# CHILDREN OF THE MOUNTAIN

## BOOKS 1 TO 3

www.rahakok.com
@rahakok

Visit www.rahakok.com to download *The Shoebox* and *The Map*, the free companion ebooks to the *Children of the Mountain* series.

*Also by R.A. Hakok*

Viable

# AMONG WOLVES

# 1

MARV SITS OPPOSITE ME, the gun on the kitchen table between us, still wrapped in the Ziploc bag. Outside the wind gusts, rattling the windows in their frames. I must have sat here a thousand times, but now it's as if I'm seeing it for the first time. The ceiling stained and cracked from snowmelt, exposing the wooden lathes behind. The counters stripped for firewood, the cupboards underneath long since laid bare.

I didn't think it would end like this. But then I guess that's what most people must think, when this moment comes. Because that's what death does, my sixteen-year-old brain is only now beginning to realize. It comes at you from behind, just like it did with Mom, and Miss Kimble, and Benjamin. And then suddenly it's there, laying a cold hand on your shoulder, forcing you to turn around and look it square in the eye. And who can be ready for that? I mean, sure, we all know we're going to die, someday. All those souls that ever lived, and not a single exception. But nevertheless, it's a sort of knowing that doesn't bear too much scrutiny. Something best not examined for too long, like staring up at the sun. Back when we still had a sun, of course. So instead you shove that uncomfortable truth all the way to the back of your mind. Something to worry about later, when you're older. But not today. Never today. Until of course, today *is* the day.

My eyes flick back to the table. The gun's still sitting there, next to the map Kane gave us. I wonder if it's the same one he used to kill Benjamin, and the little girl in the closet, in Shreve. It looks the same. There's a silencer screwed into the barrel, just like the one I saw him bring to her forehead, right before he squeezed the trigger.

Marv follows my gaze but makes no move to pick it up. I don't think I could reach it before him. I've seen how fast he is. But what's stranger is that I don't think I'll even try. It's like my brain's been flooded with a big cold rush of absolutely nothing at all. I am now that rabbit, its ears flattened, its limbs splayed, its heart dark and tharn, just waiting for the inevitable end. The only thought that pops into my head is something I've read somewhere, about how you never hear the shot that kills you.

Something to do with the bullet travelling faster than the sound it makes. But Marv's sitting only a couple of feet away from me. And then there's the silencer. Does it slow the bullet down? Is that how it works? I wonder if that'll make any difference.

Marv nods at me.

'Aw'ite boy, get to talkin'.'

I guess I must look a little confused. He has to know what I saw. I'm not sure what he can want me to talk about.

'Don't act bixicated, now, Gabriel. I ain't got neither the time nor the patience.'

Bixicated. That's a Marv word for stupid. I've heard it more than once since I started going outside with him. And to tell the truth I do feel a little stupid right now. Didn't Kane warn me, right at the beginning? And yet I let it come to this. How did I not see this was how it would end? I guess Mags was right all along; I'm not as smart as I like to think I am. I wish more than anything that I could see her again, just one more time. She'll never even know how it happened. The only truth she'll get is whatever story Marv chooses when he returns without me. And what's worse is she'll believe it, just like we all did with Benjamin.

My eyes flick around the room again, as if the cheap plywood paneling, buckled and curling with the damp, might somehow show me a way out of this. They come to rest on a spray of black mildew that's climbing the wall near the back door.

And so, because I don't want these to be the last things I see, I start to talk.

*Thirteen days earlier*

*

THE BOLTS CLUNK BACK and I wait. The electric motors whine as they slowly begin to push the four tons of carbon steel back into the darkness. There's no need to count. It takes thirty seconds, always thirty seconds. I count anyway.

A draught of cold air from the tunnel hits my face and I feel the familiar knot in my stomach. I take a deep breath, but my chest feels tight, constricted, like there's a cinder block resting there. The blessing that Kane gave earlier in the chapel, the one he always gives before we go outside, runs through my head. It does little to calm me down. I can hear my heart hammering, beating a wild tattoo against my ribcage. Inside my thermals a bead of sweat breaks free from my armpit and slowly trickles down my side. I tell myself there's nothing to worry about. I've done this dozens of times before. Hundreds.

There's already enough of a gap, but I stay where I am. The motors are still working, protesting under the load as the three feet of hardened steel continues its slow outward arc. They didn't always sound like that; they hummed gently, back when we first arrived. I wonder how many more winters they'll give us. Scudder says it's okay; they aren't even necessary. The blast door is balanced on its hinges; once the bolts have been recessed it can just be pushed back. I don't know if I believe him.

Marv appears behind me and I hesitate a moment longer before finally stepping through. The current that electrifies the door is cut as it opens and I touch my hand to the cold metal as I pass. I don't know when I first started doing that, but now it's a ritual, something to appease the tunnel gods.

The bulbs in the bulkhead lamps that haven't blown have long-since been scavenged, but enough light spills out from behind the door to illuminate the greenstone granite. I tell myself it's a big tunnel; at least thirty feet across, curving up to a crown fifteen feet above me. A mesh of brace wire covers the walls, held in place by iron bolts sunk twelve feet into the rock. But the shrill voice inside my head that won't be silenced until we're outside reminds me that we're deep inside a mountain. And right now Claus insists on knowing how the hell *chicken wire* can be expected to hold back the countless tons of rock above us.

The blast door reaches the end of its travel and stops. There's a moment's silence while the gears switch and then the motors re-engage, drawing it slowly back in. The darkness creeps forward, sensing it can now reclaim the part of the tunnel it was forced to relinquish. Claus is jabbering for the flashlight so I switch it on, even though the tired battery pack is only capable of producing a narrow cone of pale, watery light. The fickle yellow beam plays against the damp walls, the brace wire casting strange shadows against the roughhewn rock, making it seem like the tunnel is shifting, alive. Claus really doesn't care for that, but he shuts up when I ask if he'd rather we do without it. I follow the beam as here and there it catches scrawled names, notes etched into the granite. *Rigger '52. Go Steelers. Gina. Eagles suck!* All that remains of those who built Eden.

Behind me the blast door closes with a final dull clang. There's one last burst from the motors as they slide the bolts into place before falling silent. I think I hear a half second of static as the door is once again electrified, but that's probably just my imagination.

My breath's coming shallow and fast now. It sounds loud in my ears. Marv grabs my shoulder and I start inside my parka.

*Ready to go?*

I tear my eyes from the walls and nod into the darkness. The tunnel to the east has caved in so we go left. There's an elevated walkway to my right but I prefer to stay on the road. Claus doesn't like to be close to the walls.

I begin. One thousand and fifty-three paces to the west portal. I always count down on the way out. The counting helps; by nine hundred my breathing's eased a little and I strain for the first marker. Soon I hear it, the *splat-splat-splat* of dripping water, the sound echoing in the dark confines of the tunnel. Snowmelt, trickling down through the mountain. Seventy paces later my boots splash through the puddles and I shine my flashlight upwards. The beam finds the huge blast vent, the opening to a concrete shaft that leads five hundred feet straight up to the surface. A tangle of rusting pipes suspended from the roof zig-zags off into the darkness.

The tunnel runs arrow straight for the next two hundred and ninety paces before finally starting to curve left. From the curve it's only eighty-five more to the junction, but Claus reminds me that this is the worst part. If it's possible it seems darker now, the inky blackness taking on a weight, a heft, that threatens to smother me. I tell myself we're halfway there. Left is the old pedestrian walkway, long since sealed. We go right. Another seventy-five paces to the puddles that mark the second vent, and after that we hit the outer tunnels that lead, like the prongs of a giant horseshoe, to the western portals. Scudder says they were designed that way to divert the blast away from Eden's core.

The portal to the right's completely collapsed, so we take the other, following the horseshoe around. From here only three hundred and forty paces to the exit. It's colder now. I think I can even feel a breeze. I quicken my pace, fighting the urge to break into a run.

With seventy paces to go the tunnel finally straightens. The last section has partially collapsed here too, but a small amount of light seeps in near the roof, silhouetting the two figures cowled up in their parkas next to the scanner. Even from this distance I can tell it's the twins, their size distinguishing them from any of the other Guardians. One of them struggles to free his considerable bulk from the confines of the plastic chair he's wedged himself into and steps towards me. As he gets closer I can see it's Hamish. Behind him Angus is finishing what's probably his second breakfast of the morning. Something that resembles a HOOAH! from an MRE carton disappears into his mouth in a single bite.

Hamish glances briefly in Marv's direction then turns to me, pointing to a wooden trestle table sitting next to a walk-through security scanner.

'Bag.'

I know what Hamish is up to. Claus senses the end of the tunnel, the promise of open sky beyond. He doesn't want to be held up now.

'You're supposed to check us when we come back in, Hamish. Remember?'

Hamish looks momentarily confused and I take the opportunity to step past him. But Angus is already out of his chair, blocking my way. He brings himself up to his full height, folding a pair of meaty forearms over what's already a really impressive gut for a seventeen-year old. We're about the same height, and Angus has never liked that; he's used to people having to look up when they're talking to him. Unfortunately that's where any similarity between us ends; Angus has to outweigh me by a hundred pounds. And then there's the billy club he's wearing on his hip.

With what I hope passes for a weary sigh I slide the backpack off my shoulder and hold it out. Angus grabs it with one huge dimpled paw, fumbles with the plastic buckles and then upends it, sending the contents spilling out onto the table. A first aid kit from the infirmary. A fifty pack of latex gloves in a cardboard dispenser. Bottle caps and rubber stoppers of various sizes, all packed in a zippy. A plastic canteen filled with water. A couple of MREs, enough to last us until tomorrow night, assuming we don't find any food. Quartermaster used to give us spares in case the weather moved in and we couldn't make it back, but now we just get what we need to see us through quarantine. That's only seven items, not quite everything. Angus gives the bag a final shake, as if he's read my mind, although of course this isn't possible; I suspect most days Angus has difficulty reading his own mind. A small stick of UV block finally frees itself from the recesses of the backpack and skitters off the table into the dirt. I pick it up and patiently place it back on the table. Angus stares at the contents for a while longer, then motions me through the scanner.

I leave the flashlight on the table; it'll stay here for the return trip. Then I step through. There's nothing on me to set it off, obviously. The parka's zip pull and snappers have been replaced with plastic, as have the eyelets on my boots. Angus looks annoyed, like he was actually expecting me to try and take something metal *out* of Eden. He takes one of the MRE cartons from the table and then with one fleshy forearm he sweeps the remaining items onto the ground, tossing my backpack into the dirt after them. Behind him Hamish's round face splits into a grin, revealing teeth that can't have more than a nodding acquaintance with the toothbrush.

I open my mouth to protest, but then close it again; there's no way I'm getting that MRE back now. Instead I pick up the bag and dust it off, carefully replacing the remaining contents. When I'm done Angus lumbers over to the small fridge that sits on the other side of the scanner and removes a couple of Tupperware containers. Each has a name printed on a strip of masking tape across the top; another length runs all the way around the edge of the lid to prove it hasn't been tampered with. He looks from one box to the other, his lips silently forming the letter 'G', as he tries to decide which is mine. Much as I enjoy Angus's adventures with the alphabet it's a relief when he finally gives up and tosses both to me; we could be here a while otherwise, and Claus is anxious to be outside now. I hand Marv's over to him, rip the tape from the container marked 'Gabriel' and pop the lid. Inside is a large, crudely fashioned crucifix on a simple chain. I lift it over my head and drop it inside my thermals. The metal's cold against my skin.

We collect our snowshoes and respirators from the elevated walkway, where we left them when we came in last. As usual Marv's standing back, waiting for me to go first. I should just start making my way up the mound of rubble towards the exit, but instead I turn around and look back into the tunnel. Angus and Hamish have settled their ample rumps back into the plastic chairs and are already dividing up the MRE they've taken from my backpack.

'Get you ladies anything while we're out there? Lipstick? Tampons?'

Hamish goes back to looking confused; I realize he may not know what a tampon is. For a second Angus looks like he might haul himself out of the seat again, but then he thinks better of it and just gives me the finger. It's the wrong finger, but there's no doubt what he was going for.

I turn back to the collapsed portal. Snow has drifted in, covering the rocks near the top. I pull a pair of mittens from the parka's deep side pockets and start to climb. Claus doesn't like that we have to wriggle between loose rock and the roof of the tunnel for the last twenty yards, but the end is now in sight.

At last I crawl free and stand.

*

HEAVY THUNDERHEADS hang low on the horizon, threatening the dawn that's reluctantly taking shape to the east. Nevertheless, I can't help but stare up in wonder. After a week inside the mountain the sky appears boundless, a roiling gray dome of almost incomprehensible size. I've already applied UV block in the locker room. Just because no one's seen the sun in over a decade doesn't mean it isn't still there, tracking its deadly path behind the clouds. I pull the hood up on the parka, and slide a pair of ski goggles down over my eyes. The tint in the lens turns the world an ominous red.

It always takes Marv forever to make his way through the final collapsed section of the tunnel; I've already strapped on my snowshoes by the time he scrabbles free and stands beside me.

'That weren't smart, Junior. Them boys're just spoiling for a fight.' Marv's from Hager, where apparently not all consonants have equal rights. It comes out *spawlin' firra faht.*

'Yeah I know Marv, it just slipped out. Sorry.'

He looks at me for a long moment, as if deciding whether to call me on the lie.

'Well, alright.' *Aw-ite.* 'But mind that mouth of yours in future, y'hear? That pair may be dumber'n dirt, but I still wouldn't fancy your chances.'

I nod. To tell the truth I'm a little surprised. Marv's what Mom would have called a strange fish; he doesn't normally talk much, especially in the mornings. The first year, after I got chosen, he can't have said more than a dozen words to me. I don't think it was anything personal; I guess he just didn't want another partner after Benjamin died. But you scavenge in pairs, that's the rule. He's opened up a bit since, but still most of the time our conversations are limited to grunted acknowledgements, the occasional spare and functional command. Whole sentences like this are huge. I decide to press my luck.

'Much on your list?'

Marv's pulling on his respirator, muffling the response, but I'm pretty sure I hear the word *bullshit.* He turns away from me to strap on his snowshoes, signaling that the conversation is over.

I drop my respirator on the ground and kick some snow over it, then dig into the pocket of my parka for the surgical mask I've brought from the infirmary. Kane says we have to wear the respirators on account of the ash in the snow, but the respirator and Claus don't get on well together. I asked Marv once where the ash came from and he said it was because of the *awl fars.* It took me a while to figure out what he meant, but now I know. Wells in the Middle East, Venezuela or Kazakhstan, maybe even as close as Texas or North Dakota, that have been burning unchecked for the last decade, pumping untold tons of soot and ash into the atmosphere, blocking the sun. Kane says the world will stay cold until God has forgiven us, but I like Marv's explanation better. It'll be like this until the fires burn themselves out.

From the portal the land rolls gently down to the turnpike. The day we arrived this was all forest, but now the fields are almost completely bare, only the occasional gnarled trunk, long since dead, pushing stubbornly up through the thick gray shroud that covers everything else. We head off down the slope towards the handful of twisted, blackened stumps that used to be the tree line.

Our first stop is the farmhouse, halfway between the portal and the 'pike. It's where we stash gear we can't bring back into Eden, and where we sit out quarantine afterwards. It's not much to look at. Most of the clapboards have been stripped for firewood, and inside the living room's burned out, exposing the rafters above. But for the most part the roof's held, and even though it smells of damp and rot the bedrooms are dry. We pick up the things we'll need. All the metal items go in separate Ziploc bags with the openings taped. Marv wears a knife on his belt. I'm not allowed to have one, but the leatherman I carry has a blade. Marv also has a pistol, which he keeps in another zippy in the outside pocket of his parka. He doesn't think I know, but I've seen it.

As soon as we've collected our gear we set off. We're not going far today. Providence, the closest town of any size to Eden, is only nine miles to the west, so we should be back by nightfall. There hasn't been a fresh fall in a few days and the snow's settled. Good tracking skiff, Marv calls it. I think Marv used to hunt a lot, before.

It's heavy going at first, but once we get down to the highway it gets a little easier. The virus did a pretty good job of quieting the roads, so the first section of the 'pike's pretty clear of traffic. We only come across the occasional car, parked up on the hard shoulder, or sitting at a weird angle in the middle of the road. I used to play this game, when I first started going outside, identifying the make and model from the shape of the mound of snow it was buried under. I'd scrub snow off the back to check the badge, to see if I was right, while Marv marched on ahead. I don't do it anymore; it's not much fun when you're playing by yourself.

Besides, I know all the cars on the turnpike now.

We make good time until we reach Devil's Run and then there's a section where the drifts have piled deep so we switch to single file, taking it in turns to break trail. It's hard work, and I feel myself starting to sweat inside the parka in spite of the cold. Marv's pace never slows; his legs continue to rise and fall, following a tireless, mechanical rhythm. Marv's lean, wiry; I suspect he could lope along like this all day. Raw-boned and hatchet-faced, Jack would have called him. But pretty fit for an old guy, all the same. Tell the truth I'm not exactly sure how old Marv is, but he was already at Eden when we arrived, so I'm guessing at least thirty-five.

We stop every hour for frostbite checks. Marv says the cold's a vicious bitch; it can mess with your thinking, so you have to treat it with respect. I lift my goggles onto my forehead and close my eyes and Marv checks my nose and cheeks, then I do him. I check carefully, even though the scraggly red beard that covers most of the bottom half of his face makes it harder than the blond peach fuzz he has to contend with. Afterwards we sit in silence, our breath escaping in frosted plumes as we sip water from our canteens. A couple of minutes later Marv gets up without saying a word and we set off again.

We hit the blockade about a mile outside town. A semi and a school bus, parked cheek to jowl across the 'pike. Sometimes when the drifts are high it looks like you could walk right up over the rig's hood, but we always go out wide on the hard shoulder. Marv says there's no point taking chances; if the metal's been contaminated your boot could go right through. It'd be easy to break a leg that way, and then you'd most likely be done for, like Benjamin. I guess he's right.

Once we're past the blockade it's not far to the intersection where the town proper begins. The traffic light gantry's collapsed, the virus-weakened metal no longer able to bear the weight of the gantry arm, one end of which is now buried in the snow in the middle of the highway. A little further up on the left there's Calhoun's Auto Park. The sermon-style sign guarantees the best prices in the tri-state area, and no money down credit approval, but I don't think that deal's on the table anymore. There's a WalMart a little further along, behind the big Sunoco gas station on the right. Marv doesn't like working the malls, although sometimes we have to. He says most were built with steel bar joists and metal deck roofs; those that haven't already collapsed are primed to. That's okay with me; I've never liked the malls much either. I suspect they're not as bad as the hospitals, but they still got hit pretty hard in the last weeks, before it all finally quieted down for good. I guess everyone went there first to grab what they needed when it was clear the lights weren't coming back on and it was every man for himself.

The Walmart's where I saw my very first body. A regular guy, just sitting right there in the canned foods aisle, all dried and shrunken inside his rotting clothes. There was a hole bigger than a dinner plate in the middle of his chest where somebody had let rip with something large bore, maybe a shotgun, nubs of bone and frozen cartilage poking through around the edges. What was left of his fingers were still clutching a jar of Luxardo Gourmet Maraschino Cherries that may or may not have been the source of the disagreement. After I'd finished throwing up I asked Marv whether we should do something. Marv just shrugged and said the ground was too cold to bury anyone. Besides, there were too many of them to worry about. We've been back to the Walmart a few times since. Maraschino guy's still there.

When we get as far as the Hardee's Marv stops and pulls a map out of his pocket. He uses it to mark off the places we've covered. Today we're starting a new street.

Stricklen Avenue turns out to be just like everywhere else in Providence. Single story brick and shingle ranch houses for the most part. Nothing grand or fancy, just a succession of little L-shaped boxes, sitting squat as frogs under low-pitched gable roofs. A scrub of ground between portico and road, a flagpole or a basketball hoop for ornamentation. A pickup or an old Taurus parked up out front, long since sunken onto its tires under the snow.

We take the first house on the right. Marv pulls back the screen and checks the front door, but it doesn't budge. Could be that whoever lived there is still inside, although more often than not the houses have been abandoned. People still locked up when they left though, like maybe they thought they'd be back some day. Or perhaps it was just force of habit. Either way, it's not a problem. A window or a patio door's normally the easiest way in. Failing that, a pry bar or a bolt cutter will usually do the trick. I carry both in my pack.

We make our way around the back and let ourselves in through the kitchen. Marv heads straight for the basement, while I check the cabinets for food. He does the dark places, that's the rule, which is just fine with me. I'd have no interest in that, even if it weren't for Claus.

The kitchen's a bust, but then it normally is. Sometimes we find cans, like SpaghettiOs, or soup, or beans, but we can't bring those back into Eden so Marv and I eat them out here, as long as they're still good. You can normally tell just by looking whether the metal's contaminated, but Marv says you have to test by resting your boot on the top and gently pressing down. If it's bad it'll split right open before you apply more than a couple of pounds of pressure.

After the kitchen I head straight for the bathroom. That's where you'll pick up a lot of staples anyway: toothpaste, soap, shampoo, deodorant (roll-on or stick, not the aerosols, obviously). It's where you'll find the other stuff too, the things I need that aren't on Quartermaster's lists. Today I'm in luck. I find what I'm after right there under the sink in the very first house we check: three boxes of ProSom and half a dozen blister packs of Ambien. There's an unopened container of Tylenol in the cabinet with the tamper seal still intact. I shove that into my backpack as well.

When I make my way into the living room I find a bottle of Glenfiddich just sitting on the floor by a moldering armchair. The label says single malt, and there's almost two thirds left. With liquor generally what wouldn't burn got drunk, so this is pretty rare. I unscrew the metal cap and chuck it, and then remove the tamper ring with the leatherman I've brought from the farmhouse. None of the plastic caps I have fit, but one of the rubber stoppers works just fine. I wedge it in tight and slide the bottle into my backpack.

I don't bother checking the bedrooms; the pills and the whisky mean it's a good bet their former owner's still in residence. Nine times out of ten people that saw out their days at home ended up dying under their duvets. I've gotten used to seeing dead bodies, mostly. The dried out corpses with the covers tucked up around their necks, the remnants of hair and long-rotted flesh staining the pillow, they don't hold the horrors they used to. But I certainly don't go looking for them.

I make it back out to the porch first. I pull an aerosol from my backpack and spray a red 'X' on the front door. It's important to have a system, so you don't waste time working the same place twice. I could just move on to the next house, but Marv says we have to stay within what he calls hollerin' distance, so I sit down to wait for him.

We make good progress along Stricklen and the morning passes quickly. I hit the jackpot in the last house we check. Right there on the mantle there's a paperback, *The Girl With The Dragon Tattoo* by some guy called Stieg Larsson. The yellow cover's tatty, the spine's creased and bowed and most of the pages are dog-eared, but it looks intact. It's important to check; it's not like you can just wander off to your local Barnes and Noble to find another copy if it turns out the last page is missing. I flip it over and read the back. My heart sinks as I realize it's the first book in a trilogy, and I sit for a while on the floor, turning it over in my lap, trying to decide whether or not to keep it. On the one hand it's been a while since I've had something new to read, and the description on the cover makes it sound exciting. But I've always had a problem with not knowing stuff, and there's no punishment more cruel or unusual than not finding out how a good story ends. Mags would get angry with me for even considering leaving it; she'd take it, just to get whatever of the story she could. That's because she doesn't get to read anymore, though.

In the end I come to a decision and put the book in my backpack. Then I head outside and sit on the step, cowled up in my parka, waiting for Marv to finish up in the garage. The wind's blowing snow across the street, covering the tracks we made to get here; in an hour they'll be gone completely.

A few minutes later Marv appears in the doorway. His pack's looking pretty full, so I'm thinking maybe we're done. Besides, it's almost lunchtime. From here the choices are Burger King, the Golden Corral or back to Hardees. I hope it'll be the Corral; we ate at the Burger King last time.

You've got to mix things up a little.

*

MARV TAKES US BACK to Burger King, but that's okay. It's been looted like everywhere else, another reminder of the chaos of those final weeks. The main window's smashed, large cracks spiderwebbing out from a central impact point, like someone threw something big and heavy, maybe a trashcan, at it. The glass held, though, so at least we're out of the wind. The door's another story. All that's left is a mostly empty frame, hanging askance on one of its hinges, the last of the glass gripped in fragments around the edges and in the corners. Broken shards crunch under my boot as I walk in. There's a little drift, but the snow only reaches a couple of feet inside. We grab our usual booth near the back.

Neither of us has found anything, so it's the MREs we've brought. MREs are field rations they used to give to soldiers apparently. Eden was stocked with them when we arrived, but I have to go pretty far back into stores to find shelves that aren't empty now. I think we've been inside the mountain far longer than anyone was expecting.

Marv's got beef ravioli and I've drawn chicken pesto pasta. I don't care much for pesto. It sticks with me and we've got the hike back ahead of us, but I know Marv's not going to want to trade his beef so I don't even bother asking. The packet's already been opened, the end folded back over and taped shut, which means there'll be no HOOAH! for dessert either. I pull off the tape and upend the drab brown plastic, gently shaking the contents onto the table. Various cartons and sachets spill out. Some crackers and cheese spread. Instant coffee, sugar and creamer. I don't care for coffee so I slide those over to Marv. A plastic spoon. The spoon will burn if you're in a pinch and need something to start a fire. A chewing gum. Sachets of salt, pepper. A tiny bottle of Tabasco. The Tabasco makes the food taste more interesting, but I learned early on not to trust it.

I find the cardboard carton that holds the meal, and remove the plastic packet containing my chicken. I tear the top off the heater pouch, and slide the packet inside, adding a little water from my canteen to start the reaction. It soon starts hissing, telling me it's getting to work. I slide the pouch inside the cardboard carton the meal came in and balance it against my backpack. The sachet with my cheese spread's frozen from the hike out so I slide it down into the carton to defrost it. Then I tuck the flap back down to keep the heat in and wait for it to do its magic. In a couple of minutes it's done. You can make a bowl out of the thick plastic outer wrapper the MRE came in by folding the lip back on itself a few times, but your food goes cold pretty quickly out here so I prefer to just scoop it straight out of the packet.

We eat in silence. It's not bad, I suppose, as long as you mix it right.

The packet tells you that MRE means Meal, Ready to Eat, but I like to come up with other words the initials might stand for. It's kind of like a game, to see if I can get Marv to smile. I haven't managed it yet, but I think I'm getting closer. While he's having his coffee I try out Meal Refusing to Exit. This is one of my better attempts. It works because if you eat too many of them MREs make you constipated. We all found that out the hard way (you see what I did there?) the first few months in Eden. I'm rewarded with the faintest twitch, a slight upturn at the corner of his mouth that's about as close as Marv gets to smiling.

When he's done with his coffee Marv pulls out a cigarette and lights up. I asked him once whether the tobacco still tastes okay after all this time. He just grunted and said he's had worse. The smoke drifts across the table and I have to blink it out of my eyes, so I use the excuse to pick up our litter and bag it. I'm not sure why we bother. The world's full of trashcans that were left out for a collection that never came; a little more's not going to make any difference. But Marv says I have to.

When Marv's done with his cigarette he slides out of the booth and we set off back towards the farmhouse. It's late afternoon but it's early fall, I think September, so we have a few hours of light left. The weather's still holding, but the wind's picked up while we were having lunch, and now it blows hard into our faces, biting at any area of exposed skin, forcing us to lean into it. My backpack's full and I have to keep shifting it to stop the straps cutting into my shoulders.

We're Indian file a lot of the way back, taking it in turns to walk in each other's footsteps. The tracks we made on the way out this morning have already completely disappeared. I focus on the steady sound of my breathing behind the thin cotton mask. Pounding the snow like this for mile after mile lets your mind slip out of gear and idle, even though Marv says I have to pay attention. Somehow I get to thinking about the people who left Providence, and where they might have gone. I guess some of them must have travelled east on this road, hoping to pick up US15 south. Most would have stayed put until the weather turned, and by then getting out on foot would have been a whole lot more difficult. I doubt many would have made it; there's probably bodies under the snow, right where we're walking. I wonder what it'll be like if it ever thaws. Will the cold have preserved them, like the furies? I try not to have thoughts like that. You can't unthink things. But sometimes I can't help it.

By the time we arrive back at the farmhouse we're starting to lose the light. Marv heads straight for his room. He closes the door behind him and a second later I hear the key turn in the lock. My room's a little further down the hall. It's small and smells musty, but even though a section of the ceiling's fallen through it's dry, and it doesn't look like anyone ever died in the bed, so there's a lot to be grateful for. I have an old hurricane lamp that I fill with a mix of gas and motor oil. The black smoke it throws off smudges the air and stings my eyes, but the guttering flame is just enough to read by. I prop my backpack against the wall in the corner and take out *The Girl With The Dragon Tattoo*. Before this morning I hadn't found anything new in a while so I've been reading *Dune* again. I'll have to finish that first, now that I've started it. It's sort of a rule. That's not a problem though; *Dune's* a great story, and besides I don't have much left. I dig under the bed for the box where I hide the books I've found and pull it out.

I have some work to do first, though. I take a moment to listen, making sure Marv hasn't moved from his room. Mostly I don't see him again until we're done with quarantine and ready to head back into Eden. But sometimes after it's gone dark he comes back out and I hear him moving around in the hallway outside my door.

Tonight it's quiet. I dig into the backpack and remove the pills I scavenged from the house earlier, along with the other items I'll need. I pull off my mittens and snap on a pair of latex gloves. The blister packs have aluminum foil on one side. It looks okay, but you can't be too careful.

I twist the lid off the Tylenol container, breaking the seal, and remove the inner cap. Then I carefully empty the contents onto my bed. Starting with the ProSom, one by one I pop the pills from their individual bubbles into the bottle. After a few minutes I'm starting to lose feeling in the tips of my fingers so I stop to rub my hands together, but it's hard to generate friction wearing the latex gloves. Once the last of the pills have been transferred to the container I push some cotton wool in, tamping it down so it sits on top. Next the Tylenol go back. By now my fingers are pretty numb and I spill a few, but it doesn't matter, most find their way in. There's no way to replace the foil cap on the container without it looking obvious, so I don't bother. A tiny dab of superglue from a tube I keep in the bedside table between the threads on the inside of the cap and I twist it back on. The last job is to glue the tamper seal back in place. I use the end of a matchstick to apply the glue, then hold the seal in place with my fingers. When I'm happy it's set I rip off the latex gloves and jam my hands into my armpits underneath the parka to warm them up. It hurts a little as the blood creeps back into my fingers, but that won't last long. Once normal feeling's returned I hold the Tylenol container up to the flickering flame and examine the job I've done. Satisfied, I place it back in my backpack.

I pick up *Dune* and thumb to the page I've marked. I'd already got to the duel between Paul and Feyd-Rautha the last time we were out, and it takes me only a few minutes to finish. I debate whether I need to re-read the appendices, but decide against it on the basis that they're not really part of the story, even though I know this is sort of cheating. I reach for the tattered copy of *The Girl With The Dragon Tattoo*. I hold it up to the lamp, studying the creases in the bowed and battered spine by the faltering light, savoring those first moments, the promise of the story to come. Then with bated breath I flip to the first page and start to read.

*

ELIZA WILKES HAD NOT MEANT to end the world that day.

That day or any other day for that matter, for Eliza was not a wicked person. She wasn't, to borrow a phrase her father had always favored, crazy as a bullbat. That would come, soon, when the fury came upon her, but for now at least no demons tormented her, no voices whispered that only she could hear. She was neither fanatic nor zealot, radical nor martyr. She was a God-fearing woman, that much cannot be denied, and in truth Eliza may have held her faith a little stronger than most. But her heart had never secretly yearned for the fire or the brimstone. The pastor had surely called it right when he said the world was full of sinners, and Eliza noted with sadness that these days most tended to lack the good grace to even try and hide it. But for all their weaknesses she bore her fellow man no grudge, and she certainly wasn't going to be the one to pick up that first stone. God had created us in his image, and as such we were all deserving of His forgiveness. Heathen or heretic, mankind was not evil, a blight to be purged.

Neither was Eliza possessed of any authority that might mark her out as a destroyer of worlds. She hadn't, at least until now, wielded any power. Her colleagues knew her as Liz, and she worked in a cubicle, the same cubicle she had been assigned when she first joined the agency. Seven years of diligent analysis had resulted in a single, minor, promotion, two years before. Eliza suspected it was unlikely she would be promoted again, and in this she was more right than she could know. But she was, for the most part, content. The work suited her meticulous nature. She no longer hankered for a place on one of the inspection teams. She didn't need to go out and see the world; it was just fine that it should come to her.

Which it did, in the form of the Super B glossies that landed on her desk each morning, high resolution images taken by observation satellites sitting in patient heliosynchronous orbit hundreds of miles above the earth. Hers was the painstaking task of analyzing those images, grid square by grid square, searching for anything that might have changed, anything that might seem out of the ordinary. The steam rising from a turbine housing. The foam residue on a riverbank where thermal pipes vented during low tide. The rate at which snow melted on a roof during winter. She pored over dark smudges. She scrutinized discolorations that appeared on pipes, near chimneys, beside overflow valves. She measured the dimensions of buildings, estimated their height from the shadows they cast, even the depth of their foundations as they were being laid. These and a hundred other things that to most people would seem meaningless, inconsequential. And then she would file a report, detailing what she had found, carefully cross-referencing the relevant co-ordinates. Occasionally a question would come back, a request for clarification, for further analysis. But mostly that was it. She filed the report and moved on to the next glossy, safe in the knowledge that somebody else would decide what action, if any, needed to be taken.

And yet here she was, sitting in the back seat of the Paektusan, thousands of miles from the safety of her cubicle. Their small convoy had set out before dawn. Streetlights were not a priority in a country struggling to generate sufficient electricity to meet its daily needs and they had made their way out of the sleeping city in darkness. She had asked the driver to turn the heater up, and inside the tired old sedan it was stuffy. Beside her on the back seat Jan was snoring gently. Jorg, the tall Norwegian, sat in front. His eyes were closed, but from where she sat Eliza couldn't tell if he too was sleeping.

She had not been able to sleep, however, even though she was exhausted. The headaches were definitely getting worse; the Tylenol she was now taking every couple of hours no longer seemed to be having any effect. And so she had stared out of the window, the fingers of one gloved hand gently kneading her temple, watching as the city woke from its slumber. Here and there thin people in drab, gray clothes emerged from the doorways of crumbling apartment blocks, beginning another day.

She still couldn't believe that she was here. It was she who had spotted it, of course. The reactor had been re-commissioned. But the cooling tower that had been demolished years before had never been rebuilt, which meant they had to be pumping water from the Kuryong to cool the core. There had been requests for more imagery, for further analysis, as soon as her report had been digested. But she could have told them, without troubling archives for the glossies. She had been studying that river for years; she knew it wasn't a reliable source. It flooded during the late summer rains, every year, without fail. Then the riverbed would shift, silting up the collecting cisterns. The winters were even worse: it either dried up altogether or froze. She'd put it all in her report, of course, the grid squares precisely cross-referenced, as usual. It was an old reactor, graphite-moderated, like Windscale had been, and Chernobyl. If they couldn't pump enough water to cool the core it was only a matter of time before the same thing happened here. *That* had really got their attention; for the next few days she'd barely had a moment to herself as satellites were re-tasked and stacks of fresh images found their way to her cubicle. In spite of the excitement she had found herself wishing for things to return to normal.

That hope would prove forlorn. Eliza did not know it, but she had been chosen. She would be the first; her fate was already sealed. In a few short hours, if things went according to plan, she would shake hands with the man she had been sent to meet. The irony that it might begin with such an ancient gesture of peace had not yet occurred to Eliza.

For if that were to happen things would, all too literally, be out of her hands.

*

A LONG, COLD DUSK is settling over the world as we make our way back up to the portal. On top of the mountain the transmitter tower maintains its silent watch. Gray snow lies in skiffs between the bristling antennae and the long-dead microwave relays.

Marv makes me go first into the tunnel, as usual. I always call ahead when we're returning, so whatever Guardians are on duty know I'm coming, just in case. Then I take my backpack off and use it to push the snow in front of me as I wriggle my way in over the rubble. Claus has been quiet while we've been out, but now we're back in the mountain he's letting me know he's really not happy to be home.

It doesn't take my eyes long to adjust to the gloom. Tyler and Eric have replaced Angus and Hamish in the plastic chairs; they get up as I come in. Eric grabs the flashlight I left on the table by the scanner yesterday morning. He flicks it on as he walks over towards me.

I drop my backpack on the ground and lift the crucifix by the chain from underneath my thermals. Eric takes it between two latex-gloved fingers and holds it up, twisting the links so the old metal turns slowly, reflecting the pale yellow light from the flashlight's dying battery. Satisfied there's no sign of contamination, he places it in the plastic Tupperware with my name on it and snaps the lid in place. Fresh tape goes around the edge to seal it, then the container goes back in the fridge.

As usual Marv's taking his time coming through the collapsed section of the tunnel. Finally I hear him climbing down the rubble behind me. Tyler's waiting to check his crucifix, but Marv just ignores him, taking another moment to let his eyes get used to the darkness.

I walk through the scanner, the backpack in my hand. When I'm through Eric takes it off me and opens it, carefully placing the contents on the table. I try not to stare as he shakes the bottle of Tylenol, but after a cursory examination he puts it back with the other items. Next he picks up the bottle of Glenfiddich and examines the neck, to make sure I've not inadvertently left the tamper ring in place. I tell myself not to get annoyed at this, but, seriously, does he think I'd make a mistake like that? Then it too gets replaced. A quick glance over the other stuff I've brought back and Eric nods to let me know he's done.

I hesitate before returning the items to my backpack.

'Some new stuff there, still in the packets.'

Eric just nods and chooses a toothbrush, which disappears into the pockets of his black overalls. Tyler helps himself to a roll-on deodorant. That's the way things work here. They don't take much; I don't mention it to Quartermaster. Besides, Eric and Tyler aren't the worst. At least they waited for me to offer.

After I've repacked my backpack I wait for Marv. When he's done I collect the flashlight from the table and we make our way into the darkness of the tunnel. I begin the count, but Claus has already started up, reminding me that the cold will have played havoc with the old batteries. What will we do if it fails when we're in the tunnel? Telling him that Marv has another flashlight, that I know these tunnels like the back of my hand, has little effect. The inky darkness provides the perfect screen on which he can conjure images of whatever it is Marv goes looking for in the dark places, of the bodies waiting just under the snow out on the turnpike.

I keep walking, the constriction in my chest getting tighter with each step. The count's upwards as we head back into the mountain. At three hundred and forty we leave the horseshoe and a few moments later my boots are splashing through the puddles that mark the first blast vent. By the time we're turning left at the junction the fear's twisting my insides. I tell Claus we're halfway home, but this is the darkest part of the tunnel. What would happen if the flashlight were to die now? The tunnel curves right and I strain for the sounds of dripping water that will let me know we're approaching the second blast vent. At last I hear it; moments later my boots splash through meltwater and I'm on the home stretch. From here the tunnel's straight as a die until the blast door.

Finally we arrive. A keypad sits to one side, the keys underneath the stubby metal hood glowing in the darkness, waiting for the sequence of letters and numbers that will start the open cycle. But Marv and I don't get the code, so instead I push the intercom, trying to appear calm while I silently beg whichever Guardian's on duty to hurry up and let me in. Somewhere above me a camera will be focusing, so I hold the flashlight up to my face. After what seems like forever there's the heavy clunk of the bolts receding and the whine of the electric motors as the huge metal door begins to open. Just a few seconds more.

As soon as the gap's wide enough I squeeze through and dump the backpack on the floor. I sit on the bench that lines one side of the anteroom, letting my breathing return to normal. To the left there's the showers and beyond the scanner room. Claus, momentarily relieved to be out of the tunnel, starts up again at the thought. I'll let Marv go first; that'll give him some time to calm down.

No such luck. The speaker mounted to the wall behind me squawks into life and I hear Kurt's tinny voice.

'Keep moving, Gabriel.'

'Marv's going through first. I'll be right after him.'

'*Now*, Gabriel.'

One day Kurt will take over from Peck as leader of the Guardians, and you can see he's already feeling his way into the role. I'm tempted to ignore him, just to piss him off. There's no way he'd come down here, and even if he did, what could he do? But Kurt has a talent for working out your weaknesses, and I don't want him to find out about Claus. That's something he could certainly use against me.

With a sigh I get up and head for the locker room. A number of plastic crates have been stacked against the wall and I strip off, packing my parka, boots and backpack separately, filling the last crate with the rest of my clothes. A roll of tape has been left on one of the lids and I tear off several long strips and use them to seal the rims. Each crate will be scanned separately. The parka and boots will be returned to my locker in time for the next trip; the backpack will go directly to Quartermaster in the stores. The thermals I'll pick up later; they'll need to be washed before I go out again.

I removed the pills from the backpack before I sealed the crate and now I slide them into the pocket of a threadbare cotton robe that's hanging on the wall and step in to the showers. Thanks to the reactor hot water's at least one thing we're never short of in Eden. The steaming jets feel good after the cold of the tunnel and I linger as long as I can. When I can't put it off any longer I get out and towel myself dry. Then I throw on the robe and make my way next door.

The scanner sits in the center of the room, the light from the single working bulkhead lamp reflecting dully off its polished metal skin. From its hollow center a narrow platform extends, like it's been waiting for me. I look up at the camera mounted high on the wall, its red light blinking back at me. Kurt will be watching so I can't look like I'm afraid, but nevertheless I hesitate for a moment before taking off the robe and laying back on the platform's cold vinyl. Electric motors start to whir underneath me as they move the platform into the machine's dark interior and I have to force myself to remain calm. We're almost all the way in and I can tell Claus is working up to a regular hissy fit. I guess I could have taken something to take the edge off; half of one of the pills I've brought back would do the trick. But I'm determined not to go down that road unless I really have to. As the platform slides home and I'm fully enclosed Claus dials it up several notches.

I grit my teeth, willing him to calm down. The scan lasts exactly nineteen and a half minutes (guess how I know). I tell him we can deal with that rather than give Kurt the satisfaction of witnessing a meltdown. He quietens for a moment, but then threatens to lose it again as the banging starts. I know there's nothing to worry about. The scanner's just a big magnet; the sounds it makes are just pulses of electricity being fired through the coils, causing them to vibrate, and the field it generates will destroy any trace of the virus. Still, it's like being inside an oil drum that someone's pounding with a jackhammer. I spend the next twenty minutes trying to think of anything else I can while Claus writhes and twists inside my head with every new vibration.

At last it's over and the platform slowly starts to slide back out. I wriggle my way along it and jump off before it's finished its travel, no longer caring whether or not I look relaxed. By the time I've put on the t-shirt and overalls I changed out of this morning I'm a bit calmer. I transfer the pills from the robe into the pocket of my overalls and head out into Eden.

*

WE CALL IT EDEN but I don't think that's its real name. At least I don't think that's what it was called before. Besides, from the stories Kane reads to us on Sundays Eden was supposed to have trees and grass and animals, and in here it's just steel and rock. It's like you're in a giant granite igloo that someone's built a little metal town inside, a weird Flintstones version of a snow globe. Except the snow's on the outside of course.

I remember thinking it was impressive, back when we first arrived. I mean, it must have taken them years to dig it all out. The roof of the cavern's an easy sixty feet at its highest, with enough space for twelve buildings, most of them three stories high, laid out in a four-by-three grid. It's not what you'd call pretty, though. For the most part the buildings are just featureless boxes, sections of steel plate welded together and bolted to iron frames. You can't see it from here, but the frames sit on giant underground springs that allow them to absorb the shock of a nearby detonation. Miss Kimble said they used to build skyscrapers like that on the outside too, in cities that were prone to earthquakes. I sometimes wonder if earthquakes are still happening in those places, like they did before. I guess they must be. There's just no one around to worry about them anymore.

None of the buildings have windows, just a single large bulkhead door hanging on thick, buttressed hinges. In the center of each a name's been stenciled, the paint now chipped and faded with age. On Front Street there's the mess and the infirmary as well as a disused administration building and what used to be the command center, back when there was still something to command. Behind that, on Main, or what we call Juvie Row, there's another four buildings. The doors there just read Dormitories 1 through 4. That's where we sleep. We'd all easily fit on one floor of one of the dorms, but boys and girls can't share, obviously, and the Guardians bunk by themselves, so we're spread over the first three. Dorm 4's been empty for years. That's where Miss Kimble died.

It's dinnertime so right now Eden's narrow concrete streets are deserted. The thought of food makes my stomach grumble; we didn't find anything outside and the MRE Angus took was my quarantine ration, so I haven't eaten yet today. I cross Front Street and head for the mess. I hesitate for a moment, my hand resting on the bulkhead door's large latch handle. From inside I hear the muted clink and scrape of cutlery, the occasional murmur of conversation. After the tunnel and the scanner I'm not much in the mood for company, but my stomach growls again so I push the handle down and step inside.

It looks like pretty much everyone's here. The Guardians have occupied their usual table by the door; a few of them glance up as I enter but the rest remain hunched over their trays. The other Juvies are gathered around two tables at the far end of the room. I look for Mags among the gray overalls at the girls' table, but I don't see her so I head up to the counter.

Fran smiles at me and spoons mash from a steel serving tray that's sitting under a heating lamp onto my plate. Mags says there's really only two food choices in Eden – take it or leave it – and that pretty much sums it up, at least if you're a Juvie. It's always potatoes for dinner; it's the only vegetable the farms can produce. Jake's tried to get cabbage and beets to grow, with seeds Marv and I brought back from the Farmers' Union Co-op out by Cauldron, but they wouldn't take. We have to supplement our diet with vitamin pills, but at least those are pretty easy to find; I guess they weren't high on most people's list when the looting started. Twice a week we also get something from a can to go with the potatoes. Tonight it's meatballs in tomato sauce, although the only way you'd know this is if you were to read the label, which for most of my Juvie brethren isn't an option. I pick up my tray and head over to the boys' table.

I take my usual seat at the end. I don't feel much like talking and besides, there aren't that many topics of conversation in Eden that haven't already been rehearsed to death. There's only so many times you can listen to how many brace bolts someone tightened, or the state of the plastic skirting on the growing benches over at the farms. When I got chosen to go scavenging with Marv there were a lot of questions about that, and for a while all everyone wanted to hear about was how cold it was and how there were dead bodies everywhere. But even that stopped being interesting after a while, and now I think the other Juvies would rather I didn't talk about it. Everyone knows that when the food runs out we'll need to leave here, but the weather's not showing any sign of changing, and for all its faults Eden's a lot better than being outside. Besides, there's only one subject anyone's interested in now. The last of us turns sixteen next month and then we'll all find out who our matches are. Sometimes it's hard to believe that time is almost upon us, that we've really been in Eden that long.

I've barely sat down when behind me I hear the clunk of the latch handle and the groan of the bulkhead door opening. I don't need to turn around to know it's Kurt. We've been eating the same meatballs for the last ten years, but suddenly the conversation dies and everyone's staring hard at the trays in front of them, as if they've just found something new and interesting there. Out of the corner of my eye I see him appear at the end of the table. He spends a few moments just standing there before he speaks.

'The President wants to see you, Gabriel.'

'Great, I'll be there soon.'

'*Now*, Gabriel.'

I look up from my tray. I wasn't going to say anything, really, but then I see the way he's looking at me through those pickets of lank brown hair, a lazy grin playing across his plump lips, and whatever hope I might have had of holding my tongue vanishes like a frosted plume of my breath out on the turnpike. I drop my fork. It clatters loudly as it lands in the steel tray.

'What's the rush, Kurt? Is there an emergency? Have Angus and Hamish been eating the toilet paper again?' I hear a nervous snicker from somewhere further along the table, quickly cut short as Kurt glares down at whoever was laughing. 'Tell you what, why don't you run back and ask the Old Man whether whatever he wants to talk to me about is so urgent I can't take five minutes to finish my meatballs.'

That certainly solves the problem of people staring down at their trays; meatballs aren't the focus of anyone's attention any more. Excitement's a rare commodity in Eden and all eyes are now on the drama unfolding at our table. I have a long, uncomfortable moment to consider whether it might not have been smarter to heed Marv's advice from yesterday, outside the portal. I'm vaguely aware that Mags has walked into the mess with Jake. They're both looking over to see what's going on.

I'm bluffing, of course. But I'm pretty sure I know what Kane wants to talk to me about, which means I also know that Kurt won't run back to him now. Kurt enjoys throwing his weight around, but this time he's overstepped. He's been given a simple instruction, a message to pass on and he's added his own 'Moses come down from the mountain' urgency to it. If he hurries back to Kane to report me it's him that'll look like the asshole. And Kurt's just about smart enough to realize that.

I pick up my fork and turn my attention back to my meatballs, pretending to ignore him. Kurt stares at me for a long while, seething, then turns and storms back across the mess. The bulkhead door clangs shut behind him and a few seconds later conversation slowly resumes.

From the other side of the room Mags flashes me a smile.

*

ONCE KURT'S LEFT I finish eating as quickly as I can and make my way down to Back Street. Kane's request might well be routine, but it doesn't do to keep him waiting. I might occasionally run a smart mouth, but when it comes right down to it I'm a respecter of authority, an obeyer of the rules. When push comes to shove I'll toe the line. I think most of us are like that. And then there are some that aren't. Mags is one of them; she just isn't wired that way. But then I guess that's why she does so much penance.

The roof of the cavern starts to come down back here, and the last row of gray metal boxes run to two stories, not three. Kane lives in the one on the end; he's got it all to himself. I check I haven't spilled any of the meatballs down the front of my t-shirt, then I rap gently on the metal door. After a long moment there's the sound of footsteps approaching from somewhere inside, then a clunk as the latch is pressed down and it opens.

Kane's a big man, as tall as me, and broad in the shoulders. Other than the mane of white hair, carefully combed back, and a thickening at the waist and the jowls, age doesn't appear to have diminished him. He's one of those guys that'll be walking around, back ramrod straight, until the day they lower him into the ground. His suit's neatly pressed, as always, the silk tie perfectly knotted, and his shoes look like they've been freshly polished. He looks, well, presidential. But it's more than just that. It's hard to explain, but he has this authority. I've never heard him raise his voice in Eden, not once. It's like all he has to do is whisper and everyone just shuts up and listens.

'Gabriel. Thank you for dropping by.' Kane's from Galveston and he's got that Southern accent, deep and rich, like the maple syrup that goes on our pancakes in the mornings. I don't feel like I've been summoned. I feel like I'm making a social visit, like I wandered over of my own free will, as a courtesy to him.

'A pleasure, Mr. President.'

He steps back from the door and I follow him in. Inside it's the same riveted metal floors and steel panel walls you find everywhere else in Eden, but that's pretty much where the similarity ends. Here there's rugs on the floor and pictures on the walls. A pair of leather sofas and a couple of matching armchairs occupy the center of the large room. Old-fashioned lamps with actual shades sit on occasional tables, throwing out a soft yellow glow instead of the harsh glare of the dorms' bulkhead lights. And up against one wall, a whole bookcase full of books. It's the only place in Eden where you'll find them. I don't count the tech manuals Scudder has over at the plant. These look like books you might actually want to read.

The air's thick with the rich, slightly sweet aroma of Kane's cigars. I managed to find an almost full box of Padróns for him a few months back. He sent for me afterwards, to thank me in person; he said they were the best he'd ever smoked. They were sealed up tight in a box he called a humidor, so I guess maybe they were still good after all this time, but possibly he was just being polite. I've been looking for more for him ever since.

'Please, son, sit down.' Kane points to one of the sofas, then sits opposite. He's poured a glass of cherry Kool-Aid for me and there's an apple-cinnamon HOOAH! next to it.

The leather feels good as I sink into it, old but supple. It beats the hard plastic chairs in the mess or the thin mattress on my cot. My gaze inadvertently wanders over to the bookcase. So many books, and all in one place. I sometimes wonder what it would be like to walk over there and run my fingers along the spines, letting them stop where they will; to pick one at random and bring it back to the comfort of one of these armchairs. But then I catch myself and force my eyes back to the Kool-Aid and the candy bar in front of me.

Kane's already begun, so I don't think he's noticed. I've missed what he's said, but the rising inflection suggests a question and it's always the same thing he asks first. As usual I shake my head, and he nods. When I first started going outside I was sure I'd find someone. Or at least evidence that people were still out here: smoke on the horizon; fresh tracks in the snow; the faint glimmer of a fire through a silted window. But in five years I've never seen so much as a single footprint to suggest there's anyone else left out here. Alive, I mean. I know the little girl in the closet in Shreve doesn't count.

Of course Kane already knows we didn't find anyone; if we had he'd already have heard about it. He's pretty clear on what we have to do if that happens: lay low then come right back to Eden and report to him as soon as we can manage it without being seen. He says if there's anyone still left outside after all this time they're likely to be desperate, dangerous men, lawless and Godless. That's why he has Peck train the Guardians, to protect us.

Kane has other questions too, and I answer them between bites of my HOOAH! and sips of Kool-Aid. Where Marv and I have been; whether it's getting harder to find things; whether I think we'll need to start venturing further. He listens to what I have to say, and that feels good; it's one of the reasons I like visiting him. As usual he asks about the weather. Was there any sign of the storms coming? What about the snow? Does it still have ash in it?

He always asks about Marv last. I think Kane likes Marv, or at least he cares what happens to him, which, now that I think about it, might be different. His questions are always kind, but sometimes it's like he's enquiring after a once-faithful dog that's started to froth a little around the muzzle. When I was first chosen to replace Benjamin, Kane sent for me and told me that Marv had been a fine soldier, a man who had performed difficult service for his country. But he had seen things that no one should have to see and now he was a little bit broken, and I should take that into account when forming my opinion of him. He also told me it was my job to keep an eye on Marv, and to report back to him every once in a while on how he was doing. I've never mentioned this to Marv. I'm not sure how he feels about Kane, but I don't think Marv's the kind of person who'd care much for anyone looking over him, even if they meant well.

When we're done discussing Marv there's a pause in the conversation. Soon there'll be small talk for a while, and then he'll thank me again for coming, and that'll be my cue to exit. But first there's one more thing.

'Did you find me some?'

I nod, reaching into the pocket of my overalls for the container. I pull it out and place it on the table, pushing the plastic Tylenol bottle across the glass towards him. He's asked me to be discreet about the pills, which is why I don't tell Marv, and why I smuggle them past the Guardians. I don't think anyone would blame him for needing them though, not even Marv. I wouldn't be able to sleep either, if I'd had to do what he did. I mean, Kane's the reason the world is how it is outside, why nothing works anymore, why there's a gaping hole where something called the O-Zone used to be. But if he hadn't done what he had, if he hadn't defeated the virus, it would have been so much worse.

Kane looks at the container for a moment, but makes no move to pick it up. I always pay close attention when I hand him his pills. I've been watching for it, the look Jack used to get, but so far there's nothing. Kane says we're the Chosen Ones, and that's why we were saved. But he's the one who brought us here, the one who holds Eden together.

We can't afford for him to unravel.

*

IT WASN'T JUST KANE, of course; it was Miss Kimble that saved us too. If it hadn't been for her first grade class on civics and government we wouldn't even have been there in the first place.

It's not the sort of thing you'd expect is it? I mean, don't get me wrong, coloring in pictures of Uncle Sam and the Statue of Liberty sure beat having to do math problems. Even listening to Miss Kimble talk about the constitution and democracy and our civic duty was better than having to do regular schoolwork. Some of it even made sense. Like power and authority, and who had it (principal Delaney, the teachers, even the bus driver) and who didn't (kids, for the most part). And I got it when Miss Kimble said that you weren't free to just do whatever you wanted whenever you felt like it, like cutting in line, or bullying people. I noticed she looked long and hard at Kurt when she said that bit. But something that might be useful when the world's about to end? Hardly likely, right?

Miss Kimble said she was surprised when she found out, because she claimed she didn't remember applying. But she must have, because she got a letter from our Congressman saying we'd been accepted. A tour of the White House. Not the whole thing, obviously. You can't just have seven-year olds wandering around the Oval Office, spilling their juice boxes on the carpet and hiding boogers under the President's chair. But we'd get to see some of it. And more importantly, it was a day out of school.

Tell the truth, I actually didn't mind school that much. Sure, I wasn't one of the popular kids. I wasn't, as Miss Kimble put it in my first end of term report, *well integrated socially*. But it had only been a couple of months and I've always been a slow burn; the other kids would come round to liking me eventually. And besides, it meant I still got to see Mags every day, which was cool.

Still, though, visiting the White House was going to be special. The whole class had been excited for weeks. Even Angus and Hamish, who I suspect were only vaguely aware of what was going on in Miss Kimble's class most of the time, and who would have had real difficulty finding what they called 'Warshington' on the map, unless you'd left a Twinkie next to it.

I was living with Sam and Reuben at the time. They were an older couple. They'd never had any children of their own so they took in kids like me. Reuben taught at the local community college and Sam was a writer. Mom would have liked them, I think. Their house was an old brownstone out in Sparrow's Point. A little run down, always a little cluttered. They had books everywhere – stacked two deep in shelves, on window sills, even in random piles on the floor – and they never seemed to mind if I picked one up and looked at it. The place smelled of coffee and bagels, and when it was raining out, their spaniel, Jackson. They seemed, I dunno, relaxed. Comfortable in their skin.

I'd been out of Sacred Heart a couple of months by that point. I still had to go back once a week for my therapy session. Mr. Cartwright was a nice man with a big beard and an obvious corduroy problem. He said we'd made some real progress. He'd suggested early on that I give my fear a name, so that I could reason with it. I chose Claus. (Get it? Yeah, I know, but cut me some slack, okay, first grade, remember?). In my defense, I'd been dubious about this idea of Mr. Cartwright's from the beginning. It turned out I was right. Mr. Cartwright's long gone of course, but Claus is still with me all these years later. And now as well as this really useful fear of dark, enclosed spaces I get his whiny voice in *my* head whenever *he* feels like it.

On a more positive note the bedwetting was under control, mostly, and I'd been trying really hard to keep a lid on my newly-christened claustrophobe. I guess I was hoping Sam and Reuben might want to keep me around. Not that it would matter, as it turned out. Baltimore got hit in the first strikes, so the issue of what to do longer term with their periodically incontinent charge was one that Sam and Reuben never had to face. I hope it was quick for them.

Anyway, I'd been really excited about going to the White House that day. I'd hardly slept a wink the night before, and for once it wasn't because of Claus. We'd all been worried for weeks that it was going to get cancelled. Looking back I guess things had been unraveling for some time, but when you're a kid you don't always get what's going on in the world of adults. There were glimpses of course, clues. Reuben and Sam hadn't cared much for the T.V. before, but now the set in the kitchen was tuned to CNN all the time. Sometimes they'd just stare at it in silence, or Sam would put her hand to her mouth and Reuben would shake his head.

It was the same in school. One of the other teachers would come into our classroom in the middle of a lesson and whisper something to Miss Kimble and she would look down at the floor while she listened. And then she'd ask a question, or simply close her eyes. Sometimes she'd leave the room and we'd hear them talking outside, and when she'd come back in she'd have on this big smile that stopped somewhere south of her eyes. One day Principal Delaney came into our class and took Miss Kimble out. When she came back a few moments later her eyes looked red, like she'd been crying, and this time there wasn't even a smile. She told us the President had died and the school would be closed for the rest of the week. When I heard that I was sure our trip to the White House was going to get cancelled.

But somehow it wasn't. I guess with all that was going on they must have just forgotten to tell us not to come.

*

THERE'S STILL AN HOUR to go until curfew when I leave Kane so I head back to the mess. Maybe Mags will still be there.

She's deep in conversation with Beth when I walk in, so I don't think she sees me. I resume my seat at the end of the boys' table. The discussion about who's going to get matched with whom is still going strong. Everyone has their own top five, of course, but there's general agreement on who the most attractive girls in Eden are, so there's quite a bit of overlap. The exact order is a subject of continuous debate, however. Mags has actually risen up the rankings quite a bit since she decided to grow out her mohawk.

Eventually Beth gets up and leaves and I catch Mags' eye. She throws me a look and I nod back. She gets out of her seat right away and heads for the door that leads out into the corridor where the toilets are. None of the Guardians seem to be looking over, but I wait a couple of minutes before following her out, just in case. I head straight for the stairwell, taking the steps two at a time. Mags is waiting for me on the third floor landing; she's already removed the hex bolts in the access panel above her head. The first time we tried this she had to steal an Allen key from Scudder's toolbox so we could loosen them. Now we just make the bolts finger tight when we replace them, so they're easy to unscrew next time.

I check there's no one on the stairs or the landing below, then I slide the panel out of the way. The metal screeches a little as it shifts, but then it's done. Mags gets into position and I put my hands around her waist and lift her up. When we first started doing this I used to have to help her because she couldn't reach. But the ceilings are low in Eden and Mags is a lot taller now, so I think she could probably manage it by herself. Not that I mind. Boys and girls aren't supposed to touch of course, but there's no one up here to see us. Besides Mags doesn't weigh much and she always smells good, of soap and warm cotton. Tonight there's something else as well, a deep, rich aroma that I realize I've noticed before. It's annoyingly familiar, and yet I can't immediately place it. I feel like if I just stood here a little while longer it would come to me, but Mags has already disappeared into the ceiling so instead I haul myself up after her. I slide the panel back into place behind me so no one will know we're here. There's a narrow crawl space that we have to negotiate on our hands and knees. Claus really doesn't care for it much, but in no time we're at the other end and Mags is pushing aside the second access panel that opens onto the roof.

I pull myself through and stand. The cavern's granite dome is right above my head; if I were to reach up it feels like I could almost touch the mesh of brace wire covering the rock there. The mess is close to the center of the cavern and its metal roof sits directly under the main vent, a shaft not much more than a couple of feet square that rises all the way up through the rock to the mountain's surface, hundreds of feet above us. I try not to think about what it would be like to be trapped in the tight confines of that shaft, but as usual I can't help it; all it takes is the sight of the vent's dark concrete-lined opening to trigger that image.

I slip off my boots and step carefully over to the corner. Mags is already waiting for me, her feet dangling over the edge, the arc lights bolted to the cavern roof casting multiple shadows around her. I wish she wouldn't sit so close. I make out like it's because I'm worried somebody on Front Street might look up and see us, but that's not it. Nobody ever looks up in Eden; as long as we keep our voices down there's little chance we'll be spotted up here. The real reason is that weird feeling I get, that tingling sensation that travels up from my private parts to the pit of my stomach, when I see her perched right on the edge like that. I sit down beside her, a little further back from the edge, and slowly shuffle forward.

'So what was all that with Kurt?'

I shrug.

'He was just being an asshole.'

Mags nods. She gets Kurt better than most. He's always reporting her to Kane for something.

'What were you guys talking about after dinner?'

I hesitate. I like talking about most things with Mags. Our conversations are rarely stilted or awkward, and I don't have to worry about keeping my vocabulary on a tight leash, so no one figures out I'm reading on the outside. But somehow she never wants to discuss this. I know if I tell her she'll just go quiet, or stare off into the distance as if she's seen something sad there. I don't understand; it's the only thing anyone talks about in Eden now. I mean, how can you not be interested in who you're going to be matched with?

Mags must sense my reluctance because she doesn't call me on it. There's a long pause, then she changes the topic.

'Did Lena talk to you?'

I shake my head, no.

'Well, she's going to come ask you to get her something from outside.'

I already get Lena things from the outside that Mags doesn't know about, so this must be something different.

'Do you know what?'

'Nope, she wouldn't say.'

'Do you know if she has anything to trade?'

Mags makes an exasperated sound and I realize I've inadvertently strayed into difficult territory.

'You'll never get it, will you Gabriel?'

We've had variations of this conversation before, so I think I know what she means. But then there's a whole bunch of things Mags thinks I don't get, which makes it a pretty broad question. I do know she's annoyed with me though; Mags only uses my full name when she's pissed at something I've done. I figure it's best to hedge my bets and feign ignorance.

'Get what?'

She turns around to look at me.

'There's only us left. You can't just look out for yourself anymore. Maybe there'll come a day when you need something and you don't have anything to trade.'

I shrug. I really don't see that happening; Marv and I are the only ones that go outside. But I know from past experience that pointing this out won't help. It'll just earn me a *that's-really-not-good-enough* look that even I won't have trouble deciphering.

We sit there for a while, not saying anything. Eventually Mags breaks the silence.

'So, did you find anything new?'

'Yeah. A book by this guy Stieg Larsson. Seems good so far. You're going to love the heroine. Want to start now?'

She nods and the tension immediately drains out of the conversation. This is our thing. She needs the stories as much as I do, but books aren't allowed in Eden, at least not for Juvies. So I relay whatever I'm reading on the outside. Actually, it's not as easy as it sounds, especially if I haven't finished the book myself. But I think I'm getting better at it. The trick is knowing what to summarize and where to recount as much of the detail as I can remember.

We probably only have a few minutes, so I dive straight in, explaining how the story begins with the delivery of a pressed white flower to an old man. The old man's been receiving flowers from the same mysterious source each year for almost forty years. Because we're short on time I cut through Blomkvist's trial pretty quickly. When we get to Dragan Armansky's security firm and the introduction to Lisbeth Salander I linger, trying to recall as accurately as possible Larsson's description of the difficult young punk heroine with the piercings and the tattoos. When I describe her hair – short as a fuse, Larsson had written – I notice Mags' fingers reaching for her own cropped locks.

We've just got to Salander's meeting with the lawyer Frode when the curfew buzzer sounds and we both scramble for the hatch. When we get back down to the third floor landing Mags heads straight for the stairs while I replace the bolts in the access panel. As she reaches the top step she turns around and makes me promise to meet her on the roof after dinner tomorrow so I can finish telling her what I've read.

*

I'VE KNOWN MAGS the longest. Since my first day at Sacred Heart, before Miss Kimble's class even.

Sacred Heart was where I got sent after Jack got busted. A social worker called Mrs. Gruber took me back to the house and helped me pack some clothes in a bag. She let me keep a photograph of Mom that I used to have on my nightstand, but I didn't get to bring anything else. There wouldn't be space where I was going, Mrs. Gruber said.

I remember the sign outside, the day she drove me there. *The Sacred Heart Home for Children*, it announced, in once-white letters set against a faded blue background. A large woman with a deep, booming voice met us at the door and introduced herself as Mrs. Wilmington. Mrs. Gruber said Mrs. Wilmington was in charge and I had to do exactly as she said.

After Mrs. Gruber had left Mrs. Wilmington gave me the tour. The hallways were tiled and smelled of furniture polish, and underneath it of dust and old newspapers. There was a large dining hall, with long tables and wooden benches, where meals were served, and two large dormitories, one for boys and one for girls, each filled with rows of narrow, neatly made cots. The tour ended in the day room, which was empty. Mrs. Wilmington explained that the other children were out, but they'd be back later. She said she had things to do and so I should amuse myself until it was time for supper.

I asked Mrs. Wilmington whether there were any books that I could read. She smiled broadly, like I had done something good instead of just asking for what I wanted, and brought me to the far corner of the day room to a single, narrow bookshelf she rather grandly called the library. Mom used to take me to the library, back when we lived in New Orleans, and it was *way* bigger than this, but I decided to keep that fact to myself. Mrs. Wilmington pointed to the lowest shelf, where the books for young kids were kept. It was a bunch of crap like *Fox and Rabbit Are Friends* and *Flapjack's First Full Moon* and *Skippyjon Jones in Mummy Trouble*, but I said thanks anyway, because that's just being polite. I'd already seen some of the books for older kids on the higher shelves that looked way more interesting.

I hadn't noticed when I first entered the room, but there was a girl sitting on the ground by the shelves, a battered paperback in her lap. Her head was down, buried in her book, and her dark brown bangs obscured her face, but I remember thinking she seemed about my age. She didn't look up when we arrived over, not even when Mrs. Wilmington boomed hello at her.

It was pretty clear she didn't want to be disturbed, so after Mrs. Wilmington left I worked my way along the shelves looking for something to read. There were a few promising titles, even some stuff Mom had read to me. *The Lord of the Flies, Robinson Crusoe, The Adventures of Tom Sawyer.* A few well-thumbed *Harry Potters* (I've never really cared much for Harry Potter, but I get that I'm in the minority here. Or at least I was. Now I'm not so sure). In the end I plumped for *The Hobbit.* I'd already read it but it's a good story and I guess right then anything familiar seemed like just the ticket. I sat down on the ground at what I thought was a respectable distance and started to read.

After a while I was aware that she was looking at me. I don't know how long she'd been doing it. I was already at the bit where the dwarves arrive unannounced at Bilbo's and The Sacred Heart Home for Children had receded some time ago. When I looked up she didn't look away. She just held my gaze with those large brown eyes of hers. After a while she nodded at the book in my hands, an almost imperceptible gesture whose meaning was nevertheless instantly clear. I had made a good choice.

I recognized the paperback she was reading from the cover: *Watership Down.* It was the same one Mom had owned. We had discussed who the rabbit on the front was. I thought it was General Woundwort, because of the teeth and the dark silhouette. Mom thought Woundwort would be bigger and scarier. Her money had been on Hazel, but there was no way Hazel looked like that. Mom hadn't often been wrong, but when she was she could be way out there.

I guess I must have mumbled something similar back. Then we both went back to reading. At some point she got up and walked off in the direction of the kitchen, taking *Watership Down* with her (Never leave anything lying around here, she warned me solemnly, shortly afterwards). A little while later she reappeared with two glasses of milk, *Watership Down* still clutched under her elbow. She placed one of the glasses next to me and we continued reading.

It turned out Mags had arrived only a few weeks before, and so she was new to Sacred Heart, like me. But not, it seemed, to places like Sacred Heart. I asked her how she'd come to be here and she just looked at me for a while, as if deciding whether she might have misjudged me after all. Then she explained that that was the number one rule: no one ever talked about why they were here. I didn't really understand at the time, but I figured she'd been bouncing around foster homes longer than I had and therefore knew how stuff worked, so I just nodded. When I asked her why she wasn't out with all the other kids she said she'd had all her privileges removed for doing something naughty. She didn't elaborate. I would come to learn that Mags' privileges existed in a state of near-permanent suspension, and that for the most part that seemed to suit her just fine.

Sacred Heart turned out to be not that bad. A general air of neglect hung over the place, but the staff seemed nice, although with the exception of Mrs. Wilmington most of them didn't seem to have been there very long. There was a lot of routine, and not much in the way of privacy. Everyone had chores, but when you were done with those you could hang out in the day room. TV was restricted to one hour a night, unless your privileges had been removed, in which case you had to go to the dorm.

And it was exactly like Mags had said that first night we'd met. Nobody ever wanted to discuss how they'd ended up there, only when they were leaving and how. Those who still had parents talked about how they'd come back for them one day. Mags explained this to me with something approaching pity, which made me think she was like me and didn't have that particular hope to cling to. For the rest of us it was what our new parents might be like. It was the younger kids who found foster homes faster, but even the older children didn't stay in Sacred Heart indefinitely. You were just there while they fixed you up, got you started on your therapy and then you got shipped out again. For most of us it was a month, two tops.

Not for Mags, though. Everyone knew she was going to be the exception. Like one of those dogs at the pound they can't find a home for because it keeps biting people.

*

A PALE WINTER SUN had been inching over the snow-capped mountains to the east as they finally joined the expressway that cut through the coastal plain, connecting the capital with Huichon to the north. It was less than a hundred kilometers to their destination, but potholes rendered the seventy kilometer per hour speed limit irrelevant and progress had been slower than she had expected, even travelling in the right hand lane reserved for party officials. At least there had been little traffic. Only an occasional military vehicle, belching smoke with every gearshift as it lumbered along in the other lane.

It had taken over an hour to reach Anju, but then they had rounded a bend in the road and Eliza caught her first glimpse of the vast Ch'ongch'on as it emptied into the Yellow Sea. The slowly rising sun glinted off the waters, sending fresh shards of pain into the space behind her eyes. She searched in her bag for her sunglasses, fumbling them on.

The first night, after she had cracked the ampule, she had been feverish, alternating between shivers and sweats, but since then the chills seemed to have settled in for the long haul. She was bundled up inside her coat and hat in spite of the hot air blasting out of the old car's vents and yet her very bones still ached with the cold, like they had been hollowed out and filled with ice water. Her hands were the worst. She had kept her gloves on, of course, but it didn't seem to make any difference. She just didn't seem to be able to keep them warm.

Once they had crossed the river the road turned inland and she must have finally dozed off for a little while, for when she woke the landscape outside had changed and she noticed they were slowing. The car ahead, the one containing Mike Etchells, the other member of the inspection team, and Kenny Lee, their translator, was indicating right. It took a minute for her to find the small faded green sign, partially obscured by vegetation, and to recognize the symbols that indicated their destination.

The convoy's progress slowed further as they left the expressway behind. Stones piled in small mounds by the side of the road suggested the potholes were a problem here too, although it didn't look like they'd been tended to in a while. She guessed it just wasn't a priority. She knew from the images the satellites sent her that the mountainous interior to the north was sparsely populated. They'd passed only the occasional ox-drawn cart since they'd left the highway.

The bouncing of the car's tired suspension finally woke Jan. He looked out of the window, taking a moment to assess where they were before turning to her. The fingers of one hand had been pressed to her temple, trying to massage the pain away, but now she let them fall into her lap. She had taken particular care in the bathroom that morning. She didn't normally wear makeup. Vanity was a sin of course, and besides, Eliza had long since given up believing there was any point. *You can't make a silk purse out of a sow's ear*, as her mother had been fond of reminding her. But thankfully she carried some basic items in her bag for emergencies. There was no disguising the way her cheeks had hollowed, or the fact that her eyes seemed to have sunken back into their sockets. But foundation had softened the dark circles underneath, and lipstick covered the grayish hue her lips had taken on overnight. When she was done she thought she looked like one of those painted harlots on the television that her mother liked to rail at, but it was better than the alternative. Nevertheless, Jan had taken one look at her in the hotel's tired lobby and had almost insisted that she go right back to her room and call a doctor. She had assured him that she was fine, and in the end he had relented. But she could see the concern on his crumpled face now.

'How are you feeling?'

'Oh, I'm fine. My own fault for drinking the water.'

She offered him her best smile, trying not to wince as the effort produced a fresh burst of pain behind her eyes. She remembered at the last moment to keep her mouth closed. The ulcers that had first broken out across the roof of her mouth had now spread all along her gums. She didn't need him to see that.

Jan Rasmussen shook his head.

'You really should have known better, Liz. You were told that the water isn't always properly treated. You don't want to be hospitalized here.'

He sounded annoyed, but she had worked for him long enough to know her boss was simply worried. She stared out of the window, pretending to focus on a small group of villagers, bundled up in an assortment of drab rags, already at work in a nearby field. She watched their breath hanging white in the morning air as they hacked away at the frozen earth. They looked as cold and miserable as she felt.

Well, just a few more hours and then it would be over. She told herself her discomfort was a small price to pay if she were successful. She'd witnessed enough in the few days she'd been here to convince herself that this was the right thing. The pastor had been right; sanctions would never work. In almost seven decades all they seemed to have done was impose hardship on the country's already long-suffering population. She knew from the frequent briefings they received at the agency that military intervention wasn't an option either. It wasn't the Chinese. Beijing had grown just as tired of its neighbor's antics as everyone else, and without the backing of its northern ally the regime was effectively defenseless. The old Soviet radar-controlled batteries left over from the war wouldn't be any use against cruise missiles or stealth bombers.

No, the problem was that they just didn't know where to target.

Enriched uranium simply had too weak a radiation signature; it was too easy to hide underground, to move from place to place. She had analyzed images from Hagap, Kumchangni, Hamhung and a dozen other locations that had been identified as potential enrichment sites. But there had been nothing to prove that these places didn't simply serve some other innocuous purpose. Jorg had joked that they could just as easily be giant storage facilities for statues of the goddam Dear Leader. Eliza didn't care much for blasphemy, but she had almost laughed out loud when the tall Norwegian had said that.

This however, this could work. She had faith that, if it were God's will, it would. And to think, it was she who would have made it happen. What did they call it when they sent those drones in to take out just one building? You saw it all the time on CNN. The grainy black and white footage overlaid with blinking icons as the laser-guided missile silently closed in on its mark. A targeted strike. That's what she was.

But unlike those missiles she would not cause anyone any harm. Not even Pak. She had been quite clear on that score from the very start. She was not one of those people like Jack Bauer – one of her favorite shows, in spite of all the awful things that man did – who could weigh up the good her actions would ultimately do and determine whether a certain measure of sacrifice could be justified. She knew there were parts of the Bible you had to read figuratively, no matter what the pastor might say. Jonah hadn't really spent three days in the belly of a whale and she doubted Noah had actually managed to round up two of every animal and herd them onto a big wooden boat when the rains began to fall and the Euphrates started to flood. She was pretty sure however that Thou Shalt Not Kill *was* one of those parts you *were* supposed to take literally; she certainly hadn't noticed any exceptions in the footnotes the last time she'd picked up her copy of the King James. But the pastor had assured her she didn't need to worry. The nanovirus the scientists had developed was very specific; it acted only on the bonds between the atoms of certain metals. It was entirely harmless to humans.

Eliza was not a scientist. She had however learned enough from her time at the agency to understand a little about the materials from which reactors were constructed. Uranium, plutonium or thorium for the fuel rods, of course, and zircaloy, steel or magnesium for the cladding. The centrifuges in the enrichment facilities would have maraging steel rotors, the casings would be machined from high-strength aluminum alloys. Pressure vessels and steam generators required radiation-resistant metals and stringent weld specifications to ensure they were capable of withstanding the intense, long-term radiation to which they would be exposed. How could the virus know how to target only those components that were safe to fail?

The pastor had spoken slowly and patiently, as if explaining a topic of considerable complexity to an audience that could not possibly hope to comprehend. And in truth Eliza had not understood. Electrostatic forces, conduction electrons, metallic bonding; it all meant little to her. When she had asked more questions she thought the pastor had sounded a little irritated. In the end he had simply told her that it was better that she did not know all of the details. He would do everything in his considerable power to protect her, of course, but her mission – he had actually called it a *mission*, which had made her feel a little bit like that delightfully wicked Jack Bauer – was not without some element of risk. He was after all sending her out among the heathens; she would be as a sheep among wolves. And if the wolves were to discover her, to question her, well then her innocence would be her defense. Eliza preferred the Old Testament, but she had always had a liking for that passage from Matthew. And when the pastor had spoken those words it had made her feel like she was doing a brave thing.

Of course she hadn't felt very brave. The thought of leaving her cubicle and travelling to this far-flung, Godless corner of the world had caused her more than one sleepless night since she had learned what she must do. But after the initial shock a small part of her had also been excited. She would finally be joining one of the inspection teams; at last she would get to visit one of the places she had been studying for so long. And think of the good she would do if her mission – *and yes, it was a mission, wasn't it?* – was successful. You so often heard it said, but here she had the opportunity to do something that would actually make the world a better, safer place.

Who was she to say no?

*

THE MORNING BUZZER sounds, and the lights in my cell come on. I think I was in the middle of a dream about Alice. Girls other than Mags didn't use to matter to me so much, but in the last year they've taken on a significance I'm not sure I fully understand. I don't know why I'm dreaming about Alice though; she's not in my top five. That's the thing with dreams, though: you just don't get to decide what they're about. For a second I try and shunt whatever I can into memory, to be examined later. But it's no use; the details are already evaporating. Within a few seconds I can't even be sure what was happening with Alice in the dream.

I hate the buzzer; everyone does. We've been waking up to it for ten years, but you don't ever get used to it. There's a speaker in each cell, recessed in the riveted ceiling behind a mesh grill that's locked down with hex bolts. I've tried disconnecting it of course; it wasn't that hard once Mags got me the right Allen key. But that still leaves the speakers in the corridors, and in the cells adjacent. And sound carries in Eden; it's like the steel walls were built to amplify the slightest noise. I'm the only one bunking on the top floor, of course, so I could just disconnect *all* of the speakers up here. But that would be pushing it. Kurt searches the cells during the day when we're at work, hoping to find something he can report. He's never been given to excessive flights of imagination, but that's just the sort of thing he'd spot.

Finally the buzzer shuts off and soon I can hear the sounds of feet hitting steel on the floors beneath me as Eden awakes. I showered when I got in last night so I can afford a few more minutes rack time before I have to get up, although now that I'm awake Claus is letting me know he's ready to get going. I've latched the top cot up so at least there's nothing hanging over my head, but the tiny cell's still way too cramped for his taste.

I roll off the cot and stand, taking care not to whack my head off the bulkhead lamp bolted to the ceiling. The metal floor's cold and I shift from foot to foot while I pull on the last clean t-shirt from the small upright locker and struggle into the patched and fraying overalls that hang on the back of the door. I sit back on the thin mattress to pull on socks and the canvas work boots that complete the Juvie uniform.

I step out of my cell into a narrow, low-ceilinged corridor. When we were still living in New Orleans Jack took me to see the USS Alabama. This place has the same feel as that old battleship had when you were below decks, all steel plate, riveted bulkheads and hatch doors. Claus doesn't like it much, but then I don't think he'd have made a very good sailor. I head for the stairs and join the small crowd of yawning Juvies spilling out on to Main Street, making their way over to the mess to grab something to eat before morning prayer. Claus feels better as soon as we're outside. It's all relative of course; he never really lets me forget that we're inside a hollowed out mountain. But at least out here it's bright, and the rock's several stories above my head.

As usual Kurt leads the Guardians to the front of the food line, but I'm happy to hang back and wait until they've filled their trays and taken them to their usual table by the door. The breakfast menu in Eden's not much more extensive than dinner; it's always either scrambled eggs or pancakes. I've never cared much for eggs, even the real ones Mom used to make, and the powdered substitute they get from stores just produces this watery mulch that looks like the paste Miss Kimble used to give us when we were doing art. If I had to choose I'd opt for pancakes, even though the mix is so old the pancakes haven't risen in years. It's like eating the cardboard center from a toilet roll. But at least you can smother them in maple syrup. That doesn't seem to go off, ever.

Thankfully it's Amy's shift in the kitchens this morning, so I'm not constrained by the regular breakfast menu. Amy owes me for a tube of acne cream I got for her last month. That's a demand item, not surprising given the demographic here in Eden. It's also one of the things that you've got to come to me directly for; stuff like that will never find its way on to one of Quartermaster's lists. From the fresh outbreak across Amy's forehead and cheeks it looks like the cream I got her's not working. I don't operate a returns policy, obviously, but I make a mental note to fetch her a different brand next time she asks.

Amy smiles when she sees me and asks what I want. She's really nice, but she's got these crazy prominent teeth, which, when you throw the acne into the mix is why, like Alice, she's never come close to making it into my top five. I really hope she's not my match. I've been trying to think of a way to raise the topic with Kane during one of our chats, to see if I can influence things, before any unfortunate decisions get taken. It's a tricky one. I mean, it's all supposed to be decided in accordance with God's divine will of course, so I don't want it to seem like I'm trying to interfere or anything. That might not go down well. But still, if you don't ask, right?

I decide on maple sausages and Amy heads back into the kitchens. I check that none of the Guardians are looking over and then I follow her. She comes out of the pantry a few moments later with an MRE and hands it to me with another smile before returning to serve the last of the stragglers still wandering up from the chapel. I tear open the plastic outer wrapper and remove the meal pouch. There's also a packet of blueberry granola and a cinnamon pop tart inside. The pop tart goes in my overalls pocket for later. The sausage patty slithers out of the foil pouch onto my plate. I remember the sausages Mom used to make being, well, *sausage*-shaped, but hey, beggars can't be choosers.

While the microwave's doing its thing I wolf down the blueberry granola. It's got milk powder already mixed in, so you've just got to add a little water and you're good to go. I'm just scooping the last of the blue sludge out of the bottom of the packet when the microwave pings to let me know the sausage is done. The square patty comes out of the oven spitting and hissing like it's mad at me for something. It doesn't look that appetizing but it's actually not that bad. I'm just finishing the last bite when the buzzer for morning prayer sounds. I stack the plate in the back of one of the big industrial dishwashers, gather up the other packets and wrappers from the MRE and dispose of them in the trash. It's important to get rid of the evidence. If Kurt found out about my *à la carte* breakfasts I'd definitely get reported. Kane likes me, and I get him his pills, so I doubt I'd get in that much trouble. But Amy might cop for some more serious penance, and then I'd be back to eggs and pancakes for a while, no matter how much zit cream she owes me for.

I wait in the kitchen until everyone's left the mess and then slip out, joining the back of the group making their way down towards Back Street. We file into the chapel and take our usual seats in the wooden pews, girls on the left, boys on the right, the Guardians in their black overalls filling the rows at the back. It takes a second for my eyes to adjust to the gloomy interior after the glare of the cavern's arc lights. Kane's already up on the altar, watching us shuffling in, his hands resting on either the side of the pulpit. A plain wooden cross hangs behind him, but otherwise the metal walls are bare, save for a single piece of framed needlework that hangs, yellowing, to one side. *Ora et Labora* it reads. I asked Kane once what those words meant. Prayer and Work, he said. Prayer and Work.

As soon as the last person's found their spot Peck closes the door behind us and we begin. The pews are hard and after a few minutes everyone's fidgeting in their seats. To be fair to Kane he does try and mix it up a little, but most days the message is the same. We're God's Chosen Ones, all that's left of His flock; when the time is right it'll be our job to go out and multiply, to fill the earth and conquer it. It won't be easy. He says we'll be like the first disciples, who were sent forth as sheep among wolves. That's his favorite passage; he uses it all the time, even though it's from the Gospels, which isn't where he mostly goes for his material.

I think he's just trying to inspire us, but Mags thinks it's a stupid thing to keep saying. None of the Juvies have set foot outside since we got here, so there's already enough anxiety about what it'll be like when that time comes, especially with the stores the way they are and no sign of the weather changing. I've told her there aren't any actual wolves out there any more, they would have starved a long time ago, but she just says that's another good reason not to run on about them at every end and turn. I'm not sure it's such a big deal, but she says it's easier for me, because at least I know what it's like outside, and not knowing is always the scariest thing.

*

KANE SAYS IT WAS GOD'S WILL that we were saved. But on the morning of what we would afterwards call the Last Day it was the same tired yellow school bus that stopped at the end of the street and picked me up. I've often thought there had to be a more reliable way of making sure His Chosen Ones got to where we needed to that morning. But then Kane's always telling us the Lord likes to move in mysterious ways, so maybe this was just one of them.

I'd never cared much riding the bus, of course, and maybe that's part of why I've always considered it such an unsatisfactory chariot for our salvation. I like rules, you see. There's a definition to them, a certainty. With rules you know where you stand. And on the bus there were no rules. I mean, there *were* rules, obviously, like sit in your seat, and don't distract the driver, and don't hock a loogie on the kid sitting in front of you. It's just that there was no way of enforcing them. The driver had to watch the road, which meant unless you were in the front couple of rows you were off his radar. Any further back and whatever rules might in theory have existed carried no more weight than the graffiti that was scrawled on the back of the narrow bench seats.

Mom used to have this thing she'd quote about troubles. Or maybe it was sorrows. She'd say that when they came it was not as single spies but in battalions. I think that's also true of assholes. They like to travel in packs. And on the school bus the pack sits at the back.

That morning when I got on the seats near the front were all taken so I made my way down the aisle. There was a soft hiss behind me as the door closed, then a crunch of tired gears as the driver popped the clutch and I had to steady myself as the bus lurched out into traffic. I hadn't even sat down and he'd already forgotten about me. A couple of kids looked up as I passed, but I wasn't of interest and they quickly returned to whatever private mayhem they had been involved in before I got on.

The first free seat that morning was two-thirds of the way down – deep into asshole territory – but there was little choice so I made for it. As I got closer I saw that Kurt was sitting in the row behind the spot I'd chosen. That was bad news. Kurt was mean even back then. I tried not to make eye contact, but I was aware of him staring at me through that lank brown hair of his, that lazy grin hovering over those fleshy lips. As I got to the seat in front of him I saw him lean across the aisle and say something I didn't catch to Angus and Hamish, who as usual had managed to squeeze themselves into the row opposite. The Fat Twins looked up at me and brayed with laughter.

I scooched in, clutching my bag to my chest to make room for Mags when she got on. After a minute or so Kurt leaned forward and said 'Hey, dork, read any good books lately?' I felt myself flush, but I continued to stare out the window, pretending not to have heard, clinging to the hope that maybe he would soon tire of his game. But a few seconds later he repeated it, louder this time.

The bus shuddered to a halt outside Sacred Heart and Mags got on and made her way down the aisle. Things seemed to have gone quiet in the seat behind and for a moment I allowed myself to think that maybe my tormentor had just gone back to whatever asshole things he had been doing before I got on.

But then it started again. It was the same line – like I said, Kurt's never been burdened with an overactive imagination – only now he said it loud enough for the kids in the seats around us to stop what they were doing and focus on this latest drama. Even Mags turned to look at me. I continued to stare straight ahead, committed to my strategy, thinking there were only a couple more stops before we got to the school.

It went quiet again for a while and then I heard the unmistakable sound of Kurt slowly filling the back of his throat and a second later I felt something thick and wet, with the consistency of warm jello, splat into the back of my neck. It stayed there for a moment, before slowly start to slide down inside my shirt. I tugged the sleeve of my sweater down over my thumb and furiously tried to wipe it away. Across the aisle the Fat Twins were howling with laughter. This time everyone in the seats around us joined in.

Beside me Mags opened her satchel and pulled out a book. Nobody ever read on the bus, so she could only be doing this to hide her embarrassment. But she made no attempt to open it and the book just sat there in her lap, the fingers of her left hand loosely curled around the base of the spine. My face was still bright red, and I didn't want to catch her eye, but the book intrigued me and I risked a sideways glance. It was an old hardback edition of *Black Beauty*. I'd noticed it on one of the shelves of what Mrs. Wilmington had rather grandly termed Sacred Heart's library the day I'd arrived.

With my humiliation complete Kurt turned his attention to Mags. It was clear he planned to use the same approach. At first Mags ignored him, just as I had. Angus and Hamish had figured out what was coming and were giggling in anticipation. I remember thinking I had to do something. Surely I couldn't allow this to happen to her as well? But when I heard the same horrendous hawking sound I stayed rooted in my seat, just waiting for the inevitable to happen.

And suddenly I noticed Mags wasn't sitting next to me anymore. When I turned around to check where she'd gone I saw she'd stepped out into the aisle. For the briefest instant I thought she was going to commit the cardinal sin and tell the bus driver. But as I looked around I saw she was facing in the opposite direction, towards the back of the bus. The slim hardback was raised across her small body, like she was a tennis player getting reading to deliver a backhand. For one frozen instant she held it there, and I could see the fingers that had been curled lightly around the base of *Black Beauty's* spine were now gripping it so tightly that they had turned white. Then in one smooth movement she brought the book down and around, hard. It caught Kurt square across the jaw, with a *Thwap!* that cut through the general sounds of mayhem coming from further down the bus. There was a moment of silence while everyone who wasn't already following the drama looked around to see what had happened.

One side of Kurt's face was already turning red; I could feel the sting from where I was sitting. His mouth had dropped open and the gob of phlegm he had been about to launch at Mags was hanging in mid-air, suspended from his chin. His eyes were welling up and tears were only seconds away, waiting for the shock to dissipate and the reality of what had just happened to him to sink in.

Mags stood in the aisle, *Black Beauty* still grasped in one hand, waiting to see if her work was done. Angus and Hamish had recoiled in their seat, as if they really didn't want to be this close to the action any more. Their eyes were wide and their mouths formed perfectly matching 'O's, and for an instant all I could think about was Barney and Rubble, the two goldfish that Mom had let me keep in my room when she had still been alive.

And then Kurt started bawling. Mags waited a moment longer and then calmly sat back down, as if the commotion behind her was happening somewhere else entirely. I remember her taking a moment to inspect Black Beauty's cover, and then, satisfied no damage had been done, she placed it carefully in her satchel.

Kurt's wailing continued all the way to school. When we arrived in the parking lot the older kids got off, because it was only the first graders that were going to Washington that morning. Miss Kimble was already waiting in the yard with the rest of the class who hadn't come in on the bus and Kurt scrambled up the aisle and went straight up and told her what Mags had done. I was pretty sure the trip would be cancelled then; it already seemed like it had been hanging by a thread for weeks. Miss Kimble came onto the bus and asked Mags if she had done what Kurt had said. When Mags said she had Miss Kimble looked hard at her and at Kurt and then just said she would be taking it up with Mrs. Wilmington when we got back. As it turned out Miss Kimble wouldn't be talking to Mrs. Wilmington about anything, ever again. But of course none of us knew that at the time.

Kurt gave Mags a wide berth for a long time after that. He reports her for a lot of stuff now, more than any of the rest of us, even me. And occasionally, when he thinks no one's looking, I catch him staring at her in a way that scares me. Like he's just biding his time. Like nothing has been forgotten.

*

AFTER BREAKFAST I head over to the stores. That's where I work, when I'm not out scavenging, that is. Everyone works in Eden, six days a week, from lights on to curfew. When we're not in the chapel praying that is. *Ora et Labora*. Whoever hung that sign knew exactly what Eden was all about.

The stores occupy a separate cavern off the old pedestrian tunnel that leads from the western end of Front Street out to the power plant and beyond the armory. The walls are the same roughhewn granite you find in the main cavern, but instead of a dome the space that's been carved out of the rock here is narrow and long, with a high, vaulted roof. The only light comes from the single bulkhead lamp that still works, by the door; further back they're all dead, the bulbs either blown or removed for the main cavern or the farms, just like out in the tunnels. Rows of riveted metal shelves reach from the concrete floor all the way up to the ceiling, maybe twenty feet above my head, stretching all the way into the darkness at the back.

I work for Quartermaster. The stores are his domain, and that makes him pretty important. Everything that was here when we arrived, everything the farms produce, everything that Marv and I bring in, it all goes through him. I can get you some things, mostly small items, stuff that he won't bother with. But for anything else you need in Eden, it's Quartermaster you have to talk to.

He's already here when I arrive, sitting behind a large metal table to one side of the bulkhead door. He's an impossibly fat man with a perpetually vexed, wide-eyed expression on his jowly face. If it wasn't for the fact that he's completely bald he'd look like a big, bad-tempered barn owl. He pretends to ignore me for a while, continuing to work on the sheet of paper in front of him on his makeshift desk. The top half of the page is already covered with his neat script, which means his latest list is almost finished. We'll be going out again shortly.

The lists are of things Quartermaster wants us to get outside. When I get a new one I always scan it quickly, to see if there's anything different, although I have to try not to make it seem like that's what I'm doing. It's always the same stuff. Food of course, although nothing in cans, which rules out most of what little's still out there. Vitamin pills. Toothpaste. Soap. Deodorant. Shampoo. Laundry detergent. Tampons. Maalox and Dulcolax (both for Quartermaster; I don't think he's learned his MRE lesson yet). Toilet paper's always a demand item.

I'm not sure we really need the lists anymore, but I think Quartermaster likes making them. The letters are always impeccably proportioned, the items always equally spaced, even when the paper he's using isn't lined. It's like he's laid a ruler down and written on it, although I know he can't have – his lower case descenders are always perfect. I'm pretty sure he does this on purpose. I think he believes the word shapes are important to me. Mags says that's good though; it means he can't suspect about the books I have on the outside.

I don't think I'd mind the lists so much if we didn't have to go through the routine of identifying each of the items he's written down every time he gives me a new one. I must have seen hundreds of Quartermaster's lists by now, and they're all pretty much the same. But still he has to make sure I understand every word, like I'm some slow-witted child. Sometimes I really have to bite my tongue. It's not that I know *all* the words. Occasionally I'll come across something new in a book I'm reading that I need to look up, which is why I keep a dictionary under my bed in the farmhouse. But I certainly don't need help with things like 'soap' and 'toilet paper'. I've complained to Mags about this but I don't get much sympathy; she thinks I need to keep my vocabulary on a much shorter leash as it is. So I play along. On those rare occasions when something shows up on one of his lists that I haven't seen before I put on my best stumped face, like a chimpanzee being asked to do a particularly complicated puzzle. With a sigh Quartermaster will explain what the word is, and then he'll walk me through the alternative names he's written down, and the word shape for each. When he's done with his explanation I count slowly to five, and then I finish with a tentative smile or a nod to let him know I've got it. Sometimes I'll even do my baffled primate act for a word I should know, and he'll have to get up from his desk and fetch a stick of deodorant or a bottle of shampoo so he can show me what he means. I figure the exercise is good for him; it's the only time he ventures back among the shelves any more, and I can't remember the last time I saw him in the vicinity of one of the ladders.

Quartermaster finally looks up from his list. My backpack's already made its way over from scanning; it's sitting on the floor, next to Marv's. It probably got dropped off hours ago, but Quartermaster likes to wait until I arrive to go through what we've brought back. He motions to it and I lift it onto the desk. His sausage fingers work the plastic snaps and zippers with surprising dexterity; one by one he removes the contents, lining them up in front of him. His movements become more and more agitated as he gets deeper into the pack; by the time he's removing the last items they're diving in and out like fat little hummingbirds. Every so often he glances up at me and I can tell he's working himself up to complain about how little I've brought back, even though the pack was almost full. But then his fingers find the bottle. He pulls it out slowly and holds it up, examining the label. A single malt's a rare treat, and whatever rebuke he was getting ready to deliver has already begun to evaporate by the time he sets it on the desk. Right now I suspect he'd rather I wasn't even here.

Well, I can certainly oblige with that.

'I was thinking of doing the rounds this morning. Seeing what we might need, you know, before we get locked down.'

Quartermaster tears his eyes off the whisky and looks up at me. His voice is unusually high-pitched for a man of his size.

'Yes, yes, Gabriel. If you had given me the chance I was about to tell you to do that.'

I mumble sorry and make for the door before he has a chance to change his mind. My hands are already on the latch handle when I hear my name again.

'Aren't you forgetting something?'

His hand flutters dismissively over the items he's unloaded from my backpack. I return to the desk and start gathering them up, returning them one by one to the pack. I notice the bottle of Glenfiddich has already been separated from the herd; he doesn't want me taking that anywhere. When I'm done I sling the pack over my shoulder and pick up Marv's from beside the desk.

'Now Gabriel, I'll be busy with this list for a while.' He makes a show of straightening the single sheet of paper he'd been working on when I arrived, but before he can help himself his eyes shift back to the bottle. 'It would be appreciated if you could try not to make too much noise back there.'

I nod, then make my way in among the shelves.

Quartermaster won't care how long I'll be; he's going to be occupied for a while. All the same, I don't plan to linger. It's not as bad as outside in the tunnel, but Claus still doesn't care for it much back here. It's dark, and the roof might be high, but the metal shelves form narrow canyons that are altogether too tight for his taste. You don't get to choose where you work in Eden.

When I've gone far enough in I set the backpacks down on the dusty concrete. Each section has a ladder, to allow you to climb up to the higher shelves. I pull the nearest one over, the heavy steel vibrating as it slides reluctantly on its runners. Paint still clings in the corners of the steps and on the undersides, but elsewhere years of use have worn the treads back to the metal.

I open my backpack first and start removing items. The only light comes from the single bulkhead lamp by the door, where Quartermaster sits with his whisky and his list, but it's just enough for me to make out what I'm doing. Any further along and I'd probably need a flashlight, but Marv and I don't bring back enough in a season to make that necessary. Soon winter'll be on us and what little we've stashed will start retreating back towards the entrance again.

It wasn't like this when we first arrived. The bulkhead lamps above shone bright back then, and the shelves were all stocked, stacked floor to ceiling with boxes and crates and drums containing all kinds of food and other things we'd need. But that was years ago. They're mostly empty now, except for a half-dozen or so sections way off in the darkness near the end wall. All that's left is racks of old metal, the surfaces dented, scuffed, scratched, the rivets worn smooth. I won't have much trouble finding space for what we've brought back.

When I'm done with my pack I open Marv's and start removing the items he's collected. I have to hold them up to the light from the entrance to read the labels. When the lamps first started to wink out and there were no more spares to replace them I asked Marv why we didn't just go looking for more outside. He just told me not to act bixicated. Nothing like that works out there anymore, on account of what Kane had to do to defeat the virus. I sometimes wonder what it must have been like to have been outside when it happened, to have watched the missiles, wave after wave of them rising from their bunkers on columns of fire. To have seen the night burn white with the light of a thousand suns as they reached their detonation altitude, in the same moment the pulse they released plunging everything beneath into everlasting darkness.

*

AFTER I'M FINISHED stacking shelves I make my way over to the farms. There's always stuff Jake needs, although by now I know almost as well as he does when they're likely to be running low on something. But doing the rounds gets me out of stores, so there's no need for Quartermaster to know that. Besides, I think he prefers it if he thinks the help's not that bright.

The farms were Benjamin's idea. Not everyone was convinced we even needed them, in the beginning. I guess the stores looked all nice and full when we first arrived, so it was less obvious. But Benjamin was pretty smart. Even back then he was worried that we might be in here longer than anyone was expecting. His first request wasn't for much - just half a dozen fluorescent light tubes, a roll of heavy duty garbage bags and for Quartermaster to start saving him any containers that looked like they might hold water - so I think he was a little surprised when it got turned down. I guess Quartermaster didn't care much for receiving lists from Benjamin, rather than the other way around. But then of course Quartermaster had been the Secretary of Defense, and Benjamin was only a corporal.

Benjamin kept submitting his requests, but he didn't get any further, at least for a while. I don't think Kane liked the idea much at first, which can't have helped. The Bible mostly talks about crops being planted in soil, and ripening in sunshine, and so when Benjamin said you didn't actually need either of those things it probably didn't sound like it was part of any plan God might have for us. But Benjamin bided his time, and in the meantime he collected what he could get his hands on without having to go through Quartermaster. You'd see him sometimes in the mess, washing out used food cartons, or over in the tunnels by the furnace, sifting through the piles of garbage that were waiting to be burned. And then later, when we realized there was no sunshine anymore, and the ground outside had become frozen and irradiated, Kane sent for him and Benjamin laid out his plans again. And this time Kane prayed on it for a while longer and in the end he told Quartermaster and Scudder to give Benjamin whatever help he needed.

The farms are a lot bigger now. I think Benjamin would have been pleased. They take up three of the inner tunnels between the old diesel plant where Marv lives and the reservoir. The smell drifts out to meet me even before I leave the main cavern, growing stronger as I head further into the gloom. As I approach the first of the side tunnels I can see that the fluorescents are off. I stop at the entrance and look in. A couple of flashlight beams bounce around in the darkness near the back and I can just about make out what looks like Stephanie and maybe Beth moving among the growing benches. The plants need both light and darkness to grow, so each tunnel has an eight-hour night cycle. That's when the roots get sprayed and the catch trays are emptied; if you let too much light get to the tubers they come out green and you can get sick if you eat them.

Claus has no interest venturing into the darkness, so I hang back near the entrance and call in as nonchalantly as I can to see if either of them has seen Jake. There's some discussion I can't make out and then Beth shouts back that he's probably in the next tunnel, dealing with the harvest.

I head farther along, away from the main cavern. The smell's much stronger now. It's not bad, once you get used to it: deep and rich, of the liquid fertilizer they use, and of things growing. As I approach the second tunnel I can see the lights are on and it's a hive of activity. But then the farms are always busy. It takes about two months from first chits for a crop to be ready to be picked, but Jake staggers the planting so they're bringing one in every couple of weeks.

As I step into the tunnel I see the skirts around the sides of the nearest bench have been lifted and Lucy and Jen are crouched down, carefully removing the potatoes from underneath. Lucy stands as I walk by, stretching out her back, and I catch a glimpse of a plant that's yet to be harvested. It's weird, seeing the roots just hanging there, the fat white tubers suspended in darkness, like some alien food. I check out the drying tables where the newly picked potatoes will sit for a few days to allow the skins to set before they get bagged and transferred to stores. Only half the tables are covered, and Lucy and Jen are almost at the end of the bench. Not a great crop; Quartermaster won't be happy.

It's not Jake's fault, of course. He runs everything on a pretty tight schedule, making sure the growing benches are always fully utilized; a little further along Alice has already started moving seed potatoes from the chitting trays into the bench Lucy and Jen are harvesting, and at the next bench over a handful of Juvies are at work cutting back haulms that have withered or yellowed, getting ready to bring in another crop. Still, it never seems to be enough. I counted the sacks we've got in stores only a few days ago. Winter's coming and we're lower than we've ever been.

Jake reckons the problem's the lights. He says Benjamin told him we should be replacing the tubes every year, as they dim. But there aren't any more spares in Eden, so we can't do that obviously. Instead Jake makes sure the tubes are kept spotlessly clean, so none of the light gets lost that way. He's also fashioned shades from scraps of aluminum foil scrounged from the kitchens and even the inside of foil packets taken from MREs, to reflect more light onto the plants. That was clever. I think Benjamin would have been proud of what he's done.

I find Jake near the back of the tunnel. The top of his gray overalls is tied loosely around his waist and there's a twenty-gallon water butt slung effortlessly over one shoulder. He's not quite as tall as me but he's broader, a hulking mass of muscle barely contained by his t-shirt. I guess hauling water up from the reservoir all day will do that for you. Even Angus and Hamish are careful around Jake. All the Juvies like him though, especially those who work in the farms. It pisses Kurt off no end. He's always trying to find something to report him for.

Jake looks up when he sees me and offers me a brief smile, but I can tell he's not happy. He slides the water butt off his shoulder and beckons me over to one of the growing benches. The plants are about a foot tall, which means they should be ready to harvest in a few weeks. The shoots look thin, though, and the leaves are smaller than they should be. As I look closer I can see that the edges have curled inwards, and most are dappled with brown spots. Jake pulls back one of the black plastic skirts, which he would never normally do while the lights are on. When I look inside I see why. The tubers hanging from the roots are shriveled and useless.

He lets the skirt fall back and looks up at me.

'Whole crop's like this.'

Jake's normally pretty upbeat, but right now he looks on the verge of despair. He knows how much Eden depends on what the farms produce.

'What's causing it?'

He shrugs his shoulders. 'Was hoping you might be able to tell me.'

I've got no idea, but my mind's already shifting gears, trying to work out how I'll find the solution. The libraries got turned over pretty bad when people started looking for things to burn, so I doubt there'll be any point looking for the answer there. But this whole area was farmland before, and there's no shortage of agricultural stores within scavenging range. They were mostly left alone, too. Whatever I need to fix this will probably just be sitting right there, on a shelf or in a storeroom somewhere, just waiting for me to pick it up. It'll just be a case of walking the aisles, trying to find a carton or a container with a description that matches the symptoms Jake's plants are showing. I realize I'm excited. It may not sound like much, but I've always liked puzzles and there's precious little else in the way of mental stimulation around here.

'Can you write me down a list of everything you've noticed? What the leaves look like, the roots, the tubers. Anything you can think of that's not normal. In as much detail as possible.'

It's out before I have time to think about it. Jake shoots me a strange look, like I've just asked him to map out the schematics for Eden's nuclear reactor. Mags is always reminding me that being able to read isn't the same as being smart, and she's right; Jake's certainly not stupid. He's been taking care of the farms since Benjamin died, and that can't have been easy. The plants need to be watered, fertilized and given periods of light and darkness according to a precise schedule that changes as they grow. It was a lot for him to remember, when Benjamin didn't come back.

But of course Jake can't write out a list of the symptoms; I suspect he can barely spell his own name. He glances around quickly, as if making sure no one else is close enough to have heard.

'Did Mags…?'

I don't register the words right then. I'm too busy beating myself up for being so careless. Jake isn't the type to go running to Kane to report me, so I doubt any real harm's been done, but that was stupid. I tell him I've just been going over one of Quartermaster's lists and I must have gotten a little confused. All I meant to ask was whether he'd noticed anything else that was wrong. Jake shakes his head, but he's still looking at me oddly, so I tell him I have to go. I promise I'll check in before I'm due to go out again, maybe take one of the plants with me.

It isn't until later that I think about what he actually said when I first asked him to make a list of the plant's symptoms. And why his first thought when those words came out of my mouth might have been of Mags.

*

AFTER THE FARMS I head over to the infirmary. I like to make sure it's stocked, especially coming up to winter, when Marv and I won't be going out. I'm not sure how much good it'll do, though. We don't have a doctor in Eden, which sooner or later is going to be a problem. Thankfully most of the injuries we've had so far have been cuts and bruises, the occasional sprain. I'm not sure what we'd do if there was anything worse. I certainly wouldn't want Scudder rummaging around inside me looking for my appendix. Kane says we should have faith that God will protect his Chosen Ones, but that didn't do Benjamin much good, did it? I don't say that out loud of course. There's a thin line between calling it the way you see it and blasphemy, and that's one thing there's little tolerance for in Eden. Still, I can't help but think how easy it would be for what happened to Benjamin to happen again. I made it my business to find a book on first aid, as soon as I started going outside. I keep it in the farmhouse, under my bed, in the box with my other books. I've read it cover to cover several times, but I'm still not sure I'd know what to do if anything bad were to happen.

The infirmary looks like it's in pretty good shape. We're running a little low on Band-Aids and antiseptic but I can pick those up on the next trip. There's no shortage of pharmacies out there, and people kept stuff like that in their homes too, so there's no need to go near the hospitals, which is just as well. Marv says we have to give those a wide berth.

I eat the pop tart I saved from breakfast on my way back to the stores. Lena catches up with me just as I'm finishing the last bite and pulls me into the darkness of one of the side tunnels. Claus doesn't like that much, but I tell him to be quiet. Lena's quite pretty, in a delicate, elfin sort of way. She features in almost everyone's top five, so I reckon it'd be okay if Kane decided she were my match. Although lately it looks like she's losing weight - she looks even more lost than usual inside her overalls - and this morning there are dark circles under her eyes, like she hasn't been sleeping well.

Once we're far enough back into the tunnel she steps a little closer, her gaze shifting back to the entrance to make sure we can't be seen. Her voice drops and I have to bend down to hear what she has to say. Her breath smells of toothpaste, but there's a trace of something sour underneath it, like she's just been sick.

'Did Mags speak to you?'

I nod.

'If I ask you for something from the outside can I trust you not to tell anyone?'

I think about this for a while. I can't see how it can hurt. Whatever Lena wants, if I'm not comfortable getting it I'll just tell her.

'Yes.'

'Not even Mags. Do you swear?'

'Sure.'

'Say it.'

'Okay. I swear.'

Lena looks at me for a long time, as if weighing up whether she can really trust me. I'm not sure if she ever comes to that conclusion. When I think about it later, back in my cell, I think she probably just realizes she doesn't have any other options.

'Is there something you can get me on the outside that will let me know whether I'm pregnant?'

At first I think I've misheard, but when I blurt out 'What?' it's like someone's just cut the strings on a puppet and Lena slumps to the floor and bursts into tears. I don't know how to deal with this, so for a long time I do nothing. In the end I sit down next to her on the concrete until her sobbing finally subsides.

When she's done she wipes her eyes with the back of her hand and looks up at me. I'm trying to think of something comforting to say, that it'll all be okay. But if she really is pregnant I can't see how it will be. I'm not sure what to say so I figure it's best if I stick to what I know.

'Well, I'm pretty sure there are tests out there. I've seen them on the shelves in the pharmacies. They'll be old, but they might still be good. I don't think they're that big. As long as there's no metal in them I should be able to find a way to smuggle one in past the Guardians.'

Lena looks up at me like I've just offered her salvation. I guess Mags is right: not knowing is probably a torment in itself.

'Can you get me one?'

'Sure. I can try. How far along are you?'

Lena looks at me blankly.

'I think the tests only work if you've been pregnant a while. When did, em, you and the father, when did it happen?' I realize I'm blushing. For once I'm thankful for the tunnel's darkness.

Lena looks down at the floor.

'There isn't a father. I've never been with anyone.'

I'm not sure what to say to this. I've always assumed the whole virgin birth thing was a one-time deal, and Mags says she has her suspicions about that too. I don't have much (okay, any) actual experience in this area, but the subject does come up surprisingly frequently in the books I read. I'm pretty sure you need to have had sex to become pregnant.

'But then, I mean, how can you be?'

Lena just bursts into fresh floods of tears. Between sobs I gather that she's been getting sick for the last couple of weeks and she hasn't had her period in over two months. If it's possible my face turns a deeper shade of crimson as I learn this last piece of information, but my embarrassment is mixed with relief. There must be lots of things that can account for those symptoms. Okay, granted, I don't know any of them, but they must exist; if she hasn't had sex with anyone it's bound to be that. When I tell her she seems to cheer up a bit. I promise to try and get her one of the tests anyway, just to put her mind to rest. She dries her eyes on the sleeve of her overalls and picks herself up off the floor. I'm about to head back out when she grabs my arm. This takes me by surprise a little, and even though we're by ourselves in the tunnel I can't help looking around to make sure no one's seen.

'Did you get me any?'

I hesitate for a second then reach into the pocket of my overalls and pull out a couple of pills I held back from Kane. It's not just the President who has trouble sleeping. Lena came to me shortly after Kane did, back when the nightmares first started.

'Careful with the ProSom. It's stronger than what I got you last time.'

She looks down at the two small pink pills in her hand, like it'll never be enough. I do have a couple more, and when she looks at me like that I'm tempted to hand them over, but I don't. She won't be the last to ask.

'When are you going out again?'

When I say I don't know she looks crestfallen so I add it probably won't be long. I tell her I'll try and get her some more then.

She closes her fingers around the pills and tells me thanks. Then she shoves her hand into the pocket of her overalls and heads back towards the farms.

*

I KNOW WHAT YOU'RE THINKING, but it's not like that, not really. I mean, the stuff on Kane's list is just medicine, to help you sleep. And I'm not doing this for money or anything; I don't even trade the pills for favors. Well, mostly. But nevertheless, the irony isn't lost on me. I've somehow managed to end up like Jack.

I don't think Mom would be entirely happy with how that turned out. But then I don't think Mom'd be happy with how a lot of things turned out, and besides, she's not around anymore. She died a long time ago, almost a year before we came to Eden. It was cancer. She didn't even know she had it until right at the end. I've thought about it a lot and I think that was a good thing. The not-knowing I mean. Not the cancer. Obviously.

When Mom died I was left with Jack. Jack wasn't my real dad or anything, so I guess he could have taken off right then, and to be fair to him he didn't. Still, all things considered I'm not sure Jack was great parent material. But then I guess Mom hadn't planned on leaving me when she did, so it wasn't really her fault.

Jack'd never had what you'd call regular employment. He made money selling guitars he built. Mostly that seemed to involve buying the parts cheap on the internet and then doing stuff to them to make it seem like they were old so he could describe what he was selling as 'vintage'. Mom would get mad at him sometimes and accuse him of trying to cheat people, but Jack would just look hurt and say he was only trying to create the most authentic product he could for his customers.

He had a workbench in the garage, back when we lived in New Orleans. I wasn't allowed to fool around in there on my own on account of the chemicals, but if Jack was working sometimes I'd go watch him. It was the smells I remember most. Naphtha, rubbing alcohol, the white frost that comes out of a can of compressed air when you hold it upside down and press the nozzle. Even hair dye. He had a special solution he used to use on the metal bits from the guitar. The bridge, the jack plate, the covers on the pickups, even the studs that held the strap in place, they'd all go in mason jars he'd fill with it. I think Jack's special solution was actually just the stuff you used to buy in the hardware store to clean concrete. I was with him once when he went to the Home Depot and asked for the biggest container of it they had, even though I'd never once seen Jack lift a finger to do any sort of cleaning in our yard.

After Mom died Jack moved us back to Maryland, where he was from. We rented a small house in a rundown street in a place called Dundalk. It wasn't as nice as where we'd lived in in New Orleans, but I figured I really wasn't in a position to complain. Jack had taken Mom's death pretty hard, and I had to cut him some slack for that, because I was missing her too. But looking back I reckon this wasn't Jack's first time because it seemed he picked it up again pretty easy. At first he'd make me play outside or he'd send me to my room, so I wouldn't see him. But I could tell. He'd get that look in his eye, the one I watch for when I give Kane his pills, and for a while at least not much else seemed to matter.

He'd stopped working on his guitars by then. Or maybe he just wasn't doing them right anymore and people had stopped buying them. I don't know exactly when he started dealing to fund his habit. Even by the end I doubt it was much; Jack had always been small time. But soon people I didn't recognize were coming over to our house. They all had the same look Jack used to get, and none of them seemed to have read the memo that said my room was off limits. Jack was generally too out of it to do anything at the time, but I guess he must have known what was going on because at some point he started sending me up to the attic. I used to beg him not to. The roof didn't have any windows and there wasn't even a light. But he said I had to go because it was the only place he could be sure I would be safe.

I think Jack felt bad about that. He found me an old metal flashlight, the kind that took six of those fat batteries. It was so big I could barely get my hand around it. I'd hold it to my cheek in the darkness; the smooth, cold metal used to calm me down. Sometimes if he had some cash he'd ask me what I wanted, as a treat. I always asked for batteries for the flashlight, even if he'd just got me some. I think Jack was disappointed I never asked for the stuff he thought kids would want. But he'd buy me the batteries anyway.

It got so I was spending a lot of time up there. Jack had packed away everything of Mom's the day she died, and there was a box of her books, just sitting among the rafters. At some point I turned to them, to make the hours pass a little easier. It was Mom that had shown me how, long before Miss Kimble's class. She used to say that reading was one of life's great pleasures and that it was never too soon to start. She was right, of course, although it was hard at first, figuring it out. Even then I loved everything about it, from the compact heft of the paper to the way the pages smell when you hold a book under your nose and riffle them. But mostly it's the magic of turning marks on a page into images, sounds, feelings; a whole other world into which you can escape when the one around you isn't to your liking. Sometimes I'd imagine it was her in the attic, reading to me. The darkness didn't seem to matter quite as much then; the sound of her voice had always made me feel safe.

When I read now I sometimes think it's still Mom's voice I hear inside my head, but it's hard to be sure. I don't really even remember what she looked like anymore. I used to have a photo of her, but it got left on the school bus that morning, so I don't have it now. I know she was tall, and blonde, like me. She smiled a lot. And she used to call me kiddo. *Hey, kiddo, want a story?* Or *Time for bed, kiddo*. But when I close my eyes and try to picture her face there's no coherent image, only a hazy montage of feelings, moments, gestures, like fragments of a dream that's already fading. I play them over in my head anyway, so I don't lose what's left of her, and for the feeling they provide. Like stoking the embers to get the last of the warmth from a dying fire.

I reckon it was something similar that did for Jack in the end, too. He liked to get high listening to her favorite song, and one of the neighbors must have called the cops because of the noise. They found him crashed out in the sitting room with a bunch of his junkie friends, *Wish You Were Here* blaring out of the stereo. Jack got sent to prison after that, and I ended up in Sacred Heart. Sometimes I catch myself wondering what Jack's doing now. But that's just stupid.

He's dead, like all the rest of them.

*

ELIZA OPENED HER EYES.

They were on a gravel road. Stones crunched under the tires and spat up into the wheel arches, almost drowning out the creak and groan from the tired springs as the Paektusan shuddered and bounced over the corrugations. Her body now ached in sympathy with the pounding at her temples. The muscles across her shoulders and down her back felt as though they had been bound tight in rusty razor wire, and her joints felt like they had been emptied out and filled with ground glass. Each jolt and lurch from the car's overworked suspension seemed like it was being transmitted directly into her protesting spine.

She couldn't understand why she felt so terrible. The pastor had warned her that she might suffer a reaction. Even though the virus was harmless to humans it could nevertheless trick her immune system into producing antibodies, a bit like when you got the flu vaccine in winter. Well, this certainly didn't feel like any flu jab she'd had before. She'd tell him when she got back; he was bound to want to - what was the word Jack Bauer would use? - debrief her. Maybe there was something the scientists could do to lessen the effects, in case they needed to use it again.

She looked out the window. She wished she could speak with him now, but the cellphone he had given her had only been set up to receive calls. She doubted it would work out here anyway; she hadn't had a signal since they'd arrived. She had brought it though, just in case. In truth she hadn't let it out of her sight since that first afternoon.

It had arrived at her cubicle in an unmarked Jiffy bag. Her name had been printed on the front, but when she had turned the bag over there had been no return address. She had checked with the post room of course, but there had been no record of a courier delivery for her. Where the package had come from had been a mystery, and the phone had sat on her desk all afternoon while she had tried to work out what to do with it. And then without warning it had rung. The shrill tone had startled her, sending her hand flying to the silver crucifix around her neck.

The phone continued to ring, but Eliza had hesitated. The screen was lit up, but whoever was calling had withheld their number and she was unsure whether or not she should pick it up. But then her mother had always told her she needed a little more snap in her garters, and so with a deep breath she had reached for it, pressing the screen to accept the call.

She had recognized the voice immediately, even though it had been years since they had last spoken. She was not to use his name; that was the first thing he had said, cutting her off even as she was about to do just that. The phone he had sent her was secure, but you could never tell who was listening. Eliza had stood up from her chair, peeking over the partition like a prairie dog, her heart already racing as she checked the adjacent cubicles for potential eavesdroppers. But as usual nobody had been paying attention to her.

God had revealed His plan for her, the pastor had continued, as she lowered herself back into her seat. She needed to prepare herself. She was to be entrusted with a great task; soon she would be going on a journey. Eliza had no wish to contradict a man as important as the pastor, but she had nevertheless felt compelled to explain that that just wasn't possible. All she did was analyze satellite imagery; she'd never set foot outside her cubicle in all the time she'd worked for the agency. Surely the pastor would know that; it was he who had got her the job after all. But he had simply told her not to worry. She just needed to be ready.

Three weeks had passed. She had kept the cellphone with her at all times, just as the pastor had said she should, but after that first call it had remained silent. She had begun to believe he had realized his mistake after all. How could she be going anywhere? Even if she were to request a transfer to one of the inspection teams and Jan were to approve it (a very big if, right there; none of her previous applications had been accepted) her first assignment would not be for months.

And then an inspection had been announced. Word had spread quickly though the office, for the timing was unusual. The agency was already stretched thin, with teams committed to Pakistan, Iran and Russia in the coming weeks. When she had read the destination Eliza had felt a small surge of pride, followed immediately by a flash of concern. It was her report that had led to this. But what if she had been wrong? What if she had misinterpreted what she had seen? Maybe the reactor hadn't been restarted after all. It didn't occur to her then that this might have anything to do with the pastor's call, and so when her name had appeared at the bottom of the list of inspectors that had been posted a few days later Eliza had been stunned. She wasn't used to visitors at her cubicle, but she had spent the rest of the day fielding questions from colleagues who stopped by to ask what was happening. All she could say was that she honestly didn't know.

She still hadn't believed she was going anywhere however, even then. It didn't matter what the list said; Jan would never permit it, and he was deputy director general, the agency's chief inspector. The agency reported to the Security Council but technically it was independent. The pastor was an important man, and he had clearly been able to pull a few strings to get her a job there, but not even he could hope to influence its decisions.

And of course Jan hadn't allowed it. He had called her into his office that very afternoon. It had not been a long meeting; Jan Rasmussen was not a man to waste his time with niceties. He was sorry for any confusion that might have been caused; he would certainly be looking into how it had happened. But regardless of what had been posted, she would not be joining the inspection team. Yes, it was her report that had flagged the issue, and her work, as usual, had been thorough, her conclusions supported by the evidence. But this was not a suitable assignment for someone without field experience. If she still had ambitions in that direction they could certainly talk about it, but that discussion would be for the future.

She had returned to her cubicle, aware that everyone was looking at her. She had to admit she had been more than a little relieved. Of course Jan was right. She had no business on that or any other inspection team.

But when a week later her name had still not been removed from the list Eliza had begun to wonder. The cellphone had remained silent ever since that first call, but maybe the pastor had not been mistaken. Maybe he had meant her after all. She had become more certain of it in the weeks that followed, when Jan's objections were repeatedly overruled. In the end it was Jan himself who had confirmed it. He had called her into his office again and explained that she would be joining the inspection team. It was a temporary appointment and her responsibilities would be limited. She would not be required, or expected, to do anything other than take notes.

There was one additional task she would have to perform, of course; one that even Jan could not know about. The pastor had revealed it to her when he had called that very evening. Other than that, she would do as her boss had requested and stay out of the way.

She only wished she had been allowed to let him know why she had been placed on the team. It wasn't that she craved praise or recognition. The pastor had explained that her part in this must remain unknown, and that did not concern her in the slightest. She was doing God's will, and that was all that mattered; her reward would be in heaven.

It had not occurred to Eliza that it was the road to an altogether different place that was normally paved with such laudable intentions.

*

WE'RE BACK OUTSIDE three days later. Quartermaster needs us out often now, while the weather's still holding, to get us through the months when Eden will be on lockdown.

We're headed east for Shiloah, although I'm not exactly sure why; it's much smaller than Providence, little more than a wide place in the road, and we've already taken whatever was there to be had. But Quartermaster says we haven't been that way in a few months and Kane wants us to check it out before winter sets in. I tell him Jake needs me to visit a farm supplies store and there's none in that direction, but he says that'll have to wait. At least it'll be another short trip, but day hikes mean early starts and late returns, so we'll be gone before breakfast. On the upside I'll be missing prayers, although Kane insists I stop by the chapel for a blessing to compensate. It's always the same before we go outside, his favorite passage; I know the whole verse by heart at this stage. *Behold, I send you forth as sheep in the midst of wolves: be ye therefore cunning as serpents, and harmless as doves.* I guess it rhymes, sort of, and I do like the cunning as serpents bit, but as pep talks go it's definitely not his best work. To tell the truth after all this time I think I'd be quite happy to see anything alive out there, even if it was a wolf. Marv'd probably just want to shoot it though.

Dawn's seeping into the sky, like water into an old rag, as I scramble out of the portal. It's snowing, gray flakes twisting and tumbling out of the gloom, but not heavy enough to turn us back. The wind picks up as we make our way down to the turnpike, blowing in from the east, driving the snow. We pass the occasional house, set back from the road. Some are still intact, the roofs swaybacked under the weight of years of snow, but most have sections of shingle missing, or walls that have been stripped to the studs. A few are burned to the ground, just a charred chimney breast or a blackened gable wall standing alone in what I guess used to be the yard.

It's not unusual to see places like that. I guess when some folks saw what was coming they just decided it wasn't worth going on. And when that final cigarette fell to the ground and the carpet began to smolder or the drapes began to burn there wouldn't have been anyone to call the fire department. Not that I reckon anybody would have been answering by then; the world was already well on its way to winding down. But mostly I don't think that was the way it happened. A lot of the newer places didn't even have fireplaces, not that that seemed to matter. You'll often find scorch marks against one wall or in a corner, all the way up to the ceiling, where someone's tried to set the furniture alight. By the end it seems like people were lighting fires everywhere.

I guess they just couldn't get warm.

I spot the church long before we hit the town. It sits at a crook in the road on our way in, an old stone-built structure with an imposing steeple that towers over the squat houses below. Sometimes Marv and I eat lunch in the bell tower. On a clear day from up there you can see for several miles back along the turnpike, and all the way east out to the Catoctin Mountain Highway. Today the wind's too high, and besides, there'll be nothing to see, what with the snow, so we walk on into town.

Shiloah's just a collection of sad one- and two-story dwellings clustered on either side of the street, the wooden sidings long stripped for firewood. Most of the windows have been broken, and those that remain are carrying a decade of grime. Out front, flags hang weather-faded and tattered on peeling flagpoles. Red crosses mark the places we've scavenged on previous trips. There's little point going back in to any of those, so we keep heading east.

There's a small pharmacy on Main Street. I let Marv get a little way ahead of me and then I slip inside. It's been turned over pretty bad, but there's a stack of pregnancy tests just sitting there on one of the shelves near the back. I pick one and scan the instructions. It seems pretty simple. The kit's old, well past its expiry date, so it probably won't work. But then Lena's not actually pregnant, so it really doesn't matter. I open the box and shove a couple of the sticks into the pocket of my parka. On my way out I pick up a handful of Band-Aids and some antiseptic, and a couple of bottle of vitamins from a display stand that's been knocked over, just in case Marv asks what I was doing. I catch up with him further along the street, looking in the window of the Shiloah Gun Exchange. The sign says its open and currently selling the Frederick County Fireman's gun calendar. But the window's smashed and I don't need to step inside to know there's nothing left worth taking.

We trudge out of town past a veterinary clinic. I've already checked it out on a previous trip so we keep moving. Up ahead a Jubilee Foods advertises premium meats and fresh seafood, but the roof's collapsed so we don't go in. I realize this is as far east as I've been. Marv keeps going. The road climbs gently for half a mile and then we hit a blockade, just like the one outside Providence. A big semi's parked lengthways, right across the road. Behind sits a school bus, its nose half in a ditch, the back end canted up, like a large animal down on its knees.

I trudge up to the rig, excited, while Marv continues around on the hard shoulder. The snow's drifted all the way up to the top of the hood, but you can see it's one of the ones with the sleeper cab, just from the outline. I'll need to be quick. Marv doesn't like me going near so much metal; that's how Benjamin died. But that won't happen to me. I know to be careful.

I knock some snow off first, and step up on the gas tank to check the exhaust stack, the big horns on the roof. The chrome's good, a little dull, but definitely not contaminated. I head back toward the front and scoop the snow off a section of the windshield and look inside. Most people didn't die in their vehicles; I guess it was just too cold for that. But there's always the chance with a big sleeper rig like this that I'm peering into someone's tomb. Today I'm in luck, however; the cab seems empty. I dig out the snow around the bottom of the door so it'll open, revealing the logo. *Ducheyne Trucking Co.* out of Charles Town, West Virginia. I release my boot from the snowshoe and test the door with the toe. The metal seems solid.

I reach for the handle. It's locked, but I was hoping for that. It means no one's been here before me. I shrug the backpack off my shoulder and reach inside for the pry bar. The sound of the driver's window breaking is shockingly loud in the cold silence, and for an instant I forget where I am and look around in case anyone's heard. The moment passes and I'm left feeling a little foolish. I reach in and pull the handle. The door's iced up but with a little tugging it opens.

It's dark inside, even with the door open and the snow cleared from part of the windshield. I quickly go through the glove box and the center console. A road atlas, spiral bound, well-used but in good condition. I tear a few pages out for kindling and leave the rest. There's a number of stow holes and cubbies in the sleeper cab and I start sifting through them, hoping to find a book. But all I turn up is a decade-old *USA Today*, the pages faded yellow. Better than nothing, I guess; there might be something in there. I fold it carefully and place it in my backpack. I clamber back out of the rig and strap on my snowshoes. I take a second to scrape the snow off one of the school bus's windows as I pass, in case some kid's left a schoolbag inside, but there's nothing there either. Marv's already cresting the next hill and I have to hustle to catch up with him.

Marv stops us when we get as far as the highway. We eat our MREs in silence in the McDonald's at the intersection, staring out at the long concrete sweep of the on-ramp. An Exxon, the forecourt canopy collapsed onto the pumps under a blanket of snow, sits kitty corner opposite. Marv seems even quieter than usual, and then I remember that this is where Benjamin broke his leg clambering over a car. It must have been a bad break, because Marv told Kane he bled out in minutes. He's buried out there in the snow somewhere.

When we're done eating Marv says there's little point going any further, so we turn around and head back, our backpacks light. Quartermaster won't be happy with the haul, and he certainly won't remember that I told him so, but at least we'll be out again soon. And I've had a thought about how I can get in Kane's good books, maybe use it as an opportunity to open up a conversation about my match. Most of the pills on the list he's given me I can lay my hands on easily enough. The ketamine he says he prefers is harder. I've always thought I'd need to visit a hospital for that, and Marv says we're not going near one of those anytime soon. But the vet's we passed on the outskirts of town has given me an idea.

It's late afternoon when we make it back to the farmhouse. Marv heads straight to his room, but I sit at the kitchen table for a while, wrapped up in my parka, and watch through the window as darkness draws down over the world. Outside the wind howls, rattling the silted panes in their frames. My muscles ache pleasantly from the day's hike, but it's too early to turn in. Then I remember the *USA Today* I found in the rig. I dig the old newspaper out of my backpack and start looking through it while there's still some light.

Nobody knows where the virus came from, not even Kane. He says it was God punishing us for straying from His path, but even if he's right, that's not really a satisfying answer, is it? I tried asking Marv about it, but he's not very forthcoming either. He says I should just forget it. The world's never going back to the way it was, so there's no point spending time worrying about what caused it; whoever dealt that hand they've probably already got what was coming to them, and then some. I guess he's right. But that's not how it works, is it? Someone telling you not to think about something just makes the curiosity burn that much brighter.

So I've started a scrapbook, to help me figure it out. When I say scrapbook, it's actually more of a shoebox. I keep it with the books I've found, under my bed. Whenever I come across a newspaper or a magazine that has something in it about the virus I clip it out and place it with the others I've collected. Sometimes if I find an article that describes what the world was like before, in those days when a plane crashing or a ferry sinking still felt like a disaster, I'll keep that too.

Tell the truth I haven't managed to figure out much. When it got cold people burned whatever they could get their hands on, and anything like a newspaper that could have been used to get a fire going would have been in demand. What little survived those first months has mostly turned to mulch in the ten years since. I've found a few things from that last couple of weeks, in that window when trash collection had stopped but papers were still being printed, at least for those that still took their news that way. By then things were pretty grim. In other countries there were reports that the emergency services were collapsing, that hospitals were being over-run. There were stories of mass burials, photographs of bodies being dumped in the sea. Oil wells in the Middle East were ablaze, and no attempts were being made to bring the fires under control. One by one whole countries were going dark.

I remember what Miss Kimble told us about how the virus had somehow found its way on to Air Force One and how the President had died, and Sam and Reuben watching on T.V. as Kane was sworn in. I have this clipping that describes how the President's security advisors had wanted to close the borders right then. That had never been attempted before and Kane had resisted, saying it was a drastic measure, and not one to be taken lightly. But by then I guess people were afraid and the newspapers were clamoring for something to be done and in the end he agreed. The order said anyone attempting to cross on foot would be shot on sight; aircraft entering U.S. airspace would be forced down. For a while it looked like it might work, that we might somehow hold it together. And maybe we would have, if it hadn't been for the strikes. Nobody knows where they came from either, but on the morning of the Last Day a handful of missiles found their way through our defenses, the warheads leveling targets up and down the eastern seaboard. I guess that was just one thing too many. Soon after that reports started coming in of outbreaks from Seattle right across to Miami. The cities were hit the worst. Interstate exchanges began collapsing under their own weight, bridges fell into rivers, skyscrapers listed and crumbled as the virus ate away at the metal holding them upright.

But it wasn't just things that the virus attacked. I think it was what it did to people that was the scariest.

*

THE SCHOOL BUS was quieter than usual as we made our way into the capitol that morning. Of course Miss Kimble was there now to keep things under control, and we'd just had the near miss with Kurt and Mags, so everyone was trying especially hard to behave. I remember there being a few more kids out that day than usual, too. I noticed it when Miss Kimble called roll. I guess their parents decided to keep them at home, where they thought they'd be safe. They probably meant well, but how wrong can you be?

Traffic was light on the beltway, and most of it seemed to be on the other side, heading in the opposite direction. As we were crossing the Key Bridge there was a thunderous roar from above that rattled the bus's old windows, and suddenly thirty small faces were pressed up against the glass, staring up at a formation of fighter jets screaming by overhead. It was very exciting. Everyone was shouting and pointing and making whooshing sounds. Miss Kimble told us all to get back in our seats. She seemed pretty tense.

At the White House we had to leave everything in the bus, but Miss Kimble said it would be safe. It turned out she wasn't right about that, but I guess it wasn't her fault; I don't think there was any way she could have known. We all wanted to go right in but Miss Kimble made everyone visit the restrooms in the visitor center first because there were no bathrooms open to the public once you were inside. Looking back I really don't know why they ever thought that tour was appropriate for first graders.

When we were all done Miss Kimble ushered us into the security line. There were three security checkpoints, and she had to show her ID and the invitation letter to the Secret Service agents at the first two, and then as we got closer we all had to go through a metal detector. While we were waiting in line Mags tapped my shoulder and pointed up at the snipers on the roof, which was neat. A sign at the start had said we could expect to wait in line for forty-five minutes, but that day it looked like we were the only group going through, which was cool, because it took us way less than that.

And then finally we were in. The tour consisted of walking through a bunch of ornately-furnished rooms, where everything smelled clean but old at the same time. There were only seven rooms that you were actually allowed to see, plus a bunch of hallways and corridors. Other rooms were roped off, but you could peek inside as long as you didn't get too close. The names mostly made sense – the Blue Room was blue, the Red Room was red, and the China Room really did have loads of china in it. There wasn't a guide, but there were signs everywhere describing what you were looking at, and Miss Kimble said the Secret Service agents would answer questions if we put our hands up first and asked politely. I wanted to ask where the books in the library all came from, but the agent in that room seemed distracted so I didn't.

The tour went quickly. We had just finished in the Green Room (yep, green) and were filing out into this big red-carpeted hallway, making our way back down the stairs when there was a commotion in front of us. A Secret Service agent with a coil of wire tucked behind his ear had stopped Miss Kimble from going any further. Everyone was keen not to miss this latest excitement; the class quickly piled up on the steps behind her. There were sounds of protest behind me and I turned around just in time to see Kurt shove Lena out of the way and then elbow his way past me to stand near the front. I looked at Miss Kimble to see what she was going to do. It's the kind of thing she would normally have been all over, but I guess right then she was preoccupied with the agent who was holding us on the stairs. Kurt just stared at me for a long moment, to see whether I was going to be a problem. Once he was satisfied I wasn't he turned his attention back to the drama unfolding in front of us.

A bunch of Secret Service agents were walking briskly down the hall. They all had earpieces in, like the man who was holding us on the stairs, and a few of them were talking into the cuffs of their jackets. Behind them was a tall silver-haired man in a dark blue suit surrounded by even more agents. Mags asked me if I knew who he was. She didn't get much T.V. time at Sacred Heart, on account of her privileges being in a state of near permanent suspension, but I recognized him from the news shows Sam and Reuben would watch. He was the new President of the United States.

As they were walking through the President noticed us and stopped to ask the Secret Service agent next to him, a man with deep-set gray eyes and dark hair cut to little more than stubble, who we were. One of the other agents was urging the President to move along; I thought I heard him say that there wasn't much time. And then for the first time I heard the *wop-wop-wop* of rotors, faint, as though they were still some way off.

The President ignored the agent who was trying to hurry him. Instead he turned to the man with the short dark hair and in a voice that was soft and smooth and yet still loud enough for us all to hear he said 'Randall, they're children, I won't just leave them here.' The man with the short dark hair turned to the agent holding us on the stairs and asked how many of us there were. The agent relayed the question into his microphone and then pressed his finger to his earpiece, but while he was waiting for a response Miss Kimble answered over the top of his head.

'Thirty, Mr. President.'

We all pressed forward. Kurt asked what was happening in a loud voice but this time Miss Kimble was on top of it and just hushed him.

The silver-haired man appeared to consider for a moment.

'How many people will fit in Marine One, Randall?'

'Fourteen, Mr. President. But we've got the Defense Secretary riding with us, and at least one Secret Service detail. Which leaves only eleven seats.'

'That's eleven adults, though. And then there's the decoy.'

'Yes, Mr. President.'

'We'll make them fit. Randall, can you speak with their teacher and get them out on to the south lawn. Once we're outside we can organize how we're going to get them all on the helicopters.'

The Secret Service agent with the short dark hair came over to Miss Kimble and pulled her to one side. Miss Kimble told us to wait where we were. A second later she was back. She had that smile that we'd gotten used to seeing in the last few weeks and when she spoke her voice seemed shaky, like it was about to break. She told us there had been an emergency and that we were going out onto the lawn in front of the White House, the one we had seen on the way in. It was going to be like a fire drill at school, did we remember those? There were nods all around. Fire drills were an escape from the tedium of lessons and therefore generally warmly regarded.

'Good. Now everybody has to find a partner – the person standing next to you – and hold hands.'

There was some shuffling on the stairs as people figured out who their partner would be. I felt Mags slip her fingers inside my hand. Behind Miss Kimble another Secret Service agent stepped up to the President.

'Mr. President, Marine One has touched down. We need to go. Now.'

The President nodded to let him know he had heard, but he didn't move. Miss Kimble was still giving us instructions, raising her voice against the sound of the helicopters outside. I could see the door to the White House lawn behind her. I just wanted to make a break for it.

'Okay, now we walk out in double file, as quickly as we can, but we stop when we get out onto the lawn.'

She smiled again, as if to reassure us, but it was that same smile that didn't come close to reaching her eyes. The Secret Service agent on the stairs stepped out of the way and we followed Miss Kimble down past him. I'd never been good at that hinterground between ambling and flat out sprinting; once we got moving it was all I could do not to run. Miss Kimble made us stop again out on the lawn and form two lines. There were lots more men in suits outside, all with sunglasses and earpieces. Soldiers were fanning out, weapons shouldered, scanning the skies.

Directly in front of us two green and white helicopters squatted on the lawn like huge bugs, their rotors still spinning, the wash flattening the grass. 'United States of America' was painted in big white letters on the tail section of each. There were two doors in their long fuselages, one at the front near the cockpit, the other in the middle. As we made our way outside these were dropping down, the inside of the door offering steps up into the helicopter's fuselage.

Miss Kimble was walking between us counting heads. When she was satisfied no one was getting left behind she returned to the front and turned to face us. She had to shout to make herself heard above the sound of the rotors. Our row would walk quickly towards the Secret Service agent standing in front of the helicopter on our left and he would tell us which set of steps to go up. The row that had formed up behind Kurt, Angus and Hamish would make for the helicopter on the right.

The agent Miss Kimble had pointed to was already beckoning me forward and I started toward him without waiting to hear if there were any more directions. The wash from the huge rotors pulled at my clothes and tugged at my hair. Somewhere along the way fire drill fever gripped me and I lost the ability to comply with Miss Kimble's instruction to walk. I simply squeezed Mags' hand tighter and ran for all I was worth.

The agent directed us to the stairs on the left, next to the cockpit, where a marine sergeant in dress uniform was waiting. I could make out his white belt, his shiny black shoes, the brass buttons on his tunic, even the colored ribbons and medals pinned to his breast. He was standing stiffly to attention, but I thought he looked scared. I was close enough now to count the riveted panels on the pristine green paintwork of the fuselage. The smell of burnt fuel filled my nostrils and the roar from the engines made me want to clamp my hands over my ears, but I couldn't let go of Mags.

At last we were at the steps. Mags grabbed for the railing and pulled herself up. I clambered up after her. Through the perspex cockpit window I could see the pilot craning his neck, staring intently at the skies. In my haste to negotiate the steps I stumbled, but a strong hand grabbed me by the neck of my sweater and I was lifted effortlessly and shoved into the belly of the helicopter.

Inside it was surprisingly cramped, and for a second Claus balked at moving any further forward, but there was too much adrenalin rushing through me for my legs to stop now. A long couch-style row of seats took up one side of the cabin. Two leather armchairs, facing each other, were on the other side, each embossed with a fancy seal. The windows had curtains and there was even a reading lamp on a small table at each end of the couch, with a shade, like you'd see in a regular house. Mags had already found a spot; she scooched over as I stumbled into the cabin to make room for me. Within seconds all the seats had been taken, except the two marked with the seal, which we figured belonged to the President and maybe Miss Kimble or another grown up. Kids were still piling in, sitting on each other's laps or finding a spot on the floor to squat down.

From where I was sitting I could see out of the window. I saw the marine snap a salute at the President who returned it quickly as he hurried towards the front of the helicopter. A second later he appeared in the cabin and took one of the seats opposite us. The Secret Service agent the President had called Randall bounded up the steps behind him.

The whine of the engines had increased as soon as the President was on board; we lifted off even as the Secret Service agent was latching the door. Out of the window I could see the other helicopter also rising into the air. I looked around. Miss Kimble wasn't with us, which meant that's where she had to be. I suddenly remembered that I'd left my schoolbag with the photo of Mom inside it on the bus.

The Secret Service agent was leaning into the cockpit. I heard him tell the pilot that the destination had changed and to maintain radio silence and not to worry about the shell game, just to get us there as quickly as possible. I didn't know what any of that meant. Then the helicopter banked sharply and the agent had to brace himself against the bulkhead as he made his way back into the cabin to join us.

*

BECAUSE SHILOAH WAS A BUST we're done with quarantine early, so I'm back in Eden in time for movie night.

It actually sounds more exciting than it is. There's an old screen hanging from the ceiling in the mess; I guess people used to watch stuff on it while they ate, before, although Mom always used to say that was the height of bad manners. Anyway, a few years after we arrived Carl found a disc in a desk drawer over at the power plant, and when Mags put it into the slot in the side of the TV it worked. It's a horror film, *30 Days of Night*; every Friday after dinner we put it on. We've all seen it countless times by now.

I could look for more films outside, obviously. I don't think people were using those discs much anymore, but I'm pretty sure if I searched I could find some, maybe in a thrift shop or a vintage store somewhere. I'd have to put some thought into how I'd smuggle them past the Guardians, but I'd be happy to give it a go. The worst that could happen is that Kane would find out about movie night and we'd lose the one film we've all seen scores of times already. But we discussed it and it was decided that the risk was too high. So instead we all hang around the mess after dinner on Friday nights and watch the same film, over and over. I'm not sure being inside Eden this long has done much for my Juvie brethren's sense of adventure.

Right now we're sitting at the tables, waiting for the last of the Guardians to leave. There's never enough time between dinner and the curfew buzzer to fit in the entire film, but whether or not we'll be able to finish the part we didn't see last week depends on how quickly Jason and Seth get out of here. They finished eating a while back, but they've been sitting at the table talking ever since; for the last twenty minutes everybody's been stealing glances in their direction, willing them to leave.

At last they stand and make for the door. There's normally some milling around afterwards as people turn their seats around to face the screen, or get up and head for the bathrooms; in some ways we're still the first grade class that arrived here almost a decade ago. Tonight however the toilet breaks have all been taken care of while we've been waiting, so in a few moments we should be good to go.

Michael gets up and heads for the door, which means the movie'll be starting soon. He's our lookout; he'll let us know if Peck or one of the Guardians comes snooping around. There's a roster, so everyone takes a turn. Except me, of course; there's always somebody willing to trade my spot for a favor, something I can get for them from the outside. Mags says I'm missing the point. Scavenging is what I'm supposed to do, like the guys who work in the farms or for Scudder, or Amy and Fran in the kitchens. I've tried to explain that's not how it works, but I never get very far; if there's one thing I've learned it's that there's no point trying to convince Mags of something when she's set her mind against it.

Fran stands up from the girls' table and makes her way over to the TV screen. She's the current custodian of the disc. We pass it around so the risk of Kurt finding it on one of his cell inspections is spread among us. She slips the DVD from the pocket of her overalls and slides it into the slot in the side of the screen. The conversation dies down a little as the movie takes off where we left the inhabitants of Barrow last week, but soon we're up to full chat again.

It's a little annoying, actually. The mess has metal walls like everywhere else, so we need to keep the volume on the TV turned all the way down. But that means you can only hear what's going if it's generally quiet and you're sitting close to the screen. Which means anyone sitting more than a few feet away just chats among themselves anyway. And with everyone in the room talking even those sitting near the front can't hear. I figured out how you can play the movies with subtitles, but nobody liked it. Most of the Juvies can't read enough to make it even close to worthwhile and the text obscures the picture so they find it distracting. On the upside, we've all gotten pretty good at lip-reading.

I normally try and pay attention. It's actually a pretty good film. It's about these vampires that target this tiny, isolated town in northern Alaska that gets (you've guessed it) thirty days of polar night each year. I looked Barrow up in the atlas I keep under my bed in the farmhouse. It's an actual place. I sometimes wonder whether somewhere like that might have escaped the virus. It's possible I guess; it's certainly far enough out of the way. And living that far north they'd be used to the cold. Perhaps there's a whole townful of people up there who also think they're the last people alive on the planet.

Tonight I'm a little bit distracted, however. I've been looking for Lena to give her the test sticks I brought back from Shiloah, but she wasn't at dinner. And Mags hasn't shown up yet either. I'm sure Mags'll be here soon, though. We've all seen the film scores of times so it's not like you need to be around for the start to figure out what's going on. I've taken a seat at the back, near the door, even though I don't like sitting so far from the TV, because you can't hear anything at all. But there's a better chance of keeping the spot next to me free for when she arrives.

Up on the screen the vampires are roaming around Barrow hunting the humans. They're freaky. They have solid black irises that cover almost the entire eye, and their mouths are full of small, sharp teeth. It makes them look like sharks. They're intelligent, especially the leader, Marlow. But when they scream at each other it's different, almost feral. I wonder if that's the sound the furies made, before Kane silenced them for good.

The latch on the door clunks and everyone turns around, but it's only

Jake. He works late at the farms so he's never here for the start, but tonight he's later than usual. He heads into the kitchens and comes back with a tray of mashed potatoes and finds a seat. A few minutes later the door opens again and this time it's Mags. She mustn't have noticed that the seat next to me is free because she grabs a tray and brings it back to the girls' table. Jake looks over at her as she sits down. He's unaware that I'm looking at him and for a long time he doesn't shift his gaze back to the screen. I've noticed more of the guys paying attention to Mags since she decided to grow her hair back, so I guess I should be used to it. Still, though, for some reason Jake staring at her like that makes me feel strange.

On the screen the vampires have started to burn down the town to prevent any survivors from telling the world what happened. The conversation dies down to a murmur as we settle in for the finish. It's a good ending, although I'm not sure how realistic it is. Would Eben really make the sacrifice he does, turning himself into a vampire to defeat Marlow and save Stella? I mean, what's the point in winning her back if you're just going to get burnt to a crisp come sunup?

*

METAL'S ALL AROUND US in Eden. It's the first thing our feet touch when we roll out of our cots in the morning, the last thing we stare up at at night before the lights go out. So it was hard to believe at first, when Miss Kimble told us we had metal inside us too, that our bodies needed it to survive. The iron in our blood was the main example, she said, but there was also zinc, copper, manganese, chromium and a host of others with names that were hard to pronounce and even harder to remember. That was why the virus didn't just attack things, like cars and trucks and bridges and buildings. It could infect us too.

Only the virus didn't just want to destroy our bodies, the way it collapsed skyscrapers or crashed airplanes. It was like it meant to hotwire the person it had infected, to replace their internal wiring with its own. Most that became infected died anyway. It turns out the virus's circuits were way faster, and our bodies had never been designed for that kind of speed.

Those few who did manage to survive the initial stage of the virus became known as the furies. Some said it was because the real name of the thing that destroyed us was the ferrovirus. Others maintained it was because early on the symptoms had been mistaken for the final, furious, stage of another virus that had once terrorized us. One normally delivered at the frothing jaws of a maddening dog.

I'm glad I wasn't outside in those last weeks, before Kane did what he had to to shut them down. The newspapers said they only came out at night, their newly silvered eyes sensitive to even the smallest amounts of light. Once the sun had set they would emerge in their droves, however, driven from whatever dark daytime lair they had chosen by an insatiable desire to feed, to replenish the blood the virus had stolen from them.

I've only ever seen one once.

It was up in Shreve. We'd been working this house, an unremarkable single story rancher set a little ways back from the road. Marv had already warned me to stay out of the dark places of course, but I was still new to the business of scavenging back then and I hadn't yet figured on everything that might include.

We'd gone in through the front door and Marv had headed straight down to the basement. I'd checked the kitchen and bathroom and turned up nothing more than a mostly spent tube of toothpaste and a bottle of cherry antacid for Quartermaster. I'd already figured out that if you knew where to look there were still books to be had on the outside, and I had this house's former occupants pegged as readers. So instead of waiting for Marv out on the stoop I'd headed for one of the bedrooms. By then I'd had several encounters with the not-so-recently departed, enough to make me wary. I hadn't found anything to suggest any of the former residents were still in occupation, though, and when I pushed the door open with the toe of my boot and peered through the crack I could see that the bed was empty, so I went in.

The paper that still clung to the walls, water-stained and sagging, suggested this had probably been a child's bedroom. The bed was small and there was a rectangular patch of brighter color above it where a poster might once have hung, shading the now mildewed wall. But the nightstands had been empty, the drawers yanked out and ransacked long before. I'd knelt down on the damp carpet and lifted the sham, but there was nothing under there either.

It was as I was getting up that I noticed the closet. At first I didn't know what was wrong, only that I had this feeling, the faintest twinge, like I'd just walked through a cobweb, only inside my head. I get it sometimes, mostly on the outside. It's like a spidey-sense. So I looked around the room trying to figure out what might have set it off. And that's when I noticed it. Every other door or drawer had been pulled open, but the door to the closet was shut tight. I walked around the bed and opened the door, not expecting to find much more than a bunch of moldering clothes and rotting shoes.

A few items of clothing still hung from plastic hangers, obscuring my view, so I didn't notice, right off. But as soon as my eyes adjusted to the darkness I saw her, sitting in back of the closet, her face pressed up against the wall. Her cheeks were sunken and hollowed and there were dark circles around her eyes. The hair that framed her face was white and brittle, like an old person's, but when I looked closer I could see that she couldn't have been much older than we had been when we first came to Eden. The dress she still wore hung in tatters from her emaciated frame and her skin where it showed through was the color of ash, like the snow outside. But there wasn't a trace of decay. She looked for all the world like she was sleeping.

At first I was certain that I had found someone alive. I screamed for Marv. He always said we had to stay within what he called hollerin' distance and a few seconds later I heard the sound of his boots coming down the corridor and then he burst into the room and the next thing I knew I was being lifted by the straps of my backpack and bundled out the door and into the hallway outside.

He said I was to go outside and wait for him. When I told him I didn't want to he cuffed me. It was just the once, and the only time he's ever done it, before or since. I don't even think he was trying to hit me very hard. My eyes brimmed, nevertheless. I think it was the shock as much as anything; it was so fast I never saw it coming.

I went outside and sat on the porch for a while, blinking back the tears, determined not to cry in case he came back out and saw me. My cheek was still smarting, and my eyes burned with the sheer injustice of it. It was me who had found her, after all. Why should he get to keep her to himself?

Curiosity soon overcame my indignation, however. I couldn't go back into the house, so I crept around the side and checked the windows until I found the bedroom where the little girl had been hiding. As quietly as I could I cleared the snow from a section at the bottom of one of the panes. The glass underneath was coated with a decade of grime, which made it pretty hard to see through, and I didn't want to risk alerting Marv to my presence by trying to wipe it off. In the end I settled for a small section that was a little bit cleaner than the rest and pressed my face to it.

Marv had his back to me, but the first thing I noticed was that he had removed the glove from his left hand. In the other he held a pistol. The pistol was wrapped in a Ziploc bag, but it looked like there was a long metal cylinder attached to the end of the barrel. Marv was holding it so the muzzle was only inches from the girl's forehead, but she didn't seem aware. She was just sitting there in the closet with her eyes closed, her face pressed up against the wall, exactly how I had found her.

With the hand he'd freed from the glove Marv reached inside his parka. When it re-emerged it was holding the hunting knife he wears on his belt, only he was holding it the wrong way, with the blade pointed upwards. I was considering whether I should knock on the window and let him know in case he accidentally cut himself, but then I saw him run the ball of his thumb along the bottom of the blade. A moment later a fat drop of blood welled up along the cut. Without taking the gun off the girl he smeared the blood along the tip of the knife. Then he moved it closer to the girl's face so that it was only inches from her nose.

For a long time nothing happened. Then suddenly it looked like the girl went really stiff. It was hard to be sure through the dirt on the windowpane, but it seemed like the muscles in her tiny jaw had started to work, clenching and unclenching like she was grinding her teeth. Her eyes stayed closed, but for a second I thought something might have moved behind her eyelids. And then her mouth dropped open a fraction and she started to make small movements with her head, almost like she was trying to snap at the knife, except that something invisible was holding her head in place, preventing her.

Marv didn't move. He just bowed his head slightly. There was no sound, but he must have squeezed the trigger because suddenly a neat black circle appeared in the center of the girl's forehead and a second later her jaw stopped twitching.

I didn't want Marv to know I had been spying on him, so I ran around to the front of the house and sat on the step to wait. When he came back out a few minutes later there was no sign of the pistol. As we walked away from the house I asked him whether the girl had been alive. He didn't answer me at first but when I asked him again he just said not to act bixicated.

*

THE FLIGHT FROM THE WHITE HOUSE to Eden didn't take very long. We all sat in silence, the only sound that of the helicopter's straining engines. Mags held my hand; I remember her looking at me with those solemn brown eyes. Opposite us the President stared out of the window. Every so often he would check his watch.

We landed in the middle of a road in front of the entrance to a large tunnel that led into the side of a mountain. The Secret Service agent with the short dark hair got up to unlatch the fuselage door as we started to descend and was lowering it even as the wheels of the helicopter touched the tarmac. Then he was gone, bent low against the downdraft from the rotors as he ran across the road. With the doors open it was loud inside the helicopter again and the President had to shout to make himself heard. He told us when we got outside we were to run as quickly as we could towards the tunnel and not to look anywhere else.

Mags was out first. I clambered down the steps behind her, jumping the last few. The President must have gone back to open it because the other door in the helicopter's fuselage dropped down and a moment later kids were spilling out there too. I could hear the second helicopter, the one that had to have Miss Kimble on board, coming in to land just behind us.

Two soldiers stood on guard at the mouth of the tunnel, their rifles held close to their chests. One of the soldiers was enormous, the largest man I think I had ever seen. His skin was the color of coal, and in his huge hands the rifle looked like a child's toy. The other soldier was white, and normal-sized, with reddish brown hair cut so tight that his pale scalp showed through at the sides. He wore dark wraparound shades that hid his eyes completely, but his narrow face bore a pinched, unhappy expression.

When he saw us the black soldier's face split into a wide smile, revealing rows of incredibly white teeth. He crouched down and beckoned us towards him. The other man was also waving us towards the tunnel, but his expression remained taut, his hand movements impatient. I grabbed Mags' hand and ran towards the friendly black man.

As we got closer the huge soldier told us to keep moving further into the tunnel. His voice was very deep, like the low rumble of thunder, but he spoke gently, only raising his voice sufficiently to be heard above the thrum of the rotors outside. Claus baulked for a moment at the idea of heading into the mountain, but Mags just gripped my hand and pulled me on. And then as we were about to step through the portal the shadows on the ground suddenly shifted, as if a very bright light had been turned on behind me. There was no sound. The soldiers immediately raised their hands to shield their eyes, even the one who had sunglasses on. I started to turn around to see what had happened but the huge black man told me to keep facing into the tunnel as there might be more flashes that could hurt our eyes.

More kids ran in, followed at last by Miss Kimble. Her face was ashen and I noticed her hand was trembling as she moved it over our heads, counting silently. We'd already been counted before we got on the helicopters so I wasn't sure why she was doing it again, but it looked like it was important to Miss Kimble to have something to do at that moment, and I know counting can really help.

The President made his way past us. I heard him ask Miss Kimble if everyone was here, and I saw her nod shakily. He told her to start leading us into the tunnel. Mags asked where we were going. I was expecting Miss Kimble to shush her, like she had shushed Kurt on the stairs in the White House. Mags hadn't raised her hand or anything, and this was the President after all. But Miss Kimble didn't say anything. Instead she just looked at him, like this was a question she'd really like to know the answer to as well. The President said we were going somewhere safe until things were better outside. Miss Kimble paused for a moment, as if considering this, and then she nodded quickly, as if to herself, and told everyone to find a partner and follow her. From outside I could hear the pitch of the helicopters' engines increasing again as they prepared for take off. As we set off I stole one final glance behind me. The President was standing to one side of the tunnel, discussing something with the Secret Service agent with the short dark hair and a very fat bald man who must have arrived on the second helicopter with Miss Kimble. The two soldiers were stood at the entrance, staring out, the difference in their sizes even more obvious in silhouette.

Behind them a large mushroom-shaped cloud sat on the horizon, slowly unfurling itself into what had previously been a clear blue sky.

That first walk into the mountain took what seemed like forever, but I guess that's often the case when you don't know where you're going or how far ahead your destination lies. I counted one thousand five hundred and seventy-two steps that morning, but of course my legs were a lot shorter back then.

When we reached the blast door Claus bridled at the thought of going further. The lights in the outer tunnels were working back then, of course, so it was less scary than it is now, and I didn't yet know about the cavern, only that what I could see from where I was standing looked a lot smaller and narrower than where I already was. Mags waited with me, still holding my hand, while everyone else filed inside. In the end there was just the two of us. We stood there in silence until the two soldiers who had met us outside when the helicopters had landed came walking up the tunnel. The narrow-faced one stepped past me.

'What's up, Junior? Waiting for a invite?'

The huge black soldier that we would later come to know as Benjamin crouched down beside me. I notice for the first time a gold signet ring on the little finger of his left hand. The ring bore a black shield with a white eagle's head under a banner that read *The Screaming Eagles* above and *101$^{st}$ Airborne* below.

'Don't mind him. He's just being an asshole. What's the problem, little man?'

Mags told him I didn't like tight spaces. I thought he might laugh at me then but instead he just nodded.

'Me either.'

I looked at him skeptically. How could this huge man be scared of tight spaces? For someone that big surely every space was going to be tight. But he didn't seem to be making fun of me.

'It's okay once you get in there, I promise. Besides if someone like me'll fit, a little dude like you'll be just fine.'

I was the last one through the door that day. It was already closing as I stepped over the threshold. The electric motors hummed gently under the load back then; they didn't whine and strain like they do now. Except when Benjamin took Miss Kimble out, a few months later, the blast door wouldn't be opened again for almost two years. I wouldn't see daylight again for another three after that.

It was the last day any of us would see the sun.

*

ELIZA CHECKED HER WATCH. They'd been travelling for just over two hours; it couldn't be much further now. She looked out of the window. Trees obscured the view on both sides, but now and then there were gaps and she could make out water beyond. It had to be the Kuryong. The pale winter sun reflecting off its surface hurt her eyes, even behind her sunglasses. Her mother had suffered terrible migraines, as far back as Eliza could remember. When they arrived she would retreat to her darkened bedroom for days on end, and then Eliza would have to tiptoe around the house as they both waited out the pain. Back then she had never understood how a thing so warm and wondrous as God's own sunshine could bring such suffering. But now she knew.

They passed under a low stone bridge and inside the car it turned dark, momentarily revealing her reflection in the window. It took a moment for her to recognize the face staring back at her and when she did she almost recoiled in horror. It had only been a few short hours and yet she looked far worse than she had this morning. When had she cracked the ampule? Had that been yesterday or the day before? Why was it so hard for her to remember?

The inspection had originally been scheduled for Monday, she was certain of that; the file had said that Pak would be there on that day. She could work back from then. The pastor had told her that it would take a few hours for the virus to activate, which meant it had to have been Sunday when she took it. Yes, that was right. It was the first time in as long as she could remember that she had missed service (*Good Sabbaths make Good Christians* her mother had always said) and she remembered retiring early to her small hotel room for an hour with her bible before she broke out the ampule the pastor had given her. The liquid inside had tasted incredibly bitter, and it had had a strange consistency – slick, metallic, like she imagined mercury might taste. At first she had struggled not to throw up what she had just swallowed; she had had to brush her teeth several times to banish the worst of the taste from her mouth. But it was done. She was ready.

And then later that evening Jan had called her room. Their visit had been delayed. No reason had been offered, no revised date had been set. He had told her this was not unexpected. The regime had a history of expelling weapons inspectors; they were simply flexing their muscles, demonstrating their power. There was nothing to do but wait.

She told herself not to worry. The virus would remain active in her system; the pastor had explained there was sufficient iron in human blood to sustain it almost indefinitely. Soon she would be contagious however, and he had told her it would be better if she were not identified as the source. The virus was not an effective airborne agent; it would take prolonged exposure to contract it that way. But it was easily transmitted by touch. So she had donned the silicone gloves they had provided and waited in her room. She would have liked to have gone back to her King James - a verse or two from Psalms had always calmed her down - but she wouldn't touch the holy book now that she was infected, even wearing the gloves. And so she had turned on the small TV that sat in the corner of her room. There was only one channel, alternating between reports from the national news agency and movies in Korean, but at least it was a distraction.

When Jorg and Mike had tried to coax her out for dinner later that evening she had told them she was feeling under the weather, which by then had been true. Her muscles had begun to ache and she was alternating between shivers and hot flushes, like she was coming down with the flu. She had gone to bed early. At some point in the early hours her fever had broken and from then on she had just felt cold. Her hands and feet were the worst; whatever she did she didn't seem to be able to warm them up. At some point she had crawled out of bed to put more clothes on, and then she had curled up in a tight ball under the blankets with her fingers jammed into her armpits. She thought she might have managed an hour of sleep before the first of the pre-dawn light had crept into her room. She had climbed out of bed, hugging her hands to her sides, to close the threadbare curtains. Outside a rheumy, bloodshot sun had just begun to show itself above the horizon. It was still mostly obscured by the thick layer of smog that clung to the city like a shroud, but the light had troubled her eyes. She desperately wanted to climb back under the covers, but the hotel had warned them when they checked in that the water only ran hot for half an hour each morning, and the thought of bathing in cold water was more than she could bear. The face that had stared back at her from the small mirror above the sink had been pale and gaunt. Her skin had seemed gray, and deep shadows had appeared around her eyes. Her hair – normally her best feature – had been limp, lifeless, and for the first time she had noticed strands of white among the black. Not just one or two, but all along her parting and liberally salting her temples. How had she missed those before?

And she had been so tired. But then she thought that was probably just to be expected. She wasn't used to long flights; she must still be suffering from jet lag. She had climbed back under the blankets and had slept most of the morning, only getting out of bed to eat the soup she had ordered from room service. She hadn't really been hungry, but at least the bowl had been warm. She had cupped it in her hands, grateful for anything that might banish the cold from her fingers, even for a little while.

She had returned to bed and dozed fitfully through the afternoon. She woke that evening with a monstrous headache, like someone was pounding white-hot nails into her temples. The muscles along her jaw ached, like she had been grinding her teeth in her sleep, and there were ulcers across the roof of her mouth. She no longer checked her reflection when she went to the bathroom; the glimpses she now inadvertently caught worried her. Her eyes seemed to stare back at her from deep in their sockets, the patches underneath so dark that it almost looked as though she had smeared lampblack there, like those baseball players you sometimes saw on the TV. Her hair looked so brittle she was afraid it might snap should she run a brush through it.

The cellphone blinked uselessly at her from the nightstand. She wished she had a way to contact the pastor. Maybe something had gone wrong; surely this couldn't be normal? She had retrieved the ampule that contained the antivirus from her suitcase, and had been considering breaking it open when the telephone beside her bed had rung. It was Jan. They were leaving for Yongbyon first thing in the morning. Did she feel well enough to come? She had insisted she was fine, trying her best to inject a cheery tone into her voice. A little upset stomach, nothing more.

She had replaced the handset. So that was it. She had been tested, and she had almost been found wanting. But while she might have wavered she told herself she had not fallen. She would see this through. She had put the ampule back in its container, reminding herself of the pastor's words:

She had been chosen. God's plan for her had been revealed.

Now they seemed to be slowing again. Eliza opened her eyes, squinting behind her sunglasses as the morning sun set off fresh flares of pain behind her eyes. Ahead the car with Mike and Kenny was turning onto a concrete bridge. From the back seat of the Paektusan she could see a soldier in the drab olive tunic of the KPAGF emerging from the guard post, a rifle slung over one shoulder, a black fur ushanka perched on his head.

They were here.

*

IT'S SATURDAY NIGHT and I'm sitting in the chapel, waiting to be called down to confession. Everybody has to go, even the Guardians. Kane starts right after dinner, but there's thirty of us to get through so it can go on pretty late. He always hears confessions from the boys first, so at least I won't be waiting around as long as Mags. She probably won't get back to her cell until well past curfew. It's the only time in the week that's allowed.

When we first arrived in Eden Kane asked each of us what faith we'd been raised in. I was pretty sure I hadn't been raised in any. I'd asked Jack once and he'd said we were Pedestrians, which meant that when we saw a church we were allowed to just walk on by. He'd laughed long and hard when he'd come up with that one, but I figured it wasn't the answer Kane was looking for, so when it got to my turn I answered Catholic. I figured if there were questions I might be able to remember enough of the stuff from my time at Sacred Heart to fake it. But Kane had just said that was close enough for government work and moved on.

There'd been confessions at Sacred Heart too. We had to go before Mass on Sundays. The confessional was this ornately carved wooden booth that sat to one side of the altar. You went in, closed the door behind you, made the sign of the cross and knelt down in front of this grille that had a crucifix hanging over it. Behind the grille was a sliding wooden screen, and on the other side of the screen, in the next compartment, sat the priest. Once you went in the screen slid back, and you told the priest how long it had been since your last confession and all the bad stuff you'd been up to since. It was dark inside, and you had to whisper your sins, which I guess made it hard for the priest to figure out who it was unburdening themselves. Claus hated the confession box, so I always kept my list of transgressions short. I figured God being God he probably knew what I'd been up to anyway.

It's very different in Eden. After dinner on Saturdays we all go down to the chapel and he sends for us one by one. When it's your turn you walk down Back Street to his house and you go in and sit opposite him in those comfortable leather chairs and tell him what you've been up to. There's no darkened box, no grille, no screen. I guess there's little point in keeping it anonymous now that there's so few of us left. Whatever the reason, Claus much prefers it.

There's only one rule: you always have to confess something, even if it's been a slow week. Kane says we're all sinners but it's okay as long as you admit your sins and ask for forgiveness. This is comforting, although it does seem like a huge get-out-of-jail-free card. But hey, if those are the rules, who am I to argue? I've been having something of a special on impure thoughts for a while now, so finding something to confess is less of a problem for me. You can also mention someone else's sins, to help them out. Kurt's very good at that. He's always confessing stuff about Mags.

When you're done remembering all your sins Kane tells you your penance and then he gives you absolution. The penance you get varies depending on what you've confessed to, but for the most part it's having to say more prayers. I tend to go straight back to the chapel afterwards to get it over with. If you've done something particularly bad, or if you refuse to recognize what you've done is a sin, penance can be worse, like being confined to your cell. Mags gets that a lot. She was in her cell for a whole month after she got the mohawk. She said Kane couldn't tell her which rule she'd broken by cutting her hair that way and so she wasn't going to say she was sorry she'd done it. But that's just Mags. When I said earlier that she was like that dog in the pound that keeps biting people, I didn't mean it like she's mean or anything. She just doesn't get out of the way of trouble. I used to think it was because she didn't see it coming, but now I know it's not that. To her, things going smoothly doesn't compensate for that small piece of yourself you give up every time you back down. She's right I guess, and I try to be more like her. But if you're not built that way it's not always easy.

Absolution's the important bit of course. It means your sins are forgiven. I think it even works for mortal sins, like the one Miss Kimble committed. Miss Kimble was nice. I don't like the thought of her suffering eternal damnation. I'd like to think she had a chance to confess, although I don't see how she could have.

After you've been absolved of all your sins you get a drink of Kool-Aid and a HOOAH! as a treat. I think Kane got this idea from Benjamin. There are still several barrels of Kool-Aid powder in stores, although Lena thinks it's going off because she says sometimes it tastes funny. I'm not sure about that; mine's always fine. The regular supplies of HOOAH!s ran out years ago, so now Quartermaster has me strip them from the MRE cartons, which means I no longer get one for dessert when Marv and I go out scavenging.

Once I've finished the penance Kane gave me I head back to my cell, but Claus is restless. It's often like this after I've been outside, but I'm beginning to suspect Claus may be getting worse. It's hard to judge when the problem's inside your own head, though. I try not to think about what it'll be like in a few weeks when winter sets in and we're shut in here for months on end. At least we're back out again tomorrow. The storms can't be far off now, and Quartermaster wants one more haul before Kane locks Eden down. I reminded him again about what the farms need but he says it doesn't matter; we're only to go as far as Providence.

I have other plans, however. I checked the Yellow Pages I keep out in the farmhouse when we got back from Shiloah and there's a farm supplies store right next to a veterinary clinic on the other side of Ely. It'll probably be my last chance to get what I need to put me in Kane's good books before I attempt a conversation about my match. Ely's a bit of a hike, so we'll be out overnight, but the way Claus is acting up right now that suits me just fine.

I've asked Marv, obviously. I was thinking I might get some resistance, just because Ely's farther, and the storms could hit us any day now. But he just grunted, which in Marv-speak is as close as you get to an okay. I think Marv likes the farms, at least as much as Marv likes anywhere in Eden. Mags said she sees him over there sometimes, when we're not out scavenging. Scudder keeps Mags pretty busy, so it surprised me that she'd had time to help Jake out. When I asked her afterwards what she'd been doing over there she looked away for a second and then changed the subject, like she didn't want to say.

We've an early start tomorrow so I could really use the sleep, but Claus isn't happy with being confined and he's showing no sign of settling down. In the end I decide to go outside. Not *outside* obviously, but up on the roof. There's an access panel above the third floor landing that leads to a crawl space, just like in the mess. I grab my pillow and blanket and crack the door to my cell. It's after curfew so no one should be wandering around, especially up here, but I check anyway before stepping out. The main lights are out but the safeties remain on, casting the narrow corridor in shades of gray and green. The metal amplifies the slightest sound but I've learned to tread softly. A few seconds later I'm standing under the access panel. It only takes me a moment to unscrew the corner bolts, then I gently slide it to one side. I wince as the metal screeches, but it's just once, and not loud enough to travel down to the floors below. I push my bedding into the space above the ceiling and climb up after it. Within moments I'm standing on the dorm's flat metal roof. The steel plate makes it cold, but I'm not boxed in so Claus much prefers it. I choose a spot, spread out my blanket and lie back.

In Eden days and nights are defined by the arc lights bolted to the cavern roof. The main lights are cut fifteen minutes after the final buzzer and now the cavern is dark, except for the pale yellow glow cast by the bulkhead lamps dotted around the walls. It's not like the place is a riot of color in the daytime, but with the arc lights off it's like whatever little there is drains from the place. There's the occasional sound of footsteps from the street below as one by one the last of the girls head down to Kane's for confession, but after a while even that ceases and then for a long time there's nothing. Outside the storms might be raging, but inside the mountain it's always deadly quiet at night, like the whole world's gone to sleep.

Which I guess in a way it has.

I've almost drifted off when the sound of footsteps on the streets below brings me back. I know straight away it's not a Guardian patrol. Angus and Hamish are on duty tonight and they stomp around like a couple of trolls at a barn dance. Whoever this is, they're moving quietly, stopping every few seconds to listen, almost like they're trying not to be noticed. At first I think it's probably just Marv. We don't see much of him in Eden; he's got a cot in the old diesel generator room, and mostly he keeps to himself over there. He used to show up at mealtimes, but he doesn't even do that anymore. I think now he comes into the kitchens at night and fixes himself something. If I'm up on the roof I sometimes see him, long after curfew, walking down Front Street towards the mess.

Tonight the footsteps are coming down Back Street though, so it can't be him. I roll off my blanket and crawl to the edge of the roof to get a better view. But whoever it is they're moving along the edge of the building, sticking to the shadows. When they get to the corner they pause for a long moment. I shuffle along the edge as quietly as I can, waiting to see who will emerge beneath me.

Finally someone steps out into the street and a second later I recognize the cropped dark hair. It's Peck. He's carrying something bulky over his shoulder, although whatever it is the weight doesn't seem to bother him much. He walks right underneath me and in the dim light it takes a moment for my sleep-fogged brain to decipher the shape. It's the gray overalls of a Juvie. Their size and the cascade of long brown hair that hangs down from the collar means it can only be Lena. She looks like she's fast asleep. The farms have been putting in a lot of hours getting the harvest in, and she'll have been waiting for ages in the chapel, so I guess she must have nodded off during confession. Kane's probably told Peck to carry her back to her cell rather than wake her, which I guess explains why he's not walking around with his usual iron-heeled stride. Seeing Lena reminds me I still haven't given her the tests I brought back from Shiloah. I've stashed the sticks in the infirmary, so Kurt won't find them if he searches my room. I doubt he'd know what they were for, but he'd be certain to bring them to Kane, which might lead to some awkward questions.

I watch as Peck edges up to the corner of the building and stops, checking no one's on the street before crossing. Once he's slipped back into the shadows on the other side I return to my blanket.

I'm fast asleep moments later.

*

I THINK THE FIRST FEW MONTHS were the worst for all of us. And in one way I had it a little easier. I was still missing her, but by the time we got here I'd had almost a year to get used to the fact that Mom wasn't around. For most of the other kids that loss was fresh. Don't get me wrong; I was sad I wasn't going to see Sam and Reuben again. But I'd only known them for a little while, and there was always the chance they weren't going to want to keep me anyway, so it's not the same.

That's not to say that Claus wasn't being a royal pain in the ass about the whole living-inside-a-mountain situation. But at least we weren't sleeping by ourselves in the cells, not at first anyway. I have Miss Kimble to thank for that. The first night she set up cots on the ground floor of Dorm 4 and brought us all there. She and Benjamin took turns staying up, keeping an eye on us, comforting those that woke up crying for parents or brothers or sisters. That's how it was for a long while.

At some point Miss Kimble tried to start classes again. It was important for our education to continue she said, and if nothing else it would give us something to do, something to take our minds off what had happened. It would be what she called a coping mechanism. But Kane said that lessons could wait; we'd been through enough. Besides, he added, there weren't any schoolbooks in Eden. Miss Kimble said she didn't need books to teach us, but Kane wouldn't be moved. I think he must have listened to what she'd said though, because a few days after she first mentioned coping mechanisms we each got assigned chores. Mostly it was just cleaning up; loading and unloading the dishwashers, sweeping the floors in the dorms, cleaning the kitchens. The sort of stuff Mags and I had had to do in Sacred Heart.

As soon as we were done with our chores most of us would head over to the eastern tunnels to see what Benjamin was up to. As soon as Kane gave him the green light Benjamin had gone straight back to Quartermaster. In addition to the light tubes and garbage bags he had originally requested he told Quartermaster he would need to dismantle several sections of the stores' metal shelves. I don't think Quartermaster cared much for that, but now that Kane had given his support there wasn't much he could do. Benjamin brought the sections he had taken apart out to the east of the main cavern where he had commandeered one of the side tunnels, and reassembled them into long waist-high benches. He borrowed the tools he needed from Scudder and we all watched as he drilled holes in the top at regular intervals, which he explained were necessary for the plants' shoots to grow through. The mesh grating that would hold the roots in place underneath he fashioned from sections of catwalk he'd found in the old diesel power plant. He cut the garbage bags he'd gotten from the stores into sections that he hung around the outside of each bench, forming skirts that fell all the way to the floor. The assortment of tubs and containers he had collected sat underneath; these would catch the excess fertilizer that would run off the roots after they were sprayed. The last job was to hang the fluorescent lights above each bench that Benjamin said would take the place of the sun.

Kane visited the farms a lot in those early days. He seemed pleased with the progress Benjamin was making. One thing he was adamant about was that there would be no work on Sundays, though. There was service of course, right from the beginning, and sitting upright on the chapel's hard wooden pews without talking or fidgeting wasn't necessarily a relief from the week's labors. After we were done with service Kane would read to us from the Bible, as a treat. The stories weren't that great, but I guess it was better than no stories at all.

When the benches were finally ready Benjamin brought the seed potatoes he'd been storing in his cell. When Jake asked where he'd got them Benjamin said he'd taken them from a sack he'd found in the pantry on the day we'd arrived and had wrapped them in newspaper so they'd keep. He took a handful of the tubers and cut them in quarters, making sure each segment had at least a couple of eyes. Then he left them to stand underneath the fluorescent lights for a couple of days so that they could sprout shoots that he called chits. When he was happy that the chits were sturdy enough he showed us how to place them onto the mesh grating, directly underneath the holes he had drilled in the top of the bench. Then the black plastic skirts were closed to allow the tubers to germinate in the dark.

It was around the time we were helping Benjamin to place his first crop into the growing benches that Miss Kimble raised the idea of giving us lessons again. This time Kane said he'd thought about it some more and there wouldn't be any lessons, or at least not the kind we might have been receiving before. There was no longer any reason for them, he said. The world had changed; all the things we might have needed to learn before would no longer be of any use, so there would be little point filling our heads with it. He would need time to think about what sort of education might best suit the very different future that now awaited us. I could tell Miss Kimble wasn't happy about that at all.

Meanwhile things were busier than ever at the farms. The roots that were now growing through the grating had to be sprayed regularly, and that had to be done by hand. Benjamin had rescued a dozen or so plastic spray bottles from the garbage and these he filled with a fertilizer solution he had made from used coffee grounds, molasses and white vinegar he had found in the stores, and ash from the furnace. The final ingredient he said he needed for his homemade fertilizer was pee. Thankfully with a class of first graders on hand this hadn't been a problem. Of course the plants needed to be sprayed when the lights were off, just like now. When I told Benjamin I didn't like going into the tunnel in the dark he said it was okay. Instead he put me to work bringing water up from the reservoir and making sure the spray bottles were always filled.

Morning prayers found their way into our daily routine around the same time that those first roots appeared through the grating inside Benjamin's growing benches. It seemed like we were doing almost as much *ora* as *labora* by then. Years later, leafing through an old magazine I'd found out in Providence for items for my scrapbook, I came across a piece on the woman who had been President before Kane. Most of it was about her, and I was on the verge of tearing it up for kindling when I came to a paragraph about him. I didn't understand all the words, but the gist of it was that Kane had been an unusual choice as her running mate, given his 'fervently held evangelical beliefs'. The reporter described him as powerfully charismatic and said that he had been a formidable campaigner, particularly in somewhere called the Bible belt, where the President had struggled for support. (I tried to find the Bible belt in my atlas, but it wasn't there, so I'm thinking it was somewhere new). The article also said Kane had been a preacher before he ran for office, and something of a firebrand, and that was what had contributed to what it described as the potency of his appeal. I didn't know what firebrand meant so I had to look it up, later, back in the farmhouse. I'm not so sure they got that bit right; maybe the reporter just didn't know him as well as we do. Kane's certainly charismatic, but I've never heard him raise his voice in Eden, not even once. It made sense that he might have been a preacher before though, so I guess they got that bit right. And I suppose it was only natural that he would go back to that life now that his other, brief, one as President was over. Maybe that was his coping mechanism.

The first shoots appeared through the holes in Benjamin's growing benches a couple of weeks after we had placed the seed tubers inside. We all gathered in the tunnel that everybody was now calling the farms to watch. Benjamin didn't seem very happy, though. The shoots were pale and spindly and he said the leaves were the wrong color. He dropped the lights closer to the tops of the benches and left them for a few days. But that just turned the leaves brown and shriveled the edges, so he raised the tubes back up again. That was a little better, but the leaves were still too dark and he said it wasn't right that they curled under at the edges. In the weeks that followed he persevered, fine-tuning the height at which the tubes should be hung, experimenting with the amount of light and darkness the plants received each day, adjusting the composition of his fertilizer mix.

Miss Kimble was spending a lot of time over at the farms by then. She and Benjamin seemed to get on really well, so we'd see her over there most days. Even though we were now busy most of the time you could tell she hadn't given up on reintroducing lessons; it seemed like she'd take any opportunity to try and teach us something. When I first heard that Benjamin wanted to put pee on the plants he was trying to grow I told him I thought he was making a big mistake; Sam had always complained to Reuben that the grass never grew in the spot in the garden where Jackson liked to squat. But Miss Kimble said that urine (which she explained was just another word for pee) was a valuable source of chemicals called nitrogen, phosphorous and potassium, all of which were things that plants needed to grow. And when Jake asked Benjamin why the plants he was trying to grow kept dying and Benjamin said it was because they didn't like the artificial light from the tubes as much as they liked the sunshine they were used to, Miss Kimble started to explain that this was because the plants had evolved to use natural sunlight over billions of years. Kane happened to be passing through the farms as Miss Kimble was telling us this and for an instant I saw his eyes narrow, like he was annoyed with her for something, but he said nothing. Later he explained to us that it was just because Miss Kimble had made a mistake about evolution.

She may have been wrong about evolution, but I think Miss Kimble was probably right about coping mechanisms. Nobody cared much for the chores Kane assigned us, but it was good that we were busy in those first months, our days occupied by menial, repetitive tasks that crowded out the loss and stifled the pain, at least while you were doing them. I don't think it works forever though. Sooner or later the chore always ends, and even if there's another one waiting for you before you know it the curfew buzzer's sounding. And then the lights are dimmed and you have to return to your narrow cot or your small cell by yourself.

It was Benjamin that found her. One morning she just didn't come down for breakfast. When by lunchtime she still hadn't been seen Benjamin went to her room, in case she'd fallen sick. She'd taken a cell upstairs in Dorm 4, above where we were all sleeping. She hadn't locked the door, so when he knocked and there was no answer he just let himself in.

I guess Miss Kimble hadn't found the coping mechanism she'd needed. The blood had pooled around her, collecting in the rivets, in the seams where the metal plates joined. Benjamin spent two days scrubbing the floor so I'm sure it's perfectly clean, but we all moved out of Dorm 4 that afternoon and no one's slept there since.

Kane held a funeral for her the following Sunday. A funeral's basically like a regular service, only even longer. We had one when Mom died. He said some nice words, which made it seem like he'd known Miss Kimble longer than any of us.

The furnace is out in the eastern tunnels, between the old diesel power plant and the farms. Scudder fires it up once a week, to burn the regular waste Eden produces. Benjamin insisted on taking Miss Kimble's body outside, however. He said she would have wanted that. Kane didn't want to open the blast door. He said we couldn't be sure it was safe outside. But Benjamin wouldn't take no, and in the end Kane relented and said he could go as long as Peck went along to protect him. Marv wanted to go too, but Kane said it was enough that Benjamin was risking his life.

I don't know where Benjamin buried Miss Kimble. I guess Peck might. It was after the weather had changed, so the ground would have been hard by then.

*

WE LEAVE EARLY the following morning. Kane isn't happy that we're going out on a Sunday but winter's just around the corner now and every day might be critical. I get summoned to the chapel for the long version of the sheep among wolves on account of the fact that I'll be missing service, but then finally it's over and I can go. When I stop by the stores Quartermaster grumbles at giving us the extra MREs for what should just be a day hike, but I explain how easy it would be to get stranded out there this close to winter and in the end he relents. Claus manages to throw his usual tantrum in the tunnels, but then we're outside and I'm staring at another grainy dawn that's struggling to take shape over the lifeless hills to the east. Down at the farmhouse we add a couple of sleeping bags to our regular scavenging kit and then we set off.

The wind's dropped and it's eerily quiet. It's snowed since we were last out and we're trudging through drifts, Indian file, even on the turnpike. Marv keeps looking up. The sky's still heavy with it. There aren't many houses along this stretch of the highway and you don't want to get caught away from shelter in a snowstorm. But after three miles it's still holding and we leave the 'pike and head south on 491. The going's no easier here, but at least it's flat. I haven't been this way before. I ask Marv if he has and he just nods behind his respirator. I've no idea whether that means since we came to Eden or before. He doesn't seem to want to elaborate, but that's just Marv.

The road's a lot narrower than on the highway. I'm guessing under the snow it's just two-lane blacktop, and not much of a hard shoulder to speak of. You can tell it used to cut through woodland, but now all that's left on either side are bare and blackened trunks poking up through the gray, the ones closest to the road hacked God knows how long ago for firewood. When it's snowed like this the mile markers are mostly covered, so it can be hard to know exactly where the road is. You can normally work it out by following the telephone poles, but occasionally there are stretches without them. I don't know if they fell in the storms or were cut.

After a mile or so we come to a railroad crossing, the top of the dead lights just visible above the snow. Marv says we've entered Maryland; he pronounces it *Merlin*, like the wizard. I'm not used to Marv just saying things, and the unexpected sound of his voice in the cold silence startles me. I stop and look around while he marches on ahead. I don't see a sign, but I guess he just knows. Sometimes, something simple like Marv announcing we've crossed into another state causes the enormity of it all to suddenly hit me and I realize it's not just Providence or Shiloah that's like this. It's the whole of America, and beyond that probably the rest of the world.

An hour after we cross into Maryland we arrive at Fort Narrows. From the road I can see row after row of low brick buildings that look like they might once have been barracks, the snow drifted almost up to the eaves of their roofs. Marv tells me to wait out on the road while he goes in. There's a big *No Trespassing* sign, but I don't think anyone's going to call him on it.

We stop for lunch a little after. Marv chooses an old house with lap siding, a wraparound porch and a shingle roof. From the road it looks in fair condition, but as we get closer I can see the boards around the porch have been pried loose, exposing the studs and insulation underneath. The front door's busted open and the snow's drifted in a couple of feet. Still, it's the best shelter we've seen in a while and beggars can't be choosers.

I check out the kitchen while Marv goes down into the basement. There's a single jar of something sitting in the middle of one of the shelves in the old Frigidaire, but it's covered in a coat of furry gray mold that prevents me from even recognizing what it might once have been. I check the cupboards but they're bare. A chipped, stained mug sits on the counter, the only thing that remains.

I join Marv in the living room. He's already digging an MRE out of his backpack. We don't bother with a fire, and I eat my chili beans in silence. I've been working on Might Require an Enema, but it seems a little clunky, and in any event not sufficiently removed from my recent Meal Refusing to Exit masterpiece to stand on its own. I bag our trash and we set off again.

Outside there's still no wind and the bleak landscape has a silence to it that's unsettling. After a couple of miles we stop at a rise in the road. Just ahead there's a junction, the red of a stop sign just visible above the snow. I stare at it while Marv gets our bearings. It's faded but anything of color's welcome out here.

We head down to the junction and Marv takes us right. He stops again to check a mile marker, all but buried in a drift. We continue on, lumbering through open country, slowly cresting rolling hills, trudging into the shallow troughs between. All is barren, lifeless, only the occasional bare and blackened tree poking up through the gray snow to mark the way. I think how easy it would be to get lost in a place like this.

A couple of miles further on we come to a small crossroads at a dip in the road. There's a white sign with neat black letters poking out of the snow. The Zion Lutheran Church, it says, and beneath it, *Little Is Much If God Is In It*. Kane always says God is everywhere, but then Kane hasn't been outside since the Last Day. I sometimes wonder if God is in anything here anymore.

It begins with a single flake, drifting down out of nothing. Soon there are more, twisting and falling out of a leaden sky, until you can't see much more than fifty feet ahead of you. A little further on we come to the church. There's not much shelter and I can see Marv eyeing it as we pass, weighing the refuge it would provide against the unrelenting track of the sun behind the clouds. In the end he decides against it and we push on. We need to make Ely by nightfall and there's still a ways to go.

The snow keeps falling, heavier now, like a gray curtain pulling around us. Marv's checking the road markers more frequently. The outline of a fire truck separates itself from the gloom; we're on it almost before I see it. There's nothing to indicate how it got to be where it is; it just looks like it reached the end of its journey and has stood here ever since.

At last we come to a large weathered green sign. *Welcome to Washington County*. I ask Marv if we're close and he just grunts behind his respirator, but I think it's a yes. We take a left onto I-64 and the road opens up. Billboards stand in dead fields, advertising things that no longer exist. Some have collapsed, the metal supports weakened by rust or virus, the wind and the storms doing the rest.

We come to an intersection. The veterinary clinic's straight on, still a few miles down the highway. Ely's signposted to the right. The snow's still falling heavily, the collapsed traffic light gantry almost drifted out of sight. Nightfall's a few hours away yet, but dusk has already begun, and the temperature's dropping. Marv decides we should grab some shelter and sit it out. We can collect what we need in the morning.

We trudge into town. Long-abandoned houses sit lonely on empty lots, the spines of their roofs bowing under the weight of years of snow. Most have been stripped of their siding, the walls lying open to the studs. A large, squat brick building announces itself as the Ely High School, Home of the Leopards. Out front a tattered stars and stripes hangs on a peeling flagpole.

Marv leads us to a hotel on the corner of Main Street. There's a Dixie Diner opposite; a faded sign in the window says they're advertising for a grill cook. Inside the lobby smells of damp and rot and the plaster on the ceiling's bellied in swags where snowmelt's found its way in from the floors above. In the far corner there's a fireplace. The mantel and surround have already been removed, but most of the paneling's still attached to the walls. I set about prying it off and breaking it into pieces that will burn while Marv heads out to see if anything can be scavenged from the diner.

When I think I've got enough I go off in search of something to get the fire going. We each carry a couple of butane lighters and a squeeze bottle of accelerant in our backpacks. An even mix of diesel and gas works best. A small squirt would be enough to get the flames to catch and I'm tempted to use it instead of venturing out into the snow again. But Marv says the bottle's only for emergencies; I'll get in trouble if he finds out I've used it without at least looking for an alternative. I find a small plastic soda bottle on the floor behind the reception desk and use the blade from the leatherman to hack off the top. Then I zip my parka up and head back out. I've brought the length of plastic tubing I carry for siphoning gas, but I'm not planning to use it unless I have to. There's nothing worse than the taste when the first draw hits the back of your throat.

I find a recovery truck around back of Skeeter's Auto Parts, the fuel tank slung low behind the cab. I punch a hole in the bottom with the leatherman and wedge the cut-off plastic soda bottle into the snow underneath. I loosen the fuel cap to start the flow and wait. The diesel's cold and it runs like molasses, but eventually the bottle fills. I plug the hole. No sense in wasting; we might need to light the fire again in the morning.

Marv's already back in the lobby when I return. He's found a couple of tins of steak and gravy pie filling and some canned peaches so maybe we'll have an alternative to the MREs. I set to work lighting the fire. We've saved the plastic spoons from lunch and I fill them with a little of the diesel. I have to coax it a little, but soon I'm watching the flames climb upwards through the broken lengths of paneling, the strips of damp wood spitting and hissing as they catch.

Marv's already opened the cans. Sometimes what's inside will have spoiled, even if the metal's good. You can tell as soon as you open them: the smell'll be so bad it'll make you want to throw up; that's one way to get rid of your hunger, at least for a little while. But tonight we're in luck. Marv sticks the cans straight in the flames and I watch as the labels char and burn. I once stuck a tin of SpaghettiO's in the fire without thinking to pierce the top. It was right after I first started going outside, so I didn't know any better. Thankfully Marv noticed the metal swelling up and kicked it out of the coals before it went off like a grenade. He didn't let me eat that night or the following day during quarantine, so I'd learn my lesson. It worked though. I've never done anything stupid like that again.

My stomach growls as the smell of steak and gravy fills the room. Soon the sauce's bubbling and we fish the tins out with the leatherman pliers, slurping the pieces of steak straight from the can. I spill some down my parka but it tastes heavenly. I haven't eaten this well in I don't know how long.

Marv climbs into his sleeping bag after dinner. I'm tired as well, drowsy from the pie filling and the warmth of the fire. I could easily drift off, but instead I wait until I hear Marv snoring and then I dig *The Girl With The Dragon Tattoo* out of my backpack. I wouldn't normally have risked bringing it with me, but time outside is precious now. This could be our last trip before Eden gets locked down for winter and who knows when I'll have a book in my hands again, when I'll next have new stories to tell Mags?

I open the cover and thumb to the page where I left off.

I half-wake in the middle of the night from a dream I don't remember. I sit up and scan the room, charting gray shapes and darkness against memory to try and place where I am. The fire's died down and it's cold. Marv mutters something in his sleep then goes quiet again.

Sometimes when I wake like this it takes me a moment to tell whether it was the dream that was real or the world I'm waking into. In those few precious seconds it's possible to believe that things aren't the way they are, that what we're left with isn't real. That this cold, broken world has no more substance to it than the dream from which I'm waking, or the books into which I sometimes escape.

*

IT'S STILL SNOWING OUTSIDE when I wake the following morning, large ashen flakes tumbling down out of a sullen sky. Marv's already up, standing by the door, but you can't even see across the street. When he comes back he says we'll sit it out for a while, see if it eases. A few blackened lumps of charcoal are all that remain of the fire, but I can't be bothered to build it up again and Marv doesn't make me. We sit huddled in our sleeping bags eating the peaches he found in the diner. By the time it finally starts to slacken off it's already mid-morning. We pack up quickly. We've draped our gear near the fire overnight so it's mostly dry. I wash with melted snow I strain through a spare surgical mask, but I'm still tangy with sweat from yesterday's hike as we set out.

We leave Ely and head back out towards the highway. The tracks we made coming in the day before are already gone. The clouds are never thin enough to allow even the faintest of shadows, but this morning seems scarcely light at all. I look back after a few minutes; already the buildings are little more than charcoal smudges behind us.

We go right at the intersection and follow the road for a couple of miles until I spot a sign for the veterinarian's and the farm store. The wind's picked up and it seems to have gotten even darker. Quartermaster will expect his usual haul so Marv says he's going to go check out the Food Lion opposite while I get what I need for the farms. He tells me not to hang around; we've already lost a chunk of the morning and it looks like the weather's closing in again. If I'm not finished by the time he returns we're heading back, whether or not I've found what I need.

I scramble down the snow-covered embankment. The clinic's in a collection of single story buildings set back from an access road. The farm store sits next to it, its high parapet walls towering over the adjacent lots. I had planned on looking for something for whatever's affecting Jake's crop first, but Marv's warning's got me worried. I tell myself it won't take me long to find what I need for Kane in the vet's; I can tend to what the farms need right after.

All that's left of the door to the clinic is an empty frame, a few fragments of glass still gripped in the corners. I unstrap my snowshoes and step through, taking a moment to let my eyes adjust to the gloom. For some reason I'm suddenly uneasy, and there's that scratchy feeling I get inside my head that tells me something's not right. I look around, letting my gaze drift over the room, taking in the details. There are large spatters of blood on the floor, but it's long-dried, brown with age. Somebody's walked in it while it was still fresh, though; they've tracked it across the floor after them. That can't be what has spidey fussing, though; there's far worse than a little decade-old blood to be found in any Walmart or Piggly

Wiggly you care to wander into. I think of Maraschino guy, still clutching that jar of cherries with what's left of his frozen fingers. I look around again, trying to work out what's wrong. But nothing presents itself.

There's a small waiting area, a counter a receptionist would have sat behind. A single bloody handprint marks the center of the counter, as if someone had steadied themselves there. Spidey pings a little at that, but for some reason it doesn't concern me as much as the footprints. I feel like whatever's wrong is right there in front of me, like if I just wait here a little while longer the piece of information I'm missing will float to the surface. I don't have time for that, though; I need to figure out where the clinic stored its drugs, and I need to do it before Marv returns from the Food Lion. I force myself back to the task at hand.

There's a corridor to the left, with doors to what look like offices on either side. The sign behind reception says the operating room is to the right. I see a single door, at the end of a darkened hallway. That seems like a better bet, but for some reason I'm reluctant to follow the trail of bloody footprints down towards it. For the first time I notice there's a set of prints coming back out, too. I tell myself at least I won't have to face a body in there, but somehow that doesn't calm spidey like it should. From outside there's a flash of lightning, bright enough to bathe the small lobby in white light, followed seconds later by a peal of thunder. Marv will have heard it too; he'll be wrapping things up in the Food Lion, even if he's not done with his list. I shuck off my backpack and pull out the pry bar, telling myself it's because I'll need it to open the cabinets inside. I take a deep breath and hurry towards it, shoving my way through the swing doors, trying to ignore the bloody handprint in the center of the push plate.

A large stainless steel operating table occupies the center of the room. Against the nearest wall a row of glass-fronted cabinets, the glass reinforced with crisscrossed safety wire. The doors are locked, but behind the glass I can see shelf after shelf of medicines. That's where I'll find what I need. I can't help but notice the floor, however. The bloody footprints go around the table to the other side, and then return. Spidey is going spaz. We're no longer talking pinging. It's now like the *whoop!whoop!whoop!* sound a submarine makes when it's diving like crazy to avoid the depth charges dropping all around it.

I force my attention back to the cabinets. In the second one I see a whole shelf stacked with 50mg vials of Ketalar. Bingo. The lock resists the pry bar for a few moments, but then it gives with a loud crack. I shuck off my backpack and scoop in whatever's there. Kane will be pleased. There's loads, probably enough to see him through the winter. This will be even better than the cigars I found for him.

Time to get out of here. But instead of heading for the door I hesitate. I can't leave without knowing what's behind the operating table. I stare at it a moment longer, the pry bar still in my hand, as if the decision hasn't already been made, as if I still have some choice in the matter. And then I slowly make my way around, trying to avoid the prints left by bloody boots that, at one point many years before, made a similar journey.

It's a spent shell casing I see first, then the boot. Only this time there's no lapse, no mental fumbling while the different parts of my brain reach out to each other and finally make the connection. I see it straight away. The steel eyelets have been removed, just like on the boots I'm wearing. I tell myself that doesn't have to mean anything. Once people understood about the virus they might have taken similar precautions. But I don't really believe it, just like I didn't believe the footprints leading out of the theater might mean there wouldn't be a body in here. The reality is I've seen my share of corpses, and none of them had bothered to do that before. Why would they? There weren't any safe zones out here, at least not before Kane scorched the skies. Marv and I carry metal all the time, when we're outside, scavenging. The only reason we strip it from our boots and our clothing is to get back inside Eden.

Now that the connections are forming there's no stopping them. The reason I knew something was wrong the moment I stepped into the lobby is floating up, only for once I don't want it to come to the surface. I tell myself I could still head for the door, but instead I take another step so that I can finally see what's behind the operating table.

And there it is, just as I knew it would be. A body, once large, now shrunken inside a huge gray Canada Goose parka. A parka just like mine. The metal snaps have been cut out, the zipper pull replaced with a plastic one. From the state it's in it looks like the body's been here a long time. What brought him here is obvious. A bullet hole, punched through the right breast pocket; he probably came in to try and patch himself up. The zipper's pulled most of the way down, and when I use the end of the pry bar to push back the lapel I find a similar hole in thermals that were once white, but are now caked in chocolate-brown blood.

My eyes travel back up to the man's face. What skin is left there, now mostly clinging in small patches to the cheekbones and around the jawline, is dry as leather, and dark as coal. Maybe it's that fact that makes the clenched teeth look so white, even after all this time. In the middle of his broad forehead is a bullet hole to match the one in his chest. Otherwise the face looks much like all the others I see, all dried up and caved in, the eyes long rotted out of their sunken sockets.

I don't need to see the signet ring on the little finger of his bony right hand to know who this is. The ring's caked in his blood, but if I were to scrape it off I'd find a black shield and a white eagle's head, and a banner that reads *The Screaming Eagles*, and underneath, *101st Airborne*.

I open my backpack and pull out a spare Ziploc bag. I turn it inside out and use it to gently pull the ring off his finger. The skin has long since fallen from the bones, leaving only tendons and ligaments, dried taut as wire. The ring slips off easily and I fold it into the bag and slide the plastic zipper closed and place it in the side pocket of my parka.

As I'm standing I hear Marv's voice. He's out on the highway shouting for me. But I've already made the connection. It's the boots. Or more precisely, the boot prints made by the person that stood right where I'm standing and put a round in Benjamin's forehead. That's the reason spidey has been going ape ever since I set foot inside. The diamond pattern in the center of the sole. The deep lugs around the outside and on the heel. The boots Benjamin's wearing are just like mine; the tread's a crisscross waffle, stippled, with narrow indents around the edges. But I know the prints made by the boots Benjamin's killer wore. I've seen them countless times, in the dust of the tunnel floor by the portal, in the snow whenever we unstrap our snowshoes, even in the locker room inside Eden.

And the person who owns those boots is standing outside, shouting at me to quit stalling and come on out.

*

ELIZA'S PULSE BEAT in her throat like the flutter of an insect wing.

Ahead the barrier had been raised and the lead car was moving forward. Moments later their Paektusan was also advancing through the checkpoint. The guard maintained his salute, but she could feel his eyes, staring down into the car as they drove past. Her hand went to her chest, her fingers searching for the familiar shape of the crucifix resting against her skin under her blouse.

She looked out of the window, trying to get her bearings. She still found it hard to believe she was actually here. How many hours had she spent in her cubicle, poring over satellite images of this place? Her first thought was that it was huge. Even though she had meticulously measured each of the buildings from the glossies it was clear now that the true scale of the facility had escaped her. Row after row of featureless concrete structures, stretching as far as the eye could see. It reminded her of the closed nuclear cities at Sarov and Ozersk she had studied when she had first joined the agency.

They drove past a steam plant, and then what looked like a workshop. Several buildings with rows of small windows squatted opposite; probably accommodation for those working here. In front a memorial, and then a structure on her left whose purpose was not immediately obvious, the traditional Hanok-style roof incongruous among the huge blocks of gray concrete towering over it.

The convoy stopped in front of a drab building and they were ushered out. She had to hold her hand up to shield her eyes as the car door opened. It was winter; the sun was still barely above the horizon. How could it be this bright? Her legs had gone to sleep on the journey. Pins and needles stabbed up from the balls of her feet and she winced at the pain, reaching a hand out to steady herself against the car door as she climbed out. Once she judged it was safe to let go she jammed her hands deep into the pockets of her coat, clenching and unclenching her fingers to try and warm them up.

They were led up some steps, past a bronze statue of the Dear Leader. She hadn't been able to warm up inside the car, even with the heater blasting, but now she was outside it felt bitterly cold. A guard held the door open and she stepped into a tiled lobby. It seemed to be only marginally warmer in here, but at least she was out of the sun's merciless glare. They were led down a dark corridor and shown into a small meeting room. She felt her heart quicken. Would he be here? Could it be over this quickly?

She closed her eyes, trying to picture his face from the photos the pastor had sent her. The file had been waiting one evening after she had arrived home from work, just sitting there on the kitchen table in her small apartment. She had flipped the brown envelope over, but of course there had been no return address, no clue as to how it had arrived there. Inside there had been no note, no covering letter, just a thin dossier on the man she would meet. Pak Soon Ok, the regime's chief nuclear scientist. Trained in the 'nineties in Russia, he had risen quickly through the ranks to become one of the regime's favored sons. He would have unrestricted access to every one of their nuclear sites; the file said he spent most of his time travelling between them, making sure his various projects were proceeding according to plan. Once infected, he would quickly contaminate each of the enrichment facilities and in one stroke they would have achieved what decades of crippling sanctions had failed to accomplish. She had asked the pastor what would happen then, and he had explained that as soon as they had confirmation that the virus had done its job it would be deactivated remotely. Eliza thought he had sounded a little vague on how this might happen, but afterwards she thought she remembered him referring to satellites.

The impoverished country's ambitions to generate electricity from nuclear power would also be thwarted, of course, and she had had some misgivings about that. Everyone had seen the satellite images of the North at night, an almost perfect absence of light, sandwiched between the glittering constellations of the South and China. And now she had experienced the power shortages first hand she knew how bad things really were. But the pastor had quoted to her from one of her reports (she had felt a little surge of pride at that, even though she knew it was sinful). Hadn't she herself warned of the dangers of the outdated gas-graphite technology they still used? It was only a matter of time before an incident at one of the reactors, and if that were to happen radioactive materials would be spread over a potentially vast area. Surely it could only be a good thing that those facilities would be shut down as well? Besides, the pastor had added, once it was confirmed that her mission had been successful the international community would fall over itself to provide aid. It was true that there might be a little immediate hardship, but that could not be helped if a much greater good were to be accomplished. And she should rest assured that the good she would be doing in the longer term would be immeasurable.

It all depended on Pak being here, on her being able to meet him and initiate some form of physical contact. The virus could be transmitted through the air, but to be certain of contamination it would need to be inhaled over a period of hours. Even if, God willing, she were to meet Pak she might only be in his presence for moments. No, she would have to shake his hand.

Eliza stepped into the small conference room, her heart racing. Half a dozen men were already waiting, but a quick glance around told her that

Pak was not among the group assembled. A slight man of about sixty with a high forehead and a scrawny, wattled neck stepped forward, blinking continuously behind a pair of thick, black-rimmed glasses. He introduced himself as Dr. Hyun Jang Yop, the director of the facility. He spoke hesitantly in English, explaining that he would be responsible for their tour, which would follow after a short introductory briefing. One by one he introduced his colleagues. All older men - Eliza guessed the youngest was in his late fifties - each bowed in turn at the mention of his name. Their clothes looked worn; the cuffs and collars of their shirts were frayed, their shoes were scuffed.

The last man to be introduced was younger. Dr. Hyun introduced him simply as Mr. Kun, a representative from the General Bureau of Atomic Energy, adding nervously that the facility reported to the Bureau. Kun gave a shallow bow. Eliza noticed he had a much nicer suit than Dr. Hyun. His shoes looked new and they had been freshly polished.

Hyun invited them to sit and then went to a flip chart in the corner to begin his presentation. Jorg and Mike had taken their jackets off, but Eliza kept her gloves and hat on, her coat buttoned up. It was so cold in here. She fumbled with the briefcase she had brought, retrieving a pad. Jan had told her it was her job to take notes, but her fingers were numb and she struggled to grip the pen. The pain behind her eyes had abated slightly now that they were inside, but it still felt like someone was grinding glass back there.

Thankfully Dr. Hyun was brief. Soon they would visit the reactor they had enquired about. They would have the opportunity to inspect the pumping station that was drawing water from the river. After lunch they would be driven to a separate part of the facility to see the centrifuge plant. Mr. Kun spoke up, telling them that they would need to leave all cellphones, cameras or other recording devices in this room for the duration of their visit. Reluctantly Eliza removed the cellphone the pastor had given her from her pocket and placed it on the table. She noticed for the first time that it was dead, which was a little strange. It had been charging on her bedside table all night and she hadn't used it since they had left the hotel that morning.

As they left the room Dr. Hyun asked whether anyone wanted to visit the restrooms before they began. Eliza followed the signs down a narrow corridor. She had hoped for a dryer, so that she might at least warm up her hands before they had to go back outside, but there was only a single paper towel dispenser. She slipped off her gloves and ran the hot tap for a minute, testing it with one finger, desperate for anything to banish the cold from her aching fingers. But the water ran lukewarm at best.

As she turned off the tap she caught a glimpse of herself in the mirror. Her sunglasses hid how her eyes had sunken back into their sockets, the dark circles underneath, but there was no disguising her hollow cheeks, the ashen tone of her skin. And when she pulled back her hat she saw that the hair at her temples was now mostly white. Only a few more hours, she told herself, and then, God willing, it would be over.

She dry-swallowed a couple of Tylenol and went back out to join her colleagues.

*

I HEAR MARV again and I call back to him, trying to keep the fear out of my voice.

*I'm coming.*

There's no point trying to hide; he knows I'm in here. He'll have seen the tracks leading down the embankment, onto the access road. There's no other set heading back out. If I don't return to the highway soon he'll come looking for me.

I quickly check the pockets of Benjamin's parka, but they're all empty. I take another look around the operating theater, but nothing else seems obviously out of place. I feel like there's still something here I'm missing, but I don't have time to search properly.

I go back out into the reception area, following the trail of bloody prints Marv's boots made as he left. My eye catches the glove print on the counter again, and just as spidey pings me another warning it occurs to me that Benjamin wouldn't have needed to go anywhere near there if he was on his way to the operating room. I hurry over, aware that any second Marv might decide to come down here to see what's keeping me. A bunch of papers lie strewn across the workstation that sits behind the raised countertop. I'm about to move on when the corner of something blue poking out from underneath catches my eye. It's a *Standard Oil* road map. A ragged hole has been punched through the bottom corner, and the area around it is stained a deep russet brown, the pages stuck together with long-dried blood. I start to open it but the paper's weakened along the folds from countless openings. If I try and examine it now it'll probably just disintegrate, and besides I don't have time. I hear Marv calling again. I quickly refold it, sliding it as carefully as I can into the inside pocket of my parka.

I pick up my snowshoes where I left them by the busted door and make my way back out. It's noticeably darker outside than it was when I went in to the clinic. Gray clouds hang low and heavy in a restless sky, and I hear the rumble of thunder, closer now. Up on the highway Marv doesn't look pleased. He's waving at me impatiently, telling me to hurry up. I hesitate a moment longer and then I start making my way up the embankment.

'What kept you Junior? I've been standing up here hollerin' for the last ten minutes.'

I tell him sorry, that I didn't hear him above the wind and the thunder.

'What were you doing down there anyway? I thought you were going to the farm store.'

I mumble something about remembering some meds we need for the infirmary. Marv stares at me for a long moment, like he's trying to work out what I've really been up to.

'Well, aw'ite. No time for that now, though. Weather's movin' in fast. We got to hoof it.'

As if to make his point there's a flicker of light from deep inside the clouds, followed a second later by a clap of thunder, much louder than it was only minutes ago. I start inside my parka, even though I knew it was coming. Marv doesn't seem to notice. He points to a couple of plastic bags by his feet.

'I've split what I found in the Food Lion. That there's your share. I ain't haulin' it for you.'

I slide my backpack off my shoulders and start transferring items into it. It's all the usual stuff. Somewhere at the back of my mind I note that there's no treats for Quartermaster, which means he'll be in a bad mood with me. That's if I ever see Quartermaster again, of course.

Marv doesn't wait for me to finish. With one last look at the sky he turns and heads north along the highway, back the way we came yesterday. I finish loading my backpack and sling it onto my shoulder.

I don't know what else to do, so I follow him.

The storm chases us north for the rest of the afternoon, the intervals between the shudders of lightning and the peals of thunder growing shorter and shorter as it steadily runs us down. Marv sets a pace I haven't seen before, and it takes everything I have just to keep up, even though he's the one who's breaking trail. The thermals I wear are supposed to wick the sweat away, but soon they're overwhelmed and it's running freely down my back and thighs. I unsnap the throat of my parka, hoping that it'll allow me to gulp some more air through the mask I wear. Any thoughts of making a run for it are forgotten. I couldn't hope to outpace him. My focus narrows to the task of fitting my snowshoes into the tracks he leaves.

The snow holds off until we're back on 491, but then it suddenly darkens and heavy ashen flakes start to tumble out of the churning sky. Visibility drops to a hundred yards, then fifty, then twenty-five. The world around us now appears only briefly, out of a gloom rent by streaks of lightning.

Marv's pace eases a fraction, and for the first time since we set off I start to get my breath back. My mind is spinning, chasing itself in panicky circles. He must know what I've just seen. The only explanation I can come up with for why he's even allowing me to get closer to Eden is the same reason the cat doesn't immediately dispatch the mouse. And that doesn't bear thinking about. I look around. Perhaps I should take my chance now; maybe I can lose him in the storm. But then what? There is no destination other than Eden. I can't beat Marv to it and if he gets there first he can just wait for me to arrive. I resign myself to the fact that, for now at least, my only option is to follow Benjamin's killer into the darkness.

Just as I've reached that conclusion Marv leaves the road and heads towards a single story house set a little ways back from the road. It sits among what once would have been a stand of trees, but are now little more than a collection of bare and blackened stumps. A narrow porch wraps around the front and a trellis, intertwined with what might have been rose bushes, braces the front steps. A small part of me, apparently unaffected by my current predicament, is surprised the trellis hasn't been stripped and broken down for firewood. Was it the thorns that made it not worth the effort, or was it just randomly spared? The rest of me wonders if this is where he'll do it. Maybe he was hoping I'd make a break for it, out on the road, but now he's grown tired of waiting.

Marv walks up on to the porch and opens the screen. I watch as he tests the door behind. He doesn't bother with the pry bar, just takes a half pace back and aims a boot at a spot near the handle. There's the sound of wood splintering and the lock gives, the door lurching inwards on its hinges. He steps over the threshold and then he turns to look at me. Lightning strikes somewhere nearby, bathing him briefly in stark white light, the shadow of the doorway black around him. The air suddenly smells like it's been burned.

'What's up, Junior? Waiting for a' invite?'

It occurs to me that those are the exact words he said to me ten years ago, right before I first set foot inside Eden. I look around, weighing my options. I don't see any, so I follow him in.

Marv's already broken out an MRE when I get inside, so I do the same. While it's heating up I scout the place. Scavenging requires a certain low-grade thinking, the only kind my adrenalin-addled brain is capable of right now. It also means I have an excuse not to be in the same room as him, at least until I manage to compose myself. Out on the highway the goggles and mask hid my face. Now that we're inside I have to take them off and I'm worried what I've seen in the clinic will surface in some readable way there.

I move from room to room, letting my eyes roam over what's on offer. I find a plastic quart bottle of Fireball that's two-thirds full. The label shows a demon with flames for hair, spitting fire. There's a bottle of Jack Daniels with maybe a third left sitting next to it. I transfer the Jack to a small plastic Coke bottle that's lying on the floor and shove both in my backpack. Then when I can't put it off any longer I return to the living room and sit on the floor to eat. I don't have much of an appetite, but I'm shivering inside my sweat-soaked thermals now, and at least the food's warm. I stare at the wall as I dig into the carton with my plastic spoon, risking only the occasional sideways glance in Marv's direction. Outside the storm continues to rage, the windows shaking in their frames with the strength of it. Marv doesn't bother with either coffee or cigarettes. I barely have time to bag our trash before we set off again.

When we return to the road the sky's a churning soup of gray and black, the clouds occasionally lit from within by flashes of light. Now and then the lightning breaks free to stab the ground below, but the snow's falling too heavily to make out exactly where it strikes. My thoughts are still caught in an endless loop; I'm unable to make sense of anything I think I know. At some point in the snowstorm we must pass the fire truck, and Fort Narrows, and the railroad crossing, but I don't recall seeing any of them. The first I know we're at the junction where 491 hits the turnpike and I realize we're not far from home. The snow's still falling but it seems to have eased a little; the thunder and lightning are further off now. Somewhere behind the clouds the sun must be setting, because a darkness drawing in from the west is replacing the storm's gloom. If Marv's planning to have sport with me he'll need to do it soon.

But he doesn't. He leads us back to the farmhouse, and as usual heads straight for his room. I wait in the kitchen for a long time after I hear the key turning in the lock, wondering what I should do. I could go back up to the portal right now. We were only supposed to be going as far as Providence, so the Guardians might not realize I haven't been out long enough to finish quarantine. But they'd certainly think to ask why Marv wasn't with me, and even if I can make up a story to get past whoever's on duty I'd still have to explain myself to Kane when I tell him about Benjamin and Marv. And skipping quarantine's something I could get in a lot of trouble for, regardless of what I've brought back for him from Ely.

In the end I decide against it. I go to my room and move the bed against the door.

*

THE NIGHT CRAWLS past.

I stay awake, listening for any sounds coming from Marv's room. I've taken the pry bar and the leatherman from my backpack and placed them on the bed next to me. The leatherman has a knife; I keep the blade sharp. I take out the squeeze bottle of gas and the butane lighter, but then put them back again. I figure I'm as likely to set myself on fire as Marv if he tries to attack me.

I'm exhausted from the hike back, but sleep won't come; the faintest sound from outside, the wind howling under the eaves or gusting against the window panes, is enough to set me off. At some point I must drift off, because I wake with a start to a noise from the hallway, right outside my door. Marv's come back out of his room and is pacing up and down, like he sometimes does. I reach for the leatherman and flick the blade out, holding it in front of me. Marv's footsteps go up and down the corridor a few times more, and there are other sounds, too, like he's scratching at the floor out there. Eventually it stops and he returns to his room. I hear a key turning in a lock and it goes quiet again, except for the sounds of the storm still raging outside.

Finally somewhere behind the clouds the sun rises and another gray day breaks over the dead fields outside my window. I've brought my quarantine MRE in with me, so I don't need to leave the room. There's an empty Coke bottle in the closet in case I need to pee, but I reckon the hike back from Ely yesterday has sweated most of the fluid out of me. I'll probably be good if I just sip water from my canteen.

I pull out *The Girl With The Dragon Tattoo*, but I'm struggling to focus on the words on the page. In the end I put it down and instead try and figure out why Marv might have wanted to kill Benjamin. They were both at Eden when we arrived, so they must have known each other before. I don't know how well, though. It could have been years, or just a few weeks. I don't remember them being particularly friendly. But then Marv's not particularly friendly with anybody.

I begin to wonder whether I've made a mistake about the boot prints. I don't think so though. I mean, I've seen them often enough. But even setting that rather large detail aside, if Marv didn't kill Benjamin in Ely why would he have lied and told everyone that he'd broken his leg and died out past Shiloah?

The room slowly darkens as the sun completes another cold transit over our lifeless world. I hear a key turning in a lock outside in the hallway and I jump when Marv's fist thumps loudly on my door. My hand's already reaching for the knife, but then I realize he's just letting me know quarantine's over and it's time to return to Eden. I stash the signet ring I took from Benjamin under my bed, still wrapped in the Ziploc bag I used to pull it off his finger. Marv's already waiting for me in the kitchen and we head out. The storm's moved on a little, but it's still pounding the hills in the distance, lightning stabbing down from the thunderheads above. I strap on my snowshoes and we set off up the slope.

When we get to the portal Marv stands aside as usual, waiting for me to go inside. For once I'm not complaining. I wriggle through the collapsed section of tunnel, pushing my backpack ahead of me, trying to ignore Claus's whining about being back underground. I've got my story ready about the vials of ketamine I've brought back for Kane; I've already told Quartermaster the infirmary needs stocking and so if any of them think to check with him that should hold water. I doubt they will though. The Guardians are generally lazy, so I'm pretty relaxed about whatever lies I might have to tell. As I scramble over the last section of rubble I realize I haven't called ahead to announce my presence.

It's not much darker in the tunnel than it was outside and by the time I reach the end of the collapsed section my eyes have already adjusted. Jason and Seth are on duty. I was hoping for Tyler and Eric, but at least it's not the Fat Twins. I place the backpack on the ground and lift the crucifix by the chain from underneath my thermals. Seth reluctantly gets out of his plastic chair, wanders over to the quarantine fridge and snaps on a pair of gloves.

'We were expecting you back last night.'

My nerves are already frazzled from finding out about Benjamin, I can't have slept more than an hour last night, and to top it off Claus is already letting me know I'm in for a doozy of a hissy-fit once we start back into the tunnel. It's a real effort to keep the tone out of my voice.

'Haven't you heard the weather outside? We had to get out of the storm.'

Seth just grunts, like he really doesn't care. He gives the crucifix I hand him a cursory inspection then dumps it in the plastic Tupperware with my name on it. Once he's taped the edges the container goes back in the fridge. Marv still hasn't come through. I don't know what he finds to do in there, but for once I'm happy that he's not right on my tail.

I walk through the scanner, the backpack in my hand. Seth takes it from me and empties the contents on to the table. The small glass vials I've brought back for Kane clink against each other as they come to rest among the other items Marv's scavenged from the Food Lion. Seth picks one of the vials up and spends some time holding it between his fingers, pretending to read the label on the side. I wait patiently while we go through this charade. Unless the label somehow now says 'Seth' there's little chance of him being able to figure out what it says, let alone work out what it's for.

I hear Marv making his way down the rubble behind me. Jason gets up out of his chair and Seth takes it as his cue to put the vial back on the table. He moves on to the plastic bottle of Fireball. He won't be able to read the label on that either, but the fire-breathing demon seems to amuse him. He makes a show of examining the cap and tamper seal (yes, Seth, plastic, I checked) and then finally he puts it back on the table. Without saying a word he grabs a bottle of shampoo and slips it into his pocket and we're done. I quickly return the other items to my backpack.

I collect the flashlight I left yesterday morning and make my way into the darkness without waiting for Marv. The count begins as soon as I flick it on. Soon I'm leaving the horseshoe behind, and then my boots are splashing through the puddles that mark the first blast vent. The pale beam provides little comfort now, and Claus is already fretting about what sitting in the cold for two days has done to the batteries. Left at the junction, the darkest part, and it's no longer images of the bodies waiting just under the snow out on the turnpike my mind conjures out of the inky blackness. It's Benjamin, lying on the cold floor of an operating theater in a small veterinary clinic out past Ely. And the person who's standing over him, the toe of one boot resting in a dark puddle of his blood, is in the tunnel right behind me.

I stop for a second, listening for his footfalls in the darkness. I think I hear something, but it's hard to tell above the pulsing of blood in my ears, the hammering of my heart. Surely he won't do anything now we're inside? I pick up the pace, just in case. By the time I reach the second blast vent I'm almost running. Claus is urging me on and I'm on the verge of abandoning thought and bolting blindly into the darkness. I wipe a hand across my face and somehow force myself to slow down.

At last I reach the blast door. I lean on the intercom button, holding the flashlight under my face so whoever's inside can see it's me. After what seems like forever there's the heavy clunk of bolts receding and the whine of the electric motors as the huge metal door begins to open, allowing light from inside to seep out into the tunnel. A few more seconds and the gap will be wide enough. I give one final look back. I think I see a flashlight in the distance.

I squeeze through and head straight for the shower room. I strip off, dump my clothes on top of the nearest crate, and step under the steaming jets, scrubbing away the sweat and grime of the last couple of days, and with it some of the bitter tang of fear. My breathing finally starts to return to normal. The hot water feels good, but I don't linger. As soon as I'm done I step out and towel myself dry. I transfer the vials and the whisky into the pockets of the threadbare robe and place my outside clothes in the plastic crates stacked against the wall, remembering at the last minute to remove Benjamin's map from the pocket of my parka. Then I snap the lids in place and hurriedly seal the rim with tape. I've just finished when I hear the water coming on in the shower behind me.

Claus gets to twitching at the sight of the scanner, but I'm safe now. Marv won't do anything here; he knows there are cameras. I lay on the vinyl-cushioned platform and wait while it delivers me into the dark heart of the machine.

*

THE SCAN FINALLY ENDS and the platform slides out. I head to the locker room and change into a clean t-shirt and gray overalls. The ketamine, the quart of Fireball, the small plastic Coke bottle of Jack and Benjamin's map all get distributed among the overall's pockets, then I head out into the safety of Eden. It's already after curfew, and the main cavern's dark , with only dim glow from the bulkhead lamps to light the empty streets.

I'm about to cross Front Street and head for the dorm when I hear voices, drifting up from the pedestrian tunnels. I stop and listen. They're too far off to make out words, but it doesn't sound like the usual murmur of conversation. I'm tired and my mind's still reeling from what I've learned about Marv; I should just head back to my cell. But something about the voices is wrong. I glance behind me, into the corridor that leads back to the locker room. I have time; he'll be in the scanner for at least another ten minutes.

I creep down the tunnel, trying to make as little sound as I can. The glass vials in my pocket clink against each other with each step I take. I wish I'd thought to bring something to wrap them in, when I was back in the farmhouse, but there's nothing I can do about that now. I continue to edge forward, keeping to the granite wall. As I pass the stores the voices grow louder. They seem to be coming from the cavern that houses the power plant. There's definitely something in the tone that suggests tension, an argument.

As I reach the entrance to the reactor cavern I see Angus and Hamish. Their backs are to me, and whatever exchange is taking place is happening on the other side of them. The overalls in Eden are generously cut and Angus and Hamish have both opted for the largest size we have in stores. Nevertheless they fill them out impressively; I can't see what's going on behind them.

I hear a voice that sounds familiar. It belongs to a girl and it's raised, like whoever it is they're angry, but there's fear there too. Suddenly Angus steps forward, raising his arms and in the instant before he grabs her I see that it's Mags. Kurt's standing opposite, that wolfish grin playing across his lips. Mags tries to evade him, but Angus has surprised her, and he manages to get his arms around her before she can step out of the way. He lifts her off the ground easily, pinning her arms to her sides inside his. She tries to kick, but Angus just squeezes her tight, forcing the air out of her.

I feel something inside me clench like a fist and the next thing I know I'm running towards them. The bottles in the pockets of my overalls swing freely as the liquid inside sloshes around; the glass vials I've brought back for Kane rattle loudly, jostling against each other. None of that matters. I'm no longer trying to be quiet. I might even be shouting, but right now it's unclear whether that's happening inside my head. I don't have a plan other than to make Angus put Mags down.

Hamish turns around and looks at me. There's a long pause while the small walnut that passes for his brain works out what's happening and then his vacant features rearrange themselves into a smile, like this is a moment he's been waiting for. He steps into my path, raising a meaty forearm. I'm focused on batting away the sausage-like fingers reaching out to grab me, so I can get to Mags. I never see the other arm, the one that's slipped the billy club from the belt around his waist.

He doesn't bother to swing it.

I used to own a bike, back when we lived in New Orleans. Jack picked it up for me, when Mom said I was old enough to learn. It wasn't new. In fact I'm guessing from the way the paint was chipped and the chrome was pitted and spackled that I was only the latest in a long line of kids to take custody of that Schwinn. But I loved it, from the moment I first laid eyes on it. This wasn't a child's bicycle, with training wheels and streamers trailing from the handlebars. It was a real bike, with racing tires, and gears and drop handlebars.

Mom got angry with Jack when she saw what he'd brought back. True, it was a shade big for me. Even with the seat dropped all the way my feet lost contact with the pedals long before they reached the lowest point in their revolution, which meant I would have to ride it standing up. But I was already taller than everyone in my class, with limbs that suggested I might have been at least part daddy long-legger. And I was in the middle of yet another growth spurt. In no time it would fit me perfectly. If she made Jack take the Schwinn back to the thrift shop and get me another, in a matter of months I'd be stuck with a bike that was too small, and who knew when one like this might come along again. So I pleaded with her to let me keep it. Jack chimed in, saying he'd fix the Schwinn up good as new. Whether or not she believed him the promise was enough to make Mom relent.

In the end Jack did little more than oil the chain and set me off. I struggled with that bike from the first. It was heavy, and the frame was a little out of true, which meant it wobbled dangerously until I could manage to build momentum. And momentum brought its own set of problems. Riding the Schwinn would have been a precarious proposition even for an older kid, with longer legs and a season or two in the saddle. The gears were treacherous; I learned early on not to touch them. Even when not provoked they couldn't be trusted, dropping my privates sickeningly close to the crossbar each time they slipped. The back brakes did little other than squeal, no matter how hard you squeezed. The fronts were apt to pitch you over the handlebars if you as much as thought about applying them.

In the end my love affair with the Schwinn ended abruptly, a few short weeks after it had begun. Mom had told me that I was only to ride in the park, and so I had walked around the block, waiting until I was safely out of sight to mount it. I had already mastered the art of getting the bike up to speed and this Saturday morning I was standing high and proud on the pedals, lord of all I surveyed, deftly adjusting my balance as the Schwinn swayed and wobbled beneath me.

I felt the tension disappear from the chain an instant before it broke. I instinctively grabbed for the front brakes, squeezing them for all they were worth. Applied by themselves they would have tipped me clean over the handlebars, and after the obligatory tears I would have limped home to Mom oozing blood from a skinned forehead or a grazed knee. But this morning the Schwinn had something else in store for me. The chain jammed in the spokes as it flailed itself free, and even as I applied the front brakes I could feel the back wheel lock, the old tire getting ready to smear a thick line of rubber onto the concrete as it skidded. Instead of doing what I was expecting and catapulting me over the handlebars I was shot straight forward. Without thinking I stuck my feet out wide for balance.

The stem is the part of a bicycle that connects the handlebars to the front fork. The Schwinn's was machined from a single piece of aluminum that rose several inches out of the steering tube and then goose-necked forward at an acute angle to the handlebars. Like most kids of my age I was no stranger to cuts and bruises, the almost daily interaction between skin and asphalt that leaves knees scraped and elbows grazed. But when the aluminum elbow of the Schwinn's stem made contact with my still-developing testicles I experienced a pain that I had not thus far in my brief existence conceived as possible. A pain I was happy to say I had not experienced since.

Until now.

Hamish doesn't raise the club he's pulled from his belt. Some small reptilian part of his underused brain tells him that he doesn't need to. He just keeps it low as I run headlong towards him, waiting until the last moment to ram the end forward.

A sickening pain explodes between my legs, so excruciating that I can't even cry out. I don't even remember falling, or hitting the ground. One minute I'm running towards Mags, the next I'm collapsed in a hunching, writhing, bug-eyed pile, clutching my crushed testicles. My world has tilted through ninety degrees and Hamish is standing over me. I'm dimly aware that he's swinging the club, like he's just warming to his task. He raises it again, high above his head this time, and I hear Mags scream, but even though I know what's coming I'm incapable of moving my hands from between my legs.

Then suddenly Hamish isn't standing above me anymore. The world performs another axis-shift, or maybe this time it's just Hamish, and suddenly he's lying on the ground next to me, his face only inches from mine, an expression of mute surprise on his large bovine face. Somewhere (above my head? to the left?) I hear the wooden club clattering harmlessly to the ground.

There's another shout (Angus?) and a second later I'm vaguely aware of a thud as something large and soft hits the concrete, this time behind me. Kurt says something but his voice has taken on a high-pitched, reedy quality and I can't make out what it is. A second later there's the sound of footsteps rapidly receding as he runs off in the direction of the main cavern.

Then Mags is kneeling above me. If I could speak I'd tell her all I want is to be left alone. I just need to lie here on the floor rocking backwards and forwards for a while.

'Aw'ite. On your feet, Princess.'

I can't see him, but it's Marv's voice I hear. It occurs to me that Mags won't like being called Princess, but then I realize it's me he's talking to. A second later I feel strong hands under my armpits and I'm being hauled to my feet. I think I'm going to vomit. It passes, but even then the best I can manage is a hunched over chimp-like crouch. One hand rather fetchingly refuses to leave my crotch, but I manage to throw the other over Mags' shoulder and let her take some of my weight.

Angus is already on his feet, eyeing Marv warily from what he believes to be a safe distance. If I could speak it might occur to me to tell him that there probably are no safe distances from Marv. Hamish is still down, winded. His mouth's opening and closing and I'm reminded of that morning on the school bus, and Barney and Rubble, the goldfish that Mom used to let me keep in my room.

'You okay to get him back to his dorm? These boys won't bother you no more.'

Mags nods. Marv just says *Aw-ite* and then without another word he heads off into the tunnel.

*

BY THE TIME we make it to the end of the pedestrian tunnel I'm feeling a little better. My privates still feel like a dump truck's run over them, but I manage to remove my hand from that area which I'm hoping helps with the whole sex-crazed simian look. And somehow I'm exquisitely conscious of Mags' arm around my waist, the pressure of her slender body against mine. I don't know how many times I've boosted her through the hatch onto the roof of the mess, but somehow this feels deliciously new, and yet at the same familiar. She feels the way I think I had always known she would feel, but this is the first time I remember thinking about her like this.

We stop when we get to Front Street. I think I could probably walk by myself now but I keep my arm draped around her shoulder. After we pass the mess she makes to go right, towards Juvie Row and the dorms. Because I don't want it to end I blurt out:

'Want to head up on the roof?'

It's way after curfew, although I suspect it'll be a few hours before Angus and Hamish think about venturing out again. Still, after all that's happened today I should be longing for the safety of my cell. But excitement is a rare and addictive commodity in Eden, and right now I feel awake, alive, more alive than I've ever felt. Somehow I think it has as much to do with being here with Mags than any of the other things that have happened to me today.

Mags only hesitates for a moment, then she turns us back towards the mess. I check there's no one on Front Street while she gently turns the latch handle. There's a soft clunk and then we're in, making our way down the narrow metal corridor towards the back stairs. The stairway's too narrow for both of us so Mags goes first, padding silently up the steps ahead of me. I follow, more slowly, lifting my leg gingerly for each one. When I get to the third floor landing she's already undone the hex bolts on the access panel and is pulling herself up into the crawl space without waiting for my help. I follow her up.

When we get out onto the roof she heads for her usual spot over by the corner. I choose a place as close as my nerve will allow, a little further back from the edge. The plastic bottles in my overalls threaten to jab me in the crotch as I lower myself into a sitting position next to her. I take them out and set them on the roof between us.

'What're those?'

I explain to her that I bring back stuff like this for some of the grown-ups. Mags looks at me for a second like she's just learned something new but she can't decide whether it's a good or a bad thing. Then she reaches for the quart of Fireball and picks it up. She examines the label for a moment, then twists the cap off and holds the bottle to her nose. The spicy-sweet aroma of cinnamon drifts over. She doesn't ask, she just holds the rim to her lips and tilts her head back. She closes her eyes as she takes a sip and I realize I'm staring, noticing, as if for the first time her long dark lashes, the high planes of her cheekbones. She holds the whisky in her mouth for a second like she's deciding whether she likes it or not, then swallows. After a moment she hands me the bottle.

All the whisky I've brought back for Quartermaster or Scudder over the years, you'd think I might have tried some. But I haven't. I think it was the smell. That smoky, earthy, woody and yet somehow sweet aroma that would escape when I'd replace the metal cap with something from my backpack, it never appealed to me. But Mags is holding the bottle like it's somehow a challenge. I take it and raise the neck to my lips. The whisky hits my tongue and for a second all I can think of is these candies Jack would sometimes buy me to make up for the attic, large red cinnamon-flavored jawbreakers you could make last for hours. And then the raw sweet alcohol hits, searing its way down my throat. I swallow and it feels like my insides are on fire. I try not to cough, but my eyes are watering and it seems like some of the whisky has found its way down the wrong pipe. I take a second, fake, sip hoping Mags doesn't notice. Then I pass the bottle back.

'So what were you doing out after curfew?'

She just shrugs.

'I was worried when you and Marv didn't come back last night. I figured I'd hang around the pedestrian tunnel and see if you came in later on. It's no problem avoiding Angus and Hamish, you can hear them a mile off. I can't believe I let Kurt sneak up on me though.'

Mags takes another sip of the Fireball.

'So why were you out so long?'

I open my mouth to explain about Ely, and Benjamin, and Marv. I desperately want to tell her everything that's happened. But then I realize I can't. I still don't understand why Marv has let me come back, now that I know his secret. But I saw what he did to Benjamin, how he took care of Angus and Hamish, without even breaking a sweat. If I tell Mags and he finds out she knows then she won't be safe either, even here inside Eden.

'Weather moved in. Caught us by surprise.'

Mags looks at me for a long moment as if she's trying to decide whether it's worth calling me on whatever it is I'm not telling her. Then she takes another sip and hands me back the bottle. I take another swallow, longer this time. The whisky no longer burns. I feel it flowing through me, warming me from the inside. The pain in my testicles has dulled to a numb ache.

Mags shuffles back from the edge, so that she's sitting closer to me. Her dark brown hair falls forward and she brushes it out of her eyes. The mohawk's growing out but it's still a boy's cut. It suits her actually, accentuates the line of her jaw, the curve of her neck. I catch her scent, of soap and cotton and something else, something deep and rich, that I noticed before, as I boosted her up into the crawlspace the other night. My head feels fuzzy, like my brain's been wrapped in cotton wool, like my thoughts are coming to me through the maple syrup that goes on our pancakes in the mornings, but suddenly I realize where I've smelled it before. The farms. And then, with that first connection made the rest follow, tumbling through the Fireball fug all at once.

How she knew Marv had been spending time over there, and how she had looked away when I had asked her about it. All the times she and Jake have shown up late for dinner recently. And the way he was staring at her in the mess the other night, when he thought no one was looking.

Mags and Jake.

And suddenly I realize something other than the whisky is twisting inside me, burning my gut.

She asks whether I want to catch her up on *The Girl With The Dragon Tattoo*. I have a lot to tell her about Vanger and Frode, and Blomkvist's relationship with Erika Berger and Lisbeth Salander and the despicable Bjurman. I've been looking forward to it. But instead I tell her that I'm too tired. She looks at me for a long moment with those large brown eyes, wondering what has suddenly changed. Then she picks herself up. I stand next to her, feeling awkward.

She reaches up and pulls my head down. Her lips brush against mine. They feel unbelievably soft. I can make out the smell of cinnamon and whisky on her breath, and underneath it, from some time ago, toothpaste. I'm a little stunned. Mags has never kissed me before. Come to think of it, nobody's ever kissed me before.

'What was that for?'

'For what you did in the tunnel tonight.'

With that she turns and walks over to the access panel and lowers herself down into the crawlspace, leaving me to wonder what's just happened.

I sit up on the roof for a long while after she's gone. I don't know how to make sense of it. It's like something that was once familiar is now suddenly different and raw, like the way it feels when you probe the space where a tooth just fell out with your tongue.

I suspect the Fireball's not helping, but I pick up the bottle anyway and take another sip. The vials of ketamine clink softly as they shift in the pocket of my overalls. I reach in to check; miraculously none of them seem to have broken. I was going to use them to start a conversation with Kane about my match. I even had a list worked out. My top five. I've ranked them, Mr. President, in case you care, but basically any of these will do. Until this evening Mags wasn't even on it, she never has been. She was different.

And now suddenly she *is* my list.

How can that be? Did I get these other feelings just now? Or did I always have them and just never realize it? I mean I've always liked Mags. She was my friend. She *is* my friend. So why does it suddenly feel so different? And why do I care so much about whatever she's doing with Jake? Just thinking about it brings back that sudden gnawing anxiety, that freezing, burning sensation just beneath my ribcage. It can't be the Fireball, can it? Is this what alcohol does to you?

I pull the blue and red *Standard Oil* road map I took from Benjamin from the breast pocket of my overalls, desperate for anything that will distract me from thoughts of Mags and Jake. There's the hole, an almost neat puncture through the center of the top half, where Marv's bullet punched its way through the folded over sheets on its way to one or more of Benjamin's internal organs. I examine it with the tip of my finger, feeling the edges the bullet tore as it passed. The cover is stained a deep russet brown, the pages stuck together with dried blood. Tiny flakes drift lazily to the ground as I open it out, carefully prying the sections apart. The paper was already weak along the folds from countless openings. Here and there Benjamin had taped it, but the adhesive, like Benjamin's blood, has long since dried, and the tape falls away easily.

I spread it out on the metal roof. The front says it's a map of the north-eastern states, from Maine all the way down to Virginia, but it actually covers parts of Canada as far north as Quebec, the eastern seaboard from Maine all the way down to North Carolina and as far inland as the Mississippi. A single route is marked in red ink, long since faded, a more or less straight line south-south-west from a spot right on the Pennsylvania/Maryland border that I know is Eden, to somewhere that has no marking on the map, but which is identified in Benjamin's looping script as the Mount Weather Emergency Operations Center. Three other locations are marked, in the same faded red ink. The first is a place called Mount Poney, near Culpeper, Virginia, which is almost directly south of Mount Weather. The second, Greenbrier in West Virginia, is further south again, and what looks like a hundred or so miles inland. The final one is all the way down in North Carolina. Beside each location is a sequence of twelve letters and numbers. At the bottom, off the map, there's a list of a half-dozen or so other names, each with its own long code. I trace the route Benjamin has marked with my fingertip. From the scale in the bottom left corner it looks like a journey of sixty or so miles. It runs right through Ely; he must have been following it when Marv tracked him down and killed him.

I've spent the hike back from the clinic trying to put all the facts I know together inside my head, like they're the pieces of a puzzle. But nothing makes sense. Why would Marv have killed Benjamin? And why, after he'd gone to the trouble of making up a story about how he died out past Shiloah, would he let me just wander into the clinic where he must have known I'd find his body? And then why let me back into Eden so I can run and tell Kane what he's done? I stare at the map, hoping that something there will help me solve the puzzle. It doesn't. No matter how I turn each piece over in my mind, no matter how I shake them and worry at them to see what might fall out, nothing comes to me. In the end I pick the map up, taking care to reassemble the sections back along the original folds. Then I place it back in the breast pocket of my overalls and make my way down off the roof.

When I get back to my cell I pull off my boots and climb out of my overalls. I'm exhausted from the day's hike and my crushed testicles ache numbly. The whisky hits as I collapse on the narrow cot and the cell walls start a slow revolution around me in the darkness. But still my mind won't let me slip into sleep. It demands to know what I'm going to do about Marv, and Kane, and Mags, and Jake.

*

IT'S HARD TO GAUGE the passage of time with nothing to mark out the hours after lights out. At some point I drift off, but when the buzzer sounds the following morning it feels like I've only been asleep for a few minutes.

I climb off the cot and collect my overalls from where I dumped them on the floor the night before. There's a dull throb behind my eyes and my mouth feels like I've spent the last hour siphoning diesel out of a rusty tank. I think this might be my first hangover. I'm beginning to see why Quartermaster's always in such a foul mood.

I grab a towel from the locker and make for the showers. I linger under the jets for as long as I can. Sometimes solutions to problems I've been mulling over the night before float to the surface as I let my mind go slack and the hot water wash over me. But this morning there's nothing. I'm still as confused as I was when I finally fell asleep sometime just before dawn.

I join the crowd heading over to the mess. I slather the cardboard pancakes Amy forks onto my tray with maple syrup in the hope that the sugar will help with my hangover. Then the buzzer sounds again and we're shuffling down to Back Street for morning prayer. I catch Mags' eye outside. She throws me this sidelong glance that I can't decipher and then she's caught up with the crowd filing into the chapel. I slide along my usual pew. The cold, hard wood does nothing for my bruised privates and I shift uncomfortably in my seat for the duration of the sermon. Mags is sitting on the other side of the aisle, two rows in front of me. Kane's telling us again about how we're the Chosen Ones, how it'll soon be our time to venture out among the wolves, but I'm not really paying attention. I keep stealing glances at the nape of her neck, the angle of her jaw, the soft curves of her ear.

I'm feeling no better by the time I make my way over to stores. Quartermaster's in a filthy mood, even for him. He makes me stand in front of his desk while he unpacks my backpack, complaining continuously about how little I've got to show for two days' scavenging. I suspect he's mostly pissed that that was our last outing and I haven't brought him anything; I guess it's going to be a long winter for Quartermaster as well. The plastic bottle of Jack Daniels weighs down the pocket of my overalls but I have other plans for that. I could have given him the Fireball, but that got used up giving me this headache and the gnawing feeling I get in my stomach every time I think about Mags and Jake. So I just stand there, giving him my best contrite-chimp look. Eventually he grows tired of chewing me out. He tells me to go sort out the few items we brought back and then get out of his sight.

It doesn't take me long to find spaces on the shelves for the stuff Marv scavenged from the Food Lion. As soon as I'm done I make myself scarce before Quartermaster can find me another task. I need to figure out what to do about Marv and Benjamin and the map. If I'm going to tell Kane about it I can't delay. I keep thinking about how Marv saved Mags and me from Angus and Hamish. But then I see him standing over Benjamin's body, the pistol in his hand, the blood that's puddled on the floor already growing sticky with the cold as it slowly seeps between the lugs of his boot. I can't see how I can avoid telling Kane about it, but first I'll go talk to Sergeant Scudder, see if I can work out for myself why Marv might have wanted to kill Benjamin.

I bump into Leonard in the tunnels on my way over to the plant; he tells me Scudder's underneath the reactor, checking the dampers. Claus's been quiet since we got back in, but he's not best pleased with this news. Most of the buildings in Eden are mounted on huge springs that were designed to cushion them from the effects of a nearby blast. So far I've managed to avoid going down among them. Mags has told me what it's like, though: it's basically a Claus nightmare.

Leonard leads me back into the cavern where last night I had my altercation with Hamish and directs me to a checker-plated access hatch. He pulls a small t-bar from a pocket in his overalls, inserts it in a slot in the hatch, gives it a quarter turn and lifts the panel up. I peer down into the gloom. Claus is telling me I should just wait until he's left and then follow him out; we can always come back later. But this can't wait. I need to talk to Scudder so I can figure out what to tell Kane about Marv, and Benjamin, and the map. I promise Claus we won't be long. I'll find Scudder, ask what I need and get out.

I sit on the edge of the hole and after only a moment's pause lower myself down, feeling for the rungs with the toes of my boots. When my feet hit concrete I realize there's not enough headroom to stand. I take a deep breath, then crouch down and start off in the direction Leonard indicated.

It's not long till I reach the springs. Each one is huge, several feet in diameter and maybe a shade under five feet tall, compressed by the weight of the reactor above. It's like you can sense the tension in the coiled steel. It gets darker as I move away from the hatch; I guess replacing bulbs that have blown down here wouldn't have been anyone's priority, even back when we had spares. I realize I should have brought a flashlight. Claus is jabbering for me to go back and get one, but I reckon Scudder can't be far; I might as well get this over with.

I keep going, deeper and deeper among them. Soon I'm surrounded; behind me the hatch is no longer visible and all I can see are row after row of springs heading off into the darkness in all directions. At last I find him. He's hunkered down next to a an old metal work lamp, adjusting one of the dampers. He looks up as I approach. Scudder's a big man, beefy; his broad apple-cheeked face splits into a smile, like he's pleased to see me. He'll know I've just been outside, probably for the last time before winter. He'll be hoping I've brought him something.

I sit down on the dusty floor and ask what he's doing. Partly it's because I'm actually curious, but mainly it's because it's making conversation and Mags reckons I should do this more often, rather than just coming straight out and asking the question I really want the answer to. The ache I've had all morning flares up again as I think about her, but I force those thoughts from my mind and instead try and focus on what he's saying. He starts to explain how the dampers are there to counteract the effect of the springs; they'd keep everything stable if the shockwave of a nearby detonation were ever to shift the thousands of tons of nuclear power plant sitting directly above me. Claus threatens a minor spaz when he hears that, but I hush him. Marv and I have scavenged most of the territory within a twenty-mile radius, so I know there wasn't a strike anywhere near Eden. It's one of the few things we've got to be grateful for, I guess. Still, it's good to know that if that had happened we'd have been okay. But when I mention this to Scudder he just chuckles.

'Nah, son. It might seem like a big mountain but the reality is there's just far too little rock above us. Might have been okay in its day, but it couldn't have withstood a hit from a modern warhead.' Scudder's from Baltimore. *Bawlmer, Merlin.* He's got the same respect for consonants as Marv, so warhead comes out as *ward.* It takes me a moment to work out what he means.

'That's why they mothballed it, I guess.' He rests a hand on one of the huge springs. 'All these are good for now is keeping me busy.'

I get that weird scratchy feeling inside my head, like walking through cobwebs, as if something he's told me doesn't make sense. But Claus is playing up too much to let me focus on it.

Scudder takes a quick look around to check we're alone.

'So, did you bring me anything?'

I dig the plastic Coke bottle filled with Jack Daniels out of my overalls. Quartermaster would have just bitched about it, but I know Scudder will be fine with cheap whisky. He lowers himself down to the ground, resting his back against one of the springs, and unscrews the cap. He waits a second, as if he's anticipating how the amber liquid will taste when it hits the back of his throat. Then he takes a long slug.

I sit on the ground a few feet away. Claus is urging me to get on with it, but I wait. I want Scudder to loosen up a little first. I watch as he takes another long pull of the Jack and closes his eyes, resting his head back against the huge metal coils.

'Sergeant Scudder.'

Scudder opens his eyes.

'Hmmm?'

'I've noticed Marv's been kinda down lately.'

'Not his usual chatty self you mean?' Scudder snorts briefly at his own joke, then takes another hit from the Coke bottle. I smile.

'Yeah. But I've been a bit worried about him. He's been quiet, even for Marv. Like something's on his mind. I was wondering. Was it around this time of year that Benjamin died?'

I know it wasn't, at least according to Marv's version of events. But I want to get Scudder on to the topic. Jack used to say people like to talk. If you want to find things out sometimes the best thing to do is to nudge them in the right direction and then just sit back and listen.

Scudder takes another long swallow from the bottle. He purses his lips, like he's thinking.

'Nope. Benjamin died in the fall, little over four years after we got here.'

I already knew this but I nod, as if considering. Scudder raises the Coke bottle to his lips again.

'But they were friends, Marv and Benjamin I mean.'

'Well, they certainly spent enough time together. Hard to avoid people down here isn't it? But I'm not sure how close they were apart from that. They were cut from very different cloth those fellas. You wouldn't suspect it from the size of him but Benjamin wasn't really much of a soldier. He was an engineer, with the Signal Battalion. You know, making sure all the radio stuff worked.'

Maybe I shouldn't have let Scudder have all the whisky. He's got that bit wrong. But then it was all years ago now, so it's not surprising he wouldn't remember all the details. Benjamin was with the 101st Airborne. He was wearing that ring, the one with the black shield and the Screaming Eagles banner, the day we arrived. I know because I took it off his finger out in Ely not a couple of days ago.

'Marv, now, he was the real deal. Syria, Iran, Nigeria. You name it, he'd been there. Then he lost his shit out in one of those places so they had to ship him back. Only thing he was fit for after that was standing guard somewhere nobody ever thought we'd need. Still, I guess it worked out okay for him.' Scudder takes another slug of the whisky and then goes quiet, as if considering for the first time whether Marv's fate really had been better than the alternative.

'But they didn't argue, Marv and Benjamin?'

Scudder lifts the Coke bottle up. The whisky's going down quickly. He frowns at it for a little while, like he's disappointed. He raises it to his lips again, but this time he only takes a sip.

'Nope, can't say I ever saw them fall out much.' He pauses again. 'At least until that teacher of yours showed up that is.'

I nod, like somehow I understand. In reality that's just thrown another variable into a problem I wasn't even close to solving before. But then I think of how I feel about Mags being with Jake. Benjamin and Miss Kimble spent a lot of time together and they seemed to get along really well. Marv doesn't really get on with anyone. Is it possible Marv killed Benjamin because he was jealous?

Claus is urging me to get out there, but I have one more question. The next bit needs to be handled carefully.

'Sergeant Scudder, did you ever hear of a place called Mount Weather?'

Scudder puts down the bottle and stares at me for a long while, like he's trying to figure out where I'm going with this. In the end he just lets out a small sigh, like he can't be bothered trying to work out the link. Kids say stupid unconnected shit all the time.

'Sure. It's another place like this. Somewhere in Virginia I think.'

He takes one last long slug from the Coke bottle, draining it. He puts one hand out to the springs to steady himself as he stands. I hope there's nothing too demanding on his work detail for the rest of the afternoon. Then he screws the cap back on the bottle and tosses it away. I hear it bounce off one of the springs and then come to rest somewhere in the darkness. I stare after it for a moment then get to my feet. If Marv were here he'd make me go find it and put it in the trash, but I'm not scrabbling around down here looking for it.

*

I'M ON MY WAY over to see Kane when Lena catches up with me. With all that's been going on I'd forgotten about her. Now that I've decided to tell Kane about the map I really just want to get it over with, but I figure it'll be as quick for me to fetch her the tests I brought back for her from Shiloah as it would be for me to explain why I don't really have time now. I look around; everyone's at work so the cavern's empty. Nevertheless I tell her to wait in the mess while I pick them up from the infirmary.

She's sitting at the girls' table when I return, her hands folded in her lap. I fish the sticks out of the pocket of my overalls. Her eyes widen a little as I explain she has to pee on one end and then wait five minutes. She looks at me for a while like I'm making this up, but I promise I'm not and besides what choice does she have but to believe me? The instructions are printed right there on each one, but she won't be able to understand them. I tell her how to read the results. It couldn't be easier; a second pink line under the one that's already there means she's pregnant. There won't be one of course. The strips are at least a decade old, so they probably don't work anymore. And besides, Lena can't be pregnant. But at least if she takes the test she'll stop worrying about it.

She asks if I have any more pills, but I don't, so she shoves the sticks into the pocket of her overalls and leaves.

I wait a few minutes after Lena's gone, just to make sure no one sees us leaving the mess together. Then I head straight down to Back Street.

It's Kane who answers the door when I knock. He stands in the doorway, looking at me for a second, like he doesn't know what to make of me being there. Then he smiles and steps back to let me in.

'Come on in, come on in. Randall, Gabriel's here.'

This is why I like visiting Kane. He always makes it seem like I'm a pleasant surprise. I step inside. As always it strikes me how much nicer it is here; what a difference it makes to have rugs, and pictures on the walls, and a bookcase full of books. Peck's sitting on one of the sofas, eyeing me the way I'd imagine a hawk would watch a field mouse that'd just wandered out of its hole directly under its flight path. I hadn't counted on him being here; I wonder if I should come back, when Kane's alone. But then he points to the empty armchair opposite and asks me to sit. I comply, feeling myself sink into the old leather.

'Well son, to what do we owe the pleasure?'

I glance over at Peck, who's still studying me suspiciously.

'Oh don't worry about Randall, son. Anything you have to say to me you can say in front of him.'

'Yes, Mr. President. Well, we just got back from a sca- … from being outside that is, and well, I found this.' I reach into the breast pocket of my overalls for the map I found on Benjamin and hand it over.

Kane takes the map. I watch as he carefully unfolds it, laying it out on the coffee table in front of him. He reaches into the inside pocket of his jacket and fishes out a pair of reading glasses. Peck has already leaned in. It's hard to miss the holes the bullet that killed Benjamin made as it travelled through each of the map segments, the repeating pattern of the stains of his blood. Kane shoots Peck a look, no more than a shifting of the eyes, but in that moment I see something I haven't seen in all the years we've been here. For the briefest instant I could swear Peck looks scared.

'Where'd you find this, son?'

I hesitate. Kane's voice hasn't changed. It's the same kindly tone that greeted me when I arrived, like he's just asked me where I'd found the car keys he'd been looking for all morning. I feel my heart pick up. I can hear it thumping, like I'm about to go out into the tunnel; it seems like it's so loud Kane and Peck must be able to hear it too. Mom used to say when in doubt tell the truth, but that's what you have to tell kids, or there'd be mayhem. I really doubt she had this kind of situation in mind. Nevertheless, part of me does just want to tell Kane everything, and let him figure it all out. But that's not what I've decided to do. It's a big thing to accuse someone of murder, and in spite of all the evidence against Marv there are still too many things that just don't make sense.

'Well, Mr. President, we weren't exactly where we were supposed to be.' I feel the vials of ketamine shift against themselves in the pocket of my overalls. I want to tell Kane that I was only out in Ely because of him, but in spite of what he's said about speaking freely in front of Peck I'm not certain he'd want me to disclose his secret. 'The farms are having a problem with one of their crops, and I had an idea for where I might find something to help them. So we, well, me, I mean, I, decided we should go to Ely because I read in the Yellow Pages that there was a farm supplies store there. Anyway, while I'm looking I find this dead guy and he's got this map on him.' I point to the bullet-holed, bloodstained map spread out on the coffee table, like there might be another map nearby that somehow also fits that description. I realize I'm babbling, desperate for this incomplete version of the truth to be accepted, but I don't seem able to stop myself.

Peck leans back in his armchair. He's regained his composure, and he's staring at me with those deep-set gray eyes like I'm that field mouse again.

'Did you recognize the man you took the map from?'

I've been expecting this question, so I don't hesitate with my answer.

'No, I don't think so. Of course there wasn't much left of him. Most bodies you find are like that. Even with the cold.'

What I've said about bodies decomposing is true. I figure I can always backtrack on this if I need to; claim I've thought about it some more and now I think maybe it was Benjamin.

Peck just nods, apparently satisfied.

'And what do you think the map means, son?'

I allow myself to relax a little. The tough questions are over. And part of me likes that Kane is asking my advice on things again.

'Well, I'm not sure Mr. President. But I thought maybe this Mount Weather place was like Eden, you know.' I don't mention that Scudder actually told me this, not fifteen minutes ago; I want Kane to think I've worked it out by myself. 'And it seems like this guy, whoever he was, was keen to get there. If it was a place like here then maybe there'd be supplies there. Maybe even other survivors.'

Kane seems to consider this for a while.

'Well, might be, might be. There were a few places set up like Eden, before. It's been so long I've forgotten where they all were now, but I dare say we'll have some information on it. Randall, after we're done with Gabriel here why don't you run along over to command and see if there's anything over there in the files. Now, Gabriel, have you mentioned anything to anyone else about this?'

I shake my head, no.

Peck's looking at me closely again. 'Not even Marvin?'

I shake my head again, vigorously this time.

Kane nods. 'Good, good. I don't rightly know what to make of this yet, but let's not go getting anyone's hopes up before we know more shall we? I mean even if it is what you think, it's an awfully long way.'

He's already standing, getting ready to show me to the door. Before I can stop myself I blurt out: 'It's sixty miles, Mr. President. Marv and I could be there in three days, four tops.'

He looks at me. There's a smile hovering over his lips, but I can't tell whether he's amused or annoyed.

'Well I'm sure you could. I didn't mean to doubt you, son. We are blessed to have resourceful young men like you here in Eden to take care of us. I am always saying that. The Yellow Pages, indeed; how clever. Isn't that so, Randall?'

Peck smiles in agreement, but it's a thin crease of the lips that barely touches the lower half of his face. Peck just has one of those faces that wasn't built for smiling.

As I step back out into the main cavern it feels like a weight's been lifted from my shoulders. I've definitely done the right thing, and I might even go as far as to say I've been smart about it, too. Kane knows about the map now, and at the same time I've managed to buy some more time to work out what to do about Marv.

*

I'M LYING ON MY NARROW COT, staring up at the rivets in the cell's low metal ceiling. I tried to find Mags earlier but she didn't come into the mess for dinner, not even later, after Jake had arrived. When I asked Amy if she'd seen her she said she'd just taken a tray to her cell. Kurt reported her for being out after curfew the night before and so she's doing penance. Being caught out after the buzzer's pretty serious; I probably won't see her for a week.

I stopped by the infirmary on the way back from speaking with Kane and hid the vials of ketamine in one of the cabinets behind the other out-of-date medicines. They should be fine there until I get a chance to give them to him. I was going to use them to start a conversation about my match, but now I'm not sure what to do about that. I could just ask Kane to let it be Mags, of course. But somehow that doesn't seem like such a great solution if she really wants to be with someone else. And to make matters worse Jake asked me over dinner whether I'd had any luck finding out what was wrong with his crop. When I told him I hadn't he looked disappointed, but he thanked me anyway for trying. I felt pretty bad about that, even though I'm mostly annoyed with him about the whole Mags thing.

I'm too wired to sleep, and Claus is letting me know he isn't happy with being confined. He still hasn't forgiven me for bringing him down under the reactor among the springs. In the end I decide to head up on the roof. I grab my pillow and blanket and step out of my cell. It's long after curfew so the main lights are out but the safeties are on, bathing the corridor in their soft green glow. The metal feels cold under my bare feet as I make my way past the stairs to the access hatch. I undo the bolts at each corner with my fingertips then gently slide the panel to one side and push my bedding up into the crawl space. A few moments later I'm lying on my blanket staring up at the brace wire-covered granite above me.

With everything that's happened the last few days my brain's starting to feel frazzled, overloaded, like there's just too many different things to focus on. The sound of footsteps drifts up from the streets below and I roll off my blanket and crawl to the edge of the roof, happy for the momentary distraction. Eric and Tyler are on duty tonight and they walked by not ten minutes ago, so I don't think it'll be them. I inch closer to the edge, waiting for whoever it is to emerge from the shadows beneath me.

A figure appears at the corner of Main Street, but whoever they are they're sticking to the shadows, so I can't make out a face. I shuffle as quietly as I can along the edge, trying to get a better view, but by the time I shift position they're already on Front Street heading into the pedestrian tunnels to the west of the main cavern. I return to my blanket. Twenty minutes later I'm still pondering what to do about Marv and Benjamin when I hear the footsteps again, this time coming back out of the tunnels towards Front Street. I crawl back along the roof to the front of the building and catch a glimpse of the same figure as they walk between the stores and the mess. I watch for them to pass between the other side of the mess and command, but they never re-emerge. I wait. Five minutes pass, then ten. I'm beginning to doubt myself; if they sprinted past the mess they might have made it over the next cross street before I got to the other side of the roof. Or maybe I just missed them in the darkness.

It feels like well over an hour before I hear the footsteps again, this time coming back down from Front Street towards me. I scramble back towards the front of the roof and watch for whoever it is to emerge from the shadows on the other side of Main Street; from here I'll have the perfect vantage point as they cross. It's unlikely they'll think to look up, but nevertheless I lay as flat as I can on the metal roof, with just the top of my head poking over the edge. The footsteps stop on the far side of the street and a figure steps out slowly, checking left and right. For the briefest instant I catch a glimpse of a face in profile before he crosses Main Street and ducks back into the darkness.

It's Peck.

But what was he doing? The western tunnels house the stores, the power plant and the armory. The stores are locked at night and only Quartermaster has a key, although I guess Peck could have got it from him. But whatever he might've wanted there, why not wait until the morning? There'll be nobody over at the power plant at this time of night, so there'd be no point going there, either. That just leaves the armory. Peck has access to that whenever he wants; there's no need to go skulking around after dark. I return to my blanket and ponder all of this for a while, but nothing's making sense any more, and it feels like Peck's nocturnal wanderings should be the least of my concerns. Later I'll wish I'd spent more time thinking about what he might have been doing in that hour when I lost him on Front Street behind the mess.

But there was no way then that I could have known.

*

DAWN BREAKS SUDDENLY in Eden. There's no gentle transition, no attempt to replicate the sun's slow rise above the horizon. I wake to the sound of the buzzer and a second later the arc lights come on, instantly flooding the cavern with their harsh white glare.

It takes me a couple of seconds to realize I'm still on the roof. *Crap.* I always return to my cell before the lights come on; people will already be climbing out of bed, emerging from their cells for another day of work and prayer. Soon the corridors will be crawling with Juvies heading for the showers.

I grab my blanket and pillow and bolt for the hatch that leads off the roof. I'm not panicking yet. I'm the only one who bunks on the third floor, so it's unlikely anyone will come up to check my cell, at least for a while. But then I remember the access panel is directly above the stairwell that connects all three floors. If there's anyone on the landing as I climb down all they need to do is look up and they'll see me.

I scramble through the crawl space as quickly as I can, pushing my bedding in front of me. When I get to the access panel I slide it aside an inch. The metal screeches as I shift it, but the sound's lost among the noises drifting up from the floors below. I look down to the stairwell. The floor below's empty, but Juvies are starting to pass by on the landing beneath. The clutch towels under elbows, yawning, rubbing sleep from their eyes. At least no one will be looking up.

I slide the panel all the way to one side, as quietly as I can. I wait until the coast is clear and then push my bedding through, shifting myself into position on the edge. As I'm getting ready to lower myself down Carl appears on the landing. I'm already committed so I let go and drop, but in my haste I land badly. There's a loud clang as I hit the steel floor hard, then a sickening rush of adrenalin and I feel something in my ankle give. I just manage to kick my blanket and pillow out of sight before he looks up.

'Gabe, you asshole. You scared me.'

'Sorry. Missed the first step.'

He just shakes his head and mutters something about me being a klutz. Thankfully he's still half asleep and doesn't notice the open access panel above my head. I quickly slide it back into place before someone else appears on the landing. I'll replace the bolts later, when there's less people around.

Now that the shock of the fall's passed my ankle's starting to hurt. It's definitely sprained, I may even have torn something there. I pick up my bedding and hobble back to my cell to drop it off. Then I grab a towel and head for the showers.

The mess is already crowded when I arrive. My ankle's still throbbing; I'll go over to the infirmary right after prayers and bandage it up. Amy's on duty and I consider asking her to get me an MRE, but instead I just load a tray with pancakes and ladle maple syrup over them. I limp back to the boys' table with it and take my usual place at the end.

I've barely sat down when the conversation dies. All around me Juvies are staring hard at their mulchy eggs or their cardboard pancakes. I look up and see Kurt walking over with Angus and Hamish in tow. The grin that's playing across his lips seems even wider this morning. As usual I pretend to ignore him until he's standing right behind me.

'The President wants to see you, Gabriel.'

My foot's really hurting, so I'm in no mood for Kurt's usual swagger. I open my mouth to tell him I'll go see the President when I'm done with breakfast, but then I stop. He's looking up and down the table, confident. He has Angus and Hamish with him for a reason. He wants me to challenge him. Clearly this time Kurt *has* been told to come and get me urgently. I pause for a second longer then stand up from the table, ignoring the sudden pain that shoots up from my ankle as I put weight on it.

'Sure, Kurt. Happy to oblige. I was done anyway. I don't think I can face any more of these pancakes.'

In truth I haven't even touched my plate, and my stomach's growling. But it's almost worth it to see the smile disappear from his face as he realizes he won't get to have Angus and Hamish drag me out of my seat in front of everyone.

I follow him out of the mess, trying not to let my limp show.

When we get to Back Street Marv's I'm surprised to see Marv's already there; he rarely ventures into the main cavern, at least during the day. Kane must have sent Peck to fetch him. He looks over at me when I walk in and his eyes narrow a fraction, like he's wondering what hand I've had in all this. Meanwhile Kane turns to Kurt.

'Thank you for fetching Gabriel, Kurt. I am much obliged. Now I'm sure you have important things to attend to.'

Kurt looks peeved that he's being excluded from whatever's going on, but he's smart enough not to mistake Kane's pleasantries for anything other than a dismissal. He throws me a sullen look then lets himself out. When he's gone Kane turns back to Marv and me.

'Thank you both for coming on such short notice. I've been thinking about this map you brought us Gabriel.'

Marv turns to me. *What map?* I want to explain, but before I get a chance Kane continues.

'I'm sorry Marvin, forgive me. Gabriel came across a map when you were outside last.' He turns to Peck who hands him a map that Kane passes on to Marv. It's not the map I brought back, however. It has the same blue and red *Standard Oil* cover, but this one looks new, and there's no bullet hole, no bloodstains. While Marv's unfolding it Kane continues.

'It's directions to a place called Weather Mountain.' (It's Mount Weather, actually, but I decide it's better to hold my tongue.) 'I had quite forgotten about it, but Randall checked the records and you were right Gabriel, it is another facility just like Eden, about sixty miles from here.' He turns to me with a smile. 'That map you brought in last night was quite on its last legs, son. It literally fell apart as we were refolding it after you left. Thankfully we had a newer one here. I've retraced the route exactly.' He turns back to Marv. 'It's a long way but Gabriel thought you might be able to make it. I don't want to ask you to try anything foolhardy, of course. But if you thought it were possible it seems like it would be worth one last trip outside to visit this Weather Mountain before I have to lock us down for winter.' He shakes his head. 'None of us expected to be in Eden as long as we have been, and unfortunately the weather outside shows little sign of changing. If this place had been stocked like here then it might present a solution to our problems. And of course it's always possible there are other survivors there.'

Marv studies the map for a long moment, like he's considering.

'Hunnert klicks? Long ways with the weather that's coming. And how do we get in if'n we get there?'

'The blast door here in Eden opens on a twelve-digit alphanumeric code. That means it's made up of both letters and numbers.' I think I see Marv's eyes narrow again, like he doesn't need Kane to explain to him what alphanumeric means, but maybe I'm imagining it. As I've said, it's not easy to read Marv's expressions at the best of times, and most of them seem to fall on the disgruntled end of the spectrum anyway. Kane doesn't seem to notice, however, he just continues on in that soft, southern drawl. 'A code following a similar format was written on the map. We've checked our records here and as best we can tell it's the one for the blast door at Weather Mountain, or at least as it was ten years ago. I've copied the code on to the new map too.'

Marv studies the map for a moment longer then carefully refolds it. While he's doing this I ask whether they know if the keypad will still be working.

Kane switches his attention to me.

'That's a good question, son. We think it should. Weather Mountain was designed like Eden, and we know the EMP that ended the virus didn't knock us out. Peck here spoke with Sergeant Scudder last night. He thinks the power grid will be programmed to prioritize the entry systems. Now we've got to assume the worst and that the place has been abandoned all this time. Nevertheless the sergeant reckons there'll still be enough of a charge left in the emergency batteries to operate the keypad and disengage the locks on the blast door. You and Marv may need to pull the door open yourselves, but it will have been designed to be opened manually once the locks were disabled, in case of an emergency.'

Well I guess that answers what Peck was doing skulking around in the tunnels last night; Scudder must have been working late at the plant after all. Although I still don't know why I lost him for an hour in front of the mess.

'Can we have the old map as well? Just in case there's anything you've missed.'

Kane turns back to Marv and shakes his head again. It wasn't very tactful of Marv to imply that the former President of the United States might not be capable of transcribing twelve letters and numbers without screwing it up. But Kane just smiles, like he hasn't noticed.

'I'm sorry Marvin, as I said it completely fell apart when we opened it up last night. Besides, it was covered in that poor man's blood, and you can never be too careful with the virus. I had Peck put it in the furnace as soon as I had copied what was on it.'

Marv just nods, like he understands.

'How soon were you thinking of sending us out?'

'Well, we were thinking as soon as possible, what with the storms already on their way. Maybe tomorrow?'

'Tomorrow?' *Tuhmar?* 'We could lose the weather any day. Why don't we leave right now?'

I'd normally be the first to vote for an early exit but Marv's suggestion takes me by surprise. Maybe he didn't notice I was limping when I walked in. I feel like I should mention that I've just twisted my ankle, but then it was me that was bragging to Kane last night about how we could do this, so I stay quiet.

Kane looks to Peck, who just nods.

'Well, good; right now it is then. You'll have whatever supplies you need of course. Just let Quartermaster know I said so.'

Marv turns to me, an expression on his face I can't read.

'Aw'ite. Come on Junior, we'd best get going.'

*

WHILE MARV'S GETTING us provisions from Quartermaster I head over to the infirmary and strap up my ankle. I wrap the bandages as tight as I can, trying to remember what else I read about sprains in the first aid book I keep out in the farmhouse. When I'm done I rifle through the cabinets and grab some Tylenol. The label says to take them with food, but I shake a couple of pills out of the container and dry swallow them straight away.

Marv's already in the locker room changing when I get there. As soon as he's done he grabs his backpack and heads out without saying a word. Marv's never been big on pleasantries, especially in the mornings, but I'm starting to feel a little anxious. I tell myself he's probably just annoyed at me because I didn't tell him about the map, but now I'm beginning to wonder if I haven't misjudged this. I hadn't planned on being outside with him again this side of winter; I thought I'd have that time to work out what to do. Maybe I should have told Kane that it was Benjamin's body I took the map from after all.

I catch up with him at the blast door. The cycle's already started, the four tons of carbon steel committed to its slow outward arc, the electric motors whining under the load. A blast of cold air from the tunnel hits my face and there's that familiar knot in my stomach, the heavy weight constricting my chest. But now it's accompanied by a new fear. A fear that I may just have screwed up, badly.

A conversation I had with Kane years ago, when I first started going outside, floats into my head. Kane had said Marv had once been a fine soldier, but he had seen things that no one should have to see and now he was a little bit broken. And what had Scudder said, yesterday, when we were down among the springs? Marv had lost his shit while he'd been off fighting in one of those places, and the only thing he'd been fit for after was standing guard at some mothballed bunker. Is that it? I mean, everyone knows Marv's a bit strange. But can he be that messed up that he's forgotten what he did to Benjamin? And what will happen to me if he remembers?

My stomach sinks as it occurs to me that maybe he's already remembered. I'm about to limp out into the darkness of the tunnel with a killer who now suspects I know his secret. And the outside is dangerous; everyone knows that. Anything can happen, just like it did to Benjamin. Nobody would suspect Marv, particularly on a hike like this, where we're going way outside our usual territory. He could just make up some story, and nobody would think to question him on it. I feel a cold sweat break out inside the thermals I'm wearing.

The door has swung out enough for me to step through into the tunnel, but I hesitate. It's not too late for me to go back and tell Kane everything.

Or I could just say I've twisted my ankle and I'm not ready to go out. That's what I'll do. But even as I have that thought I feel a strong hand at my back, pushing me forward, and I comply, like one of those English rabbits, stupefied by their own fear. I hear the voice I think is Mom's in my head, a phrase that she read to me from that book. *But for all they looked so fine their hearts were dark and tharn.* Marv used to be a hunter. He'd know all about that. I can just see him shining a light into an animal's eyes, slowly unslinging a rifle from his shoulder. He doesn't even need the flashlight for me. The tunnel and the darkness will do just fine.

I stumble out. I try to touch my hand to the blast door as it continues its slow outward arc, but Marv has a tight grip on my shoulder, and for once the tunnel gods go unappeased. The motors pause while the gears switch and then they re-engage and the blast door starts to draw closed behind me. The light begins to fade, the darkness once again reclaiming the part of tunnel it was momentarily forced to give up. I fumble for the switch on the flashlight. I realize that the hand that's holding it is shaking. The weak cone of light it throws shudders over the damp, brace wire-covered walls.

The blast door closes with a final clang, and I start. There's one last burst from the electric motors as they slide the bolts into place before they fall silent. Marv's already shoving me forward again. I should be thinking about how I can get out of this, but instead I start the count.

We walk in silence. My breath's coming shallow and fast now, the sound of blood crashing through my veins loud in my ears. We're passing under the blast vents, about to head into the darkest part of the tunnel before I realize something else is wrong. The count's not right; I'm way off. It takes me another moment to figure out it's my ankle.

I tell myself it'll be okay. Marv won't do anything until we get outside. I can still throw myself on the mercy of the Guardians at the portal. It'll be embarrassing, but right now that's the least of my worries.

We reach the horseshoe, make our way around it, then the tunnel straightens for the last time. It's colder now. I feel the familiar breeze on my face and ahead it seems to get a little lighter. I think I can make out the table and the scanner. It takes me a moment longer to figure out that there are no Guardians here. Kane said he didn't want anyone knowing we were going out to try and find Mount Weather. Peck must have pulled them back.

If Marv is surprised by this turn of events he doesn't show it. I leave the flashlight on the table, for the return trip I now know will never happen. I go through the motions of taking our crucifixes from the quarantine fridge. The metal feels cold against my skin as it slides inside my thermals. I pick up my snowshoes and even the respirator I never bother to wear, and start up the mound of rubble towards the final, collapsed section of the tunnel. I clamber over the snow-covered rocks near the top, only vaguely aware that I've forgotten to put on my gloves. At last I crawl free and stand.

Heavy clouds hang low on the horizon, the undersides shuddering with light as a storm pounds the hilltops in the distance. But here outside Eden the wind's dropped and it's eerily quiet.

I'm waiting, like I always do, for Marv to clear the last section of the tunnel, when it occurs to me I haven't even had the chance to say goodbye to Mags. Suddenly I crash headlong into the realization that I will never see her again, and in that instant several thoughts occur to me all at once. The first is that she is the only thing I will truly miss about this place. The second is how ridiculous she would find it that I am just standing here, like that stupid rabbit, simply waiting for the end. The final thought is that this is not what she would do. She would never have let it come to this, of course. But if by some magic of the tunnel gods she were to find herself here, now, she wouldn't be standing patiently, waiting for her executioner to emerge from the darkness. She would kick and scream and rage, no matter how futile it might be.

It's that last thought that finally breaks the spell. I look around. There's nowhere to hide. I could run, but I won't get far, at any rate not with my ankle the way it is. In any event, I need to get back inside Eden, to explain to Kane that it was Benjamin that I found with the map; that it was Marv who killed him. Which leaves only one option. I drop the respirator and bend down to grab a rock from the snow, just as Marv finally crawls free.

He sees the rock immediately. Unfortunately at the same moment I realize why it's always taken Marv so long to clear the last section of the tunnel. There's a pistol in his hand, a silencer already screwed into the muzzle. It looks like it's the same gun he used to kill the little girl, all those years ago in Shreve, and I have a second to wonder if it's also the one he used on Benjamin. It's still wrapped in the Ziploc bag he's used to stash it, no doubt under some of the rocks in the final collapsed part of the tunnel, but I doubt the plastic will affect the bullet's trajectory in the slightest should he decide to pull the trigger.

I drop the rock.

Marv just nods. 'Good call, Junior. Although I'm glad you finally decided to grow a pair. Maybe tanglin' with Hamish the other night did you some good after all.' He waves the gun in the direction of the farmhouse. 'C'mon, let's go.'

I reach into the pocket of my parka for the surgical mask and my gloves, but Marv just grabs me by the arm and shoves me forward. I don't even have time to pull up my hood. I suddenly can't remember whether I applied UV block in the locker room. For this to be a concern now seems laughable. It's looking very unlikely I'll die out here from melanoma.

We make our way down through the fields towards the turnpike. Marv keeps looking over his shoulder, back towards the portal. The snow's deep and he's not making any allowances for my ankle with the pace he's setting. Whenever I show any signs of slowing he shoves me on. By the time we reach the farmhouse it's throbbing badly.

He pushes me into the kitchen, motioning for me to sit at the table. I comply. I'd love to tell you I have a plan for how I get out of this, but I don't. Part of me's just relieved to take the weight off my foot.

'Aw'ite boy, get to talkin'.'

I'm confused. He has to know what I saw, in the clinic. I'm not sure what he can want me to talk about.

'Don't act bixicated, now, Gabriel. I ain't got neither the time nor the patience.'

I look around the kitchen, the cheap plywood wall paneling curled and buckled with the damp, the counter stripped for firewood, the cabinets long since emptied of anything that might provide sustenance. My gaze lands on a spray of black mildew that's climbing the wall near the back door.

My heart sinks as I realize these are the last things I will ever see.

*

THE TOUR BEGAN on the banks of the river, in front of an ancient concrete structure that Dr. Hyun explained was the old research reactor.

The sun was so bright that Eliza found it hard to concentrate on anything; every time she opened her eyes beyond the narrowest squint a blinding white pain seared across her cortex. She thought she heard Jorg speak, his tone suggesting a question, but she didn't catch what he had said, and then Hyun was saying something about the Soviets no longer supplying them with fuel rods. She knew she should be taking notes, but she just couldn't bear to take her hands from inside the pockets of her coat. She wasn't sure her fingers would grip a pen even if she did; she couldn't feel them anymore. Her feet were just as bad. She shifted her weight from one to the other, trying not to draw attention to herself.

Hyun led them on, past the bridge they had driven over that morning to enter the facility. Ahead the huge concrete bulk of the production reactor loomed, and then mercifully they were in its shadow and the pain behind her eyes abated a little. Now that she could look at it properly she was stuck by how large it was. It was hard to tell without windows, but she thought at least ten, maybe twelve stories high. Had she measured it from the glossies, back in her cubicle? She felt like that was something she would have done, but right now she couldn't remember. The steel exhaust tower that extended from the top reached up for what looked like a similar distance beyond, but it was hard to be sure; she couldn't bear to look up into the blazing white sky long enough to tell. Well, OBSAT 34 was directly above; when she got back to her cubicle she would order up a glossy and check. Maybe she'd even request one with her in it, to keep as a souvenir.

Wouldn't that be a thing?

She looked around again. Off to one side of the reactor was the structure housing the turbine and generator. She definitely recognized the power line towers she had identified from the satellite images. And there, the elevated vent pipes that ran around the outside of the reactor building. Even from here she could see the plumes of white steam. She had been right; the reactor had been restarted.

Dr. Hyun was pointing to a spot down by the water's edge where a large pipe emerged from the bank. The river was low and Eliza could see the foam residue she had noted in her report. Steam rose from the opening as vent water from the reactor flowed into the river. She forced herself to focus on what he was saying. Something about a secondary cooling system. But all she could think was how good it would feel to walk down to the bank and wade into those steaming waters.

The next thing she knew they were inside. She had no memory of having entered the building. One minute she had been standing on the banks of the Kuryong, the next here she was, in what looked like the reactor's control room. She checked her watch. It said just after ten, but that couldn't be right, could it? It had to be much later than that. When she looked more closely she could see that the second hand was no longer moving. She had no idea how much time she had lost.

It was no warmer inside, but at least the light no longer hurt her eyes so much. The smell was overpowering though, a complicated raft of hard metallic smells that packed the air, almost more than she could stand. Was that normal? She looked over at Jan and Jorg but neither gave any appearance of being troubled by it.

From the outside the reactor had looked like it had been based on a nineteen-fifties British design. Now that she was inside she could see the Soviet influences everywhere. The equipment seemed old, outdated. Jan asked a question about the amount of plutonium they could expect to harvest from the spent rods and she saw Hyun look to Mr. Kun for permission to respond. Kun scowled back, but after a brief pause he nodded and Hyun answered. Then Dr. Hyun was hurrying them along, casting nervous glances back at Mr. Kun as they left the reactor hall behind. She took one last look around to make sure she had not missed Pak anywhere, then she followed the group out.

After the reactor hall they passed through what looked like a pump room. Large bore pressure pipes, their joints connected by thick bolts, ran along the walls and ceiling. It was impossibly loud and the smell of metal was once again overpowering. She counted two operators, both wearing ear protectors. Neither was Pak. It was too loud to ask questions. And then she was standing outside again, her ears ringing.

Hyun led them to a concrete structure he identified as the spent fuel storage pool. It looked disused, like it had been abandoned some time ago. She hoped no one was going to ask a question. They wouldn't find Pak here, and it was bitterly cold; she was shivering inside her coat and her jaw had started to spasm, clenching and unclenching uncontrollably. She caught Jan staring into the pool, as if he had seen something sad there. A thin sheet of ice covered the water, but as she followed his gaze she could see that many of the stainless steel canisters in which the fuel rods had been packed had been cracked open, the seals removed. He had been one of the inspectors that had overseen the original decommissioning; he was looking at his work undone. She wanted to tell him that it would be okay.

God willing, today she would fix this.

After the spent fuel storage pool Hyun brought them back to the administration building for lunch.

Eliza found herself struggling to keep up with the group. Her head was pounding and the sun seemed to have grown even brighter; it was like the whole sky was ablaze. She felt a moment of light-headedness as she approached the steps that led up to the building. Her fingers fumbled for the railing, closed around it. Jorg appeared at her side, asking if she was okay. She waved him away, telling him she was fine.

A wide variety of food had been laid out on the conference room table. Her eyes scanned the various plates and dishes. Her appetite had not returned, but she had been hoping for something to warm her up, perhaps a bowl of steaming broth to hold between her frozen fingers. But nothing among the bowls of tofu, pickled vegetables, and noodles appeared hot. The smell of garlic and ginger was overpowering. A wave of nausea hit her and for one horrible moment she thought that she might throw up on the table.

Dr. Hyun appeared at her side, offering her a smile. He had noticed her during the tour. She did not seem well. Was she feeling alright? Could he get her something? She told him she was fine, just a stomach bug she had picked up in Pyongyang. He pointed at the kimchi, explaining that it was soaked in a chili brine and flavored with bean paste. The chili was especially good for colds. He picked up a bowl, spooning a large portion onto a plate, presenting it to her with both hands.

Eliza had never cared much for foreign fare, but she knew food shortages were common here. The mountainous terrain was poorly suited to farming, and what little foodstuff could be imported was far too expensive for most Koreans to afford. The spread that had been laid on for them would be something that Dr. Hyun and his colleagues were unlikely to see again for a very long time. It would be rude of her to refuse.

She picked up a piece of the fermented cabbage, placing it gingerly in her mouth. The flavor was strong, tangy and salty. The chili burned the ulcers that now lined her gums and covered the roof of her mouth, but she forced herself to chew, then swallow. Her stomach lurched, threatening to return the kimchi immediately, but she managed to hold it down. Hyun smiled, seemingly satisfied, and left to speak with Jan.

Eliza excused herself and made her way as quickly as she could to the restrooms. Thankfully they were still empty. She chose the nearest stall and ran towards it. The fluorescent tubes embedded in their long ice cube tray fixtures cast a harsh, shadowless light, but at least the toilet seemed clean. She dropped to her knees on the cold tiles, not bothering to slide the bolt into place behind her. She thought she was going to be sick, but after a while it passed.

She rested her head against the partition, her hands still gripping the sides of the bowl. Every inch of her ached miserably. She didn't think she had ever been this tired; she wanted to just lie down on the floor and sleep. Had she read that this was how you died of hypothermia?

Did you just stop caring about the cold?

She came to with the fluorescent light flickering on and off.

Her headache, the bone-numbing cold in her hands and feet, they were all still there, but somehow she seemed distant from them now. And there was a strange taste in her mouth. She ran her tongue across her teeth and gums. Rich, sticky, metallic, but not altogether unpleasant. She licked her lips and looked around. It took her a moment to realize what was wrong. She was no longer in the stall. For some reason she was perched on all fours on the counter that ran along the wall opposite. How had she gotten up here?

She climbed down slowly, noticing for the first time the bloody handprint she left on the rim of the sink as she eased herself back to the floor. Had she hurt herself getting up there? She looked down at her hand. It was smeared with blood, but when she examined it she couldn't find a cut. The fluorescent light above her head continued to flicker and buzz, like it was about to fail.

Her sunglasses were lying in the middle of the floor. She bent down to pick them up. It was then that she noticed the blood on the door to the stall where she had first gone to be sick. The door was ajar. She stood in front of it for a long moment, then slowly pushed it back.

Inside a soldier in the drab olive uniform of the KPAGF lay slumped against the toilet. His eyes were open, staring sightlessly up at the ceiling where the lights continued to flicker in their trays. It looked like he had been attacked by a wild animal. His throat had been torn out, nubs of cartilage and one shocking white corner of his jawbone poking through around the edges of the ragged wound. The top of his tunic was soaked in blood. It covered the walls of the cubicle in great arcing sprays and collected in slowly congealing pools on the tiled floor.

Eliza's hands flew to her face in horror. She wanted to scream but something stopped her, the part of her fractured mind that already knew what had happened here. She slowly removed her hands from her face, only partly surprised to find that they came away tacky. She slowly turned around to look in the mirror behind her.

The lower half of her face and neck were covered in blood, too. Her teeth were stained with it. The deep circles around her eyes were now black, and the strands of hair that escaped from under her hat were completely white. But it was something else that caused a strangled cry to escape her lips. The pupils that stared back at her were impossibly dilated. And they were no longer dark. They flashed silver, reflecting the flickering light above.

She heard Jorg's voice, calling to her from outside.

She stood up and flushed the toilet in the next cubicle, calling back that she'd be out in a minute. Her blouse was stained with the guard's blood and she tore it off, burying it in the bin. She rinsed the blood from her face and neck, no longer caring about the cold. She grabbed swatches of paper towels from the dispenser and ran them under the tap. Then she closed the stall door and wiped it down. After that she cleaned the blood from the sink top. When she had done as much as she could she flushed the paper and checked her reflection again. There was blood on her jacket but the material was dark. With the buttons done up and her scarf wrapped around her neck nobody would know she wasn't wearing a blouse.

She tucked the strands of white hair that had escaped back up under her hat and replaced her sunglasses, then hurried back outside to join the others.

*

BIXICATED.

Is it even a word? I don't think so. It was one of the first things I looked up when I added the dictionary to the collection of books I keep under my bed. I couldn't find it, and I tried every spelling I could think of. My eyes flick back to the gun on the table. I realize now's probably not the time to pick Marv up on it, however.

'How'd you really come across that map, Junior?'

I don't know why he needs to hear it, but Marv doesn't look like he's in any mood for a debate. Truth is there's not much to say. I tell him about finding Benjamin in the vet's on I-64 out beyond Ely. How he'd been shot, and had most likely dragged himself in there to fix himself up. When I describe how whoever shot Benjamin must have followed him in to finish him off it's like a shadow passes over Marv's narrow features, and his eyes go dark, like those vampires who came to that little town in Alaska. I wonder if he's remembering. Either way, I figure it's my cue to stop talking. The seconds stretch out until maybe a minute has passed; in my seat it feels longer. Finally Marv comes back from wherever he's been. He asks me where Benjamin had been shot. When I tell him there was a bullet hole in the center of his forehead he just repeats the word, only it comes out shorter, like *fard.* He asks me how I knew it was him. Had I searched him thoroughly? Did I find anything else on him? Were there dog tags? When I tell him about the signet ring he just closes his eyes. He's gone for a long while this time. At last he comes back.

'Can you walk?'

Probably not far, but I nod anyway. I might be new to this, but I'm a quick study. When the person asking the questions has a gun it seems the correct answer's invariably yes.

''Kay. We don't have much time. Have you stashed food anywhere?'

I shake my head. *We were supposed to stash food?*

'S'aw-ite. I have enough for both of us. Did you eat enough breakfast?' My brains are scrambled from the sudden change in direction and it takes me a moment to decode *Jeet-nuf breffist?* from Marv-speak to English. When I finally get there I figure he doesn't need to hear that I haven't eaten since lunch yesterday, so I just nod again.

'Good. Go on and grab your gear. If you need to change your shorts I've got spares. We're outta here in five minutes.'

I don't need to take him up on this last offer, but I won't pretend it wasn't a close run thing. I limp to my room as quickly as I can and gather up my scavenging kit. I transfer the leatherman into the side pocket of my parka where I can get to it quickly. The pry bar's too big, but I make sure it's sitting on top of the backpack. And in what seems like an act of insane optimism I grab *The Girl With The Dragon Tattoo* and stuff it in too. I guess there's no accounting for decisions you make at times like this, but I realize I really want to know what happens to Lisbeth Salander. When I think I've got everything I snap the backpack closed and head back to the kitchen.

Marv's right behind me with an armful of MREs. He dumps them on the table. As he's heading back to his room he shouts over his shoulder to take the ones we got from Quartermaster that morning out of his backpack and replace them with the one's he just brought in, and to be really careful not to mix them up. I'm beginning to wonder if Marv's lost it again, like he did out in one of those places where he was fighting, before Eden. But I do as he asks. He returns a moment later, just as I'm finishing swapping out the last of the rations. The pistol's nowhere in sight, but instead there's a hunting rifle with a telescopic sight slung over his shoulder, which doesn't make me feel any better. He's already heading for the back door when I realize we've left the map Kane gave us on the kitchen table. I figure it might be important so I tell him. He says we won't be needing it, but that makes no sense so when he's not looking I go back and grab it anyway.

We strap on the snowshoes and head off. The label on the Tylenol container says to wait four hours between taking them, but my ankle's hurting like a bitch so I've dry swallowed a couple more in my room. Once we get to the turnpike Marv goes east, towards Shiloah. I'm pretty sure this isn't the way that was marked on Benjamin's map, but I'm not feeling brave enough to start questioning his sense of direction so I stay quiet. The fresh snow means it's heavy going and we're single file from the start. Marv sets a punishing pace, faster even than the trip back from Ely when we were trying to outrun the storm. He's breaking trail, his legs rising and falling like pistons, pounding the deep snow. I bound my ankle tight in the infirmary and so far it seems to be holding, but I don't know how long I'll be able to keep this up. I've unsnapped the neck on my parka so I can suck in more air, but I'm already sweating inside my thermals, in spite of the cold. I tell myself I just need to keep it up a little longer; even Marv can't maintain a pace like this for long.

Every couple of hundred yards he slips the rifle off his shoulder and spins around to scan the landscape behind us through the sight. The first time he does it I think he's fixing to shoot me for not keeping up and I stick my hands up in the air. He just tells me to put them down and not to act bixicated. I don't understand who he can be looking for. Nobody goes outside but Marv and me.

But I have no breath left for questions, and even if I did I doubt I'd get any answers.

Marv doesn't ease the pace until we reach the old church that sits on the edge of Shiloah a couple of hours later.

I stand outside in the lee of the steeple, my hands on my knees, trying to catch my breath, while he scans the road behind us through the rifle. When he's done he lowers it and motions me towards the arched doorway. One of the doors is gone and the other hangs on its last studded hinge. I step through. The font's been knocked over and there's a pile of ash in the vestibule where someone's lit a fire with the hymnals. Inside the high windows are darkened with snow, but raw cold daylight tumbles in from a large hole in the roof. All around long wooden pews sit in silent disarray. The ends of a few are charred black, evidence of failed attempts to set them alight. Further back the altar sits in darkness.

Marv motions with the rifle to a narrow set of steps that wind up to the bell tower and I start to climb. Moments later I step out into the belfry. The church sits at a crook in the road and when the wind's low like now from the top you can see for several miles back along the turnpike. After the hike out here I'm just happy to sit and get my breath back. My ankle's killing me so I prop it up on one of the parapets, like I remember the first aid book said I should. Marv unslings the rifle and uses the scope to scan the road as far as the horizon. Apparently satisfied, he sits back down.

My stomach growls loudly, reminding me I haven't been fed in almost a day. Marv digs into his backpack and throws me a HOOAH! from one of the MREs. I'm not a big fan of peanut butter; on any other day I'd ask if there was another flavor on offer - Kane always picks me out an apple-cinnamon for our chats - but I'm not about to push it. I tear off the wrapper and the bar's gone in a couple of bites. I wash it down with water from my canteen and swallow another couple of Tylenol.

When Marv stands up to check the road again I risk a question.

'Who're you looking for?'

He says nothing for a long time, just continues to look through the sight on the rifle. Eventually he mutters 'Hopefully no one.'

I have other questions that I want to ask. Why'd you kill Benjamin? Was it because you went crazy? Are you planning to kill me? But I figure that's probably my allowance for now. I'll work up to those.

Marv snaps his backpack shut and hoists it on to his shoulder.

'Aw'ite. Let's get goin'.'

I feel like I've just sat down, but I comply. I hobble down the stairs from the bell tower. We sit on one of the pews downstairs to strap our snowshoes on and then head back outside.

We walk through town. The wind's still low and the tattered, weather-beaten flags hang limp on their peeling flagpoles. I wasn't expecting to be back here this side of winter. But then this morning I wasn't expecting to leave the kitchen in the farmhouse, so I'm not complaining.

The road out of Shiloah climbs gently towards the intersection. Marv still keeps swiveling around to check behind us every few hundred yards, but he's eased the pace a little. Nevertheless my ankle's protesting at the incline. We pass the Jubilee Foods, its roof still collapsed, and haul out on the hard shoulder to get around the school bus and the rig that blockade the road a little further on. The HOOAH! Marv threw me up in the bell tower's done little more than whet my appetite. I'm thinking maybe he plans to stop us up at the McDonald's where we had lunch the other day, but he just walks on through the intersection, making his way out wide around the collapsed traffic light gantry, and then we're following the long concrete sweep of the on-ramp down to what the sign says is US15, the Catoctin Mountain Highway, a big, straight, flat section of road, I'm guessing three lanes in each direction. The drifts aren't as bad here and we can walk side by side. After a mile or so I gather up the courage to ask where we're going.

'Mount Weather.'

'The way marked on Benjamin's map's shorter.' About six miles shorter, actually.

'Yup.'

I wait a while for an explanation, but there's none forthcoming.

'Did you kill Benjamin?'

For the first time Marv stops and just looks at me.

'Now why in the hell would I do that?'

'Because of Miss Kimble. Were you and Benjamin fighting over her?'

He lets out a snort, as if I've said the stupidest thing ever. He unslings the rifle, checks behind him, then starts walking again. I stand there for a few seconds, feeling more confused then ever. Then I shift the straps of the backpack and follow after him.

We keep up a good pace and by dusk we're on the outskirts of Frederick. I've never been this far south, at least not since we came to Eden.

It looks like a lot of people lived here, once. From up on the highway I can make out the spires of a half dozen churches dotted around the edges, standing tall above the densely packed row housing clustered beneath. And closer to what must be the center, a collection of once-proud office blocks where I guess people used to go to spend their time fretting about things that stopped mattering after the Last Day. Now they list askew or askance or sit collapsed and crumbling, their virus-weakened frames no longer able to bear their weight.

The temperature's dropping; there can't be more than an hour of daylight left. We'd normally head into town to find shelter, but Marv's showing no sign of quitting the road. He walks us through a succession of interchanges until Frederick's shifted around behind us. Sometimes, if the overpass has collapsed he'll lead us up the exit, but we always end up taking the long sweep of the on-ramp back down again afterwards.

I'm beginning to wonder if he means to walk us through the night when finally he leads us up the embankment towards an uninteresting two-story building sitting right off the highway, rows of identical windows marching away round its unremarkable corners. The sign above the entrance says *Pegasus Office Supplies*. The door beneath is already smashed so we don't need to worry about breaking in. Behind the reception area there's a jungle of small cubicles; Marv chooses a spot among them to make camp. He says we can't have a fire so we heat our MREs and eat in silence. I think the first aid book said I should pack my ankle with ice, but it's too cold so I swallow a couple more Tylenol and climb inside my sleeping bag.

I'm too tired to do anything but fall asleep.

*

I WAKE IN THAT SHALLOW LIGHT just before dawn. Without a fire it's bitterly cold. Marv's still bundled up inside his sleeping bag, snoring fitfully, so I pull on my boots and parka and make my way outside. The last crumbling interchange we passed sits in the distance behind us. It's snowed again in the night and the concrete's sharp edges, the bent and twisted rebar, are once again shrouded in gray.

I head back inside. It's unusual for Marv still to be sleeping; he's normally up before me, nudging my sleeping bag with the toe of his boot to wake me from my slumber. I find some paper in a photocopier that's been overlooked and spend a few minutes twisting the sheets into tight twirls. I noticed a couple of withered trees still clinging to the embankment when we came in last night so I dig the handsaw from my backpack and head back outside to cut a few limbs. Within minutes there's a small fire going, steam rising in slow coils from the branches as I feed them to the flames. I figure Marv won't mind. The smoke's not going anywhere, and the tiny flames aren't going to give away our position to whatever demons he imagines are chasing us. I gather some snow in a charred tin mug from my backpack and set it to melt next to the fire.

It occurs to me I could just take off, head back to Eden. Binding my ankle seems to be working; it still throbs, but it's a lot better than it was yesterday. I have the map Kane gave us, the one that I picked up from the kitchen table in the farmhouse as we set out. We haven't followed the route Kane marked, but I'm pretty sure I could find my way. I'd need to do something to stop Marv coming after me, though. I could hide his boots. I'd need to do it somewhere in the building, somewhere it'd take a while for him to find them. Leaving him without boots altogether would be a death sentence, and even though I'm still not sure if he killed Benjamin I'm not ready for that.

While I'm thinking about this Marv wakes up. He winces at the light coming through the window on the other side of the room, even though between the clouds and the tint on the glass it's scarcely light at all. I've strained the snowmelt through a spare surgical mask I keep in my backpack and put the mug back in the flames. It's not a great fire, but it'll do to warm the water for coffee. When the water's bubbling I break a sachet out of one of the MRE packs and dump it in. The bitter aroma fills the air. I put on my gloves and fish the mug out of the fire and hand it over. Marv sits up, still huddled in his sleeping bag, and wraps himself around it, like he needs to extract every last ounce of the warmth that's there.

'You should've woken me earlier. We've lost half the morning.'

I just shrug. It's really not that late, and the complaint's half-hearted at best. In Marv-speak it might even mean 'Thanks for the coffee.'

'You got any of them Tylenol handy? I feel like hammered shit this morning.' I fish the blister pack out of the pocket of my parka and pop a couple into his outstretched hand.

We sit in silence while Marv slurps from the mug. When the coffee's finished he fishes out a crumpled pack of cigarettes and lights up. The smoke drifts over, burning my eyes, so I head outside and fetch an armful of snow to kill the fire. When I get back Marv's already packed his sleeping bag and is lacing up his boots.

We re-join the highway. Up ahead the gantry holding the road signs has collapsed, but there's enough of it showing above the drifts to tell us we're still heading south on 15. The overnight snowfall's made the going harder, but not bad enough for us to be single file. Marv's still stopping every few hundred yards to scan the road behind us, but he's not setting anything like the breakneck pace he was yesterday. Maybe whatever monsters he thought were chasing him when we set out from Eden have gone. The fear I had yesterday's receded a little too. I reckon if Marv was going to kill me he'd have done it by now.

For mile after mile we continue on, slowly cresting low hills, trudging into the shallows between, the foothills of the Appalachians always to our right in the distance. On each side, as far as the eye can see, nothing but empty fields, only the occasional bare and blackened tree poking up through to break the gray. Marv's not much for chatting, so we hike in silence. It's not long till my mind starts to wander. I think of Mags, cataloguing her smiles and frowns and gestures. How she had tasted when she pulled my head down to kiss me.

We eat lunch late. There're no houses along this stretch of the highway so we huddle next to an overpass where 15 splits from US340 and turns south towards Leesburg. There's little wood that would hold a fire and no place to make one and so we eat our MREs cowled up in our parkas, our backs to the cold concrete. The only time Marv speaks is to ask for some more Tylenol. Afterwards I bury our trash in the snow and we set off again.

We lumber on through the afternoon, the unseen sun tracking its way ever westward behind the clouds. We've been making slow time since we stopped for lunch. Marv's stopping for longer when he checks behind us now, and sometimes he doesn't bother to unsling the rifle and scan with the scope. I'm not complaining though. My foot's feeling a little better, but I'm glad for the break, nonetheless.

We pass through a succession of overpasses, each one collapsed. We pick our way through the rubble, taking our snowshoes off to clamber over girders, testing for rebar buried in the snow that would break an ankle or shatter a kneecap. I catch myself thinking I need to be careful;

we're miles from home now, and that was how Benjamin died.

But then I look over at Marv and a fresh jolt of fear hits me as I realize it wasn't.

Dusk's starting to settle as Marv leads us off 340 at a signpost for Brunswick. We hike into town just as the last of the light leaves the sky. A sign welcomes home America's bravest. A little further along a billboard promises live music at Cadogan's.

We stop at the edge of town. There's a large cinder block right there at the traffic circle. Marv says no need to go further, it'll do fine. I decide not to argue, but I can't help but think we could have done better. The building seems in decent shape, and the brass plaque that reads *Jonas P. Bodelmann, Funeral Home*, isn't showing any signs of the virus. But seriously? I suppose there's some perverse logic to it. At least you know for sure where the bodies will be.

We break in and set up camp in the small chapel among the scattered pews. The whole place smells of damp and rot, but otherwise it seems fine. Marv says he's not hungry; he's just going to go right to bed. He asks for another couple of the Tylenol and dry swallows them while he's unraveling his sleeping bag. I head back out with the folding saw in search of firewood.

I manage only a few withered branches from what's left of a small grove that once grew on the traffic island before I give up. I'm about to head back inside when I spot a soda machine tucked under the eaves of Jerry's Liquors opposite. I head over to check it out. Somebody's already taken a pry bar to the lock and plundered what was inside, but sometimes you can get lucky and find a can still lodged in the chute. Not today, however. I have a quick look in the store, but it's been ransacked, anything of use removed years before; there's nothing left on the shelves or in the aisles now except trash. I pick up a few pieces of cardboard to use as kindling and make my way outside.

Marv's already out cold when I get back. He sounds like he's arguing with someone in his sleep, and the muscles in his jaw seem to be working, clenching and unclenching, like maybe he's grinding his teeth. I don't think Marv sleeps well. I've considered cutting him in on the pills I get for Kane, but somehow I doubt that'd be a good idea.

I sit on the floor, my back to one of the pew ends, and start working on a fire. It takes a while for the wood to catch. It's not until my MRE's hissing away in its heating pouch and I finally look up that I notice it. One of the brass handles has momentarily caught the light from the sputtering fire, but it takes me another moment to work out what it's attached to. As I stare at it the shape separates itself from the darkness: a coffin, resting on a trestle, all the way back in the shadows farthest from the door. The casket's open. From where I'm sitting I can't see whether it has an inhabitant. I reckon it's a good bet, though. I could go and close it, but that would almost certainly involve me getting a good look at whoever's inside, so I decide to leave it alone.

Outside the wind's picked up and inside the small chapel it's cold. I sit down by the fire and pull out *The Girl With The Dragon Tattoo*, but for once I don't feel like reading. I stare into the shifting flames and think about Mags, and what happened on the roof the night before last, and how I felt when Marv pulled the gun on me outside the tunnel and I thought I wasn't going to see her again.

I don't care much for poetry, but there was a single volume of poems in the box of Mom's books that Jack had stored in the attic. Boredom must have driven me to it when the box had been depleted, the other books read and re-read. Even then it probably wouldn't have held my attention for very long. Except that, when I held it up to the old metal flashlight the spine showed signs of cracking at one point, and no other. When I flipped it over to examine the fore edge I could see Mom had folded back the corner of a single page, marking a poem by someone called Christopher Marlowe. The page was dog-eared and creased; she had clearly returned to it time and again. I imagined her fingers tracing the words as she read. A single line, the last, had been underlined. It was the only time I could remember Mom writing in any of her books.

*Who ever loved, that loved not at first sight?*

I didn't know what it meant back then. Tell the truth I'm not sure I know what it means even now. I guess whoever Christopher Marlowe was he must have been smart, for Mom to have liked his poem so much. I only know he didn't grow up in a world where you've known everyone there is to know since you were in first grade.

It's still dark when I wake the following morning. Marv's huddled in his sleeping bag, still muttering something in his sleep. I suspect he'll be mad at me for not getting him up. He said he wanted to make an early start to make up for yesterday. But I think he may be coming down with something, so I figure it's better to let him rest and recover his strength.

I banked the fire before I fell asleep, but it's died overnight in spite of it; I guess the wood was just too damp. I build it back up with what's left of the branches I collected and coax it back to life, then I grab my canteen and head out. The coffin's still there, on the other side of the room. I give it a wide berth.

When I get back Marv's awake, sitting up inside his sleeping bag by the remnants of the fire. He's got his knife out and he's checking his reflection in the blade. He sheaths it when I walk back in, but I see the dark circles under his eyes, the pallor of his skin. I make coffee and hand him a mug with a couple of Tylenol. As he's drinking it I ask how he's feeling. He just grunts. I'm considering suggesting that we hole up here for a while until he's feeling better, but as soon as he's done with his coffee he starts packing up his things. Minutes later we're back outside.

Brunswick sits on the bank of the Potomac, looking south across the river. A narrow concrete bridge spans the wide expanse of gray water, and thankfully it seems to have held. The road up to it inclines only gently, but every time the wind drops I can hear Marv breathing hard behind his respirator. When we get to the middle I stop and unsnap the throat of my parka while Marv plods on ahead. On each bank there's a rim of shelving ice, but beneath me the river's flowing gently east. I lower my hood and stand for a few minutes by the rust-pitted railings, savoring the sound. There are so few things left out here that seem alive.

When I've had my fill I pull up the hood and set off again. I catch up to him on the other side of the bridge. A faded sign shows a red bird perched on a branch between some flowers. Above it says *Virginia Welcomes You.*

All day we hike south. The road's narrow and it twists and turns for the first couple of miles, climbing steadily between gently rolling hills. Marv stops frequently now, checking for signs buried in the drift. The gradient isn't that bad, and the snow's settled since the last fall, but I can tell he's struggling. Once when I turn around he's stopped behind me and is bent over, the palms of his hands on his knees. I ask if he's okay, but he just waves the question away and sets off again.

The road continues south through a mixture of farmland and houses that sit lonely on large empty lots. Marv's still stopping to scrub snow off the mile markers, although the route's straight here and easy to follow. We pass through a place called Wheatland; a little ways on we cross the north fork of Catoctin Creek, and then shortly after the south. There's no indication we're near water other than the raised concrete barriers that suddenly appear on either side of the road.

The road briefly widens at an intersection. A sign still bolted to a gantry that's somehow survived announces we're crossing the Charles Town Pike. Dead traffic lights stare down as we pass under. A mile further on we reach a large interchange and the turnpike runs into the Harry Byrd Highway. It's already noon so we stop for lunch. The wind's staying low so we eat our MREs cowled up in our parkas under the overpass. As I'm gathering up our trash I notice Marv's hardly touched his meal. He's drinking his coffee, his fingers wrapped tightly around the cup. I offer him the last of the Tylenol and he accepts the container without saying anything. I bag our trash and we trudge up the on-ramp and start heading west.

An hour or so later the road sweeps south and we pass a large gray-brown expanse of water before it turns west again. For the next two hours it's a long steady climb uphill. Marv's pace has been dropping all afternoon, and since lunch he's been coughing continuously inside his respirator. At one point he stumbles in the snow, but when I reach out to help him up he waves me back furiously.

The road finally levels and then I see it: a small sign announcing the turnoff to the Blue Ridge Mountain Road. Underneath it another, even smaller, that says *Mount Weather EAC*. I pick up the pace, trudging through the drifts towards it, but when I look around Marv's no longer with me. He's fallen to his knees. He pulls off the respirator just as a coughing fit hits him, great wracking spasms that double him over. When I make a move towards him his hand shoots up again, warning me back. I stand there, staring down at him, helpless. Eventually the fit passes, but as he straightens up I see his face is deathly pale; the beard that used to be reddish brown is now shot through with white.

He makes no attempt to stand, just stays where he is, kneeling in the snow like he's praying. Eventually he looks over at me.

'Junior.'

'Yes Marv.'

'I ain't goin' no further.'

*

THE FIRST THING that crosses my mind is that we don't have time for this. Dusk's slipping into the sky and I can already feel the temperature dropping. We'll need to find shelter soon; there's nothing out here on the highway. But then I look down at the respirator he's cast off, the fine spray of blood coloring the snow around it. He's sicker than I thought. Maybe he's running a fever. The first aid book says sometimes that can affect your thinking.

I take a step towards him. If I can just get him on his feet maybe we can start moving again. But he waves me back furiously, grimacing with the effort of it. His teeth are stained with the blood he's just coughed into the snow.

'You stay away now, Junior. I've got it. The arn vars.'

For a second I think I've misheard. But then he unsnaps the neck of his parka and reaches inside for the crucifix under his thermals. He pulls it out and holds it in front of him, staring at it in the fading light. The metal has tarnished a deep, dull gray, like it's been sitting outside for years. As the surface catches whatever's left of the day's light I can see it's pitted and pocked, as though something's been eating away at it.

I shake my head, not wanting to believe. This makes no sense. The virus is dead, it has been for years, ever since Kane defeated it when he scorched the skies. Even so, Marv never let his guard down. He was always so careful.

'That doesn't mean anything. Maybe it just needs to be wiped down a little.'

As I say it I hear how stupid that sounds. I reach inside my thermals for the cross I wear. Marv looks over as I pull out. It's slick with sweat, but otherwise as it was when I slid it in there three days ago. He shakes his head.

'Ain't no mistake, Junior. I got it.'

He hesitates for a moment and then he lifts the ski goggles he's wearing onto his forehead. He immediately bends over, cupping one mitten to his brow to shield his eyes, like he can't bear even the little light the day has left. Then he slowly pulls back the hood of the parka. His hair is shot through with white, just like his beard. After a moment he lifts his head and with an obvious effort moves his hand away from his face, squinting at me in the failing light.

I take an involuntary step backwards, almost tripping over myself in my snowshoes. The circles around his eyes are now almost black. But it's not that that causes the breath to catch in my throat. The pupils staring back at me are impossibly dilated. And they aren't dark anymore. They flash silver, like when you shine a flashlight into an animal's eyes at night.

When he thinks I've seen enough he pulls the hood of the parka back up over his head. His features retreat into the shadow of the cowl.

'But how could you have it? The virus is dead. There's been no sign of it in all the years we've been going back outside.'

A coughing fit hits him, and for a moment he can't answer. Eventually it passes and he exhales softly.

'Virus ain't dead Junior. What Kane did knocked it back some, that's for sure. But it's still out here. I ain't ever been sure about the things: the trucks, the cars, the buildings, all the metal that got contaminated. I thought it was gone from those, although I must have picked it up from something, so maybe not. But it's there all right, in the people that were infected. In the furies. They ain't decaying like they should, which means it's still workin' away inside them, building itself back up. They can't move themselves much, yet. But eventually they'll be able to.'

An image of the little girl I found, in the house out in Shreve, floats into my head. How Marv had held the tip of the knife with his blood on it under her nose. For a long time nothing had happened, but then suddenly she had gone stiff all over and the muscles in her jaw had started to work, clenching and unclenching, like she was grinding her teeth. She had seemed like she wanted to bite the knife, but something invisible had been restraining her.

'But how did you get it?'

Marv waves his hand, like this question isn't important anymore.

'Careless, I expect. I was sure Kane would send Peck after us, but I thought if we moved quick we could stay out ahead of him. I guess with all the rushing I must have slipped up somewhere along the way, touched something I shouldn't have.'

I'm still having trouble getting my head around what I've just seen, but something he says grabs my attention.

'Peck goes outside?'

He nods. 'Not often. Only a couple of times that I've noticed. He covers his tracks pretty well, but I've been doing this longer than he has.'

I think of the blast door opening to let Peck back in and my head suddenly lights up with an idea.

'We can get you back to Eden, put you in the scanner. That'll kill it. If we turn around now we can be back in three days, maybe four tops.'

'I ain't got three days, and even if I had I ain't got it in me to make that hike anyhow. Besides, Kane'd never let me back inside Eden with the virus. Why do you think he has Peck keep Guardians out at the portal anyway?'

I look at him like I don't understand.

'The Guardians protect us from whoever might still be outside.'

Marv just shakes his head.

'It ain't that, Junior. With the tunnels collapsed we're hid pretty good inside that mountain. Besides, the blast door'd do just fine if that was all he was worried about. The Guardians are there to stop you and me trying to make it back in if'n we get infected. The scanner's just a last line of defense, in case something gets missed by those knuckleheads Peck has standing guard.'

I'm about to say something else, but Marv holds his hand up to silence me.

'We don't have much time so you need to hush up and listen now Junior. I have some things to tell you. Some of it may not be easy for you to hear, but you need to let me finish, and then think on it some later and see if'n you agree.' He wipes the back of his glove across his mouth. 'Christ, I wish I had the words for this, but that was never my thing.' He pauses, as if trying to figure where to start. 'You and the others in Eden. You're like frogs.'

In Marv-speak it's *frawgs*. There are no frogs any more so it's not a word I'm used to hearing. I'm wondering if I've misheard. I guess I must look a little confused.

'What are you? Bixicated? You do know what a frog is don't you Junior?'

I nod. Yes, of course I know what a frog is.

'Okay, well if you drop a frog into a pot of boiling water, what do you think will happen? It'll jump straight out, right?'

He looks at me expectantly, so I nod again.

'Right. But if you put the same frog into a pot of nice warm water and slowly turn the fire up your frog'll just sit there happy as a clam until he's dead.'

I'm not sure what a clam is, but I'm guessing it doesn't matter, and besides I don't want to interrupt him again, so I let it slide.

'The way Eden is, it's all wrong Junior. The confessions. The penance. Believing you're the Chosen Ones. Waiting for Kane to tell you all who you're going to be matched with. It ain't your fault you can't see it; you've never known any different. Or maybe you did once, but you were too young to remember. And Kane, well, he saved you all of course, makes you feel protected. But he's been cranking the burner up a notch at a time. And now you're all sitting in boiling water and thinking it's bath time.'

He takes a break, like the effort of explaining this has been too much for him. When he starts again his voice is lower.

'Sarah was on to him. She had him figured out from the get-go, or not long after at any rate.'

For a second I'm confused; there's no Sarah in Eden. I open my mouth to ask him what he means, but then I realize he must mean Miss Kimble. I didn't know her first name until right now.

'She spoke to Benjamin about it, but I don't think he could see it either, right back at the start. It was only when he found her in her room that he started to wonder. He never believed she killed herself; said she wasn't the type. But back then I didn't buy it. Don't get me wrong; I've never been a fan of God-botherers like Kane. Seems like they've always got something to say about how others are living their lives. Especially those like Benjamin and me.'

The look on my face must tell him I don't get his last reference. What does he mean by people like Benjamin and him? Does he mean grown-ups? He pauses for a moment, as if considering whether I need this part of the story.

'Benjamin and me, we were together Junior.'

I'm still confused. Does he mean because they were the only soldiers in Eden before we arrived? But what about Scudder? Wasn't he there too?

He looks up at me, and for an instant I think I see the silver flashing inside the cowl of his hood again.

'He was my match, Junior. Only we figured it out for ourselves, like people should. We didn't need someone like Kane to work it out for us. And we definitely didn't need him to tell us it couldn't be that way.'

Oh. *Oh*. The ring I'd found on Benjamin's finger, with the eagle and the banner; it wasn't Benjamin's. It was Marv's. I guess that's why he thought it was ridiculous when I suggested that he had been jealous of Benjamin and Miss Kimble.

'But Scudder said you started to fight with Benjamin when Miss Kimble arrived.'

When I mention this Marv bows his head a little. There's another long pause before he continues.

'We did, although not right away; Scudder's got that bit wrong. It was mostly after Sarah died that we got to arguing about what was happening in Eden. Benjamin wanted to deal with Kane right then and there. He was brave enough, and smart as a whip, but Benjamin was no soldier. I told him Kane wouldn't give up Eden without a fight, and seeing as they had access to the armory that was a fight they were likely to win. I've thought about this a lot since and I think I was right. But I also know I was scared to try. I'd already seen enough of killing to last me a lifetime. Guarding an all but abandoned bunker like Raven Rock was the only post I was fit for after I got back.'

Raven Rock? I give Marv another look, like he's lost me again.

'The place you know as Eden, Junior. Besides, Peck was watching us like a hawk those first years, especially after what happened with Sarah. So Benjamin got it into his head that if we couldn't take Eden we'd need to leave it. We knew about Mount Weather, of course. There's a few places like it scattered around, all part of what was called the Federal Relocation Arc, back then. Bunkers dug deep into the mountains of

Pennsylvania, Maryland, West Virginia, even down into the Carolinas. It's where the leaders were supposed to go in the event something like the virus happened.'

'Mount Weather's actually where Kane was supposed to be that day. Raven Rock had been removed from the Relocation Arc and mothballed decades before. But I guess whoever gave us the virus also saw to that. They must've hacked the command network. Benjamin spotted it, on the morning you all arrived. There wasn't much to do back then, so he'd been amusing himself monitoring radio transmissions. He'd intercepted a series of orders to the base commanders in each of the bunkers, telling them to evacuate immediately. Embedded in the message was a remote instruction changing the entry code on their blast doors. He wrote all the new codes down on that map you found on him.'

Marv bows his head again, takes a deep breath, then another.

'After Sarah died Benjamin was more convinced than ever that we needed to get out. But once the weather changed I knew there was no way we could make it all that way to Mount Weather, not with a bunch of young'uns in tow. I told him to sit tight, that one day you'd all be old enough to make the journey. We just needed to bide our time until then. I've never been good with kids, but Benjamin was. I told him you'd all follow him, when you were older. He wasn't much for that idea, though. He said these were the important years for children, the formative ones. Kane was already shaping your minds, molding you. Benjamin said he'd make you dependent on him, afraid of the outside; there'd come a time when you wouldn't be able to leave. In the end I couldn't stop him. I agreed to tell everyone he'd had an accident while we were out scavenging, so Kane wouldn't suspect. If Mount Weather checked out he'd come back and I'd find a way to get you all out of Eden and down there safely. When he didn't return I just assumed he hadn't made it, or maybe he had and he'd just decided to stay. I never thought Kane would send Peck after him to make sure.'

'But it was your boot prints I saw at the place where Benjamin was killed.'

He looks up at me.

'So that's why you thought I'd killed him. I've been puzzlin' over that since you mentioned it. Junior, did it ever occur to you that there might be more than one pair of the same boots out there? These are standard issue U.S. Army cold weather gear. Picked 'em up in a surplus store out in Culver. Peck probably got his in exactly the same place. Only reason Benjamin wasn't wearing the same kind was we couldn't find a pair to fit him.'

Another coughing fit hits him then. When he looks up at me there's fresh blood in his beard. He wipes it with the back of his glove then stares at the dark smear there for a long while. I'm not sure he knows he's doing it, but he's clenching and unclenching his jaw like he was in his sleep last night. At last he pulls off the glove and dumps it in the snow. He reaches into the breast pocket of his parka and pulls out a road map, just like the one Kane gave us, back in Eden.

'Before Benjamin left he made me memorize the entry codes he'd intercepted that morning. They're all written on this map. He said if he didn't make it back I had to try and get everyone out as soon as I thought it was safe. I ain't goin' to make you give me the same promise. When you get to Mount Weather if there's survivors there and they look like they're making a decent fist of it you think long and hard about stayin' put.'

He lifts his head and stares at me a while with those silver eyes to make sure I understand. I nod.

'Good. If you do decide to go back there's some stuff in my room you might find helpful. But you be careful, now. I don't know what Kane's plan was if Mount Weather checked out, but I am pretty certain he doesn't mean for anyone inside Eden to start thinking they have options that don't involve doing exactly what he says. He's smart, and if you get back he'll be watching you, close, so you keep that in mind.'

I nod again.

'And mind Peck, y'hear? If you screw up it'll be him you'll have to face. Kane might be the cause of what's wrong with Eden, but it'll be Randall he'll send for you. And when he comes there'll be no reasoning or pleading with him. I've seen his type before. Wrong or right won't come into it; it'll never even occur to someone like him to question an order he's given. The army trains men hard to make them that way, and I reckon they got their money's worth there. I'm sorry, Junior. It should have been me that had to deal with him. Not you.'

He sits there for a while. Then he reaches into the side pocket of his parka and pulls out the Ziploc bag with the gun he kept in the tunnel at Eden.

'No point in me asking if you've ever used one of these.'

I shake my head, no.

He looks at the pistol for a while as if considering. Then he tosses the bag into the snow between us.

'Well, pick it up then.'

I slide the backpack off my back and grab my cardboard box of latex gloves. I pull off my mittens, snap on a pair and carefully lift the bag up by one corner. I have to fumble with the seal on the zippy to open it. The gun's cold, heavy. The barrel has U.S. 9mm M9A3-P.BERETTA stamped on it in small letters, and there's a bunch of numbers too. I turn it over in my hands, feeling the compact heft of the blue-gray metal, the roughness of the diamond grip.

'Aw-ite. Well, it ain't so hard. It's already loaded.' He points to a small lever, at the top of the gun. 'You keep the safety on at all times, y'understand? You only flick it off if you're damn sure you want to shoot at something. Repeat it to me now, Junior.'

'I keep the safety on.'

'When?'

'At all times.'

'Good. Now, take the suppressor off, you won't be needin' it.'

I must look confused. Marv points at the metal cylinder coming out of the barrel.

'There, look. See, it just screws right out of the barrel.'

The thing Marv calls a suppressor but I thought was a silencer sticks for a moment, then loosens. I unscrew it and place it on top of the Ziploc bag.

'Aw-ite, then. Now you be careful who you show this to, but if you come across people up there you think might be no good and you don't see another way out of it you just point it up in the air and let off a round. It'll kick some, so don't let it surprise you. The sound should be enough to get most folks to turn tail, at least for long enough so you can cut out of there yourself.'

'But what if I have to actually shoot someone?'

He lifts his head. The light must hurt because he's squinting hard, now his eyes little more than narrow slits. He holds my gaze for a long moment.

'Don't. You probably wouldn't hit them anyway, unless they was close enough to take the gun off of you.'

I nod.

'Aw-ite. Well, put it away now.'

I look at the Beretta a moment longer then slide it into the side pocket of my parka. Marv pauses for a long time then, as if the effort of talking so much has finally worn him out. At last he looks up at the darkening sky.

'You need to be on your way now, Junior. Mount Weather's straight up that road; you won't be able to miss it. There's still the best part of five miles ahead of you and not long till you lose the light.'

I don't know what to say, so I pick up the map and slide it into the breast pocket of my parka. Then I just stand there, staring down at the snow. Marv slips the hunting rifle off his shoulder.

'Go on now Junior, scat.' I'm used to Marv barking orders, but the last words I hear from him are spoken softly. 'You don't want to see this.'

*

I SET OFF up the narrow road that leads away from the highway. At the first crest I stop. I try not to look around, but I can't help it. Behind me Marv's still kneeling in the snow, like he's asking forgiveness for something. It looks wrong somehow; Marv wasn't ever the type to get kneebound. I raise my hand to wave at him, but then I stop. Even if he sees me he won't answer. After a few moments I turn around and continue walking down into the dip before the next incline. A single gunshot rings out. I've been waiting for it, but it startles me nonetheless. Silence returns and after a few seconds I continue on. Tears sting my eyes; I have to blink furiously inside my goggles to clear them.

After Miss Kimble's funeral Kane said taking your own life was the worst thing that any person could do. A mortal sin, one that would stain your soul forever, that would prevent you from seeing the face of God in heaven. I asked Marv once if he thought that was true. When at first he didn't respond I wasn't surprised. Most times Marv just used to ignore what I'd say anyway; at best you might get a grunt that you'd need to interpret as a yes, a no or a maybe. By the time he finally got round to answering I suspect I'd already moved on to thinking about something else, but then he said that if God really did think like that then He wasn't worth a pisshole drilled in a snowbank and if that was the case he'd be happy to go check out the other feller, where at least it'd be warm.

I never asked him about it again. Part of it was the anger in his voice; it had shocked me. But mainly it was because what he'd said was blasphemous, and if there was one thing that never got tolerated in Eden it was blasphemy.

On Benjamin's map the Blue Ridge Mountain Road connects the Harry Byrd Highway, where behind me Marv's body lies slumped forward in the snow, to Route 50, the John S Mosby Highway, to the south. According to the map the road runs northeast-southwest, a small two-lane feeder roughly following the line between Loudoun County to the east and Clarke County to the west. Benjamin had marked the facility about halfway along it. There was nothing else on the map to acknowledge its existence, but then I guess Mount Weather was supposed to have been a secret, just like Eden.

The Blue Ridge Mountain Road continues to climb, and soon my legs are burning again, although for once I'm grateful for it. Finally the road flattens out a little and then, true to its name, snakes along the spine of the mountain range. Limbless, lifeless tree trunks poke through the gray snow, stretching away down the slopes on either side, their number suggesting a landscape that was once heavily forested. The road between them narrows until I reckon there can't even have been space for a hard shoulder. A little further on I have to track out wide around a snowplow that looks like it's slid off the road. It's tail and at least one of the rear wheels has ended up in the ditch and the front end's canted up, the blade of the plow pointing stubbornly up into the gray sky.

Behind the clouds the sun moves ever closer to the western horizon. There's little to tell where the road is now, and I'm navigating based on the gaps between the withered trunks. At some point the path I'm following traverses the ridge and starts to drop down the eastern rim of the valley. I begin to worry I've left the road behind me somewhere further up the mountain, but then the tip of my snowshoe hits something hard, metallic, buried just beneath the surface. When I dig it out it's an Adopt-a-Highway sign for Route 601. I check Benjamin's map. I'm still on track.

The road starts to climb again. A large sign, almost buried in a drift, announces I'm entering a restricted area; it says if I proceed I'm liable to be detained and searched. There are lights beneath the sign, hooded under black metal cowls, like you'd see at a railroad crossing. They're dead now, but I imagine how they must have once flashed their warning at anyone who approached. The path I'm following curves to the right, continuing its upward track. It seems to be going nowhere again, but then it straightens and crests, revealing a large clearing that straddles the mountain's spine.

I'm here.

I take a moment to look around. The facility's enclosed by a chain-link fence that rises to a height several meters above my head and is topped by a half-dozen strands of razor wire, held outwards at an angle on elbowed concrete pylons. Snow rests in kerfs along the wire, impervious to its rusted barbs.

I trudge up to the entrance. A large steel gate, mounted on runners, blocks my way. The wind rattles a faded steel sign against the bars, warning me that this is government property and I'm trespassing. I test the gate, but it's locked and won't budge. I tell myself it doesn't need to mean that Mount Weather is abandoned. There's likely to be more than one way in or out, just like there used to be in Eden. I don't have time to walk the perimeter to find it, though; the light's already almost gone. The bolt cutters make short work of a nearby section of the fence and soon I'm inside.

An empty guardhouse sits behind the gate, the drifts reaching almost to its windows. A cluster of aluminum sheds, also half buried, huddle just beyond. A single car, only identifiable by the shape of its roofline under the snow, waits patiently in the parking lot opposite. I unsnap the throat of my parka and lower the hood to listen, but there's no sound other than the wind.

Near the highest part of the compound there's what looks like a control tower. I make for it, calling out every dozen paces or so. I reckon it's best to announce my presence. There might be a Mount Weather version of Angus or Hamish lurking somewhere in one of the buildings; someone who hasn't seen a new face or heard an unfamiliar voice in as long as me; someone with a billy club, or worse. I reach into the side pocket of my parka, feeling for the pistol there.

When I make it up to the tower I stop and look around. From this vantage point I can see the installation, or at least that part of it which is above ground, laid out before me. A dozen buildings of various sizes cluster along the ridge. Two huge structures that might be water tanks squat against the tree line a little further down. Dotted here and there around the perimeter are the concrete cowls of what look like airshaft vents. And there, sitting next to a flat, open area, a tattered, faded windsock, fluttering in the wind. That must be where the helicopters that brought people to Mount Weather landed. The portal that leads into the mountain should be close by.

I make my way down to it, calling out as I go. Still there's no answer. The sky's grown dark while I've been exploring the compound and the temperature's dropping fast now. I need to find shelter, soon, but my heart's heavy with the thought of entering an unfamiliar darkness.

When I get down to the portal I see the tunnel's much bigger than it is at Eden. The entrance is protected by a large steel gate that looks like a giant guillotine, but thankfully it's still raised. The snow gathered in the tracks suggests it hasn't been lowered recently. There's no one standing guard behind it; no scanner; no makeshift quarantine fridge. No evidence at all that anyone's been here in a very long time. The tunnel simply stretches off into inky blackness.

I shuck off my backpack and dig in one of the side pockets for the wind-up flashlight I carry. The little dynamo whirs as I turn the stubby plastic handle, but the beam barely scratches the darkness. By holding the flashlight up I can see that, as in Eden, the tunnel roof is shored up with iron bolts drilled into the granite, a mesh of brace wire covering the space between. And just like in Eden an elevated walkway runs down one side. But the flashlight offers no clue as to how far into the mountain the tunnel goes, or how long it will be before I reach the blast door with the keypad.

A part of me had dreamt that when we found it the tunnel would be bathed in the light from dozens of bulkhead lamps that somehow would still be burning bright. That survivors, people who had spent the last decade eking out an existence inside a hollowed out mountain, would be waiting to welcome us in. I guess it was foolish to hold out that hope. After so many years outside, wandering through this long-dead world, it would have been too much to expect. I never thought I'd be here alone, though. It never occurred to me I might have to venture into the darkness by myself. I unsnap my snowshoes and sit down in the snow, huddled up in my parka. I stare into the tunnel's gaping maw as the light from the wind up flashlight slowly yellows and fades.

I'm not sure I can go on.

*

I SIT THERE FOR A LONG TIME while night settles around me. In the end it's Marv that makes me get up again. Or rather the thought that he will have died for nothing if I don't at least try to go inside.

I pick up the pack and hoist it onto my shoulders. I take a step backwards, winding the flashlight furiously until the small bulb is burning as bright as it ever will. And then before Claus has a chance to say anything that might make me sit down again I run screaming into the darkness. Inside my head Claus is screaming too, but on the outside I'm louder.

It doesn't last very long. The darkness isn't impressed; it holds hard against my charge. I get no further than a hundred yards in before I trip. There's a sickening moment as a jolt of adrenalin floods my already overloaded system. I throw my hands out in front of me to break my fall. For an instant I watch as the flashlight sails from my fingers and then the curb that marks the elevated walkway slams up into my ribs. The parka absorbs some of the impact, but it knocks the wind out of me nonetheless, and all I can do for long seconds is lie there, clutching my side, gasping for air.

The flashlight has come to rest on the other side of the tunnel. In spite of the pain and the panic of not being able to breathe I feel a moment of relief. At least it hasn't broken. But the cone of light it casts is already starting to shrink. I can't do anything other than lie there and stare at it, my mouth opening and closing like a fish that's just been hooked and hauled to the deck.

In the tunnel in Eden I know the fear, and I know how it changes. Sometimes, like when I'm in the darkest part, between the blast vents, it's big and panicky, like a horse that rears up, refusing to be bridled. Other times, when I'm close to the portal or to the blast door, it's smaller, like a rodent gnawing away inside me. As I lie there, unable to move, staring bug-eyed into the encroaching darkness, the fear inside me becomes like nothing I have felt before, like nothing I could hope to control. A raging elephant, trumpeting in terror as it threatens to demolish everything in its path. There's no air entering my lungs, but somehow I manage to raise my cheek from the concrete. Inch by inch I claw myself towards the light like a stood-on bug.

I don't make it before the flashlight dies. I have a moment before it finally winks out to realize this is what will happen and I beg whatever gods might be listening not to do this. But the darkness won't be bargained with. If I had breath now I know I'd scream until I was hoarse. Instead, because it's all I can do, I keep wriggling forward towards where the last afterimage of light is still dancing across my vision. When I get to the spot where I think I saw it last I reach out and start scrabbling around. At last I find it, the fingers inside my mittens closing greedily around the plastic. I clutch it to my chest, releasing the hand that's holding my ribs for a second to allow me to wind the handle. The dynamo whirs and the bulb glows orange, then yellow, finally casting a faint pool of light around where I'm lying.

Once my breath comes back I pull myself up and sit for a while by the side of the road, waiting for the adrenalin to abate and for the confused signals flooding my system to settle into pain. At last I stand. My side aches whenever I breathe in, but I don't think I've broken anything. I feel something trickle down the side of my face and I raise a hand tentatively to my temple. It stings when I touch it. When I hold the mitten up to the flashlight it's covered in blood.

I proceed more cautiously after that.

The count starts from where I fell. I inch forward into the darkness, winding the flashlight with each step. I clutch it to my chest, sweeping the road ahead in short, nervous arcs. I won't risk letting go of it again.

For one thousand three hundred and seventy paces the tunnel runs arrow straight, and I'm beginning to wonder if in the darkness I've somehow missed the blast door.

And that's when I see them. And I realize I'm not alone here after all.

*

TWO PINPRICKS OF LIGHT, there and then gone again.

I'm still not sure what I'm looking at, only that the hairs along the nape of my neck have suddenly raised like hackles. I tell myself it's probably just the beam from the flashlight, reflecting back at me as it bounces off something: the window of a guard hut, maybe. But even as I think it I know that can't be right. Whatever I just saw was right in the middle of the tunnel.

When I direct the beam back to where I saw them they're still there. Claus is jabbering at me to turn around and run back to the portal, but I know if I do that now I'll never enter this place again. So I take a deep breath and move sideways until I hit the elevated walkway. I climb up onto it and inch forward along the wall, keeping the flashlight trained on whatever's waiting in the darkness ahead of me.

There's a sound now, too; I can hear it in the lulls between turns of the flashlight's handle. At first it's hard to distinguish from the melt water dripping from the granite walls, but as I get closer it's clear this is something separate, distinct. A clicking noise. I hold the flashlight to my chest and wind the handle furiously. The dynamo whirs and for a moment the beam burns bright. And then I see it and I freeze, and for long seconds just stand there, rooted to the spot with fear.

A fury, crouched on all fours in the middle of the tunnel. Dark circles surround its eyes and its face is impossibly thin, the sunken, hollowed cheeks making it seem abnormally long. Its hair is white, wiry, and its skin is the color of the snow outside, but just like the little girl I found in the closet there's not a trace of decay. While the girl in Shreve had looked like she was sleeping, however, the creature standing in front of me has its eyes open. Its mouth is closed, its lips forming a tight gray line, but as I listen I realize the clicking sound is coming from somewhere back in its throat.

I tell myself to stay calm. Marv said the furies still can't move, and this one certainly looks like it's been hunkered here in the darkness for the best part of a decade. I shift the beam, but it doesn't move its head towards the flashlight; it just keeps staring straight ahead into the tunnel, giving no indication it even knows I'm there. But even as I try and convince myself of that spidey pings to let me know that may not be the whole truth.

I push myself up against the wall, trying to put as much space between me and it as possible as I creep forwards. The clicking sound coming from its throat seems to increase as I get closer, and I think I can make out the muscles along its jaw working now, but it's hard to be sure. The hand that's holding the flashlight is shaking pretty badly by this stage.

I'm almost level with it when suddenly it stiffens, then shudders as a quick convulsion runs through it. I let out a startled yelp, but then I remember that the little girl I found in the closet in Shreve had done exactly the same thing when Marv had held the knife with his blood under her nose. It's the cut on my forehead. It must be able to smell the blood.

The fury continues to stare straight ahead as I pass, but now it seems to be moving its head, shifting it from side to side as though tasting the air. It stays in the same place in the middle of the tunnel however, showing no signs of moving from the spot it looks like it's occupied for years. And then I'm by it, hurrying along the walkway. I keep checking behind me for a long time after the flashlight can no longer separate its hunched outline from the darkness.

At last the tunnel seems to widen and a little further on I finally come to the blast door. The flashlight's still shaking from what I've just seen, but it's obvious as soon as I play the beam over it that the door here is nothing like Eden's. It's rectangular rather than circular, and much larger, maybe ten feet tall and as much as twenty wide. I search the wall for the keypad that will hopefully grant me access. I'm relived to see it's just like the keypad in Eden, a series of plastic keys standing slightly proud of a brushed steel backplate, covered by a stubby metal cowling.

Claus is jabbering at me to hurry up, but I slide the backpack off my back and reach inside for the box of latex gloves. There's no evidence the facility's been contaminated, but then again I've just passed a fury that looks like it's been sitting out there for years, and after seeing what happened to Marv earlier I'm not about to take any chances. I realize today's not the day for having my prayers answered, but I offer a short plea to whoever might be listening that this will work. Then I pull off my mittens, snap on a glove and carefully punch in the code from the map Marv gave me.

Nothing happens. I stare at the keypad for what seems like an eternity, but the keys don't light up, the little bulb beneath doesn't flash. It gives no indication of anything other than dead circuits underneath.

Because I don't know what else to do I pull out the other map, the one I picked up from the kitchen table in the farmhouse, what now seems like an eternity ago. The memory brings with it the fear I felt then that Marv would kill me, which now seems like a betrayal. I can't help it. Memories are complicated things; they can't just be unbundled and reassembled once you know the truth. I unfold Kane's map. Maybe Marv remembered the code Benjamin gave him wrong and the President did a better job of it.

The code for Mount Weather is printed on the bottom in heavy black ink. I was expecting it to be similar to the one on Marv's map, maybe with a single transposed digit to explain why the one Marv wrote down hadn't worked. But the letters and numbers scribbled in Kane's surprisingly jagged script bear no resemblance at all to the ones Marv had written down. I hit the reset key to clear the code I've just entered. Before I even punch in the first digit there's a flicker from the red light at the bottom of the keypad, like it's deciding whether to come back to life or to fall back into the decade-long slumber from which it's just been roused. The light seems to stabilize, and then for a horrendous moment it goes out completely, before finally starting to blink at me in steady, reassuring pulses. The rest of the keypad slowly illuminates. Above me a bulkhead emergency lamp flickers to life, bathing the tunnel around the door in its soft green glow. I no longer need the flashlight to see what I'm doing. Claus breathes a small sigh of relief.

Of course, the reset button. I needed to push it to wake the keypad's circuits. I drop Kane's map and enter Benjamin's code again. When I'm done the bulb at the bottom of the keypad flashes green once, and then there's a pause. I hold my ear close to the steel, straining to hear. Finally from deep within there's a faint whine, rising to a pitch that suggests an electric motor being driven harder than its specification intended, and then a long, unpleasant, grating sound, like the teeth of cogs being pressed into unhappy service after an extended period of neglect. The pitch rises until I'm afraid the motor will burn out under the load, but then somewhere inside the door there's a heavy clunk, followed by the muted screech of metal being dragged against metal and finally the familiar sound of bolts sliding back into their recesses. The emergency light above my head dims for a moment as another set of motors come to life, and start to push the massive door out towards me. They manage no more than a couple of inches before the pitch suddenly drops and then dies, returning the tunnel to silence.

I tell myself it's okay; Scudder told Kane we could expect this. The power the electric motors were drawing was too much, so the system shut them down to preserve what's left in the batteries. At least the emergency light above my head has remained on, which hopefully means there'll now be light inside Mount Weather as well.

I grab the pry bar from my backpack and slide one end into the gap, pushing hard on the other. Nothing moves. The blast door in Eden is supposed to be balanced on its hinges; Scudder says it can just be pushed back once the bolts have been recessed. I'm not sure I ever believed him about that. And the door in Eden's about half the size of the one here.

I brace myself, leaning all my weight into the bar, feeling my boots scrabble for purchase on the tunnel's dusty concrete floor. Still nothing. The pry bar's only a couple of feet long; I need more leverage. I wind the flashlight and go searching in the darkness for something that might work better. Five minutes later I return with a length of metal pipe, slot it over the end of the pry bar and lean into it again. At first there's nothing, but then it feels like the door moves perhaps a fraction. I redouble my efforts.

Inch by inch I manage to lever the door open until there's enough of a gap to squeeze through.

There's a panel on the wall inside that operates the door, just like in Eden, but I already know there's not enough juice left in the batteries for that to work. Thankfully there's a manual control that allows it to be opened and closed once the bolts have been recessed, just as Scudder said there would be. I find the handle in a cradle by the door and slide the end into a slot in the wall nearby. An arrow above tells me it's clockwise to close, so I start winding. There's the muted grumble of gears, then the massive blast door slowly starts to creep inwards. I keep turning the handle until the door's once again flush with the wall. I can't see any way to operate the locks manually and I don't want to waste any more of whatever reserves are left in the batteries trying to get the motors to slide the bolts into their recesses. It's more important to Claus that the lights stay on.

I replace the handle in its cradle, dust off my hands. Then I pick up my backpack and walk out into Mount Weather.

*

I REMEMBER BEING IMPRESSED the first time I entered the main cavern in Eden. But as I step out of the series of antechambers that lead from the blast door I see how much larger this place is. The dozen or so buildings I saw above ground, clinging to either side of the ridge's slopes or clustered around its narrow peak, they really were just the tip of the iceberg.

Like in Eden the main cavern here is broadly dome-shaped, but that might be where the similarity ends. It's *way* bigger. The buildings sit back against the granite walls, leaving a large open area in the middle that only adds to the sense of space. As I get closer I can see that an artificial lake occupies the center, its black waters reflecting the soft green glow from the safety lamps. Streets radiate out from it, like the spokes of a wheel. They're wider than in Eden, and they have sidewalks, and streetlights. I count seven large tunnels leading out of the cavern. Their granite walls rise vertically for most of their height, like the transepts of a mighty cathedral, before finally tapering to a rounded apex that must be fifty feet above the cavern floor.

As I approach the water's edge I look up. The roof of the dome seems much higher above me. Even in the dim light Claus is almost content. I dip my hand in and smell the water. It seems fresh. It must be fed from an underground spring, like the reservoir in Eden. My stomach grumbles and I realize I haven't eaten since lunch. I shuck off my backpack and sit down to search inside for an MRE. I pull out a beef ravioli, Marv's favorite.

After dinner I feel a little better. I decide to take my HOOAH! with me and explore.

It takes me longer than I was expecting to get the measure of the place. Mount Weather's an underground city; it makes Eden seem little more than a cave by comparison. There are twenty-three buildings in the main cavern alone, more in the tunnels. They're made of metal, and just like in Eden a name has been stenciled, military fashion, near the entrance to each. But here the buildings are larger. Most are four stories high; some run to five. There are regular doors instead of the old latched bulkheads, and they all have windows.

The first place I check is the mess. The door's open and I wander in. It looks as if whoever was here on the Last Day left in a real hurry. Chairs have been pushed back, knocked over, and plates of half-eaten food, now unrecognizable under coats of furry mold, sit on tables. A pool table occupies one corner, the balls arranged haphazardly as if a game had been interrupted. There's a *Starbucks* counter that takes up an entire wall; a row of vending machines line up against another. I've just finished my

HOOAH! so I'm not hungry, but I grab a soda and a chocolate bar anyway. The soda's flat and when I peel the wrapper off the chocolate I can see the surface has turned gray. I eat it anyway. It tastes a bit stale, and it's grittier than I remember chocolate being, but it's not bad.

My forehead hurts where I skinned it in the tunnel. There's a first aid kit in my backpack; I could go back to the lake to get it, but instead I decide to go in search of the infirmary. I find a building that's more like a small hospital. On the ground floor there's several rooms with rows of empty beds, each neatly made. Upstairs I find an operating theater and a room marked Intensive Care with more beds and lots of machines, all now silent. The medical supplies are kept on the floor above. The shelves are brimming with boxes and bottles and containers of all shapes and sizes. A row of locked cabinets, where presumably the stronger stuff was kept. I find a bottle of iodine and use it to clean the cut on my forehead. It stings a little, but by the time I've taped a strip of gauze over it it's already feeling better.

I wander back outside. The letters stenciled on the next building along read 'Command, Control, & Communications'. I try the handle. It's unlocked, but I hesitate for a moment before entering. In Eden command was off limits to anyone but Kane, Peck and Quartermaster, and even though I'm miles away and there's no one here to see me it feels wrong to go in. But then I hear Mags' voice inside my head and I push the handle down and step inside. A sign on the wall tells me I've entered something called the Situation Room. Desks containing banks of computer monitors have been arranged in concentric circles stretching out from the center. Jackets hang on the backs of chairs and here and there a coffee mug sits unfinished, a skim of fungus floating on its long-cold contents. Gray, lifeless screens line the walls and hang suspended from the metal ceilings. A thick layer of dust covers everything.

On the next floor I find a television studio. The set is made up to look like a room in the White House. The cameras are pointed at a desk the President would have sat behind to deliver whatever somber news had to be conveyed to the nation. The backdrop has fake windows that give views across a tranquil lawn, the same lawn I ran across with Mags to the helicopters that morning.

From the top floor landing there's a staircase that leads to the roof. I climb up and make my way over to the edge. From up here it seems even more eerily quiet. The cavern rises to a crown that has to be at least a hundred feet above the inky surface of the lake. I feel a faint breeze and look up. Above me the familiar mesh of brace wire and rock bolts, holding back the mountain. And dotted here and there among the arc lights, the openings to vent shafts that lead up through the rock, all the way to one of the concrete cowls I saw earlier on top of the ridge.

It takes another couple of hours to explore the rest of the cavern. I find a gym, towels stiff with age still draped over long-silent treadmills. There's a morgue, thankfully unoccupied, and even a crematorium. I don't find a library, but there is a small movie theater that smells vaguely of something I think I might remember as popcorn.

When I'm done with the main cavern I start with the tunnels. Some of the walls have been shored up with concrete but most are rough-hewn granite, just like in Eden. Each tunnel accommodates more buildings. Most seem to have been designated as dormitories; inside I find row after row of cots and bunks. A few house small, self-contained apartments. Most are empty, but some look like people were living there.

At the end of one of the tunnels there's a reservoir that seems like it's been carved straight from the rock. It's impossible to tell how deep the water is or how far it stretches back into the darkness. There's a skiff moored to a hitching post near the edge. I suppose I could find out by rowing out across the lake, but Claus doesn't fancy that idea much so I move on.

The next tunnel houses the power plant. The machinery here looks newer than in Eden. Behind what I'm guessing must be the generator building sit two diesel storage tanks: huge metal cylinders, reaching almost to the roof. Checker-plated steps circle each, spiraling all the way up to a railed gantry at the top. A chain with a neatly printed sign suspended from the center warns against unauthorized entry. I step over it and start climbing, one hand skimming the railing, the other tapping the outside of the tank periodically with the end of the pry bar, listening for the shift in tone that will tell me how full they are. I'm almost at the top before I hear the hollow clang that tells me there's now only air on the other side. I make my way back down and check out the other tank. It's also full.

Other tunnels house a water purification plant and a sewage treatment facility. There's a fire station complete with a tender, sunken low on perished tires. I run my finger along the side, dislodging thick motes of dust, revealing the bright red paintwork underneath. In the last tunnel I check I find the stores, a long three-story warehouse that takes up most of the vaulted cavern. Inside metal shelves stretch from the concrete floor all the way up to the ceiling. Each is stacked with all manner of canned and dried foods, egg substitute, milk powder. I open a few containers at random to check what's spoiled. Some of it's gone bad, but a lot of what's there still seems good. There's even section dedicated to clothes. I find an aisle with boots and count row after row of pairs just like Marv's.

I haven't had a shower since we left Eden, and it's taken three days of hard hiking to get here, so I'm way past tangy. I grab a fresh set of thermals and some socks from the shelves, and a fresh bar of soap and some deodorant from the adjacent aisle and then head back to the gym.

When I turn the taps nothing comes out of the showerheads, so I grab a bucket from the kitchens and fill it with water from the lake and bring it back. The water's cold, but it feels good. There's a pile of towels in one of the storage cupboards, still folded neatly. I dry off and put on clean clothes, then I return to the infirmary, find a bandage for my ankle and bind it up tight again.

The apartments I found earlier look nice, but I don't feel like sleeping inside so instead I take blankets and a pillow from one and bring them out to the edge of the lake. I lay there, staring up in to the darkness, thinking about Marv and everything he told me about Eden and Benjamin and Miss Kimble and Peck and Kane.

*

I WAKE TO THE SAME green-tinged darkness the following morning. For a few moments I stare up at the roof of the huge granite dome above, charting unfamiliar shapes against memory until it comes to me where I am. Eden will be waking soon. This is the fourth day since Marv and I left; I wonder if Mags' penance is over yet, or if she still has more time to spend locked in her cell.

I get up and walk over to the stores with my backpack. I cut a tin of peaches from a shrink-wrapped crate and open it, eating the segments right out of the can as I wander between the shelves, transferring what I'll need into my backpack. It takes me an hour to gather everything, and when I'm done the pack's heavier than it's ever been. I hoist it onto my back, testing the straps. The canvas is old but it's strong; they should hold. I cast my eyes over the cavern one more time, then I turn and make my way back towards the exit. When I get to the blast door I slide the pack off my shoulder and lean it against the wall. I switch the mechanism and wind the handle anti-clockwise. The gears grumble as the cogs engage, but inch-by-inch they push the huge slab of hardened metal out into the tunnel.

When there's enough of a gap I slide the handle from its recessed slot and pick up the backpack. A blast of cold air hits me and I feel the familiar knot in my stomach. I tell myself it's just Claus's usual pre-tunnel jitters. But this morning Claus *really* isn't happy; he pleads and cajoles, begging me not to go back out there. There's plenty of food in Mount Weather. I could even spend the winter here; go back to Eden in the spring, when the storms are done. Spidey joins in now, letting me know that for once he agrees. There's something about the tunnel I've neglected, something important. It's the fury of course, and I certainly haven't forgotten about it. But it can't move. And at some point I'm going to have to face it, that's if I ever want to leave Mount Weather. If I ever want to see Mags again.

I touch my hand to the steel as I squeeze myself out through the gap, then I rest the backpack against the tunnel wall while I search for the slot that takes the handle on the outside. It takes another few minutes to wind the door back in and when it's fully recessed I leave the handle in place.

I hoist the backpacks onto my shoulders, shifting the straps until the weight's evenly distributed, and then I tighten them so the pack sits high. I take a deep breath and start walking back towards the portal.

I spent ten minutes inside the blast door winding the flashlight, so when I flick it on the beam's as bright as it will get. I keep turning the handle every few steps, however, just to be sure.

I don't have a precise count for the number of paces from when I passed the fury to the blast door. I've thought about it and I reckon three hundred, give or take. I start the count when I switch the flashlight on.

It'll be facing the other way of course, towards the portal, so the beam won't catch its eyes this time, which means I'll see it later. When I get to two hundred and fifty I move up onto the walkway, keeping the flashlight trained on the center of the tunnel. By the time I've counted two seventy-five I'm expecting to see something, but there's still nothing. In the lulls between winding the flashlight I strain to pick out the sound it was making, trying to separate it from the *splat-splat-splat* of melt water dripping off the brace wire. It's hard to hear anything above the sound of my own breathing and the thump of my heart, however. I cleaned the cut on my forehead again, just before I left. I reckon the iodine and the fresh bandage I've covered it with should mask the smell of my blood. I know it shouldn't matter; the fury won't be able to move. But I'd much prefer it if it didn't even know I was there.

We're at three hundred now and there's still no sign of it. I hold the flashlight to my chest and wind it furiously. The dynamo whirs and the beam grows brighter for a few moments, pushing the narrow cone of light a few feet further out into the darkness. I stop again to listen, but I can't make out anything other than the sound of water dripping from the tunnel walls.

By the time I get to three hundred and fifty I'm beginning to think maybe I got the count wrong. But spidey says that's not it; it's not the count that's wrong. There's something else, something about the brace wire. The mountain and the tunnel and the brace wire. But my mind is already giving in to the darkness. It's like all the pieces I need to solve the puzzle are laid out before me, but whenever I try to assemble them it wrenches itself away from the obvious, unthinkable conclusion.

It's the scuffling I hear first. I turn around and wind the flashlight again, shining it back into the darkness behind me. The quivering beam finds nothing, however. I tell myself it's just a trick of the tunnel, the sound of my own boots, echoing back at me from the curved granite walls. But my hackles are up again and spidey's desperately trying to get my attention. *The brace wire.*

I resume my progress towards the exit. There's nothing for a dozen paces and then I hear it again, closer this time. I spin around, pointing the light into the inky blackness. Again there's nothing, but this time I think I hear the scuffling continue for a fraction of a second after I've stopped.

I look back towards the portal. The tunnel curves right before it ends at the guillotine gate; I think I can just see the faintest glimmer of light ahead of me in the distance. I pick up the pace. Claus is begging me to abandon caution and break into a flat out run, but I resist. I'm winding the flashlight only intermittently now, trying to keep my footfalls as light as possible to allow me to strain for the slightest sound.

I hear it again, much closer now. I turn around, still stumbling backwards towards the exit, and shine the light behind me, trying to control the shuddering beam. For the first time it catches something, twin flashes of silver, there for the briefest instant and then gone again. It's more than Claus can take. I turn and sprint, my arms and legs pumping. The backpack's heavy, but adrenalin is flowing through me and I barely feel its weight. The beam from the flashlight cuts through the air in short, jittery arcs, bouncing off the walls. Ahead the tunnel's definitely growing lighter. Claus is begging me to run faster, but I can't help turning around for another glance.

And that's when I see it, and I stop, transfixed. A stream of warm urine runs down my leg inside my thermals. This is fear like I had never known it before. Not the sweaty-palmed anxiety of the scanner or the dry-mouthed fear of the tunnel, but abject terror, visceral panic. Marv had thought the furies were still incapable of movement, but he was so very wrong about that; this one's moving with almost inhuman speed. The clothes that hang in tatters from its spider-thin frame flap as it bounds on all fours towards me, like some demented hellhound.

I remember the gun. I reach into the pocket of my parka and pull it out. I have to fumble off my mittens; I feel them bounce off their tethers as I slide my finger into the trigger guard. I point the barrel into the tunnel and pull.

Nothing happens. And then I recall what Marv told me about the safety. I have to drop the flashlight to flick the lever with my other hand and then I raise it again and fire into the blackness at the point where I thought I last saw the creature's eyes.

There's a sharp crack, loud in the confines of the tunnel. The grip whacks itself against the fleshy part of my thumb as the pistol rears up. I bring it down and fire again and again into the darkness, my finger now spasming mindlessly.

The tunnel reveals itself in a series of flashbulb images, black and white snapshots of the fury's knuckle-skimming gait, captured for an instant by the pistol's muzzle flash as it bounds towards me. I have no idea where the bullets are hitting. I hear one shriek and whine as it strikes the tunnel wall and ricochets off into the darkness.

The smell of gunpowder fills the air. I don't know how many bullets I've fired or how many I had to begin with. I don't think I've managed to hit it once and it's almost on me now, close enough now that I can make out its features. The lips that yesterday formed a tight gray line are pulled back impossibly wide, its teeth working furiously.

For the second time I turn and run. Terror lends me speed I didn't know my legs were capable of; I almost make it to the portal before it hits me. I feel a sudden weight across my shoulders as it lands on the backpack, and a second later I hear the snapping of slavering jaws inches from my neck. I'm pitched forward, caroming off the granite wall, but somehow I manage to stay on my feet. I know it can't last. The fury's lunging forward again and again, straining to get at my neck, but my hood and the backpack are getting in its way. I'm trying to free myself from the straps but they're too tight; they won't let me extricate myself. And then finally I lose my balance and I'm pitched forward, careening and tumbling out of the tunnel, underneath the guillotine gate and out into the gray morning light.

In a fit of blind panic I struggle free of the straps and stagger away, only to fall again as my boots sink into the first drift of snow. I struggle to pick myself up, then flop down again, flailing in the deep powder. The parka's hood's ridden up and my vision's limited to a narrow tunnel directly in front of me. I struggle to pull it back down, expecting at any moment to feel the weight of the fury landing on me again.

I finally manage to get to my feet and yank the hood back. My backpack's lying on the ground by the guillotine gate. The fury's curled up in the snow a few feet away from it, keening and howling like a berserk animal caught in the jaws of some invisible trap. Its emaciated arms are wrapped around its head and its face is pushed into the gray snow, like it's trying to burrow its way out of whatever hell it's suddenly found itself in.

I look down and realize I'm still holding Marv's gun. I take a few steps closer so I'm standing no more than a couple of yards from it. The fury ignores me, caught up in its own private torment.

The hand that's holding the gun's shaking so much that the first shot misses. I guess Marv was right about that. I steady it with my other hand and fire again. Soon my finger takes over the function of my adrenalin-flooded brain. It continues until the magazine's empty and the only sound is the dry, impotent click of the hammer falling for the final time.

I let the gun drop from my fingers and walk over to collect my backpack.

*

I REACH THE INTERSECTION where the Blue Ridge Mountain Road hits the highway later that morning. Marv's still there, slumped forward in the gray snow. There's been a fresh fall, but not enough to cover him completely. There's nothing I can do, so I don't stop. I don't think he would have minded.

I reckon it's too soon to show, but I've been checking the crucifix anyway. I don't think the fury managed to lay a hand on me anywhere inside my parka, but then Marv didn't think he'd been infected either. I'm guessing he would have been pretty mad at me for not paying attention to what Claus, or spidey, or whoever else lives in my head was trying to tell me, back in the tunnel, and he would have been right. That *was* bixicated. Of course Mount Weather's wire-braced tunnels would have shielded anything inside from what Kane did to defeat the virus; he told us as much before we left. I haven't decided yet what to do with what Marv told me about Eden, but if I do manage to make it back I'll need to be a whole lot smarter than that.

A big storm chases me north out of Virginia. I spot it as I'm crossing the Charles Town Pike. All along the horizon behind me the sky's a churning soup of gray and black, the clouds occasionally lit from within by diffuse flashes, violent shudderings of light. I hoist the pack high onto my shoulders and hoof it. The intervals between the bolts of lightning and the peals of thunder grow shorter and shorter until finally it catches up with me just as I'm coming into Brunswick. It's still afternoon but it suddenly turns impossibly dark and heavy ashen flakes start to tumble out of the sky. I scramble onto the concrete bridge that spans the Potomac, one hand clinging to the rust-spackled railing as I stumble across. By the time I reach the middle I can no longer see the river beneath me. I find an old railway car sitting idle on a siding down by the bank on the other side. The metal's badly corroded but it's rust and not the virus so I crawl inside.

I hole up there for two nights while the storm rages. The world outside appears only briefly, out of a darkness rent by streaks of lightning. At one point it strikes so close to the car that the inside is briefly bathed in stark white light, and for a little while after the air smells charred.

I sit with the crucifix in my lap. Every few minutes I wind the flashlight and check for any sign that the metal's changing. By the second night it's still showing clear and I'm starting to breathe a little easier. I lay my head down and grab the first sleep I've managed since I quit Mount Weather.

I wake the following morning to the sound of the river and look outside. The storm's moved on while I've slept. It's ahead of me now, to the north, sitting so low on the horizon that it's hard to tell where earth ends and sky begins. Now and then the lightning breaks free, splitting the gloom, stabbing down at the barren hilltops below.

I pack up my gear, strap on my snowshoes and set off up the slope after it.

I reach the farmhouse by the turnpike just as the light's starting to fade on the fifth day. I unload my backpack and stash what I've brought from Mount Weather in the kitchen. I count the cartons as I stack them, even though I know exactly how many I brought. Marv said he had some as well. Hopefully together it'll be enough.

I head down the hall towards his room. The door's locked, but that's no obstacle; the pry bar has me in a matter of seconds. Inside it's surprisingly neat. The bed's made, the nightstands are free of clutter and the windows even look like they've been wiped down recently. I check in the drawers but all I find is a photo of him and Benjamin, taken some time before the Last Day. They're both in fatigues, standing outside what I'm guessing must have been the east portal. Marv's giving the camera his usual thousand-yard stare, but Benjamin's broad white smile makes up for it. I slide the photograph into the inside pocket of my parka. I figure Marv'd be okay with me having it.

When I check the closet I find parkas, boots and thermals in a range of sizes, together with an assortment of ski goggles, gloves, mittens and snowshoes. It looks like there's enough here for everyone in Eden. MRE cartons are stacked in neat piles on the floor. There's probably sufficient, even without what I've brought from Mount Weather. Marv must have been foregoing his quarantine rations for quite some time, probably ever since he made his promise to Benjamin to get us out.

I head straight back up to the portal waiting for my own quarantine to be done. The crucifix has been clear for five days now, so I'm pretty sure the fury didn't get me. When I get to the hole in the snow where you enter I unsnap my snowshoes and slide the backpack off my back. The storm that's passed ahead of me has dropped fresh snow and I start clearing it from the spot where I always stash my respirator. I have to hunt around for a little while, but then my fingers find the rubber strap and I pull it out.

I almost miss it at first. I'm about to call ahead to let the Guardians know I'm coming through, but then I give the respirator a shake to clear the snow that's collected inside, so whoever's on duty doesn't figure out I haven't really been using it. The filters on both sides of the mask detach and fall silently into the snow. When I turn the mask over and hold it up to catch the last of the light I see why.

I let the mask fall from my fingers and take an involuntary step backwards.

I sit in the kitchen for a long time, wrapped up in my parka. The storm's passed but the wind still blows, rattling the silted panes softly in their frames. The muscles in my legs ache from the long hike back from Mount Weather, and my shoulders are sore from the backpack's straps, but I barely notice. I stare out the window, watching as outside dusk settles.

The retaining rings on my respirator, the ones that held the filters in place, they'd corroded through completely. What little was left of the once sturdy mounts was pitted and pocked, the metal that still clung there a dull, lifeless gray. My respirator had been infected with the virus. And yet it had never left Eden.

Marv and I were never meant to make it back from Mount Weather.

It had to have been Peck. I saw him the night before we set out. I watched him from the roof as he made his way into the tunnels that lead to the power plant, when he must have gone to talk with Scudder. And then I lost him for an hour in front of the mess. The corridor that leads to the blast door is right opposite. I think of the girl in the closet in Shreve. How many others like her must there be out there, how many countless dark places? Peck must have gone outside to find a fury so that he could contaminate our respirators.

But Peck wouldn't have done this by himself, would he? What had Marv said? It would never occur to a man like that to question an order he'd been given. And if that was true it seems unlikely he'd have made up one of his own.

Which means it had to have been Kane.

And with that knowledge comes the grim realization that I can never return to Eden. I'd never make it past the portal; the Guardians will have orders not to let me in. Nobody will be coming out, either, not for months. The storms are already here; it won't be long now till Kane locks the bunker down, if he hasn't done that already.

And if I can't get in how can I hope to get Mags or any of the other Juvies out?

I finally get up from the table and head down the hallway to my room. I light the hurricane lamp next to my bed. The smoke smudges the air, stinging my eyes, the guttering flame throwing familiar shadows across the sagging wallpaper. I lie back on the narrow bed and stare up at the water-stained ceiling. Outside a gust of wind rattles the window. A draught of cold air blows in through a hole in the plaster where the laths show through.

An idea flashes into my head and I sit upright, immediately appalled by what it would mean. There has to be an alternative. I lay back down to try and think of one, but an hour later I'm still drawing a blank. I fish the stub of a pencil and a scrap of paper from my bedside table, pick up the lamp and go back into the kitchen. Right now all I have is the germ of a plan, and needless to say Claus already hates it. All the things that might go wrong run through my mind, competing for my attention; I set the lamp on the kitchen table and start to write them down. Only when I can think of nothing else do I start to make a list of all the things I'll need.

If this is going to work, I can't afford to overlook a single thing. I'm going to have to be *way* smarter than I was in the tunnel at Mount Weather, or after I found Benjamin in the clinic in Ely. Smarter even than Kane. The words of his blessing float into my head, and for once they're fitting. If this is going to work I'm going to have to be the most cunning serpent in all of Eden.

When at last I'm finished I head back to my room and climb back into bed. Sometime in the early hours I drift off, but the sleep that finally comes is filled with dreams of what lies ahead.

The grudging light from another gray dawn seeps through my bedroom window a few hours later. I feel like I could pull the musty covers over my head and sleep through the day. But I can't wait another week, not with winter already here. It has to be tonight. I get dressed and step out into the hallway. And that's when I notice it.

The farmhouse has old wooden floors, the kind that are held down by square-cut, wrought-head nails. The nails were hammered deep into the wood; what little's visible of the tops has long since blackened with age, making them hard to spot. In the living room where water comes in through the roof several of the boards have sprung free, the old iron no longer up to the task of holding the water-buckled wood in place. In my room there's less water damage, but nevertheless the planks have shifted, lending the floor a warp and a weft that's immediately noticeable underfoot. Marv's room must be an extension because the floors are concrete, and level as a billiard table. I noticed it yesterday as soon as I walked in.

But right where I'm standing, in the hallway outside my room, the floors are wooden. And yet they're solid, without a hint of movement. When I bend down to examine the boards I can see why. The nails have been replaced with screws. The heads have been recessed and covered with what looks like lampblack, so unless you were to look closely you'd never tell the difference. And then suddenly I realize what Marv was doing all those nights, pacing backwards and forwards outside my room. I pull the leatherman from my pocket. The screws slide out easy. I lift one of the boards.

The space beneath the floor is filled with wooden crates. I reach for the closest one and open it.

*

BY THE TIME dusk is falling I'm as ready as I think I can be.

I got back less than an hour ago and my legs are sore from the hike, but I can't worry about that now; if things go according to plan I'll have all tomorrow to rest up. Marv had already thought of most of the things I'd need, but there were a few final items he couldn't have anticipated, so I've spent the day making one final trip out to Providence.

A dozen large garbage bags fill the kitchen; it takes several trips to move them into position up by the tree line. I cover them loosely with snow, but I don't bother to hide them any better than that; there's a good chance that whoever comes out tomorrow night will need to find them without me. When I return to the kitchen after I've made the last run it's empty, save for my backpack and one of the wooden crates I found under the floorboards. Between them they should have everything I need. I keep thinking there's something I've forgotten, but I must have been through the list twenty times in my head on the hike back from Providence. If there is I can't think of it.

I wait until almost the last of the light's left the sky to make my way up the slope. The wind's picked up, and for once I'm glad of it. I circle around, giving the portal a wide berth until I'm a little ways above it, then I take off my backpack and inch my way down towards the tunnel entrance with the crate tucked under one arm. Peck may venture outside from time to time, but I'm pretty sure the Guardians don't, and I doubt that anyone in there could hear me above the wind. Still, I'm nervous. When I've got as close as I dare to the opening I bury the crate in the snow, just above the crown of the tunnel. I mark the spot with a rock, in case someone other than me has to find it when the time comes. Then I crawl back up to where I've left my backpack.

I start the count at twenty, to account for the fact that I'm already above the portal. Counting normally helps, but it's doing little to pacify Claus now, even though we're still outside. He knows what's coming. I focus on the steps I'm taking, trying my best to ignore him. I've been thinking about it since the idea came to me last night, and I don't see another way. I wish I did.

I follow an imaginary line from the portal behind me to the transmitter tower that sits on top of the mountain. I find the first one about a third of the way up the slope, almost completely covered by the snow. I try and imagine Eden, its caverns and tunnels laid out beneath me, inside the mountain. It's three hundred and eighty paces from this point in the tunnel to the left prong of the west portal, and that includes the curve of the horseshoe. But that distance is measured flat, and I'm climbing upwards, following the contours of the mountain, so it makes sense that my count now would be higher. I realize that there must be a way to work this out more precisely; an equation, some formula that would confirm I'm where I think I am. The people who built Eden would have needed to know things like that. It occurs to me that understanding that formula would probably be satisfying, and not just because I need it now.

It takes me a while because it's almost completely buried in a drift, but I find the second one within twenty paces of where I think it should be, slightly to the north of the line I've drawn between the transmitter tower and the portal. I climb farther up the mountain, this time heading straight for the tower. In the end I find the third vent easily. The snow's melted all around it, revealing the concrete cowling and the metal grille that covers the opening leading deep into the heart of the mountain. I was expecting this. The first two vents drop down into the outside tunnels, which are always cold. It's not exactly warm in Eden's main cavern, but the temperature's higher than it is in the outside tunnels, and it's that warmer air that's caused the melt around this vent.

I hope.

Claus is jabbering away inside my head, making it difficult to concentrate. What if I've got it wrong? What if this isn't the right shaft? There must be others, ones that drop down into different parts of Eden. The power plant would also generate heat, and what about the furnace? He's right of course, and I wish I'd had the opportunity to test this. It could have been done so easily. Some innocuous object dropped into the opening would have told me whether the shaft was clear, where it ended. But it's too late for that now.

I look up the mountain again, measuring the distance to the transmitter tower, and then back down to the portal. One thousand and fifty-three steps to the outside from when I step into the tunnel. There's only one vent in the main cavern, directly above the mess. I imagine a line from the portal to that building, how that line might arc up through the rock to the surface of the mountain where I stand. The light's almost gone from the sky, but there's still just enough to see, and from here I have a good vantage point. No other concrete cowlings are visible; there are no other areas denuded of snow within sight. This has to be the right one.

The bolts holding the grille in place are rusted, but I've brought an adjustable wrench and with a little effort I remove them. That simple, repetitive task calms Claus a little, but as soon I set the grille to one side, exposing the dark maw of the shaft he kicks off again. I pull the wind-up flashlight from the pocket of my parka. I give the handle a dozen quick turns and lean into the vent's hood, pointing the beam down into the darkness. The shaft's not much more than a couple of feet square, its concrete walls black with the dust and grime that's settled on them over the years. The light reaches no further than a dozen feet into the darkness, but over that distance the shaft seems to descend at a roughly forty-five-degree angle.

I lift the coil of climbing rope I've been carrying off my shoulders and lay it on the ground. I loop one end around the vent's hood and secure it. At the other end I've tied a series of double knots; they'll warn me the rope's running out. It's six hundred feet, the longest one I could find in Providence's only camping store. I figure that should be more than enough to get me to the bottom of the shaft. I spent my last half hour in the farmhouse at the kitchen table, marking it out in ten-foot intervals with a sharpie. A double line indicates fifty feet, a triple, one hundred. I figure having something to count on the way down might help keep Claus off my back.

According to Mags the air in Eden is processed, drawn in through huge shafts to the ventilation plant out beyond the reservoir where it's filtered before huge fans circulate the newly scrubbed air back through the cavern and tunnels. But the shaft I've chosen is an exhaust vent, so in theory there should be less to obstruct my way. Nevertheless, Eden's a bunker, an underground fortress. Whoever designed it won't have left an easy way in. The concrete hood looks like it can be sealed at the surface, but there's bound to be something more once I get in there. There'll be no space to turn in the shaft; I'll need to lower myself in headfirst so that my hands are free to deal with whatever I come across. That means that once I've started my descent I'll be committed. If I hit an obstacle I can't find a way through, even after only a few yards, I probably won't be able to pull myself back out.

I open my backpack and take out the bolt cutters and a small hacksaw and transfer them to a canvas bag, along with the leatherman and the wrench. I've tied bootlaces to the bag and my flashlight, looping the end of each to create a lanyard that will slip over my wrist. I can't afford to accidentally drop any of these items. The shaft's too narrow for the backpack to fit on my back; it'll need to come down after me.

I sit back on the snow to wait. It shouldn't be long to curfew now. I tell myself my plan will work. If there's a weakness, it's the next bit; I've no idea what I might find on my way through the mountain. I've spent the hike out to Providence thinking about everything that might go wrong once I'm in there, in the dark confines of the shaft. I've prepared for what I can. I run through my list one more time, all the same, to make sure there's nothing I've forgotten. Then I go through it again.

When I realize I can't put it off any longer I stand, unzip my parka and shuck it off. I'd probably linger but then the cold hits, galvanizing me into action. I can't stand like this for long, and to put the parka back on would be to admit defeat; if I do that there's a good chance I'd never take it off again. Inside my head Claus is screaming, telling me there has to be another way. But there isn't. Not unless I want to leave Mags and the rest of the Juvies to their fate with Kane, and spend the rest of my days either holed up by myself somewhere like Mount Weather, or wandering this frozen wasteland looking for survivors that most likely don't exist.

I bundle the parka up and push it into the backpack. I pull the drawstring tight and close the plastic snaps. Then I position it on the lip of the vent and tether it to my ankle. I pick up the coil of rope and drop it into the shaft, watching as it slithers down into the darkness. I'm wearing a harness I found in the same climbing store where I picked up the rope. I'm not sure it was designed for this, but the canvas cinched tight around my waist and thighs seems sturdy. I make a loop in the rope and slip it through the carabiner's spring-loaded gate to allow me to control my descent.

I'm already starting to shiver, so I wind up the flashlight and pay out some line through the harness. Then, before I have a chance to think any more about it I coil a loop of rope around my ankle to slow my fall, place my arms above my head against the shaft walls and slide headfirst into the darkness.

*

THE ROPE AROUND MY ANKLE works itself free almost immediately, but the first part of the descent is actually gentler than I was expecting. I find I can brake simply by bracing the toes of my boots against the walls, leaving my hands free to wind the flashlight. Claus is seriously unhappy about being inside the vent shaft, but the feeling that I can stop if I need to is helping to calm him down a little.

It's hard to gauge in the darkness, but after a hundred feet the downward angle of the shaft seems to increase. I'm definitely starting to pick up speed. The rope is whirring gently through the harness and I have to jam the toes of my boots harder and harder into the walls to slow my descent. With my right hand, the one not holding the flashlight, I grab the rope and pull it away from me, tightening the loop I've fed through the carabiner. That stops me, but it's hard to maintain a smooth descent. I find myself jerking headlong into the darkness in a series of fits and starts, trying to control each slide so that it isn't longer than the distance I can see ahead of me. It gets harder as the downward angle of the shaft increases. Needless to say Claus isn't pleased with my progress.

At one hundred and seventy feet I hit the first obstacle. I think I notice a slight easing of tension in the rope ahead of me, but I continue to jerk downwards in twenty-foot bursts. My attempts to slow my descent become increasingly frantic as I see the rope ahead of me spooling up against something in the darkness. I pull hard with my right hand, the muscles in my legs straining to jam the toes of my boots against the smooth concrete walls. I stare into the darkness, desperate for a glimpse of whatever I'm hurtling towards that might be blocking the shaft ahead. The flashlight finally illuminates a rust-pitted metal grate, not unlike the one I removed from the vent hood up on the surface. I come to a shuddering halt with my face only inches from it.

My first thought is that if the bolts that hold the grate in place are on the other side I'm finished; the hacksaw I've brought will never cut through these bars. But by the grace of whatever cousins of the tunnel gods hold dominion here they're not. I brace myself against the grate with my left hand, freeing my right to work on the first bolt. It's seized solid. I check each corner in turn and they're all the same; it's possible they haven't been replaced since Eden was built. With just one hand to work the wrench it's hard work. I start with the bolt I tried first, alternately pulling then pushing, yanking the head this way then that in an attempt to loosen it. Soon the sweat's running freely, in spite of the chill; salty beads of it that roll from my scalp and sting my eyes. I see it in the beam from the flashlight, dropping from my face to splash on the bars or fall through into the darkness beyond.

I pause every few minutes to wind the flashlight and wipe my brow. Inside the gloves I'm wearing I feel a large blister form at the base of my thumb, then burst. I ignore it. For what seems like an age I attack the same bolt, pleading with it to give. It won't be bargained with, however. It refuses to budge, not even by the tiniest fraction of an inch. I can feel the fear starting to rise, the panicky animal inside growing in size, twisting and turning as it looks for a way to break free.

When I first got sent outside I was fascinated by the snow. We'd never had any, growing up in New Orleans. I found a magazine in this house we were scavenging. Inside there was an article about avalanches. It said that people who got caught in them could become so disorientated they would no longer be able to tell which way to dig to make it back to the surface. If that happened you should spit as much as you could and see which way the saliva ran across your face; that would tell you which way was down and which way was up. I asked Marv if that's what we should do but he just said that was bixicated. If an avalanche hit you, you'd probably die from being bounced off a rock or a tree. And even if that didn't kill you you'd be buried so quick it'd be like being frozen in quick drying cement. You wouldn't be able to move your eyelids, let alone your fingers, so figuring out which way to dig wouldn't be of much help. Claus didn't let me sleep for a long while afterwards thinking about it, and I wondered whether it might have been better if Marv had just told me there wasn't much risk of an avalanche out on the turnpike. But he hadn't, and for the longest time I thought that what he had described would be just about the worst possible way to die.

Now I see this would be worse. If I can't move this grate I'm stuck here. I could scream until I felt my vocal chords tear and it would make no difference; I'm not far enough into the mountain for anyone in Eden to hear me. I've enough water for a day, maybe two if I'm careful. But what would be the point of rationing it? I might as well empty my canteen into the darkness and let it be over sooner. If I can't get past this grate I'll die here. Whether it's in three days or four will make little difference, except for the amount of time I'll have hanging upside down in the inky confines of my tomb, going mad with fear, or thirst, or both.

I scream at Claus to shut up. I'm almost positive I do this inside my head, but afterwards I can't be entirely sure. Surprisingly it works, and for a moment it's quiet again. I take a deep breath and tell myself to calm down. It can't have been more than twenty minutes. The bolts have probably been sitting there for seventy years; it's unreasonable to think they would move so easily. It's just a matter of time.

They *will* move.

I take a swig from the canteen, trying to spill as little water as possible as I hold myself mostly upside down above the grate. Then I get back to work, ignoring the pain from my hand as the inside of my glove removes another layer of skin each time I brace the wrench against the unyielding bolt.

Finally I feel something give; a movement so slight it would be easy to believe I had imagined it. Or worse, that it might be the wrench finally starting to strip the metal from the old, rusted head. I put those thoughts from my mind and redouble my efforts. A minute later the bolt moves again, this time a fraction more, and now I know I have it beat.

It's hard to know how much time passes in the darkness of the shaft, but I reckon it takes the best part of two hours to free all four bolts. By the time the last one lifts out, my left arm, the one that's been holding my weight above the grate, is completely numb. The muscles in my right, the one that's been on wrench duty, are on fire from my shoulder all the way down to my wrist, and the flesh in the crook of that thumb feels like it's been ground into hamburger meat. When I pull back the cuff I see the lining of the glove is spongy with blood.

It takes me a surprisingly long time to maneuver the grate out of place.

After that my descent becomes a lot less graceful. My damaged right hand is only good for holding the flashlight, so I switch to my left to slow the rope through the carabiner, jerking and bouncing down the shaft, caroming off the sides like a rag doll tossed down a garbage chute. The double lines marking out fifty feet zip by. I decide to try and slow myself every thirty feet, but the muscles in my arms are fatigued from the grate and respond only intermittently, when the speed I pick up causes my body to release enough adrenalin to jolt them into action. Even then they only work in short, unreliable bursts. My boots are jammed hard into the walls of the shaft; I can feel the frantic vibration in the toes as they scrabble for purchase against the concrete. Years of wading through deep snow has made my legs strong, but nevertheless I can feel them tiring. I think I can hold this for a little while, though. I can no longer hope to stop, but maybe I can keep my speed from increasing too much before the inevitable impact with whatever lies ahead.

I watch the lines I have marked on the rope as they zip by in the flashlight's stuttering beam. The small, stubborn part of my brain that's still insisting on providing a count calls out four hundred feet, followed an instant later by four-fifty. I let go of the flashlight and grab the rope that's whirring past in front of me with both hands, trying to shut out the spike of pain from my right hand. The flashlight is still tethered to my wrist and it bounces crazily, illuminating the tunnel in a series of random flashes. Five hundred shoots past in a blur, followed by five-fifty. I'm hit by the grim realization that I will run out of rope before I get to the end of the shaft.

*

IN THE END it happens quickly. I think I see a faint glimmer of light ahead and an instant later my back slams into the concrete as the shaft shifts without warning from steep to near vertical and then widens out.

Paradoxically it's this sudden increase in downward angle that probably saves me, as being thrown against the shaft wall kills some of my speed. I have an instant to glimpse the metal roof of a building what seems like a long way below before I emerge from the roof of the cavern into a curfewed Eden. A final spike of adrenalin jolts me into action. I use whatever strength I have left to push my legs even harder against the concrete before I feel the walls of the shaft disappear as it widens into an opening. I try and tighten the grip I have on the rope whirring through my gloves. The muscles in my hand work for an instant and then release, and then I'm in open air and in sickening freefall. I wrap my arms around my head and wait for the metal that's rushing up to meet me. This won't be good.

The impact I'm braced for never arrives. Instead I jerk to a sudden horizontal halt, suspended in mid-air halfway between where the vent shaft exits into the rocky cavern above me and the metal roof of the building below. I have a second to realize that the thing that arrested my fall was the knot I'd tied in the end of the rope; it's jammed itself in the carabiner that's part of the harness I'm wearing. Then my backpack comes shooting out of the shaft behind me and sails past, missing my head by inches. I don't work out it's tethered to my ankle until it reaches the end of that tether, yanking me upright.

For a second I'm too stunned to do anything. The backpack hasn't reached the roof below. It's suspended what seems like mere inches above it, and now it's acting like a pendulum; I've already started a slow, lazy rotation that provides me with an excellent view of the dimly lit cavern beneath me. I'm relieved to see that my dead reckoning on the surface has paid off; I have come down the shaft I intended, the one that ends, or begins, depending on your point of view, directly above the roof of the mess. The arc lights are off and all around me Eden's quiet. It's surprising, given the manner of my arrival, but I think I managed to avoid making much noise as I entered the cavern. I need to get down from here though, and quickly. The Guardians patrol infrequently at night, but if one were to walk down Front Street there's always the chance they might look up and see me.

I examine the rope attached to the harness at my waist. It's jammed tight in the carabiner. The small bag with my tools is still tethered to my wrist, so I take out the leatherman and start sawing through the end of the rope just above the knot. As the knife cuts through the last strands I hold the rope above tight so I can lower myself down as gently as possible.

It doesn't quite work like that. The muscles in my arms give up almost immediately and I fall rather than lower myself onto the roof below. The backpack drops the final few inches, coming to rest on the metal with a muted thud, and I land on top of it. I lie there for a long moment, just staring up at the darkness of the shaft above.

I sit up. My right hand hurts a lot. I remove the glove as gently as I can and inspect the damage there. There's a lot of blood and the skin's raw all the way from the heel of my palm to the crook of my thumb, but I tell myself it could be way worse. I packed a first aid kit in the side pocket of the backpack; I clean the wound as best I can with water from the canteen and bandage it tight. Then I carefully unpack the rest of the things I've brought with me and lay them out on the flat metal roof. Incredibly everything seems to have survived the descent intact, even the little oil lamp I read by in my room in the farmhouse. I pick up the small Tupperware container, holding it up to the dim cavern lights to check what's inside. I'm pleased with the progress: by tomorrow it should be ready; I think Jack might even have been proud of me. I carefully repack everything except for the parka, which will be my bedding for the night, the pry bar, an empty plastic bottle into which I will pee and my battered copy of *The Girl With The Dragon Tattoo.* The lamp gets packed away last. I'll need it later.

I'm exhausted, but I tell myself there'll be plenty of time to rest tomorrow; tonight I have one more thing to do. I've no idea how long it's been since the last patrol however, so I sit down to wait for whoever's on duty tonight to come around again.

I wonder how Mags is doing. Her penance for being out after curfew must be over by now. I realize I haven't seen her in ten days; that's the longest it's been since we first met. It's okay, though; as long as she hasn't managed to get herself confined for something else I should get to see her tomorrow night.

After a little while I hear the sound of heavy footsteps, carrying up from the street below. I don't need to look over the edge to know it's Angus and Hamish, down on Front Street, doing their rounds. They make their way towards the eastern tunnels, but don't spend long there. A few minutes later I hear them back in the cavern, lumbering up Juvie Row. There's some fumbling with the latch and then the door to their dorm clangs shut and silence returns to Eden. They won't be out again for at least an hour. Now's my chance.

I grab the pry bar, walk back along the roof to the access hatch and drop myself into the familiar crawl space. I'm expecting a twinge from Claus, but he's oddly quiet; I suspect he's still in shock after the horrors of our descent through the mountain. A few seconds later I'm lowering myself down onto the third floor landing and then I'm making my way down the stairs. The kitchens sit in darkness; I tiptoe through and out into the dining area. I turn the latch handle gently, searching for the mechanism's biting point, then push the door open a crack and peer out. Eden's deserted. I step out onto Front Street, moving as quietly as I can, pressing myself into the shadows cast by the dimmed curfew lights. I cross the street and scurry into the old pedestrian tunnel, leaving the main cavern behind. I pass the stores, and the cavern where the power plant's housed. As I leave the reservoir behind I realize I've never been down here before. Claus doesn't like going farther into the tunnels than is absolutely necessary, and besides all that's ahead of me now is the armory, and that's always been off limits.

It's beyond where I was expecting, but finally I see it ahead of me in the darkness. I'm out of sight of the cavern now, so I take out the flashlight and wind it gently. The beam plays over the metal and I see immediately that this one's not like all the other bulkhead doors in Eden. My heart sinks as I see a keypad mounted to the granite next to it, its red light blinking steadily at me. And then I notice the camera mounted above my head, just like the one outside the blast door. It doesn't look like it's on right now, but I push myself up against the wall anyway. I look back down at the keypad. The red light just keeps blinking back at me, maintaining its silent guard. There are no letters, and the display only has six digits, not twelve, but there's still no chance of me getting in without knowing the code. I heft the pry bar. But of course the door won't simply open if I smash up the keypad. That would probably just cause the camera to come on and then Peck would know I was here.

I take one last look at the door then I flick the flashlight off and start back along the tunnel. I'll admit to being a little disheartened at this point, but it's probably just because I'm tired and my hand's really killing me. I tell myself this bit of the plan was never likely to work, and if all goes well tomorrow it won't matter anyway.

When I get back to the main cavern it's still quiet. I cross Front Street and return to my solitary perch on the roof of the mess.

*

I WAKE TO THE ARC LIGHTS coming on and the sound of Eden's infernal buzzers filling the main cavern. Soon familiar faces start appearing on the streets below. They congregate in twos and threes, but no one seems to be talking. One by one they start making their way towards the mess. Mags emerges from the girls' dorm. Her hands are stuffed into the pockets of her overalls and she's staring straight ahead as she walks, like she's mad about something. An irrational impulse to call out to her comes over me. I want to run down the back stairs and out into the street after her. I want to tell her what I've been doing. I want to tell her about Marv. I even want to tell her what else I've read about Lisbeth Salander. But instead I sit on my parka and watch her follow the rest of the Juvies in for breakfast.

The buzzer for morning prayer sounds shortly afterwards and they reappear and start shuffling down towards the chapel. I move back from the edge in case anyone sees me, although this morning that seems unlikely. No one's looking up; everyone seems even more subdued than usual.

The morning passes slowly. After prayer everyone disperses into the tunnels for another day of work. I follow the occasional Juvie walking along Front Street but mostly the cavern's quiet. When I figure it's time for lunch I retreat to the center of the roof and break out an MRE. I eat it cold. I'm sitting right under the vent, but I don't want to take any chances heating it up in case somebody smells the food pouch cooking.

The afternoon drags. I have nothing to do but sit and think about everything that might go wrong later. I tell myself there's no point worrying about it anymore. I'm committed now; there's no choice but to see the plan through. That doesn't help much, however. I notice I'm pacing a lot and the pee bottle's getting alarmingly close to being full.

At last the evening buzzer sounds. I watch as people file back from the tunnels to the mess. Tonight we should be back to the first installment of *30 Days of Night*, and that's my chance. Movie night's the only time in the week when all the Juvies'll be together, without Kane or Peck or the Guardians. There'll be the usual trips to the bathroom after dinner, but I'll know when the film's about to start because they'll post a lookout. Unless they've changed the roster it's Ruth's turn tonight. Once I see her I'll go down.

The minutes crawl by. It seems like it's been a while since the buzzer; they should be finishing up soon. I'm ready; I've packed everything up except the pee bottle. Marv wouldn't like me not taking care of my trash, but the bottle's full and I won't want it weighing me down later.

Suddenly I hear a noise from the other side of the roof; it sounds like it's coming from the crawlspace beneath me. I freeze, straining to hear. Someone's definitely coming. Has somebody has seen me up here and reported it to the Guardians? I thought I was being careful. I look around, but of course the roof's flat, featureless; there's nowhere for me to hide. The access panel screeches as it shifts in its frame and then it pops up and starts to slide to one side. There's no other way down, no way for me to escape. I'm trapped.

A moment later Mags' head appears. When she sees me her eyes widen in surprise, but then they narrow, like she's suddenly remembered she's angry. She climbs up onto the roof and marches over to me.

'Gabriel. What are you doing here?' *Gabriel*'s not good. That's the term Mags reserves for me when I've done something wrong.

'Hi Mags.'

'Did it occur to you to tell me before you just disappeared like that?'

I'm not sure what to say to this so instead of answering I look down over the edge. Everyone'll be done eating by now, but Ruth still hasn't emerged. Mags plants her hands on hips and tilts her head to one side.

'Somewhere you need to be, Gabriel?'

*Well, yes, actually.*

But then her expression softens as she notices my hand.

'What happened to you?'

'It's nothing. I hurt myself coming down the vent shaft.'

Her eyes harden again and I think she's going to accuse me of lying. Mags knows how I feel about dark, tight spaces; she's the only one who knows about Claus. But then she looks up and sees the climbing rope, it's newly frayed end hanging from the vent above our heads. Her gaze returns to the roof. She points at the plastic Coke bottle I've been urinating in all day. Now I wish I'd followed Marv's advice and put it my backpack.

'What's that?'

'My pee bottle.'

She looks at me in disbelief for a second and then her face scrunches up.

'Ewww!'

This is not going the way I had hoped. I still have time to notice how my heart seems to do a backflip as she wrinkles her nose when I tell her what's in the bottle.

'Listen, I promise I'll explain everything, but it makes more sense if I do it all at once, to everyone. Can we go downstairs? The film's probably already started.'

She looks at me oddly.

'Oh, right. You haven't been around since Lena confessed.'

'Confessed to what?'

'To being pregnant.'

'Wait, Lena was actually pregnant?'

'At least that's what she told Kane. How did you know?'

I wave the question away. What's more important is how I'm going to get her out if she's not with the others. I need everyone together for this to work.

'Where is she now? Is she locked in her cell?'

Mags just looks down and shakes her head.

'Kane banished her.'

'She's *outside*? Okay I need to go down and speak to everyone, right now.'

'You can't. The Guardians will still be down there. They don't leave us alone anymore now.'

'But what about movie night?'

'Movie night's finished, Gabe. Kane shut it down. He'd known about it all along apparently. He said he'd tolerated it while everyone was behaving. But then when Lena confessed, and you and Marv split and took the last of the rations…'

We only left with the MREs Quartermaster gave us, but that detail seems trivial next to the fact that Lena's outside. And without movie night the plan I came up with in the farmhouse now hangs in tatters; that was my one chance to get the Juvies out of Eden without Kane noticing. I can't get into the armory. Marv didn't think he and Benjamin could take on Kane and Peck as long as they had that advantage, and they were soldiers. And that was before Peck had the Guardians.

Mags is staring at me, like she's trying to work out what's going on.

'I think you'd better tell me everything that's happened, Gabe. And make it quick. I've only got a few minutes.'

I explain to her about finding Benjamin, and the map to Mount Weather, and the meeting with Kane and Peck, and then what Marv had done to me outside afterwards. Mags' eyes grow a little wider when I mention how he had a gun, and it seemed like he was going to shoot me. Later when I tell her about Marv being together with Benjamin the corners of her mouth lift a little, as if she approves of their act of defiance, even though I'm not sure that's what it was. A different expression crosses her face as I tell her how he died. I can tell she has a hundred questions to ask but she doesn't interrupt me once. The buzzer sounds just as I'm describing Mount Weather. She looks back across the roof.

'I have to go.'

'Already?'

'Yeah, curfew's right after dinner now.' She takes a steps towards the hatch.

'Wait.' I can't just let her go. She has to meet me again, so we can figure a new plan together. I'll need her help now to get everyone out of here. I start to say all these things but she grabs my hand, silencing me.

'You need to leave here, Gabe. You can do it tomorrow morning. Everyone will be gathered in the chapel for the ceremony. There won't be anyone at the portal. You can slip out without anyone knowing you were even here.'

'What ceremony?'

'Where we get matched. Kane moved it forward after what Lena confessed. He told us who our matches were last week.'

I don't want to know, but I can't help asking anyway.

'Did you at least get Jake?'

'Jake?'

I shrug.

'I know about you and him. All the time you've been spending over at the farms.'

She looks at me for a while, as if she's deciding whether she can tell me. In the end she must figure it doesn't matter any more.

'It's not that. I've been teaching Jake to read.'

'So who'd you get matched with then?'

Mags is sitting on the edge of the access panel. She looks away but not quickly enough. I see the tears brimming in her eyes. This is troubling. I don't think I've ever seen Mags cry.

'Kurt. I got matched with Kurt.'

*

I'VE BEEN UP FOR HOURS, just sitting on my parka, waiting. With the lights dimmed it's harder to make out the rock bolts and the brace wire, but they're there, I know it. Marv was right. Eden's a cage. It always has been.

The buzzer finally sounds and a second later the arc lights blink on, instantly bathing the cavern in their harsh white glare. I don't think I'll ever get used to that; the sudden nights, the unexpected dawns. Well, after today I won't have to. This will be my last morning in Eden.

I stand, stretch out my legs and walk over to the edge. Beneath me Eden stirs, slowly coming to life. I watch from the roof as the only people I know shuffle out of the dorms in their drab gray overalls. Nobody seems interested in breakfast. They linger on Main Street, huddled together in small groups. No one's talking. It's like it's finally dawning on them that whatever little was left of their childhood is coming to an end.

The Guardians gather on Front Street, forming a menacing black line. They stand apart, arms folded grimly across their chests or by their sides, toying with the billy clubs that hang from their belts. I return my gaze to Juvie Row. I'm looking for Mags but I don't see her, and for one awful moment I think of Miss Kimble and what happened in her cell all those years ago. Mags wouldn't do that, would she? But then she steps out of the dorm. The mohawk's back, a final act of defiance. She's done it herself. Even from up here I can see that the bit at the back is crooked.

The buzzer sounds again, calling everyone down to the chapel. I notice some of the Juvies start, as if somehow they weren't expecting it. At first nobody moves, but then at a signal from Kurt the Guardians advance and in ones or twos the small crowd begins to make its way silently towards the back of the cavern. Mags is the last to move. For a long time she stands there, beautiful and sleek and fearless, just staring back at Peck and the Guardians. It looks like she doesn't mean to follow everyone else. But she has nowhere else to go. Kurt nods to Angus and Hamish who step forward, ready to manhandle her towards the chapel, and finally she turns and starts making her way after the others.

I walk along the roof, as close as I dare to the edge, keeping pace with her until she reaches the intersection with Back Street and I can go no further. She steps into the street and then without turning she stops and raises her hand. I inch closer. She clenches her fist once, then opens it, a final wave goodbye. I want to tell her it'll be okay.

But I'm not sure that it will.

My backpack's already packed; it's waiting for me by the access hatch. I lower it into the crawlspace and jump down after it. All I leave on the roof is the bottle.

I shuffle my way along, pushing the pack ahead of me. I've already removed the bolts on the panel at the other end and it slides out of the way easily. I drop my pack onto the metal landing by the back stairs and it lands with a loud clang, but I no longer care. I lower myself down after it. I don't bother to slide the panel back into place behind me.

I hoist the pack onto my shoulder and walk calmly down the stairs, through the empty kitchen and into the dining area. I pick up one of the plastic chairs and leave it outside the door on my way out.

I cross Front Street and enter the corridor that leads to the blast door, passing the room with the scanner, the locker room and the showers. I stop at my locker and open it. There's a half spent tube of UV block and a couple of unopened spares sitting on the top shelf. I hadn't thought to bring any from the farmhouse; I wasn't planning on leaving during daylight. I leave the door to my locker open.

When I get to the blast door I hit the switch that starts the open sequence. A second later there's the familiar muted screech from inside the door as the bolts recess. Then the electric motors kick in, whining under the load as they start to push the four tons of carbon steel back. A blast of cold air from the tunnel hits my face as the door slowly arcs out into the darkness, but for the first time I don't feel the knot in my stomach. My chest feels light, my breath comes slow and even.

I feel calm.

*

ELIZA MADE HER way outside. The cars they had arrived in that morning were parked in front of the building and everyone was waiting for her. She had to shield her eyes against the searing sun as she made her way down the steps to join them.

Dr. Hyun explained that they were now going to the radiochemical laboratory. This was in a different security zone to the south, so they would need to drive. He would ride with them. Jorg transferred himself to the car in front with Mike and Kenny and Eliza took his seat upfront, letting Hyun sit with Jan in the back. Gravel crunched under the old car's tires as they set off.

Dear God, what had she done? The last thing she remembered was kneeling on the cold tiles in the stall, clutching the toilet bowl. She had blacked out and then the guard must have come in and disturbed her. She wondered how long it would be before he was discovered. She had left him in the female toilet, and she had not seen another woman at the facility all morning, so perhaps that would buy her some time. Would it be enough? They were scheduled to fly out of Pyongyang that evening. But what if he had been sent to check on her? Surely they would send someone else when he didn't return.

There had clearly been a terrible mistake. The virus was not harmless to humans as the pastor had thought. She wished to God there was some way she could contact him; he would tell her what she should do. Well, one thing was certain; she couldn't go ahead with the plan to infect Pak now. At the first opportunity she would take the antivirus. The pastor had said it would deactivate the nanites in her body almost immediately; at least then she could do no more harm.

The next thing she knew they were driving past a massive, crumbling structure that appeared to have been abandoned.

She looked around. They were no longer in the facility, but she didn't remember driving through the guard post or crossing the concrete bridge. She must have blacked out again. She stole a glance at the driver behind her sunglasses, but he didn't seem to be paying attention to her. In the back seat she could hear Hyun explaining how this was to have been a second gas graphite reactor, far more powerful than the one they had seen that morning. She breathed a sigh of relief; she didn't seem to have done anything other than drift off. But she couldn't let that happen again. She had to stay awake.

She looked out of the window, forcing herself to focus on what she saw. It seemed like whatever they had been building hadn't been finished; the cranes that had been erected had never been taken down and now they just sat there, rusting. She overheard Hyun telling Jan that the project had been close to completion, but had been abandoned in exchange for a promise from the west for light water technology. Jan asked whether there were any plans to recommence the work, but it didn't look to Eliza like much was capable of being salvaged. Even from this distance she could make out huge cracks in the concrete. The exhaust tower was badly corroded, as was the pipework and the other metal structures she could see. Hyun didn't answer for a long while. When he finally said no she couldn't tell whether he sounded angry or sad.

They passed through a guard post. A soldier in a drab olive tunic stood to attention as they drove by, a rifle slung over one shoulder. A few minutes later they pulled up outside a large modern building. The back doors opened and Jan and Hyun climbed out, but she waited until Hyun was already at the steps before squeezing her eyes shut and hurrying after them. She caught up with the group just as Hyun was leading them through glass doors into a large atrium.

She immediately excused herself and headed for the washrooms. She quickly checked that the stalls were empty, then she reached into the inside pocket of her coat, retrieving the ampule she had been carrying with her all day. She snapped the neck and tipped back the container, swallowing the contents, almost gagging as the same bitter, metallic taste as before hit the back of her throat. She forced it down and then cupped her hands under the tap and drank greedily, desperate to wash the liquid from her mouth. She no longer cared that the water might not have been treated. A little upset stomach was nothing next to whatever was coursing through her veins right now.

The group had already moved on when she made her way back out to the atrium, but she could hear Jorg's voice drifting down from above. A wide polished staircase appeared to lead in that direction. She started up it.

It hit her long before she reached the last step, a heady raft of metallic smells weighing the air so heavily it was almost a physical presence. She felt a moment of light-headedness; her vision blurred and she grabbed the railing. But then it passed. She took a moment to get her breath back and continued up the stairs, the smell getting stronger with each step.

She followed the sound of voices into what appeared to be a control room. The smell was even stronger here, so dense she thought she could taste it; she had to steady herself in the doorway before she could go in. Jorg noticed her and detached himself from the group, coming over to check she was okay. She waved him away, telling him she was fine, but she could see Jan looking over as well, a worried look on his face. She took a couple of deep breaths and the dizziness passed.

She joined the others on the far side of the room on an observation deck that looked over a long high-bay area. Now she could see what was causing the smell. The floor below was a sea of metal; there had to be literally thousands of centrifuge cascades, all neatly arranged below them in closely spaced rows, running the entire length of the hall. Each looked about as tall as a man, and was perhaps a foot in diameter. No cooling coils were visible, just smooth aluminum casings with tight bundles of tubes emanating from the top. An insulated pipe ran the length of the facility, connecting each.

She stepped back from the edge, the smell threatening to overpower her again. Did nobody else notice it? She turned back towards the bank of monitors on the far wall, pretending to examine something there, in case Jan or Jorg had seen her. And then she saw him, standing in front of one of the screens, studying whatever was displayed there. His hair was shorter, his pale scalp showing through at the sides, but the face was otherwise the same collection of sharp features she recognized from the photographs in the file the pastor had sent her. The small, flattened nose; narrow eyes that seemed to regard everything with suspicion; a mouth that seemed naturally inclined to turn down at the corners.

She looked around quickly. Dr. Hyun was busy answering some question from Jan about centrifuge design. On the other side of the room Jorg was asking Kun about enrichment capacity. No one seemed to have noticed Pak; maybe there wouldn't be an introduction after all. Kun had been hurrying them along all day.

But as she looked back she saw with horror that Pak had already stepped away from the monitor and was walking towards them. Hyun had seen his approach and was bowing furiously. She breathed a sigh of relief as she remembered what the pastor had told her. They did not shake hands here; a bow was the normal greeting. It was she who would need to initiate the contact necessary to pass on the virus, and there was no way she was going to do that now. But then she heard Pak address Jan in English and stick out his hand. Jan shook it. And then Kun was introducing Pak to Jorg and Mike and Kenny; he was clasping each of their hands in turn.

She told herself not to panic. She had been wearing gloves all day. But as she pulled her hands from the pockets of her coat she saw that they were bare. When had she lost them? She hadn't been wearing them when she had washed the horrendous taste of the antivirus from her mouth a few minutes before, and now she thought about it her hands had been bare earlier too; they had been covered in blood after she had attacked the guard. She fumbled in her pockets, hoping the gloves might somehow be there. But they weren't; she had left them somewhere, most likely in the bathroom in the administration building. She looked around desperately. Maybe it was not too late to excuse herself. But then Pak was standing in front of her. She heard Kun say her name and when she looked down Pak was holding out his hand.

She stood in front of him, not moving. Pak stared at her for a long moment. For the first time she noticed a smattering of old acne scars across his cheekbones; they had not shown up on the photographs of him she had studied. His gaze dropped to his outstretched hand and then returned to her face. For a long moment he did nothing. Behind her everyone had gone quiet. She was sure every eye in the room was on her now, watching the drama unfold. Pak's hand was still outstretched, but the thin smile had vanished from his lips and his mouth had hardened. He would lose face if she did not reciprocate. Eliza felt a heavy bead of sweat collect under her arm and trickle slowly down her side. She thought she heard Kun saying something, his tone sharp. Then Jan said her name. She forced herself to ignore it, keeping her hands by her side.

And for a moment perhaps the fate of the world hung in the balance. Maybe it was already too late. There was the guard, of course. And what else had she touched that might have accepted her deadly gift? The handle as she had flushed the toilet? The railing she had steadied herself on as she had climbed the stairs moments before? She honestly couldn't remember. Then the silence was broken by a commotion behind her and she turned around to see guards bursting into the control room, their weapons drawn. They were shouting something in Korean. Pak took a quick step backwards, distancing himself from her. Then strong hands were gripping her arms, pulling them behind her back, and an instant later she felt something cold and metallic being slipped around her wrists, the bracelets ratcheting closed until the handcuffs were tight.

Jorg towered over the soldiers; it took two of them to hold him back. Jan was remonstrating loudly with Kun, insisting that she be released, that there must have been some mistake. She wanted to tell them both to stop. She didn't understand the words the guards had been shouting in Korean, but clearly they had found the body of their comrade in the toilet. The pastor had warned her that he was sending her here as a sheep among wolves, but that wasn't right; the image of what she had done to the guard in the toilet would remain with her for as long as she lived. It was she who had been the wolf.

And then Pak took a step towards her, his hand reaching out for her breast. She tried to pull away from him, but the hands that still gripped her shoulders held her tight. His fingers closed around what he had seen there. He lifted it away from her neck, turning it over to examine it. He held it up so that everyone could see the silver cross, caked in still-drying blood. Jan was looking at her, an expression of disbelief on his crumpled face.

Pak regarded the crucifix a moment longer then let it drop, rubbing the blood from his fingers. He looked at her one last time and then turned and walked back to his desk to gather his things. He was still unsure what had happened with the crazy *waegukin*; what the guards had accused her of as they had burst in made no sense at all. But he would have to leave Kun to sort it out. A car was waiting for him outside and he was already late.

He had a flight to catch.

The last Eliza saw of Jan was on the steps of the laboratory as they drove her away. She told herself she had taken the antivirus in time; the pastor had said it would deactivate the nanites in her bloodstream immediately. And maybe she was already starting to feel a little better; when they had brought her outside the light had still been unbearable, but her hands and feet were troubling her less. They were still very cold, yet somehow it seemed not to matter so much now. Her teeth were still chattering though. Well, not chattering exactly. It was like she couldn't seem to stop grinding them together. Her jaw kept clenching and unclenching in long, shuddering spasms and occasionally a low clicking sound would escape from the back of her throat. But she was sure that now she had taken the antivirus those things would pass, too.

The pastor had lied to her about this as well, however. Three days later she would die tied to a hospital bed, surrounded by doctors who were increasingly puzzled why none of their instruments seemed to be working. In the increasingly fleeting moments of lucidity that were left to her she tried to tell them. But her thoughts when they came now were wild, raging things, her speech the incoherent grunts and howls of a wounded animal. She tried to point to it in those final moments, so they would know. It was right there, slowly dissolving on her bedside table. But no one seemed to understand. By then of course little remained of the chain and what was left of the silver cross was barely recognizable.

The ampule Eliza had been given had not contained an antidote; the scientists who had designed the ferrovirus had never been tasked with creating one. There was no need. The man Eliza knew as the pastor already knew how to stop it, and he would tend to that in time, when its purpose had been served. That act would be the final part of the plan his God had revealed to him, many years before.

For mankind had strayed too far from His path, and now things needed to go back to the way they had been, in the beginning.

*

I SLIDE THE BACKPACK off my shoulder and take out what I had planned to give to anyone who would follow me into the tunnel, laying the items out neatly on the ground. Twenty-nine pairs of gloves in an assortment of sizes; a similar number of wind up flashlights. I spent the hour before the arc lights came on sitting up on the roof on my parka, turning the plastic handles. Each should hold a full charge, enough to get us through the tunnel. There was no need for so many; not everyone needed their own. But I know the comfort of light in the darkness. I lay the two unopened tubes of UV block next to them on the concrete floor.

Those they will have to share.

The door's still opening, but I don't wait for it to finish. I know it takes thirty seconds. Always thirty seconds.

I turn around and head back into Eden.

I cross Front Street and pick up the chair I left outside the mess. I don't pause when I get to the corner of Main. Eden's deserted, just as Mags said it would be. I walk down the side of the featureless metal building where I've slept for most of the last ten years. I don't need to go in. There's nothing there I need to collect.

I stop outside the chapel and put the chair down. A single voice rings out from inside, the metal walls amplifying the deep, rich tones. With my left hand I reach into the pocket of my parka and feel inside the glass for the compact orb that's resting there. The cold metal is purposeful, reassuring.

I take a deep breath. My hand's resting on the latch handle, getting ready to push it down. Paint still clings to the underside in feeble chips but on top the metal's burnished smooth from years of wear.

And then I hear it.

Kane's favorite passage, the one we hear every morning at prayer, the one he quotes in his sermon each Sunday, the blessing he gives before every trip I've taken outside. We're God's Chosen Ones; His flock; the sheep He will soon send forth in the midst of wolves. And then it hits me. And suddenly I'm no longer calm.

I turn and sprint back the way I've just come, the parka flapping around me as I run. At Front Street a left and then I'm leaving the main cavern behind. I bark a pre-emptive *shut up* at Claus as we enter the old pedestrian tunnel, and for once he stays quiet. I run past the stores, past the power plant cavern and the reservoir, retracing my steps from two nights ago, finally skidding to a halt in front of the door to the armory. The keypad's light blinks impassively in the gloom.

*As sheep in the midst of wolves*. From the Book of Matthew. Chapter

10, verse 16. Matthew is the first Gospel in the New Testament.

I enter 011016. The red light flickers rapidly for a second, then switches to a continuous green. The camera above my head blinks into life and focuses, but right now there won't be anyone watching whatever screen my face has just appeared on. From somewhere behind the door I hear an electric motor hum, and then the sound of bolts being drawn back. Finally there's a click and the door recesses a fraction. The faint smell of oiled metal wafts out.

I push it open and step from a large tunnel into a smaller one. The walls are the same roughhewn granite as outside, the floor the same dusty concrete. I flip the switch on the wall next to the door. The bulkhead lamps bolted to the roof illuminate row after row of assault rifles, standing to attention in their racks, the blue-gray metal gleaming dully in the glare from the fluorescent lights, testament to the care that someone has taken to maintain them. A wooden stool, the seat shiny from years of use, beside the door. I wonder how many hours Peck has sat down here by himself, cleaning and oiling each weapon, carefully returning it to its place in the row. I need to find some way to disable them, but there's far more than I was expecting. I walk between the racks, looking for anything that might do the trick.

And then I see them, against the far wall. A bank of glass-fronted refrigerator cabinets. I tell myself I really don't have time to explore; I need to deal with the guns and get back to the chapel while everyone's still in there. Nevertheless I feel myself drawn towards them. I bend down to peer through the thick glass. The shelves inside are stocked with trays of ampules, stacked upright in neat plastic racks. I open the first cabinet and slide one of the trays out to get a better look. I lift one of the vials out. It contains a clear liquid that shifts sluggishly against the glass as I tilt it. Printed on a narrow label next to a black and yellow symbol is a description of the contents. It's cold in the tunnels, but I feel a bead of sweat break out high on my brow and slowly trickle down my temple as I read what's inside.

*

ON THE OTHER SIDE of the thin glass held between my trembling fingers is the thing that ended the world. Peck wasn't going outside to find a fury to infect Marv's respirator the other night. He didn't need to; the virus was right here, inside Eden, all along. My hand shakes as I gently lower the ampule back into its slot. The vials clink in the tray as I slide it back into the cabinet.

I can't leave the virus here, with Kane. Even if we somehow get out of here today, as long as he has it we'd never be safe, wherever we might go. But there are way too many of the delicate glass tubes for me to carry safely in my backpack. Even in their plastic trays they rattle precariously. And I don't know how to destroy them. Eden's furnace is adjacent to the old diesel power plant, in the tunnels that lead to the farms. But it's only run when it's needed; it'll be cold now. In any event I've no idea if it even gets hot enough to destroy what's insides those ampules. If it doesn't all I'll have succeeded in doing is contaminate Eden, and I can't risk that. I don't know whether anyone will come with me to Mount Weather. I can't even be certain I'll make it out of here today.

How much time has passed since I left the chapel? Ten minutes? More? I imagine everyone inside, kneeling in the pews, and feel myself start to panic. I have to get back before whatever ceremony Kane is conducting ends; I need the Juvies all in one place for what I have planned. I start the count at twelve minutes, just to be sure.

I look around, my eyes flicking around the room. My gaze lands on half a dozen large olive-colored plastic containers, stacked on the floor against the far wall. It looks like they were designed to hold the rifles sitting in the racks next to them. They're covered in a layer of dust, like they haven't been moved since before we came to Eden.

I pop the two heavy-duty catches on the first case and open it up. I don't see any metal inside. The lid and base fit together snugly, and a rubber 'O' ring sits in a groove that runs all the way around the rim, like it's been designed to ensure an airtight fit. The lid's lined with a thick layer of charcoal foam in an egg-crate pattern. The container itself is filled with similar foam stacked in flat sheets, each about an inch thick.

I lift the first case off its stack and place it on the floor next to the row of cabinets. I take a layer of foam out and lay it on top of the case. Then I open the nearest cabinet and very carefully withdraw one of the plastic trays from the shelf and place it near the end of the layer of foam. I pull the leatherman from the pocket of my parka, flip the blade out with my thumb, and carefully cut around the base of the plastic tray. I move the tray along the foam and do the same again until I have four equally sized rectangular holes, each matching the footprint of the plastic tray. Using the first layer as a template I cut a similar pattern in eight more sheets of foam.

Sixteen minutes.

I drop two of the foam layers I've prepared into the case and, moving as quickly as I dare, ease four of the virus trays into the prepared slots. They fit snugly. One of the uncut layers of foam fits over the top and then I repeat the process until all sixteen trays of the virus have been transferred to the plastic container. I'm about to close the lid when another thought occurs to me. I carefully pull one of the vials from its slot in the top tray and as gently as I can I peel off the label and transfer it to the outside of the glass jar in my pocket. I do the same with another five vials. When I've replaced the final ampule I close the lid and snap the latches into place.

Twenty-two minutes. This is taking too long.

I lift the case gently by its handle. Fresh sweat prickles the space between my shoulder blades as I imagine the vials inside shifting. I carry it out into the tunnel. I haven't done anything to disable the guns, but there's no time for that now. I re-enter the code, hearing the lock slide into place as the door closes behind me. I remove the screws on the keypad with the leatherman and lever it free of the wall. I flip out the blade and hack away at the wires behind until the lights on the front die.

I pick up the case and make my way as quickly as I can through the old pedestrian tunnels, back towards the cavern. The case isn't especially heavy, but the size makes it awkward. I'd like to go faster but I imagine the glass vials shifting inside with each step I take, so I compromise on a quick shuffling walk, holding the handle away from my body so I don't accidentally knock the container against my thigh. I reckon I can hold it steadier in my right hand so I switch to that, in spite of the fresh pain it causes to grip the handle.

I step back into the cavern. Eden's streets are still deserted so I head straight across Front Street and into the mess. I have to put the case down to unlatch the door, then I'm heading for the stairs, taking them two at a time. When I get to the third floor landing I place the case on the floor and shuck off my parka.

Twenty-seven minutes.

I pick up the case and slide it up through the access panel and push it out of the way. I ignore the pain from my hand and pull myself up into the crawlspace that leads to the roof. The case slides easily in front of me, but I realize when I get to the roof hatch that I don't have enough leverage to manhandle it up there from behind and there's not enough space to crawl over the top and get in front of it. I have to drag it back to the access panel by the stairs, drop back down to the landing, slide it over to the other side of the open panel and then haul myself back up and drag it behind me as I do a backwards butt-shuffle through the crawlspace back to the roof hatch.

I climb out on to the roof and pull the case through the hatch, cursing myself for not thinking that through. The count inside my head says it's now been thirty minutes since I left the chapel.

I carry the case to the center of the metal roof. The top corner has an eye molded into the plastic of the lid and rim, so it can be secured with a padlock. It looks sturdy, and just about wide enough to accommodate the climbing rope I used to come down the vent shaft.

I eye the frayed end of the rope, hanging in the air above me. I can just about touch it if stand on tiptoe. I look around but the rooftop's bare, except for the pee bottle. For a desperate moment I consider it, but then sense prevails and I'm lowering myself back into the crawlspace again. I practically drop out of the ceiling onto the third floor landing and throw myself at the stairs, taking them three at a time. I grab a plastic bucket from the kitchen and sprint back up the stairs. I throw it into the crawlspace and pull myself up after it.

By the time I'm back on the roof sweat's running down my face, stinging my eyes. I upend the bucket and place it under the shaft, then step up onto it. From here I can reach the last eighteen inches of rope, which should be enough to tie off a decent knot. I test the rope with my weight then I step down and pick up the container. It's still a struggle, even with the bucket. I need to hold the case high enough with my damaged right hand to present the rope to the eye, but feeding it through with just my left proves tricky. There's a heart-stopping moment when I almost fall off, but on the third attempt I manage it. When I'm done the case hangs suspended in mid air, gently rotating on its axis above the metal roof.

Forty-five minutes.

There's no time to admire my handiwork. I dash across the roof and throw myself into the crawlspace. I grab my parka from where I dropped it on the landing and then I'm bolting down the backstairs, through the mess and out onto Front Street.

I have one last stop to make, then I'm sprinting between Eden's metal buildings towards the chapel, struggling to pull what I need out of the parka's deep side pockets.

*

DID I CONSIDER using the virus, after I worked out the code for the armory and found it in there?

We're coming to the end and I'm hoping by now you've got a sense of who I am, if not, perhaps, how this will soon end for me. Cunning as serpents? Yeah, not so much. I think Mags got closest when she said I wasn't as smart as I like to think I am, so if that's where you came out too I reckon I'd be fine with that. After all, who is? I hope you didn't end up too much further down towards the Angus and Hamish end of the bixicated scale. If you have, maybe you'll grant me some allowance for having sat in the warm waters in Eden for so long.

But to answer your question, yes, of course I considered it. I knew the plan I took with me into the darkness of the vent shaft was a long way from foolproof, and what I was left with after I spoke with Mags on the roof the following night was downright flaky. I guess things might have worked out differently if I'd walked into the chapel with one of the ampules I'd found in the armory, but now we'll never know. The truth is I couldn't ever be sure that the Juvies were going to leave, and without that I was never going to risk it.

I push open the metal door and step into the chapel, quickly scanning the crowd. It takes what seems like forever for my eyes to adjust to the gloom after the harsh glare of the cavern's arc lights.

The Juvies fill the first three rows as usual, girls on the left, boys on the right. I find Mags at the end of one of the pews; she's turned around in her seat and is staring at me, her eyes wide with surprise. Opposite her, on the other side of the aisle, I have a second to notice Kurt glaring at me before I move on. Kane's standing behind the altar, his arms raised above his head, like I've interrupted him in the middle of a blessing. My eyes rest on him for only an instant; he's not my concern right now either. I find who I'm looking for by the last row, a lot closer.

Marv said Kane's Secret Service agent was the one to watch, and he wasn't wrong. He was on his feet as soon as I came through the door, his hand instinctively reaching inside his jacket, and now he's standing in the center of the aisle, blocking my way. A pistol has appeared in his hand and from this distance the barrel looks as wide as the portal did out at Mount Weather. I was expecting it, of course, but nevertheless I'm a little disconcerted by his speed. I have a fleeting memory of being in the back yard of our house in New Orleans and Jack showing me a lizard. I remember marveling at how it could move so quickly from one spot to another, without appearing to transit through the space between, almost like it had been drawn on the pages of a flipbook. I take a deep breath and tell myself to be calm. He must realize where I'm standing. If he's as good as Marv reckoned he'll see my face, recognize what I'm holding in my hands, before he does anything stupid.

The moment draws out. Everyone's turned around in their pews and is looking at me, their faces a small sea of wide eyes and open mouths. I hear my heart beating; it thumps against my ribcage, as if I were back in the tunnel. The sweat on my face starts to cool. I wonder if the lampblack is still in place. I applied it carefully this morning, running a finger along the inside of the glass at the base of the lamp, gently smearing it under my eyes until I thought they looked like Marv's had, just before he died. I've been running up and down the stairs to the roof, clambering through the crawlspace, manhandling the container with the virus since. Did I pause at some point to wipe the sweat from my face? I don't think so, but I can't be sure. I realize I should have taken a second to check before bursting in to the chapel. Well, too late now.

I lick my lips. I think I can still get traces of the lipstick I scavenged from the nail parlor in Providence. The sweet taste of blueberries mixes with the metallic bitterness of the ink and the salty taste of sweat. I remember the cough. In the silence of the chapel with everyone looking at me it starts out sounding pretty lame. At the risk of overplaying it I try again. This time I develop it into a series of great whooping barks. I keep my arms held high throughout. It's important that they see. The chain wrapped through the fingers of my left hand is cool, comforting. I can feel the subtle shift in weight as the crucifix at its end dances in the air with each spasm. In my right hand I'm holding the respirator. My hands are sweating; the black rubber strap feels slick between my fingers. It's a spare that I found in Marv's room, and not much like the one I had before, the one Peck contaminated with the virus, but I'm hoping he won't notice.

I straighten myself up and look around slowly. Kane's lowered his arms, but his eyes won't leave the metal cross that's dangling from my left hand. The crudely-fashioned cross has been sitting in a Tupperware filled with *Patio Wizard* since the day before yesterday, the acid slowly eating away at the metal. Even from a distance you can tell. I offer a silent prayer of thanks to Jack; I guess his special guitar-ageing solution was just concrete cleaner after all.

Everyone's still looking at me. I've prepared what I need to say, but I don't want to deliver it with Peck standing in front of me. I motion with the respirator towards the pew, the meaning clear. Peck's eyes flick to the mask dangling from my fingers and then back to my face, but he doesn't move.

Making it seem like it's an effort I raise myself up to my full height and take an unsteady step forward. My boot rings out as it comes down on the chapel's riveted floor. Peck's only a few feet from me now. I've applied Jack's special solution to the retaining rings on the respirator, so the metal there looks suitably corroded, too. But I really don't want to get any closer. When I came up with this out in the farmhouse it was only as a fallback, to maybe buy us a few more seconds if things went wrong and we were discovered making our way out of Eden. In the harsh glare of the cavern's arc lights I doubt it would take longer than that to see through my crude Halloween makeover. Even in the dim light of the chapel I'm not sure how close an inspection it will bear.

I force the words out as I exhale so they sound tired, breathless.

'Sit down, Randall.'

At the same time I unclench the fingers of my left hand, letting the chain slide through. I finish with a grimace, revealing my final party trick. That's assuming there's enough of the red ink from the pen I was chewing on the roof earlier this morning still to be visible.

Peck's eyes flick to the crucifix, and then to my stained teeth, but still he doesn't move. I let the chain slide further, so now it's dangling precariously from the edge of my outstretched finger. At last I hear Kane from behind him on the altar.

'Randall. Sit down. Now!'

Peck keeps the gun on me as he eases back into his pew. The deep-set eyes that stare back at me over the barrel are gray as the snow and cold, reptilian. Kane steps around the altar and comes forward to stand at the top of the aisle.

'Gabriel.' The voice is deep and rich, soothing, like it always has been. He says my name like it's a satisfying solution to a riddle, like right now I'm the person he most wants to see in the whole world. 'You don't look at all well. Why don't we see if we can't get you some help?'

'I don't need any help. I have something to say. Then I'll be leaving.'

I don't wait for his permission to begin. I'm not sure how long I can keep this up. I look around at the assembled faces. I've thought about what I need to say to convince them. I've decided to just lay it out like Marv did with me. Except I don't think I'll use the bit about the frog. That would just lead to too many questions, and there's no time for me to explain. I take a deep breath and begin.

'Marv's dead. He told me something before he died, and now you all need to hear it.' I pause, taking a moment to look around at their faces. I was hoping for more of a reaction. There are a few downward glances, and I see Jake close his eyes, but mostly the news of Marv's death is being processed, accepted. I guess most of them hardly knew him. Marv kept pretty much to himself out in the old diesel plant; some of them won't have seen him for years.

'It isn't right, what's happening here. We shouldn't be letting anyone tell us who we have to be with. That's something we should decide for ourselves, later, when we're ready.'

I hear my voice shaking, the words that come out threatening to falter.

But there are a few murmurs that sound like agreement. Then Kane speaks, silencing them. His tone is still kind, but overly patient, like he's being forced to repeat something that's already been explained countless times before.

'Now son, I understand how difficult this is, but we've been through it all before. We don't have time to wait until you're all old enough to settle on the right choices.'

I hold his gaze for a long moment. Now that the word's about to come out of my mouth I can't believe none of us thought to ask it before.

I raise my voice and ask him why.

*

KANE STARES AT ME, like maybe he hasn't heard what I just said.

'Why what, son?'

'Why isn't there time?'

'Because it's God's will. It's all there in the Bible, right there at the start. The very first book of Genesis. "And God blessed them, and said to them: Be fruitful, and multiply, and replenish the earth, and subdue it: and have dominion over the fish of the sea, and over the fowl of the air, and over every living thing that moves on the earth."'

I see nods of recognition from the assembled faces, murmurs of agreement. They've heard this so many times before. It's familiar, and maybe that familiarity is enough to provide comfort. And the voice that delivers the message is rich, smooth, reassuring. I'm not getting through to them.

'But there are no fish in the sea. There's no birds in the air. There's *nothing* out there. We're probably the last things left alive on this whole frozen planet. So what's the rush? Why can't we wait to choose for ourselves? If God wants things done quicker then why doesn't he just cut us some slack and push the defrost button on his big heavenly microwave?'

There's a collective intake of breath from the Juvies at this heresy. But for the first time Kane doesn't seem to have an answer. The smile stays fixed on his face, but an exasperated sigh escapes his lips and I notice his eyes narrow a fraction.

'Listen, son we can all see you're not well. You probably don't know what you're saying. We all hoped the virus had been destroyed, nobody more so than me. But it was always possible it might still be out there, somewhere, waiting for someone to stumble across it. Well, it looks like you found it. Now I'm sorry to hear about Marvin, but it's not too late for you. We can put you in the scanner and fix this.'

'Marv's dead because you had Peck put the virus in his mask before we went out. You had him put the virus in my mask too.' I hold up the respirator I've brought in with me, showing everyone the job Jack's magic solution has done on the retaining rings. 'Only I never brought mine with me. It stayed here, right outside Eden, the whole time. Whatever killed Marv came from in here.'

There's a series of gasps from Juvies. In spite of what Kane had done to defeat it, there was always a lingering fear that somewhere out there the virus might somehow have survived. But at least in Eden they had believed they were safe.

'Well that's just nonsense, son, and now you're scaring everyone. Nobody knows where the virus came from. But you should know better than anyone the precautions we take to make sure that evil stays out of here.'

I hold my arm up further, allowing the strap of the respirator to shuffle back along my forearm so it's resting in the crook of my elbow. Then I slip my hand into the parka's side pocket. The vials of Ketalar I picked up from the infirmary clink together as my fingers closed around them. I pull my hand out and hold it, palm up, for him to see. Kane just looks at me, a slightly puzzled smile on his face.

'Why, what you got there, son?'

'Why don't you come and have a look?'

He hesitates. He doesn't want to come closer, but he can't appear afraid. His dominion over us has always depended on keeping us in fear, on him remaining calm, assured.

He steps down off the altar. From behind me I hear Peck calling out to him to stay back, but Kane holds a hand up to silence him. I feel the sweat prickling my shoulder blades. I don't need to turn around to know Peck's finger will have tightened around the trigger of the gun he has pointed there.

Kane steps into the aisle. The same wide smile is fixed on his face, but his eyes betray his nervousness. It's me he's afraid of though, the infection he thinks I carry, not what I have in my hand. His faith in the armory to protect his secret remains; he hasn't yet considered the possibility that I've found a way in. He takes a few steps towards me, then he stops and makes a show of searching in the inside pocket of his suit for his reading glasses. That's fine; close enough. I give him a wan smile, showing what I hope are a row of blood-stained teeth, and cough into the back of my other hand for added effect. Kane flinches but it's barely noticeable. To his credit, he stands his ground.

'You'll excuse me if I don't come closer, son. You look like ten miles of bad road.'

I bend down and roll the vials along the aisle towards him. The glass ampules clink and clack over the riveted metal. One of them comes to a halt a few feet from where he's standing. He leans in for a closer look, but doesn't make any move to pick it up. The vials of Ketalar are a slightly different shape, but the liquid inside's the same color, or at least close enough not to be able to tell in the chapel's dim light. I've switched the labels for the ones I peeled off the ampules I found in the armory. I'm hoping that's all Kane will focus on, but I realize I'm holding my breath as he bends down to examine it.

He narrows his eyes to read what's written on the small label. It takes him a couple of seconds, followed perhaps by an instant of disbelief. And then the realization hits and he steps back quickly, like a man who's just found out he's walked barefoot into a nest of vipers. He recovers quickly though, and when he speaks again he's forced the smile back on his face.

'I don't know what you got there, son, but it isn't the virus.'

My heart sinks. Whatever scenarios I had thought through, back in the farmhouse, and later, up on the roof of the mess, whatever game plan I had for how this would play out, we've strayed well outside those boundaries now. Kane knows the Juvies can't read. There's no way they'll be able to tell what's in any of the vials. I look over at Mags. She's the only one. But if I ask her to read out what's written on one of those labels I'll have given away her secret too, and there's still no guarantee the Juvies would take her word over Kane's. I look around at the assembled faces. If I can't find a way to make them believe me I'll have failed; Marv and Benjamin will have died for nothing. I think of Marv, unslinging the rifle from his shoulder as he knelt in the snow by the turnoff for the Blue Ridge Mountain Road. Of Benjamin, lying on the floor of the operating theater out in Ely, Peck standing over him with the pistol, the blood growing sticky with the cold as it crept between the lugs of his boots.

And just like that it hits me, what I need to do.

I take a step forward and place the toe of my boot on the nearest vial, feeling it squeeze up into the rubber sole.

'If it's not the virus you won't mind if I do this.'

Kane's unable to tear his eyes away, but he doesn't say anything. I press down harder. He hesitates for a fraction of a second longer then throws both arms up and takes a half-step towards me.

'Wait! Alright, stop! Stop! For Chrissakes take your foot off that goddam thing before you kill us all.'

I look around. I think it was the shock of hearing Kane's profanity as much as his admission, but whatever the reason everyone's looking at him now, not me. And I think they're finally starting to see. I'm not sure it's enough, though. I'd like to think whatever faith they had in him has been holed below the waterline, but even if it has, the truth of this is so big it'll take a while for it to sink in. And that's time I don't have. I leave my boot where it is, and turn to face the Juvies.

'These glass tubes hold the virus, the one that destroyed everything. There's shelves full of them, right here, in Eden, in the armory. Kane made us think that he saved us from it, that he was protecting us. But the virus was his doing, all along.' I turn back to face him. 'I want you to tell us why you did it.'

'You want to watch that mouth of yours, son, or I'll trim your tail feathers for you. I'm the President of the United States. I don't take my orders from you.'

I press down on the vial. The glass squeals as it grates against the metal.

Kane looks down at my boot, then back up into my face. He shoots me a look, an expression of such fierce, glassy anger that for a second my blood runs cold. When he speaks again the tone is no longer deep and rich. It's harsh, brittle.

'Yes, I did it, God damn you. It was the Lord's will. He spoke to me, told me how it had to be. We had strayed too far from His path. The world needed to be cleansed, to be purged of evil, so it could begin again.' He raises one hand, his finger sweeping the small congregation. 'You should all be grateful. I didn't have to pick you. I could have chosen another group of little brats to save.'

Of course. It hadn't occurred to me until that very moment, but Kane had to have known we would be at the White House on the Last Day. Which meant he had to know what would happen that morning; he had to have known it months before.

No, not just that.

'The strikes; you planned them. All so that you could take us with you to Eden, make us believe you had saved us. It was you who killed our families.'

Kane's mouth opens to answer me, then closes again. I leave my boot where it is for a moment longer before slowly lifting it off. I turn to address the twenty-eight young faces that have been watching the drama unfold from the pews.

'We don't have to stay here. There's another place; Benjamin left a map to show us the way. He wanted to take us there himself, but when Kane found out he had Peck kill him.'

Kane looks up at the mention of Benjamin's name. He's struggling to regain his composure, but when he speaks again his voice is still angry.

'Benjamin was a sodomite! An unbeliever! There is nowhere else.'

'That's not true. You all knew Benjamin. He was kind and smart. And the place he found for us, it exists; it's called Mount Weather. I've been there, just a few days ago. It's like Eden, only bigger, and the stores are full, like when we first arrived. I'm leaving for it, right now. Any of you who want to join me are welcome.'

This is the moment. I look around me, trying to read their faces, but all I see is indecision, fear. They've just had a taste of what Kane really is; they've caught a whiff of the brimstone. But all they know is Eden. They haven't been outside in over a decade, not since the world changed, became the thing they've been taught to fear more than anything.

Kane sees it. When he speaks again a semblance of the former calm has returned to his voice. And now it's no longer me he's addressing, but the Juvies.

'Winter's already here. The storms have arrived. And Gabriel's sick. If you follow him out there you'll all die.'

'That's not true. I can get us there. We'll be fine. It'll only take us three, maybe four days. There's places we can stop along the way to shelter. I have warm clothes for everyone, and there's food for the journey.'

I'm desperate for them to believe me. My eyes move over the faces, offering what I hope is a reassuring smile. Until I remember my bloodstained teeth and stop. But one by one the Juvies look down, or away. I search out Mags' face; the Mags I know is never unsure or hesitant. I hold out my hand, beckoning her forward; if I can just get her some of the others might follow. But now that the moment has arrived, I see the same fear in her face that I recognize in the others. She stares at my outstretched hand for a long time before she too drops her gaze.

That's it then. Mags was always the bravest of us; if I can't convince her there's no hope. Kane smiles down at me from the altar. He knows he's won. There's nothing for me to do but leave and try to get as far from Eden as I can before he sends Peck for me.

I turn around and start walking for the chapel door.

*

MY HAND'S ALREADY on the latch. Behind me I hear a single boot ring out on the metal floor and when I look back over my shoulder I see Mags standing in the aisle. She's there by herself for a long moment and then Jake steps out of his pew and stands behind her. It doesn't even bother me that he's resting a hand on her shoulder.

Jake's the turning point. One by one the other Juvies from the farms join him. First Lucy, then Alice, followed by Beth, then Stephanie, Lauren, Jen and Beverley. From the other side of the aisle Carl and Simon join them. There's a loud thud as Leonard trips over the end of the pew and almost falls, but Jake catches him. One by one the others follow until soon all that's left are the Guardians and Peck. Tyler hesitates for a second and then separates himself from the other black overalls.

'Is that offer open to us as well?'

I nod. He steps out into the aisle and a moment later Eric follows him. Out of the corner of my eye I see Kurt nodding, almost imperceptibly, and then he joins the group at the back, beckoning to Angus and Hamish to follow him. The other Guardians stay where they are. I'm not pleased by this, and looking around at the faces crowded into the aisle I can see I'm not the only one. But I can't exclude them. I figure there's enough of us to handle the three of them if they cause any trouble.

I walk out of the chapel into the harsh glare of the cavern's arc lights. I toss the respirator away. The Juvies form up around me on Back Street. I close the door to the chapel and turn the latch, hearing the lock thunk into place, then drag the plastic chair I took from the mess over and wedge it under the handle. It won't hold them for long, but all I need is a few minutes. Just enough time to get us through the tunnel.

I look up. Everyone's staring at me. They all look frightened, unsure of what to do next. I tell Mags to run to the power plant to see if she can convince Scudder to come with us; we could use him to get Mount Weather up and running. I warn her not to delay. If he doesn't say yes immediately she's to come straight back without him; I'll be waiting for her in the locker room. Then I lead the rest of the Juvies up towards the mess. As we reach Front Street I realize there's one more thing I need to do, so I tell everyone to grab a flashlight and some gloves and head out into the tunnel. Mags and I will catch up with them long before they reach the portal, but I grab Jake and give him the directions he needs for the junction and the horseshoe anyway. As soon as I see them making their way through I turn and run down Front Street, towards the eastern tunnels. Once I reach the farms it takes me only a moment to transfer a tray of seed potatoes from the chitting shelves into one of the empty hessian sacks that's sitting nearby and then I'm sprinting back through the tunnels towards the main cavern. By now Mags will be waiting for me. But when I get to the locker room she isn't there. When I step back out into the main cavern to look for her I understand why.

Kurt's standing in the middle of Front Street, a gun in his hand. Peck must have slipped it to him as we left the chapel. There's a triumphant look on his face.

'You didn't really think I'd want to join you, did you Gabriel?'

I see Kane and Peck and the rest of the Guardians making their way up from the chapel behind Angus. I risk a quick glance upwards. The plastic case containing the vials of the real virus is still suspended in mid-air, rotating lazily under the vent shaft. Nobody's noticed it yet.

Peck comes up behind Kurt and slips his hand over the gun. There's a second's hesitation, like Kurt doesn't want to relinquish this new power he has, then he lets Peck take the gun and steps back. If Peck has any sense he'll pay attention and see that for what it is, a taste of what lies ahead. But the moment was fleeting, so brief I suspect he may not have noticed, and to tell the truth I'm slightly relieved the gun's back under his control. I slip my left hand into the side pocket of the parka, closing my fingers around the last item there.

Kane turns to Kurt. 'Where're the rest of them?'

'They went out in the tunnel, Mr. President. All except Mags. She went off to the power plant. Hamish has gone to get her.'

'Alright. Well done, Kurt.'

Kurt's grin spreads even wider.

'Do you want me to go out and get them?'

Kane considers for a moment.

'No, there's no rush. We'll get to that when we're good and ready. They don't know where they're going, and even if they did they'd never venture outside without this buck here to lead them. We'll just let them shiver out there in the tunnel awhile until we're ready to bring them back in.'

He turns back to me.

'So what was your plan from here, son? You're not in the tall cotton anymore. That's concrete beneath your feet now. Randall here could drop you and you'd just die twitchin', causing no harm to no one. We'd just cover you with a rubber sheet and drag you outside.'

There's a commotion off to the right and I see Hamish appearing out of the pedestrian tunnel. As he steps into the light I see he's grabbed a handful of Mags' Mohawk. His fingers are twisted tight into her hair; he's practically dragging her along behind. It hasn't all gone his way, though; there's blood flowing freely from his nose.

Kane turns around and lets out a short, humorless laugh. While everyone's focused on Hamish and Mags I slide the jar out of my pocket and slip it behind my back.

'She's a wild one, isn't she? Look what she's done to that big bear.' He turns back to Kurt. 'You sure you want that one, son? It's not too late to pick you out another.'

Kurt just smiles at me with that wolfish grin, like we're back on the school bus.

'No, sir. She'll do fine. I believe I can teach her manners.'

'Well, alright. Rather you than me.' He turns back to me. 'What's the matter, cat got your tongue? I always thought you were the smart one, but maybe not so much. I can't see you figuring your way out of this.'

I take a step towards him. The chain's still wrapped through my fingers; the crucifix clinks against the glass as I lift the jar up for him to see. Peck barks an order at me to step away, but I ignore him. He's left it too late. The time to shoot me has come and gone.

Kane looks at the mason jar in my outstretched hand. Inside is a drab metal orb with a single thin yellow band all the way around the top, the words 'HAND, FRAG, DELAY, M67' stenciled around the center. It's from the crate I found under the floorboards in the hallway outside Marv's room. It wasn't just clothes and boots Marv had been stashing for this day.

I hold it up, so Peck understands. I pulled the pin before I slid the grenade into the mason jar on the roof this morning. The only thing holding the safety lever in place now is the glass. If he shoots me I'll drop the jar and it'll shatter.

*

KANE TRIES TO TAKE a step backwards but I follow him. The instructions that were printed on the side of the crate said the effective radius was fifty feet. Out of the corner of my eye I see Hamish has found just enough sense to stop; Mags isn't in range. Everyone else – Kane, Peck, Kurt, Angus, me – will go down and not get back up again. I call over to Hamish to let Mags go but Peck shouts over and tells him to bring her closer instead. In the end Hamish does neither; he just stays where he is, his fingers still twisted through her hair.

Peck hasn't taken his eyes off the mason jar.

'There's a five second delay on that grenade. That's a long time if you keep calm. What makes you think I can't just shoot you, grab the grenade and toss it far enough away so that it doesn't hurt anyone?'

I shake the jar gently. Rattling around inside are the broken pieces of a glass vial. The pale liquid that was inside the vial is now swirling around in the bottom of the jar, spattered around the bottom half of the grenade. It's ketamine, of course, the same as the vials I showed Kane in the chapel. But Peck doesn't know that.

'Look around you, Randall. Doesn't matter where you throw it, the shrapnel will still hit metal somewhere. And those fragments are now contaminated. As will you be, as soon as you touch that grenade. Kane might let you into the scanner. Marv wasn't so sure about that, when his time came. It's made of metal too you know.'

I hold Peck's gaze for a long time. I can see him working it through, just as I did, two nights ago, sitting in the kitchen in the farmhouse, pretending it had come to this and I was in his shoes. As long as he believes I have the virus the smart thing is to let us go. Right now, in here, I have an advantage. Once we're outside that's gone and he can deal with us at his leisure, like he did with Benjamin.

Peck reaches a decision. He doesn't lower the gun, just flicks it in the direction of the blast door. He calls over to Hamish to let Mags go as well.

Hamish releases his grip on Mags' mohawk. She turns and kicks him as hard as she can; I can hear her boot connect with his shin all the way over here. Hamish howls and reaches out to grab her, but she's already ducked out of reach.

I wait until she's left the cavern and then follow her out to the blast door. When I catch up with her she's already pulled on a pair of gloves and has picked up a flashlight. I pull the *Standard Oil* map Marv gave me from the breast pocket of the parka and hand it to her, together with the sack I took from the farms. The map has all the information Benjamin intercepted on it, the access codes to all of the underground facilities on the Federal Relocation Arc, to every place like Eden that might still be holding survivors. There's also a list of instructions for what she needs to do at the portal. I tell her to wait until she gets outside to read it.

I grab her hand as she steps towards the blast door.

'One more thing. As soon as you get everyone outside take Jake and head up the mountain towards the transmitter tower. You'll find the vent shaft I came down the other night about two-thirds of the way up. The rope will still be there. There's a case attached to the other end. Pull it up, but carefully. Inside is Kane's virus.'

She shoots me an uncertain look.

'Aren't you coming with me?'

'Sure. I'll be right after you. Someone has to stay to close the door, though.'

She looks at me suspiciously. 'Promise?'

'You think I want to stay in here with Kurt and Angus and Hamish?'

She laughs, but I can see her eyes starting to brim. A single tear dislodges and slides down her face, lingering on her chin. She reaches up and pulls me down to her. For the second time in my short life I get kissed by a girl, and not just any girl. This girl. In spite of what is to come, for a moment it fills me with a happiness so complete it's stupefying.

'Careful, you don't want to smudge my makeup.'

She smiles.

'I'll be waiting at the portal. You hurry.'

I don't know what to say, so I just nod. She slips out through the blast door into the darkness and is gone.

Then I start the count, as it turns out for the last time. Only it's not for me this time, it's for Mags.

*

KANE APPEARS at the other end of the corridor, all by himself. I don't have to think too hard to work out where Peck and the Guardians have gone.

He looks at me for a long time. When he speaks it's like he's regained something of his former composure. The honeyed Southern accent is back, smooth and rich and deep, but there's a wildness around his eyes that wasn't there before, and I'm guessing won't be leaving anytime soon.

'Nothing's changed, you know. Everything I said a few minutes ago, it all still holds. You'll never make it out. And without you to lead them no one's going to set foot outside that tunnel. I'll have them all back in here within the hour, bleating for forgiveness, for things to go back to the way they were. But that can't happen now.' He pauses, like he wants me to consider what he's just said. 'You realize that, don't you; what you've done? You've just made their lives a hell of a lot more difficult than they ever needed to be. As long as they trusted me to protect them keeping them in line was easy. Now that's gone I'll need to give them something to really be afraid of. Not just some stories about the outside and a scary film to watch every once in a while.'

I try and keep the surprise from registering on my face; I don't want to give Kane the satisfaction. I guess it doesn't work.

'Oh, did you think it was just chance that the only film you could ever find in here was one about bogeymen roaming around a frozen wilderness? Come on, son, I had you pegged for smarter than that.'

'You're wrong. They'll make it. They're stronger than you think.'

'Perhaps one or two of them might be. I can see I'll have to deal with that girl right off. We can't have someone else popping up to lead the sheep once you've been taken care of. Kurt won't be pleased of course; he really has a thing for her. But I reckon he'll be alright with it as long as I let him be the one to do it.'

Another expression must pass across my face then. Kane smiles at me from the other end of the corridor.

'Now, don't tell me you're sweet on her too. My, but that girl is popular. Can't say I see it myself.'

There's something in the way he says it that makes me think of Peck carrying Lena back from confession that night, and how she had always thought the Kool-Aid Kane gave her tasted funny. I'd always watched for signs that Kane was becoming addicted to the pills I brought back for him. But of course I needn't have worried. He'd never wanted them for himself.

Peck appears at his side before I have a chance to say anything else. Kane's final instruction is simple; he doesn't even look at me as he delivers it, he just points down the passageway.

'Randall, don't fail me again. I don't want him to make it out of the tunnel.'

He turns and walks back into the main cavern. The Guardians crowd into the corridor a moment later. They're each holding rifles, the newly oiled metal gleaming dully under the corridor's lights. I guess my hatchet job on the keypad didn't keep them out after all.

Kurt pushes his way to the front, Angus and Hamish following closely behind. He's wearing his usual grin, but now he looks as restless as a hyena. Angus and Hamish just seem eager to use the new toys they've been given; their dimpled fingers keep sliding in and out of the trigger guards, as if they can't wait for it to begin. Behind them some of the other Guardians look a little less easy, but I've no doubt when it comes down to it they'll do as they're told. I hold the mason jar up, a reminder of why we're all here. The corridor's metal, as is the blast door. They keep their distance.

I've slowed the count inside my head to account for the fact that Jake's leading a large group and they'll be scared, but it's already at five hundred. They should be approaching the first junction. Mags will still be in the straight section but she's fast; she'll catch them quickly.

I nod at Kurt, giving bravado my best shot.

'So Kurt, who do you think you'll be matched with, now that everyone else is gone? Angus or Hamish?'

I hear a snicker from somewhere back in the corridor, quickly cut short as Kurt turns around to glare at whoever was laughing. Peck offers me a tight smile, like he already knows the outcome and he's bored with this already. Kurt looks back at me. He makes a show of aiming his rifle at my chest.

'You any idea how to use that thing?'

This time Kurt just smiles, like the wolf anticipating the lamb. It's Peck who answers.

'Oh, it's not that hard, Gabriel. They don't even need to shoot straight. We've all the ammo we need, and with a nine-man line in a tunnel that size I doubt we'll even need to change clips before we bring you down. I wouldn't be in any rush to step out there if I were you. Tell you what though, put the jar down and I'll have them finish you quick. That's the best deal you're going to get today.'

After that I keep quiet and count. When I reach three hundred and fifty I picture Jake at the horseshoe, herding the Juvies left. Mags will be right on their heels, if she hasn't caught them already. If I were to leave now I might catch them just as they get to the portal. It's tempting, and for a moment I consider it.

But Peck's right. I know that tunnel better than any of them. Five hundred and ten paces to the first curve, and for that distance I'll have nowhere to hide from the hail of bullets they'll send after me. There's no way I'm going to make it. If I leave now then the Guardians will be on the Juvies before the three minutes the instructions on the map ask Mags to wait are up.

I keep counting.

Time's up.

I don't want to step out into the tunnel. I picture myself a few minutes from now, bleeding out on the cold concrete as Peck stands over me and aims his pistol, just like he stood over Benjamin.

But I can't stay here. Before I have time to think about it I push the button to commence the close sequence. The electric motors kick in, whining under the load as they slowly start to pull the four tons of carbon steel back out of the tunnel. Kurt takes an involuntary step forward, eager for the hunt to begin, but Peck places a hand on his chest, holding him back. I count the seconds. It takes thirty. Always thirty.

I lift the crucifix over my head, the cold weight of the chain around my neck familiar. My heart's beating fast, but the beats are regular. There's the usual knot of fear in my stomach, but something's different. I suddenly realize I'm about to step into the tunnel and Claus is silent. Now that I think about it I haven't heard from him since I came down the vent shaft. I'm afraid, more afraid than I think I've ever been, but not of the tunnel, or of the darkness. I just don't want to die in there.

The blast door's almost closed; it's time for me to go. I shuck off the parka; I'll be faster without it. The cold air from the tunnel bites immediately, but soon I won't feel it.

*

THE BLAST DOOR'S closing fast. At the last second I step through and bend down to roll the mason jar along the corridor behind me. Peck's kept the Guardians far enough back to be out of danger, but I'm hoping it'll buy me another second or two. I hear the clatter of machine gun fire and the whine of bullets ricocheting off metal behind me. Then I'm off into the darkness as the last of the light from inside Eden leaves the tunnel.

The fear's twisting and turning inside me, all big and panicky. It wants me to bolt, to run, and now I let it. My legs are strong; years of trudging through drifted snow have made me fit. I can run faster and longer than any of the Guardians. But not their bullets.

The flashlight is already on and the light bounces off the tunnel walls, cutting through the darkness in wild arcs as my arms pump, propelling me forward. The shadows cast by the brace wire jerk this way and that, almost making it seem like the tunnel is vibrating as I race down it. Behind me I hear the blast door close with a final clang. There's one last burst from the electric motors as they slide the bolts into place and then fall silent.

Even now Peck will be hitting the button to recommence the sequence, and in a few seconds the motors will start up again, re-opening the blast door. I reckon I have at best thirty, maybe thirty-five seconds before Peck or one of the Guardians steps into the tunnel and starts firing. Less if they think to recess the bolts manually. If they do that then Angus and Hamish will probably have the door open again in half that time.

I pick up the *splat-splat-splat* of dripping water, the sound drifting towards me out of the darkness. I know the first puddles are at eight hundred and seventy, and the tunnel stays straight for another three hundred paces beyond. Moments later my boots splash through the meltwater that's trickled down through the blast valves from the surface.

Suddenly I hear shouts behind me, and then the first rattle of gunfire echoes down the tunnel. I toss the flashlight as far as I can, hoping it'll give them a target to aim for. It skitters across the concrete and bounces up onto the elevated walkway, illuminating the greenstone granite there.

I leave the double yellow lines that run down the middle of the tunnel and make for the opposite side of the road, charging headlong into the darkness. I hold out my hand, letting my fingertips bounce over the brace wire, tracing the contours made by the rock beneath, my guide in the inky blackness. I don't let myself think what will happen if I fall here, like I did in Mount Weather.

The tunnel's alive with the sound of gunfire now. I make the mistake of glancing back over my shoulder. The muzzle flashes leave pinwheels and starbursts swirling and exploding across my vision, but not before I see the skirmish line Peck has organized. I imagine Kurt marching forward through gunsmoke, the recoil slamming the butt of the gun into his shoulder over and over. He won't be able to see me but it won't matter. All he needs to know is that I'm ahead of him somewhere in the darkness. His finger will hold the trigger down until the gun jams or he needs to reload.

Bullets are whipping through the air all around me now, as the Guardians find their range. Rounds slam into the walls and hit the roof, in front as well as behind. I feel a disturbance in the air as something whirrs past my ear. A bright sound rings out in the darkness to my left, like a hammer hitting rock, and something sharp slices my cheek. I feel blood start to trickle down my face.

Fear spurs me on, forcing my arms and legs to pump faster, and for a dozen paces I pick up speed. But I'm chewing through whatever reserves I have left. I can pound snow for hours on end, but I'm not used to sprinting. My lungs are pumping like bellows, my throat burning with each breath.

My fingers lose the left wall. At first I think I've just stumbled off course, and I stagger back towards it, skinning my thumb as I find the granite again. But then the wall disappears for the second time, and suddenly it occurs to me that the tunnel is finally starting to curve around. I know this happens at five hundred and forty. I'm less than half way to the portal, but now at least the tunnel walls will offer me some protection. I force myself to remember the count. There's a junction eighty-five paces further on, the halfway point, the darkest part. The tunnel's straight again for another hundred and fifteen paces to the right and then it hits the outer tunnels that lead to the portal. I'd already passed the first blast vent when the Guardians entered the tunnel, which means I was over two hundred paces ahead of them. If they're maintaining a line in the tunnel they'll have to move at the pace of the slowest. The distance can't have shrunk. All I have to do now is hold it and I might be okay.

And then something tugs hard at my leg, spinning me around on an impossibly complicated axis. The tunnel floor comes crashing up to meet me and my temple hits something cold, hard, unyielding. My head bounces once and then comes to rest.

*

IN THE DARKNESS it's hard to tell whether I've passed out, and if so, for how long. Without the flashlight the blackness is so complete it threatens to enfold and smother me. I feel like I should spit, to figure out which way is up, but something tells me that's wrong, for something else entirely. So I just lay there, dazed. An unknowable amount of time passes. At least there's no pain. It actually feels good not to be running, although a voice inside my head that I think I call spidey but maybe it's Claus because it's Claus who speaks to me in the tunnel is telling me I should. I'm aware of something warm running down my leg inside my pants. I remember the fury in the tunnel at Mount Weather. An image of the pee bottle, sitting on the roof of the mess building, flashes into my head, followed by a flush of shame. But I don't think it's that. It takes another indeterminate amount of time for me to realize I've been shot.

Sounds return slowly, chaotic bursts of machine gun fire from somewhere off in the darkness. Rounds zip and whine through the air above, striking the walls of the tunnels like hail on a tin roof, occasionally close enough to sting me with shards of granite. I'm having a hard time working out which direction the bullets are coming from. I can't see muzzle flashes. I must have made it around the curve of the tunnel.

I shake my head in a desperate attempt to clear it. I need to get out of here. But for the first time I'm not sure where in the tunnel I am; I only know I need to get away from the clatter of gunfire. I try to stand but a shear of pain shoots up my leg as soon as I move it. I cry out into the darkness and collapse back to the hard ground. The flow of blood down my leg increases. My sock is sodden with it; it squelches inside my boot as I draw my leg behind me.

The wall. The wall was on my left side. But the voice I call spidey or maybe Claus is saying no, I can't trust that. I pick myself up by force of will and stand, more slowly this time, reaching out in the darkness, inching towards granite I hope is there. The boot that's carrying my weight hits the high curb of the walkway and I go down again. The sounds of machine gun fire seem a lot closer now.

And then flashlight beams appear around the curve of the tunnel from an unexpected direction and I only have a second to realize I was going the wrong way after all. A light shines in my face, blinding me. I raise my hands, maybe to block it, or perhaps to deflect the inevitable bullet. As if my fragile fingers have that power. I think of Maraschino guy, sitting in the frozen foods aisle at Walmart, still clutching his gourmet cherries, and wonder if that was also his final act.

Strong hands grab me under my armpits, haul me up.

A familiar voice (*Hey, kiddo, want a story?* No, wait, that's not right) asks if I can walk and I nod, even though I'm not sure it's true. Whoever it is doesn't believe me and I'm hoisted over broad shoulders. I smell cotton, and underneath it the dark, rich smell of the farms. We set off at a trot, like my weight is insignificant. I try and count the steps but my head is bouncing, making it difficult. I think I was at the curve of the tunnel when I got shot. From there I know it is eighty-five paces to the junction.

I try and turn my head to see. The curve of the tunnel wall behind us is now just about visible, the outline faintly illuminated by the strobing muzzle flash from the Guardians' rifles. But then we're at the junction and turning right. Jake's still showing no sign of slowing, but I can't see how we'll make it. It's one hundred and fifteen paces to the horseshoe. Except Jake's shorter than me, which means it'll be more. I have no way of knowing exactly how much. It bothers me not to know.

The muzzle flashes re-appear long before we get there. Whoever's carrying the flashlight ahead of us extinguishes it and we're back in darkness again. Jake doesn't speed up or slow down, he just keeps the same pace, as if the bullets whipping through the air around us were no more troublesome than bottle flies meandering past on a summer's day. Back when there were bottle flies, of course. And summer days. It occurs to me at some point that I'm Jake's human shield. But then all things considered it's hard to complain.

By some miracle of the tunnel gods we reach the horseshoe unmolested. Jake takes the left prong, following the curve around. From here it's three hundred and forty of my paces to the exit, but the arc of the tunnel should keep us protected from our pursuers for most of that. Jake allows himself to slow a fraction. The gunfire's a constant, the tunnel walls carrying the sound to us, but it seems to have become more sporadic, as if the Guardians are finally trying to conserve ammunition. Blood's still trickling down my leg from where I've been shot; I can feel it puddling in the toe of my boot. I feel cold. I wonder if that's something I should be worried about. But then I remember I'm in the tunnel without a parka. It would be strange if I didn't feel cold.

The tunnel straightens. It seems to get a little lighter. We're close now; I think I can feel a breeze. I hear voices in the distance. Jake finally pulls to a halt next to the rubble where the west portal's collapsed and sets me down as gently as he can on the table next to the scanner. A host of concerned faces appear above me, but I wave them away. There's no time.

I get Jake to help me off the table. My head swims for a second as I stand upright. My vision grays and a wave of nausea hits me. I think I'm going to throw up, but then it passes. I grab Mags and tell her to start leading everyone up the rubble towards the exit. I can see the fear in their faces and later I think some might have stayed then, but for the sound of gunfire from the tunnel, getting closer with each moment, herding them out.

Mags goes first and one by one the rest of the Juvies follow her until there's only me and Jake left. I tell him he'll need to go ahead of me, that way if I can't make it by myself he can pull me out. He hesitates for a moment, then he launches himself up the pile of rocks.

I follow him up, hobbling up the rubble. As usual I have to wriggle between loose rock and the roof of the tunnel for the last twenty yards. It's slow going; I have to grit my teeth to stop from crying out as I drag my injured leg over a rock that juts proud of the rest. By the time I reach the snow that's drifted in from the last storm eager hands are reaching into the tunnel to grab me, and I'm manhandled the last few yards towards the exit.

Jake pulls me upright and I lean on him to stand. The sun's been up for a few hours, but it's a shallow light that coats the lifeless hills. I look around at the motley horde I've delivered from Eden, refugees shivering inside their thin polyester overalls, as far as I know most of what remains of all humanity. They're huddled together on the side of the snow-swept mountain, squinting up into an alien sky. I understand what they're seeing. After a decade inside the mountain the sky overhead must appear boundless; a roiling gray dome of almost incomprehensible size.

There's no time to lose. I call Mags over and tell her to get everyone down the slope. I point her to the line of gnarled stumps that used to form the tree line. They'll find garbage bags filled with parkas buried in the snow nearby. I don't wait to see if they've headed in the right direction; for now anywhere away from here will do. The crackle of automatic fire from inside the tunnel is getting louder; the Guardians are already in the last section of the horseshoe. I turn around and start digging in the snow just above the crown of the portal. My fingers are already starting to turn numb when they brush the crate that was hidden under the floorboards outside Marv's room. I scoop the snow away from it and lift the lid. Inside are seven more orbs like the one I brought into Eden with me.

I explain to Jake what we need to do. We divide the grenades between us and he scrambles over to the other side of the portal. I can already hear bullets ricocheting off the rubble as the Guardians fire indiscriminately up towards the exit. With fingers trembling from the cold I pull the pin on the first grenade and toss it into the darkness. On the other side of the portal Jake does the same. One by one the rest of the grenades follow; Jake's already running off down the mountain as I send the last one in. I hobble down the slope after him as quickly as I can, ignoring the pain from my leg as I try to put as much space as I can between me and the opening before the first one explodes.

Five seconds; Peck said it was a long time.

It's not.

The grenades detonate in a series of barking concussions. The first grabs me like a fist. I feel the heat of it on my back and then it squeezes, forcing the air from my lungs, spinning me around and tossing me down the mountain. I have a second to glimpse a gout of orange flame erupting from the portal, like fire belched from a dragon's mouth, as I sail backwards through the air. Then the crown of the tunnel blows out and I land flat on my back, chunks of smoldering debris raining from the sky to hiss in the snow all around me.

## EPILOGUE

IT TOOK US A LOT LONGER than I had planned to make it to Mount Weather, even taking the shorter route that Benjamin had marked on the map.

We spent the first night camped out at the farmhouse. It seemed strange to be so close to the place we had escaped from, but Mags checked the tunnel and said the blast had sealed it up; nobody would be coming out anytime soon. She took Jake and Tyler and they went up to find the vent shaft and recover the case containing the virus. Jake found Lena's body on the way back down, huddled up inside her parka not far from the portal. I guess even after Kane had banished her she'd been too frightened to stray far from Eden. Jake buried her in the snow just beyond the tree line.

The bullet tore a ragged gash along the outside of my thigh, but the wound wasn't deep and nothing was broken. Mags bandaged it up tight, but even so I wasn't fit to walk any distance. When we set off the following morning I still wasn't good for more than an hour's hike at a time, even with Jake to help me. We spent our third night on the road in Ely, all huddled together around the fire in the lobby of the hotel where Marv and I had stopped less than two weeks before. The next morning as we made our way out of town I left the highway and hobbled down the embankment to the clinic where I had found Benjamin. He was still there, lying on the floor behind the operating table. I cleaned the ring I had taken from him so that you could see the white eagle and read the inscription on the banner underneath. Then I placed it back on his finger. I think Marv would've liked that.

A storm appeared behind us on the horizon that afternoon, just as we were scrambling around the overpass where our route south out of Ely ran into I-70. Within an hour the sky to the north had become a churning soup of thunderheads; we were lucky to make it into Boonsboro before it hit. We huddled for shelter in the lobby of the Susquehanna Bank, with nothing to do but sit and watch the world outside appear again and again out of a darkness rent by lightning. The Juvies were all pretty frightened; none of them had seen a storm in all the time we'd been in Eden. They started inside their parkas with every shuddering flash and recoiled inside the cowl of their hoods with each crash of thunder that followed. Two days later it passed, as storms always do, and we hit the road again, following it south as it raged ahead of us.

The weather stayed clear after that. We hit the Blue Ridge Mountain Road on the morning of the tenth day after our escape from Eden.

We're settling in well, all things considered. There's plenty of food in the stores but Jake's already taken over one of the far tunnels. It took him less than a week to build the first growing bench and now there are several rows of them. Everyone's getting involved, even me. Jake reckons we'll harvest our first crop next month.

It took Mags a couple of days to get the power up. She's been studying the tech manuals, but she says getting the reactor restarted's most likely beyond her. Not that it matters. There's enough diesel to last us many years, as long as we're careful.

I don't think we'll be here that long, though. Kane knows where we are, and he's not the type to leave us alone. Besides, he's going to have a hard time repopulating the world with what's left of the Guardians. He won't venture out over the winter, but as soon as the weather breaks he'll send Peck for us, and I doubt he'll come alone. If we're still here by then it'll be time to post a watch.

There are places we can go, however. We have the map Marv gave me, with all the facilities that were part of the Federal Relocation Arc marked on it, and Benjamin's entry codes for each one. There's a whole archipelago of bunkers dug into the mountains or buried deep underground, stretching all the way into North Carolina. Culpeper, Virginia and Greenbrier, West Virginia are the two closest. Come spring I'll head out and try and find them. Mags says she'll come with me.

She insisted on bringing my books from the farmhouse. I don't keep them under the bed anymore; the apartment we chose has a bookshelf. She's read them all and is currently working through a stack she's collected from what was left behind when Mount Weather was evacuated. The Juvies all know to bring her anything they find first; I have to wait until she's done before I get to read any of those. After ten years she says it's only fair.

We're pretty busy during the days but in the evenings I'm helping her teach anyone who wants to learn how to read. It'll take a while, I reckon, and in the meantime movie night's been re-instated. Mount Weather's small theater has a decent collection of films, so we're finally getting to see something new. *30 Days of Night* still gets played a lot, though.

My leg's healed now, so I go out whenever it looks like we'll get a few days' clear weather between the storms. There's no real need; Mount Weather has most everything you could want. It's not about being inside, either. That doesn't bother me anything like it used to, and I haven't heard from Claus since the night I climbed down the vent shaft to get back into Eden. I just like going out; I guess old habits die hard. And there are a few things, like Amy's zit cream, that we haven't been able to find in the stores. I don't ask for trades any more, though.

The first time the weather lifted I hiked the Blue Ridge Mountain Road north as far as the Harry Byrd Highway. I looked for Marv's body but I couldn't find it; by then the storms had covered him up completely. I cut a couple of branches from a stand of spruce-fir that was still clinging to the escarpment and tied them into a cross. I stuck it in the snow where I thought I'd left him and hung the crucifix I brought from Eden on it.

I've been out there a few times since, even though there's not much to scavenge on that stretch of road and what little there was I've had. When I get as far as the highway I sit down in the snow next to the cross and tell Marv how we're getting on. He doesn't respond, but then that was never Marv's speed. Sometimes, if the wind's blowing right I think I can hear him calling me bixicated, just for thinking that he might.

# THE DEVIL YOU KNOW

LIGHTNING SPLITS THE DARKNESS, and for a second I can see.

I grab the last piece of rebar and haul myself over the edge. Beneath me the river has already disappeared; there's just a black chasm into which the snow twists and tumbles. Ahead the storm drives the drifts in long, shifting ridges that snake across the road, clearing everything in their path. I tell myself that's a good thing; soon my tracks will be covered too. But the truth is this is bad, far worse than I had counted on.

I'd like to rest after the climb, but there's no time for that now. I untie the snowshoes from my pack and step into them. It hurts as I ratchet the straps tight. I can no longer tell if it's from the cold or the bindings.

I should never have let them take my boots.

I look down. The plastic I've used to wrap my feet still seems to be holding, but I can see the duct tape starting to fray where the straps have worked against it. That's not good, but there's not much I can do about it. I lift my head and set off into the blizzard.

The wind blows hard, making me fight it for every step. My hood's zipped all the way up but still it finds its way in, squeezing tears from my eyes that freeze on my cheeks, biting at the exposed skin there. I curse it for a bitch, but it pays me no mind. It just snatches the breath from my lungs and gusts even harder.

I hug the parka tighter around me. The cold is raw, relentless. Normally pounding the snow like this would keep it at bay, but somewhere down on the river it's managed to slip inside; I can already feel the chill from my sweat-soaked thermals seeping into my core. My teeth are chattering and I don't seem to be able to stop them. I try to focus on the sound of my breathing behind the thin cotton mask, anything to shut it out. But I can't. Marv used to say the cold was a vicious bitch, that it could mess with your thinking. I need to remember that. I don't reckon it'll be hard. Because the cold is an onslaught. It refuses to be ignored.

Bitch. Bitch. Bitch.

*Bitch.*

I lift a snowshoe up, place it down again. One foot in front of the other, that's the trick. If I just keep doing that I can make it. But the drifts are getting deeper. The crash barriers I was following earlier have already disappeared; all I have left are the mile markers. I use the flashes to search for them, but they're getting harder to find. I need to hurry, before they get covered over too. I can't afford to get lost out here.

I pick up the pace. The snow senses it; it swirls around me, faster now, all I can see in the flashlight's faltering beam. I wind the stubby plastic handle anyway, until I imagine that's somehow what's working my legs and as long as I keep turning it they'll keep rising and falling, like it's the key stuck in the back of some clever clockwork toy. I keep that up for what seems like a long time, but might be less. Then I catch an edge and stumble, landing awkwardly in a drift.

Bitch.

I lay there for a while, getting my breath back. At last I push myself up and kneel in the snow. I'm trembling quite badly, long shuddering spasms that run up and down my spine and rattle my teeth together. I don't think I was down for that long, but when I set off again my legs no longer seem to want to do my bidding. The muscles there have stiffened; they don't want to work, no matter how much I twist the handle. I give up on the flashlight and jam my hands up into my armpits. Maybe it'll warm them a little. But it doesn't seem to make any difference. Inside my mittens my fingers have tightened into claws.

The sky flares again, followed by a deafening crash as the heavens are rent asunder. The storm's on me, the gap between lightning and thunder no more than a heartbeat. In the instant before darkness returns a gap opens, revealing a shotgun shack, set back from the road. I stop, stare at it. The shelter it offers is a gift; Marv would curse me for not taking it. But I can't. I have to get back; Mags can't be another night in there. An image returns, the only one I can summon, one I would burn from my eyes if I could. Forced onto her toes, her feet scrabbling for purchase on the smooth tiles as the noose tightens around her neck. The muscles along Truck's arms bunch as he hoists her up. I hear him grunt with the effort of it, but he holds her there and I would kill him if I could but there's nothing I can do to stop it. I turn my head from the shack and face back to the road. The wind howls and the gray curtain closes around me again and it is gone.

How could I have been so stupid? I had been sure that the world that waited for us outside was empty; that once we escaped all we would need to concern ourselves with was staying out of Kane's way. It hadn't occurred to me that there might be others out here.

Others worse than he was.

I try and put that thought from my mind. It won't help me, and I have other things to concern myself with. I don't even know where they're keeping her; I'll need to figure that out once I get inside. First I have to find the blast door. I try and work out where it might be from what I know of the hallways and corridors above, anything to take my mind off the bone-piercing cold. It should be easy enough, but after a few minutes I give up and return to the simpler business of placing one foot in front of the other. Anything more complicated seems beyond me.

I trudge on, stumbling through the deepening drifts like some lock-limbed Frankenstein's monster. I search the darkness ahead for the next sign. I think it's been a while since I found one, although when I try and remember I'm not entirely sure. I'm beginning to worry I've strayed from the road, but then the sky strobes again, revealing a tractor-trailer that's jack-knifed, its cargo strewn across both lanes. Did I pass it on the way out? I think so, but I can't be sure. I stagger up to it, feeling for its outline so I can make my way around.

I leave the truck behind. I'm moving much more slowly now. My limbs feel like they're seizing. Lifting each snowshoe has become a gargantuan effort, requiring all my powers of concentration. At least my feet no longer hurt. Actually I can't feel them at all. I realize I've stopped shivering. I wonder how long ago that was, but I can't remember. I don't know if it's a good or a bad thing.

Bitch?

Lightning strikes again, somewhere nearby, followed immediately by a crack of thunder, and for a second the world around me is bathed in stark white light. And in that instant I see something ahead, a small corner of metal almost buried under the snow. I stare at it absently. I know what it is, but for some reason it won't come to me.

A mile marker.

That's it.

The markers are important, I know that. I'm just not sure why. Maybe if I make my way over towards it it'll come to me. My frozen fingers reach for the flashlight's handle, getting ready to wind me forward, but there's nothing there. That thought is troubling, but eventually I let it be and focus on lifting one foot, setting it down again. But the sign seems to be further away than I first thought. I'm beginning to wonder if I've missed it when the front of my snowshoe catches something hard, just under the surface. I trip and fall into a thick quilt of gray snow. I lay there for an unknowable amount of time, just listening to the pounding of my heart as it slows. My blood feels like it's thickening in my veins, like when you tap the sump of an engine for oil to mix with gas for the fire.

Fire.

A fire would be nice.

For a while that thought occupies me, but there's another that hovers annoyingly at the edge of my consciousness, refusing to let me be. I can't stay here. There's something I have to do. Something important. I try to push myself up, but my mittens just sink into the powder and it seems like far too much of an effort to extract them. I let my head fall forward again. The snow crunches softly against the hood of my parka and I lay still. Whatever I was worrying about recedes, washed away by a wave of cold exhaustion. If I can just rest here for a little while everything will be okay. The wind howls, pushing the swirling snow over me, slowly covering me up. I feel the last of my body's heat leaching out into the thick, enveloping flakes.

It occurs to me that maybe I should be scared now. But fear is a concept that floats somewhere just beyond my reach, just like the numb hands that lie buried beneath me in the snow. Somebody I once knew called Martin (Marlin? *Marv*in) once told me something important. He said I had to mind the cold because it was vicious.

But Marvin was wrong.

The cold's not really anything at all. It's an emptiness; an absence of things. An absence of heat, of warmth.

An absence of caring.

Bitch.

*Ten days earlier*

*

DAWN'S LITTLE MORE than a faint gray smear on the horizon as I step out of the tunnel. I look through the bars of the half-raised guillotine gate, my eyes searching for the tattered windsock that hangs beside the control tower. It was gusting yesterday, but the wind's eased overnight and now it shifts only occasionally. Heavy thunderheads lumber along the spiny mountain ridge beyond, carrying what I hope will be the last of the big winter storms east. I know what Marv would say: it'd be safer to hold off another week. But I figure anything we get this late in the season should blow itself out in a day or two, and we've already waited long enough.

I look back over my shoulder. The Juvies have gathered to see us off, but I can tell they're already anxious to get back inside. They wait inside the shadow of the tunnel, reluctant to step into the grainy pre-dawn light. Most of them haven't been outside since we arrived.

I've tried to warn them. We're not safe here. As soon as the weather clears Kane will send Peck for us, I know it. They used to listen; when we first arrived it was all any of us could think about. But back then the memories of our escape were still fresh. As the days slipped into weeks and those became months things began to change. Nobody wants to talk about Kane now. I've heard more than one of them say that maybe Peck won't even come.

I should have seen it. Outside the storms might have raged, but inside the mountain life was good. No morning buzzer to jar them from sleep; no endless hours in the chapel; no curfew forcing them back to a cramped cell at night. There isn't even much in the way of chores anymore, least not for those who don't care to do them. Jake had his growing benches up and running within weeks of our arrival, and the truth is we don't need those; anything any of us might want is right there in the stores for the taking. Now I want to bring them away from all that, and all I can offer in return is Marv's map; an uncertain destination and until we find it, the promise of cold and hunger.

So I figure if I'm to have any chance of convincing them to move, first I'll need to find somewhere for us to go. I've already made the hike out to Culpeper, the nearest facility in the Federal Relocation Arc, a network of underground shelters stretching all the way through Pennsylvania, Maryland, Virginia and down into the Carolinas. It was less than sixty miles so I was there and back inside a week, even allowing for a day holed up against the storms on the way out.

The bunker was just where the map said it would be, carved right into the side of the mountain, its squat bulk waiting patiently for me behind a rusting razor wire fence. Silent guard towers watched down as I cut a hole in the chain-link and pushed my way through. Lead-lined shutters covered the narrow, recessed windows, sealing them tight, but Benjamin's code worked just fine on the blast door, just like it had at Mount Weather.

Culpeper was no use to us however; I don't think it had even been designed for people. The ground floor housed nothing but banks of long-dead servers, here and there the occasional computer terminal, all covered in a thick layer of dust. A wide metal ramp led down to a huge subterranean vault. Row after row of pallets, each stacked four or five deep, stretching all the way back into darkness.

I dug out my flashlight and cranked the handle as I made my way between them. Each was packed with shrink-wrapped bales. The blade on the leatherman sliced through the plastic easily, releasing a pristine wedge of green bills, bound tight and stamped with a seal that said Federal Reserve Bank of Richmond. I wandered the aisles, freeing a bundle from each of the bales until I had a collection of presidents and founding fathers from Washington to Franklin that put me in mind of Miss Kimble's civics and government class all those years ago. I saved one of each to show Mags and piled the rest in the middle of the floor. I figured they might do for kindling, but it turns out money doesn't burn so well after all. I left early the following morning, the best part of a week gone and nothing for my efforts but a first grade show and tell.

Most of the Juvies had already been against leaving Mount Weather, but even those that might still have been worried enough about Kane to consider it lost their enthusiasm when they heard what I'd found at Culpeper. Jake asked me what I thought Marv would do and I had to admit I didn't think he'd have led us out without a destination either, so that settled it. Mags and I will head south for Sulfur Springs, the location of The Greenbrier, the next facility on the map. It's all the way down in West Virginia, I reckon a seven-day hike each way, but if it checks out we'll be that much further from Kane, so maybe it's for the best. It means we'll be gone at least a couple of weeks, though; more than enough time for Peck to get here from Eden if Kane has a mind to send him early.

I've told them they need to post sentries while we're gone. I wanted them all the way out on the Blue Ridge Mountain Road, where Marv's buried. That's how we got here from Eden, and it's the route I reckon Peck will choose too, when he comes. It's a good spot; from up there you can see for miles along the highway in either direction. But no one wanted to hike out that far so we finally settled on two-hour shifts in the control tower on top of the ridge. They'll have next to no warning when he shows, but I guess it's better than nothing. Jake's worked out a roster. He says he'll make sure it gets done.

I've already applied UV block back in the apartment so I pull my hood up and slide a pair of ski goggles down over my eyes. As soon as Mags has said the last of her goodbyes we snap on our snowshoes and walk out underneath the gate. Marv's gun weighs down the side pocket of my parka. I almost wasn't going to bring it. It's heavy and besides, the magazine's empty. Mount Weather has an armory just like Eden's, but the door's locked and the only code Marv gave me was for the blast door. I considered heading back up to Fort Narrows to look for some more bullets; I reckon that's where Marv had been getting the stuff he'd been stashing under the floorboards in the farmhouse. But it's the best part of a two-day hike each way, and right now I figure that's time better spent looking for somewhere to move us. Besides, I can't see how I'll need them. Mount Weather and Culpeper were both abandoned, and in all the years I was scavenging I never saw so much as a single print in the snow to suggest there's anyone else waiting for us out there.

I look back over my shoulder one last time, but most of the Juvies are already heading back into the tunnel. Soon only Jake remains, just standing there in the shadow of the portal, watching as we leave. I raise my hand but it takes him a moment to wave back, like it wasn't ever my departure he'd come to see.

We make our way out of the compound. Dotted here and there around the perimeter are the concrete cowls of the airshaft vents that lead deep into the mountain. Mags has figured out how to seal them from the inside, so at least when Peck comes he won't be getting in that way. I guess that should be a comfort, although I can't see why he'd go to that trouble. Kane will send him out with the same code for the blast door that Marv gave me.

The first of the morning light's finally seeping into the sky, like water into an old rag, as we trudge up to the entrance. The gate towers over us, on either side a high chain-link fence stretching off into the distance, its rusting diamonds topped by a half-dozen strands of razor wire. It all looks formidable, but I know it won't hold them long. I find the section I opened with bolt cutters the day I first arrived and pull the wire back for Mags to step through.

*

FOR THE FIRST SIX MILES we follow the road south along the ridge. There hasn't been a fresh fall in a few days and the snow's settled. Good tracking skiff, Marv would have called it. Our path descends gently then flattens, snaking along the spine of the mountain. At some point we cross over and drop down onto the western rim of the valley. There's little to tell where the road is now, but I've hiked this way several times over the winter and I have to stop only occasionally to make sure we're still on the right path.

I break trail while Mags follows in my footsteps, her breath rolling from her in short frosted puffs. She seems excited; she kept asking me whether I thought we'd have time to go looking for books. She's read everything we have in Mount Weather and the few trips I've made out over the winter have yielded little new, just a single weary copy of *A Prayer For Owen Meany* I lucked into on the way back from Culpeper. She finished it the same day I returned. I've told her to keep her pack light, but I'm pretty sure it's found its way in among the supplies I laid out for her.

I watch as she stops to takes a swig from her canteen. I'm glad to have her with me, but the truth is I'm more nervous about this than she is. For the first time I think I understand why Marv was reluctant to take me out with him after Benjamin died. I've spent the last few weeks trying to remember everything I learnt from him. I even dug out the first aid book I used to keep under my bed in the farmhouse and read it through again, cover to cover. But what if I forget something? What if I screw up and get us lost, or worse? Mags says I should stop worrying, and maybe she's right. The worst of the storms have passed and we're both carrying enough MREs for several weeks, more than enough to get us to The Greenbrier and back without having to worry about finding food along the way.

We've been tracking steadily downhill for maybe an hour when we come to a road sign. I scrape off the ice; the rusting metal underneath says we're approaching the highway. I tell Mags it's time for frostbite checks. She unsnaps the respirator, lifts her goggles onto her forehead and closes her eyes. I study the faint smattering of freckles that run along her cheekbones underneath those long, dark eyelashes. There's little wind but the cold still bites at every inch of exposed skin and I know I should hurry. Nevertheless I can't help but pull down the surgical mask I still prefer so that I can kiss her.

'Hey! Pay attention. I thought you said we had to take this seriously.'

I offer her a sheepish grin and lift my goggles onto my forehead so she can check me. A moment later I feel her arms slip around my waist and she leans in to me and I feel her lips, soft and warm, back on mine. We've barely left and already I find myself wishing we could just forget about Kane and turn around and go back to the warmth of our small apartment.

The mountain road ends quarter of a mile later and a long, straight section of highway, two, maybe three lanes in each direction, stretches off in both directions. The wind's stayed low and it's eerily quiet. I look up. The storms might be moving on, but the skies are still heavy with snow. When I hiked out to Culpeper a week ago I took the road east from here. I haven't ventured west yet, but I doubt there'll be much in the way of shelter, least not along the highway.

We make our way down. The snow's heavier now and we're trudging through drifts, Indian file, from the get-go. The road inclines for a mile or so and for the next hour it's a long steady climb uphill. I listen to the sound of Mags' breathing as she follows in my tracks. She's been in Mount Weather's gym over the winter preparing for this, but my legs are longer than hers and I can already feel them burning with the effort.

Eventually the road crests and levels and we come to a faded sign that says *Ashby Gap* and beneath it *Welcome to Clarke County.* We sit next to it in the snow, our breath escaping in white plumes as we sip water from our canteens. A wide, open valley stretches out, gray and cold and lifeless, beneath us. I search the shrouded landscape for anything of color but there's nothing.

We stop for lunch where US340 crosses the highway. The wind's picking up again, blowing the gray snow across the road, already starting to cover the tracks we've made behind us. Up ahead the traffic light gantry's collapsed, the virus-weakened metal no longer able to bear the weight of the gantry arm, which now lies buried in the middle of the intersection. It's deep enough to step over, but I take us out wide around it anyway. What Kane did to the skies means it shouldn't be a threat, but you can never be too careful.

I ask Mags where she wants to eat and she takes a moment to weigh the options. There's a McDonalds right there, a faded red flag with the arches fluttering next to a tattered stars and stripes, but she chooses a Dunkin' Donuts that sits kitty corner opposite. It's been turned over like everywhere else, but overall it looks in better shape than the other places currently competing for our business. We trudge up to the entrance and step out of our snowshoes. The door's definitely seen better days; all that's left is a mostly empty frame, the last of the glass gripped in fragments around the edges and in the corners. Broken shards crunch under our boots as we walk in.

I get our MREs heating while Mags stares out the busted window at a panel van that's settled on to its tires under the snow. I can tell she's taking it in, processing it, so I don't say anything. It used to happen to me sometimes, even after I'd been scavenging for a while. Sometimes something simple like an abandoned car or a faded road sign will cause the enormity of it all to suddenly hit you, and you realize the way the world once was is nothing more than an idea now, a place to be visited in memories but never again found.

*

AFTER LUNCH MAGS fixes herself a coffee and I use it as an excuse to bag our trash. I've never cared much for it; sometimes, if I haven't eaten, the bitter aroma's almost enough to turn my stomach. Tell the truth I'm not sure Mags started out with much of a taste for it either. I think it's something she taught herself to like because we weren't allowed to have it while Kane was in charge.

When she's done we strap our snowshoes back on and take 340 south. The road narrows to two lanes but stays mostly flat. After we've been on it for an hour it swings west and then we hit another junction. The road switches back and forth for a while, then it straightens and starts a gentle incline. As we make our way slowly up it I see a sharp corner of something that looks metal, way too tall to be a vehicle, just beyond the next crest.

I used to be good at working out what was buried under the drifts just from the shapes they made in the snow; when I was scavenging with Marv there wasn't a car or truck on the turnpike I couldn't name just from a glimpse of its roofline. But whatever this is has me stumped. I stare at it as we approach, trying to figure it out, but it's not till the road levels and I can see the extent of it laid out before me that I realize what I've been staring at.

It's a plane, or at least what's left of one. It was the tail I spotted first, but now I see the whole rear section's detached itself; it lies across the road, blocking our way. I stop and gaze at the impossible sweep of it, jutting up into the gray sky. As I look around I see another piece of the fuselage has reached its final resting place a few hundred yards beyond, but it, too, ends abruptly, incomplete. I scan the fields on either side. There's wreckage from the crash scattered all around, but no sign of the missing cockpit.

I start down towards it. Mags makes to follow, but I tell her to wait until I've checked it out. The drifts probably conceal a multitude of twisted, charred metal; there's no sense both of us venturing in amongst it till I've found a path through.

As I get closer the debris is everywhere and I slow down, picking my way around whatever's lying under the snow. I pass something that might be an engine, sitting at a haphazard angle on the hard shoulder, a length of wing still attached. A little further along on the other side of the road there's a giant set of wheels, the strut broken off and poking skyward. Finally I draw level with the section of fuselage I first saw. It tilts forward at an improbable angle, like it has crumpled on impact. This close it's huge; it towers over me. I step around its jagged-edged side and look up into the darkened interior, realizing, too late, my mistake.

There used to be an amusement park in Baton Rouge. I don't remember now how I'd gotten wind of its existence – TV probably – but I'd pestered Mom for weeks to take me, and in the end she'd relented. Jack had driven us. Mom said I was too young for any of the really interesting rides, so I'd spent the morning sitting in little plastic teacups or astride smiling elephants with huge ears and tiny hats, all the while loading up on soda and cotton candy and dreaming of the ride I really wanted: *The Intimidator*. You could hear the screams from that all the way across the park. I figured there was little point even putting in a request for something like that, but I guess Jack must have worked it out because as soon as she went looking for the rest room he grabbed me by the arm and we doubled back. The person handing out the tickets looked at me funny, and I figured then we were sunk. But I've always been one-part daddy long-legger and when I stood against the board there was no denying I was tall enough to ride the ride.

The Intimidator was a monster: there had to be a dozen cars, each wide enough to accommodate six abreast. I remember the restraining bar coming down onto my lap and locking in place, and the never-ending *clunk-clunk-clunk* as it slowly climbed all the way up to the top and started to roll. I can still hear the shrieks from the cars ahead as one by one they disappeared until it was our turn and then the first sickening moment of free-fall and somewhere before the loop-the-loop I threw up pink cotton candy all over my shoes.

Now as I stare up into what remains of the cabin it's like I'm back there, in that amusement park. It's not the oxygen masks, dangling like plastic fronds, twisting this way and that in the wind, or the luggage bins that hang open above, their contents disgorged into the snow. It's the passengers, or at least what remains of them. They're still strapped to their seats, and now they just hang there, like they've come to an abrupt halt on the world's most gruesome roller coaster ride.

I tear my eyes from it and look back up the road to where Mags is waiting. I've seen my share of dead bodies; I can't say I care much for it, but it doesn't bother me anything like it used to. I'll never forget my first, though, the guy clutching the jar of Maraschino cherries in the frozen foods aisle of the Walmart back in Providence. I'll spare her that for as long as I can.

I turn my snowshoes around and retrace my steps through the wreckage. I tell her it's not safe, we have to go around. She glances over my shoulder, at the tracks I've already plotted, and then looks at me. I know what she's thinking. She's desperate for something new to read, and the luggage scattered in the snow will be a treasure trove. But in the end she just says okay and we make our way out into the fields, giving the plane a wider berth than I can possibly justify.

We spend the first night in a Waffle House that sits next to the long concrete sweep of the on-ramp at the interchange with I-81. We passed a Comfort Inn on the way up, a strip of rooms two stories tall horseshoed around a long-emptied swimming pool. The walls were brick, and the roof looked like it had mostly held, which meant that some of the beds might even have been dry. I could see Mags looking at it as we walked by, the sky slowly darkening around us. I knew what we'd find in there, though. When the weather changed and people finally figured out they had to get themselves south the motels got busy. But by then it was cold and few of those that had taken to the roads had prepared for it. Most that checked into places like that never checked out again.

We cut some firewood from a stand of thin black trees perched on the edge of the highway and head inside. The wood's damp so I head out to find fuel and something that'll work as kindling while Mags checks the kitchen for anything that might have been missed. When I come back in she's already built the fire. I go to light it but she says she wants to, so I hand her a stack of flyers I found in the Comfort Inn's lobby and a small soda bottle of gas I siphoned from a Honda in the parking lot that had been overlooked. She examines the flyers for a moment and then scrunches them up. She pours the gas into one of the plastic spoons we saved from the MREs we had at lunch and places it underneath the kindling, just like Marv showed me. Then she takes a lighter from her pocket and strikes the wheel. The lighter's new, fresh from the stores, but still it takes a dozen tries before it sparks, which makes me think I should have checked it before we left. But finally it catches and she cups her fingers around it and offers it to the spoon. The flames slowly climb up into the crumpled flyers and then start to lick at the wicker of blackened limbs above.

She steps back, proud of her work. But the wood's damp and it hisses and steams, sending slow coils of white smoke rising into the air. It throws off little light and even less warmth, and we eat our MREs wrapped up in our parkas and then quickly transfer to the sleeping bag I've unfurled next to the fire. It's cold, and my muscles ache from the day's hike, but I have been looking forward to this moment all day. After a winter together in Mount Weather I know exactly how we fit together. As I slip my arm around her shoulder she seems tense, however. I figure she's still working through all the things she's seen so I don't say anything. It's a long time before she speaks.

'Is it the same everywhere?'

'Everywhere I've been.'

She nods, like this is the answer she was expecting, but doesn't say anything more. I try and inject a cheery tone into my voice.

'But then Marv and I never really went that far. It could be different somewhere else. Maybe further south.'

It's full dark outside now and what remains of the diner's scattered furniture sits like so many humped gray shadows around us. The fire's already dying down; only a handful of scattered flames survive among the embers. She reaches for one of the branches and stirs what's left of the damp wood. Red sparks rise in a shudder and then disappear in the blackness overhead.

'You can't protect me from all of it, Gabe. Sooner or later I'm going to see something.'

'I know but…'

She turns around and props herself up on one elbow so that she can look at me.

'But nothing. Marv didn't stop you from seeing things, did he? I think it'll be better if I get it over with.'

I don't know what to say, so instead I slip out of the sleeping bag and bank the fire. Sometimes my feelings for her ambush me, threatening to crush my chest with the whole weight of them. When I climb back in beside her again she slips one arm around me and closes her eyes.

I lay awake for a long time staring up into the darkness after she's drifted off to sleep, just thinking about what she's said. The fear that I may have done something foolish and selfish and dangerous by bringing her out here with me settles cold and heavy inside my ribcage.

Mags is smart, and brave, braver than any of us, but she can't understand yet what she's asking for. There's a whole world out there, filled with things that are too terrible to contemplate. And no good will ever come now of seeing them.

*

I-81 WINDS ITS WAY through the middle of a wide, flat valley. For the next four days we hike south, slowly cresting low rises, trudging into the shallows between, the gray foothills of the Appalachians always to our right in the distance, the Blue Ridge Mountains on our left. There's little on either side of the highway but dead fields, only the occasional bare and blackened tree poking up through the shroud, the remains of recent falls lying in skiffs in the crooks of the branches and along its stunted limbs. Most of the interchanges we come to have collapsed. The crumbling concrete has been softened by the snow, but I know its sharper edges, its bent and twisted rebar, lies waiting for us underneath. We pick our way slowly through the rubble, taking our snowshoes off to clamber over girders, testing for metal buried in the snow that might break an ankle or shatter a kneecap.

Most days we take our lunches huddled under an overpass rather than wasting time searching for anything better off the highway. We eat our MREs cowled up in our parkas, our backs to the cold concrete. Each evening as the banished sun tracks westward towards the horizon we leave the road in search of shelter, gathering what little wood might hold a fire and then curling up inside our shared sleeping bag next to it.

And then finally, just as we're about to lose the light on the fourth day we spot the junction where I-64 splits from I-81 and turns west for Lexington and Charleston, the road that will take us to Sulfur Springs and The Greenbrier.

That night we sleep in the Rockbridge County High School, a concrete two-story that sits, bleak and grim, atop a low embankment. The parking lot opposite is filled with school buses like the one that brought us to the White House on the Last Day. They line up in neat rows, sunken onto their perished tires under a blanket of gray snow.

It's already growing dark outside as we climb the steps to the entrance. The door's not locked and we snap off our snowshoes and make our way in. It sighs closed behind us, sending a soft stir of echoes down the empty hallway. We head up the staircase and make camp in what used to be the library. I noticed a couple of withered trees still clinging to the embankment when we came in so I dig the handsaw from my backpack and head back outside to cut a few limbs while she checks the shelves to see if anything's been left behind.

On my way back in I stop at the noticeboard in the hallway, looking for something that might serve for kindling. A faded flyer announces try-outs for the Wildcats. Next to it a sign reads: *Lexington County Fire and*

*Rescue* and underneath it *Volunteers Needed!!!* In the space underneath where you're supposed to put your name somebody's written *It won't help*. I pull both notices down and stuff them in the pocket of my parka.

When I get back upstairs Mags has a small fire going. I hand her the branches I've collected and one by one she feeds them to the flames. Afterwards we eat our MREs and then climb into the sleeping bag. She pulls *Owen Meany* from her pack, but before she has a chance to open it she's fast asleep.

I half wake from a dream I don't remember. Dawn's not far off, but the fire's died down and it's cold. I reach for Mags, but she's no longer lying next to me. I sit up and slowly scan the room, rubbing sleep from my eyes while I chart gray shapes and darkness against memory to try and place where I am. I find her at the window, wrapped in her parka, staring out.

I climb out of the sleeping bag, picking my way between the scattered chairs to stand behind her. For some reason I'm suddenly feeling uneasy, and there's that scratchy feeling I sometimes get inside my head when something's not right. Spidey's been dormant all winter, but now he's back and telling me I need to pay attention.

Without saying a word she points to a spot between two of the school buses. At first I don't see anything, and I'm beginning to wonder what it is she's looking at. But then I catch it. Little more than a shifting of shadows at first, so slight that at first I think I might have imagined it.

Until I see it again.

*

WHEN I FIRST STARTED going outside, all those years ago now, I had been sure I'd find someone. Or at least evidence that people were still out here. A smudge of smoke on the horizon; fresh tracks in the snow; the faintest glimmer of a fire through a silted window. But in all my time with Marv I never saw so much as a single footprint to suggest there was anyone else out here. Kane used to say that if we were to happen upon others while we were scavenging we were to give them a wide berth; that if there was anyone still left after all this time they'd most likely be desperate, dangerous men, lawless and Godless. Of course a lot of what Kane told us wasn't true, I know that now. But still it's those words that go through my head as I watch the three men step from the shadows between the school buses.

Now that they're out in the open I can see that at least two of them have rifles. They hold them across their chests, the barrels pointed down, just like I remember Marv and Benjamin carrying their guns on the day we arrived at Eden. They cross the parking lot and then the one in the middle, the one who doesn't seem to be armed, stops and looks up. The fire died down hours ago, and the glass is coated with a decade of grime, so I know he won't be able to see us here, but nevertheless I find myself shrinking back under the weight of that gaze. He turns his head, as if saying something to his companions, and then looks over his shoulder, back in the direction of the highway. For a brief moment I allow myself the hope that they'll pass us by. But when they set off again it's towards the embankment, and the steps that will lead them to the entrance.

I whisper to Mags that we need to go. She nods once, then starts gathering her things. While she's wriggling into her pants I pull on my boots, not bothering with the laces. I stuff our sleeping bag into my backpack and hoist it onto my shoulder. We're already at the stairs when she stops and says she's forgotten her book. But it's too late to go back for it now so I grab her hand and moments later we're running down a wide hallway past row after row of metal lockers. At the end I turn right and follow the signs marked Fire Exit. Somewhere in the darkness behind us I hear the sound of a door being opened. I think they're coming in the way we did last night, but I don't stop to make sure.

We take a left and a right and then there's another long corridor. We run down it, a set of double doors with a push handle slowly separating itself from the gloom at the end. A sign says the door's alarmed, but that's not what's worrying me now. I reach for the bar, convinced it won't move and that we'll be trapped. But it sticks for just an instant then gives with a loud clunk, announcing our presence to whoever's behind us. I push against it, no longer worried about being quiet, but the door only opens a fraction. I look down and see why: snow's drifted up against the bottom on the other side. I lean my shoulder into it and shove, feeling my boots scrabble for purchase on the tiled floor. It opens a little further, enough now for Mags to squeeze through. I step back and she disappears into the gap just as a dark shape appears at the end of the hallway behind us and shouts something. I shuck off my backpack and push it through then force myself after it.

I stagger out into the snow. As I close the door behind me I see a hasp that was designed to take a padlock. I don't have one of those, but the pry bar's sitting right on top of my backpack; it'll do to hold it shut while we get clear of whoever's chasing us. But as I'm bending down to reach inside I hear Mags cry out and I stop and look up. For the first time I notice there's a huge shape standing in front of me, silhouetted against the first of the morning light. It takes me a moment to work out that it's a man. His size and the bushy blond beard covering the bottom half of his face makes him look like the world's largest Viking. He's got Mags pinned to his side under one gigantic arm. She's struggling to break free, but it's like he doesn't even notice.

I drop the pack and fumble inside the pocket of my parka for the gun. There's no bullets of course, so right now I'm hoping that Marv was right when he said most people would just turn tail at the sight of it. But the man-mountain that's holding Mags doesn't show any sign of doing that. I take a step closer and point the gun at his head, but he just blinks once and continues to stare back at me.

I hear something slam into the door behind me. There's a pause and another crash and the sound of wood splintering and when I look back over my shoulder the three men we saw in the parking lot are standing there. The hoods on their parkas are up and the throats are fastened so I can't make out their faces. I see enough in the second before I return my gaze to the Viking to realize that exactly none of their weapons are pointed at the ground any more though. I flick the safety on Marv's gun, trying to stop my hand from shaking.

'Whoa now, son. Steady with that before someone gets hurt.'

The voice is deep, slow and calm. I risk another glance behind me. It's the man in the middle who's spoken. His parka's unzipped, and I catch a glimpse of something silver hanging low on one hip as he steps forward, but his hands are empty. His hood's up, and even though it's barely light out he's wearing sunglasses. He raises his hands and holds them out, palms up.

'Tell him to let her go first.'

'Sure thing. Hey Jax, why don't you do like the kid here says and put the girl down?'

The Viking waits for a moment, like he's processing that instruction, then he releases Mags. She takes a quick step away from him and stops, fists balled at her sides inside her mittens, like she's considering what punishment the giant deserves for having had the temerity to pick her up. I catch her eye and shake my head. She pauses for a moment and then backs over towards me.

'Okay kid, now how about lowering that sidearm? I know Jax there must look like a pretty tempting target, but trust me now, that's an opportunity you'd do well to pass on. If you shoot him with anything less than a fifty cal you're just going to piss him off.'

I look back over my shoulder again. The man who seems to be in charge unsnaps the throat of his parka and slowly lowers his hood. The shades he's wearing are old, the kind with dark, round lenses and leather side blinkers, so I can't make out his eyes. His hair's short, and silver as Kane's. In place of a respirator he's got a simple black bandana, and now he pulls it down revealing a lean face that looks like it might have been cut straight from the same granite as Eden's tunnels. A thick mustache covers his upper lip and then angles down almost to his jawline.

The lines that bracket his mouth deepen as he smiles. He reaches up, slowly removes the sunglasses. One eye is covered with a patch, but the other squints back at me from underneath an eyebrow that's surprisingly dark given the color of his hair. He motions to the other two men to lower their rifles.

I glance over at Mags, but her expression's hard to read. I'm sensing we'll be having a conversation about why I suddenly have a pistol I hadn't previously disclosed, but that's for later; right now I need to work out what to do about our immediate situation. The men might have lowered their weapons, but seeing as my gun's the one without bullets I doubt we'll be shooting our way out of this.

I look at the men surrounding us. They're all wearing the same parka, what appears in the scant light to be a mix of greens and grays in a pixelated camouflage pattern. The zip pulls and the snappers have all been replaced and when I glance down at their boots I see it's the same with the eyelets; they've been swapped out for plastic too. Spidey grumbles a little at that but it's vague, non-directional, and right then I think he's just fussing; my parka and boots are rigged the same after all. I look over at the man with the silver hair who seems to be their leader. His hands are still raised and for the first time I spot the patch velcro'd high on his arm. I look around at the others and see they're each wearing the same familiar flag. I allow my hopes to lift a little. These men are soldiers, just like Marv and Benjamin were.

I take one last look around and then flick the pistol back to safe and slide it back into the pocket of my parka. The man who seems to be in charge whistles softly through his teeth, then lets his hands drop to his sides. As he does so his parka slides forward, once again covering the pistol on his hip. He smiles at me like he's relieved, but something in the way he does it makes me think the Viking may not ever have been in danger, even if Marv's gun had been loaded.

He gestures to the door we've all just come through.

'Alright, then. Now what say we make our introductions inside?'

*

WE HEAD BACK INTO the school. The three soldiers we first saw coming up to the entrance lead the way. Mags slips through the busted door after them and I follow. There's a groan and the sound of wood parting company from hinges as behind me the giant they called Jax ducks his head and squeezes his bulk into the inadequate gap. I can't help but look back at him. Benjamin always seemed huge, but then I guess we were small when we knew him. There's no doubt that this man is bigger. He doesn't say anything, just meets my gaze and stares back at me with these flat blue eyes.

When we get to the staircase the soldier with the eye patch turns to me as if looking for direction. I point up the stairs towards the library.

'Alright. I'm guessing you didn't have a fire goin'?'

The fire we had burned down overnight. I shake my head no.

'Do you have the makings of another?'

'We used the last of the wood we cut last night.'

'Fair enough. Jax, run outside and gather us up some, will you? Go on now. You're making the kid here nervous.'

The Viking looks at me for a long moment, then lumbers off towards the entrance. I keep my eye on his back until he's out the door, then start up the stairs. The soldier with the eye patch and the silver hair walks beside me.

'Don't mind Jax none; he's just interested in you is all. We ain't seen anyone new in years so I expect he'll stare some until he gets used to you. Boy's not right in the head.' He taps one temple as if to emphasize his point. 'His understanding never got much beyond what the movie people would have called soft focus.'

I nod like I get it, but in spite of his words I still find the Viking's size unsettling. We return to the library where Mags and I spent the night. One of the soldiers takes up station by the door and the other heads over to the window. The one who so far has done all the talking drags a couple of plastic chairs into the middle of the room and motions for us to sit. I hesitate a moment and then take a seat. Mags looks at the chair like she's considering it but remains standing. If the soldier cares whether she sits or not he doesn't show it, he just grabs another chair for himself and straddles it backwards, facing us. The parka falls open again, this time offering me a longer look at the pistol on his hip. It seems old, like it might be an antique. The metal's dull, and the grip that sticks out of the holster's inlaid with something cut from the tusk or bone of some long-dead animal, something that might once have been white but which years of use have stained a deep yellow. As I look closer I can see there's something scrimshawed there: a vulture or a buzzard or some other carrion bird.

The soldier reaches into his parka, pulls out a crumpled pack of Camels and holds it forward, like he's offering me one. I shake my head.

'I know, filthy habit, right? Still, I guess you gotta die of something.'

He shakes a cigarette out of the packet, places it in his mouth, and goes digging in his pocket for something to light it. He has a habit of squinting, which together with the mustache, the bandana and the piece of hardware on his hip puts me in mind of a gunslinger from the old west.

His hand reappears holding a book of matches. He tears one off and strikes it, and for a second before he cups the flame to the end of the cigarette it shows me a long, puckered burn scar that runs down one side of his neck and disappears under his collar. The creases in his narrow face deepen as he takes a drag, then exhales a jet of smoke through the side of his mouth. The tang of stale tobacco drifts over and for a moment the smell reminds me of Marv.

'Alright then, introductions. I'm Hicks. That there Mexican-lookin' fella with a face like the north end of a southbound mule is Ortiz.' He nods in the direction of a shorter, stockier man with caramel skin and dark, hooded eyes who's taken up station by the door. Ortiz flips Hicks the finger but manages a smile back in our direction.

'You've probably figured out the big fella's name's Jax. And the runt of the litter over there's Kavanagh. Everyone calls him Boots, though.'

The last soldier he points to has greasy brown hair and a scrub of beard that barely covers his chin. He hardly looks old enough to be wearing a uniform; back in Eden I reckon he might have edged out Alice as my main market for zit cream. He blinks continuously behind thick glasses with heavily taped rims that look like they haven't been cleaned more recently than the window he's standing in front of. He offers me a distracted smile and then goes back to staring at Mags.

'So what're your names?'

'I'm Gabriel but everyone calls me Gabe. And that's Mags.'

'Nice to meet you Gabe. And Mags. What's that short for, darlin'?'

I wince. Hicks doesn't seem to mean any offense by it but I could have told him Mags won't like being called darling.

'Just Mags.'

'Alright then Gabe short for Gabriel and Mags short for Mags, are you hungry? We have food. Can't say it's great, but we're happy to share it.'

I'm about to answer, but Mags just says: 'No thanks. We have our own.'

Hicks looks over at her and then down at the floor. The MRE cartons from last night's meal are still lying there, next to the remains of the fire. I didn't have time to bag them before we high-tailed it out of here.

'So I can see.' The cigarette held loosely between his fingers continues to burn; he hasn't taken another drag since he first lit it. He looks at Mags for a while, then at me, then back to Mags again. 'You pair look well fed. Where you been hiding out?'

I open my mouth to answer, but Mags beats me to it again.

'How did you find us?'

'Just lucky I guess. We picked up your tracks out by the highway, followed them in here. Almost missed you, though. I reckon another hour and the wind would have covered them over. Which way you headed?'

'Some place called The Greenbrier.'

Hicks exchanges a look with the soldier he called Ortiz and smiles.

'Well then it is your lucky day; that's where we've come from. Matter of fact we're headed back there now. We'll be happy to bring you with us. Are there any more of you?'

Mags says no, but Hicks looks at me for a long moment, like he's trying to work out what the real answer to that question might be. I shake my head. Eventually he says, *Alright then*, but keeps studying me through the smoke that drifts languidly up from the cigarette, like maybe he's expecting something else. I figure I need to get us onto another topic so I ask him how many of them there are.

'Hmm? Oh, in The Greenbrier.' He flicks the cigarette, sending gray flakes floating slowly to the dusty floor. 'We're down to eight, all told. Mostly regular army, a couple of Rangers like me and Ortiz over there. We have a scientist though. She's working on a cure for the virus.'

'A cure?' I look over at Mags. Before he died Marv told me what Kane had done to the skies hadn't killed the virus, just set it back. That's why the furies weren't decaying; it was regrouping, he said, slowly building itself back up inside them. Marv hadn't known how long it would take but at some point he reckoned they'd be able to move again, just like the one I ran into when I first went into Mount Weather's tunnel. That would be a real problem. It's been on my list of things to worry about, right after finding a place for us that'll be safe from Kane, that is.

Hicks nods.

'Yep. She reckons she's pretty close too.'

'And how're your supplies holding out?'

Hicks looks over at Mags' question. 'The Greenbrier was stocked pretty good when we arrived and we've been managing it for the long haul, so there's enough to go around, at least for now. We've been working the surrounding towns, too. Not much left out there anymore, though.'

Ortiz touches one of our empty MRE cartons from last night with the toe of his boot. 'Sure would be good to find some more of these. If you kids have come across a stash of them anywhere on your travels we'd love to hear about it.'

Hicks holds up his hand as if to hush him. The cuff of his parka drops and for the first time I notice he's wearing something inside his liners. It looks like latex; I have a box of disposables just like them in my pack. I thought Marv was pretty careful about the virus, but even he didn't make me put those on unless I was actually fixing to touch metal.

'Ortiz are you ever not hungry? I swear you have worms. Y'ate my breakfast this morning as well as your own. There'll be plenty of time for questions when we get back to The Greenbrier. I'm sure these kids'll help us if they can.'

We hear Jax stomping up the stairs and a few moments later the door swings open. It looks like the Viking's found the small stand clinging to the embankment I took from the night before. He hasn't bothered to cut the limbs though, he's just pulled the trees up, roots and all, and dragged them back. The trunks are slender enough, little more than saplings, but the ground's been frozen solid for the best part of a decade and won't have given them up easily. Hicks drops the cigarette to the floor and crushes it under his boot.

'Goddammit Jax, now what in the hell are we supposed to do with those? We need smaller stuff for the fire, remember?'

The Viking just looks at the pile of wood tucked under his arm and then at Hicks, and then back at the wood again, taking a moment to stare at Mags and me for good measure. He drops what he's gathered on the ground and picks up one of the trees and tries to snap it with his hands. The wood's been dead for years but it's wet with snow; it bends and twists, occasionally splintering but mostly just holding, not matter how hard the blond giant tries to break it.

I dig into my backpack and set to work with the handsaw while Mags strips some of the smaller branches and starts building a fire. The soldier Hicks had called Boots watches her from his spot by the window. When it looks like there's enough he pulls a squeeze bottle from the pocket of his parka and walks over. He kneels down next to her and starts squirting the contents liberally over the branches and for a second the rich, sweet smell of gasoline hangs heavy in the air. Gas is pretty hard to come by - Marv only allowed me to use it in emergencies - but Boots doesn't seem to be rationing himself. When he's done he pulls a cheap plastic lighter from his pocket and strikes the wheel with the base of his thumb. He holds it to his face and for a moment the small blue-tinged flame reflects back off the lenses in his grubby glasses. When he presents it to the wood the gas catches with a *whumpf!* that makes me wonder how many times Private Kavanagh has had to wait for his eyebrows to grow back. I have to admit though, whatever mix he's using seems to do the trick; it's not long till the flames are licking up through the damp wood. The smoke makes me cough and I have to step back from it, but he doesn't seem to be able to tear himself away. He watches the fire as though transfixed, occasionally reaching for another branch from the pile to feed it. I guess I should be grateful for small mercies; for a few minutes at least he's not staring at Mags.

The soldiers wait while we fix breakfast. Hicks says they've already eaten but I offer Ortiz some of the sausage patty from my MRE just because he's staring so hard. Hicks shakes his head and says I oughtn't do that; I'll only teach him bad habits by feeding him from the table. Ortiz's mouth's full so he just flips him the finger again and holds out his hand for a hash brown.

As we're finishing up Hicks bends down and retrieves Mags' copy of *Owen Meany* from where she left it. Her eyes dart over to the fire. The flames are already dying down. She sets her MRE aside and stands up.

'That's not for burning.'

He looks up at her.

'Don't worry darlin', that wasn't my intention. This yours?'

She nods.

'Have you read it?'

Mags hesitates, like maybe it's a trick question. Back in Eden Kane didn't allow us to read.

'Yes.'

'It's good, isn't it? I liked the little guy; he knew what had to be done. Can't say I cared much for his friend, though. Not sure what use a man is without a trigger finger.'

He examines the tatty paperback a moment longer then hands it over. She takes it and returns it to her backpack. I scoop the last of my breakfast from its pouch, bag our trash and we set off.

*

ROCKBRIDGE COUNTY HIGH'S right off I-64, the road that Marv's map says will take us all the way to The Greenbrier.

There hasn't been a fresh fall in a few days and the snow's settled, so the going's not so bad. Hicks sets a steady pace and soon I settle into an easy rhythm. But after a while I notice Mags falling behind. I'm beginning to wonder if everything's okay; maybe she hurt herself as we were running through the school earlier. I hang back and soon the soldiers are a stretch ahead of us. I'm about to ask what's wrong when she rests a hand on my arm. Jax has taken to stopping every few minutes to gawp in our direction, but he's just finishing up a stare-break. As soon as he's eyes-forward again she unsnaps one side of her respirator. The wind's picked up a little, enough to prevent anyone ahead from hearing. Nevertheless she keeps her voice low.

'What should we tell them?'

'About what?'

'About where we've come from. Sooner or later they're going to ask again.'

Hicks and Ortiz both appear friendly, and it does seem like Jax's staring is simply curiosity. I really don't care for the way Boots has been looking at her, but these certainly don't seem like the desperate, lawless men Kane had warned of. Maybe Mags is right, though; we have only just met them.

'Well, it's either Eden or Mount Weather; we won't be able to make up a story about anywhere else that'd sound even halfway believable. I think we should just say we've come from Eden. That way at least they won't know where the rest of the Juvies are.'

She considers this for a moment. 'But if they figure out where that is and go there they'll find Kane. They're soldiers; wouldn't he still be their commanding officer? And he knows where we've gone.'

I think about this for a moment. She's right, of course, but I'm not sure it widens our options any.

'After all this time I'm not so sure they'd still take orders from him. He was the one that caused all this after all. We can prove it if we have to; we still have the virus. Besides we don't have to use Eden's real name. I don't think anyone other than Kane called it that. Even if they work out where it is by the time they get there we could be gone from Mount Weather.'

She considers this for a while. In the end she nods like maybe it's not the best plan she's ever heard, but right now she can't think of another that might be better. She snaps the respirator back over her mouth and we pick up the pace.

Up ahead the soldiers have stopped next to an RV that's come to a sideways halt in the middle of the road. Jax is using his break time to get some more staring in and now Hicks turns around as well. The Viking's gaze is blank, vacant, but with Hicks it's different; I feel like behind those blinkered shades our progress is being measured. When we catch up to them he pulls down his bandana.

'How're you two doin'?'

Mags stops and unsnaps her respirator again.

'I was finding the snow a little heavy back there. I'm fine now.'

Hicks just nods and leads us on.

We stick to the interstate as it winds its way west into the Appalachians.

The first morning we pass a succession of exit signs – Shank's Creek, Longhorn Furnace, Forge – but we don't take any of them, stopping only to warm our MREs by the side of the road. Hicks sits off to one side and sips from a thermos he pulls from his pack.

As soon as we're done eating he stands, like he's keen to get back now. I bag our trash and we set off again. For a while the road opens out and billboards compete for our attention on both sides. A decade of weather has left them faded and tattered, but it's still a riot of color compared with what we've been seeing. Then the mountains close in on us again and they're gone.

The last of the light's leaving the sky when Hicks finally leads us towards an off-ramp. We make our way into a small town called Covington in almost darkness. I'm not used to hiking at night; Marv always had us off the road before dusk. We may not have seen the sun since the Last Day but I guess it's still up there doing something because once it dips below the horizon it turns real cold real quick, and without a moon or even stars to light your way it'd be easy to get lost. Hicks seems to know where he's going, though. He brings us to a small brick and shingle building just off the highway. The weather-beaten sign outside says *New Hope Baptist Church*, and underneath in smaller letters, *Praying For A Miracle.*

Hicks sends Jax off in search of firewood and then heads out himself shortly after. All the Viking comes back with are a handful of blackened limbs that do little more than smoke up the place, no matter how much gasoline Boots pours on them. We huddle around the reluctant fire scooping our rapidly cooling MREs from their plastic pouches while Ortiz, Boots and Jax eat a supper of cold franks and beans. I tear the wrapper off a HOOAH! for dessert and Jax stares at me like the world's largest, dumbest wolfhound. I break it in two and toss one half over. It disappears into his beard and I have to hold my hands up so he'll believe I'm not holding out on him.

Hicks returns a little while after. He doesn't bother with dinner or the fire, just walks past us and up into the shadows by the altar. He eases himself to the ground and sits with his back to the pulpit. A quart bottle of bourbon appears from the pocket of his parka and he unscrews the cap. Boots is staring into the dwindling flames, absent-mindedly picking at a scab on the inside of his arm. He looks up at the sound but Hicks makes no move to offer it around.

The church has a small organ balcony, so I figure that's where Mags and I will sleep. As we get up Boots tears his eyes from the fire; I can feel his gaze following us as we climb the stairs. I unfurl the sleeping bag and lay it on the dusty floor. Mags has been quiet over dinner and she still hasn't said anything as we climb inside. She lays still for a while, her back to my chest, but I know she's still awake. Eventually she whispers:

'We should hide the map. It has the code for Mount Weather on it.'

I nod. She closes her eyes and rests her head against my shoulder, like having decided this is a comfort. But it's a long time before she finally drifts off.

I wake from an uneasy sleep sometime in the middle of the night. The fire's gone out so there's little to see, but something's stirring down below. I hear footsteps as someone makes their way down the aisle, then the door at the back of the church opens and from outside there's the sound of retching. After a while it stops and then for a long time silence returns to the darkness.

I'm beginning to think whoever it was has snuck back inside without me noticing when I hear the door opening again. I ease my arm out from under Mags' head. She mumbles something and then shifts in her sleep, like whatever's troubling her has found its way into her dreams, but she doesn't wake. I slip out of the sleeping bag and creep over to the balustrade. My eyes have adjusted as much as they will, but without a fire there's nothing but inky blackness. I strain to hear. Whoever's moving around down there seems to be retracing their steps up the aisle. There's a pause and some shuffling sounds as they settle themselves, then the dry rasp of a lighter wheel being struck and Hicks' face suddenly appears out of the darkness as he holds the flame to the end of a cigarette and draws on it. He's about to extinguish the lighter, but then something causes him to stop. He turns and looks up in my direction. I suddenly feel the need to announce my presence; like I've been caught spying on him. I raise my hand to wave down, but then I stop myself. I'm hidden behind the balustrade, in total darkness; there's no way he can see me up here. After a moment he lets the lighter go out so that all that remains is the glowing red tip.

I creep back to the sleeping bag and climb inside.

*

HE'S THE LAST ONE NOW.

Still they keep the lights off. He's told them they don't bother him, that he's not like the others, that he'd rather have them on. He's told them more than once; he mentions it every time one of them comes down. He wants them to believe it, even though it's not really true anymore. When they put the flashlight on him it hurts now.

He doesn't have a name, or if he does he doesn't remember it. He's heard the doctor refer to him as Subject 99 and sometimes the mean soldier sings snatches of a tune that has the words Johnny 99 in it. He wonders if his name might be Johnny. The mean soldier doesn't have a nice voice, but the boy who might be Johnny likes the song anyway. Sometimes after they've gone he hums it to himself in the darkness, even though he doesn't know what an auto plant is or if Mahwah's even a real place or for that matter what Ralph was thinking mixing Tanqueray and wine if it can get you in that kind of trouble. He asked the doctor once whether his name might be Johnny, but when she wanted to know why he couldn't think of a reason other than the song and so he said he wasn't sure. The doctor never answered him. But after that the mean soldier didn't sing anymore. And the next time he came down he glared into his cage like he was mad at him for something, and then he put his food tray on the ground and spat in it. He had to eat the food anyway, even though he wasn't really hungry. Because not eating your food is a sign, like not looking at the doctor's flashlight, and he doesn't want to go to the other room.

He's been here a very long time. He doesn't know how long exactly, because days don't mean much with the lights off. But definitely a long time. He wasn't always here. He's sure of that, even though he doesn't know where he might have been before. He doesn't remember anything about it. The doctor says he needs to try and he wants to, he really does, and not just to please her. But it's no use. It's like whatever was before is behind some thick gray curtain in his mind and there's just no way to pull it back, no matter how hard he tries.

He thinks the room he's in now is underground. There are no windows, although of course he knows that doesn't prove anything. It's definitely at the bottom of a long flight of stairs though, because he can hear the soldiers' boots ringing off the metal each time they descend. Sometimes he counts the steps. The highest he's ever got before the door opens is eighty-nine, but the first ones are always really faint and it's possible there are more he's not hearing.

He can always tell who's coming. The mean soldier's boots are the loudest. He can hear their lumbering *thunk-clang* echoing down the stairwell for ages before he reaches the bottom. It's the mean soldier he sees the most, because he's the one who brings his food. He always carries the stick and he looks at him like he's some sort of dangerous animal in a poorly built cage. He doesn't need to be afraid, though. Johnny 99 would never hurt him, ever, he's told him that. But still he makes sure to keep all the way to the back of the cage while the tray gets pushed through the slot at the front. They don't bother to heat the food, but that's okay; they're still bringing it, which is the main thing. He always eats everything they give him, even if he's not hungry, or if he suspects the mean soldier has done something to it. That way they'll know he's still fine and doesn't need to go in the next room, with the others.

The other soldier comes down, too, although it's been a while now since he visited. His footsteps are much quieter; sometimes he makes it all the way down the stairs without Johnny even hearing and the first thing he knows the door at the end's opening and he has to scurry to the back of his cage. The other soldier doesn't bother with a stick or even a flashlight. He just sits there in the darkness, studying him through the bars. When he's done he gets up and leaves without saying a word.

The doctor doesn't come as often as she used to either, now there's only him left. And sometimes when she does she just shines the light into his eyes and then leaves without saying anything and he's disappointed. But other times there are questions. He has to answer them as truthfully as he can, which he does, he always does, even though most of the time he just can't remember. He's not allowed to ask any questions of his own, even though he has so many and sometimes it feels like he might burst with the not knowing. That would ruin the experiment the doctor says. He must try and remember himself. It's really important.

He knows he is sick, like the others were. That's why he can't remember. But the doctor says the medicine she gives him will make him better. He has to drink it all, every last drop, even though it makes him feel like he's going to throw up. The medicine didn't help the others, though. He watched each of them take it and one by one they all changed.

98 was the last, and she turned a long time ago now. Her cage had been directly opposite; she'd been there when he'd first woken up. He doesn't remember much about before he got sick, but he remembers that. He had been very frightened then. He can see quite well now; his eyes have grown used to the darkness. But back then he hadn't been able to see anything. He hadn't known where he was, or what he was doing, here, in this tiny plastic enclosure.

98 had calmed him down. She'd whispered that it would be okay, but for now it was important that he be quiet. That was one of the rules, she'd said. If the mean soldier caught you making noise he'd come down and put the lights on and even though Johnny 99 hadn't minded the lights back

then it would drive some of the others, the ones who were already turning, crazy.

Well, crazier.

Later 98 had taught him the other rules as well, like going to the back of your cage whenever the soldiers came down and never, ever putting your hand through the bars. There were more rules than that, but those were the main ones. You couldn't forget them, even for a second. If you did the mean soldier was apt to pay you a visit with the stick.

He misses 98. She had been nice to him. It had frightened him when the doctor had come down and shone a light into her cage and he had seen her for the first time. How could anyone's eyes be like that? But after a while he had gotten used to it and then it hadn't bothered him so much. He wonders if he looks now like 98 did then. There aren't any mirrors in his cage, no surfaces that might give back even the faintest reflection, so he doesn't know. His arms and legs seem very thin and pale, but then he is small, and it is always dark down here, so maybe that is normal.

98 lasted a long time, longer than any of the others. But then one day the mean soldier started taking her food away untouched, and a little while after that she had started acting up whenever the doctor had shone a light into her cage. Johnny 99 had tried to calm her down, just like she had done when he had first arrived. That had seemed to help a little, at first. But then the doctor would come down with the flashlight and that would set her off again. After that Johnny 99 knew it wouldn't be long. There's never much time left after you change.

It was the mean soldier who came to get her, with the catchpole and the stick. Johnny 99 hadn't been able to look. He'd pushed himself to the back of his cage and covered his head with his hands when it happened. He is ashamed of that because 98 was his friend, although in the end he doesn't think she knew who he was anymore.

Johnny 99's decided that won't happen to him. He'll keep taking the medicine and eating the regular food, even if he doesn't feel like it, and he won't flinch or look away when the doctor shines a light into his eyes, even if it hurts.

That way they'll know.

He's not like the others.

*

WE'RE ON THE ROAD AGAIN at first light. If Hicks' head is hurting from the bourbon he's not showing any sign of it; the pace he's setting doesn't slacken. The morning passes much as the day before did: a succession of frozen landscapes, like a series of old black and white photos. We hike through each, aiming for the bend or the crest that will show us the next. When the time comes we eat by the side of the road, huddled up in our parkas. Hicks' stomach must still be feeling delicate from the whisky; he just sips from his thermos and lets another cigarette burn down between his fingers. I'm beginning to wonder if Hicks is actually a smoker or if he's just worried what the world's lacking right now is a steady supply of ash.

When we're done eating I bag our trash and bury it in the snow and we set off again. The road inclines for a couple of miles and when it finally crests we come to a small green sign, almost buried under a drift, that reads *Greenbrier County*. A little further on a high gantry that's somehow survived rust and storm and virus spans the highway. A large sign mounted to it says *Welcome to West Virginia* and underneath *Wild and Wonderful*.

A mile or so after the sign the road fishhooks and then passes over what looks like train tracks. Beneath us, maybe a hundred yards back in the direction we've come, I can just make out the entrance to a tunnel. Ashen drifts reach almost all the way up the curved walls, almost hiding it completely. Hicks knocks snow off the guardrail then throws a leg over and drops down a steep embankment on the other side, sliding his way to the floor of a narrow ravine. Ortiz goes next and then I shuck off my backpack and follow him. A second later Mags gets to her feet beside me and dusts herself off, followed a little too closely by Jax, who arrives in an avalanche of snow. Boots spends a while looking down at us until Hicks loses patience and barks at him to hurry it up. He slips as he's clambering over the guardrail and tumbles down the slope, shedding his goggles and respirator on the way down. The drifts are deep at the bottom and Hicks has to send Jax to dig him out. He finally gets to his feet, furiously wiping snow off his glasses. It might be the first time they've been cleaned since he got fitted for them.

The track curves around for a half mile or so and then straightens. The ravine widens out and we pass a short siding, a corroded railcar sitting idle against the buffers. In the distance I can see what looks like a long shelter, the roof timbers swaybacked under the weight of snow, running the length of what I'm guessing was once a platform. As we get closer a faded Amtrak sign says *Sulfur Springs*.

We leave the railway tracks behind us and make our way through a parking lot to the road. There's a station house, almost buried under a blanket of gray snow, its small porch supported by two red and white pillars. The paint's faded and peeling but they look like candy cane and for a moment it puts me in mind of a story Miss Kimble used to read to us about these kids who get abandoned in a forest by their ne'er-do-well father and then stumble on a witch. Miss Kimble said it was a classic, but it always seemed kinda lame to me. I mean, really, we're supposed to believe the witch wants to eat these two kids, even though she lives in a house made of nothing but Hershey's kisses and Reese's peanut butter cups? Mags said she liked it though, because in the end the witch gets her ass thrown in an oven.

On the other side of the road two matching sections of wall curve inward to a pair of large stone gateposts, marking an entrance. The gatepost on the left has started to crumble, but the other's mostly intact. The once-white paintwork's flaking badly, but the sign there's still legible. The dark green cursive announces that we have arrived at *The Greenbrier*. Underneath, in neat capitals, it says *America's Resort.*

Hicks leads us between the gateposts and we start up a long driveway. I'm beginning to think there's been a mistake. I look over at Mags and I can see she's thinking the same thing. The facility listed on Marv's map definitely shared the name on the post, but it was supposed to be a bunker. And then as the road curves around I finally get my first glimpse of The Greenbrier and I'm sure of it.

I stop, pushing my goggles up onto my forehead. Beside me Mags does the same. It's like we're back at the White House on the Last Day. But it's clear even from this distance that The Greenbrier is much, much bigger; almost too big to take in in a single glance. The front is dominated by a huge portico, four massive columns supporting a low triangular gable that slopes down to a flat roof. I count five, no, six stories, rows of tall, dark windows marching off in each direction. They continue around on both sides, the wings forming a giant squared-off horseshoe that surrounds what must once have been the gardens. A line of tattered, weather-faded flags hang from poles that jut from the first floor balustrade.

We set off again, hurrying to catch up to the soldiers. As we get closer I see a dark shape squatting on the lawn, covered under a thick mantle of snow. I keep looking at it as we hike up to the entrance. The outline is unfamiliar, and it takes me a while to figure out that it's a helicopter. It's way bigger than the one that brought us to Eden, though, and it has two sets of rotors, not one. The first are mounted on a tall hump above the cockpit; the second rest on top of a tail section at the back and sit even higher above the long, riveted fuselage. The thick blades hang down under their own weight, the tips almost touching the gray powder. As we walk past I can see that the loading ramp at the back is down; snow drifts up into the darkened interior.

On the other side of the helicopter a path has been cleared. We step into the shadow of the portico; the colossal columns tower over us as we bend down to undo our snowshoes. I notice a camera mounted high on the wall above the entrance. As I watch its red light blinks once, then goes dark again. There's something about that that doesn't seem right, but Hicks is already making his way inside so I kick the snow off my boots and follow him through a set of double doors into a huge lobby.

And for a moment all I can do is stare.

*

KANE'S HOUSE IN EDEN always seemed luxurious. The sofas and armchairs where we would sit for confession were so much more comfortable than the plastic chairs in the mess or the chapel's wooden pews; the soft glow from the reading lamps so much kinder than the glare from the cavern's arc lights. But underneath the rugs the floor was the same riveted metal my feet would touch first thing in the morning; behind the pictures that hung on his walls were the same welded panels I'd stare up at from my cot before the curfew buzzer each night.

This place couldn't be more different. I look around, slowly taking it all in. Large black and white marble tiles stretch off in all directions, like I'm standing on a giant checkerboard. Above me a massive chandelier hangs from an ornate ceiling. The crystals are covered in dust, but they still manage to catch the last of the day's light coming through the lobby's tall windows. A wide, carpeted staircase leads down to a lower level; next to it another spirals upwards. And scattered everywhere, items of furniture. Dustsheets shroud much of it, but here and there something has gone uncovered. A pair of armchairs, the pattern on the upholstery like the feathers of a giant, exotic bird. A tall wooden clock, its golden face intricately carved, the pendulum beneath now still.

But what strikes me even more than these extravagances are the colors. Eden was steel and rock; a handful of small, windowless metal boxes huddled together inside a cavern dug deep into a mountain. It had no need for cheery tones; no part of it had been designed with joyful times in mind. What little there was got washed out by the arc lights, or faded to grainy shadow once the curfew buzzer sounded and those were cut. Mount Weather might be bigger, and more modern, but ultimately its purpose was no different. It existed solely to get whatever remained of humanity through its darkest hours.

It's not like that here. As I look around I see large colorful paintings hanging from wallpapered walls; thick red carpets climb the staircases and from underneath the dust cloths the once-vivid fabrics of sofas and armchairs peek out. The patterns may have faded with time, and here and there the paper on the walls is starting to peel. But even in the failing evening light this place is a riot of blues and greens and pinks and reds.

The thought I had as I caught my first glimpse of The Greenbrier from outside returns: Hicks has brought us to the wrong place. The facility marked on Marv's map was supposed to be a bunker. After ten years I know what those look like, and whatever this place might be, it isn't one. I'm about to ask him about it when he looks over and points at my boots.

'You'll need to take those off. Doc doesn't like us tracking dirt in from the outside.' Spidey pings a warning at this. But as I look over at Ortiz I see he's already removed his and is stacking them on a nearby bellhop cart next to his rifle. Beside him Jax is hard at work on his laces, a task that seems to be consuming all of his powers of concentration.

I hesitate for a second then undo my boots and hand them over. Hicks flips one over to check the size and then adds them to the cart. Mags frowns like she's not happy about this either, but in the end she does the same. He disappears down the stairs and comes back a moment later with a pair of trainers for her and some slippers with *The Greenbrier* embroidered on the front for me.

'Sorry kid, nothing in your size. You'll have to give me that sidearm now too. All weapons get locked away here. Doc don't allow guns inside the house. No exceptions.'

Marv's gun's not loaded anyway, so unless I'm planning to hit someone with it it's not going to be much use. I reach into the pocket of my parka and hand it over.

He takes it out of the Ziploc bag and ejects the magazine. Then he pulls the slide back and checks the chamber for a round. When he doesn't find one he looks up at me and raises an eyebrow in what I think might be an expression of amusement, but maybe not. Behind him Jax has finally worked out how many times the bunny has to hop around the tree before his footwear comes off. He stands up and lumbers off through the lobby like he's suddenly remembered somewhere important he has to be. Ortiz grabs his backpack and hauls it into the corner with the others. He collects the giant's outsized boots from where they've been discarded and adds them to the others on the bellhop cart, then he sets off down the corridor with it. Hicks follows him into the gloom.

Boots blinks at Mags behind his glasses and asks if she wants dinner. She looks at me. I'm not sure I care much for more of Private Kavanagh's company, but we've hiked a long way since lunch and my stomach's already betrayed me by growling loudly at the mention of food, so I shrug my shoulders and nod. He digs into his pack and pulls out a packet of boil-in-the-bag frankfurters and a tin of beans.

We follow him across the lobby and down a long, wide hallway. Tall windows look out onto what I'm guessing would once have been the gardens, where now the gray outline of the helicopter squats in the dying light. The muffled sounds of conversation drift up from somewhere ahead of us on the right.

Boots stops in front of a set of double doors and holds one open for Mags to go through. I follow her into a huge dining room. Two rows of sculpted columns support a high ceiling, at least a dozen chandeliers like the one in the lobby hanging between them. Large, ornate mirrors that would once have reflected the light back line the walls, their surfaces spackled black with years of neglect.

Most of the furniture's been stacked neatly in one corner, but in the center a single table remains. I see Jax already seated at it, his broad back to us. Three other men sit with him, all in uniform, the remains of a meal spread out in front of them. The soldier at the head of the table seems to be giving forth on something, but he stops mid-sentence as we step in, a smile splitting his face.

'Well, look what we got here.'

*

THE OTHER TWO MEN turn around in their seats, and for a long moment no one speaks. Boots is over at a sideboard fiddling with the knobs on a camping stove, trying to get the burners to light. He doesn't seem to be having much success and without gasoline I wonder how much longer it's going to take him.

One of the men inclines his head to the soldier at the head of the table, the one who first spotted us.

'Damn but that boy looks tall enough to hunt geese with a rake, don't he Truck?'

I'm not sure what to say to that, but Boots has finally managed to get the stove going and now he scurries across the room and darts in front of us, anxious not to relinquish control of his prize. He pulls out a chair for Mags and motions for her to sit. I slide myself into the next one along before he has the chance to claim it for himself. Across the table Jax is loading a rubbery-looking frankfurter into his mouth whole. He stares back at me as he chews on it. It's unclear from those flat blue eyes whether he recognizes us from before or not.

Boots makes the introductions. The soldier at the end of the table who looked like he was holding court when we came in is a big man, thickset, although the way his sweat-stained fatigues hang on his frame suggests he was once even larger. His sleeves are rolled up and he rests a pair of meaty forearms on the table. A pair of dark eyes examine us from underneath thick eyebrows that almost meet in the middle. The lower half of his face is dominated by a large jaw and heavy jowls that are darkened with stubble. Taken together his features lend him the appearance of a big old bulldog, perhaps fallen on hard times. His fatigues say his name is Truckle, but Boots introduces him as Truck. His bottom lip bumps out and he pokes at something there with his tongue for a second. Then he spits a long stream of something brown into a cut-off plastic soda bottle at his elbow, offering us a yellow gap-toothed smile.

The soldier to his left who commented on my height is thin, wiry. He smiles as it's his turn to be introduced, but his eyes keep darting back to Truck, like he's less interested in us than in the larger man's reaction to our presence. The name patch on his breast reads Wiesmann but Boots calls him Weasel. The smile flickers a little at that, like it's not a name he cares much for. I have to admit it's pretty apt though. The sharp, inquisitive eyes and overbite don't call to mind someone you'd leave in charge of the henhouse.

The third man's name is Rudd. He looks older than the others seated around him. What little hair he has left is gray, and cut to a brisk military stubble. Deep horizontal lines have grooved themselves across his forehead; more bracket his mouth, which seems naturally inclined to pull down at the corners. He seems dour, stern; hard-eyed and humorless. He looks up briefly at the mention of his name, his puffy eyes narrowing to slits, and then returns to the more serious business of digging a plastic fork into his plate of beans. His fatigues are frayed and patched, and like the other soldiers they seem to hang on him, like they once belonged to a bigger man. But at least they seem like they've been washed recently.

With the introductions over Boots heads back to the sideboard to check on our food. The heavyset man he introduced as Truck reaches into his breast pocket and extracts a small metal tin with the words *Grizzly Wide Cut* stamped across the lid, a picture of a bear above. He raps it on the table a couple of times and then pops the lid and works three fingers deep into the tobacco, pulling out a thick wad. As he holds it up to his nose I notice a small, grubby bandage taped to the inside of his arm, in the same spot Boots was picking at last night. He inhales deeply, then places the tobacco between bottom lip and gum. He works his lip in and out a few times to get the juices flowing, smacking them together in satisfaction. When he's done he replaces the lid on the tin and leans backs in his chair.

'So Huckleberry, where y'all from?'

The accent's southern, but not polished or polite like Kane's was. Maybe it's the tobacco he's just placed in his mouth, but he slurs over his consonants, omitting some altogether, instead choosing to linger lazily on the vowels. The nickname I seem to have acquired comes out *Huck-a-beh-ree*.

I tell him we're from a place called Eden. His eyebrows knit together as if he's thinking hard about where that might be. It looks like he might be building up to ask some more questions, so I decide to head him off with one of my own first. Boots has just set a plate with an anemic looking frankfurter and a spoonful of watery beans in front of me. I pick up a plastic fork and point at it.

'So, is this all you have left?'

Truck's face hardens and he spits another stream of brown tobacco juice into the container at his elbow.

'Franks and beans not good enough for you, boy? Some might say you're lucky we're sharing with you at all.'

I open my mouth to explain that I didn't mean to cause offense; I was just asking a question. The food actually smells okay; I've certainly had worse. But Mags beats me to it. She pushes her plate out in front of her, the contents untouched. I see what's coming and put my fork down with a sigh.

'You needn't worry. We have our own food; we won't need to trouble you for any of yours.'

Boots pipes up behind me.

'It's true Truck. They've got a bunch of army rations on them. All sorts of flavors.'

'Is that so?' Truck's gaze shift from Boots back to Mags. 'And just where are y'all headed, miss?'

'South.'

'South, is it?'

'Yes. We'll be moving on soon.'

The soldier Boots introduced as Weasel turns to the big man I've just managed to rile with my unfortunate question.

'Just like all the others, right Truck?'

'Right, Weez, just like all the others.'

But he stares at me as he says it, his tongue still working the tobacco he's got tucked behind his lip. Beside him the older man whose fatigues say his name is Rudd looks up long enough to cut me some stink-eye and then goes back to rounding up stray beans with his fork. The atmosphere around the table's definitely turned a little frosty after my attempt to divert Truck from questions about Eden. I'm trying to figure out how to get us back on track when from somewhere else in the building there's a sound like a lawnmower being started. It catches, revs for a couple of seconds then settles into a languid idle. Around the room emergency lights flicker to life. I see Mags looking up as well. The chandeliers' dusty crystals reflect the soft glow, but that's not what's caught my attention, and now I realize what was bugging me about the camera above the entrance, when we came in. We're above ground, and this place can't have been shielded. I look across the table.

'How do you still have lights?'

Truck's busy getting the wad of tobacco situated and for a while the question goes unanswered. I wait while he pokes at it with his tongue, until it finally looks like he's got it in a good place.

'Lights is it, Huckleberry?'

I nod.

'Well, that was the Doc. Dare say you'll meet her later.'

He looks at me and smiles, but somehow it's not an expression that makes me feel like he's warming to me again.

'Yep, the Doc she's a smart lady, alright. Right after we got here she had us go room to room and strip the bulbs, along with anything else she thought we might need that would have been affected by the burst. Afterwards we had to replace fuses, some of the wiring, but once we got it all hooked up again most things came back. 'Course we only run the genny on the emergency circuit now, to save fuel.'

There's something troubling me about his answer, but before I can get on to that I hear Mags ask another question.

'You said we were headed south like the others. You've had survivors come through here before?'

Rudd shoots a sour glance in her direction, but then just goes back to spearing the last of the beans on his plate. Truck eyes him for a moment and then looks down the table at her.

'Oh, sure. Whole bunch of 'em. When we first got here Doc had us hike out to the interstate, put signs up, the whole works. For a while that brought us a steady stream. Nothing for a long time now, though. Until you, that is.'

He looks back at me as he says this, and it seems like the twinkle's returned to his dark eyes. A half-smile bends his lips and he pokes the wad of tobacco around some more with his tongue.

'What happened to them?'

Rudd looks up from his plate again and this time he looks like he might be about to say something. But just as he opens his mouth Truck spits a thick wad of tobacco into the container at his elbow. The plastic bottle tips over and dark juice splashes the sleeve of the older man's fatigues. He stands up as though he's just been scalded.

'Dammit Truck.'

'Aw, sorry, Pops. And all over your good Class A's as well. Guess you'll need to tend to that. Lickety-split now. Could be an inspection any minute.'

Rudd pushes back his chair and makes for the door, rubbing his sleeve and muttering under his breath. Truck's gaze follows him across the room. It stays there until the door's closed behind him. Then he looks back at me and winks.

'That old coot's been in the service since Jesus was a corporal and he's still wound tighter than a duck's asshole.'

The smile's still playing across Truck's lips but it's gone again from his eyes.

'And what happened to the survivors?'

'Oh, they just moved on. I guess they never took to the place.'

Boots has been staring at Mags, but as Truck says this he finds something interesting to study on the table. Weasel just grins. I'm about to ask Truck if he knows where they went when behind me the door opens. I look over my shoulder and Hicks is standing there.

He says Doctor Gilbey will see us now.

*

WE GET UP FROM THE TABLE. I can see Jax already eyeing the franks and beans we're leaving behind. I'm halfway to the door when from behind me I hear Truck's lazy drawl.

'Be seein' ya, Huckleberry.'

I turn around and he winks at me. Next to him Weasel's still grinning. Boots is picking at the spot on his arm he was working over last night, like he's making a point of not looking up.

Hicks heads back towards the entrance. Outside night has fallen and the temperature's dropping; I can see our breath as we follow him down the hallway. But if the cold's bothering him he isn't showing it. He's wearing his glove liners but he's shed his parka and without its bulk he looks painfully thin. I guess Dr. Gilbey's 'no firearms' policy doesn't apply to the sergeant, either; his gun belt's still strapped around his waist, the old silver pistol slung low on his hip.

When we get to the lobby the bellhop cart has returned, but our boots are nowhere in sight. Hicks leads us past a bank of elevators and down a long, dark corridor. Most of the emergency lights are out here and those few that remain flicker and buzz, like the bulbs inside are close to failing. We pass a succession of double doors. Some are closed, but others hang ajar. I look in as we walk by. The banquet halls and ballrooms behind sit in darkness, the furniture under the drop cloths so many gray shapes in the gloom.

Ahead of us a thick red rope hangs from a pair of brass stanchions, blocking the way. Hicks stops before we get to it and turns to a door on the right. A varnished wooden sign above reads *The Colonial Lounge*. He knocks once and from somewhere inside I hear a muffled 'Come'. He opens the door and we step into a large semicircular room. Tall, arched windows stare back at us from between heavy silk drapes, the night-darkened glass reflecting the quivering light from the handful of emergency lamps that remain on. Large pink flowers with bright green leaves adorn the walls and as I look up I see another chandelier hanging from a high, domed ceiling. Beneath its dusty crystals more items of furniture, scattered across the checkerboard marble just like in the lobby. Most hide themselves under gray dustsheets, but the shapes are easy to make out. Chairs, sofas, occasional tables, lamps; in the corner what looks like a piano. In the middle of the room three high-backed chairs have been arranged around a low table.

I look around, confused; I thought I heard somebody telling Hicks to come in, but there doesn't seem to be anyone here. I walk over to one of the windows. The snow's drifted up, obscuring the panes near the bottom, but higher up it's only found purchase in the corners. I cup my hand to the glass and peer out. Tables and chairs have arranged themselves haphazardly around something that might once have been a fountain; large plant pots sit empty under a blanket of gray snow. It all seems cheerless and vacant now, but I can imagine how it must once have been to stand here and look out onto that terrace, with sunlight streaming in through the windows.

'It has lost some of its former glory, hasn't it?'

I turn around to face the voice behind me. A slender woman sits in one of the chairs, her back to the door we just came through. Her head doesn't come close to clearing the top of the chair, but that's not why I've missed her. The white lab coat she's wearing has been washed so often it's hard to distinguish from the dustsheet that covers the chair she's sitting in. Above it her skin is wan, pale, and the hair that frames her narrow face is the color of ash. Even the eyes that regard me over the top of her narrow, metal-rimmed glasses are gray. It's like she's an almost perfect absence of color.

'Dorothy Draper, wasn't she just a genius?'

She speaks in clipped, precise tones, each syllable enunciated perfectly. The accent is foreign, but immediately familiar. It's the same one Mom was going for when she'd read to me from the book about the English rabbits.

The expression on my face must tell her I have no idea who Dorothy Draper is however. She smiles, a barely perceptible lift of her thin lips, and raises one hand from the arm of the chair to gesture around the room.

'Romance and Rhododendrons. It was her theme for The Greenbrier.'

This doesn't get me much further; I've no idea what a rhododendron is either. I look over at Mags for help. She shrugs and says 'The big pink flowers on the wall, Gabe.'

The woman looks over at Mags, as if noticing her for the first time.

'Yes dear, very clever. A big flower. The state flower of West Virginia in fact. So delightfully pretty.' She sits forward in her chair, as if sharing a secret. 'They'd burn it all if I let them, you know. Wouldn't you Sergeant?'

Hicks' voice drifts out from somewhere in the shadows behind her.

'Yes ma'am, I believe I would.'

'Every stick of furniture, each beautiful painting, traded for an instant of light, a few moments' warmth. The world is so full of old and broken things now. I just can't bear to let a treasure like this place go.'

Outside the wind gusts, rattling the windows behind me in their frames. It's cold in here, and even though I like that there are colors, some of the furniture actually looks kinda ugly, so maybe I'm inclined to side with Hicks on this one. After my unfortunate comment in the dining room I figure that's an opinion best kept to myself however.

'Please, do have a seat.' She points to the chairs opposite. On the table in front of her a porcelain teapot and three matching teacups wait on a tray. The rims of the saucers are trimmed with gold and what looks like the same pink flower adorns the teapot and each of the cups.

'My name is Doctor Myra Gilbey.' As she lifts the teapot and starts to pour the light catches something silver circling her neck. But the pendant that hangs from the delicate chain that shows itself just above her lab coat spells out the word Amanda, not Myra. 'And you must be Gabriel and Magdalene.'

I catch Mags rolling her eyes at that, but she doesn't say anything. Dr. Gilbey's busy serving us tea so I don't think she notices. I take a seat while Mags looks around the room one more time.

She passes me one of the cups. It shifts in the saucer as I take it and for a moment I'm afraid I'll drop it. I'm not used to drinking out of anything so delicate.

'I'm afraid I can't offer you milk or sugar. Sergeant Hicks does what he can, but unfortunately there are limits to even his considerable talents. We must accept our lot and live as barbarians.' She looks at me and smiles again, but this effort's not much more convincing than the last. It's an expression that just doesn't come naturally to her, like she's had to teach herself to do it, and maybe somewhere along the way she's lost enthusiasm for the practicing.

Mags finally sits down. Dr. Gilbey holds up one of the cups, but she just shakes her head.

'We thought this place was a bunker. But it's just a big hotel.'

Dr. Gilbey finishes pouring her own tea while she answers.

'Oh, The Greenbrier has its secrets, my dear, she just hasn't revealed them to you yet. This is indeed a hotel, once perhaps America's finest. But for thirty years this is also where your politicians would have come in the event of a nuclear war.' She sets the pot down. 'That was the genius of it, you see. Everything hidden right where you could see it, all in plain sight. The entire wing you're in now actually sits on top of a huge bunker. It was decommissioned decades ago of course, and then for a quarter of a century it simply sat idle. It was only re-activated when it became clear that places like this would soon once again be needed. I'm not sure any of your leaders ever made it here, however. There was only one poor soul waiting for us when we arrived.' She looks up. 'I believe you've met Private Kavanagh.'

There's a noise from behind her as Hicks opens the door to let himself out. Dr. Gilbey leans forward in her chair.

'Excuse me for a moment, will you?' She turns her head, even though she's not tall enough to see over the back of the chair. 'Sergeant Hicks?'

There's a pause and Hicks steps out of the shadows.

'Yes, ma'am.'

'Could you wait outside? I'll need to speak with you when I'm done here.'

'Ma'am.'

The door closes behind him. Dr. Gilbey raises the cup to her lips, takes a sip and returns it to its saucer. She looks at me again but for a long moment she says nothing and for some reason I feel uncomfortable, like I'm being sized up, examined. It's Mags who breaks the silence.

'You're not American?'

Dr. Gilbey turns her head to answer and I'm released from her gaze.

'Oh good Lord, no.'

'But Hicks obeys your orders.'

'Yes.'

'So how's that?'

Dr. Gilbey gives Mags a look like she's not used to being the one who answers questions.

'Well, my dear, as it turns out I hold the rank of colonel in what remains of your armed forces. Does that surprise you?'

I'm not sure Dr. Gilbey's expecting an answer to that. Mags takes a moment to consider what she's just heard and then says 'Yeah, sort of.'

'And why might that be, dear? Is it my diminutive size? Or the lack of uniform? Or because I'm British?'

Mags just looks back at her and shrugs inside her parka. *Take your pick.*

I sense this conversation might soon be headed the way of the franks-and-beans misunderstanding with Truck earlier. I put on my sweetest smile and try to steer us back to safer waters.

'That sounds like an interesting story Dr. Gilbey, you becoming a colonel I mean. How exactly did it come about?'

Dr. Gilbey looks at Mags a second longer, then turns her attention back to me.

'Well Gabriel that's kind of you to say, but it was all rather mundane, actually. I was a virologist. A rather good one, if I do say so myself.' She smiles again. I kind of wish she'd stop; she's not getting any better at it. 'I used to carry out research for your government, at a place called Fort Detrick. I don't suppose you've heard of it?'

I have, as it turns out, but I reckon owning up to that might give Dr. Gilbey a clue as to where we've come from so I just shake my head. Fort Detrick's one of the places marked on the map Marv gave me. It's right off the Catoctin Mountain Highway, the route we took when he brought me to Mount Weather. But there's no code written next to it so I figured it wasn't a bunker. It always puzzled me why he'd gone to the trouble of circling it, though.

'Well, no matter. When it became clear how serious the situation was becoming the powers that be moved me to Atlanta, to the Centers for

Disease Control, and put me in charge of the efforts to find a cure. Shortly afterwards that facility was brought under the control of the military and they made me a colonel. I'm not sure it was entirely legal, but then when you're the President I suppose you can pretty much do as you please.'

I exchange a look with Mags.

'So you took your orders from President Kane?'

The tea cup's on its way to Dr. Gilbey's lips but at the mention of Kane's name it stops, and a look of cold, glassy anger crosses her face. In spite of her size I feel a shiver run through me that has little to do with the cold.

'I did, once. If he were still alive I doubt there's an order that man could give that I might follow now. I only hope he met the end he deserved.'

*

DR. GILBEY RETURNS the cup to its saucer and places it on the table beside her. When she looks up again the anger has gone.

'Well, enough about me. So where have you two come from?'

I'm glad now that Mags made us get our story straight before we arrived. I tell her we're from Eden.

'Eden? I'm not sure I'm familiar with it.' She looks at me, and again I get the feeling that I'm being assessed, evaluated. 'Well, wherever it is it looks like they were feeding you there. Whatever made you want to leave?'

'We didn't care for the way the place was being run.'

Dr. Gilbey looks over at Mags as she says this and then simply says *I see*, although I don't know how she can.

'And who's in charge there?'

I glance over at Mags again. I wasn't going to mention Kane, but Dr. Gilbey's reaction to his name earlier seemed genuine. I guess Mags must think the same because she nods.

'President Kane is the person in charge of Eden.'

Dr. Gilbey's eyes widen and she stares at us for a long moment. The wind suddenly picks up, howling around the terrace outside. Then just as quick it dies down and the shrouded silence of the Colonial Lounge settles around us again, the only sound the occasional flicker and buzz of the emergency lights. Dr. Gilbey seems to regain her composure. She reaches for the teapot and starts to pour herself another cup of tea. But as she does so I can see the hand that lifts the pot is shaking.

'So Kane is still alive. You must tell me everything.'

I start at the beginning, explaining how we came to be at the White House on the Last Day, and how we fled in helicopters with Kane when the bombs started to fall. I notice her leaning forward in her seat at the mention of Miss Kimble and our class of first graders, but mostly she just listens while I tell her about Eden and our time there, every now and then raising the cup from its saucer to take a sip. I finish by recounting Kane's plans for us. I confine the details of our escape to just Mags and me, so she won't wonder where the rest of the Juvies might be hiding out. When I'm done she stares at me for a long moment.

'Why, what an adventure you've both had.' She pauses a moment. 'And you say there are more of you, in this place you call Eden? How many?'

'There were thirty of us in Miss Kimble's class. Kane exiled Lena and she died outside in the cold.'

'And you two managed to escape. How brave. But twenty-seven others remain. Twenty-seven children.' She shakes her head. 'Why how awful.'

Her interest seems genuine, but somehow the last sentence seems like an afterthought, as though something else is preoccupying her.

'And tell me dear, how did you know to come here?'

I explain how Marv told me about it. I don't mention that he gave me a map to other places like The Greenbrier, and Benjamin's codes to get us into each of them.

'I see. And this Marvin, did he tell anyone else about The Greenbrier? Is there any chance others will know to come here too?'

I shake my head. 'Marv's dead. He only told me about it.'

'What a pity.' She takes another sip from her tea. 'And what do you plan to do now?'

I hesitate. The truth is I don't know. I can't see there's much for us here; the soldiers barely seem to have enough supplies for themselves. But we need to do something about Peck; if we just return to Mount Weather we'll be no better off than when we left. An idea's coming to me, but I'll need to discuss it with Mags first. She seems to have already made up her mind, however.

'We'll be moving on. It seems like you've already got enough mouths to feed here.'

Dr. Gilbey glances over as she says this, and for an instant I think the eyes behind the thin metal glasses narrow, but it's so brief that later I convince myself I've imagined it. When she looks back at me she's doing her version of smiling again.

'Well you must do as you see fit, of course. Surely there's no need to rush to a decision, though. Supplies are certainly tight, but it's been years since we've had visitors; it would be a shame to see you leave so soon.' She raises the cup to her lips again. 'And tell me, where will you go?'

'I guess we'll keep heading south, see if we can find any other places like this, where there might be more survivors.'

She pauses, as if considering something, and then turns to me.

'Gabriel, maybe you could speak with the Sergeant. I believe he's scouted most of the area around here. You might be able to ask him what he's found.'

'Do you know if he ever made it to a place called Fearrington?'

Fearrington's the next facility marked on Marv's map. It's all the way down in North Carolina, more than two hundred and fifty miles from where we are now. We don't have supplies to make it there and back on this trip, but if I can find out something about it maybe our visit to The Greenbrier won't have been wasted.

'Is that one of the places your friend Marvin told you about?'

I nod. She pauses, as if she's considering it.

'I'm not sure. It certainly rings a bell, but then the Sergeant has been to a lot of places. I'm sure if he can help you he will.' She brings her hands together, like she's reached a decision. 'Well, it's getting late and you've had a long journey. You must both be simply exhausted. Rooms have been prepared for you in the hotel.'

'You don't all live in the bunker?'

Dr. Gilbey looks over at Mags again.

'No, dear, the bunker is strictly off limits; I need it for my work. Besides, the rooms up here are so much nicer than the dormitories down there.'

'Hicks said you were working on a cure for the virus.'

'Yes, dear, I have been since before we arrived here. But I really think that's enough questions for now. Magdalene, you'll be sleeping over by the North Entrance. And Gabriel, we've got a room for you with the other men near the front of the house.'

My disappointment at these arrangements must show. Dr. Gilbey looks at me over the top of her glasses.

'Now, Gabriel, whatever relationship you and Magdalene might be having I'd suggest you take care not to flaunt it while you're here. The men haven't seen a woman other than me in a very long time. I will speak to them of course, but I think it's wise that we put Magdalene in a part of the hotel that is uninhabited. I hope it's an unnecessary precaution, but…'

She spreads her hands, leaving the sentence unfinished. Maybe she has a point. I've sort of gotten used to Jax's staring, but I remember how Boots had looked at us as we climbed the steps to the balcony in the church in Covington.

She turns her head again and calls for Hicks. A second later the door opens and he steps in.

'Ah, yes, Sergeant, would you be so good as to show Gabriel and Magdalene to their rooms? And have Corporal Truckle assemble the men.'

*

WE FOLLOW HICKS down the corridor back towards the entrance. It's colder now than it was earlier, but he still isn't feeling the need for a parka. When we get to the lobby he tells us to wait. Outside the wind occasionally gusts against the doors and from somewhere below us I can hear the drone of the generator, but otherwise The Greenbrier's quiet. Mags hugs her arms to her side and stomps her feet on the marble. I take a step closer, meaning to wrap my arms around her, but then stop myself. Hicks will be back in a minute and I'm mindful now of what Dr. Gilbey said about how we should act around the soldiers.

Hicks returns a few minutes later carrying a flashlight and we set off across the checkerboard marble, this time in the opposite direction to the dining room Boots brought us to earlier. We climb a wide staircase, the thick carpet muffling the sound of our footsteps. None of the emergency lamps are on up here, but there's just enough light from the lobby below to make out a landing. Long hallways stretch off into darkness in both directions. Hicks chooses one and we follow him down it past rows of numbered doors. The inky blackness quickly wraps itself around us; we've barely gone a dozen paces and already I'm no longer able to see a thing. The flashlight was still in his hand coming up the stairs but it's like he's forgotten he has it, and the wind-up I normally carry's downstairs in my backpack. I feel Mags slip her hand into mine.

'How many rooms are there, Sergeant?'

There's a pause then Hicks' response comes back from somewhere in front of me.

'More than seven hundred, all told.'

There's no more to his answer, and we go back to walking in silence. I resist the urge to reach out with my free hand for the wall I know must be there. Instead I strain for the sound of his footfalls ahead.

We continue on for what seems like a long time. We're mostly heading in the same direction but occasionally we round a corner, or climb or descend a flight of stairs. Hicks must know where he's going but this place is like a labyrinth; it'd be easy to lose your way in the darkness. After the first turn I start to count our steps, just like I used to do in the tunnel in Eden.

At last I see something that might be the faintest sliver of light, and in front of me Hicks' outline once again separates itself from the darkness. As we get closer I can see it's coming from underneath a door. Hicks stops when he gets to it and reaches for the handle. We follow him into a large room. A fire burns in the fireplace and someone's pulled the dustsheets off the furniture. A large four-poster bed sits against one wall.

Hicks turns to face us.

'I expect you two'll have things to talk about.' He hands me the flashlight. 'Your room's on the first floor above the lobby, at the top of the stairs. Reckon you can find your way back?'

I nod.

'Good. Don't be long now; I'll be listening for you.'

He turns to leave.

'Sergeant Hicks?'

He stops, one hand resting on the door handle.

'Dr. Gilbey said you had been south of here.'

I think I see his jaw shift from side to side, but he makes to move to turn around. The light from the fire catches the ridges on the puckered scar tissue that runs down one side of his neck.

'That's right.'

'She said you might be able to tell us whether there's anything there. You know, anywhere like this, where there might be other survivors.'

He turns around and squints back at me for a long moment. There's an expression on his face I can't read.

'She did, did she?'

I nod.

'It's getting late. You can ask me your questions in the morning.'

He leaves, closing the door behind him.

Mags looks over at me.

'Well that was helpful.'

She shucks off her parka and slides down to sit on the carpet, her back to the bed. I sit down next to her and slip my arm around her shoulders. She leans in to me and I feel a warm happiness that has little to do with the fire easing itself through my whole body. It's been a while since we've had to obey a curfew and I don't care much for it. But I'm grateful to Hicks for giving us some time alone.

We stay like that for a while, just staring at the flames. It's actually a pretty good fire. The soldiers must be cutting timber; the logs are big, and they've had time to dry. They crack and spit in the flames, sending flurries of red sparks swirling up into the chimney. Eventually Mags speaks.

'What did you think of Doctor Gilbey?'

'She certainly doesn't seem to care much for Kane.'

'Yeah, but didn't she seem creepy to you?'

I shrug. Dr. Gilbey was a little odd, but then the whole world's messed up. I'm not sure what even counts as normal anymore.

'She's been living in this place with a bunch of soldiers for ten years. It'd be strange if it hadn't affected her a little.'

Mags considers this for a while, but I don't get the impression she's buying it.

'I'm not sure this place is any better than Mount Weather, Gabe.'

'Yeah, I think you might be right. But we're not safe there; it's way too close to Eden.' The idea that was coming to me downstairs resurfaces. 'Maybe we could do a deal with Dr. Gilbey; have her send some of the soldiers back with us to Mount Weather to scare Peck off. They seem to be running low on supplies and we have plenty to share.'

Her brow creases, like this isn't something she'd be happy with.

'I'm not sure. What about that guy Truck? He just seems like an asshole.'

'Truck's probably okay. I just got off on the wrong foot with him with that comment I made about their food. Anyway, it wouldn't have to be him. One or two of the others would be enough. I mean, look at the size of Jax. And I bet Hicks is pretty handy with that gun.'

She doesn't say anything. I know she's not convinced, but I don't want to return to Mount Weather with nothing, and Fearrington's simply too far for us to check out on this trip. I've been running through our provisions in my head and we can't stretch the supplies we have left for a hike of that distance, even if we ration them. That means we'd have to scavenge as we went. I might risk it if it was just me, but this is Mags' first time out and I don't mean to bring her anywhere without food enough to get us home.

For a long while neither of us speak. There's a sound from the fire as one of the logs shifts in the grate. Outside the wind picks up; it gusts against the window, rattling the glass in its frame. She shivers against me and I pull her tighter.

'I guess you'd better get back to your room.'

But she makes no move to stand so instead I slip my hand under her chin and bend down to kiss her. Her parted lips meet mine and even though their taste is familiar to me now I experience that same moment of fascinating breathlessness I always get when they first touch. It's as though I'm suddenly aware of everything at once, the pressure of her lips and the taste of her mouth and the warmth from the fire on my cheek and its light through my closed eyelids and the breath we share as we pull away before it starts again.

She twists around and slides underneath me. Her fingers slide up into my hair and curl into it, drawing my face down to hers. I kiss her on her mouth, under her jaw, above her collarbone, lingering there for a few seconds. Her skin is soft and tastes of salt from the day's hike. I trace a line with my lips from the hollow of her throat to that spot on her neck that always makes her sigh.

I feel her hands tighten around my waist and suddenly something has changed. Her kisses are deeper, no longer gentle. After what happened with Lena we know to only go so far, but it's always Mags that has to stop us. But now it's like she wants me to go on and it's suddenly scary because I don't think I can be trusted. All I ever want is more.

I feel her hands twist into my thermals and pull them up. Cold air slips across my skin in spite of the fire but her fingers are warm. I shiver as they brush over my skin just above my belt and then slide around and up my sides. Her fingertips trace a line over my ribs; I feel them rising and falling with the bones there.

I breathe her name against the side of her neck, gently at first and then more urgently as I feel the last of what little self-control I began with evaporating. At last she stops and I bury my face in her neck and hold her tight, just breathing in her smell. I'm aware of every inch where our bodies are touching, the angle of her hips, the rise of her ribcage. Eventually she slides a hand up into my hair and tugs gently and I lift my head a fraction. Her eyelashes flutter against my cheek as she opens her eyes.

'You becoming immune to my charms Gabe?'

If only she knew. If you asked me what I know of hunger I would tell you, *All there is*. But not like this. There is no satisfaction here; each taste of her just leaves me wanting more.

Across the room the fire's slowly burning down, the flames that remain scattered among a nest of quaking embers.

'You'd better get going.'

'You going to be okay here by yourself?'

'Yeah, 'course. I'd prefer it if you were staying though.'

I bend my head down to kiss her, but this time before I get too far she tugs my hair again.

'Go on, get out of here. Hicks'll be waiting up for you.'

I stand and make my way to the door. I check for a lock on the way out but there's only one of those keycard readers, its circuits long since fried by what Kane did to the skies to stop the furies.

*

I MAKE MY WAY BACK towards the lobby, following the cone of light cast by the flashlight as it meanders down the never-ending hallway ahead of me. Tell the truth I'm dragging my feet a little; all I really want to do right now is turn around and go back to Mags' room so we can pick up where we just left off. But Dr. Gilbey's in charge so I guess we have to do as she says while we're here. Whatever, it'll not be for long. Mags is right; there's nothing to keep us. Tomorrow morning I'll find out from Hicks what he knows about Fearrington, and then we can be gone.

I'm more than a little distracted replaying what just happened with Mags over in my head, so I'm not really paying attention. I don't realize there's someone standing a little further down the corridor, just out reach of the beam, until he speaks.

'Well how y'all doin' there Huckleberry?'

The voice makes me start. I jerk the flashlight up. It casts ugly shadows, distorting Truck's already lumpen features. I hear a tapping sound and when I look in that direction I see something flashing in his hand. It's the tin of chewing tobacco. He spins it then grabs the edge between his thumb and finger, rapping the lid once with his pinkie. *Spin. Tap. Spin. Tap.* For the first time I notice a small bird tattooed in the crook of his thumb. As he flips the tin the muscles there flex, making it seem like it's moving.

'Fine, Truck.'

The tin stops mid-spin.

'*Corporal* Truckle.'

Yeah, I guess Mags called it; Truck is just an asshole. I'm tired, and hungry, and pissed at not being able to stay with Mags and generally not in the mood for whatever back-of-the-school-bus entertainment he has in store for me.

'Sure. Well, good night Corporal Truckle.'

I take a step towards him but he makes no move to get out of my way. I'm close enough now to smell his breath. It reeks of frankfurter and chewing tobacco, and underneath it something else: the smoky, sweet smell of whisky.

He goes back to flipping the tin over in his fingers.

'Weez here said I was rude to you earlier, at dinner.'

At the mention of his name Weasel steps out of the darkness behind him and grins at me. Great. Somehow I doubt he's here to witness Truck deliver a heartfelt apology.

'Didn't offer you any of my dip.' He holds up the tin.

'Yeah, well, thanks, but I don't think I'd like it.'

'But you've never tried it. It's Wide Cut, see? Only the best.' His hand flips the tin again. *Spin. Tap. Spin. Tap.* 'You sure?'

'Positive, thanks.'

'Well then, suit yourself. Whaddya say, Weez? Do you think that girlfriend of his'll want some? Perhaps she'll be more friendly to us?'

I glance behind me in the direction I've come. There's no way Truck or Weasel would actually do anything, would they? But Dr. Gilbey was already worried about the effect Mags might have on the soldiers; that's why she's sleeping all the way out here by herself. In a room without a lock. And they've been drinking. I back up a step.

'Okay, maybe I will try some.'

Weasel looks disappointed, but Truck just flashes me that gap-toothed smile. He spins the tin one more time and then pops the lid and holds it out. The pungent aroma fills my nostrils. I reach over and tentatively stick my thumb and index finger into the tobacco. It's moist, spongy; I feel it slide up under my nails. I'm trying to extract the smallest amount I can when without warning Truck's other hand darts out and closes around my wrist.

'Grab yourself a decent pinch there, boy.'

I work a lump of the tobacco free and pull it out as quickly as I can. It smells pretty gross, but how bad can it be? I hesitate for a moment then place it in my mouth against my gum, like I saw him do earlier at dinner.

At first there's not much, just a little warmth on the inside of my lip. But then I feel the juices start to build, and it's like a faucet's been turned on in my mouth. I look around, but I have nowhere to spit. Saliva wells up over my lip and runs down my jaw. Loose bits of tobacco have started to break off. They float around my tongue; I can feel them start to slide down my throat.

Beads of sweat break out on my forehead and my stomach does a slow forward roll. My head feels light and my heart starts to race and suddenly I'm on my hands and knees, still clutching the flashlight, as what little's left of the MRE I had for lunch comes flying out of my mouth onto the carpet along with a dark brown wad of tobacco. I continue to retch long after my stomach's expelled the last trace of it. Above me Truck's still chuckling, but somewhere along the way Weasel's stopped. Now I hear him whisper:

'Whaddya say, Truck; shall we go pay the girl a visit?'

I feel something inside me harden, and my head empties of all thoughts but one. I spit the last of the tobacco and wipe my chin with the back of my hand. The corridor's narrow here; it's as good a place as any. I glance up. Weasel's still standing behind Truck, so he'll have to wait his turn. I slide my hand into the parka's side pocket, my fingers slipping around the metal they find there. The blade opens easily under my thumb; I feel it lock into place. It's already halfway out when from somewhere further along the corridor I hear a familiar drawl.

'What're you fellas doing over this side of the house?'

Truck turns around.

'Aw, now nuthin' for you to concern yourself with, Sarge. We was just funnin' with young Huckleberry here is all.'

'Time for you boys to be in bed I reckon.'

I hear a *Yes, Sarge* from Weasel as he turns and scurries down the hallway. Truck makes no move to follow him.

'You might want to think on now, Hicks. Those stripes on your shoulder don't mean what they used to.'

'Maybe not, but this pistol here stands for the same as it always did. Any time you'd like a closer look at it, Corporal, you be sure to say.'

Truck casts one last look in my direction, then he hitches up his pants and makes his way off into the darkness.

I fold the blade back into the leatherman and let it slip from my fingers. My hand reaches for the flashlight and I get to my feet. I'm not really paying attention to where the beam goes and it slides off the wall and catches Hicks standing in the middle of the corridor. He squints and raises one hand as if to deflect it.

'Get that damn thing out of my face.'

'Sorry.'

I point the flashlight back at the floor. The beam circles the mess of mostly-digested MRE and ground tobacco that's already starting to seep into the thick red pile. Hicks looks at it and then back up at me.

'You'll need to get that squared away before Doc sees it; she'll have a shit-fit if she finds you've puked on her carpet.' He glances behind him along the hallway, then looks back at me again. 'But first let's go check on that girl of yours.'

*

MAGS IS STILL UP when we get back to her room. Her brow creases as I tell her about Truck and Weasel. She looks over at Hicks.

'It was lucky you showed up when you did.'

He shrugs.

'Luck had little to do with it. I was watching to see what that pair would do. I doubt they'll be back, but all the same I'd rest easier if you slept in the bunker tonight.'

Mags looks over at me and I nod. Dr. Gilbey might be a little creepy, but she'll be safer down there with her than out here by herself. It only takes a moment to gather up her things. I sling her pack over my shoulder and we follow Hicks down the corridor.

When we get back to the Colonial Lounge Dr. Gilbey's gone. The rope hanging from the brass stanchions blocks our way, but Hicks just steps over it and continues on. A little further along the corridor ends in a wide staircase. A sign says *The Exhibition Hall* with an arrow pointing straight on. We make our way down a long flight of steps. At the bottom a short passageway opens abruptly into a huge room, bigger than the dining hall we were in earlier. Garish wallpaper covers the windowless walls for most of their considerable height, but otherwise everything's plain, without any ornamentation other than the flickering emergency lights.

Hicks crosses the floor. He stops on the other side under a bulkhead lamp and feels along the wall with his fingertips. When he finds what he's looking for he pushes and a panel pops out. Dr. Gilbey said The Greenbrier had its secrets, and now I see what she meant. The busy pattern does a good job of hiding the seam; you'd need to be right up against it to see it.

He slides his fingers behind and pulls, and a whole section of fake wall concertinas out, revealing a deep alcove behind. Set back in the shadows there's a steel vault door. It's no taller than a regular door, and maybe only half again as wide. A large latch handle sits in the center. Above it the words 'Mosler Safe Co.' have been impressed on the metal.

There's a small intercom mounted flush to the wall on one side. Hicks pushes the button. There's a burst of static and then Dr. Gilbey's voice, rendered tinny by the small speaker, drifts out.

'Yes, Sergeant?'

'There's been an incident, ma'am. I need you to open up.'

There's a long pause and then from somewhere inside the buzz of an electric motor and the sound of bolts being recessed. Hicks grabs the handle and pushes it down. There's a heavy clunk and he pulls the door out towards us.

The doorway's not that wide, but behind it I can see a long, low-ceilinged corridor. A single fluorescent tube halfway along its length flickers, casting just enough light to see to the end. From this point all pretense of luxury or grandeur has been dropped, and in its place familiar concrete and steel.

A door at the end of the corridor creaks open and Dr. Gilbey steps through.

'What's the reason for this disturbance, Sergeant?'

'Just a little trouble with the men, ma'am. Nothing for you to concern yourself with. All the same I reckon it'd be safer if the girl spent the night in the bunker.'

Dr. Gilbey looks at Mags and simply says, *I see.*

'Can I stay with her?'

She switches her gaze to me.

'Is the boy in any danger, Sergeant?'

'I don't believe so ma'am. It was the girl they were interested in.'

She looks at me for a long moment and I get the feeling I had earlier, in the Colonial Lounge, like I'm being sized up, examined.

'I'm afraid not, Gabriel. As I explained earlier the bunker is strictly off limits; one of you down here will be quite enough.' She turns to Mags. 'Now Magdalene, you'll need to confine yourself to one of the dormitories. No exploring. Is that clear?'

Mags nods.

'Alright. Well, come along then.'

I hand Mags her backpack. She takes it from me and leans in to kiss my cheek.

'Take care, okay?'

'I'll be fine. Sergeant Hicks is right next door.'

I watch as she follows Dr. Gilbey down the cheerless corridor. She pauses for a moment at the end and gives me one more backward glance. Then she steps through into shadow and is gone.

*

IT'S STILL EARLY when I wake the following morning. I climb out of bed, rubbing the sleep from my eyes. Mags was right; there's nothing for us here, and after what happened with Truck and Weasel last night I don't care to linger. I'll find out from Hicks what he knows about Fearrington and then we can be on our way.

His room's next to mine but there's no answer when I knock, so I make my way down to the lobby. There's no one there either. The bellhop cart's returned, but our boots are nowhere in sight. I head for the dining hall but the only person there is Jax, just sitting by himself at the table. He looks up as I enter but doesn't say anything, just stares back at me with these flat blue eyes and then goes back to shoving frankfurters into his bushy Viking beard. I return to the lobby and take the long corridor down to the Colonial Lounge. The door's open. Outside the first of the day's light's already settling over the terrace, but it doesn't look any more appealing than it did in darkness. Beyond the frozen fountain there's a low, crumbling wall and then the ground slopes upwards into hillside. Blackened trees poke through the gray snow. The ones nearest the house have been felled, but it looks too neat to be the work of storms. I guess that's where the soldiers must be collecting their firewood.

There's still no sign of Hicks, but Mags will be up by now; I might as well go get her. I step over the rope and head for the stairs to the Exhibition Hall. The emergency lights are off; it grows darker as I descend. I'm halfway across the floor when I hear the voice.

'Lookin' for something Huckleberry? Some more dip maybe?'

I start; I hadn't realized there was anyone down here. As my eyes adjust to the gloom I see Truck, sitting at a table in the far corner. He holds up the tin of Grizzly and smiles.

I glance behind me, half expecting to see Weasel, but the stairs are clear. I turn back to face him.

'I want to go into the bunker.'

'The bunker is it?'

He pokes the wad of tobacco behind his lip with his tongue and squirts a stream of tobacco juice into a cut-off plastic soda bottle on the table.

'Yeah, the bunker.'

'Well, Huckleberry, if that's what y'all are after look no further. You're already in it.'

I'm beginning to think Truck might have been left on the Tilt-A-Whirl too long as a baby. But then I remember what Dr. Gilbey told us about The Greenbrier, how everything here was hidden in plain sight. The Exhibition Hall has no windows. And you have to come down a long flight of stairs to get to it. I look back at the entrance. The wallpaper distracts your attention from it, but you can see how thick the walls are.

'That's right, Huckleberry; maybe you ain't as dumb as you look after all.'

He stands and hitches up his pants.

'Can't let you in, though. Doc's a regular night owl; she won't be up for hours yet. And she don't like being disturbed.'

It's clear I'm not going to get anywhere with Truck so I leave the Exhibition Hall and continue my search for Hicks. I find him in the lobby, kneeling on the marble floor in front of the gold-faced clock, fastening the snaps on his backpack. He looks up when he sees me. The shadow of the portico darkens The Greenbrier's entrance but he's already wearing those funny sunglasses with the leather side-blinkers.

'Sergeant Hicks, can I talk to you?'

'Now's not a good time, Gabriel. Got some things to pick up for the Doc. Maybe when I get back.'

I look over towards the entrance. I need to find out what he knows, but I wasn't planning on hanging around; I was hoping for us to be gone as soon as Mags gets out of the bunker. He finishes with his pack and looks up.

'You can join ne if you want. I'll answer your questions on the way.'

'Where are you going?'

'Just to Lynch.'

'Is it far?'

He shakes his head.

'Next town over.'

I look back in the direction of the Exhibition Hall.

'The girl will be fine, if that's what you're worried about. I'll leave word you've come with me.'

I've nothing to do until Dr. Gilbey opens the bunker, so I guess I might as well use the time to find out all I can about Fearrington. I run up to my room and grab my backpack. I take the stairs back down two at a time, smearing UV block across my face as I go. When I get back to the lobby my boots are on the bellhop cart. Hicks is already making his way outside.

Our snowshoes are where we left them when we came in yesterday evening; the Greenbrier's massive columns tower over us as we snap them on. The day's already as bright as it means to get, but it's little more than a grudging half-light that spreads itself over the ashen landscape beyond. Hicks takes some time fussing with his sunglasses, making sure the blinkers sit flush. When he's done he adjusts his bandana and draws the hood up over his head; his face disappears into the shadow of the cowl.

We make our way past the helicopter. There hasn't been a fresh fall, but the temperature must have dropped overnight because the snow's covered with a skin of ice. Our snowshoes crunch through it, sinking deep into the soft powder underneath. Hicks sets a quicker pace than I was expecting and soon I'm sweating inside my parka. In snow like this Marv and I would have taken it in turns to break trail, but Hicks seems happy enough on point and if he means to keep this up I don't plan to argue with him over it. There's not much scope for conversation, but I figure that's okay; there'll be time later on to ask him what I need.

At the gates we turn right. We've not gone more than a couple of hundred yards when the road curves around and a large gray structure rises up on our left, a bell tower marking it out as a church. The long roof's swaybacked with the weight of snow and in places it's been breached, what remains of the rafters poking through around the edges. A large, arched doorway stares vacantly back at us as we pass; one of the doors there is gone and the other hangs inward on its last hinge. A weather-rotten sign says *St. Charles Borromeo* and lists times for service underneath.

We follow the road as it winds its way westward through the mountains. After a mile we pick up water. It's little more than a stream, for the most part frozen solid and covered over by snow. It meanders beside us, switching back and forth as we trudge on. We cross it three times, but on each occasion the bridge has held. Shortly after the road dips under the interstate but Hicks shows no sign of switching trails and we continue on.

I'm beginning to wonder just how far Lynch is when we hit water for the fourth time. The road inclines gently up to the bank, but even from a distance it's clear this is no stream; beyond a narrow rim of shelving ice a wide, gray river flows sluggishly south, the dark waters thick and oily with the cold. As we get closer I can see that the bridge is out; it's collapsed into the water no more than a quarter of the way into its span on either side. Hicks doesn't alter course. He marches right up to where the concrete ends, slides off his backpack and bends down to unsnap his snowshoes. As soon as he's tethered them to his pack he shoulders it again and disappears over. I inch forward and look down. There's a fifty foot drop to the river and I get that weird sensation in the pit of my stomach, like when I'd go up on the roof in Eden with Mags and she'd perch herself right on the edge. Beneath me Hicks is making short work of the climb; he's already most of the way down.

I step out of my snowshoes, tie them to my pack and follow him, wishing I'd paid more attention to the route he was taking. Once I start I realize it's actually not that bad, however. A rust-pitted guardrail follows what once must have been the road almost the whole way to the water, and for the most part it seems to have held. The twisted metal jutting here and there from the concrete offers a choice of hand- and toeholds.

Hicks is waiting for me at the bottom. From down here the river looks even wider than it did up on the bridge. A small wooden skiff bobs lazily in the water, moored to a section of rebar that protrudes from the rubble just above the waterline. He rolls back an old tarpaulin that's covering it and stands to one side so I can get in. It pitches alarmingly as I throw my leg over the side. I quickly find a spot and sit down, gripping the sides tight with my mittens. He casts us off and jumps in after me. As soon as he's got himself settled he lifts a pair of oars and dips them into the gray water. The wind's picked up a little since we set off and the waves lap steadily against the shallow sides. By the time we reach the middle I've got my breath back, but Hicks looks like he's having to fight the current and I figure this isn't the time to start asking questions, so I just sit there, holding the sides, watching as he works the oars. Before long what remains of the bridge on the other side looms over us. I feel the prow crunch into ice and a second later nudge bottom. I climb out and wait while he ties the mooring line off to another piece of rebar.

I'm thinking he might want to rest for a few minutes but he doesn't. I follow him up the other side and we continue on.

*

HICKS' PACE DOESN'T SLACKEN after the river but even so it's already well past noon by the time we hike into Lynch. There's not much to it, jus a little one-stoplight town, the shop windows we pass darkened, broken, those that remain silted with a decade of grime. He finally stops in front of a small wooden building with a sign outside that reads *The Livery Tavern*. He says we'll be spending the night here.

I guess I don't look too happy about that.

'Took us longer than I expected to get here.' He says it like if it wasn't for me he might have been here sooner, although I don't see how that's possible; we got here pretty quick, given how far it is. He holds up a hand. 'Don't worry about the girl; she'll be safe enough in the bunker with the Doc till we get back.'

He digs in his pocket and hands me a slip of paper with a dozen items written on it. He doesn't ask whether I can read, he just says to get what I can; he'll answer my questions when I return. He steps inside, leaving me alone on the street.

I look at the scrap of paper again. I hadn't planned on having to trade for the information I need but there's nothing difficult there, and the faster I get done the more time I'll have to ask him about Fearrington.

I adjust the straps on my pack and set off.

I get back to the Livery Tavern a few hours later.

I unsnap my snowshoes, kick the powder from my boots and make my way inside. The curtains are drawn and it takes a few seconds for my eyes to adjust to the gloom. Hicks is sitting at a long wooden table in the center of the room. He nods in my direction as I set the backpack down, but makes no move to get up. The thermos he had on the way back from Covington's open in front of him, but otherwise the table's bare.

My eyes shift to a large stone hearth in the corner, still banked with ash from the last time it was used. I'm tired but outside dusk's already settling; I should really get a fire going. I'm a little surprised Hicks hasn't bothered to light one; it's freezing in here. I guess he just doesn't feel the cold like a regular person. His parka's unzipped and as he reaches for the flask I can see he's taken his gloves off too; all he's wearing are his liners.

I shuck off my backpack and get to work. It doesn't take long; everything you might need is stacked neatly to one side. I guess the soldiers must scavenge here regularly enough to keep places like this provisioned.

My stomach's reminding me I haven't had breakfast or lunch so as soon the flames are licking up through the wood I dig in my backpack for a can of roast beef and gravy I found while I was out. I hold it up to Hicks but he just shakes his head and says he's already eaten. Even if I'd had a bellyful of cold franks there'd be no way I'd turn down a meal like this. But hey, his loss. I take the top off the can and pop it in the fire. The label chars as the flames lick up the sides and soon the gravy's bubbling away, filling the room with its thick, rich aroma. My mouth's already watering; I can barely wait. As soon as it's ready I fish it out with the leatherman's pliers and take it back to the table. I grab a plastic spoon from my pack and start slurping the pieces of meat straight from the can. Within seconds I've burned the roof of my mouth in at least two places.

Hicks picks up the thermos, lifts it to his lips and takes a sip. He grimaces like he doesn't like the taste much, then nods in the direction of my pack.

'Looks like you did good.'

I've just taken a spoonful of hot gravy so it takes me a moment to answer.

'Yep, got everything on your list.' And something that wasn't: a pint bottle of bourbon with the tamper ring still in place. I don't think it's the brand he was drinking the other night, but the Sergeant strikes me as more of a pragmatist than Quartermaster. I reckon it'll do to get him in the right frame of mind for the discussion I mean us to have.

'Who taught you how to find stuff?'

Between mouthfuls of roast beef I tell him about Marv and how we used to go out and get things for the others in Eden.

'Eden. You mentioned that when we picked you up yesterday. Where'd you say it was again? Somewhere north of here?'

I don't want to get on to the topic of where Eden might be so I just nod and turn my attention back to the can. But he doesn't seem satisfied with that answer.

'Do you remember any of the names of the towns you and Marv used to scavenge? Trapp? Briggs? Linden?'

Those are all places near Mount Weather. I shake my head.

'I don't think so. I'm not sure. I don't read so well.' I catch him glancing over at my backpack, now full of items from the list he gave me, so I add: 'I mostly go by the word shapes.'

He squints across the table at me for a while, like he's trying to figure out where the truth in that statement might be. I go back to digging in the can. In the end he must decide it's not worth pushing me on it.

'So what happened to him, this Marv fella?'

'He died.'

'How'd that come about?'

'He caught the virus while we were out scavenging. He killed himself before he could do me any harm.'

'He get it from a fury?'

'No, Marv was too careful for that. It was President Kane. He put it in his respirator the last time we went out.'

If Hicks is surprised by this he doesn't show it. He just takes another sip from the thermos.

'Doc says you and the girl plan to move on.'

I shrug. Probably.

'That's a pity; we could use you. Where'll you go next?'

'South, I guess.'

'You don't have provisions enough to get very far.'

I tilt the almost empty can of roast beef in his direction.

'We'll get by.'

He takes another swig from the thermos and works his jaw from side to side as if to say *Maybe. Maybe Not.* I think he's about to say something else, but he doesn't. I reckon this is as good a time as any to start getting the information I need. I fish the bourbon from my pocket and slide it across the table. He looks at it for a long while, and I think I catch a look like the one Quartermaster used to get when I'd bring him back something like that. But in the end he just shakes his head.

'Thanks kid, but me and bourbon don't get on like we used to.'

Well, worth a try. For a few moments I go back to scraping bits of burned beef from the bottom of the can.

'I heard there was another bunker, just outside Pittsboro, in North Carolina. Some place called Fearrington. Dr. Gilbey said you might have been there.'

The thermos is halfway to his lips again, but it stops at the mention of Fearrington.

'How'd you come to know about that, anyway?'

I tell him Marv told me about it, which is close enough to the truth.

'Remarkably well informed fella, this Marv.'

The thermos continues its journey to his lips. He takes another sip, winces, then sets it down again.

'So, do you know anything about it?'

He nods.

'It was our first stop, after Atlanta.'

*

I SET THE CAN of roast beef I've been working on aside.

I remember a scrap of newspaper I dug out of a fireplace, not long after I started going outside with Marv. It was little more than a headline and a date, a corner of grainy black and white photo and a couple of column inches that had somehow escaped the flames. I don't know why but I kept it anyway, put it with the other clippings I'd collected. I'd go through them, when I was in my room in the farmhouse, sitting out quarantine, trying to figure out how our world got to be the way it is. Mags brought them with us to Mount Weather, but they've sat in a shoebox under the bed all winter. I guess I've had other things on my mind, and besides, that mystery's been solved: it was Kane, all of it.

I'll never forget that charred headline though. It was about Atlanta.

It simply read Our Last Stand.

'Were you there?'

Hicks just nods but doesn't say anything further. I remind myself I came here to find out what he knows about Fearrington, but now we're here for the night I have time and I figure it'll be easy enough to bring us back to that topic when I need to.

'What was it like?'

He doesn't say anything, just reaches into his parka and pulls out a crumpled pack of Camels. He lights one and exhales a plume of smoke that disappears into the gloom.

'How old're you, kid?'

'Seventeen. Almost.'

'Close enough.' He pushes the bourbon across the table towards me. 'Don't care much for drinking by myself.' He raises the thermos.

I want him to keep talking so I pick up the bottle and unscrew the cap. It smells like wood and smoke and leather sofas and the cigars I used to get for Kane. I take a small sip. It's smoother than the Fireball I shared with Mags on the roof of the mess back in Eden, but it makes my eyes water, nonetheless.

Across the table Hicks is staring into the hearth, like maybe he's trying to figure out the right place to start. There's a soft crack as a branch shifts in the fire. A handful of sparks rise in a swirl and then disappear up into the chimney.

'It was a bad business. We'd already lost New York, Philly and DC to the strikes. Detroit fell to the virus a few weeks later, then Chicago. After that it was like dominoes. Pittsburgh, Columbus and Indianapolis went dark within days of each other, then Charlotte and Nashville. Each city that fell pushed a new wave of them south towards us; they flooded in through the Carolinas along 85 and through Tennessee down 75.' He stops and looks over at me. 'You came down 81, right? Probably all the way from up near Reliance?'

Reliance is a small town just a little ways west of the Blue Ridge Mountain Road, not far from Mount Weather. I saw signs for it on our way down.

'I'm not sure. We came through a lot of places.'

He waves the question away, like it doesn't matter. He picks up the thermos again and gestures at the bottle with the cigarette. I take another sip. The bourbon hits the back of my throat and burns its way down. It's all I can do to keep from coughing.

'Well, whatever. Where you started's not important. Point is you were on the road a while, right? Maybe a week, give or take a day?'

Mags and I made much better time than that; we were only on I-81 for four days. But I nod anyway.

'Right. Well, imagine what that road would have looked like with a million other people on it, all of them towing carts, pushing barrows, shopping trolleys, whatever they could find. That's enough people to stretch back along 81 almost as far as you travelled it. Helluva lot of people.'

I nod again, like I understand, but in truth there's been so few of us for so long I have trouble imagining what a hundred people all together might look like, let alone a million.

He raises the thermos and looks over at the bourbon.

'Am I drinking by myself here kid?'

I take another sip and he continues.

'It was the rumor that brought them, of course. I don't know where it started, but pretty soon that didn't matter anymore. We heard it from each new batch that arrived. The scientists were close to finding a cure, they said; they were working on it right here in Atlanta. The government would never let the city fall. This would be where we'd turn it around. Hell, I'd heard it so often I think some days I even believed it myself.'

He looks over at the fire again and shakes his head.

'Back then we still had power of course, and a little heat, a few lights, it goes a long way. The army patrolled the streets at night and during the day the grunts went house to house clearing out any furies that were holed up inside. Infantry trains for urban combat so they were good at that, and south of Home Park and east of Decatur was pretty much fury-free. It felt like we were winning, or at least holding our own. Who knows, maybe if we'd had a little longer to prepare.'

Outside the wind gusts under the eaves and then settles. The cigarette continues to burn between his fingers, but it's like he's forgotten he has it now.

'But that was time we never had. Those that had survived had taken to the freeways, and they were leading the furies right to us. There wasn't nothing we could do about that, so the brass figured we might as well use it to our advantage. 75 and 85 come together just north of the city and I guess when they looked at their maps it seemed like a good spot, so that's where we picked to make our stand. The sappers stretched concertina wire right across the highway, just north of the 17th Street Bridge. Behind that they lined up the tanks, the Bradleys, Strykers, the Humvees with the roof-mounted fifty cals. They basically emptied out Fort Benning; it was everything we had. All the other roads into and out of the city were blocked off. Jersey barriers, shipping containers, school buses, you name it; we used anything we could lay our hands on. After that it was just a matter of waiting. The survivors would bring them to us, and we'd end it.' He gives a short, humorless laugh. 'Sure wasn't how that worked out.'

He takes another sip from the thermos and nods at the bourbon.

'How're you getting on with that?'

I hold up the bottle, surprised to see there's already a couple of fingers missing. I take another hit. It's definitely getting easier. I feel it warming my insides as it slides down.

'Ortiz and I had picked ourselves out a spot on the roof of the Wells Fargo building, right by the interstate. We had orders to take out the first ones to show themselves. Brass thought it'd be good for morale. The grunts had always liked having us watching over them when they were on door-kickin' duty.'

'We'd walked both highways that morning, placing our rangefinders. It was a shade over twelve hundred yards to the Peachtree overpass where the interstates came together. Not an easy distance to make, especially with the light. But Ortiz and I were the best sniper team in the 75th; on a good day with him spotting for me I could shoot the ticks off a hound at a thousand yards. The Win Mag was waiting on a tarp at my side. I'd always favored the SR-25; you don't have to work a bolt so it's faster. But at that sort of distance the 'Mag shoots tighter groups.'

He flicks the cigarette, sending ash see-sawing down to the floor.

'So we're sitting up there, waiting, our comms dialed in to the AC-130 that's patrolling above. They haven't seen anything yet, but it's early and besides the infrared they're using never worked well on the furies; they're just too damn cold. Soon as it turns dark and they start making their way down the highway I figure we'll hear about it, though.'

'The last of the stragglers make their way through the gaps in the razor wire and I can see the engineers getting ready to close it up. Down on the line the grunts are waiting behind sandbags, just smoking or cleaning their weapons. Ortiz and I had stopped to chat to a few of them when we'd been down there earlier. The mood was pretty good. The general consensus was that brother fury didn't have a prayer. Once we opened up with all that firepower he wouldn't know whether to shit or go blind.'

He lifts the thermos and I take another hit from the bourbon. I run my tongue across the roof of my mouth; I can no longer tell where I burned it.

'The sun starts to set and the arc lights the engineers have rigged all along the highway come on, lighting up the kill zone. A cheer drifts up, for a few moments drowning the drone of cicadas that's been building since dusk.' He lifts the hand that's holding the cigarette and points it at me. 'Something's bothering me about that, mind, but right then I can't put my finger on what it is.'

'Well, we don't have long to wait after that. Ortiz taps me on the shoulder and points in the direction of the overpass. When I look through the scope there's a single fury, crouched on all fours, right in the middle of the road. It's moving its head, shifting it from side to side like a dog scenting the air, you know how they do.'

I nod. That's exactly what the one I ran into in Mount Weather's tunnel had been doing. A shiver runs down my spine and I take another sip of bourbon. Hicks squints at me for a moment, then he continues.

'I know what's troubling it, of course. Ortiz and I had scrounged a half-dozen blood bags from a casualty clearing station they'd set up on 14th. We'd sprayed the area under the overpass when we'd been up there placing our markers; I figured it might give me a few extra seconds to make the first shot. Ortiz is already calling it in so I take the 'Mag off safe. The scope's dialed out for the range so I just line the sights square on its forehead and squeeze, and a second later the top of its head comes off, like I'm shooting melon at the fair. We'd been ordered to ditch the suppressors so everyone down on the line could hear and my ears are ringing, but right away I can tell something's not right. Only minutes before they'd been whoopin' and hollerin' like Rapture just because somebody'd turned the lights on, but now there's not a sound other than the damn cicadas. I look up over the top of my scope, but I can't see a thing. I never cared much for the night vision the army gives you; at that sort of distance it's more hindrance than help. But the light's fading fast now and I can't make out whatever it is has the grunts spooked, so I reach up and switch it on. The arc lights lined up all along the highway cause it to flare out at first, but after a second it calms down. And then I see it.'

He reaches for the thermos again.

'You ever been to Atlanta, kid?'

I shake my head.

'Well, for a city, it's got a lot of trees. They start immediately north of the point where 75 and 85 come together.'

He trails off, as if remembering.

'Infrared may not work so good on the furies, but let me tell you: night vision works like a treat. All along the tree line it lights up their silver eyes like it's Christmas.'

*

HICKS TAKES ANOTHER SIP from the thermos and leans back in his chair. Outside the tavern darkness has drawn down over the world, but I've barely noticed. I look over at the hearth. The fire's burned low; there's little more than a handful of scattered flames among the embers. I should go build it up, but whether it's the roast beef and gravy or the liquor my insides feel pretty warm, and I really want to hear what happens next.

Hicks sets the thermos back on the table.

'Where was I?'

'The furies. They were in the trees.'

'Right. Well that's when it hits me. That noise I'm hearing, drifting up to us from the tree line. I'd mistaken it for cicadas. We were coming into summer, but of course it had already turned cold by then, so it couldn't have been that; we hadn't heard insects in weeks. It was the furies. Have you heard the sound they make?'

I take another sip of bourbon.

'It's like a clicking, from back in their throat.'

He squints across the table at me.

'You must have gotten pretty close to one, to tell that.'

I nod.

'Yeah, just last year.'

He looks at me again, and then at the bourbon, like he's trying to work something out. After a moment he raises the thermos to his lips and continues.

'Well anyway, I guess me shooting the first one must have set the rest of them off because they're breaking cover now, just swarming out of the trees and onto the highway. I get to work with the rifle. I've got my eye in and they're dropping, but there's just too damn many of them; I can't crank the bolt fast enough. I grab the SR-25 and start squeezing off rounds. Down on the line it's gone deathly quiet, and when I stop to reload I see why. They're knocking out the arc lights as they come; it's like they're bringing the darkness with them.'

An image floats into my head, unbidden. A black and white snapshot of Mount Weather's tunnel, the fury lit by the muzzle flash as it bounded towards me, and for a second the terror I had felt in that moment returns. I take another swig of bourbon to banish it.

'There's a few pops from the grunts now, but they're just wasting ammo. Even if their hands were steady they couldn't be expected to make shots count, not at that distance, not on things that move that quick.'

'As I'm jamming another magazine into the rifle I hear a noise and look up. A Warthog's banking around from the east. It opens up with that massive gun in its nose and for a few seconds it's like God Himself has taken a weed whacker to the tree line. The Comanches come whining in, right on its heels, sending their Hellfires streaking down towards the overpass. But the things coming down the highway don't even seem to notice what's going on behind them.'

'The AC-130 that'd been spotting for us earlier drops altitude and now tracer rounds from its mini guns are lighting up the sky, too. Down on the line the tanks and the Bradleys have finally gotten in the game. A few moments later the Humvees and the Strykers join in with their chain guns and their fifty cals. The noise is deafening. Down on the highway it's just carnage. I lay the rifle up. There's no point; nothing could get through that. And for a second I think, *They were right; this* is *where we'll stop them.* But then Ortiz taps me on the shoulder and points.'

He stops to take another hit from the thermos and I realize I'm leaning forward.

'What did he see?'

He glances at the bottle of bourbon. I raise it to my lips and take another swig so he'll get back to the story.

'Remember what I told you about Atlanta, kid?'

I nod. 'The trees.'

'Right. Well, those trees weren't just in front of us, they were all around. Sure, for a couple of blocks on either side of the highway it was mostly concrete. But pretty quickly the skyscrapers and the offices give way to regular neighborhoods and then the trees are back, spreading right out into the suburbs.' He looks across the table. 'We assumed because the furies were following the survivors that they'd stick to the interstate. But nobody thought to check with brother fury whether that was his plan. Turns out it wasn't, because now they're breaking cover on both sides.'

'The Comanches pull back and head out to the sides and begin laying down fire. A few seconds later the AC-130 hauls off to join them. Down on the line they're trying to move whatever of the armor they can around to face the flanks, but it's chaos, and now there's less fire going forward and the furies are getting through again. I jam another clip into the SR-25 and get back to work. It's no good, though. The first of them hits the razor wire without even slowing. The ones behind immediately start climbing over, struggling and thrashing and tangling themselves up in the barbs. But the weight's compressing the coils, and now others are clambering over the top. The first few make it through and crash headlong into the last of the arc lights and there's that moment, where you know it's all going to get decided.'

He lifts the thermos to his lips, like he's about to take another sip, then decides against it and puts it back down.

'Some of the Humvees have got their headlights pointed up the highway, so I can still make out a little of what's going on. That virus may be contagious, but let me tell you son, nothing spreads faster than panic. The grunts had been trained to fire in short, controlled bursts but there's little of that now. I see one kid, can't have been much older'n you, step out from behind his sandbags, switch his M4 to auto and just open up into the wire. He's empty in no more than a couple of seconds. They're on him before he's fumbled a fresh clip out of his flak vest.'

'The line collapses pretty quick after that. There's just too many of them. The Warthog's still circling, but the fire from the AC-130's more sporadic now, like it's trying to conserve ammo. Then I see the Comanches banking around, heading back to base to reload. By the time they return it'll be over. The furies are spilling out over the freeway guardrails, jumping down onto the streets below. I mean, you've seen how quick they move, right?'

I nod. He holds the thermos up, looks at me.

'Where'd you run into yours? A hospital?'

I take another sip of the bourbon and shake my head.

'Marv said we had to stay clear of the hospitals.'

'Smart fella.'

'So what happened?'

'Well, I crank the scope till it bottoms out and then step up onto the ledge so I can fire directly down into them. But before I can get a shot off I hear a roar and when I look up there's an F-16 coming in on afterburners. It drops down low as it approaches the highway and I know even before I see the bomb detach that it's over. Somebody's called it. The pilot's already banking away and I don't wait to see where it'll hit, I just shout at Ortiz to take cover. I guess it must have been a bunker buster because a second later it's like the ground's turned to jello and the next thing I know the air's sucked from my lungs and I feel the rifle ripped from my hands. The windows on the north side of the building blow out and a great plume of dust and dirt rises up into the sky like a geyser. The last thing I see before I'm hurled back from the edge is one of the Humvees being tossed through the air like a child's toy.'

He reaches for the thermos and I raise the bourbon to my lips again.

'I'm not sure how long I lay there, after, just staring up into the sky. I can't hear a thing. Now and then a chopper passes overhead, but I guess Ortiz and me don't look like a good bet, because none of them are stopping. By the time I finally manage to haul myself up the blinking landing lights are almost all the way to the horizon and I don't reckon any of them'll be coming back. Ortiz is still out of it. I look over the edge; the streets below are swarming. I figure we're not going anywhere till dawn, so I sit down to wait.'

'My ears are still shot so it's a good thing I'm facing east or I might not have seen the Chinook lifting off from CDC. I dig in my pack for a flare and then jump up on the ledge and start waving it above my head for all I'm worth. At first I don't think it's coming, but then finally it swings around and dips its nose in our direction.'

'Only takes it a couple of minutes to reach us. The Chinook's too big to land on the roof, so the pilot holds it in a hover and drops the ramp at the back. I hoist Ortiz onto my shoulder. There's a bunch of grunts inside waving at me to pass him up. I still can't hear worth a damn so I've no idea what they're saying, but then I see the look on this young red-haired kid's face change. I turn around and there's a couple of furies on the roof behind me. I guess I've attracted them, waving the flare around and hollering like an idiot. They're already running at me so I heave Ortiz up. The SR-25 I was using earlier's long gone, but the 'Mag's at my feet so I reach down for it. The elevation's still set for a distance shot and there's no time to dial it back, so I just hold it low and squeeze. The gun rises up and when it drops again one of them's disappeared, but the other's still coming. I figure I don't have time to reload so I ditch the rifle and reach for my sidearm.'

'And?'

The cigarette between his fingers has burned down to a butt. He drops it to the floor and crushes it under his boot.

'Turns out I just wasn't fast enough.'

*

'WHAT HAPPENED?'

He pulls the throat of his parka back and turns his head so I can see the long, ugly scar that runs down one side of his neck.

'Doc's what happened. The Chinook had been sent to fetch her and whatever equipment they could salvage from her lab, bring her someplace where she could continue working on a cure. Truck and his boys were her escort. They were all for shooting me then and there, but she said there was a chance, if we were quick. She burned the skin off where it had touched me. Then they stuck me in one of the plastic cages they'd taken from her lab, to see whether I'd turn. My lucky day I guess.'

He reaches for the thermos, glancing over at the bottle of bourbon I'm holding as he does it.

'So where'd you run into yours, then, if it wasn't in a hospital?'

'A tunnel.'

He pauses, like he's thinking about this.

'Probably had to have been shielded, for it to have survived the burst. Was it at that Eden place you and the other kids were holed up with Kane?' But before I have a chance to agree he waves that possibility away. 'Nope, can't have been, not if it was just last year. You and Marv, coming and going all that time, you'd have run into it long before then.'

I'm not ready for the turn the conversation's taken. I take another swig from the bottle while I work out what to say. Hicks seems okay, and he did save me from Truck and Weasel, but I hadn't planned on telling him about Mount Weather. I rack my brains for another answer but my head's fuggy from the liquor and for a long moment there's nothing. At last something pops into my head and it doesn't seem like anything better's following on its heels so I seize it.

'It was at a place called Culpeper.'

He takes a sip from his thermos, then works his jaw from side to side, like he's figured there's something not quite right with my story.

'How'd you say you came down here again? On 81?'

Even as I'm nodding I realize Culpeper's nowhere near I-81. It takes me a couple of seconds to stumble onto an excuse.

'Yeah, but I took us off the highway looking for food and then we got lost in a snowstorm and ended up wandering around a bit.'

He squints at me a while, like he knows I'm not telling him the truth and he's trying to work out whether to call me on it. In the end he must decide to let it go.

'Well, it can happen. So how'd you get away from it?'

'It chased me out into the light and I shot it.' I'm anxious to move on from my lie so I stick to the short version. I figure he doesn't need to know that I must have missed it a dozen or more times in the tunnel, and once more outside, when it was just lying there in the snow. Or that I was so afraid I peed myself in the process.

He raises the thermos again and looks at me, but I realize I can't have any more bourbon. I hold the bottle up and take a false swig, just enough to wet my lips.

'And the helicopter brought you to The Greenbrier?'

He shakes his head.

'The Greenbrier wasn't the plan, at least not at first. Doc was supposed to be headed for North Carolina.'

*That* was what I was supposed to be finding out from Hicks all along. With everything that had been going on in Atlanta I'd almost forgotten.

'The bunker at Fearrington?'

He nods.

'If you were thinking of checking it out I can save you the bother. Nothing for you there, kid.'

'You've been inside?'

He shakes his head and reaches for the thermos again.

'We landed but the place was locked down. None of the codes Doc had worked.'

'Yeah, Kane changed them all, the day he brought us from the White House to Eden.'

As soon as it's out I realize my mistake. Hicks' flask is almost at his lips but when I mention the codes it stops in midair.

'Your friend Marv tell you that too?'

I nod.

'He didn't happen to give you the new ones did he?'

I shake my head, perhaps a little too quickly. *Crap*. I really can't be trusted with liquor. I ask him another question, to keep him from dwelling on the subject.

'What'd it look like, from the outside?'

He stares at me for a moment before answering.

'Can't rightly say. I was lying at the bottom of a cage designed for something no bigger than a chimpanzee, pretty much out of it on the painkillers the Doc had given me. Ortiz saw it though; he'd come around by then. He told me later it was nothing special; just a guard hut and a couple of concrete buildings. But then Doc said most of it was underground anyway. The silo was supposed to go down thirteen stories.'

'And you never went back there, after?'

'Why would we do that? We had no way in.'

I was expecting it, but I'm a little disheartened nonetheless.

'Doc's fallback was The Greenbrier. It was touch and go whether we'd even make it; we'd used a lot of our fuel getting out to Fearrington. Later when we checked the tanks for anything that might burn there was nothing. I reckon we must have landed on fumes.'

'How'd you get in? Wasn't it locked down too?'

'That was our one piece of good fortune that night. Turns out someone was still inside. Young Private Kavanagh had been part of the guard detail that got posted there when they reactivated it. They got the evacuation order, but somehow he got himself trapped inside. As soon as his squad stepped outside they got overrun. He said he saw it all on the monitors. Shook him up pretty bad, so bad he wouldn't let us in at first. It was only when Doc explained she was working on a cure for the virus that he changed his mind.'

'Is she close, to a cure I mean?'

'She says she is. Not sure there's anyone left who can call her on it, though.'

He takes another sip from the thermos and goes quiet for a long while, just staring into the hearth. The fire's almost burned down and the tavern's turning cold. I pull my parka around me.

'Alright kid, time to hit the sack. Early start tomorrow.'

I get up, a little unsteadily, and make my way over to my backpack to get my sleeping bag. This hasn't worked out how I'd hoped. I've wasted a whole day coming out with Hicks; Dr. Gilbey already knew as much about Fearrington as he did. That bit's bothering me, too. I mean, how could she not remember it? It might have been ten years ago, but it was supposed to be where she was going to continue her research. She must have expected to spend months, maybe even years there.

Surely you wouldn't just forget something like that?

*

SHE'S WAKING UP!

He's so excited he can barely contain himself. He's been watching her since the mean soldier brought her down earlier. For a long time she just lay there, a dark shape curled up on the floor of the cage, and at first he wasn't even sure she was breathing. But he just saw her move, he's sure of it.

He creeps forward until his face is only inches from the bars, even though he knows this is against the rules. They put her in the cage next to 98's, so she's almost directly opposite. It looks like she's wearing the same dark overalls he is, which must mean...

There! She just moved again! Without thinking he presses closer to the bars. He would jump with excitement if he could, but the cage is too low and all he can manage is a small shuffling dance. He takes a deep breath and forces himself to be still. He must be calm now. If she's like he was when he first arrived she'll be frightened. She won't know where she is or what she's doing down here in the darkness.

She props herself up on one elbow and shakes her head, as if she's trying to clear it. They've shaved her hair. He runs his hands over his own shorn scalp, remembering how that had felt when he had first woken up.

She opens her eyes and slowly looks around. He knows she won't be able to see much, not yet, but nevertheless he shrinks back a little further as her eyes glide over his cage. He doesn't want to scare her, the way 98 had frightened him when he had first seen what she looked like. But then she looks right at him and his heart leaps with joy. Her eyes are still normal. She will probably be here for a long time.

Her hands reach forward and grasp the bars of the cage, and for a moment she explores them, testing the thickness of the plastic, its strength. Her fingers move to the edges and she finds the hinges and then she searches on the opposite side for the release. She's wasting her time of course. He knows where the catch is, but there's no way it can be reached from the inside.

She must figure that out because after a while she gives up and instead grips the bars with both hands and pulls. When that doesn't work she braces herself against the sides and starts kicking. That won't do any good either; the plastic's strong. He saw everything that 98 did to the cage in the end, and still it held. But she's making a lot of noise and now he's worried; if she keeps this up the mean soldier will come down, and then there'll be trouble. He creeps to the front of the cage and tries to hush her, just like 98 did with him when he first arrived. It takes her a moment to notice, but then she stops and looks right at him. He knows she probably can't see him but he retreats from the bars anyway.

'Who's there?'

That's a difficult question when you're not sure of your own name. He thinks about it for a moment and then figures Johnny 99 will do for now.

She repeats the name, like she's testing the sound of it.

'Well Johnny, hello. I'm Mags. Do you know where I am?'

That question is difficult too, so instead of answering he tells her she needs to be quiet. But she doesn't seem to get it, because she just asks more questions. As quickly as he can he explains that making noise isn't allowed; even talking like this is bad. She must go to the back of her cage and be still, or the soldier will come. That finally seems to work, because for a moment she says nothing.

'So the soldier comes if I make noise?'

He nods. Yes, yes. At last she's getting it. But then she just starts kicking the bars again and shouting, and she won't stop no matter how much he pleads with her. Soon he hears footsteps on the stairs outside and he knows it's too late now. He scurries to the back of his cage, presses himself into the corner and starts counting. He must have missed the first few steps because of the racket the girl's making; he only gets as far as eighty when they stop, and then the door at the end of the room opens with a soft groan.

He tells himself it might be okay. Maybe the mean soldier won't do anything to her this time. She's new; she couldn't be expected to know about the rules yet. He hears the sound of his boots on the concrete, growing louder as he marches towards them between the cages. The beam from his flashlight bounces ahead of him, getting stronger with each step. Moments later grubby fatigues appear in front of his cage, the bottoms tucked into a pair of large boots. He's got the stick; he's holding it behind his back; Johnny 99 can see the two metal prongs that protrude from the end of the black plastic. The girl mustn't have noticed it yet because she doesn't move away. She just looks up at him.

'Corporal Truckle. What am I doing in here?'

The mean soldier doesn't say anything. He just pushes the stick through the bars. There's a flash of blue light and the girl cries out once but doesn't let go. Her hands grip the plastic tighter as the muscles in her arms spasm. Johnny 99 covers his head with his hands so he won't have to see. Surely the soldier will stop soon. But he keeps jamming the stick through the bars. Soon the air smells like it's burning.

Before Johnny 99 knows what he's doing he's shuffled forward to the front of the cage. He shouts at the mean soldier to stop.

The soldier hits the girl one more time with the stick and then uses it to push her way from the bars. She slumps to the floor of the cage, twitches once and then lies still.

The last thing Johnny 99 remembers is the blue light arcing between the metal prongs as the soldier turns around to face him.

*

I WAKE SOME TIME just before dawn. When I look over at the table I see Hicks is already up, sitting in the same spot where I left him last night. I banked the fire before I went to bed but it's died anyway and now it's bitterly cold. He doesn't seem to care, though. He's just staring into the dead hearth, occasionally sipping from his thermos.

My head hurts a little from the bourbon, but in spite of it I'm feeling better than when I went to bed last night. I still don't understand how Dr. Gilbey could have forgotten about Fearrington, but maybe it doesn't matter; Hicks has already told me as much as I need to know. It might not be the underground city Mount Weather is, but thirteen stories should be plenty big enough for the twenty-three of us that are left. And if Dr. Gilbey had planned to go there to continue her work on a cure it must have been stocked. It'd put us far from Eden too, with The Greenbrier between us, and that could be to our advantage. There's clearly no love lost between Dr. Gilbey and Kane.

I climb out of my sleeping bag, already starting to feel excited. It'll be a long hike for the Juvies, but now that winter's almost over they can manage it. I'd really like to go there first to check it out, but the shortest route I can figure puts it seven days away, which means three weeks at the earliest before we could be back in Mount Weather. Even if we had supplies for the trip that's too long; Peck might already be on his way. Besides, Benjamin's codes have worked everywhere else I've been; there's no reason they shouldn't work there.

I get a fire going and open a can of devilled ham I picked up yesterday for breakfast. I offer some to Hicks, but he says he's already eaten. Must have been hours ago, because I can't smell any of it. He must be a night-grazer, like Marv used to be. Whatever, more for me. I scoop the last of the ground meat from the tin, bag our trash and start packing up my kit.

It can't be much after noon as we pass through The Greenbrier's crumbling gateposts, but already it seems like the day's darkening. Hicks cups one glove to his forehead and squints up at the thunderheads gathering along the horizon to the south.

'Weather's comin'.'

I follow his gaze. The sky there's got a mean look to it. I wonder what this is going to do to our plans. Storms like this right at the end of winter rarely last long, but now that I know what we have to do I don't want to lose any more time at The Greenbrier.

The breeze is quickening, sending flurries of gray snow dancing up the loading ramp into the helicopter's cargo bay as we pass. Up at the house the tattered flags snap and flutter on their flagpoles. We stop under the portico to remove our snowshoes and head inside. I shuck off my backpack, swap my boots for The Greenbrier slippers that are waiting for me on the bellhop cart and head straight for the corridor that leads to the bunker without waiting for Hicks. I'm hungry from the hike back, but I can eat later; right now I just want to let Mags know I'm back and that I've found us somewhere to go.

When I get to the Exhibition Hall it's empty. I see Truck's makeshift spittoon sitting on the table, brimming with dark tobacco juice, but thankfully there's no sign of him. I walk over to the corner and search for the panel he opened. It's not easy to find, even now I know where to look, but eventually I locate the join in the gaudy wallpaper.

I push the panel and it pops out, allowing me to fold it back. In the recess behind the vault door waits. Flecks of paint still cling to the underside of the handle, but on top the metal's burnished smooth from years of wear. I hesitate for a moment and then press down. The mechanism's stiff and the handle reaches the end of its travel with a heavy clunk, but the door doesn't budge.

I look at the intercom. Truck said Dr. Gilbey didn't like to be disturbed, but I don't care; soon we'll be gone, and then we'll never see these people again. My finger's already on the button when I hear a voice behind me.

'Whaddya up to there, Huckleberry? Want to see if your little friend can come out to play?'

I turn around like I've been caught doing something I shouldn't. Truck's standing at the bottom of the stairs.

'I want to see Mags.'

He hitches up his pants and crosses the Exhibition Hall towards me.

'You'll see her soon enough I expect.' He says it with a smile that sends a chill through me. 'Right now Doc ain't in there, though, so I can't let you through.'

I sigh. Why couldn't Kane just have released a virus that infected assholes? I tell myself it'll be fine. Hicks will sort this out. I just need to get him.

I leave Truck in the Exhibition Hall and make my way back up the steps to the long corridor, taking them two at a time. There's something about the way he smiled at me when he said I'd see Mags soon that's got me worried now. As I'm passing the Colonial Lounge I hear voices coming from within. They're muffled by the heavy door, but there's no mistaking Dr. Gilbey's clipped, precise tones. I stop outside.

'But you haven't brought me one in months.'

I hesitate for a moment. There's clearly somebody else in there with her, and Dr. Gilbey's not the sort of person you just barge in on. My hand's hovering over the door when I hear Hicks' drawl.

'I know, ma'am, but…'

I don't wait for him to finish. I knock once, harder than I intended to. There's a long pause and then I hear Dr. Gilbey say 'Come'.

I open the door and step in. The same three high-backed chairs wait in the center of the room but now they're empty. I scan the room and find her standing by one of the tall windows, looking out at the terrace. She turns to face me. In the scant light that filters through the silted panes she seems older. Her skin looks thin, fragile, almost translucent; like if it were to get much brighter you might be able to see clear through to the bones there. The hair that frames her face is so fine that when she turns her head the contours of her skull show.

'How long were you standing out there?'

'Not long at all. I mean, I was just walking past.' I turn to Hicks. 'Can I see Mags now?'

There's a moment of silence that draws out for longer than it should. Off in the distance lightning flashes across the darkening sky and for a second the light from it plays across the lenses of Dr. Gilbey's narrow glasses. She exchanges a look with Hicks and it's as if a large, dark void has suddenly opened up under my breastbone.

'Gabriel, son, you'd best sit down. There's something the Doc needs to tell you.'

I feel my throat tighten and for a moment I think I may not actually be able to breathe, but somehow I manage to stammer out a question.

'What is it?'

Dr. Gilbey purses her lips.

'You must prepare yourself, Gabriel. There's been a terrible accident.' But the voice that delivers this news is brusque, matter-of-fact. 'I told Magdalene she had to stay in the dormitory, but it seems she didn't listen. For some reason she took it upon herself to break into the laboratory last night. I found her this morning.'

'Gabriel, son, she's been infected.'

*

THE ROOM SEEMS TO SPIN around me and it's like I've been delivered straight into one of those nightmares where nothing's right and you know it and all you want is to wake up but you can't.

'You need to bring me to her.'

Dr. Gilbey shakes her head.

'I'm afraid that won't be possible, Gabriel. Magdalene was quite distraught. I've had to give her something to help her rest. I don't expect her to regain consciousness for a day or two.'

'As soon as she comes round you can see her, son.'

Dr. Gilbey's eyes narrow and she gives Hicks a sharp look, like this is not something she had approved. She tucks her lower lip, like she's about to deliver a rebuke, but Hicks cuts her off and in spite of what I've just heard gratitude wells up in me for him.

'Ma'am, with all due respect the kid needs to see the girl. Until we know how this happened I don't think you want to risk another accident in the lab, do you? When she comes to we'll bring her out here.'

He turns back to me.

'Son, I know this looks bad, but there's hope. Doc's close to a cure. And in the meantime she has medicine that can suppress the virus. Slow it way down.'

I look at Dr. Gilbey.

'How long does she have?'

'Unfortunately it's very difficult to say, Gabriel. Right now her body is attempting to come to terms with the virus, but very soon it will try and reject it. When that happens Magdalene is going to become quite unwell.'

'But she's young, and healthy. That's in her favor, right?'

'Yes, Sergeant, that is indeed fortunate. The chances are that she will pull through.'

'And then what?'

Dr. Gilbey folds her arms across her chest. She stares at me for a long moment before answering.

'Well assuming she does indeed survive the initial infection the physical symptoms – the changes to hair color, the silvering of the retina – will manifest themselves. Given the pathology of the virus acute degradation in long-term memory then unfortunately becomes inevitable, even with the drugs I'll be giving her. But I've had some success in staving off the more extreme personality changes.'

She stops, like she's done answering the question. I see Hicks' jaw tighten, but when he speaks his tone is calm, patient, as though he's grown used to drawing blood from this particular stone.

'Ma'am, the kid needs a timeframe.'

Dr. Gilbey purses her lips, like she's already provided all the information that could possibly be expected of her. But Hicks keeps squinting at her and in the end she just sighs.

'Well, as long as she keeps taking the medication I dare say I can prevent her ultimate transformation for quite some time.' She pauses, like this time she might not go on, but finally she continues. 'For someone of Magdalene's age, months, possibly even longer.'

I nod, like I'm taking all of this in, but in reality my mind's reeling, still refusing to believe what I've just heard. I realize Hicks and Dr. Gilbey are both looking at me, like they're expecting me to say something.

'What can I do?'

Dr. Gilbey folds her arms across her chest and studies me. For a moment it's like I can almost see the calculations being performed behind those gray eyes.

'Well, Gabriel, I have been working on a prototype for an antivirus. But before I can risk giving it to Magdalene it has to be tested.'

'You need to help me find more furies, son. They have to be live ones though, functioning, like the one you ran into in that tunnel. The ones that had their circuits fried by what Kane did are no good to us.'

'Is that what you were out looking for, when we ran into you?'

He nods.

'We were on our way back from a hospital over in Catawba. Those are our best bet for finding what Doc needs. There's places in them that would have been shielded, just like in the bunkers.'

Marv said we had to give the hospitals a wide berth. I always assumed it was on account of the bodies, but I guess he must have figured out what Hicks has.

'How many do you need?'

She walks over towards me, her heels clicking on the checkerboard floor.

'As many as you can get me, dear. The more I can test the antivirus the lower the risk to Magdalene when I give it to her.'

I look over at Hicks.

'How many have you found so far?'

He pauses, like this isn't an answer he much wants to give.

'Not near enough.'

'How many?'

'Seven. Four that we've managed to bring back.'

'And how many hospitals have you been to?'

'Pretty much everything within a two-day hike of here.' When he sees I need a number he adds: 'Twenty-five.'

He scratches his jaw.

'Yeah, it ain't good. I'll be honest with you son, the odds are long that a fury would have been hanging out in one of the shielded areas when the burst went off. Kane detonated the missiles at night, when most of them would have been out hunting. And there's another thing, just so you know what you'd be signing up for.'

He looks up, fixing me with a stare from his one good eye, like this is something I need to pay attention to.

'First few we caught we just walked up to them, zapped them with the baton then slipped a plastic gunny sack over their heads; it was all over long before they came out of whatever hibernation they put themselves in when they run out of food. Last couple of times they've come to much quicker. They're getting to be a real handful.'

I think of the fury that chased me out of Mount Weather's tunnel. Even the thought of going into whatever dark place we have to to find one of those things makes my blood run cold. But then I remember the last time I saw Marv. The sunken shadows around his eyes, his pupils impossibly dilated, flashing silver where the light caught them. The way his jaw worked, clenching and unclenching as he fought to control the madness that would soon be upon him.

I can't let that happen to Mags.

'How soon can we start?'

*

HE COMES TO SLOWLY.

Somebody's calling to him. It sounds like the girl but he lies still, keeping his eyes closed, trying to decide if it's a trick. There's something poking into his side. It takes him a second to work out it's the food tray; he can feel the ridges and hollows of the compartments through his overalls, the soft squelch as the congealed beans press into the thin material. The tray is uncomfortable but if he moves it hurts more, so he stays where he is.

He's had the stick before, but not for a long time now, and never this much. He lets his mind go to all the places where he thinks the prongs may have found him. His ribs definitely got the worst of it, but there's something wrong with his insides too; it feels like somebody's scrambled them all up. He wonders how many times the soldier hit him. He doesn't remember anything after the first one. The stick makes his mind go blank, like someone's found the switch that turns him off and flicked it. The soldier normally loses interest soon after that happens. He doesn't remember that from his own beatings, of course. By then he's gone; he's nothing; just a rag doll lying on the floor of the cage, with no more sense of what's happening to him than a stuffed toy set upon by an agitated dog. But he's seen the soldier use the stick on the others, and afterwards he can feel all the places he's been hit. Right now there's too many to count. The soldier must have been really mad to keep working him like that.

The girl's still calling to him. He opens his eyes a fraction. She's sitting by the bars, clutching her side like that's where it hurts too. And now he hears another sound: footsteps on the stairs outside, still faint, but getting closer. He starts the count, even though he doesn't know how many he's already missed. He suddenly realizes how close he is to the front of his own cage; he'll get in trouble if the soldier finds him here. He picks himself up, keeping his movements as small as possible to avoid fresh flares of pain. The tray that's stuck itself to his overalls detaches and clatters to the floor.

The girl must hear the sound because she shifts her head in his direction and asks if he's okay. When he replies his voice is little more than a croaked whisper.

'Yes, but we have to be quiet now. He's coming back.'

He sees her nod in the darkness, like she finally understands. She moves away from the bars. Good; she's learning. He shuffles to the back of his cage and presses himself into the corner to wait.

The soldier's boots echo off the metal, growing louder as he descends. When he reaches the bottom there's a pause and a click as the locks disengage and then a distant groan as the door opens. Somewhere at the end of the row of cages there's the faintest glimmer of light and then the sound of the soldier's boots scuffing the concrete, accompanied by something else: the hollow *clack-clack-clack* of plastic hitting plastic as he drags the stick along the bars. The beam's getting brighter; it bounces along the aisle as he approaches. Johnny 99 pushes himself as far as he can into the shadows and tries not to cover his eyes. The cone of light stops outside his cage and then stretches out as the soldier places the flashlight on the ground. A plastic tray gets pushed through the slot in the front of his cage. The soldier uses the end of the stick to slide it forward, but he doesn't withdraw it afterwards.

Johnny 99 eyes the prongs nervously. He doesn't even want the food; he'd have no interest in it even if he hadn't seen the remains of a wad of tobacco floating among the congealed beans. But in one of the tray's compartments, next to his water, there's the container with his medicine. The soldier rattles the stick impatiently against the sides of the slot but makes no move to pull it back.

'C'mon 99. Don't keep me waiting.'

The soldier will get annoyed if he doesn't take his medicine but the metal prongs are only inches from the tray and he doesn't want to go near them. He hesitates another moment and then reaches out as quickly as he can and snatches the container back into the darkness.

The soldier chuckles and then draws the stick back out. Johnny 99 unscrews the cap and drinks the contents. He gags as the bitter, metallic liquid hits the back of his throat and that causes a fresh burst of pain from his ribs, but he presses his lips tight together and forces it down. The soldier will get really mad if he throws up the medicine and he has to go back up the stairs and get him another. He reaches for the plastic cup of water and washes the taste from his mouth. He'll try and eat some of the food later, because that's what you have to do so they'll know you're still okay and don't need to go to the other room. But he doesn't think he can manage any of it now.

He screws the cap back on the container and places it near the front of his cage so the soldier can collect it. But the soldier has already lost interest in him. He bends down in front of the girl's cage and slides another food tray through the slot there. Johnny 99 stays back, keeping himself hidden in the shadows so the girl doesn't see him. He really hopes she doesn't do anything to provoke the soldier. But she seems to have learned her lesson. She's crouched all the way at the back, just like he told her.

The soldier squats in front of the bars.

'How you doin' in there, darlin'?'

Johnny 99 can hear the smile in the soldier's voice. He pushes the girl's food forward with the stick. The girl backs up, like she's frightened of the prongs too, but then without warning she launches herself forward.

The soldier's taken by surprise; he manages to yank the stick back through the slot, but as he staggers backwards he trips over his own feet and lands heavily on his elbows. His boots scrabble for purchase on the concrete as he tries to push himself out of the way. The girl's hands shoot through the bars, but he's just done enough to get himself out of her reach. Her fingers miss him by inches.

For a long moment the soldier just sits in front of Johnny 99's cage, his chest rising and falling inside his sweat-stained fatigues. Strands of his hair have fallen across his forehead and his cheeks are flushed, but there's something else that's bothering Johnny 99 now, a smell so heavy, so pungent that it makes him feel dizzy.

The soldier slowly picks himself up. He squats down in front of the girl's cage again, only this time he keeps his distance. The girl makes no move to step back from the bars.

'So, Corporal, you're scared of me.'

The soldier reaches for the flashlight, and that's when Johnny sees it. The arm of his fatigues is ripped. He must have done it scrambling backwards to put himself beyond the girl's grasp. His elbow pokes through the tear in the fabric.

Something flickers inside him, a feeling he has not had for so long that at first he does not recognize it. The pain from his ribs is forgotten. He crawls to the front of the cage, even though some rapidly receding part of him knows this is not allowed. His hands slip between the bars (*definitely* against the rules, *definitely*), reaching out to the pale flesh that shows through the torn fabric. The baton's right there. The boy knows he will be in trouble if he is caught now, but he is unable to stop himself. He is mesmerized by the heavy beads of bright red blood that have welled up all along the skin where the soldier has scraped his elbow on the concrete.

The soldier smoothes back the strands of hair that have fallen across his face, oblivious to the small hands that reach out through the bars of the cage behind him.

'And have you figured out why yet, Miss Smartybritches? I guess you must have to pull a stunt like that. But just in case you haven't, you've got the same thing he has.'

The boy's fingers stretch out, but just as they're about to touch the soldier's arm the soldier reaches for the flashlight. He swings it around and shines it into his cage. Johnny 99 scrabbles back as far as he can, but there's nowhere to hide from the cruel beam. He pulls his hands up to block the light, but in the moment before he squeezes his eyes shut he catches a glimpse of the girl's face as she sees him for the first time. Her eyes widen and in that instant something passes behind them, a recognition of the horror the soldier has just described. The soldier holds the beam on him a few seconds longer then points it along the aisle and sets it down. When Johnny dares to open his eyes again the soldier's reaching into his pocket. He pulls out a plastic vial just like the one he's just given him.

'See this here?' He holds it up so the girl can see. 'This is Doc's medicine. Take it every day like you're supposed to and the thing you've got inside you slows right down. Could take it months before it gets a good hold on you, years even. Look at 99 over there. He's been with us a long while, haven't you, boy?'

Johnny 99 thinks the soldier means to shine the light on him again. He raises his arms and tries to push himself further into the corner. But the soldier makes no move for the flashlight. He's preoccupied with the plastic container. He turns it over in his fingers, watching as the pale liquid shifts sluggishly against the sides.

'But see, without it, with the dose you've had, you'll turn in three days, four tops. And Doc hasn't figured out how to make people change back yet, so when that happens I have to come back down here with the baton and the catchpole and take you next door. Want to know what happens in there?'

The soldier waits for a response. When he doesn't get one he continues anyway.

'Well, first Doc takes a bone saw to the top of that pretty little head of yours and scoops out all the bits that interest her. After that, if you're still ticking, of course, there's another cage waiting for you, on the far side. You think it's nice in here? Just wait till you see what we got for you in there.'

He pauses to let this sink in, then he holds up the plastic container again.

'Now Doc says I have to watch you take this. I even have to fill out a little report, give her the exact time I saw you swallow it.'

'That's a lot of responsibility for a man with your abilities, Corporal. Let me know if you need any help.'

Johnny 99 thinks he hears her voice waver as she says it but even so he's never heard anybody talk back to the mean soldier before. He covers his face with his hands, afraid of what will happen next. The soldier's fingers reach for the stick and this time they close around it. For a moment he hefts it like he means to use it, but then he stops.

'Well that's very kind of you, sugar, but I think I can manage. Now, today my report's going to say you had yourself a hissy fit and refused to take your medicine. We'll see how you feel tomorrow. Maybe if your attitude improves I'll let you have one of these.'

He holds the container up a moment longer then slips it back in his pocket.

'Or then again maybe I won't.'

*

THE NIGHT CRAWLS PAST.

I'm tired but sleep won't come and so I just sit on the floor in my parka, staring out at the gathering storm. Outside the weather's worsening. Along the horizon the sky's restless with lightning; it shudders inside the clouds, occasionally breaking free to stab down at the ground below.

When I got back to my room I threw up the ham I ate for breakfast. I went back to the bathroom twice more until there was nothing left. There was a knock on my door soon after and when I opened it Hicks was standing there with a rifle. He said there were things I needed to learn. I followed him down to the dining room and he sat me down at the table and laid the rifle in front of me. It was called an M4, he said. He showed me how to check it was safe and then he taught me how to strip it. He made it look easy; it's like his fingers knew what to do without him even watching then. It took me a while to get the hang of it, but soon I could break it down until it wasn't more than a collection of receivers, assemblies, pins and springs. He made me memorize the names of each, and where they fit in relation to each other, so I'd be able to put it back together again afterwards.

When he was happy I could do that he handed me a dozen cotton swabs and a small plastic container of something that said *Weapons Oil Arctic* on the front. Every component had to be inspected, wiped down and oiled, he said. The gun already looked pretty clean to me but he said pretty clean wouldn't cut it: the tiniest grain of dirt could screw up the mechanism or prevent the firing pin striking the tail of the bullet. I thought of Marv's pistol, buried for weeks in the snow outside Mount Weather where I dropped it after I shot the fury. I doubt it would have worked even if I'd had bullets for it.

I set to with the swabs. He watched me for a while and then he reached down to his hip and slid the pistol he carries out of its holster. He laid it on the table and started emptying the bullets from the chamber. We worked in silence. When I finished with the last piece he had me reassemble the rifle and then he inspected it. He said I hadn't wiped the bolt carrier down properly. He told me to strip it and start again.

The bolt carrier was fine; it was the last thing I checked before I put the rifle back together. I reckon Hicks was trying to give me something to do, something to keep my mind from turning to what I had just learned, and I guess I should be grateful to him for that. But all I could think of as I sat there surrounded by slides and springs and receivers, the smell of the oiled metal heavy in the air, was Eden's armory. The assault rifles standing to attention in their racks, the blue-gray steel gleaming dully in the glare from the overhead lights. The bank of refrigerator cabinets against the back wall that for a decade housed the virus that ended our world.

The same virus that now works its way through Mags' veins.

Outside the wind howls, rattling the silted panes in their frames. The fire in the grate slowly burns down and one by one the quaking embers die. I don't bother to stoke it, I just wait in the darkness, letting the room turn cold around me.

Hicks says it'll be okay. The medicine Dr. Gilbey's giving Mags will keep her from turning until she can find a cure. But all I can think of is Marv. Marv had been strong, but he didn't last the three days it took us to hike the Catoctin Mountain Highway to the Blue Ridge Mountain Road.

I go back to watching the storm. As long as it stays to the south of us we'll leave in the morning. There's a big hospital out in Blacksburg. It'll be a hard hike through the mountains, but Hicks reckons we can be there in a little over a day if we push. It has a radiology department. There's a good chance we'll find what Dr. Gilbey needs there.

The thought of going looking for one of those things that attacked me in Mount Weather's tunnel scares me almost more than I can bear. But that's what I must do now, for as long as it takes Dr. Gilbey to find a cure for Mags.

*

WE SET OFF AT FIRST LIGHT. Ortiz and Jax are already waiting in the lobby when I get down. Ortiz asks if I want breakfast but I don't think I can eat so I just shake my head and hoist my pack onto my back. Hicks hands me a rifle and I sling it over my shoulder.

We leave The Greenbrier and head for the interstate. The storm continues to pound the horizon but it's keeping its distance, so we press on into Virginia and pick up a road the sign says is the Kanawha Trail. From there it's a steep climb. Hicks doesn't let the pace drop and soon my legs are burning, but I'm glad for it. No one speaks. That suits me fine, too.

We stop for lunch by the side of the road at a place called Crows. Ortiz and Jax share a pack of cold frankfurters between them while Hicks just sips from his thermos. I'm not feeling hungry but he says I have to eat, so I dig an MRE out of my pack and set it to warm. When it's done I pick at it for a while and then hand the pouch to Ortiz. While he's scooping out the remains Hicks picks up the cardboard carton my meal came in. He packs it with snow and then hands it to Jax.

'Take that down the road and place it on the guardrail, just in front of that first tree.'

He looks at me.

'Alright, on your feet. Time for your first lesson with the rifle.'

I stand.

'Show me your trigger finger.'

I slide off my mitten and hold up my right hand. The cold bites immediately, even through the liners I'm wearing. He reaches over and grabs my index finger. A short knife with a serrated edge appears in his other hand. Before I have a chance to protest he tucks the tip of the blade into the liner at the crook of the first joint and slides it forward. The knife must be sharp; the material puts up no resistance as it slices through. He withdraws the blade, folds it back into its handle, and just as quickly it disappears back into his parka.

'You always need to be able to feel the trigger. Now you can poke your finger out when you need to take the shot and slide it back in again when you're done.

I hold my hand up and examine the liner, still a little shocked by the speed with which it happened. There's a slit that reaches almost up to the tip of the glove.

He reaches for my backpack and sets it down in the snow in front of me.

'Alright now, lay down.'

I snap off my snowshoes and lie behind the pack. He squats next to me and sets the rifle down so the barrel rests across it. He tells me to take hold of it. It feels a little weird at first; the thick down of the parka makes it hard for the stock to sit snug into my shoulder.

'Push it a little bit forward and away from you, then tuck it back in to get it at the right spot. That's it.'

Down the road Jax is placing the MRE carton on top of the guardrail, packing snow around it. When he's done he turns around and starts lumbering back towards us.

Hicks pulls a clip from his pocket, thumbs in three bullets and hands it to me. I slide it up into the housing and feel it lock into place. He points to the charging handle and tells me to pull it back to load the first round into the chamber.

'It's a shade under a hundred yards to that carton. The scope's zeroed to that range. Take a look.'

The rifle feels cold against my cheek, even through the thin cotton of the mask. I squint through the sights, adjusting my aim until the center of the crosshairs settles on the cardboard container. Jax is already safely out of the way so I poke my finger through the slit Hicks made in my glove liner and start to slide it onto the trigger.

'Did I tell you to do that yet?'

I slide my finger back out of the trigger guard.

'Alright, first take a long deep breath and let it out. Now remember to keep looking through the scope after you take the shot. You'll want to see where the bullet lands.'

I nod.

'Take the weapon off safe, but only one click, mind. You want it on semi, not auto.'

I find the switch with my thumb and slide it forward one notch.

'Good. Now you're set.'

The metal feels cold as I curl my finger around it. I realize my heart's pounding. I slowly start to squeeze, feeling the slack come out of the mechanism. All of a sudden there's a loud crack and the rifle thumps back into my shoulder before I'm ready for it. The parka absorbs most of the recoil but nevertheless it startles me and I allow the muzzle to jump. By the time it settles back down again it's all over. I have no idea where the bullet's gone. All I know is the MRE carton remains exactly where Jax placed it on the guardrail, unmolested.

'Alright, shift your shoulder forward for me. That's it; make sure your body's leaning into the stock. Now remember you need to hold the gun on target long enough to see where the bullet hits.'

I put my cheek back to the metal, once again finding the carton through the scope. I breathe out slowly, squeezing the trigger as the air slips from my lungs, and this time when the gun jumps I'm ready for it.

The muzzle rises up a little but not much and I catch a puff of snow behind and to the right of the carton where the bullet lands.

Hicks unsnaps the throat of his parka and pulls down his bandana. He just stands there for a moment, like he's checking something. When he's done he holds his hand out for the rifle.

'That'll do for now. Wind's picking up and I haven't shown you how to compensate for it. No point in wasting bullets.'

I remember the thing that chased me out of Mount Weather's tunnel. I kept firing Marv's pistol at it, but not a single bullet found its target. This gun might be the only thing standing between me and whatever we find in Blacksburg tomorrow. I need to know I can do it.

'There's a round left. Let me try one more time.'

Hicks squints down at me. For a moment he looks like he's going to say no, but then he just shrugs.

'Alright.'

This time I pull my mask down so I can feel the wind on my face. I imagine it blowing across the tracks we made, slowly filling in the prints left by our snowshoes. I put my cheek back to the rifle. Without the thin cotton the freezing metal bites the flesh there, but I ignore it. I look through the scope, finding the carton again. I see how the wind picks up the snow, swirling the flakes in little eddies over the guardrail, dancing them around the cardboard. I shift the barrel a fraction so the crosshairs hover in the air no more than a hand's breadth to the left then I exhale slowly and squeeze. I feel the recoil, but this time I'm on it and the muzzle barely moves. For an instant I smell burnt gas; it mixes with the sweet scent of the gun oil and then just as quickly the wind carries it away. Down the road the carton disappears from the guardrail in a puff of snow.

]Behind me Ortiz whistles.

'Damn, Sarge. The kid might just have a talent for this.'

*

IT'S THE FOOTSTEPS he hears first, just like always. He looks across at the girl. She still hasn't moved from the back of her cage. She went there after the mean soldier left and she hasn't stirred since.

He shuffles himself away from the bars and starts the count. There's something different, now: not one set of footsteps but two. He closes his eyes and concentrates on separating them. The first is definitely the lumbering *thunk-clang* of the boots the mean soldier wears. But the second are lighter, quieter; the footsteps of a much smaller person. He knows immediately who they belong to.

It's been a while since the doctor visited. He casts a guilty glance in the direction of the food tray that sits, untouched, near the front of his cage. He had meant to eat some of it, but he thought he would have more time. He wonders if he should try now. He scurries forward and lifts the plastic spoon from the congealed mess of beans and tobacco, but then thinks better of it. He only has moments; he'll be able to manage a mouthful at best. And recently the food has started to make him feel like he might throw up, even when the mean soldier hasn't done anything to it. It will be worse if the doctor thinks that the food is making him sick.

The count reaches eighty-nine and somewhere off in the darkness he hears the click as the locks disengage and a soft groan as the door is opened. Across from him the girl has moved to the front of her cage and is looking out through the bars. He shuffles back into the corner and listens. The doctor is coming first; the heels she wears click hollowly on the hard floor. He can hear the soldier's boots scuffing the concrete in her wake, the beam from the flashlight he carries dancing between the rows of cages. He keeps his eyes open, making an effort not to squint. He does not want the doctor to know the light bothers him.

She stops in front of his cage. Her face appears in front of the bars as she bends down to look in, but it's a perfunctory examination and for once he is grateful. She turns around to face the girl. The soldier catches up and stands beside her, the stick held loosely by his side. Johnny 99 wishes the girl would go to the back of her cage like she's supposed to, but she doesn't. She just sits there holding the bars.

'Do I need to have the Corporal place you in restraints?'

The girl considers this for a moment and then shakes her head.

'Good. He told me you refused to take your medicine yesterday.'

The girl looks up at the soldier.

'That's not how I would have described it. We had a misunderstanding over his use of the cattle prod.'

The doctor *tsks* her disapproval.

'Yes, he is something of a blunt instrument, aren't you Corporal?'

'Ma'am.'

She turns to the soldier and holds out her hand. He passes her the stick. Her fingers slide along the shaft, all the way to the metal prongs that protrude from the end. The girl doesn't move, but she watches the doctor closely.

'They are such ugly things, aren't they? Do you know we found them here? I suppose the powers that be – the powers that *were* I should say – anticipated a certain amount of unrest, even among their appointed representatives. They have proved quite useful, though. Those infected with the ferrovirus are quite susceptible to the effects of electricity, far more so than the rest of us.'

'Was it you, who gave it to me?'

'Yes, dear, and no doubt you feel aggrieved. What you need to understand is that I really had no alternative. We are running very short on time. The electromagnetic pulse Kane thought would destroy the virus did not have that effect. I could have told him of course, had he thought to consult me. It is so much more resilient than he ever gave it credit for. But then the man was always such a buffoon. The only real surprise is that he was capable of conceiving a plan of such scope in the first place.'

The doctor regards the baton a moment longer and then hands it back to the soldier.

'But I digress. The net result of course is that the infected were not permanently disabled; they have merely been temporarily incapacitated. At some point, I suspect not very long from now, they will begin to wake from their slumber. And when that happens there will be nowhere for you or Gabriel or anyone else who might still be alive out there to hide. So you see my dear, in a sense your fate was already sealed. I just speeded the process up a little in the interest of finding a cure for all of us.'

The girl's brow furrows as the doctor explains this.

'You didn't come down here to give me that speech so you could feel better about what you've done.'

'Quite right dear, well said. Let's cut to the chase, shall we? The reason I am here is Gabriel.'

'Does he know?'

'That you have become infected? Yes. He thinks you accidentally contracted the virus while trespassing in my laboratory. I know dear, another awful deception; no doubt you are horrified. But if I could just have your attention for a few more minutes; this is really rather important. I have developed several prototypes of an antivirus, but unfortunately I am lacking subjects on which to test them. If it were not for Sergeant Hicks' intervention Gabriel would already be down here with you. But the Sergeant has convinced me that your young man can be more valuable to us on the outside. I have therefore agreed to give him a short trial. He has left this morning with the other men to try and find a suitable subject for my experiments.'

'What do you mean, "a suitable subject for your experiments"?'

'Why, a live infected, of course.'

The expression on the girl's face doesn't change, but Johnny 99 thinks he sees her grip on the bars tighten. If the doctor notices she shows no sign of caring.

'As long as Gabriel proves himself useful he won't have to join you down here. He has however insisted on seeing you, and against my better judgment I'm considering having you brought out to him, assuming of course that he returns. Would you like that, Magdalene?'

This seems to take the girl by surprise. She looks up at the doctor.

'Yes.'

'Good. You will need to maintain the fiction of how you came to be here, of course. Do you understand?'

The girl nods.

'Very well. Corporal Truckle will come down to prepare you. You will do exactly as he says or the next time you see Gabriel he will be in the cage next to you. Is that clear?'

The girl nods her head again, but doesn't say anything. The doctor is about to turn away when she speaks.

'Can you do it?'

'Do what, dear?'

'Find a cure for Kane's virus.'

The doctor pauses for a long moment, and when she finally answers it seems to Johnny 99 that she is speaking to herself as much as to the girl.

'It is a truly remarkable piece of engineering; so incredibly tenacious. You only have to look at how little time it took to supplant us as the dominant organism on this planet.' She looks down at the girl. 'But yes, given enough time and an adequate supply of subjects on which to test my work, I can find a cure.'

'What makes you so sure?'

'Because the virus isn't Kane's, my dear. It's mine.'

*

WE REACH BLACKSBURG the morning after. We pick up signs for the hospital on the outskirts of town, following them up a winding access road. Cars mount the sidewalk at haphazard angles; others sit abandoned where they came to rest, their trunks agape like startled mouths.

Stonewall Hospital waits for us atop a low promontory. What must once have been an imposing structure now lies in ruin. One entire wing seems to have crumbled under its own weight; to the west it ends abruptly in a mound of broken concrete and twisted rebar. On the other side things seem to have fared only slightly better; the roofline dips alarmingly at various points as whatever was bracing it there has succumbed. Rows of dark windows march off towards the last remaining corner, staring down at us as we approach.

Marv always said we had to stay clear of places like this, so I've never set foot inside one. I've read enough from the newspaper articles I used to collect to imagine what they must have been like, though. The hospitals were where the virus cases were taken, at least at first, before anyone knew what we were dealing with. Later they would work it out, but by then of course it was too late. There were reports the military took to targeting them in the end, in a last desperate attempt to halt the spread. I can't say if that was true. I only know that if it was it didn't work.

Hicks leads us towards a tall atrium that juts from the center. The steel uprights have buckled and now they list drunkenly, the large glass panes that would have once completed that part of the structure long since released from their frames. The parking lot's full, a sea of humped gray shapes resting silent under a blanket of snow; we have to pick our way through. As we get closer I can see an ambulance has crashed into the entrance, coming to rest half-in, half-out of the lobby. The rear doors hang open. A gurney that looks like it might have been ejected from the back pokes out of the snow nearby.

We unsnap our snowshoes and make our way in. Hicks goes first. The Viking follows, pressing himself up against the ambulance's paneled flank as he squeezes past. I'm beginning to wonder whether Jax even realizes there's been a virus; maybe to him the world seems just like how it's always been. Ortiz goes next, but at least he shows the good sense to give the once-contaminated vehicle a wider berth.

I hang back. I've been preparing myself for this, but now I hesitate. The fear of what we will find in here rises up, coiling around my insides, settling in my stomach like ice water.

I take a deep breath and step through. Inside it's darker; I lift my goggles onto my forehead and look around. A sign on the wall says to use the hand sanitizer provided, but the dispenser's been ripped from the wall and is nowhere in sight. Over in the far corner a soft drinks machine lies on its side, its front smashed, the contents long since plundered.

The soldiers have already taken off their backpacks and set them on the ground. I shuck mine off too. Hicks removes his gloves and unzips his parka. He draws the pistol from the holster on his hip and starts rotating the cylinder, checking each of the chambers in turn. When he's done he steps over to a directory that's hanging from the wall behind reception.

Ortiz draws a long black stick from his pack, like one of the billy clubs the Guardians used to carry in Eden, except for the two metal prongs protruding from the end. Hicks told me the furies don't care much for electricity; a single jolt should be enough to knock one out long enough for Jax to bag it. As I watch Ortiz holds the baton up and thumbs a switch on the handle. An arc of blue light jumps between the prongs. He looks at me and then over to Hicks.

'Remind me again why this ain't the kid's job?'

Hicks doesn't take his eyes off the wall.

'Gabe'll get his turn. But first he's going to watch how you do it.'

He turns to me.

'You ready?'

I nod, mostly because right now I don't trust myself to speak. I sling the rifle off my shoulder and pull the handle back to load a round into the chamber, like he showed me.

'Alright. Just keep your eyes peeled and try not to shoot anything you don't mean to.'

I tell myself I can do that.

'Jax, you got the bag?' The Viking's huge fist finally emerges from his backpack gripping a large sack made of thick black plastic.

'Okay then. Let's get this done.'

We follow Ortiz down a long hallway into darkness, our footfalls the only sound in the cold silence. I can hear my heart hammering, beating wild inside my ribcage. I check each doorway and alcove we pass, my eyes darting into the shadows, searching for whatever might be waiting for us there.

At last the corridor ends, and another runs off at right angles. Ortiz stops to get his bearings. There's a map stuck to the wall next to me, above a drinking fountain. I shoulder the rifle and dig in my pocket for the flashlight. The little dynamo whirs as I turn the stubby plastic handle, but before the bulb has the chance to warm Hicks growls at me to turn it off.

Up ahead Ortiz must have figured it out because he holds the stick up and signals left. We follow him around the corner. I see him reach inside his parka and a second later a cone of red light appears in front of him, casting the corridor in shades of crimson and black.

A bank of elevators appears out of the gloom. As we approach I can see that the doors of the last one are open. I'm not in control of the flashlight so it takes me a moment to figure out why. The body of what once was a man is holding them open. He's lying there inside his rotting clothes, all shriveled and drawn, what little remains of his flesh cloven along the bones. His ligaments have dried taut as wires, curling him up into a tight ball. We step around him and continue on.

The beam from the flashlight settles on an abandoned gurney ahead of us. It's sitting at an angle across the corridor in front of what looks like a nurse's station. Something that might once have been a woman lies slumped over it, little more than the trellis of a person, the hide stretched over the bones all dried and shrunken inside what's left of her uniform. The wheels of the gurney are locked. Their screeched complaint echoes down the corridor as Ortiz pushes it out of the way.

We make our way further into the darkness. There are more bodies now, strewn about like so much flotsam and jetsam. Sometimes they lie by themselves, other times they huddle together, a frieze of heads and limbs and torsos, so many that we have to pick our way between them. I try not to look down as I step over them, but I can't help it. All their faces are alike, the same rictus grins and gray, rotting teeth and hollow eyes.

I thought I was used to seeing stuff like this, from the years I spent scavenging with Marv.

It turns out I'm not.

*

THE HALLWAY ENDS at a door with a sign for a staircase above. Ortiz opens it with the toe of his boot and points the flashlight into the crack. He peers after it for a long while, then pushes it open and disappears through. Hicks follows him.

We make our way down the concrete stairwell, the sound of our boots echoing and rebounding around us. It gets colder as we descend; every time Ortiz exhales now I see his breath hanging red in the air in front of him. Hicks pulls off his liners and starts slowly opening and closing his hands, flexing his fingers.

Eventually we reach the bottom. Ortiz opens another door and steps through. We follow him into another corridor, this one mostly free of bodies. More doors lead off to the left and right. We come to a section where the wall's blown out. Jagged fragments of metal, what looks like the remains of an oxygen tank, have embedded themselves in the concrete. More lie scattered across the floor. They clink against each other as Ortiz moves them out of the way with his boot.

Up ahead the corridor opens into what seems to have been a makeshift ward. On both sides cots stretch off into darkness. Ortiz stops and raises the stick in the air and we wait while he slowly scans from left to right with the flashlight. It looks like there was a fire here. The paint on the walls has blistered and the floor and ceiling are covered in a thick layer of soot. As the beam slides over the beds I can see that the bodies that lie there are just so much charred meat, their blackened skin stretched over their bones, their faces split and shrunken on their skulls. The air down here is stale, spent, and for once I'm thankful; the smells that remain are mercifully faint.

We move forward again. To the right another row of cots, this time untouched by flame. But the bodies that lie strapped to the beds are different from the ones we saw in the corridor upstairs. Scraps of clothing hang in rotten tatters from their cadaverous frames, but as the beam from Ortiz's flashlight slides over them I can see that underneath the skin is the color of the snow outside, and unblemished by decay. They look just like they're sleeping. I close my eyes and take a deep breath, gathering what remains of my courage around me. When I open them again Hicks has already moved on ahead.

The corridor ends at a set of large double doors underneath a sign that says *Radiology*. A glass panel, reinforced with criss-crossed safety wire, sits in the center of each. Ortiz holds his flashlight up and peers through for a long time before he finally goes in.

The first door we come to is ajar. A small plaque in the center says *Darkroom*. Ortiz pushes it with his boot and it creaks back. He points the flashlight inside. The beam slips over a series of shallow stainless steel tanks. Racks hanging haphazardly from the ceiling cast strange shadows against the walls. When he's satisfied there's nothing hiding among them Ortiz motions with the baton and we continue on.

We make our way slowly down the corridor, checking each room as we go. As we get to the end a large sliding door stretches across one wall, from floor to ceiling. Ortiz shines the flashlight across the metal. Leprous patches spread across it, almost obscuring a yellow and black radiation warning sign. A panel to one side that looks like it would once have lit up reads *X-Ray In Use*. Ortiz tries to slide the door out of the way, but it's slipped off its track on one side and won't budge.

Hicks turns to Jax.

'Well don't just stand there. Go on and help him.'

The blond giant steps forward and bends down, slipping his fingers under the door. It groans in protest as he takes its weight and then there's a loud metallic clang that echoes along the hallway as he lets it fall back onto its track. He grips one edge with a huge glove and pulls. The runners screech in protest, but inch by inch the door slides back until there's a gap large enough for a person to fit through.

Hicks' fingers move closer to the pistol on his hip. He tells me to be ready, so I press the rifle to my cheek. I take a deep breath to try and steady the barrel, but my hands are shaking too much for that to work.

Ortiz picks up the flashlight and shines it into a large, tiled room. Some of the tiles have peeled away, revealing a dark surface that shines dully as the light slides over it. A table where people would have had their X-rays taken waits in the center; even from here I can see how badly corroded the metal is. There's a cubicle in the far corner from where the machine would have been controlled. The glass is broken; it gives back fractured carmine images as Ortiz points the beam at it. After a moment he steps inside, continuing to sweep the room. I wait, holding my breath. My insides feel like they've been scooped out and replaced with *Reddi-wip*. But there's nothing. He turns around and motions to Hicks that we can move on.

As I step back to let him out I catch a glimpse of something, slipping from behind the operator booth. Ortiz has his back to it; he hasn't noticed yet. My eyes widen but for a second I just stand, paralyzed with fear, the gun heavy and useless in my hands.

Hicks must see it now too, or maybe he just reads what's written on my face. If he's shocked he doesn't show it: his expression doesn't alter. But then I reckon Hicks is the kind of person who does his freaking and starting mostly on the inside. By the time I open my mouth to stammer a warning he's already shoving me out of the way. The hands that were empty a moment ago now hold a pistol.

Ortiz finally realizes something's wrong an instant before Hicks starts firing. I'm expecting it, but the noise the old gun makes is loud in such a confined space and I jump. The inside of the room reveals itself in a series of flashbulb images. The fury suddenly on top of the X-ray table, lit for an instant by the flare from the muzzle. Dark circles surrounding silvered eyes, thin lips pulled back wide. Sparks fly and a bullet shrieks and whines off the metal where an instant before it was perched. The next time Hicks fires the flash catches it in midair as it launches itself. I think I see the bullet graze its shoulder, but it barely seems to notice.

Ortiz has dropped the flashlight and is desperately trying to bring the baton up to ward off the attack, but he's left it way too late. Long, thin fingers are already clawing at his neck; its teeth snap furiously.

Hicks adjusts his aim and fires one last time, and this time the bullet finds its mark. The fury releases its grip and drops to the floor. The burnt stench of gunpowder hangs heavy in the air. Hicks steps into the room.

'Did it get you?'

Ortiz doesn't respond. He just stares at the thing lying there on the floor, the beam from the discarded flashlight casting ugly red shadows across its contorted features. Hicks grabs him by the shoulder and repeats the question. When he still gets no answer he unsnaps the throat of Ortiz's parka and pulls the collar back. A second later his hand falls away. Ortiz finally seems to come back from wherever he's been. He tears his eyes off the fury and looks up at Hicks.

'How bad is it, man? Can you fix it?'

Hicks looks for a moment longer and then just shakes his head. Ortiz just nods, once, like he understands.

'You know I can't go back, Sarge, not like this.'

I see Hicks raise a finger to his lips. Without turning around he tells Jax to get me out. But I just stand there, rooted to the spot with fear. The Viking steps in front of me and extends one huge arm. At last I tear my gaze from the fury and allow myself to be shepherded back in the direction of the stairwell. I've barely made it a half-dozen paces when a single final shot rings out and then it goes quiet again.

*

THE STORM THAT'S been keeping its distance for the last couple of days looks like it's finally coming our way. It's still too far off to hear the thunder, but the sky behind us crackles with lightning.

Hicks picks up the pace. There's no talking and the hike back passes in cold silence. When we finally stop to eat he sits apart and sips from his thermos. I break out an MRE but I'm not hungry and after a few mouthfuls I hand it to Jax.

I wonder if he blames me for what happened to Ortiz. Maybe if I hadn't frozen when I first saw that thing crawl out from behind the booth he could have been saved. Well even if that's true there's nothing I can do about it now. The fact is Ortiz is dead and we have nothing to show for it. It's already been days since Mags was infected. The best I can hope for is that the storm will shift course and Hicks will want to take us out again soon.

Only next time it'll be my turn to step into a darkened room with a baton and wait for one of those things to come at me.

It's long after dark when we make it back to The Greenbrier. The storm hasn't switched direction. All afternoon it's followed us, growing steadily closer, and now the lightning is accompanied by the low rumble of thunder. It'll be with us tonight, tomorrow morning at the latest.

The flags snap and flutter on their flagpoles as we make our way up to the entrance. We pass under the massive portico and remove our snowshoes. The camera above me blinks as I open the door and step through. A flurry of snowflakes follows me inside.

I take my mittens off and rub my hands together to get some feeling back into my frozen fingers. The emergency lights are on and from somewhere down below I hear the low thrum of a generator. Hicks has already shucked off his backpack and is unzipping his parka. He still hasn't said a word to me. Whether or not he holds me responsible for Ortiz I need something from him now. I undo my boots and bring them over to the bellhop cart.

'You promised you'd let me see Mags.'

He looks at me for a long moment.

'Yes, I did.'

He hands me Ortiz's rifle.

'Get that cleaned, yours too. I'll come find you when we're ready.'

I sling the rifles over my shoulder and head for the dining room. The Viking is already sitting at the table when I walk in. He looks up from his plate of franks, his flat blue stare following me as I cross the room.

When we first met Hicks said Jax was harmless, but after what happened in the hospital I'm not so sure. Marv warned me when Peck came for us there'd be no reasoning or pleading with him, and I wonder if it'd be any different with the Viking. I saw the look on his face when Hicks told him to get me out of there, after the fury got Ortiz. It was the same vacant expression I'd pretty much gotten used to. But I think I know how it would have gone if I hadn't complied.

I go to work, trying not to look over at him. At some point he finishes eating. He stares at me a while longer then gets up and lumbers off in the direction of the door without saying a word. When I'm done with Ortiz's rifle I start stripping down mine. When they're both clean I reassemble them and then just sit there and wait.

Hicks shows up not long after. He says they're ready for me. I follow him back through the lobby and then down the long corridor that leads to the Colonial Lounge. When we get to the Exhibition Hall Dr. Gilbey's already there. She turns around and gives me a tight-lipped smile. Behind her the screen's been pulled back. The emergency lamp bolted to the wall above it flickers, casting the alcove behind in intermittent shadow. I can see the vault door's open, but little beyond. I start to cross the hall to join her, but she holds up a hand.

'That's far enough, Gabriel.'

She turns back towards the entrance to the bunker.

'You can bring her out now, Corporal.'

Hicks puts a gloved hand on my arm.

'Prepare yourself, son. They've had to bind her.'

At first there's nothing and then I hear a shuffling coming from the darkness and for an instant all I can think is that it's the same sound the fury that was stalking me in Mount Weather's tunnel made. The footsteps grow steadily louder until eventually something steps out of the shadows.

Her head's been shaved, her almost-black hair a stubbled furze. A strip of duct tape covers her mouth and there's a thin plastic noose around her neck. She's wearing dark overalls that seem several sizes too big for her. The cuffs are rolled up and her hands are held together at her waist, like they've been cable-tied there. There are more plastic restraints binding her ankles.

Her eyes scan the room for a second before they find me. There are worrying shadows there, but when she turns her head I can see the pupils are dark, just like they've always been.

She continues to shuffle forward until she clears the door and then she stops and Truck steps out from behind her. The noose around her neck's attached to a long pole, the kind of device you might see being used to round up strays for the pound. Truck's gripping the other end with both hands, his tongue working the wad of tobacco that's tucked behind his lip. He glances over at me and I think I catch a trace of a smile, like maybe this is a show he's glad he got tickets for.

I look back at Mags.

'Are you okay?'

She nods, once, a terse gesture.

I turn to Hicks.

'Take the tape off. I want to talk to her.'

Hicks' eyes never leave her. His voice remains calm, but the tips of his fingers don't stray far from the pistol on his hip.

'Can't do that son.'

Mags' eyes flick over to Hicks then back to me, like she's trying to work something out.

'How… how did it happen?'

It seems like a stupid question, but it's the only one I can think of right now.

Dr. Gilbey slips her hands into the pockets of her lab coat and turns to face me.

'Well, I blame myself, of course, Gabriel. It was an unforgivable error.' She shakes her head, but it's a brusque gesture, sterile and unconvincing. 'I asked Magdalene to remain in the dormitory, but I didn't think to lock her in there. I thought she could be trusted not to wander off. After I had gone to sleep she must have taken it upon herself to explore.'

I look back at Mags. The expression on her face hasn't changed, but I recognize that look in her eyes. She's furious. She glances over at Hicks, like she's checking whether he's still watching. Her eyes switch back to me one last time and for a second she holds my gaze, like she's trying to tell me something. Then without warning she throws herself forward towards Dr. Gilbey. It happens so fast she catches Truck by surprise.

For all his size he recovers quickly. He yanks the pole back towards him and then lifts it up. I see the noose tighten around her neck; her head jerks backwards and she's forced onto her toes, her feet scrabbling for purchase on the tiles. The muscles along Truck's arms bunch as he hoists her up and I hear him grunt with the effort of it, but he holds her there and in that moment I know I would kill him if I had the means. I take a step forward but I make no more than that. Something grabs my arm and in the same instant I feel a pressure against my thigh and then the room's spinning around me; the next thing I know I'm lying on my back staring up at the Exhibition Hall's ceiling. I try to get up but Hicks has a knee on my chest, pinning me there; for someone so thin he's surprisingly strong. He fixes me with a stare from his one good eye while he barks an order at Truck to set Mags down. Truck hesitates for a second and then lowers the pole. She drops to her knees, gasping for breath.

If Dr. Gilbey is shaken by this she doesn't show it. She slowly removes her hands from the pockets of her lab coat and folds them across her chest. She nods at Truck.

'Take her back inside Corporal.'

Hicks looks up for a second.

'Gently, Truck.'

He lifts the pole and Mags gets unsteadily to her feet. She manages one last glance in my direction before she's herded back through the door and in that second our eyes meet and I nod.

The emergency lights flicker, like they might go out, then steady. Hicks watches the door for a second more, then looks back down at me.

'If I let you up will you be calm?'

I nod and a moment later I feel a weight lifted from my chest as he stands. He holds out a gloved hand to help me up.

'Now I know today was rough. That was to be expected, your first time and all. But you can't give up. She needs you now, son. And trust me, it'll get easier.'

I nod again, so he'll think I'm listening, but the truth is I'm not. I know what I have to do now, and it doesn't involve following him into another hospital to look for one of those things that attacked Ortiz. I need to be by myself to work this through, though. I glance over at Dr. Gilbey and then back at him.

'How soon can we go out again?'

*

THE GIRL HAS BEEN GONE for some time now, but still the scent lingers.

It was worse before.

After the doctor left she sat quietly for a while. Then without warning she leaned back and kicked the bars. He had been worried she was going to bring the mean soldier down again, but she only did it once, and afterwards she went to the back of her cage and sat there for a long time without moving. When she finally stirred it was only to reach for the food tray and he had been happy then because he thought maybe she was going to eat something. But all she took was the plastic spoon. He saw her wipe it on her overalls and a little while later he thought he heard a sound like plastic splintering.

It was shortly after that he smelled it. Faint at first, fainter than when the soldier had hurt his elbow right in front of his cage, but growing stronger with every passing minute. He felt the now-familiar knot in his stomach, felt it begin to twist, to gnaw at his insides. He pushed himself all the way to the back of his cage and covered his face with his hands to try and shut it out. It was no use, though. The scent was still there; it slipped between his fingers, filling his nostrils, sliding down the back of his throat until he could almost taste it. There was no way to escape it.

It had been a relief when the soldier had come to take her away.

He had watched as she had put on the restraints. She had glared at the soldier when he had slid the catchpole into the cage, but in the end she had let him slip the noose over her head and bring her out. She had been a little unsteady on her feet at first, and at one point as the soldier had led her towards the door he had heard her stumble and the soldier had cursed. It had taken her a long time to climb the stairs.

Now he hears footsteps again and he knows she is returning. She descends very slowly, but then finally he hears the click as the locks disengage and then the door opens and moments later there's the soft shuffle of her feet on the concrete as she approaches. The beam from the soldier's flashlight bounces ahead of them down the aisle. It seems brighter than it was earlier; he screws his eyes shut against it. The footsteps stop in front of his cage and there's the sound of the latch being sprung and the door opening. The scent returns, thankfully fainter now than it was before. He opens his eyes a fraction, just in time to see the soldier's face appearing at the bars. He reaches into the breast pocket of his fatigues, pulls out a container of the medicine and tosses it in.

'Here, take that while I sort her out.'

Johnny 99 shuffles forward and collects the medicine while the soldier manhandles the girl into her cage. After what happened the other day he's taking no chances. He keeps a tight hold on the pole so that her head's pulled back against the bars while he undoes the restraint that loops around her waist. Then he lifts the noose over her head and slides it out and latches the door closed. The girl raises her cuffed hands to her neck and rubs there.

The soldier squats in front of her cage. He reaches into his pocket and takes out another container of the medicine.

'Now before I give you this I think you owe old Truck here an apology for all the trouble you've been causing.'

The girl stares at the container. It reminds Johnny 99 he has to take his own medicine, or the soldier will be mad at him. He unscrews the cap and raises the vial to his lips, bracing himself for the bitter taste.

The girl shakes her head.

'I wonder what's going to happen to you, Corporal, if you have to go back to the doctor and tell her you couldn't get me to take my medicine again? Seems like having someone down here is important to her.' She looks up at the roof of the cage, only inches above her head. 'Would someone like you really fit in one of these?'

But the soldier just returns the container to his pocket. When he speaks again Johnny 99 hears the smile in his voice.

'Oh darlin', I ain't going to tell the Doc any such thing. This time my report'll say you drank it all down.'

He looks at the container the soldier's just given him. That's twice the girl will have missed her medicine. He searches his cage for the plastic cup his water comes in and quickly transfers half the contents of the vial to it, then he pushes the cup into the shadows behind him.

The soldier nods at the cuffs on the girl's wrists and ankles as he gets to his feet.

'And you can stay in those for a while. Might teach you some manners.'

He turns around to face the boy, banging the bars with the toe of his boot.

'You done in there yet?'

He makes a show of draining what remains in the plastic container, then he places it near the front of his cage and backs away. Without water to wash it away the taste is overpowering. He presses his lips tight together and concentrates on not returning what he's just swallowed to the floor of his cage. The soldier doesn't seem to notice. He rummages in his pocket for a Ziploc bag, wraps it around his hand and uses it to pick up the spent vial. He holds it up to the flashlight to check it's empty, then presses the seal closed and stands. The beam recedes as he makes his way back down the aisle. The door opens with a soft groan and then there's a click as the locks engage, followed seconds later by the distant sound of boots on metal as he starts to climb the stairs.

He waits a long time after the last footstep's faded to silence. When he's sure the soldier isn't coming back he picks up the cup and slides it out between the bars, pushing it across the concrete with his fingertips. If he lies down and stretches out he can get it almost halfway across the space between the cages. When he can get it no further he pulls his arm back through the bars and whispers to the girl to let her know what he's done. She lies on the floor of her cage like he did and slips her hands out through the bars. Her arms are longer than his so the cup should be within her grasp, but her wrists are still cuffed together, which limits her reach. And he almost forgets that she can't see either; the first time she manages to get her fingertips to it she almost knocks it over. He shuffles to the front of his cage and whispers directions. She pulls her hands back through the bars, adjusts her position and tries again. This time her fingers wrap around the plastic and she pulls it back in.

He watches as she lifts the cup to her lips and drinks the medicine. When she's done she bends over to retch and for a moment the boy thinks she will be sick and it will all have been for nothing. But then it passes and she leans back and runs her fingers around the inside of the cup. When she's extracted the last of whatever's there she sets it down and looks out through the bars. She still can't see in the darkness, so she's not looking right at him when she says it, but it doesn't matter. She whispers thank you, that she won't forget it.

And that makes him sad.

Because he knows she probably will. She can't have long now. In a few days she'll get sick and then the gray curtain will come down and everything she knew from before will be gone.

*

THE INTERVALS BETWEEN flash and thunder grow shorter as outside the storm bears down. The sky's roiling now, tortured. Lightning shudders inside the thunderheads, lighting them up all the way back to the horizon. The wind howls around the giant columns and gusts against the window, shaking the glass in the flaking frame.

I should get some rest for what lies ahead, but instead I sit on the floor in my parka, just staring out into the darkness. All I can see is Mags, forced onto her toes, her feet scrabbling for purchase on the Exhibition Hall's smooth tiles. I bury my face in my hands and breath, trying to banish the image, but it won't leave. My fingers still smell of the gun oil I've been working with all day. Right after I got to see her Hicks took me into the dining room and sat me down at one of the tables. He brought a bunch of weapons up from the bunker and laid them out in front of me. It was rifles mostly, but there were some pistols too, including one I recognized as Marv's Beretta. I already knew how to strip the M4s, but he showed me how to break each of the other guns down too. When that was done I set to work with a toothbrush and a stack of cotton buds, working the solvent up into the breech, swabbing out the chamber and bore, wiping each part down before finally setting it aside to dry. While I worked he told me where we'll go next. There's a big hospital over in Roanoke, apparently. He reckons it'll take us three days to hike it. We'll set off as soon as the storm clears.

I don't plan on being around for that. I'm still not sure what part he has in all of this, but I know now that Gilbey's not to be trusted. As Truck was hauling Mags off her feet Hicks took his eyes off her for a split second to deal with me. I guess that was what she must have been hoping for. And in that instant she turned her hand toward me and I saw what was written there. A single word scratched into her palm, the dried blood spelling out only three letters.

*Run.*

So that's what I intend to do. My backpack rests against the wall, ready to go. While everyone was at dinner I snuck down to the lobby and went through the soldiers' gear for the items I'll need. I've spent the last hour fashioning boots to replace the ones I surrendered to the bellhop cart when we came in earlier. I've wrapped the slippers Hicks gave me with strips torn from the blanket on my bed. Sections cut from one of Jax's plastic gunny sacks go around the outside, held in place with the last of the duct tape from my scavenging kit. They don't look pretty but they seem warm enough and the plastic seems tough. Hicks had meant for Jax to carry a fury back inside it, so I guess it must be. They'll have to do until

I can find better.

From outside there's another flash, followed a few seconds later by a clap of thunder. Out of habit I count the seconds between, but that's not what I'm waiting for now. The soldiers came up from dinner almost an hour ago; I heard them talking in the corridor outside. One by one they slipped off to bed, and then it got quiet, the only sounds those of the approaching storm. Hicks knocked on my door a little while later with a plate of franks. I didn't feel much like eating, but I took them anyway. I'll need the sustenance. I have a long night ahead of me.

Across the hallway Truck starts to snore. I wait fifteen minutes to make sure he's completely out of it, then I grab my bag. I used a drop of gun oil on the hinges earlier and the door opens without a sound. I cross the hall. The thick carpet muffles my footsteps, but nevertheless I tiptoe down the stairs. The generator gets cut after dinner so the emergency lights are off, but the flashlight stays in my parka. I make my way across the lobby in darkness. Outside the sky flares, briefly bathing the shrouded furniture in harsh white light. The sound of my makeshift boots scuffing the marble seems loud, but I don't think it'll carry far enough for anyone to hear it, and besides, the storm's kicking up enough of a racket now to cover it. The wind pushes against the entrance door as I open it and I have to hold tight with both hands to prevent it slamming behind me.

It's colder than I was expecting; the wind snatches the breath from me almost before I have a chance to exhale it. I slide the thin cotton mask up over my mouth and fasten the throat of my parka. It's too dark for goggles and the icy snow stings my eyes. I zip the hood all the way up, but the wind whips and tugs at it, threatening to dislodge it even before I've left the shelter of the portico.

My snowshoes are where I left them when we got back. The huge columns tower over me as I slide my makeshift boots into the bindings and ratchet them tight. I've already fixed the soldiers' guns; it was a stroke of unexpected luck Hicks fetching them up for me to work on earlier. Now I pull out the leatherman and hack through the straps on their snowshoes, then toss them off into the darkness. They're bound to have spares so it probably won't do me much good, but I figure every minute I can put between us now will be worth it. When I've taken care of the last of them I shift the backpack so it sits high on my shoulders, tighten the straps and set off.

It's slow going. Until I get out of sight of the house I'm relying on the lightning to show me the way, but between the flashes I'm blind. I grope my way around the helicopter, listening for the creak and groan of its rotors as they twist and flex in the wind. It takes me what seems like forever to reach the road, but finally I'm passing between The Greenbrier's gateposts. I dig in my pocket for the flashlight. The dynamo whirs as I crank the stubby handle. The bulb glows orange, then yellow, finally casting a faint pool of watery light that hardly seems worth the effort.

I take a right and follow the road, grateful that at least now the wind's at my back. Breaking trail keeps me warm for a while, but it doesn't take long for the cold to find its way inside my parka and through the extra layer of thermals I'm wearing. My makeshift footwear's not as warm as the boots I surrendered either; I can already feel my toes tingling. But then that was to be expected. I tell myself I can handle a little bit of cold, and at least the sacking seems to be keeping the snow out. I've barely made it past the church before I begin to sense a more serious problem, however. The duct-taped plastic has no structure to it. When I tried them out in the room my improvised footwear seemed comfortable enough, but of course that was before I strapped on snowshoes and started pounding drifts. Now the hard plastic of the bindings cuts into my feet with each step.

There's little I can do about that now. I need to keep moving; the corrugated crash barriers I'm relying on to show me the way are already disappearing under the drifting snow. I stop and dig out each signpost, every mile marker, even where I'm fairly certain I'm on the right track. The storm will get worse before it gets better, and I can't afford to get lost out here.

*

IT TAKES ME THREE HOURS to reach the river, almost twice as long as when Hicks and I hiked it the other day. The flashlight shows only the icy flakes that swirl past me in the darkness and I end up missing the sign for the bridge. Before I know it the road underneath me has disappeared and there's a sickening jolt as I feel one foot sinking through into empty air. I try to back up but the tails of my snowshoes dig in and I lose my balance. The wind gusts, like it means to send me over, and for a second it seems like it might succeed. I stagger backwards, arms flailing, and land awkwardly in the snow, pushing large chunks of it over the edge as I scramble back to safety.

I lie there for a moment, just staring up into the shuddering sky. I can't stay here. The storm's almost on me, the gap between lightning and thunder already little more than a heartbeat. I pick myself up and inch forward again. When I've gone as far as I dare I point the flashlight down, but I can't see the water. There's just a black chasm into which the driven snow twists and tumbles. I bend down and unsnap my snowshoes. My feet are already numb with the cold, but it's a relief to step out of them nevertheless. I tie them to the outside of my pack and start to climb down the rubble.

At the river the skiff bobs and jerks against its tether. I pull off the tarp, shuck off my pack and take out the rope. The length I keep with my scavenging kit would never have done, but with what I've taken from Jax's and Weasel's packs I should have enough. I tie one end to the mooring point, throw the rest into the boat and climb in after it. I take a moment to steady myself then cast off, using one of the oars to push the skiff off the bank, like I saw Hicks do. I'm not as practiced at this as he was though, and it pitches and dips alarmingly as I struggle with the current. The windup torch sits meekly between my feet, its yellowing beam only sufficient to illuminate the rope that's slowly paying itself out into the dark water behind me.

Stroke by stroke I work my way across the churning waters. The wind kicks up icy spray; waves lap furiously against the prow and crash against the sides. My arms are soon burning, but in the darkness between flashes it's hard to tell how much progress I'm making. At last I hear a creak and a second later the front of the boat rides up as it crunches into something. Above me lightning strobes, for a second illuminating the crumbling remains of the bridge towering over me. One more pull on the oars and the prow nudges concrete and comes to an unsteady halt. I climb out and carry the end of the rope to the piece of bent-back rebar Hicks used as a mooring point on this side. I feed it through and tie it off to the metal eye that's bolted to the prow, then clamber back in and push off again. It takes me a while to turn the boat around, but as soon as I'm pointed in the right direction I ship the oars; I can use the rope to pull me back now. I brace my feet against the sides and start grabbing armfuls of it. The wind that was at my back on the way out is in my face for the return. Even in the lee of the bank I can feel its strength.

There's a blinding flash of light, followed by a crash of thunder and for a second the sky above me reveals itself, a seething maelstrom of grays and blacks, lit from within. Heavy flakes start to tumble and swirl out of the darkness. The visibility drops, like a thick curtain pulling itself around me, and soon I can barely see the front of the little skiff as it pitches through the waves. The wind wants to push me back but I refuse to let it. With each armful of rope I curse it. The thermals I wear are supposed to wick the sweat away but they're already overwhelmed, and soon it's running freely down my back and sides. I look down into the boat. Only half a dozen loose coils remain and I'm beginning to wonder if I'll make it. Then finally just as the last of them starts to unwind I feel the bottom nudge something.

I pick up the torch and wind it. The beam shows me nothing more than swirling snow, but when I point it over the side I see chunks of ice bobbing up and down in the dark, agitated water. I must be close to the bank. I grab an oar and feel for the bottom. Waves are lapping furiously at the sides, but it's no more than a couple of feet deep. The rope's tied to the hook on the prow; if I untie it to give me the extra few yards I need I'll lose the end in the water and then this will have been for nothing. I give one more pull. The boat moves forward and I feel the hull grate over something that might be rubble. The last of the rope slips over the side.

I look down at my makeshift boots. The duct tape's fraying where the snowshoes' bindings have worked against it, but the plastic underneath seems to be holding. I've wrapped several strips of tape around the top where my pants go into the boot, and the material there is waterproof. It should be enough.

I stand up. The boat rocks dangerously as my foot sinks into the icy water. The surface is uneven and I stumble, but in a couple of steps I'm up on the bank. I grab the tarp from where I left it by the water's edge and step back into the shallows to bundle it in, resting the oars on top so the wind can't catch it. I take the bottle of gas I stole from Boots' pack and douse the thick canvas. I cup my hand around the lighter. It takes a dozen or more tries for it to hold flame, but eventually I get the tarp to light.

I step back out of the water and start to pull the boat across the river. The flames creep up over the sides, like a funeral pyre. For a while I can follow it, but before long the storm has swallowed it whole. I keep grabbing armfuls of rope until eventually I feel resistance. I give one last heave to make sure it's grounded, then I find a loose lump of concrete and wrap the end of the rope around it several times and tie it off. I go down to the water's edge and heft it as far as I can into the river. The wind drowns the splash; I never hear it. The rope sits on the water for a second and then slowly slips beneath the surface as the concrete sinks to the bottom.

I open my pack and grab some of the firewood I brought from my room. I use the last of Boot's gas to light it. The wind harries the fragile flames, threatening to snuff them out, but whatever he adds to the mix makes it tenacious. I huddle close but it's too small for any warmth. I tell myself that was never its purpose, but the truth is I need it now. My makeshift boots seem to have kept the water out, but inside my feet ache with the cold. The exertion that warmed me on the crossing is working against me now, too; inside my parka I can feel my sweat-soaked thermals cooling against my skin. I set an MRE to heat. As soon as it's ready I wolf down the half-mixed contents before they too have a chance to give up their warmth. When I'm done I scatter the packets that came in the carton around, wedging them under crumbling concrete or impaling them on rebar until the area around me is strewn with trash.

The fire's already burning down and I'm starting to shiver, but at least down here I'm mostly sheltered. I look up. Above me the wind howls over the collapsed bridge, sending flurries of powder tumbling over the edge. I'd like to stay a little longer, but that's not possible. I need to get back now.

Hicks told me Gilbey had a code to get them into The Greenbrier, except that when they got there it didn't work. There's no keypad for the vault door in the Exhibition Hall, though; it only opens from the inside. Which means there must be another door somewhere, one that *will* take a code. I don't know where that might be, but my guess is finding it won't be too difficult; it'll be big, way bigger than the one I've already seen. The blast doors at Eden and Mount Weather and Culpeper were all large enough to drive a truck through, and there's no reason The Greenbrier should be different. Places like that needed to be stocked after all.

Once I find it what's on Marv's map should get me in, just like it has everywhere else I've tried. I don't have that map on me of course; it's tucked behind a pipe organ up on the balcony of a little chapel in Covington. But that doesn't matter. I've studied it often enough over the winter that all I have to do is close my eyes and I can see the twelve numbers and letters Marv had written there.

I stand, hoist the backpack onto my shoulders and pull the straps tight. My makeshift boots feel heavy and when I look down I see they've iced up from when I stepped into the river. I knock the worst of it off and then slowly start to climb back up.

This will be the last night Mags spends in that bunker.

*

EXCEPT THAT'S NOT HOW IT WORKS out of course, but I guess that bit you already knew. I don't think it was the plan. That was as good as I could have come up with in the circumstances, and on a different night it might even have seen me through. It was the storm. I just didn't account for how bad it would get on the way back.

Without Marv's map it's hard to be sure, but I reckon it's a little shy of six miles from the spot where the bridge gave out to what remains of The Greenbrier's gates. I don't know how many of those I made in the end, only that it wasn't enough. Not that it matters. One mile or five, the truth is the storm had me beat before I hauled myself back up from the river; it just took me a little while longer to figure that out. I guess Marv was right: the cold really is a vicious bitch; it can seriously mess with your thinking. I only wish I had learned that lesson in time.

I'd like to tell you she was the last thing I thought of, as the drifting snow covered me over and the last of my body's heat leached out into the soft, enveloping flakes. But she wasn't. By the time my head came to rest in that gray powder I couldn't have told you where I was headed or why.

*

IT IS THE FOOTSTEPS that bring him back, echoing down the stairwell. He doesn't know how many he has missed, but he suspects a lot because they are loud, as though their owners are already right outside the door.

He hears the lock click and he opens his eyes. Although somehow he doesn't think his eyes were actually closed, it is just that now it is his turn to use them again. Weird. He blinks and looks around the cage. He feels like he has been away somewhere, although he knows that is impossible. For as long as he can remember the cage is all that there has been.

Something is wrong.

Down here in the darkness time has little meaning; it is difficult to say where one part of it begins and another ends. But that unrelenting sameness makes it easy to tell when a piece has gone missing, like it just has. He can't have fallen asleep, can he? He doesn't sleep anymore. He hasn't in a very long while.

Something is definitely wrong.

The door is already opening. The girl must have heard it too because she's sitting up, waiting. He tilts his head to one side and sniffs the air. The scent from her cage is weaker now, but still, infuriatingly, there.

Somewhere at the end of the row a flashlight comes on. The doctor's heels click sharply on the concrete as she approaches, like she's angry; he can tell from the soldier's shuffling gait that he's struggling to keep up. He suddenly realizes his face is still pressed against the bars. He scurries back to his corner. Moments later the hem of a lab coat appears in front of his cage, glaringly bright in the flashlight's beam. The soldier's grubby fatigues arrive seconds after, the bottoms spilling over the tops of his boots.

The doctor bends down to check on him, but it's a cursory examination. She glances at the untouched tray and turns to the soldier.

'No more food for 99, Corporal. And you'd best prepare a cage in the other room.'

'Yes ma'am.' The boy can't see the soldier's face but he thinks he detects a trace of a smile in his voice, like this is a task he might relish.

The doctor takes a couple of plastic containers from her pocket and slides one through the bars and then he is forgotten as she turns around to face the cage opposite. The girl starts to inch forward but the soldier raps the bars with the stick.

'Stay right where you are, missy.'

The doctor bends down.

'Magdalene, show me your hands.'

The girl hesitates for a moment and then raises her cuffed wrists. The doctor leans forward so that she can see what's written there. The boy sees it too and now he understands what the girl has done and where the intoxicating smell has been coming from.

'Very clever, dear.' The doctor turns to the soldier. 'You didn't think to check her hands, Corporal?' The soldier's boots shuffle awkwardly on the concrete but he doesn't say anything.

The doctor slides the container through the bars and takes a step back. The girl reaches forward and grabs it, like she's worried that at any moment she might change her mind. It takes her a moment to unscrew the cap with her wrists still bound together but she manages it. She holds the container to her lips and drains it, gasping with the taste.

'Well, Magdalene, it appears Gabriel has taken your advice. He wasn't in his room this morning when Sergeant Hicks went in to check on him. Every indication is that he has absconded.'

The girl wipes her mouth with the back of her hand and says *Good.*

'Do you really think so, dear? I have to say, it doesn't say much for his devotion to you, does it? And how far do you think he will get? He set off into a blizzard, without footwear. The best we can hope for now is that the storm clears and he can be found before he succumbs to hypothermia. I will have to remove those appendages that he will inevitably lose to frostbite, and then, assuming of course that he recovers, he will join you down here.'

The girl doesn't look up. She stares at the floor of her cage for a long while. When she finally speaks her voice is little more than a whisper.

'Only someone like you might consider that to be the best that could be hoped for.'

The doctor lets out an exasperated sigh.

'And perhaps you would prefer that he die out there in the cold?'

He strains to hear the girl's response, but she has nothing to say to this. She just crawls to the back of her cage and turns her head away.

*

FROM SOMEWHERE FAR AWAY in the darkness I hear my name. The voice is familiar, but muffled, like it's coming to me from deep under water. I really don't want to open my eyes. There's an immense coldness lodged inside me, but I'm too tired even to shiver; I just want the voice to go away so I can sleep. For a moment it recedes, once again becoming distant. But then it returns, and this time it's insistent.

I manage to open one eye a fraction. A large wooden crucifix hangs at an angle on the wall in front of me, the loin-clothed figure nailed to it looking only marginally less comfortable than I feel. All around me long wooden pews sit in silent disarray. It takes long seconds to process these clues, but at last I have a conclusion I think I might be willing to stand over: I'm in a church.

I wonder how long I've been out. The windows closest to me are darkened with snow, and at least where the panes remain intact, years of silt and grime, so it's hard to tell. Further up there's a gaping hole in the vaulted roof. The section of sky that shows itself looks bruised, restless, but the storm seems to have mostly blown itself out.

A while then. A day, maybe more.

My breath hangs white and heavy in the air above me. Somebody's covered me with their parka, but it's still bitterly cold. I smell burning and realize there's a fire. I shift my gaze and now I see the smoke, rising upwards in slow, lazy coils from somewhere behind me. I try to sit up so I can move myself closer, but my limbs are stiff, unresponsive, like I haven't used them for years.

'Best stay where you are. Don't want to warm you up too quickly.'

I try to turn my head in the direction of the voice, but even that small act seems beyond me; the muscles in my neck respond to my commands with only the vaguest of twitches.

'When I was stationed up in Fairbanks we had a soldier fall through the ice. By the time we fished him out he'd been in there for almost half an hour. We walked him all the way back to camp and then some idiot thought it'd be a good idea to give him a hot drink. Stopped his heart in a second.'

I'm not sure I could stand right now, let alone walk. The hot drink sounds really good though. I wonder what Hicks keeps in that thermos he always has on him. I reckon if I was offered some I might take my chances.

I hear him getting up and the next thing he steps into view. It must be his coat that's covering me because he's only wearing his thermals. Without the bulk of the parka he looks painfully thin, but if the cold's bothering him he's not showing any sign of it. He squints down at me with his one good eye.

'How're you feeling?'

I manage to croak an okay. The truth is I hurt everywhere. The pain's worst in my hands and feet; it's like someone's driving hundreds of tiny needles into my skin. He kneels down next to me and reaches for my wrist. I feel his fingers slide inside the cuff of my mittens, underneath the liner, and press lightly there. I don't know what he's doing, but whatever it is I don't have the strength to resist.

'Pulse's almost back to normal.' He withdraws his hand and pulls the parka back over me. His eyes drop to my cheeks. 'Picked yourself up some frostbite too, although I've seen worse. That was a damn fool thing you did, setting off into weather like that.'

Part of me wants to tell him I know; that I was taught better than that; that I only did it because I was desperate and needed the storm to cover my tracks. But this explanation seems impossibly long and I'm far too tired to give it, so instead I just ask where I am.

'St. Charles.'

It takes me a moment to remember that's the name of the church just a little ways west of the entrance to The Greenbrier. Close then. But I guess that doesn't matter now.

'So what was your plan, son? Clear everybody out of The Greenbrier, then while we're off looking for you, you sneak back in and get the girl?'

I don't know what else to say. It was a bit more complicated than that, but what he's just said sounds like a pretty fair summary of it. I nod.

'Well, if it makes you feel any better it was working. Right up until the part where you almost froze to death, that is. You were lucky I found you when I did.'

He stands and steps over to the fire. I hear the hiss from the damp branches as he adds more of them to the flames.

'Were you the only one sent after me?'

'Nope. Doc was pretty riled up when you split. Soon as the storm broke she had everyone out looking for you, even Pops.'

'Are they back yet?'

'I doubt it. They were headed north along the river when I parted company with them. Truck's plan was to pick up 64 and continue on after you. He's probably somewhere south of Lynch by now. Man's as ignorant as the day is long, but he's backwoods raised, so he knows how to follow a trail. I figure when he doesn't find you by tonight he'll cut his losses, come back.'

'How did you know I hadn't headed south?'

Hicks turns back and looks at me.

'You think being a soldier's just about shooting stuff, son?' He shakes his head. 'Our enemies stopped putting on uniforms long before I signed up. Most important part of it's figurin' out who those folks are, and what they might be about to do next. If you can't tell that you've no business being anywhere near a gun.'

'I saw the look on your face when Truck hitched the girl off her feet. I knew it then; no way you were leaving without her, no matter what she might have written on her hand. Having you clean them weapons was just a test. Once I saw you'd removed the firing pins I knew you were fixin' to bolt. Nice touch with the boat though. Even had me doubting you for a moment there. But then I saw the wrappers you left scattered around, down by the river. You left them so they wouldn't blow away; so we'd find them. Somebody taught you different'n that though, didn't they? Because you've been bagging your trash since the first time we met, and habits like that are hard to break. Damn stupid if you ask me, the way the world is now. But you learned it, so it's what you do.'

Hicks is still speaking but I'm only half-listening. Another, more important, thought is coming to me now. Something's wrong; we're right across the road from The Greenbrier, but for some reason I'm not already back there.

'So what do you mean to do with me?'

Hicks returns to one of the pews and sits down.

'Well that depends on you, son. I figure you wouldn't have gone to all this trouble if you didn't have a plan for breaking the girl out of the bunker and getting her to a cure. If you do I'd be mighty interested in hearing it.'

I look up. I'm still not sure whether I can trust him. But right now I'm not sure I'm long on other options.

'In Eden we had a scanner. One of those machines like in the hospital, basically a big magnet. Marv and I had to go in it each time we came back inside. It was supposed to destroy any trace of the virus we might have picked up while we were outside.'

Hicks looks down at me, like he's considering this.

'Did you mention any of that scanner stuff to the Doc?'

I shake my head. He scratches his jaw, like maybe that's not a bad start.

'This Eden place, are you sure you can find it? 'Cause if you don't mind me saying you seemed a little vague on its location when we spoke earlier.'

'I can find it.'

He nods.

'Fair enough. And what makes you think they'll let you in when you get there?'

I can't see Kane ever letting us in, certainly not once he figures out Mags is infected. But I reckon Hicks doesn't need to hear this part yet. Besides, that's not the bit that worries me. I've found a way in before; I'm sure I can do it again. It's getting back out afterwards that'll be the trick, and right now I don't know how I'm going to do that. But I'll worry about it later. If I can't get Mags into the scanner it won't matter anyway.

'I can get us in.'

'Alright then. I might have some questions for you about that, but first things first. What was your plan for getting back into The Greenbrier?'

'The bunker has to have another entrance. Something bigger, like maybe where the supplies would have been brought in. It'll have a keypad.'

He nods.

'There is. It's round back of the West Virginia Wing. We tried it when we first got here but the codes the Doc had didn't work. It hasn't been opened since.'

'I have a code that should work.'

I told Hicks earlier that Marv hadn't given me any codes, but if he remembers this he doesn't call me on it. Instead he squints down at me for a long moment, like maybe I'm being re-evaluated.

'And how about you? How far do you think you can walk?'

Right now I'm not sure I can even stand.

'As far as I have to.'

He shifts his jaw like maybe he doesn't believe it, but he doesn't say anything.

'Alright then, you'd best rest up. I'm going to fetch your boots. We'll see what shape you're in when I get back.'

He stands up and heads for the entrance. Outside the day's already darkening.

'Hicks, wait.'

He turns around.

'Why would you help us?'

'I have my reasons.'

I shake my head.

'You'll have to do better than that. I'm done taking people at their word.'

He doesn't say anything for a long while, just stares down at me like he's making his mind up about something. Eventually he must come to a conclusion because he reaches up with one gloved hand to the patch over his eye. I'm expecting an empty socket, maybe a scar, evidence of whatever it was that took the sight from him there. It won't bother me to look at it; I've seen my share of things like that, and worse. But what I see when he lifts the patch causes the breath to catch in my throat.

He's squinting hard, like he can't bear even the little light the day has left, but there's no mistaking it: the pupil that looks back at me is impossibly dilated. And it's not dark, like his other eye. It flashes silver, like when you shine a flashlight into an animal's eyes at night. When he thinks I've seen enough he pulls the patch back down.

'Turns out Doc didn't get it all. She has me on her meds, to suppress it, but I know it's there, working its way through me, building itself up, just like in the furies that got themselves fried by the burst. It's not a feeling I much care for. So maybe we can do each other a favor. You bring me with you and I'll help you get the girl out of the bunker, buy you the time she needs when we get to Eden.'

He turns back towards the doorway.

'I'll be back with your boots. You can give me your answer then.'

*

I LOOK OVER at the church's arched entrance for a long time after Hicks has left. One of the doors is missing and the other hangs inward on its last studded hinge; beyond the growing darkness beckons. I'm right across the road from The Greenbrier. I wonder if I should take my chances while he's gone.

I sit up slowly. My feet are still wrapped in the scraps of blankets I tore from my bedding, but the plastic sacking and duct tape have been removed. I spot the remnants of my makeshift footwear on the other side of the fire, lying in a puddle of melt water. I guess Hicks must have cut them off while I was out of it. Well, that settles it. Even if I had tape they're beyond repair, and without boots I'm not going anywhere. I have little choice but to wait for him to come back.

I shuffle backwards and lean myself against one of the pews. I'm not sure what to make of what I've just learned. It makes sense, of course, now that I know. It's not just the silver hair, or how gaunt he looks. I've never seen him eat, or sleep. I wonder if it explains how quick he is too. The articles I collected for my shoebox said the virus hotwired those it infected, that it replaced their internal wiring with its own. Except that the virus's circuits were way faster than ours had ever been designed to be.

Well, infected or not, right now I need his help, and not just to fetch me my boots. He's been inside the bunker, which means he'll know where Mags is being held, so I won't have to search the whole place looking for her. My spirits lift a little at the prospect of seeing her again, and for a moment I put aside what might happen afterwards and allow that thought to sustain me.

I'll need to watch him, though. I still don't even know how Mags came to be infected, only that Gilbey's version of it isn't to be believed. However it happened I tell myself Hicks can't have been part of it; he was with me the whole time. And if all he was planning to do was deliver me back to Gilbey he could have just done that already. There would be no need to bring me here.

But even if he means to help us he has the virus; I'll need to be careful. I look down and suddenly realize it's his parka that's draped over me. The snaps have been cut out, the zipper replaced with plastic, and I suspect every other trace of metal will have been removed from it. Nevertheless I throw it off me like I've just found it crawling with fire ants.

Without the extra layer it's cold and in spite of Hicks' warning I shift myself a little closer to the fire. Even the faint warmth it casts is intoxicating. My entire body aches, but my hands and feet are the worst. I pull off my mittens and liners and examine the damage. Small blisters dot my fingertips and the flesh there feels waxy and hard, like it's been frozen. When I try and curl my fingers into a fist I can manage little more than a claw. I relax my hand again and feel along my cheeks. The skin there's the same.

It's my legs I'm most worried about though; I'll need them soon. Outside dusk's already settling. Hicks said Truck would probably have given up looking for me by now. If that's the case he'll be back in The Greenbrier tomorrow. Which means I'll need to break Mags out of the bunker and get us away from here before then.

I start unraveling the strips of blanket I'd used to wrap my feet. As the last of them falls away I see the slippers underneath are striped with blood. I pull them off as gently as I can and examine the damage. It looks worse than it is. The snowshoes' hard plastic bindings have done some work, but the cuts don't look deep. I clean them as best as I can and then cover them with bandages from the first aid kit I keep in my backpack.

When I'm done I lever myself up onto the pew. Even that small effort exhausts me and I have to rest before I can continue. When I try to stand it's like my legs have gone to sleep; I can't trust them to bear me up. I lower myself back onto the pew and start massaging my thighs with my frozen fingers.

I'll try again in a little while.

It's hours before Hicks returns, but suddenly there he is, standing in the doorway with a pair of boots in one hand and an extra set of snowshoes in the other. The last of the light's already left the sky; there's little to see behind him other than darkness.

I ease myself back down onto one of the pews to take a break. Things are a little better than when he left. I'm able to hobble around now; I can make it almost the length of the aisle before I need to sit down again. Pins and needles still stab up from the balls of my feet with every step, but at least that means feeling's returning.

He drops the boots at my feet and sets the snowshoes on top of his pack.

'Did you have any problems?'

He shakes his head but doesn't elaborate.

I figure I've earned dinner so I reach into my backpack for an MRE. I tear the top off the heater and slide the packet with my meal in it inside. I add a little water from my canteen to start the reaction and then lean it against the side of the seat. It starts hissing, telling me it's getting to work.

Hicks sits down on one of the pews opposite. His gaze shifts to the fire and I catch him eyeing the bloodstained remains of the slippers I left there. When he looks back at me there's an expression on his face that's not hunger but maybe something not too far removed, a memory of what that feeling once was. I point at the MRE in case he wants one, although now that I know what's wrong with him that seems foolish. He just shakes his head and reaches for the thermos, unscrews the cap and raises it to his lips.

My dinner's as warm as it's going to get so I pick up the pouch and start scooping out the contents. Outside the wind gusts, sending a flurry of gray flakes tumbling down through the gaping hole in the rafters.

'So what will you do after?'

What I really want to know is whether I can trust him to help me get Mags out of The Greenbrier and back to Eden. But there's little point asking a question like that flat out, so I figure I'll come at it sideways. *Softly, softly, catchee fury.*

'One problem at a time, kid. I reckon we have our work cut out for us just getting you and the girl back to wherever this Eden place is.'

I take a mouthful of mostly-mixed chili beef.

'Yeah, but you must have thought about it. You'll never be able to come back here. Won't you miss the others?'

Hicks sighs, like he's resigning himself to answering my questions.

'Less than you might think. Truck's got a mean streak in him wider than a four-lane highway; I'm not sure his own mother ever missed that man. Weasel's no better. I told you they were all for shooting me on the roof in Atlanta and tossing Ortiz out the back of the chopper, just in case. You've seen what Jax is like – it's been a long time since all of his dogs were barking – and Pops can't be much more than a quick look down the road behind him.'

'And Boots?'

He takes a sip from his thermos and grimaces at the taste.

'Yeah, Private Kavanagh. Seems harmless enough, right? You know we found him at The Greenbrier, the night we arrived?'

'You said he got locked inside when the order to evacuate came and then couldn't figure a way to let the other soldiers back in.'

He squints at me over the top of the thermos.

'Yep, that's what he told us. The button's right there by the door of course. Big green thing, hard to miss, even with those Coke bottles he wears for glasses.' He takes another sip and holds the thermos up. 'A suspicious mind might wonder whether Private Kavanagh saw the writing on the wall and figured the supplies in the bunker might stretch a lot further if they didn't have to be split quite so many ways. You remember I told you it took us a while to convince him to open up when we arrived.'

I nod. Hicks had said it was only when Boots found out Gilbey was working on a cure that he let them in.

'Well, I might not have told that part exactly how it happened. Boots didn't give a damn about no cure. He only agreed to let us in when Doc threatened to contaminate the bunker if he didn't.'

'And what about Dr. Gilbey? She saved you.'

'She did, and I'll always owe her for that. But something's changed.' He sets the thermos beside him on the pew and looks at me, as if deciding something. 'I'm not sure your girl getting infected was an accident, Gabriel.'

I put the spoon down.

'Doc runs things too tight for something like that to have just happened.' He shakes his head. 'I guess I should have seen it coming. She's been down in that bunker by herself this last ten years, thinking of nothing but finding a cure, and that's a heavy load for one person to bear. Could be you and the girl showing up pushed her over the edge, or maybe she'd already taken that step a while back and I hadn't noticed.'

He raises the thermos to his lips and takes another sip.

'Well, if it's true it can't be excused. And I can't have anything more to do with her.'

*

IT'S STILL A FEW HOURS till dawn when we set off.

Away from the fire it's cold. I've zipped the parka all the way up, but it bites at my frostbitten cheeks through the thin cotton mask. I sit on the steps in the shelter of the church's arched doorway and strap on my snowshoes. I've bandaged my feet tight and my legs feel a lot better; I can make half a dozen circuits round the inside of the church now without having to rest. That's not much, I'll grant you, but you've got to look at where I started from just a few hours ago. And as Hicks says, one problem at a time. The first thing is to get Mags out of that bunker. After that we'll see how many miles I have in me.

Hicks takes us west on route 60, away from The Greenbrier's gates. We walk in silence. I'm beginning to wonder where we're going when he cuts off the road and switches back onto what looks like it was once little more than woodland trail. The wind's died and the only sounds are of my breathing and our snowshoes crunching through the ice-slicked powder. Limbless, lifeless trunks push up through the snow on either side, closing around us as we start to climb. I'm keeping to Hicks' tracks but inside my boots my feet are starting to hurt. I'm more worried about my legs though. The slope's not that bad, but already I can feel the muscles there tiring.

The path inclines, skirting around the hill that sits behind The Greenbrier. We've been following it for maybe fifteen minutes when ahead of us a low concrete structure slowly separates itself from the darkness. Snow's banked high against its featureless sides. More sits in heavy layers on its flat roof.

A large funnel-like entrance cuts into the hillside. The drifts have gathered deep between its walls, almost obscuring a huge metal gate at the end; only a series of rectangular vents near the top point to its existence. A rusting sign warns against trespassing. Another carries a faded symbol of a lightning bolt, and underneath the words *Danger High Voltage*.

Hicks hikes up to the gate. I'm wondering how we're going to get it open, but he just starts scooping snow from a spot near the center. I kneel down next to him and join in. My hands have loosened up a little, but it still hurts to work my fingers. Thankfully Hicks is making a better job of it and soon I can make out the outline of a smaller door set into the steel. When he's cleared enough snow he reaches for the handle. The door sticks in its frame, but after a little pushing it gives and then swings inwards with a dull metallic groan. Gray powder tumbles in.

I unsnap my snowshoes and follow him through into darkness. He pulls a flashlight from his parka and flicks it on. A cone of red light illuminates a square concrete-lined tunnel maybe twice as high as I am tall that ends abruptly at a massive blast door. Two huge buttressed hinges bear its weight, the only other ornamentation six circular steel plates bolted to the wall above. I'm not sure what purpose they serve, but the shadows cast by the bolts make them look like giant clocks.

Hicks shines his flashlight at a spot on the wall. A stubby metal cowling stands proud of the concrete.

'You're up kid.'

As I step closer I'm relieved to see the keypad's just like the ones in Eden and Mount Weather. I pull off my mittens and hit reset to clear whatever might still be stored in the circuits from when Gilbey tried this, years ago. The dusty plastic keys slowly illuminate, and a red light at the bottom blinks on. There's a gentle whirring from above my head as a camera focuses. I glance up.

'Don't worry about that. Doc's the only one in there and she'll be sound asleep.'

I tell myself it's just jitters, like I'd get when I was about to step into Eden's tunnels, but somehow in spite of Hicks' words it feels like we're being watched. I close my eyes and the section of Marv's map that showed The Greenbrier, complete with the code he had written next to it, appears before me. I carefully punch in the twelve numbers and letters. There's a pause and then the light underneath the keypad switches to green. From somewhere behind the door I hear a faint whine, rising in pitch as electric motors that have lain dormant for a decade shake off their slumber and get to work. Moments later there's a grating sound, like the teeth of cogs being forced into service. The pitch of the motors increases and then from somewhere inside the door there's a heavy clunk, followed by the muted screech of metal being dragged against metal and finally the familiar sound of bolts sliding back into their recesses. Another set of motors come to life, slowly pushing the dull, cold steel towards me. When it reaches the wall the motors suddenly die and silence returns to the darkness.

I follow Hicks into a long, straight tunnel. Large-bore pressure pipes run along the walls; more hang from the ceiling. Behind me, above the blast door, huge vents have been drilled through the thick concrete. Each one houses a fan, the heavy metal blades protected behind mesh screens. The steel plates I noticed on the other side were covers, allowing the bunker to be sealed off.

We make our way into darkness, our footsteps echoing off the walls. I start the count. Here and there Hicks' flashlight picks out cardboard boxes, their sides stamped with the names of the supplies they once contained. Each is empty now, the contents long since consumed.

It's two hundred paces before the tunnel ends at a door marked *Decontamination*. Another camera bolted to the concrete above blinks down at us as we pass under it. We enter a shower room. Nozzles protrude from the walls on either side, making the space seem narrow. The flashlight's beam paints everything in shades of crimson so it's hard to tell what color the tiles actually are. If I were forced to guess I'd hazard blue.

The decontamination area ends and we step into a long corridor. From somewhere off in the distance there's the low drone of a generator. Safety lights hum gently, bathing the painted walls in shades of gray and green.

Doors lead off to the left and right, each room's purpose stenciled, military fashion, above. We pass a series of numbered dormitories. Some of the doors are open; inside I can see row after row of steel bunk beds. A large but cheerless cafeteria comes next, and then a smaller lounge area, stacks of decade-old magazines still arranged neatly on the coffee tables. After that an infirmary with a dozen or so beds, and then a room with a large mural of the White House, a lectern on a podium in front of it, a television camera standing ready to transmit the news of what's just happened to those who might have survived. A little further along two drab halls filled with chairs that look like the auditorium where Miss Kimble used to bring us for assembly. The sign above one reads *Senate* and the other *House of Representatives*. Dusty pictures of men I recognize from her first grade civics and government class hang from the walls.

The door at the very end says *Power Plant*. The thrum from the generator increases as Hicks pushes it open. I follow him into a cavernous room and up onto a narrow metal gangway. A tangle of pipes snakes above my head; tanks, pumps, generators and other assorted machinery crowd into the space below. At the end of the walkway we step through another door. The noise from the plant recedes as it closes behind us.

Steel stairs spiral down into darkness, the beam from Hicks' flashlight sweeping the concrete as we descend. The steps continue for longer than I was expecting, but at last we reach the bottom. I look around. A single door leads out of the shaft we've just come down. Hicks steps over to it and punches a code into a keypad. There's a muted click as the lock releases and he pushes the door open.

*

I FOLLOW HIM into a long, low-ceilinged room. Plastic cages stacked two deep line the walls on either side. Hicks hands me the flashlight.

'Stay right here. I'll be back in a minute.'

He opens a door to what looks like a storage room. I have a second to glimpse rows of empty shelves and then he disappears inside, closing the door behind him.

I shine the flashlight along the rows of cages. They're all empty now, but I wonder what used to be kept in them. Hicks said when they took him off the roof in Atlanta Gilbey had put him in something that had been designed for a chimpanzee. These certainly look like they were built to hold a creature of about that size. I haven't seen an animal since Jackson, Sam and Reuben's dog, on the morning of the Last Day. I also assumed whatever survived the strikes froze to death in the months that followed, but now I wonder if there are any still left down here.

I point the flashlight into the darkness, but it doesn't reach very far. I figure there has to be another room at the end of this one. Maybe that's where Mags is. Hicks said to wait, but I want to let her know that I'm here, that she'll soon be free. I start to make my way down the aisle.

The beam slides over the bars, causing the shadows behind to shift and merge, so when I first see it I almost miss it. A small plastic tray, the kind that might once have held a TV dinner. I bend down to examine it through the bars. The compartments are all empty save one; in it there's what looks like a scoop of beans, long cold, the sauce congealed. I'm about to move on when something causes me to shine the light further into the cage. And that's when I see him. A small boy, lost inside dark overalls that are way too big for his tiny frame, pressed into the shadows at the back. His hands cover his face, but I can see his head is shaved; his scalp looks pale, almost gray. He slowly splays his fingers, revealing a pair of solemn eyes that stare back at me, the large silver pupils reflecting the crimson beam from Hick's flashlight.

I take an involuntary step backwards, my mind already measuring the gap between us, trying to work out whether more might be called for. He doesn't appear threatening, though. He makes no move towards me, just continues to watch from the spot he seems to have picked out for himself in the corner. After a moment he raises one impossibly thin arm and points behind me.

I turn around and shine the light into the cage opposite.

She's lying curled up on the floor, asleep. She's wearing the same dark overalls as the boy, but her wrists and ankles have been bound. I bend down as quietly as I can, suddenly afraid to wake her. What if she opens her eyes and I see what I've just seen in the cage opposite? I take a deep breath.

'Mags.'

She looks up and as she blinks back the sleep I feel relief wash through me. The shadows under her eyes seem a little heavier than they were earlier, but that's probably just the flashlight. The pupils are dark, human. She picks herself up, a little awkwardly because of the restraints. Her hands reach for the bars, but then she remembers, and quickly pulls them back.

'Gabe. What are you doing here?' Her eyes narrow. 'And what happened to your face?'

At first I'm not sure what she means; it takes a second for me to work it out.

'Oh, frostbite. I guess I got careless.'

'Does it hurt?'

It does a little, but I shake my head.

'This is what happens when I'm not there to watch over you. What are you doing here? I thought I...'

There's a noise from behind me and her eyes dart down the aisle between the cages.

'Gabe, you need to get out of here.'

Her voice is low, urgent. I look over my shoulder, but it's just Hicks walking towards us carrying a large plastic crate with the number 100 stenciled on it. I turn back to Mags.

'It's okay. He's helping us.'

He sets the crate down on the floor.

'I thought I told you to stay put.'

He looks at me for a long moment like he's deciding whether he's done taking me to task over wandering off, but then he must figure we have more pressing matters to attend to. He squats down next to me and looks at Mags.

'Now we need to do this my way. Understood?'

She looks at him as if she still doesn't know what to make of this, but in the end she just nods. He turns to me and I realize I'm expected to answer too.

'Yeah, sure.'

He looks into the cage.

'You got a blade on you?'

I nod.

'Well give it to me then.'

I hand him the leatherman; he thumbs out the knife.

'Alright, now move to the front of the cage and slide your hands through.'

I keep the blade sharp; it doesn't take him long to cut through the plastic at her wrists. When he's done he passes it through the bars. While she's working on the cable ties at her ankles he unsnaps the lid on the crate, pulls out a set of thermals and hands them to her. 'Change into those. Go on now, nobody'll look at you.'

She hesitates a moment, then starts unsnapping the fasteners on her overalls. I turn away, but when I hear her wince I glance back over my shoulder. Mags has always been thin, but not like this. Even in the scant light I can see the bones along her side, the play of muscles across her stomach. And before she pulls the thermals down over her head I catch a glimpse of something else: a chain of dark, ugly welts, tracking from one hip up her ribcage to her shoulder.

I turn away, but I feel something, also dark and ugly, welling up inside me. The best we can hope for now is that we get away from this place and never see Truck or any of the other soldiers again. I know there may be no limit to the things I would do to the person that has inflicted those marks on her, however.

When Mags is done changing into her thermals Hicks passes a pair of latex gloves and a roll of duct tape through the bars.

'Put those on and tape the cuffs to your wrists.'

She snaps on the gloves and then uses her teeth to tear a couple of strips from the roll.

'Alright. Now I'm going to let you out. But you need to do exactly as I say until we're outside. Got it?'

Mags looks up from wrapping the tape around her wrists. I can tell she doesn't care much for the instruction, but she agrees. She eyes the leatherman, but Hicks just shakes his head so she leaves it behind her on the floor of the cage. He unlatches the door and swings it open. She crawls out and stands, a little unsteadily at first.

'We ready?'

She nods in the direction of the cage opposite.

'What about him?'

Hicks looks over. The fury presses itself further back into the shadows.

'What about him?'

'We can't leave him here.'

'We can and we will.' He turns to me, like this is something I need to pay particular attention to. 'You think Doc's just going to let this go? Truck's probably already figured out you gave him the slip, which means he'll most likely be back here in a few hours. With a bit of luck it'll be too late for them to set out after us right away, but even so I reckon we'll have a day's head start at most. Boots will slow them down, and that might just be enough if you two can keep the pace. But not if we're hauling that thing along. It's been in there so long it probably can't even stand straight.' He looks into the cage. 'Besides, it's about to turn. I reckon it's got a day or two left at most.'

The fury glances up as he says this, but Hicks doesn't seem to notice. Right now all I care about is getting Mags out of here and back to Eden as quickly as possible, and what he's saying makes sense.

'Mags, you sure?'

She nods. 'I'm not leaving without him Gabe.'

I look down into the cage. Its eyes are still freaking me out, but it doesn't seem like it means us harm. If what Hicks says is true and it's about to turn I really have no interest in bringing it with us, however. But I also recognize the tone in Mags' voice. Once she's set her mind on something there's little can be done to change it.

'Hicks, we have to take the kid.'

'Aw hell Gabriel, it's not a kid. Might have been once but not anymore, and certainly not in a few days from now when it's looking at you like you're a side of prime rib and I have to put a bullet in it.'

The fury shakes its head as it hears this, but Hicks isn't even looking at it now.

'They don't sleep, you know. Which means you won't be able to either. How long do you think you'll be able to keep that up?'

'Gabe, I'll watch him.'

Hicks turns to Mags.

'And who'll watch you, darlin'? Christ. Here, gimme your flashlight.' I dig the windup from the pocket of my parka and hand it to him. He points it into the cage and cranks the handle. The dynamo whirs and the bulb glows orange, then yellow, finally casting a faint pool of almost-white light that barely reaches the back of the cage. The fury instinctively presses itself even further back, raising its arms to block the beam. But then it realizes what Hicks is doing and drops them again. Its eyes narrow to slits, but it holds its head up and forces itself to squint back.

'See that? And that's just something you'd pull from a crackerjack box.' He tosses the flashlight back to me. 'In a couple of days it won't be able to stand the daylight. What do you plan to do then? Cut it loose? Or were you planning on another moonlight stroll, son?'

I look back at Mags, but her expression hasn't changed.

'We're taking it, Hicks. You can come with us or let us go.' I watch him close as I say it, though. Because there's a third choice, of course. He could just stop us, right now, and make his peace with Gilbey. His fingers don't stray any closer to the pistol on his hip, but I can see him working through the options himself. In the end he shakes his head like he's trying to figure out just where this all went wrong.

'Alright, alright.'

He looks at Mags and the cage he's just sprung her from and then back at me, like he's deciding which of us is less likely to cause him trouble.

'Gabriel, you remember that first room we passed as we came in? In there you'll find a crate with 99 on the side of it. Bring it to me. And come straight back y'hear? No exploring this time.'

I hurry off down the aisle, winding the flashlight as I go. I get to the storage room he meant and step inside. The ceiling's low and I have to duck my head to avoid hitting it off the bulkhead lamps bolted to the concrete. Rows of shelves line the walls on either side. For as far as I can see with the flashlight they look empty, but the beam doesn't stretch as far as the wall at the end.

I find a single crate a little further back, the number 99 stenciled on the side of it. It looks like it's been sitting there a while. I drag it down, dislodging a thick layer of dust. Motes drift lazily through the beam, settling on the concrete floor.

I'm about to turn back but something makes me point the flashlight further along the aisle. Up against the back wall I can see stacks of empty crates, just like the one I'm holding. They're nested inside one another, so only the bottom crate in each stack is visible, but it looks like they each have a number stenciled on the side too.

Spidey's been keeping up a low-level grumble ever since the camera by the blast door, but he takes it up a notch at that, and maybe then I should have paid more attention. But something else catches my eye. I set the crate I'm carrying down and make my way towards it.

All the way back in the darkness there's one more crate. It looks just like all the others, but as I get closer I can see it's not. This one doesn't have a number stenciled on it; it has a name instead.

It says Amanda Gilbey.

*

MAGS HAS ALREADY pulled on her pants and is lacing up her boots as I return. The fury's moved closer to the front of its cage. It peers out through the bars, its eyes shifting nervously between me and Hicks.

I set the crate down and unsnap the lid. Inside there's everything it might need – jacket, gloves, boots, even a small pair of goggles. Spidey really hasn't been happy since I went back into the storage room and now he grumbles about this too. But I'm still a little distracted by the other crate I saw in there, and mostly just keen to get us out of here, so I hush him.

Hicks unlatches the cage and swings it open. But the fury shuffles toward the back and won't come out. It keeps staring up at him, its eyes filled with mistrust. Mags looks up from unpacking the crate.

'Sergeant, why don't you stand back a little further?'

Hicks squints down at her like he doesn't believe this is where his orders are coming from now, but in the end he just sighs and does as she says. The fury hesitates a moment longer and then crawls out. It looks around uncertainly. Squatting on all fours like that it looks like a miniature version of the thing that attacked Ortiz. For a second the memory of the fear I felt in the hospital twists my insides and I wonder if Hicks is right and we're making a terrible mistake.

Mags bends down next to it.

'Can you stand, Johnny?'

It grips the side of the cage and tries to pull itself upright, but all it manages is a chimp-like crouch. She has to help it into the clothes from the crate. When she's done Hicks tears several strips of duct tape from the roll and hands them to her.

'Seal the cuffs of the mittens to the arms of the jacket. Last strip's for its mouth.'

Mags looks like she might be about to argue, but Hicks just shakes his head.

'We're done discussing this. It's that or I go fetch the catchpole.'

She turns back to the fury.

'It'll be okay Johnny. Just till we get out of here.' She tapes up its mittens. It doesn't object as she stretches the last strip across its lips.

We leave The Greenbrier the way we came in.

Mags holds the fury's hand as we climb the stairs back to the upper levels. It manages them without too much difficulty; by the time we reach the top I think it might already be standing a little taller. When we enter the plant room it cranes its neck, swiveling around to take in each detail, like it wants to look everywhere at once. Hicks keeps a close eye on it as it steps up onto the metal gangway, but it just grips Mags' hand and follows her across. We leave the plant room and make our way down the long corridor in silence. We pass through the decontamination showers and then we're back out in the tunnel.

I counted two hundred paces from this point when we were coming in, but somehow it seems longer on the way out. The camera above the entrance door is still blinking as we pass under it; I keep looking back over my shoulder long after the little red light has been swallowed up by the darkness. At last I spot the circular vents and the huge blast door pushed up against the concrete ahead of us. We step through into the chamber between it and the outer gate. The access door where we came in is still open. Hicks stops and reaches into his pocket. He pulls out a small plastic container and hands it to Mags.

'Take this. It'll taste like the worst thing imaginable, but I guess you already know that by now.'

She stares at him for a moment, like she's working something out. Then she unscrews the cap, but instead of raising it to her lips she bends down and hands it to the fury.

'Drink that Johnny. Quickly now.'

'Aw, you can't be serious.' Hicks looks at me for support, but I can't help him. The fury hesitates, like it's unsure what it should do.

'Don't worry; the sergeant has another one for me.'

After only a moment's pause it knocks it back. Mags holds her hand out for another of the vials. Hicks looks at her like he's wondering whether any promise of a cure might be worth this, but in the end he digs into his pocket and hands one over. She unscrews the cap and lifts it to her lips. I watch as her face contorts and she bends over and clutches her stomach like she might have to throw up but after a moment it passes. She wipes her mouth with the back of her glove and reaches for the fury's mitten.

'Come on, let's get you into some snowshoes.'

As soon as she's gone Hicks grabs my arm and pulls me back into the tunnel. He reaches into his pocket and hands me four more containers like the ones he just gave to Mags.

'She needs to take one of these a day. Try and give them to her at the same time each morning.'

I slip the vials into the pocket of my parka.

'Aren't you coming with us?'

He shakes his head.

'That's all of the Doc's medicine I could lay my hands on. If she insists on sharing it there's only enough for another two days. I'm guessing that's not near enough time to get you where you're going?'

It took us more than six days to get here from Mount Weather and

Eden's further north again. I shake my head.

'Alright. I'm going to stay here, see if I can't pick up some more. You plan on going back the way you came down, right?'

I nod.

'If there's anything more you remember about the location of this Eden place Gabriel, now'd be a really good time to tell me. Make it a helluva lot easier for me to find you if I knew where you were headed.'

He looks at me hard for a while, but I just shake my head.

'Fair enough. Well, stick to the interstate for as long as you can. If you have to get off it for any reason leave me a sign. I'll catch up to you soon as I can.'

He steps back over to the wall and hits the switch to start the close sequence. A second later the electric motors kick in, whining under the load as they slowly start to pull the huge blast door back from the wall.

He looks over my shoulder again. Mags is still over by the access door strapping the fury into a pair of snowshoes, so she's got her back to us. His hand slips into the pocket of his parka. He hesitates for a moment and then passes me something cold and heavy wrapped in a Ziploc bag. I don't need to look down to know what it is.

'There's a round in the magazine; all you need to do is pull the slide back to chamber it. You remember how to do that, right?'

I nod.

'Good. Now when they turn it's quick, like someone's just flicked a switch inside them. If you so much as think that might be about to happen you don't hesitate, no matter what the girl says. Y'hear me?'

I nod again.

'Alright. Best be on your way then. I'll see you on the road.'

I have to step out of the way of the blast door as it inches its way across the concrete. When I turn around to look back into the tunnel he's already gone.

*

DAWN'S STILL SOME TIME OFF as we leave the bunker and outside it's bitterly cold. I can see Mags' breath smoking with it; she hugs her arms to her sides and stamps her boots to warm up. The fury doesn't seem to notice. It just stares at the blackened stumps poking through the ashen snow, like they're the most wondrous things it's ever seen.

My feet got a break from the snowshoes while we were inside, but as soon as I snap them back on I can feel the bindings pressing into the cuts I have there. Right now I'm more worried about the shape my legs are in however. They were tiring badly on the way up here; I wonder how far I'll be able to make it. But as I look over at the fury I realize that's going to be the least of our problems.

Marv wasn't ever big on actual explanations for stuff; I picked up pretty much everything I needed just from watching him. Even so, it didn't take me long to work out snowshoes. There's really not a lot to it. You have to raise your legs a little higher than usual, because the powder gives. And the shoes are bigger than your regular boots so you need to widen your stride to keep from tripping over yourself. But that's pretty much it. The Juvies certainly didn't set any snowshoeing records on our way from Eden to Mount Weather, but even they got the hang of it before too long.

That's not how it's going to be with the fury, though. As I watch it taking its first tentative steps I begin to realize the trouble we're in. The recent storm's brought fresh snow, but even without it the drifts up here'd be too deep for its short legs. And to make matters worse the snowshoes are too big; every time it lifts one of them it almost can't help but bring it down on the other. Neither of those things are the real problem, however. It's just like Hicks said; whatever time it's spent in the cage is preventing it from standing upright, and if it can't do that it'll never keep its balance in snow like this.

I think about it for a moment and then I take the handsaw from my pack and trudge up the hill. My recently thawed fingers are still clumsy and I struggle with the blade, but I return a few minutes later with a couple of the straightest looking branches I can find. I hand them to Mags and she shows it how to plant the makeshift poles. When it looks like it's got the hang of it we set off through the trees, following the path Hicks and I took coming up.

It takes us a long time to make it back to the road.

Once we get there I keep us to the tracks Hicks and I made on the way here, but after the church there's no choice but to start breaking trail. My snowshoes sink into the deeper powder. With each step now I can feel the bindings digging into the cuts across my feet.

We continue on, stopping regularly to dig the fury out of the drifts. It seems to take forever, but eventually I see The Greenbrier's crumbling gates up ahead. We cross the road. The station house stares back at us from behind its candy cane pillars. We make our way past it and down onto the railway line.

The sides close up around us, and with nowhere to go the snow deepens again. Our pace slows further. By the time we reach the siding where the corroded railcar rests against the buffers the sky's already getting brighter. It's still barely light at all, yet whenever I turn around now I catch the fury trying to raise its arms to shield its eyes. Every time it tries it loses its balance and pitches over and we have to stop and haul it upright.

The I-64 overpass appears around a bend. Beyond I can just see the crown of the tunnel as the track continues on through the hill. We've been traveling an hour and I doubt we've covered a half-mile. I can already feel the muscles in my legs burning, and inside my boots my feet are killing me. Even Mags seems to be struggling. In the heavier drifts she favors her side, like drawing breath is causing her pain.

The first of the day's light slowly seeps over the top of the shallow ravine as somewhere behind the gray clouds the sun finally rises. I walk us under the overpass. The fury collapses in the snow, relieved to be back in shadow. I ask Mags for the roll of duct tape Hicks gave her to bind it, back in the bunker. She hesitates a moment, like she's not sure what I'm planning, but then she digs it out and tosses it over. I pull off my gloves. I work as quickly as I can but my fingers are still numb from their recent freezing and thawing and it takes me longer than it should to tear several short strips from the roll and stick them to my sleeve of my parka.

When I have enough I step closer and tell the fury to hold its head up. It looks at me uncertainly, then at Mags. She says it'll be okay. It hesitates a moment and then tilts its face up to me. I pull a piece of tape from my sleeve, trying to ignore the silver eyes that stare back at me through the goggles. I work as quickly as I can, masking the lens so that only the narrowest slit remains through which light can enter. As I'm stretching the last piece into place the surgical mask Mags gave it slips down. Its skin is gray, the color of the snow, but the tape that Hicks insisted Mags place over its mouth in the bunker is missing. She must have removed it before we set off.

I yank my hand back like I've just burned it, but it just continues to stare back at me through the slit in its goggles. I glance over at Mags, hoping she hasn't noticed. I fumble my fingers back into the mittens, trying to pretend nothing was wrong.

We make our way up the slope and onto the highway.

*

ALL MORNING WE TRACK EAST on I-64. It's early yet but I keep looking around, hoping to see Hicks cresting a hill or rounding a corner behind us, but there's no sign of him. I tell myself it's early yet.

I stop us every hour for frostbite checks. Mags doesn't let me stand too close and she keeps her eyes open. When she looks up at me I try not to stare at the darkening circles there, but I can't help it. It's only been a few hours but already they seem worse than when we were back in The Greenbrier. I tell myself that's just being outside, in what passes for daylight. As long as she keeps taking Gilbey's medicine she'll be fine.

We take our lunch an hour after we cross into Virginia. There's no shelter on this stretch of the highway so we sit in the snow in the lee of a road sign and set our MREs to warm. I'm just grateful to have some time out of the snowshoes. Something inside my boot feels slick, like I might be bleeding again.

The fury picks a spot for itself a few feet away and slumps down into a drift. Mags asks it if it wants anything, but it just looks up at her like it's figuring out if it needs to worry about its answer and then shakes its head. She unwraps a HOOAH! and hands it over anyway. It sniffs at the candy bar, then lets it fall into its lap.

I catch her wincing as she sits back down. I ask her what happened to her ribs but she just goes quiet and says it's something best forgotten about. We finish our MREs in silence. As soon as she's done she gets up. She walks over to the fury and pulls it to its feet and I watch as they set off down the highway. I gather our trash, step back into my snowshoes and hobble after them.

Hicks said Truck would probably wait until morning to come after us. I pray he does. But even so I don't know how we can hope to stay ahead of him, limping through the snow like three broken things.

Darkness is threatening to overtake us as we take the exit for Covington, the town where we stopped with the soldiers on the way out to The Greenbrier. I'll need to go back to the church to retrieve Marv's map, but we won't be sleeping there. If the soldiers are on the road they could be here later tonight, and it's the first place Truck would check.

I spot a low brown-brick building with a sign that says US Army Reserve Center right off the interstate. We make for it as the last of the light leaves the sky. Mags gets a fire going and we sit on the floor under a poster of a soldier that says *Does Your Future Look As Exciting As Ours?* while our MREs heat. The fury picks a spot on the other side of the room. It's still working on the HOOAH! Mags gave it for lunch. Each time I look over it raises it to its lips but by the time we're finished with our MREs the candy bar remains largely untouched.

I roll out the sleeping bag Mags and I used to share. There's an awkward moment while we both stare at it, then she says I should take it. She says she'll sleep in her parka; it's not that cold. It's freezing in here; the thought that she may already not be able to feel it scares me, so I announce in a voice that's supposed to be authoritative but I suspect just sounds a little hysterical that she has to have it. I tell her I need to go back out to get Marv's map anyway. There's a Walmart right on the other side of the highway. I'll pick up another while I'm gone.

I head for the door before she has a chance to argue.

It's long after dark when I limp back to the center. Mags is propped up against the wall in her sleeping bag, *Owen Meany* open in her lap. The fury sits in the corner, where it was when I went out. She looks up at me as I step inside.

'How'd you do?'

I tell her I did pretty well, which isn't so far from the truth. I've recovered Marv's map from the church; it's back where it belongs in the pocket of my parka. And I've managed to find us a bunch of things in the Walmart that we could use.

She smiles, but she looks tired.

'Want to get some sleep while I take the first shift?'

I shake my head. We've agreed we'll take it in turns to watch the fury. I'm pretty beat, but there's a few things I need to do first.

'Wake me in a couple of hours, okay?'

I nod. Within seconds she's curled up inside the sleeping bag, fast asleep.

The fire's burned down, so I set to work coaxing it back to life. From across the room the fury watches me. The branches hiss and steam as I feed them to the flames, but eventually they catch.

I lay the sleeping bag I found down close to the spot Mags has chosen and dig into my pack for the first aid kit. I take off my boots and socks. Blood's soaked through the bandages so I remove them and clean the cuts with water from my canteen, then smear them with some Neosporin I found in the Walmart and tape fresh dressings in place. When I'm done I toss the bloodied bandages in the fire, climb into the sleeping bag and lean back against the wall. My eyelids feel heavy, but I need to stay awake. I take Marv's map from the pocket of my parka and spread it across my lap.

Hicks said to stay on the interstate, but we've been on the road since before dawn and I reckon we've barely covered fifteen miles. In a few short hours Truck and the other soldiers will set off from The Greenbrier, assuming they're not on the road already. If they hike sunup to sundown they should be able to cover thirty miles in a day, even dragging Boots with them. At that rate they'll be on us before we even reach I-81. I take the flashlight from the pocket of my parka and wind the stubby handle. The dynamo whirs and the bulb glows, finally casting a faint pool of yellow light across the familiar folds and creases. I turn the map over to find Covington and for a moment I forget where I'm pointing the beam. It slides across the wall and for a second is reflected back by a pair of silvered eyes. The fury turns its head away and buries its face in its hands.

My heart jumps and a cold flush of fear snaps me upright. Somehow outside, in the daytime, it's just a kid, no bigger than we were when Kane brought us to Eden. But now, here in the darkness, it's something much more than that. Or less.

I extinguish the beam and refold the map. As I'm returning it to the pocket of my parka my fingers brush the object Hicks handed me earlier. I take it out. The sweet smell of the gun oil drifts up as I remove Marv's pistol from the Ziploc bag. The magazine slides out easily when I press the switch. I feel along the top for the bullet and lever it out with my fingertips. Nothing pops up to take its place. Just one then. I push the round back in with my thumb and slide the magazine back up into the handle. The fury looks at me as it clicks into place, and for a moment the light from the fire catches its eyes. It holds my gaze for a moment, like it knows what that sound means.

I slip the gun inside my sleeping bag and settle back against the wall to wait.

*

I WAKE WITH A START and the feeling that I've just cried out in my sleep. The dream's already fading, but I remember a tunnel, and a shrill voice I haven't heard in a long time, urging me to run faster. I blink sleep from my eyes, worried I might still be there. But I'm not. I'm sitting upright, my back to the wall, the frigid air pressing against my sweat-soaked thermals. I must have drifted off while I was supposed to be watching the fury. I quickly look over but it's where it was earlier, huddled in the corner on the far side of the room. Mags is curled up in her sleeping bag next to me.

The fire's dead and black on the ground and it's cold. It's still sometime before dawn, but I know I won't sleep again so I get up and head outside for more firewood. Mags is awake when I get back. I set a couple of MREs to heat and then get to work on a fire. She asks the fury if it wants anything, but it just holds up the HOOAH! it's been working on since yesterday and says it's fine.

When we're done with breakfast I hand her one of the little plastic vials Hicks gave me. She takes it, unscrews the cap and finishes it with a grimace, then holds her hand out for another. I hesitate. I know the path she means to commit us to; I've known it since she demanded the second container from Hicks on the way out of the bunker yesterday. But what if he can't get us more medicine? There's only three of the vials left. With the pace we're setting that's not even enough to get her to Eden, and that's as much as I care about. I glance over to the other side of the fire. The fury's got its knees hugged to its chest, but I can see it watching to see what I'll do. I don't intend it harm, but Hicks said it's only a day or two from turning, which means anything we're giving it now is just a waste. I guess that's not the way Mags sees it though. She reaches out to touch my arm, but then thinks better of it and pulls back.

'Gabe?'

I look back at her.

'Listen, you either give me another container or the next one I get I'm just going to give to him anyway. But it's not going to come to that, is it?'

In the end I relent and she takes the medicine and hands it to the fury. I pack up our gear while she gets it ready. The Walmart had a big outdoors section and I picked up a pair of hiking poles to replace the branches I cut for it. I also found ski goggles with a darker lens and a kid's jacket with a hood like a snorkel. The goggles are for an adult so they're a little big, but Mags adjusts the strap and they seem to stay on. I've taped the lens like before, leaving only a small slit through which light can enter. Mags hands it the jacket and it tries it on. It fits okay and she gets to work taping its gloves. It can't grasp the zipper pull with its mittens on so she has to help it. Its face disappears inside the hood as she slides it all the way up.

Dawn's just starting to creep into the sky as we set off. The fury hangs back inside the shadow of the doorway and Mags has to coax it out. It still doesn't want to look directly at the light, but it manages to hold its head at a more hopeful angle than anything it could muster yesterday.

I had another look at Marv's map over breakfast. Route 220 out of Covington stays parallel to I-81 for most of its length. We can follow it almost as far as we need to north and then rejoin the interstate for the last couple of days and it doesn't look like we'll have added much to our journey. I discuss it with Mags as we head down to the highway and she reckons we should take it. I stick a patch of duct tape to the exit sign so Hicks knows which way we've gone.

We follow I-64 east for a third of a mile or so. The road crosses a wide river the map says is the Jackson and then a little further on we come to an embankment that drops down onto railway lines. According to the map they'll take us north out of town as quickly as 220 and I figure if Truck's looking for places we might have gotten off he'll check the roads before anything else.

I hang back while Mags takes the fury on ahead. I watch as they make their way down the slope. It seems to be doing better with the snowshoes this morning. I don't know if it's the poles I got it or the darker goggles, but it's managing to stand almost upright now; it only fell once on our way out here. Just as I'm thinking this it snags an edge and goes head over heels down the embankment. Mags catches up to it and digs it out, then they set off again.

I shuck off my backpack and set off after them, dragging it behind me to smooth out our tracks until we get to the first bend.

The railway line follows the river for a ways and then it continues north while the dark, brooding waters wind out west. About a mile from the interstate we come to a set of signals; the hooded lights hanging from the rusting gantry arm stare down at us as we pass underneath. After that the track opens up. Endless rows of rusting tank cars sit silent in their sidings, hauled to their final resting place by huge locomotives. They tower over us from under a blanket of gray snow as we walk between them.

We leave the tracks at a railroad crossing. The barriers are down and an arrow points to a sign that says a train is coming, but we don't wait for it. The Jackson curves back around to greet us as we rejoin 220 and leave Covington behind. The road hugs the eastern edge of the valley, rising and falling as it winds its way north into the Appalachians. I keep looking over my shoulder, hoping for Hicks' lean, rangy form to appear around a bend behind us. But that morning there's nothing.

Sometime around noon we come to a pickup that's slid off the road.

There's been no other shelter for miles so I break the window and we climb inside to eat our lunch. There's a narrow bench seat in the back and Mags holds the door open to let the fury in. It looks up like it might join us but I guess it's not feeling sociable because it turns around and slips into the back under the tarp. We eat quickly and set off again as soon as we're done.

The wind drops and the same gray clouds that were scudding across the mountain tops this morning now just hang there like they've no place better to be. We come to a narrow bridge; a ribbon of ash-choked water flows sluggishly south underneath us as we cross. If we're where we're supposed to be on the map this should be the Jackson again, but this river seems much smaller than the one that accompanied us out of Covington. I spend some time looking for a sign, but there's none.

The road runs true for the next few miles and then it veers west through a break in the ridge at a place called Gulley Run. I can't see any mention of it on Marv's map, and that's not the direction I think we should be headed. I spend some time looking for mile markers to make sure we're still following the right path, but the snow's drifted deep here and I can't find any.

I look back over my shoulder. Behind us the valley's straight enough to see for miles, but there's nothing. Hicks should have caught us by now; I'm beginning to worry he missed the tape I left on the exit sign. He told us to stay on the interstate as long as we could, but I reckon he meant I-81, and we never made it that far. I wonder if he would even have been looking for directions that soon.

In front the valley stretches out for miles, barren and lifeless, without even a barn or a stand of trees to break the emptiness. Have I made a mistake, bringing us this way? With the pace we're setting we can't hope to outrun the soldiers, and there's no shelter here; nowhere to hide; no way out but on or back. If Truck manages to pick up our trail at Covington and they follow us in there we'll be trapped.

I stop and pull out the map again, pretending to examine it while I consider our options. It doesn't take me long to realize we don't have many. If we turn around now we could march right into them, but that's not even my main concern. As I reached into my pocket my fingers brushed the last two containers of Gilbey's medicine. Enough for just one more day if Mags keeps sharing. Eden's still maybe five days ahead of us, at our best pace. Without Hicks I don't know how I'm going to get us there in time to save her; I only know we don't have time to backtrack. I fold the map and point ahead, like I know where we're going. The truth is the road I've put us on is looking like a bad call, but there's nothing to do now but keep following it.

All afternoon we continue north. I look for mile markers but find none.

I'm still stopping us every hour for frostbite checks, although I'm not sure why, other than for the break it provides. I don't think Mags can get frostbite anymore, and I already have it. I dread it now, the moment she lifts her goggles on to her forehead. I find myself staring at the darkening shadows under her eyes, trying to convince myself they're not getting worse, but struggling to find the evidence of it.

As dusk settles we pass a row of mailboxes, only their rusting tops visible above the snow. We'll need shelter soon, but there's no sign of the homes to which they once belonged. I stop to search them. I tell Mags I'm looking for kindling but in reality I'm desperate for anything that might tell us where we are. But there's nothing.

Darkness falls around us. The temperature's dropping fast and I'm starting to panic. We haven't passed shelter since the pickup where we ate lunch, and that's too far behind us now to contemplate. At last we come to a widening in the road that somebody has bothered to name Mustoe. It doesn't show on Marv's map, but that doesn't matter; as we round a bend I spot a small farmhouse, set back a ways from the road. We trudge up to it as the last of the light leaves the sky. I haven't managed to replace the pry bar I lost at the hospital, but as we get closer I can see I'm not going to need it; the door's already busted open. It looks in a sorry state. If we had alternatives I'd walk us on by, but we are beggars now not choosers. I unsnap my snowshoes and bring us inside.

*

HE SITS IN THE CORNER, one wrist held up to his mouth. His small teeth probe for the edge of the tape binding the mitten to the cuff of his jacket, unaware that that is what he is doing. The candy bar the girl gave him sits untouched in his lap; there is nothing there that holds his interest. He knows what he wants now, but he doesn't dare admit it, even to himself, because that might make it real.

Across the room the fire has died down and it is dark, but he can see perfectly well. The girl lies curled up in her sleeping bag. She mumbles in her sleep, like something is troubling her. She watched him earlier, while the boy slept. He asked her where they were going. She said they were going to bring him somewhere and fix him. He hopes it isn't far. He heard what the soldier with one eye said, when he pulled the boy back into the tunnel and gave him the thing that smells of oil and metal. He does not want that to happen. But it is there, all the time now, gnawing at him, twisting his insides. If it would just stay out of his head he thinks he might be able to brace himself against it. It doesn't, though. It slips between his thoughts, wrapping itself around them, until he can no longer be sure which are his own and which belong to it.

The days are a little better. As long as they are outside the wind carries their scent away, and he has other things to focus on, like planting his poles, and placing his snowshoes in the tracks the boy has made for him, and shielding his eyes from the light. The light is cruel, but he sees it has a purpose: its terrible brightness helps to keep the other thing, the thing inside him, at bay. Now it is dark, and there is nothing to do but sit and wait. His thoughts – *its* thoughts – are free to roam where they will.

His gaze shifts to the boy. He sits on the other side of the small kitchen, his back against the wall. He is still awake, but it will not be long now; his head has already fallen to his chest once. Even as he watches it slumps forward again.

He shifts his head to one side and tastes the air. He remembers the way the girl used to smell, when they were back in the cages and she cut her hand. But her scent is becoming less interesting to him now.

Not the boy, though; that it is getting worse. It was overpowering earlier, when he was changing the bandages on his feet. The thought of it makes the hunger rise up inside him now, so sudden and strong it surprises him.

*He could sit closer. Just a little. There would be no harm in that.*

He stops working on the cuff of his jacket with his teeth and places one hand on the floor, preparing to shuffle himself forward. For a moment it seems like he will succumb to the blackness, but instead he shakes his head to clear it and pushes himself back into the corner. He brings his wrist to his mouth again.

He likes the boy. He made him poles so he could manage the snow, and he tried to fix his goggles so the light wouldn't hurt his eyes so badly, even though he was scared.

His teeth find the edge of the tape, start to work it free.

He wishes the boy wasn't frightened of him.

But maybe it is good that he is.

*

IN THE DREAM I'M BACK in the tunnel. It is strange but familiar, a mix of Eden and Mount Weather and maybe other tunnels as well, ones that will lead to places on Marv's map I have not yet visited.

I'm in the darkest part. The blackness wraps itself around me, threatening to smother me. There's a flashlight in my hand, but it's so big I'm struggling to get my fingers around it. I look down and see why; it's the one Jack got me for when I had to go up in the attic. I hold it in both hands and flick the switch to turn it on, but of course it doesn't work. I press it to my cheek, because that used to calm me down, but something's wrong. The metal that used to be smooth now feels rough against my skin. I hold it out in front of me, and then I see why: large, scaly patches where the virus has taken hold. Even as I watch it eats through the metal, revealing the fat batteries nestled together inside.

I toss the flashlight away, horrified that I had held it to my face. And that's when I hear it: its scuffling approach echoes up through the darkness behind me. Ahead in the distance I think I can just make out the faintest sliver of light. I start running for it but somehow I don't seem to be making any progress. It's like the darkness has a substance, a heft, that pushes against me, holding me back. The sound is getting louder; any second now I'll feel its weight across my shoulders. I try to turn around, but something prevents me. I keep running, but the end of the tunnel's not getting any closer. And then I feel it: long, bony fingers, closing around my leg, and that's when I scream.

I wake with a start. The fire's gone out and the sweat's already cooling on my skin. I scan the room, peering into the blackness for angles, shapes, anything to prove I'm no longer in the tunnel. But without the fire I can't make out a thing.

I reach for the flashlight I left beside the sleeping bag. The dynamo whirs as I crank the handle. The fury's still sitting in its corner. It raises its hands to ward off the beam, but for an instant I catch the reflection from its eyes as it squints back at me. I keep the flashlight trained on it a second longer, then lay it on the ground.

I don't care much for sleep after that. I just sit there, staring into the darkness, trying to figure out what we're going to do. It's been two days since we left The Greenbrier, more than enough time for Hicks to have caught up with us. Something's gone wrong and I have to face it now: we can't rely on him to bring us more of Gilbey's medicine. My hand reaches inside the pocket of my parka for the two containers that remain. I tell myself it'll be okay; she's been taking whatever's inside those vials ever since she got infected. Some of it will still be in her system, and that has to count for something. If we ration what's left maybe I can still get her there before it's too late.

That thought does little to soothe me, however, and in the end I can't sit there any longer with my thoughts. It's still early but I get up and start rebuilding the fire. Mags must have been awake too, because as soon as I start moving around she sits up in her sleeping bag.

I set a couple of MREs on to heat and we eat them in silence. She doesn't seem much interested in what's there, though; she picks at it for a while, then pushes it aside in favor of her coffee. I take one of the little plastic containers from my pocket. She holds her hand out, but I don't pass it to her right away. I know what I have to do now. Hicks was right. I've already waited too long for this.

'Gabe.'

'No, you need to listen to me now, Mags. I've thought about this. You can only take half of it. The rest we'll save for tomorrow. That'll give us enough for four days. In that time I can get us there.'

'And what about Johnny?'

I shake my head.

'I'm not giving you any more to give to it.'

Her eyes flick to the container. For a moment she looks like she's considering wrestling it from me. I'm much bigger than she is, but I doubt that would stop her from trying; I suspect the only thing that does is the knowledge that she'd probably infect me in the process.

She looks back at me.

'You have to promise me, just half, then you'll give it back?'

She doesn't say anything. Eventually she nods once, like she understands.

I hand her the vial and she unscrews the cap. She raises it to her lips and tilts her head back. When she's swallowed half of it she stops and replaces the cap. I hold my hand out for it, but instead of giving it back she tosses it across the room. The fury hesitates for a moment and then picks the container up. It looks at me like it's wondering what it should do, but before I have a chance to say anything she turns to it.

'Drink it Johnny.'

It casts one last glance in my direction then unscrews the cap and drains the remainder of the liquid.

We pack up our things and leave the farmhouse without speaking.

For the next two days we hike north. Soon after we set off on the first morning a ridge rises up in front of us and the valley forks left and right. I take out Marv's map but it isn't clear which way we should go so I take us east, figuring that's the general direction we need to be headed. But after a couple of miles of heavy drifts the road runs out and we have to turn back.

We eat lunch by the side of the road, not much further on than where we started. I want to say something about what happened earlier but I'm not sure what so we sit apart and spoon the cooling mix from the MRE pouches in awkward silence and then pack up our things and continue on. We pick up a river that Marv's map says is the south branch of the Potomac and at some point after we must cross into West Virginia, but there's no sign to welcome us. As night bears down we stop at a small chapel sitting at a crook in the road just outside a place called Durgon. Its cinder block sides are crumbling and the corrugated roof looks like it may not have many more seasons left in it, but Mags has been slowing all afternoon and I'm not sure how many more miles she has in her.

I get a fire going and start fixing dinner, but she says she isn't hungry. She just climbs into her sleeping bag and tells me to wake her when it's her turn to stand watch. The fury waits until she's asleep and then asks for something to bind itself with. I toss it one of the cable ties I stole from Jax's backpack. I guess it already has somewhere in mind because it picks it up and slopes off into the darkness, and later when I check it's tethered itself to a radiator. In the night I hear it struggling and the following morning its restraints look like a dog's been chewing on them, but the plastic's held. Mags frees it as soon as she wakes up. As she's sipping her coffee I hand her the last of Gilbey's medicine and ask her not to share it but she does anyway and there's nothing I can do to stop it.

We set off shortly after. I check the road, but it's empty. I don't know what's happened to Hicks, only that he isn't coming. Today we'll get off 220 and finally start heading east. If we can keep up this pace I figure another four days' hike to Eden. There's no more of Dr. Gilbey's medicine left, and Mags has been on half rations since yesterday. All I have left to cling to now is that she won't change as quickly as Marv did.

The valley bends east. A grainy, reluctant dawn's seeping into the sky, and for the first hour we find ourselves hiking into it. The light troubles the fury, but there's little I can do about it, even if I cared. The road eventually curves north again into Morose, the biggest town we've seen since Covington. As we reach the outskirts it inclines slowly to a bridge. Underneath us the gray water burbles, but I don't bother unsnapping the throat of my parka to listen.

I'm just desperate to get us off this goddam road I've put us on.

We take our lunch in a *Shop 'n' Save* right next to the on-ramp for the highway. We eat quickly and set off as soon as we're done. We're finally heading in the right direction, but now the Appalachians stand in our way; we'll have to hike through them to get back on I-81.

After we quit the town the road runs flat through a long narrow valley that looks like it was once woodland, then starts to climb. A sign sticking out of a drift says the place is called Culkin, but it's another place too small to show on Marv's map. There's little in the way of shelter and we lose the light and have to backtrack a mile to a farmhouse we passed at a bend where the road crosses water. The door's shut but the lock's weak in rotten wood and it doesn't stand to my boot. I get a fire going and break out our MREs, but Mags says not to make her one; she's just going to go right to bed. She asks for a couple of Tylenol and I give them to her with a cup of coffee. She swallows them and then disappears inside her sleeping bag. The fury's found a spot for itself by a downpipe in the far corner. I hand it a cable tie and check to make sure it binds itself securely, then I turn in.

I lay awake for a long time, just listening to the sound of the house creaking in the cold. From time to time there's a scuffling from the far corner as the fury struggles against its restraints, but then long stretches of silence. Sometime in the early hours I drift off, but the sleep that finally comes is filled with dreams of dark, endless tunnels and faceless things, long and bent and spider-thin, that stalk me through them.

*

I'M UP BEFORE DAWN next morning. Mags is still curled up in the sleeping bag next to me. We have another long day ahead of us so I figure I'll let her rest. I build up the fire with the last of the wood I cut the night before, but the branches are damp and in the end I have to use a little of the gas to get it going.

While our MREs are heating I dig the tin mug I carry from my pack, fill it from my canteen and stick it among the coals. When the water's bubbling I tear open a packet of coffee and dump it in. The bitter aroma fills the room. I put on my gloves and fish the mug out of the fire then take it over to where she's sleeping.

She's pulled the sleeping bag up over her head and is balled up inside it. I set the mug down and gently shake her shoulder through the material. Her bones feel thin, sharp, and that frightens me, but I leave my hand where it is while she slowly wakes up. I miss even this contact. At last she sits up, drawing the sleeping bag around her.

'You okay?'

'Yeah.' She winces as she hugs her knees to her chest. 'Sore. Must have pulled a muscle yesterday.'

The fire's not casting much light. Even so I can't help but notice how dark the shadows around her eyes have become. I look away quickly.

'What is it?'

'Nothing.' I look back at her and force a smile back on to my lips. 'Here.'

I reach for the steaming cup. She searches for her own mug so I can transfer the contents. As she holds it up the surface catches what little light the fire's offering; the tin's pitted and pocked, like something's been eating away at it. I pour the coffee in and stand up quickly, muttering something about needing to get more water. I grab our canteens and head for the door.

The first of the day's light's just beginning to creep over the horizon as I step outside. I stumble into the snow, pulling my parka on as I go. A wire fence runs from the back of the farmhouse and I follow it, only stopping when I feel the snow giving way to shingle under my boots. I squat down and dip our canteens. The gray water bubbles over the stones. I can feel the cold coming off it, yet I leave them there long after they've filled.

My eyes are burning, but I refuse to let the tears come. That's for children and there's no place in the world for those anymore. So instead I scream. A long, throat-rending howl, wordless and incoherent; nothing but anguish and rage. I yank the canteens out of the water and pummel the wet river gravel with my fists. I keep it up until my arms ache, until my lungs burn with the effort.

But there's no one listening. No one to bargain with, no one to curse, no one to whom she even matters other than me, and I gave up whatever power I had in this when I handed her the last of the containers. I stand up and wipe my eyes with the back of my hand. Behind me the wind gusts. The fence wire's cold and it creaks in the staples. If there's a more godforsaken sound I'm not sure what it is.

When I get back to the farmhouse Mags has already packed her sleeping bag and is lacing up her boots. She's freed the fury and taped its mittens. I hand her one of the plastic canteens.

'Thanks. Hey, I thought I heard something outside. Everything okay?'

I nod and then busy myself with my backpack, not trusting myself to speak. Her MRE lies untouched next to the remains of the fire.

The Appalachians rise up in front of us. At first the gradient's not that bad, but then it steepens and even though the snow's settled since whenever it last fell the going's heavy. The road sweeps one way then the other as it winds ever upwards, but always it seems the wind is in our faces.

The morning's no brighter than the ones that have gone before, but the light seems to be troubling Mags now. After an hour we stop for a break. I tell her it's time for frostbite checks, but she just shakes her head and asks for the tape. She tears a couple of strips from the roll and starts masking her goggles, just like I did with the fury's. We set off again as soon as she's done.

Sometime around noon we come to a deep ravine. A single crumbling column is all that remains of the bridge that once spanned it, its rust-streaked concrete sides jutting from the snow at the bottom.

The slope's steep and the fury struggles from the get-go. It reverts to the crouch it had when we first stepped out of The Greenbrier, nervously inching its way down. I watch as once again it stumbles, miring itself in a bank of deeper powder. Mags starts to turn herself around to help it, but she's exhausted, barely able to lift her own snowshoes clear of the snow.

Inside my mittens my hands tighten into fists. We don't have time for this. I tell her to keep making her way down; I'll go dig it out. I start to climb back up, but with each step I feel the frustration that overcame me down by the river returning, and now it has a focus. When I reach it I grab the throat of its jacket and yank it out of the snow. It weighs next to nothing; I lift it clean off its feet as I haul it upright. And for a second I hold it there, as another thought slips darkly into place. This thing has no future; in a day or two it'll change and then we'll leave it tethered somewhere or maybe it'll surprise us and I'll need to pray I'm quick enough to put the bullet Hicks gave me in it. But meanwhile I'm letting it destroy what little chance I have left of saving her.

I glance down the slope. It's still a long way to the bottom. Beneath me the bridge's one remaining support rises up from the ravine floor. Long, twisted spines of rusting rebar poke through its crumbling concrete sides.

'Gabe.'

Mags has stopped and is looking up at me.

'Everything okay?'

I nod, slowly setting it down. I pick up its poles from where they've lodged themselves in the snow and hand them over.

It takes us an hour to make our way to the bottom, another two to climb back up the other side.

After that the road narrows. It continues to ascend, more sharply now, and for hours we hike ever upwards, towards a ridge that never seems to get any closer. The wind strengthens, whipping the snow into eddies, sending it dancing in gray flurries around us, filling in our tracks almost as soon as we make them. Finally, just as dusk's slipping into the sky, the way flattens a little and crests. A large rig lies on its side, the timber it was carrying scattered across both lanes. We sit with our backs to the logs for shelter, our breath escaping in frosted plumes as we sip water from our canteens. The fury picks a spot on the far side of the road and hunkers down, watching me suspiciously from inside its hood. I could care less. I'm well beyond worrying about its feelings now.

I gaze out into the failing light as the wind swirls snow around me. The jagged peaks that rise up on the other side of the valley are the Blue Ridge Mountains. I reckon we're no more than a day's hike from Mount Weather.

Except that's not where we're headed; our destination's still several days' hard hiking to the north. I look beside me at Mags. Her head's resting on her knees, her arms hugged tight across her chest. An emptiness colder than the coming darkness settles inside me as I realize we're never going to make it.

Night's already drawing down as we set off again. I've checked the map and the first place we'll come to is called Devil's Backbone, but we still have a way to go to get to it and I can already feel the temperature dropping.

The road snakes along the spine of the ridge for a while and then we begin our slow descent into Virginia. I spot our shelter miles before we reach it: a long, low building with a tall spire that juts up into the darkening sky like a needle. An enormous storage tank sits on the other side of the road, a narrow staircase spiraling up around its ribbed metal sides.

By the time we finally hike down off the mountain the day's long gone and what's left is iron cold, kettle black. Mags is stumbling through the drifts now, and for the last hour she's been coughing inside her respirator, just like Marv was doing, right before he quit. I try and put that thought from my mind. Getting us to our next destination; that's all I need to focus on now. Anything else is for after. And then as we turn off the highway I hear a voice, from somewhere just beyond the reach of the flashlight's beam.

'Turn that damn thing off.'

I point the beam at the source of the growled greeting and look up. A lone figure sits next to a large sermon sign. Some of the plastic letters are missing, but enough remain to make out what it used to read: *The Devil's Backbone Church of Christ*. His one good eye squints back at me as he stands.

I don't think I've ever been happier to see a person.

*

HE RAISES THE THERMOS to his lips and takes a sip.

'Yep, I saw your sign.'

It's just Hicks and me, sitting on either side of the fire. Mags is curled up inside her sleeping bag, already fast asleep. I made her eat some of an MRE after she took the medicine Hicks brought with him, just so she'd be able to keep it down. The fury's in a room behind the altar, cable-tied to a radiator.

'Gilbey had herself kittens when she found out you'd busted the girl out of the bunker. Truck was none too happy you'd fooled him either. It didn't take no orders from the Doc; I've never seen him so keen to head back out. He tracked you as far as Covington, but lost your scent soon after. I wanted to follow you up 220 but he was headed back that way to try and pick up your tracks and I figured that was my chance to cut free. I told them I'd continue on to I-81 in case you'd gone that way while they doubled back to see if they could pick up where you'd gotten off.'

'How'd you know to wait for us here?'

He takes another sip from the thermos.

'I didn't. I took a chance that your Eden was a place called Mount Weather and that's where you were headed. Round about here's where you'd be thinking of getting off if that were so.'

I shake my head, perhaps a little too quickly.

'I don't know about any Mount Weather. We're going further north.'

He squints at me over the thermos.

'Well, I guess I called it wrong then. Not that it matters, seeing as I found you.'

'Where are Truck and the others?'

Hicks shrugs.

'Can't say for certain. My guess is he picked up your trail out of Covington, followed you up the mountain road. Boots will be slowing them down some, but I'd say they're half a day behind us at most.'

'You had no problems getting more medicine?'

Hicks shakes his head.

'Doc wants you both real bad. She doesn't want the girl turning before she can get her back in a cage.'

He looks over at Mags.

'She doesn't look good. How long was she without meds?'

'She had none today until you got here. A half dose yesterday and the day before.'

He whistles softly through his teeth.

'Doc said Truck might have been holding back on her too.'

I look up at this.

'She'll be alright, though, now that she's got more of Gilbey's medicine.'

I say it as certainly as I can, but there's a pitiful tone to my voice; I can hear it. I'm not asking a question; I'm a child seeking reassurance.

He takes a sip and puts the thermos back down.

'Doc's medicine don't work like that, son. It holds back the virus, slows it down. It can't undo the damage it's done. We'd best get her to this Eden place soon as we can. How much further is it?'

'Ninety miles. Mostly interstate.'

'And you're sure you can find it? Without a map or nothing?'

I do have a map; it's in the inside pocket of my parka. But I don't need it now.

'I scavenged that area for five years. North of Hager I know like the back of my hand.'

'We're going to Maryland?' He says it *Merlin*, just like Marv used to.

I shake my head.

'Pennsylvania. Just over the state line.'

He rubs his jaw, like he's working something out.

'What kind of time you been making?'

'Maybe thirty miles a day.' In reality it's been more like twenty. On a good day, twenty-five. Only we haven't had so many of those lately.

'Three days. She ain't got that long. Can't you go any faster?'

'I can.' My feet are mostly healed now; Marv and I could do forty miles in a stretch if we had to.

'And the girl?'

I nod, but only because I need it to be so. This last couple of days Mags has been struggling, and I know it won't get better until I get her to Eden. I think of Marv on that last hike out to the Blue Ridge Mountain Road. I tell myself it doesn't matter. She never weighed much, even before, and I'm used to hiking with a full backpack. If I have to I'll carry her.

'So what's been slowing you down?'

I don't say anything but my eyes flick in the direction of the altar.

Hicks takes another sip from his thermos. He stares back at me for a long moment.

'Alright then. Well if we push I reckon we can be at this Eden place night after tomorrow. It'll involve a couple of long days and we'll have to hike through the night some, but I'm guessing you'll not object to that.'

He screws the lid back on the thermos and stands up.

'What are you going to do?'

But he doesn't answer. He just nods at my sleeping bag.

'Best get some rest, kid. Early start tomorrow.'

*

THE DOOR OPENS and the boy watches as the soldier enters. Light from the fire seeps into the room, for a moment bringing with it traces of color. The soldier closes the door softly behind him and everything is gray again.

The soldier's carrying a flask. He sets it down on the ground. The boy wonders whether he means to just sit and watch him, like he used to when he was in the cage. But then the soldier reaches into his pocket. When he pulls his hand out he's holding something between his fingers. He draws his thumb over it and a short cruel-looking blade folds out of the handle and clicks into place.

The boy tugs at the plastic binding his wrists but the soldier has ratcheted the ties tight and they don't budge. He shuffles backwards, pushing himself further up against the radiator.

The soldier crouches down in front of him.

'Don't worry. I ain't here to hurt you.'

The soldier doesn't smell like the boy, or how the girl used to, but there's the trace of something on his breath. The boy feels dizzy for a moment. Something unwelcome wakes and stirs inside him.

'Hold still now.'

The soldier slides the point of the blade between his wrists. The blade must be sharp because it slices through the plastic without the soldier having to work it. The cable tie drops to the floor. The boy places his hands in his lap and rubs his wrists.

The soldier examines the knife for a moment, then tosses it away like it is no more use to him. It skitters across the floor, bounces off the baseboard and comes to rest in the corner. He steps back and sits down opposite, next to the door. As he leans back against the wall his parka falls open. The shadows are dark but the boy can smell the oiled metal that hangs there.

'I figured it was time we had ourselves a chat.'

The soldier reaches up and flips his eye patch and the boy sees now why he smells different. The soldier is like him. Or at least part of him is.

The soldier reaches for the thermos.

'You like the girl don't you?'

The boy nods his head warily. He does like the girl. She got him out of the cage. She's going to bring him somewhere and fix him. He only hopes it won't be much farther.

The soldier picks up the thermos. The fingers of one hand close around the lid while the other steady the base. He starts to unscrew it.

'You know she's not well don't you?'

The boy nods his head again. He's sorry about what's happening to the girl now. He remembers what it was like. The headaches. The pain. Like the blood in his veins had been drained and replaced with something else, something cold and hot at the same time.

The lid completes its final revolution and the soldier places the thermos carefully to one side. He pulls back the parka and now the boy can see the gun nestling in its holster. The soldier removes the lid and places it on the ground.

It takes a second for the smell to reach him but then the boy's jaw clamps shut and the muscles there clench in a long, shuddering spasm. He feels something flare and writhe inside him, a compulsion so fierce, so complete that it threatens to bend his very bones if he does not obey. The fingers that were resting in his lap a moment ago curl into claws. He places them on the ground and tilts his head, scenting the air. The smell hangs so heavy that he can taste it; it feels slick in his throat. The thermos is only a few feet away. He leans toward it, the way a ravenous dog might approach its wounded prey.

He is almost lost to it now, but the part of him that is still the boy is vaguely aware that the soldier's hand has reached inside his parka. With an almighty effort he pushes himself back. His fingers will not unbend so he places them in his lap and pulls his knees up so they cannot be seen. The soldier's hand lingers over the pistol a moment longer, then he slowly withdraws it.

'Not as far gone as I thought you'd be by now.' He picks up the lid, places it back on the thermos and begins to screw it shut. 'All the same, you ain't got it in you to make it where we're headed.'

The smell recedes but still it lingers. The soldier is talking, but the boy can barely pay attention to what he is saying now. He continues to stare at the thermos. The muscles along his jaw ache, but he does not seem able to relax them.

'Hey, stay with me now.'

The soldier holds his hand in front of his face and clicks his fingers. The boy finally tears his eyes off the thermos and looks up.

'Thing is, the girl ain't got much time. If we hustle I reckon I can get her there before she turns. But not if we have to haul you with us. Only she's not going to leave you behind. And the boy won't go against her. So the way I see it...'

The soldier leaves the sentence for him to finish.

'You want me to leave.'

The soldier nods.

'I do. Find somewhere dark. Hunker down. It'll be over soon enough.'

'What will it be like?'

The soldier doesn't say anything for a long time, just stares at the child sitting opposite him in the darkness.

'I've thought about that a lot. Can't say I have an answer for you, though. Don't plan to find out myself.' He pulls back the parka so the handle of the gun is once again visible. 'Maybe it'll be like going to sleep. Do you remember that?'

The boy nods.

The soldier pulls the patch down over his eye. He picks up the thermos and stands.

'I'll leave the door open for you.'

'Are they going to fix you?'

The soldier stops at the door. For a long moment he just stands there with one hand on the handle. The boy thinks he's going to turn around but he doesn't. At last he just shakes his head.

'There's no fixing me, kid.'

*

IN THE DREAM I'm back in the tunnel. The scuffling echoes towards me along the curved granite walls. I know it's somewhere behind me in the darkness, but always when I try and see it something stops me; an invisible restraint that prevents me from turning my head. I reach down to wind the flashlight, but when my fingers turn the stubby plastic handle nothing happens.

I look up. I think I can just see the faintest glimmer of light, somewhere ahead of me in the distance. I try to run, but it's like I'm wading through deep snow. I hear it again, much closer now. The tunnel's definitely growing lighter, but I know I'm never going to make it.

I feel a sudden weight across my shoulders as it lands on the back, and a second later I hear the snapping of jaws inches from my neck. I'm pitched forward; I feel my shoulder bounce off brace wire, but somehow I manage to stay on my feet. I know it can't last. It's lunging forward again and again, straining to get inside the parka, but my hood and the backpack are getting in its way. I'm trying to free myself from the straps, but when I reach down I realize they're not straps but its arms.

And then finally I lose my balance and I'm pitched forward, and suddenly I'm no longer in the tunnel but tumbling out into gray morning light between two crumbling gateposts. I don't need to read the sign on the flaking paintwork to know where this place is. My boots sink into the drifted snow and I fall forward, flailing in the deep powder.

Behind me the fury's keening and howling like an animal caught in a trap. Its emaciated arms are wrapped around its head and its face is pushed into the gray snow, like it's trying to burrow its way out of whatever torment it's suddenly found itself in.

I look down and realize I'm holding Marv's gun. There's only one bullet; I can't afford to miss like I did in the tunnel at Mount Weather. I take a step closer, using my other hand to steady my aim. My finger slips through the trigger guard and I take a deep breath. There's a sharp crack as I squeeze. The grip whacks itself against my palm and the pistol rears up. A neat black circle appears in the back of the fury's head and it stops moving.

The thick, sulfurous smell of gunpowder fills my nostrils and for the first time I begin to realize something's very wrong. I let the gun fall from my fingers.

I look down again. The fury's head is shaved on both sides. But in the center there's a familiar strip of hair, once so dark it was almost black, now shot through with white. Blood, thick with the cold, wells up from the hole the bullet has made. It trickles down her neck and drops into the gray snow.

I wake with a start. Hicks is standing over me shaking my shoulder.

'Time to get up. Lot of ground to cover today.'

I blink sleep from my eyes. The dream's evaporating, but not quickly enough. I look around. It's still at least an hour till dawn and cold. I banked the fire but it's died overnight. There's no wood left so I pull on my boots and parka and head outside to find some more. When I get back Mags is awake, sitting up with the sleeping bag pulled tight around her.

I dump the meager collection of branches I've gathered on the ground and busy myself with the fire. The wood's damp and won't light, but for once I'm glad of it. The fury's gone, and soon I will have to tell her. I don't know what Hicks said to make it leave, but I can guess. When he came back from behind the altar I closed my eyes and pretended to be asleep. I heard it, though, soon after, making its way to the back of the church. I didn't stir from my sleeping bag as the door opened and it stepped out into the wind.

I fiddle with the branches for longer than I need to and then finally I use some of the gas and they catch. The withered limbs hiss as I feed them to the flames, sending up coils of dense gray smoke that smell of decay. I fill the mug with water from my canteen and place it among the smoldering branches.

What little heat the fire's offering draws Mags closer. She sits next to me, cowled up inside the sleeping bag, the faint light playing across her features. I don't want to look at her, but I can't help it. The circles under her eyes are almost black now, and underneath her cheeks have sunken in, sharpening the angles of the bones there. The water's starting to bubble so I mix in a packet of coffee and fish out the charred mug. She reaches for the cup she uses. As she holds it up so I can transfer the contents I see the virus's scabrous advance; I doubt it'll hold liquid much longer. The cup disappears inside the sleeping bag and she huddles around it, like she needs to extract every last ounce of the warmth that's there.

'How're you feeling?'

She takes a sip of the coffee.

'So-so.'

'Just a couple more days. Hicks reckons we can be there tomorrow night.'

I take a couple of MREs from my backpack and start unwrapping them. She shakes her head.

'Not for me.'

'Mags.'

'It's too early, Gabe. I'll eat later, when we've been on the road a while. Promise.'

I hand her one of the plastic containers. She picks it up, unscrews the cap and raises it to her lips. She hesitates a moment and then knocks it back with a grimace.

'Have you given Johnny his yet?'

I don't know what to say, so I stare down at the MRE that's hissing away at my feet.

'Gabe?'

Hicks voices carries over to us from somewhere behind me in the darkness.

'It's gone. Left in the middle of the night.'

'Gone where?'

Hicks steps out of the shadows. He's holding the thermos in one hand.

'Can't say that I know.'

Mags throws back the sleeping bag and gets to her feet. She has to steady herself on one of the pews.

'Didn't you try and stop him?'

She doesn't wait for a response; she's already pulling on her boots.

'Mags. Maybe it's for the best.'

She stops what she's doing. And what scares me then isn't the dark circles under her eyes, or the way there are hollow shadows where her cheeks used to be. It's the way she's looking at me, like I've said something that has surprised her, and now I'm being re-evaluated.

'He's not a bird with a broken wing, Gabriel. He's a child, just like we were, when Kane took us.' She points at Hicks. 'And when I was in that cage and one of *his* soldiers wouldn't let me have Gilbey's medicine that child gave me his.'

She reaches for her parka and then turns around to look at me again.

'Don't you see? We can't allow ourselves to think like them, like there might be some reason that makes it okay to do bad things to people.'

She goes back to gathering up her things. I stare down at the floor. I doubt I could feel any worse than I do right now. Hicks looks at her like he's just starting to figure out what he's gotten himself into.

'Alright, calm down now. It can't have gone far. I'll go find it.'

'No.'

'I thought you wanted it back.'

'I do want *him* back. I just don't trust *you* to do it.'

She looks back at me.

'Are you coming with me?'

I don't know how I've let it come to this, but there's only one thing now that might save us. I look up at her and slowly shake my head.

'No, Mags, I'm not.'

*

I SAY GOODBYE to them by a faded red *Do Not Enter* sign at the top of the off-ramp, just as dawn's taking shape over the mountains to the east. Hicks passes me a handful of the plastic containers with Gilbey's medicine. I ask him how many he has left for Mags and he says plenty but I make him take them out and show me anyway. He says they're going to try and make it to a place called Falling Waters by nightfall. It's a little town just off the interstate a mile or so shy of the Maryland state line. There's a small church that sits at a bend in the Potomac; they'll wait for me there till sunup. He sets off down the ramp. Mags hangs back.

'Thank you for doing this.'

I look down at the snow.

'I knew-' I realize I'm about to say *it* but at the last minute I stop myself '-he was going to go. I didn't stop him either.'

'Yeah, I figured. Thanks anyway.'

She reaches out one mitten like she means to take hold of my hand, then thinks better of it. She's about to pull it back when I grab it. She looks up at me.

'Take care, Gabe. Find him quickly then catch us up.'

She turns around and sets off after Hicks. I watch her making her way down to the interstate as I hike across the overpass. The wind's picked up. It swirls the snow around her. The highway curves around to the east not long after the off-ramp joins it and within minutes she's gone.

I turn my attention back to finding the kid. I told Mags I'd know where to look for him, that I'd find him faster on my own. But that was just to get her to leave with Hicks. The truth is I'm no Marv, or Truck. And whatever tracks the kid might have laid down earlier, the wind's long covered them.

I tell myself it won't be difficult. All I have to do is put myself in his shoes and try and figure out where he would have gone. Truck's hot on our heels so I doubt he'll have gone back the way we've come. He knows we were headed north on I-81, so it's unlikely he'd choose that way either. Taking the interstate south would certainly get him out of everyone's way, but as I look at it stretching out for miles behind me I figure he'll have passed on that too. He'll only have had a few hours to find somewhere to hole up before it got light, and there's nothing that might pass for shelter that way as far as the eye can see. That only leaves east. The map says there's a town on the other side of the highway. I tighten the straps on my backpack and make my way down towards it.

I start checking houses as soon as I leave the interstate. He struggles with the snow so he won't have gone far, and out here by the highway it's sparsely populated, just the occasional dwelling set back from the road. I don't even have to check all of them. He's too small to go clambering through windows and he doesn't have the means to force a lock, so he'll have been looking for somewhere that's already been broken into. I allow my hopes to rise a little. It won't be long until I find him.

But as I get closer to town roads start branching off to the left and right, each one lined with squat little boxes, and a lot of them have busted front doors. I begin to realize the enormity of the task that lies ahead. It might have taken Marv and me all day to work a single street like this when we were back in Eden; I have to find him in the next couple of hours if I'm to have any hope of catching Mags and Hicks.

I make my way up to the next house along, a single story brick and shingle with a sagging snow-laden roof, trying to figure out how else to narrow my search. Darkened windows stare back at me as I trudge up to the screen door and unsnap my bindings. And that's when it hits me: he'll have taken his snowshoes off outside. That should speed things up considerably. I'll still have to hike up to each stoop or porch to check, but at least I won't have to venture inside.

An hour and three streets later and I still haven't found him, though. I cross the road and start up the next one along. The house on the corner is burned to the ground, just a charred chimneybreast standing alone in what I guess used to be the yard. The next one's not much better; the walls have been stripped to the studs and when I look up there's little left of the roof between the gables. But the third house looks more promising. The boards have been pried off, exposing the insulation underneath, but otherwise it looks in decent shape, and I can see the front door's open. An old Bronco, long since sunken onto its tires, sits at a haphazard angle on the scrub of ground that might once have passed for lawn. There's no tracks to tell anyone's been here, but when I walk around to check the porch I find what I'm looking for: a pair of red snowshoes, already almost covered with snow. Another hour and I might have walked on by.

I climb the steps. The front door's ajar; I push it back and look in. There's no mistaking which way he's gone; the prints left by his small boots stop at a door near the end. The pair of hiking poles I got him lie abandoned next to it.

I unsnap my snowshoes and step inside. There's little to distinguish this place from the countless others like it I've scavenged over the years. The wallpaper's peeling from the walls and the ceiling's stained and cracked, in places the wood behind showing through. I call out but there's no answer, so I make my way down the hall and open the door. A narrow staircase winds down into darkness. I pull the flashlight from my pocket and turn the handle, but the beam doesn't extend much beyond the first few steps.

It was Marv's job to scavenge the dark places, that was the deal. Claus may not live inside my head anymore but I'd be grateful for that arrangement now, just the same. I call out again. Still there's no answer, and now that's beginning to worry me, too. He has to be down there. I wonder if he's already turned. Hicks said it could happen at any moment, and when it did there'd be no warning; it'd be like a switch had been flipped. I look behind me at the busted door. Spidey's offering all sorts of helpful suggestions, most of them variations on a single theme: let's get out of here and catch up with Mags and Hicks, tell her we couldn't find him. I'd be lying if I said I wasn't tempted.

I pull off my mittens and slip my hand into the pocket of my parka, feeling for Marv's pistol. I take it out and pull the slide back to chamber the only round it holds.

I take a deep breath and start down the stairs.

*

I HAVEN'T MADE more than a couple of steps when the toe of my boot catches on something and I stumble. I grab for the railing to steady myself and almost drop the gun. The beam from the flashlight briefly shows a pair of ski goggles, the lenses taped, before they skitter off down the stairs and are lost to darkness.

I stand there for a long moment, my heart pounding, my breath white and heavy in the air in front of me. Once I've calmed myself a little I continue my descent. When I reach the bottom stair I stop and look around. In the corner nearest to me there's a small furnace, the flue pipe snaking up to a rough hole cut into the low plasterboard ceiling. A washing machine and dryer sit side by side next to it, a pile of moldering clothes heaped in a laundry basket on top. Cardboard boxes have been stacked against the wall opposite. Snowmelt's got to them, turning the card to mulch, spilling their contents across the concrete floor.

My pulse is still racing but the fading beam refuses to show me any further so I inch forward, the flashlight in one hand, the gun in the other. My finger's already slipped through the slit Hicks cut in my liners and now it curls around the trigger. I slide the safety, feeling it click under my thumb.

I advance slowly, sweeping the darkness in front of me with the flashlight. It slowly illuminates a small boy, his knees pulled to his chest. He looks asleep, just like the little girl I found, in the closet in Shreve, all those years ago. She hadn't been able to move, but still Marv had grabbed the straps of my backpack and hauled me away, like he'd found me with my hand out to a maddening dog.

Johnny's not like that girl, though. He may not have gotten the hang of snowshoeing yet, but he can move just fine. My eyes flick to the floor. His mittens lie discarded, the frayed remnants of the duct tape still clinging to the cuffs.

The flashlight's starting to dim. I raise the gun and level it at his head. My hand's shaking a little and I only have one bullet, but I reckon from this distance not even I could miss. My finger tightens around the trigger. I feel the last of the slack come out of it.

'Johnny.'

I hold the pistol on him, waiting for his reaction. For a long time there's nothing and then his eyes fly open, flashing silver as they catch the beam. The muscles in his jaw are working now, clenching and unclenching, as though he's grinding his teeth. Just like the little girl in the closet was doing, after Marv held the knife with the blood on it under her nose.

I call his name again, louder. At last his face softens. He raises one hand to ward off the weakening beam and squints back at me.

'Didn't you hear me calling you?'

He nods.

'It was the other one's turn. I had to push him out of the way.'

I don't care to dwell on what that might mean. I reach into the pocket of my parka and toss him one of the plastic vials. It bounces across the dusty concrete floor and comes to rest at his feet.

'Take that then put your mittens back on. We've got to get going.'

He looks at the container but makes no move to pick it up.

'The girl sent you back for me.'

He doesn't say it like it's a question, but I nod anyway.

'The soldier said I was holding you up. Maybe it'd be better if you went back and told her you couldn't find me.'

The truth is it might. I don't say that, though. Instead I tell him Mags has gone on ahead; before we start worrying about slowing her down first we'll need to catch up. A look of concern crosses his small face as he hears this.

'The girl isn't with you?'

I shake my head.

'She and Hicks set off up I-81 this morning. We'll meet them on the road.'

His brow furrows and he reaches for the container. He unscrews the cap and downs the liquid inside, grimacing with the taste. He reaches for his mittens. As I'm taping them up he looks at me.

'The soldier's like me you know. You shouldn't trust him.'

We head back out to the porch. The kid hangs back in the shadow of the doorway, looking up at the darkening sky. The wind's picked up since I went inside; there's definitely more weather coming. I tell myself Hicks will know to find shelter before it hits, and besides, there's nothing I can do about that right now; I just need to focus on keeping us ahead of it. Storms this late in the season normally blow themselves out after a day or two. But right now that's time I can't afford.

I coax the kid out and we snap on our snowshoes and make our way back up to the interstate. I can see he's trying, but we're moving far too slowly. It's already well past noon. At this rate it'll take us most of the night to reach Falling Waters.

I'm waiting at the top of the on-ramp for him to catch up when I happen to look back in the direction we came that morning. The snow's drifting across the road; I can barely make out the church where we spent the night. But then the wind drops and in the instant before it picks up again I spot movement. I tell myself it could be anything: the weakening light playing tricks with my eyes; some random piece of debris blowing across the highway. Part of me already knows better than that, however.

I motion to the kid to stay where he is, then I crouch down and edge up onto the overpass, staring at the spot where I thought I saw something. For what seems like an eternity there's nothing and then I see it again, closer now. Four figures walking line abreast towards us. Even at this distance Jax's bulk is unmistakable.

I glance behind me at the small figure waiting in the middle of the road. By the time I get him down the on-ramp they'll be at the interstate. We'd never make it around the bend in time, and even if we did they'd spot us on the next straight. My feet are mostly healed; if it was just me there's a chance I could outrun them. But not with the kid. I cross to the guardrail on the other side. It's a near vertical drop to the road below.

I tell him we're going over. He shuffles forward and looks down suspiciously then turns back to me.

'Go on. The snow's deep. It'll be fine.'

He takes one more look and then clambers up onto the guardrail. He stops on the top like he's about to change his mind so I grab his parka and push him over. A second later I hear a soft *whumpf* as he disappears into a drift in a cloud of snow. I glance around. There's no time to do anything about the tracks we made getting up here. They shouldn't be visible from the other side, so as long as Truck doesn't take it on himself to cross the interstate he shouldn't see them. I unsnap my snowshoes, throw my leg over and the next thing I know I'm falling into soft powder.

It takes me a moment to dig myself out, then I find the kid and drag him under the overpass. We scooch behind one of the concrete pillars and wait. A few minutes later four figures appear at the top of the off-ramp on the other side of the highway, right by the *Do Not Enter* sign where I stood and said goodbye to Mags a few hours ago. They stop for a long moment as if in discussion and then the one who might be Truck bends down. He stays like that for a while, like he's looking for something in the snow. Hicks said Truck was backwoods raised, but I don't care if he was suckled by bluetick coonhounds, there's no way the tracks we made this morning will still be visible. At last he stands up again and they start down onto the interstate.

We watch them until they disappear around the first bend.

*

ALL AFTERNOON WE FOLLOW the soldiers up I-81. Mostly we keep to the median, always making sure there's a turn in the road between us. On the long straight stretches we have no choice but to wait them out and then hustle to catch up. In the low ground between north- and southbound lanes the snow's drifted deep and it's heavy work. The kid's making a real effort to keep up, but our progress is painfully slow.

The sky darkens; it has a mean look to it now. A churning mass of thunderheads crowds along the western ridge and then moves down into the valley behind us. The wind picks up. It blows off the mountains, driving the snow across the highway, filling in the soldiers' tracks until only the deeper indentations made by Jax's snowshoes remain. There's little shelter from it, even in the gulley.

We pass a succession of exits but Truck shows no sign of quitting the interstate. Just as dusk's settling we come to a long, straight section that inclines steadily. I break a HOOAH! from one of the MRE cartons and watch as they slowly trudge away from us in the failing light. The kid's happy for the rest, but I'm worried we'll lose their tracks and stumble into them waiting for us, so I climb out onto the road and lay prone in the powder to watch. Just as I think they're about to disappear over the next crest I see them heading for the off-ramp.

It takes us the best part of an hour to catch up to where they got off. Night's almost on us and I'm having trouble picking out Jax's prints now; if I hadn't seen them take this exit I reckon I'd have walked us on by. Deep inside the clouds lightning shudders and for the first time I hear the low rumble of thunder, still some ways off, but doubtless headed our way. We make our way up to the interchange. A familiar Exxon sits at the top of the off-ramp, its forecourt canopy collapsed onto the pumps under a blanket of snow. I realize this is where Mags and I first got on I-81, almost three weeks ago now. I take us up to the Waffle House where we spent the night. It's just as we left it, the door leaning inward on its one remaining hinge. I tell the kid to wait inside, I'll be back soon. He stares at the busted door, but makes no attempt to comply.

'Where are you going?'

'To find where the soldiers are sleeping, see if I can't figure a way to hold them up.'

I spotted a sign for a Holiday Inn as we were leaving the highway. I reckon Truck will have seen it too. There's a good bet that's where they'll be.

'I want to come with you.'

'Well you can't.'

This comes out a little harsher than I intend. But it's already full dark, the temperature's dropping and I don't need to look at the map to know we've not made it a dozen miles today. Falling Waters is still the best part of a day's hike ahead of us, and there's a storm coming. And on top of that I have to think of something to stop the soldiers from catching up with Mags and Hicks. So right now I don't have time to spit, much less worry about whether the kid might get lonely if I leave him by himself for twenty minutes.

'Are you going to use your flashlight?'

I'm tempted to tell him to quit acting bixicated, but instead I just shake my head.

''Course not. They might see it.'

He stares at me as I start back towards the road. I've gone barely half a dozen paces when I hear him behind me again.

'You're going the wrong way.'

I turn around. He's pushed the goggles up onto his forehead. One arm is extended and a small duct-taped mitten is pointing at right angles to the direction I was taking.

'I can see the big soldier's prints. They went that way.'

I don't know how he can make anything out in this darkness, but he seems pretty certain and I have nothing to go on other than the Holiday Inn sign so I beckon him forward and tell him to lead on. We follow what's left of Jax's prints across the interchange and down an access road on the other side. Lightning flares and the kid drops his poles and scrambles to pull his goggles back down, but I've seen what I need. Ahead there's a sign that says *Welcome To The Rest Easy Motel* and underneath *Low Extended Stay Rates!* Behind it a flat-roofed building two stories tall overlooks a small parking lot. From a window on the ground floor the soft glow of firelight seeps out onto the snow outside.

We hike up to a door on the corner that says *Reception*. I tell the kid to wait. He hunkers down against the wall and I make my way across the parking lot. An old Taurus sits under a blanket of snow in front of the room the soldiers have taken. Next to it there's a pickup, parked at a hasty angle, its tailgate still down. I snap off my snowshoes and creep between them, painfully aware of the sound my boots are making as they crunch the powder. When I draw level with the pickup's fender I stop and look out. The faint orange light from a fire escapes from behind a set of grubby curtains. For a long moment I just listen, but I can't hear anything above the sound of the approaching storm. I take a deep breath and break cover, crossing the walkway to crouch underneath their window. I stop again, straining to hear. But there's nothing. I start brushing snow aside with my mittens.

I had hoped to find four pairs of snowshoes, but I guess the soldiers have learned their lesson from when I took my leave of The Greenbrier.

Well, it was worth a try. I have no other plan for stopping them, so the only thing to do now is cut out of here and try and put as much distance as possible between us overnight. I'm about to head back to where my snowshoes are waiting when lightning flares again, followed closely by the heavy rumble of thunder. I hear a voice from inside.

'Sure is getting nasty out there, Truck.'

On the other side of the window the curtain twitches. I have half a second to press myself under the sill before it gets pulled back and Weasel's face appears at the grimy pane above me.

I hold my breath. I don't dare move. If he looks down now he's bound to see me.

'You sure they ain't gotten off here?'

'Weez, I told you. They ain't left the interstate.' *Innuh-stay*. There's no mistaking Truck's drawl.

'I dunno. Maybe we missed somethin'. Doc was sure they was headed for Mount Weather.'

'We didn't miss nuthin'. Why don't you make y'self useful. Go out and cut us some more firewood.'

'Aw, Truck. It's nasty out there. Why can't Jax do it?'

'Because I told you to. Go on now. I ain't goin' to tell you again.'

The curtain closes and from behind the door I hear footsteps and then the sound of something being moved out of the way. I crawl towards the adjacent room, but when I reach up for the handle the door's locked and won't budge.

There's no time to find another hiding place, so I throw myself into the gap between the Taurus and the pickup. I figure I might be able to squeeze under one or other of them, but their tires have long since given out and there's no way I'll fit, so instead I shuffle forward and press my face into the snow. Through the gap between the pickup's front wheels I see the door opening. Light from the fire inside spills out, followed a moment later by the aroma of cooking frankfurters. I haven't eaten since the HOOAH! out on the interstate and my stomach betrays me with a growl so loud I'm sure Weasel will hear it and come to investigate. But just then from inside I hear Truck barking another order.

'Dammit Weez, shut the door. You're letting all the heat out.'

A pair of black boots fills my vision as Weasel steps out of the room, then the light from inside disappears as he closes the door behind him. I hear him mutter a curse and then he bangs something with his hand and finally a cone of pale yellow light blinks into existence, illuminating the stretch of walkway visible to me through the pickup's wheels. A large rubber flashlight appears on the ground a couple of feet from the fender. The beam shines right under the truck, showing me its perished tires, its rusted springs. A pair of snowshoes drop to the snow and a second later Weasel bends down and starts fiddling with the straps. I'm close enough to see the repairs he's had to make to them from my last hatchet job. I hold my breath. If he lowers himself just a little further he can't help but see me. But if I try and move he'll hear me for sure, so I just lay there, holding my breath, and wait.

He's almost done with the second snowshoe when the beam from the flashlight suddenly goes out. He curses again and then picks it up and shakes it. It flickers back to life for a second and then dies.

'Piece of shit.'

He bangs it against the wall, hard. The beam returns and he goes back to work. When he's done he stands and picks it up, returning the underside of the pickup to darkness. The yellow cone moves to a spot somewhere further along the walkway, mercifully in a direction away from where the kid's hiding. A second later Weasel's boots disappear from view as he sets off after it. When I'm sure he's gone I pick myself up and peer over the hood. He stops at the end of the walkway in front of a soft drinks machine and bends down to check the dispensing tray. When he finds nothing he hits the front of the machine with the flashlight and moves on.

I wait to make sure he's not coming back and then retrieve my snowshoes. My hands are shaking a little so it takes me a second or two longer than it should to strap myself in and then I set off for where I left the kid. His head pokes out from around the corner as I approach and I wave at him to follow me.

Moments later we're making our way out of the parking lot, back towards the interstate.

*

THE NEXT BIT'S MY FAULT.

In my defense, after my near miss with Weasel I suspect there's little more than adrenaline pumping through my veins. But instead of taking a couple of deep breaths to calm myself I slide over and let it climb up into the driving seat. It doesn't take it long to find the fast pedal, and soon it's goosing it like it doesn't particularly care for the gas miles we'll have to show for it later.

I set off at a pace the kid'll never be able to match. He doesn't say anything of course, just lets me push on ahead, with every step putting more and more space between us. Maybe he figures I'll slow down soon enough. Or perhaps he reckons he's being ditched again, because that's just how things seem to be working out for him lately.

I tear across the parking lot, still hell-bent on setting a new Shenandoah County snowshoeing record. Lightning flares, briefly illuminating the sign we passed on the way in, and beyond it I see the access road that'll bring us back up to the interchange. I tuck my head down and make for it. I don't look behind me to see if the kid's keeping up, because, like I said, right then there's a wide-eyed lunatic with his hair on fire behind the wheel of the Gabemobile.

Just as I'm coming up to the sign a dark shape steps out from behind. It takes me a moment to work out it's Weasel. I guess he must have struck out behind the motel and doubled back to try his luck finding firewood out here. His flashlight's given out on him again and he's just standing there shaking it to try and get it to come back on. There's a second where he still hasn't seen me and I have time to wonder whether I might yet be able to duck back into the parking lot. Then the sky lights up again, bathing us both in stark white light.

The only consolation I have is that he seems every bit as startled as I am. He steps backwards and would probably have ended up on his ass in the snow if there wasn't a station wagon parked up behind him. He stumbles against the wing and drops the flashlight he's been screwing with. It lands in the snow on the hood and suddenly blinks back to life. There's a moment where we both just stare at each other, then he's scrabbling in the pocket of his parka while I ditch my mittens and reach for Marv's Beretta. He gets there first and pulls out the handsaw he's brought with him, but the thick gloves he's wearing prevents him levering the blade out of the handle. He fumbles with it for a while and then in his frustration he throws it, but from his aim it's unclear whether he meant to hit me or just be rid of it. It sails off into the darkness. I hear it plop in the snow somewhere behind me as I pull out the gun.

'Damn. I knew it. I just *knew* it. You did get off the highway. What you up to Huckleberry, sneakin' around here? Trying to mess with our snowshoes again?'

I raise the pistol a fraction, like this isn't his hour for having questions answered.

'You got a bullet in there this time? Bet you ain't. I'll *bet* you ain't.'

He pushes himself off the station wagon and takes a step towards me.

I pull the slide back and tilt the Beretta forward. The flashlight half-buried in the snow on the station wagon's hood must be throwing off just enough light for him to see into the chamber because he takes a step backwards and raises his hands.

'Alright, alright. Take it easy now.'

I risk a quick look behind me. The kid's disappeared, probably run off into the darkness at the sight of one of the soldiers. I'll worry about finding him later. I return my gaze to Weasel. A thin smile's spreading across his face.

'You ain't gonna pull the trigger.'

I haven't actually figured out what I mean to do yet, but that option's definitely not been cleared from the table. I raise the gun and point it at his chest.

'I worry you're putting too much stock in our friendship, Weasel.' I emphasize the last word on purpose. The smile flickers for a second and I see his features harden. He shakes his head.

'Nope. I'm countin' on you not wanting more company than you already got right now. Gunshot's a pretty distinctive sound, Huckleberry. Loud, too.' He nods in the direction of the motel. 'Truck'll hear it. What, you think he's in there right now watching TV with the volume turned all the way up?'

I realize he has a point. Even if there was more than just one bullet in Marv's gun there's no way I want Truck and the other soldiers out here hunting for me with their automatic rifles. But I can't take him with me. And I can't let him go back to the motel. They'd be on me just as quick.

There's another flash and for an instant the parking lot lights up again. A crash of thunder follows moments after and out of habit I log the gap. Storm's close now. It occurs to me that the thunder would probably mask the sound of the gunshot, if I timed it right. I curl my finger around the trigger, feeling the cold metal through the slit in the liner. All that's left is to figure out if I have it in me to pull it.

Turns out that's a question that'll need answering before the night's out, but not right now. Lightning crashes again and this time, on the roof of the station wagon, where a moment ago there was nothing, something crouches. I have just enough time before it goes dark again to recognize the kid. He's pulled his hood back and his over-sized goggles hang around his neck. He looks just like a smaller version of the thing that attacked

Ortiz in the hospital. Something must show on my face because Weasel turns around and looks behind him, just as the kid slides down the windshield onto the hood.

A strangled cry escapes his lips. He tries to step away from the car but his feet get all tangled up in his snowshoes and this time there's no saving him. He stumbles sideways, his arms pinwheeling, and ends up on his back in the snow. The kid jumps off the hood and lands on all fours next to him. Weasel's got a hand to the fender and is already trying to haul himself upright, but the kid just narrows his eyes to slits and moves his face close. He lets go of the fender with a whimper and quits.

I slide the pistol back into my pocket and reach for a cable tie.

'Alright Johnny, let him up now. We got to get going.'

But he ignores me, continuing to hold his face inches from the soldier's, tilting his head from side to side like he's tasting the air. I'm beginning to wonder if I've been hasty putting the gun away. Suddenly the sky strobes again and he starts. He fumbles for his goggles, pushing them back up.

'You okay?'

He fiddles with the strap for a while, making sure they're on right, then he nods. It's hard to tell what's going on behind the taped up lens, but I'm beginning to suspect there's more than one person inside that little head of his now. And the kid who just answered my question may not have been whatever was crouched on the roof of the station wagon just a moment ago.

*

WEASEL DOESN'T GIVE us much trouble after that, at least not for a while. He holds his hands meekly out in front of him while I cable tie them together. When I'm done I collect his flashlight from the hood. It's temperamental but the beam's way stronger than the little wind-up I keep in my pocket so I figure I'll have use for it later, at least while the batteries hold. I motion forward with it and he starts walking ahead of us up towards the interchange. I keep the gun on him the whole time, but I doubt he even notices. Every few steps he looks over his shoulder to check if the kid's still behind us.

There's a KFC next to the on-ramp and I head for it. I don't have to worry about breaking in; all that's left of the door is a mostly empty frame, all buckled and bent around the lock where a long time ago somebody took a pry bar to it. There's a little drift, but the snow only reaches in a couple of feet. A sign over the entrance just says *Hungry?*

I'd prefer somewhere a little harder to find, but right now the kid and I need to be gone. I tell him to wait in the restaurant and he climbs up into one of the booths. Weasel starts to perk up a little now it's just me and him and I have to push him through a set of swing doors into the kitchens. I set his flashlight down on one of the counters. The light flickers for a second but then steadies.

'Truck'll find me.'

'Yeah, I know.' I'm kinda counting on it actually. The jury's still out on whether I might have been able to put a bullet in him back in the parking lot, but I'm pretty sure I don't have it in me to tie him up somewhere and just leave him to starve.

'Then we'll come get you, Huckleberry. Just you wait. You're goin' in a cage. I'm going to come visit you every day. You and…'

He stops.

'The girl. Where's the girl? She ain't with you, is she? Where's she at, Huckleberry?'

I push him forward again, but he turns around to face me, and now there's a triumphant look on his face.

'Did she turn already, is that it? She did, didn't she?' He lets out a whoop. 'God-*damn*! How was that? You didn't have to shoot her did you?'

Probably wasn't Weasel's smartest move. I'm tired and cold and hungry, and given where my dreams have been going lately that was just way too close to the bone.

So I punch him.

I've never actually hit someone before. Afterwards, when I think back on it, I'm pretty sure I don't do it right. In *Thirty Days of Night* Eben rams his fist right through the back of Marlow's skull and it doesn't seem to bother him at all. But later my hand will hurt, a surprising amount. I guess Eben had already turned into a vampire by that point. And *Thirty Days* was a film, of course, and not real.

I guess if I'd been smart I would have swung at him with the flashlight. But right then there's just a satisfying crunch as my knuckles connect with his nose and for the second time that evening Weasel ends up on his ass. By the time I step over him and grab the hood of his parka, blood's already running freely down his face. He's holding his cuffed hands to his nose to try and stanch the flow but it drips between his fingers as I drag him into the storeroom, falling in heavy red drops that spatter on the tiled floor.

It doesn't take me long to bind him. Once I'm happy he won't be able to free himself I tear off a strip of duct tape and go to place it over his mouth. He fusses a little at that so I pinch his busted nose. He howls, spraying blood and mucus all over my liners and the cuffs of my parka, but this time when I approach him with the tape he holds still. He has two final words for me as I stretch it over his lips, and as you've probably guessed those words are not *Happy* and *Birthday*. For good measure I tear off an extra-long strip and wrap it all the way round the back of his head and spend a few more seconds tamping it down. I doubt it'll hush him any better, but it'll be fun when Truck eventually finds him and has to pull it off. When I'm done I search him for anything we might use. There's a pocketknife that looks like it's seen better days but I've been looking for a blade since the leatherman got left behind in The Greenbrier so I take it. The only other thing I find is a radio. Weasel's no longer in a position to call for help, but I figure better safe than sorry. I transfer it to my parka and step back out into the kitchen.

The flashlight's on the counter where I left it, but when I pick it up the beam finds the kid, crouched on the floor next to the spot where Weasel fell when I hit him. I guess he must have heard the ruckus and followed me in. His eyes narrow and I point it away quickly.

'Come on, we need to get going.'

He gives no sign that he's heard me. The beam flickers again and threatens to go out but then steadies.

'Johnny, come on.'

He looks up at me slowly, like he's coming back from a far away place. Eventually he picks himself up and slouches off in the direction of the door.

Outside the weather's worsening. I watch it through the broken door as we strap on our snowshoes. The kid seems a little distant, but right then I'm mostly focused on getting us back on the road. It won't be long before Truck starts to wonder what's happened to Weasel. I reckon he'll send Jax or Boots looking for him first, and if they don't find him he'll come himself, and sooner or later – I'm hoping later – he'll be found. I need to put some distance between us before that happens. The wind's already covering the tracks we made getting up here, but I bend down to sweep the snow that's drifted in clean of our prints too. When I'm done I grab Weasel's snowshoes and we set off towards the interchange.

The world reveals itself frequently now, out of a darkness rent by lightning. The sky's restless with it. Towering thunderheads crowd into the valley behind us and hang low along the ridges on either side. The storm lights them from within, occasionally sending blue-white forks to stab down at the mountains below.

We pass the on-ramp but don't take it. The interstate's too exposed; the storm'll be on us before the night's out and I don't want to get caught without shelter. According to the map route 11's less than a quarter mile west and it runs pretty much parallel all the way up as far as Falling Waters, where by now Mags and Hicks will be waiting.

We make our way up on to the overpass. The wind's merciless. It blows straight up the valley, drifting the snow across the road in front of us, forcing us to lean into it. I stop in the middle and dump Weasel's snowshoes over the guardrail. I wait until we're on the other side before I allow us his flashlight. It flickers and starts but the beam's much brighter than the wind-up I carry and I'm glad of it.

We head into town and turn north onto 11, but even with the wind at our backs it's still bitterly cold. The night's sharp with it now. My hood's zipped all the way up but it finds its way in regardless, biting at any inch of exposed skin like a thousand tiny needles. I have to keep us out in it if we're to have any chance of catching Mags and Hicks, but I don't plan to make the same mistake I did when I quit The Greenbrier. I reckon I'll walk us for a couple of hours then rest for a while, get a fire going and warm up before we set out again.

*

WE MAKE IT AS FAR as a place called Winchester before the cold finally drives me off the road. We haven't come as far as I'd hoped. The kid's slowed down a lot. He seemed to be coping better with the drifts earlier, when we were coming up the interstate. Since we left Weasel in the KFC it's like he's regressed to that chimp-like crouch he had when we first left the bunker.

We head through the center of town on what looks like the main drag. I spot what we need, right on the corner: a First Citizens Bank with an ATM lobby. There'll be nothing in there worth having - the banks mostly got passed over for anywhere that might have had food or fuel - but I'm not here to scavenge. All I'm looking for now is somewhere to shelter.

I make my way in, drop the armful of dead branches I hacked from a stand on the way into town and shuck off my backpack. The kid pushes his way through the door behind me and skulks off into darkness on the other side of the lobby. I don't see anywhere to bind him so I don't bother. We won't be here long.

There's a trashcan in the corner, overflowing with ATM receipts. I scoop out a handful for kindling and then dig out the squeeze bottle of gas I carry and douse the sorry-looking pile of firewood. Marv said I had to keep the gas for emergencies, but I figure this qualifies; one look at the blizzard that's building outside tells me it's no time to be walking the streets looking for fuel tanks that might have been missed. I pull off my mittens, fish in my pocket for the lighter and fumble with cold-numbed fingers to spin the wheel. After a few attempts the gas catches and I lean in and hold my hands as close as I dare.

The wood's damp and once the gas has burned off the flames die down quickly. I shuffle myself closer, but the sad excuse for a fire's doing little to ward off the cold so I unzip my parka and jam my hands up into my armpits instead. I flex my fingers a few times to get the blood flowing. My knuckles are starting to hurt where I hit Weasel, but at least that means feeling's returning. I turn my attention to dinner. While my MRE's hissing away I fill the mug I carry with water from my canteen and nestle it among the flames. I upend the carton and go searching among the various items that tip out for a packet of coffee. I really don't care for the taste, but it's warm and Mags says it keeps you awake, and right now those are both things I need.

A few minutes later I've wolfed down something the packet said was meatballs in pasta and I'm staring out the grimy window, letting the mug warm my fingers, when something inside my parka squawks. It takes me a moment to work out it's the radio I took from Weasel. I dig in my pocket and hold it up. For a while there's just static, but then I hear Truck's voice, rendered tinny and distant by the small speaker. It's clear they haven't found him yet. Good. I leave the radio on the ground beside me while I finish the coffee. I hear Truck a few more times and then for a long time there's nothing.

Outside lightning bathes the intersection in its harsh white glare, briefly illuminating a sign on the gantry arm that points east along route 7. A half-day hike in that direction would bring me to the turnoff for the Blue Ridge Mountain Road, to the spot where I left Marv and made my way on to Mount Weather, the place that over the winter became our home. For a moment I allow myself to wonder if I'll ever see it again, but then I stop. It doesn't matter. The only thing I care about in what's left of this world is somewhere ahead of me, hopefully already most of the way through West Virginia, waiting to cross into Maryland. I reckon another three hikes like the one we've just done and we'll catch up to them.

The radio's still hissing static. I pick it up, slip it back in my pocket and drain the last of the coffee. I call over at the kid to let him know we're heading out again.

We meet up with I-81 a mile or so outside town. We pass underneath it and continue north on route 11.

I keep looking behind me, worried about what's coming our way. I no longer need to count the gap between flash and crack to know how close the storm is now. The wind shrieks down the valley with seemingly little to get in its way. It drives the snow in long, shifting ridges that span the width of the road. The kid's really struggling with the drifts. He can barely make it a hundred yards without falling, and each time I have to go back and haul him upright.

Sometime after the underpass Weasel's flashlight blinks out for the last time and I toss it into the darkness. The cold's relentless. Whatever warmth had managed to seep into my fingers from the fire evaporated within minutes of stepping outside again. I switch the little windup between my hands so I can keep one of them jammed up into my armpit at all times. I'm not sure it's doing any good. Inside my mittens my fingers tighten; I have to keep opening and closing them to make sure they'll wind the stubby handle.

We pass a collection of buildings huddled tight around a junction. A CITGO gas station sits opposite a diner, a faded red Coca Cola sign still clinging bravely to the wall. Up ahead there's something big, lying on its side across the road. The snow's drifted high around it, disguising its shape. I stop and stare at it while I wait for the kid to catch up. Back in Eden I used to know every car, pickup and rig on the turnpike just from the shape it made under the powder, but the best I can muster now is fallen dinosaur. I wonder if it's the cold, starting to affect my thinking.

Maybe we should stop here, find a place to warm up. But we haven't even made it to West Virginia yet, and Mags and Hicks will be all the way through it now, getting ready to cross the Potomac into Maryland come first light. We'll never catch them if we keep stopping. Lightning flashes somewhere close by, and I catch a glimpse of a set of huge double tires, poking up into the sky at the end of a thick axle. From there I finally figure it out: it's a cement truck.

I look around. Behind me the kid's gone down in a drift. I pick up my snowshoes and start making my way back towards him. The wind's definitely getting stronger; it fights me with every step. I grab hold of his arm and pull him to his feet. We set off again but we don't make it far before he's mired once more. I turn around to dig him out then grab his parka and drag him behind the truck. We sit in the snow, our backs to the underside of our temporary shelter. The wind howls around it, sending snow up into the sky in furious flurries.

'This isn't working. We'll never catch Mags like this.'

I say it mostly to myself, so I'm surprised he hears; even in the lee of the fallen monster it's surprisingly loud. He looks at me for a long time then just nods, like he understands.

'It's okay.'

And then I realize that he expects me to leave him here. I shake my head.

'No, I mean I'll need to carry you. Just till the drifts get a little better.'

He shakes his head, but I'm not paying attention. I'm already shucking off my backpack, making a list of the things I'll need.

Now I know what you're thinking: chalk another one up to the bitch, right? But I don't reckon it's that. It's cold, for sure, almost more than I can stand now, but as far as I can tell I'm still thinking straight.

I certainly know what Hicks would say, and I'm not sure Marv's views on the subject would be much different. But the truth is neither of them are here. I told Mags I'd bring him back, and that's certainly a part of it, but perhaps not the main part. If he's as close to turning as Hicks reckons it's probably not going to end well for him, whatever I do. But if that's how it's to be maybe I want it to be somebody's doing other than mine.

The wind gusts shrill through a gap in the cement truck's chassis and I have to shout to make myself heard.

'Are you feeling okay?'

He hesitates for a second and then I think I see him nod inside his hood.

I slip off my mittens and dig in my pocket for the roll of duct tape. It takes a while for my fingers to find an edge, but eventually I manage to tear off a strip. I stick it to the sleeve of my parka and then pull the zipper on his jacket down. But when I go to stick the tape over his mouth he shakes his head and pulls away. I guess right there is where I should have thought it through some more, but I just figure he doesn't care for being gagged any more than Weasel did. I'm about to explain this bit's not up for discussion when he holds out his hand. I pass him the tape. The mittens he's wearing make it difficult and the wind's certainly not helping, but in the end he manages it. I zip his hood back up then start transferring the things I'll need from my backpack to the parka's large side pockets.

He squirms a little as I pick him up and hoist him onto my back, but then the lightning flashes and he grips tight and buries his head in my parka. The arms around my neck feel no thicker than the branches I cut for firewood, but they're surprisingly strong. I stand. He weighs less than my pack would after a day's scavenging. We'll make much better time now; I don't know why I didn't think of this earlier.

Okay, a little bixicated there, maybe. But in my defense, it wasn't an altogether terrible idea.

There was just one kinda important thing I forgot.

*

WE CROSS BACK INTO West Virginia at a place called Ridgeway. It's somewhere approaching the middle of the night and the cold has turned cruel now. With each step I curse it through chattering teeth.

I stop us at the first place we come to, no more than a hundred yards over the state line. A sign above the door with a grinning pig's head says *The Hogtied* and underneath it *Cold Beer To Go!* A single pickup, buried deep under a decade of snow, waits patiently in the parking lot. I stagger up to the entrance. The outer door hangs askance in its frame, but the inner one seems to have held. I guess the cold's finally getting to the kid because he continues to cling tight even after I bend down to let him off; I have to pry his arms from around my neck and slide him to the ground. He crouches there for a second and then scurries off inside, the door swinging shut after him.

A single withered tree still pokes through the snow on the other side of the road. I dig the handsaw from the pocket of my parka and cross over to cut a few limbs but I'm having trouble gripping the handle and it's slow work. When I think I've finally collected enough wood for a fire I head inside.

The Hogtied's not a big place. To one side there's a bar. The shelves are empty, anything that could have been drunk or been used to start a fire long since removed. The wall behind was once mirror but the few shards that still cling there now just throw back crazed reflections as the beam from the flashlight slides over them. Across the room a dozen or so booths crowd around a small pool table, the balls arranged haphazardly as if a game had been interrupted.

There's no sign of the kid. Maybe I should have given some thought to that, but I figure his mouth and mittens are taped and right then I'm too cold and too tired to go looking for him. I make my way over to the nearest booth. Snowmelt must have found its way in through the ceiling, because the floorboards are buckled; they flex and groan under my boots. I dump the firewood on the ground and sit next to it, already fumbling in my overladen pockets for the squeeze bottle of gas. I know I should really check behind the bar before using it; there could be a bottle of liquor back there that's been missed. But the shelves look empty and now I'm down I'm too tired to get up again. I fumble off the cap and squirt a measure Private Kavanagh would have been proud of over the blackened branches. Within minutes there's a small fire going, steam rising lazily from the hesitant flames.

I dig out Weasel's radio to see if there's any news on the search, but all I get is static. As I set it down I spot a corner of a newspaper that's been missed, tucked underneath the table behind me. In different times that would have been treasure, but now I just twist the pages into tight twirls and feed them to the fire. I hold my hands as close as I dare, desperate to catch whatever heat's thrown off before it's lost to the cold.

The soft hiss from the radio is somehow soothing and I feel my eyelids growing heavy. I can't afford to nap; if I do I may not wake for hours. I dig the mug from the pocket of my parka, fill it with water from my canteen and set it among the flames. We're making better progress now I'm carrying the kid. If I can keep it up there's still a chance I might catch up to Mags and Hicks before morning.

When I reckon the water's as hot as it's going to get I tear the top off a packet of coffee and dump it in. The dark, sour aroma mixes with the smoke from the fire and the damp, moldering smell of The Hogtied. I put on my gloves and fish the mug out of the already dwindling flames. I need to drink the coffee to wake me up, but right now the warmth soaking into my frozen fingers feels good. I lean back against the booth.

I'll just close my eyes for a moment.

*

HE SITS IN THE CORNER in darkness. The restroom is small, windowless, a single stall occupying most of the available space. Its door is missing, or maybe there never was one. A steel urinal runs the length of the wall opposite; holes dot the space above where a vending machine once hung. Graffiti spreads across the crumbling plaster, competing with the sprays of mildew that climb from the tiled floor.

The air is musty, stale, freighted with a decade of enclosed decay, but he doesn't notice. His hood is pulled back and his goggles lie discarded among the garbage strewn across the floor. He purses his lips and drags the back of one mitten across the tape at his mouth, trying to lift an edge.

A door opens in the next room and he looks up. The boy has come back inside. The door closes again, the sound of the storm abating. There's the creak of boots on floorboards and a few moments later the sweet cloying smell of gasoline and then the damp smokiness of fire.

None of these things are important.

He resumes his work on the tape.

There was something on the boy's jacket. He smelled it earlier, in the restaurant, and afterwards, when they stopped in the bank. Outside the wind was strong and it carried the scent of it away into the swirling darkness. But now they are back inside the heavy, coppery aroma sings to him.

The blood, on the tiled floor of the kitchen where they left the soldier; somehow some of it must have gotten on the boy's jacket. Just thinking about it now causes the hunger to well up in him, so sudden and strong the muscles in his stomach twist and coil with it.

He drags the mitten across his mouth again and this time a corner of the tape lifts. He feels for it with his fingers, but it is too small yet for them to find purchase. Soon. He goes back to work.

It is stronger now, the thing inside him; it will not allow itself to be confined much longer. It is a large animal, straining on a fraying leash, a tether that cannot hope to hold. He has felt its claws, raking his insides, desperate to tear its way out. He is ashamed of what he will do when that time comes, and yet giddy with the anticipation of it.

More of the tape lifts and this time when he reaches for it with his mittens his fingertips grasp it. He rips it off, letting the spent tape fall among the litter scattered at his feet. His small teeth set to work on his mittens. Soon they too lie discarded.

He shuffles over to the door and opens it a crack. Over by one of the booths the boy is sleeping. He will do it now. But as he steps through lightning flares, for a moment bathing the inside of The Hogtied in stark white light. He raises his hands to his eyes to block the light, but he is too late, and for a second the blinding glare pushes the thing inside him back.

He blinks and looks around, unsure of how he came to be here, but certain of what he had been about to do.

Outside the storm is getting worse. The wind is shrill; the door shudders in its frame with the strength of it.

The soldier with one eye was right.

He must go now, quickly, before it is too late.

*

THERE'S A CRASH of thunder, loud enough to rattle the Hogtied's remaining windows in their frames. I wake with a start.

This time when I pulled the trigger I saw her face. It takes me a moment to figure out it was just a dream and there's an instant where relief washes through me. But then the lightning flashes again and I see him, crouched on the other side of the fire, his small shoulders hunched up like whatever carrion bird is etched into the handle of Hicks' pistol. He shrinks back at the flare and his eyes close to slits, but they never leave me. As soon as it darkens again he inches forward, taking a cautious step around the dying fire. The tape on his mouth's gone and as I look down at the small hands splayed out in front of him I can see that so too are his mittens. His palms rest flat on the water-buckled boards, but the fingers are curled into claws.

I fumble in the pocket of my parka. The forgotten mug of coffee slips from my lap, spilling its now-cold contents across the floor. His eyes flick to it for a second, then return. My fingers close around the grip; I feel the compact heft of the metal as I pull it out. The round's already chambered from earlier. I level it at him and flick the safety forward.

He tilts his head to one side, regarding the gun with animal interest. I slip my finger inside the trigger guard, feeling it curl around the metal there. I shout his name and he pauses, like some part of him remembers. But then he sniffs the air and takes another step forward. I can see the muscles along his jaw working, clenching and unclenching, like he's grinding his teeth.

Hicks told me this moment would come, and that when it did I shouldn't hesitate. I push myself back against the booth and take aim at his head. I squeeze gently, feeling the last of the slack go out of the mechanism. But at the last second I shift the barrel to the left. There's a sharp crack and the muzzle flares.

I drop the gun and hold my hands up, ready to hold him off. But his face has softened. He blinks uncertainly, looks at me and then at the door.

After that the kid and I have a chat. I tell him I'm not going to shoot at him anymore and he promises in turn to warn me if he's feeling he might get like that again, although if Hicks is right and it's like a switch being flipped I'm not sure how much stock I can put in that. The bottom line is I need to start being a lot more careful than I've been so far tonight.

I fetch his mittens from the restroom and he puts them back on and then I tape them to the cuffs of his jacket and hand him an extra strip for his mouth. I use a little of the water from my canteen to scrub the front of my parka and then I mix up a paste with coffee powder and the contents of one of the little bottles of Tabasco that comes in the MREs. I work it into the material everywhere I think Weasel's blood might have gotten on it. It smells really bad, but then that's the point.

When I'm done I hold out the parka and ask him if it's any better. He sniffs it and nods his head warily. I'm not so sure, though. I suspect the kid may not have long now till whatever's inside him takes over for good. I feel his tiny body stiffen as I haul him onto my back, just like the girl in the closet did when Marv held the knife with his blood on it under her nose.

The wind's strengthened while we were inside. It shrieks around The Hogtied and I have to lean my weight into the door to open it. As I step outside I look up into the skies. I'm not sure how long I was asleep, but the storm's used the time well. It's almost on us now.

I point us north and we set off. Lightning strikes all around, the intervals between flash and clap so short as to defy the counting. At least when it flares I can see though, and for the next hour I search those half-seconds of light for road signs, telephone poles, abandoned cars; anything to mark our place in the world.

The cold is raw, an onslaught. It claws my fingers inside my mittens, threatening to crack the bones there with the sharpness of it. I pull the zipper up as far as it will go and tuck my chin to my chest but I have no defense against it; it slips inside the parka with absurd ease. The muscles across my shoulders and back tighten; soon they ache and grind like the cogs of a long-neglected machine.

There's another strike, so close that for an instant it smells like the air has been charred, and the road in front of us is briefly bathed in stark white light. The heavens crash, like they're being torn asunder. The kid starts, but then he grips my shoulder and I know this is something different. I set him down and he crouches there, wrestling with whatever other thing is locked inside his head. He's like that for a while and I'm beginning to wonder if he's ever coming back. But then he looks up and nods inside his hood and I bend down and let him clamber back up again.

We don't make much more than a handful of miles before the storm finally catches us. Soon heavy flakes are tumbling and twisting out of the tortured sky. The wind picks them up and drives them, swirling them around us in furious flurries.

I can't see worth a damn now and the cold's so bad I'm struggling to wind the flashlight's stubby handle. We're nowhere near as far as I'd like us to be, but we'll have to take shelter. There's a town up ahead. I figure we'll stop, get another fire going, maybe let the storm blow itself out for an hour or so.

I feel the kid squeeze my shoulder. I reckon he needs some more alone time so I start to bend down to let him off, but instead he lifts one mitten from around my neck and points. A flash of lightning illuminates a sign close to road that says *Pikeside Bowl.* I ask why he wants to go that way, but even if he can hear me over the wind I realize he can't answer through the duct tape. He just keeps pointing in the same direction.

We need to get inside and I guess this place will do as well as any, so I turn off the road. I pick my way between the cars in the parking lot, heading for where I assume I'll find the bowling alley. Another flash illuminates a low flat-roofed building straight ahead of us, the only feature along its squat length a covered entranceway. In the instant before it goes dark again I spot a familiar figure, sitting in a chair behind the glass.

I stagger up to the entrance and push the door open; a flurry of flakes follows me in. As I bend down to let the kid off he raises an eyebrow but doesn't pass further comment on it.

'Been watching for you. Figured you'd get off the interstate once you saw the storm coming.'

'Where is she?'

He motions behind him and I look over his shoulder. There's a fire going by the counter where you rent shoes. Mags is curled up tight inside her sleeping bag next to it. I go to step around him but he holds one gloved hand out to stop me.

'Best let her rest. She's had a long day.'

He looks down at the kid.

'You had any problems with it?'

I shake my head.

'Alright. Let's get it tethered then.' He reaches down, but the kid takes a step back and moves behind my leg. All I want now is to sit as close as possible to Mags and the fire and sleep, but instead I find myself saying I'll take care of it.

'Suit yourself. There's places at the back you can tie it.'

The glow from the fire doesn't stretch much beyond where Mags is sleeping. I wind the flashlight and head down the way Hicks said. Screens hang from the ceiling, their gray surfaces thick with dust. Behind them rows of wooden lanes stretch off into darkness. I take the kid to the nearest one.

'Alright here?'

He nods and sits on the floor next to one of the machines that returns the bowling balls.

I take out Weasel's knife and make an incision in the tape around one cuff so it can be lifted then I rip it off. Once he has a hand free he removes the tape from his other wrist and finally his mouth and then he feeds his arms through the rack. I pass him a cable tie that's already looped and he slips his hands through and ratchets it tight with his teeth. When he's done he holds them up to let me see.

I walk back to the lobby. I just want to sleep now, but there's something I need to know first. Hicks is still sitting in the chair by the entrance, where I left him.

'How's she doing?'

He holds the thermos up to his lips and takes a sip, like he's considering the question.

'This is as far as we could make it.'

I'm not sure what that's supposed to mean. I'm deciding whether I want to know more when he speaks again.

'Virus has gotten a good hold of her, son. I'm not sure how much longer she can hold out, even on Doc's meds. Only hope now is we get her to that scanner of yours quickly.'

I look back at where Mags is lying by the fire. We haven't come as far as I'd hoped, but if the storm clears overnight and we start out early I reckon we can still make it to Eden by tomorrow night. I just need one more day.

Hicks gestures in the direction of the bowling lanes where I've left the kid.

'Any problems finding it?'

I look back at him and shake my head.

'I ran into Truck and the others as we were coming back on to the interstate.'

He raises an eyebrow.

'And how'd that work out? I guess not so bad seeing as you're here and they're not.'

I tell him about following the soldiers off I-81 at the Fairfax turnpike and how I accidentally bumped into Weasel while trying to steal their snowshoes.

He takes another sip from the thermos.

'So what happened to him? There still a round in that weapon I gave you?'

I shake my head.

'There isn't, but Weasel's still alive if that's what you're asking. Or at least he was when I left him tied him up in a KFC out by the interchange. I figure Truck'll find him eventually; might just take him a while though. I dumped his snowshoes off the overpass. Unless they're carrying spares that should slow them down a bit too.'

Hicks just nods.

'You did good. Mind if I take that pistol from you now, though? Firearms make me nervous.'

I dip my hand into my parka and fish Marv's gun out. He pulls the slide back and tilts the Beretta forward so he can see the chamber's empty, then he thumbs the switch and ejects the magazine. When he's satisfied he slips it into his pocket.

'Alright, best you get some rest. It's only a few hours till dawn and we've got a long hike ahead of us tomorrow.'

I head back to where Mags is sleeping, unfurl my sleeping bag and climb into it. The fire's dying down and I don't have it in me to go out for more wood to build it up again. I pull the parka over the top and close my eyes.

I'm already drifting down in to that place where thoughts no longer cohere when something in my pocket squawks. It occurs to me I never told Hicks about the radio, but when I look up he's no longer in his seat and I'm too tired to go searching for him now. The last thing I think I hear before the weight of exhaustion pulls me under is a staticky voice that can't possibly be right and then I'm gone, dragged into a deep and mercifully dreamless sleep.

*

IT'S STILL SNOWING when I wake, large ashen flakes drifting down out of a sullen sky, but the storm seems to have mostly played itself out. Hicks is back in his seat by the entrance, keeping watch over the humped gray shapes in the parking lot.

I've slept longer than I intended to. I sit up and look around. Beside me Mags is still curled up in her sleeping bag. I'm desperate to wake her but I figure Hicks is right; it's best if she rests as much as she can. We have a long day ahead of us if we're to make it to Eden tonight.

A few lumps of charcoal are all that's left of the fire so I pull on my boots and parka and make for the door. I mutter a good morning at Hicks, but he just looks back at me from behind those blinkered shades and goes back to staring out at the lot. When I get back Mags is sitting up, the sleeping bag wrapped around her. She's got her back to me but I can see she's rubbing her temple.

I sit down next to her and start building a fire.

'How're you feeling?'

She lets her hand fall back inside the sleeping bag and turns to offer me a wan smile.

'Okay, I guess.'

It's barely light out but she's squinting. The circles under her eyes are black now. I force myself to smile back. She pulls the sleeping bag tighter around her.

'Is it colder this morning?'

It's not but I nod anyway.

'Yeah, but I'll soon have a fire going.'

'Did you find Johnny?'

'He's in the back. I'll go get him as soon as I'm done here.'

'Is he okay?'

The news that I'd found him seemed to cheer her up a little, so I don't mention what happened in *The Hogtied.* I set to work on the fire. As soon as it's lit I put water on to boil and hand her one of Gilbey's containers. She washes it down with the coffee and then asks me for a couple of Tylenol but shakes her head at breakfast.

As soon as I'm done with my MRE I head down to the lanes to cut the kid loose. The scant light that filters in through the entrance doesn't make it much beyond the fire and I find myself dragging my heels as I make my way back into the darkness. Tell the truth I'm worried what I'll find. But as my eyes adjust to the gloom I can see he's right there where I left him, sitting on the ground hugging the thick metal rails of the ball return machine. I don't want to give up Weasel's knife so I go looking for anything else that might do to free him. I find a box cutter in one of the drawers behind the refreshments counter; the blade's rusty, but it'll do the trick. I ask him if he's okay and he hesitates for a moment but then gives me a thumbs-up. As I lean in to cut the plastic ties I can see he's been working on them and it doesn't take much for me to finish the job. I throw the 'cutter away and hand him his medicine. When he's taken it he asks for a strip of tape for his mouth then he puts his mittens back on and I tape them too, making sure to add a couple of extra turns for good measure. I start to make my way up to where Mags is sitting by the fire but he holds back.

'What's wrong?'

He points up towards the entrance and I understand. He's already wearing his goggles, but I guess they're no longer enough. I tear another strip of tape and cover the remaining slit then zip his hood all the way up. I bend down and hoist him onto my back and we make our way up to join Mags. She looks up when she sees us and her eyes widen.

'It's okay, he's taped pretty good. This is how we got here last night.'

I set him down next to her. She looks over at Hicks, but he just shakes his head like he wants no part of it and goes back to eyeballing the parking lot.

We pack up our things and get ready to leave. Outside the storm's moved on, but the powder's soft and deep from the fall overnight. I hoist the kid onto my shoulders. He wraps his arms around my neck and buries his head in my parka and we set off.

All morning we trek steadily north. Hicks takes us out to the interstate at the first opportunity. We can't be that far from Hager and I think sticking on 11 might have been faster, but I don't reckon there's much in it so I don't argue the point. The road curves this way and that but at least it stays pretty flat. I keep checking behind me to see how Mags is doing. Hicks is breaking trail and I'm following in his footsteps, so the snow she's treading's as packed as it's going to get, but before we've gone much more than a mile she's struggling.

We pass an exit sign for Falling Waters and shortly after there's a succession of overpasses. The last of them has collapsed and we have to take off our snowshoes and pick our way down through the rubble. Hicks clambers up the other side. I let Mags go ahead of me; I can hear her breathing hard inside her respirator as I follow her up. When we reach the top I ask if she wants to take a break, but she just shakes her head and waves Hicks on.

The road swings east for a couple of miles and then starts a long, slow descent. We come to a faded yellow sign that says *Maryland Welcomes You* and a little ways further on we reach the Potomac. There are separate bridges for east- and westbound traffic; the westbound crossing's given way but thankfully ours has held. I stop in the middle and wait by the guardrail for Mags to catch up. Beneath us the river flows sluggishly south.

We reach Hager soon after. Hicks stops at a large stone church on the far side of town. A bell tower with a tall steeple looms over us as we trudge up to the entrance and unsnap our snowshoes. Two heavy oak doors bar our way, but they're not locked and we step through into a darkened foyer, our boots shedding snow on the cold stone. Stained-glass windows sit high on the walls on both sides but they're silted with grime and admit little light.

Hicks chooses a spot near the door and sits with his back to the wall. I set the kid down and ask how he's doing. He hesitates for a moment then nods tentatively so I unzip his hood.

'It's pretty dark in here.'

He lifts the goggles onto his forehead and squints around. But then he catches Hicks pulling the thermos from his backpack and scurries off into the shadows.

There's a stack of hymnals that have been missed that'll do for a fire; I gather them up and use the last of the gas to get it going. Mags wraps herself around the coffee I make but shakes her head when I offer her an MRE and just asks for a couple more Tylenol. While she's taking them I go through her pack and throw out whatever she won't need to lighten the load. She looks like she might object when I find *Owen Meany* so I jam it into the inside pocket of my parka instead. When I'm done Hicks raises the thermos to his lips and looks over at me.

'How much further we got, kid?'

'We're close. I reckon we can be there tonight.'

'So what's the plan?'

'We go in as soon as we get there.'

'Sure you're up to that? You won't need to rest up or nothing?'

I don't need to look over at Mags to see how she's doing. She started coughing again as we were coming into Hager, and that worries me. The kid's no better; he's barely holding it together now. He's been squeezing my shoulder for the last hour, asking to be set down, but we don't have time to wait while he sorts himself out. I shake my head.

'Fair enough. You have the code for the blast door?'

I don't, but I nod anyway.

'Alright. And what'll we face when we get in there?'

I hesitate. The truth is I don't know. Up until now my main concern's been that Kane would send Peck to Mount Weather for us at the earliest opportunity. Now if I'm going to get Mags to the scanner I'd much rather he and the Guardians weren't in there waiting for us. But they could well be, and I guess Hicks deserves to know what he's up against.

'Kane's secret service agent, Randall Peck.'

'He any good?'

'Yeah.'

'Anybody else?'

He already knows about Kane. Quartermaster used to be the Defense Secretary but I suspect it's been a while since his fingers fitted a trigger guard. I tell him about Scudder. He was a soldier too, even though he was mostly Eden's maintenance guy.

'That it?'

'And maybe six Guardians.'

'Guardians?'

'Kids like us that Peck has trained. He used to keep two of them at the portal. Another two patrolling inside.'

'Armed?'

'They could be.'

Hicks shifts his jaw, like he's considering this.

'Alright, then. Well, it's your show from here.'

*

WE TAKE I-64 EAST out of Hager. For a long while the highway runs straight. Giant billboards clutter the fields on either side. Most have collapsed, the metal supports weakened by rust or virus, the wind and the storms doing the rest. Those that still stand look down on us as we pass, their tattered hoardings showing weather-faded images from a world that no longer exists.

The road finally starts to curve north and we pass a Food Lion, and then a little further on I spot the farm store, its familiar parapet walls towering over the adjacent lots. Next to it's the veterinary clinic where I found Benjamin, what now seems like a lifetime ago. We come to a junction. A collapsed traffic light gantry lies across the intersection, almost drifted out of sight. I take us out around it but we keep to the road. Less than a mile further on I find what I'm looking for: a sign, mostly buried under a blanket of snow, that says US491 above an arrow that points right. On the other side of the road there's another, its message hidden under a thick crust of snow and ice. Hicks stops in front of it and scrapes it off while Mags catches up. He stares at it for a moment and then turns to me.

'Raven Rock. Is that it kid? Is that where Kane's been holed up all these years?'

I shrug my shoulders like I don't know, but I do. Marv told me Eden's real name just before he died. Hicks looks at the sign some more and then shakes his head.

'Well I'll be damned. You have to hand it to him. I'd forgotten that place even existed. Suspect most folks had; must be fifty years since they mothballed it. No-one would have thought to look for him there.'

We turn off the highway. The road narrows until there can't be more than two lanes of blacktop under the snow, and at times it's hard to know if we're still on it. I follow the telephone poles, but there are stretches where they've fallen or been cut and then I'm down to picking my way through the bare and blackened remains of the trees, searching for anything that might look familiar.

The light's already slipping out of the sky. I reckon we've only got maybe ten more miles to go, but from here most of it's uphill. Mags is coughing behind her respirator now, pretty much all the time. The kid's been squeezing my shoulder for a while to let me know he needs time to de-fury himself so I bend down and let him slide off while she catches up. He stumbles off to the other side of the road and crouches down in the snow.

Hicks stops beside me and points back down into the valley. I follow his finger. It takes me a while but then I spot them: four figures side by side, about a mile into that long straight stretch of road out of Hager. They can't be more than seven or eight miles behind us. There's little wind, nothing to cover our tracks. Truck'll have no problem spotting where we've gotten off.

Mags stops beside me and unsnaps her respirator. She bends over, the palms of her hands on her knees, trying to catch her breath. I want to ask her if she's okay but that's a question without any meaning to it now so I don't.

'I'm sorry. We have to keep going.'

She stays like that for a while, like maybe she hasn't heard me. But then she nods once and hauls herself upright.

One by one I tick off the landmarks I remember. An old house with lap siding and a wraparound porch where Marv and I stopped for lunch. The fire truck whose final journey somehow ended out here in the middle of nowhere. The white sign by the crossroads at a dip in the road, its once-neat black letters spelling out *The Zion Lutheran Church*, and underneath, *Little Is Much If God Is In It*.

We come to a junction, the red of a stop sign just visible above the snow and I stop to dig out a mile marker. I'm pretty sure I know the way from here, but night's falling and it would be easy to get lost. I can't afford to lead us wrong now.

As we set off again Mags stumbles. She kneels in the snow and unsnaps the respirator, trying to catch her breath. Hicks stares back down the road into the gathering darkness then looks over at me.

'How much farther?'

I figure a mile, maybe a shade less, to the state line and another beyond that to the turnpike. From there three more to Eden.

He whistles softly through his teeth but doesn't say anything. He doesn't need to. The soldiers are running us down. Sometimes on the switchbacks I can see their lights now, always closer.

I bend down to Mags.

'We need to go.'

She nods and gets to her feet. As she clips the respirator back in place the filter on one side detaches and falls silently into the snow; when I look at it I can see the steel retaining ring on that side has given out. I dig in my backpack for one of the spare cotton masks I carry while she unfastens it. As soon as she's tied it on we set off again.

We continue on past Fort Narrows. From the road I can just make out the barracks, row after row of low brick buildings, the snow drifted almost up to the eaves of their roofs. I'm pretty sure this was where Marv was getting the things he'd stashed under the floorboards up at the farmhouse.

There are things in there I could use, but I can't stop now to go looking for them. Hicks has promised to buy us the time we need when we get to Eden. I'll have to rely on him for that.

The road curves around and we come to a railroad crossing, the top of the dead lights just visible above the snow. I don't know exactly when it happens because there's no sign, but shortly after that we return to Pennsylvania.

*

IT'S WELL AFTER DARK when we leave the turnpike and start making our way up the mountain. We're close now but I'm not sure how much more Mags has left in her. The 'pike was mostly flat, but even there she was struggling to put one snowshoe in front of another. And she's coughing continuously, just like Marv was in the end. We don't do frostbite checks anymore, but I've seen the blood that flecks the cotton mask I gave her to replace the respirator. The kid's in bad shape too. He doesn't squeeze my shoulder now; he just grips tight and butts my neck with his head, like he's trying to find a way in. I'm not sure setting him down would do any good, even if we had time for it. There may not be much left of him in there anymore.

We pick our way between the withered trunks that poke through the gray snow. As we pass the farmhouse where Marv and I used to store our scavenging gear Mags stumbles again. She tries to push herself back up, but it's like she's used the last of whatever strength she's been saving to get this far. I turn around and start back down the slope to help her up but Hicks gets there before me and extends a gloved hand. She looks at it as if she means to wave it away, but then she reaches up and allows him to pull her to her feet.

We stop at what used to be the tree line and I scan the darkness. I know the portal's somewhere up there ahead of us. It's little more than a hole in the side of the mountain, though, barely wide enough for a man to squeeze through. Even in daylight it's hard to spot. I guess that's what Kane must have been hoping for when he had Peck collapse the tunnel entrance.

Hicks points down the slope.

'Don't mean to rush you kid.'

On the turnpike four lights have appeared around the curve of the mountain. I look back up, desperately searching for our way in. I used to find it by lining myself up on the transmitter tower, but it's way too dark to see those bristling antennae now. I'm beginning to wonder whether Kane's re-opened it. Maybe the Juvies were right all along; maybe he never meant to come after us and all this was for nothing. But then I see something: the faintest glimmer coming from a spot not more than a hundred yards further up. Hicks has spotted it too.

'Is that it?'

I nod. He looks down the mountain at the lights making their way along the turnpike. He studies them for a moment and then turns to face me.

'The tunnel. How long?'

'One thousand and fifty-three paces.'

He raises an eyebrow, like it's high time for me to start providing useful information.

'How long will it take you to get through?'

Flat out, with fresh legs, I reckon I could clear the tunnel in a couple of minutes. I look at Mags. She's exhausted; she won't be running any part of it. And first I'll need to deal with whoever's waiting for us at the portal.

'Fifteen, maybe twenty minutes.'

He looks down the mountain at the approaching soldiers.

'Yeah, I doubt we've got that. If Truck catches us in there it'll be like shootin' fish in a barrel.'

He unzips his parka and reaches inside for the pistol.

'Best you get going then. I'll hold them off here long as I can. Let me have the code for the blast door so I can follow you in.'

'I don't have it.'

'What?'

He raises the gun like suddenly he might have a different target in mind, one much closer. I hold my hands up.

'It's okay, I know how to get us in. Peck always keeps a couple of Guardians posted at the portal.' I point up at the spot where light's escaping through the snow. 'That'll be their fire. Give me Marv's pistol. I'll make them open it.'

'You and I need to put some serious work into our communication, kid.' He says it without a trace of humor, like he's come too far for such a threadbare plan, but he digs in his pocket and tosses me Marv's Beretta. There's no clip and when I pull back the slide the chamber's empty.

'Yeah, there ain't no bullets. If you'd thought to tell me this was what you were planning maybe I could have brought some.' He slides his pistol back in its holster. 'And don't think I'm sending you in there with an empty gun either. We'll have to take our chances with Truck.'

I slip the Beretta into my pocket and we continue up the hill. The glow from whatever fire the Guardians have got going grows stronger as we approach. Another coughing fit grips Mags and she drops to her knees in the snow. I have to pry the kid's arms from around my neck, but once he's off my back he calms down a little and just crouches down in the snow. Hicks stands over him while I unsnap his snowshoes and then I help Mags with hers. When I'm done I slide Marv's gun from my pocket.

'Wait here okay? I'll call for you when I'm ready.'

Another coughing fit hits her. When she's done she just nods.

'Don't worry. This'll all be over soon.'

I take one last look down the mountain. The flashlights have already left the turnpike and are starting up the slope.

Hicks gestures for me to go first, just like Marv used to, so I lower myself through the hole in the snow and start crawling down the rubble, trying to make as little noise as possible. This was when I'd call ahead, so whoever was on duty would know I was coming, but I won't be doing that tonight. I inch forward through the darkness, the empty gun cold and heavy in my hand. I tell myself it'll be okay; the Guardians at the portal didn't used to carry anything more than billy clubs and there'd be no reason for that to have changed in the months since our escape.

Kane can't have imagined we'd ever try and come back.

*

TURNS OUT I NEEDN'T have fretted, at least not on that score. There's only one Guardian waiting for us as we make our way down into the tunnel. It's Angus, and he's fast asleep in one of the plastic chairs, snoring fitfully. There's a sizable fire at his feet. He's got his boots so close to it that I reckon the rubber soles might be in danger of melting.

Something's not right, though. The Guardians didn't ever come out to the portal by themselves. And I don't think I've ever seen Angus and Hamish separated. I look around, checking I haven't missed anything, but everything else seems normal. The step-through scanner waits where it always has. There's an old familiar flashlight sitting on the table next to it, the light from the fire reflecting softly off its scarred metal sides.

Angus sleeps on, oblivious. His ample rump's wedged pretty tight in the chair, but in the firelight his face looks thinner than I remember. Without the farms they'll have been relying on what was left in the stores, and I know better than most how little that was. I guess it's been a lean winter in Eden.

I wait until Mags and the kid have made their way down to wake him. In different circumstances the look on his face might even have been comical. He blinks several times at the gun and then does a double take as he sees Hicks standing next to me. But it's not until he sees Mags and Johnny that his eyes really widen. After that he's like a steer that's just been shown the branding iron; it's hard to get him to focus on much else. In the end I have to get her to take the kid over into the corner just so he'll pay attention to me.

'Where's Hamish?'

His eyes flick over to Mags and Johnny.

'Inside.'

'Why's he not out here with you?'

'We're the only ones left. Peck took all the other Guardians and went looking for you.'

It's the thing I've been worrying about all winter, but right now I can't imagine better news.

'How long have they been gone?'

Angus's gaze returns to the kid.

'Hey, focus. You want me to bring him back over here?'

His eyes snap back to me.

'No, no. Don't do that. This morning. They left this morning.'

'Why aren't you and Hamish with them?'

He looks down at his boots.

'Peck said we was too outta shape.'

'So who's in there? Just Kane, Quartermaster and Scudder?'

He cuts another glance in the direction of Mags and Johnny and then shakes his head again.

'Sergeant Scudder's gone with them too.'

We're so close now; the scanner's right at the other end of the tunnel, only minutes away. All that's left is to get us inside.

'So how do you get back in? Did Kane give you the code for the blast door?'

I know even before I'm done asking that can't be it. Kane would never trust the codes to any of the Guardians, and even if he had, this knucklehead wouldn't be able to remember it. Angus shakes his head again, confirming my suspicions.

'I buzz Hamish on the intercom.'

I point the gun at him.

'Alright, on your feet.'

I lift the old flashlight from the table and stomp out the fire. No point in making it easy for Truck to find us. I still haven't figured out what we're going to do about the soldiers, but I'll worry about that once we're inside. Only Hamish and the blast door stand in our way now, and for the first time in days I allow myself to hope. Suddenly getting Mags her scanner time seems like it might just be possible.

Turns out I couldn't have been more wrong.

*

HAMISH SHOWS LITTLE MORE resistance than Angus did. His eyes narrow when I step through the blast door and then widen again at the sight of the gun. He reaches for the club on his hip and for a moment it looks like he might try something, but then he sees Hicks. When Mags and the kid step out from behind me his mouth drops open and he stumbles backwards against the wall and slides to the ground.

The spot Hamish has picked out for himself's as good as any, so I tell Angus to take a seat next to him. I start digging in my pocket for cable ties to bind them both, but Hicks just says to get Mags to the scanner; he'll take care of it. Behind me the electric motors continue to whine, still winding the four tons of carbon steel out into the darkness. I point him to the large button on the wall that starts the close sequence but he just nods.

'Go on now. I got it.'

I follow Mags and the kid through the locker room and the showers to the scanner. She's already killed the lights and it waits in the darkness, the faint glow that follows me in reflecting dully off its polished metal skin. From its hollow center a narrow platform extends, like it's spent the long winter months just sitting there hoping for my return. I look up at the camera mounted high on the wall. The red light's blinking but if what Angus has told me is true there shouldn't be anyone in the control room looking at the screen.

She sits on the platform and beckons the kid over. He looks at her dubiously and then sniffs the air around the machine, but eventually he takes a seat next to her. She unzips his parka then wraps an arm around his narrow shoulders and lays back down, pulling him close. He struggles a little at first and I step forward, ready to pry him off her if I need to, but she holds a hand out and shakes her head. He seems to calm down after that. She gives him a moment to settle and then nods at me to begin.

There's a big red button on the wall that will stop the scan in an emergency, but to start it you have to go next door, to the control room. I've never actually been in there, but I figure operating the machine can't be that difficult; Kurt managed it for years after all. I step through into a small, windowless room. A desk with a bank of screens and a keyboard built into it sits in the center, a microphone on a long angled stalk jutting from its surface. I flick the switch on the side and all three screens come to life. The one on the right shows a grainy black and white feed from the camera next door, but with the lights off it's hard to tell what's going on in there. On one side of the keyboard there's a row of switches and on the other a large green button with the word 'Start' written on a piece of tape above it. The plastic around it looks grubby, like it's the only part of the apparatus that ever got touched. I press it and the switches light up all at once and then start flickering in seemingly random order. Lines of information scroll up the center screen, too quickly for me to read. A digital counter next to the button I've just pressed blinks to life and displays nineteen minutes and thirty seconds.

On the screen showing the feed from the camera I can just make out the platform retracting, drawing Mags and the kid into the machine's interior. She's holding him tightly to her, keeping his arms pinned to his sides inside hers. He doesn't struggle, almost like he finds the close darkness soothing. The platform slides in the last few inches and another light on the panel comes on. The digits on the counter flash several times and then it starts counting down.

There's a long pause and then from the next room I hear it, like someone's started up with a jackhammer on an oil drum. It's loud, even in here, and I wonder how the kid's taking it. As he sat next to her on the vinyl I heard Mags explaining there was nothing to worry about; that this was the machine that would fix him. He seemed calm, but the child that got that explanation only a few moments ago may not be the one who's in there with her now.

I watch as the display slowly counts its way down. After a minute of nothing happening I figure the scanner's on its version of autopilot and doesn't need my help anymore. I get up from the console and step back into the corridor. The banging sounds even louder out here. I was going to head out to the tunnel, but now I look towards the cavern. There shouldn't be anyone in there. Kane and Quartermaster are the only ones left, and they'll be asleep. But it'll only take a second to check, and I figure better safe than sorry. As I walk along the corridor the sounds from the scanner recede. When I get to the end I stop and strain for anything that might suggest our presence has been detected, but there's nothing. I step out onto Front Street. It's long after curfew and the arc lights are off, but the dim glow cast by the handful of bulkhead lamps that remain on is enough to see by. The windowless metal boxes; the narrow concrete streets, the domed, brace-wired roof; it all seems familiar and yet somehow strange. We've only been gone a few months, but after a winter in Mount Weather this place seems small, cramped. I wonder how we ever spent ten years here.

I take one last look then turn around and walk back to the scanner room. I don't need to check the control panel to tell me how many minutes are left on the scan; the timer inside my head's done that count often enough, and it's been running since I pushed the button to start it. The volume builds as I approach, once again becoming deafening. I shout in to Mags to check she's okay. There's no answer, but I know what it's like in there; I doubt she can even hear me. I peer into the machine's dark interior. It's no use, though; with the lights off I can barely make out the soles of her boots. It doesn't seem like she's having any difficulties with the kid, however; there's no sign of him struggling.

I take one last look and then make my way back out towards the tunnel to check on Hicks. As I step into the shower room I suddenly realize how exhausted I am.

But that doesn't matter. We've done it. The scan's already almost halfway through; in a few minutes Mags and the kid will be free of the virus. I have no plan for getting us out, after, but I'm not sure I need one. With Eden locked down we're safe. Truck won't be able to pull the same trick Gilbey did to get into The Greenbrier. The blast door's electrified, and even if it weren't it'd take a long time for the virus to eat through that much metal.

We can sit it out if we have to.

He can't wait out there forever.

*

IN MOUNT WEATHER'S MAIN CAVERN, nestled between the infirmary and the gym, there's a building that stands head and shoulders above those around it. The plaque on the outside says 'Command, Control, & Communications'. I checked it out when I first arrived, but I don't think it got much in the way of visitors after that. In Eden that building was off limits to anyone but Kane, Peck and Quartermaster, and even though we were miles away and they were stormbound I guess to most of the Juvies it still felt wrong to go inside.

We were all pretty busy those first few weeks anyway. When Mags started the generators up it got crazy for a while. I guess when the order had come the facility had been evacuated in a real hurry, because a lot of stuff got left on. For a while after the power came back we did nothing but run around switching everything off. We ended up getting most of it, but Mount Weather's not small and inevitably things got missed. If it was a hair dryer or something with an electric motor it'd run for a few days before it'd burn itself out, and then maybe a smoke alarm would sound. But that was the worst of it. We were lucky.

I guess nobody thought to check Command though.

Once things settled down I brought Mags over there. I remembered a staircase from the top floor landing that led to the roof. I figured we'd take a blanket and look up at the mesh of brace wire and rock bolts spread across the cavern's huge dome, and maybe it'd be like when we'd sneak up on the roof of the mess in Eden.

But as we stepped inside we were met by a pulsing red glow, coming from behind the door to the Situation Room. When we went to investigate we found a large glass and metal sign, the kind that lights up from within, mounted high on the wall. It blinked slowly, flashing a single word: DEFCON1. Neither of us knew what that meant so we started trawling through the user manuals that had been left behind in case it might be warning of a problem with our new home. Turns out it wasn't that at all.

DEFCON stands for Defense Readiness Condition, apparently. DEFCON1 means maximum readiness; that sign was only meant to light up when nuclear war was imminent. I climbed up on one of the desks and tried to disconnect it but the box was sealed and so we just closed the door behind us and left. I didn't go back, afterwards, but I used to think about that sign from time to time. At some point the bulb will give out, but as far as I know it's still blinking away in there, letting us know things have gotten pretty much as bad as they can and we're probably all screwed.

As I make my way through the showers a draft of cold air hits my face and spidey dials it up to DEFCON1, so suddenly that it stops me in my tracks. This isn't a faint twinge, that vague walking-through-cobwebs scratchiness I sometimes get inside my head when something's not right. It's like somebody's just poured ice water down my spine.

I've done the walk out to the tunnel often enough to know what's wrong, but I don't want to believe it. So instead I just stand there, straining to hear. It's no use, though; the racket from the scanner drowns out everything else. I take a deep breath and creep forward, slowly making my way into the next room. Narrow metal lockers stand in tired rows around me, their surfaces dented and scarred. But it's no good; I still can't hear a thing.

Ahead there's the door that leads to the chamber where I left Hicks with Angus and Hamish. It's still ajar from when I came through earlier, but from here I can't see past it. I inch towards it, hoping to catch a glimpse of what's waiting behind. As I get closer a sliver of the tunnel's darkness finally shows itself, enough to confirm what the draft I felt in the shower room had already told me: the blast door's still open. I'm about to stick my head around to get a better look when something impossibly large, clad in the gray-green of a camouflage parka, steps into view on the other side, then disappears again.

Cold fear floods through me and I take a step backwards.

Jax.

The soldiers are inside.

Behind me the scanner's still banging away. I need to turn it off, immediately; the sound will draw them. I seize that idea, mostly because it involves fleeing, and before I know it I'm running back towards the showers.

But then I stop.

I have to be smarter than that. I need to think this through.

There's no way they haven't already heard. And there's only one way into Eden anyway. They'll be there soon enough, whether or not I let the scanner run.

Besides, I can't shut it off. The scan needs twenty minutes. Mags has been in there for less than half of that.

I need to buy her some time.

But how? There's only one door between the blast door and the scanner room: the one right in front of me. I don't need to check the handle to know it doesn't lock.

I turn around, looking for anything I might use to brace it. But there's nothing. The lockers are empty and the only other thing in here's a stack of plastic crates our clothes used to go in when we came back from the outside.

From the next room I hear the sound of boots and I duck behind the door, pressing myself up against the wall. Through the gap between door and frame I see Truck step into the doorway, only feet from where I'm hiding. He pokes at the wad of tobacco he's got tucked behind his lip for a while before he speaks. He has to shout to make himself heard above the din from the scanner room.

'Hey Huckleberry, what's with all that bangin'? You back there? If you are Weez here wants a word with you. He's mighty pissed at you for bustin' his nose like that.'

I don't give myself time to think, I just take a deep breath and slam the door in his face. There's a startled curse from the other side, but before he has a chance to open it again I grab the nearest locker and tip it over. It pitches sideways and crashes to the floor. I send the one next to it the same way; I'm already reaching for the one after before it's even got itself settled. There's not much in the way of method to it; I'm just trying to put as much metal in front of that door as I can. One by one they topple, bouncing off each other, occasionally popping their locks, until the last of them comes to rest. When I'm done my heart's pounding, threatening to drown out the racket behind me. I step back and examine my handiwork. It's as good as I could have hoped for: the door's mostly hidden under a haphazard heap of metal. Lockers pile on top of each other all around it, three and four deep.

From behind the carnage I think I hear the handle dip. The door shifts a fraction as someone on the other side tests it, but then it stops. Whoever's there tries again but when it moves no further they let go.

The next thing I hear is Truck's voice.

'Is that it? You done in there, Huckleberry? You'd better have something more than that. Because we're coming for you now, boy.'

There's another pause. And then without warning something crashes into the other side of the door. There's the groan of hinges about to part company from frame and then the screech of metal on metal and I stare in disbelief as my entire barricade shifts back a couple of inches.

I bend down to brace the locker nearest me just as Jax slams into the door again. This time I feel the impact in my arms. There's another shriek and I'm pushed backwards, my boots scrabbling for purchase on the tiles.

He hits the door again and this time I stand up and back away from it. I can't hope to hold them here. The gap's already almost wide enough for someone to squeeze through.

I run back to the scanner room. The noise is deafening, louder even than the sounds of Jax's assault on the barricade behind me. My hand hovers over the emergency stop button. Mags has barely had half the time she needs in there, but I can't wait any longer. They'll be through in moments.

I hit the button and the banging from the machine stops immediately. There's a pause and then a loud click as the locks disengage. My ears are ringing but behind me I hear the Viking slam into the door once more.

The electric motors start up and the platform slowly starts to slide back out. I bend down and call to Mags that we have to go; the soldiers are coming. But there's no response. I grab her leg and squeeze, calling her name again, louder this time.

Beneath me the platform continues to slide out, finally revealing her face. Her eyes are open but they stare up sightlessly. She doesn't respond when I shake her shoulder. Her lips part and a single, bloodstained stream of saliva drips from the corner of her mouth and begins to pool on the vinyl beneath her cheek.

The platform reaches the end of its travel and stops. The arm she has draped around the kid falls away and he slips out from underneath it and slides to the floor.

*

WHAT HAVE I DONE?

The scanner was supposed to rid Mags of the virus but instead it's fried her circuits, just like the girl in the closet in Shreve.

From behind me there's another crash and now a sustained shriek as Jax pushes the lockers back the final few inches.

The soldiers will be here in seconds. We have to go. I look down at the kid, lying on the floor. I can't carry both of them.

I bend down and pick up Mags, surprised at how little she weighs. She doesn't resist as I lift her off the platform. Her head falls back and her cheek comes to rest against my neck. The skin there feels impossibly cold.

I take one last look at the kid and then I set off down the corridor towards the cavern. I step out into the dim glow from the emergency lights. Eden's narrow concrete streets are still deserted.

I glance along Front Street, my mind racing. I need to put her somewhere safe from the soldiers until I can figure out what to do. In front of me there's the mess. Its bulkhead door is stout, the buttressed hinges thick; I doubt even Jax could breach them. But the door doesn't lock and there are few places in there to hide other than up on the roof. I consider it for a second and then discount it. I can't count on that way being open to me.

I make for the old pedestrian tunnels, leaving the main cavern behind. The darkness slips around me, and for once I am glad of it. I pass the stores, the power plant cavern and the reservoir, finally coming to a halt in front of the door to the armory. Scudder must have fixed it because the red light at the bottom of the keypad is blinking. I only pray he didn't think to change the code.

I enter 011016, the verse from the Book of Matthew that was Kane's favorite. The light flickers rapidly for a second and then switches to continuous green. From somewhere behind the door I hear an electric motor, and then the sound of bolts being drawn back. Finally there's a click and the door recesses a fraction.

I step inside and lay her on the ground. The light switch is where I remember it. The air's still heavy with the smell of gun oil, but when the bulkhead lamps flicker to life they illuminate mostly empty racks. Only a couple of assault rifles still stand to attention near the back, the dark metal gleaming dully in the pale yellow glow.

I close the door and kneel down beside her. Her breath comes in short, irregular gasps. Occasionally her throat convulses weakly, as if she's having trouble swallowing. I turn her onto her side because that's what the first aid book I used to keep under my bed in the farmhouse said you had to do. Her lips are tinged with blue. I touch my hand to her cheek, no longer caring whether she might still be infected. The skin there feels frozen. I shuck off my parka and cover her with it. It seems futile, but I don't know what else to do.

I close my eyes, trying to remember anything else I read in the first aid book that might be useful right now. But there's nothing. The only thing I can think of is Hicks. He's been living with the virus for ten years. If anyone knows what to do for her it'll be him.

Spidey doesn't think this is much of an idea, even by my standards. He reminds me that I left Hicks to close the blast door and now the soldiers are inside. It had to have been him who let them in.

I look back down at Mags, lying on the floor under my parka.

He might still be willing to help her. He told me Gilbey wanted us both back, real bad. And there's something else I might be able to trade. I bend down and take the map from my parka and slip it into my pants pocket. I grab one of the guns from the rack and a magazine from a crate on the shelf. It slides up into the slot and clicks home.

I take one last look at Mags and then step out of the armory. I re-enter the code and wait while the motors slide the bolts back into place. Then I shoulder the rifle and run back to the main cavern.

*

THE SOFT GLOW from the curfew lights appears around the curve of the tunnel. As I draw level with the stores I slow down and inch along the granite, trying to be as quiet as possible. I'm straining for any sound but all I can hear is the thumping of my heart, the pulsing of blood in my ears. When I get to the end I stop. From here I can see all the way down Front Street. Eden still looks deserted.

I step out of the darkness and dart around the side of the mess, pressing myself into the shadows. I take a couple of deep breaths and follow the building's riveted steel down as far as Juvie Row.

I halt at the corner and look down the street. The second dorm along's where I used to bunk. I make my way towards it, stopping at the end of the mess building to check the way's still clear before scooting across. When I reach the door I place my hand on the latch and gently press down, feeling for the mechanism's biting point. There's a soft clunk as it engages and then a gentle groan as the door swings out on its hinges. I step inside. The main lights are out but the safeties are on. The air is musty, stale, like no-one's been in here in months.

I make my way past the showers and head straight for the stairs, taking the steps two at a time. The metal amplifies the slightest sound but I know how to tread softly and I pad silently up, the rifle bouncing on my shoulder as I ascend. When I get to the third floor I stop and reach up for the access hatch above my head, feeling for the bolts with my fingertips. Thankfully they're still loose and within moments I've removed the last one. Out of habit I check there's no one on the stairs or the landing below and then I slide the panel out of the way. The metal protests a little as it shifts, but then it's done.

I unsling the rifle, slide it into the crawl space and pull myself up after it. Moments later I'm climbing out onto the roof. The cavern's granite dome is right above me. I keep as low as I can until I reach the front of the building and then lie down on the cold metal.

The mess blocks my view of the corridor that leads to the tunnel. Its roof would have offered a better vantage point, but as I look over I can see I was right not to try it. The pee bottle I left there after my descent through the vent shaft is gone. If Peck found that it's a good bet he would have locked down the hatch too.

I turn my attention back to the narrow strip of Front Street I can see. There's still no sign of the soldiers. They should be in here by now; I wonder what's keeping them. Just as I'm thinking this I hear a shouted warning and a second later there's a loud bang followed by a muffled crump and plumes of dust belch from the corridor that leads to the blast door.

A few moments later the arc lights flick on, instantly bathing the cavern in their harsh white glare. I wait, trying to work out what's happening. Soon I hear footsteps from somewhere behind me, near the back of the cavern. I crawl over to the side of the roof just in time to see Kane marching up from Back Street.

He's not the President I remember. The mane of white hair, normally so carefully combed back, is wild, unruly, and the heavily stubbled face underneath looks gaunt, stretched. His suit is crumpled, and there's no tie; I think it's the first time I've seen him without one. His back's as straight as ever though, and in spite of the unkempt air he cuts an imposing figure as he strides up towards Front Street.

There's another sound from the back of the cavern and as I look around again I see Quartermaster, struggling to catch up. He's still a large man, but a shadow of his former self. I guess no belt's gone untightened over the winter months.

I turn my attention back to Kane. He's already reached Front Street. He must see something I can't because he stops mid-stride and raises himself up to his full height.

'What's going on here? Who are you men?'

There's a pause and then I hear a familiar voice. The accent's Southern, just like Kane's, but it has none of the charm or polish.

'Well look who we got here.'

From around the side of the mess Truck steps into view. He's still wearing his parka but now it's unzipped. In one hand there's a dark shape that can only be a pistol.

'I'm your commander-in-chief, soldier. You will address me as Mr. President or sir. And holster that sidearm.'

Truck makes a show of hitching up his pants, then he turns his head and spits a stream of something brown onto the dusty concrete to let Kane know what he thinks of that. Just as he does this Quartermaster rounds the corner, huffing and puffing.

'And if it isn't the *De*-fense Secretary.' Truck turns back to Kane and points the gun at his chest. If Kane flinches from up here I can't see it. 'It's your lucky day, Mr. President; Doc said we was to bring you back alive.' He holds the pistol there a moment longer and then swings it in Quartermaster's direction. 'Doc never said nuthin' about you.'

There's a loud bang. Quartermaster's mouth opens even wider and he staggers backwards, clutching his chest. His legs give out and he collapses in the middle of the street. Kane watches but makes no move to help. For a few seconds Quartermaster continues to stare up at the cavern, his chest rising and falling beneath his hands. Then he draws one final gasp, lets it out, hitches in a smaller one and just quits. His chest stops mid-heave and settles slowly.

Truck slides the pistol back into its holster and adjusts his pants again.

'Boots, bring the President here out into the tunnel and put him with the others, willya?'

Private Kavanagh appears and takes the President by the elbow. Kane shows no sign of resisting as he's led away. I tear my eyes off Quartermaster. Down on Front Street Truck's issuing more orders. He turns around and points a finger at somebody behind him.

'Jax, you go find the girl now. Well, I don't know. Try behind you for a start.' A second later I catch a glimpse of the Viking as he appears briefly on the other side of the mess before he lumbers off into the pedestrian tunnel.

I haven't seen Weasel yet, but I'm guessing he won't have strayed too far from Truck's side. I don't know where Hicks is, but with Jax off looking for Mags and Boots out by the blast door I figure the soldiers are about as split up as they're going to be. I'm not sure when I'll get a better chance. I don't have much in the way of a plan, other than to get Hicks to Mags before she gets any worse. For now that will have to do.

Seconds later I'm lowering myself down onto the landing. I head down the stairs as quietly as possible and make for the door. I push it open a crack and peer out. Main Street's still deserted. I step out and cross quickly to the other side. The arc lights have banished the shadows and there are few places to hide so I press myself up against the side of the building anyway and inch forward towards Front Street. When I get to the corner I stop. Quartermaster's lying right there, still staring up at the cavern's granite dome, his blood already darkening the dusty concrete beneath him. I slide the rifle off my shoulder. I pull the handle back to chamber the first round and raise it. My thumb slides up and flicks the switch that takes it off safe.

I take a deep breath and step out onto the street.

Truck's got his back turned, so at first he doesn't notice me. On the other side of him I see Weasel. He's holding one of the electric batons in one hand; his other's gripping the end of the catchpole. The noose is around Johnny's neck, but the kid's as he was when I found him and Mags. It looks like they've had to drag him out here.

Weasel's eyes narrow as he spots me. A dark purple bruise has spread itself across the bridge of his nose and there's a neat rectangle of angry-looking skin around his lips where the duct tape's been pulled off. It looks like a chunk of hair's missing from above his ear too. He raises the baton and points it at me. The arc lights catch the two ugly metal prongs that protrude from the end.

'Hey Truck, behind you.'

Truck turns around to face me. He pokes the wad of tobacco around with his tongue then rests his hands on his hips and squirts another stream of brown juice onto the ground.

'Well what have we got here? Looks like Huckleberry's found his-self a weapon.'

I keep the rifle pointed at him and take a step forward.

'Where's Hicks?'

A half-smile creases Truck's lumpen features; his dark eyes twinkle with amusement.

'Well wouldn't you like to know?'

If staring into the business end of the rifle's bothering Truck he's not letting on. Maybe he reckons I don't have it in me to do this. I think of how I found Mags in the cage, the marks I saw across her ribs. I doubt he could be more wrong.

'I would.'

Trucks stares at me for a long moment and then fishes in his pocket. My finger tightens on the trigger, in case he's about to try something, but when the hand re-emerges it's holding a radio. There's a squawk of static as he presses a button on the side of it and just like that I realize how stupid I've been.

'Hey Sarge, come on out willya? Huckleberry's here lookin' for ya.'

*

THERE'S A LONG PAUSE and then Hicks appears at the end of the corridor that leads to the blast door. He squints up at the arc lights then takes a moment to look around the cavern, like I'm not even there.

'So this is Eden. Yep, I can see why you left.'

He turns his gaze to me.

'You let them in.'

I don't need him to answer. A half-memory's already floating to the surface, something that even now I might dismiss as little more than a fragment of a mostly-forgotten dream. The last thing I heard on Weasel's radio as I fell asleep by the fire in the *Pikeside Bowl.* It was Hicks' voice, not Truck's. He must have had a radio too. There was never any need for Truck to track us. As long as we were with Hicks they knew where we were all along.

'You've been playing us, getting us to lead you here.'

He takes a step out onto Front Street. His hands are held clear of the pistol on his hip but his parka's unzipped and his gloves are off. I suddenly realize I've got the rifle pointed in the wrong direction; he's far more dangerous than either Truck or Weasel. I swing the barrel around so it's leveled at his chest. He doesn't seem to care.

'Now, son, you might want to take a moment to consider where'd you'd be if it weren't for me. Doc was all for sticking you in a cage right away, with the girl. She's a smart woman, the Doc, but she's never been much for the bigger picture. Maybe if she were she wouldn't have been so quick to come up with something like the virus. Only one use for an abomination like that.'

He shakes his head ruefully and takes another step towards me.

'But what's done is done. All that matters now is cleaning up the mess as best we can. And for that Doc needs warm bodies, and lots of them. And I needed you to bring me to them.'

*Warm bodies, and lots of them.*

And that's when it hits me, the thing that was bothering me when he first took me into the bunker to find Mags. All the empty cages. The crates stacked against the back wall in the storage room. With all that's happened since I haven't thought on it, but now I see. There were never enough live infected. Hicks flat out told me when I asked him how many they'd managed to capture.

'It wasn't just Mags. All the other survivors that found their way to The Greenbrier. Gilbey used them for her experiments too.'

Hicks shakes his head, like he's disappointed in me.

'Survivors? Son, the state most of them were in when we found them they wouldn't have lasted the month. It's like Doc says: it's all just a question of timing. But you're right on one score: this place was always the prize.'

He looks around the cavern again.

'Except there's no one else here is there? Wasn't just you and the girl who fled; you got them all out, didn't you? Probably stashed them someplace nearby and then went looking for somewhere with a little more distance from that fella.' He inclines his head in the direction of the tunnel, where Boots has just taken Kane.

'It's Mount Weather isn't it?' He raises a hand as if to dismiss the question. 'S'alright, you don't need to say. Has to be. That story you fed me out in Lynch needs a little more work by the way. I've been to Culpeper. It doesn't even have a tunnel.'

He takes another step in my direction. There's not much more than twenty feet between us now.

'There's still a way out of this for you, though. You and the girl. Where is she by the way?'

I guess he must see the look on my face as he mentions Mags.

'Aw hell, you've already put her through haven't you? I thought you'd have the sense to test it first.' He nods in the direction of Johnny. 'I mean son, what'd you think would happen?'

I shake my head, like I don't want to hear it.

'She just didn't get enough time in there. We're going to put her through again.'

'Wouldn't do no good. Besides, what'd you think that explosion was?'

I stare at him in disbelief.

'Why would you do that?'

But he just sighs, like he's weary of explaining how stuff works to me.

'Haven't you been listening to a thing I've been telling you? There weren't enough bullets in the world to stop those things, back when we still had people to shoot them. There certainly aren't enough scanners. What're you going to do, son? Drag every last one of them in here and wait while they go through individually?'

I hadn't given it any thought; there was only ever one person I cared about curing. But that's still no reason to destroy it. And then I remember the storage room in the bunker. There was only one crate on the shelves other than the kid's. It had said Amanda Gilbey on the side.

'Dr. Gilbey has a daughter that's infected. She's doing all this to try and save her.'

He smiles at me.

'Well, you're finally getting it. If the scanner had've saved your girl there's a chance it might have worked on Amanda, and I couldn't risk that. I told you: the Doc's our only hope now. I can't have her losing focus.'

'But you didn't even wait to see if it would work. You could have put yourself through first.'

He shakes his head again and when he looks back at me the smile's gone.

'Son, the things I've done I don't deserve a cure. I'll get what's coming to me, and that pretty soon. But there are things that need taking care of first.' He looks around the cavern one more time then returns his gaze to me.

'So this is how it's going to be: Jax is going to find the girl, then you and she and those two we found in the tunnel and Kane and whoever else is still hiding out in here are coming back with us. But first we'll take a visit to Mount Weather. I have a deal for you, though. You give me whatever codes you might have and when we get there, if they work, I'll let you go. You have my word on that. You can head on down south. Do whatever you want with what little time we've all got left. I swear I won't say a word. Your friends'll never even know it was you who sold 'em out.'

'But you'll infect them with the virus, put them in cages like you did to Mags?'

'Aw hell, kid, pay attention. If Doc doesn't find a cure for the virus they're done for anyway. We all are. You just gotta think about yourself now. Do you want to wind up in one of those cages? And that's not even the worst of it. You haven't seen what Doc does to them in that other room.'

But I'm not even listening to him anymore. I raise the rifle. The cold metal presses against my cheek.

'You're going to help me with Mags and Johnny and then you're going to let us walk right out of here. And you're going to forget you ever even heard of Mount Weather.'

Hicks shakes his head. He shifts his reaching arm a fraction. The parka falls back, exposing the pistol.

'You're overplaying your hand here kid. None of that's going to happen. You think maybe because you got lucky with that MRE you can hit me? You'll get maybe one shot, assuming you don't freeze up of course. Took you three to hit that carton, remember? And it wasn't shooting back at you.'

I reach up with my thumb. The rifle's already off safe, but I snick it forward one more notch, to its final position.

'You're a lot closer than that carton, Hicks. And I've got thirty shots actually. All I have to do is hold the trigger down, right? Like that rookie down on the line in Atlanta? I may not hit you with the first few. But I doubt I'll miss with all of them.'

Hicks' expression doesn't change, but for the first time I think Truck looks a little nervous. The smile disappears from his face. His eyes shift to

Hicks and then back to me again. He takes a step back towards the pedestrian tunnel.

Hicks squints at me for a long moment, like he's reassessing the situation.

'Fair enough, if that's the way you want it. Corporal, the kid'll empty that clip in a little over a second. If I don't get him first you take him down. Understand?'

Out of the corner of my eye I see Truck draw his sidearm.

'And then you find the girl and bring her back to the Doc. She might still have use for her. Kane will tell you how to get into Mount Weather. I don't care much for how you get that information from him.'

'Sure thing, Sarge.'

My heart sinks. He's right of course. Kane has the same codes Marv gave me, and I've no doubt he'll hand them over once Truck goes to work on him. He'll take the Juvies back to The Greenbrier, whether or not I shoot Hicks. Mags will either die in the armory or she'll end up in that other room he was talking about. I'm not sure which would be worse.

And then from the depths of the pedestrian tunnel I hear a sound like something very large pounding metal. Hicks must hear it too.

'Looks like Jax has found your girl. Last chance, kid.'

The pounding continues, echoing up from the darkness. Hicks turns his head a fraction, but his one good eye never leaves me.

'Private, go down there and see what that idiot's up to.'

Weasel drops the catchpole and starts off into the tunnel.

For long seconds there's nothing but the sound of Jax pounding on the armory door. And then without warning something bursts out of the darkness. It's moving too quickly and at first all I see is a blur as whatever it is hits the light. Then I catch a single snapshot of Mags, barefoot, suspended in the air as she swings whatever it is she's holding. And in that moment I'm back on the bus we took to the White House on the Last Day. But instead of an old hardback copy of *Black Beauty* it's the gray metal stock of a rifle that arcs downwards towards its target. There's a dense crunch as it connects and a large wad of tobacco sails out of Truck's mouth along with something that might be a tooth. She doesn't wait for him to land; by the time he hits the concrete she's already closed the distance to Hicks. She comes to a stop with the barrel inches from the back of his head.

'What was that switch you were talking about, Gabe?'

I don't answer her. I suspect I'm wearing the same slack-jawed expression Truck is right now. She glances over at me.

'Never mind. I don't think I'm going to need all of my bullets.'

*

I KEEP THE GUN TRAINED on the soldiers while Mags binds their wrists. She works her way quickly along the pew. None of them resist. Hicks just looks bored; the only time he shows interest is when I take his pistol. I earn a look that tells me the cable ties probably won't be holding him for long.

Truck's still out of it. A long strand of something brown drips from the corner of his mouth, searching for a place to settle on his fatigues. Even in the chapel's gloomy interior I can see his cheek's swelling up nicely, and there's a nasty bruise spreading along his jaw. When he finally comes to I suspect it's going to hurt something mean. It'll be a while before he thinks of tucking a wad of Grizzly there.

Weasel's already back with us. He's got a bruise just like Truck's to go with the one across his nose, but he's traded his front teeth for it. I think it makes him look better, although I doubt he agrees. He stares at me with barely concealed contempt while Mags slips a cable tie around his wrists. He cusses at her as she ratchets it tight. The general gist is that it's cutting off the circulation, but there's a lot of extra words in there it'd be easy to take offense to. When she's done she picks up the baton and zaps him in the neck with it. He yelps but after that he stays quiet and goes back to glowering at me while she moves on to Boots.

The Viking's the only one not present and accounted for, but he'll do just fine where he is. Mags came around just in time; she was headed back to the cavern when she heard him making his way along the tunnel towards her. She retraced her steps and hid in the darkness beyond the armory. Even for someone with Jax's limited faculties the open door was too much of a temptation. She waited for him to wander in and then locked it behind him. Once Hicks gets free he'll get the code out of Kane, but by then I mean us to be gone.

Mags finishes up with Boots and crosses the aisle to tend to the President. He's been quiet since we dragged him in from the tunnel, but now as he sees her approaching he raises his hands and backs himself up along the pew. I suspect it's not so much what's in her hand as the dark shadows under her eyes and the way her cheeks are sunken in. She holds the baton up and flicks the switch on the grip. Blue light arcs between the prongs; he stares at it for a second then lowers his arms and slides them behind his back. When she's done I see her reach inside his jacket and slip something into her pocket. Whatever she's taken, he doesn't fuss over it. He just looks up at the single piece of framed needlework that hangs, yellowing, from the wall. I don't need to read it to know what it says. *Ora et Labora*. I'm not sure about *labora* but I suspect his days of praying may be just about to start.

Mags comes over to stand next to me.

'All done?'

'Almost.' She reaches over and pulls the dog tags from Boot's, Truck's and Weasel's necks and slips them into her pocket next to whatever she took from Kane.

'Let's get out of here.'

As we reach the door I hear Hicks' drawl from behind me.

'Be seein' you real soon, kid.'

I stop.

I told Mags we should shoot them, every last one. I told her it'd be the smart thing. We wouldn't have to worry about Dr. Gilbey and without Kane I wonder if Peck would be so interested in finding us. But Mags said that wasn't how we were going to go about things, and she has more cause to want it than I do, so I agreed.

But now as I hear Hicks's words I know he's one more thing we'll never be rid of. I slide his pistol out of the gun belt I took from him. The cylinder clicks around as I thumb the hammer back. Mags reaches out and puts a hand over it.

'I got this.'

She walks back down the aisle and stands in front of him.

'No, you won't, not if you're smart. But I worry you're not, Sergeant, so pay attention now. You needn't bother with Mount Weather; by the time you get there we'll be long gone. And there's something else you might want to consider before you set off looking elsewhere for us. Gilbey's not the only one with the virus. We have trays and trays of it. Ask him if you don't believe us.' She points across the aisle at Kane. 'If I so much as suspect you're taking an interest in us we'll pay The Greenbrier another visit, and this time we won't come empty-handed. We have the code for the bunker. Remember that.'

We close the door to the chapel behind us and head back up to Front Street. The sound of Jax pounding on the armory door echoes up from the depths of the pedestrian tunnel.

The kid's sitting by the corridor to the blast door, where we left him. He rubs his eyes, like he's just been woken from a deep slumber, and squints up at the arc lights, like maybe they're too bright. For a second I think I catch a flash of silver, but when he looks at me I see the pupils there are dark, human.

I tell Mags I have one more thing to attend to, so she takes him by the hand and leads him out to the tunnel. I head over to the command building and make my way inside. It doesn't take me long to find what I'm looking for and then I'm back out on Eden's narrow streets. Quartermaster's still lying on the dusty concrete where Truck shot him. I look down at him for a moment, then I step around him and leave the cavern for the last time.

The scanner room's in ruins. Hicks was as good as his word; there's little left of the machine that's recognizable. Its polished metal skin is twisted and charred, like a giant can that someone's stuck in the fire without remembering to stick a hole in first.

I walk through the showers and into the locker room. I have to pick my way over the remains of the barricade to get out. Mags is already kneeling by the open blast door, going through the soldiers' backpacks for what we'll need. I figure she's got that covered so I head out into the tunnel.

Angus and Hamish are propped up against the wall outside, their arms cable-tied to the brace wire above their heads. I pull out the knife I took from Weasel. Their eyes widen and as I kneel down I detect a sharp odor. During the course of the evening's entertainment I think one or other of them has had an accident in their overalls. I sigh. To think I used to let these clowns intimidate me.

I hold my hands up.

'Alright, settle down; I don't mean to hurt either of you. I'm just going to use this to cut your restraints. But before I do I need you to listen.'

I remind myself to take it slow. The message I have for them isn't complicated, but I'm dealing with a pair of intellects rivaled only by the plastic that's currently binding their wrists.

'Those soldiers you saw earlier, they've killed Quartermaster. You can go back inside and have a look if you don't believe me. Kane's in the chapel with them right now. We've tied them up, but I doubt it'll take them long to get free. Before that happens Mags and I intend to be on the other side of the portal, and we mean to blow it behind us, like we did last time.'

I pause to let this sink in.

'Now it seems to me that you've got a couple of choices. You can go back in there and rescue Kane and afterwards take your chances with the soldiers. Or you can leave now with us.'

They look at each other. It seems like Angus is custodian of the family brain cell today. He turns back to me and his face gets as close to thoughtful as I suspect it ever does.

'Where are you going?'

'Mount Weather.' I get a blank expression for that. 'The bunker where the rest of the Juvies are.'

'And we can go there with you?'

I shake my head.

''Fraid not. I'm going to draw you a map of the route Peck and the other Guardians have taken. If you stick to it you should be able to find them.'

Hamish looks at me.

'You want us to go get Peck?'

I nod.

'I do. And when you find him you need to give him a message. You need to tell him the soldiers you met earlier have Kane and they mean to bring him to a place called The Greenbrier.' I see the worried look on Angus's face. 'Don't worry I'll write it all down; all you have to do is show it to him. But you need to tell Peck if he wants to save Kane he'll have to hurry. I don't think the person they're bringing him to see is a fan of the President's work.'

Angus comes to a decision quicker than I gave him credit for. He looks up to his wrists and I cut him free. While I'm working on Hamish Mags appears at the blast door. She holds up an olive colored metal orb, just like the ones from the crate I found under the floorboards in the hallway outside Marv's room when we first escaped from Eden.

'They brought loads of them. Should be plenty.'

I stand up and put the knife away.

'Alright, let's get out of here.'

*

HEAVY CLOUDS HANG LOW on the horizon, threatening the dawn that's reluctantly taking shape to the east.

Behind us the farmhouse burns. The flames have already made their way up into the roof; thick black smoke coils up from the rafters, smudging the morning sky. Whatever Marv had stashed under the floorboards went up like the Fourth of July, but we don't stay to watch. Peck has a day's start on us.

We make our way down to the turnpike, picking our way between the gnarled trunks. There hasn't been a fresh fall and the snow's settled. Good tracking skiff, Marv would have called it. We've barely made it a hundred yards before Hamish has his first yard sale, all the same. Angus is faring a little better but I can already hear him breathing hard behind me.

I stop when we get down to the road and wait while Mags and the kid continue on. Angus trudges up to me a few minutes later, his face beet red. He bends down, his hands on his knees, gasping for breath. Hamish is still coming down the slope. He's already covered head to toe in powder, but from the way he's driving his snowshoes I suspect he has at least one more tumble in him before he joins us on the 'pike.

When Angus gets his wind back I hand him a piece of paper. On one side there's the message I want them to give to Peck, on the other a simple map. We didn't meet anyone on the way up, which means he must have taken the Catoctin Mountain Highway, the route Marv and I followed when we first went to Mount Weather. Angus looks at the paper and then back up at me.

'It's not hard. You just stick on this road till you hit a town called Shiloah. A little ways beyond it there's a big highway. Turn right when you get to it. If you hike sunup to sundown you should be on it maybe a couple of days before you need to start looking for the first sign. Don't worry too much about the names. I've written down all the numbers you need to look for.'

Angus looks dubiously at the map and then the road.

'Can't we come with you?'

I shake my head. Benjamin's way through Ely's shorter, but it's a harder hike. And we need to travel fast now if we have any chance of getting to Mount Weather ahead of Peck and the Guardians.

Angus looks crestfallen. His brow furrows; I can see him searching for something to say that might convince me. Eventually he raises one arm and points down the road at the kid.

'We won't hold you up no more than that.'

I look at Johnny. The snowshoes are way too big for him; I'll definitely have to find him another pair. There's no getting around how short his legs are, either. Whatever way you cut it he's going to struggle when the drifts get deep. I turn back to Angus.

'Yeah, but him I can carry.'

Angus stares forlornly down the 'pike.

'You'll be okay. Just keep an eye on the skies and remember to get off the road before it turns dark.'

There's nothing else to say so I shift the straps on my backpack and set off after Mags and the kid. When I reach the first bend I look over my shoulder. Hamish has joined Angus now. They're both standing in the middle of the road where I left them, staring down at the map.

I catch up with Mags. The going's not bad along this stretch and we can walk side by side. The kid marches on ahead. The snow might have settled, but I suspect it'll not be long before he tires of breaking trail.

'You think they'll be alright?'

I turn to look at her.

'Yeah. The way's easy and they have most of the soldiers' supplies. There shouldn't be any more storms. I can't see them catching Peck and the others, though.'

'Guess that's up to us then.'

I nod.

'You think it'll work?'

'Without weapons Hicks'll have no choice but to return to The Greenbrier. And all Peck cares about is Kane. I reckon as soon as he finds out the soldiers have him he'll forget about Mount Weather and strike out after them with the Guardians. While they're working things out between them we can be gone.' I pause. 'As long as Peck believes us.'

'He will. We have something of Kane's, and the soldiers' dog tags.'

I look over at her.

'That was clever, taking his glasses. I wish I'd thought of it.'

'Don't feel bad. I thought we'd got that straight. You're the tall one. I'm the smart one. Remember?'

She stops and lifts the goggles onto her forehead. I've given her a fresh cotton mask to replace the one she was wearing on the way up. She pulls it down and smiles at me.

'Frostbite check?'

We've barely come a quarter of a mile so there's really no need. But I reckon if I ever turn that invitation down you can take Hicks' pistol and shoot me where I stand.

She tilts her head back and closes her eyes. Her skin's already losing its gray pallor and the shadows under her eyes are fading; I can already see the faint smattering of freckles that run along her cheekbones underneath those long, dark eyelashes. I pull down my mask so that I can kiss her and a moment later I feel her arms slip around my waist. The rifle slides off her shoulder but she ignores it and for the next few moments at least the cold is forgotten. Eventually she pushes me away and slings the rifle back onto her shoulder. She pulls the mask up and sets off again.

I stand in the middle of the road for a moment, watching her walk away. Sometimes I worry that the feelings I have for her will be our undoing. That the world we live in now is too dark and gray and cold to abide them. That it will keep trying until it finds a way to do us harm.

I pull my mask back up. Underneath my thermals the dog tags shift against my skin. I told her we should each wear a set because that's what Marv and I used to do, when we went out, with the crucifixes. She said she wanted Truck's and the kid asked for Weasel's so I ended up with Private Kavanagh's. I already checked hers this morning, while she slept. Now I reach for the chain and pull out the ones I'm wearing, holding them up to the scant morning light. They're as they were when I slid them in last night, but I reckon it's still too soon to show.

Mags said Gilbey told her that the virus was far more resilient than Kane had ever given it credit for; that it would do anything to ensure its survival. Not even what Kane did to the skies could stop it.

I watch as she marches off towards the kid who's waiting for us further up the turnpike. She says she feels better than ever. She's still way too thin, but her appetite's back, or at least part of it. She didn't seem to care much for the MRE I made her for breakfast, but she wolfed down the HOOAH! that came with it, and then went looking for mine.

I tell myself the field the scanner created had to be stronger than whatever Kane's missiles did, way up in the skies, and even though she didn't get the time in there she was supposed to, what she did get was enough.

But the truth is I don't know. I don't understand how any of it works. I can't tell you why the scanner brought Mags and the kid back, when all the others out there in the dark places just got their circuits fried. Perhaps it has something to do with the medicine she was taking. Or maybe once you're gone so far there's just no coming back and they hadn't yet crossed that line.

I hope that's it.

I'm not so sure, though.

The newspaper reports I used to collect said it was like the virus meant to hotwire the person it had infected, that it wanted to replace their internal wiring with its own. Except that the virus's circuits were way faster, and our bodies had never been designed for that kind of speed. All I can think of is how high she jumped in that moment when she appeared out of the pedestrian tunnel; how quickly she closed the gap to Hicks after she had dealt with Truck. I've seen how fast Hicks is and she got the drop on him, like she wasn't even trying.

And that's what worries me.

I take one last look at the dog tags and drop them back inside my thermals. The wind's already chilled the metal. It feels cold as it comes to rest against my skin.

# LIGHTNING CHILD

WE TAKE BENJAMIN'S ROUTE, south through the mountains. We have just the one pack between us and I've lightened it for the hike, but there's the rifles, and where the drifts run deep the kid needs carrying.

I count off the landmarks we pass. The barracks at Fort Narrows. The veterinarian's outside Ely, where I found Benjamin's body. The Susquehanna Bank in Boonsboro that sheltered us from the storms after we fled Eden. We don't stop at any of them. We have to make time now. Peck has a start on us.

The first day we make it almost to the state line before darkness and cold run us off the road. We crest a shallow rise and I spot a small church in the valley below, sitting right on the banks of the Potomac. It has little to recommend it, but we've passed nothing else for miles, and I can't see anything better on the stretch beyond the river. I catch Mags eyeing it, weighing the shelter it'll provide against the shrinking sliver of gray to the west that still separates earth from sky. She turns back to the road, like she means go on, but I pull the mask I wear down and call to her through chattering teeth. It'll do for the few hours we mean to be here. I wait while she considers what I've said, hoping she doesn't call me on the rest of it. Truth is we've pushed hard to get this far; I'm not sure how much more I have in me now. Eventually she nods, points her snowshoes in the direction of the chapel.

There's no need for the pry bar; the door's already hanging back on its one remaining hinge. She heads off with the kid in search of wood for a fire while I make my way inside. I shuck off my pack and start tending to our dinner. My fingers are numb from the cold; it takes longer than it ought to get the cartons open and our rations assembled. I'm still working on the last of them when she returns, dumps what she's gathered on the floor and sets to work, stacking firewood and kindling with practiced ease. I add water from my canteen to the MREs, spilling as much as I manage to get into the cartons, then I shuffle myself as close as I can to the smoldering branches and listen as the chemical heaters do their work, hissing away as they slowly thaw our food. As soon it's passable warm I tear the top off one of them and start wolfing down what's inside. Mags waits a little longer before she opens hers, then starts poking around half-heartedly at the contents. When I've had the last of mine I throw the empty pouch on the fire. The foil shrivels and for a second the flames flicker brighter as it's consumed. I hold my hands close for whatever heat they'll allow, but already they're dying down again.

The wind howls around the gable, rattling the door against its frame. I pull the parka tighter around me. I'm exhausted, bone weary, but it's been worth it. We've come farther than I thought possible when we first set out this morning; farther than I ever hiked in a day with Marv. At first light we'll cross the river and then we'll be back in Virginia, with no more than twenty miles between us and the Blue Ridge Mountain Road.

I wonder where Peck is tonight. Angus said he'd set out with Kurt and the other Guardians yesterday morning. We didn't run into him on the way up with Hicks, so he must have taken the Cacoctin Mountain Highway. That road is easier, but it's longer, and he's no reason to push hard. If we can maintain the pace we managed today there's a chance we might yet overhaul him, make it back to Mount Weather before he arrives. I glance over at the rifles, propped against the wall. If we can do that maybe we can hold the tunnel, keep him out. For a moment I allow myself that hope. Truth is I have no other plan.

I take a final swig from the canteen and announce I'm turning in. But when I go to stand the muscles in my legs have stiffened; I have to reach for one of the pews to haul myself upright. I glance over at Mags while I steady myself, but she's busy fixing herself a coffee and hasn't noticed. On the other side of the fire the kid's focused on a HOOAH! he's liberated from one of the MRE cartons. I watch as he pushes the candy bar up inside its wrapper, then takes to gnawing away at the end of it with those little teeth of his. I'd gotten into the habit of tethering him while we slept; it feels a little strange to have him roaming free now. He looks up at me for a moment, like maybe his thoughts have run that way too, then he turns his attention back to his meal.

I undress quick as I can and climb inside the sleeping bag, pulling the quilted material tight around me. Mags is still sitting by the fire, swirling her coffee as she stares into the flames. When we set off this morning I thought she looked better; that the shadows under her eyes had faded a little, that maybe the angles of her cheekbones were a little softer. But now I'm not so sure.

I tell myself it's just the firelight. Besides, it's early yet; barely a day since she came through the scanner. She didn't get the time inside it it'd been set for, but there's no way she's still sick. I've seen firsthand what the virus does to a person. Marv had been strong, and by the end he hadn't been able to lift a boot from the snow. When she took her turns breaking trail earlier it was all I could do to keep up.

I hold on to that thought for a while. It should bring me comfort, but somehow it doesn't. My mind keeps returning to the image I have of her, bursting out of the pedestrian tunnel. The way she had moved had been…unnatural. She had dealt with the soldiers, each in turn, without so much as a break in her stride. Even Hicks; she'd been on him before he'd barely had time to twitch.

I lie there for a while, trying to work out what it might mean. But it's no use; sleep's already plucking at my thoughts, unraveling them before they have a chance to form. I feel my eyelids growing heavy. I reach up for the dog tags I lifted from Boots. It's too early to tell yet, I know. I run my fingers over them anyway, testing for imperfections that weren't there this morning. Other than the letters pressed into the metal the thin slivers of steel are still smooth.

I close my eyes.

I'll check hers later, when she's sleeping.

*

WE'RE ON THE ROAD AGAIN before dawn. Mags takes the pack and rifles while I follow behind, carrying the kid on my shoulders. If breaking trail tires her she doesn't show it; her pace doesn't slacken, not even on the inclines. My legs are longer, and I have years of pounding the snow to my name, but I feel like it's me who's holding us up now.

We make good time, but it's already stretching into the afternoon before we catch our first glimpse of the Harry Byrd Highway. I set the kid down at the top of the on-ramp and search the snow for signs anyone's passed while I get my breath back. But there's nothing, far as the eye can see. The wind's been squalling all morning, however; if they came by more than an hour ago it'd already have wiped their tracks clean.

Mags adjusts the straps on her pack and sets off again. I hoist the kid back onto my shoulders and follow. From here it's a long steady climb and for the next hour I focus on her boots as they rise and fall ahead of me, following a tireless, mechanical rhythm, like she could do this all day. At last the road levels and off in the distance I see it: a faded blue sign announcing the turnoff to the Blue Ridge Mountain Road.

I catch up to her by a stand of spruce-fir that still clings stubbornly to the embankment and pull the mask I wear down to gulp in air. The thin cotton's iced up where I've been breathing through it, and for some reason that sets spidey off. Mags asks if I'm ready. I don't have my wind back yet so I just nod and she takes off again.

I'm about to follow when I spot something out of the corner of my eye: a length of chain, tangled up in one of the branches that poke through the snow. The old steel crucifix I used to wear, the one I placed on Marv's grave. Mags is already halfway to the first crest, but I just stand there, staring at it. I don't know what waits for us ahead, but I get the strong sense that whatever it might be, I won't be passing this way again.

I hesitate a moment longer then reach down, pull it free. I shake the chain to clear the powder from it, then I slip it into my pocket and take off after her.

The mountain road climbs sharply from the highway and soon my thighs are burning. When we reach the ridgeline it flattens enough that I consider setting Johnny down, but ahead Mags has picked up the pace so I just tell him to hang on. We follow the road along the spine of the mountain range, picking our way through the lifeless trunks that push up through the snow on either side.

Somewhere far behind clouds the color of gunmetal the sun's already dipping towards the horizon, but we're close now. We round a bend and I see a familiar sign, its dead lights hooded under black metal cowls, announcing we're entering a restricted area. We continue upwards for another half-mile and then finally the road straightens and levels. The trees fall away and we find ourselves in a large clearing that straddles both sides of the ridge.

Ahead there's the chain-link fence, the coils of razor wire above held outwards on rust-streaked concrete pylons. I stop and search its length for signs of a breach, but there's nothing. Spidey doesn't care for it, all the same. He starts pinging a warning, but like earlier it's vague, non-directional. Mags has already found the section I opened with bolt cutters the day I arrived. She slips through, holding the wire back for the kid. I set him down and he follows her in. While he's putting his snowshoes back on I unsnap the throat of my parka and lower the hood to listen. But the only sound's the wind, rattling a faded *No Trespassing* sign against the bars of the gate.

Mags unslings one of the rifles and hands it to me. We leave the guardhouse behind us and make our way into the compound. I scan the perimeter, counting off the concrete cowls of the airshaft vents as we pass. The snow on top of each is undisturbed, but that means even less than the absence of tracks out on the highway. Kane had the codes to the blast door for each facility in the Federal Relocation Arc; Peck wouldn't have planned on making his entrance the way I got back into Eden.

The control tower rises from the highest point of the ridge, its roof bristling with antennae. Dark windows slant outwards from the observation deck, staring down at our approach. The Juvies were supposed to post a watch while we were gone; if anyone's up there they're bound to have spotted us by now. I keep my eyes on the doorway, waiting for it to open. But no one comes out to greet us.

On the far side the helicopter landing pad, the tattered windsock snapping and fluttering on its tether. Spidey dials it up a notch as we hurry past. The temperature's dropping fast now, but that's not what's quickening my stride. We're almost at the portal.

The path curves around then straightens and at last I see it.

In the lee of the tunnel where the wind hasn't yet had chance to smooth it the snow's all churned up, a wide confusion of snowshoe tracks. Beyond I can see the guillotine gate. It's been lowered, a last desperate attempt to keep them out.

It hasn't worked.

The gate hangs inward at a defeated angle. The metal's twisted, charred; on one side it's jumped its runners. The bars that remain grin back at me, spare steel teeth in a gaping maw.

Behind the tunnel stretches off into inky blackness.

*

MAGS PUSHES HER GOGGLES up onto her forehead. She unsnaps her snowshoes and makes for the gate. I reach for her wrist.

'Maybe you should wait out here, with the kid.'

She makes no move to withdraw her hand, but for a second the shadows around her eyes that yesterday I thought were fading seem to grow a fraction darker. She tilts her head.

'You have a plan you're not sharing with me, Gabriel?'

As it turns out, I don't. I've had the last two days to come up with something, to figure out what we might do if Peck beat us here. But I've got nothing. Whatever hopes I had rested on us making it here ahead of him, finding a way to keep him out.

I shake my head.

'Then you're going to need me in there.'

She doesn't say it like there's much else needs discussing but she waits anyway, letting me work it through for myself. And the truth of it is she's right. It wasn't me who saved us, back in Eden. She took care of the soldiers, single-handed. All I did was let them in and then stand back and watch, for the most part of it slack-jawed, while she went to work.

She holds my gaze a second longer, then she just says *Okay*, and slips her hand from mine.

We make our way into the mountain. The darkness closes around us, swallowing us whole; soon I can no longer make out Mags or the kid in front of me. If not being able to see is a hindrance to either of them they aren't showing it; their footfalls grow steadily softer until I can no longer hear them above the sound of my own breathing.

I reach in my pocket for the flashlight, but then stop; it'd only mark us out to whoever might be watching for our approach. Instead I shoulder the rifle and shuffle over to the elevated walkway, groping for the guardrail. My fingers close around it and I set off again, lengthening my stride, anxious not to slip any further behind. The tunnel runs true for a ways and then I feel the rail start to curve. When it straightens again I start the count. For a long time there's nothing but my footsteps and the occasional drip of melt water, rendered distant by the darkness. At last I think I catch a glimpse of something: the tiniest grain of light, and soon Mags' silhouette once again separates itself from the darkness. She's farther than I had imagined, but at least now I can see again. I relinquish my grip on the guardrail and take off after her.

With each step the light grows, the mote becoming a sliver, then a slender shaft, until at last I can make out the blast door ahead. It juts into the tunnel at an unfinished angle, as though it has come to an unexpected halt, its trajectory interrupted. A pale glow spills out from behind, casting soft brace-wire and rock-bolt shadows over the roughhewn granite.

Mags moves closer to the wall, leaning forward to peer around the massive steel frame. She stays like that for a long moment, then disappears inside without saying a word. I shuck off my mittens and unsling the rifle, whispering to the kid to wait. I guess he mustn't care much for that plan, however, because he squeezes past me and takes off after her.

I follow them through the series of antechambers that lead in from the tunnel. Mags stops at each doorway to listen, moving forward again only when she's satisfied there's nothing waiting behind. When we reach the entrance to the main cavern she suddenly holds up a hand and I freeze, my nerves jumping like bowstrings. For long seconds she just stays like that. Eventually she whispers back at me over her shoulder.

'Hear that?'

I close my eyes, trying to quiet the pounding of my heart while I strain for whatever it is she's heard. But it's no use; I can't make out a thing. I shake my head.

I watch as she slips silently into the cavern. I take a deep breath and scurry across the street after her, my eyes darting this way and that for any sign of Peck or the Guardians. When she reaches the first of the buildings she stops. The kid crouches next to her. He angles his head up, one mitten cupped to his brow against the glare of the arc lights. His mouth opens in wonder and for a second I see this place as he must, as I did when I first arrived here. The huge, domed roof, the high vaulted tunnels; how much bigger it is than what we had known before.

Mags sets off again, keeping tight to the buildings for the thin shadows they provide. We pass the mess and cross to the infirmary, and now for the first time I hear it, too: a soft sound, intermittent, like water splashing. It echoes faintly off the cavern walls, in and out of the tunnels, making the source hard to pinpoint. There's only one place it can be coming from, though.

As we get closer to the lake the sound gets louder, and now in the space between there's something else, almost too soft to hear, like a gasped breath. I tap Mags on the shoulder and point. She nods, like she's already had the same thought. Mount Weather's tallest building, *Command*, is right there. From up on the roof we'll be able to see everything in the cavern laid out beneath us.

We hurry over to the entrance. I sling the rifle onto my shoulder and gently press down on the handle, feeling for the mechanism's biting point. There's a soft click as the lock releases and then we're inside. A sliver of red light pulses intermittently from underneath a door at the end, but otherwise the corridor's dark. The air smells fusty, stale, like it hasn't been disturbed in months. Mags pushes by me, making for the stair. The kid follows, padding silently up the steps behind her.

I follow, my boots squeaking softly on the tread plate. When I get to the top floor she's standing on tiptoe under the access panel that leads to the roof, the fingers of one hand reaching up for it.

'Wait, let me.'

I rest my rifle against the wall and undo the latch. The hatch swings down with a groan and a narrow metal ladder slides out on rollers. She already has her foot on the bottom rung before it reaches the end of its travel; in a few quick steps she's disappeared through. The kid squints up after her, like he doesn't much care for the lights burning from the brace-wired roof. And for a second I think I catch a glimpse of something; something I thought I saw earlier, in Eden's cavern, when he came back to us from wherever the scanner had sent him: a flash of silver, there and then gone again, like a fish under water. I feel the breath catch in my throat, but when I look closer his pupils are dark. It was just my own eyes playing tricks with me after the gloom of the stair.

I whisper to him to wait on the landing and this time he nods, like he might do just that. I turn and follow Mags out onto the roof. As my head clears the hatch I see her, standing on the ledge, looking down. I start to make my way over to join her, but when I glance over again she's already headed back towards me. Her lips have hardened into a tight line, and above her eyes are blazing. I step into her path, mouth opening to ask what's wrong, but I'm far too slow; the fingers that were meant for her shoulder close on thin air. I turn around to call after her, but she's already disappearing through the hatch behind me.

*

IT MIGHT HAVE WORKED OUT differently if I'd gone after her, right then, although all things considered I doubt it. But I'm only a few feet from the edge now, and curiosity takes over, insisting I witness firsthand whatever it is she's just seen. I step over to the edge, look down into the cavern, and then I'm running back across the roof too. I know even as I lower myself through the hatch I have little hope of catching her; she's long gone, the echoes of her boots already dying on the stair. I lean over the rail and call out, loud as I dare, but if she hears she's past heeding me. She hasn't even bothered with her rifle; it leans against the wall where she left it to go up on the roof. I snatch mine from beside it, shouting over my shoulder at the kid to stay where he is. There's no time to check if he means to comply.

I take the steps two, three at a time, the weapon bouncing on its strap as I bound after her. At the bottom the door swings open and I burst onto Mount Weather's bright, wide streets. Ahead of me she's broken into a silent sprint, heading for the lake.

I slide the rifle off my shoulder and take off after her, fumbling with it as I go. It feels no more familiar to my hands than when I leveled it at Hicks in Eden's cavern, a couple of days ago; the time I've had with it since doesn't seem to have deepened the bond between us. I get a grip on the charging handle and yank it back to chamber the first round, desperately trying to remember everything he told me about shooting it. The only thing I can recall is the bit about getting my breathing under control and there's little chance of that happening, so instead I grip it tight and run as fast as I can, trying not to think about what might happen after.

Ahead of me Mags has already disappeared around the corner. I reach the end of the sidewalk and then I'm clear of the last building and out in the open, a wide strip of concrete the only thing now between me and the water. I raise the rifle, press the stock to my cheek. My mind registers what I see as a series of freeze-frame images, presenting each in turn.

Up ahead the Juvies, kneeling in short, uneven rows. Their heads are bowed; here and there shoulders shake with tears. To one side, Tyler and Eric, the two former Guardians who fled with us here, also on their knees, their hands bound behind their backs. A beefy, apple-cheeked man stands over them, shifting his weight from one foot to the other, like he might not care for his current station. Scudder. But he's of little concern to me right now.

Another group, right at the water's edge. Zack, Jason and Seth, the other three Guardians. They're bent over a fourth person, lying on his back between them. His face is covered by a rag, but there's only one person it can be; no one else in our group approaches that size. A final figure stands over him, a rifle slung over his shoulder. Kurt. He's pouring water from a jerry can onto the cloth, a smile playing across his lips as he does it. Now and then he flicks his head back, clearing strands of lank hair from his eyes. Jake struggles furiously as the water hits the rag; it's taking all three of the Guardians to hold him down.

My eyes return to Mags. She's almost on them, but miraculously no one's spotted her yet; they're all preoccupied with what they're doing to Jake. That won't last; any second now all hell's going to break loose. I look around, desperately scanning the cavern for the one person I haven't found.

'Alright, let him up. We'll see if he'll tell us now. Kurt, pick me out one of his favorites, just in case he's still not feeling co-operative.'

*There.*

I swing the rifle in the direction of the voice. He stands to one side, hands clasped behind his back. He's facing away from me, out onto the lake, but there's no mistaking that iron-heeled stance. I sprint towards him, bringing the barrel up as I run. A few more yards and he'll be close enough that I might even stand a chance of hitting him.

Kurt takes his time emptying the last of the water from the jerry can. When he's done he turns around, takes a step back towards the Juvies and reaches down, grabbing a fistful of blond hair I think belongs to Lauren. She squeals as he drags her to her feet.

Peck's the danger; I shouldn't take my eyes off him, not even for a second. But any moment now Kurt's going to spot Mags, and he has a weapon. Even as I think it he finally sees her, bearing down on him. His mouth opens and he starts to slip the rifle off his shoulder, but he's left it far too late. She grabs the barrel, wrests it from him with absurd ease, and in the same motion swings the stock around high. There's a crunch as it connects with his nose and he drops, so quickly he might as well have been shot.

He's no longer a threat, I know it even before he hits the ground. But there's something happening with Mags now, and for an instant I'm unable to look away. Kurt's lying at her feet, hands cupped around his busted nose. It looks like it's a gusher; fat drops of blood are already spilling from between his fingers, spattering the sidewalk. Peck's right there, no more than a handful of yards behind her, but if that's a concern she gives no sign of it. She just stares down at Kurt as though transfixed.

I finally tear my gaze from her and swing the rifle around. My thumb remembers the safety of its own accord; it flicks the selector even as my finger slips over the trigger. But Lauren's still on her feet and Mags is in the way now, too. I open my mouth to shout at her to get down, but the warning dies on my lips. Peck takes a step to the side, placing her squarely between us, and I sense whatever chance we had for this going our way evaporating. In the end I never even see where it comes from.

One second his hand's empty.

The next it's holding the unmistakable shape of a pistol to the back of her head.

*

I SKID TO A HALT among the Juvies.

Mags still grips the weapon she took from Kurt. Peck barks at her to drop it, but she pays him no mind; from the way she holds it it's unclear whether she's even aware she has it.

I start to inch forward, but Lauren's standing in front of me, blocking the way. Her eyes are wide, her hair a bird's nest of tangles where Kurt has used it to drag her to her feet. I hiss at her to sit down. She starts at my voice, like she didn't realize I was there, and then she bobs her head, once, a quick up and down that suggests there's nothing she'd like better than to oblige. She makes no move to sit, though, just keeps staring straight ahead, like the part of her brain that might be in charge of processing that instruction has flipped the sign from *Open* to *Out to Lunch* or possibly even *Gone Fishin'*. A few of the Juvies glance up in my direction, but for the most part they keep their heads bowed, their eyes fixed on the ground.

Mags continues to glare down at Kurt, seemingly unaware of the gun held to her head. Peck shifts his gaze from her to me then back again, as though he's assessing which of us is most likely to cause him trouble. He takes another half-step to the side. He needn't have bothered. Even if my hands were steady there's no way I'd risk that shot. He tells her to drop the rifle again, this time jabbing the pistol into the back of her neck for good measure.

*That* gets her attention.

Her eyes flick to the side and I see her tense. And for a second I think she might be about to try something very foolish. An image pops into my head, from a dream I had, not three nights back, sleeping on the floor of the church in Devil's Backbone. And for a moment I'm not in Mount Weather's cavern. I'm stood between a pair of crumbling gateposts at the end of *The Greenbrier's* long driveway. I can see the blood welling up from the hole the bullet has made. It trickles slow down her scalp to drip into the snow. In the dream it was me who had pulled the trigger, but if she keeps this up the outcome will be no different.

I lower the rifle.

'Mags.'

Her eyes jump to me and I think I catch a flicker of recognition there, but the pistol Peck has pressed to her neck's not helping. I call her name again, louder this time. Her eyes close, stay that way for a long moment, and when they open again it's like she's come back from wherever it is she's been. The Secret Service agent shouts at her to drop the rifle she's holding. She glances at it then lets it slip from her fingers. It clatters uselessly to the ground.

Peck turns to look at me, his eyes gray as the snow outside and just as cold. He pushes the pistol forward, pressing the muzzle into the back of her head.

'Alright, you can lay yours down too, Gabriel. Nice and easy now.'

Mags looks at me and shakes her head, but the Secret Service agent just reaches for her parka and yanks her backwards towards him, jamming the gun into the nape of her neck. Her eyes narrow, like she's struggling to contain whatever it was I saw there only seconds ago. She closes her eyes again and I hold my breath, but when she speaks her voice is calm.

'I wouldn't do that if I were you.'

'Really? And why's that?'

'Because I'm infected.'

A few of the Juvies raise their heads and there's the sound of fresh struggling from the water's edge. Peck doesn't seem impressed by any of it, however.

'Nice try, but Gabriel's already played that card, remember? I'm not falling for it again.'

She shrugs.

'Suit yourself.'

For a long moment his eyes don't leave me, but then without warning they flick to her, and when they return for the first time I think I see doubt there. He glances over again, allowing his gaze to linger a little longer this time. She's got her back to him, but even from behind he must see how thin she looks. He hesitates a moment longer, then shifts the gun back a fraction. His free hand reaches forward to spin her around, but then he thinks better of it. He takes a slow step backwards, barks another order.

'Hands behind your head. Interlace your fingers.'

She does exactly as he says.

'Alright, turn around. Nice and slow.'

His eyes move to her face and for a split second I see his expression change. Under the glare of the arc lights there's no mistaking it; this isn't some Halloween lampblack stunt, like the one I pulled in Eden. He takes another step back. The gun stays pointed at her, but his eyes drop to the barrel, betraying him. He's not wearing gloves. Would the few seconds he had it pressed to the back of her head have been enough?

'On the ground. Now.'

She lowers herself to her knees, her hands still behind her head.

'We didn't come back for you, Randall. And right now you shouldn't be wasting your time worrying about us, either. You'd do better to concern yourself with how you're going to save your boss.'

Peck's eyes narrow at the mention of Kane, but he doesn't say anything. He looks distracted, like he's trying to work out how long he has; how quickly the virus might move through the metal in his hands.

Mags keeps talking.

'You came down the Catoctin Mountain Highway didn't you?'

She doesn't wait for a response.

'I know you did, because we've just come from Eden too. We left the President in the care of some men. Soldiers. Serious types. They've already killed Quartermaster. If you let me show you what I have in my pocket I can prove it.'

Peck appears to consider this for a while, but his thoughts seem elsewhere. The gun doesn't move from her head, but his eyes keep returning to it, like it's something he'd be mighty keen to be rid of. Eventually he tells her to go ahead.

Mags reaches inside her parka and pulls out Kane's reading glasses. She holds them out for him to see.

I start to inch forward again. Mags is finally out of the way, but Lauren's still on her feet, just waiting for the first bullet to find her. I whisper at her to get down, but she just hitches in a breath and stays right where she is.

Peck's staring at Kane's glasses. He gives an almost imperceptible shake of his head, like he might not believe it. I take another step, racking my brains for something to say that will convince him.

'They're planning to bring him to somebody you might know. Dr. Myra Gilbey.'

At the mention of Gilbey's name Peck's eyes flick back to me.

'She's the one who infected Mags. She didn't seem a big fan of the President. My guess is he can expect similar treatment, soon as they get him back to her. They'll be on their way by now. They left right after us.'

'Where are they headed?'

I shake my head.

'You'll get that information when we're outside.'

Peck looks at Mags again, then back at me. He brings the pistol closer to her forehead, but this time he makes sure not to touch her with it.

'You tell me where they're bringing Kane, Gabriel. You tell me right now, or so help me I'll end her.'

I take a deep breath, then shake my head.

'In a couple of days she'll be done for anyway, just like Marv. I've seen how that goes, and it's not pretty.' His eyes flick to the barrel again. ''Fact, you'd probably be doing her a favor.'

There's fresh commotion from out by the lake as the Guardians struggle to restrain Jake. Mags looks over her shoulder and I see her brow furrow, like she may not much care for how I'm playing the hand she's dealt me either. I take a step closer. Lauren's standing right in front of me, so close I could rest the rifle on her shoulder if I chose. Still she doesn't move.

'But then I'd shoot you.' I raise my voice, so those out by the water can hear. 'And Kurt here, and all the rest of you, too, for good measure. And the President would still be with those soldiers on his way to Dr. Gilbey.'

Lauren's mouth drops open and she turns and stares at me over her shoulder, wide-eyed. Peck doesn't seem as impressed, but I can see him working through his options. I summarize them for him, just in case he's having a slow day.

'Randall, you've nothing to lose. If we're lying you can just come back in a week and we can do this all again.'

*

THE LAST OF THE LIGHT'S already slipping from the sky as we make it out to the portal.

Kurt eases himself through the ruined guillotine gate, his hands still clutched to his nose. He shuffles over to where Scudder and the Guardians are waiting and then turns to glare back at Mags and me. I ignore him; right now I have a much bigger fish to fry. Peck still has a pistol held to her head, but he doesn't look any more content with that situation than I am. His eyes keep flicking to it like it's a grenade he's holding, and he's just noticed the pin's not where it ought to be.

'Alright, we're outside, like you wanted. Now where're they headed?'

'First I want the map Kane gave you, the one with the code to this place on it.'

'That wasn't part of the deal.'

'Well it is now. Think about it, Randall. If Kane's still in Eden you can get it from him again. We don't know how to change them. If we did we'd have done it already, wouldn't we?'

He hesitates, like he's considering. I don't want him to dwell on it too long, or he might think to wonder just why *I* want the map from him. He can't know it, but the last thing I did before we quit Eden was take a trip along Front Street, to the command building. I figured Kane had to have his own list of codes for the bunkers in the Federal Relocation Arc, and I couldn't risk that list falling into Hicks' hands. Finding it turned out to be easier than I had expected; it was sitting right there on top of a filing cabinet, like he'd just had it out and hadn't yet bothered to put it away, which I guess was probably just the way of it. I checked the drawers and there was no other, but that doesn't mean he wouldn't have thought to stash a copy somewhere else. If he didn't, though, then whatever codes he gave his Secret Service agent when he was setting out for Mount Weather might be the only ones not in my possession.

I flick my eyes in Mags' direction.

'Hey Randall, how long do you think it's been since you jabbed her with that pistol?'

He waits a second longer then reaches inside his parka with his free hand and takes out a blue and red *Standard Oil* map, just like the one Marv gave me, and tosses it over. It lands in the snow at my feet.

'Now put the gun down and I'll tell you where they're headed.'

His eyes shift to the pistol, and for a second I think he might just do it, he wants rid of it that much. But instead he shakes his head.

'Yeah, that's not happening, Gabriel.'

'Let Mags go back inside, then. Once she's safe I'll tell you where they're taking him. You can keep your gun on me.'

'Gabe.'

'It's alright Mags, I know what I'm doing.'

I say it with way more confidence than I feel. But I've had the walk through the tunnel to think about how this might play out, and I figure this is as good an outcome as can be hoped for. Afterwards I'm not sure if I blinked and I missed it or if he was just that quick, but one moment the pistol he's holding is pointed at her head, and the next I'm staring down the business end of a Beretta just like Marv's. I was ready for it, of course, at least as much as you can be ready for something like that, but nevertheless I'm a little thrown by the speed with which it happens.

My finger's been resting on the M4's trigger all the way out through the tunnel, but as soon as Mags steps out of the way I tighten it, until there's nothing left in the mechanism. With my thumb I reach up and snick the selector to its final position, the one that Hicks said would empty the clip in a little over a second. I don't dare take my eyes off Peck, but I have one more instruction for Mags.

'When you get back to the cavern fetch the other rifle from the roof and wait by the blast door. If you see anyone other than me you let rip. Tunnel that straight, it won't matter whether you manage to shoot straight. Right, Randall?'

If Peck remembers that those were his words to me on the day we fled Eden, he gives no sign of it. His eyes drop to the pistol he's holding, then return to me.

Mags looks from one of us to the other, like she's unsure what to do.

'Mags, take the map and go, now.'

She hesitates a second longer then bends down to pick it up, and just like that she's gone.

Peck stares at me over the barrel of the Beretta.

'Alright Gabriel, she's safe. Now tell me, where are they taking the President?'

I don't answer; in my head I'm counting.

He pushes the gun closer, until the muzzle seems like it's only inches away.

'I mean it now, start talking.'

I keep up the count, trying to not to let my gaze get drawn into the barrel; from this distance it looks about as wide and as dark as the portal must from the other side of that guillotine gate. When I think Mags has had enough time to make it to the blast door I tell him the soldiers are headed for The Greenbrier.

'West Virginia?'

I nod.

He drops the pistol into the snow, scoops up a handful of powder and starts scrubbing his fingers with it, like that might somehow help. I keep the rifle trained on him while I explain the rest of it.

'There's five of them. I reckon they'll be somewhere along I-81 by now. Angus and Hamish are coming down the Catoctin Mountain Highway. They'll tell you everything I just did, save you going all the way back to check.' I nod in the direction of the gate. 'You'd best be on your way, now, before you lose any more of the light. There's a farmhouse almost at the end of the ridge road, maybe a quarter mile back from the highway. It's your best bet for shelter.'

He wipes his hand on the front of his parka and pulls on a mitten.

'That's twice I've underestimated you now, Gabriel. Best you don't count on there being a third.'

He squeezes through the gate and joins the others. I watch as they hike up towards the control tower, and then one by one disappear into the gathering darkness. I stay like that for a while, just staring after them. At last I lower the rifle, sling it over my shoulder. Without something to occupy them my hands take to shaking. I have to press them together to get them to stop.

'I'm not planning on ever seeing you again, Randall.'

*

'HAVE THEY GONE?'

I turn around to see Mags and the kid standing behind me. I guess my attention must have been elsewhere; I didn't hear either of them coming back through the tunnel.

'Yeah, I think so.'

She looks past me, out to the control tower. I bend down to pick up the pistol Peck discarded. I wipe the snow from it then thumb the button to eject the magazine and slip it into my parka. I rack the slide to clear the round in the chamber, just like Hicks showed me, and pocket that too. The gun's safe, but I spend a while longer fussing with it. There's a question that needs asking, I know it; I'm just not sure I'm ready for the answer. In the end I just blurt it out.

'Mags, what happened in there, with Kurt?'

The kid tilts his head to her, then back at me. She opens her mouth as if to respond, then stops and looks over my shoulder, back into the tunnel. For a long while there's nothing and I'm working up the courage to ask her again, but then I hear footsteps, drifting up out of the darkness. They grow steadily stronger until at last I see the beam from a flashlight, jittering around the curve of the tunnel.

She turns and makes her way over to the mangled gate, leaving my question unanswered. The kid looks up at me then scurries off after her, just as Jake's bulk separates itself from the darkness. He stops next to me, his chest heaving, like he's been running. His hair's still wet from the lake and blood trickles slowly from a cut above his eyebrow. More of it oozes from his lip.

'You okay?'

He keeps his eyes forward, on the gate, where Mags is standing with the kid.

'I'm fine.'

'You should head back inside, have someone take a look at those.'

'I said I'm fine, Gabriel.'

His voice is terse, like somehow what I've just said has annoyed him.

I slip Peck's pistol into the pocket of my parka.

'Alright, but turn that off if you mean to stay.' I point to the flashlight he's carrying. 'If anyone's still out there it'll give them something to aim at.'

Out at the gate the kid shakes his head.

'It's okay. The dangerous man's gone. They've all gone.'

Jake stares at him for a second, like this pronouncement hasn't eased his mind any. He kills the flashlight, returns it to his pocket. Mags turns to face us.

'Do you think they'll be back?'

I shake my head.

'No, at least not tonight. Did you see the look on Peck's face when he heard Gilbey's name? He knows her.' I turn to Jake. 'We should have someone stand watch, though, just in case.'

His eyes narrow at the suggestion.

'We *were* posting guards, Gabriel.'

I'm not sure what I've done to piss him off; I'm pretty sure I just saved everyone. But right now I have other things on my mind. I hold my hands up.

'Hey, I never said you weren't. There was nothing you could have done anyway. Peck had the code for the blast door, and they had guns.'

He looks down at the snow and grunts, but he doesn't seem mollified.

Mags makes her way back from the gate. She stops in front of Jake and looks up at the cuts on his face. 'Gabe's right, you should have someone take a look at those. We'll take first watch, right Gabe?'

'Sure.'

The truth is I'm exhausted, but my nerves are still jumping; I suspect it'll be a while before I've any chance of sleep. And I need some time alone with her now, to find out what just happened in the cavern.

'Are you sure you're okay?'

I open my mouth to tell him I'm good, but then realize the question wasn't meant for me.

She nods.

'I'm fine.'

'So you're not…?'

'Infected? No, not any more. I was, but Gabe got me back to Eden in time.'

He glances over at me, then goes back to staring at her. Eventually he says: *Okay, then* but makes no move to go back inside. I pull my parka tighter around me.

'Jake, can you send Tyler and Eric out to relieve us in an hour?'

He doesn't say anything and at first I'm not sure he's heard me. When at last he delivers his answer he does it without taking his eyes off Mags.

'We had a roster worked out. They pulled a shift earlier.'

'Well, get them to do another. Unless there's someone else in there you think can be trusted with a rifle?'

It comes out a little harsher than I intend, but it's not getting any warmer out here. And there's something about the way he's looking at Mags that's starting to piss me off now, too.

He looks at me like he means to argue some more, but then Mags steps between us, rests a hand on his arm.

'Please, Jake.'

His eyes drop to her hand and the fight seems to go out of him. He nods once, says *Alright*, then turns and walks off into the tunnel.

*

THE CONTROL TOWER LOOMS over us as we make our way up to it from the portal. The door at the base is open; it creaks as it shifts back and forth in the wind. I step inside, digging in my pocket for the flashlight while Mags and the kid start up the narrow steps. I crank the handle, but as the bulb starts to glow it splits, swims in my vision. My head grows suddenly light and for a second it feels like whatever has been keeping me going since The Greenbrier, it might choose now to desert me. I reach for the handrail, hold it for a half-dozen breaths, then follow Mags and the kid up the stair.

The smell of smoke hits me as I climb the last steps and when I sweep the observation deck with the flashlight the beam finds the blackened remains of a fire in the center. Mags is already at work rebuilding it from wood that's been stacked nearby, so I make my way over to one of the large windows that lean outward from the consoles beneath.

I cup a hand to my brow and peer through the glass, already beginning to realize the futility of the task I've assigned us. In daylight from up here you'd be able to see every part of the compound, but now it's dark I can't even make out the tattered windsock by the helicopter landing pad, not twenty yards from the base of the tower.

The kid clambers up onto the workstation next to me. I catch his reflection in the darkened glass and for a moment I study him, just squatting there on his haunches. It doesn't mean anything, I know; I guess he just got used to sitting that way from all the time he spent in one of Gilbey's cages. But crouched like that, the pale skin stretched over his bare scalp, the deep shadows that still circle his eyes and darken his sunken cheeks, he reminds me of the thing that attacked Ortiz, in the basement of the hospital, in Blacksburg. I shiver inside my parka, an involuntary action not entirely prompted by how cold it is up here. If the kid notices he doesn't let on. He presses his face closer to the glass.

'What are you looking for?'

'Any sign Peck's coming back.'

He looks up at me.

'Which way will he come?'

I point towards the far side of the compound, in the direction of the steel gate.

'That way, I think.'

He looks puzzled.

'You mean where we came in, earlier?'

I nod.

'It's over there.'

He raises an arm, one small mitten extending to a spot to the right of where I know the guardhouse to be. I open my mouth to correct him. I can't see the gate now, of course, but I've been here all winter and I know this place like the back of my hand. But then I remember tracking the soldiers as they took the Fairfax Pike off I-81, and how he had been able to follow Jax's prints in the snow, long after I had lost them.

I stare out into the featureless darkness.

'Johnny, what can you see out there?'

He looks up at me again, like he doesn't understand. Then he just says: 'Everything.'

Mags has a fire going, so I make my way over to it while the kid keeps watch from his perch up on the workstation. There's a crate of MREs sitting next to the firewood. I pick a couple from the top, open them up, shake out the contents. I get the chemical heaters working on the food pouches then I toss the kid a HOOAH! He doesn't seem fond of regular rations, but since he came through the scanner he seems to like the candy bars just fine. He snatches it from the air and busies himself with the wrapper. As soon as he's got it open he takes a bite and goes back to staring out of the window.

When the heaters are done hissing I tear the top off one of the pouches and start poking around at what's inside. The question I asked down by the portal went unanswered, and I haven't yet worked myself up to asking it again. I keep glancing over at Mags. She doesn't seem much interested in her food either. After a while she sets the MRE aside and reaches for the chain around her neck. She pulls out Truck's dog tags, turns them over in her fingers. The light from the fire plays over the metal. It's dull, tarnished by age, but otherwise fine, with no sign of the virus.

'You want to know what happened, back in the cavern.'

I nod.

'I don't know. It was weird. When I saw what they were doing to Jake, up on the roof, I got so mad. I …' She pauses, like she's searching for the right words. 'Part of me knew what I was doing, and that it was stupid. But I was so angry.' She hesitates again. 'I just couldn't help myself.'

She looks at me for a moment and then away, and I get the feeling that whatever she's told me isn't the whole of it. I glance over at the kid. He's staring down from his perch on the workstation, like he's suddenly developed an interest in the conversation we're having. She slips the tags back inside her thermals.

'I'm sorry.'

'It's okay. It all worked out.'

She shakes her head.

'It's not, though. We need to be smarter than that. *I* need to be smarter than that.'

I'm not sure what to say, so I don't say anything. She picks up her mug, swirls the coffee.

'What do you think it means?'

Truth is I'm not sure. I tell myself her anger has always been a quick thing, long as I've known her. It can burn hot and high, like a gasoline fire, but it dies down after just as fast. There's a small, faithless voice inside my head that's not content with that explanation, however. It starts to whisper that this was different. I hush it and it goes quiet for a moment, but then it shows me an image: her standing over Kurt, like an animal over its kill, transfixed by the sight of the blood spilling from between his fingers.

She's looking at me, waiting for my answer. I reach for the empty MRE carton, feed it to the fire. The cardboard curls, blackens as it's consumed.

'I don't think it means anything. You're fine, the tags prove it.' I say it with confidence, like there could be no doubt. But I can already hear the voice inside my head, getting ready with its next objection. I have no interest in hearing it, so I keep talking.

'It's been two days now, more than enough time for the virus to show. If it's anything it's probably just an aftereffect of being infected. I suspect Gilbey could tell you.'

I realize I've started to babble so I stop.

She looks into the flames then raises the mug to her lips, drains the last of her coffee, sets it on the ground.

'Let's not go back and ask her.'

There's a silence that stretches on for longer than it ought, and then from somewhere below the groan of a door being opened, followed by the sound of boots climbing the stair. A few moments later Tyler and Eric appear, bundled up in their parkas, their breath smoking in the cold. Tyler steps into the observation deck, but Eric hangs back by the door.

I get to my feet. My legs have stiffened, sitting by the fire; they protest as I stretch them out.

'Sorry to make you guys pull another shift.'

Tyler holds up a hand. When he smiles his teeth are surprisingly white against his ebony skin.

'It's all good, Gabe. I reckon Eric and me were next in line for the treatment Jake was getting. We were glad you showed up when you did.'

His gaze shifts to the windows and for the first time he notices the kid, crouched on one of the consoles underneath. The smile falters.

'Not sure what you expect us to see out there, though.'

I step over to where Johnny's looking out through one of the large panes and tap him on the shoulder, tell him to shift over. He looks up at me, like he doesn't understand: there's windows on all sides; I could choose any of them to look out of. I want the Guardians to see I'm not nervous of him, though, so when he doesn't move I shoo him out of the way. He shuffles across to the next console, goes back to staring out. I lean closer to the glass, but all I can see is my own reflection there. I cup a mitten to it. It makes no difference. Beyond there's only impenetrable blackness.

'Yeah, I'm sorry. When I asked Jake to send you out I hadn't thought it through.'

Tyler keeps his eyes on the kid a moment longer, like he's still distracted by him, then they return to me.

'No worries, Gabe. Like I said, we were just happy to see you.'

I start to make my way back to the fire, but then an idea comes to me. I turn to the kid.

'Johnny, how're you feeling?'

He looks at me uncertainly.

'Okay.'

'Not too tired?'

He shakes his head.

'Want to keep Tyler and Eric company for a while?'

He hesitates for a moment and then nods, but I catch the two former Guardians exchanging a look. Eric steps away from the door.

'Nah, Gabe it's okay. Really. We can manage.'

Tyler turns to me.

'Gabe, seriously, we got this. Sounds like you guys have had a long day. I'm sure…Johnny…needs his rest.'

The kid stares at me with those solemn eyes, waiting for a decision. The Guardians really don't want to be left with him and I can't say as I blame them; I'd be nervous too if I'd just met him. At least Tyler used his name, which is more than he got from me on our first encounter. What Mags said earlier is right, though: we need to be smarter now, and having someone up here who can actually see would make a lot of sense. The wind picks up, gusts against the glass. Peck's not coming back tonight, however. I'll give it a couple of days, let them get used to him; maybe catch Tyler by himself, explain the situation. I beckon the kid down.

'C'mon Johnny, let's go back inside.'

He jumps off the console and hurries over to stand next to Mags.

I take one last look out into the darkness and then make my way towards the door.

*

MY LEGS HAVE SEIZED worse than I thought; I hobble down the control tower's stair, clutching the railing for support. Mags asks if I'm okay, but I tell her I'm fine; just a little sore from the hike. The truth is we pushed hard getting back here; hotfooting it all the way from Eden has taken more of a toll than I had figured.

She holds the door open for me at the bottom and I follow her back to the tunnel, jealous of her easy, loose-limbed gait. I watch as she slips effortlessly through the ruined guillotine gate. I squeeze myself between the charred, twisted bars, wincing as I stand on the other side. She holds an arm out, says I can lean on her, but I shake my head and tell her I'll be fine; the walk will do me good, stretch out the muscles in my legs a little. The truth is I just want to snap my fingers and be back in our apartment.

She sets off into the darkness, the kid trotting along beside her. I flick on the flashlight and limp after them. The tunnel seems to have lengthened since I walked it with Peck earlier, but at last we reach the blast door. I shuffle through, leaving her to close it up. Just a little further and then I'll be able to take off my boots, lie down in a bed, *an actual bed*, and sleep for as long as I care.

But as I step into the glare from the cavern's arc lights it's clear that's not going to happen. All the Juvies are there, like they've been waiting for us to return. As soon as they see me they rush forward. Only Jake hangs back. He's changed his bloodied t-shirt but there's a sullen bruise spreading across his cheek and his lip's already swelling up where Peck or one of the Guardians split it. He stares at me like these things, and whatever else might currently be ailing him, I'm the certain cause of it.

The Juvies crowd around, bombarding me with questions.

'Where's Peck?

'Is he gone?'

'Will he be coming back?'

I close my eyes for a moment, letting their questions wash over me. I'm a little overwhelmed; I don't know who to answer first. But then suddenly everyone goes quiet. I turn around. Mags is standing at the entrance to the cavern, and for a second I see her as they must: head shaved; cheeks sunken, hollowed; the shadows under her eyes, still dark enough to convince Peck she was carrying the virus. The kid appears beside her. He looks even worse; like a fury in miniature. He slips back behind her leg, clearly uncomfortable with the attention. She reaches for his hand and the Juvies part quickly to let them through. I catch her eye as she passes; their reaction hasn't gone unnoticed. She takes Johnny over to where Jake's standing by himself. There's a long pause and then the clamor starts up again.

'Where did you go?'

'Were you really back in Eden?'

'What's happened to Kane?'

'Is it true Quartermaster's dead?'

I hold my hand up for quiet and the chatter dies. Answering their questions piecemeal is going to take forever; it'll be quicker if I start at the beginning. I lower myself to the sidewalk. When the last of them have settled around me I take a deep breath and begin. I tell them about the soldiers following our tracks to the high school in Rockbridge, and how we went back with them to The Greenbrier and met Dr. Gilbey. There are a few gasps when I recount what Gilbey had been doing to survivors who'd had the misfortune to make their way there, and when I get to the bit where she put Mags in a cage and infected her with the virus they all shift around and take to staring at her again.

I press on quickly, describing how we escaped and fled to Eden so she and Johnny could go through the scanner and be cured. I linger on that detail for a while, letting it sink in, but I notice more than one head turning in her direction, like they may not trust the work I've told them the machine's done. I finish with how Mags saved us from Hicks and the other soldiers, but in my version she spends a lot more time skulking around in tunnels and far less bursting out of them like Wonder Woman. When I'm done an uncomfortable silence settles, and for a long moment I'm not sure how to break it. In the end it's Lauren who does it for me. She stands up, offering me a broad smile.

'Well, we're just relieved you made it back safely, Gabe.'

Her voice is calm, assured; her eyes bright, clear. It looks like she may even have found time to run a brush through her hair. The Juvies all turn to look at her, and I realize I'm not the only one who's shocked, and not just by the transformation from the shell-shocked stupor I witnessed earlier. I think that might be more words than I've heard Lauren speak all in one go, long as I've known her. Eden wasn't exactly a social place, of course; between work, chapel and curfew there wasn't a lot of time left for just shooting the breeze. Not that you'd ever accuse Lauren of that. She always made a point of sitting apart in the mess, her head down over her food; as soon as she was done she'd hurry back to her cell, long before the buzzer had a chance to announce curfew. I can't remember her showing up for movie night either, except when it was her turn to be custodian of the disc, and even then often as not she'd just hand it over and disappear. I suppose I'd always assumed she was a little like me; just not one of those kids who was, as Miss Kimble put it in what would turn out to be my last ever end-of-term report, *well integrated socially*.

She presses her hands together and turns to Mags.

'You too of course, Mags.'

I feel a sudden rush of gratitude to her for that. She looks down at Johnny, adopting the tone you'd use for a shy three-year-old.

'And what's your name?'

The kid just stares back solemnly.

'I don't know.'

Her smile doesn't falter, but I'm not sure she knows what to make of his answer. He looks at her for a moment and then he tilts his head and his nostrils flare, like he's scenting the air. And for an instant it puts me in mind of the fury that was waiting for me outside, in the tunnel, when I first came here. It's a subtle gesture, though, barely perceptible. I don't think anyone's noticed.

The kid studies her a moment longer.

'You needn't be scared. I won't hurt you.'

Lauren lets out a nervous laugh, like he's said something funny. I glance around at the Juvies. If the kid's intention was to put them at ease I'm not sure it's worked. I quickly add that we've been calling him Johnny.

Lauren studies him a moment longer. The smile remains, but it seems a shade less certain than it was a few moments before. Then she turns to me and her face suddenly grows serious.

'You warned us this would happen, Gabe. You said Kane would send Peck, but we didn't pay attention. I think we all might be more willing to listen now.' She looks around, gathering support from the faces assembled around her. To my surprise I see heads nodding, murmurs of agreement. 'So tell us, what should we do?'

Twenty-three young faces swivel in my direction, waiting for an answer. Even Jake seems keen to hear what I have to say. I'm a little taken aback. I wasn't expecting to be having this discussion, here, now, in front of everyone. Tell the truth I'm not sure what we should do. Before The Greenbrier I was pretty certain we needed to leave. But a lot has changed since then. I tell Lauren the only thing I can: I don't know.

It's obvious this isn't an answer the Juvies care much for. For the next few moments they're all talking over each other.

'But you've been out there.'

'You escaped from Gilbey and the soldiers.'

'And you got rid of Peck.'

'He'll be back.'

'Should we leave?'

'Where should we go?'

'Just tell us what to do.'

'Yes, tells us.'

I close my eyes. Right now I just want to lie down and sleep for as long as I can. It's Lauren who comes to my rescue once again. She holds her hand up for silence.

'We're being unfair. Gabe's obviously tired.' She looks around at the Juvies, and then back to me, offering another smile. 'Why don't we let you sleep on it? I'm sure you'll have thought of something by the morning.'

And just like that I hear myself saying that I will.

*

I SLEEP LATE for the first time in weeks. When I finally wake I lie there for a long while with my eyes closed, counting up all the places it hurts. At last I gather up the strength to lift my head and look around the tiny apartment. Mags is long gone; only the faintest aroma of the coffee she made earlier still lingers. I let my head fall back to the pillow. It feels like my entire body's been worked over with a hammer. I don't understand: we both made the same hike. How come she isn't she suffering like I am?

The low, faithless voice inside my head has an answer for that, but I hush it before it gets the chance to give it. I reach one hand up for the chain around my neck, follow it down to the tags I wear, run my fingers over the pressed metal. Still smooth, and this is the third day. If the scanner hadn't done its work it'd be showing by now.

I lie there a few minutes longer, then I drag myself out of bed and limp into the shower. For a long time I just stand under the steaming jets, letting the scalding water soothe my aching muscles. When I step out I feel a little better. I towel myself dry and grab a clean t-shirt and a set of overalls from the closet, the first fresh things I've had on in days.

I gather up the clothes I left strewn across the floor on my way to bed the night before. My parka feels heavier than it should. I lift the flap on the big outer pocket and take out the Beretta Peck dropped in the snow the night before. I turn it over in my hands. Ash has dried on the metal from where it fell in the snow. More will have found its way inside; it'll need to be stripped and cleaned. Hicks would have had me do it soon as I got back last night, but there was no way that was happening; I barely made it to the bed before I passed out.

I reach for the backpack and lift out the pistol I took from him, still wrapped in the gun belt. I unravel it slowly. The leather's worn, stained dark from years of use. I draw the gun from the holster and run my fingers over the metal, dull with age, the dark carrion bird scrimshawed into the yellowing handle. The etching looks like it's been done by hand. I wonder if it was him who carved it, or someone before.

I turn it over in my hands. Compared to the Beretta it looks ancient; an antique. I asked him once why he'd chosen something so old for a weapon. His answer was simple: he said it was because when he needed it to, he knew it'd work. Bitter cold or blazing heat didn't matter much to a gun like that, he said. It'd been riding on somebody's hip for the best part of a hundred years, and if there was anyone left in another hundred it'd probably be doing the same. I slip the pistol into its holster, roll the belt around it, then return it to my pack.

The clock on the stove says it's noon. My stomach sends an audible reminder that I haven't yet had breakfast, and that needs tending to, as a matter of urgency. I check the cupboards but of course they're bare, so I head out into the cavern and make my way over to the mess.

It doesn't occur to me until after I've pulled the door back that this might have been a mistake; it's lunchtime, and most of the Juvies are here. They all look up as I enter. I remember too late the promise I gave: that I'd have an answer for them as to what we should do. I glance over my shoulder. I feel like turning tail, but it's already too late for that. So instead I step inside, making my way quickly between the tables to join the end of the food line.

Things have calmed down a little from last night, but still everywhere I look someone's smiling or saying hi. It's a little weird; I'm not used to this much attention. Back in Eden there were a few moments in the sun, figuratively speaking of course, like when I started going outside with Marv. Everyone wanted to know how that was, at least at first. And then later, when I brought us here. That brief burst of popularity didn't last very long either, though; I lost it not long after we arrived, trying to convince them we needed to run away again. But now it's like there's been a poll overnight and I've just been elected President.

I grab an MRE from the stack on the counter, then stand in line for one of the microwaves. Amy insists I go in front of her and won't take no for an answer, so I smile a thank you and then pop the food pouch in and twist the dial. It pings to let me know it's ready and then I beat a hasty retreat for the farthest table. I pick a spot at the end and sit down, hoping to be left alone. I've barely freed the plastic fork from its wrapper when I hear a screech as the chair opposite's pulled back.

'Hey, sleepyhead.'

I look up to see Lauren setting her food down. She flicks her hair over one shoulder and sits, offering me a smile, and once again I'm struck by how different she is, not just from the Lauren Kurt dragged to her feet last night, but from the Juvie I knew before. Back in Eden we all spent a lot of time discussing who our matches might be; it was pretty much the only game in town as far as conversations went, unless you wanted to hear how many brace bolts someone had tightened that day, or the state of the plastic skirting on the growing benches over at the farms. Everyone had a list, a top five, and who should or shouldn't be on it was the subject of near-continuous debate. Lauren never made mine, and I don't recall her ever featuring on anyone else's either. Looking at her now, for the life of me I can't understand why, though. Somehow, whether by accident or design, she just managed to spend all those years in our collective blind spot.

I mumble hello and then turn my attention back to my Shredded BBQ Beef. She looks over at the carton and then holds hers up.

'Hey, snap!'

She opens the flap and starts arranging the packets neatly in front of her.

'So I stopped by this morning, but Mags said we should let you rest.'

I spear a strip of beef and say something about being pretty tired. Lauren murmurs sympathetically, but then her eyes shift up and down the table, as though she's checking whether anyone's in earshot. She leans forward, lowering her voice.

'Are you sure she's okay, Gabe? Mags, I mean. She doesn't look well.'

I nod.

'She was pretty sick, after Gilbey gave her the virus. That's why we had to go back to Eden, so she could go through the scanner. She's fine now.' Lauren stares at me across the table, doubtful. I feel the need to add something. 'The virus can't survive that.'

I say it with more certainty than I feel. Lauren doesn't seem convinced either.

'It's just that yesterday, that thing with Kurt. She seemed, well, a little strange.'

Crap. Most of the Juvies had been on their knees, their eyes fixed on the ground, and I had hoped that had gone unnoticed. Lauren had been on her feet, of course, but she'd seemed pretty out of it. I guess not as much as I'd thought.

'She was just mad about what they were doing to Jake. You know how Mags can be.'

She nods, but she still seems unsure.

'She's fine, Lauren. Trust me.'

Her eyes dart down the table again.

'But how can you be so certain?'

I put down the fork and reach inside my t-shirt for the dog tags. I hold them up for her to see.

'We each wear these. The metal shows the virus. I check hers every day. If she was sick I'd know it.'

She reaches across the table. Her fingers hover in the air for a second, like she's unsure, and then she runs them over the pressed steel.

'Who was Private…Kavanagh?' She pronounces it slow, one syllable at a time.

'One of the soldiers we ran into.'

She looks into my face and her eyes brighten.

'A soldier. And you took them from him.'

I doubt she'd be as impressed if she got a look at Boots, or if I told her it was all Mags' doing anyway, so I keep those bits of the story to myself. She stares at the tags a moment longer and then lets them go. I lift the chain and slip it back inside my t-shirt, feeling the metal settle against my chest. Her eyes linger there for a moment and then she looks up at me again.

'So have you had a chance to think about what we do now?'

Truth is I've still got no idea, but I find myself saying I've had a few thoughts.

'Great. After lunch I'll get everyone together so we can hear them.'

*

I FINISH EATING and set off in search of Mags.

I meet Leonard on the far side of the lake, coming out of one of the tunnels. He almost runs right into me, like something's got him spooked. I ask him if he's seen her. He glances over his shoulder, jabs a finger back in the direction he's just come, then hurries off towards Main Street, like he has urgent business there.

I find her over in the fire station, showing Johnny the tender. The kid sees me first. He gives me a wave then goes back to staring at his reflection in the fire engine's huge chromed wheels. She looks up, offers me a smile. The shadows around her eyes are still there, but they seem a little better than they were yesterday. The whispering voice inside my head isn't happy with that, however. It reminds me of what I saw by the lake. I remind myself what I told her, last night: whatever happened with Kurt, it wasn't important; just an aftereffect of being infected. But somehow that explanation doesn't seem to have gained traction in the hours since I first gave it; it seems no more plausible under the glare of the arc lights than it did up in the darkness of the control tower.

She slips her hands into the pockets of her overalls.

'I was beginning to wonder if we'd see you today.'

'Yeah, I was pretty beat. Weren't you tired?'

She shrugs.

'Not really. I got a couple of hours' sleep, then Johnny and I went out to relieve Tyler and Eric. Jake came out at first light and warmed up a couple of MREs for us.'

I guess I should be happy she's eating, but for some reason the news that it's Jake who's fixing her breakfast doesn't make me feel that way. I turn away before those unpleasant thoughts have a chance to show on my face.

'Everything okay?'

'Um, sure.' I can see she's not buying it, though, and I don't care to admit to her what's really bothering me, so I switch topic before she can figure it out.

'Hey, is it just me, or does everyone seem a little weird since we got back?'

'How so?'

'I dunno; it's like everyone suddenly wants to be my friend.'

Even as I say it I remember how the Juvies had looked at her last night, when she came back in; how quickly they had parted to let her through. We both take to staring at the kid while I search for something to say. He seems oblivious, still mesmerized by his own reflection. He reaches up to touch the chrome, but before his fingers can get there she takes hold of his hand.

'We're not going to touch things, remember? At least not for a few more days.'

He looks up at her and nods, then goes back to studying the hubcap.

'Lauren stopped by earlier, while you were sleeping.'

'I know. I just ran into her in the mess. She's going to organize a meeting this afternoon, so I can tell everyone what to do.'

Mags raises an eyebrow.

'Lauren? Organizing a meeting? With people?'

'I know, right? I guess she's got a point, though. Peck's not gone for good, and I doubt Gilbey's forgotten about us either.'

'So what are you going to say?'

I shake my head.

'I'm not sure. Hicks knows we're here, and now Peck does too. We have to assume that at some point one of them's going to be back for us.'

She doesn't say anything for a while, like she's thinking. Then she reaches into the pocket of her overalls and fishes out the map we took from Peck. She unfolds it, holding it up to the fire truck's flank. I take a step closer.

'What are you looking for?'

She points a finger at the sole location marked there – ours. Next to it a single twelve-digit code, the letters and numbers scrawled across highways and mountain ranges in Kane's spiky script. She turns to me like I should get the significance, but I don't.

'It looks like our President didn't trust his Secret Service agent with more than one code.' She looks up at me. 'And you've got his master list, the one with all the others written on it.'

I nod. The list I retrieved from the command building, just before we left Eden, is back in our apartment, sitting in the inside pocket of my parka, next to the map Marv gave me. And for a second I allow myself to believe it. We might be safe here. But then I shake my head. Truth is we've never been that lucky.

'He's bound to have made a copy.'

'Maybe.' She says it like she's not so sure.

'If he has we've got to assume he'll give it up, if he hasn't already.'

She folds the map and slides it back into her pocket.

'So where do we go? Fearrington?'

'It's the only place we know anything about.'

'But?'

'I don't know. I was all in favor of it before, when we thought it was only Kane we had to worry about. Now there's Gilbey, too. With all the questions I asked she'll have no problem figuring out that's where we'll go next. And if Kane gives her the codes we'll be no safer there than here.'

I stare at the dusty concrete. The Juvies are expecting an answer from me, and I'm no closer to giving it to them.

She hesitates a moment, like she has something to say.

'What is it Mags? If you have any suggestions I'd be sure happy to hear them.'

*

THE JUVIES GATHER BY THE LAKE, in the same spot where the night before they had knelt and watched Jake being interrogated. They arrive in ones and twos, taking their places by the water's edge. There seems no order to it, and yet when they're done somehow Mags has ended up off to one side with the kid, separated by a wide stretch of concrete that does not seem of her choosing. The Juvies chat quietly among themselves, but every now and then I catch one of them cutting a nervous glance in her direction.

Jake's the last to arrive; I spot him on the far side of the lake, making his way back from the farms. There's a fresh bandage above his eye and the bruise that had begun on his cheek has sunken into the socket, lending him the appearance of a large, muscle-bound raccoon. He takes a seat next to Mags, close enough that it annoys me.

I give him a chance to settle and then I get to my feet. The last of the conversations die and an expectant silence takes their place. I let my gaze roam the familiar faces. We sure don't look like much, huddled beneath the massive granite expanse of the cavern's dome. But this is it; all of us except Tyler and Eric, who are outside standing watch. I went out to the control tower earlier and set out for them the choices I now plan to lay out for the rest of the Juvies, so they'd have the same say as everyone else. When I was done Tyler was quiet for a while, like he was considering everything I'd just told him. I was expecting questions, but all he said was he was fine with whatever I reckoned was for the best. Eric plumped for that option too, although I think that was mostly because it was what Tyler had just said. That wasn't how I meant it to go, but if nothing else it gave me a chance to rehearse what I plan to say now. I clear my throat and begin.

'Well, there's been no sign of Peck, so I guess it's safe to assume he's gone, at least for now.'

Murmurs of relief greet that news. I wait for a moment for things to go quiet again.

'I doubt it's the last we'll hear from him, though, so we need to work out what we do next. As I see it we have a couple of options. But before we get into that I think we need to agree on something. There's only twenty-four of us left.'

That earns me a bunch of confused looks. Reading might not be their strong suit, but there's so few of us we all know what our number is, and since we quit Eden it's been twenty-three. I hear someone whisper *the little fury*, but I don't catch who says it. Mags shoots a look in Ryan's direction, but if he notices he has the good sense not to return it. Everyone else turns to stare at the kid who promptly takes to studying the square of concrete between his feet.

I raise my voice and continue on.

'So whatever we choose, we have to agree that we all stick together.'

That was Mags' idea. She didn't think it should be up to me or anyone else to tell the Juvies what to do next, however much they might appear to want it. It was high time they got used to making decisions for themselves, she said, although it probably made sense to start with an easy one, on account of how little practice they'd had in recent years. That was smart; I see it now. All around me heads are nodding in agreement, like they're pleased with themselves. I pause to let that sink in before I go on.

'Okay, well, our choices are pretty simple: we can stay right here and see what happens, or try and find another home.'

'Shouldn't we just go, before they comes back?' Amy looks around plaintively, as though in spite what I said at the outset she expects Peck to reappear at any moment. Jake just shakes his head.

'That's what we're here to discuss, Amy.'

Lauren glances over in his direction and for a second I see her eyes narrow, like somehow what he's said has vexed her. But when she turns back to me her features have softened again.

'So where would we go, Gabe?'

'Well, Marv's map has the location of a half-dozen bunkers, but I think it comes down to just one: a place called Fearrington. It's the only one we know anything about, and besides, the rest are all much farther away.'

'So where is it?'

'North Carolina.'

A few vague glimmers of recognition greet that piece of information, but mostly all I get are blank stares. Kane never showed much interest in our education, and geography was certainly no exception to that; so long as we could find the farms and the chapel that was about as much as he cared for. Perhaps we should be grateful for small mercies. Who knows what he might have taught us otherwise? A man like that that, it's quite possible he believes the world's flat and dragons patrol Virginia's southern borders.

Ryan asks how far it is. I catch Amy glancing over at the entrance to the cavern, like depending on my answer she might be considering setting off right after we're done here. The map is in my pocket, but I don't need to take it out to give him an answer. I've already worked out the route we'd take. US15 would certainly be quickest - it's pretty much a straight shot. But that would bring us uncomfortably close to The Greenbrier. I have no idea how things will play out between Peck and Hicks, but whichever of them prevail it won't be long before they come looking for us, and we certainly can't risk running into them on the road. So instead we'll head out east to hook up with I-95, which we can follow south as far as Richmond. From Richmond I-85 will take us almost all the way there. It's longer, and mostly interstate, so the pickings along the way will be slim, but it'll be safer. I tell Ryan the best part of three hundred miles.

I see the Juvies exchanging nervous glances. I guess that must sound like a distance. Probably because it is.

'How long would it take?'

I figure Mags and I could do it in ten days. Maybe less, if I could find a way to match the pace she's been showing since she came through the scanner. The Juvies won't travel anything like that fast, however, at least not judging by how long it took us to make it here from Eden.

'Three weeks, give or take.'

More uncertain looks. That's twice as long as it took us to get here, and none of them recall that journey with any affection. They all remember fleeing Eden, though, the fear they had felt stepping out into icy wind, snow that had stung like needles. And later, when the storms had chased us off the road, cowering in an abandoned gas station or trash-strewn bank lobby while the lightning split the sky outside. Most haven't set foot beyond the portal since we first arrived.

'Winter's over now, though. If we decide to leave it's as good a time as any to go.'

I say it with a reassuring smile, but it doesn't seem to work. I see Lauren casting her eye over the assembled faces, gauging their reactions.

'How long before Peck comes back, Gabe?'

I shrug.

'I can't say. I'm not even sure it'll be Peck who comes back.'

She gets to her feet.

'But somebody will come for us, right? If not Peck then those soldiers.' She looks around at the faces now staring up at her. 'The ones who infected Mags with the virus, who put her in a cage?'

The Juvies all turn to Mags as she says it, but I keep my eye on Lauren. I see what she's doing. The Juvies are scared of the outside; no amount of comforting words is likely to overcome that, and she knows it. She plans to give them something else instead, something to be even more afraid of. She looks at me, waiting for an answer to her question.

'Yes, I believe so. Someone will be back.'

'Then we should leave. Soon, before they get here.'

Jake shoots her a disgruntled look.

'Sit down, Lauren. We haven't decided we're going anywhere yet.'

Even now, part of me expects her to retake her seat. The Lauren we all knew before would have done just that. But then that Lauren wouldn't ever have gotten to her feet in the first place.

She turns to face him, and for a second I almost feel sorry for Jake.

'Haven't you been paying attention, Jake? It's not safe here.'

'You think I don't know that?' He points to the spot by the water's edge where the Guardians had held him down. 'It was me there, last night, Lauren, not you.'

'Then you should know better than anyone we can't stay here. Peck could be back any time, or if not him then someone worse. Gabe's already warned us once.'

Jake glances over at me, his face darkening with anger. He looks at Mags, like he might have something to say, but then he checks himself.

'We've just got the farms set up. If we leave now we'll be throwing away a harvest.'

Lauren throws her hands up in the air, like she can't believe what she's just heard. She lets out a bitter laugh.

'And *that's* what you care about? We don't even need the stupid harvest.'

Now Jake's on his feet as well.

'We thought we didn't need the harvest when we were back in Eden. But the food ran out there.'

Lauren just rolls her eyes and looks to me for support. The truth is she's sort of right. We don't need the harvest, at least not here; what's in the stores will last the few of us who are left several lifetimes, even if we're not careful with it. But that's also missing the point. The real question isn't whether we need the harvest *here*; it's whether we'll need it wherever we go next. Hicks said Fearrington was thirteen stories underground, which should be plenty big enough, but the truth is I have no idea how well provisioned it might be. Gilbey had planned to continue her work there, which I'm hoping means it was stocked for her arrival. But I have no idea for how many, or for how long.

From somewhere near the back Leonard slowly raises a hand, like we're back in Miss Kimble's class.

'What happens if we stay here and Peck comes back?'

Jake takes it on himself to answer.

'We'd have to defend this place.'

It's clear Lauren doesn't think much of this plan. She shakes her head.

'That didn't work well yesterday, did it?'

'We have guns now.'

'But none of us know how to use them.'

'Tyler and Eric do. So does Gabe.'

'And what chance do you think they would have against Peck? He's a Secret Service agent. He killed Benjamin, remember? And Marv. And they were soldiers.'

Jake's still on his feet.

'I'd rather face Peck than whatever else might be waiting for us out there.' He raises a finger and jabs it at me. 'Gabe took Mags out there and he almost got her killed.'

Some of the Juvies go back to staring at Mags, but most look at me. I feel my face redden. I don't have anything to say, because the truth of it is, Jake's right. Mags is looking out onto the lake, like she's trying to work something out. After a few seconds she turns back around and when she speaks again it's to me.

'Why don't you tell them what you know about Fearrington, Gabe? Maybe it'll help us all decide.'

'Yeah, what's it like?'

I clear my throat.

'Well, I've never been, obviously.'

That earns me a bunch of uncertain looks, and I realize it may not have been the best place to start. I press on quickly.

'We did learn a few things about it from the soldiers, though. It's an underground silo. It goes down a long way, but even so it'll be nowhere near as big as here. There aren't many of us, though, so it should be enough space.'

'And we can definitely get in?'

I nod.

'Yes, we can get in.'

Jake looks at me like he wouldn't take my word for it if I were to suggest the water in the lake behind him might be wet.

'You just said you've never been. You can't know that.'

I'm still stinging from his last comment, and now I feel myself growing angry. I take a deep breath, making an effort to keep it from showing in my voice.

'The codes on the map Marv gave me have worked everywhere else I've been. There's no reason they shouldn't work there too.'

Jake folds his arms across his chest, like he's not happy with that answer.

'But you don't know.'

Lauren shakes her head.

'What would you do, Gabe?'

The Juvies quiet down. I see the ones in the back leaning forward to listen.

'Well, we like it here; there's loads of space and more supplies than we need. I took Kane's codes with me from Eden, and we have the one he gave to Peck too, so maybe next time he comes he won't find it quite so easy to get in.' I look over at Mags, but her expression's hard to read. 'I wouldn't count on it, though. Kane might have made a copy, and even if he hasn't there's a chance Peck will remember the code.'

Jake snorts at that.

'That's nonsense. Those codes are way too long for anyone to remember.'

Afterwards I regret what I do next, but right then I can't help myself; it feels like I haven't been able to catch a break from him since we got back from The Greenbrier. I reach into the pocket of my overalls and take out the tattered roadmap with the *Standard Oil* logo on the cover.

'What's that?'

'It's Marv's map, the one with the entry codes for all the facilities in the Federal Relocation Arc written on it.' I hold it out to him.

He looks at it suspiciously, like he knows what's coming next. He doesn't want to take it, but he has little choice; everyone's eyes are on him now.

'Open it up.'

He unfolds it slowly.

'Choose one.'

He stares at me for a long moment and then turns his attention to the map. I watch as he studies each of the locations there, searching for the one to test me. At last he looks up and says *The Notch.*

The Notch is the codename for a bunker at a place called Bare Mountain, just outside a town called Hadley, Massachusetts. It's way north, certainly not anywhere I'd planned on us ever visiting. But that's okay. I've studied that map often enough over the winter that all I have to do is close my eyes and I can see the twelve numbers and letters written next to each of the locations marked on it. I call out the code he's asked for. When I'm done there's silence. I ask him if I've got it right.

He looks down at the map for a second, then starts to fold it up again.

'That doesn't prove anything.'

But now everyone's talking at once again.

'Peck still has the code.'

'He's bound to come back.'

'Or the soldiers.'

'They could already be on their way.'

'We need to leave, now.'

I glance over at Mags, but this time she doesn't meet my gaze. Lauren smiles triumphantly. I hold my hands up again for silence, only this time it's longer coming. At last things quiet down again.

'Has anybody got anything else to say?'

The Juvies look at each other but nobody speaks.

'Jake?'

He glares at me for a moment and then just shakes his head.

'I guess we should vote then. Everyone in favor of leaving raise your hand.'

Amy's arm's in the air almost before I've got the words out. Lauren raises hers too. Jake just shoves his hands into the pockets of his overalls. A couple of the Juvies who worked with him in the farms vote to stay too, but everyone else is in favor of quitting Mount Weather.

There's no need for a tally, but I do it anyway. Jake doesn't wait to hear the final result. He gets up while I'm still counting and marches off in the direction of the farms.

*

TWO DAYS LATER we gather by the lake again. This time there's little chatter. The Juvies wait, fiddling nervously with flashlights or adjusting the straps on their goggles, while Mags heads over to the plant room to power everything down. After a few minutes the faint background hum of the generator dies, leaving an eerie silence in its wake, and then one by one the arc lights blink out. There's a moment of darkness after the last of them shuts off and I hear a gasp that might be Amy, then the safeties kick in, bathing the cavern in their green glow.

We start making our way out. I wait at the blast door, standing to one side as they file by, leaning into the straps of their packs against the unfamiliar weight. I've loaded each till the seams were straining and the snaps would barely close. We have a long hike ahead of us, but if I've counted right we should be carrying enough for a return journey on short rations, should we need to make it.

The last of them leave and for a while I can still hear their footsteps, slowly receding as they shuffle off into the tunnel, and then it goes quiet again. I'm beginning to wonder where Mags has got to when she appears at the end of the corridor, pulling on a wool beanie. It's the first time I've seen her wearing one, but then her hair's yet to grow back and it'll be cold out there. The kid's got one too; he keeps reaching up to touch it, like it bothers him. She must have taken a detour to the stores, to pick them up. I would have fetched them for her, if she'd asked, but then I've hardly spoken to her since the vote. This last few days she's spent all her waking hours over at the plant. Seems like it's taken almost as long to shut Mount Weather down as it did to get it up and running.

I hit the button to start the close sequence. There's the shrill whine of electric motors, then the familiar grumble of gears as the blast door commences its final inbound journey. Mags steps past me, out into the tunnel. Her pack's no less full than the others', but if the weight troubles her she doesn't show it. The pockets of her parka bulge suspiciously, too. I told her we'd have to leave her books behind - they were a luxury we couldn't afford - but I suspect a few of her favorites from the bookshelf have managed to stow themselves away, all the same. The kid hurries through after, like he's worried we might choose this moment to leave him behind. I stand there for a while after they've gone, just staring back into the cavern. Everything seems just like it did when I first arrived. Soon it'll be like we were never here.

I take a final look then follow them out. The Juvies' lights are already stretching off into the dark, quivering like fireflies as they make their way towards the portal. The soft glow spilling out from behind the blast door shrinks as the thirty tons of carbon steel slowly rumbles inward. Mags reaches into the side pocket of her parka and retrieves a flashlight. She cranks the handle to get the bulb burning then holds it out to the kid. He looks up at her, like he's unsure what to do, and I think I catch something passing between them. But then he nods, a quick bob of the head, as though he's remembered, and takes it from her. Another dynamo whirs as she winds one for herself, then she looks over at me.

'Ready?'

'You go on. I have to fetch it.'

'Alright. Be careful.'

They start out after the others, and for a moment I just watch them. The kid holds his flashlight low, aimless, like he's already forgotten he has it. Mags points hers ahead, slowly sweeping the tunnel floor. But there's something measured, mechanical, in the way she does it. It makes me wonder whether she needs it any more than he does.

The pitch of the motor drops, then dies. Behind me the sliver of light from inside winks out as the blast door clangs shut for the last time. I dig the windup from my pocket and crank the handle, then set off in the opposite direction.

From the blast door I count two hundred paces then I point the beam up onto the raised walkway and start scanning the concrete there. A little further along I find what I'm looking for: a shallow pile of rubble, stacked indifferently against the tunnel wall. I clamber over the railing and start lifting rocks from the top until my fingers settle on the olive-drab plastic of a rifle case. Not the most secure hiding place, but then the Juvies wouldn't have it inside. I can't say as I blame them.

I keep clearing debris until the entire container's exposed, then I play the flashlight over it. The plastic's a little scratched but otherwise it appears intact, and when I run the beam along the seal the rubber seems to have held. I brush the dust from the two heavy-duty catches and check they're still tight. I don't plan on popping them; I already know what's inside: Kane's stockpile of the virus, stolen from the armory on the day we fled Eden. I'd rather not have to bring it with us, but I don't reckon we have a choice. Its whereabouts was one of the things Peck was trying to get out of Jake when we interrupted him, so there was the proof, if we'd needed any, that Kane hadn't just forgotten about it. We can't risk leaving it behind for him to find.

I clear the last of the rubble then reach for the handle and lift it upright. Sweat prickles the skin between my shoulder blades as I imagine the delicate glass tubes shifting in their trays, clinking against the hard plastic that holds them in place. I'll need to get used to that. I have a long way to haul it.

I adjust my grip on the handle and set off after the others.

It's not long till I see the Juvies' flashlights ahead of me again. Those in front are already starting to wink out, as one by one the beams are lost to the curve of the tunnel. Soon I can hear the boots of the stragglers, scuffing the dusty concrete. And then I'm rounding the bend. Ahead lies the portal.

Outside the first reluctant grays of dawn are spreading slowly through the compound. Mags and the kid stand by the mangled remains of the guillotine gate. Tyler and Eric wait on the other side, next to the elevated walkway, their breath smoking in the cold. Something about that sets spidey off, but as usual there's no explanation why he's fussing. The only thing I can figure is the rifles they each carry, slung over their shoulders, but somehow that doesn't seem like it.

The rest of the Juvies are huddled further back, inside the arch of the tunnel, staring out. No one seems keen to venture farther. I make my way between them. They look up at me as I pass, their faces tight, anxious. I catch Lauren's eye. She smiles but it's fleeting, uncertain, like even she might not be sure of the course upon which we're about to embark. It's not been two days since we decided, but I suspect if I were to call another vote, right now, we might end up turning around and going back inside.

And maybe that wouldn't be the worst decision.

Our destination is farther than I've ever been, and a long way from certain. What if Fearrington's not what I've assumed? What if we make it there and Marv's codes don't work? What if I can't even get us there?

The dark windows of the control tower stare down through the twisted bars. Behind, clouds the color of coal dust squat low along the spiny mountain ridge.

Mags comes to stand next to me. She asks if I'm ready.

I'm not sure I have an answer for her, so instead I grasp the charred metal and squeeze myself through.

*

IT TAKES US ALL OF THAT FIRST MORNING just to clear the Blue Ridge Mountain Road. We stop for lunch in a barn just off the John S Mosby highway. The Juvies huddle at the back and eat quickly, their eyes darting over to where Mags and the kid are sitting by the door. Afterwards we cross the highway and continue south, into the mountains. I keep us to the valley floor, where the going's easiest, but our pace doesn't improve.

About an hour into the afternoon I stop at the crest of a shallow rise and set the container down in the snow, making sure it's settled before I release the handle. Mags pulls down the bandana she now favors in place of a respirator and asks if everything's okay. I tell her it's fine; I'm going to wait here a minute while the rest of them catch up. She should go on.

She looks at me for a moment, then pulls her mask back up and sets off again. I stand next to the kid, staring at the raggedy line of Juvies shuffling up the incline. They stumble through the drifts like a herd of indifferent turtles, lifting their snowshoes high, flapping them around like the good Lord Himself might not be sure where they mean to set them down. I have some sympathy for the chronically uncoordinated; long as I can remember it seems like my own limbs have been a measure too long for the body they came with, and rarely under any semblance of control. But this is unwarranted, even by those standards. Had it been this way when we set out from Eden? That trip had certainly taken an unconscionable length of time for the miles we had covered, but I don't remember it being this bad.

The kid pushes his goggles up on his nose. They're the ones I got him after we escaped The Greenbrier, when the light was troubling him. They were meant for an adult, so they're way too big on him, but they were the only ones that were dark, which at the time was important. He's removed the tape I bound the visor with, but I still can't see a thing through it, so I have no idea what he might be thinking. I'm about to ask when without warning he points his poles around and takes off after Mags.

I turn my attention back to the Juvies. One by one they drag themselves up the rise, snowshoes crunching clumsily through the ice-slicked snow. When they get to the top they shuffle on by, eyeing the drab olive container at my feet with suspicion. I wait till the last one has passed, then I reach down for it and set off after them.

I wonder what Marv would have made of it. I come to the conclusion he'd probably have shot one of the stragglers, for the example it might provide. I return to that idea more than once as the afternoon slips by, far faster than our progress.

The thought of it becomes sorely tempting.

We keep heading south, winding our way between peaks with names like Hardscrabble, Pignut, Watery, Lost. Our progress continues, painful slow. The Juvies stop often, and when they do it's always as one; it seems like we can't cover much more than a mile without a snowshoe that needs fixing or a bladder that needs to be emptied. Getting them to their feet again after is the devil's own work.

As evening draws in I take us off the road. I hiked this stretch, back when I visited Culpeper, so at least I know where to bring us for shelter. I choose a gas station just outside a place called Marshall. I head around back to find a place to stash the virus while the rest of them shuffle inside. When I join them Mags already has a fire going. The Juvies have arranged themselves on the far side of it, as though some line only they can see divides their territory from that assigned to her and the kid. They huddle close as they dare to the smoldering branches, picking at half-warmed rations, occasionally casting nervous glances over the reluctant flames. I pass around the first aid kit and then get to work on my own meal while they tend to whatever blisters or chafes have been earned that day. There's little in the way of chatter. Those that are done unfurl their sleeping bags and turn in, until soon there's only me, Mags and the kid left.

The kid finishes the HOOAH! I've given him, then he curls up on top of his sleeping bag and closes his eyes. Seconds later he's out. When we were leaving The Greenbrier Hicks warned me he wouldn't ever sleep, but the scanner seems to have cured him of that; since he came through he's developed a knack for it, almost like an animal. It's rarely for long, though - mostly little more than a catnap - but deep, complete. For the next while he'll be dead to the world; you could stand over him clashing cymbals and I doubt he'd stir.

I dig out the map and spread it on the floor, checking how far we've advanced by the light from the dying flames. It looks even less impressive measured that way. Mags sets her ration aside. She hesitates a moment, then reaches over and rests a hand on my shoulder. She says it'll be okay, I just need to be patient. It's only the first day; they'll soon settle to it, find themselves a pace. She says it was no better when we first quit Eden.

I don't recall it that way, but when I point this out she says I probably can't be relied on to remember on account of recently having being shot and not being that much use in a snowshoe myself. I'm not convinced, though. I mutter something about us being no better than those English rabbits.

'English what?'

I start to fold the map.

'Rabbits. They weren't built for long marches, either. It says so, right at the beginning, when Hazel and Fiver and the others first set out from the Sandleford warren.'

She looks at me like she has no idea what I'm talking about.

'"They spend all their lives in the one place, never traveling more than a hundred yards at a stretch. They prefer not to be out of distance of some sort of refuge that will serve for a hole."' I'm sure I have some of the words wrong, but I think it's pretty close. I think I can even hear Mom's voice in my head, reading them to me. 'It's from *Watership Down*, remember?'

She shakes her head.

'Was it among the books we had at Mount Weather?'

'No, but…'

I stop, mid-sentence. An uneasy feeling settles low in my stomach, that she would even ask. I could name every single volume we had on the bookshelf in our tiny apartment: the books I brought with me from under my bed in the farmhouse outside Eden; the ones that had been left behind by those who had fled when the bunker had been evacuated; the few paperbacks I managed to scare up on the scavenging trips I took whenever the storms would ease. She knows what was there as well as I do, better even. She'd read and re-read every single book on it, countless times over the long winter.

I look over at her. She smiles.

'Then I don't think you've told me that one. Sounds like a good story.'

She shifts a little closer, like she might be ready to hear it.

I'm not sure what to say. Every story I have, Mags already knows it. When I'd find a new book on the outside I could barely get back to Eden quick enough so we could go up on the roof of the mess and I could tell her about it.

But she's right, of course; I never did tell her that one. I didn't need to. It was the book she was reading when we first met, all those years ago, in the day room of the Sacred Heart Home for Children.

*

THE THREE DAYS THAT FOLLOW continue much as the first.

The snow's settled deep in the valleys, and for the most part we're forced to hike Indian file. Mags breaks trail out front while I spend my time at the rear, with the dawdlers and the lollygaggers. At first we switched up every few hours, but that didn't work so well. The kid insists on being at her side and the Juvies found it hard to concentrate on the road ahead with him on their heels. I asked if she got tired, breaking trail all day. She said she didn't. Truth was she felt great, better than ever. The morning after we quit Marshall she lifted Truck's dog tags from inside her thermals and tossed them. There was no need for them she said; it'd already been five days since she came through the scanner, and that was plenty of time for the virus to show. I pulled the cross I took from Marv's grave from my pocket and handed it to her. I explained how it'd been mine, when I used to go outside scavenging. I said it had always brought me luck, and I wanted her to have it. She studied it for a while, then she smiled and slid it inside her thermals. Afterwards she kissed me.

I felt bad about lying to her like that, but her not remembering about the rabbits worries me almost as much as what happened with Kurt in the cavern. I tell myself I've forgotten things along the way too, important things. At some point in the years after the Last Day I stopped being able to call up Mom's face. The voice points out that's not the same, however; I still remember I *had* a Mom. I have no answer to that, so I take to asking questions, probing for gaps in what she should know. Herding the Juvies all day there's little opportunity, but in the evenings, after we've found shelter and they've gone to sleep, there's plenty of time. The further back I go the sketchier she gets on the detail. After a while her answers grow short, like I'm being annoying, or maybe she suspects something is missing and it's the not-knowing that vexes her, so I stop. I wait till she's gone to sleep and then I check the cross. I do it every night, but the metal remains clear, or at least I find no marks other than the ones I put there with the *Patio Wizard* I used to fool Kane. I tell myself whatever work the virus has done, the scanner's put a stop to it.

It has to have.

The kid doesn't remember a thing from the time before he got sick.

Just shy of noon on the sixth day after we quit Mount Weather we hit a little no-stoplight place name of Warren. The Juvies have been dragging their snowshoes all morning; we've barely made a half-dozen miles since we broke camp, and I don't see us doing better with the afternoon. I catch her looking back at the long straggly line of them stretched out behind us, like even she may be beginning to doubt they have it in them to make this journey.

We wait out front of a *Gas 'n' Go* while they catch up. The kid stares off into the distance, fiddling with the strap on his goggles. Something's gotten into him today, too. We hit our first properly deep drifts earlier, not long after we broke camp. I bent down to pick him up, like I'd done countless times before, but he just stopped and shook his head, then set off again, without so much as an explanation. There were stretches where he was barely able to lift his snowshoes high enough to clear the snow, so I asked him again, but for some reason he wouldn't contemplate taking a ride. If it was just the three of us I might have made him, but the truth is it's not him that's holding us up now.

I turn around and look at the road ahead, watching as it winds its way through the valley floor. There's little of anything for what looks like miles, not even a barn or a stand of blackened trees to break the emptiness. This is as far as I've been; after Warren we'll be in new territory. I worry what that will mean for our progress. I can't risk keeping us out after dark, not in a place like this. From now on as soon as the sun starts dipping towards the horizon we'll need to turn over what remains of the day to finding shelter.

I guess Mags must have had the same thought, or maybe mine are just easy to read, because she announces she's going on ahead to find us somewhere to spend the night. I'm not sure I like that idea. I didn't particularly care for how he delivered the message, but Jake had one thing right: it's not safe out there; that much was true even before I learned the world's not as empty as I once thought it was. And there's another part to it, too; one I don't care to admit. The outside, scavenging, finding us places to stay - that's *my* job; it's maybe the only thing I know how to do. If anyone has to hike out to find us shelter, it should be me.

I don't say that last bit out loud, of course. Realizing how things might sound to others has always been what you'd call a development area for me, but even I can see that's not the kind of reasoning that's apt to appeal to Mags. So instead I remind her of the rule. You always scavenge in pairs. There are no exceptions.

She shakes her head.

'We can't both go. One of us needs to stay with them.'

'Then I'll do it.'

She hesitates for a moment, like she's trying to figure out a way to say what she has to.

'It makes more sense for it to be me. I can cover more ground than you.'

She waits to see if I have anything to say to that, but I don't. After a few seconds she pulls up her hood, like it's decided.

I tell her to wait. I shuck off my pack and set it down in the snow, then dig in one of the side pockets, pull out a Ziploc bag. I have to take off my mittens to break the seal. For an instant there's the sweet smell of gun oil before the wind snatches it away again. I reach inside for the pistol Marv gave me and hold it out.

'It's already loaded. I took the bullets from the gun Peck left behind.'

She hesitates for a moment, then takes it from me. I show her how the safety works and how to chamber the first round. There's a soft *snick-snick* as she racks the slide. I cleaned and oiled it before we set off, so the mechanism should be good. She examines it for a moment, then closes her fingers around the grip. It looks too big for her hand.

'I don't know how to shoot it.'

'You just point and squeeze. There's not much more to it.' I say it with a shrug, like I might have spent my formative years terrorizing cattle towns alongside Billy the Kid and his Regulators, rather than counting tins for Quartermaster in Eden's stores. I see her eyeing the pistol, like she's not sure she really wants it, so I give her the talk Marv gave me, about how if she comes across people she thinks might be no good she should just point it up in the air and let off a round. That would be enough to get most folks to turn tail he said, although even as I hear myself repeat those words I wonder. I can't help but think it'd take more than a loud bang and a puff of gun smoke to get someone like Hicks to cut and run.

She checks the safety again then slides the pistol into the pocket of her parka, shifts her bandana back in place and sets off. I watch as she hikes out ahead. I wasn't sure at first, but I've been watching her these past few days and I know it now. Her strides are measured, deliberate, like she's checking herself, holding back; like she could go faster than she's showing me. Even so, she's breaking trail with a pace I doubt I could match. She's almost at the first bend when I hear the crunch of snow behind me. I turn to see Jake, hurrying up the slope. He draws level, unsnaps his respirator, but it's a few seconds before he has breath enough to ask his question.

'Where's she going?'

'To find us shelter.'

He looks up at me, incredulous.

'You...you just let her go? All by herself?'

I don't know what to say to that, so I don't answer, I just keep watching her. More of the Juvies are arriving now, huffing and puffing their way up the incline. They gather round, making sure to keep a respectable distance back from the kid. Jake pulls his goggles onto his forehead and stares at me, waiting for an answer.

'You want to stop her Jake, be my guest.'

He glares at me a moment longer, then points his snowshoes in the direction of the *Gas 'n' Go*. One by one the others follow until there's only me, Lauren and Johnny left.

For a while we watch Mags. As she nears the bend her stride seems to lengthen, and for the last few seconds before she disappears it's almost as though she's bounding through the snow. Then she's gone and there's nothing left but her tracks, the shallow indents already softening with the wind.

Lauren takes a step closer. For a while she says nothing, but then she turns and looks up at me.

'Is that normal?'

I don't answer. The truth is I'm not really sure what that means any more. She rests a mitten on the arm of my parka, squeezes once, then follows the others into the gas station.

*

WE LEAVE THE MOUNTAINS BEHIND, the serried peaks giving way to low, rolling hills that are much more to the Juvies' liking. They find themselves a pace, just like Mags said they would. It's barely faster than the one they set out with, however.

A week after we quit Mount Weather we pick up the interstate, a wide, furrowed scar winding its way through endless frozen wasteland. For mile after mile we cleave to it, trudging ever south. We pass exits for places called Thorn, Golan, Ruther, but take none of them. Our days take on a pattern. We start early, covering what miles we can while legs are fresh. When we stop for lunch Mags leaves us. I eat with the kid while the others huddle together in the far corner of whatever gas station or truck stop we're favoring with our custom, although sometimes he waits outside, watching the road like he expects her to come back. Afterwards I lead us on again, but slower now. With little to do but coax the stragglers and watch for her return the afternoons drag. Each evening we trade the highway for whatever roadside diner or motel she's found for us, only to rejoin it the following morning.

I watch Mags for any sign of what I saw that first night back in Mount Weather, but there's nothing, or at least nothing I can detect. If anything she grows quieter; it's almost like with every day that passes now she draws a little further into herself. I ask her what it is, but she says nothing. I think I can guess, though. Sometimes with dusk settling I spot places from the highway that look like they might do for shelter, but she just shakes her head and says they're not for us. I don't ask her why, because I know. She's already been inside. It used to be Marv's job to check the dark places, and for a short while after he died it became mine.

Now that job is hers.

On the morning of our thirteenth day on the road we see our first sign for Richmond, the almost-halfway point in our journey, but for the rest of that day and the next it remains always ahead of us, seeming to get no closer. At last we round a long curve in the interstate and an exit sign for the city hoves into view. I pick up the pace, ignoring the protests from behind me. Mags has been gone since early; I'm keen to catch up with her and get the Juvies to shelter while there's still a few hours left in the day. I know from the newspaper articles I used to collect that the city got hit in the strikes, but Marv's map shows it was a big place, once; there's bound to be something left I can scavenge, maybe stretch out our supplies a little. They could certainly use it; we've not been making near the time I had allowed when we quit Mount Weather. It'll probably be the last opportunity we get, too. South of Richmond we join interstate again, and that'll bring us all the way into North Carolina.

The kid senses the new urgency and sets off, his head bent to the snow. When he gets to the off-ramp he scurries straight up it without so much as a backward glance. I'm about to holler at him, but then he stops of his own accord and waits while I make my way up to join him.

From the interchange the land falls away before us and then lays flat, as far as the eye can see. I scan the horizon while I wait for the Juvies to catch up, searching for any hint of what lies ahead: a crumbling skyscraper, a listing apartment building, even the spindly jib of a tower crane; anything to break the featureless gray. But there's nothing, or at least as close to it as makes no difference.

As soon as everyone's gathered we set off again. The few buildings we pass now are little more than husks. I stare up at one as we trudge by. It's been stripped to its skeleton, its walls blown out, what little remains of its insides strewn with blackened debris. Spidey's been quiet since before we quit Mount Weather, but now he starts up again. It's low level, a not-so-urgent rumble I could probably drown out if I put my mind to it. But for once I understand what's got him on edge. I'm used to how the world is now; I've seen the work the virus has done. This is different, though; a manner of destruction I have not witnessed before. The Juvies sense it too. They grow quiet, like this place, the very air we're breathing, is thick with despair.

I spot a sign ahead. The gantry arm leans towards us, like something has pushed it over. The paint is blistered, making what's written there hard to read; it may say *Downtown*, but there's not enough of the letters left to be sure. As I pass underneath I look up. On the side facing the city the metal has been scorched black.

We start to hit traffic. At first just a vehicle here or there. A tractor-trailer on its side, the molten remains of its tires still clinging to the rims. The shell of a four-by-four, front wheels stuck in the low gully of the median, rump pointing skyward, like a steer down on its knees and waiting for the bolt gun. I drag my hand across its flank, dislodging an armful of ashen snow. Underneath the paintwork's bubbled, just like the sign.

More now, but all the same, until soon the road's choked with burnt-out wrecks, the glass blown from their windows, their insides melted. They rest on their sides or on their roofs; others protrude from the snow at improbable angles, like they were little more than *Hot Wheels*, held to the fire and then scattered, the work of a sulking child.

We keep going. Soon we have to pick our way between them, our progress slowed by the weight of carnage. A stake-bed's impaled itself on the sheared iron of a guardrail; the kid ducks under but the rest of us have to squeeze past its slatted sides, one at a time. Up ahead he stops by the hood of a semi that's somehow managed to stay on its wheels and points forward with one mitten, like he's seen something there. When I catch up to him he turns to look up at me through his outsize goggles.

I set the container with the virus down in the snow. What I thought to be a low rise in the road is in fact the rim of a shallow crater; it stretches off on both sides, almost as far as the eye can see. Within its ragged circumference there's nothing left but the scorched char-pits of foundations exposed by the blast, mercifully filling with snow.

I let my gaze linger for a few moments, taking in the details of the cauterized bowl that was once a city. Nothing stands that might offer shelter. We have no choice but to cross, however; it's already too late to contemplate going around.

I wait for the last of the stragglers to join us then I start making my way down. The sides are steep; I hold my hand out to the kid but he just shakes his head, like he wants none of it. Without markers it's hard to tell where the road once was, so we just keep heading south. I keep my eyes on the opposite rim of the crater, expecting Mags to appear there at any moment. She would normally have returned to us by now, but I tell myself not to fret; she'll have had to travel farther than usual to find us somewhere to pass the night.

By the time we've hauled ourselves over the lip on the far side there's little left of the day. I can already feel the temperature starting to drop, so I pick up the pace, and for once there are no complaints from behind me. A couple of miles further on we reach a river Marv's map says is the Appomattox. A low concrete bridge, squat, ugly, but sturdy enough to have survived the blast, spans the sluggish gray waters. On the far side a lone figure, making her way towards us.

Nobody looks back as we cross.

*

WE PASS THAT NIGHT in a *Target* Mags has found for us just north of a place called Chester. I don't much care for the malls but she says it's the best there is, at least within any distance the Juvies might be capable of reaching this side of noon tomorrow. It makes me wonder how far ahead she's been.

I stand by the entrance as they unsnap their snowshoes and file inside. We've been on the road longer than usual and they look pretty beat. When I've counted the last of them in I head off to find a place to stash the virus. By the time I return there's already a fire going by the checkouts. I head down one of the aisles, making my way towards the back of the store, where Mags is waiting with the kid.

That was Lauren's idea. She took me to one side, not long after Warren, and suggested it'd be for the best. It wasn't her, she said; she felt bad even bringing it up. But the truth was the kid was making some of the others nervous. I can't say it was altogether a surprise. I remember how I'd felt, the first time I laid eyes on him, crouched at the back of his cage in that basement room in The Greenbrier's bunker. His appearance has improved a little since, but the truth of it is he's still pale as a sheet, coat hanger thin, and the shadows around his eyes are proving a lot more stubborn than Mags'. That habit he has of dropping to all fours persists, too. I know there's nothing in it; it's just from all the time he spent in the cage. It doesn't exactly set a mind at ease, however.

I wasn't sure how Mags was going to react, but she just said okay, almost like she'd been expecting it. I told her what Lauren had said to me: it wouldn't be for long. The Juvies'll get used to him, same as I did. It's the same as with the snowshoes. We just have to give them time.

I watch as he chooses a spot not far from us and rolls out his sleeping bag. Mags hands him an MRE carton and he lifts the flap and upends it, searching among the pouches and packets that spill out for the HOOAH! he favors. He tears the wrapper with his teeth and pushes the bar up; it's gone in a couple of quick bites. He spends a moment examining the foil for crumbs and then looks over at me hopefully. I wait until Mags is busy fixing herself a coffee and then dig mine from the carton. She'll be mad if she catches me; she says we have to wean him off them, get him on the food pouches, even though it's been a while since she finished one of her own. He's yet to show much interest in those, though, and he'll never get to a regular size if he doesn't eat.

When she's not looking I toss the candy bar over. He snatches it from the air and it disappears without a sound, I think up the sleeve of his jacket, but it happens too quick for me to be sure. Then he curls up on top of his sleeping bag and closes his eyes. Seconds later he's out.

I finish my meal and climb into the sleeping bag. The floor is hard, even through the quilted material, but I guess I must be more tired than I had figured; as soon as I lay my head down I feel my eyelids growing heavy. I hear the zip being drawn back and Mags slips in beside me. She takes off the beanie she wears and sets it on the ground.

I drape my arm around her, my fingers tracing a line across the taut curve of her stomach. She still has weight to gain back, but then I tell myself she was always thin. My fingertips come to rest on the angle of her hip. The skin there is chilled, like it's been left outside the sleeping bag. I shiver.

'You cold?'

She shakes her head but I pull her close anyway, hoping to warm her up. I'm already slipping down into that place where your thoughts unravel and you lose yourself to sleep. Without thinking I press my lips to the back of her head.

She lies there for a moment, not moving, then slowly lifts one hand and runs her fingertips across her scalp where I've just kissed it.

'It's not growing back, is it?'

I brush my lips over the skin there and tell her I hadn't noticed. The low, faithless voice inside my head pipes up before I have a chance to silence it.

*Liar.*

She just shakes her head.

'It's not, least not as quickly as it should. Back in Eden, when I had the mohawk, I'd have to shave it every couple of days.'

I slide my hand up from her waist. I checked the crucifix I gave her last night, while she slept, but now I reach for it again. I run my fingers over the crudely-cast metal, relieved to find the surface unchanged. For a long time she doesn't say anything, but I can tell she's still awake. The scanner gave the kid back some semblance of sleep but for Mags it's the opposite; I don't reckon she gets much more than an hour a night now.

She glances over at the small form curled up on the other side of the fire. He hasn't stirred, but she lowers her voice anyway.

'I don't think Johnny's hair's growing back at all. What do you think it means, Gabe?'

I kiss the back of her head again.

'I don't think it means anything.'

That answer doesn't seem to placate her any more than it does the voice inside my own head. It feels like it has something to say, but this time I hush it before it has a chance to get going. There's no way she's sick. No way. Whatever chance I might have had when we first set out, I couldn't hope to keep up with her now. I reckon it'd be the same with the kid, too, if it wasn't for those little legs of his.

She shifts around inside my arms.

'How old do you think he is, Gabe?'

The question takes me by surprise.

'I dunno. He doesn't look much older than we were, when Kane brought us to Eden.'

'But that would mean he would have to have been born after the Last Day.'

I say something about it being possible. It is of course, but somehow I'm not sure I believe it, any more than I reckon she does. Truck told us the survivors who found their way to The Greenbrier had shown up not long after everything had fallen apart. Before we arrived they hadn't seen anyone in years.

An image pops into my head, unbidden, of the girl I found in the closet in Shreve, all those years ago. I hadn't thought on her in a long while. I can still picture her, though; her face pressed to the backboard; the dark circles around her eyes; her ashen cheeks sunken and hollowed. Her hair had been white and brittle, like an old person's, but I remember thinking the same thing about her as I just did about Johnny: she couldn't have been much more than a first-grader. I wonder now if I got that right. I hadn't been scavenging more than a few months back then, but it had already been six winters since the Last Day. Kane scorched the skies not long after we first went inside the mountain, which meant she had to have been in that closet ever since. The dress she was wearing had hung in tatters from her tiny frame, but what remained of it had still fitted, like she hadn't grown in all that time.

There's a soft crack as a branch shifts in the fire. A handful of red sparks rise in a swirl and then disappear. Mags looks over at the kid but he's still out of it.

'I asked him how long he was in that cage. He said he didn't know. He said it was hard to tell down there, in the darkness.' She pauses. 'A long time, I think. Months. Maybe even years.'

She doesn't say anything for a while. When she speaks again it's like it's mostly to herself.

'I don't know how he did it. I was only there for a few days and...'

She doesn't finish, just lets the sentence hang there in the darkness. I feel her shudder.

'I don't think I could do that again.'

I pull her close and tell her she won't ever have to. And right then I mean it, as much as I think I've meant anything in my whole life. Not that that matters. I should know better by now. The world doesn't bend itself to hopes and prayers, leastways not any I might have to offer.

I'll learn, though, soon enough.

Promises like that I simply have no business making.

*

HE WAKES FROM A DEEP AND DREAMLESS SLEEP, his eyes blinking wide. The transition is sudden, jarring, like someone has found the switch inside that works him and flicked it on. For long seconds he stares into the darkness, his pulse racing. Until his brain reboots he is empty, just breath and heartbeat and blood pumping, with no memory of who he is, what he might even be. Slowly it comes to him, in fragments at first and then all at once, a rush of sights, sounds, smells; what little he remembers. He presses his cheek to the sleeping bag, inhaling the warm, slightly musty odor. The quilted fabric does little to soften the hard floor, but it is a comfort nonetheless. He knows where he is now, and it is not the cage.

He blinks again, more slowly this time, his heart finally beginning to calm. He doesn't know how sleeping was, before, but somehow he doesn't think it was like this. He wonders if he will ever get used to it.

He lifts his head, taking in his surroundings. On either side rows of empty shelves, stretching off into gloom, the aisle between scattered with discarded packets, wrappers, here and there an abandoned shopping cart. Everything cast in grainy shades of gray, except around the fire, where a few motes of color still remain. He looks over to where the boy and the girl are sleeping. The boy's breath rolls from him in slow plumes, hangs for a moment in the still air, then vanishes. He cups one hand to his mouth and exhales slowly, watching. But there's nothing; his breath doesn't smoke like that. He wonders what it means.

Something shifts among the embers, then settles. The fire is dying. An idea comes to him, sudden, exciting: he could go outside and find more branches, build it back up. He knows how; he has watched the girl. He sits up. He won't sleep again tonight, and morning is hours away yet; it would certainly help pass the time. There is something about the idea that thrills him, too. For a very long time he wasn't allowed to go anywhere.

He looks along the aisle, towards the entrance. That is where the others are, though; he would need to walk right past them. He stares in that direction for a long while, watching for any sign of movement. It seems like they are all asleep now, but it is hard to be sure. He knows how to be quiet; he is very good at it. But what if the door is noisy and he wakes them?

It is better if he stays away, that was what the girl had said. Just until they got used to him. She had smiled then, but it wasn't her usual smile. There was something sad about it. And she had looked away right after, like she wasn't sure how much she believed it either.

It wasn't her idea, he knows that. It was the girl with the blond hair. He heard her, talking to the tall boy. It wasn't her she said; it was some of the others. She didn't mind him at all.

But she does, he can tell. The girl with the blond hair might be more afraid of him than any of them. She pretends not to be, and she is quite good at that. She smiles whenever she looks at him, so it never shows on her face, and she keeps it from her voice. He can smell it, though, every time she is near. Her fear has a bitter odor. She spreads it among the others with her questions, at night, when they huddle by the fire. She thinks he can't hear her if she whispers, but he can.

*Earlier, did you see...?*

*Gabe says they're cured, but...*

*How can that be normal?*

He looks back at the fire, already little more than a handful of embers, nestling in ash. It doesn't matter; he doesn't need it. The cold doesn't bother him, not really. If it did he could climb inside the sleeping bag, like the others do. He won't do that, though. The thick material is soft, but he does not like to be confined.

He remembers the candy bar the boy gave him. He reaches into his sleeve and takes it out, opening it slowly. He means to make it last, but it is too delicious and in a few bites it is gone. He pulls the wrapper apart, searching for crumbs. When he's certain the last of them have been had he puts it on the fire, watching as the foil shrivels with the heat. For a second the flames flicker bright around it as it is consumed, then they too disappear, as quickly as they came.

His gaze shifts to the trash-strewn aisle.

He doesn't have to go that way, of course; he could head towards the back of the store instead. There won't be firewood there, but maybe he'll find something else; something on the shelves that's been missed. The tall boy checked earlier and said there was nothing, but he might have more luck. He feels himself growing excited again. Maybe even another candy bar.

He gets up slowly, taking care not to make a sound. At the last minute he remembers the flashlight. He doesn't need it, of course, but it makes the others feel better, that's what the girl says. He picks it up and winds the handle slowly. The little motor inside hums; moments later the bulb glows orange, then yellow.

He sets off down the aisle, picking his way carefully among the debris. He is only tall enough to check the bottom shelves, but there's nothing there; everything has long since been stripped, plundered. After a while he gives up and just walks. The flashlight hangs at his side, already forgotten.

He wonders how long it will take the others to get used to him. The girl said not long, but he's not sure about that. He sees how they look at him. Mostly they pretend he's not there, but sometimes they can't hide it, like when the tall boy had bent down to carry him through the deep snow. They had stopped and stared, as though the idea of it was appalling to them. He won't let himself be carried anymore. It would just be another way for them to see he is different, and if they think he's different they won't ever get used to him. Besides, he's much better with the snowshoes now. He never falls down, and it's only when the drifts get really deep that he struggles. It's just because his legs are short, and there's nothing he can do about that.

He reaches the end of the aisle. The shelves give way to long racks of clothes. Some have been knocked over, the garments that once hung there lying in heaped disarray, but most still stand. He holds his hands out as he makes his way between them, letting his fingers brush the moldering fabrics.

A sudden flicker of light ahead, there and then gone again. He freezes and for a dozen hurried heartbeats peers into the grainy gloom. But it is only a mirror, for an instant catching the beam from the forgotten flashlight. He continues on, making his way towards it between the racks. As he gets closer he can see that the glass is broken. Only a few shards still remain, gripped by the frame; the rest have fallen to the floor. They crunch under his boots as he steps up to it.

He tilts his head to one side, studying his fractured reflection. He is still getting used to it. He does not remember what he looked like before, of course, and there were no mirrors in the cage; no surfaces that might have offered even the faintest clue as to his appearance. Sometimes when they are outside he catches himself in the darkened glass of an abandoned storefront, but it is never for very long and he is always masked, hooded, his eyes hidden behind the dark goggles he wears.

He leans a little closer, reaching up with the cuff of his jacket to wipe the dust away. The beam from the flashlight wanders and for an instant the eyes that stare back at him flash silver.

His heart races; he glances over his shoulder, worried that somebody might have seen. But there's no one there; they're all still sleeping. He winds the flashlight and raises it, more slowly this time. When he finds the right angle he holds it up, forcing himself not to squint.

How long will it take them to get used to *that*?

A long time, he suspects. He remembers how frightened he had been when the doctor had come down and shone a light into 98's cage and he had seen her eyes for the first time. And he is much braver than they are.

He lowers the flashlight and closes his eyes for a moment, thinking. He reaches for the goggles that hang around his neck and pushes them up. They are a little big but the girl has adjusted the strap so they mostly fit, and the lens is dark; the tall boy got them for him when he was sick, to help with the brightness. He raises the flashlight again, but this time the goggles do their work; now there is nothing to see. He moves the beam closer, tilting his head this way and that until he is certain of it. Then he turns around and starts making his way back towards the fire.

It was lucky he found the mirror. He does not care to think about what might have happened if one of the others – especially the girl with the blond hair – had noticed first.

The thought that he might still be sick does not occur to him. He feels fine. And he has the metal tags he wears around his neck, the ones they took from the soldier. He checks them all the time and they never change. The tall boy says that proves it; the thing inside that made him dangerous has gone.

Well, not gone, exactly.

But not in control anymore.

Definitely not.

*

SOUTH OF WHAT WAS ONCE RICHMOND the interstate has little to say for itself, and for mile after mile we trudge on through empty, snow-shrouded flatlands. The days run one into the other. On the twenty-third morning after we set out from Mount Weather, when by my earlier reckoning we should already have arrived at our destination, we finally quit Virginia. The other side of the state line proves no more bountiful than what preceded it. Our packs grow light. I have the Juvies empty them, so I can check what we have left. I had counted on us arriving at Fearrington with enough food for a return journey on short rations, should we need to make one. I'm not sure exactly where it's happened, but somewhere along the way we've passed the point where that might have been possible.

We keep trudging on, ever south. Mags has to work hard to find us shelter now. Mornings she sets off before we've broken camp. I spend the days herding the Juvies along a stretch of interstate no different from those that have gone before. Afternoons I watch for her return, but often dusk's settling by the time I spot her hiking back towards us. Sometimes she says there's nothing we can reach with what remains of the day and we have to backtrack. I asked her once how far she goes when she leaves us but she just said *a ways* and wouldn't be drawn on it.

That's how she is most of the time now: quiet, withdrawn. Evenings she eats what little she cares for from her MRE and turns in without saying more than a dozen words. At first I tell myself she's just tired, on account of all the extra miles she's putting in, finding us shelter. I'm not sure that's it, though. I wait up each night until she passes into whatever it is she calls sleep, and then I check her crucifix. That crudely cast cross has become my talisman. I remember how Marv's had been, before he died. The virus had only had a couple of days to work on it, but already it had been pitted and pocked, like something had been eating away at it. Hers is always the same: the metal no different than how it was when I lifted it from his grave.

We pass our fifth night in North Carolina in a *Red Roof* she finds for us just outside of a place called Heavenly that has no business trading on that name. As day breaks we rejoin the interstate and point our snowshoes south once again. For once Mags won't be leaving us. Our next milestone is Durham, and barring calamity we should reach it before nightfall. Place that size there should be no shortage of places to sleep.

The drifts aren't bad along the first stretch so we can walk side by side. I settle in next to her, the kid between us. I make a few attempts at conversation, but she seems more comfortable with silence so I let it be.

The kid looks up at her through those outsize goggles, then back at me. He wears them day and night, now; I can't recall the last time I saw him without them. I wondered about that when he first started doing it; I was worried it might be his eyes bothering him again. But when I mentioned it to Mags she got mad. She said I should stop trying to find problems where there were none. If it was the light that was troubling him why would he have taken to wearing them at night? I couldn't find a flaw with that, so I quit asking. I watched him close for a few days, all the same.

The morning slips by, our progress no better or worse than the days that have gone before. With each crest in the road I find myself scanning the horizon, eager for my first glimpse of the city. We're embarked on the last leg of our journey now. We'll be in Durham by evening and Fearrington's no more than a day's hike beyond; even accounting for our laggard pace we should be there by nightfall tomorrow. I should be relieved, but now that we're almost at our destination I'm nervous. I glance over at the pack Mags is carrying. It bears little resemblance to the one she set out with. Whatever rations we have left, they won't see us back to Mount Weather. Not even close.

I look behind me at the long, raggedy line of Juvies stretched out behind me on the interstate. We all voted, but I know the truth of it. They're here because of me, a bunker marked on a map a dead man gave me, and the things I told them about it: that I'll be able to find it; that Marv's codes will work to get us in; that there'll be food there to sustain us.

If any of those things prove false we're in a whole heap of trouble.

Sometime just shy of noon we pass an exit sign and not long after an overpass appears around a bend in the road. Ahead the interstate stretches off into the distance, with no apparent end to it. If we stayed on it would bring us all the way to 501, which in turn runs right by Fearrington. But the way I mean to take us – south through the city – is more direct; I reckon it could shave as much as a day off our journey. Our supplies could certainly use that, but mostly I just want to see what waits for us here. There was no mention in the newspaper clippings of Durham being hit in the strikes, but then there was no confirmation it had been spared either, and what we saw in Richmond has been on my mind since we came through it. Our new home's going to be a lot smaller than Mount Weather was. Even if it's stocked like I've assumed we're going to need things, and Durham's where I'll be coming to get them.

I lead us off the highway. At the top of the exit ramp a lone semi blocks the intersection; it looks like it was in the middle of executing one final turn when something called a halt to its advance. As I get closer I see what: the traffic light's given out just as it was passing under, staving in the roof of the cab. A single cluster hangs from the end of the collapsed gantry arm, creaking and groaning as it shifts in the wind.

From the junction the road slopes down. Drive-thrus line up one after the other on either side, their once-garish signs competing for our attention. A decade of weather has left them faded and tattered, but it's still a riot of color compared with what we've been seeing on the highway. My heart sinks in spite of it; the Juvies may not have much reading between them, but they remember enough to know what those signs mean. Behind me I hear the first of them asking whether it's time yet for lunch.

I turn my snowshoes around, but the rebellion's already caught hold. I look up to the sky. It's not yet noon but somewhere behind the clouds the sun will soon be contemplating its downward course. We're close to Durham now, though, so I guess I shouldn't sweat it. I call after them twenty minutes, knowing it'll be an hour if I'm lucky. They set off in the direction of a flat-roofed building the sign out front identifies as *Bojangles' Famous Chicken 'n' Biscuits*, a spring in their stride that's been sorely lacking all morning.

I shake my head and start to follow their tracks. As I enter the parking lot I get that familiar scratchy feeling, like stepping through cobwebs, only inside my head. Spidey's been quiet for days, but now something's woken him up. He hasn't yet reached for the alarm button, but he's telling me he's not happy about something, all the same. I stop, for the first time paying attention to the sorry-looking diner the Juvies have chosen. The roof's a little heavy with snow, but no worse than the Speedway or the Taco Bell on either side of it. It gives no indication it's likely to quit on us, least not until we're done with lunch.

Mags asks if everything's okay. I hesitate a moment then nod and we continue making our way towards the entrance. The door hangs back on its hinges and when I look closer I can see scratches around the lock where somebody's had at it with a pry bar. Spidey pings again at those, but the marks are old and he's giving no other clue as to what's suddenly getting him antsy. I set the container with the virus down and bend to my bindings. Mags is already out of hers and making her way in. I hear the snow crunch behind me and when I turn around the kid's standing there. He stares at me for a moment then follows her.

I step out of my snowshoes and join them inside. It takes a second for my eyes to adjust to the gloom, but when they do I see the Juvies have spread themselves across the available booths. There's still space left if they would bunch up and let us in, but no-one's showing any sign of that. They keep their eyes down, making busy work of unwrapping their rations. A few even shuffle closer to the end. I've been taking my lunches with the kid since she started hiking out to find us shelter, so I've kinda gotten used to it. It's been a while since she ate with us during the day, however, and now it seems like it's bothering her. I look for Jake - he can generally be relied on to find a spot for Mags - but he's got his back to the door and hasn't spotted us yet. I tap her on the shoulder, point to a couple of stools at the counter.

'Those'll do.'

She makes no move towards them. She stares at the Juvies a moment longer then she says she's not hungry; she's going to go on, find us somewhere to pass the night. Her voice is low, barely a whisper, but there's an edge to it that wasn't there a moment ago. I start to tell her there's no need. We're close now; as long as Durham isn't like Richmond there'll be no shortage of places there. But then I stop. Her hands remain by her sides, but her fists are clenched, and when my eyes return to her face her expression has hardened. And there's something else there too, something that makes me take a step back.

I tell her we'll catch up with her soon as we can. She pushes past me without saying a word and hurries outside. The kid runs after her like he means to follow, but then stops. We both watch as she crosses the parking lot, bounds up the embankment and rejoins the highway. Whatever efforts she had been making to conceal her pace, those are forgotten now; it's not long till she's little more than a speck in the distance.

I stand in the doorway after she's gone, uncertain what to make of what's just happened. I head back into the diner, choose a stool at the counter and shuck off my pack, but before I can sit Lauren sees me and waves me over. A space has miraculously opened up next to her; as I watch she shuffles in to make more room. I'm not sure what else to do, so I head over and sit. She hands me her canteen. I use a splash from it to get the heater in my ration working then hold the bottle to my lips and take a sip. The water's sharp with the cold; I can taste the ice crystals. I close my eyes and for a second, for no reason I can fathom, I'm sitting next to Mags outside a *7-Eleven*, the sun warm on my face. There's a white van in the parking lot, *The Sacred Heart Home for Children* printed in blue cursive along its side. I can feel the Big Gulp clutched to my chest, the first spike of brain-freeze from the soda I've just drunk too fast already on its way. Next to me Mags giggles, holds her hands out for it. I try to hold the memory, but then my head gives an involuntary shake and it's gone. I pass the canteen back, feeling the water I've just swallowed settle cold in my stomach.

Lauren smiles at me as she takes it.

'Not much longer now.'

*

AS SOON AS THE LAST food pouch has been emptied I get the Juvies to their feet and hustle them towards the door. The kid's waiting for us out in the parking lot. He looks up when he sees me, happy that we're on the move again. He scurries back to the interchange and disappears around the stricken semi without so much as a backward glance. I set off after him, but the Juvies show little interest in keeping up; it's not long till they're stretched out in their usual vagabond line behind me.

I ease back, resigning myself to their pace. My pack is light, barely worth the mention. With each step the container with the virus swings on its handle, but after weeks on the road I've grown accustomed to it. It hardly troubles me anymore; fact is there are days I even find it soothing. Marv said you always had to pay attention, but often, pounding the snow like this, with nothing to do but herd the Juvies along mile after mile of interstate my mind will slip out of gear and settle to an idle.

I'd be happy for it to do that now, but it won't.

I look at Mags' tracks, stretching out in front of me. I wonder how far ahead of us she is already. Probably in the city by now, the speed she took off. I tell myself it doesn't have to mean anything. Her crucifix is still clear; I checked it only last night. She's just pissed the Juvies are still being that way with her and the kid. She'll calm down soon enough; by the time she comes back to us she'll be fine.

The voice isn't going to let me have that, though. As my snowshoes crunch into the shallow indentations she's left it takes to whispering.

*There was something else, though. You saw it.*

My head dips inside the hood of my parka, before I can stop myself. Because the truth is I did.

*Something behind her eyes.*

Yes.

*Like with Kurt. Almost as though…*

Almost as though whatever she was battling with then was back.

We make our way into Durham.

I keep following the tracks she's left, not really heeding much around me other than the occasional street sign. Little by little gas stations and strip malls give way to row houses with small yards, and then low-slung modern buildings. Spidey takes to grumbling again, but there's no sign here of the fire-blackened concrete, the blown out walls, we saw in Richmond, so I hush him. We crest a shallow rise and I catch my first proper view of Durham's skyline. Off in the distance small clusters of lonely high-rises huddle together, dotting the horizon. They seem in poor shape, listing this way or that or lying collapsed in rubble, the metal that once braced them virus-weakened, no longer able to bear the weight of concrete. They are a relief, nonetheless; proof that the devastation we witnessed earlier has not been visited here too.

Our pace slows the closer we get to the center. The Juvies stop at each cross street, craning their necks at the slowly disintegrating buildings, like each one we pass is a wonder. I stop often to let the stragglers catch up, making sure my charges don't get too strung out behind me. The streets get busy. Vehicles rest where they've been abandoned, their trunks popped, their doors agape. Others have mounted sidewalks, or folded themselves around light poles. Around Eden the virus did a pretty good job of quieting the roads, but then Providence, Shiloah, Ely, those were all small towns. It doesn't look like that was the way of it in the cities. Beyond the blast crater Richmond's streets were clogged, and it's no different here; Durham's final traffic jam appears to have been a doozy.

The wind's picked up a little while we've been making our way in and Mags' tracks are already fading. The kid runs farther ahead, following her prints as though fearful they'll be wiped clean before he's able to find her again. For once I'm less anxious about her return. She'll be back with us when she's ready; there's no shortage of places here we might hole up for the night. Best she takes the time she needs to sort out whatever's going on inside her head.

Every now and then spidey pings at something he refuses to share but I keep going, navigating the wrecks largely on autopilot, committing the occasional landmark to memory, until eventually the burned-out hulk of a tractor-trailer blocks our path. I lose Mags' tracks in a drift just this side of it, then I find them again, veering off through the parking lot of a VA medical center. The lot's full, a sea of humped gray shapes sitting silent under a thick blanket of snow. The building on the far side of it's in bad shape, even by the standards of what surrounds it. Its roofline sags pitifully and one entire wing has collapsed to rubble, twisted rebar poking out through the concrete like the ribs of a decaying carcass. Marv always kept us away from places like this. After what I saw in Blacksburg I can't say as I'd fault him for it.

I set the container with the virus in the snow while I wait for the Juvies to catch up. It's a relief Durham's not how Richmond was, but I can't say I'm much looking forward to working it, all the same. It might have been an okay place, once, but a straight shot of ferro, followed by a few hectic weeks of looting and then a decade of neglect has put paid to that. There's no shortage of hospitals here either; we're not halfway through yet and I've already counted a worrying number of them. They're easy to spot, even from a distance; that was where the virus did its best work. I stare up at the crumbling remains of the VA. Rows of dark, broken windows march off towards its edges, and for a second I think I see movement behind one of them. But when I look there it's just the wind, tugging at the curtains. They flap uselessly, snagging on the edges of glass that still cling to the frames.

I wonder if it's all the hospitals that have been making spidey so antsy. I mull it over for a little while, but somehow it doesn't seem quite right. I look around, trying to work out what else it might be. It feels like it's right there, all around me; if I could just focus for a moment it'd come to me.

Lauren's snowshoes crunch the snow beside me.

'Something wrong?'

I let my gaze linger a moment longer then shake my head.

We make our way down into the parking lot, picking a path between the abandoned cars. I call back to the Juvies not to touch anything. What Kane did to the skies should have struck the virus from the metal, but this close to a hospital I certainly don't plan on taking chances. I breathe a sigh of relief when the last straggler clambers back up the embankment on the far side and we're through. I do a quick head count and then we set off again.

The kid's already picked up Mags' tracks, so I let him lead the way. Spidey's bleating grows louder, but I'm having no better luck working out what has him riled than earlier, so I just do my best to drown him out. A half-dozen blocks south of the VA I stop outside a Walgreen's while I wait for the Juvies to catch up again. I'm staring at my reflection in the darkened storefront, when for no good reason my gaze shifts from the glass to the wall nearby, settling on a section of concrete there.

I stare at it while my brain slowly joins the dots. And then a spike of adrenalin sends my heart racing.

*

I SWING BACK TO THE DOORWAY, silently cursing myself for not paying more attention. I check again, to be sure I haven't imagined it. But there's no mistake. My eyes jump to the next building along. Another. Across the street, more, all around us, everywhere I turn, obvious now that I know what to look for.

How long have I been missing them?

I look ahead at the prints Mags has left in the snow, and for a second I consider just taking off after her. I take a deep breath, tell myself to calm down; I need to think for a moment, try not to do something stupid. Lauren's been following in my tracks. She comes to a halt behind me.

'What's wrong?'

I tell her to get everyone off the road. Her eyes go wide and her mouth opens, like she might have a question, but something in the tone of my voice must convince her this isn't the time to have it answered. She turns around and starts ushering the Juvies into the Walgreen's.

I set the container with the virus down in the snow and turn my attention back to the street. Up ahead the kid's stopped. He looks at me, wondering why we're no longer following. I hold up a hand and beckon him to join us, quick. He hesitates for a second, eyeing what little's left of Mags' tracks like he doesn't care to give them up, but then he swings his poles around and starts making his way towards us.

Lauren's already herded most of the Juvies into the store as I begin retracing our steps. Jake calls out to me as I pass and asks what's wrong. I tell him I'll explain when I return; for now he needs to follow the others inside.

I make my way back the way we've come, ignoring his protests. I remember I have Hicks' pistol, and for a moment I consider getting it out. But that would require digging around for it in my backpack, and in any event, it's not loaded. I don't plan to go far. A block or two, no more. Just enough to be certain.

The kid must have missed the memo about the Walgreen's; before I've gone more than a hundred yards I hear his snowshoes behind me. I turn around to find him looking up at me. I point back to where Lauren and Jake are herding the last of the Juvies out of sight, but he doesn't budge, just stares at me through the darkened lens of his goggles. I hold my mittens to my lips and he nods, once, like he understands. I set off again. He follows carefully in my tracks, watching as I search each doorway. When I reach the corner I cross over and check the next block, then the one after, just to be sure.

Tyler and Eric are the only ones still on the street when I return. They stand one on either side of the entrance to the Walgreen's. They've both slung the rifles off their shoulders. Behind them the Juvies huddle together back in the shadows. They press forward when they see me, anxious to know what's going on. Lauren squeezes her way to the front.

'What is it, Gabe?'

I point a finger at the wall.

'We've been passing them for a while.' That must have been what spidey was pinging at, in the parking lot of the Bojangles. 'Probably since we left the highway.'

She stares at the wall for a second and then her mouth draws taut. Behind her the Juvies crane their necks, anxious to see. There's more than one puzzled expression; not all of them have figured out as quickly as she has what the red 'X' sprayed across the concrete means.

'It's a scavenging mark, just like Marv and I used to leave on the places we'd visit, so you don't waste time working the same spot twice.'

From somewhere back in the shadows Amy pipes up.

'Maybe they're from a long time ago?' She says it hopefully, like all she wants right now is for me to tell her it's so. She's not the only one looking for that comfort; I hear others behind her, murmuring in agreement.

I reach up. Like everything else the wall's coated with a decade of grime. When I rub it the red comes off easy under my fingers.

'Paint's sitting on top.' I dust it from my mitten. 'I've been back a few blocks. The marks are older that way.'

Lauren continues to look at the wall.

'They live somewhere to the north.'

I nod.

'That'd be my guess. They come into the city to find what they need; probably been doing it a while. Each time they have to venture a little bit farther.'

'We could have walked right past them.'

I look over at Amy again. Her eyes are wide now, panicky as cattle. She sounds close to tears. The rest of the Juvies are exchanging worried glances. None of them need to be reminded what happened when Mags and I ran into the soldiers.

'I don't think so.' I say it with as much confidence as I can muster. I'll need to leave them now, to go find Mags, but before I do that I have to calm them down. Nothing spreads faster than panic, that's what Hicks had said, and right now the Juvies look no more than a couple of quick heartbeats from a stampede. 'I haven't seen any other tracks.' I'm sure I wouldn't have missed those.

I shuck off my backpack and set it on the ground. I undo the snaps and reach inside. My fingers find what they're looking for – a heft of cold hard steel, wrapped in old leather. I pull the pistol out and start to unravel the gun belt.

Lauren's gaze drops to the holster, and for a second it's as if her eyes brighten. She takes a step closer and looks out onto the street, following what remains of the prints Mags has left. She rests one hand on my shoulder and bends closer, lowering her voice. Behind her the Juvies shuffle forward, anxious not to miss whatever's being discussed.

'Should we be going on, Gabe? I mean, wouldn't it be safer to head back? It's like you said: we didn't pass anyone on the way in.'

Jake narrows his eyes at that suggestion, but most of the others are nodding in agreement. I look up into their anxious faces, uncertain what to say. The truth of it is I don't know. I have no idea who's working this place, or how many of them there are, or what their intentions might be towards strangers. All I know is whoever they are they most likely come from somewhere behind us, and we haven't yet reached the limits of their territory. Lauren could be right; they might be a few blocks ahead of us, even now. And if that's the case Mags will already have run into them.

I loop the belt around my waist and buckle it, feeling the weight of the pistol settle against my hip.

'You might well be right, Lauren. That's why everyone's going to wait here while I go find Mags. I don't expect I'll be long; she should have been coming back to us anyway.'

*Unless she's already run into whoever's out there.*

Jake pushes himself to the front.

'I'll come with you.'

I shake my head.

'I'll be quicker on my own.'

It comes out harsher than I intend, but I don't have to explain it in a way that might save his feelings. I make for the door before he has a chance to argue.

Tyler and Eric are still standing guard by the entrance. Eric looks twitchier than I would have cared for. His eyes won't settle in one place and his finger darts in and out of the trigger guard like it expects to have business there soon; I daresay Hicks would have a thing or two to say about his gun manners. Tyler seems calmer. He clutches his rifle to his chest, the barrel held low, his eyes slowly sweeping the street. For a second he reminds me of Benjamin, waiting for us by the portal on the day we arrived at Eden. I pull him to one side on my way out.

'Can you keep watch out here, at least till it gets dark.'

He nods.

'They'll want a fire, but make them wait as long as they can, and then light it all the way in back, away from the windows. If I'm not back you stay here tonight, and then first thing tomorrow you head back to the highway. We'll find you on the road.'

'Don't worry Gabe, I got this.'

'Alright. See you soon.'

*

I SET OFF, following what's left of Mags' prints. Before I've got to the end of the block I hear the crunch of snowshoes behind me and I turn around to find the kid on my tail. I point in the direction of the Walgreen's, but he says no. I tell him he has to, I have no time for this now, but he just shakes his head and stares up at me through his goggles, like it's me who's holding things up. I can't think of anything to do other than shoot him, and tempting as that seems right now there's a good chance someone'd hear it.

'Alright then, but this time you have to stay behind me. And don't fall back. I'm not joking now; I'm not waiting on you.'

He bobs his head like he understands.

I check the streets are empty and then dart across, quick as I can. I meant what I said; I'm not making any allowances for his size. He's as good as his word, though. He follows hard on my heels; my snowshoes have barely cleared their tracks before I hear him stepping into them.

I keep us to the sidewalk, pressed to the buildings for what little cover they provide. The paint marks continue, growing fresher with each one we pass. A half-dozen blocks south of where I left the Juvies I stop. I realize I haven't heard the kid's snowshoes in a while. When I look behind me he's come to a halt under the faded yellow star of a Hardee's. I raise my hand to hurry him on, already cursing under my breath, but something in the way he's crouched gives me pause. I turn my snowshoes around and make my way back. I find him bent over a familiar shape in the snow. A discarded rattle can sits on top of a shallow drift, only a light dusting of windblown powder covering it. He lowers his head to it again, wrinkling his nose at the smell, but when I pick it up I don't get anything. The paint's still bright on the nozzle, however, like it's not been long since it was used. I drop the can and we continue on.

The marks are everywhere now. I slow us down, checking doorways, entrances, even the silted windows above, trying not to start each time I catch my reflection in the darkened glass of an abandoned storefront. Up ahead a delivery truck's mounted the curb, barring our progress. Mags' prints go up it then disappear. As I get closer I can see two words, scratched into its ice-crusted flank in letters each a foot high.

GO BACK.

I scurry forward and peer over the crumpled hood. A hundred yards beyond the block ends at another street. There's a *KwikPrint* on the corner, its weather-faded awning snapping and fluttering in the wind.

Beyond I can just make out what looks like another set of tracks, coming out of the east. The wind's already flattening their edges, but they can't be any older than hers; whoever made them must have passed through right about the time she did. I look back down at the prints I've been following, trying to stay calm.

She had time to leave a message, which means she saw them before they saw her. Probably. I look down at the snow. Other than the prints she's left, and the set running up the middle of the cross street, it's smooth, unmarked. There's no way she would have let someone take her without a struggle, and there's no sign of that.

So where is she?

I feel the kid tugging at the sleeve of my parka. He points a mitten in the direction of the *KwikPrint*, and then without warning he takes off towards it. I hiss at him to come back, but he's showing no greater inclination to heed what I say now than he did earlier. He crosses the street and disappears into the store. I hesitate a second longer then break from the cover of the truck and hurry after him.

The tattered awning flaps above my head as I step under it, into the shadow of the entrance. It takes a moment for my eyes to adjust to the gloom, but when they do I see a familiar figure, standing by the window. The kid's already out of his snowshoes, crouching next to her. I unsnap my bindings and hurry over to join them. She presses a finger to her lips.

'Didn't you see…'

I don't wait for her to finish, just throw my arms around her, hold her tight to me for a long while. Eventually she taps my arm.

'Hey.'

I wait a moment longer then let her go. She turns back to the window, but not before I catch what might be a smile. It occurs to me it's not an expression I've seen much of recently.

She looks over my shoulder, back towards the entrance.

'Where are the others?'

'As soon as I spotted the paint I got them off the street and came looking for you.' I hadn't intended it, but I realize that does sound pretty heroic, in a *Last of the Mohicans* sort of way. That was one of Mags' favorite films, back in Mount Weather, so I decide not to go into detail on how many blocks I had to pass before I finally noticed the big red X's sprayed on pretty much every building since we left the highway. I can't see how Hawkeye would have missed something like that.

She leans a little closer to the pane and goes back to looking out. Large cracks zig-zag their way across the glass, and what's not broken is coated with grime, all of which makes it pretty hard to see. I find a section that's a little cleaner than the rest and press my face to it.

'So what are you looking at?'

She points at a *Save-A-Lot* kitty corner opposite.

'The two men I almost ran into, coming up the street, they went in there. That was over an hour ago now. They haven't come out yet.'

For the next twenty minutes we keep watch in silence. Outside the day starts to darken, and I wonder if, whoever it is we're waiting for, they've settled in for the night. But then Mags and the kid both stir. I cup one mitten to the glass and peer out, holding my breath. At first I don't see anything, but a few seconds later there's movement by the doorway and a tall man steps into view. He's bundled up in so many clothes it's hard to tell much about him other than his height. He looks up to the sky, then gestures to someone else to hurry up. There's a pause and a second, shorter, man steps into view. He adjusts the straps on the pack he's carrying and then both set off up the street, Indian file.

I follow them until they're out of sight and then I step back from the window. An idea's starting to form, but I'll need to be quick. I glance at my pack, propped against the wall. I shouldn't need it; I don't mean to be gone that long. I start making my way towards the door.

Mags turns to look at me.

'What are you doing?'

'Going after them.'

She stares at me like I've taken leave of my senses.

'You're *what*?'

'Okay, I know how it sounds, but just think about it a second. Fearrington's going to be small; we know that, right? If we're lucky there'll be basic supplies, food, water, but probably not much else. Which means pretty soon I'm going to have to find us stuff. Marv's map says this is the only place of any size within a day's hike. The fact that someone else is working this place doesn't have to be a problem; I can stay out of their way, *as long as I know where they're going to be*. Now the marks I spotted earlier made me think whoever they are, they're coming out of the north.' I point out towards the *Save-A-Lot*. 'But the tracks those men made came out of the east and now they're headed west. I just need to follow them a little ways to figure out which it is. Otherwise sooner or later I'm going to end up running into them again, just like you almost did. Only next time I may not be so lucky as you were.'

She looks at me a while, like she's considering this. I guess she must see some sense in it, because she reaches for her backpack.

'Alright, I'll come with you.'

I shake my head.

'You need to get back to the others. I left them in a Walgreen's a dozen blocks back the way we came. The kid knows where it is.'

I see her weighing what I've just said. She doesn't look convinced.

'Some of them might be starting to fret by now.' *Might?* If Amy isn't already the proud mother of kittens I'll be amazed. I figure it's best not to overdo this last bit, however; Mags knows the Juvies every bit as well as I do. She thinks on it some more. In the end she nods reluctantly.

'Alright, but not far, okay? Seriously, Gabe - don't make me come looking for you.'

*

THE TWO MEN from the *Save-A-Lot* are already half a dozen blocks distant by the time I step outside. I watch from the shelter of the *KwikPrint*'s doorway to make sure they're not in the habit of checking behind them, then I wave Mags and the kid onto the street.

She steps into her snowshoes, pulls up her hood. She's about to set off but then she turns and grabs my arm.

'I mean it, Gabe: be careful, okay?'

'Don't worry; I'll be back here long before you. If I'm not bring the others as far south as you can while there's light, then find somewhere to hole up. I'll come find you.'

I watch until she and the kid have disappeared around the delivery truck, and then I turn my attention back to the two men. They're already little more than a couple of charcoal smudges, mostly lost to the swirling snow.

I pull off my mittens, unzip my parka and reach for the pistol on my hip. I saw no sign of a rifle slung over either man's shoulder, but I don't plan on taking any chances, all the same. I pry the hammer back and lever the loading gate open, then jiggle a round from the cartridge loops on my belt, drop it into the chamber and move the cylinder on a turn. The cold finds its way through my liners fast; by the time I'm pushing the last one home the tips of my fingers are starting to lose feeling.

I drop the gun back in its holster, pull on my mittens and poke my head out, just as my quarries disappear up a side street. I set off after them. My heart's beating a little faster, but as I cross the street I realize most of it's excitement. I meant what I said to Mags: I'm not going to do anything stupid. I don't plan on following them far, just enough to see which way they're headed. It'll make a welcome change from herding the Juvies down mile after mile of interstate. For the first time in weeks I feel useful.

I hurry along the sidewalk, keeping my eyes on the single set of prints they've left in the snow. When I get to the spot where their tracks veer off I stop and peer around the corner. I still haven't seen any sign they're checking behind them, but I hold back anyway, watching as they trudge steadily away from me. Maybe this is going to be even easier than I had counted on. They're headed north now. If they show no sign of deviating from their current course by the time I lose them again I'll take it as their destination and call an end to the pursuit.

I wait five minutes, then ten. I catch only occasional glimpses of them now, through gaps that open in the drift. I lift my goggles onto my forehead, squinting into the windblown snow, but it doesn't help. The sightings grow less frequent, and for a long while I don't see them at all. And then, just as I'm about to turn around and head back to the *KwikPrint* the wind drops, and for a second before it picks up again I see them cutting across the street, like they mean to leave it. I look up to the gunmetal sky. There's not much left of the day, but this might be my only opportunity to figure out where it is they're coming from. I hesitate a second longer, then pull the goggles back down and set off after them again.

For the next half hour I follow the men as they wind their way through the city. After the first few turns I think I have a sense of the general direction in which they're headed, but then suddenly their route seems to lose all reason. They switch this way then that, at times doubling back, until I start to wonder whether they know themselves where they're going. The wind strengthens. It drives the drifts in long, shifting ridges that snake across the road, clearing their prints; I have to keep shortening the gap between us to keep them in sight. They seem oblivious to my presence, however, and in any case the flurries of snow that obscure them will keep me hidden too.

They disappear down yet another cross street and I hurry to catch up, but when I get to the corner and peer around there's no sign and for a moment I think I've finally lost them. I look up. The sky's darkening and I can feel the temperature beginning to drop; I think it might be time to cut my losses and turn back. But then through a gap in the snow I see a flashlight wink on, followed moments later by another.

I set off after them again. Tracking their beams is easier so I allow myself to drop back a little, more comfortable now that I can keep a block between us. They finally seem to have found a heading they're happy with, too. The road begins to incline, and from the signs we pass it looks like we're almost back at the interstate. Ahead of me the flashlights stop and then perform a complicated little dance. I wait, peering into the gloom, trying to work out what's going on. After a few seconds the beams resume their onward march. I creep forward again, more slowly now, until I reach the interchange. Ahead the gantry arm from a stoplight lies collapsed in the snow, blocking my path; the light show I've just witnessed must have been them clambering over it.

The wind's strengthening; already there's little left of their tracks. I stand at the foot of the overpass, my arms hugged to my sides, watching the intermittent pinpricks of light until they finally lose themselves to the swirling snow. I've seen as much as I need to, though. I look around. I'm farther north than I expected and dusk's already settling; it's too late to go looking for Mags and the others now. I'll find somewhere to shelter for the night, catch them on the road tomorrow.

I make my way down off the interchange. There's a *U-Haul* lot right across the street. A single-story cinder block with a faded sign above squats in one corner, and as a bonus the door's already ajar, saving me the bother of busting it open, which is just as well given that the pry bar's sitting in my pack, back in the *KwikPrint*. I point myself toward it, already looking forward to the fire I'll soon have going.

I unsnap my snowshoes at the entrance and push the door back. The floor's dusty, scattered with debris. A long counter stretches the length of the far wall. There's a metal box mounted behind, its lock pried open, keys still hanging from hooks inside. Next to it a whiteboard, marked with the comings and goings of vehicles. To one side a stack of packing boxes that look like they'll hold a flame. I'm in luck; I won't even need to go outside again for firewood.

I step inside, pulling what remains of the door closed behind me. The sound of the wind recedes. But as I bend to undo my bindings I hear a soft *snick-snick* and I freeze. It's a sound I have recently come to know; the sound of the slide being pulled back on a handgun, as its owner chambers the first round.

*

A COLD KNOT OF FEAR tightens my stomach. I raise my hands and turn around to face a thin black man, bundled up in an assortment of rags. A pair of dark eyes, the whites tobacco yellow, stare back at me from deep in a wide, angular face. He holds the pistol he's just cocked sideways in front of him, at a flat angle, his finger already curled around the trigger. The muzzle's close enough that even in this light I can read the words *Smith & Wesson* stamped along the barrel.

Hick's pistol rests useless against my hip, under my zipped-up parka. The idea that I might draw it and fire a round in the air, and that that might frighten him off, suddenly seems laughable.

'Why you been following us?'

My mind races, searching for something to say. I can't tell him anything that'd make him think there's more than just me. I also really – and I can't stress this enough – *really* don't want to get shot.

'I…I thought you might have some food.'

His lip curls in a derisive grin, revealing a mouth full of gold teeth. If it was his intention to put me at ease, it doesn't work. There's something cruel, feral about it; a malice that infects the whole of his face. He inclines his head to one side, but the pistol doesn't move.

'Does it look to you like I might have any to spare?'

That sounds like a rhetorical question, but I shake my head anyway.

'You strapped?'

I stare at him blankly. I have no idea what he means.

'Are you packing?'

I'm still not sure what he wants me to say. My eyes flick over my shoulder. He must see I'm not carrying a backpack.

'Do-you-have-a-wea-pon?'

He says it one word at a time, punctuating each syllable with a short, agitated jab of the pistol into my chest. I nod quickly, desperate for him to stop doing that.

'Yes. Yes. Under my coat.'

'Take it out. Nice and easy, now.'

I unzip the parka and reach down to the holster, pulling Hicks' pistol out with my fingertips. When he sees it he whistles through his gilded teeth and snatches it from me. He stares at it for a moment and then it disappears inside one of the many folds in his clothing.

'Belt too.'

I unbuckle the gun belt and hand it over.

'Anything else?'

I start to tell him about Weasel's knife, but he's already rummaging through my pockets. He finds the blade, examines it for a second and then that goes the way of the pistol. My heart sinks when he takes out Marv's map, but all he does is study the cover for a moment and then toss it. It occurs to me now, too late, that I never thought to make a copy. Kane's master list of codes for each facility in the Federal Relocation Arc is sitting in the outside pocket of my pack, back in the *KwikPrint*, but without the map showing the bunker's location Mags might never find it. I glance down to where it lies, discarded, on the dusty floor. The snow outside will be wiped clean of my prints long before she'll think to come after me. How will she know to look for it here?

'That it?'

I nod.

'Travellin' a bit light aintcha?'

I don't know what to say to that so I just nod again.

'Alright, hold out your hands.'

An already looped length of cord appears from one of his pockets. He pulls off my mittens and slips it over my wrists, drawing it tight. He runs the cord around a few more times, passing it between my hands in a neat figure of eight, and then ties it off with practiced efficiency, like he's done this before. He tests the knot. The work's good; I can already feel pins and needles pricking my fingertips. Satisfied, he picks up one of my mittens, removing a tattered, fraying glove so he can try it on. The fit must be close enough because he pulls off the other, smiling at me like he's happy with the trade.

I bend down to recover the gloves he's discarded, but he just pushes me in the direction of the door before I have a chance to retrieve them.

His accomplice waits for us up on the overpass. He's thin, like the first one, and no better groomed, but taller, a raggedy scarecrow of a man. He grips a flashlight in each hand, the yellow beams describing stretched out circles in the gray snow. The one with the teeth pushes me forward towards him. The scarecrow shifts a flashlight and holds me in its beam while he looks me up and down. The first man smiles, his eyes wet with excitement. The light from the beam glitters off the gold caps that crowd his mouth.

'Look what I found, Mac. Just wait till Finch sees him. Just you wait.'

The man called Mac pulls down something that might once have been a scarf. His skin is even darker than his companion's, the eyes that stare back at me black as coals. A patchy beard, straggled and unruly, salted with gray, covers the lower half of his face.

'Quit your yappin', Goldie. It's getting late, and we have a ways to go yet.'

*

WE LEAVE THE INTERSTATE behind and continue north. Crumbling strip malls slowly give way to houses with yards, then snow-covered fields. After a couple of miles the road branches at a water tower and we take the westerly fork. We keep to it for what seems like a long time. I close my eyes and try to recall what was on the map for this stretch, but as far as I can remember there wasn't much of anything. I really hope we don't have much farther to go. The last of the light's already draining from the sky and the temperature's dropping fast now; I can feel the ice-crust forming on the powder beneath my snowshoes. I flex the muscles in my wrists to keep the blood flowing, but the cord's too tight; my fingers are already numb. All I can do is I hold them to my face and blow into them to try and keep them warm.

We continue on, following the beams from the flashlights. The tall man stays quiet, but the other one, the one with the impressive dentistry, likes to talk. He keeps it up without pause. Mostly it's variations of the same thing, repeated over and over. Somebody called Finch is going to be very happy to see me. That seems to bode well for him, although it's unclear yet what it might mean for me. I find myself wishing for our destination in spite of it. Anything to get out of the bone-splitting cold.

We trudge up a long, straight section and then, just as I think we're about to start down into the shallow beyond, Mac takes a turn I hadn't even spotted was there. I search for a sign, any clue as to where we might be headed, but there's nothing. The road narrows to little more than a track. We follow it for an hour, maybe more, our snowshoes crunching through the ice-slicked snow as it winds ever upward. At last we reach the ridgeline and now I see what must be our destination. In what little remains of the light I can make out little more than its size: a huge, walled fortress, sitting alone in the valley beneath us.

We make our way down towards it. Goldie grows more excited. He pushes me forward, jabbering continuously, barely stopping to draw breath. As we get closer I can see that the fortress's high stone walls are topped with tangled coils of barbed wire. A guard tower stares down from each corner. The nearest one on the western side looks like it's been set ablaze; there's little left of its structure other than a few charred beams, poking up into the darkening sky.

My heart sinks as I realize a building like this could only have one purpose.

Mac sets course for a tall iron gate that dominates the closest side. A rusting sign above confirms my fears: it announces we have arrived at *Starkly Correctional Institution*. Kane used to say if we were to happen upon others while out scavenging we were to give them a wide berth; that if there was anyone still left after all this time they'd most likely be desperate, dangerous men, lawless and Godless. Our President had his reasons for keeping us fearful, I know that now. But it gives me little comfort that my captors may not have had much of the law about them, even before the world fell apart.

We stop in front of the entrance. The gate towers above us; it must be three times as high as I am tall. Mac steps up to a smaller door set into the thick, riveted metal and pounds on it with his fist. After a long pause a latch slides back. A second later from somewhere behind there's the sound of bolts being drawn and the door creaks open.

I bend to undo my snowshoes. Goldie's eager to get inside now; he snaps at me to hurry, but my frozen fingers aren't up to the task of working the bindings. I finally manage one, but the second proves more stubborn. In the end he loses patience and shoves me. I trip over the foot that's still tethered and stumble forward. I try to get my hands out in front of me, but they're bound together and slow with the cold. My head bounces off the edge of something hard and then I'm falling through the door. I land awkwardly on the other side and just lay there for a moment, stunned, staring up at a wire-mesh sky. I feel something wet trickling down one side of my face, already growing sluggish in the frigid air. I raise my hands tentatively, trying to direct them to the spot. It takes longer than it ought. When I hold them out in front of me they're smeared with blood.

Something tugs at my boot and then rough hands grab me under my arms and haul me to my feet. I look around. I'm in some sort of holding pen. In front there's a step-through metal detector, like the one we had in the tunnel in Eden; beyond it a barred gate. Somewhere off in the darkness an indifferently muffled generator chugs away, marking out uneven time.

A small man sits in a glass-fronted booth, off to one side. At his elbow a low flame gutters in something that might once have been a candle, but is now little more than a pool of wax. The glass is pocked with frosted impact points, thin cracks spider-webbing out from the center of each. The pane seems to have been designed with such an assault in mind, however, because it's held.

Mac shucks off his backpack and approaches the booth. A metal tray slides out. He pulls a handgun from his coat, ejects the magazine and drops both in. Goldie does the same with his weapon, then digs in his pocket for Hicks' pistol. He pushes it up against the glass.

'I got to show this to Mr. Finch.'

The man behind the glass appears to consider the request for a moment, then simply says *Bullets*.

Goldie studies the pistol, turning it over in his hands, like he doesn't know how to work it. After a moment he holds it out to me, an irritated expression souring his dark features. My fingers are too numb to do it for him, so I explain through chattering teeth how he has to pull the hammer back to open the loading gate and then use the plunger to eject each round from its chamber. He struggles with it for a while before Mac steps over and takes it off him with a grunt. His fingers work the mechanism smoothly, rotating the cylinder so that one by one the bullets rattle into the bottom of the tray. When it's empty the man behind the glass draws the tray back. Goldie holds his hand out sullenly, and after a brief pause Mac gives the pistol back. It disappears into the folds of his clothing and then I'm being shoved forward again, in the direction of the metal detector. I tell him the dog tags I wear will set it off. He cusses me a few more times while he stops to yank them from my neck, and then I get pushed through.

Mac takes his turn after me. There's a loud beep as Goldie steps up to it. He turns to the man in the booth and pulls back his lips, pointing to his teeth.

'C'mon, man. Every time?'

There's a pause and then the gate buzzes and I'm hustled through into a large open area, a hundred yards or more on a side, like the keep of an old castle. A long gray building, three stories tall, its slab sides dotted with tiny slit windows, holds the center. A path's been cleared through the snow from the holding pen towards it. A handful of smaller structures huddle together at the base of the prison's high stone walls. By what little remains of the day's light it looks a hard place, devoid of either warmth or color, and I can't see how its appearance will have improved much by morning. Assuming I'm around to see it, that is.

Goldie pushes me towards a stout wooden door that looks to be the entrance to the main building. Mac holds it open and I step inside. A metal stair zig-zags up into darkness. He turns to his companion.

'Bring him through. I'll go tell Finch.'

His boots clang up the stair. Goldie grabs me by the elbow, drags me along a short corridor that opens into a huge, dimly lit hall. As my eyes adjust to the gloom I can see it's open, all the way to its high, vaulted roof. Around the sides iron landings protrude from the gray stone and beyond I can just make out rows of cell doors. Most sit in darkness, but here and there the soft glow of candlelight seeps out from within. Shadowy figures lean against the railings in ones or twos, talking in low murmurs, here and there the glowing red tip of a cigarette passing between them. I feel the weight of their stare as I enter.

A long wooden table stretches off into shadow, candles in various stages of decomposition punctuating its length. Flames gutter in the shells of a few, but most are unlit. Goldie pulls out a chair near the end and manhandles me into it, then places Hicks' pistol on the table nearby.

He stands to one side, grinning down at me.

'Mr. Finch'll be down soon, don't you worry.' A giggle escapes his lips, like he can barely contain his excitement.

I stare down at the table. My head's starting to hurt from where I banged it, but I suspect whatever injury I've picked up there is soon going to be the least of my worries. I don't know who Finch is, but I can't say I share Goldie's excitement at the prospect of meeting him. There's not much I can do about that, however, so instead I tuck my frozen hands into my lap and sit there, awaiting my fate.

*

I DON'T HAVE LONG TO WAIT.

From somewhere behind and above there's the creak of a door being opened and then the slow, uneven clang of hard shoes on metal. The sound echoes through the hall, reverberating off the cold stone. The footsteps reach the end of the landing and take to the stair. They become more deliberate as they descend, until at last they reach the bottom. There's a pause and then they start up again, growing louder as they make their way toward me. And now the hollow click of heels is punctuated by another sound, an intermittent *clack* as something other than shoe leather strikes the concrete.

The footsteps come to a halt, right behind my chair. There's a long pause and then a short, neat man, dressed in a dark suit and tie, appears before me, leaning on a wooden cane. His graying hair is parted carefully to one side, and a pair of horn-rimmed spectacles perch precariously on his thin nose. He's flanked on either side by two much bigger men. The one on the left is burly, barrel-chested. An impressive gut hangs over his belt; a beard, wide like a shovel, adds to his scope. The other man is equally large, but whereas his companion looks like he might be running to fat, this one is muscular, powerful. His shaved head sits directly on a pair of broad shoulders without a discernible neck to separate the two.

The one with the beard steps forward, pulls out the chair at the head of the table. The smaller man I assume to be Finch lowers himself into it, then holds the cane up for the bearded one to take. He settles back in the chair, carefully placing one knee over the other. The cuff of one pant leg hitches up as he does it, revealing a polished wingtip. He rests his elbows on the arms of the chair, steeples his fingers, and for a long moment just studies me over them. Then without warning he leans forward and reaches out a hand. The fingers are narrow, delicate, the nails clean, recently clipped. He smiles, revealing a perfect picket fence row of teeth.

'Garland Finch.'

The voice is low, soft like velvet, and yet somehow intense. For a few seconds I just stare at the hand, unsure what to say. There is something about him that is different, other. It's like he's wrong for this place; like he doesn't belong here. At last I stammer out my name. He repeats it, rolling the word from his tongue, almost like he's tasting it. I lift my hands from my lap to take the one he's offering, but it's a little difficult with my wrists tied together. He looks down at my bonds and his face wrinkles with displeasure. He tilts his head to one side.

'Mr. Goldie?'

The man with the teeth scurries forward out of the darkness.

'Yes, boss?'

Finch nods at my wrists.

'Why is Gabriel bound, Mr. Goldie?'

Goldie looks at me, and then at Finch, then back at me again, like he might not understand the question. The man who, for all his diminutive size, is clearly in charge of this place sighs. When he speaks it is patiently, as if to a slow-witted child.

'What do I detest more than anything Mr. Goldie?'

Goldie bobs his head, like he knows this one.

'Bad manners, boss.'

Finch looks at my bonds again, as if his point has been made.

Goldie leans closer, bows his head, so it's next to Finch's ear. He points at the pistol that sits in front of me on the table. His voice drops to a whisper.

'But boss, we found that on him.'

'Well no doubt he was carrying it for his own protection, Mr. Goldie. And I can't say I blame him, with hooligans like you running around untethered.' He smiles at me, apologetically. 'I'm sure he doesn't mean to use it on us, do you Gabriel?'

I shake my head.

'No, certainly not.'

*At least not without the bullets it came with.*

Goldie's mouth opens, like he might be about to protest some more. Finch closes his eyes and raises one hand to his brow. His narrow fingers press between his eyebrows, as if stanching a headache.

'Mr. Goldie.'

He doesn't raise his voice, but for those few syllables the tone changes. It loses all its softness and takes on a hard, flinty quality. From the dark balconies above there's a sound like I remember the rustling of leaves, as though the men there have suddenly all decided to draw breath at precisely the same moment.

Goldie's jaw snaps shut with an audible click. He hurries forward, fumbling in his pocket; Weasel's knife appears between his fingers. I hold my hands up. He slips the end of the blade between my wrists and starts sawing at the cord like his life depends on it. A few moments later the severed ends drop to the table. I rub my wrists, wincing as the blood returns to my fingers.

Finch looks at me as if embarrassed. He waits while I flex my fingers and then holds out his hand again. When he speaks his tone is once more pleasant.

'A pleasure to meet you, Gabriel.'

I shake his hand. The fingers that slip into mine feel slight, fragile, like there may be nothing more substantial than the bones of birds beneath the skin there.

'You will have to forgive Mr. Goldie. It may not surprise you to learn that he has a long and troubled history with firearms.'

Goldie's already retreating, clearly anxious to be out of our presence, but the man with the beard steps forward, blocking his way. He folds a pair of meaty forearms across his chest and stares down at the shorter man.

Finch tilts his head to one side, the thinnest of smiles playing across his lips.

'Mr. Goldie, I do believe you've forgotten something.'

Goldie pauses then turns around and scurries back to the table. He deposits Weasel's knife next to Hicks' pistol, then hurries away again.

Finch turns back to me and shakes his head ruefully.

'You will need to be more careful with your possessions while you are with us, Gabriel.' He shifts a little closer, speaking into the back of his hand, as though the comment is intended for me alone. 'There is a regrettable criminal element.'

His fingers brush the knot in his tie. I'm struck again by how neat he appears. There's not a thing out of place. Even his shoelaces look like they might have been pressed.

'Now tell me: how have they been treating you?

'Uh, fine, I guess.' At the last moment I remember his comment about manners. 'Thank you for asking.'

He smiles, but then something catches his attention. He leans forward, studying my face.

'I do hope that cut on your forehead wasn't caused by one of these ruffians.'

From somewhere off in the darkness I hear Goldie's voice again. He speaks quickly, tripping over the words, like he's anxious to get them out. Seems like the pitch might be a shade higher than it was just moments before, too.

'Wasn't me, boss. He fell of his own accord, coming in through the gate. Clumsy! Clumsy! I tried to help him, yes I did. Swear to God.'

Finch's eyes narrow at the lie; he lifts one finger and starts tapping the arm of the chair, like it vexes him. Nothing in our brief history should make me care for Goldie's wellbeing, but for some reason I can't fathom I nod, confirming his story. Finch stares at me for a long moment, his fingernail still marking out time. Then without warning he stops, spreads his hands, and the smile returns.

'Well I'm glad to hear it. Now, Gabriel, we were just about to eat. Will you join us for dinner?'

The inquiry sounds genuine, like I'd be free to get up and walk out if I chose. It's too late to go anywhere till morning, of course, but the fact that he makes it seem that way lifts my spirits a fraction, all the same.

'Um, sure.' I remember his comment about manners, and what Goldie said about them not having any food to spare. 'I'm afraid I don't have anything to contribute, though.'

Finch waves the idea away, like he wouldn't hear of it.

'Nonsense, you are our guest.' He tilts his head in Goldie's direction.

'Mr. Goldie, please run and tell Mr. Blatch we shall have one more for dinner.'

'One more for dinner, right boss.'

'And let him know he may serve whenever he's ready.'

*

GOLDIE'S FOOTSTEPS RETREAT as he scurries off on his errand. Those on the landings take it as their cue to join us. They shuffle down the stairs and across the hall, approaching the table cautiously. The positions they assume seem well rehearsed, though, as if this is a ritual they have performed countless times before. Finch introduces each as they step into the faltering candlelight. The names continue as more men emerge from the shadows; soon I've given up any hope of keeping them straight in my head and all I have is the count. The last two to arrive – thirty-six and thirty-seven – are the small man I saw in the booth as we came in, who Finch says is Mr. Culver, and Goldie's tall raggedy companion who he calls Mr. MacIntyre. None of these men look like they're carrying any extra weight. Their lips are parched, cracked, their faces chiseled gaunt by hunger. They keep their eyes down, focusing on the bowl and spoon each has brought with him. The two large men who entered with Finch are the last to sit, taking places on either side of him at the end of the table. Their size marks them out in contrast. The muscular man Finch introduces as Mr. Knox. The heavy one with the beard he calls Mr. Tully. If Finch had been the warden of this place I'm guessing Knox and Tully must have been two of his guards.

There's the dull groan of a door being opened somewhere behind me, followed by the quick, shuffling footsteps of someone hefting a load. I look over my shoulder, just as a long streak of a man with a narrow bloodhound face enters, struggling under the weight of a large metal pot. The table creaks as he sets it down at Finch's elbow. His mouth puckers into a frown as he sees me.

'I didn't know we was having guests.'

Finch offers me an apologetic smile. *You can't get the help*. He leans forward, as if sharing a secret.

'You will have to forgive Mr. Blatch, Gabriel. He is quite the genius in the kitchen, but he harbors an intense dislike for surprises. He will cluck like an old hen if I propose the slightest change to our dinner plans.' He turns to the cook. 'Now, Mr. Blatch, we must remember our manners.'

Blatch mutters something and then lifts the lid off the pot. Steam rises up, quickly disappearing into the darkness above. It smells of something that might once have been meat, but is now so diluted as to defy the identifying.

Finch leans forward and inhales theatrically.

'Why, it smells simply divine. Mr. Blatch, you may serve.'

Empty bowls make their way up the table. Blatch slops a ladle of piping hot liquid into each and then passes it back down. It's pretty cold in here; whatever it is he's serving won't hold its heat long. But nevertheless everybody waits patiently. When the last bowl has been placed in front of Finch Goldie steps from the shadows, fusses with a napkin for his lap, then scurries off again. The warden raises his spoon.

'*Bon appetit*, gentlemen.'

I'm not sure what that means, but the men seem to take it as a sign they can finally chow down. They bow their heads, each concentrating on his bowl with uncommon intensity. From somewhere behind me there's the chug of a starter; a motor sputters complainingly, then settles to a lump idle. And for a second I think of The Greenbrier, and how the lights had come on in the chandeliers at a similar sound. I look around at the stone walls, the iron landings, the barred cells behind. This place could hardly be more different.

A scratching sound brings me back. It's followed by the popcorn-crackle of an old record and from off in the darkness the thin, reedy strains of music drift out from a rattling speaker. It's a woman singing, in a language I don't understand. To hear music is a strange thing, and for a few seconds I just sit there and listen.

Goldie returns from the last of his errands and takes a seat a little further down the table. He leans forward, lowering his head to the soup, and starts slurping at it with a determination that's impressive to behold. Drops spill from his lips, running down his chin. He runs a grubby sleeve across his mouth, returns it to the table. The warden looks down the table at him and sighs.

'Mr. Goldie.'

Goldie looks up.

'Yes boss?'

'No uncooked joints on the table, if you please.'

Goldie withdraws his arms from the table. His chin drops to his chest and he tucks his offending elbows into his lap.

'Sorry, boss.'

He returns his attention to the broth, his fervor only slightly diminished by the reprimand.

Finch picks up his own spoon, but then he just holds it over the bowl and turns to me, as if waiting for me to go first. Tell the truth the broth doesn't look that appetizing, but I remember what he said about manners, so I try some. If Blatch was aiming for equal parts watery and greasy he's nailed it. There's little chunks of something gray that might once have been meat floating in it, too, but without the can they came out of it's hard to tell what it might be. It does have a certain flavor, though. I look up from the bowl and Finch is still staring at me. I hadn't really noticed it before, but his eyes are the palest of blue, and for the briefest instant it's almost as if they burn a little brighter. He holds my gaze a moment then leans forward to sip his soup. When he's done he dabs at his lips with the napkin.

'Another triumph, Mr. Blatch, I do declare.'

I point my spoon in the general direction of the music.

'You have power?'

'Well, after a fashion.' He smiles down the table at the small man who was sat behind the booth in the holding pen. 'Mr. Culver was able to work his magic on a couple of old diesel generators we found in one of the sheds; he has an aptitude for that sort of thing. Fuel is hard to come by, of course, so we must be frugal. But music is so good for the digestion, don't you think?'

I have a better vocabulary than any of the Juvies, except maybe Mags, but sometimes the warden uses words and I don't know what they mean, except maybe from how he uses them. I think I can guess *frugal* from the context but I make a mental note to look it up, next time I'm in the vicinity of a dictionary.

'Can't say that I know.'

Finch looks at me for a moment, like he's considering this, then goes back to his bowl. I take another mouthful of the broth. Maybe it's just because I'm hungry, but the taste's kinda growing on me.

'So, Gabriel, what is it that brings you our way?'

I keep my eyes down for a moment. I knew sooner or later this question was coming, but my heart quickens a little nevertheless. I dip the spoon in the bowl and swirl the greasy liquid around, trying to sound as unconcerned about my answer as possible.

'Oh, I was just passing through. I noticed Mr. Goldie and Mr. Macintyre's prints and thought I'd follow them, see where they were headed.' I look up from my bowl, adlibbing a little to make it seem natural. 'I wouldn't normally have done that; I mostly make it my business to stay out of the way of others. But I haven't had a square meal in weeks and I was getting a little desperate.'

The warden's spoon is on its way back into his broth, but now it stops, and when he looks up at me his expression has darkened unpleasantly. I wonder if I've taken it too far. There's not much left of the rations we set out from Mount Weather with, but I haven't had to skip a meal yet, and compared to most of the wraiths sitting around the table I must look like I've been living high on the hog. Finch fixes me with those piercing blue eyes and for a moment it's as if I can't quite catch my breath. I want to look away, but somehow I think that would be a bad idea. Off in the shadows the woman's still singing, but otherwise it seems like the room's suddenly gone very quiet. The warden starts tapping his spoon against the rim of the bowl, slow, methodical, but in a way that's completely out of kilter with the music. The sound it makes seems as loud and deliberate as a hammer pounding an anvil.

'You were lucky you ran into us. City's not a place to be, least not after dark.'

Finch stops his tapping. His gaze stays on me a moment longer, then shifts down the table to Mac. At first I'm just relieved for the interruption, but as his words sink in I realize that's where Mags and the others are right now; she won't have got them clear of it before nightfall. I keep my eyes on my broth, trying not to let the concern show in my voice.

'What…what do you mean by that?'

Mac's spoon hovers over his bowl, but he doesn't look up. In the end it's the warden who answers for him.

'Oh, don't mind Mr. MacIntyre, Gabriel. He has the constitution of an old woman.'

Across the table Goldie giggles and then goes back to slurping his soup. I want to dismiss the tall convict's warning, but there's something about it that sticks with me. I remember the feeling I'd had, as we had made our way through the parking lot of the hospital, that we were being watched. I stare at Mac, but now he won't meet my gaze.

'Have you seen something, Mr. MacIntyre?'

For a long while he doesn't respond, then eventually he just shakes his head.

'No.'

Finch leans forward in his seat. The smile has returned.

'You really shouldn't worry, Gabriel. You're perfectly safe with us, all the way out here in the willy-wags.'

*

THE THIN CLINK AND SCRAPE OF CUTLERY continues as all around me the prisoners concentrate on extracting the last of the broth from their bowls. Then one by one my dinner companions get up from their chairs, gather their utensils and shuffle off into the shadows, returning to their cells. Further down the table Goldie cuts a glance in the warden's direction then lifts his to his lips, tilting his head back for the dregs. I look down at my own bowl, surprised to see it's almost empty. I guess dinner was just the soup, then. I scoop out the last of it and set the spoon down. I could definitely eat more, but there's been no mention of seconds and seeing as I'm freeloading anyway I say it was the best I've tasted and I couldn't fit another mouthful. Finch seems happy with that. He dabs at his lips with his napkin and smiles.

'It is kind of you to say, Gabriel. Now, I would love to stay and chat but unfortunately I have an errand to run.' He smiles, as if a pleasant thought has just occurred to him. 'But if you'd care to join me I can offer you a tour of our humble facility.'

I have nothing else planned for the evening so I say that would be nice. Tully gets to his feet and pulls the chair back for his boss while Knox fetches his cane. Hicks' pistol is still sitting on the table in front of me, next to Weasel's blade. I glance at them uncertainly. Finch follows my gaze then flutters a hand in their direction.

'Oh, by all means bring those with you.'

He accepts the cane Knox proffers, leaning his weight on it to stand. When he's got his balance he limps off. Tully lifts a candle from the table and lumbers after him. Knox glares at me as I reach for the gun and knife, but the warden was clear, so I shove both into my pocket and hurry after him.

We leave the main hall and enter a long, dark corridor. Iron-braced doors punctuate the stone at seemingly random intervals. Most are shut, but some hang ajar. I look inside as we pass. Behind one, rows of industrial-sized washing machines and tumble dryers, sitting gape-mouthed in the darkness. Another opens to what might once have been a pantry, but the shelves that line the walls now are dusty, bare.

Finch's heels and cane click-clack ahead of us, the sounds echoing along the passageway. The air grows thick with the smells of grease and smoke. We arrive at the kitchens, where I guess Blatch must cook up his masterpieces. The warden stops outside and sends Tully in to retrieve something while we wait. The candle he carries casts unreliable shadows, but I can make out things as he passes. Rows of steel countertops, stretching back into darkness. An assortment of pots and pans, their surfaces blackened from years of use, stacked precariously underneath. A collection of knives, saws, cleavers, the candlelight briefly playing over the honed steel. And for an instant in the far corner something long and gray, hanging from an old hook. I peer into the darkness, but Tully has already moved on with the candle and whatever it might be is lost again to shadow.

Finch shifts his weight on the cane.

'So tell me Gabriel, what is it you like to do with your free time?'

He says it like taking in a show, or visiting a museum or learning to play the piano might all be perfectly acceptable responses, so at first I'm not sure what to say. There hasn't been much in the way of free time since we quit Mount Weather, but there was enough of it over the winter for me to remember what having a spare hour feels like. I take a moment to sift through the possibilities. It doesn't take me long to settle on the answer I reckon is least likely to get me into trouble.

'Mostly I like to read.'

Finch looks up and once again I find myself caught in that piercing gaze. He continues to stare at me, as though measuring my age against the truth in that statement. One finger hovers over the head of his cane, as though he means to start that tapping thing again. But then the smile broadens.

'Well said, well said. There is nothing like a good book, is there?' He holds a hand up. 'Why, the library is right on our way. You must let me show it to you.' He raps the cane once on the stone floor, as though it's decided, then inclines his head in the direction of the kitchens, raising his voice a fraction. 'If Mr. Tully ever sees fit to return to us, that is.'

Moments later Tully emerges from the shadows carrying a battered looking metal flask, a length of fraying cord looped around the handle, and we set off down the corridor again. At the end there's a turn and a half-flight of stairs. I wait while Finch hobbles up them and then I follow his click-clacking footfalls down an even narrower passageway that ends in a small wooden door. He stops in front of it and reaches into his suit pocket, pulling out a key chain on which there must be a dozen keys. He selects one and inserts it deftly into the lock; the cylinders turn with a soft *snick* that suggests they have been oiled recently. He returns the keys to his pocket and opens the door, ushering me in with exaggerated courtliness.

I step through. It takes a moment for my eyes to adjust, but when they do I find myself in a square, high-ceilinged room. Two slender windows punctuate one wall, their grimed glass recessed behind thick iron bars. In daylight I'm guessing they would give views out onto the prison yard, but my gaze doesn't linger there; something else has caught my attention. The walls that remain are lined with shelves that stretch from floor to ceiling. Each is crammed, two and sometimes three deep, with books. Hundreds of them, maybe even thousands, more than I've seen in one place since the Last Day.

From out in the hall I hear the warden telling Tully and Knox to wait, and then the sound of the door being closed, but I just continue to stare. At some point I become aware that Finch is watching me. I turn to face him, my mouth still open.

'How...how did you get so many?'

The warden leans on the cane, his other hand holding a candle he's taken from one of the guards. He smiles at the question, but not like earlier. Now it's as if his whole face shines with it, as though he's inordinately pleased with himself.

'Well, it wasn't all my doing, of course. The prison had a library before I was assigned here, although that was such a shabby collection as to be hardly worth the mention. Autoshop manuals; back copies of *The Reader's Digest*.' He waves the memory away, as though it causes him displeasure. 'I set to work immediately, of course. You wouldn't believe the letters I wrote, Gabriel. Senators, Congressmen, none were spared. But my pleas fell on deaf ears. Society is rarely at its most enlightened when it comes to the treatment of the incarcerated, and more books just wasn't where our representatives felt the public's hard-earned tax dollars needed to be spent. I cultivated a circle of more forward-thinking correspondents, and from time to time there would be a bequest from a private collection. There was the occasional donation from a public library. But this,' he raises the cane, an expansive gesture encompassing the room and everything in it, 'only really started to take shape later, ironically when things started to go wrong on the outside.'

I look at him for an explanation.

'It's the men you see.' He smiles again, as though embarrassed by this revelation. 'They were grateful when I took it upon myself to release them, and they know how much I enjoy something new to read. So when they go outside, searching for supplies, they keep their eyes open.'

My eyes continue to roam the shelves, now and then lighting on a familiar volume. When at last I'm done my gaze shifts to one of the corners. There's a chair there, sitting back in the shadows. I had ignored it in favor of the books at first, but now I see it's no ordinary piece of furniture. Heavy, wooden, almost like a throne. The legs, arms, back are all made of stout timber, worn smooth with time. A large metal cap hangs from a hinged bracket above, a rubber cable wide as a hosepipe feeding into the top. Thick leather cuffs with heavy buckles circle the arms; more straps extend from round the back.

The warden follows my gaze.

'Ah, I see you've found Old Sparky.'

He hobbles up to it, setting the candle down on one of the arms. The guttering flame illuminates a spring-loaded clamp, bolted to one of the legs. The gate's open; inside I can see thick nubs of metal, bound together with rubber. Another cable runs from the base of it, snaking away across the dusty floor.

'It is a rather disagreeable piece of furniture, isn't it? It occurred to me to have it moved, but it turns out it is rather comfortable.' He turns and looks at me and for a second the smile twists, becoming slightly predatory. 'Would you like to try the hot seat?'

I stare at him for a moment. The chair doesn't look like it works, but all the same I can't think of anything I'd like less.

Finch shakes his head.

'No, of course not. Forgive me. How macabre.'

The part of my brain responsible for these things adds *macabre* to the list of words I need to look up. The warden lifts his cane, pointing it around the room.

'You said you liked to read, Gabriel. Tell me, do you have a favorite? You never know; I might just have it.'

I examine the shelves again, considering his question. There are so many to choose from. But then a spine I recognize catches my eye. It's the book about the English rabbits; the one Mags had, that first day we met, in Sacred Heart. Finch follows my gaze.

'Ah, *Watership Down.*' He hobbles over and slips it from its place. 'An intriguing choice.' He holds it up for a moment, turning it over in his hands. It's the very same edition, the one with the rabbit Mom thought was Hazel but I know to be General Woundwort, hunched in silhouette on the cover. Its ears are folded back, its teeth bared.

The warden leans forward.

'How the world looks at the bottom of the food chain. From the ass-end of the totem pole, so to speak. It really is quite a frightening read, isn't it?

It's been a long time since I read it, but I know the story well: Fiver's visions, of fields covered with blood; Bigwig caught in the snare, the wire slicing into his neck as he had struggled against it; the Owsla, the warren's secret police, and how they had ripped Blackavar's ears to shreds as punishment for trying to escape.

I nod.

'I hadn't thought about it that way, but I guess you're right.'

He shakes his head.

'I'm surprised anyone ever considered it a suitable book for children.'

He runs his fingers over the cover and then takes a measured step closer, holding it out to me.

'Why don't you hold on to it tonight? The hours can be long after dark. It will help you pass the time till morning.'

*

WE LEAVE THE LIBRARY.

The warden hands Knox the candle and then swings the door closed behind him, making sure to lock it. He returns the keys to the pocket of his suit and sets off down the passageway, back the way we came, heels and cane *click-clacking* off the dark stone. Tully picks the flask from the floor, gathers up its tether and sets off after him. We rejoin the hallway that led up from the kitchens. As we get to the end a door separates itself from the gloom. Knox hurries ahead to hold it open and I follow Finch through into another long corridor. This part of the prison is no more uplifting than the rest, but it does seem like it might have been more recently constructed: the walls and floor are concrete, not stone, and smooth; fluorescent tubes nestle in dusty ice cube tray fixtures set back in the low ceiling. At the end a guard booth waits, its thick glass reinforced with criss-crossed safety wire. Beyond, a large, barred gate. A sign above reads *High Security*; another *Maximum Control Unit*. A third warns against unauthorized entry.

We step through into yet another corridor. Cells with narrowly-spaced bars line one side, the doors hanging inward on their hinges. The metal is smooth; the locks sleek; I see no hole that might fit a key. Behind there's a small, windowless space, hardly big enough to be called a room. A narrow metal cot takes up most of the floor, a stainless steel toilet the only other furniture. It's been a while since I had Claus inside my head, but now a memory of him stirs, shudders. This would not have been a good place to spend time.

Finch turns to me, as if he's read my mind.

'Yes, it is rather unpleasant, isn't it? What you have to realize Gabriel is that Starkly was where society sent its most undesirable undesirables, its most obdurate felons.' I add *obdurate* to my dictionary list. 'Most were housed upstairs, in the main cellblock, where we ate dinner earlier. But for some, the worst of the worst, the most irredeemable class of criminal, there was this place.'

I stare through the bars. I wonder if any of the men I've just had dinner with were confined here. I guess some must have been. Goldie must have been a shoe-in for the *Most Obdurate Asshole* award; Blatch had a mean look about him, too.

'And you just released them? Weren't you worried what they might do?'

Finch's mouth stretches out in a curious way, that might perhaps have been meant for a smile.

'Well, it was a risk, I'll grant you, but a calculated one. I didn't know each of the inmates personally of course, at least not at the time. But in my position I did have the advantage of access to their prison files, which in most cases were quite detailed. So I felt like I understood them, their strengths and weaknesses, their distastes and peccadilloes, how they had each come to be in a place like this.'

*Peccadilloes?* If I get out of here and can lay my hands on a Scrabble board I reckon I might be unbeatable.

The warden hobbles a little closer, leans over his cane.

'Some were deeply unpleasant men, there is no denying it. Most, however, were merely unsuited for the world, at least as it was then. And there was a truth to be faced. The very nature of their incarceration had changed. The society to whom they had once owed a debt no longer even existed. There was no longer anywhere for them to escape to, either; no better place they were forbidden to be.'

He holds one hand up.

'Besides, what else was I to do? Leave them in their cells and simply allow them to starve?' He shakes his head, as if answering his own question. 'How inconceivably barbaric.'

I nod. I remember how I had worried about leaving Weasel tied up in the KFC when Johnny and I were fleeing for Eden. As nasty a piece of work as he had been, I hadn't wished that end on him either.

Finch looks at me then, and for a second it's like he's just peered into my thoughts and read what's there.

'Good. So you understand.'

He turns and continues down the corridor, the candle throwing long flickering shadows ahead. I take one last look into the cell and follow him.

'Of course that's not to say we haven't had our difficult times. There have been misunderstandings. But I feel we've put those behind us now.'

We approach the end of the row. The last cell door's shut, secured by a length of chain and a heavy padlock. And now I understand the reason for the flask Tully's carrying. It makes sense there might have been one or two of Starkly's inmates who were beyond redemption; felons so dangerous not even a man like the warden could get comfortable releasing them. As we get closer I can see a strip of tape running down the center of the floor in front of the bars. Spidey doesn't care much for that, but I tell him to hush; whoever's still locked up back there, they seem secure. Ahead of me Finch stops. A chair has been placed in front of the cell, on the safe side of the taped line, but he chooses not to sit. Instead he turns to Tully, pointing to a spot on the ground with his cane.

Tully passes the candle back to Knox and slowly starts to unscrew the lid of the flask. He places it on the ground, taking a surprising amount of care for a man of his size, then pushes it forward with the toe of his boot.

For a moment nothing happens, then I think I see something shift in the shadows, but Knox is holding the candle too far back for me to see all the way into the cell. I lean forward for a better look, just as long, spider-thin fingers shoot through the bars towards me.

*

I STAGGER BACKWARDS, but something large, unyielding, blocks my retreat. I hear a grunted protest as I step on Knox's foot, and then a rough hand plants itself between my shoulder blades and shoves me forward. My boots scrabble for purchase as I try and get out of the way, but the fingers that shot through the bars have already closed greedily around the flask. The battered metal container clangs loudly as it's yanked back and then it's gone, swallowed whole by the shadows, the only evidence there was anything there a small amount of whatever was inside that's slopped over the rim, darkening the concrete. I take a breath, waiting for my heart to steady. It all happened so fast that if I'd have blinked there's a good chance I'd have missed it. Except I didn't; in that split second I saw what was there, lurking in the darkness behind. I look over at Finch.

'You...you captured one?'

'Well, it would be more accurate to say he fell into our lives.' He turns around, gesturing with one hand. 'Bring the candle over, Mr. Knox, so Gabriel can see.'

Knox hesitates. He eyes the bars warily, as though for all his size he's reluctant to come any closer. But after a moment's pause he does as he's bid and steps forward with the flame. The swaying light creeps into the cell. Spidey's still sounding a klaxon inside my head, but this time I'm ready for it. My breath catches in my chest as the candle reveals the cell's sole inhabitant, all the same.

The men I met at dinner were all painfully thin, but this final specimen appears inhumanly so. Rags that were once clothing hang from its emaciated frame. Here and there gray skin pokes through, stretched tight over bones like sticks; the contours of its skull showing clearly through what little remains of its hair. Its eyes narrow to slits at the candle; it clutches the flask to its chest and tries to shuffle away. But there's only so far it can go, so instead it turns and bares its teeth. The pupils that glare back through the bars are unmistakably dilated; they glow silver as they catch the light.

'Yes, our friend was an infected.' Finch turns to me. 'In one sense we were fortunate, during those difficult times, in being so far out of the way here; we were generally untroubled by visitors of his kind. But somehow this one found us. Or rather we found him, just lying out there in the yard.' He looks over at me and says *No, really*, as if I had somehow challenged his account of it. 'He had managed to scale the walls and I suspect was up to no good in one of the guard towers when something must have caused him to fall.'

The creature in the cage raises the flask to its lips, which for some reason I can't fathom sets off a fresh chorus of alarms from spidey. It tilts its head back slowly, continuing to regard us with animal mistrust. Drops of something dark spill from its lips and run down its chin.

'It was Kane, scorching the skies. That's what did it.'

I say it mostly to myself, but after a moment I realize Finch is leaning forward on his cane, looking at me expectantly.

'The missiles, the ones the President launched. The explosions caused some sort of pulse that was intended to defeat its kind.'

The warden raises a finger to his chin, strokes it thoughtfully.

'Why, yes, the timing would certainly fit. I didn't witness that event myself of course; I was otherwise occupied at the time. But I've heard stories, from the men. And it was the very next morning I found him, just lying out there, in the yard, so still that at first I was sure he was dead.'

I think of the little girl, in the closet in Shreve, and how peaceful she had looked, too. At least until Marv had held the knife with his blood on it under her nose.

The fury drains the last of whatever's in the flask and lets it fall to the ground. It clanks hollowly as it hits the concrete, then comes to rest. It's hard to think straight, what with the sirens going off in my head, but there's something very wrong about this; something that doesn't sit with what I know of the virus.

Tully steps forward and picks up the end of the cord. I watch as he reels the battered container in, pulling it back through the bars. He waits till it's safely over the line then bends to retrieve it. Spidey kicks it up a notch as he replaces the lid, and now the sound inside my head's like a fire truck, trying to force its way through a clogged intersection. A dark thought pushes itself forward. The flask's ribbed metal sides are dented, scarred, but that's the extent of the damage there. I look over at the bars. They're smooth, untarnished.

The room tilts on some axis I did not know it possessed. I feel the blood drain from my face. I hear a voice that might be mine, asking a question I'm not yet sure I'm ready to have answered.

'It's…it's not infectious?'

Finch turns to look at me.

'Why, how very observant of you, Gabriel. Yes, our friend here can no longer transmit the virus.'

'You…you're certain?'

'Quite. We had to be, before we could risk letting him into a place like this, which is why the poor fellow spent so long in the hotbox. Besides, he's been down here for almost a decade.' He taps the bars with the tip of his cane. 'If he was still capable of passing on the virus I'm sure we would know about it by now.'

I'm aware he's still talking, but the warden's voice seems to be coming to me from somewhere distant. My mind's running around in herky-jerky little circles, trying to fit this new piece of information into what I thought I knew of the virus.

The metal was how you could tell. Every time you go outside it was the same: you strip as much of it from you as you can, the rest you wrap in plastic. But there was always a single piece – a cross, dog tags – left exposed, worn next to the skin, so you would know if you'd been infected. That was how it always was, from my very first scavenging trip with Marv to the last time I saw him, on his knees in the snow, slinging the rifle off his shoulder.

I look into the cell. The fury glares back at me through the bars.

But this creature, it gives the lie to all that. And that can mean only one thing: the crucifix Mags wears, the one she took from Marv's grave, it doesn't prove a thing.

Beside me Finch is still speaking. I force myself to pay attention; there may be something I can learn, something that might help make sense of it. I replay his words in my head.

'What's a hotbox?'

He stops and looks at me, and I think his eyes narrow a fraction, like whatever he was just saying he might not care for my interruption. But after a brief pause he answers.

'A throwback to an even less enlightened time in the history of our nation's penal system, Gabriel. It's a wooden box, little bigger than an outhouse, dug into the earth. Most institutions of Starkly's vintage would have had one. Their position was chosen quite carefully; somewhere in the middle of the yard, a spot that would never catch the shade. A man shackled out there for a day in the Carolina sun would literally bake to death. The sun had abandoned us by then of course, so there was little danger of that fate befalling our friend here. I regretted it nonetheless; the hotbox is an unpleasant spot to spend any amount of time.'

'When…when did he come around? Was it recent?'

Finch looks at me quizzically, and this time there's a longer pause before his answer.

'A week before you arrived.'

'Tell me about it.'

I remind myself I need to be careful; he's watching me closely now. I remember his comment about manners from earlier and add a *Please*.

'Why as chance would have it I was right here when it happened.'

He says it nonchalantly, like it was the funniest of coincidences, but I find myself glancing behind him to the chair pushed up against the wall, the seat shiny from use. I wonder how many hours the warden has spent down here over the years, just staring into that cell. He stares at the fury for a moment before continuing.

'Not that there's much to tell. One minute he was lying on the cot, the very same as he had been the past ten years. The next he's crouched on the floor, wide awake, like someone had just flicked a switch inside him.'

He tilts his head, leans forward on the cane.

'I must say, you seem remarkably well informed on this subject, Gabriel.'

I start to say something about it being a guess, but if that's the story I'm selling I'm not sure the warden's buying it. He starts doing that thing with his fingernail on the head of the cane again. It was Gilbey who warned me that we may not have long, but I don't plan to get into that with Finch. I turn my attention back to the cell, keeping my gaze on the thing crouched against the far wall while I rack my brains, searching for some answer that'll get me back on safer ground. The light catches its silvered eyes and it shifts its jaw, like it's grinding its teeth. And for a second I think of Marv, as he was right at the end. I turn back to the warden.

'I had a friend, once. He reckoned his kind weren't altogether done for; that one day they'd rise up again. If it was the same thing put them all under, it'd make sense they'd come back at about the same time too. This is the first sign of it I've seen, and I've been watching. Makes me think it had to be have been recent.'

Finch continues to stare at me, as if weighing the truth in that statement, and what else it might be I'm not telling him. There's something in that piercing gaze that makes me want to keep talking. It's like I can't help it.

'What Mac…Mr. MacIntyre said earlier, at dinner, about there being something in the city…'

Finch's hand shoots up before I have a chance to finish.

'Mr. Knox, Mr. Tully, would you be so good as to give us a moment?'

Knox and Tully exchange a look, then they turn around and lumber back in the direction of the guard booth.

The warden leans forward on his cane.

'You must forgive me, Gabriel; interrupting you like that was rude. But it is a little early to jump to such conclusions. If the men were to get wind of this – as yet unproven – theory of yours I suspect it would be difficult to convince any of them to return to Durham.' He spreads his hands. 'And we are rather reliant on the city for the few meager supplies it provides.'

'I understand, Mr. Finch.' I glance down the corridor. Knox and Tully are out of earshot, but I drop my voice anyway. 'If the furies really are waking up, though, we're in for a whole heap of trouble.'

He studies me a moment longer, then at last he switches his gaze back to the cell.

'Yes, they are rather formidable creatures, aren't they?'

'That'd be one way of putting it.'

The warden gives his head a little shake and smiles.

‘Oh you must look past that ferocity, Gabriel; those inhuman sanguinary appetites.’ He hobbles forward, shuffling across the line that’s taped to the ground, and points the cane through the bars. The creature crouched by the back wall glances up at this new intrusion and raises its lip in a snarl. But if Finch is afraid of it he gives no sign. When he turns to look at me it’s as if his eyes have brightened again.

‘Regard our friend here. Hardly much of a physical specimen, wouldn’t you say? And yet he was able to scale Starkly’s walls without difficulty, and even to survive a fall from one of its towers.’

He holds the cane up a moment longer, then lowers it.

‘Physically we are such a sad case in comparison. Look at us. Frail, fragile things, with our small, blunt, teeth, our delicate claws. In a fair fight we have never been a match for any animal approaching our size. It was only our intellect that placed us at the top of the food chain. And see how precarious that position has proven.’

He leans forward, his face only inches from the hardened steel. The fury curls its lip one more time, then turns its head to the wall. The warden smiles indulgently at it, as though it were a favorite pet.

‘Remarkable.’

He shakes his head, then shuffles back over the line. He looks up at me and the smile broadens, revealing that perfect picket fence row of teeth. Later I tell myself it’s just the shadows the candle was throwing. But for a second it seems like there might have been a few too many of them.

*

WE MAKE OUR WAY BACK to the main cellblock, where earlier we sat for dinner. I follow the warden as he hobbles up the metal stair to the second floor, then makes his way slowly along the landing. Here and there back in the shadows a candle still flickers, but most of the cells are dark. He finally stops outside a barred door that hangs open. I look inside. There's not much in the way of comforts, just a metal bunk with a threadbare mattress, a steel bowl for a toilet. I guess I should be thankful for small mercies. At least he's not putting me down in the basement with the fury.

He points with the cane. I hesitate for a moment, then step inside. The door creaks on its hinges, then clangs loudly as Knox pulls it closed. Finch gestures to the guard to hand me the candle then he reaches into the pocket of his jacket for the bunch of keys he carries. I tell him there's really no need, but he insists; he says he'll sleep better knowing I'm safe. I can't see how I have much of a choice in the matter so I say that'll be fine. He selects a key, inserts it into the lock and turns it. The bolt closes with a heavy clunk.

He returns the keys to his pocket, wishes me a pleasant evening, then points his cane along the landing. I stand at the bars for a while, listening to the slow shuffle and clack of his retreating footsteps. When at last they've faded to silence I set the candle on the ground by the leg of the bunk and sit.

The copy of *Watership Down* shifts in the pocket of my parka and I take it out, run my fingers over the familiar cover. I glance through the bars to check there's no one watching, then I hold it under my nose and riffle the pages, like I used to do when I'd find something new. I close my eyes and inhale the book smell, and for a second I'm not sitting on a metal cot in the main cellblock of Starkly Correctional Institution. I'm in the day room of the Sacred Heart Home for Children. A single shaft of dusty sunlight filters through a high window above, and the air smells of furniture polish and old newspapers. There's a girl sitting opposite me. Her head's down, buried in a book, the same one I'm holding. Her dark brown bangs obscure her face, but I know in a moment she'll look up, and I'll see her for the first time. I try to hold that image but I can't, and just as quickly as it came it vanishes again. I open my eyes and Starkly returns.

I lay back on the thin mattress. The cot's not long enough and I have to raise my knees to get my feet on it. I stare up at the bunk above, watching as the candle makes the shadows cast by the rusting springs shift and merge. There are things I need to consider now, but I'm not ready for that, not yet, so instead I open the cover. Another world waits for me in there, one where everything is still as it was when I first met her, and right now that's what I need. I turn to the first page, forcing myself to concentrate on the words.

Without anything to mark it the time draws out. Starkly grows quiet, save for the sound of the wind outside, moaning against the walls. A draft finds its way into my cell, disturbs the flame. For a moment it flickers, threatens to go out, then steadies again. I look down, surprised to see that the candle's almost done; all that remains is a charred wick in a shallow puddle of wax. But when I look back to the page I realize I've got no further than the paragraph I began on.

I set the book down. It's no use. The thing I saw, down in the basement, it will not be ignored. The truth of what it means drags at my brain, like a fishhook.

I've been checking Mags' crucifix every night since we left Mount Weather. All the other stuff - how quick she is now; how she can see in the dark; how her skin is always cold - I'd convinced myself none of it mattered. The metal was how I'd know; as long as it stayed clear she wasn't going to end up like Marv.

The low, faithless voice has been quiet for some time, but now it whispers.

*That's not true, though, is it?*

It reminds me of something Gilbey told us; something I knew all along, but chose not to dwell on. The virus was a truly remarkable piece of engineering, she said, incredibly tenacious; so much more resilient than Kane ever gave it credit for. He fired all the missiles he had, but all that did was render those carrying it unconscious. For years it's been waiting, slowly building itself back up inside them, just like Marv thought. And now it's ready to return, and those that had it once are no different from how they had been before.

I lay my head down on the cot, letting that truth wash over me.

Kane scorched the sky; tore a hole in it; made the night burn bright with the force of a thousand explosions. And still he couldn't defeat it. What did Mags get? A few minutes in a glorified magnet; a machine designed to look inside you. Not even the time it had been set for.

How could I have ever hoped that would be enough?

*

HE PICKS HIS WAY through the darkened mall. On either side vacant stores, their trash-strewn aisles stretching back into gloom. He tries a few, searching the dusty shelves for anything that might have been missed. But there's nothing. Each has been ransacked, stripped of anything that might provide warmth, sustenance. In one he finds a box of plastic lighters, sitting by the cash register. He lifts one out, tries it. For a while it just sparks and he's about to toss it, but then finally it catches, holds. He stares at the blue-tinged flame until the metal grows hot, then he lets it die.

He steps back outside to resume walking the concourse. This is what he does now, while the others are sleeping. The girl does not like him wandering off by himself, so he has to wait until she has fallen asleep, too. She doesn't sleep for long now, hardly more than he does, so he can't go very far. But that's okay. He uses the time he has to explore. He likes it.

He makes his way through the food court. Packets and wrappers litter the floor, but there's nothing among them worth having. Occasionally he holds the lighter up, thumbs the wheel. He does not need it, any more than the flashlight in his pocket. But he likes the soft glow of the flame, the way the plastic feels warm in his hand after.

He finds an escalator, climbs it to the level above. He follows the walkway, examining each storefront he passes. A soft drinks machine lies toppled over, its front pried open. He checks the insides in case a can has been forgotten, like he's seen the tall boy do. The chute is narrow, but his arm is small and he can reach almost all the way up inside. There's nothing there, though, so he continues on.

He wonders where the tall boy is right now. He was supposed to have caught up with them already, but he hasn't. When they returned to the print store his pack was still there, right where he had left it. The girl stared at it a while then knelt to rummage in one of the side pockets. She took out a folded piece of paper, opened it to check something, then slipped it inside her parka. She stepped over to the counter, returning with a sheaf of paper. She pulled the stub of a pencil from her pocket and bent to scribble a note. When she was done she tucked it under one of the straps then headed back out to where the others were waiting. She led them on, picking her way between the cars and trucks that clogged the streets. Every few paces she would turn to check behind, but for the rest of that evening the road had stayed clear.

They had arrived at this place just as night was falling. The boy with the curly hair had brought them inside while she waited out on the road. When at last it had turned dark and there was no chance the tall boy might still be coming she had come in. The others already had a fire going, a way back from the entrance, where the flames would not be seen, but the girl showed no interest in joining them. She stayed by the doors, keeping watch over the parking lot. He could hear the others, whispering.

*What's she doing out there?*

*Can she see in the dark, too?*

*How can she stand to be so far from the fire?*

But if she heard she paid little attention. Some time later the boy with the curly hair had come out to join them. He had hugged his parka tight to him and his breath had smoked in the cold. He said she should come inside, that the tall boy would be alright. The girl nodded, but when he returned to the fire she made no move to follow.

He completes his circuit, returns to the escalator. Trash is strewn everywhere here; he has to pick his way among it as he makes his way up the ribbed steel stairs. At the top a single large room, stretching back into darkness. On one side a long counter; a sign above that would once have lit up. Large posters hang from the walls or lie curled on the floor beneath.

He heads for the counter, treading decade-old popcorn into the mulchy carpet as he goes. The glass is dusty; he has to wipe it with the sleeve of his jacket to see inside. He presses his face to it, hoping to spot a candy bar that's been missed. But the cabinet's empty. This place has been plundered, like everywhere else.

He holds the lighter up, cranks the wheel; his reflection appears in the glass. He turns his head to one side, studying it. He thinks it is a little better. The shadows around his eyes are finally fading, but enough of them remain to lend his face a hollow, sunken-in look. He is used to it now, but somehow it still feels unfamiliar, like this is not how he is supposed to look.

'Hello there.'

His fingers scrabble for the goggles hanging around his neck. In his haste to pull them up he drops the lighter and it blinks out, returning the room to grainy shades of gray.

He turns around slowly, still fiddling with the strap. A boy stands there, staring down at him, his hands stuffed into the pockets of a tattered leather jacket. The hood on the sweatshirt he wears underneath is pulled up, but there's enough of his face showing to suggest it's amusement that shapes his pale features. He turns his head, as though addressing someone behind him.

'Hey, check out the shades on this little dude.'

A girl appears at his side. Her hair is cut in a ragged bob; without the lighter it's hard to tell what color it might be. She wears a denim jacket with buttons pinned to the front. Underneath a dark t-shirt with a snaggle-tooth skull. Where the neckline dips he can see her collarbones. Her skirt is short and her legs are bare; they end in a pair of dirty high-tops. She tilts her head, her jaw working continuously. She flashes him a smile, says

*Hey, cutie*, and goes back to chewing her gum.

One by one others step out of the shadows, until there are maybe twenty of them, arranged in a loose semicircle around him. Some are not much bigger than he is. None seem older than the girl, or the tall boy.

His brow furrows. He had not heard them, any of them. He can always hear the others, even when they are trying to be quiet.

The boy with the hood takes a step closer, squats down in front of him. His jeans are faded, his boots scuffed. He takes his hands from the pocket of the leather jacket and waves them in front of him, quick, almost too fast to see. A candy bar appears where before there was nothing. He holds it out.

'Y'all looking for this?'

He stares at the candy bar for a moment, then reaches down for the lighter instead. He holds it up, thumbs the wheel. The boy's pupils glow in the flame. He leans in, his eyes locked on the lighter, then pulls back the hood on his sweatshirt, revealing a shock of white hair.

'That's right, little dude. Just like you.' The boy holds his arms out, gesturing to the others gathered around him. 'We all are.'

He keeps his thumb on the lighter, holds it up. The girl cocks her head, pulls a face, goes back to chewing her gum. In the flame he can see her hair is bright pink, the same shade as the lipstick she's wearing.

The lighter grows too hot to hold and he snaps it off, returns it to his pocket where it glows like a coal against his leg. The boy's eyes turn dark again. His hand still holds the candy bar.

'It's alright.'

He hesitates a moment then takes it, peels the wrapper. The chocolate inside is gray with age. It tastes gritty, stale, but not altogether bad. He finishes it quickly. The boy smiles, like he's pleased.

'Want a drink?' He turns to his companions, not waiting for an answer. 'Hey, somebody gimme a soda.'

From somewhere back in the shadows there's the rasp of a zipper being pulled and a second later a can gets passed forward. There's the faintest of hisses as the boy pops the tab, hands it to him.

He takes a sip. What little gas is left stings his nose, makes his eyes water. It's so sweet it makes the roof of his mouth tingle. He takes a large gulp, then another, and another, until it's gone. He stands there for a moment, then belches loudly.

The boy laughs.

'Little dude likes it. Y'all got a name, little dude?'

He's about to tell them what he told the girl with the long blond hair, back in the mountain place: he doesn't know. But then he remembers how that went.

'They call me Johnny.'

The girl with the pink hair tilts her head again. She frowns, as though something about that answer doesn't sit right with her.

'And is that your name?'

He shrugs. The boy and the girl exchange a look he can't figure, then they both turn back to him.

'Well, Johnny, I'm Vince. And this is Cassie.'

The girl curtsies, flashes him another smile.

'Please-ta-meetcha.'

He holds up the can and the candy bar wrapper.

'Where did you find these?'

'Oh, around. You just need to know where to look.' He winks. 'Hey, Johnny, come with me.'

The boy with the leather jacket leads him back towards the escalator. When they reach the guardrail he leans over, points down. Far below, towards the entrance, the cherry wink of a campfire; a collection of gray shapes, huddled around it.

'Those friends of yours?'

He hesitates. He's not sure what he should say. The girl is, for certain. And the tall boy, although he's not down there right now. He's less certain about the others.

'Some of them are.'

'Got it. Probably haven't known them long, am I right?'

He nods. That bit is true.

'And where are y'all headed?'

He pauses again. When he was in the cage the doctor said it was important to answer questions truthfully. He's not sure what he should say now, however. The place where they're going, the place that'll be their new home, he thinks it's supposed to be a secret. He doesn't know exactly where it is, anyway, except that it's close, but he's not even sure he's allowed to say that much. He considers it a few seconds more and then settles on an answer he thinks should be okay.

'South.'

'Y'all don't plan to stay here, then?'

He shakes his head.

The girl with the pink hair folds her arms across her chest.

'Told ya, Vince, no need to get your panties all up in a bunch. Just passin' through.'

The boy holds his hand up, like he wants her to be quiet.

'And what about the other one, the tall one, the one who took off after those men. Will they wait for him?'

He shakes his head again.

'He's going to follow us.'

'Wouldn't count on it, kid.'

The boy's features twist in irritation.

'Shut up, Cass.'

The girl rolls her eyes, goes back to chewing her gum. The boy turns to face him again. The smile returns.

'Sure about that, Johnny? The bit about heading south, I mean. Y'all definitely don't plan to stay here?'

He shakes his head and the boy's smile widens.

'Do you live here?'

The boy with the leather jacket goes back to staring at the campfire.

'Oh, here and there. Wherever we want.' He pauses a while and his face grows serious. 'You could stay with us, if you like.' He nods at the empty soda can. 'There's more of those. Loads more. We could show you how to find them.'

He shakes his head. The girl will be done sleeping soon. If she wakes and finds him gone she'll worry.

'I have to get back.'

The boy spreads his hands, like he understands.

'Alright. Well, Johnny, it was sure nice to meet y'all.'

He's not sure how he feels about having met them, so he just says thanks for the soda and the candy bar and hurries out onto the escalator.

He's barely made it back to the level where the others are sleeping when he hears a sound from somewhere off in the shadows. He turns towards it and the girl with the pink hair is there, waiting inside the entrance of a *Tastee Freez*. He looks back at the escalator. He came straight down; he's not sure how she made it here ahead of him. He opens his mouth to ask, but she presses a finger to her lips, beckons him over. He glances towards the fire then hurries over to join her. The gum she was chewing earlier has gone. She looks around nervously.

'What you said up there, about moving on, did you mean it?'

He nods.

She looks relieved.

'That's good. Vince, he doesn't care much for warmbloods.' She glances out towards the entrance. 'Although all things considered Vince might not be the worst of your problems.'

He's not sure what she means by anything she's just said.

'What are warmbloods?'

The girl nods in the direction of the campfire.

'Your friends.'

'Why doesn't he like them?'

She tilts her head, like she's not sure what to make of his question.

'You kiddin' me, right? You don't remember what it was like?'

He shakes his head. He doesn't remember anything from before.

'Their kind, they hated us.' She keeps her voice low, but it grows hard. 'They wanted us dead, every last one, even those that had stopped being sick. They sent their soldiers, to hunt us down.'

He does know about soldiers. He remembers the mean one, with the zap stick; how he had looked at him, when he had come down with his food, like he was a dangerous animal, in a poorly built cage.

'It was Vince who saved us. Found us places to hide. Then the first winter came and that was it for their kind. Not enough of them left to be a threat to us anymore; for a long time now it's just been the men from the prison. They come into town every once in a while, looking for food. Makes Vince mad as hell. Me and a few of the others, we try and discourage them. The warmbloods, they're kinda dumb; they have to mark the places they've been, otherwise they forget. Makes it real easy to figure where they'll go next.' She shakes her head. 'We strip whatever might be left before they get there; don't leave them hardly anything. But still they keep coming back.'

She inclines her head towards the campfire.

'So where'd you meet these ones?'

'They were living inside a mountain.'

She raises an eyebrow at that, but if she has more questions she doesn't ask them.

'Known them long?'

He shakes his head.

'But they're treating you okay?'

He hesitates a second then nods.

'Even the ones with the guns?'

He nods again.

'That's good.' She goes quiet for a moment, like she's thinking about something. 'Hey, Johnny, do you plan to say anything? About meeting us, I mean. Only I don't think it'd be a good idea if one of them was to take it into their heads to try and find us. You know, like the tall one did, going after those prisoners.'

He thinks about that a moment, then shakes his head. When the tall boy comes back he doesn't want him going off again.

'Alright.'

He looks back towards the entrance. The girl will be up soon. He's already been gone too long.

'I'd best get back.'

'Sure thing.'

She reaches in her pocket, holds out a candy bar. He hesitates a moment then takes it from her. As he turns to make his way back towards the entrance, she reaches for his shoulder.

'Hey Johnny, they're not your kind anymore. You know that, right?'

*

I DON'T SLEEP MUCH the rest of that night. I pick up the book again, but I make no more progress with it. The candle burns down, spends a little while working out whether it means to keep going, then simply winks out. After that it's just a matter of counting out the hours until at last somewhere far behind the clouds the sun rises and another gray dawn breaks over Starkly's walls.

Sounds drift into my cell - the creak of mattress springs, the scuff of boots on stone, the clang of metal - as around me the prison slowly wakes. I sit on the edge of the cot, waiting, but it's a long time before anyone comes to release me. At last I hear Finch's shoes and cane on the landing outside. I'm standing by the bars when he appears.

'Good morning, Gabriel. And how was your night?'

Truth is I've had better, but I remember how he feels about manners so I tell him I slept just fine. He smiles, like he's pleased to hear it. He reaches into the pocket of his jacket for the keys and takes them out, selecting one for the lock. He's about to insert it, but then he hesitates.

'I must say, it has been pleasant having you here with us. I feel like we have got along terribly well. It is nice to have someone who shares the same interests. Much as I have come to care for them, my charges are not the sort for whom a literary discussion is the preferred mode of entertainment.' He pauses, and for a second his pale eyes grow a little brighter. He presses his lips together, in what might be a smile. 'Tell me, would you give some thought to staying with us a little longer?'

The key hovers by the lock. I glance down at it, wondering how much of a bearing my answer might have on whether I'll be leaving this cell today.

'It's a kind offer, Mr. Finch, it really is. But I reckon I should be heading on.' I feel the need to say something more, to offer him a reason why. 'I heard there were survivors, down south. Won't be long now till winter's on us again and I have a ways to go yet if I'm to find them before it gets here.'

The smile flickers. One finger hovers over the head of the cane, taps it twice, then comes to rest.

'I want to thank you for everything, though. For the meal, and for lending me this.'

I hold up the copy of Watership Down.

'Of course, of course.'

He inserts the key in the lock, turns it, then stands back to let me out. I step past him onto the landing. Knox and Tully are waiting a little further along, by the stair.

I hand him his book.

'How far did you get?'

'Not very.' I glance back into the cell at the puddle of wax that used to be a candle.

He looks down at the paperback. His fingers fiddle restlessly along the edges, as though he is deciding something. In the end he pushes it back towards me.

'Why, you must have it, to take with you. To remember us by.'

I start to tell him I couldn't, but my hands betray me; they're already reaching for it of their own accord. Any book is a treasure, but this one means so much more.

'I insist. And who knows, maybe someday you will be in a position to do me a similar favor.'

He says it like he expects our paths to cross again, but the truth is I have no plans to return to Starkly. I figure there's little mileage to be had in pointing that out, however.

'Well, if you're certain.'

He nods, once. But when I go to take the book from him his fingers suddenly tighten around it. I look up and something has changed, a hardening of whatever is behind his eyes.

'Maybe I shouldn't take this from you, Mr. Finch. Books are hard to come by, and it's obviously one of your favorites.'

And just like that it's as though whatever spell he was under has been broken. He pushes the book into my hands.

'Nonsense. I won't hear of it, Gabriel. Never let it be said that Garland Finch was an Indian giver.'

We make our way down the stair. The mittens Goldie took from me are waiting on the table where the night before we sat for dinner. There's no mention of breakfast, and I don't enquire after it. I wasn't certain when I checked in last night I'd ever be checking out again, so all things considered I reckon I'm up on the deal.

I exchange goodbyes with the warden in the hall. He says his leg's no good in the snow, but Mr. Goldie will show me to the gate. Goldie bobs his head and smiles broadly, as if nothing could conceivably bring him greater pleasure.

I follow him outside. I can't say daylight's improved Starkly any, but then my expectations weren't high to begin with. Goldie jabbers at me all the way to the holding pen. Mostly it's how sorry he is about our misunderstanding; how he hopes I don't hold it against him. I tell him not to give it another thought, but he keeps up his jawboning regardless. His apologies don't put me much at ease. I haven't known him long, but I'm pretty sure remorse isn't among this particular inmate's limited catalog of feelings.

He holds the gate open and I step through. Culver's sitting behind the pockmarked screen, just like he was when I came in last night. Goldie bangs on the glass with the side of his fist and the tray slides out. He hands me the gun belt and then busies himself gathering up the bullets that were emptied from Hicks' pistol while I loop the leather around my waist and cinch the buckle. When I'm done he hands me the cartridges with a smile. I slip them into my pocket while he runs on ahead to work the bolts on the door set into the main gate.

I take one last look back into the yard. Finch is still standing by the entrance to the cellblock, leaning on his cane. He holds one hand up to wave me goodbye. I hesitate for a moment then return the gesture. Behind me the last of the bolts slide back and I hear the door swing inward.

My snowshoes are waiting, right where I left them. The snow's been wiped clean of the tracks we made coming down, but that's okay; I'll be able to find my way just fine without them. I tighten the bindings and set off. I think I hear Goldie's voice calling after me, but whatever he says is lost to the wind. I don't turn around; if he has parting words for me I don't need to hear them.

I don't stop until I've crested the ridge. I pull off my mittens and dig in my pocket for one of the bullets Goldie handed me as I was leaving. I angle the tail to the light, searching for what I thought I saw there earlier. I hold it under my nose, to be certain. I check each of the others, to make sure there's no mistake.

There isn't. They're all the same. Dollars to donuts the ones nestling in the gun belt's cartridge loops won't be any different.

I weigh the bullets in my hand one last time, then throw them as far off into the snow as I can.

*

IT'S ALREADY EDGING into the afternoon by the time I find my way back to the interstate. I glance behind me then hurry up onto the overpass. The pistol shifts on my hip underneath the parka as I make my way across. There's not many things I can say I'm grateful to Hicks for, but he did show me how to check a weapon, and that included the ammunition that went with it. The primers on the cartridges that were returned to me had been soaked in something, from the smell my guess'd be oil, to make sure they wouldn't fire.

It's possible Goldie did that on his own initiative, of course, but somehow I doubt it. I've seen nothing to change the impression I had on our first meeting: there's little more to him than a fast mouth run by a slow brain. Which means it was the warden told him to do it, and that's a lot more worrisome. I could offer you three guesses as to why he'd go to that trouble when it'd be just as easy to have Culver hold back the bullets in the first place. But unless your name's Angus or Hamish I doubt you'll need more than one.

Nope, he wanted me to walk out of those gates feeling good and relaxed, like my dealings with Starkly Correctional Institution and all its inmates were firmly in the rearview. And there's only one reason I can think of for that: he means to send someone after me, to see where I'll go. Could just be idle curiosity, of course. I guess even with all those books time must sit heavy on your hands in a place like Starkly. I wouldn't bet on it, though. Well, I've been fooled by that trick before. I certainly won't be falling for it again.

I make my way down off the overpass and head straight for the U-Haul. I cross the lot and hike up to the low cinder block where Goldie jumped me. The door hangs back on its hinges, just how I left it. I snap off my snowshoes and step inside. Marv's map's lying on the floor. I return it to its rightful place in my pocket and make my way back to the interchange.

I need to get back to Mags and the kid now, quick as I can. Someone will be coming down that road after me, however, and I can't lead them right to the Juvies. I lift my goggles onto my forehead. On either side the highway stretches off into the distance, far as the eye can see.

One way looks as good as the other so I choose left, then set off down the on-ramp. The wind picks up, but not enough to clear my tracks. For now that suits me. I want whoever's following to pick up my trail. At first I swing around every few paces, expecting to find the dark shapes of whoever Finch has sent on the road behind. But each time it's empty, and after a mile or so I allow myself to relax a little. My thoughts return to what I saw at Starkly.

I have a theory now about the virus, of sorts. I reckon the furies that found themselves somewhere that was shielded the night Kane scorched the skies, those ones can probably still pass it on. Hicks certainly seemed to think so, and if he was wrong about that he put Ortiz to his end unnecessarily, after he got attacked by that one in the basement of the hospital in Blacksburg.

For those furies that were out in the open when the missiles detonated it might have been different, however. The pulse that was released didn't strike the virus from them, and it's been building its way back up inside them all this time, just like Marv suspected. Whatever ability they had to transmit it was lost, though. The crucifix Mags wears, I can't rely on that anymore.

I tell myself none of it means she's going to get sick again. The voice has been quiet since I quit the prison, but now it pipes up. It wants to know about all the other things: how quick she is now; how she can see in the dark; how her skin is always cold.

*How she was with Kurt.*

It seems like it has a lot more to say on the subject, but I hush it. None of that has to mean anything either. It's already been weeks since Mags and the kid came through the scanner, and they're both still fine.

If something was going to happen to them it would have done so by now.

I stick to I-85 as it winds its way west. I pass the exit for 501, the road that would take me south to Fearrington, but I don't take it. About a mile further on the interstate elbows north at a place called Eno and shortly after runs through what must once have been forest. I slow down. This is far enough. If I'm going to find my way back to the Juvies I'll need to cut south again, and here looks as good a spot as any. I have no backpack to drag in my wake, so I take out Weasel's blade and cut a branch from the withered remains of a tree that's still clinging to the embankment. I return to the center of the highway and keep going until the gnarled trunks on either side are as densely packed as I think they're apt to get, then I quit the road, using the branch to sweep the snow behind me. When I reach the tree line I look back. I doubt what I've done would've fooled Marv, or Truck, but with a little help from the wind it might do. It'll have to. Right now it's as much as I can manage.

I head cross-country for a while until I hit a little place name of Blackwood. I stop on the far side of town, lift my goggles onto my forehead and look west. From here I could go directly south to Fearrington, but I have one final detour to make. My backpack's sitting in a print store, south side of Durham. I don't care much to go back to the city, not after what I learned in Starkly, but there are items in it, chief among them the box of bullets for Hicks' pistol and the list of codes for each facility in the Federal Location Arc I took with me from Eden. There's a good chance Mags will have taken the list with her when she returned with the Juvies, but I can't be certain of that. There's no information on it that isn't already in my head, but Mac and Goldie were scavenging right across the street when Mags ran into them.

I can't take the risk that they'd find it.

Traffic clogs the streets as I approach the city. I pick my way among the wrecks. The buildings grow taller the closer I get to the center. I keep looking up, thinking I catch movement behind the darkened windows, but each time I check there's nothing.

I arrive back at the *KwikPrint* just as the last of the light's slipping from the sky. My pack's right where I left it, propped against the wall in the corner. There's a note from Mags sitting on top, saying she's taken the Juvies on ahead. I'm sorely tempted to head right back out after them, but it's too late for that. There's no way I'd catch up, not with the head start they have; I doubt I'd even make it out of the city. Better to rest up, get back on the road early.

I head back to the entrance to check the street again, then wedge the door shut. I return to my pack and break out one of the last of my MREs. While it's heating I search the aisles. I find a few cardboard boxes and a ream of paper in the storeroom that's been overlooked, enough for a fire. I set it in back, as far from the windows as I can. When I've got the paper lighting I break down the boxes and feed the pieces to the flames while I wait for my ration to heat.

Soon as my food's passable warm I tear it open. I haven't had anything but watery soup since the night before and I'm ravenous. I don't lift my nose from the pouch until there's nothing but a half-dozen sorry-looking beef ravioli left in the bottom. I lean back against the wall, wipe my mouth with the back of my hand, then reach for the canteen to wash down what I've just eaten.

As I unscrew the cap I glance up, just in time to see a flash of something through the silted glass of the storefront as the first of them come for me.

*

THE CANTEEN SLIPS from my fingers. It hits the ground, teeters drunkenly as the contents slosh around inside, then topples. Water spills from the neck, darkening the dusty floor, but that's not my concern now; I'm already on my feet, running to the window. I press my face to the cracked pane. A single flashlight beam, jitterbugging its way down the street as whoever's behind it picks their way between the abandoned cars.

*How did they find me so soon?*

I waste precious seconds staring at it in disbelief, watching the beam grow steadily closer. It looks like just the one, but I've been fooled by that trick before. I snap myself out of my stupor. How they found me matters little now. I turn back to the fire. It's too late to worry about extinguishing it, so instead I reach down for Hicks' pistol. The grip is still unfamiliar, but the heft gives me courage, at least until I remember it's not loaded. I rush over to where my backpack rests against the wall and upend it, scrabbling through the items that spill out for the box of ammunition. I pry the hammer back and fumble the loading gate open. I shake the bullets onto my palm, not caring that most of them end up on the floor. I've been inside long enough for my fingers to have thawed, but haste makes them clumsy; it takes an inordinate length of time to jiggle each cartridge into its slot, rotate the cylinder and push the next one home. The last bullet slides into place just as I hear a sound from outside. I look up. The beam's come to a halt right in front of the store.

I snap the gate closed and cock the hammer, just as a lone figure steps up to the entrance. The flashlight makes it hard to tell who it might be, but from his height I'm pretty sure it's Goldie's companion, Mac. He raises both arms above his head. The wind's gusting and he has to shout to make himself heard.

'I don't mean you no harm. I only want to talk.'

'Is it just you?'

'It is.'

He turns his head, like he's checking for something further up the street, then looks back to the door.

'I'd appreciate if you'd hurry up and let me in. You can shoot me inside just as easy as out.'

I hesitate a moment, weighing my options, then I call back that he can enter. The door opens and he stumbles in, a flurry of snow swirling around him. He pushes past me and makes straight for the fire, paying little mind to the pistol I have on him. He drops to his knees, shuffling as close to it as he can, his hands held out like he would grasp the flames to him if he could.

When he's warmed himself enough he pulls the scarf he's wearing down and turns to me. If he has a weapon I don't see it, but I certainly don't plan on taking any chances. I make a show of leveling the gun at him, trying to keep my hand steady.

'It's loaded, so you know. And not with the bullets I left Starkly with.'

I nod in the direction of my backpack where the ammo box lies on its side, a dozen cartridges scattered in the dust around it. His eyes dip to it and then return to stare at me.

'Fair enough. Just remember I walked in with my arms raised. Don't know why I'd have done that, if I planned to hurt you.'

I don't have a good explanation for that, but I see no upside in dropping my guard just yet, either.

'How'd you track me here?'

He shakes his head.

'Didn't have to. You weren't carrying a pack when we picked you up. A person wouldn't get very far without supplies, not out here. I reckoned you must have stashed it somewhere after you picked up our trail. Seemed like a good bet you'd come back for it. I figured I'd just retrace the route Goldie and me took earlier, see if I got lucky.'

He looks around the room. His gaze settles on the remains of my MRE, sitting by the fire.

'Don't suppose you'd be done with that?'

I wasn't, actually, but the dark eyes that flick back to me are filled with so much hunger I tell him he can have it. He holds my gaze a moment longer, then grabs the pouch as though he expects me to change my mind at any moment. I watch as he pulls off his mittens and sets to, using his fingers to scoop what was left there into his mouth. It doesn't take long. When he's got the last of it he runs one finger round the inside and licks it clean. Then he reaches for the carton it came in and upends it. The various packets inside tip out. He seizes on the HOOAH! and looks at me for approval. I nod, watching as he tears the wrapper open. The candy bar disappears in a couple of bites. He talks as he sifts through the remainder of the carton's contents.

'I'm here to give you a warning. You and whoever else you're traveling with.'

I start to deny it, but he just shakes his head.

'You might have done enough to fool that bonehead Goldie, but not me, and certainly not Finch.' He finds a ketchup and tears the corner, squirting it straight into his mouth. His eyes close for a moment, and then his tongue darts out to lick the corner of his chapped lips.

'Alright; have it your own way. Probably best I don't know anyway.' He nods at the fire. 'You can sit if you want. Ain't nobody else coming, leastways not tonight.'

I think on that for a while. It sounds like he's telling the truth, but I shake my head at the invitation anyway.

'Suit yourself.'

'How many of you did Finch send after me?'

'Six. We split up when we hit the interstate. Goldie took the rest of them off after the tracks you laid down. He'll follow them till they run out, just like I expect you intended.'

He checks the last of the packets, grunts at nothing in particular, then breaks out the little plastic toothpick that comes with each meal. He sets to work with it on a row of chipped yellow teeth.

'Why does the warden care where I go?'

He stops what he's doing and looks up at me slowly, like he doesn't understand. Then his eyes crease with humor. I watch as a slow smile spreads across his face.

'Garland Finch? The warden?' He gives a snort, like what I've said amuses him. 'What gave you that fool idea?'

'He said he was.'

'You sure about that?'

I open my mouth to tell him I am, but now that I think back I can't recall him ever saying as much, at least not specifically. I guess I just assumed from the way he talked, his suit, the shoes, the bunch of keys he carried.

He gives a shake of his head, goes back to work with the toothpick.

'I doubt it. Hard to know what rules a man like that lives by, but I ain't ever heard him tell no lie. He considers it the height of bad manners.'

I run back through our conversations in my head, trying to find any other evidence for my assumption.

'He said he released you all.'

He worries at something with the pick a moment longer, then runs his tongue over the front of his teeth.

'Well, that he did.' When he looks up at me again his mouth is doing something that might be a smile, but this time it doesn't stretch to his eyes; those have darkened considerably. 'Eventually.'

'So who was he, then?'

He picks up the empty MRE box and turns it over in his hands like he means to check inside it one more time. His eyes stay there a moment longer, then he looks up at me.

'Only the most dangerous man ever to set foot through the gates of Starkly prison.'

*

HE SHAKES THE CARTON one last time to be sure, then shoves it onto the fire. The flames grow brighter for a second as they consume the card, then die down again.

'How old are you, anyway?'

I tell him seventeen. Truth is I'm not quite there yet, but I figure an extra year goes a lot better with the pistol.

'So you was what, when it all ended? Six? Seven? I guess you would hardly have been outta diapers when they caught him.'

'Caught him? You mean he's just a prisoner?'

I don't mean no offense by it, words just have a habit of coming out of me that way. Mac's mouth hardens at the comparison. He rakes the embers with the side of his boot; sparks rise in a shudder and die in the blackness overhead. He leans toward me, and when he speaks again there's an edge to his voice that wasn't there before.

'Don't let the cane and that gimp leg fool you, kid. Garland Finch, he ain't like nobody else.'

'What...what was he in for?'

'Murder.' He pauses while he goes to work with the pick again. 'Not that that'd distinguish a man in a place like Starkly; ain't nobody ever been sent there on wino time.' He shakes his head. 'No, what set Garland Finch apart was the manner of his crimes. They reckon he was responsible for more than a hunnerd deaths, all told. Nobody's exactly sure how many, of course. They never did find a single body.' He smacks his lips like he's finally dislodged whatever he was hunting for. 'Probably because he ate 'em.'

At first I'm not sure I've heard him right, and for a few seconds my brain does that thing where it replays the words, trying to work out an alternative meaning that more closely fits with what I know of reality. Mac mustn't notice, or maybe he doesn't care, because he keeps talking.

'Starkly was a mean place to do time, maybe the meanest, so I guess it made sense they'd send him to us. The *warden*,' he looks over at me as he says it, 'was a prime asshole by the name of Stokes. Prided himself on being a real hardcase. But even Stokes was smart enough to know what he was dealing with, with a man like Garland Finch. He didn't take no chances. Soon as he arrived he emptied out HCON. All those who'd been down there – the snitches, the punks, the chesters, anyone who'd earned himself a stretch in solitary, even those on death row – he transferred back into the general population, so Finch would have the place to himself. Said it was for his own protection.' He gives a short, humorless laugh at that. 'First five years he was with us no one even laid eyes on him.'

'So how did he come to be in charge?'

Outside the wind moans, rattling the door in its frame, then settles down again. For a long moment Mac just stares into the fire, like he's considering whether he wants to tell me the next part. When he speaks again his voice has lowered.

'Whole world got turned on its head, is how.' He goes quiet, for longer this time. I begin to wonder if that's as much explanation as I'll get when without warning he hitches in a breath and starts talking again.

'You wind up in a place like Starkly, you try not to think too much about the world outside. How it's going on without you. Ain't much comfort to be had in that. There was the TV, of course, least for the hour each day Stokes allowed it. We knew from the news reports that things had taken a turn for the bad, but we figured it'd pass. The President had been on. The scientists were working on a cure, she said; wouldn't be long till they had it sorted.'

'The warden, he's a cautious man, though. He sticks the entire prison on lockdown. No one in or out; no visits, no furlough; hell, we weren't even allowed into the exercise yard. Can't say anyone cared much for that; more time in your cell's not something a con wishes for. Stokes, he says it's temporary; just till it all blows over.'

He prods the embers with the toe of one boot, sending another rush of sparks swirling up into the darkness.

''Cept things didn't seem to be getting no better, on the outside. Wasn't long before we're beginning to feel it, too. Starts with a few of the COs not showing up for their shifts. The screws were a mean bunch, so that didn't seem no bad thing, least not at first. It gets worse, though. Soon the warden's saying he doesn't have enough men to watch us at mealtimes, so we'll be taking our food in our cells, for the foreseeable.'

He leans forward, holding his hands a little closer to the dying fire.

'The future's something a con in a place like Starkly dwells on even less than what's going on outside. Mostly you teach yourself *not* to think on it. But by now the wise blood's starting to wonder how much longer our room service is going to hold out.'

He looks up at me.

'Well, the answer to that question was: not much. Starts with just a meal here and there being skipped, but before long getting fed's proving to be the exception rather than the rule. Never thought I'd miss a single one of those assholes, but that first morning no guard shows up to walk the block I knew it: we were screwed. The TVs in the main block are on, day and night now - I guess whoever was last out the door didn't bother to turn them off - but the coverage is getting pretty sketchy. Most of the channels have shut down and the ones that are still broadcasting are showing the same bulletins, over and over. It was pretty clear: the world outside had fallen apart. Wasn't nobody goin' to care much about a bunch of prisoners, stuck in some Godforsaken place out in the middle of nowhere.'

He takes a breath, lets it out slow.

'Once that realization sinks in all hell breaks loose. Cons start banging on the bars, hollerin' for the warden, the guards, Jesus; anyone they thought might listen. It stays like that for a couple of days, then all of a sudden it turns eerily quiet, 'cept for the few TVs that were still on, just pumping out static now.' He points a finger at nothing in particular, as though remembering. 'That was strange. Starkly hadn't ever been a peaceful place, even at night.'

He pauses, and for a while he just stares into the flames. Outside the wind gusts, rattling the door on its hinges, and he returns from wherever he's been.

'I'd been stashing food for a while; anyone with any sense had. What little I'd managed to squirrel away didn't last long, though. After that it was just a matter of taking to your cot, to wait for the end. Days passed like that; I can't say how many, so don't ask; by then they were just blending into each other. Then one night all sorts of weird shit starts happening. Outside the skies go white, like it's the middle of the day, only brighter. I was pretty sure I was trippin', you know, on account of not having eaten for so long. It stays like that for a while, the light comin' and going' in waves, like fireworks. Some of those that had found religion start hollering like it's Rapture. Then just as sudden as it lit up everything dies: lights, TV, the works. Starkly gets its final curfew.'

He goes quiet again, for longer this time. I realize I've let the pistol drop to my lap. I look down at it, then over at him. I don't reckon he means me any harm, so I ease the hammer back down.

'So how did you get out?'

'It was like Finch said. He let us out.'

'But how did he escape?'

'He was being held separate, remember, over in HCON.' He looks up. 'You must have seen it, when he was givin' you the tour? I bet he showed you that thing he keeps down there, too, didn't he?'

He grunts, like he doesn't much care for Finch's pet fury.

'It was the only modern part of the whole compound. They built it when the state designated Starkly a supermax. The cells had those fancy electronic locks, magnetic.' He wiggles his fingers in the air as he says it, as though as far as he was concerned they might have worked on magic rather than electricity. 'So when that weird shit happens in the sky and everything with a circuit gets fried, those locks, they just give up. The doors down in HCON spring open and Garland Finch he walks right out, free as a bird.'

'And he released you.'

Mac nods, only this time he doesn't say anything, just takes to staring into fire again. When at last he speaks his voice is little more than a whisper.

'That he did, eventually. First he walked the block, though, up and down with that leg of his, setting it out in terms he thought we'd understand. The world was a changed place, he said. Lean times were upon us. There were truths to be faced, hard ones. There wasn't going to be enough to feed everyone, and something had to be done about that, starting right then. So he'd come to a decision. He'd only let one man out of each cell, and only when there was nothing left of the other.'

*

I HEAR THE WORDS but my brain chooses not to accept them. I look over at Mac, hoping he's going to offer some alternative explanation for what I've just learned. Any other explanation.

'Yeah, at first we didn't think he was serious, either. But once you've known Garland Finch a while you realize that's not his style. You learn to take him very seriously.' He shakes his head slowly. 'He was every bit as good as his word, too. There were upwards of four hundred cons in the main block of Starkly, most of us two to a cell. When the last of those doors were opened what was left counted for not much more than a hunnerd-fifty. Weren't no cell where more than one man crawled out.'

The truth of what's he's told me finally sinks in. I stagger to my feet and take a step backwards.

'You *ate* your cell mates?'

I can hear the revulsion in my voice even as I say it. Mac looks at me over the fire, fixing me with a stare that makes me wonder if I should have kept the pistol cocked after all. He keeps his voice low, but there's a hardness to it now that reminds me why a man like him might have ended up in Starkly in the first place.

'You'd do well to keep that tone from your voice, boy. You prob'ly think you understand hunger 'cuz you had to skip a meal every now and then. You ever tried to eat the ticking out of your mattress? You ever spend your days praying for a roach to wander by your cell so you can slap your boot on it, maybe wash it down with a handful of water from the toilet bowl? You try that for a week or two, we'll see just what you would and would not do.'

He glares at me for a long moment, the embers from the fire burning red in his eyes. I tighten my grip on the pistol, reaching my thumb down to cover the hammer.

'Whatever shit I done, you think I deserved that? You think any of us did? Hell, I didn't even have that long. My time was short.'

'You were about to be released?'

He shakes his head.

'I wasn't ever going to see the outside of Starkly's walls. I had my ticket for the Big Bitch. The Stainless Steel Ride.'

I stare at him blankly; I have no idea what he's talking about.

'I was due to be executed. It was okay, though; I'd made my peace with it. When the time came the state was going to pay up for some expensive pharmaceuticals to take me over the line.'

He prods the fire with the toe of his boot again.

'I didn't sign up for any of it.'

His voice trails off and for a long while neither of us speak. My mind's still baulking at what I've just heard. I gaze into the fire, trying to make sense of it.

'But why would he do something like that? If he was worried about food he could just have released a bunch of you, forced you to leave, let you take your chances outside.'

Mac shakes his head.

'I thought about that a lot, after. What Finch done, it wasn't just about thinning our numbers, see. I think he figured he could give us a taste for it.'

He shakes his head, quick, like he's denying it.

'He sends us out, looking for supplies, but we never bring back enough. I guess the city had been picked over long before we got to it.

I'm not sure why he's telling me this, but all of a sudden I get a feeling, deep in the pit of my stomach. He keeps talking, but now it's like whatever he's about to tell me I'm not sure I want to hear it. It's too late for that, though. There's a part of my brain that's already racing ahead, working it out.

*He said Finch released a hundred and fifty of them from their cells. There was only thirty-seven when we sat for dinner.*

'And then there's the winters, when we can't hardly go out at all.'

*As I had passed the kitchens, something gray, back in the shadows, dangling from an old hook.*

'So when it gets tight we have ourselves a lottery. Supposed to be the same odds for everyone, but I doubt you'll ever see Tully or Knox's name get drawn. Nobody thinks it's going to be them. Until it is.'

I feel the blood draining from my face as I realize what he's telling me.

'The soup…'

He nods.

'Best not to think too hard 'bout what ends up in Blatch's cookpot.'

I stagger backwards but I don't make it as far as the door. Next thing I know I'm on my knees, still clutching the pistol, as what's left of the beef ravioli I had earlier comes flying out of my mouth. I continue to retch long after my stomach's expelled the last trace of it. When I think I'm finally done I wipe my mouth with the back of my hand and return to the fire.

Mac's still sitting, staring into the flames. He looks over at me as I take a seat. Whatever anger was there earlier has gone.

'I'm sorry, kid. I shouldn't have laid that on you. No reason for you to have to carry that around.'

I set the pistol down beside me. If I don't learn one more thing about Starkly for as long as I live I reckon it'll still be too soon. We sit in silence for a while, then Mac picks up the toothpick again. He digs around for a while till he finds something, holds it out to examine it, then goes back to work. One by one the embers wink out, until there's only a handful left, nestling among the ashes.

'So what do you mean to do?

He stretches his hands out to the fire.

'I done what I came to, which is give you a warning. I don't know how many of you there are, or where you're hidin' out, and I don't care to. Garland Finch has taken an interest in you, and believe me that ain't no good thing. If you've any sense you'll clear out of here, quick as you can, and you won't ever show yourself again, least not anywhere within a couple of days' hike of Starkly, or Durham, or anywhere else he might send us looking for you.'

'And you'll just head back?'

He nods.

'First light. I'll say I followed your tracks south into the city, but then I lost you. Goldie and the others'll tell the same story. You let me have that book he gave you it might go a little easier on me.'

I reach into my pocket for the copy of *Watership Down*, but as I pull it out I find myself hesitating, reluctant to hand it over.

'Won't he wonder how you came across it, if you couldn't find me?'

He shakes his head, like he's already thought about this.

'I'll tell him you tossed it, before your trail went cold.'

I stare at the cover a moment longer, then hand it over.

'I appreciate it. Man sure loves his books. You find him one, your name don't go in the lottery for a while. I'm surprised he let you leave with it.'

He looks over at the backpack lying against the wall. Most of its contents lie scattered on the floor from when I upended it looking for the bullets.

'Maybe you could spare one of those food cartons, too? You know, for the journey back.'

I open my mouth to tell him I don't have any extra to spare, but then I see how he's staring at me. He has the look of a man who's been on the wrong end of every deal going for longer than he can remember. I nod. He reaches for the closest one and it disappears inside his coat.

'Much obliged.'

Outside the wind gusts against the front of the *KwikPrint*, harder this time. There's a loud crack as it flexes the fractured pane. Mac spins around and takes to staring at the window. I remember how he had hurried in off the street when he first arrived, like he was more concerned about what might be out there than he was with the gun I had on him.

'What you said over dinner last night, about the city not being safe after dark. What did you mean? Have you seen something?'

He stares at the window a little longer then turns back to the fire.

'No, not exactly. It's just sometimes, when I'm out…I dunno…I get this feeling. Like I'm being watched.'

I remember thinking the same thing, when we cut through the parking lot of the VA medical center, on our way down through Durham. I tell him what Marv told me; how he reckoned the furies weren't gone for good; that one day they'd rise up again.

He studies me for a long moment without saying anything.

'Your friend one of them scientists?'

I shake my head.

'Then how could he know?'

But there's no conviction in his words; it's like he's only saying them because he needs it to be so. I consider telling him about Gilbey. She *is* a scientist, probably the only one left whose opinion counts for a damn, and she thought the same as Marv. I don't, though. Doesn't seem like he's trying to trick me into talking about stuff I'd do better to keep to myself, but if I'd been a little more suspicious of Hicks from the get-go things might have been different. Besides, I don't need to mention what happened at The Greenbrier to convince him.

'The fury Finch keeps, down in the basement.'

'What of it?'

'It's awake.'

He looks up at me like he's not sure what he's supposed to do with that information.

'When did that happen?'

'Just last week, according to Finch. He doesn't want anyone to find out about it. Says it might discourage those he sends out scavenging.'

'Son of a bitch.'

His eyes shift back to the street. He looks like he might be about to say something, but then he just takes to staring at the ground between his boots.

'Why are you going back to Starkly, Mac? I mean, why don't you just stay away yourself?'

He shakes his head.

'First thing Finch'd do is send Goldie and a few of the others out for me, then I'd wind up on the sharp end of Blatch's knife, for sure. Besides, where would I go? That place is all I got; it's all any of us got. Nuthin' else left on the outside, not anymore.'

His voice drops and he glances around furtively, as though someone might be listening.

'Besides, I reckon Garland Finch's time's getting short. There's not many of us left now, so that lottery of his ain't lookin' like the deal it used to. I reckon it won't be long before some of the brothers take it on themselves to bump titties with Knox and Tully. I figure I just gotta keep my head down, bide my time, pray my number don't come up in the meantime.'

*

When I wake the following morning the fire's died and the room's bitter cold. I draw the sleeping bag tight around me and watch as my breath rolls out in fat, white plumes. It hangs above my head for a few seconds before vanishing into the frigid air. I wipe the sleep from my eyes and look around. There's no sign of Mac. My gaze flits to the backpack, resting against the wall on the far side of the blackened remains of the fire. I climb out of the sleeping bag and hurry over to check the contents, but nothing's missing beyond what I offered him.

I get dressed quick as I can, then pack up my things. I don't bother with breakfast. I'm anxious to be on the road now, and besides, my appetite hasn't yet recovered from what I learned about Starkly. I hoist the backpack over my shoulder and head outside. A single set of tracks leads away from the *KwikPrint*, the wind already softening their edges. I stare at them for a moment and then point my snowshoes around and set off in the opposite direction, picking my way between the abandoned wrecks that clutter the street, swinging around every few paces to check behind me. A few blocks south a sign points to the turn for 501, but I don't take it. I plan to stay off the main roads, least till I'm well clear of Durham. It's a fair bet Goldie and the other men Finch sent are already out there somewhere, looking for me. I have no intention of making it easy for them.

Listing high-rises give way to crumbling warehouses and then finally to darkened strip malls as I make my way out of the city. Little by little the roads start to clear. I pass a *Kmart*, squatting long and low on the far side of a vast parking lot. Mac said there was little left here; that the city had been picked clean. I don't think he was lying to me about that, not with how thin he and most of the other inmates were, but I'd like to go in and check what's on the shelves, all the same, to see for myself. Seems strange there wouldn't be something worth scavenging, not in a place this size. There'll be time for that later, though. Right now I need to get back to Mags and the others.

One by one the last of the malls drop away and the road snakes out into open country. I follow it as it curves this way then that, trudging up each incline, hurrying down into the shallows between. When at last I reckon I'm far enough from the city, I cut west and start heading back towards 501. An hour later I pick up the highway and turn south again. I keep checking behind me, but less often now. The road stays clear.

Morning stretches into afternoon, then evening. As dusk's getting ready to settle I come to a large wooden yardarm, poking up through the snow just off the hard shoulder. The sign that hangs there shifts back and forth, creaking in the wind. Its paint is flaked, peeling, the timber underneath split, rotten black, but there's just enough of the faded cursive left to tell me I'm entering Fearrington Village.

I hurry on by, following the highway into town. It doesn't take me long to get the measure of the place. It's little more than a wide spot in the road; not even a diner or a gas station, just a couple of stores clustered around a stoplight, most of their windows broken, those that remain thickened with grime. I make my way quickly through. There'll be time later to explore, but I can't say as I hold high hopes for what I'll find for us here.

I pass another sign on my way out, this one buried in a drift. I bend down and scrub snow from the metal until I can read what's there.

*Mount Gilead Church Road.*

I recognize the name; according to Marv's map the bunker waits somewhere down that way. I'm about to point my snowshoes around when I stop. Mags has the list of codes she took from my backpack, but without the map I'm carrying there'd be little hope of her finding the bunker. It's more likely she'd have chosen a spot close, got the Juvies off the road, then settled in to wait for me.

I take another look along Mount Gilead. I can't see anything that way that'd do for shelter, so I turn back to the road I've been following. A little further along, right on the edge of town, a single low brick building, set a little ways back from the highway, its roof heavy with snow. I stare at it a moment longer then start making my way towards it.

As I get closer I see a weather-faded sign: *The Suntrust Bank.* Out front a small parking lot, empty save for a lone sedan, sunk on its tires under a blanket of gray powder. The snow is smooth, undisturbed, but that doesn't mean anything; if the Juvies got here more than a few hours ahead of me the wind would have taken care of their tracks. I scan the building again, more slowly this time. A narrow ATM lobby stretches the length of the front. To one side of the entrance the corner of something pokes from a drift. I don't have to stare at it long to work out what it is: the container with the virus.

I start to make my way down off the highway then I stop, remembering how twitchy Eric had been with his weapon when I'd left them in Durham. I pull my mask down and call out, like I used to do with the Guardians when I was about to crawl back into Eden's tunnel. There's a pause, then movement from back in the shadows and a second later the kid scampers into the lobby. He drops to a crouch in front of one of the ATM machines and raises a hand like he means to wave but then he stops, the gesture interrupted. He tilts his head. It's hard to tell on account of the goggles he wears, but it looks like he's checking the road behind me.

Tyler shows next, cradling his weapon to his chest, followed by Eric.

The rest of the Juvies crowd into the lobby after them, staring out as I make my way through the parking lot. I wait for Mags to appear, but there's no sign of her. As I bend to snap off my snowshoes Lauren pushes her way to the front.

'Gabe; thank God. I was…' She stops herself. 'I mean, we were all worried about you, of course. What happened? Did you find out where those men were coming from?'

I open my mouth to tell them about what happened at Starkly, but just then Jake appears at her shoulder. From the look on his face it's clear not everyone's as happy to see me as she was.

'Where's Mags?'

'She's not with you?'

He shakes his head.

'She brought us down here last night. First thing this morning she went back out looking for you.'

'Which way was she headed?'

It's a stupid question; I know it before I'm done asking. Where else would she go? I'm already re-fastening the bindings on my snowshoes even as he points behind me, north, back towards the city.

Lauren hugs her arms to her sides.

'What are you doing?'

'There are men there, looking for me.'

The Juvies' eyes shift as one, out to the parking lot, like I've just pointed to a horde of them, gathering behind the sedan. Jake mutters something under his breath I don't catch.

Lauren takes a step closer.

'Wait, Gabe; are you sure it makes sense to go back out? I mean, it's already getting late. I'm sure Mags will be here soon.'

I stop for a second. What Lauren's saying makes sense. Mags knew there were others out there; she would have been careful. When she doesn't find me in the city she'll go looking for shelter, somewhere to hole up for the night.

I look up to the darkening skies. That might be more than I'll manage. I doubt I'll even make it back to where I joined 501 before I lose the light, and there was little in the way of shelter along that stretch; I know because I've just hiked it. Marv certainly wouldn't be taking us out again, not this close to nightfall.

But that doesn't change the fact that she's up there right now, while Goldie and whoever else Finch may have sent are looking for me. I finish tightening the straps on my snowshoes and point them in the direction of the highway, before I can think of any more reasons not to go. The kid's still crouched in front of the ATM. He looks up at me through those outsize goggles he wears.

*You should warn them.*

I'm not sure how to do that, though, and right now I don't have time to figure it out. I turn to the Juvies crammed into the narrow lobby.

'Go back inside, all of you, and stay out of sight.'

They don't need to be told twice. The ones closest the door are already tripping over themselves to get out of the lobby.

I wait till Eric's gone back inside then I call Tyler over.

'Can you stand watch while I'm gone?'

His brow furrows.

'You really think they'll find us, all the way out here?'

I let my gaze linger on the highway a moment longer than it needs to before I answer, like I'm giving serious consideration to his question.

'I hope not. But there *are* men out there looking for me. I've left a trail, and if Mags is on her way back here she'll be doing the same. That's how the soldiers found us last time.'

He looks to the road, like he's considering what I've just told him.

'Alright.'

'One more thing.'

I turn to the kid.

'Johnny, will you stay out here and keep watch with Tyler?'

He hesitates for a moment, then turns his head in Tyler's direction. It's hard to tell behind those dark goggles, but it looks like he's taking in the rifle held across his chest. Tyler glances down at him then looks back at me.

'It's okay, Gabe, really. I got it.'

I shake my head.

'I need him out here as much as I need you, Tyler.' I lower my voice, not wanting the others to hear. 'The truth is he can see in the dark like you can't.'

Tyler cuts another glance in the Johnny's direction and I see his grip on the rifle tighten, like I've just disclosed the kid's favorite food is Juvie-brain and he hasn't been fed in an age. But then he nods, once, like he's getting himself straight with it.

'Alright.'

I pull my goggles down and set off across the parking lot. I can't see how anyone's coming down this road for us, not so late in the day, and if they are I'll run into them first. But at least out here the kid'll be away from the others. And Tyler will watch him close, without me having to tell them why.

As I pass the buried sedan I glance back towards the lobby. The kid's settled himself underneath one of the ATMs. Tyler stands by the entrance, the rifle still clutched to his chest.

It'll be fine. Tyler's calm. He won't freak easy, not like Eric, or one of the others. I tell myself that's why I chose him, and there's truth to that. The voice pipes up as I make my way up the embankment and rejoin the highway. It thinks there might be another part to it, too, whether or not I care to admit it.

*It wonders whether I picked Tyler because he has a gun.*

*

I CAN'T RIGHTLY SAY what my expectations might have been for the rest of that evening, only that they weren't met.

Not even close.

I've barely gone a mile when a lone figure appears around a bend in the road, not twenty yards ahead of me. She stops when she sees me, shifts her goggles onto her forehead and pulls down her mask. For some reason spidey pings at that, but as usual there's little explanation for it, so I put it down to the same surprise I'm feeling at finding her so soon. By the time I've shifted my brain back into gear she's already closed the gap between us. She stands there for a moment, then throws her arms around me. I grunt as the air's squeezed from my lungs.

'Easy.'

She doesn't let up.

'Asshole. You had me worried.'

Eventually she releases her grip.

'It's getting late. We should head back.'

I shuffle my snowshoes around and we set off back towards *The Suntrust Bank.*

'So what happened? Where were you?'

I tell her about getting surprised by Goldie and how he and Mac brought me to Starkly to meet Garland Finch. I describe how I took dinner with the inmates, but I don't go into detail on what might have been in Blatch's cookpot. I'm not sure I mean to tell anyone about that, ever, not even Mags. I describe the tour of the prison I got from Finch afterwards, including the library and the copy of *Watership Down* he gave me, but when the time comes I don't mention what I saw in the basement there either. It'd not take her long to work out the significance of a fury being held behind metal bars, and I haven't yet made up my mind how to tell her about that, or even if I mean to. I finish up with the warning Mac gave me about staying clear of Durham.

'I didn't see anyone there.'

'How far'd you go?'

'Just to the print store. When I saw your backpack was gone I figured you were on your way back down to us and somehow I'd missed you on the road.'

We walk for a while in silence. The *KwikPrint* was on the south side of Durham, but that's still more miles than anyone should have been able to cover in a day.

*A normal person, you mean.*

I tell the voice to be quiet. Up ahead the sign for Fearrington shifts on its yardarm; beyond it the stoplight and the turn off for the Mount Gilead Church Road.

'I guess the city's off limits then?'

I nod, still a little distracted.

'Unless we want to risk running into more of Finch's men.'

I tuck my thumbs into the straps of my pack, suddenly aware of how little heft there is to it; it weighs hardly more than the canvas it's made of.

This place I'm bringing us to, it'd better be stocked.

Mags stops, turns to look at me. It takes me a moment to realize I've said the words out loud.

'You want to see if we can find it?'

'Now?'

She nods.

I take a look down the Mount Gilead Church Road. Dusk has already settled over the snow-shrouded fields; it won't be long till darkness draws down behind it. I know what Marv would say; we've already pushed our luck enough for one day. But according to the map in my pocket the bunker's only a mile or so east of here.

I turn back to face her.

'I do.'

*

WE SET OFF INTO THE FAILING LIGHT. I scan the road ahead for signs. It curves east for a while, then straightens again. The bunker should be somewhere around here, at the end of a lane neither Marv nor the map had bothered to name. Up ahead I spot a turnoff that seems in about the right place. I push my goggles onto my forehead. A narrow track runs through open fields for a couple of hundred yards and then ends at what was once dense woodland. I look across the empty snow, my breath smoking in the cold as I try and decide what to do. The temperature's falling fast now; there's not much of the day left to us.

Beside me Mags pulls down her mask. Spidey pings again, like he did when I first saw her earlier, and it seems like he has something more specific he wants to say, but I'm too busy trying to stop my teeth from chattering to focus on whatever it might be. I ask her what she can see. She doesn't say anything for a while, but then eventually I just get *Trees*. She goes quiet again.

'How far down there was it supposed to be?

I don't need to get the map out to give her an answer.

'Not far. Half a mile maybe.'

I stamp my snowshoes, trying to keep warm. She looks at me for a moment, like she might be measuring my ability to go on. In the end she must come to a decision because she pulls her mask up again.

'Let's give it another ten minutes. If we haven't found anything by then we'll turn back. Okay?'

'Alright.'

I open my mouth to ask her if she's cold but she's already off, a new purpose to her stride. I try to keep up, but by the time we're halfway across the field she's already more than a dozen paces ahead of me. She doesn't slow for the tree line, just disappears among the gnarled trunks. I hesitate for a second and then follow her in. Long-dead trees push up through the snow on either side; their blackened limbs swiping at my parka as I make my way deeper into the wood. Darkness quickly fills the space between, until there's little to see but the moldering remains of those closest to whatever trail she's following. I'd get out the flashlight, except I don't want to fall any further behind, so instead I try and focus on the sound of her snowshoes crunching the ice-crusted powder. They're getting harder to hear above the sounds of my own breathing. The air is sharp with the cold now; it burns my lungs. This is crazy. I'm about to call out to her to suggest we go back when I realize that she's stopped.

As I catch up I see something ahead, jutting from the ground to waist height, blocking the way. She brushes snow off it, then turns to look at me. I dig in my parka for the flashlight, fumbling with the stubby handle while I get my breath back. Spidey pings again as the beam spreads, but I'm too distracted by what she's found to pay attention. I play the light over the obstacle, trying to keep my hand steady against the cold.

A barrier, the kind that rises right out of the road, the rusting metal painted in wide yellow and black stripes. On either side a high fence stretches off as far as the shuddering beam will allow. A single weather-faded sign hangs forlorn from the chain-link. It says we're on government property and right now we're trespassing. Beyond it the trees stop, as abruptly as they began.

We clamber over the barrier and make our way into the compound. A small guard shack squats on the far side, the snow drifted high against its aluminum sides. It's almost full dark now and inside my parka I'm shivering so hard my teeth are rattling together. I crank the flashlight again, the fingers inside my mittens already stiffening with the cold. The dynamo whirs and the bulb grows momentarily brighter, but the beam soon reaches its limit and won't be pushed further; all I can see are the tracks Mags is making in the snow. She seems to know where she's going, though, so I give up on winding the handle and follow her. A rusting pole appears out of the darkness; a tattered windsock shifting back and forth on its fraying tether. This must be where Gilbey and the soldiers landed in their helicopter, all those years ago. I look around for other landmarks that might confirm it, but find none.

Ahead the ground starts to incline and soon I can make out a raised embankment. As we get closer a pair of giant concrete cubes slowly emerge from the darkness. I play the flashlight over their sides. The beam won't stretch all the way to the top, but from what I can see it seems like the concrete sweeps inward to a point in the center, almost like a huge dish has been molded there.

Mags makes for the space between, where a narrow funneled entrance cuts into the ground. I can just make out the top of a metal door, right at the end. A camera stares down from a rusting bracket above, its single lens cataracted with ice.

She steps forward and starts scooping snow from in front of the door. I hang back a moment then join in, but my hands are numb with cold and I end up spilling as much as I clear. When we've managed to clear an area big enough for the door to open I stand back and crank the flashlight again, trying to hold the beam steady. It's little more than a Hobbit hole, hardly bigger than the vault door in the Exhibition Hall back at The Greenbrier. A large wheel handle sits at its center. The only other feature is a small window at eye level above. It's about the same size and shape as a letterbox, its metal surround held in place by heavy bolts. The thick glass is rimed with ice; I scrub it clear with the edge of my mitten and shine the flashlight inside, but I can't see a thing.

I search the wall to one side, relieved to find a keypad just like the one in Eden. I clear the snow from around the cowling and hit the reset button. For a moment nothing happens, but then there's the faintest of flickers from the light at the bottom, like it's deciding whether it cares to rouse itself from its decade-long slumber. The light gradually grows brighter, and then for a heart-stopping moment it goes out, before finally returning to blink at me in long, steady pulses. The rest of the keypad slowly illuminates.

I close my eyes and the section of Marv's map that showed Fearrington, complete with the code he had written next to it, appears before me. I start to punch in the sequence but my fingers are shaking so badly I keep having to start over. After the third attempt Mags taps me on the shoulder. I step away and call them out so she can do it.

She enters the twelve letters and numbers and stands back. The light underneath switches from red to green, and then there's a pause. A faint whine rises from somewhere behind the door, builds to complaining pitch, and then from deep within there's the grinding of gears. The handle in the center of the door begins a hesitant, anti-clockwise rotation. For a few seconds there's the muted screech of metal being dragged against metal as bolts slide back into their recesses, then it reaches the end of its travel with a loud clunk. Silence returns once again to the darkness.

I grab the wheel with both hands and pull but the door allows me only a fraction and then immediately retreats, like there's something else holding it in place, preventing it from opening. I kick the last of the snow from the base and try again, this time bracing one boot against the concrete to the side. Behind me I hear Mags asking if she can help, but I just keep yanking desperately at the handle. At last I think I feel something give. I renew my efforts. It takes a few more frantic tugs, but at last there's a soft sucking sound and the door finally surrenders, swinging back out towards me with a dull metallic groan.

*

I WIND THE FLASHLIGHT and shine it inside. A thick rubber seal runs around the edge of the recessed frame, explaining its unwillingness to yield. Beyond there's a small chamber, no taller or wider than the entrance. At the end another heavy steel door, identical to the first.

I step in. The air smells fusty, stale, like it hasn't been disturbed in years. I play the beam over the walls. The metal looks old, its surface covered with tiny whorls, scratches, the dull patina of age. The floor is steel grating, and when I point the flashlight upwards it finds more of the same. In the hatched shadows behind I can just make out the curving blades of what look like ventilation fans.

I step up to the inner door and try the handle, but it won't turn. I search the frame for a keypad; there's none. Instead a large green button protrudes from the wall, the plastic cracked, faded, the word CYCLE stenciled above. I push it, but nothing happens. I wait for a few seconds, listening, then try again. This time I press my ear to the cold steel, straining for any sign of activity within. But there's only the sound of my breathing.

I point the flashlight at the edges. Another strip of rubber compressed between door and frame, just like the one behind me. I grab the wheel and lean into it. The soles of my boots squeak as they compress against the grating but it won't budge, not even a fraction.

I step back and hit the button, harder this time, feeling the panic begin to rise. We can't have come all this way to be denied entry now. Mags rests a hand on my shoulder.

'Gabe.'

I turn around. She looks back at the door we've just come through.

'Let's try closing that one. Maybe the inner door isn't designed to open unless the outer one's shut.'

'Okay. Yeah. Good idea.'

She reaches for the handle to pull it shut.

'Wait.'

I dig in my pocket for Marv's map, but my fingers are numb with the cold and I have to fumble with it to pull it out. I look up. My breath hangs heavy in the air between us, and suddenly I understand what spidey's been trying to tell me since we left the Juvies. Because it's only my breath I see, roiling yellow in the flashlight's faltering beam. I stare at her, studying her slightly parted lips, the almost imperceptible flare of her nostrils as she exhales. There's no mistake; her breath is clear.

*I wonder what that means.*

'Gabe?'

It doesn't have to mean anything. She's not freaking out like you are, that's all. Besides, right now I have other things to worry about. If I don't get this door open we could freeze out here.

*You might. She won't.*

I squeeze my eyes shut and to my surprise it works; when I open them again the voice has gone.

'Gabe, you okay?'

I nod, hold the map out to her. The faded blue-red cover with the Standard Oil logo trembles in my hand. I tell her through chattering teeth to go back outside.

She looks at me like she means to argue, but I shake my head.

'W-who knows how much juice is left in the b-batteries? If they die before the cycle's c-complete I need you out there to f-figure a way to get me out.'

She hesitates for a moment like she doesn't care much for this plan. I guess she can't think of a better one, though, because in the end she takes the map and steps back outside.

I pull the door closed behind her, turning the wheel to lock it. This time when I hit the button there's a series of muted clicks, followed by more silence. I hold my breath, waiting for something else to happen. After what seems like an eternity there's a buzzing sound from above my head and I point the flashlight up just in time to see the fans in the ceiling start to rotate. They stutter at first, but then the pitch builds until they're nothing more than a blur. I feel a pressure in my ears as the air's sucked out of the tiny chamber. The motors run for a while then die, and for a long time after there's more silence. I'm starting to think there might not have been enough left in the batteries to complete the cycle after all, when at last I hear a click from the door in front of me and then the whine of another motor, followed by the low grinding of cogs as the mechanism grumbles through its internal processes. In front of me the handle slowly starts to turn, and from inside the door there's the familiar sound of bolts working their way home. When the wheel reaches the end of its travel it stops and silence once again returns to the small chamber.

I press my shoulder to the steel and push. It takes another couple of tries to break the seal on the inner door, but in the end it gives just like the outer one did. I shout over my shoulder that I'm in. I've no idea whether she can hear me through the steel, but I tell her to wait while I find a way to open the door manually.

I step out of the airlock into a tiled area, no wider than the chamber I've just left. A fat metal drain in the center of the floor; a showerhead, round like a sunflower; a metal chain you'd pull to make the water flow. A sign on the wall with instructions. Beyond the decontamination area, a concrete passageway stretches off into darkness. I find a metal hatch, low on the wall. It opens with a creak, revealing a handle with the word

OVERRIDE stenciled in red above, an arrow telling me the direction it needs to go. The mechanism's stiff, but after a little coaxing I get it to move. I step back into the airlock, and this time when I grasp the outer door's wheel it turns. I keep winding it until the bolts have been drawn back. I push the door open and Mags joins me.

We make our way along the passageway, following a run of rust-spackled pipes that hang from the low ceiling. No more than a dozen yards from the entrance it ends abruptly at a narrow concrete-lined shaft. A short walkway with guardrails on either side leads out to a metal staircase that spirals down into darkness. I shine the flashlight over the edge, but the drop is deeper than the beam will show me. I stand there for a second, inhaling the spent air. It feels dank, clammy. There's something else, too: a smell, heavy, unpleasant, drifting up from the depths.

'Everything okay?

I nod, make my way out onto the gangway. The metal looks old, worn, just like in the airlock. It groans worryingly as it accepts my weight, but it doesn't feel like it's about to give, so I keep going, out to the stairs. When I reach them I rest a hand on the rail. Paint still clings to the underside, but on top the steel's burnished smooth from years of use. When I point the flashlight down at the tread plate it's the same there: in the corners the raised diamonds still show; in the center where my boots fall there's little left but their outlines.

I start down. Inside my head I begin the count, measuring our progress in steps descended. The shaft is tight, the walls close enough to touch. Small vents punctuate the concrete at intervals I take to be equal to a floor, the area beneath each streaked brown with rust. I shine the flashlight on one. My breath still smokes in the beam, but less than above; already it feels a little warmer. I pull off a mitten and stretch my hand out to the grille. A gentle breeze slips between my fingers.

We continue on, round and round, each spiral taking us deeper into the bunker, our footfalls echoing and rebounding off the concrete as we descend. The walls get no closer, but somehow the shaft seems to press in, becoming more confined the lower I go. I push that thought from my mind and focus on the count. By the time I've reached two hundred I'm beginning to worry. I lean over the railing and point the flashlight down into the blackness below, desperate for evidence of anything other than this never-ending spiral. But the beam finds only more steps.

I pick up the pace. My hand skims the rail and my boots ring out on the tread plate, sending little clouds of dust shivering through the flashlight's herky-jerky beam that disappear off into darkness. I can feel my heart beating faster, but not from the effort of our descent. Hicks said the silo was only thirteen stories deep. I had assumed each of those would have living space, like the floors of a tall building, only buried underground.

But what if for most of it there's just this stair?

*

AT LAST I THINK I SEE something below me and I force myself to slow down. After a few more turns the stair drops through a grated ceiling and the shaft opens out. A narrow gangway juts into emptiness. I lean over the handrail. Beneath me the stair continues its spiraling descent, but the flashlight's no match for the inky blackness; I have no idea how much farther it goes.

A bead of sweat breaks free inside my thermals and trickles down my side. It's definitely warmer down here. I unzip my parka and step onto the catwalk, pointing the beam ahead. The gangway joins the stair to what looks like a doughnut-shaped floor that surrounds the shaft on all sides.

I make my way across. On the far side metal desks, lined up in neat rows that stretch back into darkness, their surfaces crammed with gauges, switches, readouts. Swivel chairs sit neatly under each. There's something not right about that, but I can't work out what it might be, so instead I lean closer and wipe dust from a few of the dials. The markings look old, antiquated. I continue along the row until I reach the end. The wall curves around gently, punctuated here and there by more grilles like the ones I saw in the shaft. But when I hold the flashlight up the surface isn't concrete; it has a dull luster, like it's sheathed in something metallic. In the yellowing beam it looks green, but in a different light it might also be blue.

'Copper.'

I turn around, surprised to see Mags standing right there. I hadn't heard her come up behind me. Her hood's pulled back and she's taken her mittens off. She reaches a hand out to the metal.

'It was on the walls of the plant room in Eden, too. Scudder said it was put there to shield the machinery from the effects of a pulse, like what Kane did, when he scorched the skies.'

I study her face. I can't see her breath, but then when I look in the flashlight's beam I can't find mine either. I take off my mittens, reach for her cheek. Her skin feels cold, but then we have just come from the outside.

She pushes the hand away.

'Hey, we're supposed to be checking this place out, remember?'

But as she turns her head away she flashes me a smile.

We head back to the stair and keep going down. The next level's similar to the first, only in place of the workstations there's stacks of what looks like computer servers, mounted on thick rubber shocks. A rat's nest of wires trails from the back of each; more snake along the floor; others hang in thick bunches from the low ceiling. The machines look clunky, old, like they belong in a museum.

We return to the shaft and continue our descent. The level below was clearly the mess. I count four long tables, each bolted to the floor. Chairs are tucked neatly underneath, just like upstairs. Something seems wrong with that, too. I stare at them for a while, but I have no more success figuring out what than I did earlier, so in the end I move the flashlight along. The beam finds a row of industrial-looking ovens, mounted on heavy springs. Large stainless steel hoods hang down, their elbowed vent pipes disappearing into the ceiling above. To one side, counters where food would have been prepared. Further along, rows of metal shelves, stacked with pots, pans, bowls.

I return my attention to the nearest table and play the flashlight over the scuffed metal. Mags takes a step closer, runs a finger across it, dislodging thick motes of dust that swirl through the beam before starting their lazy descent to the floor.

'It all looks so tidy. Do you remember how long it took us to clean up in Mount Weather?'

And then I see. Mount Weather's mess had been, well, a mess. The tables had been covered in plates of half-eaten food; the chairs had been pushed back, knocked over. We knew why, of course. On the morning of the Last Day Kane had contacted the base commanders of each of the facilities in the Federal Relocation Arc and ordered an emergency evacuation; anyone inside would have left in a big hurry. Afterwards he'd changed the codes on the blast doors remotely, preventing anyone from getting back in. Thankfully Benjamin had been listening, and had thought to write the new codes down, so that years later Marv could hand them to me.

There's no evidence anything like that happened here. The tables are bare, the chairs lined up neatly underneath. I point the flashlight over at the shelves. Plates, bowls, cups, all in perfect stacks; everything squared away, just so. I look back at Mags, but she's already worked it out.

'Whoever was here had plenty of time to tidy up before they left.'

I nod. It'll be good not to have to clean up like we did in Mount Weather. But there's something about it makes me feel uneasy, all the same.

We make our way back to the stairs and keep going down. The next level is stores. Metal shelves stretch back into darkness, all the way from the central shaft back to the silo's copper walls, like the spokes of a giant wheel. I'm relieved to see most are packed tight with boxes. I play the beam over the nearest one. The cardboard's old, speckled with mildew, but the faded letters printed on the sides are still mostly legible.

*U.S. Army Field Rations ~ Type C.*

I point the flashlight along the row. They're all the same. I drag one down. I don't need Weasel's blade; the adhesive's long dried; the tape lifts easily when I get a finger to it. Inside, small cans, each large enough for maybe a single meal. I lift one out and examine it. The contents are stamped, military-fashion, on the lid: the tin I've chosen says *Meat Stew with Vegetables*. I examine the sides but there's no further clue as to what animal it might have been taken from. If it's like Eden it won't resemble anything in God's creation; the army seemed to have only the vaguest grasp of what food actually tasted like. But cans are good; as long as the seals have held what's inside shouldn't have spoiled. I drop the one I've been inspecting back into its slot and return the box to its place on the shelf.

We head back to the main shaft. The floor below looks like it's been given over to provisions as well. From the stair my flashlight won't reach between the shelves, but when I set foot on the gangway to cross Mags says there's no need; it all looks the same as above. We continue on. The air grows heavy around us. I catch the smell I picked up when I first came through the airlock again, stronger now.

We wind our way down, deeper into the silo. The levels beneath the stores house the dorms. I count the cells as we cross the gangway: twelve to a floor. I push the door back on the nearest one, lifting my boot over the raised threshold. Inside is shaped like a slice of pie, narrow near the front, wider towards the back. Two metal-framed cots hinge down from the wall, just like in Eden. There's no more in the way of comforts than there was in our first home either, just a single bulkhead lamp mounted high on the riveted steel opposite.

I step back out, return to the shaft. Mags says the floor below looks identical to the one above so we stick to the stair. The next level down is ablutions. We find rows of narrow stalls, shower cubicles barely big enough to accommodate a body. The plumbing is rust-streaked, crusted with grime; by flashlight it all looks pretty grim. Here and there a rubber joint has given out, but most of it seems to have held. Beyond the final stall a row of washbasins, bolted to the silo's curving wall. Above each a square of steel that would once have served as a mirror.

I try one of the faucets, but it won't budge, so I move along to the next. It's seized solid, too. Mags steps up to the basin beside me and grasps the handle. For a second it looks like it won't yield either, but then she adjusts her grip and it turns with a low metallic groan.

She looks at me and smiles.

'Weakling.'

'You just got an easy one.'

We wait. At first there's nothing and then from somewhere above the sound of pipes clunking and shuddering. Finally something brown that might be water spits and sputters from the pipe in chaotic bursts. It doesn't look very appealing, but Mags says it's probably okay; at least whatever passes for a reservoir here hasn't run dry or frozen. She lets the water run until the stream steadies and starts to flow clear, then she shuts the faucet off and starts making her way back to the main shaft. I check she's not looking then I try the next one along, but I can't get it to turn any more than I could the first two. I wipe my hand on the outside of my parka and follow after her.

Beneath the showers the stair spirals down through another couple of turns then ends at a floor made of sections of thick, riveted steel. A large metal hatch, a wheel handle in its center, like the kind of thing you'd find on a submarine, waits for us at the bottom. I grasp the handle with both hands and heave it open, then point the flashlight through the opening. A narrow ladder drops to a grated landing; beyond, more steps.

I climb through the hatch and we rejoin the stair. There are no more floors now, just a single cavernous space. The sound of our footsteps changes, taking on a hollow, watery reverberation. The air is thick, the smell pungent.

I wind the flashlight until the dynamo hums and the bulb's burning bright as it can. I hold it out over the handrail, sweeping the darkness as we descend. Large-bore pressure pipes, their surfaces spackled with rust, circle the walls; others crisscross the open space between. Here and there gangways leave the stair, extending out to machines in an assortment of shapes and sizes. In the yellowing beam they all look old, decrepit.

Behind me Mags steps off onto one of the narrow catwalks. I turn around to see where she's going, but she's already lost to the darkness. I'm about to point the beam after her to light the way, but then I remember she doesn't need it. I lose her footsteps and for a few seconds there's nothing, but then I hear a tapping from somewhere above me that sounds like she's checking the level in one of the tanks. I stand there for a moment, uncertain what to do. I've had several weeks now to get used to how she and the kid can manage without the light, but the truth is I still find it a little unnerving.

I wind the flashlight and continue my descent. Less than a turn of the stair later the tread plate suddenly becomes slick and I feel my boot slide from under me. A jolt of adrenalin rushes my system and I grab for the handrail. The flashlight slips from my fingers, clatters off down the stair.

I take a deep breath and pull myself upright. From somewhere above I hear Mags, asking if I'm okay.

I call back that I'm fine.

I look down. The flashlight's come to rest on a narrow landing a few steps beneath me. I make my way down to retrieve it, gripping the handrail tighter now. I pick it up. The lens is cracked and when I shake it there's a rattle that wasn't there before, but at least it still seems to be working. I wind the handle. There's an unhappy grinding from somewhere within and for a moment the bulb flickers, but then it brightens. I point it over the edge. The beam reflects back off something dark, oily, and I see why the steps have suddenly become so treacherous, and where the smell's been coming from. Beneath me the staircase disappears into water. The bottom of the silo's flooded. I hold the beam close to the slowly undulating surface, but there's no way to tell how deep it is.

I shout up at Mags. A moment later her voice echoes back to me from somewhere in the blackness above. I point the flashlight to where I thought I heard her, and for a split second the beam picks out two pinpricks of silver, there and then immediately gone again.

The blood in my veins turns to ice water. An image flashes before me: a dark shape, spider-thin, slipping from behind an operator booth, and for a moment I just stand there, paralyzed with fear, just like when that thing attacked Ortiz in the basement of the hospital in Blacksburg. And then I'm bounding back up the stair. My mouth opens to shout a warning, but what comes out is wordless, incoherent. I feel Hicks' pistol bouncing on my hip, but the narrow steps are treacherous and I need my reaching hand for the rail.

Mags must sense the alarm in my voice because I hear her boots above me now, hurrying across the gangway. She meets me where it joins the stair.

'What's wrong?'

I push past her and point the flashlight along the catwalk, searching for the thing I saw only seconds ago. But the gangway's empty, at least as far the beam will show me. I inch forward, holding it out in front of me. My other hand drops to the haft of the gun. Ahead the fuel tank Mags was checking slowly separates itself from the darkness, its rusting flanks disappearing up into the gloom. I keep going, all the way out to the silo's curving walls.

'What is it, Gabe?'

I sweep the beam over the guardrails, the grating, the blue-green copper. This is where it was, right here, I'm sure of it. But there's nothing; nowhere for anything to hide. I lift my hand from the pistol's grip, letting it slide back into the holster.

I feel her hand on my shoulder and I start. Another possibility occurs to me then, settling cold in my stomach. I swing the flashlight around, but she's too fast. Her hand closes around my wrist, so quick it surprises me. She pushes the beam away before I have a chance to see.

'Hey! Careful with that.'

She stares up at me, a quizzical expression on her face.

'You look like you've seen a ghost. What's wrong?'

I manage to stammer out something about the silo being flooded. She holds my hand for a second longer then lets it go.

'*That's* what freaked you out? I could have told you there was water down here as soon as we came through the airlock.'

She turns around and steps out of the beam, disappearing into the darkness beyond. I think I hear her boots on the stair, but it's hard to tell above the sound of my own breathing. When I point the flashlight over the guardrail it finds her crouched by the water's edge. She studies the oily surface for a moment, then comes back up to join me.

'It's okay. This far underground they'll have had to pump the water out, just like we did in the deeper parts of Eden. With the power off all this time it's seeped back in, that's all. Once we get the generator running the pumps should kick in and clear it out.'

I nod, like this is good news. She looks at me strangely, like she's wondering what it is I'm not telling her.

'Well, I guess we've seen as much as there is'. She dusts her hands off. 'Ready to head back up?'

I nod again, still distracted by what I think I've just seen. She studies me a moment longer, like she's still trying to work it out, then heads for the stair.

*

WE MAKE OUR WAY BACK up to the hatch, clamber through, then rejoin the spiraling stair. When we reach the mess I set the flashlight down on one of the tables and start digging in my pack for the last of my MREs while Mags wipes the dust from the old steel. I open the cartons, add a little water from my canteen to the chemical heaters to start the reaction and then leave the pouches to warm. When they're ready she tears the foil off one and starts poking at the contents with the plastic fork that came in the packet. She skewers something the carton says is a Chicken Chunk and holds it up.

'Hey, I've been meaning to ask. Do these taste funny to you?'

'Like what?'

'I dunno. Stale?' She shakes her head, like that's not it. 'Dull. Boring. Like it's missing something?

I shrug. My meal tastes like every other one I've had. She goes back to digging half-heartedly in the pouch for a few moments then abandons the Chicken Chunks in favor of the HOOAH! that came with them. I steal a glance across the table as she removes the wrapper. The flashlight with its freshly cracked lens sits further along the table. The sorry puddle of light it casts is slowly receding, but it's enough to see by. She looks okay; still a little thin perhaps, but the shadows have all but gone from her eyes. She finishes the candy bar and looks over at mine.

I slide it across the table towards her. She flashes me a smile and then unwraps it. When she's done she busies herself fixing a coffee. We haven't bothered with a fire, so all that's left to warm the water is the heater from the MRE carton. She takes a sip, grimaces, then looks around the room.

'So what do you think?'

My mind's elsewhere, still fretting over what I think I saw in the plant room, so at first I miss what she says. She glances around, the gesture clearly meant to encompass more than just the mess. She looks at me expectantly.

'Well, it's thirteen stories, just like Hicks said. He just forgot to mention most of them don't start until you're almost that far underground.'

She raises the mug to her lips, letting her gaze rove one more time. I find myself stealing glances at her eyes, searching for anything unusual there. But there's nothing. The memory of what I thought I saw in the plant room is already growing less certain. Did I imagine it? Was it just my own eyes playing tricks on me?

I'm waiting for the voice to chime in; it seems like just the sort of thing it would have an opinion on. But for once it stays quiet.

'It seems old, doesn't it? Maybe even older than Eden was. What do you think they built it for?'

I force myself to pay attention.

'I dunno. This far underground, the shielding on the walls, the way everything's mounted, it was definitely built to survive a blast. It must have something to do with that equipment up there.'

She takes another sip from the coffee, sets it on the table.

'There's bound to be a set of manuals. I bet they'll tell us.'

She looks right at me. Her pupils are definitely wide, but then the only light we have is from the flashlight's tiny bulb. And they're dark, normal, with no trace of what I thought I saw, earlier.

I must have imagined it. It was pitch black down there, after all. And I had been staring into the floodwaters. Maybe what I saw was the afterglow of the flashlight, reflected off the oily surface.

That would explain it.

I wait for the voice to contradict me, but it remains silent.

A trick of the light, that's all it was.

I nod to myself, as if to confirm it. I'm being foolish, letting my imagination run away with me. And right now there are plenty of other things I need to concern myself with. I look at the handful of tables arranged around us. I certainly wasn't expecting anything on the scale of Mount Weather, but this place is smaller than I had imagined. *Way* smaller. The dorms only sleep forty-eight, and that's assuming two people bunking together, which would be pretty cramped. *Seriously* cramped. I'm not sure the cells are even as big as the ones we had in Eden.

'It certainly doesn't look like it was designed to hold many people.'

I say it mostly to myself. Mags reaches for the mug again, raises it to her lips.

'Good thing there aren't many of us, then. At least it's warm, and there's food, and water. As long as we have those things we can make it work.'

Two levels devoted to stores *is* good. Not a lifetime's worth of food, but several winters at least, as long as we're careful. I realize I should feel better about that than I do.

'Yeah, but only cans. Isn't that strange?'

She shrugs.

'I guess. I'm just glad we won't have to clear out stuff that's spoiled. Do you remember how long that took us in Mount Weather, and we didn't have that stair to contend with.'

I nod, still a little distracted.

'I'll need to check the stores, properly.' There's bound to be other things we'll need. And now that Durham's off limits I have to figure out where else I can go to get them.

She reaches across the table for my hand.

'You can do that tomorrow. Come on, let's go pick out our room.'

She drains what's left of her coffee while I bag our trash, and then we head back out on to the stair. I stop to charge the flashlight. The handle sticks and grinds for a few turns, like there's still something amiss with its innards, but then the bulb brightens. I point it along the gangway, but Mags has already disappeared into the darkness. I hesitate a moment then set off after her. When I reach the dorms she's waiting for me by the guardrail.

'Okay, which one?'

I sweep the light over the bulkhead doors that circle the landing. The cells all look identical, so I settle on the closest one.

'Excellent choice.'

She pushes it open and steps through, but instead of following her in I wait. It's been weeks since we've been alone together, without either the kid or the Juvies nearby. I should be looking forward to this. But somehow I can't help my thoughts returning to what I thought I saw in the plant room earlier.

I shake my head.

I'm being stupid.

I take a deep breath and step over the threshold.

The cots bolted to the walls are too narrow to share so she takes the thin mattresses off, lays both side-by-side on the floor, then latches the frames out of the way. I unpack our sleeping bag while she wriggles out of her thermals and slips under the quilted material. I set the flashlight down so I can get undressed, not paying attention to where I point it. Her eyes narrow at the beam, and in the second before she reaches to turn it away I glimpse again what I had almost convinced myself I had imagined down in the plant room.

I freeze, one foot still caught in the leg of my pants, but she's busy pointing the flashlight at the wall and doesn't notice. The pale cone of light reflects dully off the tired steel. Even as I watch it shrinks, the weakening bulb shifting from yellow to orange as it dies.

'Hurry up, slow poke.'

I finish getting undressed, making much more of a deal than I need to of folding my clothes. She props herself up on one elbow, watching my progress from inside the sleeping bag.

'Really? *That's* your priority right now? Should I be worried, Gabe?'

She says it like it's a joke, but when I look down the smile that goes with it is less certain. She holds back the flap. I don't know what else to do so I climb in beside her.

The flashlight flickers for a few seconds, steadies, then finally blinks out. For a moment afterimages of the dying bulb swirl across my vision, then they too fade, leaving only blackness. I close my eyes then open them again, like I do when I'm trying to get them to adjust. It makes no difference, though; I can't see a thing. We lie there for a while, barely touching, then she takes my wrist, guides my hand to her side. After a moment she moves it down to her hip. Where there should be cotton my fingers feel only skin.

I think of the nights I have spent since we quit Eden, trying to find a way past that narrow stretch of material; the daylight hours spent in contemplation of how it might be achieved. My efforts never came to anything. Whatever subtlety, distraction or boldness I attempted, the result was always the same: my hand would gently be relocated elsewhere.

I let my fingers rest where she has placed them.

All I can think is how cold she feels.

She murmurs something I can't make out, shifts closer. I feel her arms slip up behind my neck. Her face is only inches from mine but the darkness is complete, impenetrable; I can't make out anything there.

*But she can see you.*

She stretches up, pressing into me, and now I feel her breath on my neck. An image appears, unbidden, the flashes of silver I saw earlier. I feel myself tense.

She pauses. I screw my eyes shut, trying to push it away, but the image reappears, and this time the voice returns with it. It effects a drawl, the last thing Hicks said to me as we stepped out of The Greenbrier's tunnel.

*When the time comes there'll be no warning. It'll be like a switch has been flipped.*

I know it's Mags, but I can't help it. As she leans in to kiss me again I flinch.

She stops.

'What's wrong, Gabe?'

My heart's pounding and there's a tightness in my chest, a weight, just beneath my ribcage, like I'd get when I'd go out in the tunnel in Eden.

'Nothing. I…I guess I'm just a little tired.'

I feel her pull back. I can't see a thing, but in my mind's eye I picture her, examining my face, searching it for proof of the lie I've just told. It won't be hard to find. I'm sixteen years old; most of the time it feels like I was standing *way* too close to the front of the line when hormones were being handed out. Nobody knows that better than Mags. This isn't an invitation she'd ever have expected to be declined.

She exhales slowly, and then for what seems like an eternity there's just the darkness and the weight of her stare. Finally she turns around. I slip my arm hesitantly around her waist, but this time she doesn't press back into me.

*

HE SITS ON HIS SLEEPING BAG, his back to the wall. The lobby is small, narrow. A row of bank machines at one end, their long-dead screens gray, filmed with dust. At the other a small trashcan, lying on its side. Scraps of crumpled paper spill out onto the moldering carpet.

The remains of his meal lay spread out around him. He picks at the pouch's contents with the plastic fork. The girl says he has to eat as much of it as he can, so he takes another bite. He tells himself it's not so bad. It doesn't taste of much at all, really, but if you stir it like she showed him at least it's not gritty, and that helps.

He looks out into the parking lot. The girl was supposed to be back by now. The tall boy's gone to get her. He wonders if he should have told him about the others he met, in the shopping mall. But then the boy might have tried to find them, and the girl with the pink hair said that wouldn't have been a good idea.

He takes another forkful of the food, chews it slowly. Even mixed up properly it's not as nice as the candy bar. He eyes the HOOAH!, still in its wrapper, sitting on the sleeping bag next to his goggles.

The boy with the dark skin is gone now, so he doesn't have to wear them anymore. The boy stayed as long as he could, but eventually it got too cold and he had to go back inside. He offered to make him a fire. The girl lets him build them so he's gotten quite good at it. He knows how to stack the firewood and where to place the kindling, and to blow on the flame when it catches to so it will spread up through the branches and not die. But the boy said they couldn't have one, not out here. Somebody might see.

He looks out to the parking lot. The wind has picked up; it sends snow swirling around the abandoned car.

A fire would have been fine. No one could be out in that.

At least not one of them.

He likes the boy with the dark skin, though. He seems okay. He was nervous at first, even though he tried not to show it. But after a while he rested his gun against the wall and sat down. Not close, but not as far as he could have sat either. He even spoke to him a few times. Mostly just to ask what he could see, so not a conversation exactly, but better than silence. Much better. Back in the cage he wasn't allowed to talk at all.

The other boy came out to them a few times, but he never stayed long. He kept to the far corner, clutching his rifle, and pretended to stare out into the darkness. He was pretty scared. He could smell it, even from all the way at the other end of the lobby.

After the boy with the dark skin went back inside he could hear them, whispering their questions.

*What was it like?*

*Did it say anything?*

*Weren't you frightened?*

The boy who stayed in the corner said he wasn't; he had a gun. The boy with the dark skin told him to shut up. After that it had gone quiet again.

They'd get used to him, that's what the girl said.

But it's been a long time now.

Outside the wind gusts against the glass, flexing the pane. He catches his reflection as it shifts. Maybe if he looked more like them. He tilts his head, studying the still-unfamiliar face that stares back at him. The grimy glass makes for a poor mirror, but it shows him enough. The shadows that darken his eyes seem to be fading at last, but slowly. He reaches up, takes off the cap the girl makes him wear, runs the fingers of one hand over his scalp. He feels something there, like the beginnings of stubble. It is hard to tell just by looking. The hair that grows there is white, just like his skin. He can't be sure, but he doesn't think that was the color it was, before.

He looks down at the food pouch, eyeing it guiltily. He will definitely finish it later. He hesitates for a moment and then reaches for the candy bar. He's busy tearing at the wrapper with his teeth, so at first he doesn't hear the footsteps. Then the door creaks open behind him. He drops the HOOAH! and scrabbles for his goggles just as the beam from a flashlight dances into the lobby.

The boy with the curly hair steps through, zipping up his parka.

'What're you still doing out here?'

He turns away from the light while he sorts out his goggles. Once he's got them situated he looks back at the boy and says he's keeping watch.

The boy hugs his arms to his sides and glances back over his shoulder, to where the others are huddled around the fire.

'Aren't you cold?'

He shakes his head. The truth is he's not. It is colder out here, but it doesn't bother him. Not really.

The boy stands there for a moment, as though he's considering that. He steps back into the other room but then he returns, carrying an armful of branches from the firewood they collected earlier. He dumps them on the ground and then heads over to the corner and bends to the trashcan.

'We're not supposed to have a fire.'

The boy doesn't look up from his task.

'Nobody's coming now.'

He returns with a handful of crumpled ATM receipts. The flames are reluctant at first, but slowly they creep up through the kindling and then start to lick at the wicker of blackened limbs above. When he's certain they've caught he sits back on his haunches and dusts off his hands, but he makes no move to leave. He watches the fire for a while, as though measuring his work.

'So what's with your eyes? Are they troubling you?'

He shakes his head. The tall boy asked him that too, when he first started wearing the goggles. But the truth is they're not, or at least nothing like they used to. The light outside sometimes hurts, but only in the very middle of the day, and even then not much. When he's wearing his goggles he hardly even notices it.

'Why do you wear those all the time then?'

He shrugs. The boy looks at him for a while like he might press him on it, but he doesn't.

'Is it true you can see out there?'

He hesitates. Being able to see in the dark is another way he's different. But the tall boy already told the boy with the dark skin about that, so they probably all know by now. He nods.

The boy stares into the fire for a while as though he's considering this. He looks like he has another question he wants to ask, but it takes a long time for him to get to it.

'Mags too?'

He's not sure what to say. He's pretty certain the girl doesn't want the others to think she's different, any more than he does. That's why she wears the cap and pretends with the flashlight. But he doesn't think this boy means her any harm. He sees how he looks at her, when he thinks no one's watching. Sometimes he feels a little sad for him.

He nods again.

The boy with the curly hair keeps looking at the fire. Eventually he says *Okay, then*, as if to himself, and then he gets up and goes back inside.

*

I OPEN MY EYES SLOWLY, still fuggy with sleep. The cold darkness, the thin mattress, the unyielding steel, all are familiar, and in those first uncertain moments between sleeping and waking I think I'm back in my cell in Eden, waiting for the buzzer to sound, and everything that has happened since we left, all just fragments of a dream that, however vivid, will soon begin to fade.

I pull the sleeping bag around me. Not so much a dream as a nightmare. I close my eyes and wait for it to recede. The dream is stubborn, however; I find myself wishing for the bulkhead lamp to blink on and banish it. But for long seconds nothing happens. I open my eyes again as it slowly begins to dawn on me where I am.

I stretch out one hand, sweeping the cold metal for the flashlight. I pick it up and crank the stubby handle. It graunches a complaint but after a few turns the bulb starts to glow, slowly illuminating my cramped sleeping quarters. I play the beam over the worn steel. Even with the bunks latched out of the way it feels tight in here, confined. The reluctant cone of light continues its journey, coming to rest on a pile of clothes by the door. I stare at them for a moment, vaguely aware that something's not right. Far too neatly folded for my hand. And Mags certainly isn't in the habit of picking up after me.

Mags.

The thought of her brings everything else back. I swing the flashlight around, but I'm alone. I struggle out of the sleeping bag, pulling my clothes on as I stagger out to the landing.

I waited until she'd lapsed into whatever passes for sleep for her now, then I checked her crucifix again. I had no reason for doing it other than habit; I already knew what I'd find. After that I just lay there, waiting, trying to keep images of things I have seen in dark places from popping into my head. She woke with a start some time later. I listened while her breathing calmed, pretending I was asleep. I don't think she was fooled, but she mustn't have had anything to say to me either, because she didn't call me on it. For a long while we just stayed like that, not speaking. I hadn't meant to, but I guess at some point I must have drifted off.

And now she's gone.

I lean over the guardrail and call out to her, but the only answer I get is my voice echoing back up through the silo. I tell myself there's no reason to be concerned. She'll have got bored just lying there and gone off to do something, maybe see if she can find those manuals she was talking about, that's all. But my heart's beating a little faster than it should as I cross the short gangway and start down the stair.

The steps spiral down, past the dorms below, then the showers. I call out as I go, but still there's no answer. The voice pipes up; it has something it wants me to see. It shows me a long tunnel, a flashbulb image of something pale, impossibly thin, bounding towards me. I screw my eyes shut, trying to banish it, but the voice grows bold with the darkness. It shows me another. The basement of a hospital this time; a dark shape slipping from behind an operator booth.

I grip the handrail.

I'm being stupid. It's Mags. She wouldn't hurt me.

Marv this time, on his knees in the snow, silver eyes staring back at me from inside the shadow of his hood as he slips the hunting rifle from his shoulder. My hand drops to my hip. I realize I've left Hicks' pistol back in the cell.

The voice wonders whether it might be a good idea to go fetch it.

I put that shameful thought from my mind and climb through the hatch into the plant room. At the bottom of the ladder I pause, listening. I think I hear a sound now, drifting up from below. A tapping: hollow, metallic. It stops for a second and then resumes.

I rejoin the stair. Every few steps I call out; still there's no answer. I keep following the flashlight around, forcing my boots to continue their downward journey. The air grows thick, dank. I feel like I should be close to the bottom, but I've forgotten to count, so I can't be certain. I listen for the sound of lapping water. It's hard to hear over my own breathing, though.

The tapping grows louder. It seems to be coming from the end of one of the gangways. I point the flashlight there, but whatever might be causing it is beyond the beam's reach. I crank the handle. Something inside grinds in protest and then the dynamo whirs; for a few seconds the bulb grows brighter.

I step off the stair and make my way along the catwalk. An access panel lies propped against the guardrail, the old steel dented, scarred. I find her just beyond it, lying on her back on the metal grating, peering up into the belly of one of the ancient machines, an assortment of tools spread out around her. There's a windup flashlight among them, but she must not have need of it because she's allowed it to go out.

I call her name again. There's a pause and then she puts down whatever it is she's working on and starts to wriggle herself out. My heart races again as she sits up, but she gets a hand up to ward off the beam before I have a chance to see whatever might be there.

'Point that somewhere else, will you?'

I hesitate for a second, then let the beam fall to the grating.

'What is it, Gabriel?'

The long form of my name; never a good sign.

'I...I was calling for you.'

‘I heard.’

I want to say something about what happened last night, about what I saw in Starkly, about what might be about to happen to her. But how do you begin with that? *Hey Mags, guess what? The scanner I thought would cure you? Yeah, it didn't do that after all. Turns out you and the kid both still have one-way tickets to Furytown.*

In the end I just point the flashlight at the generator and ask if she needs help.

She tilts her head and stares at me for a moment, like she wants to know if that's really the question I want answered. When I don't come up with another she just shakes her head and slides back under the old machine.

I tell her I'll go back and fetch the others, then. But the only answer I get is the sound of the tapping resuming.

*

I CLIMB BACK UP THROUGH THE HATCH, trading the plant room's depths for the compressed levels above. At the dorms I step off, grab my parka and backpack from the cell, then continue my spiraling journey up through the silo. When I reach the concrete shaft I pause to crank the flashlight. The handle sticks but then the bulb burns brighter, throwing confused shadows over the rust-streaked walls that shift and merge as I climb. Tight spaces don't bother me anything like they used to, but there's a weight that has lodged itself behind my breastbone, an ache that is at the same time hollow and heavy, just like I'd get when I'd step into Eden's tunnel. I quicken my stride, anxious to be outside again now.

At last the shaft ends and I hurry along the passageway and into the airlock. I push back the outer door, step outside, and for a moment I just stand there, waiting for that feeling I'd get when I'd crawl out through the portal, like an invisible burden had been lifted. But the weight in my chest remains.

I look up to the sky. Somewhere off to the east dawn's already breaking. The light that filters through is gray, flat, but sufficient to grant me my first view of our new home. There's not much to look at. Blackened trees circle the compound, pressing themselves up against the rusting chain-link, like they might still hold a grudge for the clearing they were once forced to concede. The part of Mount Weather that was above ground was busy with buildings: storage sheds, a barracks, a motor pool, the control tower; even a hangar for a helicopter, but here there's nothing other than the two huge concrete cubes that guard the entrance and a single tattered windsock, clanking listlessly against its pole. I guess I shouldn't be surprised. Mount Weather was an underground city; the silo's only a fraction of its size. I can't escape the feeling something's missing, all the same; something that should be here, but isn't.

I pull my hood up and set off, heading for the gap in the fence that marks the entrance. When I reach the guard hut I stop and turn to scan the compound again, but whatever it is won't come to me, and right now I have other things on my mind. I clamber over the security barrier and make my way in among the trees, following the tracks Mags and I made last night. Without them I'm not sure I'd be able to find my way, even in what passes for daylight. I don't know how she managed it, in the dark.

*Yes you do.*

An image, sudden, unwanted: a pair of silvered pupils, caught for an instant in the flashlight's beam.

I squeeze my eyes shut against it. It doesn't mean she's sick. She can't be. I've seen firsthand what that looks like: by the end Marv wasn't able to lift a boot from the snow. She hiked all the way to Durham and back in a day, a distance he couldn't have covered at his best, and it took nothing from her; I couldn't keep up with her last night.

I hold tight to that thought as I pick my way between the withered trunks. But whatever comfort it might bring, the faithless voice won't allow it. It starts to whisper.

*Hicks was pretty quick, too, remember?*

Hicks knew he had the virus, though. He told me he could feel it, working its way through him. Mags says she feels fine.

The voice shows me another image. This time it's Finch's fury, crouched at the back of its cell. I shake my head, desperate to dislodge it. If that were going to happen it would've happened already. It's been weeks since she and the kid came through the scanner.

I have little more than hope to back that theory up, however, and the voice knows it. I try and hush it, but it won't be quieted. It has things to say now, and it means to be heard.

*You thought it would be that easy?*

I know what's coming next. I shout at it to shut up, but it makes no difference; it carries on regardless.

*Kane launched every missile he had, enough to turn the night sky bright as day.*

I quicken my pace until my snowshoes are pounding the snow. But the voice is in my head; it can't be outrun any more than I might hope to silence it.

*Hicks had it burned from his flesh, but that didn't work either.*

I reach the end of the woods, strike out into open fields.

*Gilbey's a* scientist. *She knows more about the virus than anyone. She* invented *it. She's been searching years for a cure and she hasn't found one yet.*

*You really thought* you *could do better?*

I force my legs to work faster, anything to escape it. My lungs burn with the effort. Sweat soaks my back, my legs, more than my thermals can hope to wick away. It runs down my face inside my goggles, stinging my eyes. I yank down the thin cotton mask I wear, desperate for more air. And still the voice continues, over and over, a never-ending loop inside my head.

*You think the few minutes you got Mags in the scanner could do what Gilbey couldn't?*

*How could you?*

*You don't understand how it works, any of it.*

*You're just a* kid.

I have no answer for any of it. I only know what happened to Marv, and Hicks and Finch's fury can't happen to her.

There's no reason.

It just *can't*.

I keep it up for as long as I can. My legs are accustomed to the snow, but not the pace I've set them. I feel the muscles there come to the end of their endurance, become unreliable. I catch an edge with a snowshoe, stagger into a drift. I throw my hands out against the fall, but I land awkwardly, my arms sinking deep into powder. I stay like that for a while, just sucking in air. The voice has finally fallen silent, but its work is done. A cold darkness wraps itself around my heart.

At last I struggle to my feet. Snow has found its way inside my mittens; it sticks to my cheeks, my mask, my goggles. I don't bother to dust it off. I point my snowshoes toward the road, but my knees have turned to rubber. It takes longer than it ought to make it the final few hundred yards back to the SunTrust Bank.

As I stagger into the parking lot I see the kid, sitting by himself in the ATM lobby. He stares at me through those goggles. I should have paid more attention to that, I see it now. When did he first take to wearing them at night? I try to remember, but the days since we left Mount Weather have blended into each other and I can't be sure. I unsnap my snowshoes, meaning to go in and ask him about it, but as I step out of them Jake appears at the door, blocking my way. He looks past me, over my shoulder.

'Where's Mags?'

I tell him we went to check out the bunker; that she's back there right now, working on getting the power back on. He stares at me like I might have sprouted another head overnight.

'Seriously, you just left her, by herself? What if something's hiding in there, like when you went to Mount Weather?'

Something hiding.

If only he knew how absurd that sounds. I feel something inside my chest start to convulse, and I realize I might actually laugh. I can feel it, bubbling up inside me. I have to grit my teeth to suppress it.

Mags *is* that thing, you muscle-bound moron.

Or soon will be.

Jake's still glaring at me, waiting for an answer. In the room behind the Juvies have stopped whatever they're doing to tune in to this latest drama. I take a breath, start to explain that it's okay. Fearrington wasn't that big; we checked everywhere. It's clear he doesn't care much for that explanation, however. He turns on his heels and heads back inside before I've got more than a couple of words out. I stand there for a moment, aware that the Juvies are all watching me.

I feel the heat rising in my cheeks. I follow him inside, meaning to make him listen to what I have to say, whether or not he cares to hear it. But before I've made it half way across the room Lauren steps into my path. She slips one hand through my arm and the next thing I know I'm being led over to where the rest of them are huddled around the fire.

'So, Gabe, what's it like?'

I look at her, distracted, for a moment unsure what she means.

She tilts her head, smiles.

'The bunker?'

I glance over at Jake. He's stuffing his sleeping bag into his pack.

She squeezes my arm and I feel the anger beginning to subside. I study the faces gathered around me. They stare up, anxious for details of our new home.

'Well it's a little smaller than Mount Weather.' *Way* smaller. 'But there's food, and water.'

I'm not sure what else to say. I find myself repeating the words Mags told me, the night before, in Fearrington's mess.

'I…I think we can make it work.'

*

WHILE THE JUVIES ARE PACKING UP I head back out to the lobby. The kid's sitting under one of the ATMs, smoothing out a candy bar wrapper he's picked up from somewhere. I check no one's within earshot then I squat down next to him, ask how he's feeling. He nods and says fine, but when I reach for his goggles he pulls back.

'You have to let me.'

He looks at me uncertainly.

'It'll be alright, I promise.'

I lift the goggles onto his forehead. He squints a little against the light but keeps his eyes open. I dig in the pocket of my parka for the flashlight and crank the handle. It grinds for a turn, then the bulb starts to glow. When it's as bright as I can get it I hold it close. The beam barely competes with the light filtering through the clouds, but when I shift it back and forth I catch a glimpse of what I knew I'd find there. I was ready for it, but my heart picks up a little all the same.

'You're feeling okay, though? No different?'

He shakes his head.

'Are you going to tell the others?'

I think about that for a moment. There's no prizes for guessing how the Juvies will react if they find out about Mags and the kid; there's a good chance they'll make them leave. I'm not prepared for that, not yet. I shake my head, tell him to put the goggles back on. He pulls them down, settles them in place.

I flick the flashlight off.

'You'd let me know, wouldn't you? I mean if you felt even a little bit strange?'

He nods, then reaches inside his jacket for the dog tags he wears. He holds them up. The thin slivers of pressed steel rotate slowly on the end of their chain. The metal's still smooth, but I hadn't expected it to be otherwise. I examine them, mostly because he seems to want me to, then I tell him to put them away.

The Juvies have no tricks up their sleeve; there's no sudden burst of speed they've been holding back to carry us over the finish line. For once I'm grateful for it. I have some thinking to do before I bring them to our new home.

I settle to their pace, letting my snowshoes follow the trail I left on my way back to the Suntrust Bank. The kid runs on ahead. Every now and then he stops and turns to look at me, like he's wondering what's holding us up. The Target, outside Warren, not long after we set out; that's when he took to wearing them night and day. How many weeks ago now? Four? More? I really should have paid more attention.

He says he feels fine, but I'm not sure how much comfort I can take from that. The voice has an answer. It replays Hicks' words, the same ones I heard last night, in the cell with Mags.

*There'll be no warning. It'll be like a switch has been flipped.*

It shows me the thing that got Ortiz again, in the basement of the hospital in Blacksburg. How fast it had moved; not even Hicks had been quick enough to save him. I imagine what something like that would be like, loose inside the silo. I set the container with the virus down in the snow, pull the mask I wear down, take a breath, then another. I can't let my thoughts get dragged that way; no good will come of it.

I pick up the container and set off again. There has to be a solution; something I can do to fix this. I call up everything I know about the virus, anything Marv ever told me, anything I read in the newspaper clippings I used to collect, anything I might have heard Hicks say. It doesn't take long; there's not that much. I lay it all out in my head anyway, examining each piece of information, like I'm trying to find a place for it in a puzzle. It does no good, other than to remind me how little I understand of any of it. I keep returning to the same conclusion. There's only one person who might be able to help: the person who knows more about the virus than anyone; the person who invented it.

The one who infected Mags in the first place.

That can't be the answer, though, and even if it is, there's no way I'd ever convince Mags to come with me back to The Greenbrier. Not after what happened to her there.

I pull the mask back up and set off after the kid.

There has to be another way.

I just need to figure it out.

It's already late morning by the time we make it to the Mount Gilead Church Road. I lead the Juvies single file across the open fields and in among the trees, picking my way carefully between the withered trunks, until at last I spot the raised security barrier ahead. I wait with the kid while one by one they clamber over. When the last of them has made it in I look down at him. The barrier's too high for him to clear; it's almost as tall as he is. But when I hold out my arms to hoist him up he just shakes his head.

I tell him he can make his own way over then. I throw my leg over and slide down the other side. I send the rest of them off in the direction of the two concrete cubes, then I pick up the container with the virus and bring it behind the guard shack. I set it down in the snow, lay it carefully on its side and scoop armfuls of powder over it until there's no trace of the olive drab plastic. I'll need to come up with a better hiding place, maybe somewhere deep in the woods, where it'd never be found. That's for later, though, once I've got the Juvies inside.

I head back, planning to haul the kid over the barrier if I have to. But when I make my way around front of the guard shack he's standing on top of it, holding his snowshoes. He looks at me for a moment then slides down the other side, steps back into them and starts making his way across the clearing. I stare at the barrier a moment longer, unsure how he did it, then set off after him.

Up ahead the Juvies have gathered by the entrance. I follow the tracks they've left in their wake, a swathe of churned up snow cutting through the smooth, unmarked powder. Sometimes when your mind's focused elsewhere solutions to other problems you didn't even think you were still working on float to the surface. It suddenly occurs to me what's missing from the compound.

Vent shaft covers.

I look around, searching for the telltale bumps in the snow, but there's nothing. Those grilles in the shaft were definitely for ventilation; I could feel the breeze when I placed my hands over them. The pipes must lead to the surface somewhere; if not inside the perimeter then maybe beyond the fence, among the trees. I look at the blackened trunks pressing up against the chain link, wondering whether that's something I should be worrying about too. But the vents were way too small for someone to crawl down. No one's getting into Fearrington the way I snuck back into Eden.

I unsnap my snowshoes and make my way into the narrow opening. The keypad accepts the code and I haul the blast door open. As I step into the airlock I realize I'm holding my breath. I'm hoping for the lights in the passageway beyond to be on, but when the inner door swings back it's to darkness. Mags hasn't got the power back on yet.

*Assuming that's what she's still working on.*

I tell the voice to hush. The kid's still fine. He got the virus way before she did; carried it far longer. It makes no sense she'd turn before he did.

*You're sure about that? He was taking Gilbey's medicine a long time too, remember?*

I close my eyes, pushing that thought from my mind.

'Everything okay, Gabe?'

When I open my eyes Lauren's standing next to me, a concerned look on her face.

I nod quickly.

'Yeah. Absolutely. Just letting my eyes adjust.'

The kid squeezes past, hurries along the corridor. When he gets to the stair he pushes the goggles up onto his forehead and looks over. He stays like that for a moment and then starts down the shaft without so much as a backward glance; by the time I reach the gangway I've already lost him to the turn of the stair. The pitter-patter of footsteps drifts up, echoing off the concrete. He hasn't bothered with his flashlight, but if the darkness impedes him he shows no sign of it.

Lauren leans over the guardrail.

'How does he…?'

She says it softly, under her breath, so I doubt the question's directed at me. Which is just as well, seeing as the answer I have isn't one she'd much care to hear. Behind her the Juvies are already crowding into the corridor. I dig in my pocket for the flashlight and hold it up.

'The power's still out. You'll need these.'

There's the inevitable shuffling while they fumble in pockets or backpacks for the windups they each carry, but finally I hear the whir of the first dynamo being cranked, followed seconds later by others. It rises to a soft drone then one by one the flashlights blink on, casting overlapping shadows that shimmy and bounce along the passageway's concrete walls.

We make our way out onto the stair. The old metal complains at the weight of so many boots, but it holds steady. Behind me flashlights curl up into the darkness, a raggedy helix of fireflies. I lead them down. For a long while there's just the long drop of the concrete shaft, but finally we reach the upper levels and the silo opens out.

Mags must hear us coming, or maybe the kid fetches her, because when we reach the mess she's waiting. She sits on one of the tables, her boots dripping water onto the worn tread plate. Her fingernails are dark with something that might be grease or maybe engine oil. A smudge of it marks her cheek, another her temple. A single flashlight rests on the table next to her, the yellowing bulb casting weary shadows over the scuffed steel. The kid stands to one side, watching our approach.

She looks up as she sees me, but her expression's hard to read. Behind me the Juvies continue to file down out of the darkness. As they see her they come to a shuffling halt and a dozen flashlights swing in her direction. I hurry across the gangway and stand in front of her. I turn to face them, holding a hand up against the beams.

'Hey, point those somewhere else, would you?'

There's a moment's hesitation, then one by one the beams drop. The Juvies hang back, gathered on the gangway or bunched up on the stair; no one seems keen to follow me into the mess. I step to one side, her cue to go on. But for a moment she just stares at me, like she's wondering what the point of all that was.

'Well, there's plenty of diesel.' She pauses, then continues. 'The problem is the generator; the flooding's done more damage than I thought.' Uneasy murmurs greet that news; fuel or not, if we can't get the power on this is going to be a shorter stay than any of us had bargained for. She raises her voice. 'I think I can fix it; it might just take a while.'

'Like when we got to Mount Weather,' I add, like anyone needs reminding of the bright, underground city I traded us for this place. 'It took a few days to get everything working there too, remember?'

I study the faces crowded onto the gangway, assembled on the stair. They've already seen as much as they need to of our new home and I can tell they don't care for it. It's right there in their furrowed brows, the turn of their mouths, expressions even I can read. I can't say as I blame them. I don't care much for it either, and it was me who brought us here.

Mags lifts the flashlight from the table and stands, then makes her way past me to the stair. The kid hurries after her, like he's worried he might get left behind. When she reaches the gangway she stops. It takes a second for Lauren to realize she means to get by and then there's confusion as she tries to get out of the way. Those behind shuffle back, pressing themselves against the guardrail or retreating up the stair. Mags takes a step back, allowing Lauren and a few of the others forward into the mess. When the gangway's clear she squeezes the kid's shoulder and they cross. For long seconds their boots echo up out of the darkness and then it goes quiet again.

'Okay, well, I guess we'd best get settled in. Dorms are three levels down. Everyone gets their own…' - I'm about to say *cell* but catch myself just in time - '…room.' I don't have it in me to sound cheery, and even if I did, I'm not sure it'd do much good.

There's a pause and then those nearest the front turn towards the stair. As they start to make their way down I remember I'm not done; I have one more piece of bad news for them. I'd prefer not to have to deliver it so quick on the heels of their arrival, but there's really no helping it. I take a step forward, hold a hand up.

'But before you go I need you to empty your packs.'

Jake looks at me suspiciously.

'Why?'

'I still need to do a proper count, but I reckon there's food here to last us a few winters, as long as we're careful.' I pause, letting that one piece of good news sink in. 'But it's in cans.'

A groan travels up the stair. After a decade in Eden they know all about C-rations. What comes in the MRE pouches may not be great, but it's way tastier than anything you'll find in a tin, at least one that has *U.S Army* stamped on it.

Lauren looks around, and I get the sense that's she's taking a measure of things, like she did by the lake in Mount Weather, right before we voted to leave.

'Why can't we just finish off what we brought, Gabe? I mean we're here now, right? We've made it. We'll be eating out of cans soon enough.'

I see heads nodding, murmurs of agreement. I close my eyes. Maybe she's right. There can't be much of our travelling rations left, now; does it really matter if we eat the last of them? I have a much more immediate problem to worry about.

It's Jake who answers for me.

'Because at some point we'll be leaving again, Lauren. And when that time comes every ounce of food we can carry will matter. So all of you, just do as he says: hand them over.'

The Juvies shuffle to the tables and start unloading their packs. When the last of them have been emptied there's even less than I had hoped for, just a few pitiful stacks of cartons. Jake looks at each for a few seconds, like he might be counting what's there. He turns to me.

'Just to be clear though, these are for when we leave.'

A few of the Juvies look puzzled, but I have no trouble working out what he means. In Eden MREs were in short supply. Marv and I used to get them from Quartermaster, for when we'd go out scavenging. I also had my own deal going on with Amy and some of the other Juvies who worked the kitchens; they'd get them for me in exchange for stuff I'd fetch from the outside. But for everyone else they were rationed pretty tight; before Mount Weather I doubt Jake or any of the other Juvies who worked the farms had seen one in years.

I shake my head.

'I'll be eating the same food as you while we're here, Jake. We all will. Nobody's getting any special treatment.'

He holds my gaze a while longer, like he's not sure how satisfied he is with that answer, but in the end he just points his flashlight toward the stair and starts making his way down. One by one the others follow, until there's no one left in the mess but me and Lauren. Eventually she swings her pack onto her shoulder and goes to follow them. As she's about to step off the gangway she stops and turns around, offering me an apologetic smile.

'I'm sorry, Gabe. I didn't mean to cause trouble, about the food, I mean. I just thought…'

'It's alright, Lauren.'

She stands there for a second, then she bobs her head, smiles again.

'It'll be okay, you'll see.'

I nod, like of course she's right. She looks at me for a second longer, then turns and sets off down the stair after the others.

*

I WALK OVER to one of the tables, drag out a chair. I slump into it and sit there for a while, just staring at the scuffed steel.

What just happened, with Mags and the flashlights, that was close. Until I've figured out what to do I need to find a way to keep her and the kid apart from the others, as much as possible. The flooding in the plant room, maybe it'll turn out to be a blessing. She'll be working on the generator till she gets it running; after that there'll be other machinery needs fixing too. Who knows how long that might take? The kid, he won't leave her side, and the Juvies won't venture down there; they'll want to stay out of her way, much as they can. I think of them just now, shoving themselves back up the stair to let her pass.

It's hardly a plan, but it'll have to do while I come up with one. I push the chair back, head for the gangway. I make my way down, not really sure where I'm going, just letting my boots find their own way. When I look up again I'm at the stores. I stop. Row after row of metal shelves, each laden with boxes, stretching back into darkness. I had planned to inventory what's there anyway, and counting things has always helped. Maybe it'll be like with the vent shaft covers earlier, outside in the compound. If I can just take my mind off Mags and the kid, even for a little while, perhaps the answer will come to me.

I cross the gangway and step in among the shelves. I tear a strip of card from the lid of the nearest box and make my way along the aisle, a nub of pencil from my pocket in one hand, the flashlight in the other. I shine the beam over the stacked rations, wiping dust from their flanks so I can read what's printed there. Occasionally I drag one down, to confirm the contents match, but mostly I keep counting, not wanting to give my thoughts a chance to catch up. When I reach the end of the first aisle I hurry on to the next without stopping. It doesn't take me long to finish the upper level. As soon as I'm done I move down to the one below.

A half-hour later I come to the end of the last shelf. I look back along the stacks of boxes. It took me the best part of a week to go through everything that was in Mount Weather's stores, and when I was done my lists had filled a notebook. I glance down at the card. My scribbles don't even cover one side of it. Aside from a single ammo can of *Sterno*, a box of candles and a couple of crates of bottled water it's canned food, and more of it. There's only three meals to choose from: *Ham and Eggs*, *Meat Stew with Vegetables* and *Beans with Frankfurter Chunks in Tomato Sauce*. We're going to be mighty sick of those by the time we're done, but as long as I haven't messed up the counting there should be enough to last us a couple of winters, maybe three if we're careful.

I drag a final box off the shelf and set it on the floor. Motes of dust tumble through the flashlight's beam, see-sawing down to settle on the worn tread plate. The flap says meat stew and when I look inside the contents are a match. I lift one of the cans out and hold it up to the flashlight. The metal looks dull, tarnished. Mags said she thought this place was at least as old as Eden, and I've seen nothing that'd make me doubt that view. I reckon Fearrington must have been abandoned long before the Last Day, mothballed, just like Eden had been, before Kane decided he had a use for it after all. It would explain how we found it: nothing on the shelves that might spoil and everything else just so, with no trace of a hurried evacuation. I point the flashlight down the aisle, playing the beam over the stacks. If that's right then what's on these shelves has been sitting here for half a century, maybe even longer.

I hear noise on the stair and when I look up Jake's silhouette's standing on the gangway. One by one the other Juvies appear behind him. From their faces it's pretty clear they haven't found anything in the lower levels to make them feel any better about their new home.

I return the tin to its slot and close the flap, then pick up the box and slide it back into place. Jake looks past me to the shelves.

'So how does it look?'

'Three winters.'

He repeats it, like he's testing what I've just told him, or maybe he's simply contemplating spending that much time in a place like this.

'You're sure?'

I am, but I find myself looking down to the strip of card anyway.

'Long as we're careful.'

'We should start work on some growing benches, then.'

I catch Lauren rolling her eyes at that, but I tell him I think it's a great idea. Setting the farms up again will be a lot of work, and if the Juvies are busy up here there's even less chance they'll go wandering down to the plant room to check on Mags.

I say he can take this level. There's as much space as he'll find anywhere in the silo and the shelves should provide him with the materials he'll need; all we have to do is move what's on them. He looks at me for a moment, then steps past to examine the closest one. He runs his fingers over the steel, testing the bolts that hold the shelves to the uprights, like he's trying to find a problem with what I've offered. I guess he mustn't see one, because he starts organizing the Juvies into groups, then dispatches them into the aisles.

I stand back and watch as they go to work. I have to hand it to him; it's all pretty efficient. The Juvies at the end are already lifting boxes down, passing them along and out to the landing, where others are waiting to stack them by the guardrail.

I glance back at the stair. Forming a line up to the level above would have been better, but I'm not about to suggest it. Now that he's got a project Jake almost looks happy again; he's dragging boxes off the shelves and tossing them along the line like there's little he'd rather be doing. I pick up the closest one and start making my way towards the gangway with it.

Neither of the Guardians got assigned a place on one of Jake's chain gangs and now Tyler steps forward, like he means to help. As he reaches for a box another thought occurs to me. I tell him to hold up.

'Listen, I'm sorry to have to ask, but can you and Eric take the rifles and stand watch outside?'

Eric's face falls. The silo may not have a lot going for it, but being inside where it's passable warm beats being out in the cold.

'I'm sorry; I know we just got here, but the journey took us way longer than I expected. Peck will have reached The Greenbrier not long after we set out; whatever went down between him and Hicks, that'll have played out long ago. One or other of them's probably on the road already. We can't let them surprise us.'

'Alright, Gabe, you got it. C'mon Eric.'

'And when you come back in, leave the rifles up in the airlock, yeah? It's the only way in. Makes no sense having them down here.'

He nods.

'Sure thing.'

I watch as they both set off back up the shaft. It's not long till I've lost them to the turn of the stair and all that's left is the echoing clang of their boots on metal. Soon that too fades.

I hoist the box back onto my shoulder.

What I said about Peck and Hicks is true, and it's reason enough for wanting to post a guard. But there's another part to it, one I scarcely dare admit to myself.

I don't know how long I have before Mags and the kid go the way of Finch's fury. That moment lies an unknowable amount of time ahead, but it's on its way; I'm as certain of that now as I once was that the dog tags and crucifix proved otherwise.

And if that time comes before I've figured out how to stop it I need the two Juvies with the rifles to be as far from her as possible.

*

I SET TO WITH THE BOXES, hauling the rations Jake and the others are clearing from the shelves up to the level above.

It's harder work than I had anticipated. The print on the side says fifty pounds, but it soon starts to feel like a lot more. I learn quick to check bottoms and seams. The damp air's got to the old card, and some of the boxes are no longer up to the task of holding their contents together.

After a few trips Lauren decides her time's better spent helping me than among the shelves, on one of Jake's details. I tell her I'm fine, but she just shakes her head and says Jake has enough helpers already, and I look like I could use the assistance. Problem is two people's not sufficient for a chain. and the stair is too narrow for more than one person. We try it for a while, but each time we meet and I have to squeeze past her it's awkward. I suggest maybe it'd be better if she worked on clearing space from the shelves above instead. For a split second her face rearranges itself into an expression I can't quite read, but then just as quick the smile returns. She says *Sure* then turns and disappears up the steps, the hank of her ponytail swinging after her.

Without Lauren to distract me I settle into a rhythm, of sorts. My thoughts return to Mags and the kid. I run through everything I know about the virus again, but at the end of it the conclusion's no different than it was on our way here: Gilbey's the only one who might be able to help. There's no way I'll get Mags to go back to her, but maybe I don't need to. Gilbey has medicine, medicine that can hold back the virus. Not forever, certainly, but a long time. Hicks must have been taking it since he got infected, back in Atlanta, and that was ten years ago now. The kid almost as long, if Mags is right about the time he spent in that cage. It's a long way from a cure, I know it, but right now I'd take it, in a heartbeat.

I return to the level below, pick another box from the nearest stack, heft it onto my shoulder.

Problem is Gilbey's not just going to give it up, though, not without wanting something in return.

Something big.

I make my way back up the stair. As I'm crossing the gangway Lauren appears from between the shelves. She collects another box from the end of one of the rows, flashes me a smile. I hear Hicks' drawl in my head even before she's disappeared back into the darkness.

*Warm bodies, and lots of them.*

Eden was the prize; that's what he told me, that night in the main cavern, right before Mags burst out of the tunnel. It's the only reason Gilbey had been willing to let her and the kid go: Hicks had promised he'd get her the rest of the Juvies if she did.

I stand there considering it, for perhaps longer than I ought. I can't give up the Juvies for Mags, though.

But maybe I don't have to.

I slide the box I'm carrying off my shoulder and set it on top of a stack next to the guardrail.

How many inmates had I counted at Starkly?

Thirty-seven; half again our number. Would that many warm bodies be enough for Gilbey? Would she trade me as much as I could carry of her medicine for their location?

I start off down the stair again.

She might.

I spend the rest of the afternoon trying to think of anything else I have to offer, anything she might want instead. But there's nothing. Starkly's my best shot.

My only shot.

I tell myself it's not like they were innocent men, any of them. Murderers for the most part. *Ain't nobody ever been sent to Starkly on wino time,* those were Mac's exact words. If Finch were in my shoes he'd do it, in a heartbeat, I have no doubt of that. He'd do it and sleep sound that night, and all those that followed. Only one reason I walked out of that place alive, and that's the same reason I escaped The Greenbrier. Finch knew I was travelling with others; he wanted me to lead him to them so there'd be more for Blatch's cookpot.

I set the box I'm carrying on top of the nearest stack and start making my way back down.

We may not be done with him yet, either. He'll keep sending Goldie and those other men out looking for me, hoping they'll pick up my trail. Looked at that way it'd be no more than self-defense. I'd simply be making sure they were dealt with before they got around to finding us.

Little more than a question of timing, really.

Even as I think it I realize that was exactly how Hicks managed to get himself straight with what Gilbey had done to Mags, and Johnny, and all the other survivors that had found their way to The Greenbrier.

I tell myself this is different. It's only information I'd be offering; just the fact of their existence, a location, nothing more. Given enough time Hicks might even have stumbled on to them by himself. He was out looking for subjects for Gilbey to experiment on when he ran into Mags and me, after all. And Starkly's not that far from The Greenbrier.

Even if I give him the location, it's not like I'd be sealing their fate. That place is as much fortress as prison now; there's no certainty Hicks would even be able to find a way in, let alone overcome those inside. And Finch would be a more than capable adversary. *The most dangerous man ever to set foot through Starkly's gates*, that's what Mac had said.

These and a dozen other excuses run through my head as I heft one box after another up the stair. I try each on for size, hoping to find the one that'll make the decision sit that bit easier. None of them do, no matter how many I come up with; no matter how I dress them up.

I can't even pretend I'd be doing it to fix the world, like Gilbey, or Hicks. It might not even save Mags, while we're at the business of truth-telling. Most likely it'll just postpone the inevitable. I'll do it, all the same; I've known that since the idea first came to me. I'll trade the thirty-seven souls living inside Starkly's walls if it means there's even a chance to save her, maybe the kid too if I'm lucky and can make it back in time. And there's only one reason when it comes right down to it: those other people don't mean anything to me, and she does.

I think of Gilbey; the necklace around her neck, the one that belonged to her daughter, Amanda; the box in the storeroom with her things inside. Hicks told me he'd blown up the scanner just in case it could have been used to cure her, to make sure Gilbey wouldn't lose focus. It occurs to me then that all the terrible things she did, it would have begun just like this: weighing the value of a life, one she cared about more than anything, against others, less important to her. I can't know the exact circumstances of it, but in the end those matter little.

That first step she took would have been no different to mine.

This is how she would have gotten started.

*

I KEEP GOING, hefting one box after another onto my shoulder, planning my return to The Greenbrier as I haul each up the spiral stair.

If I cut cross-country, hike sun-up to sundown, I reckon I can reach Sulphur Springs in six days, maybe five. I don't know how long it'll take Gilbey to prepare all the medicine I'll need, but I'll have to assume a few more. Coming back will take longer. I'll have to return via Starkly, to prove my side of the deal. I could show them on a map, but I can't see Hicks taking me at my word. He'll want to see it for himself. That's when he'll try and double-cross me, like he did in Eden, but this time I'll know it's coming. Assuming I can figure a way to get away from him, it'll take me another couple of days to get back here. All that means I'll be gone two weeks, maybe a shade longer. Mags must have that time. The kid's already had that eyeshine thing the best part of a month and he hasn't turned yet. Hers has just started.

I step off the gangway and look around. Boxes are still stacked four- and five- deep waiting to be taken up, but the shelves behind are mostly bare; Jake's already started dismantling the first of them. Upstairs the last of the empty spots have been filled and now Lauren's placing boxes anywhere she can find space – in the aisles, at the end of the rows, against the railing that circles the shaft. Another day at most and I reckon the stores will be all squared away. It'll take Jake a little longer to get the farms up and running, but I won't hang around for that. I'll leave at first light, whether or not Mags has the power back on. I'll tell the Juvies I'm heading out scavenging; Jake will need things to complete his growing benches, so they'll buy that. I'll leave a note for Mags; something she won't find until after I'm gone. I'll need to warn her to start tethering the kid again, too. I have no way of knowing how long he might have left.

I set the box I'm carrying on top of a nearby stack. I can't say I'm excited about the prospect of returning to The Greenbrier, but I've had long enough to think of an alternative now to realize there isn't one coming.

I hear the sound of boots on metal, echoing through the silo, and I look up. Tyler and Eric, returning from outside. Their footsteps grow steadily louder, until at last a pair of flashlights materialize on the railing above and begin circling their way down through the darkness. Moments later Tyler appears around the curve of the stair, still bundled up in his parka. His eyebrows are white with ice; more of it thickens his lashes. The crystals stand stark against his ebony skin.

'We stayed out as long as we could, Gabe. I can't see anyone coming tonight.'

Behind him Eric nods quickly, like he's worried I might yet send them back to the guard hut. He asks through chattering teeth whether we've eaten yet.

I shake my head.

'You're just in time.'

I reach for a box sitting atop a nearby stack. The writing on the side's faded, obscured by mildew, but enough remains to make out *Beans with Frankfurter Chunks in Tomato Sauce*. That was as close as we got to a favorite in Eden; it'll do for our first meal here. I pick it up, hold it out to him.

'Bring this up to the mess while I fetch something to heat them up.'

He takes the box, cradles it to his chest, sets off up the stair.

Lauren emerges from the shelves, dusting her hands on the front of her pants. She flashes me a smile.

'Somebody mention food?'

I nod.

'Yep. Can you go and tell the others?'

She hesitates, one foot on the gangway. The smile remains, but now it looks hesitant, uncertain. She looks at me, like she's waiting for confirmation. I suddenly remember.

'Just Jake and the others. Mags will be busy with the generator; she won't want to be disturbed. I'll bring her something later myself.'

Her expression relaxes and she disappears off down the stair.

I make my way back in among the shelves. The mess has a couple of large industrial-looking ovens, but like everything else here they're useless without power. I spotted something while I was going through our supplies that should help, though. I return to the aisle where I thought I saw it and there it is, peaking out from between two mildewed cardboard boxes: an ammo can with the word *Sterno* stenciled across the top. I drag the old metal container out, spring the catch and lift the lid, reaching inside for one of the little blue fuel blocks. There were a couple of crates of them in Eden, back when we first arrived; Marv would bring a handful with us each time we'd go scavenging. They were useful to get a fire going, or if we managed to scare up a tin of something on the outside. They smell pretty bad when you light them, but what's here should keep us in warm meals until Mags can get the power back on. I fasten the catch, sling the container over my shoulder and head back to the stair.

Word about dinner spreads fast; the Juvies are already making their way up as I step out from between the shelves. I cross the gangway and join the last of them. When we reach the mess I deposit the *Sterno* on the table next to the box of cans. They gather round, anxious to find out what's on offer now that MREs are off the menu. A few like Jake might have enough reading to be able to make out what's printed there, but for most I suspect the letters stenciled on the mold-spackled cardboard might as well be hieroglyphics.

I pull back the flaps, reach inside and lift out one of the tins, setting it on the table. The Juvies press forward, looking on expectantly. Lauren hands me a can opener. I figure I'll get the first of the tins heating and then bring something down to Mags and the kid while she sees to the rest. I press the opener into the lid, but the cutting wheel's dull with age and for a second the metal resists. I squeeze the handle tighter and finally it gives with a high-pitched squeal, like a whistle being blown. It keeps that up for a couple of seconds then settles to a sharp hiss.

The Juvies lean closer, puzzled looks troubling their faces. I know what's wrong, though; I've heard that sound before. I grab the pierced can. The opener unclamps itself from the rim, clatters to the floor. No time to retrieve it. I toss the can into the box and scoop it off the counter, thinking if I'm quick I might just make it. But the Juvies are all around, blocking the way.

Beside me Amy reaches for the table, and out of the corner of my eye I see Fran, one hand already clapped to her mouth. I held my breath as soon as I heard, but now I catch the first whiff of it too: a vile smell, the rank odor of decay. A hot acid rush hits the back of my throat and my stomach feels like it's about to do something that could well be projectile. I grit my teeth and swallow hard, then shove my way through them.

The Juvies have finally figured out something's wrong. They clear a path for me, but it's too late. Behind me I hear the first of it: the strained sounds of retching, followed seconds later by something wet spattering on metal.

I push my way out onto the gangway and start up the stair. I have no thought other than to get the box as far away from the others as possible, but as I follow the steps up past servers and workstations into the concrete confines of the shaft, a simpler reality displaces that goal. I'm never going to make it all the way on a single lungful of air.

I set the box down, press my face to one of the rusted grilles and breathe deep. When I've had enough I take the pierced can, cover the hole with my thumb and carry on, stopping close to a vent whenever I need to take another breath. When I get to the airlock I spin the wheel, shoulder the outer door open. I've come up without my parka and the blast of icy air bites immediately, finding its way through my thermals with ridiculous ease. I toss the can out and heave the door closed, then set off back down the stair to retrieve the box of unopened cans I left behind.

I'm sweating as I make it back to the airlock for the second time. I drop the box in the corridor outside, open the access panel and yank the handle back, cancelling the override. I drag the box into the chamber, close the inner door behind me and hit the green button to start the cycle. It's only as the ceiling fans stutter to life that I realize I've left the can opener back in the mess. I dig in my pocket for Weasel's blade and unfold it, holding it over the first of the lids. Above me the fans are turning faster; I wait for them to get up to speed and then I start puncturing metal. The tins squeal like pigs as they're stuck, the high-pitched shriek quickly settling to an angry hiss that's mostly drowned out by the thrum of the fans. When they finally shut down I hold my breath and wait for the cycle to finish. As soon as it's done I open the outer door and toss out whatever's bad.

The third time I run the fans they start up as usual but never really get beyond half-speed, and when I cycle the airlock for the fourth time they manage no more than a dozen lazy rotations before grinding to a halt. Whatever juice was left in the batteries, I've had it; I can no longer rely on them to purge the chamber of the stench that escapes from each can I puncture.

I yank the recessed handle to the over-ride position then head back into the airlock and open the outer door. The wind blows snow around the thick steel, sending it dancing into the small chamber in furious flurries. I work quick as I can, but within minutes the fingers that grasp the blade are starting to go numb. I grip the knife in both hands and stab at the lids that remain, puncturing as many as I can while my breath holds, tossing those that hiss or squeal out into the snow before the smell has a chance to linger.

When there are no more tins left in the box I stagger to my feet and pull the outer door closed again. My fingers have already begun to claw and it takes me longer than it should to turn the wheel handle. As soon as it's done I slump to the floor and jam my hands into my armpits. I lean back against the frigid steel and stare at what remains of the cans I hauled up the stairs.

This isn't good.

I'd figured on some spoilage, maybe a few tins in each box where the seal had failed. But nothing like this. There were enough cans in that box to keep us in lunches or dinners for the best part of a week. I count up what's left: barely enough for a single meal.

I glance back towards the inner door. The Juvies are waiting for me to return. If they see how few cans I've been able to save they'll freak.

I take a deep breath, tell myself to calm down. I gather up the cans and begin placing them inside the cardboard. That was just one box; the others won't be like it. They can't be. I reach for a tin, examining the ragged hole Weasel's knife has made in the lid. Problem is there's no way to be sure, not until each one's been opened.

I place the can with the others and look around, as if the answer might somehow be found among the scuffs and dents that scar the airlock's walls. But the old metal is unhelpful; if it has the answer it refuses to reveal it.

My breath starts to come quicker so I screw my eyes shut, try to bring it back under control. It's okay; there's no need to panic yet. I'll bring another box up, try some more cans. As long as those aren't spoiled then there's a good chance this was just a stupid, unlucky box.

I gather up the last of the tins, place them with the others sitting at the bottom of the box. I get to my feet. I feel a little better now that I have a plan, but mostly I just want to run down to the stores and grab another box, right away. That'll have to wait until after the Juvies have gone to bed, however. There's no sense letting them know about this, not yet.

Not until I'm sure.

*

THEY'RE ALL WAITING in the mess when I return. I step off the stairs, clutching the box with the cans I managed to salvage to my chest. I make my way over to the table. The surface has been wiped clean, but the tang of vomit remains. From the looks on some of the faces I'm guessing it was more than just Fran and Amy lost whatever they had last eaten. I set the box down, aware that everyone's staring at me.

'It was just a random can. What are the odds it'd be the first one we opened?'

I say it like it really was the funniest of coincidences. Lauren smiles back, but she might be the only one. I start unloading the punctured tins.

'I've brought down enough for our meal tonight.' I stack the cans neatly to one side, trying to sound casual. 'The rest I've left up in the airlock.'

I figure I'll be safe in that lie. The airlock's all the way at the top of the shaft; the Juvies have no reason to venture anywhere near it, at least not tonight. Lauren picks up the can opener and sets to work on the already punctured lids. I keep talking.

'Yeah, I reckon I'll open them up there and bring down what we need each day. Better safe than sorry, right?'

Another smile. It goes unreturned, just like the last one. Jake gives me a funny look, like he's already suspicious of my story.

Lauren removes the lid from the first of the cans and empties its contents into a metal bowl she picks from a stack on the counter behind her. The beans hold the shape of the can for a while, then slowly start to collapse.

I pop the catch on the ammo can of Sterno and free one of the little blue fuel tabs from its wrapper. I take the tin Lauren just emptied and start punching holes in the side with Weasel's knife, just like Marv showed me. When I figure there's enough to let the air flow through I take one of the tabs and drop it in. I dig in my pocket for a lighter and hold the flame to the fuel until I'm sure it's caught, then I set it on the table and place the bowl on top.

Tyler's been watching and now he gets to work on the cans Lauren's discarded. Before long there's a dozen of the makeshift stoves, each with a tin of congealed franks and beans resting on top. My eyes are watering from the fumes, but the little *Sterno* tabs are doing their job; I can already see the sauce in the first of the bowls starting to bubble. The beans that float in it look a little anemic, and I seem to remember there being more in the way of franks in our rations back in Eden, but at least our first meal here won't be cold.

One by one the Juvies shuffle forward to collect a bowl. They take them off to other tables, away from the still lingering smells of vomit and the stinging odor from the fuel blocks. They eat in silence, their heads bowed. I hear spoons scraping metal before I've handed out the last of them, then the dull screech of chairs being pushed back. Nobody seems inclined to linger.

Good; the sooner they leave the better.

My beans are already cooling, but I force myself to go slow. Cleaning up the mess outside the airlock, that can wait till morning; as long as I'm up there before Tyler and Eric, everything will be fine. The other part of it won't, though. I need to fetch another box of cans up from stores, to convince myself that first one was just a fluke, a random piece of bad luck.

One by one the Juvies finish eating and make for the stair, until soon there's only Lauren, me, Jake, Tyler and Eric left. Across the table Jake gets to his feet. He brings his bowl to the counter, mutters a goodnight and then heads for the gangway. Tyler takes a final mouthful of beans, sets his spoon down, wipes his mouth with the back of his hand.

'Guess I'll be turning in too. See you both tomorrow.'

Eric leaves with him. I watch as the two Guardians make their way toward the stair. For a while the sound of their boots echoes up out of the darkness and then those too fade.

I go back to pushing the last of my frankfurter chunks around with the spoon, pretending to study the greasy patterns they make in the congealing sauce. Lauren's already done with her bowl, but she's showing no sign of getting up. I will her to go downstairs with the others, but she doesn't move.

In the end I drop my spoon into the bowl.

'Well, I reckon I'm done, too.'

But when I glance across the table she's still sitting there, just looking at me.

'It'll be okay, Gabe. Really. Things will seem a lot better after we've had a good night's sleep.'

I nod, like I believe it.

She hesitates for a second and then reaches across the table and places her hand over mine, like Mags did, when it was just the two of us here, last night.

I glance over at the counter, to where the last of the makeshift stoves are burning.

'Mags and Johnny; we forgot to bring something down for them.' I look back at her. 'Hey, would you…'

I was only meaning to ask if she'd mind if I tended to that, but I never get the chance to finish the sentence. She draws her hand back, and for an instant the smile becomes uncertain, like maybe she's worried I was going to ask her to do it for me. She gets to her feet, a little faster than I guess she means to. Her chair teeters like it might fall; she holds a hand out to steady it.

'Well I guess I should let you get to that.'

She makes for the gangway without waiting for my reply.

*

HE SITS ON THE NARROW CATWALK, his elbows resting on the bottom guardrail, his feet swinging into empty space below. The flashlight the girl gave him lies on the grating, next to his goggles. It went out hours ago, but he hasn't bothered to wind it.

Far below he hears her, at work on one of the machines. It's the important one, she says, the one that will make this place run again. He asked her if she could fix it and she said she thought she could. He hopes she can. He's not so sure, though. The girl is smart, he knows that. But not everything can be fixed. And most things down here smell old, broken.

He rests his chin on the metal and stares out at the silo's curving walls. He hasn't been to many other places, at least not that he remembers, so he doesn't have much to compare this place to. There was the place inside the mountain, where the girl and the tall boy brought him first. He had been very sick when they arrived, though, and they had left right after, so his memories of that place are broken, incomplete, like when he first woke up in the cage.

They had gone to the other place next, where the rest of them had been living. It had been much nicer there. Inside a mountain too, just like the first, except it hadn't felt like it. It was *way* bigger, for a start. He liked that. He spent a long time in a box not large enough even for him; he does not care for tight spaces anymore. It wasn't safe there, though, that's what the tall boy had said. The man with the gray eyes and the gun had left, but he would probably be back.

And now they are here. He lifts his head and looks down, past the catwalks that crisscross beneath, all the way to the bottom, to the rusting machines rising from the oily floodwaters. He wrinkles his nose at the smell.

This place isn't so nice.

He returns his gaze to the gangway. His new perch is okay, though. He chose it carefully. It is the highest of the walkways, passing through a space for the most part uncluttered by pipes or cables, yet still far enough beneath the ceiling above that he does not feel it pressing down on him.

The plant room falls quiet and he realizes the girl has stopped whatever she was doing. He wonders if she is finished. It has been a while since he ate and he thinks he might be hungry. He has decided he will finish all of the food in the pouch today, before he opens the candy bar. That will make her happy. He listens, waiting to hear her boots on the stair. But then the tapping resumes as she goes back to work.

He hears another sound and he looks up, following the steps that spiral towards the ceiling. All afternoon he has listened, straining for any sign that one of them might be about to come down. It was difficult at first. The sounds in this place are unreliable; they echo, bouncing off the curving walls, so it is hard to tell their source. But he thinks he is getting the hang of it.

There has been no one, though, not even the tall boy. A little while ago it seemed like they all stopped what they were doing and then there was the hollow clang of boots as they took to the stair. He scrabbled for his goggles, but when he listened closer the sounds were heading up, not down, and he had relaxed again. Soon after there had been a commotion, and just one of them – he thinks maybe the tall boy; he knows his footsteps well – had set off up the steps, only this time he had been running. Soon after there had been a smell; faint at first, but growing steadily stronger. It was horrible; he had to bury his face in his hands to try and block it out.

Things stayed quiet for some time after that. When at last the boy had returned other smells had started to drift down. Those had been all jumbled up, and it had taken him a while to untangle them. There had been smoke, that one had been easy. But not the thick, wet odor of the branches he is used to. This had been different: a sharp, peppery smell that had burned his nostrils and stung his eyes. And underneath the smoke, something cooking. Not like the food they normally eat, though, the kind that comes in the plastic pouches. This was different. Not a bad smell exactly, at least not bad in the way the first one had been. But there had been something about it, something familiar, that at the same time had made him feel uneasy.

The girl must have noticed the smells too, because she had stopped whatever she had been working on, and for a long while the whole silo had gone quiet except for the occasional noise from above, much more subdued now: the thin clink and scrape of cutlery; the dull screech of a chair being drawn back. Then the sound of boots on metal again as the first of them had started to make their way down through the silo. He had reached for his goggles again, but it soon became clear none of them planned to venture beyond the hatch. For a while that had continued until he had been sure the last of them had gone to bed.

Now somebody *is* coming down, however. Their footsteps are awkward, like they're carrying something, but it's the tall boy, he's sure of it. They continue, past where they should have stopped if he were going to bed, like all the others. He looks down, searching the plant room's depths. The girl continues to work on the machine. Maybe she hasn't heard yet.

The footsteps grow closer, stop. There's a long pause and then the hatch creaks open and he sees the wink of a flashlight above. Food smells, stronger now. It is the tall boy, bringing them something to eat. He tilts his head, scenting the air. There's something about the smell that is unsettling, but that doesn't matter. He'll eat the food and then there'll be a candy bar for after, maybe two; the tall boy always gives him his. For a second the thought consumes him. He picks himself up and scurries along the catwalk. It's only when he nears the end that he realizes he's left his goggles behind. He looks up, just as the flashlight appears on the handrail where the ladder drops through the ceiling. A shape appears, but it is nothing more than a shifting of shadows behind the light, a movement in darkness not even his eyes can penetrate. It is definitely the tall boy, though; he is certain of it now. The flashlight starts circling its way down. He glances back towards the goggles. He still has time to fetch them. But then he remembers. He doesn't have to wear the goggles around the tall boy, not anymore.

He already knows.

The footsteps come to a halt just above his perch, on the far side of the column supporting the stair. The boy calls the girl's name. The sound echoes off the walls, but she doesn't answer. For a long moment the boy waits, and then he continues, more slowly now. He takes the last few steps around and then peers over the guardrail, canting his head to one side, as though listening. The boy is right at the end of the gangway, only a handful of yards away, but he hasn't seen him yet. It is too dark for his eyes.

The boy bends down. There's the soft clank of something metal being laid on the grating. He has to shift his grip on the flashlight to set the second bowl down. As he does he loses control of the beam; it darts along the catwalk.

The light is a surprise and for a second all he can think is that he must not look away. Because not looking at the flashlight is a sign, just like not eating your food.

The boy's eyes suddenly grow wide. He drops the bowl, takes a startled step backwards. The bowl clatters to the grating, for a second teeters on the edge like it might go over, then rights itself.

The tall boy bends down, pulls the bowl back.

'Jesus, Johnny. You scared me.'

He tilts his head, testing the air. He knows. He can smell it.

The boy glances over his shoulder, as if reassuring himself that that way is still clear. He reaches in his pocket for a couple of spoons, sets them next to the bowls, then takes another step back.

'Listen, I have to go. Can you make sure Mags gets one of those?'

The boy turns and hurries back up the stairs, not waiting for an answer. Seconds later there's the sound of his boots climbing the ladder and then the creak of the hatch closing behind him.

He picks himself up and crawls along the gangway.

The bowls sit side by side on the metal grating. He bends over the closest one.

His brow furrows as he sees what's there.

*

I MAKE MY WAY slowly down through the narrow shaft, the flashlight sweeping the gray walls. A vent grille appears in the beam, long fingers of rust staining the concrete beneath. I'm not sure how far I've come. For once I'm not counting, simply following the yellowing cone of light as it circles the spiral stair.

This is bad.

*Really* bad.

The first box I picked at random, from nowhere near where I got the franks and beans. I chose ham and eggs. I figured I'd open just what was needed for the Juvies' breakfast. That'd be enough. It's pretty cold up in the airlock, so whatever I tried would keep until morning, and that way there wouldn't be any waste.

The smell from the eggs was even worse than the franks and beans. I tossed the shrieking cans out as quick as I could, but without the fans to clear it the stench was overpowering; the first time I threw up I barely made it out to the snow. After that I dragged the box close to the airlock's outer door, trying to ignore the icy wind that howled around the edge of the thick steel. When I was done I heaved it closed again and counted up what remained. There wasn't enough for a single meal. Not even close. I had to make another two trips to the stores, just to give me the numbers I needed for breakfast.

That's four boxes I've opened now, each worse than the last. Assuming the rest are like that we won't make it through a single winter, let alone two or three. Our food will run out long before the storms break.

The thought makes me want to throw up again. I stop and reach for the handrail. My knees fold underneath me and I slump to the narrow step. I rest my forehead against the cold steel and wait for it to come. But there's nothing left. After a while I get to my feet again and continue on, letting my boots find their own way down the spiraling stair. The voice starts to whisper. It reminds me of what Mac said, about how things got in Starkly when the food ran out.

It won't get to that. I'll figure something out.

I keep going, following the flashlight around, fighting to stop the panic from rising.

One problem at a time. There's enough cans in the airlock for the morning. It's too cold outside to clear the ones I had to discard from in front of the blast door, but I'll head back up first thing and deal with those. All I need to do now is bring another box of franks and beans up to the airlock, to replace the one I opened first.

The concrete ends and the silo opens out to silent rows of

workstations. When I drop to the level beneath I stop among the dusty server stacks and listen. But the mess is dark, quiet. I continue on, treading as lightly as I can. At the stores I step onto the gangway. The old metal groans under my boots as I cross, but I learned in Eden how to tread lightly; the sound won't carry to the dorms.

On the other side boxes circle the central shaft, piled high against the guardrail. The shelves start beyond, stretching back into darkness. They're crammed tight, the empty spots from earlier now filled; Lauren's already started stacking boxes against the walls at the end of each row. And this isn't all of it; there's more yet to come up.

I stop in the middle of the gangway, then reach for the strip of card in my pocket, the one with the inventory of our supplies. Back in Eden it was Quartermaster's responsibility to keep track of our provisions, and because I'd worked with him all those years, in Mount Weather it became mine. It'll be no different here. Most of the Juvies don't have enough reading to know what's printed on the side of the boxes.

I stare at the stacks, my mind already starting to sketch out the bones of the deception. Boxes waiting to be opened can go in the decontamination area next to the airlock, and in the passageway beyond. I can stash them in other places too: under the workstations and between the banks of servers on the levels above. The airlock's where I'll keep the cans I've already checked. It's hardly convenient, having them all the way up there, but after what happened in the mess earlier, when I opened that first tin, there won't be any objections.

I feel a glimmer of insane hope.

As long as I make sure the Juvies have sufficient food for the time I'll be gone nobody needs to know. Not yet. Not till I get back from The Greenbrier.

I return the strip of card to my pocket.

I'll make a start tonight.

The flashlight's about to die so I wind the stubby handle. It clicks and grinds but after a few turns the bulb brightens, then takes to flickering. I give it a shake, as though that might solve the problem, then I step in among the shelves and start probing the dusty boxes with the faltering beam.

It doesn't take me long to find the one I'm looking for. I drag it down, crouching over it to check the contents are match. But as I lift the flap I suddenly realize I'm not alone. I stagger to my feet, startled, take a quick half-step backwards. I hadn't heard anyone on the stair. I point the flashlight along the narrow aisle. There are two figures standing between the shelves.

Mags raises a hand to ward off the beam. The kid peeks out from behind her. He's put his goggles back on.

The flashlight continues to flicker. Mags waits until I've pointed it down, then she takes a step closer.

'What're you doing, Gabe?'

I can't help an incriminating glance at the box at my feet.

'I...I was just bringing some cans up to the airlock. For tomorrow's breakfast.'

Her eyes drop to the lid. The cardboard's mildewed but the print's legible through it: *Beans with Frankfurter Chunks in Tomato Sauce*.

She looks at me, waiting for the rest of it.

'...and dinner. Thought I'd get a head start on tomorrow.'

So far I'm still within spitting distance of the truth; now would be a good time to let her know about our supplies. I can almost feel the relief that would come with it. But if I tell her about the cans she'll insist on getting the others involved, and who knows what will come of that? I certainly can't wait around to find out; I need to set out for The Greenbrier as soon as possible. Before I'm aware I've even made a decision I hear myself repeating the same thing I told the Juvies earlier.

'Yeah, one of the cans in the first box we opened had gone off. So I'm going to open all of them up there. Just to be safe.'

This time I notice the lie slips out a little easier than before. But then I guess lying's no different to most things: to get good at it just takes practice. I think I even manage a smile.

The flashlight falters, like it might die, then steadies, goes back to flickering. She looks at me like she's trying to work out what it is I'm not telling her. I don't want her dwelling on that too long, so instead I ask what her *she's* doing in the stores. I hadn't practiced that one, however, and it comes out weird, like I'm accusing her of something.

'I came up to get something for Johnny.'

I glance down to the kid, then back to her.

'I brought food down, for both of you.'

She cants her head to one side and looks at me, like that's something else she wouldn't mind an explanation for, as long as we're on the subject. When I don't say anything she continues.

'Yeah, I saw.'

She doesn't raise her voice but there's an edge to the way she says it, like there's a whole litany of things wrong with what I've done. She stares at me for a long moment, like she's waiting for my thoughts on the subject. When it's clear I don't have any she continues.

'You didn't stop to think what it was you were giving him?'

The kid looks up at her, mumbles something about it being okay, he's really not that hungry. Mags pays him no mind.

'Cold beans, Gabe?'

The kid says the beans weren't actually cold, not really, but she ignores that too. I guess I'm a little distracted, or maybe I'm having a slow day, because I'm still not sure what she means.

'That's what Truck was feeding him, in the cage. You couldn't have found something else?'

I'm not sure what to say to that. I open my mouth to explain, but then realize I've got nothing, so I close it again.

'Well I guess it just didn't occur to you.' She glances at the shelf. There's a box that has *Meat Stew* stamped on the side right by her head. 'It's okay. One of those will do.'

She reaches for it and now I feel a spike of fear. I've no reason to believe the contents of that box will be any different to the four I've already opened tonight. I step forward, placing a hand across the box's flank. It happens to be the one holding the flashlight.

Her eyes narrow at the beam, like it troubles her, but not enough to make her step away. And for long seconds I just stand there, transfixed. Her pupils are wide, and what's behind them glows, incandescent. This close it's not silver, though, but palest gold.

I stammer out something about there not being enough. Her eyes flick to the boxes stacked all around us, then return to me.

'Then I'll trade him what I'm having for breakfast, Gabriel.' She says it slow, like she's trying to figure out how deep this new streak of asshole goes.

She stares back at me. I want to look away, but I can't. I shake my head.

'I already told the others: no one's getting special treatment. That goes for you and the kid too. I'm sorry. Franks and beans is what we have. He'll just need to get used to it.'

She takes a step closer, and for a second I think she might just take the box anyway.

*And you might not be able to stop her.*

The kid grabs hold of her arm and says it's okay, he's not hungry.

She keeps looking at me, her eyes shimmering with something that might now be rage. The kid says it's okay again, louder this time. She holds my gaze for a second longer then lets her hand fall from the box.

'C'mon Johnny, let's go.'

*

HE HURRIES AFTER THE GIRL, out of the shelves, past the stacks of old, tattered boxes that push up against the guardrail. As they cross the gangway he remembers his flashlight. The girl said they should use them whenever the others are around, but hers hangs forgotten from her wrist, bouncing on its tether as she takes to the stair. It died on the way up from the plant room, but she hasn't bothered to wind it.

He follows her as she makes her way around, quickly dropping through the level below. Boxes line the guardrail here too, just like above. Beyond, more shelves, stretching back into grainy shadow. Most are empty now, the closest ones already in various states of disassembly. The girl said they were going to grow things here. Food. He's not really sure what that means. The only food he's ever known comes in cans, packets, wrappers.

She keeps going down, passing silently through the floors where the rest of them are sleeping. Most of the doors are shut, but here and there one has been left ajar. The soft night sounds they make drift out from behind.

He feels bad. He should have just eaten what was in the bowl. Not eating your food is a sign; he knows that, better than anyone. How could he have forgotten? Does the tall boy think he's getting sick again? Is that why he was scared, just now?

But that doesn't make sense. The tall boy checked his dog tags; they prove it. And he had been frightened earlier, too, when he first brought the food down, before he could have known he wasn't going to eat it. He hadn't been wearing his goggles then, of course. But he didn't think he had to, not in front of the tall boy. He already knew.

They leave the dorms behind. He doesn't know what to make of any of it, and something behind his eyes feels scratchy, now. He raises one hand to his goggles, then stops. He knows what that feeling means, and rubbing them won't help. He just needs to rest. Only one more floor and the hatch and then he will be back on his perch, high above the machines, and he can sleep, just like they do.

But when the girl reaches the next gangway she suddenly stops. She stands on the stair for a moment, listening, and then she crosses, quickly disappearing among the narrow stalls. He hesitates, unsure what to do, then he follows, making his way between the dark cubicles. He finds her standing in front of the row of washbasins.

She steps up to the nearest one and places her flashlight on the lip of the shallow basin. She leans forward, examining her reflection in the square of steel above. Her fingers probe the skin under her eyes. He wonders what she's looking for. It may still be a shade darker there, but it's hard to tell now. Those shadows have all but disappeared.

When she's done examining her eyes she turns her attention to the rest of her face. A smudge of grease marks one cheek; another follows the line of her jaw. She reaches for the faucet. It sticks for a moment, but then turns with a dull groan. There's the sound of pipes clunking and then water spits from the tap, quickly steadying to a stream. She cups her hands under it, then brings them to her face and starts scrubbing at the marks there with the cuff of her overalls.

When she's finished she shuts off the faucet and checks her reflection again. She hesitates for a moment then pulls off the cap she wears and sets it on the washbasin next to the flashlight. She leans closer to the mirror. Her hair is growing back faster than his, but after all these weeks it's still little more than stubble. A wide swathe of it darkens the top of her head, continuing all the way back to the nape of her neck. She lifts one hand, runs her fingers over it. She tilts her head first this way, then that, examining the sides. He follows her gaze, trying to work out what she's doing. At first he thinks it hasn't grown back as quickly there. But then he sees it's not that; it's just that what's there is flecked with white.

And then at last he thinks he understands. He hesitates a moment then lifts the goggles from his face, settles them around his neck. He reaches for the flashlight and starts to wind the handle. The dynamo whirs and after a few seconds the bulb begins to glow. The tangle of rubber-jointed pipes throw complicated shadows against the wall behind.

The girl looks down to see what he's doing. He holds the flashlight up, pointing it back towards himself. The beam isn't that bright, but his eyes have grown accustomed to the darkness and he has to force himself not to squint. When he thinks he has the flashlight in the right place he looks up so she can see.

The girl's eyes widen; she starts to take a step backwards. He quickly reaches for the tags he wears and holds them up. The slivers of pressed metal hang in the beam, slowly twisting at the end of the beaded chain.

Her gaze flicks from his eyes to the tags, then back again.

When he thinks she's seen enough he holds the flashlight out to her. She stares at it for a long moment. At first he's not sure she understands, or maybe she doesn't care to. Then she takes it from him.

She turns back to the mirror and holds it up, searching for the right angle, just as he did. When she finds it she stops, and for a long time she stays like that. Then she closes her eyes. She leans forward, her hands grasping the side of the shallow washbasin.

He tells her it's okay. They're not sick. The tags, the cross she wears; they prove it. He starts to tell her what she told him, back when they first set out. The others, they'll get used to it.

But then he stops. He's not sure that last bit's really true. It's been a long time since they left the mountain place. And now the tall boy is frightened of them, too.

Perhaps it’s like the girl with the pink hair said, in the shopping mall.

Their kind, maybe they’re just too different after all.

*

WHEN I RETURN TO THE DORMS they're dark, quiet. I push back the door to the cell, half expecting to find Mags in there, waiting for me. But it's empty. Tell the truth I'm a little relieved. I don't think I've ever seen her as mad at me as she was earlier, down in the stores, and I haven't got the words to make it better. I step inside, wind the flashlight and set it on the ground, then lower myself onto the thin mattress next to it.

My legs ache, my shoulders are numb from hefting boxes and I've lost track of the times I've been up and down the stair. But the first part of it's mostly done. Enough of the rations are now distributed between the upper floors of the silo and the corridor by the airlock that it'll be impossible for anyone to keep track of what we have, even if they wanted to.

I lean back against the cold steel. All I want to do is climb into the sleeping bag, curl up into a ball and pretend none of this is happening. But I can't. Up on the surface dawn can't be more than an hour away. I can't let Tyler or Eric find all the cans I've had to toss out of the blast door.

I'll go back up there soon, bring the Juvies down their breakfast, let the Guardians know I'll take their shift. They can stay in the silo, help Lauren with whatever of the boxes still need moving. I can't see either of them objecting to that. Soon as I've dealt with the discarded tins I'll set to work opening more. When I've got enough to last through the time I mean to be away I'll leave. It shouldn't set me back more than a few hours.

I'll just take a little rest first. I feel my eyes start to close so I sit up straight, blink them open. I can't afford to drift off. My backpack leans against the wall by the door; the cell's small enough that I can reach it just by leaning forward. The snaps are already undone and I reach inside. Hick's pistol sits on top, wrapped in the gun belt. I lift it out, set it down beside me. Cartridges nestle in their loops, the stamped brass ends glowing dully in the flashlight's waning beam.

I return to the backpack. In a Ziploc bag buried near the bottom there's the container of gun oil I took from Hicks' pack before we left Eden, the worn nub of a toothbrush and a half dozen cotton swabs. I part the seal, shake the contents onto the floor next to the gun belt. The smell of the oil wafts out. I reach down for the pistol, draw it from its holster. The carrion bird etched into the grip feels rough against my palm. I turn the pistol over in my hands, pointing the muzzle up so I can get to the base pin.

I still need to work out what to do with the Juvies, when I get back. I look over at the pack. The map Marv gave me is in the side pocket, but I don't need to take it out to know what it'll tell me. There are only two locations on the map I haven't yet been.

The first is a facility called The Notch, at a place called Bare

Mountain. It's the one Jake tried to test me on, when we were deciding what to do about Peck.

*Would they have voted to leave if you hadn't risen to the bait?*

I push that thought from my mind. What's done is done; wishing things were different won't make it so, no matter how much I'd like it to. I just need to figure out a way to make it right.

I turn my thoughts back to the map. Bare Mountain's no good. It's all the way up in Massachusetts, even farther north from Mount Weather than we are south. The second facility is a place called North Bay, on the shores of a small body of water called Lake Nipissing, about a third of the way up Ontario's eastern border. It might as well be the far side of the moon; whatever chance we have of reaching Massachusetts, there's no prospect of us making it to Canada.

I jiggle the base pin free, set it aside and slide out the cylinder.

In the bottom corner of the map, in Marv's careful hand, there's a list of codes for other places. *Crown*, *Cartwheel*, *Corkscrew*, *Cannonball*, *Cowpuncher*; each name less likely than the one before. A few have lines drawn through them. Marv didn't get round to explaining why he'd done that, but I reckon those were places that got hit in the strikes. Whether I'm wrong or right on that score makes little difference. There's no corresponding mark on the map for any of them, which suggests either Marv didn't know where they were, or they weren't on it. Either way, I have no hope of finding them.

I pick up the container of gun oil and one of the cotton swabs and set to work on the back of the cylinder, where the ratchet touches the frame.

The last code given is for a facility called Cheyenne Mountain. It's not marked on the map either, but at least for Cheyenne I understand why: Marv's written *Colorado* after it. I'd need to find an atlas to check, but I think that's way out west somewhere.

The Juvies don't have it in them to make any of those places, even if we had the supplies for it. And why would they trust me to embark on such a journey, anyway? I know even less about those places than I thought I knew about here. There's every chance each one is just the same: ancient, mothballed, long-abandoned relics; their machines all broken, whatever supplies might still be there long since spoiled. Mount Weather might be the only place left where we ever stood any chance of surviving, and I led us away from it.

I need to get them back there.

It's less of a decision, more a lack of other options. A measure of relief comes with having arrived at it, all the same.

I set the swab down, reach for the toothbrush. I turn the cylinder over and start on the chambers, working the bristles up into each. The smell of the oil fills the tiny cell. I think of the wooden stool I found behind the door, in Eden's armory, the seat shiny from years of use, testament to the hours Peck must have sat down there by himself, tending to each weapon. I think I understand now. The ritual is somehow calming. I hold my hand to my mouth, stifling a yawn.

There's not much time. Winter's still a couple of months off, but I can't risk them getting caught out in it; I need them back inside before the first of the storms arrive. The journey down took over a month, which means I have four weeks, no more; by then they need to be back on the road. The good news is they should be able to follow the route we took coming down, for the most part. I can't risk sending them back through Durham, of course, not with Finch's men out looking for us, but finding another way around won't be difficult, and it shouldn't add much to the journey; once they're clear of the city they can rejoin the interstate and from there it'll be easy. They've hiked that road already; they know where the shelter is to be found. The interstate has another advantage, too, one I hadn't appreciated before Starkly. Whatever might be starting to wake up out there, the danger will be in the towns, not out in open country.

I finish with the cylinder, wipe it down, set it to one side.

Supplies will be a problem. There's precious few of the MREs we set out with left, maybe enough for the first couple of days, but not much more than that. I can't rely on there being anything worth scavenging along the way, either, even if they knew how to find it. Which means they'll have to survive on whatever they can take from here.

Pounding the snow's hard work; I figure even on short rations each of them will need three cans a day, which means a hundred apiece for the trip. Plus basics: canteen, sleeping bag, fixings for a fire. A heavy load; more than they set out from Mount Weather with.

*You think they'll manage?*

They'll have to.

I'll need to do something about the cans, to make sure they last, even with the lids punctured. I can't risk them eating food that'd make them sick; there's no place for that on the road. The holes I can reseal, like I used to do with the containers with Kane's medicine, when I was smuggling them back into Eden. Wax should do the trick; there's a box of candles in the stores. The cold will help. At night they can leave their packs outside. Maybe I can rig something up for during the day; line the insides with garbage sacks, pack it with snow.

*How do you think they'll take the news that they're leaving again?*

I pick up the pistol and set to work on the barrel.

I'm not going to tell them, not until I get back from The Greenbrier.

*And you're certain, about the other thing? About not going with them?*

I lean back against the steel, close my eyes.

I am.

*

I WAKE TO DARKNESS. At first I think it's still the middle of the night and all I want to do is drift back down to sleep. But then through the metal walls I hear the muted sounds of others stirring.

I lift my chin from my chest, wincing as an unexpected jolt of pain shoots down my neck. I reach up with one hand to rub it. Something I didn't realize was there slips from my fingers. It lands in my lap, the weight of it startling. I open my eyes to try and make sense of it, but the blackness is complete. I struggle with simple concepts like up and down for longer than a right-minded person has any business doing, but eventually I work out I'm sitting upright. I rub my eyes, trying to clear the sleep from them. The smell of gun oil is heavy on my fingers. Hicks' pistol. I must have fallen asleep cleaning it.

I reach out with one hand, find the flashlight, wind it slowly. The mechanism grinds out its now-familiar complaint but eventually the bulb glows, spreading its light slowly over the steel.

The pistol's reassembled and loaded; there's brass in each of the chambers bar the one under the hammer, just like Hicks showed me. The box of ammunition I stole from him sits nearby, but the mattress it was resting on last night is gone. I glance up at the door. I closed it behind me when I came in, but now it's ajar.

Mags.

She must have been here at some point while I slept. I think of her, staring down at me in the darkness. I wonder what it means that she took the mattress. It can't be good, but the sounds from the adjacent cells are growing louder, reminding me I have things to attend to. I'll worry about that later. First I need to find Tyler and Eric, let them know I'll be standing guard this morning.

I slip the pistol into its holster, loop the gun belt around my waist, tighten the buckle and make for the stair.

I hurry up to the airlock, load one of the boxes with enough of the ham and eggs for the Juvies' breakfast and return to the mess. I get the Sterno stoves lighting and start transferring the yellow mulch the Army reckoned would stand for ham and eggs to the tin bowls. The first of the bowls is already starting to bubble by the time I see the Juvies' flashlights circling the stair. One by one they shuffle out of the darkness, take a bowl and make their way over to the tables.

Lauren comes over to stand next to me, an expression of concern troubling her features. She rests a hand on my arm.

'Gabe, you look exhausted.'

'Yeah, couldn't sleep.'

'I noticed the stores as I came up. Seems like you were busy last night.'

I shrug, hoping to get her off the topic.

'Figured I might as well be useful.' I notice the two Guardians on the gangway. 'Hey, Tyler, Eric, can you guys help Lauren with the boxes this morning? I'll keep watch outside.'

Lauren's face rearranges itself into a frown, but Eric seems relieved. Tyler asks if I'm sure.

'It's only fair. You guys were out yesterday.'

Jake takes one of the bowls off its stove.

'What about Mags? Is she coming up?'

A few of the Juvies raise their eyes from their bowls, like they're waiting for my answer. I shake my head.

'No, I…she said she was in the middle of something with the generator. I'll bring her and the kid their breakfast before I head outside.'

Jake looks at me for a moment like he's not sure what to make of this, but then he collects a spoon and heads over to one of the tables. Lauren lifts a bowl from its makeshift burner.

'Don't you want to eat first?'

I look down at the yellow mulch she's offering. Truth is I've never cared much for eggs. The powdered substitute we had in Eden bore more than a passing resemblance to the paste Miss Kimble used to give us when we were doing art, and what's in these cans looks like it's from no better stock.

I shake my head.

With what I have planned for the day I doubt I'd be able to keep it down anyway.

I bring a couple of bowls down to the plant room. The kid's sitting on the same catwalk where he'd startled me the night before. He looks up as I make my way around the stair. After what happened in the stores I'm not sure what to say to him so I just leave the bowls on the grating nearby and ask him to bring one down to Mags.

A few minutes later I'm back in the airlock. The wind's picked up overnight. I can feel it, pushing against the blast door as I heave it open. Gray flakes swirl around the edges and dance into the narrow chamber.

I smear UV block across my cheeks and then pull up my hood. Outside the snow is littered with the cans I tossed out of the airlock. I pick up one of the cardboard boxes and start gathering them into it. The contents have frozen overnight so there's hardly any smell, and what little remains the wind carries away, but I pull the cotton mask I wear up over my nose anyway. When the box is full I snap on my snowshoes and set off through the compound, cradling it to my chest. The tattered windsock snaps angrily on its tether as I pass.

At the guard shack I rest the box on the raised security barrier while I clamber over, then pick it up and carry on. I follow the trail for a while, until the gnarled, blackened trunks grow thick around me. I glance back over my shoulder to make sure no one's watching, then I turn off the track and start making my way deeper into the wood. Dead branches whip and claw at my parka as I squeeze myself between them. After a few minutes I arrive at a small gap in the trees, hardly big enough to count as a clearing. I glance back over my shoulder. Somewhere a little further from the trail would be better but I'm in a hurry now, so I upend the box and dump the cans into the snow.

A couple more trips and all the tins I threw out of the airlock have been relocated to the place I've found for them in the woods. When I've disposed of the last of them I collect the container with the virus from behind the guard shack and carry it out there too. I bury it in a drift a little way off to one side then I go back to the airlock and start over, opening cans from the boxes I brought up last night. I come up with a system: I puncture each tin on the bottom, in the crevice between rim and base, where it's harder to spot. For those handful of cans in each box that haven't spoiled a drop of candlewax seals the hole. I get pretty good at it. By the time I've done a dozen of them I doubt anyone would notice, unless they were told where to look.

When I get to the bottom of the first box I go outside, collect the spoiled cans from in front of the airlock and ferry them off into the woods. I'm about to turn around and head back but then I stop, pick one of the cans from the pile and set it in the crook of a tree. The clearing's mostly sheltered from the wind, so I don't need to spend much time digging it in. I turn around and measure out ten paces. That's not very far in snowshoes, but I reckon it makes sense to start with a realistic goal.

I slip off my mittens and unzip my parka. The gun belt sits low across my hips, the old pistol snug in its holster. I take a deep breath, let it out slow, watching it turn white before it's carried away. I picture how Hicks was, in the hospital in Blacksburg, when the fury attacked Ortiz. I was looking right at him, but it happened so fast all I have now are a series of disconnected images. One second his hand had been empty, the next there'd been a pistol there. A burst of shots in rapid succession, his off hand little more than a blur as it worked the hammer, his other pumping the trigger, just like one of those gunslingers from the movies.

I flex my fingers against the cold, then reach down and practice sliding it out. The pistol feels heavy, awkward in my hand. I bring it up slow, keeping the hammer down and my finger away from the trigger until I've got the barrel pointed roughly where I think I need it to be. I doubt I'll get the drop on anybody that way, but at least I'll stand a chance of walking away with all my toes accounted for afterwards.

I reach for the hammer with my thumb. The mechanism's stiff and it takes some effort to cock it. I settle the sight back on the can and squint down the barrel, lining the blade at the end with the groove at the back so that both rest on the target. A random gust of wind picks up the snow, swirling the flakes in little eddies around the tree, but I have no thoughts of correcting for it. I just hold the grip steady as I can and slowly squeeze the trigger. The hammer snaps forward before I'm ready for it. There's a loud bang and the pistol bucks, jumping skyward with the recoil.

When the smoke clears the can's where it was, undisturbed, just like the tree it was resting in, and as far as I can tell, all the others that surround it. I have no idea where the bullet went.

I return the pistol to its holster. I tell myself it'll be alright; I'll have more time to practice with it on the road.

Besides, my plan doesn't depend on me being a sharpshooter.

The stack of cans inside the airlock grows steadily. By mid-morning the passageway that leads to the shaft is once again clear of boxes, but I reckon I'm done. There's enough rations there now to last the Juvies while I'll be gone.

I gather up the last of the spoiled cans and set off across the compound. If there was any doubt before, there can be none now; most boxes had no more than a handful of cans that could be saved. I have no reason to think what's down in the stores will be any different. I don't need to check the card in my pocket to know that's nowhere near enough to see the twenty-four of us through the winter.

A gust of wind picks the windsock up, sets it clanking against its pole as I pass.

What's there should stretch for three, though.

When I return from The Greenbrier I'll send the Juvies back to Mount Weather. Mags, the kid and me will stay here for the winter. I doubt there'll be too many objections to that, not after they find out where I've been, and why I went there.

I reach the security barrier, rest the box on top of it.

When the storms clear I'll find Mags, the kid and me somewhere else to go.

*That's months from now. You're certain Gilbey's medicine will see them through till then*?

I have no answer for that, so instead I clamber over and set off into the woods on the other side.

*

I'M HALFWAY DOWN THE SHAFT from the airlock when I hear something like a cough from way down deep in the silo. I stop to listen. For a long moment there's silence and then I hear it again. On the third go it catches, sputters, almost dies, and then settles into a lumpy rattle. A few seconds later the bulkhead lamp closest to me flickers to life. I look over the railing, just in time to see others coming on beneath me.

I hurry down, taking the steps as quickly as I can. The noise grows louder as I drop out of the shaft into the silo's upper levels. I continue round the spiral stair. All around me bulkhead lamps are lit. Here and there a bulb has blown, and more than a few falter like they're on the verge of it. But enough are burning to bathe the ancient workstations, the dusty server stacks, in their soft yellow glow.

When I reach the farms the Juvies are gathered around the guardrail. They lean over, eyes fixed on the source of the sound, but none seem keen to investigate. I continue past them, round and round the spiral stair. Jake's waiting for me at the bottom. He stands by the open hatch, like he wants to go down, but something's giving him pause. I peer into the plant room's depths and now I see what's troubling him. Above me the silo's lit up like Christmas, but below there's only inky blackness.

'Why would the lights not be on down there?'

He says it without looking up, like maybe the question's not meant for me. Whether it is or not there's a voice inside my head that's ready with an answer.

I don't wait to hear it. I unzip my parka and lower myself through the hatch, searching for the rung of the ladder with the toe of my boot. When my feet touch the grating I step off and reach into my pocket for the flashlight. I hesitate. Now that I'm down here Jake's question's got me thinking too. Mags might not need the lights, but that's no reason to turn them off.

*Unless they bother her.*

I look up through the hatch, but Jake shows no sign of following me, so I rejoin the stair and start making my way down. I go more slowly now, probing the gangways I pass with the beam. I find the kid in his usual spot, sitting by the guardrail, his legs dangling over the edge. He looks up as the flashlight finds him, then goes back to staring down into the darkness.

I continue on, calling out to her as I go. The harsh clatter from the generator grows louder; soon I have to raise my voice above it. I can feel the reverberations in the handrail now, too. I keep sweeping the darkness with the flashlight until finally I spot her, halfway out along one of the gangways, right on the edge of the beam. The top of her overalls are tied around her waist and she's working a pipe wrench almost as long as her arm, tightening the mounting bolts at the base of one of the ancient machines. The muscles across her narrow shoulders cord with the effort as she leans into it.

I call her name one more time and she stops what she's doing, hoists the wrench onto one shoulder. The air is thick now, humid. Her skin gleams with sweat; the thin cotton of the vest she's wearing clings to it.

She waits till I've lowered the flashlight, then turns to look at me. The beanie she's been wearing ever since we quit Mount Weather is gone, but the mohawk's back. It looks like it's been done recently, too; there's a nick just above her ear where she's pressed too hard with the razor.

*I wonder what that means.*

'What do you want, Gabriel?'

The long form of my name again, but there's no trace of the anger I heard in her voice last night. Mostly she just sounds weary, like she might not care any more. I can't decide if that's worse.

'I dunno, I…' I glance around, searching for something to say. 'Why is it dark down here? The lights are on in the rest of the silo.'

It's her turn to look away.

'I stripped the bulbs from the bulkhead lamps. Jake'll need them for his growing benches.'

I want to tell her that no, he won't. The Juvies won't be here to see a single crop from the farms; they'll be gone long before he has a chance to plant the first chits. But she can't know those things, not yet, so instead I just shrug.

'Well, you did it.'

She inclines her head. Maybe.

'What's wrong?'

She hesitates a moment then sets the wrench down and walks toward me. I back up to let her by and then she sets off down the stair without saying another word. I assume she has something she wants to show me, so I follow her. When she reaches the bottom she makes her way out onto the last gangway. This close to the generator the racket is deafening, but I can just make out another sound, underneath it. I point the flashlight over the railing. Beneath me the steps disappear into water. Where it was still before the oily surface is agitated now, countless ripples splashing and lapping off the metal below.

Mags is waiting for me by the clattering machine, so I follow her out onto the catwalk. The thin mattress she took from our cell lies spread out on the grating. I have to step over it to join her.

This close to the machine it's hot. I unzip my parka. Her eyes drop to the pistol at my waist. They linger there for a second then she looks up at me again. She says something, but it's just moving lips. I bend down to hear what she's saying. She hesitates a moment and then leans in. This close to the machine she has to shout to make herself heard.

'This is the one I got working. The other's beyond fixing.'

I feel her breath on my neck. I have to force myself to concentrate. My eyes just want to follow the chain from the crucifix as it disappears inside the neck of her vest.

'Okay, but we can manage with just one generator, though, right? I mean without all that equipment up there to run?'

She nods.

'Yeah, but that's not the problem.'

She looks at me like I should understand, but I don't. She hesitates again, then takes my arm by the cuff of my parka and directs my hand to the casing. I can feel the heat, now, radiating from the metal. And something else: a thrumming, heavy in my fingertips. When I lay my hand flat it travels up through my palm until my whole arm is vibrating.

'Something in there's not right.'

'Can you fix it?'

She looks doubtfully at the shuddering machine.

'I might be able to, if I took it to pieces. I've watched Scudder break down all sorts of things. But there's no guarantee I could put it back together again, after. We'd need fresh seals, gaskets, lubricant. Is there anything like that in the stores?'

I shake my head, no. I'm not even sure where I'd start looking for some of that stuff on the outside.

'So how long will it last?'

She returns her gaze to the generator.

'I don't know. As long as it doesn't get any worse it might hold out for years. It could give up on us later today.'

I close my eyes while I digest this latest piece of bad news. It may not matter for the Juvies; in a couple of weeks they'll be on their way back to Mount Weather. Mags, the kid and me, we won't be making that journey with them, however; this will be our home for the winter. I hadn't figured on spending those long months without heat, or light. I don't care much to think about what that would be like.

She steps away from the machine, back into the shadows. When she returns she's carrying a cardboard box.

'I'll need to run the generator for a while to clear the flooding. Those vibrations will work things loose pretty fast, so I'll be staying down here to keep an eye on it. Okay?'

I nod, still a little distracted by what she's just told me.

'Good.' She hands me the box. Inside are the bulbs she's removed from the bulkhead lamps. 'And Gabe, I'll be busy, so maybe it'd be best if I wasn't disturbed. Can you let the others know?'

I doubt they'll need telling, but I nod again anyway.

‘Sure.’

Her eyes drop to the mattress for a second.

‘That means you too.’

She turns away before I have a chance to say anything.

‘You can leave rations for Johnny and me by the hatch. If you can see your way clear to swapping out his franks and beans for something else I’d appreciate it. Hard enough to get him to eat regular food in the first place.’

*

I MAKE MY WAY BACK up through the plant room.

I have to balance the box of light bulbs on my shoulder to climb the ladder. Jake's waiting for me at the hatch. I hand it to him.

'She thought you'd need these.'

I expect questions about that, but I don't get any. He just stares at the box.

I swing the hatch closed, but the noise from the ailing machine is only slightly reduced. It travels up through the silo with little to stop it, like the walls had been designed to hold it in, to amplify it.

'Is everything alright?'

'There's a problem with the generator. She doesn't want to be disturbed.'

'What does that mean?'

'It means she doesn't want anyone going down there, Jake.'

I don't have time to explain it further, even if I had a mind to. Things are worse than I thought. Mags knows something's wrong with her; that's why the lights are off, why she's shutting herself down there, making sure everyone stays away. I'm not sure how much time I have, but it's probably a lot less time than I counted on.

I set off up the stair, taking the steps two at a time. At the dorms I step off and run across the gangway to my cell. I never really got around to unpacking, so it takes only seconds to stuff what I'll need into my backpack. I return to the stair and continue on up.

When I reach the farms the Juvies are still gathered around the guardrail. Jake's with them, still carrying the box I gave him. He calls out to me from the gangway.

'Hey, where are you going?'

Their eyes settle on me, waiting for an explanation. I glance behind them. Growing benches in various stages of completion stretch back into shadow; it won't be long until the first of them are ready. Too bad they're wasting their time; those benches will never see a harvest. They give me the excuse I need, however.

'Outside.' I nod in the direction of the benches. 'Those look almost done, and now Mags has the power back on.' I point to the box of bulbs he's carrying. 'You're going to need more than what's there to get the farms up and running.'

He hesitates a moment, then sets the box down. He reaches into his pocket and pulls out a scrap of paper, holds it out to me.

'Here. I made this.'

I take it from him and unfold it, pretending to study his large, careful handwriting while he stares at me, waiting for questions. Some of his spellings are pretty out there, but there's nothing I can't make out or guess at; I know as well as he does what he needs. Most of the important stuff – garbage bags for the skirts; aluminum foil to wrap the lights; containers he can use as drip trays – I could probably pick up right there in Fearrington Village. But I have no more intention of telling him that than I do of actually looking for anything on his list. I stuff the scrap of paper into my pocket.

'I'll be gone a while.' Nobody seems interested in asking why, but I have an explanation ready so I deliver it anyway. 'Now that Durham's off limits I'll need to go further afield to find everything. Mags is having problems with the generator so she's going to stay down there till it's fixed. She said it'd be better if she wasn't disturbed.'

A few of the Juvies exchange glances at that, like they already suspect there's more to it than I'm telling them. It doesn't matter; all that matters is that they stay away. I search the faces for the one I'm looking for.

'Lauren, are you mostly done sorting out the stores?'

She nods.

'Good, because I'll need Tyler and Eric to stand watch outside again.' I find the two Guardians. 'Get your coats and follow me up. I'll see you in the airlock.'

I return to the stair before any of them have a chance to ask questions. I make my way past the mess and the upper levels, into the concrete shaft. When I reach the airlock I shuck off my backpack and count in two weeks' worth of supplies. Soon as that's done I grab an empty cardboard box and set it on the ground. I dig out the list Jake gave me, flip it over and start scribbling a note for Mags. It explains everything: what I saw at Starkly, what I think that means for her and the kid, what I intend to do about it. When I'm done I place it at the bottom of the box and then start stacking tins of *Meat Stew* and *Ham and Eggs* on top. As long as she doesn't think to empty the box it'll be a week before she finds it. By then it'll be too late to stop me, even with the pace I know she's capable of.

I'm transferring the last can when I hear Tyler and Eric on the stair. A few moments later they step into the airlock, rifles already slung over their shoulders.

I get to my feet.

'I'll be relying on you guys to bring food down for the Juvies while I'm gone. You need to check each tin up here before you bring any down. Make sure the fans are running first. Most seem to be good, but every now and then you'll hit a bad one.'

I've left a few tins I haven't checked among the stacks, to make sure that they will. Word will soon spread that it's not safe to test rations outside the airlock. I don't want the Juvies thinking they can just wander into the stores for a box whenever they feel like it.

'No worries Gabe, we got it.'

I bend down and pick up the box I've filled with cans for Mags and the kid.

'Can one of you bring this to the plant room? Don't worry - you don't need to go down there. Just leave it by the hatch and she'll come get it.'

*

I HURRY ACROSS THE COMPOUND, clamber over the security barrier, and make my way into the woods.

I have less time than I thought. I need to get Mags some of Gilbey's medicine, quick. The Greenbrier's due north from Fearrington, a distance just shy of two hundred miles. I reckon I can make it in five days if I go as the crow flies, which I intend to do. That means going through Durham, which I had hoped to avoid, but tacking west around the city would add the best part of a day to my journey, and that's time I don't have. I tell myself it'll be okay, long as I'm careful. I'll stay off the main roads, out of the way of whoever Finch might have out looking for me. I'll give the hospitals a wide berth, too. Most of those I spotted on the way down were close to the center anyway, and there's no reason for me to venture in there.

I make it to the outskirts with little of the day's light left to spare. Depots and warehouses line the road on either side, their windows silted or smashed, their corrugated roofs sagging under the weight of snow. I hurry between them, searching for somewhere that'll do for shelter.

As night falls I spot a junkyard, nestling between a railway siding and a cluster of squat gas tanks. I stop in front of it and peer through the fence. Vehicles lie in haphazard piles, their doors missing, their trunks agape. It looks like they were once stacked five or six high, but whatever attempt at order there was before has long succumbed - only here and there a few teetering columns remain. Dotted among the wrecks are other shapes, dark, hulking: huge, tracked machines with powerful hydraulic limbs, raking claws; elsewhere the square-toothed jaws of giant, slab-sided compactors. They all rest silent now, their operator compartments deserted, filling with snow. It's a sorry-looking spot and no mistake, but I couldn't hope for better. Nobody in their right mind would bother to scavenge a place like this; stands to reason they wouldn't come looking for me here either.

The gate's padlocked, but the fence has been breached before; it doesn't take me long to find a spot where the chain-link's parted company from the uprights. The wire scratches and claws at my parka as I squeeze myself through. I find what I'm looking for near the back, behind an old Airstream trailer: an unremarkable cinder-block with a low, sloping roof. The temperature's dropping so I hurry towards it, already contemplating the fire I'll soon have going. I reckon it'll be safe enough to light one; the building's set well back from the street, hidden from view by the piles of vehicle carcasses that clutter the lot.

I make my way up to the entrance and step out of my snowshoes. When I try the door it's locked, but the wood in the frame is old and doesn't stand long to the pry bar. I hurry inside, a little windblown snow following me in. I close the door behind me and wind the flashlight. The beam shows me an open space, laid out like a waiting room. Threadbare sofas push up against the walls, low tables slung between them, here and there an armchair. Beyond, almost at the end of the flashlight's reach, a long wooden counter that runs the width of the room. What looks like tall metal shelves behind, stretching back into darkness.

Spidey's antsy about something, but as usual he's not sharing the detail. It seems pretty low-level, though, and he's been on edge ever since we made it back to the city, so I shuck off my backpack and prop it against the busted door. I step over to one of the sofas and sit. The cushion sags and I can feel the springs beneath, but at least the fabric's dry. There's even a stack of magazines, neatly arranged on one of the tables. I won't even have to go searching for kindling.

I sit there for a moment, just listening, but there's nothing except the sound of the wind outside. I glance over at the counter, the shelves beyond. This wasn't a place folks would have chosen to live, before, so I can't see how anything'll be waiting for me back there. I guess I'd better go check it out, all the same. I hesitate, watching my breath hang in the flashlight's yellowing beam. It's been a while since I've had to do this. These past weeks it had become Mags' job, on account of it was she who was finding us shelter. I didn't like that it fell to her to do that, but I can't say I missed it much, either.

I look over at my backpack, resting against the door. I'll tend to it once I've got my dinner on. I undo the snaps, dig out one of the cans I've brought, hold it up to the flashlight. There's no sign of leakage; the wax I've used to seal the hole's still doing its job. I shouldn't get my hopes up, though; it hasn't yet been a day. We'll see what shape the tins are in in a couple of weeks, when I get back to Fearrington.

If *you get back to Fearrington.*

I return to the pack and pull out one of the Sternos and a makeshift stove. There's no point doubting myself now; it's the only plan I've got. Gilbey will go for it; there's no reason she wouldn't. All I'm asking is for some of her medicine. Hicks was ready to cut me a deal for the location of the Juvies; what I'm offering this time is even better.

I don't care to revisit what that might mean for the current inhabitants of Starkly prison, so instead I busy myself opening the can and setting up the jury-rigged burner. When it's done I fumble in my pocket for the lighter. Seconds later the little blue Sterno tab is aglow, filling the air with its acrid fumes.

I step back while it warms my meal. I'd like to get started on a fire, but spidey's still jangly about something or other so I wind the flashlight and make my way back to the counter. On the far side rows of wide-spaced metal shelves, stretching all the way up to the ceiling.

I hesitate a moment, then step in among them. On either side, high as the flashlight will show me, car parts: springs, shocks, mufflers, body panels, here and there what looks like an entire engine; the innards pulled from the vehicles outside. I head further back, letting the beam sweep the laden shelves. After a dozen or so paces cardboard boxes take the place of hubcaps and chromed fenders. I set the flashlight down and pull one out. A few motes spiral lazily through the faltering cone of light. Spidey takes it up a notch at that, and for once I'm way ahead of him. I run a finger along the shelf, then hold it up. Hardly any dust. When I check the floor it's the same, almost like it's been swept recently.

I lift the flap on one of the boxes, point the flashlight inside. I'm expecting more car stuff, so at first when I see what's there I think it's my eyes playing tricks on me.

Candy bars.

Scores of them, maybe hundreds. *Hershey's*; *Twizzlers*; *Oreos*; *Peanut Butter Cups*. A dozen other names, some I haven't seen in more than a decade.

I pull out a *Butterfinger* and hold it up to the light, then tear off the wrapper. The chocolate is gray and when I take a bite it tastes a little gritty, but otherwise it's fine. I check a couple of other boxes from higher up on the shelf. The contents are all the same. I pocket the *Butterfinger* and reach for a box from the other side of the aisle. It feels heavier, and when I drag it down I see why. Inside, instead of candy bars, soda cans, packed most of the way to the lid. I lift one out, pop the tab. The soda's flat, but it's good all the same; way nicer than the snowmelt from my canteen that tastes of plastic and ash and the cloth I've used to strain it.

I take another sip and return my gaze to the boxes stretching up into darkness. At last, a piece of good luck. Candy bars are way lighter than tins. If all the boxes are like the few I checked there should be more than enough here to see the Juvies back to Mount Weather, without me having to worry about whether some stupid wax seal will hold.

I finish the *Butterfinger*, pocket the wrapper. I wonder who stashed all this stuff here, though, and what happened to make them just abandon it? I return the box of sodas to its place on the shelf and start off again, the beam dancing ahead of me down the aisle. The cardboard boxes continue for a while and then stop, as abruptly as they had begun. At first I think the shelves beyond are empty, but when I shine the flashlight further along I see they're not. The beam catches a familiar shape, just beyond the next upright: a pair of stockinged feet. Spidey bleats a warning, begging me to run, but instead I stop, take a breath. It's been a while since I've come across a dead body, but it's hardly my first. Over the years I've seen my fair share of them, grown as used to the experience as I expect a person can. I can't say I'm thrilled at the prospect of finding another, but I'm certainly not about to abandon a find like this over it.

I take a breath, steady the flashlight. At least the mystery of who stocked this place has been solved. I have to hand it to them: they picked a good spot to hide their stash, a place no one would think to check; the fact that it's gone undiscovered all this time is testament to that. I guess they set up camp right next to it, presumably meaning to guard it against those who would have taken it from them. At some point along the way the cold's had another idea, however, and the cold, being a vicious bitch, has prevailed: they've frozen to death, long before they had a chance to consume what they'd gathered. I shift the beam forward, trying to ignore the fresh caterwauling inside my head as it shows me a pair of hands, folded neat across a shallow rise of chest. It's a girl, or at least once was. A girl no older than I am. The light slides up over collarbones thin as pencils, to a slender neck. Spidey's pinging like crazy now, and at last I start to realize my mistake. This is no corpse. Her skin is pale, smooth, unblemished by decay. She looks just like she's sleeping.

I cover the windup with my hand before the light can land on her face, afraid that it might wake her. Spidey's pleading with me to get out of there, but instead I glance over to the other side of the aisle. Another one, a boy this time, hands just the same, neat across his breastbone. I slowly angle the flashlight up, sweep it carefully over the shelves above.

On either side, more of them, as far as the beam will show me.

*

I TAKE A QUICK STEP backwards, then another, my heart racing. Looks like these furies are all still out of it, just like the ones in the basement of the hospital in Blacksburg, but after what I saw in Starkly I might not be willing to bet the farm on it. I turn around and hurry back towards the counter. Outside night's already fallen; under normal circumstances I wouldn't even be contemplating a fresh search for shelter. I'll have to take my chances, however; I don't plan on spending another minute under the same roof as whatever's back there.

But as I step from between the shelves I stop. The door I thought I had closed behind me when I came in hangs ajar, and when I look there's no sign of the backpack I had propped against it. That's not what has spidey dialed all the way up to DEFCON 1, however. I glance over at the sofa. The little Sterno's still burning away in its makeshift stove. The flame is low, the light it casts next to useless, but sufficient to show me a dark shape, hunched over it.

I freeze and for a dozen heartbeats just stand there, staring. The figure on the sofa doesn't move, least not as far as I can tell. I can't even be sure it's seen me. I realize I'm still holding the soda can I took from the shelves. I set it on the counter as quietly as I can and reach down for the pistol. As my fingers close around the grip whatever it is that's sitting there looks up from the flame.

'Hey! How're y'all doin?'

The hand on the pistol relaxes a fraction and I allow myself to exhale. I shine the flashlight in the direction of the voice. The hood of a sweatshirt covers his head, hiding his face, but whoever this latest interloper in the run of poor choices that has become my life might be, at least he's not like one of those things in back. I know this for one simple reason: furies can't talk.

That undeniable piece of logic does little to calm spidey, however. I try to quiet him as I make my way around the counter, but with little success. The figure on the sofa speaks again.

'My name's Vince, by the way.'

I hold a finger to my lips then use it to point behind me.

'Nice to meet you Vince, but you need to keep it down now. There's a bunch of furies back there.'

I half expect him to up and bolt for the door at this news, but instead he looks past me, into the shelves, like he's considering what I've just said. After a moment he just says *Good to know*, then gestures at the can of franks and beans bubbling away on the stove.

'This yours?' He leans forward. 'Sure don't smell very good.' He shakes his head, as if to confirm it. 'Hey, y'all wanna see something neat?'

He doesn't wait for my answer, just pushes up his sleeves and places his hands over the makeshift stove. His arms look thin, like he may not have eaten recently. He flips them over, so his palms are facing down, then starts moving them in slow interlocking circles, like he's a magician, performing a trick. His hands speed up, going faster and faster until they're a blur. After a few moments he pulls them away with a flourish. The stove's still there, the remnants of the Sterno burning away inside it. But the can that was sitting on top a moment before has disappeared.

'Pretty neat, huh?'

He keeps his head down, but I get the feeling he's waiting for a reaction, maybe even some applause. I just stand there with the flashlight, uncertain what to do. I begin to wonder if there's something not right with him, like maybe not all his dogs are barking. I know he heard what I said, because he responded to it.

'Alright, let's see what else y'all got in here.'

He bends forward and reaches down between his knees, his hand disappearing into something that looks like it might be my backpack. He pulls out a can, appears to study it for a moment, then discards it. It clatters noisily to the floor.

I glance over my shoulder, nervous that something back there might have heard.

'Hey, stop that now. We got to get out of this place.'

He keeps rummaging through my pack, like he doesn't hear me, or if he does he doesn't care. I take a step closer.

'Listen, friend, I don't know what your deal is, but I mean to be on my way, and if you have any sense you'll come with me. It's not safe here, you might want to trust me on that.'

He doesn't lift his head from the pack. Instead he pulls out another can, sends it sailing over his shoulder. It crashes to the floor somewhere behind him.

'Hey, quit that! I mean it now. That's my stuff.'

'It's only fair. That candy bar y'all ate was ours. The Coke you drank, too.' He pulls out another can, tosses it. 'And then there's the door you busted.'

*Ours*? Does he live here, among the furies? That'd make him crazier than a sprayed roach, and I don't care much to tangle with an insane person. Spidey's begging me to just cut my losses and get out of here. I glance over at the door, then back at the hooded figure hunched over my backpack, still pulling stuff out it. But I can't just leave; I need what's in that pack to get me to The Greenbrier.

I pull the pistol from the holster and hold it up so he can see.

'Hey, asshole! That's enough. I mean it now; I have a gun.'

If he hears me he gives no sign of it. Another tin gets discarded, skitters across the floor, rolls noisily off into darkness. I level the pistol at him, like I mean business. He continues to ignore me, so I lever the hammer back with my thumb. There's a loud click as it locks into position.

That finally seems to get his attention. The hood lifts a fraction, like he might be considering what I've just said. He tilts his head to one side and raises his voice.

'Y'all hear that, Cass? Sundance here says he's got a gun.'

I'm wondering if whoever he's talking to is real or just a figment of his imagination, when all of a sudden out of the corner of my eye I catch movement, a shifting in the darkness, almost too fast to comprehend. My brain's still contemplating what instructions it might want to issue to the rest of my body when I feel the pistol wrenched from my hand.

I snap my head around, startled. Where a second ago there was nothing now a girl stands. She's wearing a denim jacket, a bunch of buttons pinned to the front: *This Is Not The Life I Ordered; Stare All You Want; Bite Me;* a bunch of others I can't read. Beneath it a short skirt, scruffy-looking high-tops. Her hair is cut in a ragged bob. In the flashlight's yellowing glow it seems orange, maybe even pink. Her bangs hang down, hiding most of her face, but where they end I can see her jaw working. She turns the pistol she's just taken from me over in her hands, points it at the ground, squints along the barrel.

'Hardly a gun, Vince. More of an antique.'

I point the flashlight at her. She looks at me sideways through the strands of hair – definitely pink – that fall across her face.

'What, you couldn't have found something older?'

She lowers the hammer, studies the pistol a moment longer, then with a flick of her wrist sends it spinning towards the sofa. My eyes twitch left, trying to follow the shallow arc it takes, but I'm *way* too slow. By the time I catch up Vince is already on his feet, and now he's standing atop the low table. He snatches it from the air with an almost alarming grace.

I take a step backwards, finally beginning to realize how wrong I've got this. I swing the flashlight in his direction. The beam shows me faded jeans, snugged down over a pair of scuffed work boots, a leather jacket. The sweatshirt he wears underneath has an eagle's head on it and the words *Lynyrd Skynyrd.* I don't know what that means; it doesn't even sound like English. I hesitate for a second and then angle the flashlight up. The beam slips into the cowl of his hood, suddenly setting his eyes ablaze. He narrows them a fraction, but doesn't look away.

He steps down off the table and pulls back the hood, revealing a shock of white hair. His face splits into a lopsided grin. If it was his intention to reassure me with that gesture, he's missed the mark, and by some margin. He regards me the way a fox might a chicken that's just wandered into its den, all of its own accord.

I stand there, rooted to the spot, just staring back at him.

He holds me in his gaze a moment longer, then he looks over my shoulder and whistles through his teeth.

*

THERE'S A SOUND FROM BACK IN THE DARKNESS, faint, like I think I remember the flutter of birds' wings, and when I swing the flashlight around others are appearing from among the shelves. They take up positions all around me, by sofas or armchairs or backed against the wall. Others hop up on the counter, like it's nothing to them. Some are small, little bigger than the kid. With the exception of maybe Vince none seem older than I am. They keep coming, one after another, until I count maybe twenty.

When the last of them has emerged I turn back around. Vince is standing right in front of me now. I take a half-step backwards, surprised by his sudden proximity. I hadn't heard him step closer.

'So y'all are the one the prisoners been out looking for.' The smile disappears and his face creases into a frown, like something's troubling him. He leans in, tilts his head, like he's testing the air, then looks over at the girl. 'Why ain't he more afraid of us, Cass?'

My brain's still trying to come to terms with what I'm seeing, but I realize he's right. My heart's doing a little giddy-up, for sure, but there's something else, another feeling, for the most part keeping the fear in check. It takes me a moment to recognize what it is.

Relief. I'm almost light-headed with it. The stuff with Mags and the kid, I've had it all wrong. They're not sick anymore, not like Marv was. They're on their way to becoming whatever Vince and Cass and all these others are.

The girl with the pink hair shrugs, like she could care less. She takes to studying a fingernail that's already been bitten back to the quick.

'I dunno, Vince. Could be he's too dumb to realize the fix he's in.'

The once called Vince looks me up and down, like he's considering this.

'Could be, Cass, could be. He sure don't look that bright, even for a warmblood.' He glances around, as though waiting for a reaction from the others. 'Tall enough though, ain't he?' He leans back on his heels, cups one hand to his mouth. 'Hey, up there! Y'all got a name?'

I shake myself from my stupor, manage to stammer out an answer.

'Gabriel. Gabe.'

He stares up at me for a moment, like he's considering that. I feel like I should say something. I have so many questions, but my mind's still running 'round in herky-jerky circles, which makes it hard to put them in any sort of order.

'What are…I mean, how did you come to be this way?'

The one called Vince holds my gaze a second longer then turns to the girl with the pink hair.

'Where's this guy been, Cass?'

She doesn't look up from her fingernails.

'Hidin' out inside a mountain, Vince.'

I open my mouth to ask how she knows that, then close it again. Vince has slipped his finger through the trigger guard on Hicks' pistol and has taken to spinning it, slow lazy rotations, first this way then that. It seems like I should pay attention to that.

'So waddya think, should we hand him over to them?'

Cass just shakes her head.

'You could, Vince, but it'd be a mistake. I keep telling you: the prisoners, they ain't a problem. Hell, they don't even know for sure we exist. That'd soon change if you give this one to them, though. You can be sure he'd tell them where we're at, too.'

Vince's face scrunches into a scowl and he glares at me, like I've already done the thing I've been accused of.

'What should we do with him, then? Give him to the crazies?'

*Crazies*? I look over at Cass, but she's already shaking her head.

'You don't want to get them any more riled up than they already are.'

Vince stops twirling the pistol for a second and looks at her.

'I ain't afraid of their kind.'

She flicks the hair from in front of her face

'I never said you was. All the same.' She hesitates a moment then looks up from her fingers, cuts a glance at the pistol. 'You let me have that back, I'll take care of him for you.'

Vince looks at her.

'Y'all would?'

She takes a step closer, nodding quickly.

'You were right about this one, Vince; I can see it now. He's different. Pokin' his nose in where it don't belong; stealin' our stuff; wavin' his gun around at us.'

A slow smile spreads across Vince's lips, like he likes the way that sounds. I start to explain I hadn't been looking for them; that me stumbling in here was just chance. He swings the pistol in my direction so fast it makes my head spin.

'Now y'all just need to stay quiet while us grown-ups discuss this.' He looks back at the girl. 'Sorry about that, Cass. Rude. Go on, now.'

'Like I said, Vince, you had it right, before. I should've just let you deal with him, with all of them, back when we had the chance.'

Vince waits a moment, like he's thinking on it, then he tosses her the gun. She catches it effortlessly then waves it in the direction of the door, like whatever she has planned for me, she's anxious to be getting on with it.

'Alright, let's go.'

I open my mouth, meaning to protest my innocence again. I get rewarded with a jab of the pistol to my ribs. Not hard enough to hurt, but the speed of it surprises me. I step towards the door. As I pass Vince he leans in. His nostrils flare and then his face creases into a smile.

'Hey, Cass - I think he's finally startin' to get it.'

*

OUTSIDE IT'S ALREADY FULL DARK; the cold bites before I've even stepped through the door. My snowshoes are where I left them, up against the wall. Cass pokes around in the snow a little further along, then picks up what looks like a tennis racket, the bindings improvised out of duct tape. Her fingers are bare, but if the temperature bothers her she shows no sign of it. She bends to retrieve another then drops both to the ground and steps into them.

Vince appears in the doorway behind me.

'Where y'all bringin' him?'

'The railway line.'

'Why don't y'all just do it right here?'

'Really? You wanna have to step over him every time we go outside?'

Vince scratches his head, like he's considering this. The thought of him stepping over my frozen corpse brings home to me the trouble I'm in, and I feel the first quickening tendrils of panic wrap themselves around my insides, urging me to bolt. I take a deep breath, push the fear back down. I wouldn't make it more than a half-dozen paces. I'll go along with the girl, for now. Wherever she means to take me, I have a better chance away from the rest of them.

I step into my snowshoes without waiting for an instruction. Vince watches me. He waits till I'm done tightening the straps, then points at my feet.

'Hold up now. Fancy snowshoes like that are hard to come by. It's not far to the fence. He can walk it.'

Cass gives a little shake of her head, sighs.

'Alright, you heard him.'

I bend down and unsnap the bindings, step out of them. My boots sink into the snow, but not too deep; the trailer provides a measure of shelter and in front of the building the snow hasn't had the chance to drift. I stamp my feet, anxious now to get moving. It won't be long before the cold makes my limbs unreliable, and however I plan to escape, I need to do it before that happens. Cass waves the pistol into the darkness, motioning me on. I wind the flashlight and set off, following the direction she's indicated. Vince and the rest of them hang back by the door, watching.

Beyond the trailer the snow deepens. Within a few paces it's above the tops of my boots; I have to lift my knees high to clear the drifts. It's an effort, but at least it'll keep my muscles warm, least for a while. I risk a glance behind me. Cass isn't close enough that I might try reaching the gun.

*And you think if she were you could take it from her?*

I might not care to hear it, but a part of me knows the voice is right. I've seen how quick she is. I'll have to be smarter than that. I wait till I reckon we're far enough from the others then I stop, pretending like I need to get my breath back.

'So what are you, exactly?'

I say it mostly for something to say, to get a conversation going while I come up with a plan. But even as I hear the words I realize part of me desperately needs to know. Satisfying my curiosity doesn't seem to be high on Cass's list of priorities, however. She just tilts her head and shows me the gun, like *Really, this is what you want to talk about, now?*

I start forward again.

'But you're some kind of fury, though, right?'

I don't expect a response; my brain's already trying to come up with something else to say that might distract her. This time her answer comes back quick, however, and now there's an edge to it.

'Wrong.'

I stop again, like I need another rest. I try to turn around so I can face her, but the snow's up around my knees and it's too much effort. I look over my shoulder. She's a little closer, maybe, but still keeping her distance. I don't know how much farther the railway line is, but whatever I'm planning on doing, I'll have to get to it soon. The fingers that grip the flashlight are already starting to ache with the cold.

'You must have been once, though, to be the way you are.'

She brings the pistol up, in a single fluid motion. It happens too fast for me to see it, but I hear a click as the hammer cocks.

'You're just as dumb as all the rest of them.'

I'm not sure who *the rest of them* might be but I jerk my hands up, worried she means to shoot me right here.

'Sorry!' I pause, trying to choose my next words carefully, worried they might be my last. 'I didn't mean anything by it, really. I don't understand how it works, any of it. I want to, though. I have these friends…'

The gun drops a fraction.

'The one you call Johnny?'

I want to ask how she knows about the kid, but it seems like she might be about to tell me something else, something more important, and I don't want to interrupt her.

'He'll be fine. It's not him you should be worrying about right now.'

'How…how do you know?'

I wait for an answer, but I don't get one, so instead I search for something else to say, a line of questioning less likely to get me shot. Maybe it's the cold - I can feel its barbs sinking into me now, slowing me down - but I can't think of anything. I raise my hands a little higher.

'So I get that you weren't a fury. You must have been infected, though, right? I mean, to be the way you are.'

She doesn't say anything for a moment.

'I was. I'm not any more.'

'But, how?'

'That thing with the sky.' She shrugs her shoulders. 'I don't remember much more than how bright it was. But when I came to I wasn't sick anymore. None of us were.'

She pokes me in the ribs with the gun again.

'Alright, Gabriel, question time's over. Start movin'.'

The snow's settled around my legs and it takes longer than it ought to work my boots free. When I finally manage it I set off again, lumbering through the drifts in the direction she indicates. I'm shivering inside my parka now, in spite of the effort it takes to keep moving. Cass isn't exactly dressed for the outdoors, but if the cold's bothering her she gives no sign of it.

'S-so, are there more…more of you, then?'

She shakes her head.

'We're all there is.'

The virus does its work quick, I know that; there's only a small window between being infected and turning. What Kane did to the skies would have had to coincide with that. Still, though; something about what she's said doesn't seem right.

'Isn't…isn't that s-strange?'

'What do you mean?'

I don't answer her right away. I sense we're getting close to wherever she means to take me, and I need to draw her in. This might be my last chance.

'It j-just doesn't seem enough. N-not for a city…the s-size of Durham.'

She goes quiet and for a while I'm not sure I'm going to get an answer. I shuffle around to face her. Her eyes narrow at the flashlight, but she doesn't look away. The gun's pointed square between my shoulder blades; behind it her expression has hardened. I begin to suspect I've made a terrible mistake continuing with my questions.

'There used to be more of us, but then the soldiers came. They didn't care; they hunted us down, just the same as the crazies. First winter took care of them, though; took care of all of you. Your kind aren't a threat to us anymore. There's only a handful of you left now, hanging on to life outta little more than habit. Soon enough you'll be gone.'

She gestures for me to move on.

My teeth are chattering, and I don't seem able to stop them. I start to tell her what I was trying to explain to Vince, back inside: I wasn't looking for her, or any of them. I was on my way to The Greenbrier, to trade the prisoners for a medicine for Mags and the kid. A pointless errand, seeing as it turns out neither of them need it. I don't get very far into the story before she cuts me off.

'Save your breath. I'm not interested.'

I lift a boot from the snow, stumble forward. Somewhere in the darkness ahead I think I hear the creak of fence wire, and when I point the flashlight that way it finds a stretch of chain-link. There's a section right in front where it's been breached, the diamonds cut, pulled back to create a gap.

I feel the panic rising up inside me as I realize this must be where she means to do it. I freeze, trying to think of something to say, anything to make her change her mind. Something hard jabs into the space between my ribs.

'Quit stallin'.'

I shuffle forward until I can feel the snow crumbling under the toes of my boots.

'Okay, that's far enough.'

I point the flashlight down but there's nothing, just a black chasm into which the snow twists and tumbles. This is it, then. The end of the road. I meant to do something, to fight, to run, but I've left it too late. There'll be no struggle. No last-minute attempt to overpower my executioner, to wrest the pistol from her grip. I can't even turn to face her; my boots are wedged too deep in the snow. I hold my arms out.

'Listen, Cass, y-you don't have to do this. Just...just let me go and I p-promise, you'll never...'

I don't even get to finish the sentence. There's a bang, shockingly loud, and something hits me hard, right between the shoulder blades, knocking the wind from me. My mouth opens in surprise, even as the force of it pitches me forward.

And then I'm falling, breathless, into darkness.

*

NOW, YOU COULD SAY I'M NOT OLD ENOUGH to know for sure, but I reckon there are moments in your life you don't ever forget, no matter how long you live. You take those snapshots because the thing that happened in that moment is significant, remarkable. It can be something good; something you desperately want to cling to. Or the opposite: something so terrible your mind just won't let go, much as you might wish for it. Memories like that don't fade, or dim, because every time you call them up the details get etched a little deeper, until each is a record cut so deep it will endure a lifetime. I have a few of them. Sprinting hand in hand with Mags across the White House lawn on the Last Day. The first time she kissed me, on the roof of the mess, back in Eden. My first glimpse of the fury in Mount Weather's tunnel, bounding towards me out of the darkness.

One of those moments is from the farmhouse outside Eden, the place Marv and I would visit, before we'd head out scavenging. I didn't know it then, but it was the last time I'd be there with him. He was sitting opposite me in the kitchen. There was a pistol on the table between us, wrapped in a Ziploc bag. I was afraid, certain he was about to shoot me with it. A question had popped into my head, nevertheless; in the circumstances a stupid, pointless curiosity. I'd read somewhere, in a book or maybe a magazine, I forget now, how you never hear the shot that kills you. Something to do with the bullet travelling faster than the sound it makes.

These shots I hear just fine.

The pistol booms a second time, even as I'm falling. A third shot follows, fast on its heels, and an instant later something hits me, hard, like a hammer, from a direction I wasn't expecting. The impact is even more shocking than the first. I feel something inside me give, even as the force of it spins me around. I open my mouth, but there's no air left in my lungs to give voice to the cry. My shoulder bounces off something unyielding and I land heavily. Pain explodes up the side where the second bullet found me, sending starbursts swirling and exploding across my vision. The sheer magnitude of it threatens to overwhelm me.

Another shot rings out, but I don't even have it in me to flinch. I just lie there, like a stood-on bug, waiting for the bullet to find me. A pause, a final shot, and then a thud, directly above. Snow rains down on my head and then it grows quiet, save for the crunch of powder beneath me as I rock back and forwards, trying to force air into my lungs. Each attempt sends a fresh spike of pain down my side, but I can't stop; the need to breathe again overrides everything else.

After what seems like an eternity I manage a shallow, hiccupped breath, then another. My mind switches to the task of gathering reports of the damage I've suffered. The pain isn't so bad where I got hit first, between my shoulder blades, but rather worryingly I think I can feel something wet trickling down my spine there. The real action's coming from my side, however. The pain there is medieval; it feels like someone's jammed a pry bar between my ribs, spread them, then ripped my lungs out through the gap between.

For a while I just lie there, rocking back and forth, mouth agape; marveling that somehow I'm still alive. The cold seeps inside my parka, wraps itself around me. It's oddly soothing. Little by little the pain starts to recede, becoming almost distant.

I know what comes next, though. I can't stay here. I need to find shelter; I've already been outside too long.

I lift my head from the snow. I'm not even sure where I am; it's too dark to make out anything. The flashlight's still tethered to my wrist, but I don't want to wind it. Cass might still be up there, considering whether she needs to come down and finish me off. Instead I reach out a hand, grope around in the snow. There's an excruciating reminder from my side that all is not well there; I have to push my face into the snow to stifle a cry.

When the pain subsides I try again, this time making my explorations gentler. I seem to be lying on a narrow metal ledge; if I brush away the snow I can feel the small, ridged diamonds of tread plate just beneath the surface. When I stretch a little farther my fingers close around metal. The upright of a guardrail? I wriggle towards it. The movement causes fresh agony from my side, making my head swim, but inch by inch I haul myself upright.

I take a couple of shallow breaths then shuffle along the ledge, one hand gripping the rail, the other clutched to my ribs. After a few steps the walkway ends at what feels like a narrow metal door. I grope around until my fingers brush something that might be a handle. It sticks a little as I press down then turns. I lean my shoulder into it and stumble inside, pull it closed behind me.

I reach into the pocket of my parka for the flashlight. I hesitate a moment then give the handle a couple of slow turns, just enough to get the bulb glowing. It shows me a small cabin, a cushioned seat mounted on a thick pedestal, a footrest at its base. Beyond a narrow windscreen, the glass dark with snow. I brave a few more turns of the windup. The bulb grows brighter, revealing a control panel, busy with levers, switches, dials. *Engine Start*, *Brake Power*, *Throttle*, *Dynamic Grade.* A plate riveted above says *GM Electro-Motive Division* and underneath *La Grange, Illinois.*

Cass said she was bringing me to the railway line. I must be in the cab of a locomotive.

I lean against the seat and gently unzip my parka. Each movement sends fresh bursts of pain down my side, but all things considered I'm in way better shape than I should be, considering I've just been shot.

Twice.

I remove a mitten and feel along my ribs on the side I was hit. When I hold my fingers up to the flashlight I expect them to come away sticky with blood, but somehow they're dry. My spine feels cold, damp, but I'm beginning to think that might just be snowmelt.

She was right behind me. How could she have missed?

She couldn't have, not from that range.

She must have shoved me off the ledge, then fired Hicks' pistol up into the air to convince Vince she'd done as she promised. Just my luck I found a freight train to break my fall.

But why would she spare me?

I think on that for a while, but can't come up with a reason, other than the desire any human might have not to end the life of another.

*Except she's not...*

I hush the voice before it can get going. Whatever her reasons, I can't be here when the sun comes up. I look down at my boots. Without snowshoes I won't be going very far, though. My first thought is to try and make it back up to the junkyard, steal back the ones Vince stole from me. It doesn't take me long to realize that dog's not for hunting. I don't think I fell that far, but I doubt I have it in me to climb back up, not with my ribs the way they are. Vince and the others can see in the dark, too, and if they're anything like Mags and the kid are now they won't be much for sleeping. If one of them spots me I'll be done for.

I wind the flashlight and look around the tiny cab. A newspaper, yellow with age, lies folded beneath the windshield, the headline proclaiming the end of days. An old thermos on its side next to it. I move the beam along. A drop-down seat, a sidewall heater bolted to the wall, what looks like a locker between them. I squat in front of it, wincing at the protest from my busted ribs, and slide the latch. Inside there's a pair of work gloves and a large metal flashlight, the end furred where the batteries have leaked. Next to it a single spiral-bound volume, thick with dog-eared pages. I reach in and lift it out. Across the front, printed in large letters under a GM logo: *Locomotive Engineers Manual*. I consider it for kindling, but it's way too small and poorly ventilated in here for a fire, and cracking the door would defeat the purpose. I'm sorely tempted nonetheless. I might be out of the wind, but there's little to the cab's walls. It's like an icebox in here.

I take the items out, one by one, set them aside. In the darkness behind the beam finds an old hinge-top toolbox, the metal dented and scarred. My side hollers again as I reach for the handle. I slide it towards me as gently as I can, unsnap the catches and shine the flashlight inside. A motley collection of tools: screwdrivers, wrenches, a claw hammer. A socket set on a rust-spackled rail, half of the sockets missing. Underneath, a large roll of silver duct tape, a rattle-can of WD-40.

I sit back on my heels, considering. I look over at the heater again. A length of hose runs from the underside, back towards the control panel. I reach over and work the end free. The rubber's old, but when I flex it it doesn't split.

I reach into the toolbox, pull out one of the wrenches, hold it up for size.

It might just work.

*

HE JERKS FROM SLEEP, eyes wide like saucers, blinking in his surroundings. In every direction unfamiliar metal, stretching and twisting and spiraling off into grainy shadow. He reaches for the mattress, clutching the musty fabric, waiting, heart pounding, for the memories to come back. One by one they return, slow at first, disjointed, then all in a rush.

He lies there for a while, letting his breathing slow, then he sits up, shuffles himself over to the edge. It is quiet now, only the occasional wheezing gasp from the air purifiers to punctuate the silence. It was louder earlier, with all the machines running. *Way* louder. The roar from the old diesel generator had been deafening. He had fled to his perch and covered his ears with his hands, but it had done little good; there was no escaping it. The noise was a physical thing, a vibration he could feel in his chest, his teeth. The girl said she was sorry but they needed to clear the flooding. He watched as inch by inch the waters dropped, until at last beneath the oil-slicked surface you could make out the huge springs on which the silo rests. Once the pumps had done their work the girl shut the machine down, but it had taken a while for his ears to stop ringing.

The hatch had creaked open shortly after. A voice had called down, asking if anything was wrong. It was the boy with the curly hair. He had sounded nervous. The girl had shouted back that she needed a few hours with the generator off, so she could tend to whatever had worked its way loose. He should go back up, use the time to get some sleep.

He hears her now, working on it. He rests his chin on the guardrail and for a few minutes just stares out into the darkness, listening.

He hears another sound, different, and he lifts his head. At first he thinks it is the girl, starting the machines up again. But he knows the noises they make – the shrill whine of the starter; the way the generator coughs before it catches; the labored whine from the bilge pumps. That wasn't one of them.

He tilts his head, trying to determine where it's coming from. His ears are no longer ringing, but the sounds in this place are difficult and he's not used to them yet. He's pretty sure it's not something the girl is doing; he doesn't think it even came from down there. He looks up towards the hatch. It's not one of the others either; they have yet to stir. It seemed almost like it came from within the walls. He picks himself up and scrabbles along the gangway. When he reaches the end he presses one ear to the metal and waits, holding his breath.

Again, louder this time. A muffled crump, like an explosion, from somewhere on the other side of the curving wall, followed immediately by another, then a third. He feels a tickle in his nose, like he might sneeze, and when he looks up he sees a fine rain of dust, filtering through the grille above his head.

He looks down. Beneath him the girl is still at work on one of the machines; she hasn't heard it yet. He scampers back across the gangway and climbs the stairs, padding lightly up the worn tread plate, until he reaches the ladder that leads to the hatch. He clambers up the rungs and pushes the hatch up, poking his head through. He doesn't like being up here, where the others are, but he's pretty sure they are sleeping now.

He stops, listening.

Another sound: faint, intermittent, the ringing chime of metal striking metal. But uneven, not mechanical. And coming from somewhere else, somewhere…

He scurries back down the ladder and rejoins the stair, his hand skimming the railing as he descends. He continues, round and round, all the way to the bottom. He jumps off the last step, splashing through the last six inches of groundwater the pumps have yet to clear. On either side of him huge springs, each several feet in diameter. Even compressed by the weight of concrete and steel above the coiled steel is higher than he is tall.

The girl has her back to him. She stands ankle deep in floodwater, working on one of the dampers, leaning her weight into a wrench. She turns at his approach, swings the wrench on to her shoulder. She wipes her forehead with the back of her hand and looks down.

He points to his ear and then up, up. She looks at him for a moment, her brow furrowing. She cocks her head to one side and closes her eyes. She stays like that for a moment and then her expression changes. The wrench slips from her hands. She's already at the stair before it hits the water.

He catches up to her at the console. Her hands move over the switches, then she reaches underneath, transfers something to the pocket of her overalls. She takes off again, bounding up the steps, taking them two at a time. The machines that scrub the silo's air draw one final wheezing breath, exhale, then fall silent.

He follows on her heels, dropping to a crouch so he can keep up. At the dorms some of the others have emerged from their cells. They stand on the landing, looking up, their faces anxious. Others peek out from behind the narrow cell doors, blinking sleep from their eyes. They can hear it now too. The boy with the curly hair hurries across the gangway like he means to confront her, but she just shouts at him to get out of the way and he freezes, lets her pass.

By the time they reach the upper levels she's already several turns of the stair ahead of him. She continues up into the shaft without pausing. The sound is louder now; it echoes down towards them, reverberating through the long drop of darkness above.

He reaches the gangway at the top of the stair, hurries along the narrow passageway, into the shower room beyond. At last he finds her, standing by the inner door. Sweat glistens her shoulders, but her breathing is calm, regular. She pauses a moment, listening, but there is only the same, persistent clanging. She takes hold of the handle. The wheel grumbles through a rotation, reaching the end of its travel with a heavy clunk. She pulls the door back and steps into the chamber.

The clanging grows louder.

He follows her into the airlock. At the outer door she pauses, as though steeling herself. She reaches up and slides the hatch back, leaning forward so she can see through the narrow slot.

The clanging stops.

Something in her face changes and she steps away from the door. She closes her eyes, one hand clenching into a fist at her side. After a long moment she takes a deep breath and returns to the slot, gesturing at whoever's on the other side of the door to back up.

He tugs at the leg of her overalls.

'What is it?'

She closes the hatch and squats down in front of him.

'The man who was at Mount Weather, he's found us. I have to go outside to talk to him.'

Her eyes flick over his shoulder.

'I need you to go back in there and stay out of sight. Whatever happens you don't come out. Okay?'

He is frightened now, but he nods anyway.

She reaches into the pocket of her overalls, pulls out the handgun she collected from the console. She pulls back the slide, checks something above the grip, then tucks it into the back of her waistband. She turns to the outer door, spins the handle until the locks click, then pushes it back. A flurry of wind-blown snow swirls through the opening and then she steps through, pulling it closed behind her.

*

I STOP ON A BLUFF overlooking a place the map says might be Calvander. My right boot has worked itself loose again; it'll need tending to before I can go any further.

I lower myself into the snow and set to. The mittens make for clumsy work. I have to pull them off to remove the tape that's frayed, but once that's done it's a quick job to rebind the boot at toe and heel. The other one still seems solid. I add a couple of strips anyway, then lean back to admire my handiwork.

Not the prettiest, but with a little luck these repairs will see me back to Fearrington. It was Cass gave me the idea, or rather those tennis rackets she had jury-rigged into snowshoes. They looked like nine parts hope, one part Hail Mary, but they seemed to do the trick all the same. I figured with what was available to me in the locomotive's cab I should be able to come up with something similar. Didn't need to be anything fancy; whatever I could throw together only needed to get me back to the bunker.

The rubber pipe I pulled from the sidewall heater, that would do for the base. I cut it into two lengths, both about as long as my leg, then bent each back on itself and taped the ends together until I had a pair of teardrop-shaped loops that looked about the right size. A couple of the smaller wrenches across the midsection of each, the ends bound in place, to give it some structure; a place for my boots to sit. Then a shedload more tape, wrapped tight around the frame I had constructed, and my makeshift snowshoes were starting to take shape. I considered working up bindings, just like the ones Cass had on hers, but in the end I figured there was no need for anything so fancy. They only needed to last me one trip; it'd be far easier just to stretch the tape over my boots before I set out.

When I was done I propped my newly constructed footwear against the door and reached for the newspaper. I might not be able to use it for a fire, but the paper would at least provide some extra insulation to get me through the night. I began tearing pages from it, crumpling them up and stuffing them inside my parka. When I couldn't fit anymore I pulled the zipper up as far as it would go, tightened the drawstrings on my hood, hugged my knees to my chest and sat there to wait for the dawn.

I return the remains of the tape to my pocket and get to my feet, wincing at the pain from my busted ribs. I set out before the first gray smear of dawn had begun to trouble the horizon, but with my side the way it is and the stops I've been making to fix my footwear I certainly haven't been setting any snowshoeing records. If I can hold to this pace, though, I reckon I can be back at Fearrington before the afternoon's out.

I lift a snowshoe high to clear a drift. Underneath my parka Hicks' pistol shifts in its holster. It was sitting on the roof of the locomotive when I stepped outside; Cass must have tossed it down after she was done emptying it. My backpack's gone, however, which means the only ammunition I have left for it is what's tucked into the gun belt's loops, less than a dozen shells all told.

My ribs ache with every breath. I have no food, not even a canteen. And when I get back to the bunker I'll have to come clean to the Juvies: admit to the lies I told about our food and break the news that we'll be leaving again, not even a week after we arrived.

But it doesn't matter, any of it.

Behind the mask I feel the corners of my mouth pull upwards into a smile.

I can scarcely believe my luck.

I don't have to go back to The Greenbrier. I don't have to convince Gilbey to give me any of her medicine, and I don't have to trade Starkly's inmates for it. Mags and the kid, they don't need it.

They never have.

I think back to the newspaper reports I used to collect, when I was out scavenging with Marv. Among them was an interview with a scientist, one of those tasked with studying the virus, in the hope of coming up with a cure. The world had come to know ferro as a weapon, she said, something that had been designed to kill. But what she'd seen didn't support that theory; the way it worked was just too complicated for that to be its purpose. She reckoned those that had become infected, it was like the virus meant to rebuild them, on the inside, to replace their internal wiring with its own.

Problem was the circuits the virus meant us to have were *way* faster, and our bodies had never been designed for that kind of speed. Most people who got infected simply didn't survive. Those few that did became something else, a transformation you'd be hard pressed to consider an improvement.

Except it didn't have to go that way - Vince and Cass and the others from the junkyard are the proof of it. If the virus got interrupted before it overwhelmed you, before you turned, there's a chance you could become something else.

Something better.

Faster.

Stronger.

Getting Mags and the kid back to Eden and into the scanner, it must have done that for them. I don't understand how exactly, but that doesn't matter now. Once the Juvies understand they'll stop being afraid. We can all return to Mount Weather together.

I pick up the pace, ignoring the protests from my side. There's already several weeks' worth of rations in the airlock; it won't take long to add enough to that for the journey back. We can be on the road within a couple of days, and safely back inside the mountain long before the storms arrive.

*

THE HANDLE COMPLETES ITS ROTATION and comes to a jerky halt. He stares at the metal door, undecided. The man with the gray eyes is dangerous, he knows that; the girl shouldn't be out there alone with him. He hesitates a moment longer and then steps into the airlock, crossing quickly to the outer door. The slot is too high, so he drags a box of cans over from the stacks that line the wall and steps onto it. He has to go up on tiptoe, but now he can see.

The girl is standing in front of the door, her back to him. A little way beyond the dangerous man waits, his arms held out from his sides. He's holding something in one hand. The glass is thick, rimed with ice, so it's hard to tell, but it doesn't look like a gun. At his side is a boy he also recognizes, from that night inside the mountain. He stares at the girl through strands of lank brown hair. His nose looks funny, like what the girl did to it, it didn't set straight. A lazy grin plays across his lips. Three others kneel in the snow in front of him, their heads down, their hands behind their backs. The two on either side he knows immediately; it's the boy with the dark skin and the other one, the one who goes outside with him to guard the silo. There's a third figure between them, a bag over his head. The plastic blurs his features, but he thinks he recognizes him. It's one of the two large boys from the first place inside the mountain they visited, the place that had the machine, the one that fixed him. He can't tell which of them it might be, however, because those boys were difficult to tell apart.

Behind him he hears noises as others reach the top of the stair and start making their way along the passageway. The girl with the blond hair is the first into the airlock. When she sees him she comes to a sudden halt and shouts at those behind who are still trying to push forward. The boy with the curly hair squeezes past her and steps up to the door. He shuffles over to make room for him. The boy cups one hand to his brow and presses his face to the slot.

'What's she doing out there, without a parka? She'll freeze. And what's…'

He stops midsentence and takes a sudden step backward. His hands drop to the handle.

'She said we were to wait.'

'That's Peck. I'm not leaving her out there with him.'

He grips the wheel, but the girl has set the lock; when he tries to turn it it just clanks against its stop. The sound is loud inside the small chamber. Outside the girl must hear it too. She doesn't turn her head, but one hand slides behind her back and she splays her fingers.

*Stay.*

The boy with the curly hair doesn't say anything, but after a moment he lets go of the handle and presses his face back to the glass.

Outside the dangerous man is saying something to the girl. The man's voice is muffled by the thick steel, but he can still make out most of his words.

'...need to watch carefully now...not do anything stupid.'

The man turns and nods at the boy with the grin. He steps behind the large boy in the middle. The large boy looks frightened, but the boy with the grin lays one hand on his shoulder, like he means to reassure him, and that seems to calm him down. With his other hand he reaches for a corner of the plastic, pinches something there, then takes a quick step backward.

For a moment nothing happens, and then the large boy's eyes suddenly go wide and his whole body convulses. Something white that looks like foam spews from his mouth, spraying the inside of the bag. He tries to stand but fails in the attempt, and instead falls forward, landing face first in the snow. He twitches once, twice, and then goes still.

The girl reaches behind her back, draws the gun. For a second the man's expression changes, like the speed of it might have taken him by surprise, but then he recovers. He raises his hand and now he can see the thing he's holding is a radio.

'Those explosions you may have heard, they were grenades, dropped into each of the vent shafts to open them up. Jason, Seth, Zack, Sergeant Scudder, they each have a canister of the same stuff that just did for Angus there. Some sort of nerve agent Gilbey had us pick up from Fort Detrick. It's nasty business, make no mistake.' His eyes drop to the body lying in the snow. 'Only took the tiniest little capsule of it to do that.' He holds up the radio. 'They're waiting for me to tell them whether or not to drop those canisters down the shafts.'

The girl takes aim at the man's head.

''Course if they don't back hear from me, or if they hear a gunshot, their orders are to drop them anyway.'

The girl pauses for a moment, like she's considering this.

'What do you want?'

'Why, you. And the other one Gilbey had been working on, the little one.' He turns to the boy beside him, the one with the grin. 'What'd she say his name was, Kurt? 99?'

The one called Kurt smiles, nods.

'That's it.'

The man raises his voice, as if he's addressing not just the girl now.

'Gilbey doesn't care about the rest of you anymore. She's only interested in the two who were infected and found themselves a cure.'

He hears murmurs from behind him as this news makes its way back along the passageway. The boy with the curly hair tells them to be quiet.

Outside the girl still has the gun trained on the dangerous man.

'You working for Gilbey now, Randall?'

'I serve at the pleasure of the President, little girl, same as I ever did. I guess you thought you were being smart, sending him back to her like that? You think a man like Kane wouldn't be able to cut himself a deal?' He looks at her for a moment, as though he's expecting a response. When he doesn't get one he continues. 'So here it is: I fetch you and the kid back, she lets him go.'

The girl shakes her head.

'You won't drop those canisters. If you do you'll kill us all. And if I'm dead you have nothing to bring back to Gilbey.'

The man just stares back at her.

'You might want to think that through a second. Without you and the kid Kane's dead anyway. Or worse. So you decide. What's it to be?' He raises his voice again. 'You and the kid, or everyone in there dies.'

'You can't have Johnny.'

'I'm not sure you're in any position to be making demands.'

The man nods at the boy he called Kurt. He pulls a plastic bag from his pocket and takes a step towards the boy with the dark skin who's still kneeling in the snow. The girl shifts her aim and he freezes. The smile disappears from his face.

'You can't have him because he's already dead, Randall. He turned the same day we left Eden. Gabe had to put a bullet in him. His body's lying in a ditch, not more than hundred yards from the railroad crossing, right there on the other side of the state line. Go look for yourself if you don't believe me. Should be easy enough to find.'

The dangerous man studies her for a long moment, as if considering. In the end he nods.

'Well, Gilbey said that might happen. I guess you'll just have to do then.'

The girl nods, like she understands. She lowers the gun.

'I need to gather my things.'

She turns back towards the entrance.

The dangerous man calls after her.

'Don't be long.' He holds up the radio, as if to make his point. 'I'm not in a patient mood.'

*

THERE'S A SERIES OF CLICKS as the girl enters the code, then the grumble of gears and the handle starts to turn. He steps off the box. There are too many of them in the room beyond the airlock and he doubts they will let him hide among them, so he scurries over and crouches behind the stacked rations. A second later the door swings back and the girl steps inside. She grabs the wheel and pulls it closed behind her.

The boy with the curly hair steps forward.

'That was just to buy some time, right? I mean, you have a plan, don't you?'

He says it like he needs it to be so. The girl looks past him, into the faces pressed into the passageway beyond the airlock. Her eyes settle on one near the back.

'Amy, can you run down to the dorms and fetch my backpack? My parka too; it's behind the door.'

There's a pause and then the sound of footsteps, growing softer as they descend the shaft.

The boy shakes his head, like he doesn't want to believe it. His mouth opens, but he looks like he's struggling to arrange words into sentences. He finally manages to get one out.

'You can't go with them.'

The girl with the blond hair had pushed herself back among the others, but now she steps forward again.

'She has to, Jake. You heard what Peck said. It's her or all of us.'

She looks around. A few murmurs of agreement, but most of them just stare down at their boots. She points a finger in his direction.

'The little fury; he should go too.'

He does not want to go back in the cage, and for a moment the thing inside him takes control. He snaps his head around, bares his teeth. The blond girl yanks her hand back like it's just been burned. The smell of her fear flares in his nostrils.

He feels the girl's hand on his shoulder.

'Johnny's not coming with me, Lauren. I hear that suggestion again, though, and someone else will be.'

The girl with the blond hair glares back, but after that she stays quiet.

The girl digs in the pocket of her overalls, retrieves the nub of a pencil. She glances around, searching for something to write on. Her eyes settle on the boxes. She tears the lid from one, presses it against the wall.

The boy with the curly hair looks around, desperate for something to say that will change her mind.

'What about the airlock? We can move the cans; hide in here.'

The girl doesn't look up from what she's doing.

'We'd never all fit. And even if we did, then what? If Peck dumps whatever that stuff is into the vent shafts the whole silo will be contaminated. We couldn't go back inside.'

Footsteps echo up the shaft as the girl she sent to get her clothes returns. There's only one thing left that might convince her. He doesn't want to say it out loud, but he also doesn't want her to leave with the dangerous man, and he's running out of time.

He takes a step closer, tugs at her overalls. His voice drops to a whisper.

'The doctor will take you into the other room.'

As soon as it's out he's sorry. Of course the girl knows this. The pencil stops scratching its way across the card and she closes her eyes as the fear rises up in her. He can smell it now. She takes a deep breath, stepping down hard on it so she can concentrate. The nib of the pencil returns to the paper, resumes its path. When she's done she reaches inside her vest and lifts out the crucifix. She presses it into his hand with the note.

'Give that to Gabe when he gets back.'

The girl she sent to get her things appears among the others, her face flushed. They part quickly, letting her through. The girl takes the backpack she offers, undoes the snaps and starts pulling out what's inside. When she finds her thermals she stops, lets the pack fall to the floor. She takes the gun from the waistband of her overalls and hands it to the boy with the curly hair, then starts to undress.

There's a loud clang as something strikes the blast door and her eyes flick that way. She shouts that she's coming, then goes back to putting on her clothes. When she's done dressing she pulls on her boots, laces them up, stands. She reaches for her parka and steps over to the door.

'Coming out.'

She closes her eyes, bracing herself, and then turns the handle.

The seal breaks with a soft sigh and she pushes the door back, slipping through without a backward glance. It closes behind her. There's a series of clicks as she enters the code and then the grinding of gears as the handle turns to lock it.

He drags the box of cans back over, steps up on it, peers through the slot.

She stands in front of the entrance, her arms held out at her side, while the boy named Kurt checks her for weapons. When he's done he pulls her hands behind her back, loops something around her wrists, ratchets it tight. Then he bends down and does the same to her ankles.

'You planning to carry me all the way back, Randall?'

The dangerous man doesn't answer. He says something into his radio. There's a long pause and then he sees the girl tense. Moments later the huge soldier with the beard and the empty eyes appears, lumbering through the compound. The dangerous man points at the girl. She tries to back up, but her legs are bound. He lifts her as if she weighed nothing, throws her over his shoulder.

The dangerous man unzips his parka and reaches inside. The girl sees what's coming and starts to struggle, but the huge soldier holds her easily. There's a single gunshot and the boy with the dark skin slumps forward into the snow. The other boy stares at his body for a second, then tries to get to his feet. The man adjusts his aim and fires again. He joins the other two in the snow.

'What are you doing? We had a deal.'

The dangerous man returns the pistol to his jacket.

'I said Gilbey wasn't interested in the rest of them. I never said anything about Kane. He doesn't much care for being betrayed.'

*

I FOLLOW A TWO-LANE FEEDER Marv's map says is the old North Carolina highway south from Calvander. My snowshoes start to unravel in a serious way just outside a place name of Dogwood and I lose more time than I would like fixing them. Somewhere far behind the bruised clouds the sun reaches its peak and starts tracking for the horizon, but I'm close now. In a few miles I'll pick up 501, and from there it's not much more than an hour's hike to Fearrington.

I spot the tracks not long after I join the Mount Gilead Church Road: a wide swathe of churned up snow, cutting across the field from the woods that surround the bunker, then turning south. That many prints, at first I think it must be the Juvies. They wouldn't have left Fearrington without me, though, not unless something very bad had happened. And why would they have taken off in that direction if they had? The only places they know are north of here. I stare at the tracks a while, trying to make sense of it. Then I spot a set of prints, off to one side, indentations so deep they could only belong to one person. I feel something in my chest tighten.

I take off for the trees, the pain in my side forgotten. Branches swipe at my parka, but I pay them little mind. I clamber over the security barrier and stagger into the clearing.

It's Tyler I see first, his frozen corpse face down in the snow. Eric's lying on his side a little further on. His head is turned away, the gray powder beneath stained dark with his blood.

I find Angus last. His hands have been cable-tied behind his back, just like the others, but his method of execution was different. I bend closer to examine the bag that's been taped around his neck. He stares back at me through the clear plastic. His eye are wide, the whites bloodshot, the pupils little more than pinpricks. There's something around his mouth that looks like foam. More of it sprays the inside of the bag.

I head for the blast door, fumbling my mittens off to punch in the code. I heave it open, step inside, close it behind me. Someone must have canceled the override because I have to wait for the airlock to cycle. At last the fans die and the wheel on the inner door rotates. I push it open. The corridor beyond is lit, but the bulkhead lamps are dimmed and I don't hear the generator, which means they're running off the batteries. A backpack I recognize as Mags' lies on its side. The snaps are undone; items of her clothing lie strewn across the floor.

I hurry through the showers and out onto the stair. I make my way down the concrete shaft, taking the steps two at a time.

The Juvies are gathered in the mess. They sit around the tables, but no one's talking. Some have their heads in their hands, others stare down at their boots. A few glance up as I step off the gangway, but most keep their eyes down, unwilling to look at me. I seek out Lauren, ask her where Mags is. For a moment she meets my gaze, then she looks away again without saying anything.

I return to the stair. I find Jake by himself in the farms, tightening the bolts on one of his growing benches. I call across to him from the gangway.

'Where is she?'

He shakes his head, but doesn't look up from what he's doing.

'I couldn't stop them.'

I hurry past him, down to the plant room, still not wanting to believe it. I climb through the hatch, calling out to Mags as I clamber down the ladder. The kid's waiting for me on the landing below.

'Is she down there?'

But all he says is he's sorry.

He hands me something, wrapped in a scrap of card. It's the crucifix she wore. I study it for a moment then turn the card over, read the message she's left.

*

I PUSH THE BLAST DOOR OPEN and stagger out, pulling my goggles down as I go. I grab a pair of snowshoes from the pile by the entrance. I stare at Angus's corpse as I adjust the bindings to my boots. The wind's drifting gray flakes over his body, already starting to cover him up.

I had a hand in it, what happened to him. It was me who sent him off after Peck, him and Hamish. And now he's been returned; a reminder from Kane to the rest of us: the price of betrayal. Tyler and Eric lie slumped forward in the snow next to him, bearers of the same message.

I sling Mags' pack onto my back. There's little heft to it, but it has everything I'll need. Behind me I hear Jake shout something, but whatever he says is lost to the wind. I set off across the compound, heading for the gate. He catches up to me at the security barrier, grabs my shoulder.

'Are you going after them?'

I shake my head. That would be pointless.

'Then what?'

I can't bring myself to say it out loud. Instead I tell him to follow me.

I turn and throw my leg over the barrier, dropping into the churned up powder on the other side. I hear him scrambling over behind me. I follow the trail for a dozen paces and then push my way in among the gnarled, blackened trunks. The branches claw at my parka but I stagger on, snowshoes crunching through the drifts until at last I reach it. Jake steps into the small clearing seconds after me. He stops and stares at the tins that litter the ground.

'What's this?'

I cross to the far side of the clearing, drop to my knees. I tell him about the cans while I dig. If he has thoughts about why I chose to hide the truth of it from them he keeps them to himself.

My fingers hit something hard. I scoop the snow away in handfuls, revealing a familiar olive drab container. I work my way quickly around the edges. When the lid is clear I sit back on my heels. Behind me Jake leans a little closer.

Sweat prickles the skin between my shoulder blades as I pop the catches. The case hasn't been opened since we fled Eden and the lid is snug; I hear the contents shift inside as I try and lever it open. I hesitate. What if something inside has broken? But that concern seems trivial now, absurd.

There's a soft sigh as the seal gives. I lift the lid. The inside's lined with a layer of charcoal foam, molded in an egg-crate pattern. Beneath, sheets of the same dark material, square cutaway sections accommodating the trays I took from the cabinets in Eden's armory. I examine the neat rows, each vial standing to attention in its individual slot. None of them seem damaged.

I pull off my mittens. The cold bites but I hardly notice. I reach inside for one of the tubes. Behind me I hear Jake take a step backwards.

'Gabe! What are you doing?'

My hand shakes as I lift out the delicate vial, clinking the glass against the hard plastic of the tray. I hold it up, examining it in the ashen light. The liquid inside shifts sluggishly against the glass.

I tell him what I mean to do. Just hearing the words out loud is enough to make my blood run cold. I realize how scared I am; how much I don't want to do this.

I stare down at the vials, lined up neat in their trays. I reach down, lift another one out, hold it up to him. An unspoken plea.

*If there were two of us.*

He stares at it for a moment and then takes a step backwards. His eyes drop to the ground and he shakes his head.

'I…I can't.'

I slip the vials into my pocket.

'Alright.'

I close the lid, snap the catches.

'You were right, Jake; coming here was a mistake. I thought I could put it right, but it's on you now.'

I reach inside my parka, pull out Marv's map, hand it to him.

'You need to get the Juvies back to Mount Weather.'

He takes it from me, studies the cover for a moment, then slips it into his pocket. As we make our way back I explain what he needs to do with the rations, how to seal the cans that can be saved, the route he needs to take to avoid Durham. I talk quickly because there's not much time. When we reach the trail I turn to leave but he calls after me.

'Gabe, I'm sorry, for giving you a hard time, about everything. About Mags. It's just…she's…I mean, I always thought…'

'I know.'

'But when they came for her I couldn't do anything either.'

'It's alright, Jake, really. I have to go.'

I set off through the woods, the only sound my breathing and the crunch of my snowshoes. The trees end and I strike out across open fields, following the tracks Peck and the others have cut through the snow. When I reach the junction where the Mount Gilead Church Road runs into 501 I stop. Their tracks swing south, and for a long moment I just stare after them.

I wasn't to come after her; that's what her note had said. It would do no good.

I can't argue with that. Peck, Kurt, Scudder, the Guardians, Jax; there's just too many of them. All I have is an old pistol I can't shoot worth a damn and a handful of bullets.

I have no hope of beating them.

Not like this.

I reach into my pocket for one of the vials. But as I unscrew the cap I feel my resolve start to slip away.

The voice inside my head is pleading with me now. It shows me image after image, of things I have seen in the dark places, of creatures once-human, now pale and bent and spider-thin, their minds lost to whatever bloodlust or rage now consumes them.

Before I can lose my nerve I lift the vial to my lips, tilt my head back and drink what's inside. The taste is a shock: like nothing I have ever experienced before. Bitter, metallic, like how it might taste if you melted down aluminum foil, only a thousand, thousand times worse. I drop to my knees, my stomach already heaving. I cover my mouth with my hand and swallow hard to stop myself throwing it right back up.

I wait until the urge has passed, then look up to the skies. I reckon I have at best three hours of daylight left. There's a Walmart just this side of Dogwood; I passed it on my way down. If I hustle I reckon I can make it by nightfall. I don't have a second to waste; the clock's ticking now.

When I told Jake my plan he looked at me like I'd lost my mind.

But I'm not crazy.

Not yet.

I reckon I have three days before that happens.

*

I MAKE IT TO THE WALMART not long after dark. The door's already busted open. I hurry inside and dump the firewood I gathered behind the checkouts.

My side still aches from where I belly-flopped onto the freight train, but it's not the only place now. The muscles in my back and legs are getting in on the act, too; they feel all sprung out of joint, strained and achy. I tell myself it's from the hike, but there's a headache brewing just behind my eyes that says otherwise, and it seems like it means business. I resist the urge to pull the dog tags from around my neck to check them. There'll be nothing to see yet; this is only the first day.

I don't much feel like eating, but I'll need my strength for what's to come, so I get a fire going and break out one of the MREs I took from the stores before I left Fearrington. While the chemical heater's doing its work I walk the aisles looking for something to dull the pain. But there's nothing; the shelves have been stripped bare. I wish I'd thought to bring some Tylenol with me, but then I remember my first aid kit's still with my pack, in a junkyard south side of Durham.

I head back to the fire and wait for my dinner. When the carton stops hissing I tear open the pouch and poke around at the contents, but I don't manage to finish more than a few mouthfuls. I set it to one side, thinking maybe I'll feel like it in the morning, then I climb inside my sleeping bag. The branches I managed to gather on the way up were black and moldering, and once the Sternos I use to get them lighting are spent they do little more than smoke up the place. I shuffle as close as I can regardless, but they provide little comfort.

It's only been a few hours, but already I feel it coming. I thought I'd have longer. I wonder if I should have waited another day to take the virus. There was never time for that, though. Even if he takes the long way around to avoid the mountains Peck'll be back at The Greenbrier in a week, no more.

I can't let him get there before me.

The fever sets in not long after I take to my sleeping bag. It rises in ominous waves that break and crash against my body, growing larger with each set. I know this is just the beginning, but already I feel worse that I ever thought possible. One minute I'm shivering, long shuddering spasms running up and down my spine, rattling my teeth together. The next I'm burning up, my back and legs drenched with sweat; heavy, salty beads of it roll from my scalp, into my eyes and mouth. And through it all, a jack-hammer of a headache that no amount of Tylenol could hope to tame.

Sometime in the early hours the fever breaks, and the chills settle in for the long haul. I drag my parka over the top of the sleeping bags and throw more Sternos on the fire, but it does little good. My bones ache with the cold, like someone's hollowed them out and packed the space there with ice. My hands are the worst. I try rubbing them together, but with the latex gloves I've taken to wearing it's hard to get the friction.

Exhaustion finally overcomes me and I drift off, but it's thin, sketchy dreams that haunt my sleep. Some are familiar: of dark, endless tunnels and faceless things, long and bent and spider-thin, that stalk me through them, a shrill voice I haven't heard in a long time, urging me to run faster.

Others are new.

In one a girl with pink hair shakes me awake, but when she sees what I've done her eyes go wide and she staggers backwards, disappearing into the night. That dream seems more real than the rest, but later when I check I can find no evidence she was ever there.

When I wake the following morning the fire's died and it's bitter cold. My thermals are drenched and for a while I just lie there, shivering, barely able to contemplate getting out of my sleeping bag. I feel hammered hollow. My head aches like someone's trying to drive a spike into the space behind my eyes; my muscles feel like they've been strung with razor wire. Not even a day has passed since I drank what was in the vial. How could Marv have lasted the hike to Mount Weather? It suddenly occurs to me I may have miscalculated. I assumed Marv got the same dose I took, but the truth of it is I have no idea how much of the virus Peck gave him. And it was put in his respirator, not swallowed straight like I took mine.

The realization jars me into action. I might not have three days, or anything like it. I clamber out of the sleeping bag and start gathering up my things. Last night's food pouch lies next to the blackened remains of the fire, but I don't even look at it. As soon as I'm packed up I head outside and rejoin the road.

I make my way north through the city, my head down, my arms held tight to my sides, shivering inside my parka. I stumble into the drifts; struggling to lift my snowshoes high enough to clear even the shallowest of them. After what seems like hours I finally come to the *U-Haul*, where Goldie surprised me with the gun. The low cinder block that once served as the office sits on the far side of the lot. The door's still open; it swings back and forth on its hinges in the wind. I stagger up onto the overpass and continue on, leaving Durham behind me.

By the time I reach the stretch of highway I think I remember the day's already dying. I trudge along it, searching for the turnoff. There's no sign, and I have to backtrack a couple of times before I find it. The road narrows to little more than a track, then starts to incline. Each step now is a Herculean effort.

When I finally reach the ridgeline I rest for a dozen breaths, my hands on my knees. My lungs burn, my sides pumps like a bellows. Inside my parka my thermals are soaked with sweat; it runs freely between my shoulders, down my back and thighs. I shuck off Mags' backpack, fumbling for the snaps. My fingers sing out in protest, like someone's packed the space between my joints with ground glass. I take out what I need and cover the canvas over with snow. Then I pick myself up and stumble down into the valley. The gray fortress grows steadily closer, until finally its stone walls are looming over me. I stagger up to the gate and pound my fist on the rusting iron. For a long time there's nothing, and then the sound of movement behind and the hatch slides back.

A pair of eyes appear at the slot. It takes a moment for Goldie to recognize me, and then his mouth drops open and for a moment he's at a loss for words. I don't care to let him get started. I hold up the Ziploc bag with the handful of books Mags brought with her from Mount Weather.

'I have something…for Mr. Finch. Tell him…it's important…tell him he needs to come out and see me.'

I push the bag through the slot before he has a chance to object. There's a pause and then the hatch snaps shut. A wave of exhaustion hits me, threatening to drag me under. I put my hand out to the wall for support, but it's not where I expect it to be and I end up slumping into the snow. My head falls between my knees and for a long time I just sit there, sucking in air in long, rasping gasps.

At last from somewhere above my head there's the clang of bolts being drawn back. I stagger to my feet just as the smaller door set into the gate creaks inward. Goldie beckons me forward and I stumble over the threshold into the holding pen. I glance over at the guard booth. The small man Finch had called Culpeper (*no, that's not right; Culver*) watches me closely from his seat behind the pock-marked glass.

Goldie tells me to wait, then he hurries off into the yard. I stand there for what seems like an eternity, shivering in the cold. I'm not sure how long I can trust my legs to hold me upright. It feels like they could give out again at any moment.

At last the gate buzzes and I look up, just as Tully steps through. He stands to one side, holding it open. Moments later Finch appears in a heavy overcoat, the collar trimmed with fur, a thick scarf wrapped around his neck. The hands that grasp the cane are clad in soft leather. I have the same thought I had when I first saw him: that he is other, exotic, not of this place.

Knox steps into the pen after him, holding the Ziploc bag with Mags' books. Behind him I can see other figures making their way across from the main building. They gather around the holding pen and take to staring at me through the wire.

Finch leans forward.

'Gabriel. What a pleasant surprise. I really hadn't expected to see you back here so soon.' He looks me up and down, slowly. 'But I must say you do not look the better for our time apart. You have something of a desperate air to you.'

'I brought you a present, Mr. Finch.'

'Yes. I received your books. Very thoughtful, very thoughtful indeed. It was quite unwise for you to deliver them in person, however. But I like you, Gabriel, I really do. And so I will accept your gift, and give you something in return, as good manners dictate. A piece of advice. One you have no doubt already received, but for reasons I cannot quite fathom, have chosen to ignore. Best you leave here, right now, this very instant. And never return. Lest you wish to find yourself in Mr. Blatch's cook pot, like our friend the recently departed Mr. MacIntyre.'

I shake my head.

'The present's not the books, Mr. Finch. That was just to get you to come out here. The present's me.'

I reach in my pocket. A pistol appears in Knox's hand and he steps forward, but Finch waves him back. My fingers close around the second vial of the virus I brought with me from Fearrington. It's sealed up in a zippy, just like the books. I pull it out slowly, hold it out in front of me.

Tully steps forward and takes it from me. He hands it up to Finch, who examines it for a long moment.

'Now where did you come by this?'

'I've infected myself with one just like it.'

There's a rustle of uneasy murmurs and the inmates who have been gathering on the other side of the wire shift back, like they may not trust the protection the holding pen offers. Finch just stares at me, his expression implacable. I can see I have his attention now, though, and that's good. My plan depends on it. It sends a chill through me, all the same, one that has little to do with the approaching night, or whatever is coursing through my veins. The curiosity of a man like Finch is not something to be wished for lightly. It's the kind of thing that makes a snake slip its head into a bird's nest; that will lure the fox into the henhouse.

'And tell me, Gabriel, why would you have done something as foolhardy as that?'

For starters, in case you had thoughts of adding me to the cook pot, like you did Mac. I don't say that out loud, however; Finch might take it as rude. Besides, there's no need. He'll already have worked that bit out for himself.

'Somebody has taken something from me, Mr. Finch. Something important; more important than all the rest of it. And I mean to have her back. But to do that I need your help.'

He looks at me a moment longer then snaps his fingers. There's a commotion behind him and I see a chair being passed forward. Goldie hurries to the gate to collect it. He makes sure it's settled in the snow, then he wipes the seat with the cuff of his jacket. Finch orders another for me and he fetches that too. My chair doesn't get a wipe-down and I notice he steps back smartly as soon as it's been delivered. I slump into it, grateful that I no longer have to stand. Two of the other prisoners roll an old oil drum into the pen. They busy themselves building a fire inside it while Finch goes back to studying the vial. The prison's walls offer some shelter against the wind, but the air's turning frigid nonetheless. I get up to drag my chair closer, but Knox steps forward and waves me back with the pistol. I sit back down and clutch my arms to my sides against the cold.

When the flames are licking up over the rim Finch turns his gaze back to me.

'Well then, you must tell me what you need, Gabriel. But I warn you, this time you will have to be more honest than on our last encounter. You must tell me absolutely everything.' He holds a finger up. 'If you lie to me, if you leave out so much as the smallest detail, I'll know, and it won't go well for you. Do you believe that?'

I nod, because I do.

'Good.'

He leans back, crosses one leg primly over the other.

'You may begin.'

*

DUSK SETTLES OVER THE YARD. On the other side of the wire more fires are lit.

I tell them everything. The Last Day, the White House, how Kane brought us to Eden. The ten years we spent there, our escape to Mount Weather. How Mags and I went looking for another home for the Juvies and instead found Dr. Gilbey and the soldiers. I describe our escape from The Greenbrier, first to Eden and then to Mount Weather, our journey south to Fearrington. How Peck found us there.

One by one the fires burn down. More wood is brought out, dumped into the drums, sending showers of sparks swirling up into the darkness. I talk till there's little strength left in my voice, and it feels like I'm croaking out whispers. The prisoners shuffle closer to the mesh, anxious not to miss the details of my story.

I leave out nothing, just as Finch warned me. A low murmur rumbles around the outside of the pen as I tell of my plan to trade them for the medicine I thought I needed for Mags, but Finch holds up a hand and it dies just as quick.

When I've divulged the last detail I lay out what I mean to do and the things I need from him to get it done. I tell him what I'm offering in return. When I'm finished he remains quiet for a long moment, the light from the fire playing across his glasses.

'That is indeed an interesting proposition, Gabriel. You have certainly given me a lot to consider. You must let me sleep on it.'

I want to remind him not to take too long, but to a man like Finch that might appear impolite, so I hold my tongue. I've already told him what happened to Marv, and I was very specific about how little time that took.

'But what to do with you in the meantime?' He looks around the holding pen. 'I can't just leave you here. And I'm afraid I can't offer you one of the cells either. There is simply far too much metal for someone in your condition.'

I glance behind me.

'It's alright, Mr. Finch. There's a farmhouse, up on the ridge. I can spend the night there, come back at first light.'

He shakes his head, offering me an apologetic smile.

'I'm afraid I can't have you just roaming around outside, either, Gabriel. You seem lucid right now, but from what you've told me the progress of the virus can be somewhat…unpredictable. Our friend in the basement seemed to have little difficulty scaling our walls, and he is a rather fragile specimen next to you.'

He presses one gloved finger to his lips, as though considering the dilemma, then his eyes brighten.

'Ah, I think I have it.' He turns his head. 'Mr. Goldie.'

Goldie appears at his shoulder.

'Yes boss.'

'Do you think you and a couple of the men could open up the hotbox for me?'

Torches are lit from the fire pits; the inmates set to work with shovels. Finch watches their progress for a while and then gestures for the Ziploc bag with the books I've brought him. He opens one and starts flicking through it. I hunch forward in the chair, desperate for whatever I can get of the fire's warmth. Tully and Knox keep their pistols trained on me the whole time. I can't see how it's necessary; I'm not sure I have it in me to stand, let alone do them harm.

When enough snow has been cleared Goldie hurries over to fetch us. Finch hands the book back to Knox and retrieves his cane while Goldie holds the gate open for him. Tully waves me up with the gun.

As I get to my feet the pain in my head flares; it feels like my skull might explode with it. My vision narrows and for a moment I'm unsure if my legs will bear my weight. I get no offer of assistance from either of Finch's minders. The hulking inmates keep their distance, unwilling to come any closer.

I stumble across the yard to where the prisoners have gathered. They have the look of a crowd that's gathered for a lynching, or to see a heretic get burned. They part before me, those with torches holding them out as though to ward off the evil I have brought into their midst. I lower my head as I pass among them. It hurts to look directly at the flames now.

Finch stands to one side of a newly excavated hole. I shuffle up to the edge and peer down at the hotbox. There's little more to it than a rectangle cut into the frozen dirt, no wider than a grave, and not quite as long. A wooden trapdoor sits back against the snow. The timber is rough, gapped, but the hinges and bolt look sturdy. Tully gestures with the pistol for me to get in. I glance over at Finch, but he just spreads his hands in an expression of apology.

'I am sorry, Gabriel. I'm afraid it's the best I can offer.'

I ease myself to the ground, sit on the edge and lower myself down. It's not quite deep enough for my height; I have to hunker low as they close the door until all that remains of the light from their torches is what seeps through the gaps in the timber, barely enough to let in the air a man might need to breath.

The wood creaks as someone steps on it to slide the bolt into place, and then one by one the prisoners leave for their cells, taking what remains of the light with them.

I press my hands to the sides in the darkness. I'm glad there's little more than the memory of Claus left inside me. I don't think he would have cared much for this.

I find if I scrunch myself up I can just about sit, and so I settle to the bottom, my back flat to the rough planks behind me, knees pressed to my chest. Finch said the hotbox had been put there to punish inmates, back when Starkly was first built. Its location was chosen with that purpose in mind: slap bang in the middle of the yard, where for most of the day not even the prison's high stone walls would have offered any respite from the Carolina sun. A man left in here for a day would literally bake to death, he said. Right now that doesn't sound so bad.

I close my eyes and press my mittens to my temples, trying to drive out the pain in my head. I think about where Mags might be tonight. The note she left me is in the inside pocket of my parka, but I don't need to take it out. I've read it over in my head so many times I know every word by heart.

*Gabe*

*Peck is here, with Kurt and the other Guardians. He just killed Angus, right in front of me. Whatever it was he used, it was quick; there was nothing I could do to stop it. Peck said they had canisters of it. They're going to dump it into the vents unless I go with them. Gilbey thinks I'm the key to the cure she's been working on, so Kane's done a deal with her: if Peck brings me back she'll let him go.*

*I'm not going to let that happen. Truck told me a little of what Gilbey does in that other room, when I was in the cage. I won't be something for her to experiment on.*

*When you read this you might think of coming for me, but you need to be smart now. There's too many of them. And there's something else. I think you've begun to suspect, but you can't know the extent of it. I'm not sure I know it myself. I'm not the person I was before. I can do things now. So you see, I stand a better chance by myself.*

*Besides, you have another job, you and Jake. Once I get free Peck will come back; he has no other choice. You can't still be in Fearrington when that happens. You need to get the Juvies somewhere else, somewhere safe.*

*I know you can do it.*

*M*

I want to believe it, that she'll find a way to escape before they get her back to The Greenbrier. But that's not the way it's going to go. Those were Jax's prints I saw; there was no mistaking them. They mean to bind her tight, like they would a fury, carry her back.

The tracks were headed south, but that road curves west soon after. My guess is they'll follow it as far as Greenboro. From there they can pick up

220 and then it's a straight shot all the way up to I-64. They might be on it already; it's been two days since Peck arrived at Fearrington. He'll push hard to get back, to set Kane free. He should be able to make good time, too. It's mostly flat country, at least until they're past Blacksburg. Carrying Mags won't slow them down. I doubt Jax will even notice her weight.

I start to feel the panic rise. I need to get there before them; if I let them take her back inside it's over. I take a deep breath, push it back down. Finch said he needed to sleep on it, but he'll go for it, I know he will. I saw the look on his face when I told him about Mags and Johnny, and what the scanner did for them. I figure by sometime tomorrow I can be on my way again. Peck has a head start on me, but Starkly's almost a day closer to The Greenbrier than Fearrington. I saw how fast Mags was, after. Whatever time I've lost coming here I can make it up on the road.

*Assuming you survive what comes before?*

A fit of shivering hits me, rattling my teeth together. When it finally subsides the voice is quiet again.

I can't let myself dwell on that. What it might be like. Whether it will even work.

I tell myself it just has to.

*

HE WAITS UNTIL THE REST OF THEM HAVE GONE THROUGH, then steps into the airlock. The outer door is open; he can see the snow beyond, littered with cans. He holds his breath and hurries out, picking his way among them. The wind carries most of the smell away, but it is still pretty bad. He finds a spot away from the others and sits to strap on his snowshoes, keeping his head down. The sky is gray, brooding, but after the darkness of the plant room it seems impossibly bright.

The girl with the blond hair pulls up her hood, hoists her pack onto her back and starts making her way towards the gate. The three bodies that lie in front of the entrance are mostly covered over now, only their outlines visible. She takes a wide path around them all the same. One by one the others follow until there's only him and the boy with the curly hair left. The boy heaves the blast door closed and turns the handle to lock it. He tightens the bindings on his snowshoes and then they both set off through the clearing after the rest of them.

At the guard shack they stop, waiting for those ahead to climb over the barrier. Nobody speaks; there's only the crunch of snow as one by one they shuck off their packs and clamber over. When it's his turn the boy with the curly hair reaches down for him. The others are already shuffling into the woods so he lets himself be picked up. The boy climbs over after him, then tells him to wait. He disappears in among the blackened trunks and when he returns he's holding the green plastic case the tall boy carried with him on the way down. They set off into the woods. Before long the trees end and they make their way out into open fields. The others are strung out in a raggedy line ahead of them, lifting their snowshoes high as they trudge through the deeper powder.

When she reaches the road the girl with the blond hair waits for them to catch up. The others gather around, hands gripping the straps of their packs tight as they lean into them, their breath smoking in the cold. The boy with the curly hair stops, sets the container down. He pushes his goggles onto his forehead, turns his gaze south. There's little to see that way; the wind has already scrubbed the snow of the tracks they made. He bends down, his fingers tracing the crusted outline of what might once have been a snowshoe print.

'They need our help.'

The boy's voice is low, barely a whisper, as if he's talking to himself. He shuffles a little closer.

'Do you have a plan?'

A troubled look crosses the boy's face. He shakes his head.

'Plans were more Gabe's thing.'

He says nothing for a while.

'Perhaps if we follow them something will come to us.'

The boy's eyes don't leave the tracks, but he nods his head, like he's reached a decision. He calls the girl over. The others start shuffling their snowshoes around, anxious to know what's happening.

'Lauren, I'm going after Peck. We can't leave Gabe to do this by himself.'

She lifts her goggles onto her forehead and stares at him in disbelief.

'You're crazy, Jake. You know what he meant to do. You can't help him now, either of them. You'll just get yourself killed as well.'

The boy reaches into his pocket, like he hasn't heard. He pulls out a map, holds it out to her.

'I marked the route Gabe told me to take. It shouldn't be hard to follow; mostly it's the way we came down. Can you get them back?'

The girl takes the map, opens it out. She pretends to study it, but her eyes are elsewhere. She points down.

'And what about him?'

The boy with the curly hair looks undecided.

'I don't…'

He doesn't wait for him to finish whatever he was about to say. He tells him he'll need him. He's the only one who's been there. Inside. He knows it's sort of a lie, even as he says it. He doesn't remember much from that place, mostly just the cage. But as frightened as he is of going back, he is certain he does not wish to stay with the others.

The boy stays quiet for a long moment, considering. Eventually he reaches a decision.

'I'm taking him with me, Lauren.'

The girl folds up the map, slips it inside her parka. She says *Alright.* It's hard to tell behind the mask she wears, but he thinks she might be smiling.

*

I HUDDLE AT THE BOTTOM OF THE PIT, my knees tucked up to my chest, shivering like a beaten dog. It doesn't seem like sleep will ever come, but at some point I must drift off.

I'm not sure how long I'm out, only that when I wake it's still dark outside. The wind's picked up again. It blows ashen flakes through the gaps in the timber that settle on my parka. I slide off one of my mittens and reach inside my thermals for the dog tags. I poke my finger through the slit in the liner (*I wonder when that happened. I keep my gear pretty good*) feeling for any changes in the metal. But the only imperfections I can feel are ones I think I recognize.

I pull the mitten back on and just sit there, counting out the seconds as they tick into minutes and those slowly become hours. The cracks in the trapdoor grow visible again, as somewhere off to the east the first lifeless grays of dawn break over the horizon.

It won't be long now. I pull my hood back, making an effort to stop my teeth from chattering so that I'll be able to hear whoever Fitch sends to let me out. But there's nothing other than the wind. I press my back to the plank sides. The cold has crept into my muscles, stiffening them; they cry out in protest as I shuffle myself upwards. I stay like that for a little while, one ear pressed to the timber, just listening. It's not long until the muscles in my legs are trembling, however. I slump back down to the bottom of the box before they give out.

An hour passes, two. Far above the clouds the sun continues its slow pass over Starkly's stone walls, its crumbling watchtowers. The gaps between the planks are narrow, but somehow inside the hotbox it gets uncomfortably bright. I shuffle my head as far back into the parka's hood as I can and close my eyes.

Finch said he needed to sleep on it, but it's been light for hours now. I don't understand. Has something caused him to change his mind? Maybe he thinks it's too dangerous to let me into the prison. There are things he could do, to make it safer. I try to remember whether I made that clear, last night, in the holding pen. But when I search for the details of what I told him they're muddled, fragmented, like a conversation held years before and not revisited since.

I feel an uneasiness growing inside me.

That was only a few hours ago.

*Mags had forgotten all about Watership Down.*

*The kid can't remember a thing from before he got infected.*

I tell myself it was because I was sick, exhausted, but what the voice said has me worried. I close my eyes, trying to ignore the pounding in my head while I call up the map Marv gave me. I can picture it. Blue and red. It had a logo across the front. But when I try and picture it I can't remember what it said. *Something Oil. Shell*? There were fourteen facilities in total; seven on the map itself, another seven listed in his neat hand at the bottom. Thirteen codes between them; we never had one for Eden, I'm sure of it. But when I try and list them off I manage no better than ten. The codes are wrong, too. I used to be able to just close my eyes and they'd appear, but now the letters and numbers are fuzzy, indistinct, and when I read them out it seems like parts are jumbled up.

All winter I studied that map. I knew it like the back of my hand.

What else might be slipping away?

The Juvies. I list their names, girls first, then boys.

Mags, Ruth, Angela, Beth, Fran, Amy, Jen, Beverley, Lucy, Stephanie, Alice. Jake, Tyler, Eric, Kyle, Michael, Ryan, Carl, Nate, Leonard, Kali.

That's twenty-one. Including me, twenty-two.

Somehow that doesn't seem right. But when I run through the names again the number doesn't increase.

There were thirty of us in Miss Kimble's class.

Six of the Guardians stayed behind when we fled Eden. Kurt, Angus, Hamish, Zack, Jason, Seth.

Twenty-four.

There was a girl that died. I can picture her face. She was pretty; she made me nervous. She asked me to get her something once, from the outside. Her name is on the tip of my tongue but I can't remember. I'm almost positive it was Lauren, but it might have been Laura.

Twenty-four less Lauren would leave twenty-three. Twenty-three sounds right. I'm almost positive that's how many we were over the winter.

So who am I missing?

I go back over the names again, but no matter how many times I list them out the count remains at twenty-two.

I've known each of the Juvies for almost as long as I can remember. How can I have forgotten one of them? But the answer is obvious; I don't need the voice to tell me. The thought of it suddenly fills me with dread, a terror I have not felt since Claus. I need to get out of here, before I lose anything else to whatever is coursing through my veins.

I struggle to my feet, my knees popping like dud firecrackers. I brace my shoulder against the trapdoor and push for all I'm worth. The old timber creaks, but the hinges and bolt are stout, designed to resist attempts like this. I slam my shoulder into the wood, over and over, until at last a coughing fit takes me and I have to stop.

I slide back down to the bottom of the box and pull my parka tight around me. I start to make lists of everything I remember. Not just the Juvies, or what was written on Marv's map, but everyone and everything I have ever known. Books I have read, the characters in each. Articles I found about the virus. Places I have been, before the Last Day, and since. Things I would carry in my scavenging kit. Flavors of MRE. I recite each out loud, one item after the other. When I get to the end of a list I come up with another. When I can think of no more things to list I go back to the first one and start over.

The light coming through the trapdoor grows steadily brighter. I shrink back inside my hood, pull the drawstrings tight and continue on, stopping only to holler at Finch from the bottom of the hotbox. But the rest of that day I don't hear from him.

Dusk settles slowly over the yard. Little by little the pain behind my eyes abates, enough that I might even sleep. I don't allow it; I'm afraid of what I might lose to the darkness if I let it take me again. So instead I sit there, rocking backwards and forwards as I work my way through my lists.

As the last of the light slips from the sky I shuffle my way up to the trap door and call out to Finch, but a coughing fit forces me back down before I can get very far into it. I continue hacking until I can taste the blood in my throat and when I slump back down it feels like something inside me has broken.

I reach for the dog tags, probing the slivers of pressed metal with my fingers. They feel rough now, grainy. We're coming to the end of the third day since I infected myself. Whether Finch ever intended to let me out of this box, soon it won't matter. Because the same thing that's eating away at the tags is gnawing away at me now, too, hollowing me out from the inside. I can feel it, stripping away what's there so it can rebuild me, rewire me, make me the way it wants me to be. Not just flesh and bone, muscle and sinew, but the important stuff, the things I know, the memories I have.

The things that make me who I am.

*

I WAKE TO A LOUD THUD as someone jumps down onto the trapdoor. I open my eyes to scorching brightness. I squeeze them shut again, yank my hood forward.

*Where am I?*

I reach a hand out uncertainly. Rough planks beneath me, on all sides.

A shuffling noise from above and I feel flakes drifting down through the gaps in the timber. The muscles along my jaw ache, like I've been grinding my teeth, and when I run my tongue along the roof of my mouth there are ulcers there. I cough painfully, spitting to clear the blood from my throat.

There's the scratch of bolts being drawn and then whoever is up there steps away again. I remember where I am just as the door swings up and a flood of searing white light fills the box. I raise my arms above my head, trying to get away from it. Strong hands reach down, grab me. From somewhere behind them I hear a voice I think I recognize.

'Easy now. Finch said we was to be gentle with him.'

The voice giggles, like this might be funny.

My hood slips back as I'm dragged from the hotbox. I screw my eyes tight against the blinding glare, but not before I glimpse a man with golden teeth. The grin he's wearing dissolves; his eyes go wide as he sees my face.

Then I'm being hauled across the yard. I try to straighten my legs, but they've seized and won't unbind; I can manage only the small, mewling steps of a newborn, unaccustomed to the business of walking. I give up, allow myself to be carried. The toes of my boots drag through the snow, leaving shallow furrows in the gray powder. I let my head hang down. The parka's hood falls forward, mercifully returning me to the shadow of its cowl.

We pass through a door and beneath me snow gives way to stone. It feels no warmer inside, or maybe I have stopped noticing the cold, but at least I'm out of the merciless light. I'm dragged through the cellblock, into a dark passageway, past kitchens and laundry. I lift my head a fraction. The smells are stronger here, a complicated raft of odors. Concrete replaces stone and the corridor narrows, forcing whoever is carrying me to press closer. Their smell is tight-packed, overpowering; a pungent blend of breath and sweat and clothes long unwashed.

And something else, underneath all of those things.

I lift my head a fraction, wrinkling my nose at it. A sweet, coppery aroma fills my nostrils and I feel something flicker inside me. Ahead the man with the gold teeth continues to jabber away, but I can barely pay attention to what he's saying. I am suddenly aware that I have not eaten in days. An image flashes before my eyes, of an earlier visit to this place. The thing I had glimpsed, back in the shadows, dangling from an old hook, as I had passed the kitchens.

And for a second something flares, writhes inside me, a compulsion so fierce, so complete, that it might bend my very bones if I do not obey. Inside the hood my jaw clamps shut and the muscles there clench in a long, shuddering spasm.

The men carrying me are breathing hard. They walk with the quick, shuffling steps of those hefting a difficult load; every now and then I hear one or other of them grunt with the effort. My weight's not enough to trouble men like that. I tilt my head to one side, slowly, so they don't notice, and then I see why: they hold me awkwardly between them, out at arm's length, like I'm a hundred and fifty pounds of sweating nitro on a bumpy road.

I let my head fall back down. Inside my mittens my fingers curl into claws.

They are right to fear me.

I am weak now, and they are strong.

But soon that will change.

We pass through a metal gate. To one side a guard booth, the glass reinforced with safety wire. Another corridor. The bars of cell doors, each ajar.

I'm dragged into a large, candlelit room. Thick drapes line one wall, as though we are on a stage. In the center on a raised plinth there's a heavy wooden chair, almost like a throne. I don't think I've been in this room before, but the chair is familiar.

Next to it a small man, kneeling by an old diesel generator, tools scattered around him. My boot catches on a thick rubber cable that snakes across the dusty floor and then I'm being hauled up onto the platform, lowered into the seat. I'm stripped of my parka. Thick leather cuffs fold themselves over my forearms.

The men who have been carrying me each take a side. They work quickly. Fingers cased in thick rubber hold my head to the back of the chair. The one with the beard leans in and there's that smell again, slick in the back of my throat, so strong I can almost taste it. He reaches under my arms, pulls a thick strap across my chest, feeds the end through a heavy buckle.

From behind me I hear a *tut-tut* at the big man's handiwork.

'I think that will need to be a little more secure Mr. Knox'.

A pause and the one called Knox steps forward again. My spine is pressed into the back of the chair and I feel the air squeezed from my lungs as he pulls it tight. He steps away smartly, but the smell of him lingers.

I lift my head. A small, neat man stands by the wall, clutching something to his chest.

Him I know.

Finch.

He hobbles forward.

'You must forgive the delay, Gabriel. Rest assured, Mr. Culver here has been working around the clock since we last spoke.'

He holds up the thin volume, offering me a better look. The pages are dog-eared, tattered but I can read what it says on the cover: *North Carolina Department of Corrections*, and underneath, *Modular Electrocution System Operating Manual.*

My boots and socks are being removed. I look down. The top of a large, domed head, glistening with sweat. I feel the leather around my shins being tightened.

Finch leans forward on his cane.

'Yes, Mr. Culver has been quite the wonder; we would have been lost without him. Inverters; capacitors; regulators; I had no idea this could be so complicated. We've had to improvise a little, of course. The chair has not seen use in decades; it was in need of considerable repair. And then there's the matter of the voltage. Too low and I fear this simply may not work; too high and the body will simply combust.'

He splays his fingers, demonstrating that effect, then sets the manual down and pulls on a pair of rubber gloves. He takes my head in his hands, more gently than the other men did. His brow knots with concern.

'I have to say you're not looking very well, Gabriel. I do wish you could have given us more notice, so that we might have been ready for you.'

He turns to the man bent over the generator.

'Mr. Culver, are you almost done? I really think we should proceed without delay.'

He turns back to me, reaches for my neck. The one he called Knox steps forward to restrain me, but Finch sends him away with a flutter of his hand. He grasps the chain there, lifts it gently over my head. He holds the dog tags out, examines them for a moment. As the dull metal catches the light I can see it's pitted and pocked, like something's been eating away at it.

The other man, the one with the beard, holds out a thick garbage bag and Finch drops them in.

He turns around and Knox passes him a set of hair clippers, the kind you work by hand. The metal is cold where he presses it to my scalp. He works his way gently from front to back. The clumps of hair that fall to my lap are shot through with white. When he's done he carefully brushes the last of it away, dropping the clippers into the bag with the dog tags.

Then he reaches above my head for the metal headpiece that hangs there. There's a dull creak as it swings forward on its bracket.

He turns around and points to a bucket on the floor.

'Mr. Tully, if you would be so kind.'

The man with the beard whose name is Tully dips his hand into the bucket and hands him a sponge. He places it on my head and lowers the metal cap. Another strap goes under my chin. He tightens it. Water streams down my face, stinging my eyes. It runs down my neck, inside my thermals.

Finch pulls a handkerchief from pocket of his suit and mops my brow.

'I am sorry, Gabriel.'

Another sponge wets my shin and I feel something cold, metallic, close around my ankle, the hard nub of an electrode pressing into the bone there. Tully sops up the excess water with a rag. When he's done he dumps it into the bucket.

Culver makes some final adjustments to the generator and then hurries up onto the platform clutching a thick rubber cable. More water runs down my forehead, wetting my cheeks, as he attaches it to the headpiece.

Finch steps off the platform.

'Are we ready, Mr. Culver?'

He looks back at me.

'Would you care for a blindfold?'

I shake my head.

Culver returns to the generator, bends over it, grasps something there, pulls. It takes several goes before the motors catches, then it sputters to life and settles into a lumpy idle. He retreats to the far side of the room, like he may not have as much faith in his handiwork as Finch made out. The two large men join him.

Finch steps over to the wall and flicks a switch on a large console. A moment later there's the whir of an exhaust fan somewhere above my head. His hand moves to a large lever. He looks at me for a long moment and then pulls it down. There's a loud bang. A sharp, acrid smell fills the room, like burning metal.

The hair on the back of my neck stands straight up and suddenly every muscle in my body tenses all at once and it feels like I'm on fire. I try to scream, but my jaw has clamped shut and won't open. I can think of nothing save the pain and in that instant I know there may be nothing I would not sacrifice, no one I would not give up, to make it stop.

And then, mercifully, I'm gone, carried off into oblivion on a bolt of white lightning.

*

HE WALKS DOWN THE HALLWAY. The floor is dusty, littered with debris. Once-colorful posters hang from the walls, the edges lifting, curling with damp. Here and there withered pieces of rubber that might once have been balloons dangle from faded ribbons.

The boy with the curly hair said this place was a school, once. When they climbed the steps out front he had shone his flashlight up above the entrance and read the words there out loud, slow, like he was uncertain of them. *Stoneville Elementary*.

They hiked all day, until it got dark and it was too cold for the boy to continue. He lit a fire with branches he had gathered from outside while the boy warmed a couple of the cans with the little blue squares that sting your eyes. The boy wolfed his down, but he had only picked at his before setting it aside. When the boy was done with his own tin he had looked over and asked if he meant to finish it. He was worried the boy might think he was sick, but he only seemed interested in what was left of his ration, so he handed it over. He watched hopefully in case there might be a candy bar in return, but there wasn't. The boy took to his sleeping bag as soon as he was done eating.

The boy is sleeping now. It will be hours before he wakes and they can set off after the girl again. The boy says they are making good progress, but he's not so sure. They have been on the road for two days already, and they have yet to see any sign of the dangerous man. They have a map the boy found in a gas station. He takes it out and studies it whenever they come to a sign. He spells each word, checking them carefully against what's written there, as though he doesn't trust the directions he gives himself. At night he traces the route they have taken with his finger. It has been mostly flat so far and the snow has settled, so he can go quickly. The boy tries to keep up, but he has to wait for him a lot. Tomorrow they are going to cross into another place the boy says is called *Vir-gin-ya*. He asked the boy if that is where the doctor and the soldiers live. The boy said it wasn't, but they are closer.

He wanders into one of the classrooms. In the center of the room rows of tiny desks, facing a large chalkboard. A couple of crudely-drawn pictures still cling to the walls, but for most the tape that held them up has long since failed and they lie scattered across the floor. He makes his way in, pulls back one of the small chairs, takes a seat. A piece of plastic is peeling from the edge of the desk he has chosen. He pulls at it and it lifts easily, revealing the board underneath.

He's not sure what they will do if they ever catch up to the dangerous man. There has been no more talk of that since they left the others. At night the boy takes out the gun the girl gave him. He turns it over in his hands, studying it, but it doesn't look like he knows how to use it.

It is good they are going after the girl, though, even if they don't have a plan yet for what they will do if they find her. The boy explained to him what the tall boy intended to do. He doesn't think that is a very good idea at all.

He sits there for a while, just staring up at the row of letters written across the top of the chalkboard. When the boy studies the road signs they pass the names that are written there are foreign to him, alien. But there is something about the way these letters have been arranged that is familiar, pleasing even. He looks up at them from the desk for a long time.

Eventually he gets up, makes his way out of the classroom. And for a second as he steps back into the hallway the colors return and he hears sounds: laughter; voices; the squeak of sneakers on polished floor. Somewhere in the distance a bell is ringing. At the end of the corridor a woman stands, waving to him. Her lips move and although he can't hear what she is saying he knows she is calling to him. He stares at her for a moment. Her hair is long and brown, except where the sun catches it and it turns gold. Her eyes are dark, smiling. But in spite of all these differences he recognizes her immediately.

He starts to run towards her but in a blink the colors are gone again, replaced with silent shades of gray. He stands in the middle of the empty, trash-strewn hallway and looks around, confused.

Has he been in this place before?

He tries to bring the woman back, but all he can see now is 98, as she was when he knew her, crouched in the cage opposite his: her head shaved, her cheeks hollow, her eyes dark and sunken, except when the doctor would shine the flashlight on her and they would flash silver.

The woman he just saw at the end of the corridor, it was her, though; he is sure of it. She had been calling his name. His real name. He couldn't hear her above the other sounds, so doesn't know yet what it might be.

Only that it isn't Johnny.

*

I COME TO SUDDENLY, like someone's just flicked a switch inside me. The experience is abrupt, jarring, and for a few seconds I just lay there, blinking in the gray half-light, awake but empty, unsure of what I am now, or who I might have been before.

There's a strange taste in my mouth, like metal. A smell, too: charred, sulfurous. I look around. The room I'm in is small. Concrete on three sides, the fourth, bars. The narrow cot I'm lying on takes up most of the floor. At the foot of the bed a toilet, without seat or lid. Above it a steel mirror, bolted to the concrete. Otherwise the walls are bare. Something's wrong, though, not with the room, but…

It takes me a moment to work it out. There's no color, just gritty, ashen tones. Everywhere I look it's the same, just grainy shadows, shades of gray and black.

Is this how I see things now?

A helpful voice inside my head suggests that's the wrong question. It wonders how I'm seeing anything at all. I look around the cell again. The voice has a point. There are no windows. The corridor beyond the bars is dark.

I sit up slowly, noticing for the first time that my ankle is bandaged. There's a sensation there I recognize as pain, but somehow it's distant, unimportant. For a moment another memory – *the creak of a hinge closing; something hard, metallic pressing there* – threatens to break the surface, but then slips under again.

From somewhere outside my cell, the fitful chug of a generator. A different memory shifts, slowly uncoiling itself. But when I reach for it it retreats, just like the first.

I stare down at my ankle again. I wonder if I am injured anywhere else. I roll my shoulders. The smell becomes momentarily stronger. I tilt my head to one side, testing the air, trying to work out where it's coming from. It's heavy, cloying. It clings to my nostrils, so thick and rich it's almost a taste.

The generator grumbles away in the background, its lumpy clatter muted by the concrete between us. I probe for a little while longer and then all of a sudden it hits me.

*A heavy wooden chair. Leather straps, tight across my arms, chest.*

Something bad. I was afraid.

*A metal cap for my head.*

A tumble of memories now, each more vivid than the one before.

*Cold water streaming down my cheeks, the briny taste of it in my mouth.*

*A small man with pale eyes and a cane, his hand on a lever.*

*The hairs on the back of my neck rising on a wave of gooseflesh.*

*A loud bang and an instant of unbearable pain.*

Suddenly I'm standing. It happens so fast I put a hand out to steady myself. But it's unnecessary. There's no dizziness, no disorientation. I stare down at the thin mattress, at the shallow indentation where I was just lying.

What just happened?

I don't remember deciding to get up. I was thinking about it, and the next thing…

I bring the back of my wrist to my nose.

I know what the smell is, now.

I hold out my hand, flex my fingers.

Have you ever smelled burning flesh?

Have you smelled your own?

It's not just the smell, though; I realize I can feel every singed hair, every inch of bruised, charred skin. My mind isn't ready for this; it baulks at the sheer volume of information, the absence of control. There's another part of me, however, an older, animal part, the part that never cared to trade tooth and claw for reason and intellect.

That part is already rejoicing.

I return my gaze to the bars, just as the last of the memories slot into place.

Mags.

I can't be here.

Next thing I know I'm standing at the front of the cell, barely aware of the sequence of actions that brought me here. I grasp the thick steel, but it won't budge. A voice inside my head, familiar, but somehow calmer, quieter, tells me I should pay attention to that. The rest of me's already busy shouting. At first my cries come incoherent, wordless, but soon they settle around a name:

*Finch.*

I keep it up for what seems like an eternity. At last from somewhere off in the darkness I hear the soft *click-tap* of heels and cane on concrete. As they get closer I can make out the heavier footsteps of two others behind him. I can smell them now too, the faint odor of their sweat. From the end of the corridor there's the sound of a gate opening, and then a flicker of candlelight. It grows steadily brighter, bringing with it traces of color.

At last Finch appears in front of my cell. The men take up positions on either side of him. I know their names. Tully and Knox.

Finch leans forward on his cane, regarding me through the bars.

'And how is the patient feeling?'

'How long was I out?'

He waves the question away, as if it is unimportant.

'*How long?*'

'A matter of hours.'

'You need to let me go.'

'All in good time, Gabriel. All in good time.'

'No, *now*. I've shown you it works. That was the deal.'

He shakes his head.

'You are back with us, and that is indeed encouraging. A proof of concept, so to speak. But you offered *me* a transformation, not merely the right to preside over yours. Rest assured, once your part of the bargain has been satisfied I will release you.'

'She doesn't have that time.'

His pale eyes grow brighter, but he just shakes his head again, more slowly this time.

'I'm sorry, Gabriel. We had a deal. A man's word is his bond, and I mean to hold you to yours.'

I feel a rage then, sudden and terrible, rising up inside me. I grip the bars tight, press my face to the cold steel. The quiet voice warns me that this will do no good, but the fury in me drowns it out. My lip curls upwards in a snarl.

'Let me out, you son of a bitch.'

Finch's face hardens, his features twisting with appalling suddenness. He raises a hand and the one called Knox steps forward, shoulders tight, his muscle-bound body following a simple program his much smaller brain has not yet thought to re-evaluate. He raises his hands, cracks his knuckles, signaling the ease with which he could snap my bones.

The quiet voice speaks again, telling me it is still not too late. There is another game to play here, a smarter one.

*Just step away from the bars.*

The other part of me is in no mood to heed that advice, however. I tilt my head to one side, watching the big man's approach with disdain. He moves so slowly.

The voice sighs. For now it cannot compete with the anger. Instead it puts itself to better use, measuring distance against the reach of my arm.

*Not yet.*

*Wait.*

*Wait.*

I relax my grip on the bars. He's still coming forward, as yet unaware of the mistake he's made. I allow him one more step before I reach through - *very fast, oh, so very fast* - and slip my hands behind his head. His eyes widen, only now beginning to sense the trouble he's in. I feel the first hint of his resistance, but he's left it far too late. I grasp tightly, bracing my feet against the steel, then yank him towards me. There's a soft crunch as his face slams into the bars and he goes limp. I hold him there for a second then release my grip, letting him slump to the floor.

Tully takes a quick step back with the candle, showing more intelligence than I had earlier allowed him. Finch's expression doesn't change, but his eyes seem to shine. I jab a finger at him.

'You let me out. You let me out *now*.'

For a long moment he doesn't budge. Then without warning he lifts the cane and takes a step closer. He glares back at me through the bars, and now those pale eyes seem hot enough to strike sparks from the steel. When he speaks again his voice has lost all of its softness.

'You should take care not to offend me, Gabriel. If you do you will have to stay in there until I feel better towards you.'

He holds my gaze for a long moment. Then without warning he steps back. His voice softens again.

'Well, I believe it is time. Mr. Tully, if you please.'

Tully sets the candle down. When he turns back towards me he's holding a familiar metal flask, a length of fraying cord looped around the handle. He sets it on the ground, pushes it forward with the toe of his boot. Finch taps it with his cane.

'To sustain you.'

Tully slips his hands under Knox's shoulders and starts dragging his limp form down the corridor. Finch continues to examine me through the bars. The flickering candle casts ugly shadows over his face.

'I have to say, Gabriel, I don't much care for your new look.'

He lifts the cane, points it through the bars.

'I fear we may have left you out there in the yard a little too long.'

*

AFTER FINCH HAS GONE I retrieve the candle from where Tully left it and bring it to the back of the cell. Above the toilet there's a small square of stainless steel, bolted to the concrete. I hesitate for a second, then step in front of it. Years of neglect have left the metal dull, but it shows me enough.

The eyes that stare back at me from the mirror have sunken deep into shadow. The virus has taken a knife to the rest of my face, too, carving away my cheeks, sharpening my jaw, thinning my nose. I run my hand over my newly-shorn scalp. It's done its work there as well; my fingers can trace every curve and angle of the bone beneath.

Finch was right. I've definitely looked better.

I lean a little closer, holding the candle up. It takes a few seconds to find it, but when I tilt my head just the right way I catch a flash of something behind, like a fish, knifing through water. I was expecting it, but it's a shock nonetheless.

I return to the cot, but I can't settle. I'm not tired, and even if I were I couldn't sleep now, assuming that's still a thing I do. If Finch was telling the truth about how long I was out it'll be four days since Peck took Mags from Fearrington. By now they'll be well into Virginia, more than half way back to The Greenbrier.

I can't be here.

I return to the bars and start shouting. That does little except rile up the fury in the cell next to me, but I keep it up for a while regardless. Eventually I grow tired of listening to my voice just echo off into darkness. I don't have it in me to sit still, so instead I take to pacing the thin strip of concrete between bed and wall. The generator continues to chug, marking indifferent time with its lumpy idle. I return to the bars every now and then to call out to Finch, but I don't hear from him. The candle burns low. At some point I start to feel a scratchiness behind my eyes. When I rub them it doesn't ease it, and before long an overwhelming tiredness comes over me. I lie down on the cot.

Seconds later I'm out.

I come to some unknowable time later, eyes blinking wide. For a while I just lie there, staring up into grainy darkness, heart pounding, while my brain reboots. When at last the memories return I look around. The candle's little more than a guttering flame in a puddle of wax, but it's still lit. I can't have been out for that long. I jump off the bed and start hollering for Finch again, but I get no more response than I did earlier. I return to pacing, back and forth between cot and wall, even though there's barely a couple of strides to it. Soon after the candle burns down, flickers out.

After that it grows hard to keep time straight.

Sometime in what I judge to be evening of the following day, but which could in reality be earlier or later, I finally hear a sound. I stop to listen. A metallic squeak, listless, languid, like a wheel in need of grease; faint with distance, but growing louder. I rush to the front of the cell and press my face to the bars.

It reaches the end of the corridor, stops. The gate creaks open and it resumes, accompanied now by footsteps. A glimmer of light and moments later Culver appears, a candle in one hand, a jerry can in the other. Seconds later Finch follows in an old wheelchair, his cane across his lap. He doesn't look well. His head's been shaved; shadows deepen his eyes and his already narrow features look stretched, gaunt. Knox stands behind, a strip of tape stretched across his busted nose. He glares back at me from the raccoon eyes that go with it, but keeps both himself and his charge to the far wall, well out of reach. There's no sign of Tully.

I beg with Finch to let me out, but he has just the one word for me: *Patience.*

He delivers it without looking in my direction and then his wheelchair passes beyond the stretch of corridor visible from my cell and is gone. I hear their procession come to a halt at the end. The noise from the generator builds as the door is opened, then drops again as it closes behind them.

I grip the bars, straining to hear. It seems like they're in there for a long time.

Suddenly the pitch from the motor increases, like someone's goosed the throttle, and I think I hear the whir of a fan. Seconds later there's a deafening bang, and I start, even though I'm expecting it. The diesel engine drops back to an idle for a few minutes and then suddenly picks up again. There's a second bang. Was that part of the plan? Did they have to jolt me more than once? I have no way of knowing.

A little while later the door at the other end of the corridor opens. A burning smell fills the air.

Culver appears in the corridor outside my cell. I call out to him to release me but he scurries on by, his head down. Finch follows a few moments later, slumped forward in the squeaking wheelchair. Knox pushes him past my cell without stopping. I plead with him to let me out, but he ignores me too.

I keep shouting after them to come back, long after they've gone.

But none of them ever do.

*

IT WON'T BE MUCH LONGER NOW, that's what I tell myself.

At least at first.

A man's word is his bond, those were Finch's very words. I repeat them over and over as I pace the narrow stretch of floor between cot and wall. People lie, I know it, but Mac said that was one of the few rules Finch abided by. As soon as he comes to he'll release me. It can't be much longer. I was only out for a couple of hours, and I'm sure I was sicker than he looked, going in.

I try and work out where Mags will be by now. Far as I can tell we're coming to the end of the fifth day, which should put them north of Boones Mill, maybe even as far up as Roanoake. Peck will take them the long way around, to avoid going over the mountains, I'm sure of it. That'll add time to their journey. It'll be three days yet before they're back at The Greenbrier.

I can still make it.

As the hours slip by I start to doubt myself, however.

I return to the bars to listen for any sign of my release. But all there is is the listless chugging from the generator.

What if something went wrong and Finch didn't survive? He certainly didn't look well when they wheeled him out. Maybe Culver and Knox took the opportunity to be rid of him? But if that was their intention surely they could have done it easier than with the chair? And where was Tully during all this? Is he gone for good? Is it only Knox, now? I begin to wonder if what I did to him wasn't a mistake. If Finch doesn't survive I could be relying on his kindness to let me out of here.

The voice inside my head says *I told you so.*

I return to the front of my cell and take to hollering again. It does me little good. My cries echo down the corridor, but nothing ever comes back. All that's left in their wake is the distant drone of the generator.

A night passes, then, as best I can tell, another day. I take to reciting the lists I made in the hotbox. My recollection of Marv's map does not improve, and the number of Juvies' names I can remember never gets higher than twenty-two, but I do not seem to have lost anything more as a result of my time in the chair.

I think.

Truth is I have no way to be sure.

I still shout for Finch, but less frequently now; nothing ever comes of it. Peck will already be in the foothills of the Alleghenies; the day after tomorrow they'll be back at The Greenbrier. Whatever Gilbey has planned for her after that, I'm going to be the best part of a hundred and fifty miles away when it happens, with the whole of the state of Virginia between us.

And these bars.

I have failed. The certainty of it settles beneath my ribcage, a gnawing hole in my gut that has little to do with the hunger that has now started to plague my waking moments. I feel the anger building inside me, that I will be powerless to stop it.

The voice inside my head tells me to stay calm, that no good will come of letting that other part of me back in charge. But sometimes the feelings of rage and despair grow too strong to be resisted. When that happens it's like a barrier descending, inside my head, and that part of me capable of directing my actions is trapped behind it. The barrier's not a solid thing, like a blast door or the roadblock that rises out of the ground at the entrance to Fearrington. It feels more like the wire that braces Eden and Mount Weather's tunnels. It allows me to see through well enough, but while its down it's like my hands are off the controls, my role reduced to that of passenger, spectator, while the other side of me does what it must to vent its fury.

To my surprise that part proceeds mostly in silence. There are no howls of rage, no wordless, incoherent cries. Mostly I grit my teeth and take to testing my strength against the steel. That bears no more fruit than my hollering does, however. The cell has been designed not just for those who were content with their captivity. It meets each of my assaults with its own patient resolve, happy to wait until the last of them has been spent.

The creature in the next cell stays quiet for the most part, but when I take to shouting or to wrestling with the bars it stirs, and for a while after my anger has been spent and I have returned to my cot I hear it, scuffling backwards and forwards on the other side of the wall that separates us.

The hours slip by; I give up on keeping them straight. When my eyes grow scratchy I sleep, or whatever absence of consciousness now passes for that. I can't say I care for it much. I don't think it lasts for long, but without the candle I have no way of knowing. Only one thing I'm certain of now: no one's coming to let me out. Dead or alive, Finch won't be keeping his side of the bargain. I eye the flask he left, sitting outside my cell. I tell myself I won't drink from it, but the truth is I could have rolled it further along the corridor, put it out of my reach, once and for all, if that really was my last word on the subject. I remember what Mac said, that night in the print shop. I might have skipped a meal here and there, but I hadn't yet come to understand hunger. I stare at the flask a moment longer, then go back to pacing.

That time might not be far off now, however.

*

THEY FINALLY CATCH UP to the soldiers three nights later. Or at least two of them.

They enter a town with dusk upon them. All day they have hiked in the shadow of mountains that seemed to grow no closer, but now in the fading light they suddenly loom high over them. The boy with the curly hair checks a road sign against the map he carries. He says this place is called Salem, and beyond it lies the interstate. That way is easier, but longer. Or they can continue north, into the mountains. Tomorrow they will have to decide.

The boy chooses a small church for shelter. He knows there is something wrong as soon as he steps inside. A smell packs the air: thick, sweet, and for a moment he feels something inside him stir. The boy dumps the branches they have gathered on the floor and shucks off his backpack, seemingly unaware.

He glances down at the bundle of moldering sticks. It is his job to light the fire. He is good at it, and so the boy lets him. That task will have to wait, however. He peers into the grainy shadows, trying to locate the source of the smell, but there is nothing. There is no mistaking it, though; it is strong; almost overpowering. It makes him think of another church and the soldier with the patch over his eye, opening a flask, sliding it towards him. The thing inside him clenches again at the memory, and this time he has to work harder to force it back down.

He tilts his head, testing the air. It seems to be coming from somewhere in the back. He crouches down, making his slowly way between the scattered pews, checking each as he goes.

He finds the first of them lying on the floor at the end of one of the long wooden benches. It is one of the men from the night they arrived at the first place inside the mountain. Not the dangerous man, with the gray eyes and the gun, but the other, the one who had been standing by the lake while the others had held the boy with the curly hair down and poured water on him. He lies propped against the wall. His cheeks were red before, but all the color has drained from them now. His parka is open and a large bandage has been taped to one side of his neck. The material is dark, sodden with his blood. His eyes are closed, but now and then his chest rises and a fresh bead of it breaks free from underneath the gauze, trickles down his neck.

The thing inside him struggles, and for a moment all he can do is stare while he wrestles with it. At last he calls out. The boy must sense something is wrong from the tone of his voice. He drops the kindling he is gathering and comes running. When he sees the man lying on the ground he bends down next to him.

'Sergeant Scudder.'

For a moment there is nothing, but then the man's eyes flutter open. He sees the boy and then his eyes shift to him, grow wide. He tries to get up, but he is too weak.

'It's okay. He won't hurt you.'

The man's eyes suggest he doesn't believe it. He stares like that a moment longer, then croaks for water.

The boy fetches his canteen and holds it to his lips. The man sips greedily, but most of it runs down his chin, mixing with the blood on his neck. When it seems like he is done drinking the boy lifts the canteen.

'What happened?'

The man's eyes flick to the boy, then return to him. He takes a shallow breath, whispers a single word: *Waiting*.

'Someone was waiting for you?'

The man nods.

'Here?'

The man points over in the direction of altar. The boy reaches for his flashlight, but he has already seen them. Two more bodies. The nearest is one of the boys from the lake. The other he doesn't think he recognizes, but it takes him a moment to be certain. The sunken eyes and hollowed cheeks make it seem familiar, but then everyone looked like that when he was in the cage.

The boy cranks the flashlight's handle. As the beam settles on the nearest body he mouths the word *Seth*. He lets it linger there for a moment, then moves it along. When it finds the second one the boy jumps to his feet. He drops the flashlight and starts fumbling in his pocket for the gun the girl gave him.

The man shakes his head.

'Already dead. Peck. Shot it.'

The boy picks up the flashlight. He stares at the creature lying on the floor for a long moment, like he might not trust what the man has told him. After a few seconds he slowly returns the gun to the pocket of his parka. His eyes return to the man.

'Mags? Was Mags okay?'

The man closes his eyes, nods. He raises a finger, points to an old metal radiator mounted to the wall.

'Tied up, right there.'

He holds his hand there for a while, like it's important. Then he lets it fall to his side, as though the effort has exhausted him. He shakes his head.

'Showed no interest in her. Would've…had to step right over her to get by.'

*

THE FLASK FINCH LEFT ME remains untouched, but I find myself eyeing it each time I reach the bars now, so I give up on pacing and take to the cot. I stare up at the ceiling, listening to the sound of the generator. The last few hours it's been running ragged. The motor will hunt for a while, up and down, like someone's tweaking the throttle, or it'll take to sputtering, like something's caught in the pipes. It always seems to right itself, however. Even as I listen it coughs, once, twice, like it's clearing its throat, then returns to its languid drone.

I close my eyes. Peck will be on the home straight by now; tomorrow evening they'll be back at The Greenbrier. My fingers grip the side of the cot as I imagine Truck dragging her into that other room. The curtain inside my head starts to descend as the anger builds, pushing aside the feelings of helplessness and despair. The voice speaks, telling me to breath. I prefer its measured tones to the craven whispers of whatever it has replaced, but I can't help but think it's being far too relaxed about this. I wonder if whatever lives inside my head has gone native. Hicks said the furies put themselves into some sort of hibernation when they ran out of food. Maybe it's looking forward to that.

*No.*

The generator takes to coughing again, for longer this time. Eventually it settles, but the chugging drone has become lumpier, more erratic.

*Are you ready?*

I sit up slowly.

Ready for what?

The motor catches, and for a second revs, like it's been goosed. Then without warning it simply dies. There's a moment's silence, followed by a loud click from the front of my cell as the lock releases. I watch for a second in disbelief as the door slowly swings back on its hinges, and then I'm on my feet.

But as I step out into the corridor I freeze. A little further along I can see my parka, draped over the back of the chair Finch had placed in front of the fury's cell. The rest of my clothes are resting on the seat, neatly folded, my boots side-by-side underneath. None of those things are what's giving me pause, however. The door to the cell next to mine: there's no sign of the chain that once held it fast, and now it hangs open, too. I guess my lock wasn't the only one to release when the generator died.

I stare at it for a moment. Has the creature Finch kept there already escaped? But even as I think it I catch movement from the shadows behind. I watch as it slips through.

It looks up as it sees me, and for long seconds we both just stand there, no more than a half-dozen paces apart, each waiting to see what the other will do.

My eyes flick past it, to the corridor beyond.

I don't have time for this. I take a deep breath, getting ready to run at it.

*Wait.*

*On the floor; look.*

I glance down, not daring to take my eye off the creature in front of me for more than a second. The flask Finch left is right at my feet. When I look up again I see the fury's gaze has shifted there too.

I slide it forward with my foot. As soon as it's within reach the creature snatches the flask up, then hurries back into its cell. It pushes itself into the corner and busies itself with the lid. Its eyes dart to me one last time, then it lifts the battered metal container to its lips, tilts its head back and starts to drink. Drops of something dark trickle from its lips, falling from its chin to spatter the concrete.

I'm already reaching for my parka when the smell hits me. My head snaps back to the cell, and for a moment I'm rooted to the spot, transfixed; all I can do is stand there and stare. Something inside me awakens, uncoils itself. I know what it would have me do. The creature in the cell senses it; its lip curls and it snarls back at me from the shadows. It is a puny thing, though, pathetic; it will be no match for me. I take a step towards it. Inside my head the brace wire shutter starts to descend.

*No.*

I grip the bars, wrestling for control. But the smell is maddening; it takes everything I have not to rush into the cell, rip the flask from the creature's hands.

*You have somewhere else to be now.*

It shows me an image: Mags, forced onto her toes, her feet scrabbling for purchase as the noose tightens around her neck. The muscles along Truck's arms bunching as he hoists her up.

And now the rage has a different focus.

I take a step backwards, then another. I grab my parka and boots from the chair and set off along the passageway at a run.

At the top of the stairs concrete gives way to stone and I stop to pull on my boots. I take a couple of deep breaths as I tighten the laces, still trying to clear my head. I'm not sure what almost happened back there but whatever it was I can't allow it again, least not till I'm clear of Starkly's walls. I shuck on my parka and make my way down the hall, past laundry, kitchens, pantry, straining for sounds ahead.

When I reach the cellblock I stop again. My luck seems to be holding; Starkly's quiet as a morgue.

*Too quiet.*

The voice is right. It might still be dark outside, but there's nothing; no snores, no dream-laden grunts, none of the other night sounds the prisoners would make. Only the tinny silence of emptiness, the occasional gust of wind against stone outside.

If this is a game Finch is playing with me I don't understand it. He either means to let me leave or he doesn't. I take a deep breath and step through the door, making my way across the open expanse of cellblock quick as I can. I hold my breath, expecting at any moment to be challenged. But there's nothing, and then I'm out in the yard, crunching through snow. Ahead lies the holding pen. I pull back the gate and step inside. The pockmarked booth is dark, empty. I make my way towards the access door set into the towering main gate and slide back the bolt. The hinges creak as I heave it open. I don't bother to close it behind me. My snowshoes are waiting where I left them, propped against the wall outside. I step into them, ratchet the straps tight and then I'm gone.

I stop on the ridge overlooking the valley long enough to dig up Mags' backpack from where I buried it on my way in. I strap on the gun belt, sling her crucifix around my neck, and then I'm off again, bounding down to the highway with a pace I can scarcely believe.

I take the straightest route I can figure, cutting cross-country where I figure it might save me a quarter mile, less. I'm a five-day hike from The Greenbrier with at best two days to cover that distance. I don't trouble myself with whether it can be done. I just point myself north and make my strides as long and fast as my legs will allow.

One by one the miles fall under my snowshoes. I pass through places with names like Prospect, Blanch, Vandola, but don't stop in any of them. The day grows uncomfortably bright. I keep my head down, cupping my hands to my goggles when I need to raise it to study the road ahead. At last, somewhere far behind the clouds, the sun starts tracking for the horizon. As dusk settles I quit North Carolina and continue on into Virginia.

Neither darkness nor cold will stop me now.

Just before dawn I get that scratchiness behind my eyes that tells me I'll soon need to sleep. I fight it for as long as I can, but soon my vision starts to narrow and things that cannot be there appear in what remains, making me think what I see now might not be trusted. Up ahead a shotgun shack sits just off the highway, gray snow banked against its dilapidated sides, more pressing down on its corrugated roof. A padlocked gate hangs rusting between two crumbling posts, but I don't trouble myself with it; only a few broken staves remain of the fence that once completed its sad perimeter.

The front door's already busted open, so there's no need to unsling

Mags' pack for the pry bar. I snap off my snowshoes and climb the steps. The boards are waterbuckled, sprung; they creak under my boots as I yank the screen door back. Ahead there's a narrow hallway, the wallpaper mildewed, peeling; the ceiling cracked, crumbling, the laths poking through behind.

I don't bother with a fire, just find a spot on the floor and lay my head down. My eyes close and seconds later I'm gone.

By evening of the second day I'm most of the way through Virginia. The flatlands are behind me now, and in front the Appalachians rise up, their snow-capped peaks scraping the underbellies of the clouds that hang ominous and low over them. I arrive at a place called Salem with dusk falling and hurry through it, looking for the interstate beyond. Peck will have cut east from here in search of one of the low passes that wind their way through the valley floor. But the quickest way's north, into the mountains.

I make my way across the overpass and continue on, what little color there is leaching away as darkness settles around me. Beyond the road climbs steeply, switching back on itself as it twists ever higher, each ridge gained merely a foretaste of the one to come. For the first time I begin to sense the limits of my newfound endurance, but it's alright. My legs only need to hold a little longer. I am closer now than I could have hoped.

Just as night's getting ready to be done the road finally levels and I arrive at a place called Crows, where I stopped with the soldiers on our way to the hospital in Blacksburg. My eyes have been feeling gritty since Catawba, and for the last hour the darkness has had a dreamlike quality to it. I find a gas station and curl up behind the counter. I figure I'll close my eyes for twenty minutes, be on my way again before sunup.

*

HE SITS IN THE DARKNESS, staring out. Beyond the station house's candy cane pillars the parking lot is mostly empty. The boy with the curly hair huddles in the corner, bundled up in his parka. They cannot have a fire and inside the crumbling station house it is cold.

It has been two days since they found the other two, in the church. The man called Scudder didn't last the night. He listened from across the room as his breathing grew ragged, then just before dawn he hitched in a final gasp, something inside his chest rattled, and it settled for the last time.

Before he died the man told the boy which way they had taken the girl. They picked up their tracks later that day and have been following them ever since, always staying out of sight, occasionally catching a glimpse as they crested some distant hill, but mostly just following their prints in the snow. Yesterday evening, as the last of the light was leaving the sky, they saw them ahead in the distance, trudging up an off-ramp as they exited the highway. He hurried to catch up, leaving the boy with the curly hair behind. But then he had been forced to watch, helpless, as they had marched through the crumbling gates and up towards the big house.

He looks out into the parking lot. It is still dark, but already he can sense the approaching dawn. The girl will be back in the cage by now. How long will it be before the Doctor takes her to the other room?

'We have to go inside.'

He says it mostly to himself, but across the room the boy lifts his head from his knees.

'H-how? We c-can't get in. You saw yourself. Those were s-soldiers up at the entrance to the bunker. They had rifles.' He holds the pistol up. 'I d-don't even know how to shoot this!'

He goes back to staring out the window. The boy is close to giving up; he can hear it in his voice. He is afraid too. He tells himself the tall boy will know what to do, when he gets here. Except he should have been here already, and now they are out of time.

He looks out at the parking lot. His eyes fall on a long-abandoned car, waiting patiently under a blanket of snow right in front of the station house. He gets up, crosses the floor. He clears a spot on dusty, trash-strewn floor with his mitten then sits next to the boy.

'There's one more thing we can try.'

They hurry through The Greenbrier's gates and start up the long driveway. The tracks they are making will be fresh, but that cannot be helped; if they stick to the churned up snow no one should notice. Behind him the boy stumbles uncertainly, feeling his way through the darkness.

They cannot have the flashlights and dawn is still some time away; it is not light enough yet for his eyes.

The road curves around, finally revealing the massive building. He makes for a dark shape that squats on the lawn in front of the entrance's towering columns. As they draw close he leaves the tracks they have been following and hurries towards it. The huge rotors hang down under their own weight, the tips almost touching the powder. They creak and groan as they flex in the wind.

He makes his way along the fuselage, all the way to the back. The loading ramp is down and snow has drifted up into the darkened interior, settling deep in the gaps between the cargo bay's ribs. Webbing adorns the bellied walls; thick ratchet straps hang from the riveted ceiling, twisting in the wind.

He unsnaps his snowshoes and makes his way inside, heading for the front. For a machine so large the cockpit is surprisingly cramped. Two high-backed seats side by side, only a narrow space between, busy with controls. He clambers over the frame, using the straps of the harness to swing himself into one of the seats. A console sweeps around in front of him, crammed with dials, gauges, their surfaces white with frost. More levers sprout from the floor between his feet. Snow darkens the canopy, but here and there a section remains clear. He presses his face to the closest one.

He hears footsteps staggering up the ramp, and seconds later the boy appears at his shoulder, shivering. He looks down into the crowded cockpit, eyes the narrow space between the seats, then decides against it.

'This is c-crazy. It won't work.'

He ignores him, continuing his search. Stress patterns craze the curving perspex, making it hard to see, but outside dawn is finally breaking; a reluctant light slowly congeals over the ashen snow. Without warning the wind catches one of the huge rotor blades, dips it down in front of them. He shifts in his seat so he can see around it, then stops, points. Behind him the boy leans forward, following his outstretched hand. A puzzled look troubles his face.

He points again, jabbing at a spot all the way back in the shadows.

And then the boy sees it too.

On the far side of the massive columns a red light blinks once, then goes dark again.

*

I WAKE WITH A JOLT, blinking furiously at unfamiliar surroundings while my brain reboots. Then the memories load and I jump up, rush outside. My legs have stiffened while I slept, but I have no time for that now; dawn's already spreading itself over the spiny ridges to the east. They'll loosen on the road.

I pick up the Kanawha Trail, beginning a hurried descent into West Virginia. I haven't been on the road more than half an hour when up ahead I spot a weather-beaten sign for the interstate. The switchback mountain trail I'm following crests and at last I can see it below me, snaking its way through the valley floor. I quit the track for the steeper but more direct route through what would once have been forest, my snowshoes sending small avalanches of powder tumbling down the slope ahead of me as I bound between the blackened trunks, Hicks' pistol bouncing against my leg with each stride.

The trees come to an abrupt end and I stop and scan the highway below for any sign of them. The road's clear in both directions, but it doesn't take me long to spot where they've passed through: a wide swathe of tracks out of the east, at least seven or eight abreast. They've beaten me here.

I hurry down the embankment and join the highway, searching the snow for the deeper indentations Jax will have left, but it's so badly chewed I can't pick them out. I bend down, tracing the outline of the nearest one with my fingers. The edges are crisp, well-defined; the wind can't have had more than an hour to smooth them out. They must have come through here earlier this morning. There's still a chance I can head them off.

I pick up the pace. The wake of freshly-churned snow leaves the interstate a mile later, at an exit marked 60, but I stay on, searching for the quicker route Hicks took when he first brought us this way. Soon after the turnoff the road fishhooks and then passes over a railway line, just as it exits a tunnel. I throw my leg over the guardrail and drop down the embankment on the other side. I hit the bottom in a cloud of powder and take off along the narrow ravine, pounding through the deeper drifts with as much speed as I can muster. The track curves around for a half-mile or so and then finally straightens. Ahead there's a short siding, a corroded railcar sitting idle against snow-covered bumpers, and beyond in the distance a long shelter, roof timbers swaybacked under the weight of snow. I hurry towards it. A faded Amtrak sign, the words barely visible under a crust of ice and snow, tells me I've arrived.

I leave the tracks behind and hurry through the parking lot. But as I come to the station house I stop. A set of fresh prints exit from between the candy cane pillars that mark the entrance.

*What was someone doing in there?*

I follow the prints out to the road. On the other side two sections of wall curve inward to a pair of crumbling gateposts. The tracks head in that direction, but the mystery of who made them is already forgotten; something else has caught my eye.

The snow between the gates has been disturbed. A swathe of tracks, wide, just like the ones I ran into up on the highway less than an hour ago. I hurry across the road, thinking there might still be time to head them off before they reach the house. But as I get closer I can see the prints here are faint, the edges smoothed by wind, the hollows already mostly filled in by the driven snow.

These tracks are old; whoever made them came through a while ago. I stare at them for a long moment, not understanding. And then my heart fills with dread as off to one side I spot the deeper set I have been looking for.

I'm too late.

They already have her inside.

*

I STARE DOWN AT JAX'S PRINTS, not understanding. The tracks I picked up out on the interstate were fresh. But these are a day old, maybe more.

I point my snowshoes around and start heading west on 60, away from The Greenbrier's gates. My legs are tiring, but I force them on, pounding the snow harder than ever. The road slowly curves around. A huge gray structure rises up on my left, its breached roof and disintegrating bell tower familiar from the time I spent there with Hicks. I barely notice. The thought of what Gilbey might have done with the time she's already had fills me with rage.

When I reach the trail I cut off the road and switch back, making my way in among the blackened trunks. The path starts to incline as it skirts it way around the hill that sits behind The Greenbrier. The muscles in my legs send a warning that they might not be expected to keep this pace up much longer, but I pay it no attention. I strain for any sounds from the trail ahead, but there's only my breathing and the crunch of my snowshoes through the ice-slicked powder.

The track widens and a low concrete structure slowly separates itself from the trees. Snow drifts high against its featureless sides; more of it rests in heavy layers on its flat roof. The woods seem still but I stop, forcing myself to listen. And that's when I hear it: from somewhere up ahead, the low murmur of conversation.

I slip off my mittens and slowly unzip my parka.

I start forward again, forcing myself to go slow. The track curves around and now I see them, in front of the entrance to the bunker: two figures, bundled up in parkas, their breath smoking in the cold. A fire burns between them. They stand close, holding their hands out to the flames. One has a rifle slung over his shoulder; the other doesn't appear armed. Neither has seen me yet, but that won't last. My hand drops to the pistol on my hip. I start to draw it from its holster.

*No.*

The voice shows me an image: a small clearing; a can nestling in the crook of a branch, untroubled by the bullet I had just fired at it.

*It's too far.*

*You can't let them raise the alarm.*

I let the pistol slide back into its holster. I raise my arms out from my sides and start making my way up towards them.

It's Boots who spots me first. He looks up from the fire and calls out to his companion, who turns to face me. My head's down, my face hidden in the shadow of the hood's cowl, but Weasel seems to have little trouble working out who it is. He slings the rifle off his shoulder, but keeps it low.

'Well, there he is. Hicks said you'd show up.'

I keep trudging up the path towards him, my arms outstretched. He takes a step away from the fire, unconcerned by my approach.

'You're too late, though. Doc's already begun.'

He smiles, revealing a gap where the stock of Mags' rifle dislodged the teeth there. There's a cruelty to the expression that seems to infect the whole of his face and I feel something harden inside me, that he would take pleasure from this. I feel an overwhelming urge to break into a run, to launch myself at him, to claw the grin from his face.

The voice inside my head tells me to wait. It starts to measure out the distance between us. The count helps calm me down.

*Good.*

Weasel turns to his companion. Private Kavanagh is at least showing the good sense to look nervous.

'Just look at him come, Boots. Must be keen to get himself into one of those cages.'

He turns back to face me.

'Is that right, Huckleberry? You been missing us?'

I keep walking towards them. My hands are still held out from my sides, but now I slowly start to flex my fingers. Behind the soldiers the entrance to the bunker slides into view. A section of the huge metal gate at the end is already visible; the outline of a smaller door set into the steel. A rusting sign above, a faded symbol of a lightning bolt.

*They have no idea.*

'What's the rush, Huckleberry?'

The smile's still there, but for the first time I hear nervousness in Weasel's voice. His thumb reaches for the safety, even as his finger slips through the trigger guard. With his other hand he reaches down for the charging handle.

*Just a few steps more.*

'Hey! You just hold it right there, now.'

*Alright. That'll do.*

I exhale slowly, forcing my heart to slow. In the skip between beats my hand reaches for the pistol. I lift my head and the hood falls back, for the first time revealing my face.

Weasel's smile vanishes like a breath in the wind. His eyebrows reach for his hairline and he starts to bring the barrel up. The rifle's still at half-mast, but in his panic he squeezes the trigger anyway. Flame bursts from the muzzle, the snow between us erupting in an arc of exploding powder that tracks its way ever so slowly towards me.

I slide the pistol from its holster, my thumb already reaching for the hammer. I feel the tension in the mechanism, the click as it locks in place, and then the barrel appears before me and there's nothing to do but squeeze. There's a loud bang and the pistol jumps with the recoil, sending my first shot high and wide. A puff of snow behind and to the left tells me where the bullet lands and I see now how right Hicks was to tell me to watch for it; that part *is* important. Adjusting for it is child's play, and then it's just a matter of waiting for the cylinder to rotate, placing the next round under the hammer. It seems to take forever, but at last I hear it click into place.

The second bullet catches him in the neck, snapping his head back. His legs give out from under him and he slumps to the ground.

I swing the pistol around, searching for Boots, but he hasn't moved. He stands, rooted to the spot. He stares back at me, eyes wide with fear.

I keep the pistol on him as I draw level with Weasel. There's a ragged hole where his throat once was. He holds a hand there, trying to stanch the flow. He opens his mouth, but nothing comes out except a low gurgle and a pink cord of saliva. He looks up at me a moment longer, like he doesn't yet believe it, then a dull blankness slides over his eyes and he just flickers out like a candle.

I stand over him for a second, watching the blood slip from between his fingers to stain the snow beneath. Something twists inside me at the sight of it, but the voice repeats the message it gave me in Starkly: *there's no time for this; I have things to do*; and this time I heed it quicker. I turn to face Boots.

'What he said about Gilbey, is it true?'

He stares at me blankly, like he's having trouble processing the question. He seems more scared of me than the pistol I have on him, so I grip the throat of his parka and draw him close.

I ask again, and this time he bobs his head, quick.

'You'd best not be here when I come back out.'

*

I HOLSTER THE PISTOL and bend down to unsnap my snowshoes, then hurry inside. Behind me I hear the crunch of snow as Boots stumbles off into the woods, but I don't bother to check which direction he's taking. The blast door's open, resting all the way back against the wall on its huge, buttressed hinges. Beyond it the tunnel stretches off into grainy gloom.

High in the corner the red light of a camera blinks once, then goes dark. The voice wants me to wait, to think this through. Hicks is expecting me, and there's no cover that way, nowhere to hide.

But I'm already sprinting. With each step I expect to hear the first crack of gunfire, but somehow it never comes. I make it to the door marked *Decontamination* unharmed and pass under another camera bolted to the wall above, entering the showers. Rusting nozzles protrude from the tiles, narrowing my path, and then I'm through, stepping into a long corridor. Safety lights hum, adding shades of green to the gray. From somewhere off in the distance there's the low drone of a generator.

I run towards it, past dormitories, a cafeteria, infirmary, drab halls filled with chairs. The thrum from the generator increases as I open the door to the power plant. I make my way up onto a narrow gangway, my boots clanging on the metal grating. I push through another door at the end; the noise from the plant recedes as it closes behind me. I hurry down the stair beyond, taking the steps two and three at a time, but the descent seems to take forever in spite of it. At last I reach the bottom. A single door leads out of the shaft, a keypad to one side blinking out its silent guard.

I try it, but it won't budge, so I shuck off my backpack, reach inside for the pry bar, and start to attack the lock. It has been designed to resist such attempts, however: the gap between door and frame is narrow, the edges reinforced with steel. There's nowhere for the bar to get purchase.

My efforts grow increasingly frantic, as I imagine what Gilbey might be doing right now to Mags in that other room. Inside my head I feel the brace wire starting to come down. I drop the pry bar and draw the pistol, level it at the lock.

*No! They'll hear.*

I squeeze the trigger. There's a bang, loud in such a confined space, and the gun bucks in my hand. Sparks fly from the lock and there's the whine of a ricochet. The shaft fills with the smell of gunpowder.

I take a step back and aim my boot at the lock. There's the sound of wood splintering, and this time I feel it give. It yields on the third kick and I burst through into a familiar room: long, low-ceilinged, plastic cages lining the walls on either side.

I leave everything behind me and set off at a run, the cages little more than a blur on either side. Halfway along I think I catch the briefest glimpse of something, a shape, drawing back into the shadows behind, but I don't stop. Whatever might be there isn't my concern now.

The room ends at another door. I brace myself, getting ready to charge it. The voice inside my head pleads with me to slow down; it tells me I can be quiet and still go quickly. But it is small now; it struggles to make itself heard. It goes silent for a moment, then it says the one thing that might cut through the maelstrom: her name.

*You'll be no good to her if you get yourself caught.*

I manage to reassert some semblance of control just as I arrive at the last cage. I skid to a halt in front of the door and reach for the handle. To my surprise there's no resistance; it isn't locked. I push down, more gently than I would have thought possible only seconds before.

The door opens with a soft groan and I step through into a smaller room, its only feature a row of black metal chambers set into the wall at waist height. Each has a large latch handle, the words *Crematex Incinerator Corp.* stamped in raised letters above. I pass quickly between them. Most of the chambers are closed, but near the end one of the doors hangs outward on its hinges. I catch a glimpse of charred concrete behind as I hurry past.

The next room's like the first, long, low-ceilinged, rows of plastic cages stretching off into gloom on either side. The ones closest the door are empty, unremarkable, but as I make my way deeper among them that changes.

The first one I come to has the number 98 stenciled along the top. Inside a gray shape crouches. A scar circles the top of its shaved scalp, the tissue puckered and rucked around the edges. Its shadowed eyes are open, but it just stares out, unblinking, giving no indication it knows I'm there. On a shelf above rests a large glass jar. Inside, something gray and folded, cut in cross-section, hangs suspended in clear liquid.

The cages beyond are all the same; I make my way quickly among them. A sound drifts towards me out of the darkness now, faint, muffled. I can't be certain if it was there earlier, or if it just started up.

I hold my breath for a moment, listening. It's high-pitched, like the whine of a mosquito, only regular, mechanical. And then I feel my throat constrict as I realize what it is.

*

HE STANDS AT THE TOP of the loading ramp, peering out. The wind gusts around him, sending flurries of gray snow dancing up into the helicopter's darkened cargo bay. He tilts his head to one side, scenting the air, listening for any sound. But there's nothing. The sun has been up a while now. They can't wait any longer.

On the other side of the helicopter a path has been cleared through the snow. He makes his way down the ramp and scurries along it, making sure to keep his head low. He does not want to be seen. Not yet.

As he approaches the front of the massive building he slows. Peeling flagpoles jut from the second floor balustrade, the tattered flags that hang there snapping and fluttering in the wind. Ahead, recessed in shadow, the wide entrance door, and above, mounted high on the wall, a single camera. Its red light blinks once, then goes out.

He glances back at the helicopter. The boy with the curly hair stands by the cargo door, watching his progress. A worried look troubles his face. He does not think this is a very good plan; he only agreed to it because he could not think of another.

He returns his gaze to the entrance. The lobby's dark windows stare down menacingly. His heart races, fluttering inside his small ribcage like a trapped moth. He does not want to go back in the cage. He looks at the helicopter again. It is not too late; he could still turn around. He and the boy could hide there for the hours of daylight that remain, and then escape together under cover of darkness.

But that would mean leaving her in there.

He closes his eyes and takes a deep breath, summoning his courage. There is not as much of it as he had hoped; already far less than there was when he left the helicopter, just moments ago. Before even that has the chance to desert him he stands, takes several quick steps into the shadow of the portico.

The colossal columns tower over him. He makes his way between them, continuing up the steps to the entrance. He stands on tiptoe and peers through the door, but beyond the lobby is dark, empty. Above the light on the camera blinks, then goes out again.

His heart is pounding; he can hear it now, hammering away inside his chest; it is all he can do not to run. He closes his eyes, tries to push the fear back down, like he saw the girl do in the airlock.

He takes a deep breath and steps under the oblong box mounted to the wall. He lifts his goggles onto his forehead and looks up. The camera's single mechanical eye stares down at him impassively. He raises his hands above his head, waves them hesitantly. The light blinks and he almost bolts, but then it goes out again.

He keeps his arms above his head while he watches through the glass for any sign of their approach. The doctor wants him back; the dangerous man said so, when he came to take the girl away. As soon as they see he's here they'll come out for him. He needs to lead them away, to give the boy time to go inside and find her.

He looks up into the camera. But how much longer should he wait? Surely they've seen him by now. He imagines them, sprinting along whatever corridors and passageways lay beyond, only seconds from bursting into the lobby. The muscles in his legs tense at the thought. He mustn't let them catch him.

A soft whirring from above, barely audible above the sound of the wind. His eyes flick upwards, just in time to see the camera's iris narrow as it focuses on him.

His hands reach up for his goggles even as he bolts for the path that's been cleared through the snow. He takes the steps in short, urgent strides and then his feet are crunching powder. For a second he thinks he hears something behind him, a sound that might be the thud of boots on stone, but he forces himself not to look back – surely they can't be here already?

The thought of it spurs him on; he tucks his elbows tight to his sides and runs for all he is worth. When he reaches the spot where he left his snowshoes he steps into them and drops to a crouch, fighting the impulse to look over his shoulder while his fingers works the straps. As he tightens the last one he hears the clunk of a handle and the unmistakable clatter of a door being thrown back on its hinges. There's a harsh shout and then he is on his feet, mittens bouncing on their tethers, arms and legs pumping as he scrambles up the embankment and takes off into deeper snow.

*

I DRAW HICKS' PISTOL and break into a run, ignoring the vacant stares from the cages on either side as I sprint towards the source of the sound. The room seems to stretch out, like I might never reach the end, but eventually a door separates itself from the gloom ahead. The voice begs me to be careful, but it is small now, drowned out by the shrill whine that grows louder, the rage that builds with each step.

I reach the door, crash through it without slowing. I find myself in dazzling brightness; instinctively raise a hand to shield my eyes. The sound is coming from somewhere in front of me, but the light is so intense I can't stand to look directly at it. My entrance seems to do the trick, however; the pitch drops as whatever's causing it is switched off.

A complicated raft of smells pack the air. The sharp tang of disinfectant, the coppery aroma of blood, the burn of an electric motor. And underneath it something else, stale, familiar. The voice inside my head really wants me to pay attention to that but I can't, not till I've found her.

The light's too bright to look at so I squint into the corners, trying to gather details. The room is square, wider and higher than the one I've just left. Counters run most of the way around the walls. A sink, a microscope, other equipment I don't recognize. Above, shelves, stacked with bottles, jars, other containers, an array of glass and ceramic, all gleaming in the brilliance. To my right a doorway, or maybe a large alcove, a dark curtain hiding whatever's behind.

I force my gaze back to the center. What looks like an operating table, its angular surfaces ablaze under a huge domed light hanging down from above. I catch a glimpse of movement on the other side of it and I step forward, narrowing my eyes against the glare. I point the pistol in the direction I thought I saw it.

'The light; turn it off.'

'It bothers you?'

A long pause and then the light is cut, leaving only the soft glow from a handful of bulkhead lamps bolted to the walls. Pinwheels and starbursts swirl and explode across my vision, but if I squint past them I can make out shapes.

She's lying in front of me, wearing only a surgical gown. A thick Velcro strap circles her waist; cuffs bind her wrists and ankles to the table. Her head has been shaved and a dotted line that looks like it might have been drawn there with a sharpie circles her scalp. A metal clamp holds it in place. A trickle of blood where the screws have pierced her skin.

I call her name but she doesn't respond. I search her face for any sign she knows I'm there, but her eyes have been taped shut.

I look up, for the first time seeing Gilbey. She studies me over her glasses, the rest of her face hidden behind a surgical cap and mask. In her hand some type of electric saw, the jagged-toothed disc still spinning as it grinds slowly to a halt.

'What have you done to her?'

She pulls the mask down.

'Nothing, yet. I was just about to begin.'

I step forward, touch her shoulder.

'Mags.'

'She can't hear you.'

I point the pistol across the table, still struggling to keep the rage from bringing down the brace wire.

She holds up her hand, says *Wait.* My vision is still swimming with color, but it's almost like the instruction isn't meant for me. The voice inside my head concurs; something is wrong.

*She should be afraid of you, but she's not.*

She sets the saw down.

'You've infected yourself.' She tilts her head, as though considering her own statement. 'You saw what it did to her; thought it might give you a chance against the soldiers. Reckless, given how little you could possibly understand of the pathology, but there's a certain logic to it. It is what the virus was designed for, after all.'

She takes a step around the table, then stops. She looks down at Mags and then back to me, as though another thought has just occurred to her.

'You're no longer contagious; you wouldn't have touched her like that if you were. How did you manage it?' She looks up, not waiting for my answer. 'I'm guessing an electrical shock of some sort?' She leans closer, studying me over her glasses. 'It looks like you may have overdone the voltage.'

'Wake her up, now.'

'I can't.'

She points at a metal stand beside the table. A plastic drip bag hangs from a hook. A tube snakes down from it, entering her arm just below the elbow.

'She'll be out for a while yet. I had to give her quite a large dose. The changes to her physiology were…profound.'

I point the pistol at the straps.

'Then untie her. I'll carry her.'

She just ignores me.

'And how do *you* feel, Gabriel?' She studies me over the rims of her spectacles. 'You seem lucid, but perhaps not entirely…in control?' She pinches the bridge of her nose, shakes her head. 'The delivery mechanism: that was always the problem. The virus was supposed to shut itself down, once the remap had been completed, once the subject's central nervous system had been optimized. We could never get it to do that, however. It always seemed to want to keep on going.'

I raise the pistol, thumb back the hammer.

'I said untie her.'

Gilbey's eyes flick to the gun, then for an instant they cut right and narrow. She gives the briefest shake of her head, but something's wrong; the gesture is far too calm.

*That's because it's not meant for you.*

I hear a sound from behind me and suddenly there's that smell again, stronger than before. Too late I recognize what it is. Stale sweat, and underneath it, tobacco.

I turn around, just as Truck steps from the shadows behind me, a baton in one hand. He lunges forward with it, an arc of blue light dancing between the metal prongs.

*

I TRY TO BACK UP, but the operating table's in my way, blocking my retreat, so instead I swing the pistol around. The speed of it takes him by surprise, and for an instant I see the shock re-arranging his features. But even as my finger tightens around the trigger, I know it won't be enough. I feel the prongs of the baton pierce the thin material of my thermals, jabbing hard into my ribs, just as the last of the slack comes out of the mechanism. The pistol bucks in my hand and in the same moment there's an instant of pain, quickly cut off as some internal circuit breaker I didn't know I had gets tripped.

Darkness rushes in from the corners of my vision and the ground beneath my feet lurches alarmingly. I hear the gun clatter to the floor and then my legs give way and I'm falling in some indescribable, slantwise direction. I expect to hit wall, but instead I feel something soft give way behind me. I reach for it with the hand that still seems to work and for a second thick material passes between my fingers, but I can't get a grip on it. I feel something sharp slam into my back, and then the floor comes rushing up to hit me.

I lay there for a moment, uncertain whether I am still conscious. I think I might be. Afterimages of the light from the other room swirl across my vision, but the darkness beyond is not complete; it has texture, grain. From somewhere on the other side of it I hear voices, furry, indistinct.

'...have to do that, Corporal?'

'...bastard shot me.'

I shake my head, trying to clear it, but it's like someone's ripped out a bunch of the wires inside me, and now nothing works like it should. The right side of my body seems to have switched off completely. I try to push myself up, but the arm there is limp, useless; it ignores whatever messages my brain tries to send it. My other side's better; I can still feel things there, enough to tell me I'm trapped against something hard, with ridges, presumably whatever I fell against on my way to the floor. I reach out with my hand. My fingers close around plastic.

I turn my head in that direction. The bars of a cage. When I look down I can see a section of the floor has been marked off with tape. I stare at the striped perimeter for a moment. It reminds me of another place. There was tape on the floor there, too, but the bars were metal, not plastic. I'm still trying to make the connection when I hear a shuffling sound behind me and then a single click, low and guttural. The hairs on the nape of my neck raise like hackles.

A face presses itself to the bars, only inches from mine. What once might have been a girl, not much older than I am now. The furies that occupied the cages in the other room seemed unaware of my presence, but this one knows I'm here. It stares back at me from deep, shadowed eyes, its nostrils flaring. I lie there, not even daring to breathe. After a few seconds it retreats.

The curtain I fell through is pulled back and Truck stands over me, the baton loose in one hand. The shot I fired before he zapped me has torn a gash in his fatigues and the material there is already dark with his blood. More of it runs down inside his sleeve and drips from his fingers. I feel something flicker inside me at the sight of it, but weaker then before, like the jolt I took from the baton has disabled it, too.

Truck takes a step closer. Unfortunately my bullet doesn't seem to have impaired him significantly. He wipes his hand on his pants leg, then tightens his grip on the baton, flicking the switch with his thumb. I watch as blue-white electricity sizzles between the prongs. Gilbey appears at his shoulder.

'He's no use to me dead, Corporal.'

'Don't worry, ma'am, I ain't going to kill him. Just going to mess him up a little. You can have him when I'm done.'

He smiles down at me, his face a mask of dull, lazy violence.

There's a soft, scrabbling sound beside me and I glance over. On the other side of the bars the fury has stiffened like a dog on point. It stares out, the muscles along its jaw clenching and unclenching, its fingers slowly raking the floor of the cage.

Truck doesn't seem to have noticed; it's dark in the alcove, and right now he seems more preoccupied with the vengeance he's about to extract from me. He takes another step towards me, thumbing the switch on the baton's handle again. I slide my good hand along the top of the cage, like I mean to pull myself up.

'That's it, Huck, you try that. Just make it that much more fun for me when I put you down again.'

I grasp the front, like I mean to do just as he says, but at the last second I shift my hand over. For a second Truck's brow knits together as he tries to work out what I'm doing, then he raises the baton, brings it down hard. There's a sickening crunch and I hear myself scream as the bone in my finger snaps like a twig. I pull my hand back, but he's too late; I've already released the catch. The gate springs open and the fury bounds out, teeth bared. Truck staggers backward, surprisingly fast for a man of his size. He raises the baton to ward off the attack, but Gilbey steps between them and grabs it, trying to wrest it from him.

'Don't! You'll hurt her!'

The fury's on her in an instant. I hear something clatter to the floor and then all three of them disappear from view.

I lie there for a moment, cradling my busted hand to my chest as I wait for the pain there to subside. To my surprise it quickly settles to a dull throb. I haul myself slowly to my feet. My right arm's still useless, but a measure of feeling seems to have returned to the leg on that side. I grab hold of the curtain and peer through. The fury has dragged its kill into the shadows underneath the operating table. It looks over at me, its jaw dark with blood, then returns to its meal. I watch to make sure it's settled, then turn my attention to the rest of the room. On the other side of the table, pressed up against the counter, stands Truck, one hand held to his injured arm. He shifts his gaze to me for a second, then his eyes dart back to the fury.

The pistol I dropped lies on the floor. I bend down to recover it. Mags is lying on the operating table, still unconscious. I'll need to get a lot closer to the fury if I'm to free her. I tell myself it'll be alright. It had the chance to attack me, when I fell against its cage, and it didn't. The one in the basement of Starkly was just the same; it paid more attention to the flask Finch left than it did me. Maybe whatever I am now isn't of interest to them.

I'm not sure I'm ready to trust everything to that theory, however, so I grip the pistol with the fingers I have that still work and pry the hammer back. It's awkward work getting the middle one through the trigger guard, but it gives me the courage I need to shuffle closer. The fury glances up as I start to advance and I freeze, but after a few seconds it returns to feasting on Gilbey. I hold the pistol on it a little longer, then take a deep breath and step up to the table.

I set the gun down, trying to ignore the grunts and snaps coming from by my feet. I start with the needle on her arm, removing the tape that holds it in place, sliding it out as carefully as I can. Then I turn to the clamp that's holding her head. I have to feel with my fingers for the screws, but one by one they come free. A trickle of her blood wets my fingertips as I withdraw the last one.

Truck watches me close, his eyes darting between the pistol and what's going on under the table. As I move on to the straps at her ankles he takes a step away from the counter. I shift my hand to the gun.

'You don't want to test me, Truck, not today.'

I can't be sure if it's me or the fury at my feet that's keeping him back, but he returns to the wall, glares at me for a while, then hitches his pants up and starts pacing, a slow shuffle back and forth along the length of the counter, like a wounded bear. There's a crunch and a wet sucking sound as beneath the table the fury takes another bite out of Gilbey. Truck's gaze flicks to the floor and back again, but he comes no closer.

I go back to Mags' restraints. The Velcro's tricky to manage one-handed, with the digits I still have at my disposal, and every now and then Truck gets a look in his eye and I have to pick up the pistol and show it to him again, but eventually I get the last cuff open. There's a couple of sensors stuck to her skin, but they come off easy.

I spot a roll of tape on the counter, like the kind Gilbey's used on Mags' eyes, sitting on top of a spiral bound notebook. I slip the tape into my pocket, adding the notebook for good measure. Then I slide my good arm underneath her and hoist her onto my shoulder. Truck shuffles forward, but I'm ready for him; I snatch the pistol up before he gets close enough to rush me. I back up slowly, watching as he starts to inch his way around the table.

He doesn't get very far before the fury lifts its head, flicks it in his direction. A single click, low and menacing, emanates from somewhere deep in its throat. I grip the pistol, getting ready to switch aim if I have to, but it's not me that's caught its attention. Truck freezes, unwilling to come any closer.

I take the opportunity to make our exit. The heel of my boot clips the baton he dropped, sending it clattering against the baseboard, but the fury pays it little mind; it returns to its meal, like I'm not even there. I put my shoulder to the door and then I'm out, letting it swing shut behind me. I set the pistol on the ground, lay Mags down as gently as I can and return to the door. I push it open with the toe of my boot, checking that the fury's still busy chowing down on Gilbey, then I bend down to retrieve the stick. On the far side of the operating table Truck hitches up his pants and hisses across the room at me.

'Hey! So that's it? You're just going to leave me here?'

I nod.

'I haven't killed you, which is more than you deserve.' I glance down at the fury, then point the baton at the alcove. 'If I were you I'd think about finding myself somewhere to hole up. Might want to do it quick, while it still lets you.'

I hold his gaze for a second longer then back out. Last I see of Truck he's taken my advice and is shuffling along the wall in the direction of the curtain and the plastic cage behind.

The door closes and I look over my shoulder. Mags hasn't stirred from where I set her down. I wonder how much longer she'll be out of it. Behind her rows of cages stretch off into the gloom. I think of how I found her, the first time I rescued her from this place; the dark, ugly welts Truck had inflicted with the same baton, branding her from hip to shoulder. And for a second the anger flares again, only this time I'm not sure it's the thing the virus put inside me that twists with it. This feels familiar; something that was there all along.

I pick the baton up, turn back to the door, slide it through the handles.

I make sure to wedge it in tight.

*

I SIT ON THE FLOOR next to Mags and reach for the pistol. The finger Truck broke is already starting to swell, but as long as I don't ask too much of it it doesn't hurt that bad. I wonder if that's the virus's doing too.

It doesn't change the fact that my chances of hitting anything that doesn't oblige by positioning itself at the end of the barrel and holding still are slim, however, so I use the tape to bind my busted finger to the middle one, just like I remember reading in the first aid book I used to keep under the bed in the farmhouse outside Eden. When I'm done I return the pistol to its holster. My right arm's starting to tingle, but that appears to be as much as it can be relied upon to do. The leg on that side feels rubbery, unreliable, too, but for now at least it seems to be obeying the messages my brain's sending it.

I hoist Mags onto my shoulder and start retracing my steps. I make my way between the cages, ignoring the vacant stares from those hunched on the other side of the bars. Then we're past them, hurrying through the crematorium, and finally back in the first room. I hobble towards the door at the end, my thoughts already on the stair beyond. But halfway along something catches my eye and I stop.

On the floor of one of the cages, a plastic food tray. I balance Mags on my shoulder and bend down for a better look, making sure to keep a respectful distance from the bars. A large shape crouches on the other side of the tray, too big for the dimensions of his confinement. His head's been shaved and when he looks up his eyes are sunken, dark. The face that used to soft, round, has angles to it now, and there are deep hollows where his cheeks used to be. It is familiar, nonetheless.

'Hamish?'

He shifts uncertainly at the mention of his name.

'Angus?'

I shake my head.

'No Hamish. It's Gabe.'

He says my name a few times, as though testing it. I think there's a glimmer of recognition there, but it's hard to tell. He shuffles forward, looks up at me hopefully.

'Is Angus coming?'

'Angus is dead, Hamish. I'm sorry.'

As soon as the words are out I wish I could take them back. It's as if his face is held together by a number of unseen bolts and each of them has suddenly been loosened a turn. His head drops.

I feel the need to say something, to explain.

'It was Peck who killed him, but it was my fault. I should have known, when I sent you both back to him…'

He looks up. The face that was slack a moment ago has tightened again. He whispers a single word.

'Peck.'

'Yes, Peck, but it was me...'

'Peck.'

I try again, but there's no point. The name seems to be all he's capable of now; he just keeps repeating it over and over, like it's the only thing he cares to hold on to.

I glance along the aisle, towards the broken door. Hicks is still up there, somewhere, together with Jax and whoever else remains of the soldiers. Kane, Peck, and the Guardians, too. By now they must realize something's wrong; they're probably already looking for us. I hesitate for a moment and then get to my feet. I take a step toward the exit and then stop, turn around and press down on the latch. The spring releases and the gate opens a fraction, but Hamish doesn't come out. I make my way between the cages. When I reach the door I check behind me again, but the aisle remains empty.

I lay Mags on the floor and step into the storage room. All her stuff's there, in a plastic crate just inside the door. For a second I consider trying to dress her, but it'd take too long with my hands they way they are; I'm not even sure I'd be able to manage it. I'll worry about it when I get us outside. Her backpack's where I left it, against the wall. I stuff her things into it, then lift her onto my shoulder again, grab the pack and start up the stair.

It takes longer on the way up than coming down, but at last I can hear the thrum of machinery above, growing louder with each step. As we near the plant room she stirs on my shoulder, starts to struggle. I whisper to her to stay still.

'Gabe?' Her voice is thick with the anesthetic. 'Where are we?'

'Still in The Greenbrier. We'll soon be out.'

'I feel weird.' She shifts her head. 'I can't see.'

'There's tape on your eyes, that's all. Just hold on to me and as soon as we get to the top I'll take care of it.'

'Okay.'

At last the stair ends. I push the door open a crack. The clatter from the generator increases, but when I peer through our luck seems to be holding; the gangway ahead is still empty. I carry her up onto it, set her down on the metal grating. She reaches up to her face but her movements are clumsy, uncoordinated.

'Here, let me.'

I kneel down in front of her. It takes a while, but I finally get an edge of the tape between the thumb and third finger of my good hand and gently lift the tape from one eye, then the other.

She looks up at me, blinking. It takes her a moment to focus and then she breathes in sharply and recoils, pressing herself back against the railing.

I turn away quickly; I had forgotten what I look like now. I grab the backpack and start pulling out her clothes, anxious for something that will keep me from seeing that look on her face again. I feel her hand on my arm. She reaches up, touches my cheek.

'I'm sorry. I…I was just surprised. What happened?'

I clear my throat, not sure I trust myself to speak.

'I'll tell you later. Right now we need to get out of here.' I hand her her clothes. 'Put these on.'

She looks down, for the first time realizing what she's wearing. Her fingers fly to her scalp.

'It's okay. She didn't get a chance to do anything.'

She probes the skin there a moment longer, like she may not believe me, then she picks up her thermals and starts putting them on. Her movements are still awkward. I try to help, but the best I can manage is to hand her stuff. She pulls on a boot while I reach for the other.

'What's wrong with your arm?'

'Truck. He zapped me with the baton.'

I look down at it, hanging useless by my side. It used to be numb, but now if I concentrate I think I can feel a prickling sensation, like pins and needles, in my fingertips. I tell myself that has to be a good sign.

She finishes tying the laces while I close the pack and heft it onto my shoulder

'Do you think you can walk?'

'I'm not sure.'

I hold out my good arm. She grabs my wrist and I pull her to her feet. But when she tries to take a step her legs buckle and she has to reach for the railing behind her.

'It's alright, I got you.'

I slip my arm around her waist and we make our way slowly across the gangway and down the steps on the other side. I open the door a fraction and peer through.

The safety lights still hum, bathing the walls in their green glow, but the corridor that was empty when I came through earlier now has a body in it. Or to be more precise, a pair of legs; the rest of whoever it is has been dragged into one of the dorms. The boots are missing, but the fatigues tell me it's one of the soldiers. I stare at them for a moment, trying to work out who it might be. It's not big enough for Jax, but it could be any of the others, except maybe Weasel, unless someone's bothered to haul him in from outside. It might even be Hicks, although I can't see how we'd ever be that lucky.

I whisper to Mags that we need to go. She holds on to me and together we step into the corridor. The noise from the plant room recedes as the door closes behind us.

As we get closer more of the torso becomes visible. I can read the name above the breast pocket of his fatigues now, but I no longer need it. This is the man the other soldiers called Pops. The deep lines that bracketed his mouth and grooved themselves across his forehead have softened in death, but his eyes are wide with surprise, like whatever it was he last saw, he wasn't expecting it. A single bullet hole punctures the middle of his forehead, a trickle of darkening blood snaking its way into the gray stubble at his temple.

Mags looks up at me.

'What happened to him?'

'I don't know.'

I dip the toe of my boot in the dark puddle of blood that surrounds the back of his head. It's still tacky.

'Whatever it was, it wasn't long ago.'

*

WE LEAVE THE CORRIDOR and enter the decontamination chamber. The nozzles that protrude from the tiles make it hard to walk side by side. Mags says she's okay, but when I let go of her she sways alarmingly and has to reach for the wall to steady herself. I slip my arm back around her waist and we continue on, shuffling sideways between the pipes. Behind us the door to the bunker closes, robbing the cramped passageway of color. When we make it to the end I tell her to hold on to something; I need my hand to work the handle. I push down; the door creaks softly as it swings out into the tunnel.

I put my arm around her again and we step through. But when I look up I stop. Ahead of us in the tunnel, a pair of flashlights, quivering in the darkness. I glance back the way we've come, but there's no light that way that might reveal us to whoever it might be. I stare at the beams for a moment, trying to work it out. They don't seem to moving away. It's like they're just standing there, waiting.

'What is it?'

'Someone in the tunnel.'

'Can you see who?'

I shake my head.

'Probably the ones who did for Pops.' I look up at the pipes that hang down from the roof, running straight out into darkness. It's the same all the way to the blast door; there's no cover in there. 'Maybe we should find another way out.'

I say it mostly to myself, but I hear her whisper back to me.

'Who had to quit so you could be in charge of smart decisions?'

I open my mouth to respond, but before I get the chance I sense movement behind us. I feel Mags tense at my side. Without warning a light flicks on, momentarily blinding me, and I have to turn my head away. My brain sends a message to my reaching hand, but it just twitches uselessly. I squint into the glare, trying to see who's behind the flashlight, but all I can make out is the muzzle of the pistol it's pressed up against.

'Cute.'

I may not be able to see his face, but that voice I know.

*Peck.*

He points the beam at Mags for a second and then returns it to me.

'Hell, Gabriel, what have you done to yourself?' He holds the flashlight on me a second longer, then whistles into the tunnel. From off in the darkness a voice answers, faint with distance, but immediately familiar.

'Who is it, Randall?'

'Someone here you might want to see, Mr. President.'

I force myself to look into flashlight, trying to gauge the distance to his gun. I have one mostly good hand, and I'm fast now, fast enough that I might even be able to surprise someone like Peck. He's standing just far enough away to make the outcome uncertain, however. And then there's Mags. She can barely stand, let alone be counted on to step aside from a bullet.

The lights in the tunnel grow brighter as Kane and whoever's with him make their way back towards us. I glance into the decontamination chamber, searching for another way out. Colors are still swirling across my vision from the flashlight, but for an instant I think I see a sliver of green.

'I warned you not to underestimate me, Gabriel.'

I ignore him and instead screw my eyes shut, trying to clear the comet tails and starbursts. The light I thought I saw at the end has gone, if it was ever there.

Peck shifts the gun a little closer; I feel Mags grip me tighter.

'Hey, do I not have your attention?'

'Sure. I heard you. Underestimate.'

My eyes flick back to the showers, but now there's only darkness. For a second I could have sworn I saw the door at the other end open, though.

Kane's getting closer, his footsteps growing louder as they echo towards us out of the tunnel. I peer into the gloom, trying to make out who's with him, but I can't see beyond their flashlights.

I risk another glance into the decontamination chamber. This time I think I see movement. One of the soldiers? I only glimpsed it for a second, but the shape I saw didn't look big enough for Jax, and that only leaves Hicks. I'm not sure how his arrival will play out any better for us. And then I catch a sound. I glance over at Peck. I don't think he's heard it yet. I squeeze Mags' waist and shuffle backwards.

'Hey, where do you think you're going?'

'Nowhere, Peck.'

I say it loud. My voice echoes back at me from the chamber. I take another step away from the Secret Service agent.

'Hold it right there, Gabriel.'

The flashlights coming down the tunnel are almost on us, and for a second one of the beams slips into the narrow chamber. The light shifts over tiles, nozzles, for an instant lands on a pair of silver eyes, moves on.

I back up again. Peck moves forward, and now he's the one standing in front of the doorway.

'Godammit Gabriel, I'm serious. Move again and I'll shoot you where you stand.'

'Okay, Peck.'

This time when his name comes back from the showers the echo isn't right. His brow furrows and he looks at me, momentarily puzzled.

'Sorry, Randall.'

The pistol drops a fraction and his eyes flick into the chamber, then widen.

'You son of a…'

If he gets another word out I never hear it. I grab Mags tight and drag her backwards even as Hamish appears in the doorway. He sees Peck and lunges forward, hands outstretched, reaching for the Secret Service agent's throat.

*

PECK RECOVERS SURPRISINGLY QUICKLY. He takes a step backwards, wheeling around to face the new threat. His gun comes up, his finger already curling around the trigger, even as Hamish slams into him. They stumble backwards together then both go over, hitting the ground with a dull thud. Hamish is the bigger of the two, even now, but there's no finesse to his attack, only frenzy, fury. His teeth snap, his fingers clawing at the Secret Service agent's neck. At last he finds purchase there, lifts his head in both hands, slams it back down. There's a sickening crunch, then a muffled bang as the pistol goes off.

Hamish grunts once and slumps forward, the last of the life already going out of him. Peck makes no move to push him off. His eyes are open, but they stare up sightlessly. A pool of blood spreads from the back of his head, darkening the dusty concrete.

I look up to see Kane, striding out of the tunnel, a camouflage parka flapping around him. The tag on the breast says it once belonged to Pops, and I'm guessing that's where he got the boots he's wearing too. They look out of place on him, but then I realize this is the first time I've seen him out of a suit. He comes to a halt a few feet away. Kurt appears beside him a moment later, a rifle clutched to his chest.

Kane studies his Secret Service agent for a moment then slowly turns his gaze to Mags and me. Last I saw of him was in Eden's chapel, when we left him with the soldiers. He hadn't been himself then, as though the wind had been knocked out of him by the events of the day. He looks like the President we always knew now, though. He brings himself up to his full height.

'Gabriel.' His lip curls in distaste, like the mention of my name causes him displeasure.

I slip my arm out from around Mags and step in front of her. Feeling's starting to return to my fingers, but I still can't rely on them do my bidding. I don't think Kurt notices. He stares at me, slack-jawed, his mouth open, like he's not sure he believes what he's seeing.

Kane glances down at the pistol.

'Unwise of you to keep that sidearm holstered, son.'

I take a step closer, my eyes still on Kurt. His finger hovers over the trigger, but he hasn't yet swung the rifle in my direction.

'There's no rush, Mr. President. I'll draw it when I'm good and ready.'

I shift my shoulder back a fraction so my fingers rest over Hicks' pistol, trying to make it seem natural.

Kane studies me for a moment, like he's making his mind up about something, then he turns to the Guardian.

'Shoot him, Kurt, and let's get out of here.'

I ignore him, addressing myself instead to Kurt. I raise my good hand and point my taped fingers behind him, into the tunnel.

'You and Peck must have come in the same way I did, earlier.' I don't wait for him to confirm it. 'You'll have seen Private Wiesmann on your way in, then. You remember Weasel, don't you, Kurt? Small, kinda ratty-looking? Has a big hole where his throat used to be? He tried to shoot me earlier, too. Didn't work out so well for him.'

I wait a second for that to sink in.

'Did Kane ever tell you what the virus was designed for, Kurt? I just found out, from Dr. Gilbey. It wasn't meant as a weapon, least not the way the world got to experience it. They were trying to create a better soldier; someone faster, stronger. More resilient.' I hold up the hand that still works, slowly curl it into a fist. For a second the pain from my busted finger is excruciating, but then something inside me shuts it down.

'And that's exactly what it does; it rewires you, makes you all those things.' I stare at my hand a moment longer, then let it fall to my side. 'You could ask Gilbey yourself, she'd tell you. If I hadn't killed her, that is. Her and Corporal Truckle.'

I leave him a moment to digest those details, then I glance down at the gun on my hip.

'See, Kurt, if I wanted I could draw this pistol, put a bullet right between your eyes, have it back in its holster before you even knew you'd been hit. I'm new to the killing business, though, and it's been a busy day. So I reckon I'll wait till you swing that rifle in my direction. I figure that way I'll sleep a little easier tonight.'

Kane's eyes narrow, like he's not buying it. He turns to Kurt, his tone impatient.

'If he was going to do something he would have done it already. Finish them both and let's go.'

I ignore him, keeping my eyes on the rifle Kurt has clutched to his chest.

'Ready whenever you are, Kurt.'

I try to flex the fingers of my right hand, and this time I think I feel them wiggle. Kurt's gaze drops there.

'Maybe we should just get out of here, Mr. President.'

Kane lets out an exasperated sigh, and for a second I think he might take the weapon and do this himself. But he doesn't. He simply shakes his head and then turns and walks off into the tunnel.

Kurt calls over his shoulder.

'What about Randall, Mr. President? I-I think he's still breathing.'

Kane doesn't stop. His voice drifts back up to us through the tunnel, already growing hollow with distance.

'He's beyond saving. That other one was infected, so he'll have it now too. Come along.'

Kurt looks down at Peck, then his eyes return to me.

The voice inside my head warns me against it, but I can't resist. I wave my good hand in his direction, like he's dismissed.

'Listen to your master, Kurt. Best you run along now.'

He starts to follow, then his face twists and he jabs a finger at me.

'Freak.'

I lean forward, offering him a smile. My features the way they are now I'm guessing that brings him no more comfort than I intend it to. He takes a quick step backwards, and when he speaks again there's fear in his voice.

'I'm warning you, both of you: you'd better not follow us.'

He holds up the rifle as if to make his point, but I notice he takes care not to point it at me. I spread my good hand, a gesture of supplication. To my surprise the other manages something vaguely similar.

He takes another step backwards, then without warning he turns and runs off after Kane.

I watch their flashlights until they're little more than pinpricks in the darkness.

*

WE MAKE OUR WAY through the decontamination chamber, back into the bunker. The safety lights are still burning, but other than Pops the corridor remains empty. Mags squeezes my side and points to the left, to a door with a push bar marked *Emergency Exit*.

'That's the way we came, the first time Gilbey brought me down here.'

I push on the bar, half-expecting an alarm to sound, but it just creaks open. We step through into a concrete stairwell and start climbing. Mags seems a little steadier on her feet now, but it's slow work all the same. When we reach the first landing I stop and try to splay my fingers. They twitch, like they want to do my bidding, but the messages my brain's sending still aren't getting through right. Mags watches, then her gaze shifts to the pistol, nestled in its holster.

'Is it true, everything you said back there?' She studies the floor a moment. 'It's not that they didn't deserve it, after all they've done. And I know what it feels like, to be so mad...'

Her voice trails off and she looks up at me, waiting for an answer.

'I shot Weasel, just like I said. It was that or he was going to shoot me. Gilbey's dead, too. I didn't kill her, but I did release the thing that did. I meant it for Truck, but she got in the way. As for Corporal Truckle, as far as I know he's still alive, most likely holed up in one of those cages they put you and Johnny in, hiding from it. So, no, I didn't kill him either. I just didn't save him when I had the opportunity.'

I look away as I say the last bit, because there's more to it than I've let on, and I don't want her to see it in my face. I wonder what she'd think if I told her about the baton I slipped through the door handles, or why I might have chosen to do something like that.

We continue up the stairs. At the top there's another door and then a long, low-ceilinged corridor. A single fluorescent tube hangs from the ceiling, the light it throws barely sufficient for its length. Beyond, set back in the shadows, a familiar vault door, a large latch handle at its center.

We make our way towards it. I press down on the handle and the door creaks back into darkness. I reach out with my hand, feeling for the join, and then push. The section of fake wall pops out, concertinas, allowing me to slide it sideways. We step into the Exhibition Hall.

An emergency lamp flickers above my head. Shadows from the concrete pillars that brace the high ceiling shift against the walls. The garish wallpaper does well to hide the fact that we haven't yet left the bunker, a fact I mean to remedy without delay. On the far side of the room stairs lead up to the Colonial Lounge. Beyond there's a long passageway and then the lobby, all that now stands between us and getting out of this place.

We're halfway across when I hear a sound. Mags must have caught it too; she freezes at my side.

Something appears at the bottom of the stairs. A dark shape, the contours unfamiliar, until I realize it's not a single person but two: one lean, rangy, the other of much heavier build. The larger one reaches the foot of the stairs, stumbles into the flickering light and now I recognize him. He's bent forward, an arm twisted high behind his back. The thinner man stands behind, shoving him on.

Hicks.

It's less of a shock than I was expecting; I guess deep down I knew the chances of us getting out of here without running into him were slim. His prisoner's more of a surprise, however. By now Jake should be somewhere in Virginia, leading the Juvies back to Mount Weather.

Hicks pushes him forward a few more steps, then stops and looks at me.

'You shouldn't have come back.'

I feel the anger bubbling up again, that he would say something like that.

'You didn't leave me that choice.'

He nods, like he understands.

'I figured.' He squints at me, shifts his jaw from side to side. 'You've been busy.'

He says it without an explanation of what he means. Could be the way I look now, or that Mags is free. Maybe he found Weasel outside. It might be all of it.

I slide my arm behind my back and try to flex my fingers again. This time they tighten, like they want to do my bidding, but the signal my brain's sending's still getting jumbled somewhere before if reaches them.

Mags looks over at Jake.

'Are you okay?'

Jake looks scared, but he nods.

She turns to Hicks.

'So what do we do now, Sergeant?'

The voice warns me against saying anything rash, but its influence is already waning as the anger builds inside me. I don't wait for him to respond.

'He'll let Jake go and step out of our way, if he knows what's good for him.'

I don't need the voice to tell me that's not going to happen, though. That's just not who he is; I doubt there's ever been a single thing in his life he wouldn't have sacrificed on the blessed altar of getting the job done. I think of Mags, and Johnny, all the others he helped put in cages. And for what? To comply with an order he'd been given, years ago, by some politician or general long since dead.

The thought of it makes me even angrier.

'I'm warning you, Hicks. Get out of our way now. I haven't come this far to die in the trying.'

Mags squeezes me, letting me know she needs me to be quiet now. I hear her say the one thing that might change his mind.

'Gilbey's dead, Sergeant. Whatever you thought you were doing here, it's over. There's no point anymore.'

Hicks stares at her for a moment, then looks at me for confirmation. I feel Mags squeeze my side again. I'm not sure I can be trusted to speak, so I just nod. And for a moment it seems like it might work. He sags, like the weight of the world has just settled on his shoulders; like there may be nothing holding him up anymore but the clothes he's wearing. But then he shakes his head.

'Godammit son, do you know what you've done?'

And with that whatever hope there was for us all to walk out of the room evaporates. The anger returns, and this time there's no hope of holding it back.

What *I've* done?

I spit the words out, with as much venom as I can muster.

'Something you should've, a long time ago.'

He rocks back on his heels, like I've just slapped him. Whatever strength had abandoned him a moment ago, something else takes its place now: a cold indifference, as though he cares little about what happens next, only that there is business yet to finish.

He lets go of Jake.

I slip my arm out from around Mags, hiss at her to get out.

She opens her mouth to protest, but I tell Jake to take her. He hesitates, then hurries over. I push her towards him, not daring to take my eyes off Hicks.

'Gabe, wait…'

I don't want to hear what she has to say. I bark at them both to leave. She starts to struggle, but Jake picks her up easily, starts carrying her towards the stair.

Hicks shifts his arm and the parka falls back, exposing a pistol, just like Marv's. He works his jaw from side to side.

'Whenever you're ready, kid.'

And just like that it hits me, sudden and absolute. This is it; I have embarked on the final seconds of my life. And for a moment the shock of it displaces even the rage. I look past Hicks to where Jake is dragging Mags up the stairs. The sight of it triggers a final burst of memories: the first time I saw her, in the dayroom of the Sacred Heart Home for Children, a tattered paperback cradled in her lap; sneaking up to the roof of Eden's mess before the curfew buzzer sounded, to tell her the stories I had found on the outside; the first time we kissed. And with them an instant of unbearable sadness. Because these are things I want so much.

Hicks' hand hangs loose at his side, his fingers still hovering over the steel on his hip, the instrument that will take this away from me. And just like that the anger returns, hardening my will. The calm voice lets go, ceding control to the older part of me, the part that takes care of heartbeat and breath, tooth and claw. The part nature built first to keep my ass alive.

Behind me the emergency light flickers. My nerves are already jumping like bowstrings; it's all it takes. The muscles in my hand twitch, and then it begins.

Time slows, is replaced by something else. Hicks' fingers are already closing around his weapon. When I saw him, in the basement of the hospital in Blacksburg, after Ortiz got surprised by the fury, I could scarcely believe how fast he was. *Shrapnel*-fast. One instant his hand had been empty and the next there had been a pistol there. I told Mags afterwards I didn't think even Peck would have been a match for him, and now I see the truth in that.

It wouldn't have been close.

My brain's sending furious messages to my own hand, but it still hasn't moved, and yet I know with cold certainty that even now I could beat him, if I weren't for what Truck had done to my arm.

The anger grows, becomes a rage, a fury.

And at last I feel something there.

Purpose.

My hands dips for the holster.

Too late.

Hicks has already drawn the Beretta. He brings it up in one smooth motion, sudden and terribly deadly. I can see the barrel now, wide, like a tunnel. He can't miss, not from this distance.

And then my own pistol is in front of me. I feel its weight, the coldness of the steel, the contours of the grip, the subtle give in the trigger, the punch of the recoil. There's the pepper-smell of gunpowder and then I'm stepping through it and it's gone, even as I squeeze again.

I stride forward, keeping my finger tight on the trigger, my off hand fanning the hammer back, over and over. The bullets shake him, like a sapling in a blizzard, and then I'm standing over him, the last round fired and all there is the dry click of the hammer hitting an empty chamber. The pistol slips from my fingers and I let out a howl, wordless and incoherent, of relief, or rage, or sadness, I can't be sure.

I feel something touch my arm and I spin around, still struggling to drag my brain out of the torrent of adrenalin.

Mags.

She bends down and collects the Beretta from where Hicks has dropped it. Her brow furrows and she looks up, like she's deciding whether to show me. She hesitates a moment then holds it out.

I take it from her, not understanding. She points to a spot at the back, between the grip and the rear sight, and then I see.

The safety.

It was never off.

*

I RELOAD THE PISTOL with the last of the bullets from the gun belt while Jake explains how he's come to be here. His skills don't lie in storytelling; he's done before I've dropped the final cartridge into its chamber. I snap the gate shut and return the pistol to its holster.

We're not done yet.

The kid's plan to empty out The Greenbrier worked, at least as well as could be expected; Jake said he took off with Jax and a couple of the Guardians on his tail. I can't see how that will have gone well for him. The kid's quick, but his legs are short; no way he'd be able to outpace The Viking, not in the snow. I need to go find them. First we need to get clear of this place, though; if there's anyone still left inside they'll have heard the gunfire.

But when we reach the lobby there's just a single figure waiting. He stands in the center of the checkerboard marble, hands clasped behind his back, staring up at the chandelier that hangs from the high ceiling. He looks over as we enter.

'Ah, Gabriel.'

'Mr. Finch?'

He's wearing the overcoat with the fur-trimmed collar he had on that night in the holding pen. The hem is splashed with dirt, like he has travelled a distance in it.

He turns to Mags.

'And this must be Mags.' He holds out a hand. 'I am delighted to meet you, my dear. Gabriel has told me so much about you. My name is Garland Finch.'

Mags eyes him suspiciously, then takes his hand. He offers Jake a smile, then gestures to a pair of armchairs that sit either side of a tall wooden clock.

I look around uncertainly, still not sure what's going on. Through the lobby's tall windows I see a handful of dark shapes, bundled up in rags, making their way towards the entrance.

'I'm sorry Mr. Finch, but we have business to attend to. There's a friend of ours still unaccounted for.'

He flutters his fingers, like this should not be a concern.

'Oh, don't fret on his account, Gabriel. I expect he'll be with us presently.'

I'm not sure what he means by that, but now more men are gathering outside and I have yet to figure out how to get us by them, so I follow him over to the chairs. His heels click on the marble. There's no sign of the cane and only the merest hint of a drag in his stride. He stands in front of the clock, taking a moment to admire the carvings on its golden face, then bends to the nearest chair and lifts the drop sheet that covers it. The upholstery is patterned like the feathers of some colorful bird. He brushes the dust from it and motions for Mags to sit. She hesitates then takes a seat. He points me towards the other one.

'I'll stand, if it's all the same to you, Mr. Finch.'

'As you wish, Gabriel, as you wish.'

He chooses a spot on the sofa opposite, carefully placing one knee over the other, then looks up at me. The spectacles are gone. Without them his eyes seem an even paler shade of blue.

I glance back towards the entrance. What looks like the entire population of Starkly Correctional Institution now seems to be waiting outside. I realize it must have been their tracks I saw this morning, out on the interstate, not Peck's.

'When did you send them out?'

Finch's lips crease in a smile.

'The morning after you showed up.'

'You were always going to go for it.'

He nods.

'I do hope you will excuse the subterfuge.' He spreads his hands. 'Only when I heard you speak of this place, it seemed like an opportunity too great to pass up.'

He leans forward and his expression changes, as though an unpleasant thought has just occurred to him.

'You didn't have any designs on it yourself, did you?'

I shake my head. I can't imagine anything worse than spending another night here.

'Good, good. I would hate for us to fall out over it.'

'You held me in that cell, though.'

He spreads his hands by way of apology.

'Yes, but your incarceration was only temporary. I assumed you would need our help, and I needed time to get these fellows here. You will forgive me Gabriel, but your plan did seem a little…threadbare.' He looks over at Mags, then back to me again. 'Although I have to say, you seem to have managed admirably.' He gestures in the direction of the Exhibition Hall. 'What will we find back there?'

'Just bodies, for the most part. There's a level beneath the plant room; you might want to be careful when you go check it out. One of the furies got free. It has a soldier trapped down there.'

He stares at me a moment, like he's trying to work out whether there's a part of it I'm not telling him, but then he just says, *I see.*

There's a commotion from outside and I look over in time to see Jax being dragged forward. His arms have been bound, but nevertheless it's taking Tully and three of the other inmates to hold him. Behind him I see

Zack and Jason. It looks like they've found Boots, too. There's no sign of Kurt or the President.

Goldie appears at the entrance, presses his face to the glass. Finch waves him in and he enters the lobby, pushing the kid in front of him. The kid sees Mags and makes to run over to her, but Goldie grabs him by the shoulder, holding him back. Mags gets to her feet; there's an expression on her face that suggest Goldie had best take care what he does next.

The fingers of my reaching hand flex involuntarily. There's still a few pins and needles there, but my arm seems like it might finally be ready to do my bidding. It doesn't change the fact I only have five bullets to my name, though.

I look over at the kid.

'You okay?'

He nods.

'That one's our friend, Mr. Finch. We'll be needing him back.'

Finch leans back on the sofa. His fingers brush the knot of his tie.

'You know it's not wise to get between a predator and its meal, Gabriel.'

Mags' expression hardens at his words. I catch her eye.

*Let me take care of this.*

'I know, Mr. Finch. But this time I'm afraid I'm going to have to insist.'

My hand settles on the haft of the pistol, but I make no move to draw it. The voice speaks softly.

'I'll trade you for him, though.'

*Good.*

'And what is it that you have to offer me, Gabriel? More books?'

I shake my head.

'Something much better than that, Mr. Finch.'

I lean forward, whisper it into his ear.

He sits still for a moment, then turns his head to look at me.

'I'm not sure, Gabriel. You know what they say: a bird in the hand. And that one looks tasty.'

But his eyes are sparkling as he says it; I know I have him.

'Oh, you wouldn't find him palatable, Mr. Finch. Trust me on that.'

He lifts a finger, starts tapping the arm of the sofa with it.

'You're not putting me on are you, Gabriel?'

I shake my head.

'I know better than to lie to you, Mr. Finch.'

He beckons Goldie forward. I take him off to one side, tell him which way Kane was headed. He looks at Finch for confirmation then hurries back outside. Moments later he leaves, taking half a dozen of the prisoners with him.

Finch gets to his feet, smoothes the front of his overcoat.

'Well then, it appears our business is concluded. Will you be joining us for dinner? It appears we have plenty to go around.'

'I don't think so, Mr. Finch. We'll be on our way, if it's all the same to you.'

He nods, ushers us toward the entrance. At the door he stops and turns to Mags.

'Well my dear, it was a pleasure to make your acquaintance.'

The smile doesn't waver, but as he says it he grabs her by the wrist, so fast it surprises me. His other hand darts inside his coat. Mags' eyes narrow and she starts to pull away, but it's clear whatever Finch is up to he's caught her off guard too.

My fingers don't wait for an instruction from my brain. I have the pistol clear of its holster and pointed at his head with the hammer cocked before his hand has a chance to re-emerge. He pauses, then slowly pulls out a small package wrapped in brown paper, tied up with string. He places it in her hand.

'Something Gabriel would have wanted you to have.'

She hesitates a moment and then pulls the string. The paper falls away and inside is a book. On the cover a dark rabbit, hunched in silhouette, its ears folded back, its teeth bared. The copy of *Watership Down* he gave me on my first visit to Starkly.

I return the gun to its holster.

'That wasn't smart, Mr. Finch. I could have killed you.'

He spreads his hands.

'It was a risk, but I had to know.'

I'm not sure I understand. A smile creases his lips.

'You do remember our discussion, Gabriel? The totem pole; where we each stand on it.' He leans a little closer and the smile becomes wistful. 'I think I could have been a little braver, with that gift you gave me. Held out just a little longer.'

Mags wraps the book back up in the paper and slides it into the pocket of her parka. Jake holds the door open for her and the kid and they step outside. I'm about to follow them, but then Finch rests a hand on my arm.

'I have enjoyed our time together Gabriel, I really have. Probably best that our paths don't cross again, wouldn't you agree?

'I would, Mr. Finch.'

He nods.

I push the door back and step into the shadow of The Greenbrier's massive portico.

'Gabriel.'

I turn around.

Finch is standing in the doorway, his hands clasped behind his back. I remember what I thought, the first time I laid eyes on him, in the cellblock of the Starkly Correctional Institution: that he was other, exotic; that he did not belong in a place like that. Perhaps it's The Greenbrier's outward splendor: the towering columns; the sweeping staircases; the paintings that hang from its gaily-colored walls. Or maybe it's the darkness that for so long has lurked just beneath that polished veneer. Either way, Garland Finch no longer seems out of place. It seems like he is home.

'What is it, Mr. Finch?'

'That flask I left you; did you happen to try any of it?'

'No, Mr. Finch, I did not.'

He smiles, then turns to go back inside.

'Good for you, Gabriel. Good for you.'

*

OFF IN THE DISTANCE a lowering cloud gives sudden birth to a sliver of blue-white light; seconds later the low boom of thunder rumbles through the valley. I look up into the darkening sky. To the east thunderheads the color of charcoal, heavy with the snow they carry, drag their swollen bellies along the peaks. Storms are coming; it won't be long now until the first of them are upon us.

I pause to let Jake catch up while Mags continues on ahead, the kid following close in her tracks. It's been ten days since we quit The Greenbrier and she's yet to ask me what it was I offered Finch to let him go. I guess she doesn't need to. There was only the one thing I had to trade, and she knows it. When we had Kane and Hicks and the other soldiers all tied up in the chapel in Eden, after she'd come through the scanner, I told her I was ready to shoot them, and be done with it. And looking back at how things have turned out, I can't say as that would have altogether been a bad thing. Those we spared then are dead now, or worse, and there are a few, like Tyler and Eric, and Angus and Hamish, who might still be alive if I had. But she stopped me. She said that wasn't how we were going to do things now.

This time she didn't raise a finger.

Still, though, I can't help but wonder if she'd have done it any different, in my shoes. I can't see how she could. Sometimes there just aren't any good choices, even if you see the world the way Mags does.

I turn back to Jake, watching as he struggles towards me through the drifts. I doubt he has much left in him now. I can't fault him for it. He doesn't have the pace we do and I've been pushing hard, hoping to get us most of the way back before our rations ran out.

Tell the truth I never thought we'd manage to stretch them out as long as we have; the MREs I brought with me from Fearrington weren't ever intended for four. But something's changed since Starkly. I can get by on much less than I used to need, even pounding the snow all day long. Mags and the kid, too. Jake's been getting the lion's share of what we have.

I've been reading Gilbey's notebook at night, searching for clues as to how the virus works, what it's done to make us the way we are now. Most of what's she written I just don't get, and I doubt any dictionary I might find down the road will help with that. But occasionally there's something, a paragraph, a sentence, even just a single word, I can make sense of.

On one page she'd scribbled *Fuel* above a bunch of equations, underlining it several times for good measure. The rest of what followed looked like so much gobbledygook and I was about to flip the page, when among the jumble of symbols I spotted a word I recognized from years of studying the backs of MRE cartons: *calories*. It appeared more than once in the pages that followed.

Food is like fuel, same as diesel for the generator or branches for the fire, only for our bodies; that much I already knew. I always figured it got used up when you did stuff, like running around, or hiking through the snow. Turns out I had that bit wrong, however. According to what followed in Gilbey's notes for the most part it goes to regulating your body temperature, keeping you warm. And if I've understood her right, Mags, the kid and me, we don't need that anymore.

MRE doesn't stand for *Magically Replenishing Eats*, all the same, and I've yet to figure out the workings of that loaves and fishes trick Kane would sometimes sermonize about, when he was trying to convince us what was left in Eden's stores would be enough to see us through the winters that lay ahead. We split the last of the cartons yesterday morning. Ever since there's been nothing but the snowmelt in our canteens.

I'm not worried, though. An hour ago we quit the John S Mosby highway for the Blue Ridge Mountain Road. There can't be more than a couple of miles left between us and Mount Weather now. By nightfall we'll be there.

Jake's still struggling up the incline. I look behind him. All along the horizon lightning flashes inside the clouds, occasionally breaking free to stab down at the peaks below. I count the seconds until the thunder reaches us. Still distant, but getting closer. Back in Eden I used to dread the winters, the long months spent locked up inside a mountain. But this one I'm looking forward to. I've had enough of the world outside to last me a good long while. I'm ready to be home now.

Jake finally draws level then pulls down his mask and bends over, hands on his knees. When he's got his breath back he reaches for his canteen. He unscrews the cap, raises it to his lips, but there's little left. He tilts his head back and upends it, shaking the last few drops into his mouth. I dig mine from the side pocket of my pack and hold it out to him. He stares at it a moment, then he says he's okay.

I take a swig. I can't say as I blame him. I'm not sure I'd accept a drink from someone who looks the way I do, either. Things are a little better than when I first caught my reflection, in the cell, back in Starkly: the dark circles around my eyes are beginning to fade and I think I've gained back a little of the weight I lost to the virus, in spite of the short rations we've been on. My hair's yet to start growing back, however, and the deep grooves where my cheeks used to be persist. Mags says she likes them – she reckons they lend my face character - but I'm not so sure about that. All in all there's a little too much of the night about me.

I screw the cap back on, return the canteen to my pack.

'Good to go?'

He nods once, pulls his mask up and we set off again.

For the next mile the road continues to climb, but then it finally flattens and, true to its name, starts to snake its way along the ridge. Withered trunks poke through the snow on either side, stretching off down the slopes into the valley below. The gap between them narrows until there's little to tell where our path might be, but if Mags is uncertain of our path she doesn't show it; she leads us on without slowing.

As dusk settles we come to a large sign, almost buried in a drift. The lights above are hooded under black metal cowls, the kind you'd see at a railroad crossing, the lenses rimed with ice. It says we're entering a restricted area and should turn back. Beyond the road curves to the right. We follow it around and then it straightens and crests, revealing a large clearing straddling the mountain's spine.

We've made it; we're home.

The main gate rises up from the snow in front of us, a high chain-link fence topped with razor wire stretching off into the distance on either side. Mags has already found the section I opened with bolt cutters the day I first arrived. The kid follows her in. I bend down to squeeze myself through, then hold the wire back for Jake.

We make our way into the compound. Up ahead the control tower juts from the highest point of the ridge. A flash of lightning illuminates the sky behind, briefly silhouetting the antennae that bristle from its roof, the awkward gray shapes of the microwave transmitters. On the far side of it is the portal. When I first came here part of me had hoped that I would find it bathed in light; that survivors, people who had spent the last decade eking out an existence inside a hollowed out mountain, would be waiting to welcome me in. But as I look up what I see is a thousand times better.

Behind the tower's tall, angled windows, the soft glow of firelight.

Mags has seen it too. She turns to look at me.

'The Juvies; they made it back.'

Jake pushes his goggles onto his forehead. He's exhausted, starving, but I hear the smile in his voice.

'They've been posting a watch.'

We hurry up towards it, calling out as we go. As we get closer I can see the door's been left open; it creaks back and forth on its hinges in the wind. I keep my eyes on it, waiting for a familiar face to appear there. But no one comes down to greet us. As I get closer I see a single set of tracks, leading off in the direction of the tunnel.

We make our way past the tower, down to the helicopter landing pad. The tattered windsock snaps and flutters on its tether. Beyond it the path curves around one final time and at last I see it.

The gate that Peck blasted open has been repaired, returned to its runners. Where the bars couldn't be bent back into shape strands of razor wire have been strung across them, covering the gaps. A heavy chain and sturdy padlock secure it to the frame. Behind the tunnel stretches off into grainy shadow.

Mags stares into the darkness while I call out to whoever might be there. When there's no answer she turns around, makes her way back up to the control tower. The kid watches uncertainly, like he can't decide whether he should follow. She returns a few moments later.

'A fire's been lit, but there's nobody up there.'

I turn back to the gate and resume shouting. After a few seconds Jake joins in. The last of the light's leaving the sky and the temperature's starting to fall, but for a long while there's nothing except our own voices and the wind. And then at last the sound of footsteps, drifting up through the tunnel. Jake keeps hollering; he hasn't heard them yet. I hold a hand up and he falls quiet.

Moments later a single flashlight appears around the corner, making its way slowly towards us. The beam is brighter than a windup has any business being; I can't make out who's behind it. As they draw closer I raise a hand to ward it off. For once Jake's eyes serve him better.

'It's Lauren.'

She stops, still some distance back from the gate. Jake takes a step towards the bars.

'Lauren, thank God. We were beginning to think we'd have to spend the night in the control tower.'

She keeps the flashlight on me.

'We didn't think you'd be back.'

'I know. We have a lot to tell you. Let us in.'

Jake's voice is trembling with the cold now, but she makes no move to come closer. She holds the light on me a little longer then just shakes her head.

'I can't do that.'

I join Jake at the bars.

'What do you mean?'

'I'm sorry. We all decided. The way you are now. We can't take the chance.'

'But we're no danger to you.' I'm not sure what else to say so I reach inside my thermals for the crucifix, hold it up to the light. 'See?'

'I'm sorry.'

Something about the way she says it makes me think she's not though, not really. Beside me Jake clutches his arms to his sides.

'You can't do this, Lauren! You can't! We have no food, nowhere to go.'

This time her answer comes quickly, like she's had time to think about it. The walk through the tunnel, maybe. My guess is probably longer than that.

'There are rations in the control tower. You can take whatever's there.'

I feel myself growing angry, that they would do this; that a handful of MREs is the best they would offer. *I* found this place. They're here because of me. I lower my hand and stare through the bars, wanting her to see my eyes. Her face is hidden behind the light, so I can't see her reaction. But I can smell her fear, a bitter, acrid thing, not unlike the Sterno tabs we would burn to warm our food.

I reach for the bars. Inside my head the voice calls out a warning.

*Careful.*

*Look.*

I shift my gaze from the beam, back into the shadows. Afterimages from the light are still swirling across my vision, but I see a pair of cables, snaking up from the snow to the elevated walkway that runs down one side of the tunnel. They end at the terminals of a large battery that sits there.

Lauren must have followed my gaze.

'We've electrified it, just like the blast door in Eden. We don't want any trouble. It'd be best if you all just went on your way.'

I unzip my parka, start to reach inside for the pistol. Before I get to it Mags steps between us.

'You'll let Jake in. He was never infected.'

Lauren glances over at Jake, but she's already shaking her head, like that decision might have been made some time ago, too.

'No. We can't be certain.'

Mags slips off one of her mittens.

'You misunderstand me, Lauren. I'm not asking.'

I see what she means to do, but when I try to warn her she just turns to me, shakes her head. She reaches for a strand of the razor wire, runs a finger along it, as though testing it. Then she chooses a spot between the barbs, grasps it, and slowly twists. There's a jangling sound as the wire goes taut, and then it snaps with a *ping*. She pulls the strand from the bars, holds it up.

'Is that it? You really think what you've done here will keep us out?'

She lets the wire fall to the snow. Lauren stares at it for a moment and now when her eyes return to Mags they're wide with fear.

'So this is what's going to happen, Lauren. We're going up to the control tower to get those rations. You're going to let Jake in, and then you're going to *run* and fetch us Marv's map. When we come back if Jake's still out here, or if that map's not waiting for us, I'm coming in, and you're the one I'll be looking to for an explanation.'

Lauren nods quickly.

'Okay. Okay.'

Jake stumbles forward, shaking his head.

'No. They have to let us all in. Otherwise I'm coming with you.'

Mags turns to face him.

'No, you're not, Jake. Winter's almost here. Gabe, Johnny and me, we can survive on the outside now, but you can't. Besides, they need you in there.' She glances through the bars. 'Even if they don't realize it yet.'

We make our way up to the control tower and fill our packs with the MREs. When there's no more space left we strip the HOOAH!s from the cartons that remain and start stuffing them into the pockets of our parkas, as many as will fit. As we open the last of them I catch Mags flexing her fingers.

'Is your hand okay?'

She nods.

'It's fine, just a little numb. The battery was old, probably lifted from the fire truck. Between that and the cold I figured what little charge it still held wouldn't be enough to do me serious harm.'

I close the snaps on my pack.

'They have no right to banish us. We should go back, make them let us in.'

She doesn't say anything for a moment, but then she reaches over, grabs my hand.

'I've had longer to think about this than you, Gabe.' She looks over at the kid, then back to me again. 'The truth is the Juvies aren't going to get used to the way we are now, no matter how much time we give them. I wish it were different, but it's not. So you can go back inside if you want to. But I'm not sure it's for me, or Johnny. We just don't care to go on living with people who don't want us there.'

When we return to the portal the tunnel's deserted. Marv's map's waiting at the foot of the guillotine gate, wrapped in a Ziploc bag. I pick it up, transfer it to the inside pocket of my parka. Mags and the kid start back up the path, but for a few moments I just stand in front of the bars, staring into the darkness.

There's a crack of thunder, louder than the ones that have gone before, and I glance up. Lightning shudders through the thunderheads above, a warning of the wrath to come. Mags told Jake we could survive out here, but I have less confidence in that than she does. She and the kid are the only things left in this cold, broken world I care about, however, so I take one last look into the tunnel then turn around and follow them.

By the time I reach the gate they're already waiting for me on the other side. Mags holds the wire back and I squeeze through to join them. She pulls her hood up, turns to look at me.

'So where are we going to go?'

The remains of the tracks we made coming up stretch off into the trees. We could go back, but what lies that way is already known to us. None of it is any good.

I let my gaze follow the ridge in the opposite direction, the road I came up when I first arrived here. There are places on Marv's map that way, places I never thought I'd have to visit. I know little of them, but I'm not sure what other options we have.

I reach up for my goggles, slide them down.

'North.'

I hope you enjoyed the first three *Children of the Mountain* books.

I'm currently working on *The Last Guardian*, the fourth book in the series. If you'd like to be notified when it will be available, or indeed if you'd just like to say hi, please get in touch through the contact page at www.rahakok.com. I love getting emails from readers.

If you'd like to read the newspaper clippings Gabriel collects to try and figure out what happened to the world, or follow his progress on the map Marv gave him, you can download each free at www.rahakok.com.

But before you go…

It's hard to overstate how important reviews are to an indie author, so if you enjoyed the adventure and you have a moment to spare could I ask you post one? A sentence or even a couple of words will do just fine!

Thank you!

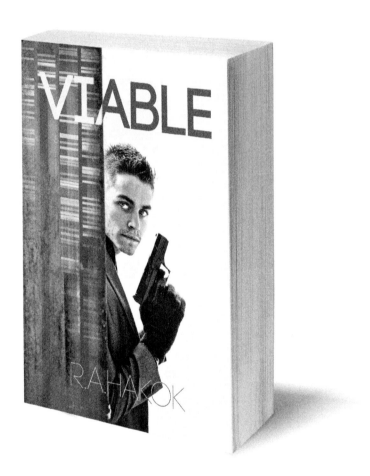

Printed in Great Britain
by Amazon

33780549R00468

# A complete body of planting and gardening. Containing the natural history, culture, and management of deciduous and evergreen forest-trees; Also instructions for laying-out and disposing of pleasure and flower-gardens Volume 1 of 2

William Hanbury

*A complete body of planting and gardening. Containing the natural history, culture, and management of deciduous and evergreen forest-trees; ... Also instructions for laying-out and disposing of pleasure and flower-gardens; ... To which is added, the manne Volume 1 of 2*
Hanbury, William
ESTCID: T100906
Reproduction from British Library
Dedication dated Dec. 1, 1769. Originally published in weekly numbers, starting 9 December 1769; according to The Morning Chronicle and London Advertiser, it was published in two volumes on 6 August 1773 (Henrey).
London : printed for the author; and sold by Edward and Charles Dilly, 1770-71 [i.e.1773].
2v.,plates ; 2°

ECCO

Eighteenth Century
Collections Online
Print Editions

**Gale ECCO Print Editions**

Relive history with *Eighteenth Century Collections Online*, now available in print for the independent historian and collector. This series includes the most significant English-language and foreign-language works printed in Great Britain during the eighteenth century, and is organized in seven different subject areas including literature and language; medicine, science, and technology; and religion and philosophy. The collection also includes thousands of important works from the Americas.

The eighteenth century has been called "The Age of Enlightenment." It was a period of rapid advance in print culture and publishing, in world exploration, and in the rapid growth of science and technology – all of which had a profound impact on the political and cultural landscape. At the end of the century the American Revolution, French Revolution and Industrial Revolution, perhaps three of the most significant events in modern history, set in motion developments that eventually dominated world political, economic, and social life.

In a groundbreaking effort, Gale initiated a revolution of its own: digitization of epic proportions to preserve these invaluable works in the largest online archive of its kind. Contributions from major world libraries constitute over 175,000 original printed works. Scanned images of the actual pages, rather than transcriptions, recreate the works ***as they first appeared.***

Now for the first time, these high-quality digital scans of original works are available via print-on-demand, making them readily accessible to libraries, students, independent scholars, and readers of all ages.

For our initial release we have created seven robust collections to form one the world's most comprehensive catalogs of 18$^{th}$ century works.

*Initial Gale ECCO Print Editions collections include:*

***History and Geography***
Rich in titles on English life and social history, this collection spans the world as it was known to eighteenth-century historians and explorers. Titles include a wealth of travel accounts and diaries, histories of nations from throughout the world, and maps and charts of a world that was still being discovered. Students of the War of American Independence will find fascinating accounts from the British side of conflict.

***Social Science***

Delve into what it was like to live during the eighteenth century by reading the first-hand accounts of everyday people, including city dwellers and farmers, businessmen and bankers, artisans and merchants, artists and their patrons, politicians and their constituents. Original texts make the American, French, and Industrial revolutions vividly contemporary.

***Medicine, Science and Technology***

Medical theory and practice of the 1700s developed rapidly, as is evidenced by the extensive collection, which includes descriptions of diseases, their conditions, and treatments. Books on science and technology, agriculture, military technology, natural philosophy, even cookbooks, are all contained here.

***Literature and Language***

Western literary study flows out of eighteenth-century works by Alexander Pope, Daniel Defoe, Henry Fielding, Frances Burney, Denis Diderot, Johann Gottfried Herder, Johann Wolfgang von Goethe, and others. Experience the birth of the modern novel, or compare the development of language using dictionaries and grammar discourses.

***Religion and Philosophy***

The Age of Enlightenment profoundly enriched religious and philosophical understanding and continues to influence present-day thinking. Works collected here include masterpieces by David Hume, Immanuel Kant, and Jean-Jacques Rousseau, as well as religious sermons and moral debates on the issues of the day, such as the slave trade. The Age of Reason saw conflict between Protestantism and Catholicism transformed into one between faith and logic -- a debate that continues in the twenty-first century.

***Law and Reference***

This collection reveals the history of English common law and Empire law in a vastly changing world of British expansion. Dominating the legal field is the *Commentaries of the Law of England* by Sir William Blackstone, which first appeared in 1765. Reference works such as almanacs and catalogues continue to educate us by revealing the day-to-day workings of society.

***Fine Arts***

The eighteenth-century fascination with Greek and Roman antiquity followed the systematic excavation of the ruins at Pompeii and Herculaneum in southern Italy; and after 1750 a neoclassical style dominated all artistic fields. The titles here trace developments in mostly English-language works on painting, sculpture, architecture, music, theater, and other disciplines. Instructional works on musical instruments, catalogs of art objects, comic operas, and more are also included.

FRONTISPIECE.

C. Wale inv. del. Isaac Taylor sculp.

A

# COMPLETE BODY

OF

# PLANTING and GARDENING.

CONTAINING

The NATURAL HISTORY, CULTURE, and MANAGEMENT of

DECIDUOUS and EVERGREEN FOREST-TREES;

With Practical Directions for RAISING and IMPROVING

WOODS, NURSERIES, SEMINARIES, and PLANTATIONS,

AND THE

Method of Propagating and Improving the various Kinds of DECIDUOUS and EVERGREEN SHRUBS and TREES proper for ORNAMENT and SHADE

ALSO

Instructions for LAYING-OUT and DISPOSING of

PLEASURE and FLOWER-GARDENS,

Including the Culture of Prize-Flowers, Perennials, Annuals, Biennials, &c

LIKEWISE

PLAIN and FAMILIAR RULES for the MANAGEMENT of a

KITCHEN-GARDEN,

Comprehending the NEWEST and BEST METHODS of Raising all its different Productions

TO WHICH IS ADDED

The Manner of PLANTING and CULTIVATING

FRUIT-GARDENS and ORCHARDS

THE WHOLE FORMING A

COMPLETE HISTORY of TIMBER-TREES,

Whether raised in FORESTS, PLANTATIONS, or NURSERIES,

AS WELL AS

A GENERAL SYSTEM of the PRESENT PRACTICE

OF THE

FLOWER, FRUIT, and KITCHEN GARDENS.

---

By the Rev WILLIAM HANBURY, A M

Rector of CHURCH-LANGTON, in LEICESTERSHIRE

---

IN TWO VOLUMES

---

VOL I

---

THOU, LORD, HAST MADE ME GLAD THROUGH THY WORKS AND I WILL REJOICE IN GIVING PRAISE FOR THE OPERATIONS OF THY HANDS! Psalm xcii 4

---

LONDON

Printed for the AUTHOR,

And sold by EDWARD and CHARLES DILLY, in the Poultry

MDCCLXX

✓

TO

HIS SACRED AND MOST EXCELLENT MAJESTY

GEORGE THE THIRD,

BY THE GRACE OF GOD,

OF GREAT-BRITAIN, FRANCE, AND IRELAND,

KING,

DEFENDER OF THE FAITH,

DUKE OF BRUNSWICK AND LUNENBURG,

ELECTOR OF HANOVER,

ARCH-TREASURER AND ELECTOR OF THE HOLY ROMAN EMPIRE,

&c &c &c.

THE ENCOURAGER OF MERIT,

THE PATRON OF ARTS AND SCIENCES,

THE PROMOTER OF VIRTUE,

THE FATHER OF HIS PEOPLE,

THIS WORK

IS HUMBLY INSCRIBED,

BY

HIS MAJESTY'S MOST LOYAL,

MOST OBEDIENT, AND MOST DEVOTED

SUBJECT AND SERVANT,

Church Langton,
Dec. 1, 1769.

William Hanbury.

THE

# P R E F A C E.

THE profits and ſatisfaction attending Planting and Gardening are ſo univerſally known and acknowledged, as to render it needleſs to expatiate upon that ſubject, or to urge their practice from thoſe motives An attempt, however, to ſet them in the beſt and cleareſt light muſt prove no unacceptable preſent to the Public, and the Explanation of the beſt Methods of Practice muſt be productive of general utility

Numbers of books have been written within theſe few years on different parts of Planting, Botany, or Gardening, all of which are extremely defective, their plan of execution being both unnatural and abſurd

To treat the plants, as they ſtand arranged in the different claſſes of the ſcience, is certainly a good method for a treatiſe ſolely on Botany, but ſhould by no means be adopted in a Book of Gardening, where the unlearned but uſeful Gardener would be puzzled to find out the ſorts for his purpoſe, among the hard names, titles, claſſes, and technical terms of the Science

One Author, who has dignified his work with the appellation of A GENERAL BOOK of GARDENING, deſcribes only about half a dozen flowering trees or plants every week, as they ſucceed in order of blow throughout the year, and out of the great variety of cultivated plants with which Nature has enriched our globe, has inſerted the culture of not more than three hundred, except a few articles for the kitchen-garden, and the like, to complete a number

Another performance has appeared under the form of a Dictionary, though nothing can be more injudicious than to compoſe a book of this nature dictionary-wiſe for to arrange the various genera ſo widely different in their natures, in an alphabetical order, is very bad, but to continue all the ſpecies, of what kind ſoever, under their reſpective genera, muſt be ſtill worſe One ſpecies of a genus may, perhaps, be an annual, the next a perennial, a third a tree, and the fourth an uſeful eſculent for the table This, perhaps, may require the heat of a ſtove, That be hardy enough for the coldeſt ſituations, whilſt another may demand the moderate protection of a green-houſe, or thrive very well abroad under a warm wall

*Is it not extremely abſurd, to have* plants *of* ſuch different conſtitutions, though agreeing in their fructification, thus promiſcuouſly blended together in a work deſigned for practical uſe? Where an Author, indeed, confines his ſubject wholly to Botany, ſuch a method is tolerable, but in a book of Gardening is inſufferable, becauſe in the latter all the trees and plants for the different purpoſes of Gardening ought to be ſelected, that they may appear at one view, ready for uſe, and preſent themſelves in full array to ſuit thoſe palates which are moſt inclined to reliſh them There are numbers in the kingdom whoſe Gardening conſiſts only in the management of a ſmall ſtove, there are many whoſe ſole buſineſs is the care of a green-houſe, ſome, perhaps, ſhall employ themſelves entirely in laying-out and managing wilderneſs-quarters, ſhrubberies, &c, others in the culture of perennial flowers, annuals, and ſuch ſhed-flowers as more peculiarly diſtinguiſh a perſon by the appellation of FLORIST, whilſt the well-managing country-ſquire, ever attentive to the culture of foreſt-trees, and the improvement of his eſtate, laughs at the admirers of flowers, and in the old trite pun tells us, he likes " no flower like a cauliflower"

The different taſtes of various people at once ſhew the abſurdity of thoſe plans for a General or Complete Treatiſe of Gardening, hitherto offered to the Public, the execution of which is as prepoſterous, as their practice is in many caſes erroneous Varieties are aſſerted with great confidence to be real ſpecies, ſpecies are often arranged under wrong genera, and obſolete tities are ſtill retained. Indeed, conſidering the great alteration which has lately been introduced into the ſyſtem, (in the laſt edition of the SPECIES PLANTARUM) and the many new genera and ſpecies that have been added to it, together with the former abſurdities in other books, every reader muſt evidently perceive the neceſſity of ſetting thoſe articles in their proper light, and the great want of a Complete Body of Planting and Gardening.

Should the reader enquire into my pretenſions for attempting ſuch a work, I can only anſwer, That they are founded on the great experience I have had in every branch of the art. Gardening is a ſcience for which I have ever had a natural inclination, that very early in life put me upon the practice of it, and induced me to join with it the ſtudy of philoſophy. The Gardener and Philoſopher are two diſtinct characters, neither of them, merely as ſuch, are qualified to write a Book of Gardening. The Gardener may underſtand the practical part, but be totally ignorant, or at leaſt poſſeſs only a ſmattering, of the philoſophical; while, on the other hand, the Scholar in his purſuit of knowledge acquires great ſkill in the philoſophical, but knows nothing of the practical part. Neither of theſe ſeparately, nor a Society of theſe ſeparately, are qualified to write a Book of Gardening. The philoſophical and the practical departments muſt unite; and when practice is joined to the ſtudy of philoſophy, then, and then only, inſtructions or directions for the culture of trees, plants, &c. may be depended on.

How far I have ſucceeded in theſe purſuits, my extenſive nurſeries have given ſufficient proof to the world. They were raiſed with a deſign to eſtabliſh a charity, which, by the bleſſing of God, has proſpered; and to render this more general, there was no part of gardening which I omitted. I not only raiſed all curious foreign trees, ſhrubs, tender exotics, perennials, and annuals, but fruit-trees of all ſorts, foreſt-trees, and every article in the kitchen way. My extenſive correſpondence abroad enabled me to procure every ſort of ſeed; my extenſive nurſeries, ten in number, ſtanding upon near forty acres of ground, and in four different pariſhes, afforded a proper ſituation in one or other for moſt of them; and my ſucceſs in the whole has been ſo great, that many hundred thouſand trees, ſhrubs, and plants, have been raiſed; and every one who has ſeen them has given teſtimony of their excellence, luxuriance, and beauty.

Fraught with ſuch practice and obſervation, I determined to compoſe the Work I now offer to the Public, which is arranged or diſpoſed in Two Volumes, in the following manner.

## VOL. I. BOOK I.

After a ſhort Introduction to Botany, or an explanation of the technical terms uſed in the deſcription of the roots, ſtems, leaves, fructifications, &c. of the different trees and plants, together with the Twenty-four Claſſes of Sir Charles Linnæus's excellent Syſtem, ſucceeds BOOK I. divided into Four Parts, which contain,

I. The hiſtory, culture, and management of all hardy deciduous Foreſt-Trees proper to improve a gentleman's eſtate.

II. ———— Aquatics, or ſuch timber-trees as flouriſh beſt by the ſides of rivers, and in moiſt places.

III. ———— Evergreen foreſt-trees.

PART IV. Relates to woods and fences; and contains inſtructions for raiſing woods with variety of foreſt-trees; for the management and improvement of old woods; for making fences; and the manner of raiſing quick.

Having amply treated of the different trees neceſſary to occupy an eſtate, the next diviſion of the Volume, or BOOK II. contains Four Parts.

PART I. Treats of deſign in Gardening, or the method of laying-out the ground for the general purpoſes of beautifying the environs; with directions for the preparation and management of the ſeminary and nurſery, as well as rules for grafting, budding, layering, and propagating trees from ſuckers and cuttings.

PART

PART II Contains the history and culture of hardy deciduous foreign trees and shrubs proper for the wilderness, &c with their titles in the Linnæan system. In

PART III The reader will find hardy evergreen trees and shrubs treated in the same manner

PART IV Gives directions concerning climbers

In these two divisions are included the history, culture, and management of all the hardy trees and shrubs of the known globe, which deserve to be propagated

BOOK III is divided into Two Parts

PART I Comprehends a treatise of such perennial flowers as are more peculiarly called Prize Flowers, such as the polyanthus, auricula, tulip, carnation, &c

PART II Treats of hardy perennial flowers in general, the countries in which they abound in a state of nature, their time of flowering with us, their culture, management, &c &c Their classes and titles in the Linnæan system are also given

Such are the articles which complete the First Volume.

VOL II BOOK IV

PART I Treats of annuals and biennials in general, the manner of raising them to blow fair, and the places proper for them in the pleasure-garden

PART II Relates to the green-house and green-house plants, or such as will live in our climate, with protection only from cold weather in winter

PART III Treats of the stove and stove plants in general, or such as will not thrive in this climate without the assistance of actual fire

BOOK V

Includes the culture and management of the Kitchen-Garden in general, shewing in

PART I The method of raising all sorts of plants which fall under that denomination for the table

PART II The doctrine of hot-beds, hot-walls, forcing-frames, &c

PART III The management of the pine-apple plant, melons, strawberries, and all low sorts of fruit

BOOK VI and Last,

Contains the culture and management of fruits and fruit-trees

PART I Treats of wall fruit-trees, such as vines, peaches, nectarines, apricots, plums, cherries, pears, apples, &c the manner of raising them, planting them out for bearing, pruning, and after-management.

PART II Of orchards, of trees proper for them, the manner of planting them, and after-management

PART III Gives directions for gathering of fruit, and the method of preserving it

Such are the materials that compose this Work, which I have endeavoured to arrange in such a manner as to render the whole a useful, natural, and Complete Body of Planting, Gardening, and Botany

And as mixing the botanic with the gardening part, has a great tendency to create confusion, and embarrass the unlearned gardener, rather than assist him in his labours, those two divisions of the science are preserved distinct In the department relating to Forest-Trees,

as

as it relates to the improvement of estates, rather than the information of the judgment in philosophical researches, I have introduced very little of botany, and have only pointed out the classes of those trees, as they stand in the Linnæan system.

In the succeeding part, where plants of all sorts are raised for pleasure or philosophical observation, short descriptions are given, and the culture of their respective trees, shrubs, or plants, are laid down in a plain, familiar, and easy manner, for practical use: then follow the titles of those plants, and the characters of their fructification; and as in one species other varieties are often contained, which have been titled by former botanists as distinct species; as the same plant has been variously named by the several eminent botanists in different ages of the world, and as the knowledge of those titles may convey a still better idea of each species under consideration, the most important names are given, as they occur in the works of the most learned botanists, from that father of natural history, THEOPHRASTUS, to the botanists of the present age.

In short, I have omitted no circumstance which I thought likely to render this an entertaining as well as useful book, in which gardeners may meet with ample instructions for the practical part of every branch of their art; gentlemen are duly directed in the right method of improving their estates by planting of timber-trees; the florist is instructed how to win the prize at a feast; those who are fond of hardy perennial flowers and annuals, may know what they are, and how to raise them to advantage; those also who are attentive to the still more delicate method of preserving and rearing fine green-house and stove plants, will meet with fruitful helps; and those who love to regale their palates will find themselves not disappointed, by pursuing the rules laid down for raising the various esculents of the kitchen-garden.

Neither is this work serviceable for the above purposes only; it is designed likewise for readers of natural history in general. Ladies who are fond of such researches, and gentlemen who have no inclination to put the practical parts into execution, may here see the natural history of the different trees, shrubs and plants; be acquainted with their nature, know the country in which they naturally abound, their uses, &c. so that I have the presumption to hope, that whoever peruses this Work either as a gardener, an improver of his environs, or a philosopher only, will not find himself disappointed in his expectations.

And to him who is any ways exercised in these employments, results the sweetest satisfaction and pleasure. They conduce to innocence, by employing that time in laudable, which would otherwise probably be spent in trivial, pursuits; they are a means of prolonging life; they enlarge the capacity, and inspire us with the utmost praise and gratitude to God.

Here we see how the Almighty *openeth his hand, and filleth all things living with plenteousness!* Hence flow the necessaries, the conveniences, the pleasures of life! Hence are extracted those healing balsams, which relieve the accidental and natural infirmities to which frail human nature is subject! It is the omnipotent Creator alone who giveth remedies to heal our sicknesses, but he does not give them without exacting labour on our part, and requiring that we should investigate his wonderful works, well knowing, that we cannot study them without daily signatures of his almighty power, and constant manifestations of his sovereign goodness.

The study of Nature affords real wisdom, and yields delight unknown and inconceivable to those who have not made the trial. Here the wise, the serious, and religious mind dwells with rapture. *The works of the Lord are done in judgment from the beginning, and from the time He made them, He disposed the parts thereof. He garnished his works for ever and ever; and in his hand are the chief of them unto all generations: they neither labour, nor are weary, nor cease from their works: none of them hindereth another, and they shall never disobey his word: therefore the Lord looketh on the earth, and filleth it with his blessings.*

Glory then be to God for his all-bounteous liberality, and for disposing human hearts to imitate his divine perfections, who enableth human understanding to trace his almighty power in the works of his creation, who accepteth of their praise and thanksgiving, and declareth, that those who honour him, he will honour.

INTRODUCTION

A SHORT

# INTRODUCTION TO BOTANY:

OR, AN

# EXPLANATION

OF THE

# BOTANIC TECHNICAL TERMS

Which will frequently occur in the Course of this Work

TOGETHER WITH THE

## Different Classes, &c. of the LINNÆAN SYSTEM.

THOUGH an explanation of the technical terms of Botany may seem foreign to a Treatise on Planting and Gardening, as a person may arrive at great skill in the latter without any knowledge of the former, yet there is such a close connection between the noble science of Botany and the delightful art of Gardening, that the relish for the one is improved and heightened by having a perfect knowledge of the other The Botanist and the Gardener are two distinct creatures, but when the Gardener, after having attained to the achmé of his art, proceeds farther, when he scrutinizes into the characteristics, examines the different sexes, with the difference and number of the male and female parts in the hermaphrodite flowers, and investigates minutely the vegetable system, he will proportionally receive additional pleasure in every executive branch of his first studied art

To allure him to these pursuits is one design of this Work, and the more effectually to accomplish that end, the botanic and practical parts are kept as distinct as possible, that one may not clash with the other, but leave every reader at liberty to sit down with the practical knowledge only, or make himself master of the abstruser parts of the science

A gentleman, at his first entrance on the study of the science of Botany, will be startled, perhaps, at the many seemingly bombastic words and pedantic expressions used in the description of the flowers, leaves, and stalks When he looks for the description of a flower, and is told that "the *calyx* is *permanent*, that the *corolla* consists of a certain number of *crenated petals*, the *stamina* of numerous *capillary filaments*, with simple *antheræ*, &c &c" he is equally surprised and disgusted with expressions which leave him as wise as they found him

They may indeed appear very strange and uncouth at first, but, after he has waded into the depths of the science, he will not only perceive their propriety and use, but will afterwards with difficulty form his mouth, much less his pen, to make use of any other words

In the prosecution of this work I shall introduce as few of these words as possible, that the Gardener may not be embarrassed and perplexed in his practical work But as I shall all along have a view to the science of Botany, and make my performance equally serviceable to the attainment of the knowledge of both arts, I cannot avoid giving the description of flowers, &c in their own terms

In the part relating to Forest-Trees, very few of these words make their appearance, and only the class in which each genus is ranked in the Linnæan system, is chiefly pointed out

In that division relating to trees for ornament and shade, as they are numerous, and more peculiarly attract the attention of the philosopher, they will more frequently occur, and by thus introducing them gradually into the description of flowers and plants, the curious observer will insensibly acquire a knowledge of both arts I have been, however, very careful to let them have no other place than in the description

As the root is the life of the plant, and first receiver of all the vegetative juices, I shall begin with explaining the different terms used for the variety of roots, shall next proceed to the stalk, leaves, and flowers, and then conclude this Introduction with a concise explanation of the different classes, &c of the Linnæan system

# Of ROOTS

A ROOT *(Radix)* conſiſts of two parts, the one aſcending, the other deſcending The aſcending part ſerves to raiſe the branches, leaves, and fructification, and is the ſtem of the plant, the deſcending part is that which ſtrikes into the ground, and conveys nouriſhment to the plant

Roots are principally divided into three claſſes, Bulbous, Tuberous, and Fibrous, which alſo have their diviſions

## I BULBOUS ROOTS

Are uſually of a large, roundiſh, ſolid figure, have fibres at the baſe, and conſiſt of the following ſorts

Plate I fig 1 Fig 2 — 1 A *ſolid* bulb ſignifies a root forming one entire uniform lump of matter Plate I fig 1 repreſents ſuch a bulb, and fig 2 is the ſame bulb cut acroſs horizontally through the middle

Fig 3 Fig 4 — 2 By a *tunicated* bulb is underſtood ſuch bulbs as are formed of many coats, ſurrounding each other Fig 3 is a repreſentation of this bulb, and fig 4 is the tranſverſe ſection of the ſame bulb

Fig 5 — 3 A *ſquamoſe* bulb expreſſes a bulb formed of ſeveral ſcales or flakes lying one over another, as in fig 5

Fig 6 — 4 A *duplicate* bulb is compoſed of two ſolid bulbs joined in one, as in fig 6

Fig 7 — 5 *Aggregate* bulbs are ſeveral little bulbs cluſtered together Many of theſe are often found very ſmall, not larger than a grain of corn, and, from their having a ſimilar appearance, are alſo ſometimes called *granulous roots* For a repreſentation of this root ſee fig 7

## II TUBEROUS ROOTS

Theſe ſorts of Roots conſiſt of a large and fleſhy ſubſtance, though without the characters of the bulbous kinds Their figure is irregular, and they are thicker than the ſtalk they produce Tuberous Roots are ſaid to be,

1 *Seſſile*, when they adhere or ſit cloſe to the baſe of the ſtalk

2 *Pendulous*, if they are found ſuſpended, as it were, at the ends of fibres See fig 8 and fig 9 — Fig 8 & 9.

3 *Faſciculated* when the knobs are in bundles

4 *Palmated*, when the parts ſpread out, in form of the hand

## III FIBROUS ROOTS

By Fibrous Roots are implied ſuch as conſiſt of many ſlender bodies, which divide at the ſtalk, and branch out in many directions Being the moſt common of all the ſorts of Roots, they require no figures to explain them Fibrous roots are termed,

1 *Perpendicular*, when they run ſtraight into the ground It is this ſort to which the gardener applies the name *tap-root*

2 *Horizontal*, when they creep and ſpread under the ſurface

3 *Carnoſe*, if they are ſomewhat fleſhy or thick

4 *Capillary*, when the roots are very thin and fine, like hairs

5 *Simple*, when they run all the way undivided

6 *Branched*, when the root divides, and ſends forth ſmaller roots

7 *Hairy*, when their ſurface is covered over with exceeding ſhort and fine fibres

# Of the STALK and TRUNK

THE only difference between the Trunk and Stalk is, that one is applicable to large trees, the other to plants, and both are uſed to expreſs that part which ariſes immediately from the root, receives nouriſhment from it, and produces and ſupports both the leaves, flowers, and fruits

Trunks or Stalks are of four kinds, known by the reſpective names of *Caulis*, *Culmus*, *Scapus*, and *Stipes*

## I CAULIS

The principal, and by far the greateſt, part of Stalks fall under this denomination, and may be ſaid to be either Simple or Compound

Simple is a term applied to ſuch Stalks as ariſe undivided from the root to the top and Compound includes all thoſe which ſoon divide into branches

A Stalk is ſaid to be,

1 *Naked*, when it is furniſhed with no leaves

2 *Folioſe*, when leaves are its ornament

3 *Flexuoſe*, when it turns different ways, or the ſtem changes its direction at every joint

4 *Erect*, when the ſtem riſes up ſtraight

5 *Oblique*, when it grows aſlant

6 *Ramoſe*, when it ſends forth lateral branches When theſe ariſe upwards, the term is *aſcendant*, when they are ſpreading, *diffuſe* when the arms are large, they are called *brachiate*, when there are very many branches, *ramoſiſſimi* *fulcrate* is the term for ſuch branches as are ſupported, and *proliferous* for thoſe which ſend forth branches from the center of the apex

7 *Voluble* Stalks are thoſe which ſpirally twiſt round other plants

8 *Reclinate*, is applied to thoſe which bend towards the ground

9 *Procumbent*, to thoſe whoſe directions are horizontal, and lie on the ground

10 *Repent*, to ſuch as creep along the ground, and put out freſh roots at all the joints as they ſhoot along

Stalks are denominated,

11 *Sarmentoſe*, when they are repent, long, and are bare of leaves

12 *Round*, when of a round ſhape

13 *Ancipital*, if double-edged, or they make two oppoſite angles

14 *Trigonous*, when they form three angles

15 *Tetragonous*, if they are ſquare

16 *Pentagonous*, if they form five angles

17 *Polygonous*, when they have many angles

18 *Triquetrous*, when they have three plain ſides

19 *Sulcate*, if furrowed

20 *Striate*, when ſtreaked, or marked with hollow lines

21 *Scabroſe*, when rough, having numerous projecting points

22 *Glabroſe*, if they have a ſmooth ſurface, and,

23 *Villoſe*, when they are hairy or ſhaggy

A Stalk

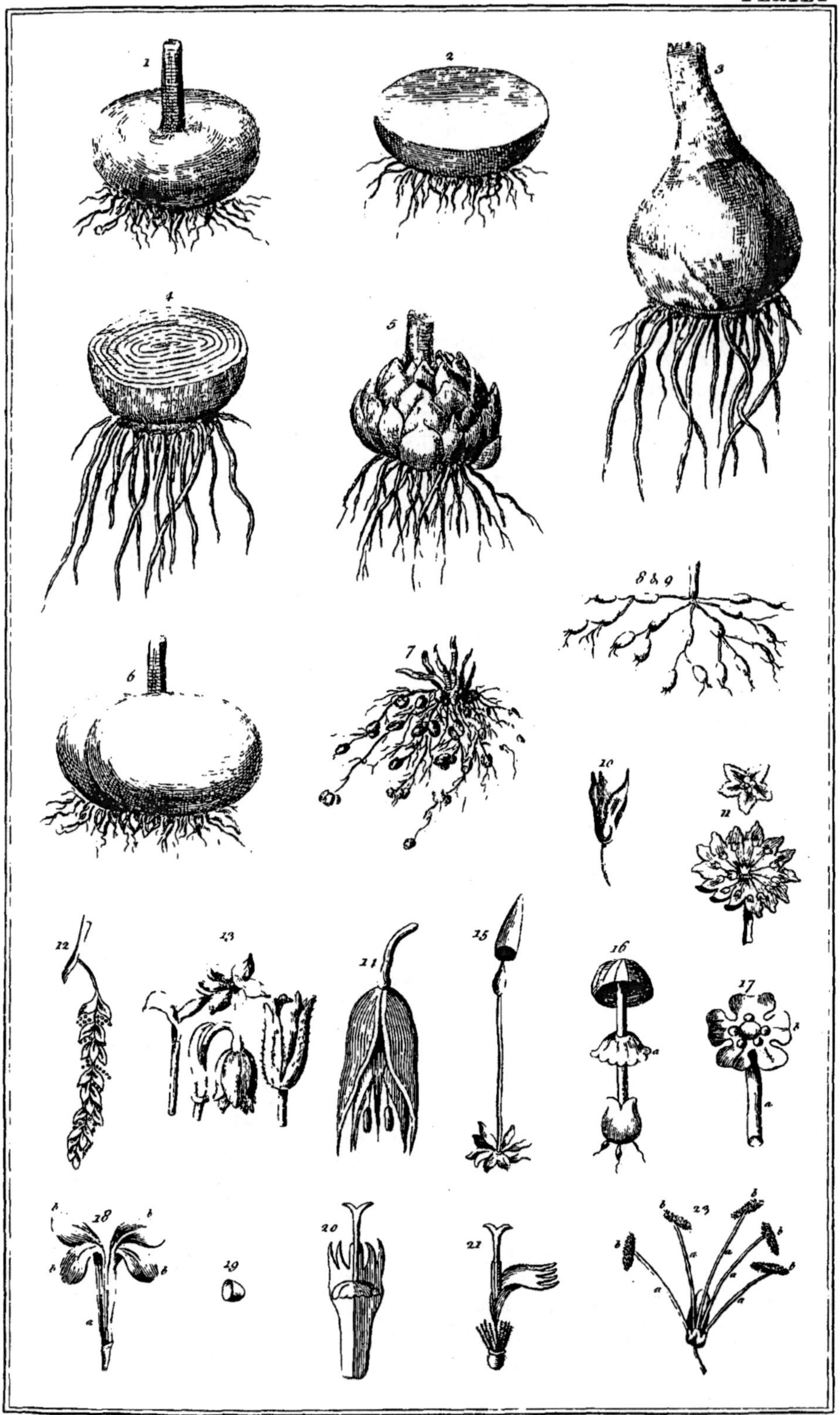


I Lodge

A Stalk is called,
24 *Hispid*, when the roughness is of an higher degree, so as to be bristly or pinching
25 *Annual*, when it is of only one year's duration
26 *Perennial*, when it continues for many years
27 *Dichotomous*, when it is forked, or divided into two others
28 *Distichous*, when the branch divides into two series of branches
29 *Subdivided*, when they are again divided without order, into a multitude of branches

## II CULMUS

This division comprizes all stalks of corn or grass, which are said to be,
1 *Nudus*, if naked, or without leaves
2 *Foliose*, when furnished with leaves
3 *Ramose*, if branched
4 *Articulate*, when they are connected by many knots
5 *Equal*, when they have no such articulation, and,
6 *Squamose*, when they are scaly

## III SCAPUS

Comprehends those Stalks which rise immediately from the root, without branches, and support the flowers and fructification, such as those of the Hyacinth, Narcissus, &c

## IV STIPES

Includes the Stalks of the different sorts of *fungi*, *filices*, and *palms*, and is used also to express that slender part which elevates the pappus of downy seeds

# Of the FULCRA of PLANTS

FULCRA are such parts of plants as tend to preserve, support, and strengthen the others They are of seven sorts, and are known by the various names of *Pedunculus*, *Petiolus*, *Stipula*, *Bractea*, *Cirrhus*, *Pubes*, and *Arma*

## I PEDUNCULUS

By this is understood such little stalks as grow from the branches of a plant, and support the flowers or parts of fructification, and these are said to be,
1 *Cauline*, when they are produced from the stem
2 *Axillary*, when growing from the wings or angles made by the leaves and branches, or the branches and the stem
3 *Terminal*, when terminating the branches
4 *Radical*, when they arise immediately from the root
5 *Solitary* when they are single
6 *Sparsed*, when they are found thin
7 *Conglobate*, when there are many together
8 *Conglomerate*, when in clusters
9 *Spicate*, when these peduncles are found in spikes, and,
10 *Racemose*, if in bunches

All these sorts of pedicles are to support the parts of fructification, and have their terms in that office Thus, a pedicle is said to be,
1 *Uniflorous*, when it sustains only one flower
2 *Biflorous*, when it supports two
3 *Triflorous*, if it sustains three
4 *Multiflorous*, when it sustains many flowers, and,
5 *Numerous*, when it supports a great number

As to structure, they are,
1 *Filiforme*, slender
2 *Teres*, taper
3 *Triqueter*, three sided
4. *Articulate*, jointed, &c

## II PETIOLUS

Is a stalk that supports the leaf, as the peduncle does the fructification

## III STIPULA

This expresses that small scale situated at the base of the footstalks of some leaves Two of them are generally attendant on a bud, one growing on one side, the other on the opposite, though some plants have only one, and a great number none at all Their situation is usually on the outside, though they are sometimes found placed on the inside of the leaves They are of different figures, growing in some plants free or loose, in others close, in some they are deciduous, in others permanent

## IV BRACTEA

This expresses a floral leaf, which is attendant on the flower, comes out along with it, and is of a different shape and colour from the other leaves of the plant

## V CIRRHUS

Is a tendril or clasper, by which the plant supports itself, by fastening to other bodies

## VI PUBES

Of this there are eleven sorts, called by the names of *Pili*, *Lana*, *Barba*, *Tomentum*, *Strigæ*, *Hami*, *Glochides*, *Glandulæ*, *Utriculi*, *Viscositas*, *Glutinositas*, all of which have their offices assigned them
1 The *Pili*, or hairs on the surface of plants, serve as excretory ducts
2 *Lana*, or wool on the surface of many plants, screens them from the extreme violence of the sun's rays
3 *Barba*, a beard, is several hairs ending in a point, and serves probably for the same uses as the *pili*
4 *Tomentum*, down, affords protection to plants against too much heat, wind, or cold
5 *Strigæ*, with their stiff bristles guard the plant against animals
6 *Hami*, are three pointed or crooked bristles or hooks, which lay hold of and fasten themselves to animals as they pass by
7 *Glochides*, are the small points of the pubes of plants
8 *Glandulæ*, are little glands which serve for the secretion or excretion of the humours
9 *Utriculi*, are glandular vessels full of secreted liquor
10 *Viscosites*, is a clammy matter, lodged on the surface of some plants
11 *Glutinosites*, probably expresses the same kind of matter, in a higher degree

## VII ARMA

This term is more peculiarly meant to express the arms or weapons of plants, which Nature has granted them for their defence They are of four kinds *Aculei*, *Furcæ*, *Spinæ*, and *Stimuli*:
1 *Aculei*, are those prickles or sharp points which are fastened only to the rhind of plants, and are easily torn off.

2 *Furcæ*,

2 *Furcæ*, are thoſe ſharp two or three-tined forks, which are a guard to plants againſt animals of all kinds. The gooſeberry-buſh, barberry, &c. are plentifully furniſhed with theſe weapons.

3 *Spinæ*, are thoſe ſharp thorns or prickles which firmly adhere to certain parts of plants for their defence. Of ſome they are found on the branches, of others on the leaves; they occupy the calyx of ſome plants, and poſſeſs the fruit in others.

4 *Stimuli*. Theſe kind of weapons are uſually called Stings: they wound the hand and naked parts with venomous punctures, and thus frequently occaſion the plant to remain unmoleſted. The common nettle, for inſtance, is a plant plentifully furniſhed with theſe weapons.

## Of the LEAVES.

THE Leaf is the next part of the plant which offers itſelf for deſcription. The Leaves may be ſaid to be the lungs of the plant: they are its great ornament, attract and tranſpire the air, and ſupport the vegetable life in the ſame manner as the lungs do the animal.

The different ſhapes of Leaves are ſo numerous, that the number of terms expreſſing them all muſt conſequently be very great. I ſhall briefly explain the moſt material, and illuſtrate each with a figure, which will be the eaſieſt and moſt effectual method of making them perfectly underſtood.

Leaves are divided into three claſſes, viz. Simple, Compound, and Determinate.

### I. Of SIMPLE LEAVES.

By Simple Leaves are to be underſtood all ſuch as grow ſingly on a footſtalk. And if we conſider theſe with regard to their circumference, they are ſaid to be,

Plate II. fig. 1. 1 *Orbiculate*, when a leaf is of a round figure, the extremity of the ſides being equally diſtant from the center.

2 *Subrotund*. This term is applicable to a leaf nearly orbiculate, and differs from it only in being broader or larger in one part or other. Fig. 2.

3 *Oblong*, expreſſes a leaf the length of which is more than twice the breadth, and the two points are narrower than the ſegment of a circle. Fig. 3.

4 *Oval*, a leaf in form of the ellipſis, or oval. Fig. 4.

5 *Ovate*, a leaf ſhaped like an egg. Fig. 5.

6 *Obverſely ovate*, an egg ſhaped leaf, whoſe ſmaller end is fixed to the footſtalk. Fig. 6.

7 *Cuneiform*, is a leaf in form of a wedge, that is much longer than it is broad, and from the top is gradually narrower. Fig. 7.

With reſpect to angles, a leaf is denominated,

8 *Lanceolate*, when it is in the ſhape of a ſpear, is oblong, and narrows gradually from the middle to each end, where it terminates in points. Fig. 8.

9 *Linear*, when the ſides are nearly parallel, and are ſometimes narrowed at the two ends only. Fig. 9.

10 *Acerose*, when the leaf is linear and perſiſting. Fig. 10.

11 *Subulate*, when it is in the ſhape of an awl, i.e. very narrow, but broader at the baſe, and contracting gradually into a point. Fig. 11.

12 *Triangular*, is a leaf which forms three angles, the two loweſt of which are on a level with the baſe. Fig. 12.

13 *Quadrangular*, a four-cornered leaf, or *Quinquangular*, a leaf whoſe ſides are ſtraight, and make five angles. Fig. 13.

14 *Deltoide*, a leaf that has four angles, of which thoſe at the extremities are further diſtant from the center than thoſe of the ſides. Fig. 14.

With reſpect to the *ſinus*, a term uſed to expreſs the openings or cavities in leaves, they are called,

15. *Reniform*, when a leaf is in ſhape of the kidney, being hollowed at the baſe, without any angle, and almoſt round. Fig. 15.

16 *Cordiform*, or *Cordated*, is an heart-ſhaped leaf, ovated, hollowed at the baſe, and which has no angles. Fig. 16.

17 *Obverſely cordated*, a leaf like the former, differing only in having the oppoſite end fixed to the footſtalk. Fig. 17.

18 *Lunulate*, a leaf like an half moon, hollowed at the baſe, and which has two curve angles. Fig. 18.

19 *Sagittate*, a leaf ſhaped like the head of an arrow. Fig. 19.

20 *Cordato-Sagittate*, a leaf like the former, except that the ſides are convex. Fig. 20.

21 *Haſtated*, a javelin-ſhaped leaf. It is triangular, the ſides and baſe are hollowed, and the angles ſo expanded as to appear like an halbert. Fig. 21.

22 *Panduriforme*, a leaf ſhaped like a violin. It is oblong, broader at both ends than in the middle, and, like a violin, it is cut in deeply in the ſides. Fig. 22.

23 *Bifid*, a leaf divided into two parts at the top. Some leaves are divided either into three, four, five, or many parts; and the reſpective terms for each are, *Trifid*, *Quadrifid*, *Quinquifid*, *Multifid*, &c. Fig. 23.

24 *Lobate*, a leaf divided to the middle into parts, which are ſeparated from each other, and have their borders bounded; and from the number of theſe lobes, either two, three, four, or five, a leaf is ſaid to be *Bilobe*, *Trilobe*, *Quadrilobe*, *Quinquelobe*, &c. Fig. 24. is a trilobe leaf, by which an idea of the reſt may be formed. Fig. 24.

25 *Palmate*, a leaf in form of an hand open, being divided into ſeveral parts from the top to the middle, or to the baſe. Fig. 25.

26 *Pinnatifid*, a leaf which has three, four, or more lateral ſinuſes, ſeparated by long horizontal parts. Fig. 26.

27 *Laciniate*, a leaf which has ſeveral ſinuſes down to the middle, and the lobes that ſeparate theſe not ſmooth, but jagged or indented at the edges. Fig. 27.

28 *Sinuate*, a leaf full of ſinuſes or hollows on the borders, divided by ſhortiſh lobes. Fig. 28.

29 *Sinuato-dentated*, a leaf of the ſame figure with the former, except that the lateral lobes are narrower. Fig. 29.

30 *Retrorſo ſinuated*, a leaf with ſinuſes at the ſides, the lobes which divide them are pointed, and turned towards the baſe, like the beards of an arrow. Fig. 30.

31 *Lyrate*, a lyre ſhaped leaf. It is divided into tranſverſe ſegments, the upper ones are larger than the lower, and the lower are further aſunder. Fig. 31.

32 *Partite*. This term is uſed to expreſs ſuch leaves as are ſeparated down to the baſe; and if they are divided into two, three, four, five, or many parts, they are ſaid to be *Bipartite*, *Tripartite*, *Quadripartite*, *Quinquepartite*, *Multipartite*. Fig. 32. is a quinquepartite leaf, and from this an idea of the others may be formed. Fig. 32.

Directly oppoſite to all the diviſions in a leaf, of what kind or nature ſoever, is an *entire* leaf (*integrum*), which is one without diviſions, having no ſinuſes nor openings.

I ſhall

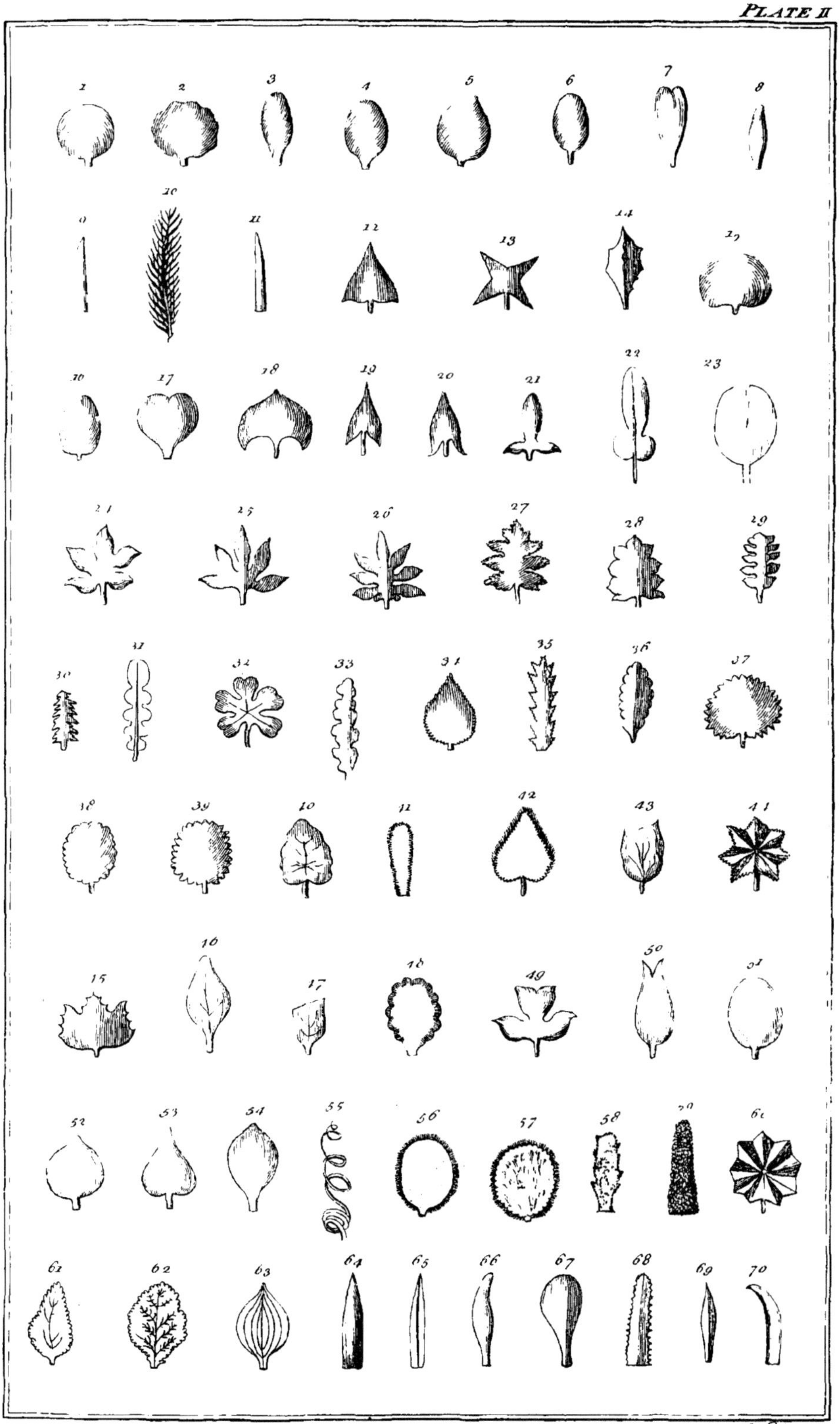

J. Lodge sculp

I shall now proceed to the terms expressive of the borders or edges of leaves, which are said to be,

33 *Dentate*, when the borders of the leaf end with horizontal points, of the same matter Fig 33 with the leaf itself, and are separated from one another

34 *Serrated*, when the edges are notched like a saw These points form acute angles, and bend towards the top of the leaf, but if they point towards the base, the leaf is termed *retrorsum serratum*, i e sawed backwards *Obtuso-serratum* is applied to such leaves as are indented in the same manner, but whose indent- Fig 34 ings are obtuse and weak, and,

35 *Duplicato-serratum* means those leaves which have a two-fold serrature, the less upon the Fig 35 greater

A Leaf is termed,

36 *Crenated*, whose borders are so indented that they turn neither towards the top nor the base, and whose indentures are contiguous to Fig 36 each other

37 *Acutely crenated*, when the indentings are Fig 37 sharp at the ends

38 *Obtusely crenated*, when the notches are Fig 38 rounded

39 *Duplicato-crenated*, when there are small Fig 39 crenatures upon the larger

40 A *Repandous* leaf signifies one whose border is marked the whole length with short lobes, each of which is a segment of a circle, and the Fig 40 sinusses between them are obtuse

41 *Cartilaginous*, a leaf whose edge is distinguished from the other part of it by a thick or Fig 41 fleshy substance

42 *Ciliated*, a leaf whose edge is surrounded Fig 42 with parallel hairs, like those of the eyelid

43 *Lacerated*, a leaf whose edge is composed of seemingly torn segments, of different shapes Fig 43 and figures

44 *Crisped*, or *Curled*, is a leaf curled or Fig 44 fringed at the edge

45 *Erose*, a leaf whose border appears to be Fig 45 gnawed

46 An *entire* leaf (*integerrimum*) is one free Fig 46 from indentures of all sorts in the borders

When the points or endings of the Leaves constitute the terms, they are denominated,

47 *Truncate*, when the point of a leaf seems to be cut off, its extremity being in a transverse Fig 47 line

48 *Retuse*, is a blunt leaf, whose top is Fig 48 terminated by an obtuse sinus

49 *Præmorse*, is also another blunt leaf, whose Fig 49 top is terminated by an open sinus

50 *Emarginated*, is a leaf indented at the top Leaves of this kind are said to be *obtusely emarginated*, when the indenting is terminated on each side by obtuse points, and *acutely emargi-* Fig 50 *nated*, when the points which form the indentings are acute

51 *Obtuse*, a leaf terminated by the segment Fig 51 of a circle

Fig 52 52 *Acute*, a leaf terminated by a sharp point

53 *Acuminated*, is one whose extremity is Fig 53 sharp, like the point of an awl

54 *Obtuse pointed*, is when the summit of the leaf is obtuse, and is terminated by a sharp Fig 54 point

55 *Cirrhose*, is when the leaf ends in a clasper, Fig 55 or tendril

When we consider a Leaf with respect to its superficies, it is called,

56 *Tomentose*, when covered with such fine hairs as cannot singly be distinguished by the naked eye, and which cause the surface to appear Fig 56 like velvet, or downy

57 *Pilose*, when the surface is so hairy that the hairs may be separately distinguished *Hirsute* and *Villose* also express such kinds of leaves, but the former is chiefly applicable to such as have hairs rough and strong, and the latter to those which have their surfaces covered with hair, like Fig 57 shag

58 *Hispid*, a stinging leaf, having its surface covered over with such hairs as strike into the Fig 58 flesh, and are broken off

59 *Scabrous*, a leaf whose surface is covered over with little and irregular tubercles

60 *Aculeate* A leaf is so called when the surface is covered with sharp and prickly points, strong enough to wound the flesh

61 *Spinose*, is applicable to a leaf whose surface is armed with thorns

62 *Nitid*, expresses a smooth and glossy leaf

63 *Papillose*, a warted leaf, having its surface covered with small protuberances, or vesicles Fig 59

64 *Plicate*, a leaf which appears plaited, the surface rising and falling in angles, Fig 60

65 *Undulate*, a waved leaf

66 *Rugose*, one whose veins are sunk deep, and the surface appears wrinkled Fig 61

67 *Venose*, a leaf whose surface has a great number of branched vessels like veins, running through it Fig 62

68 *Nervose*, a leaf which has simple vessels, that extend themselves from the base to the extremity without branching Fig 63

69 *Naked*, expresses a leaf the surface of which is every where smooth and equal

With respect to the substance of Leaves, they are said to be,

70 *Teres*, that is, nearly cylindrical Fig 64

71 *Tubulose*, or hollow within This, however, cannot be perceived, unless cut across

72 *Carnose*, that is, full of pulp, or of a fleshy substance

A Leaf is styled,

73 *Membranaceous*, when it has no pulp between the membranes of which it is composed

74 *Depressed*, when it has the mark of impression on one side

75 *Compressed*, if it has the same sort of mark on both sides

76 *Plane*, when the surface is every where level and parallel

77 *Convex*, if the middle rises higher than the sides, and,

78 *Concave*, when the middle is hollowed, or lower than the sides.

79 A *canaliculate* leaf is one channelled the whole length Fig 65

80 *Ensiforme*, a compressed leaf, and edged like a sword, with an high rib running down the middle

81 *Acinaciforme*, a compressed fleshy leaf, shaped like a spear point, one of whose edges is narrow and convex, the other broader and radled Fig 66

82 *Dolabriforme*, a leaf shaped like a hatchet, it is compressed, roundish, obtuse, projects outwards, with a sharp edge, and is almost cylindrical and taper towards the lower part Fig 67

83 *Linguiforme*, a depressed obtuse fleshy leaf, in the shape of a tongue, it is convex, and is commonly cartilaginous at the edge Fig 68

84 *Trisquete*, a leaf with three flat sides, which gradually grow smaller from the base to the point, where it is usually awl-shaped Fig 69

85 *Trigonal*, a three cornered leaf, like the former, but the sides are channelled or hollowed, and the ribs are sharp and membranous Leaves of this kind are called *tetragonal*, *pentagonal*, when, instead of three, they have four or five ribs

86 *Sulcated* is a term used when a leaf has a number of longitudinal ridges, and as many obtuse sinusses between them Fig 70

87 *Striated*, a leaf with a number of slight longitudinal furrows on its surface

88 *Carinated*, a leaf shaped like the keel of a boat, the under part of the surface being prominent, the upper concave

These are the principal terms made use of for expressing Simple Leaves I proceed now to explain those applicable to the second division of Leaves, called,

## II COMPOUND LEAVES

When several small Leaves are united to one common pedicle, or footstalk, all these form a Compound Leaf The result of this combination of small Leaves on a footstalk constitutes nothing more than an *entire folium*, which is then properly so called, whilst the word *foliola* is expressive of the smaller Leaves so united

A Compound Leaf, strictly speaking, is one formed of a single series of Simple Leaves, growing together on one common footstalk But besides these, there are the *Decompound*, as also the *Supradecompound*

With respect to Compound Leaves, they are denominated,

Plate III fig 1 — 1 *Binate*, when formed only of two folioles on one footstalk

Fig 2 — 2 *Ternate*, when three small leaves stand upon one footstalk

Fig 3 — 3 *Digitate*, if a leaf has several folioles growing regularly on the same footstalk, which spread themselves in a fingered or hand-shaped manner, nevertheless, when there are only two or three leaves on a footstalk, and ought therefore to be called *Binate*, *Ternate*, &c they are often classed under this denomination

4 *Articulate*, when the base of one leaf grows on the top of another

5 *Pinnate*, when many little leaves are ranged along on each side of the common footstalk, like wings The various sorts of Pinnated Leaves are said to be,

Fig 4 — *Pinnated with an odd one*, when the leaf is terminated by a single foliole

Fig 5 — *Pinnated abrupt*, that is, terminated neither by an odd leaf nor tendril

Fig 5 — *Oppositely pinnated*, when the small leaves stand opposite to each other

Fig 4 — *Alternately pinnated*, if the small leaves stand alternately

Fig 6 — *Interruptedly pinnated*, when the small leaves are alternately unequal

Fig 7 — *Cirrhose*, or *cirrhated pinnated*, if the winged leaf, instead of ending with an odd foliole, terminates with claspers, or tendrils

Fig 8 — *Decurrently pinnated*, if three folioles have borders running along the petiole from one to the other

Fig 9 — *Membranaceous pinnated*, when a winged leaf resembles the preceding, except that the footstalks are membranaceous and articulated

Fig 10 — *Conjugated pinnated*, when the winged leaf is composed of two folioles only, placed opposite

I now proceed to treat of DECOMPOUND LEAVES, by which are understood those Leaves whose footstalks divide themselves twice before they are ornamented with leaves

Fig 11 — 1 *Duplicato-ternate* is a term used to express a sort of these leaves, which have three little leaves on a footstalk, and each of these leaves is ternate This leaf is often called *bipinnate*

Fig 12 — 2 *Duplicato pinnate* is a double-winged leaf, being composed of leaves that are themselves pinnate *Pinnato-pinnate* and *bipinnate* are terms also used to express this leaf

Fig 13 — 3 *Pedate* is a leaf with a divided footstalk, which has some small leaves on its inside, foot-fashion

4 *Bigeminate* is when the petiole divides into pairs, and connects four folioles on its top

The next sort of Leaves are those called SUPRADECOMPOUND, by which is meant a leaf whose footstalk is divided more than twice before it is ornamented with folioles.

Fig 14 — 5 *Triplicato-ternate* expresses a leaf of this kind, and is one whose footstalk divides into three branches, each of which is garnished with flowers, that are also each of them ternate *Ternato-ternate* and *triternate* imply the same sort of Leaf

Fig 15 & 16 — 6 *Triplicato-pinnate* is a leaf whose footstalk bears many folioles, which are each of them bipinnated When a leaf of this kind is terminated by two folioles, it is said to be *abrupt*, when by an odd leaf, it is called *triplicato-pinnate with an odd leaf* Fig 15 and 16 represent these two leaves, the former figure being a representation of the first, the latter of the second

I come now to the third division in which Leaves are classed, namely,

## III DETERMINATE LEAVES

By Determinate Leaves is understood those which are considered without any regard to their own structure or figure, but are known from their direction, place, insertion, and situation on the parts of plants

With respect to their direction, Leaves are said to be,

1 *Inflex*, when a leaf in growing turns its point towards the plant — Fig 7 a

2 *Erect*, when it makes an acute angle with the stem — b

3 *Patent*, when it makes a larger angle with the stem than the other, nearly approaching to a right angle — c

4 *Horizontal*, when it forms an exact right angle with the stem, and grows parallel to the horizon — d

5 *Reclinate*, when it grows downwards, so that its extremity is lower than the base — e

6 *Revolute*, when its upper part rolls itself downwards — f

7 *Adverse*, when the sides turn towards the south, and not towards Heaven

8 *Oblique*, when the base looks towards Heaven, and the summit towards the horizon

9 *Adpress*, when the disk approaches the stem

10 *Dependent*, when it points to the earth

11 *Radicant* is a leaf that strikes root

12 *Natant* expresses a floating leaf, and,

13 *Demerse*, a leaf sunk beneath the water's surface

When we consider a leaf with respect to its place, we mean that part to which it is fastened, and in this sense a leaf is denominated,

1 *Seminal*, when it comes up directly from the seed — Fig 18 a

2 *Radical*, when it grows directly from the root, and not from the stalk, of a plant — b

3 *Cauline*, if it grows on the stalk — c

4 *Rameous*, when it grows on the branches — d

5 *Axillary*, if it grows between the branches and the stem — e

6 *Floral*, when it grows with the flowers — f

With regard to its insertion, a Leaf is called,

1 *Peltate*, or *peltated*, when the footstalk is fixed to its side, and not to its edge, thereby somewhat resembling a shield — Fig 19 a

2 *Petiolate*, when the footstalk is fastened at the margin of the base — b

3 *Sessile*, when a leaf grows to the branch, without any footstalk — c

4 *Decurrent*,

PLATE III

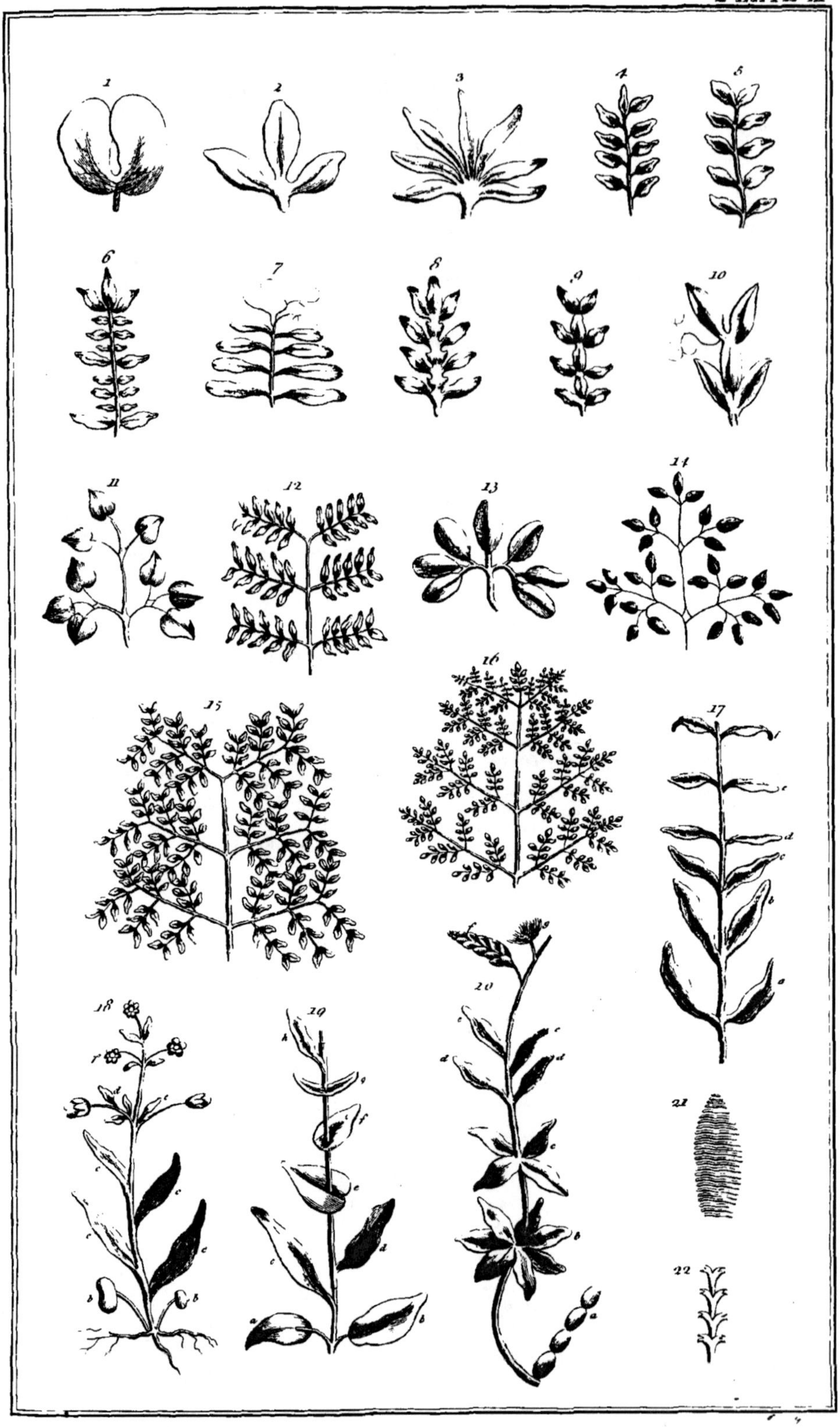

4. *Decurrent*, when the baſe of a ſeſſile leaf is
Fig 19 *d* extended downwards, along the ſtem
5 *Amplexicaule*, when the baſe of a leaf
—— *e* wholly ſurrounds the ſtalk
6 *Semi-amplexicaule*, when the lobes of the baſe are too ſhort to ſurround the ſtalk
7 *Perfoliate*, when the baſe of the leaf ſurrounds the ſtalk, without any of the edges ad
—— *f* hering to it
8 *Connate*, when the baſes of leaves unite,
—— *g* ſo as to appear one
9 *Vaginant*, when the baſe of a leaf is of a
—— *h* cylindrical form, and ſurrounds the ſtalk
In reſpect to the ſituation or diſpoſition of Leaves on plants, they are ſaid to be,
1 *Articulate*, when one leaf grows on the top
Fig. 20 *a* of another
2 *Stellate*, when ſix or more leaves grow at a
—— *b* joint, in a ſtar-like manner
3 *Ternate*, when leaves grow three at a joint, ſurrounding the ſtalk
4 *Quaternate* and *Quinternate* expreſs ſuch leaves as have four or five growing in this manner, and when there are more than this number,
—— *c* *Stellate* is the proper term Fig 20 *c* is *quaternate*; from which an idea of the reſt may be formed
Leaves are termed,
5 *Oppoſite*, when they grow on each ſide the ſtalk, exactly oppoſite to each other Fig 20 *d*
6 *Alternate*, when they grow ſingly one above the other —— *e*
7 *Sparſe*, when they grow irregularly, and without order, all over the plant
8 *Confert*, when they grow in cluſters, ſo cloſe as to leave hardly any ſpace between them
9 *Imbricate*, when they lie over each other, like the ſcales of fiſhes —— *f*
10 *Faſciculate*, when they grow in cluſters proceeding from the ſame point —— *g*
11 *Diſtich*, when the leaves are ranged along two ſides of the branches only
12 *Frondis* is the term for ſuch Leaves as make the whole of the plant, as, for inſtance, the Fern kind, one leaf of which makes a plant: It is divided into ſeveral other little leaves, and the fructification is placed on the back of them Every leaf of this kind is called *frondis*, and not *folium* Fig 21 is *frondis pinnatus*, and fig 22 Fig 21 & 22
*frondis articulatus*

## Of the FLOWERS and FRUIT

A FLOWER and its Fructification are ſaid to conſiſt of the following parts, namely, *Calyx*, *Corolla*, *Stamina*, *Piſtillum*, *Pericarpium*, *Semina*, and *Receptaculum* The four firſt belong to the Flower, and the three laſt to the Fruit I ſhall explain each in their order

### I CALYX

Is the termination of the outer bark, and ſuſtains the other parts of a flower It is called the Flower cup, and the various ſorts are known by the ſeveral names of *Perianthium*, *Involucrum*, *Amentum*, *Spatha*, *Gluma*, *Calyptra*, and *Volva*
1 *Perianthium* is a Calyx that ſurrounds the Flower It is compoſed of ſeveral parts, or of
Plate I one part cut or divided into ſegments, and is
fig 10 the moſt common of all the ſorts of the Calyx
2 *Involucrum* is a Calyx at a diſtance from the
Fig 11 Flower, and belongs to umbelliferous plants Its ſituation is at the foot of an umbel, which, if it be an univerſal one, the *involucrum* is called by the ſame name, or, if it be partial, then this kind of Calyx is called a *partial involucrum* It is alſo ſaid to be *monophyllous*, *polyphyllous*, &c according to the number of leaves of which it is compoſed.
3 *Amentum* is what is uſually called a *Katkin*
Fig 12 It is compoſed of a multitude of male or female flowers, faſtened to an axis, having their proper ſcales, which ſtand for Calyces
4 *Spatha* is a cup made in form of a ſheath, being compoſed of a membrane faſtened to the ſtalks, which burſts longitudinally to exhibit the
Fig 13 flowers
5 *Gluma* is the ſort of Calyx which belongs
Fig 14 to corn and graſs. It is formed of one, two, or more valves; and in ſome ſorts is ſmooth, in others rough, ſome are deeply coloured, and many have tranſparent borders
6 *Calyptra* is the Calyx of moſſes It is of
Fig 15 a membraneous compoſition, very thin, uſually of a conic figure, or ſhaped like a hood, and its ſituation is over the antheræ, or parts of fructification
7 *Volva* is the Calyx of the *fungi* It is mem-
Fig 16 branaceous, and torn on the ſides. Fig 16 is a muſhroom, and *a* its Volva

### II COROLLA

Is the next part of the Flower that offers itſelf for our conſideration, by which is implied the part that ſurrounds the organs of generation, and is chiefly compoſed of one or more coloured leaves, called petals This is the moſt beautiful and conſpicuous of any part of the Flower, and is the termination of the inner bark in that pleaſing form
A Corolla is ſaid to be,
1 *Monopetalous*, when it conſiſts of one piece only, and theſe alſo have terms deſcriptive of their parts The lower part is called the *Tube*, and the upper part the *Limb* Fig 17 *a* is the Fig 17 *a*
tube, and *b* the limb —— *b*.
Monopetalous Flowers are denominated,
*Campanulate*, when ſhaped like a bell
*Infundibuliform*, when ſhaped like a funnel
*Hypocrateriform*, when ſhaped like a ſalver
*Rotato-plane*, when they are plane and wheel-ſhaped
*Ringent*, when gaping, &c
A Corolla is termed,
2 *Dipetalous*, *Tripetalous*, *Tetrapetalous*, &c when it conſiſts of two, three, four, &c petals or parts, and,
3 *Polypetalous*, when it conſiſts of many parts The narrow part is called *Unguis*, and the upper ſpreading part *Bractea*, or *Lamina* Fig 18. *a* Fig 18 *a*
the unguis, *b* the bractea —— *b*
4 *Nectarium* is a part belonging to the Corolla, and is of various figures and ſhapes Its Fig 19
uſe is to hold the honey juice belonging to the Flower
5 *Corollula* is a term for thoſe little florets which conſtitute the whole of a compound Flower, and is ſaid to be,
*Tubulate*, when it conſiſts of a bell-ſhaped limb, that is divided into four or five parts Fig 20
*Ligulate*, when it has only a flat narrow limb, which is either entire, or divided into
three or five parts Fig 21

### III STAMINA

Another part of the Flower is the Stamina; by which is underſtood the male organs of generation.
The Stamen is compoſed of two parts, a *filament* and an *anthera*

1. The

1 The *Filament* is a slender body, serving to support the anthera, and connect it with the Flower. It is of various forms, and has terms expressive of its different shapes. It is said to be *Capillary*, when it is like hairs, *Subulate*, when awl shaped, *Cuneiform*, when in the shape of a wedge, *Emarginate*, when nicked, *Spiral*, when screw-shaped, *Reflex*, when bent back, and *Hirsute*, when hairy. Filaments are sometimes unequal, and sometimes irregular; sometimes very long, at other times very short. Their situation in different Flowers is also different.

2 *Anthera* is what is elevated by the filament, and is the essential part of the Stamina. It contains in it the male *farina*, which it discharges when arrived at maturity, for the impregnation of the plant. The Anthera varies in shape, and the terms expressive of such varieties are, *Angulate*, when they are cornered, *Sagittate*, when arrow-shaped, *Cornute*, when horned, *Oblong*, *Globose*, &c when they are of those figures.

Plate I Fig 2, Fig 23 *a* the filament, *b* the anthera

## IV PISTILLUM

A fourth part of the Flower is the Pistil, by which is meant the female part of generation.

The Pistillum is composed of three parts: The *Germen*, the *Style*, and the *Stigma*.

1 *Germen* may properly enough be said to be the uterus in plants. Its situation is at the bottom of the Pistil, it contains the embryo seeds, and is of various shapes.

2 *Style* is placed on the germen, and serves to elevate the stigma. Some Flowers have no Style, but in those which have, it is of various shapes. Like the filaments, the Style is called *Subulate*, *Capillary*, *Cylindric*, *Angulate*, &c when it is of those figures. Its *Lacinia* also is said to be *Bifid*, *Trifid*, *Quadrifid*, *Quinquifid*, &c when it is found to be such.

3 *Stigma* is always seated on the top of the style, if there be any; if not, then always on the top of the germen. It is composed of a viscous matter, and its office is to receive the farina from the anthera, and break it for the discharge of the proper parts to the germen, for the impregnation of the seeds. It is of various shapes and figures, and is said to be *Globose*, when round, *Capitate*, when headed, *Obtuse*, when blunt, *Ovate*, when shaped like an egg, *Emarginate*, when notched, *Truncate*, when lopped, *Orbiculate*, when rounded, *Peltate*, when like a shield, *Cruciform* when shaped like a cross, *Coroniform*, when shaped like a crown, *Canaliculate*, when channelled, *Uncinate*, when hooked, *Concave*, when hollow, *Angulate*, when cornered, *Striate*, when streaked, *Plumose*, when feathery, &c. The *Lacinia* also of the Stigma are *Revolute*, when rolled back, *Convolute*, when rolled together, and they are called *Sexpartite*, *Multifid*, &c according to the number of their divisions.

Terms to express the opening for the discharging of the seeds when ripe, are, if at the apex, *Quadridentate*, *Quinquedentate*, *Decemdentate*, &c when it split into four, five, or ten segments, or, if they open at the base, sides, &c they have terms of this kind expressive of their meaning.

## V PERICARPIUM

The next part is called the Pericarpium, which belongs to the fruit. It is what encloses the seeds, and is the germen of the pistil enlarged. It is divided into eight sorts, which are distinguished by the terms, *Capsula*, *Siliqua*, *Legumen*, *Folliculus*, *Drupa*, *Pomum*, *Bacca*, and *Strobilus*.

1 *Capsula*, is a hollow Pericarpium, composed of one or more dry elastic valves, which open in a determinate manner to discharge the seeds when ripe. It often consists of several cells, which are separated from each other by partitions called *Dissepiments*, and a membranaceous substance, denominated *Columnella*, connects the with the seeds.

Different Capsules are named according to the different circumstances attending them. If a capsule consists of one cell only, it is termed *Unilocular*, if of two, *Bilocular*, if of three, *Trilocular*, (and when it is trilocular, and each cell contains a single seed only, it is called *Tricoccous*), if of four, *Quadrilocular*, if of five, *Quinquelocular*, if of six, *Sexlocular*, if of many, *Multilocular*.

When it is composed of two valves, it is said to be *Bivalve*, when of three, *Trivalve*, when of four, *Quadrivalve*, when of five, *Quinquevalve*, &c.

They are of different figures, and are said to be *Triquetrous*, *Tetragonous*, *Pentagonous*, when they have three, four, or five sides. They are termed *Turbinate*, when narrowing like a top, *Inflate*, when swelled or puffed out, *Membranaceous*, when composed of thin membranes, &c.

It opens sometimes at the base, sometimes on the sides, but most usually at the top, and bursts in as many different ways as there are valves of which the Capsule is composed.

2 *Siliqua*, is a Pericarpium composed of two valves, having the seeds fastened alternately to each suture, and is usually called a *Pod*.

3 *Legumen*, is a Pericarpium of two valves, and differs from the other in that the seeds are arranged along one suture only.

4 *Folliculus*, is a Pericarpium of one or two valves, growing longitudinally, and has not the seeds fastened to it.

5 *Drupa*, is a Pericarpium without a valve, being composed of a soft, fleshy, succulent pulp, having in the middle of it a nut or stone.

6 *Pomum*, is a Pericarpium composed of solid, fleshy pulp, having in the middle of it a capsule, or seeds enclosed in membranaceous coverings.

7 *Bacca*, is a Pericarpium without valve. It consists of a succulent pulp, in the middle of which are many naked seeds.

8 *Strobilus*, is a Pericarpium formed of an amentum.

## VI SEMINA

The sixth part of Fructification is the seed, in which is contained the rudiment of a new vegetable.

The seeds are of different figures, situations, substances, sizes, numbers, &c in the different plants.

Their diversity of shape is expressed in terms similar to those of the leaves, that is, they are said to be *Cordiform*, when heart-shaped, *Cinct*, when girt, *Reniform*, *Ovate*, and *Echinate*, when kidney shaped, egg-shaped, prickly, &c.

With respect to their situation, in some plants they are fastened to a columnella, in others they are placed on receptacles, in some affixed to the suture, and in others dispersed within a pulp. Their substance is denominated *Osseous*, *Callous*, &c when bony, tough, &c and they are called very small, middle sized, or large, according to the appearance they present.

When a Seed is produced singly, the plant is said to be *Monospermous*, when there are two *Dispermous*, when three, *Trispermous*, when four, *Tetraspermous*, &c.

A Seed is composed of the following parts: *Corculum*, *Cotyledon*, *Hilum*, *Arillus*, *Corona*, and *Ala*.

1 *Corculum*, is the heart, essence, or first principle, of a new plant within the seed. Its situation

situation is within the cotyledon, and it consists of a scaly part, called *Plumula*, which ascends, and a plain part, named *Rostellum*, which descends

2 *Cotyledon* is a side lobe of the seed, and is porous, bibulous, and perishable

3 *Hilum* is the scar, or external mark of the seed, where it was fixed to the fruit

4 *Arillus* is the outer coat of the seed, which falls off of itself

5 *Corona* is the crown or down on seeds, by which they are wafted to a considerable distance It consists of either *Calyculus*, the calyx of a floret, or *Pappus*, a down elevated by a stipes, though other prominent parts or appendices of some seeds are often classed under this denomination The *pappus* is said to be *Capillary*, when simple and filiforme, *Plumose*, when feathery, soft, and compound, *Paleaceous*, when chaffy, and *Stipitated*, when elevated on a stipes

6 *Ala* is a membrane fixed to some seeds, by which they are made to fly and disperse

All these parts, however, are not common to all seeds, so that a seed may, in a strict sense, be said to consist only of the *Corculum*, containing the *Plumula* and *Rostellum*

## VII RECEPTACLE

Is the basis or support of the other parts of the fructification When it is the basis of the Fruit only, it is said to be the *Receptacle of the Fruit*, when of the Flower, the *Receptacle of the Flower*, when it is common to both Flower and Fruit, the *Receptacle of the Fructification*, and when it connects many florets, so that the taking away any would cause irregularity, it is then termed *Receptaculum commune*, or common Receptacle

The Common Receptacle, therefore, chiefly relates to compound Flowers, and, for the elevation of the florets, it assumes different figures, Sometimes it is found of a conic figure, sometimes convex, sometimes flat, &c and then the terms *Conic*, *Convex*, *Plain*, &c are applied to it

It varies also in its surface, and has appellations also to express the difference in this respect It is called *Punctate*, when dotted, *Villose*, when shaggy, *Setose*, when bristly, *Paleaceous*, when chaffy, &c

# Of INFLORESCENCE

INFLORESCENCE is the term expressive of the different ways in which flowers are joined to the plant by the peduncle

The sorts of Inflorescence are called by the respective names of *Verticillus*, *Capitulum*, *Spica*, *Corymbus*, *Thyrsus*, *Racemus*, and *Panicula*

1 *Verticillus* expresses such flowers as grow in whirls, or surround the stalk, like the radii of a wheel

2 By *Capitulum* is meant that the flowers are closely connected in a roundish knob or head

3 *Spica* implies that the flowers grow in spikes, or are alternately placed, without peduncles, on a simple stalk When the flowers are all turned one way, it is called *Spica secunda*, when both ways, *Spica disticha* A Spike is also said to be *Incurvate*, when crooked, and *Spiral*, when the flowers are arranged spirally along the stalk

4 By *Corymbus* is understood that the flowers growing in clusters, on their own separate peduncles, are so disposed as to form a sphere A bunch of ivy berries is properly a Corymbus

5 *Thyrsus* is when the flowers grow loosely on the stalk, in an ovate form

6 *Racemus* is applied when the footstalk is branched, or divided into others, closely supporting the flowers or fruit in an oblong form A bunch of grapes is a Racemus

7 *Panicula* is used when the footstalk of the flowers or fruit are variously subdivided It is of two sorts, *Diffuse* and *Coarctate* A *diffuse* panicle is when the pedicles are spread asunder, a *coarctate* is when they grow pretty close together

HAVING thus explained the principal terms of art used for the description of the different parts of trees and plants, I shall proceed now to the System itself

THE

# SEXUAL SYSTEM.

## CLASS I.

Plate IV fig. 1

### MONANDRIA.

THE word *Monandria*, by which Sir Charles Linnæus has distinguished his first class of plants, is formed of the Greek words *μονο*, *unicus*, and *ανηρ*, *maritus*, implying that the flowers or plants of this class contain only one male stamen. In the explanation of the parts of a flower, it has been shewn, that the stamina consisted of a filament, and an anthera placed at its top, which are the male organs of generation. Hence the reader will perceive, that every flower which has only one filament, with its anthera, belongs to this class, as having only one stamen, or male part, to perform the office of generation. However, it must be observed, that a female part must not be wanting, otherwise, the flower will belong to another class. So that all flowers ranged under the title Monandria are hermaphrodites, having both male and feminine parts on the same flower. These also are divided into two or more orders, according to the style, or female part, that belongs as well as the male to the same flower.

The First of the Orders belonging to this class is called

#### MONOGYNIA,

A word formed of the Greek *μονος* and *γυνη*, *mulier*, by which is understood a plant having only one style, or female part, that has the organs of generation. Whenever, therefore, a flower is found to consist only of one stamen and one pistil, that is, of one male and one female part, it is an hermaphrodite flower, and naturally falls under the class and order *Monandria Monogynia*.

#### ORDER II.

#### MONANDRIA DIGYNIA.

This order comprehends those plants whose flowers have two styles and one filament, the word *Digynia* being compounded of the above-mentioned *γυνη* and the numerical word *δις*, signifying *two*. So that by this compound word, *Digynia*, is meant a flower with two styles, or female organs of generation. Whenever, therefore, a plant is found with two styles and one filament, it must be ranked under the class and order *Monandria Digynia*.

## CLASS II.

Fig. 2.

### DIANDRIA.

THE meaning of this word may be easily understood, as it differs from the first only in the derivation of the numerical term, which instead of one, expresses twice that number. So that the plants belonging to this division have in every flower two stamina, as well as one or more styles. This class consists of three distinct orders.

#### ORDER I.

#### DIANDRIA MONOGYNIA.

Comprehends those plants whose flowers are furnished with two stamina and one style only.

#### ORDER II.

#### DIANDRIA DIGYNIA.

Includes such plants as have two styles, as well as two stamina, in each flower.

#### ORDER III.

#### DIANDRIA TRIGYNIA.

Contains those plants that have two stamina and three styles in each flower.

## CLASS III.

Fig. 3.

### TRIANDRIA.

THE numerical word of this class being formed of *τρεις*, *tres*, signifying three, plainly points out such plants as have three stamina in each flower.

This class comprehends three orders.

#### ORDER I.

#### TRIANDRIA MONOGYNIA,

Includes those plants whose flowers have each three stamina and one style,

#### ORDER II.

#### TRIANDRIA DIGYNIA,

Those whose flowers have each three stamina and two styles, and

#### ORDER III.

#### TRIANDRIA TRIGYNIA,

Such plants as have three stamina and three styles in each flower.

CLASS

PLATE IV.

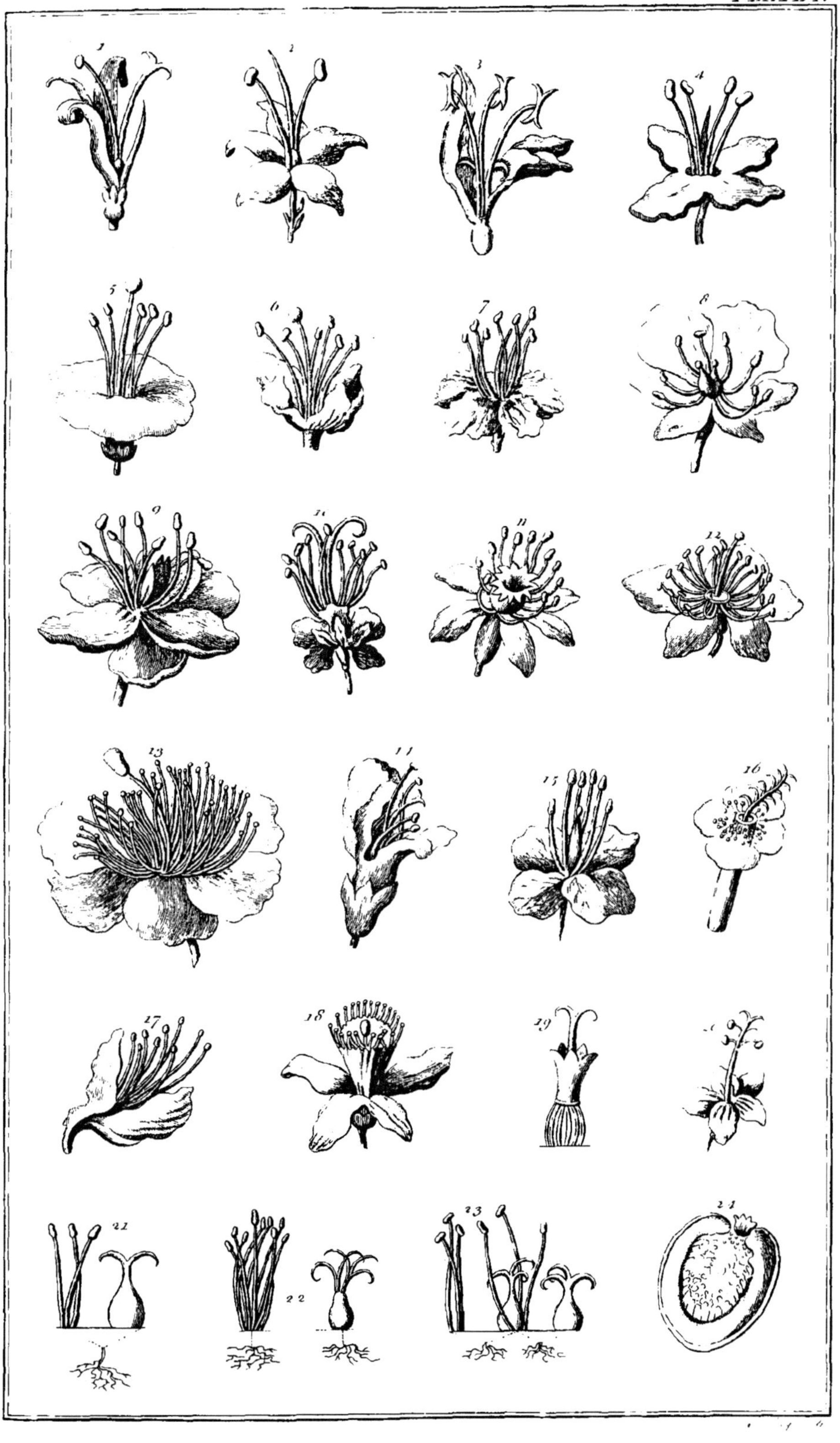

## CLASS IV

Plate IV fig 4

### TETRANDRIA

THE Greek word τεσσαρες, *quatuor*, having a ſhare in the compoſition of this term, evidently implies that it comprehends thoſe plants whoſe flowers have each four ſtamina They are all hermaphrodite flowers, and are arranged in three orders

ORDER I

TETRANDRIA MONOGYNIA,

Comprehends thoſe plants whoſe flowers have four ſtamina and one ſtyle only

ORDER II

TETRANDRIA DIGYNIA,

Comprizes thoſe plants whoſe flowers have each four ſtamina and two ſtyles

ORDER III

TETRANDRIA TETRAGYNIA,

Includes all thoſe whoſe flowers have in each four ſtamina and four ſtyles

## CLASS V.

Fig 5.

### PENTANDRIA

THE word πεντε being compounded with the uſual ſubſtantive ανηρ, *vir*, plainly informs us, that in this claſs are comprehended all thoſe plants whoſe flowers have each of them five ſtamina Its orders are ſix

ORDER I

PENTANDRIA MONOGYNIA,

Includes thoſe plants whoſe flowers are furniſhed with five ſtamina and one ſtyle

ORDER II

PENTANDRIA DIGYNIA

This order contains thoſe plants whoſe flowers have each five ſtamina and two ſtyles,

ORDER III

PENTANDRIA TRIGYNIA,

Comprehends thoſe plants whoſe flowers have each five ſtamina and three ſtyles

ORDER IV

PENTANDRIA TETRAGYNIA,

Comprizes ſuch plants whoſe flowers have each five ſtamina and four ſtyles

ORDER V

PENTANDRIA PENTAGYNIA

Under this order are arranged ſuch plants as have in every flower five ſtamina and five ſtyles, and under

ORDER VI

PENTANDRIA POLYGYNIA,

Are claſſed thoſe plants whoſe flowers have in each of them five ſtamina and many ſtyles

## CLASS VI.

Fig 6

### HEXANDRIA

THE Greek alphabet again points out the number of ſtamina in the word expreſſive of this claſs, which conſiſts of ſuch plants as have in each flower ſix ſtamina, and is divided into five orders

ORDER I

HEXANDRIA MONOGYNIA

This order comprehends ſuch plants whoſe flowers have each of them ſix ſtamina and one ſtyle only

ORDER II.

HEXANDRIA DIGYNIA,

Includes ſuch plants as have in every flower ſix ſtamina and two ſtyles

ORDER III

HEXANDRIA TRIGYNIA,

Takes in plants whoſe flowers have each ſix ſtamina and three ſtyles

ORDER IV

HEXANDRIA TETRAGYNIA,

Comprizes thoſe plants which have each ſix ſtamina and four ſtyles in each flower, and

ORDER V

HEXANDRIA POLYGYNIA,

Contains thoſe plants whoſe flowers have each ſix ſtamina and many ſtyles

## CLASS VII.

### HEPTANDRIA

Plate IV Fig 7

THIS word directs us to look for ſuch flowers as have each ſeven ſtamina. Of this claſs there are four orders

ORDER I

HEPTANDRIA MONOGYNIA

This order denotes thoſe plants whoſe flowers have ſeven ſtamina and only one ſtyle

ORDER II

HEPTANDRIA DIGYNIA,

Includes thoſe which have as many ſtamina and two ſtyles in each flower

ORDER III

HEPTANDRIA TETRAGYNIA.

Under this order are arranged the plants containing ſeven ſtamina and four ſtyles; and to

ORDER IV

HEPTANDRIA HEPTAGYNIA,

Belong thoſe with ſeven ſtamina and ſeven ſtyles in each flower

## CLASS VIII.

### OCTANDRIA

Fig 8

IN this claſs, in which one more is added to the number of filaments, are contained ſuch plants as have in each flower eight ſtamina The orders of this claſs are four

ORDER I

OCTANDRIA MONOGYNIA

The plants of this order are ſuch whoſe flowers have eight ſtamina and only one ſtyle

ORDER II.

OCTANDRIA DIGYNIA,

Includes thoſe whoſe flowers have each eight ſtamina and two ſtyles

ORDER III

OCTANDRIA TRIGYNIA,

Comprehends ſuch as bear flowers that have each eight ſtamina and three ſtyles, and under

ORDER IV

OCTANDRIA TETRAGYNIA,

Are arranged thoſe whoſe flowers have each eight ſtamina and four ſtyles

## CLASS IX

### ENNEANDRIA

Fig 9

THE Greek word expreſſive of the number *nine*, forming a part in the compoſition of this term, evidently points out this claſs to comprehend thoſe plants whoſe flowers have each nine ſtamina The orders are only three

ORDER I

ENNEANDRIA MONOGYNIA,

Contains thoſe plants whoſe flowers have each nine ſtamina and one ſtyle To

ORDER II

ENNEANDRIA TRIGYNIA,

Belong thoſe which have nine ſtamina and three ſtyles in each flower, and to

ORDER III

ENNEANDRIA HEXAGYNIA,

Thoſe plants that have in every flower nine ſtamina and ſix ſtyles

## CLASS X.

### DECANDRIA

Fig 10

THE Greek numerical term uſed in the compoſition of this word beſpeaks this claſs to conſiſt of ſuch plants as are furniſhed with ten male parts or organs of generation It conſiſts of five orders

ORDER I

DECANDRIA MONOGYNIA,

Such plants as have in every flower ten ſtamina and one ſtyle

ORDER II

DECANDRIA DIGYNIA

Of this order are thoſe plants that have in every flower ten ſtamina and two ſtyles

ORDER III

DECANDRIA TRIGYNIA,

Includes thoſe plants whoſe flowers have ten ſtamina and three ſtyles

ORDER IV

DECANDRIA PENTAGYNIA,

Contains ſuch as have ten ſtamina and five ſtyles, and

ORDER V

DECANDRIA DECAGYNIA,

Comprizes thoſe plants that have in every flower ten ſtamina and ten ſtyles

CLASS

## CLASS XI

Plate IV Fig 11

### DODECANDRIA

THIS claſs comprehends all ſuch plants whoſe flowers are each of them furniſhed with twelve or more ſtamina Their orders are five.

#### ORDER I

DODECANDRIA MONOGYNIA

To this order belong thoſe flowers that have each twelve ſtamina and one ſtyle

#### ORDER II

DODECANDRIA DIGYNIA,

Includes ſuch as have twelve ſtamina and two ſtyles

#### ORDER III

DODECANDRIA TRIGYNIA,

Takes in thoſe flowers that have twelve ſtamina and three ſtyles

#### ORDER IV

DODECANDRIA PENTAGYNIA,

Such as have twelve ſtamina and five ſtyles.

#### ORDER V

DODECANDRIA POLYGYNIA,

Comprehends flowers with twelve ſtamina and many ſtyles

## CLASS XII.

Fig 12

### ICOSANDRIA

THE word *Icoſandria* is compounded of the numerical Greek word εικοσι, *twenty*, and the uſual ſubſtantive ανηρ, ſignifying that the ſtamina of the flowers are uſually about that number It is not the number of ſtamina in the reſpective genera, however, that alone conſtitutes the characteriſtic of this claſs we muſt pay due regard to the place of their inſertion, for they are always fixed either to the inſide of the calyx or to the corolla ſo that whenever we meet with a flower containing many ſtamina faſtened to the inſide of the flower-cup in this manner, we may be certain it belongs to this claſs We may farther obſerve, that the calyx of the flowers is always formed of a ſingle concave leaf, and that the corolla is faſtened by the ungues to the inſide of the calyx

The orders are five

#### ORDER I.

ICOSANDRIA MONOGYNIA

This order conſiſts of thoſe flowers that have only one ſtile and about twenty ſtamina, fixed, as was before obſerved, either on the inſide of the calyx or corolla

#### ORDER II

ICOSANDRIA DIGYNIA,

Comprehends ſuch flowers as have two ſtyles, and about twenty ſtamina, ſtationed in the aforeſaid manner

#### ORDER III

ICOSANDRIA TRIGYNIA

To this order belong thoſe plants that have the ſaid number of ſtamina with the above characters, and three ſtyles

#### ORDER IV

ICOSANDRIA PENTAGYNIA,

Includes ſuch flowers as have five ſtyles

#### ORDER V

ICOSANDRIA POLYGYNIA,

Comprizes thoſe plants whoſe flowers have the uſual number of ſtamina, fixed as was before obſerved, and many ſtyles

## CLASS XIII.

Fig. 13

### POLYANDRIA

THIS word, which is compounded of the Greek πολυς, *many*, and the uſual ſubſtantive, plainly implies that the flowers have in each of them many ſtamina, like the flowers of the former claſs, which might indeed be arranged under this, if their ſituation was not different In the former they are fixed to the ſides of the cup, in this, to the receptaculum So that whenever we ſee a number of filaments, that is more than twelve, faſtened to the receptaculum, and have no connection with the cup, we may be aſſured thoſe flowers belong to this claſs, the orders of which are ſeven

#### ORDER I

POLYANDRIA MONOGYNIA,

Comprehends thoſe plants whoſe flowers are each furniſhed with numerous ſtamina and one ſtile only

#### ORDER II

POLYANDRIA DIGYNIA

The genera belonging to this order are ſuch as have in every flower many ſtamina and two ſtyles.

### ORDER III

### POLYANDRIA TRIGYNIA,

Comprehends thoſe plants whoſe flowers have numerous ſtamina and three ſtyles

### ORDER IV

### POLYANDRIA TETRAGYNIA,

Comprizes ſuch plants as have numerous ſtamina and four ſtyles in each flower

### ORDER V

### POLYANDRIA PENTAGYNIA,

Includes ſuch flowers as have many ſtamina and five ſtyles

### ORDER VI

### POLYANDRIA HEXAGYNIA,

Contains thoſe flowers that have many ſtamina and ſix ſtyles, and under

### ORDER VII

### POLYANDRIA POLYGYNIA,

Are arranged all plants whoſe flowers are furniſhed with numerous ſtamina, ſtanding on the receptacle, and have numerous ſtyles

## CLASS XIV.

## DIDYNAMIA

Plate IV. no 14

THIS claſs received the appellation *Didynamia* from δις, *bis*, *twice*, and δυναμις, *potentia*, *power*, becauſe part of the ſtamina have a power ſuperior to the other The flowers of this, like thoſe of the fourth claſs, have only four ſtamina, with this difference however, that in the claſs we are now deſcribing, two of the ſtamina are always ſhorter than the others, are placed together, and are connivent, ſo that whenever we find a flower which has four ſtamina, two of which are ſhorter than the others, we may conclude the plant to be of the claſs *Didynamia*

Farther, flowers of this claſs are diſtinguiſhed from thoſe of the fourth, and all others, by the following characteriſtics

1 The calyx is a monophyllous, erect, tubular, permanent perianthium, divided into five unequal ſegments

2 The corolla is monopetalous and erect, the baſe is tubulated, contains the honey, and does the office of a nectarium The limb is for the moſt part ringent, the upper lip ſtraight, the lower patent and trifid, and the middle one the broadeſt

3 The filaments of the ſtamina are four in number, linear, inſerted in the tube of the corolla, and inclining towards its back, and the inner or two neareſt, are the ſhorteſt They are all parallel, and rarely exceed the length of the corolla. The antheræ are commonly hid under the upper lip of the corolla, in pairs, and reſpectively connivent

4 The piſtillum conſiſts of a germen, uſually placed above the receptaculum, and of a ſingle filiform ſtyle, bent with the filaments, uſually placed between them, a little exceeding them in length, and ſlightly curved at the top, having a ſtigma for the moſt part bifid

5 The pericarpium is either wanting, or elſe chiefly bilocular

6 If there is no pericarpium, the ſeeds are four in number, and lodged in the bottom of the calyx If there be a pericarpium, they are then more numerous, and fixed to a receptacle in its center

The genera of this claſs are arranged into two orders

### ORDER I

### DIDYNAMIA GYMNOSPERMIA,

Expreſſes the genera of this claſs which have naked ſeeds, the word *Gymnoſpermia* being compounded of the Greek γυμνος, *naked*, and σπερμα, *a ſeed*

### ORDER II

### DIDYNAMIA ANGIOSPERMIA,

Includes ſuch plants of this claſs as have their ſeeds incloſed in a pericarpium the word *Angioſpermia* being formed of the Greek αγγειον, *vas*, *a veſſel*, and σπερμα, *a ſeed*

## CLASS XV.

## TETRADYNAMIA

Fol.

THE word *Tetradynamia* is formed of the Greek τεσσαρες, *quatuor*, *four*, and δυναμις, *potentia*, *power*, and comprehends thoſe plants whoſe flowers are each furniſhed with four long and two ſhort ſtamina Beſides this, they have the following ſtructure

1 The calyx is an oblong perianthium, compoſed of four oval, oblong, concave, obtuſe, connivent, deciduous leaves, which are gibbous at the baſe, and the oppoſite are equal In theſe flowers the calyx is a nectarium

2 The corolla is called cruciform, and conſiſts of four equal petals Their ungues are plain, ſubulate, erect, and a little longer than the calyx, the limb is plain and obtuſe, the laminæ widening outwards, and hardly touching one another The petals are inſerted in the ſame circle with the ſtamina.

3 The ſtamina are ſix awl-ſhaped erect filaments, of which the two oppoſite ones are the length of the calyx, the other four are ſomewhat longer, but are nevertheleſs ſhorter than the corolla The antheræ are ſomewhat oblong, acuminated, ſwelling at the baſe, erect, having their apices leaning outward There is a nectariferous gland, which is variouſly formed in the different genera, Its ſituation is at the baſe of the ſhorter filaments, ſo that theſe, having a ſmall curvature to avoid preſſing upon it, gives occaſion to their being ſhorter than the others

4 The piſtillum conſiſts of a germen ſituated above the receptacle (daily growing longer) a ſtyle, either of the length of the longer ſtamina, or none at all, and an obtuſe ſtigma

5 The pericarpium is a pod formed of two valves, and often containing two cells It opens from

from the base to the top, and has the dissepiment prominent at the apex beyond the valves, which before performed the office of a style

6 The seeds are roundish, nutant, alternately and longitudinally immersed in the dissepiment The receptacle is linear, surrounds the dissepiment, and is lodged in the sutures of the pericarpium

Of this class there are two orders

ORDER I

TETRADYNAMIA SILICULOSA

ORDER II

TETRADYNAMIA SILIQUOSA

The first order comprehends those plants whose pericarpium is a silicular or short round pod, the second those that have long pods

## CLASS XVI

## MONADELPHIA

Plate IV fig 16

THIS class comprehends those plants whose flowers have stamina that coalesce or unite in one body, so as to form a kind of column It is denominated *Monadelphia* from μονος and αδελφος, *frater*, on account of this fraternity or union

Flowers with such united stamina have the following structure

1 The calyx is a perianthium always present, persisting, and frequently double

2 The corolla consists of five obcordate petals, the sides of which lap each over the other, contrary to the motion of the sun

3 The filaments of the stamina are all united below, but distinct above, and the exterior filaments are always the shortest The antheræ are incumbent

4 With regard to the pistillum, the receptacle of the fructification is prominent in the centre of the flower The germina are erect, rotato-articulately surrounding the top of the receptacle, the styles unite in one body below, and form one substance with the receptacle, but above, they are divided into as many distinct threads as there are germina The stigmata are patent and slender

5 The pericarpium is a capsule divided into as many cells as there are pistils The figure is various in the different genera

6 The seeds are reniform

The orders of this class are three

ORDER I

MONADELPHIA PENTANDRIA

This order comprehends those plants whose flowers have five stamina, united together at their base

ORDER II

MONADELPHIA DECANDRIA,

Includes those that have ten stamina, all united into one common body downwards, and

ORDER III

MONADELPHIA POLYANDRIA,

Those plants whose flowers have each many stamina, which coalesce at the base, in the same manner

## CLASS XVII.

## DIADELPHIA

Fig 17

AFTER knowing the meaning of the title of the former class, this, which comprehends such plants as have two columns or different bodies in every flower, formed by the coalescence of the filaments at their bases, will be easily understood

The classical characteristics are,

1 The calyx is a monophyllous, campanulated, withering perianthium, gibbous at the base, affixed below to the peduncle, obtuse above, and melliferous, the rim is divided into five acute, erect, oblique, and unequal parts, the lower odd segment being longer than the others, the upper pairs are shorter and farther asunder, the bottom of the cavity, which is always moist with an honey-dew, incloses the receptacle

2 The corolla is termed *papilionaceous*, unequal, and the several petals which form it have names peculiar to themselves, by which they are distinguished, such as,

1 *Vexillum* literally signifies a standard, and implies a petal which covers the rest This is large, incumbent, and plano-horizontal, its unguis is inserted into the upper margin of the receptacle, approaches to a roundish figure when out of the calyx, is nearly entire, and a ridge rising above the surface runs all along it, making the petal appear as if compressed downwards The part of this petal next to the base approaches to a semi-cylindrical figure, and embraces the parts under it The disk of this petal is depressed on each side, but the sides of it nearest the margin turn upwards where the halved tube ends, and the halved limb begins to unfold itself, there are behind two concave impressions, prominent below, and compass the alæ, which lie under them

2 *Alæ*, or wings, are two equal petals, one on each side of the corolla, and placed under the vexillum Their margins are incumbent, parallel, roundish, oblong, and broadest externally, their upper margin is straight, the lower spreading into a kind of roundness, the base of each is bifid, the unguis is inserted into the side of the receptacle, of about the length of the calyx, and the upper portion is shorter and inflexed

3 The *Carina*, or keel, which is the lowest petal, is often bipartite, and situated between the alæ, under the vexillum It is shaped like a boat, is concave, and its sides are compressed, its base is mutilated, and the lower part is drawn out into an unguis, the length of the cup, and inserted into the receptacle, but the upper and side segments

segments are shorter, and interwoven with that part of the wings which is of a similar shape. The sides of the Carina in shape resemble those of the alæ, and their situation is nearly alike, except that they are lower, and stand more inward. The line which forms the Carina is continued nearly straight to the middle of the petal, and then gradually rises into a segment of a circle; but the marginal line is continued straight to the extremity, and there meeting the carinal, they terminate obtusely.

3 The stamina called *Diadelphous* are two filaments of different forms, one of which involves the pistil, and the other lies upon it; the inferior or lower surrounds the germen, and from the middle downwards is membranaceous, cylindric, and splits longitudinally upwards, where it terminates in nine subulate parts, which resemble the shape of the carina, both in length and flexure, of which the intermediate radii are alternately longer by pairs. The upper filament is subulato-setole, covering the suture of the former filament, is simple, incumbent, always to it in situation, is gradually shorter than it, opens from it at its base, and so causes a passage on each side to the honey. The antheræ on both the filaments are ten in number; one is on the upper filament, and the other nine are on the lower, one standing on each of the radii. They are small, equal in size, and terminate the radii.

4 The pistillum is single, and grows out of the receptacle within the calyx. The germen is oblong, nearly cylindric, slightly compressed, straight, and the length of the cylindric part of the lower filament, by which it is involved. The style is subulato-filiforme, ascendant, withering, and of the same length and situation as the radii of the filaments, among which it is placed. The stigma is downy, the length of the style from the part turned upwards, and placed immediately under the antheræ.

5 The pericarpium is an oblong, compressed, obtuse, bivalve legumen, having two longitudinal sutures, one above, the other below, both straight. The upper one, nevertheless, descends near the base, and the lower one ascends near the apex; and the legumen opens at its upper suture.

6 The seeds, which are few, are roundish, smooth, fleshy, pendulous, and have a prominent embryo near the point of insertion. When the ova are discharged, the cotyledons preserve the form of the halved seed.

7 The proper receptacles of the seeds are very small, short, and attenuated at the base, obtuse at the disk, oblong, inserted lengthways in the upper suture of the legumen, in an alternate manner, so that when the valves are parted, one half of the seeds adhere to one, and the other half to the other.

The genera of this class are arranged into four orders, according to the number of the antheræ in each, and are as follow.

ORDER I.

DIADELPHIA PENTANDRIA,

Includes those plants whose flowers have each two filaments and five antheræ,

ORDER II.

DIADELPHIA HEXANDRIA,

Those that have two filaments and six antheræ,

ORDER III.

DIADELPHIA OCTANDRIA,

Those which have two filaments and eight antheræ, and,

ORDER IV.

DIADELPHIA DECANDRIA,

Those flowers that have ten antheræ on the filaments.

## CLASS XVIII.

## POLYADELPHIA.

Fig. 18

THIS class comprehends those plants whose flowers have each many setts of monadelphous stamina. The flowers are of no particular form; the genera belonging to it are few, and the orders are three.

ORDER I.

POLYADELPHIA PENTANDRIA,

Comprehends such plants as are each furnished with five stamina in every sett.

ORDER II.

POLYADELPHIA ICOSANDRIA,

Consists of those that have twenty stamina in each sett, and

ORDER III.

POLYADELPHIA POLYANDRIA,

Of those which have many stamina in each sett.

## CLASS XIX.

## SYNGENESIA.

Fig. 19

THE word *syngenesia* is formed of the Greek συν, *simul*, and γενεσις, *generatio*, and comprehends those flowers whose antheræ coalesce, and form a tubular body or cylinder, through which the style rises, uniting, as it were, in their manner to perform the office of generation together. The flowers of this class are flosculose, or compound flowers, being composed of numerous florets, or *flosculi*, with the following characters.

1 The calyx is a small permanent perianthium, often divided into five segments. It is seated on the apex of the germen, and becomes the crown of the seed.

2 The corolla is monopetalous, with a very long and narrow tube, situated on the germen. The sorts of these florets are,

1 The *tubulate* kinds, which have campanulate limbs, divided into five reflexed patent segments,

2 The

2 The *Ligulate* kinds are those whose limb is narrow, plain, turned outward, entire at the top, or divided into three or five segments or else truncated, and

3 The *Neuter*, implies those floscules where the limb and tube, as it often happens, are wanting

3 The filaments of the stamina are five in number, capillary, very short, and inserted in the neck of the corollulæ, having the like number of linear erect antheræ, which join at their sides, and form a tubulate quinquedentate cylinder, of the same length as the limb

4 The pistil consists of an oblong germen, seated under the receptacle of the floscule, of a filiform erect style, the length of the stamina, perforating the cylinder formed by the antheræ, and of a stigma, divided into two revolute patent parts

5 There is no true pericarpium, though in some genera we meet with a kind of coriaceous or leathery coat

6 The seed is single, oblong, often tetragonous, but usually smallest at the base It is either coronated, or with the crown wanting This crown is of two kinds, either formed of a downy matter, or the perianthium If it is composed of the former, it is either sessile, or stands on a stipes, and consists of many rays disposed in a circular order, which are sometimes simple, sometimes radiated, and sometimes ramose When the corona is formed of the perianthium, it is such as I have shewn under the first article Calyx

The composite or flosculose flower, which is formed by an arrangement of a number of these florets or floscules, has,

1 A calyx, which is a perianthium, containing the floscules and the receptacle This is contracted when the flowers are fallen, and is expanded again, and thrown back, when the seeds are ripe It is said to be *Simple*, when it surrounds the florets only with one series of leaves; *Imbricated*, when it consists of a great number of scales, the exterior of which are gradually shorter, and cover part of the interior, and *Augmented*, when double, or if it consists of one long equal series of segments, that surrounds the floscules, and another shorter series, that surrounds the base of the others that are interior

2 The disk of the common receptacle, that receives the sessile florets, is either concave, plane, convex, pyramidical, or globose The surface of the disk is sometimes naked, and has no inequality, except being sometimes covered with slight dots or punctures, sometimes it is villose, *i e* covered with erect hairs, and sometimes it is paleaceous, or covered over with subulate, linear, compressed, erect paleæ, which serve to part the florets

The calyx and the receptacle, however, contribute little to the essential characters of a compound flower, because in some genera one or other is wanting It consists in the coalescence of the antheræ into a cylinder, together with the seed being single, and placed below the receptacle of the floret

Compound flowers are of several sorts, and consist of,

1 Tubular hermaphrodite florets, both in the disk and the radius

2 Tubular hermaphrodite florets in the disk, and tubular female ones in the radius

3 Tubular hermaphrodite florets in the disk, and tubular neutral ones in the radius

4 Tubular hermaphrodite florets in the disk, and ligulate hermaphrodite ones in the radius

5 Tubular hermaphrodite florets in the disk, and ligulate female ones in the radius

6 Tubular hermaphrodite florets in the disk, and ligulate neutral ones in the radius

7 Tubular hermaphrodite florets in the disk, and naked female ones in the radius

8 Tubular male florets in the disk, and naked female ones in the radius

9 Ligulate hermaphrodite florets, both in the disk and the radius

The genera of this class are arranged into six orders

### ORDER I

SYNGENESIA POLYGAMIA ÆQUALIS,

Comprehends those compound flowers of which the florets are all hermaphrodites

### ORDER II

SYNGENESIA POLYGAMIA SUPERFLUA,

Consists of those plants the flowers of whose disk are hermaphrodites, and those of the radius females

### ORDER III

SYNGENESIA POLYGAMIA FRUSTRANEA,

Includes such plants as have the florets of the disk hermaphrodites, and those of the radius neuter,

### ORDER IV

SYNGENESIA POLYGAMIA NECESSARIA,

Such plants as have the flowers of the disk male, and those of the radius female,

### ORDER V

SYNGENESIA POLYGAMIA SEGREGATA,

Such as have several perianthiums, or distinct and separate cups, within the general calyx, and to

### ORDER VI

SYNGENESIA MONOGAMIA,

Belong such plants whose florets are simple.

## CLASS XX

## GYNANDRIA

Plate IV fig 20

THE word *Gynandria* is compounded of the Greek *γυνη*, *mulier*, and *ανηρ*, *vir* The flowers belonging to this class are such as have the stamina placed either upon the style itself, or the receptacle elongated into the form of a style, supporting both the pistil and stamina.

The genera of this class are arranged into seven orders

### ORDER I

GYNANDRIA DIANDRIA,

Consists of such plants as have two stamina growing on the style

The flowers of this order are known by the following characteristics

1 The germen is always contorted

2 The petals are five, the two interior ones are connivent, and form a helmet, the lower labium of which becomes a nectarium, and serves for a pistil and a sixth petal

3 The style grows to the interior margin of the nectarium, in such a manner that neither it nor its stigma can hardly be distinguished

4 The filaments are two, very short, having antheræ on each, which are narrower, lower, naked, and divisible like the pulp of a Citrus These

These are covered by little cells that are open below, and grow to the interior margin of the nectarium.

5. The fruit is a trivalvate unilocular capsule, which opens in the angles under the carinate ribs.

6. The seeds are scobiform, *i. e.* like sawdust, numerous, and fixed to a linear receptacle in each valvule.

ORDER II.

GYNANDRIA TRIANDRIA,

Includes those flowers which have each three stamina growing on the style.

ORDER III.

GYNANDRIA TETRANDRIA,

Consists of such flowers as have four stamina growing on the style. To

ORDER IV.

GYNANDRIA PENTANDRIA,

Belong such flowers as have five stamina growing in the same manner.

ORDER V.

GYNANDRIA HEXANDRIA,

Comprehends such flowers as have each six stamina growing upon the style.

ORDER VI.

GYNANDRIA DECANDRIA,

Includes those flowers that have ten stamina growing on the style.

ORDER VII.

GYNANDRIA POLYANDRIA,

Comprehends such flowers as have many stamina growing on the style.

## CLASS XXI.

## MONOECIA.

Plate IV. fig. 21.

THE word *Monoecia* is compounded of the Greek μονος, *solus*, and οικος, *domus*, and was applied to this class on account of its comprehending those plants that have distinctly on each both male and female flowers. These are also called *Androgynous* plants. The orders are eleven.

ORDER I.

MONOECIA MONANDRIA,

Includes those monoecious plants of which the males are furnished each with one single stamen.

ORDER II.

MONOECIA DIANDRIA,

Comprehends those whose male flowers are each supplied with two stamina, and

ORDER III.

MONOECIA TRIANDRIA,

Such as have stamina in each of their male flowers. To

ORDER IV.

MONOECIA TETRANDRIA,

Belong those monoecious plants whose flowers have each four stamina, to

ORDER V.

MONOECIA PENTANDRIA,

Such as have five stamina in the male flowers, to

ORDER VI.

MONOECIA HEXANDRIA,

Those whose flowers have each six stamina, to

ORDER VII.

MONOECIA HEPTANDRIA,

Such male flowers of this class as are each furnished with seven stamina, and to

ORDER VIII.

MONOECIA POLYANDRIA,

Those male flowers that are each furnished with numerous stamina.

ORDER IX.

MONOECIA MONADELPHIA,

Includes those monoecious plants whose male flowers are furnished with monadelphous stamina, or such as are united into one body.

ORDER X.

MONOECIA SYNGENESIA,

Comprehends such monoecious plants the antheræ of whose flowers are united, and

ORDER XI.

MONOECIA GYNANDRIA,

Such as have the stamina of the male flowers gynandrous, being situated upon a kind of imperfect style.

## CLASS XXII.

## DIOECIA.

Fig. 22.

THIS class is called *Dioecia* from δις, *bis*, and οικος, *domus*, which implies two habitations. The plants of which this class consists are such as bear male and female flowers separately, that is, every species belonging to it has male and female flowers on separate or distinct plants, and not male and female flowers on the same plant. The orders are fourteen.

ORDER

ORDER I

DIOECIA MONANDRIA,

Consists of such plants as have male and female flowers on distinct plants, and whose male flowers have only one stamen,

ORDER II

DIOECIA DIANDRIA,

Of such as have male and female flowers on distinct plants, with two stamina on the male flowers

ORDER III

DIOECIA TRIANDRIA,

Comprehends such dioecious plants as have three stamina

ORDER IV

DIOECIA TETRANDRIA,

Includes such plants as have male and female plants distinctly, and whose male flowers have four stamina

ORDER V

DIOECIA PENTANDRIA

The plants belonging to this order have male and female flowers on separate plants, with five stamina on the male flowers

ORDER VI

DIOECIA HEXANDRIA,

Comprehends such male flowers of this class as have six stamina, and

ORDER VII

DIOECIA OCTANDRIA,

Those that have eight stamina To

ORDER VIII.

DIOECIA ENNEANDRIA,

Belong such dioecious plants the male flowers of which have each nine stamina, to

ORDER IX

DIOECIA DECANDRIA,

Such as have ten stamina, to

ORDER X

DIOECIA DODECANDRIA,

Such as have twelve stamina, and to

ORDER XI

DIOECIA POLYANDRIA,

Those male flowers that are furnished with numerous stamina

ORDER XII.

DIOECIA MONADELPHIA,

Takes in those dioecious plants the male flowers of which have monadelphous stamina, or such as are united or grow together in a body

ORDER XIII

DIOECIA SYNGENESIA,

Comprehends such as have the antheræ of the male flowers united

ORDER XIV

DIOECIA GYNANDRIA

The stamina of these dioecious plants are seated on a sort of imperfect pistil

## CLASS XXIII

## POLYGAMIA

Plate IV Fig. 23

THIS class comprehends those plants which bear hermaphrodite flowers, together with male or female flowers, or both And from such variety of impregnation it is that this class gained the above appellation, *Polygamia*, which is formed of the Greek πολυς, *multus*, and γαμος, *nuptiæ* The orders are three

ORDER I

POLYGAMIA MONOECIA,

Consists of such plants as have the polygamy on the same plant

ORDER II

POLYGAMIA DIOECIA,

Comprehends such as have the polygamy on two distinct plants

ORDER III

POLYGAMIA TRIOECIA,

Includes such as have the polygamy on three distinct plants

## CLASS XXIV.

## CRYPTOGAMIA

Fig 24

THE title of this class is compounded of the Greek word κρυπτος, *occultus, concealed*, and γαμος, *nuptiæ, nuptials*, plainly indicating that the plants belonging to it have their fructifications concealed, or at least not very obvious to view

The genera of this class have of all others the least to do with gardening, they being seldom cultivated for pleasure, as consisting of ferns, mosses, flags, and mushrooms The orders are four, known by the respective Latin names of those plants, *Filices, Musci, Algæ*, and *Fungi*

ORDER

### ORDER I

### *FILICES*, FERNS.

Ferns which belong to this order are called dorsiferous plants, on account of their fructifications being on the back of the leaf

The calyx of these plants is a squamma that grows on the back of the leaf, and opens on one side Under this there are pedunculate globules, each of which is girt with an elastic ring, which, breaking elastically, sheds a dust

The plants of this order are arranged according to their situation under their *operculæ*, or little covers, the parts of fructification not admitting of any regular distinction

### ORDER II

### *MUSCI*, MOSSES

The fructifications of these plants also can be but imperfectly distinguished The antheræ have no filaments, the seed is a naked corculum, without cotyledon or tunic, &c They are distinguished according as the antheræ have, or are destitute of, a calyptra, according to the situation, &c.

### ORDER III

### *ALGÆ*, FLAGS

These have their leaf, stem, and root joined together, and the characters of the fructification are yet still more imperfectly known

### ORDER IV.

### *FUNGI*, MUSHROOMS

The certain fructification of these plants also is altogether unknown

THESE are the twenty-four classes into which the Genera of Plants is arranged by the celebrated Sir Charles Linnæus There is no flower yet discovered which is not found to belong to one or other of them, and by the due exercise of the rules hereafter to be given, I trust that a novice in botany will soon be able to make a general collection, and class every plant with the exactest propriety

A COMPLETE

A

# COMPLETE BODY

OF

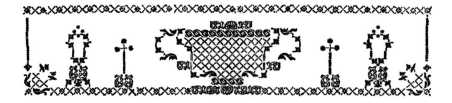

# PLANTING and GARDENING.

## BOOK I.

## PART I.

### Of DECIDUOUS FOREST-TREES.

### CHAP. I.

### *QUERCUS*, The OAK-TREE.

THE Oak, the glory and pride of all our woods, demands our firſt attention, whether we conſider it as being largeſt in ſize, or the variety of uſes for which it is employed.

Derivation of its generical name.

The word *Quercus*, its generical name, is altogether of uncertain original, though ſome have been weak enough to deduce it from κερχω, to exaſperate, whet, make ſharp, or rough, a derivation which to me conveys no meaning. But its Latin appellation, *robur*, ſignifying ſtrength, is, I think, applied with peculiar propriety to this tree, on account of its being ſo durable, ſtrong, and laſting.

Duration of the timber.

If we look at theſe venerable trees when full-grown, they ſeem to nod at Time, and even to laugh at his threats; and if we conſider the duration of its timber when felled for uſe, we have reaſon for amazement as well as thankfulneſs. The time an oak will ſtand before its total decay, is ſuppoſed by many to be more than a thouſand years; and if we reflect, that in the animal creation ſeveral creatures continue to a great age, the texture of whoſe frame is extremely frail and brittle; nay, that man himſelf, *whoſe fleſh is graſs*, and *whoſe breath is in his noſtrils*, frequently holds out an hundred years; we have ſufficient reaſon to ſuppoſe the hardy oak will endure more than ten times as long.

The timber of this tree, of all others, is the longeſt before its total decay. The true heart of oak, if kept dry, never rots; but when Time, the devourer of all things, has run his full length upon it, the outward particles firſt begin to diſſolve and give way, and ſo on until the whole is conſumed, which will not happen in many hundred years. In this lies the difference between the timber of the Spaniſh cheſnut and the oak, which comes the neareſt to it in duration. The timber of the cheſnut firſt decays in the center, and by ſlow degrees carries its diſtemper to the outward part; ſo that a beam of a Spaniſh cheſnut may externally appear ſound and firm, when it is almoſt conſumed; whereas the diſeaſe of the oak timber ſhews itſelf firſt on the out-ſide, ſtill retaining the heart, but nevertheleſs is in a ſtate of diminution until the whole is conſumed.

Uſes to which it is applied.

The uſes to which the timber of the oak may be applied, are almoſt infinite. If we look into our ſolemn temples, we find their chief wooden ornaments of this material, not only the

the pews, the beams, &c but alſo the carved works preſent themſelves of this wood, in a ſolemn, pleaſing, and awful view —— Its ſuperlative uſes are ſo well known in houſe-building, and various kinds of carpentry, as to need no deſcription In ſhort, it is applied to make laths, pales, ſhingles, cooper's ware, wainſcot pannels, wheel ſpokes, pinns, pegs for tyling, ſpars, piles for water-works, mill-wheels, knee timber for ſhipping, &c

Valuable qualities of the branches, bark, root, agaric, and leaves

Neither is the timber only of this tree to be valued, the branches are excellent for the fire, or to make charcoal, the bark proves ſerviceable to the tanner, the root is uſed by the joiner, of which he makes ſeveral inſtruments, the agaric, &c is known in the ſhops, the leaves alſo have their ſalutary uſes, and the acorns are almoſt a ſufficient motive for the planting of this tree, were there no other, ſince they are reputed the beſt food for ſwine or deer, will fatten them the ſooneſt, and enhance the flavour of the meat

The acorn excellent food for fattening ſwine

The goodneſs of the Weſtphalia hams is ſuppoſed to be owing to the ſwine feeding on acorns, for there, ſays Evelyn, no young farmer is permitted to marry until he can bring proof that he has planted as many oaks as will produce acorns ſufficient to feed his ſwine In England, and particularly Leiceſterſhire, the Poor, who gather them for their hogs to eke out the beans, feel the benefit of the few ſtraggling trees amongſt us, and I know ſeveral gentlemen who have oak woods, fatten as many hogs in them as are ſufficient for their families a whole year, a ſpecies of œconomy worthy of imitation Sir John Danvers, of Swithland in this county, and Donatus O'Brien, Eſq of Blatherwicke in Northamptonſhire, informed me, that they, every year, fatten as many hogs as will ſerve their families with that kind of meat Their method is this In September they buy in their hogs, which are of the ſhort-legged breed, commonly called the Berkſhire breed theſe generally coſt about eight or nine ſhillings each They are immediately turned into the woods, and no farther care taken of them, until the time of their ſlaughter, which is about the feaſt of St Thomas, when they will be worth near twenty ſhillings a piece —Sir John generally kills all his at the ſame time, when the hams are ſet apart for drying, and the other parts are ſalted down in leaden ciſterns, which he has for that purpoſe, and where, he informs me, they would keep good, if there ſhould be occaſion, for two years

Some inſtances of the amazing ſize to which this tree will grow

The ſize to which the oak will grow is amazing Evelyn has recorded ſome that were remarkable in his time He mentions an oak in Weſtphalia which ſerved for a caſtle and a fort, another one hundred and thirty feet high, and thirty feet in diameter, a third in the duke of Norfolk's park at Workſop, which ſpread almoſt three hundred yards ſquare, and three oaks in Dennington park near Newbury, called the King's, the Queen's, and Chaucer's oak, the firſt of which was fifty feet high before any bough or knot appeared, and cut five feet ſquare at the but-end, all clear timber, the other two were remarkable for their ſize and beauty —— Dr Plot, in his Hiſtory of Oxfordſhire, takes notice of an oak between Courtney and Clifton, which ſpread from one extent of the boughs to the other eighty-one feet, ſhading in circumference nine hundred and ſixty yards ſquare, and under which two thouſand four hundred and twenty men might commodiouſly ſtand in ſhelter, of another at Magdalen college, the branches of which in his time ſhot ſixteen yards from the ſtem, and alſo of another at Boycoate, that extended its arms fifty-four feet, under which three hundred and four horſes, or four thouſand three hundred and ſeventy-four men might conveniently ſtand

But it is unneceſſary to produce any farther inſtances of the oak's amazing growth, ſince there are few perſons who have not ſeen or heard of ſuch wonderfully-pleaſing productions of Nature

The appearance of the oak is undoubtedly the moſt ſolemn of all trees Religious rites were wont to be performed under its branches Every one knows that the Druids always ſacrificed under the oak, and that the miſletoe of it was held moſt ſacred, which occaſioned this line of Ovid,

*Ad viſcum Druidæ, Druidæ cantare ſolebant*

Nay, from their conſtant dwelling within oak groves, and their celebrating no ſacrifice or divine ſervice but under its branches or leaves, they doubtleſs acquired the name of Druids, from the Greek word δρῦς, which ſignifies an Oak

Deſcription of the Druids ceremonies in gathering miſletoe

Pliny gives the following account of their ceremonies in gathering the miſletoe "The "Druidæ (ſays he) eſteem nothing in the world "more ſacred than miſletoe, and the tree where-"upon it groweth, ſo it be an oak —— Now "this you may take by the way Theſe prieſts "or clergymen chooſe on purpoſe ſuch groves "for their divine ſervice as ſtand only upon "oaks Nay, they ſolemnize no ſacrifice, nor "celebrate any ſacred ceremonies, without "branches and leaves thereof, and indeed, "whatſoever they find growing to that tree, be-"ſides their own fruit, they eſteem it as a gift "ſent from Heaven, and a ſure ſign that their "God himſelf, whom they ſerve, hath choſen "that peculiar tree And no marvel, for miſle-"toe is rarely to be found on the oak, but, "when they meet with it, they gather it de-"voutly, and with many ceremonies Firſt, "they principally obſerve that the moon be juſt "ſix days old, for upon that day they begin "their months and new years, yea, and their "ſeveral ages, which have their revolutions "every thirty years, becauſe ſhe is thought "then to be of great power and force ſufficient, "and is not yet come to her half light, or end "of her firſt quarter They call it in their lan-"guage All-heal (for they have an opinion "that it healeth all maladies whatſoever) Now, "when they are about to gather it, after they "have duly prepared their ſacrifices, and feſti-"val cheer, under the ſaid tree, they bring "thither two young bullocks, milk-white, whoſe "horns are then, and not before, bound up "This done, the prieſt, arrayed in a ſurplice or "white veſture, climbeth the tree, and with a "golden bill cutteth off the miſletoe, and they "beneath receive the ſame in a white caſſock "Then fall they to kill the beaſts aforeſaid "for ſacrifice, mumbling many orations, and "praying, that it would pleaſe God to bleſs "this gift of his, to their good unto whom he "hath vouchſafed to give it Now this con-"ceit have they of miſletoe thus gathered, that "what living creature ſoever, otherwiſe barren, "drinketh thereof, it will preſently thereupon "become fruitful, alſo, that it is a ſovereign "remedy againſt all venom "—By ſo ſtrange an infatuation were mankind actuated in thoſe days! —The miſletoe of the oak is now ſcarce, indeed I have made it my buſineſs to ſearch for it in oak-woods, where it grows common on the white-thorn, crab-tree, &c but without ſucceſs, and I have made ſtrict enquiry of thoſe who have quantities of miſletoe, but could find none who ever ſaw it growing upon the oak

Varieties of the oak

There are great varieties of oaks in our woods, I have counted near forty, differing in ſome reſpect or other, in a very ſmall ſpace ſome have

had

OAK had large acorns, others ſmall, ſome have been oblong, others round ſome grew upon ſhort foot-ſtalks, others on thoſe that were very long, ſome had ſmall leaves of a paliſh green, others very large, and of a reddiſh hue theſe are accidental varieties, the effects of ſeed, and when full grown are all invariably our true, honeſt, Engliſh heart of oak

Claſs in the Linnæan ſyſtem

The oak, in the Linnæan ſyſtem, is ranked in the claſs and order *Monœcia Polyandria*, which comprehends ſuch plants as have male and female flowers on the ſame plant, the male flowers having numerous ſtamina Of this family alſo is the ever green oak, the cork-tree, the American oaks, &c which will be all duly treated of in their proper places

Time of putting forth its flowers

We may expect to find flowers on the common oak tree in the ſpring, though there is no exact time for the opening of the flowers or leaves, which depends much on the backwardneſs or forwardneſs of the ſeaſon, or the difference of the ſituation or ſoil on which the trees ſtand One oak I have obſerved in full leaf, and at the ſame time another, which has been near it, has had no ſuch appearance, owing to the coldneſs or poverty of the ſtratum on which it ſtood, and which would have been unperceived, had not the tree ſhewed it But notwithſtanding this, obſervation and experience teach us, that theſe differences are very inconſiderable, and that the oak which is moſt backward in putting forth its leaves, generally retains its verdure the longeſt in the autumn In general, the flowers which are of a yellowiſh hue, begin to open about the 7th of April about the 18th the leaves appear, at which time the flowers are in full bloom, and about the 6th of May the leaves will be quite out, and remain until the autumnal froſts come on

Oaks generally raiſed in woods

Oaks are generally raiſed in vaſt quantities together called Woods, where they thrive beſt, and arrive to a greater height than in hedge rows, &c We ſeldom ſee a good oak in a hedge-row they generally throw out large lateral branches, and form a ſpreading and beautiful head, but the trunk is for the moſt part very ſhort; whereas in woods they draw one another up, and thus ſociably aſpire to ſuch an height, as to be ſufficient to anſwer any purpoſes in uſe

Various are the opinions of mankind about the raiſing a wood of this tree Some think they ſhould never be removed, but remain where the acorn was firſt planted, others, again, believe that a wood ſhould be raiſed by ſmall plants of oak taken from a nurſery

As each of theſe methods has its advantages, I ſhall therefore lay down rules, and ſhew the beſt mode of proceeding in raiſing an oak wood both ways, that every one may chooſe that which he likes beſt

And firſt to raiſe a wood from plants, which muſt be raiſed for the purpoſe, after being obtained from the ſeeds

Method of raiſing a wood from plants

In order to raiſe plants from the acorns or ſeeds, let a proper ſpot in the ſeminary be prepared againſt the ſeeds are ripe The ſoil ſhould be loamy, freſh, and in good heart, and the preparation is made by well digging of it, breaking all clods, clearing it of weeds, roots, large ſtones, &c The acorns ſhould be gathered from the ſtraighteſt, moſt thriving, and beautiful trees, and if they remain until they fall off of themſelves, they will ſucceed ſo much the better

Having a ſufficient quantity of well ripened acorns for your purpoſe, proceed to prepare your beds in the ground that is juſt got ready for their reception Mark out the beds with a line, four feet broad, and let there be an alley between each bed two feet wide, rake the earth out of the bed into the ſpaces deſigned for the alley, until the bed be ſunk about two inches deep, ſow your acorns in the bed, about three inches aſunder, and gently preſs them down with the ſpade Skim the earth that had been raked into the alleys over the acorns, until it is raiſed about two inches above them, then, after having dreſſed up the bed and alley, and gently preſſed it down with the back of the ſpade, proceed to the next bed, and ſo on until the whole is finiſhed After this ſet traps at proper diſtances, all over the beds, for if the mice find them out, they will ſoon deſtroy the greateſt part the crows alſo, ſhould they diſcover them, will have their ſhare As ſoon as theſe latter are perceived to take to them, ſome of them muſt be ſhot, and hung upon gibbets *in terrorem*, with their wings expanded, and their bills pegged open, in which ſhould be put ſome gunpowder, in order to produce the better effect OAK

In the ſpring of the year the plants will appear above ground, and in theſe beds they may remain for two years, without any farther trouble or care than keeping them clean from weeds, and now and then refreſhing them with water in very dry weather

When the young trees are two years old, they will be of a proper ſize for planting out Let us ſee in what manner the ground deſigned for the wood is to be prepared to receive them And for this the beſt and only true way is by trenching, or double digging, as deep as the ſoil will allow, all over but as this would be a very expenſive proceeding, and conſequently would be practiſed by few, I ſhall point out another good method of preparing the ground for the reception of oak plants for the raiſing a wood This is to be done by proper ploughing, and, if you chooſe it, the year before it is planted it may bear a crop of oats, barley, or turneps By this means the ſward will be effectually rotted, and the ſoil become more pliable for the other preparations After the crop is off, let the ground be plowed very deep, and then harrowed with an heavy harrow to break the clods about the end of October, let it be plowed again croſs-ways, and harrowed as before This is the ſeaſon for planting of the ſets; for the ground, by being thus croſs-plowed deep and harrowed, will be in proper order for their reception The manner of planting the ſets is as follows

Firſt, carefully take the plants out of the ſeed-bed, ſhorten the tap-root, and take off part of the ſide-ſhoots, that there may be an equal proportion of ſtrength between the ſtem and the root If the wood is deſigned to be but ſmall, ten, twenty, or thirty acres, then lines may be drawn, and the trees planted in rows, four feet diſtance from row to row, and the trees two feet aſunder in the row each line muſt have a man and a boy for planting The man having a good iron ſpade in his hand, and the ground being made light and pliable with croſs-ploughing and harrowing, ſtrikes his ſpade into the earth cloſe to the line; he then takes out his ſpade, and gives another ſtroke at right angles with it, when the boy having a parcel of plants under his left arm, takes one with his right hand, and is ready to put it into the crevice the ſpade made at the ſecond ſtroke after this the man gently preſſes the mould to it with his foot, and thus the young oakling is planted He proceeds in the ſame manner to the next, and ſo on till all is finiſhed An active man will, with his boy, plant fifteen hundred or two thouſand in a day, and while theſe are planting, others ſhould be employed in taking up freſh ſets from the ſeed-bed, ſorting them, and preparing their roots. In ſhort, a ſufficient number of hands

OAK

hands should be set to every part of this work, that the whole may be carried on with dispatch, for it cannot be too soon before the ground is furnished with its plants, after it is in readiness to receive them, neither can the plants be put too early into the ground, after they are taken up from the seminary.

Those plants which are nearly of the same size should be made to occupy a large quarter together, and the weakest may be rejected, if there are enough for the purpose, or they may be left in the seminary a year longer, to gain strength.

Hitherto we have supposed the woods to consist of about thirty or forty acres, but when they are designed to be extensive and large, to stand on one, two, or three hundred acres of ground, then it would be proper to have a pair of wheels made with scoops for the opening of the holes, which must be drawn by an horse. — The centers of the rims of these wheels must be exactly a yard asunder, the wheels must move upon an axis, drawn by the horse in the shafts, the rims or fellies of the wheels must be near a foot broad, and in these rims must be screwed at a yard distance, scoops made of hardened metal; so that when the wheels are drawn by the horse, holes are scooped for the young plants at three feet asunder in the rows, which being also at an interval of three feet, the plants will stand at a yard distance from each other every way. Then the Poor may be employed, and men, women and children soon taught to put in the plants, which have been prepared by the gardener as before directed, into the holes, and close the ground about them properly.

The trees, either for small or large plantations, being in the ground, the first care will be, to fence it well from cattle, and even, if possible, from rabbits and hares. The next should be, to keep them clear from weeds, that the young plants may not be incommoded in their vegetating progress. Some land is more prolific of weeds than others, but in all they must be carefully watched, and destroyed at their first appearance. In small plantations hoeing may do, but where the plantations are large and noble, a double shelving plough must be provided, and when the weeds are got two or three inches high, this must be drawn exactly down the middle of each row, by horses with their mouths muzzled, somebody leading the foremost horse: this plough will effectually throw a ridge each way, so that the edge of it will be almost contiguous to the plants, on either side. This being done, the whole surface of the ground is changed, and the weeds are all buried, except a few, perhaps, about the stems of the plants, which a man following the plough should be ready to cut or pluck up. In this manner the ground may lie until a fresh breed of weeds present themselves, and in the furrows on the ridges, three inches high, when a common plough should be provided to go up one side of the row and down the other, to plough the ridges made by the double shelving plough into their former places, men following with hoes to destroy such weeds as are near the stems of the trees. Thus will the whole scene be changed again, the ground will appear as new tilled, and in this condition it may remain until the weeds call for the double shelving plough a second time, which must also be followed alternately with the common plough, as occasion may require. By this means the ground will not only be kept clean of weeds, but the earth, by constant stirring, will be more replete with vegetating juices, the gentle showers will produce their good effects, the sun will have his influence, and all the powers of vegetation will combine to nourish and set forward the infant oak. This work must be repeated every year, until the oaks are of a height sufficient to destroy the weeds, which may be, perhaps, in four or five years, according to the goodness of the ground in which they are planted.

Thus have you a wood planted with young oaks taken from the nursery or seed-bed. I shall now proceed,

*Method of raising an oak wood from acorns*

Secondly, to the raising of an oak wood from the acorns. Having the ground prepared as before directed for the reception of the young oak plants, and having a sufficient quantity of acorns, all gathered from under the most vigorous, healthy, and thriving trees, proceed to their planting in the following manner.

Let lines be drawn across the ground for the rows, between which let there be four feet distance; but if the plantations are to be very large and the ploughs are designed to be used for keeping the ground clear, the rows should be no farther than a yard asunder, and then the acorns must be set at a greater distance from one another in the rows. Then having sticks rounded properly to make the holes, plant them by the side of the lines, at the distance of about one foot asunder, or one foot and an half, if there is an interval of three feet only between the rows; let them be put about two inches deep in the ground, and see that the earth is properly closed by the prepared stick, to prevent the mice or crows from injuring them. If a person wants a quantity of young oak-sets more than what are designed for his plantation, they may be raised at the same time, thus. Let him draw drills across the ground, and sow the acorns in these drills about four inches asunder, where the young plants, after they are come up, may remain for two years, and be then drawn out, leaving plants at about one foot asunder in the rows, and these also should be thinned, taking out every other or the weakest plant, after they have stood about three years.

The first year after sowing these acorns, the weeds must all be kept down with hoeing and hand-weeding, and this must be done early in the spring, before the weeds get too strong to hide the tender plants, which would occasion many of them to be destroyed in cleaning. It is also the cheapest, as well as neatest husbandry, to take weeds down before they get too large, for though the ground may require an additional hoeing in the season, yet the weeds being hoed down when young, a man may hoe over a greater quantity of ground in a day, and the weeds themselves, being tender, immediately die; whereas those weeds that are grown old and strong, frequently grow again, especially if rain falls soon after, perfect their seeds in a little time, and thereby poison the soil of the whole plantation.

The second year of their growth, in such extensive plantations as require them, the double shelving and common plough may be made use of, as before directed, to cultivate and keep the ground clean, and this culture may be afforded the ground until the plants get so large that it will not be in the power of the weeds to injure them.

Having thus given directions for the raising of woods, both by the young sets and the acorns, I now proceed to its future management, which will be the same in both.

*Of the after management of the plants*

And, first, the rows being four feet asunder, and the plants two feet distant in the rows, or else the rows a yard asunder, and the plants every way a yard distant from each other, they may stand in this manner for about twelve or fourteen

years,

OAK

years, when every second plant may be taken out, and sold for hoops or small poles. Now, though I say in twelve or fourteen years the plants will be fit for these purposes, yet this is not to be a general rule, as the difference of the land's goodness will make a great variation in the growths of the plants. And consequently, if the trees take to growing well, they will want thinning sooner. This business, therefore, must be left to the care of him who is entrusted to manage the plantation.

After every second plant is taken away, let the roots be grubbed up, not only because they will pay for grubbing as fire-wood, but that there may be more room given to the standing plants, freely to extend their roots.

The plants being now four feet asunder each way, will require no more thinning for seven or eight years longer, when the healthiest and best-thriving trees must be marked to stand for timber, and the others cut down for poles, and their roots should remain to produce future under-wood. If the wood stands on twenty acres, I would advise to perform two acres of this work sixteen years after it is planted, two acres more the next year, and so on until the wood is wholly gone through. By this means the trees designed for timber will not be too much thinned at a time, so as at once to expose it to the cold winds, which would give a check to their growth, but there would be an annual sale of two acres, for ten years together, of which the owner would taste the sweets. And this should be a rule, To contrive the cutting, whether the woods be great or small, so as to have a fall of this under wood every year, whilst the trees designed for timber, being at about thirty feet asunder, will shower in at length immense riches. The under-wood will produce our present gains, which will not be inconsiderable, whilst the timber will prove fortunes for our descendants. That this is an effectual way of doubling and securing estates to families is well known. Many a gentleman of a profuse turn has saved his estate by the fall of his timber, which had been carefully planted by his provident ancestors.

Woods raised from plants grow soonest and fastest.

Woods raised from plants will grow the fastest, and come to perfection soonest, and altho' some have asserted the contrary, experience proves it to be true. Some will tell you, that they have tried both ways, and that those from the acorn, without being removed, outstrip the others considerably. When this has happened, I am certain the acorns have had the best land, or the oak plants were very bad ones. An oak has generally a tap root, which goes straight into the earth, if not removed; when removed, this tap root is shortened, and when the tree is planted, the roots strike out from the side, and, being nearer the surface, receive the vegetating juices of the earth in greater quantities.

Oaks raised from acorns grow slowly, but are the best timber.

Those trees raised from the acorn without removing, on account of the tap-root striking down into the ground, where there is less nourishment, grow slowly, but are, when they arrive at timber, the best, being generally fuller at heart, and more compact, strong, and lasting.

Method of training oaks for standards.

Such gentlemen as are desirous of oaks to plant out for standards, either in parks or in fields, for clumps or for avenues, must train them in the following manner.

Having raised them in the seed-beds as was before directed for woods, and having stood two years in the seed-bed, a piece of good ground must be prepared for their reception, where they must grow until they are of a size sufficient to be planted out where they are designed to remain. This ground must be trenched, or double dug, then, taking the plants out of the seed-bed, prepared as was before directed, let a man and boy plant these upon this new double dug ground, at the distance of two feet row from row, and a foot and half asunder in the rows. Every winter, until the plants are taken out of this nursery, the ground should be dug between these rows, and this is what gardeners call *turning-in*. They will require no other pruning, than taking off any unsightly side shoot, or, where the tree is inclined to be forked, to take off the weakest branch. Nor is any other precaution necessary, until the time of their being planted out to continue, which must be done as follows.

OAK

First, carefully take the trees out of the nursery, and then prune the roots, which must be done by holding the plant in your left hand, that the stroke of the knife in the right may so cut the bottom of the root, that the wound may be downwards, next, take off all bruised and broken parts of the root, and, having holes prepared, in the figure of a circle, three feet in diameter and a foot and half deep (the sward being worked and chopped small in the bottom of the holes, and some mould laid to cover it), plant the trees in such a manner that the top of the root may be nearly level with the surface of the ground. Let the finest of the mould, that which was under the turf, be to lap the root in, and, after the earth has regularly filled the hole, let it be pressed down with the foot, to settle it properly to the root. A little litter should be laid over the root, to prevent the wind and sun from drying the mould, and thereby retarding the growth of the trees, especially if the planting is deferred till the spring. The plants should likewise have proper stakes, to secure them from the violence of the winds, or if they are planted where cattle or deer can come at them, they should be properly hurdled. After this, they will require no farther care. Not an hatchet or knife should come near them. Pruning off tender branches is the destruction of this tree, as well as others.

Oaks grow tallest in woods.

Oaks will not aspire to such height or fineness of trunk, when planted in these places, as in woods, but they will form most beautiful heads, their shade will be extensive and large, and the number of acorns they bear will be very great, to the heightening of the flavour, as well as fattening both hogs and deer.

Soil in which the oak principally delights.

The oak will grow and thrive upon almost any soil, provided the ground and the trees be properly prepared and planted, though we cannot suppose that the growth will be equal in all the sorts. A rich deep loamy earth is what oaks most delight in, and in such they will arrive at the greatest magnitude in the fewest years, though they grow exceeding well in clays of all kinds, and on sandy and gravelly ground.

We have experience of their being extremely luxuriant, thriving, and of great variety, where the ground is a clay, especially if it be alternately a red, white, and blue sort, and we have many instances of their growing to a monstrous size, where the soil is no other than a rock-sand.

Time most proper for felling.

The time for cutting down the oak is limited by act of parliament to the spring, after the sap is flowing, that they may with more ease peel off the bark for the tanners use. But it is observable, and with great reason too, that the timber of these trees will not be so good or so durable as if they had been cut down in the dead of winter, when the sap was at rest. The French, knowing this, take the bark off the tree standing, and let it remain till the winter following, and altho' the timber of these will not be quite so good as that of those which were felled in winter, yet it is a very laudable example, and worthy of our imitation.

# C H A P. II.

## *ULMUS*, The ELM-TREE.

THE Elm is the next tree which offers itſelf to our conſideration, and it deſerves this place, whether we conſider the uſefulneſs of this tree when growing, its beauty or its bulk, and the many purpoſes its timber will at laſt ſerve, when felled for uſe.

*Various uſes of the elm when growing*

The uſes of the elm when growing are various. There is none more proper to plant to break the violence of the winds, and defend an habitation; no tree is more ſerviceable to form high and towering hedges, which may be kept clipped and neat, if required, to ſhelter what is wanted; there is no ſhade more wholeſome than that of the elm; and what conſtitutes a peculiar excellence in this tree is, that it may be removed, even when twenty years old, with all reaſonable hopes of ſucceſs to that where ſhade or ſhelter is wanting, either may be obtained in a little time.

*and beautiful appearance*

The beauty of the elm is no leſs remarkable. The procerity of the ſtem, and the waving head of the true Engliſh elm, untrimmed and unlopped, ſtrike the imagination, whilſt the large arms and ſpreading branches of the Wych elm make an agreeable contraſt.

*Inſtances of its extraordinary bulk*

The bulk the elm will grow to is very great, being next in ſize to the oak. We read of an elm on Blechington-Green in Oxfordſhire, in the cavity of which a poor ſtrolling woman was delivered of a child; of another on Binſey-Common, which was ſix yards diameter next the ground; and of a third in Sir Walter Bagot's Park in Staffordſhire, which when felled lay forty yards in length, and was in diameter at the ſtool ſeventeen feet: and the monſtrous trees we ſee in different places, ſtill luxuriant and thriving, induce us to believe the moſt extraordinary accounts.

*Purpoſes to which the timber is applied*

The timber of theſe noble trees, when cut down for uſe, ſerves for many purpoſes. The wheelwright finds his advantage in cutting it into naves or hubs, axletrees or fellies, and it is more uſed than aſh for broad-wheel waggons, &c. They are not only uſeful for ſmaller utenſils, as handles for ſaws, &c. but alſo larger conveniencies, as ſideboards in kitchens, dreſſers, &c. and, being moſt laſting where it lies continually wet, it is very proper for water works of moſt ſorts, as for pumps, aqueducts, mills, pipes, &c. Add to all theſe, our laſt remains are generally repoſited in coffins made of this wood.

*Derivation of the name*

*Time when the flowers blow and leaves open*

The name *Ulmus* is formed of the Greek word ὕλη, *lignum*, wood; and its ſtation in the Linnæan ſyſtem is in the claſs and order *Pentandria Digynia*, there being in each flower five ſtamina and two ſtyles. The flowers are in full blow about the beginning of April, and the leaves open about the middle of the ſame month; but the ſeeds are not ripe before the beginning of June.

*Principal ſorts of elm propagated for timber*

There are many ſorts of this tree, but thoſe principally propagated for timber are,

1. The true Engliſh elm.
2. The narrow leaved Corniſh elm.
3. The Dutch elm.
4. The black Worceſterſhire elm.
5. The narrow-leaved Wych elm.
6. The broad-leaved Wych elm.
7. The upright Wych elm.

Elms are propagated by layers, by ſeeds, and by grafting them on their own kinds.

*Method of propagating elms by layers*

In order to propagate them by layers, proper ſtools for the purpoſe muſt be firſt obtained; to procure which, let a piece of good ground be double dug, and plant elms of about four or five feet high over it, at the diſtance of about ten feet. If they make good ſhoots in the firſt year after, they may be cut down early the ſpring following; if not, they ſhould remain two years before they are headed for ſtools, which ſhould be by cutting them down to within half a foot of the ground. After they are cut down, they ſhould be ſuffered to grow undiſturbed for two years. The ground between the ſtools muſt be dug in the winter, and conſtantly hoed as the weeds ariſe in the ſummer; and at the end of that time, that is two years, the branches growing from theſe ſtools will be fit for layering, which may be performed thus: Excavate a piece of ground wide enough to receive a whole branch, and let the hollow be about half a foot deep; then ſplaſh the branch with a knife, near the body of the ſtool, that its head may be more readily brought into the prepared place. Next, thruſt an hooked ſtick into the ground, to hold it cloſe; take off all the ſuperfluous branches, which croſs and would otherwiſe incommode thoſe that are to be continued. After this, cut all the remaining young branches acroſs half through with the knife, turn the edge towards the end, ſlitting it about half an inch. When this is done on all the young branches, the mould ſhould be gently put amongſt them, and every one of them ſhould have their ends bent towards the ſtool, that the ſlit may be open. Laſtly, having the whole vacuity filled with its own mould, ſmooth and even, take the end of each twig off that peeps above the ground, down to one eye, and the branch ſo layed will afford you as many plants as there are buds peeping out of the ground. Proceed in like manner to the other branches of the ſame ſtool, then to the next ſtool in order, and ſo on until the whole buſineſs of layering is finiſhed.

By the autumn following, theſe layers will have taken root, and many of them will have made a ſhoot of near a yard in length. It is now neceſſary to take them from their ſtools, and plant them in ſome double dug ground in the nurſery. They ſhould be ſet in rows three feet aſunder, and the diſtance allowed them from each other in the rows ought to be a foot and a half. Here they may ſtand till they are planted out where they are to remain, with no farther trouble than digging the ground between the rows every winter, and in the ſummer carefully watching thoſe which ſhoot out two branches at the head, and nipping the weakeſt of them off.

After the layers are taken up, the ſtools muſt have all the wounded parts, occaſioned by the former ſplaſhing, taken away; the old branches alſo ſhould be cut off, pretty cloſe to the ſtem; and in the ſpring they will begin to ſhoot out freſh branches again, for a ſecond layering, which will likewiſe be ready to have the ſame operation performed the ſecond year after. And thus may this layering be performed on theſe ſtools every other year. But nurſerymen who would raiſe great

great quantities of trees this way, ſhould be provided with two quarters of ſtools, to come in alternately, ſo that from one or other of them they may annually receive a crop

*Method of raiſing elms by ſeeds,*

Another, and by far the moſt expeditious method of raiſing elms, is by ſowing the ſeeds, but this practice chiefly reſpects the Wych elms, the ſeeds of the others very rarely ripening in this country In order, therefore, to obtain a good quantity of theſe elms, let the ſeeds be gathered the beginning of June, it being the time when they are full ripe When gathered, ſpread them three or four days to dry, for if they were to be ſown immediately after they were gathered, they would rot Having been ſpread about that time, and the mould, which ought to be freſh and good, being in readineſs for their reception, mark out your beds four feet wide, and let the alleys between them be a foot and a half or two feet broad Rake the mould out of the beds until they are about an inch deep, riddle that which came out of the beds into them again, until the bottom of each bed is raiſed half an inch (*i e* half filled) with riddled mould, then gently preſs the mould down with the back of the ſpade, and ſow the ſeeds thinly all over it with an even hand, covering them down with fine earth about half an inch deep When the ſeeds are all ſown this way, the beds ſhould be hooped, and covered with mats, to be ſhaded in that hot ſeaſon of the year, and they ſhould alſo ſometimes be refreſhed with water Part of the young plants will come up in about a month, or ſooner, the others not till the ſpring following From the time the ſeeds are ſown to their appearance above ground, whenever rain falls be careful to uncover the beds, and as ready to cover them again when the ſcorching beams of the ſun break out About the end of Auguſt, the mats ſhould be wholly taken away, that the plants may be hardened against winter The ſpring following, a freſh breed will preſent themſelves among thoſe that came up the ſummer before All the ſummer following they ſhould be conſtantly kept free from weeds, and watered as often as dry weather ſhall render it neceſſary, and in October or ſpring they may be planted out in the nurſery, at the diſtance before preſcribed for the layers, and afterwards ſhould be managed like them

*and by grafting*

Grafting is the next method of propagating elms, all the ſorts of which may be encreaſed this way The ſtocks for the purpoſe ſhould be the broad-leaved Wych elm, which muſt be raiſed from the ſeed, and planted out as before When they have grown two years in the nurſery, they will be of proper ſize to receive the graft, and the laſt week in January is the beſt time for the work If a large quantity of elm ſtocks are to be grafted, procure ſix men in readineſs for the purpoſe The buſineſs of the firſt man is to take the mould from the ſtem of the ſtocks, with a ſpade, down to the root, laying the top of the root bare, the next man is to follow him with a ſharp pruning-knife, cutting off the heads of the ſtocks, and leaving the ſtumps to be grafted only about two inches above the root, the third man is the grafter himſelf, who having his grafts cut about four or five inches in length, all of the young wood, and ſuch as has never bore lateral branches, in a diſh, takes out one of them, and holding it in his left hand, the taper end being from him, with the knife that is in his right he takes off a ſlope about an inch and half or two inches long, and if the grafter be an artiſt, it will be cut as true as if wrought by a plane This done, he makes a ſmall cut acroſs, nearly at the top of the ſlope, and then proceeds to prepare the ſtock to receive it, which is effected by ſloping off a ſide of it, of the ſame length with the ſloped graft, that the parts may fit as near as poſſible He then makes a cut nearly at the top of the ſtock downward, to receive the tongue he had made in the graft, and having properly joined them, he proceeds to the next After the grafter follows a perſon with baſs matting, cut into proper lengths, and with theſe he ties the grafts pretty cloſe to the ſtock The fifth man brings the clay, which ſhould have been prepared a week or longer before, and well worked and beaten over, mixed with a fourth part of horſe-dung, and ſome chopped hay, in order to make it hang the better together With this he ſurrounds the graft and the ſtock Laſtly, the ſixth man comes and cloſes the clay, ſo that there may be no probability of its being waſhed off Two or three rows being grafted, let an additional hand or two be employed, either in drawing the earth up above the clay, ſo that it may be wholly covered, or digging the ground between the rows, and levelling it ſo that nothing of the performed work may appear, except the tops of the grafts, above ground The danger of froſt renders this precaution highly neceſſary, for if it ſhould be delayed a night or two, and ſharp froſts ſhould happen, the clay will moſt of it fall off, and thus the work will require to be repeated, whereas, when it is lapped warm in the manner directed, there will be no danger of ſuch an accident

A good workman with the above mentioned neceſſary aſſiſtance, will graft about fifteen hundred ſtocks in a day In the ſpring, the buds will ſwell, diſcloſe, and ſhoot forth nearly as ſoon as thoſe of the tree from which they were taken By the latter end of June, they will be ſhot a foot, or about a foot and half when they ſhould be freed from the clay, the matting ſhould be alſo taken off, and themſelves left to ſport at eaſe with all the vegetative powers At this time, of thoſe which have put forth two ſhoots, the weakeſt ſhould be taken up, to ſtrengthen the other, and to lighten the head, which would otherwiſe be ſubject to be broken off by high winds By autumn the ſhoot will have grown about a yard in length, and in the winter dig the ground between the rows

In this place they may remain till they are of a ſize to be planted out for continuance, with no other trouble than what was directed for the layers, namely, keeping them clear of weeds, digging between the rows in the winter, at the ſame time taking off all very large ſide-branches, and in the ſummer pruning off ſuch young ſhoots, in the head, as may have a tendency to make the tree become forked

*Grafting a valuable improvement of the Engliſh elm*

This practice of grafting will be found a valuable improvement of the Engliſh elm, if we conſider the nature of the Wych elm, on which it is grafted Firſt, the Wych elm will not only grow to the largeſt ſize of all the ſorts, but will grow the faſteſt However, this is not to be wondered at, if we examine the root, which we ſhall find more fibrous, and the pores larger and in greater numbers than in any of the other elms Now, as all roots are of a ſpongy nature, to receive the juices of the earth for the nouriſhment and growth of the tree, that tree muſt neceſſarily grow the faſteſt whoſe root is moſt ſpongy and porous, and therefore the true Engliſh elm, being ſet upon the root of the Wych, a greater quantity of nutriment is received from the earth for its encreaſe, in proportion as the root of the Wych elm is more ſpongy and porous than that of its own ſort Thus the Engliſh elm, on this baſis, will arrive at timber

many

ELM

many years sooner than those raised by layers, and be also forced to a greater size. If we consider too that the roots of the Wych elm will imbibe such juices as are proper for the growth of its own sorts, timber thus raised must be better, as the wood of the Wych elm is so excellent in its kind as to answer the purposes of all the other kinds.

Soil most proper for the elm

The elm will thrive best on a rich pasture-ground, moist and loamy, though those that have been grafted upon poorer soil will grow well, as the Wych elm is of a hardy nature, for the pores of the roots being very large, it is not so delicate in the filtration of its juices, but takes in all, both coarse and fine.

All sorts of elms not to be planted for woods

All the sorts of elms, the Wych excepted, are not so proper to be planted for woods. Nature having designed them rather for hedge-rows, and the borders of open fields. For this purpose, they should be planted in October, or early in the spring. In planting them, observe not to set them too deep, let the roots be even with, or rather above the surface, and a bank raised to keep the sun from drying the roots. Previous to this, the holes should be dug a foot and half deep, and three feet broad, the turf must be worked to the bottom of the holes, and then earth put in to raise it up to the proper height the tree is to be planted. The leading shoot of the tree is to remain untouched, and no other pruning is required than to take off the side-branches which are largest, and leave only what are sufficient to draw the sap, and this must always be in proportion to the goodness or badness of the root. The roots will require no farther pruning than taking off all the wounded parts. After the trees are wholly planted, they must be staked, and secured from cattle and deer.

Banks, or near old hedges, an improper situation

I would by no means advise the planting of these trees on banks, or very near old hedges, as they will make a very small progress in many years. Let them be set at least four or five yards from such situations, and they will grow extremely well. But where a gentleman owns the whole demesne, it will be better to plant them on the ditch side, as they will there meet with the moisture they delight in, and consequently the encrease will be proportionably greater.

Wych elm thrives best in woods

The Wych elm is by no means proper to plant in hedge-rows or open fields, as it will throw out monstrous large arms, and thereby appear not so beautiful as the English elm. Few of these, therefore, should be planted, unless it be to make a contrast with the others. This tree, however, is very proper to be planted for woods, for, being near each other, they will aspire like the oaks, no great arms will be produced, but a clean noble trunk will present itself, to a great height.

Directions to plant an Ulmarium

Whoever is desirous of having an *Ulmarium*, or a wood of these elms, must let the plants be raised in the seminary as before directed, and afterwards be planted in the nursery. The rows need not be wider than two feet, nor the plants above a foot asunder, if ground is scarce, as they must be soon taken from hence, to form the wood. When they are about three or four feet high, they will be of a proper size for this purpose. The ground should be prepared ready for their reception, which I would advise to have done by double digging; but if this should be thought too expensive, and the plantation is designed to be very large, let it be plowed all over very deep, with a very strong plough, that the turf or rich soil at the surface may be worked down, in order to receive the roots of the plants when they strike, and send them forth with more vigour. This being done, make the holes all over the ground, in the manner before directed, only, as these trees are not so large as those planted for standards, they need not be so wide, a foot and a half will be sufficient, and if there be any turf, see that it is chopt small at the bottom of them. If the best mould, designed to lap the roots in, is not very pliable or fine, it will be proper to let the holes lie open some time, and the mould be exposed to the sun, rain, and frost, which will greatly mellow it, and render it more fit for the purpose. The distance of these holes should be two yards. Having taken the trees out of the nursery, cut off all large lateral branches, and shorten the other side-shoots, in proportion to the root, and having also taken off all the bruised parts of the roots, proceed to plant them. After this, they will require no farther care till their branches begin to touch one another, when they should be thinned, by taking away every second, or rather the less thriving trees all over the plantation. Thus they may continue until the branches meet again, when they should undergo a second thinning, grubbing up always the old roots, and so on, to the pleasure and profit of the owner, till the trees are arrived at maturity, when they will be noble, lofty, and valuable.

Best time for felling the timber

The best time for cutting down the timber of the elm is in the dead of winter, when the sap is at rest, and if this be exactly observed, the timber will be more durable and strong.

## CHAP. III.

### *FAGUS*, The BEECH-TREE.

THE Beech, which I have chose to succeed the elm, is a beautiful as well as valuable tree. The leaves are of a pleasant green, and many of them remain on the branches during the winter, when they present themselves of a brown colour, for which reason this tree is highly proper to shelter habitations, and such places as require to be screened from violent winds.

The beech succeeds well in woods or open fields

The beech may be planted either in woods or open fields, in both which stations it grows to a large height, and carries a trunk of a proportionable bulk. By hedge-rows and the borders of fields they expand their branches to an amazing extent.

Proper for parks, &c.

There is no tree more suitable for parks, lawns, wilderness quarters, clumps, &c. as its shade is generally esteemed wholesome, and what encreases its value is its mast, which contributes greatly to the fattening swine and deer, no contemptible motive for planting trees of this kind, for, besides the expectation of their valuable timber, you have the benefit of an annual crop,

BEECH

crop, which is not inconſiderable. With what chearfulneſs then may a perſon ſet about propagating theſe trees, when he reflects that in a few years they will not only begin to defray his expences by their own produce, but continue it annually, with an additional increaſe, till they are full grown to timber, and muſt be cut down for uſe.

*Purpoſes to which the timber is applied*

The wood of the beech has a fine grain, and is therefore uſeful to make ſeveral curious inſtruments diſhes, trenchers, buckets, trays, &c. are made of it by the turner, for the houſewife, whilſt it furniſhes the huſbandman with ſhovels, grafts for his ſpades, handles for hatchets, &c. The bellows-maker finds his account in this wood, and it is equally ſerviceable for chairs, ſtools, bedſteads, dreſſer-boards, coffins, &c.

*Derivation of its generical name*

The generical name of this tree, *Fagus*, is derived from the Greek word φαγω, *I eat*, and the propriety of this derivation is apparent, as the maſt in all ages has in ſome meaſure, but particularly in the earlier times, been the food of ſome part of mankind.

*Claſs and order in the Linnæan ſyſtem*

The Fagus belongs to the claſs and order *Monoecia Polyandria*, there being both male and female flowers on the ſame plants, and the male flowers having many ſtamina.

*Time when the flowers blow and leaves open*

The buds of the beech-tree begin to open about the fifteenth of April, and the leaves will be out about the twenty-firſt. The flowers begin to ſhew themſelves about the ninth of May, and by the firſt of June they will be in full blow. They are ſucceeded by the maſt, an angular fruit, which is ripe in the autumn.

*Method of propagating the beech,*

The manner of propagating this tree is thus. Gather a ſufficient quantity of maſt, about the middle of September, when it begins to fall, ſpread them upon a mat, in an airy place, for ſix days, to dry, and after that you may either proceed to ſowing them immediately, or you may put them up in bags, in order to ſow them nearer the ſpring, which method I would rather adviſe, as they will keep very well, and there will be leſs danger of having them deſtroyed by mice or other vermin, by which kinds of animals they are greatly reliſhed.

BEECH

The ground being ready for the ſeeds, line your beds out four feet wide, with alleys at a foot and a half or two feet broad, for this is the propereſt width of raiſing the ſeeds of all ſorts of foreſt-trees, let the earth be raked out of each bed, one inch deep, and, after having levelled the bottom, and gently tapped it down with the ſpade, ſow the ſeeds all over it, even and regular; then tap them down with the back of the ſpade, and cover the mould over them an inch deep. In the ſpring of the year, many of the young plants will make their appearance, whilſt others will not come up till the ſpring following.

After they have been two years in the ſeminary, they muſt be planted in the nurſery way on ſome double-dug ground. The rows ſhould be two feet and a half aſunder, and the plants at eighteen inches diſtance in the rows. The rows ought to be kept clean of weeds in the ſummer, and dug between every winter. Here they may remain till they are to be planted out for continuance.

If they are deſigned for ſtandards in fields, parks, &c. they muſt grow till they are of a proper ſize, when they ſhould be carefully taken up and planted in the ſame manner as was ordered for the elm.

If they are deſigned for woods, the ground muſt be prepared in the ſame manner as I have directed for the Wych elm, they ſhould be planted at the ſame diſtance, of the ſame ſize, and thinned accordingly.

*which thrives well upon moſt ſoils*

Theſe trees will flouriſh very well upon moſt ſoils. Upon ſtony ground and chalky mountains they grow very well, upon the declivities, ſides and tops of hills, they flouriſh amazingly, and at Gumley, where I have a large nurſery, they are all healthy, and ſhoot ſtrong, on that white clay. In ſhort, they may be cultivated to great advantage on moſt barren places, if they are firſt of all raiſed on ſuch, as well as to ſtill greater profit, where the land is of a higher value.

*Time moſt proper for felling the timber*

It is almoſt needleſs to mention, that the time of cutting down the timber of this tree is in the dead of winter, the time when the ſap is wholly at reſt.

## CHAP. IV

## *FRAXINUS*, The ASH-TREE

WE come now to the Aſh, whoſe timber (the oak only excepted) ſerves for the greateſt variety of uſes of any tree in the wood. Its Latin appellation, *Fraxinus*, is of doubtful derivation, and we have no Greek word from which we can with propriety deduce it. Virgil calls the aſh the moſt beautiful tree in the woods, and whoever entertains the ſame opinion now, ſhould take care that its chief reſidence be there. For this tree, beautiful as it is, ought by no means to be planted for ornament in places deſigned to be kept neat and clean, becauſe the leaves, which are large and noble, fall off of themſelves, with their long ſtalk, very early in the autumn, and by their litter deſtroy the beauty of ſuch places. If they are conſtantly taken away, there is a conſtant ſucceſſion falling, and if they are ſuffered to remain, the worms draw them into the ground, and render the ſpot by no means pleaſing.

*Derivation of its generical name dubious*

*The aſh moſt proper for woods and parks,*

But altho' this tree is not well adapted to plant near gravel walks and places deſigned for pleaſure, it is very proper not only for woods, but to form clumps in large parks, or it may be ſet out for ſtandards in any place that is not tillage land, on which it ſhould never be planted, becauſe the dripping of the leaves is extremely injurious to corn, and the roots have the greateſt tendency to draw out the ſtrength of the ground.

*Is a quick grower*

The quick growth of the aſh, as well as value of the timber, is a great encouragement to propagate it. Evelyn mentions an aſh in his time, that in forty years from the key was ſold for thirty pounds ſterling, and altho' we never can expect the ſame ſucceſs, yet we ſhall find our profits in raiſing theſe trees will be very great.

*Uſes for which the timber is ſerviceable*

The wood of the aſh is uſeful for almoſt every inſtrument in huſbandry. Plows, harrows, axletrees and wheel rings, balls, and oars, are made

ASH

made of this wood. It is proper for pullies, handles, screws for tools, spade-trees, &c. The poles are excellent either for spars, coopers hoops, or hop-yards. In short, waggons, carts, ladders, &c. are mostly composed of it.

Class and order in the Linnæan system.

This genus of plants is ranked in the class and order *Polygamia Dioecia*, the polygamy being on two distinct plants.

Time of the flowers and leaves opening.

The curious observer of Nature will find the flowers of the Ash begin to open about the sixteenth of April, and about the twenty-second they will be in full blow. The leaves, also, of many trees by this time will be out, though others will not shew their foliage till the middle of May.

Manner of propagating the tree,

Let us now see in what manner this tree is to be propagated, whether for standards, spinneys, or woods. In the first place, gather the keys from some young, thriving, healthy trees; and, having ground prepared for the seminary, let beds be made as has been before directed; but in these let them be sown soon after they are gathered, in an even regular manner. In the second spring after this, the plants will come up, for they generally lie two years. In this bed they may remain till the spring following, and, if designed for woods, they should be pricked out, in the nursery way, about a foot square, and so may stand for two years.

for standards or clumps,

If the plants are designed for standards, or for clumps, &c. it will be proper to let them remain two years in the seed-bed, and then be planted in the nursery, in rows one yard asunder, and at two feet distance in the rows. After taking them out of the seminary, the tap root must be shortened, as also the side-shoots; but by no means diminish the leading bud, for this is the chief operator in drawing the sap and setting the juices afloat, so that if this be cut off, the young plant will not only want the chief promoter of its growth; but, being vastly pithy, is then liable to great injuries. Indeed, it is amazing to see what surprizing shoots some ashes have made the first year, though cut down when planted. But this should be no argument for continuing the practice; it only shews how strongly the powers of vegetation operate in this tree. After they have stood in the nursery till they are of a proper size, they may be planted in those places where they are designed to remain.

for spinneys,

If a spinney of these plants is wanted for poles on some moist ground, it must be carefully trenched, to drain off the superfluous moisture, and the ground should be laid out in beds fit for planting, six feet broad. Along each of these beds may be planted three rows, which will be two feet asunder, and the plants must be at two feet distance in the rows. The young plants proper for this work are such as have been raised in the seminary, and pricked out in the nursery for one or two years. Such places as these, which hitherto have hardly produced any profit to the owner, will be now greatly improved, since he will have a growing stock on the ground, which will pay him as much as he gets by his best pasture. For I have known an acre of poles, thus planted, in less than twenty years sold for more than a hundred pounds.

or for woods.

If a large wood of these trees is intended to be planted, the ground may bear a crop of oats, barley, or turneps, the year before; and after that is carried off, it should be ploughed deep with a very strong plow, and harrowed well with a heavy harrow, to break the clods. But before the plants are planted, which should be in the latter end of October, the ground should be ploughed crossways, and harrowed as before.

Having thus prepared the ground, let lines be drawn across it, three feet asunder, and let the plants be set in these lines, at the distance of two feet. [illegible] work may be performed by a man and boy, as was shewn under the article Oak.

After they are planted, the double-shelving plow may be made use of, to throw the mould each way to cover the weeds, and the common plow afterwards introduced, to plough the mould into its former place, the horses all the time being muzzled. This work may be continued at proper seasons two or three years, after which they will require no farther care than to keep out cattle, &c.

As the quickness of their growth will depend on the goodness of the soil, the number of years from the first planting to the first fall will vary accordingly, though, if the wood be large, I would advise to have the first fall of poles very soon, that there may be an annual sale till the wood has been wholly cut down, and this should be so contrived, that the year after the last quarter is cut, that which was first begun on may be ready for a second falling. This will happen at an interval of about fifteen or twenty years, by which time the poles will be large. But, if they are wanted for smaller purposes, the fall should be proportionably sooner.

After the first fall, great care should be taken to grub up the worst stools where they are too thick, for now every stool will send out four or five branches. But before any are grubbed up, a proper number should be pitched on to grow to timber, and these should always be such trees as are the largest, most healthy, and thriving. So that whilst the owner is reaping his annual crop of poles, these, like an estate in reversion, may pour in a tide of wealth upon him in after years.

ASH

The ash will grow exceeding well upon almost any soil, and the best time for felling the timber is in the winter months, from November to February. For if it be cut later, it is not only subject to a worm which greatly damages the timber, but the bark will divide from the stools, to their great detriment.

The ash grows well on almost any soil. Best time for felling its timber.

It is observable, that pollards should always be lopped in the spring, and it is further to be remarked of these, that when the head of a pollard begins to be hollow, the body then enters upon a state of decay, so that if this is designed to be useful, the pollard should be then wholly cut down.

Pollards should be lopped in the spring.

Pollards are of great service where fuel is scarce. A few of these trees will turn out many loads of lop, and the wood of them makes the sweetest of all fires, and will burn well either green or dry.

One caution more let me give with respect to these trees. Do not let the interval between their lopping be too great. If the branches be suffered to grow to a very great thickness, the taking them off will proportionably injure the tree.

CHAP.

# CHAP. V

## *PLATANUS*, The PLANE-TREE.

*Principal sorts of the plane-tree, which are adapted to avenues, Lawns, &c.*

THERE are ſeveral ſorts of Plane-trees, the principal, however, are the Oriental, the Occidental, and the Black Spaniſh. They are all delightful trees for avenues, and afford an excellent ſhade in walks deſigned for that purpoſe. They are alſo proper to be planted for ornamenting lawns, parks, &c. and, as they grow to great timber-trees in a few years, they will be equally advantageous to the owner for profit, they may therefore be alſo raiſed either in ſimple ſtandards, clumps or woods.

*Derivation of the generical name.*

The plane tree, *Platanus*, is ſo called from the Greek word πλάτυς, which ſignifies *broad*, because the leaves of this tree are of an extraordinary breadth and as the fewneſs of the branches of trees is always in proportion to the breadth of the leaves, Pliny might juſtly obſerve, that no tree defends us ſo well from the heat of the ſun in ſummer, or admits its rays more freely in winter.

*The plane tree greatly eſteemed by the Romans.*

The plane tree was in great eſteem among the antients, particularly the Romans, who having obtained them from the Levant, planted them in places deſigned for contemplation and philoſophy. To theſe plantations their greateſt orators, philoſophers, and ſtateſmen repaired, with extraordinary pleaſure and ſatisfaction, and teſtified their fondneſs of theſe trees by frequently irrigating them with wine inſtead of water.

*Extraordinary inſtance of Xerxes fondneſs of it.*

But among all the inſtances of antient fondneſs of this tree, that of Xerxes is the moſt remarkable. Being on his march, with ſeventeen hundred thouſand men, and meeting with an oriental plane-tree, of extraordinary beauty and figure, he ordered his whole army to halt for ſome days, that he might feaſt himſelf with admiring its pulchritude and procerity. Ælian and other authors tell us, that he ordered all his own jewels, gems, bracelets, &c. as well as thoſe of his concubines, and his ſatrapes or nobles, to be placed about it, and became ſo enamoured with it, as to appear totally unaffected concerning the fate of his great expedition, and to have wholly forgot the intereſt and honour of his arms, calling it "his miſtreſs, his minion, his goddeſs." And, when he was forced to leave it, he cauſed the figure of it to be ſtamped on a gold medal, which he wore continually about him.

*Singular marks of reſpect paid to this tree in France.*

In France plane-trees have likewiſe been treated with ſingular marks of reſpect, for ſo greatly were they admired, after being firſt obtained from Rome, and ſo deſirous were the principal nobility of having their eſtates diſtinguiſhed by theſe trees, that a law was enacted prohibiting all perſons under a certain degree of honour from planting them, and ſo prized was their ſhade, that they exacted a tribute from any native who preſumed to ſit under them. In England, I only wiſh to ſee them receive ſo much reſpect as to be planted with other trees, either in fields, parks, lawns, or woods.

*Inſtances of its ſurprizing growth.*

The plane-tree will grow to a monſtrous ſize, inſomuch that we read of one belonging to the emperor Caligula, which, when hollowed, made a room large enough for the regalement of ten or twelve perſons, with their waiters. The Hon. Paul Dudley, Eſq. in a letter to the Royal Society, ſays, he obſerved in New-England an occidental plane-tree nine yards in girth, which continued its bulk very high, and that, when felled, it made twenty two loads of wood. The timber has not been much proved with us, but the Turks uſe it for building their ſhips, ſo that I think it will not only make good boards, but anſwer all the purpoſes of the lime, ſycamore, horſe-cheſnut, willow, &c. for which uſes, as it is a very ſwift grower, it juſtly deſerves to be planted.

*The timber uſed by the Turks for building ſhips.*

*Claſs and order in the Linnæan ſyſtem.*

The plane tree produces both male and female flowers, and as the male flowers have numerous ſtamina, its claſs and order is *Monoecia Polyandria*. The flowers are ſo ſmall as to be ſcarcely viſible, and come out late in the ſpring. The buds of the leaves of the oriental ſort begin to ſwell about the fourteenth of May, and the leaves will be quite out by the latter end of the ſame month. The leaves are divided into ſix or ſeven ſegments, and are very large and palmated. The fruit is a large rough ball, which has occaſioned this tree ſometimes to be called the Button-Tree. It is a native of the Eaſt, and is called by Bauhine *Platanus Orientalis*.

*Time of the leaves of the oriental plane-trees coming out.*

*The occidental,*

The occidental plane tree is a native of North-America. Its leaves are larger, but come out at the ſame time with the other. I have meaſured leaves of this tree, and found them fourteen inches broad. It produces the ſame ſort of flowers, and perfects its ſeeds in the autumn. This alſo has had the name of Button-Tree given to it.

*and black Spaniſh ſorts deſcribed.*

The black Spaniſh plane-tree differs from the others, in having the ſegments of the leaves narrower, and the bark of the young ſhoots of a dark brown.

*Method of propagating the oriental and black Spaniſh plane-trees.*

The oriental and black Spaniſh plane-trees are propagated from ſeeds, when they can be eaſily procured, but whoever enjoys not this convenience, muſt have recourſe to layers. The ground proper for the ſeminary ſhould be moiſt and ſhady, well dug, and raked till the mould is fine, then, in the autumn, ſoon after the ſeeds are ripe, let them be ſcattered over this ground, and the ſeeds raked in, in the ſame manner as turnep-ſeeds. In the ſpring, many of the young plants will come up, though you muſt not expect the general crop till the ſecond year, the ſpring after which they may be taken out of the ſeminary, and planted in the nurſery in rows one yard aſunder, and at one foot and a half diſtance in the rows. Here they may remain, with the uſual care of digging between the rows and keeping them clean, till they are of ſufficient ſize to plant out for good.

Where the ſeeds of theſe trees cannot be procured, layering muſt be the method of propagation. For this purpoſe, a ſufficient number muſt be planted out for ſtools, on a ſpot of earth double dug. After they have ſtood one year, they ſhould be cut down, in order to make them throw out young wood for layering. The autumn following, these ſhould be laid in the ground, with a little nick at the joint, and by the ſame time twelve months after, they will be trees of a yard high, with a good root, ready to be planted out in the nurſery, where they may be managed as the ſeedlings, and as the ſtools will have ſhot up freſh young wood for a ſecond operation, this treatment may be continued *ad libitum*.

The [illegible]

PLANE

Manner of propagating the occidental plane-tree

The occidental plane-tree is propagated by cuttings, which, if they are taken from ſtrong young wood, and planted early in the autumn, in a moiſt good mould, will hardly fail of ſucceeding. They are generally planted thick, and then removed into the nurſery-ground, as the layers of the other ſort. But if a large piece of moiſt ground was ready, the cuttings might be placed at ſuch a diſtance as not to approach too cloſe before they were of a ſufficient ſize to plant out for good; and this would ſave the expence and trouble of a removal. The oriental plane-tree will grow from cuttings, but not ſo certainly as this; and whoever has not the convenience of proper ground for the cuttings of either to take, muſt have recourſe to layers with this tree alſo, which, indeed, is always the moſt effectual and ſure method.

PLANE

Situation proper for the various ſorts of plane trees

Plane trees delight in a moiſt ſituation, eſpecially the occidental ſort. Where the land is inclined to be dry, and plane-trees are deſired, the others are to be preferred. But in moiſt places, by the ſides of rivulets, ponds, &c. the occidental makes ſuch ſurpriſing progreſs as induces me to think, that it might be ranked among the Aquatics, without any impropriety.

# CHAP. VI.

## *PINUS LARIX*, The LARCH-TREE.

THE Larch, which is one of thoſe trees that ſhed their leaves in the autumn, preſents its ſtem and branches of a pleaſing whitiſh colour, thereby cauſing, amongſt other trees, an agreeable variety.

A ſwift growing tree,

The larch is a very ſwift-growing tree, inſomuch that I have known it ſhoot near five feet in a year. Its branches are ſlender, and hang downwards. The leaves are of a light green, and, like the cedar of Lebanon, are bunched together, like the pencils or little bruſhes of painters.

and proper for woods of all ſorts

Altho' the larch is originally a native of the Alps and Appennine mountains, yet it is a very proper tree to plant in clumps, or in woods of all ſorts with us; though it is not quite ſo ſuitable to be planted out for ſingle ſtandards, as the thin pendulous branches at the top of the tree are ſometimes very long, and overload the principal ſhoot. Theſe, aſſiſted by violent winds, frequently bring down the head of the tree, and bend it in ſuch a manner as never to recover its former procerity. Whoever, therefore, plants them for ſtandards, either in parks, lawns, fields, &c. ſhould every year obſerve the leading ſhoots of his trees, and mark ſuch lateral branches as have a tendency to grow large. Theſe ſhould be either ſhortened, or wholly taken off, in order to lighten the leading ſhoot, to prevent its curvature.

Uſes of the timber

Many encomiums have been beſtowed on the timber of the larch; and we find ſuch a favourable account of it in antient authors, as ſhould induce us to think it would be proper for almoſt any uſe. Evelyn recites a ſtory of Witſen, a Dutch writer, that a ſhip built of this timber and cypreſs, had been found in the Numidian ſea, twelve fathoms under water, ſound and entire, and reduced to ſuch a hardneſs as to reſiſt the ſharpeſt tool, after it had lain ſubmerged above a thouſand four hundred years. Certain it is, this is an excellent wood for ſhip and houſe building. At Venice this wood is frequently uſed in building their houſes, as well as in Switzerland, where theſe trees abound. So that, without all doubt, the larch excels for maſts for ſhips, or beams for houſes, doors, windows, &c. particularly as it is ſaid to reſiſt the worm.

In Switzerland, their houſes are covered with boards of this wood, cut out a foot ſquare; and as it emits a reſinous ſubſtance, it ſo diffuſes itſelf into every joint and crevice, and becomes ſo compact and cloſe, as well as ſo hardened by the air, as to render the covering proof againſt all weather. But as ſuch covering for houſes would cauſe great devaſtation in caſe of fire, the buildings are confined to a limited diſtance, by an order of police from the magiſtrates. The wood, when firſt laid on the houſes, is ſaid to be very white; but this colour, in two or three years, is changed, by means of the ſun and reſin, to a black, which appears like a ſmooth ſhining varniſh.

The turners abroad are very fond of the wood of this tree for their uſes. It poliſhes exceeding well, and is of a very ponderous nature.

Its generical name of uncertain derivation

The larch-tree is now found to be a ſpecies of *Pinus*; and as the old word *Larix* is of uncertain derivation, I ſhall not pretend to trace its origin.

Time when the flowers blow and leaves open

Its buds begin to open in the end of March; and it ſhews its flowers in the month of April. They are male and female, of a red or white colour, and in the form of cones, which by degrees loſe their colour, and grow into the real cones that produce the ſeeds, and which will be ready for gathering in November.

Method of propagating this tree

In the winter, therefore, let a ſufficient quantity of theſe be procured, and kept till the ſpring of the year. Juſt before ſowing, let the cones be opened or torn into four quarters by a knife, the point of which muſt be thruſt exactly down the center, ſo that the ſeeds in their reſpective places may not be damaged. Formerly, great pains were beſtowed in getting at the ſeeds, by cutting off the ſcales of the cones ſingly, and letting the ſeeds drop. This occaſioned great expence to thoſe who wanted a quantity of ſeeds; ſo that it is wholly laid aſide now, for the more eaſy method of opening them with knives, and then threſhing them. A certain price is generally allowed per thouſand to the poor for opening them. When a ſufficient quantity is opened, they ſhould be threſhed in a room, which will divide the ſcales, and diſlodge the ſeeds, without injuring many of them. Three thouſand cones will generally produce about a pound of good ſeeds. The cones being ſufficiently broken, and the ſeeds threſhed out, they ſhould be winnowed or ſieved, to have clear ſeeds; after which they will be ready for ſowing.

Let the ſeminary conſiſt of a ſpot of fine light earth, and let the ſeeds be ſowed in beds a quarter of an inch deep. In the ſpring, when the plants appear, they ſhould be gently refreſhed

with

LARCH with water in dry weather, and carefully kept clean of weeds during the whole summer. By the autumn they will not have shot more than an inch or two, and in spring they should be pricked out in beds about three inches asunder. The spring following, they must be taken out of these beds with care, and planted in the nursery-ground, three feet asunder in the rows, and two feet distance, and here they may remain until they are fit to plant out for good, which will be about the second or third year after.

If they grow well in the nursery, I would advise to plant them where they are to continue after having attained two years strength in that place, if the ground can possibly be prepared for their reception, since these trees always thrive best when removed small from the nursery; if they are of a sufficient size not to be injured by the weeds; if they are smaller, the owner must keep them clean.

Previous to the planting of these trees for good, the ground should be double dug, if only clumps or small plantations are wanted; but whoever is desirous of having large tracts of them, must content themselves (as the expence of double-digging would be so great) with making holes two or three feet wide, and deep as the soil will permit, and then planting them in these holes, lapping their fibres in the finest mould with the greatest care. The top of the root should be even with the surface of the ground, and only a few of the side-branches should be taken off, about a foot or two feet high, in proportion to the height of the tree planted, near the root. As the branches near the head will be left there, if the tree is of any tolerable height, they will cause it to be shaken down by the violent winds. For its security, therefore, a stake must be driven into the ground, and the tree should be tied fast to it with a hay-band. LARCH

The larch-tree will grow extremely well on almost any soil, as well as in clays of all sorts; it thrives amazingly on the declivities of hills, and sides of high mountains; is sufficiently tough to resist the severest cold, therefore proper for all exposed places. And, as the timber is so valuable, and its growth so quick, it is a tree which may be propagated to the great advantage of the owner. The larch thrives well upon all soils. Is a quick grower.

* * *

# CHAP. VII.

## *FAGUS CASTANEA*, The CHESNUT-TREE.

THIS beautiful tree deserves to be ranked with timber-trees of the first class, whether we consider its ornamental appearance when growing, or its uses when felled. The leaves are large, of a pleasant green colour, and in the autumn turn to a golden yellow; so that in that declining season, amongst the different tinges of the wood, this is very conspicuous, and makes an agreeable contrast. If these trees are planted in large wilderness quarters next the walks, or in woods by the side of the ridings, and are left untrimmed, as they ought to be, they will be feathered to the bottom, and not only make a beautiful appearance, but all the summer will hide those naked and crooked stems of other trees, in the plantations and woods, which might present themselves disagreeable objects to the beholders. This tree was formerly cultivated in this island in greater quantities than at present, and appears to have been the chief timber, in earlier times, used for building. Many antient houses in London, it is plain, were built of this wood; and Fitzstephens, who wrote in the reign of Henry II. mentions a large forest which grew on the North side of the city. His words are, *Proxime patet foresta ingens, saltus nemorosi ferarum, latebræ cervorum, damarum, aprorum, & taurorum sylvestrium*, &c. Situations proper for this tree.

It were greatly to be wished, that the antient spirit of propagating the chesnut could be revived, as the timber is excellent in its kind, being as valuable as the oak, and in many respects superior to it; and, like that king of our woods (for this title the oak must still retain), also yields the industrious planter an annual crop. The nuts of this tree are equally well liked by the deer, and by many other animals are even preferred to the acorn. Nay, I know several people who are fond of the nuts, especially when roasted.

The uses of the timber of this tree, like that of the oak, are almost universal. It is not only excellent for all sorts of building, but is also serviceable for mill timber, and water-works; so that if pipes bored of this wood lie constantly under ground, they will endure longer than the elm. Of the chesnut are made very fine tables, stools, chairs, chests, and bedsteads. It is preferred for the making all sorts of tubs and vessels to hold liquor; and in this respect it is superior to the oak, because, when once thoroughly seasoned, it is not subject either to shrink or swell, but will constantly maintain an equal magnitude of bulk; and for this reason the Italians make their casks and tuns for wine of this wood. For smaller purposes it has its superior advantages. Poles of this tree for hops, vines, &c. will last longer than of any other, and stakes of the underwood will remain nearly twice as long as that of any other sort. Uses to which the timber is applied.

This excellent tree, formerly called *Castanea*, for now it is made a species of *Fagus*, is supposed to have taken its name from Castanea, a city of Thessaly, where it used antiently to abound. Derivation of its generic name.

In the botanic system it is ranked in the class and order *Monoecia Polyandria*, as the same tree will produce both male and female flowers, the male flowers having many stamina. Class and order in the Linnæan system.

The male flowers of the chesnut are collected in long catkins, and begin to open about the ninth of May. The buds usually open about the fourteenth of April, and in six or seven days after the leaves will be quite out, and remain green till the twelfth of October, when they will assume their fine yellow colour. Time of the flowers and leaves coming out.

The culture of the chesnut is as follows. Having provided a sufficient quantity of nuts, throw them into water, to know whether they are found and good. The found ones will sink to the bottom, whilst the others will shew themselves Manner of propagating this tree.

CHESNUT ſelves to be faulty by ſwimming. This method ſhould be always practiſed, that you may be certain of your ſeeds, whether they are Engliſh ſowed, or come from abroad. Indeed, in our cold damp ſoils, cheſnut-trees ſeldom perfect their ſeeds here; but where they do, our Engliſh trees produce very good ſeeds for the purpoſe, though it is generally allowed that thoſe brought from Portugal and Spain are better.

The goodneſs of the nuts being thus proved, and having a ſufficient quantity of ground properly prepared for the ſeminary, in the month of February let drills, about a foot diſtance from each other, be made acroſs this ground, about four inches deep, in which let the nuts be placed, at about four inches diſtance, throughout every drill.

In the ſpring, when the young plants appear, they ſhould be kept clean from weeds, and as often as any weeds preſent themſelves, they muſt be plucked up during their ſtay in the ſeminary, which ought to be two years from the time of ſowing.

A ſeminary of theſe trees, planted in this manner, ſhould always be hand weeded, becauſe, being pretty near each other, it would be dangerous to introduce a hoe among them, for fear of hurting the tender rhind, which would greatly injure the plants ſo wounded.

The plants, having ſtood in the ſeminary two years, muſt be carefully taken up, all the ſide ſhoots taken off, and the tap root ſhortened; then, having ground in the nurſery double dug, let them be planted in this ground in rows, which ſhould be two feet and a half or three feet aſunder, and let them at leaſt one foot and a half diſtant in theſe rows. The beſt time for doing this work will be the latter end of February, for if they are planted in October, the ſevere froſts will be ſubject to throw the young plants out of the ground before winter is over. A year after they have been planted in the nurſery, it will be very proper to cut every one of them down to within an inch of the ground, which will cauſe them to ſhoot vigorouſly with one ſtrong and ſtraight ſtem. Without this treatment, they are very ſubject to grow ſcraggy and crooked, and to make but ſlow progreſs, ſo that where they do not take well to the ground, and ſhoot promiſcuouſly, they ſhould be cut down according to this direction; after which they will ſhoot ſtrongly, and overtake thoſe that never underwent this operation, though planted ſome years before them, in a very ſhort time.

In this nurſery they may remain four or five years, when they will be fit to plant out, with no other pruning than taking off very ſtrong ſide-branches, and ſuch as have a tendency to make the tree forked. The only trouble the ground will occaſion, will be keeping it clear of weeds, and every winter digging between the rows.

After they are of a ſufficient ſize to be planted out for ſtandards, either in fields, clumps, wilderneſs quarters, or avenues, they ſhould be carefully taken out of the nurſery, and having holes dug three feet ſquare, and a foot and a half deep, with the turf chopt ſmall at the bottom of each hole, and all the bruiſed parts of the roots taken off, the fineſt mould ſhould cover the fibres, obſerving always to plant them no deeper than the ſurface of the ſoil. After this, they may be turfed round to keep them ſteady againſt the winds. The beſt ſeaſon for this work is October.

Directions for raiſing a wood of cheſnut trees. Where a wood of theſe trees is wanted, they ſhould be raiſed in the nurſery way, according to the former directions; and when the plants are about five feet high, they will be of the propereſt ſize for the purpoſe; for they will then not be ſo large as to require ſtaking, nor yet ſo ſmall but that they will be out of the reach of hares, rabbits, &c. Therefore, as ſoon as the trees are about this height in the nurſery, let the ground deſigned for the wood be ploughed deep with a very ſtrong plow, that the uppermoſt and beſt part of the ſoil may be laid as low as poſſible, to be of greater nouriſhment to the tree, when it receives its tender fibres. The diſtance theſe trees ſhould be planted from one another ought to be two yards, and this will be a proper diſtance for them to grow up to poles; when they ſhould be cut down, only leaving a ſufficient number of the beſt and moſt thriving trees for timber. Thus, whilſt the latter are making their progreſs to a larger bulk, being left at a diſtance of near twenty feet, the poles will, at the interval of fourteen years from the firſt planting, reward the owner's toils with no inconſiderable profits; and if they are cut down within about a foot of the ground, there will be ſtools for another crop of poles, which will be ready for a ſecond cutting in about ten years. So that every ten years the planter will taſte the ſweets of his labour, while his expectations are ſtill augmented, as to the advantage of his family in after-times. If the plantation is large, I would adviſe to begin the firſt fall of poles ſo early, and to defer the laſt ſo late, that the year after the laſt fall the ſtools of the firſt-cut poles ſhall have ſent forth poles ready for a ſecond cutting. Thus the proprietor will not only enjoy the benefits of an annual ſale, but the country will not be glutted with too great a quantity of poles at a time, and conſequently they may be ſold at a better price.

Such are the directions I would give for raiſing a wood of theſe trees, which I take to be better than planting the nuts, and letting them remain; not only becauſe the plant is then ſubject to a tap root, which ſtrikes directly into the ground beyond the reach of nouriſhment, and conſequently muſt in proportion grow ſlower, but alſo becauſe the expences will be leſs. While they are in the nurſery, a vaſt quantity of them will ſtand upon a ſmall ſpace of ground, and conſequently be raiſed at a ſmall expence; but when the nuts are planted with a deſign to remain, the whole extent of the ground intended for the wood muſt be kept clear of weeds till the plants are of a ſufficient ſize to defend themſelves againſt them, and while young they will be ſubject to be deſtroyed by hares, rabbits, &c. But if any perſon is deſirous of raiſing a wood immediately from the nuts, the ground ſhould be prepared in the manner directed for the oak, and the nuts planted about three inches deep in rows near a yard aſunder, and at half a yard diſtance in the rows. After they come up, they muſt be kept clear of weeds, by ploughing, hoeing, or ſome other way, for four or five years, till they are out of their reach. When they get too cloſe, every ſecond ſhould be taken away; and this thinning ought to be continued till they are at proper diſtances for ſtools, when the poles ſhould be cut down, and the moſt thriving trees left for timber.

Grows well on almoſt all ſoils and ſituations. The cheſnut will thrive on almoſt all ſoils and ſituations. It will grow beſt, indeed, in a rich loamy land; but it will ſucceed very well on that which is gravelly, clayey, or ſandy. All mixed ſoils are ſuitable to it, as well as expoſed and bleak places, and the declivities of hills.

Time moſt proper for felling the timber. The time for felling the cheſnut-tree is in November and December, when the ſap is inactive. The timber then felled will be proportionably more durable than if cut down in the ſpring.

CHAP.

## CHAP. VIII.

## *ÆSCULUS, HIPPO-CASTANUM,*

## The HORSE-CHESNUT-TREE

*Its appearance described*

THIS is a tree of singular beauty and use. The leaves are large, fine, and palmated, and seen very early in the spring. It is naturally uniform in its growth, forming its head, if left to Nature, into a regular parabola. In the spring it produces long spikes of natural flowers, and altho' in the autumn its leaves fall off pretty early, it makes amends by exhibiting its nuts of a beautiful brown colour, some on the ground, some falling, and others just peeping out of their cells.

*At what time and from whence it was brought into Europe*

The horse-chesnut is a native of the East, and said to have been brought into Europe in 1610, at which time also the laurel was introduced into the English gardens. But we have reason to believe that this tree was brought from Constantinople, and made a denizen of England, almost an hundred years before the abovementioned period. But be this as it may, certain it is, we are now blessed with it in great plenty, and it may be easily raised in quantities by the nuts, for any use wanted.

*Situations most proper for this tree*

These trees are very proper to be planted for avenues or walks, though I know it has been objected by some, that its leaves fall early in the autumn. But if they duly considered that it shoots out earlier in proportion in the spring, and remembered the beautiful flowers and nuts it produced, this objection, I think, would vanish.

The horse-chesnut-tree is extremely well adapted to parks, not only because it grows to a large size, and forms a beautiful regular head, thereby at a distance striking the imagination with a pleasing surprize, but on account of the quantity of nuts it produces, which are excellent food for the deer in the rutting season. So that in parks where great numbers of deer are kept, I would recommend these trees to be planted in abundance. They are likewise very proper for the boundaries of open fields, to terminate views, &c. and though there are no deer to eat the nuts, yet the swine are equally delighted with them, and will fatten greatly with such provender.

*Uses for which the timber is serviceable*

The wood is useful for most sorts of turners ware, and as the trees grow to a great magnitude, they sell for those purposes at so great a price as to make them well worth the planting, for the sake of the timber.

*Derivation of the generical names*

*Æsculus*, the new name for the horse-chesnut, is derived from *esca, food*, the nuts of this tree being eatable, or food for many creatures. The old word, *Hippo-Castanum*, by which it is most known, is a compound word, formed from the Greek word ἵππος, *a horse*, and the Latin word *castanea, a chesnut*. The word ἵππος was added to *castanea*, because the nuts prove very beneficial to disordered horses. It is one of the chief remedies in Turkey for horses troubled with violent colds, coughs, hard-wind, &c. for the cure of which they give them the nuts of these trees ground to flour, in their provender.

The buds of this tree, before they shoot out leaves, become turgid and large, so that they have a good effect to the eye, by their bold appearance, long before the leaves appear. And what is peculiar to the horse-chesnut is, that as soon as the leading shoot is come out of the bud, it continues to grow so fast, as to be able to form its whole summer's shoot in about three weeks or a month's time. After this it grows little or nothing more in length, but thickens, and becomes strong and woody, and forms the buds for the next year's shoot.

*Time when the flowers blow and leaves open. Class and order in the Linnæan system*

The flowers are in full blow about the twelfth of May, and on fine old trees make a pleasing appearance. They have seven stamina and one style, which shews the tree to be of the class and order *Heptandria Monogynia*. Sir Charles Linnæus altered the old title to that of *Esculus*, and to this genus he has joined the *Pavia* of Boerhaave.

*Manner of propagating the tree*

The horse-chesnut is propagated from the nuts. In autumn, therefore, when they fall, a sufficient quantity should be gathered. These should be sown soon afterwards in drills, about two inches asunder. If the nuts are kept till spring, many of them will be faulty, but where the seminary-ground cannot be got ready before, and they are kept so long, it may be proper to put them in water, to try their goodness. The good nuts will sink, whilst those which are faulty will swim, so that by proving them this way you may be sure of good nuts, and have more promising hopes of a crop.

In the spring the plants will come up, and when they have stood one year they may be taken up, their tap-roots shortened, and afterwards planted in the nursery, and managed in the same manner as was directed for the Spanish Chesnut.

When they are of sufficient size to be planted out for good, they must be taken out of the nursery with care, the great side-shoots and the bruised parts of the roots should be taken off, and then planted in large holes level with the surface of the ground, at the top of their roots, the fibres being all spread and lapped in the fine mould, and the turf also worked to the bottom. A stake should be placed to keep them safe from the winds, and they must be fenced from the cattle till they are of a sufficient size to defend themselves. The best season for all this work is October.

After the trees are planted, neither knife nor hatchet should come near them, but they should be left to Nature to form their beautiful parabolic heads, and assume their utmost beauty.

*Soils in which it thrives best*

The horse-chesnut, like most other trees, delights most in good fat land, but it will grow exceeding well on clayey and marley grounds. I have seen large trees, luxuriant and healthy, in very cold, barren, and hungry earth. In short, it is not very nice in its diet, but may be planted in most places to the owner's satisfaction.

*Best time for felling its timber*

When this tree is fit to be felled, let it be done in November or December, those being the best months for this purpose, when the sap is at rest.

CHAP.

# C H A P. IX.

## *JUGLANS*, The WALNUT-TREE.

A vulgar error refuted

THE Walnut is another tree that pays the industrious planter in a double way, by its annual produce when standing, and by its valuable timber when felled. It has been generally supposed, that the walnut will grow many years before it bears nuts, insomuch that I have heard it spoken as a proverb "That whoever plants the nuts must never expect to live to reap the fruit the tree will produce." But this discouraging saying is so far from having any just foundation, that the walnut produces fruit, if the soil is proper for it, almost as soon as any tree I have known to bear plentifully, five years from the nut. I saw an instance of this kind at Thorpe-Langton, in the garden of Charles Roberts, Esq. where I observed a young walnut, in the spring, coming out of the ground from a casual nut, and by the autumn it had shot more than a foot. In the following spring, it shot with two strong stems, upon which I desired the weakest of these stems to be taken off, which was accordingly done. The third year, it made another good shoot, and thickened in proportion in the stem, so that it became a fine straight tree, of near seven feet. The fourth year it formed a head consisting of several branches, some of which were near half a yard long. And in the fifth year it produced a very full crop of walnuts. But as no the walnut-tree-planter should not expect his trees to bear in so short a time as this, it being a very rare circumstance, and what may seldom happen, yet I would by no means have him discouraged by the vulgar observation, that, "Whoever plants walnuts must not expect to see them bear fruit." The expectation of the fruit is a great motive to the planting of these trees, and indeed it is the principal reason with many, who plant them only for the sake of the annual crop they will afford. But where the view is extended equally to the annual crop, the ornamenting the environs, and the timber in the end, there is a greater foundation of expectation, hope, and pleasure.

Places in which it is proper to be planted

The walnut is a very proper tree to be planted for avenues leading to gentlemen's houses, for clumps in parks, or for odd trees, for, when planted singly, walnuts will throw out large and spreading arms, and thereby form a noble outside head, and they will have a fine effect, if they are in this manner properly disposed. This tree is suitable also for being planted by the borders of fields, hedge-rows, and even by the sides of the banks near ploughed land, for it has this peculiar property, that it will not send its roots so near the surface as to incommode the plowman. It is even said that walnuts are so far from destroying the crop which grows under them, that they rather cherish and keep it warm.

Purposes to which the timber is applied

The timber of the walnut is extremely good, but improper to make beams to support great weights, being subject to break, and of a very brittle nature. It is well adapted, however, for wainscot, being finely grained, as well as for tables, chests, boxes, bedsteads, stools, &c. Coach wheels, and the bodies of coaches, are made of this wood. Gunsmiths and drum-makers use it: the first for gunstocks, the other for the rims of drums. The cabinet-maker also is fond of it for inlayings, &c. as the wood is beautifully streaked. For these purposes it exceeds all our other English timber, and is the most durable, having this property, that the worm will never take it.

There are several sorts of walnut, of foreign growth, which are excellent timber; but that species called the Black Virginian Walnut is by far the best and most beautiful wood. I shall enumerate the several kinds of these trees when I come to treat of trees of foreign growth, though I cannot help throwing out this hint to the timber-planter, That if he can procure the nuts of the Black Virginian sort from abroad, and manages them according to the directions for the English walnut, this will afford him a valuable timber as any we have, the oak itself not excepted.

Class and order in the Linnæan system

Time of the flowers and leaves opening

If the botanist examines the flowers, he will find the walnut belong to the class and order *Monoecia Polyandria*. The flowers generally begin to open about the middle of April, and will be full blown by the middle of the month following, before which time the leaves will be all quite out.

Proceed we now to its raising and culture. If the fruit of these trees are greatly coveted, the utmost care should be taken to gather the nuts from those trees which produce the best sorts, and altho' the varieties of walnuts are only seminal variations, yet there is the greater chance of having a succession of good nuts, if they are gathered from trees that produce good fruit. The maxim holds good in animals. The finest breed would degenerate if attention was not paid to the sorts for brood, and the like care should be extended throughout the whole system of planting, whether for fruit or timber. If for timber, we should be solicitous to gather the seeds from the healthiest, the most luxuriant and thriving young trees. If for fruit, from those which produce the largest and best kinds.

Having marked the trees that produce the finest nuts, either for thinness of shell or goodness of taste, when they have begun to fall they will be ripe enough for gathering. But as collecting them by the hand would be tedious, they may be beat down by long poles prepared for that purpose.

Having procured the quantity wanted, let them be preserved, with their husks on, in sand, till the beginning of February, which is the time for planting them. This is to be done in the following manner:

Method of propagating this tree.

Let drills be made across the seminary, at one foot asunder, and about two inches and a half deep, and let the nuts be put in these at the distance of about one foot. In the spring the young plants will come up, and here they should continue for two years, being constantly kept clean of weeds, when they will be of a proper size to plant out in the nursery. The ground should be prepared, as has been always directed, by double digging; and the trees being taken out of the seminary, and having their tap-roots shortened, should be planted therein, in rows two feet and a half asunder, and the plants at a foot and a half distance. Here they may remain with the same culture as has been all along directed for the management of timber trees,

WALNUT trees, till they are of a proper ſize for planting out for good.

If they are deſigned for ſtandards to be planted in fields, &c. before they are taken out of the nurſery they ſhould be above the reach of cattle, which may otherwiſe wantonly break their leading ſhoots, though they do not care to eat them, on account of their extraordinary bitterneſs. They ought likewiſe to be removed with the greateſt caution, and the knife ſhould be very ſparingly applied to the roots. They muſt alſo be planted as ſoon as poſſible after taking up; and this work ſhould be always done ſoon after the fall of the leaf, in the manner directed for planting out the preceding ſtandard timber-trees.

If theſe trees are intended to form a wood, for which purpoſe they anſwer extremely well, I would adviſe to take them out of the nurſery when they are about three or four feet high, and to plant them about three yards aſunder; and, after their heads begin to touch, they ſhould be thinned, as has been before directed. By this means, theſe large and branching trees will be drawn up, with a beautiful ſtem, to a great height. At the laſt thinning of the trees, the ſtandards ſhould be left at about thirty feet diſtance. But if the owner expects to reap the benefit of the fruit, the diſtance he ought to leave them ſhould be ſeven or eight feet more. Thus will the planter have a wood of walnuts every year rewarding him with its produce (which is always ready money, being ſold to the people who ſupply the markets), till they are full grown to timber, and muſt be felled. WALNUT

Soils ſuitable to this tree

The ſoil this tree delights in is a rich loamy earth. It thrives exceedingly in chalky and marly ground, and will grow very well on the ſides of ſtony and chalky hills, and alſo in vales by the ſides of pits, highways, &c. In all theſe ſoils and ſituations it will grow to an exceeding great bulk, and every year produce plenty of fruit, which is another motive, as I ſaid before, for propagating it.

# CHAP. X.

## *TILIA*, The LIME or LINDEN-TREE.

THERE are three or four ſorts of this tree, though thoſe we chiefly propagate for timber are known by the titles of the Common Lime and the Red twigged Lime. Theſe are varieties only of the ſame ſpecies; becauſe the ſeeds of one ſort will frequently produce the other. Thus, ſeeds gathered from the red-twigged trees frequently produce plants of the common ſort; and thoſe that have come up the true red-twigged kind, and have been raiſed and planted out as ſuch, have been found to run away from their colours, and change into the common green twigged ſort.

Its appearance deſcribed

The lime is a handſome pictureſque tree, forming a beautiful cone by its branches, and maintaining its body taper and ſtraight; and, as it will grow to a monſtrous ſize, it is very

Situations proper for it

proper to be planted for avenues, to terminate the bounds of lawns, and to make a variety in places deſigned for relaxation of mind. And altho' the leaves fall off very early in the autumn, yet it immediately makes amends for this by exhibiting its beautiful red twigs; for which reaſon the red twigged lime ſhould always be preferred for theſe purpoſes; ſince, notwithſtanding it will ſometimes run away from the colour, this is not often the caſe. It has alſo other properties to recommend itſelf to ſuch ſituations. The ſhade is excellent; the branches are ſo tough as ſeldom to be broke by the winds; and if any of them ſhould want occaſionally to be taken off, no tree has its wound ſooner healed over.

A quick growing tree

The lime is a remarkable quick-growing tree; and as it will come to timber ſoon, it certainly deſerves to be planted on that account, as the wood ſerves for many purpoſes, and begins now to be very dear.

Inſtances of its ſurprizing growth

This tree will likewiſe grow to a monſtrous ſtature and bulk, inſomuch that I have read of ſome that have meaſured eight or ten yards round; and I know ſeveral which are ſo large, healthy, and thriving, that they ſeem to bid fair for the ſame bulk.

The timber of the lime tree, altho' it be of a ſoft nature, has nevertheleſs a variety of uſes. It is an excellent wood for carved works; and therefore is in high eſteem with carvers, who frequently make ſtatues and curious figures of it. Architects alſo form models of buildings of this wood, which being of a very light and tough nature, and not ſubject to ſplit, is extremely proper for yoaks, and uſes of that kind. It likewiſe makes very good bowls, diſhes, ſpoons, &c. for which purpoſes the turners buy it.

Claſs and order in the Linnæan ſyſtem

The lime tree is of the claſs and order *Polyandria Monogynia*, there being in every flower numerous ſtamina and one ſtyle only.

Time when the flowers blow and leaves open

The flowers of this tree begin to open about the fifteenth of May, and will be in full blow by the thirteenth of July, when they appear of a white colour, and have a very fragrant ſmell. The leaves begin to open about the twelfth of April, will be quite out by the eighteenth of the ſame month, and fall away very early in the autumn.

Method of propagating the lime tree

I come now to its culture. There is only one good way of raiſing it, which is from the ſeeds. For thoſe trees raiſed from layers or from cuttings never grow ſo handſome or ſo faſt, nor are any ways equal to thoſe raiſed in the ſeminary by the ſeed.

To proceed, then, to this buſineſs. Let the ſeeds be gathered from thriving healthy trees of the true red twigged kind; and then by far the greateſt part of the young plants will be of that ſort. The ſeeds will be ripe in October; and let a dry day be made choice of for gathering them. As the ſeeds grow at the extremity of the branches, and as it would be tedious to gather them with the hand, they may be beaten down by a long pole, having a large winnowing ſheet, or ſome ſuch thing, ſpread under the tree to receive them.

When you have got a ſufficient quantity, ſpread them in a dry place, for a few days, and then ſow them. The manner of ſowing them

LIME

muſt be the ſame as has been directed in ſeveral of the preceding articles, i. e. Having a fine ſpot of rich garden-ground, and having the mould made fine by digging and raking, let it be raked out of the beds about an inch deep. Theſe beds may be four feet wide, and the alleys a foot and a half. After the mould is raked out, the earth ſhould be gently tapped down with the back of the ſpade, to make it level, then the ſeeds ſhould be ſown, at about an inch aſunder, all over the bed, and likewiſe gently preſſed down, as well as covered about an inch deep. After the bed and the alley are neated up, the ingenious gardener muſt proceed to the next, and ſo on till the whole is finiſhed.

In the ſpring of the year the young plants will make their appearance, when they ſhould be conſtantly kept clean from weeds, and gently watered in very dry weather. In this ſeminary they may ſtand for two years, when they will be fit to plant in the nurſery, at which time they ſhould be carefully taken up out of the ſeminary, their roots ſhortened, and the young ſide-branches, if they have ſhot out any, taken off. They muſt be planted in the nurſery-ground in rows, two feet and a half aſunder, and one foot and a half diſtant in the rows. Here they may ſtand till they are of proper ſize to be planted out for good, obſerving always to dig between the rows every winter, and conſtantly to keep the ground free from weeds.

*Soil ſuitable to this tree*

The lime-tree will grow well on almoſt any ſoil or ſituation, but if planted in a rich and loamy earth, wherein it (like moſt other trees) chiefly delights, the growth of it will be almoſt incredible. This ſhould be a great motive to the planting of this tree, which will in a very few years ſufficiently reward the induſtrious planter.

*Derivation of its generical name*

The generical name, *Tilia*, ſeems to be derived from [illegible], *folium Eſt eb uno ramoſa & folioſa*. Miller ſays, very abſurdly I think, the lime is called *Tilia* of *telum*, *a dart*, becauſe its wood is uſed in making darts.

# CHAP. XI.

## *ACER PSEUDO-PLATANUS,*

## The GREATER MAPLE or SYCAMORE-TREE.

THE Sycamore is a large growing tree, and adapted to encreaſe the variety in our woods and hills. It is very proper, if kept down, for underwood, becauſe it ſhoots very faſt from the ſtools, and makes excellent fuel.

*Situations proper for this tree*

There is no tree more proper than the ſycamore to form large plantations near the ſea, for the ſpray, which is prejudicial to moſt trees, ſeems to have no bad effect upon this, and it thrives in ſuch places better than any tree I know.

*It endures many years*

The ſycamore is not only a large timber-tree, but will ſtand long on the ſoil before its decay. This may be ſeen from what St. Hierom ſays, who lived in the fourth century after our Bleſſed Lord, and is undoubtedly to be believed, namely, That he ſaw the ſycamore-tree which Zaccheus climbed up, to ſee our Saviour ride in triumph to Jeruſalem. This was a long time for a tree of ſuch quick growth and ſo ſoft a wood to remain, and it probably was far from being decayed at the time St. Hierom ſaw it, not to mention, that it might have ſtood many years, and was probably grown to a large tree, at the time our Bleſſed Saviour entered into the city of Jeruſalem.

*The juice makes a good wine*

The ſycamore being wounded exudes a great quantity of liquor, of which is made good wine.

*Uſes to which the timber is applicable*

The timber of this tree, being light and tough, is very proper for waggons, carts, plows, harrows, &c. though for theſe purpoſes it is not quite ſo good as the aſh. It is excellent, however, for diſhes, bowls, ſpoons, trenchers, ladles, &c. for which uſes the timber ſells well to the turner.

*Time when the flowers and leaves open*

The ſycamore is in leaf about the thirteenth of April, and about the twenty-fifth the flowers will be in full blow. They are ſmall, and their colour ſeems to be between white and a green. Upon examination, there may be found both male and hermaphrodite flowers, which ſhews this tree to belong to the claſs and order *Polygamia Monoecia*.

*Method of propagating the ſycamore*

The propagation of the ſycamore is very eaſy. In the autumn, when the keys are ripe, they may be gathered, and in a few days after ſown, as has been directed for the aſh, &c. In the ſpring the plants will appear, and make a ſhoot of about a foot and a half by the autumn following, if the ground of the ſeminary be tolerably good, and they are kept clean from weeds. The ſpring after they come up, they ſhould be planted in the nurſery, in rows two feet and a half aſunder, and their diſtance in the rows muſt be one foot and a half. Here they may remain till they are big enough to plant out for good, with no farther trouble than taking off unſightly ſide branches, and ſuch as have a tendency to make the tree forked, except digging between the rows, which muſt always be done every winter.

*Soil proper for it*

This tree will grow upon almoſt any ſoil, and from its quickneſs of growth, as well as hardineſs juſtly deſerves propagation.

## CHAP. XII.

### *ACER CAMPESTRE*, The COMMON MAPLE-TREE.

THE Common Maple does not grow to ſuch a large ſize as the ſycamore, though its timber is of greater value

Extraordinary value ſet upon this wood by the antients

We meet with high encomiums on this wood among the antients Pliny gives us many, and Virgil introduces a prince himſelf ſitting on a maple throne The firſt mentioned author highly commends the maple growing in the different parts of the world, and extols many of them which were remarkable for their fine grain Indeed, the fineneſs of the grain ever governs the value of the wood In former times, ſo mad were people in ſearching for wood curiouſly wrought, which is ſometimes to be found repreſenting figures, nay, birds, beaſts, &c that they ſpared no expence in procuring it to be made up into ſuch little ornaments as beſt pleaſed their own taſte But when boards big enough for tables were found of this curious-veined wood, the extravagance in purchaſers was incredible We read of a table which coſt ten thouſand ſeſterces, and of another that fetched fifteen thouſand; nay, of one being ſold for its weight in gold And altho theſe were adapted to the purſes of princes, and thoſe of a lordly rank, yet all mankind have been extravagantly eager in purchaſing tables which have been curiouſly veined and ſpotted

The maple ſeldom planted in quantities to form woods

The maple is ſeldom planted in ſuch quantities together as to form woods, but where they appear in plantations, they are generally cut down for underwood, for which purpoſe they anſwer extremely well, as they ſhoot away from their ſtools very faſt, and make excellent fuel

but generally in hedgerows

Uſes of its timber

The largeſt trees are generally found in hedge-rows, where they are occaſionally to be met with all over the kingdom Their timber with us is deemed excellent, and is uſed for ſeveral curious purpoſes, ſuch as muſical inſtruments, inlayings, &c For the making of turnery ware alſo, ſuch as diſhes, bowls, trays, &c it is ſuperior to moſt other wood

Time when the flowers and leaves open

The flower-buds of the maple begin to open about the ſixth of April, and the leaves will be out about the eighteenth The flowers will be full blown about the eleventh of May, and the ſeeds will be ripe in the autumn

Method of propagating this tree

If a quantity of theſe trees are wanted, they may be raiſed in the ſame manner as the ſycamore, and managed accordingly

Soil proper for it

They will grow on almoſt any ſoil or ſituation, and the beſt month for felling it is January

## CHAP. XIII

### *ACER PLATANOIDES*, The NORWAY MAPLE-TREE

Its appearance deſcribed.

THE Norway Maple will grow to a great timber tree, and therefore ſhould be raiſed to encreaſe the variety in our plantations The leaves are of a ſhining green colour, look beautiful all ſummer, and die to a golden yellow in the autumn This tree perfects its ſeeds with us, ſo that it may be raiſed in the ſame manner as the ſycamore, from the keys It may be alſo propagated by layers and by cuttings, which, if planted in a moiſt ſoil in the autumn, will grow Theſe ſhould be ordered in the nurſery way, as was before directed, and managed till they are of a ſufficient ſize to be planted out for good

Reaſons why this tree ſhould be planted

Theſe trees being ſcarce, have been hitherto ſeldom planted, unleſs in wilderneſs-quarters for ornaments, &c But as it is a very quick grower, arrives at a great bulk, and the timber will anſwer all the purpoſes of the ſycamore, the raiſing it, even for this uſe, as well as ornament and variety, ſhould not be neglected

Situation proper for it

The Norway maple is reckoned among our beſt trees for ſheltering habitations

## C H A P XIV

## *ACER NEGUNDO*, The ASH-LEAVED MAPLE-TREE.

Its properties,

THE Aſh-leaved Maple-tree is a quick grower, arrives to a large timber tree, and is admirably adapted to cauſe a beautiful variety in our woods, though it is not proper to be planted in expoſed places the branches being ſubject to ſplit when attacked by violent winds

and appearance deſcribed

The leaves are of a pale green colour, moderately large, and fall off pretty early in the autumn

Uſes of its timber

The timber is extremely uſeful for turners uſes, and, like the Norway maple, ſerves for all the purpoſes of the ſycamore

Method of propagating this tree

It is propagated by ſaving the keys, which this tree, though a native of Virginia, perfects in our country

It is alſo propagated by layers, or by planting the cuttings, in a moiſt ſituation, in the autumn

## C H A P XV

## *PRUNUS CERASUS*, The CHERRY-TREE.

THOUGH all the various ſpecies of Cherry-trees afford very good timber, yet none are equal to the black-cherry or wilding, which is far ſuperior to all the other kinds, and therefore is the only ſort I ſhall introduce for a foreſt-tree

Derivation of the generical name

The word *Cerafus* is Greek, and ſuppoſed to be derived from X..., *Chereſium*, a town near the Black Sea, where this tree grew wild, and from whence it was ſent into the different parts of Europe Italy was the firſt nation of Europe bleſſed with cherry trees

When firſt introduced into Europe

Lucullus brought them there from Pontus, after he had overcome Mithridates, king of that place, in the year of Rome 683 About a hundred years afterwards, ſome of theſe trees were introduced into Europe

The fruit of the cherry-tree ſhall be conſidered in another place At preſent, I ſhall confine my obſervations to the wilding, the black, and little red, which are the beſt trees for ornament and timber, and are alſo very proper for ave-

Situations proper for this tree

nues leading to houſes where they are deſired, for parks, for clumps, or for woods

Where theſe trees are properly diſpoſed in lawns, parks, or fields, they ſtrike the imagination in the ſpring by their flowers, which will appear all over the whole trees of a milky white In the autumn they afford a crop, and if the owner is inclined to ſell it, he may without trouble meet with purchaſers enough, who buy the fruit for the markets The fruit of the black-cherry-tree is ſuppoſed by many to be ſuperior in taſte and flavour to moſt of the other ſorts of cherries The flowers afford great relief to the induſtrious bee, and whoever is delighted with the muſic of the feathered choir, can deviſe no method ſo proper to invite them, as to tempt them with the fruit of this tree, on which the blackbird regales, and the thruſh feaſts

Neither are theſe ſweet-ſinging birds the only part of the feathered creation who are fond of this fruit, for ſwarms of jackdaws, magpyes, jays, &c will carefully watch the ſeaſon, and contend for their ſhare

The timber of the cherry tree is of a reddiſh colour, which makes it more valuable than many other ſorts, on that account, to the turner, who applies it to various uſes Tables of this wood look well, inſomuch that I have known ſome which have been taken for a coarſe mahogany And, as the timber is ſo beautiful, and the purpoſes it may be applied to are ſo various, these motives ſhould be ſufficient to induce us to raiſe this tree, were there no other

Uſes of the timber.

Time when the flowers and leaves blow

The buds of the cherry-tree begin to open about the twenty-ninth of March, and the flowers will be in full blow about the eighteenth of April Upon examination, you will find more than twenty ſtamina and only one ſtyle, which ſhews it to belong to the claſs and order *Icoſandria Monogynia*, to which claſs moſt fruit-trees of the higheſt eſteem belong The plum tree and the cherry-tree are both of the ſame family, and the wood of the former is valuable on many accounts Such as are deſirous of raiſing plum-trees for the ſake of their timber, may do it in the ſame manner as the black-cherry-tree, which is performed as follows

Claſs and order in the Linnæan ſyſtem

Method of propagating this tree

When the fruit is quite ripe, having a ſufficient quantity for the purpoſe, let the ſtones be placed in beds of light ſandy earth, in the manner before directed, about one inch deep The ſpring following the young plants will appear, and all the ſummer ſhould be kept clear of weeds, and in dry weather refreſhed with water In this bed they may ſtand two years, if the firſt ſummer's ſhoot has not been favourable, though, if they have ſhot pretty ſtrong, it would be beſt to take them out of the ſeed bed the autumn following After they are taken up, the tap rooted plants ſhould have them ſhortened, but none muſt have their leading bud taken off They ought afterwards to be planted in the nurſery, in rows two feet and a half aſunder, and one foot and a half diſtant in the rows, where they may remain till they are of ſize to plant out for ſtandards, with no other trouble than keeping them clear of weeds, and digging between the rows in winter

Soils ſuitable to it.

This tree delights in a light ſoil, but as it will grow on poor ground better than moſt others, it is propagated by many for that reaſon

CHAP

## CHAP. XVI

## *CRATÆGUS*, The MAPLE-LEAVED SERVICE-TREE.

Its appearance described

THE Maple-leaved Service-tree, which is inclined to be a large-growing tree, where it likes the situation, is naturally of an upright growth, though it sends forth large arms in hedge-rows, and in open places It will grow to about fifty feet high

This tree springs up naturally in our woods and hedges, and is found in many parts of Germany, Switzerland, and Burgundy

Fruit relished by some persons

It bears excellent fruit, which being gathered in the woods, tied in bunches, and exposed for sale, not only proves grateful to many persons, but likewise affords a maintenance, in the autumn, to those poor people who make it their business to gather it

Uses for which the timber is serviceable

The timber is very valuable, being hard, and useful for millwrights, who greatly covet it. The turners also seek after it, on account of its whiteness, and beautiful appearance in whatever purposes they apply it This wood serves likewise for larger uses, in buildings of most sorts, being often sawed into planks and boards, and the carpenters use it occasionally for most parts of their business

Manner of propagating this tree

These trees are propagated by grafting or budding, either upon plum stocks, quinces, medlars, or thorns But in order to raise them for timber, they should be propagated from the berries, which should be sown in the autumn, soon after they are ripe, in a border of fine mould, covering them down a full inch deep They will remain in the ground till the second spring after sowing, before the plants come up When they make their appearance, they should be watered, if the weather proves dry, and be constantly kept clean from weeds

When they have stood in the seed-bed one year, the strongest plants may be drawn out, and planted in the nursery-ground, one foot asunder, and two feet distant in the rows, whilst the weakest may remain in the seed-bed another year to gain strength, before they are set out in the like manner,

When they have been in the nursery two years, they should be planted out for good Nevertheless, they may remain longer, if they are wanted for standards

If they are designed at first for standards, they should be allowed a greater distance in the nursery-ground The ground between the rows must be dug every winter, and the weeds constantly hoed down as they arise in the summer, which is all the trouble these plants will require

Situations proper for this tree

This is a very useful tree, not only for woods, but to be planted singly in parks and open places, where it will form a large spreading head, afford great beauty from the flowers (which will be out in May), and regale the palates of those who like them, by the fruit (which will be ripe in autumn)

Time of the flowers blowing and fruit ripening

Class and order in the Linnæan system

In every flower there are about twenty stamina and two styles, which entitle this tree to the class and order *Icosandria Digynia*

## CHAP. XVII

## *MORUS*, The MULBERRY-TREE.

Derivation of its generical name

ALTHO' the word *Morus* is derived from the Greek word μαυρος, which signifies *black*, because the fruit is generally of that colour, yet it is that sort called the White Mulberry-tree which I propose to treat of in this place, as being, of all others, the most deserving the name and title of a forest tree

Places in which it is proper to be planted

This tree will grow to a large size, and is very proper for walks and avenues, or for clumps or standards, either in fields or parks, since, by encreasing the variety, it consequently enhances the beauty of such places

Its appearance described

The leaves are of a clear light green, and the fruit is of a paler colour than any of the other sorts, which makes it take the name of the White Mulberry This tree possesses the peculiar property of breeding no vermin, either growing or cut down, neither does it harbour any sort of caterpillar, the silk-worm only excepted, whose food is its leaves

The mulberry-tree was very earnestly recommended by king James to be planted in great quantities, to feed these worms, in order to have silk of our own for working And indeed, if we consider what vast revenues the silk manufactory brings in to other states, we shall find an undertaking of this nature worthy of a princely care and assistance All recommendations, however, have hitherto proved fruitless, and no more trees have been planted than what have been sufficient to keep a few worms for a gentleman's pleasure and amusement A plain proof of our indolence and inattention, since it is observable, that where these trees will grow and flourish, there the silk-worms will prosper also

Soils in which it thrives best

The mulberry-tree delights chiefly in a light dry soil, though I have several growing luxuriant and strong at Gumley, on a white clay In short, I think it would thrive in most soils, provided they are not too wet So that there is very little land in this kingdom which might not be planted with these trees, to a national advantage, even by the maintaining of silk-worms, and introducing the manufacture of raw silk

This ought to be a sufficient motive for the planting of this tree, were there no other, and

I make no doubt, if we were to plant them for the beforementioned purpoſe ſolely, our pains would be rewarded with ſucceſs. Abroad, the leaves of theſe trees, which are farmed out at a great annual rent, are not ſtripped off the branches ſingly, but young branches are generally ſheared off with the leaves on, and this renders them better for the worms, and leſs injurious to the trees.

But if the planter is not influenced by theſe reaſons, yet he ſhould think this tree worth propagating for the timber, as it will laſt in water as long as the moſt ſolid oak, and is very durable in every kind of uſe. The carpenter and the joiner know its value, and each apply it to various purpoſes in their reſpective buſineſſes. It is uſeful alſo in ſmaller matters, for the making of wheels, hoops, bows, &c. and its lop is excellent fuel.

*Uſes to which the timber is applied.*

The leaves of the white mulberry open in the ſpring, conſiderably ſooner than the other ſorts; and the male flowers having four ſtamina, as alſo male and female flowers at ſeparate diſtances, proves it to belong to the claſs and order *Monoecia Tetrandria*.

*Time of leaves coming out.*

*Claſs and order in the Linnean ſyſtem.*

This tree is propagated two ways, from ſeeds, and by layers. Where the former can be procured, it is the moſt expeditious way of raiſing great quantities; and whoever has a correſpondence in the South of France, or in Italy, may through that channel obtain them. Having the ſeeds ready, let a fine warm border of rich mellow earth be prepared, and let this border be hooped, in order to ſupport mats to defend the young plants, when they appear, from froſts. If no ſuch border can be eaſily had, it will be proper to make a gentle hot-bed, and cover it with rich fat mould. This alſo muſt be hooped, as the border. Then ſow the ſeeds in little drills, about a quarter of an inch deep. The middle of March is the beſt time for this work; and when the young plants appear, which will be in about ſix weeks, they muſt be conſtantly covered with the mats in the night, if any appearance of froſt preſents itſelf, as there often is at that ſeaſon. During the ſummer they ſhould be kept clear from weeds, and covered from the extreme heat of the ſun while the hot months continue. Whenever any cloudy or rainy weather approaches, the mats ſhould be always taken off, that the plants may enjoy the benefit of it. By thus carefully nurſing the beds, keeping them clear from weeds, watering the plants in dry ſeaſons, covering them from the parching ſun, and uncovering them again in the night, cloudy or rainy weather, the plants by autumn will be got pretty ſtrong, though not ſo ſtrong as to be left to themſelves. The following winter they will require ſome care. When the froſts approach they muſt be carefully covered with the mats, as in the ſpring; for without this protection, many of them would be deſtroyed, and the greateſt part killed, at leaſt down to the ground. In this bed they may ſtand two years, when they will be ſtrong enough to plant out in the nurſery. The ground for this purpoſe being double dug, the young plants ſhould be ſet in rows, at two feet and a half diſtance, and one foot and a half aſunder in the rows. Here they may remain till they are of a ſufficient ſize to plant out for good. The ground ſhould be dug between the rows every winter, and they muſt be conſtantly kept clear of weeds; and when they are to be planted out for ſtandards, it ſhould be done in the manner already directed for the elm, &c.

*Method of propagating this tree.*



Another method of propagating this tree is by layers. Whoever has not the conveniency of obtaining the ſeeds, muſt procure a number of plants to be planted for ſtools. The ground on which theſe ſtools are to ſtand ſhould be double dug, and the trees may be planted for this purpoſe two yards aſunder. The ſize of the ground, and the quantity of trees for the ſtools, muſt be proportioned according to the number of plants wanted; though the reader ſhould obſerve, that a few ſtools will ſoon produce many layers, as they throw out plenty of young branches, when the head is taken off. Having a ſufficient quantity of ſtools that have ſhot forth young wood for layering, in the beginning of winter perform this buſineſs, as follows. Let the earth be excavated around each ſtool, and let the preceding ſummer-ſhoot be ſlit at a joint, and laid therein; a peg would be proper, to keep them from being torn up, and the fine mould ſhould fill the interſtices; the ground muſt be levelled, and the young twigs cut down to one eye above the ſurface, that it may juſt appear above the ground. Such is the method of layering this tree; and whoever performs the operation in this manner, will find in the autumn following, that the plants will have all taken good root, and made a conſiderable ſhoot in the ſtem. Theſe plants will be now ready for the nurſery-ground, in which they ſhould be planted and managed in the ſame way as the ſeedlings. The ſtools, the ſecond year after, will have exhibited a freſh crop of young wood for layering. And thus may this operation be performed every ſecond year, till the deſired quantity is raiſed.

Such is the method I would recommend for the raiſing of this uſeful and noble tree. A tree well adapted to the beautifying our environs; a tree which would do honour to our nation were there public-ſpirited patriots who would encourage the planting of it in large quantities, for the worms and ſilk; in fine, a tree whoſe wood when felled ſerves for many purpoſes better than moſt other ſorts.

## CHAP. XVIII.

## *CARPINUS*, The HORNBEAM-TREE.

THE Hornbeam is ſo far from being a contemptible tree, that it will ſerve for as many purpoſes as almoſt any tree of the foreſt. It will grow to the height of ſeventy feet, or more, if it delights in its ſituation, and is very proper to be planted in parks, either for ſtandards or clumps, becauſe it will be ſecure from the teeth of the deer, who will leave this tree unmoleſted, whilſt they will tear off the bark, and deſtroy moſt others, unleſs they are well

*Situations moſt proper for this tree.*

well hurdled until they have attained ſufficient ſize and ſtrength to reſiſt their teeth.

There is no tree more proper than the hornbeam for hedges, it being a tonſile tree, and growing feathered to the bottom, and as it will aſpire greatly, may be trained up to what height the gardener pleaſes.

As the leaves continue all winter, this affords excellent ſhelter to other trees, and as the branches are ſo tough as to reſiſt the winds, and the tree is of quick growth, it is very proper to be planted for theſe purpoſes. The birds alſo repair in ſevere weather, as well as in tempeſts, to the hornbeam, for ſhelter under its leafy branches. So that whoever is fond of ſinging-birds, and the muſical warblings of the feathered tribe, ſhould never be without plantations of this tree, which they may fly to as an aſylum, when the howling winds and northern tempeſts roar.

**Derivation of its generical name.** The word *Carpinus* is ſuppoſed to be deduced from the Latin verb *carpere, to gather* or *crop*. For my own part, I profeſs not to ſee much propriety in this derivation.

**Purpoſes to which the timber is applied.** The timber of this tree is of a very tough and flexible nature, and is uſeful not only for turnery ware, but for making of mill cogs, yoaks, heads of beetles, ſtocks and handles of tools; and where it is cut down as underwood for the fire, it burns admirably well.

**Time when the flowers blow and leaves open.** The leaves of the hornbeam begin to open in the latter end of March, and will be quite out by the middle of April, and the flowers are in full blow towards the end of that month. **Claſs and order in the Linnæan ſyſtem.** Upon examining the latter, we find both male and female, and that the ſtamina are twenty in number, which indicates this tree to belong to the claſs and order *Monoecia Polyandria*.

**Manner of propagating the tree.** There is only one good method of propagating this tree, which is from the ſeeds. Some have recommended raiſing them by layers, but trees raiſed this way will never grow ſo tall nor ſo ſtraight as thoſe propagated from the ſeeds, neither are they fit for any other uſe than to be planted for hedges.

In the autumn the ſeeds will be ripe; when, having gathered a ſufficient quantity for the purpoſe, let them be ſpread upon a mat a few days to dry. After this, they ſhould be ſown in the ſeminary-ground, in beds four feet wide, with an alley of about two feet, in the manner directed for raiſing the aſh. In this bed they muſt remain till the ſecond ſpring before they make their appearance, and all the ſummer they lie concealed, the weeds ſhould conſtantly be plucked up as ſoon as they peep, for if they are neglected they will get ſo ſtrong, and the fibres of their roots will be ſo far ſtruck down among the ſeeds, as to endanger the drawing many ſeeds out with them, on weeding the ground. After the young plants appear, they ſhould conſtantly be kept clear of weeds during the next ſummer; and if they were to be now and then gently refreſhed with water in dry weather, it would prove ſerviceable to them. In the ſpring following they may be taken out of theſe beds, and planted in the nurſery, at the ſame diſtances, in the ſame manner, and managed as before directed. Here they may remain till they are of a ſufficient ſize to plant out for ſtandards.

But if a wood of theſe trees is deſired, I would adviſe their ſtanding two years in the ſeminary, by which time they will have acquired greater ſtrength, and be better able to reſiſt the weeds, &c. Where a wood of hornbeams is deſired, I ſay, let the ground be firſt prepared by a crop of oats, barley, or turneps, and then ploughed very deep after theſe are off, with a ſtrong plow, and well harrowed, to break the clods. Juſt before planting, let it be ploughed again croſſways, and harrowed as before. After taking the young plants out of the ſeminary at two years old, let them be planted in rows acroſs this ground, four feet aſunder, and two feet diſtance in the rows, having firſt prepared their roots, and plucked off all ſide-ſhoots. They ſhould be kept clean of weeds till they are out of their reach, either by hoeing or ploughing. When they get too thick, every other plant in the rows ſhould be taken away; and in this manner you ſhould continue to thin them as often as their heads touch, till they arrive at maturity.

This is the method I would recommend to raiſe a wood of theſe trees, where rabbits and hares may be kept out. But where there are many of theſe animals, it will be proper to raiſe them firſt of all in the nurſery, till they are about four or five feet high, and then having the ground ploughed deep with a ſtrong plow, in order to turn the beſt ſoil under to feed the roots, let them be carefully planted two yards aſunder each way. Where hares and rabbits cannot be kept out, I ſay, this muſt be the method. They muſt be firſt raiſed till their leading-ſhoot is out of their reach; for although deer will reject hornbeams, yet the above-mentioned animals are very voracious of them, and whenever theſe have taken off the tops, they ſeldom make ſtraight fine growing trees after, unleſs the plant be cut down to the ground. This I woefully experienced in one of my plantations at Gumley, where having planted a fine quarter of near ten thouſand one year old from the ſeed-beds, the winter following the tops were almoſt all eat off by the hares and rabbits. I headed part of them down to the ground, and let the other remain. Thoſe which were headed, the ſummer following made a fine ſtrong ſtraight ſhoot, whilſt the remainder ſhewed their tendency to become ſcraggy, forked, ſtocked, and manifeſted every ſymptom which would render the tree incapable of any uſe, except for hedges only. Finding myſelf compelled to practiſe ſome expedient to ſecure our nurſery from the hares another ſeaſon, I ſent out people to deſtroy them, but to no effect. Very few were to be found, ſo inconſiderable were their numbers, and yet ſo capable were theſe few of doing great miſchief. I perceived myſelf under a neceſſity, therefore, of raiſing ſuch plants on the ground as I knew they were fond of, and accordingly ſowed parſly, ſingle pinks, coleworts, &c. which ſerved by way of dampers to them; ſo that tho' I experienced ſome damage the winter following, yet it was very trifling. Thus this fleet, little, and otherways innocent and harmleſs animal proves more deſtructive to our young plantations than any other beaſts of venery, the deer only excepted. I muſt own, I have never perceived our vines to be touched, which has perhaps been owing to the number of plants better adapted to their palates, though they were of old deſtructive to vineyards, ſince the Bacchanalians teſtified their reſentment by always having at the Feaſt of Bacchus a hare roaſted upon a hazle ſpit, becauſe the root of that tree was looked upon as peculiarly injurious to the vines.

**Grows well on almoſt all ſoils and ſituations.** The hornbeam will grow in almoſt any ſoil or ſituation. It will not only thrive well on good, but on barren land, and even on ſtiff ground and in clays. It delights in cold hills, and all bleak and expoſed places, ſeems to rejoice in reſiſting the winds, and prides itſelf in guarding its neighbouring trees. In all ſuch barren and expoſed ſituations this tree is proper to be planted; and may be cultivated to great advantage.

CHAP.

# CHAP. XIX.

## *CELTIS*, The LOTE or NETTLE-TREE.

*The dark-fruited nettle trees recommended for woods, &c.* THE dark-fruited Nettle-trees, of which there are two remarkable kinds, one with black, the other with a dark purple fruit, are the sorts I would have introduced into our woods and plantations, whether designed for pleasure or profit.

The black-fruited nettle tree is a native of Italy, and abounds also in the South of France, and in Spain, in which places it grows to a great size. The other, with dark purple fruit, belongs to North-America, and likewise thrives to a great bulk.

*Its appearance described.* The nettle trees grow with large, fair, straight stems, their branches are numerous and diffuse, their bark is of a darkish grey colour, their leaves are of a pleasant green, three or four inches long, deeply serrated, end in a narrow point, nearly resemble the leaves of the common stinging-nettle, and continue on the trees till late in the autumn. So that one may easily conceive what an agreeable variety this tree would make in places designed for pleasure or profit, in wilderness quarters or woods, in open fields or enclosures, in parks or lawns. Add to this, that its shade is admirable.

*Uses of its timber.* The wood of the lote-tree is extremely durable. In Italy they make their flutes, pipes, and other wind instruments of it. With us, the coachmakers use it for the frames of their vehicles. It is very tough and pliable, and therefore useful for every thing which requires such wood; nay, of the very root of this tree are made hafts for knives, tools, &c.

*Time of the flowers opening. Class and order in the Linnæan system.* The flowers of the nettle-tree appear in the spring, but generally decay before the leaves have grown to their full size. There are hermaphrodite ones, and males, which shews this tree to be of the class and order *Polygamia Monoecia*. The hermaphrodite flowers have five stamina and two styles, but no petals; and the fruit is a drupe, of the size of a black cherry, in which is contained a single kernel. The male flower has but one stamen, and no petals. So that these trees receive little advantage from their flowers, which only serve to attract the philosopher's notice, as well as to answer the purposes of generation.

*Time of the leaves opening.* The leaves are late in the spring before they shew themselves, but they make amends for this, by retaining their verdure till near the close of autumn, and then do not resemble most deciduous trees, whose leaves shew their approaching fall by the change of their colour, but continue to exhibit themselves of a pleasant green, even to the last, just before they fall; insomuch that I have observed a nettle-tree in my garden, at the end of November, which has had the appearance of an evergreen, and in a few days afterwards not a leaf has remained on it. But at the same time I must remark, that I had another when this was in its verdure with never a leaf on the branches; and yet there was no apparent difference either in soil or situation.

*Method of propagating this tree.* Nettle-trees are propagated from seeds, which ripen in England, if they have a favourable autumn, though I have observed that the best seeds are imported from abroad, and are always most certain of producing a crop. I have received seeds of the dark-purple-fruited sort from North-America in the spring of the year, which have been preserved in sand, and have come up in less than a month after sowing. However, those who have no correspondents to furnish them with foreign seeds, must content themselves with what can be procured at home. Indeed, if the autumn be fine, the seeds of our English trees will grow very well, and whoever has a few large trees, may gather seeds enough for his purpose.

These seeds should be sown, soon after they are ripe, either in boxes, or in a fine warm border of rich earth, a quarter of an inch deep, and in the following spring many of the young plants will appear, though a great part often lie till the second spring before they shew their heads. If the seeds in the beds shoot early in the spring, they should be hooped, and protected by mats from the frosts, which would nip them in the bud. When all danger from frosts is over, the mats should be laid aside till the parching beams of the sun get powerful, when, in the day-time, they may be laid over the hoops again, to screen the plants from injury. The mats should be constantly taken off every night, and the young plants should never be covered either in rainy or cloudy weather. During the whole summer, these seedlings should be frequently watered in dry weather, and the beds kept clean of weeds, &c. In the autumn, they must be protected from the frosts, which often come early in that season, and would not fail to destroy their tops. The like care should be continued all winter, to defend them from the same enemies. This caution may be necessary, tho' not absolutely so, if the situation is tolerable. I generally leave them to themselves in November, when the sap is at rest, and have hitherto found them shooting out in the spring, though they have had the severe trials of long and hard frosts, in our exposed situation at Church-Langton.

In this seminary they may remain, being kept clean of weeds and watered in dry weather, till the end of June, when they should be taken out of their beds, and pricked in others at six inches distance. And here let no one be startled at my recommending the month of June for this work, for I have found by repeated experience, that the plants will be then almost certain of growing, and will continue their shoots till the autumn; whereas I have ever perceived, that many of those planted in March have frequently perished, and that those which did grow made hardly any shoot that year, and shewed the early figure of a stunted tree.

In June, therefore, let the ground be well dug, and prepared for this work, and let the mould be rich and good. But the operation of removing must be deferred till rain comes, and if the season should be dry, this work may be postponed till the middle of July. After a shower, therefore, or a night's rain, let the plants be taken out of their beds, and pricked out, at six inches distance from each other. After this, the beds in which they are planted should

LOTE

ſhould be hooped, and covered with mats when the ſun ſhines, but theſe muſt always be taken away at night, as well as in rainy or cloudy weather With this management, they will have ſhot to a good height by the autumn, and have acquired ſo much hardineſs and ſtrength as to need no farther care than to be kept clear of weeds for two or three years, when they may be planted out in places where they are to remain, or ſet in the nurſery, to be trained up for large ſtandards, to be planted in fields, parks, &c

Beſt ſeaſon for planting lote trees

The beſt ſeaſon for planting out theſe ſtandard trees is the latter end of October, or beginning of November; and in performing that operation, the uſual rules muſt be obſerved, with care

The ſoil well upon moiſt ſoil

The ſoil for the lote tree ſhould be light, and in good heart, and the ſituation ought to be well defended, the young ſhoots being very liable to be deſtroyed by the winter's froſts

## CHAP XX

## *SORBUS*, The MOUNTAIN ASH, or QUICKEN-TREE

Its appearance deſcribed

ALTHOUGH this tree will not grow to the largeſt ſize, yet it is one of the moſt beautiful trees of our woods Its growth is naturally upright and ſtraight, its bark ſmooth, and of a pleaſant browniſh and greyiſh green colour The foliage is delightful, being compoſed of ſeveral narrow ſharply-ſerrated lobes, beautifully arranged along the mid rib, and terminated by an odd one Theſe have a fine effect, and diverſify the ſcene, as in the ſpring they appear of a hoary colour The flowers alſo, which grow in large bunches, and are remarkable for their ſweet ſcent, contribute greatly to the beauty of this tree But above all, their berries ſtrike the eye with ſurprize and pleaſure During the firſt part of the winter, they appear all over the tree of a beautiful light red colour I have known thoſe who have been unacquainted with the *Sorbus*, take it at a diſtance for a tree covered with red flowers, which they have expreſſed great ſatisfaction to ſee in that dead ſeaſon

Situations proper for it

But nobody muſt expect to have theſe trees covered with their profuſion of berries long, unleſs it be on ſuch as are planted in court yards, or places where the birds dare not venture to approach, for theſe are ſo voracious of the berries, that they will devour them even before they are ripe The blackbird and the thruſh are their chief deſtroyers, ſo that quicken-trees ſhould be planted for their ſupport by thoſe who are delighted with their warbles, eſpecially as the berries will come in to ſucceed the wild cherry, &c

Uſes to which the timber is applicable

This tree will grow to a ſize large enough to be ſawed out into planks, boards, timber, &c and as its wood is ſaid to be all heart, it is excellent for wheelwright's works of all ſorts, for the making of tools for the huſbandman, goads, &c

In the North of England and Wales the mountain-aſh is very common, it abounds in hedge-rows, as well as woods, and the traveller is regaled by the ſweetneſs of the flowers in ſpring, while his eyes are feaſted by the delightful appearance of the red berries in winter In the Southern part of the kingdom it is not very common

Time when the flowers and leaves blow

The buds of the quicken-tree begin to open in the beginning of April The leaves will be quite out by the middle of the month, and the flowers will be full blown by the ſixth of May There are in each flower female parts of generation, and twenty males, inſerted into the calyx, which ſhews this tree to belong to the claſs and order *Icoſandria Trigynia*

Claſs and order in the Linnæan ſyſtem

Previous to the propagating of this tree, care muſt be taken to procure ſome ſeeds that are thoroughly ripe, which will be attended with ſome trouble, unleſs there be great quantities of them, or they grow ſo near a houſe that the birds dare not approach otherwiſe they will effectually deſtroy them before they are ripe, to the great mortification of the intended planter In order, therefore, to ſecure the fruit from theſe enemies, the trees muſt be netted, as well as ſome of the birds ſhot, and hung up with other ſcarecrows *in terrorem*

Method of propagating this tree

Having procured a ſufficient quantity of berries, they ſhould be ſowed, ſoon after they are ripe, in the ſeminary, about half an inch deep, in beds made as has been before directed They frequently lie till the ſecond ſpring before they make their appearance, and, in the ſpring following, may be planted out in the nurſery I need not repeat that the ſeminary ſhould be kept clear of weeds, and that the young plants in dry weather now and then ought to be refreſhed with water, neither need the gardener be reminded, that after they are planted in the nurſery way, digging the ground in the rows muſt be obſerved every winter, taking off all ſhoots alſo which would make the tree forked, and keeping the weeds hoed in the rows, till they are of ſufficient ſize to plant out where they are intended to remain

When theſe trees are fit to be planted out, let them be taken out of the nurſery with as much care as poſſible let the wounded parts of the root only be taken off, and ſee that the hole be made large enough, that the turf may be worked down to the bottom of it, in order to nouriſh the tree, and promote its ſhooting off healthy and ſtrong at the firſt Afterwards, let it be well ſtaked to prevent its being blown aſide by the winds, and well fenced to ſecure it from cattle, deer, &c and then left to Nature The beſt time for this work is the latter end of October

Although I have hitherto recommended the raiſing of this tree from the ſeeds in the foregoing manner, yet it will take very well from layers, ſo that whoever cannot procure the berries, and has a few of theſe trees, may cut them down cloſe to the ground, when they will throw out many ſtools, and if the year

QUICKEN

following theſe are laid in the ground in the ſame manner as carnations, they will have taken good root in one year But trees cultivated this way will not grow ſo ſtraight and handſome, neither will they arrive at ſo great a magnitude as thoſe raiſed from the ſeeds.

Soils ſuitable to this tree

The quicken-tree will grow upon almoſt any ſoil, either ſtrong or light, moiſt or dry It flouriſhes both on the mountains and in the woods, it is never affected by the ſeverity of the weather, being extremely hardy; and if even planted on bleak and expoſed places, it grows exceeding well These excellent properties, as well as others, ſhould engage our notice, and demand our attention

# C H A P. XXI

## *B E T U L A*, The B I R C H - T R E E

THE Birch is a foreſt-tree of humble growth, but nevertheleſs, if permitted, will arrive to a tolerable ſize It is excellently well calculated to diverſify the ſcene, and makes a pleaſing variety among other trees, either in winter or ſummer

Its appearance deſcribed

In the ſummer it is covered over with beautiful ſmall leaves, which are of a pleaſant green, and by every breeze of air are pleaſingly waved on their ſlender twigs In the winter it appears conſpicuous, by preſenting itſelf with its body covered over with a whitiſh bark, which has a good effect

Situations proper for this tree

Theſe trees, therefore, may be planted in parks, lawns, &c to encreaſe the variety, as well as in woods or coppices, to be cut down for profit

Uſes of its timber

Of the wood of this tree are made diſhes, bowls, ladles, and ox yoaks for the huſbandman It is alſo applicable to larger uſes, and is highly proper for the fellies of broad-wheel waggons, it being interlocked ſo as not to be cleaved I have been informed by an old experienced wheelwright, that old birch-trees cannot be cleft, as the grains run croſſways, and that he prefers it for ſeveral uſes in his way to moſt wood, and as I have ſeen ſeveral of theſe trees more than two feet ſquare, the timber of the birch may perhaps be of more value than it has hitherto been eſteemed

The lopping of the birch makes excellent fuel, as well as the beſt of brooms The bark is of a very durable nature The Swedes cover their houſes with it, and it laſts many years The inner fine bark was, before the invention of paper, antiently uſed for writeing, and of the ſap is made a wholeſome wine, ſalutary, it is ſaid, for conſumptive perſons, and ſuch as are frequently afflicted with the ſtone and gravel

Derivation of the generical name

The word *Betula* ſeems to be formed of the old Britiſh name *Bedw*, and, without all doubt, this is an indigenous plant, claiming Britain for its original ſoil and country.

Time when the flowers blow and leaves open

The leaves of the birch-tree will be quite opened by the beginning of April The flowers will appear in full blow by the twenty-ſeventh of that month, and about the eleventh of September it will have formed catkins

Claſs and order in the Linnæan ſyſtem

Both male and female flowers are found on this plant, and the male flowers with four ſtamina, which ſhews this tree to belong to the claſs and order *Monoecia Tetrandria*

Method of propagating the tree from ſeed

There are two good ways of propagating this tree, either from layers or ſeeds If from ſeeds, they ſhould be carefully gathered in the autumn, before they are dropped from their ſcales, which will happen ſoon after they begin to open Theſe ſhould be carefully ſown in the ſeminary, about a quarter of an inch deep, and, after they are come up, ſhould be carefully cleanſed from weeds for the firſt ſummer The ſpring following they may be planted out in the nurſery The rows muſt be two feet and a half aſunder, and the plants a foot and a half diſtance in the rows Here they may remain till they are of a ſufficient ſize to be planted out for good

and from ſtools.

Whoever has not the conveniency of procuring the ſeeds, may ſoon raiſe a great quantity by layers from very few ſtools Having planted ſome ſtools for this purpoſe, and having headed them down to the ground, let them remain two years before they are layered By this time each branch will have a great quantity of fine-ſhoots, which being ſplaſhed and laid in the ground, every twig will grow, and make a fine plant, fit to be planted out in the nurſery by the autumn following Theſe plants ſhould be taken from the ſtools, and planted as the ſeedlings, and the ſtools ought to be refreſhed with the knife, by taking off the old ſplaſhed wood, and preparing it to throw out with vigour freſh ſhoots for a ſecond operation, which ſhould be repeated every two years

After the plants are of a ſize fit to be ſet out for good, they may be planted upon almoſt any ground with ſucceſs, for (the birch being a native of Britain) they reliſh all ſorts of ſoils ſhe affords her vegetable offſpring

All ſoils ſuitable to it

They will thrive extremely well on all ſorts of barren land, whether it be wet or dry, ſandy or ſtony, marſhy or boggy They ſow themſelves ſometimes, and come up in places where hardly any other tree will grow To what advantage, then, may many parts of this iſland be planted with this tree, particularly ſuch as have the advantage of large rivers, where the wood may be ſent off by water, for where water carriage may be had, the broom-man will be a conſtant purchaſer for theſe trees; who will ſend whole barges full of brooms, made of their bruſh, to the different parts of the kingdom

Profits of planting it for the broom-man

Whenever coppices of the birch are planted, with a deſign to be ſold to the broom-men, the plants ſhould be taken out of the nurſery, and ſet five feet aſunder, and in eight years they will be ready to cut, when an acre, if it has ſucceeded well, will be worth about ten pounds After this, the trees may be cut every ſix years, when the acre will be of the ſame value If plantations of this tree are intended for hoops and ſmaller uſes of huſbandry, they will ſupport a cutting for theſe purpoſes every twelfth year, and will be worth more than twelve pounds per acre Thus may ſuch land as is not worth a ſhilling an acre be improved with birch trees, as

BIRCH improvement so much the greater, as the nature of the tree will admit of its being raised and planted out at a very small expence. Indeed, if the ground was good enough to bear a crop, by being ploughed the mould would be better prepared for it to strike in; but where this cannot be done, the plants may be taken out of the nursery, when they are out of the reach of weeds, and then planted; and no farther care need be taken of them than keeping out cattle, till they are fit for cutting. The best season for planting out the birch, if it be on a dry ground, is autumn; but if it be in a wet soil, the spring is preferable.

For the benefit of such as desire to make birch-wine, I have taken some pains to procure a receipt, and have at length met with one, in a noted Treatise on Cookery; which a lady assures me is very valuable. It differs very little from Mr Evelyn's, and is as follows.

Receipt for making birch-wine

"THE season for procuring the liquor from the birch trees is in the beginning of March, while the sap is rising, and before the leaves shoot out; for when the sap is come forward, and the leaves appear, the juice, by being long digested in the bark, grows thick and coloured, which before was thin and clear.

"The method of procuring the juice is, by boring holes in the body of the trees, and putting in fassets, which are commonly made of the branches of elder, the pith being taken out. You may, without hurting the tree, if large, tap it in several places, four or five at a time, and by that means save from a good many trees several gallons every day. If you have not enough in one day, the bottles into which it drops must be corked close, and resined or waxed. However, make use of it as soon as you can.

"Take the sap, and boil it as long as any scum rises, skimming it all the time. To every gallon of liquor put four pounds of good sugar, and the thin peel of a lemon. Boil it afterwards half an hour, skimming it very well; pour it into a clean tub, and when it is almost cold, set it to work with yeast spread on a toast. Let it stand five or six days, stirring it often. Then take such a cask as will hold the liquor, fire a large match dipt in brimstone, and throw it into the cask; stop it close till the match is extinguished. Tun your wine, lay the bung on light till you find it has done working; stop it close, and keep it three months, then bottle it off."

## CHAP. XXII.

## *PRUNUS PADUS*, The BIRD-CHERRY-TREE.

THE American Cluster-Cherry is that species of the Bird Cherry which I would have introduced into our woods. And indeed, we shall see good reason to admit a few of these trees at least, if we consider that it is a fine upright tree, that it will grow to the height of thirty or forty feet, and that its wood its extremely serviceable.

Situations proper for this tree. Its appearance described.

This tree will make a pretty variety either in parks or lawns, and will look well, if planted out any where for standards. The bark is of a dark brown colour, and the leaves are of a shining green, of an oval figure, serrated on their edges, and continue on the branches late in the autumn. The flowers are large and white, growing in long bunches, and are succeeded by a black berry, of which the birds are very fond.

Class and order in the Linnæan system.

The botanist, on examining the flower to distinguish its class, will find the stamina to consist of twenty or thirty filaments, of an awl-shaped figure, with roundish antheræ, nearly the length of the corolla, which consists of five roundish patent petals, inserted into the edge of the calyx. He will find only one style, which is filiforme, of the length of the stamina, and crowned with one entire obtuse stigma. The class, therefore, to which this tree belongs is apparently *Icosandria Monogynia*.

The wood is very valuable, is much used by the cabinet-makers, will polish very smooth, and displays beautiful veins, both black and white. So that though this does not equal many other forest trees in size, yet it will not only encrease the variety, but make some amends for this defect by the value of its timber. Uses of the timber.

This tree is a native of North-America, and must be raised from seeds; for those reared from layers seldom succeed well, and will neither grow so straight nor tall as those propagated from seeds.

In order, therefore, to obtain young plants, beds of light earth must be prepared in the autumn, in which the seeds should be sown about half an inch deep. In the spring following the young plants will appear; and during that summer must be kept clean of weeds, and watered in dry weather. In the succeeding spring, they must be planted out in the nursery, a foot asunder, and two feet distance in the rows; where they may stand, with only the usual care, till they are fit to be planted out for good. Method of propagating this tree.

The bird-cherry-tree will thrive well in most soils, provided they are not too dry. It affects a moist situation; and in such places will arrive at the greatest height. Soils proper for it.

# CHAP. XXIII.

## *CORNUS*, The CORNELIAN CHERRY-TREE.

EVERY perſon deſirous of having a great number of different ſorts of trees in his plantations, will be eager, I think, to give the Cornelian Cherry-tree a place, as it ariſes to upwards of twenty feet in height, and its wood is not only very valuable, but very early in the ſpring, even in the beginning of February, produces great quantities of ſmall flowers introducing, as it were, the flowery tribe. This muſt produce a pleaſing effect in plantations of all kinds, whether deſigned for pleaſure or profit.

*Time when the flowers appear.*

On account of the early flowering of this tree, though there is nothing very valuable in the flowers, it has always been introduced into wilderneſs quarters, places deſigned for pleaſure, ſhrubberies, &c. and the botaniſt, on examination, will find it to belong to the claſs and order *Tetrandria Monogynia*. Neither does the *Cornus* exhibit its flowers merely for amuſement. It likewiſe affords a good crop of fruit, which, in the month of September, will appear all over the tree, of a red colour. This fruit is much liked by ſome, whilſt with others it is in little eſteem, though it makes very good tarts, for which purpoſe it is by many people preſerved. Theſe cherries are uſed in medicine, both as an aſtringent and cooler, and the *rob de cornis* is an officinal preparation of the fruit of this tree.

*Situations moſt proper for this tree.*

*Claſs and order in the Linnæan ſyſtem.*

The timber of the cornel tree is white, very durable, as well as ſolid and hard, and, beſides the uſes it has in common with other trees, is much recommended for wheel-works, pins, wedges, &c. It is ſaid to laſt as long as iron, and as this tree will grow to a conſiderable bulk, I would recommend to have a few in every plantation.

*Uſes of its timber.*

The word *Cornus* is derived from the Latin *cornu, a horn*, and is ſo called *ob corneam duritiem*, on account of the horn-like ruggedneſs or durableneſs of its timber.

*Derivation of the generical name.*

The cornelian cherry-tree may be raiſed from the ſeeds, or by layers, the former of which is the beſt method. Theſe ſhould be ſown in the autumn, ſoon after they are ripe, or they will not come up till the ſecond ſpring, and ſometimes, when the intermediate ſummer has proved very dry, they will not appear till the ſummer after. So that great care ſhould be uſed to get theſe ſeeds into their beds as ſoon as poſſible, or if the work cannot be done before the ſpring, and the plants do not come up, the beds ſhould be left undiſturbed for at leaſt the two ſeaſons following.

*Method of propagating this tree.*

When the plants have made their appearance, they may ſtand in the ſeed-beds a year or two to acquire ſtrength, during which time they ſhould be kept clean of weeds, and in dry weather watered. After this, they ſhould be planted out in the nurſery, in rows, where they may remain, with the uſual care, till they are fit to be planted out for good, the beſt ſeaſon for which is the autumn.

The cornelian cherry-tree is a native of Miſnia, Auſtria, and ſome other places, but grows very well with us, and may be planted with ſucceſs on moſt ſoils.

*Soils proper for it.*

# CHAP. XXIV.

## *CORYLUS*, The HAZEL or NUT-TREE.

THE Hazel is the laſt of the foreſt-trees of this ſort I ſhall introduce here, and the reaſon of its being placed in this order is, that it is one of the loweſt in growth, and is ſeldom planted out for ſtandards, but is generally cut for underwood, or planted in coppices for poles, &c. which will grow twenty or thirty feet high.

*Situations proper for it.*

The wood of the hazel is very uſeful for ſpars, hoops, fork-handles, &c. alſo for leſſer uſes, as walking-ſticks, angle-rods, ſpringes to catch birds, and the wood-cutter knows its ſuperlative ſervice to him, in making the beſt ſort of withs and bands for faggoting.

*Uſes of its timber.*

This tree derives its name *Corylus* from the Greek word κόρυλος. It hath alſo another name, *Cavellana*, ſo called from *Cavella*, a town in Campania, where it abounded in great quantities. But I think it might as well have been called *Anglicana*, as our woods in general are ſtocked with no tree in greater quantities than they are with this.

*Derivation of the generical name.*

If you want to ſee the flowers of the nut-tree, you muſt look for them early, for they begin to open about the twenty-third of January, and in a month's time after will be in full blow. They are ſmall, but of a beautiful red colour. In the middle of September the catkins of this tree, which belongs to the claſs and order *Monoecia Polyandria*, are formed.

*Time when the flowers open.*

*Claſs and order.*

Whoever is deſirous of having a coppice of hazels, ſhould be provided with nuts in the autumn. Theſe muſt be preſerved from mice and vermin till February, in a moiſt place, to keep the kernels from ſhrivelling. Then, having your ground well ploughed, and harrowed to break the clods, let them be ſown in drills drawn acroſs the ground, at one yard diſtance, the nuts ſhould be planted about two inches deep, and placed in the drills about one foot aſunder. When the young plants come up, it is natural to ſuppoſe they muſt be kept clear from weeds, and this they ſhould be, in the manner before directed, till they are out of their reach

HAZEL reach Where the plants stand too thick, they should be properly thinned, the weakest must always be taken away And this thinning ought to be continued till they are a yard asunder each way

A Coryletum also may be made of setts; but not as Virgil says,

*Plantis edurae coryli nascuntur*

The setts should be raised from the nut in the seminary, where they must be sown so thin as that they may not incommode one another till they get about a foot and a half or two feet high I advise this, to save the trouble and expence of planting them out in the nursery way From this seminary they may be taken in the autumn, and planted all over the ground designed for them, one yard asunder In about twelve years they will be fit to cut down for poles, but they will be ready for a second fall much sooner, and may be cut every seventh or eighth year, when their stools will send up strong and vigorous shoots HAZEL

Soils suitable to this tree. Whoever is anxious to procure a quantity of these trees, need not be concerned about their succeeding in his soil or situation, be it what it will, as they will thrive well on mountains or in vales, and prosper extremely both in dry or moist, in cold or barren, in rocky or sandy grounds

# PART II.

# Of AQUATICS;

## OR,

## British Trees proper to be planted by the Sides of Rivers, Ponds, Bogs, &c.

## CHAP. I

## *POPULUS*, The POPLAR-TREE.

THE Poplar demands the first place amongst the Aquatics, whether we consider the quickness of its growth, or the magnitude to which it will arrive And altho' this tree is styled an Aquatic, yet it will grow exceeding well, and attain an extraordinary bulk in a few years, on tolerably dry ground in fields, pastures, &c

Three species of poplar only recommended for timber-trees. There are many species of the poplar, though I shall recommend only three to be planted for timber-trees These are, the white poplar, known by the name of the Abele-tree; the black poplar, so called from a black circle perceived at the center of its trunk when felled, and the trembling poplar, or Aspen tree

Situations proper for this tree. All these sorts of poplars, especially the white or abele, are very proper for walks and avenues at a distance from (especially if the soil be moist), but are by no means fit to be planted near, houses, or the pleasure-garden, not only as the catkins, down, &c make a prodigious litter, but because they are very subject to send out quantities of suckers, which will come up, and greatly injure and deface gravel walks, &c

which is a quick grower. If any person is desirous of having a shew of timber in a few years, he will find these trees favourable to his wishes If the soil is tolerably good and moist, they will aspire to the height of thirty feet, or more, in six or seven years So that such houses as stand low and exposed, may have shelter and shade in a very little time

Valuable properties of its timber. The poplar grows to a large timber-tree, and its wood is now esteemed of greater value than formerly Being exceeding white, the boards are on that account sought after, by many neat and curious people, for flooring Few woods are so little liable to shrink or swell as this, which makes it very proper for wainscoting of rooms The boards and timber of this tree are extremely durable, if kept dry, and the poles may be used for spars, &c which will last many years, when cleared of their bark Poplar poles have been esteemed of little value for these purposes, people having found by experience that they generally decayed in a few years This, however, was owing to some part of the bark being left; which in a few years becomes a proper nidus for animalculæ, that hatch in great quantities, and soon eat away the strength of the spar, whereas, had the bark been taken off at first, it would have remained sound and good

POPLAR

Uses to which the timber is applied.

The wood of this tree is greatly sought after by the turner, for being very white, it makes the finest sorts of dishes, bowls, &c. Being likewise extremely light, it is proper to make one-horse carts, the use of which is so well known, that few gentlemen at present are without them. The bellows-maker finds his account also in this wood, and the heel maker converts it into heels and soles of shoes. The poles are not only proper for spars, as was before observed, but the smaller sort may be used for vines, hops, &c. and the lop answers very well for the fire.

Derivation of its generical name.

The word *Populus* is derived from the Greek verb παιπάλλω, *to shake*, because the leaves of the different species of this tree, especially those of the aspen, are more easily shaken than any other. By the least breeze of wind, nay, even in a seemingly perfect calm, their leaves will alternately shew their horny and other sides; and those of the aspen have almost always a constant trembling motion: insomuch that this species of poplar has been distinguished from the others by the name of *Populus tremula*.

Class and order in the Linnæan system.

Time when the flowers blow and leaves open.

The flowers of the poplar are, both male and female, on distinct plants, and the male flowers have eight stamina, which entitles it to the class and order *Dioecia Octandria*. The male and female flowers are both arranged into an amentum. In the beginning of April they make their appearance, though the aspen flowers will be full blown by the twenty-second of March. The male flowers appear first, and the female about a week after. The catkins are about three inches long. Soon after the female flowers come out, the males drop off the tree, and in about five or six weeks after the female will have ripe seeds, which are sometimes dispersed by the winds to a considerable distance.

The method of propagating the different sorts of this tree is the same in all, so that the directions must be general, and the timber of each is nearly valuable. I shall only observe, that whoever plants them in places for ornament, should form the mixture so as to produce the most pleasing effect. For these trees judiciously intermixed form an agreeable variety.

The appearance of the white,

The trunk of the white poplar is straight, and covered with a smooth whitish bark. The leaves are about three inches long, and stand upon footstalks about an inch in length. They are indented at the edges, are of a dark-green on the upper surface, but white and woolly underneath. They are usually quite out by the eighteenth of April.

black,

The leaves of the black poplar are not so large as the former, their colour is a pleasant green, they are heart shaped, and appear about the twenty second of April.

and aspen poplar described.

The leaves of the aspen are smaller than those of the black poplar. They stand upon long slender footstalks, which renders it, of all the other sorts, the most tremulous, are roundish, and smooth on both sides, but do not make their appearance before the beginning of May.

Method of propagating this tree.

The propagation of the poplar tree is very easy. It will grow from cuttings, setts, truncheons, &c. though I by no means approve of the planting of truncheons, as has been often practised on boggy places, because I have always observed, that plantations of these luxuriant trees, attempted to be raised in this manner, have been frequently stocked, and very unpromising, and that the most promising trees have never equalled, in goodness or beauty, those planted with regular trees raised in the nursery.

In order, therefore, to obtain a quantity of poplars, proper to be planted in avenues or clumps, by the sides of rivulets, bogs, or any other places where they are desired, you must get a piece of ground double dug for the nursery. If the trees wanted are to be planted for good in a watery situation, this nursery ground should be pretty near it; but if they are designed for pasture-grounds, fields, or such as have no more than a common degree of moisture, the soil of the nursery should be proportionably drier.

POPLAR

The latter end of October is the best season for planting the cuttings, though they will grow if planted in any of the winter months. They should be all of those last year's shoots which have been vigorous, or at least not older than two years wood. These cuttings should be one foot and a half in length, and must be planted in the nursery-ground in rows, a yard asunder, and at a foot and a half distance from one another. They should be planted a foot in the ground, while the other half must remain to send forth the leading shoot. Now, in order to have one leading shoot only, in summer these plants should be carefully looked over, and all young side-branches nipped off, in order to encourage the leading branch. After this, no farther care need be taken of them than keeping them clean of weeds, and digging between the rows in the winter, till they have attained a proper size to plant out for good, which will be in two years, if they are designed to form small woods or spinneys, in boggy or watery ground.

If they are wanted for standards, for fields, sides of rivers, &c. they may remain in the nursery another year, when they will not be too large for that purpose, but may be taken out of the nursery and planted, and in a few years they will make a surprising progress, so as to be worth, in about twenty or thirty years, as many shillings, or more, a-piece.

Directions for forming a coppice of poplars.

In order to form a coppice of these trees, if the land be not so boggy but that it may be ploughed, a crop of oats or other grain may be got off it the preceding year of the planting, and in the autumn it would be a still greater advantage, if, just before the planting, it was to be ploughed again, as by this operation it would be rendered lighter, and the weeds, &c. would be buried. Having prepared the ground, let the two-year old plants be taken out of the nursery, and planted one yard asunder. It will be proper to continue hoeing the weeds down for the first year. Afterward, they will require no farther trouble till the time of cutting, which may be done in seven years from the first planting, and every four or five years after they may be cut for poles, firewood, &c. The quickness of these trees growth, and their value when cut, even for these purposes, greatly augment the value of the land planted with them. Nay, by this means boggy or marshy ground will produce more per acre than the best pasture or feeding land, a consideration which should stimulate every gentleman possessed of a large quantity of such sort of land, which brings him in very little, to improve it in this manner, and the improvement will be the greater, in proportion as the scarcity of wood in his neighbourhood is greater or less. If the ground for these plantations be so boggy as not to admit of ploughing and sowing, then the planter must be contented with taking the plants out of the nursery, and setting them in holes at the aforesaid distance, and they will thrive surprisingly even in this way.

Every gentleman desirous of having plantations of large trees of the sorts I have recommended, should plant them as before directed, at one yard asunder, and when their heads begin to interfere with and incommode one another, every other tree should be taken away, which will sell very

well

*POPLAR*

well for large poles, and the remainder ſhould be left to grow for timber But though I adviſe every other tree to be taken away, I would not have this caution too ſtrictly obſerved I only mean to have the weakeſt and leaſt thriving eradicated, and if two fine luxuriant trees ſtand together, and others leſs promiſing on each ſide, let the weakeſt be taken up And thus they ſhould continue to be thinned as often as they grow too cloſe, till you have a plantation of timber poplar-trees

I muſt not forget to give another precaution to the poplar planter; viz That after theſe trees are planted out for good, he ſhould never ſuffer a tree to be ſtripped up, nor even a ſide branch taken off, for by doing this, the progreſs of the tree will be ſtopped for ſome years, whereas, if theſe are permitted to remain, they powerfully attract the nutritious juices, and help to ſupply the trunk, as well as themſelves, in ſuch plenty, as to contribute ſurpriſingly to its encreaſe, both in bulk and height

## CHAP. II

## *BETULA ALNUS*, The ALDER-TREE

*Derivation of its generical name*

THE word *Alnus*, the former name of this tree, ſhews it to be an aquatic, being derived from the Latin verb *Alo*, *to nouriſh* or *feed*, and was applied to this plant on account of the extraordinary nouriſhment it receives from river and watery places

*Places in which it is proper to be planted*

The uſes of the alder tree when growing are, to ſecure the banks of rivers from being waſhed away, and confine the water in its proper channel, when, by frequent torrents, the banks wear away, and the courſe widens For theſe purpoſes no tree is more proper than this, for as it conſtantly ſends forth ſuckers from its loweſt roots, which are numerous, ſtrong, and compact, it will effectually prevent the banks from being undermined by the current

Theſe trees are alſo very uſeful to form hedges on boggy or ſwampy ground, where they may be ſo trained as to make a fence of a conſiderable height to divide ſuch places, and which to the eye will have a good appearance

They may be planted to enliven the ſcene, in clumps or woods, in places where they are wanted to make a proſpect compleat, even though the ſituation be cold, wet, or damp for they will grow ſurpriſingly in the moſt abject weeping parts of foreſts, water-galls, &c Indeed, where ſituations are low, ſome of theſe trees may be planted for ſhade, as they are allowed to be very wholeſome, and are ſaid to nouriſh whatever grows under them

*Height to which it grows and purpoſes to which the timber is applied*

The alder-tree will grow to the height of about thirty-five or forty feet, and its timber is very valuable for works intended to lie conſtantly under water, where it will harden, and laſt for ages It is ſaid to have been uſed under the Rialto at Venice, and we are told that the moraſſes about Ravenna were piled with this timber, in order to lay the foundation for building upon

The firſt veſſels we read of were made of the wood of theſe trees, which are thought to have given the firſt hint towards navigation

*Tunc alnos primum fluvii ſenſere cavatas*
Geo I

*Nec non & torrentem undam levis innatat alnus*
*Miſſa Pado*——— Geo II

We uſe the timber now for pumps, ſluices, water-pipes, troughs, piles, &c which purpoſes it ſuits admirably well It is alſo proper for making of wooden heels for ſhoes, ſo that where this trade is carried on there will be a certain ſale for theſe trees The turners likewiſe apply it to various uſes

*Time of the flowers coming out*

*Claſs and order in the Linnæan ſyſtem*

The flowers of the alder tree will be in full blow about the twenty ſixth of March They have both male and female ſeparately on the ſame plant, and the ſtamina of the males are four, which ſhews it to belong to the claſs and order *Monoecia Tetrandria* The catkins are formed about the ſixteenth of September The flowers have no beauty to recommend the tree, affording pleaſure only to the botaniſt, and curious obſerver of Nature But the leaves are moderately large, and of a deep green The bark alſo, being ſmooth, and of a purpliſh colour, makes this tree have an agreeable effect among others, in all ſorts of plantations of the watery tribe

*Its appearance deſcribed*

*Time of the leaves opening*

Its leaves begin to open about the ſeventh of April

*Method of raiſing a coppice of alders from young trees*

The alder-tree is generally planted for coppice wood, to be cut down every ninth or tenth year for poles Theſe coppices are raiſed either from truncheons or young trees, the latter of which I greatly prefer In order to obtain a quantity of trees for this purpoſe, ſome ſuckers ſhould be taken out of the meadows where the alder-trees grow, and where there is no fear of their being found in plenty Theſe ſhould be planted on a prepared piece of ground, and afterwards headed down for ſtools By the ſucceeding autumn, they will have ſhot out many young branches, which may be layed in the ground, and by that time twelve-month they will have taken root; when they ſhould be removed from the ſtools, and planted in rows, to ſtiffen, and acquire a ſufficient height to be above the weeds, when planted in the places where they are to remain In one or two years time, they will be ſtrong enough to be planted out for good, and, if the coppice is to ſtand upon boggy or watery ground, they may be removed from the nurſery, and having made holes all over the ground, ſhould be planted at three feet aſunder Here they may ſtand for ſix or ſeven years, when every other tree ſhould be taken away, and the reſt cut down for ſtools The ſtools will then be ſix feet aſunder, and as each ſtool will throw out many young branches for poles, they ought not to ſtand at a nearer diſtance Every ninth or tenth year will afford a fall of theſe trees for poles, and in performing this operation, they ſhould be taken off ſmooth and fine, ſo that the ſtool may not be damaged, or hindered from producing a freſh crop

The

ALDER or from truncheons

The other, less eligible method, though perhaps least expensive, is planting of truncheons, which should be three feet long. Two of these feet must be thrust into the ground, having first widened a hole with a crow, or some such instrument, to prevent the bark being rubbed off by the foot. The distance at which these should be set, is one yard. But, at the time of the first falling, the planter must not expect to remove every other tree. Many of the truncheons will not grow; neither have I ever seen a coppice raised this way so luxurious and beautiful as those reared from regular plants.

After these truncheons are first planted, the weeds should be kept down, till they are shot out of their reach. And after every fall, in the following winter, the stools ought to be looked over, and all the weak side-branches taken off. This will strengthen those which are already the strongest, and will enable them to shoot up more vigorously for poles. ALDER.

Age most proper for felling.

Alders planted by the sides of rivers, brooks, &c. may be cut every eight or ten years, which will produce good profit, as well as keep the river in its proper channel.

# CHAP. III.

## *SALIX*, The WILLOW-TREE.

IT is generally allowed, that few trees grow faster than the Willow. Indeed, its generical name, *Salix*, which is taken from the Latin verb *salio, to leap* or *jump*, plainly alludes to this tree bounding, as it were, in a very few years, to the greatest height.

There are many kinds of the willow, which are propagated for various purposes, according to their nature. Some are designed to be cut every year, for the basket-makers; some every third year, for hurdles; some are propagated for poles, and others for the sake of their timber; though I would recommend always to have some of these trees in plantations for amusement and shade; not only on account of their forming an agreeable variety, but as their shade has been antiently reputed chaste, this may perhaps inspire pious meditations on that cardinal virtue.

Uses for which the timber is serviceable.

The uses of the different sorts of willow and sallow, put together, are almost infinite. They are converted into baskets, flaskets, sieves, bands, lattices, cages, hampers, cradles, handles for rakes, forks, mops, &c. hop poles, chairs, gunstocks, half-pikes, shoemakers lasts, heels, clogs for pattens, goldsmiths and apothecaries boxes, trenchers, trays, dressers, cart-saddle-trees, harrows, bodies of coaches and waggons, &c. &c.

The sort proper to be planted for timber has an exceeding fine grain, is smooth, polishes well, and being sawed into boards makes the most elegant sort of flooring and wainscoting; for which purposes I have known a tree of the common willow, the wood of which is exceeding white, sold for between five and six pounds, that grew from being originally a common hedge-stake.

Class and order in the Linnæan system. Time of the flowering and leaves opening.

The botanist will find the willow to belong to the class and order *Dioecia Diandria*, and will see a great variety of them in the hedges and fields, woods and bogs. The flowers of that species called the sallow make their appearance about the eleventh of March, when they will be full blown; and the leaves will be out by the seventh of April. The leaves of the weeping willow are to be seen about the first of that month; the buds of the white willow by the tenth of April will be swelled, and by the eighteenth the leaves will be quite out, and the flowers full blown. The catkins of the sallow are formed about the fifth of October.

I proceed now to shew the method of raising these trees for their various uses. And, first, to raise a good ozier-bed.

Manner of raising a good ozier bed.

Previous to planting, the ground should be dug over, or ploughed, the latter of which is not so beneficial as the former, though least expensive. The cuttings must then be procured; and altho' they should consist chiefly of the true ozier kinds, yet other sorts must be introduced into this ozier-bed, to make it compleat, and more useful to the basket-maker, who will want the different sorts for the different purposes in his trade. Besides the true ozier, of which the plantation is chiefly to consist, there must be the sallow, the long-shooting green willow, the crane willow, the golden willow, the silver willow, the Welsh wicker, &c. by which names they are best known.

The cuttings should be of two-years wood, though the bottom parts of the strongest one-year's shoots may do. They ought to be two feet and a half long, a foot and a half of which should be thrust into the ground, and the other foot remain for the stool. These cuttings should be put in at two feet two inches distance each way; and all the summer following the weeds must be kept under; the summer after that also the tallest of the weeds should be hacked down. The willows must continue growing for three years, when they should be all cut down to the first-planted head. They will sell well to the hurdle-makers, and there will be a regular quantity of proper stools left, to exhibit an annual crop of twigs, which will be worth five or six pounds, or more, per acre, to be sold to the basket-makers. But the prices of the twigs are greater or less, in proportion to the nature of the situation. Watery ground, by the sides of navigable rivers, planted in this manner, will produce a greater price per acre, because there are generally near such places greater numbers of basket-makers, and having the conveniency of water-carriage, the twigs may with ease be sent to distant quarters.

Plantations of these kinds may not only be regularly made to great advantage on watery land, by the sides of rivers, but the very islands, or any part where there is mud or earth, may be planted this way, to the great profit of the proprietors, which would otherwise produce nothing

WILLOW

nothing. And here ſuffer me to give one caution in the planting of theſe places. Let the rows, which ſhould always run the ſame way with the ſtream, be at a greater diſtance from each other, and the cuttings proportionably cloſer in the rows. I adviſe the diſtance of the rows being greater in theſe places, that the floods may have free liberty to carry off ſedge, filth, &c. which would otherwiſe be detained by the ſetts, to their great prejudice.

Plantations of willows deſigned for hurdles, &c. ſhould be raiſed in the ſame manner as the preceding, and cut every ſecond or third year, which will be a great improvement to all ſorts of boggy or watery places.

Plantations of willows to be cut down every ſix or ſeven years for poles, ſhould likewiſe be raiſed by the abovementioned method, remembering that the diſtance the ſetts ſhould be placed at ought to be greater, viz. one yard aſunder.

Method of raiſing a Salictum

To raiſe a *Salictum*, or a plantation of willows for timber, the ground alſo muſt be dug or ploughed, and the cuttings for this purpoſe ſhould be of the laſt year's ſhoot. They ought to be a foot and a half long, and a foot of each ſhould be thruſt into the ground, at the diſtance of three feet each way. At the latter end of May, or the beginning of June, the plantation requires to be looked over, when ſuch ſetts as have ſhot out many branches ſhould have them all taken off, except the ſtrongeſt leading ſhoot. All this ſummer and the next the weeds muſt be kept down. Afterwards, the trees will demand no farther care till the time of thinning, which will be in about five or ſix years. When the branches interfere with each other, the weakeſt tree ſhould be grubbed up and taken away, to make room for the remainder. In five or ſix years more they will require a ſecond thinning. In this manner they muſt be continued to be thinned as often as they approach to touch one another, till the trees are arrived to their full maturity. By planting the cuttings a yard aſunder at firſt, and afterwards thinning of them, they not only draw each other up, and by that means aſpire to a great height, but the plants taken away to make room for the ſtrongeſt will be a conſiderable ready ſale for poles, &c.

The common white and red willow recommended for plantations

The ſorts uſed for plantations of theſe trees have hitherto been our common white and red willow. Theſe, however, ſeem now to give place to more ſorts, which have been lately introduced. A few years ago I ſaw in the public papers an advertiſement of a willow which would grow large enough for maſts of ſhips, &c. in twenty or thirty years, and in another paper there was an account, that theſe trees might be ſeen in full maturity at one Squire Angel's, about three miles from Weſtminſter-Bridge. I went to examine them; but when I came found them the common white willows, which, having liked the ſituation, had grown to a great ſize and beauty. I enquired out the author of the advertiſement, but found he knew nothing of the nature of theſe willows, and that he had his account from a baſket-maker near Weſtminſter-Bridge. Upon applying to the baſket-maker, he diſavowed knowing any thing of the trees growing by Mr. Angel's, but ſaid he had two ſorts of willows, which would anſwer in every reſpect to the firſt advertiſement, that they were of all others the freeſt ſhooters, that they were not ſo ſubject to rot in the ſides as the large white willow-tree, but that they would grow ſound to timber fit for maſts of ſhips, &c. in leſs than thirty years. He added, that he had the cuttings many years ago brought him from the coaſt of France by a captain whoſe name I have forgot. I immediately procured ſome cuttings of theſe ſorts, which grow to a miracle, and ſeem as if they would anſwer the promiſed expectation, ſo that now theſe are the trees of which our future timber-plantations ſhould conſiſt. Nay, whether they are deſigned for the baſket-makers or for hurdles, they ought to have their ſhare, and ſhould always be preferred to be planted out for ſtandards for lopping, by the ſides of rivers, rills, ditches, &c. The cuttings of theſe two ſorts have been diſperſed into almoſt every quarter of England, ſo that there is no doubt but that in a few years the planting of them alone for timber will become general, as they may be encreaſed at pleaſure, by every ſlip or twig.

Setts proper to be planted by the ſides of ditches, &c. for pollards, ſhould be nine feet in length, two feet and a half of which muſt be thruſt into the ground, having firſt prepared the way by driving down a crow, or ſome ſuch inſtrument, to prevent the bark, though the end be ſharpened, from ſeparating from the fleſh. After they are planted, they ſhould be thorned from cattle, and in five or ſix years they will be fit for lopping, and thus may be continued to be lopped every fifth or ſixth year, to the improvement of ditch-ſides, water-gutters, &c. were it only for the fuel, as it emits little ſmoke, is remarkably ſweet, burns pure and clear to the laſt, and is therefore proper for ladies chambers, and ſuch people as are curious in procuring the ſweeteſt ſorts of fire.

Willows ſhould be planted in the autumn, and may be continued all winter, but ought never to be deferred longer than the month of February, as the following year's ſhoots would not only be retarded, but the ſtools from whence they were taken greatly injured. — Beſt ſeaſon for planting willows

Theſe are the principal of the Engliſh Aquatics. But beſides theſe, there are many others, of foreign growth, which might be introduced into all moiſt places, to the great advantage of the owners, ſuch as the Deciduous Cypreſs, the Swamp-Pine, &c. whoſe culture is exhibited in their reſpective places.

# PART III.

## Of EVERGREEN FOREST-TREES;

O R,

## Such as retain their Verdure during the Winter Months.

### CHAP. I

### *PINUS CEDRUS,* The CEDAR-TREE of LEBANON

Introductory observations

THE Cedar of Lebanon is now very justly ranked with the Pines, an arrangement which the practical gardener perhaps will not approve at first, nevertheless, he will soon be acquainted with the propriety of the station it occupies in the present system

This antient and glorious tree, famous for being celebrated in Holy Writ, is a native of the mount whose name it bears, though that is not the only place where it naturally grows, for it is found upon Mount Taurus, Amanus, &c but not in great quantities, and indeed, Mount Lebanon seems to be the chief seat of its residence Solomon is said to have brought a great number of cones from Lebanon at the time he fetched the wood for the building of the Temple, and to have raised great quantities of these trees in Judæa

Many nations are possessed of this tree, though it has been cultivated in England very sparingly till of late years when its superlative beauties, as well as the value of its timber, attracted the planter's attention And as we have many trees in this country which bear cones that perfect their seeds, we may propagate it with spirit, since we shall no longer be at the extraordinary expence of procuring the cones from Mount Lebanon, as those of our own growth, though not so large, produce seeds which come up very well

It appearance described

The cedar tree is not only noble and of large bulk, but the branches are produced in a most agreeable form, growing horizontally, and spreading themselves abroad in a free and singular manner, so that the allusion of the Royal Psalmist is natural and easy, when he saith, *She spreadeth forth her branches as the cedar-tree*

The leaves of the cedar grow in pencils, like the larch, and the extremities of its branches are declining These contribute to give it, wherever planted among other beauties, a most pleasing effect, especially when, waving with the wind, they alternately discover the upper and under green, thereby exciting admiration in the curious observer of Nature's works and as this tree is so beautiful, noble, and lofty, every one must see the propriety of planting it for pleasure grounds of all sorts, as well as for timber In short, they will find no tree better adapted to beautify their environs, or that will exhibit a more pleasing appearance in parks or open places, or in terminating views, &c

Valuable properties of its timber

It is unnecessary to enlarge upon the value of the timber of the cedar It was greatly used in the building of Solomon's temple, which at once convinces us of its superlative excellence It is said to continue found for two thousand years, and we are told, that in the Temple of Apollo at Utica there was found cedar-wood of that age The magnificent temples of the Pagans, as well as those of the true God, were chiefly built of this famous timber The statue of the Great Goddess at Ephesus was made of this material, and if this tree abounded with us in great plenty, it might have a principal share in our most superb edifices The effluvia constantly emitted from its wood are said to purify the air, and make rooms wholesome Chapels and places set apart for religious duties, being wainscotted with this wood, inspire the worshippers with a more solemn awe It is not obnoxious to worms, and emits an oil which will preserve cloth or books from worms or corruption The sawdust will preserve human bodies from putrefaction, and is therefore said to be plentifully used in the rites of embalming, where practised

Extraordinary marks of veneration paid to the remaining cedars of Mount Libanus

There are said to be a few cedar-trees remaining still upon Mount Lebanon, which are preserved with a religious strictness For we are informed, from the Memoirs of the Missionaries in the Levant, that upon the day of the Transfiguration, the patriarch of the Maronites (Christians inhabiting Mount Libanus) repairs to these cedars, attended by a number of bishops, priests, and monks, followed by five or six thousand of their religious from all parts, where he celebrates that festival which is now called "The Feast of Cedars" We are also told, that the patriarch officiates pontifically on this solemn occasion, that his followers are particularly mindful of the Blessed Virgin on this day, because the Scripture compares her to the cedars of Lebanon and that the same holy father threatens with ecclesiastical censures those who presume to hurt or diminish the cedars still remaining

Ir

*CEDAR. Differ in accounts of travellers respecting the number of cedar-trees remaining on Mount Libanus. Number mentioned to be standing by Rauwolf,*

It is strange that travellers should vary so much in their account of the number of these remaining trees, and this difference has occasioned some persons to believe they cannot be numbered, like the stones which compose our Stonehenge on Salisbury-Plain.

Rauwolf, who lived near a century ago, says, that he counted upon this Mount twenty-six trees only, twenty four of which grew in a circle, the other two standing at a small distance. He also remarks, that their branches seemed to be decayed with age, and that he could find no young trees coming up to succeed them.

*Maundrel,*

Maundrel, another traveller, acquaints us, he saw only sixteen trees remaining on this Mountain, some of which were of prodigious size, and that having measured one of them, he found it twelve yards six inches in circumference. He adds, that there were several others of a smaller size.

*Le Brun,*

Monsieur Le Brun, another gentleman who visited this place, observes, that he counted thirty six trees on Mount Libanon when he was there.

*and Thompson.*

Thompson, in his Travels, relates, that when he arrived at the cedars, not far from the highest part of Libanus, he found many of them remarkable for their age and prodigious bulk, and that there were many young ones of a smaller size. "Of the old ones, which are large, says he, there are only sixteen, one of which we measured, and found it near thirteen yards in circumference, and its branches spreading every way round it for about forty paces. Five or six yards from the ground, the trunk divides itself into five limbs, each of them as big as a large tree." He adds, however, that there are few of the cedars of these vast dimensions.

But perhaps it may be said, that, by dwelling upon these particulars, I digress from my purpose. I shall therefore proceed to the culture and management of this celebrated tree.

*Method of propagating this tree.*

Having procured the cones, whether from the Levant or of our own growth, the seeds, a little before sowing, should be got out in this manner. Let a hole be bored with a passer exactly up the center of each cone, from the base to the apex, put them into a tub of water, where they may remain till the next day, then having a wooden peg, rather bigger than the passer, let it be thrust down the hole, and it will so divide the cones, that the different scales may be taken away, and the seeds picked out. In doing this, great care must be taken not to bruise and hurt the seeds, which will then be very tender.

The soil in which you sow these seeds should be rather of a sandy nature, or, for want of this, some mould taken fresh from a rich pasture, and sieved with a little drift sand, will serve the purpose.

Having the mould and seeds ready, in the beginning of March let the latter be sown in pots or boxes near half an inch deep. In about seven or eight weeks the plants will come up, when they should be removed into the shade from the heat of the sun, where they may stand, but not under shelter, all the summer, during which time they should be kept clean of weeds, and watered now and then. In the winter season they must be removed into a warmer situation, or, if it is likely to prove very severe, they should be sheltered either by mats, or removed into the greenhouse, or covered with an hotbed frame, for they are subject to lose their young tops at first, by the severity of frosts.

*CEDAR.*

In the beginning of April following, these plants may be pricked out in beds four inches asunder, and if the weather proves dry, they should be shaded and watered, till they have taken root, after which they will want little shading and less watering. Indeed, nothing more is required than keeping them clean from weeds, and covering the ground so as to keep it moist, and prevent its chapping by the sun's rays. In these beds they may remain two years, when, in the spring, they should be transplanted to the nursery, where they may remain till they are planted out for good.

During the time they are in the nursery, and after planting out, many will frequently have a tendency to droop in their leading-shoot. As soon, therefore, as this is perceived, an upright stake must be driven into the ground, to which the shoots should often be tied with bass matting to keep them in their upright growth. This, however, will not always effect it, for I have known some, after being tied, so effectually turn the shoot downwards over the bandage, though loose, as to appear as if they were beat down on purpose. The larch tree, which is nearly allied to this species, will sometimes rebel in this way, as has been observed. So that I think it would not be amiss, in both cases, whenever they first discover any signs of such a tendency, to lighten the head, by nipping off the extremities of some few of the largest branches.

When these trees are planted out for good, they should be left to Nature, after being properly fenced. Not a knife nor a hatchet should come near them, lopping even their lowest branches is so injurious, that it both retards their growth and diminishes their beauty.

*Grows well on almost all soils and situations.*

The cedar of Lebanon will grow well in almost any sort of soil or situation. As a proof of this, we need only observe, that in its native situation the roots are during part of the year covered with frost and snow, for in the month of December the snow begins to fall, and the Mount remains frozen and covered with snow till the month of April, when it begins to melt, and continues thawing till the end of July, by which time it is all vanished. And here I cannot help remarking the goodness of Divine Providence over all his creatures throughout the globe, and particularly to the neighbouring inhabitants of this Mount, for by causing the snow to fall and remain on it during the winter months, and to melt in the heat of summer, it thus forms rivulets, and affords water to the inhabitants dwelling in the vallies below, who would otherwise experience a fatal want of this useful element.

From this tree thriving well in such a place we learn, that few soils or situations, as above observed, disagree with it, so that, as we have cedar-trees which bear cones in great plenty, it is to be hoped, that gentlemen of fortune will not be contented merely with beautifying and ornamenting their environs with them, but will plant them for profit, even on their most bleak and barren hills and mountains.

Thus may every gentleman have a Mount Libanus of his own, to his great respect and praise in particular, as well as, were there many of them planted throughout the kingdom, to the honour of the nation in general.

CHAP.

# CHAP. II.

## *PINUS SYLVESTRIS*, The PINE, or SCOTCH FIR-TREE.

*Situations proper for this tree.*

THAT species of the Pine called the Scotch Fir is the hardiest of all the sorts, and is most proper to be planted by the sides of high hills, to beautify and enliven the scene in that dreary season when Nature looks comfortless and ghastly, as well as in woods for the sake of its timber. By these the eye will be relieved, and the imagination cheared, when, after looking on the deciduous and seemingly weeping part of the creation, it is turned to a plantation of these trees, which will represent a perpetual spring, or the sweet encreasing verdure of the summer months. The Scotch fir, therefore, is a very proper tree for plantations of all kinds, whether great or small, though I must own a few of them together are far from producing such a pleasing effect as large plantations, neither can I recommend planting out a few odd ones for standards, either in fields, lawns, or parks.

The species of pine I am treating of is called by us the Scotch Fir, because it grows naturally on the Highlands of Scotland, where the seeds falling from their cones come up and propagate themselves without any care. But it is not in Scotland only that these trees thrive naturally, for they grow spontaneously in Denmark, Norway, and Sweden.

*All soils suitable to it.*

And tho' from the above instances it would seem that they delighted principally in these northern parts, yet when the plants are properly raised and planted out, no climate comes amiss to them, for they will thrive and grow to be good timber trees in almost any part of the world.

*Uses to which the timber is applicable.*

The timber of the Scotch fir is what we call Deal, which is sometimes red, sometimes yellowish, but chiefly white, and in all the colours is a wood of high value and worth. Every one knows the use of these deals for flooring, doors, and wainscotting; for trees to lay under the leads in churches, which being always kept dry, they will last almost as long as oak; for boxes or chests, for masts of ships, and so many other uses, both in the shipwright's, joiner's, and carpenter's way, that it is needless to recite them.

*Derivation of the generical name.*

The generical word, *Pinus*, is formed by the change of a letter, namely *t* into *n*, in the Greek word πιτυς, which signifies *a pitch tree*, and the tree is so denominated, because of some species of it pitch and tar are made.

*Class and order in the Linnæan system.*

The flowers of the pine are, both male and female, on the same plant, and as the stamina are joined in one body at their base, the tree is entitled to the class and order *Monoecia Monadelphia*.

*Time when the flowers and buds appear.*

The flowers of the Scotch fir begin to open by the twenty-second of April, and will be in full blow by the seventh of May. By the eighteenth of April, the buds of this tree will be greatly swelled, and soon after it begins its shoot with such rapidity, as to be able to perform its whole summer's shoot by the beginning of July; for this tree, near to the horse-chesnut, makes its summer's shoot in the least time, and altho' it is often a yard in length, yet is this effected in little more than the space of two months. The remaining part of the summer is employed in strengthening itself, and forming the eyes strong and bold, to push vigorously a second course in the months of May and June following.

*Manner of propagating this tree.*

The Scotch fir is propagated by seeds, of which their cones afford great plenty. In order to get them out, the cones, which must be gathered in winter, should be preserved till the month of July, when, in a hot day, they should be all brought forth, and exposed to the utmost heat of the sun. This will occasion their scales to open, so that the seeds will easily shake out. A large carpet or oil-cloth is a very proper thing to lay them on, which will save the seeds that drop by turning the cones; for as often as the scales on one side of them are opened, the other side should be turned to the sun, to receive the same effect.

This is the method of procuring great quantities of these seeds, which will be ready to sow the spring following. But when numbers of these cones are obtained, and a gentleman, having his ground ready for their reception, is unwilling to wait another year before he sows his seeds, as there will be little sun by the time they should be sown, the cones may be laid before a gentle fire at some distance, which will occasion their scales to open, and the seeds to fall out of their cells. However, this manner of procuring the seeds is not so good as the former, because some of them will be in danger of being scorched, though the utmost care be taken; so that I would advise, when it is practised, not to wait till all the scales of each cone are opened, but, as soon as a few begin to gape, to beat what seeds you can out, and then proceed to the next in like manner, till you have got seeds sufficient. By this means, the fire will not have time to injure the seeds much, and you may be certain of what you have being pretty good. Here I take it for granted you are not in want of cones. If there are few cones, and many seeds are wanted, the additional labour of cutting off the scales close to the center must be applied.

But to proceed. Having obtained a quantity of good seeds, the best season for sowing them is the middle of March. The weather ought to be warm, and dry at the time, and the mould fine and light. Beds should be made in the seminary three or four feet wide, and the seeds must be sown in these at a little more than a quarter of an inch deep. In about six weeks, the young firs will appear with the husk of the seeds on their heads, and now is the time to watch them carefully; for if the sparrows and other birds once take to them, they will destroy every plant as it comes up; nay, so fond are they of the husks on the young plant's first appearing, that having once tasted them, no scarecrow will terrify them, or arts keep them off. In order, therefore, to secure your crop of firs, it would be proper to have them, soon after they are sown, well netted, and strings of sewelling drawn across, that before they have any temptation, the birds may be frightened to other quarters,

ters, and the plants at their firſt appearance remain unnoticed by them As ſoon as all the plants are come up, and have parted with the huſks off their heads, the nets and ſewelling may be taken off, for the ſeedlings will be then entirely out of danger

All this ſummer they will need no farther care than being kept clean from weeds, and in the latter end of March, or beginning of April following, they ſhould be taken out of theſe beds, and pricked in others three or four inches diſtance At the time of their being firſt pricked out, being one year old from the ſeeds, you will find they have made no ſhoot, but are ſlender plants with ſmall weak eyes, and by the ſpring following, being two years from ſowing, few of them alſo will have made a ſhoot, but they will have employed this ſummer in ſtrengthening the eye in order to make a bold puſh the ſummer enſuing, which will be in height about half a foot The ſpring after, they ſhould undergo a ſecond removal, into the nurſery, where they ought to be planted a foot aſunder, and at two feet diſtance in the rows, and this ſummer they will have ſhot another half foot In the ſpring following, being now four years old, and one foot in height, if the ground deſigned for the plantation is ready, and there are no rabbits or hares, they may be planted out for good But where theſe animals can get to them, I would adviſe their remaining in the nurſery another year or two, till they are out of their reach, as I have frequently known plantations of theſe ſmall plants wholly deſtroyed the winter after planting by hares, &c It, therefore, they are ſuffered to remain another year in the nurſery, having acquired ſtrength of body, they will make a ſhoot that ſummer of near two feet, ſo that the plants, at five years old, will be about a yard high, which is a good ſize for removing

If they ſtand another year, till they are ſix years old, they will ſhoot about two feet more, and be near five feet in height But here it is to be obſerved, that the larger theſe trees grow, the more difficulty there will be in removing them, and where they are of a tolerable height, many will be loſt in their removal, though the utmoſt care be taken Having, however, fixed on the height of your trees, according to the nature of your ground, or your ſecurity from hares, &c and the ground having borne a crop of grain, if it is to be planted with trees a foot or two high, muſt be ploughed to bury the weeds, and the plants ſhould be ſet one yard aſunder But if you intend to plant it with larger plants, there will be no occaſion for ploughing, as they will be out of the reach of weeds, only let holes be made, and the trees ſet one yard aſunder all over it And altho' this may appear too cloſe, yet as there will be a great hazard of loſing many of theſe large trees, the growing ones by the ſpring following may probably ſhew themſelves not too near However, this ſhould not diſcourage thoſe gentlemen who are deſirous of having an immediate ſhew, for if the plants be properly removed every two years in the nurſery way, they may be tranſplanted with reaſonable hopes of ſucceſs, even at a great height Neither ſhould they be alarmed becauſe a large tree and a ſmaller being ſometimes planted together, the ſmall one has quickly overtaken the large one, and outſtript it, for though this may happen, yet the cauſe is eaſily demonſtrated The larger plant might have taken ſuch footing in the nurſery, that the removing it was like tranſporting a man into a different clime, ſo that if ſuch a tree lives, it will be ſome years before it can recover itſelf ſo as to make a good ſhoot But where firs have been regularly removed every two years, a ſmall one can never overtake a larger, if the ſoil and ſituation be equal Both will make a ſmall ſhoot the firſt year, the next year's will be longer, and in this manner they will keep their regular diſtance, as I have found in many experiments I have made of theſe trees, by planting of different growths at the ſame time I have hitherto perceived them to maintain their ſtation, if the larger had always been properly removed Nay, I have ſome few growing at preſent, that have been planted this way for trial, in which the large ſeem to be much finer trees in proportion And what wonder? for being kept removing every two years, they not only throw out a great number of fibres, but ſtrengthen in the body In this always conſiſts the difference between plants properly raiſed in the nurſery, and thoſe that have never been tranſplanted The former will ever be thick at the bottom, and continue tapering to the top, like an acute cone, with a ſmall baſe, whereas the latter will always have very ſlender ſtems, even when the tree is at a great height, which ſhews the neceſſity of pricking theſe plants out in the ſeminary the ſpring after they come up, and of continuing to remove them every two years, till they are planted out for good

The beſt ſeaſon for making plantations of theſe trees is early in the month of September, for if they are planted in the beginning of that month, they will have taken to the ground before the winter comes on, and having the mould thoroughly ſettled by the winter's rains, &c to the roots, ſhould a dry ſpring afterwards happen, they will receive leſs injury from the drought March alſo is a good time for removing theſe trees, nay, they may be tranſplanted in any of the winter months with tolerable hopes of ſucceſs But whenever this is done, they muſt be taken out of the nurſery with great care, the holes ſhould be ready made, that they may be out of the ground as little time as poſſible, and in planting them, the fineſt mould ſhould be laid to their fibres, which ought to be ſpread in their proper places, that they may not be clotted together, which would cauſe them to get mouldy If theſe precautions are obſerved, and the earth be afterwards gently preſſed down with the foot to ſettle it firm, there will not be much fear of the plants ſucceeding

(Margin: September beſt ſeaſon for planting theſe trees, and March moſt proper for tranſplanting or removing them)

After the plantation is made, it will require no farther trouble or expence than keeping the fences good (unleſs the trees be ſo large at firſt as to require being ſtaked, to prevent their being blown aſide by the winds, which I by no means adviſe) till they want thinning Not a ſingle under-branch ſhould be cut off, for the growth of the tree will be retarded in proportion to the number of branches taken away In about ſeven years, the plantation will want thinning This, however, muſt be done ſparingly at firſt, only the weakeſt trees and the underlings ſhould be cut out, that the remainder may ſtill ſtand pretty cloſe, to draw one another up to a greater height, for it is the length of this wood when felled that greatly enhances its value Two or three years after you may repeat the operation of cutting down ſuch trees as appear unhealthy, for there will be no occaſion of grubbing up their roots, as they will never ſhoot out again And in this manner a few of the weakeſt may be cut out every year, which will ſell well for ladders, ſcaffolding poles, &c Thus ſhould the plantation be continued to be thinned as often as you ſee occaſion, till the trees are grown to their full maturity, which, by being raised in this manner, will aspire to a prodigious height, be as straight as an arrow, and consequently of more value for masts of ships boards, &c

Soils in which it thrives best

The Scotch fir will thrive upon almost any soil or situation It grows fastest, indeed, in a rich moist soil, but it makes surprizing progress in clays of all sorts, it will grow upon the tops of mountains and rocks, where there is little more than the crevices for the roots to strike into, and I have known it extremely luxuriant in little islands in the midst of ponds, it shews no disdain to all sandy and stony ground, and will succeed on barren heaths, where hardly any thing but heath or furze will grow Considerations which deserve the serious attention of every one possessed of such land, as he may by this means improve it to a great amount

# C H A P. III

## *PINUS PINEASTER*, The WILD PINE-TREE

THE *Pineaster* is another species of Pine which grows to a monstrous size, and therefore claims a place in all sorts of evergreen timber plantations, whether designed for pleasure or profit, and altho' the wood is not quite so valuable as that of the Scotch fir, yet it has its uses This pine is a quick grower, has long leaves of a pleasant green colour, and is therefore well adapted to enhance the beauty by encreasing the variety of evergreen plantations

A fast growing tree

Affords pitch turpentine and resin

This tree affords pitch, turpentine, and resin An oil of turpentine is distilled from the common sort, and in this operation, that which comes first pure and good, is the spirit of turpentine, whilst what is found remaining in the still is the common resin

The *Pineaster*, when it grows large, is subject to throw out large branches, especially where there are few of them and this has occasioned the tree's being disliked by some persons But as these branches, though appearing naked, have a pleasing majesty, awe, and grandeur, and the leaves are larger, thicker, and longer than the Scotch fir, these additional perfections make amends, in my opinion, for the seeming defect of such large branches presenting themselves unfurnished with leaves

Uses to which the timber is applicable

The timber of the wild pine is serviceable in many parts of carpenters and joiners work, it is useful for the wainscoting of rooms, may be sawn into good boards for flooring, and altho, as was before observed, it is not quite so valuable as the Scotch fir, yet is this tree by no means to be neglected planting on that account, as the purposes for which its wood is wanted are many and various

The Pineaster a native of Italy, and used for covering houses in Switzerland

The *Pineaster* is a native of Italy, though it abounds in the South of France, and in Switzerland, where there is great plenty of these trees, the inhabitants cut them into shingles for the covering of their houses, which soon becomes so compact and close, by the sun's diffusing the resinous substance, as to be proof against all weather

Manner of propagating this tree

This tree may be raised in the same manner as the Scotch fir, and the cones should be prepared, and the seeds obtained, according to the directions given for that tree They should also be sown at the same time, and in about six weeks the young plants will appear They will have made a short shoot this summer, and in the middle of the ensuing one, they should be pricked out in the nursery, in beds at a foot asunder each way Rainy and cloudy weather is the time for this work, and as the sun at that season frequently breaks out in hot gleams, so as to destroy the young-planted trees, the beds should be hooped for their preservation, and covered with mats, till they have taken root I do not doubt but that advising the planting of trees in the middle of summer, when the winter has always been reputed the only time for that work, will appear strange to many But I can certainly inform such sceptics, that I have planted these trees, in fine moist weather, hooping and matting them in the heat of the day, uncovering them in the night, refreshing them with gentle waterings as they required, I have planted the young trees, I say, in this season and in this manner, not only with success, but many of them have seemed not to droop, as if they had never perceived their removal After your plants are taken to the ground, they will want no farther care than keeping them clean of weeds, till the latter end of August, or beginning of April twelve month following, in either of which months they should be planted out for good, if possible and if the ground cannot be got ready for their reception, they must undergo a second removal in the nursery way, otherwise almost all will be sure to die when planted out, for it is difficult to make this tree thrive when grown pretty large, if it has not been used to constant moving

The distance at which these trees should be set from each other when planted out for good ought to be one yard, and they should be afterwards thinned, and managed as was directed for the Scotch fir

The wild pine will thrive, when once it has taken to the ground, in almost any soil So that whoever is desirous of encreasing the variety of his evergreen timber plantations with these trees, need not be anxious about the nature of the ground in which they are to stand. Thrives well upon most soils

## CHAP. IV.

### *PINUS STROBUS*, The WEYMOUTH PINE-TREE.

*Situation moſt proper for this tree.*

THIS is a tree of admirable uſe and beauty, and well adapted for huge evergreen plantations of any kind. If it is planted in parks or open places, we find it growing up remarkably ſtraight, with annual ſhoots of two feet or more in length. The leaves are of a fine green colour, long and ſlender, beautifully adorning their branches, and the bark is perfectly ſmooth and fine. Properties which entitle this pine to be ranked in the firſt claſs of the moſt beautiful trees of this tribe.

*Height to which it grows.*

But theſe are not the only reaſons why the *Pinus Strobus* ſhould be planted. I am now treating of timber trees, and this tree ſurely claims a place on that account, as it will grow to a prodigious magnitude, more than a hundred feet high, and makes ſuch excellent maſts for ſhips, that the legiſlature, in the reign of Queen Anne, enacted a law enforcing the encouragement of the growth of theſe trees in America, where they abound.

Weymouth pines were ſparingly propagated in England till of late years, on account of the great price of their ſeeds, which were all imported from abroad, and ſold extremely dear; but as ſome trees have been introduced into our Engliſh gardens near forty years ago, we have now plenty of ſeeds perfected in our own country, not only from thoſe of the old ſeſt ſtanding, but from younger trees, ſo that as the ſeeds may be eaſily obtained, I entertain hopes this pine will be raiſed in proportionably larger quantities.

*Uſes to which the timber is applied.*

This tree is called in North America, where it grows naturally, the White Pine; and reaſon will ſuggeſt to every man, that the timber is not only ſerviceable for the navy, but for other uſes, as it certainly is for flooring, wainſcoting, boxes, bellies for harpſichords, and muſical inſtruments of all ſorts, doors, bolts, &c.

The cones of this tree for the ſeeds ſhould always be gathered in the winter, for being very long and looſe, the ſcales will open and emit the ſeeds at the earlieſt influences of the ſpring ſun; ſo that unleſs timely care is taken to gather them from the trees ſoon enough, a ſeaſon may eaſily be loſt.

*Method of propagating the tree.*

The ſeeds of the Weymouth pine are larger than thoſe of the Scotch fir, and in order to raiſe the young plants, it will be proper to ſow them in pots or boxes, which may be removed into the ſhade after the plants are come up, when the ſun's rays are violent. If they are ſown in beds of fine light earth, they ſhould be hooped, and conſtantly covered with mats from the ſun's heat, and as carefully uncovered when he ſets. In about ſix or ſeven weeks after ſowing, the young plants will appear, when they ſhould be regularly guarded from birds, as was directed for the Scotch fir, otherwiſe all your ſeeds, time, and trouble, will be loſt; for if the birds take to them at their firſt coming up, and are unmoleſted, they will not leave a ſingle plant.

The plants being now above ground, the weeds ſhould be conſtantly picked out, as they appear, leſt the fibres of their roots mixing with thoſe of the firs, many of theſe latter be drawn out with them. In dry weather they ſhould be refreſhed with water. But this muſt be done ſparingly, and with the utmoſt caution; for as the ſtems of the young plants are very ſlender, by over watering they are frequently thrown aſide, which they hardly ever recover. Thus I have known gentlemen, who, in attempting to raiſe theſe trees, have ſeen the young plants go off without perceiving the cauſe; and the more watering and pains they have taken, have found the plants periſh in this way more and more, to their great mortification and aſtoniſhment.

In the ſpring following theſe plants ſhould be pricked out in beds half a foot aſunder each way; and here they may ſtand two years, when they may be either planted out for good, or removed into the nurſery, at the diſtance of one foot aſunder, and two feet in the rows. If the plantation is to conſiſt of ſmall plants, which are the beſt if hares and rabbits can be kept out, the ground ought to be prepared as was directed for the Scotch fir, and the plants managed accordingly; but if it is to be formed of larger trees, they muſt be raiſed by removing in the nurſery every other year, like the Scotch firs, and when planted out for good ſhould receive the ſame management, till they arrive at their full maturity. If care has been taken of them in the nurſery, they may be removed at a conſiderable height with great aſſurance of ſucceſs; for it is much eaſier to make this pine grow than any of the other ſorts. So that where they are wanted for ornament in parks, open places, &c. a ſhow of them may be made in a little time.

*Soils proper for it.*

The ſoil the Weymouth pine delights in moſt is a ſandy loam; but it likes other ſoils of an inferior nature; and altho' it is not generally to be planted on all lands, like the Scotch fir, yet I have ſeen it luxuriant and healthy, making ſtrong ſhoots, on blue and red clays, and other ſorts of ſtrong ground. On ſtony and ſlaty ground, likewiſe, I have ſeen ſome very fine trees. So that I believe whoever is deſirous of having plantations of this pine, need not be curious in the choice of his ground.

## CHAP V

### *PINUS TÆDA*, The SWAMP-PINE-TREE

*Situations proper for this tree, Its appearance described*

THE Swamp-Pine is a very large-growing tree, and is highly proper, as its name imports, to be planted in moist places

The leaves are long, of a delightful green colour, three issue out of each sheath, and adorn the younger branches in great plenty

*Uses of its timber*

The timber is of equal value with most of the other sorts of pine, either for boards, traces, or any carpentry uses

*Method of propagating this tree.*

Its propagation is the same as the Weymouth pine, and the planting out, and after-management of the trees, should be exactly similar

*Soils proper for it.*

It will grow well on all upland and dry grounds, but its chief delight is in moist places Here the owner will plant them to the greatest advantage, and if there are contiguous hills planted with Scotch firs and other kinds, the different greens will produce a delightful contrast

## CHAP VI

### *PINUS PINEA*, The STONE-PINE-TREE

*Its appearance described*

THE Stone-Pine is a tree of which there should be a few in all plantations of ever greens It will grow to a considerable height, and arises with a straight and fair stem, though with a rough bark The leaves will contribute to the diversifying of the scene, as they differ in colour from any of the preceding sorts, and are arranged in a different manner The cones which it bears are monstrously large, and, being noted, strike the eye by their bold appearance when hanging on the trees, and afford pleasure upon being more closely examined, from the beautiful arrangement of their scales They produce a kernel as large as an almond, and as sweet to the taste Formerly they were kept in the shops, and sold for restoratives, but are at present neglected

*A native of Italy*

*The kernels salutary in coughs &c*

This tree is a native of Italy, where the kernels are served up in desserts at the table, and as they are known to prove salutary in colds, coughs, consumptions, &c I think this tree ought to be propagated for the fruit

*Uses for which the timber is serviceable*

The stone-pine may be sawed into good boards, tho the timber is generally allowed not to be quite so valuable as the before-mentioned sorts The colour is not the same in all trees, some exhibiting their timber of a very white colour, others again are yellower, and smell stronger of the turpentine The yellow sort is allowed to be the better of the two, though, doubtless, they are both useful to the joiner and the carpenter for many purposes in their way

*Method of propagating this tree*

These trees are all raised from the seeds, which may be procured from their large cones by the help of a vice, for this will so effectually break the cones, without hurting the seeds, that they may be taken out with pleasure The cones should be fresh, not older than a year or two at farthest, or the seeds will not be good for altho' it has been asserted, that the seeds of pines in general will keep in their cones many years, yet the cones of this species of pine are an exception, as the seeds are rarely found good after the cones are one year old

The season for sowing these seeds is the middle of March The weather being fine, and the ground fit for working, they should be sown about half an inch deep, in beds of fine light earth In about seven weeks the plants will appear, which must be kept clean of weeds, and now and then watered in dry weather till July, by which time they will have made a tolerable shoot In the month of July they should be taken out of the seed-beds, and pricked in others four inches asunder Rainy and cloudy weather must be made choice of for this work, and after they are planted, the beds ought to be hooped, in order to be covered with mats in the heat of the day, which, however, should be always uncovered in the night When they have taken to the ground, further covering will be needless, and here they may remain, with only now and then watering, and keeping them clear of weeds, till the spring twelvemonth following, when, in the beginning of April, they should be planted out in the nursery, in well prepared ground, a foot asunder, and at two feet distance in the rows Here they may stand two years, and then should be planted out for good. But if the trees are desired to be larger before they are brought to the spot where they are to stand, they must be kept constantly removing every two years in the nursery, for without this management this is a very difficult tree to be improved

*Soils suitable to this tree*

The stone-pine delights in a sandy loam, though, like most other pines, it will grow well in almost any land However, I would never advise the making large plantations of this tree, yet a few of them should always be admitted, to encrease the variety and strike the imagination, as the timber is useful

*Situations to which it is adapted*

They are also very proper for clumps in parks or lawns But, as I said, I would never advise the making large plantations of them, as the Scotch and Weymouth pines are more easily raised, and their timber is much more valuable

CHAP

# CHAP. VII.

## *PINUS ABIES*, The COMMON SPRUCE-FIR-TREE.

THE *Abies*, the *Larix*, and the *Pinus*, which have always been looked upon as different genera, are now very juſtly claſſed with the pines.

The Spruce Fir is a beautiful tree, as well as valuable for its timber. It grows to a prodigious height, on which account the appellation *Abies* was formerly given to it, from the Latin word *Abeo, to ſpring* or *advance*, and with the ſame propriety the Greeks called this genus ..., which ſignifies *height*, from the verb ..., *to advance*.

Derivation of the generical name.

This tree is a native of Norway and Denmark, where it grows naturally, and is one of the principal productions of their woods. It is alſo found growing in the Highlands of Scotland, where it adorns thoſe dreary mountains with its conſtant verdure.

A native of Denmark and Norway.

The timber is the white deal, a wood univerſally known for its utility.

The timber is the white deal.

From this fir pitch is extracted, which is known to ſerve for many common uſes in life.

Pitch extracted from this tree.

The manner of propagating this tree is nearly the ſame as that ordered for the Scotch pines, only this will more eaſily grow when of a large ſize, and conſequently will not require removing ſo often in the nurſery.

In the middle of March, therefore, having got the ſeeds out of the cones (which are very long) as has been directed, let them be ſown in a North border, for when they come up, by being conſtantly ſhaded all the ſummer in ſuch a ſituation, they will ſhoot much ſtronger and be better to prick out the ſpring following in the nurſery. In about ſix or ſeven weeks after ſowing, the young plants will appear, when they ſhould be ſcreened with the uſual care from the birds, which otherwiſe would ſoon deſtroy them. By the autumn, many of theſe young plants, if they are kept clean from weeds and watered in dry weather, will have ſhot three or four inches, and in ſpring they ſhould be carefully taken out of their ſeed-beds, ſo that the fibres may by no means be broken off or injured. Being thus cautiouſly taken up, they ſhould be as carefully planted in the nurſery-ground, at the diſtance of one foot aſunder each way. Here they may remain, with keeping them free from weeds, for three years, when they ſhould be ſet out in the places where they are deſigned to remain. But if larger trees are deſired for this purpoſe, they ſhould be taken up and planted in the nurſery, a foot and a half aſunder, in rows two feet and a half diſtant, where they may ſtand, if required, till they are ſix or eight feet high, without any other removing. When they are ſet out for good, they may be planted, with tolerable hopes of ſucceſs, for the ſpruce-fir is not ſo nice or difficult in ſhifting its quarters as any of the other ſorts of pines. But though theſe trees may be tranſplanted at a good height, I would always adviſe removing them to the places deſigned for them with all poſſible diſpatch, as they are more certain of growing, and will recover the check occaſioned in all trees by removal in leſs time.

Manner of propagating this tree.

The better the ſoil is, the faſter will the ſpruce-fir grow, tho' it will thrive very well in moſt of our Engliſh lands. In ſtrong loamy earth it makes a ſurpriſing progreſs, and it delights in freſh land of all ſorts, which never has been worn out by ploughing, &c. though it be ever ſo poor.

Soils ſuitable to this tree.

It is not proper to plant theſe trees near great towns, becauſe they cannot bear the ſmoke, which changes their colour into that of a dirty green, or rather a ſort of black, ſtops the progreſs of their growth, and proves very injurious to them. All the ſorts of fir ſuffer in ſome reſpect this way, but the ſpruce more remarkably.

Situation improper for it.

# CHAP. VIII.

## *PINUS PICEA*, The SILVER-FIR-TREE.

THE Silver-Fir-Tree is another ſpecies of this genus, of admirable procerity and beauty.

It grows naturally in moſt parts of Germany, particularly about Straſburg, and adorns the Scotch mountains in moderate plenty.

A native of Germany, &c.

It affords the turpentine, which we have conſtantly imported from Germany in large quantities every year.

Yields turpentine.

The timber is a yellowiſh deal, of equal goodneſs with any of the other ſorts, and applied like them to ſuch various purpoſes and uſes as are well known to every reader.

Uſes of the timber.

Theſe trees are raiſed by ſowing the ſeeds in a ſhady border, about the middle of March. They will readily come up if the ſeeds are good, but as this is not often the caſe, eſpecially if theſe are procured from the ſeedſmen, they ſhould be ſown very cloſe, otherwiſe you will be certain of having a very thin crop. The ſucceeding ſummer the plants will require no trouble, except keeping them clean from weeds, and the ſpring after that they ſhould be pricked out in beds at about four inches diſtance from each other. Here they may ſtand for two years, when they ſhould be planted in the nurſery, in rows a foot aſunder

Method of propagating this tree.

SIL. FIR. aſunder every way. The year, or at fartheſt two years, after they have been ſet in the nurſery, they ſhould be planted out for good; for if they are continued longer, many of them will die when planted out, and thoſe which grow frequently loſe their leading-ſhoot, and meet with ſo great a check as to be hardly able to get into a good growing ſtate for ſeveral years.

*SIL. FIR. Grows well on almoſt all ſoils and ſituations. Situations proper for it.*

The ſilver-fir is exceeding hardy, and will grow in any ſoil or ſituation, but always makes the greateſt progreſs in a good rich loamy earth.

It is highly proper for parks and open places, not only as being a large, beautiful, upright tree, but as the leaves on their under-ſide are of a ſilvery white, while the upper ſurface is green, this contraſt cauſes a delightful effect.

# CHAP. IX.

## *CUPRESSUS*, The CYPRESS-TREE.

THE Cypreſs, though hitherto ſet in plantations of evergreens deſigned more for pleaſure than profit, is a tree which ought to have its ſhare in plantations or foreſt-trees intended for emolument. Indeed, in evergreen wilderneſs quarters no tree makes a more agreeable variety than this. The leaves are of a pleaſant darkiſh green colour, and the growth of the whole tree is pyramidical.

*Its appearance deſcribed.*

*Situations proper for this tree.*

Theſe trees are peculiarly proper to be planted near temples, or ſacred ſtructures of any kind, as they give ſuch buildings a pleaſingly ſtriking appearance; for by exhibiting them through their narrow tops, each tree forming itſelf, as it were, into a pyramid of dark green, they make a ſweet contraſt to the white colour of the temples, &c. near which they ſtand.

Beſides being thus proper for places of a religious kind, they are much more valuable for their ſalutary properties. The aromatic effluvia continually emitted from them, are allowed to render the air more healthy, and prove a ſpecific for the lungs.

*which emits aromatic effluvia that prove ſalutary to the lungs.*

The Male Spreading Cypreſs is ſaid to be poſſeſſed of theſe properties in an eminent degree; and we are told, that in the iſland of Candia, where theſe trees uſed anciently to grow in great quantities, the phyſicians frequently ſent their patients, conſumptive perſons eſpecially, or thoſe troubled with weak lungs, to live among them for ſome time; from which they ſeldom failed of receiving great benefit.

Neither are cypreſs-trees adapted only to ornament and improve the air in wilderneſs quarters near habitations, &c. they are alſo proper for clumps or lawns, or to terminate views at a diſtance. In ſhort, they have their beauties every way, and in every place.

*The male ſpreading cypreſs particularly recommended for plantations.*

What is called the Male Spreading Cypreſs grows to the largeſt ſize, and is therefore the ſort I would recommend for timber-plantations; though the others ſhould have a ſhare, to increaſe the variety. This tree is diſtinguiſhed from the common ſpecies by not growing in ſuch a beautiful pictureſque form, but its branches are more ſpreading and irregular, as its name imports.

*Purpoſes to which the timber which is of great value is applied.*

The timber of the cypreſs, which is of the higheſt value and uſe, is of a very ſonorous nature, and therefore proper for muſical inſtruments, baſſoons, German flutes, organ-pipes, &c. It is ſaid to reſiſt the worm or moth, and to be proof againſt all putrefaction; and if we conſider the purpoſes it has been anciently applied to, we ſhall be better enabled to judge of its value. Plato is ſaid to have preferred it to braſs, to write his laws on. The bridge built by Semiramis conſiſted of this timber. The doors of St. Peter's church at Rome were made of this wood, and laſted from Conſtantine the Great to the time of Pope Eugenius IV. who changed them for braſs, though they were as freſh and entire as if they had been new, notwithſtanding they had ſtood there many hundred years. The cheſts of the Egyptian mummies are made of this tree; and Thucydides tells us, that the Athenians always uſed to bury their heroes in coffins made of it. The gopher-wood mentioned in ſcripture, of which the ark was built, is thought by many to have been the cypreſs; a conjecture for which there is ſome foundation, as thoſe parts of Aſſyria where the ark is ſuppoſed to have been built, has ever ſince the Deluge produced theſe trees in great plenty.

The cypreſs grows naturally in the iſlands of the Archipelago, the Levant, and ſeveral other parts of the world. The word is ſuppoſed to be formed of *Cypariſſus*, the name of a beautiful young man, whom the poets feign to have been changed by Apollo into a cypreſs tree. But I rather think it comes from κυω, *to produce*, and παρισος, *equal*, becauſe the branches are all equally produced. It affords male and female flowers on the ſame plant, and belongs to the claſs and order *Monoecia Monadelphia*.

*Derivation of the generical name.*

*Claſs and order in the Linnæan ſyſtem.*

*Method of propagating this tree.*

The manner of propagating the cypreſs is as follows. A warm border, or well ſheltered beds, ſhould be prepared for the purpoſe, after having been well worked, turned over, and mellowed by the froſts all winter. The ſoil of this border, or beds, ſhould be ſandy; and if it is not naturally ſo, ſome drift ſand may be brought to mix with it, and worked all over the bed, at leaſt ſix inches deep. Having the border prepared, the mould being ſmooth and fine, let a ſmall part, ſufficient to cover the ſeeds, be taken out, and then let the bed be raked ſmooth and fine. After this, ſow the ſeeds all over it pretty thin; for if they are ſown too thick, the roots get matted together, ſo that the plants cannot be removed out of the ſeed-bed into the nurſery, without great danger of loſs. The ſeeds being now ſown regularly over the bed, riddle the mould that was taken out, over them, not quite half an inch thick. The beginning of March is the beſt time for this work, and by the beginning of May, if the ſeeds were good, the plants will come up. If the month of April ſhould prove very dry, as it often happens, the beds may have now and then a gentle watering, and

*CYPRESS.* and it will help to bring the plants up. After they have come up, if the summer should not prove very dry, they will require little watering, and even in the greatest drought twice a week will be sufficient for them, provided it be done in the evenings. This is the only care they will require the first summer, except being kept clean from weeds. In the winter, if the place where they are sown be tolerably well sheltered, they will stand it very well, though it should prove severe, as I have many times experienced; but where the situation is not well sheltered by plantations, to break the violence of the frosty black winds, they must be screened, otherwise many will be lost. It is the black frosts, attended by high winds, which will destroy these plants; so that where there is not shelter enough to break their edge, the beds should be hooped over, and covered with mats during that severe weather.

The ensuing summer the plants may remain undisturbed, when they will require no watering, and no further care, except weeding. The spring following, being then two years old, they should be set out in the nursery, exactly at two feet square. In taking them out of the seed-bed, some earth should be taken with the roots. The latter end of March is the most proper time for this work, and if the weather should prove dry and cold, as it often happens, the March winds blowing, the work must be deferred till rainy or cloudy weather; for without these precautions, you will find this a difficult plant to remove. After they are planted out in the nursery, they may be now and then watered in dry weather, kept clean from weeds, and thus may stand till they are of a sufficient size to be planted out for good.

*Directions for raising a Cupressetum.* The ground intended for a *Cupressetum* may the preceding year bear a crop of grain, and the winter before it is planted be ploughed with a strong plow, to destroy the weeds, and lay the best soil downwards.

After this, holes should be made all over at two yards distance. The plants must be taken out of the nursery with as much mould with the roots as possible, and carefully planted in their holes. If these trees are designed for coppice wood, they will be fit to cut in fifteen or twenty years; for I am informed, that the cypress succeeds very well in coppices, though I must own I never experienced the effect of cutting down large trees. If the plants are designed for timber, when they get too close they ought to be proportionably thinned, and should undergo a second thinning as often as they touch each other, till they arrive at their full size.

The cypress has been cultivated in many parts of the world for the sake of its timber, and it was a custom in some islands in the Archipelago, at the birth of a daughter, to plant a *Cupressetum*, or grove of cypress-trees, to be given her for her portion. Hence every plantation of this kind was called *Dos Filiæ*, or a daughter's dower. If the gentlemen of these kingdoms were to imitate this practice, they might give their daughters good portions without incumbering the estate, by leaving their fortunes to be paid by the eldest son out of it, thereby oftentimes keeping him in poverty and slavery the greatest part of his life.

*Soils which it delights in.* The soils which the cypress delights in are many and various. It grows exceeding well in good rich land, and makes surprising progress in my Gumley plantations, where the soil is a poor hungry white clay. But above all, it seems to feast in gravelly and sandy ground, in which it will arrive to a great bulk in a few years. So that whoever is possessed of such land, may plant it with cypress to his own great emolument, as well as beautifying and ornamenting the country for the pleasure of the public.

## CHAP. X.

## *QUERCUS ILEX*, The EVERGREEN OAK-TREE.

THE *Ilices*, or Evergreen Oak-Trees, together with the sorts of cork-trees, are undoubtedly species of the *Quercus*, as their characters testify, being found, upon examination, to be the same in all respects, altho' they were always reputed, till the new system was published, to be distinct genera. There seems to be many species of the *Ilex*, though we have great reason to believe, they are no more than varieties, as I have sown acorns of the same tree which have produced plants very different, especially with respect to the leaves. The leaves of one tree have been very narrow and long, of a second more rotund, of a third deeply indented, of a fourth is full of prickles almost as the holly; whence I think it is natural to infer, that the different sorts of these trees are not distinct species, but only varieties of one common genus, the *Ilex*; the different sorts of which are very beautiful trees, and highly proper for evergreen plantations of all kinds. They make an agreeable variety in evergreen wilderness quarters, produce a pleasing effect in clumps, and have their value in evergreen timber-plantations designed chiefly for profit.

*Places in which it is proper to be planted.*

## *QUERCUS SUBER*, The CORK-TREE.

I EQUALLY recommend the cork-tree and the evergreen oak for planting, under this article, as they may be both equally propagated to the owner's advantage.

*Derivation of the generical name.* The word *Suber* is derived *à subeo, quod mergi nequit, sed subit*.

*Uses to which the timber is applied.* The timber may be sold for many uses, and is serviceable for pins, wedges, chairs, stocks of tools, mallet heads and beetles, palisadoes, axle-trees, and many purposes in building. It affords excellent fuel, and makes the best and most lasting charcoal. In Spain, where these trees abound, their charcoal is chiefly made of it. The *Suber*, or cork-tree, and the *Ilex*, are nearly equally serviceable for the above uses, besides which, the former affords the cork, so generally serviceable

*CORK. Various uses of cork.*

able both by sea and land. It is useful to the merchants for securing liquors, and without this material the country would be ill supplied with fish by the fishermen, who require it for their nets. Besides, it has other valuable properties, which are too numerous to be inserted here, but which are nevertheless known to the inhabitants in countries where these trees abound. The poor people in Spain lay it to tread on instead of carpets. It is often used for coffins, which, being lined with a resinous composition, are said to preserve the bodies longer uncorrupted. It makes very good soles to shoes, being dry and light, and indeed is every where preferred, particularly by old people, for this purpose, to leather.

*Manner of taking off the cork from the tree.*

The manner of taking off the cork from the tree nearly resembles our method of stripping off the bark of our oak for the tanners use. When it is taken from the tree, it is pressed flat before the fire, and weights laid upon it to keep it in that state, after which it will always remain so. The oldest trees afford the best cork, which will, every seven or eight years, yield a crop. The month of July is the time for this work, when the sap is in its highest flow; but dry weather must be made choice of, because should much moisture fall upon the *cuticula*, or tender rhind, at that time just exposed, the tree might be endangered, which will be so far from being injured by the bark being taken off, if the weather is dry, that it is even necessary to have this operation performed to preserve it in health and growth. The tender rhind is sufficient to perform the offices of the bark in trees, and unless the cork be taken off, the tree will become stunted, and decay in a much fewer space of years than those that have yielded their crops for use. The cork of young trees is of little value; however, to render the future cork of these trees good, it would be proper to have them decorticated when about ten or twenty years old, for this will refresh the tree, and the cork will at every after peeling become better and better.

*Ashes of the cork proper in the bloody flux, and piles.*

The ashes of the cork are said to prove salutary in the bloody flux, and, being mixed with fresh butter, to afford an ointment which has been found a sovereign remedy for the piles.

*Method of propagating evergreen oak and cork trees.*

The manner of propagating both the preceding sorts of trees is by the acorns, which are to be managed in the same manner as our English oaks, to which I refer the reader, and shall only observe in this place, that it is difficult to excite them to grow when they are removed; that, contrary to most trees, they may be transplanted with greater hopes of success when the plants are four or five feet high than when they are seedlings; and that, after all, if the ground can be properly prepared, it will be better to sow these acorns in places where they are to remain, as they will sustain a great check in their growth, and the loss of many trees be endangered, by their removal.

*In what countries this tree grows naturally.*

The cork-tree grows naturally in Portugal and Spain, in Italy, and the South of France; it is found likewise in New England, and the coldest parts of Biscany. And in most of these places also the evergreen oaks grow.

*All soils suitable to the cork and evergreen oak trees.*

Both these sorts of trees will grow upon almost any ground. Rocky mountains, stony heaths, &c. where hardly any thing else will thrive, may be planted with them to advantage. And altho' the reader, in the preceding articles, will find many trees which particularly delight in such soils and situations, yet the cork and evergreen oak should have their share, especially if the planter can purchase the acorns or setts at the same price as the other sorts. Indeed, where neither seeds nor setts of any particular tree can be procured, others must be sought for that will suit the same land, to supply their place. There are more sorts of trees than one which will grow well in any soil; and the planter's first care should be to consider what trees will thrive best on his ground. Some people entertain a notion, that no trees deserve planting except oaks, ashes, and elms. Nay, I know several gentlemen who, having tried these upon some ground, and finding them not to succeed, have become disgusted, quitted the pursuit, and left the land altogether uncultivated for the future. Let every planter, therefore, consider, that the different soils of the kingdom have plants peculiarly adapted to them, and thence be induced to study the nature of his soil, with the trees proper for it, to assist him in the knowledge of which is one part of the design of this work. Would every gentleman pursue this plan, and in his plantations always keep this consideration in view, our number of forest-trees would be encreased, the smallest portion of land would be then planted with trees proper to its nature, we should have timber for every use, and the pleasure resulting from such beauty and variety would call for the warmest thanks and praise to that Allwise and Beneficent Creator, who has formed trees of different structure, according to the various soils, in order to grow and flourish for his creatures' service.

## CHAP. XI.

## *JUNIPERUS*, The JUNIPER-TREE.

THERE are many species of the Juniper, but the sort I would chiefly recommend to be planted for the sake of the wood is the large blue-berried juniper-tree, commonly called the Red Virginian Cedar, which is a tree of admirable use, and, altho' a foreigner, will thrive exceedingly well in our climate. The beauty

*Situations proper for this tree.*

of this tree is apparent to all beholders, and at once convinces them how excellently it is calculated for enlivening the scene, and ornamenting places of all kinds, whether the pleasure-garden or wilderness, parks or lawns.

*Its appearance described.*

Its growth is upright, the branches form a beautiful cone, and, if left unsprigged, the tree will be feathered to the very base. It grows to near forty feet high, and the timber is valuable for many excellent and rare uses. It will continue sound and uncorrupt for many ages, being possessed of a bitter resin which prevents the worms from attacking it.

*Uses of its timber.*

The wood may be converted into utensils

JUNIPER

utensils of most sorts, as well as applied to a great part of the uses, to which the cypress is adapted. It is remarkable, however, for being of a very brittle nature, and is therefore not proper to be introduced into buildings where any great weight is to be lodged. Nevertheless, in Virginia and Carolina, where they abound, these trees are used in structures of all kinds, with this precaution; and the inhabitants prefer the timber to most other wood for wainscoting their rooms, and building of vessels.

I think it unnecessary to enlarge farther on this tree and its uses. Those who are desirous of having variety of timber-trees in their plantations, from what has been said will doubtless be inclined to allow this a place; I shall therefore proceed to its culture.

Method of propagating this tree

The seeds must be procured from Carolina or Virginia; they are generally brought over by the latter end of February, or beginning of March, and should be soon after sown in beds of light sandy earth; but if the soil is not naturally so, drift sand must be mixed with the common mould, to make it such. These beds should be made fine by digging and raking, and then a small share taken out for covering the seeds after they are sown. The bottom of the beds ought to be raked level, before the seeds are sowed; the mould taken out of the beds should be riddled over the seeds, and be of a quantity sufficient, when riddled over, to cover the seeds half an inch deep. After this the beds must be dressed up, and the business is done.

In about twelve months after being sowed, the plants will appear; for it rarely happens that any come up sooner. During the summer they lie in the ground, they must be cleared of weeds, which, if neglected even a short time, by striking in the fibres of their roots amongst the seeds, may, when drawn, bring the seeds out with them, and thus endanger the loss of the seminary.

The spring following, when the plants appear, the same care in weeding must be observed; and during dry weather the following summer, they should be now and then watered. With these cautions, they may stand two years, when they should be planted out in the nursery, at two feet asunder each way. The ground in which they are to remain till they are planted out for good, should be nearly the same, if possible, with the land designed finally to receive them.

Directions for forming a plantation of the Virginian cedars

If a large plantation of these trees is required, the ground ought to be first ploughed with a strong plow, to turn the best soil downwards; holes should be made all over it, at two yards distance, and the trees taken out of the seminary the latter end of September, with as much mould to the roots as possible. Moist weather must be made choice of for this work; and if the dry weather should continue till that season, as frequently happens, it will be proper to defer it till a fall of rain; otherwise the pores of the roots will be in danger of being closed, to the great hazard of the tree. But though I advise autumn for the planting out these trees, yet if the ground cannot be got ready by that season, the end of March or beginning of April is no improper time for this business; nay, I have planted them out in all the winter months, with success. I mention this, that no person may be discouraged if his ground cannot be prepared against any particular time. I have also planted them out soon after Midsummer, with the greatest success; and I am certain, if moist weather should happen at that time, it would be the best season for their removal.

A plantation of these trees being made, at two yards distance, will require no farther care than keeping down the weeds for three or four years, after which they will be strong enough to resist their utmost efforts, and will every year be better enabled to destroy them. When the trees begin to touch and incommode each other, they should be thinned; which operation should be repeated as often as occasion requires, till they are fit for the general fall.

Soil suitable to this tree

Plantations of these trees may be raised upon most sorts of land. I have some now extremely thriving and luxuriant on a stiff wet red clay; and those planted at Gumley, on a hungry white clay, shew how well they like such kind of earth. Nevertheless, a sandy earth is their general soil; and in such land we may be pretty certain of their making surprising progress, especially if it be fresh, and has not been exhausted.

This is the principal sort of this genus I would recommend to be planted for timber. But being on the article *Juniperus*, I shall now mention two other sorts, of much humbler growth, but which may nevertheless be admitted in small quantities into evergreen plantations, if the owner is desirous of having great variety, especially as the wood of both species is valuable. These are the Common Juniper, and that known by the name of the Swedish Juniper.

The common juniper

The common juniper is a native of England, and, what is very remarkable, in the soil where these trees come up naturally, which is for the most part chalky or sandy, they seldom rise higher than four or five feet, by their manner of growth seeming to testify that they have been forced into such places, and that they by no means relish them; whereas seeds taken from these, and sown in different soils, have produced plants so superior to their originals, that they appear to be of another species. I have in my own garden juniper-trees of the common sort, which rise with straight and upright stems, make strong shoots every year, and at present promise to become as large trees as the Swedish juniper.

And Swedish juniper described

The Swedish juniper, the other sort under consideration, will grow to the height of fifteen or seventeen feet. Its branches grow more erect, and the leaves are rather narrower, than those of the English tree. It is, however, very beautiful, and is found growing wild in Sweden, Denmark, and Norway.

Valuable properties of the juniper

The wood of the juniper-tree is of a yellow colour, and, for its size, inferior in value to none. It is a fine aromatic, and in rooms where it is used, causes a wholesome perfume. It is naturally endued with salutary qualities, and spoons made of it are allowed to be wholesome to the mouth. When converted into spits, the wood is said to give the meat roasted on them a delicious flavour. It is likewise valuable for all sorts of carved work; and when large enough for small tables, chests, boxes, drawers, &c. its exceeding value for these uses may be easily seen.

Method of raising the juniper tree

Juniper-trees may be raised in the same manner as the Virginian cedars, only be careful to get them in the ground as soon after the seeds are ripe as possible; for if this precaution is observed, they will come up the spring following; whereas, if they are neglected till the spring, they will not appear till the spring after that; and sometimes a great part of them will remain till the second, and even third season, before they come up.

After the plants are come up, they should be treated exactly as the Virginian cedars, only their distance in the nursery need not be so great,

JUNIPER great, a foot asunder in the rows, and rows at two feet distance, will be space sufficient. When they are to be planted out for good, a ball of earth should be taken with each plant, otherwise there will be great danger of losing many of them.

The beginning of October is the best season for planting out these trees in moist or cloudy weather; and if a spot of ground is designed peculiarly for them, they should be planted at no more than one yard asunder, and afterwards managed as the Virginian cedars, till they are arrived at their full maturity and growth, and are fit for felling. JUNIPER

March is deemed the best season for felling the juniper-tree, and it is observable, that trees felled in that month afford their timber of a more grateful and sweet odour. Best time for felling its timber

## CHAP. XII.

## *TAXUS*, The YEW-TREE.

Purposes for which this tree was chiefly planted. THE Yew-Tree has been generally cultivated for the pleasure-garden, both to clip into the figures of beasts, birds, &c. and also for hedges. Whoever is pleased with such figures in his garden can raise no tree more proper for his purpose, as the branches and the leaves may be clipped and fashioned into almost any form or shape. But as this method is now pretty exploded, and as every one who makes the least pretension to taste must always prefer a tree in its natural growth to those old fashioned monstrous figures, the yew is chiefly planted for wilderness quarters, as also for hedges, for which last use it is excellently well adapted, as no tree bears clipping so well.

Notwithstanding the yew-tree has been chiefly planted for the above uses, I wish to have some cultivated for the sake of the timber, as it is extremely valuable, and the trees may be raised on cold barren lands, which are of little or no value. Such places might not only be made beautiful to the owners, but, when the trees become ready for felling, the profit would be ... be inconsiderable.

Uses to which the timber is applicable. The wood of the yew-tree is of a very hard and durable nature, but has nevertheless been used for ... bodies of lutes, theorbos, and other musical instruments, which are almost exploded amongst us. Bows were frequently made of yew:

—— *Ityraeos taxi torquentur in arcus.*

We now cut it up for pins and wedges, wheels and pullies. It is found also to be proper for mill cogs, and for all things, as to make axle-trees beyond comparison. Posts of this wood set in moist ground will stand for ages. And as it is particularly ... for these and other purposes of the like nature, and is of a beautiful reddish colour, its timber sells at a proportionably greater price.

Derivation of its generical name. The word *Taxus* is derived from the Greek ..., which signifies *poison*, because the leaves of this tree are of a poisonous nature. It has been distinguished by the name of *Taxus Lethifera, the death-bringing Yew*, and was anciently used in compounding poisons. It has ever been looked on as a symbol of mortality, for which reason it has been planted in church-yards, amongst the dead, to remind people, as it were, of their approaching fate. And indeed, I have seen many noble trees growing in church-yards, which, when felled, would have been extremely valuable.

It has been thought dangerous to turn cattle into fields where yew trees grow, but I believe no beasts will touch them, unless compelled by extreme hunger. It is true, several have lost both horses and cows by their eating the leaves of this tree. But this accident must be attributed either to the abovementioned cause, or to the gardener having thrown the clippings carelessly in places where cattle come, who, particularly cows, will eat them when about half dry as greedily as new hay. By such an accident, viz. a gardener's having thrown the clippings of a yew-tree over the wall, a neighbouring farmer of mine lost seven or eight of his best cattle: which ought to be a caution to all gardeners, whenever these trees are cut, to be careful that the clippings be either carried in for the fire or buried.

The yew-tree is a native of Britain, and most parts of Europe. The flowers are very inconsiderable, and of a yellowish cast. They will be in full blow in the beginning of March; and the botanist will find them to belong to the class and order *Dioecia Monadelphia*. Time when the flowers blow. Class and order in the Linnaean system.

From the berry, which succeeds the flowers, the tree is raised. These berries are surrounded by a beautiful bright red pulp, which makes the tree have a fine effect. They are ripe in the autumn, and are greatly liked by the birds.

Manner of propagating this tree. In the autumn, when the seeds are ripe, a sufficient quantity should be gathered; and being first cleared of their mucilage, let them be sown neatly, in beds about half an inch deep. By being thus expeditious in planting them, many will come up the next spring; whereas, if the seeds are kept out of the ground till February, the plants will not appear until the spring after. During the summer the beds must be kept clean from weeds; and if the weather should prove very dry, now and then watered. This will promote the growth of the hidden seeds, and at the spring may be expected a general crop.

The plants being come up, no other care will be necessary, for two years, than keeping the beds weeded, and refreshing them in dry weather with gentle waterings. After they have gained strength in these beds by standing two years, a piece of ground must be prepared for them, in which they should be planted at a foot asunder. Here they may stand for three or four years, and may be then planted where they are designed to remain, or set out in the nursery in rows two feet asunder and three feet distance in the rows, in order to be clipt, or trained for hedges or other purposes, or raised to a good size to be planted out for standards.

Every

YEW.

Every person desirous of having a plantation of yew-trees should plough the ground deep, to turn the sward downward in order to afford nourishment to the tree when the root strikes into it, and he should also plant them a yard asunder, and continue thinning them as often as they touch each other, till they are arrived to their full growth.

*Yew best proper for.*

This tree being a native of Britain, agrees well with most of our English soils; but as yews will grow to be large trees, even thirty or forty feet high, in the most barren, cold, and damp places, they certainly deserve the attention of those planters who are possessed of such places.

# CHAP. XIII.

## *ILEX*, The HOLLY-TREE.

*Its appearance described.*

THE Holly is another tree of singular use and beauty. If planted for ornament, it makes a handsome appearance in clumps of evergreens. Its broad and prickly leaves, which are of a chearful green colour, form an agreeable contrast with others of a different hue; and this is still heightened, if the tribe of the variegated kinds be admitted to encrease the variety. The red berries which continue on the trees the greatest part of the winter, add to their lustre; and the procerity of their growth renders them inferior to none, and superior in beauty to most evergreens of this class. But as I profess to treat of trees more for use than beauty, I shall enumerate some of the properties of its timber, by which its value will be best known, and afterwards, as usual, proceed to its culture.

*Height to which it grows.*
*Uses for which the timber is serviceable.*

The holly will grow to about thirty feet high, and its timber when felled is of all others the whitest. It polishes well, and is valuable for inlayings, and several sorts of cabinet work. Hones to set razors on are made of this wood, which likewise excels for all sorts of hardy uses, as bolts and bars for doors and gates; nay, hinges have been fabricated of holly instead of iron, which have answered very well, and lasted long. The millwright finds no timber excel it for his purposes; and it furnishes the turner, when he can procure it, with the whitest and finest ware in his way. But it would prove endless to enumerate the various uses of this valuable wood, which not only serves for some of the elegant conveniences of life, but also surpasses many in articles of lower or common uses, as pins for blocks, handles to tools, flails, carters whips, &c.

*A native of Britain.*

This useful and beautiful tree is a native of England; and although it is found in most parts of Europe, we boast it to be peculiarly an indigenous plant of Britain. It was formerly called *Ilex Aquifolium, quod acutis in folium habet*; and indeed, these sharp leaves, which are oblong, oval, and prickly at the points and about the edges, make a handsome appearance on their flexible branches, equally of a beautiful green colour, and which grow from a noble upright stem, covered with a smooth greyish bark. The flowers exhibit nothing remarkable; they are of a greyish white, and Nature's observer will see them in blow the latter end of April and in May, and will find them to belong to the class and order *Tetrandria Tetragynia*. The berries, which succeed the flowers, are first green, and afterwards of a beautiful red when ripe, which is in the beginning of October.

*Time when the flowers are in blow.*
*Class and order in the Linnæan system.*

*Method of propagating this tree.*

The manner of propagating the holly is nearly the same as the yew, only as the plants never appear until the second spring, instead of sowing the berries immediately, as was directed for the yew, they may be buried in the ground, then taken up, and sown the autumn following. If the plants are sown as soon as they are gathered, they will undoubtedly come up the spring twelvemonth after, and this would be the most eligible, as well as the surest way of obtaining a crop, could you be certain of guarding them from mice during so long a space of time; for these animals, when once they find out the seeds, will soon, unless they are exterminated, effectually destroy a whole seminary. If the planter is not averse to run this hazard, the best method will be to sow the seeds soon after they are ripe. During the following summer the beds must be kept clean of weeds, traps must be constantly set for the mice; and, if the season should prove dry, it would assist the growth of the seeds to give them now and then a gentle watering. These precautions being observed, the plants will come up in the spring following.

I cannot think that burying the plants one year in the ground is so good a method as the preceding, because I have frequently known them not to come up till the spring after their being sown; nay, if they are taken out of the ground, and sowed late in the spring, or the spring should prove a dry one, this would be almost certain of being the case, at least of far the greatest part of them. Thus a whole year would be lost. However, if the seeds have been buried, let them be taken up in October; and having some light fine mould for the seminary, let beds be made four feet wide, with an alley between each bed, a foot and an half broad. In those beds let the seeds be sown half an inch deep, and carefully covered from the mice; and after being dressed up, for safety let some traps be set. In the spring, when the plants appear, no weeds should be suffered to incommode them; and if the seminary be naturally dry, they should be sometimes watered; but if the soil is rather inclined to be moist or damp, little water should be given them, because in such places they do not require it.

Two years must elapse with no other care or trouble than these precautions, when being two years old seedlings, in the spring they should be taken out of the beds, and planted in the nursery in rows a foot asunder, and two feet distance in the rows. Here they may stand, being kept clean of weeds and dug between the

rows

HOLLY

rows every winter, till they are of a sufficient size to be planted out for good.

*Manner of raising a plantation of holly trees,*

If any person is inclined to enrich the variety of his evergreen plantation, by having one of holly, he should take them out of the nursery when they are large enough to overpower the weeds, and having ploughed his ground, he may plant them any time from the beginning of September to the middle of March, at a yard asunder. They may be afterwards managed as has been directed for the preceding trees of a similar nature. If the land designed for hollies is naturally dry, I would advise to get them into the ground early in the autumn, that the winter rains, &c. may thoroughly settle the earth to the roots, to prevent their suffering greatly if it should prove a dry spring. If the land is of a moist nature, the planter need not be very anxious about the time or the winter in which he makes his plantation of hollies.

*which thrive well upon most soils*

The holly being an indigenous plant of Britain, will grow in almost all our English soils. We have few hollies in Leicestershire, a circumstance which somewhat surprizes me, as I am certain this tree would flourish exceedingly in any land in this county. Those in my nurseries at Gumley shew how well it likes a hungry white clay, and those growing in a strong loam at Tur-Langton testify their delighting in such sort of land. In short, a person need not be very anxious about their succeeding in almost any soil. The woods in Warwickshire afford plenty of holly trees, Staffordshire also abounds with them, and it is observable, that where there has been a charcoal fire, the ground seldom fails of producing a great crop of these trees, from the seeds which accidentally fall on the spot. All these places have soils of a different nature, which, like a true Briton, seem to disdain no food of British production. However, the holly seems more peculiarly to abound in such situations as those above-mentioned, and also takes a great liking to all sorts of coal-ground, for about Coleorton, Ashby, the pits near Nun Eaton, and most other places where coal is gotten, this tree is generally found in great plenty.

HOLLY

*The leaves, reduced to powder, prove salutary in the stone and fluxes*

Its leaves, when dried to powder and drank in white wine, are said to prove serviceable in the stone and fluxes. The bird-lime is a composition of the bark of this tree, which being very useful to gardeners, I shall insert the receipt for preparing it from Evelyn.

*Receipt for making bird lime*

"PILL a good quantity of holly bark about Midsummer, fill a vessel with it, and put to it spring water, then boil it, till the grey and white bark rise from the green, which will require near twelve hours boiling, then take it off the fire, separate the barks, the water first being well drained from it, then lay the green bark on the earth, in some cold vault or cellar, covering it with any sort of green and rank weeds, such as dock, thistles, hemlock, &c. to a good thickness. Thus let it continue near a fortnight, by which time it will become a perfect mucilage, then pound it all exceedingly in a stone mortar, till it be a tough paste, and so very fine as no part of the bark be discernible. This done, wash it accurately well in some running stream of water, as long as you perceive the least ordure or motes in it, and so reserve it in some earthen pot, to purge and ferment, scumming it as often as any thing arises for four or five days, and when no more filth comes, change it into a fresh vessel of earth, and reserve it for use, thus: Take what quantity you please of it, and in an earthen pipkin add a third part of capon's or goose grease to it, well clarified, or oil of walnuts, which is better. Incorporate these on a gentle fire, continually stirring it, till it be cold, and thus your composition is finished. But to prevent frosts (which in severe weather will sometimes invade it on the rods) take a quarter of as much oil of petroleum as you do of grease, and no cold whatever will congeal it."

# CHAP. XIV.

## *PRUNUS*, The LAUREL-TREE.

THE Laurel-tree, though hitherto chiefly used for wilderness quarters of evergreens, hedges, concealing of old walls, &c. will nevertheless, if properly trained, arrive to a tree of a considerable bulk, and not only affords useful timber, but is very proper for avenues, &c. particularly as its evergreen, noble broad leaves, and the manner of its growth, cause a pleasing effect in such uses, as well as when they are planted in suitable places purely for their timber.

*Situations most proper for this tree*

The laurel will grow to about thirty feet high, and the leaves, which are sometimes five or six inches long and three broad, being likewise of a firm structure and even at the edges, garnish the branches of the tree in such a manner as would excite our admiration, did not the frequency of this noble plant diminish our respect. The laurel therefore should be raised for pleasure and profit. In all our evergreen wilderness quarters, this ought to be one of our chief trees, large walks may be ornamented with them, as well as avenues in some particular places (such as lead to a temple, green house, or some building in large gardens, for I do not assert that they are proper for avenues leading to the front of gentlemens seats). They should also have a share in evergreen plantations designed for profit, and likewise in all deciduous plantations, as they will grow exceeding well under the drip of other trees, and make good underwood. And though there are many sorts of deciduous trees better adapted for underwood than this, yet whoever is desirous of ornamenting his wood should admit a few of these, especially by the borders of them, and along the sides of the ridings, which will increase the variety of leaves, and difference of green in summer, and will also produce a delightful effect in winter, when, though other trees are despoiled of their honours, these still retain their leafy verdure.

Neither

LAUREL

Neither is this the only delight it affords, by thus *ornamenting woods, wilderness quarters, &c* its berries are rich food for blackbirds, thrushes, and other sorts of whistling birds So that where these trees abound, there will be plenty of these feathered songsters to entertain the owner with their warbles

Uses of the timber

The wood of the laurel-tree, though not so hard as some of the preceding sorts, is nevertheless very valuable for most kinds of turnery ware, and is much sought after by the joiner and cabinet-maker, who use it for many purposes in their way

Time of the leaves opening

The young leaves of the laurel-tree will begin to open about the tenth of March, and be quite out before the middle of April The flowers are white, and though small, yet being clustered together, they make a tolerable appearance But the berries afford the greatest beauty, being large, rather oblong, and when ripe very black

Derivation of its original appellation

This tree was formerly called *Lauro-Cerasus*, a word compounded of *laurus* and *cerasus, the cherry-bay* Linnæus has now made it a species of the *Prunus*, which has been objected to, because, it is said, no sorts of the cherry will grow upon plum-stocks, nor plums upon cherry-stocks, whereas real species of the same genus will unite, when properly grafted or budded on each other, and as none of these sorts will take upon each other, therefore in making these cherries only a species of the *Prunus*, which were always before looked upon as different genera, he is here supposed to have exceeded the bounds of Nature This observation put me upon trying the experiment Accordingly, having a sufficient quantity of plum-stocks proper for the purpose, I grafted the different sorts of cherries on them at different times in the spring, and my success was, they grew exceeding well, shot near a yard the succeeding summer, and were then proper plants either for dwarfs or espaliers

A native of the East When first brought into Europe

The laurel is a native of the East, and grows naturally about the Black Sea It was first brought into Europe by Clusius, in the year 1576, but being easily propagated, is now spread over Italy, and the greatest part of Europe, and is found every where amongst us in our gardens

Method of propagating this tree from seeds,

The laurel is propagated either from the seeds or cuttings If the former method is practised, the seeds must be gathered from the trees when they are full ripe This will be known by their being quite black, which is generally about the beginning of October These seeds should be sown directly in beds of light earth, half an inch deep, which must be afterwards hooped over, to be covered in very severe frosts A hedge of furze bushes also should be made around them, to break the force of the freezing black winds, and secure the seeds, together with the mats, from being destroyed This is a much safer method than covering the beds with litter, which, if neglected to be taken off when the frost is over, will retain the rains which generally succeed such weather, sodden the beds, and make them so wet as frequently to destroy the whole of the expected crop The seeds being sown, and preserved with the above care, will appear in the spring During the following summer they should be kept clear of weeds, as well as watered in dry weather, and all the ensuing winter they must remain untouched in their beds, the furze-hedge still standing till the frosty weather is past; for if these young seedlings are planted out in the autumn, the major part of them will be in danger before the winter is expired, of being thrown *out of the ground by the frost*; and not only so, but of being really killed by it, as they are not very hardy at one year old In the spring, therefore, when the bad weather is ceased, let them be planted out in the nursery ground, in rows two feet asunder, and the plants a foot and a half distance in the rows, where they may stand till they are planted out for good

LAUREL

Trees raised from seeds generally grow more upright, and seldom throw out so many lateral branches, as those reared from cuttings, nevertheless, as the expectation of a crop from seeds has so often failed, notwithstanding great care has been used, and as the difficulty of procuring the seeds, and preserving them from the birds, has been very great, the most certain and expeditious method of raising quantities of these trees is by cuttings, and is as follows

and from cuttings

In the month of August the cuttings should be gathered, about a foot and a half in length They will thrive the better for having a bit of the last year's wood at the end, though without this they will grow exceeding well The under leaves should be cut off a foot from the thick end of the cutting, which must all be planted about a foot deep in the ground, the other half foot, with its leaves, being above it No distance need be observed in planting these cuttings, which may be set as thick as you please, though the ground for raising them should be sheltered, lest the winds, which are frequently high at this time of the year, or soon after, loosen the plants just when they are going to strike root, if not wholly blow them out

The weather when the cuttings are to be planted should be either rainy or cloudy and if no showers should fall in August the work must be deferred till they do; for if cuttings are planted in August when the weather is parching and dry, they will be burnt up, without great care and trouble in shading and watering Neither is cloudy or rainy weather only to be recommended in planting these cuttings, but a shady situation also, either under a North wall, or in beds which are covered the greatest part of the day with the umbrage of large trees This shady situation is very necessary for them, since, though the weather be rainy and cloudy when they are planted out, yet should it prove fair afterwards, the sun will soon dry up the moisture at that season, and endanger the plants, if they are not constantly watered and protected with a shade, which at once shews the expediency of pitching on a spot where such a conveniency is natural

If these cuttings are planted in August, they will have taken root before winter, especially if they have shade, and water in dry weather, but they should remain undisturbed till the spring twelvemonth following, in order to acquire strength to be planted in the nursery During the summer, they will require no other trouble than watering in dry weather, and being kept clean from weeds, and by the autumn they will have made a shoot of perhaps a foot or more in length In the beds, nevertheless, they may remain till the spring, when they should be all carefully taken out, and planted in the nursery, as was directed for the seedlings

October the best season for planting

When these trees are to be planted out for good, any time during the winter will be proper for this work, though I would recommend the month of October as the most favourable season The ground ought to be prepared for their reception by ploughing, and they should be planted in holes made all over it, at one yard asunder When they begin to touch each other, do

LAUREL

do not immediately thin them, but suffer them to remain unthinned two or three years longer, by which means they will draw one another up to regular stems. When you begin to thin them, it must be done sparingly, and in small quantities, only taking out a weakly plant here and there, to make room for the more vigorous shooting of the others, lest the cold, entering the plantation too much at once, should retard its growth, if not wholly destroy it.

Plantations of this tree should be thinned sparingly, and with caution.

The danger of losing these plants is, I believe, only when they have been used to grow close, and the cold is suffered to rush in upon them all of a sudden; but where they have been planted on bleak or exposed places singly, I seldom ever knew a plant of this tree killed by the cold. However, let these plantations be continued to be thinned with caution till the general fall.

Grows well on almost all soils and situations.

The laurel is now so far naturalized to us, as to grow well in almost any of our soils or situations. So that plantations of this tree may be made in any place where there is a conveniency. In Italy there are numerous woods consisting entirely of these trees; and altho England at present cannot boast of many plantations of this kind, yet his grace the duke of Bedford has set a noble example to men of fortune, at Wooburn, where he has planted one hill solely with laurels, which thrive exceedingly; as do those also which are mixed in great quantities with his other evergreens, throughout his whole plantations.

LAUREL. The berries wholesome,

Altho' the berries of the laurel have been looked upon by many to be pernicious, they are nevertheless very wholesome, and may be eaten by those who like them without danger of injury; and when put into brandy, they make a good sort of ratafia. Those also have laboured under a mistake who have hitherto supposed the leaves to be endued with any noxious quality; for by many experiments they are found to be not only innocent, but even salutary; which circumstance being now generally known, they are used in custards, &c. to which they give a most agreeable flavour.

and leaves salutary.

Thus much for this noble evergreen, at present the pride only of our wilderness quarters and gardens; but which, it is hoped, will shine upon our hills in woods; a tree worthy of our attention, as well as deserving of the extraordinary deference shewn it by the antients, who used it, together with the bay, in crowning triumphant generals, poets, &c.

*Tu sacros Phœbi tripodas, tu sidera sentis,*
*Et casus aperis rerum præsaga futuros.*
*Te juvat armorum strepitus, clangorque tubarum;*
*Perque acies medias, sæv que pericula belli,*
*Accendis bellantûm animos, te Cynthius ipse,*
*Te Musæ, vatesque sacri optavere coronam.*
*Ipsa suis virtus te spem proponit alumnis,*
*Tantum servat tibi alma pudor, & bona fama.*

RAPINUS.

## CHAP. XV.

## *LAURUS*, The BAY-TREE.

THE Bay-Tree is at once a fine aromatic as well as evergreen, and has hitherto been seldom planted except for the sake of the leaves, or to add to the variety of evergreens in wilderness quarters. For these purposes, indeed, this tree is extremely proper; and as it will grow in shades, and under the drip of trees, is excellently adapted, like the laurel, for ornamenting the borders of woods, especially as it adds a lively chearfulness to such places at all seasons.

Situations proper for this tree.

But whoever considers that this tree will mount to a large size, will find that it ought to be raised for more considerable purposes. It will grow to thirty feet in height, with a trunk of two feet in diameter; and consequently may be planted for proper avenues like the laurel, or raised for the sake of its timber.

Height to which it grows.

The wood of the bay-tree is not very valuable; so that plantations of it should be few and small in proportion. Indeed, this tree ought to be planted chiefly with a view to make the greater variety. However, the timber may be used for all the purposes of the laurel, and is greatly coveted by the turner, joiner, and cabinet-maker.

Uses of its timber.

The leaves of the bay tree begin to open about the middle of March, and will be quite out by the beginning of May. They stand close, are about three inches long and two broad, are hard, rigid, and of a deep green colour; so that any one will know how to dispose of these trees so as to make the most agreeable variety. The flowers, which are of a light yellow colour, make no show. They have generally nine stamina and one style, which shews the plant to belong to the class and order *Enneandria Monogynia*.

Time of the leaves opening.

Class and order in the Linnæan system.

The generical word, *Laurus*, is derived from the Latin verb *lavo, to wash* or *purge*, not only as this tree was very powerful in purging and cleansing of the blood, but was used by the antient heathens in their religious purifications. It was dedicated to Apollo, and was planted before the gates of emperors and pontiffs. Its branches were made into garlands for triumphs, &c. and were conjectured to be eat by the Sybils, &c.

Derivation of the generical name.

The bay-tree is a native of Italy, though it grows in most parts of Europe, and is very common in almost all our gardens, especially in old ones, which seldom fail of exhibiting some very large trees of this species.

A native of Italy.

This tree is propagated by layers, or the berries. In order to raise a quantity of these trees by layers, some stools should be planted for the purpose; and after these are shot about a yard high, the branches must be brought down to the ground in the winter, all the preceding summer's shoots laid on it and pegged down (being first slit in the joint), and the leaves taken off, which would otherwise be under ground. In one year's time these layers will

Method of propagating this tree from layers.

will have taken root, and in the ſpring they ſhould be taken up, and planted in the nurſery a foot aſunder, in rows two feet diſtance After they are planted out, if the weather ſhould prove dry, they muſt be conſtantly watered, for without ſuch care, it is difficult to make this tree grow After they are well taken to the ground, they will require no farther trouble than keeping clean from weeds, and digging between the rows each winter, till they are planted out for good

Directions for raiſing it from the berries

In order to raiſe this tree from the berries, they ought to hang on the trees till about January before they are gathered A well-ſheltered ſpot of ground for the ſeminary muſt be made choice of, and having the mould ſmooth and fine, they ſhould be ſowed ſoon after they are gathered in beds, or drills, rather more than half an inch deep Towards the cloſe of the ſpring the plants will come up, and during ſummer muſt be duly attended, by watering and weeding In the winter following, their ſheltered ſituation muſt not be truſted to, to defend them from the froſt Furze buſhes, or ſome ſuch things, ought to be ſtuck in rows, between the beds or drills, to guard them from the black froſts Indeed, without this precaution, if the winter ſhould prove very froſty, few of the young ſeedlings will be alive in ſpring

During the following ſummer, weeding and watering muſt be obſerved, and the winter after that they ſhould be defended with covering as before, for they will be ſtill in danger of being deſtroyed by ſevere froſts In the enſuing ſpring, the ſtrongeſt may be taken out of the ſeed beds, and planted in the nurſery way, though if they have not by that time made good ſhoots, it will be adviſeable to let them remain in their beds till the third ſpring, for a ſmall plant of this kind is with more difficulty made to grow than one which is larger

When they are planted in the nurſery, the diſtance which ſhould be allowed them is the ſame as the layers, a foot aſunder and two feet diſtance in the rows, and this will not be found too cloſe, for notwithſtanding the greateſt care is exerted in planting them in the nurſery, even making choice of rainy and cloudy weather, which muſt always be obſerved in ſetting them out, many of them will be loſt by being tranſplanted After they are thus planted out in the nurſery, whether layers or ſeedlings, they muſt be ſtill watered in dry weather, kept free from weeds, and the rows dug between every winter You will even find, that thoſe plants which ſuffer leaſt by being tranſplanted will have met with a check, which they will not recover in two or three years, and till they have acquired new ſtrength they ſhould not be taken from the nurſery, but when they appear to be good ſtuff plants, and the year before had made a vigorous ſhoot, they will be then proper plants for planting out for good Holes ſhould be got ready for their reception, and as ſoon as the firſt autumnal rains fall, the work ſhould be ſet about, eſpecially if the land be gravelly or dry, but if it be moiſt, the ſpring will do as well Being now planted at one yard diſtance, they will make a poor progreſs for two or three years more but after this, when they have overcome all theſe difficulties, they will grow very faſt, and arrive to be good trees in a few years

Soils ſuitable to this tree

Altho' this tree flouriſhes well in all old gardens, where the ſoil has been rich and deep, and loves the ſhade and ever dripping of trees, it thrives nevertheleſs exceedingly well in our hotteſt gravels and ſands, and, after it has ſurmounted the hardſhips of tranſplanting, will grow in ſuch ſituations extremely faſt, and arrive to a large bulk

The berries an excellent carminative and uſed in medicine

The berries of this tree are poſſeſſed of many extraordinary qualities, being an excellent carminative, and much uſed in medicine

## CHAP XVI

## *BUXUS*, The BOX-TREE

Situations proper for this tree

THIS is a very proper tree to encreaſe the variety in quarters of evergreens, and places deſigned for pleaſure, and altho' it is a ſlow grower, and never arrives to any very large ſize, yet the value of its timber is ſuch as ſhould induce every perſon poſſeſſed of cold and barren hills, from which he reaps little benefit, to plant them with theſe trees, for on the declivities of ſuch places they will grow as well as in any other ſituation, and after the expence of the planting, and keeping the weeds down two or three years, is over, the charge attending a plantation of this ſort, even including the annual rent of the ground, will be very inconſiderable But it will prove a good eſtate in reverſion either to the owner's children or grandchildren, as the value of box-wood is much ſuperior to that of any other tree, being not ſold by the meaſure like other timber, but by the weight, at a certain price per pound

Uſes to which the timber, which is extremely valuable, is applied

The box-wood is ſo heavy that it will ſink in water, and ſo hard as to be excellent for innumerable ſorts of utenſils Of what ſuperlative value is it for theſe diminutive purpoſes! rulers, rolling-pins, tops, pegs for muſical inſtruments, ſcrews, cheſſmen, bobbins, ſpoons, nutcrackers, combs, &c Weavers ſhuttles are made of this wood, and peſtles, beetles, and mallets, cut out of it are highly valued, but the engravers and mathematical-inſtrument makers buy it for a great variety of uſes in their way In ſhort, whoever has plenty of this wood will have a number of purchaſers, who will be glad to buy it by the pound for different curious uſes

Derivation of the generical name

This tree derives its name, *Buxus*, from the Greek πύξος, which ſignifies *a box tree*, and is ſo called from the verb πυκάζω, *denſo, to thicken*, becauſe this wood is of all others the cloſeſt and moſt compact

Claſs and order in the Linnæan ſyſtem

The flowers of the box-tree, which are of a yellow colour, make no ſhow, and are unnoticed by all, except the botaniſt There are male and female flowers on the ſame plant, and the male flowers have four ſtamina, which ſhews this tree to belong to the claſs and order *Monoecia Tetrandria*

The

BOX. A native of Britain.

The box tree is a native of Britain, and grows wild in many parts of England. It may be propagated by cuttings as follows.

Manner of propagating this tree from cuttings.

The month of Auguſt is the beſt time for planting, if any rain falls. If none ſhould happen, then the work muſt be deferred till it does. Indeed, the cuttings may be planted with ſucceſs any time in the winter, even till the middle of April; but it is moſt prudent, if the ground is ready, to have this work done as ſoon as the firſt autumnal rains fall.

Theſe cuttings ought to be of one and two years wood, ſhould be about a foot long, rather more than the half of which muſt be planted in the ground in the manner directed for the laurel. A ſlip of the laſt year's wood ſtripped from an older branch, is an excellent ſett, of which there will be little fear of its growing. The cuttings for the firſt raiſing of theſe trees ſhould be at about four inches diſtance in the beds; and after they are planted, will need no trouble except watering in dry weather, and keeping clean from weeds, till about the third year after planting; for in all that time they will not be got too big for the ſeed-beds.

Seaſon for tranſplanting theſe trees.

The ſeaſon for tranſplanting theſe trees from the ſeed-beds to the nurſery is any time from Auguſt to April, though if they are to be tranſplanted early in the autumn, or late in the ſpring, moiſt weather ſhould be made choice of for this purpoſe.

The diſtance theſe plants ſhould be placed at in the nurſery muſt be a foot aſunder and two feet in the rows; and here they may ſtand till they are planted out for good.

The box-tree may be alſo propagated from ſeeds; and trees raiſed this way will often grow to a larger ſize. In order to raiſe this tree from ſeeds, let them be gathered when they are quite ripe, and juſt ready to burſt out of their cells, and ſoon after ſow them in a border of light ſandy earth, about half an inch deep. In the ſpring the plants will appear; though it ſometimes happens that they lie in the beds one whole ſeaſon before they come up, eſpecially if they happen to have been kept long before they were ſowed after being gathered. If they ſhould not appear in the ſpring, the beds muſt remain undiſturbed till the next, only keeping them free from weeds, and now and then giving them a gentle watering in dry weather. After they have made their appearance, they ſhould ſtand two or three years in the ſeed bed, the firſt of which will require attendance by watering in dry weather. When they are ſtrong enough to plant out, they may be ſet in rows in the nurſery, as was directed for the cuttings.

BOX. Method of raiſing it from ſeeds.

When they are planted out for good, they ought to be ſet a yard aſunder, and thinned afterwards as the owner ſees neceſſary.

Soils in which it delights.

The ſoils and ſituations theſe trees will thrive in are pretty general. They will not only grow in vales, but on the declivities of cold and barren mountains. On Box-Hill, near Darking in Surry, which takes its name from theſe trees growing in great abundance thereon, there were formerly trees of a great bulk and ſtature, which are now chiefly deſtroyed. This hill is a chalky ſoil, mixed with gravel; and as box-trees grew naturally on this ſituation, it ſhews this ſoil to be moſt natural to them; though they thrive exceeding well at Gumley, in that white clay, and ſucceed as well at Langton, in our ſtiff loam. In ſhort, they flouriſh in all our Leiceſterſhire clays, and hardly any ſoil comes amiſs to them.

## CHAP. XVII.

## *THUYA*, The ARBOR VITÆ TREE.

THE Arbor Vitæ, like ſeveral of the preceding trees, has hitherto been only raiſed for ornament; though if we conſider that it is a tree which will ariſe to between forty and fifty feet high, and that the wood is very valuable, it might with good reaſon be planted for the ſake of the timber alſo.

There are three ſorts of the arbor vitæ, the Common, the Chineſe, and the Sweet ſcented American arbor vitæ; the two latter of which, eſpecially the Sweet-ſcented, are at preſent very rare, and altho' they probably will grow to as great a ſize as the Common, I ſhall leave them till I come to treat of the trees proper to form a complete wilderneſs of evergreens, propoſing at preſent to confine myſelf ſolely to the Common arbor vitæ.

The Common arbor vitæ tree only treated of in this chapter.

This tree, as I before obſerved, will ariſe to above forty feet in height, ſtraight and fine; and the wood is reddiſh, firm, and reſinous. So that we may eaſily judge of its value for curioſities of moſt ſorts, when worked up by the reſpective artificers of turnery, joiners, cabinet-makers, &c.

Its appearance deſcribed. Purpoſes to which the timber is applied.

The arbor vitæ is a native of North-America, but having been long introduced into our gardens, it produces plenty of ſeeds here, and ſeems to thrive as well in our ſoils as in thoſe of North-America.

A native of North-America.

The ſtrong ſmell of the leaves, and ſweetneſs of the wood of this tree, has occaſioned it to be called *Thuya*, from the Greek Θυω, *odoramentum, a perfume* or *ſweet thing*; and the wood being very laſting, as well as ſweet, has occaſioned it to be called the Life-Tree, *Arbor Vitæ*, or *Tree of Life*.

Derivation of its generical name.

The American ſweet-ſcented arbor vitæ which is a ſort lately introduced into our gardens, ſeems to claim the greateſt right to theſe derivations. The ſeeds were procured me, from Penſylvania, by my late worthy friend Peter Collinſon, Eſq; F. R. S. to whom alſo I was indebted for many curious plants, which I have raiſed from ſeeds, and which he procured me from the above-mentioned province, and other parts of the New World.

Time when the flowers open.

The flowers of the arbor vitæ come out early in the ſpring, but make a mean appearance. They are adorned by no corolla, have male and female flowers ſeparately on the ſame plant; and their claſs and order are *Monoecia Monadelphia*, the ſtamina being connected into one body.

Claſs and order in the Linnæan ſyſtem.

The arbor vitæ is to be propagated either from ſeeds, layers, or cuttings, the former of

which

ARB. VIT.

which produce the beſt trees, though the two latter methods of propagating are more generally practiſed.

Method of propagating this tree from ſeeds,

In order to propagate this tree from ſeeds, theſe laſt ſhould be gathered as ſoon as they are quite ripe, which will be by the beginning of October. They muſt be ſown in pots or boxes of light fine earth, being covered about a quarter of an inch deep. The boxes ſhould immediately after be put in a well-ſheltered place, ſo that the ſeeds in them, whilſt they are preparing to diſcloſe, may not be deſtroyed by violent froſts. Being thus protected till the month of February, they muſt be brought out, and ſet along a South wall, that the ſun warming the mould may ſet the powers of vegetation at work; and whenever ſevere weather is expected, they ſhould be removed into their ſhelter, but muſt be brought out again when the fine ſpringing weather returns. With this care, the plants will come up in the ſpring; whilſt, without it, they frequently lie till the ſecond ſpring before they make their appearance, by which neglect one year is loſt.

When the young plants are up, and all danger of the froſt is ceaſed, they ſhould be ſet in the ſhade where they can have the free air; and in this place they may remain all ſummer. During that ſeaſon, little water ſhould be given them; keeping them clean from weeds is the principal trouble they will cauſe. By the autumn they will have made a poor ſhoot; for this reaſon they ſhould continue in their pots or boxes, which muſt be placed in the ſame ſheltered ſituation they had at firſt, where they may remain all winter. In the ſpring they may be brought out into the ſun again, to reap the benefit of his influence at that ſeaſon; and if they are ſet in the ſhade at the beginning of May, to remain there all ſummer, it will forward their growth. The ſpring following, being then two years-old ſeedlings, they ſhould be taken out of the boxes, and planted in beds nine inches aſunder. Here they may ſtand two years, before they are ſet in the nurſery. When they are taken from theſe beds with this intent, a moiſt ſeaſon ought always to be made choice of, and they ſhould be planted a foot and a half aſunder, and two feet and a half diſtance in the rows, where they may ſtand till they are ſet out for good.

layers,

In order to propagate this tree from layers, the ground ſhould be dug, and made light round about the ſtools, and the branches laid down ſo deep as that the top eyes may but juſt peep above the ground, all being of the young wood. But if it ſhould ſo happen, that a few of the laſt year's ſhoots on the branches ſhould have ſhot out vigorouſly, and that there are many healthy twigs which would make good layers, that are not ſo long; in order to have the greater plenty of layers, and that the ſhorter ſhoots may not be buried, it will be proper to ſhorten the longeſt, ſo that, being all laid in the ground, their noſes may juſt appear above the ſurface. This will be a means of preſerving every twig, and conſequently of propagating the greater number of plants from the ſame ſtool. When theſe plants are layered, the ſhoots ought to have a gentle twiſt or a ſmall nick; for without this they will not always ſtrike root. Nay, if the land is ſtrong and heavy, it is great odds but you find them without root, as you laid them, only grown bigger. Thus will one year be loſt, which ſhews the neceſſity of obſerving theſe precautions. Being layered in this manner in the autumn, by the autumn following they will have taken root; and in the ſpring, when the ſevere froſts are paſt, they may be taken from the ſtools, and planted in the nurſery, at the diſtance directed for the ſeedlings.

and cuttings.

In order to propagate theſe trees from cuttings, young ſhoots ſhould be taken from the trees in Auguſt, if rain has fallen; if not, the buſineſs muſt be deferred till it does; for work of this kind ſhould never be performed till the early autumnal rains have fallen upon the earth, and made it cool and moiſt. All theſe cuttings ought to be of the laſt year's ſhoots, and if a bit of the old wood be left at the end of each, it will encreaſe the certainty of ſucceſs.

Situation and proper ſoil for this tree.

The ſituation theſe cuttings ſhould have ought to be ſhady and well ſheltered, and the ſoil in which they are planted, to enſure the greater ſucceſs, ſhould be a red loam. They may be planted almoſt as thick as you pleaſe; not more, however, than four or five inches aſunder, in rows; the rows may be a foot and a half diſtance from each other; and after they are planted, a little litter may be laid between the rows, to keep the froſt out of the ground in winter, and the ſun from over drying them in the ſummer. This litter will not only keep down the weeds, but will ſave the trouble of watering, which will be much better for the plants; for theſe young plants, juſt ſtriking root, do not much like watering, at leaſt not in great plenty, as it often cauſes the tender fibres to rot at firſt ſtriking, and ſo deſtroys the young plant. In one year theſe cuttings will have good roots; ſo that the litter may be taken away, and the ſurface of the earth turned over in the ſpring, which will cheriſh the plants, and prepare them to ſhoot vigorouſly the ſucceeding ſummer. In the autumn, being then two years old, they may be taken up, and planted in the nurſery, at the diſtance directed for the ſeedlings and layers. After they are planted in the nurſery, they will require nothing more than the uſual care of keeping them clean from weeds, and digging between the rows in winter, till they are planted where they are to remain.

Beſt ſeaſon for planting out.

October is the beſt month for planting out theſe trees, though any of the winter or ſpring months will anſwer. When they are planted, they ſhould be ſet a yard aſunder, and thinned and managed as has been all along directed for others which are nearly of the ſame growth.

# PART IV.

## Of WOODS and FENCES.

### CHAP. I.

### Of WOODS in General, with Directions for raising them with Variety of FOREST-TREES.

Introductory observations.

HAVING finished the method of propagating those forest-trees which are most useful, and shewn in what manner they may be raised, either for standards, clumps, wilderness quarters, or woods, of each respective species, I come now to treat of Woods in general, or such large plantations as may consist of the different sorts of trees, blended promiscuously, without seeming order, as in wilds, forests, &c.

The [illegible] decline of our wood lands [illegible].

Few isles were formerly more blessed with woodlands of these kinds than Britain, but now, alas! there seems to be almost a total decay, a general demolishment of those venerable landmarks of antiquity which have hitherto so powerfully defended us from invasion, and secured us free, *still dwelling under our own vine, and eating every one under his own fig-tree*. And as we seem at present to be almost destitute of materials to mend any future breach in these bulwarks of our nation, these wooden walls, as it were, this circumstance should alarm every true son of Britain for his safety, and it would well become the Legislature to stop the farther progress of this growing evil. But as those who are invested with this power reap a greater benefit, in proportion to the violence of the tables, we have too much reason to fear little alteration will be made on that head, until it be too late, and our nation is left without a defence.

Henry VIII the first destroyer of our forests.

The first attack of any consequence made upon our forest-trees was in the reign of Henry VIII when that ambitious and turbulent prince, not contented with sacrilegiously demolishing and appropriating to his own use the revenues of the religious houses throughout the kingdom, which the piety of the first British Christians had founded, seized on the forests also, and raised vast sums from the annual sale of their timber. This calamity, however, was little felt by the nation in that early time, our timber was found growing so universally over the whole island, that it was not in the power of a few years to have injured us, had the contagion been then stopped. But from that æra the decay of our timber bears its date, and its diminution seems to have encreased gradually ever since.

From whence [illegible] of the decay of our timber may be dated.

The next general onset, that threatened a total dismantling of his majesty's forests, was under the grand Usurpation, when those blood-thirsty mock saints fastened upon our growing and wrought timber. They not only entered our solemn temples, cut down the carved work with axes and hammers, and deformed the *Beauty of Holiness*, but set upon the forests with so much fury, that, had their power continued much longer, hardly any of them would have been preserved. But the loss of their authority was what they apprehended, and therefore, like free-booters, they sold all the timber as fast as they cut it down. It was at this æra, that a mortal blow was given to our forests, which have ever since continued to be gradually dismantled, insomuch that at present some have little other appearance of forests than the bare names.

But the most mortal blow was given to our forests in the time of the Usurpation.

But the demolishing of his majesty's forests was not the only injury which the nation sustained, the contagion has diffused itself, either in a greater or less degree, throughout the kingdom. The spendthrift heir has cleared his estate of trees, to supply his extravagancies, the griping miser has eagerly felled his woods, to add greater heaps to his ill-gotten treasure, whilst other powerful owners, possessed of neither of these extremes, through inattention have suffered their timber to lessen insensibly, and having taken no care to plant others for the succession, many goodly estates have now scarcely any woods left.

Other causes which have contributed to the decline of our timber.

At once, therefore, to rouse the inattentive, and instruct them in the best method of improving their estates by planting, is one of the objects of this work. Plantations merely for the sake of the timber have scarcely ever been attempted, the design of all our modern ones being chiefly for shade and ornament. For this purpose, I have in the preceding chapters laid down the manner of raising our different useful timber-trees, since nothing but a general plantation of all sorts of serviceable trees can sufficiently recompense for the hitherto almost general waste and destruction of our woods.

Leicestershire [illegible] deficient in this necessary article.

Though this evil has been general, yet the contagion seems to have made the greatest havoc in Leicestershire, in which extensive county there are very, very few woods left, a loss which every inhabitant sensibly feels, when he pays for the least stick he wants for use. To the Leicestershire people, therefore, I more peculiarly address myself, and exhort them to improve their estates by planting, which will not only turn out to their own profit, but the present age will be indebted to them for ornamenting the county, and posterity will have reason to hold their memory precious.

But notwithstanding the present scarcity of wood in Leicestershire, this county always seems to have been extremely barren of timber, altho there is no land in the kingdom more proper for raising the different sorts of useful forest trees, than the soil in general is. I russet, a versifier ...

though no land more proper for useful forest trees.

WOODS in the reign of Henry VIII complains of this inattention, and as his reasoning is honest, pertinent, and has already been quoted by Evelyn, in his Discourse on Forest-trees, I shall insert his verses on this subject

Ancient poem from Tusser in Henry VIII's reign on the advantages of inclosure and planting

I

" Example by Leicestershire,
" What soil can be better than that
" For any thing heart can desire?
" And yet doth it want ye see what,
" Mast, covert, close pasture, and wood,
" And other things needful as good

II

" More plenty of mutton and beef,
" Corn, butter, and cheese of the best,
" More wealth any where (to be brief),
" More people, more handsome, and prest,
" Where find ye (go search any coast)
" Than there where inclosure is most?

III

" More work for the labouring man,
" As well in the town as the field,
" Or thereof (devise, if you can)
" More profit what countries do yield?
" More seldom where see ye the poor
" Go begging from door to door?

IV

" In woodland the poor men that have
" Scarce fully two acres of land,
" More merrily live, and do save,
" Than t'other with twenty in hand
" Yet pay they as much for the two
" As t'other for twenty must do
" If this same be true, as it is,
" Why gather they nothing by this?"

Thus earnestly, even in that fruitful age of timber, were the advantages of inclosure and planting enforced, and if there was reason for it in those days, how much more so now, when, I dare venture to assert, there is not the thousandth part of the trees standing in the kingdom as there were in the times when Tusser lived.

However, my design is not to spend too much time in exhorting people to plant, it is chiefly to instruct those who are already attached to this pleasing art So that I shall proceed to give directions for the raising of woods with the variety of forest-trees

Directions for raising woods with the variety of forest trees

If the wood is to be extensive, the soil may greatly vary in that compass Some parts of it may be mountainous, others boggy, some consist of a light sand, others of a stiff clay This variation will often happen in the compass of some hundred acres When it does, the ground must be looked over, to allot the different sorts of trees to those soils in which they succeed best, and which may be easily known from perusing the preceding sheets

If the soil be in general of an even nature, then may oak, chesnut, Wych elm, beech, ash, and all the foregoing sorts of deciduous trees, have nearly an equal share, the largest-growing trees, and such as seem to succeed best in the soil, to grow for timber-trees, the others to compose the underwood

Having wholly considered the nature of the land, the seeds of all the sorts proper for it are next to be procured The year before planting, the ground should be ploughed, and sowed with a crop of turneps, to turn the sward and mellow the land, which will be still farther improved by these turneps being eat off by sheep Some old writers on planting have advised to get two or three successive crops of grain off the land, and after that to sow it again with oats, mixed with the seeds of the trees This advice, however, is certainly very absurd, as well as dangerous for the ground having born three or four crops, without any manure, its strength will be almost exhausted, so that when the seeds of the trees grow, they will only have vigour sufficient to make their appearance, and for want of proper juices to set them forward, will often become stunted, never grow fast, and hardly in any age make a wood of timber The weeds also will prove another check to them, which they will not overcome in many years, for I take it for granted, that those who have recommended the raising of woods this way, never intended they should be weeded In order, therefore, to have your young wood shoot healthy and strong from the first, the ground should bear no more than a crop of turneps to mellow it, and these should be eaten off with sheep, to enrich the land, for it has been remarked, that as the first year's shoot of the young plant from the seed is, so it continues to flourish in proportion during the future growth of the tree An observation which the folly of those persons strongly points out, who, for the sake of two or three crops of grain, yearly occasion the ruin of what they intended to raise

The seeds being procured, should be laid by in proper and secure places, till the month of February The acorns and nuts must be preserved from mice and vermin, and all the other sorts kept as directed under their respective heads, till that time As soon as the turneps are eaten off, which ought to be as soon as possible, the ground should be ploughed over with a good strong plow, and afterwards harrowed with a strong harrow to break the clods In the beginning of February it should be ploughed again across with the same plow, and harrowed as before, after which it will be fit for sowing And here I must observe, that though I direct this work to be performed in February, yet if the plantation is to be large and extensive, and there be a necessity for it, it may be done all winter The season for sowing our forest tree seeds, is from the time they are ripe till the spring But I prefer February, as a month in which, if the business abovementioned is done, the weeds will appear later in the spring, and in less quantities than if the land had been undisturbed since October Besides, the seeds would be secure from vermin, if kept till that season; and consequently after they are sown, will require less attention, for it is incredible to think, as soon as they are committed to the ground, notwithstanding the greatest care has been taken to cover them safe, what swarms of crows, mice, and other vermin, will attack them all over the whole seminary Whenever, therefore, the plantation is designed to be so extensive as to require a whole winter's work, the number of acorns, nuts, and such seeds as vermin are fond of, ought to be doubled, or more, to be sown first, for these animals will not only live upon them all winter, but will carry them to a distance, and lay them up in hoards for their future relief

The ground being ready for sowing, the seeds should be all mixed together, nearly in equal quantities, the oak only excepted, of which there ought to be a greater share The ash also has been so far distinguished, that it has been held as a fundamental rule in making such plantations, that every third seed should be an ash key But this rule every planter may vary from or retain, according to his own taste, or the timber that is most wanted in his parts

The

The ſeeds being mixed, according to the taſte of the owner, or the nature of the ground, the ridings are next to be marked out. Theſe I would adviſe to be large, if the plantation is of great extent, eſpecially the capital ones, that the air may be admitted freely when the trees come to grow, which will refreſh the plants, render them more hardy, and cauſe them to ſhoot forth with greater vigour. It is impoſſible to aſcertain the breadth of theſe ridings, which muſt always be in proportion to the extent of ground planted, though I muſt obſerve, if any planter ſhould think his ground loſt by having them wide he is miſtaken. The woods will be rather improved by this means, for the wideſt ridings may annually be made to bear a crop of oats, or other grain, and this ſtirring of the land will alſo prove of great ſervice to all the trees growing within ſome diſtance of the borders. It is almoſt unneceſſary, I think, to inform the planter, that the width of the riding need not be ſo ſtrictly obſerved when the plantations are on mountains and high hills, ſince ſuch exalted ſituations will always naturally have air in greater plenty than levels. It is ſufficient, therefore, that places are left for paſſage and carriage. The grand capital ridings being marked out, other inferior or narrower ones ſhould be ſet out, in ſuch a manner as to divide the whole wood into quarters, of not more than four or five acres. But this rule is not to be obſerved too ſtrictly. The eye ſhould be caſt around, to ſee what diſtant objects preſent themſelves, and thoſe ſmaller ridings which lead from the capital ones ſhould be ſo contrived, if poſſible, as to exhibit the view of a church, caſtle, windmill, or ſome agreeable object, which will at once equally pleaſe and ſtrike the imagination. And this may certainly be done, for though ſome of the quarters by that means be too large, yet they may be divided by ſmaller ridings, that they may have alſo a due proportion of air.

This work being performed, we now proceed to ſowing.

The ground being mellow and light, the clods broken by ploughing and harrowing, and the roots of all large weeds, ſuch as docks, &c. picked out and deſtroyed, let lines be drawn and drills made acroſs each quarter, three or four inches deep, and let the drills be one yard aſunder. Men or women, boys or girls, may be inſtructed how to ſcatter the ſeeds (being firſt mixed together) promiſcuouſly in theſe drills, and after they are ſown, a ſufficient number of hands ſhould be employed in covering them up and finiſhing the work. After the ſeeds are all got into the ground, traps muſt be ſet for the mice, ſcarecrows made, and the whole conſtantly guarded with a gun till the plants appear, which will be in the ſpring, when raiſed from the acorns, nuts, &c. Aſh-keys will remain in the ground till the ſecond ſpring before they come up, ſo that they will give the oak the advantage of one year's ſhoot before them. This ſuperiority, however, happens very fortunately, as the aſh ſhoots faſter than the oak at firſt, but the young oakling having this year's ſtart, will maintain its place, if it likes the ground, keep pace with the aſh, and be found of the ſame height, or nearly, when the fall of underwood is made.

After the drills for the ſeeds are made, it will be proper to ſtick pegs in the rows, for theſe pegs will be a guide to the hoers, who muſt conſtantly keep the ground clear from weeds, till the plants are of a ſufficient ſize to deſtroy them. The earlieſt and moſt attentive care muſt be excited the ſpring after the ſeeds are ſown, to hoe the weeds down between the rows as the plants ſpring up, and to pick thoſe out with the hand which ſeem to be over the ſeeds, and to which you will be directed by the pegs. After the plants have made their appearance, the pegs will be of no uſe, the ſcarecrow will loſe his office: the attention muſt now be directed to keep down the weeds that ſummer, and the ſummer following eſpecially. The ſucceeding ſpring the aſh keys, mountain aſh-berries, &c. will ſend forth their young plants, and if they are kept clear of weeds all the ſummer, by the autumn following they will make a pretty appearance. You will then ſee the whole tribe of foreſt-trees juſt ſprung out of their mother earth, and preſenting themſelves, ſtill weak and helpleſs, ſtill capable of being deſtroyed by weeds, rabbits, hares, or vermin, without the attention or tender nurſing of the planter, who muſt guard them with watchful care, and inceſſantly labour to ward off thoſe evils. In this defenceleſs ſtate they will remain till they attain proper ſize and ſtrength. But they will ariſe in ſuch ſwarms, if the ſeeds are good, as to be unable to be maintained in their places by their common mother, ſo that if any other plantation is to be made, they may be properly thinned, and planted out in the nurſery way to acquire ſtrength. Thus, for the ſame trouble, an infinite number of plants of all ſorts may be raiſed, either to form any other plantation, or be ſold to defray the expence of what has been already done. But if no more planting can be afforded, and no ſale is to be had, the owner need not give himſelf much trouble about them, or be at any further expence in drawing or tranſplanting. The moſt vigorous and thriving plants will deſtroy the weakeſt and the underlings, and a ſufficient quantity of trees will be found at the firſt under-wood-fall to reign more or leſs predominant.

Having kept the plants clean from weeds till they are out of their reach, no other care will be required than keeping the fences good till the time of the firſt fall. This ſhould always be determined by the ſize of the wood, and the demand likely to be made for the materials. If the wood ſtands upon ſeveral hundred acres, and at the fall both faggots and poles can be ſold, then let a great part of it be cut down, if the ground is good, at eight or ten years growth. The year following another ſhare ſhould be taken, and the ſucceeding year another, and ſo on, that when the laſt quarter is cut, that which had the firſt fall may be ready to cut again, obſerving always to have an annual ſucceſſion. But this fall muſt always be governed by the nature of the country, to ſupply it with ſuch timber as it moſt wants. If larger poles and wood are wanted, the falls ſhould be of leſs extent, and may be ſo managed that the return of each may be made in eighteen or twenty years. If ſmaller poles, faggot-wood, &c. are moſt wanted, then the annual fall may be of greater extent, and the returns of each may be every ſix, ſeven, eight, ten, twelve, or fourteen years, according to the judgment of the owner.

In every fall care muſt be taken to leave the moſt vigorous and thriving trees for timber. If the final ſtandards are deſigned to be all oak, there will be more than ſufficient for the purpoſe, all healthy and ſtrong; if of different ſorts of trees, a luxuriant tree of what ſort ſoever muſt be left, whether oak, aſh, cheſnut, beech, or elm. Theſe ſtandards may be left pretty cloſe the firſt fall, but every ſucceeding fall they muſt be thinned, and this thinning muſt be continued as they encreaſe in bulk, till they arrive at timber.

*WOODS.*

*Method of raising a wood of young plants [illegible]*

Such is the method of raising a wood from the variety of seeds. Another way is to raise them of young plants from the nursery. Whoever, therefore, is desirous of raising his wood in that manner, must sow the seeds of the respective trees in a seminary, as has been directed under each article. When these plants have been two or three years, according to the shoots they have made, in the seed-beds, they may be taken out for the purpose. This is always to be understood when woods are to be of a remarkable extent; for when they are to be of small compass, the plants from the seed-beds should always be planted out in the nursery way, to stand two or three years to acquire strength, before they are set out for good. But the trouble and expence of this method would be too great for large plantations. Therefore, the plants being of tolerable strength in the seed-beds, and the land being prepared by bearing a crop of turneps the preceding year, to kill the sward, and by ploughing and harrowing afterwards to make the mould fine, as was ordered for the seeds; I say, the plants may now be taken out of their respective beds, and having shortened the tap roots, and taken off the side-branches, a sufficient number of men and boys should be ready to plant them in the manner I directed for the oaks, in rows one yard asunder, and at two or three feet distance in the rows.

*Advantages attending plantations made the above way.*

Plantations made this way have these advantages. If the soil appears to vary much when it comes to be turned up, the planter having young trees of all sorts ready, will know how to vary them as the soil changes, and suit every tree by planting it in such land as best agrees with its own nature. There will be no fear or danger of the plantation's being destroyed by mice or vermin. A small seminary will afford trees to plant out a prodigious tract of land; and when plantations are made this way, little expence is caused by weeding: for altho' the plants must be kept clear of weeds till they are above their reach, yet that will be in a very little time, and a double shelving plow may be used for part of the purpose.

The advantage of sowing the seeds where they are to remain, is at once to get rid of all the trouble of transplanting them from the seminary, which is very considerable. But how far this trouble balances with that of scarecrowing, and close weeding for many years, every planter is at liberty to judge.

*Other directions to be observed in raising woods.*

But in making these plantations, whether by seeds or young trees, another thing must be observed, in order to render them charming and delightful; the borders must be planted with evergreens, such as laurels, bays, &c. which will form a more pleasing and greater variety of greens in the summer, and make a sweet contrast between their constant verdure and the naked stems of the other in winter. Flowering trees and shrubs also should have their share in the borders of woods, such as lilacs, laburnums, spindle-trees, dogwoods, syringas, viburnums, spiræa frutices, &c. Neither will these be trees serviceable only for ornament, but at each fall the wood of most of them will be found to have a more than ordinary value, for several curious uses. The timber, or even branches, of the laburnum is so ponderous, that it will sink in water; and that wood is generally esteemed of most value which is the heaviest. The spindle-tree also is a very hard wood, and is used not only for inlayings, but the musical-instrument-makers make jacks for spinnets and harpsichords, fiddle-sticks, &c. of it. The dogwood will serve for mill cogs, bobbins, skewers, &c. besides, the charcoal of this tree is of all others the best, if not the only good sort, used for the making of gunpowder. The viburnum deserves planting, if for no other purpose than the sake of making bands, which it makes the best and most pliant of any tree. Other flowering-trees also have their uses more or less: at least they have this in common with all others, the fire; which will be something, besides beautifying and ornamenting the places, from fall to fall. But the manner of raising these plants must be sought for under their respective heads, among such trees as are more peculiarly designed for ornament and pleasure.

*Further cautions necessary in the making of woods.*

Another thing is to be observed at the first making of woods. If they are of large extent, there will probably be pits, bogs, and marshy ground. These pits, if they are not filled up, should have their edges planted with truncheons of willow, &c. The bogs and the marshy ground ought also to be set with small truncheons of poplars, or other aquatics; but where the plow cannot come, and it is not too boggy, the turf should be first turned under by digging with the spade before the cuttings are planted, upon part of which should be the cuttings of the sallow, as that wood always sells readily to the turner, for making of spickets, fassets, &c. Some cuttings of elder likewise should be planted, for they will grow this way like a willow, not only on account of its wood, but of its medicinal qualities.

*Valuable properties of the elder tree.*

The elder-tree, if permitted to stand long, will grow up to firm timber, and is valuable for mill-cogs, butchers skewers, and all sorts of tough uses. Most people know the medicinal properties of the elder, and how wholesome the young buds are when eaten in gruel in the spring. The flowers too afford a fine pickle, and the berries a useful wine. These useful purposes, joined to the value of its wood, justly entitle this tree to a place in our plantations. And these are the only places for elder trees at a distance, where they are hardly ever seen, except when sought after for use; for they should by no means be planted in pleasure-grounds, or near habitations, as their very large flowers in the spring afford a strong disagreeable scent, which is generally supposed to be unwholesome.

*Planting recommended on account of its advantages to every person;*

Thus have I given the rules and method of forming a complete wood; a work so advantageous to the nation in general as well as beneficial to the family of the planter, that it is much to be wished every man would set about it, in proportion to his fortune. Those persons who have neither land nor money to plant large tracts, may nevertheless dedicate some share of what they have to this work, especially as a very little planting upon an estate will be sufficient to double its value to the next generation.

*but more especially to men of large fortunes, &c.*

But this duty is more peculiarly incumbent upon our nobility, men in power, and such as enjoy large fortunes. The wants of the nation call upon them for this supply; and their exerting themselves for this purpose would shew them possessed of a truly noble and patriotic spirit. How many thousand acres of waste ground are there in the kingdom belonging to these men of superior class, which now produce nothing, that may be profitably improved this way! Surely did they rightly consider, they would immediately set about this useful work. They would carefully look over their whole estates, search out every useless bog, and plant it with poplars, or other aquatics. They would examine all the waste ground, and set apart some for the use of the cottagers, and employ the most barren and useless this way. They would soon cover the

WOODS.

their barren mountains, fruitless sands, and worthless heath ground, with trees. And if I should by any means be successful in rousing their attention, and putting them upon this profitable work, the same pleasure will result to me from this reflection, as to one who has contributed something towards the safety of the nation in general, as well as the benefit and profit of each respective individual throughout the kingdom.

WOODS.

# C H A P. II.

## Of the Management and Improvement of OLD WOODS.

AS I cannot without pleasure behold, and with pleasing reflection look upon an old wood, that has been left undestroyed, so I cannot but be somewhat concerned to see the carelessness and negligence of the owners of many of them, who pay so little regard to their preservation, as to leave them exposed to all external accidents of men and beasts. I have seen many an ancient plantation with the underwood ruined, by its owner's carelesly permitting his tenants without controul, or servants for his own use, to cut down poles, or such hedge-wood as is required on their farms, or on his own occupied estate. If either himself or tenants want a few poles for rails, they are immediately sent to the wood, and, in order to have them of the size required, they will for the purpose pick out and hackle them off of as many different stools, if not take a young oakling or ash, that would have grown to keep up the succession of timber. By thus taking off poles at different times, and in that injudicious manner, the stools in a few years will be ruined. Many will be wholly killed, and those which do but just survive, and make any shoots, will always send forth those shoots few and weak in proportion. Thus have I known woods that were formerly thick and good, and which abounded with trees of all the proper sorts, by this bad indulgence, or wicked licence, to tenants or servants, bereft of all their valuable underwood, and made thin of other excellent trees, by such ignorant and careless persons, who, under the pretence of wanting gates, posts, &c. will seize upon a vigorous and thriving oak as soon as a stunted one, which would serve as well for the purpose, and which perhaps grows too near a fine tree, and ought to be taken away, to make room for its greater progress. Thus gentlemen, receiving little present benefit from their woods, remain unroused from their lethargy, and look upon the future advantages of planting to be very inconsiderable, and the expence [illegible] first attending it to be very great.

[illegible margin note]

There are others again, who neglect their fences, and carelesly suffer cattle of all sorts to browse upon the tender twigs. This is an effectual way of stopping the progress of a whole plantation, large timber trees only excepted, for the cattle cropping the leading shoots and branches of the trees, or the rubbing of sheep, &c. against their stems, being venomous, will so retard their growth, and make whatever does grow so knotted and bad, that they will hardly ever make any considerable progress, without being cut down, in order to shoot healthy and fresh from their stools. This is an evil which the great planter as well as poet, Virgil, cautions us to avoid, in these beautiful lines.

*Texendæ sepes etiam, & pecus omne tenendum est*
*Præcipuè dum frons tenera imprudensq; laborum*
*Cui, super indignas hyemes, solemq; potentem,*
*Sylvestres uri assiduè capreæq; sequaces*
*Illudunt. Pascuntur oves, avidæq; juvencæ.*
*Frigora nec tantum canâ concreta pruinâ,*
*Aut gravis incumbens scopulis arentibus æstas;*
*Quantum illi nocuere greges, duriq; venenum*
*Dentis, & admorso signata in stirpe cicatrix.*
Geo. II.

Virgil's caution on this subject.

Next, fenc'd with hedges and deep ditches round,
Exclude th' encroaching cattle from thy ground,
While yet the tender gems but just appear,
Unable to sustain th' uncertain year;
Whose leaves are not alone foul winter's prey,
But oft by summer suns are scorch'd away;
And worse than both, become th' unworthy browze
Of buffalos, salt goats, and hungry cows.
For not December's frost that burns the boughs,
Nor dog-days parching heat that splits the rocks,
Are half so harmful as the greedy flocks;
Their venom'd bite, and scars indented on the stocks.
DRYDEN.

There are too many planters who carelesly suffer their woods to be injured this way, little considering, that if a head of cattle break into a close of grain just ready for mowing, the mounds should be immediately repaired, to keep them out, and forgetting that his wood, which is of so much more value than a crop of grain, and which will turn so much more to his advantage, should call for his more immediate care and security. Thus, instead of raising up more woods in the room of those which have been destroyed, no care has been taken to preserve those that were left, but many of them have been almost brought to destruction, by these and other means. To repair, therefore, those which are decayed, and make the best of those that still remain in tolerable order, is the design of this chapter.

Design of this chapter.

Whoever is possessed of a wood of any kind, and is desirous of making the best of it, let him carefully, first of all, go over it, and mark such trees as are decaying, or are incapable of future improvement, for the axe; for if this is neglected, he will not only lose the interest of the money which these would make, but part of the principal also, as these will annually get worse and worse, and consequently become of less value. Whenever, therefore, you find trees in your wood that have many of their top branches rotten and decayed, it is a certain sign that the trees

General rules and directions for the preservation and improvement of old woods, &c.

trees are at their full growth, and though they should not appear very large of the sorts, yet from these bad symptoms we may conclude, that they will afterwards make very little progress. Neither are those trees alone to be taken away that are arrived at their full growth, but such also as are found to be in a state of decay; likewise those which discover any hollowness, side-crevices, or holes in which the water may sink, and such as the wood-peckers have seized; for the wood-peckers holes are a certain sign of the decay of those trees in which they are found; and therefore they, amongst all others of this sort, are to be taken away, to make room for others, as well as make the loss the less.

After having cut down the unimprovable timber trees, and those that were in a state of decay, the next thing required is to observe the underwood, and see in what condition it is, or in what manner it has been used. If the stools are thin all over the ground, and the standards but sparingly scattered, it should be properly planted, that no ground may be lost. If the cattle have been used to go into the wood, especially if before the underwood was out of their reach, nothing but a general fall of the underwood should immediately ensue; for by this means the stools would be refreshed, and they would send forth shoots vigorous and strong, which would soon overtake any other part of the wood that should be left uncut. Thus may this wood continue for the future to undergo its regular fall, which will abundantly repay the owner for his care in fencing, and protecting it from other accidents.

If the wood be thin, sparing of underwood, and other trees, but yet contains so many as that they ought not to be grubbed up for further planting, then may it be improved and thickened in the following manner. Let the more vigorous shoots that are in the middle of the stools, be properly taken off, and those which grow on the outside splashed for layering. Hornbeam, birch, elm, hazle, and most of the sorts of underwood, will grow this way; and by this means a thin wood, in a few years, if the stools are not at too great a distance, may be made to be as thick as it is necessary. In performing this work, the ground should be dug round each stool, at the distance the young wood of each respective branch will fall. If the stools be at twenty feet distance, branches of eight or nine feet of each may be splashed and layered, so as that when they have taken root, they will be near enough to form stools of themselves, whilst the shorter branches may be brought down this way, to make the wood as thick as necessary. The layering of these plants requires no other art than layering the younger branches in the ground as has been directed, and they will afterwards take root, and shoot up. Quintus Curtius has recorded of the *Mardorum gens*, that by planting trees this way upon their borders, they gave a vigorous check to the force of Alexander, which I shall quote, to shew how surprisingly a plantation may be thickened and implicated this way. *Arbores densæ sunt ex industria consitæ, quarum teneros adhuc ramos manu flectunt, quos intortos rursus inserunt terræ, inde velut ex alia radice lætiores virent trunci. Hos, qua natura fert, adolescere non sinunt, quippe alium alii quasi nexu conserunt, qui ubi multa fronde vestiti sunt, operiunt terram. Itaque occulti nexus ramorum velut laquei perpetuâ sepe iter cludunt*, &c.

Your wood being gone over, and layered this way, the next thing to be observed is the larger vacancies, where the stools being at such a great distance, the branches cannot be layered so near but that ground must be still lost. All these vacancies should be dug, and planted with setts of willow, sallow, poplar, &c. which will always be good for cutting, either for poles, hurdles, or fuel. They will grow very well in such places, especially if the ground be moist, and will pay sufficiently for the charge of digging and planting. If the interstices be very large, and the trees and stools be forty, fifty, or sixty feet asunder, then, after the ground is dug, young plants may be introduced from the nursery, of elm, hornbeam, birch, and most of the other sorts, and these may be planted in the vacant places, observing always at the same time to sow a few acorns, ash keys, &c. amongst them; and if at the time this layering was performed, a few of these seeds were to be near the layers, where the ground had been dug, the future value of the wood would perhaps be none the worse.

These things being done, you will have an old worn out wood metamorphosed into new stuff, which must cause great pleasure to observe the change, as well as afford the owner afterwards a great profit. A year or two after this work is finished, the weeds should be plucked up, which may grow amongst the layers, setts, or plants, especially stinging-nettles, which are sometimes subject to grow in old decayed woods. If this should happen to be the case of the wood you are about to improve, they should be all picked out when the ground is first dug, for layering and planting. The first fall of these woods should be early; it ought not to be deferred longer than five, six, or seven years. For it will be necessary not to have the fall longer deferred, that the new-raised plants from the layers, &c. may be themselves formed into proper stools, the transverse branches that came from the old stools in order for their layering, taken off, and the old stools, if they are almost worn out, and there be young ones sufficiently thick to supply their places, grubbed up, or else refreshed by the axe. The tree being thus stripped of all its external incumbrances, will shoot vigorous and strong, amongst the other smaller stools against the next fall. But this is not all, by this early fall the underwood will be made thicker; and if after this, as we are upon the article of felling woods, the underwood should appear too thin, the fall, for the future must afterwards be repeated the oftener, which will still be an help towards thickening such places. In all falls whatever, a sufficient quantity of young plants, whether they proceeded from the acorn or trees from the nursery at the first improving the place, should be left to grow to timber to succeed the old ones and keep up the succession; and as often as these get too close they must be thinned, the weakest and least thriving being always taken away.

In all the falls of underwood of whatsoever plantation, let the trees be cut near to the ground, to form the future stools, and let them be neatly sloped off, smooth and clear. For this purpose such persons as have been used to the work should be made choice of, as the inexperienced are subject to haggle and leave the stools with broken bark and rugged sides. After the fall is over, let the poles, &c. be carried into the different ridings for loading, for I would have no carting or waggoning amongst the stools; and if the ridings are not sufficient to contain the quantity, let those that are first sold, whether poles, hedge-wood, or faggots, be brought to the waggons standing in the ridings and there loaded. And if the ridings be cut, and each of these quarters be of the size I directed in the foregoing chapter, the trouble of this will not

be

WOODS be great, to the preservation of the stools, and the benefit of the future crop

If the sale does not go currently on to fetch them all away soon after falling, then let the remainder be brought into the ridings, and each quarter cleared of all small boughs, twigs, chips, &c This the quarters will be left neat and clean, and will afford no temptation for any persons to go amongst the stools, which, when shooting in the spring, may have an eye knocked off, that would otherwise have grown by the next fall to a good pole

Thus have you rules for managing and improving an old, neglected, and thin wood, and the hints for felling and carting should be taken for all, and used in every cutting of what nature soever

Directions for the planting of closes and hedge-rows

Neither is the improvement of the woods a gentleman's only concern he should also have regard to the proper planting of his closes and hedge-rows, and this might be done without any expence For suppose a man was to go over his estate, and mark out for the axe such trees as are at their full growth, and employ the money, or a share of the money these sell for, to purchase young standard trees, to be set regularly, near the hedge rows of the respective closes When an estate is to be improved this way, I would advise the planting them on the ditch-side of the hedge And if they are obliged to be planted on the bank-side, I would advise their being set at some distance, especially if the hedge be old, for then the banks are often very dry, and the old roots of the hedge have taken such close and strong possession of the ground, that the young roots of the fresh planted trees will be many years before they make their way to get a head, and consequently all this time the tree is embarrassed, and its progress stopped, whereas those planted on the ditch-side have fewer difficulties to encounter The roots of the hedge will not be in such plenty, and the trees will stand cooler, and would begin their progress soon after planting, which they would continue with so much vigour as to arrive at timber sooner by many years than if they had been planted on the other side Thus might a gentleman beautify and improve his estate without any loss, only cutting down such trees as are incapable of farther improvement, and which would afford this way so many more in their room, to be improving and enlarge the succession Nay, if a gentleman was unwilling to fell his timber-trees, the venerable ornaments of his estate, though at their full growth, he might take away all useless stunted trees, all unsightly dodderels, and employ the money these sold for in other uses WOODS.

If these methods were to be observed in general, the nation would be improved, without any sensible expence of individuals. But this we can hardly ever expect to become universal, as a kind of *vis inertiæ* seems to have seized so great a share of mortals How often have I wished that an act of parliament might be made, to enforce something of this kind! Laws and statutes to oblige people to plant are made and observed in many nations, but have been miserably neglected in ours

Some acts, indeed, for the preservation of timber, have been made, but I believe they have been very badly put in execution King Ina enacted a law against burning of trees, inflicting a punishment on any who set fire to them, besides a mulct of three pounds, which was no inconsiderable sum in those days Moreover, if any person clandestinely cut wood, he was fined thirty shillings, and the sound of the blow of the axe was sufficient conviction for the purpose. There was an act also in Edward the Fourth's time, to limit the distance of the falls of underwood, and another in Henry the Eighth's time, obliging cattle to be kept out of woods, &c till a certain time after the fall It is probable, this prince's care was owing to his having tasted the sweets of planting In the reign of Queen Elizabeth other laws were made, or the former ones confirmed But what is greatly wanting now is a law as I before observed, obliging every person to plant a certain proportionable number of trees, as well as all the preceding laws renewed to ensure their future safety

Acts made in former reigns for the preservation of woods,

recommended to be amended and enforced in hepreten

# CHAP. III.

## Of Fences, and the Manner of raising Quick

Introductory observations

As I am now upon the subject of forest-trees, it must not be expected that I say any thing here of such trees as are proper to make hedges to divide wilderness quarters, or places designed more peculiarly for pleasure, a list of these trees, and their management, will come in another place At present, I shall treat of such fences as are proper for the security of woods and enclosure

Directions for making fences of walls and pales

Walls and pales, such as are used round parks, are certainly good fences; but the raising of these is more the business of the mason and carpenter than of the planter, though I cannot help observing, that whoever has sufficient plenty of oak wood to make a fence of the latter, that the thinner the wood for paling is cleft, the longer the pales will last, as they will be lighter, and not subject to sink under the pressure of their own weight, and if the rails to which they are fastened be cut triangular, to shoot off the wet, and the posts be not too far asunder, a fence of this kind will last, with very little repair, near fifty years These are the sorts of fences chiefly used round parks, for keeping in of the deer, both fallow and red, and are generally seven or eight feet high, the height proper for the purpose Some stuff is saved by cutting every other pale shorter by about a foot than the rest, which, in going round a large park, will not be inconsiderable As these are fences seldom made use of for common plantations or woods, I shall proceed to the different sorts of fences more peculiarly proper for these purposes, which are hedges

First,

*FENCES. Method of raising a hedge of elders,*

First, hedges may be made of elder to be immediate fences, if the ground be moist and good. Ditches may be made four feet wide, and the banks stuck with cuttings of this tree, having the ends first sharpened, to prevent the bark from peeling. They may be five, six, or more feet long, according to what fence is wanted, and may be stuck about a foot asunder, and wattled along the top. If this work is done early in winter, they will all grow, and will form an immediate fence for the succeeding summer.

Another way of planting these cuttings is chequer-wise, and if they are stuck rather sloping in the banks, and wattled as before, they will be an immediate fence. In wattling these trees, care must be taken not to bind them too strait, or too near the top, to impede the shooting of the uppermost eyes of the plants in the spring. The elder setts would be better without it. I only recommend a light wattling, to make a more immediate show of a fence, in order to answer the purpose the better.

*which are improper to be planted near gardens,*

Of all the sorts of fences, though they are the soonest raised, those made of elder are the meanest and least beautiful, not only as they shoot very irregular, but emit a strong disagreeable scent, especially when in blow, and if used near gardens, they will fill them with young elder trees, occasioned by the seeds falling from the old trees, which will be as troublesome as weeds to extirpate. I mention hedges of elder of this kind only to shew that, and in what manner, they may be raised, leaving every one to do as he shall think proper.

*Hedges of alder recommended for boggy and wet land.*

Other sorts of fences, on different ground, may be made of alder, and for the following situations I would recommend it, viz. On boggy and wet lands, that are constantly grazed with the larger cattle. Such places may be divided with planting truncheons of alder, even ten or twelve feet long, and if the proprietor has enough of them to plant them pretty close, they will in such places soon become a strong and good fence.

Again, another sort of fence is to be made of the furze bush. This also makes an indifferent hedge, but is nevertheless useful for ground opposite to the foregoing sort, namely, on dry and sandy banks, where hardly any thing else proper for a hedge will thrive.

*Manner of raising a hedge of furze-bush,*

In order to raise a hedge of this kind, the mould must be dug along the top of the bank, and the whole laid level and smooth. Then, having procured a sufficient quantity of the seeds of the furze-bush, they should be sown in the autumn, covering them over with fine mould about half an inch deep. They will readily come up, will want little weeding in such a situation, and will soon grow to be a fence. But they are liable to be destroyed by severe winters, and sometimes it happens that part of the hedge only is killed, while a share of it will shoot out again from the bottom. The gaps must be repaired by sowing the seeds as before, or planting of setts. But such hedges ought never to be thought of, unless for sandy, dry, barren places, where nothing else will grow, for they have a beggarly look, make a very bad fence, and may be justly reckoned among the worst of hedges.

*which is proper only for sandy, dry, barren places.*

*Hedges made of black-thorn not approved, and why.*

Again, the black-thorn is a tree of which hedges may be made, but I can by no means relish them for this purpose, as they throw out such an innumerable quantity of suckers as to over run the ground near which they are planted. Add to this, that their main stems, when cut, frequently die, and thereby lose their effect. However, their thorns have some superlative advantages over others. They make the best dead hedges, when cut, in the world. Their wood is of a very hard nature, which makes it durable, and being armed with many long, hard, and sharp thorns, will remain the longest of any unmolested either by hedge-breakers or cattle.

*FENCES. The thorns of this tree however have some superlative advantages over others;*

Faggots also of this tree are by far the best of any to be laid under ground for drains, for being of an hard nature, and excluded the external air, they will lie, for the draining of land in such places, found for a long time. Whoever, therefore, is possessed of land which requires several ground drains of this sort, or is any other ways desirous of raising hedges of this tree, must pursue the following method.

*and its faggots are to be preferred for ground drains.*

*Method of raising a hedge of black-thorns,*

Let a ditch be made four feet wide, and the mould and turf be laid on one side, to form a bank. The turf on the bank-side should be first taken off, and may be placed on the farther side, to keep up the mould that came out of the ditch, and this may be so done as to appear like a regular border. The mould out of the ditch being broken and made fine with the spade, and being regularly supported on each side with turfs, two drills should be made the whole length, and the sloes should be sown in these drills pretty thick, and then covered up close. The best time for this work is December, when the sloes are full ripe.

If no bank or ditch is required, then may the ground which is marked out for the hedge be well dug, one yard wide, the turf being all well turned to the bottom and covered, the drills made, and the sloes sown and covered up as before. This work being done, or rather before it is done, a good stake hedge, or other fence, should be made on each side, and when the plants come up they should be constantly kept clean of weeds. By thus continuing and keeping the fences good, an hedge may be raised this way in a little time.

*which will grow sooner from seeds than setts.*

This is the best and most expeditious method of raising an hedge of these plants. It is the most expeditious, because the plants, after they have been one year up, will shoot faster than any that have been planted with setts, and it is the best way, as the hedge will never be so subject to send out such quantities of suckers as those that have been raised from setts. This will preserve the real plants healthier and stronger, for the continual spawning of these plants makes them weaker, the nourishment being drawn from them, and this may be one reason, why these main plants so frequently die when the hedges come to be set.

*Hedges, however, raised from setts preserve hares better, and afford greater plenty of thorns.*

However, altho' I have recommended sowing the seeds, as they will make the most beautiful and best hedges in the least time, and are not so subject to fill the ground with their spawn, yet whoever wants to cut annually plenty of these thorns for use, or is desirous of having plenty of hares, &c. should raise his hedges from setts taken from other hedges, for these will in a short time spread their roots to a good distance, and will in a few years, especially if the ground was to be dug or ploughed after the plants get strong, form a kind or stratum of black thorns eight or ten yards wide the whole length of the ground, which will afford the planter plenty of thorns for his use, as well as prove an excellent preservative to the hares, for they can sooner blink the dogs, and ensure their safety in such hedges as these, even than in large woods. So that whoever is desirous of having plenty of this sort of game, and cannot easily keep off over-grown coursers, cannot more effectually obtain it, unless he almost woods his whole estate, than by raising hedges on it of this kind. And if the land is not

FENCES

not very dear, though ſuch a ſhare of it ſhould be taken up by ſuch broad hedges, as it were, yet the thorns that may be annually cut will more than pay for the rent of the ground they have all along occupied.

*The holly a proper tree for fences*

Again, another ſort of tree proper for a ſtrong fence is the holly, a beautiful evergreen, and not only adapted to this purpoſe, but to make hedges in the pleaſure-ground, &c. The ſmall progreſs that the holly makes towards a hedge for two or three years after planting, has diſcouraged ſome, perhaps, from attempting to raiſe them, who would otherwiſe have been glad to have had their eſtates ornamented and improved with hedges of theſe trees.

*Objections to the uſe of it in fences*

But I would deſire every one to conſider, that all young trees make a ſmall progreſs at firſt, and that the holly, though none of the [illegible], will afterwards make ſtrong ſhoots, and if the plants have been properly raiſed in the ſeed-beds, and not gathered wildings from the woods, after two or three years gentle pace, they will puſh forward, and if they like the ground, they will grow to a tolerable hedge, nearly as ſoon as quick. However, I dare venture to affirm, they will require fencing not more than two years longer than white-thorn quick! For the leaves being very [illegible] and ſharp, protect them from being eat by the cattle. So that one ſhould think a perſon would not be unwilling to wait a year or two extraordinary for a hedge of this beautiful evergreen, which will form a very ſtrong fence, and be the beſt ſhelter in winter for both man and beaſt.

*Manner of raiſing a holly hedge*

The manner of raiſing a holly hedge is as follows. Let the plants be taken out of the ſeed-beds two or three years old, or if they had been pricked out for a year or two, they would be ſo much the better, and ſurer of growing. The ground for the hedge ſhould be well dug, and cleared of all roots both of weeds and trees. If the hedge is to be made upon a level, the turf, or upper ſurface, ſhould be thrown to the bottom and covered up, the ground being trenched a yard broad the whole length. It will be then ready for planting, which may be done any time in the winter, though if the ground be of a very dry nature, the ſooner it is done in the autumn, after the autumnal rains have fallen about the beginning of October, it will be ſo much the better, for then the winter rains will cloſely ſettle the mould to the roots, and thereby make them in leſs danger of ſuffering by the future drought. If the ground be of a moiſt nature, then March is a good time for this work. After the hedge is thus planted, nothing more is required than keeping it clear from weeds, and fenced from the external injuries of cattle, till it is of a ſufficient ſize to defend itſelf, and conſtitute a fence, which will be in eight, nine, or ten years, according as the plants have taken to the ground.

*Another way of raiſing the ſame hedge*

Another way of raiſing a holly hedge is by ſowing the berries. Whoever, therefore, is deſirous of raiſing his hedge this way, ſhould, a year before he attempts it, procure his berries, and bury them in the ground like haws, and in October the ground on which the hedge is to be raiſed ſhould be well dug or trenched, the turf covered cloſe to the bottom, and all weeds and roots cleared off. Having thus made the mould fine and clean, let two drills be drawn along it, at about a foot aſunder, and the berries which had lain in the ground all ſummer be taken up and ſown in theſe drills, about an inch and a half deep. They ſhould be regularly covered up, and ever after conſtantly kept weeding.

FENCES

*Remarks on this latter method of raiſing holly-hedges*

This is a very good way of raiſing hedges of theſe trees, if you have luck, that is, if the plants come up in the ſpring. But of this there is great hazard; for I have very often known berries that have been buried a whole year, and then ſown with the utmoſt care, not appear till the ſpring twelvemonth afterwards, a few plants excepted; and that the greateſt part has lain in the ground even till the ſpring after that before they made their appearance. Nay, in my nurſery-ground at Gumley we can hardly ever get theſe plants up, without being buried a year in the ground, and lying a year in the beds. This is a ſort of white hungry clay; in which, nevertheleſs, they thrive exceedingly afterwards. And if a gentleman who is deſirous of raiſing his hedge from the immediate ſeeds, ſhould find after ſowing that they have a tendency to make this long reſt, what a hazard is there of his expectations of a future hedge being abortive! for the mice, &c. are particularly fond of the kernels of theſe berries, ſo that if they once take to them, they will purſue them in the drills, and never leave (unleſs they are deſtroyed themſelves) till they have deſtroyed them all. Add to this, that as theſe places may be at a diſtance, and not immediately under the inſpection of the maſter-gardener, to watch and guard againſt theſe dangers, and the ſeeds lying ſo long as a whole ſeaſon or two before they come up, the danger is very great of their being found out and deſtroyed by theſe little animals.

*to which there are many objections*

There are other motives for not raiſing theſe hedges from ſeeds ſown in the places, namely, the fences muſt be kept up two or three years longer than will be required for thoſe planted with good ſtrong ſets, eſpecially if they have been before removed. Beſides this, the charge of weeding will be conſiderably greater, for after the ſeeds are ſown in the drills, early in the ſpring the young weeds muſt be plucked up as often as they appear, in the ſame manner as in a regular ſeminary, otherwiſe they will over-run and deſtroy the plants as they come up, and if they ſhould not happen to appear the firſt ſpring after ſowing, the continuing of this work ſo minutely for a ſeaſon or two will be an expence not inconſiderable. However, whoever ſows his ſeeds in this manner for a hedge, muſt keep them clean of weeds. After they are come up, they muſt be picked out with care, and the mould now and then ſtirred, to admit the gentle ſhowers, &c. to refreſh the young plants. This care alſo muſt be hereafter proportionably obſerved, and the fences kept good, till they themſelves become a fence, and are proof againſt cattle and other accidents.

*Holly-hedges particularly recommended for the diviſion of fields and paſtures, and why*

Altho' holly-hedges have hitherto been raiſed chiefly to be kept ſheared, &c. in the pleaſure-ground, yet as they will make ſo ſtrong and durable a fence, I would ſeriouſly recommend them for the diviſion of fields and paſtures, eſpecially if in view of a gentleman's houſe. For what pleaſure muſt it give the inhabitant to ſee the country wear a different and more pleaſing aſpect than what it had been accuſtomed to during the winter months! What ſatisfaction too muſt it afford the owner, when in his own houſe, to view his eſtate thus ornamented with uſeful fences, to ſee it diſtinguiſhed from the neighbouring ones by its evergreen hedges exhibiting their never failing verdure in the moſt dreary ſeaſon! And what farther ſatisfaction muſt it be to him to find, if he walks abroad at that ſeaſon, they will ſo effectually defend him from the churliſh winds, that he may reap the benefit of the air, without feeling the effects of its diſagreeable blaſts! Add to this, that his cattle

cattle alſo will be ſecured and defended from the injuries of the weather by them. Theſe are motives which ſhould induce gentlemen to raiſe at leaſt ſome hedges of theſe trees, eſpecially if they are in view of their own houſes.

*The crab-tree proper to make a good fence.*

Again, another tree proper to make a good fence is the crab tree, which is of very quick growth, and will make a ſtrong fence in a few years. There is no particular property in this tree for which I ſhould recommend it for hedges more than another, only it is of quick growth, and affords crabs for verjuice, and the proper number of trees may any time be grafted, either with uſeful family apples, or ſuch as are fit for cyder. Whoever, therefore, is deſirous of raiſing a crab tree-hedge muſt do it either from the plants or kernels. If from the kernels, the ground ſhould be trenched all along, one yard broad, and the turf well covered down, and all roots whatſoever taken out. Then having the mould fine, and fit for working, let a drill be made the length of the ground, exactly in the middle of it. The drill ſhould be but about an inch and a half deep, and may be made broad at the bottom with the hoe, even half a foot wide, and laid ſmooth and level the whole length. The kernels, which ſhould be procured from the crab-mills, muſt be ſown all along this broad drill, if the huſks are not ſeparated from the kernels, pretty thick, otherwiſe you will be in danger of being deceived, as there may be fewer kernels amongſt the huſks than what appeared to be. This done, they ſhould be covered down about one inch and a half deep, or if two drills be made, a foot aſunder and the ſeeds ſown, they need not be made ſo wide, and if the plants come regularly in both, it will be rather better than in one broad drill, as they will have more room. The time for this work is during the whole winter, though if it be deferred till January it will be better, as the mice, &c. will have then leſs time to find them out and deſtroy them. This is a misfortune which often attends endeavours to raiſe hedges from ſeeds, after all the trouble of preparing and fencing, few plants have appeared, the vermin having in the mean time, unnoticed, deſtroyed the kernels that were the rudiments of the future hedge. So that whoever attempts the ſowing of kernels for this purpoſe ſhould directly ſet traps, and afterwards ought frequently to look over the ground, to ſee if the mice have made a beginning, or whether they have burrowed where the kernels are, and followed the drills. If they appear to have diſcovered them, traps muſt be multiplied, or poiſon laid. The plants will come up in the ſpring, and will afterwards occaſion no other trouble than the uſual care of weeding and fencing.

*Directions for raiſing this tree from the kernels;*

*or from ſetts.*

Whoever is deſirous of raiſing his hedge from ſetts, ſhould ſet apart a piece of ground for the ſeminary, and having it well trenched or dug, the mould being made fine, beds ſhould be marked out with a line, four feet wide, with alleys one foot and a half broad. In theſe beds, the mould being raked out, the kernels, being firſt procured from the crab-mills, may be ſown, and covered over an inch and a half deep, and after the beds are neated up, a few traps ſhould be ſet. In the ſpring the plants will come up, and if the ground is good, and the weeds kept down, they will be ſtrong enough by autumn to be taken up, and planted out for hedges, otherwiſe they may ſtand in theſe ſeed-beds till the autumn following, when they will be very ſtrong plants, and may be then uſed for the purpoſe. Ground planted with ſuch ſtrong ſetts as theſe, if they take rightly to it, will ſoon have a good ſtrong hedge, which will prove a fence againſt almoſt any thing, though theſe hedges at firſt are often kept down by the hares, eſpecially where they abound, for theſe animals are ſo fond of the ſhoots of either crab or apple-trees, that ſetts planted for hedges have frequently had their whole year's ſhoots almoſt entirely eat off the winter following by them, ſo that if this ſhould happen to any future new-planted crab tree-hedge, it ſhould be gone over in the ſpring with the ſhears, and all the envenomed ends of the twigs taken off, that they may ſhoot out again vigorous and freſh.

*The white-thorn another ſort of tree proper for hedges.*

Again, the laſt ſort of tree proper for a hedge I ſhall mention is the white thorn. This is the moſt general hedge of the kingdom, and is of all others the beſt and moſt profitable, as they require to be often ſplaſhed, to keep them thick at the bottom and in good order, and every cutting affords excellent thorns for dead hedges, as well as fuel. In order, therefore, to raiſe an hawthorn hedge, haws ſhould be gathered in October or November, and theſe muſt be either buried or ſown ſoon after. The hawthorn is a plant that will not come up till the ſecond ſpring, which is the reaſon why they have been generally buried in the earth, or kept in ſand, during one ſummer. Though if the planter will be at the trouble of plunging them into a good heat of dung, and keep the bed hot till the beginning of March, this fermentation will prepare them to ſprout, and if they are then carefully ſown and covered over with fine mould, will come up in the ſpring.

*Directions for raiſing a white-thorn-hedge.*

This method is to be practiſed by thoſe only who want ſmall quantities. But as quick may be bought all over the kingdom at a very eaſy rate, the raiſing it will merit no one's attention, unleſs he does it for the ſake of experiment.

*Method of raiſing a quantity of quick.*

In order to raiſe a quantity of quick, there is only one method generally practiſed, namely, by firſt burying the haws, and taking them up to ſow the October following, though there is another way, more preferable, namely, by preparing the beds, and ſowing the haws ſoon after they are gathered. Whoever purſues the former method, having gathered what quantity of haws will anſwer his purpoſe, ſhould, in ſome bye-corner of the kitchen-garden or nurſery, dig an hole or pit, capacious enough to receive them, ſome of the earth which came out of the hole, after the haws are put in it, ſhould be laid upon them, and being thus carefully covered down, they may remain there till October. Then, having ground well dug, and cleared of the roots of all troubleſome weeds, and the mould being fit for working, the beds ſhould be made for the haws. Four feet is a very good width for theſe beds, as they may be eaſily reached over to be weeded; and if the alleys between be each one foot and a half wide, they will be of a good ſize.

The beds being marked out with a line, ſufficient mould muſt be raked out, to cover the haws an inch and a half deep. This being done, and the bottom of the beds being made level and even, the haws ſhould be ſown, and afterwards gently tapped down with the back of the ſpade, and then the fine mould, which had been raked out of the beds, muſt be thrown over them, covering them an inch and a half deep. In the ſpring the plants will come up, and in the ſummer following ſhould be kept clear of weeds, though it does ſometimes happen, that few of them will appear till the ſecond ſpring after this, nay, I have ſometimes known, even after the greateſt care has been taken, of burying, taking up, and ſowing them, that the

crop

FENCES

crop has been very thin till the third spring after, when an additional quantity of young plants have shewn themselves, which makes the other method, to avoid this hazard, more eligible, namely, to sow the seeds soon after they are ripe.

Having procured the haws, let them be sown soon after, in the same manner as has been directed for those that have been buried, and all the summer following let the beds be constantly kept clean from weeds, which must be regularly picked out as often as they appear, for if they are neglected till they acquire any size, the very roots will draw out the haws with them, and so proportionably destroy the seminary. But it may, perhaps, be objected, that by following this method, the rent of the ground and the expences of weeding for one year will be wholly thrown away. To this I answer, As to the rent of the ground, it will be inconsiderable, since a small spot will raise many hundred thousands, and the expences of weeding the beds, especially if they are made of new ground, will not be very great. Add too, that in return for these small disadvantages, by pursuing this method, you are pretty sure of having a crop the succeeding spring, the haws lying near the surface in the warm beds, during the whole summer, about an inch and a half or two inches deep will be prepared by the interchangeable influences of the showers and sun, to clit, and will not only come up in the spring, but will make so strong a shoot by the autumn following, if the land is good and they are kept free from weeds, that they will be the best sorts of plants, and of the best size to plant for a quickset-hedge.

The method of planting a quickset hedge is so well known to every practical gardener, and there are so many people called quickers, who make it their sole business during the winter, if they can get work, that it may seem needless to say any thing upon that subject, nevertheless I cannot help blaming them for making, and some authors for recommending such large ditches as are commonly used. And lest it should be expected by some of my readers, I shall lay down a few general rules for planting and ordering a quickset-hedge.

General rules for planting and ordering a quickset hedge.

Now by a quick hedge, in an extensive sense, may be understood all growing hedges of what sort or nature soever, but, in a customary and more confined sense, by quickset hedges are meant those raised from the setts of the white-thorn only. In order, therefore, to raise a quickset-hedge, the plants should be taken out of the seed beds, at one or two years old. Those of one year's growth, if they have shot strong in the seed bed, will be good stuff for the purpose, and afterwards make rather a more beautiful and regular hedge, though those that have stood in the seed-bed two or three years, or have been before pricked out, will shoot stronger when planted, and often grow to a fence sooner by a year, though perhaps not in such an even and regular manner.

Having made choice of your quick, lines are to be laid to mark out the ditches, which ought not to be more than three feet from the bottom row of quick to the opposite side of the bank, that is, they should be only one yard wide. This is the properest size for the ditches, as they will then afford a sufficient quantity of mould to cover the quick. It may be needless to mention, that a row of turf, cut even and well, is to be laid at the edge of the ditch which is to form the bank side, and that the quick being headed and the roots pruned, are to be laid along these turfs, at about half a foot asunder, that the best mould is to hill up the roots, and that a second row of even cut turfs is to be laid to the necks of the young plants to be planted with another row, to make two in number, that the plants in this row also are to be about half a foot asunder, that they are not to be opposite to the other plant, and that each is to be set to answer the middle of the vacancy of the other row. All these rules are generally known, so that I chiefly observe, that if the ditch is three quarters of a yard wide only, as is practised by some, such a ditch can never afford mould enough to plant the quick and secure it in a dry season, unless it be in naturally moist ground, for as that which comes out of the ditch is laid on the contiguous turf to plant the quick in, and this not being sufficient properly to crown the quick, if it should happen to prove a very dry summer, the earth in which the quick is planted being so little, and lying thin upon the turf, will let the sun and the wind into it, and destroy it. So that in order to have a sufficient quantity of mould, to secure the quick from these accidents, the ditch should be one yard wide at top, and the slope tolerably large, which will make it very narrow at bottom, to hinder the mould on the face of the ditch from being liable to tumble or be worked down.

FENCES

This then is the best size for the ditch, though ditches for ring fences may be four feet wide, but care must be taken at the same time, not to overload the quick, as a ditch of this size will afford too much earth to be laid on it. Four inches depth of soil is sufficient to crown the quick, unless it be a very dry soil; if so, a little more, and this should be laid flat over it, in order to retain such moisture as falls. So that when the quick is covered with the best of the mould, which lay nearest the turf, in this manner, the rest may be laid on the opposite side of the ditch, called the Free board, and this will help to make the fence the greater.

The quick being thus planted, nothing more is to be observed than keeping it well fenced from cattle, and regularly weeded as often as occasion requires, and if the hares, the first season or two after being planted, have cropped the tops, which they certainly will do if there be any, it should be gone over with the shears, and the ends of the envenomed twigs taken off. Nothing more, I say, need to be done than continuing this care till the hedge be fit for splashing, which will be in about six years.

The ways of splashing of hedges and ordering them are different, according to different customs in different parts, though I think none better than the method practised among us. I shall lay down the rules for splashing and ordering a hedge, but they must be put in practice by none except those who have been used to the business. These are the only men to do the work dexterously, and by constant practice, a labourer has been known to exceed the greatest artist. One Grant, a labourer, in my parish, is a living instance of this truth, who for his dexterity in managing of a hedge, or from the vast load of wood he will carry home with him in an evening, has acquired the nick-name of Hedge Stakes. I mention this to destroy the custom, or recommend a much better method than permitting the hedgers to carry a bundle of wood home with them every night, namely, by allowing them something more per day. This is a privilege they claim about us and in other parts, which ought to be broke, though at the expence of additional wages, as it is a temptation to a man, and, if he is not conscientiously honest, he will often cut such branches as ought to be left for the good of the hedge, if he finds they will answer this purpose.

But to return. Having now your hedge about six years old, we come next to the splashing it. And

FENCES. Directions for ſplaſhing a quickſet hedge.

And to this, firſt, the under row of quick neareſt the ditch muſt be entirely cut off, cloſe to the ſide of the bank, ſmoothly ſloped, without being higgled &c. ſo that there will be only the uppermoſt row remaining. The plants in this row being about half a foot aſunder, every third plant, or as many as will leave them about the diſtance of ſtakes for hedges, ſhould be cut within about a yard of the ground, and the others ſhould be what they call Jointed, i. e. cut down to half that length, within a foot and a half of the ground: leaving, nevertheleſs, a ſufficient ſhare of branches for wattling the talleſt, which will then be as ſtakes to ſecure the fence. The height of theſe living ſtakes, I ſay, is generally about a yard, though this ſhould be no abſolute rule, but muſt be according to the ſtrength of the hedge. If it is a very ſtrong one, they may be left a little longer, if weak, proportionably ſhorter; and if it ſhould appear, that it will after ſplaſhing be too weak for a fence, the work muſt be deferred till the next year. Having now left ſome to be as ſtakes, at about the diſtance of thoſe that are generally ſet for ſtake-hedges, having jointed others, i. e. cut them within a foot and a half or two feet of the ground, and having left a ſufficient number of branches for wattling, they ſhould be then ſplaſhed and wattled between the high and low ſtandards, to make the back fence. After this, the ditch being ſcowered completes the whole. I cannot but give this general caution, to leave no more branches for wattling than what will be juſt neceſſary for the good of the fence. It is the ruin of a hedge to have too much wood ſplaſhed and laid down in it. Cutting wood makes wood, and it is this that will continue your hedges for ages, make them thick at the bottom, and afford thorns for uſe. The hedge being thus ſplaſhed, and the ditch ſcowered, it will be then a fence, though if there are cattle that will crop the tender ſhoots as they ſpring in the ſummer, it may be proper to prick a few thorns, or make a ſlight ſtake-hedge along the edge of the ditch. The expence of this will be but trifling. It may keep them off on that ſide for a year or two, and the dead thorns may afterwards be uſeful for fuel. The other ſide will want little guard, though where gentlemen deſire to ſee their hedges grow free and uninterrupted, and if there be large cattle, ſuch as bullocks, &c. I have often known a ſingle poſt and rail run the whole length, which has effectually ſecured it from all ſuch inſults. But this is to be practiſed only by thoſe who have wood enough for the purpoſe. (In feeding-ground where there are bullocks, if there are no rails, the hedges muſt be cut higher, and a greater quantity of wood ſplaſhed among the uprights, otherwiſe they will tear them to pieces, both with their horns and mouths.) In ſeven or eight years the hedge will be fit to cut again; which ſhould be done on the crown ſide, and in this ſecond cutting, the top row ſhould be cut up to the bottom, and the under row ſhould be ſo cut as that ſtakes may be left, and joints and wattling as before. The ditch, this time of cutting, will want no ſort of fencing, let the cattle in the field be what they will; but it may be proper to guard the tender ſhoots, as they grow on the top-ſide, with a ſlight ſtake-hedge. Half an acre of thorns will do near two acres this way; and they will be afterwards uſeful for fuel. And now if there be tolerable conveniency for making a ſingle poſt and rail along it, it will be more wanted than at the cutting before, eſpecially if there be large cattle. After this, theſe hedges may be cut every ſeven or eight years, and a crop of thorns obtained this way; obſerving always, in future cuttings, that every hedge ought to be cut twice on the ditch-ſide for the other's once.

FENCES. Rules for improving old hedges.

This is the beſt way of raiſing and ordering a quickſet-hedge. As to ſuch old hedges as gentlemen may find on their eſtates, theſe alſo may be improved, with proper management. If there are gaps in the hedges, theſe may be filled by ſplaſhing branches from the adjacent parts each way, and layering them in the ground, which will grow and form ſtools for themſelves. Tho' if there be many gaps, or large, I would rather adviſe the planting them with good ſtrong quick, bringing freſh ſoil at a diſtance from the paſture, to fill them in. If the hedge has no real large gaps, but is rather thin, then all ſtraggling branches near the hedge may be cut down, or ſo ſplaſhed into it as to thicken it, if it is wanted. Hedges of this kind ſhould be cut often; for the oftener this is done, they will become the thicker and better. At every ſplaſhing of theſe hedges, let them be cut ſo low as to be but juſt a fence; for this alſo will make them the thicker and grow the better. At every ſplaſhing, ſhoots on the oppoſite ſide of the ditch, and in it, ſhould be taken away, unleſs there be a neceſſity of bringing ſome of the latter into it, to thicken it; and all roots of traveller's joy, briery, elder, &c. ſhould be grubbed up. At every ſplaſhing of hedges, the ditches ſhould be well ſcowered, mould laid to the ſide of the quick, whether old or young, to nouriſh it, and keep up the branches, and afterwards pricked with thorns to ſecure it from cattle. By obſerving theſe rules, and others which a perſon's own reaſon will ſuggeſt, an old hedge may be made to become a very ſtrong fence, though it never will be a beautiful hedge. If the ſtumps are very old, and only few on the banks, I would rather adviſe the grubbing them all up, and planting it afreſh. The roots will pay for the grubbing. In doing of this, freſh turf and ſoil are to be brought at a diſtance.

A neceſſary caution in ſtopping gaps.

Before I conclude this chapter, I cannot but caution all againſt one bad practice; and that is, when a ſmall gap is made in a hedge, by a ſheep or cattle creeping through, I have many times ſeen a bunch of thorns thruſt into this gap, to ſtop it. But this is what by no means ſhould be done; for by thruſting dead wood in this manner into a hedge, the dead wood will choak the young ſhoots of the live, and hinder them from filling the places. So that when gaps of this kind are obſerved, hedges of dead wood ſhould be made round ſuch holes, at a diſtance, for the fence, and ſmall branches of live wood drawn acroſs, in order to grow the holes up and thicken the hedge.

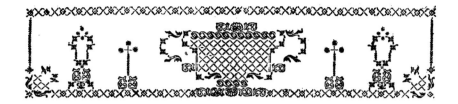

# A COMPLETE BODY OF PLANTING and GARDENING.

## BOOK II.

## PART I.

### Of DESIGN in GARDENING;

WITH

DIRECTIONS for the PREPARATION and MANAGEMENT of the SEMINARY and NURSERY,

AND RULES FOR

GRAFTING, LAYERING, and PROPAGATING TREES from SUCKERS and CUTTINGS

### CHAP I

Of the Method of Laying-out the GROUND for the general Purposes of BEAUTIFYING the ENVIRONS

NOTHING affords more real and unsullied satisfaction to the mind, than those amusements which are practised in the pleasing solitude of rural retirement The consequences are attended with no remorse, no upbraidings of conscience On the contrary, the mind is naturally led to form a just judgment of things, the calmness and composure which it then possesses, causes it to pry into the works of Nature, and seeing with what wisdom and astonishment she acts, is irresistibly led to the profoundest returns of praise and gratitude to the Great and All-wise Author of the Creation.

Reflections such as these will be the natural result of a retreat from the noise and bustle of the world, to the tranquil scenes of rural solitude But though these may be the consequences of such a change, yet the situation, wherever it happens, is capable of higher improvement, and greater objects to assist our meditation, may be introduced to make our continuance lasting, and fetter us, as it were, in such places with the overflowing pleasures of rural delights Plantations are objects that have no small share in these inducements, for a noble house, seated on the declivity of a hill, without protection or this kind, will be exposed to every ruffian blast of wind, and the scene itself, unless thus ornamented, will exhibit, especially in the winter

winter ſeaſon, a wild, comfortleſs, and dreary appearance But by the proper diſpoſing of plantations, every ſituation may be benefited, ſhelter from tempeſtuous ſtorms in winter may be procured, ſhade, in the raging heat of the ſummer months, may be obtained, the ſcene will be enlivened, and from ſuitable contemplations on the variety of trees and plants, their different manner of leafing, ſhooting, and flowering, the heart may be mended, and induced to acknowledge, *how wonderful the Great Author of Nature is in all his works, and that in wiſdom he hath made them all*

To point out ſome hints for ornamenting the environs of a houſe in the moſt uſeful and pleaſing manner, is the propoſed ſubject of this part, whilſt the manner of raiſing the variety of hardy trees, both foreign and Engliſh, proper for the purpoſe, will be explained in the Second Part of this Book But what rules can be given, which can be ſtrictly obſerved? The variety of ſituations will require as many different plans One houſe is ſeated on a high hill, whilſt another ſtands in an humble vale, This ſhall have the advantage of a noble and extenſive proſpect, whilſt That is ſecluded from all view, and can ſcarce be ſeen an hundred yards from the foundation But though much will depend upon the genius of the deſigner, in adapting every thing to the nature of the place and ſituation yet ſome general rules muſt be obſerved to furniſh the ground all around, be the ſituation what it will

Manner of laying out lawn, And, firſt, ſuppoſing the ſite to be tolerably good, with a large park before the houſe, fifty or ſixty acres of ground muſt be left for a lawn, and if the park or eſtate ſhould extend to a diſtance, and at the farther ſide terminate the proſpect, the open may be continued to the utmoſt extent; at the verge of which trees ſhould be planted, that the imagination may conceive the view to be ſwallowed up in wood, and if theſe trees are planted in a curve that is concave to the houſe, the effect will be more ſatisfactory and ſtriking

Though I mentioned this lawn to be in the front of the houſe, yet there are ſome points in view in which it produces a more pleaſing effect than in others, and there are ſome in which a lawn ought by no means to be introduced Neither ſhould every lawn conſiſt of fifty or ſixty acres, but muſt always be proportioned to the extent of the ground

With regard to the ſituation, if the houſe ſtands ſouth-eaſt, as this is the moſt favourable aſpect with us, a lawn in ſuch a front has every charm and advantage to render it deſirable and pleaſing It may, indeed, if there is an abſolute neceſſity, be on the weſt ſide of the houſe, but that is not near ſo well, as the weſterly winds will then have free acceſs to it, and not only greatly injure the houſe, but prove deſtructive in the ſpring to the tender bloſſoms of peach-trees, &c But if the weſt ſide of a houſe is a bad aſpect for the ſcite of a lawn, the north ſide is much worſe, nay, this is a point in which it ſhould never be admitted, as the houſe will thereby be conſtantly expoſed to the boreal blaſts and piercing guſts of theſe ſearching winds

Diametrically oppoſite to the nature of a lawn is that of a plantation, which muſt be placed in a variety of forms, and at proper diſtances all over the eſtate Amongſt theſe plantations, that which is termed a Wilderneſs muſt have the firſt

and planting wildernesses place, nay, as our ornamental trees are of two ſorts, deciduous and evergreen, I would have a wilderneſs of each ſort planted, to make the greater variety, and cauſe a verdure in one or other during the whole revolution of the twelve months I would by no means adviſe to mix the evergreen with deciduous trees in the ſame plantation, but recommend them to be continued ſeparate, as the uniformity in each will be kept up, and the appearance of both preſent a bolder look. Theſe wilderneſs quarters may be made on each ſide of the lawn, that of the deciduous trees on the one ſide, whilſt thoſe of the evergreen may occupy the oppoſite part, and the extent of theſe plantations may form a part of the bounds to the lawn, which ſhould have no regular figure, but vary according to the nature of the ground in which it is deſigned to be This will produce a ſweet variety in the ſummer months, to behold from the houſe the different ſhades and tinges of the green leaves, and in the winter months will afford an agreeable contraſt, during that dreary ſeaſon, on the one ſide to view the deciduous trees, diveſted of their honours, emblems of our approaching fate, whilſt, on the other ſide, the eye is relieved by the proſpect of the evergreens, ſtanding as a perpetual ſpring, and appearing juſt ſymbols of immortality,

In planting theſe wilderneſſes, care muſt be taken, in the firſt place, to plant them in ſuch places, and in ſuch a manner, as not to hinder a diſtant proſpect The worſt point in view of a proſpect ſhould be the place for the wilderneſs, though this is not ſtrictly to be obſerved, for altho a wilderneſs may be planted in ſuch places where the proſpect is indifferent, yet it ought to be, if poſſible, where, from the recluſe walks and winding mazes of ſuch plantations, a perſon may at once break out, and command the beſt view the ſituation will afford If, therefore, from the nature of the ground, the wilderneſs cannot with any propriety be planted next to the lawn, the lawn muſt be bounded by other trees, planted in clumps, and other irregular ways And as I would have the length of the lawn extend as far as the proſpect, there to terminate with plantations of trees, planted in a concave manner, ſo, where the pleaſure-ground is to ceaſe, and paſture is to commence, I would propoſe an ha-ha to be drawn acroſs, by digging of a ditch five or ſix feet deep, ſloping it off on the farther ſide, and building a perpendicular wall on the ſide next the houſe This will be a very good fence againſt all cattle, whilſt nothing of that kind can be ſeen at a diſtance, which would appear very unſightly

Another thing to be obſerved, with reſpect to the ſituation of wilderneſſes, is, that they be planted at a proper diſtance from the houſe, not too far off, which might cauſe a wearineſs in ladies, and others, in the ſummer months, before they experienced the refreſhment of ſhade, nor yet too near the houſe, as the number of trees may contract a dampneſs, and render the places unwholeſome

In planting of a wilderneſs, walks ſhould be left of a ſize proportioned to the extent of ground on which it is to ſtand They ought to be ſerpentine, winding in an eaſy manner throughout the whole works, and ſhould on a ſudden, if poſſible, as I before obſerved, lead into a large grand walk, which commands a view of the circumjacent country This would not fail to ſtrike the imagination, and fill the mind both with pleaſure and ſurprize

Another thing to be attended to with reſpect to walks, is, that they ſhould be ſo contrived as ſeldom to croſs each other, and beſides the grand walk abovementioned which they are inſenſibly to lead to, the plantation muſt be ſo laid out, that all along they ſhould now and then lead into opens of different ſorts, one of which may be a ſmall circle, with a ſeat placed for reſt, another walk may lead to an octogon piece of graſs, in in the middle of which is a ſtatue, a third open may be a baſon, in which a ſmall fountain plays, if a perſon has a taſte for ſuch ornaments, but I think theſe ſpouting fountains trifling, if not ridiculous, and in all large wilderneſſes a graſs plat of a conſiderable ſize ſhould be contrived to be near the middle of it, in which a tent may be ſtruck, or ſome building erected, for regalement in hot weather

With reſpect to the quarters that are to be planted, they ſhould be of a ſize large enough to hold a ſufficient number of trees to intercept the view of any two walks, i e there muſt be ſo many trees as to prevent a perſon walking in one from ſeeing the company walking in another The largeſt growing trees ſhould be always planted in the middle of the quarters, the loweſt next the walks, and the different growths ſhould be ſo placed, one next the other, as that the heads of the loweſt, and the next, may hide the ſtems of the talleſt, forming at the ſame time a beautiful amphitheatre And here let me obſerve that all the trees muſt retain their natural growth, and are by no means to be either clipped or ſheered but ſhould naturally form their waving heads with the pleaſing luxuriancy and beauty in growth

But notwithſtanding theſe are the rules for planting of wilderneſs quarters and walks in general, yet in every wilderneſs there ſhould be a walk or two of another ſort, called a Cloſe Walk, in which the talleſt trees ſhould be planted near the edges, to form a gloomineſs, and abſolute ſhade, and be more peculiarly proper for contemplation and retirement After every thing is effected thus far, to finiſh the whole, perennial flower roots of all ſorts ſhould always be planted among the trees in the quarters, and if for a few years before the trees cover the ground, ſome annuals be planted amongſt them, they will render the places exceedingly delightful, and afford an additional livelineſs to the new plantation

*[Margin: Every wilderneſs ſhould have a cloſe walk]*

As to the ſorts of trees proper for wilderneſſes, both evergreen and deciduous, theſe will be deſcribed hereafter, ſo that whoever is deſirous of avoiding the expence or trouble of making a general collection of the different ſorts, may have ſuch only as beſt ſuit his taſte, or thoſe that he can with the greateſt eaſe raiſe to anſwer his purpoſe

*[Margin: Method of improving old plantations]*

Hitherto we have ſuppoſed a houſe deſtitute of all contiguous plantations, and have therefore given directions for ſupplying this deficiency, as far as will be ſufficient to conſtitute ſuch parts of them as may be termed the Wilderneſs-works, and bounds to the Lawn But many houſes may luckily have near them ſome plantations of old trees of one kind or other, which the care of their owners predeceſſors had happily provided When this is the caſe, if there be a number of grown trees to cover a tolerable piece of ground, or as many as will be ſufficient to conſtitute what may with propriety be called a Grove, then may ſuch a plantation be ſoon formed into a place of delightful retirement And though this may be ſo contrived as in many reſpects to anſwer the purpoſes of the above-deſcribed wilderneſſes, yet ſuch wilderneſſes, notwithſtanding, ought to be planted in that manner with young trees, and at the ſame time the deſign carried on, with ſerpentine walks, &c through this grove of grown trees, in order to make the greater variety

Whenever, therefore, the environs of a ſeat are to be beautified, and a grove of trees of this kind is found growing there, the firſt thing to be obſerved is, whether it intercepts a fine proſpect If it does, the part which obſtructs the view ſhould be taken away, for nothing affords more pleaſure and ſatisfaction to the mind, than a noble and extenſive proſpect, which muſt therefore by no means be concealed If the grove happens to ſtand too near the houſe, alſo, it muſt undergo the ſame fate, for no plantations of any kind ſhould be too near an habitation, as they naturally contract a dampneſs, and render the places unwholeſome Where theſe groves happen to be in proper places, a few ſerpentine walks may be ſo contrived as to lead through or twiſt between the trees in ſuch a manner as to cauſe few of them to be cut down By this method the whole will appear more natural, and if an old ſturdy oak ſhould happen to fall in the middle of a walk, if the walk be widened on each ſide, and the oak left ſtanding in the middle, it will produce a good effect

The ground amongſt the old ſtandards ſhould have all old ſtumps or ſtools grubbed up, it ought to be dug, and cleared of the roots of all ſtrong and noxious weeds, and ſhould be then planted with roſes honeyſuckles, ſweet-briars, &c which will afford an agreeable fragrance If it be the owner's taſte, he may introduce laurels, bays, and ſuch evergreen plants as will grow under the drip of large trees Perennial flowers, annuals, &c may alſo be introduced to complete the whole Thus an old plantation may at once be converted into a place of the ſweeteſt retirement, ſhade is already prepared in the hotteſt ſeaſon, the gloomineſs occaſioned by the full-grown trees affords the calmeſt ſolitude and theſe plantations will prove the ſame to us as groves were to the Antients, who held them ſacred, and from their being gloomy, dark, and ſhady, called them, by a beautiful figure, *Luci, a non lucendo*

Thus far we have proceeded in our ornamental plantations Before we proceed any further to plant others, we muſt fix upon proper ground both for the flower and kitchen garden The ſize of the former ſhould always be in proportion to the greatneſs of the collection of curious flowers intended to be planted in it The extent of the latter ſhould in the ſame manner be proportioned to the greatneſs or number of the family

*[Margin: Proper ſituation for gardens pointed out]*

Now theſe gardens ſhould always be made in ſuch places as are beſt adapted for the purpoſe, excepting always the front of a houſe, for as in one or both of them there muſt be walls, &c for fruit, were they to be placed before the houſe, every perſon's imagination will ſuggeſt how diſagreeable theſe objects will appear, when compared with a beautiful lawn bounded with trees both evergreen and deciduous Gardens, therefore, ought never to appear in the front of a houſe, but ſhould be made in places where the ſoil is naturally good and where the elevation is not ſo high as that the plants may ſuffer by the drought in ſummer, or cold in winter, nor yet ſo low as to be ſubject to overflowing, damps, &c which often generate vermin, and render the productions unwholeſome But the manner of chooſing proper ground, and making theſe gardens, will be treated more amply hereafter, at preſent I ſhall only obſerve, that the kitchen-garden ought, for the conveniency of dung, to be as near the ſtables as poſſible, which ſhould always be at a diſtance from the houſe, and that theſe gardens, together with the finiſhed lawn, wilderneſſes, groves, &c will take up a large ſhare of the ground adjoining to the houſe

Theſe things being effected, in order to complete the ſcene, the eye muſt be carried on to a diſtance, to ſee what is deficient, and what redundant

*Farther obſervations and rules for beautifying the environs of a houſe.*

dundant. All unſightly dodderels which hinder the view, or happen to grow where there ought to be a plain, ſhould be grubb'd up, and other trees muſt be planted in ſuch places, and in ſuch a manner as to complete the ſcene in the moſt pleaſing taſte. Indeed if the ſituation naturally exhibits a boundleſs proſpect, ornamented with woods and water, diſtant villages and churches, and old ruins, it is a fortunate as well as happy circumſtance, ſince nothing more is then required to be done than ſetting off the ground that falls within the vortex of a morning walk in the following manner. Clumps and plantations may be ſo ſtationed as ſometimes to intercept the view, ſo that every time the eye breaks from theſe it is ſtruck with freſh pleaſure. A great part of the wilderneſs-walks ſhould have no proſpect, whilſt on a ſudden a perſon is unexpectedly led into a large and ſpacious walk commanding the ſcene, at the end of which if a temple or ſome edifice be erected, it will appear noble. I am by no means ſo having many of theſe temples, as their appearance is no ways adequate to the expence in building, neither do I greatly reliſh the playing of fountains, and the expenſive forms of ſea horſes, dolphins, &c. A gentle rill, trickling by the ſide of a hill from an upper ſpring, naturally winding its moſſy courſe to the diſtant vales, affords the moſt pleaſurable ſenſation, becauſe it is pure nature, unſtudied, and without art. Nature muſt be imitated in all our works. Art ſhould appear to have no connection with our plan. A clump of trees muſt be placed in ſuch an eaſy or irregular manner, as if Nature had thrown it there; and where gentle meanders and gliding ſtreams naturally trickle down the ſides of hills, &c. they ſeem to have been formed for real ſatisfaction and pleaſure. Indeed, a magnificent long gravel walk, commanding the circumjacent country, may be admitted, but then this is chiefly to cauſe the greater variety, and afford the homely garb of Nature, that appears thro' the other works, a greater ſimplicity and pleaſing luſtre. For the ſame reaſon, the ſtatue of Neptune in his chariot, attended by the Naiades, Tritons, &c. may be fixed in the center of large waters, by thoſe who do not regard the expence. As to the playing of fountains, if the owner is fond of ornaments of this kind, and has a good reſervoir at a great height he may indulge his taſte. Indeed, a noble jet d'eau, as the French term it, of this kind, exhibits a pleaſing ſpectacle; but where there is no conveniency of having them very large and elegant, all thoughts of them ſhould be laid aſide: for I muſt own, that the playing of ſmall fountains to me preſents both a trifling and puerile appearance. The gardens in Portugal and Italy abound with jet d'eaus, where they are looked upon as extremely ornamental; but there is a good reaſon why they ſhould pleaſe and prevail there more than with us, as the heat in thoſe countries, eſpecially in ſome parts, is often exceſſive in the midſt of ſummer, and the playing of theſe fountains in great plenty occaſions a real coolneſs in the air, to the great relief and refreſhment of the inhabitants.

Theſe things being effected in this plain and eaſy manner, the buſineſs is done, the ſeat is complete, with its environs, and where the ſituation is ſuch as I am deſcribing, happy is the man, if poſſeſſed of real virtue, who is the owner of ſuch an eſtate. If the proſpect be extenſive, and woods and other objects at a diſtance are wanting, he can only lament the loſs, and if water alſo is deficient, he muſt ſit down with the ſame. In ſome grounds the latter may be ſupplied, and water brought on the eſtate at a ſmall expence. A diſtant meadow, bounded by riſing grounds, through which a brook conſtantly runs, may be eaſily thrown under water, and will not only have a pleaſing effect to the view, but afford plenty of fiſh for uſe.

*Hints for ſupplying a deficiency of water,*

Water-falls, caſcades, &c. may alſo be made at an inconſiderable expence, and will appear ſolemn and natural, if no very large current runs down the vale, and the deſcent be tolerably great.

*as well as making water-falls, caſcades,*

A river may be cut in a flat plain, if there be land ſprings, or a ſmall brook, to ſupply it with water; and a piece of water of this kind may be made to have all the appearance of a real river, winding its courſe in a ſeemingly natural and eaſy manner.

*rivers*

Lakes alſo may be made at no great coſt. Where a brook runs between two hills, either with a ſmall, or a pretty great expence; proper heads to each being made, they may be carried by a beautiful climax even to the top of a mountain. Thomas Selwen, Eſq. of Maidwell in Northamptonſhire, has at once ſhewn his taſte and ingenuity, and to what a height of perfection lakes of this kind may be brought. The ground of this gentleman's lakes is of a tolerable deſcent; is bounded on each ſide by riſing land, at the top of which is a ſpinny. The hilly ground is narrow at the neck, and ſo continues proportionally to widen at a conſiderable diſtance, ſo that the head of the largeſt lake being made, others alſo may be made, even till you arrive at the top of the ſpring, each head forming a beautiful caſcade. But when a work of this kind is undertaken, all other ſprings muſt be ſought for, drains muſt be laid, and every additional help of water muſt be introduced to add to the caſcade, and ſupply the lakes in greater plenty. Theſe lakes ſhould be cut in a gentle ſerpentine manner, and not with too many turns and windings, becauſe they make the appearance ſtiff and unnatural. This rule too ſhould always be ſtrictly obſerved in making the abovementioned artificial rivers. The grand head, alſo, of the lakes ſhould be planted with trees, either evergreen or deciduous, or both, which will hide the banks and render the appearance both natural and eaſy.

*and lakes*

Though ſome general rules may be given for ornamenting places well ſituated, and which enjoy theſe conveniences for improvement, yet, where the ſeat happens to be in a vale, or the proſpect in front of it is indifferent, if it be ſo ſituated as that one part of it exhibits a fine view, whilſt the other preſents diſagreeable objects very near; I ſay, a ſeat that has ſuch a low ſituation, with no proſpects, can only be ornamented within the compaſs of its own ſhort view; tho' if by eaſy aſcents from the houſe you arrive, at no very great diſtance, to the top of a hill that commands the circumjacent country, a ſerpentine walk may lead to this place from the houſe, and plantations in the wilderneſs way may be made, leading to the top of this riſing ground, where the ſpectator breaking at once imperceptibly from the recluſe of groves, &c. will be equally ſurpriſed, delighted, and entertained with the proſpect. Plantations alſo with walks of different ſorts may be carried on over this riſing ground, or ſuch part of it as the owner ſhall think proper. The intermediate ſpace around the houſe, to the top of the riſing ground, will be taken up with the gardens and other works, whilſt thoſe ſpots which are not thus occupied, ſhould be ornamented with clumps, well ſtationed; and the brow of the hill all round ought always to be planted with ſome ſort of trees; for where a proſpect is ſhut, trees at the fartheſt end ſhould be planted. By this means

*Directions for improving a ſeat with a low ſituation*

means the imagination will be so far from entertaining the idea of an abrupt stoppage, that it will be filled with the beautiful images of woods, groves, &c continued imperceptibly without end

*Disagreeable objects must be concealed from the view by trees*

Whenever any disagreeable objects present themselves to view, such as dove cotes, old barns, &c such places are always to be hid with trees, and as it should be a rule to plant trees to conceal disagreeable objects, so it should also be a maxim to take away every tree that intercepts the view of an agreeable object, which would appear from some capital point

*Pleasing objects to terminate views recommended*

Of all buildings, a distant church is the most pleasing object to set off a prospect, whether it exhibits a stately tower, or a steeple like an obelisk, at the utmost verge of the intermediate space These objects naturally bring on us the calmest thoughts of our duty, and rouse us to a sense of our dependance A monastic cell should never be concealed, it inspires us with a love of solitude and religious retirement, and is a standing monument of injured piety and decayed magnificence That whimsical machine a windmill is also no undesirable object It affords a rural scene, replete with industry, innocence, and simplicity, and fills the mind with an idea of plenty Broken rocks and craggy clifts likewise have their uses in proper places, and contribute much both to the beautiful and sublime

As many of these objects, therefore, as possible, are always to be brought in, and exhibited to some point or other, whilst the contrary objects are to be kept from the sight Rocky and barren grounds, if near the house, and of short extent, are always to be hid, but where rocky mountains and heathy ground is carried on to a great distance, it will make an agreeable contrast on one side of the view, with that of fertile plains, rich pasture, woods, and water, on the other Whenever, therefore, this happens to be the case, the view of such an object is by no means to be intercepted, as it will cause the greater variety, though if land of this nature takes in too large a portion of the whole, some of it must be properly planted to hide the redundancy, whilst the most agreeable parts should be left open, to bear an exact proportion with every thing else in view, and afford the more agreeable contrast

These are some of the laws which are to be observed in ornamenting the environs of a gentleman's seat But as the situation of different houses varies so widely, the curious designer is only to judge how to put these rules in execution, and adapt every thing to the nature of the ground and situation he is to improve But in all situations whatsoever, Nature is to be studied and followed, and our art never pleases so much as when it makes her appear most pure and simple

*Images should be [illegible]*

The old fashion of images seems to have been lately revived amongst us I have no objection to them, if properly disposed, nay, they are certainly an ornament, and are useful in works of this kind A statue of a Grecian warrior brings in to our mind the idea of his noble exploits, whilst the modern fashion of haymakers, mowers, &c affords no other idea than rural simplicity and rustic industry Sylvanus and Feronia, the god and goddess of woods, may have their images properly stationed in such places, where also should be placed a statue of Actæon, admonishing all hunters to *take heed* lest they be devoured by their own dogs The images of Jupiter, Mars, and Bellona, with their attendants, may be stationed on proper and ornamental pedestals, in the midst of the grandest opens The figures of Minerva, Pallas, and Vesta, inspire reflections on wisdom and chastity Æolus will make a bold appearance on the top of a high hill, terrace-walk, or mount, whilst the goddess Vallentia will ornament the vales Tellus, goddess of the earth, Pytho, goddess of eloquence, the three Destinies, &c may be properly stationed by those who have a taste for these ornaments, and Flora and Chloris, Daphne and Rusina, are always an ornament to the flower-garden If any statues are placed in the orchard, they should be those of Ceres and Pomona and the Hesperides The closest walks and most private recesses may have an image of Mercury, or of Harpocrates and Angerona, the god and goddess of silence, and if Aristæus, the patron of bees, be admitted, his station should always be where an apiary is found

*Heathen deities which images may be placed with propriety in certain situations*

Other devices also, such as artificial hares, &c both in their forms and in a sitting posture, I have seen disposed about plantations for pleasure, which have been so natural as to have deceived many The introducing statues, and objects of this kind, to ornament the environs, entirely depends on the taste of the owner Whoever is pleased with such ornaments, let him have them in reasonable plenty whoever has no relish for them, has a taste which will save him a great expence, that may be laid out to much better advantage

As the nature of situations, ground, gentlemens taste, &c are so various, that no rules which may be laid down are to be strictly observed, as the designer must adapt the nature of the situation, as near as can be, to the above rules and the owner's taste (which ought to be, though in many respects contrary to the strict rules of gardening, indulged), what I have said upon this subject may suffice I shall therefore proceed next to give the reader some directions for the Preparation and Management of a Seminary and Nursery, as well as lay down general Rules for grafting, budding, layering, and propagating Trees from Suckers and Cuttings

CHAP

# CHAP. II.

## Of the SEMINARY.

General observation.

THE most natural, direct, and general way of raising trees and plants is from seeds. In order to this, proper soils must be prepared for them, as suitable as possible to their respective natures; and when the ground is ready, and properly furnished with the embryo plants, it is properly and significantly called the Seminary.

Seminaries are of different kinds, according to the nature of the seeds to be raised. The florist has his separate seminary, filled with pots and boxes for his seeds, and reed-hedges and walls for shade; the dealer in tender plants has a part appropriated for hot beds, in order to raise trees and plants from such seeds as will not vegetate, or at least come to any perfection in this country, without such assistance. Other nice articles in gardening must have seeds and soils suitable to their birth, or the attempting them had better be entirely omitted. Proper directions for these, however, shall be given under their respective heads, where the gardener will see what soil they require, and what care is necessary to cause them to vegetate properly, to commence good trees; he will also be taught what part of the seminary must be appropriated to them, what methods are to be taken, and expedients used in the whole process. So that by the

Explanation of what is to be understood by a seminary.

Seminary here is to be understood a piece of ground large enough to contain all the seeds that will grow in beds in the open air, and the manner of preparing it properly for their reception; but the particular ways of sowing them, when they vary from common practice, will be mentioned under their respective articles.

The parts which constitute the seed have been explained in the Introduction, where the gardener may see what a seed is, and what it consists of. The only further caution necessary to be given him in this place is, to see that the seeds are good, well ripened and preserved, fresh, and (if possible) gathered from the most healthy, thriving, and best bearing trees of the best sorts, for when these precautions are taken, and seeds of such excellence can be obtained, your after-trees will be proportionally more valuable, the fineness of your collection will be enhanced, and your own reputation as a gardener held in greater esteem.

Caution in the choice of seeds.

Of its size.

The size of the seminary should be in proportion to the quantity of seeds to be raised; the land should be good, and the situation ought to be warm, and well defended, for many trees, though hardy enough afterwards, are nevertheless frequently tender when young.

And situation proper for it.

The situation of the seminary should be as near the nursery as possible, though if this is not convenient, neither the seminary nor the nursery need be stationed near the house or other works. Let, therefore, a fertile mead or rich pasture, lowly situated, be sought after for the purpose, in a place not conspicuous to the view from any part of the pleasure garden, if possible; and if this cannot be had, let it be intercepted with trees, stationed a little either on one or both the inner parts at leisure, so as to give it the appearance of plantation.

Low situations recommended and why.

I choose to have the seminary low, because these situations are always the warmest, and it will receive additional warmth from the trees intended to conceal it; and I recommend it to be a rich soil, because the seeds will grow better in it, and will make finer trees afterwards; so that when the situation is not well defended, and the soil rich, the one must be assisted with plantations or hedges and trees all round it, and the other by the addition of good rotten dung.

Manner of preparing the ground for the reception of the plants, &c.

Having fixed upon the place for the seminary, let it be double dug, working the sward to the bottom; nevertheless, if the soil be too shallow for double digging (for you ought not to go below the depth of the natural mould) you must be content with digging it only a spit and a half deep. We may suppose this work to be done in the winter. In the spring, as the weeds arise, they must be constantly kept down, and about Midsummer, if the soil is not naturally very rich, some rotten dung should be spread all over the surface of the ground, which should be then trenched or double dug afresh. The sward by this time will be rotten, and by bringing it up to the surface, it will be reduced to a finer mould, and better qualified to answer the purposes it is designed for in the autumn. From Midsummer until September the ground must be kept clean from weeds, and just before the seeds are committed to it, it should be double dug afresh. At this time the parts must be wholly incorporated; the rotten dung found at the bottom must not be made wholly to occupy the top, neither must the rotten part at top be laid all in the bottom, but the whole must be mixed as equally as possible, which may very easily be done, though double dug, by the careful attention of the person employed about this business. When this is done, the ground must be levelled, and the beds laid out for the different purposes wanted, reserving nevertheless, such a proper portion of it as will be wanted for the reception of those seeds which are to be sown in the spring.

What sorts of trees, &c. are to be raised in the seminary.

In this seminary should be raised all the sorts of forest trees, hardy flowering shrubs, and American plants, also all sorts of shrubs for the grafting and budding the different sorts of fruit-trees, likewise all perennials which are raised from seeds, and require removing before they are planted out for good. Biennials also which will bear transplanting are to be raised here, whence they are to be removed into their proper places in the flower garden.

Which must have different apartments for the different sorts of seeds.

The seminary must be divided into different apartments, for the different sorts of seeds, according to their nature. Those seeds that are to be sown in autumn should be in a part by themselves, those in the spring in another. These also must again be separated. Seeds which remain until the second spring before they come up should be all sown in beds contiguous to each other, and those also which often continue three years, must be sown by themselves, that the whole spot may be kept separate, entire, clean from weeds, and the dormant seeds no way incommoded by the trampling of labourers and persons

ſons employed in aſſiſting in the proper management of thoſe plants which have come up from ſeeds the firſt ſpring.

Soon after any of the apartments have performed their office of exhibiting the plants, and theſe are all taken off for the nurſery, the ground ſhould be double dug, and lie fallow the ſummer following, manuring it with rotten dung, and double digging it about Midſummer as before. In the autumn it will be ready to be ſowed afreſh; but this ſhould always be with ſeeds of a different nature from thoſe by which it was before occupied.

*The ſeminary ſhould be fenced where hares, &c. abound.*

One caution, however, ought to be obſerved from the firſt ſetting out, or at leaſt from the firſt ſowing of the ſeeds. If rabbits or hares abound in or about the place where the ſeminary is deſigned, it ſhould be fenced with pales, walls, or any other fence, to keep them out, otherwiſe they will cauſe great devaſtation, by devouring the ſeedlings as they come up, or will ſo crop and ſtunt them, as that many of them will hardly ever be made to become good trees afterwards.

*What the author means by freſh ſeeds.*

I have before cautioned the gardener to ſee that his ſeeds are freſh. By freſh ſeeds I mean ſuch as are not too old to grow. Melon and cucumber ſeeds four or five years old I call freſh, becauſe then they will be more ſuitable for the gardener's purpoſe, in raiſing his cucumbers and melons. Cabbage, colewort, convolvulus, &c. of two or three years old, I alſo call freſh ſeed, becauſe it will grow and anſwer for me as well as if it had been only one year old. But I call the generality of ſeeds old that have been kept longer than the ſpring after they were ripe. The far greateſt part of ſeeds is good for little after this time; ſo that the gardener is cautioned to procure good ſeeds for his ſowing in the autumn or ſpring of the preceding ſummer's growth. Such ſorts as he may venture to keep a longer time out of the ground, and which will grow very well after they are one year old, ſhall be ſpecified in the ſeveral articles in which the reſpective plants are diſcuſſed.

## CHAP. III.

## Of the NURSERY.

*The meaning of the word explained.*

BY the Nurſery is meant a ſpot appropriated for the reception of the young plants, whether ſeedlings, layers, ſuckers, or cuttings, where they are to be kept in proper training until they are fit for the purpoſes wanted, and from whence they are to be removed to the places of their final deſtination.

*Situations proper for it.*

There is no neceſſity that the ſituation of the nurſery ſhould be near the houſe or gardens; though the nearer it is to the latter the better; or rather, if it is continued to be a part of them it will afford variety, and form a ſweet contraſt with the wilder ſcenes, to many who think nothing more beautiful than a well ordered nurſery, replete with the various trees, riſing with an healthy ſprightlineſs and vigour.

Whoever has this reliſh for the nurſery, let him fix it on the outſide of the wilderneſs-quarters, leading inſenſibly into it by an obſcure winding walk. But he who thinks a nurſery too formal to bear a part with the native eaſe and rural wildneſs of the other ſcenes, may fix it in any place out of view; or it may be ſo ſtationed as to appear a riſing wood at a diſtance, when ſuch an object is wanted to make a ſeat the more agreeable.

*which ſhould be fenced where hares and rabbits abound.*

In either caſe, it would be well to have the ſeminary as near the wilderneſs-quarters as poſſible. Its ſituation, however, ſhould be ſtill in the fartheſt part from view, and if there are many hares and rabbits, as there generally is where plantations of any extent are carried, the nurſery as well as ſeminary ſhould be paled round, to keep them out, or there will be no end of the devaſtation they will cauſe among your riſing blood of tender trees, eſpecially when a ſnow happens. If few of theſe animals infeſt a ſituation, ſo as to make the expence of paling the nurſery in a manner needleſs, the beſt way will be to ſow a large quantity of ſeeds of the ſingle pink, parſly, &c. on which they will feed, and which will in a great meaſure, though not wholly, preſerve your young trees from their venomous teeth. This expedient I uſed with ſucceſs on firſt raiſing my plantations at Gumley; for before I practiſed it, though very few hares were to be found, I uſed to have many thouſand plants deſtroyed or maimed in one ſeaſon.

*Soil for the nurſery cannot be too rich.*

The ſoil cannot be too rich for the nurſery, even though the trees are to be tranſplanted to an indifferent one afterwards; and it is a vulgar error to think otherwiſe. Reaſon dictates that young trees growing luxuriantly in the nurſery will be more active in drawing the juices; the ſpongy parts and pores of the roots will be more dilated for their reception; and their admiſſion will be beſtowed in larger quantities, than when, on poorer land, ſo ſmall a quantity of nutriment is afforded as hardly to keep the plant in a growing ſtate. A luxuriant tree, therefore, having the veſſels dilated as much as poſſible, will be better enabled to draw in the coarſeſt food in the pooreſt ſoils; whilſt young trees, on the contrary, raiſed on bad land, having the veſſels contracted, will be a long time, even after they are removed to a rich ſoil, before they attain to a vigorous growing ſtate. And as this is ſuggeſted by reaſon, experience confirms it to be true.

*A freſh ſoil always proper for a nurſery.*

One ſort of ſoil, however, is never improper for a nurſery, whether rich or poor, if it be moderate paſture; viz. a freſh ſoil, or an untilled paſture, having the turf dug to the bottom, and covered with the other parts. In a freſh ſoil, therefore, though the land be poor, foreſt-trees of all ſorts will make amazing progreſs; hardy American plants, flowering ſhrubs, evergreens, &c. will do the ſame. Fruit-trees ſhew they reliſh it, and will thereby be better qualified for the rich border in the kitchen-garden, or the ſhort

short bitten turf of the orchard. Nevertheless, though plants will thrive well in a poor soil if it be fresh, they will succeed still better if the soil be rich. A gardener, however, need not be over anxious about the soil of his nursery, but may place it where it suits his convenience, or best coincides with his other works, provided there be turf to be thrown into the bottom for the roots to strike into. If the situation be low, warm, and well defended, it will be better, but if the nursery is to consist wholly of hardy trees, little regard need be paid to water, for they will want none, if planted out at proper times. Or indeed, if they did, who could support the fatigue of watering fifty, sixty, or a hundred thousand trees? No water is found at my dry plantations at Gumley, and though hot summers frequently followed the planting out many thousand seedlings the winter before, few, if any of them were found to droop or suffer by the drought.

Directions for the preparation and management of a nursery

Having fixed upon a proper place, therefore, large enough to contain the quantity of trees wanted, in the first place let it be well fenced, either with hedges sufficient to keep out cattle, or pales or walls to keep out rabbits or hares, for without such defence a nursery will be soon demolished.

Then trench the land all over, turning the turf down to the bottom of the trench, and covering it with the other mould, and in doing of this, be sure dig no deeper than the natural soil, for if you go ever so little below it, that lying at the top will be ready to surround the roots of the different trees and plants as they are brought from the seminary, and will retard their striking root at first, if not totally kill them.

When the whole is thus trenched or double dug, which must be in September, the surface should be smoothed, and it should be laid out in quarters for the different trees which are intended to occupy it. A walk should lead directly down the middle, which may be broader or narrower according as it is designed for use, though it ought not to be gravelled, as in removing of trees with the mould at the roots, the soil, by always falling upon and mixing with the gravel, will destroy its property.

Having made your central walk, however, with or without gravel (for it is not absolutely forbid, if gravel is near at hand and a person chooses it), proceed to divide the other parts. Let the richest part of the whole nursery be appropriated to stools for the production of plants by layers, and the poorest for common flowering-shrubs, and such other ligneous plants as have a natural tendency to grow low. Let the forest trees occupy one part, the fruit-trees another, and take care to plant such trees, shrubs, &c contiguous to each other, as will probably be removed together at the time of drawing, that the whole spot may be cleared at once, and put in a condition for another planting, or applied for different uses.

What the before described nursery is to consist of

I do not design this to be a nursery for the offspring of bulbous roots, that thrive best in the kitchen garden, a quarter of which should be appropriated to that service. The nursery under consideration is to consist of trees of all sorts, whether seedlings, layers, suckers, or cuttings, and in this they are to be kept for training, until they are proper for the uses for which they are designed.

Rules for planting the seedling, &c. of flowering shrubs, fruit trees and forest trees,

Lines should be drawn in which they are to be planted, and the distance they should be allowed from each other ought to be according to their natures, or the size they are required to grow to before they are removed. Flowering shrubs should be generally planted a foot asunder in the rows, at an interval of two feet between row and row, and fruit-trees of most sorts at about the same distance, if designed for dwarfs, if for standards a little farther asunder. Forest-trees also should vary in their distance, according to the size at which they are to be taken up. When they are to be removed early, they need not be planted farther from one another than the dwarf fruit-trees, if they are to grow to common standards, the rows should be at two feet and a half distance, and the plants two feet asunder in the rows, and when they are to grow to large standards, to be planted in parks and open places, they should not be nearer than one yard from each other every way. But the proper distances for timber-trees in the nursery, for their different uses, has been already shewn under their respective heads, the others will succeed in order, as they occur in the course of this Work, with the manner of taking them out of the seminary, shortening their taproots, planting, &c.

and managing the ground till,

The ground between the rows must be regularly dug every winter, and kept clean from weeds by good hoeing every summer, and this is all the trouble the nursery will require till it be finally cleared of its produce.

and after it is finally cleared of its trees.

If the ground is rather poor, after it is finally cleared of its trees, the nursery should be made in a fresh place. If it is tolerable pasture-ground, as soon as a quarter is cleared off, it should be fallow a summer or two, during which time it should be kept clean of weeds, well manured, and double dug every winter, or if there be plenty of dung, it may have an extraordinary supply of that, and be then made to bear a crop or two of kitchen stuff, and after that planted afresh.

The nurserymen near London often plant savoys coleworts, &c between the rows in the nursery, for the supply of the markets. But this is a practice that ought not to be imitated every where, for unless your soil be naturally as rich as that near London, and you have as great plenty of dung at hand to keep it so, you will soon exhaust the strength of your nursery ground, and render it unfit for trees, or any thing else.

CHAP.

# CHAP. IV

## Of GRAFTING

*Various uſes of this art pointed out,*

GRAFTING is one of the moſt uſeful arts belonging to the gardener's practice It is the method by which the various ſorts of curious and rich fruits are preſerved in their kind, and multiplied, it is an operation by which trees of foreign growth may be made to flouriſh on their kindred ſtocks which are inhabitants of Britain, it is the art by which trees of all ſorts may be made to grow to a larger ſize, or contracted in their natural growth, to ſuit the various purpoſes for which they may be wanted and by which the number of beautifully variegated trees may be augmented, and one tree, with its delightfully ſtriped leaves, may be made to form as many new trees as the number of young branches are of which it is compoſed In ſhort, it is the method by which many elegant ligneous tender plants for the green houſe and ſtove are encreaſed, of more hardy kinds for the wilderneſs quarters and ſhrubberies, of larger trees for our timber plantations, or fruit-trees for our orchards, and is of general utility in gardening

*which tho well known, is believed not to have been much practiſed by the antients*

Grafting was well known to the antients, though I can hardly believe the practice of it was ſo much uſed as is generally imagined, or the ſtrange tales they tell us of figs and mulberry-trees, plums and cheſnuts, walnuts and ſtrawberry-trees uniting by grafting, &c would have been in thoſe early ages refuted, and thoſe unexperienced authors expoſed, who, either too credulouſly relying on the aſſertions of the common gardeners of thoſe times, or ſervilely copying from other writers, erroneouſly publiſhed for truth ſuch ſtrange and unnatural alliances

*General obſervations on the practice of this art.*

Experience has taught us, that, in general, the different ſpecies of any genera will grow by grafting upon each other, but this is not ſo ſtrictly to be depended on, as to induce us to believe the practice may be made univerſal Some trees, which agree perfectly well in their general characters, are with ſo much difficulty brought to unite, that the attempt does not deſerve the labour There are ſpecies of different genera which will grow upon each other *Cratægus*, *Sorbus*, *Meſpilus*, and *Pyrus*, are inſtances of this, which, in all their ſpecies, may be multiplied by grafting upon one another

In general, however, the ſpecies of one genus only are found to grow well upon each other by grafting, and even among theſe there is generally one ſpecies, or a variety of one ſpecies, better adapted to afford ſtocks to graft upon than another Witneſs the black-cherry ſtock, for cherries of all ſorts, the muſcle-plum ſtock, for the different kinds of plums, and for the reception of peaches and nectarines, which, though generally performed by budding, ſeldom live long, unleſs they are worked into proper ſtocks of the muſcle plum tree The ſtocks, however, for each kind will be ſet forth under their proper heads, in the courſe of this Work, for general and direct practice, leaving it to thoſe gentlemen who have leiſure for experiments, to try their ſucceſs on the moſt unlikely kinds, and ſee how far they are to be brought into uſe I have grafted cherries on the muſcle-plum ſtocks, which have ſhot more than a yard the firſt year, and bore the ſecond I have budded peaches upon the ſloe-tree, and they bear well Theſe, however, were done only for experiment, and though I ſucceeded, yet I would not recommend it to be followed in general uſe Cherries ſucceed better upon their own ſtocks, and peaches diſdain almoſt all plums except the muſcle

As the ſtocks proper for each kind will be ſet forth under each article, ſo will the preparation of the ground, method of raiſing them, planting them out, ſuitable grafts, &c be alſo exploited However, I cannot help obſerving here, for it cannot be too often repeated, That the beſt grafts are generally the middle of the laſt ſummer's ſhoots, and that they ought to be taken from the healthieſt trees and the beſt bearers, whenever we regard the flowers or fruit, for it is with trees, even when raiſed by ſeeds, as with animals the offspring often inherits the perfections or defects of the parent, and if this happens when trees are raiſed from ſeeds, with greater reaſon may we expect to find it continued by a branch of the ſame tree inſerted into the ſtock of another

*Which are the beſt ſeaſons for this operation.*

The different trees, and the different ways of grafting, frequently require different times of the year for the operation of the reſpective ſorts, though, in general, grafting ought to be performed in February It is uſual chiefly to perform it in March That month, indeed, is well adapted for apples, or the like, but cherries ought to be grafted early in February, or in January Plums alſo ſhould be grafted in January, The different methods of the operation may vary the ſeaſon a little, but grafts of almoſt all kinds will grow, if the work be performed in the autumn

*the ſucceſs of which will depend greatly upon the dexterity with which it is performed*

The ſeaſon, however, is not ſo much to be depended upon for ſucceſs, as the dexterous performance of the art If the parts are nicely joined, according to the directions that will be given, and ſo cloſely guarded with the clay as to riſk no injury from the wind, ſun, and rain, they will in general grow, be the time of the operation when it will But if the ſun or air penetrate to the cloſed parts, that glutinous or cementing matter which ſoon flows for their uniting, becomes quickly evaporate, the parts dry, and the graft ſoon after withers and dies away The ſtocks alſo, as low as the ſloped parts, are killed, and Nature, by a freſh *conatus*, ſends forth freſh ſhoots near the bottom of the ſtock, all of which ſhould be rubbed off, except the ſtrongeſt, or beſt-placed, to be ready for budding the ſummer following, or for undergoing a freſh operation of grafting the ſpring after

*Air ſun, and rain to be carefully kept from penetrating to the parts united*

Much wet alſo, though not ſo very dangerous as the admiſſion of the ſun and wind, is nevertheleſs injurious to young grafts if not kept out It deſtroys the cementing property of the flowing juices, liquefies them, retards their motion, as well as corrupts and diſables them for the offices Nature deſigned them, whence it follows, that the death of the graft muſt quickly enſue

Other evils, of ſtill leſs dangerous conſequence, attending, have ſome tendency to deſtroy the graft which are frequently injured, if not destroyed, by frosts, cold, insects, and flies.

graft before it is well taken to the stock. Frosts and cold, nay insects and flies, will seize on the buds as they disclose early in the spring. The former by nipping them, and the latter by contaminating the juices, and repeatedly feeding on them as fresh supply of food is afforded, will by degrees weaken, and at length kill the graft.

From frosts and cold grafts are not to be protected, unless for housed plants, but must endure all weathers. As to the insects and flies, which will often regale on their tender buds, when the nursery is unfortunately situated where such animalcula abound, these are not so easily guarded against as the still more dangerous enemies, though in other respects, friends to vegetation, air, sun, and rain, which, however, may be effectually kept out from the united parts of the grafts and stocks by preparing a proper mortar to surround the parts.

Preparation of a mortar to preserve the graft from the injuries of air, sun, and rain.

This mortar should be made of loamy soapy earth, or if that cannot be procured, a binding clay of any soil will be sufficient. It should be laid on an heap, and to this should be added, a fourth part of horse-dung from the stable, with some chopt hay of the finest sort, which also should be in readiness. The clay should be well beaten on a floor, or large door, for two days successively, and as it becomes too dry, should be still moistened with water. At every beating it should be worked over as the threshers do barley, driving it before them beating poles or flails, then it should be beaten over the top, until it becomes flat, after that it should be laid on a long heap again, and beaten as before. The repetition of this ought to be more or less, as the nature of the clay requires it. But we may suppose for the first day it ought to be beaten over eight or ten times, the next morning the chopt hay must be added, trampling it in, and beating it together as before. This must be repeated about half a dozen times, always moistening it with water as often as necessity requires it, and by that time your grafting clay will be in proper order to surround the grafts. As soon as it is in readiness, and you are provided with a sufficient quantity of bass strings and proper tools, the business of grafting should be next entered upon.

Grafting is performed various ways, according to the nature of the stocks to receive the grafts, called,

1. Whip-Grafting,
2. Cleft-Grafting,
3. Crown-Grafting,
4. Cheek-Grafting,
5. Side-Grafting,
6. Grafting by approach, or Inarching.

## I. WHIP-GRAFTING.

Method of performing whip grafting.

THIS is by far the best method of any of the kinds of grafting, and is the only art practised by nurserymen for raising fruit-trees of all sorts. It is always performed on small stocks, and is called Whip-Grafting because the grafts and the stocks are sloped and fitted to each other, in the manner of carters whips, anglers rods, or the like. The grafts proper for this operation are the well ripened wood of the last summer's shoots, and the stocks may be from the thickness of a goose-quill to an inch diameter, though the nearer they approach to the former the better. The proper tools for this practice are, a good grafting-knife and new bass matting strings, cut into lengths about a foot and a half long, or shorter or longer according to the size of the stocks they are to surround, though woollen yarn and rushes are sometimes used. The grafts should be in a dish for readiness, and the stocks should be headed, or cut off just above some clear place of the bark, where you intend to place the graft. The manner of this operation has been already set forth under the article *Ulmus*. The stalk must be sloped an inch, an inch and half, and sometimes two inches, according to the length and strength of the graft. It must be made with a steady hand, at one stroke if possible, and a cut quite across it, parallel to the horizon, must be made into the wood of the stock. The cion should be cut in a similar manner, it must be held in the left hand, with the smallest end from you, and then, with the right, a slope must be made quite through, of the same length with the slope on the stock. A cross nick, called a Tongue, should be made to fit that on the stock, and they should be joined together, fixing the tongue of the one into the opening of the other. They will grow up without this tongue on the cion, and horizontal cut on the stock, if the parts are applied closely to each other, but this method is more effectual for keeping the grafts in their proper places at first, strengthening the parts afterwards, and for preventing their being broken off by the winds. The graft being fixed in its proper place on the stock, must be next tightly bound with bass strings, then clay must be applied, made to surround the whole, and be well closed at the top and bottom, to prevent its falling off. And if the clay has been well worked, according to the preceding directions, there will be little danger of that, it will sit hard, be impregnable to any weather, will answer for all the purposes and ways of grafting, and be much superior to the pretended grafting wax, which, in that cold season when such business is performed, is with much difficulty and trouble kept to a proper degree of warmth, and which, by sitting so close, is with as much difficulty removed from its post, after it has performed the necessary operations of its function.

When the grafts are in a good growing state, which will be in May, though sooner or later, according to their first growing, the clay should be wholly taken away, but not the bass strings, which must still remain to keep the graft in its position, and prevent its being blown out by the strong winds. When the parts swell, and seem to be too much confined by the strings, it is usual to slacken them, but this is unnecessary trouble, as well as a great fatigue to nurserymen who graft ten or twenty thousand trees in a season. Let them remain a little longer untouched, and when the parts are so swelled that the bass strings seem to confine them too much, and threaten a stoppage of the juice, then let the strings be wholly taken off, for by that time the parts will be all properly united, though it will be necessary to lighten the head, if more than two shoots are made from the eyes or buds, for by that means the winds, without the use of many precautions, often cause great devastation before the end of summer in the different quarters of the lately-grafted trees. If a graft was designedly long at first, and three, four, or more shoots have been made for any intended purpose, it will be adviseable to thrust a stake or strong stick into the ground to fasten it to, otherwise the odds are great against it, but that it is blown out of its socket, before the leaves are fallen, by the high winds.

From the first appearance of shoots from any part of the stocks, they must be carefully rubbed off, otherwise they will rob the grafts of their nourishment, and bring on weakness and death. This work must be repeated as often as the appearance of fresh buds on the stocks makes it necessary, and must be observed for all the sorts of grafting. Thus your trees will un-

interruptedly

terruptedly arrive at perfection, and will be in good order by the autumn following to be planted out for good

## II CLEFT-GRAFTING

*and cleft grafting*

CLEFT GRAFTING may be performed on small stocks, but is generally used for such as are too large for whip grafting, and also for the increase of curious plants which have much pith, such as jessamines, vines, figs, elders, &c The tools necessary for this operation are, an hand-saw, a mallet, chissel, grafting knife, strings, &c If the stocks are not too large, they may be cut off with a slope, like the former method, if they are large, they may be sawed off, in either case, a chissel must be applied to the back part of the slope, which must be beat down with the mallet, so as to cause a fissure or cleft of size sufficient to receive the graft The graft being cut in form of a side wedge, having one side sharpened like a knife, but the back or bark part broad, must be inserted into this fissure or cleft, joining the rhinds of both as equally as possible While this is doing, the cleft should be kept open with the chissel, which being taken away, each side of the cleft will squeeze the graft and hold it close This being done, it must be bound with bass strings, to keep it in its position, and also must be clayed like the others, to ensure safety to the grafts from the sun, rain, and wind When the grafts are well united to their stocks, and shew signs of health and good growth, the clay may be removed, and about a week or ten days after the strings, for the tree is then made

## III CROWN-GRAFTING

*On what trees this method is usually practised*

THIS method of grafting, which is used chiefly for large trees, is practised in Herefordshire, Worcestershire, and other cyder counties, for the increase of their cyder apples in the hedge-rows, &c and is called crown grafting, because the large tree or stem being cut horizontally, and the grafts inserted into the side, have a crown-like appearance It is also called shoulder-grafting, rhind-grafting, and has other names in different counties

*Method of performing the operation of crown grafting*

For the performance of this operation, which is usually in March and sometimes in April, a good saw should be provided, and the upright stems or branches must be sawed off horizontally The crown is to be pared smooth, then having a sufficient number of good grafts in readiness, they should be cut on the side, so as to form a shoulder, and from that they should be sloped off to the opposite side, the length of an inch, an inch and a half, two inches, or more, if you think it necessary Your grafts being thus sloped flat on one side, and having a shoulder to rest on, will be properly prepared to be inserted into the stock This must be done by raising the bark of the stock, and thrusting down the graft, that the shoulders may rest on the crown of the stock The number of grafts for each stock, stem, or head, must be in proportion to its size, and after they are all inserted, the whole must be tied tight and clayed over, to prevent the parts receiving injury from the sun and wind

*which is said to be the most ancient of all the modes of grafting*

This is said to be the most ancient of all the methods of grafting Pliny says, the antients were afraid of cleaving the stocks But be this as it will, it appears their fears were soon dissipated, for cleft grafting is described and recommended by Theophrastus

*An objection to this practice obviated*

The chief objection to this practice is, that the grafts are for a longer time liable to be torn off by the winds, therefore, when this is practised, they should, for four or five years, be tied to proper supporters At the time of the performance of the operation also, the graft may be in some measure let into the stock by taking out, at the time of raising the bark, a small quantity of wood, with a small chissel provided for the purpose The graft will unite full as soon as if the wood had never been taken away, and, by being made to occupy the interstice, the whole will be sooner incorporated, and less liable to suffer injuries from that quarter Crown-grafting may also be performed by making several clefts in the stock, and inserting the graft, round the top, as is done in cleft grafting

## IV CHEEK-GRAFTING

*Manner of performing cheek-grafting*

TO perform this operation cut the stock horizontally, and smooth the top with the knife, then make a slope on the side an inch, an inch and a half, or two inches deep, according to the size of the graft, in the manner practised for whip grafting, next, cut the graft on the side opposite to the lowest bud, to make a shoulder It should be cut but a small way in, and sloped gradually to the point, making the slope of the graft the same length with the slope on the stock, that they may more exactly fit Afterwards, place the graft on the stock, its shoulder resting on the crown of it, tie it tight with bass strings; clay it like the others, and the business is done

## V SIDE-GRAFTING

*Its uses*

THE use of Side-Grafting is to fill up the vacant parts of trees by inserting grafts into the sides of the branches, without heading them down

*The operation of side grafting explained*

In the performance of this work, mark the best parts of the branches for the reception of the grafts, where their direction will be proper for filling the head, and let the number be rather more than is necessary to furnish the tree with a full head, that a sufficient quantity may remain in case some should miscarry, slope off the bark on the side with some of the wood, in the manner practised for whip grafting, cut the grafts to fit as nearly as possible, join the parts, tie them with bass strings, apply the clay, and the greatest part of your grafts will grow soon, furnish your tree with a beautiful head, and if the performance be for the sake of fruit, great variety of fruit on the same tree may be obtained this way, for no two grafts may be of the same sort, if you choose it

## VI GRAFTING BY APPROACH, OR INARCHING

*Grafting by approach a certain though no a good method,*

THIS is a certain, though by no means a good method of grafting, and is chiefly used to multiply such trees as are with difficulty made to grow, either by any of the former ways of grafting, or by budding, and as it is a sure method, it is also used where there is a scarcity of plants, to prevent the young shoots being lost, in case they should not grow by the common operations

A tree that is to be multiplied this way, must have a certain number of young plants set round it for stocks When they are grown of proper height, they must be headed, and each of them must receive a young shoot of the growing tree The operation may be performed by sloping the parts, and making a nick, in the manner of whip-grafting, or it may be done by making a cleft, and inserting the branch, in the manner of cleft-grafting In either case, bind it tight with bass strings, and clay it over, let a strong stake be be thrust into the ground, to faſten it to, and prevent its being diſlocated by the winds, and they will perfectly unite The year following, or two years after, if you chooſe it, the ſtock being a proper baſis for the graft, and able to ſupply it with ſufficient nouriſhment, it may be then cut off from the parent plant, and after ſtanding one year more, to become a ſtrong plant, may be removed to the place where it is deſigned to remain

Inarching is not recommended to be practiſed often and why

Altho this is a ſure method of practice, I for the moſt part found trees grafted in this manner thrive ill, be ſlower in growth, and leſs beautiful, than thoſe raiſed by whip-grafting The part alſo where the ſtock and graft were joined, was always turgid and unſightly, ſo that this operation, unleſs for the above reaſon, ſhould be rarely practiſed It was a method I at firſt uſed to multiply my variegated oaks, Eaſtern hornbeams, &c but after I had a number of plants, I grafted them by the common way, and the beauty of the plants raiſed by the latter method ſo far ſurpaſſed the former, that a compariſon could not be made

The beſt ſeaſon for this operation

Inarching is generally performed in April or May, though it may be done with ſucceſs in the winter or, in ſhort, at any time of the year

There are ſeveral other methods of grafting, none of which deſerve mentioning after thoſe already deſcribed, ſuch as taking off the bark of a branch with the buds, cutting away the bark alſo of the ſtock of the like ſize and figure, then inſerting the bark from the branch in the room of that which was on the ſtock, binding it with ſtrings, and claying the parts, leaving only the buds out to be ready for ſhooting

Grafts of the ſame fraternity as the ſtocks will unite with little or no trouble

Grafts of the ſame fraternity as the ſtocks, if applied to the outward part of the bark, will frequently grow, and in time coaleſce with the whole ſtock, and grafts applied to the wood only, without touching the bark of the ſtock, will grow, in ſhort, when the ſtocks and grafts are ſuitable to each other, if the parts are almoſt any-how applied to each other, they will unite I had an inſtance of a bough of about an inch diameter, being broken by the winds from a large ſycamore tree This falling with the ſmall end, or young branches, on the ground, the thick end or part where it was ſlipt from the tree (for it was a ſlip) reſted upon the trunk of the tree, near the bottom It ſoon joined itſelf to the bark on the trunk, and, by Midſummer following, became ſo perfectly united, that it required a ſtrong pull, with a jerk, to part them This ſhews how ready parent-trees are to adopt ſimilar offspring; and probably from ſuch inſtances the antients were induced to believe, that all trees might be made to grow on one another

When the grafts are in a growing ſtate, the ſtocks ſhould be conſtantly freed from ſide-ſuckers, &c With regard to their after-management, that will be ſhewn of courſe under the reſpective articles

# CHAP. V

## Of BUDDING

Difference between budding and grafting explained, both which operations are peculiarly adapted to different ſorts of trees

BUDDING, commonly called Inoculating, is only a different way of grafting, and is the inſertion of the buds, inſtead of grafts, into proper parts of the tree By this method, ſome ſorts of trees are beſt multiplied though the inſertion of grafts is much preferable to budding for many kinds Cherries, for inſtance, ſhould always be grafted, and not budded, or they will for the moſt part gum, canker, and ſooner die off Peaches, nectarines, apricots, &c are always propagated by budding, for though they may grow by grafting, yet they will gum, canker, and ſoon die off, whilſt apples, pears, plums, &c ſucceed equally well by budding or grafting The beſt method of practice for propagating the different trees for budding or grafting will be ſhewn under their reſpective articles, as they ſucceed in order in the courſe of this work, together with the variation of time, which is very little, for all the trees, or ſhrubs, that are to be multiplied this way

August the beſt month for performing his buſineſs and why

The beſt time of budding of every tree I know is in Auguſt, from the beginning to the end of that month, though the middle, or latter end, is better than the beginning If the ſtocks are budded much earlier, great numbers of the buds will ſhoot the ſame ſummer, the conſequence of which will be, that the wood, not having time to be duly ripened, will be killed by the firſt hard froſt that happens Thus your too early hopes will be ſuddenly diſappointed In order to guard againſt this evil, ſome are in a great hurry to get their budding over, beginning in June, or earlier, if the ſap runs freely in the ſtocks, and the buds are ſufficiently mature to be taken from the cuttings, that they may have time to ſhoot ſtrong, and be enabled to reſiſt the winter's cold Theſe they call ſpring-ing-buds, to diſtinguiſh them from the latter, which are not improperly termed Dormant-buds; hereby thinking that they gain a year by their early application to the buſineſs However, they are greatly deceived, for trees worked this way ſeldom ſucceed, even though they ſuffer no injury from the winter's froſt But this is a bare ſuppoſition, for, in general, the wood from the ſpring budding will be ſo ſpongy and ill-ripened, that a ſevere winter will deſtroy a whole plantation, eſpecially if it be on a ſtrong, wet, or damp ſoil, and even ſhould they ſucceed and ſurvive the winter, they will ſhoot very weak the ſummer following, often gum and canker, and, if this is practiſed for peaches and nectarines, will be infinitely inferior in the autumn, to the one-year's ſhoots which have ſprung directly from the dormant buds the preceding ſummer

Determining, therefore, upon the month of Auguſt as the beſt ſeaſon for this operation, unleſs for ſome few green-houſe or ſtove plants, which may be protected from cold, or aſſiſted with artificial heat, proceed to the operation, being provided with good budding-knives, baſs-ſtrings, &c

Five

Five perſons ought to be employed, if large quantities of fruit or other trees are to be worked, the firſt in gathering the cuttings and numbering the ſorts, the ſecond in clearing the ſtocks from all external branches, the third in inſerting the buds, the fourth in tying them with the baſs ſtrings, the fifth in placing the number-ſticks, and finally booking them, that no miſtake may afterwards be made as to the ſorts.

*Directions for gathering and managing the cuttings*

The cuttings ſhould always be taken from the moſt healthy and thriving trees; and, in fruit-trees, they ſhould be taken from the healthieſt, moſt thriving, beſt-bearing, and beſt ſorts of fruit which can be procured. Cloudy weather, or early in the morning before the ſun is riſen, or evenings, is the beſt time for this buſineſs, though where large quantities of trees are to be worked, it muſt be performed all day long indiſcriminately, as the weather happens. As the cuttings are gathered, the leaves ſhould be taken off, leaving only a quarter of an inch of the ſtock, the unripened ends alſo ſhould be cut off, the cuttings ſhould be then numbered, in order to be booked, kept in wet moſs, and covered from the ſun, until they are removed to the quarter where they are to be worked up.

*Method of performing the operation of budding deſcribed*

The operation is as follows. Cut the bark on the north ſide of the ſtock, in a ſmooth place, horizontally, quite through to the wood, then with the point of your knife make a perpendicular ſlit, to meet it in the middle at right angles, half an inch, an inch, or more deep, according to the nature of the bud that is to be inſerted. Next, proceed with all expedition to take off the bud. For this purpoſe, hold the thin end of your cutting near you, in your left hand, and with the knife in your right ſlope off the bud. It muſt enter about half an inch or an inch below it, muſt be directed nearly half way through the cutting, and may be continued half an inch and more on the neareſt end. Then, hold the bud in your left hand firm, and with the right thumb and finger ſtrip out the wood from the bark of the bud. In doing of this, the eye is frequently loſt, when it is good for nothing, and muſt be thrown away. If the eye is retained, it is a proper bud to be inſerted, alſo if a little of the wood remain about the eye, it will be never the worſe, though if the eye is perfect, there will be no occaſion of wood to promote the growth of the bud. Afterwards, clap the end of the cutting between the lips, take the bud in your left hand, and with the back of the knife in your right divide the bark on the ſtock, thruſting the haft from the tranſverſe cut downwards on each ſide, let in the bud, thruſting it down to the bottom of the ſlit, cut off the bark of the bud at the horizontal ſlit, to let it in, and then, if you have hands to go on with the different parts of the buſineſs ſeparately, proceed to the next; and let the tyer, having his baſs ſtrings (firſt ſoaked in water to make them pliable) in readineſs, tie it pretty cloſe from below the perpendicular ſlit to above the horizontal cut, covering the whole with the ſtrings, to exclude the air, ſun, and wet, except the eye of the bud, which ought to be left eaſy, free, and juſt preſſed with the ligature only, to unite the parts, but not ſo cloſely that there may be danger of the bud's ſuffering by too ſtrict a bandage.

This is the whole myſtery of Inoculation, which ſhould always be performed with diſpatch, to prevent the parts from drying, and, indeed, ſo ſpeedily may the ſeveral ſteps be taken, that a good workman will bud upwards of two thouſand ſtocks in a day, if he is regularly ſupplied with cuttings, and proper perſons to tie after him.

*Farther directions in the art of budding*

In about ten days or little more, you may ſee which buds have taken, by the healthy appearance they will retain, if united to the ſtock. Soon after this, it is generally adviſed to looſen the ſtrings, to prevent the bark's being too much bound. But this is needleſs expence and trouble. Let every thing alone until the middle or end of September, when you may take off all the ſtrings, leaving the buds at eaſe in their now proper and own ſtocks, and if the bark of ſome ſhould be ſwelled, and appear injured by long confinement, it will ſoon recover itſelf, and be little if any the worſe. In March, or early in April following, the ſtocks muſt be cut off juſt above the buds, and not three or four inches higher, as is commonly practiſed, for this will draw the nouriſhment from the root which would otherwiſe be communicated to the bud, by the repeated efforts to put out new ſhoots, though they are continually rubbed off. The reaſon alledged for leaving four or five inches length of the ſtock above the bud is, that the young ſhoot may be tied to it, and ſupported in caſe high winds ſhould happen. To this it may be anſwered, that it will not be a ſufficient ſupport to many ſtrong ſhooting trees, which will ariſe more than ſix feet in one ſeaſon from the bud, by being tied with a baſs ſtring ſo near the baſe, many thorns, medlars, fruit and other trees, will often in one ſeaſon from the bud grow to this height, and if the ſituation is bleak and ill-defended, a ſtrong ſtick ſhould be thruſt down by each plant, to which it ſhould be faſtened, otherwiſe there will be great danger of its being blown out of its ſocket before the end of ſummer.

With regard to the lower ſhooting trees, there will be no occaſion to leave a part of the ſtock above the bud to faſten them to, and protect them from high winds, for there will be little or no danger of their ſuffering from that quarter. At the time of heading, therefore, to avoid future trouble, let the ſtocks be cut down exactly above the bud, ſloping it off from the back part to the top of the bud, ſo that when the bud commences a ſhoot, it may appear as if Nature had deſigned it to ſpring from that ſtock only, and as if it had never been brought there by art. Rub off all ſide-buds from the ſtock as often as they appear, take off all ſuckers from the roots which may ariſe, keep the ground clean from weeds all ſummer, and by the autumn your buds will have uninterruptedly arrived at all poſſible perfection, when the plants may be taken up, and removed to the places where they are deſigned to remain.

*The different heights at which flowering, fruit dwarf, and ſtandard trees ſhould be budded*

Flowering-trees may be budded at any height to form the moſt beautiful heads, at the diſcretion of a judicious operator, fruit-trees muſt be budded in different places, according to the purpoſes they are deſigned for, dwarf trees three or four inches above the ground, that the branches may at firſt be trained low to the wall, and ſtandards ſix feet from the ground, or higher or lower as they are wanted.

*The north the beſt ſide for inſerting the bud*

I always preferred inſerting the bud on the north ſide of the ſtock, if there is a proper place for it, as, by being in the ſhade, it will be leſs liable to be dried by the ſun before it is united to the ſtock. A ſmooth part of the ſtock ought to be pitched on, though no regard ſhould be paid to its being fixed on a bud or gem of the ſtock, which the antients univerſally believed to be eſſential to the ſucceſs of the operation. This plainly proves that Theophraſtus, Virgil, and other early writers on the ſubject, were better philoſophers than practical gardeners, and wrote in theory more than from experiment and obſervation.

When

*Moiſt moſs uſed to convey cuttings to a diſtance*

When cuttings are to be conveyed a conſiderable diſtance, there is no occaſion for tin pans, with a ſocket to hold water, in which to place the cuttings in an upright poſition. Cuttings, if they are taken from the trees early in the morning, may be conveyed with ſafety in moiſt moſs from any part of England to the other, and being lapped in that cloſe manner, will not only be conveyed with greater eaſe, but be leſs liable to bruiſes and other accidents, than when tumbled about in watering-pans provided for that purpoſe.

When the cuttings arrive at the place where they are wanted, they ſhould be ſet an inch or more deep in water, perpendicular, and ſhould be worked up as ſoon as poſſible. When there are plenty of cuttings, the beſt buds ſhould always be taken, which are for the moſt part about the middle of the cutting, thoſe near the extremity being ill ſhaped, and thoſe on the thick end being generally ſmall, and having the wood hard, are rarely taken off with good eyes. When the cuttings are few, however, and the ſtocks numerous, you muſt begin as near the ſmall end as the wood, tho' ſoft, will ſeparate from the bark, leaving an eye, and you muſt proceed to the others regularly, ſloping the buds off ſometimes obliquely, ſometimes your cuts muſt be ſhort, ſometimes narrow, and ſo you muſt proceed to the laſt bud on the thickeſt end of the cutting, that no bud may be loſt, for it is not abſolutely neceſſary to take a certain ſhare of the bark with the bud, it is the eye only that produces the future plant, though the more bark there is with it the better.

When cuttings of choice fruit-trees are ſcarce, nurſery-men who want to raiſe large quantities for ſale ſhould uſe every bud which ſhews any probability of taking, for tho' the greateſt part of them may die, his trouble only, which is trifling, is loſt, the ſtocks remain where they are, and will be ready for grafting the ſpring after, and if they ſhould not be wanted for grafting, they ſhould be headed down to the ground, and as they ariſe again in the ſpring, all the ſide-ſhoots ſhould be taken off, leaving only the ſtrongeſt in the center, which will be admirably adapted to undergo the freſh operation of budding the Auguſt following.

## CHAP. VI.

## Of LAYERING.

LAYERING is another and admirable way of propagating trees and plants, and whereas *grafting and inoculating chiefly reſpect the* variety of fruit-trees, and ſeeds timber-trees, layering is applicable to the encreaſe of almoſt all ſorts of ſhrubs, flowering trees, evergreens, and the like, the proper rules for which ſhall be given under their reſpective articles.

*What are the proper ſubjects for layering*

Layering on different plants may be performed at all times of the year, though, in general, the beſt ſeaſon for it is the autumn. Nevertheleſs, it may be done ſucceſsfully for the moſt part in the winter or ſpring, and ſuch plants as are found not to take readily by being layered at that ſeaſon, ſhould be layered in June or July, while they are tender, and performing their ſummer's ſhoot.

*Autumn the beſt ſeaſon for this operation*

Layering may be performed different ways, and trees of different texture are with different degrees of difficulty made to ſtrike root. It is chiefly the young ſhoots of the preceding ſummer that the operation ſhould be performed on, though all wood of looſe texture or a ſpongy nature, if ſeveral years old, will grow very well.

The different ways of layering are,

*The different ways of layering*

1. By only making a ſmall cavity and laying the ſhoot, whether young or old, in it, covering it over with fine mould. No other trouble than this ſlight layering is neceſſary for the encreaſe of numbers of trees, ſuch as vines, viburnums, laurels, &c.

2. By twiſting the ſhoots and ſlightly breaking the bark, numerous trees, which would not ſo readily take by the former method, will emit roots from the bruiſed parts, and if the work be performed in the autumn, will commence good plants by the autumn following.

3. By thruſting an awl through the joint, the young ſhoots of many trees will ſooner emit fibres from ſuch wounded part, than if they had been otherwiſe laid in the ground, and in the courſe of the ſummer-months will commence good plants, fit to be taken off and planted out.

4. Cutting our ſome ſmall ſlips of bark, about a joint, will facilitate the ſhoot's ſtriking root, and cauſe it the ſooner to commence a plant.

5. Twiſting of wire round the ſhoot, and pricking it in each ſide with the awl, has been recommended. I ever found the twiſting unneceſſary trouble if the places were pricked with the awl, as the fibres always proceeded from the wounded places, and not from the parts ſurrounded by the wire, nevertheleſs, it may be ſerviceable in ſome caſes, if the binding is not too hard, and the bark bruiſed or broken only with the wire. From ſuch bruiſed parts fibres will come out, and then the pricking with the awl may be omitted.

6. Slit-layering, or that operation generally known among gardeners by the name of Tongue-Layering, is the moſt univerſal, the beſt, and the ſafeſt way of layering trees and plants, and is the only method to have recourſe to when the former fail. It is known to every floriſt, who layers his carnations this way, and is practiſed by all gardeners for almoſt all ſorts of trees which are not known to take by the ſimple method of barely laying the ſhoots in the ground.

*Slit or tongue-laying the beſt and ſureſt method*

Tongue-layering is performed by cutting with the knife half way through the ſhoot at right angles with it, and then turning the edge of it upwards, in a perpendicular direction, along the middle of the ſhoot, half an inch, an inch, or more, according to the nature of the ſtock that is to be layered. The horizontal cut in carnation layering is always at a joint, and is for the moſt part practiſed by making the cut at a joint or end, where the performance is on trees. The more elegantly to perform this, make the horizontal cut half through, take out the knife and

*That operation deſcribed*

and a little below that cut, on the heel of the underwood, taking it off, and drawing the edge of the knife up the middle to the above length. By taking the heel of the underwood off, the tongue or bottom of the layer will ſit more at eaſe, and by being ſurrounded with mould, will be the better diſpoſed to ſtrike root, ſhould the parts by any accident be made to cloſe again. The ſhoots being cut in this manner, ſhould be next pegged down into the ground, a place being hollowed for the purpoſe, then the point of the layer ſhould be brought forward, pointing towards the ſtem of the plant, which will ſeparate the tongue from the other part of the branch, and to keep it at a diſtance, a ſmall chip, or ſuch-like thing, may be inſerted near the top of the ſlit, to keep it open. The mould muſt now be applied, and after heading the layer down to within one eye or more of the ground, the buſineſs is done.

Trees that are layered muſt have the ground mown and kept clean from weeds.

In all layering watering muſt be applied in ſummer, to keep the ground moiſt, if dry weather ſhould happen. The ground muſt always be kept clean from weeds, and there are few trees in compariſon, if layered this way, and with this management in the autumn, which will not be fit to take up the autumn after.

Theſe are the various ways of layering trees, and by which they may be multiplied. In order to raiſe great quantities, a ſufficient number of trees ſhould be ſet, to be headed down for ſtools. The ground, previous to planting, ſhould be double dug, and the diſtances they ought to be ſet from each other ſhould vary according to the ſize, height, or manner they are intended to grow before they are layered. The autumn after planting, each tree ſhould be headed to within a few inches of the ground, and the ſummer following it will afford you plenty of young ſhoots proper for layering in the autumn.

It is beſt to wait two years before you layer many trees; and why.

Nevertheleſs, in many trees it will be the beſt way to wait two years before you layer them, as each ſtool will afford you ten times the number of layers for the purpoſe, and the ſhoots being then many of them ſide ſhoots, and weaker than the ſtrong ſhoots from the ſtool the autumn before, will for the moſt part more readily ſtrike root. For it is obſervable, that in vigorous ſtrong ſhoots, though only of one year's growth, after they have been layered a twelvemonth, even by ſlit-layering, the end of the divided part has only ſwelled, and ſtruck no root, whereas ſmaller branches on the ſame tree, in the ſame ſpace of time, have ſtruck good root, and commenced plants fit to be taken off and removed to the nurſery.

If the tree has grown from the ſtool two years, it muſt be ſplaſhed, to bring the head and branches down to the ground. All branches which croſs, crowd, or any ways incommode each other, muſt be taken out, the ground ſhould be excavated, and the head of each branch brought into the hollow, pegging it down firmly with a ſtrong peg. The ends of the young ſhoots muſt be alſo ſhortened, for one eye only, for the moſt part, ought to be out of the ground, if you can tell how they will fall, as it will be a ſafer way to do it before the ſlit is made than afterwards. Then the ſlit, or twiſt, or whatever method you chooſe, muſt be entered upon, and when all the branches have undergone the operation, the mould muſt be carefully brought in among them, filling all the interſtices, and levelling the whole ſo that an eye of each may juſt appear above ground, and if ſome ſhoots were before improperly ſhortened, it may be now done, holding it ſteady with the left thumb and finger, and cutting off an eye above the ground with the right. When the ſtool is completely layered in this manner, proceed to the next, and ſo on till the whole is completed.

By waiting two years after the heading of the plant for the ſtools, ſtools which perhaps would hardly have afforded you ſix plants will now yield ſixty, or more, which is a ſufficient encouragement for patience, nay, it is what ought to be practiſed by nurſery-men, or gentlemen who want to raiſe large quantities of trees for ſale, or to be planted out on their own eſtates.

And when this is the caſe, two quarters of ſufficient ſize ſhould be planted for ſtools, which coming in alternately, one with another, there may be an annual crop of layers for the purpoſes wanted.

As ſoon as the layers are taken off, all ſcraggy parts ſhould be cut off from the ſtools, the heads ſhould be refreſhed with the knife, and two years after each ſtool will have afforded you a ſufficient quantity of branches to be layered afreſh, during which time the ground ſhould be dug between the ſtools every winter, and in ſpring and ſummer the weeds ſhould be hoed and cleared off, as often as they make their appearance.

Manner of bringing down a tree to the ground on its ſide.

Trees of much larger growth than two or three years may be ſplaſhed, brought down, and layered in this manner, and when they are grown too large for ſplaſhing, or the nature of the wood will not bear ſuch an operation, they may be thrown on their ſides. In order to effect this, the mould muſt be cleared away from the roots, on the ſide you intend the head to be brought down, and on this ſide a ſufficient number of the roots muſt be cut, that the tree may be brought to the ground, leaving proper roots to continue it in a growing ſtate, but for this very few will be ſufficient. When the tree is brought down, all the young branches are to be layered in the former manner, and the year following, after they are taken off, the tree may be ſet upright again, cutting off all ſcraggy parts, ſide-branches that had been beat down, &c. and if you put freſh mould to the roots, it will put out as freſh as ever, and may, if you pleaſe, afterwards undergo a ſecond operation in the like manner. If magnolias, or large leafy evergreens, are layered in this manner, and the place is not well defended, it will be highly proper to make a ſtake-hedge of good height, at a ſmall diſtance, otherwiſe the high winds having power on their large leaves, will frequently break them off before they have taken root.

Layers may be procured from trees of any ſize, by building ſcaffolding of proper height, to ſupport tubs or pots filled with good earth, in which to layer the young branches. But this method is never practiſed unleſs on ſome very ſcarce tree, which is deſired to be continued in its upright ſtate, in as much beauty as poſſible. Neither, indeed, does it deſerve to be adopted, unleſs on ſome ſuch extraordinary occaſions, not only on account of the expence of building the ſcaffolding, but of the conſtant trouble there will be in keeping the mould in the pots of a due moiſture, for being elevated in that manner above the ground, it will dry very faſt, and if it is not conſtantly watered, there will be little hope of your layers ſtriking root in any reaſonable time.

# CHAP VII

## Of SUCKERS

*Some trees may be multiplied very faſt by ſuckers*

NO inconſiderable ſhare of the vegetable world may be multiplied very faſt by the ſuckers which they produce Some are ſo very fertile this way, as to extend their roots to, and ſend forth young plants at, a conſiderable diſtance from the tree, and others again produce ſuckers in ſuch plenty, that, if not taken off, they will over-run and deſtroy every thing that is near them

*which will afford good plants*

*All theſe, with proper management, will afford* you good plants Let them be dug up in October, and be well pruned, cutting off all the knobbed thick parts, leaving a few fibres only to the ſucker that is to be planted If the ſucker has no fibres except thoſe which proceed from the knobbed thick creeping root that produced it, do not retain that woody tranſverſe part for the ſake of the fibres, but ſlip off the ſucker from that thick part, and plant it, even though it ſhould have no fibres belonging to it, for the lower part of it having been under ground, and contiguous to the root, will be very ſpongy, and much ſooner ſtrike root than any cutting from the upper parts of the tree

*Method of preparing their roots*

As you thus prepare their roots, ſhorten their length to a foot and half, or two feet, according to their natures, and the fibres they are poſſeſſed of at the bottom Then proceed to planting them in the nurſery ground observing always to plant the beſt rooted ſuckers by themſelves, and thoſe which are more dubious of growing likewiſe by themſelves, as well as much cloſer together

*and planting them*

During their ſtay in the nurſery, if the uſual care of weeding be afforded them in ſummer, and the ground be dug between the rows in the winter, they will in a little time commence good plants, and may be, any time in the autumn, winter, or ſpring, taken up, when they are trained ſuitable for the purpoſes wanted

By the time they are removed, they probably will ſhew a tendency to emit freſh ſuckers, all ſuch prominent parts, therefore, ſhould be rubbed off, and not cut off at the time of planting out, as Nature will ſooner follow the bent in ſuch efforts, than when inſulted by the parts being rubbed off by the finger and thumb

*Objections to this practice answered*

The raiſing trees of any ſorts from ſuckers has been objected to by many, becauſe, ſay they, trees raiſed from ſuckers will proportionally be more productive of ſuckers again than thoſe raiſed any other way But for this reaſoning there is little foundation, as I ever found that trees which naturally (and it is the nature of many ſorts) put out ſuckers, never fail to afford you plenty of them, if the ſoil is ſuitable, let them be raiſed from layers, ſeeds, or by any other method, and I am pretty certain, that if all the horizontal points are cut off in the manner I have directed, ſuch a ſucker will make a plant as little adapted to put out freſh ſuckers, as if it had been a layer or a ſeedling

What might incline people to this notion was, that they have obſerved trees raiſed from ſeeds very long before they produced ſuckers But they ſhould conſider, that no tree or plant will produce ſuckers till it is of a ſuitable ſize or ſtrength for the purpoſe, any more than animals can produce young before they are of proper age, and let them plant a ſeedling that is grown ſtrong, a layer of the ſame ſtrength, and one which has been raiſed from a ſucker, exactly of the ſame ſize, and with the ſame number of fibres to the root, and they will find that the ſeedling or the layer will not be behind-hand with the other in producing ſuckers, if they have all alike ſoil and ſituation, for it is peculiar to them to ſport under the ſoil in this manner, and Nature will ever act agreeably to herſelf, if not ſtopped in her progreſs by art

*Soil proper for trees planted to produce ſuckers*

When trees of any ſort are to be planted in order to produce ſuckers for multiplication, they ſhould have a rich light ſoil, and in ſuch a ſtation they will put forth ſuckers in abundance, and afford an amazing encreaſe

When trees which are ſubject to throw out ſuckers are planted out for ornament, the ſuckers ſhould be conſtantly cleared away from the roots as often as they are produced, otherwiſe they will rob the parent plant of its nutriment, diminiſh its beauty, and in a little time over run every thing that is near it

CHAP

# CHAP. VIII

## Of CUTTINGS

A Large ſhare of the vegetable creation may be alſo multiplied by planting only their ſlips or cuttings in the earth, and affording them management ſuitable to their reſpective natures Some trees grow ſo readily this way, that it is the only method practiſed to raiſe any deſired number of plants The willow, the alder, the poplar, &c in all their varieties, are inſtances of the larger kinds, whilſt the ſage, the roſemary, the rue-plant and ſouthernwood, are ſome inſtances of the lower ligneous plants that, every common houſewife can inform you, are with the utmoſt facility multiplied by ſlips These will grow if planted at any time of the year, but ſuch as will not prove ſo obſequious to your diſcipline, you muſt indulge in the ſeaſon they require to be ſet in, the autumn for ſome, the ſpring for others, the early part of the ſummer for one plant, and the latter end of it for another

*What trees grow moſt readily from cuttings*

Some, again, muſt not only have their ſeaſons ſuited to them, but even require other help to put them in their growing ſtate The hardieſt ſorts will proceed with ſhade and water at firſt, on which account ſuch cuttings ſhould always be planted in a ſhady border Some muſt have the aſſiſtance of a ſlight hot bed, others a ſtrong degree of warmth, to promote their taking root, and by ſuch aſſiſtance, numbers of our tender exotics are multiplied, obſerving always to afford them water, ſhade, and light For though the eſſentials towards vegetation are generally ſaid to be heat, moiſture, and ſhade, a fourth ought to be added, viz light, which is highly neceſſary for exhilarating the plant, and cauſing it to aſſume an healthy and ſprightly look Others, again, grow beſt without any aſſiſtance, and are encreaſed by planting the cuttings, in the ſummer, in pots, and placing them in a ſhady part of the greenhouſe, with the windows open Of this the myrtle is an inſtance, and this is the only good way by which it can be raiſed in plenty

*Some trees however, will require aſſiſtance, whilſt others thrive beſt without any help*

The various methods, however, will come of courſe under their ſeparate articles, as well as the various parts that are moſt ſuitable for propagation, the older wood of one ſort, the young ſhoots of another, and the leaves of a third, ſome muſt be long, for larger purpoſes, others ſhort, when they are to figure in the dwarf way, and the reſt ſhould be ſuitable to the various purpoſes for which they are deſigned Thus eaſily may a large part of the vegetable creation be multiplied, the particulars of which ſhall be ſet forth under their reſpective heads So that by cuttings, layering, grafting, and budding, all the curious varieties, whether reſpecting beauty or uſe, are prepared and encreaſed in their proper kinds whilſt by ſeeds the whole produce of Nature is to be raiſed, and freſh varieties produced

I ſhall now proceed to the Method of raiſing the Variety of Trees, both evergreen and deciduous, proper for Ornament and Shade, and which are to be propagated by one or other of the former methods

PART

# PART II.

## OF DECIDUOUS TREES PROPER FOR ORNAMENT and SHADE

## CHAP I

## *ACER*, The MAPLE-TREE

AS I ſhall arrange the different genera of deciduous trees proper for ornament and ſhade in an alphabetical manner, according to the generical name of each, *Acer*, the maple-tree, firſt preſents itſelf to our conſideration

The ſpecies of *Acer* are,

Various ſpecies of the maple

1 The Common Maple
2 Greater Maple, or Sycamore
3 Aſh leaved Maple
4 Norway Maple
5 Montpelier Maple
6 Cretan Maple
7 Scarlet-flowering Maple
8 Sugar Maple
9 Tartarian Maple
10 Mountain Maple

1 2 3 4 Theſe have been already treated of as foreſt trees

General deſcription of the leaves &c and properties of the Common Maple and Sycamore

1 2 The Common Maple and the Sycamore are hardly ever planted as ornamental trees in the wilderneſs, unleſs it be where there is a deficiency of other ſorts They are common and known every where, and the leaves of the Sycamore, though beautiful on their firſt appearance, are for the moſt part, on the approach of hot weather, eat full of holes by inſects, and rendered unſightly, which makes this tree to be ſtill more diſregarded It affords, however, admirable ſhade; and is peculiarly uſeful in ſome ſituations, eſpecially near the ſea, where it reſiſts the ſpray, and thrives amazingly There are two remarkable varieties of the Sycamore, one with large broad leaves, and keys of more than double the ſize of the Common ones, and another with variegated leaves The Striped leaved Common Maple and the Striped Norway Maple are alſo found in our nurſeries

the Aſh leaved and Norway Maple

3 4 The Aſh-leaved and the Norway Maple, in the common ſorts, are much ſought after for ornamental plantations, as being of foreign growth Their ſituation ſhould be amongſt the talleſt-growing trees, and there they will afford a pleaſing variety The leaves are naturally of a good green colour, ſmooth, large, and of a thin conſiſtence The leaves of the Norway Maple are as large or larger than thoſe of the Sycamore, their edges are acutely and more beautifully indented, they are not ſo liable to be eat by inſects in the ſummer, and in the autumn they die to a golden yellow colour, which cauſes a delightful effect by the colouring at that ſeaſon, when the different tints of the decaying vegetable world are diſplayed A ſeaſon by ſome perſons thought ſuperior to any in the year, the ſpring itſelf not excepted, and therefore many in their collections are more peculiarly attentive to have ſuch trees as diverſify the ſcene in the moſt beautiful manner at that time, by diſplaying the moſt lively colours in a dying ſtate The flowers alſo of the Norway Maple are very beautiful They come out early in the ſpring, are of a fine yellow colour, and ſhew themſelves to advantage before the leaves come out They are frequently ſucceeded by keys, but generally drop off before they come to maturity

5 Montpelier Maple grows to about twenty feet high, and is a very beautiful tree The leaves are compoſed of three lobes, are of a ſhining green, a thickiſh ſubſtance, and retain their verdure later in the year than moſt of the other ſorts The flowers come out in the ſpring, but have very little beauty, their blow is ſoon over, and ſometimes they are ſucceeded by ſeeds which come to perfection in our gardens

of the Montpelier maple

6 Cretan Maple This grows to about the height of the former The leaves are downy, compoſed of three lobes, and grow oppoſite to each other on long downy footſtalks The flowers come out in the ſpring, are inconſiderable to the floriſt, and are very ſeldom ſucceeded by good ſeeds in England

Cretan maple

7 Scarlet-flowering Maple Of this there are two ſorts, called, 1 Virginian Scarlet-flowering Maple,

Scarlet flowering maple

Maple, and, 2. Sir Charles Wager's Maple. Both of theſe are propagated for the ſake of the flowers, which are of a ſcarlet colour, and come out early in the ſpring. The leaves are compoſed each of five ſharp pointed lobes, which are ſlightly indented or ſerrated. They are ſmooth, of a pale green on their upper ſurface, glaucous underneath, and they grow on long, ſimple, taper, reddiſh footſtalks. The flowers come out in cluſters from the ſide of the branches, and the botanic characters, which follow their titles, indicate their ſtructure. They appear in April, and the ſeeds ripen in June. The ſort called Sir Charles Wager's produces larger cluſters of flowers than the others, on which account it is in moſt eſteem.

Sugar maple. 8. Sugar Maple is a large-growing tree, will arrive at the height of forty feet, and has broad thin leaves, divided into five principal parts, which are again indented or cut at the edges into ſeveral acute ſegments. Their ſurface is ſmooth, of a light green colour, whitiſh underneath, and they grow on pretty long footſtalks. The flowers come out in the ſpring, about the time of the Norway Maple, and they are ſucceeded by long keys, which ſometimes ripen in England. In America, the inhabitants tap this tree in the ſpring, boil the liquor, and the fæces afford a uſeful ſugar. The Sycamore, the Aſh-leaved and the Norway Maples alſo abound with a ſaccharine juice, from which I make no doubt but a uſeful ſugar might be prepared.

Tartarian maple, 9. Tartarian Maple will grow to upwards of twenty feet high. The leaves are heart-ſhaped, undivided, and their edges are unequally ſerrated. The flowers come out from the wings of the leaves, in longiſh bunches; they appear early in the ſpring, and ſometimes are ſucceeded by ripe ſeeds in our gardens.

and Mountain maple. 10. Mountain Maple. The ſtalks of this tree are ſlender, covered with a whitiſh bark, ſend forth ſeveral red branches, and grow about fifteen feet high. The leaves are three-lobed, pointed, and are unequally and ſharply ſerrated. The flowers come out in longiſh bunches, in the ſpring. They are of a greeniſh yellow colour, and are ſucceeded by ſeeds which (like thoſe of the Norway Maple) generally fall off before they are ripe.

Method of propagating theſe ſorts of maple from ſeeds. Theſe ſorts are all propagated firſt by the ſeeds, but as they do not always all ripen in this country, the beſt way will be to procure them from the places where they naturally grow.

A cool ſhady part of the ſeminary ſhould be appropriated for the purpoſe, the mould ſhould be made fine, beds ſhould be marked out four feet wide, and in length proportionable to the quantity, and in theſe the ſeeds ſhould be regularly ſown, ſifting over them about half an inch of the fineſt mould. When the plants come up they muſt be kept clean from weeds, and frequently watered, and this work muſt be duly attended to all ſummer. The ſpring following, the ſtrongeſt may be drawn out, and planted in the nurſery, in rows two feet aſunder, and at the diſtance of a foot from each other in the rows, leaving the others in the ſeminary to gain ſtrength. The ſpring following they alſo muſt receive the ſame culture; and in the nurſery they may remain, with no other trouble than keeping the ground clean from weeds in the ſummer, digging between the rows in the winter, and taking off all ſtrong and irregular ſide-ſhoots, till they are planted out for good.

Notwithſtanding theſe are the general laws of raiſing all the ſpecies of *Acer* from ſeeds which come from abroad, the culture varies with reſpect to the Scarlet flowering Maple, when the ſeeds are gathered at home. This ſpecies brings its ſeeds to maturity the beginning of June in our gardens. They ſhould be then gathered, and after having lain a few days to harden, they ſhould be ſown in beds of the fineſt mould, and covered only a quarter of an inch deep. The beds ſhould be hooped, and covered with mats in ſcorching weather, but in rainy and cloudy weather ſhould always be uncovered. In about a month or ſix weeks, a great part of the plants will appear, but the far greateſt ſhare will not come up before the ſpring following. When the ſummer-plants firſt ſhew themſelves, they ſhould hardly ever ſee the ſun in his full beams. The ſeeds muſt be conſtantly covered with the mats in the day-time, unleſs cloudy and rainy weather happens, when they ſhould always be uncovered; in nights alſo no mats muſt be over the plants, that they may have all the benefit of the refreſhing dews, air, and cooling ſhowers. When theſe latter do not fall, watering muſt be duly attended to, and this is all the trouble they will require for the firſt ſummer in the ſeed bed. The ſummer following, they may be wholly expoſed to all weather, being only kept clean from weeds, and watered in dry weather, and the ſpring after that, the ſtrongeſt may be ſet out in the nurſery way, like the former ſeedlings. MAPLE. Manner of raiſing the Scarlet flowering maple.

Trees raiſed from ſeeds will grow faſter, and arrive at greater height, than thoſe raiſed from layers; but they will not produce ſuch quantities of flowers, which makes the latter method more eligible for thoſe who want theſe plants for a low ſhrubbery.

2. By layers all the ſpecies of this genus are to be propagated, though it is never practiſed for the Common Maple and the Sycamore. The young ſhoots may be any time laid down in the autumn, winter, or early in the ſpring. By the autumn following, they will have ſtruck root, and become good plants, when the ſtrongeſt may be ſet out in the places where they are to remain, whilſt the weakeſt may be planted in the nurſery, like the ſeedlings, for a year or two, to gain ſtrength. All the ſpecies of this genus may be propagated by layers.

3. By cuttings alſo theſe trees are to be propagated. But this method is chiefly practiſed on the Aſh-leaved and Norway Maples, which more readily take root this way. The cuttings ſhould be the bottom parts of the laſt year's ſhoots. They ſhould be taken off early in October, and planted in rows in a moiſt ſhady place. The ſpring and ſummer following, they muſt be duly watered as often as dry weather makes it neceſſary, and be kept clean from weeds. By the autumn they will be fit to remove into the nurſery, though if the cuttings are not planted too cloſe, they may remain in their ſituation for a year or two longer, and then be ſet out for good, without the trouble of being previouſly planted in the nurſery. Maples may alſo be raiſed by cuttings,

4. By budding, grafting, and inarching likewiſe maples are to be propagated. But the other methods being more eligible, theſe are never practiſed, except for the variegated ſorts and the large broad leaved kind. This latter is to be continued no otherwiſe than by budding it on ſtocks of the Common Sycamore, for the ſeeds, though ſo large themſelves, when ſown afford you only the Common Sycamore in return. and by budding, grafting, and inarching.

Seeds of the variegated kinds, however, when ſown will produce you variegated plants in return, which renders the propagation of theſe ſorts very expeditious, where plenty of ſeeds may be had.

Where theſe are not to be obtained, in order to propagate theſe varieties by budding, let ſome plants of the Common Sycamore, one year old, be taken out of the ſeminary, and ſet in the

MAPLE

Method of propagating the variegated kinds of maples by budding.

nursery in rows a yard asunder, and the plants about a foot and half distance from each other in the rows. Let the ground be kept clean from weeds all summer, and be dug, or, as the gardeners call it, *turned in*, in the winter, and the summer following the stocks will be of a proper size to receive the buds, which should be taken from the most beautifully-striped branches. The best time for this work is August, because if it is done earlier, the buds will shoot the same summer, and when this happens, a hard winter will infallibly kill them. Having, therefore, budded your stocks the middle or latter end of August, with the eyes or buds fronting the north, early in October take off the bass matting, which before this time will have confined the bark and pinched the bud, but not so as to hurt it much. Then cut off the stock just above the bud, and dig the ground between the rows. The summer following, keep the ground clean from weeds, cut off all natural side buds from the stock as they come out, and by autumn, if the land is good, your buds will have shot forth, and formed themselves into trees five or six feet high. They may be then removed into the places where they are designed to remain, or a few of them only may be drawn out, leaving the others to be trained up for larger standards, to serve for planting out in open places, or such other purposes as shall be wanted.

The Striped Norway maple should be budded on stocks of its own kind. What soil is most proper for variegated plants.

The Striped Norway Maple should be budded on stocks of its own kind, for on these they take best, and both kinds are not very liable to run away from their colours. Variegated plants in general must be planted in poor, hungry, gravelly, or sandy soils, to feed the disease which occasions their beautiful stripes, and cause it to be more powerful. But these trees shew their stripes in greater perfection in a good soil. The plant, though in sickness, has the appearance of health, the shoots are vigorous and strong, the leaves are large, less liable to be hurt by insects, and the stripes appear more perfect, natural, and delightful, than those on stunted trees growing on a poor soil.

Titles of the different species.

1 The Common Maple is styled, *Acer foliis lobatis obtusis emarginatis*. In the *Hortus Cliffortianus* it is termed, *Acer foliis tripartito-palmatis lacinus utrinque emarginatis, cortice sulcato*. Haller calls it, *Acer foliis sub trilobis, lobis obtuse incisis*. Caspar Bauhine, *Acer campestre & minus*; Gerard, *Acer minus*; Parkinson, *Acer minus & vulgare*; and Vaillant, *Acer campestre & minus fructu rubente*. It grows naturally in hedges, thickets, woods, &c. in England, and most countries of Europe.

2 Greater Maple, or Sycamore. This is, *Acer foliis quinquelobis inæqualiter serratis, floribus racemosis*. In the *Hortus Upsaliensis* it is termed, *Acer foliis quinquelobis acutis obtuse serratis, petiolis canaliculatis*; in the *Hortus Cliffortianus*, *Acer foliis palmatis obtuse serratis, floribus sub apetalis racemosis*. Caspar Bauhine calls it, *Acer montanum candidum*; Dodonæus, Gerard, &c. *Acer majus*; and Parkinson, *Acer majus latifolium, Sycomorus falso dictum*. It grows naturally in England, Austria, and Switzerland.

3 Ash leaved Maple is, *Acer foliis compositis, floribus racemosis*. Plukenet calls it, *Acer maximum, foliis trifidis & quinquefidis, Virginianum*. It grows naturally in Virginia and Pensylvania.

4 Norway Maple is, *Acer foliis quinquelobis acuminatis acute dentatis glabris, floribus corymbosis*. In the *Hortus Cliffortianus* it is termed, *Acer foliis palmatis acute dentatis, floribus corollatis dichotomo-corymbosis*. Caspar Bauhine calls it, *Acer montanum, tenuissimis & acutissimis foliis*; Cammerarius, *Acer major*; and Plukenet, *Acer montanum, orientalis platani foliis atro-virentibus*. It grows naturally in Norway, and several of the northern parts of Europe.

5 Montpelier Maple is, *Acer foliis trilobis integerrimis glabris*. Caspar Bauhine calls it, *Acer trifolium*. It grows common near Montpelier.

6 Cretan Maple is, *Acer foliis trilobis integerrimis pubescentibus*. Tournefort calls it, *Acer orientalis, hederæ folio*; and Alpinus, *Acer Cretica*. It is a native of the East.

7 Scarlet flowering Maple is, *Acer foliis quinquelobis subdentatis subtus glaucis, pedunculis simplicissimis aggregatis*. In the *Hortus Upsaliensis* it is termed, *Acer foliis quinquelobis acuminatis acute serratis, petiolis teretibus*. Herman calls it, *Acer Virginianum, folio subtus incano, flosculis viridi-rubentibus*; and Plukenet, *Acer Virginianum, folio majore, subtus argenteo supra viridi splendente*. It grows naturally in Virginia and Pensylvania.

8 Sugar Maple is, *Acer foliis quinquepartito-palmatis acuminato dentatis*. It inhabits Pensylvania.

9 Tartarian Maple is, *Acer foliis cordatis indivisis serratis lobis obsoletis, floribus racemosis*. It grows naturally in Tartary.

10 Mountain Maple is, *Acer foliis trilobis acuminatis serrulatis, floribus racemosis*. It grows naturally in Pensylvania.

Class and order in the Linnæan system.

*Acer* is of the class and order *Polygamia Monoecia*, and the characters are,

The characters.

1 CALYX is a monophyllous, permanent perianthium, plane and undivided at the base, but cut at the top into five acute, coloured segments.

2 COROLLA is small, not much larger than the calyx, and is composed of five oval, obtuse, spreading petals.

3 STAMINA are eight very short, awl shaped filaments, with simple antheræ. The farina is cruciforme.

4 PISTILLA, in the hermaphrodite flowers, consists of a compressed germen, immersed in a large, convex, perforated receptacle, a filiforme style which daily encreases in length, and two very slender, sharp-pointed, reflexed stigmas.

5 PERICARPIUM is two roundish compressed capsules, which join at their base, and are terminated each by a large membranaceous wing.

6 SEMINA. The seeds are single and roundish.

It is observable, that on the first opening of these flowers, the stigmas only appear, and that the style afterwards by degrees grows out, &c.

CHAP.

# C H A P. II

## *ÆSCULUS*, The SCARLET-FLOWERING HORSE-CHESNUT.

*Species.*

THERE are only two ſpecies of this genus

1 The Common Horſe-Cheſnut

2 The Scarlet-flowering Horſe-Cheſnut

In the Part relating to Foreſt-trees I have ſhewn the culture and management of the Horſe Cheſnut-tree, a tree not only valuable for the ſake of its timber, but for the beautiful appearance it makes, both in the manner of its growth, the leaves, flowers, and the nuts, but as this will grow to ſeventy or eighty feet high, it muſt have a ſhare in the largeſt plantations now under conſideration

2 The Scarlet flowering Horſe-Cheſnut is of a much humbler growth, and therefore proper for ſhrubberies, to mix with trees of nearly its own ſize

*The Scarlet-flowering Horſe Cheſnut deſcribed*

The Scarlet flowering Horſe-Cheſnut will grow to about fifteen or ſixteen feet high, and there is a delicacy in this tree that makes it deſirable The bark of the young ſhoots is quite ſmooth, and the growing ſhoots in ſummer are of a reddiſh hue The leaves are palmated, being pretty much like thoſe of the Horſe Cheſnut, only much ſmaller, and the indentures at the edges are deeper and more acute The lobes of which they are compoſed are ſpear-ſhaped, they are five in number, are united at their baſe, ſtand on a long red footſtalk, and grow oppoſite by pairs on the branches, which are ſpread abroad on every ſide The flowers come out from the ends of the branches The firſt appearance of the buds is in May, though they will not be in full blow till the middle of June They are of a bright red colour, and conſequently have a pleaſing effect among the vaſt tribe of yellow-flowering ſorts which ſhew themſelves in bloom at that ſeaſon They continue in ſucceſſion for upwards of ſix weeks, and ſometimes are ſucceeded by ripe ſeeds in our gardens

There are two ways of propagating this tree First, by budding it upon the young plants of the Horſe Cheſnut

*Method of propagating it by budding*

These ſtocks ſhould be raiſed as was directed in that article They ſhould be planted in the nurſery way, a foot aſunder, and two feet diſtant in the rows, which ſhould be kept clean of weeds, and muſt be dug between every winter till the operation is to be performed After they have ſtood in the nurſery ground about two years, and have made at leaſt one good ſummer's ſhoot, the ſummer following is the time for the operation Then, having your cuttings ready ſoon after Midſummer, if an immenſe quantity of inoculating is not to be done that ſeaſon, evenings and cloudy weather ſhould be made choice of for the work Whoever has a great number of trees to inoculate, muſt regard no weather, but keep working on, to get his buſineſs over before the ſeaſon ends, and indeed, a good hand will be always pretty ſure of ſucceſs, be the weather what it will Having your cuttings ready at this time, I ſay, work the buds into the ſhoot that was made the laſt year, and manage them as has been directed under the article of inoculating If the ſtocks were healthy, the ſummer following they will make pretty good ſhoots, and in a year or two after that will flower This is one method of propagating this tree, and thoſe plants that are propagated this way will grow to a larger ſize than thoſe raiſed immediately from ſeeds

*and by ſeeds*

2 This tree alſo may be propagated by ſeeds, which will ſometimes ripen with us, and may be obtained out of our own gardens The manner of raiſing them this way is as follows Let a warm border be prepared, and if it is not naturally ſandy, let drift ſand be mixed with the ſoil, and in this border let the ſeeds be ſown in the month of March, about half an inch deep After this, conſtant weeding muſt be obſerved, and when the plants are come up, if they could be ſhaded in the heat of the day, it would be much better Theſe, with now and then a gentle watering in a dry ſeaſon, will be all the precautions they will require the firſt ſummer The winter following, if the ſituation is not extremely well ſheltered, protection muſt be given them from the hard black froſts, which will otherwiſe often deſtroy them So that it will be the ſafeſt way to have the bed hooped, to cover them with mats in ſuch weather, if the ſituation is not well defended, if it is, this trouble may be ſaved, for even when young, they are tolerably hardy In about two or three years, they may be removed into the nurſery, or planted where they are to remain, and they will flower in three or four years after The uſual nurſery care muſt be taken of them when planted in that way, and the beſt time for planting them there, or where they are to remain, is October, though they will grow exceeding well if removed in any of the winter months, but, if planted late in the ſpring, they will require more watering, as the ground will not be ſo regularly ſettled to the roots, as if they had been planted earlier

*Titles of the different ſpecies*

1 Horſe-Cheſnut is entitled, *Æſculus floribus heptandris* In the *Hortus Cliffortianus* it is termed ſimply *Æſculus* Cluſius calls it, *Caſtanea folio multifido* It grows naturally in Aſia, and was brought firſt into Europe in the year 1550

2 Scarlet flowering Horſe-Cheſnut is, *Æſculus floribus octandris* Plukenet calls it *Saamouna piſonis ſ ſiliquifera Braſilienſis arbor, digitatis foliis ſerratis, floribus teneris purpureis*, Boerhaave and others, *Pavia* It grows naturally in Carolina, the Braſils, and ſeveral parts of the Eaſt

*Claſs and order in the Linnæan ſyſtem The characters*

*Æſculus* is of the claſs and order *Heptandria Monogynia*, and the characters are,

1 Calyx is a ſmall, tubulous, monophyllous perianthium, indented in five parts at the top

2 Corolla conſiſts of five roundiſh, plain, patent, waved, unequally-coloured petals, which are broad and folded at their extremities, narrow at their baſe, and are inſerted in the calyx

3 Stamina are ſeven declining awl ſhaped filaments, of the length of the corolla, having upright antheræ

4 Piſtillum conſiſts of a roundiſh germen, an awl-ſhaped ſtyle, and an acuminated ſtigma

4 Pericarpium is a roundiſh, coriaceous, trivalvate capſule, containing three cells

6 The ſeeds are uſually two, large, and of a roundiſh figure

C H A P.

# CHAP. III

## *AMORPHA*, BASTARD INDIGO

AMORPHA, or Bastard Indigo, is a plant now well known, being to be found in most shrubberies, even where there is but moderate collection It has been encreased in great plenty, both by layers and seeds, ever since it began to be known among us, which was about the year 1724 at which time Catesby sent over the seeds from Carolina

*Where the tree should be planted* This tree ought not to be planted in the middle of large quarters amongst tall-growing trees, as it would by them be soon overpowered and lost, its growth being only about ten feet Neither should it be planted singly, or in exposed places, for there many disadvantages will be the consequence

*Its beauties and defects pointed out* This tree has its beauties, but it has other ill effects to detract from its value The leaves are late in the spring before their foliage is fully displayed The ends of their branches are generally destroyed by the frost, or, if they recover it, they have the appearance of being dead, whilst other plants testify their effects of the reviving months

*and the leaves flowers &c described* But notwithstanding these defects, this tree has some other good properties that in part make amends for them The leaves, when out, which will not be before the middle of May, are admired by all They are of a pleasant green colour; are very large, beautifully pinnated, the lobes being arranged along the stalk by pairs, and terminate by an odd one The flowers are of a purple colour, and shew themselves in perfection with us the beginning of July They grow in spikes, seven or eight inches long, at the ends of the branches, and are of a singular structure In order to make this tree have its best effect, it should be planted among others of its own growth, in a well-sheltered situation, by which means the ends will not be so liable to be destroyed by the winter's frosts, then branches will not suffer by the violence of the winds, and as it is subject to put out many branches near the root, these indelicacies and imperfections will be concealed, whilst the tree will shew itself to the utmost advantage when in blow, by elevating its purple spiked flowers amongst the others in a pleasing view

*Method of propagating this tree by seeds,* This tree may be propagated two ways, first, by seeds, which must be procured from America, where the plant is a native, for they do not ripen with us in England We generally receive the seeds from thence in February, and they should be committed to the ground as soon after as possible They will grow in almost any soil that is tolerably good, though the more sandy it be, it will be the better After they are come up, they should have the usual care of seedlings for a year or two, and then be planted, either where they are to remain for good, or else in the nursery, where they will in a year or two make strong plants

*and by layers* This tree may be also propagated by layers, and this operation I would have performed the latter end of summer, whilst the sap is in motion, for if it is deferred until winter, the branches are then so exceeding brittle, that it will be with difficulty they are brought down, without breaking, a proper depth into the earth Let the utmost care be taken, or many of the young branches that would have made layers will be lost. In summer, then, let the branches be brought down while they are pliable; and by the autumn twelvemonths after they will have taken root, and be fit to remove

*Title of this tree* Thus much for the culture of this plant, which has been distinguished by the title, *Barba Jovis Americana pseudoacaciæ foliis flosculis purpureis minimis Barba Jovis Caroliniana, Pseudoacaciæ foliis, &c* It is now in the modern catalogues known by the title *Amorpha*, of which we have but one known species

*Class and order in the Linnæan system* This plant belongs to the first division of the third order of the seventeenth class, entitled, *Diadelphia Decandria* It has been shewn, in the Explanation of the Classes, that the flowers under the title *Diadelphia* are papilionaceous, and that the corolla of each consists of a vexillum, alæ which are two in number, and a carina, but what is very singular in this genus is, that both the alæ and the carina are wanting The characters of the flowers are these

*The characters* 1 CALYX is a monophyllous, tubulous, cylindric, turbinated perianthium, which is divided into five obtuse parts at the top, that are erect

2 COROLLA As the alæ and carina are wanting, we must observe the vexillum, and this we find oval, concave, and erect, and inserted between the two upper segments of the calyx

3 STAMINA The title of the class and its order, point out the nature and number of the stamina These are of unequal lengths, with simple antheræ

4 PISTILLUM The pistil consists of a roundish germen, of a subulated style (the length of the stamina), and of a simple stigma

5 PERICARPIUM is a lunulated, reflexed, compressed pod, which is unilocular

6 SEMINA The seeds are generally two in number, and their figure is reniforme

CHAP

# CHAP IV.

## *AMYGDALUS*, The ALMOND-TREE

WE are now come to a genus that is one of the greatest ornaments to our gardens in the early spring The species, and their varieties, are all worthy of our admiration and invite us into the gardens, even when the chilling air forbids to move

Species of this genus. The species of this genus are only three in number, though the varieties are many They are,

1 The Common Almond
2 The Dwarf Almond
3 The Peach-tree

Description of the Common Almond tree. 1 The Common Almond-tree will grow to near twenty feet high, and whether planted singly in an open place, or mixed with others in clumps, wilderness-quarters, &c shews itself one of the finest flowering-trees in nature Those who never yet saw it, may easily conceive what a noble appearance this tree must make, when covered all over with a bloom of a delicate red, which will be in March, a time when very few trees are ornamented either with leaves or flowers No ornamental plantation, therefore, of whatsoever kind soever, should be without plenty of almond trees, and if they are planted on a grass plat, or any where near a parlour window, they will afford a most pleasing sight during the blow, to ladies, &c who are unwilling or unable to stir abroad until the spring has made farther advances Neither are the beauties of the flowers the only thing desirable in this tree The fruit would render it worthy of planting, were there no other motive It ripens well, and its goodness is not unknown to us

White flowering Almond. The White flowering Almond, well known in our nurseries as a variety of this species, and is cultivated for the sake of the flower and the fruit, though the flowers are inferior to the others Neither is this tree so proper to plant singly in open places, or near windows, for the show of its flowers, for although they come out early, yet the whole bloom is subject to be taken off in one night's nipping weather, which frequently happens at that season Its station, therefore, should be in wilderness quarters, in well-sheltered places, and in such it will flower exceedingly well, and shew its white blossoms to great advantage When it is designed for fruit, it should be set against a south wall, in a well-sheltered place, otherwise there will be little hopes of success

the Dwarf Almond; 2 The Dwarf Almond Of this tree there are two sorts, the single and the double Both grow to about four or five feet high, and are in the first esteem as flowering-shrubs The single sort has its beauties, but the double kind is matchless In both, the flowers are arranged the whole length of the last year's shoots, their colour is a delicate red, and they shew themselves early in the spring, which still enhances their value

and the Peach tree 3 The Peach tree has hitherto been planted against walls for the sake of the fruit, but as I hardly ever knew a person who was not struck with the beauty of the flowers when in full blow against a wall, why should it not have a share in wilderness quarters and shrubberies, amongst the sorts of almonds, &c ? It may be kept down, or permitted to grow to the height of the owner's fancy, and the flowers are inferior to none of the other sorts Add to this, they frequently, in well sheltered places, produce fruit which will be exceedingly well flavoured, and thus the owner may enjoy the benefit of a double treat

The above observations respect the single peach, with regard to the double-flowered, it is generally propagated for ornamental plantations, and is universally acknowledged to be one of the finest flowering-trees yet known Against a wall, however, these trees are always the finest, and if they have this advantage, they are succeeded by very good fruit

All these sorts are propagated by inoculating them into plum-stocks, in August The stocks should be first planted in the nursery, when of the size of a straw, and the first or second summer after they will be ready to receive the bud The usual method of inoculation must be observed, and there is no danger of success, though it may be proper to observe, that the double blossomed peach should always be worked into the stocks of the muscle plum The two sorts of Dwarf Almond may also be propagated by layers, or from the suckers, which they sometimes send forth in great plenty — Method of propagating the different sorts of almond-trees

1 The Common Almond tree is styled, *Amygdalus foliis petiolatis, serraturis infimis glandulosis floribus sessilibus geminis* Caspar Bauhine calls it, *Amygdalus sylvestris*, Dodonæus, *Amygdalus*, and Tournefort, *Amygdalus amara* It grows naturally in Mauritania — Titles of this tree,

2 The Dwarf Almond is titled, *Amygdalus foliis petiolatis basi attenuatis* Plukenet calls it, *Amygdalus Indica nana* Amman, *Armeniaca Persicæ foliis, fructu exsucco* It is a native of Asia Minor

3 The Peach-tree is styled, *Amygdalus foliorum serraturis omnibus acutis, floribus sessilibus solitariis* Caspar Bauhine calls it, *Persica molli carne & vulgaris*, and Camerarius, *Persica rubra* It is not certain in what part of the world the peach-tree grows in a state of nature

*Amygdalus* is of the class and order *Icosandria Monogynia*, and the characters are, — Class and order in the Linnæan system The characters

1 CALYX is a monophyllous, tubular, deciduous perianthium, that is divided at the top into five obtuse patent segments

2 COROLLA consists of five oblong, oval, obtuse, concave petals, inserted in the calyx

3 STAMINA are thirty erect slender filaments, shorter than the corolla, and inserted in the calyx, having simple antheræ

4 PISTILLUM consists of a roundish hairy germen, a simple style the length of the stamina, and a capitated stigma

5 PERICARPIUM is a large, villose, roundish, sulcated drupe

6 SEMINA The seed is an oval, acute, compressed, furrowed, netted, punctated nut

## CHAP V

## *ANAGYRIS*, The STINKING BEAN TREFOIL.

Species

THERE is only one known species of this genus, and this admits of a few varieties The more remarkable ones are,

1 The Oval Broad-leaved *Anagyris*
2 The Narrow leaved *Anagyris*

This shrub described

*Anagyris* is a shrub of about ten feet growth The leaves are different in the different varieties In one sort they are oval, and moderately broad, in the other they are oblong and narrow, but all of them are hoary The flowers are produced from the sides of the branches, in May, like those of the *Laburnum* They are numerous, of a bright yellow colour, but seldom succeeded by good seeds in these parts

Method of propagating it by seeds

The best method of propagating these plants is by the seeds, which should be procured from the countries where they ripen well Sow them in a border of good rich earth, in a well-sheltered place, and sift over them about half an inch of fine mould March is a very good month for this business and when the plants appear, if the weather proves dry, frequently give them water, keep them clean of weeds all summer, and at the approach of winter prick round the beds some furze bushes very close These will break the keen edges of the black winds, for common frosts these plants bear moderately well In the spring let them be set out in the nursery-ground, at a foot distance from each other Here let them stand a year or two, and they will be of a proper size to plant out for good

and by layers

These plants may also be propagated by layers For this purpose, a few plants should be set for stools Let them grow one summer, to get good hold of the ground, and then head them down The summer following they will make strong shoots, which in the autumn should be layered They will readily strike root, and by the autumn following will be good plants The weakest of these may be set out in the nursery-ground for a season or two, but the strongest may be immediately planted out for good

Titles of this tree

There being no species of this genus, it stands simply with the name *Anagyris* Van Royen calls it, *Anagyris floribus lateralibus*, Caspar Bauhine, *Anagyris fœtida* It grows naturally on the mountains of Italy, Sicily, and Spain

Class and order in the Linnæan system The characters

*Anagyris* is of the class and order *Decandria Monogynia*, and the characters are,

1 CALYX is a campanulated perianthium, divided at the top into five segments, the upper being much deeper cut than the others

2 COROLLA is papilionaceous

The vexillum is obcordated, broad, emarginated, and is much longer than the calyx

The alæ are oblong, oval, plane, and longer than the vexillum

The carina is upright, and longer than the alæ

3 STAMINA are ten parallel, distinct, assurgent filaments, with simple antheræ

4 PISTILLUM consists of an oblong germen, a simple assurgent style, and a hairy stigma

5 PERICARPIUM is a large, oblong, roundish, obtuse pod, which is a little reflexed at the point

6 SEMINA The seeds are reniforme, and there are usually about six or eight in each pod

## CHAP VI

## *ANDROMEDA*

THE next tree in the order of alphabetical succession is *Andromeda*, a genus to which no English name has yet been given This shrub's known species are,

The species of Andromeda

1 Virginian Andromeda
2 Canada Andromeda
3 Maryland Andromeda

Virginian Andromeda described

1 Virginian Andromeda is a branching shrub, about four feet high The leaves are oblong, pointed, plane, and are placed alternately on the branches The flowers come out in panicles from the ends of the branches They are of a pale yellow colour, and their general characters indicate their structure They come out in July, but are rarely succeeded by good seeds in England

2 Canada Andromeda is a low branching shrub, hardly a foot and a half high The leaves are oval, spear-shaped, obtuse, reclined on their borders, and possessed of numerous small punctures The flowers grow in short leafy spikes from the ends of the branches Their colour is white, they appear in July, and are seldom succeeded by good seeds in this country

There is a variety of this species, with oval obtuse leaves, of a thick substance, and which, in mild seasons, continue on the plants all winter

3 Maryland Andromeda This is a shrub, about two feet high, sending forth several ligneous stalks from the root The leaves are oval, entire, of a pale green colour, and grow alternately on short footstalks The flowers come out in small bunches from the points of the stalk They are of a greenish colour, come out in June and July, and are sometimes succeeded by five cornered capsules, full of seeds, which, nevertheless, seldom ripen in England

These

ANNONA the Papaw Tree

Method of raising these plants from seeds,

These plants succeed best upon boggy and moist grounds You must procure the seeds from the places where they grow naturally, a year before which a boggy or the moistest part of your garden should be dug, and the roots of all weeds cleared off As the weeds begin to arise, so constantly should the ground be again dug, and sea or drift sand should be plentifully mixed with the natural soil By this management till the seeds arrive, the ground being made tolerably fine, the seeds should be sown very shallow in the moist or boggy land, or if the land should be so boggy that it cannot be easily worked, so as to be proper for the reception of the seeds, then let a sufficient quantity of soil from a fresh pasture, mixed with drift sand, be laid over the bog, and let the seeds be sown therein The bog will in time absorb this soil, but the seeds will come up, and this is the most effectual method of procuring plants of this kind from seeds The first year after they come up, they should be shaded in very hot weather, and after that they will require little or no care

or by layers or suckers,

Another method of encreasing these shrubs is by layers, or suckers, so that whoever has not the conveniency of procuring the seeds from abroad, should get a plant or two of the sorts he most likes These he should plant in a boggy situation, and in a very little time he will have encrease enough, for they throw out suckers in prodigious plenty, if they like the situation, and to a great distance These may be taken off, and planted where they are to remain

and their names

1 Virginian Andromeda is titled, *Racemis secundis nudis paniculatis, corollis subcylindricis, foliis alternis oblongis crenulatis* In the *Hortus Cliffortianus* it is termed, *Andromeda foliis ovatis acutis crenulatis planis alternis, floribus racemosis* Catesby calls it, *Frutex foliis serratis, floribus longioribus spicatis subviridibus, spicis pentagonis*, and Plukenet, *Vitis idaea Americana, longiori mucronato & crenato folio, floribus urceolatis racemosis* It is a native of Virginia

2 Canada Andromeda is, *Andromeda racemis secundis foliaceis, corollis subcylindricis, foliis alternis lanceolatis obtusis punctatis* Gronovius calls it, *Cistus Ledon s Andromeda, floribus monopetalis parvis albis tubulosis spicatis in summis ramulis dispositis, foliis & facie vitis idaeae, capsula unica sicca quinquepartita*, and Buxbaum, *Chamaedaphne* It grows naturally in Virginia, Canada, Siberia, and Ingria

3 Maryland Andromeda is, *Andromeda pedunculis aggregatis, corollis cylindricis, foliis alternis ovatis integerrimis* Gronovius calls it, *Andromeda foliis ovatis, pedunculis fasciculatis, capsulis pentagonis apice dehiscentibus*, and Plukenet, *Arbuscula mariana brevioribus euonymi foliis pallide virentibus, floribus arbuteis ex eodem nodo plurimis spicatim uno versu erumpentibus* It grows naturally in Virginia

Class and order in the Linnæan system The characters

*Andromeda* is of the class and order *Decandria Monogynia* and the flowers have these characters

1 CALYX is a coloured, permanent perianthium, divided into five small acute parts

2 COROLLA is a bell shaped petal, cut at the top into five reflex segments

3 STAMINA are ten awl shaped filaments, shorter than the corolla, to which they are affixed, having two horned nutant antheræ

4 PISTILLUM consists of a roundish germen, of a cylindrical permanent style longer than the stamina, and of an obtuse stigma

5 PERICARPIUM is a roundish pentagonal capsule, consisting of five valves, has five cells, and opens in the angles

6 SEMINA The seeds are many, roundish, and bright

# CHAP VII

## *ANNONA*, The CUSTARD-APPLE-TREE

The species of this tree named the Papaw tree only proper for our plantations

THERE are many species of *Annona*, but only one will suit our purpose for our hardy plantations, and that is known by the name of the *Papaw*-tree, nay, this species itself is not very hardy at first, but must be carefully nursed for a few years whilst it is young, before it is permitted to have a share in the sort of plantations now under consideration

Its appearance, &c described

The Papaw is a tree that will grow to about sixteen or eighteen feet in height The leaves are large, and shaped like a spear, and they fall off pretty early in the autumn The flowers, which will shew themselves in the beginning of May, are a kind of chocolate colour, tinged with purple and grow two or three fruit on a footstalk The fruit is large, and never ripens in England, but in the countries where it grows naturally, it is eaten by the meanest of the inhabitants The difference of its shape from that of a pear is, that its widest part is nearest the footstalk, and it contains a number of large seeds lying in a row

It is a native of Maryland, Carolina, Virginia, and the Bahama-Islands, and from thence we have the seeds brought, by which numbers of plants are annually raised

Method of raising this tree

The manner of raising them is thus Let a bed be prepared in a moistish part, that is exceedingly well sheltered, and naturally sandy, or inclined thereto If the soil is opposite to this, let a fourth part of drift sand be mixed with the mould, and having obtained the seeds from abroad, sow them in this bed about half an inch deep, letting the seeds be at some distance from each other It is probable they will come up in the spring, though they sometimes remain till the second, nay the third spring before they make their appearance When this happens, the beds must be weeded all the time, and the mould at the surface gently loosened, if it should be inclined to crust over After the plants are come up in the spring, no other than the usual care of seedlings need be taken, until the autumn, when the beds must be hooped over, to be covered with mats at the approach of any frost, and the gardener must constantly observe the weather, whether the air hath the least tendency to it, that he may cover the bed over, for

for one night's hard froſt, while they are ſo very young, would deſtroy them all. With this careful eye he muſt conſtantly watch over theſe plants all winter. He muſt double his covering as the froſt encreaſes, and muſt always uncover them again in mild and open weather. The ſecond winter, the ſame care muſt be obſerved, though ſo ſtrict an eye will not be neceſſary; for though they will be ſubject to be deſtroyed by hard froſts, yet if a gentle froſt ſhould catch them unawares to the gardener in the night, there will not be much danger of their ſuffering, for they will be got tolerably ſtrong by the ſecond ſummer's ſhoot. They will, nevertheleſs, be too tender to ſtand the brunt of a winter's froſt for a year or two after that, and conſequently, muſt have a proportional ſhare of this care on every year during these months. By this time the plants will have grown to be tolerably ſtrong, and may be taken up and planted where they are to remain, though their ſituation ſhould be well defended; for a ſevere froſt in an expoſed place would ſtill overpower them, tho', now they have grown to be of larger ſize, they are hardy enough.

If a perſon has the conveniency of a green-houſe, or ſome ſuch room, he may ſow his ſeeds in boxes or pots, filled with maiden earth from a rich paſture, mixed with drift ſand. Theſe boxes or pots ſhould be afterwards plunged into the natural mould, in a ſhady part of the garden, and the autumn after the plants are come up, they may be removed into the green-houſe, where they will be naturally protected from the [illegible] of weather. This protection may be afforded them every winter, till they are ſtrong enough to defend themſelves, when they may be turned out of the boxes or pots, mould and all, into the places where they are deſigned to remain.

The names *Annona* and *Papaw* are both barbarous expreſſions of the country where the tree naturally grows. It has been called *Guanabanus*; but the word *Annona* is more eligible, as having a more harmonious and agreeable pronunciation.

The title of the Papaw-tree is, *Annona foliis lanceolatis, fructibus triſidis*. Cateſby calls it, *Annona fructu luteſcente levi ſcrotum arietis referente*. He ſays it grows common in the Bahama-Iſlands, that its uſual growth there is in height about ten or twelve feet, and that the ſtem is in thickneſs about the ſmall part of a man's leg. Titles

There are many other ſpecies of *Annona*, which will come under conſideration among plants that require artificial heat, and many of which afford admirable fruit to the natives of the countries where they grow naturally.

*Annona* is of the claſs and order *Polyandria Polygynia*, and the characters are, Claſs and order in the Linnæan ſyſtem. The characters.

1. CALYX is a ſmall perianthium, compoſed of three heart-ſhaped, concave, acuminated leaves.

2. COROLLA conſiſts of ſix cordated ſeſſile petals, of which the three interior are the ſmalleſt.

3. STAMINA. Hardly any filaments can be obſerved, but there are a great number of antheræ on each ſide of the germen.

4. PISTILLUM conſiſts of a roundiſh germen, placed on a roundiſh receptacle, and of numerous obtuſe ſtigmata, having viſible ſtyles.

5. PERICARPIUM is a large, oblong, oval berry, of one cell, having a ſquammous and punctated rind.

6. SEMINA. The ſeeds are many, oval, oblong, ſmooth, hard, and are placed circularly.

## CHAP. VIII.

## *ARALIA*, The ANGELICA-TREE.

ANOTHER tree that requires a more than common care in nurſing, till it is of ſize and ſtrength ſufficient to be planted out for good in the open ground, is that ſpecies of *Aralia* called the Angelica-tree, a tree of no extraordinary beauty, but which ſhould have its ſhare in plantations to make the greater variety, as its appearance both in winter and ſummer is different from that of moſt other trees. The height to which this tree will grow, if the ſoil and ſituation wholly agree with it, is about twelve feet, and the ſtem, which is of a dark brown colour, is defended by ſharp ſpines, which fall off in May; the very leaves, which are branching, and compoſed of many wings, and are of a pleaſant green colour, have theſe defenders, which are both crooked and ſtrong, and ſtand as guards to them till the leaves fall off in the autumn. The flowers are produced in large umbels from the ends of the branches. They are of a greeniſh yellow colour, and their general characters indicate their ſtructure. They make their appearance the end of July or beginning of Auguſt, but are not ſucceeded by ripe ſeeds in our gardens.

The ſpines which are on the branches and the leaves admoniſh us, for our own ſafety, not to plant this tree too near the ſides of frequented walks; and the conſideration of the nature of the tree, which is rather tender at the beſt, directs us, if we have a mind to retain the ſort, to plant it in a warm and well-ſheltered ſituation, where the piercing froſts, come from what point they will, will loſe their edge; for without this, they will be too tender to ſtand the teſt of a ſevere winter, though it has often happened, that after the main ſtem of the plant has been deſtroyed, it has ſhot out again from the root, and the plant by that means been both encreaſed and preſerved.

This tree will what gardeners call *ſpawn*; [illegible] after digging among the roots young plants will ariſe, the broken roots ſending forth freſh ſtems; nay, if the roots are planted in a warm border, and ſhaded in hot weather, they will grow; but if they are planted in pots, and aſſiſted by a moderate warmth of dung, or tanners bark, they will be pretty ſure of ſucceſs, ſo that the propagation of this tree is very eaſy. But the general method of propagating it, and by which the beſt plants may be had, is from ſeeds, which muſt be procured from America, for they do not ripen in England; and, after having obtained them, they muſt be managed in the following manner. The time that we generally receive them is in the ſpring; ſo that againſt their coming we muſt be furniſhed with a ſufficient number of large pots. Theſe, when the ſeeds are come, muſt be filled with fine mould, which, if taken from a rich border, will do very well. The ſeeds muſt be ſown in theſe pots as ſoon as poſſible after their arrival, hardly half an inch deep, and then the pots ſhould be plunged in a warm place their whole depth in the ſoil. Care muſt be taken to break the mould in the pots, and water them as often as it has a tendency to cruſt over; and if they are ſhaded in hot weather, the plants will frequently come up the firſt ſummer. But as this does not often happen, if the young plants do not appear by Midſummer, the pots ſhould be taken and plunged in a ſhady place; nay, if they ſhould, there will be ſtill more occaſion for this being done, for they will flouriſh after that better in the ſhade; and the deſign of plunging them in a warm place at firſt was only with a view of ſetting the powers of vegetation at work, that, having natural heat, artificial ſhade alſo may be given them, and water likewiſe, the three grand neceſſaries for the purpoſe. The pots, whether the plants are come up in them or not, ſhould be removed into ſhelter in October, either into a greenhouſe, ſome room, or under an hotbed-frame; and in the ſpring, when all danger of froſt is over, they ſhould be plunged into the natural ground their own depth in a ſhady place. Thoſe that were already plants will have ſhot ſtrong by the autumn following; and if none of them have appeared, they will come up this ſpring; and whether they are young ſeedlings, or ſmall plants of a former ſummer's growth, they muſt be conſtantly kept clean of weeds and duly watered in the time of drought; and this care muſt be obſerved until the autumn. In October they muſt be again removed into ſhelter, either into a greenhouſe, &c. as before, or fixed in a warm place, and hooped, that they may be covered with mats in froſty weather. In the latter end of March following, they ſhould be planted in the nurſery way, to gain ſtrength before they are planted out for good. The ground for this purpoſe, beſides the natural ſhelter, ſhould have a reed-hedge, or ſomething of the like nature, the more effectually to prevent the piercing winds from deſtroying the young plants. In this ſnug place the plants may be ſet in rows, in each of which rows furze-buſhes ſhould be ſtuck the whole length; and all theſe together will enſure their ſafety. But here one caution is to be obſerved, not to ſtick the furze ſo thick, but that the plants may enjoy the free air in mild weather, and not to take them away too early in the ſpring, leſt, being kept warm the whole winter, and being deprived of their protection, a cutting froſt ſhould happen, as it ſometimes does even in April, and deſtroy them. Weeding, and watering in dry weather, muſt be their ſummer's care. They may be ſtuck again with furze-buſhes in the winter; though it will not be neceſſary to do it in ſo cloſe a manner; and with this care, ſtill diminiſhing in proportion the number of furze buſhes, they may continue for three or four years, when they may be ſet out for good in the warmeſt parts of the plantation.

With this management theſe plants will be inured to bear our winters, in well-ſheltered places.

Titles. The ſpecies now under conſideration is diſtinguiſhed by the title, *Aralia arboreſcens, caule foliolisque aculeata*. In the *Hortus Cliffortianus* it is termed, *Aralia caule aculeato*. Commeline calls it, *Angelica arboreſcens ſpinoſa, ſ. Arbor Indica fraxini folio cortice ſpinoſo*; and Plukenet, *Chriſtophoriana arbor aculeata Virginienſis*. It grows naturally in Virginia.

Claſs and order in the Linnæan ſyſtem. *Aralia* is of the claſs and order *Pentandria Pentagynia*; and the characters are,

The characters.

1. CALYX. The flowers are collected into a roundiſh umbel, having a very ſmall involucrum. The perianthium is very ſmall, placed on the germen, and indented in five parts.
2. COROLLA conſiſts of five oval, acute, ſeſſile, reflexed petals.
3. STAMINA are five ſubulated filaments, the length of the corolla, having roundiſh antheræ.
4. PISTILLUM conſiſts of a roundiſh germen, ſituated below the calyx, and of five very ſhort permanent ſtyles, with ſimple ſtigmas.
5. PERICARPIUM is a roundiſh, ſtriated, coronated berry, of five cells.
6. SEMINA. The ſeeds are ſolitary, hard, and oblong.

# CHAP. IX.

## *AZALEA*, AMERICAN UPRIGHT HONEYSUCKLE.

THERE are two ſpecies of this genus, very proper to join in our ſhrubberies, and which are worthy of our culture and care. They are,

Species of this tree.

1. The Red American Upright Honeyſuckle.
2. The White American Upright Honeyſuckle.

Deſcription of the Red American Upright Honeyſuckle, 1. The Red American Upright Honeyſuckle has ſeveral ſtems ariſing from the ſame root, which will grow to ſeven or eight feet high. The leaves are of an oval figure, ſmooth, entire, and placed alternately on the branches. The flowers are produced in cluſters from the ſides of the branches, on long naked footſtalks. Their colour is red, and they are agreeably ſcented; each compoſed of a long naked tube, cut at the top into five ſpreading ſegments. They will be in blow in July; but they ſeldom ripen their ſeeds in our gardens. There is a variety of this, with yellow flowers.

and the White American Upright Honey-ſuckle. 2. The White American Upright Honeyſuckle. From the root of this ariſe ſeveral ſlender brown ſtems, to three or four feet high. The leaves are spear-shaped, narrow at their base, have a rough border, and grow in clusters. The flowers terminate the branches in clusters, coming out between the leaves. They are finely scented, and each of them has a tube of near an inch long, divided at the top into five segments, two of which are reflexed. Their colour is white, with a bar of yellow on their outside; they will be in blow in July, but are never succeeded by seeds in our gardens.

These sorts are propagated by layering the young shoots; and for this purpose, a slit must be made on each, as is practised for carnations. The autumn is the best season for the work. When your layers have struck good root, they may be removed into the nursery, and planted in lines at a small distance from each other, where after having stood a year or two at the most, they will be proper plants to be set out for good.

These sorts also propagate themselves very fast; for as they throw up many stems from the same roots after they have stood a few years, some of these may easily be taken off, with some root to each, and either planted in the nursery-ground or the places where they are to remain.

1. The Red American Upright Honeysuckle is titled, *Azalea foliis ovatis, corollis pilosis staminibus longissimis*. Gronovius calls it, *Azalea ramis infra floribus nudis*; Plukenet, *Cistus Virginiana, periclymeni flore ampliori minus odorato*; Colden, *Azalea erecta, foliis ovatis integris alternis, flore luteo pilloso praecoci*. In the *Hortus Cliffortianus* it is termed, *Azalea scapo nudo, floribus confertis terminalibus, staminibus declinatis*. It grows naturally in the dry parts of Virginia.

2. The White American Upright Honeysuckle is titled, *Azalea foliis margine scabris, corollis piloso-glutinosis*. Gronovius calls it, *Azalea ramis infra floribus foliosis*; and Plukenet, *Cistus Virginiana, flore & odore periclymeni*. It grows naturally in Virginia.

*Azalea* is of the class and order *Pentandria Monogynia*; and the characters are,

1. CALYX is a small, erect, coloured, permanent perianthium, divided at the top into five acute segments.

2. COROLLA is a single bell-shaped petal, divided at the top into five reflexed parts.

3. STAMINA are five free filiforme filaments, inserted into the receptacle, having simple antheræ.

4. PISTILLUM consists of a roundish germen, a filiforme permanent style the length of the corolla, and an obtuse stigma.

5. PERICARPIUM is a roundish capsule, formed of five valves, and containing five cells.

6. SEMINA. The seeds are numerous and roundish.

# CHAP. X.

## *BERBERIS*, The BERBERRY-BUSH.

TO the height of about ten or twelve feet grows the Berberry, a plant well known in England, for the excellent pickle it affords; for there is a double advantage arises from planting this tree: for it not only affords pleasure in common with others, from its stature, the manner of its growth, flowers, fruit, &c. wherever we meet with it, but the fruit serves in itself for pickling, which are not only esteemed by most, and are very wholesome, but are likewise excellent garnish to many able dishes at the table. The Berberry should be planted in great plenty in woods at a small distance from an habitation. For these thick bushes will afford food for the winged songsters, who, in return, will entertain you with their warbling notes. But they should not be planted in too great quantities near much-frequented walks, as their flowers afford a smell that proves to many disagreeable.

Besides the common Berberry, there is a sort without stone; and although it does not always exhibit its fruit entirely without stone, yet this is the sort chiefly propagated for the use of the berry. There are also the Berberry with white, and the Berberry with black fruit. All these are only varieties; and the two last by no means deserve propagating in respect to the common Berberry, as they are not only bad bearers, but likewise are much inferior in beauty to that lively scarlet of which the fruit of the other is possessed. The root of the Berberry-bush is yellow, and the inside bark of the stem is also of the same colour, with a white pith. The branches are armed with sharp spines, which generally proceed by threes with the leaves. The colour of these is of a pleasant pale green, and when bitten they afford an acid taste. The leaves of this tree are not very large, being no more than about an inch or an inch and half long, and about an inch broad. They grow alternately on the branches, and are nearly oval, with serrated edges. The flowers, which are yellow, stand in long clusters on pedicles. They will be in full blow in May, and are succeeded by berries, which are first green, and afterwards of a bright red colour, which will be in September, when they are fit for use.

Whoever examines the Berberry will find it answer these characters. A tree worthy of propagation, not only to attract the attention of the philosopher, and for the use of its berries, but for its farther excellent qualities and uses in medicine. Its root is said to be an aperient; the inner bark is taken for the Jaundice, &c. Conserves are also made of the fruit, which are good against fluxes; and other excellent properties belong to this tree, with which physicians are best acquainted.

Besides the common Berberry, with its varieties, there is another distinct species, called the Box-leaved Berberry. It grows only to about a yard or four feet high, and is possessed of many sharp spines at the joints. The leaves are like those of the box-tree, between which the flowers come out, on slender footstalks. But as this sort never produces any fruit in England, and being also liable to be killed by hard frosts, it is seldom propagated in our gardens.

Method of propagating the Berbery by ſeeds

The propagation of the Berbery is as follows: When a quantity of the common Berbery is wanted, the beſt way is to raiſe it from the ſeeds, which ſhould be ſown, ſoon after they are ripe, in a bed made in any part of the garden. Theſe will frequently remain till the ſecond ſpring before the plants come all up, till which time the beds ſhould be weeded as often as the weeds appear; for if they are neglected ſo as to get ſtrong, by pulling them up many of the ſeeds will alſo be drawn out of the bed by their roots. After the plants have grown one year in the ſeed-bed, they ſhould be planted out in the nurſery, where they may remain for four two years, when they will be fit to plant out for good. This is the moſt expeditious method of raiſing a large quantity of theſe trees, when wanted.

by layers,

Another method of propagating the Berbery is by layers, a method by which all the ſorts may be encreaſed, and in the performance of which, no other art or trouble need be uſed, than laying the branches down in the ground, without either ſlit or twiſt. If this is done any time in the winter, by the autumn following they will have taken good root, the ſtrongeſt of which layers will be then fit to plant out for good, whilſt thoſe that are weaker may be planted in the nurſery-ground, to gain ſtrength.

and by cuttings

The cuttings alſo of theſe trees will grow, for if they be planted in October, in a moiſtiſh good earth, they will moſt of them ſtrike root, ſo that the propagation of this tree by any of theſe ways, is very eaſy. Whoever is deſirous of the Box-leaved Berbery, muſt afford it a warm dry ſoil, in a well ſheltered place.

1. The common Berbery is titled, *Berberis pedunculis racemoſis*. In the *Hortus Cliffortianus* it is termed, *Berberis ſpinis triplicibus*. Cammerarius calls it, *Berberis vulgaris ſ. Creſpinus*; Caſpar Bauhine, *Berberis dumetorum*, and Gerard, *Spina acida ſive oxyacantha*. It grows naturally in woods and hedges in England, alſo on Mount Lebanon, and ſeveral parts of the Eaſt.

Titles of theſe ſpecies

2. Box-leaved Berbery is named, *Berberis pedunculis unifloris*. Caſpar Bauhine calls it, *Berberis Alpina Cretica*, Tournefort, *Berberis Cretica, buxi folio*, and Alpinus, *Lycium Creticum*. It grows naturally in Crete.

Claſs and order in the Linnæan ſyſtem

*Berberis* is of the claſs and order *Hexandria Monogynia*, and the general characters of the flowers are,

Characters

1. Calyx is a patulous perianthium, compoſed of oval, concave, coloured, deciduous leaves, which are narrow at their baſe, and are alternately ſmaller.

2. Corolla conſiſts of ſix roundiſh, concave, oval, patent petals, that are hardly larger than the calyx.

The nectarium is compoſed of two roundiſh coloured parts, faſtened to the baſe of each petal.

3. Stamina are ſix erect, compreſſed, obtuſe filaments, having two antheræ faſtened to their tops.

4. Pistillum. The germen is cylindrical, and the length of the ſtamina; there is no viſible ſtyle, but an orbicular ſtigma, that is broader than the germen, and ſurrounded with an acute border.

5. Pericarpium is a cylindric, obtuſe, umbilicated berry, of one cell.

6. Semina. The ſeeds are two, oblong, cylindric, and obtuſe.

# CHAP. XI

## *BETULA*, The BIRCH-TREE.

Species

THE ſpecies of this genus are,

1. White, or Common Engliſh Birch.
2. Black Virginian Birch.
3. Canada Birch.
4. Dwarf Birch.
5. The Alder-tree.

Deſcription of the White or Common Engliſh Birch

1. The White or Common Engliſh Birch is well known every where, and its uſe and beauty in profitable plantations has been ſet forth in the place where it claims a right among the Britiſh foreſt-trees. In wilderneſs quarters alſo it may be introduced, as it will cauſe a pleaſing effect by its white and ſpeckled bark; but neither this nor any of the ſucceeding ſpecies muſt be expected to afford much beauty from their flowers, they being catkins, and unnoticed by any but thoſe who are intent on Nature's productions.

of the Black Virginian Birch

2. The Black Virginian Birch, being of foreign growth, is propagated for wilderneſs and ornamental plantations; but as it begins now to become pretty common, it is to be hoped it will ſoon make a figure among our foreſt-trees, it being equally hardy with our Common Birch, and will arrive at a much greater magnitude.

This ſpecies will grow to upwards of ſixty feet in height. The branches are ſpotted, and more ſparingly ſet in the trees than the Common ſorts. The leaves are broader, grow on long footſtalks, and add a dignity to the appearance of the tree; and as it is naturally of upright and ſwift growth, and arrives at ſo great a magnitude in a few years, prudence will direct us to let it have a ſhare among our foreſt-trees, to plant them for ſtandards in open places, as well as let them join with other trees of their own growth in plantations more immediately deſigned for relaxation and pleaſure.

Varieties of this ſpecies

There are ſeveral varieties of this ſpecies, differing in the colour, ſize of the leaves, and ſhoots, all of which have names given them by nurſerymen, who propagate the different ſorts for ſale, ſuch as, 1. The Broad leaved Virginian Birch, 2. The Poplar-leaved Birch, 3. The Paper-Birch, 4. The Brown Birch, &c.

Canada Birch

3. Canada Birch. This grows to a timber-tree of ſixty or more feet in height. The leaves are heart-ſhaped, oblong, ſmooth, of a thin conſiſtence, pointed, and very ſharply ſerrated. They differ in colour, and the varieties of this ſpecies

Varieties of this species

species go by the names of, 1 Dusky Canada Birch, 2 White Paper Birch, 3 Poplar leaved Canada Birch, 4 Low-growing Canada Birch, &c The bark of this species is very light, tough and durable, and the inhabitants of America use it for canoes.

Description of the Dwarf Birch,

4 Dwarf Birch This is a low branching shrub, about two feet high The leaves are round, and their edges are serrated It hardly ever produces either male or female flowers, and is chiefly coveted when a general collection of plants is making

and Alder tree

5 The alder-tree has been treated of among the Aquatics, and if ever it is admitted into the pleasure-ground, it should be stationed in the most distant, the moistest, and coolest parts of the works It admits of some varieties, however, which are sought after for curious collections such as, 1 The Long-leaved American Alder, 2 The White Alder, 3 The Black Alder, 4 The Hoary-leaved Alder, 5 The Dwarf Alder The Dwarf Alder grows common upon bogs, and is with difficulty preserved in gardens, unless the soil be naturally moist and wet The others are names assigned them from the different colours of the leaves and bark, except the first sort, so titled from its long leaves

Names of its varieties

Long-leaved American Alder described

This is a beautiful variety, worthy of a place in any collection, and deserves to be continued in the form it assumes, which may be done by layering or planting the cuttings It will grow to about thirty feet high. The branches are slender, smooth, numerous, and of a dark-brown or purple colour The leaves are long, and dispossessed of that clammy or glutinous matter which is peculiar to those of the common alder They are smooth, oval, spear shaped, indented, and give the tree an air of freedom in its luxuriant state Add to this, they continue on the tree till very late in the autumn I have known them on the tree the latter end of December, and that it has been taken for an evergreen

These being the different species of *Betula*, with their varieties, proceed we now to their culture

The method of propagating all these sorts (the foreign ones, viz the common alder and birch tree having been already treated of) is, from seeds We receive the seeds from America, where they are natives, and if we sow them in beds of fine mould, covering them over about a quarter or an inch deep, they will readily grow

Method of propagating the above sorts of birch from seed,

During the time they are in the seminary, they must be constantly weeded, watered in dry weather, and when they are one or two years old, according to their strength, they should be planted in the nursery, in rows, in the usual manner Weeding must always be observed in summer, and digging between the rows in winter, and when the plants are about a yard or four feet high, they will be of a good size to be planted out for the wilderness quarters A part, therefore, may be then taken up for such purposes whilst the remainder may be left to grow for standards, to answer such other purposes as may be wanted

by layers,

2 These trees may also be propagated by layers, and this is the way to continue the peculiarities in the varieties of the different sorts A sufficient number of plants should be procured for this purpose, and set on a spot of double dug ground, three yards distance from each other The year following, if they have made no young shoots, they should be headed to within half a foot of the ground, to form the stools, which will then shoot vigorously the summer following, and in the autumn the young shoots should be splashed near the stools, and the tender twigs layered near their ends They will then strike root, and become good plants by the autumn following, whilst fresh twigs will have sprung up from the stools, to be ready for the same operation The layers, therefore, should be taken up, and the operation performed afresh If the plants designed for stools have made good shoots the first year, they need not be headed down, but splashed near the ground, and all the young twigs layered Thus may an immediate crop be raised this way, whilst young shoots will spring out in great plenty below the splashed part, in order for layering the succeeding year This work therefore, may be repeated every autumn or winter, when some of the strongest layers may be planted out, if they are immediately wanted, whilst the others may be removed into the nursery, to grow to be strong plants, before they are removed to their destined habitations

and by cuttings

3 Cuttings also, if set in a moist shady border the beginning of October, will frequently grow But as this is not a sure method, and as these trees are so easily propagated by layers, it hardly deserves to be put into practice, except for the alders the cuttings of which will grow, and soon become good plants, without farther trouble

Titles of the different species

1 The White or Common English Birch is titled *Betula foliis ovatis acuminatis serratis* In the *Flor Lapponic* it is termed, *Betula foliis cordatis serratis*, Caspar Bauhine and others call it, *Betula* It grows naturally in woods, hedges, and moist places in England, and most of the colder parts of Europe

2 Black Virginian Birch is, *Betula foliis rhombeo-ovatis acuminatis duplicato-serratis* Gronovius calls it, *Betula foliis ovatis oblongis acuminatis serratis*, and Plukenet, *Betula nigra Virginiana* It grows naturally in Virginia and Canada

3 Canada Birch is, *Betula foliis cordatis oblongis acuminatis serratis* Gronovius calls it, *Betula julifera, fructu conoide, viminibus lentis* It grows common in Virginia and Canada

4 Dwarf Birch is titled, *Betula foliis orbiculatis crenatis* Amman calls it, *Betula pumila, foliis subrotundis* It grows naturally on hilly, boggy, and moist places in Lapland, Russia, and Sweden

5 Alder-tree is titled, *Betula pedunculis ramosis* In the *Flor Lappon.* it is termed simply, *Alnus* Caspar Bauhine calls it, *Alnus rotundifolia glutinosa viridis*, also, *Alnus folio incano*, and, *Alnus folio oblongo viridi* It grows common in England, most parts of Europe, and in America

Class and order in the Linnæan system

*Betula* is of the class and order *Monoecia Tetrandria*, and the characters are,

I The male flowers are disposed in a cylindrical katkin

The characters

1 CALYX The common amentum is on every side imbricated, loose, and cylindrical Each scale of the katkin possesses three flowers, which have two very minute scales situated at the sides

2 COROLLA The compound flower consists of three florets, which are equal, and fastened to the disk of each of the calycinal scales The proper floret consists of one very small patent petal, divided into four oval, obtuse segments

3 STAMINA of the florets are four very small filaments, having didymous antheræ

II The female flowers are collected in a cylindrical katkin, like the male

1 CALYX The general amentum is imbricated The calycinal scales are affixed to the axis,

axis, divided into three parts, are every way opposite, concave, heart-shaped, pointed, short, and each contains two flowers

2 COROLLA There is none visible

3 PISTILLUM consists of a small oval germen and two bristly styles the length of the calycinal scales, having simple stigmas

4 PERICARPIUM There is none The seeds are lodged under the scales of the katkin

5 SEMINA The seeds are single and oval

# CHAP XII

## *BIGNONIA*, The TRUMPET-FLOWER

THERE are many species of *Bignonia*, but one only properly belongs to this place, which is commonly known by the name *Catalpa*, a tree not only hardy, but in every respect desirable in our choicest collections, where the extent of ground will permit all trees of tolerable growth to have a share The *Catalpa* will arrive at the height of about thirty feet and as the stem is upright, and the leaves fine and large, it should be planted as standards in the midst of openings, that it may without molestation send forth its lateral branches, and show itself to every advantage in view These openings, nevertheless, should be such as are well sheltered, otherwise the ends of the branches will be destroyed by the severity of the winter's frost, which will cause an unsightly appearance, and the leaves being very large, make such a resistance to the summer's high winds, as to occasion whole branches to be split off by that powerful element

The bark of the *Catalpa* is brown and smooth, and the leaves are cordated They are about five or six inches in breadth, and as many in length They stand by threes at the joints, are of a bluish cast, and are late in the spring before they come out The flowers are tubulous, their colour is white, having purple spots, and yellowish stripes on the inside They will be in full blow in August, but are not succeeded by good seeds in England

Method of propagating this tree by cuttings, Whoever has the conveniency of a bark bed, may propagate this tree in plenty by the cuttings, for being planted in pots, and plunged into the beds in the spring, they will soon strike root, and may afterwards be so hardened to the open air, that they may be set abroad in the shade before the end of summer In the beginning of October, they should be removed into a green house, or under some shelter, to be protected from the winter's frost In the spring, after the bad weather is past, they may be turned out of the pots, and planted in the nursery-way, in a well sheltered place, and if the soil be rich, and rather inclined to be moist, it will be the better Here they may stand for four or five years, the rows being dug in winter, and weeded in summer, when they will be of a proper size to plant out for good

These cuttings will often grow in a rich, shady, moist border, so that whoever can have plenty of them, should plant them pretty thick in such a place, and he may be tolerably sure, by this way, of raising many plants

And by seeds *Catalpa* is also propagated by seeds, which must be procured from America, where the tree is a native After they arrive, they should be sown in a fine warm border of light rich mould, or else in pots or boxes If they are sown in the border, they should be shaded in the heat of summer, if in pots or boxes, they may be removed into shady places It often happens that the seeds do not come up till the second spring, and if they were to have the assistance, at that time, of a moderate warmth of dung, it would promote their disclosing, and cause them to make stronger shoots than they otherwise would have done If they have the benefit of the dung, they should not be kept covered longer than the middle of May, and whether they have this help, or are left solely to the efforts of unassisted Nature, either in the pots, boxes, or borders, they should be watered in dry weather, shaded from the heat, left exposed to all rainy and hazy weather, and as constantly kept clean of weeds all the summer The planter will perceive that more than common care is to be taken of these seedlings during the following winter If they grow in the border, it should be hooped to be covered with mats, to protect them from the frosts, if they are sown in pots or boxes, they may then be removed into the greenhouse, or placed under some hotbed-frame, or other shelter, to be protected from extreme cold If the seedlings are pretty strong, they may be planted, at the latter end of March, in the nursery-way, if not, it would be proper to let them remain another year, either in their beds, pots, or boxes, whereby they will grow stronger, and be less subject to be destroyed, either by drought, weeds or the succeeding winter's frost Being now planted in the nursery-way, their after-care and management is the same as that of those young plants which were raised from cuttings

The word *Catalpa* is a barbarous expression of the inhabitants of South Carolina, where it principally abounds, and the name expressive of the whole species, *Bignonia*, was given it by Tournefort, in honour of Abbé Bignon, librarian to Lewis XIV and a man of extraordinary abilities in learning Origin of the title Bignonia

This species is titled, *Bignonia foliis simplicibus cordatis, caule erecto, floribus diandris* In the *Hortus Cliffortianus* it is termed, *Bignonia foliis simplicibus cordatis* Brown calls it, *Bignonia arborea, foliis ovatis verticillato-ternatis siliqua gracili longissima*, Catesby, *Bignonia urucu foliis, flore sordide albo, intus maculis purpureis & luteis adsperso, siliqua longissima & angustissima*, Plumier, *Bignonia arbor, folio singulari undulato, siliquis longissimis & angustissimis*, and Duhamel, *Bignonia Americana, arbor syringæ cæruleæ folio, flore purpureo* It grows naturally in Carolina Titles of this genus

*Bignonia* is of the class and order *Didynamia Angiospermia*, and the characters are, Class and order in the Linnæan system

*The characters*

1 CALYX is a monophyllous, erect, cyathiform perianthium, divided into five segments

2 COROLLA is one bell-shaped petal The tube is very small, and the length of the calyx The body of the flower is very long, swelling underneath, and of an oblong campanulate nature The limb is divided into five segments, the two uppermost of which are reflexed, and the three under ones spread open

3 STAMINA are four subulated filaments, shorter than the corolla, and of which two are longer than the others, having oblong, reflexed antheræ

4 PISTILLUM consists of an oblong germen, of a filiforme style of the like situation and figure with the stamina, and an headed stigma

5 PERICARPIUM is a bivalvate pod, containing two cells

6 SEMINA are numerous and compressed They have on both sides wings, and lie over each other in the pod in an imbricated manner

## CHAP XIII

## *CALYCANTHUS*, ALLSPICE-TREE.

A VERY different tree from the last described is *Calycanthus*, a shrub which seldom grows, at least with us, to more than about five feet in height, and is at present not very commonly met with in our English collections The height of the tree directs us to the class it must be ranked with, though more than ordinary care must be taken in setting it out for it a warm dry soil and situation, otherwise we shall be in danger of losing it in the winter, as it is of too tender a nature to resist, without shrinking at, our northern blasts

*This tree described*

*Calycanthus* is a shrub of no regularity in its growth It divides into many branches irregularly near the ground They are of a brown colour, and being bruised emit a most agreeable odour The leaves that garnish this delightful aromatic are of an oval figure, pointed They are near four inches long, and are at least two and a half broad, and are placed opposite by pairs on the branches At the end of these stand the flowers, of a kind of chocolate purple colour, and which are possessed of the opposite qualities of the bark on the branches They stand single on their short footstalks, come out in May and June, and are succeeded by ripe seeds in England

*Method of propagating*

The propagation of this species is not very difficult, though more than a common care must be taken, after small plants are obtained, to preserve them till they are of a size to be ventured abroad The last year's shoots of this tree, laid in the ground, the bark especially being a little bruised, will strike root within the compass of twelve months, particularly if the layers are shaded, and now and then watered in the summer's drought In the spring they should be taken off, and planted in pots, and if these are afforded a small degree of heat in a bed, they will strike so much the sooner and stronger After they have been in this bed a month or six weeks, they should be taken out In the heat of the summer they should be placed in the shade, and if the pots are plunged into the natural ground, it will be so much the better At the approach of the succeeding winter's bad weather, the pots should be removed into the greenhouse, or some shelter, and in the spring may resume their old stations, and this should be repeated till they are of a proper size and strength to be planted out for good If the pots in which they were first planted were small they may be shifted into larger a spring or two after, and, when they have got to be pretty strong plants, they may be turned out, mould and all, into the places where they are to remain By this care of potting them, and housing them during the severe weather in winter, the young crop will be preserved, otherwise, if they are planted immediately abroad, the first hard frost the ensuing winter would destroy them all Tanner's bark about their roots will be the most proper security, as they are at best, when full grown, but tender plants, and must have the warmest situation and the driest soil Add to this, *Calycanthus* is a very hard tree to make grow when of a tolerable size, so that by raising these plants in pots, they may be turned out, even at their most mature state, the mould full at their roots, without their drooping

*Titles of this genus*

This species is titled, *Calycanthus petalis interioribus longioribus* Duhamel calls it, *Butneria anemones flore* and Catesby, *Frutex corni foliis conjugatis, floribus instar anemones stellatæ, petalis crassis rigidis, colore [illegible] rubente, cortice aromatico* In Miller's Dictionary it is termed, *Basteria foliis ovatis oppositis, floribus lateralibus, caule fruticoso ramoso* It is a native of Carolina, where, from its aromatic odour, the inhabitants have given it the name of Allspice

*Class and order in the Linnæan system*

*Calycanthus* is of the class and order *Icosandria Polygynia*, and the characters are,

*The characters*

1 CALYX is an urceolated, squarrose perianthium, composed of many spear shaped, coloured folioles, which have the appearance of petals

2 COROLLA There is none The calycinal folioles are all the flower consists of

3 STAMINA are numerous awl-shaped filaments, inserted in the neck of the calyx, having oblong sulcated antheræ growing to their tops

4 PISTILLUM consists of numerous germina, and the like number of awl-shaped compressed styles the length of the stamina, with naked stigmas

5 PERICARPIUM There is none The calyx thickens into an oval berry or fruit, and contains the seeds

6 SEMINA The seeds are many, and caudated

CHAP

*Calycanthus*

# C H A P XIV

## *C A L L I C A R P A.*

The shrub described

CALLICARPA is a shrub of low growth, seldom arising higher than five feet The branches are numerous, and produced irregularly The oldest are of a brown colour others that are younger of a pale green, while the youngest are hoary, soft, slender, and very tough

The leaves are roundish, acute, pointed, and are near three inches in length They are of a *hoary cast*, being, like the *youngest shoots*, covered with a kind of woolly matter They stand opposite by pairs on moderate footstalks, and their edges are made delicate by beautiful small serratures The flowers are produced in whirls round the twigs, at the setting-on of the leaves, and are of a reddish purple colour Each flower separately is small and inconsiderable, though the whole number of which the whirls are composed form, together with the leaves and nature of the growth of the tree, a singular and pleasing aspect Their appearance is usually in July, and they are succeeded by succulent berries, which are at first red and afterwards of a deep purple when ripe

Method of propagating by cuttings

*Callicarpa* is propagated by cuttings, layers, or seeds When by cuttings, they should be planted, in the spring, in a moist sandy border As the hot weather comes on, they should be constantly shaded, and watered if the bed is not naturally very moist, and by this means many of the cuttings will strike root, and become good plants

Layers

By layers, which is a certain method, these plants may also be encreased If a few plants are obtained for this purpose, they should be planted in a warm well sheltered situation, and if the soil be naturally sandy, it will be the better The autumn after their stools have shot forth young wood, these young shoots should be laid in the ground, and by the autumn following they will be fit to take off, either for the nursery, or where they are to remain for good

and seeds

Numbers of these plants may also be obtained by seeds These we receive from abroad They should be sown in a warm border of sandy earth, a quarter of an inch deep The beds should be shaded from the heat of the sun, and now and then gentle waterings should be given After the plants are come up, shade and watering must be continued, and the spring following the beds should remain undisturbed, for many of them will not appear before then At the approach of winter, the beds should be hooped, to be covered with mats in very frosty weather, and this care being observed for about two winters, while they are in the seed bed, they may in the spring be taken up, in order to be planted in the nursery ground The places designed for these plants to gain strength in, should be well sheltered, and the soil should be naturally sandy and warm, for these plants are rather tender when young, though afterwards they are hardy enough If, therefore, no such place is naturally found, they should be enclosed by reed-hedges, or some such shelter, and if the soil is not naturally sandy, a mixture of drift or sea-sand will greatly promote the growth of the young plants

Titles of this genus

There being no other species of this genus, it stands singly with the name, *Callicarpa* Dr Mitchel calls it, *Sphondylococcos*, Du Hamel, *Burchardi*, Plukenet, *Anonymos baccifera verticillata, folio molli & incano, ex America*, Catesby, *Frutex baccifer verticillatus, foliis scabris latis dentatis & conjugatis*, Miller, *Johnsonia*, and Gronovius terms it, *Frutex foliis amplis subrotundis acuminatis ex adverso binis, viminibus lentis infimis quasi lini canitie tectis* This grows naturally in many parts of America, but particularly in Virginia and Carolina

Class and order in the Linnæan system The characters

*Callicarpa* is of the class and order *Tetrandria Monogynia*, and the characters are,

1 CALYX is a monophyllous, bell shaped perianthium, that is divided at the edge into four short erect segments

2 COROLLA is monopetalous and tubular, having the limb cut into four obtuse, patent parts

3 STAMINA are four filiforme filaments, twice the length of the corolla, with oval, incumbent antheræ

4 PISTILLUM consists of a roundish germen, of a filiforme style that is thicker upwards, and of a thick obtuse stigma

5 PERICARPIUM is a smooth globular berry

6 SEMINA The seeds are four, oblong, hard, and compressed

C H A P

# CHAP. XV.

## *CARPINUS*, The HORNBEAM-TREE.

Species.

THERE are only two real species of this genus.

1. The Common Hornbeam.
2. The Hop Hornbeam.

Common Hornbeam.

Whoever refers to p. 23 of Book I. will soon see what share the Common Hornbeam should have in all sorts of plantations, whether for profit or pleasure. It is not only valuable to be planted on account of its timber, but it seems peculiarly adapted to the plantations now under consideration, for by the leaves remaining on the trees all winter, how well do they break the winds, and what excellent shelter do they afford to the tenderer plants! Where there are plenty of Hornbeams, you may walk at ease in the highest winds, and may thus reap the benefit of the fresh air, without receiving its insults. Thus do these trees afford protection to man, birds, and tender plants. But when a collection is making in a small tract of ground, of a plant or two of a sort, to exhibit the products of Nature, one or two plants of the Hornbeam may be sufficient with the rest. If the place is to be surrounded, which indeed it ought to be, with tall trees for shelter, then the Hornbeam should be used for this purpose, and for the reasons before given, there are no trees more proper than this.

When they should be planted.

But where large plantations of wilderness-works are making, a considerable share of these trees, among those of their own growth, should be admitted, in proportion to the liking the owner has for them. No more need be said to recommend this tree, its uses and its beauties being well known. But besides the valuable sort called the Common Hornbeam, this species sports into the following varieties, viz.

Varieties of Common Hornbeam.

The Eastern Hornbeam.
Flowering Hornbeam.
American Hornbeam, all of which afford variety and pleasure.

The Eastern Hornbeam arrives to the least height of all the sorts, about ten feet is the highest of its growth, and it looks pretty enough with trees of the same kind. The leaves are by no means so large as the Common sort, and as the branches are always closer in proportion to the smallness of the leaves, where a low hedge is wanted of the deciduous kind, this would not be an improper tree for the purpose, either to be kept sheared, or suffered to grow in its natural manner. The bark of this sort is more spotted than that of the Common.

The Flowering Hornbeam is the most free shooter of any of the sorts, and will arrive to be as large as the Common Hornbeam only excepted, for it will grow to be thirty or forty feet high, and ... large trunks, useful when felled for many purposes. The branches of this tree are less spotted ... spots than any of the other sorts. The leaves are very rough, of a dark green colour, and are longer than the Common sort. The property which the Common Hornbeam is possessed of, of retaining its leaves all winter, ... belong to this sort, the leaves of which fall off in the autumn, with other deciduous trees.

American Hornbeam is a more elegant tree than any of the former sorts. The branches are slender, covered with a brownish speckled bark, and are more sparingly sent forth than on any of the others. The leaves are oblong, pointed, and of a palish green, and are nothing near so rough as the Common Hornbeam, though the flowers and fruit are produced in the same manner. I have two or three more varieties of this species, which have arisen from seeds sent me from America.

2. Hop Hornbeam is of taller growth than the Eastern kind. It will arrive to the height of twenty feet, or more. The leaves are nearly the size of the Common sort, and some people admire this tree on account of the singular appearance it makes with its seeds, before they begin to fall. There is a variety of this tree, which grows to thirty feet high, shoots freely, has long rough leaves like those of the elm, and long sh... yellow-coloured flowers, called the Virginian Flowering Hop Hornbeam. Hop Hornbeam.

These different sorts of Hornbeam are to be propagated by layers, for which purpose a few plants for stools must be procured. The stools of the Eastern Hornbeam should be planted a yard, and the other sorts a yard and a half, or two yards asunder. After the plants have made some young shoots, they should be layered in the autumn, and by that time twelvemonth they will have struck root, at which time, or any time in the winter or early in the spring, they should be taken off, and planted in the nursery-way, observing always to brush up the stool, that it may afford fine young shoots for fresh layering by the autumn following. The distance the plants should be allowed in the nursery need be no more than one foot in rows that are two feet asunder, and there they may stand, with the usual nursery care of weeding and digging the rows in winter, until they are to be planted out for good; though the Virginian Hornbeam will frequently send forth two shoots, which will seem to strive for mastery in the lead. When this is observed, the weakest should always be taken away, otherwise the tree will grow forked. Method of propagating these trees.

1. The Common Hornbeam is titled, *Carpinus squamis strobilorum planis*. Caspar Bauhine calls it, *Ostrya ulmo similis, fructu in umbilicis foliaceis*; Gerard, *Betulus sive Carpinus*; Parkinson, *Ostrys sive Ostrya*; and Dodonæus, *Carpinus*. It grows naturally in England, and most parts of Europe, also in America. Titles.

2. Hop Hornbeam is, *Carpinus squamis strobilorum inflatis*. Caspar Bauhine calls it *Ostrya ulmo similis, fructu racemoso lupulo simili*; Micheli, *Ostrya Italica, Carpini folio, fructu longiore & breviore nabitione*; and Plukenet, *Ostrys cognata* ... *Virginiana*. It grows naturally in Italy and Virginia.

*Carpinus* is of the class and order *Monoecia Polyandria*; and the characters are, Class and order in the Linnæan system.

I. Male flowers are collected in a cylindrical katkin. The characters.

1. Calyx. The common katkin is on all sides loose and imbricated. The scales are oval, concave, acute, ciliated, and each contains one flower.

2. Co

2. COROLLA. There is none.

3. STAMINA are usually about ten very small filaments, having compressed, hairy, bivalvate, didymous antheræ.

II. Female flowers in the same plant are disposed in an oblong, imbricated katkin.

1. CALYX. The scales are spear-shaped, hairy, reflexed at their top, and each contains one flower.

2. COROLLA is one bell-shaped petal, cut at the top into six segments, of which two are larger than the others.

3. PISTILLUM consists of two very short germens, each having two long capillary styles, with simple stigmas.

4. PERICARPIUM. There is none. The katkin becomes large, and at the base of each scale is lodged the seed.

5. SEMEN. The seed is an oval, angular nut.

## C H A P. XVI.

## *C E A N O T H U S*, N E W - J E R S E Y - T R E E.

The leaves of this tree used in Jersey as tea.

Its appearance described.

THIS species of *Ceanothus* commonly goes in our gardens, &c. by the several names of the *Red Twig*, *Carolina Shrub*, &c. but the name *Jersey-Tree* is with propriety given this plant, as the leaves are used by the inhabitants of Jersey, where it naturally grows, as tea. The height to which it will grow in our country is about three feet. The stem, which is of a pale brown colour, sends out branches from the bottom. These are thin, flexile, and of a reddish colour, which may have occasioned this tree to go by the name of *Red Twig*. The leaves which ornament these branches stand on reddish footstalks, about half an inch in length. They are oval, serrated, pointed, about two inches and a half long, and proportionably broad, and have three nerves running lengthways from the footstalk to the point. They are of a light green colour, grow irregularly on the branches, and not opposite by pairs, as has been asserted. They are late in the spring before they shoot. The flowers grow at the ends of the twigs in clusters. They are of a white colour, and when in blow give the shrub a most beautiful appearance. Indeed, it seems to be almost covered with them, as there is usually a cluster at the end of nearly every twig, and the leaves which appear among them serve as ornaments only, like myrtle in a distant nosegay, though Nature has denied them this, to give the plant a genteeler and more complete shape. This tree will be in full blow in July, and the flowers are succeeded by small brownish fruit, in which the seeds will sometimes ripen in England.

Method of propagating it by seeds.

The propagation of this plant is both by seeds and layers. If from seeds, a compost should be made, consisting of soil from a fresh pasture, which has been got a year before at least, and laid in a heap, with the sward with it, to rot. This should be often turned over, which will break the clods, rot the sward, and make the mixture more even. The whole being now converted to a fine mould, let a third part of drift or sea-sand be added, and that being well mixed together will be a proper compost for the reception of the seeds. Having the seeds ready, which, if procured from abroad, should have been preserved in sand, let them be sown as soon as possible after their arrival, in pots or boxes of this compost, about a quarter of an inch deep. The pots or boxes may be removed into a shady place, and in the summer should be set in the shade, [illegible] will come up the first spring. The winter following, the boxes must be placed under shelter in great frosts, and early in the spring the young plants will appear, when it will be proper to put them under a hotbed frame, or in some place where they may be secured from the nipping spring frosts. However, it must be observed, that each weather [illegible], and the plants kept under cover only in that severe time. In fine open weather they should have all the advantage of the sun and spring showers, which will bring them forward vigorous and strong. Too much watering should not be given these plants the succeeding summer, and the pots and boxes, the winter following, should be placed in a well sheltered situation, and should be either hooped to be covered with mats, or put under a hotbed frame, or else in the greenhouse, in frosty weather; for at that time one night's frost will endanger the whole crop. The spring following, they should be planted in separate pots, when all danger of frost is over. Each pot should be plunged into the natural ground in a shady border, where they may remain the whole summer. The winter following, care must be taken to preserve the plants from the frost, for they will still be in danger of being destroyed by it; and after they have been in their pots two or three years, they may be then turned out into the places where they are to remain for good, as they will then be hardy enough to endure almost any weather, though the soil in which they are planted ought to be warm and well sheltered; for they keep growing pretty late in the autumn, and unless they have these advantages, the ends of the shoots will be often destroyed by the early frosts, which sometimes come early and without notice in the season.

and by layers.

Another method of propagating these trees is by layers; though it is sometimes with difficulty they are made to strike root. The best time of layering them is in the summer, just before they begin to flower. At that time lay the tender twigs of the spring shoots in the earth, and nip off the end which would produce the flowers. By the autumn twelvemonth following, some of them will be rooted, though you must not expect roots to them all. [illegible] success will be better than common [illegible] stool, however, they must all remain until the spring, when they should be taken off, and the best rooted and the strongest be planted in the nursery, [illegible] and well shel-

ſheltered place, where they are to remain, while the bad rooted ones and the weakeſt ſhould be planted in pots, and if theſe are plunged into a moderate warmth of dung, it will promote their growth, and make them good plants before autumn In the winter they ſhould be guarded againſt the froſts, and in the ſpring they may be planted out where they are to remain, or, if the ground is not ready, may remain in the pots longer [illegible]

*Titles of this tree*

This ſpecies is titled, *Ceanothus foliis trinerviis* In the *Hortus Cliffortianus* it is termed, *Celaſtrus inermis, foliis ovatis ſerratis trinerviis, racemis ex ſummis alis longiſſimis*, and in the Upſal Catalogue, *Ceanothus corymbis folio longioribus* Plukenet calls it, *Evonymus, jujubinis foliis, Carolinenſis, fructu parvo fere umbellato*, and Dr Commelin, in the *Hort Amſt Evonymus Novi Belgii, corni fœminæ foliis* It grows naturally in Virginia and Carolina

*Ceanothus* is of the claſs and order *Pentandria Monogynia*, and the characters are, *Claſs and order in the Linnæan ſyſtem* *The characters*

1 CALYX is a monophyllous, turbinated, permanent perianthium, having the limb divided into five acute ſegments, which cloſe together

2 COROLLA conſiſts of five equal, roundiſh, compreſſed, obtuſe, patent petals, that are rather ſmaller than the calyx

3 STAMINA are five ſubulated, erect filaments, which are the length of the corolla, placed oppoſite to the petals, and have roundiſh antheræ

4 PISTILLUM conſiſts of a trigonal germen, cylindric ſemitrifid ſtyle the length of the ſtamina, and an obtuſe ſtigma

5 PERICARPIUM is a dry, trilocular, obtuſe berry

6 SEMINA The ſeeds are oval, and lie ſingly in each cell

## C H A P XVII

## *C E L T I S*, The N E T T L E - T R E E

THERE are only three ſpecies of this genus yet known

*Species of this genus*

1 The Common Black-fruited Nettle-tree

2 The Occidental, or Purple-fruited Nettle

3 The Oriental, or Yellow-fruited Nettle-tree

The two firſt, as foreſt trees, have been treated of in the foregoing Book, where the reader will ſee them deſcribed, the figure they will make, and the places they ought to occupy in the plantations now under conſideration

*Deſcription of the Oriental Nettle-tree*

3 The Oriental, or Yellow-fruited Nettle-tree The height to which this ſpecies will grow is no more than about twelve feet, and the branches are many, ſmooth, and of a greeniſh colour The leaves are ſmaller than thoſe of the other ſorts, though they are of a thicker texture, and of a lighter green The flowers come out from the wings of the leaves, on ſlender footſtalks They are yellowiſh, appear early in the ſpring, and are ſucceeded by large yellow fruit, which occaſions this ſpecies to be diſtinguiſhed by the above appellation

*Culture of this ſpecies*

The culture of this ſpecies is the ſame, and the plants may be raiſed in the ſame manner, as the other two ſorts, ſet forth in the Firſt Part, to which, to avoid repetition, I refer the reader, only I muſt admoniſh him, to let this all along have a peculiarly dry ſoil, and a well-ſheltered ſituation, otherwiſe it will not bear the cold of our winters

*Titles of this tree*

1 The Common Black-fruited Nettle-tree is titled, *Celtis foliis ovato-lanceolatis* Caſpar Bauhine calls it, *Lotus fructu ceraſi*, Cammerarius, *Lotus ſ Celtis*; and Lobel, *Lotus arbor* It grows naturally in the ſouth of Europe, and in Africa

2 Purple-fruited, or Occidental Nettle-tree is, *Celtis foliis oblique ovatis ſerratis acuminatis* Tournefort calls it, *Celtis fructu obſcurè purpuraſcente*, Gronovius, *Celtis procera, foliis ovato-lanceolatis ſerratis, fructu pullo*, and Ray, *Lotus arbor Virginiana, fructu rubro* It grows naturally in Virginia

3 Yellow-fruited, or Oriental Nettle-tree is, *Celtis foliis obliquè cordatis ſerratis ſubtus villoſis* Tournefort calls it, *Celtis Orientalis minor, foliis minoribus & craſſioribus, fructu flavo* It grows naturally in the Eaſt

*Celtis* is of the claſs and order *Polygamia Monoecia*, and the characters are, *Claſs and order in the Linnæan ſyſtem* *The characters*

I Hermaphrodite florets are ſingle, and above the male, and of theſe,

1 CALYX is a monophyllous perianthium, divided into five oval, patulous, withering ſegments

2 COROLLA There is none

3 STAMINA are five very ſhort filaments, having oblong, thick, quadrangular, four-furrowed antheræ

4 PISTILLUM conſiſts of an oval, pointed germen the length of the calyx, and two long, awl-ſhaped, patent, downy, reflexed ſtyles, with ſimple ſtigmas

5 PERICARPIUM is a roundiſh unilocular drupe

6 SEMINA The ſeed is a roundiſh nut

II Male flowers are ſituated below the former, and are of a ſimilar ſtructure with reſpect to the Calyx, Corolla, and Stamina, which are all they conſiſt of, the other parts being wanting

C H A P.

# C H A P XVIII

## *CEPHALANTHUS*, The BUTTON-WOOD

THERE is only one ſpecies of this genus, which is called the Button-Tree, from the flowers and fruit having the appearance of This tree deſcribed a kind of globular button It is a ſhrub of about five or ſix feet in height, and deſerves a place in all collections among thoſe of its own growth It is not a very buſhy plant, as the branches are always placed thinly in proportion to the ſize of the leaves, which will grow more than three inches long, and one and a half broad, if the trees are planted in a ſoil they like The leaves ſtand oppoſite by pairs on the twigs, and alſo ſometimes by threes, and are of a light-green colour Their upper ſurface is ſmooth, they have a ſtrong nerve running from the footſtalk to the point, and ſeveral others from that on each ſide to the borders Theſe, as well as the footſtalks, in the autumn die to a reddiſh colour The flowers, which are aggregate flowers, properly ſo called, are produced at the end of the branches, in globular heads, in July The florets which compoſe theſe heads are funnel-ſhaped, of a yellow colour, and faſtened to an axis which is in the middle

The propagation of the Button-Tree is from Method of raiſing this tree from ſeed, ſeeds, which we receive from America Theſe ſhould be ſown as ſoon as they arrive, and there will be a chance of their coming up the firſt ſpring, though they often lie till the ſpring after before they make their appearance, when they will come up in vaſt quantities, if the ſeed is good No extraordinary trouble need be taken in preparing any particular compoſt for theſe ſeeds, for they will grow in good garden-mould of almoſt any ſoil, though if there be ſoil that was taken from a freſh paſture, and duly turned, it will be better The method of ſowing the ſeeds is as follows Let a bed or two, in proportion to the quantity of ſeed, be made, and if there is any part of the garden that is inclined to be rather moiſt, though not wet, if the bed is made here, it will be the better A ſmall quantity of the mould being taken out of the beds to cover the ſeeds, the earth being made fine, and the bottom of the beds ſmooth and level, ſow the ſeeds, and riddle the mould over them about a quarter of an inch thick Then neat the beds up, and if the plants do not appear in the ſpring, it will be proper to riddle a ſmall quantity of earth again over the beds; otherwiſe the ſun and wind, by drying and blowing, will, before the ſummer is over, lay great part of the ſeeds bare Theſe beds will require no other trouble all ſummer than weeding; and this ſhould be performed at very ſmall intervals; for if the weeds are permitted to get ſtrong, they will in drawing pull up many ſeeds alſo with their roots The ſummer after theſe plants come up, they ſhould be watered in dry weather, and if there ſhould be a ſucceſſion of it, ſo as to cauſe the ground to crack and open, the beds ſhould be hooped and covered with mats in the heat of the day, and as conſtantly uncovered in the evening This will not only prevent your loſing many plants, but will make them all more vigorous and ſtrong In theſe ſeed-beds they ſhould remain two years, for if they are planted the firſt autumn, they will be ſo ſmall as to be thrown out of the ground by the firſt froſt, nay, even if they remain in the ſeed-bed, they will ſuffer this fate, if there be much cold weather in the winter Let, therefore, the beds be hooped and covered in very ſevere froſts Thus there will be no danger of their ſuffering by the inclemency of the ſeaſon, for although theſe trees are very hardy, yet the ſeedlings of moſt ſorts, like tender infants, require ſome nurſing The autumn twelvemonth after the plants come up, or any time during the winter, they ſhould be removed into the nurſery, and planted there at one foot aſunder, in rows of two feet wide, and, in two or three years more, they will be good plants for the ſhrubbery, or thoſe places where they are to remain Any time in the winter or ſpring will do for their removal, though the month of October is the beſt, and if there is a moiſt place in the garden, be careful to plant ſome in it, for there they will arrive at a greater height, and will ſhew their flowers and leaves proportionably larger and fairer

This ſhrub is alſo propagated by layers If or by layers or cuttings the young ſhoots are laid in the autumn, they will have ſtruck good root by the autumn following, and may be then taken up, and ſet in the places where they are deſigned to remain Cuttings of this tree, alſo, planted in the autumn in a rich, light, moiſt ſoil will grow, and by that means alſo plenty of theſe plants may be ſoon obtained

This ſpecies is titled, *Cephalanthus foliis oppoſitis terniſque* In the *Hortus Cliffortianus* it is Titles of this tree termed, *Cephalanthus foliis ternis* Plukenet calls it, *Scabioſa dendroides Americana ternis foliis caulem ambientibus, floribus ochroleucis* It grows naturally in North-America

*Cephalanthus* is of the claſs and order *Tetrandria Monogynia*, and the characters are, Claſs and order in the Linnæan ſyſtem The characters

1 CALYX The florets are collected in a globular head, and there is no general perianthium, but the Calyx of each floret is an angular, infundibuliforme, monophyllous perianthium, divided into four ſegments at the top

2 COROLLA The general flower is equal, and each floret is one funnel-ſhaped acute petal

3 STAMINA are four filaments, inſerted in the petal, and are ſhorter than the limb, having globular antheræ

4 PISTILLUM conſiſts of a germen ſituated below the flower, a ſtyle that is longer than the corolla, and a globular ſtigma

5 PERICARPIUM There is none

6 SEMINA The ſeeds are ſingle, large, pyramidical, and woolly

The Common Receptacle is globular and hairy

CHAP.

# CHAP. XIX.

## *CERCIS*, The JUDAS-TREE.

Species. THERE are two species of this genus: 1. The Common Judas-tree. 2. Canada Judas-tree; and both these have their varieties, which are equally desirable by those who would make a collection of the greatest number of sorts.

Description of the Common 1. Common Judas-trees differ in the height of their growth in different places. In some they will arrive to be fine trees, of near twenty feet high; whilst in others they will not arise to more than ten or twelve feet, sending forth young branches irregularly from the very bottom. The stem of this tree is of a dark greyish colour, and the branches, which are few and irregular, have a purplish cast. The leaves are smooth, heart-shaped, and roundish, of a pleasant green on their upper surface, hoary underneath, and grow alternately on long footstalks. The flowers are of a fine purple colour, and their general characters indicate their structure. They come out early in the spring, in clusters, from the side of the branches, growing upon short footstalks; and in some situations they are succeeded by long flat pods, containing the seeds, which, in very favourable seasons, ripen in England. Some people are fond of eating these flowers in sallads, on which account alone in some parts this tree is propagated. The varieties of this species are, 1. The Flesh-coloured; 2. The White-flowered; and, 3. The Broad-podded Judas-tree.

and the Canada Judas tree. 2. Canada Judas-tree will grow to the size of the first sort in some places. The branches are also irregular. The leaves are cordated, downy, and placed alternately. The flowers usually are of a pale reddish colour, and show themselves likewise in the spring, before the leaves are grown to their size. These too are often eaten in sallads, and also make an excellent pickle. There is a variety of this with deep red, and another with purple flowers.

The pleasure which these trees will afford in a plantation may be easily conceived, not only as they exhibit their flowers in clusters, in different colours, early in the spring, before the leaves are grown to such a size as to hide them; but from the difference of the upper and lower surface of the leaves, the one being of a fine green, the other of a hoary cast, so that on the same tree, even in this respect, is shewn variety, an improvement whereof is made by the waving winds, which will present them alternately to view.

Method of raising this tree. As these species will not take root by layers, they must be propagated by seeds, which may be had from abroad. They are generally brought us sound and good, and may be sown in the months of February or March. Making any particular compost for their reception is unnecessary; common garden mould, of almost every sort, will do very well. And this being well dug, and cleared of roots, weeds, &c. lines may be drawn for the beds. The mould being fine, part of it should be taken out, and riddled over the seeds, after they are sown, about half an inch thick. Part of the seeds will come up in the spring, and the other will remain until the spring following; so that whoever is desirous of drawing the seedlings of a year old to plant out, must not destroy the bed, but draw them carefully out, and after that there will be a succeeding crop. However, be this as it will, the seeds being come up, they must be weeded, and encouraged by watering in the dry season, and they will require no further care during the first summer. In the winter also they may be left to themselves, for they are very hardy, tho' not so much but that the ends of the branches will be killed by the frost, nay, sometimes to the very bottom of the young plant, where it will shoot out again afresh in the spring. Whoever, therefore, is desirous of securing his seedling-plants from this evil, should have his beds hooped, in order to throw mats over them in the hard frosts. This, I say, may be done; but where a multiplicity of business is carried on it may be omitted, for there will be plants both hardy and good. In the latter end of March, or beginning of April, the plants having been in the seed-bed one or two years, they should be taken out, and planted in the nursery. The distance of one foot asunder, and two feet in the rows should be given them. Hoeing the weeds down in the summer must also be allowed, as well as digging between the rows in the winter. Here they may stand until they are to be removed for good; but they must be gone over in the winter with the knife, and such irregular branches taken off as are produced near the root, by which management the tree may be trained up to a regular stem.

Such is the culture of the species of *Cercis*; sorts that are not to be omitted where there are any pretensions to a collection. Besides, the wood itself is of great value; for it polishes exceeding well, and is admirably veined with black and green.

Titles. 1. The Common Judas-tree is titled, *Cercis foliis cordato-orbiculatis glabris*. Caspar Bauhine calls it, *Siliqua sylvestris rotundifolia*; and Dodonæus, *Arbor Judæ*. It grows naturally in Portugal, Spain, Italy, and the South of France, also in the East.

2. The Canada Judas-tree is, *Cercis foliis cordatis pubescentibus*. Ray calls it, *Ceratia agrestis Virginiana, folio rotundo mucronato*; and Tournefort, *Siliquastrum Canadense*. It is a native of Canada, Virginia, and most parts of America.

Class and order in the Linnæan system. *Cercis* is of the class and order *Decandria Monogynia*; and the characters are,

The characters. 1. CALYX is a very short, melliferous, bell-shaped, monophyllous perianthium, convex at bottom, and indented in five parts at the top.

2. COROLLA consists of five petals inserted in the calyx, and these form the appearance of a papilionaceous flower.

The alæ are two petals, fastened by long ungues, and bend upwards.

The vexillum is one roundish petal, situated under the alæ.

The carina consists of three petals, which close in form of a heart, are affixed by their

their ungues, and encloſes the parts of generation

The nectarium is a filiforme gland, ſituated under the germen

3 Stamina are ten diſtinct, awl-ſhaped, declining filaments, of which four are longer than the others, having oblong, incumbent, aſſurgent antheræ.

4 Pistillum conſiſts of a narrow, ſpear-ſhaped, pedicellated germen, a ſtyle the length and ſituation of the ſtamina, and an obtuſe aſſurgent ſtigma

5 Pericarpium is an oblong, obliquely-acuminated pod, of one cell

6 Semina The ſeeds are few, roundiſh, and annexed to the upper ſuture

## C H A P XX

## *CHIONANTHUS*, The SNOWDROP-TREE.

CHIONANTHUS has two Engliſh names, the Snowdrop tree and the Fringe tree The former was given it on account of the flowers being remarkably white, the latter becauſe they appear fringed, being cut, or deeply laciniated, into many parts This tree will grow to the height of about fifteen feet, and, until late years, was very rarely to be met with in our gardens The ſtem of it is rough, and of a dark-brown colour The leaves are large, ſhaped like a laurel, broad and roundiſh, of a fine deep green on their upper ſurface, but rather hoary The flowers come out in bunches, in May, from every part of the tree They are of a pure white, and, in the places where it grows naturally, this muſt be a moſt delightful plant, for at that ſeaſon it exhibits its white flowers in bunches all over it, ſo as to reſemble a tree covered with ſnow The few trees we have ſeldom flower, and even when they do, the flowers are few, and make no great figure Whoever is deſirous of raiſing this ſhrub, muſt plant it in a moiſt part of the garden, which is well defended with other trees, for there he will have a chance of ſeeing the flowers (which are ſucceeded by black berries, of a moderate ſize) in more plenty, and in greater perfection

*Deſcription of and proper ſituation for the Snowdrop-tree*

The culture of this tree is not very eaſy, for if we attempt to propagate it by layers, there are with difficulty made to ſtrike root, and if we obtain good ſeeds from abroad, great care and management muſt be uſed, to raiſe them to be ſtrong plants, fit to be ſet out for good By layers and ſeeds, however, this tree may be encreaſed, and when layers is the method adopted, let the plants deſigned for ſtools be ſet in a very moiſt place, where the ſoil is rich and good After theſe ſtools have thrown out young ſhoots, they ſhould be layered in the autumn If there be many twigs of the ſummer's growth to be layers, different methods may be uſed on the different twigs; for no one that ever I experienced could be depended on, and yet they have grown by almoſt all One time the layering has been performed by a ſmall ſlit at the joint; another twig has had a gentle twiſt, ſo as to juſt break the bark; a third has been wired The ſlit-layers, after three or four years, have only ſwelled to a knob, without any fibres; while the twiſted parts have ſhot out fibres, and become good plants. At other times, the twiſted part, after waiting the ſame number of years, has ſtill remained in the ground as a branch without any root; whilſt the ſlit-twig, in the mean time, has become a good plant The like uncertainty I have ever found to attend the other manner of layering To propagate the Snowdrop-tree this way, every method ſhould be uſed, and then there will be a greater chance of having ſome plants, but, at the beſt, you muſt not expect them with good roots, until they have lain in the ground about three years, for it is very rarely that they are to be obtained ſooner The layers ſhould be taken from the ſtools the latter end of March, and planted in pots Theſe ſhould be plunged into a hotbed, and, after they have ſtruck root, ſhould be uſed to the open air In May they may be taken out, and plunged in the natural ſoil, in a moiſt ſhady place When the froſt comes on, they ſhould be removed into the greenhouſe, or ſet under a hotbed frame for protection, and in the ſpring they may be turned out of the pots, with the mould, into the places where they are to remain, which ought to be naturally moiſt and well ſheltered

*Method of propagating the Snowdrop by layers*

This tree may alſo be propagated by ſeeds. Theſe we receive from America, in moſt parts of which it is found more or leſs growing naturally, though we cannot always have them good Having, however, got the ſeeds, let them be ſown in large pots, about half an inch deep, and if the mould to receive them is a ſtrong, ſandy loam, it will be the better. After the ſeeds are ſown, the pots ſhould be plunged their whole depth into the ground, in a moiſt ſhady place; and no other care need be given them than weeding and watering until the winter following, for I never knew them, by any art, come up the ſpring they were ſown in In the autumn theſe pots ſhould be removed into the greenhouſe, or under an hotbed-frame, until March, at the beginning of which month a good hotbed ſhould be made, and the ſeeds plunged therein This will promote their growth; and after they are come up, the glaſſes muſt be ſhaded in the heat of the day, and proper air and water conſtantly afforded them The heat of the beds being out, and the plants being uſed to the air, the pots ſhould be plunged into a moiſt ſhady place as before, and weeded and watered during the ſummer At the approach of winter they ought to be brought into ſhelter, and then alſo frequently watered; for this is what they like; and for this reaſon I recommend the ſowing them in large pots, that there may be a greater quantity of mould, which will not dry ſo ſoon as in ſmall pots The ſummer following they muſt reſume their old ſtations; and the winterly care muſt be obſerved for

*and by ſeeds*

for two or three seasons, by which time the seedlings will be got tolerably strong In the spring the pots should be emptied, and the plants set in separate pots, which should also be plunged into an hotbed to forward their growing After that, the usual treatment should be bestowed on them till the spring, when they may be turned out, with the mould, into the places where they are to remain

Titles

This species is titled, *Chionanthus pedunculis trifidis trifloris* In the *Hortus Cliffortianus* it is termed, *Chionanthus* Petiver calls it, *Amelanchier Virginiana, lauroceraʃi folio* It grows naturally in most parts of North-America

Claſs and order in the Linnæan ſyſtem

*Chionanthus* is of the claſs and order *Diandria Monogynia*, and the characters are,

The characters

1 Calyx is a monophyllous, erect, acuminated, permanent perianthium, divided into four parts

2 Corolla is one funnel-ſhaped petal, the tube very ſhort, ſpreading, and the length of the calyx The limb is cut into four very long, narrow, erect, acute ſegments

3 Stamina are two very ſhort, ſubulated filaments, inſerted in the tube, having heart-ſhaped, erect antheræ

4 Pistillum conſiſts of an oval germen, of a ſimple ſtyle the length of the calyx, and of an obtuſe, trifid ſtigma

5 Pericarpium is a roundiſh, unilocular drupe

6 Semina is a ſingle and ſtriated nut

## C H A P XXI

## *C L E T H R A*

WE are now come to another plant whoſe ſtation ſhould be in a moiſt part of the garden, and whoſe culture is nearly the ſame as that before deſcribed, though it may with greater eaſe be propagated by layers *Clethra* has yet no Engliſh name It grows naturally in Virginia, Carolina, and Penſylvania, like our alder, by the ſides of rivers and watry places

Deſcription of this ſhrub

*Clethra* is a ſhrub, with us, of about four or five feet, though I am informed, in the above places, it is ſometimes found ten feet high The branches it ſends forth are not numerous, and theſe are garniſhed with leaves, which are ſpear-ſhaped and ſerrated They are about three inches long, an inch and a half broad, and have ſhort footſtalks *Clethra* uſually flowers in July, though I have known it in blow both in Auguſt, September, and October The flowers are produced at the ends of the branches, in long ſpikes They are white, and poſſeſſed of a ſtrong ſcent *Clethra*, at preſent, is not very common in our gardens It is deemed a curious plant, and ought to make one in every good collection

Method of propagating Clethra by layers,

The culture of this ſhrub is both by layers and ſeeds The plants deſigned to be encreaſed by layers ſhould be ſet in the moiſteſt part of the garden, and managed like thoſe of the preceding article, though there will not be near the difficulty of making them ſtrike root, for I have known them, when layered in autumn, have good roots by the autumn following Whenever theſe plants are layered, they muſt be conſtantly watered in dry weather through the ſummer, and if ſhade be afforded them, it will be the better Their future management may be like that of the preceding article, to which, to avoid repetition, I refer the reader

by ſeeds,

Theſe trees may alſo be raiſed by ſeeds, which ſhould be ſown and managed exactly the ſame as *Chionanthus*, only they may be planted out in the nurſery way the ſpring after they come up They will grow eaſily, and if they are placed in a ſhady moiſt place, well ſheltered, leſs trouble in potting, &c after they are ſtrong ſeedlings, of a year or two old, than what ought to be afforded the Snowdrop tree, will do for them

and by ſuckers

Theſe ſhrubs will very often ſend out ſuckers, by which it may likewiſe be propagated Theſe may be taken off in the autumn, if they have good roots, and planted out in the nurſery-way, if they have not, they ſhould be let alone till March, then taken up, and planted in pots of good loamy ſoil, and afterwards plunged into a moderate warmth of dung, which will promote their growth The autumn following they will be fit to plant out for good

Titles

There is no other ſpecies of this genus yet known It ſtands, therefore, with the name ſimply, *Clethra* Plukenet calls it, *Alnifolia Americana ſerrata, floribus pentapetalis albis in ſpicam depoſitis* It grows naturally in Virginia, Carolina, and Penſylvania

Claſs and order in the Linnæan ſyſtem

*Clethra* is of the claſs and order *Decandria Monogynia*, and the characters are,

The characters

1 Calyx is a monophyllous, permanent perianthium, divided into five oval, erect, concave ſegments

2 Corolla conſiſts of five oblong, erecto-patent petals, that are longer than the calyx, and broadeſt toward their extremities

3 Stamina are ten ſubulated filaments, the length of the corolla, having oblong, erect antheræ

4 Pistillum conſiſts of a roundiſh germen, of a filiforme, erect, permanent, encreaſing ſtyle, and a trifid ſtigma

5 Pericarpium is a roundiſh, trivalvate, trilocular capſule, encloſed in the calyx

6 Semina The ſeeds are many and angular

CHAP

# CHAP XXII

## *COLUTEA*, BLADDER-SENA

THERE is only one hardy, permanent ſhrubby ſpecies of this genus, called the Bladder-Sena, but it ſports in the following varieties, all of which are beautiful in their kind, and afford delight both by their flowers and leaves, viz

Varieties of this ſpecies

1 The Common Bladder-Sena
2 The Oriental Bladder-Sena
3 Pocock's Bladder-Sena
4 The Red podded Bladder Sena

Deſcribed

1 The Common Bladder Sena is the talleſt grower of all theſe ſorts It will arrive to the height of about ten or twelve feet The branches are of a whitiſh colour, which diſtinguiſh it in the winter, and the leaves in the ſummer have a pleaſing effect They are pinnated, the folioles are oval, and indented at the top, they conſiſt of ſometimes four, ſometimes five pair, placed oppoſite, and are terminated by an odd one The flowers are of the butterfly kind They are produced in June, July, and Auguſt, in cluſters, are numerous, of a yellow colour, and the footſtalk that ſupports them is long and ſlender The flowers are ſucceeded by large inflated pods, like bladders, which catch the attention of thoſe who have never before ſeen them This tree has variety enough of itſelf to make it eſteemed, but it ſhould always be planted among other trees of the ſame growth, to break the force of the ſtrong winds, not but that it is hardy enough to reſiſt our ſevereſt winters, but the branches will eaſily ſplit, which will make it unſightly, unleſs they are ſheltered in ſome degree by other trees This ſort will ripen its ſeeds in the autumn

2 The Oriental *Colutea* will grow to the height of about five or ſix feet The branches of this tree alſo are greyiſh, and the leaves pinnated, as well as terminated by an odd one, and the lobes are obverſely cordated and ſmall The flowers are reddiſh, ſpotted with yellow, and grow from the ſides of the branches on footſtalks, each of which is formed ſometimes with two, ſometimes with three flowers This tree is extremely hardy, and as it does not grow to the ſize of the Common ſort, nor in ſo luxuriant a manner, the branches will not be ſo liable to be ſplit off by the winds, and therefore the precaution neceſſary for that, in this ſort may be the leſs obſerved

3 Pocock's Bladder-Sena is another variety, of lower growth than the Common ſort The leaves are pinnated, and the folioles ſtand oppoſite by pairs in both the kinds They are indented in the ſame manner at the top, neither can I perceive any other difference between this and the Common Bladder-Sena, only that the one is larger than the other, and the flowers come out earlier in the year

4 The Red podded Bladder-Sena is alſo a variety, which will happen in common to all the ſorts, more or leſs, when raiſed from ſeeds

These trees are all very eaſily raiſed by ſeeds Any time in the ſpring will do for the work, tho' the month of March is the beſt ſeaſon, and no other compoſt will be required than garden-mould of almoſt any ſort, dug and raked fine If the ſeeds are ſown about half an inch deep, they will come up like corn in a month or two after Keep the beds weeded until the ſpring following, and then plant them out in the nurſery-way, obſerving always to ſhorten the tap-root which they often have In a year or two they will be good and proper plants for the ſhrubbery — Method of propagating the different ſorts of Colutea by ſeeds,

Theſe trees may alſo be propagated by layers; and that is the method we generally practiſe with Pocock's ſort, to continue it in its low growth — and by layers.

Bladder-Sena is titled, *Colutea arborea, foliolis obcordatis* Caſpar Bauhine calls it, *Colutea veſicaria*, and Dodonæus, *Colutea* Commelin calls one variety, *Colutea Africana, ſennæ foliis, flore ſanguineo*, and another ſtands with the title in Miller's Dictionary, *Colutea foliolis ovatis integerrimis, caule fruticoſo* It grows naturally in the ſouth of France, in Italy (particularly about Mount Veſuvius), and in many parts of Auſtria. — Titles

*Colutea* is of the claſs and order *Diadelphia Decandria*, and the characters are, — Claſs and order in the Linnæan ſyſtem The characters.

1 CALYX is a monophyllous, erect, bell-ſhaped, permanent perianthium, indented at the top in five parts

2 COROLLA is papilionaceous The vexillum, alæ, and carina vary in their figure, in the different ſpecies

3 STAMINA are diadelphous (nine of which are joined, the other ſtands ſingle) having ſimple antheræ

4 PISTILLUM conſiſts of an oblong, compreſſed germen, a riſing ſtyle, and a linear, bearded ſtigma

5 PERICARPIUM is a large, broad, inflated, membranaceous pod, of one cell

6 SEMINA The ſeeds are many, and kidney-ſhaped

CHAP.

# CHAP. XXIII.

## *CORNUS*, The CORNEL-TREE.

Species of this tree.

THE ſhrubby ſpecies of this genus are only three in number, called,

1. Cornelian Cherry-tree.
2. Common Dogwood.
3. Virginian Dogwood.

Cornelian Cherry-tree treated of before.

1. The Cornelian Cherry-tree has already been treated of in Book I. where the reader will ſee the method of propagation, together with its uſe and beauty in plantations of every kind. No more, therefore, need be ſaid of this ſort here; for after having read that deſcription, he ſees where and in what manner it ſhould be placed, among others deſigned for plantations of pleaſure. But beſides this, there are other ſpecies and varieties of *Cornus*, which do not arrive to that height, and which, on moſt accounts, deſerve to be admitted into wilderneſs-quarters, ſhrubberies, &c.

Deſcription of the Common Dogwood.

2. The Common Dogwood is well known all over England, as it grows naturally in moſt parts of our kingdom; but a few of theſe trees, nevertheleſs, may be admitted, nay, they ought to have a great ſhare in wilderneſs-quarters, if they do not grow common near the place where the plantation is to be; for the young twigs are red, eſpecially in winter, which look pretty at that ſeaſon, as do alſo its flowers and leaves in the ſummer. The redneſs of theſe young ſhoots has occaſioned this ſort to go by the name *Bloody-twig*. The leaves are about two inches long, and an inch and a half broad. Theſe have large nerves, which terminate in a point, and they often die in the autumn to a reddiſh colour. The flowers are white, produced in umbels at the ends of the branches, and are ſucceeded by black berries, like thoſe of the buckthorn, but have in each only one ſtone. The wood of this tree makes the beſt kind of charcoal in the world for gunpowder. It is brittle, exceedingly white, and when growing is covered with a dark brown bark, the twigs being red.

and the Virginian Dogwood.

3. Virginian Dogwood will grow rather higher than our Common Dogwood. The twigs are of a beautiful red. The leaves are obverſely cordated. The flowers are produced in a large cymbus, having a large involucrum. Their colour is white, they come out in May and June, and the berries ripen in autumn.

Varieties of theſe ſpecies.

From theſe ſpecies, the following beautiful varieties figure in our nurſeries, viz. Female Virginian Dogwood, American Blue-berried Dogwood, White-berried Dogwood of Penſylvania, and Swamp Dogwood.

deſcribed.

Female Virginian Dogwood, during the winter months, exhibits its branches of ſo beautiful a red colour, as to diſtinguiſh itſelf to all at that ſeaſon. It grows to eight or ten feet high; though the leaves are ſpear-ſhaped, acute, nervous, and in the autumn die to a fine red. The flowers come out in umbels, at the ends of the branches. They appear in May and June, and the berries ripen in the autumn.

The American Blue-berried Dogwood arrives at the height of about eight or nine feet. The twigs of this tree alſo are of a delightful red. The leaves are larger, oval, and hoary on their under-ſide. The flowers are white, come out in umbels from the extremity of the branches, and are ſucceeded by large, oval, blue berries, which make a fine appearance in the autumn.

White-berried Dogwood arrives at the ſame ſize with the others. The young ſhoots, like thoſe of the others, are of a beautiful red colour during the winter. Like them, alſo, it produces its white flowers in large umbels in May; but they are ſucceeded by white berries in the autumn.

Swamp Dogwood grows naturally in moiſt places, almoſt all over America, and it will grow with us in almoſt any ſoil or ſituation. The leaves of this are of a much whiter colour than any of the other ſorts, though the flowers and fruit are produced in the ſame manner.

I have ſeveral other ſorts, which I raiſed from ſeeds that I received from Penſylvania. Some have white ſtalks and hoary leaves, ſome very narrow leaves and ſlender twigs, others very broad leaves, ſome with large bunches of flowers, others with ſmall ones. The time of blooming in the different ſorts alſo varies; ſome come into flower early in May, whilſt others again do not exhibit their bloom before Auguſt.

One method of propagation is common to all theſe ſorts of *Cornus*, though this may be effected three ways; by ſeeds, layers, and cuttings. The ſeeds of the Common ſort ſhould be ſown in the autumn, ſoon after they are ripe, and theſe will come up in the ſpring. The ſeeds of the American ſorts we generally receive in the ſpring. Theſe ſhould be ſown directly; but they will not come up till the ſpring following; nor would thoſe of our Common ſort, if they were kept until the ſpring before they were ſown. No particular art is required for theſe ſeeds. They will grow in common garden-mould of almoſt any ſort, though the richer it be the better. This muſt be made fine, cleared of all roots, weeds, &c. and the ſeeds ſhould be ſown about half an inch deep. The ſpring after the plants come up, they ſhould be planted in the nurſery, at a ſmall diſtance from each other, where they may ſtand for two or three years, and then be planted out for good. Method of propagating theſe ſorts by ſeeds,

Theſe trees may alſo be eaſily propagated by layers; for after having obtained ſome plants for the purpoſe, if the ſhoots that were made the preceding ſummer be only laid in the ground in the autumn, they will have good roots by the autumn following. Theſe may be taken off, and planted in the nurſery for a year or two, as the ſeedlings; and the ſtools being cleared of all ſtraggling branches, and refreſhed by the knife, they will make ſtrong ſhoots for a ſecond operation by the autumn following. by layers,

By cuttings likewiſe theſe ſorts may be propagated. This work ſhould be done in October; and the cuttings for the purpoſe ſhould be the ſtrongeſt part of the laſt year's ſhoot, that had ſhot vigorouſly from a healthy ſoil. If theſe are cut into lengths of about a foot long, and planted in a moiſtiſh ſoil, two parts deep, they will grow and make good ſhoots the ſummer following; and by cuttings.

following, and these will require no removing before they are planted out for good

Titles of the 1 ... species. 1 The Cornelian Cherry-tree is titled, Cornus arborea ... Clusius calls it, Cornus mas ... Caspar Bauhine, Cornus hortensis mas, also, Cornus sylvestris ... It grows naturally in the hedges of Austria

2 Common Dogwood, or Bloody twig, is, Cornus ... Dodonæus calls it Virga sanguinea ... Bauhine, Cornus femina This grows in most parts of Europe, Asia, and America

3 The Virginian Dogwood is, Cornus arborea, ... This is the Cornus ... Virginiana, floribus ... Plukenet It is a native of Virginia

Class and order in the Linnæan system. Cornus is of the class and order Tetrandria Monogynia, ...

1 CALYX The common involucrum is composed of four coloured, oval, and deciduous leaves, the opposite ones being smallest. The characters

The perianthium is deciduous, very small, situated on the germen, and indented in four parts

2 COROLLA consists of four oblong, acute, plane petals, smaller than the leaves of the involucrum

3 STAMINA are four subulated, erect filaments, longer than the petals, having roundish incumbent antheræ

4 PISTILLUM consists of a roundish germen situated below the ... of a filiform style the length of the corolla, and of an obtuse stigma

5 PERICARPIUM is a roundish, umbilicated drupe

6 SEMEN is an oblong nut, of two cells, each of which has an oblong kernel

# CHAP XXIV

## CORONILLA, JOINTEDPODDED COLUTEA, or SCORPION-SENA

THERE are several low ligneous species of this genus, though only one proper to join in the shrubbery with other hardy plants, viz the Scorpion Sena

The shrub described. The Scorpion Sena sends out numerous irregular branches, from the root and on all sides the oldest and most woody of which are of a greyish colour, whilst the youngest are smooth, and of a dark brown The leaves are pinnated, and constitute a great beauty in this shrub, being of a pleasant green, and are composed of three pair of folioles, which are terminated by an odd one, these stand opposite on the midrib, and each has an indenture at the top These leaves, by a proper fermentation, will afford a dye nearly like that of indigo However beautiful as the leaves are, it is the flowers which constitute the beauty of these shrubs, and indeed, of all the shrubby tribe, there is none more striking or pleasing than this when in full blow This usually happens in May, when it will be covered all over with bloom, the shrub itself appearing as one large flower divided into many lofty spikes, for the flowers come out all along the sides of the branches by the leaves, on long footstalks, each supporting two or three flowers, which are butterfly shaped, of a yellow colour, and large in proportion to the size of the shrub They are succeeded by long slender pods, in which the seeds are contained This shrub often flowers again in the autumn

There is a variety of it, of lower growth called Dwarf Scorpion-Sena

This beautiful shrub is very easily propagated, either by seeds, layers, or cuttings, any of which may be easily made to grow

Method of propagating it by seeds. 1 By seeds These should be sown, in the spring, in beds of common garden mould, made fine, and cleared of the roots of all weeds, &c They should be covered about half an inch deep, and, if a very dry spring does not ensue, they will be up in about a month or six weeks If this should happen, the beds must be now and then watered, and shaded from the heat of the sun, which sometimes is very intense and parching, even at the beginning of May They may stand in the seed-bed two years before they are taken up all which time they will want no other care than weeding, and if they have watering the first summer, should it prove a dry one, they will grow the faster After this, they may be taken out of the seed bed, planted in the nursery way, and in about two or three years will be good plants to join in the shrubbery

2 By layers This business may be performed any time in the winter, but as the shrub sends forth numerous branches, many of them should be taken off, and only such a number left, as that they may be laid into the ground without crowding one another The branches should be of the last year's shoot, and the operation should be performed by a gentle twist, so as just to break the bark, for without this I have found them in the autumn just as they were when layered, and with this, they have always struck root, so as to be fit to take off the winter following These layers should be planted out in the nursery, and after having stood about two years, they also will be grown to be good plants — layers,

3 By cuttings The cuttings should be the strongest of the last year's shoots They should be planted close, in October, in a shady border of good fine mould If the spring and summer prove dry, watering must be afforded them every other day, and by this means many plants may be raised If the cuttings are planted close and most of them grow, they should be thinned, by taking up so many as may leave the others at a foot or more asunder, and these plants also, thus taken up, should be set out in the nursery ground — and cuttings.

a foot asunder, in rows at a foot and a half distance, where they must stand until they are taken up for good.

Titles of this genus. Scorpion-Senna is titled, *Coronilla fruticosa, pedunculis subtrifloris, corollae unguibus calyce triplo longioribus, caule angulato.* Cammerarius calls it, *Colutea scorpioides*; Caspar Bauhine, *Colutea siliquosa, sive Scorpioides major*; also, *Colutea siliquosa minor*. It grows naturally about Vienna and Geneva, also in Italy, and the South of France.

There are some other species of *Coronilla*, which are shrubby plants, and which will thrive abroad in warm situations, in mild winters; but I durst not introduce them here amongst hardy shrubs, as the hazard of losing them is very great.

Class and order in the Linnæan system. *Coronilla* is of the class and order *Diadelphia Decandria*; and the characters are,

1. CALYX is a very short, compressed, erect, monophyllous perianthium, divided into two parts. The characters.

2. COROLLA is papilionaceous. The vexillum is heart-shaped, and reflexed on both sides. The alæ are oval, obtuse, join at the top, but open below. The carina is rising, sharp pointed, compressed, and often shorter than the alæ.

3. STAMINA are diadelphous. Nine of the filaments are united, the other stands separate; and their antheræ are simple and small.

4. PISTILLUM consists of an oblong taper germen, a setaceous rising style, and a small obtuse stigma.

5. PERICARPIUM is a very long, taper, jointed pod.

6. SEMINA. The seeds are many.

## CHAP. XXV.

## CORIARIA, The TANNER's SUMACH,

## Commonly called The MYRTLE-LEAVED SUMACH.

The description. THE Myrtle-leaved Sumach is a shrub of low growth, seldom arising to more than four or five feet high. The bark is of a brown colour, and spotted. The wood is very brittle, and very full of light pith. The young shoots are produced in great plenty from the bottom to the top. They are square, and come out three or four together, from one side of the stem, whilst the other side is often furnished with an equal number. The leaves resemble some of the sorts of myrtle, which gave occasion for its being called the Myrtle-leaved Sumach. They are oblong, pointed, of a bright green, and stand opposite by pairs on the twigs. The flowers are both male and female, on different plants. They are produced in spikes, at the ends and sides of the branches, and have little beauty to recommend them. The tree is planted, however, as a flowering shrub, amongst others of its own growth; but the place in which it is set should be well sheltered; for notwithstanding this is a very hardy shrub, yet the ends of the branches are often killed in the winter, which makes the plant unsightly in the spring.

Method of propagating it. The propagation of the *Coriaria* is very easy. Nothing more need be said, than after having obtained a few plants, to plant them in a lightish soil of any sort. Here they will propagate themselves in great plenty; for they will (what gardeners call) *spawn*; i. e. their creeping roots will send forth many young plants, at more than three yards distance from the real plant. The strongest of these may be taken up, and planted where they are to remain, whilst the weaker may be set in the nursery-way, to gain strength, before they are set out for good. In this easy manner may plenty of these shrubs be obtained; and every winter after they are taken up, if the mould about the mother-plant be raked smooth, and weeded in summer, she will afford you a fresh crop by the autumn following, which may be taken off and planted as before.

Titles of this genus. The title of this shrub is, *Coriaria foliis ovato oblongis*. In the *Hortus Cliffortianus* it is termed, *Coriaria*. Bauhine calls it, *Rhus myrtifolia Monspeliaca*; and Lobel, *Rhus plinii myrtifolia Monspeliensium*. It grows naturally about Montpelier in France, and is used there by the tanners for tanning of leather, which occasioned its being called Tanner's Sumach. This plant, especially the bark, is said to be possessed of many excellent virtues, and is good medicine in epilepsies, &c. The leaves afford an ointment which is powerful in stopping gangrenes; and the seeds, pounded, mixed with honey and oak-coals, are good against the piles. Valuable properties of this plant.

Class and order in the Linnæan system. Male and female flowers are found upon different plants, and the stamina of the male flowers are ten in number. From hence we know the class and order to which it belongs are *Dioecia Decandria*.

The characters of the male flowers are,

The characters. 1. CALYX is a very short perianthium, consisting of five oval, concave leaves.

2. COROLLA consists of five petals, like the calyx.

3. STAMINA are ten filaments the length of the corolla, with simple oblong antheræ.

The characters of the female flowers are,

1. CALYX is a very short perianthium, composed of five oval, concave leaves.

2. COROLLA is composed of five cuspidated, calyciform, connivent petals.

3. PISTILLUM consists of five compressed germina, and of the like number of long setaceous styles, with simple stigmas.

4. PERICARPIUM. There is none. The petals become fleshy, form an angular berry, and enclose the seeds.

5. SEMINA are five, and reniform.

# CHAP. XXVI.

## CORYLUS, The HAZEL or NUT-TREE.

Species.

THERE are two species only of this genus:
1. The Common Nut-tree.
2. The Byzantine-nut.

Common Nut-tree.

1. The Common Nut-tree is so well known as to need no description; we have before treated of it as a forest-tree; we are now to see in what manner it should have a place in our wilderness-quarters. The Common Nut-tree includes all the varieties of sorts that are to be found in our woods and gardens, such as the large clustered red filbert, white filbert, &c. These are varieties only of one species; for I have planted the nuts of all the sorts, and sorts of all kinds have been produced from them. These varieties, however, have a great effect, even by their leaves, as well as in the difference of the fruit they produce; for the leaves of that sort called the Red Filbert are of a much darker colour than the others, and in the mixing of which they make a pleasing contrast with those of a lighter hue. Few of the sorts of nut-tree should be admitted among the choice shrubs; they ought to be stationed in the coarsest parts of the largest wilderness-quarters with those of their own growth, which will be about twenty, or thirty feet. The Common Nut-tree should not by any means be admitted; only those that produce the choicest fruit should have a share. The former may serve for underwood in the wilds or forests, &c. whilst the latter, tho' with no more beauty in the flowers or leaves than those, feast the eye, by exhibiting their clusters in different forms and shapes, as well as regale the taste by their improved kinds. The white filbert, then, the red filbert, the Spanish nut, and the great cob-nut, are the sorts we should propagate. These are all worthy to be planted for the sake of the fruit, so that they will answer in both respects in their places.

Description of the Byzantine Nut-tree.

2. The Byzantine-nut. This is distinguished from the other species chiefly by the stipulæ, which are very narrow and acute, whereas those of the Common Nut are oval and obtuse. It differs also in the size of its growth, the true Bizantine-nut tree seldom growing higher than four or five feet, and hence the name *Dwarf-nut-tree* has been used to this plant. In other respects, it is like our Common Nut-tree; it flowers at the same time, the fruit is produced in clusters, and it ripens accordingly.

Method of propagating the different sorts.

The propagation of nut-trees by seeds has been already shewn, but whoever is desirous of multiplying the real kinds, and continuing them in their sorts, must get some plants of the real kinds, which he must set for stools. They will grow on almost any soil, and the young twigs, being laid in the ground in the autumn, will have struck root by the autumn following. These should be taken off, and planted in the nursery, a foot asunder, and two feet distant in the rows, and if there be any young shoots made the intermediate summer, they also may be laid down, or the plant headed within half a foot of the ground, to send forth young shoots for a second operation the autumn following. By this means the sorts may be propagated and kept distinct, for the seeds sown of any of them will not in general come to good, though it is observable, that from the best nuts there will be the best chance of having good nuts again, and I have known some few trees, raised from seeds, which have produced nuts better than those they were raised from. This may, perhaps, induce a gardener desirous of obtaining a great variety to try this method, when he may extirpate the worst sorts, and, if any should be worthy of it, may propagate the others in the manner directed.

1. The Common Nut-tree is titled, *Corylus stipulis ovatis obtusis*. Caspar Bauhine calls it, *Corylus sylvestris*; Fuchsius, *Avellana nux sylvestris*. The varieties of it go by the names of, *Corylus sativa, fructu albo minore*; *Corylus sativa, fructu oblongo rubente*; *Corylus sativa, fructu rotundo maximo*; *Corylus fructibus in racemum congestis*. It grows naturally in our woods and hedges, and in the like situations in most parts of Europe. Title.

2. Byzantine-nut-tree is titled, *Corylus stipulis linearibus acutis*. Bauhine calls it, *Avellana peregrina humilis*; Clusius, *Avellana pumila Byzantina*; and Hermann, *Corylus Byzantina*. It grows naturally near Constantinople.

*Corylus* is of the class and order *Monoecia Polyandria*; and the characters are, Class and order in the Linnæan system. The characters.

I. Male flowers are collected in a long katkin.
1. CALYX. The common katkin is cylindrical and imbricated. The scales are narrow at the base, broad at the top, obtuse, inflexed, and cut into three segments, of which the middle one is much the broadest, and each scale contains one flower.
2. COROLLA. There is none.
3. STAMINA are eight very short filaments, fastened to the inner side of the scale, having oval, oblong, erect antheræ, that are shorter than the calyx.

II. Female flowers are included in the bud, sit close to the branches, and are distinct from the males in the same plant.
1. CALYX is a two-leaved, coriaceous, erect perianthium, the length of the fruit, and lacerated at the margin.
2. COROLLA. None.
3. PISTILLUM consists of a very small roundish germen, and of two setaceous, coloured styles, longer than the calyx, with simple stigmas.
4. PERICARPIUM. There is none.
5. SEMINA. The seed is an oval nut, that is shaved at the base, and a little compressed and pointed at the top.

CHAP.

# CHAP. XXVII.

## *CRATÆGUS*, The WILD SERVICE-TREE.

Species.

THE real ſpecies of this genus are,
1. The Common Hawthorn.
2. L'Azarole.
3. Aria Theophraſti, or White-leaf tree.
4. Maple-leaved Service tree.
5. Virginian Thorn, commonly called Cock-ſpur-thorn.
6. Virginian L'Azarole.
7. Gooſeberry-leaved Virginian Thorn.
8. Green-leaved Virginian Thorn.

Theſe ſpecies comprehend numerous varieties, of great uſe and beauty in our wilderneſs quarters, and different parts of our works.

Common Hawthorn.

Varieties of this ſpecies deſcribed.

1. The Common Hawthorn. This admirable and uſeful ſpecies ſports in the following varieties: The Large Scarlet Hawthorn, the Yellow Haw, the White Haw, the Maple-leaved Hawthorn, the Double-bloſſomed Hawthorn; the Glaſtonbury Thorn.

The Large Scarlet Hawthorn is no more than a beautiful variety of the Common Haw. It is exceedingly large, oblong, perfectly ſmooth, and of a bright ſcarlet, and, from the additional ſplendor it acquires by the berries, it is propagated to cauſe variety in plantations for obſervation and pleaſure.

Yellow Haw is a moſt exquiſite plant. The buds at their firſt coming out in the ſpring, are of a fine yellow, and the fruit is of the colour of gold. The tree is a great bearer, and retains its fruit all winter, cauſing a delightful effect in plantations of any kinds. It was originally brought from Virginia, is greatly admired, and no collection of hardy trees ſhould be without it.

White Haw is but a paltry tree, compared with the former. It hardly ever grows to the height of the Common Hawthorn, is an indifferent bearer, and the fruit is ſmall, and a very bad white.

Maple-leaved Hawthorn will grow to be near twenty feet high, and has very few thorns. The leaves are larger than the Common Hawthorn, reſemble thoſe of the maple, and are of a whitiſh green colour. The flowers are produced in large bunches, in June, and are ſucceeded by remarkable fruit, of a ſhining red, which looks beautiful in the winter.

Double-bloſſomed Hawthorn produces a full flower, and is one of the ſweeteſt ornaments in the ſpring. Nature ſeems to have peculiarly deſigned this ſort for the pleaſure garden, for though it be the Common Hawthorn only, with the flowers doubled, yet it may be kept down to what ſize the owner pleaſes, ſo that it is not only ſuitable for wilderneſs quarters, ſhrubberies, and the like, but it is alſo uſeful for ſmall gardens, where a tree or two only are admitted. Theſe beautiful double flowers come out in large bunches, in May, and the tree is ſo good a bearer, that it will often appear covered with them. Their colour, at their firſt appearance, is a delicate white. They afterwards die to a faint red colour, and are frequently ſucceeded by ſmall imperfect fruit.

Glaſtonbury Thorn differs in no reſpect from the Common Hawthorn, only that it ſometimes flowers in the winter. It is ſaid to have originally been the ſtaff of Joſeph of Arimathea, that noble counſellor who buried Chriſt. He, according to the tradition of the abbey of Glaſtonbury, attended by eleven companions, came over into Britain, and founded, in honour of the Bleſſed Virgin, the firſt Chriſtian church in this iſle. As a proof of his miſſion, he is ſaid to have ſtuck his ſtaff into the ground, which immediately ſhot forth and bloomed. This tree is ſaid to have bloſſomed on Chriſtmas Day ever ſince, and is univerſally diſtinguiſhed by the name of the Glaſtonbury Thorn. I have many plants that were originally propagated from this thorn, and they often flower in the winter, but there is no exact time of their flowering, for in fine ſeaſons they will ſometimes be in blow before Chriſtmas, ſometimes they afford their bloſſoms in February, and ſometimes it ſo happens that they will be out on Chriſtmas Day.

L'Azarole thorn.

2. L'Azarole. The L'Azarole-thorn will grow to be fifteen or ſixteen feet high. The leaves are large, nearly trifid, ſerrated, and obtuſe. The flowers are large, come out in May, and, in the different varieties, are ſucceeded by fruit of different ſize, ſhape, and reliſh.

Varieties.

The principal varieties of this ſpecies are, The Azarole with ſtrong thorns, the Azarole with no thorns, the Jagged leaved Azarole, the Oriental Medlar.

Aria Theophraſti.

3. Aria Theophraſti, or White-leaf-tree. The Aria Theophraſti, called the White leaf-tree, will grow to be more than twenty feet high. This tree is engaging at all times of the year, and catches the attention, even in the winter, for then we ſee it ſtand, though naked of leaves, with a fine ſtraight ſtem, with ſmooth branches, ſpotted with white, at the end of which are the buds, ſwelled for the next year's ſhoot, giving the tree a bold and fine appearance. In the ſpring the leaves come out of courſe, and look delightfully, having their upper ſurface green, and the lower white. Their figure is oval, they are unequally ſerrated, about three inches long, and half as wide. Several ſtrong nerves run from the mid-rib to the border, and they are placed alternately on the branches, which appear as if powdered with the fineſt meal. The flowers are produced at the end of the branches, in May, they are white, grow in large bunches, having meally footſtalks, and are ſucceeded by red berries, which will be ripe in Autumn.

Maple leaved Service.

4. Maple leaved Service tree. The Maple leaved Service is a large growing tree. It will arrive to near fifty feet, and is worth propagating for the ſake of the timber, which is very white and hard, and is uſeful for millwrights, and many purpoſes of that kind. This tree grows naturally in ſeveral woods in England; and it is the fruit of this ſpecies that is tied in bunches, and expoſed for ſale in the autumn. It is gathered in the woods, and by ſome perſons is much liked. The leaves in ſome degree reſemble thoſe of the maple tree in ſhape; their upper ſurface is a fine green, their under hoary, and they grow alternately on the branches. The flowers

flowers come out in May, exhibiting themſelves in large cluſters at the ends of the branches They are white, and are ſucceeded by the afore ſaid eatable fruit, which, when ripe, is of a brown colour, and about the ſize of a large haw This ſpecies ſhould be ſtationed in the largeſt parts of the wilderneſs quarters, among tall growing trees

*Cockſpur thorn* 5 Cockſpur thorn The Virginian Cockſpur-thorn will grow to about twenty feet high. It riſes with an upright ſtem, irregularly ſending forth branches, which are ſmooth, and of a browniſh colour, ſpotted thinly with ſmall white ſpots It is armed with thorns, that reſemble the ſpurs of cocks, which gained it the appellation of Cockſpur-thorn In winter, the leaf-buds appear large, turgid, and have a bold and pleaſant look among others of different appearances In ſummer, this tree is very delightful The leaves are oval, angular, ſerrated, ſmooth, and bend backwards They are about four inches long, and three and a half broad, have five or ſix pair of ſtrong nerves running from the midrib to the border, and die to a browniſh red colour in the autumn The flowers are produced in very large umbels, making a noble ſhow, in May, and are ſucceeded by large fruit, of a bright red colour, which have a good effect in the winter

*Varieties* The principal varieties of this ſpecies are, The Cockſpur-hawthorn with many thorns, the Cockſpur-hawthorn with no thorn, the Cockſpur with eatable fruit

The latter was ſent me from America with that name, and I have raiſed ſome trees of the ſeeds, but they have not yet produced any fruit, ſo that I cannot pretend to ſay how far it may be deſirable, though I have been informed it is reliſhed in America by ſome of the inhabitants there

*Berries produced by this ſpecies good food for ſwine, deer, &c.* All the ſorts of Cockſpur-hawthorns are not only beautiful in plantations of all kinds, but their berries are excellent food for ſwine, deer, &c which ſhould gain them a place in the park and diſtant fields If they are ſet in clumps in the park, and fenced with oak pales, which will laſt till they are ſtrong enough to defend themſelves, they will be highly ornamental in thoſe places, be very ſtrengthening to the bucks in the rutting ſeaſon, and enhance the flavour of the doe-veniſon, or, if they are ſet in diſtant fields or woods, they will prove admirable food, with the leaves, for ſwine, bring them forward, and cauſe their meat to be firm and well reliſhed

*Virginian L'Azarole* 6 Virginian L'Azarole. This ſpecies will grow to be near twenty feet high The ſtem is robuſt, and covered with a light coloured bark The branches are produced without order, are of a dark brown colour, and poſſeſſed of a few long ſharp thorns The leaves are ſpear-ſhaped, oval, ſmooth, and ſerrated; of a thickiſh conſiſtence, and often remain on the tree the greateſt part of the winter Each ſeparate flower is large, but as few of them grow together, the umbels they form are rather ſmall They come out in May, and are ſucceeded by large dark-red coloured fruit, which ripens late in the autumn

*Names of its varieties* The varieties of this ſpecies are, The Pear-leaved Thorn; the Plum-leaved Thorn, with very long, ſtrong ſpines and large fruit, the Plum-leaved Thorn, with ſhort ſpines and ſmall fruit.

*Gooſeberry leaved Virginian Hawthorn.* 7 Gooſeberry-leaved Virginian Hawthorn This ſpecies grows to about ſeven or eight feet high. The branches are ſlender, and cloſely ſet with ſharp thorns The leaves are cuneiforme, oval, ſerrated, and hairy underneath The flowers are ſmall, and of a white colour They are produced from the ſides of the branches, about the end of May; and are ſucceeded by yellow fruit, which ripens late in autumn

*Variety* There is a variety of this, called the Carolina Hawthorn, which has longer and whiter leaves, larger flowers and fruit, and no thorns

*Green leaved Virginian Thorn* 8 Green leaved Virginian Thorn The ſtem and branches of this ſpecies are altogether deſtitute of thorns The leaves are lanceolate, oval, nearly trilobate, ſerrated, ſmooth, and green on both ſides The flowers are white, moderately large, come out the end of May, and are ſucceeded by a roundiſh fruit, which will be ripe late in the autumn

*Method of propagating theſe ſpecies* The reſpective ſpecies are all propagated by ſowing of the ſeeds, and the varieties are continued by budding them upon ſtocks of the white-thorn This latter method is generally practiſed for all the ſorts, though, when good ſeeds can be procured, the largeſt and moſt beautiful plants are raiſed that way

*by ſeeds,* In order to raiſe them from ſeeds, let theſe be ſown, ſoon after they are ripe, in beds of freſh, light, rich earth Let alleys be left between the beds, for the conveniency of weeding, and let the ſeeds be covered over with fine mould, about an inch deep The ſummer following, the beds muſt be kept clean of weeds, and probably ſome few plants will appear But this is not common in any of the ſorts, for they generally lie till the ſecond ſpring after ſowing before they come up At the time they make their appearance they muſt be watered, if the weather proves dry, and this ſhould be occaſionally repeated all ſummer They ſhould alſo be conſtantly kept clean from weeds; and in the autumn the ſtrongeſt may be drawn out, and ſet in the nurſery-ground, a foot aſunder, in rows that are two feet diſtant from each other, while the weakeſt may remain until another year During the time they are in the nurſery, the ground between the rows ſhould be dug every winter, and the weeds conſtantly hoed down in the ſummer, and this is all the trouble they will require until they are planted out for good, which may be in two, three, or more years, at the pleaſure of the owner, or according to the purpoſes for which they are wanted

*and by budding* Theſe trees are eaſily propagated by budding alſo, they will all readily take on one another; but the uſual ſtocks are thoſe of the Common Hawthorn In order to have theſe the beſt for the purpoſe, the haws ſhould be got from the largeſt trees, ſuch as have the feweſt thorns and largeſt leaves, and they ſhould be ſown and managed as has been directed for raiſing of quick After they are come up, and have ſtood one year in the ſeed bed, the ſtrongeſt ſhould be planted out in the nurſery, a foot aſunder, and two feet diſtant in the rows, and the ſecond ſummer after, many of them will be fit for working The end of July is the beſt time for this buſineſs; and cloudy weather, night and morning, are always preferable to the heat of the day Having worked all the different ſorts into theſe ſtocks, they may be let alone, until the latter end of September, when the baſs matting ſhould be taken off. In the winter the ground between the rows ſhould be dug, and in the ſpring the ſtock ſhould be headed about half a foot above the bud The young ſhoots the ſtocks will always attempt to put out, ſhould be as conſtantly rubbed off, for theſe would in proportion ſtarve the bud, and ſtop its progreſs With this care, I have known ſeveral of the ſorts ſhoot ſix feet by the autumn; and as they will be liable to be blown out of their ſockets by the high winds which often happen in in the summer, they should be slightly tied to the top of the stock that is left on for the purpose, and this will help to preserve them. Your plants are now raised, and they may, any winter after this, be removed for good.

Titles of the species

1. The Common Hawthorn is titled, *Cratægus foliis obtusis subtrifidis serratis*. Caspar Bauhine calls it, *Mespilus, apii folio, sylvestris spinosa, sive Oxyacantha*; Dodonæus, *Oxyacantha, sive spina acuta*. It forms our hedges, and grows naturally all over Europe.

2. L'Azarole. This is titled, *Cratægus foliis obtusis subtrifidis subdentatis*. Caspar Bauhine calls it, *Mespilus apii folio laciniato*; John Bauhine, *Mespilus Aronia veterum*. It grows naturally in Italy and the south of France.

3. Aria Theophrasti, or White leaf-tree. This is titled, *Cratægus foliis ovatis inæqualiter serratis subtus tomentosis*. Caspar Bauhine calls it, *Alni effigie, lanato folio major*; John Bauhine, *Sorbus Alpina*; Ray, *Sorbus sylvestris Anglica*; and Dalechamp, *Aria*. It grows naturally in England, and most of the cold parts of Europe.

4. Maple leaved Service tree is titled, *Cratægus foliis cordatis septangulis lobis infimis divaricatis*, in the *Hortus Cliffortianus* as it is termed, *Cratægus foliis cordatis acutis lacinulatis acutis serratis*. Caspar Bauhine calls it, *Mespilus, apii folio, sylvestris non spinosa, seu sorbus torminalis*; John Bauhine, *Sorbus torminalis & Cratægus Theophrasti*; and Cammerarius, *Sorbus torminalis*. It grows naturally in England, Germany, Switzerland, and Burgundy.

5. Cockspur Hawthorn is titled, *Cratægus foliis ovatis repando-angulatis serratis glabris*. Caspar Bauhine calls it, *Mespilus Virginiana, apii folio, rutilo*; Plukenet, *Mespilus, apii folio, Virginiana spinis horrida, fructu amplo coccineo*; and Ray, *Oxyacantha spina sancta dicta*. It grows naturally in Virginia and Canada.

6. Virginian L'Azarole is, *Cratægus foliis lanceolato ovatis serratis glabris, ramis spinosis*. Plukenet calls it, *Mespilus aculeata pyri folia denticulata splendens, fructu insigni rutilo, Virginiensis*; and Clayton, *Mespilus pruni foliis, spinis longissimis fortibus, fructu rubro magno*. It grows naturally in Virginia.

7. Gooseberry leaved Virginian Thorn is titled, *Cratægus foliis cuneiformi ovatis serratis subangulatis subtus villosis, ramis spinosis*. Gronovius calls it, *Mespilus inermis, foliis ovato-oblongis serratis subtus tomentosis*; Frew, *Mespilus Caroliniana, apii folio, vulgari similis major, fructu luteo*; and Plukenet, *Mespilus Virginiana, grossulariæ foliis*. It grows naturally in Virginia.

8. Green leaved Virginian Thorn is, *Cratægus foliis lanceolato ovatis subtrilobis serratis glabris, caule inermi*. Gronovius calls it, *Mespilus inermis, foliis oblongis integris acuminatis serratis basi sinuatis utrinque viridibus*. It is a native of Virginia.

Class and order in the Linnæan system

*Cratægus* is of the class and order *Icosandria Digynia*; and the characters are,

The characters

1. CALYX is a monophyllous, permanent perianthium, cut into five concave, patent segments.

2. COROLLA is composed of five roundish, concave, sessile petals, that are inserted in the calyx.

3. STAMINA are twenty awl shaped filaments, inserted in the calyx, having roundish antheræ.

4. PISTILLUM consists of a germen situated below the flower, and two filiforme, erect styles, with capitated stigmas.

5. PERICARPIUM is a roundish, fleshy, umbilicated berry.

6. SEMINA. The seeds are two, longish, cartilaginous, and distinct.

# CHAP. XXVIII.

## *CUPRESSUS*, The CYPRESS-TREE.

CYPRESS-TREES, which in general are evergreens, deserve propagating both for their timber and the improving such kinds of plantations, but there is one species distinct from the others, which sheds its leaves in the autumn, called the Deciduous Cypress tree, which tree is worthy of propagation, both for the use of its timber, and for the improving plantations for pleasure. The Deciduous Cypress has been many years in the English gardens, though even yet it is not grown common, being to be found only in some few collections. It will grow to near sixty feet high, if stationed in a place suitable to its nature. It is very hardy in respect to cold, and a share of the moistest part of the plantation must be allotted it. In Virginia and several parts of America, where this tree is a native, it is a real aquatic, being found growing to a very large size in places wholly covered with water; and with us, if planted in watery places, by the edges of rivers, ponds, springs, &c. it will be more luxuriant, and will proportionally arise to a greater height and bulk than if planted in a dry soil. This tree in the summer has a little the resemblance of an evergreen, and the leaves have a pleasing effect, appearing in some respects like some sorts of the Acacias, and these are the chief inducements for its admission into the pleasure ground.

Description of the Deciduous Cypress tree

This sort is to be propagated by seeds and by cuttings. The seeds we receive from America; and if they are sown and managed as was directed for the Cypress in the former Book, certain success, if the seeds are good, will attend them.

Method of propagating this tree by seeds,

The other method of propagating this tree is by cuttings. These should be planted, in October, in a moist sandy soil. Many of them will grow, though I never could yet obtain a general crop; and they should be kept clean of weeds the summer following, as well as the summer after that. In the autumn, or any part of the winter, they should be planted out in the nursery; and, if they are to stand there a considerable time, they should be allowed a good distance; for they will grow, with proper care, when removed at a large size. If any part of the nursery ground is moister than the other, they must have a share of it. The ground should be constantly dug between

and by cuttings

tween the rows every winter, the weeds hoed down in summer, and, when planted out for good, these trees should have moist places, in consequence of what has been before observed

Titles of this species. This species of Cypress has the title, *Cupressus foliis distichis patentibus* Plukenet calls it, *Cupressus Virginiana, foliis acaciæ cornigeræ paribus & deciduis* Catesby names it simply, *Cupressus Americana*, and Commeline, *Cupressus Virginiana, foliis acaciæ deciduis* It grows naturally in Virginia, Carolina, and in many parts of America

Class and order in the Linnæan system. *Cupressus* is of the class and order *Monoecia Monadelphia*, and the characters are,

The characters. 1 Male flowers are disposed in an oval katkin

1 CALYX The common katkin is oval, and the flowers are placed thinly in it The scales are about twenty, roundish, peltated, opposite, and each contains one flower

2 COROLLA There is none

3 STAMINA There are no filaments, but four antheræ, which adhere to the bottom of the scales

II Female flowers are collected in a roundish cone

1 CALYX The common cone is roundish, and contains about eight or ten flowers The scales are opposite, oval, convex, and each contains one flower

2 COROLLA There is none

3 PISTILLUM The germen is hardly visible Under each calycinal scale there are numerous concave points, which serve for styles

4 PERICARPIUM There is none The round cone, containing the seeds, opens into roundish, angular, peltated scales

5 SEMINA The seed is a small, angular, sharp-pointed nut

# CHAP. XXIX

## *CYTISUS*, The TREFOIL-TREE

OUR gardens are enriched by the species of *Cytisus*, and additional pleasure added to the spectator by the beauty and variety they all afford Most of them are of a shrubby nature but as many are low growing kinds, and others tender, these shall be reserved for the flower-garden, selecting for our present purpose

Species.
1 Smooth Round-leaved *Cytisus*
2 Black *Cytisus*
3 Tartarian *Cytisus*
4 *Laburnum*

Description of the Smooth Round-leaved Cytisus. 1 Smooth Round-leaved *Cytisus* will grow to the height of about five or six feet The branches are numerous, erect, very brittle, and covered over with a smooth brown bark The leaves are small, and of a fine green They are nearly of an oval figure, and grow by threes on the twigs, on some branches they sit quite close, on others they grow on very short footstalks The flowers grow at the ends of the branches, in short spikes They are of a fine yellow, come out the beginning of June, and when in full blow the shrub will appear almost covered with them The seeds usually ripen in August

the Black, 2 Black *Cytisus* will arrive to about the height of the former, and naturally divides into many branches The bark is brown, and the young shoots are of a greenish red The leaves resemble trefoil They are smooth, and grow three together on brownish footstalks, the folioles are of an oblong oval figure, and their upper surface is of a dark-green, but they are paler underneath The flowers are produced in long, erect, close spikes, at the ends of the branches They are of a beautiful yellow colour, come out in July, and when in full blow make a fine appearance The seeds ripen in the autumn

and the Tartarian Cytisus. 3 Tartarian *Cytisus* The stalks are shrubby, branching, green, and grow to three or four feet high The leaves are oval, oblong, smooth, and of a whitish green colour The flowers come out in close heads from the ends of the branches, in May They are of a light-yellow colour, and have a cluster of leaves under them, they are sometimes succeeded by short woolly pods, containing the seeds

There is a variety of this species, with naked stalks, smaller leaves and flowers, rather earlier in the spring, usually called the *Siberian Cytisus* Variety

4 The *Laburnum* is a large-growing tree It will aspire to the height of near forty feet, and is one of the most noble trees our gardens afford It will form itself into a fine head, and the branches are smooth, of a pale green colour, and possessed of a few greyish spots The leaves stand by threes on long slender footstalks Each of these is oblong and entire, their upper surface is smooth, and of a shining green, but their under surface is more inclined to be downy The time of this tree's flowering is May, and the effect can hardly be conceived which it will have, when it appears covered with its long pendulent bunches of flowers, of a delightful yellow Each flower that helps to compose one sett is tolerably large of itself, and the common stalk to which they adhere by their own separate footstalks is often a foot or more in length, so that the appearance must be most noble, when it exhibits these long series of flowers hanging down from almost every part of the whole head Laburnum described

Thus useful is this tree for ornamenting plantations for pleasure But this is not all, the timber when felled is exceeding valuable It will arrive in bulk in proportion to its height, and the timber is both heavy and hard, and of a fine colour, inclined to yellow The very branches of this tree are so ponderous as to sink in water It polishes extremely well, and is so much like to green ebony, that it is called by the French *Ebony of the Alps*, where the tree grows naturally And as the timber is so valuable for many sorts of rich furniture, this should arouse the timber-planter's attention; for it will grow to be a timber tree of more than a yard in girt, in almost any poor and stony soil, where other trees will hardly grow, let the situation be Its valuable timber [illegible] what it will. And how enchantingly ornamental must large quarters or clumps of these trees appear, either by the borders of other woods, or in parks, and at the same time the expectation of the timber-crop [illegible]d.

*Other sorts of Laburnum.* There are some other sorts of *Laburnums*, of equal or more beauty than the preceding. One is called the [illegible] *Laburnum*, another the [illegible]. The leaves of these are larger, and the bunches of flowers longer, and the individual flowers [illegible] which the bunches are composed proportionally larger. There is also another sort, with smaller leaves and bunches longer than the common, which difference it always preserves from seeds, and this being planted among the common sort, will afford the greater variety.

*Method of propagating them from seeds.* One method of culture is common to all these sorts of *Cytisus*. It is to be performed both by seeds and cuttings. When by seeds, common garden-mould, well dug, and cleared of the roots of all weeds, will do for their reception. They should be sown in the spring, in beds made up, about half an inch deep, and in about six weeks the young plants will appear. Nothing more will be necessary, than keeping them clean from weeds during the summer, unless the weather proves very dry, if it does, a little watering sometimes will be proper. The spring following, the *Laburnums* should be planted out in the nursery, but the other sorts should stand in the seed-bed two years, to gain strength, before they are taken up. These should be planted a foot asunder, and two feet distant in the rows, but the *Laburnums* ought to have a much greater distance, especially if they are designed to be trained up for standards.

*or by cuttings.* Another method of encreasing these sorts is by cuttings. October is the best month for the work, and the cuttings may be planted either a foot [illegible], and two feet asunder in the rows, so that they need not be removed till they are taken up for good; or they may be set very thick, and those which have taken up the winter following, [illegible] planted out in the nursery way, at distances [illegible] proportion to the time they are to stand.

*Derivation of the name Cytisus.* This genus has the name *Cytisus* given it because it grew naturally in vast quantities on an island in the Archipelago, called *Cythnus*.

1. Smooth Round-leaved *Cytisus* is titled, *Cytisus racemis erectis, calycibus brevibus [illegible], foliis floralibus sessilibus*. Caspar Bauhine calls it, *Cytisus glaber, foliis subrotundis, pediculis brevissimis*; J. Bauhine, *Cytisus glaber, siliqua lata*. In the *Hortus Cliffortianus* it is termed, *Cytisus foliis [illegible] [illegible] [illegible]*. It grows naturally in France, Italy, and Spain.

2. Black *Cytisus* is titled, *Cytisus racemis simplicibus erectis, foliolis ovato oblongis*. Caspar Bauhine calls it, *Cytisus glaber nigricans*; Clusius, *Cytisus IV*. It grows naturally in Austria, Bohemia, Italy, and Spain.

3. Tartarian *Cytisus* is, *Cytisus floribus umbellatis terminalibus, calycibus [illegible]*. In Miller's Dictionary it is termed, *Cytisus floribus capitatis, foliolis ovato-oblongis, caule fruticoso*. Caspar Bauhine calls it, *Cytisus incanus, folio oblongo, Apulus*; and Clusius, *Cytisus V*. It grows naturally in Siberia, Austria, and Italy.

4. *Laburnum* is titled, *Cytisus racemis simplicibus pendulis, foliolis ovato-oblongis*. Caspar Bauhine calls it, *Anagyris non fœtida major Alpina*; J. Bauhine, *Laburnum [illegible] [illegible] anagyridi similis*. It grows naturally in Helvetia, Sabaudia, and most parts of Europe.

*Class and order in the Linnæan system.* *Cytisus* is of the class and order *Diadelphia Decandria*, and the characters are,

*The characters.*

1. Calyx is a very short, bell-shaped perianthium, obtuse at the base, and divided into two lips. The upper lip is bifid and sharp-pointed; the lower lip indented in three parts.
2. Corolla is papilionaceous.
   The vexillum is oval, rising, and reflexed on the side.
   The alæ are straight, obtuse, and the length of the vexillum.
   The carina is bellied and sharp-pointed.
3. Stamina are diadelphous and assurgent. Nine of them are joined together in a body, the other stands single, and their antheræ are simple.
4. Pistillum consists of an oblong germen, a simple rising style, and an obtuse stigma.
5. Pericarpium is an oblong, obtuse, rigid pod, narrow at the base.
6. Semina. The seeds are few, reniform, and compressed.

# CHAP. XXX.

## DAPHNE, MEZEREON.

THE species of *Daphne* are all low shrubs, and when proper situations are found for the different sorts, they afford a pleasing variety, and some of them are highly valuable on account of the fine fragrance they possess. The species for this place are,

*Species.*

1. *Mezereon*, or Spurge Olive.
2. Flax-leaved *Thymelæa*.
3. *Cneorum*, or Cluster-flowered Spear-leaved *Daphne*.
4. *Tarton Raire*, or Cluster-flowered Oval-leaved *Daphne*.
5. Alpine *Chamelæa*.
6. *Thymelæa*, or Milkwort-leaved *Daphne*.
7. Small Hairy Portugal *Daphne*.

*Description of Mezereon.*

1. *Mezereon*. Of this elegant plant there are four sorts: 1. The White, 2. The Pale-red, 3. The Crimson, and, 4. The Purple flowering; and they have each every perfection to recommend them as flowering-shrubs. In the first place, they are of low growth, seldom arising to more than three or four feet in height, and therefore are proper even for the smallest gardens. In the next place, they will be in bloom when few trees, especially of the shrubby tribe, present their honours. It will be in February, nay, sometimes in

in January, then will the twigs be garnished with flowers, all around, from one end to the other. Each twig has the appearance of a spike of flowers of the most consummate lustre; and as the leaves are not yet out, whether you behold this tree near, or at a distance, it has a most enchanting appearance. But this is not all; the sense of smelling is peculiarly regaled by the flowers, their spicey sweetness is diffused around, and the air is perfumed with their odours to a considerable distance. Many flowers, deemed sweet, are not liked by all; but the agreeable inoffensive sweetness of the *Mezereon* has ever delighted the sense of smelling, whilst the lustre of its blow has feasted the eye. Neither is this the only pleasure the tree bestows; for besides the beauty of the leaves, which come out after the flowers are fallen, and which are of a pleasant green colour and an oblong figure, it will be full of red berries in June, which will continue glowing till the autumn. Of these berries the birds are very fond; so that whoever is delighted with those songsters, should have a quantity of them planted all over the outsides of his wilderness quarters.

No particular place should be assigned these shrubs; they ought to be in every place, and in great plenty, amongst those of their own growth; particularly, if rows of them were planted near frequented walks on each side, the circumambient air would be perfumed, to the delight of all. The leaves are said to be a strong cathartic.

Method of raising this species. Before I proceed to another species, I shall shew the culture of this sort. It ripens its seeds with us, and may at any time be easily obtained, if these are secured from birds. Previous, therefore, to sowing, the healthiest and most thriving trees, of the White, the Pale, and the Deep red sorts, should be marked out; and as soon as the berries begin to alter from green, they must be covered with nets, to secure them from the birds, which would otherwise devour them all. The berries will be ripe in July; and due observance must be had to pick them up as they fall from the trees, and to keep the sorts separate. As soon as they are all fallen, or you have enough for your purpose, they may be then sown. The best soil for these plants is a good fat black earth, such as is found in kitchen gardens that have been well manured and managed for many years. In such soil as this they will not only come up better, but will grow to a greater height than in any other. No particular regard need be paid to the situation; for as this tree is a native of the northern parts of Europe, it will grow in a north border, and flourish there as well as in a south; nay, if there be any difference, the north border is more eligible than the south. The ground being made fine, and cleared of roots of all sorts, the seeds should be sown, hardly half an inch deep. The mould being riddled over them that depth, let the beds be neated up, and they will want no other attention until the spring. I have sometimes had these seeds remain in the ground two years; but for the most part they come up the spring after sowing, and the seedlings will require no other care during the summer than weeding, and gentle watering in dry weather. After they have been in the seed-bed one year, the strongest may be drawn out, and planted in the nursery, to make room for the others; though if they do not come up very close, it would be as well to let them remain in the seed-bed until the second autumn, when they should be taken up with care, and planted in beds at a foot asunder each way. This will be distance enough for these low-growing shrubs. October is the best month for planting them out for good; for although they will grow if removed any time between then and spring, yet that will certainly be a more proper season than when they are in full blow.

Such is the culture of this sweet shrub. The other species of this genus require a different management.

Description of the Flax-leaved Thymelæa. 2. Flax-leaved *Thymelæa* seldom grows higher than three feet. The branches are very slender, and ornamented with narrow, spear-shaped, pointed leaves, much like those of the common flax. The flowers are produced in panicles at the ends of the branches. They are small, come out in June, but are rarely succeeded by seeds in England.

Cneorum. 3. *Cneorum*, or Cluster-flowered Spear-leaved *Daphne*. This rises with a shrubby, branching stalk, to about a foot or a foot and a half high. The leaves are narrow, spear-shaped, and grow irregularly on the branches. The flowers are produced in clusters at the ends of the little twigs. They make their appearance in March, are of a purple colour, and possessed of a fragrance little inferior to that of the *Mezereon*; but they are seldom succeeded by seeds in England.

Tarton Raira. 4. *Tarton-raira*, or Cluster-flowering Oval-leaved *Daphne*. This rises with a woody stalk to the height of about two feet. The branches are numerous, irregular, tough, and covered with a light-brown-coloured bark. The leaves are oval, very small, soft to the touch, and shining. The flowers are produced in clusters from the sides of the stalks. They are white, come out in June, and are succeeded by roundish berries, which seldom ripen in England. This sort should have a dry soil and a warm situation.

Alpine Chamælea. 5. The Alpine *Chamælea* will grow to the height of about a yard. The leaves are spear-shaped, obtuse, and hoary underneath. The flowers come out in clusters from the sides of the branches, and are very fragrant. They appear in March, and are succeeded by red berries, that ripen in September.

Milkwort leaved Daphne. 6. *Thymelæa*, or Milkwort-leaved *Daphne*, will grow to the height of about a yard. The stalks of this species are upright, branched, and covered with a light-brown bark. The leaves are spear-shaped, smooth, and in some respect resemble those of milkwort. The flowers are produced in clusters from the sides of the stalks. They are of a greenish colour, have no footstalks, appear in March, and are succeeded by small yellowish berries, which will be ripe in August. This sort requires a dry soil and a warm situation.

Small Hairy Portugal Daphne. 7. Small Hairy Portugal *Daphne*. The stalks are ligneous, about two feet high, and send forth branches alternately from the sides. The leaves are spear-shaped, plane, hairy on both sides, and grow on very short footstalks. The flowers have very narrow tubes, are small, and make no great show. They come out in June, and are not succeeded by ripe seeds in England.

This shrub, in some situations, retains its leaves all winter in such beauty, as to cause it to be ranked among the low-growing evergreens; but as in others it is sometimes shattered with the first black winds, it is left to the Gardener whether to place this shrub among the Deciduous trees or Evergreens.

Situations proper for the sorts. The *Cneorum* and the Alpine *Chamælea* are very hardy, and will grow in the coldest situation; but the other sorts should have a warm soil and a well-sheltered site, or they will be subject to be destroyed in bad weather.

Method of propagating them. All these sorts are with some difficulty propagated and retained. They will by no means bear removing, even when seedlings; and if ever this [illegible], not one in an hundred must be expected to grow. Only are raised by seeds, which we receive from the places where they grow naturally; and he who is desirous of having these plants, must manage them in the following manner:

Let a compost be prepared of these equal divisions, one fourth part of [illegible] both, one fourth part of [illegible], another of [illegible], some large, others smaller, and the other part of maiden earth, from a rich pasture. Let these be mixed all together, and [illegible] large pots. In each of these pots put a seed or two, about half an inch deep, in [illegible] of the mould. We receive the seeds in the spring, so that there is little hopes of their coming up until the spring following. Let, therefore, the pots be set in the shade all the summer, and in the autumn removed into a warm situation, where they may enjoy every minute of the sun's rays all winter. In March let them be plunged into a moderate hot-bed, and the plants will soon after appear. This bed will cause them to be stronger plants by the autumn; and when all danger of frost is over, they may be uncovered wholly, and permitted to enjoy the open air. In the autumn, they should be removed into the greenhouse, or [illegible] an hot-bed-frame all winter, and in spring, they should be placed where they are to remain, moulding them up the height of the pot, the pots also being sufficiently broken to make way for their roots, as they shoot, and then left to Nature.——The situation of the four tenderer sorts must be well sheltered, and if it be naturally rocky, sandy, and dry, it will be the better; for in the places where they grow naturally, they strike into the crevices of rocks, and [illegible] where there is hardly any appearance of soil.

This second method of obtaining these shrubs [illegible], by sowing the seeds in the places where they are to remain. The situation [illegible] the bove-[illegible] mould should be [illegible] seed or two sown [illegible] should be stuck down [illegible] to the place where they [illegible]. The [illegible] care must be observed, [illegible] to pull up the weeds as often as they appear, for if they are permitted to get [illegible] root they will pull up [illegible]. In the spring following, [illegible] the plants will appear [illegible] the [illegible], they should be watered in [illegible], and, for the first winter or two, should have some furze bushes pricked all round them, at a proper distance, which will break the [illegible] of the frosty winds, and preserve the [illegible] plants until they are strong enough to defend themselves.

1. [illegible] Spurge Olive, is titled, *Daphne* [illegible] *foliis lanceolatis* [illegible]. In the [illegible] it is termed, [illegible]. Caspar Bauhine calls it, *Laureola folio* [illegible] *Laureola femina*, [illegible], *Daphnoides*, Gerard, *Chamælea* [illegible], and Tournefort, *Thymelæa* [illegible] *Laureolæ femina*. It grows common in England, and in most of the northern parts of Europe.

2. Flax-leaved *Thymelæa* is, *Daphne panicula terminali, foliis linear-lanceolatis acuminatis*. Sauvage calls it, *Daphne foliis lineari-lanceolatis basi angustioribus, racemo* [illegible] *terminali*; Clusius *Thymelæa*, Caspar Bauhine, *Thymelæa foliis lini*, and Gerard, *Daphne floribus racemosis, foliis linear-lanceolatis acuminatis* [illegible]. It grows common in many parts of Italy, Spain, and about Montpelier in France.

3. *Cneorum*, or the Cluster-flowering Spear-leaved *Daphne*, is, *Daphne floribus congestis terminalibus sessilibus, foliis lanceolatis nudis*. This Caspar Bauhine calls, *Thymelæa affinis facie externa*. Matthiolus and Clusius call it *Cneorum*, and Sauvage, *Daphne humifusa, foliis oblongis, flores sessiles* [illegible] *subcingentibus*. It grows naturally in Switzerland, Hungary, upon the Alps and Pyrenean Mountains.

4. *Tartonraira*, or Cluster-flowering Oval-leaved *Daphne*, is, *Daphne floribus sessilibus aggregatis axillaribus, foliis ovatis utrinque pubescentibus nervosis*. Caspar Bauhine calls it, *Thymelæa foliis candicantibus serici instar mollibus*, and Lobel, *Tartonraire Gallo-provincia Monspeliensium*. It grows naturally in many parts of France and Italy.

5. The Alpine *Chamælea* is, *Daphne floribus sessilibus aggregatis lateralibus, foliis lanceolatis obtusis subtus tomentosis*. Gesner calls it, *Daphne* [illegible], *foliis* [illegible]. Tournefort, *Thymelæa* [illegible] *folio, pediculis* [illegible]; Caspar Bauhine, *Chamælea Alpina, folio* [illegible]; Haller, *Thymelæa floribus* [illegible], *folio* [illegible]; Lobel, *Chamælea Alpina* [illegible]; Ray, *Chamælea* [illegible], *folio utrinque* [illegible], *flore albo*; and Plukenet, *Thymelæa* [illegible] *folio & flore*, [illegible]. It grows naturally on the Alps of Switzerland, in Geneva, Italy, and Austria.

6. *Thymelæa*, or Milk-wort-leaved *Daphne* is, *Daphne floribus* [illegible], *foliis* [illegible], *caulibus* [illegible]. J. Bauhine calls it, [illegible]; Caspar Bauhine, *Thymelæa foliis polygalæ glabris*; Sauvage, *Daphne floribus* [illegible] *simplicissimos*; and Plukenet, *Thymelæa* [illegible], *pediculis* [illegible] *foliorum ortum* [illegible]. It grows naturally in Spain and the south of France.

7. Small Hairy Portugal *Daphne* is, *Daphne foliis sessilibus* [illegible], *foliis lanceolatis* [illegible]. Tournefort calls it, *Thymelæa* [illegible] *Lusitanica, polygoni folio*. It grows naturally in Portugal and Spain.

This genus is of the class and order *Octandria Monogynia*; and the characters are, | Class and order in the Linnæan System.

1. CALYX. There is none.
2. COROLLA consists of one funnel-shaped petal, the tube of which is cylindric, imperforated, and longer than the limb. The limb is divided into four oval, acute, plane, patent segments.
3. STAMINA are eight short filaments, inserted in the tube, being alternately lower, and having roundish, erect, and bilocular antheræ.
4. PISTILLUM consists of an oval germen, a very short style, and a depressed, plane, capitated stigma.
5. PERICARPIUM is a roundish berry, of one cell.
6. SEMEN is single, roundish, and fleshy.

CHAP.

# C H A P. XXXI.

## *DIOSPYROS*, The DATE-PLUM.

TWO ſpecies of tolerable growth belong to this genus:

Species.

1. The Indian Date-Plum.
2. The Piſhamin Plum.

Deſcription of the Indian Date-Plum,

1. The Indian Date-Plum will arrive at the height of more than twenty feet, and is an excellent tree for ſhade. It riſes with an upright ſtem, and the young branches are covered with a ſmooth whitiſh bark. The youngeſt twigs ſtand alternately on thoſe of the preceding year, and the buds for the next year's ſhoot begin to ſwell ſoon after the fall of the leaf. The leaves are of two colours; their upper ſurface is of a delightful green, and their lower of a whitiſh caſt. They are of an oblong figure, end in a point, and are in length about four inches and a half, and near two inches broad. They are placed alternately on the branches, and ſeveral ſtrong veins run alternately from the mid-rib to the borders, which are entire. Theſe leaves will be of a deep green, even when they fall off in the autumn. The flowers are hermaphrodites and males on different plants, and have little beauty to recommend them. They are pitcher-ſhaped, and grow ſingly on very ſhort footſtalks, on the ſides of the branches. They are of a reddiſh colour, and are ſucceeded by largiſh black berries, which are eatable, like the medlar, when in a ſtate of decay.

and the Piſhamin Plum.

2. The Piſhamin Plum will not aſpire to the height of the former ſpecies, tho' it will ſometimes grow to be near twenty feet. The branches of this tree are whitiſh, ſmooth, and produced in an irregular manner. The leaves are very large and beautiful, about five or ſix inches long, and three broad. Their upper ſurface is ſmooth, and both ſides are of a beautiful green. They are of an oblong figure, end in a point, grow irregularly on the branches, and ſeveral veins run irregularly from the mid-rib to the borders, which are entire. They fall off in the autumn, at the coming on of the firſt froſts, when their colour will be that of a purpliſh red. The flowers, like thoſe of the other ſort, have no great appearance, but are ſucceeded by a fruit, which is eatable, when, like medlars, it is in a ſtate of decay.

Method of propagating this tree.

Both theſe ſorts are propagated from the ſeeds, which we receive from abroad, in the ſpring. The compoſt proper for their reception is maiden earth, from a rich paſture, dug up ſward and all a year before, which has been three or four times turned to rot the ſward. This being made fine, a fourth part of drift or ſea-ſand ſhould be added, and being all well mixed, the ſeeds ſhould be ſown in pots or boxes, three quarters of an inch deep. The pots ſhould afterwards be placed in a ſhady place during the ſummer, for the ſeeds rarely come up until the ſecond ſpring, and in the autumn they ſhould be removed into a well ſheltered place, where they may enjoy the benefit of the ſun all winter. In the ſpring the plants will come up; and if they are aſſiſted by plunging the pots into a moderate hotbed, it will make them ſhoot ſtronger, though this is not abſolutely neceſſary. All the ſummer they ſhould ſtand in a ſhady place, where they may have free air; and, if the weather proves dry, they ſhould be watered every other evening. At the approach of winter, they ſhould be removed into the greenhouſe, or placed under an hotbed-frame, or ſome ſhelter, and, when all danger of froſt is over, they muſt be put in the ſame ſhady ſituation as in the former ſummer. In the winter alſo they ſhould be hooped as before, and in ſpring may be planted in the nurſery ground. Their plants, when they get tolerably ſtrong, are very hardy; though even then the ends of the branches are ſubject to be killed; ſo that when they are ſeedlings, or very young, they will be in danger of being deſtroyed by the froſts, which makes the above directed care and protection neceſſary till they have gained ſtrength.

Titles.

1. The Indian Date-Plum is entitled, *Dioſpyros foliorum paginis diſcoloribus*. Van Royen calls it, *Dioſpyros foliis utrinque bicoloribus*. Caſpar Bauhine, *Lotus Africana latifolia*; alſo, *Lotus Africana anguſtifolia ſive femina*. Cammerarius, *Pſeudo Lotus*; alſo, *Lotus Africana altera*. In the *Hortus Cliffortianus* it is termed, *Dioſpyros foliis utrinque diverſi coloribus*. It grows naturally in Africa, Italy, and the ſouth of France.

2. The Piſhamin-Plum is entitled *Dioſpyros foliorum paginis concoloribus*. In the *Hortus Cliffortianus* it is termed, *Dioſpyros foliis utrinque concoloribus*. Plukenet calls it, *Guajacana loti arboris effigie Virginiana Piſhamin dicta*; Cateſby, *Guajacana*; Caſpar Bauhine, *Lotus Africana ſive Indica*; Boerhaave, *Guajacana anguſtiore folio Piſhamin dicta*; and Gronovius, *Dioſpyros floribus dioicis*. It grows naturally in Carolina, Virginia, and in many parts of North-America.

Claſs and order in the Linnæan ſyſtem.

*Dioſpyros* is of the claſs and order *Polygamia Dioecia*, it having hermaphrodite and female flowers on the ſame plant, and male flowers on others. In the hermaphrodites,

The characters.

1. CALYX is a large, monophyllous, permanent, obtuſe perianthium, divided into four parts.
2. COROLLA is one large, pitcher-ſhaped petal, divided into four acute ſpreading ſegments.
3. STAMINA are eight very ſhort, ſetaceous filaments, that are ſlightly joined to the receptacle, having oblong antheræ, which are deſtitute of farina.
4. PISTILLUM is a roundiſh germen, a ſingle quadrifid, permanent ſtyle longer than the ſtamina, and an obtuſe bifid ſtigma.
5. PERICARPIUM is a large globular berry, of eight cells, placed on the large patent calyx.
6. SEMINA. The ſeeds are ſingle, roundiſh, compreſſed, and very hard.

In the male flowers on the diſtinct plants,

1. CALYX is a ſmall, erect, acute, monophyllous perianthium, divided into four parts.
2. COROLLA is one pitcher-ſhaped coriaceous, tetragonous petal, cut into four roundiſh, revolute ſegments.
3. STAMINA are eight ſhort filaments, inſerted in the receptacle, having long, acute, twin antheræ.

## CHAP. XXXII.

## *ELÆAGNUS*, The WILD-OLIVE.

WE are now come to a tree that affords as great a variety in ornamental plantations as any I know. The leaves of most trees are possessed of a verdure, and occasion variety by the difference of greens they exhibit, as well as their figure, during the summer, but the leaves of the plant under consideration are white, especially the under side, and stand upon white twigs, so that the tree by these exhibiting its silvery head, causes at once astonishment and pleasure. *Its appearance described.*

It will grow to be near twenty feet high, and the branches are smooth, and of a brown colour. The preceding year's shoots are white and downy, and the silvery leaves are placed irregularly on them. These are of a spear-shaped figure, about two, and sometimes three inches long, and three quarters of an inch broad, and are as soft as satin to the touch. Neither is summer the only time the leaves afford us pleasure. They continue on the tree great part of the winter, so that the effect they cause, when other trees are despoiled of their honours, may be easily conceived. The flowers appear in July, but make no figure. They are small, and come out at the footstalks of the leaves, their colour is white, and they are possessed of a strong scent. The fruit that succeeds them much resembles a small olive.

*Variety.* This shrub has a variety, with yellow flowers.

*Method of propagating this tree.* The culture of both varieties is very easy. They are propagated by cuttings, which must be of the last summer's shoot. But in order to have them proper for the purpose, a sufficient number of trees must be fixed on, from which the family is to be encreased. They must be headed near the ground in the winter, which will cause them to make strong shoots the succeeding summer, and these shoots afford the cuttings. They should be taken off in the autumn and cut into lengths of about a foot each, three parts of which should be set in the ground. They may be planted very close, and in the autumn following removed into the nursery, where they should be set a foot asunder, and at two feet distant in the rows, or, if there be ground enough, they may be planted thinner, and so will want no removing until they are set out for good. The best soil for these cuttings is a rich garden mould, inclined to be moist, and in a shady place, and in such a soil and situation almost every cutting will grow. The tree itself is exceeding hardy, and will afterwards shoot vigorously, in almost any soil or station.

The word *Elæagnus* is formed of the Greek ἐλαία, *an olive*, and ἁγνὸς, *a tree*, *the chaste tree*, the leaves resembling those of that tree, and the fruit that of the olive. *Derivation of the generical name.*

The title of the Wild-Olive is, *Elæagnus foliis lanceolatis*. In the *Hortus Cliffortianus* it is termed simply, *Elæagnus*. Caspar Bauhine calls it, *Olea sylvestris, folio molli incano*. It grows naturally in Bohemia, Spain, Syria, and Cappadocia. *Titles of this tree.*

*Elæagnus* is of the class and order *Tetrandria Monogynia*, and the characters of the flowers and fructification are, *Class and order in the Linnæan system.*

*The characters.* 1. CALYX is a monophyllous, bell-shaped, deciduous perianthium, rough on the outside, coloured within, and divided at the top into four segments.

2. COROLLA. There is none.

3. STAMINA are four very short filaments, that are inserted below the divisions of the calyx, having oblong incumbent antheræ.

4. PISTILLUM consists of a roundish germen, situated below the receptacle, of a simple style, a little shorter than the calyx, and a simple stigma.

5. PERICARPIUM is a smooth, oval, obtuse drupe, having a puncture at the top.

6. SEMEN is an oblong, obtuse nut.

## CHAP. XXXIII.

## *EVONYMUS*, The SPINDLE-TREE.

NO good collection should be without all the sorts of Spindle-trees, not on account of the figure their flowers exhibit, which is indifferent, but on account of the beauty of their leaves and natural growth, and more particularly the extraordinary beauty and singular appearance of their fruit, in the autumn, and good part of the winter.

There is only one real deciduous species of the Spindle-tree, but the principal varieties of it are,

*Varieties of this species.* Deep Red berried Narrow-leaved Spindle-tree.
Pale Red berried Spindle-tree.
White-berried Narrow-leaved Spindle-tree.
Broad-leaved Spindle-tree.
Variegated Spindle-tree.

The Narrow-leaved Spindle-tree will grow to be sixteen or eighteen feet high, will aspire to an upright stem of this height, and will naturally form itself into a regular head. The bark of the stem is of a dark brown, but those of the first and second years shoots are smooth, and of *described.*

of a fine green, the white-berried ſort eſpecially, which differs from the red-berried in this reſpect, as the ſhoots of that are browner. The leaves are ſpear-ſhaped, of a fine deep green colour, about three inches long and an inch and a half broad, moſt ſlightly ſerrated, and placed nearly oppoſite on the branches. The flowers have little beauty to recommend them. They are ſmall, and of a greeniſh colour, produced in ſmall bunches from the ſides of the branches, the latter end of May, the bunches hanging on long footſtalks, and are ſucceeded by fruit, which conſtitutes the greateſt beauty of theſe plants. The ſeeds are of a delightful ſcarlet; four are contained in each veſſel, and theſe opening, expoſe them to view all over the head of the plant, ſome juſt peeping out of their cells, others quite out, and ſticking to the edge, and theſe veſſels being in bunches on long pendulent footſtalks, have a look which is ſingularly beautiful. The ſeed-veſſels of the firſt-mentioned ſort are of the ſame deep ſcarlet with the ſeeds, thoſe of the ſecond, of a paler red, thoſe of the third are white, which, together with the twigs of the latter being of a lighter green, conſtitute the only difference between theſe ſorts, for the ſeeds themſelves of all the ſorts are of a deep ſcarlet.

The Broad-leaved Spindle-tree is a variety of the Common Spindle-tree, though it will grow to a greater height than either of the other ſorts. It will arrive at near five and twenty feet high, and the branches are fewer, and the leaves broader. The young ſhoots are ſmooth, and of a purpliſh colour, and the buds at the ends of them, by the end of October, will begin to be ſwelled, and be near an inch long, preparing for the next year's ſhoot. The leaves are much larger than thoſe of the other ſorts, being, on a thriving plant, near five inches long and two broad. Their figure is like the other, though rather inclined to an oblong oval. Some are moſt ſlightly ſerrated, of a light green, ſtand oppoſite by pairs, and fall off much ſooner in the autumn, before which their colour will be red. The flowers make an inconſiderable figure, though they are rather larger than the other ſorts. The ſeeds that ſucceed them with their veſſels alſo are proportionably larger, and many of the common footſtalks to each bunch will be four inches, which cauſes a more noble look in the autumn; though the others are equally pleaſing, as the flowers are produced on the Narrow-leaved ſorts in greater plenty. Add to this, the berries of the Broad will fall off long before the others.

There is but one good method of propagating the Spindle-tree, and that is by ſeeds, though it may eaſily be done by layers or cuttings, for if the young ſhoots be laid in the ground in the autumn, they will have ſtruck root by the autumn following, and if cuttings are planted in the autumn in a moiſt rich earth, that is ſhaded, many of them will grow, but neither of theſe methods will produce ſuch fine upright plants, or that will grow to ſuch a height as thoſe raiſed from ſeeds, though they will be every whit as prolific of flowers and fruit. Whoever has not the convenience of procuring the ſeeds, let him improve theſe hints, if he has got a plant or two, which will be ſufficient for his purpoſe. Whoever can get the ſeeds, had better never attempt thoſe arts.

Method of propagating this tree by ſeeds,

The ſeeds ſhould be ſown in the autumn, ſoon after they are ripe. They will thrive in almoſt any ſoil or ſituation, if it be made fine and clear of the roots of all weeds, &c though if it be a fine garden-mould, it will be the better. They ſhould be ſown three-fourths of an inch deep. It ſeldom happens that more than a few odd plants come up the firſt ſpring, the beds muſt, therefore, remain untouched until the ſpring twelvemonth after ſowing, only conſtant weeding muſt be obſerved. At that time the plants will come up very thick, and all the ſummer they muſt be weeded. In this ſeed-bed they may ſtand two years, and be then planted out in the nurſery, where they may remain, with no other care than weeding and digging between the rows in winter, until they are planted out for good.

and by budding

The Broad-leaved ſort will take very well by budding it on the Common. The ſtocks for this purpoſe ſhould be planted out when they are one year's ſeedlings, and by the ſummer twelvemonth after they will be fit for working, ſo that whoever has young plants of the Common ſort, and only one of the other, may encreaſe his number this way.

Valuable properties of the timber of this plant

The wood of theſe trees is very valuable, eſpecially the Common ſort. It is very white, and makes excellent jacks for harpſichords. Muſical inſtrument-makers alſo uſe it in many other things. Tooth-pickers made of this wood are ſaid not to damage the teeth. It makes likewiſe good ſcewers, and the beſt ſpindles in the world, which occaſions its taking the denomination, Spindle-tree. *Evonymus* is ſaid to be hurtful to animals, and is ſo called by Antiphraſis, of ευ, which ſignifies *good*, and ὄνομα, *a name*.

Derivation of the generical name

The Broad-leaved Spindle-tree will not continue in the kind, when raiſed from ſeeds, as has been aſſerted. Miller ſays, he has raiſed many of theſe ſhrubs from ſeeds, and has never found them alter to the Common ſort. I am almoſt induced to queſtion his veracity, at leaſt, he has been very lucky in his experiment, for I have raiſed thouſands of them for ſale (there being hardly any ſhrub more called for), and ever found the ſeeds of the Broad-leaved Spindle-tree to come up the Common Narrow-leaved ſorts, which I was very punctual about at firſt, becauſe if they could be raiſed from ſeeds, it would ſave much trouble in budding, grafting, and planting cuttings, the only methods by which the Broad-leaved ſort is to be continued and encreaſed.

Titles

This ſpecies is titled, *Evonymus floribus pleriſque quadrifidis*. J Bauhine calls it, *Evonymus vulgaris, granis rubentibus*, alſo, *Evonymus latifolius*. Cluſius holds the Narrow and Broad-leaved ſorts as diſtinct ſpecies, and calls one, *Evonymus* I *ſ latifolia*, the other, *Evonymus* 2. In the *Hortus Cliffortianus* it is termed, *Evonymus foliis oblongo ovatis*. Gerard calls it, *Evonymus Theophraſti*, and Parkinſon, *Evonymus vulgaris*. It grows naturally in hedges and woods in England, and moſt parts of Europe.

Claſs and order in the Linnæan ſyſtem

*Evonymus* is of the claſs and order *Pentandria Monogynia*, and the characters are,

The characters

1 CALYX is a plane, monophyllous perianthium, divided into five roundiſh, concave ſegments.

2 COROLLA conſiſts of five oval, plane, patent petals, that are longer than the calyx.

3 STAMINA are five awl-ſhaped, erect filaments, ſhorter than the corolla, joined to the germen, having didymous antheræ.

4 PISTILLUM conſiſts of an acuminated germen, of a ſhort ſimple ſtyle, and an obtuſe ſtigma.

5 PERICARPIUM is a ſucculent, five-cornered, coloured capſule, containing five cells.

6 SEMINA. The ſeeds are ſingle, oval, and of a deep ſcarlet colour.

# CHAP XXXIV

## *FAGUS*, The BEECH and SPANISH CHESNUT-TREE.

Species

THERE are only three species of this genus

1 The Beech-tree

2 The Spanish Chesnut

3 The Dwarf Chesnut, or Chinquepin

The Black Chesnut-tree and the Beech-tree have been fully treated of in the former part of this Work among the forest trees, where the curious planter may see the method of raising them, as well as in what manner these trees should be placed in plantations of the largest size All that remains to be mentioned in this Chapter is, to recommend the Striped-leaved Spanish Chesnut to those who are fond of variegated trees, and to describe the species of *Fagus* called the Dwarf Chesnut, or Chinquepin

Description of the Dwarf Chesnut

The Dwarf Chesnut grows to about eight or ten feet high The stem is of a brown colour, and divides into several branches near the top The leaves are of an oval, spear-shaped figure, acutely serrated, with a hoary cast on their under side The flowers come out in the spring, in slender knotted katkins They are of a greenish yellow colour, and are very seldom succeeded by ripe seeds in England This tree is very hardy, and thrives best in a moist soil and shady situation

Method of propagating

The method of raising the Dwarf Chesnut is from seeds, which we receive from America These should be planted in drills, as soon as they arrive, of rich garden-mould, in a moistish bed If the seeds are good, they will come up pretty soon in the spring After they appear, they will require no trouble, except keeping them clean from weeds, and watering them in dry weather They may stand in the seed-bed two years, and be afterwards planted in the nursery-ground, at a foot asunder and two feet distance in the rows, and here when they are got strong plants, they will be fit for any purpose

The variegated Chesnut is multiplied by budding, grafting, or inarching it in stocks of its own kind

Titles of this genus

1 The Beech-tree is titled, *Fagus foliis ovatis obsolete serratis* Caspar Bauhine and others call it simply, *Fagus* It grows naturally in England, and most parts of Europe, also in Canada

2 The Chesnut tree is, *Fagus foliis lanceolatis acuminato-serratis subtus nudis* Cammerarius calls it, *Castanea*, Caspar Bauhine, *Castanea sylvestris*, also, *Castanea sativa* It grows naturally on the mountainous parts of the south of Europe

3 Dwarf Chesnut is, *Fagus foliis lanceolato-ovatis acute serratis subtus tomentosis, amentis filiformibus nodosis* Van Royen calls it, *Fagus foliis ovato lanceolatis serratis*, and Plukenet, *Castanea pumila Virginiana, racemoso fructu parvo in singulis capsulis echinatis unico*, also, *Castanea Americana, foliis aversa parte argentea lanugine villosis* It grows naturally in North America

Class and order in the Linnæan system The characters

*Fagus* is of the class and order *Monoecia Polyandria*, and the characters are,

I Male Flowers

1 CALYX is a monophyllous, awl-shaped perianthium, divided into five segments

2 COROLLA There is none

3 STAMINA There are about a dozen setaceous filaments, of the length of the calyx, having oblong antheræ

II Female flowers

1 CALYX is a monophyllous, acute, erect perianthium, indented in four parts

2 COROLLA There is none

3 PISTILLUM consists of a germen situated within the cup, and of three subulated styles, with simple reflexed stigmas

4 PERICARPIUM is a large, roundish capsule, (formed of what was the calyx) armed with soft spines

5 SEMINA The seeds are two

It may be proper to observe, that the male flowers of the Beech-tree are digested into a globular form, whereas those of the Chesnut form a cylindric amentum, and the male flowers of the Chinquepin are a still more slender and knotted katkin The figure of the fruit, also, of the Beech and Chesnut-tree are very different, the latter being a roundish nut, whereas the former is three sided, irregular, and pointed

# CHAP XXXV

## *FRAXINUS*, The ASH-TREE

Species of this tree

THERE are only three real species of this genus, viz

1 The Common Ash

2 Flowering Ash

3 American Ash

Common Ash

1 The Common Ash, though propagated as a timber-tree, should, nevertheless, have a share in our largest quarters in the plantations under consideration, for although these trees exhibit no blow of flowers worthy the notice of any person but a botanist, yet their large compound leaves make a noble figure in summer, and their upright stems, with the grey colour of the bark, have a noble and pleasing effect in winter

Of

Varieties of this species

Of this species there are three varieties, which are much coveted by those who are fond of variegated plants, viz The Silver-striped, the Gold striped, and the Yellow coloured Ash The colours of these trees are good, and make a beautiful appearance among those of the larger-growing variegated kinds

Flowering Ash

Varieties described

2 Flowering Ash The varieties of this species are, the Virginian Flowering Ash, and the Dwarf Ash of Theophrastus

Virginian Flowering Ash, when in blow, is inferior in beauty to few of our flowering trees It will grow to near thirty feet in height The branches of this sort, in the winter, have nearly the same appearance with the Common, only they are, especially the youngest, more inclined to a black cast The buds also which will begin to swell in the autumn, are of that hue The branches will not burn, when green, so well as those of the Common Ash The leaves are of a fine green, smooth, serrated, and consist of about three or four pair of folioles, placed a good way asunder along the mid rib, and they are usually terminated by an odd one The mid rib is long, but not straight is jointed, and swelling where the leaves, which fall off early in the autumn, come out The flowers are white, and produced in May, in large bunches, at the ends of the branches I have had this tree, the second year from the bud, produce, on the leading-shoot, a tuft of flowers, and although this is not common, yet, when it gets to be about ten feet high, almost every twig will be terminated with them The flowers exhibit themselves not in a gaudy dress, but in a loose easy manner, all over the tree, which, together with the green leaves peeping from amongst this white bloom, makes the appearance extremely pleasing I have never yet known the flowers to be succeeded by seeds

Dwarf Ash of Theophrastus is, as the name imports, a low tree for the Ash tribe, about fourteen or fifteen feet is the height it generally aspires to The branches are smooth, and of a darkish green The leaves also are pinnated, of a dark-green, and serrated on the edges, but proportionably smaller than those of the Common Ash The flowers of this sort make no show, though they are possessed of petals necessary to complete a flower, which are denied the Common Ash

American Ash. Varieties described

3 American Ash The varieties of this species are, Manna Ash, White Ash, Red Ash, Black Ash, and New-discovered Ash

Manna Ash will grow to about twenty feet high I have had it shoot eight feet the first year from the bud, though I never knew it shoot more than two feet in a summer afterwards The bark of the young shoots is smooth, of a brownish green, and has a few greyish spots The leaves are composed of four or five pair of folioles, placed on a straight mid-rib, which are of a fine pleasant green, and more acutely and deeply serrated than any of the other sorts The flowers make no show They are partly the colour of the Common Ash, and are produced, like them, early in the spring, before the leaves appear From the leaves of this tree the Manna of the shops is collected

White Ash is so called from the whitish colour of the young branches in winter They are spotted all over with many white spots, which makes their colour that of a lightish grey This sort will arrive to about thirty feet high, and the branches are strong, and produced in an irregular manner The folioles which compose the leaves are of a light green, and obtusely sawed on the edges They seldom consist of more than three pair, with the usual odd one, which has a long point, and these are placed far asunder, on the mid rib These leaves fall off early in the autumn, when they are of a whitish colour This, together with the grey branches, makes the tree have a whitish look The flowers are produced in the spring, and make no show This sort is commonly called the New England Ash

Red Ash The Red Ash is a stronger shooting tree than any of the former, the Common Ash excepted The branches, which are fewer, are smooth, and the young shoots are of a reddish colour in the autumn The leaves of this sort make the most noble figure of any of the others; for although they are seldom composed of more than three pair of folioles, besides the odd one, yet these are exceeding large, especially the odd one, which will be sometimes six inches long, and three and an half broad The pair next it, also, will be fine and large, though they diminish in size as they get nearer the base of the footstalk These folioles are distinctly sawed on their edges, are of a fine light-green during the summer, and in the autumn die to a red colour, from which circumstance, together with that of their red twigs, this sort takes the denomination of the Red Ash It has its seeds very broad, and is commonly called the Carolina Ash

Black Ash we receive from abroad by that name, though it is difficult to see the propriety of its being so called The colour of the shoots is nearly like that of the White Ash, but they shoot stronger, and promise to form a larger tree. The leaves are large, and ribbed underneath, of a very dark green, and die to a still darker in the autumn The folioles are not so large as those of the Red sort, but they quit the tree about the same time The keys are very broad, and, when we receive them, of a blackish colour

New discovered Ash I received from Pensylvania, where it was discovered growing in the woods near Philadelphia The keys are very small and flat, and come up in a fortnight after being sown The young shoots of this sort are covered with the same kind of bark as the White Ash, and the leaves nearly resemble those of the Black Ash, though they are not quite so large

Method of propagating the different sorts by seeds,

All the sorts of foreign Ashes are easily raised, if the seeds can be procured from abroad We often have them in February, and if they are sown directly, they will sometimes come up the beginning of May, though they generally lie, or at least the greatest part of them, until the spring following The beds may be made in any part of the garden, and almost any sort of garden-mould, made fine, will do for the purpose After the seeds are sown, they will want no other care than weeding, until the plants are a year or two old in the seed-bed, when they may be taken up, and planted in the nursery, at the usual distance of a foot asunder, and two feet in the rows, which will be sufficient for them till they are taken up for good

and by budding

Budding is another good method of propagating these trees, so that those who have not the convenience of a correspondence in the countries where they grow naturally, should procure a plant or two of a sort, and should raise young Ashes of the Common sort for stocks, as has been directed under that article among forest-trees These stocks should be planted out in the nursery, a foot asunder, and two feet distant in the rows When they are one year old, and grown to be about the thickness of a bean-straw, they will be of a proper size for

for working. A little after Midsummer is the time for the operation, and care must be observed not to bind the eye too tight. They need not be unloosed before the latter end of September. In March, the head of the stock should be taken off, a little above the eye; and, by the end of the summer following, if the land be good, they will have made surprising strong shoots, many of them six feet or more.

The variegated kinds are only encreased this way; for the keys of these being sown, produce the Common green-leaved Ash in return.

Titles of the different species.

1. The Common Ash is titled, *Fraxinus foliolis serratis, floribus apetalis*. In the *Hortus Cliffortianus* it is termed, *Fraxinus floribus nudis*. Caspar Bauhine calls it, *Fraxinus excelsior*; Dodonæus, *Fraxinus*. It grows common in hedges and woods all over England, and most parts of Europe.

2. Flowering Ash is, *Fraxinus foliolis serratis, floribus corollatis*. In the *Hortus Cliffortianus* it is titled, *Fraxinus floribus completis*. Caspar Bauhine calls it, *Fraxinus humilior, sive altera Theophrasti, minore & tenuiore folio*; John Bauhine, *Fraxinus tenuiore & minore folio*; and Morison, *Fraxinus florifera botryoides*. It grows common in many of the southern parts of Europe.

3. American Ash is, *Fraxinus foliolis integerrimis, petiolis teretibus*. Catesby, in his History of Carolina, terms it, *Fraxinus Carolinensis, foliis angustioribus utrinque acuminatis pendulis*. It grows naturally in Carolina and Virginia.

Class and order in the Linnæan system. The characters.

*Fraxinus* is of the class and order *Polygamia Dioecia*; and the characters are,

I. Hermaphrodite flowers.

1. CALYX. Either none at all, as it sometimes happens, or else a small, monophyllous perianthium, divided into four acute parts.

2. COROLLA. Either none, as in the Common Ash, and some species, or else four long, acute, erect, narrow petals.

3. STAMINA are two erect filaments, much shorter than the corolla (where that is found), having on them erect, oblong, four-furrowed antheræ.

4. PISTILLUM consists of an oval, compressed germen, an erect cylindric style, and a thickish bifid stigma.

5. PERICARPIUM is a compressed key, enclosing a single seed.

6. SEMEN. The seed is spear-shaped, membranaceous, and compressed.

II. Female flowers.

The characters are exactly the same with those of the hermaphrodite flowers, the stamina only being wanting.

## C H A P. XXXVI.

## *GENISTA*, BROOM or DYERS WEED.

Description of, and proper situation for the different species.

THE garden is enriched by many species of the *Genista*, which are all plants of admirable beauty, but of low growth; and though most of them are shrubs, it seems difficult to say with certainty, whether they have a greater right to the flower garden or the shrubbery. For my part, I think they have a claim, at least most of them, to both places; for the shrubby sorts are of low growth, and at the time of blow will be beautifully covered with flowers, and therefore are by no means improper to mix in the larger flower-garden; and in the shrubbery no plants are more proper than these to mix with the lowest growers, near walks, &c. in the edges of the quarters. All the sorts of *Genista* are proper for either place, except the Sagittated Broom, an herbaceous plant, and two or three others, which grow but to a few inches high, and that sweet sort called the Canary Broom, which requires the protection of the greenhouse.

Species.

The shrubby sorts of this genus are,

1. The Portugal Broom.
2. The *Genista Tinctoria*, or Dyers Broom.
3. Branching Broom.
4. Dwarf English Broom.
5. German Prickly Broom.
6. Prickly Spanish Broom.
7. Purging Broom.
8. *Cytisus* of Montpelier.

These are all distinct species, and some of them have varieties, which in some degree add to the beauty of the collection.

Portugal Broom described.

1. The Portugal Broom is one of the larger growers. It will arrive to be five or six feet high, and the branches are very slender, tough, and for the most part three-cornered and jointed. The leaves end in three points, and are small, though some of them will be produced by threes, in such a manner as to be entirely trifoliate leaves, whilst others again are often found single. By the beginning of May, this shrub will be in blow. The flowers, which are yellow and of the butterfly kind, are each very large. They grow from the sides of the branches, and wings of the leaves, singly, on short footstalks, and are produced in so free and easy a manner, that they may not improperly be said to have a genteel appearance. They are succeeded by pods, in which are contained kidney-shaped seeds, that will be ripe in autumn.

Varieties.

There are two varieties of this species of Broom, one with larger, the other with narrower leaves, both of which are sought after by those who are fond of having great varieties. These sorts are the least kinds, and require a sheltered situation.

Dyers Broom. Varieties described.

2. The Dyers Broom. Of this species there are two varieties, one of which has a narrower leaf, and grows more upright, the other is more spreading in its branches. Their natural growth is about two or three feet high, and their branches are taper and channelled. The leaves are of a lanceolated figure, and placed alternately on the branches. These branches will produce spikes of yellow flowers in June, in such a manner, that though each individual flower is but small for those of the butterfly kind, the whole shrub will appear covered with them, to the pleasure of all beholders. These flowers are

are succeeded by pods, which will have ripe seeds in the autumn.

Description of the branching Broom.

3. Branching Broom, as the name indicates, is a plant whose branches spread abroad, and decline towards the earth's surface. The main stalk is beset all over with tubercles, and the leaves that ornament the slender branches are obtuse and spear-shaped. The flowers, which are yellow, are produced at the ends of the branches, in spikes, in June; and they are exhibited in such profusion as to make a delightful show. They are succeeded by pods that ripen their seeds in autumn.

Dwarf English Broom.

4. Dwarf English Broom has many beauties to recommend it to the gardener, though it grows common in many of our barren heaths. In these places, it goes by the common name of *Petty-Whin*. All the sorts of our choicest cultivated plants grow wild in some parts of the globe, but lose nothing of their value because they appear thus spontaneously. Why then should this, because it is common in some parts of England, be denied admittance into gardens, especially those that are at a remote distance from such places, as it has many natural beauties to recommend it? It is a low plant, seldom growing to be more than two feet high; on which account no garden is so small but it may be there planted, if the commonness of it be no objection to the owner. This shrub has some single, long spines, though the flower branches are entirely free from them. The leaves, like the shrub, are proportionally small, of a lanceolated figure, and grow alternately on the branches. The flowers, which are of a fine yellow, are produced the beginning of May, in clusters, at the ends of the branches, and are succeeded by thick short pods, in which the seeds are contained.

German Prickly Broom.

5. German Prickly Broom will grow to be about a yard high. The shrub is armed with many compound spines; the branches are slender and numerous, though those that produce the flowers are entirely free from spines. The leaves of this sort, also, are small, and of a lanceolate figure, and grow alternately on the branches. The flowers are produced in plenty at the ends of the branches, in June. They are of the colour and figure of the others, and are succeeded by pods, in which the seeds are contained.

Prickly Spanish Broom.

6. Prickly Spanish Broom will grow to be five or six feet high. This shrub is possessed of many compound spines, though the branches that produce the flowers are entirely free from them. The leaves are exceeding narrow, many of them being no wider than a thread, but very hairy. The flowers are yellow, produced in May, in clusters, at the ends of the branches, and are succeeded by hairy, compressed pods, in which the seeds are contained.

Purging Broom.

7. Purging Broom. This is a low plant, sending forth numerous, taper, striated branches, which spread themselves every way. The leaves are spear-shaped, obtuse, simple, and downy underneath. The flowers are yellow, come out in May and June, and are succeeded by compressed pods, containing ripe seeds, in September.

and the Cytisus of Montpelier.

8. *Cytisus* of Montpelier rises, with an erect, shrubby, branching, striated stalk, to the height of about a yard. The leaves are trifoliate, oval, and hairy underneath. The flowers come out on leafy footstalks, from the sides of the branches. They are of a bright yellow colour, appear in June, and are succeeded by hairy pods, containing ripe seeds, in September.

Method of propagating these sorts.

The best way of propagating all these sorts of *Genista* is by seeds; and if these are sown soon after they are ripe, they will come up either in the spring, and make better plants by the autumn. They should only stand one year in the seed bed before they are transplanted. They should be taken up in the spring, and planted out for good, in ground properly prepared for such small plants; for the less they are removed, so much the better will they thrive, as they naturally grow with long strong stringy roots, that do not love to be disturbed; on which account, if places in the plantations were to be marked out, the mould made fine, a few seeds of the different sorts sown, and sticks set as guides to prevent their being hoed or dug up, plants that have been thus raised, without removing, will shoot stronger, and flower better, than any that have been brought from the seed-bed or nursery. After they are come up, if there be too many in a place, the weakest may be drawn out, and only two or three of the strongest left, which will cause them to flower better and stronger.

Titles of this genus.

1. Portugal Broom is titled, *Genista ramis triquetris subarticulatis, foliis tricuspidatis*. Caspar Bauhine calls it, *Chamægenista caule foliato*; Tournefort, *Genistella fruticosa Lusitanica latifolia*; also, *Genista frutescens Lusitanica angustifolia*. It grows common in Portugal and Spain.

2. Dyer's Broom is, *Genista foliis lanceolatis, glabris ramis striatis teretibus erectis*. Caspar Bauhine calls it, *Genista tinctoria Germanica*; Clusius, *Genista tinctoria vulgaris*; and Gerard, *Genistella tinctoria*. It grows naturally in Germany, also in many parts of England.

3. Branching Broom is, *Genista foliis lanceolatis obtusis, caule tuberculato decumbente*. Caspar Bauhine calls it, *Chamægenista foliis genistæ vulgaris*; also, *Genista ramosa, foliis Hyperici*; also, *Chamægenista Pannonica*. Clusius terms it *Chamægenista Pannonica*. It grows naturally in Hungary, Germany, and in many parts of France.

4. Dwarf English Broom is, *Genista spinis simplicibus, ramis floriferis inermibus, foliis lanceolatis*. Caspar Bauhine calls it, *Genista minor aspalathoides*; Gerard, *Genista aculeata*; Parkinson, *Genistella aculeata*; and Dodonæus, *Genista* [illegible]. It grows naturally in most heathy ground in several parts of England.

5. German Prickly Broom is, *Genista spinis compositis, ramis floriferis inermibus, foliis lanceolatis*. Caspar Bauhine calls this, *Genista spinosa minor Germanica*; and Rivinus, *Genistella spinosa*. It is a native of Germany.

6. Prickly Spanish Broom is, *Genista spinis decompositis, ramis floriferis inermibus, foliis linearibus pilosis*. Caspar Bauhine calls it, *Genista spinosa minor Hispanica villosissima*; also, *Genistella Monspeliaca spinosa*; and J. Bauhine, *Genistella montis ventosi, spinosa*. It grows naturally in Spain, and some parts of France.

7. Purging Broom is, *Genista spinis terminalibus, ramis teretibus striatis, foliis lanceolatis simplicibus pubescentibus*. John Bauhine calls it, *Genista, seu Spartium purgans*. It grows naturally near Montpelier.

8. *Cytisus* of Montpelier is titled, *Genista foliis ternatis subtus villosis, pedunculis lateralibus subquinquefloris foliatis, leguminibus hirsutis*. In the former edition of the *Species Plantarum* it is termed, *Cytisus floribus lateralibus, foliis hirsutis, caule erecto striato*. Tournefort calls it, *Cytisus Monspessulanus, medicæ folio siliquis densè congestis & villosis*; and Clusius, *Cytisus sylvestris candicans*. It grows naturally in Italy, and about Montpelier in France.

Class and order in the Linnæan system.

*Genista* is of the class and order *Diadelphia Decandria*; and the characters are,

The characters.

1. CALYX is a small, tubulous, monophyllous, bilabiated perianthium. The upper lip is deeply cut

cut into two ſegments, the lower one is unequally indented in three parts.

2. COROLLA is papilionaceous.

Vexillum is oval, acute, wholly reflexed, and remote from the carina.

Alæ are oblong and looſe, and ſhorter than the vexillum.

Carina is erect and emarginated, and longer than the vexillum.

3. STAMINA are ten filaments, joined together, ſituated on the carina, having ſimple antheræ.

4. PISTILLUM conſiſts of an oblong germen, of a ſimple aſcending ſtyle, and an acute involute ſtigma.

5. PERICARPIUM is a roundiſh, turgid, bivalvate pod, containing one cell.

6. SEMINA. The ſeeds are reniforme.

## CHAP. XXXVII.

## *GLEDITSIA*, TRIPLE-THORNED ACACIA.

*Deſcription of this tree.* WE are now come to a tree that aſpires to near forty feet in height, and is in every reſpect ſo ſingular and beautiful, as to attract the eye of the moſt incurious. Its growth is naturally upright, and its trunk is guarded by thorns of three or four inches in length, in a remarkable manner. Theſe thorns have alſo others coming out of their ſides at nearly right angles. Their colour is red. The branches are ſmooth, and of a white colour. Theſe are likewiſe armed with red thorns, that are proportionally ſmaller. They are of ſeveral directions, and at the ends of the branches often ſtand ſingle. The young ſhoots of the preceding ſummer are perfectly ſmooth, of a reddiſh green, and retain their leaves often until the middle of November. Although there is a peculiar oddity in the [illegible] and poſition of the ſpines, yet the leaves conſtitute the greateſt beauty of theſe trees. They are doubly pinnated, and of a delightful ſhining green. The pinnated leaves that form the duplication, do not always ſtand oppoſite by pairs on the middle rib; the pinnæ of which they are compoſed are ſmall and numerous, no leſs than ten or eleven pair belong to each of them, and as no leſs than four or five pair of ſmall leaves are arranged along the middle rib, the whole compound leaf conſiſts often of more than two hundred pinnæ of this fine green colour. They ſit cloſe, and ſpread open in fine weather, though at the approach of bad weather, they will droop, and then their ſurfaces nearly join, as if in a ſleeping ſtate. The flowers are produced from the ſides of the young branches, in July. They are a greeniſh katkin, and make little ſhow; though many are ſucceeded by pods, that have a wonderful effect, for they are exceeding large, more than a foot, and ſometimes a foot and a half in length, and two inches in breadth, and of a nut-brown colour when ripe, ſo that the effect they occaſion, when hanging on the ſides of the branches, may eaſily be gueſſed.

*Variety.* There is a variety of this ſpecies, with fewer thorns, ſmaller leaves, and oval pods. It has exactly the reſemblance of the other, though the thorns being not ſo frequent, and the pods being ſmaller, each containing only one ſeed, this ſort loſes that ſingular effect which the other produces by them.

*Method of propagating this tree.* The culture of theſe beautiful and noble trees is not very difficult. We receive the ſeeds from America in the ſpring, which keep well in the pods, and are for the moſt part good. They generally arrive in February, and, as ſoon as poſſible after, they ſhould be ſown in a well-ſheltered warm border of light ſandy earth. If no border is to be found that is naturally ſo, it may be improved by applying drift ſand, and making it fine. The ſeeds ſhould be ſown about half an inch deep, and they will for the moſt part come up the firſt ſpring. If the ſummer ſhould prove dry, they muſt be conſtantly watered, and if ſhade could be afforded them in the heat of the day, they would make ſtronger plants by the autumn. A careful attention to this article is peculiarly requiſite, for as the ends of the branches are often killed, if the young plant has not made ſome progreſs, it will be liable to be wholly deſtroyed by the winter's froſt, without protection. And this renders the ſowing the ſeeds in a warm border, under an hedge, in a well ſheltered place, ſo neceſſary; for there theſe ſhrubs will endure our winters, even when ſeedlings, and ſo will require no farther trouble; nay, though the tops ſhould be nipped, they will ſhoot out again lower, and will ſoon overcome it.

It will be proper to let them remain two years in the ſeed bed, before they are planted out in the nurſery. The ſpring is the beſt time for the work. Their diſtances ſhould be one foot by two, the rows ſhould be dug between every winter, and, being weeded in ſummer, here they may remain, with no other particular care, until they are ſet out for good. Theſe trees are late in the ſpring before they exhibit their leaves, but keep ſhooting long in the autumn. They ſhould not only join in wilderneſs quarters, with others of their own growth, but ſome of them ſhould be planted ſingly in opens, &c. where they will excite admiration, by their triple ſpines, fine leaves, and large pods.

*Titles.* The Triple-thorned Acacia is titled *Gleditſia ſpinis triplicibus axillaribus*. In the Upſal Catalogue it is termed Triple *Gleditſia*; in the *Hortus Cliffortianus*, *Caſalpinoides foliis pinnatis & duplicato pinnatis*. Mitchell calls it, *Melilobus*; Derham, *Gleditſia ſpinoſa*; and Plukenet, *Acacia Americana, abrui folio, triacanthos*; and Cateſby, *Acacia, abruæ folio, triacanthos, capſula ovali unicum ſemen claudente*. It grows naturally in Virginia and Penſylvania.

*Claſs and order in the Linnæan ſyſtem.* *Gleditſia* is of the claſs and order *Polygamia Dioecia*; and the characters are,

The male flowers are collected in a long, compact, cylindric katkin.

*The characters.* 1. CALYX is a perianthium, compoſed of three ſmall, acute, and ſpreading leaves.

2. Co-

2 COROLLA consists of three roundish, some petals, which spread open, and are shaped like the leaves of the calyx. There is a turbinated nectarium, the mouth of which grows to the parts of fructification.

3 STAMINA are six filiform filaments, longer than the corolla, having oblong, incumbent, and compressed antheræ.

Hermaphrodite flowers are situated at the end of the same catkin with the males.

1 CALYX,
2 COROLLA and Nectarium,
3 STAMINA, are all like the males.
4 PISTILLUM,
5 PERICARPIUM,
6 SEMINA, like the females.

Female flowers, which are produced on different plants, are disposed in loose katkins.

1 CALYX is a perianthium, the same as the male, but it consists of five parts.

2 COROLLA consists of five long, acute, erect, patent petals. There are two short, thread-like nectariums.

3 PISTILLUM consists of a broad compressed germen (longer than the corolla), a short subulated style, and a thick stigma.

4 PERICARPIUM is a very large broad, compressed pod, having in it many transverse partitions, and replete in each division with a pulpy matter.

5 SEMEN is single, roundish, hard, bright, and surrounded by the pulp.

## CHAP. XXXVIII.

## GUILANDINA, The BONDUC or NICKAR-TREE.

THERE is one species of this genus which will bear the cold of our winters in the open air, called the *Dioiceous Bonduc*, or *Nickar-tree*. *This tree described.* The stem is erect, firm, often twenty feet high, and sends forth several branches, which are covered with a smooth, bluish, ash-coloured bark. The leaves are bipinnated, and the folioles are large, smooth, entire, and ranged alternately on the mid-rib. The flowers are dioiceous, there being male and female on different plants, and the general characters shew their composition. They appear in July or August, but are very rarely succeeded by seeds in England.

*Method of propagating this tree by seeds,* This species is propagated by seeds, which must be procured from the places where the tree naturally grows. The seeds are very hard, and often lie two years before they make their appearance, so that if they are sown in common ground, the beds must all the time be kept clean from weeds. In the autumn it will be proper to stir the surface of the mould, but not so deep as to disturb the seeds. In the spring the plants will come up. All summer they must be kept clear from weeds, watered in dry weather, and in the autumn the strongest may be planted out in the nursery, at the usual distance, while the weakest may remain another year in the seed-bed to gain strength.

The seeds also may be sown in pots, and plunged into a hot-bed. This will bring the plants up the first spring. After they make their appearance, they must be hardened by degrees to the open air, and have the same treatment as the former kinds of seedlings.

*by layers,* This tree may likewise be propagated by layers. These must be the smaller shoots of the last year's wood. The operation must be performed by making a slit, as is practised for carnations, and the best time for the business is the autumn.

*and by cutting the root.* By cutting the root, also, this tree may be encreased. In order to this, bare away the earth from the top of the root, then, with the knife cut off some parts of it, leaving them still in the ground, and only directing their ends upwards. Then cover the whole down lightly with mould. The parts that have been separated will shoot out from the ends, and come up as suckers all round the tree. If dry weather should happen, you will do well to water them all the summer, and in the autumn they may be removed to the place where they are designed to remain, which ought always to be in a light dry soil, and a well sheltered place.

*Titles of this species.* This species is titled, *Guilandina inermis, foliis bipinnatis basi apiceque simplicibus pinnis*. Du Hamel calls it, *Bonduc Canadense polyphyllum, non spinosum, mas & femina*. It grows naturally in Canada.

*Class and order in the Linnæan system.* *Guilandina* is of the class and order *Decandria Monogynia*; and the characters are,

*The characters.* 1 CALYX is a monophyllous bell-shaped perianthium, cut at the brim into five, equal, spreading segments.

2 COROLLA consists of five spear-shaped, concave, sessile, equal petals, which are rather longer than the calyx, and inserted in it.

3 STAMINA. There are ten awl-shaped, erect filaments, inserted in the calyx, which are alternately shorter than each other, and have obtuse incumbent antheræ.

4 PISTILLUM consists of an oblong germen, a filiforme style the length of the stamina, and a simple stigma.

5 PERICARPIUM is a rhomboid, swelling, compressed, unilocular pod, having a convex suture on the upper side, containing one cell, and divided into many partitions by transverse valves.

6 SEMINA. The seeds are osseous, roundish, compressed, and lodged singly in the different apartments.

# CHAP XXXIX.

## *HAMAMELIS*, The WITCH-HAZEL

The ſhrub deſcribed

THE Witch-Hazel is a ſhrub of about four feet in growth, and will conſtitute a variety among other trees, though there is no great beauty in it, except what is afforded by the leaves These are placed on the branches, which are numerous and ſlender, in an alternate manner, and much reſemble thoſe of our Common Hazel, that are known to all The flowers make no ſhow, but perhaps the time of their appearing, which happens in winter, in November or December, when they will be produced in cluſters from the joints of the young ſhoots, may make the plant deſirable to ſome perſons Nothing farther need be ſaid to the gardener concerning this ſhrub which Nature ſeems to have deſigned for the ſtricter eye of the botaniſt, ſo that we ſhall proceed to its culture

Method of propagating it by ſeeds,

1 It is propagated by ſeeds, which muſt be procured from America, for they do not ripen here An eaſterly border, well defended from the north and weſterly winds, is beſt for their reception, for these plants when ſeedlings are rather tender, when older, they are hardy enough They will grow in almoſt any kind of good garden mould, made fine, and they ſhould be covered about half an inch deep They never come up before the ſecond ſpring, and therefore, during the ſummer the weeds muſt be plucked up as faſt as they appear, otherwiſe they will ſoon ſtrike their roots in plenty amongſt the ſeeds, and then, in drawing them up, you will be apt to draw out the ſeeds with them They will come up the ſecond ſpring, and if it ſhould prove dry, watering muſt be afforded them In the heat of ſummer, alſo, if they could be a little ſhaded, they will prove the ſtronger plants for it by the autumn In the winter, it will be neceſſary to prick furze-buſhes on the ſide expoſed, to break the eaſterly, or any other froſty winds that may happen By this means, the plants will be ſecure, and, after having ſtood two years in this ſeed-bed they ſhould be planted in the nurſery They ſhould remain in the ſeed-bed, I ſay, two years, for many of the ſeeds will not come up ſometimes even until the third ſpring after ſowing Thus may many plants be ſaved

2 This tree may alſo be propagated by layers, so that whoever has not the conveniency of procuring the ſeeds from abroad, having obtained a plant or two, may increaſe them this way The operation ſhould be performed on the twigs of the preceding ſummer's ſhoot These ſhould be ſlit at the joint, and a bit of chip, or ſomething, put in to keep the ſlit open If these ſtools ſtand in a moiſtiſh place, which these ſhrubs naturally love, and are layered in the autumn, they will have ſhot root by the autumn following, and may be then either planted out in the nurſery, or where they are to remain for good — and by layers

As there is no other ſpecies of this genus, it ſtands with the name ſimply, *Hamamelis* Mitchell calls it, *Trilopus*, and Plukenet, *Piſtacia Virginiana nigra, coryli foliis* It grows naturally in Virginia — Titles

*Hamamelis* is of the claſs and order *Tetrandria Digynia*, and the characters are, — Claſs and order in the Linnæan ſyſtem

1 CALYX is a triphyllous involucrum, the two folioles of which, that are interior, are roundiſh, ſmall, and obtuſe, the third, which is outward, is large, and of a lanceolated figure The perianthium is double The exterior conſiſts of two ſmall roundiſh leaves the interior of four leaves, which are oblong, obtuſe, and equal — The character

2 COROLLA conſiſts of four linear, equal, very long, obtuſe, reflexed petals There are four nectaria adhering to the petals

3 STAMINA are four narrow filaments, that are ſhorter than the calyx, having bicornate, inflexed antheræ

4 PISTILLUM conſiſts of an oval hairy germen, and of two ſtyles the length of the ſtamina, with capitated ſtigmas

5 PERICARPIUM There is none

6 SEMEN is an oval, hard, ſmooth, obtuſe, ſulcated nut, ſituated in the calyx

# CHAP XL

## *HIBISCUS*, The SYRIAN KETMIA

MANY parts of the garden are ornamented by the various ſpecies of *Hibiſcus*, but that which is neceſſary for our preſent purpoſe is what is commonly known by the name of *Althæa Frutex*, a ſhrub of ſingular beauty and variety, which flowers late in the autumn Of the *Althæa Frutex* there are ſeveral ſorts, as,

Varieties of the Althæa Frutex

The White *Althæa Frutex*
The Red-flowering *Althæa Frutex*
Yellow-flowering *Althæa Frutex*
Pale Purple-flowering *Althæa Frutex*
Deep Purple *Althæa Frutex*

All these, though ſuppoſed to be only ſorts of one ſpecies of *Hibiſcus*, afford wonderful varieties to the gardener They will grow to the height of about ſix feet Their branches are not very numerous, they are ſmooth, and of a whitiſh colour The leaves are of a pleaſant green, and grow — Deſcription of this tree grow on ſhort footſtalks irregularly on the branches They are of an oval, ſpear-ſhaped figure, ſerrated at the edges, and many of them are divided at the top into three diſtinct lobes The flowers have longer footſtalks than the leaves, and come out from the ſides of the young ſhoots with them; inſomuch that the young ſhoots are often garniſhed with them their whole length The Common Mallow produces not a bad flower, did not its commonneſs render it unnoticed The flowers of theſe ſpecies ſomewhat reſemble it in ſhape, but by far exceed it both in ſize and ſplendor of colour, and each has a greater variety, inſomuch that though they are termed Red, White, Purple, &c from the colour of the upper part of the petals, yet the lower part of all of them is very dark, and ſeems to ſhoot out in rays in directions towards the extremity of each petal Auguſt is the month we may expect to be entertained with this bloom, though, in ſtarved cold ſoils, the flowers rarely ever appear before September

This beautiful ſhrub may be propagated by two methods

Method of propagating this tree by ſeeds, 1 By ſeeds, which we receive from abroad Theſe ſhould be ſown in a bed of light ſandy earth, and if it is not naturally ſo, drift ſand muſt be added, and if ſome old lime-rubbiſh, beat to powder, be alſo mixed with it, it will be the better Having worked them all together, and made the bed ſmooth and fine, the ſeeds ſhould be covered about a quarter of an inch deep The ſituation of this bed muſt be in a warm well-ſheltered place that the young plants may not ſuffer by froſts the firſt winter Any time in March will do for the work, and in about ſix weeks the young plants will come up In the heat of ſummer, it will be proper to ſhade them, and if conſtant waterings are afforded them in dry weather, they will acquire greater ſtrength and vigour by the autumn At the beginning of November, beſides the natural ſhelter of theſe beds, it will be proper to prick furze buſhes at a little diſtance all around, to break the keen edge of the black froſts, which otherwiſe would deſtroy many of them the firſt winter After that, they will be hardy enough for our ſevereſt weather They ſhould ſtand in their ſeed beds two years, and all the while be weeded and watered in dry weather The ſpring is the beſt time for planting them out in the nurſery, where no more diſtance need be allowed them than one foot

by layers, 2 Theſe plants may be propagated by layers, for which purpoſe the ſtools ſhould be headed near the ground, to throw out ſome good ſtrong ſhoots the following ſummer Theſe ſhould be laid in the ground, the bark being broken, or cut at one or two of the joints, and they will have ſtruck root by the autumn following, when they may be taken up, and planted in the nurſery, like the ſeedlings, and a ſecond operation performed on the ſtools

and by cuttings Theſe plants may be raiſed alſo by cuttings, for by planting them in a ſhady border, many of them will grow though I never found this to be a certain method

Title The true title of this ſpecies is, *Hibiſcus foliis cuneiformi ovatis ſuperne inæquali-dentatis, caule arboreo* Caſpar Bauhine calls it, *Althæa arboreſcens Syriaca*, and Cammerarius, *Althæa arboreſcens* It is a native of Syria

Claſs and order in the Linnæan ſyſtem This genus is of the claſs and order *Monadelphia Polyandria*, and the characters are,

The characters 1 Calyx is a double perianthium The outer cup is compoſed of many narrow permanent leaves the inner is of one leaf, which is cyathiforme and permanent, and cut at the brim into five acute ſegments

2 Corolla conſiſts of five obcordated petals, that join at their baſe

3 Stamina are numerous filaments Theſe coaleſce below, and form a column, higher they expand, and all have reniforme antheræ

4 Pistillum is a roundiſh germen, and a filiforme ſtyle longer than the ſtamina, and is cut upwards into five parts, having on each of them a capitated ſtigma

5 Pericarpium is a capſule formed of five valves, and containing five cells

6 Semina The ſeeds are reniforme

# CHAP. XLI

## *HIPPOPHAE*, SALLOW THORN, or SEA-BUCKTHORN

THERE are two real ſpecies of the Sea-Buckthorn to encreaſe our variety

Species of this genus
1 The European Sea-Buckthorn
2 The American Sea-Buckthorn

Deſcription of the European 1 The European Sea-Buckthorn will grow to the height of about twelve feet, and ſends forth numerous branches in an irregular manner Their colour is that of a dark brown, and on them a few ſtrong and long ſharp ſpines are found, nearly like thoſe of the Common Buckthorn This tree is chiefly admired for its ſingular appearance in winter, for the young ſhoots of the preceding ſummer are then found thickly ſet on all ſides with large, turgid, uneven, ſcaly buds, of a darker brown, or rather a chocolate colour, than the branches themſelves Theſe give the tree ſuch a particular look, that it catches the attention, and occaſions it to be enquired after, as much as any ſhrub in the plantation About the end of February theſe turgid buds will be much larger, and a little before their opening, upon ſtriking the tree with a ſtick, a yellow duſt, like brimſtone, will fall from them Though ſome think the beauty of this ſhrub to be diminiſhed after the leaves are opened, yet theſe have their good effect, for they are of two colours Their upper ſurface is of a dark green, their under hoary, they are long and narrow, entire, have no footſtalks, nearly like thoſe of the roſemary, tho' rather longer and broader, and they are placed alternately all around, without any footſtalks, on the branches They continue on the tree green and hoary late, ſometimes until the beginning of December, and at length die away to a light brown The flowers are

are of no consequence to any but Nature's strict observers There will be male and female on distinct plants They are produced in July, very close by the sides of the young shoots, the male flowers appear in little clusters, but the females come out singly They are succeeded by berries, which, in the autumn, when ripe, are either of a red or yellow colour, for there are both those sorts

*and the American Sea Buckthorn*

2 Canada Sea Buckthorn will grow to about the same height as the other species, nearly, the same dark-brown bark covers their branches, and, except the figure of their leaves, which are oval, this plant differs in few respects from the European Sea Buckthorn

*Method of propagating them*

Both these sorts may be propagated by cuttings of the young shoots, planted in a shady border, in October, though the most certain method is by layers If the trees to be encreased are of some years growth, the ground should be dug and made fine, as well as cleared of the roots of bad weeds, &c all around The main branches may be splashed, and the young twigs that form the head laid in the ground, taking off their ends with a knife, that they may only just peep If this work be performed in the autumn, they will be good rooted plants by the autumn following, when they may taken off, and either planted in the nursery, or where they are to remain

Both these sorts are subject to spawn, and throw out many suckers, sometimes at a good distance from the plants, so that by this method they propagate themselves But these plants are not so good as those raised from cuttings or layers, as they will soon throw out a greater quantity in a similar manner, thereby over-running the ground

*Titles of the ...*

The title of the European Sea Buckthorn is, *Hippophae foliis lanceolatis* In the *Flora Lapponica* it is termed, *Hippophae* Tournefort calls it, *Rhamnoides florifera, salicis folio*, Clusius, *Rhamnus 2*, C Bauhine, *Rhamnus salicis folio angustiore, fructu flavescente*, and Parkinson, *Rhamnus primus Dioscoridis Lobelio, sive littoralis* It grows upon the sandy sea shores of most parts of Europe

2 American Sea Buckthorn is, *Hippophae foliis ovatis* It grows naturally in Canada

*Class and order in the Linnæan system*

*Hippophae* is of the class and order *Dioecia Tetrandria*, and the characters of the flowers are,

*The characters*

I The Males

1 Calyx is a monophyllous perianthium, divided into two roundish, obtuse, concave, erect parts, which close at their points

2 Corolla There is none

3 Stamina are four very short filaments, with oblong angular antheræ, of equal length with the calyx

II Females

1 Calyx is a monophyllous, oval, oblong, tubulated, clavated, deciduous perianthium, divided at the top into two parts

2 Corolla There is none

3 Pistillum consists of a small roundish germen, of a very short simple style and of an oblong, thick, erect stigma, twice the length of the calyx

4 Pericarpium is a globular berry, of one cell

5 Semen is single and roundish

# CHAP XLII

## HYDRANGEA

*Its characters described*

THERE is only one species of this genus, neither has any English name yet been given to it It seldom grows to more than a yard or four feet in height, and affords as much pleasure to those who delight in fine flowers as it does to the botanist It forms itself into no regular head, but the branches of which it is composed shoot chiefly from the root These, when young are for covered and green, when old, of a fine brown colour They are very large for their height, as well as very full of pith The leaves are a great ornament to these plants, being also very large, and having their upper surface of a fine green, and their under with a downy Their figure is nearly shaped like a heart, but ends in an acute point, and their size will prove according to the nature of the soil they grow in On a dry soil they will often be no more than two inches long and scarcely an inch and a half broad, but, in a moist rich soil, they will frequently grow to near four inches long, and two and three quarters broad in the widest part They are serrated at their edges, and are placed on long footstalks, opposite to each other, on the branches But the flowers constitute the greatest beauty of these plants, for they are produced in very large bunches, in August Their colour is white, and the end of every branch will be ornamented with them They have an agreeable odour, and make such a show all together as to distinguish the shrubs even at a considerable distance With us, however, they are seldom succeeded by any seeds

*Method of propagating this tree*

To encrease this singular and beautiful plant is very easy than to keep it within bounds for the roots creep to a considerable distance, and send up stalks which produce flowers, so that these being taken off, will be proper plants for any place It likes a moist soil

*Title*

There being no other species of this genus, this shrub stands with the term simply *Hydrangea* It grows naturally in Virginia

*Class and order in the Linnæan system*

*Hydrangea* is of the class and order *Decandria Digynia*, and the characters are,

*The characters*

1 Calyx is a small, monophyllous, permanent perianthium, indented in five parts at the top

2 Corolla consists of five equal roundish petals, that are larger than the calyx

3 Stamina are ten filaments, longer than the corolla, and are alternately longer than each other, having roundish didymous antheræ

4 Pistillum consists of a roundish germen, placed under the receptacle of the flower and

of two short styles, at a distance from each other, with obtuse permanent stigmas

5 PERICARPIUM is a roundish didymous capsule, on which are two beaks like horns, formed by the permanent styles It is made angular by many veins, coronated by the calyx, divided into two cells by a transverse partition, and has an aperture between the two beaks for the discharge of the seeds

6 SEMINA The seeds are numerous, angular, sharp-pointed, and very small

# C H A P. XLIII.

## *HYPERICUM*, St JOHN's WORT

THE garden receives great ornament from the different species of the St John's Wort, but the sorts most proper for the shrubbery are,

Species

1 Shrubby Stinking St John's Wort, or Goat scented St John's Wort

2 Canary St John's Wort

Description of the Shrubby St John's Wort

1 Shrubby St John's Wort Of this there are several varieties The Common is a beautiful shrub, near four feet in height The branches are smooth, of a light brown, and come out opposite by pairs from the side of the strongest stalks, and these also send forth others, which alternately point out different directions The leaves are of an oblong, oval figure, grow opposite by pairs, and sit very close to the stalks These being bruised, emit a very strong disagreeable scent The flowers are yellow, and make a good show in June and July, for they will be produced in such clusters, at the ends of the young shoots, that the shrub will appear covered with them They are succeeded by oval black coloured capsules, containing ripe seeds, in the autumn

Varieties of this species

There is a variety of this species, which will grow to be eight feet high The stalks are strong, the leaves broad, and the flowers large, and being produced in great plenty, causes it to be a valuable shrub for the plantation There is another variety with variegated leaves, which is admired by those who are fond of such kinds of plants There is also a variety dispossessed of the disagreeable smell, which causes it to be preferred by many on that account

Canary St John's Wort described

2 The Canary St John's Wort is a shrub of about six or seven feet high The branches divide by pairs, and the leaves, which are of an oblong figure, grow opposite by pairs, without any footstalks The flowers come out in clusters from the ends of the branches They are of a bright yellow, have numerous stamina, which are shorter than the petals, and three styles They appear in July and August, and are succeeded by oval roundish capsules, containing the seeds

Method of raising these sorts from suckers,

No art need be used in propagating these shrubs, for having obtained a plant or two of each, they will afford encrease enough by suckers Having stood about three years, the whole of each plant should be taken up, and the suckers and slips which root that this may be divided into, may reasonably be supposed to be twenty in number The strongest of these may be planted where they are to remain, whilst the weakest may be set out in the nursery to gain strength

Other method

These shrubs may also be propagated by seeds, which ripen well with us, and will come up with the common care, nay they will often shed their seeds which will come up without sowing, especially the last sort, of which I have had seedlings in such plenty about the old plant, that, unless they had been destroyed, they would have over run the ground to a considerable distance

Titles of the species

1 Shrubby Stinking St John's Wort is titled, *Hypericum floribus trigynis, staminibus corolla longioribus, caule fruticoso ancipiti* Tournefort calls it, *Hypericum foetidum frutescens*, Dillenius, *Hypericum foetidum frutescens minus*, Caspar Bauhine, *Androsæmum foetidum, capitulis longissimis filamentis donatis*, and Clusius, *Tragium* It grows naturally by the sides of rivers in Sicily, Calabria, and Crete

2 Canary St John's Wort is, *Hypericum floribus trigynis, calycibus obtusis, staminibus corolla brevioribus, caule fruticoso* Commeline calls it, *Hypericum frutescens Canariense* [illegible] and Plukenet, *Hypericum frutescens Canariense* [illegible] *ramosum, copiosis floribus*, [illegible] It is a native of the Canaries

Class and order in the Linnæan system

*Hypericum* belongs to the class and order *Polyadelphia Polyandria*, and the characters are,

The characters

1 CALYX is a permanent one divided into five oval, concave permanent segments

2 COROLLA consists of five oblong, oval, obtuse, patent petals

3 STAMINA are numerous capillary filaments, which are joined together at their base into three or five distinct bodies, having small antheræ

4 PISTILLUM consists of a roundish germen, and of three usually, though sometimes of only two, or five simple distant styles, the length of the stamina, with simple stigmas

5 PERICARPIUM is a roundish capsule, with the same number of cells as the styles of the flower

6 SEMINA The seeds are numerous and oblong

CHAP

# CHAP. XLIV.

## *JASMINUM*, The JESSAMINE-TREE.

THERE are several sorts of Jessamines, of admirable beauty and scent, but those best adapted to our hardy plantations are,

Species.
1. The Common White Jessamine.
2. The Yellow Jessamine.
3. The Italian Jessamine.

Description of the Common White.
1. Common White Jessamines have usually been planted against walls, &c. for the branches being slender, weak, and partly, by such assistance they have arrived to a good height: though this shrub is not the most eligible for this purpose, as its branches, which are numerous, are covered with a brown dirty-looking bark, and afford shelter for snails, spiders, and other insects, which in winter, when the leaves are fallen, will give them an unsightly look; and if they are clipped and kept up to the wall, as the flowers are produced from the ends and wings of the shoot, the same will of course be sheared off, so that little bloom will be found, except what is at the top of the tree. I do not mean, however, to dissuade those people who are fond of it from planting it against walls. It naturally requires support, tho' attended with those defects; and it may be planted amongst shrubs in wilderness quarters, to appear to great advantage. It should keep company with the lower kind of shrubs; and whenever the branches grow too high to support themselves without nodding, and discover their rusty stems, these should be taken off from the bottom. There will always be a succession of young wood, and these young shoots, which are covered with a smooth bark, of a delightful green colour, also exhibit their leaves and bloom. The leaves are pinnated, and very beautiful. They grow opposite by pairs, and the folioles are usually three pair in number, besides the odd one with which each leaf is terminated. They are all of a dark strong green colour, are pointed, and the end one is generally the largest, and has its point drawn out to a greater length. The flowers are produced from the ends and joints of the branches, during most of the summer months. They are white, and very fragrant, but are succeeded by no fruit in England.

There is a variety of this sort with yellow, and another with white striped leaves.

the Yellow,
2. The Yellow Jessamine is often planted against walls, pales, &c. as the branches are weak and slender, and it will grow to be ten or twelve feet high, if thus supported. It may, however, be planted in wilderness quarters, in the same manner as the other, where it will contribute much to the beauty of those places. The young shoots are of a fine strong green colour, angular, and a little hairy. The leaves are trifoliate, though sometimes they grow single. They are placed alternately on the branches, are of a thick consistence, smooth, and of a fine deep green colour. These leaves, in well sheltered places, remain until the spring before they fall off, so that this plant may not be improperly ranked among Evergreens, especially as the young shoots are always of so strong a green. The flowers are yellow, and do not possess the fragrance of the preceding sort. They are produced in June, and the blow is soon over, but they are succeeded by berries, which, when ripe, are black. These have occasioned his sort to be called by some persons the Berry-bearing Jessamine.

and the Italian Yellow Jessamine.
3. The Italian Yellow Jessamine is, of all the sorts, best adapted to a shrubbery, because it loses part of its beauty, if nailed to a wall. It is naturally of lower growth, and the branches are stronger, fewer in number, able to support themselves in an upright position, and are angular. The bark is smooth, and of a fine deep green colour. The leaves grow alternately. They are chiefly trifoliate, though some pinnated ones are found upon this shrub. The folioles are smooth, and of a fine strong green. They are much broader than the preceding sorts, and often continue till spring before they drop off, so that this shrub, on account of the beautiful green of the young shoots, might have a place among Evergreens. The flowers are yellow, and much larger than those of the other sorts. They are produced in July, and are sometimes succeeded by berries; but I never yet knew them come to perfection. This species is very hardy, and has grown in the most exposed places in our plantations, resisting the severest frosts for many years.

Method of propagation.
Little need be said concerning the culture of these plants, for they will all grow by layers or cuttings. So that if either way be pursued in the winter, you will have plenty of plants by the autumn following. The cuttings, however, must have a moist good soil, and should be shaded and watered as the hot weather comes on, the beginning of summer. The Common Yellow Jessamine may be propagated by the seeds; but it naturally sends forth such plenty of suckers as to render it needless to take any other method for its increase; for these being taken off, will be good plants; nay, if it is planted in borders, they must be annually taken for use, or thrown away, or they will overspread every thing that grows near them. The Yellow and White-striped leaved Jessamines are propagated by grafting, budding, or inarching, into stocks of the Common White. They are rather tender, especially the White, therefore must have a warm situation. The Yellow-striped is the most common and least beautiful, and may be encreased by layers and cuttings, like the plain sort.

Titles.
1. The title of the Common White Jessamine is, *Jasminum foliis oppositis pinnatis*. Caspar Bauhine calls it, *Jasminum vulgatius, flore albo*; and others, *Jasminum album*. This plant, though so hardy and common with us, is a native of India.

2. The Common Yellow Jessamine is, *Jasminum foliis alternis ternatis simplicibusque, ramis angulatis*. Caspar Bauhine calls it, *Jasminum luteum, vulgo dictum bacciferum*; and Dodonæus, *Trifolium fruticans*. It grows common in the south of Europe, the Cape of Good Hope, and in most parts of the East.

3. The Italian Yellow Jessamine is, *Jasminum foliis alternis ternatis pinnatisque, ramis angulatis*. In the *Hortus Cliffortianus* it is termed, *Jasminum*

fo-lis

*foliis alternis ternatis acuminatis*, and Caspar Bauhine calls it, *Jasminum humile luteum* It grows common in Italy

*Jasminum* is of the class and order *Diandria Monogynia*, and the characters are,

1 Calyx is a monophyllous, tubular, oblong perianthium, divided at the edge into five erect, permanent segments

2 Corolla consists of a single petal, the tube of which is long and cylindrical, and the limb is divided into five spreading segments

3 Stamina are two short filaments, having small anthers, within the tube of the corolla

4 Pistillum consists of a roundish germen, a filiforme style the length of the stamina, and a bifid stigma

5 Pericarpium is a smooth oval berry, of two cells

6 Semina The seeds are two, large, oval oblong, convex on one side, and plane on the other

## C H A P XLV

## *I T E A*

THERE is only one species of this genus, which is a plant of about five or six feet in growth, that well deserves a place in a collection of shrubs about that height (This shrub described) The branches are numerous, and produce irregularly all around The leaves with which they are ornamented are of a fine green colour, gentle serratures possess their edges, their figure is that of a spear, and they grow alternately on the twigs But the flowers constitute the greatest beauty of these shrubs, for they are produced in July, at the ends of the young shoots, in large erect spikes Their colour is white, and as most of the branches will be terminated by them, the tree itself appears, at a distance, like one large bunch of white flowers So delightful is the variety which Nature furnishes for our contemplation and pleasure

The culture of this beautiful shrub is not very easy, tho it may be propagated by seeds and layers (Method of propagating it by seeds) We receive the seeds from abroad They should be sown in pots or boxes of fine loamy earth, mixed with drift or sea sand, and these should be plunged up to the brim in the moistest part of the garden, where they may remain till the spring after, for the seeds seldom come up the first year In March, therefore, the pots should be taken up, and plunged into an hotbed, which will promote the growth of the seeds, and make them become stronger by the autumn After the heat of the bed is over, they may be put in the same moist places again The plants ought to be constantly weeded and watered, and in the autumn should be removed into the green house, or placed under an hotbed-frame, to be protected in severe weather This care should be continued through the next winter also In the spring, a damp day being made choice of, and a moist part of the nursery being well prepared, they should be taken out of the pots or boxes, and planted at about a foot asunder, which will be distance enough for their standing two or three years, when they will be of a sufficient size to be planted out for good

2 These trees are also propagated by layers (and by layers), for which purpose, some of them should be planted for stools in a moist rich soil The young shoots of the preceding summer should be laid in the ground in the autumn and in order to make them strike root, a little wire should be twisted pretty close round the bud, where the root is desired to be This will impeding the motion of the sap the succeeding summer, will occasion them to swell in those parts, and strike root There are other methods by which the operation may be performed, but I ever found this the most expeditious and best

This genus, of which there are no other species, and to which no English name has been given, is distinguished by the name simply, *Itea*, and Mitchel calls it, *Diconangia* It is a native of Virginia, from whence we receive the seeds (Titles of this species.)

*Itea* is of the class and order *Pentandria Monogynia*, and the characters are, (Class and order in the Linnæan system. The characters)

1 Calyx is a very small, oval, monophyllous, permanent perianthium, divided at the top into five acute, coloured segments

2 Corolla consists of five long, spear shaped petals, inserted in the calyx

3 Stamina are five awl shaped, erect filaments, the length of the corolla, and inserted in the calyx, having roundish incumbent antheræ

4 Pistillum consists of an oval germen, a permanent cylindrical style the length of the stamina, and an obtuse stigma

5 Pericarpium is an oval, unilocular capsule, much longer than the calyx, and mucronated with the permanent style

6 Semina The seeds are numerous, small, oblong, and very bright

 CHAP

# CHAP XLVI

## *JUGLANS*, The WALNUT-TREE

THE real hardy distinct species of this genus are,

*Species of this tree*

1 The Common Walnut-tree
2 The Black Virginian Walnut
3 White Virginian Walnut
4 Pensylvanian Walnut

*Common Walnut* 1 The Common Walnut-tree has been already treated of in the former Book, among forest-trees, to which the reader is now referred, where he will see in what manner these large growing trees should be stationed in ornamental plantations

*Black Virginian Walnut* 2 The Black Virginian Walnut will grow to be a large timber-tree, as big as the Common sort The young shoots are smooth, and of a greenish brown The leaves are produced irregularly They are large and finely pinnated, being composed of about eight, ten, twelve, and sometimes fourteen pair of spear-shaped, sharp pointed folioles, which are terminated by an odd one, sawed at the edges, and the bottom pair are always the least The flowers, which make no show, are collected in a cylindrical katkin There are both male and female on the same plant but they give pleasure only to the curious botanist They blow early in the spring, and the females are succeeded by nuts of different sizes and shapes The nuts of the Common sort have a very thick shell, enclosing a sweet kernel They are furrowed, and of a rounder figure than those of the Common Walnut

*Varieties* There are many varieties of this species, and nuts of different sizes, like those of the Common Walnut, will always be the effect of seed Some will be small and round, others oblong, large, and deeply furrowed You must expect also to find a variety in the leaves, some will have no scent, others will be finely perfumed Hence the names, Common Virginian Walnut, Aromatic Walnut, Deeply-furrowed-fruited Walnut, &c have been used to express the different varieties of this species

*White Virginian Walnut* 3 The White Virginian Walnut, called the Hickery-nut, is a tree of lower stature, seldom rising more than thirty or thirty five feet high, though the sort called the Shag-bark is the strongest shooter The young shoots of all are smooth The leaves are also pinnated, though some of them are small, the number of folioles being from two or three pair to six or seven, besides the odd one with which they are terminated The folioles are of a pleasant green colour, narrowest at their base, and serrated at their edges The flowers are no ornament, and the nuts are small, hard, and of a white colour

*Names of its varieties* The sorts of this species go by the various names of Common Hickery-nut, Small-fruited Hickery-nut Shag-bark Hickery nut, &c

*Pensylvanian Walnut* 4 Pensylvanian Walnut This species grows to about the height of the former The [illegible] are very long, being composed of about eleven pair of folioles, besides the odd one with which they are terminated The flowers [illegible] yellowish, come out at the [illegible] the other, and are succeeded for the most part by small, roundish, hard-shelled fruit, though the fruit will be of different sizes in the different varieties

The method of propagating these trees is from the nuts, which we receive from America, where they grow naturally These must be sown as soon as they arrive, in the manner directed for raising the Common Walnut Their after management must also be exactly the same, therefore, to avoid repetition, I refer the reader to the Chapter in Book I which treats of this tree

*Title* The title of the Common Walnut is, *Juglans foliolis ovalibus glabris subserratis subæqualibus* Dodonæus calls it, *Nux Juglans*, Caspar Bauhine, *Nux Juglans, sive regia vulgaris* The many sorts of it have been distinguished by such titles as these, *Nux Juglans fructu maximo*, *Nux Juglans fructu teneri & fragili putamine*, *Nux Juglans bifera*, *Nux Juglans fructu serotino*, &c It is not certain in what part of the world the Common Walnut-tree naturally grows

2 Black Virginian Walnut is, *Juglans foliolis quindenis lanceolatis argute serratis, exterioribus minoribus gemmulis supra axillaribus* Herman and Catesby call it, *Nux Juglans Virginiana nigra*, and the other sort is by authors styled, *Juglans nigra, fructu oblongo profundissime insculpto* It grows naturally in Virginia, Carolina, and Maryland

3 White Virginian Walnut is, *Juglans foliolis septenis lanceolatis serratis impari sessili* Parkinson and Catesby call it, *Nux Juglans alba Virginiensis* Gronovius entitles it, *Juglans alba, fructu ovato compresso profunde insculpto durissimo* [illegible], and Plukenet, *Nux* [illegible] *alba* [illegible] *fastigio* [illegible] The Shag-bark variety, in the *Flora Virginica*, is termed, *Juglans alba fructu ovato compresso, nucleo dulci, cortice squamoso* It grows naturally in Virginia

4 Pensylvanian Walnut is, *Juglans* [illegible] *alterni breviore* It grows naturally in Pensylvania, and many parts of North America

*Class and order in the Linnæan system* *Juglans* is of the class and order *Monoecia Polyandria*, and the characters are,

I Male flowers are digested into an oblong katkin

1 CALYX The common amentum is cylindrical, and loosely imbricated, being composed of scales having spaces between them, each containing one flower

2 COROLLA is an elliptical, plane petal, divided into six segments

3 STAMINA are many very short filaments having erect acuminated antheræ, the length of the calyx

II Female flowers grow in small clusters, sitting close to the branches, having no footstalk

1 CALYX is a very short, erect, quadrifid petal [illegible] situated in the germen

2 Co

2 Corolla is an acute, erect petal, rather larger than the calyx, and divided into four parts

3 Pistillum conſiſts of a large oval germen, ſituated below the calyx, and two very ſhort ſtyles, with large, clavated, reflexed ſtigmas

4 Pericarpium is a large, oval, dry drupe, of one cell

5 Semen is a large, roundiſh, netted, furrowed nut, nearly divided into four cells The kernel is compoſed of four lobes, and is variouſly furrowed

# CHAP XLVII.

## *LAURUS*, The BAY-TREE

THOSE who are unacquainted with the different ſpecies of the various genera, may at firſt be ſtartled to find the article *Laurus* in this place, but I muſt give my readers to underſtand, that there are ſome ſorts of *Laurus* which ſhed their leaves, and beautifully contribute to the variety of deciduous trees, not ſo much by their flowers, as by the nature and fine colour of their leaves and bark, and the circumſtance of their being alſo ſcarce plants, renders them in other reſpects the more valuable and deſirable

The ſorts, then, of the Bay-tree proper for the plantations we are now treating of are,

Species

1 The Deciduous Bay

2 The Benjamin-tree, falſly ſo called

3 The Saſſafras-tree

Deſcription of the Deciduous Bay,

1 The Deciduous Bay, on a moiſt rich ſoil, in which it principally delights, will grow to be about ſixteen feet high, but in ſome ſoils, that are poſſeſſed of the oppoſite qualities, it will hardly arrive at half that height The branches are not very numerous, but they are ſmooth and of a purpliſh colour, look well in winter, and in ſummer exhibit their leaves of an oval ſpear-ſhaped figure They are about two or three inches in length, are proportionally broad, and placed oppoſite to each other on the branches Their upper ſurface is ſmooth, and of a pleaſant green colour, whilſt their under is rough and veined The flowers are ſmall and white, make no figure, come out from the ſides of the branches in May, and are ſucceeded by large red berries, which never ripen in England So that, not to mention the leaves in ſummer, which are very pretty, and the colour of the bark, which makes a variety in winter, it is the ſcarcity of this plant which makes it valuable

the Benjamin-tree,

2 The Benjamin-tree will grow to a much larger ſize than the other and its branches are rather numerous They are ſmooth, and of a fine light green colour The leaves are oval, acute, near four inches long, and two broad, their upper ſurface is ſmooth, and of a fine light-green colour, but their under ſurface is venoſe, and of a whitiſh caſt When bruiſed, they emit a fine fragrance The flowers make no figure They are ſmall and yellowiſh, come out from the ſides of the branches, in little cluſters, and are ſucceeded by large blackiſh berries, which never ripen in England

and the Saſſafras tree

3 The Saſſafras-tree The wood of the Saſſafras is well known in the ſhops, where it is ſold to be made into tea, being eſteemed an excellent antiſcorbutic and purger of the blood A decoction of the leaves and bark is alſo ſaid to poſſeſs the ſame virtues, and is drank by many perſons for thoſe purpoſes This tree will grow to nearly the height of the others, though the branches are not ſo numerous Its bark is ſmooth, and of a red colour, which beautifully diſtinguiſhes it in winter, whilſt the fine ſhining green of its leaves conſtitutes its greateſt beauty in ſummer In these, indeed, there is a variety, and a very extraordinary one Some are large, and of an oval figure, others are ſmaller, and of the ſame ſhape, whilſt others again, are ſo divided into three lobes, as to reſemble the leaves of ſome ſorts of the fig-tree Their edges are entire, their under ſurface is of a whitiſh caſt, their footſtalks are pretty long, placed alternately on the branches, and die to a red colour in the autumn The flowers are ſmall and yellowiſh They are produced in cluſters on longiſh pedicles, and are ſucceeded by blackiſh berries, which never ripen in England

Method of propagating this tree by ſeeds,

One method of culture is common to theſe three ſorts of trees and that may be performed two or three ways, but the beſt of all is by the ſeeds Theſe we receive, from the places where the trees grow naturally, in the ſpring They ſhould be preſerved in ſand, and, as ſoon as they arrive, ſhould be ſown in largiſh pots, an inch deep The ſoil for their reception ſhould be taken from a rich paſture at leaſt a year before, with the ſward It ſhould alſo be laid on in heap, and frequently turned, until the ſward is grown rotten, and the whole appears well mixed and fine If the paſture from whence it was taken near the ſurface is a ſandy loam, this is the beſt compoſt for theſe ſeeds, if not, a ſmall addition of drift or ſea ſand ſhould be added, and well mixed with the other mould After filling the pots with this ſoil, the ſeeds ſhould be ſown an inch deep and then they ſhould be plunged into common mould up to the rim If the ſoil be naturally moiſt, it will keep them cooler, and be better, and if the place be well ſheltered and ſhaded, it will be better ſtill Nothing more than weeding, which muſt be conſtantly obſerved during the ſummer, will be neceſſary, and in this ſituation they may remain until the March following, about the middle of which month, having prepared a good hot bed, the pots ſhould be taken up and plunged therein Soon after the ſeeds will come up, and when the young plants have ſufficiently received the benefit of this bed, they ſhould be enured by degrees to the open air Weeding and watering muſt be obſerved during the ſummer, and, at the approach of the cold weather in the autumn, they ſhould be removed under an hotbed frame, or ſome cover, to be protected from froſts during the winter In the ſpring, when the danger is over, they ſhould reſume their firſt ſtation, namely, the pots ſhould be plunged up to the rim, as when the ſeeds were firſt

first sown, and if this place be well sheltered, they may remain there all winter; if not, and severe frosts threaten, &c. should be taken up and placed under cover as before. After they have been thus managed three years from the seeds, they should be taken out of the pots with care, and planted in the nursery ground, at small distances, where they may remain until they are strong enough to be set out for good. By sowing the seeds in pots, and assisting them by a hotbed, a year or less is saved, for I hardly ever knew them come up, when sown in a natural border, under two years from the seeds; nay, I have known them remain three, and even some plants to come up the fourth year after sowing; which once shews the preference of the former practice, and should caution all who have not such conveniences, not to be too hasty in disturbing the beds when the seeds are sown in the natural ground, especially if they are not well preserved in mould or sand, there may be some years before they appear. Indeed, it is the long time we are in obtaining these plants, either by seeds, layers, &c. that makes them at present so very scarce among us.

2. These plants may also be encreased by layers, but very slowly, for they will be two, and sometimes three, or even four years, before they have struck out good roots; though the Benjamin-tree is propagated the quickest by this method. The young twigs should be laid in the ground in the autumn, and I ever found that twisting the wire round the bud, so as in some degree to stop the progress of the sap, and taking away with a knife a little of the bark, was a more effectual method of obtaining good roots than by the slit or twisting, especially when practised on the Sassafras tree.

3. Plants of these sorts are likewise sometimes obtained by suckers, which they will at times throw out, and which may be often taken off with pretty good roots; but when they are weak, and with but few fibres, they should be planted in pots, and assisted by a moderate heat in a bed. With such management they will be good plants by the autumn, and in the spring may be planted out any where.

4. Cuttings of these trees, when planted in a good bark bed, and duly watered, will also oftentimes grow. When this method is practised, and plants obtained, they must be enured by degrees to the open air, till they are hardy enough to be set out for good.

1. The Deciduous Bay is entitled, *Laurus foliis enervosis obovatis acuminatis annuis, ramis supra-axillaribus*. Gronovius calls it, *Laurus foliis lanceolatis enervibus annuis*; also, *Laurus foliis enervibus ovatis utrinque acutis*. Catesby, *Cornus foliis salicis Laurinæ acuminatis, floribus albis, fructu jasminis*. It grows naturally on swampy places, and by the sides of brooks, rivers, &c. in Virginia.

2. The Benjamin-tree is, *Laurus foliis enervis ovatis utrinque acutis integris annuis*. Commelin calls it, *Arbor Virginiana, citreæ vel limonii folio, Benzoinum fundens*; and Plukenet, *Arbor Virginiana, pishamin folio, baccata Benzoinum redolens*. This is a native of Virginia and Pensylvania.

3. The Sassafras is *Laurus foliis integris et trilobis*. Plukenet and Catesby call it, *Cornus mas odorata, folio trifido, margine plano, Sassafras dicta*; also, *Cornus mas Sassafras laurus foliis ...*. C. Bauhine calls it, *Sassafras arbor, ex Florida, ficulneo folio*. It grows naturally in Virginia, Carolina, and Florida.

*Laurus* is of the class and order *Enneandria Monogynia*; and the characters are,

1. CALYX. There is none.

2. COROLLA consists of six oval, acuminated, concave, erect petals. The nectarium consists of three acuminated, coloured tubercles, standing round the germen.

3. STAMINA are nine compressed, obtuse filaments, standing in order by threes, having antheræ which adhere to the edge of the upper part of the filaments on both sides.

There are two roundish glands, which are fixed by a very short footstalk to each filament of the inner order near the base.

4. PISTILLUM consists of an oval germen, a simple equal style the length of the stamina, and an obtuse, oblique stigma.

5. PERICARPIUM is an oval, acuminated drupe of one cell.

6. SEMEN. The seed is an oval, sharp-pointed nut.

# CHAP. XLVIII.

## *LAVATERA.*

THE *Lavatera* affords several species of a shrubby kind, which will grow to be large plants, and make a great show at a distance, but, at the same time, are very improper for the wilderness, on account of their short lived nature, some of them continuing only about two or three years, and then dying, leaving a vacancy in the places which they used to occupy. Nevertheless, as they are very beautiful plants, and in some warm sandy situations continue for many years, we will venture to introduce them in this place, at the same time laying no restraint on the discerning horticultor, but leaving him to judge, from the nature of his soil and situation, whether he will have them among his shrubs, or reserve them for the warmer parts of the flower garden, to be regularly raised, like other large growing plants of that duration. The species then are,

1. The Common Mallow-tree.
2. Trilobate Mallow-tree.
3. Five-lobed Mallow-tree.
4. Shining leaved Mallow-tree.

1. The Common Mallow-tree is a well known plant. It usually grows to eight or ten feet high, and in a rich soil will grow to twelve, or more. The stem is thick and strong, and divides near the top into several branches, which are closely ornamented with large downy leaves; they are soft to the touch, plaited, and their edges are cut

cut into many angles The flowers are produced in clusters, from the wings of the leaves, in June, and there will be a succession of them until late in the autumn Each flower has its separate footstalk Their colour is purple, their shape like that of the Common Mallow; and they would cut a great figure, were they not much obscured by the largeness of the leaves The whole tree has a noble look and its continuing for about three months in flower makes it very valuable But though its short-lived continuance is much to be regretted, yet Nature seems to have made some amends for this, by furnishing it with good seeds in such great plenty, for by these thousands of plants may be soon raised, nay, they will sometimes shed themselves, and come up without any art But when they are to be regularly sown, let it be done in April, in the places where they are designed to remain, and they will flower the summer after Though this plant is called a biennial, in some warm dry situations the stalks become hard and woody, and the plants will continue to produce flowers and seeds for many years

Varieties There are several varieties of this species, the leaves of some being round and indented, others acutely cut, others waved These among old gardeners go by the names of the Round-leaved, Waved-leaved Mallow tree, &c All of them will cause variety, and their station must be in open places in wilderness-quarters, at a distance from the walks, or rather, more properly, as their lives are of short continuance, at the back of large borders in the pleasure garden Quitting these, we will proceed to some other sorts, which must be placed near the edges of the wilderness-quarters, among low shrubs, being very beautiful flowering shrubs, of low growth, that will continue flowering for many years The species for this purpose, then, with its varieties, is called,

Trilobate Lavatera. 2 The Trilobate *Lavatera* This species is very ornamental in the front, or among the low shrubs in the wilderness quarters, or when stationed in large borders in pleasure gardens, as it is naturally of low growth, seldom rising to above four or five feet high It has rather a large spreading root, in proportion to the size of the shrub The branches are numerous, and of a palish green colour, and the leaves are of different figures, though chiefly trilobate, or composed of three lobes, that are indented on their edges They vary much in their size, some being larger, some smaller, and some more divided than others Their colour, when the plant is in perfect health, is a very pleasant green, but they will often shew themselves a little variegated, at which time you may be assured the shrub is in a sickly state This often does not continue long, and the plant will assume its former verdure, and as frequently and very speedily relapse into its weak state, which shews that, though hardy with respect to cold, it is rather of a sickly nature in this country The flowers are produced singly, on short footstalks They grow from the joints, at the bosoms of the leaves; three or four of them will appear at each joint, and being large, they make a fine show in August, the time of flowering

Varieties There are varieties of this species, differing in the shape of the leaves and size of the flowers, which still have names among old botanists

Five lobed Lavatera 3 Five-lobed *Lavatera* is a distinct species from the preceding, though it differs little from it, except in the nature of the leaves, each of which is composed of five lobes, that are hastated, or pointed like a spear, and in the flowers of this shrub being smaller They will be in full blow in August, and there will often be a succession of them till the early frosts advance

Varieties in its leaves The leaves of this species vary Some are shaped like briony, others are nearly round, and the lobes of others are very acute Hence the names Briony leaved, Round-leaved, Acute-leaved Mallow tree, &c have been used to express them

Shining leaved Mallow 4 Shining-leaved Mallow-tree grows to about the height of the former The leaves are large, septangular, plaited, downy, white, and glisten towards the sun The flowers are produced in bunches, from the ends of the branches They are shaped like those of the Common Mallow, come out in July, and continue in succession until the end of autumn

Varieties of this species The varieties of this species go by the names of Waved-leaved, the Common Spanish, the Sulphur leaved Mallow-tree, &c

Method of propagating the three last sorts, These three sorts are easily propagated by cuttings, which should be planted, early in the spring, in a shady border of light rich earth Many of them will grow, and the plants may stand two or three years before they are removed to the places where they are designed to remain

and best way to propagate all the species The best method of propagating all the sorts is by seeds, and by this way fresh varieties may be obtained The seeds should be procured from Spain, where the plants naturally grow, for none, except the first sort, ripen well here Having got a sufficient quantity, sow them in a border of light, fine, rich earth, about the middle of March They will easily come up and nothing but weeding and watering in dry weather will be required until the spring after, when they should be planted in nursery-lines, there to remain until they are set out for good The leaves of all the sorts continue until the frosts come on, so that if an open winter happens, they will continue in verdure the greatest part of the season

Titles 1 The Mallow-tree is entitled, *Lavatera caule arboreo, foliis septemangularibus tomentosis plicatis, pedunculis confertis unifloris axillaribus* In the *Hortus Cliffortianus* it is termed, *Lavatera foliis septemangularibus obtusis plicatis villosis, caule fruticoso, floribus ad alas confertis* Dodonæus calls it, *Malva arborescens*, and Caspar Bauhine, *Malva arborea veneta dicta, parvo flore* It is a native of Italy

2 The Trilobate *Lavatera* is entitled, *Lavatera caule fruticoso, foliis subcordatis subtrilobis rotundatis crenatis, stipulis cordatis, pedunculis unifloris aggregatis* In the *Hortus Cliffortianus* it is termed, *Malva foliis subcordatis trilobis obtusis serratis villosis* Van Royen calls it, *Lavatera foliis subcordatis emarginatis obsolete trilobis crenatis petiolo brevioribus, stipulis cordatis*, and Plukenet, *Althæa fruticans Hispanica, aceris Monspessulani incanis foliis, grandiflora saponem spirans* It is a native of Spain

3 *Lavatera* with five lobes is called, *Lavatera caule fruticoso, foliis quinquelobo-hastatis, floribus solitariis* In the *Hortus Cliffortianus* it is named, *Lavatera foliis quinquangularibus acutis crenatis lacinia media productiore* Caspar Bauhine calls it, *Althæa frutescens, folio acuto, parvo flore*, Plukenet, *Althæa frutescens, folio acuto virente molli, flore speciosa*, and Lobel, *Althæa arborea Olbia in Galloprovincia* It is common in the south of France

4 Shining-leaved Mallow is, *Lavatera caule arboreo, foliis septemangularibus acutis crenatis plicatis tomentosis, racemis terminalibus* Morison calls it, *Malva foliis mollibus undulatis in margine superius incis sulphureis ad solem splendentibus donatis*, also, *Malva Hispanica* It grows in Spain and Portugal

Class and order in the Linnæan system. The characters.

*Lavatera* is of the class and order *Monadelphia Polyandria*, and the characters are,

1 CALYX is a double perianthium The exterior is formed of one leaf, which is semitrifid, obtuse, permanent, and short The interior is also of one leaf, this is quinquifid and permanent, and more acute and erect than the other

2 COROLLA consists of five obcordated, plane, patent petals, which coalesce at their base

3 STAMINA are numerous filaments, joined below, and form a cylinder, above they are loose, and inserted into the corolla Their antheræ are reniform

4 PISTILLUM consists of an orbicular germen, and a short cylindric style, crowned by many bristly stigmas

5 PERICARPIUM is composed of numerous small capsules, formed into a round head, and covered in front by a hollow shield

6 SEMEN In each of these capsules is contained one kidney shaped seed

## CHAP XLIX

## LIGUSTRUM, The PRIVET

THE Privet is very far from being destitute of beauties to recommend itself to a Collection, though the commonness of it will not suffer us to permit more than a few plants there It grows almost all over England in our hedges, is known to all, and has been, and is still by some, planted to make hedges, though there are a great many other sorts more proper for that purpose However, a Collection ought to have a few plants of the Privet for it has its beauties in many respects, and is by some held in great esteem

Description of the Privet

The Privet will grow to the height of about ten or twelve feet The branches are very numerous, slender, and tough, covered with a smooth grey bark, and, when broken, emit a strong scent The young twigs are generally produced opposite, and alternately of contrary directions on the older branches The leaves also are placed opposite by pairs in the same manner They are of an oblong figure, small smooth, of a dark green colour, have a nauseous disagreeable taste, and continue on the trees very late The flowers are produced in close spikes, at the ends of the branches, in May, June, and often in July They are white, very beautiful, but disagreeably scented, appear in May, June, and July, and are succeeded by black berries, which in the autumn will constitute the greatest beauty of this plant, for they will be all over the tree, at the ends of the branches, in thick clusters They are of a jet black, and will thus continue to ornament it in this singular manner during the greatest part of the winter

The culture of the Privet is easy, for it may be increased,

Method of propagating this tree by seeds

1 By the seeds and by this way the strongest plants may be obtained The seeds, soon after they are ripe, should be sown in any bed of common garden-mould made fine They ought to be covered about an inch deep, and all the succeeding summer should be kept clean of weeds; for the plants never, at least not many of them, come up until the spring after After they are come up, they will require no other care than weeding, and in the spring following may be planted in the nursery-ground, where they will require very little care besides keeping the weeds down, until they are taken up for good

by layers,

2 These plants may be encreased by layers, for the young shoots being laid in the ground in the autumn, will by that time twelvemonth have taken good root, the largest of which may be planted out for good, and the smallest set in the nursery, to gain strength

and by cuttings

3 Cuttings, also, planted in October, will strike root freely, and if the soil is inclined to be moist, and is shaded, it will be the better for them, especially if the succeeding summer should prove a dry one If these cuttings are thinly planted, they will require no other removing till they are set out for good If a large quantity is desired, they may be placed close, within about two or three inches of each other, and then taken up and planted in the nursery the autumn following, to remain there until they are wanted for the above purpose

Proper situation for it

The Privet, of all other trees, will thrive best in the smoke of great cities, so that whoever has a little garden in such places, and is desirous of having a few plants that look green and healthy, may be gratified in the Privet, because it will flourish and look well there It will also grow very well under the shade and drip of trees

Titles of this species

The Privet stands with the simple title, *Ligustrum* C Bauhine calls it, *Ligustrum Germanicum*, others, *Ligustrum vulgare* It grows naturally in Italy, Germany, England, and almost all parts of Europe

Uses of its berries and leaves

The berries of the Privet were formerly used in dyeing, and for making of ink The flowers and leaves have excellent virtues, and are used for many purposes in medicine

Class and order in the Linnæan system The characters

*Ligustrum* is of the class and order *Diandria Monogynia*, and the characters are,

1 CALYX is a small, monophyllous, tubular perianthium, divided at the top into four erect, obtuse segments

2 COROLLA is an infundibuliforme petal The tube is cylindric, and longer than the calyx The limb is cut into four oval, patent segments

3 STAMINA are two simple filaments, that are placed opposite to each other, having erect antheræ almost the length of the corolla

4 PISTILLUM consists of a roundish germen, a very short style, and of a bifid, obtuse, thickish stigma

5 PERICARPIUM is a smooth, roundish berry, of one cell

6 SEMINA The seeds are four, convex on one side, and angular on the other

CHAP

# CHAP. L.

## *L I Q U I D A M B E R.*

THIS genus affords two of the finest tall growing trees we receive from abroad.

These trees described

They will grow to be thirty or forty feet high, and, except the flowers, which make little show, they have every other perfection to recommend them. They are tall, upright, well growing trees, and naturally form themselves into a beautiful head. The leaves are of a shining delightful green, and both species of this shrub possess an excellent aromatic fragrance, which chears and revives the head and spirits.

The two species of the *Liquidamber* are distinguished by the names of,

Species

1. Virginian, or Maple leaved *Liquidamber*.
2. Canada *Liquidamber*, or Spleenwort leaved Gale.

Description of the Virginian

1. Virginian, or Maple-leaved *Liquidamber*, will shoot in a regular manner to the above-mentioned height, having its young twigs covered with a smooth, light brown bark, whilst those of the older are of a darker colour. The leaves grow irregularly on the young branches, on long footstalks. They resemble those of the Common Maple in figure, the lobes are all serrated, and from the base of the leaf a strong mid rib runs to the extremity of each lobe that belongs to it. They are of a lucid green, and emit their odoriferous particles in such plenty as to perfume the circumambient air, nay, the whole tree exsudes such a fragrant transparent resin, as to have given occasion to its being taken for the Sweet Storax. These trees, therefore, are very proper to be planted singly in large opens, that they may amply display their fine pyramidal growth, or to be set in places near seats, pavilions, &c. The flowers are of a kind of saffron colour. They are produced at the ends of the branches, the beginning of April, and sometimes sooner, and are succeeded by large round brown fruit, which looks singular, but is thought by many to be no ornament to the tree.

and the Canada Liquidamber

2. Canada *Liquidamber*, or Spleenwort leaved Gale. The young branches of this species are slender, tough, and hardy. The leaves are oblong, of a deep green colour, hairy underneath, and have indentures on their edges alternately, very deep. The flowers come out from the sides of the branches, like the former, and they are succeeded by small roundish fruit, which seldom ripens in England.

Method of propagating both sorts by seeds

The culture of both these species is the same, and may be performed by seeds or layers; but the first method is the best. We receive the seeds from America in the spring. Against their arrival a fine bed, in a warm well sheltered place, should be prepared. If the soil is not naturally good, and inclined to be sandy, it should be wholly taken out near a foot deep, and the vacancy filled up with earth taken up a year before, from a fresh pasture, with the sward and all well rotted and mixed by being often turned, and afterwards mixed with a sixth part of drift or sea sand. A dry day being made choice of, early in March, let the seeds be sown, and the finest of this compost riddled over them a quarter of an inch deep. When the hot weather in the spring comes on, the beds should be shaded, and waterings given often, but in very small quantities, only affording them a gentle, nay, a very small sprinkling at a time. Miller says, the seeds of these plants never come up under two years. But in this compost, and with this early management, I hardly ever knew it longer than the end of May before the young plants made their appearance. The plants being come up, shading should still be afforded them in the parching summer, and a watering every other night, and this will promote their growth, and cause them to become stronger plants by the autumn. In the autumn, the beds should be hooped to be covered with mats in the severe frosts. These mats, however, should always be taken off in open weather, and this is all the management they will require during the first winter. The succeeding summer they will require no other trouble than weeding; though, if it should prove a very dry one, they will find benefit from a little water now and then. By the autumn, they will be grown strong enough to resist the cold of the following winter, without demanding the trouble of matting, if the situation is well sheltered; if not, it will be proper to have the hoops prepared, and the mats ready, against the black northern frosts, which would endanger at least their losing their tops. After this, nothing except weeding will be wanted; and in the spring following, that is three years from the time of their first appearance, they should be taken up (for I would not have them removed before, unless some of the strongest plants be drawn out of the bed) and planted in the nursery, a foot asunder, and two feet distant in the rows. Hoeing the weeds in the rows in the summer, and digging them in the winter, is all the trouble they will afterwards occasion until they are planted out for good.

2. These plants are easily encreased by layers. and by layers
The operation must be performed in the autumn, on the young summer's shoots; and the best way is by slitting them at the joint, as is practised for carnations. In a strong dry soil, they will be often two years or more before they strike root; though, in a fine light soil, I ever found them to take freely enough. By this method good plants may be obtained, though it is not so eligible as the other, if we have the conveniency of procuring the seeds.

1. The title of the Virginian, or Maple-leaved Title
sort, is, *Liquidamber foliis palmato-angulatis*. Plukenet and Catesby call it, *Liquidamber arbor seu Styraciflua aceris folio*; Ray, *Styrax aceris folio*; Caspar Bauhine, Gronovius, and others, simply, *Liquidamber*. It grows naturally in the uliginous parts of Virginia and Mexico.

2. Canada *Liquidamber* is, *Liquidamber foliis oblongis alternatim sinuatis*. In the *Hortus Cliffortianus* it is termed, *Myrica foliis oblongis alternatim sinuatis*. Petiver calls it, *Gale mariana, asplenii folio*; and Plukenet, *Myrti Brabanticae affinis Americana foliorum laciniis asplenii modo divisis*. It grows common in Canada and Pensylvania.

This

Claſs and order in the Linnæan ſyſtem. The characters.

This genus is of the claſs and order *Monoecia Polyandria*, and the characters are,

I. The male flowers are numerous, and collected into long, conical, looſe catkins.

1. CALYX. The common involucrum is formed of four leaves, which are oval, concave, and caducous, and alternately ſhorter.

2. COROLLA. There is none.

3. STAMINA are very ſhort and numerous filaments, joined together into a body, which is convex on one ſide, but plane on the other, having erect, didymous, four-furrowed, bilocular antheræ.

II. Female flowers form a globe, and are ſituated at the baſe of the male ſpike.

1. CALYX. The involucrum is the ſame as in the male, but double. The perianthium of each is oval ſhaped, angular, and verrucoſe.

2. COROLLA. There is none.

3. PISTILLUM conſiſts of an oblong germen faſtened to the perianthium, and of two tubulated ſtyles, with recurved downy ſtigmas.

4. PERICARPIUM conſiſts of a number of oval unilocular capſules, that have two valves at the top, are acute, ligneous, and collected into a globular body.

5. SEMINA. The ſeeds are many, bright, and oblong.

# CHAP. LI.

## LIRIODENDRON, The TULIP-TREE.

Deſcription of this tree.

THE Virginian Tulip-tree is a very curious foreign plant, or the largeſt-growing ſort. In thoſe parts of America where it grows common, it will arrive to a prodigious bulk, and affords excellent timber for many uſes, particularly, the trunk is frequently hollowed, and made into boats ſufficient to carry many people, and for this purpoſe no tree is thought more proper by the inhabitants of thoſe parts. With us, it may be ſtationed among trees of about forty feet growth, beſides others which ought to be placed ſingly in large opens, and in the fineſt graſs plats, where a few odd trees of different ſorts are promiſcuouſly thrown. The Tulip-tree riſes with an upright trunk, covered with a grey bark. The branches, which are not very numerous, of the two years old wood, are ſmooth and brown, whilſt the bark of the ſummer's ſhoots is ſmoother and ſhining, and of a bluiſh colour. They are very pithy. Their young wood is green, and when broken emits a ſtrong ſcent. The leaves grow irregularly on the branches, on long footſtalks. They are of a particular ſtructure, being compoſed of three lobes, the middlemoſt of which is truncated in ſuch a manner, that it appears as if it had been cut off and hollowed at the middle. The two others are rounded off. They are about four or five inches long, and as many broad. They are of two colours, their upper ſurface is ſmooth, and of a ſtronger green than the lower. They fall off pretty early in autumn, and the buds for the next year's ſhoots ſoon after begin to ſwell and become dilated, inſomuch that, by the end of December, thoſe at the ends of the branches will become near an inch long, and half an inch broad. The outward lamina of the leaves are of an oval figure, have ſeveral longitudinal veins, and are of a bluiſh colour. The flowers are produced with us in July, at the ends of the branches. They ſomewhat reſemble the tulip, which occaſions its being called the Tulip-tree. The number of petals of which each is compoſed, like thoſe of the tulip, is ſix, and theſe are ſpotted with green, red, white, and yellow, thereby making a beautiful mixture. The flowers are ſucceeded by large cones, which never ripen in England.

Method of propagating it.

The culture of the Tulip-tree is very eaſy, if the ſeeds are good, for by these, which we receive from abroad, they are to be propagated. No particular compoſt need be ſought for, neither is the trouble of pots, boxes, hotbeds, &c. required. They will grow exceeding well in beds of common garden mould, and the plants will be hardier and better than thoſe raiſed with more tenderneſs and care. Therefore, as ſoon as you receive the ſeeds, which is generally in February, and a few dry days have happened, that the mould will work free, ſow the ſeeds, covering them three quarters of an inch deep, and in doing of this, obſerve to lay them lengthways, otherwiſe, by being very long, one part perhaps, that of the embryo plant, may be out of the ground ſoon, and ſo the ſeed loſt. This being done, let the beds be hooped, and as ſoon as the hot weather and drying winds come on in the ſpring, let them be covered from ten o'clock in the morning till ſun-ſet. If little rain happens, they muſt be duly watered every other day, and by the end of May your plants will come up. Shade and watering in the hotteſt ſummer muſt be afforded them, and they will afterwards give very little trouble. The next winter they will want no other care than, at the approach of it, ſticking ſome furze-buſhes round the bed, to break the keen edge of the black froſts, for I ever found ſeedlings of this ſort very hardy and ſeldom to ſuffer by any weather. After they have been two years in the ſeed bed, they ſhould be taken up and planted in the nurſery, a foot aſunder, and two feet diſtant in the rows. After this, the uſual nurſery care of hoeing the weeds, and digging between the rows in the winter, will ſuffice till they are taken up for good.

Titles of this genus.

The title of the Tulip-tree is, *Liriodendron foliis lobatis*. It has been called, *Tulipifera*, a very proper name. Hermann calls it, *Tulipifera arbor Virginiana*, and Plukenet and Cateſby, *Tulipifera Virginiana, tripartito aceris folio, media lacinia velut abſciſſa*, also, *Tulipifera Caroliniana, foliis productioribus magis angulosis*. It grows common in moſt parts of North America.

Claſs and order in the Linnæan ſyſtem.

*Liriodendron* is of the claſs and order *Polyandria Polygynia*, and the characters are,

1. CA-

The characters

1 CALYX The proper involucrum is compoſed of two triangular, plane, deciduous leaves The perianthium alſo is deciduous, and is compoſed of three oblong, concave, patent leaves, reſembling petals

2 COROLLA is bell ſhaped It is compoſed of ſix petals Theſe are obtuſe, channeled at their baſe, and the three outer ones are deciduous

3 STAMINA are numerous, linear filaments, ſhorter than the corolla, and inſerted in the receptacle of the fructification, having narrow antheræ that are faſtened longitudinally to their ſides

4 PISTILLUM conſiſts of numerous germina, formed into a cone, having no ſtyle, but a globular ſtigma ſituated on each of them

5 PERICARPIUM There is none, but the ſeeds are ſelected imbricatum wiſe into a body in ſhape of a cone

6 SEMINA are numerous They are angular on their inſide, acute and compreſſed at the baſe, and each ends in a ſpear-ſhaped ſquamma, which takes its riſe from the acute angle on the under ſide

# C H A P LII

## *L O N I C E R A*, The H O N E Y S U C K L E

LONICERA now ſwallows up many genera of old authors, ſuch as, the *Diervilla*, the St Peter's Wort, the Upright and the Trailing Honeyſuckles, &c How many beautiful ſorts are here preſented to our view! and how different is the appearance they make in the garden! The ſpecies, with their varieties, form a tolerable collection, and each has ſome ſtriking beauty to recommend it Though it muſt be owned the flowers of the Upright ſorts of Honeyſuckles make little ſhow, yet there is an elegance in them which is vaſtly pleaſing They are of low growth, and naturally form themſelves into a neat upright head, whilſt the Trailing ſorts, which we call Woodbines, not only feaſt the eye with the profuſion of beautiful flowers with which they are covered at the time of blow, but regale the ſmell with a fragrance inferior to none of the flowery tribe The Woodbines, however, belong to another part of this Work, whilſt the ſpecies proper for this place are,

Species of this genus.

1 *Diervilla*
2 St Peter's Wort
3 Upright Blue berried Honeyſuckle
4 Upright Red berried Honeyſuckle
5 Black-berried Upright Honeyſuckle
6 Fly Honeyſuckle
7 Pyrenean Dwarf Cherry
8 Tartarian Honeyſuckle, or Dwarf Cherry with heart-ſhaped leaves

Diervilla deſcribed

*Diervilla* is a ſhrub of about the height of three or four feet The branches are few, and larger in proportion than the height of the ſhrub, they are very full of pith, and when broken emit a ſtrong ſcent The leaves are placed oppoſite by pairs, on ſhort footſtalks They are near three inches long and about half as broad, of an oblong heart ſhaped figure, finely ſerrated, and end in acute points Their upper ſurface is ſmooth, and of a fine green colour, their under is lighter, and has five or ſix pair of ſtrong nerves running irregularly from the midrib to the borders The flowers are produced in looſe bunches, both at the ends and at the ſides of the branches Each is formed of one leaf, the tube is long, and the top is divided into five parts, which turn backward They are of a yellow colour, and will be in blow in May, and ſometimes moſt of the ſummer months Theſe flowers are ſucceeded, in the countries where they grow naturally, by black oval berries, each containing four cells *Diervilla* forms an agreeable variety amongſt other ſhrubs of its own growth, though the flowers make no great figure It is very hardy with reſpect to cold, and may be planted in any part of the nurſery where it is wanted

Method of propagating this tree from ſuckers,

No art is required to encreaſe this plant, it ſpawns, and thus propagates itſelf in great plenty Theſe ſuckers ſhould be taken up in autumn, and planted out in the nurſery After remaining there a year or two, they may be taken up for good

and by cuttings

This tree may be alſo encreaſed by cuttings Theſe ſhould be planted in October, very cloſe, if a quantity are wanted By the autumn following, they will have good roots They may be taken up and planted in the nurſery, like the ſpawn, for a year or two, and then ſet out for good Plants raiſed this way will not be quite ſo ſubject to throw out ſuckers as the others

St Peter's Wort deſcribed

2 St Peter's Wort St Peter's Wort will ariſe to the height of about four or five feet The main ſtems are ragged, and of a dirty dark brown The branches are numerous and ſhort, though oftentimes it ſends out ſome trailing ſlender branches which will grow to a great length The leaves of this ſhrub conſtitute its greateſt beauty They are very numerous, ſmall, about half an inch long, and of an oval figure Their footſtalks are exceeding ſhort, and they ſtand oppoſite by pairs on the ſlender branches They die in the autumn to a dark brown The time of this plant's flowering is Auguſt The flowers grow round the ſtalks They are ſmall, of an herbaceous colour, and make no figure

Manner of encreaſing it from the trailing branches,

The culture of St Peter's Wort is very eaſy If a ſpade full of mould be thrown over each of the trailing branches, any time in the winter, they will by the autumn following have ſtruck root, and theſe may be planted out in the nurſery, to ſtand until they are of a proper ſize to be planted out for good

and by cuttings

This ſhrub may be alſo propagated by cuttings, and in order to obtain good cuttings for the purpoſe, the year before the plants ſhould be headed near the ground, which will make them ſhoot vigorouſly the ſummer following Theſe young ſhoots muſt be the cuttings to be planted October

October is the best month for the work, and if they are planted in a moistish soil, and have a shady situation, they will have taken good root by the autumn If they are planted very thick, as cuttings commonly are, they should be all taken up, and planted in the nursery a foot asunder, and two feet distant in the rows, but if the living cuttings are no nearer than about a foot, they may remain without removing until they are planted out for good

Description of the Upright Blue-berried,

3 The Upright Blue-berried Honeysuckle is a shrub of about four feet in growth The branches are round, smooth, and of a reddish-purplish colour The leaves are oblong spear-shaped, of a fine green, and stand opposite by pairs on the branches The flowers, which are white, are produced in May from the sides of the branches, and are succeeded by blue berries, that will be ripe in August

Red-berried

4 The Upright Red-berried Honeysuckle will grow to the height of about five feet The branches are very upright, the young shoots are angular, and covered with a brown bark The leaves are tolerably large, spear-shaped, a little resemble those of the mock-orange, and grow opposite to each other The flowers are produced from the sides of the branches, on long footstalks They are of a red colour, come out in April, are each succeeded by a pair of red berries, which will be ripe the end of July or early in August

Black-berried,

5 Upright Black-berried Honeysuckle differs from the Blue-berried only in that the seeds of this are black, and grow two together, whereas those of the Blue-berried are single and distinct Except this, there is hardly any difference to be perceived

and Fly Honeysuckle

6 Fly Honeysuckle will grow to the height of about seven or eight feet The bark on the branches is of a whitish colour, which causes a variety, and makes it distinguished in the winter season The leaves, which are placed opposite by pairs, are downy, and of an oblong oval figure The flowers are white and erect They are produced from the sides of the branches, in June, and are succeeded by two red berries, which will be ripe in September

of the Pyrenæan Dwarf Cherry

7 The Pyrenæan Dwarf Cherry is but a low shrub It seldom arrives to more than a yard in height The branches are produced irregularly The leaves are smooth, oblong, and placed opposite by pairs The flowers are white, produced from the sides of the branches, on slender footstalks, in April, and are succeeded by roundish berries, which will be ripe in September

and the Tartarean Honeysuckle

8 Tartarean Honeysuckle, or Dwarf Cherry with heart-shaped leaves, is a shrub of about three or four feet high Its branches are erect, like the upright sorts and it differs in few respects from them, except that the leaves are heart-shaped It exhibits its flowers in April, and these are succeeded by twin red berries, which will be ripe in August

These are the Upright sorts of *Lonicera*, to which one method of culture is common, and that may be performed two ways

Method of raising these sorts by seeds,

1 By seeds Common garden-mould, dug fine, and cleared of the roots of all weeds, will serve for their reception In this the seeds should be sown soon after they are ripe, about half an inch deep After the beds are neated up, they will require no other care until the spring, when the weeds should be picked off as fast as they appear Some of the plants by this time will have come up; but the far greater part will remain until the second spring before they shew themselves, so that the beds must be entirely untouched until at least two years after sowing They will require no care all this time, except being kept clear of weeds, though if watering be afforded them in dry weather, it will be the better After they are all up, and have stood a year or two in the seed-bed, they may be taken up and planted in the nursery, at small distances, and in two or three years, they will be of a proper size to plant out for good

and by cuttings

2 All these sorts may be also propagated by cuttings These should be planted in October, in any sort of garden-mould that is tolerably good If a quantity is wanted, they may be placed very close, and a small spot of ground will hold thousands If the place be shaded, it will be a great advantage, as most cuttings are in danger of suffering by the violence of the sun's rays before they have struck, or whilst they are striking root The winter following, they may be all taken up, and planted out in the nursery, a foot asunder, and two feet distant in the rows, where they may stand until they are taken up for good

Observations on the Trailing sorts

The Trailing sorts of the *Lonicera* should be next considered, but these belong to another part of this Book, which treats of Trailing and Climbing Plants Nevertheless, it must be observed here, that Honeysuckles are not to be excluded low shrubberies and gardens, for as they may be trained up to a stem, kept low, managed in what manner, and reared to what size the owner pleases, for these reasons they have always had a principal share amongst shrubs and in flower gardens, as well for the beauty of their flowers, as for the delightful odours they emit all around, especially after a shower, in the evening, or in cloudy weather The gardener, then, should have plenty of all the different sorts which he will find for his purpose among the Climbing plants, in the shrubbery, near frequented walks, and also those that are more peculiarly designed for private retirement, for by their exhalations the animal spirits will be comforted and revived, and proper reflections introduced of that Almighty and Good Being, who *affordeth food for all cattle, and green herb for the use of man*

Let us now see the titles of these respective species in authors

Titles of these species

1 The title of *Diervilla* now is, *Lonicera racemis terminalibus, foliis serratis* In the *Hortus Cliffortianus* it is termed, *Diervilla* Tournefort calls it *Diervilla Acadiensis fruticosa, flore luteo* It grows naturally in Nova Scotia and Acadia

2 St Peter's Wort is, *Lonicera capitulis lateralibus pedunculatis, foliis petiolatis* In the *Hortus Cliffortianus* it is termed, *Lonicera pedunculis axillaribus capitatis, foliis petiolatis* Dillenius calls it, *Symphoricarpos foliis alatis* It grows naturally in Virginia and Carolina

3 Upright Blue-berried Honeysuckle is, *Lonicera pedunculis bifloris, baccis coadunatis globosis, stylis indivisis* Van Royen calls it, *Lonicera pedunculis bifloris villabiatis, baccâ singulari globosâ integerrimâ*, Caspar Bauhine, *Chamæcerasus montana, fructu singulari cæruleo*, and Clusius, *Periclymenum rectum, fructu cæruleo* It grows naturally in Switzerland

4 Upright Red-berried Honeysuckle is, *Lonicera pedunculis bifloris, baccis coadunatis didymis* In the *Hortus Cliffortianus* it is termed, *Lonicera pedunculis bifloris, foliis ov[illegible] integris* C Bauhine calls it, *Chamæcerasus Alpina, fructu rubro gemino, duobus punctis notato*, Van Royen, *Lonicera baccis bifloris con[illegible], f[illegible] bilobatis*, Clusius, *Periclymenum rectum qu[illegible]*, and Gesner, *Chamæcerasus* It grows naturally on the Savoy, Helvetian, and Pyrenean Mountains

5 Black-berried Upright Honeysuckle is, *Lonicera pedunculis bifloris, baccis distinctis, foliis ellipticis integerrimis* Gesner calls it, *Periclymenum [illegible] nigrum*, Caspar Bauhine, *Chamæcerasus*

*cerasus Alpina, fructu nigro gemino*, J Bauhine, *Periclymenum rectum, folio serrato*; and Clusius, *Periclymenum rectum* 2 It grows common on the Alps and Swiss Mountains

6 Fly Honeysuckle is, *Lonicera pedunculis bifloris, baccis distinctis, foliis integerrimis pubescentibus* In the *Hortus Cliffortianus* it is termed, *Lonicera pedunculis bifloris, foliis ovatis obtusis integris* C Bauhine calls it, *Chamaecerasus dumetorum, fructu gemino rubro*, John Bauhine, *Periclymenum rectum, fructu rubro*, and Dodonæus, *Xylosteum* It grows common in the hedges and woods in most of the coldest parts of Europe

7 Pyrenæan Dwarf Cherry is, *Lonicera pedunculis bifloris, baccis distinctis, foliis oblongis glabris* Van Royen calls it, *Lonicera pedunculis bifloris, baccis distinctis, floribus infundibuliformibus, ramis divaricatis*, and Tournefort, *Xylosteum Pyrenaicum* It grows naturally on the Pyrenæan Mountains

8 Dwarf Cherry with heart shaped leaves, or Tartarean Honeysuckle, is, *Lonicera pedunculis bifloris, baccis distinctis, foliis cordatis obtusis* Amman calls it, *Chamaecerasus fructu gemino rubro, foliis glabris cordatis* This species grows naturally in Tartary

*Lonicera* is of the class and order *Pentandria Monogynia*, and the characters are, (Class and order in the Linnæan system. The characters)

1 Calyx is a small perianthium, situated above the germen, and divided into five parts

2 Corolla consists of one tubulous petal The tube is gibbous and oblong, the limb is divided into five segments, which turn backwards, and one of them is more deeply serrated than the rest

3 Stamina are five awl shaped filaments, nearly the length of the corolla, having oblong antheræ

4 Pistillum consists of a roundish germen placed below the receptacle, a filiforme style the length of the corolla, and of an obtuse capitated stigma

5 Pericarpium is an umbilicated, bilocular berry

6 Semina The seeds are subrotund and compressed

## CHAP LIII.

## *MAGNOLIA*, The LAUREL-LEAVED TULIP-TREE

BESIDES that grand and noble evergreen the Laurel-leaved Tulip-tree, there are three sorts of this genus that shed their leaves in the winter, and which, of all others, ought to be introduced into our present collection These sorts are distinguished by the names,

(Species)
1 Small *Magnolia*
2 Long-leaved *Magnolia*
3 The Umbrella-tree

All these sorts are at present very scarce, and where they are found, greatly enhance the value of the collection

(Description of the Small Magnolia)
1 The Small *Magnolia* grows with us to about the height of ten or twelve feet The wood is white, and the branches, which are not very numerous, are covered with a smooth whitish bark The leaves are tolerably large, and of two colours, their upper surface being smooth and of a fine green, whilst their under is hoary They are of an oval figure, have their edges intire, and often continue the greatest part of the winter before they fall off the trees The flowers are produced at the ends of the branches, in May Their colour is white, and the petals of which they are composed are concave and large, so that, together with the numerous stamina in the center, they present a beautiful appearance They are also remarkable for their sweet scent, and are succeeded by conical fruit, which never ripens in England, but in the places where they grow naturally, a singular beauty and oddity is added to their trees by the fruit, for their seeds are large, and lodged in cells all around the cone When quite ripe, these are discharged from their cells, and hang each by a long narrow thread, causing thereby an uncommon and pleasing effect

(the Long leaved Magnolia)
2 Long-leaved *Magnolia* will grow to be near twenty feet high The wood of this sort is yellow, and the branches are covered with a smooth light bark The leaves are very large, being near ten inches long, their figure is oval, spear-shaped, and all end in points The flowers, which are produced in May, are white, and composed of twelve obtuse petals, which, together with the number of stamina, make a good show These also are succeeded by conical fruit, which never ripens in England

(and the Umbrella tree)
3 The wood of the Umbrella-tree, which grows to about twenty feet in height, is more spongy than any of the other species of *Magnolia* It is called the *Umbrella-tree* from its manner of producing the leaves, for these are exceeding large, and so produced as to form the appearance of an umbrella The flowers of this sort also are white, and the number of petals of which each is composed is about ten They are succeeded by fruit of a conical figure, with many cells all round for the seeds, which never ripen in England

All these sorts may be propagated by seeds, layers, and cuttings By the first of these methods the best plants are raised, though it is a very tedious way, and must be followed with great patience and trouble

(Method of raising this tree by seeds)
We receive the seeds from those parts of America where they grow naturally These are always preserved in sand, but, nevertheless, will not always prove good As soon as possible after they arrive, which is generally in February, they should be sown in pots, about half an inch deep The best compost for them is, a fresh loamy earth, mixed with a fourth part of drift sand, and the seeds should be thinly sown in each pot After this is done, the pots should be plunged up to the rims in the natural mould, under a warm hedge, where they may reap the benefit of the sun during the month of March and part of April, but when the rays of the sun begin

begin to be ſtrong and powerful, and dry the mould in the pots very faſt they ſhould be taken up, and plunged again up to the rims in a ſhady border By the end of May, if the ſeeds were good, the plants will come up, and all the ſummer they muſt be conſtantly attended with weeding and watering At the approach of winter, they ſhould be removed into the greenhouſe, or placed under ſome cover, but in mild weather ſhould always have the benefit of the open air and gentle ſhowers In March, the pots with their ſeedlings ſhould be plunged into an hot-bed to ſet them forwards Tanners bark is what the hotbed ſhould be compoſed of, and as much air as the nature of the bed will allow, ſhould always be afforded them Water alſo muſt be given pretty often, though in ſmall quantities, and the glaſſes muſt be ſhaded in the heat of the day After this, about June, they ſhould be inured to the open air watering muſt ſtill be afforded them, and this is what they require during the ſecond ſummer It has been a practice to plunge the pots into an hotbed ſoon after the ſeeds are ſown, but this is a very bad method, for the young plants being thereby forced, grow thin and ſlender, and are ſeldom made to live longer than the firſt year The ſecond ſummer's management alſo has uſually been, to plant the ſeedlings in March, in little pots, and then plunge them into a hotbed, but this is alſo a very bad way for theſe ſeedlings, whether raiſed on hotbeds or the common ground, will be ſmall, and not of conſiſtence ſufficient to carry the juices, though the powers of vegetation are aſſiſted by an hotbed Thus, hardly any of them ſurvive this early tranſplanting This having been the general practice, theſe plants have been always thought very difficult to preſerve the ſecond year, whereas all thoſe difficulties vaniſh, by obſerving the above-directed method, for by letting the ſeeds have only the natural ſoil they will the firſt ſummer be formed into young plants, which though ſmall, will nevertheleſs be plants, and healthy Thus being in the ſpring in their natural ſtate, with their pores open to receive the nutritious juices, and not having ſuffered by being tranſplanted, the hotbed will ſo help them, that they will be pretty plants by the autumn At the approach of winter, they muſt be removed again under cover, and the former aſſiſtance of an hotbed ſhould be afforded them, and this ſhould be repeated until the plants are grown to be a foot or more in length The ſpring following, the mould ſhould be turned out of the pots, and ſhaken from the roots, and each plant put into a ſeparate pot For theſe, an hotbed of tanners bark ſhould be ready, which will promote their growth, and make them healthy and fine During the time they are in the bed, they ſhould be ſhaded, and about Midſummer the pots may be taken out, and placed in a ſhady border The winter following, it will be proper to houſe them in ſevere froſty weather, but always obſerve to place them abroad in mild ſeaſons In March they may be turned out of the pots, the mould hanging to the roots, and planted with that in the places where they are to remain

by layers. 2 Theſe plants may be alſo propagated by layers The young ſhoots in the autumn are moſt proper for the purpoſe, and I ever found that a gentle twiſt, ſo as juſt to break the bark about the joint, was a better method than any other in practice Theſe will ſometimes ſtrike root in one year, and ſometimes you muſt wait more than two before you find them with any After they have ſtruck root, and are taken up, the beſt time for which is March, I would recommend to plant each ſeparately in a pot, and plunge them into an hotbed, as directed for the ſeedlings, and by the ſpring following, they will be good ſtrong plants for any place

3 Theſe plants may likewiſe be encreaſed by cuttings, by which they may be procured in plenty, if a perſon has the conveniency of a good ſtove and without one this method ſhould not be attempted Theſe cuttings ſhould be planted in pots, and after they are ſet in the ſtove, muſt be duly watered and ſhaded By obſerving theſe directions, many of them will grow After this, they ſhould be brought by degrees to the open air the winter following ſhould be placed under an hotbed-frame, or ſome ſhelter, and in the ſpring planted out for good and by cuttings.

Theſe plants often retain their leaves, eſpecially when young, all winter, or the greateſt part of it, in ſome ſituations, and in ſuch they may paſs for evergreens

1 Small *Magnolia* is titled, *Magnolia foliis ovato-oblongis ſubtus glaucis* In the *Hortus Cliffortianus* it is termed, *Magnolia foliis ovato-lanceolatis* Dillenius calls it, *Magnolia lauri folio ſubtus albicante*, Plukenet, *Tulipifera Virginiana, laurinis foliis aversa parte rore cæruleo tinctis, conibaccifera*, and Ray, *Laurus tulipifera, baccis calyculatis* It grows naturally in Virginia and Penſylvania Titles

2 Long-leaved *Magnolia* is, *Magnolia foliis ovato oblongis acuminatis* In Miller's Dictionary it is termed, *Magnolia foliis ovato-lanceolatis acuminatis perennis* Cateſby calls it, *Magnolia flore albo, folio majore acuminato haud albicante* It grows naturally in Penſylvania

3 Umbrella-tree is, *Magnolia foliis lanceolatis, petalis exterioribus dependentibus* In Miller's Dictionary it is termed, *Magnolia foliis lanceolatis amplissimis annuis* Cateſby calls it, *Magnolia amplissimo flore albo, fructu coccineo* It grows naturally in Carolina, and in Virginia, tho' ſparingly

This genus is of the claſs and order *Polyandria Polygynia*, and the characters are, Claſs and order in the Linnæan ſyſtem The characters

1 CALYX is a perianthium compoſed of three leaves, that have the reſemblance of petals Theſe are oval, concave, and deciduous

2 COROLLA conſiſts of nine oblong, concave petals, that are broad at the extremity, but narrower at the baſe

3 STAMINA The filaments are numerous, ſhort, acuminated, compreſſed, and inſerted into the common receptacle of the piſtils, below the germens The antheræ are linear, and grow on each ſide the filaments

4 PISTILLUM conſiſts of numerous, oval, oblong germina, with very ſhort, recurved, contorted ſtyles, and longitudinal hairy ſtigmas

5 PERICARPIUM is an egg ſhaped ſtrobilus, compoſed of compreſſed, roundiſh, almoſt imbricated, acute, ſeſſile, cluſtered, permanent, unilocular capſules, each being formed of two valves, and open outwardly

6 SEMINA The ſeeds are roundiſh, baccated, ſingle in each capſule, and hang by ſlender threads from the hollow of the ſcales of the ſtrobilus

CHAP

# CHAP LIV

## *MELIA*, The BEAD-TREE.

Its appearance &c describ d

THE Bead tree is a large plant In its native country it will grow to the ſize of one of our pear-trees, and there is no doubt, if our ſoil and ſituation ſuited it, that it would arrive to near that magnitude with us The trunk is covered with a grey bark, and the young branches, which are not very numerous, are quite ſmooth and green The leaves are a very great ornament to this tree They are compound, and very large, the whole leaf being a foot and a half, and ſometimes near two feet long Each is compoſed of a great number of folioles, which are all terminated by an odd one These little leaves have their upper ſurface of a ſtrong ſhining green their under is paler, and their edges are indented The flowers are produced in July, from the ſides of the branches, in long cluſters They are, ſeparately, ſmall, of a bluiſh colour, very fragrant, and each ſtands on a long footſtalk The flowers are ſucceeded by a yellow fruit, tolerably large, in which ſome nuts are encloſed, uſed in the Catholic countries to compoſe ſome ſorts of roſaries, on which account this tree is called the Bead-tree

It is generally preſerved in winter as a greenhouſe plant and indeed a few plants of this fine ſhrub ought always to be introduced in ſuch places deſigned for trees as are proper for them The reaſon of its being treated as a greenhouſe plant is, becauſe it is rather of a tender nature, and as the plants are not yet very plentiful in England, to this may be added, the deſire of preſerving thoſe few a perſon has obtained But notwithſtanding the Bead tree's being looked upon as a greenhouſe-plant, ſome Gardeners have ventured to ſet them abroad againſt warm walls, where they have ſtood the winter, and flouriſhed exceeding well, others have planted them out in well-ſheltered places only, where they have flouriſhed, and ſtood the brunt of many a ſevere winter What inclines me to introduce the *Melia* amongſt our hardy trees is, that I have planted it in an open cold expanſe, in a naturally damp and moiſt ſoil, where it has flouriſhed for more than ſeven years, and diſplayed its beautiful foliage every ſummer, to the great pleaſure of all beholders This treatment and practice, however, muſt be uſed with caution, and whoever ventures to plant them abroad muſt have a dry ſoil, as well as a warm and well-ſheltered ſituation, and then nothing but our hardeſt froſts will deprive the owner of theſe treaſures But, were they more tender, and if a perſon has no greenhouſe, it will be worth while to venture the planting a few abroad, though there ſhould be little chance of his keeping them longer than two or three winters, as they are ſcarce plants with us, and the leaves, the only beauties the tree can afford in that time, are compounded in ſuch a manner as to afford admiration and pleaſure

Care and trouble muſt be uſed before we can raiſe theſe plants to be of ſufficient ſtrength and hardineſs to defend themſelves, when planted out for good They are all to be raiſed from ſeeds, and theſe are to be procured from the places where they commonly grow, which is in moſt of the Catholic countries

Method of propagating this tree

Theſe ſeeds muſt be ſown in pots, filled with light ſandy earth, half an inch deep, the end of March This done, the pots ſhould be plunged into a bark bed, which will cauſe them to come up When the plants appear, they muſt have plenty of air and water, and the open air muſt be afforded them pretty ſoon in the ſummer, that they may be hardened before winter After they are taken out of the beds, they ſhould be ſet in a ſhady place, and every other day watered till the autumn, and at the approach of winter, they ſhould be removed into the greenhouſe, with the hardieſt of thoſe plants In April following, the plants ſhould be taken out of the pots, and each planted in a ſeparate ſmall pot, and after this is done, they ſhould have the benefit of the bark-bed as before, to ſet them a-growing Care muſt be taken to give them ſufficient air, and not to draw them too much, and after they are well entered upon a growing ſtate, they muſt be hardened to the open air as ſoon as poſſible, and the pots taken out, and plunged up to the rims in a ſhady border, which will prevent the mould in the pots drying too much They will require little watering, if this method be uſed, during the ſummer, and at the approach of winter, they muſt be removed into the greenhouſe as before, or placed under a hot-bed-frame, or ſome ſhelter The next ſpring they muſt be ſet out with other greenhouſe-plants, and managed accordingly, and removed into the houſe again with them Every other year, they ſhould be ſhifted out of their pots, with the earth to their roots, and planted in larger, and by thus treating them as greenhouſe plants, and letting them have larger pots as they encreaſe in ſize, till they are ſix or eight years old, they will arrive to be good ſtrong trees Then in April, having made choice of the drieſt, warmeſt, and beſt-ſheltered ſituation, there they may be planted, taking them out of the pots with all their mould, which if done with care, they will never droop on being removed

Titles of this tree

The title of this tree is, *Melia foliis bipinnatis* In the *Hortus Cliffortianus* it is termed, *Melia foliis decompoſitis* Dodonæus calls it, *Azedarach*, Caſpar Bauhine, *Arbor fraxini folio, flore cæruleo*, and Cammerarius, *Pſeudo-ſycamorus* It grow naturally in Syria, and is now very common in Portugal, Spain, and Italy

Claſs and order in the Linnæan ſyſtem

*Melia* is of the claſs and order *Decandria Monogynia*, and the characters are,

The characters

1 CALYX is a very ſmall, monophyllous perianthium, that is divided into five erect, obtuſe ſegments

2 COROLLA conſiſts of five long, narrow, ſpear ſhaped, patent petals There is a cylindric nectarium of one leaf, which is the length of the corolla, and much indented at the brim

3 STAMINA are ten very ſmall filaments, inſerted into the top of the nectarium, having

having oblong and ... that do not rise above

4 Pistillum consists of a conical germen, a ... style the length of the nectarium, and ... quinquevalve stigma

5 Pericarpium is a soft globular drupe

6 Semen The seed is a five-furrowed, roundish nut, of five cells, in each of which is a single oblong kernel

## CHAP LV

## *MESPILUS*, The MEDLAR.

NOTWITHSTANDING the sorts in old ... under this article are so numerous, the following are the only real species yet ... of this genus

Species

1 The Medlar
2 Arbutus-leaved Medlar
3 Amelanchier
4 Canada Medlar
5 Dwarf Quince
6 Bastard Quince

Description of the Dutch Medlar

1 The Medlar, commonly called the Dutch Medlar, in some situations grows to be a moderately large tree It grows irregularly, and the branches are frequently crooked The leaves are spear-shaped, large, entire, downy underneath, and grow on very short channelled footstalks The flowers, which grow singly from the sides of the branches, are very large, and of a white colour They come out the end of May, and are succeeded by that well-known fruit called the Medlar

Varieties of this species

The varieties of this species are,

The Pear-fruited Medlar, and

The Nottingham Medlar

These are plants of more upright growth than the Dutch Medlar Their leaves are narrower, and their flowers and fruit smaller

Of the Arbutus-leaved Medlar

2 Arbutus-leaved Medlar This is frequently called, Virginian Wild Service tree, with an Arbutus Leaf It is a shrub about six feet high frequently sending forth many suckers from the root, and branches from the sides of the plant The leaves are spear shaped, downy underneath, and indented They grow alternately on very short footstalks Their upper surface is a fine green colour, though white below, and they die to a purple colour in the autumn The flowers are produced in bunches from the ends and sides of the branches They are small, white, come out in May, and are succeeded by a dusky brown fruit, like the common haw which will sometimes ... ripe in the autumn

American ...

3 Amelanchier The stalks of this species are slender, branching a little, and grow to about four feet high The young branches are of a reddish purple colour and the whole plant is altogether destitute of thorns The leaves are oval and serrated about three quarters of an inch long, half an inch broad, green on their upper surface, and woolly underneath The flowers are produced in bunches from the ends of the branches Their colour is white, and they are succeeded by small black fruit, of a sweetish taste, which will be often ripe in the autumn

This is a beautiful shrub, and in different parts goes by the various names of the Dwarf Black-fruited Medlar, the New-England Quince, *Petit Pear*, &c The young shoots which support the flowers are woolly underneath, but this by degrees wears off, and they soon become of a purple colour, which remains all winter

Canada Medlar,

4 Canada Medlar This shrub, which rises to about five feet high, is free from thorns, and divides into a few branches, which are smooth, and of a purplish colour The leaves are oval, oblong, smooth, slightly serrated, and grow on long slender footstalks The flowers are white, and terminate the branches in small bunches They come out in May and are succeeded by a purplish fruit, hardly so large as the common haw

Dwarf Quince,

5 Dwarf Quince grows to about four or five feet high The branches are few, smooth, and of a reddish purple colour The leaves are oval, entire, and grow on very short footstalks The flowers are produced, two or three together, from the sides of the branches, without any footstalks They are small, of a purplish colour, come out in May, and are succeeded by round fruit, of a bright red colour when ripe in the autumn

and the Bastard Quince

6 Bastard Quince This species grows to about four or five feet high The branches are few, smooth slender, and covered with a purplish bark The leaves are oval, smooth, serrated, or ... yellowish green, and grow on pretty long footstalks The flowers are produced in small ... from the wings of the stalks, and between them are long narrow bractee, which fall off before the flowers decay Both flowers and bractee are of a purplish colour The fruit is small, and of a red colour when ripe

All these sorts are to be raised from the seeds, from layers, and by budding them upon hawthorn stocks

Method of propagating ... by seeds,

The seeds should be sown in the autumn, soon after they are ripe, in a bed of good earth, in a moist part of the garden They usually lie two years before they make their appearance, during which time the bed must be kept clean from weeds When the plants come up, they must be frequently watered, if dry weather should happen and this should occasionally be repeated all summer Weeds must be eradicated as they arise, and in the autumn, winter, or spring, the strongest plants may be drawn out, and set in the nursery ground, a foot asunder, in rows two feet distant from each other, whilst the others may remain in the seed beds a year longer, to gain strength

In the nursery, the Medlars should be trained for standards, if designed for fruit, or they may be headed to any height if for other purposes, while the lower kinds will require no other management than keeping them clean from weeds, and digging the ground between the rows in winter

These

How raised. These plants may be also raised by layers, especially the last sort. The young branches should be laid early in the autumn, and by the autumn following many of them will have struck root, when they should be taken up, and planted in the nursery ground, like the seedlings, to remain there for a year or two, before they are set out for good.

The best method. But the most expeditious, and by far the best, way of raising these sorts is, by budding them upon stocks of the white-thorn. The haws to raise the stocks should be gathered from such trees as are the largest, shoot freest, and have the largest leaves and fewest thorns. When the stocks are one year old they should be set in the nursery at the broader distance. By the end of July, many of them will be ready for working, when they should be budded in the usual way, and they will take; seldom any other method than this is practised for raising of Medlars, and the other sorts, when growing on so firm a basis as the white-thorn, will be larger, have a better look, and be more fertile in flowers and fruit.

Titles of the four first species. 1. The Medlar is titled, *Mespilus inermis, foliis lanceolatis subtus tomentosis, floribus sessilibus solitariis*. Caspar Bauhine calls one sort of it, *Mespilus Germanica, folio laurino non serrato*; and another, *Mespilus, folio laurino major*. Dodonaeus names it simply, *Mespilus*. It grows naturally in many of the southern parts of Europe.

2. Arbutus-leaved Medlar is styled, *Mespilus inermis, foliis lanceolatis crenatis subtus tomentosis*. Hermann calls it, *Sorbus Virginiana, folio arbuti*; Breynius, *Sorbus aucuparia Virginiana, foliis arbuti*; and Tournefort, *Crataegus Virginiana, foliis arbuti*. It grows naturally in Virginia.

3. Amelanchier is titled, *Mespilus inermis, foliis ovalibus serratis, caulibus hirsutis*. In the *Hortus Cliffortianus* it is termed, *Mespilus inermis, foliis ovalibus serratis, aristis*. Caspar Bauhine calls it, *Alni effigie, lanato folio, minor*; and Clusius, *Vitis Idaea III*. It grows naturally in Austria, France, and Italy.

4. Canada Medlar is titled, *Mespilus inermis, foliis ovato-oblongis glabris serratis*. Gronovius calls it, *Mespilus inermis, foliis subtus glabris serratis ... ovatis*. It grows naturally in Canada and Virginia.

5. Dwarf Quince is, *Mespilus inermis, foliis ovatis integerrimis*. Caspar Bauhine calls it, *Cotoneaster folio rotundo non serrato*; Lobel, *Chamaemespilus cordus*; and Clusius names it, *Chamaemespilus Gesneri*. It grows naturally on the Pyrenees, Ararat, and in many of the cold parts of Europe.

6. Bastard Quince is titled, *Mespilus inermis foliis ovalibus serratis glabris, floribus capitatis, bracteis caducis linearibus*. In the *Hortus Cliffortianus* it is termed, *Crataegus foliis ovalibus utrinque glabris, plicatis inaequaliter serratis*. Caspar Bauhine calls it, *Cotoneaster folio oblongo serrato*; and Clusius, *Cotoneaster fortè Gesneri*. It grows naturally on the Austrian and Pyrenean Mountains.

Class and order in the Linnaean system. *Mespilus* is of the class and order *Icosandria Pentagynia*; and the characters are,

The characters.

1. CALYX is a monophyllous, permanent perianthium, divided into five concave, patent segments.
2. COROLLA is five roundish, concave petals, inserted in the calyx.
3. STAMINA are twenty awl-shaped filaments, inserted in the calyx, having simple antherae.
4. PISTILLUM consists of a germen situated below the flower, and of five simple, erect styles, with capitated stigmas.
5. PERICARPIUM is a globose, umbilicated berry, having the connivent calyx at the top.
6. SEMINA. The seeds are five, osseous, and gibbous.

# CHAP. LVI.

## *MORUS*, The MULBERRY-TREE.

THE different species of the Mulberry tree, together with all the sorts of them that can be procured, may be admitted in small quantities, to increase the variety in a collection, and this they will do by their appearance in winter, when divested of their leaves, as well as more so by them in the summer months. Indeed it is principally for the variety they occasion on these accounts, that I would recommend to have some of them, for the flowers make no figure. There are male and female on the same plant. The male is nothing but a katkin, and the females attract the attention of none except the curious botanist. These trees, considered as fruit trees, belong to another Part, tho' it may not be amiss to observe here, that by these also they add much to the variety in the autumn, among the different plants that will exhibit their seeds with their vessels of different shapes and colours.

Species. The species, then, of the Mulberry-tree, of which a few may be admitted, are,

1. The White Mulberry.
2. The Black Mulberry.
3. The Paper Mulberry.
4. Virginian Mulberry.

White Mulberry. The first of these species has already been treated of as a forest-tree, in Book I. where the reader may see its nature, use, and culture, and from which he will be enabled to judge of the number of these trees he should like to have in his Collection.

Black Mulberry. The second sort is the Common Mulberry-tree of our gardens, and is too universally known to need any description. It is principally cultivated for the fruit, and in ornamental plantations a few of them will be sufficient to make the collection general, as well as to be ready at all seasons for the notice and observation of the curious philosopher.

Variety. There is a variety of it, with jagged leaves, which makes it esteemed on that account, but the fruit is smaller than that of the common sort.

Description of the Paper Mulberry. 3. The Paper Mulberry is so called because the inhabitants where the trees grow naturally make paper of the bark. It will grow to the

the height of about thirty feet, and exhibits its fine large leaves of different shapes, many of them being divided into several lobes, whilst others again are entire. They are of a fine strong green colour, though the under surface is paler than the upper. The flowers, as has been observed, are male and female, and the females are succeeded by small black fruit. It is the bark of the young shoots of which the paper is made, and for this use it is cultivated much in China, as well as Japan, where large plantations are raised. The plants are headed to within about a foot of the ground, and every year the crop of the summer's shoots is taken.

and the Virginian Mulberry

4. Virginian Mulberry-tree will grow to be thirty or more feet high. It sends forth many large branches, and the bark of the young shoots is of a blackish colour. The leaves are larger than the Common Mulberry, and rougher, though in other respects they somewhat resemble them. It produces plenty of katkins, in shape like those of the birch tree, and the female flowers are succeeded by a dark reddish fruit. This is a very scarce plant at present, and is coveted by none but those who are desirous of making their collection general.

Method of propagating the different sorts

The manner of propagating the White Mulberry has already been shewn under that article, in the former Book. That method being exactly practised, either by seeds or layers, will raise all the other sorts; so that nothing need be added here, except referring the reader to that chapter, after first informing him, that by cuttings also all the sorts may be propagated, and this may be done two ways.

1. By cuttings planted in the autumn. These should be strong shoots of the last year's wood, and if the tree to be encreased is not in so flourishing a state as to make such shoots, it should be headed the year before, and you will have cuttings proper for your purpose. The strongest shoots are the best; and October is the best month for the business. They should be a foot and a half long, and must be planted a foot deep, in a shady well-sheltered place, and a moist soil well worked and fine. By this method many good plants may be raised.

2. These trees may also be encreased by cuttings planted in the summer. The latter end of June, or the beginning of July, is a proper time for the work, and the management must be as follows. Having a sufficient number of pots ready, the cuttings, or rather slips, from the trees, should be gathered, and planted in these pots, in any sort of common garden mould made fine. After this, they should have a good watering, and the pots be plunged up to their rims in the stove. Here, if water and shade be constantly afforded them, they will strike root and become good plants. It may be proper to observe farther in this place, that cuttings planted in pots in March, and managed this way, will readily grow. After they have struck root, they may be hardened by degrees to the open air. They should remain under cover in the pots all winter, for they will be rather tender at first, by being so nicely nursed; but in the spring, when all danger of frost is over, they may be turned out, with the mould, either in nursery-lines at a foot distance and two feet asunder in the rows, or else in the places where they are designed to remain for good; for they will be hardy enough, after growing openly this summer, to be in little danger of suffering by almost any weather.

The respective titles of these species are,

1. The White Mulberry is, *Morus foliis oblique cordatis lævibus*. Caspar Bauhine calls it, *Morus fructu albo*; Dodonæus, *Morus candida*. This sort grows naturally in China, and is much cultivated in many parts for the feeding of silk-worms. — Titles

2. The Black or Common Mulberry is, *Morus foliis cordatis scabris*. Caspar Bauhine calls it, *Morus fructu nigro*; and Dodonæus simply, *Morus*. It grows naturally in Persia, and in the maritime parts of Italy.

3. Paper Mulberry is, *Morus foliis palmatis, fructibus hispidis*. Kæmpfer calls it, *Morus sativa, foliis urticæ mortuæ, cortice papyrifera*; others, *Morus papyrifera sativa Japonica*. It grows naturally in Japan.

4. Virginian Mulberry is entitled, *Morus foliis cordatis subtus villosis, amentis cylindricis*. Plukenet calls it, *Morus Virginiensis arbor, loti arboris instar ramosa, foliis amplissimis*; and Gronovius, *Morus foliis subtus tomentosis, amentis longis dioicis*. It grows naturally in Virginia.

*Morus* is of the class and order *Monoecia Tetrandria*, and the characters are, — Class and order in the Linnaean system. The characters

I. The male flowers are collected in a katkin.

1. CALYX is a perianthium divided into four oval, concave parts.

2. COROLLA. There is none.

3. STAMINA are four subulated, erect filaments, longer than the calyx, having simple antheræ.

II. In the female flowers,

1. CALYX is a perianthium composed of four roundish, obtuse, permanent leaves.

2. COROLLA. There is none.

3. PISTILLUM consists of a cordated germen, and two awl-shaped, long, rough, reflexed styles, with simple stigmas.

4. PERICARPIUM. There is none. The calyx becomes a large, carnose, succulent berry, full of tuberances.

5. SEMINA. The seeds are single in each tuberance, oval, and acute.

CHAP

# C H A P. LVII.

## *MYRICA*, The CANDLEBERRY-MYRTLE.

MYRICA affords us three or four species, of a most fragrant odour, and on that account, as well as others, demands admittance into pleasurable plantations of any kind. These are,

*Species of the tree*

1. The Candleberry-Myrtle.
2. The Gale, or Sweet Willow.

*Candleberry Myrtle described*

1. The Candleberry-Myrtle is a shrub about five feet in growth. Many slender branches are produced from the stalk. They are tough, smooth, and of a yellowish brown, having the older spotted with grey spots. The leaves grow irregularly on them all round, sometimes by pairs, sometimes alternately, but generally at unequal distances. They are of a lanceolated figure, and some are serrated at the top, whilst others have their edges wholly entire. They stand on very short footstalks, having their upper surface smooth, and of a shining green colour, whilst their under is of a more dusky colour. The branches of the old plants shed their leaves in the autumn, but the young plants, raised from seeds, retain them the greatest part of the winter, so as during that season to have the appearance of an evergreen. But this beauty will not be lasting, for they shed their leaves proportionally earlier as the plants get older. There are both male and female trees of this sort. The flowers are small, of a whitish colour, and make no figure, neither does the fruit that succeeds the female, which is a small, dry, blue berry, though produced in clusters, make any show. So that it is from the leaves this tree receives its beauty and value, for these being bruised, as well as the bark of the young shoots, emit the most refreshing and delightful fragrance, that is exceeded by no myrtle, or any other aromatic shrub that I know of.

*Variety*

There is a variety of this species, of lower growth, with shorter but broader leaves, and of equal fragrance. This grows commonly in Carolina, where the inhabitants collect a wax, of which they make candles, and which occasions its being called the Candleberry tree. It delights in a moist soil.

*Description of the Gale*

2. The Gale, or Sweet Willow, is a shrub of about the same growth with the other. The branches are tough and slender, and covered with a smooth yellowish brown bark. The leaves are of the same figure with the other, though not so large. They are placed on the same irregular manner on the branches, and when bruised, like them, emit a delightful and refreshing scent. The flowers, which will appear in July, and the berries, which succeed them in clusters, make no figure to any except a botanist, so that where the science has no share in view, it is on account of its fragrance that it is propagated. This sort grows naturally upon bogs, in many parts, particularly the northern parts of England, so that when it is desired to be in the shrubbery, the moistest parts should be assigned it.

*Method of propagating these sorts by seeds*

Both these sorts may be propagated by seeds or layers. The seeds of the Candleberry-Myrtle, and the Spleenwort leaved Gale, we receive from abroad, those of the Sweet Gale, from the bogs where they grow in England. The best way is to sow them in boxes of earth from a rich pasture, well broken and fine. They should be sown about half an inch deep, and when the hot weather comes on, should be set in the shade. They will often remain until the second year before they come up, especially those seeds that come from abroad. If the boxes are set in the shade, and the plants come up, they will require no other trouble the first summer than keeping clean from weeds, in winter they should be removed to a warm hedge or wall, where they may enjoy the benefit of the sun. In the following spring they will come up in plenty. In the beginning of May they should resume their shady situation, and this summer they will require no other trouble than weeding and watering in dry weather. In the winter they should be removed into a well-sheltered place, and this may be repeated two years, when, in the spring, they should be taken out of the boxes, and planted in the nursery, at about a foot asunder.

*layers,*

2. These sorts may be also easily propagated by layers, for this operation being performed on the young wood in the autumn, will occasion them to shoot good roots by the autumn following, many of which will be then good plants, fit for any place.

*suckers,*

3. These plants may likewise be encreased by suckers, for many of them often throw them out in vast plenty, so that these being taken out, the strongest and best-rooted may be set out for good, whilst the weaker, and those with less root, may be planted out in the nursery.

*and cuttings*

4. These trees will also grow by cuttings, tho' I never yet could have a crop to my liking this way. But this should not deter others from trying every expedient that may tend to improve the art.

*Titles*

1. The Candleberry-Myrtle is entitled, *Myrica foliis lanceolatis subserratis, caule arborescente*. In the *Hortus Cliffortianus* it is termed, *Myrica foliis lanceolatis subserratis, fructu baccato*. Plukenet and Catesby call it, *Myrtus Brabanticae similis Caroliniensis baccifera, fructu racemoso sessili monopyreno*; and the latter also, *Myrtus Brabanticae similis Caroliniensis humilior, foliis latioribus & magis serratis*. It grows naturally in Carolina, Virginia, and Pensylvania.

2. The Sweet Gale is, *Myrica foliis lanceolatis subserratis, caule fruticoso*. In the *Flora Lappon* it is termed, *Myrica foliis lanceolatis, fructu sicco*. J. Bauhine calls it, *Gale frutex odoratus septentrionalium*; Caspar Bauhine, *Rhus myrtifolia Belgica*; Parkinson, *Rhus sylvestris, sive myrtus Brabantica vel Anglica*; Gerard, *Myrtus Brabantica, sive eleagnus cordi*; and Dodonaeus, *Chamaeleagnus*. It is found growing common on bogs in many parts of England, and also in most of the northern parts of Europe.

*Class and order in the Linnaean system*

*Myrica* is of the class and order *Dioecia Tetrandria*; and the characters are,

*The characters*

I. The Male Flowers.

1. CALYX. The amentum is oval, oblong, loose, and imbricated on all sides. The scales are concave, moon-shaped, obtusely acuminated, and each contains one flower. There is no real perianthium.

2. COROLLA. There is none.

3. STA-

3 STAMINA are four, and in some sorts six, short, erect, filiforme filaments, having great didymous antheræ, with bifid lobes

II The Female Flowers

1 CALYX The same as in the male

2 COROLLA None

3 PISTILLUM consists of an oval germen, and of two filiforme styles, longer than the calyx, with simple stigmas

4 PERICARPIUM is an unilocular berry

6 SEMEN The seed is single

# CHAP LVIII

## *NYSSA*, The TUPELO-TREE

IN the *Nyssa* I present the curious searcher after an extensive Collection with an account of a tree that is yet scarce in our gardens, tho' the seeds have for some years been commonly sent from several parts of America, with others of that extensive country's growth It is called the Tupelo tree, of which there are two principal varieties

Varieties

The Entire-leaved Tupelo tree

The Serrated leaved Tupelo tree

described

The Entire leaved Tupelo tree, in its native Country, will grow to be near twenty feet high, with us, its size will vary according to the nature of the soil or situation In a moist rich earth, well sheltered, it will bid fair for twenty feet, in others, that are less so, it will make slower progress, and will in the end be proportionally lower The branches are not very numerous, and it rises with a regular trunk, at the top of which they chiefly grow The leaves are of a lanceolated figure, and of a fine light-green colour They end in acute points, and are very ornamental, of a thickish consistence, soft, grow alternately on pretty long footstalks, and often retain their verdure late in the autumn The flowers, which are not very ornamental, are produced from the sides of the branches, growing sometimes singly, sometimes many together, on a footstalk They are of a greenish colour, and in the countries where they naturally grow, are succeeded by oval drupes, inclosing oval, acute, furrowed nuts In England, I have never yet seen them produce fruit

The Serrated leaved Tupelo tree grows usually to near thirty feet high, and divides into branches near the top like the other The leaves are oblong, pointed, of a light-green colour, and come out without order on long footstalks The flowers come out from the wings of the leaves, on long footstalks They are small, of a greenish colour and are succeeded by oval drupes, containing sharp-pointed nuts, about the size of a French olive

Method of propagating the tree

The propagation of these sorts is from seeds, which we receive from America As soon as they arrive, they should be sown in large pots of light sandy earth, one inch deep The Gardener, (who must not expect to see any plants come up the first spring) after this work is done, should plunge his pots up to their rims in the natural ground, and if it be a moistish place, it will be the better Weeding must be observed all summer, and a few furze bushes ought to be pricked round the pots in November, which will prevent the ground from freezing, and forward the coming up of the seeds In the next spring, the pots should be plunged into an hotbed, and after that the seeds will soon come up As much air as possible, and watering, should be afforded them, and they must be hardened soon, to be set out The pots should be then plunged to their rims again in the natural mould, where they may remain until October Watering must be given them, and they should also be shaded in the heat of the day In October, they should be housed, with other greenhouse plants, or else set under a hotbed-frame, or some other cover, all winter The third spring they should be taken out of the larger pots, and each planted in a smaller, in which their growth may be assisted by a gentle heat in a bed, but if they are planted up to the rims in a moistish place, and shaded in dry weather, they will grow very well Though by this time they may have become hardy, yet it will be proper to shelter them the winter following in bad weather They will require little more care during their stay in the pots, which may be either two, three, or more years, if they are large enough, when in some spring they may be turned out, with the mould, into the places where they are to remain, which ought always to be moist and well-sheltered

The Tupelo is distinguished by no other title than, *Nyssa* In the *Hortus Cliffortianus* it is termed, *Nyssa foliis integerrimis* Catesby calls it, *Arbor in aquâ nascens, foliis latis acuminatis & dentatis, fructu eleagni minore*, also, *Arbor in aquâ nascens, foliis latis acuminatis & non dentatis, fructu eleagni minore*, Gronovius, *Nyssa pedunculis multifloris*, also, *Nyssa pedunculis unifloris*, and Plukenet, *Cynoxylon Americanum, folio crassiusculo molli & tenaci* It is a native of North America, where it grows plentifully in moist watery grounds Titles

*Nyssa* is of the class and order *Polygamia Dioecia*, and the characters are, Class and order in the Linnæan system The character

I Male Flowers

1 CALYX is a perianthium, divided into five patent segments

2 COROLLA There is none

3 STAMINA are ten awl-shaped filaments, that are shorter than the calyx, having didymous antheræ, the length of the filaments

II Hermaphrodite Flowers

1 CALYX is the same kind of perianthium as the male, and sits upon the germen

2 COROLLA There is none

3 STAMINA are five erect, subulated filaments, with simple antheræ

4 PISTILLUM consists of an oval germen situated under the receptacle, of a subulated incurved style, longer than the stamina, and an acute stigma

5 PERICARPIUM is an oval drupe, of one cell

6 SEMEN is an oval, acute nut, marked with longitudinal furrows, angular and irregular

CHAP

## C H A P LIX

## *ONONIS*, The REST-HARROW

THERE are many species of *Ononis*, all of which are very beautiful plants, though some are deemed very troublesome weeds, both in the garden and the field, particularly that well-known sort, which, by its creeping and strong roots, is very troublesome, and so hinders the husbandman in his tillage by frequently stopping his ploughs, harrows, &c as to occasion its being called Rest-Harrow These sorts, however, produce very beautiful flowers, though the sight of them is the less desirable in the field, as they generally possess the most barren and poorest of soil at once shewing their fair flowers, and the beggary of the land in which they grow

There is one species however, of a shrubby nature, which more peculiarly attracts the attention of the Gardener, called the Purple Shrubby Rest-Harrow This is a flowering-shrub about a yard in growth The branches are numerous, slender, and covered with a purplish-brown bark, having no spines The leaves are trifoliate, grow irregularly on the branches, sit close, are narrow, spear shaped, and their edges are serrated The flowers come out in panicles from the ends of the branches They are of the papilionaceous kind, and their general characters will indicate their structure They stand on long footstalks, usually three on one They are large, red, appear in May, and are succeeded by short turgid pods, which will have ripe seeds by July or August

*This shrub described*

This sort may be propagated by the seeds Common garden-mould of almost any soil, made fine, will do for the purpose The beds should be made and the seeds sown in March, and covered about half an inch deep In May the plants will appear, and all the summer they must be weeded, and duly watered in dry weather In the spring they should be taken out of the seed-bed, and planted in the nursery, a foot asunder, where they may stand a year or two, and then be planted out for good

*Method of propagating it*

As the seeds of this sort ripen exceeding well with us, a few may be sown in different parts of the garden, and sticks placed for a direction Where there are too many come up to grow together, they may be drawn, and transplanted for other places, or thrown away, if plenty of seeds can always be had, and thus may these plants be raised in their proper places, without the trouble of removing

The title of this species of *Ononis* is, *Ononis floribus paniculatis, pedunculis subtrifloris, stipulis vaginalibus, foliis ternatis lanceolatis serratis* Dodart calls this species, *Anonis montana praecox purpurea frutescens*, also, *Anonis purpurea frutescens non spinosa*, and Morison, *Anonis purpurea verna praecox frutescens, flore rubro amplo* It grows common on the Alps and other mountainous parts of Europe

*Titles of this species*

*Ononis* is of the class and order *Diadelphia Decandria* and the characters are,

*Class and order in the Linnæan system The characters*

1 CALYX is a perianthium divided into five narrow, sharp pointed segments, which are a little arched and raised upwards, except the lower one, which is situated under the keel

2 COROLLA is papilionaceous

The vexillum is heart shaped, striated, depressed on the sides, and larger than the other parts

The alæ are oval, and much shorter than the vexillum

The carina is acuminated, and rather longer than the alæ

3 STAMINA are ten filaments formed into a cylindrical body, having simple antheræ

4 PISTILLUM consists of an oblong hairy germen, a simple assurgent style, and an obtuse stigma

5 PERICARPIUM is a rhombeous, turgid, hairy, unilocular pod, formed of two valves

6 SEMINA The seeds are few, and kidney-shaped

## C H A P LX

## *PHILADELPHUS*, The SYRINGA or MOCK ORANGE.

THERE are only two real species of the *Philadelphus* These are called,

*Species*

1 The Syringa, or Mock Orange

2 The Carolina or Scentless Syringa

*The Syringa Varieties described*

1 The Syringa, or Mock Orange, admits of three remarkable varieties Common Syringa, Double Syringa, and Dwarf Syringa

The Common Syringa, or Mock Orange, is a very beautiful shrub, about six feet in growth It sends forth numerous branches from the root, which are brittle and full of pith These also send out others from their sides that are shorter, stand generally opposite by pairs, and are alternately of contrary directions These younger shoots are slender, jointed, and covered, some with a smooth pale-brown bark, others with a smooth bark of a darker colour The leaves are large, and placed opposite by by pairs on short footstalks They are of an oval, spear-shaped figure, or a strong green colour, and have the flavour of a cucumber Their edges are unequally indented, their surface is rough, and they fall off early in the autumn This shrub, by its flowers, makes a fine figure in May and June, for they are produced in clusters both at the ends and from the sides of the branches They are of a fine white colour, and exceeding fragrant The petals of which each is composed are large, spread open like those of the orange, and then forming bunches, which stand each on its own separate short footstalk, and being produced in plenty all over the shrub, both at once feast the eye and the smell The eye by the pleasing appearance it will then have, the smell, as the air at some distance will be replete with the odoriferous particles constantly emitted from those fragrant flowers These flowers, however, are very improper for chimneys, water-glasses, &c in rooms, for in those places their scent will be too strong and for the ladies in particular, often too powerful

The Double-flowering Syringa is a low variety of this species, seldom rising to more than a yard high The description of the other belongs to this sort, except that the leaves and branches are proportionally smaller and more numerous, and the bark of the shoots of a lighter brown It is called the Double-flowering Syringa, because it sometimes produces a flower or two with three or four rows of petals whereas, in general the flowers, which are very few, and seldom produced, are single They are much smaller than those of the other, and you will not see a flower of any kind on this shrub oftener perhaps than once in five years It is hardly worth propagating on this account, so that a few plants only ought to be admitted into a collection, to be ready for observation

The Dwarf Syringa is still of lower growth than the other, seldom arising to more than two feet in height The description of the first sort still agrees with this, only that the branches and leaves are still proportionally smaller and more numerous, and the bark is still of a lighter brown It never produces flowers

Description of the Carolina Syringa

2 The Carolina Syringa is the tallest grower by far of any sort of the Syringa, and makes the grandest show when in blow, though the flowers are destitute of smell It will grow to about fourteen feet in height, the branches are numerous and slender, and the bark on the young shoots is smooth and brown The leaves also are smooth and entire, and placed opposite by pairs on longish footstalks The flowers, which are produced at the ends of the branches, are of a fine white colour, and being larger than those of the first sort, have a noble look

The propagation of all the sorts of *Philadelphus* is very easy They are encreased by layers, cuttings or suckers

Method of propagating this tree by layers,

1 The most certain method is by layers, for the young twigs being laid in the earth in the winter, will be good-rooted plants by the autumn following

cuttings

2 These plants may be encreased by cuttings, which being planted in October, in a shady moist border, many of them will grow, though it will be proper to let those of the Carolina sort remain until spring, and then to plant them in pots, and help them by a little heat in the bed By this assistance hardly one cutting will fail

and by suckers

3 They may be also encreased by suckers, for all the sorts throw out suckers, though the Carolina Syringa the least of any These will all strike root, and be fit for the nursery ground Nay, the Double flowering and the Dwarf sorts are always encreased this way, for these plants having stood five or six years, may be taken up and divided into several scores All the plants, however, whether raised from layers, cuttings, or suckers, should be planted in the nursery-ground to get strength, before they are set out for good They should be planted a foot asunder, and the distance in the rows should be two feet After this, they will require no other care than hoeing the weeds, until they have stood about two years, which will be long enough for them to stand there

Titles of this genus

1 The title of the first sort is, *Philadelphus foliis subdentatis* In the *Hortus Cliffortianus* it is termed, *Philadelphus* Clusius calls it, *Frutex coronarius*, and Caspar Bauhine, *Syringa alba, sive Philadelphus Athenaei* The place where this grows naturally is at present uncertain

2 The Carolina Syringa is entitled, *Philadelphus foliis integerrimis* Catesby calls it, *Philadelphus flore albo majore inodoro* It is a native of Carolina

Class and order in the Linnaean system

*Philadelphus* is of the class and order *Decandria Monogynia*, and the characters are,

The characters

1 CALYX is a monophyllous, permanent perianthium, divided into four acute segments

2 COROLLA consists of four large, roundish, plane, patent petals

3 STAMINA are twenty awl-shaped filaments, the length of the calyx, having erect, four-furrowed antheræ

4 PISTILLUM consists of a germen placed below the receptacle, and of a filiform style, divided into four parts, each of which has a single stigma

5 PERICARPIUM is an oval, acuminated capsule, surrounded in the middle by the calyx It is formed of four valves, containing four cells

6 SEMINA The seeds are numerous, small, and oblong

## CHAP LXI

## *PINUS LARIX*, The LARCH-TREE

THIS delightful deciduous species of *Pinus* has been already treated of as a forest-tree in the First Book, where the reader will see its use in any place, and how desirable this tree is for the larger parts of ornamental plantations, as well as those more peculiarly designed for profit, so that after referring him to that place, it may be sufficient to observe here, that there are two or three sorts of the Larch, to help the variety The first and most beautiful of

Descrip tion of the different sorts of Larches

of all is the Common Larch, which exhibits its flowers, of a delicate red colour, early in the spring Another sort produces white flowers at the same season, and these have a delightful effect among those of the red sort, whilst another, called the Black Newfoundland *Larix*, encreases the variety, though by an aspect little differing from the others There are also Larches with greenish flowers, pale red, &c all of which are accidental varieties from seeds These varieties are easily distinguished, even when out of blow The young shoots of the White flowering Larch are of the lightest green, and the cones when ripe are nearly white The Red-flowering Larch has its shoots of a reddish cast, and the cones are of a brown colour, whilst the cones and shoots of the Black Newfoundland Larch are in the same manner proportionally tinged The cones, which are a very great ornament to several sorts of the Pines, are very little to these Their chief beauty consists in the manner of their growth, the nature and beauty of their pencilled leaves, and fair flowers, for the cones that succeed them are small, of a whitish, a reddish, or a blackish brown colour, and make no figure

Method of propagating this tree

One method of propagation is common to all these sorts This has been already treated of in the former Book; and the class, order, and description, will be given under the article *Pinus*, as a species of which genus it is now rightly looked upon, so that nothing more is necessary here than to present the curious botanist with its real, as well as the various titles by which it has been distinguished in authors

Titles

The title, then, of the Larch tree is *Pinus foliis fasciculatis obtusis* Linnæus had called it, *Abies foliis fasciculatis obtusis*, but afterwards altered it to the preceding J Bauhine calls it, *Larix, folio deciduo, conifera*, others simply, *Larix* It grows naturally in Switzerland, in some parts of Italy, and upon the Alps

## C H A P LXII.

## *PISTACIA*, The PISTACHIA-NUT, or TURPENTINE-TREE

Situations proper for this genus.

THERE are four species of *Pistacia* which will endure our winters, provided they are planted in places that are warm and well sheltered on all sides, and the frosts should not happen to be too severe The first of these must be allotted them, and the risk of the other run, for without these, they will be liable to be destroyed, and with the former precaution many of them will be lost, especially if a frosty winter should happen before they are grown to be old trees The sorts, then, are,

Species

1 The Common Turpentine-tree
2 The Pistachia Nut tree
3 The Three-leaved Pistachia, or Turpentine tree
4 The Larger-fruited Turpentine-tree

Description of the Common Turpentine-tree

1 The Common Turpentine-tree will grow to the height of about thirty feet The bark of the trunk is thick, full of cracks, and of a dark-brown colour, whilst that on the young shoots is thin and smooth The leaves are pinnated and large, of a dark-green colour, and grow alternately on the branches The folioles of which each leaf is composed are oval, spear shaped, and consist of three or four pairs, which are placed on the mid-rib, besides the odd one with which they are terminated There will be male and female flowers on different plants They exhibit their bloom in April The male flower is nothing but a katkin, and the females make no figure, so that where philosophy has no view, it is from the desire of having an extensive Collection that we procure these trees In warm countries, the leaves of the *Pistacia* continue all the year, with us, they fall off when attacked by the frosts From the trunk flows the true turpentine, in the room of which that taken from some of our Pines is generally substituted

Pistachia Nut tree,

2 The Pistachia Nut-tree is about twenty feet in height The trunk of this species also is covered with a dark-brown bark, full of cracks, whilst the young shoots are smooth, and of a light-brown colour The leaves are likewise pinnated, being composed of about two or three pairs of folioles, which do not always stand exactly opposite on the mid-rib, terminated with an odd one These folioles are large, and nearly of an oval figure Their edges turn backwards but have nevertheless a noble look The male flowers are katkins of a greenish colour, and the female flowers are very small, and produced in clusters from the sides of the branches April is the month of their flowering, and the female flowers are succeeded by the Pistachia nuts we eat

Three leaved Pistachia-tree

3 The Three-leaved Pistachia tree is of about twenty-five feet growth The bark of the trunk is very rough, and of a dark-brown colour but that of the young shoots is smooth, and lighter The leaves of this species are trifoliate The folioles are of an oval figure, of a very dark green colour, and are greatly ornamental to the plant Different trees will have male and female flowers The males are greenish katkins, and the females have no petals, are small, and make no show

and the Larger fruited Turpentine tree

4 Larger-fruited Turpentine tree will grow to be about twenty-five feet high The bark partakes more of a whitish colour, and is smoother, than those of the other species The leaves also are pinnated, but the folioles of which each is composed, are not always of the same number Sometimes there are three, sometimes five pair of folioles to form the compound leaf. These are of a paler green than any of the other sorts, of a roundish figure, and stand on longish footstalks The male flower of this species also is a katkin, and the females are succeeded by nuts, which by many are liked being eatable, like the Pistachia nuts The leaves continue on these trees great part of the year, in warm countries

Method of propagating them

The seeds of all these sorts, which we receive from abroad, should be sown as soon as possible after their arrival A compost should be prepared for them, mixed in the following proportions. Six barrows full of earth, from a freſh paſture taken from hence the ſurface be cut, with the green ſward, and well turned and rotted, three barrows of drift or ſea ſand, and one barrow of old lime rubbiſh, broken to duſt. Theſe ſhould be all well mixed together. The ſeeds ſhould be ſown about half an inch deep in pots, which may then be ſet under a warm wall or hedge, until the hot weather begins to come on, when they ſhould be removed into the ſhade, and plunged up to the rims in ſome mould. At the approach of winter, they may be removed into a warm place, and at ſpring a hot-bed muſt be prepared for their reception. As theſe plants rarely come up the firſt year, this will be a better method than to plunge them in a hot-bed ſoon after they are ſown, for even with this aſſiſtance, they will be late before they come up, will be very weak and tender, ſhooting by the autumn, and will require extraordinary ſkill and care to preſerve them, whereas, if they are ſuffered to remain unforced for one year, they will be preparing to vegetate, and of courſe will come up themſelves the ſecond ſpring, but a hot-bed will be neceſſary, as at that time it will make them ſhoot ſtronger. But the forcing muſt by no means be continued, a little only is to be given them, and they ſhould gradually be hardened to the air. Watering and ſhade all ſummer muſt be allowed them, and they ought to be made as hardy as poſſible by the autumn. At the approach of winter, when other plants are to be ſet in the green-houſe, theſe ſhould go with them, or be placed under an hot-bed frame. They ſhould be ſet out with them in the ſpring, and in May the pots muſt be plunged up to the rim in the ſhade as before. The next winter they will require the green-houſe, and in the ſucceeding ſpring they will be then two-years-old ſeedlings, at which time they ſhould be ſhaken out of the pots, and each planted in a ſeparate pot, in the ſame ſort of compoſt in which the ſeeds were ſown. This being done, they ſhould be afforded a heat in the bed to ſet them forward. After they have begun ſhooting freſh, the glaſſes ſhould be taken off by degrees, and now they will want no more hot-beds. Watering muſt be given them in dry weather, and in the autumn they muſt be removed into the green-houſe, with other plants. And thus they ſhould be treated as a green-houſe plant for four or five, or even ſix years it will be ſo much the better, obſerving always, however, in the ſpring, to ſhift them into a freſh and larger pot every other year. The plants being now five or ſix years old, and being become tolerably ſtrong and woody, may be ſet out in the places where they are to remain. Theſe, as is obſerved, muſt be warm well-ſheltered places, with a naturally dry ſoil, and if the two or three ſucceeding winters ſhould prove mild and favourable, they will by that time be grown to be very hardy, and may bid defiance to almoſt any weather. The Common Turpentine-tree and the Piſtachia Nut-tree, when grown old, reſiſt our ſevereſt froſts, and the other ſorts, though rather of a more tender nature, even if not old, will droop to none but the moſt piercing.

1. The Common Turpentine-tree is entitled, *Piſtacia foliis impari-pinnatis, foliolis ovato-lanceolatis*. Clusius calls it, *Terebinthus*, and Caſpar Bauhine, *Terebinthus vulgaris*. It grows common in Italy and Spain, and ſome parts of Africa. Titles of the ſpecies.

2. The Piſtachia Nut-tree is entitled, *Piſtacia foliis impari-pinnatis, foliolis ſubovatis recurvis*. Lobel calls it, *Terebinthus Indica Theophraſti, Piſtacia Dioſcoridis*; Caſpar Bauhine, *Piſtacia peregrina, fructu racemoſo, ſive Terebinthus Indica*, and John Bauhine, *Piſtacia*. It grows common naturally in Arabia, Syria, and India, from whence we receive the nuts.

3. The Three-leaved Piſtachia, or Turpentine-tree, is, *Piſtacia foliis ſubternatis*. Tournefort calls it, *Terebinthus ſive Piſtacia trifolia*, and Boccone, *Piſtacium mas Siculum, folio nigricante*. It is a native of Sicily.

4. The Larger-fruited Turpentine-tree is, *Piſtacia foliis pinnatis trifoliatiſque, foliolis ſubrotundis*. John Bauhine calls it, *Terebinthus Indica major, fructu rotundo*; Tournefort, *Terebinthus peregrina, fructu majore, piſtaciis ſimili, eduli*; Sauvages, *Piſtacia foliis ſæpius ternatis orbiculatis*; and Lobel, *Terebinthus major, piſtaciæ folio*. It grows naturally in Perſia, Armenia, Meſopotamia, and the ſouth of France.

*Piſtacia* is of the claſs and order *Dioecia Tetrandria*, and the characters are, Claſs and order in the Linnæan ſyſtem. The characters.

I. Male Flowers.

1. CALYX is a looſe, ſparſed catkin, compoſed of many ſmall ſcales, each of which contains one flower. The proper perianthium is ſmall, and divided into five acute ſegments.
2. COROLLA. There is none.
3. STAMINA are five very ſmall filaments, with large, oval, four-cornered, erect, ſtulous antheræ.

II. Female Flowers.

1. CALYX. There is no amentum, and the Calyx is a very ſmall, triſid perianthium.
2. COROLLA. There is none.
3. PISTILLUM conſiſts of an oval germen, larger than the calyx, and of three reflexed ſtyles, with thick hiſpid ſtigmas.
4. PERICARPIUM is an oval, dry drupe.
5. SEMEN is a ſmooth, oval nut.

## CHAP. LXIII.

## *PLATANUS*, The PLANE-TREE.

THE Plane, as a timber-tree, has already been treated of, and what has been ſaid of it before, may ſuffice to inſtruct in what places, and in what quantity, theſe ſorts ſhould be admitted into our preſent plantations. Two real ſpecies there are undoubtedly of the Plane-tree, called the Oriental and the Occidental Planes, and beſides theſe, there are at leaſt two varieties, one of which is called the Spaniſh Plane-tree, the other the Maple-leaved Plane-tree. The Species. Varieties.

leaves

Described. leaves of the former are exceeding large, and make a noble show, whilst those of the latter are smaller and in figure a little resemble those of the Maple-tree, which occasions its being so called. These add to the variety, and claim a place in plantations of all sorts. If the reader turns back to the article *Platanus*, amongst the forest trees, he will perceive that nothing more need be added here to induce him to plant these trees, or to instruct him in the method of raising them, though it may not be amiss to add, that the varieties should always be propagated by the layers or cuttings (the former of which is by much the surest method), that the variety may be still continued.

Method of propagating these trees.

1. The Oriental Plane-tree is entitled, *Platanus foliis palmatis*. Caspar Bauhine calls it simply, *Platanus*; Parkinson, *Platanus Orientalis verus*; others, *Platanus Orientalis*. It is found growing naturally in Asia, and many parts of the East.

Titles of this genus.

2. The Occidental Plane-tree is titled, *Platanus foliis lobatis*. Catesby calls it, *Platanus Occidentalis*, and Parkinson, *Platanus Occidentalis, sive Virginiensis*. It grows naturally in North-America.

*Platanus* is of the class and order *Monoecia Polyandria*, and the characters are,

Class and order in the Linnæan system. The characters.

I. Male flowers are collected into a globular katkin.

1. CALYX. There are a few very small lanulæ, which serve for calyces.
2. COROLLA is hardly discernible.
3. STAMINA. The filaments are numerous, oblong, thickish upward, and coloured. They have four-cornered antheræ.

II. Female flowers. These, which will be numerous upon the same tree, are also gathered in a roundish ball, and have for,

1. CALYX, many small squamæ.
2. COROLLA consists of many small, concave, oblong, clavated petals.
3. PISTILLUM consists of several subulated germina, with subulated styles and incurved stigmas.
4. PERICARPIUM. There is none.
5. SEMINA. The seeds are roundish, numerous, and downy at their base.

# CHAP. LXIV.

## *POPULUS*, The POPLAR-TREE.

THREE real species of the Poplar-tree have been already treated of in the First Book, where the reader will see the propagation and uses of all these sorts in the plantations under consideration. The sorts before described are,

Species.

1. The White Poplar, or Abele.
2. The Black Poplar.
3. The Tremulous Poplar, or Aspen-tree.

What has been already said concerning these may suffice, particularly as they are common and known to all, so that I shall proceed to two other species of *Populus*, which are of the greatest ornament to the larger plantations, namely,

4. The Carolina Poplar.
5. Virginian Poplar.

Description of the Carolina.

4. The Carolina Poplar will grow to be a large timber tree, and has a majestic and enchanting appearance. It is an exceeding swift grower, insomuch that I have known it shoot ten feet in the space of one summer, and to be in thickness, nearest the base, an inch in diameter. The bark is smooth, and of a whitish colour, though that on the young shoots is of a fine green. The young shoots are cornered, having five angles, and the bark of which these are composed, being extended by the future growth, leaves only the traces on the older branches of these angles; and this again gives the tree in winter a particular look; for at the base of each bud they curve over and meet. Thus there will be between every bud formed by the bark, figures like niches, as it were, of public buildings, though with an upright in the middle, at the top of each of which, like an ornament, is seated the bud, for the future shoot or leaf. These buds are only to be found on the younger branches, but the figure is retained on the bark of the older without those ornaments. But of all the trees in a Collection, none more agreeably by its leaves entertains us than this, whether we consider their colour, figure, or [illegible]. The colour is a light shining green, which is heightened in the autumn, by the strong nerves, and the large veins that issue from it, turning to a red colour; the lesser veins also being in some degree affected, occasions upon the surface a sweet contrast. Their figure is nearly that of a heart, and they are notched at the edges. But the chief majesty this tree receives is from the size of the leaves. I have measured one of the younger trees, and found the leaves ten inches long and eight broad, with a strong foot-stalk of four inches in length. These and the leaves are placed alternately on the branches, though, as the tree advances in height, they diminish in size. This species shoots late in the autumn, and these young shoots have their ends often killed in hard winters, which is an imperfection, as it causes the tree to have a very bad look in the spring, before and when the leaves are putting out. However, these last will not fail afterwards to make ample amends for the former defect. The flowers afford no pleasure to the gardener. They are only katkins, like other Poplars, and fit only for the curious botanist's inspection.

5. Virginian Poplar grows to be a large timber tree. The branches are numerous, venerable, and angular. The leaves are heart-shaped, broad, slightly serrated, and downy on their first appearance. The flowers come out in loose katkins, and make little show. They appear early in the spring, and are succeeded by numerous downy seeds, which are dispersed all about to a considerable distance.

and the Virginian Poplar.

These plants are propagated,

1. By

Method of raising these sorts by cuttings. 1 By cuttings In order to obtain proper cuttings for the purpose, the plants should be headed the year before, and a foot and a half of the thickest part of the former summer's shoots should be taken The month of October is the season; and these cuttings should be planted in a moist shady soil, one foot deep, with the other half foot above ground Many of them will grow, though it is generally allowed to be a good crop if half succeed, and as the plants to get proper cuttings must be headed the year before, the best method is to have the operation performed,

By layers. 2 By layers These must be of the last summer's shoots, and the operation ought to be performed in the autumn before they have done growing, for the sap being then in motion, they may readily be brought down, whereas, if it is deferred until winter, the young shoots are then so exceedingly brittle, that though all possible care be taken, many of them in attempting to bring them down, will be broken A small slit with the knife must be given to each, and after the operation is performed, some furze bushes should be stuck round each stool, to break the keen edge of the black frosts, and preserve the ends of the layers from being killed In the spring they should be cut down to within one eye of the ground, and by the autumn they will have struck root, and be good plants, either for the nursery-ground, or where they are intended to be set out for good

Titles 1 The White Poplar is entitled, *Populus foliis subrotundis denteto-angulatis subtus tomentosis* Dodonæus calls it, *Populus alba*, Caspar Bauhine, *Populus alba, majoribus foliis* It grows common in England and most parts of Europe

2 The black Poplar is, *Populus foliis deltoidibus acuminatis serratis* Caspar Bauhine and others call it, *Populus nigra* It grows common in moist places in England and most parts of Europe

3 The Aspen tree is entitled, *Populus foliis subrotundis dentato angulatis utrinque glabris* Dodonæus calls it, *Populus Lybica*, and Caspar Bauhine, *Populus tremula* It grows common in the moist woods in England, and most of the colder parts of Europe

4 The Carolina Poplar is, *Populus foliis subcordatis denticulatis* Catesby titles it, *Populus nigra folio maximo, gemmis balsamum odoratissimum fundentibus* Wackendorf, *Populus foliis cordatis crenatis basi nudis, petiolis teretibus*, and Gmelin, *Populus foliis ovatis acutis serratis* It grows common in Carolina, and many parts of North America

5 Virginian Poplar is, *Populus foliis cordatis, primoribus villosis* Wackendorf calls it, *Populus foliis cordatis obsolete serratis infimis serratis glandulosis, petiolis lateraliter utrinque planis*, and Gronovius, *Populus magna, foliis amplis aliis cordiformibus, aliis subrotundis primoribus tomentosis* It grows naturally in Virginia

Class and order in the Linnæan system This genus is of the class and order *Dioecia Octandria*, and the characters are,

The characters I Male Flowers

1 CALYX The catkin is oblong, cylindric, loose, and imbricated The scales are oblong, plane, and lacerated at their margin, and under each of them is situated a single flower

2 COROLLA There is no petal, but a monophyllous nectarium, turbinated at the bottom, but is at the top tubulous, oblique, and undivided

3 STAMINA are eight very short filaments, with large four cornered antheræ

II Female Flowers

1 CALYX The katkins are like those of the males

2 COROLLA There are no petals, but nectaria, like the males

3 PISTILLUM consists of an oval, acuminated germen, a very short style, and a quadrifid stigma

4 PERICARPIUM is an oval, bilocular capsule

5 SEMINA The seeds are numerous, oval, and pappous

# CHAP LXV

## *PRINOS*, The WINTERBERRY

PRINOS affords us one deciduous and one evergreen species, which will encrease the variety in our Collection The deciduous species is called the Virginian Winterberry It is a shrub of about six or eight feet in growth, This shrub described sending forth many branches from the bottom to the top, which are covered with a brownish bark The leaves are spear shaped, pretty large, of a strong green colour, lengthways serrated, and placed alternately on slender footstalks on the branches The flowers are produced at the sides of the branches, growing one or two together at the joints They make no show to the Gardener, and the general characters indicate their structure They appear in July, and are succeeded by purple coloured berries, which remain on the trees all winter, and look well

Method of raising this tree The best way of propagating these plants is from the seeds These should be sown, soon after they are ripe, in beds of fine sandy earth, and if the garden does not naturally afford such, a few barrows full of drift sand must be brought to mix with the common mould The beds being thus prepared, and made ready for sowing, the seeds should be sown about three quarters of an inch deep It is very seldom that any of the seeds come up the first spring after, if any do, there will be but few, so that all the summer they must be kept clean from weeds The spring following the plants will come up, though many will lie until the third spring before they make their appearance After they are come up, weeding and watering must be afforded them in the summer, and with this care they may remain in the seed bed two years In March, being then two years-old seedlings, they should be taken up and planted in the nursery, at very small distances, and here they may remain, with the

usual

usual nursery-care, until they are set out for good

Title — The Virginian Winterberry is entitled, *Prinos foliis longitudinaliter serratis*. Though it grows plentifully in Virginia, it is found in Pensylvania, and other parts of North-America.

Class and order in the Linnæan system — *Prinos* is of the class and order *Hexandria Monogynia*; and the characters are,

The characters —
1. CALYX is a small, plane, monophyllous, permanent periarthium, cut at the brim into six segments.
2. COROLLA consists of one wheel-shaped petal. There is no tube, but a plane limb, that is divided into six oval parts.
3. STAMINA are six erect, awl-shaped filaments, shorter than the corolla, having oblong, obtuse antheræ.
4. PISTILLUM consists of an oval germen, terminating in a style shorter than the stamina, and an obtuse stigma.
5. PERICARPIUM is a roundish berry, that is much larger than the calyx, and contains six cells.
6. SEMINA. The seeds are single in each cell, osseous, obtuse, on one side convex, and on the other angular.

# CHAP. LXVI.

## *PRUNUS*, The PLUM-TREE.

Introductory observation — THE mere Gardener would expect to find the varieties of Plums only under this generical term *Prunus*, it being the word under which he has hitherto found them arranged; but the improvements now made in botany, have taught us to bring others, that have hitherto been deemed distinct genera, and place them here, as species only of *Prunus*. The anxious searcher after truth will be surprized, no doubt, when we inform him, that the Cherry tree, the Apricot, the Laurel, &c. are only distinct species of the Plum tree. When we come to treat of the Fruit-Garden, as they differ extremely in their shape, nature, &c. in those respects, and that the honest Gardener may by no means be embarrassed, we shall treat of them separately, as distinct and different fruits, under their old titles; but here we must preserve our plan with a stricter eye to science. And this we with more pleasure follow, as we can, by this method, exhibit to him who is desirous of being a gardener only, the deciduous species of *Prunus*, without entangling him in the botanic part; whilst the botanist will be delighted to see the different species here arranged and treated of for his own or the Gardener's use, and afterwards the titles, &c. of the real species given for his instruction and pleasure.

The joining the Cherry-tree as a species only of the Plum, has been a stumbling-block to many; and the dabblers in the science have always had their objections. Miller says, it cannot be; and his reasons are that all species of the same genus will grow by grafting or inoculating upon one another; whereas, says he, the Cherry-tree will by no art be made to grow upon a Plum stock. He boasts of having had forty years experience. This is a long series of years, indeed, to be exercised in the art; and a moderate capacity may in that time attain to a great knowledge of things, as he doubtless has; but strange it is, one should think, that in so many years practice, he should not yet know how to graft Cherries upon Plum stocks. It being so confidently asserted by him and others, that they would not grow, and Linnæus arranging them as belonging to the same family, put me upon trying the experiment; and this I made with more than common care. They shot out in the spring, as well as those grafted on their own stocks; they perfectly united to the Plum-stocks, and by the autumn were grown a yard or more high, and were then fit to plant out, either for espaliers or walls. I ever found Cherries to take the best upon the Maple-Plum-stock; and to these I always found them unite with greater readiness than to the Laurel. Nay, in the spring 1762, when such an exceeding dry and parching summer ensued, as to burn away the young shootings grafts of many plants after they had shot an inch or two, in this spring, I say, I grafted several Cherries on Maple Plum-stocks, and several on the Laurel. Those on the Laurel were all burnt up as they were preparing to shoot, whilst those on the Maple Plum stocks, in defiance of all the heat and drought, shot forth vigorously, and made good trees by the autumn.

Remarks on Miller's mistake in his objection to grafting this tree

Thus has this experiment justified the great Linnæus in his arrangement of the different species under their proper genera; and at the same time it should demonstrate all of the folly of thinking to look big because they have the assurance to find fault with the greatest talents, without having understanding enough to know with certainty what they are about.

The method of grafting is exactly the same as the Elm, which may be seen in the First Book.

But to return to the Gardener who wants to know what sorts, under this head, are to be added to his Collection. The real species then are,

Species —
1. The Common Bird Cherry.
2. Virginian Bird Cherry.
3. Canada Bird Cherry.
4. Mahaleb, or the Perfumed Cherry.
5. The Apricot-tree.
6. The Cultivated Cherry-tree of our Orchards.
7. The Wild Cherry-tree.
8. The Cultivated Plum-tree of our Orchards.
9. The Bullace-tree.
10. The Black-thorn, or Sloe-Bush.

Common Bird Cherry — 1. The Common Bird Cherry is a tree of about twenty feet growth; oftentimes it rises higher. It grows [illegible] to an upright stem, and makes a handsome appearance. The bark of the older shoots is of a dark-brown, inclined to a purple colour, and is [illegible] sprinkled with a few greyish spots, while the preceding summer's shoots are smoother, and of a reddish cast. The buds early in the winter will begin to swell, for the future shoots. The leaves are large, and grow alternately on the branches. Their figure is nearly oblong. They are rough, and have their edges serrated. Their under surface is of a lighter colour than their upper, and they have two glandules at their base. Their flowers are white, and produced in May, in long bunches. A kind of spike of white flowers grows from the sides of the branches, and these waving about on every side, in a loose and easy manner, have a genteel and pleasing effect. The flowers of which these spikes are composed stand each on their own proper footstalks, that are all arranged alternately along the main stalk, which is tolerably long. These flowers are succeeded by fruit, which is a small berry, that ripens in August, at which period it will be black; but before this, it will undergo the changes of being first green, and afterwards red. When these berries are ripe, they are of a sweet, disagreeable taste, but so liked by the birds (which will flock from all parts to feed on them), as to occasion its being called the Bird Cherry; and for their sake purely many plant a more than common quantity of these trees, that they may have these feathered songsters in greater plenty.

Variety. There is another sort of this tree, called the Cornish Bird-Cherry, which differs from it in some respects, but as these differences are inconsiderable, and it is generally deemed a variety only, no more need be said of it here.

Virginian Bird Cherry. 2. The Virginian Bird Cherry has been treated of as a forest-tree in the First Book. It will grow to be thirty or forty feet high, and affords wood of admirable value. The bark is of a dark brown, inclined to a purple colour, and spotted irregularly with some greyish blotches. The young shoots are of a lighter colour, and very smooth, and the whole tree is more remote than the former sort. The leaves are oval, and of a shining green colour. Their edges are serrated, and placed alternately on the branches. They stand on short footstalks, and continue on the trees late in the autumn. Their flowers are white, and produced in May, in the same sort of long bunches as the other, and are succeeded by black berries, which are equally coveted by the birds, for whose sake only this tree also is frequently planted.

Canada Cherry. 3. Canada Bird Cherry-tree is of much lower growth than the former sorts. The branches are smooth. The leaves are broad, spear-shaped, rough, downy, and destitute of glands, like those of the former species. The flowers grow in long, branching bunches. Their colour is white; they come out in May, and are succeeded by small, round, black berries, which will be ripe in the autumn.

Perfumed Cherry. 4. The Perfumed Cherry seldom grows to be more than ten or twelve feet high. It is called *Mahaleb*, and the branches are covered with a smooth, whitish, grey bark. Their leaves are small, of a lucid green colour, of an oval figure, and stand alternately on the branches. The flowers are white, produced in May in roundish clusters, and are succeeded by berries, of which the birds also are very fond. The wood of all these sorts is much esteemed by the cabinet-makers, particularly amongst the French, as they always emit a very agreeable odour.

Apricot tree. 5. The Apricot-tree is often planted as a flowering shrub, for though it will grow to be thirty feet high, it may nevertheless be kept down to what height the owner desires. This tree, as well as most of the sorts of fruit-trees, is exceeded by few in ornament; for being permitted to grow in its natural state to twenty or thirty feet high, with all its luxuriancy of branches, covered with their delightful heart-shaped leaves, what a glorious figure will it present! But when we reflect on the fine appearance such a tree must make, early in the spring, when covered all over with the bloom of such fine flowers as those of the Apricot are known to be, this enhances the value; and either of these motives is sufficient for introducing these trees into plantations of this kind. Add to this, some of the sorts, in warm well-sheltered situations, will produce fruit when growing in this manner, as well as if planted and trained against walls, so that additional returns will be made by the fruit to the curious planter of these trees.

Cherry of the Orchard. 6. The Cherry-tree of our Orchards is too well known, with all its varieties, to need any description. And indeed were the tree scarce, or even with much difficulty propagated, every man, though possessed of a single tree only, would look upon it as a treasure. For besides the charming appearance these trees have, when bestowed, as it were, all over with bloom in the spring, can any tree in the vegetable tribe be conceived more beautiful, striking, and grand, than a well grown and healthy Cherry-tree, at that period when the fruit is ripe?

Each sort of the many kinds of Cherry-trees affords a variety, all differing in some respect in their manner of shooting, leaves, or fruit; and as these sorts are all well known, I shall only remind the curious planter, that by a judicious mixture of these trees, he will be highly benefited. Besides the numerous varieties of Cherry-trees, two in particular demand admission into the pleasure garden. The Double-blossomed and the Red flowering. Varieties

described. The Double-Blossomed Cherry-tree is a variety of our Common Cultivated Cherry-tree. The pleasing show the Common Cherry-tree makes when in blow is known to all; but that of the Double-blossomed is much more enchanting. It flowers, like the other, in May, and these are produced in large and noble clusters; for each separate flower is as double as a rose, is very large, and placed on long and slender footstalks, so as to occasion the branches to have an air of ease and freedom. They are of a pure white, and the trees will be so profusely covered with them, as to charm the imagination. Standards of these trees, when viewed at a distance, have been compared to balls of snow; and the nearer we approach, the greater pleasure we receive. These trees may be kept as dwarfs, or trained up to standards, so that there is no garden or plantation to which they will not be suitable. By the multiplicity of the petals the organs of generation are destroyed, so that those flowers which are really full are never succeeded by any fruit.

The Red flowering Cherry-tree differs in no respect from the Common Cherry-tree, only that the flowers are of a pale red colour, and by many are esteemed on that account.

Wild Cherry tree. 7. The Wild Cherry-tree is a very large growing tree. The leaves are oval, spear-shaped, and downy underneath. The flowers come out from the sides of the branches in sessile umbels. They appear rather later than the Cultivated sorts, and are succeeded by small red fruit, which ripens late in the autumn. This is often called the Wild Northern English Cherry.

Plum tree. 8. The Plum tree, with all its varieties, is so well known as to require no description. No one

red

Spotted Cistus

Purple Cortusa

Double Blossomd Cherry

need be told, that the Plum-tree is a large growing tree, and that it has a beautiful appearance in spring when in blow The fruit that succeeds the blossom is of many colours, shapes, and sizes, and the trees of the variety of sorts will be so adorned with them in the autumn, as to have a noble and delightful effect, being hardly exceeded by the cherry itself These are seldom planted any where except in orchards, but let them be set where they will, they never fail to repay the owner with pleasure and profit

Varieties The varieties which are principally designed for ornamental plantations are, The Cherry Plum-tree, the Double blossomed, the Stoneless, the Gold striped, and the Silver-striped Plum

described The Cherry Plum-tree is always planted among flowering shrubs, on account of its early flowering It may be kept down to any height, and the flowers will be produced in March, in such plenty, and so close, as almost to cover the branches It is admired by all for the early appearance of its flowers, which are succeeded, after a mild spring, by a round reddish plum, on a long slender footstalk, that has the resemblance of a Cherry Unless there is little or no frost after these trees have been in blow, it rarely happens that any fruit succeeds the flower

The Double blossomed Plum tree is another variety The flowers of this sort are exceeding double, and the twigs will be gorgeously bespangled with them in the month of May Their petals, like those of the Cherry, are of a pure white, though amongst these some filaments with darkish antheræ appear As soon as the show of flowers is over, we are not to give up all expectations from this tree, for many of them will be succeeded by fruit, which is of the same colour, shape, and taste, with the common damascene, though smaller, and is liked by many

The Stoneless Plum This is a variety that should be admitted on no other account than because the pulp surrounds a kernel, without having any stone It is a small blue plum, and those people who have it in possession, take a pleasure in shewing it as a curiosity

The two Striped sorts make a variety by their variegated leaves, on which account they are frequently sought after by the curious

Bullace tree 9 The Bullace tree is very often planted in wilderness-quarters for the sake of the fruit, for, after that profusion of luscious and rich dainties of the various sorts of fruit the autumn affords, these cause an alterative, by many persons deemed very agreeable, for they are possessed of a fine acid The fruit ought to be pulled and eaten immediately from the tree It will whet the appetite, and is generally thought very wholesome

Names of its varieties The varieties of this species are, The Black, the White, and the Red Bullace

Sloe tree 10 The Sloe-tree The Sloe bush is, without all doubt, a species distinct from either Plum or Bullace And indeed it is such a species, that, were it not for its commonness, it would be thought inferior in beauty to none of our shrubs For what can exceed the beauty of a sloe-bush in the spring, when every twig is covered all over with white flowers? Or what can surpass it in the autumn, when the same twigs are beset all around with their pretty berries? The commonness of this tree, however, causes its beauties to be unnoticed by many, and forbids us to admit any in our Collection It grows all over England, in our hedges and woods Of this sort also good hedges for fence are made, so that the most we must admit of this species is only a plant or two, for the philosopher's observation

Many of the preceding sorts being fruit-trees, their culture falls of course in another place What is necessary to be said here is, that

Method of propagating the different sorts 1, 2, 3 The Common, the Virginian, and Canada Bird Cherry, may be raised by seeds, sown and managed as was directed for the propagation of the Virginian Bird-Cherry, among the forest-trees, in the First Book The Bird Cherries may be propagated by layers also, for the young twigs being laid in the ground, without any other trouble, will strike root in one year, and may be taken up and planted in nursery lines, or set out for good These trees will also easily grow by cuttings The best time for planting them is in October If the succeeding spring and summer should prove very dry, they should be watered every evening, and it will not be improper to plant them in the moistest part of the garden They may be set very close, within three inches of each other By the autumn following they will have struck root, when they should be taken up and planted in the nursery, a foot asunder, and two feet distant in the lines, and there they may stand until they are planted out for good

4 The Perfumed Cherry is propagated by grafting or budding upon any of our cherry-stocks, the method of raising which will be set forth under that article among the Fruit-trees

5 The Apricot-tree is propagated by budding it upon the plum stock, the practice of which will be shewn under that article, in a future Book

6 The Fruit-bearing, Double-blossomed, and Red-flowering Cherry-trees, are cultivated by grafting upon stocks raised from the stones of the Black-Cherry-tree, though it may be proper to observe here, that when the Double blossomed Cherry is wanted to be kept very low, in its dwarf state, the Common Bird Cherry will be a much more proper stock to work it upon, as that sort is naturally of much lower growth than the Black Cherry tree

7, 8, 9 The Plum-tree, in all its varieties, and the Bullace tree, the Cherry Plum, the Double Blossomed Plum, and the Stoneless Plum, are propagated by grafting upon Plum stocks raised from seeds, though it is observable, that suckers of the Bullaces will grow to be trees, and produce plenty of good fruit, but these will not be so good as those grafted on the Plum-stocks, as they will be subject to throw out many suckers, and over-run the ground

10 The Sloe-bush may be obtained from the places where they grow, for from thence a sucker or two may be taken, and planted for the convenency of observation, but these will not be so good as those raised from the stones, as they will have a greater tendency to throw out suckers, and over-run the ground, unless they are grubbed up in time; so that it will be the best way to raise a few of these plants from the stones, which will not afterwards, in so high a degree, have that tendency

1 The Common Bird-Cherry is entitled, *Prunus floribus racemosis, foliis deciduis basi subtus biglandulosis* This is what stands in the *Hortus Cliffortianus* with the title, *Padus glandulis duabus, basi foliorum subjectis*, and in the *Flora Lapp Padus foliis annuis* Caspar Bauhine calls it, *Cerasus racemosa sylvestris, fructu non eduli* It grows naturally in woods and hedges in the North of England, and most countries of Europe Titles

2 Virginian or American Bird Cherry is, *Prunus floribus racemosis, foliis deciduis basi antice glandulosis*

*g'a. dulcis.* C tc by ca'ls it, *Ce afus l. t ore folio, fruct i iecen fo purpureo ejon* and Gronovius, *Cerasus sylvestris, fruct i nigricante in racemis longis pendulis phytolacce instar congestis* It grows naturally in Virginia, Pensylvania, and Carolina

3 Canada Bird Cherry is, *Prunus flor bus racemosis fol s late lanceolatis rugosis utrinque p besrent bus* Du Hamel calls it, *Cerasus pum la Canadensis, oblongo angusto folio fructu parvo*, and Pluk net, *cerasus racemosa, fo is amygdalin s, Ia rica* It grows naturally in many parts of North Ame c

4 Mahaleb, or the Perfumed Cherry, is, *Prunus flor bus corymbosis, folis ovatis* Cammerarius calls it simply, *Mahaleb*, Caspar Bauhine, *Cerasus effi us*, and J Bauhine, *Ceras s sylvestris amara, mahaleo putata* It grows naturally in Switzerland, and in many of the northern parts of Europe

5 The Apricot tree is entitled, *Prunus floribus sessilibus, folis subcordatis* In the *Hortus Cliffor* ... *us* it is termed, *Prunus fol is ovato cordat s* Caspar Bauhine calls it, *Mala Armeniaca majora* also, *Mala Armeniaca minor*, also, *Mala Armeniaca major, nucleo dulci* It is not certain in what part of the world the Apricot-tree naturally grows

6 The Cultivated Cherry-tree is entitled, *Prunus umbellis subsessi bus folns ovato lan colatis conduplicatis glabris* In the Upsal Catalogue it is termed, *Cerasus folis ovato-lanceolatis* Caspar Bauhine calls it, *Cerasus hortensis flore pleno*, also, *Cerasus hortensis, flore roseo*, also, *Cerasus alba ..*, also, *Cerasus carne tenera & aquosa*, also, *Cerasus pumila*, also, *Cerasus cordo majore*, also, *Cerasus fetrica rotunda rubra & acida*, also, *Cerasus racemosa hortensis*, &c &c It grows naturally in woods and hedges in England, and most parts of Europe

7 The Wild Cherry-tree is titled, *Prunus umbellis sessilibus, folns ovato lanceolatis conduplicatis subtus pubescentibus* John Bauhine calls it *Cerasus sylvestris, fructu nigro & rubro*, Caspar Bauhine, *Cerasus major, sive sylvestris, fructu subdulci nigro colore inficiente* It grows naturally in hedge-rows and woods in England, and many of the northern parts of Europe

8 The Plum tree is entitled, *Prunus pedunculis subsolitariis, folns lanceolato ovatis convolutis ramis muticis* In the *Hortus Cliffortianus* it is termed, *Prunus inermis, folns lanceolato ovat s* The different sorts of Plum also, like the Cherry, have been described by different titles by some authors, but those titles are now thought beneath the notice of every good botanist The Plum-tree is common in many parts of Europe

9 The Bullace-tree is titled, *Prunus pedunculis geminis, foli s ovatis subtus villosis convolutis, ramis spinescentibus* Ray calls it, *Prunus sylvestris major*, also, *Prunus sylvestris fructu majore nigro*, also, *Prunus sylvestris fructu majore albo*, also, *Prunus sylvestris fructu rubro, acerbo & ingrato* Caspar Bauhine calls it *Prunus sylvestris praecocior* It grows naturally in hedge-rows in England and Germany

10 The Sloe-bush is entitled, *Prunus pedunculis solitariis, fol s lanceolatis glabris, ramis spinosis* Caspar Bauhine calls it, *Prunus sylvestris* It grows in most every where in our hedges and woods, and in the like places in most countries of Europe

*Prunus* is of the class and order *Icosandria Monogynia*, and the characters are,

1 CALYX is a monophyllous, campanulated, deciduous perianthium, divided into five obtuse, concave segments

2 COROLLA consists of five large roundish concave, patent petals, inserted by their ungues into the calyx

3 STAMINA are from twenty to thirty subulated filaments, almost the length of the corolla, and inserted in the calyx These have didymous short antherae

4 PISTILLUM consists of a roundish germen a filiform style the length of the stamina, and an orbicular stigma

5 PERICARPIUM is a roundish drupe

6 SEMEN is a roundish, compressed nut

## CHAP LXVII

## *PTELEA*, The TREFOIL-SHRUB

Description of the Ptelea

PTELEA affords us two species, one for the stove, and another for this Collection The sort proper for our present purpose is commonly called the Carolina Shrub Trefoil This plant will grow to the height of ten feet Miller indeed says, in his Book of Prints, that it is a plant of five or six feet growth, whereas I have known it shoot higher in one summer The branches of this shrub are not very numerous, and when broken, they emit a strong scent They are brittle, though full of pith, and covered with a smooth purplish bark The leaves are trifoliate, and grow irregularly on the branches, on a long footstalk The foholes are oval, spear-shaped, of a delightful strong green colour on their upper side, lighter underneath, smooth, and pretty large when they are fully out, which will not be before part of the summer is elapsed, for they put out late in the spring The flowers are produced in bunches at the end of the branches Their are of a greenish white colour, and their general character indicate their structure They come out in June, and are succeeded by roundish bordered capsules, but the seeds seldom ripen in England

This shrub may be propagated either by seeds, layers, or cuttings

1 By seeds These should be sown in a warm border, in the spring, in common garden mould, made fine, and if the seeds are good, they will grow, and come up the first summer We generally receive the seeds from abroad, though they will in some warm seasons ripen here with us When the young plants begin to come up, which will be, if the seeds are good, by the end of May, they should be shaded and every second evening duly watered, and this, together with

ei

conſtant weeding, will be all the care they will require until the autumn At the approach of winter, it will be proper to prick ſome furze-buſhes round the bed, to break the keen edge of the black froſts They will then require no other trouble until the ſecond ſpring after they are come up, when they ſhould be all taken out of the ſeed-bed, and planted in the nurſery, a foot aſunder, and in two or three years they will be fit to plant out for good

By layers. 2 By layers For this purpoſe a number of plants muſt be planted for ſtools, and, after they have ſtood a year or two, theſe ſhould be cut down pretty near the ground By the autumn they will have made ſhoots, ſome of which will be five or ſix feet, or more, in length and theſe are the ſhoots for layering October is the beſt month for the work, and the operation is to be performed by cutting the twig half through, and making a ſlit half an inch long Any thing may be put into this ſlit, to keep it open, and after the mould is levelled all round, the longeſt ends ſhould be taken off By this method I have ever found them with good roots by the autumn following, and that the ſtools had ſhot out freſh wood for a ſecond layering At this time they ſhould be taken up, and the weakeſt planted in the nurſery, to get ſtrength, whilſt the ſtronger layers will be good plants to ſet out for good After this, the operation may be again repeated, and ſo continued annually, *ad infinitum*

and by cuttings. 3 By cuttings In order to obtain plenty of good cuttings, the plants ſhould be headed as for layering In October the young ſhoots ſhould be taken off, and cut into lengths of a little more than a foot, two thirds of which ſhould be ſet in the ground Some of theſe cuttings will grow; though I ever found this way very uncertain, and not worth the practiſing But if the cuttings are planted in pots, and aſſiſted by artificial heat, they will grow readily This, however, is not a good method, for they will be tender the firſt winter, as well as require to be protected in the greenhouſe, or under ſome cover, which will occaſion more trouble than if they had been layered By layers and the ſeeds, therefore, are the beſt and moſt eligible methods of encreaſing theſe trees

This ſpecies of *Ptelea* is entitled, *Ptelea foliis ternatis* In the *Hortus Cliffortianus* it is termed ſimply, *Ptelea* Zinn calls it, *Ptelea ſimplex*, and Plukenet, *Frutex Virginianus trifolius, ulmi ſamaris* It grows common in Virginia and Carolina Titles of this ſpecies

*Ptelea* is of the claſs and order *Tetrandria Monogynia*, and the characters are, Claſs and order in the Linnæan ſyſtem

1 Calyx is a perianthium divided into four ſmall, acute parts

2 Corolla conſiſts of four oval, ſpear ſhaped, plane, coriaceous petals, larger than the calyx, and ſpread open The characters

3 Stamina are four ſubulated filaments, with roundiſh antheræ

4 Pistillum conſiſts of a roundiſh compreſſed germen, and of a ſhort ſtyle, with two obtuſe ſtigmas

5 Pericarpium is a roundiſh, perpendicular membrane, having two cells in the center for the ſeed

6 Semen The ſeed is ſingle and obtuſe

## CHAP LXVIII.

## *PYRUS*, The PEAR-TREE

Introductory obſervations. THERE are hardly any trees of the flowering tribe which exceed the different ſorts of our fruit-trees, in that reſpect, either for majeſtic look, profuſion of flowers, or the beauty of each, ſingly conſidered But it is their commonneſs which makes them ſo little noticed, and few people ever think of their being arrayed in beauty, except when they are covered with ripe fruit The different ſorts of Pears only uſed formerly to be arranged under the generical term of *Pyrus*, but we are now taught that the Pear, the Apple, and the Quince, are all juſtly comprehended in this genus, all of which, with their ſorts, are of great beauty as well as uſe, though the former is little noticed Were the meaneſt of them to be planted in a country where no ſuch tree had before appeared, how would the inhabitants be amazed and delighted, when the branches ſhewed themſelves in the ſpring, covered with their delightful bloom? And though they may not affect us who have them in ſuch plenty in that manner, yet a man muſt be inſenſible indeed, if the commonneſs of a tree can throw ſuch a miſt over its beauties as to render them imperceptible by him Too many perſons, it is to be feared, however, are of this ſtamp, whilſt the attentive obſerver of Nature can ſee beauty and wiſdom in all its works, and that the common Crab-treee of our hedges ſtands in the foremoſt rank amongſt trees of the flowering tribe Not that I would here be thought to inſinuate, that the ſorts of Pears and Apples ought to be planted as flowering-trees in wilderneſs quarters for that purpoſe only No, we have them every-where in our orchards, where we ſhall ſee them in their greateſt perfection, and if fixed at proper diſtances, they will vary the ſcene, after turning the eye from wilderneſs ſhrubs to their beauties, ſo that all I have to do here is, to ſelect ſuch ſorts of *Pyrus* as are not common, and have always been thought deſireable in making a Collection of rare plants Theſe are,

1 The Double bloſſomed Pear Species.
2 The Twice-flowering Pear
3 The Paradiſe-Apple
4 The Fig Apple
5 The Virginian Sweet-ſcented Crab tree
6 The Quince tree

1 The Double bloſſomed Pear differs from the other ſorts only in that the flowers are double The leaves, indeed, are not ſo much ſerrated Deſcription of the Double bloſſomed Pear,



Tt

rated as some of the other Pears, nay, scarcely any serratures appear at all, except on the oldest leaves, for the younger are perfectly entire and downy. The multiplicity of the petals of this flower, are not sufficient to entitle it to the appellation of a full flower, for it consists only of a double row of petals, but as these are all large, in large clusters, and of a pure white, they entitle the tree to be called a flowering-tree, with greater propriety than the ordinary Pear can be so styled. The planter of this species is rewarded in a double effect, for as the petals are not multiplied in so great a degree as to destroy the stamina, the flowers are succeeded by a good fruit, whose properties are such as entitle it to the rank of a good baking Pear.

*Twice flowering Pear.* 2. The Twice flowering Pear. This species is sufficiently described by the title, it being a Pear that often produces flowers in the autumn, when the fruit that succeeded those of the spring are near ripe. This tree deserves to be planted both for its beauty and singularity, for it sometimes happens, though by no means constantly, that it is covered over in September with bloom and fruit. This autumnal bloom falls away, and the chilling cold often prevents its coming to any embryo fruit, but it seems to bid fair to entitle ours to the praises of that happy country, where, Virgil says,

*Bis gravidæ pecudes, bis pomis utilis arbos.*

*Paradise Apple.* 3. Paradise Apple is rather a shrub than a tree. There are two sorts of it, which gardeners distinguish by the names of the French and the Dutch Paradise-Apple. They are both low growing trees, and the only difference between them is, that the Dutch sort is rather the strongest shooter. They are chiefly used for stocks to graft apples upon, in order to make them more dwarf, so that a plant or two in a Collection, for the sake of saving they are in it, will be sufficient.

*Fig Apple.* 4. Fig-Apple has a place here for no other reason than its being destitute of the most beautiful parts of which the flowers are composed, viz. the petals. They have all the stamina, &c. but no petals, which is a singular imperfection, though by many they are coveted on that account. As the stamina and other parts are all perfect, the flowers are succeeded by a tolerable good eating Apple, for the sake of which this tree deserves to be propagated.

*Virginian Sweet-scented Crab.* 5. The Virginian Sweet-scented Crab is a native of that country by whose name it is distinguished. With us it is propagated as a foreign plant, and differs from our Crabs in the leaves, flowers, and fruit. The leaves are angular, smooth, of a fine green colour, and have a look entirely different from any of our crabs or apples. The flowers stand on larger footstalks than those of the generality of our crabs, and are remarkable for their great fragrance. This tree is seldom in full blow before the beginning of June. The flowers, when they first open, are of a pale-red, though the petals soon after alter to a white colour. They are succeeded by a little, round crab, which, of all others, is the sourest, roughest, and most disagreeable, that can be put into the mouth. The curiosity of many will prompt them to taste of these crabs,

*At sapor indicium faciet manifestus, & ora*
*Tristia tentantum sensu torquebit amaror.*

There is another sort of American Crab tree, that retains its leaves all winter, on which account it comes in of course amongst the ever-greens.

*and its Quince tree.* 6. Quince-tree. There are many varieties of the Quince-tree, which are chiefly raised for the fruit, to be used either in medicine, or to make marmalade for kitchen use. They are, however, very fine flowering trees, and no Collection should be without a few, as being not only beautiful in themselves, but as they may be planted to appear ornamental in such places where few other trees should be trusted. The Quince-tree seldom grows to be higher than eight or ten feet, and the bark on the branches is often of a kind of iron colour. The leaves are large and oval. Their upper surface is of a pleasant green colour, though often possessed of a loose downy matter, and their under side is hoary to a great degree. The flowers are produced in May, all along the branches. They grow upon young shoots of the same spring, and are very large and beautiful, for although each is composed of about five petals only, yet these are often an inch long, are broad and concave, and of a fine pale-red as they first open, though they afterwards alter to a white, and those flowers being produced the whole length of the branches, and bespangling the whole tree in a natural and easy manner, justly entitle this species to no mean place among the flowering kinds. They are succeeded by that fine large yellow fruit which is so well known, and which at a distance, on the tree, appears like a ball of gold. Indeed, these trees should always be planted at a distance from much frequented places, for the fruit, valuable as it is when properly prepared for use, has a strong disagreeable scent, that will fill the air all around with its odours, which to most people are offensive. The place Quince-trees, then, ought to have should be at some distance from walks, and they serve admirably, when planted at the edges, to hide unsightly ditches, with muddy water, &c. which conveniency will not permit to be filled up. They will exhibit their beautiful bloom in the spring, and fine fruit in the autumn.

*Method of propagating the sorts.* All these sorts will take by grafting or budding upon one another, notwithstanding what Mr Miller has alledged to the contrary. I have a tree that bears excellent apples, grafted upon Pear-stocks, and Pears grafted upon Crab stocks, that have not yet borne, so that we see Virgil is not justly censurable for saying,

*Et sæpe alterius ramos impune videmus*
*Vertere in alterius, mutatamque insita mala*
*Ferre pyrum, &c.*

The usual way is to graft the Pears on stocks raised from the kernels of Pears, and the Apples on Crab-stocks. These should be sown, even after the fruit is ripe, in beds half an inch deep, and carefully guarded from mice, which will soon destroy the whole seminary, if once found out. In the spring the plants will come up, and in the winter following they should be planted out in the nursery, in rows two feet asunder. In a year or two after this, they will be fit for working, and by this method all the sorts of Pears and Apples are propagated.

The Paradise Apple is generally raised by layers or cuttings, and all the sorts of Quinces grow readily by cuttings, planted any time in the winter, though the early part of that season is to be preferred. Though the trees will grow by layers, and new sorts may be obtained by seeds, yet experiments of this kind do not deserve trying, as they will be many years before

before they bear from seeds, and the sorts we already have are many and excellent

Titles of the different species

1, 2 The Pear-tree is titled, *Pyrus foliis serratis, pedunculis corymbosis* In the former edition of the *Species Plantarum* it is called, *Pyrus foliis serratis, pomis basi productis* Authors have distinguished the wild sort by the title, *Pyrus sylvestris*, and the cultivated sorts by the titles of, *Pyrus Bergamotta gallis*, *Pyrus boni Christiani*, *Pyrus Jesu, s moschatellina rubra*; *Pyra dorsalia eademque liberalia dicta*, &c &c The Pear-tree is found growing wild in most parts of Europe

3, 4 The Apple-tree is entitled, *Pyrus foliis serratis, umbellis sessilibus* In the former edition of the *Species Plantarum* it is called, *Pyrus foliis serratis, pomis basi concavis* The varieties go by the respective names of, *Malus sylvestris*, *Malus pumila, quæ potius frutex quam arbor*, *Malus prasomila*, *Malus sativa, fructu sanguinei coloris ex austero subdulci*, *Mala cur tipendula dicta*, *Mala sativa, fructu magno intense rubente, violæ odore*, *Poma orbiculata*, &c &c It grows common in most parts of Europe

5 The Virginian Sweet-scented Crab is, *Pyrus foliis serrato angulatis, umbellis pedunculatis* In the former edition of the *Species Plantarum* it is called, *Pyrus foliis serrato angulosis* Gronovius calls it, *Malus sylvestris, floribus odoratis* It is a native of Virginia

6 The Quince-tree is titled, *Pyrus foliis integerrimis floribus solitariis* This is by some authors called, *Malus cotonea sylvestris*, by others, *Cotonea & Cydonia* The varieties are distinguished by, *Malus cotonea major*, *Malus cotonea minor*, &c It grows naturally on the banks of the Danube

Class and order in the Linnæan system The characters

*Pyrus* is of the class and order *Icosandria Pentagynia*; and the characters are,

1 CALYX is a monophyllous, concave, permanent perianthium, divided into five patent segments

2 COROLLA consists of five large, roundish, concave petals, inserted in the calyx

3 STAMINA are twenty awl-shaped filaments, shorter than the corolla, and inserted in the calyx, having simple antheræ

4 PISTILLUM consists of a germen situated below the receptacle, and of five filiforme styles, the length of the stamina, with simple stigmas

5 PERICARPIUM is a roundish, umbilicated, carnose apple, of five cells

6 SEMINA The seeds are oblong, obtuse, acuminated at the base, convex on one side, and plane on the other

## CHAP LXIX

## *QUERCUS*, The OAK-TREE

THE Common English Oak, and all its varieties, together with the different species or foreign oaks, and their sorts, make now a great swell in our Collection, and in a numerous manner encrease the variety Our English Oak has leaves, acorns, footstalks, and cups, of different colours, shapes, and sizes, insomuch that I have been asked, by people of no great skill, the name of such an Oak and such an Oak, which they saw growing in the nursery-quarters, among those raised from acorns promiscuously gathered from our woods, and indeed they have had so different an appearance, some leaves being small and green, others large and red, others paler and more indented, as might justly induce them to ask the question The species of the foreign sorts have also their varieties, so that, upon the whole, we have a large fund of sorts from this great genus the Oak

The real deciduous, distinct species of the Oak, in the *Species Plantarum*, are,

Species

1 The Common English Oak
2 The Willow leaved Oak
3 The Chesnut leaved Oak
4 The Black Oak
5 The Red Oak
6 The White Oak
7 The Cut-leaved Italian Oak, or *Phagus* of the Greeks
8 Oak with prickly Cups and large Acorns
9 Oak with prickly Cups and smaller Acorns

Common English Oak

1 The Common Oak of our woods is so well known as to need no description, and a great many sorts of this may be obtained to encrease the variety in our larger plantations, especially whilst young; as they grow older the difference of the leaves will be less visible, and the variety occasioned by the acorns, footstalks, &c will be too inconsiderable to procure them on that account The chief pleasure, then, this variety will give, will be by the difference of their leaves, during the first ten or fifteen years after the plantation is made, and whoever is desirous of this, should mark the most opposite sorts in the summer, as they stand in the nursery lines, that they may be removed in the winter

Variety

Besides such casual varieties, there is the Striped leaved Oak, a tree in high esteem with those who are fond of variegated plants

Willow-leaved Oak

2 The Willow leaved Oak, which will grow to be a large timber tree, and is a native of North-America, is so called because the leaves are long and narrow, greatly resembling those of our Common Willow These long narrow leaves have their surface smooth, and their edges entire, and their acorns will be almost covered with their large cups

Varieties

There are several varieties of this sort, some having shorter leaves, others broader, and hollowed on the sides, some large acorns, others smaller, &c all of which are included under the appellation of Willow leaved Oaks

Chesnut leaved Oak

3 The Chesnut-leaved Oak This also will grow to be a large timber tree, and in North-America, where it grows naturally, the wood is of great service to the inhabitants It is so called, because the leaves greatly resemble those of the Spanish chesnut-tree They are about the same size, smooth, and of a fine green colour

There

Varieties. There are two or three varieties of this sort, but the leaves of all prove, that they are of the species called the Chesnut-leaved Oak, so that nothing more need be observed, than that the leaves of some sorts are larger than those of others, that the acorns also differ in size, and grow like those of our English Oak, on long or short footstalks as it shall happen.

Black Oak. 4. The Black Oak is a tree of lower growth, it seldom arising to more than thirty feet high. The bark of this tree is of a very dark colour, which occasioned its being named the Black Oak. The leaves are smooth, very large, narrow at their base, but broad at their top, being in shape like a wedge. They have indentures at the top, so as to occasion its having an angular look, they are of a shining green colour, and grow on short footstalks on the branches.

Variety. There is a variety or two of this sort, particularly one with trifid leaves, and another slightly trilobate, called the Black Oak of the Plains, the leaves and cups of all which are small.

Red Oak. 5. Red Oak. The Red Oak will grow to be a timber-tree of sixty or seventy feet high, and the branches are covered with a very dark-coloured bark. It is called the Red Oak from the colour of its leaves, which in the autumn die to a deep red colour.

Varieties. There are several varieties of this species, the leaves of which differ in size and figure, but those of the larger sort are finely veined and exceeding large, being often found ten inches long and five or six broad. They are obtusely sinuated, have angles, and are of a fine green colour in the first part of the summer, but afterwards change by degrees to red, which is mark enough to know these trees to be of this species. There are several varieties of this tree, which exhibit a manifest difference in the size of the leaves, acorns, and cups. That is the best which is commonly called the Virginian Scarlet Oak, and the bark is preferred for the tanners use before that of all the other sorts.

White Oak. 6. The White Oak. The White Oak will not grow to the size of the former, it seldom being found higher than forty feet even in Virginia, where it grows naturally. But though the timber is not so large, yet it is more durable, and consequently of greater value for building to the inhabitants of America, than any of the other sorts. The branches of this tree are covered with a whitish bark, the leaves also are of a light colour. They are pretty large, being about six inches long and four broad. They have several obtuse sinusses and angles, and are placed on short footstalks.

Varieties. There are a variety or two of this species, and the acorns are like those of our Common Oak.

Cut-leaved Italian Oak. 7. The Cut-leaved Italian Oak will grow to about the height of thirty feet. The branches are covered with a dark-purplish bark. The leaves are smooth, and so deeply sinuated as to have some resemblance of pinnated leaves, and each has a very short footstalk. The fruit of this species sits close to the branches. The cups are in some degree prickly and rough, and each contains a long slender acorn, that is eatable. This is the true *Phagus* of the Greeks, and the *Esculus* of Pliny, and in the places where these trees grow naturally the acorns are, in times of scarcity, ground into flour and made into bread.

Oak with prickly Cups and large Acorns. 8. The Oak with prickly Cups and large Acorns will grow to be as large a tree as our Common Oak, and is no way inferior to it in stately grandeur, for the branches, like that, will be far extended all around, causing, with the leaves, a delightful shade. Though the bark of these branches is of a whitish colour, yet they are nevertheless spotted with brownish spots. The leaves are of an oblong oval figure, but not very long, seldom being longer than three inches and two broad. They are smooth, and have their edges deeply serrated. These serratures are acute, and chiefly turn backwards. Their upper surface is of a fine light green colour, and their under of an hoary cast, and with these beautiful leaves each branch is plentifully ornamented all over the tree. The cups are most peculiar and singular, for they are very large, and composed of several rough, black, large scales, that lap over one another like the scales of a fish. They almost cover the acorn, though they are pretty large, narrow at the bottom, but broader higher, and have their tops flat. The Greeks call the acorns *Velan*, and the tree itself *Velanida*, and the acorns are used in dyeing.

And with smaller Acorns. 9. The Oak with prickly Cups and smaller Acorns is of lower growth than the preceding species, it seldom rising to more than forty feet high. The leaves are of two colours, their upper surface being of a fine green colour, and their under downy. Their figure is oblong, but they are so indented about the middle as to make them have the resemblance of a lyre. They are wing pointed, transversely jagged, and stand on slender footstalks on the branches. The cups of this sort also are smaller and prickly, and the acorns also proportionally smaller, than those of the preceding species.

Method of propagating these species. All these sorts may be propagated from the acorns, which must be procured from the places where the trees naturally grow. They should be sown as soon as possible after they arrive, and if any of them have sprouted, great care must be used in taking them out of the boxes in which they were conveyed. Any sort of our common garden-mould, made fine, will suit them, and they should be sown in drills, in beds an inch deep. The first spring after sowing, the plants will come up, they should be always kept clean from weeds, and if they are watered in dry weather, it will be the better. They will want no preservation in winter, for they are all very hardy, even when young. In March they should be all taken out of the seed-bed, have their tap-roots shortened, and be planted in the nursery-ground a foot asunder, and two feet distant in the rows, where they may stand, with the usual nursery care, until they are to be planted out for good. Thus easily may all these curious sorts be propagated, if we can procure the acorns from the places where they grow naturally, and which may be seen after their respective titles.

The Striped-leaved Oak is usually propagated by inarching it into the Common Oak, but it is best encreased by grafting, in the manner of the elm. In the same manner, also, any particular variety belonging to the other species may be continued and multiplied.

Titles. 1. The Common English Oak is entitled, *Quercus foliis deciduis oblongis superne latioribus sinubus acutioribus, angulis obtusis*. Caspar Bauhine calls it, *Quercus latifolia mas, quæ brevi pedicula est*, to distinguish it from another sort which he calls, *Quercus cum longo pediculo*, and Tucker and others, *Quercus*. It grows almost all over England, and is found in most parts of Europe.

2. The Willow-leaved Oak is, *Quercus foliis lanceolatis integerrimis glabris*. Ray calls it, *Quercus, seu Ilex Marilandica, folio longo angusto salicis*; Catesby, *Quercus foliis oblongis non sinuatis*, also, *Quercus humilis, foliis folio breviore*, and Plukenet, *Quercus salicis folio*. It grows in most parts of North America.

3 The

3 The Chesnut-leaved Oak is titled, *Quercus foliis ovato-oblongis acuminatis sinuato-serratis denticulis acutis uniformibus* Plukenet and others call it, *Quercus, Castaneae foliis, procera arbor, Virginiana* It grows naturally in most parts of North America

4 The Black Oak is, *Quercus foliis cuneiformibus obsolete trilobis* Catesby calls it, *Quercus folio non serrato, in summitate quasi triangulo*, also, *Quercus Marilandica, folio trifido ad sassafras accedente* It is a native of North America

5 The Red Oak is, *Quercus foliis obtuse sinuatis setaceo mucronatis* This, together with the sorts of it, stands in authors by the various titles of, *Quercus foliorum sinubus obtusis angulis lente obtusis seta terminatis integerrimis tri divisis*, *Quercus Æsculi divisura, foliis amplioribus aculeatis*, *Quercus foliorum, sinubus obtusis angulis acutis seta terminatis intermediis tridentatis margine integerrimo*, *Quercus Caroliniensis, virentibus venis muricata*, *Quercus Virginiana venis rubris muricata*, &c It grows common in Virginia and Carolina

6 The White Oak is, *Quercus foliis oblique pinnatifidis sinubus angulisque obtusis* Gronovius calls it, *Quercus foliis superne latioribus opposite sinuatis, sinubus angulisque obtusis*, and Catesby, *Quercus alba Virginiana* It grows naturally in Virginia

7 The Cut-leaved Italian Oak is, *Quercus foliis pinnato-sinuatis laciniis, fructibus sessilibus* This is the *Quercus pumila, five Esculus Græcorum*, and *Esculus Plinii*, of Caspar Bauhine It grows common in Spain, Italy, and the south of France

8 The Oak with large Acorns and prickly Cups is, *Quercus foliis ovato oblongis glabris serrato repandis* Caspar Bauhine calls it, *Quercus cerris calyce echinato, glande majore*, and John Bauhine, *Cerri glans Ægilops aspis* It is a native of Spain

9 The Oak with prickly Cups and smaller Acorns is, *Quercus foliis oblongis subovatis pinnatifidis laciniis transversis acutis, fructus sonectosis* Caspar Bauhine calls it, *Quercus calyce hispido, glande minore*, and John Bauhine, *Phagus, sive Esculus* This also is a native of Spain, and of Austria

This genus is of the class and order *Monoecia Polyandria*, and the characters are, Class and order in the Linnæan system The characters

I Male flowers are dispersed in loose katkins, and,

1 CALYX is a monophyllous perianthium, divided into four or five acute and often bifid segments

2 COROLLA There is none

3 STAMINA consist of several very short filaments, having large didymous antheræ

II Female flowers are on the same plant with the male, and sit close to the buds, and for these,

1 CALYX is a monophyllous, coriaceous, hemispherical rough, undivided perianthium

2 COROLLA There is none

3 PISTILLUM consists of a very small oval germen, and of a simple quinquefid style, longer than the calyx, having simple permanent stigmas

4 PERICARPIUM There is none

5 SEMEN is an oval, smooth, taper nut or acorn, having a coriaceous shell of one valve, and derased or shaven at the base, where it is fixed into the calyx

# CHAP LXX

## *RHAMNUS*, The BUCKTHORN

MANY genera of old authors are now made to belong to *Rhamnus* The real deciduous species proper for our hardy plantations are,

Species

1 The Buckthorn, or Purging Thorn

2 The Common *Frangula*, or Berry bearing Alder

3 Rough-leaved Alpine *Frangula*, or Berry-bearing Alder

4 *Paliurus*, or *Christ* Thorn

Purging Thorn Varieties

1 Buckthorn, or Purging Thorn Of this species there are the following varieties Dwarf Buckthorn, Long-leaved Dwarf Buckthorn, and the Common Buckthorn of our Hedges

Variety is the sole motive for admitting these sorts into a Collection The flowers have no beauty to catch the attention, though their berries, their manner of growing, the colour of their bark in winter, and verdure of their leaves in summer, court us to admit a few of them, and thereby the greatness of our Collection will be encreased

described

Dwarf Buckthorn is a shrub of about a yard high The branches grow irregular, and are covered with a blackish-coloured bark The leaves are nearly oval, though they end in a point They are scarcely an inch long, about half that breadth, and stand opposite by pairs for the most part The flowers grow on short footstalks on spurs, by the sides of the branches They are of a greenish colour, and make little show

Long-leaved Dwarf Buckthorn differs little from the other, only that it grows to be rather a larger shrub, and the leaves are longer The flowers are about the same colour as the Dwarf sort, but neither of these scarcely ever produce berries This makes them much less valuable than our Common Buckthorn, which will exhibit its black berries in plenty in the autumn, either for show or use

Common Buckthorn is well known in England Where it does not grow common about a habitation, a few of these shrubs should be admitted, for it is a well-looking tree, either in winter or summer, and its black berries in the autumn are no small ornament The Common Buckthorn will grow to be near sixteen feet high, and will send forth numerous branches on all sides These are smooth, and the bark is of a bluish colour Many strong sharp spines come out from the sides and ends of the branches The leaves are oval, spear shaped, about two inches long and one broad Their under surface is of a lighter green than the upper They have serrated edges and stand, sometimes by pairs, sometimes single, on longish footstalks on the branches. The flowers are produced in clusters from the sides of the branches, in June. Their colour is green, and they are succeeded by black berries, each containing four seeds. These berries look well in the autumn, and garnish the twigs in a pleasing manner. The *Syrupus e Spina cervina*, or Syrup of Buckthorn, is made of these berries, and is well known as a cathartic. From the juice of these berries also an admirable green colour is prepared, which is in great request with miniature-painters.

Syrup of Buckthorn made from the berries of this sort.

All the sorts of Buckthorn are easily propagated, either by seeds or cuttings. The seeds of the Purging Buckthorn may be gathered in plenty in most parts of England, but the seeds of the Dwarf sorts must be procured from abroad where they grow naturally, for they produce no seeds with us. They should be sown as soon as possible after they are ripe, in almost any kind of garden-mould made fine. They will not always come up the first spring, so that the beds must remain undisturbed and weeded during the summer. After they are come up, and have stood in the seed-bed a year or two, they may be planted out in the nursery-way, at small distances.

Method of propagating these sorts by seeds.

These plants are also to be raised by cuttings, which should be planted in the autumn, and if they are not planted very close, they will want no removing until they are set out for good. If a large quantity of these plants is wanted, and little ground is prepared for the cuttings, they may be set very close, and in the winter following taken up, and planted in the nursery way, like the seedlings. In two or three years, they may be planted out for good.

And by cuttings.

2. *Frangula*, or Berry bearing Alder. This species affords us the following varieties: Common Black-berry bearing Alder, Dwarf Berry-bearing Alder, and the American Smooth-leaved Berry-bearing Alder.

Frangula. Varieties.

The Common Black-berry bearing Alder will grow to the height of about ten feet. It will aspire with an upright stem, and produces numerous branches on all sides. The bark is smooth, of a blackish colour, and is all over spotted with white spots, which make it resemble a bluish grey. The leaves are oval, spear-shaped, and grow irregularly on the branches. They are about two inches long and one broad. Their upper surface is smooth and of a shining green, and their under surface is possessed of many strong veins that run from the mid-rib to the edges. The flowers are produced in bunches in June, each having a separate footstalk. They are of a greenish colour, and make no show, but they are succeeded by berries, which are first red and afterwards (when ripe) black, and are a great ornament to the tree.

described.

Dwarf Berry-bearing Alder is of very low growth. It seldom rises higher than two feet. The branches are of a bluish-brown, and the leaves are nearly round. They are placed on short footstalks, and many strong veins run from the mid-rib to the border. It makes no show, either in the flowers or fruit, the first being small, and the latter rarely happening.

American Smooth-leaved Berry-bearing Alder will arrive at the height of our Common sort, and hardly in any respect differs from it, either in leaves, flowers, or fruit.

3. Rough-leaved Alpine *Frangula*, or Berry bearing Alder, differs in no respect also from the Common sort, only that it is unarmed with thorns, will grow to be rather taller, and the leaves are rough, larger, and doubly serrated.

Rough leaved Alpine Frangula.

There is a variety of this species, with smooth leaves, and of rather lower growth, called the Smooth leaved Alpine *Frangula*.

Var.

The method of propagating these sorts of the Berry bearing Alder is exactly the same as that laid down for the Buckthorn, and if those rules are observed, any desired quantity may be raised.

Method of raising them.

4. *Paliurus*, or Christ's Thorn. The *Paliurus* will grow to be a tree of near fourteen feet high, and may be trained to an upright stem, which will send forth numerous slender branches on all sides. These are armed with sharp thorns, two of which are at each joint. One of these thorns is about half an inch long, straight and upright; the other is scarcely half that length, and bent backward. Between these is the bud for the next year's shoot. The bark on these twigs is smooth and of a purplish colour, and the spines themselves are of a reddish cast. The joints alternately go in and out, forming at each bud an obtuse angle. The leaves are nearly of an oval figure, of a pale-green colour, and stand on very short footstalks. They are small, being scarcely an inch in length, have three longitudinal veins, and are placed alternately on the branches. The flowers are produced in clusters from the sides of the young shoots. They are of a yellow colour, and though each single flower is small, yet they will be produced in such plenty all over the plant, that they make a very good show. June is the time of flowering, and they are succeeded by a small fruit, that is surrounded by a membrane.

Description of Christ's Thorn.

The plant under consideration is undoubtedly the sort of which the crown of thorns for Our Blessed Saviour was composed. The branches are very pliant, and the spines of it are set every joint strong and sharp. It grows naturally about Jerusalem, as well as in many parts of Judea, and there is no doubt that the barbarous Jews would make choice of it for their cruel purpose. But what farther confirms the truth of these thorns being then used, are the antient pictures of our Blessed Saviour's crucifixion. The thorns of the crown on his head exactly answer to those of this tree, and there is great reason to suppose these were taken from the earliest paintings of the Lord of Life, and even now our modern painters copy from them, and represent the crown as composed of these thorns. These plants, therefore, should principally have a share in those parts of the plantation that are more peculiarly designed for religious retirement, for they will prove excellent monitors, and conduce to due reflection on and gratitude to *him who hath loved us, and has washed us from our sins*, &c.

Of this thorn it is probable the crown of thorns for Our Saviour was composed.

These trees may be propagated by seeds and layers. The soil for the seed should be that taken from a fresh pasture, with the sward, and having lain a year to rot, and been turned three or four times, to this a fourth part of drift sand should be added, the whole being well mixed, the seeds should be sown half an inch deep. They rarely come up before the spring twelvemonth after sowing, so that the beds must be undisturbed all the summer, and kept free from weeds. After the plants are come up, they may stand a year or two in the seed bed, and be then planted out in the nursery, at the usual distance. In about three years they will be fit to plant out for good.

Method of propagating it by seeds.

These plants may also be propagated by layers, but this is not always a very easy task, and it is seldom that plants can be obtained under two years. Nicking them like carnations is a very uncertain method to be practised on these twigs, for the end of the neck where the root is expected to strike will fall, and be covered with

By layers.

a close

a close warty substance, without sending out any fibres, and the branch growing in the ground will in two or three years grow this out, and thus all hopes of a root will be lost By twisting them, also, is an uncertain method, though I have raised many plants this way, for if the twisting be too great, you kill the twig designed for the layer, and if it is too little, you may look, at the end of two or three years, and find no roots at your layers However, by a gentle twist, just breaking the bark, plants may be raised

Finding these methods precarious and uncertain, I had recourse to another, by which I obtained numbers of plants With a sharp knife I made a gentle nick or two the depth of the bark, about the bud and thorns which are at a joint Having done this in two or three places in every shoot, and having laid them in the ground, every twig had struck root, and were become good plants, by that time two years, many of which were fit to plant out for good, and the smaller proper for the nursery ground, to gain strength Proceed we now to the botanic part

Titles 1 The Common Purging Buckthorn is titled, *Rhamnus spinis terminalibus, floribus quadrifidis dioicis foliis ovatis* Caspar Bauhine calls it, *Rhamnus catharticus* Gerard, *Rhamnus solutivus*, and others, *Cervispina* The Dwarf Buckthorn, and that with a longer leaf, are distinguished simply by, *Rhamnus catharticus minor*, and *Rhamnus catharticus minor, folio longiore* The Common Buckthorn grows naturally in our hedges, the Dwarf sorts are found growing in Spain, Italy, and France

2 Berry-bearing Alder is, *Rhamnus inermis, floribus monogynis hermaphroditis, foliis integerrimis* In the *Flora Lapp* it is termed, *Rhamnus inermis, foliis annuis* C Bauhine calls it, *Alnus nigra baccifera*, Dodonæus, *Frangula*, Parkinson, *Frangula, seu alnus baccifera*; and Gerard, *Alnus nigra, sive frangula* It is common in England, and most of the northern parts of Europe

3 Rough leaved Alpine Frangula is, *Rhamnus inermis, floribus dioicis, foliis duplicato crenatis* Haller calls it, *Frangula rotundifolia ferruginea*, Caspar Bauhine, *Frangula altera polycarpos*, also, *Alnus nigra polycarpos*, John Bauhine, *Alnus nigra baccifera, rugosior folio, major* and Tournefort, *Frangula rugosiore & ampliore folio* It grows common on the Alps

4 Christ's Thorn is entitled, *Rhamnus aculeis geminatis, inferiore reflexo, floribus trigynis* Dodonæus calls it, *Paliurus*, and Caspar Bauhine, *Rhamnus folio subrotundo, fructu compresso* It grows common in Palestine, also in Spain, Portugal, Italy, and in some parts of France

*Rhamnus* is of the class and order *Pentandria Monogynia*, and the characters are, Class and order in the Linnæan system

1 Calyx There is none, though by some the corolla has been taken for it

The characters 2 Corolla consists of an imperforated petal of an infundibuliforme shape It is externally rude, and coloured on the inside The tube is turbinated and cylindric, the limb is acute, divided, and patent At the base of every division there is a very small squamula, that is inwardly connivent

3 Stamina are the same number of filaments as the segments of the corolla They are awl shaped, inserted under the squamula of the petal, and have small antheræ

4 Pistillum consists of a roundish germen, a filiforme style the length of the stamina, and an obtuse stigma, divided into fewer segments than the corolla

5 Pericarpium is a round naked berry, divided within into fewer cells than the segments of the corolla

6 Semina are single, roundish, gibbous, and compressed on one side

## CHAP LXXI

## *RHODODENDRON*, The DWARF ROSE-BAY

THE different species of *Rhododendron* are very beautiful shrubs, and extremely ornamental, where they happen to take to the places they are planted in The species proper for ornamental Collections are,

Species 1 Ferrugineous Dwarf Rose-Bay

2 Hairy Dwarf Rose Bay

3 *Chamæcistus*, or Ciliate leaved Dwarf Rose-Bay

4 Daurian Dwarf Rose-Bay

Description of the Ferrugineous 1 Ferrugineous Dwarf Rose Bay is a shrub of about two or three feet in growth The branches are numerous, irregular, and covered with a dark brown bark, having a tinge of purple The leaves are of two very different colours, the upper surface is of a fine green, but the under is of an iron colour There will be numbers of them on every twig, and they grow in a pleasing irregular manner They are of a lanceolated figure, have their surface smooth, and are little more than an inch long Their edges are reflexed, but they have no serratures, and, on the whole, constitute a great beauty when in leaf only The flowers grow at the ends of the branches, in round bunches Their petals are funnel-shaped, of a pale rose colour, appear in June, and are rarely succeeded by seeds in England

2 Hairy Dwarf Rose-Bay is a shrub of about the same, or rather of a lower growth The branches of this species also are numerous, and the bark with which they are covered is of a lightish brown colour They are ornamented with plenty of leaves, in an irregular manner They are not so large as those of the former sort, but are of the same figure, only a little more inclined to an oval They sit close to the branches, and have no serratures, but hairs on their edges like the eye-lashes Their under surface also is possessed of the same sort of hairs, which are all of an iron colour The flowers will be produced at the ends of the branches in bunches, in May These are also funnel shaped, of a light red colour, make a good show, and are succeeded The Hairy

by

by oval capsules, containing [illegible] ſeeds, in Au[illegible]

[illegible] *Chamæciſtus*, or Ci[illegible] Dwarf Roſe-Bay, [illegible] about [illegible] the branches [illegible] produced irregularly, and covered with [illegible] bark [illegible] leaves are produced in [illegible] plenty, and without order, on the branches They are oval, ſpear-ſhaped, [illegible], and the [illegible] ſurface is of the colour [illegible] The edges alſo are poſſeſſed of many [illegible] coloured hairs, which are placed like thoſe on the eyelids The flowers are produced at the ends of the branches, in bunches They are of a wheel-ſhaped figure, pretty large, of a fine crimſon colour, and make a handſome ſhow They [illegible] in June, and are ſucceeded by oval capſules, containing ripe ſeeds, in September

and the Daurian Dwarf Roſe Bay

4 Daurian Dwarf Roſe Bay is a low ſhrub, ſending forth many branches covered with a browniſh bark The leaves are broad, naked ſmooth, and come out without order on ſhort footſtalks The flowers are wheel-ſhaped, large, and of a beautiful roſe colour They appear in May, and are ſucceeded by oval capſules full of ſeeds, which do not always ripen in England

Method of propagating these

All theſe ſorts are propagated beſt by the ſeeds, and as they grow naturally on the Alps, Appennines, and other ſnowy and cold mountains, and are ſeldom made to grow and flouriſh [illegible] in gardens, [illegible] the beſt way for a gentleman who has extended his plantation, and has any part of it mountainous, hilly, or rocky, on the north ſide, to get ſome ſpots well cleared of all roots and weeds, and theſe being made fine and level, let the ſeeds be ſown therein They will want no covering, a gentle patting down with the ſpade will be ſufficient, [illegible] the [illegible] are ſo exceeding ſmall, that they will be waſhed into the ground deep enough by the firſt ſhower of rain that follows Whoever is not content with ſowing ſeeds, and covering them no more than what they will get by being patted down, muſt only lightly ſift ſome earth over them, for if they are covered half an inch, the general depth for moſt ſeeds, you muſt expect no crop After the young plants come up, they [illegible] be watered in dry weather, weeded, and in the winter protected from the froſts, which will deſtroy them And here one thing is to be obſerved, that though the north ſide [illegible] at the foot of [illegible] thought moſt proper for their growth, as being moſt ſuitable to their [illegible], yet [illegible] muſt be choſen for them that [illegible] trees and hedges to ſhelter them from the [illegible] froſts [illegible] trees, [illegible] will be liable to be deſtroyed by them, for want of ſnow, [illegible] other places, to cover them [illegible] keep them warm in the winter ſeaſon After theſe plants are come up, they ſhould be thinned, and leaving only a proper number in each reſpective place, and being protected for the firſt two or three winters, either by mats or hand-glaſſes, in the ſevereſt weather, they will be afterwards ſtrong enough to be left to themſelves, eſpecially if the places are tolerably ſheltered

If a gardener has no other ground than his ſeminary for raiſing plants, his beſt method will be to prepare a compoſt for theſe ſeeds in the following manner Take four buſhels of earth from ſome neighbouring hill, which if rocky, that neareſt the ſurface, on which the ſheep have been uſed to lie and dung, will be the beſt, but if it be of any other nature, the mould neareſt the ſurface, mixed with the following, will do very well Take ſix buſhels of maiden earth, from a rich loamy paſture, that has been dug up with the ſward, and by frequent turning is well rotted and mixed, and four buſhels of drift or ſea ſand Let theſe be well mixed together and of this let the bed be made The bed being made level and fine, the ſeeds ſown, and gently patted down with the ſpade, or at fartheſt no other covering than being gently duſted over with the fineſt mould, may be left to Nature This bed ſhould be in a [illegible] ſheltered place, and the plants after they are come up ſhould be weeded and watered in the ſummer, and protected from froſts by mats in the winter In the ſpring they may be pricked out in beds in the nurſery-ground, at a very ſmall diſtance, that they may be hooped and matted if the following winter ſhould prove very ſevere The ſecond winter they will require no other trouble than pricking furze-buſhes round the bed for their defence, and after that they may be ſet out [illegible]

1 Ferrugineous Roſe-Bay is, *Rhododendron foliis glabris [illegible], corollis [illegible] formibus* Caſpar Bauhine and [illegible] call it, *Ledum Alpinum, foliis [illegible]* [illegible] calls it, *A[illegible] adſperſo, [illegible]*, Dalechamp, *[illegible] Theophraſti*, Lobel, *[illegible] ſerifolia*, Haller, *[illegible] foliis gl[illegible], [illegible] tubuloſo* and Tournefort, *Chamærhododendros Alpina glabra* It grows naturally on the Alps and Appennines, alſo on many mountains in Switzerland, Savoy, and Piedmont

2 Hairy Dwarf Roſe Bay is, *Rhododendron foliis ciliatis nudis, corollis infundibuliformibus* Caſpar Bauhine and Ray call it, *Ledum Alpinum hirſutum* Cluſius terms it, *Ledum Alpinum*, Lobel, *Balſamum Alpinum*, Haller, *Ledum foliis glabris ciliatis ovatis, flore tubuloſo*, and Tournefort, *Chamærhododendros Alpina, villoſa* It grows naturally upon the Alps, and upon many mountains in Switzerland and Auſtria

3 *Chamæciſtus*, or Ciliated-leaved Dwarf Roſe-Bay is, *Rhododendron foliis ciliatis corollis rotatis* Cluſius calls it, *Chamæciſtus VIII*, Caſpar Bauhine, *Chamæciſtus hirſuta*, John Bauhine *Ciſtus pumilus montis Baldi*, Plukenet, *Ciſtus chamærhododendros foliis con[illegible]*, and Micheli, *Ledum foliis [illegible] ad margines [illegible], [illegible]* It grows naturally upon Mount Baldus, and near Salzburg in Germany

4 Daurian Dwarf Roſe Bay is, *Rhododendron foliis glabris [illegible], corollis rotatis* Amman calls it, *Ch[illegible] foliis [illegible], [illegible] amplo flore roſeo* It grows naturally in Dauria

Claſs and order in the Linnæan ſyſtem [illegible]

*Rhododendron* is of the claſs and order *Decandria Monogynia*, and the characters are,

1 Calyx is a permanent perianthium, divided into five parts

2 Corolla conſiſts of one petal, which is ſhaped either like a wheel or a funnel The limb is patent, and the ſegments rounded

3 Stamina are ten declined, filiform filaments, nearly the length of the corolla, having oval antheræ

4 Pistillum conſiſts of a five-cornered retuſed germen, a filiforme ſtyle the length of the corolla, and an obtuſe ſtigma

5 Pericarpium is an oval capſule of five cells

6 Semina The ſeeds are numerous and very ſmall

CHAP

# CHAP LXXII

## *RHUS*, SUMACH

THE hardy species of this genus are,
1 Elm-leaved or Tanner's Sumach
Species
2 Virginian Sumach
3 Smooth Sumach
4 Lentiscus leaved Sumach
5 Poison-Ash
6 Poison-Oak
7 Radicant *Toxicodendron*
8 *Coccygria*, or Venetian Sumach

Elm leaved Sumach

1 The Elm leaved Sumach is a distinct and noble species of *Rhus* It will grow to be about twelve feet high, and the branches are covered with a brownish hairy bark It is said that this bark is equal to that of the English oak for tanning of leather, and that the leather from Turkey is chiefly tanned with it The leaves of this shrub, which are placed alternately on the branches, have a grand look They are pinnated, and each ends with an odd foliole The mid rib of each is garnished with about eight pairs of folioles, which all terminate with an odd one The folioles of which the compound leaf is composed are oval, and not large, being scarcely two inches long, and three fourths of an inch broad, but the whole leaf makes a fine show Their colour is a light-green, their under surface is hairy, and they are sawed at their edges The flowers, which are produced in large bunches at the ends of the branches, are of a whitish colour, with a tinge of green Each is composed of many spikes, on which the flowers sit close They come out in July, but are not succeeded by ripe seeds in England, like some of the subsequent sorts The leaves and seeds are possessed of many excellent virtues They have great efficacy as styptics, and prevent mortifications and gangrenes, if either inwardly or outwardly applied, they are also admirable in fluxes, hæmorrhages, &c

Virginian Sumach Varieties described

2 Virginian Sumach Of this species there are several varieties, such as, The Common Stag's Horn, Large Virginian, and Dwarf Sumach

The Stag's Horn Sumach is so called from the younger branches much resembling a stag's horn, called the Velvet Horn It will grow to be about ten feet high, and the older branches are covered with a smooth brownish bark, in some places of a greyish colour, whilst the younger ones are covered with a hairy down, which much resembles the velvet horn of a stag The leaves have a noble look, for they are large and pinnated The folioles are oblong, and larger than those of the preceding sort, about seven pairs are set oned along the mid-rib, which are terminated by an odd one Their under surface is hairy, and they die to a purplish scarlet in the autumn The flowers are produced in June, at the ends of the branches They will be in large tufts, but make no show, though some admire them when succeeded by seeds in the autumn, for at the end of that season, even after the leaves are fallen, there will be large tufts of seeds, of a scarlet colour, left at the ends of the branches, which have an uncommon appearance

The Large Virginian Sumach differs in no respect from it, only that it shoots stronger, and grows to be larger, even sixteen or eighteen feet, and is a more regular tree The young shoots also are of a more reddish colour, and though possessed of the like hairy down, on the whole do not so much resemble those of the velvet stag's horn as the other

Dwarf Sumach differs in no respect from the Common Stag's Horn, except that it is of very low growth, seldom rising higher than three feet

3 Smooth Sumach This includes many notable varieties, commonly called, New-England, Smooth Carolina, and Canada Sumach

Smooth Sumach Varieties described

New-England Sumach will grow to about sixteen feet high, sending forth many strong shoots from the root and the sides, covered with a smooth downy bark The radical shoots will often be near an inch in diameter in one summer's growth The young branches also from the sides will be large they are smooth, though a little downy in the summer, and the bark in the winter is of a light-brown colour The leaves of this sort are the largest of any, being composed of ten or more pairs of folioles, proportionally large, and which are terminated by an odd one The flowers are produced at the ends of the branches, in large loose panicles They are of a greenish-yellow colour, and come out in June, but are not succeeded by seeds with us

The Carolina Sumach seldom rises to more than ten feet high The branches are smooth, of a fine purplish colour, and dusted over with a whitish powder The leaves are pinnated like the other, and the flowers are produced in panicles at the ends of the branches They are of a fine scarlet colour, appear in July, and are succeeded by bunches of seeds, which in autumn are of a very beautiful red, though they never ripen in England

The Canada Sumach grows to about ten feet in height, and the branches, which are smooth and of a purplish colour are dusted over, like the former, with a kind of whitish powder The leaves are pinnated like the other, and the folioles are on both sides smooth, but their surfaces are of two colours, the upper being of a shining green, whilst the under is hoary The flowers are red, and produced in July, in large panicles, at the ends of the branches They appear as if a whitish powder had been dusted in among them, which attracts notice, but their seeds do not ripen in England

4 Lentiscus-leaved Sumach The chief varieties of this species are, The True Lentiscus-leaved, and the Canada Lentiscus leaved Sumach

Lentiscus leaved Sumach Varieties described

The True Lentiscus-leaved Sumach seldom rises to more than four feet in height, and the branches are covered with a smooth brown bark The leaves also are pinnated, and are the most beautiful of all the sorts, for the folioles, though small, are of a shining green There are about four or five pairs on the mid-rib, which are beautifully arranged, having a membrane or wing on each side running from pair to pair, they are terminated by an odd one, resemble in appearance those of the Lentiscus, and are the greatest ornament of this shrub The flowers are produced in July, at the ends of the

  branches

branches They are of a greenish colour, and though produced in large loose panicles, make no great figure, neither do the seeds ripen with us

Canada Lentiscus-leaved Sumach grows to be ten feet high The leaves have chiefly the properties of the former, but are larger, less delicate, and dusted or pounced over with a whitish matter The flowers are produced in the same manner as the other They are greenish, and succeeded by seeds in England

Poison Ash. 5 The Poison Ash This is called the Poison-tree because it abounds with a milky poisonous juice, it is distinguished by the title Poison-Ash, because the leaves somewhat resemble those of the ash tree It is called also by some the Varnish-tree, being the shrub from which the true varnish is collected The Poison Ash, with us, will grow to the height of about eight feet, and the branches, which are not very numerous, are covered with a smooth light brown bark, tinged with red The leaves are pinnated, and the foholes of which each is composed consist of about three or four pairs, with an odd one These are of an oblong pointed figure, of a fine green colour, and have their edges entire In the autumn, they die to a red or purple colour, and at that time their leaves, just before they fall, make a charming appearance, some being red, others purple, others between both, the colours of the footstalks and mid ribs will also be various, thereby in the same tree affording a variety of shades The flowers are small, and make no show They are whitish, and produced in May, from the wings of the branches There will be male and female on different plants, and the female are succeeded by small roundish fruit, which seldom ripens in England

Poison Oak. 6 The Poison-Oak is a lower shrub, seldom growing to be more than four feet high The branches are smooth, and of a light brown colour It will cost the gardener some trouble to keep these plants properly, as upright shrubs, for they will send out shoots from the bottom, which will naturally trail on the ground, and strike root But these must be constantly taken off, for were they to be neglected a few years, a single plant would have spread itself to such a distance as to occupy a great space of ground, in a manner not becoming a well ordered shrubbery or wilderness The leaves of this shrub are trifoliate Each foliole has a short pedicle to itself, and the common footstalk of the whole three is very long They are of a shining green, smooth, and have their edges sometimes sinuated, though generally entire They are roundish, angular, large, and on the whole make a good show The flowers are of a whitish colour, are produced from the sides of the branches, in July, and are succeeded by cream coloured berries, which growing in the autumn, and even in the winter, after the leaves are fallen, in a kind of panicles, are by many taken notice of, and said to look very pretty

Varieties. There are several varieties of this species some with hairy leaves, some with leaves very downy, others of the upright growth In other respects their difference is inconsiderable

Radicant Toxicodendron. 7 Radicant *Toxicodendron* Of this species there are several varieties, some of which are of upright growth, though the stalks of all have, more or less, a tendency to lie on the ground, and strike root at the joints The leaves of all the sorts are trifoliate, or an oval figure, smooth, and entire The flowers are greenish, appear in June and July, and are succeeded by roundish yellow berries, which rarely ripen in England

8 The Venetian Sumach is a shrub of about ten feet growth, and has many valuable properties to recommend it The bark on the older branches is of a light brown colour, whilst that on the young shoots is smooth and of a purple hue The leaves are nearly of an oval figure, and stand singly upon long footstalks on the branches From these the tree receives great beauty They are of a delightful green, are smooth, and when bruised emit a strong scent, which by many is thought very grateful, and on that account only makes this shrub desireable The flowers are produced at the ends of the branches, in July, in a singular manner The end of the last year's shoot about that time will divide itself, and produce hair-like bunches of purplish flowers, so as to cover the tree, and in the autumn, though they do not perfect their seeds with us, these tufts will still remain, but of a darker colour, and almost cover it, on account of which singular oddness this shrub is valued by some persons The bark is used by the tanners, whilst the wood and leaves are sought after by the dyers, the former being said to give a yellow, and the latter, together with the young branches, to dye a good black Venetian Sumach.

The propagation of the Sumach is not very difficult, for the second, third, and fourth sorts, with their varieties, produce suckers in such plenty as to over-run, if not taken off, all that is near them These suckers when taken up will be each a good plant, nay, their very roots will grow, and though they be thrown upon a bed and dug carelessly in, even then many young plants will spring from them Method of propagating the different sorts.

The Poison-Oak and Radicant *Toxicodendron* also propagate themselves very fast by their trailing branches, which strike root as they go, and each of which will be a plant

The Venetian Sumach is easily encreased by layers, for the young shoots being slit and layered in the autumn, by the autumn following will be good plants, either for the nursery-ground, or where they are to be planted for good

The fourth and fifth sorts, however, do not throw out suckers in this manner, and these are to be encreased from the seeds, which we receive from the places where they naturally grow.

An east border or garden mould (made fine) should be prepared, and in this the seeds should be sown as soon as possible after we receive them The depth they will require will be about half an inch After being sown, and the border dressed up, nothing more need be done till the weeds begin to come up, which will be before the plants As often as these appear, they must be picked up, and when the hot parching weather comes on, the border must be shaded in the heat of the day, and every evening should be gently sprinkled over with water In the beginning of June many of the plants will come up, though they frequently remain, at least the greatest part of them, until the second spring before they make their appearance After the plants are come up, they will want no other care than shading, weeding, and now and then a watering during the first summer and if the winter should be severe, they should be matted, especially the Elm-leaved sort, which is rather the most tender whilst young After this they will require no other care than weeding until they are two-years-old seedlings, when, in the spring, they should be taken up and planted in the nursery ground, and in two or three years more will be fit to set out for good And here I must not omit to observe, that the other

other sorts before mentioned, which propagate themselves so fast by suckers, may be raised this way if the seeds can be obtained; and indeed, whoever has not the conveniency of procuring a few plants of each, and can have the seeds, must practise this method with them, by which he will soon procure plenty.

Titles 1. Elm-leaved or Tanners Sumach is entitled, *Rhus foliis pinnatis obtusiuscule serratis ovalibus, subtus villosis*. In the *Hortus Cliffortianus* it stands with the title, *Rhus foliis pinnatis serratis*. Caspar Bauhine calls it, *Rhus folio ulmi*, Dodonæus, *Rhus coriaria*. It grows naturally in Turkey, Italy, Spain, Palestine, and Syria.

2. Virginian Sumach is, *Rhus foliis pinnatis lanceolatis argute serratis, subtus tomentosis*. Caspar Bauhine calls it, *Rhus Virginianum*. It grows naturally in Virginia.

3. Smooth Sumach is titled, *Rhus foliis pinnatis serratis lanceolatis utrinque nudis*. Gronovius calls it, *Rhus foliis pinnatis serratis*; Dillenius, *Rhus Virginicum, panicula sparsa, ramis patulis glabris*; Caspar Bauhine, *Rhus angustifolium*; also, *Sumach angustifolium*. It grows naturally in North-America.

4. Lentiscus-leaved Sumach is, *Rhus foliis pinnatis integerrimis, petiolo membranaceo articulato*. Gronovius calls it, *Rhus elatior, foliis impari-pinnatis, petiolis membranaceis articulatis*; Ray, *Rhus Virginianum lentisci foliis*, and Plukenet, *Rhus obsoniorum similis Americana, gummi candidum fundens non serrata, foliorum rachi medio alata*. It grows naturally in North-America.

5. The Poison-Ash, or Varnish-tree, is called, *Rhus foliis pinnatis integerrimis, petiolo integro aequali*. In the *Hortus Cliffortianus* it is termed, *Rhus foliis pinnatis integerrimis*. Dillenius calls it, *Toxicodendron foliis alatis, fructu rhomboide*, and Plukenet, *Arbor Americana, alatis foliis, succo lacteo venenata*. It grows common in most parts of North-America, and also in Japan.

6. The Poison-Oak is, *Rhus foliis ternatis foliolis petiolatis angulatis pubescentibus caule radicante*. Tournefort calls it, *Toxicodendron triphyllum, folio sinuato pubescente*; Cornutus, *Hedera trifolia Canadensis*; and Ray, *Arbor trifolia venenata Virginiana, folio hirsuto*. It grows common in most parts of North-America.

7. Radicant *Toxicodendron* is, *Rhus foliis ternatis foliolis petiolatis ovatis nudis integerrimis, caule radicante*. Dillenius calls it, *Toxicodendron amplexicaule, foliis minoribus glabris*; also, *Toxicodendron rectum, foliis minoribus glabris*. It grows in Virginia and Canada.

8. The Venetian Sumach is, *Rhus foliis simplicibus obovatis*. In the *Hortus Cliffortianus* it is termed, *Cotinus foliis obverse ovatis*. Dodonæus calls it, *Cotinus coriaria*, and Caspar Bauhine, *Coccygria, sive coccygria*. It is a native of Italy, Spain, and many parts of Europe.

*Rhus* is of the class and order *Pentandria Trigynia*, and the characters are, Class and order in the Linnæan system

1. CALYX is an erect, permanent perianthium, divided into five parts. The characters

2. COROLLA consists of five oval, erect, patent petals.

3. STAMINA are five very short filaments, with small antheræ, which are shorter than the petals.

4. PISTILLUM consists of a roundish germen, as large as the corolla, with hardly any visible styles, but three small cordated stigmas.

5. PERICARPIUM is a roundish berry of one cell.

6. SEMEN. The seed is single, roundish, and osseous.

As this genus comprehends the *Rhus* and *Toxicodendron* of authors, it may be proper to observe, that the *Rhus* produces a hairy berry, with a round kernel, and that the berry of the *Toxicodendron* is smooth and striated, with a kernel compressed and furrowed.

# CHAP. LXXIII.

## *ROBINIA*, FALSE ACACIA.

THE hardy species of *Robinia* are not very numerous; but our plantations are highly improved by those few that are proper for it, they being in every respect beautiful, both in leaf and flower; neither is the variety they cause inconsiderable even in the winter, when despoiled of their former honours. The sorts by which we are benefited, then, are,

Species
1. False Acacia.
2. Caragana.
3. Shrubby *Aspalathus*.
4. Dwarf *Aspalathus*.

False Acacia 1. False Acacia will grow to the height of thirty-five or more feet. The branches are covered with a smooth purplish-coloured bark, and armed with strong spines, which are placed at the buds. Each bud, especially of the young vigorous shoots, will be generally guarded by two of these spines, one of which will be on one side, while the other will occupy the opposite place. The branches are very brittle, and in summer, when the leaves are on, are often broke by the high winds. The leaves come out late in the spring; but for this they make ample amends by the beautiful foliage they will display soon after. They are pinnated leaves, the most beautiful of all the compound sorts. The folioles of which each is composed are of a fine green; and as there are no less than nine or ten pair of them placed along the mid-rib, with an odd one, the whole leaf appears very large, and all the tree being thus ornamented has a noble look, even at that time. But this shrub will be in its greatest beauty when in flower, for these will be produced in long pendulous bunches, in June. They are of the papilionaceous kind, their colour is white; and when the tree blows freely, its head will be enchantingly covered with them; for they will hang all over it in a free and easy manner; some bunches appearing wholly in view, others again half hid by the waving leaves, that will sometimes alternately hide and shew them; at which time also, when there is a current of air, the flowers them-

selves

selves receive fresh beauty from being thus agitated. But this is not all, Nature has granted them a smell, which is very grateful, so that in an evening, or after a shower, they will perfume the circumambient air to some distance. Thus they will prove grateful to all those who will attend to their culture, as they will never fail rewarding owners of the estate by their grateful and profuse fragrance. These flowers, it is to be lamented, are of short duration, and are succeeded by pods, which in some seasons will perfect their seeds with us.

Varieties. The principal varieties of this species are, The Scentless, Prickly-podded, Rose coloured, Scarlet, Smooth-podded, &c. Acacia.

described. The Prickly Acacia with Rose coloured flowers appears to have the most material difference. It is of lower growth, the young branches, and the footstalks and very cups of the flowers, are armed with prickly hairs or spines. The flowers are produced in hanging clusters like those of the other sorts, they are large, and of a most beautiful rose-colour. They are produced later than the others, but make a noble show when in blow. They are succeeded by pods, and the variety is most beautifully characterized by this sort. The difference of the colours is chiefly pointed out by the names which are commonly used to express them.

Caragana. 2. *Caragana*, with a shrubby stalk, to the height of about eight or ten feet, sending forth several branches, which are covered with a greenish-yellow bark. The leaves are abruptly pinnated, the lobules are oval, spear-shaped, pointed, and consist of about five or six pair arranged along the mid-rib. The flowers come out from the sides of the branches, on single footstalks. They are small, of a yellowish colour, appear in May, and are succeeded by smooth compressed pods containing the seeds, which will be ripe in September.

Shrubby Aspalathus. 3. The Shrubby *Aspalathus* is a beautiful flowering shrub. Its growth will be seven or eight feet, and the branches naturally grow upright. The bark is smooth, and of a yellowish colour, but that of the youngest twigs partakes more of a purplish colour on one side, and is on the other often of a light-green with a yellow tinge. The leaves are each composed of about four foliols, which are oval and pointed. The flowers are produced in May, from the joints of the branches, upon single footstalks. They are of a fine yellow colour, and of the butterfly make, and so adorn the tree when in blow, as to render it inferior to few of the flowering shrubs. These flowers are succeeded by pods, containing ripe seeds, in the autumn.

Dwarf Aspalathus. 4. Dwarf *Aspalathus* is a pretty little shrub, sending forth several slender branches, which are covered with a golden bark. The leaves are quaternate, wedge shaped, obtuse, have no footstalks, and, unless very severe weather happens, continue on the plant the greatest part of the winter. The flowers come out from the sides of the branches on single footstalks. They are small, of a yellow colour, appear in May, and are succeeded by ripe seeds in the autumn.

Method of propagating these species by seeds. The propagation of all these sorts is very easy and may be done,

1. By seeds. If these are sown the beginning of March, half an inch deep, in a bed of any common garden-mould, plants will come up in May, which will want no other care than weeding all the first summer, and no protection of any kind in the winter, for they are all hardy enough. In the following spring they should be planted out in the nursery ground, a foot asunder, and two feet distant in the rows, and here (the three first sorts) they should not stand longer than two or three years before they are set out for good, as they will grow exceeding fast, and by that time will be perhaps six feet in height. The fourth sort being of lower growth, the plants may be pricked in beds, a foot asunder, which will be room enough for them to grow in, before they are set out for good. It may not be amiss to observe also, that the seeds of this sort often remain until the second spring before they come up, so that when they do not appear the first after sowing, the beds must be kept weeded all summer, and, if the seeds were good, there will be no fear of a crop the following spring.

2. These sorts are easily propagated by cuttings, which if planted in October in a moistish shady border, many of them will grow. Here they may stand two years, when they will be proper plants to set out for good, though we must observe, that the fourth sort may remain longer before they are set out; and as the cuttings of that sort have often failed growing, the most certain method, and what is generally practised when there are no seeds, is to encrease it by layers. cuttings,

3. The first sorts will encrease themselves by suckers, in sufficient plenty, for the old plants will spawn at a considerable distance, and afford such a quantity of fine shooting suckers, that they will be all good plants, fit to be set out for good. and suckers

Titles. 1. The False Acacia is titled, *Robinia racemis pedicellis unifloris, foliis impari-pinnatis, stipulis spinosis*. In the former edition of the *Species Plantarum* it is termed, *Robinia pedunculis racemosis, foliis impari pinnatis*; in the *Hort. Cliffort.* *Robinia aculeis geminatis*. Tournefort calls it, *Pseudoacacia vulgaris*; Ray, *Acacia Americana, siliquis glabris*; Boerhaave, *Pseudoacacia Americana, siliquis echinatis*; Plukenet, *Acacia affinis Virginiana spinosa, siliqua membranacea plana*; and Catesby, *Pseudoacacia hispida, floribus roseis*. All these sorts are found growing in most parts of North-America.

2. *Caragana* is titled, *Robinia pedunculis simplicibus, foliis abrupte pinnatis*. Amman calls it, *Aspalathus arborescens, pinnis foliorum crebrioribus oblongis*; and Van Royen, *Caragana Sibirica*. It grows naturally in Siberia.

3. The Shrubby *Aspalathus* is entitled, *Robinia pedunculis simplicissimis, foliis quaternatis sub petiolatis*. Amman calls it, *Aspalathus frutescens major latifolius, cortice aureo*. It grows naturally in Siberia and Tartary.

4. Dwarf *Aspalathus* is, *Robinia pedunculis simplicibus, foliis quaternatis sessilibus*. Amman calls it, *Aspalathus frutescens minor angustifolius, cortice aureo*. It is a native of Siberia.

Class and order in the Linnæan system. *Robinia* is of the class and order *Diadelphia Decandria*, and the characters are, The characters.

1. Calyx is a monophyllous small, bell shaped perianthium, indented in four parts, of which the three under segments are narrow, and the upper much broader and slightly indented.

2. Corolla is papilionaceous. The vexillum is large, roundish, patent, and obtuse. The alæ are oblong, oval, free, and have short, obtuse, appendices. The carina is nearly semi-orbicular, compressed, obtuse, and the length of the alæ.

3. Stamina are diadelphous (nine filaments are joined in a body), the other stands single, having roundish antheræ.

4. Pistillum consists of a cylindrical oblong germen, a filiforme bent style, and a hairy stigma.

5. Pericarpium is a large, compressed, gibbous, long pod.

6. Semina. The seeds are few in each pod, and kidney shaped.

CHAP.

# C H A P. LXXIV.

## *ROSA*, The ROSE-TREE.

Introductory observations.

WE are now come to the Rose, the pride of all our gardens. It is generally called *Flos florum*, and, if we consider the beauty of its flowers, the variety of its sorts, or the sweetness of their scent, the Rose may justly claim the precedence of all other flowers. Some sort or other of these trees are in blow from May to the end of the summer-months, but the greatest burst of all appears at a time which seems peculiarly designed for contemplation and pleasure. This season is in June and the beginning of July, when the fine lady and even the invalid are invited abroad to partake of Nature's bounties, when the farmer is preparing to reap the fruits of the earth, and the philosopher is found in the field and in the garden, making his observations.

" Now the mower whets his scythe,
" And every shepherd tells his tale
" Under the hawthorn in the dale."

The variety of these sorts is very great, and somewhat embarrasses botanists to distinguish which are varieties only, and which distinct species, but I will venture to assure my readers, that they will find more satisfaction in examining a few, than in perplexing themselves with researches after more. The real number of distinct species of the Rose, however, gives very little concern to the gardener, who sees and admires a profusion of sorts which encrease as well as add variety and pleasure to his Collection. The following, however, are held as distinct species by botanists:

Species.

1. Dog-Rose, or Hep-tree
2. Burnet-Rose
3. Scotch Rose
4. Alpine Rose
5. Eglantine, or Sweet-Briar
6. Cinnamon-Rose
7. Carolina Rose
8. Apple-Rose
9. Hundred leaved Rose
10. Gallican Rose
11. Musk-Rose
12. Long fruited Rose
13. White Rose

Dog Rose.

1. Dog-Rose, or Hep tree, grows all over England, and is never cultivated in gardens. It is, nevertheless, possessed of many beauties, if observed with due attention, and, if it was not so very common, would deserve a place in the choicest Collection. The varieties of this species are,

Names of its varieties.

The Hep-tree with Red Flowers
The White-flowered Hep-tree

Burnet Rose.

2. Burnet-Rose is a small-growing tree, seldom rising higher than one yard. The flowers are single and make no great figure, but what renders this Rose valuable is, that the leaves are pinnated in such a manner as to resemble those of the burnet, which occasions its being so called, and by which it constitutes an agreeable variety among the leafy tribe.

Varieties.

The varieties of it are,
Red-flowered Burnet-leaved Rose
Black Burnet-leaved Rose
White Burnet-leaved Rose

Scotch Rose.

3. Scotch Rose. The varieties of this species are all of low growth, and known by the respective names of,

Varieties.

Dwarf Scotch with a White Flower
Dwarf Scotch with a Red Flower
Dwarf Scotch with a Striped Flower
Dwarf Scotch with a Marbled Flower

described.

These are all beautiful flowering shrubs. The White-flowering sort will grow to the highest size, as it will commonly grow to be three feet, whilst the others seldom rise to above two feet in height. The branches are upright and numerous, and smartly set off by their beautiful pinnated leaves, for the leaves of these sorts excel those of all other Roses in delicacy, the folioles being small, of a good green colour, and arranged along the mid-rib in the manner of those of the burnet. The flowers will be produced from the branches in vast profusion, and though they are all single, they make a show inferior to few shrubs. In winter they will be full of heps that have the appearance of black-berries, and if the weather be mild, the young buds will swell early, and appear like so many little red eyes all over the shrub, which is a promise of the reviving season, and looks pretty enough. The young branches of all these sorts are exceeding full of prickles.

Alpine Rose.

4. Alpine Rose. This is usually called the Rose without Thorns, the branches being perfectly free from all kinds of prickles. They are exceeding smooth, of a reddish colour, and look well in winter. The flowers are single, and of a deep red colour. They come out in May, before any of the other sorts, and the plant is valued by some people upon that account. They are succeeded by long narrow heps, which look singular, and, together with the early appearance of their flowers, and their beautiful twigs, that are wholly free from the armature of the other sorts, cause this species to be much admired.

Sweet Briar.

5. Eglantine, or Sweet-Briar. The sorts of this species are,

Varieties.

Common Sweet Briar
Semi-double Sweet-Briar
Double Red Sweet-Briar
Maiden Blush Double Sweet-Briar
Sweet-Briar with Yellow Flowers

described.

The Common Sweet-Briar is well known all over England. The branches, which are of a reddish cast, are all over closely armed with prickles, the flowers are single, and of a pale-red colour, like those of the Common Wild Briar. The leaves constitute the value of this plant, for they are possessed of so grateful an odour, as to claim admittance for this sort into the first class of aromatic plants. The odoriferous particles they emit are sweet and inoffensive, and they bestow them in such profusion, especially in evenings or after a shower, as to perfume the circumambient air to a considerable distance. For this reason, plenty of Sweet Briars should be planted near much-frequented walks, or if the borders of these are designed for more elegant flowering-shrubs or plants, they may be stationed at a diſtance, out of view and then they will ſecretly liberally beſtow their ſweets, to the refreſhment of all. For noſegays, alſo, there is nothing more proper than ſprigs of the Sweet-Briar, when diveſted of its prickles, for theſe will not only have a good look as a fine green in the center of a poſy, but will improve its odour, let the other flowers of which it is compoſed be what they will.

Semi-double Sweet Briar differs in no reſpect from the Common, only that the flowers conſiſt of a double ſeries of petals that ſurround the ſtamina. The leaves are poſſeſſed of the ſame fragrance, but this ſort is thought more valuable on account of the flowers, which, being poſſeſſed of more petals, make a better figure.

Double Sweet-Briar. The number of petals are ſo multiplied in this ſort as to form a full flower, and it ſeems to differ in no other reſpect from the other Sweet Briars. The flowers are red, and ſo large and double as to be equal in beauty to many of the other ſorts of roſes. As by the fragrance of their leaves they afford us a continual treat during the ſummer months, as well as by their fair flowers at the time of blowing, all who pretend to make a Collection are careful of procuring plenty of this ſort.

Double Bluſh Sweet-Briar is a moſt valuable, and at preſent a very ſcarce plant. It ſeems to have a tendency not to grow ſo high as the other ſorts of Sweet Briars. The branches are green, and cloſely armed with ſtrong prickles. The flowers are of a pale-red or bluſh colour, and every whit as double as the Cabbage-Province Roſe. It cabbages in the ſame manner, and is very fragrant. No one need be told the value of a Roſe which has every perfection and charm, to the higheſt degree, both in the leaves and flowers, to recommend it.

Sweet-Briar with Yellow Flowers. The flowers of this ſort are ſingle, the petals are of a bright yellow colour, but it differs in no other reſpect from the Common Sweet Briar.

Cinnamon Roſe. 6. Cinnamon Roſe. The varieties of this ſpecies are,

Varieties. Single Cinnamon Roſe.
Double Cinnamon Roſe.

deſcribed. The Single Cinnamon-Roſe is a much ſtronger ſhooter than the Double ſort, which is better known. It will grow to be ten or twelve feet in height. The young branches are of a reddiſh colour. The flowers are ſingle, and have the ſame hue as thoſe of the Double. It is rather a ſcarce plant at preſent, on which account chiefly it is thought valuable.

The Double Cinnamon-Roſe will grow to be but five or eight feet high, and the branches are many and ſlender. The prickles are pretty numerous, and the young ſhoots in winter are of a red colour, with a purpliſh tinge. This ſort, which uſhers in the flowery tribe of Double Roſes, will be in blow ſometimes pretty early in May. The flowers are ſmall, but very double. They are of a purpliſh red, very ſweet, and have a little of the ſmell of cinnamon, which occaſions this Roſe to be ſo called, and on that account only, not to mention their early appearance, this ſort is truly deſirable.

Carolina Roſe. 7. Carolina Roſe. The varieties of this ſpecies are uſually called,

Varieties. Wild Virginian Roſe.
Penſylvania Roſe.
Pale Red American Roſe.

deſcribed. The Wild Virginian Roſe will grow to be nine or ten feet high. The branches are covered with a ſmooth red bark, and guarded by a very few prickles. It produces its flowers in Auguſt, when moſt of the other ſorts are out of blow, and is by many valued for that reaſon. The flowers are ſingle, of a red colour, are produced in cluſters, and will continue blowing from the beginning of Auguſt until October. Neither is this the ſole beauty this ſort affords us, for the flowers will be ſucceeded by heps, which in winter appear like ſo many red berries all over the ſhrub. Theſe heps ſerve as food for birds, and are therefore much frequented by thruſhes and others of the whiſtling tribe, who will be ready to uſher in, by their ſweet warbles, the earlieſt dawn of ſpring. This tree grows wild in Virginia and many parts of North-America, from whence we receive the ſeeds, and propagate it not only on ſome of the above accounts, but becauſe it is naturally an upright well growing tree, and makes a good figure in winter in wilderneſs quarters, &c. by its red and beautiful ſhoots.

The Penſylvania Roſe ſeems to differ in nothing from the former, except its ſize, it ſeeming to be a plant of lower growth, and the Pale Red ſort occaſions variety only from the lobes of the flowers.

8. Apple Roſe. This ſpecies is a curioſity, not ſo much from the ſingularity of the ſhoots, leaves, or flowers, as fruit. The ſhoots, indeed, will be ſtrong and bold, and in winter diſtinguiſh the tree from others by a degree of eminence. They are then covered with a ſmooth reddiſh bark, and the prickles which guard them are thinly placed, though thoſe are very ſtrong and ſharp. Many think this tree has a good look in winter, and value it much on that account. As to the leaves, they are nearly the ſame as the other ſorts of Roſes, but are large, and very hairy and downy underneath. The flowers are ſingle, of a red colour, and are ſucceeded by heps as large as little apples. To their account the value chiefly of this ſort is to be placed, for being thus large, they occaſion a ſingular look, and this is heightened by being all over beſet with ſoft prickles. For uſe as well as beauty this ſort is propagated by ſome, for their heps or fruit, when preſerved, make a ſweetmeat greatly eſteemed. Apple Roſe.

9. Hundred leaved Roſe. This is a very extenſive ſpecies, and includes all varieties whoſe ſtalks are hiſpid, prickly, and have leaves growing on footſtalks which are not armed with prickles, and whoſe flowers have oval, hiſpid germina and footſtalks. Of this kind are, Hundred leaved Roſe.

The Deep Red Province.
The Pale Red Province. Varieties.
The Large Cabbage Province.
The Dutch Province.
The Childing Province.
The Moſs Province.
The Great Royal Roſe.
The Bluſh Hundred leaved Roſe.
The Dutch Hundred-leaved Roſe.

The Province Roſes are all well known. The Red and the Pale Province ſorts differ, in that one is a deep, the other a pale red, the petals are larger and looſer than the Cabbage-Province, and make varieties. The Cabbage-Province is the beſt of all the ſorts, and, if its commonneſs does not detract from its value, is inferior to no Roſe. The Dutch Province ſeldom flowers freely with me, though when it does, it has a tendency to cabbage, and is of a deeper red than the Common Province. The Childing is of lower growth than any of the other ſorts, ſeldom growing to be more than four feet. It is naturally of upright growth, and the bark is brown and prickly. The flowers at firſt are globular, though they will afterwards open at top, deſcribed.

top, and diſplay their petals folded a little like thoſe of the Belgic. All theſe are beautiful roſes, and greatly ornamental either to ſhrubberies or gardens.

The Moſs-Province is a ſort that has been ſought after of late more than any of the others. Its branches are of a duſky brown, and they are all over cloſely beſet with prickles. The flowers are like thoſe of the Common Province, though they have a ſtronger footſtalk, and grow more upright. About the calyx or the flower grows a kind of moſs, which is of a yellowiſh-green colour, and by which it will be wholly ſurrounded. This roſe has not been many years known in England, and from whence it was firſt brought is uncertain. It ſeems to owe its excellence to the moſſy ſubſtance growing about the footſtalk and calyx of the flower; but were this as common as the other ſorts of Province-Roſes, that would be looked upon as an imperfection; for though this flower naturally is poſſeſſed of the ſame agreeable fragrance as the other Province-Roſes, yet this moſſy ſubſtance has a ſtrong diſagreeable ſcent, is poſſeſſed of a clammy matter, and is liked by very few.

Great Royal Roſe is one of the largeſt, though not the compacteſt Roſes we have. It will grow to be eight or nine feet high. The branches are brown, and have a number of prickles. The flowers are red, and poſſeſſed of a very grateful odour, and the petals very large. Upon the whole, this is a ſort very much coveted, and is one of the beſt roſes in England.

The Bluſh and Dutch Hundred-leaved Roſes differ in no reſpect, only that the flowers of one are of a paler red than thoſe of the other; and both theſe ſorts may contend for the prize of beauty with any of the roſy tribe. They ſeldom grow more than four feet high. The branches are green and upright, and have very few ſpines. The flowers are large, and exceeding double. Each is compoſed of numerous ſhort petals, which are arranged in ſo regular a manner as to form a compleat flower; and it is on account of the extraordinary number of theſe petals that this roſe takes the name of Hundred-leaved Roſe. We ſeem to do injuſtice to this Roſe, when we do not pronounce it the faireſt of the whole liſt; but when we reflect on the ſurpaſſing delicacy and beauty of many other ſorts, we are obliged to give the preference to none.

Gallican Roſe. 10. Gallican Roſe. Under this title are arranged all thoſe Roſes whoſe branches and footſtalks of the leaves are hiſpid and prickly, and whoſe flowers have oval, hiſpid germina, and grow on hiſpid footſtalks. Of this kind are,

Varieties.
- The Semi-double Red Roſe
- The Old Double Red Roſe
- The *Roſa Mundi*, or Variegated Roſe
- The York and Lancaſter Roſe
- The Semi-double Velvet Roſe
- The Full-double Velvet Roſe
- The Bluſh Belgic Roſe
- The Red Belgic
- The Bluſh Monthly
- The Red Monthly
- The White Monthly
- The Striped Monthly
- The Red Damaſk
- The White Damaſk
- The Bluſh Damaſk
- The Doubled Virgin
- The Marbled
- The Great Spaniſh
- The Yellow Auſtrian Roſe
- The Copper coloured Roſe
- The Double Yellow
- The Francfort Roſe

The Semi-double and the Double Old Red would be thought good Roſes, were there not ſo many others that far ſurpaſs them in beauty. They will grow to be about three or four feet high; the growth is naturally upright, and the branches, which are brown, have few prickles. The flowers are large, and of a deep red colour, but thoſe of the laſt ſort are not very double. Their odour is very agreeable, though not ſtrong, and they will be produced in great plenty. Being aſtringent, they are uſed in medicine. They cut a grand figure at a diſtance, amongſt other flowering ſhrubs. deſcribed.

*Roſa Mundi* is a variety of the Red Roſe. Its manner of growth and ſhoots are exactly like that, and the flowers are moſt beautifully variegated. The ſtripes are white, and the red is of a deepiſh colour. As the petals of which the Roſe is compoſed are very large, this ſort may juſtly be ſaid to make the beſt figure of any of the variegated kinds.

The York and Lancaſter Roſe. The flowers of this ſort are a mixture of red and white, often laid in beautiful ſtripes. This Roſe aſſumes the appearance of the Red Damaſk, excluſive of its ſtripes. The tree grows to about the ſame ſize. The flowers come out at unuſual times, and, on the whole, it is acknowledged by all to be a valuable Roſe. The flowers are frequently ſucceeded by long, ſmooth, red heps, which will ſometimes have ripe ſeeds, from which freſh varieties may be obtained.

The Semi double Velvet Roſe will grow to be about four feet high. It produces its branches in an upright manner. Theſe are covered with a greeniſh bark, and there are very few ſpines to incommode any. The petals are large, and arranged in a double ſeries, around their numerous ſtamina. They are of a delightful velvet, and cauſe both aſtoniſhment and pleaſure. Words cannot expreſs the beauties of this ſort properly, and the pleaſure is only to be felt when we ſee them in blow, and the judgment is employed in the admiration of them.

Full double Velvet Roſe is not near ſo valuable a flower as the former; for though it is nearly a full flower, yet the petals in general will not have the true velvet colour of the other ſort. Many of them will be red, and others will have a tinge of it only. This ſort, however, is ranked among our moſt valuable Roſes; and indeed, it will ſometimes produce flowers moſt enchantingly fine, being of the true velvet, and very double.

The Bluſh Belgic is another Roſe in great eſteem. It will grow to be five or ſix feet high; and the branches are greeniſh, and much armed with thorns. The flowers are very double, and of a pale-red or bluſh colour. Each is compoſed of numerous petals. Theſe are ſhort, and as they open, diſplay the manner of their foldings. The flowers are very fragrant, and this is juſtly ranked as a valuable roſe.

The Red Belgic Roſe differs from the former only in the flowers being of a fine red colour. The ſame tendency to that colour is alſo to be obſerved in the ſhoots and leaves. It is equally valuable with the other ſort, and merits a place in all Collections.

The Monthly Roſes have all the ſame manner of growing and flower, except the colour of their flowers, and therefore one deſcription is common to them all. Their young ſhoots are of a green colour, and they are all around cloſely beſet with numerous crooked, brown

ſpines

ſpines The flowers of theſe differ only in one being of a red colour, a ſecond paler, a third white, and another variegated, and there is an elegance in their form peculiar to theſe ſorts Moſt paintings in which the Roſe is introduced, has one or other of the Monthly ſorts for the purpoſe, and indeed theſe, when half blown, *i. e* before their petals are fully expanded, have an air of gentility beyond conception Their fragrance, alſo, is by many ſuppoſed to be the moſt high and ſpicy, and on theſe accounts, as well as their frequently blowing, they are very juſtly to be coveted Not that they will continue blowing every month in the year, as the name would ſeem to imply, but they will flower in May, June, and July, and often again in Auguſt and September, nay, in mild ſeaſons, I have known flowers on theſe ſorts at Chriſtmas, to the pleaſure and ſurprize of many who ſaw them

The Red Damaſk Roſe is ſo common as to need no deſcription It will grow to a greater height than moſt of the ſorts, and though the flowers are not very double, yet it ſhould have a ſhare in plantations, as it is exceeded by few in fragrance The flowers of this ſort are purgative, whereas thoſe of the Red Roſe are aſtringent

The White Damaſk will grow to be nine or ten feet high, the branches alſo are green, and beſet all around cloſely with ſpines It is called the White Damaſk, though the flowers are not ſtrictly of that colour, for they have a reddiſh tinge when they firſt open, though they afterwards turn white I have not often met with this ſort, which makes me think it to be rare at preſent

The Bluſh Damaſk differs from the former, in that the tinge of red is in a higher degree

The Virgin Roſe will grow to be five or ſix feet high The branches are green, and have no ſpines, at leaſt none ſo conſiderable as to injure the hand if drawn over the branches This is a large double Roſe, of a pale-red colour, ſhaped a little like our Common Province, and very fragrant

The Marbled Roſe poſſeſſes great merit It produces its ſhoots in an upright manner They are of a browniſh colour, and armed with very few ſpines The flowers are very large and double, and their petals are finely marbled, which cauſes it to be much admired

The Great Spaniſh is a moſt noble, and at preſent a very ſcarce Roſe Its manner of growth, and the nature of the ſhoots, are a little like thoſe of the Dutch Hundred leaved ſort The flowers alſo much reſemble thoſe of that Roſe, only they are larger, ſo that nothing more need be ſaid to recommend this ſort

The Yellow Auſtrian Roſe is one of the moſt valuable ſorts in the whole Collection The flowers are of a clear and bright yellow, and the whole ſhrub will be covered with them at the time of blow Other ſorts of the Yellow Roſe ſeldom exhibit their flowers fair, but this never fails affording them in abundance, pure and complete Each flower is of ſhort duration, but they are conſtantly ſucceeded by others, and this ſometimes during a month The ſmell of theſe flowers is a little like ſome of the ſorts of the Dog Roſe No one ever ſaw this ſort in blow who did not expreſs his ſatisfaction, ſo juſtly is it eſteemed In winter, the ſhoots are of a reddiſh colour They are pretty cloſely beſet with ſhort, brown, crooked ſpines

The Copper-coloured Auſtrian Roſe differs in hardly any reſpect from the other, except in the colour of the flowers, for the inſide of theſe is of a kind of copper colour, whilſt the outſide of their petals, is a yellow They have the ſcent, like the former, of ſome of our Dog-Roſes, and have a genteel, and, when the tree is in full blow, an enchanting look This ſort is, with great reaſon, ranked amongſt our moſt valuable Roſes

The Double Yellow Roſe What a contraſt is made in our Double ſorts, by the appearance of the Double Yellow Roſe among the variety of reds, with their different tinges! This Roſe has been hitherto found only in ſome curious Collections, and at preſent in many parts of England it is ſtill ſcarce The uncommonneſs of the colour for a Roſe, and to ſee that alſo very double, muſt catch the attention, and be ſurprizing at firſt to thoſe who never ſaw it; whilſt thoſe who have been acquainted with it, muſt ſtill remain affected with its charms This Roſe will grow to be ſix or ſeven feet high, and the branches are of a kind of chocolate brown Theſe are armed on all ſides with numerous prickles, that are pretty large and ſharp, and ſwarms of others alſo that are ſmaller will appear among them All theſe are of a yellowiſh colour, and the buds alſo in the winter, when beginning to ſwell, will exhibit themſelves of a yellow complexion The flowers reſemble in make thoſe of our Cabbage-Province-Roſe They are every whit as double, and the petals are of a fine yellow Nothing more need be ſaid of this Roſe, ſince the Reader can now form an idea of it In many ſeaſons theſe Roſes do not blow fair, ſometimes they appear as if the ſides had been eaten by a worm when in bud, at other times the petals are all withered before they expand themſelves and form the flower For this purpoſe, many have recommended to plant them againſt north walls, and in the coldeſt and moiſteſt part of the garden, becauſe, as the contexture of their petals is ſo delicate, they will be then in leſs danger of ſuffering by the heats of the ſun, which ſeem to wither and burn them as often as they expand themſelves But I could not obſerve without wonder, what I never ſaw before, *i e* in the parching and dry ſummer of 1762, all my Double Yellow Roſes, both in the nurſery-lines and elſewhere, in the hotteſt of the moſt ſouthern expoſures and dry banks, every where all over my whole plantation, flowered clear and fair Scarcely one among them was to be found with a ſhrivelled leaf, nor did I ſee any that had the appearance of the grub taking their ſides, but all in general blew as fair, as double, and every whit as complete, as the Cabbage-Province-Roſe I never obſerved the blow to be ſo generally fine before, and it is what ſeldom happens with us I mention this caſe of that extraordinary ſummer, as it ſeems to demonſtrate, that no perſon need be anxious about the ſituation of his Double Yellow Roſes, but may plant them in ſuch places where he would ſooneſt chooſe they ſhould be

The Frankfort Roſe is the moſt free ſhooter of all the ſorts of Roſes It will often throw forth ſuckers to be ſix feet high in one ſummer The bark is ſmooth, and of a lightiſh brown, the prickles are not many, but they are pretty ſtrong The flowers are very large and double, and of a purpliſh red colour, which has occaſioned this Roſe being called by ſome the Purple-Roſe There is little delicacy in this flower, and it is by many ranked amongſt the worſt ſorts, if that term may be admitted here

Musk Rose Varieties

11 Muſk-Roſe Beſides the ever-green, there are two deciduous varieties of this ſpecies, called,

The Single Muſk Roſe
The Double Muſk-Roſe

Single described

Single Muſk, or White-Cluſter, is a ſcarce and valuable Roſe The young ſhoots are covered with a ſmooth green bark, and are not poſſeſſed of many ſpines, thoſe few they have are very ſtrong, and of a dark-brown colour This ſort produces its flowers in Auguſt, in very large cluſters They are of a pure white, and the tree will continue to exhibit its ſucceſſion of flowers until the froſt puts a period to the blowing The ends of the branches are frequently killed by the froſts in the winter, ſo that early in the ſpring they ſhould be gone over with the knife, and all dead wood taken off which would have an ill look, amongſt the healthy leaves and young ſhoots

The Semi double and Double Muſk, or White Cluſter-Roſes are late-flowering ſorts They will begin blowing in Auguſt, and continue ſo till the froſt puts a period to their glories for that ſeaſon The ſtalks are covered with a ſmooth green bark, which will be armed with a few very ſtrong, brown, crooked ſpines The flowers are of a pure white, and produced in large cluſters at the ends of the branches I have counted in one cluſter, alſo in a cluſter of the Single ſort before-mentioned, more than two hundred Roſes and buds These at preſent are not common, and are much coveted by the curious

Pendulous fruited Rose

12 Pendulous-fruited Roſe grows only to about five or ſix feet high, ſending forth ſeveral hiſpid branches from the bottom to the top The leaves are compoſed of many oval folioles, arranged along the mid-rib, and their footſtalks have few or no prickles The flowers have oval, ſmooth germina, grow on hiſpid footſtalks, and are ſucceeded by long pendulent fruit, full of ſeeds

White Rose

13 The White Roſe The characteriſtics of this ſpecies are, the ſtalks and footſtalks of the leaves are prickly, the flowers have oval ſmooth germina, and grow on hiſpid footſtalks Of this kind are,

Varieties

The Double White Roſe
The Semi double White
The Dwarf White
The Maiden's Bluſh Roſe

described

The Large Double White Roſe is well known in our gardens, and perhaps has been introduced into them as long as any of the ſorts The ſpines are ſtrong, and more numerous on the branches than on thoſe of the Semi double The branches are of a greeniſh or brown colour, and the flowers are well known They are large and full, and no ſhrub has a grander or more beautiful look when in blow, being then covered all over with them The middle of June is the time we may look for this ſhow Theſe flowers are delightfully ſweet, but their ſweetneſs is different from that of moſt of the other ſorts

The Semi double White is a genteel Roſe, though only a Semi-double flower The young ſhoots are ſmooth and greeniſh, and the prickles not ſo numerous as on many of the ſorts The flowers are of a pure white, and the petals large, and theſe being arranged in a double ſeries around the numerous ſtamina, in the center, with blackiſh antheræ, form an eaſy and beautiful figure They will be ſucceeded by heps, that will often have ripe ſeeds

The Dwarf White Roſe will grow to about a yard or four feet high The bark is ſmooth and greeniſh, and the prickles are not very numerous It produces a ſingle white flower, and nothing but variety induces us to admit a plant or two of it into our collection

Maiden's Bluſh Roſe is a free-ſhooter, though I do not remember to have ever ſeen it higher than ſeven feet The bark is exceeding ſmooth, and the ſpines are few in proportion to ſome of the other ſorts The colour of one ſide of a twig will be brown, whilſt that of the other ſide will be green Such a profuſion of noble ſorts of flowers does the *Roſa* afford us, that when we view one, we think that the beſt, when another, that that excels We may gaze with admiration on moſt or the before-recited ſorts, and ſhall have reaſon for aſtoniſhment in what are to follow but ſurely we may pronounce of this that it is exceeded by no Roſe, neither are we affected by any, more than by the ſort before us They are produced in very large cluſters, and each Roſe is as large as the Common Double White Their fragrance is of the ſame nature with this ſort, and they are every whit as delicate and large As to their colour, can we juſtly form an idea of the finiſhed beauty of a young lady, who is every way perfect in ſhape and complexion, and whoſe modeſty will give occaſion (without any real cauſe) for the cheeks gently to glow Form to yourſelves an idea of ſuch a colour at that time and that is the colour of the Roſe we are treating of, before it has been too long expoſed to the air A Roſe properly termed the Maiden's Bluſh, and which all covet and admire

A large ſhare of the varieties under the tenth ſpecies, in different trees, ſhew themſelves to belong to the ninth, particularly the Old Red, which is by Linnæus expreſsly arranged under the tenth ſpecies, yet upon examining ſeveral trees, I have found the footſtalks of the leaves altogether free from prickles, and conſequently, as the germina are oval, and the flowers grow on hiſpid footſtalks, this property ſhould entitle that Roſe, and others of the ſame kind, to be ranked as varieties of the ninth ſpecies In like manner, ſome of the varieties of the ninth, in different trees, anſwer to the characteriſtics given of the tenth So that in order to know with certainty which Roſes belong to one ſpecies, and which to another, a very young plant or two of each ſort ſhould be ſet in an open, rich, well dug part of the garden, where you will find the footſtalks of their leaves furniſhed with thoſe weapons which Nature deſigned them, and in the poſſeſſion or diſpoſſeſſion of which Linnæus has made the difference of theſe two ſpecies chiefly to conſiſt — Remarks on the above arrangement

I have obſerved the Auſtrian Roſes, alſo, with ſmooth germina, hiſpid peduncles, and prickly ſtalks and leaves, which ſhould entitle them to be claſſed with the White Roſes, from all which it appears, that the ſpecific difference of theſe plants is not properly aſcertained, as ſeveral of the ſorts, in different trees, will anſwer to the titles of more than one ſpecies I have arranged them as nearly as poſſible as they appeared to me on ſome old trees growing in my home-gardens, which had been often cut for flower-pots, &c But as ſuch trees are often deſtitute of the appendices peculiar to them in their young and vigorous growing ſtate, I will not abſolutely ſay, that, in the manner they are arranged, they are real varieties of the reſpective ſpecies under which they ſtand, and belong to no other I, for my part, am inclined to think, there is but one real ſpecies of the Roſe, which is the Dog-Roſe of our hedges, and that the numerous ſorts of cultivated and wild Roſes are only varieties of it Linnæus is inclined

inclined to be of this opinion; and though he has given titles to fourteen distinct species, yet he seems to be doubtful whether Nature ever stamped upon them, or intended, any permanent specific difference to be invariably assigned them. Be this as it may, all the sorts are distinct flowers. They are the glory of our flowering-shrubs, and were the pride and admiration of former ages. Beds of Roses are celebrated by the antient poets. With these the tombs of heroes were strewed, with these priests were crowned for sacrifice, with these garlands for love were made, and wreaths wore by all for festivity. We boast more sorts than ever the antients could pretend to, their number is encreased as horticulture is improved, and whether they are distinct species, or sorts belonging to one or other of the preceding thirteen species, or varieties only of one species, it makes no difference to the Gardener, who is here presented with a catalogue of no less than sixty different sorts, for the ornament and improvement of any part of the shrubbery, wilderness, or garden.

All the sorts of Roses are to be propagated,

Methods of propagating the different sorts by layers. 1. By layers. For this purpose, in order to obtain plenty of them, a sufficient number should be planted for stools, and after these have been planted a year or two, they should be headed near the ground, which will make them throw out plenty of young shoots. In the autumn, these should be layered in the ground. The best way to do it is, by a slit at the joint, though a gentle twist will often do as well, particularly for all the sorts of Monthly Roses, Damask Roses, and Sweet Briar, which will readily take if the bark be just broke, and will often send forth roots at every joint by the autumn following. Most of the other sorts do not strike out so freely, so that amongst them, by the autumn after layering, few will be found strong enough, and with root sufficient, to be planted out for good. However, in general, they will have roots, and oftentimes very good ones. In the autumn every layer must be taken up, the stools headed up, and a fresh operation performed on the young shoots that may have shot the preceding summer. The layers that have been taken up should be planted in the nursery, at no very great distance, and the sorts should be kept separate and booked, number-sticks being made to the separate sorts, that they may be distinctly known. The Moss-Province and the Musk-Roses do not strike root so freely by layers, neither does the Apple-bearing Rose, so that for all these sorts you must often wait two years before you take off the layers from the stools, and sometimes longer, which is the reason of these plants being rather scarce, they not being to be expeditiously propagated in plenty.

[By suckers.] 2. These trees may be propagated by suckers, which most of the sorts have a natural tendency to throw out, and these may be taken up, and the strongest and best rooted set out for good, whilst the weakest may be planted in the nursery for a year or two, to gain strength. But here we must observe, that the Moss-Province, Musk and Apple bearing Roses seldom throw out suckers, so that we must not wait for them from these sorts, but must get forward with our layering.

[By seeds.] 3. The Common Sweet Briar is to be propagated by seeds. These should be sown as soon as they are ripe, in a bed of common garden mould made fine. They generally remain until the second spring before they come up, and afterwards will require no other care than weeding until the spring following, when they may be taken up, and planted in the nursery, at small distances, and in two or three years time they will be good plants for the shrubbery, wilderness, or hedges. And indeed as great quantities of these odoriferous plants are often wanted, this is the easiest and most expeditious way of raising them in plenty.

By seeds, also, the Burnet-leaved, Apple-bearing, and Red or White Scotch Roses may be raised, which are doubtless distinct species, and will preserve the sorts by seeds.

Titles of the different species. 1. The Dog-Rose, or Hep-tree, is entitled, *Rosa germinibus ovatis pedunculisque glabris, caule petiolisque aculeatis*. In the *Flor. Suec.* it is termed, *Rosa caule aculeato, petiolis inermibus, calycibus semipinnatis*. Caspar Bauhine calls it, *Rosa sylvestris, flore odorato incarnato*; Dodonæus, *Rosa canina vulgo dicta*; Parkinson, *Rosa sylvestris inodora, seu canina*; and Gerard, *Rosa canina inodora*. It grows naturally in hedges in England, and most parts of Europe.

2. Burnet-Rose is, *Rosa germinibus globosis pedunculisque glabris, caule aculeis sparsis rectis, petiolis scabris, foliolis obtusis*. It grows naturally in most parts of Europe.

3. Scotch Rose is, *Rosa germinibus ovatis glabris, pedunculis caule petiolisque aculeatissimis*. In the *Flor. Suec.* it is termed, *Rosa caule petiolisque aculeatis calycis foliolis indivisis*. Caspar Bauhine calls it, *Rosa campestris spinosissima, flore albo odorato*; John Bauhine, *Rosa pumila spinosissima, foliis pimpinellæ glabris, flore albo*; Parkinson, *Rosa pimpinella, sive pomifera minor*; and Gerard, *Rosa pimpinellæ folio*. It grows naturally in England, Scotland, and most parts of Europe.

4. Alpine Rose is, *Rosa germinibus ovatis, pedunculis sub-hispidis, caule inermi*. Caspar Bauhine calls it, *Rosa campestris, spinis carens, biflora*; John Bauhine, *Rosa rubello flore simplici non spinosa*; and Haller, *Rosa non spinosa*. It grows naturally on the Alps of Switzerland.

5. Eglantine, or Sweet Briar, is, *Rosa germinibus globosis pedunculisque glabris, caule aculeis sparsis rectis, petiolis scabris, foliolis ...*. Haller calls it, *Rosa aculeata, foliis odoratis subtus rubiginosis*; Caspar Bauhine, *Rosa sylvestris, foliis odoratis*; and Tabernamontanus, *Rosa eglanteria*. It grows naturally in England and Switzerland.

6. Cinnamon Rose is, *Rosa germinibus globosis, pedunculisque glabris, caule aculeis stipularibus, petiolis sub-inermibus*. Caspar Bauhine calls it, *Rosa, odore cinnamomi, simplex*; John Bauhine, *Rosa cinnamomea, floribus sub-rubentibus, spinosa*. It grows in the southern parts of Europe.

7. Carolina Rose is, *Rosa germinibus globosis hispidis, pedunculis sub hispidis, caule aculeis stipularibus, petiolis aculeatis*. In the former edition of the *Species Plantarum* it is titled, *Rosa foliis serratis medio tenus integerrimis*. Dillenius calls it, *Rosa Carolina fragrans, foliis medio tenus serratis*. It grows common in North America.

8. Apple-Rose is, *Rosa germinibus globosis aculeatis, pedunculis hispidis, caule aculeis sparsis, petiolis aculeatis, foliis tomentosis*. Haller calls it, *Rosa foliis utrinque villosis, fructu spinoso*; Caspar Bauhine, *Rosa sylvestris pomifera major*; Ray, *Rosa sylvestris pomifera major nostras*; also, *Rosa sylvestris fructu majore hispido*; and Parkinson, *Rosa pomifera major*. It grows naturally in England and most parts of Europe.

9. Hundred leaved Rose is, *Rosa germinibus ovatis pedunculisque hispidis, caule hispido aculeato, petiolis inermibus*. In the former edition of the *Species Plantarum* it is titled, *Rosa caule aculeato pedunculis hispidis, calycibus semipinnatis glabris*. Caspar Bauhine calls it, *Rosa multiplex media*; and Clusius, *Rosa centifolia Batavica*. It is not known where this Rose grows naturally.

10. Gill

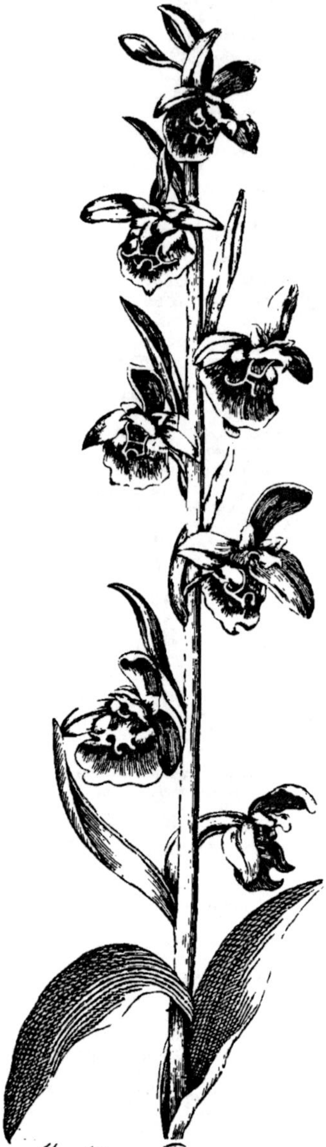

The Bee Flower

Velvet Bindweed

Double Blossomd Bramble

10 Gallican Rose is, *Rosa germinibus ovatis pedunculisque hispidis, caule petiolisque hispido-aculeatis*. Caspar Bauhine calls it, *Rosa rubra multiplex*; also, *Rosa versicolor*, and John Bauhine, *Rosa rubra, flore sempleno*, also, *Rosa prænestina alba & versicolor*. It grows naturally in most parts of Europe.

11 Musk Rose is, *Rosa germinibus ovatis pedunculisque tomentosis, caule petiolisque aculeatis*. It grows naturally in Germany.

12 Long-fruited Rose is, *Rosa germinibus ovatis glabris, pedunculis cauleque hispidis, petiolis inermibus, fructibus pendulis*. Dillenius calls it, *Rosa sanguisorbæ majoris folio, fructu longo pendulo*. It grows naturally in several parts of Europe.

13 The White Rose is, *Rosa germinibus ovatis glabris, pedunculis hispidis, caule petiolisque aculeatis*. In the former edition of the *Species Plantarum* it is called, *Rosa caule aculeato, pedunculis lævibus, calycibus semipinnatis glabris*. Caspar Bauhine calls it, *Rosa alba vulgaris major*, and Besler, *Rosa alba, flore pleno*. It grows naturally in some parts of Europe.

Class and order in the Linnæan system. The characters. *Rosa* is of the class and order *Icosandria Polygynia*, and the characters are,

1 CALYX is a monophyllous perianthium, ventricose at the base, and divided at the top into five long, narrow, lanceolate segments, two of which alternately have appendices on their sides, and the other two are alternately naked, whilst the fifth is appendiculated sometimes on one side only. [These peculiarities are always found to be more constant and certain in the Wild Briars than in any of the cultivated sorts of Roses.

2 COROLLA consists of five obversely cordated petals, the length of the calyx, into which they are inserted.

3 STAMINA are numerous short, capillary filaments, inserted into the neck of the calyx, having three cornered antheræ.

4 PISTILLUM consists of numerous germina, placed in the bottom of the calyx, and of the same number of very short hairy styles, which are strictly compressed to the neck of the calyx, and inserted into the sides of the germen, having obtuse stigmas.

5 PERICARPIUM is a fleshy, turbinated, soft, unilocular berry, formed of the fleshy base of the calyx, straitened at the neck, and retains at the top the rude segments of the limb.

6 SEMINA. The seeds are numerous, oblong, and hairy, and are on each side fastened to the calyx.

# CHAP. LXXV.

## *RUBUS*, The BRAMBLE, or RASPBERRY-BUSH.

Introductory observations. THE Brambles, which are all trailing plants unless supported, come of course under plants of that kind, though it may not be amiss to observe here, that there are some sorts that do well in plantations of upright trees, if they are staked, and tied to them with bass matting, which may be done with very little show of that nature among the leaves. If this be performed, and the luxuriant shoots stripped off as they sprout forth, they may be kept to what size is wanted, and may appear as the lowest shrubs, even if alone, in a bed in a small flower-garden. There are some sorts of the Bramble that are scarce plants, and will add to the variety, if managed this way: and there is one sort in particular so admired for its flowers, that no plantation of any kind ought to be without it. This is the Double blossomed Bramble, which will produce its flowers in such beauty and plenty that it demands admission into any place, and calls for art to check its natural luxuriancy, and qualify it for an associate among the other regular shrubs. Besides the Double Bramble, there is also the Bramble without Thorns, on which account only it is deemed curious. But to shew the beauties of this sort, it ought to have its natural run, for to train it as a shrub, and in that appearance to have no spines, is nothing extraordinary, but to see a Bramble perfectly smooth, and without prickles, raises our admiration. There is another sort of the Bramble, also, that produces white fruit, and for the same reason also as for that without thorns, it should have its free and natural growth, and consequently all these sorts will come into consideration under the Part relating to Trailing Plants, though I could not but observe thus much at present, as they may be introduced here if desired, and managed accordingly. Indeed, the Double blossomed ought to be so, it being exceeded by scarce any of the flowering-tree kind. I proceed now to an upright species of *Rubus*, which has always been propagated on account of its flowers only, and that is,

Description of the Virginian Flowering Raspberry. The Virginian Flowering Raspberry. All the sorts of Raspberries are species of *Rubus*, and are propagated for their fruit, but this sort is cultivated solely to mix with our flowering shrubs. It arises from the ground like the Common Raspberries, though it will naturally grow higher, but its growth is either higher or lower in proportion to the nature of the land or situation, as it will grow higher by two or three feet in a deep, rich, moist soil, than it will in a soil of the opposite nature. The stalks are of a brown colour, and wholly without prickles, and the strongest will divide into several smaller branches. The leaves are exceeding large for one of that height, from whence the plant derives no small beauty. They are broader than they are long, and of a fine green on both sides, the upper being of a dark, the under of a lighter colour. Each is divided into an uncertain number of lobes, which are serrated, and end in acute points. These leaves grow alternately, on footstalks that are of a proportionable length and strength to the size of the leaves; they being often eight or nine inches broad, and seven or eight in length. The flowers are produced in July, in plenty, at the ends of the stalks, and their succession will be continued for often more than two months, though

though they are always the most beautiful on their first appearance. They are of a purplish red, a colour which is very desirable at that time, when most of the other shrubs that are in blow will have yellow flowers. Each stands on a long footstalk, and many of them being collected into loose bunches, they make a tolerable figure. They are seldom succeeded by any fruit with us, and when this happens, it is of no flavour, and on that account of no value.

Method of propagating the Tree.

It is easily propagated from the suckers, which it sends forth in such abundance, that from a few plants, in a few years, almost any desired quantity may be obtained. Nay, so fast do the roots creep and send forth stalks on all sides, that unless they are constantly taken up as they grow, they will soon over-spread and choak all small plants that grow near them. The best time for taking off the suckers is the autumn, though they will grow very well if planted either in the winter or spring.

Titles.

The Virginian Flowering Raspberry is titled, *Rubus foliis simplicibus palmatis, caule inermi multifloro.* Cornutus calls it, *Rubus odoratus.* It grows common in Virginia, Canada, and some other parts of America.

Class and order in the Linnæan system.

*Rubus* is of the class and order *Icosandria Polygynia*, and the characters are,

The characters.

1. CALYX is a monophyllous perianthium, divided into five oblong, lanceolated, permanent, patent segments.

2. COROLLA consists of five roundish, erecto-patent petals, inserted into the calyx.

3. STAMINA are numerous filaments that are shorter than the corolla, and inserted into the calyx, having roundish compressed antheræ.

4. PISTILLUM consists of numerous germina, and of small capillary styles, which arise from the sides of the germen, with single permanent stigmas.

5. PERICARPIUM is a compound berry. The acini of which it is composed are roundish, and each contains one cell.

6. SEMINA. The seeds are single and oblong. The receptacle of the pericarpium is of a conic figure.

# CHAP. LXXVI.

## *SALIX*, The WILLOW-TREE, or SALLOW.

THE Willow has been treated of in the former Part of this Work, where its propagation is given, as well as a hint for some of these trees to be admitted into Plantations for Ornament and Shade. Their commonness, however, makes them neglected, else they are noble trees, and afford beauty by their shoots and leaves. The real species of them are very numerous, and the varieties of those species almost infinite. The Gardener would hardly think it worth while, nay, it would be ridiculous to attempt, to make a general collection of Willows for the pleasure garden; a task better befitting a basket-maker, or such as have much marshy ground to improve. There is, however, a wonderful variety of kinds, and a plant or two of each species may be introduced into any plantation of trees, to enrich the Collection, while the usefullest kinds may be cultivated in greater plenty by those who would make the best of every part of their estates. The real and distinct species of the Willow are,

Species.

1. The White Willow.
2. The Yellow Willow.
3. Purple Willow.
4. Sweet-scented Willow.
5. Weeping Willow.
6. Shining Willow.
7. Tri-andrious Willow.
8. Phylica-leaved Willow.
9. Almond-leaved Willow.
10. Hastated Willow.
11. Crack Willow.
12. Rose-Willow.
13. Sallow.
14. Ozier.
15. Glaucous Willow, or Alpine Sallow.

Description of the White,

1. White Willow. A few plants of the Common White Willow may, and indeed ought to have a place among the tallest-growing trees in the moistest part of the plantation, as their long and silver leaves will look exceeding well, and make a sweet contrast with the different greens of the other sorts.

Yellow,

2. The Golden Willow ought also to be sparingly stationed in the plantations, not for any extraordinary figure these trees will make in summer, but from the show they make in winter; for their bark is smooth and of a clear yellow, and in that season they have a singular and striking effect among other trees. This will not grow to near the size of the other sort.

Purple,

3. The Red Willow is a free shooter, and will grow to a size almost as large as the Common White Willow. A few of these only should be admitted into our plantations, for they have no singular look in summer; but in winter their bark appears of a red colour, which makes a pretty variety among other trees at that season; but it is, nevertheless, not near so striking as the yellow sort. I proceed now to two other sorts, which seem more peculiarly designed for ornamental plantations; and these are,

Sweet-scented,

4. The Sweet-scented Willow. This will grow to be a large timber-tree, and the branches are covered with a smooth brown bark. The leaves of this sort resemble those of the Bay-tree, and are by far the broadest of any of the sorts of Willows. They are smooth, and have their upper surface of a shining green; but their under surface is paler, and they are serrated at their edges. They emit, especially when bruised, a grateful odour; so that as an aromatic it claims a place in these plantations among others of its own growth. Indeed it deserves it; for I have known the air perfumed by the fragrance of its leaves after a shower to a considerable distance; so that it will readily join with other aromatics in perfuming the air with their spicy odours.

5. The

*Weeping.* 5 The Weeping Willow of Babylon will grow to be a large tree, and no tree is more proper to be planted by rivers, ponds, over springs, &c than this, for its slender branches are very long and pendulous; the leaves, also, are long and narrow, and when any mist or dew falls, a drop of water will hang at the end of each of these leaves, which, together with their pendulent branches and leaves, cause a most lugubrious appearance Lovers garlands are said to have been made of the wreaths of this Willow, the branches of which are very slender and pliable, and the plant itself has always been sought after for ornamental plantations, either to mix with others of the like growth in the largest quarters, or to be planted out singly over springs, or in large opens, for the peculiar variety they will occasion by their mournful look

*Shining.* 6 Shining Willow is a large-growing tree, sending forth several slender branches, which hang down, and are covered with a pale brown bark The leaves are smooth, glandulous, serrated, and of a yellowish-green colour The flowers are numerous hairy katkins, and the male flowers have two stamina only They appear early in the spring, and the females are succeeded by downy seeds, like the Common Willow

*Triandrous.* 7 Triandrous Willow is a large-growing tree, sending forth numerous, erect, flexible branches, which are covered with a greyish bark The leaves are oval, smooth, spear-shaped, acute-pointed, serrated, green on both sides, and eared at their base The katkins are long, narrow, loose, and appear early in the spring This sort is planted by the basket-makers, to mix with other kinds for their different sorts of work

*Phylica-leaved Willows.* 8 Phylica leaved Willow This is a tree of rather lower growth than the former The branches are numerous, flexible, tough, and serviceable for several articles in the basket-way The leaves are spear-shaped, smooth, serrated, and waved on their edges The flowers are long katkins, which come out early in the spring from the sides of the branches, and they soon afford a large quantity of down, which is wafted about with the winds to a considerable distance

*Variety.* There is a variety of this, with broad leaves

*Almond-leaved Willow.* 9 Almond-leaved Willow This is a Willow of the middle size, sending forth numerous, flexible, tough branches, covered with a light-green bark The leaves are spear-shaped, smooth, serrated, acute, eared at their base, and of a light green colour on both sides The flowers are oblong katkins, which turn to a light down in the summer

*Varieties described.* There are several sorts of this species, which are of inferior value to this, which is generally distinguished from the others by the name of the Old Almond-leaved Willow The branches are very tough and flexible, and when planted in the Ozier way, and grown to be one year's shoots from the stools, are very strong, and highly serviceable for the different purposes of basket making

*Hastated Willow.* 10 Hastated Willow This is a middle sized tree for the Willow kind, sending forth several long green shoots from the stools, which are very full of pith, but nevertheless tough and serviceable to the basket-maker The leaves are nearly oval, acute, smooth, serrated, sit close to the branches, and have very broad appendices at their base The flowers are an oblong, yellow katkin, and come out in the spring, from the sides of the young shoots, almost their whole length

*Crack Willow.* 11 Crack-Willow is another middle-sized tree for the Willow kind The branches are very brittle, and covered with a brownish bark The leaves are oval, spear-shaped, long, smooth, serrated, green on both sides, and have glandulous footstalks The katkins are long, slender, and the scales are loosely disposed

*Variety.* There is a variety of this species, with a yellow bark, which it casts every year, called the Almond-leaved Crack Willow Both sorts are unfit for the basket-makers use, being very brittle, on which account this species gained the appellation of Crack-Willow

*Rose Willow.* 12 Rose-Willow This is of much lower growth than the former The body of the tree is covered with a rough, yellow bark The branches are upright, tough, and of a reddish colour The leaves are spear-shaped, narrow, smooth, of a bluish-green colour, and, towards the upper part of the branches, are nearly opposite to each other The flowers come out from the sides of the branches, and numbers of them are joined together in a rose-like manner They are of a greenish white colour, and have a singular and beautiful look

*Varieties described.* There are two or three varieties of this species The leaves of one are downy underneath, the stalks of another are brittle, and the leaves are green on both sides, whilst another has its leaves of a light green on the upper surface, and glaucous underneath They are all low growing plants, and seldom cultivated for use

*Sallow.* 13 Sallow The Sallow is well known all over England, and delights in a dry rather than a moist soil It is a tree rather below the middle growth The branches are brittle, smooth, of a dark-green colour, and their chief use is for hurdle-wood and the fire, though the trunk, or old wood, is admirable for several uses in the turnery way The leaves are oval, rough, waved, indented at the top, and woolly underneath The katkins are very large, white, appear early in the spring, and are much resorted to by the bees, on their first coming-out of their hives at that early season

*Varieties.* There is a variety of this species with long leaves, which end in acute points, and another with smooth leaves, beautifully striped with white, called the Striped Sallow

*Ozier.* 14 Ozier is a tree of rather low growth, tho' the shoots grow amazingly long and strong in one year from the stools The leaves are spear-shaped, narrow, long, acute, almost entire, of a bluish green on their upper side and hoary underneath, and grow on very short footstalks This is the most propagated of all the kinds for basket-making It admits of several sorts of different value, but all are nevertheless useful to the basket-maker, who covets as many sorts of it as he can get

*Varieties.* The varieties usually go by the names of the Green Ozier, the Old Basket Ozier, Welsh Wicker, &c

*Glaucous Willow.* 15 Glaucous Willow This is a low Alpine Willow, of little use for ornament or profit The leaves are oval, oblong, entire, of a glaucous colour, and possessed of fine hairs on their under side The katkins are large, oval, of a white colour, and appear about the time of those of the Common Sallow This species is often called the Alpine Sallow

These are the chief kinds of Willows, a few of which may be brought into the wilderness quarters and ornamental plantations, as well as be cultivated for profit But besides these, there are many other species, of very low growth, seldom rising more than a foot, or a foot and half in height, an account of which shall be given among the Perennials, together with their culture, and the places proper for them pointed out

All the sorts of Willows are propagated by

Method of propagating these trees

planting the cuttings, which may be done at all times of the year, for they will grow if it is in summer, though the best season is the winter, or early in the spring, just before they begin to shoot. The cuttings should be of the last year's wood, should be in length in proportion to their thickness, and always ought to be planted in an upright position, and trained up to one stem, if designed to [illegible] with other [illegible] in ornamental plantations; for [illegible] purposes, their culture is fully [illegible] in the proper article, among the Forest-trees.

Titles

1. The Common White Willow is entitled, *Salix foliis [illegible] serratis [illegible]*. Haller calls it, *Salix foliis [illegible] lanceolatis serratis [illegible]*; Caspar Bauhine, [illegible]; others [illegible]. It is common about our towns and villages in most parts of Europe.

2. The Golden Willow is, *Salix foliis serratis [illegible]*. Caspar Bauhine calls it, *Salix [illegible]*, and Guettard, *Salix [illegible]*. It grows naturally in [illegible] parts of Europe.

3. The Purple Willow is, *Salix foliis serratis [illegible]*. Ray calls it *Salix [illegible] longo [illegible]*; Caspar Bauhine, *Salix folio longo [illegible]*, and John Bauhine, *[illegible] folio longo [illegible]*. It grows in England, and some of the southern parts of Europe.

4. The Sweet Willow is, *Salix foliis serratis [illegible]*. In the *Flora Lapponica* it is termed, *Salix [illegible]*. Ray calls it, *Salix folio laureo, seu lato glabro odorato*; Caspar Bauhine, *Salix [illegible]*, and J. Bauhine, *Salix [illegible] folio amygdalino, fragilis non auriculata*. It is to be found growing spontaneously in mountainous and marshy swampy ground in England and most parts of Europe.

5. Weeping Willow is, *Salix foliis serratis glabris lineari-lanceolatis ramis pendulis*. Tournefort calls it, *Salix orientalis, flagellis deorsum pulchre pendentibus*, and Caspar Bauhine, *Salix Babylonica, foliis [illegible]*. It is a native of the East.

6. Shining Willow is, *Salix foliis serratis glabris, floribus [illegible]*. Ray calls it, *Salix latifolia folio splendente*. It grows about Alton in Cumberland, and also Upsal in Sweden.

7. Triandrous Willow is, *Salix foliis serratis glabris, floribus triandris*. Haller calls it, *Salix foliis [illegible] utrinque glabris serratis appendiculatis*, and Ray, *Salix folio auriculato splendente flexili*. It grows in Switzerland and Siberia.

8. Phylica-leaved Willow is, *Salix foliis serratis glabris lanceolatis [illegible]*. In the *Flora Lapponica* it is termed, *Salix foliis serratis glabris oblongo-ovatis*. It grows naturally in the North of Sweden.

9. Almond-leaved Willow is, *Salix foliis serratis glabris [illegible] trapeziformibus*. In the *Flora Lapponica* it is termed, *Salix foliis serratis glabris [illegible] appendiculatis*. Caspar Bauhine calls it, *Salix folio amygdalino utrinque virente aurito*. Haller, *Salix Persicae folio*, and Parkinson, *Salix [illegible]*. It grows common in England and most parts of Europe.

10. Hastated Willow is, *Salix foliis serratis glabris [illegible] sessilibus, stipulis subcordatis*. In the *Flora Lapponica* it is termed, *Salix foliis serratis glabris [illegible] sessilibus appendiculatis*. Haller calls it, *Salix foliis glabris ovatis serratis, appendicibus latissimis*. It grows naturally in Lapland and Switzerland.

11. Crack Willow is, *Salix foliis serratis glabris ovato-lanceolatis, petiolis dentato-glandulosis*. Van Royen calls it, *Salix foliis serratis glabris lanceolatis acuminatis appendiculatis*; Ray, *Salix, folio longo latoque splendente, fragilis*; also, *Salix folio amygdalino utrinque virente [illegible]*; and Caspar Bauhine, *Salix fragilis*, also, *Salix folio amygdalino utrinque virente aurito*, and John Bauhine, *Salix spontanea fragilis amygdalino folio auriculata & non auriculata*. It grows common in England and most of the northern parts of Europe.

12. Rose-Willow is, *Salix foliis serratis glabris lanceolato-linearibus superioribus oppositis obliquis*. Haller calls it, *Salix foliis utrinque [illegible]*; Ray, *Salix humilior, foliis angustis subcaeruleis [illegible]*; John Bauhine, *Salix tenuior, folio minore utrinque glabro*, and Dalechamp, *Salix [illegible] Theophrasti*. It grows naturally, but not very common, in England; also in the southern parts of Europe.

13. Sallow is titled, *Salix foliis ovatis rugosis subtus tomentosis, [illegible] dentatis*. In the *Flora Lapponica* it is termed, *Salix foliis [illegible] ovato oblongis*, also, *Salix foliis oblongis subtus villosis [illegible]*. Haller calls it, *Salix folio rugoso obiter serrato subtus [illegible]*; Caspar Bauhine, *Salix latifolia rotunda*, also, *Salix folio ex rotunditate acuminato*; Gerard, *Salix caprea rotundifolia*, and Gmelin, *Salix foliis ellyptico-lanceolatis subtus sericeis appendiculatis*. It grows naturally in dry places in England, and most parts of Europe.

14. Ozier, *Salix foliis [illegible] lanceolato-linearibus [illegible] subtus [illegible]*. Van Royen calls it, *Salix foliis [illegible] lanceolatis [illegible] tomentosis*; Caspar Bauhine, *Salix folio longissimo angustissimo utrinque albido*; Ray, *Salix folio longissimo*; John Bauhine, *Salix foliis angustis & longissimis [illegible]*, and Gmelin, *Salix foliis [illegible] lanceolatis [illegible] integris subtus [illegible]*. It grows naturally in England and most parts of Europe.

15. Chamoeis Willow or Alpine Ozier, is, *Salix foliis integerrimis [illegible]*. Caspar Bauhine calls it, *Salix Alpina Pyrenaica*. It grows naturally on the Alps of Lapland and the Pyrenees.

This genus is of the class and order *Dioecia Diandria*, and the characters are, Class and order in the Linnaean system The characters

I. Male Flowers.

1. CALYX. The general katkin is oblong, and every where imbricated. The scales are oblong, plane, patent, and each contains one flower.

2. COROLLA. There is none. The nectarium is a small, cylindric, truncated, melliferous gland, in the center of the flower.

3. STAMINA are two erect, filiform filaments, longer than the calyx, having didymous, quadrilocular antherae.

II. Female Flowers.

1. CALYX. The katkin is the same as the males, as are also the scales.

2. COROLLA. There is none.

3. PISTILLUM consists of an oval, attenuated germen, and a style which is hardly distinguishable from the germen, having two erect, bifid stigmas.

4. PERICARPIUM is an oval, subulated, unilocular capsule, formed of two valves, and opens at the top.

5. SEMINA. The seeds are numerous, small, oval, and crowned with hairy down.

CHAP.

# CHAP. LXXVII.

## *SAMBUCUS*, The ELDER-TREE.

*Species.*

THE shrubby species of this genus are,
1. Common Elder.
2. American Elder.
3. Mountain Red-berried Elder.

*Common Elder.*

1. Common Elder. There are several sorts of the Elder-tree, that will sometimes grow to be twenty or five and twenty feet high; which as they come in of course here, I will give them, that if any suits the planter's taste, he may choose it for his purpose. They are,

*Varieties.*

The Black Elder-tree.
The White-berried Elder-tree.
The Green-berried Elder-tree.
The Parsley-leaved Elder.
The Gold-striped Elder.
The Silver-striped Elder.
The Silver-dusted Elder.

*Described.*

The Common or Black Elder is too well known to need any description. I have seen it more than thirty feet high, with a large trunk, and then it is that the wood is highly valuable. The leaves and flowers have a strong and disagreeable scent, which makes it highly improper for pleasurable plantations. The physic-garden seems more proper for these trees, the virtues of which are well known in medicine. Few cattle, nay, hardly any animal, will browse on them, so disagreeable are they to the taste of most creatures. However, they possess many excellent and rare virtues. The inner bark, the buds, the leaves, the flowers, the berries, prove sovereign remedies for many disorders, and they may be made very ornamental, if properly stationed in their plantations. They should not, indeed, be placed among other trees in any of the wilderness-quarters, nor yet near walks, for the reasons above given; but if they could be planted singly, or a small clump of them, at a distance from any place of recess, there is no tree in the world will cut a grander figure, or be more striking when in blow; for at that time they will be covered all over with large bunches of white flowers, which will assume an air of majesty at that distance, beyond any of the flowering tribe. Neither may a few of them only be stationed in this manner, but any acute corner of the plantation, that shews itself at a distance, may end with one of these trees, so that it will display its gaudy pride when in blow, and the eyes of all be feasted by its delicious appearance, whilst the sense of smelling is no way incommoded by its strong disagreeable scent.

The White-berried Elder differs from the former, in that the berries are whiter, the bark, also, of the young shoots is whiter, the buds, likewise, at their first appearance, are inclined to a whiter colour, the leaves, too, are of a paler green, and the plant in general has not such a strong disagreeable scent, though it nevertheless has a proportionable share. A plant or two only of this sort is to be admitted, merely for variety, though, where they are required for the sake of the berries to make wine, an hedge of them may be planted, in a place that is little frequented, and they will plentifully furnish the owner with berries for his purpose.

Green-berried Elder differs, in that the berries are green; the bark, also, of the young shoots is of a darker grey than that of the White; and the buds at their first appearance have nearly as dark a colour as that of the Common Elder. We must have only a plant or two of this sort for variety; and where the berries are wanted for wine, an hedge of them may be planted in some distant place, in the same manner as those of the White sort.

The Parsley-leaved Elder varies in no respect from the Common sort, except in the nature of the leaves, which are laciniated in such a manner as to resemble the leaves of some sorts of parsley. These leaves occasion a wonderful variety in wilderness-quarters among the leafy tribe; and on their account the plant is deemed worthy of a place in any Collection, though the flowers possess the same nature with the Common sort, and emit the same disagreeable scent.

The fifth and sixth sorts are distinguished by their different coloured stripes; whilst the seventh, the Silver-dusted kind, is remarkable for leaves finely powdered or dusted over, in a pounce-like manner, causing thereby a very beautiful and striking appearance.

*Description of the American.*

2. The American Elder is of lower growth than any of the above sorts, seldom rising higher than eight or ten feet. The young shoots are of a reddish colour. The leaves on the lower part of the plant are trifoliate; others are composed of about two or three pairs of folioles, terminated by an odd one. These folioles are serrated, and of a pleasant green colour; neither do they emit so strong a scent as any of the other sorts. The flowers are produced in the same manner as the foregoing, and are succeeded by berries of a reddish colour. Tho' these berries have not quite such a strong disagreeable taste as the Common Elder berries, yet they have a kind of physical flavour; nevertheless, they are liked by some persons, who are as fond of them as they are of some sorts of fruit. I have known those who were fond of eating these berries, call it the Eatable Elder Berry-tree. What was said of the first sort, recommending its being planted singly, or in small clumps at a distance, will hold good in all these sorts, which when in blow will equally have the same noble appearance as that, except the American, which is of lower growth, and consequently of less figure than the others, and as such less proper for the purpose.

*and the Mountain Red berried Elder.*

3. The Mountain Red-berried Elder will grow to about ten or twelve feet high, and is a tree that is with great justice universally admired. The bark of the young shoots is of a reddish colour, and the buds in winter will be very large and turgid, and of a still deeper red. The leaves are pinnated with an odd one; their folioles are serrated; they are placed at a good distance on the mid-rib, which is pretty long, and they die to a reddish colour in the autumn. The reddish coloured branches, with their large red turgid buds, have a singular and noble look in winter amongst other trees; and in the spring, as flowering shrubs, these trees seem to attempt to vie with any of the flowering tribe. For in April

April, and the beginning of May, they will produce their bunches of flowers at the ends of every joint of the last year's shoots. These bunches of flowers are of an oval figure, a figure in which compound flowers are not commonly produced. They are not, however, of so clear a white as any of the other sorts, being tinged with green, and although the tree will be covered with them, they have not the same striking appearance; but this defect is made amends for by the peculiar form which they assume, and the scarcity of the plant itself. Were there nothing but the above recited properties to recommend this shrub, it might justly claim admission in plenty into our choicest plantations: but these are not all its beauties. What remains is much more striking and engaging; for these oval bunches of flowers are succeeded by oval bunches of berries, that are of a deep scarlet colour. A crop, indeed, does not always ensue; but when it does, no tree is more singularly beautiful than this is rendered by them, chiefly occasioned by their colour and form, which any one must conceive to be delightful.

Elder berries used in medicine, and to make wine. The Elder chiefly used in medicine is the Common sort, together with the Dwarf Elder, called *Ebulus*, which is an herbaceous plant. Wines are made from the berries of all the sorts, which are allowed to be excellent cordials, and very wholesome. The manner of making them is so well known, that nothing need be said here on that subject. I shall, however, insert a receipt to make a wine from the flowers of Elder (copied from a much esteemed Cookery Book), which is affirmed to be very similar to Frontiniac.

Receipt to make wine from flowers of Elder. "Take six gallons of spring water, twelve pounds of white sugar, and six pounds of raisins of the sun chopped. Boil these together one hour, then take the flowers of Elder, when they are falling, and rub them off to the quantity of half a peck. When the liquor is cold, put them in. The next day put in the juice of three lemons, and four spoonfulls of good ale yeast. Let it stand covered up two days, then strain it off, and put it in a vessel fit for it. To every gallon of wine put a quart of Rhenish, and put your bung lightly on a fortnight, then stop it down close. Let it stand six months, and if you find it is fine, bottle it off."

Method of raising Elder tree. All the sorts of Elder are propagated by cuttings. These should be of the last year's shoot, and each cutting should consist of three joints, two of which must be in the ground, whilst the third is left above, to make the shoot. October is the best month for this business, and almost any soil will do, though the moister it is the better. These cuttings may be either planted very close, and removed the autumn following into the nursery-ground, or they may be planted a foot or more asunder, and then they will be of a sufficient distance until they are taken up for good, which may be any time after two years. Thus easy is the culture of these plants when known.

Titles. 1. The Common Elder is titled, *Sambucus cymis quinquepartitis, caule arboreo*. In the *Hortus Cliffortianus* it is termed *Sambucus caule perenni ramoso*. Caspar Bauhine calls it, *Sambucus fructu in umbella nigro*, also, *Sambucus fructu in umbella viridi*; also, *Sambucus laciniato folio*. Van Royen terms it, *Sambucus caule arboreo ramoso floribus umbellatis*; and Dodonæus, *Sambucus*. The Elder grows common in most parts of England though it is originally a native of Germany.

2. The American Elder is, *Sambucus cymis quinquepartitis, foliis sub-bipinnatis, caule fruticescente*. It grows naturally in Canada, Pensylvania, and Virginia.

3. The Mountain Red-berried Elder is, *Sambucus racemis compositis ovatis, caule arboreo*. Van Royen calls it, *Sambucus caule arboreo ramoso, floribus racemosis*; Caspar Bauhine, *Sambucus racemosa rubra*; and John Bauhine, *Sambucus racemosa, acinis rubris*. It grows common in the mountainous parts of the south of Europe.

Class and order in the Linnæan system. *Sambucus* is of the class and order *Pentandria Trigynia*, and the characters are,

The characters. 1. CALYX is a small, monophyllous, permanent perianthium, divided into five parts.

2. COROLLA consists of a wheel-shaped, concave petal, that is cut into five obtuse, reflexed segments.

3. STAMINA are five subulated filaments, the length of the corolla, having roundish antheræ.

4. PISTILLUM. The germen is oval, obtuse, and situated under the receptacle. There is no style, but in the room of it is a swelling glandule. The stigmas are three, and obtuse.

5. PERICARPIUM is a roundish berry, of one cell.

6. SEMINA. The seeds are three, convex on one side, and angular on the other.

## CHAP. LXXVIII.

## *SORBUS*, The SWEET-SERVICE-TREE.

Species. THIS genus consists of three notable species:

1. The Wild *Sorbus*, or Quicken-tree.
2. The Sweet-Service.
3. The Semi-pinnated Sweet-Service.

Description of the Wild Sorbus. 1. The Wild *Sorbus*, or Quicken tree, has been already treated of as a Forest-tree in the First Book, where the reader may see how desirable that tree is, not only on account of its wood, but to join in other plantations of all sorts. He will there perceive, that few trees have greater beauty, or afford greater variety; and from thence he may collect in what manner and where it ought to be stationed, in plantations for pleasure.

Sweet-Service. 2. The Sweet Service-tree is so distinguished from the other, because it produces eatable fruit, which in France, Italy, and other parts, is served up in deserts; and the tree is cultivated there solely on that account. It will grow to be larger than the Quicken-tree, and in many respects is superior in beauty to most trees. It will grow with an upright stem, and the young shoots in the summer are so downy as to appear covered with meal. In the winter they are inclined

clined to a purplish colour, and are spotted all over with whitish spots The buds at the ends of them will be turgid, preparing for the next year's shoot The leaves resemble those of the Quicken tree, but are finely pinnated, and composed of seven or eight pair of lobes, which are terminated by an odd one They are broader than those of the Quicken tree, serrated in a deeper and more irregular manner, and their under surface is of a much more downy nature The flowers are white, grow in umbels, come out in May, and are succeeded by an agreeable fruit, which is large, fleshy, and of various shapes in the different varieties

Semi pinnated Service. 3 The Semi pinnated Service This seems to be a mongrel, between the Quicken tree and *Aria* It is an upright-growing tree, and the young branches are of a whitish colour The leaves are very downy, and pinnated at the base, but the upper lobes join together, thereby forming a half pinnated leaf The flowers are white, grow in umbels, and are succeeded by bunches of roundish berries, which will be ripe in the autumn

Method of propagating the sorts. The culture of the Quicken-tree has already been given, and that culture will serve for all the sorts But in order to have good fruit of the Sweet Service tree, the best sorts should be grafted or budded upon pear or quince stocks

These trees are all very hardy, for they will grow in almost any soil, though they make the swiftest progress, and arrive at the greatest height, in a moist situation

Title. 1 The Quicken tree is titled, *Sorbus foliis pinnatis utrinque glabris* In the *Hortus Cliffortianus* it is termed, *Sorbus foliis pinnatis* John Bauhine calls it, *Sorbus aucuparia*, Caspar Bauhine, *Sorbus sylvestris foliis domesticæ similis*, and Cammerarius, *Sorbus sylvestris* It grows naturally in England, and most of the northern parts of Europe

2 The Sweet-Service is titled, *Sorbus foliis pinnatis, subtus villosis* Caspar Bauhine calls it, *Sorbus sativa*, and Clusius, *Sorbus legitima* It grows naturally in the south of France, Italy, and most of the southern countries of Europe

3 The Semi-pinnated Sweet-Service is titled, *Sorbus foliis semi-pinnatis subtus tomentosis* In the *Flora Suec.* it is termed, *Cratægus fennica* It grows naturally in Gotlandia

Class and order in the Linnæan system. The characters. *Sorbus* is of the class and order *Icosandria Digynia*, and the characters are,

1 Calyx is a monophyllous, concave patent, permanent perianthium, indented in five parts at the top

2 Corolla consists of five roundish, concave petals, inserted in the calyx

3 Stamina are about twenty awl-shaped filaments, inserted in the calyx, having roundish antheræ

4 Pistillum consists of a germen placed below the receptacle, and of three filiforme, erect styles, with capitated stigmas

5 Pericarpium is a soft, globose, umbilicated berry

6 Semina The seeds are three, oblong, distinct, and cartilaginous

## CHAP. LXXIX

## *SPARTIUM*, The BROOM.

We come now to another genus of the papilionaceous flowers, of which there are several species and varieties, and they are,

Species.
1 The Common English Broom
2 The Spanish Broom
3 The Starry Broom
4 The Single-seeded Broom
5 The Eastern Broom
6 Prickly *Cytisus*
7 Prickly Broom

Common English Broom. 1 The Common English Broom is known in most parts of England, tho' I do not remember to have seen a plant growing, in its natural wild state, within many miles of Church Langton This plant is extirpated all over England, where it naturally grows, as a pest to the land, so that we can hardly recommend to plant it in gardens, for was it to be set there, many persons would suppose it to have come up of itself, and perhaps censure the Gardener for his neglecting to root it out sooner The Common Broom, however, is a plant of admirable beauty, which, were it not for its commonness, would be sooner taken notice of and allowed It will grow to be about six feet high The branches are very flexible and numerous, they are angular, and the bark with which they are covered is of a delightful green The leaves are both trifoliate and single, the lower part of the branches producing the former, the upper part the latter The flowers are large, and produced in May, all along the sides of the last year's shoots, from the bottom to the top They stand upon short footstalks, and so ornament each twig of which the whole shrub is composed, that they have a look grand beyond expression; which is generally unobserved but by those whose delight is in observing the wisdom of God, and greatly it is manifested in the wonderful structure of the flowery tribe! These flowers are succeeded by compressed pods, containing kidney-shaped seeds, all of which are very well known

Spanish Broom. 2 Spanish Broom There are two notable varieties of this species

Varieties
Common Spanish Broom
Double Spanish Broom

described. Common Spanish Broom is a fine plant, and has been much sought after as a flowering-shrub It will grow to be ten feet high The branches are taper, placed opposite, and covered with a smooth green bark The leaves, which are not very numerous, are of a spear shaped figure, and, like the twigs, of a fine green colour The flowers are produced at the ends of the branches, in loose spikes, in July, and there will be a succession still kept up, at the end of each spike, often

often until the froſt puts a period to their blowing. The flowers of this ſort, alſo, are ſucceeded by compreſſed pods, which contain kidney-ſhaped ſeeds, and which often ripen in the autumn.

The Double Spaniſh Broom differs in no reſpect from the other, except that the leaves are very double. The manner of growing, colour of the ſhoots, and nature of the leaves, are exactly the ſame; and it produces very full double flowers. But theſe flowers do not come out ſo early as the ſingle ſort, it being often September before any of them will be in blow; and the ſucceſſion will be continued ſo ſlowly, that ſometimes not more than two or three flowers on a ſpike will be fully out before the froſts nip them for any further blow. This ſort is ſucceeded by no ſeeds.

Starry Broom. 3. Starry Broom is a low plant, ſeldom growing more than a yard high, even when it has the advantage of culture in the places of its natural growth; two feet it ſeldom aſpires to. Notwithſtanding the low growth of this ſhrub, however, it will occupy a large ſpace of ground in proportion to its ſize, for it extends its flexible branches all around to ſome diſtance. The branches of which it is compoſed are very narrow, angular, and grow oppoſite by pairs. The leaves are trifoliate, grow oppoſite to each other, and the ſolioles are awl-ſhaped, placed oppoſite, and ſpread out in ſuch a manner as to reſemble the rays of a ſtar, which occaſions its being ſo called. The flowers are produced in June and July, at the ends of the branches. They will be in a kind of ſmall cluſters or ſpikes, are of a bright yellow colour, and of the ſame figure with the former, but proportionally ſmaller. They are ſucceeded by ſhort hairy pods, in which are a few kidney-ſhaped ſeeds, which will be ripe in Auguſt or September.

Single-seeded Broom. 4. Single-ſeeded Broom. The varieties of this ſpecies are,

Varieties. The Common Yellow.
The White-flowered.

described. The Common Single-ſeeded Broom is a plant of about ſix feet in growth. Its branches, which are very numerous, and tough, are angular; and the leaves, which are not very many, are of a lanceolated figure. The flowers are produced in bunches from the ſides of the branches. Theſe bunches are ſmall; but being of a fine deep yellow colour, and alſo being in plenty all over the ſhrub, give it a beautiful look. This ſhrub blows in July; and the flowers are ſucceeded by ſhort pods, each of which contains a ſingle ſeed only, which ſeldom ripens in England.

White-flowered Single-ſeeded Broom, which is alſo called the White Spaniſh Broom, is of a more tender nature than the former ſort; yet not ſo tender but that it will thrive abroad with us, in any dry ſoil and well ſheltered ſituation, if the winters are not too ſevere. After this precaution, I would adviſe the gardener not to venture his whole ſtock of theſe plants abroad, leſt a ſevere winter ſhould take them all off, but to have a few planted in pots, and ſet under ſhelter, that, in caſe the others ſhould be killed, a ſhare of theſe may ſupply their places. The White Spaniſh Broom, then, will grow to about eight feet high; and the branches are numerous, ſlender, and tough. Their bark is of a whitiſh colour, and they are taper, almoſt like a ruſh. The leaves, which are not many, are of a lanceolated figure. The flowers are white, come out in cluſters from the ſides of the branches in July, and are ſucceeded by ſhort pods, each of which contains one ſingle ſeed only.

Eastern Broom. 5. The Eaſtern Broom will grow to about ſix or eight feet high. The branches of this, alſo, are numerous, ſlender, and tough. They are rather of a ſingular ſtructure, each of them affording ſix angles. The leaves, which are few, are of different figures, ſome being found ſingle only, whilſt others are trifoliate. The flowers are produced in July, at the ends of the branches, in a kind of ſpikes. They are of a paler yellow than moſt of the other ſorts, and are rarely ſucceeded by ſeeds with us.

6. Prickly *Cytiſus* has ſcarcely any buſineſs in this place, being generally reckoned as a green-houſe plant; but as it will bear our moderately-mild winters in a warm ſoil and ſituation, with this caution it may be introduced. It is about ſix feet in growth, and the branches are numerous, ſlender, tough, angular, and armed with long ſpines. The leaves are trifoliate, and the flowers are produced in cluſters, in June, at the ends of the branches. They ſtand on long footſtalks, are of a bright yellow, and make a noble figure. They are ſucceeded by ſhort, hard pods, which contain a few ſeeds of the ſame figure with the others. Prickly Cytiſus.

7. Prickly Broom. The ſtalk of this ſpecies is woody, and ſends forth ſeveral ſlender, prickly branches, which ſpread themſelves every way. The leaves are oval, ſmooth, and in ſome varieties hairy. The flowers are moderately large, and ſome are of a deep yellow colour, whilſt others are pale. They appear in July, and are ſucceeded by ſhort pods, containing the ſeeds, which ſeldom ripen in England. Prickly Broom.

All theſe ſorts of Broom, the Double-bloſſomed excepted, are to be raiſed from ſeeds; and one method may be obſerved for all the ſorts. The ſorts that ripen their ſeeds in England are ſuppoſed to be ready at hand; the ſeeds of the others muſt be procured from the places where they grow naturally. The firſt week in April is the beſt time for ſowing the ſeeds; and this ſhould be either in drills, or in beds half an inch deep. It will not be long before the plants appear; and as the hot weather comes on, they ſhould be ſhaded from nine o'clock in the morning till within an hour of ſunſet. Watering and conſtant weeding muſt be given them; and this is all the trouble they will require in ſummer. The reader will perceive our Common Broom to want none of this care; neither will the Common Spaniſh Broom need much of it; it is to be afforded thoſe only which are leſs common, that we may be more certain of a fuller and ſtronger crop. In the ſpring all theſe ſeedlings are to be taken up, and pricked out in the nurſery-ground, a foot aſunder, and two feet diſtant in the rows. This work muſt be done when they are one year old ſeedlings, becauſe they naturally ſend down a ſtrong tap root, which, if deferred longer, will be grown ſo big as to endanger the growth of the plant. After they have ſtood in the nurſery-ground two years, they will be good plants for ſetting out where they are to remain. Thus may all the ſorts of *Spartium* be raiſed by ſeeds; though it will be highly proper to have particular regard to the ſituation of the tenderer ſorts, ſuch as the White Spaniſh Broom, the Oriental, and the ſorts called the Prickly *Cytiſus* and Prickly Broom. Theſe may be raiſed the ſame way; but the ſoil and ſituation muſt be naturally warm and well-ſheltered, and the beds ſhould be hooped to be covered with mats in froſty weather, otherwiſe the whole crop will be in danger of being loſt the firſt winter. In the ſpring they may be planted, ſome in pots (to preſerve the ſorts), others in the warmeſt places of the ſhrubbery. Another method will not be improper to be followed in raiſing the tenderer ſorts, namely, by ſowing them in pots in April, and plunging Method of propagating the ſpecies.

plunging them in a shady border up to the rim At the approach of the first frost, they may be removed into the greenhouse, or placed under some shelter, when they will be effectually preserved until the spring, then they should be turned out, and planted in separate pots, which should be plunged in a shady border, and removed under cover in the winter By thus protecting them for a winter or two, they will get stronger, and be able to resist the cold, and then a share may be planted out in the warmest situation, whilst the others may be removed into larger pots, to be kept and treated as greenhouse-plants

Titles of the different species.

1 The Common English Broom is entitled, *Spartium foliis ternatis solitariisque, ramis inermibus angulatis* Caspar Bauhine calls it, *Genista angulosa & scoparia*, John Bauhine, *Genista angulosa trifolia*, Tournefort, *Cytiso genista scoparia, vulgaris flore luteo*, and Dodonæus simply, *Genista* It grows naturally upon barren lands in England, and most of the southern parts of Europe

2 Spanish Broom is, *Spartium ramis oppositis teretibus apice floriferis, foliis lanceolatis* Caspar Bauhine calls it, *Spartium arborescens, seminibus lenti similibus*, and John Bauhine, *Genista juncea* It grows common in Spain and Portugal, and in some parts of Italy and Sicily

3 Starry Broom is, *Spartium foliis ternatis linearibus sessilibus, petiolis persistentibus, ramis oppositis angulatis* John Bauhine calls it, *Genista radiata, sive stellaris*, Columna, *Spartium æqui colorum minimum montanum triphyllum* It is a native of Italy

4. Single-seeded Broom is, *Spartium ramis angulatis, racemis lateralibus, foliis lanceolatis* Caspar Bauhine calls it, *Spartium alterum monospermum, semine reni simili*, also, *Spartium tertium, flore albo*, Clusius, *Spartium III Hispanicum* It grows naturally in the most barren parts of Spain

5 The Eastern Broom is, *Spartium foliis solitariis ternatisque ramis sexangularibus apice floriferis* Tournefort calls it, *Spartium orientale, siliqua compressa glabra & annulata* It is a native of the East

6 Prickly Cytisus is, *Spartium foliis ternatis ramis angulatis spinosis* Caspar Bauhine calls it *Acacia trifolia*, John Bauhine, *Aspalathus secunda trifolia*, and Herman, *Cytisus spinosus* It grows near the sea coasts in the southern parts of Europe

7 Prickly Broom is, *Spartium ramis spinosis patentibus, foliis ovatis* John Bauhine calls it, *Aspalathus secunda Monspeliensis*, Caspar Bauhine, *Genista spartium spinosum minus, flore luteo*, also, *Genista-spartium spinosum majus secundum, flore pallido*, also, *Genista-spartium spinosum majus tertium hirsutum* Clusius terms it, *Aspalathus alter III* It grows naturally in Spain and the South of France

*Spartium* is of the class and order *Diadelphia Decandria*, and the characters are, Class and order in the Linnæan system

1 CALYX is a very small, coloured, cordated tubular, monophyllous perianthium, having a very short margin, marked with five denticles The characters

2 COROLLA is papilionaceous, and consists of five petals

The vexillum is obcordated, large, and totally reflexed

The alæ are oval, oblong, annexed to the filaments, and shorter than the vexillum

The carina is dipetalous, spear-shaped, oblong, hairy, longer than the alæ, and inserted into the filaments

3 STAMINA are ten unequal filaments, joined together in a body, having oblongish antheræ

4 PISTILLUM consists of an oblong hairy germen, an awl-shaped rising style, and an oblong hairy stigma

5 PERICARPIUM is a long, cylindrical, obtuse, bivalvate pod containing one cell

6 SEMINA The seeds are few, roundish, and kidney-shaped

# CHAP. LXXX

## *SPIRÆA FRUTEX*

THE *Spiræa Frutex* affords us many species, which are as beautiful as they are now frequent; insomuch that there are hardly any shrubs more common, and few that have more beauty to recommend them The species are,

Species

1 The *Spiræa Frutex*, commonly so called
2 The Red-flowering *Spiræa*
3 The *Hypericum Frutex*
4 Spanish *Spiræa*
5 Gelder-Rose-leaved *Spiræa*
6 Service-leaved *Spiræa*

Spiræa Frutex

1 The *Spiræa Frutex* commonly rises to about the height of four feet The root is spreading; so that, besides the common stalks which send forth branches, others are produced from the root, called Suckers, which by the autumn will be as high or higher than any of the whole plant The bark on all these is smooth, and of different colours. That on the old stalks is red, though for the most part clouded with a dusky matter, the young shoots that grow from these stalks are lighter, though nevertheless of a reddish tinge, whilst the bark on the summer shoots, that spring from the root, are nearly white The leaves of this species are of a fine green, and grow without order on the branches They are spear-shaped, obtuse, naked, and their edges are serrated The flowers are produced in June, at the ends of the branches that grow from the main stalk, and before these have done blowing, the suckers that arise from the roots will exhibit their flower-buds at the ends These are generally larger and fairer than those that were before in blow, and by these suckers a succession of flowers is often continued even until late in the autumn The flowers are produced in double-branching spikes, which are larger downwards, diminish gradually, and end with an obtuse spike at the top They are of a pale-

pale red colour, and though separately each flower is small, yet being produced in their thick spikes, four or five inches long, they have a good look. These flowers, with us, are succeeded by no ornamental seeds. The vigorous shoots of this shrub that arise from the roots are very tough, pliable, and tiner, and make the best tubing switches, for the summer, of any plant that grows.

Red flowering Spiræa

2. The Red flowering *Spiræa* will grow to the height of about four feet, and the branches are covered with a purple bark. The leaves grow on these without order. They are of an oval, lanceolated figure, and unequally serrated. Their upper surface is of a fine green colour, but their under is downy. The stalks, also, are possessed of a good share of this mealy kind of matter. The flowers are produced in July, at the ends of the branches, in double branching spikes, like the former, and being of a bright red colour, make a fine appearance.

Variety

There is a variety of this species, with white flowers.

Hypericum Frutex.

3. The *Hypericum Frutex* will grow to the height of about five or six feet, and its beauty and elegance beyond description, not so much from its natural form of growth, or the colour of the bark, or leaves, as from the flowers, for the branches are produced irregularly. The older shoots are covered with a dark brown bark, the younger shoots are smooth and lighter, and are tinged with red. The leaves are small, though of a pleasant dark green colour, they are produced irregularly on the shrub, and have their edges entire. The flowers are produced in May, almost the whole length of the branches. They are of a white colour, and though each flower is separately small, yet they are collected in umbels that sit close to the branches, which being thus ornamented their whole length, scarcely any thing but flowers, besides the main stalks, are to be seen, so that the shrub has the appearance of one continued flower branched out into as many different divisions as there are twigs, for every twig at a little distance will look like a long narrow spike of flowers, and these being all over the shrub, of a pure white, the show they then make is enchanting.

Spanish Spiræa

4. Spanish *Spiræa* will grow to be about four feet high, and the branches, which are produced irregularly, are covered with a dark brown bark. The leaves are small, of a pleasant green colour, and serrated at their ends. The flowers are produced from the sides of the branches, in May. They grow in roundish bunches, are of a whiter colour than, and being produced nearly the whole length of the branches, make a charming show like the preceding sort, from which this species very little to differ, without being strictly examined.

Guelder Rose leaved Spiræa

5. Guelder Rose leaved *Spiræa*. Of this species there are two varieties, called,

Virginian Guelder Rose.

Carolina Guelder Rose.

Varieties described

Virginian Guelder-Rose will grow to be seven or eight feet high. The branches are covered with a dark brown bark, which peels off in the winter, and discovers an inner, which is smooth, and of a lighter colour, so that in winter this shrub has a very ragged look. The leaves resemble those of the common currant-bush, which has occasioned its being called by some the Currant leaved Guelder Rose. They are for the most part lobed like them, though all the leaves will not be alike, some being divided into more than three lobes, whilst others are scarcely divided at all. They are serrated at their edges, are of a palish green colour, and placed irregularly on the branches, on long green footstalks. The flowers are produced in June, at the ends of the branches. They are white at their first opening, and afterwards receive a reddish tinge, which is still heightened before they die off. Each flower separately is rather small, but many of them grow together, each having its separate footstalks, in large umbels. The beauty of the Common Hawthorn is known to all, and it may not be amiss here, as the simile is just, and that my Reader may have a true idea of the flowers, to assure him, that each flower separately has the appearance of a single flower of the Hawthorn, and that they are produced in bunches, though not quite of the same make with them, these growing in more regular umbels. Nothing more need be added concerning this flower, for the reader may form a true idea of it. These flowers are succeeded by the same kind of bunches of reddish cornered fruit, which causes a pretty variety in the autumn.

Carolina Guelder Rose differs very little from the former sort. The branches are covered with the same kind of falling bark, though the leaves are not lobated in the same manner, for there will be of different shapes, yet most of them are nearly oval, but end in points, and are all unequally serrated round their edges. The flowers of this sort, also, are white, but grow in rounder and smaller bunches than the other. They are succeeded by the like kind of cornered fruit, which is of a reddish colour in the autumn.

Service leaved Spiræa

6. Service leaved *Spiræa* is a shrub of very low growth; a yard is the highest I ever yet knew it arrive to. The young branches are covered with a purplish bark. The leaves are beautifully pinnated, so as nearly to resemble those of the Service tree. The folioles are oblong, and generally about four pair in number. They are uniformly serrated, and exceedingly ornamental to the shrub. The flowers are white, and produced at the ends of the branches, in July, in panicles. They are seldom succeeded by seeds in England.

Methods of propagating the different sorts by cuttings,

The propagation of all the sorts of the *Spiræa* is very easy. It may be done by cuttings, for if the strongest parts of the shoots of the last summer's growth be planted in October, in a shady border, most of them will grow, and become good plants by the autumn, so that by the autumn after that, they will be very proper plants to be set out for good.

and by layers.

But if a person has only a plant or two of a sort, from which he can get but a very few cuttings, the best way is to layer them, and not hazard their growing this way, for altho' they will strike freely, yet by some unseasonable weather, I have known whole crops of cuttings of all sorts to fail. Thus, of the many thousand cuttings of all sorts I planted in the winter preceding the dry summer in 1762, very few grew, and for altho they were shaded and watered, and others planted in shady borders, yet such large cracks and chasms would open among them (as they did almost all over my plantations) as to cause watering to be of no service, nay, the more I watered them, the harder the mould was, and the chasms became greater, and notwithstanding many of the cuttings were planted in parts that were possessed of a natural moisture, yet the crevices there were larger and the ground harder, and all attempts to prevent it seemed to be in vain. Though this is the nature of the soil of few nurseries, I mention this to shew, that there is an hazard in planting of cuttings, unless the season should prove good; for this turn I had scarcely any grow. So that whatever trees will grow by cuttings,

cuttings, if a gentleman has only a plant or two and wants to have them increased, the best way is to do it by layers, and hence, of all the sorts here re-mentioned, if the twigs be but laid in the ground in the autumn, they will have good roots by the autumn following, many of which will be plants strong enough to be planted in the shrubbery, whilst the weaker may be set in the nursery ground for a year or two, to gain strength

and by suckers

Some of these sorts will throw out suckers, which will be good plants when taken up. Nay, the first sort will propagate itself fast enough this way, for after it has stood a year or two, it will throw them out so vigorously, as has been before observed, that in one summer they will grow to be as high as the whole plant, and will have fair flowers at the ends in the autumn. And here the Gardener must observe, that after this sort is planted in the shrubbery, the suckers must be constantly cleared off the old plants every winter, otherwise they will soon be so numerous and close, as to lose that beauty which always attends plants that unite with single or with few stems

Titles

1 *Spiraea Frutex* is titled, *Spiraea foliis lanceolatis obtusis serratis nudis, floribus duplicato-racemosis* Clusius calls it, *Spiraea Theophrasti forte*, Tournefort, *Spiraea salicis folio*, Caspar Bauhine, *Frutex spicatus, foliis serratis salignis*, and Amman, *Spiraea frutex folio longiore serrato, floribus rubris* It grows naturally in Siberia and Tartary

2 The Red-flowering *Spiraea* is, *Spiraea foliis lanceolatis inaequaliter serratis subtus tomentosis, floribus duplicato-racemosis* Plukenet calls it *Ulmaria pentacarpos, integris serratis foliis parvis subtus incanis, Virginiana* It is a native of Philadelphia

3 *Hypericum Frutex* is, *Spiraea foliis ovatis integerrimis, umbellis sessilibus* In the *Hortus Cliffortianus* it is termed, *Spiraea foliis integerrimis pedunculis simplicibus* Tournefort calls it, *Spiraea Hyperici, folio non crenato*, and Caspar Bauhine, *Pruno sylvestri affinis Canadensis* It is a native of Canada

4 Spanish *Spiraea* is, *Spiraea foliis oblongis obtusis apice serratis, corymbis lateralibus* Tournefort calls it, *Spiraea Hispanica, hyperici folio crenato*, and Amman, *Spiraea umbellis foliis, alias modo integro modo dentato* It grows naturally in Siberia and Spain

5 Guelder Rose-leaved *Spiraea* is *Spiraea foliis lobatis serratis, corymbis terminalibus* In the *Hortus Cliffortianus* it is termed, *Spiraea foliis trilobis angulatis, floribus corymbosis* Tournefort calls it, *Spiraea opuli folio*, and Commeline, *Evonymus Virginiana, ribesii folio capsula eleganter bullata* It grows common in Virginia, Canada, and Carolina

6 Service-leaved *Spiraea* is, *Spiraea foliis pinnatis, foliolis uniformibus serratis, caule fruticoso, floribus paniculatis* In the *Flora Petrop. Academ.* it is termed, *Spiraea foliis pinnatis* Amman calls it, *Spiraea foliis fraxini serrato, panicula, floribus albis* It grows naturally in moist land in Siberia

Class and order in the Linnaean system

*Spiraea* is of the class and order *Icosandria Pentagynia*, and the characters are,

The characters

1 CALYX is a monophyllous perianthium, plane at the base, and divided into five acute permanent segments

2 COROLLA consists of five oblong, roundish petals, inserted in the calyx

3 STAMINA are twenty or more filiform filaments, that are shorter than the corolla, and inserted in the calyx, having roundish antheræ

4 PISTILLUM consists of five or more germina, and of the like number of filiform styles, that are the length of the stamina, having capitated stigmas

5 PERICARPIUM consists of oblong, acuminated, compressed capsules, each opening with two valves

6 SEMINA The seeds are few, small, and acuminated

# CHAP LXXXI

## *STAPHYLÆA*, The BLADDER-NUT

THERE are two species of *Staphylæa* that are coveted for the wilderness-quarters, shrubberies, &c and which indeed are fine plants, and agreeably increase the variety in all plantations of that nature They are,

Species

1 The Common or Five-leaved Bladder-Nut

2 The Trifoliate Bladder-Nut

Description of the Common

1 The Common Bladder-Nut will grow to be eight or ten feet high The older branches are covered with a brown bark, that on the younger shoots is of a much lighter colour The bark is exceeding smooth, the twigs are very pithy, and when broken have a very strong scent The buds will be turgid and large early in winter, as if ready to burst out of their stipulæ, and begin their shoots, this causes the plant at that season to have an air of health and verdure, which of course must then be very pleasing The leaves are pinnated, of a light green colour, and, like all others of that nature, are very ornamental They consist of two pair of folioles, that are terminated with an odd one, which occasions this sort being frequently called the Five leaved Bladder Nut These folioles are tolerably large, oblong, pointed, and stand on pretty long footstalks The flowers are produced in long pendulous bunches, from the wings of the leaves, and are white The buds appear in the spring, almost at the first dividing of the stipulæ, though they will not be in full blow until May These flowers are succeeded by large inflated bladders, in which the seeds are contained, and have a very striking and singular look in the autumn The nuts of this tree are smooth, and said to be eaten as food by the poor people in some countries They are also used by the Catholics, who compose some of their rosaries of them

and the Trifoliate Bladder Nut

2 The Trifoliate Bladder-Nut grows to about the same height with the former The elder branches will be besprinkled, as it were, with o ei ish grayish spots The bark on the younger branches is perfectly smooth, and of a yellowish colour The buds will be swelled early in the winter, though they will not be so large and turgid as those of the former sort The leaves are trifoliate, and grow by threes on a footstalk, which has occasioned this plant being distinguished by the name of Three leaved Bladder-Nut They are of a light green colour, and the folioles are generally pretty large, oval, pointed, and serrated at their edges The flower-buds appear at the first beginning of the buds to open in the spring, which I have known to be sometimes so early as January, though the flowers will not be in full blow until May These flowers, like the former, are produced from the sides of the branches, in long pendulous bunches Their colour is white, and they are succeeded by large inflated bladders, in which the seeds are contained The seeds of both species ripen well in England

Method of propagating these sorts by seeds

These species may be propagated by seeds, layers, or cuttings The seeds should be sown, soon after they are ripe, in the autumn, three quarters of an inch deep, in almost any sort of common garden mould made fine In the spring some share of the plants will appear, though you must not expect the whole crop until the second spring following Nay, if the sowing of the seeds is deferred until the spring, scarcely any of them will come up until the spring after All the summer the beds must be kept clear of weeds, and if it should prove dry a gentle watering should be given the young plants, which will encrease their growth The spring after the remainder of the crop will come up, and the business of weeding must be continued that summer In the autumn the two years old plants should be drawn out and planted in the nursery, a foot asunder and two feet distant in the rows and in the beginning of March the one year old seedlings should be taken up, and planted in the same manner The reason of deferring the planting out of the youngest seedlings is, that, being small when planted out in autumn, they are often thrown out of the ground by the frost, and many of them lost, whereas, of larger plants there will be little danger After they have stood two or three years in the nursery, they will be good plants for any places where they are wanted

By ...

These shrubs may also be propagated by layers and this should be performed in the autumn, on the shoots of the preceding summer, by slitting them at a joint, and laying them in the ground The ... g of this slit will be necessary, or at least the well breaking of the bark, otherwise they will not strike root, and if this be done with judgment, they will have good roots by the autumn following, many of which will be good plants, and fit for the shrubbery, whilst the weaker may be planted in the nursery ground for a year or two, to gain strength One caution is to be observed If the layering is to be performed by twisting the young shoots so as to break the bark, be careful not to over do this, for being very pithy it will kill them to be much twisted, and if the bark is not well broke, they will not strike root this way

cuttings

These trees are to be encreased also by cuttings, from which they will grow very well The cuttings must be the bottom part of the last summer's shoot, which should be planted in October, in a shady border of light earth If the spring should prove dry, give them some watering, and there will be little fear but that most of them will grow

and suckers

These plants will often multiply themselves For after they have grown a few years, they frequently send forth suckers, which become plants with good roots, without any trouble, and as such, they may be taken up and planted in any place where they are wanted

Titles

1 The Common Bladder-Nut is titled, *Staphylea foliis pinnatis* Dalechamp calls it, *Staphylodendron*, Caspar Bauhine, *Pistacia sylvestris* Parkinson, *Nux vesicaria*, and others term it, *Staphylodendron vulgare* It is found growing in England and many parts of Europe

2 The Trifoliate Bladder Nut is, *Staphylea foliis ternatis* Gronovius calls it, *Staphylodendron triphyllum, racemo tripartito*, Herman, *Staphylodendron Virginianum trifoliatum*, and Morison, *Pistacia Virginiana sylvestris trifolia* It is a native of Virginia

Class and order in the Linnæan system The characters

This genus is of the class and order *Pentandria Digynia*, and the characters are,

1 CALYX is a roundish, concave, coloured perianthium, almost as large as the corolla, and divided into five parts

2 COROLLA consists of five oblong, erect, petals, and nearly resembles the calyx There is a concave pitcher-shaped nectarium at the bottom of the flower

3 STAMINA are five oblong, erect filaments, the length of the calyx, having simple antheræ

4 PISTILLUM consists of a thick germen, divided into three parts, and of three simple styles a little longer than the stamina, having obtuse, contiguous stigmas

5 PERICARPIUM is three inflated flaccid capsules, that are joined by a longitudinal suture, having sharp-pointed tops and opening within

6 SEMINA are two, hard, smooth, and almost globular

# C H A P. LXXXII.

## *S T E W A R T I A.*

This ſhrub deſcribed.

THERE is only one ſpecies of this genus, called *Stewartia*. It is a ſhrub of about eight or ten feet growth with us, and the branches, which are produced irregularly from the ſides of the main ſtem, are covered with a brown bark. The leaves are placed alternately on the branches, and are of much the ſize and make as thoſe of the cherry tree. Their upper ſurfaces are of a fine green, though they are lighter and hairy underneath, and have their edges moſt acutely ſerrated. In the beginning of June this tree will be in blow. The flowers are produced from the ſides of the branches. They are white, and ſeem to be compoſed of five large oval petals, but upon examining them to the bottom, we find them joined at the baſe. The flowers have a genteel look, are poſſeſſed of an air of delicacy, and this being at preſent a very ſcarce plant, makes it more valuable. It was named *Stewartia* in honour of the Right Hon. the Earl of Bute, as a compliment to his great ſkill in the ſcience of botany.

Method of propagating it by layers,

*Stewartia* is to be propagated by layers and ſeeds. The young ſhoots ſhould be layered in autumn, by making a ſlit at the joint, as is practiſed for carnations. In the ſpring, a tall hedge of ſome kind ſhould be made on the ſouth ſide of them, bending alſo a little towards the eaſt and weſt, that they may be ſhaded all the ſummer. In dry weather they ſhould be watered, and then they ſhould remain until the March following, when they ſhould be examined to ſee if they have ſtruck root; for ſometimes they will ſtrike root pretty freely, if ſo ſhaded and watered, and ſometimes they have diſappointed our expectations after waiting two years, though cuttings will ſometimes grow. In March, however, a ſufficient quantity of pots muſt be provided, filled with good garden mould, mixed with a ſhare of drift ſand, and the layers ſhould be taken up, whether they have ſtruck root or not, and planted in theſe pots, which muſt then be plunged up to the rims in a bark-bed. Thoſe layers that have no roots will have the parts ready for ſtriking, and this aſſiſtance will ſet them all forward, ſo that in a very little time they will become good plants. They muſt be hardened as ſoon as poſſible to the open air. For this purpoſe the pots ſhould be taken out of the beds, and plunged up to the rims in a ſhady place, and though theſe are hardy trees, it will be proper to take the pots up, and remove them into the greenhouſe, or under ſome ſhelter, for the firſt winter. At the latter end of March they may be turned out of the pots, with their mould, into the places where they are wanted for good.

and by ſeeds.

Another method of propagating theſe plants is from ſeeds, which we receive from abroad. Theſe ſhould be ſown in pots of light earth, about half an inch deep, and the pots ſhould be plunged up to the rims in a bark bed, where all the advantages of heat, water, and ſhade, muſt be afforded them; for without theſe requiſites, it is not often that they will grow. After they are come up, ſhade and watering muſt be conſtantly given them, neither muſt the hardening them to the open air be too long deferred. When this is done, the pots ſhould be taken up and plunged up to the rims in a ſhady border, and in the autumn they ſhould be removed into the greenhouſe, or placed under an hotbed-frame during the winter. In the ſpring, the plant ſhould have the benefit of the bark-bed as before, have conſtant ſhade and water, and be again hardened to the open air, then they ſhould reſume their former ſtations in a ſhady border, and in the autumn be removed into the greenhouſe as before. This method muſt be practiſed for the year following, for even when they are three-years old ſeedlings, it is not often that they are large plants. Being now three years old, each plant muſt be ſet in a ſeparate pot in March, and a bark-bed prepared for them, in which they muſt be plunged. This will forward their ſtriking root, and promote their growth, eſpecially if water and ſhade be ſtill allowed them. Theſe muſt be hardened again as uſual, and the pots plunged up to the rims in a ſhady border, to prevent the mould drying, and in the autumn they ſhould be ſet in the greenhouſe with the other plants. They will by this time have become pretty good plants. At the end of March, they may be turned out of the pots, with the mould, into the places where they are deſigned to remain for good. It will be proper to water and ſhade them during the firſt ſummer, after that they will require no more care, the plant being naturally hardy enough, and when it has taken to the ground, and got to any ſize, will be in little danger of ſuffering either by heat or cold.

Title of this tree.

There being no other ſpecies of this genus, it ſtands ſimply with the name, *Stewartia*. Michell calls it, *Malacodendron*. It is a native of Virginia.

Claſs and order in the Linnæan ſyſtem.

*Stewartia* is of the claſs and order *Monadelphia Polyandria*, and the characters are,

The characters.

1. CALYX is a monophyllous, permanent perianthium, divided into five oval, concave, patent ſegments.
2. COROLLA conſiſts of five large, equal, oval, patent petals.
3. STAMINA. The filaments are numerous, ſlender, coaleſce into a cylinder at the bottom, and are ſhorter than the corolla, to which they are connected at their baſe. The antheræ are roundiſh and incumbent.
4. PISTILLUM conſiſts of a roundiſh hairy germen, and of five filiforme ſtyles the length of the ſtamina, with obtuſe ſtigmas.
5. PERICARPIUM is a five-lobed juiceleſs apple, containing five cells.
6. SEMINA. The ſeeds are ſingle, oval, and compreſſed.

# CHAP. LXXXIII.

## *STYRAX*, The STORAX-TREE.

Situation proper for this genus.

OUR plantations muſt never be without the *Styrax*, if any dry, warm, well ſheltered place is to be found in them, as it is ſo delightful an aromatic as to be exceeded by few, either in the wood or flowers, and has alſo ſcarcity to recommend it, not to mention the deſire which muſt naturally poſſeſs even the incurious, of being maſters of a tree ſo famous in medicine as the *Styrax* is known to be. There is only one objection to the admiſſion of this plant, and that is, its being thought too tender for the cold of our winters, as it has hitherto been treated like a greenhouſe-plant, or at moſt a few only have been planted againſt warm walls, to be covered with mats, &c. at the firſt approach of danger. This, I muſt own, has with good reaſon been the treatment of theſe plants. But if they are raiſed and treated as hardy greenhouſe plants, for the firſt ſix or ſeven years, when they will be ſtrong and woody, they may be planted in the warmeſt parts of the wilderneſs, where they will grow, and endure the cold of our ordinary winters very well, and will every winter get harder, and conſequently undergo leſs danger of ſuffering by hard weather. But to proceed to its deſcription.

Deſcription of this tree.

The *Styrax*, in its native places of growth, will arrive to be more than twenty feet high; with us, twelve or fourteen feet is the height we may expect it to grow to. The branches are covered with a ſmooth greyiſh bark, and the younger ſhoots are of a reddiſh colour. The very wood of this tree is finely ſcented, and in Turkey and other places where it naturally grows, that fragrant reſin called Storax exſudes from its trunk, an inciſion being firſt made. The virtues of this reſin are well known, and the tree is conſidered valuable on that account. The leaves which ornament the ſlender branches, that are produced without order all around, are of a moderate ſize, and of an oval, pointed figure. Their edges are a little waved, though free from ſerratures. They grow on ſhort footſtalks, without any order, being ſometimes by pairs, ſometimes ſingly, keeping nothing but irregularity, with which they thus in a pleaſing manner ornament the plant. They a little reſemble the leaves of the quince-tree, and are of two colours, their upper ſurface is of a lucid green, but their under is hoary, and this difference of colours makes a good contraſt, eſpecially when waving with the wind, on this charming ſweet ſcented tree. The flowers are produced in June, from the ſides of the branches, in bunches; ſeven or eight flowers will conſtitute a tuft. Their form and colour ſomewhat reſemble thoſe of the orange tree, and their odours are diffuſed all around. Theſe flowers are ſucceeded by no fruit with us, ſo that the acme of its beauty is when it is in full blow.

Method of propagating this tree.

The propagation of the *Styrax* is from ſeeds, which we receive from abroad. Theſe muſt be ſown an inch deep, in pots of light ſandy earth, which pots ſhould be plunged in a ſhady well-ſheltered place, there to remain until the ſecond ſpring after ſowing. In March the ſeeds will be ready to ſprout, and to aſſiſt them, it will be neceſſary to take up the pots, and ſet them up to the rims in an hot bed. When the plants come up, all convenient air muſt be given them, often water, and they ſhould be hardened ſoon to the open air. They ſhould be then ſet abroad in the ſhade, and in the winter ſhould be removed into the greenhouſe, and placed under ſhelter. In the ſpring it will not be neceſſary to force them a ſecond time in the hot bed, for if the pots be ſet in a ſhady place up to the rims, and now and then a little watering afforded them, the plants will grow very well, and make good ſhoots that ſummer. Like greenhouſe-plants, at the approach of winter, they muſt be removed into ſhelter, and in ſpring they muſt be ſhook out of theſe larger pots, and each planted in a ſeparate ſmall pot, and being well watered, if they are plunged in a hot bed, it will ſet them growing finely. After they have had help this way, they muſt be ſoon hardened, and the pots taken up, and ſet up to the rims in mould in a ſhady place. In winter they ſhould be placed in the greenhouſe as before, and this method muſt be continued for ſix or eight years, treating them exactly as hardy greenhouſe plants, and ſhifting them into freſh pots, as their encreaſe of ſize by growth requires. By this time they will be woody and ſtrong, and may then, the beginning of April, be turned out of the pots, with the mould, into the places where they are deſigned to remain. If the ſoil be naturally dry and warm, and the place well ſheltered, nothing but very ſevere froſts will injure them, eſpecially after having ſtood a winter or two, and thereby become proportionally harder and larger.

*Styrax* is a genus without any other ſpecies, and is titled ſimply, *Styrax*. Caſpar Bauhine calls it, *Styrax folio mali cotonei*; and Cammerarius, *Styrax*. It grows naturally in many parts of Italy, particularly about Rome, is very common alſo in Paleſtine, is found in plenty in the hotteſt parts of Syria, and grows wild in moſt parts of the Eaſt.

*Styrax* is of the claſs and order *Decandria Monogynia*; and the characters are,

1. CALYX is a ſhort, cylindric, erect, monophyllous perianthium, indented in five parts at the top.

2. COROLLA is one petal, of an infundibuliforme ſhape. The tube is ſhort and of the length of the calyx. The limb is large and patent, and divided into lanceolate, obtuſe ſegments.

3. STAMINA are more than twelve erect, awl-ſhaped filaments, placed in a circular manner, and inſerted in the corolla, having oblong erect antheræ.

4. PISTILLUM conſiſts of a roundiſh germen, ſituated below the flower, a ſingle ſtyle the length of the ſtamina, and a truncated ſtigma.

5. PERICARPIUM is a roundiſh drupe of one cell.

6. SEMINA are two roundiſh, pointed nuts, convex on one ſide, and flat on the other.

CHAP.

# CHAP. LXXXIV.

## *SYRINGA*, LILAC.

THERE are many ſorts of the Lilac, which are exceeded by few other plants, in the beauty or grandeur of the ſhow they make when in blow, which excels almoſt any thing of the flowering-tree kind; though their commonneſs occaſions their being neglected by many perſons; a crime which ought never to be committed againſt theſe plants, and which is ſtill rendered more heinous, as their flowers poſſeſs, beſides majeſtic beauty, a very delightful fragrance. Though the varieties are numerous, the real diſtinct ſpecies are only two,

Species.

1. Common Lilac.
2. Perſian Lilac, or Perſian Jeſſamine.

Common Lilac.

1. Common Lilac. The varieties of this ſpecies are,

Varieties.

The Purple Lilac.
The Blue Lilac.
The White Lilac.

Perſian Lilac.

2. Perſian Lilac. The varieties of this ſpecies are called,

Varieties.

The Common Perſian Lilac, or Perſian Jeſſamine.
The White Perſian Lilac.
The Blue Perſian Lilac.
The Cut-leaved Perſian Lilac, or Perſian Jeſſamine.

General deſcription of the ſorts.

The firſt three ſorts have nearly the ſame majeſtic grandeur peculiar to them all; and as the colours of the flowers are quite oppoſite, as the titles ſet forth, there are hardly any three diſtinct ſpecies which afford varieties more pleaſing, or make a greater or ſtronger contraſt.

The Purple Lilac generally riſes to the higheſt ſize of any of the three ſorts, though the height of all of them is either greater or leſs, according to the ſoil in which they are planted. The Purple, in good, light, rich earth, will grow to be ſixteen or twenty feet high; and the others, in the ſame ſort of mould, nearly as high. The Purple Lilac is naturally of an upright growth, though it ſoon divides into branches; and theſe alſo, as the tree grows older, into others, all of which are covered with a ſmooth browniſh bark. All winter the plant has a bold and healthy look, occaſioned by the large and turgid purpliſh buds, which will have begun to ſwell early the preceding ſummer, and which will burſt forth into leaf ſoon in the ſpring following. The leaves are large and ſmooth, and of a pleaſant dark-green colour. They are of an oval, cordated figure, end in acute points, and grow oppoſite by pairs on the branches. The flowers will be produced in May, at the end of the ſame ſpring's ſhoot, in very large and almoſt conical bunches. They are of a purpliſh colour, are cloſely placed, and the number of which each bunch is compoſed is very great. I have meaſured a bunch of them which has been a foot long; and can any thing be thought to excel ſuch a profuſion of flowers, in its aggregate ſtate, of which each cluſter is compoſed! But many of theſe flowers appear all over the tree, mixed in an eaſy manner, among the delightful leaves, ſome peeping as it were above them, and ſeveral reclining their tops, to make the appearance ſtill more free and eaſy. The value of theſe flowers is ſtill heightened by their delightful fragrance; and when their blow is over, which will be in a fortnight or three weeks, they have paid us their tribute, except what they afford from their leaves and manner of growth; for they are ſucceeded by ſeed-veſſels, of ſuch a colour and nature as none but the curious botaniſt can find any pleaſure in obſerving.

The Blue Lilac differs in no reſpect from the Purple, except that the branches are rather more ſlender and leſs erect, and that it ſeldom riſes higher than twelve or fourteen feet. The branches are covered with a ſmooth browniſh bark; and the buds in the winter will be turgid like the former, tho' ſmaller, and they, as well as the young ſhoots, will have a blueiſh tinge. The leaves are exactly like the preceding ſort, tho' they will have a caſt with blue. The flowers are produced in May, in not quite ſuch large bunches as the former ſort; the bunches will be alſo looſe. They are of a fine blue colour, and admirably ſcented; and the preference is to be given with juſtice to neither of theſe trees.

The White Lilac ſeems rather a ſtiffer plant than the Blue, and the branches grow more erect than any of the ſorts. The young branches are covered with a ſmooth light-coloured bark; and in winter the buds, which will be large and turgid, are of an herbaceous yellow colour, by which this ſort at that ſeaſon may eaſily be diſtinguiſhed from the others. The leaves are of the ſame figure and nature, though their colour is lighter, thereby making a variety. The flowers are of a fine white colour, and are produced in the ſame kind of large cloſe panicles as the others, which ſtand upright. They are very fair, and in the bunches are ſet very cloſely together, which cauſes them to be more erect than either of the two former ſorts. Thus may any perſon who has never ſeen theſe trees form an idea of their beauty when in blow; which will be very early, when the plants are ſmall; for they will begin flowering at the height of four or five feet, and will every year after afford greater plenty of flowers as they advance in growth. The bunches generally grow by pairs, two at the end of the ſame ſpring ſhoot, though of unequal ſize, the one being generally much larger than the other.

2. Perſian Lilac.

The Common Perſian Lilac ſeldom grows higher than five feet, and is deemed a moſt delightful flowering-ſhrub. The branches are long, ſlender, flexible, and covered with a ſmooth browniſh bark, with a blueiſh tinge, on which are often ſeveral yellowiſh punctules. The buds will be large and turgid in winter; and the leaves and flower-buds will come out early in ſpring. The leaves are of a lanceolate figure, of a fine green colour, and grow oppoſite by pairs on the branches. The flowers will be in full blow before the end of May. They are of a blueiſh colour, and are produced in the ſame kind of panicles as the other ſorts, though they will be ſmaller and looſer. Their odour is more heightened than that of the others; and the ſhrub, on the whole, is very valuable, though now pretty common. The long flexible branches have a natural tendency to hang downwards, and when in blow their bunches of flowers will greatly encrease this tendency, on which account it will be proper to place a few sticks to support them, which may be disposed in such a manner as to escape notice, unless by the nicest examiner; and this will be proper, as the seeing the branches tied to sticks in full view, would shew a degree of baldness which would not look well.

White Persian Lilac will grow to the same height with the former. The leaves, buds, and shoots are of a lighter colour. It produces its flowers at the end of May, in the same kind of panicles as the other, though these are of a white colour, and possessed of the same delightful odour. This is all the variety this shrub will cause from the other.

Blue Persian Lilac differs from the preceding in that the flowers are of a deep blue colour, thereby causing an admirable variety on that account.

Cut-leaved Persian Lilac affords the greatest variety by its leaves, though the bark is rather darker, and the twigs seem slenderer, and are still more inclined to bend downwards. The leaves of this sort are divided almost to the mid-rib, into an uncertain number of segments; and as this occasions them to have a different, an unfrequent, and singular look, the value of the plant is much heightened on that account, particularly as it is in no respect diminished in the elegance and fragrance of its flowers.

Method of propagating these species by layers. The best way of propagating all these sorts is by layers; for if this work be performed in autumn, on the young shoots, they will be good plants by the autumn following. This method is particularly to be preferred in the three first sorts of Lilacs, as they naturally throw out such plenty of suckers as to weaken, unless constantly taken off, and diminish the beauty of the mother-plants. Plants raised by layering will be less liable to throw out suckers, and consequently will be more valuable. The common way, indeed, is to take up the suckers, and plant them in the nursery for a year or two, and then set them out for good: but these plants will not be so valuable as the others, as they will be more liable to produce suckers, which to the gardener, when he has got a sufficient stock of plants, are often very troublesome.

Suckers, The Persian sorts being less liable to put up suckers, may not only be encreased by layers, but when they do throw out any, the suckers may be taken up, and deemed good plants.

Cuttings. Cuttings of these sorts, also, planted in August, in a shady moist place, will often grow.

The Persian Lilacs never produce seeds with us, but the first three sorts do, and by these the plants may be encreased; which also is a good method. The seeds ripen in the autumn, and in October they should be sown. They are rather small, and therefore the mould of the bed should be very fine, and they should be covered over lightly. In the spring they will come up, and will want no other care than weeding. In the spring following they may be planted in the nursery, a foot asunder, and two feet distant in the rows, and here they may stand two or three years, when they will be of a proper size to plant out for good, and will flower in a year or two after. The differences of all these three sorts are generally permanent from seeds, so that a person may sow them with reasonable hopes of obtaining the like kinds of sorts the seeds were gathered from. and seeds.

Titles. 1. Common Lilac is titled *Syringa foliis ovato cordatis*. Old authors have distinguished the three sorts according to their colours; thus, Caspar Bauhine calls the Blue Lilac, *Syringa caerulea*, and so of the rest. It grows naturally about Persia, and also in some parts of Egypt.

2. Persian Lilac is, *Syringa foliis lanceolatis*. In the *Hortus Cliffortianus* it is termed, *Syringa foliis lanceolatis integris*, also, *Syringa foliis lanceolatis integris dissectisque laciniatis*. Caspar Bauhine calls it, *Ligustrum foliis laciniatis*. Tournefort, *Lilac laciniato folio*. Plukenet, *Syringa Babylonica, foliis dissectis densioribus foliis*, and Cornutus, *Agem-lilac Persarum*. It grows common in Persia.

Class and order in the Linnaean system. *Syringa* is of the class and order *Diandria Monogynia*; and the characters are,

The characters. 1. CALYX is a small, tubulated, monophyllous, permanent perianthium, divided at the brim into four parts, which are erect.

2. COROLLA consists of one funnel-shaped petal. The tube is cylindric and very long, and the limb is divided into four narrow, obtuse, patent, revolute segments.

3. STAMINA are two very short filaments, placed within the tube of the corolla.

4. PISTILLUM consists of an oblong germen, a filiforme style the length of the stamina, and a thick bifid stigma.

5. PERICARPIUM is an oblong, compressed, acuminated capsule, formed of two valves, and containing two cells.

6. SEMINA. The seeds are single in each of those cells. They are oblong and compressed, acuminated at each end, and have a membranaceous border.

## CHAP. LXXXV.

## *TAMARIX*, The TAMARISK.

THERE are two species of *Tamarix* which are allowed to be very ornamental to shrubberies, called,

Species. 1. The French Tamarisk.

2. The German Tamarisk.

Description of the French. 1. The French Tamarisk will grow to the height of about fourteen feet. The branches are few, and spread abroad in an irregular manner, some being upright, others horizontal, whilst others decline with their ends towards the earth. The bark is smooth, and of a deep red or purplish colour next the sun, but on the opposite side of the branch of a pale-brown. The leaves are rather of a pale-green, and very beautiful.

They

They are very narrow, and upon examining them we find them ſcaly in ſome degree. The flowers will be produced in plenty at the ends of the branches. They grow in ſeemingly very large looſe panicles, but on examining them, we find that each is compoſed of numerous compleat flowers, which grow in ſpikes, and are produced near the extremities of the branches on the ſlender twigs all around. Each of theſe ſpikes ſeparately is but ſmall, and they are of a pale-red colour. The flowers of each ſpike are exceeding ſmall, and the number of ſtamina is five, which differs from the other ſpecies by only having half the number. This ſort flowers in July, and I have known it in full blow in September, and ſometimes in October, and even November, when the weather has been all along mild. Nothing ornamental ſucceeds the blow.

and the German Tamariſk. 2. The German Tamariſk is of lower growth, ſeldom aſpiring higher than eight or ten feet. It is a more regular tree than the former, as the branches naturally grow in an upright poſition. They are very brittle, are ſcented, and covered with a ſmooth yellowiſh bark. The leaves have a ſcaly appearance, and ſtand much cloſer together than thoſe of the other ſort. They are of an exceeding light-green colour, and very ornamental. The flowers are produced in July, at the ends of the branches, in long looſe ſpikes. Each ſeparate flower is ſmall, though much larger than the other ſorts, and is poſſeſſed of ten ſtamina, which are alternately ſhorter. Theſe ſpikes attract the attention when in blow, and are acknowledged by all to have a fine look; neither is their noble appearance loſt when the flowers are faded, but it is continued in the ſpikes even until the ſeeds are ripe, which then ſeem to diſſolve into a ſhattered down and ſcales.

Method of propagating theſe ſorts. The culture of theſe ſorts is very eaſy. Every cutting will grow that is ſet in winter, and will be a good plant by the autumn following. The encreaſing of theſe ſorts by layers has been recommended, but this is bad advice, not only as being unneceſſary trouble, when they will grow ſo freely by cuttings, but becauſe layers of this tree very often will not ſtrike root at all. I have layered them, and found them, after lying two years, without any roots, and the wound being grown up, differed from the other branches only in that the mould had a little altered the colour of the bark, which ſhould warn all perſons who want a ſtock of theſe plants to beware of layering; and this, no doubt, they will do when I aſſure them, the cuttings will ſtrike root as freely as thoſe of the common willow. The beſt time for the work is October, though any time of the winter will do. The cuttings ſhould be of the laſt ſummer's ſhoot, and a moiſt part of the garden is moſt eligible for them to be planted in. In two years, they will be good plants for the wilderneſs or ſhrubbery, and may then be planted out in almoſt any ſoil, though they beſt like a light moiſt earth, eſpecially the German ſort, as in other countries, where it grows naturally, it is generally found in low watery grounds.

Titles of this genus. 1. The French Tamariſk is titled, *Tamarix floribus pentandris*. In the *Hortus Upſalienſis* it is termed, *Tamarix pedunculis ..., floribus pentandris*. John Bauhine calls it, *Tamarix major*, Caspar Bauhine, *Tamarix altera, folio tenuiore, ſive Gallica*, and Lobel, *Tamar ſeu Narbonenſis*. It grows naturally in France, Italy, and Spain.

2. German Tamariſk is, *Tamarix floribus decandris*. Caſpar Bauhine calls it, *Tamarix fruticoſa, folio craſſiore ſive Germanica*, and Lobel, *Tamariſcus ...* It grows naturally in low overflowed places in Germany.

Claſs and order in the Linnæan Syſtem. *Tamarix* is of the claſs and order *Pentandria Trigynia*, and the characters are,

The characters. 1. CALYX is a permanent perianthium, ſhorter by half than the corolla, and divided into five obtuſe, erect ſegments.

2. COROLLA conſiſts of five oval, concave, obtuſe, patent petals.

3. STAMINA are five or ten capillary filaments, with roundiſh antheræ.

4. PISTILLUM. The germen is acuminated, there is no ſtyle, and the ſtigmas are three, oblong, revolute, and plumoſe.

5. PERICARPIUM is an oblong, acuminated, three cornered capſule, longer than the calyx, formed of three valves, and containing one cell.

6. SEMINA. The ſeeds are numerous, very ſmall, and downy.

# CHAP. LXXXVI.

## *TILIA*, The LIME or LINDEN-TREE.

Species. THERE are only two ſpecies of this genus:

1. European Lime-tree.
2. American Lime-tree.

European Lime tree. 1. European Lime-tree. What has been ſaid of the Lime amongſt the Foreſt-trees, in the Firſt Book, may ſerve here, as the reader will there plainly ſee how well this noble tree is adapted for plantations of all ſorts. One real ſpecies of our Common European Lime is all we have, though of this there are three or four varieties, as,

Varieties

The Narrow-leaved Mountain Lime.
The Broader-leaved Mountain Lime.
The Elm-leaved Lime.
The Green-twigged Lime.
The Red-twigged Lime.

deſcribed. All theſe are very inconſiderable differences, and though, if nicely obſerved, they cauſe ſome variety, yet that is ſo ſmall as not to deſerve much pains to procure them, except the Red-twigged ſort, which of all others is the moſt beautiful, becauſe, when diveſted of their leaves, its young branches exhibit their fine, ſmooth, red bark all winter, which has a pleaſing effect in all places; though in the younger plants this effect will be more ſtriking and delightful, as the bark only is red of the laſt year's ſhoots, and the ſmaller the plants are, the more of theſe and the leſs of older wood the compoſition of the tree will be; whereas, when the trees get older and large, the twigs will be ſhorter and leſs viſible, and though ſtill of a red colour, yet

yet not of so delicate a red as the young plants on their bark at first wear. Sometimes these trees will run away from their colour, and grow with green branches; but as this is not common, the Red-twigged sort must be still allowed to be preferable to all others, and the seeds of this must always be sown for the raising of sorts. As to the varieties with great, rough, or small leaves, I have no objection to a person's finding them out for the Collection if he chooses it; and what has been said on Lime-trees in the Former Book, will teach the curious planter the uses of all these sorts, and how they are to be stationed in plantations of every kind; so that I proceed now to the other species of the genus, which is at present not very common in our gardens, called,

American Lime-tree. 2. The American Linden-tree. Of this species also there are a variety or two, which indeed differ very little in appearance from those of our Common European sorts, for the leaves are heart-shaped like the others. There are a larger and a smaller-leaved sort. Their edges are finely serrated, and end in acute points. These beautifully cordated leaves that thus run into acute points, have their under surface of a paler-green than their upper. The larger-leaved kind is by far the finest sort, and the branches vary from all others of this genus, in that they are covered with a dark-brown bark. The flowers excite no attention in the Gardener; but the Botanist is delighted when he finds they are furnished with nectaria, whereas the flowers of our Common Lime-tree have none. The flowers are produced in bunches like our common sort, but make no better figure. They are very fragrant, and are succeeded by coriaceous capsules, containing the seeds.

Method of propagating them by seed. The culture of the Lime-tree has already been sufficiently shewn under that Chapter in the Former Book. Seeds are there recommended as the best method, and this should be practised for raising the American sorts as well as our own; though if we have not the conveniency of procuring the seeds from abroad, a few plants must be obtained. These should be planted in a light rich soil, if such can be had, for in such they will shoot the strongest, though almost any other will do. After these plants have stood a year or two, they should be headed near the ground, for stools. They will then shoot out many young branches from these, which may be layered in the autumn; though if they stand two years there will be greater plenty of young twigs for layering, for every shoot of the first summer will the year following divide into several. When the layering of these is to be performed, which ought to be in the autumn, the strong two-years shoots must be brought down, and if they are stiff and do not bend readily, they must have a gentle plash with the knife near the bottom, a slit should be made at the joint for every one of the youngest twigs, and their ends bent backwards that the slit may keep open. This being done, the mould must be levelled among the layers, and the ends of them taken off to within one eye of the ground. The business is then done; and the autumn following they will have all good roots, many of which will be strong, and fit to plant out for good, whilst the weakest may be removed into the nursery-ground, in rows, to gain strength.

All the sorts of Lime-trees will also grow from cuttings; but this I ever found to be an uncertain method; and if it was more certain, plants raised either by them or layers are not near so good as those raised from seeds, which way ought always to be practised where they can be obtained. Where that is not to be done, any art must be used to obtain some few plants; and if the gardener should happen to procure a cutting or two of the American sorts, set them in pots, and plunge them in the bark-bed, let him water and shade them, and they will be sure to grow; and these he may afterwards encrease at pleasure. and cuttings.

1. The European Lime or Linden-tree is entitled, *Tilia floribus nectario destitutis*. Authors have hitherto distinguished the sorts by titles expressive of them in this manner, thus, Caspar Bauhine calls it, *Tilia femina, folio majore*; also, *Tilia montana maximo folio*; also, *Tilia femina, folio minore*; Ray, *Tilia foliis molliter hirsutis, viminibus rubris, fructu tetragono*; also, *Tilia ulmi folio, semine hexagono*; Gesner, *Tilia urbana*; Tilli, *Tilia Bohemica, foliis minoribus glabris, fructu oblongo utrinque acuminato minime costulato*; and John Bauhine, *Tilia vulgaris Platyphyllos*. It grows naturally in England, and most parts of Europe. Titles of these species.

2. American Lime-tree is titled, *Tilia floribus nectario instructis*. Gronovius calls it, *Tilia foliis majoribus mucronatis*; Plukenet, *Tilia, amplissimis glabris foliis, nostrati similis*. It is a native of Virginia and Canada.

*Tilia* is of the class and order *Polyandria Monogynia*; and the characters are, Class and order in the Linnæan system. The characters.

1. Calyx is a concave, coloured, deciduous perianthium, divided into five parts, and nearly the size of the corolla.

2. Corolla are five oblong, obtuse petals, crenated at the tops.

3. Stamina are numerous (thirty or more) awl-shaped filaments, the length of the corolla, having simple antheræ.

4. Pistillum consists of a roundish germen, a filiforme style the length of the stamina, and a five-cornered obtuse stigma.

5. Pericarpium is a coriaceous, globular capsule, of five valves, containing five cells, and opening at the base.

6. Semina. The seeds are single and roundish. Though the cells are five, it is seldom that more than one seed in the capsule is ripened; and this so occupies the room of the others, that, to the less cautious observer, the capsule appears to be unilocular.

CHAP

# C H A P LXXXVII.

## *VIBURNUM*, The WAYFARING-TREE.

THE *Viburnum*, the *Tinus*, and the *Opulus*, of authors are now found to be of the same family, and accordingly are all included under the generical word *Viburnum*. The *Tinus* affords us three of the finest sorts of flowering evergreens; and the deciduous species for this place are,

Species. 1. The *Viburnum* (commonly so called), or Wayfaring tree, or Pliant-Meally-tree.
2. The Serrated-leaved *Viburnum*.
3. The Virginian Entire-leaved *Viburnum*.
4. The Black Haw.
5. The Marsh Elder.
6. Maple-leaved *Viburnum*.
7. Bastard *Cassine*, Cassioberry-bush, or South Sea *Thea*.

Wayfaring tree. 1. The Wayfaring-tree will grow to be twenty or more feet high, though it may be kept down to any height desired; and in such gardens as are at a distance from the places where it grows common, and in which it has not been before observed, in such gardens, I say, it is enquired after, and attracts the attention of those who walk therein, almost as much as any shrub in the whole Collection. The branches are not very numerous, and in winter they are covered with a smooth greyish bark, inclined to a brown colour, especially near the bottom of the shoot. The younger, as they shoot, are white and downy, and the ends, especially in winter, feel soft and woolly. The branches are long, and exceeding tough. They will often shoot near six feet from the bottom in a year; and where they grow common, they make the best bands for faggotting; and even where they do not, the young squire will steal a shoot out of the shrubbery for riding switches, for which they are excellent, for the summer's use. The leaves are very large, heart-shaped, very full of large veins, and have their edges serrated. Their upper surface is of a dark green colour, but their under is white and like cotton; and they are placed opposite by pairs on the branches. The flowers are produced at the ends of the branches; the buds will be formed the preceding summer, which continue to get larger in the autumn, all winter they will be in a state of encrease, and at that season they terminate the ends of the branches like so many rough buttons. The flowers, when out, will be in large umbels, to form which these buds encrease in size all spring, but shew little of what may be expected from them until about May, when they begin to divide, and shew that they are growing to be bunches of flowers. In June, they will be wholly out, and formed into large umbels; they are of a white colour, and have a most noble look. These flowers are succeeded by berries, which are also ornamental, and cause variety; for they will be first of a fine red colour, and afterwards of a deep black.

Varieties. There is a variety of this sort, with more oval leaves, but the differences are very inconsiderable in all respects.

There is also the Striped-leaved *Viburnum*, which is coveted by those who are fond of variegated plants.



2. The Virginian Serrated-leaved *Viburnum* is so called because the leaves are more beautifully serrated than any of the sorts. It is at present not a very common plant with us, and is in much esteem by all persons of true taste. Its growth, leaves, and flowers, are not so large as the former, but they are of a more genteel growth. It will grow to the height of about ten feet. The bark is smooth and of a light colour, and the leaves are of a fine light green. They are tolerably large, though nothing like those of the other sorts, and stand on longish footstalks, which give them a fine air. They are strongly veined, and have their edges finely serrated. They are of a roundish, oval figure, and are placed opposite by pairs on the branches. The flowers are produced in June, at the ends of the branches, in very large round bunches. Their colour is white; they appear in June; and are seldom succeeded by any berries in England. Virginian Serrated

3. Virginian Entire-leaved *Viburnum*. The sorts of *Laurustinus* are evergreens, and have all entire leaves; but this species with entire leaves agrees in every respect in description with two sorts, one of which sheds its leaves in winter, whilst the other retains its verdure during that season. The deciduous kind grows to about ten feet high. The younger branches are covered with a smooth, deep red bark, whilst those of the older are smooth, and of a dark brown colour. The leaves are pretty large, and of a delightful shining green on their upper surface, but their under is paler, and much veined. They are of a lanceolated, oval figure, though their ends are rounded; their edges are entire, and they stand opposite by pairs on the branches. The flowers are produced in July at the ends of the branches in large umbels, their colour is white, and they have much the resemblance of those of the common *Laurustinus*, though they are rather smaller. They have a genteel look, and are succeeded by berries, which never ripen with us. and Entire-leaved Viburnum.

4. Plum-leaved *Viburnum*, or Black Haw. This species, for the most part, goes by the name of Black Haw, because the fruit a little resembles that of the Haw, though of a black colour. It will grow to be about ten feet high; and the branches are covered with a smooth reddish bark. The leaves are oval, and not so large as any of the other sorts, being seldom more than two inches long, and proportionally broad. They are of a light pleasant green colour, and have their edges finely serrated. Their footstalks are pretty short, and they grow for the most part opposite by pairs on the branches. The flowers are produced in June, at the ends of the branches, in large umbels. Their colour is white, but they are seldom succeeded by berries in England. Plum-leaved Viburnum

5. Marsh Elder. Of this species there are two notable varieties: Marsh Elder.

Marsh Elder with Flat Flowers. Varieties.

Gelder-Rose.

The Marsh Elder with Flat Flowers will grow to be a tree near twenty feet high. The young branches are covered with a smooth and almost described.

Fee white

white bark They are often produced oppoſite by pairs, tho' in general they are of an irregular growth The young ſhoots will be cornered, and this is more perfect in the more vigorous ones, being compoſed of five or ſix flat ſides The leaves are large and ornamental, of a fine green colour and a ſoft contexture, compoſed of three large lobes, which are jagged at their edges, and grow on glandulous footſtalks In autumn theſe leaves have exquiſite beauty, for they die to ſo fine a red, as to have a ſtriking effect at that ſeaſon The flowers are produced in large umbels, the beginning of June, all over the tree and have a grand look Each umbel is compoſed of very many hermaphrodite flowers, which of themſelves make no great figure, but they are ſurrounded by a border of male flowers, which are white, and are ſo ornamental to each buſh as to throw a luſtre over the whole tree Neither does this ſhrub ceaſe to exhibit its beauties when the flowers are over, for beſides what it affords by its leaves which are inferior to few other trees, both in ſummer and autumn, the hermaphrodite flowers will be ſucceeded by fine ſcarlet berries, which will grow in ſuch large bunches, and be produced in ſuch plenty all over the ſhrub, as to give it in appearance ſuperior to almoſt any thing of the berry kind, and were it not for its commonneſs, this would, on their account only, be ranked amongſt trees of the firſt value

The Gelder-Roſe is a variety only of the preceding ſort, its original was accidental and it is kept up and continued by culture in our gardens The nature of the ſhoots, and ſize of the tree, together with the colour of the bark, differ in no reſpect from the former The leaves alſo are of the ſame form, are produced in the ſame manner, and die away to the ſame delightful red in the autumn The variety this ſort occaſions, then, is by the flowers, and by theſe this variety is ſo great, as to be exceeded by ſcarcely any two diſtinct ſpecies whatſoever They are produced in the beginning of June, all over the tree, in large globular bunches Each bunch is compoſed of numerous male flowers, of the ſame nature with thoſe that ſurround the hermaphrodite flowers of the former ſort Their colour is white, like thoſe, but being produced in large globular heads, and in great plenty, have a much finer appearance And indeed it is delightful to ſee this tree uſher in the month of June, as it were, with its glorious flowers, which will then at a diſtance have the appearance of balls of ſnow, lodged in a pleaſing manner all over its head The common people, who with artleſs taſte often call things properly enough by outward appearances (the criterion only by which they can judge), have not improperly named this the Snowball-tree, the Queen-Cuſhion, &c by which cant terms it has been long known amongſt them The flowers of the Marſh Elder being hermaphrodites, as has been obſerved, are ſucceeded by ornamental bunches of ſcarlet berries, but theſe being all male flowers, are ſucceeded by no fruit, ſo that though this ſort exceeds the former in the beauty of its flowers, that, in return has the preference by its autumnal ſhow of fruit

Maple leaved Viburnum

6 Maple-leaved *Viburnum* This is a middle-ſized ſhrub, ſending forth ſeveral branches, which are tough, and full of pith The leaves are compoſed of three principal lobes, like thoſe of the Maple-tree, and grow on ſmooth footſtalks The flowers come out from the ſides of the branches, in umbels Their colour is white, they appear in June, and are rarely ſucceeded by ſeeds in England

Baſtard Caſſine

7 Baſtard *Caſſine*, Caſſioberry-buſh, or South Sea *Thea*, is rather tender, will grow to about ten feet in height forming itſelf into a buſh by riſing with three or four ſtems, and ſending forth numerous branches from the bottom to the top The leaves are of an oblong, lanceolated figure, ſerrated, grow oppoſite by pairs, and continue on the trees until the nipping froſts come on, inſomuch that in the early part of the mild winter, they have been taken for an evergreen Theſe leaves are of an exceeding bitter nature, if chewed, tho' it is ſaid that an infuſion of them proves efficacious in removing pain, bracing a relaxed ſtomach, and reſtoring a loſt appetite The flowers are produced in bunches from the ſides of the branches Their colour is white, they appear at the end of July and are ſucceeded by red berries in the autumn Whenever this plant is to have a ſhare in a Collection, a naturally warm dry ſoil, that is well ſheltered, muſt be ſought for it otherwiſe there is a chance for loſing it again or if the plant is not wholly deſtroyed, the young branches will be killed, and the tree ſo hurt with the winter's froſt as to have rather a bad appearance with others in the ſpring

Method of propagating the different ſorts

The firſt ſix ſorts are very eaſily propagated, either by ſeeds, layers, or cuttings No particular art need be uſed for the ſeeds, whether they be of the ſorts of our own ripening, or of thoſe we receive from abroad A border of common garden-mould made fine will be ſufficient, though it may be proper to obſerve, that many of them will lie until the ſecond ſpring before they appear The beds, before and after the plants are come up, will want nothing except weeding, and when they are a year or two old, they may be planted in the nurſery, at ſmall diſtances, and in two or three years more they will be fit to plant out for good

They are all eaſily propagated by layers alſo, for if branches are pegged down, and the mould any how thrown on them, they will have plenty of roots by the next autumn, and moſt of them will be good plants for almoſt any place This freedom, however, ſhould be given to none but thoſe of our own country, for the American ſorts, as being ſtrangers, demand more care and neatneſs in the performance

They are alſo eaſily propagated by cuttings, for the young ſhoots of theſe trees cut into lengths, and planted in a moiſt garden ſoil, in the autumn, will any of them grow, and this is our common method of propagating them So that if a perſon has only a few plants of the American kinds, the beſt way is to make uſe of encreaſing them by layers

If a large quantity is wanted, the beſt way is to raiſe the Marſh Elder by ſeeds As the Gelder-Roſe is a male flowering variety, and never produces any ſeeds, it muſt always be propagated by layers or cuttings, by which the variety will always be preſerved

The ſeventh ſpecies is propagated by layers The young ſhoots are fit for this purpoſe, and when they have taken root, if they are planted in pots, and protected for two or three winters until they are grown ſtrong plants, either in a greenhouſe, under a hotbed frame, or ſome cover, there will be leſs danger of loſing them than by planting them immediately in the nurſery, or where they are to remain for good However, a perſon who has not theſe conveniences, muſt fix on the warmeſt and beſt ſheltered ſpot he can find, and having prepared the ground, let the layers be taken from the old plants in the ſpring, if the weather be moiſt, it will be ſo much the better, and let him plant them in the nurſery,

ſery, row by row, at two feet aſunder In the ſummer, they ſhould be watered in dry weather, and when the winter froſts begin to come on, the ground ſhould be covered with peaſe-ſtraw almoſt rotten, old thatch, or tanners bark, to keep them from penetrating the roots By this means many of the plants will be preſerved, and this care may be repeated every winter until they are planted out for good But this is not ſo good or ſo ſafe a method as potting them, and managing them as before directed, for they may be then turned out of their pots, when wanted, mould and all together, without feeling the effect of a removal The Cape Phillyrea is propagated in the ſame manner, only the plants are too tender to ſtand out thro' our winters, ſo muſt always be preſerved in the greenhouſe

Titles 1 The title of the *Viburnum* is, *Viburnum foliis cordatis ſerratis venoſis ſubtus tomentoſis* In the *Hortus Cliffortianus* it is termed ſimply, *Viburnum* Caſpar Bauhine calls it, *Viburnum vulgo*, Dodonæus, *Lantana*, and Gerard, *Lantana ſive Viburnum*. It grows naturally in the hedges about Buckingham, in many parts of Hertfordſhire and Bedfordſhire, and in ſome parts of Leiceſterſhire It delights chiefly in a chalky or marly ſoil, and, in ſhort, in ſuch places it is generally found growing in the hedges in moſt of the northern parts of Europe

2 The Virginian Serrated leaved *Viburnum* is, *Viburnum foliis ovatis dentato-ſerratis plicatis* It is a native of Virginia

3 Virginian Entire leaved *Viburnum* is, *Viburnum foliis integerrimis lanceolato-ovatis* It is a native of Virginia

4 Plum leaved *Viburnum*, or Black Haw, is, *Viburnum foliis ſubrotundis crenato ſerratis glabris* Plukenet calls it, *Meſpilus prunifolia Virginiana non ſpinoſa, fructu nigricante*, and Vaillant, *Viburnum Canadenſe glabrum* It grows common in Virginia and Canada

5 The Marſh Elder is, *Viburnum foliis lobatis, petiolis glanduloſis* In the *Hortus Cliffortianus* it is termed, *Opulus* Caſpar Bauhine calls it, *Sambucus aquatica, flore ſimplici*, alſo, *Sambucus aquatica, flore globoſo pleno*, Dodonæus, *Sambucus paluſtris*, Parkinſon, *Sambucus paluſtris ſeu aquatica*, and Gerard, *Sambucus aquatilis ſeu paluſtris* It grows for the moſt part in moiſt watery ground in moſt parts of Europe, though I have often found it in hedges, on the ſides of dry hills, full of berries, and very beautiful

6 Maple-leaved *Viburnum* is, *Viburnum foliis lobatis, petiolis lævibus* Gronovius calls it, *Opulus* It grows naturally in Virginia

7 Baſtard *Caſſine*, Caſſioberry-buſh, or South-Sea *Thea*, is, *Viburnum foliis ovalis crenatis glabris, petiolis eglandulatis carinatis* Du Hamel calls it, *Viburnum phillyreæ folio* In Miller's Dictionary it is termed, *Caſſine foliis ovato-lanceolatis ſerratis oppoſitis deciduis, floribus corymboſis* It grows naturally in Virginia and Carolina

*Viburnum* is of the claſs and order *Pentandria Trigynia*, and the characters are, Claſs and order in the Linnæan ſyſtem

1 Calyx is a very ſmall permanent perianthium, indented in five parts The characters

2 Corolla is a campanulated petal, half cut into five obtuſe, reflexed ſegments

3 Stamina are five ſubulated filaments, the length of the corolla, having roundiſh antheræ

4 Pistillum The germen is roundiſh, and placed below the receptacle There is no ſtyle, but in the room of it, a turbinated glandule The ſtigmas are three

5 Pericarpium is a roundiſh berry, of one cell

6 Semina The ſeeds are ſingle, oſſeous, and nearly round

# C H A P. LXXXVIII.

## *VITEX*, The *AGNUS CASTUS*, or the CHASTE-TREE.

Introductory obſervations THIS tree has been famous in all ages for its rare and excellent virtues, it being believed to be poſſeſſed of ſuch qualities as to conduce much to the excellent virtue of Chaſtity Hence it has interchangeably gone by the names of *Agnus Caſtus*, Chaſte-tree, or ſome other term expreſſive of that Virtue The Athenian Matrons always lay on beds of the leaves of this tree, when they celebrated the pious rites of Ceres, and ſo univerſal, antiently, was the belief, that a ſecret influence, conducive to the retaining of Chaſtity, was lodged in it, that not only the common people, and thoſe of moderate learning, but the moſt illuſtrious and greateſt ſcholars of antiquity believed the ſame, and vouched it as matter of fact Dioſcorides, Pliny, Theophraſtus, &c are amongſt this number So ſtrongly did Superſtition prevail, that no ranks of men, even the moſt learned and judicious, were free from her ſervitude With us it may have the ſame effect, by leading us to due reflections on that excellent virtue, and the real honour and happineſs which will always be the conſequence of preſerving it

The word *Vitex* is now at the head of this genus, of which there are four or five real ſpecies, but the ſpecies I would principally recommend for this place is that which has always been called the Chaſte-tree Of this there are two varieties

The Broad-leaved Chaſte-tree Varieties

The Narrow-leaved Chaſte-tree

One deſcription will nearly ſerve for both ſorts, though it has been obſerved, that the Narrow-leaved ſort will grow to be the talleſt For my part, I never yet ſaw one more than ſix feet, and to about that height both ſeem to have a tendency to grow The branches are produced from the bottom and ſides of the ſtalk They are very pliable, and the joints are long It is difficult to expreſs the colour of the bark, to ſay it is grey is not proper, and to ſay it is brown is not true, it is of a colour between both, tho', in different ſoils, the bark of ſome trees will be of a darker colour than others The leaves described, are

are digitated, being composed of several folioles, which so unite at their base in one common footstalk as to resemble an open hand These folioles are of a dark green colour, and their number is uncertain, being five, six, seven, and sometimes eight They are narrow, and the longest grow always in the middle, whilst the shorter occupy the outsides This character is common to both the sorts, tho' it is observable, that the folioles of the Broad-leaved sort are both shorter and broader, which occasions its being so called Their edges are also serrated, whilst those of the Narrow-leaved are intire, and in this the most important difference of these plants consists The flowers of both sorts are produced at the ends of the branches, in whorled spikes These spikes are pretty long and their colour is that of a blush purple They appear in September and October, and are not succeeded by seeds in England Each individual flower is inconsiderable, but the whole spike makes a pretty show, and the circumstances of their flowers being produced late, even often when most other flowers are over, as well as being also very fragrant, greatly heighten their value The early frosts often destroy the beauty of these spikes, before and when they are in full blow, so that it is no wonder their ornamental fruit seldom, if ever, succeeds them

There is a variety of each kind with white flowers

Method of propagating this tree by layers, The propagation of these sorts is easily done, either by layers or cuttings The young shoots being layered, any time in the winter, will have roots by the autumn following, though it will be proper not to take them up until the spring, as they shoot late in the autumn, and have often their ends destroyed by the frosts When this work is deferred till the spring, all the killed ends may be taken off, and all danger from severe frosts being over, they will meet with no check in their preparing to shoot The removing of these trees in the spring, however, is not absolutely necessary, for it may be done any time in the winter, though the cutting off the dead ends should be deferred until the latter end of March, when they should be gone over with the knife, and cut down to within an eye or two of the ground, whether planted in nursery-lines, or finally set out for good

Plenty of plants may be soon raised by cuttings About the middle of March is the best time for planting them, and they should be set in a shady border of good light garden-mould Nothing but weeding, and now and then watering, will be required all summer, though if the place is not naturally well sheltered, they must be defended from black frosts by sticking plenty of furze bushes all around them If this be judiciously done, it will take off the keen edge of those winds sufficiently, and will occasion much less trouble and expence than reed hedges, &c All these plants are very hardy, but they require this protection, to preserve the young shoots Here they may grow until they are planted out for good, and if it be a moist, light, rich soil, and a well sheltered situation, they will like it the better — and by cuttings

The Chaste tree is titled, *Vitex foliis digitatis, spicis verticillatis*. In many authors it stands with the title simply, *Vitex* Caspar Bauhine calls it, *Vitex foliis angustioribus cannabis modo dispositis*, and distinguishes the other by the title, *Vitex latiore folio*, also, *Vitex folio serrato*, and John Bauhine, *Vitex folio serrato* It grows naturally in marshy moist places in some parts of France, Italy, and Sicily — Titles of this tree.

*Vitex* is of the class and order *Didynamia Angiospermia*, and the characters are, — Class and order in the Linnean system

1 Calyx is a very short, cylindrical, monophyllous perianthium, indented in five parts — The characters

2 Corolla consists of one ringent petal. The tube is slender and cylindric The limb is plane and bilabiated, and both lips are divided into three segments, of which the middle is broadest

3 Stamina consist of four capillary filaments, a little longer than the tube, of which two are shorter than the other, having versatile antheræ

4 Pistillum consists of a roundish germen, a filiforme style the length of the tube, and two awl-shaped patent stigmas

5 Pericarpium is a globular berry of four cells

6 Semina The seeds are single and oval

## CHAP LXXXIX.

## *ULMUS*, The ELM-TREE

THE Elm is a tree so well known as to need no description, and the numerous sorts, whether real species or varieties, present themselves, one or other, in almost every hedge in this kingdom The Narrow-leaved Dutch Elm grows the most common in Leicestershire, and this is the slowest grower and worst-looking tree of all the sorts, but the timber by far exceeds all the others in value The sort called the Wych Elm occupies the hedges in most parts of the north of England, which occasions its being called by many the Northern Elm This is the swiftest grower, and will arrive at the greatest bulk of any of the sorts, and its timber is excellent, though it least of all ought to be planted for avenues, or by the sides of walks, hedge-rows, &c as in such places it will naturally throw out great arms, and grow irregular, and consequently appear less beautiful than many of the other sorts But when many of them are planted in clumps, or set for woods, no tree is more proper, as they naturally there draw one another up, and will aspire, with an upright stem, to a great height, so that when these trees are to be admitted, it must be to join in clumps at a distance, and occupy the middle of the largest quarters, where they will rear their heads amongst others in an agreeable manner, and in the end, when any alteration is made, and the plantation cut down, they will repay the owner by their own value The Upright English Elm is the most picturesque and beautiful of all the sorts — Description of the different sorts

sorts It grows naturally in the hedges in most parts of the south of England, which occasions its being distinguished by many by the name of Southern Elm Of all the sorts this is the least proper for woods, tho' none is more fit for ornamental plantations of any kind If clumps or woods of the Broad-leaved Wych Elm are planted, their borders should be ornamented by two or three rows of this sort all round, that their picturesque manner of growth appearing at a distance, the same idea may be conceived of the whole plantation This sort also is adapted for avenues or rows, for making of hedges, or single standards, though I must own a Wych Elm, growing singly in the midst of a large park, with its diffused branches, has a very good effect Neither are the upright growth and size of this tree its chief good properties, it has others to recommend it to ornamental plantations Its buds swell the largest and open the soonest in the spring of any of the preceding sorts, which is motive enough for this Elm to have the preference in plantations for pleasure But no more need be said of it every experienced gardener knows its beauty and uses, and can hardly err in planting it

The Cornish Elm is a sort well known in the gardens, and for some uses it has the preference of all the sorts It grows in the same picturesque manner as the English Elm, though it will not arrive at the same magnitude The leaves are nearly of the same figure, though smaller, and the branches are proportionally more in number Its buds swell, and the leaves will be out as early as the English, whence it may be easily seen, that no sort is more proper for hedges that are to be kept at a certain height, or for such as are not wanted to be of the utmost height tree will grow to For these highest kinds of hedges let English Elms be planted, as they will grow to rather an higher size

It would be endless, as well as needless, to enumerate the sorts of Elms I have counted in my time more than twenty, in woods, hedges, &c that have fell in my way, when in quest of plants I have, from suckers of the most beautiful and promising sorts, propagated them in our nurseries, first planting them for stools, and then preparing them for layering, but I have since discontinued their encrease, and now scarcely raise any sorts besides the Upright English Elm, and the Broad-leaved Wych Elm, a few of the Cornish Elm for hedges excepted, as I always found the true English Elm the most beautiful, and the Wych the most valuable of any of the sorts Not but the timber of the English Elm is of excellent value, very fit for staves, &c But that of the Wych is what they call more locked, and consequently more proper for all kinds of wheelwright's works, and other large uses, to which the timber of the Elm may be applied

I observed, that the timber of the Narrow-leaved Dutch Elm excels, as being very hard and tough, and will answer any purposes of the other sorts, for though I have seen large trees of this sort upon some ground, yet in general they are of smaller growth, and though they will shoot fast for the first twenty years, they will in general afterwards become stocked, and remain so, so that little more in any age or ages may be expected from them If we add to this, that their growth is extremely straggling and unpleasing, and that they produce their leaves the latest in the spring, this sort, of all others, surely is the least worth propagating, though its wood is of superior value But this rather belongs to the First Part, about Forest-trees, and it would not be amiss for the reader to look over what has been said there I must particularly refer him to the culture of Elms, which is amply shewn in that Part, and which it would be only needless repetition to describe here It must not be forgot, however, to remind the Gardener, that there are Striped-leaved Elms of all the sorts, such as, the Yellow-striped Wych Elm, the White-striped Wych Elm, the Yellow-striped English, the White English, the Golden-leaved English, the Striped Narrow-leaved Dutch, and the Silver-dusted, &c all of which have a beautiful effect, as variegated trees, to those who are fond of such kinds of plants, and which may all be encreased by layers, or grafting them upon stocks of the plain sorts

The Common Elm is titled, *Ulmus foliis duplicato-serratis, basi inæqualibus* Linnæus formerly agreed with other authors in calling it, *Ulmus fructu membranaceo* In the *Hortus Cliffortianus* it is termed, *Ulmus fructu membranaceo* Caspar Bauhine calls it, *Ulmus campestris & Theophrasti*, and Dodonæus, *Ulmus* It is found growing, more or less, in one or other of its varieties, in hedges, about villages in most parts of Europe. Title

*Ulmus* is of the class and order *Pentandria Digynia*, and the characters are, Class and order in the Linnæan system

1 Calyx is a monophyllous, turbinated, rough, permanent perianthium, coloured on the inside, and cut into five erect segments The characters

2 Corolla There is none

3 Stamina are five subulated filaments, twice the length of the calyx, having short, erect, four furrowed antheræ

4 Pistillum consists of an orbicular, erect germen, and of two reflexed styles, shorter than the stamina, with downy stigmas

5 Pericarpium is a large, oval, dry, compressed, membranaceous drupe

6 Semen The seed is single, roundish, and slightly compressed

# CHAP. XC.

## *ZANTHOXYLUM*, The TOOTHACH-TREE.

THIS tree is diſtinguiſhed by the Engliſh name of Toothach tree, becauſe, in the countries where it grows naturally, the bark of it is ſaid to prove of great ſervice to the inhabitants, in the cure of the toothach.

*The ſhrub deſcribed.* This tree grows in many parts of America, and the different parts of that continent furniſh us with trees varying in ſome reſpect or other. It grows to the height of about twelve feet, and the bark is rough, and armed with ſhort thick ſpines. The leaves are its greateſt ornament, for they are pinnated, are of a ſhining green on their upper ſurface, and yellowiſh underneath, and grow without order on the branches. The folioles are ſpear-ſhaped, long, four or five pair are terminated by an odd one, and the whole leaf has much the reſemblance of thoſe of the Maſtich tree. The flowers come out in looſe panicles, from the ends of the branches. They are ſmall, and of little figure, having no petals, though the coloured ſegments of the calyx have been taken for petals. They are ſucceeded by roundiſh unilocular capſules, containing the ſeeds, which hardly ever ripen in England.

*Variety.* There is a variety of this genus, with leaves compoſed of oval, oblong folioles, and having prickly mid-ribs, which difference is permanent from ſeeds. They are numbered in the nurſeries as two diſtinct ſorts, the firſt is called the Lentiſcus-leaved Toothach tree, the other the Aſh-leaved Toothach-tree.

*Method of propagating this tree.* Theſe trees are propagated from the ſeeds, which we receive from abroad, and theſe are ſeldom leſs than two, and often three or four years before they come up. They muſt be ſown as ſoon as poſſible after their arrival, an inch deep, in largiſh pots, filled with a good, light, ſandy compoſt; and after that the pots may be plunged into ſome natural ſoil, in a ſhady place, and there left undiſturbed, except having conſtant weeding during the next ſummer and winter. The ſpring following they may be taken up and plunged into an hotbed, and this will bring up many of the ſeeds. They muſt be next hardened by degrees, and afterwards plunged into their former ſtation, to remain there until autumn. In the enſuing winter they muſt be preſerved in the greenhouſe, or under an hotbed frame, and in the ſpring they ſhould have an hotbed as before, and then you may expect to ſee the remainder of the whole crop. The ſame management muſt be repeated until the ſpring following, when they muſt be all ſhaken out of the pots, and each be planted in a ſeparate pot. Watering ſhould be given them, to ſettle the mould to the roots, and they ſhould be plunged into a hotbed as before. After this they muſt be hardened to the air, and ſet abroad in a ſhady place. Your plants are now raiſed, but they ſhould be treated as greenhouſe plants for two or three years after, when, in ſome ſpring, they may be turned out of their pots, with their mould, into the places where they are deſigned to remain. The places allotted them ſhould be naturally warm and well ſheltered, for although they are tolerable hardy when old, they require protection at firſt, and with this, nothing but the ſevereſt winters can deſtroy them.

*Titles of this genus.* The Toothach-tree is titled, *Zanthoxylum foliis pinnatis*. In the *Hortus Cliffortianus* it is termed, *Zanthoxylum*. Cateſby calls it, *Zanthoxylon ſpinoſum, lentiſci longioribus foliis, evonymi fructu capſulari*; and Du Hamel, *Fagara fraxini folio*. It grows naturally in Jamaica, Carolina, Virginia, and Penſylvania.

*Claſs and order in the Linnæan ſyſtem.* *Zanthoxylum* is of the claſs and order *Dioecia Pentandria*, and the characters are,

*The characters.*

I. Male Flowers.

1. CALYX is a perianthium, deeply divided into five oval, coloured ſegments.
2. COROLLA. There is none.
3. STAMINA are five awl-ſhaped, erect filaments, that are longer than the calyx, having didymous, roundiſh, ſulcated antheræ.

II. Females.

1. CALYX. The ſame as the males.
2. COROLLA. There is none.
3. PISTILLUM conſiſts of a roundiſh germen, and an awl-ſhaped ſtyle longer than the calyx, having an obtuſe ſtigma.
4. PERICARPIUM is an oblong capſule, formed of two valves, and containing one cell.
5. SEMEN. The ſeed is ſingle, roundiſh, and ſmooth.

PART

Arbutus, the Strawberry Tree

# PART III.

## OF EVERGREEN TREES PROPER FOR ORNAMENT and SHADE

## CHAP. I.

## *ARBUTUS*, The STRAWBERRY-TREE

TWO species of this genus are very ornamental to our Plantations of Evergreens

Sorts 1 Common Strawberry, or *Arbutus*

2 Oriental Strawberry-tree, the *Andranche* of Theophrastus

Common Strawberry tree 1 Common Strawberry-tree, or *Arbutus* The *Arbutus* has been a tree of great note, from the earliest times down to the present The Greeks and Romans held it in high esteem, nor there is there scarcely any tree which more frequently occurs in the writings of their poets, or that has more exercised our modern critics in explaining its meaning The Greeks call the fruit of this tree μημαικυλον, and it was universally believed, that the fruit together with beech-mast and acorns, were the food of the first race of men, when living in woods, before the different sorts of grain were in use Lucretius speaks thus

*Quod sol, atque imbres dederant, quod terra crearat*
*Sponte sua, satis id placabat pectora donum*
*Glandiferas inter curabant pectora quercus*
*Plerumque, & quæ nunc hyberno tempore cernis*
Arbuta *Puniceo fieri matura colore*

And Ovid also says,

*Arbuteos fœtus montanaque fraga legebant*

No wonder, therefore, that this tree should be so often mentioned by the antient poets, and that, notwithstanding they were extremely ignorant of its true nature, they should have said things of it contrary to all reason and experience They have told us of its uniting by grafting with the walnut-tree, also of some other strange marriages of trees, which we find unnatural, and which never can be made to come together This has been the occasion of much ridicule to some, and has greatly puzzled our modern critics in their examination Virgil, speaking of the operation of grafting, calls this tree the *Arbutus horrida*, and to hear the different reasons given by critics for its being so called, is at once sufficient to cause one to laugh at their folly, and for ever to put one out of conceit with all modern criticism Ruæus says, "The epithet *horrida* was given this shrub, because of the fewness of its leaves" But certainly Ruæus, when he wrote this sentence, had never seen the shrub, for its branches are plentifully ornamented with leaves Martyn thinks it was so called because of the ruggedness of its bark Now the bark of the branches of this tree is smooth, and although that on the older stems is loose and falling, yet it is far from being so rugged as to deserve the epithet *horrida* Dr Hill, modestly, though it is equally ridiculous as the preceding, throws in his conjecture, and at the same time seems ashamed of it He says, *Horridus* is sometimes put for *Jejunus*, which being used here, the meaning of *Arbutus horrida* is the Hungry Arbute "And this tree, says he, may be so called from its readiness to unite with so strange a cion as a walnut" But enough of such criticisms!

Taking leave, therefore, of the old Greeks and Romans, let us see what sorts of this tree are proper for our plantations And here we are entertained with some of the finest evergreens that Nature has afforded us for ornament and use These are,

The Oblong-fruited Strawberry-tree Varieties
The Round-fruited Strawberry-tree
The Strawberry-tree with Red Flowers
The Double-blossomed Strawberry-tree

One description is nearly common to them all described And their inconsiderable variation is almost sufficiently shewn in the manner they stand numbered The Oblong fruited *Arbutus* will grow to be a middling-sized tree in some countries, for we read of the large uses its wood has been applied to to, such as, *Arbutea Cratis*, &c Arbutean harrows, &c With us it may be kept down to any size The main stems are covered with a light-brown bark, rough, and falling The younger branches are of a kind of purple colour, whilst the last year's shoots are of a fine red, and a little hairy The leaves grow alternately on the branches, and are of an oblong oval figure They stand on short footstalks, and the oldest leaves make a contrast with the younger, by having their footstalk and mid-rib of a fine scarlet colour They are smooth, and beautifully serrated Their upper surface (as in most trees) is of a stronger green than their under, and the young twigs are garnished with them in plenty These are beauties in common to most trees, in some degree or other, but every thing else almost of this tree that presents itself to consideration is singular The time of its flowering will be in November and December, when it is rather singular to see a tree in the open ground in full blow, and the fruit ripens by that time twelvemonth after The manner and nature of the fruit, which look like very large red strawberries, give it also a singular and delightful look, and this is heightened as they appear all over the tree among the flowers, for that is the time of its being ripe, when the flowers for the succeeding crop are fully out The flowers themselves make no great figure, they are of a kind of whitish yellow colour, and are succeeded by the above-mentioned Strawberry fruit, which will require a revolution of twelve months, before they perfectly arrive at their maturity and colour The flowers of the first sort are larger than those of the second, and the fruit is oval, and much larger than our Common Scarlet Strawberry

The second sort has its pitcher shaped flowers, which are succeeded by round scarlet fruit, as wide as they are long, and this is all the difference between these sorts

The Strawberry-tree with Red Flowers differs in no respect from the Common sort, only the flowers are red, and these constitute a variety from the other sorts of flowers, but the contrast is not so great between their fruit and them, as of the other sorts, their colour approaching too near to a sameness

The Double-blossomed Strawberry tree differs in no respect, only that the flowers are double, but this difference is so inconsiderable, that it will not be seen without looking into the flower, and even then the doubleness will appear so trifling as scarcely to merit notice, so that a plant or two, to have it said that the Collection is not without it, will be sufficient Neither ought any more to be admitted, for they will not produce the same plenty of fruit, which constitutes the greatest beauty of these trees, as the single sorts

Oriental Strawberry tree.

2 Oriental Strawberry-tree, or *Andrachne* of Theophrastus The Oriental Strawberry-tree will grow to a larger size than the other The leaves are smooth, and nearly of the same figure as the preceding sort, tho' they are larger, and have their edges undivided The flowers grow like the other sorts, are of the same colour, and they are succeeded by large, oval, scarlet fruit It is called the Oriental Strawberry-tree, because this sort grows plentifully in many parts of the East, and is useful to the inhabitants for many purposes in life

Method of propagating these sorts.

Proceed we now to the culture of those sorts that have always gone by the name of *Arbutus*, or Strawberry tree, and as these are deemed varieties only, Reason directs us, that, to continue the sorts, they must be encreased any way they will take root, but not by seeds By layers they will all grow The operation must be performed on the youngest twigs, and in some sorts they will strike root pretty freely, whilst in others they can hardly be made to grow at all But before they have lain two summers, you may scarcely venture to look for any When the roots are struck, the layers should be carefully taken off in the spring and planted in separate pots, and after well watering them, they should be plunged up to the rims in an hotbed, and this will set them forward, for without this assistance, many of the layers will be lost, since they are but bad plants to make grow After the hotbed has set them a-growing they may be taken out, and plunged up to the rims in some natural mould, to keep them cool and moist, and here they may stand for two or three years, or longer, if the pots are large enough, without ever removing or sheltering in winter, for they are hardy enough to resist our severest cold When they are to be set out for good, all the mould may be turned out of the pots hanging to the roots, and having proper holes made ready, they may be planted in them, and the plant will be ignorant of its new situation

These plants may be encreased by cuttings, which must be planted in pots, and have the benefit of a good bark-bed, in which being constantly shaded and duly watered, many of them will grow As the plants raised this way will be rather tender by being forced in the bark-bed, it will be necessary to remove them into the greenhouse, or to place them under an hotbed-frame, during the first winter and after that, the pots may be set up to the rims in the ground, and, like the layers, the plants may be turned out at a convenient time into the places where they are to remain

Proceed we next to the best way of raising the Common *Arbutus*, and that is from seeds Let the seeds be taken from the Oblong or Round-fruited sort, and plenty of both the sorts may be expected from them The seeds, which will be ripe some time in November or the beginning of December, for they will not be ripe at the same time in all places, must be then gathered, and as they should not be sowed until the spring, it will be proper to put them into a pot or jar, mixing with them a quantity of drift-sand, and this will preserve them sound and good The beginning of March is the best time for sowing the seeds and the best soil for them is maiden earth, taken from a rich pasture at least a year before, with the sward, and this, by constant turning, being well rotted and mixed, will be ready to receive them Having filled a different quantity of pots with this fine mould, let the seeds be sown and but just covered, scarcely a quarter of an inch deep A dry day should be chosen for the business, and no watering by the hand should be given them, as it will endanger the setting the mould hard in the pots Leave them abroad until some rain falls, which at that time may be hourly expected, and after that, having an hotbed ready plunge the pots therein In less than six weeks you may expect your plants to appear, when much air should be afforded them, and frequent waterings, in small quantities, gently sprinkled over them. After this, they may be hardened to the air by degrees, and the pots set up to the rims in the natural mould, in a shady place In October they should be removed into the greenhouse, or some shelter, in frosty weather, though they should always be set abroad in mild open weather In the spring they may be shook out, and planted in separate pots, and they should have the advantage also of an hotbed to set them a-growing, their future management

management may be the same as was directed for the layers When these trees are to be planted out, very little regard need be paid to the soil or situation; for they will grow almost any where, and resist our severest northern blasts One thing, however, the Gardener must constantly observe, in order to continue his trees in their beauty, viz as often as a heavy snow falls, so constantly should he go and shake the boughs, for it will lodge amongst the leaves and branches, in such great quantity, as to weigh down and split the largest branches, the deformity of which afterwards may be easily conceived Besides, many years must expire before the tree will if ever it should, grow to its former beauty, to preserve this, therefore, makes the narrowly watching these trees in snowy weather highly necessary

Titles

1 The title of the Common *Arbutus* is; *Arbutus caule erecto, foliis glabris serratis, baccis polyspermis* Caspar Bauhine calls it, *Arbutus folio serrato*, and others simply, *Arbutus* It grows naturally in Ireland, and in many parts of Europe

2 Oriental *Arbutus*, or *Andrachne* of Theophrastus, is, *Arbutus caule arboreo, foliis glabris integerrimis baccis polyspermis* Caspar Bauhine calls it *Arbutus folio non serrato*, and Clusius, *Andrachne Theophrasti* It is a native of the East

Class and order in the Linnæan system The characters

*Arbutus* is of the class and order *Decandria Monogynia* and the characters are,

1 Calyx is a very small, obtuse, permanent perianthium, placed under the germen, and cut into five segments

2 Corolla is a single pitcher-shaped petal It is plane at the base, and the rim is divided into five small, obtuse, revolute segments

3 Stamina consist of ten awl shaped, swelled filaments, about half the length of the corolla, having bifid nutant antheræ

4 Pistillum consists of a globular germen, standing on the receptacle, marked with ten dots, of a cylindric style the length of the corolla, and of a thick obtuse stigma

5 Pericarpium is a roundish berry, of five cells

6 Semina The seeds are small and hard

# CHAP II

## *ARTEMISIA*, MUGWORT.

Description of this tree

THERE is one species of this genus which is a very beautiful shrub, and hardy enough to grow in the open air, in a well sheltered place This is called the Tree Wormwood It rises, with an upright branching stalk, to the height of about six feet The leaves are its chief excellence, and of these there are two or three sorts One sort is very much divided, or cut into several narrow segments, those of the other are broader They are very hoary, and as they continue on the branches all winter, they have a singular and an agreeable effect among the evergreens at that season The flowers are small, and have very little beauty, they are collected into roundish heads, and I never perceived them to be followed by good seeds

Method of propagating it

This plant is easily raised by cuttings Plant them in May, June, July or August, in a shady place, and they will readily grow especially if they are watered a few times at the first planting In the autumn these cuttings, which will then have become good plants, should be each set in a separate small pot, and placed under a hotbed-frame, or in the greenhouse, to be preserved all winter In the spring they may be turned out into the places where they are designed to remain, which must be naturally warm and well sheltered, or they will be liable to be destroyed by the severity of the following winter In such a situation they will live for many years, though it may be adviseable to keep a plant or two in the greenhouse, to keep up the stock, if a more than common hard winter should put a period to those that are planted abroad

Title

The Tree Wormwood is titled, *Artemisia foliis compositis multifidis linearibus, floribus sub globosis, caule frutescente* Lobel calls it, *Absinthium arborescens*, and Caspar Bauhine, *Abrotanum latifolium arborescens* It grows naturally in Italy and in the East

Class and order in the Linnæan system The character

*Artemisia* is of the class and order *Syngenesia Polygamia Superflua*, and the characters are,

1 Calyx The common calyx is roundish and imbricated The scales are roundish and connivent

2 Corolla is composed of hermaphrodite and female florets The hermaphrodite florets are many, and tubulous in the disk The female flowers surround them

Each hermaphrodite floret is funnel-shaped, and cut at the top into five parts

3 Stamina of the hermaphrodite florets consist each of five very short capillary filaments, having a cylindrical anthera, indented in five parts

4 Pistilla of the hermaphrodite florets consist each of a small germen, a filiforme style the length of the stamina, and a bifid revolute stigma

In the female flowers the germen is small, the style is filiforme and longer than the hermaphrodites, and the stigma is like that of the hermaphrodites

5 Pericarpium There is none

6 Semina The seeds of both the hermaphrodite and female flowers are single and naked

The receptacle is plane, and either naked or hairy

# C H A P. III

## *ATRIPLEX*, The PURSLAIN-TREE

*Introductory observations.*

INSTEAD of an evergreen, the ſhrubby *Atriplex* may more properly be called an ever ſilvery tree, as its leaves are of a white and ſilvery colour, thereby making a good contraſt with moſt of other trees at all times Of this genus there are two ſpecies, which may not improperly be ranked with ſhrubs that retain their leaves all winter, though it ſometimes happens that they greatly loſe their beauty by the early ſharp froſts, which often nip them in ſuch a manner as to make a part of the tree if not the whole of it, appear as if dead Many trees are ſubject to this accident by the delicacy of their texture, which ſhould warn us to ſeek out proper places for all ſorts, and to repair the beauty of the trees by taking away in time ſuch branches as are rendered unſightly by the received injury The ſhrubby ſpecies of this genus, then, are commonly known and diſtinguiſhed by the names of,

*Species.*

1 The Broad-leaved Purſlain-tree
2 The Narrow-leaved Purſlain tree

*Deſcription of the Broad-leaved*

1 The Broad-leaved Purſlain-tree generally grows to about five or ſix feet, and will ſend forth its branches ſo as to ſpread around, and form a large broad buſh The young branches are covered with a ſmooth white bark, that of the older is of a light grey colour, which will be peeling lengthways, and falling, eſpecially in the ſpring The branches are exceeding brittle, and their inſide is green to the very pith, of which there is very little The leaves are ſoft, white and ſilvery, and nearly of the ſhape of the Greek letter *Delta* They have their edges entire, and look well at all times, eſpecially in winter, when they cauſe as great a variety as poſſible among thoſe trees that retain their leaves at that time This ſhrub ſeldom flowers in our gardens, and when that happens, it is poſſeſſed of no beauty to recommend it to Gardeners, ſo that for them the characters may be ſufficient

*and the Narrow leaved Purſlain tree*

2 The Narrow-leaved Purſlain-tree commonly grows to about four feet high The branches are numerous and grey, and they naturally ſpread abroad in a buſhy manner The leaves are ſilvery, though not ſo white as the other ſort, but they are narrower, which occaſions its being ſo diſtinguiſhed, and of an oval figure, and by them the ſhrub receives no ſmall ornament The flowers have little beauty for the Gardener and the general characters may ſerve to indicate their ſtructure to the Botaniſt

*Method of propagating theſe ſorts*

Theſe ſhrubs are propagated by cuttings, which will grow, if planted at any time of the year, though the beſt way is to take the cuttings in March, of the ſtrongeſt former ſummer's ſhoots, to cut them into lengths about a foot each, and to plant them a third part deep in the mould They will all readily take root, and be good plants by the autumn following In ſummer, ſlips and cuttings may be planted, but then it will be adviſeable to plant them pretty cloſe together in beds, and afterwards to hoop the beds, and ſhade them from the heat at that time They will ſoon take root, and after that will require no further trouble But until that is effected, they ſhould be watered and ſhaded in the hot weather, and the mats ſhould be conſtantly taken off in the evening, and alſo in rainy, moiſt, or cloudy weather, and by this means plenty of plants may be raiſed If it happened to be a dripping day when they were firſt planted, much trouble in ſhading and watering will be ſaved, as they may be nearly upon ſtriking root, before the weather clears up Theſe ſhrubs ſhould be always raiſed at a diſtance from farm-yards, barns, &c where there are ſparrows, for theſe birds are ſo exceeding fond of the leaves, that when once they find them out, they will never leave nor forſake them until they have entirely ſtripped the plants, and though the ſhrub will ſhoot out afreſh, yet they will as conſtantly repair to their repaſt, and will thus continue to prey upon them until they have entirely deſtroyed them I am obliged to give this precaution, becauſe all my plants of theſe ſorts are thus conſtantly eat up by the ſparrows in my Gardens at Church-Langton, as often as I plant them, ſo that I am obliged to keep them at Gumley, and in my other diſtant nurſeries, where they remain free from ſuch devourers

*Titles of the ſpecies*

1 The Broad-leaved Purſlain-tree is entitled, *Atriplex caule fruticoſo, foliis deltoidibus integris* Caſpar Bauhine calls it, *Halimus latifolius, ſive fruticoſus* Cluſius, *Halimus*, and Moriſon, *Atriplex latifolia, ſive halimus fruticoſus* It grows common on the ſea-coaſts of Spain and Portugal, and is found in great plenty in Virginia

2 The Narrow-leaved Purſlain tree is, *Atriplex caule fruticoſo, foliis obovatis* Van Royen calls it *Atriplex caule fruticoſo, foliis lanceolatis obtuſis*, Caſpar Bauhine, *Halimus, ſive Portulaca marina*, Dodonæus, *Portulaca marina*, and Ray, *Atriplex maritima fruticoſa, halimus & portulaca marina dicta anguſtifolia* It grows common on the ſea-ſhore in England, and alſo in ſuch places in many parts of the northern parts of Europe

*Claſs and order in the Linnæan ſyſtem*

*Atriplex* is of the claſs and order *Polygamia Monoecia*, and the characters are,

*The characters*

I. Hermaphrodite Flowers

1 CALYX is a permanent perianthium, compoſed of five oval, concave leaves, having membranaceous borders

2 COROLLA There is none

3 STAMINA are five ſubulated filaments, placed oppoſite to the leaves of the calyx, and longer than them, having roundiſh didymous antheræ

4 PISTILLUM conſiſts of an orbicular germen, and of a ſhort ſtyle, that is divided into two parts, with reflexed ſtigmas

5 PERICARPIUM There is none
The calyx becomes five-cornered, cloſed, and compreſſed

6 SEMEN The ſeed is ſingle, orbicular, and depreſſed

II Fe

II Female Flowers

1 Calyx is compoſed of two large leaves, which are plane, erect, oval, acute, and compreſſed

2 Corolla There is none

3 Pistillum conſiſts of a compreſſed germen, and of a ſtyle that is divided into two parts, and having acute, reflexed ſtigmas

4 Pericarpium There is none

5 Semen The ſeed is ſingle, round, and compreſſed

# CHAP IV.

## *BUPLEURUM*, SHRUBBY ETHIOPIAN HARTWORT.

THIS ſhrubby ſpecies of *Bupleurum* is known to the Gardener by the name of the Ethiopian Hartwort, a delightful low growing evergreen of itſelf, but ſcarcely hardy enough to ſtruggle with our ſevereſt weather Whenever it is introduced into plantations, it ſhould always have the advantage of a dry ſoil and a well-ſheltered ſituation, and with theſe advantages, little danger is to be feared from any weather This ſhrub had for many years been preſerved as a greenhouſe-plant, but experience now teaches the Gardener to make room there for others of a more tender nature, by planting it abroad This, however, muſt be done with the above caution, for I muſt own, I have had fine old plants, which had ſtood for ſome years had grown their ſtems woody, and ſeemed likely to defy any weather, theſe, I ſay, I have had, after growing ſome years in an open expoſure, and a good ſoil, entirely killed by a night's unexpected ſevere froſt, late in the ſpring Let this hint, then, be ſufficient for the Gardener

The ſhrub deſcribed. The evergreen ſhrub we are now deſcribing is of low growth, which makes it more valuable to many perſons It ſeldom riſes more than eight feet high, and will produce plenty of flowers before it gets to the height of one yard The bark of the oldeſt ſtems is of a brown, that on the younger ſhoots of a reddiſh colour, but this is not conſtant, for ſometimes it will be greyiſh, at others of a purpliſh blue The leaves are of a fine pale green colour, and placed alternately on the branches They are of an oblong, oval figure, and have their edges entire They are ſmooth, and being of a delicate pale-green, are very ornamental to the ſhrub The flowers are produced from the ends of the branches, in longiſh umbels They make no great figure (having but a bad yellow colour), appear in July and Auguſt, and are ſucceeded by ſeeds, which often, though not always, will ripen with us, and by which, when they do, plenty of plants may be raiſed Theſe plants, then, are to be encreaſed,

Manner of propagating it from the ſeed. 1 By ſeeds, either of our own growing, or of thoſe we receive from the ſouth of France or Italy, where the ſhrub grows naturally Theſe ſhould be preſerved with care, and a compoſt of good mould, with nearly half the ſame quantity of ſand mixed with it, ſhould be prepared for them, or if the ſoil be naturally ſandy, or is taken from a naturally rocky place, this will of itſelf do for them, for the ſhrubs grow naturally among the rocks near the ſea in many parts Let this not be taken too literally, however, for as there are ſome ſandy grounds ſo barren as ſcarcely to produce any thing, this ſort, if it is to be uſed, ſhould have a ſhare of at leaſt half of good garden-mould (what is called fat earth), and this will be a proper compoſt for its reception, for although it will grow very well in the moſt ſandy, gravelly grounds, and in ſuch ſoils will be more ſecure from danger even in the ſevereſt froſts, yet ſomething of more heart ſhould be mixed with that ſoil, for the ſeeds to make their firſt ſhoots in, that they may be healthy and ſtrong The ſeeds and mould being ready, at the beginning of March let the ſeeds be ſown in pots filled with the mould; and if theſe are ſet in a ſhady place, and now and then watered as the hot weather comes on, they will come up by May, though if the pots have the advantage of a moderate hotbed, the plants will come up ſooner, and be ſtronger by the autumn Let either of theſe methods be practiſed All ſummer the pots muſt be plunged up to the rims in a ſhady place, and in October it will be proper to remove them under ſhelter, to ſecure the plants from froſt during the firſt winter The firſt week in April they ſhould be planted out in the nurſery, at ſmall diſtances The ſoil ſhould be naturally warm and well ſheltered, and here they may remain until they are planted out for good, which ought alſo to be in warm well ſheltered places, where there will be little danger of loſing them by bad weather

2 Theſe ſhrubs are alſo propagated by cuttings The latter end of July is the time, and if the weather be moiſt or rainy, ſo much the better, if not, ſome beds muſt be well dug, and made moiſt by watering The cuttings ſhould be planted in the evening, and the beds muſt be hooped, to be covered with mats in the heat of the day On their being firſt planted, no ſun ſhould come near them, but after they have been ſet a fortnight, they may have the morning ſun until nine o'clock, and afterwards ſhading; obſerving always to uncover them in the evening, as alſo in moiſt, cloudy, or rainy weather Many of theſe cuttings will grow, and in winter it will be proper to protect them from the froſt with mats in the like manner After that they will require no further trouble until they are ſet out for good, for out of this bed they need not be taken into the nurſery-ground, unleſs they are ſet very cloſe, then, indeed, they ſhould be taken out the ſpring come twelvemonth after planting, and ſet in the nurſery-ground, at ſmall diſtances, like the ſeedlings and by cuttings.

The title of this ſpecies of the *Bupleurum* is, *Bupleurum fruteſcens, foliis ovatis integerrimis* In the Titles the *Hortus Cliffortianus* it is termed, *Bupleurum, foliis obverse ovatis in petiolum attenuatis* John Bauhine calls it, *Seseli Ethiopicum fruticosum folio periclymeni*, Caspar Bauhine, *Seseli Ethiopicum, salicis folio*; and Dodonæus, *Seseli Ethiopicum frutex* It grows naturally amongst the rocks on the coasts of the south of France, and also in some parts of Italy

Class and order in the Linnæan system. *Bupleurum* is of the class and order *Pentandria Digynia*, and the characters are,

The characters 1 CALYX The general umbel consists of about ten radii, the partial ones, which are nearly of the same number, are erect and patent

The universal involucrum is composed of many pointed leaves the partial involucrum of five leaves, which are oval, acute, and patent

The proper perianthium of each separate flower is scarce visible

2 COROLLA The general flower is uniform, each floret consists of five small, whole, inflexed petals

3 STAMINA are five slender filaments, with roundish antheræ, &c

4 PISTILLUM consists of a germen placed below the proper receptacle, and of two small, reflexed styles, with minute stigmas

5 PERICARPIUM. There is none The fruit is roundish, compressed, striated, and divides into two parts

6 SEMINA are two They are of an oval, oblong figure, convex, striated on one side, and on the other plane

# C H A P. V

## *BUXUS*, The BOX-TREE

THE Box has already been treated of in the former Book, among the Forest trees, little more, therefore, need be added here, than to set down the sorts, which will all spontaneously encrease the variety Linnæus supposes only one true species of *Buxus*, and that may be satisfactory enough for the Botanist, but the Gardener will be delighted when he finds that there are sorts, which have as different a look, and will cause as great a variety in his Evergreen plantations, as many plants that belong to different classes The sorts of Box, then, are,

Species

1 The Dwarf, commonly called the Dutch Box
2 The Broad-leaved Box tree
3 The Narrow-leaved Box-tree
4 The Gold-striped Box-tree
5 The Silver-striped Box-tree
6 The Gold-edged Box-tree
7 The Curled-leaved Striped Box-tree

Description of the Dwarf. 1 The Dwarf Box is a plant so well known as to need no description It may be planted as an evergreen shrub among the lowest sorts, though its general use in gardens is for edgings, and for keeping up the mould in borders, for which purposes no plant is better adapted, though Box-edgings of this kind are now become pretty much out of fashion, and with good reason, as they have rather a formal look, and destroy in some measure that natural and easy appearance which gardens and plantations of all kinds ought to have In little gardens, however, where walks are obliged to be gravelled to walk on, and the owner is fond of edgings, no plant will keep the mould and gravel asunder better than the Dwarf Box, a plant which Nature seems more peculiarly designed for those uses With the method of planting and managing this tree all orders of Gardeners are acquainted

Broad leaved. 2 The Broad leaved Box tree is a plant also well known This is the sort I have recommended to be planted as a forest tree, for the improvement of cold barren land What has been said before may suffice here, though I must repeat, that few trees are more proper for ever green plantations than this for it is naturally of beautiful growth The branches are numerous, and of a yellowish colour, and these being closely garnished with small, oval, shining leaves, make as great a contrast as can be conceived, and keep up the spirit of variety, when planted amongst laurels, bays, and the larger-leaved evergreens, as well as with the smaller and prickly kinds, such as hollies, evergreen oaks, &c

Narrow leaved. 3 The Narrow-leaved Box-tree is by far the most beautiful of all the sorts Of this species there are some varieties, that differ in the size of their leaves, but it is the smallest-leaved sort I mean, and as this sort is not very common, it is valued on that account It is rather of a lower growth than the former sort, and its branches are more slender and numerous It forms itself naturally into a regular head, and the whole shrub assumes an air of delicacy The leaves grow opposite by pairs, as in the other sort, but are produced in greater plenty They are very small and narrow, and their surface is not so shining as the Broad-leaved box As the branches and leaves are the only ornament these trees afford gardens, nothing further need be added to the description of this sort

Gold and Silver-striped. 4 5 The two sorts with striped leaves are the Common Tree Box variegated, though they have a different appearance in their manner of growth, as well as in their striped leaves They will grow indeed to be as tall, but the branches will be naturally more slender and weaker, and many of them will often hang downwards, which gives the tree a much different appearance from the plain Tree Box, whose branches are naturally straight and upright The leaves of these sorts being beautifully striped, makes them much coveted by all who are fond of variegated trees

Gold edged. 6 The Gold edged Box is still the True Box in the same natural upright growth The branches of this are not so weak as those of the former sorts, but are upright and strong Their bark is rather yellower than the green sort, in other respects there is no difference, except that the leaves are tipped or edged with yellow, which is thought by many to be very ornamental to the shrub

7 The

and the Curled leaved Striped Box-trees 7 The Curled-leaved Striped Box is so called on account of its leaves being a little waved This, together with the Narrow leaved, is the scarcest of all the sorts, and is indeed, like that, a very elegant shrub It is certainly a variety of the Common Tree Box, but it seems rather of lower growth Its leaves are waved, and they are variegated in such a manner as to cause the shrub to have what may be called a luscious look It makes a variety from all the others, and a good contrast with other trees, and is truly beautiful and pleasing

Method of propagating them The method of raising the Box-tree has been already shewn in the First Book, where the reader will find it may be performed by cuttings and seeds, and may see the method of putting both in practice The same method, then, must be practised on all these sorts, observing always that the variegated sorts are to be raised from cuttings, for the seeds taken from any of them, and sown, will produce the Common Green Tree Box

Titles As there is only one species of this genus, it stands simply with the name, *Buxus* Caspar Bauhine calls it, *Buxus Arborescens*, also, *Buxus foliis rotundioribus*, Dodonæus, *Buxus humilis*, and Ray, *Buxus angustifolia* It grows wild in England, and many of the southern parts of Europe

Class and order in the Linnæan system The characters *Buxus* is of the class and order *Monoecia Tetrandria*, and the characters are,

I Male Flowers

1 CALYX is a perianthium, composed of three roundish, obtuse, concave, patent leaves

2 COROLLA consists of two roundish, concave petals, resembling the leaves of the calyx, but larger

3 STAMINA are four subulated, erect, patent filaments, with erect, didymous antheræ

4 PISTILLUM There is the rudiment of a germen, without either style or stigma

II Female Flowers on the same bud with the Males

1 CALYX is a perianthium composed of four roundish, obtuse, concave, patent leaves

2 COROLLA consists of three roundish, concave petals, resembling those of the calyx, but larger

3 PISTILLUM consists of a roundish, obtuse, three cornered germen, on which are three very short, permanent styles, with obtuse, hispid stigmas

4 PERICARPIUM is a roundish capsule, of three cells It has three beaks, and opens with elasticity three ways

5 SEMINA The seeds are two in each cell They are oblong, rounded on one side, and on the other are plane

# CHAP VI.

## *CELASTRUS*, The STAFF-TREE

THERE is one species of this genus proper for this place, called the Virginian Staff-tree It is a shrub of about four

This shrub described feet in growth, rising from the ground with several stalks, which divide into many branches, and are covered with a brownish bark The leaves are of a fine green colour, and grow alternately on the branches They are of an oval figure, and have their edges undivided The flowers are produced in July, at the ends of the branches, in loose spikes They are of a white colour, and in their native countries are succeeded by very ornamental scarlet fruit, but with us this seldom happens

This shrub must have a well-sheltered situation, otherwise the leaves are apt to fall off at the approach of frosty weather

Method of propagating this tree by seed, It is easily propagated from seeds, which we receive from many parts of North-America These should be sown at least an inch deep, in beds of good fresh mould, made fine They seldom come up until the second, and sometimes not before the third spring, so that all the intermediate time the beds must be weeded, and that will be the only trouble they will require After the plants come up, they should be shaded as the hot weather comes on, from about nine o'clock; and this, together with frequent waterings in dry weather, will cause them to become strong plants by the autumn As they are very hardy, they will give no trouble the winter following, neither will they require any the succeeding summer except weeding, for it will be proper to let them remain two years in the seed-bed, not only as they will become stronger plants and less liable to be lost, but even the third spring after sowing many seeds will come up, which might have been destroyed, had the beds been disturbed sooner The first week of April, they should be planted in beds, at a small distance; and if it happens not to be moist weather at the time, they should be then watered, to settle the mould to their roots and this watering should be repeated in dry weather all the following summer After this, they will require no other care than weeding, until they are planted out for good, which may be at the pleasure or convenience of the owner

and by layers This species is also propagated by layers, and, to be concise, the work must be performed on the young wood, in the autumn, by a slit at the joint These layers may be expected to strike root by the autumn following, when they may be taken up and planted in the nursery-ground, in the same manner as the seedlings

The Staff-tree is titled, *Celastrus inermis, foliis ovatis integerrimis* Plukenet calls it, *Evonymus Virginianus rotundifolius, capsulis coccineis eleganter bullatis* It grows in many parts of North-America, but particularly in Virginia

Class and order in the Linnæan system The characters *Celastrus* is of the class and order *Pentandria Monogynia*, and the characters are,

1 CALYX is a very small, plane, monophyllous perianthium, cut into five unequal, obtuse segments

2 COROLLA consists of five oval, patent, sessile, and equal petals, which have their ends reflexed

3 STAMINA are five subulated filaments, the length of the corolla, having very small antheræ

4 PISTILLUM consists of a very small germen, which is immersed in a very large, plane receptacle, marked with ten channels, of a subulated style, shorter than the stamina, and of an obtuse trifid stigma

5 PERICARPIUM is an oval, obtuse, three-cornered, coloured, trivalvate, capsule, containing three cells

6 SEMINA. The seeds are few, oval, coloured, and smooth.

## C H A P. VII

## *C I S T U S*, The R O C K - R O S E

THE larger kinds of *Cistus*, and such as have a right to a place among evergreens, are as follow

Species.
1 Poplar leaved *Cistus*
2 Bay-leaved *Cistus*
3 Ladanum *Cistus*
4 Hoary-leaved *Cistus*
5 Gum *Cistus* of Montpelier
6 Oblong White-leaved *Cistus*
7 Sage-leaved *Cistus*
8 Waved-leaved *Cistus*
9 Sea Purslain-leaved *Cistus*
10 Spanish Round-leaved *Cistus*
11 Cretan *Cistus*
12 Spanish Narrow-leaved *Cistus*

These are all distinct species, and there are numberless varieties of them, differing in some respect or other, some having narrower, others broader leaves, in the colour of the flowers also they vary very much

Description of the Poplar leaved. 1 The Poplar leaved *Cistus* is a shrub of about six feet in height, though it begins its bloom when lower than two feet The branches have no regular way of growth, and are covered with a brown bark, which will be lighter or darker according to the different soils The leaves are cordated, smooth, pointed, have footstalks, and a little resemblance to those of the Black Poplar Old Botanists have distinguished two species of this sort, which they called the *Major* and the *Minor*, the one being of larger growth than the other, but modern improvements shew these to be varieties only The flowers are white, and produced about Midsummer, in plenty, at the ends and sides of the branches They are of short continuance, but there will be a succession kept up for near six weeks, during which time the shrub will have great beauty

Bay-leaved. 2 Bay leaved *Cistus* is an irregular branching shrub, of about the same height with the former The leaves are oval, pointed, and in the Midsummer months are very clammy Their upper surface is of a strong green, but their under is white, and they grow on footstalks, which join together at their base The flowers are produced from the ends and sides of the branches, about Midsummer They are white, and stand on naked footstalks, and being large, and produced in plenty at that time, make a good figure This species is rather tender, and requires a warm, dry soil, and a well-sheltered situation

Ladanum. 3 The Ladanum *Cistus* is so called because the Ladanum of the shops is collected from this shrub There are many varieties of it differing in the colour of the flowers, or in some respect or other, and the tree, with its varieties, will grow to be six or more feet high, though it produces its flowers and exhibits great beauty when very low It arises with a woody stem, and though it produces its branches in no regular manner, yet it has the appearance of a well-fashioned shrub The leaves are of a lanceolate figure Their upper surface is smooth, and of a fine green colour, but their under is whitish and veined They are scented, and have footstalks that join together at their base The flowers are very large and delicate, and are produced all over the shrub in plenty They exhibit themselves about the usual time Many of them are of a pure white, with a deep purple spot at the bottom of each petal, whilst others again from these afford a variety, being of a purple colour, or having their edges of a reddish tinge The beauty of this tree, when in blow, is often over in very hot weather, by eleven o'clock in the morning but that is renewed every day, and for about six weeks successively a morning's walk will be rendered more delightful by the renewed bounties which they bestow

4 The Hoary leaved *Cistus* is a shrub of about four feet high, and forms itself into a bushy head There are four or five varieties of this sort, that have been looked upon by some authors as distinct species, but Experience now teaches us better The leaves of all are hoary, but they differ often in shape, size or figure; and this has occasioned their being named accordingly, and to be distinguished by the names of, Common Hoary leaved *Cistus*, the Long-leaved Hoary Male *Cistus*, the Rounder-leaved Male *Cistus*, the Large Hoary-leaved Male *Cistus*, &c Whenever these different sorts can be procured, they by their make a variety, and in that manner contribute to make the plantations more agreeable The leaves of these sorts of *Cistus* sit close to the branches, are hairy, and rough on both sides Their figure will be different on the same plant, and be produced in different manners, those on the tops of the branches are spear shaped, and grow singly, but the lower ones oval, and are joined together at their base All of them are hoary, though some of the sorts are whiter than others, and these leaves make a good contrast with the stronger greens, during the winter months These shrubs produce their flowers earlier than the other sorts, they often shew some in May They are of a purple colour, which, in different sorts, will be stronger or lighter They fall away in the evening, but are constantly renewed, for a month or longer, by a succession every morning Hoary leaved.

5 The

Gum,

5 The Gum *Cistus* of Montpelier is commonly of about four feet growth, though, like the others, it is very beautiful when no higher than one or two feet. The branches proceed from the bottom of the plant, in plenty; they are hairy, tough, and slender. Their leaves are lanceolated, exude a very fragrant matter, are hairy on both sides, have three veins running lengthways, are of a dark-green colour, and sit close to the branches. The flowers are produced in their greatest plenty about Midsummer, and sometimes earlier, on long footstalks, at the ends of the branches. They are white, and the succession of the blow will be continued often longer than six weeks.

Oblong White leaved,

6 Oblong White leaved *Cistus* will grow to be five or six feet high, and the younger branches, which grow in an upright manner, are tough, and covered with a woolly substance. The leaves are oblong, very white, downy, trinervous, and sit close, surrounding the stalk at the base. The flowers are produced from the ends of the branches, at the beginning of June. They are large, of a fine purple colour, and look very beautiful.

Sage-leaved,

7 The Sage leaved *Cistus* is a much lower shrub, and the branches are many, spreading, and slender. The leaves resemble those of some of the sorts of sage plants. They are oval, on both sides hairy, and have very short footstalks. The flowers are produced in June, from the wings of the leaves. They are white, and stand on naked footstalks, and though they are smaller than some of the other sorts, yet being produced all over the shrub, they make a fine show.

Waved leaved,

8 The Waved leaved *Cistus* is of about four or five feet growth. The branches are very many, and spreading. The leaves are spear shaped, waved, hairy, naturally bend backwards, and grow opposite by pairs on the branches. The flowers are produced from the wings of the leaves, in June. Their colour is white. The succession will be kept up for a month, or longer.

Sea Purslain leaved

9 The Sea Purslain leaved *Cistus* is a shrub of about four feet growth, and sends forth many branches in an upright pretty manner. The younger branches are downy, and the leaves have some little resemblance to the Sea Purslain, though there are varieties of this species with broader and narrower leaves, some that approach to an oval, and others that are sharp pointed. They grow opposite by pairs, and make a good variety by their white and hoary look. The flowers are produced in June and July, on very long, naked footstalks, which support others also with shorter footstalks. They are of a fine yellow colour, and make a good figure when in blow. This is the most tender of all the sorts, and is generally treated as a greenhouse-plant, but if the soil be naturally dry and warm, and the situation well-sheltered, it will do very well abroad in our tolerably open winters. But it may be adviseable, however, to secure a plant or two in the greenhouse, that, in case a very severe winter should happen to kill those abroad, a fresh stock may be raised from the thus-preserved plants.

Spanish Round leaved,

10 Spanish Round-leaved *Cistus*. This is a branching shrub, of about a yard or four feet high. The leaves are oval, round, hairy, and placed on footstalks on the branches. The flowers come out in plenty from the tops and sides of the branches, in July. Their colour is purple, and though they are very fugacious, yet there will be a succession of them for a long time.

Cretan

11 Cretan *Cistus*. This is a branching shrub, of about the same height with the former. The leaves are spatulated, oval, enervous, rough, and grow on footstalks on the branches. The flowers are red, and they make their appearance about the same time with the former.

and Spanish Narrow-leaved Cistus

12 Spanish Narrow leaved *Cistus*. This rises with a shrubby, naked, purple coloured stalk, to about four feet high. The leaves are narrow, light, reflexed on their sides, and grow opposite to each other without any footstalks. The flowers grow in small umbels, and come out from the ends and sides of the branches, on long slender footstalks. Their colour is white, and their appearance is about the same time with the former.

All the sorts of *Cistus* are raised by seeds and cuttings.

Method of propagating these sorts by seeds

1 Seeds is the best way, as by them the most handsome plants are produced, though they will not always afford so great a plenty of flowers as the plants raised from cuttings. When they are to be raised by seeds, a moderate hotbed should be in readiness for their reception by the beginning of March, and they should be sown in drills a quarter of an inch deep. A dry day should be made choice of for the purpose, and pegs should be stuck to shew the extremity of the drills. The drills may be made two inches asunder, and the bed being heated up, no other covering will be necessary than an old mat, to guard the plants, when coming up, from the spring frosts which may happen, for if the seeds are good, you may expect many plants to appear in less than a month, at which time they should be covered in the night, but be always kept uncovered in open and fine weather. As the dry weather comes on, they must be watered moderately every other morning, and the weeds constantly cleared off, and as the summer heat increases, the mats used to guard them from the frost in the night, must change their office. They must never come near them in the night, but only protect them from the scorching heat in the middle of the day. By the latter end of August many of the plants will be four or five inches high, when they may be thinned, and those drawn out either pricked in the nursery ground, in beds at small distances, in well sheltered places or planted in pots, to be secured in the winter, and turned out at leisure. Of all the sorts, the Bay-leaved and the Sea-Purslain-leaved species, with all their varieties, require this treatment. The rest are all very hardy. Those that are pricked out in rows in the nursery will immediately strike root; and, as well as those left in the old hotbed, if they are in well-sheltered places will do without any protection. If the place is not well defended, either by trees or hedges, it will be proper to prick some furze-bushes all around, to break the keen edge of the severe frosts. Those left in the old bed should be planted out in the spring in the nursery ground, and in a spring or two after this, they should all be planted out where they are to remain; for none of these plants succeed so well if removed when grown old and woody.

and cuttings.

2 These plants are easily raised by cuttings, and plants raised this way are often the best flowerers, though their manner of growth is not always so upright and beautiful. August is the month for this work, and if a dripping day happens in that month, it must be made choice of; if not, a bed of fine mould must be prepared, and the cuttings should be planted a few inches asunder, and after that should be watered to settle the mould to them. The beds should be hooped, and the next day, as the heat of the sun comes on, they should be covered with mats. This covering should be repeated, observing

ſerving always to uncover them in the evenings, and alſo in moiſt and cloudy weather These cuttings will take root in a very little time and their after management may be the ſame as the ſeedlings

Titles of this genus

1 The Poplar-leaved *Ciſtus* is titled, *Ciſtus arboreſcens exſtipulatus, foliis cordatis lævibus acuminatis petiolatis* Caſpar Bauhine calls it, *Ciſtus Ledon, foliis populi nigræ major*, alſo, *Ciſtus Ledon, foliis populi nigræ, minor* Cluſius terms it, *Ledum latifolium 2 majus*, and, *Ledum latifolium 2 minus* It grows naturally in Spain and Portugal

2 Bay-leaved *Ciſtus* is, *Ciſtus arboreſcens exſtipulatus, foliis oblongo ovatis petiolatis trinerviis ſupra glabris petiolis baſi connatis* Caſpar Bauhine calls it, *Ciſtus Ledon, foliis laurinis*, John Bauhine, *Ciſtus Ledon latifolium Creticum*, and Cluſius, *Ledon 1 latifolium* It is a native of Spain

3 Ladanum *Ciſtus* is, *Ciſtus arboreſcens exſtipulatus, foliis lanceolatis ſupra lævibus, petiolis baſi coalitis vaginantibus* Caſpar Bauhine calls it, *Ciſtus ladanifera Hiſpanica incana*, Cluſius, *Ciſtus Ledon 1 anguſtifolius*, and Commelin, *Ciſtus Ledon, flore macula nigricante notato* It grows naturally in many parts of Spain, Italy, Crete, and in the ſouth of France

4 Hoary-leaved *Ciſtus* is, *Ciſtus arboreſcens exſtipulatus, foliis ſpatulatis tomentoſis rugoſis inferioribus baſi vaginantibus connatis* Caſpar Bauhine calls it, *Ciſtus mas anguſtifolius*, and Cluſius, *Ciſtus mas 2* It grows naturally in Spain, and in ſome parts of France

5 Gum *Ciſtus* of Montpelier is, *Ciſtus arboreſcens exſtipulatus, foliis lineari lanceolatis ſeſſilibus utrinque villoſis trinerviis* Caſpar Bauhine calls it, *Ciſtus ladanifera Monſpelienſium*, alſo, *Ciſtus Ledon foliis oleæ, ſed anguſtioribus*, and Cluſius, *Ledon 5* It grows common in the ſouth of France

6 Oblong White leaved *Ciſtus* is, *Ciſtus arboreſcens exſtipulatus, foliis ovato-lanceolatis tomentoſis incanis ſeſſilibus ſubtrinerviis* Caſpar Bauhine calls it, *Ciſtus mas, folio oblongo incano*, Cluſius, *Ciſtus mas 1*, and John Bauhine, *Ciſtus mas 4 Monſpelienſis, folio oblongo albido* It grows common in many parts of Spain, Portugal, and France

7 The Sage leaved *Ciſtus* is, *Ciſtus arboreſcens exſtipulatus, foliis ovatis petiolatis utrinque hirſutis* Caſpar Bauhine calls it, *Ciſtus femina, folio ſalviæ*, and Cluſius, *Ciſtus femina* It grows naturally in France, Italy, and Sicily

8 Waved-leaved *Ciſtus* is, *Ciſtus arboreſcens exſtipulatus, foliis lanceolatis pubeſcentibus trinerviis undulatis* Caſpar Bauhine calls it, *Ciſtus mas, foliis chamædryos*, and Cluſius, *Ciſtus mas* It is a native of Luſitania

9 Sea-Purſlain-leaved *Ciſtus* is, *Ciſtus arboreſcens exſtipulatus, foliolis duobus calycinis linearibus* Caſpar Bauhine calls it, *Ciſtus femina, Portulacæ marinæ folio latiore obtuſo*, alſo, *Ciſtus femina, Portulacæ marinæ folio anguſtiore mucronato*, Cluſius, *Ciſtus halimi folio 1*, alſo, *Ciſtus halimi folio 2* It grows common near the ſea ſhore in Spain and Portugal

10 Spaniſh Round-leaved *Ciſtus* is, *Ciſtus arboreſcens exſtipulatus, foliis ovatis petiolatis hirſutis* Caſpar Bauhine calls it, *Ciſtus mas, folio rotundo hirſutiſſimo*, and Dalechamp, *Ciſtus mas Matthioli* It grows naturally in Italy and Spain

11 Cretan *Ciſtus* is, *Ciſtus arboreſcens exſtipulatus, foliis ſpathulato-ovatis petiolatis enerviis ſcabris, calycinis lanceolatis* Tournefort calls it, *Ciſtus ladanifera Cretica*, Caſpar Bauhine, *Ciſtus Ledon Cretenſe*, and Alpinus, *Ladanum Creticum* It grows naturally in Crete and Syria

12 Narrow leaved Spaniſh *Ciſtus* is, *Ciſtus arboreſcens exſtipulatus, foliis revoluto linearibus, floribus umbellatis* Barrelier calls it, *Ciſtus anguſto libanotidis folio, flore ſingulari*, and Caſpar Bauhine, *Ciſtus Ledon anguſtis foliis* It is a native of Spain

*Ciſtus* is of the claſs and order *Polyandria Monogynia*, and the characters are,

Claſs and order in the Linnæan ſyſtem The characters

1 Calyx is a permanent perianthium, compoſed of five roundiſh, concave leaves, of which two alternate ones are ſmaller and lower than the others

2 Corolla conſiſts of five roundiſh, large, plane, patent petals

3 Stamina are numerous capillary filaments, ſhorter than the corolla, having ſmall, roundiſh antheræ

4 Pistillum conſiſts of a roundiſh germen, a ſingle ſtyle the length of the ſtamina, and a plane, orbicular ſtigma

5 Pericarpium is a roundiſh, covered capſule

6 Semina The ſeeds are roundiſh, ſmall, and numerous

## CHAP VIII

## *CNEORUM*, WIDOW-WAIL

THERE is only one ſpecies of this genus, which is known in our gardens by the name of Widow Wail It is a ſhrub of about a yard in growth, and is an excellent one for the front of evergreen quarters, where the loweſt ſhrubs are to be placed The wood of this tree is very hard, and the older branches are covered with a brown bark The ſtem naturally divides into many branches, and the bark on the youngeſt is ſmooth, and of a pale-green colour The leaves are ſmooth, of a fine dark green colour, and conſtitute the greateſt beauty of this ſhrub They are of an oblong figure, and very long in proportion to the breadth They will be two inches or more long, and about half an inch in breadth Their under ſurface is of rather a paler green than their upper, and their baſe joins to the young branches without any footſtalk The flowers are yellow, and make no great ſhow You may expect to ſee a healthy plant in blow moſt part of the ſummer They grow from the wings of the leaves, towards the ends of the branches, and are ſucceeded by the ſeeds, which grow together

This ſhrub deſcribed

ther by threes, which will be of a dark-brown or black when they are ripe

*Cneorum* may be propagated by seeds or by cuttings

Method of propagating it by seeds.

1 By seeds These should be gathered in October, and be those which have grown from the first flowers of the shrub that summer, and which will be then black, or nearly so, if ripe They should be sown in a bed of common garden-mould made fine, about half an inch deep You may expect to see your plants come up in the spring though it often happens that the greatest part of them remain until the second spring before they appear Whether your plants come up or not the first spring, let the beds remain undisturbed until the second, with only keeping them clean from weeds The second spring you may expect your whole crop, and in order to thin them, and make room in the beds, those that came up the year before may be carefully drawn out and planted in a shady border, at small distances But if in doing this, you are likely to destroy several young plants that will be then coming up, let all remain until the spring following, when they may be all taken up with care, and planted in a shady border If no such border happens to be vacant, any bed will do, though it will be necessary to secure them from the heat of the sun as that grows more powerful, until at least they have taken root and begun growing, which indeed will be very soon, if moist weather happens at the time of their being planted out If this is wanted, they should be watered, to settle the mould to the roots, and this watering must be continued until the heavens afford it in due season In this bed they may stand two or three years, and may then be planted out for good

and by cuttings

2 These plants may be encreased by cuttings, but they never make such beautiful shrubs, neither is the method worth practising if seeds can be obtained The cuttings may be planted in spring, then it will be necessary to set them in pots, and give them the assistance of an hot bed, and this will set them a growing The beginning of August also is a very good time for planting these cuttings or slips They should be planted in beds of good fine mould, and these should be hooped, and matted from nine o'clock in the morning until near sun-set Then they should be uncovered, and should remain so in all cloudy and rainy weather Most of these cuttings will grow, and there they may remain without removing until they are set out for good

Soils proper for this genus

When these shrubs are to be planted out, the most dry and gravelly spots must be chosen for them and in these places they will bid defiance to our severest weather, though in such a soil they will not grow so high as in a moist fat soil, by a foot or more, which is considerable in a shrub of such a natural low growth, but it is necessary for them to be planted in a dry or gravelly soil, because there they will be secure from injury by frosts, &c These shrubs were formerly, and, indeed, are now by many, treated as greenhouse-plants, but this is known to be unnecessary, for if they are planted in a sandy or gravelly soil, a little sheltered, hardly any weather can hurt them, nay, if they are set in a fat, moist soil (where they will grow more luxurious), even there they will endure the cold of our ordinary winters very well, and if a severe one happens, the greatest damage done to them is generally no more than killing some of the younger branches, which being taken off by the knife as soon as the bad weather is over, they will shoot out from the main stems again in the spring

Title

This shrub is styled singly, *Cneorum* Caspar Bauhine calls it, *Chamelea tricoccos*, Cammerarius and others, *Chamelea* It is found growing in dry and gravelly places in Spain, Italy, and France

Class and order in the Linnæan system

*Cneorum* is of the class and order *Triandria Monogynia*, and the characters are,

The characters

1 Calyx is a small, permanent perianthium, indented in three parts

2 Corolla consists of three oblong, spear-shaped narrow, concave, erect, deciduous petals

3 Stamina are three awl-shaped filaments, shorter than the corolla, having small antheræ

4 Pistillum consists of an obtuse, three-cornered germen, an erect firm style the length of the stamina, and a patent trifid stigma

5 Pericarpium is a dry, globular, trilobate berry, containing three cells

6 Semina The seeds are round, and single in each of the cells

## CHAP IX

## *CUPRESSUS*, The CYPRESS-TREE

Species

THE evergreen species of this genus are,

1 Common Cypress
2 Small Blue-berried Cypress
3 Cape Cypress

Common Cypress

1 Common Cypress Little need be added here after reading what has been said under this article among the Evergreen Forest-trees, where the Reader will see an account of two of the chief varieties that are most generally planted, and will thence know their use and value These shall stand first in our present order, and I will add another sort to complete the variety we may expect from this species, and then the Common Cypress, in its sorts, will stand thus

Varieties

The Female Cypress
The Male Cypress
The Smaller-fruited Cypress

described

The Female Cypress It has been observed, that this tree is of all the sorts the most beautiful and picturesque, and from thence the reader may infer the effect these pyramidical trees will have when growing stationed in almost any place, but particularly when planted to advantage in those most proper for them

The Male Cypress. It has also been remarked, that this sort is naturally of larger growth, and affords excellent timber; that its branches are more spreading, &c. and after this, nothing more need be added here, for the Reader's information.

The Smaller-fruited Cypress is still more spreading than the other, and produces its boughs in an irregular manner. If it is not crowded by other trees, and is left to Nature, it will be feathered from the top to the bottom. It will grow to about the height of the Common Cypress, and is a sort that looks well if planted singly on grass plats, &c. as well as when assisting to form clumps, or larger quarters of Ever-greens.

Small Blue-berried Cypress.

2. Small Blue-berried Cypress. This is the lowest grower of all the sorts with us; though in America, where it grows naturally, it arrives to timber, which serves for many excellent purposes. The tallest of these trees I have seen has not been higher than fifteen feet; and as this tree is encreased by cuttings, those plants raised this way seldom rise higher than about nine or ten feet. The branches stand two ways, and are pretty numerous, and the tree naturally forms itself into a regular head. The leaves of this sort also are imbricated, like the *Arbor Vitæ*, though smaller, and are of a browner kind of green than the Common Cypress. The fruit is very small, and of a blue colour, and will be produced in great plenty all over the plant. They are of the size of the juniper-berry, and much resemble it, though they are cones, and like the other species of this genus, but much smaller. When these plants are raised from seeds they will aspire to a great height, especially if planted in a moist soil; but those raised by cuttings generally have the appearance of shrubs. They are all, however, very beautiful, and greatly embellish those parts of the evergreen plantations where they are stationed.

Cape Cypress.

3. Cape Cypress. The branches of this species are numerous, slender, and spread themselves all around. The leaves are narrow, awl-shaped, about an inch long, of a light green colour, and grow opposite to each other on the branches. The flowers come out from the sides of the branches, like the Common Cypress, and they are succeeded by black fruit; but the seeds never ripen in England.

Methods of propagating the different sorts.

The method of propagating the Common Cypress has been already shewn, and by that method plenty of the Common sorts may be obtained. With regard to the Small Blue-berried and Cape Cypress, the seeds should be sown in pots or boxes. We receive them from abroad. They are very small, and seldom come up before the second spring; so that there will be less danger of their being lost if they are sown in pots or boxes, which may be set in the shade in summer, and removed into well-sheltered places during the winter. In the spring the plants will come up, and after that the Blue-berried Cypress may have the same treatment as the young seedlings of the Common sort. With respect to the Cape Cypress, the plants must be set in pots, to be housed in winter, until they are grown to be a yard high. When they are turned out into the open air, they should have a dry, warm soil, and a well-sheltered place; and even there will not ensure their safety; so that whoever is desirous of having these trees in his plantations, should have some wooden fences made, to cover them with in frosty weather; and if this is observed until they are grown of a tolerable size, I make no doubt but they will live, in a warm well-sheltered place, through our common winters.

Titles.

1. The Common Cypress, with its varieties, is titled, *Cupressus foliis imbricatis, frondibus quadrangulis*. Linnæus had called it, *Cupressus foliis imbricatis erectis*, but altered it to the former. Caspar Bauhine, Camerarius, &c. call it simply, *Cupressus*. Tournefort, *Cupressus meta in fastigium convoluta quæ fœmina*; also *Cupressus ramos extra se spargens quæ mas*. It grows naturally in Italy and Spain, but particularly in Portugal, and in the Isle of Crete.

2. Small Blue-berried Cypress is, *Cupressus foliis imbricatis, frondibus ancipitibus*. Plukenet calls it, *Cupressus nana mariana, fructu cæruleo parvo*. It grows common in Canada.

3. Cape Cypress is, *Cupressus foliis oppositis decussatis subulatis patentibus*. In Miller's Dictionary it is termed, *Cupressus foliis linearibus subquadrifariam oppositis*. It grows naturally at the Cape of Good Hope.

## CHAP. X.

## *CYTISUS*, BASE TREE TREFOIL.

Shrub described.

THIS species of *Cytisus* proper for this place is commonly known in our gardens by the name of Evergreen *Cytisus* of Naples. This shrub is naturally of an upright growth, and its common height is about six or seven feet. It may be trained up to a single stem, for two, three, or four feet high, and will naturally send out many branches, which will form themselves into a fine head. The bark on the main stem is of a grey colour, the branches also are grey with a green cast at a distance, and many of them will have the appearance of being channelled, the bottom of the grooves being of a dusky green, but their upper edges white. The younger shoots are green and streaked, and their surface is hairy. The leaves also have this property, and stand three upon a short footstalk. They are nearly of an oval figure, and have a strong mid-rib running the whole length. They are of a fine green colour, and cloath the shrub with great beauty. The flowers are of a clear yellow colour, and are shaped like those of the other sorts. They appear in June, and are produced from the sides of the branches, all over the shrub, in short bunches, so that its golden head at that time is both beautiful and striking. Neither is June the only time of its flowering; for it will often flower again in October, and, if the

the winter continues open and mild, it will ſometimes boaſt flowers in November and December. The flowers that appeared in June, which is its regular time of blow, will be ſucceeded by ſmall hairy pods, in which the ſeeds are contained, and which ripen with us very well in the autumn.

Method of propagating this tree

This ſort ſhould be propagated by ſeeds, which ſhould be ſown in the ſpring and managed as was directed for the deciduous ſorts, only it may not be amiſs to obſerve, that it will be neceſſary to plant them in the nurſery when they have ſtood one year in the ſeed bed. They ſhould be ſet about a foot aſunder, in rows at two feet diſtance, and here they may ſtand for about two years, when they ſhould be planted for good.

Titles of this tree

The Evergreen *Cytiſus* of Naples is titled, *Cytiſus pedunculis ſimplicibus lateralibus, calycibus hirſutis trifidis ventricoſo oblongis*. In the *Hortus Cliffortianus* it is termed, *Cytiſus calycibus hirſutis ſeſſilibus, pedunculis ſimplicibus breviſſimis*. Cluſius calls it, *Cytiſus*, and Caſpar Bauhine, *Cytiſus incanus, ſiliqua longiore*, alſo, *Cytiſus foliis ſubrotundis lanuginoſis hirſutis*. It grows naturally in Italy (particularly about Naples), in Spain, Auſtria, and Siberia.

## CHAP. XI.

## *DAPHNE*, The SPURGE-LAUREL.

Introductory obſervation

THIS ſpecies of *Daphne* is commonly known by the name of Spurge-Laurel, and is an evergreen which has many excellencies, as well as beauties, to recommend it to the planter. It will grow and flouriſh, if ever ſo much crouded with other ſhrubs, and the drippings of taller trees ſeem to exhilarate this plant; for in thoſe places the leaves are of a pure delightful green, without being tarniſhed by the heat of the ſun, which is one excellent property, and renders the ſhrub very uſeful to be ſet in wilderneſs-quarters, where large trees are already grown, and where few plants are to be found that will thrive under them. The other good properties of this ſhrub are as follow.

The ſhrub deſcribed

It is a low ſhrub, ſeldom growing more than a yard or four feet high, it ſends out many branches from the bottom, and theſe are covered with a ſmooth light-brown bark, that is very thick. The bark on the younger branches is ſmooth and green, and theſe are very cloſely garniſhed with leaves of a delightful ſtrong lucid green colour. Theſe leaves ſit cloſe to the branches, and are produced in ſuch plenty that they have the appearance, at a ſmall diſtance, of cluſters at the ends of the branches. They are ſpear-ſhaped, ſhining, thick, and ſmooth, their edges are entire, and this is another excellent property of this tree, that it is thus poſſeſſed of ſuch delightful leaves for its ornament. Theſe leaves, when growing under the drip of trees, ſpread open, and exhibit their green pure and untarniſhed, in its natural colour, when planted ſingly in expoſed places, they naturally turn back with a kind of twiſt, and the natural green of the leaf is often alloyed with a browniſh tinge. This ſhrub is alſo valuable on account of its flowers, not becauſe they make any great ſhow, but from their fragrance, and the time they appear; for it will be in blow the beginning of January, and will continue ſo until the middle or latter end of April before the flowers fall off, during which time they never fail to diffuſe abroad their agreeable odours, which are refreſhing and inoffenſive. In the evenings eſpecially, they are more than commonly liberal, inſomuch that a few plants will often perfume the whole end of a garden, and when this happens early, before many flowers appear, the unſkilful in flowers, perceiving an uncommon fragrancy, are at once ſtruck with ſurprize, and immediately begin enquiring from whence it can proceed. Neither are its odours confined to a garden only, but, when planted near windows, they will enter parlours, and aſcend even into bed-chambers, to the great comfort of the poſſeſſor, and ſurprize of every freſh viſitor. Theſe flowers make but little ſhow, for they are ſmall, and of a greeniſh yellow. They are produced amongſt the leaves from the ſides of the ſtalks, in ſmall cluſters, and will often be ſo hid by them, as to be unnoticed by any but the curious. They are ſucceeded by oval berries which are firſt green, and afterwards black when ripe. Theſe berries will be in ſuch plenty as to be very ornamental, but will ſoon be eaten up by the birds, which is another good property of this tree, as it invites the different ſorts of whiſtling birds to flock where it is planted in great plenty.

Method of raiſing it

This ſhrub is raiſed by ſeeds, in the ſame manner as the Common *Mezereon*. The ſeeds muſt be preſerved from the birds by nets, until they are ripe. Soon after, they muſt be ſown as is directed for the *Mezereon*. They will often be two years before they come up, during which time, and afterwards, they may have the ſame management as has been laid down for the Common *Mezereon*, until they are ſet out for good, which may be in any ſoil or ſituation, but particularly under large trees, where they will flouriſh in their natural elegance and beauty.

Titles of this ſpecies

The Spurge-Laurel is titled, *Daphne racemis axillaribus foliis lanceolatis glabris*. In the *Hortus Cliffortianus* it is termed, *Daphne racemis lateralibus, foliis lanceolatis integris*. Caſpar Bauhine calls it, *Laureola ſempervirens, flore viridi*; Tournefort, *Thymelæa lauri folio ſempervirens, ſeu laureola mas*, Dodonæus and others ſimply, *Laureola*, and *Laureola mas*. It grows naturally in woods and hedges in many parts of England, we have it growing in Brampton Wood, and among the black thorns in Deſborough-Field, in Northamptonſhire and Leiceſterſhire. It grows alſo in Switzerland, France, and upon Mount Baldus.

CHAP.

# CHAP. XII.

## *EPHEDRA*, The SHRUBBY HORSE-TAIL.

SINGULARITY as well as beauty, in the vegetable tribe, contributes its ſhare in rendering plantations delightful, not only as it encreaſes variety, but ſhould it happen to be clothed even with deformity itſelf it anſwers ſome ends, and ſerves as a foil to ſet other trees off, and cauſe them to appear with a double ſplendor. The plant before us, though ſingular, is not deſtitute of beauty, and I have choſe to introduce it in this place, becauſe it is always green, and conſequently by no means improper to join in the claſs of plants that are to form a plantation of Evergreens. The Shrubby Horſe-Tail, then, will grow to three, four, five, or ſix feet high, according to the nature of the ſoil in which it is placed; for if it be a fat moiſt ſoil, it will arrive to double the height it will attain in that of a contrary nature, and will be more ſhrubby, tree-like, will have much larger leaves, and be more beautiful. The bark of the old ſtem is rough, and of a dark, dirty colour. Theſe ſtems or branches are few, but they have joints at ſhort intervals. Many of them are protuberant, and ſend forth younger ſhoots and leaves in prodigious plenty, ſo as to cauſe the ſhrub to have a cloſe buſhy look. The older of theſe branches will have bark that is ſmooth, and of a brown, reddiſh, or yellowiſh colour, whilſt that on the younger will be of a fine green. Theſe branches are jointed and hollow, though they have often in them a kind of reddiſh pith; they ſend forth ſmaller, which are called the leaves. Theſe leaves are jointed, grow oppoſite by pairs, are alternately produced at every joint in oppoſite directions, and will thus branch out in that ſingular and horſe-tail manner, in a ſuitable ſoil, to a great length, and the beauty they will then have may be eaſily gueſſed at. *This ſhrub deſcribed.*

The leaves or ſhoots of this ſhrub being bruiſed in the winter, emit a very fetid diſagreeable ſcent, but in the ſpring when the juices begin to flow, they are poſſeſſed of a different quality. The plants in all my gardens, being bruiſed, emit a fine odour, and are by many ſuppoſed or fancied to be like that of the pine-apple; and on account of this ſcent alone, in the ſpring, this tree is by many much coveted and admired. The flower buds will appear in May oppoſite at the ſides of the joints, they grow by pairs, and by the middle of June will be in full blow, each ſtanding on very ſhort green foot-ſtalks. Male and female flowers will be found on different plants; they are ſmall, and of a yellow colour, and afford pleaſure only to the nice obſerver of the wonderful ſtructure of all the minute parts of the vegetable world. This ſhrub ſhould always have a moiſt, fat ſoil, and in thoſe places it will appear more luxuriant and beautiful. It is very hardy, and although it has been uſed to be preſerved in pots in greenhouſes, I never yet found a ſingle plant, in the moſt expoſed places, ſuffer from the cold of our ſevereſt winters. In the winter the leaves, or rather young ſhoots or joints, are of a dark, duſky green; but as the ſpring approaches, that goes off, and a fine, lively, chearful green poſſeſſes the whole plant. The old leaves fall off the latter end of April or beginning of May, at which time the tree will ſend forth young ones, and will continue to do ſo until late in the autumn.

This ſhrub is very eaſily encreaſed, for it will propagate itſelf in great plenty, eſpecially if planted in a light, moiſt ſoil. So that where a quantity is wanted, ſome plants are to be procured for breeders, and theſe being planted in good light earth, will ſoon ſpread their roots, and produce plenty of ſpawn, which may be taken off, and planted in the nurſery ground, to gain ſtrength, for a year or two, or they may be immediately, eſpecially the ſtrongeſt plants, ſet out for good. As theſe ſhrubs naturally ſpawn, and produce ſuckers in great plenty, after they are ſet out in the wilderneſs quarters for good, the ſpawn ſhould be every year taken off, and the ground dug about the roots, otherwiſe they will not only appear rambling and irregular, but they will diminiſh the beauty of the mother plants, which will by no means appear to be luxuriant and healthy. *Method of propagating this tree.*

The title of this ſhrub is, *Ephedra pedunculis oppoſitis amentis geminis*. Caſpar Bauhine calls it, *Polygonum bacciferum maritimum majus*; and Cammerarius, *Tragum*. It grows naturally on the rocky mountains, near the ſea-coaſts, both of Italy, France, and Spain. *Titles of this ſpecies.*

*Ephedra* is of the claſs and order *Dioecia Monadelphia*, and the characters are, *Claſs and order in the Linnæan ſyſtem.* *The characters.*

I. Male Flowers are collected into an oval amentum.

1. CALYX is compoſed of a few, roundiſh, concave ſcales, each of which contains a ſingle flower. The proper perianthium is ſmall, of one leaf, and half cut into two roundiſh, obtuſe, compreſſed parts.

2. COROLLA. There is none.

3. STAMINA are ſeven filaments, that coaleſce in form of a ſubulated column, having roundiſh antheræ, of which four are inferior, the other three ſuperior.

II. Female Flowers.

1. CALYX is an oval perianthium, compoſed of five ranges of leaves, which are alternately placed over each other.

2. COROLLA. There is none.

3. PISTILLUM conſiſts of two oval germina, ſituated on the perianthium, having ſimple, filiform, ſhort ſtyles, and ſingle ſtigmas.

4. PERICARPIUM. There is none. The calycinal ſquammæ ſurround the ſeeds.

5. SEMINA. The ſeeds are two, oval, and acute, convex on one ſide, on the other plane.

CHAP.

## CHAP. XIII.

## *EVONYMUS*, The SPINDLE-TREE.

AMERICA sends us one species of *Evonymus* for our evergreen wilderness-quarters, which richly deserves a place in any Collection, not only as it is a fine evergreen, but at present is not very common in our gardens. This species is known by the name of Evergreen Spindle-tree; and besides this, there is the variegated sort of it, having the leaves beautifully striped with yellow, and which will cause a variety when the variegated sorts of trees that retain their leaves are to be admitted as evergreens, and placed amongst them. These sorts grow to the height of about seven feet. The branches are slender, covered with a smooth green bark, and grow opposite by pairs at the joints. The leaves also grow opposite, are spear-shaped, and have a strong mid-rib, running their whole length. Their upper surface is of a fine strong green colour, but their under is paler. They are smooth, are lightly indented, acute pointed, and justly entitle this shrub to be called a fine evergreen. The flowers are produced in July, from the sides and ends of the branches, in small bunches. They are of no great figure; but they will be succeeded by rough, warted, red, five-cornered capsules, containing the seeds.

Description of this tree.

This species is to be propagated in the same manner as the other sorts. The best way is from seeds, which we receive from Virginia. These will be two, and sometimes three years before they appear; so that a person should not be too hasty in disturbing the beds; and after this precaution, what has been formerly said relating to the management of raising the common sorts of Spindle-trees from seeds, must constantly be observed in this species.

Method of propagating it by seeds,

By layers also, and cuttings, it may be encreased; but when the latter way is to be practised, it will be proper to plant each cutting separately in a small pot, and plunge them into a bark-bed, otherwise it is very seldom that they will grow. After they have taken root, the pots may be set in the natural mould up to the rims for about two years; then the plants should be turned out into the places where they are to remain, and they will be sure of growing.

layers and cuttings.

This species is titled, *Evonymus floribus omnibus quinquefidis*. Gronovius calls it *Evonymus foliis lanceolatis*; Plukenet, *Evonymus Virginianus, pyracanthæ foliis, capsulâ verrucarum instar asperata*; and Commeline, *Rhus Virginianum folio myrti*. In the *Hortus Cliffortianus* it is termed, *Celastrus foliis oppositis ovatis integerrimis, floribus sessilitariis*; and in the Upsal Catalogue, *Evonymus foliis lato lanceolatis serratis*. It grows naturally in Virginia.

Titles.

## CHAP. XIV.

## *ILEX*, The HOLLY-TREE.

THE hardy evergreen species of this genus are,

Species.

1. Common Holly.
2. Dohoon Holly.

1. Common Holly. If we separately consider our Common Holly, we shall find it exceeded by no evergreen, either for beauty or use. Its naturally upright growth, the grey colour of its main trunk, the smooth fine green of the younger shoots, the lively verdure of the leaves at all seasons, together with their singular make, and the fine red of the numerous berries, growing in clusters in such great profusion, demand our respect, and force us to acknowledge its eminence. Its uses are as various; for from these properties it may easily be conceived how well these trees will suit with evergreen plantations of any kind, either for clumps, or to be set out singly in large opens, where their upright stems will advance to be thirty or more feet high; and if left to Nature from the first, many of them will be feathered to the very bottom, forming as it were a kind of cone, whose base is at the ground. Its uses extend also to hedges of all kinds, either for real fences for pasture grounds, as has been shewn, or for ornamental partitions in gardens, either to be clipped, or permitted to run in its natural state. Besides, what should make us still more in love with this plant (which is, indeed, by too many the cause of its being despised), is, that it is of our own breed. Britain can boast the Holly, with all its varieties, to be her offspring. And certainly we should never wholly neglect our neighbours, for the sake of foreign guests. There are variety of evergreens of this genus; but if we enumerate the variegated kinds, here we find such a hoard of Collection as deserves infinite praise, and excites a degree of enthusiasm in a manner enchanting. The evergreen sorts, then, are,

Common Holly.

Sorts,

- The Common Holly.
- The Smooth leaved Holly.
- The Green leaved Yellow berried Holly.
- The Box-leaved Holly.
- The Hedge-Hog Holly.
- The Sawed-leaved Holly.

The variegated sorts are known in our gardens by the names of, and variegated kinds

Fair Phillis
Fuller Cream
Chohole
Milkmaid
Chimneysweeper
Partridge's Holly
Wise's Holly
Broderick's Holly
Glory of the East
Glory of the West
Cheney's Holly
Ellis's Holly
Gray's Holly
Longstaff's Holly
Bradley's best
Blotched Yellow berried
Mason's Copper coloured
Painted Lady
Bench's Ninepenny
Blind's Cream
Pritchet's
Sir Thomas Franklin's
Brittain's
Whitmel's
Bradley's Long-leaved
Bradley's Yellow
Bridgman's
Wells's
Glass's
Bagshot's
Brownrig's
Hertfordshire White
Common Blotched
Silver Hedge-Hog
Yellow Blotched Hedge-Hog
Langton Holly

described

The Common Holly is so well known that, together with what has been formerly said, nothing more is necessary to be added concerning it

The Smooth-leaved Holly is a variety of the Common sort Of the two it seems to be the strongest shooter, and bids fair for the largest growing tree The leaves are nearly oval, and most of them are entirely free from prickles, only they end in acute points This sort is commonly called the Carolina Smooth-leaved Holly But it is a native of England, and is found growing amongst the others in many parts

The Green leaved Yellow-berried Holly differs in no respect from the Common Holly, only the berries are yellow, and as this tree produces berries in plenty, which are thought by most people to be uncommon and curious, this sort, on their account, richly deserves a place, either in small or large gardens, in wilderness quarters, or plantations of any kind

The Box-leaved Holly has but little claim to be so called, for though some of the leaves be small, pretty free from prickles, and nearly oval, yet there will be so many nearly as prickly as the Common Holly as to merit no claim to that appellation The leaves, however, are small, and by them, on that account, the chief variety is occasioned

The Hedge-Hog Holly has the borders of the leaves armed with strong thorns, and the surface beset with acute prickles, a little resembling those of an hedge-hog, which gave occasion to this sort being so called by the Gardener This singularity causes great admiration in all beholders, neither is it less beautiful than singular, and this, together with the Striped sorts of it, are justly ranked amongst our Hollies of the first rate

The Sawed leaved Holly is a kind very different from any of the other sorts The leaves are as long as any of the sorts, very narrow, and of a thick substance Their edges are formed into the likeness of a saw, though they are not very sharp and prickly This is a very scarce and valuable Holly, and is by all admired

These six sorts of themselves form a Collection truly valuable, and are, as it were, some of the main supports of the honour due to our evergreen ornamental plantations, and if the variegated sorts are also to have a share, which they may properly enough (though this must be according to the owner's taste) as they retain their leaves, though tinged with variety of colours, we introduce then a fresh Collection which for variety and beauty far exceeds not only the variegated sorts belonging to any one genus, but perhaps all the variegated sorts of trees and shrubs put together

The sorts in the list are thirty six in number, all differing in colour, shape of their leaves, manner of growth, or some other respect, and though indeed the difference of many of these sorts is so inconsiderable, as to be distinguished by none but a close examiner, yet the generality of them are so widely different as to cause variety in its utmost extent for what can be more different than the Silver striped, the Gold, the Copper coloured, the Narrow leaved Cream coloured, the Broad-leaved Gold Blotched, the Silver and Gold Hedge-Hogs, are from all the other sorts, in a Collection of variegated Hollies, for they ought to be planted in clumps or in quarters by themselves? Like auriculas, polyanthuses, tulips, &c which, when set singly, make little figure, and often are passed unnoticed but when planted in proper numbers in beds, they strike the imagination, so it is with these hollies, there is no conception of the grandeur of a Collection, by seeing a few straggling plants standing singly at a distance, for though these, like an odd tulip, &c may be beautiful in themselves, they seem not qualified to present such striking grandeur as they all do, when they compose a regular quarter or clump There we see the opposite colours of yellow, white, and green, shaded in that easy way which belongs to Nature there we see the Cream, the Copper-coloured, and the Bench, blended as it were in the whole superficies There the many different sizes and shapes of the leaves, and many tings of colours, unite to cause the greater variety A Collection of variegated Hollies, planted this way, has been justly compared to a fine piece of painting, and indeed I believe there is no painting in the world that charms the imagination, or strikes the fancy, more than this What induces me to believe this is, I never yet knew a person, who, upon first viewing a quarter of these trees in our nursery, but has been forced to acknowledge their power and effect, and what is still a greater recommendation to these trees is, their beauty is in the greatest perfection in the winter months In the summer we have variety of objects, that daily present themselves in a succession, in a pleasing view In winter they are rare and scarce, but at that season the leaves of many of the sorts of Hollies will be as beautiful as several of our summer flowers, and the whole shew will have a grander figure than the summer's Collection of most sorts And here I cannot but recommend the planting of clumps of these trees amongst our quarters of evergreens, for to those, by their green colour, represent the verdure of the flourishing summer, so the Hollies will heighten the contrast, and look like a bed of flowers of the noblest blow, and thus, both will stand, truly symbolical of eternal spring or everlasting summer

But

Method of propagating the sorts

But let us proceed to the culture of all these sorts We have already shewn how the Common English Holly may be raised from the berry That method is to be practised, and plenty of that sort may be raised These are to be stocks, on which the others are to be budded or grafted, for though they will take by layers, yet plants raised that way are of little or no value, and if the berries of the variegated sorts be sown, the plants will come up plain, and be our Common English Holly Thus from Hedge Hog berries plants of the Hedge-Hog Holly are frequently raised

grafting budding

By grafting or budding, then, these sorts must be propagated, and for this purpose young stocks must be raised of the Common Holly, as has been already directed After they have stood two years in the seed bed, they should be taken up, have their roots shortened, and be planted out in the nursery, a foot asunder, in rows at two feet distance The summer following they will probably make few shoots, but the summer after that, they will shoot strongly, and when the operation is to be performed by grafting, these will be proper stocks for the purpose by the spring following The first week in March is a good time for the work Whip grafting is the method to be practised, and it must be performed on the young wood, namely, on that of the preceding summer's shoot The cions being cut true and even, and well jointed to the stock, many of them will grow, and this is a very good method of encreasing these trees

and inoculation

They may also be multiplied at pleasure by inoculation This operation is best performed about ten days after Midsummer, in cloudy weather, and for want of this, evening should be the time, and if much work is to be done, morning too may be added, nay it may be practised all day in the hottest seasons, and with good success, but this is never so eligible, unless when the multiplicity of work obliges us to lose no time The young wood of the preceding summer's shoot is proper for the purpose, and the operation is to be performed in the usual way In the autumn the bands should be loosed, and in spring the stocks dressed up, and headed two or three inches above the bud, the buds will be as early in shooting out as any of the shoots of the growing trees, and will soon become good plants for any place

Dohoon holly

2 The Dohoon Holly is an American plant, particularly of Carolina, where it grows to be nearly as large a tree as our holly does with us It naturally rises with an upright stem, which is covered with a brown bark, and this affords plenty of younger branches, whose bark is green and very smooth The leaves are pretty large, and of an oval lanceolated figure, they are of a thickish composition, of a fine green, and grow alternately on the branches Their edges are serrated, though altogether different from the Common Sawed Holly, their serratures towards the upper end of the leaf being small and sharp The leaf, on the whole, is of a fine composition, and grows on short footstalks on the branches The flowers are small and white, and a little resemble those of the Common Holly They are produced from the sides of the branches, in short thick clusters, and are succeeded by red berries, equalling those of our Common sort in beauty

The Dohoon Holly may be propagated by seeds, which we receive from the countries where it grows naturally, for the berries will not ripen, and indeed are very seldom produced, in England The best way is to sow them in pots filled with light sandy earth, as soon as they arrive, and then plunge them up to the rims in the natural mould, where they may remain until the spring following, for they rarely ever come up the first summer The spring after that the plants will appear, and if they have then the assistance of a hotbed, it will greatly help them forward They must be used to the open air soon The pots must be taken up and plunged in a shady place, and in October they should be removed into the greenhouse for the winter In the spring the plants in the pots may be thinned by drawing out the strongest, and those thus drawn should be planted each in a separate pot, and must be set forward with a hotbed as before The others, also, may be taken out at two or three years growth, planted in pots, and assisted in the same manner Every October they should be removed into the greenhouse, set out in the spring, and treated as greenhouse-plants, until they are at least five or six years old, for before then they will be hardly woody enough to venture the planting them out for good The latter end of March, when the danger of bad weather is chiefly over, is the best time for the purpose, and if they have a dry soil and warm situation, they will bear the cold of our common winters, though if a very severe winter should happen before they are got very strong and woody, it is extremely probable that all of them will be destroyed

Method of propagating it

Titles.

1 The title of the Common Holly is, *Ilex foliis ovatis acutis spinosis* Caspar Bauhine calls it, *Ilex aculeata baccifera*, and John Bauhine, *Aquifolium, sive agrifolium vulgo* It grows naturally in most of the northern parts of Europe, but particularly in Britain

2 The Dohoon Holly is, *Ilex foliis ovato-lanceolatis serratis* Catesby calls it, *Aquifolium Carolinense, foliis dentatis, baccis rubris* It grows common in Carolina

Class and order in the Linnean system The characters

*Ilex* is of the class and order *Tetrandria Tetragynia*, and the characters are,

1 CALYX is a small, permanent perianthium, indented in four parts

2 COROLLA consists of a plane petal, divided into four large, roundish, concave, patent segments, which cohere only by their ungues

3 STAMINA are four awl-shaped filaments, shorter than the corolla, having small antheræ

4. PISTILLUM consists of a roundish germen, no style, but four obtuse stigmas

5 PERICARPIUM is a roundish berry, of four cells

6 SEMEN The seed is single, hard, oblong, obtuse, gibbous on one side, and angular on the other

CHAP

# CHAP XV

## JUNIPERUS, The JUNIPER-TREE

Introductory cautions

THE Gardener little acquainted with botany, perhaps, may expect to find under this head only the Juniper tree that affords the berries of the shops for use, or perhaps at farthest a variety or two of this species But how agreeably will he be surprised, when he finds that there are nine real species of this genus, and many of them which also afford varieties for his use! The Savin and the Cedrus of old Botanists, which used to go under the old names of *Sabina*, *Cedrus*, &c are now found to belong to it But if ever he should make any advancement into Botany, he will be not only satisfied but pleased, when he finds how properly they are ranked here, being stationed as species of that genus to which Nature designed them of course to belong The real and distinct species, then, of the Juniper tree are,

Species

1 Common Juniper
2 Spanish Juniper
3 Virginian Cedar
4 Cedar of Bermudas
5 Jamaica Cedar
6 Spanish Cedar
7 Lycian Cedar
8 Phenician Cedar
9 Savin

Common Juniper Varieties

1 Of the Common Juniper there are two principal varieties, called,

English Juniper
Swedish Juniper

Described

The English Juniper, though naturally of our own growth, is very little known in many parts of England, for it grows naturally only on dry, chalky, sandy, hard, and where the soil is opposite to this, it may never be expected to be found Thus, in Leicestershire it is so little known, that when growing amongst other trees in a shrubbery, it is as much enquired after as any of the most rare and curious sorts, and indeed, when properly raised from seeds and planted in gardens, it is a pretty spreading evergreen shrub Those who have been used to see it in its wild state, on sandy, barren commons &c will have little motive to plant it, as there they will see it a mere moor, and seldom shewing a natural tendency to aspire, but when planted in a good soil, it will grow to the height of fifteen or sixteen feet, and will produce numerous branches from the bottom to the top, and will form a well-looking, bushy plant These branches are exceeding tough, and covered with a smooth bark, which, in some parts, will be falling This bark is of a reddish colour, with a gentle tinge of purple The leaves are narrow, and sharp pointed They grow by threes on the branches, their upper surface has a greyish streak down the middle, but their undersides of a fine green colour, and they garnish the shrub in great plenty This tree flowers in April and May The flowers are small, of a yellowish colour, and make no figure They are succeeded by the berries, which are of a kind of a bluish purple when ripe, which will not be before the autumn twelvemonth following

The Swedish Juniper has a natural tendency to grow to a greater height, and consequently has more the appearance of a tree than the former sort, sixteen or eighteen feet, however, is the highest it commonly grows to, and the plants raised from its seeds have, for the most part, a tendency to grow higher, and become more woody and ramose The leaves, flowers, and fruit, grow in the same manner, and are of the same nature which shews it to be a variety only Old Botanists mention it as a distinct species Caspar Bauhine asserts this, and calls one the Shrubby Juniper, and the other Tree Juniper, and he also mentions another sort, which he calls the Lesser Mountain Juniper, with a broader leaf and a larger fruit This is still a variety of the Common Juniper The leaves, flowers, and fruit, however, are much the same, though there may be some difference in the size of their growth From what has been said the Gardener will know, when he meets with them by those different names, where to plant them in suitable places

It is observable of both these sorts, that in the beginning or middle of May, when they will be in full blow, the farina of the male flowers is discharged in such plenty, that upon striking the shrub with a stick it will rise up, in a still air, like a column of white smoak and like it will be wafted with the gentlest wind, until it is lost or out of sight

Spanish Juniper

2 Spanish Juniper will grow to be rather an higher tree than the Swedish, in some soils It will be feathered from the bottom to the top, if left untouched from the first planting, or if not crouded with other trees The leaves are awl-shaped, and finely spread open They are very short, sharp-pointed, and give the tree a fine look Few besides real Botanists, or lovers of the science, take but little notice of the flowers of any of the sorts, but those of this shrub are succeeded by large reddish berries, which are very beautiful when ripe

Virginian Cedar

3 Virginian Cedar There are several varieties of this species which go by the names of,

Its varieties

Red Virginian Cedar
Carolina Cedar, &c

Described

And indeed the Virginian and Carolina Cedars are with good reason supposed varieties only, as the seeds brought from either country will produce trees of much difference in the manner of their leafing and branching Thus, these two sorts differ from one another The Carolina sort has on the ends of the youngest shoots imbricated leaves, but lower they are narrow and sharp-pointed The leaves of the Virginian sort also have these properties They are called by Gardeners the Virginian and Carolina Cedars as being brought from those countries The raised seeds which I have produced trees of very great variety, insomuch that in a small quantity I have caused no less than twenty sorts, differing in some respect or other, both in their manner of growth, nature of their leaves, colour, &c though all have a tendency to grow in a conical, picturesque form

These sorts make a sweet variety, even among themselves, and they render a place very entertaining, when properly disposed amongst others of their own ſize The Red Virginian Cedar has already been treated of in the Firſt Book, and thither to avoid repetition, the reader is referred for his further information In that general deſcription is included the ſort called the Carolina, and all the varieties to be found of these kinds, ſo that nothing more need be added here, than to remind the Gardener that he muſt not wonder if he is not delighted with the flowers, though the curious obſerver of Nature will ſee great beauty in them They are ſmall, brown, conical, and grow on the ends of the youngeſt ſhoots, in April They have the properties of flowers belonging to their claſs, and are ſucceeded by a ſmall blue or purple berry The leaves of theſe trees being bruiſed, emit a ſtrong odour, which to many is agreeable, and ſaid to be refreſhing, whilſt others perceive a different effect

Cedar of Bermudas. 4 Cedar of Bermudas is a very tender plant, and requires not only a dry warm ſoil, and a well ſheltered ſituation, but open mild winters, to make it continue through them, ſo that when a perſon is deſirous of having an extenſive Collection, then and then only are theſe ſorts to be ſought after When they are planted abroad in the warmeſt places, ſheds ſhould be made for them of boards well cloſed, and ſhould be at hand for the Gardener to cover the plants with at the firſt approach of froſty weather, and to uncover them at its departure Theſe ſheds are to be enlarged as the trees advance in height, for though they will more peculiarly want protection when young, yet a ſevere froſt, with cutting black winds, will endanger the deſtroying very full-grown trees Theſe ſheds may be made like the centinel boxes, and muſt always be of a proportionable ſize to the tree This ſpecies grows to be a large timber-tree in America, and we uſed to receive the wood from thence in greater plenty than we do at preſent It is poſſeſſed of a very ſtrong odour, and rooms wainſcoted with it are much ſcented, which to many is agreeable, but not to all; though moſt perſons agree it renders the air wholeſome We never muſt expect to raiſe this tree to anſwer any purpoſes in the timber-way, the moſt we may expect is a few only in our plantations, for variety and obſervation It is obſervable, as theſe trees advance in growth, their branches become cornered, and their leaves ſuffer a change in their nature They are narrow, ſharp pointed, and produced by threes round the branches, ſpreading open in a pretty manner The leaves afterwards grow ſhorter, and are produced by fours, without having any tendency to ſpread open The flowers are produced nearly in the ſame manner as the Virginian kinds, and are ſucceeded by purpliſh berries

Jamaica. 5 Jamaica Cedar is a very large timber-tree in Jamaica and other iſlands where it grows naturally, and is much ſought after for the building of ſhips, &c The branches are ſpreading, many are cornered, and their bark is rough, and of a brown colour The leaves grow by fours, and lie over each other They are ſmall, the older leaves are ſharp-pointed, but the younger are more oval, and many are imbricated in a manner like the cypreſs Neither the male nor female flowers, which are found on different plants, make any figure, and they are ſucceeded by a ſmall browniſh berry This is a very tender plant, though if it has a ſhed like the other, it may be nurſed until it becomes a large tree In very hard froſts, care muſt be taken to lay plenty of litter, &c round the bottom of the ſhed (which muſt indeed be obſerved for both the ſorts), to keep the froſt from penetrating into the ground The ſhed muſt be always taken off, and the litter kept from the ſtem, on the firſt return of fine open weather

6 Spaniſh Cedar grows plentifully in the country by whoſe name it is diſtinguiſhed, and is itſelf a regular growing tree, riſing in a conical form, if the branches are untouched, to the height of thirty or more feet The leaves are imbricated, and lie over each other four ways, they are acute, and of a fine green colour From theſe properties only, an idea of a fine tree may be had The flowers are inſignificant to a common obſerver, but they are ſucceeded by berries which make a good ſhow when ripe for they are very large, and of a fine black colour, and adorn the young branches in great plenty Spaniſh,

7 Lycian Cedar is as common in Spain as the former ſort, and is ſo called to diſtinguiſh it from the above, as it grows naturally, alſo, about the country ſo called It will riſe to the height of about twenty-five feet, the branches have naturally an upright poſition, and their bark is of a reddiſh hue The leaves are every where imbricated, and each is obtuſe and of an oval figure They reſemble thoſe of the cypreſs, and are very beautiful The flowers are ſucceeded by large oval berries, of a brown colour and will be produced in plenty from the ſides of the younger branches all over the tree Lycian

8 Phœnician Cedar ſeldom grows higher than twenty feet, and is a beautiful upright ſort, forming a kind of pyramid, if untouched, from the bottom It has both ternate and imbricated leaves, the under ones grow by threes, and ſpread open, and the upper ones are obtuſe, and lie over each other like the cypreſs The flowers are produced from the ends of the branches, and the fruit that ſucceeds them is rather ſmall, and of a yellow colour It is commonly called the Phœnician Cedar, though it is found growing naturally in moſt of the ſouthern parts of Europe and Phœnician Cedar

9 Savin Of this ſpecies there are three ſorts Savin
Spreading Savin Varieties
Upright Savin
Striped Savin

Spreading Savin is a low ſpreading ſhrub, the branches have a natural tendency to grow horizontally, or nearly ſo ſo that it muſt be ranked amongſt the loweſt growing ſhrubs, inſomuch that unleſs it is planted againſt a wall, or ſupported in an upright poſition, we ſeldom have it higher than two feet When it is to be planted and left to Nature, room muſt be firſt allowed for its ſpreading, for it will occupy a circle of more than two or three yards diameter, and will choak any other leſs powerful ſhrub that is placed too near it The bark on the older ſhoots is of a light brown colour, but the younger, which are covered with leaves running into each other, are of as fine a green as any ſhrub whatever Theſe leaves are erect, and acute-pointed They are placed oppoſite, and grow a little like thoſe of the French Tamariſk This ſhrub ſeldom produces flowers or berries, but when any berries do appear, they are ſmall and of a bluiſh colour It deſerves a place amongſt low-growing evergreens, on account of the fine ſtrong green of its leaves both in winter and ſummer, but it is valuable for nothing elſe, for it produces neither flowers nor fruit ornamental, and is poſſeſſed of a very ſtrong ſmell, inſomuch that being ſtirred by whatever runs amongſt it the whole air is filled with a fetid ſcent, which is emitted from its branches and leaves, and which to moſt people is diſagreeable It is in great requeſt with horſe doctors, described and cow-leeches, by which they much benefit those creatures in many disorders. The juice of it, mixed with milk and honey, is said to be good to expel worms from children, as well as, without that mixture, to destroy those in horses, for which purpose it is strongly recommended. The juice of it is reported to take away all freckles from the face, and a poultess thereof will cure scald-heads, ulcers, &c. In short, the virtues of this shrub are many, and excellent for several disorders, but it is to be feared, they are too often prostituted, and made to serve a diabolical purpose by wicked and lewd women.

Upright Savin is a delightful tree, it will grow to be twelve or fourteen feet high. The branches are numerous and slender, and give the tree a genteel air. The leaves are nearly of the same nature with the other, though they are of a darker green. The flowers are produced in plenty, but make no show, and they are succeeded by berries in such plenty as to cause a good effect. The upright tendency of growth of this tree, together with the very dark-green of the leaves, which causes a good contrast with others that are lighter, together with its not being possessed of that strong disagreeable scent of the other sort, makes it valuable for evergreen plantations, and causes it to be admired by most persons.

Variegated Savin is a variety of the former; it has not that tendency to spread like the Common, neither does it grow quite so upright as the Berry-bearing Savin. It is a fine plant, and at present rather scarce. The ends of several of the young shoots are of a fine cream-colour, nay, all the smaller branches appear often of that colour, and at a distance will have the appearance of flowers growing on the tree. In short, to those who are fond of variegated plants, this shrub has both beauty and scarcity to recommend itself.

Culture of the different sorts. The culture of the Virginian Cedars and Juniper-trees has been shewn in the Chapter of the Cedar, in the First Book, so that I have nothing more to add, except that the method directed there for the raising of Cedars, is to be observed for all the rest of the species; that the seeds of the Cedars of Jamaica and Bermudas are to be sown in pots of the fine compost, and that after they are come up, they must be planted each in a separate pot, always housed in winter, and managed as has been already directed, until they are strong enough to be set out for good. With these precautions, the culture of the first eight sorts may be followed.

The Common Savin is to be encreased by slips, which if planted almost at any time, or any how, will grow. The Upright Savin also is to be encreased by slips planted in moist weather, in August, and kept shaded and watered in dry weather afterwards. This is the best way of treating cuttings of the Upright Savin, though they will often grow if planted at any time, either in winter or summer. The Striped Savin also is to be encreased this way, though care must be always used to take off those branches that are most beautifully variegated, and such also as are entirely of a cream colour, for this will be the most probable method of continuing it in its variegated beauties. This plant is also to be raised by berries, and if these have the same treatment as the other sorts, it will be very proper, and by these the most upright and best plants are raised. Let us now proceed to the titles.

Titles. 1. The Common Juniper is titled, *Juniperus foliis ternis patentibus mucronatis baccâ longioribus*. In the *Hortus Cliffortianus* it is termed, *Juniperus foliis patentibus*. Caspar Bauhine calls it, *Juniperus vulgaris fruticosa*, also, *Juniperus vulgaris arbor*, also, *Juniperus minor montana, folio latiore, fructu longiore*. John Bauhine, *Juniperus vulgaris, baccis parvis purpureis*, also, *Juniperus Alpina*. It grows naturally in England, and in many of the northern parts of Europe.

2. The Spanish Juniper is titled, *Juniperus foliis ternatis patentibus mucronatis baccâ breviore foliis*. Sauvage calls it, *Juniperus foliis quaternis patentibus subulatis mucronatis*. Caspar Bauhine, *Juniperus major, baccâ rufescente*. Van Royen, *Juniperus foliis quaternis patentibus subulatis pungentibus*, and Clusius, *Oxycedrus*. It grows naturally in Spain, and in the south of France.

3. Virginian Cedar is titled, *Juniperus foliis ternis basi adnatis junioribus imbricatis, senioribus patulis*. Ray calls it, *Juniperus major Americana*, Plukenet, *Juniperus Barbadensis, cupressi folio, arbor præcelsa τετραγονόφυλλος*, and Sloane, *Juniperus maxima, cupressi folio minimo, cortice exteriore in tenues philyras spirales ductili*. It grows naturally in Virginia and Carolina.

4. Cedar of Bermudas is, *Juniperus foliis inferioribus ternis superioribus binis decurrentibus subulatis patulis acutis*. Herman calls it, *Juniperus Bermudiana*. It grows common in America.

5. Jamaica Cedar is, *Juniperus foliis omnibus quadrifariam imbricatis junioribus ovatis, senioribus acutis*. Plukenet calls it *Juniperus Barbadensis, cupressi foliis, ramulis quadratis*. It grows also in America.

6. Spanish Cedar is, *Juniperus foliis quadrifariam imbricatis acutis*. Tournefort calls it, *Cedrus Hispanica procerior, fructu maximo nigro*. It is a native of Spain.

7. Lycian Cedar is, *Juniperus foliis undique imbricatis ovatis obtusis*. Caspar Bauhine calls it *Cedrus folio cupressi, media, majoribus baccis*, Lobel, *Cedrus Phœnicia altera Plinii & Theophrasti*. It grows naturally in Spain, Italy, and France.

8. Phœnician Cedar is, *Juniperus foliis ternis obliteratis imbricatis obtusis*. Caspar Bauhine calls it, *Cedrus folio cupressi majore, fructu flavescente*, and Clusius, *Juniperus major*. It grows about Montpelier, and in some parts of Portugal, and in the East.

9. Savin is titled, *Juniperus foliis oppositis erectis decurrentibus oppositionibus pyxidatis*. In the *Hortus Cliffortianus* it is termed, *Juniperus foliis infernè adnatis oppositionibus concatenatis*. Dodonæus calls it simply, *Sabina*, Caspar Bauhine, *Sabina folio cupressi*, also, *Savina folio tamarisci Dioscoridis*. It grows common in Italy, Siberia, on Mounts Olympus and Ararat, and in Lusitania.

Class and order in the Linnæan system. The characters. *Juniperus* is of the class and order *Dioecia Monadelphia*, and the characters are,

I. Male Flowers.

1. Calyx. These compose a conical katkin, growing by threes, opposite, and terminated by an odd one. The squammæ serve for the calyces, and each scale is short, broad, incumbent, and affixed to the column by a short pedicle.

2. Corolla. There is none.

3. Stamina. In the end flowers are three subulated filaments, that coalesce below into one body, but those of the lateral flowers are hardly distinguishable. The antheræ are three, and are distinct in the end flowers; those of the side adhere to the scales.

II. Fe-

II Female Flowers.

1 CALYX is a small, permanent, tripartite perianthium, that grows to the germen

2 COROLLA consists of three stiff, acute, permanent petals

3 PISTILLUM consists of a germen below the calyx; and of three single styles, with simple stigmas

4 PERICARPIUM is a roundish, fleshy, umbilicated berry

5 SEMINA The seeds are three, and oblong, they are convex on one side, and angular on the other

## CHAP XVI

## KALMIA.

THERE are two species of *Kalmia* that in some places are fine evergreens and scarce plants, and, as such, in high esteem with some people, of a vitiated taste, who think nothing valuable that is common, and these are distinguished by the names of,

Species

1 The Broad leaved *Kalmia*

2 The Narrow-leaved *Kalmia*

Description of the Broad leaved

The first of these seldom rises to more than four or five feet high, and the branches, which by no means are regularly produced, are hard, and of a greyish colour The leaves are of an oval, spear-shaped figure, and of a fine shining green colour Their consistence is rather thick in proportion to their footstalks, which are but slender, and grow irregularly on the branches The flowers are produced at the ends of the branches, in roundish bunches They are first of a fine deep red, but die away to a paler colour Each is composed of a single petal, which is tubular at the bottom, spreading open at the top, and has ten permanent corniculæ surrounding them on their outside They generally flower with us in July, and are succeeded by roundish capsules, full of seeds, which seldom ripen in England In some places this is a fine evergreen, and in others, again, it often loses its leaves, and that sometimes before the winter is far advanced

and the Narrow leaved Kalmia

The second sort is rather of lower growth than the other, and the branches are more weak and tough The leaves are very beautiful, being of a fine shining green, they are of a lanceolate figure, and in all respects are smaller than those of the former sort, and stand upon very short footstalks They are produced in no certain regular manner, being sometimes by pairs, at other times in bunches, growing opposite at the joints The flowers are produced from the sides of the branches in roundish bunches, they are of a fine red colour, and each is composed of one petal, that has the property of spreading open like the former They flower in July, and are very beautiful, but are not succeeded by ripe seeds with us

Both these sorts are to be raised three ways, by seeds, layers, and suckers

Method of propagating them by seeds

1 By seeds These we receive from abroad, and for their reception we should prepare a compost, consisting of half fresh soil from a rich pasture, taken from thence a year before, and half drift or sea sand, these being well mixed, will be proper for the reception of the seeds, which should be sown in pots or boxes, half an inch deep As soon as they are sown, they should be removed into a shady place, to remain until the spring following, and all this time nothing but weeding will be wanted, for I never yet knew them come up the first summer About the beginning of March it will be proper to plunge these pots into an hotbed, and this will fetch the plants up, and make them grow strong They must be hardened by degrees to the air, and then set in a shady place Watering must be now and then given them, if the season proves dry, and at the approach of winter, they may be removed into the greenhouse, or set under an hotbed-frame, but should always have the free air in open weather In these pots or boxes they should remain until they are two years-old seedlings, when they should be shaken out, and planted in a separate pot These should be set growing by plunging the pots into an hotbed Afterwards, they may be removed into the shade, and if they are kept growing in the pots, and removed under shelter in hard weather for a year or two, they may be afterwards planted out for good

2 These shrubs are propagated by layers It should be done in the autumn, and the young wood of the preceding summer's shoot is proper for the purpose If the soil is free and light, they will strike root pretty readily, though we must sometimes wait two years before we find any But by this way the strongest plants are obtained in the least time Layers,

3 They are also encreased by suckers, for if the soil be light and fine, and is what agrees with them, after standing a few years, they naturally send out suckers in plenty These should be taken off in the spring, and those with bad roots should be set in pots, and plunged into an hotbed, to make them grow Thus will these trees encrease themselves, if we will only wait for their time, and good plants are often obtained this way and suckers

1 The Broad-leaved *Kalmia* is titled, *Kalmia foliis ovatis, corymbis terminalibus* In the *Flora Virginica* it is called, *Andromeda foliis ovatis obtusis, corollis corymbosis infundibuliformibus, genitalibus declinatis* Catesby calls it, *Chamæ Daphne foliis tini, floribus bullatis*, Trew, *Ledum floribus bullatis confertis in summis caulibus*, Plukenet, *Cistus chamæ rhododendros Mariana laurifolia, floribus expansis summo ramulo in umbellam plurimis* It is a native of Maryland, Virginia, and Pensylvania Titles

2 The Narrow leaved *Kalmia* is, *Kalmia foliis lanceolatis, corymbosis lateralibus* In the *Flora Virginica* it is termed, *Azalea foliis lanceolatis integerrimis non nervosis glabris, corymbis terminalibus* Catesby calls it, *Chamæ Daphne sempervirens, foliis oblongis angustis, foliorum fasciculis oppositis*.

*oppositis*, Plukenet, *Cistus sempervirens laurifolia, floribus eleganter bullatis*, and Trew, *Ledum floribus bullatis fasciculatis ex alis oppositis foliorum* It is a native of Pensylvania, Carolina, &c

Kalmia is of the class and order *Decandria Monogynia*, and the characters are,

1 CALYX is a small, permanent perianthium, divided into five oval, acute segments

2 COROLLA is of one petal The tube is cylindric, and longer than the calyx The limb divides into five roundish parts, which spread open On the inside are ten permanent, nectariferous corniculæ, surrounding the flower

3 STAMINA are ten awl-shaped, erect, patent filaments, a little shorter than the corolla, into which they are inserted, having simple antheræ

4 PISTILLUM consists of a roundish germen, a filiform declining style, longer than the corolla, and an obtuse stigma

5 PERICARPIUM is a roundish, depressed capsule, composed of five valves, and containing five cells

6 SEMINA The seeds are numerous

Class and order in the Linnæan system The character.

## CHAP XVII

## *LAURUS*, The BAY-TREE,

Observations and reference

THE Bay is, indeed, a noble tree, and well known in our gardens The Gardener will naturally expect to find it treated of here as a fine evergreen for wilderness quarters, a fine evergreen it certainly is, and possessed of many properties that render it more valuable than most sorts of trees for those purposes, particularly its thriving under the drip of trees, and growing strong and well though ever so crouded with other sorts But this tree has already been treated as one which deserves to be raised for the sake of the wood, in the First Book, and, to avoid repetition, the curious planter is referred to that Chapter, where every thing necessary relating to this shrub is set forth for his information, and after reading which, I believe, he will see that nothing else need be added I cannot but take notice, however, that varieties of these trees may be had from seeds, and where sorts of this kind are very different, they may be encreased by layers, for they often differ in the size or shape of the leaves, or in some respect or other I have known some with very large broad leaves, and others smaller and very narrow, some have been nearly round, others long, with their edges crisped, &c Of this last sort the greatest plenty is to be found, but they all, nevertheless, go under the name of Common Bay From what has been shewn in the above-referred Chapter, a gentleman will see how proper it will be to have a number of these trees in his plantations, and this is still encreased on account of their rare virtues, which are well known, and which will remind us of gratitude to that bountiful Being, who giveth medicine to heal our sicknesses, &c

As the culture also of the Bay-tree has been already shewn, we shall dismiss the Gardener with only giving him, with the Botanist, the titles

The Bay-tree is titled, *Laurus foliis lanceolatis venosis perennantibus, floribus quadrifidis dioicis* Caspar Bauhine calls it, *Laurus vulgaris*, Camerarius simply, *Laurus* It grows common in Italy, Greece, &c Titles

## CHAP XVIII

## *LIGUSTRUM*, The PRIVET

Remarks

THE Gardener who has been used to the different sorts of the Privet, viz the Deciduous and the Evergreen, will know the latter is only a variety of the former, and, as that has been already treated of, nothing more is necessary to observe of the Evergreen variety here, but that its branches are hardy, weak, slender, and pliable as the other sort, and that it has a tendency to grow to be a taller and a stronger tree The leaves are rather larger, more pointed, of a thicker consistence, of a dark-green colour, and that they continue on the plant so long as to entitle it to the appellation of Evergreen, though I must own I have often observed it almost destitute of leaves early in winter, especially those that were on the ends of the highest branches, which are often taken off by the first cutting winterly winds In order to have this tree keep up the credit of an evergreen, it should have a well-sheltered situation, for although it be hardy enough to bear with impunity the severest cuts of the northern blasts, on the tops of hills, craggy rocks, &c yet without some shelter, the leaves are seldom preserved all winter, and with protection it is generally allowed to be an handsome evergreen As it is a variety

riety of the deciduous sort, the same flowers and fruit may be expected

Culture It is to be raised in the same manner, by layers or cuttings, though the seeds of this sort often produce plants of the like sort, that retain their leaves

Titles Plukenet supposes this to be a distinct species from the Common sort, and entitles it, *Ligustrum foliis majoribus & magis acuminatis toto anno folia retinens* Linnæus adds nothing to *Ligustrum*, one word being sufficient for a genus of which there are found to be no real distinct species.

## CHAP. XIX

## *LONICERA*, The EVERGREEN HONEYSUCKLE.

Introductory observation THE Evergreen Honeysuckle, though a climbing plant, is nevertheless to be stationed amongst other evergreens, in wilderness-quarters of all kinds All the other sorts of the honeysuckle should be stationed among the deciduous trees and shrubs, and so managed that their appearance may agree with those of upright growth This is done by nipping off the young shoots (which would soon get rambling and out of reach), that the plants may be kept within bounds, and made to join in the Collection with great beauty Neither may they only be kept low, to almost what height is required, but they may, by fixing a stake for their support, be trained up to a stem, which will every year grow more and more woody and firm, so that in this case the eye must frequently over look the tree, to take off the young shoots as they grow out, and not permit the head to grow too large and spreading for the stem, which it soon would do without this care, and with it, the head may be so kept in order as to bear good proportion to the stem, thereby causing the tree to have the appearance of an upright ever green

Description of the best sort There are two or three sorts of Evergreen Honeysuckles which are well known The best evergreen sort is that called the Italian It has the strongest branches of all the sorts, is therefore most proper for wilderness-quarters, and is very beautiful The bark for the most part is of a purple colour, and the leaves are very large, and of a delightful shining green Toward the ends of the branches, they chiefly surround the stalks, though lower they stand opposite, and often on short strong footstalks. The flowers are very genteel, and have a delightful fragrance They are produced at the ends of the branches, in June, in whorled bunches Three or four of these bunches will often be connected, the one growing out of the other, and being of a fine red colour, with their insides rather yellow, and being produced in great plenty, make a most charming figure But this is not all, their long continuance in blow, renders these shrubs doubly valuable, for they will continue their succession until October Nay, I have often had them in mild open winters full in blow at Christmas, and the whole months of January and February These are very valuable properties, and of which very few trees or shrubs are possessed

Culture The best method of propagating the different sorts of Honeysuckles has already been shewn to be by cuttings It will be sufficient to observe here, that the present sort does not so readily take this way, so that in order to make sure of plants, the young branches must be layered, any time in the autumn or winter, and by the autumn following they will have plenty of roots, and be good plants, fit for removing to any place

The Evergreen Honeysuckles are varieties only of deciduous species, and the titles will be given as they occur in due order, among the climbing plants

## CHAP XX

## *MAGNOLIA*, The LAUREL-LEAVED TULIP-TREE.

THREE distinct species of this genus have been already treated of among the deciduous trees, another, the largest and no blest of all, is always distinguished from the

This species described rest by the name of Larger Laurel-leaved Tulip-tree In the countries where it grows naturally, viz Carolina and Virginia, it arrives to the height and bulk of a timber-tree Those countries are adorned with woods that are chiefly composed of this plant, and indeed, a wood of so noble a tree, luxuriantly shooting, flowering, and seeding, healthy and strong, in soil and situation wholly adapted to its nature, must be a sight of which we can hardly form an adequate idea, or have a just conception of its beauty or grandeur; for the tree naturally aspires with an upright stem, and forms itself into a regular head Many other trees do the same, but its most excellent properties consist of the superlative beauties of the leaves, flowers, and seeds. The leaves much resemble those noble leaves of the Laurel, from which it is so called, only they are larger, and of a thicker consistence. Many of them will be ten inches or more in length, and four broad, and all are firm and strong. Their upper surface is of a shining green, but their under is lighter, and often of a brownish colour. This tinge, which is not always found in all trees, is by some thought a great beauty, and by others an imperfection; so various is the taste of different people. These leaves are produced without any order on the tree, and sit close to the branches, having no separate footstalks. The idea we can form of one tree, of seventy or eighty feet high, plentifully ornamented with such large and noble leaves, must be very great, and will induce us on their account only to endeavour to naturalize so noble a plant to our country. But let us consider their flowers. These we find large, though single, and of a pure white. They are produced at the ends of the branches, in July, and each is composed of about nine or ten large spreading petals. They have the usual properties of those that are broad and rounded at their extremity, of being narrow at the base, and their edges are a little undulated or waved. In the center of these petals are situated the numerous stamina, which the Botanist will be more curious in observing than the Gardener. But what affects all equally alike that have the sense of smelling is, their remarkable fragrance, which indeed is of so great a degree, as to perfume the air to some distance, and if one tree, when in blow, is sufficient to effect this, what conception should we form of the odours diffused in the countries where there are whole woods of this tree in full vigour and blow! The fruit is nearly of the shape and size of a large egg; but what make it most singular and beautiful are the pendulous seeds, of a fine scarlet, which being discharged from their cells, hang by long threads, and have an effect both striking and uncommon.

Rules have been given before for raising the Narrow-leaved *Magnolia*, the same rules observed, whether for seeds, layers, or cuttings, will raise plenty of this sort; neither need any thing be added, except hinting to the Gardener, that this is more tender than the other sorts, and that from thence he should learn not to be over hasty in committing these plants to the winter's cold, and planting them out for good. Snow is peculiarly injurious to them while young, so that if the approach of such weather, they must be particularly covered; and if snow should happen to fall unawares, it should be carefully cleared off the leaves and stems. When these plants are set abroad for good, if the place is not exceedingly well-sheltered, it will be proper to have a shed at hand, which the Gardener may put together, to screen them from the severe northern frosts and the black easterly winds also, from which this shrub is most likely to suffer damage; and these frosty winds are the most destructive to it when they come early in the winter, while the shoots are rather tender; for then they are often destroyed, and the tree rendered unsightly for some time, though it will shoot out again. — *Of the propagating the plant*

When this shrub is to be encreased by layers, it will be necessary, after the operation is performed, to make an hedge of reeds, or something, at a little distance round it, to keep off the strong winds, and prevent them from blowing the layers out of the ground; for without some guard this will be in danger of being done, since the leaves being very large and strong, the wind must have great power over them.

This noble species is titled, *Magnolia foliis lanceolatis perennantibus*. In Miller's Dictionary it is termed, *Magnolia foliis lanceolatis persistentibus, caule erecto arboreo*. Catesby calls it, *Magnolia altissima, flore ingenti candido*; and Trew, *Magnolia maximo flore, foliis subtus ferrugineis*. It grows naturally in Florida and Carolina. — *Titles*

# CHAP. XXI.

## *MEDICAGO*, MOON-TREFOIL.

A TREE as different as possible from the former now comes of course under consideration; a tree that has many beauties to recommend it; a tree which has been much celebrated by the antients, and is now in great request with the moderns. It commonly goes by the name of Moon-Trefoil, or Shrubby Hoary *Medicago*. This species of *Medicago* will grow to be six or seven feet high, and divides without any order into many branches, which are covered with a grey bark. There is a delicacy in the young shoots beyond what is found in most trees; for they are white and silvery, and at the same time are covered with the finest down. These young shoots are plentifully ornamented with leaves, many of which come out from a bud. These are trifoliate, and grow on long slender footstalks. Each of these folioles is cuneiform, or shaped like a wedge; the others grow out more into a lanceolate figure, have also a whitish look, and are downy, though not to so great a degree as the young twigs on which they grow. They have a large mid-rib, which contracts the borders in the evening, and this alters their position of sides on the alteration of weather. The flowers are produced from the sides of the branches, in clusters, on long footstalks. Each of these clusters will be composed of ten or twelve flowers, which are of a beautiful yellow. They are of the butterfly kind, and are succeeded by moon shaped pods, that ripen their seeds very well. One or other of these trees is to be found in blow almost at all times. The beginning of the blow is generally said to be in April or May, and indeed then we may expect to see the flowers largest and in the greatest perfection, but I have seen flowers of these — *Description of this plant*

trees

trees in July, Auguſt, and September; and in a greenhouſe I have known them in blow all winter, which makes the tree more valuable to thoſe who are deſirous of ſeeing flowers in unuſual months

This ſhrub is by many ſuppoſed to be the true *Cytiſus* of Virgil It grows plentifully in Italy in the iſlands of the Archipelago, and many other parts, where it is eſteemed excellent fodder for cattle For this purpoſe, the raiſing of it has been recommended by ſome perſons in England, but there ſeems no probability of ſuch a ſcheme being brought to bear here; neither is it any ways neceſſary to give ourſelves the trouble to try experiments of this kind, as, ſhould it even ſucceed to our utmoſt wiſhes, we have many ſorts of fodder that will exceed it in quantity and quality, without any proportion to the extraordinary expence which muſt attend the raiſing any quantity of theſe ſhrubs, to cut for that uſe The flowers, leaves, and top ſhoots have, however, a fine peaſe like taſte, which is what, I make no doubt, moſt cattle would be fond of, and of which the inhabitants of ſome countries where it grows naturally reap the advantage, for the goats that feed on it yield a greater quantity as well as a more excellent kind of milk, from which good cheeſe is at length obtained, where theſe creatures have plenty of theſe ſhrubs to brouze upon

In our wilderneſs quarters we muſt give this tree a very dry ſoil and a well-ſheltered ſituation, for with us it is rather a tender ſhrub, and has been frequently treated as a greenhouſe-plant, and this is another argument againſt any attempt to raiſe theſe ſhrubs for fodder in England They are too tender to bear our ſevere winters without ſhelter, and ſhould we proceed in raiſing ſixty or ſeventy acres, a thorough froſty winter would deſtroy the greateſt part of them, or, if the winter ſhould not be ſo ſevere as totally to kill them, yet their end-ſhoots would be ſo nipped and damaged, that it would be late in the ſummer before they would ſhoot out and recover this injury, and conſequently ſmall crops muſt be expected

Method of propagating it by ſeeds, This plant is eaſily raiſed by ſeeds or cuttings The ſeeds ſhould be ſown in the ſpring, a quarter and half an inch deep, in beds of fine light garden mould After they are come up, the uſual care of weeding muſt be afforded them, and if they are ſhaded and now and then watered in hot weather, it will be ſo much the better The beds muſt be hooped againſt winter, and plenty of mats muſt be ready to cover the plants when the froſt comes on, and if this ſhould be very ſevere, their covering ſhould be encreaſed, or there will be danger of loſing them all In the ſpring the ſtrongeſt may be drawn out, and planted in pots, to be houſed for a winter or two, until they are got ſtrong, but where a quantity is wanted, and there is no ſuch conveniency, it may be proper to let them remain in the ſeed bed another winter, for the conveniency of being covered in bad weather, and then in the ſpring they may be planted out in the nurſery, in lines two feet aſunder, and at one foot diſtance This nurſery ſhould be in a well-ſheltered warm place, and they will be ready for tranſplanting, whenever wanted

and by cuttings 2 Theſe plants may be raiſed by cuttings If a few only are wanted for ornamenting a wilderneſs, the beſt way will be to plant theſe in pots, and ſet them up to the rims in a ſhady place, that they may have the conveniency of being houſed in winter When a quantity is wanted, they muſt take the chance of wind and weather, and the moſt we can then do is to plant them in fine light ſoil in a well ſheltered place The latter end of March is the beſt time for the purpoſe, they will ſtrike root freely, eſpecially if they are ſhaded and watered in dry weather, and from this place they need not be removed until they are ſet out for good

Titles This ſhrub is titled, *Medicago leguminibus lunatis margine integerrimis, caule arboreo* Caſpar Bauhine calls it, *Cytiſus incanus, ſiliquis falcatis*, John Bauhine, *Cytiſus ſiliquâ incurvâ folio candicante*, and Lobel, *Cytiſus marantæ* It grows common in Italy, Sicily, &c

Claſs and order in the Linnæan ſyſtem *Medicago* is of the claſs and order *Diadelphia Decandria*, and the characters are,

The characters 1 CALYX is a monophyllous, erect, campanulate, cylindric perianthium, divided into five equal, acute ſegments

2 COROLLA is papilionaceous

Vexillum is oval, whole, and reflexed

Alæ are oval and oblong, and fixed by an appendix to the carina, under which the ſides are connivent

Carina is oblong, bifid, patent obtuſe, and reflexed, and bends from the vexillum

3 STAMINA are ten filaments, with very ſmall antheræ One of the filaments is ſingle, the other nine grow together, almoſt to their ſummits

4 PISTILLUM conſiſts of an oblong, incurved, compreſſed germen, a ſhort ſubulated ſtyle, and a very ſmall terminal ſtigma

5 PERICARPIUM is a long, compreſſed, inflexed pod

6 SEMINA The ſeeds are many, reniforme or angular

# C H A P. XXII

## *MESPILUS*, The EVERGREEN THORN

This plant deſcribed THE Evergreen Thorn uſually goes by the name of *Pyracantha* It is a fine evergreen, and has been chiefly uſed to ornament or hide the ends of houſes, barns, ſtables, or other buildings that break in upon the view; and for this purpoſe no plant is better adapted, as by its evergreen leaves, cloſely ſet, it will not only keep from ſight whatever cannot regale that ſenſe, but will be to the higheſt degree entertaining by the profuſion of berries it will produce, and which will be in full glow all winter But though the hiding as well as ornamenting

menting of walls, &c has been the chief use for this tree, it is with very good reason planted as an evergreen in wilderness-quarters, where, notwithstanding its branches against walls, &c are very flexible, it will become stronger and more woody, and will diffuse its leafy branches in an agreeable manner These branches will be terminated with its fine fruit, which will glow in the quarters all winter, if they are not eaten by the birds, so that the tree before us is proper for any place A further account of this shrub is almost needless, as it is well known, there being few towns which have not an house or two whose front is ornamented with them, where they are generally kept clipped, and of which the owners are often not a little proud In such places they may be trained up, as is seen, to a great height, but when planted singly in quarters, though their stems naturally become stronger, they seldom grow higher than twelve or fourteen feet, and they will spread abroad their slender branches, and will often have a bushy, though not unpleasing form These branches are covered with a smooth bark, which is of a dark greenish brown colour, and often spotted with greyish spots, and they are often possessed of thorns, which, though not numerous, are sharp and strong The leaves are spear shaped, oval, and their edges are crenated Their upper surface is smooth, and of a fine shining green, their under is paler, and they are produced in much plenty all over the shrub The flowers are produced in bunches, like those of the common hawthorn, though they are small, and not of so pure a white They are often later before they are produced, and are succeeded by those large delightful bunches, or berries, which are of a fiery red, and which are as ornamental in the winter as any that are produced on trees of the berry bearing tribe

These plants are easily raised by the berries, or from layers The berries should be sown in any common garden-mould made fine, an inch deep, and these will remain two years before they appear, though if the berries are old ones (for they will often remain on the tree two years) they will frequently come up the succeeding spring After the plants have stood one or two years in the seed bed, in the spring they should be planted out in the nursery, at small distances, and in about two years more they will be good plants, fit for any place — Method of propagating by seeds,

They are easily propagated by layers, and this business should be performed in the autumn on the young shoots A gentle twist may be given them, though if they are only laid down, and covered with earth, they will strike root by the next autumn, nay, I have known that, by some mould being accidentally thrown on a branch which was near the ground, roots have shot from almost every joint These layers should be taken off any time in the winter; the strongest will be fit for immediate use, while the weaker may be set in the nursery, like the seedlings, and in a very little time they will grow to be good plants — and by layers.

The Evergreen Thorn, or *Pyracantha* is entitled, *Mespilus spinosa, foliis lanceolato-ovatis crenatis, calycibus fructus obtusis* Caspar Bauhine calls it, *Oxyacantha Dioscoridis, sive spina acuta, pyri folio*, Tournefort, *Mespilus aculeata, amygdali folio*, and Dalechamp *Uva ursi* It is found growing in hedges in many parts both of Italy and France — Titles

# CHAP. XXIII.

## *PHILLYREA*, The MOCK-PRIVET.

Remark — THE *Phillyrea* and the *Alaternus* present an appearance so much alike, that they are blended together, and frequently mistaken for each other, by many of our Gardeners, who are nevertheless called masters of their Art But that they may no longer labour under mistakes of this kind, it may be proper to observe, that the number of stamina are different, the flowers of *Alaternus* having five filaments with their antheræ, (which shrub is now with good reason found to be a species of *Rhamnus*), whilst the flowers of *Phillyrea* have two stamina only They not only, therefore, belong to different classes (which may perhaps be too nice a difference for some Gardeners to observe), but another obvious difference presents itself to all, who will take even the least notice, and that is, the leaves of *Phillyrea* always stand opposite on the branches by pairs, whereas those of *Alaternus* stand singly, and are produced in an alternate manner, which occasions all those plants to be called *Alaternus* Having thus set the Gardener right as to that article, let us proceed to shew him how many sorts of *Phillyrea* there are to enrich his Collection The real species are only three

1 The Oval-leaved *Phillyrea* — Species
2 The Broad-leaved *Phillyrea*
3 The Narrow leaved *Phillyrea*

1 Oval-leaved or Middle *Phillyrea* has the following varieties — Oval leaved Phillyrea

Common Smooth leaved *Phillyrea* — Varieties
Privet leaved *Phillyrea*
Olive leaved *Phillyrea*

The Common Smooth leaved *Phillyrea* will grow to be twelve or fourteen feet high, and the branches are many, the older of which are covered with a dark-brown bark, but the bark on the young shoots is of a fine green The leaves are smooth, and of a very fine green colour They are oval, spear-shaped, and grow opposite by pairs, on strong short footstalks The flowers are produced in clusters, from the wings of the young branches They are small, and of a kind of greenish white colour, they appear in March, and are succeeded by berries, which are first green, then red, and black in the autumn when ripe — described

Privet-leaved *Phillyrea* will grow to be ten or twelve feet high, and the branches are covered with a brown bark The leaves a little resemble the Privet, they are of a fine green colour, and nd grow by pairs on the branches They are of a lanceolate figure, and their edges are entire, or nearly so, for some signs of serratures sometimes appear The flowers grow like others, in clusters, in March They are whitish, and are succeeded by small black berries

The Olive-leaved *Phillyrea* is the most beautiful of all the sorts It will grow to be about ten or twelve feet high, and the branches, which are not very numerous, spread abroad in a free easy manner, which may not improperly be said to give the tree a fine air They are long and slender, and are covered with a light-brown bark, and on these the leaves stand opposite by pairs, at proper intervals, on short footstalks They resemble those of the olive tree, and are of so delightful a green as to force esteem Their surface is exceeding smooth, their edges are entire, and they also are of a thickish consistence The flowers are small and white, and, like the other sorts, make no show They are succeeded by single roundish berries

Proper ... fill a 2 The Broad-leaved *Phillyrea* will grow to be about twelve feet high The branches seem to be produced stronger and more upright than those of the former species The bark is of a grey colour, the younger branches are of a fine green colour, spotted with white, which has a pretty effect; and the leaves grow opposite by pairs They are of a heart-shaped oval figure, of a thick consistence, and a strong dark green colour Their edges are sharply serrated, and they stand on short strong footstalks The flowers grow from the wings of the leaves in clusters, in March They are of a kind of greenish white colour, make no show, and are succeeded by small, round, black berries

Varieties The varieties of this species are, the *Ilex*-leaved *Phillyrea*, the Prickly *Phillyrea*, the Olive *Phillyrea* with Slightly serrated Edges

Narrow-leaved Phillyrea 3 The Narrow-leaved *Phillyrea* is of lower growth, seldom rising higher than eight or ten feet The branches are few and slender, and they also are beautifully spotted with grey spots The leaves, like the others, stand opposite by pairs They are long and narrow, spear-shaped, and undivided, of a deep green colour, and of a thick consistence Their edges are entire, and they also stand on short footstalks The flowers, like the others, make no show They are whitish, and grow in clusters from the wings of the branches, in March, and are succeeded by small round black berries

Varieties The varieties of this species are the Rosemary *Phillyrea*, Lavender *Phillyrea*, Striped *Phillyrea*, &c

These sorts are often planted for hedges, to separate or divide the different gardens from each other, and indeed an hedge of any of these shrubs looks beautiful and well, provided it be permitted to grow in its own natural way, without clipping, &c as is too often done The custom, however, of shearing and clipping trees is now with good reason pretty much laid aside, for can there be any comparison between these trees, when in hedges, clipped in a formal manner, or when in standards, sheared into round balls, &c can any comparison, I say, be made between such formal figures, and when they exhibit their branches freely in their own natural growth, which will then shew themselves with an air free and easy, and demonstrate how kindly Nature indulges us with useful objects of these kinds, of pleasing air and beauty One use, indeed, these plants have been applied to, in which shearing them is more excuseable, and that is, in hiding old unsightly walls, &c In this case, the tree exhibits an imperfection in view to hide a greater however, I cannot but observe, when they are planted for this purpose, they may be so trained, by shortening in the winter some of the shoots that they will multiply in branches, and so will take off the unsightly look of a decayed old wall, and still (nor being clipped) retain their own beauty, by sending their slender branches free and easy the whole length and breadth The sorts of *Alaternus*, however, are equally, if not more, proper for these purposes, and the *Phillyrea* never appears more delightful than when planted among other evergreens in quarters These are the places they are chiefly adapted to, and no plantations of such kinds ought to be without them

The *Phillyreas* are to be raised by seeds or layers

1 By seeds These ripen in the autumn, and should be sown soon after The mould must be made fine, and if it is not naturally sandy, some drift sand be added, it will be so much the better The seeds for the most part remain until the second spring before they come up, and if they are not sown soon after they are ripe, some will come up even the third spring after They must be sown about an inch deep, and during the following summer should be kept clean from weeds After they are come up, the same care must be observed, and also watering in dry weather, and if the beds are hooped, and the plants shaded in the hottest season, they will be so much the better for it However, at the approach of winter they must be hooped and the beds covered with mats in the hardest frosts, otherwise there will be danger of losing the whole crop, for these trees though they are very hardy when grown tolerably large, are rather tender whilst seedlings It will be proper to let them remain in the seed-beds, with this management, for two summers, and then, waiting for the first autumnal rains, whether in September or October (having prepared a spot of ground) they should at this juncture be planted out, and this will occasion them immediately to strike root The distance they should be planted from each other need not be more than a foot, if they are not designed to remain long in the nursery If there is a probability of their not being wanted for some years, they should be allowed near double that distance, and every winter the ground in the rows should be well dug, to break their roots, and cause them to put out fresh fibres, otherwise they will be in danger of being lost, when brought into the wilderness-quarters

Method of propagating these trees by seeds

2 By layers they will easily grow The autumn is the best time for this operation, and the young shoots are fit for the purpose The best way of layering them is by making a slit at the joint, though they will often grow well by a twist being only made When the Gardener chooses the method of twisting a young branch for the layers, he must be careful to twist it about a joint so as only to break the bark for if it is too much twisted, it will die from that time, and his expectations wholly vanish But if it be gently twisted with art and care, it will at the twisted parts be preparing to strike root, and by the autumn following, as well as those layers that had been slit, will have good roots the strongest of which will be fit for planting where they are wanted to remain, whilst the weaker and worst rooted layers may be planted in the nursery-ground like the seedlings, and treated accordingly By layers

1 Oval-leaved or Mock Privet is titled, *Phillyrea foliis ovato-lanceolatis subintegerrimis* In the *Hortus Cliffortianus* it is termed, *Phillyrea foliis ovato-lanceolatis* ... Caspar Bauhin calls it, *Phillyrea* ... *folio*, and Clusius Titles

*Phillyrea* 3 It grows naturally in most of the southern countries of Europe

2 Broad-leaved *Phillyrea* is, *Phillyrea foliis cordato ovatis serratis* Caspar Bauhine calls it, *Phillyrea latifolia spinosa*, also, *Phillyrea folio leviter serrato*, and Clusius, *Phillyrea* 1 2 It grows naturally in most of the southern parts of Europe

3 Narrow-leaved *Phillyrea* is, *Phillyrea foliis linear lanceolatis integerrimis* Caspar Bauhine calls it *Phillyrea angustifolia prima*, also, *Phillyrea angustifolia secunda*, and Clusius, *Phillyrea* 4 5 It grows naturally in Spain and Italy

Class and order in the Linnæan system. The characters. *Phillyrea* is of the class and order *Diandria Monogynia* and the characters are

1 CALYX is a small, monophyllous, permanent perianthium, indented in four parts at the top

2 COROLLA consists of one funnel shaped petal The tube is very short, and the limb is divided into five oval, acute segments, which turn backward

3 STAMINA are two short filaments, placed opposite to each other, having simple erect antheræ

4 PISTILLUM consists of a roundish germen, a slender style the length of the stamina, and a thickish stigma

5 PERICARPIUM is a globular berry, of one cell

6 SEMEN The seed is single, large, and round

# CHAP XXIV

## *PHLOMIS*, JERUSALEM SAGE

Species. THERE are two hardy ligneous evergreen species of this genus, called,

1 Yellow *Phlomis*, or Jerusalem Sage

2 Purple *Phlomis*, or Portugal Sage

These species, with their varieties, can scarcely be called evergreens, as their leaves are of a downy white or hoary colour, nevertheless, they are highly ornamental to evergreen plantations in winter, by the sweet contrast they make with leaves of different sorts, and of different kinds of green

Yellow Phlomis. 1 Yellow *Phlomis*, or Jerusalem Sage The varieties of this species are

Varieties. The Broad leaved Sage-tree of Jerusalem

The Narrow leaved Jerusalem Sage-tree

The Cretan Sage-tree

described. The Broad leaved Jerusalem Sage-tree is now become very common in our Gardens, which indeed is no wonder, as its beauty is great, and its culture easy It will grow to be about five feet high, and spread its branches without order all around The older branches are covered with a dirty, greenish, dead, falling, ill-looking bark and this is the worst property of this shrub But the younger shoots are white and beautiful, they are four cornered woolly, and soft to the touch The leaves are roundish and oblong, and moderately large, and these grow opposite at the joints of the shrub on long footstalks They are hoary, to a degree of whiteness, and their footstalks also are woolly, white tough, and strong The flowers are produced in June, July, and August, at the top joints of the young shoots, in large whorled bunches They are of the labiated kind, each consisting of two lips, the upper one of which is forked, and bends over the other A finer yellow can hardly be conceived than the colour of which they are possessed, and being large, they exhibit their golden flowers at a great distance, causing thereby a handsome shew

The Narrow leaved Jerusalem Sage tree is of lower growth than the other, seldom rising higher than a yard or four feet This shrub is in every respect like the other, only the shoots seem to have a more upright tendency of growth The leaves also, which are narrower, are more inclined to a lanceolate form They are numerous in both the sorts, and hide the deformity of the bark on the older stems, which renders them less exceptionable on that account In short, these sorts are qualified for shrubberies of all kinds, or to be set in borders of flower gardens, where they will flower, and be exceeded even in that respect by very few shrubs

Cretan Sage shrub is still of lower growth than either of the former, seldom arriving to a yard in height The leaves are of the same white, hoary nature, they are very broad, and stand on long footstalks The flowers are also of a delightful yellow colour, very large, and grow in large whorls, which give the plant great beauty

2 Purple *Phlomis*, or Portugal Sage The stalks of this species are woody four feet high and send forth several angular branches, which are covered with a white bark The leaves are spear-shaped, oblong, woolly underneath, crenated, and grow on short footstalks The flowers are produced in whorls, from the joints of the branches They are of a deep purple colour, and have narrow involucra They appear in June and July, but are not succeeded by ripe seeds in England Purple Phlomis.

There is a variety of this species, with iron-coloured flowers, and another with flowers of a bright purple Varieties.

There are some more shrubby sorts of *Phlomis*, of great beauty, but these not only often lose their leaves, and even branches, from the first frosts, but are frequently wholly destroyed, if it happens to be severe They are low shrubs, very beautiful, and figure admirably with perennials, where they will not only class as to size with many of that sort, but being rather tender, may have such extraordinary care as the owner may think proper to allow them

The culture of the above sorts is very easy, either by layers or cuttings, for if a little earth be thrown upon the branches, any time in the winter, they will strike root, and be good plants by the autumn following, fit for any place Thus easy is the culture by that method Method of propagating them by layers

The cuttings will also grow, if planted any time [illegible] and cuttings time of the year Those planted in winter should be the woody shoots of the former summer These may be set close in a shady border and being watered in dry weather, will often grow

This shrub may be propagated by young slips, also, in any of the summer months These should be planted in a shady border, like sage, and well watered If the border is not naturally shady, the beds must be hooped, and covered with matting in hot weather Watering must be constantly afforded them, and with this care and management many of them will grow

*Derivation of the generical name*

The word *Phlomis* is said to be formed of the Greek word φλεγω, *to burn*, it being anciently used by the lower people to burn, to give light in the night

*Title*

1 Yellow *Phlomis*, or Jerusalem Sage, is titled, *Phlomis foliis subrotundis tomentosis crenatis, involucris lanceolatis caule fruticoso* In the *Hortus Cliffortianus* it is titled, *Phlomis involucris radiis lanceolatis villosis*, and in the *Hortus Upsaliensis*, *Phlomis involucris tomentosis lanceolatis, foliis cordatis villosis, caule fruticoso* Caspar Bauhine calls it, *Verbascum latis salviæ foliis*, Dodonæus, *Verbascum sylvestre alterum*, Tournefort, *Phlomis Cretica fruticosa, folio subrotundo, flore luteo*, and Dillenius *Phlomis latifolia capitula lutea grandi flore* It grows naturally in Spain and Sicily

2 Purple *Phlomis*, or Portugal Sage, is, *Phlomis involucris linearibus obtusis calyce brevioribus, foliis cordatis oblongis tomentosis caule suffruticoso* Caspar Bauhine calls it, *Verbascum subrotundo salviæ folio*, Plukenet, *Salvia fruticosa, cisti folio haud incano, floribus purpureis*, and Tournefort, *Phlomis fruticosa Lusitanica, flore purpurescente foliis acutioribus* It grows naturally in Portugal and Italy

*Class and order in the Linnean system*

*Phlomis* is of the class and order *Didynamia Gymnospermia*, and the characters are,

*The characters*

1 CALYX is a monophyllous, permanent perianthium, consisting of an oblong tube with five angles

2 COROLLA is of one petal, which is ringent, and the tube is oblong, the upper lip is oval, hairy, arched, and inflexed, the under lip is divided into three parts, the middle of which is largest and obtuse

3 STAMINA are four filaments, of which two are longer than the other They are hid under the upper lip, and have oblong antheræ

4 PISTILLUM consists of a quadripartite germen, a style the length of the stamina, and a bifid acute stigma

5 PERICARPIUM There is none The calyx supports the naked seeds

6 SEMINA The seeds are four, oblong, and cornered

## C H A P. XXV

## *P I N U S*, The P I N E - T R E E.

*Introductory observations*

THE species of *Pinus*, with all their varieties, which stand the glory and pride of foreign woods, are so numerous as to enrich our Collections of the tallest hardy Evergreens, more than the species of any other genus I know The various sorts strike the imagination with wonder and pleasure the height and magnitude to which they will arrive in the meanest ground, nay, on rocky hills, where there is nothing but the crevices for their roots to strike into, force our astonishment, whilst their delightful greens, together with the different tints of the many species and varieties, their natural procerity of growth and waving boughs, afford sensible and unsullied delight to the contemplative mind Many of the sorts are well known, and their beauties daily observed, as the planting them has been a fashion now for many years The environs of many a gentleman's seat have been improved by them, and my wishes are, that the spirit for planting these trees may be encreased more and more, as none are more ornamental when growing, or turn to more profit when felled But what makes them more peculiarly proper for evergreen wilderness plantations is, they are said to render the air wholesome, by the balsamic particles they emit from all parts

The best sorts for our purpose, then, which cause the greatest variety, are,

*Species and sorts*

1 Wild Pine, called the Scotch Fir-tree
2 Pineaster, or Wild Pine
3 Weymouth Pine
4 Stone-Pine
5 Cembro Pine
6 Three-leaved American Swamp Pine
7 Two leaved American Pine
8 Yellow American Pine
9 Yellow Tough Pine
10 Tough Pine of the Plains
11 Bastard Pine
12 Frankincense Pine
13 Dwarf Pine
14 Cedar of Lebanon
15 Yew-leaved or Silver Fir
16 Sweet scented Yew-leaved Fir, called the Balm of Gilead Fir
17 Norway Spruce-Fir
18 Long-coned Cornish Fir
19 White Newfoundland Spruce-Fir
20 Red Newfoundland Spruce Fir
21 Black Newfoundland Spruce Fir
22 Hemlock Fir
23 Oriental Fir

There are many other varieties, and probably real species, of *Pinus*, but the difference of all that I know is very inconsiderable from one or other of those above-mentioned, so inconsiderable, in my opinion, as to render any farther enquiry after them needless, so that I shall proceed to consider the above sorts as they stand in their regular order

*Scotch Pine*

1 The Scotch Pine, commonly called the Scotch Fir-tree, is so well known as to need no description, though it may not be improper to remind the Gardener, that the leaves grow by pairs, two being in each sheath, that they are rather

rather short, and of a strong green colour, and this hint may be sufficient for placing them properly among other evergreen timber-trees that are to ornament distant hills, or to be planted for that purpose in clumps, or in the midst of the largest quarters of the wilderness works.

Pinaster. 2. The Pinaster, or Wild Pine, is also tolerably well known. It is a large timber-tree, and naturally throws out very large arms, some of which will be nearly horizontal. Some people think these trees are very ornamental on their account, for in the winter especially they appear naked, and are of a yellowish colour, and being spread abroad thus large, and without order, in the mixture of the more regular sorts of growing Firs, they make a good contrast. The Gardener must observe, that the leaves of this sort are very large and long, and of a lighter-green than those of the Scotch Fir, which is another circumstance to direct him to its situation, and he must also observe, that those long and large leaves which ornament the younger branches only, give the tree a majestic air, and as the larger arms appear naked to view, so the younger, being thus plentifully furnished, have a noble effect, besides what beauty it receives from its numerous cones.

White Pine. 3. The White Pine, called the Weymouth Pine, is as regular and as large, or larger, a tree than any of the sorts. It is the present fashionable Pine, and has beauties enough to recommend it. The bark is smooth and soft to the touch, and though of a dusky brown colour, on the whole has a delicate look. The leaves are mostly ornamental, though their colour is nothing extraordinary, being of a kind of dusky green, but they are long and slender, and hang in so easy and free a manner, as to make one in love with the tree. These leaves grow five in a sheath, and plentifully on all sides adorn the youngest branches. The cones are long, loose, and slender, and have as little beauty as any of the sorts.

Stone Pine. 4. The Stone Pine is another delightful tree, though it will not grow to the height of the former, and the bark is rough, and on some trees of a reddish colour. The leaves are long, very ornamental, of a fine sea-green colour, and grow by two together, though the primordial ones are single and ciliated. The cones give this tree the grandest look, for they are sometimes five or six inches long, and are large, thick, and turbinated. The scales are beautifully arranged, and the whole cone is large and curious. The kernel are eatable, and by many preferred to almonds; in Italy they are served up at table in their desserts, they are exceeding wholesome, being good for coughs, colds, consumptions, &c. on which account only this tree deserves to be propagated.

Caution. It may be proper here to take notice of a very great and dangerous mistake Mr Miller has committed by saying, under this article of Stone Pine, that seeds kept in the cones will be good, and grow, if they are sown ten or twelve years after the cones have been gathered from the trees, whereas the seeds of this sort, whether kept in the cones or taken out, are never good after the first year, and though sometimes a few plants will come up from the seeds that are kept in the cones for two years before, yet this is but seldom, neither must a tenth part of a crop be expected. This caution is the more necessary, as several gentlemen who had cones, upon reading Mr Miller's Book, and finding the seeds would take no damage when kept there, deferred the work for a season or two, when they thought they should have more conveniency either of men or ground for their purpose, and were afterwards wholly disappointed, no plants appearing, the seeds being by that time spoiled and worth nothing.

Cembro Pine. 5. The Cembro Pine is a fine tree, though of lower growth than any of the former, and the leaves are very beautiful, for they are of a lighter green than most of the sorts, and are produced five in a sheath. They are pretty long and narrow, and as they closely ornament the branches all round, they look very beautiful, and render the tree on their account valuable. The cones of this tree also have a good effect on their waving heads, for they are larger than those of the Pinaster, and the squammæ are beautifully arranged.

Three-leaved American Swamp Pine. 6. The Three-leaved American Swamp Pine is a very large growing tree, if it has the advantage of a moist situation. The leaves are of a fine green colour, and are exceeding long, slender, and beautiful, three issue out of one sheath, and they closely garnish the younger branches. This is a tree worthy of propagation, whether we regard its timber, or its fine appearance when growing. Its timber is said to be equal in value to that of most sorts of the Pine, and besides, the beauty it receives from its fine, long, three-sheathed leaves, its head will be ornamented with very large cones, the good effect of which may be easily conceived.

Two-leaved American Pine. 7. The Two-leaved American Pine will grow to be a large tree, and the leaves are long, two only grow in each sheath, which occasions it being so distinguished. The leaves are of a lighter colour than many of the others. On the whole, it is a fine tree, but will make very little variety, unless closely examined. The cones of this sort are much larger, and the scales more beautifully arranged, than those of the Scotch Fir, though they are not of the size of the former. This Fir also loves a moist soil.

Yellow American, Yellow Tough Pine and Tough Pine of the Plains. 8, 9, 10. The Yellow American Pine, the Yellow Tough Pine, and the Tough Pine of the Plains, I received by those names. There is some difference in the size and shape of the cones, though that seems inconsiderable. These three sorts make very little variety among themselves, for they have nearly the same manner of growth, and though I have none that are yet grown to any large size, yet they all seem to have a tendency to throw out large arms, a little like the Pinaster. How valuable the timber may be, I cannot tell, but the younger shoots of all of them are exceeding tough, and, had we plenty, would make excellent bands for faggoting. The leaves are long, and of a yellowish green colour; there are three, and sometimes two only in a sheath. If a large quarter of these were to be planted, to be seen at a distance, by any of the darker coloured Pines, then very different shades must have a delightful effect.

Bastard Pine. 11. Bastard Pine is another sort we receive from America, though it differs very little from some of the other American sorts. The leaves are long and slender, sometimes two and sometimes three grow in each sheath. They are generally of a yellowish colour towards their base, though their ends are green. The cones are rather long and slender, and the ends of the scales are so pointed, as to occasion its being called by some the Prickly coned Pine.

Frankincense Pine. 12. Frankincense Pine is another American sort, which we receive under that name. The leaves of it are long and of a fine green colour. They are narrow, and three are contained in each sheath. They closely ornament the younger

branches

branches all round This tree, however, beautiful as it is on their account, makes little variety among the Pines, for many others look like it, but by the cones it makes a striking difference, for these are exceeding large, near as large as those of the Stone-Pine, but their scales are looser, and their arrangement is not quite so beautiful

Dwarf Fir 13 The Dwarf Pine, as its name imports, is the least grower of all the sorts of Pines It is an American plant and the leaves grow two in a sheath, these are short, and of a pretty good green colour This sort is coveted by some, on account of its low growth, but it is the least beautiful of any of the Pines, and has naturally a shabby look The cones are small, and the scales are pointed There is very little in the plant to make it desirable

There are many other sorts of American Pines, which we receive from thence with the like cant names as those of the above, which I have chose to retain, as they will probably be continued to be sent over, and that the Gardener receiving them as such may best know what to do with them In many, of those sorts I see at present no material difference, so am induced to think they are the same, sent over with different names Some of the sorts above mentioned differ in very few respects, but I have chose to mention them, as a person may be supplied with the seeds from Pensylvania, Jersey, Virginia, Carolina, &c where they all grow naturally, and having once obtained the seeds, and from them plants, they will become pleasing objects of his nicest observations

Cedar of Lebanon 14 Cedar of Lebanon The Cedar of Lebanon, which is now classed with the Pines, carries with it an idea of majestic grandeur beyond any tree belonging to Nature The history of it, in some respects, is recent in every one's memory, at least there are few who do not remember reading of the lofty Cedars, the spreading Cedars, and the many allusions and comparisons made to it in Holy Writ, and by these reflections our ideas of it are exalted, particularly when we further reflect on what is known to every one, that the wood-work of the most superb edifice that ever this world could boast, was chiefly of this material How far trees of this nature have their uses when planted, by leading the minds of their beholders to meditation and contemplation, is best known to those who are blessed with such a happy turn, but every one's own reason must tell him, that if one tree can inspire reflection more than another, those that have been most famous in history must at the first sight strike the attention, and produce the most pleasing train of ideas in the imagination The Cedar of Lebanon has been treated of in the former Book, as a Forest-tree, and to avoid repetition, thither the reader is referred There he will find how well this tree is adapted for plantations of all kinds, whether for profit or pleasure, and there he may see its description and history as also the method of raising it from seeds, the only true way to propagate it, so that nothing more need be added, except to repeat, that the more the environs of a gentleman's house are ornamented with plantations of these trees, the grander will be the improvements, to drop this hint afresh to the Gardener, that they are in their full beauty when planted singly in large parks and opens; and also to caution him, when they are to be planted in large clumps or wilderness-quarters, not to crowd them too much for unless their branches have room to spread, one of their greatest beauties will be destroyed, as having this advantage is what makes them so peculiarly elegant when planted singly as standards, in opens This precaution must be always observed, and that the planter may never lose fight of this rule, as well as for his own encouragement in virtue, let him reflect, that there is a promise, that *the righteous shall flourish, and shall spread their branches like the Cedar of Lebanon*

15 The Yew leaved or Silver Fir is a noble upright tree The branches are not very numerous, and the bark is smooth and delicate The leaves grow singly on the branches, and their ends are slightly indented Their upper surface is of a fine strong green colour and their under has an ornament of two white lines, running lengthways on each side the mid rib, on account of which silvery look this sort is called the Silver Fir The cones are large, and grow erect, and when the warm weather comes on, they soon shed their seeds, which should be a caution to all who wish to raise this plant, to gather the cones before that happens Silver Fir

16 Sweet scented Yew-leaved Fir, commonly called the Balm of Gilead Fir, has of all the sorts been most coveted, on account of the great fragrance of its leaves, though this is not its only good property, for it is a very beautiful tree, naturally of an upright growth, and the branches are so ornamented with their balmy leaves, as to exceed any of the other sorts in beauty The leaves, which are very closely set on the branches, are broad, and their ends are indented Their upper surface, when healthy, is of a fine dark green colour, and their under has white lines on each side the mid rib lengthways, nearly like those of the Silver Fir These leaves, when bruised, are very finely scented, and the buds, which swell in the autumn for the next year's shoot, are very ornamental all winter, being turgid, and of a fine brown colour, and from these also exsudes a kind of fine turpentine, of the same kind of (tho' heightened) fragrancy The tree being wounded in any part, emits plenty of this refreshing turpentine, and it is supposed by many to be the sort from whence the Balm of Gilead is taken, which occasions the tree being so called But this is a mistake, for the true Balm of Gilead is taken from a kind of *Terebinthus*, though I am informed, that what has been collected from this tree has been sent over to England from America (where it grows naturally), and often sold in the shops for the true sort Balm of Gilead Fir

This tree must be planted in a deep, rich, good earth, neither will it live long in any other sort of soil It matters little whether it be a black mould, or of a sandy nature, provided it be deep, and there is room for the roots to strike freely As these trees have hitherto been planted without this precaution and as such a kind of soil does not often fall in the ordinary course of Gardening, very few trees that have been planted many years are in a flourishing state, for if they do not like the soil, or if the roots begin to meet with obstructions, they soon begin to decline, which will be frequently in less than seven years, the first notice of which is, their leaves, which are naturally of a fine strong green colour, lose their verdure, and appear with a yellow tinge, and this colour grows upon them daily, until they look like another kind of tree Another sign of this tree being at its *ne plus ultra* is, its producing vast plenty of cones, this argues a weakness, and they generally die away by degrees soon after This is always the case where the soil does not wholly agree with them, but where it is deep and good, they will be healthy

healthy and flourishing, and produce cones for seeds.

Norway Spruce Fir. 17. Norway Spruce-Fir is a tree of as much beauty while growing, as its timber is valuable when propagated on that account. Its growth is naturally like the Silver, upright, and the height it will aspire to may be easily conceived, when we say that the white deal, so much coveted by the joiners, &c. is the wood of this tree; and it may perhaps satisfy the curious reader to know, that from this Fir pitch is drawn. The leaves are of a dark green colour; they stand singly on the branches, but the younger shoots are very closely garnished with them. They are very narrow, their ends are pointed, and they are possessed of such beauties as to excite admiration. The cones are eight or ten inches long, and hang downwards.

Long-coned Cornish Fir. 18. The Long-coned Cornish Fir is a variety of the Spruce-Fir only, and differs scarcely in any respect, except that the leaves and the cones are larger. As Gardeners generally receive it as a distinct Fir, I thought it not amiss to mention it here, though I must own the difference is so inconsiderable as to make it hardly worth seeking after; and though the cones are rather longer than the other sort, yet of that also the cones are very large, oftentimes near a foot, so that they may easily pass the one for the other, as they both hang down alike.

Newfoundland Spruce Fir. 19, 20, 21. The three next sorts are all varieties of one species, and differ so little that one description is common to them all. They are of a genteel upright growth, though they do not shoot so freely or grow so fast with us as the Norway Spruce. The leaves are of the same green, and garnish the branches in the same beautiful manner as those of that species, only they are narrower, shorter, and stand closer. The greatest difference is observable in the cones; for these are no more than about an inch in length, and the scales are closely placed. In the cones, indeed, consists the difference of these three sorts. Those of the White species are of a very light-brown colour, those of the Red species more of a nut brown or reddish colour, and those of the Black species of a dark or blackish colour. Besides this, I could never see any material difference, though it is observable, that this trifling variation seems to be pretty constant in the plants raised from the like seeds. These sorts will often flower and produce cones when only about five or six feet high, and indeed look then very beautiful; but this is a sign of weakness in the plant, which it does not often fairly overget.

Hemlock Fir. 22. Hemlock-Fir possesses as little beauty as any of the Fir tribe, though being rather scarce in proportion, it is deemed valuable. It is called by some the Yew-leaved Fir, from the resemblance of the leaves to those of the Yew-tree. It seems to be a tree of low growth with us, the highest I have ever seen any were hardly sixteen feet, and those seemed to be at their crisis of encrease. It has but few branches, and these are long and slender, and spread abroad without order. The leaves do not garnish the branches so plentifully as those of any other sort of Fir. The cones are very small and rounded; they are about half an inch long, and the scales are loosely arranged. We receive these cones from America, by which we raise the plants; though this caution should be given to the planter, that this tree is fond of moist rich ground, and in such a kind of soil will make the greatest progress.

Oriental Fir. 23. Oriental Fir. This is rather a low elegant tree. The leaves are very short, and nearly square. The fruit is exceeding small, and hangs downward; and the whole tree makes an agreeable variety with the other kinds.

Method of propagating them. The propagation of these Fir-trees has been already set forth under their respective articles in the former Book; and the sorts not mentioned there are to be raised from seeds in the same way; though, as the seeds of the American, Spruce, and Hemlock Fir are very small, a more than ordinary care should be taken of them, lest they be lost. They should be sown in pots or boxes of fine light mould, and covered over hardly a quarter of an inch. They should be then plunged up to the rims in a shady place, and netted, to save them when they first appear from the birds. If the place in which they stand is shaded, they will need little or no water all summer, unless it proves a very dry one; and being all of a very hardy nature, they will not require the trouble of covering in the winter. The beginning of July after that, the Newfoundland Spruce Fir should be pricked out in beds at a small distance, though the Hemlock Spruce should remain in the pots a year longer, as they will then be very small. After they are planted, they must be well watered, and the beds must be hooped, to be covered with mats for shade. In hot weather the mats should be put over the beds by nine o'clock in the morning, and constantly taken off in the evenings, and remain so in cloudy and rainy weather. After they have taken root, they require no further care, until they are planted out for good; which custom has taught us to do in the autumn or in the spring; but I have by much experience found, that July is a good month for planting out all the sorts of Firs; and if it be done in a wet time, and the weather should continue moist or cloudy for two or three weeks, it would be by far the best time in the whole year. Whoever, then, plants out Firs in July, unless such weather happens, must shade and water them for a month or six weeks; but as that is not to be afforded large trees of this kind, if there be many of them, their removal must be at the usual times, lest that parching time which often comes in the middle of summer burn them up before they can have time to take root. On this account, the planting of trees at Midsummer should be tenderly enforced; though I must declare, that I have repeatedly planted Scotch Firs of different sizes, some one yard and more, others six feet high, in the scorching heat, and left them to Nature, without giving them any assistance, and they have always for the most part grown. Let others, if they please, make the experiment on a few, before they venture to plant our quantities at that season.

Pines. 1, 2. The Wild Pine is titled, *Pinus foliis geminis primordialibus solitariis glabris*. Caspar Bauhine calls it, *Pinus sylvestris*. It comprehends many varieties, called by their respective names of, *Pinus maritima altera*, *Pinaster latifolius, julis virescentibus sive pallescentibus*, and, *Pinaster tenuifolius, julo purpurascente*. They grow naturally in gravelly woods in many of the northern parts of Europe.

3. The Weymouth Pine is titled, *Pinus foliis quinis margine scabris, cortice laevi*. This is, *Pinus foliis longissimis ex uno folliculo quinis*, in the Cold. Noveb. 229. Plukenet calls it, *Pinus Virginiana, conis longis non ut in vulgari echinatis*; and Tournefort, *Larix Canadensis, longissimo folio*. It grows naturally in New-England, Virginia, Canada, and Carolina.

4. Stone-

4 Stone Pine is styled, *Pinus fo' is geminis primordialibus solitariis ciliatis* Caspar Bauhine calls it, *Pinus sativa*, and John Bauhine, *Pinus ossiculis duris, fol is long s* It grows naturally in Spain and Italy

5 Cembro Pine is, *Pinus fol is qu nis lævibus* Haller calls it, *Pinus fo'is quinis, cono erecto, nucleo eduli*, Amman, *Pinus sativa, cortice fisso, foliis setosis sibrig dis ab uni vagina quinis*, Caspar Bauhine, *Pinus sylvestris montana tertia* Cammerarius, *Pinus sylvestris Cembra*, and Breynius, *Larix sempervirens, foliis quinis, nucleis edulibus* It grows naturally in the Alps of Siberia, Tartary, Switzerland, &c

6 Swamp Pine is titled, *Pinus foliis ternis* Plukenet calls it, *Pinus Virginiana tenuifolia tripilis, sive ternis plerumque ex uno folliculo satis, strobilis minoribus* It grows naturally in the swampy parts of Virginia and Canada

7 8 9 10 11 12 13 are notable varieties only of one or othe of the former species

14 Cedar of Lebanon is titled, *Pinus fol is fasciculatis acutis* In the *Hortus Cliffortianus* it is termed, *Abies fol s fasciculatis acuminatis* Trew calls it, *Cedrus foliis rig dis acuum natis non deciduis, conis subrotundis selectis*, Caspar Bauhine, *Cedrus conifera, fol is laricis*, Barrelier, *Cedrus Liban* It grows naturally on Mount Lebanon

15 16 Yew-leaved Fir is, *Pinus foliis solitariis emarginatis* In the *Hortus Cliffortianus* it is termed, *Abies foliis solitariis apice emarginatis* Tournefort calls it, *Abies taxi folio, fructu sursum spectante*, Caspar Bauhine, *Abies conis sursum spectantibus, sive mas*, and John Bauhine, *Abies femina, sive Elate telija* It grows naturally in the Highlands of Scotland, also in Sweden, and many parts of Germany

17 18 Norway Spruce-Fir is titled, *Pinus fol is solitariis subulatis mucronatis lævibus bifariam versis* In the *Hortus Cliffortianus* it is termed, *Abies foliis solitariis apice acuminatis* Cammerarius calls it, *Picea* The varieties of it go by the respective names of, *Picea major prima, sive abies rubra*, *Abies alba, sive femina*, and, *Abies minor* It grows naturally in the northern parts of Europe and Asia

19 20 21 are varieties only of one species, whole title s, *Pinus foli s sol tar is huc ustibus o tusiusculis submembranaceis* Gronovius calls it, *Abies foliis solitariis confert s ob usis membranaceis*, and Rand, *Abies Piceæ fol is brevioribus, conis minimis*, also, *Abies Piceæ fo'is brevioribus, conis parvis biunciabus laxis* It grows naturally in Canada, Pensylvania, and other parts of North America

22 Hemlock-Fir is titled, *Pinus foli s solitaris sub-emarginatis subtus linea duplici punctata* Plukenet calls it, *Abies minor, pectinatis foli s, Virginiana, conis parvis subrotundis* It grows naturally in Virginia and Canada

23 Oriental Fir is, *Pinus fol is solitar s tetragonis* Tournefort calls it, *Abies orientalis folio brevi & tetragono, fructu minimo deorsum inflexo* It is a native of the East

*Pinus* is of the class and order *Monoecia Monadelphia*, and the characters are,

Class and order in the Linnæan system The characters

I Male Flowers are disposed in scaly bunches

1 CALYX The scales serve for calyces

2 COROLLA There is none

3 STAMINA There are many filaments, which below are joined in a kind of erect column, but divide at the top The antheræ are erect

II Female Flowers in the same plant

1 CALYX They are collected into an imbricated cone, which is nearly of an oval figure The scales are oblong, persisting, rigid and each contains two flowers

2 COROLLA There is none

3 PISTILLUM consists of a very small germen, a subulate style, and a simple stigma

4 PERICARPIUM There is none The calycinal cone contains the seeds

5 SEMEN is an oval oblong nut, having a light membranaceous wing

## CHAP. XXVI

## *PRINOS*, The WINTERBERRY

Description of this plant

THIS genus consists of two species, one of which is a deciduous plant, the other an evergreen, called, the Evergreen Winterberry, *Yappon*, or South Sea *Thea* It grows to about eight or ten feet high, sends forth many branches from the bottom to the top, and the whole plant assumes the appearance of an *Alaternus* The leaves are oblong, spear-shaped, acute, serrated, of a strong green colour, and placed alternately on the branches The flowers come out from the wings of the leaves, two or three together on a footstalk They are small, white, appear in July, and are succeeded by red or purple berries, which remain on the trees all winter

Of the propagating this plant

The culture of this shrub is exactly the same as the deciduous species, to which, to avoid repetition, the Reader is referred, observing to him, nevertheless, that this species is of a more tender nature, and instead of setting out the seedlings in the nursery-ground, each should be set in a separate pot, to be placed under shelter in winter for a few years, until they are grown strong plants, and after that to be turned out, with the mould at the roots, into the places where they are designed to remain, which ought always to be in a dry sandy soil, and a well sheltered situation

Titles

The Evergreen Winterberry, *Yappon*, or South-Sea *Thea* Shrub, is titled, *Prinos foliis ovatis serratis* In Miller's Dictionary it is termed, *Cassine foliis lanceolatis alaternis sempervirentibus, floribus axillaribus* Catesby calls it, *Cassine vera Floridanorum arbuscula baccifera, alaterni ferme facie, foliis alternatim sitis, tetrapyrena* It grows naturally in Canada

## C H A P. XXVII

## *P R U N U S*, The L A U R E L - T R E E

Species

THE Evergreens of this genus are,

1 The Common Laurel

2 Portugal Laurel

Common Laurel

1 Common Laurel By this time it is to be hoped, the reader will not be ſurpriſed at finding the Laurel under the generical word *Prunus*, as it has been before obſerved, and the curious examiner of Nature, who has hitherto followed us in our botanic deſcription, will ſee how properly it is arranged as a ſpecies of that genus The Common Laurel has been already treated of, ſo that nothing more need be added here, as the reader will there ſee the uſe and beauties of this noble plant, which has almoſt every charm to recommend it, and being alſo a plant pretty well known, a further or more minute deſcription is needleſs

Varieties

The varieties of that are, The Gold-ſtriped, and the Silver-ſtriped, both of admirable beauty in the variegated tribe

Portugal Laurel

2 Portugal Laurel is a lower-growing tree than the former and though its leaves, flowers, &c are proportionally ſmaller, it is thought by many to be much the moſt beautiful the commonneſs of the one, and ſcarcity of the other, may perhaps not a little contribute to this opinion The Portugal Laurel will grow to be ſix, eight, or ten feet high, according as the ſoil in which it is placed contributes to its encreaſe The branches are produced in an agreeable manner, being chiefly inclined to an upright poſture, and the young ſhoots are cloathed with a ſmooth reddiſh bark The leaves are ſmooth and of a fine ſtrong green colour, though their under ſurface is rather paler than the upper They are much ſmaller than the Common Laurel, are of an oblong, oval figure, and have their edges ſerrated, they are of a thick conſiſtence, and juſtly entitle the tree to the appellation of a fine Evergreen The flowers are produced in the ſame manner as the Common Laurel, though they are ſmaller They are white, appear in June, and are ſucceeded by berries, which when ripe, are black, though before that they will undergo the different changes of being firſt green, then red

Culture of the other ſorts.

The culture of the Common Laurel has already been amply ſhewn The Portugal Laurel is to be raiſed the ſame way, by the ſeeds or cuttings, though I never yet found the cuttings of the Portugal to take ſo freely as thoſe of the Common, and the young practitioner, out of a good bed of cuttings, muſt expect to ſee but a few real plants ſucceed If they are planted in July or Auguſt, they muſt be ſhaded, and kept moiſt during the hot weather, and that will be the moſt probable way to enſure ſucceſs If a perſon has the conveniency of a good ſtove, the beſt method is not to plant them until the ſpring, and then many cuttings may be planted in one pot, and afterwards plunged into the bark bed, and by this means numerous plants may eaſily be obtained

Titles

1 The Common Laurel is titled, *Prunus floribus racemoſis, foliis ſempervirentibus dorſo glanduloſis* In the *Hortus Cliffortianus* it is termed, *Padus foliis ſempervirentibus lanceolato-ovatis*, and in the *Hortus Upſalienſis*, *Padus glandulis dualibus averſo foliorum innexis* Caſpar Bauhine calls it, *Ceraſus folio laurino*, Cluſius, and others, *Lauroceraſus* It is a native of Trebiſond, near the Black Sea, from whence it was brought to Europe in the year 1576

2 Portugal Laurel is called, *Prunus floribus racemoſis, foliis ſempervirentibus eglanduloſis* In the *Hortus Cliffortianus* it is termed, *Padus foliis ſempervirentibus ovatis*, and in the *Hortus Upſalienſis*, *Padus foliis glandulis destitutis* Tournefort calls it, *Lauroceraſus Luſitanica minor* It is a native of Portugal, and grows naturally alſo in Penſylvania, and ſome other parts of America

## C H A P. XXVIII

## *P Y R U S*, The E V E R G R E E N C R A B - T R E E

This plant deſcribed

AMERICA, from whence our wilderneſs quarters are furniſhed with numerous trees and ſhrubs of admirable beauty and variety, here preſents us with a crab which ſo retains its leaves in the winter, as to entitle it to be planted amongſt Evergreens It ſeems to be a variety of the ſort called the Virginian Sweet-ſcented Crab, of which an account has been already given This ſort is at preſent very rare in England, and is what I have no where met with in any Collection I have had an opportunity to viſit, neither do I find it mentioned by any writers either on Botany or Gardening Its natural growth ſeems to be not more than twelve feet, and the branches are covered with the ſame kind of ſmooth brown bark as our Common Crab-tree The leaves are long and narrow, and will often be found of different figures, for though ſome will be angular, others again are oblong, or of a lanceolate figure They are fine, ſmooth, of a ſtrong dark-green colour, and have their edges regularly ſerrated They will

remain

remain until late in the ſpring, which rather entitles this ſhrub to a place here; tho' in an expoſed ſituation, the ends of the branches will be often ſtripped of thoſe ornaments, after a few ruffian attacks of the piercing northern blaſts. So that this tree, when conſidered as an evergreen, ſhould always be planted in a well-ſheltered place, where it will retain its leaves, and look very well all winter. The leaves in the ſpring turn to a browniſh colour, and ſoon after this drop off (but this will not be till late in the ſeaſon), and make an agreeable contraſt to the pale light-green colour of the young leaves that are then growing, to preſerve the honour of the tree, in their place. The flowers grow in bunches, upon long ſh footſtalks. They appear the latter end of May, or beginning of June, and the tree will often exhibit them in pretty good plenty. At their firſt beginning to open, they are tinged with a fine red colour, which afterwards dies away, ſo that before the petals of the flowers are dropped, they will be almoſt white. Theſe flowers are ſucceeded by crabs, which are ſmall, and to the laſt degree ſour and nauſeous to the taſte.

*Culture.* This ſort, like the others, is to be grafted or budded on the common crab or apple ſtocks; though when grafted care muſt be obſerved to cut both ſtock and cion true, and join them ſtrictly according to the cut, or very few will grow. Care muſt alſo be taken in well-tempering the clay, and nicely ſurrounding the parts to be covered, and a ſtrict eye muſt be had to repair ſuch as may crack or break off; for being in the leaſt expoſed to the air before the cion and the ſtock are well joined, it will ſoon dry up the juices, and diſappoint the Gardener's expectation. The beſt time for this work is in the month of February; and, with great care and caution, they may be multiplied this way; tho' by budding I ever found them the moſt ready to take. And for this work the middle or even latter end of July is the beſt ſeaſon; for by that time the cuttings will be got ſtrong, and there will be no danger of ſhooting when the buds are joined to the ſtock that autumn. Either way being practiſed the plants reſpectively raiſed are equally good, though the operation by budding is what I always found to be the moſt certain; but this ſhould, nevertheleſs, not diſcourage the curious artiſt from making his experiments in all ways.

# CHAP. XXIX.

## QUERCUS, The EVERGREEN OAK-TREE.

As the *Suber* and the *Ilex* of old Botaniſts are found to belong of right to this genus, a large collection of Evergreens is now comprehended under the term *Quercus*, which cauſe admiration in our larger Evergreen plantations, by their procerity of growth, and the nature and diſpoſition of their leaves and branches. The real evergreen diſtinct ſpecies are,

*Species.*
1. The Cork-tree.
2. The Common *Ilex*, or Evergreen Oak.
3. Holly-leaved Oak.
4. The Kermes Oak.
5. The Live Oak.

*Remark.* Of all theſe ſorts there are varieties, particularly of the *Ilex* kind, which affords a prodigious number of ſorts by the acorns, inſomuch that in one ſeed bed of about two thouſand plants, I have by ſtrictly comparing, found near forty whoſe leaves have been different in ſome reſpect or other; ſo that if all ſuch varieties as theſe be admitted, we ſhall find comprehended under the term *Quercus* almoſt plants enough to form a little wilderneſs. But to proceed.

*Cork tree.* 1. The Cork-tree admits of two notable varieties, which are pretty permanent from ſeeds:

*Varieties.*
Broad-leaved Cork-tree.
Narrow-leaved Cork-tree.

*describ'd.* The Broad-leaved Cork-tree is a timber-tree in Portugal and Spain, and other ſouthern parts of Europe, where it grows naturally. In our preſent plantations, it ſhould be placed near the middle of our largeſt quarters, among others of about forty feet growth; and a few alſo ſhould be planted ſingly in opens, that its fungous bark may be in view; not that there is any great beauty merely in the ſight, but with us it is a curioſity, being the true Cork, and is of the ſame nature with what comes from abroad, and we uſe for bottles, &c. Thus rough and ſpongy is the bark on the trunk and main branches; but the bark on the young ſhoots is ſmooth and grey, and that on the youngeſt white and downy. The leaves are of an oblong, oval figure, with ſawed edges. Their upper ſurface is ſmooth and of a ſtrong green colour, but their under is downy. They grow alternately on the branches, on very ſhort though ſtrong footſtalks, and indeed differ in appearance very little from many ſorts of the *Ilex*. As the flowers of the *Quercus* make no ſhow, we ſhall proceed to the next ſort, after obſerving, that the acorns of the Cork-tree are longiſh, ſmooth, and brown when ripe, and of the ſize and ſhape of ſome of our common acorns, to which they are ſo much alike, as not to be diſtinguiſhed, if mixed together.

The Narrow-leaved Cork-tree is a variety only of the common and moſt general ſort; ſo that as this article requires nothing more than obſerving that the leaves are ſmaller, and as ſuch make a variety in plantations, it may not be amiſs to ſay ſomething of the Cork, which we receive from abroad, and which is collected from theſe trees.

*Of the cork.* The beſt cork, then, is taken from the oldeſt trees, the bark on the young trees being too porous for uſe. They are, nevertheleſs, barked before they are twenty years old; and this barking is neceſſary, to make way for a better to ſucceed; and it is obſervable, that after every ſtripping, the ſucceeding bark will increaſe in value. They are generally peeled once in ten years, with an inſtrument for that purpoſe, and this is so far from injuring the trees, that it is necessary, and contributes to their being healthy, for without it they thrive but slowly, nay, in a few years they will begin to decay, and in less than a century a whole plantation will die of age, whereas those trees that have been regularly peeled, will last upwards of two hundred years. Wonderful then, is the wisdom and goodness of Almighty God, and calls for our profoundest admiration, that he should not only provide for us his creatures such variety of things for use, but cause, as in this instance, what would be death to one tree, to be refreshment to another, for the supply of our necessities, and in the formation of this tree, not only causing the cork to grow, but providing also an inner bark sufficiently to nourish the tree, and even in a manner exhilarate it, as the loaded wool is shorn from the fleecy kind. To make our gardening to the utmost degree useful, we should be always exercised in these considerations, and this will inspire us with thanks of gratitude and obedience.

Ilex. 2. The *Ilex* is a well known Evergreen, of which there are many varieties, all of which add great beauty to the large quarters of evergreen trees. The bark of all these sorts is entire, and that of the young sorts smooth; but the leaves are of different shapes and composition, according to the nature of their variety. Some of them are nearly like those of both sorts of the Cork-tree, others again are nearly round and prickly, some are long, smooth, and narrow, with few indentures, whilst others are broad and much serrated. All these varieties will often proceed from acorns gathered of the same tree; nay, the leaves of the same tree will not be always alike, being often found very different on the same plant; so that a quantity of plants of this species raised from seeds, will of themselves afford wonderful variety. The acorns of all these sorts are of different sizes, though their shape is nearly the same, which is like that of some sorts of our Common Oak, but smaller.

Holly-leaved Ilex. 3. The Holly-leaved *Ilex* differs from the other sorts only that the leaves are shaped like those of the Holly-tree. They are of an oblong, oval figure, sinuated prickly, and downy underneath; but many sorts raised from seeds of the *Ilex*, will have such kind of leaves, and it constitutes no further a variety, than what may reasonably be expected from a quantity of the acorns of the *Ilex* sown.

Kermes Oak. 4. Kermes Oak. This is a low-growing tree, and a fine Evergreen. It seldom grows to be twenty feet high, and it may be kept down to what height is required. It has the appearance of some of the sorts of the *Ilex*, from which it looks to be a variety only, though doubtless this is of itself a distinct species. The leaves are smooth and of an oval figure. They are of a thickish consistence, and larger than most sorts of the *Ilex*. Their verge is indented, and many of them are possessed of small spines, and they are placed on short strong footstalks on the branches. The acorns of this sort are small, though there are to be found in our woods acorns of about the same size and shape.

Live Oak. 5. The Live Oak is an American plant, where it grows to timber. The leaves are large, spear-shaped, oval, of a fine dark green colour, entire, and placed on short footstalks on the branches. The acorns of this sort are small, though they grow in cups with footstalks like the other sorts. The wood of this tree is very useful to the inhabitants of Carolina, Pensylvania, and Virginia, where it grows naturally, being very tough and hard, and serves for many purposes that require such a sort. The acorns serve for food for the meanest people, who not only eat them as such, but, being of a very sweet nature, they are liked by persons of all ranks. From these acorns a sweet oil also is extracted, which is very good.

There are many other varieties, if not distinct species of Evergreen Oaks, which it will not be so necessary to search for here, as the sorts mentioned are the bulk of the tribe, and of themselves afford much variety, and indeed, if much cost and trouble were bestowed in procuring others, the variety would be little heightened, particularly as the pleasure received from the variation arises principally from the different forms of the leaves, for none of these trees produce flowers for ornament, and the acorns afford too minute a variety to require dwelling long on here, so that I proceed to say something of the culture of the Evergreen Oak.

Method of propagating them by seeds. All these sorts are to be raised from the acorns, in the manner which has been directed for the other sorts of Oak. The best acorns we receive from abroad, for they seldom ripen well with us, though I must own I have had tolerable good acorns of the *Ilex* that grew in England, from which I have had many good plants. The acorns which come from abroad, and which are by far the finest, often sprout in the passage, so that care must be used in taking them out of what they are enclosed in, and they should be put into the mould as soon as conveniency will permit. The pots, boxes, &c. must be set in shade after they come up; they will want nothing but weeding to the end of three years, for I would not have them taken out of the seed beds sooner, especially the sorts of the *Ilex*, for when these have been planted out of the seed-bed at one year old, they have seldom grown, and though sometimes some of them will be green, and have the appearance of growing during one summer, they will often turn brown, and gradually go off afterwards. After the plants have stood to be two or three feet high, I always found them more sure of growing when moved. I have transplanted such plants at most times of the year with success in the spring, in the depth of winter, and in the autumn, and have had them grow well when moved in July; and indeed I am pretty well persuaded there is no month in the year more proper than that for the removing of most sorts of Evergreens, provided the weather be rainy or hazy at their planting, and shade can be afforded them for some time after.

Inarching. These trees may be also encreased by inarching, for they will grow very readily this way on stocks of our Common Oak. So that having a tree or two of any of the sorts, if young Oaks are planted round each of them, after they have grown a summer or two, they will be ready to embrace the young shoots. After they are well joined, they may be cut off from the mother tree, and transplanted into the nursery ground or where they are to remain, and fresh Oaklings planted around the trees to be multiplied, and the continuance of the repetition of this may be at pleasure. In removing of the inarched plants, the time should be observed as in removing young plants of our Common Oak, as has been directed, the roots still remaining of that kind and nature.

and by grafting. These trees will take by grafting on the young stocks of our Common Oak. The stocks should be young and healthy, the cuttings strong and good, and great care must be taken in properly joining and claying them, or they will not grow; which makes the inarching more necessary, as by that

that practice no cutting is in danger of being lost

Titles 1 The Cork-tree is titled *Quercus foliis ovato-oblongis indivisis serratis subtus tomentosis, cortice rimoso fungoso* Caspar Bauhine calls it, *Suber latifolium perpetuo virens*, others, *Suber* It grows naturally in the southern parts of Europe

2 The *Ilex* is called, *Quercus foliis ovato oblongis indivisis serratis petiolis subtus incanis cortice integro* Caspar Bauhine calls it, *Ilex folio angusto non serrato*, also, *Ilex oblongo serrato folio*, John Bauhine *Ilex* [illegible], also *Smilax* [illegible], and Van Royen, *Quercus foliis oblongo-ovatis* [illegible] *integerrimis* It grows naturally in Spain, Portugal, &c

3 The Holly leaved Oak is titled *Quercus foliis oblongo-ovatis sinuato spinosis sessilibus subtus tomentosis glandibus pedunculatis* Magnol calls it, *Ilex foliis rotundioribus & spinosis, e luco granuloso* It grows naturally near Montpelier

4 The Kermes Oak is titled, *Quercus foliis ovatis indivisis spinoso dentatis glabris* Caspar Bauhine calls it, *Ilex aculeata cocciglandifera*, Commerarius, *Ilex coccifera*, and Sauvage, *Quercus foliis ovatis dentato spinosis, glandibus sessilibus* It grows naturally in France and Spain

5 Live Oak is, *Quercus foliis lanceolato-ovatis integris mucronatis* It is a native of America

# CHAP XXX

## *RHAMNUS*

THE hardy evergreen species of this genus are,

Species 1 *Alaternus*

2 Narrow leaved Buckthorn

3 Olive leaved Buckthorn

Alaternus. 1 The *Alaternus*, which used to be reckoned a distinct genus is now classed with the species of *Rhamnus*, and by it, with its varieties, our Evergreen plantations are much profited The green colour of most of them is fine, and most of their leaves are shining, and though their flowers are inconsiderable as to ornamental show, yet what heightens the value of these sorts for the evergreen plantations is, they are succeeded by berries of which the whistling birds are so exceeding fond that they will repair hither from all parts, and will render such places very delightful for though they will soon have devoured all the berries in the autumn, yet they will be accustomed to the wilderness and be ready to proclaim the first approach of spring by their [illegible], so that whoever is fond of these [illegible], indeed, who is not? should always have [illegible] such trees as are beautiful, and [illegible] for their enticement and for this [illegible] are better adapted than the sorts of [illegible]. Of [illegible], then, the principal are,

Varieties The Common *Alaternus*

The Broad leaved *Alaternus*

The Jagged leaved *Alaternus*

described The *Alaternus*, commonly so called, is a tree [illegible] known as hardly to need a description. The variegated sorts are much esteemed by such [illegible] kind of those plants There are of it, the Gold striped, the Silver Striped, the Blotch leaved, the Large and the Smaller growing *Alaternus* and whoever is for having them in plantations of the present kind, will still encrease the variety This is indeed objected to by some, as, they say, they cannot be Evergreens, others again think they are most proper, as they retain their leaves, and appear amongst others, of different colours like flowers in [illegible]. The branches of these sorts of *Alaternus* are numerous, and the younger branches are covered with a smooth green bark In winter indeed they will be brown, and some of a reddish colour, others will have their sides next the sun red, and the opposite green The leaves are oval, of a lucid green in the common sorts, and look very beautiful Their edges are crenated, and they grow alternately on the branches The flowers are produced in April, from the wings of the leaves, in little clusters They are of a greenish colour, but make no figure and are succeeded by the above-mentioned kind of berries, which are so grateful to blackbirds, thrushes, and the like kinds of whistling birds

The Broad leaved *Alaternus* is the grandest-looking tree of all the sorts It will grow to the greatest height, if permitted to shoot freely, though it may be kept down to any height wanted The leaves are the largest of any of the sorts and their edges are slightly crenated They differ little in figure from the preceding sort, being more heart-shaped They are of a fine shining strong green colour both in winter and summer, and this tree produces flowers and seeds like the other

The Jagged leaved *Alaternus* has as different a look from the other as any two evergreens whatever It is a well-looking upright tree, and the branches are covered with a smooth fine bark, which in winter is of a reddish colour The leaves, like those of all the sorts, grow alternately They are long and narrow, and are so jagged as to cause them to have a particular look Their surface is smooth and shining, and their figure lanceolate, and this, together with the nature of their serratures, cause in the tree a beautiful as well as singular look The flowers are produced in the same manner as the others, and are succeeded by berries, which are used by painters in composing some of their yellows There are variegated sorts of the Jagged leaved *Alaternus*, in both Silver and Gold stripes, which are indeed very beautiful, but they are very apt to turn green, if planted in a rich soil, so that to continue the stripes in perfection, the worst sort of hungry land should be allotted them

There are more varieties of the *Alaternus*, but their differences are so inconsiderable as scarcely to be worth enumerating All the sorts have been confounded by the unskilful with those of *Phillyrea*,

*Phylica*, which have undeservedly passed one for the other. That the Gardener, therefore, may be guarded from running again into these errors, he must observe, that the leaves of all the sorts of *Phylica* grow always opposite by pairs, whereas those of the *Alaternus* grow singly and alternately on the branches, which first gave occasion to the shrub's being so called. The Botanist will see a more material difference, when, upon examining the flowers, he finds they belong to another class.

Narrow-leaved Buckthorn. 2. Narrow-leaved Buckthorn grows to be a tree of ten or twelve feet high, sending forth several branches from the sides from the bottom to the top. They are covered with a blackish or dark-coloured bark, and each of them is terminated by a long sharp thorn. The leaves are very narrow, fleshy, astringent, of a strong green colour, and grow together in bunches on the sides of the branches. The flowers come out from the sides of the branches in small bunches. They are of an herbaceous colour, appear early in the spring, and are succeeded by large round berries, like those of the Sloe-bush, which are harsh and sour to the taste, and of a fine black colour when ripe. The fruit of this sort continues on the trees all winter, making a beautiful appearance among the narrow clustered leaves at that season. A decoction of their berries is said to be good for the gout, and, by fomentation, is greatly serviceable to paralytic, weak, and relaxed parts.

Olive-leaved Buckthorn. 3. Olive leaved Buckthorn will grow to be eight or ten feet high, sending forth numerous branches, each of which is terminated by a long sharp spine. The leaves are small, oblong, obtuse, undivided, veined, smooth, of a thickish consistence, and grow two or three together on their own separate footstalks. The flowers come out from the sides of the branches in the spring. They are small, of a whitish green colour, and are succeeded by round black berries, about the size and colour of those of the Common Purging Buckthorn.

These sorts are to be propagated,

Method of propagating the sort by layers. 1. By layers. This business must be done in the autumn, when the last summer's shoots should be laid in the ground. These will often strike root at almost every joint; though I have known them in some strong soils, upon examining them in the autumn, after being layered a whole year, without any roots, so that it would be proper to give the layer a slit at the joint, and bend it so in the ground as to keep it open, and it will have plenty of root by the autumn. Another thing to be observed is, that in order to obtain good layers, the plants designed to be encreased should be headed the year before, and this will cause them to shoot vigorously, and from these shoots the strongest and best layers may be expected, many of which will be good plants, to set out where they are to remain, while the weakest may be planted in the usual nursery-way, to gain strength.

By seeds. 2. These plants may be raised by seeds, the variegated ones excepted, so they must always be encreased by layers. The seeds will be ripe in September, or the beginning of October, when they should be guarded from the birds, or they will soon eat them all. Soon after they are ripe they should be sown, for even then they will often remain two years before they come up. The beds should be composed of fine light mould, and they should be sown an inch deep. If few or no plants appear in the spring, you must wait, and weed the beds with patience, until the spring following, when you may expect a plentiful crop. Let them stand two years in the seed-bed, with constant weeding, and frequent watering in dry weather, and in March let them be planted out in the nursery, where they will be afterwards ready for removing, when wanted. As these trees produce plenty of good seeds, by this means a prodigious quantity of plants may be soon raised, and those from seeds are always observed to grow straighter, and to a greater height than those raised from layers; so that where many of these trees are wanted for large plantations, the raising them from seeds is the most eligible method. All the sorts of *Alaternus* are very hardy, and may be planted in almost any soil or situation, but the Narrow and Olive-leaved Buckthorn should be stationed in a dry, warm, well sheltered place.

Titles. 1. *Alaternus* is titled, *Rhamnus inermis, floribus dioicis, stigmate triplici, foliis serratis*. In the *Hortus Cliffortianus* it is termed, *Rhamnus inermis, floribus polygamis, stigmate triplici, foliis serratis*. Caspar Bauhine calls it, *Phylica elatior*; also, *Phylica humilior*; and Clusius, *Alaternus* 1. 2. It grows naturally in most of the southern parts of Europe.

2. Narrow-leaved Buckthorn is, *Rhamnus spinis terminalibus, floribus quadrifidis dioicis, foliis ovatis*. Clusius calls it, *Rhamnus tertius flore virgei*; accordingly Gerard terms it, *Rhamnus tertius Clusii*. It grows naturally in Spain.

3. Olive-leaved Buckthorn is, *Rhamnus spinis terminalibus, foliis oblongis integerrimis*. Tournefort calls it, *Rhamnus Hispanicus, oleae folio*. It is a native of Spain.

## CHAP. XXXI.

## *RHODODENDRON*, The DWARF ROSE-BAY.

THERE are two species of this genus which more peculiarly offer themselves for this place, called,

Species. 1. The American Mountain Laurel.
2. Pontic Dwarf Rose-Bay.

American Mountain Laurel. 1. American Mountain Laurel is a plant so distinguished because, in America, it grows naturally upon the highest mountains, and on the edges of cliffs, precipices, &c. There it will grow to be a moderate-sized tree; with us it seldom rises higher than six feet. The branches are not numerous, neither are they produced in any order. The leaves are large and beautiful, of an oval spear-shaped figure, and a little resemble those

those of our Common Laurel They are of a shining strong green on their upper surface, tho' paler underneath; but they lose this delicacy as they grow older, altering to a kind of iron colour. Their edges are acutely reflexed, and they grow irregularly on short footstalks on the branches. The flowers are produced at the ends of the branches, about Midsummer though sometimes sooner, before which time the buds will be large and turgid, and indeed, as they begin to swell early in the autumn before, these have a good effect, and look well all winter. When the shrub is in blow, the flowers appear close to the branches, in roundish bunches. Each is composed of one petal, which is divided at the rim into five parts, one of which is dotted in a pretty manner. They are very beautiful, and alter their colour as they grow older, for at first the petals are of a very pale blush colour, which dies away to a white, but the outside, which is a peach colour, is not subject in so high a degree to this alteration. They will continue, by a succession of flowers, sometimes more than two months, but they are succeeded by oval capsules, full of seeds.

And the Pontic Rose-Bay, described. 2. Pontic Rose-Bay grows to about four or five feet high, sending forth several branches without order from the root. The leaves are spear-shaped, glossy on both sides, acute, and placed on short footstalks on the branches. The flowers are produced in clusters from the ends of the branches, each of them is bell-shaped, and of a fine purple colour. They appear in July, and are succeeded by oval capsules containing the seeds, which seldom ripen in England.

Method of propagating them. The culture of these beautiful shrubs must be from seeds, which we receive from the places where they grow naturally. The best way is to sow them very thin in the places where they are designed to remain, and if these places be naturally rocky, sandy, and shady, it will be so much the better (especially for the first sort, the second requires a moistish soil, in a warm shady place), if not, a quantity of drift-sand must be added to the natural soil, and all made fine and level. Some spots for the reception of the seeds are to be pitched on. A few seeds should be put in each, and covered about half an inch deep and then some stick stuck round them to direct to the true places, that they may not be disturbed by hoeing of the weeds, but that these may be all carefully plucked up by the hand as often as they appear, for it will be a whole year, and sometimes two or more, before the plants come up. This careful weeding must always be repeated, and after the plants come up those that grow too close may be drawn the spring following, and each set in a separate pot and then plunged into a hotbed to set them growing. The plants that remain without removing will be the strongest and best, and will be more likely to produce flowers than any other, though this seems to be a plant that will bear transplanting very well, especially if it is not to be carried at too great a distance for the roots to dry, and ball of earth be preserved to them. Whenever they are not to be raised and remain in the places, the best way is to sow them in pots filled with sandy earth, or such as is made so by at least a third part of sand being added. After the plants come up, they may be planted in separate pots the spring following, and then set forward by a plunge in the bed, and afterwards they may be any time turned out into the places where they are to remain, which ought to be in a naturally sandy situation, otherwise there will be little hopes of seeing them in any degree of perfection.

Titles. 1. American Mountain Laurel is titled, *Rhododendron foliis nitidis ovalibus obtusis venosis margine acuto reflexo petiolis florem*. In the *Amœnitates Academicæ* it is called, *Ledum lauro cerasi folio*. Catesby calls it, *Chamærhododendros, lauri folio, semper virens, floribus bullatis corymbosis*. In Miller's Dictionary it is termed, *Kalmia foliis lanceolato ovatis nitidis subtus ferrugineis, corymbis terminalibus*. It grows naturally in Virginia.

2. Pontic Dwarf Rose-Bay is, *Rhododendron foliis nitidis lanceolatis glabris, racemis terminalibus*. Tournefort calls it, *Chamærhododendros Pontica maxima, folio lauro cerasi*. It grows naturally in the East, and in most shady places near Gibraltar.

## CHAP. XXXII

## *ROSA*, The ROSE-TREE

THE Evergreen Rose is justly admired. Though it is a trailing shrub, and should of course come in among the trailing tribe, yet as it makes a good figure among Evergreens in wilderness quarters, and will form itself (if supported) into a thicket, it may as well have a place here as any where.

This species described. This shrub (if supported) will grow to a great height, and will climb up pales, hedges, &c where it will make a handsome show, but when planted singly in Evergreen quarters, it first sends its slender branches along the ground, and from these others are produced, so that by degrees it will form a bush of six feet high, or more. The compass it is to extend is to be limited, and the Gardener must be careful to nip the trailing branches, that are proceeding to exceed the given distance, and thus will this shrub have an agreeable, wild, bushy look. The bark is smooth, and the leaves are of a fine green colour. They are composed of about two pairs of folioles, that grow opposite on the mid rib, besides the odd one. The mid rib is armed with spines, and is often of a reddish colour. The flowers are produced at the ends of the branches, the latter end of July. They grow in bunches, and are single. They are of a clear white, and very fragrant, and sometimes these bushes will be covered with them, causing thereby a most enchanting look.

Culture. The culture of this sort is the same as that of the others, and it will take by layers as readily as any of them.

Titles. This species is titled, *Rosa germinibus ovatis pedunculisque hispidis, caule petiolisque aculeatis*. In the former edition of the *Species Plantarum* it is termed, *Rosa caule aculeato foliolis quinis glabris perennantibus*. Clusius calls it, *Rosa semper virens, jungermannia*, and Caspar Bauhine, *Rosa moschata sempervirens*. It grows common in Germany.

# CHAP. XXXIII.

## *RUSCUS*, BUTCHERS BROOM.

Introductory observations. RUSCUS affords us several sorts to enlarge the variety in our quarters of Evergreens; some of which will grow to be four or five feet high, whilst others are naturally of so low a growth as might raise an objection to their being admitted amongst Evergreen trees. They are, however, of all others the most fit for these places; not only as they will grow under the drip of all trees, but in such places their leaves are always of a more elegant shining green colour; or they may be ranged with the lower growing sorts, those of a yard, or four or five feet high, who will find enough to keep them company. They may be placed near the borders to help to continue the first row, then the others, according to their growth, by a beautiful climax, as it were, to succeed in order; whilst the very lowest, such as the *Hypoglossum*, may be planted near the foot of the walk, where it will be always green, and, though very low, will afford variety and pleasure. The real hardy species of *Ruscus* are,

Species.

1. The Common Butchers Broom.
2. The Broad-leaved Butchers Broom.
3. The *Hypoglossum*, or Tongued Laurel.
4. The Alexandrian Laurel.

Description of the Common. 1. The Common Butchers Broom will arise with tough, ligneous, striated, green, spreading stalks, to about a yard in height. These proceed from a large, white, tender, creeping root, which will, when the plant has remained long, be found very deep in the ground. The leaves are of an oblong figure, of a dark dusky green colour, and grow alternately on the stalks. Their edges are entire; they are of a thick stiff consistence; and their points are prickly and as sharp as a needle. The flowers grow on the middle of the upper surface of the leaves, and will be in June. They are small and greenish, and the females are succeeded by large beautiful red berries of a sweetish taste. This plant is of great use to the butchers, who gather it to make different besoms, both for sweeping of their shops and cleaning of their blocks; from whence it has the appellation of Butchers Broom. The young tender shoots of this shrub, in the spring, may be eaten like hop-tops or asparagus, and some people are very fond of them. The seeds and roots are much used in medicine.

and the Broad-leaved Butchers Broom. 2. The Broad-leaved Butchers Broom has large white roots, with long thick fibres, and from these arise pliable stalks, which will grow to be near a yard high. These stalks are of a very fine green colour, and are very tough and numerous. They produce their leaves in an alternate manner; are of a very fine shining green colour, and of a thick consistence. They are longer and broader than the other sort, their figure is oval, and they end in acute points. The flowers of this sort grow on the under surface of the leaves, near the middle. These are small, and of a greenish white. They are produced in July; and the seeds that succeed them are small and red, and will be ripe in winter.

3. The *Hypoglossum* is the lowest of all the sorts, as the stalks seldom get to above a foot high; and has very few pretensions, indeed, to be called a shrub; nevertheless, it may justly claim a place at the edge at least of all Evergreen shrubberies. The roots are nearly of the same nature with the other sorts, and the stalks are numerous and pithy. They are of a dull green colour, and striated; and they produce their leaves in an irregular manner, being sometimes alternate, whilst others again may be seen standing opposite by pairs. These leaves are of a lanceolate figure, and are of the same dull green colour with those of the stalks. They are from three to four inches long, and about one broad. They grow without any footstalks, being narrow at both ends, and their edges naturally turn towards the center of the upper surface. They are free from serratures; and from the stalk or base of the leaves run several veins the whole length, which gradually diverge from the middle, but approach again in the same manner until they all end in the point of the leaf. Each of these leaves produces another small leaf of the same shape, from the middle of its upper surface; and from the bottom of these small leaves are produced the flowers. These will be ripe in July, are small and yellowish; and the fruit that succeeds them is large and red, and will be ripe in winter. of the Hypoglossum.

4. The Alexandrian Laurel has the same kind of white fleshy roots with long thick fibres as the others; and the branches are very numerous and pliable. They are smooth and round, of a shining green colour, and produce others smaller alternately, from the bottom to the top. They will grow to be four or five feet high, and their pliable branches are nevertheless brittle near the bottom. The leaves grow chiefly on the smaller side shoots, and on these they are placed alternately. They are close to the branches, are smooth, of a delightful shining green colour, and have several small veins running the whole length, diverging from the middle, but approaching again to end at the point. They are from two to three inches long, and about one broad, are of an oblong lanceolated figure, and end in very acute points. The flowers are hermaphrodites, of the Alexandrian Laurel.

dites, and produced in long bunches, at the ends of the branches. Each of them is small, and of a yellowish colour, and they are succeeded by large red berries, which will be ripe in winter.

Variety. There is a variety of this sort, with red flowers.

This sort formerly used as wreaths. This species of *Ruscus* is supposed to be the Laurel which composed the wreaths worn by the antient victors and poets, and indeed with good reason, not only on account of its pliableness, by which it might be easily wrought for such purposes, but the wreaths on the antient busts &c seem to figure to us the leaves and flexible branches of the plant we are treating of.

Other varieties. There is another sort of *Ruscus*, which has oval acute-pointed leaves, growing by threes round the stalks, and which produce the flowers and fruit from the mid-rib on the under surface. Also another sort, with oval acute-pointed leaves, that produces the flowers from the mid-rib on the upper surface. But as these are only varieties of the above sorts, have the same kind of roots, produce the same kind of slender pliable branches, and have their flowers succeeded by nearly the like kind of berries, nothing more need be said of them.

Method of propagating these sorts by roots; All these sorts may be easily multiplied, after having obtained a plant or two of each, for their roots will encrease so fast, and will proportionably send forth such a quantity of stalks, that each of them will soon form itself into a little thicket. These, then, are to be taken up and divided, and from one original root or off-set many will be soon produced. The best time for this work is early in the autumn, though they will grow very well if divided and removed in the spring, or any time in the winter.

and by seeds. These plants are also to be encreased by seeds. This, however, is a slow way, but must, nevertheless, be practised, when the plants cannot be obtained. The beds for their reception must be made fine, and cleared of the roots of all weeds. They will require no other compost than that of good common garden-mould. They should be sown an inch and a half or two inches deep, and the beds should be suffered to lie undisturbed, for they will not come up before the second, and sometimes the main crop the third, spring after sowing. All the summer they should be kept clean of weeds, and if the beds wear away so as to endanger the seeds being laid bare, a little fine mould should be riddled over them, to supply what may be lost by wear in weeding, settling, &c. After they are come up, they will require no other care than weeding, for they are very hardy, and when they come too thick in the spring after the frosts are over, the strongest should be drawn out and planted in beds, six inches asunder. This will make room for the others to flourish; and though mention is made of removing these plants after the frosts are over, it is not because they are tender and subject to be destroyed by it, but if they are removed in the autumn, or early in the winter, being then small, the frosts generally throw them out of the ground, to the great danger, if not entire loss, of the whole stock of the new-removed seedlings. This, however, is considered by few Gardeners who have not paid dear for their experience, and is what is chiefly recommended by our modern authors, to transplant seedlings of most sorts from the beds in October, which indeed would be an excellent month, were no frosts to ensue. But good thought and experience, by fatal practice, have taught the Gardener now, to defer the removing his small seedlings until the spring, when they will not be liable to be turned out of their warm beds when they should least like it, by the rigours of the winter. But to return: After the seedlings are two or three years old, whether they have been removed or not, they will by that time be good strong plants, fit for removing, and may be then taken up and planted out for good.

1. The Common Butchers Broom is titled, *Ruscus foliis supra floriferis nudis*. Tournefort calls it, *Ruscus myrtifolius aculeatus*; Caspar Bauhine simply, *Ruscus*; Gerard, *Ruscus, sive Bruscus*; others, *Ruscus vulgaris*, &c. It grows common in woods and thickets in England, Italy, and France. Titles.

2. The Broad-leaved Butchers Broom is titled, *Ruscus foliis subtus floriferis nudis*. Caspar Bauhine calls it, *Laurus Alexandrina, fructu folio insidente*; Tournefort, *Ruscus latifolius, fructu folio innascente*; Columna, *Laurus Alexandrina, Chamædaphne*; and Dillenius, *Ruscus latifolius, fructu ex medio foliorum extra pendente*. It grows naturally on the declivities of hills and mountains in Italy.

3. The *Hypoglossum* is, *Ruscus foliis subtus floriferis sub foliolo*. Caspar Bauhine calls it, *Laurus Alexandrina, fructu pediculo insidente*; Tournefort, *Ruscus angustifolius fructu folio innascente*; and Columna, *Hypoglossum Dioscoridis, laureola Plinii*. It grows naturally in shady mountainous parts in Italy and Hungary.

4. The Alexandrian Laurel is titled, *Ruscus racemo terminali hermaphrodito*. Tournefort calls it, *Ruscus angustifolius, fructu summis ramulis innascente*. It is not certain in what part of the world this species grows naturally.

*Ruscus* is of the class and order *Dioecia Syngenesia*, and the characters are, Class and order in the Linnean system. The character.

I. Male Flowers.

1. CALYX is an erect, patent, perianthium, composed of six oval, convex leaves, having reflexed borders.

2. COROLLA. There are no petals, but there is an oval, inflated, erect nectarium, the size of the calyx, and which opens at the mouth.

3. STAMINA. There are no filaments; but three patent antheræ, sitting on the top of the nectarium, and joined at their base.

II. Female Flowers.

1. CALYX is the same sort of perianthium as that of the males.

2. COROLLA. There are no petals, but the same kind of nectarium as in the male flowers.

3. PISTILLUM consists of an oblong, oval germen, hid within the nectarium, of a cylindric style, the length of the nectarium, and an obtuse stigma, standing above the mouth of it.

4. PERICARPIUM is a round trilocular berry.

5. SEMINA. The seeds are two, and round.

CHAP.

# CHAP XXXIV

## *SALSOLA*, The STONECROP-TREE

THIS is a fine plant, looks well in any place, and may be placed amongst the Evergreens, as it retains its leaves (if well sheltered) during the winter months. This sort is commonly called the Stonecrop-tree, though in some places it is called Shrubby Blite, Shrubby Glasswort, &c but the former is the name which it most generally bears and is known by. This shrub described: The Stonecrop-tree is a shrub of about four or five feet growth. It will shoot rather higher, if permitted, but is never more beautiful than when about a yard high. The branches are numerous, naturally grow upright, are covered with a grey bark, and are very brittle. As to the leaves, they are very much like the Common Stonecrop of our walls, which is so well known, being narrow, taper, and fleshy like them. They are of the same light, pleasant green, and the branches are stored with them in plenty. The flowers make no show, neither is there any thing that is desirable to the Gardener that succeeds them. This is a very hardy shrub, but, as we have introduced it amongst the Evergreens, it may not be improper to give an hint or two for its being properly stationed. It should be set in a well-sheltered place, for although the leaves remain on all winter, yet our severe black frosts suddenly coming on them, when in an open exposed place, destroy them, and cause them to turn black, and although the shrub will shoot out again early in the spring, yet the black destroyed leaves will look very disagreeable all winter, and be as blots among others that are less subject to these disasters. One hint more may be necessary, and that is, wherever this shrub is planted, either in small or large gardens, among deciduous or evergreen trees, not to circumscribe the tree, with strings or bass mattings, in order to confine the branches and keep them closer. This will effectually destroy all the branches and leaves, if not the whole plant, for being thus closely confined, the free admission of the air will be excluded, which will cause these succulent leaves to rot and decay. This precaution is the more necessary, as their upright branches being heavy laden with such plenty of succulent leaves, are subject to be blown down from the bottom by the high winds, and as they then must of course look irregular, and may probably overspread some little plant that grows near them, it is a common thing to tie them up again to the other branches. This custom, then, for the future must never be practised, but when any of them happen to be blown down in that manner, they must be taken off and thrown away.

Method of propagating it: Nothing is more easy than the culture of the Stonecrop tree, for it is encreased by layers, cuttings, and suckers. In short, if some of these shrubs are planted they will soon send forth many stalks from the roots, and if the whole be then taken up, these without any other trouble, may be divided, and will each of them be a good plant, and thus in a few years, from a plant or two of this shrub, scores may be obtained.

Titles: The title of this genus is, *Salsola erecta fruticosa, foliis filiformibus obtusiusculis*. In the former edition of the *Species Plantarum* it is termed, *Chenopodium foliis linearibus teretibus, carnosis, caule fruticoso*. Boerhaave calls it, *Chenopodium, sedi folio minimo, frutescens perenne*, Ray, *Blitum fruticosum maritimum, vermicularis fruticosum dictum*, Muntingius, *Sedum minus arborescens*, Haller, *Lerchea foliis obtusis*, Caspar Bauhine, *Anthyllis chamæpithyodes frutescens*, and John Bauhine, *Kali species vermicularis marina arborescens*. It grows naturally on the sea coasts of England, France, Spain, and Persia.

Class and order in the Linnæan system: *Salsola* is of the class and order *Pentandria Digynia*, and the characters are,

The characters:

1 CALYX is a permanent perianthium, composed of five oval, concave, leaves.

2 COROLLA. There is none.

3 STAMINA are five very short filaments, inserted in the division of the calyx.

4 PISTILLUM consists of a round germen, a short double or triple style, and recurved stigmas.

5 PERICARPIUM is an oval capsule of one cell, wrapped up in the calyx.

6 SEMEN. The seed is single, large, and spiral.

CHAP

# CHAP. XXXV.

## *TAXUS*, The YEW-TREE.

Remarks

WHAT has been already said of the Yew-tree, in the First Book, may be sufficient for the purpose particularly as it is with us universally well known and as its culture is there very fully explained, no one will be at a loss how to arrange his plants when thus raised, either in the wilderness quarters, or hedge-rows, or for covering at a distance bleak and barren hills, either for beauty or profit. So that nothing is wanted to be added here, more than to remind the Gardener, that there is a variety of it, with very short leaves, which has a singular and very beautiful effect in ornamenting plantations, and another with Striped leaves, of great value among the variegated tribes. They are both to be encreased by layers, and the Striped sort must be set in a very barren soil, or it will soon become plain.

Title

The Yew-tree is titled, *Taxus foliis approximatis*. This tree is found in old books of Botany with no other title than, *Taxus*, though some have the epithet *vulgaris*, &c. It is a native of Britain and most parts of Europe, and grows also in Canada.

Class and order in the Linnæan system

*Taxus* is of the class and order *Dioecia Monadelphia*, and the characters are,

The character

I. Male Flowers.

1. CALYX. There is none, but a gem like a four leaved perianthium.
2. COROLLA. There is none.
3. STAMINA are numerous filaments, that cohere at the bottom, in a column longer than the gem. The antheræ are peltated and depressed, have obtuse margins, are divided into eight segments, and open on each side the base, discharging their farina.

II. Female Flowers.

1. CALYX. The same as the males.
2. COROLLA. There is none.
3. PISTILLUM consists of an oval, acuminated germen, with no style, but an acute stigma.
4. PERICARPIUM is a wasting, red-coloured, juicy berry, lengthened from the receptacle, globular at the top, and below covered by a proper coat.
5. SEMEN. The seed is single, oval, and oblong, its top is prominent beyond the berry.

# CHAP. XXXVI.

## *THUYA*, The TREE of LIFE.

THE Common *Arbor Vitæ* has been already treated of in the First Book, where its being planted as a fruit-tree is enforced. This delightful tree is worthy of all plantations, and in wilderness-quarters for ornament it should have a good share. Nothing more need be added in relation to this sort, for there the reader will see enough of its description, and may know how to rank it amongst others in his works. Besides this species, there are two others, one of more beauty, the other of better quality, though they will all arrive to nearly the same height and magnitude, and these are,

Species

2. The Chinese *Arbor Vitæ*.
3. The American Sweet-scented *Arbor Vitæ*.

Description of the Chinese

2. The Chinese *Arbor Vitæ* is a much more beautiful plant than the Common species, for its branches are more numerous, and grow in a more picturesque erect manner, and the leaves are of a fine pleasant light-green colour, whereas those of the other in winter are of a dark disagreeable green, inclined to a dusky brown, which is the worst property of this tree in the winter-season. The branches of the Common *Arbor Vitæ* are of a dark brown colour, and the bark on the young branches is smooth, the bark of the Chinese is also smooth, and of a light brown. The leaves of this sort, like the others, are imbricated, that is, they grow over each other, but they are more numerous and smaller, and grow closer together, and being of so fine a green, which continues all winter, make this sort the most valuable, though not to the rejection of the others, even in pleasurable plantations, for those cause good variety by their manner of growth, as well as the colour of their leaves. The flowers of none of the sorts have any beauty, they have males and females distinct, and the females of the Common *Arbor Vitæ* are succeeded by smooth cones, whereas the cones of the Chinese sort are rugged. They are larger than the Common sort, and are of a fine grey colour.

and the American Sweet-scented Arbor Vitæ Tree

3. The American Sweet-scented *Arbor Vitæ* is a variety, only of the Common sort, it came up from some scattered seeds at the bottom of a box I had from Pensylvania. It has the same dusky look in winter as the Common sort, though it is better furnished with branches, neither are they produced so horizontally, or hang down in the manner of the Common sort. What makes this sort most valuable is the property of its leaves, for, being bruised, they emit a most refreshing odour, which is by many supposed to be as fine an aromatic as any we have, whereas the leaves of the other sorts being bruised, to

most people are fœtid and disagreeable. Whether this property will be continued by seeds, I have not yet experienced.

Method of propagating them. I encrease it by cuttings and layers, as has been directed before, and this method of propagation is common to all the sorts.

Titles. The Chinese *Arbor Vitæ* is titled, *Thuja strobilis squarrosis squamis acuminatis reflexis*. Van Royen calls it, *Thuja strobilis uncinatis squamis reflexo acuminatis*. It grows naturally in China.

The Common *Arbor Vitæ* is, *Thuja strobilis lævibus squamis obtusis*. Caspar Bauhine calls it, *Thuja Theophrasti*; Clusius and others, *Arbor Vitæ*. It grows naturally in the moist parts of Canada and Siberia.

Class and order in the Linnæan system. *Thuja* is of the class and order *Monoecia Monadelphia*; and the characters are,

The characters.

I. Male Flowers.

1. CALYX. They form an oval amentum, grow opposite on the common footstalk, and each embraces it with its base. The calycinal squamma is oval, concave, and obtuse.

2. COROLLA. There is none.

3. STAMINA. Each floret has four exceeding small filaments, with the like number of antheræ, that adhere to the base of the calycinal squamma.

II. Female Flowers on the same plant.

1. CALYX. They form an oval cone, and each scale contains two flowers.

2. COROLLA. There is none.

3. PISTILLUM consists of a very small germen, of a subulated style, and a single stigma.

4. PERICARPIUM is an oval, oblong, obtuse cone, opening lengthways. The squammæ are nearly equal, oblong, obtuse, and convex on their outside.

5. SEMINA. The seeds are oblong, and each is longitudinally surrounded with a membranaceous indented wing.

# CHAP. XXXVII.

## *VIBURNUM, LAURUSTINUS.*

LAURUSTINUS is one of the greatest ornaments of our gardens in the winter-months, not only as it is a fine evergreen, but because, during that season, it will either be in full blow, or else exhibit its flowers and buds in large bunches, ready to burst open, in spite of all weather that may happen, and the boldness of these buds, at a time when other flowers and trees shrink under oppressive colds, is matter of wonder and pleasure. There are many varieties of *Laurustinus*, but those most remarkable are,

Varieties.

The Narrow-leaved *Laurustinus*.
The Broad-leaved *Laurustinus*.
The Hairy-leaved *Laurustinus*.
The Shining-leaved *Laurustinus*.
The Silver-striped *Laurustinus*.
The Gold-striped *Laurustinus*.

described. The Narrow-leaved *Laurustinus* is so called because, of all the sorts, the leaves of this are smallest. It is generally planted among the low shrubs, though I have known it trained up against a wall to fourteen or sixteen feet high. It produces its branches irregularly, which will grow so thick and close as to form a bush, for it hath that appearance when planted singly in open quarters. The bark in summer is green, and often a little hairy and glandulous; in winter it is frequently of a dark-brown colour. The leaves grow by pairs, standing opposite, on strong and very tough footstalks. They are of an oval figure, and their edges are entire. Their upper surface is smooth, and of a strong green colour, but their under is lighter, and a little hairy; and they are at all seasons very ornamental. The flowers are produced in large umbels, and are well known. It generally will be in full blow in January, February, March, and April, during which time it will be covered with bloom, causing a delightful effect.

The Broad-leaved *Laurustinus* differs from the former sort, in that the leaves are broader, and the roots proportionably stronger. It will arrive to a greater height than the other sorts, and the umbels of the flowers are larger, tho' they will not be produced in such plenty; it, nevertheless, makes an excellent figure.

The Hairy-leaved *Laurustinus* is as free a shooter as the other, and the leaves are frequently as large, and differs from that in scarcely any thing but that the leaves are hairy, the young shoots also are hairy to a great degree. In this respect it makes a small variety. It flowers like the other sorts, though in my gardens, I have ever observed it to blow rather later than those.

The Shining-leaved *Laurustinus* is still of about the same growth, and the leaves are large and fair. They are of an oval figure; and their upper and under surface are both shining, though their under is veined, and of a paler green. It differs only in that the leaves and young shoots are smooth, shining, and free from hairs; and being of this lucid green, force esteem. It generally flowers later than the two first sorts.

The two variegated sorts are only one or other of the above sorts, striped with white or yellow, though the sorts striped with Silver I have met with have been the Broad-leaved kinds; but the Gold-striped sort has always been the first, or Narrow-leaved kind, with leaves striped or blotched with yellow; and on these accounts, those who are fond of variegated plants covet these in their Collection.

All these sorts are easily propagated; for if in winter a little mould be any-how thrown amongst the young branches, they will strike root, and be good plants by the next autumn. Notwithstanding these plants, however carelessly the mould be thrown, will grow, it is not here recommended to the Gardener to practise that custom; it is expected that he be always neat in all his work; it is mentioned here only to shew what may be done; but let him gently lay the branches down, Culture of the different sorts.

down, strip off some of the lower leaves, and with his hand draw the mould amongst the young shoots, and leave them neated up, as if a workman had been there, and these will be all good plants by the autumn, the strongest of which may be set out for good, whilst the youngest may be planted out in the nursery, at small distances, to gain strength

Titles Laurustinus is titled, *Viburnum foliis integerrimis ovatis ramificationibus venarum subtus villoso-glandulosis* In the Upsal Catalogue it is termed, *Viburnum foliis ovatis integerrimis*, only Some authors call it simply, *Tinus*, others, *Laurus sylvestris*,—*Laurustinus*, &c Clusius and some others distinguish the different sorts by calling them, *Tinus primus*, *Tinus secundus*, *tertius*, &c It grows naturally in Italy and Spain

## CHAP. XXXVIII

## *ULEX*, FURZE, WHINS, or GORSE

Introductory reflections THERE are two species of this genus, one is an African plant, the other is European, and in England called by the various names of, Gorse, Furze, Whins, and in some places Prickly Broom There are several varieties of this species, and I introduce them in this place, not that their leaves are evergreen, for they soon fall off, but on account of the never failing strong green exhibited from their young shoots and spines, which in the winter season is in the most perfection, and at that time better adapted to mix with Evergreens, if a person is desirous of heightening his variety with a few of these plants, which, tho' common in England, are in many countries highly prized and valued as their finest flowering shrubs, and very justly too, they being possessed of such beauties and properties as are peculiar to few plants, and which the commonness of the shrub only renders unnoticed in this country

The plant described The root is hard, woody, divided, and of a whitish colour The stalks are hard woody, firm, branching, of a whitish brown colour, and four, five, six, or eight feet high The young branches are green, striated, flexible, and beset with numerous green thorns The leaves are small, hairy, pointed, come out in the spring, and soon fall off The flowers come out from the sides of the young shoots, and also from the spines, in great plenty They are large, and of a beautiful yellow colour They appear in March, April, and May, and in warm well-sheltered places will frequently shew themselves in February and earlier, but their greatest show is in May, when whole heaths will be covered with their golden bloom At this time, when they are in such plenty, they occasion a faint smell to a considerable distance They afterwards die away to a pale or whitish yellow, and are soon succeeded by oblong, straight, turgid pods, containing the seeds The principal varieties of this species are,

Varieties
1 The Common Gorse of our heaths
2 The White-flowered Gorse
3 Long Narrow-spined Gorse
4 Short-spined Gorse
5 Large French Furze or Gorse
6 Round-podded Gorse
7 Dwarf Gorse

These sorts are pretty permanent from seeds, so that if those of any one kind are sown, the plants will for the most part be similar to those from whence the seeds were taken

The seeds of Furze or Gorse are best sown in the autumn, and they will then come up early the spring following, though the business may be deferred till the spring

Of the propagating the plant The Common Furze may be propagated in poor, cold, moist land, to great advantage where fuel is scarce Whoever, therefore, is desirous of propagating tracts of Furze for fuel, for heating of ovens, burning of brick, drying of malt, or the like, should well plough the ground, and in the spring sow it with a crop of oats or barley, at the same time mixing with the oats or barley a third part of gorse seeds After the oats are off, the young Gorse will shew themselves all over the spot The summer following they will grow strong, and will soon cover the ground, and in three or four years be fit to cut for use

Titles European Furze or Gorse is titled, *Ulex foliis villosis acutis, spinis sparsis* In the *Hortus Cliffortianus* it is termed, *Ulex folio sub singulis spinis subulato plano acuto* Dodonæus calls it, *Genista spinosa*, Caspar Bauhine, *Genista spinosa major, longioribus aculeis*, also, *Genista spinosa minor, brevioribus aculeis*, Gerard, *Genista spinosa vulgaris*, and Parkinson, *Genista spinosa vulgaris, sive Scorpius Theophrasti, quam Gaza Nepam translulit*, also, *Genista spinosa minor* It grows naturally in England, Gaul, and Brabant

Class and order in the Linnean system *Ulex* is of the class and order *Diadelphia Decandria*, and the characters are,

The characters 1 CALYX is a permanent perianthium, composed of two oval, oblong concave, straight, equal leaves, which are a little shorter than the carina

2 COROLLA is papilionaceous, and composed of five petals

The vexillum is obcordated, large, straight, and emarginated

The alæ are oblong, obtuse, and shorter than the vexillum

The carina consists of two straight obtuse petals, whose under borders meet, and seem joined together

3 STAMINA are diadelphous filaments (nine of the filaments are joined in a body, the other stands separate), having simple antheræ

4 PISTILLUM consists of an oblong, cylindrical, hairy, germen, a filiforme assurgent style, and a small obtuse stigma

5 PERICARPIUM is an oblong straight, turgid pod, formed of two valves, and containing one cell

6 SEMINA The seeds are few, roundish, and emarginated.

CHAP

# CHAP XXXIX.

## *VISCUM*, WHITE MISSEL, or MISSELTOE

Introductory observations

THE Misseltoe is a very extraordinary plant, growing from the sides and branches of other trees, instead of the earth, out of which our noble Collection springs. This occasions a singularity beyond expression, and is by many thought very delightful and nice. In those countries where the Misseltoe is rarely found, it is much admired, and is to most people a very desirable plant, and even where it abounds in the hedges and woods, they have a peculiar regard for it, and seldom fail to procure some of it in the winter, by which a part of the house is distinguished. The veneration this plant has met with in all ages, particularly among the antient Druids, by whom it was held sacred, may even now contribute to its exciting our esteem, and as it is a plant out of the ordinary way of culture, every curious person will expect an account of it in a work of this nature. I have chose to introduce it here among the Evergreens, because the leaves are of a thick consistence, and continue on all the winter months. This plant is most conspicuous when growing on a deciduous tree, such as apples, crabs, thorns, &c. and on these I would chiefly recommend it, to shew Nature, and appear singular in deciduous plantations, though amongst Evergreens, notwithstanding it will appear there with less notice, it will, nevertheless, grow on the Evergreen Crab tree, and a sort of Plum leaved Thorn, which retaining its leaves until spring in well-sheltered places, is sometimes in such places planted as an Evergreen. On these and the like trees the Misseltoe will grow, and if it is wanted in evergreen wilderness quarters, these are the sorts our ingenious Gardener must pitch upon for his purpose.

Description of this plant

This plant, then, which grows on other trees, is composed of many branches, and spreads itself often as much in breadth as it may be said to advance in height, so that the form it for the most part naturally assumes is nearly round. The bark of this plant is of a yellowish colour, and the numerous branches of which it is composed usually grow by pairs, in a kind of forked manner, thus dividing themselves from the main stem very near the base all over the shrub. At the joints grow the leaves, which are oblong, or of a spear-shaped figure, but obtuse or rounded at their end. They are of a thick consistence, of a yellowish green colour, and all winter have a singular, beautiful, and odd appearance. The flowers grow in small spikes, from the wings of the branches. They are of a yellowish colour, very small, and make no figure, but are succeeded by a fine, large, almost transparent, viscous, white berry, which will be ripe in the winter.

Method of propagating it

The manner of propagating this shrub is by the berry, when quite ripe. It will grow upon apple, crab, white thorn, hazel, ash, or oak, though it is seldom found on the oak, and is what I never saw, but that it will grow upon that tree, we have the suffrage of antiquity. On the oak therefore, do not fail to try your experiments of encreasing the plant, and if your expectations fail, as I assure you the hopes are not great, from what I have experienced, nevertheless, be not discouraged, but repeat the trial for the method is easy, and common to all the sorts of trees on which it will grow. It is thus.

When the berries are fully ripe, they are to be gathered, and having marked the smooth place of a tree on which you would have them grow, one, two, or more berries are to be stuck to this smooth place, on the outside of the bark, and the viscous matter with which they are possessed will cause them to stick, and prevent their falling. If a small slit be made with a knife, through the outward bark only, and each berry lodged in this slit, it will be never the worse, for they will grow both ways. If there are berries enough, the operation may be performed on several parts of the same tree, observing always to choose the smoothest part of the bark, and in this manner it may be extended to other trees at pleasure. Many of these berries will grow, though I must own, they for the most part make but slow progress, for I have known bushes of eleven years old, and scarcely round, of little more than a foot diameter. Though this should not discourage the planter, for it sometimes happens that they so take to the tree as to form a large bush in a few years.

The Misseltoe is encreased in the woods chiefly by the birds, which carrying the berries from tree to tree, and lodging some of them, they adhere to the bark and grow.

Virtues of the Misseltoe

This plant is said to be possessed of many excellent and rare virtues, and is used in medicine for nervous disorders, &c. Birdlime is made of its berries, which being well boiled in water, and afterwards well beaten and cleared, will be fit for use.

Title

*Viscum*, which is so called on account of this glutinous quality of the berries, is entitled, *Viscum foliis lanceolatis obtusis, caule dichotomo, spicis axillaribus*. Caspar Bauhine calls it, *Viscum baccis albis*, and Cammerarius, *Viscum*. It grows upon trees in England and most parts of Europe.

Class and order in the Linnæan System characters

*Viscum* is of the class and order *Dioecia Tetrandria*, and the characters are,

I. Male Flowers

1. CALYX is a perianthium composed of four oval, equal leaves.

2. COROLLA. There is none.

3. STAMINA are four in number. There are no filaments but four oblong, acuminated antheræ, each of which grows to a lobule of the calyx.

II. Female Flowers

1. CALYX is a perianthium composed of four small, oval, erect, deciduous leaves, sitting upon the germen.

2. COROLLA. There is none.

3. PISTILLUM consists of an oblong three cornered germen, situated under the receptacle, without any style, but an obtuse stigma.

4. PERICARPIUM is a round smooth berry of one cell.

5. SEMEN. The seed is single, obcordated, obtuse, compressed, and compressed.

PART

# PART IV.

## OF

## HARDY CLIMBING PLANTS,

## OR,

## Such as are proper to be planted in the SHRUBBERY, WILDERNESS, &c.

### THEIR NATURE, CULTURE, AND MANAGEMENT.

### Of CLIMBERS.

Remark

O LORD, *how manifold are thy works! in wiſdom haſt thou made them all!* was a juſt exclamation of the Royal Pſalmiſt. And have we in the leaſt degree more cauſe to be ſilent, and not to expreſs our juſt admiration of the wonders of the creation in general, but particularly now, when our attention is more immediately engaged in thoſe of the vegetable creation. There is not a ſingle plant that grows but extols its Maker's praiſe, and diſcovers infinite wiſdom in the continuance of its kind, by the contrivance of the male and female organs of generation, which operate the ſame as in animals, and by which the ſpecies are preſerved and new varieties formed, and tranſmitted from generation to generation, and will continue to be kept up until the lateſt time. Neither is his wiſdom and power leſs manifeſt in these works of his hands, than his goodneſs and kindneſs to mankind, ſince, in the courſe of the vegetable creation, he has provided every thing that way for our uſe, contemplation, and pleaſure. The variety of foreſt trees ſerve, indeed, for all theſe purpoſes, but artificers and others poſſeſſed of hardly any reflection perceive only their great uſe, and how neceſſary they are for our ſupport, in the conveniencies of this world. The flowers poſſeſſed of fragrance and beauty, ſeem pleaſure by feaſting the eye and ſenſe of ſmelling, and attract the attention of the fine lady, the prude, the coquette, and the beau, equally with that of the philoſopher: but theſe value them only as ſuch, without ever looking farther, or conſidering the Being who thought it to endow plants for other purpoſes, as well as regaling our ſenſes of ſeeing and ſmelling. But beſides theſe two extremes that have their admirers, the one for their uſe, the other for their beauty, there is another, and by far the greateſt part of the Vegetable Creation which falls not under the notice of thoſe two claſſes of mortals, who conſtitute a very large ſhare of mankind, and they are ſuch as neither preſent you with large, fair, ſweet-ſmelling flowers, nor are hardy and ſturdy enough to be put to the uſeful purpoſes of life. Many of thoſe ſorts, indeed, fall of courſe under the inſpection of another part of mankind, who ſtudy their uſes in medicine, and know how to apply them for our remedies in ſickneſs. Theſe, as phyſicians, are obliged to ſcrutinize into their nature, and ſearch out their virtues and uſes. So that our foreſt-trees, our beautiful flowers, and our medicinal plants, have all their admirers and protectors, who know and are benefited by their virtues, beauty, or uſe. But there is a great ſhare of the vegetable tribe that affords us no beautiful flowers, that are poſſeſſed of no medicinal qualities yet known, and whoſe ſtalks or ſtems are of ſuch little conſequence as to be hardly fit for the fire. All theſe, nevertheleſs, have their beauties, have the organs of generation perfect, and afford infinite pleaſure and contemplation to another ſet of people, who delight in ſtudying the works of Nature, and ſeeing the wiſdom of the All-wiſe Creator in their formation and continuance; and this ſet have uſually been called Philoſophers, ſo that whoever pleaſes, whether a man of fortune, or an artificer, may be a philosopher, we shall not pretend to make him such in this respect, unless he delights to examine all the plants that grow on earth as well as such as excel in those kinds of virtues, for the true wisdom appears in the one as the other; and they all equally call for our wonder, acknowledgment, and praise.

Of the Climbers. To the variety of plants that seem peculiarly adapted to attract the philosopher's attention, the Climbers seem of right to belong; for none but philosophers will perceive them to be of any use. Some of them, indeed, are possessed of fair and good flowers, but these are for the most part destitute of smell, and very inconsiderable in number. Some of them are useful in medicine; but the virtues of the greatest part are either not known, or have been disused; and if we examine the whole tribe, we shall find few, if any of them that can answer any purpose in life. These plants, however, all of them afford matter of wonder and gratitude to the God of Nature, for his thus bedecking the globe with such variety of plants of variety of forms; and that these slender plants should be possessed of either a flexuose or winding nature, or furnished with tendrils to supply the defect of their weakness, and by the help of such arrive at the height Nature has limited their shoots. The delight and beauty which wilderness-quarters and plantations for pleasure receive from these plants cannot but be remarked by the slightest observer of Nature's beauties; some winding round the stems, and interweaving themselves in their branches, others, having aspired to the top of the shrub, and mounted aloft, spread about, and, at a distance, beautifully appear like a tree of a hitherto unknown genus; and others, of a lower growth, are contented to trail gently on the ground, or to attach with their embraces the lowest shrubs. All these cannot fail of giving pleasure even to those who may be deemed incurious, whilst, to the real observer of Nature's works, they afford much benefit, and raise his contemplation and wonder, gratitude and praise.

The different ways by which these weak and slender plants raise themselves to advantage have terms to express the manner in which they rise. Thus, they are said to be,

1. *Twining by the stalks*, when they spirally twist about any plant. And their manner of twining.

When they wind or twist themselves towards the left, the plant is said to *ascend, twisting according to the sun's motion*.

When they wind or twist to the right, they are said to *ascend contrary to the sun's motion*.

2. *Twining by the clasper*. Numbers of plants, whose stalks are possessed of no twining property, are nevertheless furnished with Claspers, which lay hold of, and wind about every thing that is near them.

3. *Parasitic*, when they strike root into the bark of other trees, hang upon, and gain their chief support from them.

But as the phrases respecting the different properties of stalks and their claspers have been already explained in the Introduction, I shall proceed to the Climbers themselves, and shall begin with *Bignonia*, and then treat of the others as they come of course in their order.

## CHAP. I.

## *BIGNONIA*, The TRUMPET FLOWER.

BIGNONIA affords us at least four distinct species, besides varieties, which, though tender when young, will nevertheless grow well abroad against warm walls, and in well-sheltered places; and, if the winters should prove uncommonly severe, it would be worth while to be at almost any trouble in matting and covering them, they being all plants of admirable beauty. The hardiest species are,

Species.
1. The Evergreen *Bignonia*, or Jasmine of Virginia.
2. The Quadrifoliate *Bignonia*.
3. Capreolated *Bignonia*.
4. Radicant *Bignonia*.

Evergreen Bignonia. 1. The Evergreen *Bignonia*, or Virginia Jasmine, has almost every perfection to recommend it as a climber; for though the plants are small, yet if they are trained up to a wall, or have bushes or trees on which to climb, they will mount to a great height, by their twining stalks, and over-top hedges, and even trees, and will form at a distance a great figure from the sway they will bear. The leaves of *Bignonia* are single, and of a lanceolate figure. They grow from the joints, are of a fine strong green colour, and very ornamental. But the flowers constitute the greatest value of this plant, on account of the fine odour Nature has bestowed on them, which is to so great a degree as to perfume the circumambient air to a considerable distance. These flowers are of a yellow colour, and less beautiful than some of the other sorts, which is sufficiently recompensed by their extraordinary fragrance. They grow in an erect manner, from the wings of the leaves at each joint, and their figure nearly resembles that of a trumpet. The pods that succeed these flowers are small.

Variety. There is a variety of this species, which over-tops whatever plants are near it, to a great height. The leaves are of a lanceolate figure, and grow from the joints, often four opposite. They are of a fine green; but their flowers are produced rather thinly, and stand each on its own footstalk, and are not possessed of that height and fragrance with the other.

Quadrifoliate Bignonia. 2. The Quadrifoliate *Bignonia* is another noble Climber. It arises by the assistance of tendrils, the branches being very slender and weak; and by these it will over-top bushes, trees, &c. twenty or thirty feet high. The branches, however, shew their natural tendency to aspire, for they wind about every thing that is near them, so that, together with the assistance Nature has given them of tendrils, it is no wonder they arrive at so great a height. These branches, or rather stalks, have a smooth surface, are often of a reddish colour, but [illegible] the sun, and

and are very tough The tendrils grow from the joints, they are curled, and are divided into three parts The leaves grow also from the joints, and are four in number, at each These are of an oblong figure, have their edges entire, and are very ornamental to the plant; for they are of an elegant green colour Their under surface is much paler than their upper, and their footstalks, mid-rib, and veins, alter to a fine purple Each flower is composed of one large leaf The tube is very large, and the rim is divided and spreads open These flowers being of a fine scarlet, make a noble figure They grow from the wings of the leaves, in August, two usually at each joint, and they are succeeded in the countries where they grow naturally by long pods

Capreolated, and 3 Capreolated *Bignonia* is another fine Climber, which rises by the assistance of tendrils or claspers The leaves grow at the joints opposite by pairs tho' those which appear at the bottom frequently come out singly They are of an oblong figure, and continue on the plant all winter The flowers are produced in August, from the wings of the leaves They are of the same nature, and of the shape nearly of the former, are large, of a yellow colour, and succeeded by short pods

Radicant Bignonia 4 Radicant *Bignonia* will arrive to a prodigious height, if it has either buildings or trees to climb up by, for it strikes root from the joints into whatever is near it, and thus will get to the tops of buildings, trees, &c be they ever so high This species has pinnated leaves, which grow opposite by pairs at the joints These leaves are composed of about four pair of lobes, which end with an odd one They are of a good green colour, have their edges deeply cut, and drawn out into a long point The flowers are produced in August, at the ends of the branches, in bunches They are large, and like the others are composed of one tube, but they are shaped more like a trumpet than any of the sorts They are of a fine red colour, and make a grand show, and this sort is chiefly known by the name of Scarlet Trumpet-Flower

Varieties There is another sort, called the Smaller Trumpet-Flower It differs from the other only in that the leaves and flowers are smaller, and some fancy their colour to be a finer red, the colour of the former in some situations, often approaching to that of an orange colour

Proper situation These two sorts are more hardy than any of the others, and consequently more proper to be set against old walls, &c in exposed situations They will all, however, bear our climate very well, though it would be more adviseable to set the others in well sheltered places, as they will otherwise be in danger of suffering by severe frosts especially while young, if there be nothing to break their edge

Method of propagating the first by layers The propagation of all is very easy, for if the shoots are laid upon the ground and covered with a little mould, they will immediately strike root, and become good plants for setting out where they are wanted

They will all grow by cuttings The bottom part of the strongest young shoots is the best, and by this method plenty may be soon raised by cuttings

They are to be raised by seeds, but this is a tedious method, especially of the Pinnated leaved sorts, for it will be many years before the plants raised from seeds will blow Having obtained seeds, however, the method of management is thus A spot of rich garden-mould must be pitched on, in a well sheltered place, and being made fine, and cleared of all roots of weeds, &c the seeds should be sown in beds, about half an inch deep These beds should be hooped, and as the hot weather in the spring comes on, should be shaded with mats, and have frequent watering and by this means the seeds, if good, will soon come up, and if shade and watering be afforded them during the heat of summer, it will be the better At the approach of the next winter, the strictest eye must be had to the weather, for at the approach of the first frosts, they must be matted over, especially the three first sorts, which are most tender, and this care may be repeated all winter, covering them in hard weather, and taking off the mats as soon as the weather grows mild In the seed bed they may remain two or even three years, and then be planted out for good in the leaves

1 The first of the above species is titled, *Bignonia foliis simplicibus lanceolatis, caule volubili* Van Royen calls it, *Bignonia foliis ovato-lanceolatis conjugatis integerrimis*, Catesby, *Gelsemium, sive Jasminum luteum odoratum Virginianum scandens sempervirens* and Plukenet, *Syringa volubilis Virginiana, myrti majoris folio, albo simine, floribus odoratis luteis* It is a native of Virginia Titles

2 Quadrifoliate Bignonia is, *Bignonia foliis conjugatis cirrhosis, foliolis ovato-lanceolatis, capreolis trifidis*; Tournefort calls it *Bignonia Americana, capreolis donata, siliqua longissima*, Plumier, *Clematis quadrifolia, floribus digitalis luteo, claviculis donatis*, Plukenet, *Clematis hyssopifolia, capreolis tribus foliis, Americana tetraphyllos*, and Sloane, *Gelsemium indicum hederaceum tetraphyllum, folio fibroso nodo aurantio* It grows naturally in Barbadoes, Domingo, &c

3 The third species is styled, *Bignonia foliis conjugatis cirrhosis foliolis cordato lanceolatis, foliis imis simplicibus* Breynius calls it *Bignonia Americana capreolis donata, siliqua breviore*, Zanoni *Clematis tetraphylla Americana*, and others, *Clematis Americana siliquosa tetraphyllos* It grows naturally in North-America

4 Radicant Bignonia is titled *Bignonia foliis pinnatis, foliolis incisis, caule geniculis radicatis* Rivinus calls it *Pseudo gelseminum siliquosum*, Cornutus, *Gelseminum hederaceum indicum*, Morison, *Pseudo apocynum hederaceum Americanum, tubuloso flore Phoeniceo, fraxini folio*, and Catesby, *Bignonia fraxini foliis, coccineo flore minore* It grows naturally in Carolina, Virginia, Canada, and many parts

CHAP

## CHAP II

## *BRYONIA*, BRIONY

Its description. THE White Briony is the only hardy species of this genus that grows common in our hedges and bushes It is really a fine plant, but is hardly ever introduced into gardens, which may be owing to its commonness, it growing almost every where The root is exceeding thick and large, and the branches will grow to a great length in a year, fastening themselves to every thing that is near them The leaves are large, palmated, rough, and callous on both sides The flowers are produced in small clusters, in May Their colour is white, and they are succeeded by berries, which are at first green, but afterwards (when ripe) of a fine red

A plant or two of this kind may be admitted for variety, as a climber, amongst our shrubs or bushes, but on the whole, it is very little valued and is seldom introduced, unless for philosophical observation, into any part of our works

Culture. It is propagated by sowing the berries, in the spring, where they are to remain If many of them come up the weakest must be drawn out They must be kept free from weeds until they are got out of their reach, and afterwards they will call for no trouble, for they will assist themselves, by laying hold of every thing that is near them, and add to the diversity of the scene where climbing plants are admitted It is the root of this species that is used in medicine

Titles. The White Briony is titled, *Bryonia foliis palmatis utrinque calloso scabris* Gerard calls it, *Bryonia alba*, and Caspar Bauhine, *Bryonia aspera sive alba, baccis rubris* It grows naturally among hedges and bushes in most parts of Europe

Class and order in the Linnæan system. *Bryonia* is of the class and order *Monoecia Syngenesia*, and the characters are,

The characters. I Male Flowers

1 CALYX is a monophyllous, bell-shaped perianthium, indented at the top in five parts

2 COROLLA is bell shaped, adheres to the calyx, and is divided at the top into five oval segments

3 STAMINA are three very short filaments, with five antheræ, two of the filaments having double antheræ, and the other one

II Female Flowers in the same plant with the males

1 CALYX is a monophyllous, bell-shaped, deciduous perianthium, indented in five parts at the top

2 COROLLA is the same as in the male

3 PISTILLUM consists of a germen situated under the flower, a trifid spreading style the length of the Corolla, and an emarginated spreading stigma

4 PERICARPIUM is a smooth, oval berry

5 SEMINA The seeds are few, adhere to the skin, and are nearly oval

## CHAP III

## *CELASTRUS*, The STAFF-TREE

Description of this plant. ONE species of this genus presents itself for this place, called the Climbing Staff-tree, or Bastard *Euonymus* The stalks are woody, twining, and will rise by the help of neighbouring trees or bushes to the height of twelve feet The leaves are oblong, serrated, of a pleasant green colour, pale, and veined underneath, and grow alternately on the branches The flowers are produced in small bunches, from the sides of the branches near the ends They are of a greenish colour, appear in June, and are succeeded by roundish, red, three-cornered capsules, containing ripe seeds, in the autumn

Method of propagation by layers. It is propagated by laying down the young shoots in the spring By the autumn they will have struck root, and may then be taken off and planted in the places where they are designed to remain

By seeds. They are also propagated by seeds These should be sown after they are ripe, otherwise they will be two, and sometimes three years before they come up When they make their appearance, nothing more need be done than keeping them clear from weeds all summer and the winter following, and in the spring the strongest plants may be drawn out, and set in the nursery for a year, and then removed to the places where they are designed to remain, whilst the weakest, being left in the seed-bed one year more, may undergo the same discipline

The plant is exceeding hardy, and makes a beautiful appearance among other trees in the autumn, by their beautiful red berries, which are near akin to those of the Spindle-tree, and will be produced in vast profusion on the tops of other trees, to the height of which these plants by their twisting property aspire

They should not be planted near weak or tender trees, to climb on, for they embrace the stalks so closely as to bring on death to any but the hardiest trees and shrubs

This species is titled, *Celastrus inermis, caule volubili, foliis serrulatis* Du Hamel calls it *Euonymoides Canadensis scandens, foliis serratis*, and Gronovius, *Frutex scandens ... foliis infimis, foliis profunde serratis* It resides in Canada

CHAP

# CHAP. IV

## *CLEMATIS*, VIRGIN'S BOWER

Derivation of the generical name CLEMATIS is a Greek word ſignifying *a claſper*, ſo that one ſhould expect to find all plants that climb by that means arranged under this title, but though it does not include all ſuch, yet the ſpecies of *Clematis* are pretty numerous, and to theſe the varieties being added, they form of themſelves a noble Collection of climbing plants The moſt material ſpecies, with their varieties, &c, as they are

Species commonly called,

1 Virgin's Bower
2 Virginian Climber
3 Carolina Climber
4 Oriental Climber
5 Travellers Joy, or *Viorna*
6 Evergreen Spaniſh Climber
7 Creeping Climber, or *Flammula*
8 American Sweet ſcented Climber

Virgins Bower 1 Virgin's Bower The varieties of this ſpe-

Varieties cies uſually go by the names of,

Double Purple Virgin's Bower
Single Purple Virgin's Bower
Single Blue Virgin's Bower
Single Red Virgin's Bower

As theſe ſorts are invariably continued by layers, and the variety they afford in the climbing tribe is very great and beautiful, I ſhall conſider them diſtinctly, before I proceed to the other ſpecies

described Double Purple Virgin's Bower This ſort ſtands firſt on the liſt, not only becauſe it is an admirable climber, but alſo is poſſeſſed of a large double flower It will grow to the height of twenty or thirty feet, if ſupported, and is very proper to cover arbours, as well as walls, hedges, &c The branches are of a dark-brown or duſky colour, angular and channelled The younger branches are of a fine green colour, and nearly ſquare They are very numerous, and grow from the joints of the older, and thus they multiply in that manner, from the bottom to the top of all the plant The leaves alſo grow from the joints They are both compound and decompound The folioles of which each is compoſed are of an oval figure, and their edges are entire, and in ſummer, when the plant is in full leaf, if ſet alone to form an arbour, after it is ſaid to be grown ſtrong, the branches and large leaves will be produced in ſuch plenty, as not only effectually to procure ſhade, but even to keep off a moderate ſhower, ſo excellently is this plant adapted to this purpoſe and more particularly ſo, as it will grow, when it has properly taken to the ground, fifteen or ſixteen feet in one year The flowers are of a dirty purple, but very double They blow in July and Auguſt, and are ſucceeded by no ſeeds, the multiplicity of the petals entirely deſtroying the organs of generation

The Single Purple Virgin's Bower is rather a ſtronger ſhooter than the Double, and will climb to rather a ſtill greater height The Double is only a variety of this, but, nevertheleſs, notwithſtanding the double fine flowers of the other, ought not to be neglected, for this exhibits a fair flower, compoſed of four large petals, in the center of which are ſeated the numerous ſtamina

The Single Blue Virgin's Bower produces its ſhoots, leaves, and flowers, in the ſame manner as the other, and makes a variety only in that the flowers are of a blue colour

The Single Red is of much lower growth, and ſeems of a more delicate and tender nature, not but it is hardy enough to endure any weather, but its ſhoots are weak, and ſhort in proportion They are angular, and channelled in the manner of the other, but they are of a reddiſh colour The leaves are ſmaller than the other ſorts, and the flowers alſo are ſmaller, though they make a fine variety, by their colour being red Theſe all flower at the ſame time, but are ſucceeded by no ornamental ſeeds

2 Virginian Climber The branches are ſlender and numerous, and the leaves, as in the Virgin's Bower, are both compound and decompound The folioles grow by threes, and theſe are often multiplied to form a decompound leaf of nine in number They are nearly cordated, of a good green, and ſome of them are trifid The flowers are produced in July and Auguſt, from the wings of the leaves They are of a kind of blue colour, and the petals, which are four in number, of which each is compoſed, are of a thick coriaceous ſubſtance This ſort will ſometimes ripen its ſeeds in England Virginian,

3 Carolina Climber This is by ſome called the Curled-flowering Climber, and indeed by that name it is chiefly diſtinguiſhed in our gardens It is one of the lower kind of climbers, ſeldom ariſing, by the aſſiſtance of its claſpers, to more than ſix feet The ſtalks are very weak and ſlender The leaves afford great variety, being ſometimes trifoliate and ſometimes ſingle The folioles alſo differ much, for ſome of them are found whole and entire, whilſt others again are divided into three lobes Theſe leaves are of a dark-green colour, and are produced oppoſite, from the joints or the ſtalks The flowers are produced in July and Auguſt, on ſhort footſtalks, below which a pair or more of oblong pointed leaves often grow Theſe flowers are compoſed of four thick, coriaceous, purple, curled petals, which occaſions its being by ſome called the Curled-flowering Climber This ſpecies will for the moſt part produce ripe ſeeds in our gardens Carolinian,

4 Oriental Climber is no great rambler, for, notwithſtanding its ſlender ſtalks are well furniſhed with claſpers, it is ſeldom found to climb higher than about ten feet The leaves of this ſort are compound The folioles are cut angularly, and the lobes are ſhaped like a wedge They are of a good green colour, and are very ornamental to the plant The flowers are produced from the wings of the leaves early, for it will often be in blow in April They are of a kind of yellowiſh green colour, and the petals naturally turn backwards Theſe flowers differing in colour from the above ſorts, and coming earlier in the ſpring, makes it more deſirable, as it teſtifies how many months in the ſummer are ornamented with the blow of ſome one or other ſpecies of *Clematis* The ſeeds of this ſort alſo will often ripen and Oriental Climber

Travellers Joy

5 Travellers Joy is a noble climber, and well known in many parts of England, the hedges where it abounds being frequently covered with it But its greatest singularity is in winter; at which time it more peculiarly invites the travellers attention The branches of this species are very thick and tough, sufficient to make withs for faggots, and for this purpose it is always used in the woods where it can be got These are so numerous, and produce side-branches in such plenty, which divide also into others, that they will over-top hedges, or almost any thing they can climb by, for this is the greatest rambler, if I may so call it, of all the sorts of climbers Besides the claspers with which it is furnished, the very leaves have a tendency to twine round plants These leaves are pinnated, and a variety is occasioned by them, for the foliols of some sorts are indented at their edges, whilst others are found with their edges entire They are of a bluish green, and moderately large The flowers are produced in June, July, and August, all over the plant, in clusters They are succeeded by flat seeds, each of which, when ripe, is possessed of a white hairy plume, and growing in clusters, will exhibit themselves in winter all over the tops of bushes, hedges, &c which at that time will look very beautiful and singular In countries where this plant does not naturally grow, no wilderness ought to be without some, if it be only on that account Where it grows naturally, indeed, the lane hedges, &c will for the most part afford plenty enough for observation This is the *Viorna* of old Botanists, and is called Travellers Joy from its thus ornamenting hedges, bushes, &c to the entertainment of the traveller

Spanish,

6 Spanish Climber is a fine evergreen It is but a low climber, seldom growing higher than six or eight feet The branches are very numerous, weak, and slender, but it rises by claspers, which naturally lay hold on any thing near them The footstalks of the leaves, also, will twine round twigs, &c so that they become claspers, and ensure the hold of the plant Now, if there be no hedge or plant near, by which they may lay hold and rise, they will twine amongst themselves, and as the branches are produced in great plenty, they will be so mixed one amongst another, as to form a low thicket, which makes this plant well adapted to produce variety in evergreen wilderness quarters, where, if planted singly, at a distance from other trees, it will naturally form itself into a thick bush These leaves are sometimes cut into three lobes, sometimes into two, and many of them are undivided The lobes, when most perfect, are nearly lanceolate, have their edges indented, and are of as fine a shining green as can be conceived The flowers are produced in the midst of winter, from the sides of the branches They are of a greenish colour, though inclined to a white, but the petals being pretty large, and coming at that unusual season, makes this plant highly valuable

Creeping,

7 Creeping Climber, or *Flammula*, will mount by the assistance of other plants to a good height, sometimes near twenty feet The stalks are slender and numerous, and the leaves are in this respect singular, for the lower ones are pinnated, and their edges are jagged, but the upper ones grow single They are of a lanceolate figure, and their edges are entire The flowers of this species are exhibited in June, July, and August They are white, and by some admired

and Sweet scented American Climber

8 Sweet-scented American Climber This sort will rise, by the assistance of neighbouring bushes and trees, to a great height The branches are many, spread themselves all around, and lay hold of every thing that is near them The leaves are ternate The foliols are heart shaped, angular, and nearly cut into three lobes The flowers are white, and being possessed of a most agreeable fragrance, render this climber highly proper for arbours, and to be stationed near seats and places of resort

These are all the hardy climbing species of this genus yet known The varieties of the first kind are notable, and afford as much diversity in a garden as if they were distinct species The other sorts also admit of varieties, but the difference is very inconsiderable, and makes little variety, as they nearly agree with some or other of the above sorts

Method of propagating these sorts

The culture of all these sorts is by layers, and this is best done in summer, on the young shoots, as they grow As soon, therefore, as they have shot about a yard or four feet in length, let the ground be well dug about each stool and made fine, and a gentle hollow made about a foot from the stool In this hollow let the young shoots be pressed, and covered with mould, leaving their ends out to continue growing In a very little time they will be a yard or more in length, when a second hollow may be made, at a distance from the other, and the shoots pressed down and covered with mould as before, the ends being still left out to grow On some of the long shooting sorts, this may be repeated again, and even again, and these shoots, thus layered, will strike root Many of the sorts will have good root by the autumn, and others must be waited for until the autumn following This summer method of layering is highly necessary, because some of the sorts, particularly the Virgin's Bower, if layered in winter, in the common way, will be often two whole years, nay sometimes three, before they will strike root Any time from autumn to spring the layers may be taken up, and from one stool some scores are often obtained Those with good roots may be set out for good, and every bit that has a fibre should be cut off below that fibre, and should be headed to one eye or joint above the part that had been out of the ground, and thus all the layers being collected together, should be planted in the nursery, at small distances, and in a year or two they also will be good plants for use

The Travellers Joy may be layered at any time, for the roots will easily strike, nay, they will grow by cuttings

The Evergreen Spanish Climber requires no art or trouble to encrease it, for it will encrease itself if the ground is left undisturbed a year or two, and will throw out plenty of suckers, which will have roots, and be good plants

Titles

1 The Virgin's Bower is titled, *Clematis foliis compositis decompositisque foliolis ovatis integerrimis* Caspar Bauhine calls it, *Clematitis caerulea vel purpurea repens*, also, *Clematitis caerulea, flore pleno* Clusius terms it, *Clematis altera* It grows naturally in the hedges of Italy and Spain

2 Virginian Climber is titled, *Clematis foliis compositis decompositisque foliolis quibusdam trifidis* In the *Hortus Elthamensis* it is called, *Flammula scandens, flore violaceo crasso* Ray calls it, *Clematis purpurea repens, petalis florum coriaceis*, and Petiver, *Scandens Carolinana planta, viornae folio* It grows naturally in Virginia and Carolina

3 Carolina Climber is, *Clematis foliis simplicibus ternatisque foliolis integris trilobisve* Dillenius calls it, *Clematis flore crispo* It grows naturally in Carolina

4 Oriental

4 Oriental Climber is, *Clematis foliis compositis foliolis incisis angulatis lobatis cuneiformibus, petalis interne villosis* Tournefort calls it, *Clematis orientalis, apii folio, flore e viridi-flavescente postestius reflexo* In the *Hortus Elthamensis* it is termed, *Flammula scandens, apii folio glauco* It is a native of the East

5 Travellers Joy, or *Viorna*, is titled, *Clematis foliis pinnatis foliolis cordatis scandentibus* John Bauhine calls it, *Clematis latifolia integra*, also, *Clematis latifolia dentata* Caspar Bauhine, Sloane, &c term it, *Clematis sylvestris latifolia*, Dodonæus, *Vitalba*; and Cammerarius, *Clematis tertia* It grows common in the hedges of England, and most of the northern parts of Europe It is found also growing naturally in Virginia and Jamaica

6 Evergreen Spanish Climber is titled, *Clematis cirrhis scandens, foliis simplicibus* Clusius calls it, *Clematis altera Bætica*, Tournefort, *Clematis peregrina, foliis pyri incisis nunc singularibus, nunc ternis*, and Caspar Bauhine, *Clematis peregrina, foliis pyri incisis* It grows naturally in Spain and Portugal

7 Creeping Climber is, *Clematis foliis inferioribus pinnatis scandentibus laciniatis summis simplicibus integerrimis lanceolatis* Caspar Bauhine calls it, *Clematitis, sive flammula repens*, Dodonæus and others, *Flammula* It grows naturally in the hedges about Montpelier, also in some parts of Saxony, and on the Alps

8 Sweet-scented American Climber is titled, *Clematis foliis ternatis foliolis cordatis sublobato-angulatis scandentibus, floribus dioicis* Plukenet calls it, *Clematis Virginiana Pannonicæ similis*, Albinus, *Clematis Floridensis flore albo odoratissimo*, and Gronovius, *Clematis aquatica trifoliata lati scandens, floribus albis odoratis* It grows naturally in North-America

*Clematis* is of the class and order *Polyandria Polygynia*, and the characters are, Class and order in the Linnæan system The characters

1 CALYX There is none

2 COROLLA consists of four loose, oblong petals

3 STAMINA consist of numerous awl-shaped filaments, shorter than the corolla, with antheræ growing to their sides

4 PISTILLUM consists of numerous, roundish, compressed germina, ending in subulated styles, longer than the stamina, with simple stigmas

5 PERICARPIUM There is none The receptaculum is small and capitated

6 SEMINA The seeds are numerous, roundish, and compressed The style, which is of various forms in the different species, adheres to them

## CHAP. V.

## CYNANCHUM.

THE hardy climbing species of this genus are usually called,

Species

1 Montpelier Acute-leaved Scammony
2 Round-leaved Montpelier Scammony
3 Carolina *Periploca*

Montpelier Acute leaved,

1 Montpelier Acute leaved Scammony The root is strong, creeping, and spreads itself to a considerable distance The stalks are herbaceous, twist about every thing that is near them, will grow to be six feet long, but always die to the ground in the autumn, and fresh ones are put forth from the roots in the spring The leaves are oblong, heart-shaped, acute-pointed, smooth, and grow opposite by pairs, on long footstalks The flowers come out from the wings of the leaves, in small bunches, they are of a dirty white colour, appear in June and July, but are not succeeded by good seeds in our gardens This plant, on being wounded, emits a milky juice

and Round leaved Scammony

2 Round-leaved Montpelier Scammony The root of this species is large, thin, juicy, and spreads itself to a considerable distance The stalks are herbaceous, and twine to six or seven feet high about whatever is near them The leaves are broad, reniform, roundish, and grow opposite, on long footstalks The flowers come out from the wings of the leaves, in small bunches, they are of a bad white colour, appear in June and July, and are rarely succeeded by good seeds in our gardens The stalks die to the ground in the autumn, and fresh ones arise again in the spring On wounding any part of this plant, a milky juice immediately flows.

Carolina Periploca

3 Carolina *Periploca* The stalks of this species are slender, ligneous, shrubby, and will twist about any thing to the height of about seven feet They are hairy, and their lower part is covered with a thick, fungous, cloven, cork-like bark The leaves are oval, heart-shaped, pointed, and grow opposite at the joints on long hairy footstalks The flowers come out from the wings of the leaves in small bunches They are greenish on their first appearance, but die away to a bad purple They exhibit themselves in July and August; but are not succeeded by good seeds in our gardens

Culture of the different sorts.

The two first sorts are exceeding hardy, will grow in any soil or situation, and will over-run any small plants that are near them Their situation, therefore, should be among such trees as have strength enough to admit their embraces; and their propagation is by cutting the roots in the autumn Every cut will grow, and when planted, will call for no trouble except keeping them clear from weeds, when they first shoot up in the spring.

The other is propagated by laying down the young shoots as they advance in the summer, and covering them over with some fine mould These will soon put out roots, by the autumn will be good plants, and may then be removed to the places where they are designed to remain This species is rather tender, and the soil in which it is planted should be naturally dry, warm, light, and sandy, and the situation well defended Being thus stationed, it will live abroad, and continue for many years, but if the soil is moist, rich, and ill-defended, the chance will

will be very great but it will be destroyed the first winter

Titles

1 Acute leaved Montpelier Scammony is titled, *Cynanchum caule volubili herbaceo, foliis cordato oblongis glabris* Caspar Bauhine calls it, *Scammonia Monspeliacæ affinis, foliis acutioribus*, and Clusius, *Apocynum 3 latifolium* It is a native of the south of France, Sicily, Spain, and Astracan

2 Round leaved Montpelier Scammony is, *Cynanchum caule volubili herbaceo, foliis reniformi-cordatis acutis* Caspar Bauhine calls it, *Scammonea Monspeliaca, foliis rotundioribus*, and Clusius, *Apocynum IV latifolium Scammonea valentina* It grows naturally in Spain and the south of France

3 Carolina *Periploca* is titled, *Cynanchum caule volubili inferne suberoso fisso, foliis cordatis acuminatis* Dillenius calls it, *Periploca Carolinensis, flore minore stellato* It grows naturally in Carolina, and other parts of America

Class and order in the Linnæan system The characters

*Cynanchum* is of the class and order *Pentandria Digynia*, and the characters are,

1 Calyx is a small, erect, monophyllous, permanent perianthium, indented in five parts at the top

2 Corolla is a single petal The tube is very short The limb is plane, and divided into five long, narrow segments In the center of the flower is situated an erect, cylindrical nectarium, of the same length with the corolla, and indented in five parts

3 Stamina are five parallel filaments, the length of the nectarium, having conniving antheræ, placed within the mouth of the corolla

4 Pistillum consists of an oblong bifid germen, a very short style, and two obtuse stigmas

5 Pericarpium consists of two oblong, acuminated, unilocular follicules, opening longitudinally

6 Semina The seeds are numerous, oblong, placed imbricatim, and crowned with down

# C H A P VI

## *GLYCINE*, KNOBBED-ROOTED LIQUORICE VETCH

Species

THE climbers of this genus are usually called,

1 Carolina Kidney Bean-tree
2 Ash-leaved Milk-Vetch
3 Climbing Rest Harrow
4 Maryland Kidney-Bean plant
5 Virginian *Glycine*

Carolina Kidney Bean-tree

1 Carolina Kidney-Bean-tree does not arise by the assistance of claspers, but by the twining branches, which naturally twist round any adjacent trees, nay, if trees are at ten feet or more distance from the root of the plant, its branches, being too weak to support themselves, will trail along the ground, until they reach these trees, and then they will twine their branches with theirs, and arrive to a great height Indeed, where trees are near at hand, and they begin by the first spring shoot to twist about them, they will twine up them to the height of near twenty feet This climber is possessed of noble large pinnated leaves, very much like those of liquorice The folioles are about three pair in number, arranged on their common mid-rib, and they always end with an odd one Their colour is for the most part of a lightish hoary cast, with a blueish tinge The flowers are very large and ornamental Their colour is that of a blueish purple, and their general characters indicate their structure They are produced from the wings of the leaves, in July and August, and are succeeded by long pods, like kidney beans

Method of propagating it by seeds

This fine climber is easily propagated by seeds, if there is a conveniency of procuring them from abroad, for they never ripen with us In the spring, as soon as we receive them, they should be sown, in fine beds of light sandy earth, half an inch deep They will readily come up, and all summer must have frequent waterings, and if the beds be shaded in hot weather, it will be the better In winter the beds should be hooped, and covered with mats in frosty weather And in spring the strongest may be drawn out, which will thin the bed, and make way for the others, which should stand until the next spring The plants thus drawn should be set in the nursery, at small distances, and in a year or two after, they will be good plants for any place where they are wanted

and by layers

This plant is also easily encreased by layers, for if the young shoots of the preceding summer be laid in the ground in the autumn, by the autumn following they will have struck root, when the best-rooted and strongest layers may be planted out for good where they are wanted, whilst the weaker, or those with hardly any root, may be set in the nursery, like the seedlings, to gain strength

Ash-leaved Milk Vetch

2 The Ash-leaved Milk-Vetch will twine from six to twelve feet high, according to the nature of the soil; for in a rich rare mould it will grow near double the length it will in a soil of an opposite nature These stalks die to the ground every autumn and in the spring new ones are issued forth from the roots, which are composed of many knobs, that encrease in number the longer the plant is suffered to remain The leaves somewhat resemble those of the ash tree, being pinnated almost in the same manner The folioles, which consist of three pair besides the odd one, are of an oval lanceolate shape, and being arranged opposite along the mid-rib, and terminated with a single one, form a fine leaf The flowers are produced from the sides of its twining stalks, in August They grow in small spikes, are of a reddish colour, and being of the butterfly or open blossomed kind, make a pretty good show These flowers are sometimes succeeded by pods, which never perfect their seeds with us

Climbing Rest Harrow

3 Climbing Rest Harrow is but a low plant for a climber, seldom arising higher than five feet The stalk dies to the ground every autumn,

and

and the loſs is repaired by a natural ſucceſſion preſented from the root every ſpring The leaves are trifoliate and very downy Every one knows the beauty that ariſes from leaves of an hoary nature, amongſt the variety of greens of different tinges The flowers are of the pea bloom kind, and are produced in ſhort bunches, in June and July, from the ſide of the ſtalks They are of a yellow colour, and though they are rather ſmall in proportion are very beautiful They are ſucceeded by pods, in which two ſeeds only are contained, and which will be ripe with us in September

Maryland Kidney bean plant

4 The Kidney-Bean plant of Maryland has a ſlender, annual, twining ſtalk, which will riſe to be three or four feet high The leaves are ternate and ſit cloſe to the ſtalks They are hairy, and the folioles are of an oval lanceolate ſhape, and being of a good green, make the whole ornamental enough But the greateſt ornament this plant receives is from the flowers, which are alſo of the pea-bloom kind, and are of a clear blue They are produced in June, from the ſides of the ſtalks, in fine recurved bunches, and theſe are ſucceeded by pods, which will have ripe ſeeds in Auguſt or September

Virginian Glycine

5 The Virginian *Glycine* will ariſe with its ſlender branches to a degree higher than the other The ſtalks are hairy, and the leaves with which they are ornamented are trifoliate and naked The flowers are produced from the ſides of the ſtalks, in June and July They grow in pendulent bunches, and are alſo of the butterfly kind They are very beautiful, and each exhibits a variety of colours, for the wings and the keel are white, whilſt the ſtandard is of a pale violet colour Theſe flowers are ſucceeded by compreſſed half-rounded pods, hanging by lengthened peduncles, and the ſeeds will often be ripe in September

Remarks.

Theſe perennials are all proper to be planted amongſt ſhrubs in warm and well-ſheltered places, for they are rather of a tender nature, and are often deſtroyed by ſevere froſts As the ſtalks are all annual, as ſoon as they decay at the approach of winter, they ſhould be cut up cloſe to the ground, and cleared of ſuch plants as are near them, by which they have aſpired, otherwiſe they will have a dead paltry look, and render the places inelegant, for, even in the dead of winter, neatneſs and elegance muſt be obſerved, which will not only ſhew a more promiſing expectation of a reſurrection, but the clearing away old ſtalks, &c will be better for the plants themſelves, as they would in ſome degree hinder and choak the young ſhoots as they advance in the ſpring

Method of propagating them

All theſe ſorts are propagated by the ſeeds, and this may be in the places where they are to remain, or in warm well ſheltered beds, or in pots, to be houſed for the firſt winter, if it ſhould prove ſevere They will very readily come up, and if they are ſown in the open ground, the beds ſhould be hooped at the approach of winter, to be covered with mats, in caſe it ſhould prove bad It will be proper to plunge thoſe ſown in pots, immediately after, up to the rims in the natural mould, for this will keep them cool and moiſt At the approach of hard froſts, they may be removed into the greenhouſe, and in ſpring may be turned out into the places where they are deſigned to remain Thoſe in the beds, alſo, ſhould be tranſplanted to ſuch places Their after management will be only to part the roots about every three or four years, and by this method alſo they may be all encreaſed The ſpring is the beſt time for parting of the roots, and by this way they may be multiplied faſt enough As to the firſt ſort, this method is chiefly practiſed for its propagation as it does not ripen its ſeeds here, [illegible] a conveniency of procuring them from abroad The roots of this ſort are compoſed of ſeveral tubers, and theſe being taken up and divided, readily grow and become good plants

Titles

1 The Carolina Kidney Bean-tree is titled, *Glycine foliis impari pinnatis, caule perenni* In the *Hort Angl* [illegible], it is titled, *Phaſeoloides fruteſcens Caroliniana, foliis pinnatis, floribus* [illegible] *onolon* [illegible] It grows naturally in Carolina and Virginia

2 The Milk [illegible] Milk Vetch is titled, *Glycine foliis impari-pinnatis ovato lanceolatis* In the *Hortus Cliffortianus* it is termed, *Glycine radice tuberoſa* Cornutus calls it, *Apios Americana*, Tournefort, *Aſtragalus tuberoſus ſcandens, fraxini folio*, Moriſon, *Aſtragalus perennis ſpicatus Americanus ſcandens caulibus, radice tuberoſa* It grows naturally in Virginia

3 Climbing Reſt Harrow is titled, *Glycine foliis ternatis tomentoſis racemis axillaribus bi*[illegible] *leguminibus aſperſis* Gronovius calls it, *Ononis caule volubili*, and Dillenius, *Anonis Phaſeolides ſcandens floribus flavis ſeſſilibus* It grows naturally in Virginia

4 Maryland Kidney Bean plant is, *Glycine foliis ternatis hirſutis, racemis lateralibus* Gronovius calls it, *Glycine foliis ternatis*, and Petiver, *Phaſeolus marianus ſcandens, floribus comoſis* It grows naturally in moiſt and ſhady places in Virginia

5 Virginian *Glycine* is, *Glycine foliis ternatis nudiuſculis, caule piloſo, racemis pendulis floribus fructiferis apetalis* In the former edition of the *Species Plantarum* it is called, *Glycine foliis ternatis nudiuſculis caule piloſo racemis pendulis bracteis ovatis* Gronovius calls it, *Glycine foliis ternatis, pedicellis bracteatis* It grows naturally in moiſt and ſhady places in Virginia

*Glycine* is of the claſs and order *Diadelphia Decandria*, and the characters are, Claſs and order in the Linnæan ſyſtem

1 CALYX is a monophyllous, compreſſed, bilabiated perianthium The upper lip is emarginated and obtuſe, and the under (which is longer) is trifid and acute The characters

2 COROLLA is papilionaceous

- The vexillum is obcordated, deflexed on the ſides, gibbous on the back, and emarginated at the point
- The alæ are oblong, oval towards their end, ſmall, and bend backwards
- The carina is narrow, falcated, and its point (which is broadeſt) turns towards the vexillum

3 STAMINA are diadelphous They conſiſt of ten filaments, with ſingle antheræ, nine of which filaments grow together, and the other ſtands ſingle

4 PISTILLUM conſiſts of an oblong germen, a cylindrical, ſpiral ſtyle, and an obtuſe ſtigma

5 PERICARPIUM is an oblong pod

6 SEMINA The ſeeds are reniforme

# CHAP. VII.

## *HEDERA*, IVY.

Species

THERE are two species of this genus:
1. The Ivy-tree.
2. The Virginian Creeper.

Ivy-tree. Varieties.

1. Ivy-tree. The varieties of this species are,
Common Ivy tree.
Yellow-berried Ivy.
Gold-striped Ivy.
Silver-striped Ivy.

described

Common Ivy-tree is well known all over England, and how it naturally trails either on the ground, or rises with walls or trees, striking its roots all along the sides of the branches for its support. It chiefly delights in old houses or walls; and when it has taken possession of any outside of the outer buildings, will soon cover the whole. It will make surprising progress when it reaches old thatch, and will soon, if unmolested, climb above the chimneys itself. Neither are old houses or walls what it chiefly likes to grow on; for it will strike its roots into the bark of trees, and cling to them with its never failing embraces to the very top. But above all, it chiefly affects old rotten trees or doderels; for these it will almost cover, and rear its head with a woody stem above the trunk, and will produce flowers and fruit in great plenty. There, as well as on the sides of old walls and buildings, it becomes a habitation for owls and other birds of night. There solitude itself is rendered more natural, and the poet's genius enlivened for the most solemn composition. The usefulness of Ivy, then, in Gardening is to over-run caves, grottos, old ruins, &c. to which purpose this plant is excellently adapted; and were it not for its commonness, this would be reckoned inferior to few evergreens; for the older grey stalks look well, whilst the younger branches, which are covered with a smooth bark of a fine green, are very beautiful. The leaves, also, are of a fine strong green, are large and bold, and make a variety among themselves; for some are composed of lobes, whilst others are large, and of an oval figure. The flowers are nothing extraordinary, unless it be for the figure in which they grow. This is strictly the *Corymbus*, and all flowers growing in such kind of bunches are called by Botanists Corymbose Flowers. The fruit that succeeds them, however, is very beautiful, for being black, and growing in this round regular order, and also continuing on all winter, it makes the tree singular, and, were it not for its commonness, desirable. It is observable, if Ivy has no support, but is left to creep along the ground only, it seldom flowers; but having taken possession of rails, hedges, trees, or buildings, from these it sends out woody branches, which produce the flowers and fruit.

The Yellow-berried Ivy differs from the Common Ivy in that its berries are yellow. It grows common in the islands of the Archipelago, and is at present rare with us. This is the *Hedera Poetica* of old authors.

The Gold-striped Ivy is the Common Ivy with yellow blotched leaves; though it is observable, that this sort has very little inclination to trail along the ground, or up trees or buildings, as it naturally rises with woody branches, and forms itself into a bushy head. So that this sort may be planted amongst variegated trees, or evergreens, as a shrub. Let it be set where it will, it is very beautiful, for the leaves will be a mixture of yellow and green, and sometimes they will have the appearance of being all yellow, thereby causing a very singular and striking look at a distance.

The Silver-striped Ivy is a variety of our Common sort, though the branches are naturally more slender. The leaves also are smaller; and of all the sorts this creeps the closest to walls or buildings, or is of strength sufficient to form its ligneous branches, when got to the top, to any head. This plant, then, is of all others to be planted against walls for ornament; for its leaves are very finely striped with streaks of silver, and the trees being first planted at small distances, will soon cover them all over, so as to have a delightful look. A more beautiful ornament to a wall can not be conceived, than what belongs to a wall of Charles Morris, Esq; of Loddington. It consists of these plants, which having first taken properly to the ground, and afterwards to the mortar joints, have so overspread the surface as to be a sight, of the kind superior to any I ever beheld; and I am persuaded there are few people of taste, who had seen any thing of this nature, but would be induced to have the like, even against their choicest walls. And here let it always be remembered, that whereas our Common Green Ivy is to hide and keep from view all old and unsightly walls, so the Silver-striped Ivy is to ornament all walls, even those of the finest surface.

2. The Virginian Creeper is a real species of the *Hedera*. It sheds its leaves in the autumn, and will spread itself over poles, walls, buildings, &c. in a very little time. It puts forth roots at the joints, which fasten into mortar of all sorts; so that no plant is more proper than this to hide the unsightly surface of an old barn end, or any other building which cannot be concealed from the view by trees being planted at some distance; as in one year it will shoot often near twenty feet, and, let the building be ever so high, will soon be at the top of it. The bark on the shoots is smooth and of a brown colour; and the buds in the spring, as they are beginning to open, will be of a fine red. The leaves are large and well looking. Each is composed of five smaller, which are serrated at their edges. The common footstalk is proportionably strong, and they die to a fine red in the autumn. Virginian

All the sorts of *Hedera* are to be propagated by cuttings. For these being set any time in the winter, in almost any soil, will strike root by the autumn following; and if they are permitted to remain another year, they will then be strong plants, fit to be set out for good. The Common Ivy is also to be raised from seeds; but I believe few Gardeners will want so great a quantity of these plants as to put this method in practice. Propagation

1. The Ivy-tree is titled, *Hedera foliis ovatis lobatisque*. Caspar Bauhine calls it, *Hedera arborea*; also, *Hedera major sterilis*; also, *Hedera poetica*,

*poeticæ*, also, *Hedera lauri ramis*, John Bauhine, *Hedera communis major* Parkinson, *Hedera arborea sive scandens & corymbosa communis*, and Gerard, *Hedera helix* It grows naturally in England, and most parts of Europe

2 The Virginian Creeper is, *Hedera foliis quinatis ovatis serratis* Tournefort calls it, *Vitis quinquefolia Canadensis scandens*, Micheli simply, *Helix*, and others, *Vitis hederacea indica* It is a native of Virginia and Canada

Class and order in the Linnæan system *Hedera* is of the class and order *Pentandria Monogynia*, and the characters are,

The characters 1 CALYX The involucrum of each umbel is small, and divided into many parts The perianthium surrounds the germen, and is indented in five parts

2 COROLLA consists of five oblong, patent petals, having incurved points

3 STAMINA are five subulated, erect filaments, the length of the corolla, having incumbent antheræ, that are bifid at their base

4 PISTILLUM consists of a turbinated germen, surrounded by the receptacle, of a short simple style, and a single stigma

5 PERICARPIUM is a globular berry, of one cell

6 SEMINA The seeds are five, large, gibbous on one side, and angular on the other

# CHAP VIII

## *HUMULUS*, The HOP-PLANT

OF this genus there is only that well-known species called, The Hop plant, or Hops the root of which is long, slender, and fibrous

Description of this plant The stalk is slender, round, rough, very tough, often purplish, and will twist about poles, or whatever is near it, to a great height The leaves are large, palmated, rough, cut on their edges, and grow on strong footstalks The flowers come out from the ends and sides of the stalks, in clusters, hanging downward They are of a whitish yellow colour, and strongly scented They appear in July, and the seeds ripen in August and September

Its use, The uses of Hops are very few in medicine, though they are strong, and agreeably bitter Their chief employment is in taking off the glutinous quality of malt liquor, giving it a more agreeable flavour, rendering it more wholesome, and causing it to pass off more freely by urine, for which purposes they are raised in vast quantities in many parts of England

This genus, being dioecious, admits of two principal sorts, the Male Hop plant, the Female Hop plant The Male Hop plant grows common in hedges, in most parts of England, and the young shoots in the spring, while they are tender, are eaten as asparagus, to which by many people, they are thought little inferior

The Female, which is the sort cultivated for Hops, admits of some varieties known among hop-planters by the respective names of, the Early White Hop, the Long White Hop, the Oval Hop the Long and Square Garlick Hop, all which are propagated by those who deal in this profitable article

Proper situations, Hops will grow in any soil or situation, though they chiefly love a deep, light, fat, loose, fresh earth, inclined to moisture In a fertile meadow properly prepared they will sport amazingly, but must have the sun and free air, so that if the situation is low, but full upon the sun, the current of air good, the soil fit and loose, and properly prepared, the greatest quantity and the best hops may be annually expected from such situation

and management in culture Having fixed upon the situation, the next thing to be done is to prepare the ground, and for this, if you choose to have your ground in the best order, it should lie fallow the summer before, or it may be fallowed, and about Midsummer sown with a crop of turneps, which may be eat off in the early part of the winter by sheep, for the planting need not be performed before March, and the season continues good till the middle of April Keeping the sheep thus feeding upon the turneps will enrich the spot, and bring it into better condition for the good growth of the Hop-plants

As soon as the turneps are eat off, the ground should be well ploughed with a deep strong plough, and if it be again cross-ploughed it will be the better Heavy harrows should then break the clods, and the whole should be made as fine and pliable as possible Having got the ground in readiness, the next thing is to procure the plants or sets These are cuttings which arise immediately from the roots they should be six or seven inches long, and there should be three or four good buds to each

The sorts should be all alike, that they may ripen together, for if the Early, the Middle, and the Late sorts are promiscuously blended together, the trouble must be very great in watching their ripening, and going over the Hop-ground so often as the promiscuous plantations of the different kinds of Hops, for proper gathering and curing at the time of ripening, shall require

The Early White is the first that ripens, comes first to market, and is a high-flavoured Hop, but it is a bad bearer, and tenderer than any of the other sorts The Long White comes about a week or ten days after, is a good bearer, dies to a good green, and is one of the most valuable hops The Square Garlick is a very plentiful bearer, is the most hardy of all the sorts, and comes in latest, but then it is a brown Hop, fit only for common ale, and of inferior value to any of the preceding sorts This Hop, however, is most generally raised, on account of its being hardy, and a good bearer, and is the sort with which the markets are most abundantly supplied

Having fixed upon the sorts, and being provided with a sufficient quantity of cuttings, the next thing to be proceeded on is the planting them And for this if it is a long time since the land has been ploughed, it should be ploughed afresh that the mould may work well, be fine,

and

and in good order for the reception of the plants These are generally set on little elevated spots, called Hills, at a certain distance from each other In order, therefore, to mark out the places for the hills begin at an outside, and with a line set out the outer border of your hop-ground ten or twelve feet from the hedge Parallel to this, let another line be drawn, in which the Hops may be planted The hills should be six, seven, eight, or more feet distance from each other, according to the richness of the ground, or the size of the Hop that is to be planted For the more expeditious method of marking out the places for the hills, let small bits of rag be tied on the line at any of those distances you would choose Having drawn the line straight, let a stick be thrust down by each rag for a direction, and then proceed to mark out the others in the like manner, observing always, that the hill of each row may be opposite to the middle of the interval of the other, which method I rather prefer, though some are fond of planting their Hops chequer-wise, square, or exactly opposite to each other in every direction

Having the ground set out, the best of the mould should be elevated round each stick, so as to form a small hill or bank, and it should be made level, or dished at the top If the soil is not naturally good, a sufficient quantity of well rotten dung should be in readiness to mix with the common mould at the places that form the hills, and it will afterwards invigorate the plants, cause them to shoot strong, and become plentiful bearers, though if the land be fresh, little, or even no dung, at the first planting, need be added, let its nature be what it will, the rotted turf will be superior to any dung manure, and the sweetness peculiar to fresh soils, when properly mixed and prepared, gives a healthy sprightliness to plants, and causes them to be more fruitful, beyond what can be procured from manures, though the plants thereby may be made to grow faster, become larger, and forced beyond their natural size of growth

Having the hills all raised and in readiness, either of their own natural soil, or in conjunction with well rotted dung, at the top of each hill five sets should be planted One set should be placed in the center, the other four should surround it A setting stick is always used for this business, the finest mould must surround them, and it should be pressed very close to the sides of the plants

The Hop Plantation being thus made, will call for no trouble or care until May, when the weeds will rise, and the ground will require digging in order to kill them In digging, be sure to bury all the weeds, pick out all old roots of trees, strong weeds, &c that may have escaped before, and add a little mould to each hill, that it may be of greater body, the better to support and invigorate the plants

The remaining part of the summer the weeds should be hoed down as they arise, and the sets being properly planted, and meeting with no interruption, will shoot tolerably strong the first summer, and if poled off with small poles, will bear some Hops, but they ought not to be poled the first year, it will weaken the plants, and cause them afterwards to be less vigorous All that is to be done to the binds the first summer is to twist them into a bunch at the top of each hill, and this work is generally performed in June

The winter following, the ground should be manured with well rotted dung, especially if it has been any ways old, worn out, or in bad heart at first And for this purpose, the dung or compost should be brought upon the ground in frosty weather, that the cart-wheels may not cut in to detriment the roots or the plants, but as you cannot be certain of a frost for your purpose, the best way will be to bring in your dung soon after Michaelmas, whilst the ground is hard, and for the same reason, the poles, either for sticking at first, or to renew decayed ones, are to be brought into the plantation, to be ready for use

The quantity of dung for an acre varies according to the nature of the land, or the intention of the Hop dresser Sometimes it is repeated every year, laid thinly, and applied only to the hills In this case sixteen or twenty loads will be sufficient for an acre Sometimes it is laid thick all over the alleys, to be dug in, and no less than forty load, for the purpose of such a thorough dressing, is necessary to be brought upon an acre When the land is thus dunged, the repetition need not be oftener than at an interval of three years and after this, every person must determine for himself how to manage from the nature of his land, or the quantity of dung he has annually to spare

The end of February, or beginning or middle of March, is the season for pruning, or, as it is called, Dressing the Hop plants In order to this, the earth must be cleared away from the tops of the roots with an iron picker, or some convenient instrument proper for the purpose The stocks should be then headed down, and all weak shoots and suckers should be cleared away, which being done, the stocks should be covered over with half an inch depth of the finest mould

The plants will soon shew themselves after this When they are all out of the ground, which will be in April, they should be poled Three poles are requisite for one hill the space between two of them being to the south, that the whole may the better receive the sun's beams They should be set close to the sides of the hill, and should be let down deep with an iron crow, in order to cause them to stand firm to resist the winds Their direction should not be perpendicular, but their tops should be made to spread from each other, and this will cause them to be at a greater distance, keep them from entangling and winding one among another, and render them more susceptible of the benefits to be received from the sun, air, and dews

The length of the poles should be in proportion to the goodness of the soil, from about fifteen to twenty feet is in general the height of the poles, tho' the greatest caution should be used, not to put long poles to a young or weak Hop-yard for this will not only weaken the plants, by drawing them too much but the produce will be proportionally smaller, the bearing branches being most vigorous after the binds have topped the poles, which must be a great hindrance to them, if the poles are so long that they are unable to arrive at the tops In one and the same Hop yard, poles of different lengths will be required, and the young shoots, at the time of fixing the poles, will direct the person employed in that office Those shoots which rise strong and healthy will call for the tallest poles, others, less vigorous, the middle sized poles, and the weakest the least of all And if, after all the poles of any should prove too short, taller should be thrust close to them, in order to elevate the binds to any desired height

Poles may be made of any wood if they are of sufficient length, though they are commonly of ash, birch, willow, maple, sycamore, poplar, Spanish chestnut, and oak the two latter of which ...

which are preferred, as being the more durable, but they are not ſo eaſily met with as any of the other ſorts, which are the common ſticking-poles of hop-plantations.

Hops being thus ſtuck, they will naturally wind about the poles according to the ſun's motion, and ſuch binds as do not happen to lay hold of its proper pole, muſt be directed to it with the hand, looſely tying it there with withered ruſhes, or the like ſoft and eaſily-attainable bandage, and if afterwards, when theſe binds are grown to a conſiderable height, they ſhould miſs their hold, and diverge from the pole, they muſt then, by the aſſiſtance of ſtanding ladders, be reinſtated and tied as before.

If the binds happen to run up weak, and you find the poles are too long for them, by the aſſiſtance of a ſtanding ladder you ſhould ſaw off the tops down to a proper length, otherwiſe they will be much more weakened, and the produce of Hops be very inconſiderable, and if the binds are extremely ſtrong, and much over-top the poles, it is a common practice to ſtrike off the heads with a long ſwitch, and this occaſions their throwing out numerous branches, which will be ſoon loaded with large cluſters of fine Hops.

About three vines are ſufficient for every pole, and where more than theſe are found, when the ground is old, it is cuſtomary to pull them up; when the ground is young, the practice is to wrap them together, and place them ſecurely on the middle of the hill.

The Hops being thus properly trained to their poles, and the tying ſeaſon, as they call it, being over, which will be by the end of May, the next thing to be done is digging the ground, called the Summer-digging. The firſt week in June is the beſt time for this work, and it conſiſts chiefly in digging about the hills, and laying ſome fine mould to each of them, for the better nouriſhing of the plants, and in the beginning of July an additional ſupply ſhould be granted the hills, by paring the alleys, which ſhould always be done at this time, to cauſe the whole to be neat and clean, and raiſe the hills to a proper ſize. About a week after this, or about the middle of July, they will come into blow, and the Hops will be ripe about the end of Auguſt. But before that time, you ſhould carefully watch their ripening, eſpecially the Early ſorts, becauſe, if the gathering is deferred but a little time, the greateſt danger is impending, for a ſudden ſtorm happening, breaks the branches, bruiſes the Hops, changes the colour, and conſequently diminiſhes the value. A ſtrict eye, therefore, muſt be kept upon their ripening, and the utmoſt expedition of gathering them uſed, when the ſigns of ripeneſs do appear. The tokens of ripe Hops are, firſt, their being poſſeſſed of a ſtrong Hop-like odour, ſecondly, their being dry and hard to the touch, and thirdly, when on examining the ſeeds, you find them plump, and of a browniſh colour. Theſe are the ſure ſigns of ripe Hops, and whenever you perceive the tokens, you muſt proceed to gathering with all expedition.

In order to this, fair weather ſhould firſt of all be made choice of if poſſible, and then the binds of a certain number ſhould be cut, and the poles drawn out of the ground, the quantity of binds cut at a time, ſhould be no more than what can be conveniently picked in an hour or two; and a piece of wood in form of a lever, having a forked piece of iron with teeth on the inſide, ſhould raiſe the poles, when they ſtick faſt.

In picking the Hops, great care ſhould be uſed to take no leaves or ſtalks, and a long ſquare frame of wood, called a bin, having within a cloth hanging on tenter-hooks, ſhould be ready to receive the Hops as they are picked.

This bin is uſually eight feet long and three broad, is ſupported by four legs, and over it is another piece of wood elevated at a proper height, on which the poles are laid to be picked.

Two poles are generally laid on it at a time, and at this bin eight perſons may conveniently work, four on a ſide, picking the Hops and putting them into it.

A certain number of hills ſhould be pitched on to be cleared at one time, uſually ten, eleven, twelve, or more, the bin ſhould be ſet as near the center as poſſible, and when all the poles of that quarter are picked, it ſhould be removed to the middle of another ſpot appropriated to the ſame purpoſe. The Hops ſhould from time to time be carried in coarſe bags from the bin to the kiln to dry.

The kiln is the ſame as is uſed for malt drying, and ſhould be of a ſize proportioned to the quantity of Hops to be dried. It ſhould be covered with a hair-cloth, and charcoal is the beſt fuel for drying of Hops. They ſhould be ſpread about a foot thick, or more if they are gathered dry, but if green and wet they ſhould be laid thinner, and a gentle fire, before they are ſpread, ſhould firſt warm the kiln.

After they are ſpread, a ſlow, moderate, uniform fire ſhould be continued. If it is too fierce, the Hops will ſcorch; if too ſlow, the ſweat or moiſture which the ſmalleſt heat will occaſion to the Hops, will fall on them again, and diſcolour them. The fire, therefore, ſhould be rather encreaſed as the Hops get nearer dried, in order totally to diſperſe the fumes and vapours ariſing. After they have lain nine hours they ſhould be turned, and in about two or three hours after they will be ſufficiently dried, which may be known by the brittleneſs of the ſtalks, and the eaſy-falling off of the leaves, they may be then taken away.

Proper rooms ſhould be in readineſs for their reception, in which they ſhould be repoſited, to cool and become tough, otherwiſe they will break, be almoſt reduced to powder, and much damaged by bagging. A ſpace of three weeks or a month is neceſſary for theſe purpoſes, by which time they will be ſufficiently cooled and toughened, and afterwards may be bagged for ſale.

The bags conſiſt each of four ells and a half of ell-wide coarſe cloth, and uſually contain two hundred and a half of hops.

The manner of bagging the Hops is thus. They firſt tie a handful of Hops to each corner of the bottom, in order to ſerve for handles, for the proper wielding of the bags when full of Hops. They then place the bags in the mouth of a Hole made for that purpoſe, in the floor of the upper room where the Hops lay. A hoop is next put round the mouth of the bag, on which it is to reſt in the hole. A perſon is appointed to tread down the Hops, whilſt another puts them into the bags. This he does on every ſide, and in as cloſe a manner as he can, as the Hops are thrown into the bag, and ſo continues until the bag is full, which being done, they unfaſten the bags from the hoop, let them down and cloſe up the mouths, faſtening at each corner a handful of Hops as before, to ſerve as handles, for the more convenient wielding of the bags. If Hops have been well bagged, and were properly dried, they will keep many years, but then the room in which they are placed muſt be very dry, and be frequently inſpected, that no vermin come near them, eſpecially mice, which will gnaw the bags, neſt and breed in the Hops without being noticed, unleſs a ſtrict inſpection into the bottom and back or hidden parts of the bags, at proper intervals, be made

The Dutch and Flemings have another method of drying of Hops, and various ways are practiſed in different parts, according to the cuſtom of the countries in which they have been uſed, but the difference is inconſiderable, and the ſucceſs perhaps little inferior to the before-mentioned method The Dutch lay the Hops on beds of lath, without any cloth, half a yard thick, rake the ſurface even and then kindle the fire, keeping it to a regular and conſtant heat at the mouth of the furnace only There are others who are advocates for ſpreading them leſs than a foot thick Some contend that Hops ought never to be turned, but remain undiſturbed until the whole floor is dried, while others produce reaſons againſt ſuch practices, and aſſert to the *practice of thoſe who turn their* Hops, in order to have them equally and perfectly dried

In ſhort, by the worſt of theſe methods good Hops are obtained The Dutch and Flemiſh Hops are very fine, and uſeful Hops are prepared by the moſt indirect practices The method I have laid down is chiefly practiſed in England, and how far it is excellent for the intended purpoſe, the prodigious quantity of fine Hops which are annually afforded give ample teſtimony

As ſoon as the Hop-harveſt is over, like good huſbandmen, your time ſhould be employed in taking care of your poles, and preparing your compoſt for the enſuing crop

If the poles could be kept dry under cover, they would laſt above as long again, but as this is generally impracticable, on account of the large quantities that muſt be uſed, even for comparatively ſmall Hop-yards, the uſual method is to fix three or ſix poles firm into the ground, ſetting them wide at the bottom, and binding them cloſe at the top, and then to ſet a large quantity of the others round them Thus thoſe on the inſide will in a great meaſure be protected from the wet, which may be made to be no inconſiderable number, the top and the outſide ones only being expoſed to the inclemencies of all weather

The compoſt ſhould be next prepared Horſe and cow-dung well rotted, or mixed with mould that has been taken with the turf, is the beſt compoſt that can be uſed for Hops Human ordure has been recommended, but it is too hot for Hops, which delight in cool manure, for which reaſon, pigeons dung, lime, &c ſhould rarely be uſed, unleſs on cold damp lands, when a little, being judiciouſly mixed with mould, and applied to the hills, in ſuch ſituations, proves ſerviceable

Accidents to which Hops are liable

Hops are a very profitable article, and would be much more ſo were it not for the many accidents they are peculiarly liable to, and which frequently fall on them in their riſing and flouriſhing ſtate, nip them in the bud as it were, deſpoil them of their beauty, and from a moſt promiſing expectation, afford the owner a ſad ſpectacle of deſolation and miſery For Hops ſuffer firſt from grubs, or vermin of different ſorts, at the roots, an uninterrupted ſeries of dry weather frequently cauſes the mould of the hill to become a proper nidus for theſe creatures, and then they hatch, and ſoon ſhew themſelves in amazing abundance Theſe devour the roots, and the young ſhoots as they are forming, ſo that the plantation is thereby weakened, the ſhoots prove few and inconſiderable, and ſuch as have ſhot away from theſe reptiles look ſickly and are very ill qualified to afford a crop in any tolerable plenty

Flies are a terrible nuiſance to Hop plantations Theſe frequently ſhew themſelves on the leaves in May, and will be in ſuch ſwarms the remaining part of that month, and alſo in June as to ſuck our the leaves, cauſe the plants to be come ſickly, and render them unfit for the office of affording a plentiful crop

Lice alſo frequently breed on the Hop ſhoots, and are found in amazing numbers on the ſhoots and leaves Theſe corrupt the juices, and impair, if not deſtroy, the riſing crop

A long ſeries of rainy or damp weather without a ſufficient current of air, or proper intervals of dry weather, affords too much moiſture to the plants The free and natural perſpiration is thereby impeded, the juices being ſtagnated become corrupted, the leaves and fruit grow mouldy, and large quantities of flouriſhing Hop plants are ſoon deſtroyed

A mould, called the Fen, owing to the above cauſes, or its own natural encreaſe from ſcattered ſeeds, which ſoon ripen and come to maturity, ſeize the leaves and ſhoots in great abundance, and as the ſeeds ſoon ripen and come to maturity, it frequently ſpreads itſelf through a whole plantation This contagion is the more dreadful, becauſe Hop grounds, which have been once infected with it, will ſcarcely be free from it for ſeveral years

The Mildew is alſo fatal to Hop-plantations It is a white dew, which ſhews itſelf about ſunriſe, and is moſt fatal when the Hops are in flower, for lighting on the leaves and young Hops at that time, it withers and conſumes them This deſolation is ſometimes partial, ſometimes general, whole Hop-grounds being frequently ruined by this dew, however, the plants are ſometimes relieved by rain ſeaſonably falling, which waſhes them clean, and frees them from the diſtemper

Honey-dews are another dreadful calamity that befal Hop-plantations Theſe frequently ſhew themſelves in June, and in a month's time the leaves become black, ſtink, and a direful appearance poſſeſſes the whole plant

In extreme hot weather, eſpecially after warm ſhowers, ſcorching vapours bound, by which the Hop plants are ſcalded, and deſolation brought on a conſiderable ſhare of the plantations This evil is uſually called the Fire Blaſt It uſually happens in July, and *frequently* affects the inner parts of cloſe plantations, where the atmoſphere is denſer, whilſt the outſides, and ſuch parts as have a purer and freer air, are generally free from this calamity

All theſe are evils which the Hop planter, one time or other, is pretty ſure to ſuffer, in ſome degree or other, but they are in ſome degree made amends for by the ſudden riſe of the price of Hops, which becomes almoſt inſtantaneous, on the leaſt appearance of the failure of the crops; and which will never fail to afford him a more than ordinary price for the curtailed quantity he ſhall be enabled to bring to market

There being no other ſpecies of this genus, it ſtands with the name ſimply, *Humulus* Caſpar Bauhine calls it, *Lupulus mas*, alſo, *Lupulus femina*, John Bauhine, *Lupulus mas & femina*, Fuchſius, *Lupulus ſalictarius*; Gerard, *Lupus ſalictarius*, and Parkinſon, *Lupulus ſylveſtris* It grows naturally in hedges in England, and moſt parts of Europe Title

*Humulus* is of the claſs and order *Dioecia Pentandria*, and the characters are, Claſs and order in the Linnæan ſyſtem

I Male

The cha racters

I Male Flowers

1 CALYX is a perianthium composed of five oblong, concave, obtuse leaves

2 COROLLA There is none

3 STAMINA are five very short capillary filaments, with oblong antheræ

II Female Flowers

1. CALYX The general involucrum is quadrifid and acute

The partial involucrum is oval, consists of four leaves, and contains eight flowers

The perianthium is monophyllous, oval, large, plane on the outer side, and connivent at the base

2. COROLLA There is none

3 PISTILLUM consists of a very small germen and two awl-shaped, reflexed, spreading styles, with acute stigmas

4 PERICARPIUM There is none The seed is contained in the base of the calyx

5 SEMEN The seed is roundish, and covered with a thin skin

# CHAP. IX

## *LONICERA*, The HONEYSUCKLE or WOODBINE

THE Honeysuckles, or Woodbines, are chiefly divided into three classes

Species

1 Italian Honeysuckles

2 English Honeysuckles

3 Trumpet-Honeysuckles

Italian Honeysuckle Varieties

1 Italian Honeysuckles The varieties of this species are,

Early White Italian Honeysuckle
Early Red Italian Honeysuckle
Yellow Italian Honeysuckle
Late Red-flowered Italian Honeysuckle
Evergreen Italian Honeysuckle

described

The Early White Italian Honeysuckle is that which first makes its appearance, in May The leaves of this sort are oval, and placed opposite by pairs, close to the branches, at the extremity of which the leaves quite surround it The flowers grow in bunches round the ends of the branches, and have a very fine scent Their blow will be soon over, and they are succeeded by red pulpy berries, which will be ripe in the autumn

The Early Red differs from the preceding in that the leaves are narrower, the fibres of the flowers are more slender, and it blows a little later in the spring.

The Yellow Italian Honeysuckle does not blow quite so early as the other, and the flowers are yellow In other respects it is very much like the former

Late Red-flowered Italian Honeysuckle is one of the best we have The stem is tolerably firm, the branches are few, and the leaves large, the flowers are also large, of a deep-red colour, tho' less scented than the Earlier sorts

Evergreen Italian Honeysuckle This is a stronger shooter than any of the sorts The joints are more distant from each other The leaves are large, of a thick consistence, unite and surround the stalk with their base, and continue all winter The flowers are large, of a good red colour, with some paler stripes, and often continue in blow to the end of autumn

English Honeysuckles Varieties

2 English Honeysuckle Of this species are,

The Common Woodbine of our Hedges
The Oak-leaved Honeysuckle
Red Dutch Honeysuckle
Midsummer Honeysuckle
Late German Honeysuckle
Long Blowing Honeysuckle
Evergreen Honeysuckle

The Common Woodbine is known all over England, in our woods and hedges There are still varieties of this sort, in its wild state, some having prodigious weak trailing branches, others again with tolerably woody stems Some of the flowers are whitish, others are of a greenish cast, whilst others are possessed of a reddish tinge As the flowers of none of these are nearly so beautiful as those of the cultivated sorts, only a plant or two of them should be introduced, which will cause some variety, and serve as a foil to set the others off Described

There is a variety of this species, with Striped leaves

Oak-leaved Honeysuckle is an accidental variety of our Common Woodbine It differs in no respect from it, only that some of the leaves are shaped like those of the Oak-tree, on which account it is valuable, and makes a pretty variety in Collections

There is a variety of this sort, with leaves beautifully variegated, called Striped Oak-leaved Honeysuckle

Red Dutch Honeysuckle is a very good sort It flowers in June, and will often continue in blow a month or two The branches have a smooth purplish bark, and may be known from the others even in winter, when they will appear, with their swelled buds also of that colour The leaves are of an oblong oval figure, and stand opposite by pairs on the branches, on short footstalks The flowers are produced in bunches at the ends of the branches Their outside is red, but within they are of a yellowish colour, and possessed of a delightful odour

The Midsummer Honeysuckle is very much like the former, only the stalks are more slender, of a lighter-brown colour, and the tubes of the flowers are smaller, neither are they so red It will be in blow about Midsummer, and the plant, whether set against a wall, pales, a hedge, or in the ground, will be all over covered with bloom, making an enchanting appearance to the eye, and perfuming the air all around to a considerable distance

Late German Honeysuckle is very much like the Red Dutch, only it blows later It will flower in July and August; and has all the properties of the other sorts, as to fragrance and beauty

The Long blowing Honeysuckle is still another

ther variety of the Dutch It will often exhibit flowers in June, July, and August, tho' the profusion will not be so great as that of the other sorts

Evergreen Honeysuckle is another variety, which retains its leaves all winter It often flowers late in the autumn, and sometimes, in mild seasons, retains its bloom until Christmas, which makes it still more valuable

Trumpet-Honeysuckle. 2 Trumpet Honeysuckles Of these are,

Varieties Virginian Trumpet-Honeysuckle

Carolina Trumpet-Honeysuckle

Evergreen Trumpet-Honeysuckle

described Virginian Trumpet Honeysuckle is the most beautiful of all the sorts, though Nature has denied it smell The branches are slender, smooth, and of a reddish colour The leaves sit close to the branches by pairs They are of an oblong oval figure, and their lower surface is not of so shining a green as the upper Those at the extremity of the branches near the flowers surround the stalk, through which it comes The flowers grow in bunches, at the ends of the shoot, and are of a bright scarlet colour They will often be in blow from June to October, but the flowers have no scent

Carolina Trumpet-Honeysuckle differs in no respect from the former, only that the branches are more slender, and the leaves and flowers also are proportionably smaller, thereby making a pretty variety This sort was introduced into our gardens from Carolina, as was the preceding from Virginia

Evergreen Trumpet-Honeysuckle The leaves are of a thicker substance, and continue on the plants all winter, but the flowers are of a deep scarlet, like the other, and are possessed of little or no fragrance

Manner of propagating the sort by layers The propagation of these sorts is very easy The young branches being laid in the ground any time in the winter, with no other art, will become good plants by the autumn following, and may be then taken off for use

and by cuttings But our common method of propagating these sorts is by cuttings The best month for this work is October By this way prodigious quantities of plants may be raised, and hardly any of them will fail growing So easily may these delightful plants be multiplied, when a plant of each sort is once obtained!

Titles 1 Italian Honeysuckle is titled, *Lonicera floribus verticillatis terminalibus sessilibus, foliis summis connato perfoliatis* Caspar Bauhine calls it, *Periclymenum perfoliatum*, and Dodonæus, *Caprifolium Italicum* It grows naturally in Italy, and most of the southern parts of Europe

2 English Honeysuckle is, *Lonicera capitulis ovatis imbricatis terminalibus, foliis omnibus distinctis* Caspar Bauhine calls it, *Periclymenum non perfoliatum Germanicum*, Tournefort, *Caprifolium Germanicum, flore rubello serotinum*, Gerard, *Periclymenum*, Parkinson, *Periclymenum, sive Caprifolium Germanicum*, and Merret *Periclymenum foliis quercinis* It grows naturally in England, Germany, and many of the midland parts of Europe

3 Trumpet-Honeysuckle is, *Lonicera spicis nudis verticillatis terminalibus, foliis summis connato-perfoliatis* In the *Hortus Cliffortianus* it is termed, *Lonicera floribus capitatis terminalibus, foliis summis connatis, inferioribus petiolatis* Rivinus calls it *Periclymenum Virginianum*, and Hermann, *Periclymenum perfoliatum Virginianum sempervirens & florens* It grows naturally in Virginia and Mexico

# CHAP X

## *LYCIUM*, The BOXTHORN

THERE are several sorts of Boxthorn that require housing in winter, and of which some will do abroad in mild winters, if their situation be warm and good, but there are two sorts which present themselves that bid defiance to our severest weather, and which are both natives of China, from whence the seeds were originally brought These are distinguished by Gardeners by the names of,

Varieties The Broad-leaved Boxthorn

The Long Narrow-leaved Boxthorn

described The Broad-leaved Boxthorn is a rambling plant, and will, if let alone, in a few years overspread every thing that is near it The branches are very many, and spread about in all directions They will lie upon the ground, if unsupported, and will shoot, in a good soil, sixteen feet in length in one summer Those branches that lie upon the ground will strike root, so that from every part fresh shoots will be set forth the next spring, and thus in a few years, they will occupy a large compass of ground so that whenever this plant is desired, they should be constantly kept within bounds Indeed, from its exceeding rambling nature, not above a plant or two for variety or observation should be admitted in hardly any place The branches of this plant are covered with a grey or whitish bark The leaves are of a light, whitish green, and of a thick consistence They grow on the branches, on all sides, by threes This plant, of all the sorts, is possessed of the longest spines (some of which are a foot or more in length) These spines are garnished with leaves, and on these they for the most part stand singly in an alternate manner On the branches where they grow by threes, the middle one is always the largest They are all of an oval, spear shaped figure, are very smooth, a little glossy, and often continue till the middle of winter before they fall off Besides the long leafy thorns before-mentioned, it produces many short sharp spines, of a white colour, near the ends of the shoots The flowers are produced in August, and there will be often a succession of blow until the frosts come on They grow singly at the joints, on short footstalks They are of a purplish colour, small, and are succeeded by no fruit with us as I could observe

The Long Narrow-leaved Boxthorn is also a very great rambler The branches are many, and are produced irregularly on all sides It is

possessed

poſſeſſed of ſpines, but theſe are very ſhort, and the bark with which they are all covered is pretty white The leaves are of a lanceolate figure, and are narrow and long Their colour is that of a whitiſh-green, and they grow alternately on the branches The flowers are ſmall, and appear in July, and are ſucceeded by red berries, which ripen in September, and at that time are very beautiful

Method of propagating it — The propagation of theſe ſorts is by cuttings, for they will grow if planted at any time, in any manner, and in almoſt any ſoil or ſituation, except a white clay, for they do not ſucceed well in our plantations at Gumley Even plants that have been ſet there with good roots have hardly been made to grow, and the moſt flouriſhing of them have been weak, far from rambling, have had an unhealthy look, and their main ſtems have been covered with moſs In a black rich earth, therefore, they will be the moſt healthful and moſt vigorous ſhooters, and though the cuttings will grow at all times, yet the winter-months are to be preferred for the purpoſe

Title. — Theſe ſorts are only varieties of one ſpecies, whoſe title is, *Lycium foliis lanceolatis craſſiuſculis, calycibus bifidis* Du Hamel calls it, *Jaſminoides ſinenſe, halimi folio longiore & anguſtiore*, and Shaw, *Jaſminoides aculeatum, polygoni folio, floribus parvis albidis* It grows naturally in Aſia, Africa, and Europe

Claſs and order in the Linnæan ſyſtem — *Lycium* is of the claſs and order *Pentandria Monogynia*, and the characters are,

The characters — 1 CALYX is an obtuſe, erect, ſmall, permanent perianthium, divided at the top into five parts

2 COROLLA conſiſts of one infundibuliforme petal The tube is cylindric, patent and incurved The limb is cut into five ſmall, obtuſe, ſpreading ſegments

3 STAMINA are five ſubulated filaments, ſhorter than the corolla, having erect antheræ

4 PISTILLUM conſiſts of a roundiſh germen, of a ſimple ſtyle (longer than the ſtamina), and a thick bifid ſtigma

5 PERICARPIUM is a roundiſh berry of two cells

6 SEMINA The ſeeds are numerous and reniforme

# CHAP XI

## *MENISPERMUM*, MOONSEED.

THE ſpecies of Moonſeed which preſent themſelves for our preſent purpoſe are diſtinguiſhed by the names of,

Species — 1 Canada Moonſeed

2 Virginian Moonſeed

3 Carolina Moonſeed

And altho' cuſtom has prevailed thus to diſtinguiſh them, they are all, nevertheleſs, found growing naturally, more or leſs, in all thoſe countries reſpectively, except the laſt, which is ſtill ſuppoſed to be peculiar to Carolina only

Deſcription of the Canada, — 1 The Canada Moonſeed will twine round trees to the height of fifteen or ſixteen feet, and if there be no trees near for it to aſpire by, its almoſt numberleſs branches will twiſt and run among one another, ſo as to form a thick cloſe-ſet bush These twining ſtalks are covered with a ſmooth green bark, though in ſome places they are often reddiſh, and in winter often of a brown colour The leaves are very large, and ſtand ſingly upon long green footſtalks, which alſo have a twining property, and aſſiſt the plant to climb Theſe leaves have their upper ſurface ſmooth, and of a ſtrong green colour, but they are hoary underneath They are what are called peltated leaves The footſtalk is not near the middle of the leaves, but within about a quarter of an inch of the baſe, and from thence it branches into ſeveral veins unto the extremity Theſe peltated leaves are of a roundiſh figure in the whole, though they are angular, and being large, and of a good green, make it a valuable climber The flowers are produced in July, from the ſides of the ſtalks They grow in bunches, and are of a greeniſh colour They are ſucceeded by ſeeds, which often ripen well here

Virginian, — 2 The Virginian Moonſeed differs very little from the other, except in the ſhape of the leaves, for it has the ſame kind of twining ſtalks, produces in great plenty, and the flowers and fructification are the ſame, ſo that nothing more need be obſerved of this, only that the leaves are often heart-ſhaped, and many of them have lobes like thoſe of the common ivy

and Carolina Moonſeed — 3 The Carolina Moonſeed is an herbaceous climber, and will, by the aſſiſtance of trees, riſe to be ten or twelve feet high The twining ſtalks are garniſhed with heart-ſhaped leaves, which do not divide into lobes like the others These leaves, which are of a good ſtrong green colour, have their under ſurface hairy, are much ſmaller than either of the other ſorts, and the ſpecies itſelf is of all the leaſt valuable, as it is ſcarcely ever known to produce flowers here

Culture of the different ſorts — All theſe ſorts propagate themſelves very faſt, for if they are planted in a light ſoil, their roots will ſo ſpread and multiply the ſhoots, that in a few years after planting, each of them being wholly taken up, they may be parted, often into ſome ſcores of plants, which will be fit to ſet out, the weakeſt in the nurſery to gain ſtrength, and the ſtrongeſt where they are to remain Any time from October to March will do for taking off the ſuckers or parting the roots

The young ſhoots, alſo, being covered with mould, will grow, and be good plants in one year

They may be likewiſe raiſed by ſeeds, for if theſe are ſown in the ſpring, in a bed of light earth, half an inch deep, they will come up, and require no other trouble than weeding until they are planted out for good, which will be two years after their appearance, and which may be done very well from the ſeed bed, without previous planting in the nurſery

Titles — 1 The Canada Moonſeed is titled, *Meniſpermum foliis peltatis ſubrotundis angulatis* Tournefort

fort calls it, *Menispermum Canadense scandens, umbilicato folio.* Plukenet, *Hedera monophyllos Virginiana, convolvuli foliis.* It grows naturally in Canada and Virginia.

2. The Virginian Moonseed is, *Menispermum foliis cordatis, peltatis lobatis.* Dillenius calls it, *Menispermum folio hederaceo.* It grows naturally on the sea shore in Virginia and Carolina.

3. The Carolina Moonseed is, *Menispermum foliis cordatis subtus villosis.* It is a native of Carolina.

Class and order in the Linnæan system. The characters.

*Menispermum* is of the class and order *Dioecia Dodecandria*, and the characters are,

I. Male Flowers.

1. CALYX is a perianthium composed of two narrow short leaves.

2. COROLLA. The exterior petals are four, oval, patulous, and equal. The interior petals are eight, oval, and concave.

3. STAMINA are sixteen cylindrical filaments, rather longer than the corolla, having very short, obtuse, four-lobed antheræ.

II. Female Flowers.

1. CALYX. The same as the males.

2. COROLLA. As in the males.

3. STAMINA. There are eight filaments like those of the males, with pellucid sterile antheræ.

4. PISTILLUM consists of two oval, incurved, connivent, pedicellated germina, having solitary, short, recurved styles, with bifid, obtuse stigmas.

5. PERICARPIUM consists of two roundish, reniforme, unilocular berries.

6. SEMEN. The seed is single, reniforme, and large.

# CHAP. XII.

## *PASSIFLORA*, The PASSION-FLOWER.

[illegible]

THERE are many species of this genus, the best of which I shall introduce in this place, called the Common Passion Flower. This wonderful plant, although it has been introduced into our gardens but a few years, is now grown pretty common, which indeed is no wonder, as its propagation is easy, and as a climber, or for the beauty of its flower, it has every claim to recommend itself to our notice. As a climber, it is excellently adapted for the hiding of walls, for the branches may be trained up to their tops, even if they are more than forty feet high, and the length of one summer's shoot they make is really prodigious, being often near twenty feet. But if no such walls want covering, the extraordinary beauty and singularity of the flowers oblige every person of true taste to find some situation for this plant, which I must own does best against a south wall, and ought always to be planted in the most conspicuous point of view. It may be planted also in well-sheltered places in wilderness-quarters, and will climb up other trees to a prodigious height. But as the shoots are rather tender, and subject to be killed by frosts, it is best to plant it against a warm south wall, so that if the winter should prove very severe, it may be covered with mats, and if this be observed, it will survive very hard winters. But when the plants are destroyed, even to the bottom, they for the most part in the spring shoot out afresh; so that people should not be over-hasty in pulling them up, when they have the appearance of being dead.

Description of this plant.

The leaves of this plant are palmated, being shaped like the hand, each is composed of five folioles, the middle one of which is, like the fingers of the hand, longer, and the rest are shorter in the same proportion. These folioles are smooth, and have their edges free from serratures, and all together form a noble leaf. The leaves grow from the joints, on short footstalks, from whence also the claspers come out. From the joints, also, the flowers are produced, in July, August, and September. They are well known, and in some countries serve as monitors to the religious, as shewing the instruments of our Blessed Saviour's Passion; for they bring in the leaves of some the sorts to represent the form part of it, and the contorted columns the flagella with which he was scourged.

I see no ill use to be made of this, and am for encouraging every thing that may raise in us due reflection, and awaken us to a sense of devotion and of our duty. Hear what the excellent poet Rapinus says on the Passion-Flower. Remarks.

*Fervent es etiam tum Granadilla per æstas*
*Prodit, Amazonii quam littore fluminis ortam*
*Ad nos extremo Peruvia misit ab orbe;*
*Caule ea sublimi, vallo prætendit acuto,*
*Spinarum in morem Patiens O Christe, tuorum*
*Inscripta foliis summa instrumenta dolorum*
*Nam surgens flore e medio caput alta triumphis*
*Sustinet, tollit apex clavos imitatus adunco.*

RAPINUS.

Hear also what another ingenious poet says on this subject.

*Pulcher in Americæ musco redolentior est flos,*
*Qui gerit occisi nobile stemma Dei.*
*Consecrata flagrorum cocco stat in orbe columna,*
*Circumstant granis viminea quinque notis.*
*Cum clavis residet spinosa in vertice sertum,*
*Respectus violam pingit ubique cruor,*
*Insitur ... pla te foliis penetrabile ferrum,*
*Sacrum quo fossit lancea dira latus.*
*Sed qui vul... fici flores dant poma cedente,*
*Ambrosius nascet nectar eusque sapor.*
*Portentis nostros, & consona rebus imago,*
*Adstruit antiquam clarificatque fidem*
*Missaque Pontifici Romano circuit orbem,*
*Fertque salutifera nuntia vita crucis.*
*Nam Deus omnipotens nostros tulit ipse dolores*
*Ipsius est nobis crux parcarsus. Amen.*

Upsal, 18 Dec. 1753. NIEREMBERG.

This extraordinary plant is very easily propagated, for it takes freely either by cuttings, layers, or seeds.

1. By cuttings. These should be planted in a most rich soil, at the beginning of March. The Method of propagating it by cutting.

The beds ſhould be immediately hooped, and every day, during the drying March winds and ſun, ſhould be covered with mats, and all the time they ſhould have frequent waterings in the evening. In moiſt, hazy, or cloudy weather, they ſhould be conſtantly uncovered; and with this management many of them will ſtrike root. If, through the heat of ſummer, the mats be applied, and evening waterings continued, the plants being thus kept cool and moiſt, will ſhoot to be good ones by the autumn. During the winter, the mats muſt be applied in froſty weather, and in the ſpring they may be ſet out for good.

Layers. 2. Good plants are obtained by layers, for theſe being laid in the ground in the ſpring, will have ſtruck root, and be good plants for removing the ſpring following.

and by ſeeds. 3. By ſeeds. Theſe ſhould be ſown in pots filled with fine ſandy ſoil, from a rich meadow, and theſe plunged up to the rims in a ſhady border. In theſe pots they will readily come up, and at the approach of winter ſhould be removed into the greenhouſe, or ſet under an hotbed frame. In the ſpring following they may reſume their old place, and the ſpring after that may be ſet out for good.

The after management will be, if planted to climb up trees in warm well-ſheltered places, to take away the dead ſhoots in the ſpring that have been killed by the froſts, for theſe will not only appear unſightly, but by ſhortening the branches it will cauſe them to ſhoot ſtrong and flower better. If planted againſt high walls, they muſt be conſtantly nailed up as they ſhoot; and in the ſpring following, the branches muſt be ſhortened and the others taken away. If they be reduced to about a yard or four feet in length, and all weak ſhoots cut out, you will be pretty ſure of having plenty of good bloom the ſummer after. This ſort is ſucceeded by a large, oval, yellow fruit, which alſo looks well. As this plant is rather tender, and requires mats to be nailed before it in very hard froſts, theſe mats muſt be always taken off immediately on the alteration of weather, for otherwiſe the ſtems will grow mouldy, and be deſtroyed that way. And as it is natural to lay ſtraw, dung, &c. about the ſtems to prevent the froſt penetrating the ground, this dung, &c. muſt not be laid up to the ſtem ſo as to touch it, but all round it; for if it is laid up to the ſtem the bark will be deſtroyed, and the tree killed, and alſo very little chance remain of the root's throwing out freſh ſhoots, as it often does when the plant is killed down to the ground.

Titles. This Paſſion-Flower is titled, *Paſſiflora foliis palmatis integerrimis*. In the *Hortus Cliffortianus* it is termed, *Paſſiflora foliis palmatis quinquepartitis integerrimis, involucris cordatis triphyllis*. Tournefort calls it, *Granadilla polyphyllos, fructu ovato*; Boerhaave, *Granadilla pentaphyllos, flore cæruleo magno*; Michel, *Granadilla indica ſcandens & ſempervirens, radice repente, foliis palmatis, &c.* and Sloane, *Flos paſſionis major pentaphyllos*. It grows naturally in the Braſils.

Claſs and order in the Linnæan ſyſtem. *Paſſiflora* is of the claſs and order *Gynandria Pentandria*; and the characters are,

The characters. 1. Calyx is a plane, coloured perianthium, divided into five parts.

2. Corolla conſiſts of five, ſemi lanceolated, plane, obtuſe petals, of the ſize and figure of the calyx.

The nectarium forms a triple coronet, the exterior of which is the longeſt, and ſurrounds the ſtyle within the petals.

3. Stamina are five ſubulated, patent filaments, fixed to the baſe of the germen, and to the column of the ſtyle, having oblong, obtuſe, incumbent antheræ.

4. Piſtillum conſiſts of a roundiſh germen, placed on a ſtraight cylindrical column, and three ſpreading ſtyles, with capitated ſtigmas.

5. Pericarpium is a fleſhy, oval, unilocular berry, ſitting on a pedicle.

6. Semina. The ſeeds are many, and oval.

## CHAP. XIII.

## *PERIPLOCA*, CLIMBING DOG's BANE.

THE different ſorts of *Periploca* are ſuppoſed to be poſſeſſed of noxious qualities, and, like thoſe of the Dog's Bane, are hurtful if not deſtructive to animals.

The plant deſcribed. The ſpecies for our purpoſe here, uſually called ſimply *Periploca*, or Common Climbing Dog's Bane, or Virginian Silk, is a fine climbing plant, that will wind itſelf with its ligneous branches about whatever tree, hedge, pale, or pole is near it, and will ariſe, by the aſſiſtance of ſuch ſupport, to the height of above thirty feet; and where no tree or ſupport is at hand to wind about, it will knit or entangle itſelf with itſelf, in a moſt complicated manner. The ſtalks of the older branches, which are moſt woody, are covered with a dark-brown bark, whilſt the younger ſhoots are more mottled with the different colours of brown and grey, and the ends of the youngeſt ſhoots are often of a light-green. The ſtalks are round, and the bark is ſmooth. The leaves are the greateſt ornament to this plant; for they are tolerably large, and of a good ſhining green colour on their upper ſurface, and cauſe a variety by exhibiting their under ſurface of an hoary caſt. Their figure is oblong, or rather more inclined to the ſhape of a ſpear, as their ends are pointed, and they ſtand oppoſite by pairs on ſhort footſtalks. Their flowers afford pleaſure to the curious examiner of Nature. Each of them ſingly has a ſtar-like appearance; for though it is compoſed of one petal only, yet the rim is divided into ſegments, which expand in ſuch a manner as to form that figure. Their inſide is hairy, as is alſo the nectarium, which ſurrounds the petal. Four or five of the flowers grow together, forming a kind of umbel. They are of a chocolate colour, are ſmall, and will be in blow in July and Auguſt, and ſometimes in September. In the country where this genus grows naturally, they

they are succeeded by a long taper pod, with compressed seeds, having down to their tops, but I never could perceive such to follow the flowers with us

Culture. The propagation of this climber is very easy, for if the cuttings are planted in a light, moist soil, in the autumn or in the spring, they will readily strike root Three joints at least should be allowed to each cutting They should be the bottom of the preceding summer's shoot, and two of the joints should be planted deep in the soil

Another, and a never-failing method is by layers, for if they are laid down in the ground, or a little soil only loosely thrown over the young preceding summer's shoots, they will strike root at the joints, and be good plants for removing the winter following

Derivation of the generical name. The word *Periploca* is Greek, being compounded of περι and πλοκη, because of its entangling property

Titles. This species is titled, *Periploca floribus interne hirsutis* In the *Hortus Cliffortianus* it is termed, *Periploca foliis lanceolato ovatis* Caspar Bauhine calls it, *Periploca folio oblongo*, Clusius, *Apocynum 2 angustifolium*, and others, *Apocynum foliis oblongis*, & *Periploca folio longo, flore purpurante* It is a native of Syria

This genus is of the class and order *Pentandria Digynia*, and the characters are,

1 CALYX is a small permanent perianthium, divided into five oval segments

2 COROLLA is one plane rotated petal, divided into five oblong, narrow, emarginated segments There is a very small nectarium surrounding the center of the petal, this emits five incurved filaments, that are shorter than the corolla, and are placed alternately with its segments

3 STAMINA consist of five short, incurved, connivent, hairy, filaments, having erect antheræ

4 PISTILLUM consists of a very small bifid germen a cylindrical style, and a capitated pentagonal stigma, on which are situated five oval pedicellated glandules

5 PERICARPIUM consists of two large, oblong, ventricose, follicules, having one cell

6 SEMINA The seeds are numerous, lie over each other imbricatim, and are crowned with down

## CHAP XIV.

## *RHUS, TOXICODENDRON*, The POISON-TREE.

THE general name *Toxicodendron* being now obsolete, the different sorts are arranged under the generical title of *Rhus*, as they are found to be of the same family, and there the reader will find a sort or two with ligneous trailing stalks, that are unable to support themselves without assistance, particularly the sort called the Poison Oak, which, besides the beauty it affords by its well-looking leaves during the whole summer, is desirable on their account in the autumn, when they die to a fine red, and so enlighten the shade of colours at that season, as on that account only to make it valuable, and proper to be used as a trailer, or kept down as a low shrub in plantations of any kind

## CHAP. XV.

## *ROSA*, The ROSE-TREE.

THE Evergreen Rose that has naturally a trailing property, and is well adapted either to mix with evergreens in quarters, or be used as a climber, in this Collection, has been already described, and to that place the curious planter is referred for farther information

CHAP

# CHAP. XVI.

## *RUBUS*, The BRAMBLE.

Species. UNDER this head come of courſe,

1. Common Bramble.
2. Canada Bramble.
3. Cæſian Small Bramble, or Dewberry-buſh.

Common Bramble. 1. The Common Bramble has many peculiarities and beauties to recommend it to the Botaniſt, and nothing but its commonneſs hinders moſt from diſcerning how delightfully the country is ornamented by its flowers in the ſummer, as well as by the load of noble fruit that ſucceeds them in the different tinges of green, red, and black, in the autumn. A philoſopher with delight takes his obſervations, both with reſpect to their manner of ſhooting, flowering, and fruiting; and there are plants enough every where for his inſpection, for they grow almoſt all over England, on which account they are juſtly denied admiſſion into our gardens; and when any appear by ſome caſual ſeeds they are to be extirpated, as intruders into the family of ſhrubs. Though the commonneſs, not its want of beauties, makes the culture of this plant neglected, yet there are ſome varieties of it that have both beauty and ſcarcity to recommend themſelves here. These are,

Varieties.

The Double bloſſomed Bramble.
The Bramble without Thorns.
The Bramble with White Fruit.
The Cut leaved Bramble.
The Variegated Bramble.

described. The Double bloſſomed Bramble differs in no reſpect from the Common Bramble, only, that the flowers are very double. The ſtalks, like that, are cloſely armed on all ſides by ſtrong crooked prickles, that turn backwards. They are, like that, channelled, and in the winter have ſome of a reddiſh-purple colour, others green, ſome red on one ſide and green on the other. The leaves alſo are ſhaped like the hands, and are compoſed ſometimes of three, ſometimes of five lobes. They have their upper ſurface ſmooth, and of a fine green colour, whilſt their under is of a whitiſh colour. The footſtalks that ſupport them are prickly, and a ſeries of prickles are arranged all along the midrib of each lobe. They continue on the plants moſt part of the winter, at the beginning of which they are green, but after Chriſtmas they turn brown, and ſeldom look well after. This is the deſcription of the Common Bramble, and of the Double ſort alſo, which differs in no other reſpect than in the doubleneſs of the flower. They are produced in the ſame manner at the ends of the ſhoots, each of which is exceeding double. The petals are whiter, and as a profuſion of theſe ornament the ends of moſt of the ſhoots in the ſame manner as the flowers of the Common ſort, they make a ſhow, and are beautiful beyond expreſſion. There is hardly any plant more beautiful, or more proper for any plantation than this. In the Former Part it has been ſhewn how it may be kept down, and confined to have the appearance of a flowering-ſhrub; and here, if any part of the wilderneſs is deſigned to repreſent wilds, &c. no plant is more proper than this, as it will ſhoot and run like the Common Bramble, and at the ſame time, without any appearance of deſign, will entertain you with its fair flowers. These flowers are ſucceeded by no fruit.

It will alſo thrive and flower exceeding well under the drip of trees; ſo that for old plantations, this is a uſeful plant for the under ſhrubs, as it will flouriſh where hardly any thing elſe will.

Bramble without Thorns, is not near ſo ſtrong a ſhooter as the Common Bramble, the ſhoots being more trailing and ſlender, perfectly ſmooth, and of a bluiſh colour; and on this account it is that this plant is held as a curioſity. A curioſity, indeed, it is, and many have expreſſed their agreeable ſurpriſe to find a Bramble that they could familiarly handle without hurt. The leaves of this ſort have a bluiſh tinge, and the footſtalks and midrib are entirely free from prickles. It flowers in the ſame manner as the Common Bramble, though the flowers are rather ſmaller, and are ſucceeded by black berries, on which the inſects do not ſeem to ſwarm in ſuch plenty as they do on the other ſort.

Bramble with White Fruit is deemed curious only on that account, and has often given occaſion to a hearty laugh, by a bull which has inſenſibly been made by many on their firſt ſeeing this fruit, who have cried out with ſurpriſe, "Here is a Bramble that bears white blackberries." It is, therefore, the colour of the fruit that makes this ſort coveted, though the leaves are of a lighter green than any of the other ſorts, and on that account make a variety among the leafy tribe.

Bramble with Cut Leaves differs from the Common only in that the leaves are cut in an elegant and beautiful manner. It affords a variety in no other reſpect; and thoſe that are fond of ſuch, are ſure of meeting one in this, whoſe leaves being thin and elegantly cut, make the plant have a different look from the other ſorts.

Variegated Bramble differs in no reſpect from the Common Bramble, only it is a weaker plant. The leaves are ſtriped; and it is valuable only to thoſe who are fond of variegated flowers.

2. Canada Bramble. The ſhoots of this ſpecies are long, ligneous, procumbent, rough, and hairy. The leaves are trifoliate, naked, cut at the edges, ſerrated, and grow on hiſpid footſtalks. The footſtalks of the flowers alſo are hiſpid. They come out from the ends and ſides of the branches, in July and Auguſt, and are ſucceeded by round reddiſh fruit in the autumn. Canada Bramble.

3. *Cæſius*, Small Bramble, or Dewberry buſh. The ſtalks of this ſort are weak, ſlender, prickly and trailing. The leaves are trifoliate, large, and uſually of a duſky green colour. The flowers are whitiſh, come out from the ends and ſides of the branches, in July and Auguſt, and are ſucceeded by large blue fruit, which will be ripe in the autumn, and of which an excellent wine is made. Cæſius.

All theſe ſorts will grow by cuttings. They ſhould be planted in the autumn in a ſhady border, and by the autumn following they will be fit to remove. But as a crop from cuttings Method of propagating them.

often fails, the best way will be to throw some mould over the shoots, as they strike in the spring, and when they have shot two or three feet farther, cover them afresh, and so on all summer By this means, those parts that were first covered will have either struck root, or they, together with all the others, will be preparing to strike root, so that being cut into lengths, and the parts before covered planted again in earth, and about three or four inches of the uncovered part being above ground, almost every one of the cuttings of this nature being thus prepared will grow, and thus plenty of plants may be soon obtained

Titles The Common Bramble is titled, *Rubus foliis quinato digitatis ternatisque, caule petiolisque aculeatis* In the *Hortus Cliffortianus* it is termed, *Rubus caule aculeato, foliis ternatis ac quinatis* Caspar Bauhine calls it, *Rubus vulgaris, sive Rubus fructu nigro*, Cammerarius, *Rubus*, Parkinson, *Rubus vulgaris major*, Magnol, *Rubus flore albo pleno*, and Ray, *Rubus vulgaris major, fructu albo*, &c It grows naturally in most countries of Europe

2 Canada Bramble is, *Rubus foliis ternatis, nudis, caulibus petiolisque hispidis* It grows naturally in Canada

3 *Cæsius*, or Dewberry-bush, is, *Rubus foliis ternatis sub nudis lateralibus bilobis, caule tereti aculeato* In the *Flora Lapponica* it is termed, *Rubus caule aculeato reflexo perenni, foliis ternatis* Caspar Bauhine calls it, *Rubus repens fructu cæsio*, John Bauhine, *Rubus minor fructu cæruleo*, Dodonæus, *Rubus minor*, and Parkinson, *Rubus minor, chamærubus sive humirubus* It grows naturally in moist places in England, and most parts of Europe

# C H A P XVII

## *S M I L A X*, P R I C K L Y B I N D W E E D

SMILAX affords us many species that seem peculiarly adapted by Nature for wilderness-quarters, or to mix with other trees to form any range to terminate any garden, park, lawn, or the like, for they will not only run among and grow under the drip of all trees, but in such places, if tolerably sheltered, they retain their leaves, and will commence ever greens, which property most of them will lose if planted out singly, or by themselves, in open or exposed places The species, then for this purpose are,

Species
1 The Common Rough Bindweed
2 Oriental Rough Bindweed
3 Peruvian Rough Bindweed, or Sarsaparilla
4 Canada Rough Bindweed
5 Laurel-leaved Rough Bindweed
6 Briony leaved Rough Bindweed
7 Lanceolate Rough Bindweed
8 Ivy leaved *Smilax* of Maryland

Common Rough Bindweed described 1 The Common Rough Bindweed is possessed of a long, creeping, white, fleshy root, which sends forth many slender, angular stalks, armed with strong, short, crooked spines, and having claspers If any thing is near for it to climb on, it will by such assistance arrive at the height of ten or twelve feet The leaves are cordated, end in acute points, are of a fine dark green colour, indented, have nine longitudinal veins, have their edges beset with some short spines, and are placed on tolerable long tough footstalks The flowers make no figure They are white, and are produced from the wings of the stalks, in small bunches, in June or July, and the female flowers will be succeeded by round, red berries

Varieties There is a variety of this species, which produces black berries, and from which it differs in no other respect, and which occasions its being called by Gardeners, the Black-fruited Rough Bindweed

There is also another sort, with brown fruit

Description of the Oriental, 2 Oriental Rough Bindweed is a lofty climber, for being planted near pretty tall-growing trees, it will ascend to their very tops, and proudly, by such assistance, shew itself to a great distance The roots are thick, white and fleshy, and the stalks are angular, and armed with spines The leaves are of a pleasant green colour, and are nearly of a sagittated figure They are possessed of no spines, have longitudinal veins, and their footstalks are tolerably long and tough Their flowers are whiter, and are produced in small bunches, in June and July, and the females are succeeded by round red fruit in their own countries, but not with us

3 Peruvian Rough Bindweed, or Sarsaparilla, has also white, thick, fleshy roots These send out angular stalks, that are armed with sharp spines, but they will not climb up trees to near the height of the former The leaves are smooth, being unarmed with spines They are retuse, oval, cordated, of a strong green colour, have three nerves, and grow on strong tough footstalks The flowers are produced in small bunches, from the sides of the branches They are of little figure, and the females are succeeded by a small, round, red fruit, where they grow naturally. Peruvian,

4 Canada Rough Bindweed has long creeping roots, which send forth round, slender stalks, that are thinly guarded with sharp, straight spines The leaves are reniforme, cordated, and have no spines They are broader than they are long, have five strong nerves, and short footstalks, from each of which grow two slender claspers The flowers are produced in small bunches, in June and July They will be succeeded by a small berry, which will not come to perfection here Canada

5 Laurel-leaved Rough Bindweed has round taper stalks, that are beset with spines They are of a strong green colour, and a very thick consistence They have no spines, have three nerves, are of an oval lanceolate figure, and are about the size of those of our Common Bay-tree The flowers are produced in small round bunches, in June and July, from the wings of the stalks, and these are succeeded by small black berries in the autumn This sort is rather of Laurel leaved

of a tender nature, and unless the soil be naturally dry and warm, and the situation well sheltered, they will be pretty sure of being killed in the winter

Black Briony leaved. 6 Black Briony-leaved Rough Bindweed has large, fleshy, white roots, which send forth round, taper, prickly stalks The leaves are oblong, heart-shaped, have no spines, but have many veins running lengthways Their upper surface is of a fine strong green colour, and being tolerably large they make a goodly show The flowers are produced in July, in small loose bunches, and they are succeeded by black berries

and Lanceolate Rough Bindweed 7 Lanceolate Rough Bindweed The stalks are slender, taper, and free from prickles The leaves are spear-shaped, pointed, and unarmed with spines The flowers come out in small clusters, and are succeeded by red berries

Ivy leaved Smilax of Maryland described 8 The Ivy-leaved *Smilax* of Maryland The stalks are angular, herbaceous, unarmed with spines, but possessed of claspers by which they lay hold of any thing near them for support The leaves are oval, free from spines, septemnervous, and grow on footstalks The flowers of this genus make no show, being possessed of no petals except the segments of the calyx Those of this species are very small, and are collected in small umbels They appear in June, and are succeeded by roundish berries, which seldom ripen in England

Methods of propagating these sorts These sorts are all easily propagated, or rather they propagate themselves, if a plant or two of each sort can be obtained, for they are possessed of long creeping roots, which run under the surface of the ground, and will, both near the main plant and far off, send up young ones which being taken up in the autumn or spring, or in any time of the winter will be good plants for use Thus will these plants by Nature furnish you soon with plants enough for your purpose, if one or two of each can be first procured, and planted in a light good soil, in proper beds prepared for the purpose, under warm hedges, or amongst trees in well sheltered places

They are also to be raised from seeds, which may be easily procured from North-America For their reception a place must be marked out for a bed, of a size in proportion to the number of seeds to be sown This ought to be in some open, in a large quarter of the wilderness, or in some grove amongst trees, or under a warm or between a double hedge, and as we may suppose such a spot to be over-run with the roots of the adjacent trees, and the strength of the soil exhausted, all the soil, roots, &c should be cleared away two spit deep, and good fresh soil from under the turf of a rich pasture brought in to fill this place some inches above the level of the surface, and if this be collected a year before with the sward, and by frequent turning all be rotted and incorporated together, it will be so much the better This soil or compost should be naturally sandy, but if it is not inclined to that property, a fourth part of drift-sand should be brought, and well mixed with the earth, all of which being put into the vacated place, it will then be a proper bed for the reception of the seeds In this bed the seeds should be sown two inches deep It will be best to sow them in rows thinly, sticking a peg at the end of each row, as a direction to the rows the seeds were sown in, that more than common care may be had in not disturbing the seeds in weeding the beds, for they will remain there until the second, and sometimes until the third spring before they come up, all which time they should be cleared of weeds as often as they come up, and the beds should be constantly kept moist during the summer, by good watering in dry weather Nothing more need be done to these beds until the plants come up, not a mat in winter, let it be ever so severe, need be added, for Nature will be never the backwarder in disclosing and causing the seeds to germinate, when the congenial warmth of the sun has prepared the beds and them for the purpose in the spring After the plants are come up, if the beds they grow in are so well-sheltered as to take off the edge of the black and piercing frosts, let them come from any quarter, they may be left to nature, if not, some furze bushes should be pricked pretty closely round the bed to answer that purpose In these beds they may remain, without further care for two or three years, by which time most of them will be good plants for setting out where they are to remain

1 The Common Rough Bindweed is titled, *Smilax caule aculeato angulato, foliis dentato aculeatis cordatis novem nervis* In the *Hortus Cliffortianus* it is termed, *Smilax caule angulato aculeato, foliis cordato oblongis acutis aculeatis* Caspar Bauhine calls it, *Smilax aspera, fructu rubente*, also, *Smilax aspera minus spinosa, fructu nigro*, Clusius, *Smilax aspera, rutilo fructu*, also, *Smilax aspera, fructu nigro*, and Plukenet, *Smilax viticulis aspera, foliis longis angustis mucronatis e-vibus auriculis ad basin rotundioribus* It grows naturally in the hedges of Italy, Spain, Sicily, and some parts of France Titles

2 Oriental Rough Bindweed is titled, *Smilax caule aculeato angulato, foliis inermibus cordatis novemnerviis* Tournefort calls it, *Smilax orientalis, sarmentis aculeatis excelsas arbores scandens, foliis non spinosis*, Van Royen, *Smilax caule angulato aculeato alternatim inflexo, foliis sagittatis acutis inermibus*, and Albinus, *Smilax aspera* It grows naturally in many parts of the East

3 Peruvian Rough Bindweed, or Sarsaparilla, is, *Smilax caule aculeato angulato, foliis inermibus ovatis retuso-mucronatis trinerviis* Van Royen calls it, *Smilax caule angulato aculeato, foliis ovatis acutis inermibus*, Plukenet, *Smilax viticulis asperis Virginiana, folio hederaceo lævi zarza nobilissima*, Gronovius, *Smilax caule angulato aculeato foliis dilato cordatis inermibus acutis*, and Caspar Bauhine, *Smilax aspera Peruviana, sive Sarsaparilla* It grows common in Peru, Mexico, and Virginia

4 Canada Rough Bindweed is, *Smilax caule aculeato tereti, foliis inermibus cordatis acuminatis sub septemnerviis* It grows naturally in Canada

5 Laurel leaved Rough Bindweed is, *Smilax caule aculeato tereti, foliis inermibus ovato-lanceolatis trinerviis* Catesby calls it, *Smilax lævis, lauri folio, baccis nigris*, and Plumier, *China altera aculeata, foliis oblongis cuspidatis* It grows wild in Virginia and Carolina

6 Black Briony leaved Rough Bindweed is, *Smilax caule aculeato tereti, foliis inermibus cordatis oblongis septemnerviis* Catesby calls it, *Smilax Bryoniæ nigræ foliis, caule spinoso, baccis nigris* It grows wild in Carolina, Virginia, and Pensylvania

7 Lanceolate Rough Bindweed is, *Smilax caule inermi tereti, foliis inermibus lanceolatis* Catesby calls it, *Smilax non spinosa baccis rubris* It grows in Virginia

8 Ivy-leaved *Smilax* of Maryland is titled, *Smilax caule inermi angulato, foliis inermibus ovatis septemnerviis* Ray calls it, *Smilax lævis Marilandica, foliis hederæ nervosis prælongis pediculis insidentibus, flosculis minimis in umbellam parvam congestis*, and Plukenet, *Smilax claviculata, hederæ*

*hederæ folio, tota levi, e terra Mariana* It grows naturally in Virginia and Maryland

Class and order in the Linnæan system. The characters.

*Smilax* is of the class and order *Dioecia Hexandria*, and the characters are,

I Male Flowers

1 Calyx is a bell shaped perianthium, composed of six oblong, patent leaves

2 Corolla There is none

3 Stamina are six simple filaments, with oblong antheræ

II Female Flowers

1 Calyx is the like perianthium as in the males, but is deciduous

2 Corolla There is none

3 Pistillum consists of an oval germen, and of three very small styles, with oblong, reflexed, downy stigmas

4 Pericarpium is a globular trilocular berry

5 Semina The seeds are globular, and two in number

# CHAP XVIII

## *SOLANUM*, NIGHTSHADE.

Description of this plant.

THE species which offers itself for this place is commonly called, Woody Night Shade It is found growing in our hedges and amongst the bushes in most parts of England, so that it is not so necessary for the Gardener to admit it in his Collection of shrubby plants, neither has the Botanist so great an occasion to find it arranged properly in the wilderness-quarters, amongst the shrubs, to be ready for observation, because in the compass of a small walk, it is probable he may find enough occupying their natural places of growth, and supporting themselves amongst the bushes, by which they are enabled to appear to the best advantage Were it not for the commonness of this plant, however, it would claim a principal place in our esteem, as one of those sorts that require supports to set them off, for besides the flowers, which are of an exquisite fine purple, and grow in bunches, it has many beauties to recommend it to our observation and care Daily observation, as well as the company it is arranged with to be treated of will tell you, that the branches, which are ligneous, are very slender, weak, and flexuous The leaves stand on large footstalks, and their upper ones are of an halberted figure Their beautiful purple flowers will be produced in small clusters, in June and July, and they are succeeded by oblong red berries, which will be ripe in autumn This is the Common sort, which is of all the most beautiful, though rarely ever propagated The varieties of it, however, are in great esteem with most people, and of these there are,

Varieties.

1 A variety with white flowers, which is much coveted on that account, and although these flowers are not so beautiful as the purple ones, yet the sort being a rare plant, makes it desirable, and this is the sort that is cultivated, and which differs in no respect from the purple, only in its white flowers, thereby pleasing the spectator by the variety it affords

2 The next beautiful variety of the Woody Nightshade is that with beautifully variegated leaves These plants are sedulously propagated for the sake of their finely striped leaves, so that there is scarcely a nurseryman who does not raise plenty of them for sale amongst other shrubs, and they are so generally liked, that his disposing of them will be pretty certain This plant, as has been observed, is only the Common Woody Nightshade with the leaves delightfully variegated, its flowers being of the same fine purple, and the fruit that succeeds them exactly the same

3 Another variety has thick leaves, which are very hairy This sort grows chiefly in Africa, and must have a warm situation to live through our winters It is, however, a very fine plant, and where such a situation is not found, ought to be treated as a greenhouse-plant

Culture.

All these sorts are easily propagated by cuttings, for they will grow, if planted in any of the winter months, in almost any soil or situation, and will be good plants for removing by the autumn following If the owner has only a plant or two of these, which he is desirous of multiplying with certainty, let him lay the young stalks upon the ground, and draw over them a little soil, and they will effectually be good plants by the next autumn, and this will be the surest way, as cuttings of most sorts, though they will for the most part take very well, are often attended with much hazard The variegated sort must be planted upon a poor soil, or it will be in danger of running away from its colours And here I cannot but take notice, that notwithstanding I have said they will grow in almost any soil, I never could get them to live in my plantations at Gumley, which is a white clay, for more than two or three years The bottoms would contract a moss, and the tops would die, and thus by degrees they would always die away And in my home gardens at Church-Langton, which are of a strong black mould soil, I hardly ever could keep the variegated sort from running plain So that these common sorts which every hedge-gardener knows how to propagate, and which never sell for more than three pence each plant, has occasioned me more trouble to keep up the sorts, than many curious American plants, whose culture must be studied, and whose price ever bears a proportionate rate

Titles.

The Woody Nightshade is titled, *Solanum caule inermi frutescente flexuoso, foliis superioribus hastatis, racemis cymosis* Caspar Bauhine calls it, *Solanum scandens, sive Dulcamara* and Dillenius, *Solanum dulcamarum Africanum, foliis crassis hirsutis* It grows among hedges and bushes, especially in moist places, in most parts of Europe

Class and order in the Linnæan system. The characters.

*Solanum* is of the class and order *Pentandria Monogynia*, and the characters are,

1 Calyx is a monophyllous permanent perianthium, cut half through into five erect, acute segments

2 COROLLA consists of one rotated petal The tube is very short, the limb is large, plicated, and divided into five pointed spreading segments

3 STAMINA are five very small, subulated, connivent filaments, with oblong, erect, connivent antheræ

4 PISTILLUM consists of a roundish germen, a slender style (longer than the stamina), and an obtuse stigma

5 PERICARPIUM is a roundish, smooth, bilocular berry, punctated at the top, having a convex fleshy receptacle

6 SEMINA The seeds are numerous, roundish and compressed

# CHAP XIX

## *TAMUS*, BLACK BRIONY.

OF this genus there are only two species

Species
1 Common Black Briony
2 Cretan Black Briony

Common Black Briony
1 Common Black Briony This has a very thick, fleshy root, full of a viscous juice, blackish without, white within, and from which issue numerous slender twining stalks, which wind about themselves, or any thing that is near them, and will mount, if supported, to about twelve feet high The leaves are heart-shaped, smooth, undivided, of a shining green colour, and grow alternately on the stalks The flowers come out from the sides of the stalks, in long bunches They are small, of a whitish colour, appear in June and July, and the females are succeeded by round red berries, which ripen in the autumn

Varieties
There is a variety of this with brown, and another with black berries

Cretan Black Briony
2 Cretan Black Briony This has a large, fleshy root, from which issue many slender twining branches, which, if supported, will rise to about the height of the former The leaves are trifid, or divided into three lobes They are of a good green colour, smooth, and grow alternately on the branches The flowers come out in bunches, from the sides of the branches They appear about the same time as the former, and are succeeded by the like kind of red berries

Of the propagating this plant
The propagation of both these sorts is very easy It is effected by parting the roots, or sowing the seeds

The best time of parting the roots is early in the autumn, that they may be established in their new situation before the frosts come on

The seeds also should be sown in the autumn, soon after they are ripe, otherwise they will often lie until the second spring before they make their appearance A very few of these plants in the wilderness, especially of the first sort, which grows common almost every where, will be sufficient The best way is to well-dig the ground under the trees or bushes where you choose they should grow, then put five or six berries in a place, covering them over about half an inch depth of mould They will readily come up, will twist about the trees, and shew themselves to greater advantage than when directed by art in their course

The second sort being of foreign growth is coveted, though the first being common is rarely cultivated A few, however, ought to be raised for variety and observation, and its virtues are of great efficacy in medicine The root is said to be good in dropsies, and when used by way of cataplasm to be serviceable in bruises, swellings, and black or blue marks in the flesh The young shoots afford an admirable pith The berries fetch off the tan specks, and other blemishes of the skin

Titles.
1 Common Black Briony is titled, *Tamus foliis cordatis indivisis* Caspar Bauhine calls it, *Bryonia lævis, sive nigra racemosa, cujus baccæ rufescunt, sive nigrescunt*, also, *Bryonia sylvestris baccifera*, also, *Bryonia lævis, sive nigra racemosa*, and, *Bryonia lævis, sive nigra baccifera* Dodonæus terms it, *Vitis sylvestris, sive Tamus*, Tournefort, *Tamus racemosa, flore minore luteo pallescente* Gerard, *Bryonia nigra*; and Parkinson, *Bryonia sylvestris nigra* It grows naturally among hedges and bushes in England, and in most of the southern parts of Europe, also in the East

2 Cretan Black Briony is, *Tamus foliis trilobis* Tournefort calls it, *Tamus Cretica, trifido folio* It grows naturally in Crete

Class and order in the Linnæan system
*Tamus* is of the class and order *Dioecia Hexandria*, and the characters are,

I Male Flowers

The character.
1 CALYX is a perianthium composed of six oval, spear-shaped leaves, which are spreading at the top

2 COROLLA There is none

3 STAMINA are six simple filaments, shorter than the calyx, having erect antheræ

II Female Flowers

1 CALYX is a monophyllous, bell-shaped, deciduous perianthium, situated above the germen, and divided into six spear-shaped segments

2 COROLLA There is none The nectarium is an oblong punctum, situated on the inside of each segment of the calyx

3 PISTILLUM consists of a large, oval, oblong, smooth germen, under the calyx, and a cylindrical style the length of the calyx, with three reflexed, emarginated, acute stigmas

4 PERICARPIUM is an oval, trilocular berry

5 SEMINA The seeds are two, and globose

# CHAP. XX.

## *VINCA*, PERIWINKLE.

THERE are only three real ſpecies of this genus which will live abroad in the open air, though their varieties are very great. The ſpecies are,

Species.

1. Broad-leaved Periwinkle.
2. Smaller Periwinkle.
3. Yellow Periwinkle.

Remarks.

There are no plants more proper to mix in plantations of any ſort for ornament than the different ſpecies of *Vinca*, with their varieties; but they are very improper for border-flowers, or to be planted in the pleaſure-garden only, as the flowers will be but thinly ſeen over the plant, and they will ſoon over top, without conſtantly keeping in culture, whatever plants are near them; whereas, in wilderneſs quarters, the Larger Green Periwinkle may be planted in different parts, and ſo managed as to have the appearance of a low evergreen ſhrub, which, by its pleaſant green leaves and large blue flowers, though ſparingly produced, will have a good effect; whilſt the Smaller ſort, with its varieties, may not only be made to anſwer the ſame purpoſe, though much lower, but if a quantity of them are planted together, and left to Nature, they will ſo over run the ground, and entangle themſelves with one another, and in different parts will make a *conatus* (as it were) to be uppermoſt, whilſt the other parts will be low, yet healthy and flouriſhing, that they have much the reſemblance, at a diſtance, of rock work. And as all theſe ſorts are very hardy, and will grow under the drip of trees, and flouriſh in all ſoils and ſituations, no plants are more proper to be ſet among low or higher ſhrubs, either in the evergreen or deciduous quarters, to form tufts, or beds for this reſemblance of rock work, or to be placed near other ſhrubs, by whoſe aſſiſtance their ſlender ſtalks may be ſupported to the height Nature will admit them to riſe.

Deſcription of the Large.

1. The Large Green Periwinkle has ſmooth ſtalks of a pale green colour, which, if ſupported, will ariſe to about four or five feet high; but, unſupported, the tops turn again at about two feet high, and thus at a diſtance form the appearance of a round evergreen ſhrub, of that low ſize; and when they are deſigned for this, the ſuckers muſt be always taken off, otherwiſe they will ſoon form themſelves into a pretty large bed; for they will ſend out theſe at ſome diſtance from the mother plant, and the very tops bending to the ground will often take root, which, unleſs taken away or prevented, will ſoon ſpread abroad, and take off the ſhrub like appearance of the plant. The leaves are of a delightful evergreen, and ſtand oppoſite by pairs on ſtrong footſtalks. Their edges are entire, and they are of an oval heart-ſhaped figure. They are ſmooth and ſhining, and very ornamental in the winter months. The flowers are produced from the wings of the ſtalks, almoſt all the year round; for in winter, eſpecially if the weather had been tolerably mild, I hardly ever viewed this plant without obſerving ſome flowers on it, which make it the more valuable. They are large and blue; but there will be ſometimes white ones ſeen amongſt them. They are compoſed of one petal, ſtanding ſingly on upright footſtalks. The tube is narrow, and nearly of a funnel ſhape; but their brim is large and ſpreading, ſo as to form a pretty large well-looking flower. Such are the beauties this plant conſtantly affords for obſervation.

The Common Green Periwinkle.

2. The Common Green Periwinkle has ſmooth, and green ſtalks, like the former, though they are much more weak and ſlender, and will trail along the ground, and ſtrike root at almoſt every joint. So that they will ſoon run a great way, and conſtitute the before mentioned rock work-like appearance; though if they are planted near other ſhrubs, they will riſe to two or three feet high, and will cauſe a pretty look amongſt them this way. The leaves are ſmooth, and of a fine ſhining green colour. They are of an oval figure, their edges are entire, and they ſtand oppoſite by pairs on ſtrong ſhort foot ſtalks. The flowers are compoſed of one petal. They ſpread open at the rims, and grow from the wings of the ſtalks in the ſame manner as the former, though they are much ſmaller; and as they are not ſo ſubject to flower in winter, that is another reaſon for their being held leſs valuable.

The varieties of this ſpecies are,

Varieties.

The Green Periwinkle with Blue Flowers.
The Green Periwinkle with White Flowers.
The Green Periwinkle with Double Blue Flowers.
The Green Periwinkle with Double White Flowers.
The Green Periwinkle with Double Purple Flowers.
The Gold-ſtriped Periwinkle with White, Blue, and Double Flowers.
The Silver-ſtriped Periwinkle with White, Blue, and Double Flowers.

All theſe ſorts are varieties of the Common Periwinkle; though they differ only in the colour or properties of the flowers, or the variegation of the leaves. The White-flowering Periwinkle is this very ſort, only the flowers are white; the Double Periwinkle is the ſame ſort, only the flowers are double and of a reddiſh colour; the Gold-ſtriped Periwinkle is alſo this ſort, only the leaves are beautifully variegated with a gold colour; and the Silver-ſtriped with that of ſilver; and which indeed are ſo completely done, and their ſtripes ſo little ſubject to vary or run away, that they are highly eſteemed amongſt the variegated tribe. There are Double Blue and Double White flowers belonging to both theſe ſorts, and theſe are all the hardy varieties Nature affords us from this genus.

Yellow Periwinkle deſcribed.

3. Yellow Periwinkle has a twining ſlender ſtalk, which twiſts about whatever is near it. The leaves are oblong, and not much unlike thoſe of ſome of our willows. The flowers are both ſingle and double, and thus continue in ſucceſſion from June to the end of ſummer. This ſpecies muſt have a warm light ſoil, and a well-ſheltered ſituation.

Method of propagating theſe ſorts.

The propagation of theſe ſorts may be eaſily ſeen to be not very difficult. With regard to the firſt ſort, the ſuckers it naturally ſends out may be taken up and multiplied at pleasure, and the ends of the shoots that turn again, and strike root into the ground, will be good plants when taken off. Nay, the very cuttings will grow, so that any desired number of these plants, be it ever so great, may be soon obtained. With regard to the other sorts, there is no end of their multiplying, for as they will strike root, if permitted to lie on the ground, at every joint, one good plant of each sort will produce you hundreds of the like in a season or two.

Titles. 1. Broad-leaved Larger Periwinkle is entitled, *Vinca caulibus erectis, foliis ovatis, floribus pedunculatis*. Caspar Bauhine and Dodonæus call it, *Clematis daphnoides major*; Parkinson, *Clematis daphnoides latifolia, sive Vinca pervinca major*; and Gerard, *Clematis daphnoides, sive pervinca major*. It grows naturally in many parts of England, France, and Spain.

2. The Narrow-leaved or Common Periwinkle is, *Vinca caulibus procumbentibus, foliis lanceolato-ovatis*. Caspar Bauhine and Dodonæus call it, *Clematis daphnoides minor*. Parkinson terms it, *Vinca pervinca vulgaris*; and Gerard, *Vinca pervinca minor*. It grows wild under hedges in many parts of Germany, also in France and England.

3. Yellow Periwinkle is, *Vinca caule volubili, foliis oblongis*. Catesby calls it, *Apocynum scandens, salicis folio, flore amplo plano*. It grows naturally in Carolina.

*Vinca* is of the class and order *Pentandria Monogynia*; and the characters are, Class and order in the Linnæan system.

1. CALYX is a permanent perianthium, divided into five erect, acute segments. The characters.

2. COROLLA consists of one salver-shaped petal; the tube of which is longer than the calyx. It is cylindric at the bottom, but broader higher, marked with five lines running the whole length, and has a pentagonal mouth. The limb is horizontal, and is composed of five segments, which are broadest outward, obtuse, obliquely truncated, and grow to the top of the tube.

3. STAMINA are five very short inflexed filaments, with erect, obtuse, crooked, membranaceous antheræ, that are loaded on each side with farina.

4. PISTILLUM. There are two roundish germina, to the sides of which grow two round flat corpuscles. One cylindric style is common to them both. It is longer than the stamina, and has two stigmas, the under one is orbicular and plane, the upper capitated and hollowed.

5. PERICARPIUM consists of two long, taper, erect follicules of one valve, opening lengthways.

6. SEMINA. The seeds are numerous, oblong, cylindric, and furrowed.

## CHAP. XXI.

## *VITIS*, The VINE.

Introductory observations. THE reader must not expect we are bringing in the vast train of viniferous plants, though excellent climbers indeed, and endowed with the more excellent properties of producing fruit, and affording wine of many sorts, to preserve health under proper regulations, and *to make glad the heart of man*. This plant properly belongs to the fruit garden; and what present themselves for our purpose here, are a few oddities, as they are called, or rather scarce species of *Vitis*, which are by no means valuable for their fruit; but only as climbers, and being scarce plants, must be brought in to enrich or complete a Collection of those sorts. These commonly go by the names of,

Species.
1. The Wild Virginian Grape.
2. The Fox-Grape.
3. The Parsly-leaved Grape.
4. The Pepper tree.

Description of the Wild Virginian. 1. The Wild Virginian Grape, if desired for its climbing property, should be planted amongst pretty large trees or shrubs; for, by the assistance of its well holding tendrils, it will arrive to a great height; and if the shrubs that grow near it be low-growing ones, it will entirely over-top them, and in summer, its leaves being large, almost conceal them from the sight. These large ornamental leaves have their edges indented, and are nearly divided into three lobes, tho' they are of a heart-shaped appearance, and downy on their under side. The flowers are produced in bunches, like the other species of the Vine, and they are succeeded by round, rough-flavoured, black fruit.

2. The Fox-Grape. The name of this species naturally brings the fable of the fox and grapes to the memory; and it is very common for those who are not skilled in the history and nature of plants to ask, if this species is not possessed of more excellent properties, or produces more desirable fruit, than most of the other sorts of the vine; whereas, alas! this sort is called the Fox Grape from the flavour of its fruit, which is like the disagreeable scent of a fox, and which name the inhabitants of Virginia, where it grows naturally, have given it on that account. It must, like the former, be planted amongst largish trees, for it will over-top the small ones. The leaves are large, smooth on both sides, of an heart-shaped figure, and their edges are indented. The flowers are produced in the Vine-like bunches, and they are succeeded by black fruit of the above named disagreeable flavour. Fox,

3. The Parsly-leaved Grape. The leaves of this sort are finely divided, and at a distance resemble those of parsly, tho' larger. The stem is very thick, and the shoots are strong, so that when it is planted for a climber, the tallest trees must be appropriated for its support, otherwise it will be too powerful for trees of lower growth. and Parsly leaved Grape,

4. The Pepper-tree is a weaker shooting plant than any of the others, and affords singular beauty from its leaves. Their upper surface is of a fine and the Pepper-tree.

a fine shining green colour, their under is paler, and they are composed of a multitude of folioles of the most elegant and delicate texture. The shoots will arrive to a tolerable height by their tendrils, if they have trees near for their support, but they are very liable to be killed down very low in severe winters, on which account the plant should be stationed at first in a well-sheltered place. Every spring the Gardener should carefully cut off not only the dead shoots, but shorten them within an eye or two of the old wood, which will make them shoot stronger, and the leaves will be larger and finer. The flowers are white, and are produced in bunches from the wings of the stalks, but I have never yet perceived any fruit to succeed them.

The name Pepper-tree is a cant name, and was given it without any meaning by the inhabitants where it grows naturally.

Method of propagating the sorts by cuttings, All these sorts are propagated by cuttings, layers, or suckers. The cutting must be the bottom of the last year's shoot, and if there be a bit of the old wood to it, it will be the better.

layers, When raised from layers, the young branches should be pegged down, and a little soil drawn over them. They will strike root, and become good plants by the season following.

and by suckers. Suckers may be taken from these plants, and must be immediately planted or set in the nursery, for a year to gain strength, before they are set out for good. But there is one objection to plants of this kind. They are always more liable to produce suckers again, and cause more trouble in keeping the mother plants clear of them.

1. The Wild Virginian Grape is titled, *Vitis foliis cordatis subtrilobis dentatis subtus tomentosis*. Caspar Bauhine calls it, *Vitis sylvestris Virginiana*, Plumier, *Vitis hederæ, folio serrato*. It grows common in many parts of North-America. Titles.

2. Fox-Grape is, *Vitis foliis cordatis dentato serratis utrinque nudis*. Plukenet calls it, *Vitis vulpina dicta Virginiana nigra*, and Ray, *Vitis aceris folio*. It is a native of Virginia.

3. Parsly leaved Grape is, *Vitis foliis quinatis foliolis multifidis*. Cornutus calls it, *Vitis laciniatis foliis*, and John Bauhine, *Vitis apii folio*. It grows naturally in Canada.

4. The Pepper-tree is, *Vitis foliis supradecompositis foliolis lateralibus pinnatis*. Plukenet calls it, *Frutex scandens, petroselini foliis, Virginianus, claviculis donatus*. It grows naturally in Virginia and Carolina.

*Vitis* is of the class and order *Pentandria Monogynia*, and the characters are, Class and order in the Linnæan system. The characters.

1. Calyx is a very small perianthium, indented in five parts.

2. Corolla consists of five small petals that drop off.

3. Stamina are five subulated, erect, patent, falling filaments, with simple antheræ.

4. Pistillum. The germen is oval. There is no style; the stigma is capitated and obtuse.

5. Pericarpium is a large, roundish berry, of one cell.

6. Semina are five. They are hard, roundish, and narrow at the base.

A

# COMPLETE BODY

OF

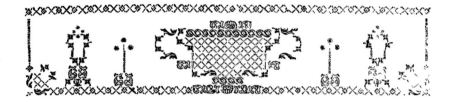

# PLANTING and GARDENING.

## BOOK III.

## PART I.

## Of PRIZE FLOWERS.

### INTRODUCTION.

Introductory Reflections.

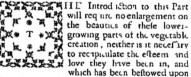

THE Introduction to this Part will require no enlargement on the beauties of theſe lower-growing parts of the vegetable creation, neither is it neceſſary to recapitulate the eſteem and love they have been in, and which has been beſtowed upon them by the wiſeſt of men in all ages, or to allure the reader into a love of what perſons of true taſte muſt naturally eſteem and admire. The purſuer of theſe ſtudies has the ſuperiority of his taſte in ſuch reſearches warranted from the practice of the wiſeſt of all men, who declares he made choice of ſuch works of the creation to be principally the objects of his obſervation, from the vaſt inferiority of the beauty and richeſt attire of the ſplendid monarch in his higheſt pomp to the beauties of one of the meaneſt plants in its natural cloathing and colours.

Our wonder is raiſed, and praiſe and adoration become neceſſary duties every time we view the Heavens, and ſee in what manner that vaſt canopy is ornamented by the number and variety of ſtars. If we take a view of our terreſtrial globe, we ſhall find the ſame cauſe for praiſe and adoration, and amongſt other things, our wonder will be excited by the vegetable works of our Great Creator, who has embelliſhed our globe with them in ſo beautiful a manner, cauſing ſome part of it to produce its ſhare of one ſpecies of plants, whilſt another is poſſeſſed of thoſe of a different nature, thereby occaſioning variety and choice. For as ſtars are to the Heavens its furniture, ornament, and glory, ſo are Flowers to the earth its ornament and glory. Plants, then, and trees, of all the inanimate creation, are moſt worthy our care and protection, and in theſe employments every part of it will turn to our profit, as there are some of them more peculiarly adapted for our encrease of knowledge, others, to bring in revenues to the industrious owners, others, to afford medicine to heal our sickness, others, to make glad the heart of man, and all to afford profit, by improving our meditation and reflection on the all-wise and Bountiful Creator of them

The number of plants that garnish our globe is very great, and new sorts are daily discovered by the curious observers of Nature, traversing the before-untracked parts, in search of such treasures We know of above a thousand distinct and different genera, and that more than twenty thousand species, besides varieties, are found growing in their natural state of wildness, on some part of the globe or other, most of which, with judgment and care, may be naturalized, and made to flourish in our gardens, under the management of a Gardener who is a real artist But we are happy in having many of the above sorts growing naturally in some part or other of our own island, and though they may, and are each possessed of their virtues, beauty, and use, yet they are what are seldom or never cultivated in gardens, so that the Gardener is not to be intimidated at the sight of that great number, as if the care of so large a family was to fall to his lot, since our cultivated sorts, though very great, fall vastly short of that number, and at the same time must give him great pleasure After having enumerated the sorts under his care, both in the wilderness and shrubbery, the annual and perennial Flower-Garden, the Physick and Kitchen-Garden, the Greenhouses, Stoves, &c what strides are made toward a general Collection of these works of Nature, which are daily encreasing in number, and which may be encreased at pleasure from our woods, heaths, meadows, &c where they grow naturally, and where most of them appear with as much beauty as many of the long cultivated sorts There is not a plant but has some part of the globe where its family flourishes in their natural state of wildness, and the most beautiful of these have ever been selected as ornaments to our gardens, and are what we call flowers Though it is common to reject such in those gardens as happen to be where they naturally grow, and to enhance the esteem of all others whose habitations are known to be at a great distance I am for having a few, however, to be admitted, though they grow wild in the next field, to be ready in their regular course for our observation, especially such as have been used to be cultivated, and are most beautiful, whilst the others may fall under inspection when engaged in the circle of a distant walk

The preceding Books of this Work have unfolded the nature and management of a large tract of the larger part of the Vegetable Creation, and the gentleman whose environs we are about to improve and beautify will find a large share of his ground properly disposed and planted, whilst the remaining part is reserved for such articles as are necessary to compleat the whole, and which come of course to be treated of in their regular order, in the course of this work So that the next thing we enter upon now is the doctrine of Flowers, their management and improvement, and the making them truely serviceable to the purposes of philosophy and pleasure For this purpose, we must fix upon a spot of ground for their reception, and properly prepare that; for it would be absurd to engage in the care of a numerous family, without having first prepared proper rooms, lodgings, &c for them. And the spot to be employed this way is, and is what ought to be, called the FLOWER GARDEN

We have supposed, that in laying out the already-planted ground, the place for the Flower-Garden, as well as that for the kitchen-garden, with room for proper seminaries, &c are left marked out for the purpose For before a spade is struck in any work of this kind, the idea of the whole is to be clear in the imagination of the designer, and committed to paper, in order to be transferred to the ground, and every thing fixed on and proved to agree, or there will be no end of alteration and confusion

Our lawn being finished, and our wilderness planted, all redundant trees in our long-standing grove being grubbed up, the winding walks leading us about those left standing, by the sides of which, roses and honeysuckles, laurels and bays, hollies and shrubs, and such perennials as will bear the drip of trees, are planted in their places, our Flower and Kitchen-Garden are next to be laid out and furnished The former is to be of a size in proportion to the greatness of the curious collection to be cultivated, and the latter in proportion to the number or greatness of the family And as the lawn, &c is to front the house if possible, so is the kitchen-garden to be as much out of sight as possible, it being more designed for use than pleasure, and the fixing on a spot quite out of view, behind the outward offices and stables, will not only be attended with the conveniency of having the dung always at hand for use, thereby saving much trouble and expence on that account, but the walls that must necessarily be built for the sake of the fruit as well as other uses, and which are now, in our improved taste, a sight not very tempting, will be the seldomer seen So that leaving a spot the most convenient, the most backward, and least in view, for our Kitchen Garden, the place for our Flower Garden must fall of course on one side of the wilderness or other and then we have only to choose the best land, under some few regulations, or to determine which side, by the superiority of its situation, aspect, conveniency of water, or the like, is the most eligible of the two *Proper situation for a garden*

No other choice, then, are we allowed, and if a gentleman is to have a garden at all, it must be in one or other of these situations How ridiculously absurd, then, are the rules given by our modern Gardeners in the choice of the soil, situation, aspect, water, &c when the situation, &c is to be such as the ground adjacent to the house affords, for we are not to travel to our garden; and yet the requisites to establish a garden are made so many and indispensible, that not one gentleman's house in an hundred, I may say in a thousand, is so happy as to have every thing for the purpose so commodious near it

First, "In the examination of the soil, says "Miller, observe whether there be any heath, "thistles, or the like weeds growing spontaneously, if they do, it is a certain sign the land "is poor" With regard to thistles, their growing naturally in a piece is as sure an indication of good land as bad, for there is no end of them all over the richest pasture, and the annual expence of mowing and keeping them down is very great And though growing of heaths, &c indicates poor land, yet such land is generally of a sandy nature, and if not to be pitched on out of choice, yet it is not wholly to be rejected, as it may with proper management be made to answer every purpose in Gardening *Observations on Miller and Hill*

And

And though the vigour and healthy looks of the large-growing trees and hedges are a sign of a good soil, they are often a sign of a bad one, for there are some soils that will not suit for Gardens in which some trees will be very flourishing and fair, whilst the trees of other hedges, though the soil be rich and good in itself, being at first stunted by being cropped by cattle, or the like, never appear healthy and thriving after However, trees and hedges growing vigorously is a good rule of judging of the soil, tho not too strictly to be adhered to, for the above reasons

Though these reasons are not satisfactory enough, though the trees all around grow vigorously and well, though there be neither heath nor thistles, nor the like weeds, but on the contrary good pasture grass, all this is only encouragement enough for us to try the depth of the soil "And for this, says Miller, dig holes 'in several places, six feet wide and four deep, 'and if you find three feet of good earth, it "will do well, but less than two will not be "sufficient" Hill says, "Let an hole be "opened four spades deep, and if it be a free, "loose, hazel earth, neither very dry nor too "moist, and continue such to the depth of the "fourth spade, it is the most perfect that can "be wished, if it be good for three spades it "will do very well, but if there be much less "than this, it is a reasonable objection" I believe such a sort of soil is very good, and very proper for a plantation or garden of any sort, but I do not know where they will have it We have as rich ground in Leicestershire as in any county of the kingdom, and I have tried our richest pastures, and have ever found the natural vegetative mould to lie no deeper than the depth of one spade, and that they always after that exhibited our Leicestershire clays It has been, nevertheless, such land as has been lett at about thirty shillings per acre for grazing, and was such as might never be objected to, nay, would claim the preference for Planting and Gardening So that if the rules laid down by those two great Gardeners were to be not very strictly adhered to, we should, at least in Leicestershire, have very few gardens But this is not all There must be the following requisites The situation, let the ground be ever so good, is neither to be on the top of an hill, nor in a vale, there must be water for cascades, canals, &c The place must command a prospect of a fine country, &c "It would, says "Miller, be egregious folly to plant a garden "where any of these are wanting"

It is not unnatural to think that this author, instead of recommending Planting and Gardening to his readers, had wrote this article on purpose to frighten them out of it, for though there are some gentlemens seats so situated as to be happy in all these requisites, yet these are to be found very seldom, and are what may be wished for rather than expected, and this should induce us to be contented with our situation, and put us upon improving it to the best advantage

But let us leave these curious designers, and proceed to the management of our own garden upon rational principles As to the spot for the purpose, having, as we may suppose, the choice of two only, that must be left to the judgment of the Gardener or owner The best soil is what I recommend, though if that be counterbalanced by other advantages, of water, prospect, and the like, there are very few who would not choose such a situation Though one thing I must observe, these articles have already been considered in that part of the Pleasure-Garden already laid out, where our serpentine walks are to lead to the finest opens, and our grandest walks, buildings, &c are to command a prospect of as much of the country as may be, so that where this is the case, it will not be found so necessary to have the Flower-Garden so situated, and then the best land, though it should happen to be low, should be ever preferred Let us suppose, then, in the first place, our garden is to be situated in a vale, but not so low as to be subject to inundations, floods, and the like, for this would be an objection indeed, but only upon the lower part of the ground, level and even, or nearly so, the house, with the wilderness, lawns, &c being upon the rising ground, fronting another aspect, and gradually declining to a distant vale We must suppose this, for it is all supposition, and the designer must correct and alter our general rules till they will best answer his purpose, let the situation be what it will Such a low situation as this for the Flower-Garden is the most happy of all others, for, in the first place, we may reasonably suppose it will be the best land In the next place, it will be the warmest in winter, and the soil will be naturally coolest in the summer, and again, there will be the most probability of having all conveniencies of water If the house happens to be built upon a level country, this will fall of course to be near one wing, if on a hill, it may lead to it by a gentle winding walk, planted with tall trees for shade, as well as honeysuckles, roses, sweetbriars, &c or the sloping part may be prepared to be a part of it, and to receive such flowers as will be shewn in their respective order to like such an aspect and situation These things being all agreed to, our ground is now to be laid out, and for this we must proceed upon a different principle than heretofore in what we have already done In the disposition of our trees, whether in our wilderness-works, woods, parks, &c we have followed Nature in the simplest state the appearance of art and form has been avoided, to render the whole more simple and pleasing In our Flower-Garden, however, the ground is to be set out in a formal manner, and the figure is to be either a square, an oblong, a triangle, an octogon, a circle, or some figure the ground will admit of, though the two former of all these are much to be preferred The outlines of this figure are to be first marked out, and the place is to be large in proportion to the number of plants it is to receive And besides this, a spot must be fixed on for the seminary, independent and distinct of itself There should be likewise a place set apart with sheds built for auriculas, &c which should be either bricked or stoned, also a place for the mixing and preparing the different sorts of compost, &c. But this latter, though it would be convenient, will not be absolutely necessary to be near the Flower-Garden, it may be near the stables, or in an unfrequented place behind the Kitchen Garden, or in any place where it cannot be seen But if this cannot be, some quick-growing trees must be planted round the borders of it to conceal it from sight, and indeed with this management it may be fixed in any place that will be most convenient for it, as thereby, if many of these trees are planted, they will not only answer the purpose of concealing the composts, &c but will form the appearance of a large clump, and may be made very ornamental A place, also, for the hotbeds, for raising such seeds as require it, should also be set out, but these may well enough be raised in some hotbeds in the place belonging to the Kitchen-Garden, as there ought never to be more than one yard, if possible, for purposes of that sort

Method of laying out the ground

But let us return to our principal garden It should

should be walled round, or fenced with a yew or holly hedge, and if a real fence from cattle is wanted besides it, a quickset-hedge, or a large ditch, at a proper distance, must be made. The hedges will be more natural, be more pleasing, and will be warmer; though the walls will be wanted, for the tenderest sorts of climbers may be nailed and trained up against them, or such hardy greenhouse-plants may be made to stand our common winters against them with little care. However, these advantages are few in proportion to the great expence of building; and as they do not look so well, draw the air, are colder in winter, and by the reflection of the rays are hotter and very troublesome to walk near in summer, I incline to an hedge fence, and, until these can be grown up, reed fences must supply their places.

Directions for digging.

The bounds of the Flower-Garden being prescribed and finished (for fencing should always be the first thing set about), the ground should be double dug, or trenched. At the bottom of each trench, or under the first spit, common mulch from a farm-yard should be laid; however, less of this in proportion will be necessary, if the soil be good and fresh, and there be a good green sward to be buried low. But tho' we direct double digging, the Gardener should not go strictly to the depth of two spades, if the soil will not require it, but only its natural depth, for the clay, or whatever is under it, should not be turned up; and if the owner should be so lucky as to have it, as Hill and Miller say, three or four spades deep, the vegetative mould should be turned up from the very bottom. Dung should be laid between each stratum, the spit nearest the top should have well-rotted dung that has been preserved for the purpose almost a year before, and as the double or triple digging is finished as you go on, a good sprinkling over the surface of the produce of the compost-yard should be bestowed upon it, or good manure, that by having lain above twelve months at least, and by frequent turnings is nearly converted to rich mould. This last will be absolutely necessary, not only as the surface of the new prepared ground will consist of what lay lowest before, and consequently be less replete with vegetative juices, but the new plants will require such a compost for their roots, to cause them to grow at first, and become luxuriant afterwards.

and laying out the ground for a Flower Garden.

The ground being thus prepared, must be next set out. And first of all, a grand gravel-walk must run straight through the middle, the full length. This walk must be of a breadth in proportion to its length, and must be regulated by the Gardener's judgment, though I cannot but caution him against making it too narrow, notwithstanding it should be of no great length; for a broad walk, especially when it is to be a principal one, always looks bold. The mould where this walk is to fall should be regularly spread over the adjacent trenched ground, which will add something to the depth of the soil. The foundation of the walk should be first laid with rubbish of any sort, such as brick ends, broken stones, slates, or the like. Upon this the gravel is to be laid a foot or more deep. It is to be highest in the middle, but so as hardly to be perceived; for walks too much rounded not only look bad, but to many people will be uneasy and troublesome to walk on. If the ground-plat for the garden be a square or a parallelogram, the gravel-walk should be laid quite round it, leaving only a large border near the wall or fence. If the plat be any irregular figure, it may be made a square or oblong for the principal quarters, whilst the smaller angles or corners on the outside of the walks may be appropriated for the taller-growing perennials, or the less beautiful flowers or physical herbs, or the like, ever making the most beautiful to show themselves in such quarters as they may be expected to be found in. Reed-hedges, if they can be obtained, should accompany each side of the gravel-walk, down the middle, and the side next the center of the garden all round; and if the ground be irregular, and is to be brought into a square by these walks, the reed hedges must be on both sides, to separate the corners and nooks, which would otherwise appear paltry and ill-looking.

Besides this general division, the garden must be divided into lesser squares by reed-hedges, not only to form the different quarters, but that especially by these hedges the whole may be kept warm in winter, and that in summer one side of them may always have shade for such plants as cannot bear the sun. In short, the space included by the gravel walks should be laid out into at least four grand quarters, and these laid out into beds. In one of these quarters should be the annuals, in another the lower growing perennials, in another those of a larger growth, and in another the bulbs. The annuals, in their quarter, should always be attended by tulips, hyacinths, and such bulbous flowers as require to have their roots taken up and planted annually, whilst the other quarters should remain undisturbed for at least two years, when most of the perennials will want to have their roots taken up and divided. Each of these quarters should be laid out into long straight beds, four feet and an half broad, with an alley between each at two feet distance. There should be a double row of flower roots for each bed, tho', among the smaller and least-spreading sorts, three rows may be set along each bed. Nothing but the Gardener's neatness in dressing up these beds will be wanted, nor a bit of any thing for edging, neither should the alleys have any thing to walk on; for without these, every thing will be the plainest and simplest, as to the beds themselves, which will set off the flowers that adorn them: but this method must be taken for the sake of future conveniences.

I have said that the ground should be laid out into four grand quarters, at least; but the reader is not to conclude, that he is to divide his ground, if large, into no more parts. More than double that number may be made, if the Collection is to be large, all square and uniform, with their beds regularly drawn out for planting. The number of annuals of each sort in that quarter, is *ad libitum*; and if show is to be made for ornament, whole beds of many of the sorts are to be planted together. For instance, what can look bolder in the autumn than a large bed of African marygolds, from seeds well sowed, full and good flowers; though there will be no other variety in their colours than that of the pale cream and deep yellow? whilst another large bed planted in the same way with the French marygolds, varies the look with beauties in their way. The different sorts of mallows arranged in a longish large bed, have a picture-like appearance; whilst the sorts of the Chinese asters, continuing their blow late in the autumn, call for our admiration and raise our delight. I mention these as an hint to the Gardener; and after that, his own judgment must direct him to set out every thing properly; for there are some annuals that are preserved chiefly for Botanic observations, and have so little show that a few of them only will be necessary, and these placed always in the least conspicuous part, and

their

there are some, again, that are not by nature to be planted many together, but only properly placed singly in corners, rising ground, or the like, such as the large double sunflower, called mallow, &c.

Rule to be observed in the distribution of perennials.

With regard to the perennials, two only of a sort will be necessary. These should be always booked, with their titles, and number-sticks, or lead, with plain figures, placed by each to a direction. A plant of a sort should be appropriated only to one quarter, whilst another quarter, at as remote a distance as may be, should be occupied by the same number of plants and sorts. These perennial quarters will require new dressing every two years, and this thing is principally to be observed. That altho' there be two quarters here to contain the same number and the same sorts of plants, one of them is to be planted twelve months after the other, and thus while one quarter is flourishing with its perennials of two years old, the other will not be so full and large, but many of them perhaps weak, so as not to shew their flowers fair, which quarter by the year following will be also in its full vigor, whilst the other being taken up, their roots divided, and removed, will make the same kind of show as that before. And thus the Gardener must alternately proceed with his perennials, not only to shew them flourishing in their different states or ages, but effectually to preserve the sorts, for were the roots of almost any plant to be divided and set out at the same time, some unforeseen accident may happen to affect these new-set out plants, and destroy them all, whereas, by this alternate method of dividing, there will always be a bed *de reserve*, to have recourse to to make up such contingencies, as well as to shew the appearance of the same plants at their different years growth.

The Gardener need hardly be told, that every time there is to be a removal of a quarter of perennials, they are not to be planted again in the same quarter, but in some other, and that the ground is to occupy a different produce. Thus the annual quarter is another year to consist of perennials, and that which was before one sort of perennials, must be possessed by another sort, or annuals, and by thus varying the quarter, the plants will always blow better, be stronger, and appear fairer, than if the ground was always to have the same sort, though the addition of new soil was to be added in ever so great a degree. At the removal of every quarter, the ground must be double or triple dug, as before, rotten dung must be laid at the bottom of each trench, and between the strata, and this will always be so converted to a state of rich mould, by the next digging of the quarter, as to be proper for the reception of the roots of new plants. So that with regard to these, one caution only remains to be given, and that is, in marking out the beds, observe to make what was before an alley, to fall out to be in the middle of the bed, and what was before the middle of the bed, an alley. This alternate method is ever to be observed, that the alleys which had lain unoccupied, and a share of the beds whose richness had been somewhat exhausted, may be made the best of, by this interchange of activity and rest.

No other general rules, with regard to the distribution of the plants, need be given, because they should be always varying, and the same quarter should never exhibit the same show for more than two years together, though one rule should be ever observed, and should become general. If the Flower-Garden is contiguous to the house, or is to be commanded from some sitting room, a large quarter near the windows should always have a good quantity of snow drops, Christmas roses, winter aconites, hepaticas, crocusses, Persian iris, and the like, to be fore-runners, as it were, of the Flora [illegible] that is to succeed them, and this will administer pleasure to the eye and much satisfaction to the mind, to behold them in their full bloom and vigor, even at a time when Nature, in every other respect, often looks dreary and uncomfortable, and will hardly permit a nearer approach for the ladies than a distant view through a window. And even then, as there will often be the intervals of sunshine and fine weather, how must this pleasure be heightened to walk abroad in a Flower-Garden in full bloom, in such months as Nature proclaims winter, and at the same time by these flowers proclaims aloud that the spring is at hand, and gives us them as pledges of our future hopes!

Besides these perennial flowers for this spot, there should be plenty of mezereons of their different sorts, almonds, and even some double-blossomed peaches, though they come in the rear of the sorts of this early nature, and if some spurge-laurels be planted, though their flowers are small and inconsiderable (but produced in vast plenty), they will nevertheless direct you to their habitation by the delightful fragrance they continually emit, especially in evenings, or after warm showers. And if some of these are planted under the window of a common sitting-room, or even a bed chamber, they will diffuse their agreeable odours to such places, and strangers who happen to come, and have not been used to them, will express their surprize and satisfaction at so unaccustomed and delicate a treat.

Observations on the introduction of pieces of water into and directions for making reservoirs of water for the use of the flower garden.

Thus may we suppose we have our Flower-Garden finished and well stocked, under such regulations, alterations, and conveniences, as the nature of the ground and situation, and the judgment of the ingenious designer, will direct. Water will be one conveniency that will be much wanted, and the judgment of the Gardener must direct him to make it the most commodious for his purpose, as he can have the opportunity of obtaining it. If a small rill from a neighbouring spring, or a little brook, glides near the spot, its course may be turned, and so directed as to become very ornamental, as well as to afford water for use. It might, perhaps, be made to divide the garden, by being made as a regular canal quite through. Grass walks then, on each side, should be well kept in constant mowing, and sportive fishes, such as play near the surface of the water, should well store it, for the entertainment of the company. If there be no running water, it will perhaps be difficult to form a canal to answer the same purposes, unless there be some land springs to keep it clean and good. However, I advise all thoughts of ornamental water to be given up in this place, unless there be a natural current, and a bason or two contrived in such places as will be most convenient to supply for watering. Indeed, if the Flower-Garden be very large, and a grand gravel walk running down the middle is crossed by another of the same nature, exactly in the center of these a bason may be formed, and tho' it may have no supply from itself or other places, by having the bottom well clayed it might be made to hold water for use, and look well. But unless you are sure it will keep its water of a perfect clearness, it is not worth while to try about it. Let a few pits or holes, that will hold water, be sunk at convenient places, out of the garden, in such spots as will not

not be in view, and let there be a door near each, for the Gardener to fetch in his supply. We can hardly suppose the water in these places to stagnate, as there are very few in which it will, if it has only a free air. However, if this should happen, such water is not to be used, and the plants must be left to struggle with the greatest drought, or have a supply elsewhere. But there is much more bustle made about watering than need to be, for if Planting of all sorts be done properly, and at proper seasons, the ground being also well prepared, there will be little occasion of watering of any sort. I have never been used to water any thing, except plants in pots, or the like (and indeed, out of the many hundred thousands I have raised, had I begun, there would have been no end of it) and hardly a plant in a hundred, in the whole collection, one with another, has failed, unless in such sorts as the land they were planted in was averse to their nature.

What hedges are most proper.

The judgment of the Gardener, under the general directions, must regulate every thing. The reed hedges, though useful and possessed of a neat look, are not too strictly to be observed, as in some places they may be very expensive, and cannot easily be had, and the repeating of such fences may cause a reasonable objection. Haw-hedges, then, to divide the quarters, as well as for warmth and shade, should be planted, neither will it be always necessary to have too many of these. If the situation be well sheltered by adjacent plantations, these may be few in proportion, and the hardiest perennials, which will be very numerous, may occupy from time to time a very large space, without any other division than their common necessary walks.

With regard to the seminary for the supply of these gardens as they shall want, it has been much recommended to let the plants first blow there, that the best sorts being marked, may be afterwards removed into the Flower Garden. This is very bad advice, and should be practised only with such flowers as must ply by the roots, and by the offsets, or the like, which are much better for removing, for in general, plants never blow so fair as they do at first from the seeds, being properly pricked out. So that if more than two plants of a sort are desired, and a number are to be planted in a bed to make a fine figure, they should be planted as close again, or more closer, in proportion to the goodness of the seeds, and the Gardener's eye must constantly go over the bed, as they begin to shew their flowers. He must then pick out all single ones by the very roots, and such as discover bad properties, which he will perceive even before they shew their flowers quite out, and by thus weeding out the bad sorts, the beds will be so thinned as to have a proper number of the best sorts only remaining, which will be always much more fair, strong, and beautiful, than if they had blown before in the seminary, and been removed from thence. This rule, however, is not always to be strictly observed in every sort, for there are some that ought always to blow in the seminary ground before they are admitted into the Flower-Garden, such as carnations, &c as there will be many of them that will not deserve propagation. The best of these, then, are to be layered and the rest thrown away, and these layers jointly will be best qualified to make a show in a large bed the summer after. As this spot is designed for the raising of seedlings of all sorts, so should the offsets of all bulbs here find proper nursing, until they are of age to blow strong and fair, when they also may be promoted to the honour of a place in the Flower Garden.

What flowers should be made to blow in the seminary before removing into the flower garden.

The spot for this nursery must be pitched on by the Gardener, where it will appear convenient, and rather out of sight, for it will not be very necessary to have it near the house or gardens. It should be well sheltered, and have water at hand. As to its lying full upon the sun, as is always recommended, I had much rather it lay full upon the shade, for the sun has destroyed more plants, especially seedlings, than our severest frosts. So that there must be walls, or yew or reed hedges, for the different seedling pots and boxes, to be placed under their shade as the young plants appear in the summer, and as to those which require whole beds, they may be hooped, and covered with mats in the heat of the day, to answer those purposes. The spot designed for shed flowers, especially auriculas, should be near the house, that their enchanting show may be ever ready to attract the ladies observation, as a long walk may not be so agreeable to them at their time of blowing, it being often before the bad weather is past.

Situation most proper for a seminary.

Thus have we now our Flower-Garden, with all its conveniences, added to our wilderness-works, which is another principal step towards completing the environs of a gentleman's seat. In this we have deviated from the modern taste, have run into form, and have approached near to the four walls of our ancestors, but the nature of this garden requires it. Shade and shelter must be had for many of the plants, the sorts must be numbered, and the places marked out and numbered over, to be found as occasion shall require, and they never can be in so commodious a manner as when they are placed in order in beds allotted for them. We have also hitherto fixed our garden in a vale, as being most proper, contrary to all modern directors, who are for the declivity of a hill facing the sun. Our situation will not only be better for the plants, but the mind of the beholder will be more closely fixed upon those objects he there visits for observation of any sort, without having it diverted with external views, and how sweetly will he then walk in the different wildernesses, now secluded by the variety of trees keeping gently growing naturally, now insensibly and on a sudden in a large spacious walk commanding an adjacent country, and furnishing every delight that way? These different gardens will mutually assist to enhance the esteem and pleasure for one and the other, and by this variety fill the mind with a constant supply of delights.

General observations on the preceding precepts.

Seats for rest must, at proper distances, stand in both these gardens, and the Flower Garden should not only have these conveniences, but they must be placed in the shade, under such trees as have been properly stationed for that purpose.

Directions as to seats,

Terras-walks are always convenient and delightful, and if the more rising part of this garden should be possessed of one, it would be called a more finished thing. The nearer this is to the house, it will be the better, though if it does not stand upon a rising ground, the expence of making such terras's will be very great, and indeed are what I think are never *taasti*, unless in making of a large fish pond, or the like, such a quantity of earth may be applied to the purpose, as otherwise could not well be disposed of.

and terras walks.

As soon as ever a terras is finished, it should be planted for shade, and our variety of forest trees will afford him choice enough for his purpose, though there are no trees more proper than our English Elm.

If

General rules reſpecting the ſituation of a flower garden

If the nature of the ſituation be ſuch that the whole of the Flower-Garden muſt of neceſſity fall on the declivity or ſide of a hill, it muſt of courſe command a ſhare of the neighbouring country, and the pleaſure ariſing from ſuch a proſpect is almoſt all the advantage it can afford us, but then it will be very bleak in winter, and hot in ſummer. The beds can never be ſo commodiouſly laid out, without the danger of the mould being waſhed away from the roots of ſome plants, while others are liable to be buried by thoſe that run with the current from the ſtill more riſing ground. And if the declivity in general be not ſo ſteep as to cauſe any danger of this ſort, it will be always very difficult walking on, and the aſcent and deſcent from place to place will be very diſagreeable. The number of gravel-walks muſt be greater, and the expence of ſteps alone would be of itſelf a reaſonable objection. Shelter, in ſuch a ſituation, is not to be obtained, for it muſt lie open to the aſpect it fronts, without the aſſiſtance of helps from plantations for its protection, and if it lies full upon the ſouth, ſouth-eaſt, or weſt, many plants that bid defiance to all cold will be burnt up in ſummer, without a more than common expence of ſhade and water. Beſides all this, I ever found ſuch a ſituation particularly to abound with inſects of all ſorts, and the diſagreeable company of ſuch ſwarms of animalculæ all ſummer will be ſure to be had, particularly the ſmother fly, ſo well known to the Gardener, and which has diſappointed ſo many peoples' expectations both in flowers and fruit. We have only one ſituation more to ſuppoſe, and which can hardly be ſuppoſed to be the lot of the Flower Garden, and that is the top of an hill. If this ſhould happen to be the caſe, bleak as it will naturally be, it may nevertheleſs be helped in that particular in a few years, by a plantation border of the quickeſt-growing trees, ſuch as beech, hornbeam, and Scotch firs, which ſhould be lined by a hedge of the Engliſh elm, and theſe elm-hedges may be continued croſſwiſe, and may divide the ground again, whilſt the yew or reed hedges ſeparate the ſmaller quarters. When neceſſity directs us to ſuch a place, all contrivances muſt be uſed to make it more ſuitable for our purpoſe, and this is an advantage that cannot ſo commodiouſly be had on the declivity of the hill, though there will be a great uncertainty of your having the conveniency of water, which will be more wanted in theſe two laſt ſituations than elſewhere.

Leaving, then, the ingenious Gardener to regulate theſe general rules by the nature of his ground, as it ſhall happen, I ſhall finiſh this head with ſome neceſſary cautions reſpecting gravel walks.

Neceſſary cautions reſpecting gravel walks

Firſt, let me again repeat, that there be a good quantity of rubbiſh at the bottom of every walk, not only to prevent weeds from growing through it, worm caſts, and the like, but to keep the pure gravel from incorporating with the under mould, &c. As any kind of ſtony, broken materials are beſt adapted for this purpoſe, they will probably be more ready to come at than gravel, and then the deeper this is laid, the ſhallower may the ſtratum of gravel be laid on it, though this ſhould not, at leaſt, be thinner than ſix inches, and on your very wide walks muſt be deeper, for the conveniency of rounding it properly, which ought to be ſufficient to drain off the wet as it comes by rain, and yet not ſo much as to make it uneaſy or diſagreeable to walk on. For a gravel-walk of ten feet width ſhould riſe in the middle about two inches, one of twenty feet, four inches, and this proportion is found by experience to be the beſt, and is to be obſerved accordingly in any width whatſoever. With this proportion too the eye will not ſee the bounding, which it ought not, neither will the feet be diſagreeably affected by walking.

There is no country in the world that abounds with ſuch fine gravel as our own, and it is by this that our walks ſo much exceed thoſe of Italy and France, though the beſt ſort is not to be found in every field, and the expence of fetching it at too great a diſtance will be ſo high as to render having it impracticable, which makes the rules given about the choice of gravel almoſt as ridiculous as the choice of the ground, whereas in both, the owner muſt be content with ſuch as Nature has afforded him, and in ſuch reſpects as it is not ſtandard proof with the gravel in other places, he muſt endeavour by art to improve it, or muſt reſt contented under ſuch diſadvantages. When the gravel is compoſed of ſmall pebbles, flints, &c. with a moderate quantity of loam, it is the moſt perfect, and a walk properly laid with ſuch a gravel will bind as hard as a rock. It is the colour of this loam that conſtitutes the beauty of a walk, and that which approaches neareſt to nature is of all others the moſt eligible and agreeable, and though we often find it of a ruſty iron colour, and a diſagreeable brown, yet it is often perfect in its kind, binds equally as hard, and is deficient in no reſpect, except in the diſagreeable caſt ſuch colours will give the walks. The gravel, however, is not to be rejected on that account, for though not quite ſo eligible, it muſt be taken and uſed as Nature's bounty. And theſe colours will often have the better effect near the places where they are taken, as the natural ſoil of the land will often be of that hue, and then this defect in the appearance of the walks is not only diminiſhed, but the colour approaches nearer to the nature of the place.

Where gravel of this ſort is wanting, there are rules for making it, that is, by mixing a quantity of ſmall pebbles, flints, &c. with a moderate proportion of clay or loam. This may do very well for a walk or two, but there will be no end of the trouble and expence of making gravel for large walks in extenſive gardens and plantations, though without a loam with pebbles they will never ſettle hard, will be looſe under the feet, and liable to be kicked about, than which nothing can be more diſagreeable walking on. Again, if there be too great a proportion of loam, this has alſo its terrible diſadvantages, for after a warm ſhower, or the like, it will conſtantly ſtick to your heels in walking, and be very troubleſome that way, and then this muſt be helped with an addition of pebbles, and the like.

The Gardener will now know how to proceed with his gravel. If he has the beſt ſort, happy will it be for him and his maſter, if the other, he will know how to mend it, though perhaps at the expence of deeply draining his maſter's purſe. But as there are ſome ſituations where gravel of no ſort is to be had near, but plenty of ſand, I ſhall ſay ſomething of ſand walks, after having firſt given directions for laying of a gravel-walk.

Directions for laying of a gravel walk

Firſt, having cleared the mould out of the place deſigned for the walk, let at leaſt three rows of pegs be ſet, of the exact height the ſurface of the walk is to be, one row exactly down the middle, which is to be the higheſt, the other at about half way, on each ſide, from the middle to the edge, for theſe will be a ſure direction to the Gardener's eye, and accuracy will be more eaſily had. Then, let the bed of coarſe

coarse gravel, broken stones, rubbish, &c be laid, and let it be rounded in the same manner as the gravel is to lay finally on its surface. By no means roll the rubbish, rake the surface only, tolerably smooth, that the gravel which is to cover it may incorporate and become one with it. As soon as this is done, and not before, let the gravel be brought from the pits, and the walks made up as soon as conveniently may be, otherwise it will lose, in a great measure, its binding property, by being exposed in the open air, for the loam which constitutes that property, like clay, after it has been some time dug up, will soon lose its strength and natural properties. Gravel-walks may be laid any time of the year, but the best season is early in the spring, and of all weather moist or rainy. The gravel must not be fine, for too fine gravel is worse than coarse. All large stones, only, are to be picked out, and it will be then fit for use. The surface must be raked quite smooth and fine, and a good rolling must be bestowed on it, both overthwart as well as lengthways, and if this be done, especially on a rainy day, it will bind as hard as a rock. No roots of perennial weeds can make their way through it, no worms can annoy it, and having the surface so smooth and hard, the seeds of annuals will either blow off, or it will be so improper a bed for vegetation, that they will either not grow, or be so weak as to be destroyed by the very next rolling. A walk thus laid will remain for years. Nor it should not be disturbed, as is the too common practice, by being thrown in ridges for the winter. And here I cannot but lament that unreasonable practice, for, first, the gravel-walks are rendered useless for a large part of the year, and at such a time when they are most wanted, for surely if they are ever necessary, it is at a season when sound walking is hardly any where else to be found. Secondly, by this exposing the gravel turned up in ridges to the open air, the loam loses its natural clamminess and binding property. And thirdly, they will be ever ready to receive the seeds of all weeds, which the wind will not fail to lodge plentifully in them. I hope these considerations, with others that every man's own reason must suggest that considers about it, will put a stop to this inconvenient, unsightly, and unseasonable practice.

Directions for laying of sand walks and where to be used.

Sand-walks may be laid in the same manner as the gravel, and this must also be proportioned with a sufficient quantity of loam, as without this it will not bind, but will be always slipping under the feet, which is both disagreeable and troublesome; and if it consists of too large a share of loam, it will stick to the heels in mild moist weather, and be troublesome that way. Indeed, when necessity obliges the walks to be of sand, they are often attended with these disadvantages, for good sand of those binding qualities is much seldomer to be met with than gravel. Sand, however, is most proper for wildernesses, and among plantations of trees of all sorts, for when these are laid with the best of gravel, the dripping of trees will in time, worse than heavy rains, impair the surface, work the loam away, and leave the pebbles uneven, naked, and disagreeable, whereas, sand is not only not subject to such disadvantages, but such walks will have more the look of nature, winding about in that easy manner as they are made to do where Nature is mostly to be imitated. Horrid, therefore, beyond conception (however useful if no others can be procured), are walks composed of pounded shells, seacoal ashes, &c. Miller says, that seacoal ashes are preferable to most materials for the walks in wilderness quarters. How much of a piece must this be with our other works there, copying Nature in her sweetest attire! How charmingly must the hue of such walks agree with the verdure and delights of the shrubby tribe, not to mention how agreeably the scent arising from such materials must coincide with the fragrance which the profusion of flowers will continually bestow?

Images, by many people, are still in very great request, and if any gentleman should happen to have Mr Miller's taste in that particular, I would advise him, to finish the character, at the end of such a walk, or in some convenient place, to fix up the statues of a group of blacksmiths.

Grass walks objected to in flower garden.

When materials for any of these kinds of walks are difficult to come at, the number of grass-walks must be multiplied, but this will be a very disagreeable necessity, especially in the Flower Garden, for, by constant use, pads, or bare paths, will be made, which will look very bad. Neither will they be so proper in evenings and mornings, the most common times for walking, these being then damp and dewy, and not only improper, but to some constitutions dangerous; and in all moist weather, especially all the winter, they are never so comfortable. So that walks of this kind especially in such places, are always to be as few as possible; though, in your larger and more open works, they look very well, approach nearer to Nature by their constant verdure, have the advantage of all other walks in being more easy for walking on in summer and hot weather, but here they are more to be considered as sheets or carpets of grass, for surely nothing can be conceived so bad as a long slip of grass, by way of a walk, running forward to a great length, which should teach us, when grass, for the convenience of walking, is to be laid, it should be broad and spreading, though the length be ever so short. Neither should the edges be limited, or kept exactly to the same breadth, but it is to be extended to the edge or border of the clump or different quarters they are designed to separate, and these, whether they are on a rising ground, forming a kind of mount or in a vale, are to have their grass-plats brought regularly to them, in an easy natural way, and if this be judiciously done, Nature will be in her proper dress, and the whole will be delightful. And in this respect, let the number of gravel-walks be ever so great, some of this kind, to divide the different quarters or opens, are always to be had. In order, therefore, to lay grass walks, plats, or carpets of this kind, let the turf be laid bare, and the roots of all perennial weeds entirely grubbed up, then let the Gardener's eye direct him to such earth as is ... where the hollows are too great, and let the lowering of one be applied to the rise of the other. After regulating these things as near as possible with a general view, let him come to a more close and narrow inspection, for the more accurately finishing the whole, and, as he finds it by the laws of proportion, let him stick pegs, the tops of which should be even with the surface the grass is to form. This being done, let the ground be raised or taken away to near the tops of the pegs, that the turf being raked and rammed down may form a level. Then sprinkle a little fine garden mould over such places as the soil has been pared off and is hard, for the root of the turf to strike into and in such places where this is to be sprinkled, for there will be no occasion in the raised parts, allowance must be made for the rise the ground will have by

Though proper in some works.

Rules for laying grass walks.

such sprinkling, which need be very small If it be late in the spring, or in the summer, a good watering, before the turf is laid, should be bestowed on it; but if it be in the winter, or early in the spring, which is the best of all times, there will be no occasion for that The turf should be laid as soon as possible after taking up, and while the ingenious Gardener is busy at this work, properly instructed hands, as every Gardener knows, with sharp turfing irons, should be engaged in taking up more for his supply, and thus the work will go regularly on until it is finished After the turf is laid, a sufficient number of hands should be employed, with broad bottomed rammers, to settle it well, and form the surface even Next a good rolling must be given it; afterwards a good watering all over, then immediately another good rolling, and the work is finished

If the turf is laid in very dry weather, or in the summer, or a succession of dry weather should happen, it will divide at the joints, lose its colour, and have the appearance of being dead But the owner need not be under great apprehensions on that account, for as the rains come on it will close again, and by degrees resume its verdure

When a large quantity of turf is wanted, to save expence, the sowing of grass-seeds has been recommended But this is a very bad way, for these walks will be many years before they will be tolerable, and will never be so fine as those that are at once made by turfing, which, tho' expensive, are from the first in their full perfection

Rules to be observed when the grass is to be sowed — When the grass is to be sowed, the properties of the ground are to be as before, only greater pains must be taken in covering the surface with fine good garden-mould, for its reception This being raked smooth, the seeds should be sown very thick, and then raked smooth and fine again Little need be done to it the first year, besides weeding It need not be mowed more than two or three times, that the roots may first get strong, by which they will be better able to spread, and mix one among another Little rolling for the first year will be required The second year, and ever after, the oftener the mowing and rolling is repeated the better, and in time, with good management, a tolerable good surface of grass may be had The chief difficulty will be to obtain good seeds: Those from a common haystack have been recommended, but they will for the most part be very improper, as they consist of all sorts promiscuously, among which will be thousands that will not do.

Method to obtain good grass-seed — The way, then, to have this method put in practice in its greatest perfection is, to mark out a piece of ground that affords the finest turf when grazed, and the purest grass for mowing. This should be laid the year before; and two or three times, or more, as regularly as weeding for a crop of grain, this piece should be gone over, and the heads of all improper seeds pulled off This grass should stand long before it is mowed, the better to ripen the seeds; and tho' the hay may not be so fine, yet there will be more of it, it may answer better for many sorts of cattle, and the seeds will be sure to be good However, I do not lay much stress upon this; for plenty of good seeds may be obtained, if cut at the usual time I am not for spoiling a crop of grass; but if the mowing be deferred only a few days, the seeds will be proportionally better There are some who are for going over the piece with sacks, when the seeds are ripe, and plucking the heads of none but the pure pasture-grass This is a sure and very good way; but it will be attended with much trouble, and the crop itself will be damaged for mowing and hay So that if a proper spot be pitched on, and the above weeding observed, no reasonable objection can be made to the seeds such hay will afford Constant mowing and rolling are the essential articles to keep grass-walks fine and in good order, and when there are large tracts of this kind, and a horse is used for the roll, he should be without shoes, and his feet be well muffled with thick woollen cloths. Where men are to draw the roll, flat shoes with no heels are ordered to be worn, but this is an over nicety, and nothing but bowling-greens call for shoes of a particular make

The greatest enemies to grass-walks are worms, to destroy which, ducks are the properest instruments If, therefore, a quantity of ducks be permitted to range in such places, they will eat the dew-worms, and prevent the mischiefs done by their casts, &c as well as be the devourers of young frogs, toads, and many other disagreeable insects

## Of SHED or PRIZE FLOWERS.

Introductory observations — WE shall treat of Perennial Flowers as they come of course in their alphabetical order, but before we enter upon these, it may not be amiss to give the management of such plants as are commonly distinguished by their being cultivated in large quantities together, to form a bed, or furnish a shed prepared for the purpose, of more than ordinary beauty and splendor To treat of these plants as distinct and separate of themselves, will by no means be improper, as there are many gentlemen of small fortunes, even in towns, nay tradesmen, whose appetites ought to be indulged in this innocent delightful way, and who having a spot of ground are for appropriating their leisure hours to the care of these sorts of plants, without having fortune, time, or room, for a more general collection, an employment truly commendable, and conducive to more peace and inward satisfaction than the frequent methods in which the generality of people consume those hours that do not immediately call for their attendance on their trades or domestic concerns, called Leisure Hours

It is a knowledge of the management and perfection of these sorts of flowers that chiefly constitutes the title or appellation of Florist, and a person claims it as his right to be so called who

who has a good Collection, and has studied and made himself master of their nature. So that this title is of small latitude, and very different from that of Botanist, which includes a knowledge of plants in general, founded upon different principles; for there are many terms, phrases, and rules, to be observed among florists that are unknown in science, and which the rigid botanists, as such, look upon as too trifling, and beneath their notice. Linnæus himself is a great enemy to such distinctions and appellations. He calls them idle nonsense, and warns all true lovers of the science from catching the infection.

*Difference between a florist and a botanist.*

But this is very harsh and implicit; for if a man has neither time, nor advantage, nor learning, nor abilities, for becoming a thorough adept in the science, is he not to amuse himself in this pleasing way, and comply with custom in such innocent distinctions? Is a man who has little fortune or [illegible] and for a general Collection, to have nothing of this noble part to employ his leisure time, and keep up the distinctions which Custom has taught him, and by which their differences are known? Nay, should not a man who has all advantages of education and fortune, one who is a thorough master of the science, and has laid out his extensive grounds in the manner we have shewn him, is he to have a few plants only of this sort for botanic observation, and like his inferior neighbours, have no general Collection? or, if he has, are not the customary names or distinction, whereby to know one sort from another, to be used? Surely they are, and are as necessary to a florist, as such, as the real titles in science are to a botanist. The manner of naming flowers affords matter of merriment more than objection, and are generally given by such Gardeners as had the good fortune first to obtain them from seeds. They are generally very pompous, being sometimes named after the heathen gods and goddesses. Sometimes a great statesman, or general, is metamorphosed into a flower, sometimes a celebrated toast; but of all the curious names, I had a very excellent carnation sent to me, entitled, "the Duchess of Hamilton's Pride."

*[illegible] terms used by florists.*

*Names of flowers.*

The florists are now become more numerous in England than has been known in any preceding age, and the culture and management of those flowers that more immediately concern them are brought to a degree of perfection never heard of before. And indeed there is now the greatest encouragement for it, more than ever was known. Gentlemen are become patrons particularly of these sorts of flowers, and many clubs have been founded and feasts established, where premiums are allowed to him who exhibits the best and fairest.

These feasts are now become general, and are regularly held at towns, at a proper distance, almost all over England. At these exhibitions, let not the Gardener be dejected if a weaver runs away with the prize, as is often done, for the many articles he has to manage demand his attention in many places. A very small shower, which may come unexpectedly, when he is engaged in other necessary work at a distance, will take off the elegance of a prize auricula or carnation; whereas your tradesman who makes pretensions to a show, will be ever at hand, can help his pots into the sun, and again into the shade, can refresh them with air, or cover them on the least appearance of a black cloud; and this will be an ease and a pleasure to him, and enable him to go to his work with more alacrity. Thus, when tradesmen have made their flowers their study, and are thoroughly acquainted with their nature, they have the advantage of being near at hand to encourage and protect them. And it is from these advantages that they often exhibit the fairest flowers, and that a weaver, or the like, will often run away with the prize at those feasts, from Gardeners of the first abilities and practice.

*A [illegible] Gardener seldom gains the prize at florists feasts.*

Flowers that more peculiarly require to be exhibited in beds, pots, or the like, in large quantities together, to form the best show their nature is capable of, and which will be the grandest and most pleasing of all the flowery tribe, are chiefly that species of *Primula*, with its varieties, called *Polyanthus*, the *Auricula Ursi*, and *Carnation*. These are fibrous-rooted plants, and it is chiefly to him who excels in his exhibition of one or other of these sorts, that the prize at feasts is adjudged.

*The sorts usually exhibited at the above feasts.*

The other sorts that are cultivated in large companies are chiefly bulbous or tuberous-rooted plants, such as hyacinths, anemonies, tulips, &c. Excellence in one or other of these, also, in many places obtains prizes; but in my neighbourhood their culture is not so general. So that we shall begin with our common Prize-Flowers, and shall proceed to other flowers, as they come of course in order.

## *PRIMULA*, The POLYANTHUS PRIMROSE

THE Gardener scarcely need be informed, that the cowslip, the oxslip, and the Common Primrose of our woods, are all very near relations of the Polyanthus. These have all their beauties, and will come of course to be considered amongst perennial flower-roots, being seldom cultivated in gardens, much less in beds for show, though there are varieties of some of these species that deserve all care and management this way, having every beauty to recommend them, and which are delightful when assembled together, uniting their common charms; and these are, the Double Yellow, the Double White, the Double Crimson Primrose, the Double Scarlet Cowslip and Oxslip. These are ornaments, indeed, to the borders of the Flower-Garden, and this hint is given to the Gardener, that he should have a bed or two of them planted in the manner we shall direct for the Polyanthus Primrose.

We are now speaking to the florist, however, let him not be offended if we inform him of the meaning of the title of this plant. It is formed of the two Greek words πολυς, *multus*, and ανθος, *flos*, and is so called from the many flowers growing together in a head from one common stalk.

*Derivation of the title.*

ſtalk. Neither need it give him much offence to be told, that the Polyanthus is originally a native of Turkey, where it ſtill flouriſhes, in the manner of the Common Primroſe with us, in all its native luxuriance and beauty.

With us, the Polyanthus is one of the moſt beautiful of all our ſpring flowers, and has other properties to make it ſtill more deſerving. One or other of theſe plants will exhibit their flowers in autumn, and even late in that ſeaſon, when few others are to be ſeen; nay, if the winter is mild, they will not fail to furniſh you with ſome of their preſents during the greateſt part of it; and every one knows the value of a flower in any tolerable degree of perfection in ſuch ſeaſons. But here it muſt be obſerved, our directions are, to plant theſe flowers in a ſhady border, as being moſt ſuitable to their nature. In ſuch ſhady borders the flowers will appear leſs frequent, either in autumn or winter, ſo that when they are deſired at thoſe ſeaſons, a warm well ſheltered border, full upon the ſouth or ſouth-eaſt, ſhould be prepared for their reception. Here they will never fail your intentions, and often flower too in ſuch quantities, as will conſtitute what may be called a tolerable good blow. When this is the caſe, the borders (which ſhould be as near the parlour or ſitting room as poſſible) ſhould be hooped, and covered with mats in the evening, and taken off again in the morning. They ſhould alſo be covered in all miſty and rainy weather, and uncovered again when it is quite clear; and with this little trouble, punctually beſtowed, their flowers may be ſeen in beauty, though perhaps not in perfection, or in very large quantities, in thoſe unexpected and unuſual months.

*Directions where theſe flowers ſhould be planted.*

To have theſe flowers, however, in perfection, all in blow at their uſual time in the ſpring, they ſhould be planted in a ſhady border; and here they will not have that tendency to blow, as in warmer places, at unuſual times; or when they do, their flower-buds ſhould be nipped off as they appear, that the root may be exhauſted of none of its ſtrength, and that all may unite in their full vigour to exhibit as perfect a blow as poſſible. The roots ſhould be at ſix inches aſunder; and the longer and broader the border is, thus properly furniſhed, the greater and more amazing will be the exhibition. The ſoil ſhould be rich with dung, well dug in and mixed the year before; and it matters very little with what ſort, for the ſoil being ſuppoſed to be ſhady and cool, that from the hall-muckhill, if it be well rotten, is not to be objected to; though it will be better if it be ſuch as is compoſed of different ſorts, ſuch as that of old thatch, ſaw duſt, ſweepings of yards, and the like, all mixed together; and if the ſoil be naturally dry and hot, the greateſt ſhare of the enrichment then ſhould be of neat dung. Any of theſe ſhould be laid on the borders, well dug in and mixed with the natural mould, and it will be well prepared for receiving the plants, without the expence and trouble of wheeling our the natural mould, and bringing in compoſt, as directed to be prepared by different authors. Theſe compoſts, however good in themſelves, are not neceſſary. The other method will do very well, and the gentleman or his pocket ſhould never be made to tire by ſuch expences as may be avoided.

*Situation, ſoil, &c. moſt proper for theſe plants.*

Though we adviſe the planting them in a ſhady border, we would not be underſtood that the ſun is of no ſervice to theſe flowers. Could it be had early in the ſpring, a little before, and at the time the flower-buds begin to ſhew themſelves, it would be of vaſt ſervice in bringing them forward. But theſe are advantages that are no ways adequate to the miſchiefs it will afterwards occaſion to theſe plants and its flowers. There are very few adapted to bear the blaze of the noon-day ſun; and it is really a ſhocking ſight to behold theſe plants that are in open warm borders ſtruck flat and deprived of almoſt all appearance of life by the ſun, as the ſummer advances. The leaves will be withered, and if the roots are not killed, they will be impaired, and not near ſo ſtrong to exhibit their blow the ſpring after. Such will be the diſadvantages attending the roots; the flowers alſo will ſuffer as the ſun becomes powerful; and where they are to ſuſtain its full blaze, the ſhow will be paſt its beauty the ſooner by ſome weeks. If the beſt flowers of theſe plants are to be ſhewn for a prize, they ſhould be covered from wet and dews, which will diminiſh their beauty and perfection; and where the owner is nice about them, the beds ſhould be hooped and covered with mats in all rainy and moiſt weather. But when a ſhow is to be exhibited at no ſtated time this will not be abſolutely neceſſary, as thoſe flowers that have ſuffered will go off, and a freſh ſucceſſion in a few days, of ſuch admirable beauty as to keep up the uſual appearance, ſucceed them.

*Method of propagating them,*

The uſual method of cultivating theſe flowers is by offſets, or parting of the roots; and if a flower is once obtained that has good properties, this is planted out by thoſe who raiſe them for ſale, to be encreaſed by the roots, and ſold, which they do now indeed at a very great rate. But this is a very bad method; and out of a thouſand old roots, parted and planted with all the art imaginable, a good blow is hardly to be obtained. There is only one method for this, and that is by ſeeds; for it is from ſeedling plants, at their firſt blow, that perfection muſt be expected, and theſe being removed afterward, will never be the ſame again. So that in order to keep up this ſtock, there ſhould be a ſucceſſion of beds, raiſed by a ſucceſſion of ſeeds, and this muſt be the method to have a good ſtock of theſe flowers. And for this, let us ſuppoſe a perſon deſtitute of any of them. He muſt hardly ever think of getting good ſeeds; he muſt raiſe them himſelf by proceeding in the following manner.

*and of procuring good ſeed.*

Let him purchaſe ſome roots of the beſt ſorts that have been raiſed for ſale; a few will do, and his general collection may come on gradually, at no great expence; but if he is deſirous to accelerate this, more money muſt be laid out in more roots, in order to obtain a greater quantity of ſeeds. A rich bed, compoſed of dung converted to a mould, with a ſmall mixture of drift ſand and the natural ſoil, ſhould be prepared for their reception; and it is from theſe plants the ſeeds are to be raiſed. If they are planted any time in the autumn, or winter, or even juſt before they flower, they will flower, and the ſeeds ripen kindly after; ſo that if a perſon has marked ſuch as he makes choice of when in blow, he may afterwards tranſplant them at his leiſure to his own beds; or if he knows the ſorts by name or character, it may ſave a year in time, by his getting them immediately into poſſeſſion, that the ſucceeding flowers and ſeeds may be his own. After the flowers are over, and the dry warm weather comes on, every other evening the roots ſhould be watered, by which means the ſeed will be fairer, and more of it will come to perfection. As ſoon as the capſules begin to open, watering muſt be left off, for the ſeeds will then be nearly ripe, at which time they ſhould be every day looked over, and ſuch heads as become quite brown, their veſſels opening, ſhould be gathered; for they will then diſcharge the ſeed, and if this care is not taken, the beſt of it will be loſt. The firſt week in June we may ſuppoſe the ſeeds

to

to be ripe, and that there will be some time between those that are first ripe and the latest, so that the first gathered should be laid on a dry warm shelf, being spread on a piece of writing paper, and the rest as they are gathered should be added to them. As soon as they are all gathered, which we may suppose to be at the distance of about eight or ten days, then is the time for their being sown, or if the seeds be many, the first gathered should be sown first, and the later should not be kept out of the ground more than three or four days after. It is necessary the seeds be dry before they are sown, but not hardened, for they will be the longer before they come up. They will do very well, if sown in a fine rich border, but that less of the seeds may be lost, as well as for other conveniences in winter, it will be best to sow them in boxes, about six inches deep, with holes at the bottom to drain off the wet. Neats dung converted to a mould, with about a fourth part of fine natural garden soil, and a fourth part of drift sand, all well mixed together, is the best for their reception, though almost any other fine rich mould will do.

The boxes should be then filled, a few oyster-shells or the like covering the holes, and the sides well shaken to settle the mould, the surface of which being smooth, the seeds should be sown, but not too thick, which would occasion many of them being lost. After this, they should be gently pressed down with a trowel, or the like, and a little mould sprinkled over them. This should be done so sparingly as to be hardly called a covering, at most it ought not to be deeper than the breadth of a barley-corn. The boxes should be next removed into the shade, and the business is done.

In about three weeks they will come up. A little watering must be given them at times all summer, and by October they will be tolerably good strong plants. As the frosts come on they should be placed under a hotbed-frame, or housed, not because they are tender, but because it will throw them out of the ground, and this will be the conveniency of sowing them in pots or boxes, rather than in open beds. When necessity, however, obliges the latter to be done, they should be hooped, and covered with mats in such weather, to preserve them from the like danger. In March, the largest of these plants should be planted out for good, in good rich borders, at about three or four inches asunder, and in the spring following they will shew their flowers.

We may suppose half of them to be not worth preserving, which is my reason for ordering them to be planted out so close, so that if every other plant be pulled up and thrown away, they will be at about six or seven inches asunder, their proper distance for remaining. At their first shewing their flowers, the bad ones should be plucked up and thrown away, and though we cannot suppose this to be every other in order, yet by taking out about half the quantity, a proper thinning will be made, and though three or four, or more, should remain together unremoved, yet the contiguous ones being taken off, room will be made for their spreading. Thus will this bed, for about three seasons, exhibit a most perfect blow, such a one as can never be obtained from offsets or removed old plants, be the sorts ever so valuable.

Caution ary remark. This shews their absurdity, and how little those persons must be acquainted with the true nature of these plants, who order them to be planted out in a nursery till they have flowered, and then the best of them marked and taken up to be set in the Flower-Garden. How absurd also is the ordering the seeds to be kept until the beginning of January before they are sown! They will seldom, then, with the best management, come up before the end of April, and will not be fit to plant out before the March after, so that a whole year is lost, besides a large share of the seeds, which will not grow so regularly if kept beyond that time. Both these erroneous practices are enforced and recommended by Mr Miller and Dr Hill, to the great loss of a gentleman's time and expectation, and to obviate which for the future is the design of these remarks. But to return.

The same boxes that had their largest plants pricked out the spring before, will have a fresh supply for planting out, and this bed will succeed the other in order. We suppose the boxes to be either large, or many of them, or these beds will be small, however, it is not so very material at first, you will have flowers ever after to produce you what quantity of seeds you require. These beds will be in their greatest perfection the second year of their blowing, the roots will be strong, and they will throw out the flowers also vigorous and strong. The third year also they will be excellent, though probably in every respect not so fair as the spring before, at the close of which their extreme beauty will be past. They will after that degenerate, and every year get worse and worse; so that seeds should be sown, and other beds should be prepared in the same manner, to succeed them.

These seeds should be collected from the flowers that have the best properties, and when that is to be done, all moderate flowers, by which is to be understood such as have been too good to be thrown away, and yet are none of the best, must be taken up as they first open, otherwise they will adulterate the others, and the seeds be little better than if they were gathered promiscuously in common.

The properties of a good Polyanthus are,

1 The stem should be upright and strong in proportion to the number of peeps it is to produce. Properties of a good Polyanthus.

2 These peeps should have short footstalks, that are strong enough to support them in an upright position, or nearly so, on their main and common basis.

3 The peeps should be large and spreading, though the size is dispensed with where the colours are exquisite.

4 The colours should be as opposite as possible in their mixture, and the fashion of any particular time determines what reigning colour is most valuable.

5 The eye should be large, clear, and bold, and the antheræ should cover the neck of the tube. This is what Florists call a Thrum-Eye. When the style perforates, and shews its stigma above the antheræ, this is called a Pin-Eye, and such a flower is rejected by all modern Florists, let its other properties be what they will.

6 It should die well, *i e* when in its decaying state it preserves its colours lively and strong to nearly the last, and of these there is a very great difference.

This last property is by many esteemed valuable, for there cannot be a more melancholy sight, or a better emblem of our own fate, than the last stage of a blow of beautiful flowers of any sort. Some sorts of the Polyanthus, however, will look well till the swelled seed-vessels appear. It is chiefly the dark or purple colours that are most possessed of this property. These colours were more sought after a few years ago than they are at present,

present, the gold and orange colours being chiefly in fashion

The doctrine of the Florist and Botanist never more disagree than in the fifth article The Florists reject a pin eyed Polyanthus, as an imperfect, despicable flower The Botanist regards such a flower as the most perfect of its sort It is the female organ of generation, and in monopetalous flowers, in its most perfect state, is longer than the stamina

Caut.o. From what has been said, the Florist must observe not to omit carefully sowing the seeds, and raising plants every two or three years, to form beds to succeed those that will be going off, for every one of those beds, after it has blowed three seasons, should be destroyed, those plants only that are remarkable for their good properties being preserved, and planted out in other places, for the beds of succession from seeds, if they are managed with the above care, will exceed all others, let them be what they will

If the old roots of every excellent sort be planted in a well sheltered bed by themselves, they will stand there as remembrances of what you have raised and will always be ready to furnish you with seeds, without the trouble of marking the best, and nipping off the worst as they appear in their common blow, and by this, fresh faces, and the best sorts too, may be ever obtained Indeed, were old roots or offsets to produce their flowers as strong and fair as seedlings, yet the latter method should be mostly practised, because you have a treasure upon the ground, of which you do not know the value; whereas you know what the others will be, even before they flower This expectation encreases your hope, and affords you pleasure, especially when it is more nearly exhausted, and the season comes on for the yet unseen beauties to appear Neither will they fail your expectations, if care has been used, nor are your hopes ever to cease, if beds are to succeed in order, which is allowed to be one of the greatest of all human happinesses, and which could never commence, in this article, were known plants only to be multiplied by culture

## *PRIMULA*, The *AURICULA URSI*, or BEAR's EAR.

Introductory observations THE pride of our English florists is the family we are now entered upon, as there is no nation that ever boasted such variety, to form a large Collection, all raised by their own industry and skill So that while the Dutch are boasting of their grand tulips, hyacinths, &c we may lay claim to a greater honour, in our improvement of these delightful plants, for the Auricula, if we regard its sweetness or odour as well as beauty, must claim the precedence, and stands in our gardens the glory of all flowers, the carnation itself not excepted The florist, perhaps, may be startled to find that the same generical word to which the Polyanthus Primrose belongs, governs also our *Auricula Ursi*, or Bear's Ear He will wonder to see these plants arranged as brethren of one family, which before were thought to have no other connection than their flowering in the spring But Science, which daily meets with improvements, directs us to make all researches, and the laws she dictates inform us, that these hitherto-supposed strangers are near relations, are brethren, or species of one common genus, which, for distinction sake, is titled *Primula*, a title that the Botanist, upon strict examination by these laws, will find to be proper, right, and just

Origin of the generical term of this species The usual word, and what has till now been used as the generic l term of this species, is simple and natural enough, the *Auricula Ursi*, the leaves resembling for the most part the ears of a bear, but this word is so corrupted by common pronunciation, that it is impossible to know its meaning as it is commonly pronounced, unless you know what has been talking about, much less to give you the reason, or convey any idea of the form of the leaf

which grows naturally on the Alps, &c The Auricula grows naturally on several mountainous parts in Europe, particularly the Alps, and even in its wild state has many charms to recommend it, and though the places where they are found to abound are covered with snow during great part of the year, yet with us, in their cultivated state, we find nothing more destructive to these plants than snow, and much wet of any sort That wonderful variety which constitutes the glory of our gardens, and grandeur of our shade or stages on which they are usually arranged, is supposed originally to proceed from the Common Yellow, though some botanists give the Purple an equal share in the origin of the family, for they make these two plants distinct species, and say, that from them our amazing variety is obtained Be that as it may, we have sorts enough, of admirable beauty, (to use the Gardeners phrase) to breed from, and from these our variety is daily multiplied, and the splendor of our Collection yearly encreased Not that we are to think of raising our show to appear at once from seeds, like the Polyanthus Primrose, for out of a thousand seedling plants, all raised from the best seeds, perhaps ten will not be found so far worth preserving as to be admitted into a Collection The present wonderful variety supposed to proceed from the common yellow and purple.

New faces are to be obtained by seeds; and the raising of these is the florist's glory With these he exults and swells at the annual feast, he calls them after his own name, and places to himself much merit on their account A new valuable flower once raised is to stand for ages, and it is the number of these of which our Collection consists They are all named, and are known to the world of florists, they are all numbered and booked, and it is by offsets, or dividing their roots, they are encreased, and the present stock kept up New faces to be obtained from seeds

Thus the culture of a collection is to be continued; till by degrees, new faces appearing, the worst sorts are thrown out to make room for them, though it will be a series of years before the admission of a new face is banished the Collection, to make room for another, which is not always the best But novelty, and prepossession in the owner's judgment, are too often the cause of the change. And thus the state of Auriculas, like other things, is ever fluctuating, and mutable.

The management of auriculas a very delicate point

The right management of a Collection of Auriculas is as nice a point as any thing the art produces, and, with the observance of the best rules, situations or the like have so strange an influence on these plants, that they will gradually die away. Hence it is that the young florist often finds himself under the necessity of furnishing himself with a stock two or three times over, before he hits upon their true and right management, notwithstanding the rules delivered to him with so much confidence from different authors. He shall have the method I have ever practised, and if his situation be high or low, damp or dry, in his practice by these rules his judgment will inform him how to humour them accordingly.

Method of culture practised by the author

The first thing he must furnish himself with is a proper compost, in which to plant them. The simple composition of neats dung and soil from a fresh pasture, taken with the sward, and drift or sea sand, is the best that can be. To every four loads of neats dung let there be added four of a rich pasture soil with the sward, and two loads of drift sand. This will be the proportion in the composition, and if to these you add one, two, or three loads of willow mould, saw-dust, rotten wood, or the like, it will be the better. This compost should be formed, and the whole turned over, at intervals, and well mixed, for at least twelve months before it is used. Once in three months will be often enough, until the last quarter, when it should be turned and mixed every month. This will be the best compost for these plants, so that we will proceed to their management.

If a Collection is already had, that has passed the season of flowering, they should be taken up, and their roots divided and planted afresh in July. This is the best time for the work, though they may be removed at any other season, and then it is that the young Florist must furnish himself with a sufficient number of offsets.

Having provided himself with a sufficient number of pots, and having his compost in readiness, in a shady place, to prevent the roots drying, &c. he is to plant a single offset in each pot, spreading the fibres and pressing the mould gently to the whole root. The tops of the roots should be level with the surface. This is an indispensible rule, for if they are planted too deep, that is, if the bottom of the leaves are below the compost soil, the outward leaves will first rot, then the next, and so on till the whole plant is lost, though it sometimes happens, that the perfect one goes, which indeed may be called the whole plant, for it rarely makes any thing ever after. When they are planted, a little water must be given them, to keep them cool, settle the mould to the roots, and prepare them for striking. After that, they should be set in the shade, but may have the morning sun until eight of the clock, or the afternoon sun from five. A quantity of slates or tiles must be laid, to keep them clear from the earth, and if the succeeding part of the summer be dry, a little water twice a week, but not oftener, should be given them, and then they may remain until the approach of winter. Nevertheless, if a very rainy autumn should happen, the pots should be laid on their sides, for nothing is so prejudicial to these plants as too much wet. The places these pots are stationed in should have a free open air, and the shade should be occasioned by a wall, or the like, and not by trees, the drippings of which will bring on destruction and death. Every now and then look over your pots, and as often as you find rotten leaves, take them away, for they will spread the contagion, and one leaf will rot its neighbour until the infection becomes general. In the autumn the strongest plants will exhibit flower-buds. These must be nipped off as they appear, which will cause the roots to be stronger and blow fairer in the spring. At the approach of winter, they should be arranged along a wall that commands a good share of sun, where they may stand in an upright position, on slates or tiles, until bad weather sets in (by which I mean much wet, sleet, or melting snow), when they should be laid on their sides, but not with their faces towards the wall, as is by some recommended, for then they cannot have the benefit of so fine and free an air, and the dampness they may contract, by having their faces towards a wall, not being immediately exhaled, they may contract a mouldiness, which will be succeeded by rottenness, &c. Whereas were they to face the free open air, though the storm may beat, yet lying sideways, there will be no danger of their suffering too much by wet, and whatever superfluous moisture they may imbibe, yet facing the sun, and having the benefit of an open air, that will soon be exhaled, and the plants and the composition in which they grow will be wholesome and in good plight.

Never make yourself uneasy let what frosts will happen. They will often reduce plants in appearance, but not kill them, and these will be more amazing in their progress of improvement as soon as such weather is past. This plant will naturally bear cold, and wet only is its greatest enemy, particularly such as proceeds from melted snow. Make not yourself, however, uneasy on that account. If the deepest snows should fall, let them remain buried until the time of thawing. Then clear away, fronting the pots, their whole length, take up the pots, brush away the snow from their surface, the roots, and leaves of the plants, and having cleared it off the slates or tiles, lay them sideways as before, and with this care your plants will receive little or no injury, though they have lain buried for weeks in the largest drifts.

In February the pots should have a new situation. They should be placed in quantities together, and the place hooped for conveniency of covering in frosty weather, against which the plants should be carefully protected, for the flower-buds will be preparing to shew themselves, and the frost will injure if not destroy them. An Auricula pot seldom if ever comes into the hand but it calls for some management. Now you must not only pick off all decayed leaves, rub away all mouldiness, if any appear, and the like, but the mould must be taken out round the sides, as deep as conveniently may be without too much disturbing the root, and the pots filled with fresh soil from the compost. This will be like a cordial to the plant, which having this fresh soil for its nourishment, will flower with more force and beauty. This then is the next stadium of the *Auricula Ursi*.

During their stay here, they should have a free air, be never covered except in frosts and heavy rains, and must always be uncovered immediately upon the return of fine weather. More than two flowers should never be suffered to belong to a root, so that while they are in this station, as they will shew their flower stems, such roots as produce more must have the weakest nipped off, and the others will be larger and fairer in proportion. It will also strengthen the offsets

again t

against the time for their commencing mother-plants.

We may suppose the curious florist has already a stage built for his plants to blow on, consisting of a flight of stairs, or shelves, arranged one above another. As soon as they begin to open, on this they should be placed, to make the greatest figure in their blow. These stages or shades are often built with all conveniencies, at a great expence, and are made to turn to any aspect, at the pleasure of the florist, who, without more trouble, can allow them any quantity of sun or shade. Be this as it will, the plants on the stage ought always to have the morning sun until ten of the clock, and no more of it. The pots on the stage must every now and then be turned, to keep their flowers in an upright position, or they will draw to one side, and such whose stalks are too weak to support their heads to advantage, must be supported with small forked sticks, placed up them, so as scarcely to be perceived. Watering-pans must be provided, with one narrow hole only at the end of their necks to convey the water into the pots without wetting the leaves or pees, which at this time would be very dangerous. Indeed the nature of these plants is such, that if wet was never to come near their leaves or flowers, they would be much the better for it. Their roots, however, must be watered in that careful manner every other morning. In a cloudy dry day they may be uncovered, but not when there is much wind stirring, for it will incommode their whole order. Neither should they be uncovered unless a person is near at hand to watch the coming-on of a shower, for should the smallest rain fall on them at this time, it will entirely deface their show. It will at once impair their colours, and wash off that profusion of delicate farina so essential to the beauty of these flowers.

After their blow is over they should be removed into one or other of their shady stations, where they should remain, with now and then a little watering, as the weather requires it, until July, when the operation of clearing the old root of their offsets, and fresh potting, is to be performed again, though it hardly need be told the practitioner, if an offset has made but little improvement, by having thrown out no others that are fit to take off, if the pot is not too small, it may remain undisturbed till the next July.

Culture by seeds. The raising these flowers from seeds is to be the constant exercise of the florist, let his Collection of named established plants be ever so great, in order to his obtaining fresh faces, which will not only tend to his own pleasure, but distinguish his diligence, and gain him applause among his brethren. In order to this, he must fix upon such flowers as he knows to have the best properties. These are to be selected from the others, and not permitted to flower in the Collection on the stage, but should be set apart to enjoy all the benefit of the air and sun, to ripen the seeds and bring them to perfection, for those flowers that have had the tender nursery of the shed will seldom be succeeded by seeds, the vessels, instead of swelling into maturity, often dying away with the flowers, or soon after. And if some of them should have seeds, by being moved early out of the shed, even before the beauty of the flowers is well over, they will be few in proportion, neither will the seeds be so fair and good. Such a number of pots, therefore, must be set apart, as will be sufficient to produce the quantity of seed desired, and amongst these no self coloured flowers must be had, those being altogether improper to breed from, let their properties be what they will. These pots should be placed where they may have the morning sun only, they must have the benefit of a free air, and warm showers contribute much to the swelling the vessels, and ripening the seeds, so that if these do not frequently happen, they must be often watered, not with the usual watering-pans, but with a rose, sprinkling them all over, like a shower of rain. In dry seasons, those pots have best ripened their seeds that have been plunged up to the rims in garden-mould. This is a good method to be practised, it will keep the roots cool, and much watering will be saved, neither need you be so careful to have their situation in that manner so shady, for, thus placed, the sun will have less power to hurt them. Nevertheless, this practice has its inconveniences. If a wet season should happen, the moisture will soon be too powerful for them, and then dangers enough will surround them, and though they may be taken up, yet probably not before they have received damage; and thus the trouble of plunging them, taking them up, &c. will not only be thrown away, but perhaps be detrimental. The practice, however, like many other things in agriculture, is good, if the season suits, and, like those practices, is capable of benefits and advantages, but still subject to disappointment and loss.

The seeds will be ripe in June, when every day, nay twice a day, the eye should be upon them, and the hand ready with a pair of scissars, to cut off the bolls as they ripen. Bags of clean writing paper, having the tops shut, should be held under, for them to drop into as they are cut off, and this will prevent the loss of any of the seeds, which will fly by being handled, especially in the afternoon; so that it will be the safest way to gather the seeds always in the morning, after the dew is off, and when the business is deferred or repeated till the afternoon, it must be with that care, and this method is to be repeated until the seeds are all gathered. They may all this time remain in these paper bags, if they are not too large, and may be hung in windows, to be thoroughly dry, or they may be laid, as they are gathered, upon a few sheets of writing-paper, on a warm dry shelf, if no animals can get near to scatter them, nor any current of air, by which they will suffer the same fate.

Immediately upon the seeds being all gathered, they should be sown, or if there be too many of them to be sown at once, the first gathered should be sown, whilst the latter may remain a few days longer, to be thoroughly dry. The compost is to be the same as for the roots, only about a sixth part of the finest sand should be added, and all well mixed together, and if there is the same quantity of the finest willow mould, it will be the better. Willow-mould agrees extremely well with the nature of an Auricula, and as this is seldom to be got in large quantities, it should not be swallowed up in the general compost, but must be laid apart to be mixed with the finest sort of it for the reception of the seeds. A sufficient number of boxes, pots, or tin pans, must be provided, which being filled with this last-mentioned compost, having holes covered with oyster shells, slates, or the like, to drain off the wet, they should be well shook to settle the mould; and having made the surface of each smooth and level, the seeds should be sown not too thick, then gently pressed down with a trowel, and a small sprinkling of water bestowed on them, and the business is done. Do not wonder at my not ordering them to be covered with mould. This is the most dangerous thing that

that attends the seeds, for if they are covered the least too much they will not grow. The first shower that comes, or the sprinkling at the time of sowing, will settle them deep enough, and if they were to lie upon the surface of such well-prepared mould, they would grow very well, even there they would germinate, and the rostellum, the principle which descends and forms the root, would naturally strike into it, whilst the plumula would form itself above the surface, and soon commence the plant.

Why the antients could not raise these plants by seeds.

It was for want of knowing this, that the antients looked upon Nature only to be capable of encreasing these plants, and thought that the raising them by seeds was not in the power of art. The reason why they always failed in their attempts was, they covered them with mould in the usual way, and it was not in the nature of the plant to break though it, so that while they were ruminating that Nature alone could multiply these plants that way, she was teaching them their true method of culture. They might observe seedlings arise near the mother-plants, without art or management, and this should have directed them, in sowing, to scatter them accordingly, and expect the like success. It does not appear, however, that they took Nature's hint, which was more, indeed, for she gave them demonstration, for we find them, not many years ago, placing the seeds in the wind, that, by its scattering them, plants might be expected, which could not be the case if sown by the hand. This superstitious practice plainly shews, they were still ignorant of the cause why the attempts of art had failed. By this method, however, many plants were obtained, and another practice gained ground, which bordered less upon superstition, and seemed to indicate they had hit upon their nature, and that was, to prepare the pots and boxes, and set them abroad until the first snows came on, then to sow their seeds upon the snow, leaving them to descend to the soil as that thawed. By this method they obtained numerous plants, and this method I am not for discouraging even now, if the seeds must be deferred sowing until winter, for although they may be hand sown as soon as there is a conveniency, yet I never knew the practice of snow sowing, though tried for experiment only, fail of producing a good crop.

Willow mould peculiarly liked by these plants.

How well these plants have liked willow-mould has been known many years. It has been in use for more than one hundred years, which perhaps is the cause why our modern books of Gardening have left off to recommend it, lest they should appear still in the beaten track. But its being so long used without any reasonable objection, is a proof why it should be continued to be recommended, it having so long given demonstration how well its nature agrees with the nature of these plants. Rotten willow, well converted to a fine mould, is excellent soil for these plants, and tho' we have given it, our seeds need no other covering than what the rain will procure them. This is a caution, to prevent their being buried. A little of this fine willow-mould, mixed with some very fine sand, may be gently dusted over them, and to make it have the best effect, it should be sprinkled so sparingly, as not to exceed the thickness of an auricula seed in depth.

The boxes, immediately upon their being sown, should be removed into a place where they can have the benefit of a free air, but no sun, except a little in the morning. If very heavy rain falls, they should be covered, and in dry weather should be watered by fine sprinkling every other morning or evening. They should be protected with nets, or wire lattice from the birds and other animals, who by the scratching, &c. would bury the seeds and incommode the whole work. In this situation they may remain until the beginning of October, by which time you will find you have a tolerable good crop of seedlings. Though nothing is so prejudicial to these young plants as the sun in its full blaze continued too long, yet a little of it at this time will refresh them, and bring them forward, so that their position should be altered, and they should be set where they can have it until eleven o'clock, and even in a few days, the young plants will shew how well it agrees with them.

A place must this month be got in readiness for their standing all winter, for they must be covered every night and always uncovered again in a fine morning. Not that it will be necessary to cover them every evening, was the continuance of fine weather certain, but for fear of accident for a mild gentle season altering to some keen cutting weather, may make great havock in the boxes, especially among the weakest seedlings, and such as may even yet be only just germinating, or forming themselves into a plant. All winter, however, they must have as much free air as possible, as little covering as will just ensure their safety, and as much sun as may be, and with this care and nursing they are to pass the winter. In March they should resume their October situation, and should have the sun no longer than about ten or eleven o'clock, as the days get longer and hot weather comes on, they should have still less of it, and if in the beginning of April they should be removed into a perfect shade, having a free air, it will be the better. The usual care of watering in dry weather must be bestowed on them, and in July the largest will be fit to transplant. This should be done in the same compost, and in the manner directed for the offsets and old roots. But as one plant in a hundred will not probably be worth preserving, there would be no end of pots for the work, and boxes may be provided with less trouble, in which they may be planted pretty close, yet if a quantity of seedlings is obtained, in order to have the better chance of raising the more good flowers, there will be hardly any end of these. So that when this is the case, beds must be marked out in the open ground, and filled with the same compost for their reception, whilst those that have a more moderate quantity may give them the better nursing of pots or boxes.

In these beds they need not be planted more than two inches asunder, so that a bed of any size will hold a prodigious quantity. A great number may be crowded into a few boxes, which will be the best for the plants. Beds are designed only for those whose wishes include the most extensive Collections. These beds should be hooped, and the plants covered with mats from the sun until they have taken root, which will not be long, and after that they will require no other care than watering and weeding. This is hinted to save trouble, for if they are covered in the blaze of hot weather all summer, it will be better, but in the winter after, no covering need be afforded them, not even protection from frosts, snow, or rains, for they will be much hardier than the old cultivated plants, though if they are covered in that weather, and have air, &c. in other, possibility of danger will be avoided. In the spring many of them will blow, but hardly one in a hundred will be worth preserving. As these

wish

worst sorts appear, pluck them up and throw them away, or plant them out as border-flowers, for nosegays, or the like, and such as are found with all properties to render them worthy to be admitted into a Collection, you may either pot immediately, or mark them, to be potted in July, when this work is to be in general done. The seedling-boxes out of which these plants had been drawn we may suppose still to be nursed, for they will have a succession of fine plants, to be set out in the same manner, by the July after, and thus is this stock to be kept up, and the sorts encreased. When a new flower is raised, the owner pitches upon a proper name, and the plant in its pot, in full blow, is generally brought to some neighbouring florists feast, to have its properties examined, and its name confirmed.

Properties of a good Auricula.

The properties of a good Auricula are,

1. The stem should be upright, of a proper height and strength in proportion to the cluster of flowers it is to sustain.

2. The cluster should be large and regular, forming a globular figure as nearly as possible, to effect which, the footstalk of each individual peep should be short, or strong enough to support it in an upright or any direction necessary to contribute to form the whole into a regular flower.

3. Each flower, or (as it is commonly called) the peep, should have a large and spreading rim, a short tube, and the neck, or top, not too wide.

4. The style, which is usually called the Pin, should not arise above the antheræ or buttons that compose the thrum.

5. The eye should be large and fair. If it be of the original colour (yellow) it will be good, but if it be of a clear white, it will be better.

6. The colours of the pin ought to be as opposite as possible, and both clear and perfect of their kind.

Remarks.

These will be always standing rules and never-failing characteristics of a good auricula, let the fashion vary or alter ever so often. The second rule points so much to perfection, that few flowers are found to answer to it strictly, and many beautiful Auriculas, worthy of attention, are found, whose bunches are loose, and though irregular, their disposition is agreeable.

Fashions, as in the Polyanthus, alter the more trivial properties at pleasure, and what is a perfection at one time or place, at another shall be called a defect. Nay, the very leaves are often by fashion made the chief characteristics of a good flower, and tho' the real flower has every perfection, if the leaves do not answer such a particular description, it is rejected. The leaves are by a florist called the Grass, a strange corruption indeed! There is, however, no harm in it, and let him indulge himself in his own terms. I am not for finding fault and discouraging him on that account. I would exhort him by all means to persevere in his employment, for I dare say, there cannot be a more innocent, a more pleasant, a more heathful, or a more natural amusement, than the care and management of such a family, which will fill the mind with pleasure, but no remorse, and improve the heart, by raising suitable ideas and due contemplation of the All wise and All powerful Creator of these beautiful works of his hands.

## *HYACINTHUS*, The HYACINTH.

The Dutch most famous for cultivating this flower.

THE Dutch pride themselves upon the Hyacinth, as the chief or mistress of all flowers, and boast that they alone are possessed of its true nature and management. Certain it is, they bring it blow to very great perfection, they raise infinite numbers from seeds, and obtain numerous fresh sorts of prodigious value, by which their stock, both in number and value, is greatly encreased, and above all, they annually finger a good quantity of our gold, for which no one can blame them, for their indutry is really commendable, and it is to them we are chiefly indebted (though by paying for them) for the many fine sorts our gardens are possessed of.

Botanic phrases and terms give little pleasure to the florist, simply as such; neither is the rigid Botanist delighted with the pompous names bestowed upon the different sorts of these flowers, however useful, but the want of some thing of this kind would breed confusion. The florist cannot be offended with me, however, upon my telling him, that all those different fine flowers on whose culture he bestows so much pains, are varieties only of one species, termed the Oriental Hyacinth, the original of which is supposed to be that with a single white flower; and that it is from the seeds of that single white flower the profusion of varieties in delicacy and grandeur proceeds.

All the different kinds of this flower proceed originally from the Oriental Hyacinth.

The Dutch excel the English gardeners in the management of these flowers.

It has been too justly lamented, that our skill in the management and ordering of these flowers falls vastly short of that of the Dutch florists, and that even after a Collection of bulbs of the best sorts are obtained from Holland, they degenerate, and every year deviate from the grand appearance they made in those gardens, plainly proving, that there has been some great defect in their management after being obtained. And tho' many ingenious Gardeners have tried various ways, invented different composts for their reception, and laid down their rules with great confidence, as if they alone had hit upon the true art, yet, alas! upon repeated trials, the success has so often failed that they have never been able to remove the complaint. This is a very interesting point, which, if once hit on, would enable the English florist to blow his old roots to advantage, raise them from seeds in as great plenty as the Dutch, and save great sums that are annually sent abroad in the purchase of what his own industry has provided him at home.

At Haarlem, in Holland, are several very ingenious florists, whose show of these flowers has rather more than equalled those of other parts. This has put our English florists, after considering the nature of the soil thereabouts, to make a mixture of our different earths, so as to resemble that in colour. But this is very bad philo-

Soils that agree in colour may yet differ in quality

philosophy, for though soils may be so mixed as *to agree very well in colour, they may be very* different in quality, and tho' the florist may have hit upon the necessary ingredients of rotten cows dung, tanners bark, and the like, yet, for want of a due mixture and management, the success has failed. Failed, I say, for though in such compost the plants have lived and flowered, even so strong as to make the Gardener pique himself upon his art, yet, to those who are thoroughly acquainted with the nature of this flower, their best flowers appear but very moderate.

Most plants will grow in a well managed border of common earth

Every plant in Nature has some particular favourite soil, in which it will grow, multiply itself, and flourish best, and there is hardly any plant that will not grow and flourish well in a well managed border of common earth. Bring a plant from the tops of the highest mountains, from between the crevices of the rocks, and it will grow in such a border, nay, take a marsh marigold from the bogs, and it will here flower the fair and clear. There are some exceptions to these, and the nature of the situation, as well as soil of their original growth, must be attended to, to make them to flourish in our gardens. Hence has arisen the invention of the prodigious number of different composts for the reception of different plants, and this is become so general, that the Gardener looks upon his art to be nothing, if some strange composition is not invented for every plant. In short, compost, to the rival of our modern writers on Gardening, are like med cines to a quack, though with this difference, a quack with a few will cure all disorders, but every plant must have a different compost invented, in the quack-puffing way, for its preservation and health. What a number of these mixtures are to be found in Miller's Dictionary, and Dr Hill, that he might by no means fall short, or rather, that his doctrine should be of more consequence the more strange the nature of its composition, for the management of about two hundred plants, has given you directions for making almost as many different composts. This is sufficient to dishearten any gentleman from having any connection with the flower garden, indeed, for there would be no end of the trouble and expence, and his compost yard, to keep them separate, ought to be as large as a field. But what is still more unpardonable in the abovementioned gentlemen, most of their composts are for such flowers as may not improperly be called Border flowers, or such as will thrive and flourish well in a common border of good garden mould. Maiden earth from a good loamy pasture ground, taken not too deep, with the sward laid in a heap, rotted and well mixed by frequent turning, will answer almost all the purposes of vegetation. Whenever any other mixture is necessary, the reader will find it under the article treated of, and the uses and value of such an earth are so well known, that both Miller and Hill thought a proper compost for the Hyacinth could not be without a share of it. But

The author an enemy to varieties of composts

Rich, fresh loamy earth destructive to a fine blow of Hyacinths

rich, fresh, loamy earth, valuable as it is for almost all plants, is, nevertheless, destructive to a fine blow of Hyacinths. They will live in such soil, encrease by offsets, and will flower, but they will fall vastly short, let whatever other ingredients be added, in beauty to those that are properly managed. *Dr Hill recommends pond-mud for these bulbs*, than which nothing is more contrary to their nature. Composts, however, tho' a greater value has been put upon them than they deserve, tho *much puffing and self-sufficiency* have been bestowed in their invention, and tho' they occasion much expence to the owner, and are of little service to the plants, are highly necessary for the proper management of many articles in Gardening, and proper skill in their nature and mixture is the Gardener's art. But the Hyacinth, of all others, requires a proper compost, without which, let not a fine show be attempted, let a person be contented with raising a few of these plants only, for nosegays and the ornament of rooms, &c.

A proper compost will be near two years in preparing, so that if a person is possessed of a parcel of bulbs, he must be content all this time to plant them in his usual way. We take it for granted that he has been accustomed to use a good quantity of sand in his mixtures, for it has been early known how well they like a light sandy soil, let this be continued, or, if he has been used to raise Auriculas in the manner directed in the preceding chapter, and has such a compost in readiness for them, that compost will do very well for his Hyacinths, and indeed is a better mixture, and more adapted to their nature, than any composition directed to be made in any book of Gardening I have hitherto met with.

Directions for preparing a proper compost

But to have this plant in the highest perfection, *four ingredients, and four only, are to form the* composition, which are, Neats dung, drift or sea sand, rotten tanners bark, and rotten leaves of trees. Let these be put together in the following quantities, which may be multiplied at pleasure.

Four loads of neats dung, which if gathered from the pasture grounds in the clots, will be better. Four loads of drift or sea sand, free from all mixture of loam or clay. Two loads of rotten tanners bark, which should have lain at least two years from use. Two loads of rotten tree leaves, and if these should be difficult to be got, vegetables and old thatch, mixed in equal quantities, and well rotted, will nearly answer the same end.

These mixtures being prepared and multiplied according to the quantity wanted, they must be brought to meliorate in a free open place where they can have all the benefit of the sun, air, and showers. This is so essential an article, that a failure in this point will bring detriment, if not destruction, to the flowers, let the composition be ever so good. Of this Van Kampen *gives us an instance, in a Dutch florist, who* having a proper mixture, laid it in an improper exposure, towards the North, where there was no sun, to avoid the unsightly appearance it *might make in the front of his house*, "The consequence of which was, says he, the utter ruin of all his Hyacinths." This, then, is principally to be observed. The compost must have the sun, and every benefit of the elements, or it will not be replete with such qualities as are proper for our present purpose. For this end, being brought into an open place, facing the south, or open to the sun, it should be laid in a long ridge, to be made into a bed about three feet deep, and this bed should be continued longer or broader, in proportion to the quantity of compost. The ridge being made, by burying the mixture, of sufficient height to form the bed of that depth, it may lie a week or ten days, then be made into the bed, a yard deep all ways, mixing the different ingredients as you go along, and, next to the procuring the composition, this is the first important step towards preparing a proper habitation for these delightful flowers.

as well as making and managing suitable beds to their flower

Twelve months before the compost is to be used, this step ought to be taken, and the materials well rotted even at that time. For were they not converted to a mould before they are used, they would be too rich, fat, and suffocating, to the destruction of the bulbs, so that unless

leſs the bark has been two years from uſe, and the cow-dung and leaves well rotted, the mixture ſhould be made of them a year and a half at leaſt, or more, before it is uſed, for in this mixture, as directed to be ordered, they will ſooner commence proper earth for the intended purpoſe.

One month after laying the mixture in a bed a yard deep, it ſhould be ſtirred, by beginning at one end, and turning it over, keeping a trench open to the very bottom, and mixing the parts well as you go along. It ſhould be laid in a bed in the ſame manner, level and even, the bottom of the former bed being at the top of this new one, and this work muſt be repeated once a month, till it is wanted for uſe. The bed is ordered to be one yard deep only, for that depth (the ſoil lying light) the ſun will penetrate, and warm it to the bottom, and every part of it will alſo receive all the benefits of the elements. The ſtirring is ordered once a month, becauſe by that time it will have ſettled, and become unfit to receive the influences of the ſun, air, and ſhowers, without being lightened again by another removal. And thus, by this repetition, every part will be well mixed, it will be of a proper degree of fineneſs, and be in every reſpect proper for uſe.

Farther rules for perfecting their cultivation.

October is the beſt month for planting the bulbs, and next to that November, for if they are planted in September, as directed by ſome Gardeners, the flower buds will appear ſo early, that all imaginable precaution will not always hinder their being injured by the ſpring-froſts. Beſides, they will be in blow too early in the ſpring, before the fine weather is well ſettled, and the roads will permit the curious to ſhew them proper reſpect, for it muſt be a great pleaſure to a generous mind, not only to feaſt itſelf with that delightful ſight, while it is continued, but to ſatisfy the curioſity and afford pleaſure to others who have it not in their power to be poſſeſſed of any thing of the like kind. In October or November, then, we may ſuppoſe the bulbs are to be planted, and one month before the place for the beds is to be marked out, the natural earth muſt be taken out at leaſt three feet deep, and ſo far muſt earth of any ſort be from mixing in the compoſt for planting of Hyacinths, that the very ſmell of it ſhould be kept from them as much as poſſible. Tho' the ſoil be removed thus deep and the compoſt put in its place, yet fumes and vapours will nevertheleſs ariſe from below it, which would be very prejudicial unleſs prevented. For this purpoſe, as ſoon as the earth is taken away to the depth of a yard, cow-dung muſt be trodden down well, or rammed cloſe, until it forms a compact conſiſtence of half a foot thick, this will prevent all vapours from ariſing, and the bulbs will be affected with no other fumes than what naturally ariſe from their own compoſt. This being done, the compoſt is to be laid upon it, and raiſed half a foot above the ſurface, even and ſmooth, ſo that its thickneſs then above the trodden-down cows dung at the bottom will be one yard. A ſouth or an eaſt expoſure is moſt proper for theſe beds, which ſhould be raiſed higher backwards, and made with a ſlope, in manner of our hot-bed-frames, for this will ſhew the flowers to much advantage when in blow. The beds ſhould be long enough to contain the number of bulbs, or there ſhould be more of them, and their breadth ſhould be near five feet, but not broader, for conveniency of managing, and this will contain five rows of bulbs, at nine inches aſunder, leaving a proper diſtance between the verge or extremity of the beds, and a wooden frame would be neceſſary, to keep the mould in its proper place. The mould is deſired to be brought into the place a month before the bulbs are to be planted, that it may be properly ſettled, that the whole may be even, and you may be ſure of the bulbs remaining at the depth you plant them. Four inches is the proper depth for the bulbs to be planted, and they may be ſet at ten inches aſunder, ſo that each bed will have five rows running the whole length.

If the number of bulbs be large, more beds muſt be provided for the early and late ſorts ſhould be kept ſeparate, and always planted together, but if the number of bulbs be not too large, the early ſorts may be planted at one end of the bed, then the next, and the lateſt at the oppoſite end. But in order to make a blow all together, plant the early flowers five inches deep, and the late ones three inches, and thus they will ſhew their beautiful bloom at the ſame time.

In order to preſerve a uniformity in blow, be ſure to ſee that the bulbs at the time of planting out are all healthy and good. If any of them have a fetid ſmell, and are ſticky, let them be thrown away as good for nothing, nay as dead. If any diſeaſe ſhews itſelf at the bottom of the bulb, or any part be bruiſed, ſearch theſe to the bottom, and with a knife take off every bit of the diſordered part, until you come to the clear white, when you may be ſure the bulb is ſound. Lay this in an airy place to dry, and the bulb is cured, but if the infection goes to the heart of the bulb, throw it away, for then the infection is paſt remedy. If the outward ſkins of any of the bulbs be bruiſed, and have contracted a mouldineſs, this is a dangerous diſorder. The cure then is to take off all the infected coats, and lay them alſo in an airy place, or in a window, to dry, and the cure will ſoon be effected. An eye muſt be had to the bulbs, from the time of taking up to the time of planting, and as thoſe diſeaſes ſhew themſelves, they muſt be healed in the above manner. If a young floriſt is now furniſhing himſelf with a new ſtock, to be managed according to theſe directions, from Holland, let them be carefully examined after importation, and if no diſorder appears in any of the bulbs, lay them all in an open airy place, to dry, for they probably will have contracted a dampneſs, which, if not removed before the bulbs are planted, may prove fatal to many of them. After all, ſuch bulbs as have been faulty, and are ſeemingly perfectly cured, it will be the beſt to plant by themſelves, in a ſeparate bed, for if the infection ſhould break out again among the ſound roots, the contagion will ſpread itſelf, the conſequence of which may be eaſily imagined. The ſound bulbs, therefore, and thoſe only, are for this beſt bed; and having them all in readineſs, let them be planted as above directed.

and for curing any diſeaſes of the bulbs

Faulty bulbs recommended to be planted in a ſeparate bed

The next precaution muſt be to guard them againſt the froſt at the approach of winter, and for this end it has been cuſtomary to cover the beds three or four inches deep with tanners bark, or the like. The Dutch practiſe this method and by their ſucceſs one ſhould think it muſt be right, but I am certain, notwithſtanding, if the froſts can be kept from the roots without this weight upon the beds for ſo long a time it would be much better, for it is often the occaſion of the bulbs rotting, or, if there was no danger of this, how much more proper would the ſoil be to ſend forth the leaves and flowers than if left open, engaging all the benefits of the ſun, air, and ſmall froſt all winter, or than when cruſhed down

Covering the beds with tanners bark, &c againſt froſts objected to and why down by a weight of tanners bark, &c. Let the young practitioner, then, observe, that it is not so much the bulbs as the striking fibres that the frost affects, so that if it should freeze so sharp as to reach the bulbs, but not penetrate so low as the bottom from whence the fibres issue, no danger may be apprehended. Let this be well remembered, and let it regulate his conduct. The bulbs will be four or five inches deep, and many winters pass which are called open winters, in which there is little or no frost, what a pity would it be to have the beds loaded during such weather? Let the intelligent Gardener consider, therefore, that, even at the setting in of frosty weather, it is very seldom that in the first night's time the frost will go so deep as five inches. Let him have fleaks drawn with furze bushes, and as winter settles in, and any night looks clear and frosty, let him set these on the windy side of the bed, or, if the evening threatens a hard frost, let him set round the beds with these well drawn fleaks. Surely, then, there can be no danger, in one night, of the bed being frozen so deep as to kill the plants, for a fence of this kind will take off the edge of a frost much better than a wall or boards, and every one must have observed, that, even in our largest frosts, when in a night's time water in rooms has been converted to ice, the frost under a close hedge has but just crusted the mould; however, if, after all, danger is apprehended, let some litter be shook over each bed.

*Surrounding the beds with well drawn fleaks,*

*Or shaking litter over them is commended as a better practice in moderate frosts,*

I have been the more particular in this, to keep off as long as possible the tan-bark from the beds, and indeed, with this management, they will pass many of our winters without danger. Let the Gardener, however, have his tanners bark, or peas straw, in readiness, for these fleaks are intended to ensure protection in small frosts, or for the first night at the setting in of great ones. If, therefore, in the morning the beds are frozen and near the evening the frost seems to be set in in earnest, then cover the beds three or four inches deep with the bark. Let the alleys or spaces also between them be well filled up at a good distance, and, lest it should grow more and more intense, let the fleaks be set round as usual, and this will be the strongest safeguard that has ever been recommended. As soon as ever it begins to thaw, take off the bark, &c. and in all open weather let the beds have all sun and air. The usual protection of fleaks in moderate frosts will probably carry them through winter, but if there should be a repetition of the former severity, a repetition of the bark covering must be had, and that must be always taken away at the first thawing. The Dutch, famous as they are, let the bark lie on till all danger from bad weather is over, and Miller, knowing this, orders the same practice. But what a pity it is to have plants and soil excluded the benefit of the elements during a great part of a mild and open winter? Nay, in such weather, Nature will be at work, and the bulbs will send out their leaves, which penetrating the bark covering sooner than was expected, would contract a disagreeable sickly yellow, which they not only seldom outgrow the whole season after, but which is often the occasion of bringing on many diseases to the plants.

*this tanners bark, &c. must be used in more severe weather*

We have accompanied the beds now, we may suppose, through the winter, the plants are come up, and longer days come on. Frosts, however, will not yet have left us, so that, as a farther safety to the flowers, the beds must be hooped, and every night they should be covered with mats, which should be taken off again at the return of morning. The Dutch make use of wooden sliders, which they draw on and off. These have a neater and better look, but I do not much relish them, as they are too apt to draw the plants, if, for fear of bad weather, they should be continued on the least too long.

By this time, we may suppose, the flower-stalks have grown to a considerable height, and the bells, though yet unexpanded, are grown large at the top. Then it is, and until their flowering is over, that they are liable to receive damage from every ruffian blast of wind, and unless they have supports to enable them to resist its insults, great havock and devastation will be made among them. So that by this time there must be in readiness a sufficient quantity of straight, narrow, well seasoned sticks. These should be about two feet long, and no thicker than what will furnish them with strength to perform their office. They should be thrust down by the side of the bulb, about half a foot deep, but not so near as to touch it. These are to be the supports of the flowers, and for this purpose, above the lowermost bell, let a loop of small, strong, yarn thread be tied, not so tight as to draw the stalk and stick into too near embraces, nor so large as to give them room to deviate, but of such a size only as will keep them parallel in their upright position. As the flower-stalk advances, and the weight of the bells becomes too great for it, a second loop must be applied, nearer the top, and a third if necessary. Then they will not only be secure from danger of the winds, but will display their charms to greater advantage in this upright position.

*Directions for protecting the flowers from violent winds,*

When a general blow is designed to be made together, the early whites and blues should be shaded in the heat of the day, to stop their forwardness. The beds also should be screened in this manner from the rays of the sun, which, of all others, it is least able to bear, as it would soon fade them, and take off their beautiful red. These screens may be made to look handsome, they may be made of very thin boards, or tin, and the best colour to paint them of is green. Thus we attend our plants until we suppose them to be nearly in blow, and now is the time to have a general shade for the whole bed. Different florists do this different ways, and if it is contrived to take up and let down in parts, and in proper places, as the nature of the flowers requires, it matters very little which way. These umbrellas should be made of canvas, and I am for having them made to cover the whole bed or beds, in a tent-like manner, that the company may walk under them, for it will be pleasant to all, in hot weather to be thus shaded, and in rainy weather they may, unconcerned about that, here indulge their fancy. It will be better for the flowers also, for they will have a larger share of air, and there will be room to draw up the sides, or let them down, as occasion requires. The late blowers will want all air and morning sun to ripen them, and these may be so contrived as to give it them, and as the heat of the day comes on, or heavy rains happen, they may be let down, and so be ever ready to assist in the Collection.

*and for shading the plants when in blow.*

With this management, these flowers will be in perfection for near a month. After they have begun to fade, and their beauty is diminished, the tents must be struck, and carefully laid up against another year, and thus with care they will last an age, so that if any persons object to the expence of them, it is but for once, and they may be also serviceable if a party should be made to partake of a cold collation, any time in the

the hotteſt months, at the top of a diſtant hill, for the ſake of viewing the proſpect, &c

But let us return a little back, examine our flowers in their progreſs towards perfection, and, like watchful phyſicians, ſee if the whole family is healthy and ſtrong Obſerve then, that a root is diſeaſed if the flower-ſtem ariſes weak and ſickly The leaves growing unequally, ſome longer than the others, and all ſhorter than thoſe of the other bulbs, is a certain ſign of a diſordered bottom A diſeaſe, and a dangerous ſymptom alſo, is, when the leaves are curled, and yellowiſh or iron-coloured ſtreaks are found in them This is a diſtemper that lies at the very heart of the plant, and can be diſcovered at no other time than when the leaves and flowers are ſhooting It is of a deadly nature, and is infectious, ſo that as ſoon as theſe ſymptoms appear, the plant muſt be immediately taken up, or, before the general time comes for taking up the bulbs, many will be infected with the ſame contagion If there be a ſcarcity of the ſort thus diſeaſed, and the bulb when taken up is found to be hard, the uſual way is to make two croſs cuts at the bottom, and plant it by itſelf, very ſhallow, and thus, though the main bulb will periſh, it will produce numbers of offsets at that time, as if to preſerve its ſpecies If the bulb upon being taken up feels ſoft, it is dead to all intents and purpoſes, and muſt be thrown away

Symptoms of a plant's being diſeaſed

Having given theſe precautions, let us now return to our bed, which has its flowers in a fading ſtate, and the canvas removed, and here we are to do nothing but deplore their fate, and with ſuitable reflections ruminate on all ſublunary things When the ends of the leaves of theſe plants, to about five or ſix inches, are turned yellow and withered, then is the time for taking them up, and this is what a floriſt calls *lifting them* He is fond of his phraſes, and would not loſe one of them, ſo we will ſpeak in his own terms When this lifting is performed, the greateſt care imaginable muſt be uſed not to bruiſe the roots, which are then full of juice, and immediately upon this, cut off their flower-ſtems and leaves cloſe to the bulb, but let the fibres remain untouched Then lay them in a dry airy place, but not in the ſun, the watry moiſture which will follow upon taking off the ſtalk will ſoon be exhaled, and the place healed, and in a few weeks their fibres will be quite withered, when they ſhould be cleared of all of them, filth, &c and the buſineſs is done until the time of planting comes on again

Method to avoid the variety of diſeaſes incident to the bulbs

This is quite contrary to the common method of practice, and to that which the Dutch ever uſe I allow it, but it is found by experience to be the only method to avoid the variety of diſeaſes that are incident to the bulbs by the common method of management The moſt dangerous of all diſeaſes is communicated to the bulbs by the ſtem and leaves; ſo that by taking thoſe off immediately upon lifting the bulbs, the communication will be ſtopped, and all contaminous juices cut off Beſides, the common method of practice often brings on deſtruction to the bulbs, and without the greateſt care will be certain to do it They are uſually covered with earth or ſand, to ripen them, as the phraſe is, they are uſually ſhaded, but if they have the leaſt ſun too much, or any thing ſhould have removed the ſhade, ſo that the ſun's full blaze be on them but a few hours in that hot ſeaſon, it will ſo roaſt and broil them that nothing but death enſues, and if heavy ſhowers and a wet ſeaſon ſhould fall upon them when they themſelves are poſſeſſed of ſo much moiſture, they will be more eaſily affected, and ſuch rains at that time will be almoſt ſure to rot them, whereas if, upon lifting, they are laid in a dry airy place, where only the morning ſun, at moſt, and no rains, can come near them, the moiſture will dry up by degrees, and this is the ſafeſt way of ripening them

The different ways of ripening them examined

And as the bulbs are in imminent danger during the uſual time of ripening, ſo are they much more ſo if ripened according to Mr Miller's directions "Raiſe the earth of your beds, "ſays he, into a high ſharp ridge, laying the "roots into it in a horizontal poſition, with the "leaves hanging out" Now muſt not any one of the leaſt diſcernment ſee the danger theſe bulbs muſt be in, ſtill at the ends of the leaves and flower ſtalks in a withering or rotting ſtate, eſpecially as he afterwards informs us (what every body knows), that "the ſtems of theſe "flowers are very large, and contain a great "quantity of moiſture, which, if ſuffered to "return into the roots, will infallibly cauſe "many of them to periſh?" After he has directed the manner of laying the bulbs with their leaves and flower-ſtems on, what follows is a reaſon why a different practice ſhould be taken, and that they ſhould be ſeparated as ſoon as poſſible This I particularly mention, that the danger of his doctrine may for the future be avoided, for it is hardly poſſible but many corrupted juices will deſcend from theſe ſtems and leaves when in a putrifying or dying ſtate, which will bring on deſtruction to many of the roots, notwithſtanding all imaginable care to prevent it

After all, the young practitioner muſt obſerve, that I am not too rigid againſt ripening the roots in their own beds, for notwithſtanding the dangers which will ſurround them at that time, if they eſcape they will have their advantages, for they will look better, and be of a finer purple caſt, which will be very material for thoſe who raiſe them for ſale The outward coat or ſkin alſo will be of a harder conſiſtence, by which they will be leſs liable to receive injury in packing to be ſent to a diſtance If the floriſt chuſes this laſt method after lifting, let the mould be raiſed on a ridge, in manner of a tillage-land, though more ſloping, to ſhoot off the wet, and on this let the bulbs be placed, with their bottoms downward, then let them be covered with the earth an inch and a half deep, and ſecured from the blaze of the ſun and heavy ſhowers This method may be practiſed, but on no conſideration let the leaves or flower-ſtems remain to them, for, beſides the above reaſon of the danger of contracting diſorders by corrupted juices from the leaves and ſtems in their decaying ſtate, there are ſeveral real diſeaſes which ſhew themſelves in theſe, and into which examination muſt be made, to find how far they are deſperate If the ſtem runs away from its real to a diſagreeable, duſky colour, it is a certain ſign of a diſtempered plant If a yellow point appears upon the ſtem it is a dangerous ſymptom, and to know how far they are mortal, whenever it appears of a ſickly yellow the diſtemper is raging But if upon cutting it lower it appears white, and of a bluiſh caſt, taking off the whole ſtem, as ordered, will be ſufficient to ſecure the bulb If the diſorder, however, runs lower, the knife muſt ſtill follow it, till the uſual healthy white of the plant appears, with its bluiſh tinge, and if the farther you cut you find it has ſpread itſelf the more, throw it away as an infectious dangerous plant.

Other ſign of a diſtempered plant

Methods of cure

There is another very dangerous diſorder that is to be cured at this time, called the Riny Sickneſs This appears in the leaves, of a ſemicircular

circular form, and of a brownish yellow colour. This distemper, which is composed of corrupted and infectious juices, will by degrees search into the bulb, and inevitably destroy it, so that to prevent this, the bulb must be cleared of all leaves and stem. From all which appears not only the necessity of clearing the roots of the leaves and stems as soon as they are taken up, and the danger of placing them in a horizontal position, but also the reasonableness of lifting the bulbs as soon as the leaves have begun to fade, which will ensure their safety from many impending dangers that might afterwards fall upon them.

We may now suppose our intelligent florist has got his bulbs well ripened and in good order. Let him preserve them, with constant inspection, from moulding, by keeping them in dry and airy places until October or November, when let him proceed, in the usual way, to prepare for the next blow. Let us now instruct him in the manner of raising these plants from seeds.

Cultivation by seeds.

The sowing the seeds of the Hyacinth is a work that ought annually to be repeated by every good florist, as it will not only keep up the stock of good flowers, but advances will be every year made towards perfection in the flower. The hopes of seeing new faces of excellent properties will afford much pleasure to the mind, even some years before they appear, and when this hope is swallowed up in the fruition of what has been long expected, it is renewed again by the pleasing hopes of a succession, and that again repeated, so that the florist's hope, the greatest of all human blessings, will be ever new and permanent, be ever swallowed up in enjoyment, and yet never exhausted. The first period will be considerable, between the sowing and flowering, but this should teach us to set a greater value upon such good flowers as shall at last reward our pains. The tediousness also should be balanced by the reflection, that it is little more than twice the time of biennials, that the gardeners of other countries make nothing of it, that when once the first period is elapsed, there will always be a succession, and if the practice can be brought to equal perfection as our neighbours the Dutch, what vast sums will annually be made to circulate among our own florists, as a reward for their industry and art, which used to be exported into foreign countries in purchase of such bulbs they can with equal goodness raise in their own gardens. A true lover of flowers, however, will want very little persuasion to set about so pleasing, so useful, and so profitable an employment, and unless a man is, in truth and earnest, a real lover of flowers, he is desired by no means to have any thing to do at least with this branch of the art, from a tending of these plants from their seedling state to their perfection in blow.

The sincere in the art, then, are desired to observe the directions that follow. First, to breed from the single flowers that have good properties, these are, of all others, the best, the semidouble next, and the double flowers worst of all. Indeed, many of the full double flowers have their number of petals multiplied in so great a degree, as entirely to destroy the stamina, so that they never produce any seeds, but there are other very double flowers, in which the stamina may be found perfect amongst the petals, and these produce seeds. Reason would seem to dictate, that seeds from such plants must be most proper for the purpose. But experience shews us, that plants raised from seeds of such double flowers are always small, the flower stalks and bells are also smaller, and are destitute in general of that bold look peculiar to the best sorts of this flower, they are not so bad, however, but a proportionable degree of imperfection will attend the seeds of the semidouble, so that it is from the finest single Hyacinth that the seed is to be collected, which will be bolder, will grow better, and from which plenty of fine doubles, and doubles, as well as singles, may be expected. Secondly, if any particular colour is wanted, such as red, blue, yellow, or the like, let the plants of the desired colour be set by themselves for seeds, for by the communication of the farina from plant to plant, if they grow promiscuously near one another, no particular colour from the seeds of any sort can be expected. Neither must the young practitioner, with the united care of keeping the sorts separate, always flatter himself that seeds raised from them will produce others of the like colour. No all our Collectors of Hyacinths conf[illegible] on species only, and the varieties will be multiplied by seeds without end. This is recommended only to gain the better chance, for if Hyacinths of any particular colour be planted by themselves, the seeds from them will probably produce many sorts, but there is much probability, that the greatest part of them will be of the same colour from whence the seeds were taken. Thirdly, it would be better if the seeds could be collected from such of the finest seedling Hyacinths that have only blown once or twice, for these young and vigorous plants always produce the best seeds, and plants raised from them are proportionably finer, and, when come to blow, will ever produce the greatest quantity of double flowers. But this is a circumstance that is too often to be wished for only, it being seldom a person may have it in his power to raise seeds from such bulbs. Any, therefore, of any age or standing, will do very well, though the others are best, when it so happens that they can easily be obtained, which a young florist cannot hope for, unless he can depend upon some obliging neighbour, until he has been in the practice for many years.

Seeds from the single flowers to be preferred.

Gathering the seeds.

Let us proceed now to the gathering of the seeds, and for this, the lifting season, or time for taking up the bulbs, being come, we find the seeds not yet ripe. They may either be permitted to remain to perfect their seeds, or they will ripen on the stalk if it be cut off, and the end planted about four inches deep of the earth in the bed. In about a fortnight the seed vessels will begin to open, and the seed being turned black is a certain sign of its being ripe. They are then to be carefully gathered, and laid to dry in an airy sunny window, where having lain for some weeks, and being perfectly dry, they should be cleared of their seed-vessels, should be lapped in clean writing paper, and laid on a dry shelf until the time of sowing.

Time for sowing them.

September is the properest season for this work, and if the quantity of seed be great, and numerous plants are intended to be raised, they should be sown in beds of the same kind of compost as them ordered for the planting the bulbs, though, if there be a scarcity of this, the auricula compost will do very well. These beds should be made four feet and a half broad, and long in proportion to the quantity of seed to be sown. They should be sown in rows, two inches deep, and at both ends of each row should be placed a stick or peg for a direction. At the setting in of winter it is usual to cover the seed beds with tanners bark, three or four inches deep, but if they were to be protected in the manner directed for the bulbs it would be better. But if they must be covered, let it be taken off with great caution, by the hand, in the end of February, and if the covering is made of leaves, instead

instead of bark, and laid a little thicker, it will as effectually keep out the frost, and less sodden the bed

In the spring the seeds will come up; and all the care they will require the first summer will be to keep them clear of weeds, and in the winter their usual protection from hard frosts must be given them

After management. The second spring the plants will appear with longer and broader leaves, and their young bulbs must be taken up before they decay, which will be so sure a direction that there will then be no danger of losing them, or if it should happen to be deferred till many of these are gone off, the rows may be followed, by the direction of the pegs, with care, and the bulbs be effectually found However, it is the best way not to defer this work until the leaves are withered, for they will be subject, in so early a prime, to many diseases, which may be prevented by being freed from their leaves in good time These young bulbs must be carefully preserved until September, when they should be planted in beds made of the before-directed compost, six inches asunder, and here they may remain until they flower, many of which will be in two years, some three, and others not before four or five years As they shew themselves, those of good properties should be marked, and lifted at the proper season, to add to the Collection whilst the worst sorts may be thrown away, which will be by far the greater number, and these will make room for the remainder as their bulbs encrease, that the plants may not be too close This method is recommended to save trouble, for it would be best to lift them every year until they blow, and throw none away until they have flowered twice, as there have been instances of very ordinary flowers, at first appearing, which, when they came to blow the second spring, have appeared with such improved colour, the arrangement of the bells has been so uniform, and their properties so excellent, that they have been ranked in the first class of value But this seldom happens and where the Collection of seedlings is great, there would be no end of the trouble of giving them the culture of the best flowers, as there probably may not prove one in a hundred worth preserving This is the method to be practised when many flowers are to be raised from much seed sown If a person has but few seeds, the best way is to sow them in pans, pots, or boxes, and, for the first and second winter, they may be secured with little trouble, by setting them in frosty weather, under hotbed-frames, and the like Let them be lifted the second summer, and planted again in September, and managed as old bulbs until they have blown twice, for out of so few plants we must stand no chance of losing a good sort to save a little trouble The worst sorts may be either thrown away or planted out in the borders of the flower-garden, for their flowers to be gathered to adorn rooms, &c whilst those of the best properties are to be admitted into the Collection

Properties of a good hyacinth. The properties of a good Hyacinth are,

1 It should not blow too early nor too late to join naturally in the early or late blowing sorts

2 The stem ought not to be too short nor too long, and of sufficient strength to support the bells in an upright position

3 The colour of the flowers should be clear and bright, and the bells large and well shaped, having their brims well expanded

4 Their pedicles ought to be short and strong, able to support the single ones in an horizontal position, and the double flowers, whose weight will not permit this, should be large, and have their middle well filled by the multiplicity of petals

5 There should be an exact proportion between the make and size of the bells, and strength of the stalks They ought to be beautifully arranged in a pyramidical or conical form, the footstalk nearest the base being longer, the rest gradually diminishing to the top, for the disposition of the bells is a property that constitutes one of the chief beauties of this flower

The first sort is rejected by florists in the same manner as sportsmen reject a hound that is too fleet or too slow for the pack. Of these two sorts, however, the latter is most to be valued, as the flowers will be the finest and largest, whilst the earliest sorts may have their uses, if not admitted into the Collection, by being planted as spring-flowers for their sake, near windows and places of constant view Remarks.

The first part of the second rule is indispensable, for if the stem be too short, a great share of the bells, however beautiful, will be hid by the leaves, and the flower itself is esteemed of little value, when destitute of that graceful appearance it would otherwise make with a proper elevation

With regard to the second part, there are many valuable flowers whose stems are not strong enough properly to support their bells, they being large and sometimes twenty or thirty in number This, though a defect, is more easily dispensed with on account of the direction before given for the due keeping of these flowers in their proper position

No Hyacinth can be deemed a good one without the third requisite

The horizontal position of the petals chiefly regards the single flowers, for a footstalk cannot be expected to be so strong as to support a large full double flower in that manner This sometimes happens, however, and the more able the footstalks are to cause the same tendency, the flower is proportionally of greater value

Symmetry and proportion constitute the chief beauty in most things, and thus it is with the Hyacinth A few bells, however beautiful irregularly placed on an ill-proportioned and almost naked stalk, will compose a flower of a very awkward appearance amongst others of different properties, and which would be so, were the extreme to be carried any other way These beautiful spikes are most enchanting, when the figure they represent is truly such, broadest at the base, and diminishing gradually to a point, and it could be wished all Hyacinths in particular had this property, but there are many, that are destitute of it, on account of others which they have in great perfection, that are admitted as very valuable flowers And indeed, though these are in general the standing properties of a good Hyacinth, yet the rules are not too strictly to be adhered to, as there are many valuable flowers that will not answer to all of them, and the florist who raises from the best of seeds must not expect to have one flower in a thousand that can, in every respect, bear the test of such criticism The laws, therefore, are left to be softened, and dispensed with at pleasure Fashion, by which most things at different times are affected, influences also the Hyacinths, and some particular sort will always have the run and be most esteemed, as being the fashionable sort, whilst others, perhaps of better properties, are less regarded But in all flowers, never was the height of fashion carried to so great a degree of absurdity, as in these flowers Strange to tell! the large Double Hyacinths have not been many years in fashion! the

Single

Single ones were only deemed valuable, and those noble full flowers were thrown away as fast as they shewed their multiplicity of petals, and loaded with the opprobrium of large cabbages This custom prevailed all over Holland and Flanders, and in most parts where these delightful plants have been propagated

# *TULIPA*, The TULIP

Introductory reflections

IMMEDIATELY after the blow of Hyacinths is over, the tulips shew themselves in all their gaudy attire Beauty and elegance are the properties of many flowers, and these peculiarly attend the before-treated-of plants, in any state of flowering, but particularly when arranged in the manner directed, in vast quantities, in sloping beds But grandeur, as well as beauty, is the distinguishing characteristic of a show of well-blown Tulips They have a tawdry splendor, but so blended with an air of majesty as to raise our wonder, and though the former at first may convey an idea of foppery, yet this is softened into the profoundest admiration on a closer examination, on finding the colours so rich and heightened, mixed and disposed in such a manner, on such large sheets, supported by well proportioned stems These together give the flower a most graceful appearance, destroy all idea of levity, and force our reason to confess, that it has perfection enough, indeed, to make us desire it

But the beauty of these flowers is not the sole good property that should recommend them to our favour That may, indeed, please the citizen, or such as never have it in their power, let their inclinations be what they will, to commence florists in an established collection

Peculiar properties of these flowers,

But there are other reasons why a florist ought to rejoice in the possession of these flowers They are attended with very little trouble What a deal of care, nursing, doctoring, managing, &c there is of the before-treated bulbs, the family of the auriculas, &c to bring them to perfection! What mixtures of compost and nice observances are to be adhered to to ensure success at the expected time of blow! But very little of these is required for the flowers under consideration They demand no other compost than such as is necessary to cause an alterative They grow in any soil or situation, provided it is not too wet, and if it is not too low, for water to settle there, their roots are subject to no injury, either from hail, frost, or snow, so that a person need not be over anxious about their safety, and, with regard to them, may rest himself satisfied and easy, let the weather be what it will

which however, have their deficiencies

Yet these flowers, valuable as they are, have their deficiencies Nature, which, at sight, seems to have given them all perfections, has denied them smell But this would be too much, for were they possessed of the fragrance of some flowers, they would so much excel the rest of their brethren as to sink them much in esteem Besides this, their short duration, when in blow, is by many looked upon as a defect, and is justly lamented They are truly emblematical of the fleeting state of things, and in particular prove that those of the greatest beauty soonest fade

This great family, for from the number of the sorts they may justly be so called, are varieties only of one species, whose botanic title may be found among the perennial flower-roots, and they are divided into the following sorts

Sorts

The Early Spring Tulips
The Double-flowering Tulips
The Whole Blowers, called Dutch Breeders
The Late Large-blowing Variegated Tulips

Early Spring Tulips described

The Early Spring Tulips are not possessed of the majestic grandeur of any of the other sorts, for their stems are short, and the flowers of most of them but very moderate Their value arises from their early flowering, several of which will be early in February, and so will continue by others in succession until the late blowers appear The flowers of the earliest blowers are placed upon very short stems, those that appear next in succession have stems longer, and this proportion is pretty nearly observed throughout the whole tulip tribe These Early Tulips should be stationed in the flower-garden near the sitting-room, to make a show early in the spring, with Crocusses, Hepaticas, Winter Aconites, Mezereons, &c and for the enrichment of this they are excellently adapted As their value chiefly consists in their early blowing, to make them as perfect as possible, they should be planted again as soon as the roots are dry and cleared of all offsets, &c at least they should be set a month before the other sorts, which the reader will find in the course of this chapter In large towns, where gardens are not to be had, these plants are chiefly used for blowing in glasses, for which they are of all the sorts best adapted It has been observed, that these are the meanest-looking flowers of all the Tulip tribe, and yet they were formerly so much in fashion, that all others were looked upon with indifference, if not despised It was for this sort the Hollanders, about a hundred and thirty years ago, were running mad, a single root sold for from two thousand to five thousand five hundred guilders Every florist has heard of the States interposing to regulate the price of these flowers by law This is really true, and I have seen an account of the act, which bears date April 27, 1637

Where they should be stationed in the flower garden

Method of propagating them

These sorts should be set in warm well sheltered places, for as the weather is often bad at the time of their flowering, they will require all protection to make them blow fair, so that if they are not naturally defended, they should be screened with mats or the like, or they will be liable to be blighted, to the destruction of the flowers, and great injury of the bulbs It is observable that these bulbs are not so hardy as the other sorts, neither do they produce their offsets in such great plenty, which may direct us to their culture As soon as their leaves decay, which will be some weeks before the other sorts,

sorts, the bulbs should be taken up, and laid in an airy, dry place, and after they are dry, and cleared of all outward slime, mould, offsets, &c they should be kept separate, in partition boxes, properly numbered, until the time of planting, which ought to be in August at farthest which will cause them to flower earlier, and give them more time to encrease by bulbs Few of these flowers blow at the same time, so that they should be kept separate, and the sorts known, and so planted in companies as to make as even a show as possible

Description &c of the Double-flowering Tulips

The Double flowering Tulips The esteem for these is hardly ever fixed and certain, for there is no one whose value ebbs and flows so often as these sorts One while they are much in fashion, large beds of them are coveted and we purchase them at a great rate from the Dutch and Flemish florists, who have them in their catalogues with pompous names Another while they are little regarded, and are set out to answer the purpose of border flowers only Anon, they are all the fashion, and then are treated with as much care as before they were neglected Neither can any reason be assigned for this it serves only to shew the caprice of the English, for they are noble, grand, well-looking flowers, and worthy of all attention and regard They are too well known to need any description, and if the double peony is to be esteemed purely for the flowers, these much more so claim that right, for the petals are of such a nature, and so multiplied, as to resemble those flowers, only they are possessed of an elegance which the other never enjoys, and their diversity of colours in their stripes and grounds renders them more beautiful than any thing that was ever seen of the peony kind The roots of these are hardier than the before mentioned early sorts, they flower later, some of them will naturally be in blow with the late variegated kinds, with which the Dutch plant them to make the variety greater, and indeed they have a very good effect, the same as the double auriculas have with the prize flowers, but this is a practice here, as in them, condemned by many of our modern florists These Tulips by no art can be made to flower so early as the before mentioned sorts, but they may be backened at pleasure, by deferring planting of the roots beyond the usual time Yet this is a very bad practice, for they never appear so fair, and consequently are not near so engaging, as when, in consequence of their being planted at the properest season, they flower naturally at their regular and due time

Whole Blowers, or Dutch Breeders described

The Whole Blowers, or Dutch Breeders These, it is to be hoped, are only temporary plants, and that they will reward the industry of the patient florist, by commencing those of the fourth class or assortment, which is,

The Late Large-blowing Variegated Tulips

The Late Large-blowing Variegated Tulips These are all broke into those beautiful stripes, from the Whole Blowers, which were first raised from seeds, (a method that has been much practised by the Dutch, from whose industry an almost infinite number of bulbs has been raised) and from which our present valuable Collection of so many thousand plants, in their varieties, have chiefly been produced The Whole Blowers are to be purchased of most florists at a very easy rate, whereas the Established Flowers run so high in price, that a large Collection at once would be out of the reach of a moderate fortune, with other expences, to accomplish So that the best way to obtain a large stock of these plants in a little time for a little money, is to purchase a quantity of Whole Blowers, and wait for their breaking into their different stripes

Different methods practised to break these flowers

There are many who pretend to several secret arts in breaking of these flowers but it does not appear that any of them are founded upon philosophy and reason Nature alone is to accomplish this work, and Art can have no other share in bringing it about, than in assisting Nature to produce the effect, and this is to be done, first, by planting them in a lean, hungry, or gravelly soil, and secondly, by causing as great an alteration in the soil as possible, every time they are planted

The first method should be practised upon the Breeders, after the bulbs are grown strong, and they have flowered once All variegations are diseases in a plant, and nothing is so proper to bring this about as a defect of nutriment It is first of all occasioned by weakness, and that weakness will be soon after attended with those sickly, but to us very desirable, symptoms of different colours breaking out by various stripes in the natural one Nature, then, alone perfects this work Plant your bulb in a poor gravelly soil, and the natural consequence will ensue

Another expedient to accomplish this desired effect is, to make as great an alteration in the soil as possible You must not expect, from the first trial of setting them in a poor soil, to have all your plants beautifully striped No, a few only will have taken the effect, and you must proceed to bring about the work in others, and so must continue from year to year until the whole is finished Let such, therefore, as remain unbroke, after flowering one year in a barren gravelly soil, be set next in a rich garden black mould, then again in a sandy earth The year after the beds for them may be made of some of the rich composts, than which none will be more proper than that for the auriculas After that, a compost may be made of an opposite nature, composed chiefly of coal-ashes, lime, rubbish, and the like, then set them in a rich garden-mould again Soils afford food for plants, the same as meat for animals, and from such sudden changes of diet, from low to high feeding, then to fall off to another extreme they had never been used to, to be obliged immediately to quit that, and have no more than the scanty allowance of mean food as at first, thus suddenly to abound in all luxuriancy and richness of diet, and as suddenly turned to their hungry starved condition, amongst animals, this would bring on diseases, and soon after death, and it will in the same manner, though perhaps not in so dangerous a degree, have a similar effect upon the plants Disease is what we not only want to bring about, but to confirm in them While they are Whole Blowers, they are found, and free from all disorder, when their beautiful stripes appear, the disease shews itself, and when they have taken sufficient hold of the plant it becomes chronical, and is not in the power of after management to remove, and then it is we have our wishes Strange as it is to be told, it is an infirmity only in the plant that makes it with us so very valuable The pleasure resulting from the hope and expectation of annually seeing fresh faces beautifully striped, makes this work agreeable, or it would otherwise appear tedious, for, with all the art that can be used, a large Collection of Whole blowers, or, as they are termed, Breeders, will sometimes take up fourteen years or more before they are all broke into established plants The Breeders are all self-coloured flowers, and have names imposed on them by the Dutch Without paying any regard to such titles, let us consider which flowers promise the fairest to answer our hopes, and for this those with white bottoms are deemed of the first class The choice of the Ba-

*guettes* are of this ſort, and they generally break into beautiful ſtripes of purple or ſky-blue, ſeparated by white ſtreaks running lengthways, ſtill retaining the purity of white in its bottom. Next to the white, the yellow bottoms are to be preferred. Of theſe chiefly are the Breeders which go by the name of the Red Dutch. Stripes of the fineſt *crimſon and reds of different ſorts may be expected* from theſe, ſeparated by ſtreams of flaming gold; though they will ſometimes break into different ſtripes, and the darkeſt coloured Tulips will proceed frequently from thoſe Yellow-bottomed Tulips whoſe petals are of a dirty red. Thoſe with dark ſwarthy bottoms ſeldom or never break at all, but there is a ſort that goes by the name of the Great Red Dutch Breeder, the bottom of which is almoſt black, and whole petals are of all reds the moſt diſagreeable and unexempting. This will often break into dark-coloured ſtripes, ſtreams of yellow will be intermingled, and different tincts of red will run the whole length. Thus Nature upon different ſubjects will operate differently, and it is from theſe diſagreeable looking ſelf-coloured flowers, raiſed from ſeeds, that our preſent valuable Collection of eſtabliſhed Tulips, and which is every year encreaſed and improved, proceeds.

Culture and management of Tulips

Proceed we now to the culture and management of theſe delightful flowers. One common culture belongs to the Breeders and the Broken Flowers, with regard to their being planted and management, though the Breeders, as has been obſerved, muſt every year have as oppoſite a ſoil as poſſible, and chiefly lean and beggarly, the better to accompliſh the great change. Broken plants ſhould always have a rich ſoil, replete with all vegetative juices, (but not too fat with dung) to keep them if poſſible in a ſtate of luxuriancy. For the floriſt will find a great diminution, both in the height and ſtrength of the ſtem and ſize of the leaves and petals, after it becomes an Eſtabliſhed Flower, from what it was before. A good Dutch Breeder, with a large ſelf-coloured flower, ſupported by a ſtrong, upright, tall ſtem, perhaps of more than a yard in height, when it becomes broken into different ſtripes through the uſage it has met with, perhaps in the beſt of ſoils, will ſhew no tendency to ariſe higher than two feet, ſo much will its natural force be diminiſhed by the weakneſs that has brought on the variegation. So that when once theſe are eſtabliſhed, and there being no danger of their recovering of that weakneſs, or running away from their colours, which ſometimes will happen, the ſoil in which they are to be planted ſhould be pretty good, to ſupport them (as it were) in their afflicted ſtate, for was this to be hungry and barren, they would be ſo ſmall that the figure they would otherwiſe make would be inconſiderable. They muſt, therefore, be planted in a good rich ſoil, and for this almoſt any ſoil of good heart will be very proper. Mould from any of the quarters in the Kitchen-Garden, that had been well dunged the year before, though it had bore a crop after, will be very good for the Tulips, eſpecially if a little drift ſand be added. Such mould may be made to ſerve one year, and after it is done with may be wheeled to its former place. Freſh ſoil from an upland paſture is excellent, and for variety ſome years they may be planted in ſuch a ſoil. The common garden mould, where the beds happen that they are to be planted, will do very well, provided it be in good heart. I mention theſe to ſave the willing floriſt the trouble of preparing ſo many compoſts where there is no occaſion. I always found them to flouriſh as fair in thoſe as any, and as they are to be every year removed, and not planted two years together in the ſame place, a ſet of changes may be rung on the different ſorts of good mould that can be come at with the leaſt trouble. Miller recommends a compoſt in which to plant theſe bulbs, Dr Hill (if he would leave out his pond-mud) directs a better. But this is unneceſſary trouble for theſe plants, the above mentioned ſimple moulds will do as well. One thing, however, muſt be obſerved, once in three or four years a compoſt ſhould be prepared for them, but then no better can be thought of than what is directed for the auriculas, and if they were now and then to have their beds made of the mould out of which the Hyacinths had been lifted, it would try whether their colours were eſtabliſhed, for it would furniſh them with every thing neceſſary to remove their weakneſs, and recover their former ſtrength. The reader will from hence learn to give himſelf no unneceſſary trouble in preparing compoſts for the Tulip, but take any good ſoil he can conveniently come at, mixing therewith, if it be of an oppoſite nature, a little drift ſand, and then proceed to prepare the beds as follows.

Method of preparing the beds

Mark out a place for the beds, of a ſize in proportion to the number of bulbs to be planted, and if its own natural ſoil be proper, let this be double dug or trenched, all roots, weeds, and ſtones cleared off, and the clods well broken, laid light, and made fine with the ſpade, but by no means riddled. When they are to be planted in a compoſt, or freſh ſoil, this is to be cleared out in the places marked for the beds, to the depth of two feet. But if the place be naturally moiſt, one foot will be ſufficient, and the mould of each bed ſhould be raiſed a foot above the ſurface of the garden, which may be ſurrounded, to keep it in its proper place, with a wooden frame. The beds for the Hyacinths were ordered to be made ſloping, as being the moſt proper to ſhew them to advantage. Theſe ſhould be differently formed. The middle ſhould be conſiderably higher than the ſides, ſo as to form an arch, and in planting of the bulbs, the talleſt growers ſhould form the middle line, the next in height the line on each ſide of it, and ſo of the reſt, to the edge of the beds, placing the loweſt ſtreaked Tulips next the ſides or alleys. And thus theſe flowers, when in blow, will form a ſemicircle, in which arrangement their ſplendor and magnificence will be amazingly heightened. They may be planted any time in the autumn or winter, but October is the beſt month for the work. The diſtance of the bulbs ſhould be eight or nine inches, or more, according to their ſtrength and nature, and they ſhould be planted about ſix inches deep. In order to have this done in the beſt manner, let that quantity of ſoil be cleared off the top of the beds, or if the beds are then making, let them be made ſix or eight inches below their intended height. Let them be rounded in the manner they are intended to be when they are finiſhed, and then with a line mark out the rows for the bulbs. In theſe lines ſet them in an upright poſition, at which time it is cuſtomary with the Dutch, and the method is practiſed by ſome of our own floriſts, who learned it from them, to ſurround each bulb with ſand. This is an excellent method, eſpecially if they are planted in common garden mould, or in ſuch compoſt as that ſand had little or no ſhare in the compoſition. If they are planted in the auricula compoſt, or made of old Hyacinth beds, it will be the leſs neceſſary, nay, I do not ſee it is the leaſt neceſſary, for they are as well without it as with it, neither ſhould I have mentioned it, only it is known to be the practice of ſeveral floriſts of

Beſt time of planting

o[illegible]lities These say it is a munition to the bulbs, but they do not want it, for nothing can hurt them but wet, which must be guarded against at the first laying-out of the beds They have, however, an advantage by it The skins of the bulbs will afterwards be finer, which may be reason sufficient to those who deal in flowers to pursue this practice The bulbs being all placed in an upright position, the earth is to be laid lightly over them, but not sifted, to the height of about six or eight inches, and after the whole is neated up the business is done They will then require no more trouble or management, except keeping them clear of weeds, until nearly the time of flowering It has been recommended by several florists to cover them in the spring, as they appear above ground, like the Hyacinths, to prevent their being injured by the frosts I have never protected any, and have ever found them liable to suffer by no external injuries of cold or heat It is customary, also, with some florists to place a stick, or wire, by the side of each bulb, to support it against the furious winds I have never given them that assistance, and never yet knew them suffer for want of it, before the heads grew large, and were near upon opening The stems are naturally strong and elastic, and I am, for the florist's encouragement, for giving him as little trouble as possible, so that if a place be well sheltered, they may be ventured nearly until the time of opening And as they must be sheltered, when in blow, from the heat of the sun, the same protection also may be made to guard them against all winds A canvas cover, of a tent-like form, large enough for the company to walk under, has been recommended as a safeguard to the blow of Hyacinths Their show is now over, and the blow of these flowers coming on in succession, let this be pitched in the same manner over the Tulips Air may be given them at pleasure, or the torrent of it stopped, by elevating or letting down the canvas All heavy rains will then be unable to molest the flowers, the raging heat of the sun will be stopped (which in a day or two would bring on the destruction of the whole blow), and the company may at any time regale themselves, in hot or rainy weather, with these pleasing productions of Nature, which may be made, by such care, to continue in splendor for a month or five weeks Thus have we employed our tent two months out of the twelve, and it may serve the like office for the carnations, besides being serviceable for regalement, on a distant hill that commands a beautiful country, in hot weather, &c

As soon as the flowers are faded, the seed-vessels must be broken off, which would otherwise greatly weaken the bulb, and when the stalk and leaves are withered, which will be before the end of June, the bulbs should be taken up with great care, that none of them be bruised They should then be laid in a dry, open, airy, shady place, and when they are quite dry, which will be in a few weeks, they should be cleared of their outward husks, filth, &c or they may remain untouched, if the place be secure, and be cleared of all these at the time of planting again, when the flowering-bulbs should be set in the usual manner, and the offsets planted in the nursery, and kept there until they are strong enough to flower

Of raising Tulips from seeds

The Gardener has begun a very tedious undertaking, when first employed in the work of raising Tulips from seeds If he has the greatest success, he will hardly get any of them to flower before seven years after sowing, and the greatest part of his crop will not bear before the eighth, nay, many of the weaker bulbs will not shew their flower-faces until the ninth, and even tenth year, and after all, he has a collection of self-coloured flowers only, termed Breeders, which may perhaps take up near twice that time before they are all fairly broke To alleviate the tediousness of this long expectation, many have recommended sowing the seeds every year, that, after the first six or seven years, there may be a constant succession, which will every year afford fresh delight This is a work that may do very well for the dealers in flowers, and those who have a constant demand for their breeding as well as other bulbs But what must a gentleman do with such an infinite number of plants as he must have in his possession by such annual sowing, in the course of a few years after the expiration of the seven? If a person raises but a thousand bulbs from his first sowing, very few of these will break properly every year, and the rest will multiply so fast by the roots, that in a few years they may be encreased to above a million in number What a stock, then, must a gentleman have, to keep every year raising from seeds, whilst the first raised are every year multiplying by the roots? the second sowing also, and then the third, &c pouring in their multiplication of numbers, &c This is the way to have a stock with a witness! So that the best, and by far the cheapest way would be to buy a parcel of Breeders at first, which usually go at easy rates These will at first afford great pleasure, from the expectation of finding many beautifully striped, and they may, as well as those that remain unbroken, be multiplied by their offsets, in no very long time, to any desired number

However, for the satisfaction of such as are desirous of engaging in the undertaking, as well as for the instruction of those who have made it their business, and have a demand for large quantities for sale, I shall now lay before them the most natural, the easiest, and best method of raising these plants from the seeds to the time of flowering

This method or practice minutely described

And, first, as to gathering the seeds These must be the produce of the healthiest, the largest, and the best kinds of self coloured flowers, or Whole Blowers Seeds from such will be surer at last of answering our expectations, for those gathered from Broken Flowers will raise plants, a far greater share of which will have flowers of different colours from their first appearance, as they will in some degree, like some animals, inherit the weakness, &c of their parents But then these colours will be far from being regular, they will be confused, and blended in so disagreeable a manner as to shew that they are, indeed, sprung from some sickly and unhealthy original The seeds are to be saved, then, from the healthiest and best-looking of all the self-coloured plants or Breeders, which are never to be covered in the time of flowering, but to be exposed to all weather, as it shall happen Their stems must be supported, to prevent their being broken by high winds, and in July the seeds will be ripe Their heads must be next gathered, being dry and opening, when the seeds will appear brown, and they must be laid upon a dry papered shelf, until the time of sowing, the best month for which is September The seeds then, and not before, should be taken out of their vessels, and sown in beds of good light earth, in rows, a stick being set at both ends of each row for a direction They should be sown moderately thin, and covered with about one inch depth of the mould

The best mould for these seeds is the auricula compost, and for want of this, some of the hyacinth compost may be added to the common mould, or if that cannot be got, and if the soil be light and good, they will come up very well in it, though if it be of a black rich nature, the mixture of a little drift sand will greatly improve it. These beds should be made in places open to the morning sun only, and in spring the plants will come up. They must be constantly kept clear of weeds, and be watered whilst their leaves are green, and this is all they will require in the first year's management.

An erroneous practice pointed out.

Before I proceed, I cannot but take notice of a very erroneous practice prescribed by Miller in the sowing of these seeds, which is by ordering them to be sown in shallow pans, or boxes, with holes at the bottom; for though the seeds will come up very well in such shallow pans or boxes, yet as the hot weather advances in the spring, let the watering be ever so often repeated, they will dry as fast, and the mould being in such small quantities will hardly be ever fit for a Tulip in its growing state; the consequence of which is, the leaves will sooner decay, and put a period to the bulbs' encrease for that year; whereas when they are sown in beds where they can enjoy all the benefit of the natural moisture, warmth, and coolness of the soil in a proper proportion, the leaves will continue longer before they decay by some weeks, and during all the time they are growing, the bulbs also are encreasing in bulk. So that to bring them forward as fast as possible, the place cannot be too shady and cool, in which the bulbs will grow to a much greater size in one year than if planted in shallow pans or boxes.

After the leaves are decayed, no more water should be given them. They must be gently cleared of weeds immediately upon their coming up, and if the surface should contract any moss, or the mould should have the least tendency to cause over, it should be stirred, and the hardened or mossy part cleared off, and some fresh soil from the auricula or the like compost sifted over the whole, to about half an inch in depth.

In the spring the bulbs will send forth their leaves broader and stronger than before, testifying at once that they proceed from a stronger original, and that their bulbs are much improved. In all dry weather they must be watered, and this must be continued until their leaves decay, when the bulbs must be taken up. If the leaves are quite gone, the pegs will direct you to the rows, so that there will be little fear of losing any. They must then be laid in a dry airy place until the time of planting again, which should be early in September. They should be set two inches asunder, in drills four inches deep, and pegs placed at the end of each row as before. The planting them so deep will cause their leaves to continue green longer before they decay in the succeeding summer, which will cause both them and their bulbs to be proportionably larger. After they are decayed, the bulbs must be taken up, and treated as before. The beginning of September, they should be planted again, at three or four inches distance, and for the same reason should be set six inches deep. These must be taken up at the usual time, the summer following, and afterwards must have the same management as the flowering-bulbs.

When these seedling bulbs have shewn their flowers, or at farthest when they are in blow the second year, all such as have not the properties of good Breeders should be plucked up and thrown away. Such whose stems appear naturally to be short, such whose petals are narrow and sharp-pointed, such flowers also that are inclined to an olive colour, or green, such also as have dark coloured bases, these either will never break at all, or when broken are of no value; there will be few of these, however, found in proportion. So that if the seeds are to be sown every year, there will be soon plenty enough of plants. When the annual sowing is to be done, as has been warmly recommended, this weeding may be more general, and all that do not at once shew themselves promising, without waiting any further, may be thrown away, as they may cause the trouble of another year's management to no purpose, and there will be plants enough without them.

As the flowers break they must be marked, to be separated from the rest of the Breeders, and after they are thoroughly broken, and commenced established flowers, they should be named and booked accordingly. Besides the naming them, they are divided into different classes by the Dutch, such as *Baguet Primo*, *Baguet rigaut*, *Bybloemen*, *Bizarres*, &c. The *Baguets* have white bottoms, and are beautifully variegated with brown, &c. The former called *Bybloemen* have also white bottoms, and their stripes are blue, violet, and blackish brown. The *Bizarres* are all yellow bottomed, and their stripes are of various colours. But there is another sort, whose stripes are of the finest red, rib, &c having white bottoms. These are very valuable, and the industrious florist may expect to find his Breeders break into sorts of different colours and beauties; so that I shall close this article by giving, in my usual way, the standard properties of this flower under consideration, and these are,

1. That the stem be tall, and proportionably large and strong. *Properties of a good Tulip.*

2. That the flower consist of six or eight petals, broad, and of a thick consistence.

3. That it be of an exact proportion with the height and strength of the stalk. If the stalk is tall and strong enough, the flower cannot be too large.

4. That the flower itself also be well proportioned, that the petals stand erect and firm, having their upper part rounded off.

5. That the stripes be bright and lively, of as opposite a nature as possible; that they be strong, regular, and distinct, arising unmixed from the bottom of the flower.

These are the properties of the finest Tulips; but there are many of great value, that are by no means answerable to them. There are many fine Tulips, admirably well broken, whose petals so fold over each other as to draw the tops nearly to a point, making the whole figure of the flower like an egg. This is a disagreeable property, but many judicious florists will dispense with it, on other considerations. So that these rules, like others, are to be softened at pleasure, and the flower not wholly to be despised or thrown away that cannot in every respect correspond in the examination. In all these flowers there ought to be no remains of the colour of the Breeder, not the least tinge left, because they are liable every year to turn to the original disagreeable self colour. But even this is not to be so much apprehended as is generally imagined, for though there be danger, there is no certainty of its happening, for I have had many delightful striped Tulips broke from the Breeders, in which the original colour has not been wholly expelled, and these have appeared very many years still retaining the original colour in the same part of the flower it appeared the year before. It could be wished this colour could be expelled at first, but I never denied them place amongst the Broken Flowers on that account, and they have never failed doing their part in contributing to the grandeur of the show. After all, there ought to be no remains, nor even stains, of the Breeding colour, and if the flower be composed of regular petals, of three distinct colours, arising from the bottom strong and unmixed, placed on a proper stem, beyond this our wishes can never go, for such a one may be said to be a Perfect flower.

# RANUNCULUS

THE florist has no English name for the flowers of this sort that more immediately fall under his protection and care. It is the generical word to which the different sorts of Crowfoot belong, but that species, which covers all the varieties of the Persian kind, goes by no other name than that of the general term *Ranunculus*, or the Persian *Ranunculus*. The word *Ranunculus* signifies a little frog, being derived from *Rana*, a *frog*, and is said to be given to this genus of plants from their delighting to dwell in moist places, where frogs love to inhabit. This is a strange derivation, but it is the best that we can come at, and at once teaches us, where the derivation of generical words is not perfectly clear, that it is the best way to let them rest without our own trifling conjectures. Some species, indeed, of this genus flourish best in moist places, whilst too much wet would be destructive to others. However, as the word *Ranunculus* stands for the genus we know what species it governs, and it serves for distinction, as the florists names do for the different sorts of flowers. As such, then, it answers our end, whether we are acquainted with its meaning or not. But where the derivation is clear, it is entertaining and instructive, pointing to some particular property or quality, perhaps, of the plant, unless named after some eminent botanist, the hearing or meeting with which must give great pleasure to every lover of the science. There are many beautiful species of this genus, that afford excellent border-flowers for general ornament, and which will be described in due course amongst the perennial flower roots. The florist expects here, purely to have his Persian sorts kept separate, that, as they are distinguished in eminence, so should they be treated as if belonging to a different family, of superior rank and condition. According to my plan, therefore, I shall suppose the florist to be possessed of a good quantity of roots, and then teach him their management and care, after that I shall instruct him in improving his collection by encreasing the varieties, by raising these delightful plants by the seeds.

Derivation of the name

And first of all for these, as for other plants, a proper soil must be prepared, but over nicety need not be observed in that composition. They require a light rich earth, and for this any good mould will do, by being made light with a mixture of drift sand, and enriched with a mixture of well rotted cows dung. Miller, lest the number of his different composts should not be great enough, has ordered a fresh one for the planting of these flowers, whereas he might have referred to several other sorts for different roots which would have done full as well for these. We admire the maiden earth from a rich pasture-ground, with the sward well rotted mixed, and wrought. This, as I have observed before, answers almost for every part of vegetation. Miller recommend it here, and we approve of it, but by fetching it away for every article we want it, we shall soon clear the grazier of a good field, so that where such is not absolutely necessary, it should not ever be even hinted at, for we are loading the curious observer of Nature in the vegetable world with such an embargo of inconveniences and expence, as perhaps will tire him in pursuit of those things, which might afford him the most pleasing reflections, and give him the greatest satisfaction in the course of his after life. A light rich earth, then, is all these plants want, and a good garden mould, whether of a black or reddish nature, which may be always procured from the kitchen-garden, and which will be always made up by the supply of manure brought there, is as proper as any thing for them. Let this be mixed with a fourth part of drift sand, and a fourth part of well rotted cows dung, and the business is done. But this is only telling the reader what will be proper if he is short of other compost, or is but a new letter upon the flower way. We have directed a compost for the auricula, for the hyacinth, &c. The auricula compost is an excellent one for these flowers, and it may be eked out by an addition of good garden-mould from the kitchen garden, or if the hyacinth compost is used, half garden mould may be added to it, and the *Ranunculus* will thrive admirably well in such composition. However, if our florist has been for some time established in the art, there is nothing better for these roots than the mould of an old hyacinth bed. Hyacinths ought never to be planted in the same bed again, and as in oeconomy these things may be put to such advantage in other use as to make the desiring of it unnecessary. Indeed, without such good management there will be no end of compositions of different sorts to be procured and after they are done with, what heaps of such used earth would be soon raised! Let, therefore, the *Ranunculi* be planted in the used Hyacinth mould, and if there should not be enough of it, add a sufficient quantity from the kitchen garden, and your roots will soon testify how well they like such a composition. And to make amends to the kitchen garden for whatever is taken from thence, make it a rule always to carry the emptyings of the auricula pots, old beds, &c for these will be excellent for the growth of vegetables for the table, and having the addition of the usual manures, will be soon wrought into the natural soil. This is there will be no diminution in that part the kitchen-

Of the management and composts proper for the Ranunculi

garden will have as many comings-in as goings-out, and the balance of power in every reſpect will be kept up and obſerved Having, therefore, a proper mould of any of theſe or the like ſorts, mark out the places for your beds They ſhould be five feet broad, and their length or number muſt be according to the number of roots Then clear out the natural ſoil to the depth of two feet, and having a wooden frame ready, one foot high in the front, and two feet and a half high in the back, fix it in its proper place, to keep up the mould that is to be raiſed above the common level The *Ranunculi* muſt be placed in a ſloping bed, like the Hyacinth, which will ſhew them to advantage, and then being thus elevated and the mould kept compact by ſuch a frame, will ſtill be an addition to their poſition The ſpace is then to be filled up with well-wrought, fine, light, rich earth, of ſome or other of the before-named ſorts This is not to be ſcreened, and it ſhould be in the beds a fortnight or three weeks before the roots are to be ſet, that it may have time firſt properly to ſettle As to the time of their being planted, it may be done any time of the autumn or winter, but there are three months that are deemed moſt proper, each of which has its advantages and diſadvantages These months are September, October, and the beginning of February If they are planted in September, they will be in full blow with the Hyacinths, they will be fair and large as their nature will admit of, and will have forty, fifty, or more flowers, belonging to a root There will be alſo the greateſt increaſe that can be in the roots, and theſe ſurely are advantages enough But the diſadvantages attending ſuch early-planted roots are, there will be no end of the trouble to keep them all winter, for without conſtant care, nurſing, and management, there will not only be a diſappointment of the blow, but the roots will be all loſt We will, however, ſuppoſe them planted at that time, and then follow them through the ſeaſon until the time of flowering

*What months are moſt proper for planting theſe flowers*

*Method of planting them*

In planting them, firſt clear off the mould of the ſurface of the bed ſufficient to cover the plants at leaſt two inches deep Then plant the roots with the crown upwards, by ſtraight lines, at ſix inches aſunder After this, let them be covered two inches above the crown, by ſpreading the earth carefully over them, and having neated up the bed the buſineſs is done In a few weeks the plants will come up, and will ſoon ſhew themſelves ſuch vigorous ſpreaders as to demand all poſſible care during the winter, for the leaves will be grown ſo large before the bad weather comes on, that they will be more liable to ſuffer by froſt, rain, or hail, ſo that having the plants in ſuch forwardneſs, ſhades muſt be put over the beds, to cover them on the approach of bad weather And this muſt be conſtantly attended to, for if they are neglected, when ſo forward as they will be ſure to be, no very hard froſt will deſtroy them, nay if this ſhould not happen, very immoderate rains falling on them will cauſe them to mould, which will bring on diſeaſes and death In March, a more than ordinary care is ſtill to be taken They will be then getting forward for flowering, and at that time nothing is more deſtructive to them than hail, ſo that they muſt be conſtantly guarded againſt all externals of that ſort, and if with diligence and attention they can be thus preſerved all winter, their blow will be the moſt perfect Art can bring them to Every good root will have forty or fifty, or more flowers, belonging to them Theſe will be large and fair, and being ſo early in the ſeaſon will continue in beauty much longer than thoſe that flower later After all, I can hardly recommend this month for planting them, for if the ſtricteſt care is not obſerved, they will be pretty certain of being killed by bad weather, and if they are protected by ſhades and coverings of mats in froſty weather, and coverings in the ſame manner in rainy weather, to prevent their moulding, if ſuch coverings are kept on too long, they will bring on the diſeaſe they were deſigned to prevent, they will more effectually procure a mouldineſs than the heavieſt rains, ſo that every thing muſt be ſo contrived as to let them have all free air as well as ſafeguard, which will be attended with much trouble and hazard, but which, if you ſucceed, will be rewarded by a very extraordinary blow, and an extraordinary multiplication of the roots

*October the beſt month, and ſureſt*

October is the uſual month for planting theſe flowers, it is the ſureſt, and as ſuch may be termed the beſt month of the two for the purpoſe The leaves will be but ſmall during the winter, and leſs liable to ſuffer by any extremity of froſt, rain, or hail They muſt be guarded, however, like the others, in bad weather, but not with ſuch great nicety Nor can hail hurt them while they are ſo ſmall, and if the taking off of the covering at a proper time ſhould be omitted, they will not be liable to mouldineſs The roots that are planted at this time will flower with the tulips, and will be very beautiful and fair, though not with the luxuriance of the others, if they have good luck It is, however, the moſt eligible month of the two for planting them, eſpecially if a perſon has a deal of buſineſs to call him off from the nice attendance the September planted roots will require to bring them to flower Miller recommends October for the planting of theſe roots, and before I quit that month, I cannot but take notice of a practice he adviſes, when the plants appear, to lay freſh earth, the ſame with which the beds were compoſed, half an inch thick, all over the beds Juſtice to the public obliges me to take notice of this, as ſeveral young Floriſts have complained to me, that by following Mr Miller's advice of covering the plants as they came up, to defend the crown of the root from froſt, as he ſays, they have had the mortification of never ſeeing them more This covering of them, tho they will ſometimes break through it, is often of dangerous conſequence, and ends in the entire rotting of the whole plants Neither would there be any ſort of occaſion for it, were the leaves ſure to reſume their ſtrength, and break through it for being planted two inches deep, they will have mould enough above the crown And though ſuch practice may ſometimes do no harm, yet as it is attended with danger, and has often proved fatal, it is beſt to omit this covering of earth, and let them be covered with mats only in ſevere froſts

*A pernicious practice of Miller exploded*

*February a good month for planting theſe flowers*

The other good ſeaſon for planting of theſe roots is the beginning of February This is called the Spring-Planting, and is the ſafeſt of all others, being attended with no hazard, for the plants will not appear above ground, to be in danger of hurt, before the very hard froſts are over, ſo that they will require no more trouble than making the beds and planting, even hooping of them will be unneceſſary, for they will want no covering, and what a deal of trouble will this ſave! The diſadvantages, however, attending this ſeaſon of planting are conſiderable Their roots will afford little increaſe, they will not blow before June, the flowers will be ſmall, and coming at ſo hot a ſeaſon, of ſhorter duration

*Diſadvantages attending it*

tion. The florist ought, however, to divide his roots between the October and February planting, nay if he has got a large quantity, and much leisure-time, they should be divided into three lots, to be planted at each of the above-named times, and then as one bed goes off another will succeed. With this management he will have a show of these delightful flowers, on one bed or other, for near a quarter of a year together.

After their blow is over, and their stalks and leaves are entirely withered, they must be taken up, and laid in a dry airy place, but by no means in the sun: and, after they are thoroughly dry, they may be cleared of all mould, offsets, &c. then put into paper bags, or laid on a dry shelf, until the time of planting is before. But this must not be in the same soil; fresh earth must always be brought, of one or other of the before-mentioned kinds, and when it has blowed the flowers, it may be wheeled into the kitchen garden, to be serviceable here.

In order to obtain good seeds, a quantity of the Semidouble *Ranunculi* are to be procured, for the full flowers never produce seeds. These must be those of the brighter colours, and a few will be sufficient, for they will produce seeds in plenty enough. As the seeds ripen, they should be gathered every day, and laid upon a sheet of white paper until the whole is gathered. Then put them into white paper bags, and hang them in a dry place until the time of sowing.

Time of sowing the seed. Miller directs the middle of August for the work, but this is very bad advice, for, if properly managed, the plants will come up by October, and if it be attended with so much trouble to preserve a collection of old plants with strong roots through the interchanges of frost and snow, rain and hail, what must it be to nurse a collection of seedlings all winter, that have a month or two only made their appearance? Keep the seeds, therefore, until the beginning of March, and then sow them in the following manner. Take some of the auricula compost, or some other of the like nature, and of this make a bed in a shady open place, sufficient to contain the seeds. Shallow pans, boxes, &c. have been recommended; but they are improper. It will be almost impossible, when the plants come up, to keep the mould in a proper degree of moisture, and we prefer beds for the same reason we do for the reception of the seeds of the tulip. Sow the seeds thinly in these beds in rows, setting a stick at each end of each row for a direction, and do but just cover them with mould. Till this time the beds must be kept moist, during the dry winds and sun of March and April weather, if it is not mingled, as it generally is, with a succession of showers, and in April the plants will come up, at which time settled dry weather often comes on, and then in particular the beds must be kept to a certain degree of moisture. We have ordered the beds to be made in the shade, and then a little sprinkling in the morning and again in the evening, with a fine rosed pan, will be sufficient, I say, a little sprinkling, and this repeated often, and it will much refresh them, but if they have too much at a time, it will endanger the rotting of the whole crop. If the beds in which the seeds are sown are not in the shade, they must be hooped and covered with mats in the heat of the day, or there will probably be soon an end to all your hopes; and if the seeds were few, and sown in pots, they may be set in the shade (but not under the drip of trees), and plunged up to the rim, and it will keep them, with proper watering, as cool as if sown in the open ground. Thus, by keeping the beds to a proper degree of moisture, the seedling plants will continue growing longer in the season, and their roots will be larger; and when their leaves are withered, they must be taken up, and managed like old roots.

The next year they will flower, when the worst sorts may be thrown away, and those of the best properties preserved, to join in the collection of established flowers.

The properties of a good *Ranunculus* are, — Properties of a good Ranunculus.

1. The stalk must be straight and strong, elevating the flower in an upright position.

2. The flower should be large and full, and very double, though the Semidoubles are by many esteemed for their fair colours, as well as for producing of seeds.

3. The colours should be as opposite as possible, bright and distinct, and disposed in small, even, straight lines.

4. The figure of the flowers ought to be regular and uniform, by the disposition and incurvature of the different petals.

A flower that has all these properties may be said to be a perfect one, though there are many valuable flowers that will not answer to all of them, so they are not too strictly to be observed. — Remarks.

To keep up and improve the collection of these flowers, the seeds should be sown every year, and for this purpose it would be proper for a correspondence to be kept up between two or three friends who can depend upon each other, after the two or three first years, for the seeds will degenerate, and will not be so good as fresh, procured from a distance. When the seeds begin to ripen, they must be watched and carefully gathered every day, until you have the whole crop, for there will be three weeks difference between the first and the latest ripe, and these should be kept in clean white paper bags, in an airy dry place, until the time of sowing.

The old Turkey *Ranunculus*, which is so well known, and which is, by our modern florists, esteemed an antiquated flower, ought to be held in more esteem than the present fashion allows it, for it is an admirable flower, as it at once strikes the eye and the mind, and the man of true taste, let the fashion for flowers be what it will, will never be without a bed or two of them. Their culture is easy; for they are much hardier than the Persian sorts, and if they are planted in February, and covered with about an inch of mould, they will reward such easy labour by charms enough when they blow in the spring, or the beginning of the summer. — Old Turkey Ranunculus recommended.

CHAP.

# *ANEMONE* The WIND-FLOWER

Introductory remarks

INFERIOR in beauty to none, though perhaps the least cultivated of any of the seven capital shed flowers, is the Wind Flower, for which no other reason can be assigned, than the inattention it has mostly met with, perhaps, in the great regard and over-care of the other sorts, and which in turn oft, and the nature of the flower duly weighed, reason would direct us to shew it more respect than it has hitherto met with, for its charms in its variety of colours are unrivalled, and its composition is of such a nature as to form (if the phrase may be allowed) a continuous beauty. There is a certain freedom or ease in this flower that is not common; they blow with those truly admired flowers the *Ranunculus* at all the times, but the proportions required to establish a compleat flower of that kind, give it rather a stiff formal look. Nothing of this is to be found in the *Anemone*, and without destroying the preceding flower, for that in its utmost perfection, the *Anemone* shews itself without that stiff look in its varieties of all colours, (yellow excepted) large and double, in all its natural luxuriance and ease, waving with every wind its petals of so delicate a texture, so soft and susceptible as to be affected by every breath of air, opening and shutting, and gently obeying the direction and impulse of such external...

Origin of the Name

The word is formed of the Greek, ἄνεμος which signifies the wind; a title which is not improperly given it on many accounts. Some suppose this name to be given it from the downy matter belonging to the seeds, which are easily blown by the wind. Pliny, and many others, suppose it not to open, except the wind blows; but this is a strange supposition, for experience teaches us, that it expands and opens most when there is the least wind and most sun. It is with most reason then called *Anemone*, or wind flower, as being easily moved, and seemingly affected by every breath of it.

This is not peculiar to the flower alone, but the very leaves and all the are liable to the same impression; and if too the downy substance attending the seeds be taken into consideration, the word *Anemone* is with great propriety given to this genus of plants.

Beautiful and delicate then as this plant is, it has other properties to recommend itself, and it demands a greater share of culture than what is usually given it; what chiefly is its hardy nature, and little trouble in the culture. So that the same encouragements which these afford to the tulip in raising them to a degree of eminence, belong equally to the *Anemone*, for it is so hardy, that nothing but such severity of weather as does not usually happen, can make them unsafe under it.

The *Anemone* is divided into two sorts, or departments.

Sorts

1. The single *Anemone*.
2. The double *Anemone*.

1. The single *Anemone* is planted chiefly for the sake of the seeds from which the double sorts are raised. It is called by the florist the parent of the rest, and he is equally anxious in procuring some of the best of these to breed from, as he is for the preservation and ordering the other sorts in their perfect state. But besides the uses of this sort in affording seeds, it is in its varieties very beautiful, and though a single flower, the petals are large and of various colours.

Indeed, there is no flower more proper to make a show in winter, and the early spring months, than the single *Anemone*, and besides a bed or two, which should be always in view of the sitting-room, a large quantity of them should be intermixed with other perennial early blowing flowers, such as crocuses, snow-drops, christmas roses, yellow aconites, hepaticas, &c. The double flowering sorts also, if unremoved and left to nature, will frequently flower at these times, so that when the delicacy and nice art of the florist is not kept up, they will do very well with ruder culture, and be ready for any discipline in perennial quarters, where general collections are raised, and where general culture only is afforded.

Double Anemone.

2. Double *Anemone*. These constitute the whole blow of Established Flowers in all their varieties and colours. The culture of both is the same, and is very easy; and having first supposed the florist to be possessed of a good quantity of roots, I shall direct him to their proper management, and then shall proceed to instruct him how to improve his collection by the most curious method of raising them from seeds.

Proper compost for them.

Having therefore a good collection of roots the chief is to have a proper soil and for their reception, and for this I would prefer one excellently adapted to their nature. To give directions therefore for a fresh compost will not only be needless, but I depending on the raising of them is fresh burthen of labour and expence. I have given the proper compost for the *Ranunculus*, and art has never yet found a more proper one for the *Anemone*, so that when a person has both these flowers, and others, for which such a composition will agree, he must at the time of mixing the parts, multiply his quantity, and make his heap in the composition large enough for the great or all supplies.

But here I must observe, that as willow mould is a material ingredient in the auricula compost, particularly for the raising them from seeds, and as it is a scarce article in many places, it should be reserved purely for those sorts for the *Auricula*, and several other sorts for which the auricula compost is ordered to be used, will do full as well without the ingredient of willow mould. This therefore is the most perfect compost for these kinds of flowers, though it is not absolutely necessary to be used, for they will grow very well, and flower fair and strong in a rich light soil or almost any sort. This I mention for the Gardener not to be discouraged if he has not a sufficient stock of auricula compost, for if he takes three or four loads of good garden mould, mixing with it two loads of cow's dung rotted to a soil, and a load of drift sand, they will grow and flower in great luxuriancy and strength. Some other composts also that have been used during a ... of garden ... is equally good, and this I mention ... to the ... to ... and ... all ... with regard to them ...

The ... compost especially is most excellent, and after it has blowed those flowers ... be ... following ... in equal quantity of good mould from the kitchen garden.

In all ... [illegible]

so, but I have had them very weak and poorly after planting them in a fresh soil with the sward rotted I verily believe the soil was too fresh, and that its not having been got long enough, and sufficiently turned, was the occasion of it, so that I am pretty certain, if such a soil is not twelve months before mixed and kept in constant turning, well-wrought garden mould will be better

The florist now may chuse for himself, and may prepare for planting his roots in such a composition as will be attended with most convenience to himself, for they will not only do well, but excel in any of the above-mentioned soils, tho' it must be said the first is to be preferred, but I have known them flower equally as well in the other sorts Let the florist, therefore, humour his composition (retaining nevertheless the like nature) for his own ease Against the next year, however, let him prepare in his composition one-eighth of good marle and let this be repeated every other year, having alternately that ingredient in the composition, if it can be easily got

Having the compost ready, a fortnight before it is to be used mark out the place for the bed, and clear the natural soil away in the manner directed for the *Ranunculus*, two feet deep, then having a wooden frame on one side one foot deep in the front, and two feet and an half in the back part, fix it in its proper place, and fill the whole with the compost This is to be done a fortnight at least before the time of planting, that the mould may settle equally, and these flowers must be planted in the same kind of sloping beds as the *Ranunculus*, not only the better to shoot off the wet, but to shew them to a greater advantage The beds should be made to face the south, tho' a south east is a good aspect, and I have ordered the beds to be elevated, chiefly for the more graceful appearance of the flowers in blow If a wooden frame is not prepared, or a person is not willing to go to the expence of it, the beds may be made and raised only in the usual way, a little rounding at the top, though if it be a damp soil in which the beds are made, it will be highly necessary to elevate them at least a foot above the level If the place be naturally dry, and they are planted even with the surface, it will be never the worse for the plants, but they will appear greatly to a disadvantage in such a low and seemingly slovenly bed

The time for planting, like the *Ranunculus* is different, according to the time the owner could wish to have his show of flowers, for if they are planted at different times, a succession of these delightful flowers may be continued for two months or more

Best time for planting. The usual time of planting, for the earliest blow, however, is in the middle of September, at which time the surface of the compost must be taken off three inches deep Lines must be then drawn, and they must be planted at the same distance, with the bud or eye upwards, as the *Ranunculus*, and they must be covered in the same manner three inches deep By the end of October the plants will come up, but will require no extraordinary trouble all the winter There are those indeed who cover them in frosty weather, and nurse them in the same manner as the *Ranunculus* but I never yet found them call for such care I ever planted them abroad, and never covered any, and yet never knew them suffer by the severest frosts, unless by those that came late in the spring, and then the worst damage was by destroying the thrum in the middle of the flower, making it appear single, so that all the care (if any) really necessary for these plants is to hoop the beds, and in the cutting black frosts to cover them with mats, taking them off as soon as the weather thaws Such trouble will not be great, and it will effectually preserve the bloom, and more than that is a task imposed on the florist which I have ever in the whole course of my practice, found needless

The crop planted in September will be in blow early in April at the time the hyacinths shine in their glory, and they will keep pace with that noble though very different flower, declining about the same time with it This is the time of planting those roots for the earliest shew, a second planting may be made in October, in the same manner, and these will be in flower before the others are gone off and for the third crop, it would not be adviseable to plant them before the month of March

Miller advises to plant them about Christmas, but this is a very dangerous time, for an *Anemone* is more liable to be destroyed by wet in winter, than any plant, and the roots being planted at that dead inactive time if much wet should happen, it will probably be destructive to the greatest part of them Nay, the only danger to the roots that I know is to be apprehended from over moisture, and although they are often proof against such a matter, yet it is sometimes their bane The best way is to defer the work until all danger on that account is past The roots planted in the end of March, should be set only two inches deep, and as their blow will be when the sun has great strength, to continue their bloom they ought to be shaded, and the late planted roots will sometimes blow as fair as those set in autumn But as their increase will be very inconsiderable, unless a person has plenty of roots, he ought to have them in the ground soon enough in the autumn, and by being repeated, they will multiply soon to any desired number for planting at any season

The time for taking up their roots is when the leaves and flower stalks are entirely dried and withered Then they are to be laid in a dry airy place, but not in the sun, and after they are cleared of all mould filth, &c they should be laid on a dry sheet, or put into some open drawers in a warm room, or they may be put into paper bags, if the place they are hung in be warm and dry, for otherwise in bags they will often contract a mouldiness about the bud or crown which will bring on distempers and death

About a fortnight before they are planted afresh, the roots should be divided, and all off-sets taken off, that the plants may thoroughly heal, which may occasion if deferred until the time of being set, a mouldiness of bad consequence They must not be divided into too many parts, if you expect a good blow the succeeding year, though if you are desirous of making your increase very great, they may be divided into as many parts as there are buds or crowns, for each of these, by being set, will become a separate plant If these plants should happen to be neglected taking up as soon as their leaves and flower-stalks are decayed, they will strike out fresh fibres, especially at the coming on of the first shower of rain, so that their time of resting must be carefully attended to If this should happen to be neglected, and they begin to strike afresh, they must be let alone for that season If an open winter should follow, many of them will blow great part of the latter end of it, and their roots by the next season of removing will have made prodigious increase Proceed we now to the method of raising these plants from seeds

The seeds should be gathered from the Single Flowers that are the largest, consist of the greatest number of petals, and have the best colours, Method of raising Anemones from seeds

 part cu-particularly the deep violet, the purple and such as are of a bright clear red These should be planted in September or October purely for the sake of the seeds, and in dry weather, during the time of their flowering, should be frequently watered, and the surface of the mould now and then stirred, which will cause them to ripen the seeds the better

In about three weeks after the flowers are faded you must begin to watch for the ripening of the seeds, for if they are not constantly attended to, as they ripen, they will be blown away, being enclosed, as has been observed, in a cottony or downy substance This attendance must be regularly given, until all the seeds are ripe, are gathered, and are well dried The beds should be next prepared for sowing, or the business should be deferred until the beginning of March The auricula mould is the best that can be thought of, and a bed in a well sheltered situation is to be formed of it, open to the south or south east Care must be taken to separate the seeds, or they will clog together and fall in lumps The best way for this is to mix them with some dry garden mould, and rub them well together, which being so thoroughly done that the seeds and mould are equally mixed and blended, sow them all together upon a bed made level and even If they were rubbed in a small quantity of mould, sow them the thinner if in a larger quantity, scatter it about in greater plenty, but not so, but that the seeds may fall rather thinly over the bed, and this is the best method of separating these seeds and sowing them even About a quarter of an inch is the covering they are to have, and the beds are immediately to be hooped to be covered with mats in the heat of the day This covering must be regularly observed every morning of an hot day, but must be taken off every evening an hour before sun set, and in all cloudy and rainy weather must never be put on If the weather proves dry, every evening a little water must be given them with a fine rosed watering pot, and this must be sprinkled about so as to fall but little heavier upon them than a good mist, for if they are carelessly watered with a common pan, the seeds will be washed out, the mould soddened, and the whole bed proportionally disordered

If these rules be strictly observed, in about six weeks or two months the plants will come up, so that the sooner this is done after the seeds are ready, it will be the better, that they may gain strength, the better to weather it through the winter At the approach of bad weather some furze bushes should be stuck round the bed, which will be all the protection they will want from common frost, for they will require only the keenest edge of the cutting winds to be taken off If the frost sets in very severe, the beds should be matted, and with this management they may pass the winter That is the best season of sowing to have these plants in greatest forwardness, though there will be some trouble in the attendance all the winter, and after all, if they are not wholly protected from frost, (which will be still additional trouble) it will throw many of the roots out of the ground If the season, as it often is, is attended with constant rains and wet weather there will be great danger of the greatest part of them being rotten So that the safest way is to defer the sowing until the beginning of March, which is the time used, as I am informed, by most of the Dutch florists of note The beginning of March, then, is another, and (if the trouble is regarded) the best season for sowing these seeds They must be sown as before directed, the beds must be hooped, and, as the drying March winds and hot weather come on, must be covered, but always left open in mild moist weather Now and then even in March, and every other night in April, if the weather proves dry, they must be watered with a fine-rosed pan, as before directed, and by the end of April, or beginning of May, the young plants will come up The weeds must be pulled up as they appear in the earliest state The days will be long, and the sun powerful, so that from nine o'clock in the morning until five in the afternoon the mats must shade the beds, except in open, mild, cloudy, or rainy weather, and when the opposite of dry hot weather happens, they must have a little water every evening This is to be their management until their leaves begin to fade, then watering is to be left off, and they may be exposed to any weather, as it shall happen None of these late sowed seedlings need be taken up the first year, unless they come too thick or in clusters, then having a bed ready for their reception, they may be thinned, before the leaves are entirely decayed, which will be destruction to the roots With these take up the mould, and about half an inch deep plant them in drills, sowing the mould with them, in the new prepared bed Thus the seedlings may be thinned at pleasure, but if they do not come up too close, the whole may be omitted until the year following But with regard to the seeds sowed the summer before, and which have had the trouble of nursing and protection all winter, and the same shade and care in the spring, their roots will be grown to rather a larger size, which will make a thinning of these more necessary, nevertheless it may be omitted, if the plants are not too thick Whether it be done or not, the beds will require no other trouble than gently stirring the surface, and sifting a little of the same compost over it, about a quarter of an inch deep This is to be done immediately after the leaves are decayed, and are cleared off, and almost upon the first showers they will begin to put out fresh fibres, and prepare for shooting, so that early in the autumn, your young family will again make their appearance above ground As the frosts come on the winter following some furze bushes are to be pricked round the bed, which should be taken away when the frost is gone, to give way for the free air in open weather, and this is all the trouble they will require all winter Most of your modern books of gardening, indeed, give orders about covering them and protecting them with much tenderness and care all the winter, but I ever found it unnecessary I always by this time found them hardy enough If a person, however, is not willing to run the same hazard, he may guard them by mats, hooping the beds, and covering them during all bad weather As the spring advances, and the weeds of course come up, they must be regularly cleared, and in all dry weather, the beds must be frequently watered, whilst the leaves are green and in a growing state As soon as they begin to decay, watering must be left off, and when they are entirely decayed, the plants must be taken up, and treated as the old roots As soon, therefore, as you have taken up as many roots as you can find, smooth the surface of the bed, and sift over it a quarter of an inch of fresh mould, and you will find a plentiful crop of it coming up early in the autumn There will be many roots that will escape the notice of the strictest eye they being small, and their natural figure and colour being very much like that of the soil in which they grow Many of these will flower the preceding spring, and most of the others being taken up

and

and managed like old roots, will at that time shew their bloom. Judgment must not, for the first year, be passed upon them with regard to their value, for I have had many blowers that have appeared very indifferent for one, two, or more years, and afterwards displayed their charms, forming complete flowers, in their different shades and colours. They ought, therefore, to be planted for at least three years successively, and then the worst sorts thrown away, whilst those of the best properties should be reserved, to join in the collection.

Properties of a good Anemone. The properties of the *Anemone* or Wind-Flower are,

1. The stalk should be large and strong in proportion to the size of the flower it is to bear.

2. The flowers should be large and very double, having the middle well filled with numerous petals, soft and delicate, and beautifully arranged in their different series.

3. The outward petals ought to be much larger than those that fill the flower, and should be rounded off in an easy agreeable manner.

4. The colours should be clear and bright, of what nature soever they are of.

5. The outward petals, and those which fill the flowers, ought to be of different colours, and the whole distinctly variegated, or else blaze and glow with variety of hues.

Remarks. The last property, being possessed of the foregoing, constitutes a perfect flower, of which we must expect but few, even by many sowings; so that these rules are not to be too strictly observed, for there are many beautiful flowers, worthy of all regard, that will not strictly answer, in all respects, to the above observations. They must, therefore, by every one be softened at pleasure, whilst the few that can stand such a test must be reckoned as perfect flowers, and valued accordingly.

Method of multiplying these flowers. Their number will be soon multiplied, as the present valuable collection of the English and Dutch florists witnesses, by parting of the roots. But in order to encrease the number of different valuable sorts, the seeds ought to be sown every year, which will afford great pleasure from hope and expectation, as well as reward us for our labours, by the appearance and perfection of those before unseen treasures. To set off a show of these flowers in the best manner, besides planting them in that sloping way which has been directed, the Gardener should have the different sorts all numbered, that he may know them at the time of planting, when he should properly chequer them, by forming a proper mixture of the purples, reds, blues, browns, whites, &c. planting among these, in the most conspicuous places, the variegated sorts, and those which shine and blaze with colours of different hues.

## *DIANTHUS*, The CARNATION.

Introductory remarks. THE last, and greatly differing from all the other shed flowers, is the Carnation, the pride of the summer, and the glory of the florists art at that season. Though strangely differing in the nature of its composition, as well as time of flowering, from the other sorts, whether we regard the root, leaves, stalk, or flower, it is inferior to few of them in the variety it causes, in the profusion of sorts, differing from each other in colour, or some respect or other. They together constitute the whole of the florists collection, and are distinguished into Free Blowers and Broken Flowers, each of which, as in the other sorts, have names for distinction imposed upon them by their different raisers, some of which are very pompous, some after the name of the place or person who raised them, and some so ridiculous as to be repeated in merriment and derision only. I have known a Carnation go by the name of the Fiery Trial, and the Bleeding Swain, and had another sent me that was called the Dutchess of Hamilton's Pride. I only mention this to warn the florist, for the future, when he raises a fresh flower, to beware of such kind of names as tend only to bring the art into ridicule and contempt.

The prodigious number of sorts of which our present collection of Carnations is composed, in all their assortments or lots, are varieties only of one species, which is the Single Carnation, or Clove Gilliflower, and it is from the seeds of this plant that Double flowers of different colours are produced, and these again improved by happy culture, until the commencement of the amazing collection of our present established flowers.

Sorts. Carnations are divided into two classes, called,

Broken Flowers.

Free Blowers.

These also have different assortments, according to the nature of their colours or stripes, and as the nature and management of all is the same, from the first planting the layer till its time of flowering, I shall begin at that period, which we may suppose to be in August, and so trace it until it shews itself in its glory the summer following.

Culture and management of these flowers. And first of all, as in others, a proper compost for this plant, which will require very little trouble, must be prepared. An old melon or cucumber bed affords proper materials to mix with some good garden-mould, or fresh, loamy, fattish soil, of double the quantity of the former, and if to this an eighth part of drift sand be added, the composition is excellent. This must be made many months before, and the whole kept in frequent turning, that the old dung may be converted to mould, and properly mixed and blended with the others, so as to form one common uniform mass. The year following the layers should be planted in the composition of the sort of mould and sand, but instead of horse, sheeps dung or cows may be added, and if to all these be added some old rotten thatch, converted to a soil, it heightens the repast for all plants of this nature. The auricula compost is excellent for these flowers, and many of the before directed sorts, to save trouble, may be used. But it may be necessary to warn the florist from admitting any of an old hyacinth-bed into his composition, which is said to bring on certain destruction to plants of this kind. Whichever of these composts be used for these flowers, he must still alter the dung in the composition for the succeeding year, and he will find the effects of it, by having stronger plants, producing larger and fairer flowers.

Having, therefore, a proper mould and layers ready for planting, it has been usual to set them in small pots, that many of the plants may be covered by a hooped frame in the severity of winter, and then in the middle of February to plant them into larger for their flowering. This method has been practised with success, but it is often attended with bad consequences, and has inevitable inconveniences. A Carnation is not naturally a very tender plant, but tenderness is brought on them by such careful nursing, so that like the true Ignoble, they can never afterwards be made to bear the winter blasts, and homely fare of the rustics. It is known to every one, that the layers we receive from France are much tenderer than those from plants of our own raising. The cause is manifest, it is the nature of their education, and not of the plant; and those we may any time for the future receive from thence must be nursed with more than ordinary tenderness and care. But it behoves us to make these, and indeed all plants, as hardy as our climate will admit, and what a world of trouble will be saved in the nursing and nice management of them in winter. Again, as layers placed under glasses are naturally made more tender, so are they more liable to destruction in the course of their after management. The design of these glasses is to secure them from bad weather in winter, and the placing them in small pots is, that numbers of them may be crowded together. What is to be done after? "Why, in the middle of February," says Miller, "you must transplant these layers into pots for their bloom." Now every one knows that the greatest danger attending these plants is the severity of the spring; and how often have we experienced of late years, that the chief of our winterly weather has happened after that time; and how well qualified will these tenderly nursed plants be, all the early part of the season, to be carried out into the open air, to grapple with every blast, and patiently endure any weather as it shall come? I have known a south east wind in March more destructive to the vegetable world, than any black frosts from the north, and I am sure if any plant has a more than ordinary protection, it should be continued until the dangers that caused it are removed, or it had better never have had it. Another inconvenience attending, though, perhaps, not a very considerable one, is a removing of these plants again in the spring, when they are in full shoot and powers of vegetation. All transplanting causes a backwardness to the progress of plants; and though a Carnation suffers as little by this with proper management, as almost any plant, yet it is a backening, and for that reason, as well as the extraordinary trouble attending, would be better to be avoided.

At the time, therefore, of your raising the layers, plant them in large pots, called Peck Pots, filled with some or other of the above composts, one to each pot, and as near the middle as possible; then give them a small watering, and set them in a shady place. By the end of October move them into the situation they are to have for the winter, which should be a well sheltered place, and the pots should be placed where the sun in the shortest days may shine on them. If the places are not well guarded by clipt hedges, or plantations, a square may be made of a reed-hedge, which will be excellent defence; and indeed, if it is a well-sheltered place, if the like kind of square with reed hedges be made, placing them in rows by the northern side upon boards or tiles, the pots themselves fronting the sun, and readily receiving the nourishment and exhilarating power of the sun and mild weather through the winter, it will be more agreeable to their nature than all the hotbed frames in the world.

If you have any French flowers, indeed, that have been used to tender nursing, that must be repeated, and such must be removed into the green-house, or under a hot bed frame or some shelter, if the weather should prove extraordinary bad; but for the other sorts the above protection is the best, and though you will often lose layers, as you will in every method of trial, yet this way it least happens, and when it does, the survivors are always the healthiest and best plants in the spring, because having weathered it out, they are dissatisfied in winter, they rejoice and exult in the pleasure of a calm and repose.

In the spring, then, supply the vacancies of dead layers, if any there be, by planting others in their room. Stir the surface of the mould, and add about half an inch more of the fresh soil from the compost yard. In this situation let them remain until the end of April, when they will require more shade, the sun by that time being so powerful, that if they were suffered to endure its full blaze and force, it would soon cause them to flag and droop; and though this would be regained every night by the influence of the dews and opposite weather, yet, on the whole, it would retard their vigorous growth. Move them, therefore, into the shade, but where they may enjoy a free air, and the morning sun till ten o'clock. Water them every other evening, and against they begin to spindle, you must be provided with a quantity of straight sticks, which if made of deal, will be lighter and better. These sticks must have small holes across, in which to place wires horizontally, to guide each spindle. These wires should one just fit the holes by their straight end, and the other should be made with a proper crook to embrace the spindle. The sticks must be placed at a distance from the layers, in proportion to the size of the flowers, and as the spindles advance, the wires must be placed for their support and protection, keeping them parallel with the sticks, and in an exact upright position. As the flower-stalks, commonly called spindles, naturally branch a little at the top, as those divisions are made, the weaker must always be taken off, so that there ought not to be above one or two flowers to each layer. A large Broken Flower will not be brought to perfection, if it has any partner in its glory; and a Free Blower ought not to have more than two proceeding from the lower root. In this situation, and with this management, they may remain until their buds are greatly swelled, and begin to open, by which time you should have erected a low stage, on which to place them for the time of flowering.

This stage should consist of a flight of seats, but built so low, that the highest row should not shew the flower when in blow, higher than about the breast high; and as they are to be supported to be exactly upright, if they were higher their beauties would not be at a view. After this hint let every one build this stage to the height he pleases.

The aspect of this stage should be full upon the south, or south east. It should not be placed too near old walls or buildings; it ought to have free air, but yet defended in some little distance from the violence of the wind from every quarter, by some sort of trees or other, which if unrestrained in its full range, will cause great devastation

vastation to those plants both before and at their time of blow.

Large shallow pans or pots should be provided, with very thick strong bottoms, well burnt, to encrease their strength. In these the feet of the stage are to be placed, and if they are placed level upon even sand or mould, made smooth and firm, it is amazing what a weight they will bear without breaking. Each of them are to be for each foot of the stage, and they are constantly to be kept full of water, to keep off earwigs and other vermin; for as the flower-buds open, these will soon find them out, will eat off the bottom of the petals of each flower, and soon end all your hopes.

It has been customary to fix hogs claws, tobacco-pipe heads, &c. upon the tops of sticks, as traps to take them and kill them. They will repair to these after their repast, but then the mischief is often past recovery done. They first eat what they think proper, bringing on thereby destruction, and then repair to these stratagems, as an asylum for their after ease and indulgence; and this is the only way of taking them, when they attack flowers planted in the full ground. But those in pots, designed for show, they ought never to come at; for the destroying of a single petal often destroys the uniformity of the flower. No method is so effectual to preserve this, as these little watering-cisterns, which cut off all communication between the garden and the stage, causing safety from those devourers to the flowers thereon. And as these stages ought not to be placed too near old walls or buildings, because they would draw up the plants, and cause them to spindle weak, so ought they not on account of these insects, for they will throw themselves from them upon the stage. Neither ought any late flowers in beds be made to grow near this stage; for it is amazing to what a great distance those creatures will throw themselves, by an elastic force, from any greater elevation. This stage must have a covering to take on and off, to give the flowers what sun is needful in their progress to perfection; and this is all that is necessary to say with regard to that article.

The pots being all upon the stage and the buds beginning to open, being arrived to their full height, or nearly so, being trained through two or three wire crooks, in an exact upright position, exactly parallel to the perpendicular sticks, and having one of the wire crooks exactly under the ball of the calyx, or pod of the flower; at this time, which we may suppose to be early in June, the flower-buds must be looked over twice a day, to direct and assist the petals in bursting open the cup properly, so as to form a compleat flower. This work, we may suppose, belongs chiefly to the Broken Flowers; for it is of these flowers I am now speaking; and unless some art and assistance be given this way, the cup will divide, and throw all the petals on one side, forming an unsightly strange flower, commonly distinguished by the opprobrium of *Bursten Flowers*, which, among the lowest class of Gardeners, for want of knowing how to manage them, are usually held very cheap.

As soon, therefore, as you perceive the cup to begin to break on one side, divide it exactly in the same manner at each of the other angles, that the petals may have free liberty to expand themselves uniformly and together, and keep the pod rising full in the middle, and in an upright position. At this time no wet must come near the flowers; they must be covered every evening at the approach of showers or mists; but they must be uncovered in fine weather, and have as much open free air as possible. The roots in the pots must be watered every evening, many of which will have side shoots fit for layering, and the sooner this is done the better, not only to have stronger layers, but as they will soon strike root, they will receive nourishment themselves, and the greater quantity will be conveyed to the flower, to make it as compleat as possible.

As the flower-bud swells and advances, many of these Broken Flowers are possessed of another bud arising in the middle of this, with green leaves, for a calyx, like those of the outward, but of a thinner consistence. The green leaves of this second bud, then, must be all carefully taken away with a pair of nippers, or the like, care being always used not to injure or bruise the real petals of either of the flowers; and when the outward petals begin to expand or open, there should be placed a round collar of dyer's press paper, or card, to keep them regular and even. This card should be cut perfectly round, and should be of a size not so large, but that the extremity of the petals may cover the edge of it, that when the flower is in full blow the edge of it may not appear. The neck also, or hole in the center, should be round, and large enough to give all the petals that compose the flower free liberty and ease to expand themselves. If the flower bud at any time is much swelled, it will be safest with a pair of scissars to cut this paper from the center to the periphery, and it may then be put on at any time, without danger of bruising the petals.

In the course of blowing these flowers, one part will often rise faster than the other. When this happens, the pot should be brought out of the shed, and a thin board or a glass placed upon the stick, to shade part of the flower, whilst the other part being exposed to the sun, may be brought forward. In the evening the pot should resume its station again on the stage, and be again treated as before, if the day is fine, that such backward part of the flower may be brought forward, so as to be all alike. As the flower advances, such of the petals as do not naturally fall so, must be regularly disposed in a beautiful series one over another, with the thin part of a quill cut smooth and narrow like a tooth picker. The middle of the flower must always be encouraged, and when a redundancy of petals appears, they must be artfully taken out, leaving only a proper number for perfection. In the course of this work the greatest nicety must be had not to bruise the contiguous petals, which will soon turn brown, and disqualify the flower for a prize. In some of the largest flowers of the Breaking kind, there will be, besides the two main buds, several others smaller also, arising almost all over the surface of the flower, attended with little green chives. These must be all carefully taken away, to give free liberty for the petals of the main flower to expand themselves in their natural order.

The well known flower called the Windsor Cutting is remarkable for this, and such flowers as these try the florist's skill, and give proof of his art. It is no very difficult matter to blow a large bursting single-podded flower, but those exceedingly proliferous ones with the multiplicity of pods, require the nicest management. Nature must be studied how she may be helped in making the flower compleat. The fullness of the middle must be chiefly studied, for the whole figure of the flower ought to be an half sphere, or globe, or nearly so. The outward petals, or those nearest the base, should form a regular surface, covering the periphery of the card or press paper. The rest should be disposed in a beautiful series, rising one over another, and filling it to the very top; and when this is done, it is a compleat flower.

It has been observed, when a redundancy of petals appears, part may be taken away This is not always to be the case, for there will often be other parts in the flower where they may be wanted, and these are to be artfully and carefully removed into such thinner parts of the flower, that the whole may be uniform, bold, and compleat When a redundancy of petals appears all over the flowers, which will sometimes happen, in these large and noble Breakers, I have frequently wholly removed the second main bud, and by that means giving way for a proper disposition of the other, which otherwise would have been too crowded, have had a most compleat flower

When the pods are single, it is not to be expected the flower will rise so full in the middle, and it is to be dispensed with, neither is a half globe to be strictly the figure of the flower we are perfectly to expect The nearer it comes to this the better, but any flower rising full in the middle, in a beautiful and regular manner, will do credit to the artist, and may be called a good flower

The Breakers and the Free Blowers have the fashion by turns The latter are now most run upon, I believe, because they occasion least trouble and few people know how to blow the other properly But there is no comparison between them, when managed with art, neither can a more enchanting sight be conceived, than a good collection of Broken Flowers, well blown and regularly disposed on a proper stage, to shew them to advantage and perfection

Free Blowers

2 Free Blowers These include all the smaller tribe of carnations, that blow the flower whole without bursting out on one side of the bud They differ in no respect from the other until the time of flowering, and then Nature tells you that little or no art need be used to blow them The same kind of stage must be erected about breast-high, with a covering to take on and off, and being fixed there, they need not be removed until their time of bloom is over Every evening, as well as the other sorts they must be watered, and at the time of flowering, nothing more is to be done than to dispose the petals, when they come in clusters, or irregularly in a uniform manner, with the same kind of quill splinters as for the other Few of them will require this, and art need not help these flowers in general, as they will usually blow according to their nature No more than one or two at most ought to be permitted to flower from each layer, accordingly all side buds and spindles ought to be picked off as soon as they appear I shall now proceed to shew the method of raising these flowers from seeds

Of raising Carnations from seeds

The greatest difficulty in this is to obtain good seeds, for when once those are got plenty of plants are easily obtained Your large Breakers scarce produce any seeds, and the fullest of the Whole Blowers seldom are made to produce any, especially your old standard flowers of note that have been long propagated by layers Seeds, therefore, are to be obtained from flowers of the best properties, and for this purpose they should always be planted in the open ground, and not in pots They should have no covering at the time of their flowering, but be constantly exposed to any weather as it shall happen Every evening plenty of water must be given them, especially if it is a dry season The water ought, as for those on the stage, to be river or pond water, or such well water as has stood two or three days to soften in the sun After the petals of the flowers are decayed, and the seed vessels begin to swell, then watering must be continued and the ground kept in a proper moisture until the seeds are nearly ripe, when this trouble may be omitted Gather the heads of your seeds, and lay them upon a dry, shady, airy shelf for a few weeks, and then put them into little paper-bags, and keep them dry until the time of sowing March is a good season for this work, and they may be sown in beds a quarter of an inch deep, or if the quantity of seeds be small, in pots or boxes filled with the same kind of fine rich earth It will not be many weeks before the plants come up, and they will require nothing more than constant weeding and watering until the August following, at which time prepare a bed for their reception of good light earth, and let them be planted in this a little more than half a foot distance Let a moist day be chosen for this business, and if none happens, defer it till it does, if it be to the middle of September, for it is amazing how readily these plants take to the ground, if removed in moist weather Let them have no guard or protection all winter, and enure them betimes to be hardy, and stout In the July following they will flower, the single ones may then be thrown away, the more indifferent ones of the Double sorts may share the same fate, or be removed into borders of the Flower-garden for nosegays or the like, whilst the fairest flowers of the best properties should immediately be layered, to join in the Collection of Stage-flowers, and their seeds also preserved and gathered for a fresh increase

The different sorts of Carnations

The whole order of Carnations, besides being divided into the two above great sorts of Classes, are arranged in lots or assortments, according to the colour of their flowers, and they are called,

1 Flakes
2 Bizarrs
3 Piquettes
4 Painted Ladies

described

1 Flakes These are at present the most in fashionable flowers, and are really very delightful The surface of their petals is adorned with two colours only, in stripes, and these are large and full, running through the whole petal

2 Bizarrs The flowers of this sort consist of more than two colours Their variegation is irregular, being in larger or smaller stripes and spots, and the different colours that compose it are three, four, or five in number

3 Piquettes These are the most numerous, were formerly in most esteem, and by many now are thought to be the most beautiful The Piquettes have always a white ground, and the additional colour is laid on in spots The spots are of different colours, small, and are often laid on in such plenty that the whole flower seems dusted with them, which has a charming effect, and renders it delightful

4 Painted Ladies These are well-known flowers, and there is by far the least variety of this sort The under part of their petals is white, whilst their upper surface is of a red or purple colour, so laid on as to appear as if really painted

These being the different classes or assortments that include the whole of the florist's collection of these flowers, I shall next lay down the properties of a good carnation

With regard to the Bursters, the fuller they are the better Art must be used to help to bring nature to perfection, and the laws directed for blowing them will direct what a flower of that nature ought to be to make it compleat

With regard to Free Blowers, as they for the most part shew themselves full, their natural properties chiefly concern them, and they are,

Properties of a good Carnation.

1 The ſtem ſhould be tall and ſtrong, in proportion to the ſize of the flower, and able to ſupport it in an upright poſition

2 The flower ſhould be large and perfectly round, with petals enough to fill every part in a regular uniform manner

3 The petals ſhould be long and broad, and of a firm conſiſtence, expanding themſelves as they open, in a free eaſy manner, and retaining afterwards that property, which more peculiarly entitles them to the appellation of Free Blowers

4 There ſhould be an exact proportion between the middle and the other parts of the flower It muſt neither riſe too high, nor yet ſo low as to form a flat ſurface, but gradually riſe ſo as to conſtitute a ſurface nearly ſpherical

5 The colours ſhould be bright, clear, and diſtinct, and diſperſed in the moſt perfect manner, to conſtitute it a flower of one or other of the above claſſes or orders

There are ſome people who take much notice of the joints of the ſtalks, and place perfection on thoſe that are the largeſt Nay, ſome make this ſo indiſpenſible, that they will gather ſeeds of no flowers but theſe whoſe ſtalks have ſtrong large joints I muſt own I could never find any thing important in this for the raiſing of the flowers, it being the good properties of the flowers, and not the largeneſs of the joints of the ſtalk, from which ſucceſs may be expected However, they give the ſtalk a ſtrong firm look, and as ſuch, tho' not eſſential, may be deemed an eligible property

Carnations, eſpecially the Whole Blowers, are very ſubject to run away from their beautiful ſtripes into their plain original ſelf-colour, and the richer the compoſt is in which they are planted, it will contribute the more towards bringing on this diſagreeable change I always chooſe therefore, to have a quantity of layers of all the ſorts planted in a bed of common garden mould, rather hungry and poor, to preſerve the ſorts, which will not only be effectual for the purpoſe, but layers taken from theſe, and planted in pots with the richeſt compoſts, to join the ſhed-flowers for ſhows, were ever more luxuriant, and flowered ſtronger, than the others So that when a perſon has plenty of layers, and garden-room enough, this is a method that ought always to be practiſed

The beſt time for layering theſe flowers is, when their ſide-ſhoots are long and ſtrong enough for the purpoſe, which is generally by the time they begin to flower The method is this

Method of layering theſe flowers

Firſt, ſtrip the intended layers of all the lower leaves, to make clear room for the operation

Secondly, ſhorten the tops of the layers an inch or two, or more, according as they are for length, but do not cut them ſo low as to affect the pee, as it is called, of the young ſhoot

Thirdly, clear away the mould all round the root, in order to bring down the layers to a proper depth for ſtriking

Fourthly, proceed then to the operation itſelf, which is thus Having a ſharp penknife, at a ſtrong joint, three or four, or more, according to the length of the ſhoot from the root, cut it exactly at right angles half through Then below this cut or joint direct your knife at right angles to that which will run lengthways, exactly up the ſtalk Let the ſlit be made half way at leaſt, or if the diſtance of the joint be ſhort, let it be continued nearly to the joint above, and thus, by performing it in this manner, the joint below will loſe one ſide of its top, which will make room for the ſquare end of the layer freely to ſtrike root, as well as be more agreeable to the nature and deſign of a layer This being done, proceed to the next, and ſo on, until all belonging to that root are finiſhed

Fifthly, the next operation is fixing them in the ground, for which purpoſe, having provided yourſelf with a ſufficient quantity of hooked pegs, bring each of them carefully down, and confine it with a peg at the joint below the ſlit, and when they are all thus managed, being brought down to a proper depth for the ſoil to ſtrike, proceed to the laſt part of the buſineſs, which is,

Sixthly, begin at a corner layer, and raiſe the head of it, drawing it gently towards the root, this will cauſe the ſlit to open, then with your right hand carefully put ſome mould at the back part, raiſing it as high as it is intended to be left, which ſhould be two or three inches above the ſlit, according to the length of the layer This will keep the layer in its proper poſture, and by thus keeping the ſlit of the Carnation open, it will more readily ſtrike root In like manner you muſt proceed to the next, and ſo on, until the whole is finiſhed Then proceed to crumble ſome fine mould between the mother plant and the layers, to the height of the mould on the outſide, and the buſineſs is done Thus will the layers have the appearance of ſo many diſtinct plants, and in about three weeks time they will really become ſo, for they will have ſtruck root, and may be planted any where The ſooner this is done the better, for the floriſt will find, that they will grow more readily when planted out early than when deferred until Michaelmas, or after, as is often the caſe The ſmalleſt fibre will be ſufficient root for a layer in the beginning of Auguſt, if it is to be planted again immediately, whereas, if removed in October, they often die, if they have not good root

This finiſhes what is neceſſary to be known with regard to the glory of our gardens, the floriſts collection, called Prize or Shed Flowers Numbers of other ſorts belong to this genus, called Pinks Sweet Williams, and beds of the Common Red Cloves ſhould be in every garden where there is room and leiſure But as there is at preſent a diſtinction obſerved between the flowers called Floriſts Flowers, and thoſe which come of courſe under the general culture of the Gardener, theſe ſhall be amply treated of under the generical name, among the Perennial Flower-Roots

# Of PERENNIAL FLOWERS.

## CHAP. I.

## *ACANTHUS*, BEAR's BREECH

OF *Acanthus* there are four or five real and distinct species, some of which are of a very tender nature, but the sorts proper for our Perennial Flower-works among Gardeners go by the names of,

Species

1 The Smooth *Acanthus*
2 The Prickly *Acanthus*
3 *Acanthus* of Dioscorides

Description of the Smooth,

1 Smooth *Acanthus* The root of this species is thick and full of fibres, and strikes very deep into the ground The leaves, which constitute the greatest beauty of this plant, are large, broad, and long and have their edges waved and indented in a manner so delightful and elegant as to excite our admiration and wonder Their colour is of a lively green, with ribs of a paler colour, and this is that graceful leaf which has been so justly celebrated in antient times The flowers form a spike, growing along the top of a moderately-long stalk These singly are small, and are by many thought to have little beauty, but on the whole they look well, being arranged for a foot in length along the top of the stalk, in a close and compact manner They will be in full blow in August, and the seeds will be ripe by the end of October

This is without all doubt the *Mollis Acanthus* of the celebrated antient poet Virgil, though it will require some difficulty perhaps to reconcile some properties he ascribes to it, and which to us seem by no means to belong to its nature It is mentioned by that author sometimes as an evergreen, but with us it has no share of that property, the difference of the climate, however, may cause the different effects in this plant It is well known, that in warm countries some plants that are annuals with us, there successfully remain for years, and others again at all times are garnished in their beauty and verdure The warm parts of Italy, &c may so far have affected this plant, as for the most part to appear in a green and flourishing state, sufficiently to entitle it perhaps to the epithet, *semper frondentis Acanthi* He calls it "a berry bearing plant," and this is no wonder, for the seed-vessels of this plant have the appearance of such But that it should be a twining plant, as he again describes it, is one of the difficulties which Virgil has put upon our modern botanists to reconcile, and which perhaps may be as difficult to be effected as his marriage of some plants by grafting, &c This has induced many to think, that by the Twining *Acanthus* he means some other plant, and some have been bold enough to pretend to know and describe it

The leaves of this species are its principal ornament, for there is nothing extraordinary in its flowers and these have been made remarkable by constituting one of the ornaments of that noble order of architecture, the Corinthian Strange is the story the antients tell us how this happened "A basket of flowers and childrens playthings, say they, being placed upon a root of this species, and being covered with a tile to protect it from the weather, the leaves and branches of the *Acanthus* sprang up, and encompassed the basket, till arriving at the tile, its course naturally became diverted, and the plant still growing, the leaves naturally bent, or turned again from the corners of the tile Callimachus, a noble Grecian sculptor, who is said to be the inventor of this order, took the hint from this, and in the same manner adorned the capitals of his order with the leaves of this plant Several entire columns are now remaining, which prove this to be the true *Acanthus* of the antients, the true leaf of this species being there found as an ornament to the capital

and the Prickly Acanthus

2 Prickly *Acanthus* Of this there are two notable varieties

Varieties

Strong spined *Acanthus*
Soft-spined *Acanthus*

described

Strong spined *Acanthus* is a noble plant, of which there are two or three sorts, that differ both in respect to the size of their leaves, flower stalks, and strength of their spines, and which by many old botanists have been taken for distinct species of each other The leaves of the strongest sort are pinnatifid, and have whitish veins, resembling those of our Lady Thistle, and are armed with very strong sharp spines The flower-stalks will arise to about four feet, and the top will be garnished by flowers in the usual manner, they beginning to blow first at the bottom, and so continuing to open as the stalk arises, so that from the beginning to the end of the first blow, the same stalk will produce flowers for more than two months together Another sort of strong spined *Acanthus* has very large pinnatifid leaves, which are deeply jagged, and have very sharp spines, each segment of the leaf having one of them for its guard There are also other varieties of this kind, all of which are delightful plants, and demand respect, [illegible] forbid too great familiarity, under pain or suffering from taking freedom Their situation must be in large borders, or in such places where smaller plants are not near, for their roots strike deep into the ground, and their leaves will soon occupy a good space They are also very proper to fill up the vacancies in wilderness-quarters and the like where they will thrive and look very well, and attract the attention perhaps as much as any thing there They will flower in July, and continue so often until September, and will perfect their seeds by the October following

Proper situation [illegible]

The soft-spined *Acanthus* has frequently been treated by Gardeners as a distinct species and [illegible]

makes a good variety for the Gardener's purpoſe The leaves of this ſort are deeply laciniated, and each ſegment ends in a ſoft ſpine They are about a foot and a half in length, and about half as broad They riſe immediately from the root, and have a thiſtle-like look, being veined, and cut into ſegments in a manner reſembling ſome of them The flower-ſtalks will ariſe to about a yard in height, the upper part is garniſhed with flowers in the uſual manner, thoſe at the bottom opening at firſt, and ſo ſucceeding until thoſe at the extremity appear in blow, to effect which will ſometimes be the ſpace of two months This ſort begins flowering early in June, ſo that flowers on the ſame ſtalk may be expected to be ſeen near the end of July The ſeeds ripen in October, by which plants are eaſily raiſed

Acanthus of Dioſcorides

3 *Acanthus* of Dioſcorides The root is compoſed of many thick fibres, which ſtrike deep into the ground The leaves are ſpear ſhaped, entire, and are prickly on their edges The ſtalks are upright, firm, and about a yard high The flowers come out from the upper parts of the ſtalks in great plenty They appear in July, and continue in ſucceſſion until autumn

Soil proper for theſe ſorts

All theſe ſorts grow naturally in woods in Italy, Portugal, Spain, Sicily, &c and are therefore very proper for wilderneſs-quarters of all ſorts, as they will thrive and flouriſh in ſhade, under the drip of trees, &c and when they are planted in borders, they ſhould be the largeſt, and at a diſtance from ſmall plants, or they will ſoon over-run them They will thrive in almoſt any ſoil or ſituation, though the Smooth *Acanthus* does beſt if it be light and inclined to ſandy

Method of propagating them by parting of the roots,

They are propagated by parting of the root, which may be done any time from Auguſt until the ſpring They will readily grow, and, if unremoved, in a few years will be ſpreading and large

and by ſeeds

They may be alſo propagated by ſeeds, which being ſown in the ſpring will ſoon appear By the autumn they will be good plants, and may be removed where they are deſigned for, though if ſuch places be marked out, and the ground made fine by digging, &c and a few ſeeds ſown here and there, about half an inch deep, ſticking a mark at each place for a direction, they will then have no need of being removed, which is the beſt way for theſe plants, as their roots ſtrike deep into the ground, and when unchecked by removal always produce leaves and flowers larger and fairer

Titles.

1 Smooth *Acanthus* is titled, *Acanthus foliis ſinuatis inermibus* Caſpar Bauhine calls it, *Acanthus ſativus, ſive mollis Virgilii*, and J Bauhine, *Carduus Acanthus, ſive branca urſi* It grows naturally in Italy, Sicily, &c

2 Prickly *Acanthus* is, *Acanthus foliis pinnatifidis ſpinoſis* Caſpar Bauhine calls it, *Acanthus aculeatus*, and Dodonæus, *Acanthus ſylveſtris* It grows common in Italy, &c

3 *Acanthus* of Dioſcorides is, *Acanthus foliis lanceolatis integerrimis margine ſpinoſis* Rawvulf calls it, *Acanthus Dioſcoridis, vel ſativus* It is a native of Mount Libanon

Derivation of the generical name

The word *Acanthus* is formed of the Greek ακανθα, *a thorn*, and is given to this genus on account of its prickly properties

Claſs and order in the Linnæan ſyſtem

*Acanthus* is of the claſs and order *Didynamia Angioſpermia*, and the characters are,

The characters

1 Calyx is a triple perianthium, compoſed of ſeveral permanent leaves, of different ſize and figures

2 Corolla The flower is of one leaf, and is unequal It is of the labiated kind, but the upper lip is wanting The tube is very ſhort, and is cloſed with a kind of beard The lower lip of the flower is broad, plane, and erect, and is divided at the extremity

3 Stamina are four ſubulated filaments, two of which are longer than the others They have oblong, compreſſed, obtuſe antheræ and theſe, together with the ſtyle, occupy the place of the upper lip

4 Pistillum conſiſts of a turbinated germen, a filiforme ſtyle the length of the ſtamina, with two acute ſtigmas

5 Pericarpium is a roundiſh capſule of two cells

6 Semina. The ſeeds are oblong, ſmooth, and fleſhy

## CHAP II

## *ACHILLEA.*

AS this genus comprehends the *Ptarmica* and *Milleſolium* of old botaniſts, the ſpecies of it are diſtinguiſhed amongſt gardeners by names very different, ſuch as maudlin, yarrow, noſe-bleed, milfoil, &c I ſhall therefore inſert them by ſuch names as they are commonly known, which will be a direction to their proper titles, which ſucceed in order after their culture, and theſe are uſually called,

Species

1 Sweet Maudlin
2 Yellow Milfoil
3 Tanſey-leaved Sneezewort
4 Southernwood-leaved Sneezewort
5 Lavender cotton-leaved Sneezewort
6 Rough-leaved *Achillea*
7 White Maudlin
8 Barrelier's Sneezewort
9 Siberian Sneezewort
10 Alpine Sneezewort
11 Bauhine's Sneezewort
12 Common Sneezewort, or Gooſe Tongue.
13 Milfoil, or Yarrow
14 Noble Yarrow
15 Cretan Milfoil
16 Egyptian Wormwood
17 Oriental Small-flowering *Achillea.*
18 Large Milfoil
19 Small Sweet ſcented Milfoil
20 Black Milfoil

Deſcription of Sweet Maudlin,

1 Sweet Maudlin This is a well known plant, being common in moſt gardens, and its virtues as a medicinal plant are pretty well known The leaves are finely ſcented, of an oblong ſpear-ſhaped figure, though rather obtuſe at their extremity The ſtalk ariſes to about two feet in height, and is well garniſhed with

with leaves, at the top of which grow the flowers in a kind of umbels These are of a yellow colour, and will be in blow in June, July, and August The seeds, by which the plants may be multiplied at pleasure, will be ripe in the autumn, and if they are carefully preserved and sowed in March, they will readily grow, and any desired number of plants may be soon raised They may be also encreased by parting of the roots, any time in autumn or spring, or even the winter will do very well for the purpose, for they will readily grow They will grow in almost any soil or situation, though it would not be adviseable to plant them in too moist a soil, because in a very wet winter the roots will be liable to be rotted

There is a variety of this species called the broad-leaved maudlin The flowers of this are in small umbels Its management is exactly the same as the former, as is also another with larger clusters of flowers, which are distinguished and much esteemed by gardeners

Yellow Milfoil

2 Yellow Milfoil This species goes by different names among gardeners, but the most common title is Yellow Milfoil The leaves are pinnated, and a little rough or hairy, the segments are very narrow, and indented, and the whole is very hoary and downy The flowers are of a bright yellow colour, and produced in June or July, and as this is naturally a low plant, seldom rising to more than a foot high, possessed of fine hoary leaves and bright yellow flowers, which often continue a considerable time in their full splendor, it is much coveted by those who have small gardens, and yet are desirous of a greater proportionable number of sorts of plants It is to be propagated by seeds and parting of the roots, like the former, though it requires a dry warm border, being subject to be destroyed by bad weather, in moist and exposed places

Tansey leaved Sneezewort,

3 Tansey leaved Sneezewort will grow to be a moderately large plant The leaves are very hoary and pinnated, and the foliols are spear-shaped, deeply cut, and serrated, and their under side is a little woolly The flowers are of a pale yellow colour, and it will be in blow in June, and continue to exhibit bloom during most of the summer after It ripens seeds with us, by which it may be propagated, or by parting of the roots, in the same manner as the former

Southern wood-leaved Sneezewort,

4 Southernwood leaved Sneezewort This plant will grow to be two feet or a yard high, and causes a good effect by its hoary leaves These are much divided, being pinnated and supradecompound leaves, and the segments are very narrow, and stand at a distance from each other The flowers are produced at the tops of the stalks, in June, in umbels They are yellow, and continue to shew themselves during most part of the summer after It is to be propagated as the other sorts

Lavender cotton-leaved Sneezewort,

5 Lavender cotton-leaved Sneezewort The leaves of this species also are hoary, indented, and bristly, the denticles are almost entire, they are awl shaped and reflexed The whole forms a very beautiful leaf The flowers are yellow, and very large, and they will exhibit bloom for a month or six weeks It is to be propagated like the former

Rough leaved Achillea,

6 Rough-leaved *Achillea* This species hath linear, indented, hoary leaves, the denticles are crenated, and the whole is unpleasant and rough to the touch The flowers are of a pale yellow, or brimstone colour, and it is to be propagated like the former

White Maudlin,

7 White Maudlin is a well known plant The leaves are lanceolated, and deeply cut, the denticles also are slightly serrated The flowers are white, and will be produced in July and August It multiplies itself very fast by its creeping roots so that a plant or two being once obtained, they may be soon encreased to any desired number

Barrelier's Sneezewort,

8 Barrelier's Sneezewort This also goes by the name of Sneezewort of *Triumfetta* This is rather a large growing plant, for it will often rise by its stalks to be upwards of a yard in height The leaves are pinnated, plain, and deeply sawed and the outermost wings are the largest The flowers are produced at the tops of the stalks in loose umbels, they are white, and are succeeded by ripe seeds, by which they may be easily propagated, as also by parting of the roots, by which method they multiply very fast

Siberian Sneezewort,

9 Siberian Sneezewort This species hath pinnated leaves, the wings are long and narrow, and at a considerable distance from each other The flowers are white, very beautiful, and are often succeeded by seeds, which being preserved until the spring and sown, numbers of plants may be easily raised

Alpine Sneezewort,

10 Alpine Sneezewort Several of the other sorts may with as great propriety be termed the Alpine as this, because many of them are found growing naturally there, but custom has stamped it chiefly on this species, so that it is become the name by which it is generally known Of itself this is a very low plant The leaves are pinnatified, plain, and obtuse, they are very hoary, and a little resemble those of the common wormwood, they grow close to the ground, and decay early in autumn The stalks, which rise but to about six or eight inches high, are terminated by flat umbels of white flowers They will be in blow in June and July, but never produce ripe seeds with us, so that unless good seeds can be obtained from the Alps, or places where it naturally grows, it is to be propagated only by parting of the roots, which may be very easily and successfully done any time in the autumn or spring

Bauhine's Sneeze wort,

11 Bauhine's Sneezewort is rather a low-growing plant The leaves are pinnated, indented, and are covered with a kind of down This gives them a very hoary look, which is to a great degree beautiful and striking The flower-stalks rise to about a foot in height, and their tops are ornamented with compact umbels of very fine white flowers Their propagation is by the usual way of seeds, or parting of the roots, by both which methods they may be speedily encreased

Common Sneezewort,

12 Common Sneezewort This is often called Goose Tongue, and the leaves are often used as a pot herb to mix with others of that nature, they are spear shaped, and very sharply serrated It is the double sort of this species that is chiefly valued for its flowers, and indeed it is deserving of it, for they are exceeding double, of a pure white, and are produced in prodigious plenty It will be in blow in July and August, and propagates itself very fast by its creeping roots, for they run under ground like those of couch grass, every knot of which will grow and become a good plant The roots, which are chiefly used in medicine, are remarkable for provoking sneezing, and being of a hot biting taste on being chewed, occasion a plentiful discharge of saliva, and frequently give ease to the tooth-ach It is found growing common in some of our woods and fields, and in some places goes by the name of Field Pellitory The variety with double flowers as often goes by the name of Double Maudlin as any other

Milfoil, or Yarrow

13 Milfoil, or Yarrow In many parts this goes by the name of Nose-bleed, but the name by which it is most generally distinguished is Milfoil, which has been given it on account of the vast number of segments of which the leaves are compos'd

composed It is a well-known plant, growing almost every where, and is never admitted into gardens, but there is a variety of it with purple flowers which is reckoned a cultivated plant, and on account of this distinction is admitted into gardens Yet it is hardly worth propagating for that reason, since at best it is but lightly tinged with purple, and this colour soon going off, the flower becomes white so that it is sought after by none, except those who thirst after a general collection, with their varieties The purple tinged sort is found growing in common with the other in many parts I have seen it in prodigious plenty near Dingley, in Northamptonshire, and from the place where they are thus found growing, the roots may be easily removed into the garden at pleasure The leaves are astringent, and are employed in hæmorrhages, diarrhœas, debility and laxity of fibres, and spasmodic hysterical complaints, and the distilled flowers afford an essential oil, of an elegant blue colour

Noble Yarrow.
14 Noble Yarrow This species has been distinguished by that name ever since Tragus, who named it *Millefolium Nobile* The leaves are doubly pinnated, and divided in a very elegant manner The pinnæ are rather at a distance from each other, and are obtuse, there are usually about seven pair on each rib, which are terminated by an odd one The midrib is a little downy, and possessed of a tinge of purple, and the whole leaf is scented not unlike the smell of camphire The stalk arises round and upright, and is garnished with leaves in an alternate manner, it is rather downy, and the flowers ornament the top in a large and irregular umbel Their colour is usually white, but there is a variety of it of a pale red colour, and another of a pale though elegant purple It will be in blow in July, and the seed will be ripe in the autumn, by which plenty of plants may be soon raised

Cretan Milfoil.
15 Cretan Milfoil This species hath very narrow downy leaves, the pinnæ are roundish or reniform, and the leaf is imbricated backward The stalk is downy, and terminated by four white flowers in the usual manner. This species is propagated as the others

Egyptian Wormwood.
16 Egyptian Wormwood This species also hath elegantly pinnated leaves, the folioles are spear-shaped, though a little obtuse, they are serrated and indented, are of an hoary look, and have, on the whole, a resemblance not unlike wormwood, which occasioned its being so called The flowers are white, growing in a kind of umbel, though I never yet knew it produce good seeds It is to be propagated in the usual manner, though it is rather tender, so should have a warm border, and a little protection in very hard winters

Oriental Small-flowering Achillea.
17 Oriental Small-flowering *Achillea* The leaves of this species are doubly pinnated, and downy, the folioles are oval and entire, and the whole forms a very elegant leaf The stalks are small and downy, and the flowers small This plant is rather tender, and requires a dry warm situation and protection in the severity of winter, in every other respect it is to be managed as the others

Large Milfoil.
18 Large Milfoil The stalk is thick, hairy, branching near the top, and two feet and a half high The leaves are large, bipinnated, hairy, auriculated at the base, and of a dark green The flowers come out in umbels from the tops of the stalks, their colour is white; they appear in June and July, and often shew themselves until the end of autumn

Small Sweet-scented Milfoil.
19 Small Sweet-scented Milfoil The stalk of this seldom rises more than four or five inches high The leaves are equally and elegantly bipinnated, and the pinnulæ are distinct, entire, and acute The flowers are formed into roundish bunches, which grow in clusters at the top of the stalk They are of a white colour, appear in June and July, and often again in the autumn The whole plant has an agreeable odour

Black Milfoil.
20 Black Milfoil The stalk is herbaceous, branching, and two feet high, the leaves are large, and composed of a multitude of narrow parts, nearly in the manner of chamomile The flowers come out in roundish bunches from the tops of the stalks, they grow on hairy footstalks, and the edges of their cups are of a black colour They appear in June and July and frequently continue in succession through August and September

Culture.
The culture of all the sorts, as has been observed, is either by seeds, parting of the roots, or slips, which will readily grow, and their titles are as follow

Titles.
1 Sweet Maudlin This is called, *Achillea foliis lanceolatis obtusis acutè serratis* It is the *Ageratum foliis serratis* of C Bauhine, and the *Balsamita minor* of Dodonæus, Morison, and others It grows common in France and Spain

2 Yellow Milfoil This is called, *Achillea foliis pinnatis hirsutis pinnis linearibus dentatis* It is the *Millefolium tomentosum luteum* of C Bauhine, and the *Stratiotes millefolia, flavo flore,* of Clusius In the Hortus Cliffortianus it is termed, *Achillea foliis linearibus pinnatifidis pubescentibus, foliolis tripartitis transversalibus media productiore* It grows common in the south of France, Italy, and Spain

3 Tansey-leaved Sneezewort is, *Achillea foliis pinnatis foliolis lanceolatis incisis serratis subtus tangentis* Tournefort calls it, *Ptarmica orientalis, foliis tanaceti incanis, semi-flosculis florum pallidè luteis,* Boerhaave, *Millefolium orientale, foliis tanaceti incanis, radiis pallide luteis,* and Vaillant, *Matricaria tomentosa & incana, Achilleæ folio, flore aureo* It is a native of the East

4 Southernwood-leaved Sneezewort is, *Achillea foliis pinnatis supra-decompositis laciniis linearibus distantibus* Tournefort terms it, *Millefolium orientale altissimum luteum, abrotani folio* It grows common in the East

5 Lavender cotton-leaved Sneezewort This is, *Achillea foliis setaceis dentatis denticulis subintegris subulatis reflexis* Tournefort calls it, *Ptarmica orientalis, santolinæ folio, flore majore,* and Vaillant, *Achillea lutea tomentosa, santolinæ folio* It grows common in the East

6 Rough-leaved *Achillea* This is, *Achillea foliis linearibus dentatis obtusis planis dentriculis crenatis* Vaillant calls it, *Achillea incana, santolinæ foliis plerumque falcatis, asperis, flore sulphureo* It grows naturally in the East

7 White Maudlin This is, *Achillea foliis lanceolatis dentato-serratis denticulis tenuissime serratis* Tournefort calls it, *Ptarmica Alpina, foliis profunde serratis,* and Herman, *Ptarmica Alpina, incanis serratis foliis* It is a native of the Alpine parts of Siberia

8 Barrelier's Sneezewort is, *Achillea foliis pinnatis planis inciso-serratis extimis majoribus coadunatis* Ray calls it, *Corymbifera millefolii amoeliæ, folio alato & laciniato,* Sauvages, *Achillea foliis bipinnatis, pinnulis linearibus indivisis,* Triumfetti, *Ptarmica Alpina, matricariæ foliis,* Haller, *Achillea, foliis pinnatis, pinnis serratis maximis, extremis confluentibus,* and Caspar Bauhine, *Dracunculus Alpinus, foliis scabiosæ* It grows naturally on the Helvetian and Italian mountains

9 Siberian Sneeze-wort This is, *Achillea foliis pinnatis*

*pinnatis pinnis distantibus lineari-lanceolatis basi sursum acutis* Gmelin calls it, *Achillea foliis pinnatis, pinnis longis acutis inferioribus sursum dente auctis glabris* It is a native of Siberia

10 Alpine Sneezewort is, *Achillea foliis laciniatis planis obtusis tomentosis* In the *Hortus Cliffortianus* it is termed, *Achillea foliis sinuato-laciniatis planis villosis nitidis obtusis* Clusius calls it, *Absinthium Alpinum umbelliferum*, Morison, *Dracunculus argenteus*, and Caspar Bauhine, *Absinthium Alpinum umbelliferum latifolium* It is a native of the Alps

11 Bauhine's Sneezewort is titled, *Achillea foliis pinnatis dentatis hirsutissimis, floribus glomerato-umbellatis* John Bauhine calls it, *Millefolium Alpinum incanum, flore speciosos*, Haller, *Achillea foliis pinnatis lanugine obductis, floribus albis umbellatis*, and Boccone, *Millefolium Alpinum tomentosum odoratum nanum* It grows common on the Alps of Siberia and Vallesia

12 Common Sneezewort is, *Achillea foliis lanceolatis acuminatis argute serratis* In the *Hortus Cliffortianus* it is termed, *Achillea foliis integris minutissime serratis* Caspar Bauhine calls it, *Dracunculus pratensis, serrato folio*, Clusius, *Ptarmica vulgaris*, also, *Ptarmica vulgaris, flore pleno*, and the Double sort he distinguishes by adding, *flore pleno* It grows common in England, and most of the temperate parts of Europe

13 Milfoil, or Yarrow, is, *Achillea foliis bipinnatis nudis laciniis linearibus dentatis caulibus sulcatis* In the *Flora Lapponica* it is termed, *Achillea foliis pinnato-pinnatis* Caspar Bauhine calls it, *Millefolium vulgare album*, also, *Millefolium purpureum majus*, Vaillant, *Achillea tanaceti folio, flore purpureo*, Parkinson, *Millefolium vulgare*, and Gerard, *Millefolium terrestre vulgare* It is found growing in meadows and pastures in most parts of Europe

14 Noble Yarrow This is, *Achillea foliis bipinnatis inferioribus nudis planis, superioribus obtusis tomentosis, corymbis convexis confertissimis* Tragus calls it, *Millefolium nobile*, and C Bauhine, *Tanacetum minus album, odore camphoræ* It grows wild in Bohemia, Helvetia, Tartary, and the south of France

15 Cretan Milfoil is, *Achillea foliis linearibus pinnis subrotundis retrorsum imbricatis, caule tomentoso* Caspar Bauhine calls it, *Millefolium incanum Creticum*, and John Bauhine, *Millefolium Creticum* It is a native of Crete

16 Egyptian Wormwood is, *Achillea foliis pinnatis foliolis obtuse lanceolatis serrato-dentatis* Tournefort calls it, *Ptarmica incana, pinnulis cristatis* Caspar Bauhine, *Absinthium Santonicum Ægyptiacum*, and Dodonæus, *Absinthium Ægyptiacum* It is a native of Egypt and the East

17 Oriental Small-flowering Ptarmica is, *Achillea foliis bipinnatis tomentosis foliolis ovatis integris* It grows common in the East

18 Large Milfoil is entitled, *Achillea fol. bipinnatis subpilosis laciniis linearibus dentatis auriculis decussatis* Caspar Bauhine calls it, *Millefolium maximum, umbella alba* It grows naturally in most of the southern countries of Europe

19 Small Sweet-scented Milfoil is, *Achillea foliis bipinnatis ovalibus nudiusculis, corymbis fastigiatis confertis* Haller calls it, *Achillea pinnis æqualibus confertis tomentosis pinnulis capillariter divisis* Barrelier, *Millefolium minimum crispum, flore albo, Hispanicum*, and Morison, *Millefolium odoratum minus Monspeliensium* It grows naturally in Helvetia, France, and Spain

20 Black Milfoil is, *Achillea foliis pinnulis pectinatis integriusculis, pedunculis villosis* Haller calls it, *Achillea foliis pinnatis, pinnis longis acutis sub-hirsutis, raro dentatis*, Caspar Bauhine, *Matricaria Alpina, chamæmeli folio*, and Clusius, *Parthenium Alpinum.* It grows naturally in the moist Alpine parts of Helvetia, Vallesia, and Austria

*Achillea* is of the class and order *Syngenesia Polygamia Superflua*, and the characters are, — Class and order in the Linnæan system The character

1 Calyx The common calyx is oval, oblong, and imbricated, and the scales are hairy, oval, acute, and connivent

2 Corolla The general flower is compound and radiated The hermaphrodite florets which compose the disk are tubular, funnel shaped, and cut at the brim into five expanded segments The female flowers, which are ranged round the border, are tongue-shaped, obcordated, patent, and cut at the top into three segments, of which the middle segment is the smallest

3 Stamina of the hermaphrodite florets are five very short capillary filaments, with a cylindrical tubulous anthera

4 Pistillum of the hermaphrodite flowers consists of a small germen, a filiforme style the length of the stamina, and an obtuse emarginated stigma That of the females consists of a small germen, and a filiforme style, with two obtuse reflexed stigmas

5 Pericarpium There is none

6 Semina The seeds of the hermaphrodite flowers are single, oval, and furnished with a kind of woolly matter, but are not crowned with down The seeds of the female flowers differ in nothing from those of the hermaphrodite

The receptacle is paleaceous and elevated The paleæ are spear shaped, and the length of the florets

# CHAP. III.

## *ACONITUM*, WOLFSBANE or MONKSHOOD.

Introductory observations

THERE are but seven species of *Aconitum*, though the number of varieties belonging to them, differing from one another in some sort or other, is very great Beautiful they all are, and worthy of due regard and attention, were it not for the poisonous properties of most of them The very smelling to the flowers has been attended with dreadful consequences, as has been asserted, which should be a cause sufficient wholly to extirpate them from all gardens, and preserve them for observation and medicine, in such places only where the skilful attend The

Common

Common Blue Monkſhood is found growing in almoſt every garden, and its diſagreeable ſmell may be the reaſon of its doing no more miſchief, for the plant itſelf is a deadly poiſon both to man and brute The Philoſophical Tranſactions give us an account of a man being poiſoned by eating ſome of this plant in a ſallad Dodonæus alſo mentions an inſtance of the like nature and of the death, attended by previous dreadful ſymptoms, it brought on ſome perſons who ignorantly eat it as a ſallad herb, and Dr Turner's narrative is well known, of ſome Frenchmen at Antwerp being killed by eating the young ſhoots of this plant for maſter wort Moſt of the ſorts are attended with this dreadful property, more or leſs, but the Blue-flowering kinds are ſaid to poſſeſs the poiſonous quality in a ſtronger degree, and after this, ſurely few will be deſirous, if any, of the Aconite to adorn their pleaſure gardens These plants are, however, eſteemed ornamental, and many of them are much uſed Some are particularly uſeful for wilderneſs quarters, as they will grow and thrive under the drip of trees, &c and for theſe reaſons demand a place here, in the liſt of Perennial Flower-roots

The ſorts of Monkſhood, then, are,

Species
1 Yellow Monkſhood
2 Small ſpiked Monkſhood
3 Blue Monkſhood, or *Napellus*
4 Yellow Pyrenean Monkſhood
5 Wholeſome Wolfsbane
6 Philadelphian Aconite
7 Syrian Aconite

Deſcription of the Yellow, 1 Yellow Monkſhood There are three or four varieties of this ſpecies, that are very ornamental plants, one or two of which will grow to a yard or better in height The leaves are palmated finely divided, large, and hairy, and the whole forms a bold well looking leaf The upper parts of the ſtalks produce the flowers in fine ſpikes They are of a yellow colour, and the general characters ſhew their compoſition They will be in blow in June, and the ſeeds ripen in September

Of all the varieties of this ſpecies, one in particular ought to be taken notice of, and is as worthy of culture as any of the ſorts This grows nearly to about a yard high, and the ſpike of flowers is much longer than any of the ſorts, and it blows exactly at the time with the other The leaves are ſmooth, and not hairy

Small ſpiked, 2 Small ſpiked Monkſhood Of this there are four or five varieties, differing in the ſize of their ſpikes of flowers, as alſo in their time of being produced The moſt elegant will grow to about two feet in height The leaves of this ſpecies are very much and very beautifully divided, and the ſegments themſelves are nearly again half cut The uppermoſt are the broadeſt, and the whole forms a leaf of more than common beauty The flowers are blue, and produced in ſpikes, in June They blow a fortnight or better after our Common Blue Monkſhood, and are ſucceeded by ripe ſeeds in September This, together with the Common Blue Monkſhood, is moſt proper to ornament the vacant ſpaces in wilderneſs quarters, where they will ſhew well at a diſtance, and be more out of danger of being gathered and ſmelled on than if planted in borders near walks, &c

Blue, 3 Blue Monkſhood, or *Napellus* Of this ſpecies there are four or five varieties, which differ greatly in appearance from one another, and are all very beautiful plants The leaves of theſe are divided into many narrow ſegments Thoſe at the top are broadeſt, and are marked with a line They are exceedingly ornamental, and afford beauty as well as by their fine ſpikes of flowers They will be in blow in Auguſt, and their colour is a ſky-blue But from ſeeds different colours have been obtained, ſo that there belong to this ſpecies the Red flowering, the Variegated, the White, &c all of a deadly nature, but which, nevertheleſs, afford much pleaſure in beholding them at a ſmall diſtance There is a ſort of this with large blue purple flowers, that will grow to about ſix feet high, and is proper to mix with perennials of that height, on the furtheſt ſide of borders, and the like The ſort called *Napellus Minor* has alſo its admirers Flowers of this ſort by ſeeds are obtained of different colours, but their deadly properties almoſt make me afraid to recommend their culture, unleſs in phyſic gardens and the like

and Yellow Pyrenean Monkſhood, 4 Yellow Pyrenean Monkſhood This is a delightful ſpecies to behold, and will ariſe, with its erect ſtalks, terminated by its fine ſpikes of flowers, to the height of three feet, or more, if in a good rich ſoil The leaves are very finely divided and the ſegments formed by the diviſions are long and narrow, but not all of a breadth, and theſe alſo are deeply notched or cut into other ſharp pointed parts The arrangement of their ſegments is ſingular, for they twiſt or fall over one another, ſo as to form the appearance of a kind of ſquammous leaf They are of a pale green, and have long footſtalks; and the whole is wild, ſingular, irregular, and yet very pretty The flowers, which are of a pale yellow colour, terminate the main ſtalk in a pretty long ſpike The branches alſo are terminated by a kind of ſhort ſpikes, each flower ſtanding on its own ſeparate footſtalk It will be in blow in July, and the ſeeds will be ripe in September

of the Wholeſome Wolfsbane, 5 Wholeſome Wolfsbane This is not only an harmleſs herb of itſelf, but is ſaid to poſſeſs the wonderful property of expelling the venom or poiſon imbibed from the other plants To theſe this is an antidote, and is reckoned a counter poiſon to all the others It is ſaid to be excellent againſt the plague, and is a ſure deſtruction to worms of all ſorts in the human body But be this as it will, I ſhould think the uſing of it muſt be attended with great danger, for it is ſo extremely like ſeveral of the other ſorts, that it may be miſtaken for them It has been preſcribed, however, and is the only ſort that is uſed in medicine, and when this is done, the root only is intended for the purpoſe The moſt ſkilful botaniſt, however, ought to put this in practice, that he may be ſure of his right ſort, and even then he ought to be intimidated, if what is ſaid of it be true, that if it grows near any of the other Aconites, it will attract their deadly quality, and will become alſo as venomous and poiſonous as thoſe Be this as it may, when a perſon has obtained the true ſort, let it be planted in a garden where there are no other ſpecies of Aconite, and then it will be the true *Anthora*, the name it has gone by for ages, and was ſo called, as being a remedy againſt the deadly poiſon of the others, which have been termed *Thora*

Philadelphian, 6 Philadelphian Aconite The ſtalk is upright, firm, taper, and about three feet high The leaves are of different properties, ſome being compoſed of three, others of five and others of many lobes They are naked, angular, indented, ſmooth, and of a good green colour The flowers come out ſingly from the ſides of the ſtalk, adorning the upper part a great way down They are of a fine blue colour, appear in July, and the ſeeds ripen in September

and Syrian Aconite 7 Syrian Aconite The ſtalks are upright, firm, taper, and about four feet high The leaves are beautifully divided, cut into many wedge-

wedge shaped segments, which are again cut into many acute parts The flowers come out in long spikes from the tops of the stalks They are of a bluish purple colour, and very large They appear in June and July, and the seeds ripen in September

The varieties of this species are,

Varieties

The Pale Blue
The Deep-blue
The Violet
The Purple

The culture of all these sorts is both by seeds and dividing the roots

Method of propagating these first by seeds

1 By seeds These should be sown in the autumn, soon after they are ripe, in beds of fresh light earth, made fine, for if they are deferred until spring, they rarely come up the first year About May the plants will appear They must be watered in dry weather, and constantly weeded, and in the autumn or spring after, they may be planted out where they are designed to remain, and these will be by far the best plants, will produce better and stronger spikes of flowers, and the colours will be more perfect than plants obtained any other way

and dividing the root

2 They may be also encreased by dividing of their roots This may be done any time from autumn till spring, and is what is chiefly practised on the common sorts, as they multiply exceedingly that way, but the flowers are seldom so fine as those from seedling plants

Proper soil and situations

They will all grow in almost any soil or situation, though the common Long spiked or Pyramidical Blue Monkshood is the only proper one to be planted under the drip of trees, so they are useful in that respect, as they may be made to occupy any desired spot

Titles

1 Yellow Monkshood is titled, *Aconitum foliis peltatis multifidis villosis* In the *Flora Lapponica* it is termed, *Aconitum foliis peltatis multifidis, petalo supremo cylindraceo* Besler calls it, *Aconitum lycoctonum flore luteo*, Cammerarius, *Aconitum II* and Caspar Bauhine *Aconitum lycoctonum luteum* It grows naturally in the mountainous parts of Italy, Austria, Switzerland, and Lapland

2 Small spiked Monkshood is called, *Aconitum foliis multifidis laciniis [illegible] partitis superne latis* Dodonæus calls it, *Aconitum cæruleum parvum*, and Caspar Bauhine, *Aconitum cæruleum minus, sive napellus minor* It grows common on the mountains of Italy and Bohemia

3 Blue Monkshood is titled, *Aconitum foliorum laciniis [illegible] superne latioribus lineâ exaratis* Lobel terms it, *Napellus verus*, and Caspar Bauhine, *Aconitum cæruleum, seu napellus* It grows naturally in Helvetia, Bavaria &c

4 Yellow Pyrenean Aconite is, *Aconitum foliis [illegible] laciniis linearibus incumbentibus [illegible]* Ray calls it, *Aconitum Pyrenaicum luteum, foliorum segmentis [illegible] incumbentibus* It is a native of the Pyrenees, and grows common in Siberia and Tartary

5 The Wholesome Wolfsbane is titled, *Aconitum floribus pentagynis foliorum laciniis linearibus* In the *Hortus Cliffortianus* it is termed, *Aconitum foliorum laciniis linearibus [illegible] ubique ejusdem latitudinis* Caspar Bauhine calls it, *Aconitum salutiferum, sive anthora*, and Cammerarius, *Anthora, sive Antithora* It grows common on the Alps and Pyrenees, and on the Helvetian and Savoy Mountains

6 Philadelphian Aconite is, *Aconitum foliis multilobis, corollarum galeis apice [illegible] longis [illegible]* It is a native of Philadelphia

7 Sirian Aconite is, *Aconitum floribus [illegible] pentagynis, foliorum laciniis cuneiformibus incisis acutis* Caspar Bauhine calls it, *Aconitum [illegible], sive napellus*, also, *Aconitum purpureum, sive napellus*, also, *Aconitum cæruleo purpureum, flore maximo, sive napellus* Clusius titles it, *Aconitum lycoctonum Tauricum*, also, *Aconitum lycoctonum Neubergense*, also, *Aconitum lycoctonum [illegible] Neubergense* It grows naturally in Siria

The word *Aconitum* is variously derived, but it most probably is taken from the Greek verb *ἀκονάω*, *to accelerate*, because it accelerates or hastens death It is called in English Monkshood and Wolfsbane, the former from the resemblance the flower hath to the figure of a hood worn by some of the religious, and the latter as being used as a bait for the wolves It is put into raw flesh, and laid where wolves frequent, which they finding greedily devour, and are killed The hunters, also, employed in the destruction of these beasts, are said to dip their arrows in the juice of these plants, which is said on their being wounded to bring on sure and certain death

Origin of the Name

*Aconitum* is of the class and order *Polyandria Trigynia*, and the characters are,

Class and order in the Linnæan system The characters

1 Calyx There is none

2 Corolla consists of five unequal petals The upper petal is galeated, tubulous, and obtuse The back of it is turned upwards, the point is bent back to the base, and in the manner of a hood covers the other part of the flower The two side petals are broad, roundish, opposite, and connivent The lower petals are oblong, and hang downwards There are two hollow nectaria hid under the upper petal They are oblique at the mouth, have a crooked tail, and are situated on long awl shaped peduncles There are six very short coloured squamulæ, placed circularly with the nectarium

3 Stamina are numerous, small, subulated filaments, which are broader at the base, turn towards the upper petal, and have small erect antheræ

4 Pistillum consists of three (though in some species five) germina, with styles the length of the stamina, crowned by simple reflexed stigmas

5 Pericarpium consists of the like number of oval awl-shaped capsules, each being formed of a single valve, and opening on the inner side

6 Semina The seeds are numerous, angular and rough

CHAP

# CHAP. IV.

## *ACORUS*, The SWEET-SCENTED FLAG

Introduc tory re marks

ALL-bountiful Nature affords us every plant for pleasure and use, and will leave us no part of our garden unoccupied, if we bestow her bounties, and manage them properly according to her laws

The plant before us grows naturally in moist, watery places, and wherever such a place is to be found in the garden, amongst others that delight in such spots, this ought to possess a share For it is a fine aromatic, and as such is worthy of regard It is also a very useful plant, for the root is an excellent stomachic, and a carminative It is said to be good against the plague, it will provoke urine, and the menses, and, in short, is a root that is in frequent use in the shops

Useful properties of this plant

Description of it

These valuable plants then, though growing naturally in shallow standing water, will grow also very well in gardens, if planted in a moist place, though they are seldom or never known to flower, unless they grow wholly in water The root is thick, spongy, and jointed, white within, of a strong smell, and a warm, bitterish aromatic taste, and these being planted in the autumn, winter, or spring, will soon become good plants

The leaves are smooth and narrow, about two feet long, and end in points, to which they diminish, growing gradually narrower from the base A thicker and more robust leaf than the rest, arises to bear the flower, this is of a paler green, has a furrowed surface, and supports the spike of flowers It will be in blow in June or July, and will continue in flower for more than a month

Of this genus, there are no other species than the plant under consideration, which makes a title for both unnecessary and absurd It stands, therefore, singly *Acorus* It is what has been by old Botanists called, *Calamus aromaticus*—*Acorus verus*, *sive calamus aromaticus officinarum*, and the like It grows in ditches and watery places in many parts of Europe, particularly in Holland, most of the ditches are full of it In England, it is found in the river Yare, near Norwich, near Uxbridge in Middlesex, near Headley in Surrey, also in Cheshire, and many parts of the North

Only one species of this genus

Title

Where found in England

Class and order in the Linnæan system

The characters

*Acorus* is of the class and order *Hexandria Monogynia*, and the characters are,

1 CALYX There is only a simple cylindrical stalk covered with flowers, termed a Julus

2 COROLLA consists of six obtuse, concave, loose petals

3 STAMINA are six thickish filaments, rather longer than the Corolla, with thick didymous antheræ

4 PISTILLUM consists of an oblongish, gibbous germen, of the length of the stamina, without any style, but a small prominent punctum, for a stigma

5 PERICARPIUM is a short triangular capsule of three cells

6 SEMINA The seeds are oval and oblong

# CHAP. V.

## *ACROSTICHUM*

THIS genus contains several species of the Fern kind, most of which are natives of the hot parts of the world, and cannot be preserved in our gardens, without more trouble than what the generality of people will allow they deserve Those which are natives of England, and which will thrive in the open borders of our gardens, are usually called,

Sorts proper to thrive in this country

1 Forked, or Horned Fern
2 Hairy Fern
3 Marsh Fern
4 Maryland Fern
5 Virginian *Acrostichum*
6 Spanish *Acrostichum*

Description of the Forked or Horny Fern,

1 Forked, or Horned Fern The root is composed of a multitude of slender, blackish fibres The stalks are numerous, slender and about three or four inches high, are divided into two or three segments at the top, and the extremities are usually bent downwards The fructifications are on the back of the plant, and they occasion the whole to be covered with a ferruginous powder, when they are in full perfection, which will be in August

2 Hairy Fern The fibres are slender, and of a dark-brown colour The leaves are numerous, nearly bipinnated, and elevated on stalks, about two or three inches high The pinnæ are blunt, undivided, grow into one piece at the base, and are hairy on their under side The fructifications are found on the back of the leaf, attended by a dusty matter, which issues from them when ripe

Hairy Fern

3 Marsh Fern The root is long, inclining to brown, and hot and biting to the taste The leaf is tender, beautifully pinnated, about six inches high, and the pinnæ are elegantly cut almost to the mid-rib, into many entire segments The fructifications are arranged on each side the mid rib along the back, and are found in perfection in August

Marsh Fern

4 Maryland Fern The root is composed of a multitude of long, narrow, brownish fibres The leaves are pinnated, the pinnæ are long, narrow,

Maryland Fern,

narrow, serrated at the top, and ranged alternately along the mid-rib. The fructifications are numerous on the back of the pinnæ, resembling a dusky, brownish matter, which proceeds from them in July and August.

Virginian Acrostichum. 5. Virginian *Acrostichum*. This is a low, elegant plant, seldom growing to more than three or four inches high. The leaves are pinnated, the pinnæ are oval, crenated, sessile, short, and upright, grow alternately on the mid-rib, and are of a silvery white on their under side. The fructifications are small on the back of the leaves, and they shew themselves in August.

and of the Spanish Acrostichum. 6. Spanish *Acrostichum*. The stalks are of a dark, purple colour, and about four or five inches high. The leaves are nearly bipinnated and spear-shaped, and the pinnæ are oval, oblong, or a thickish substance, and hairy underneath. Some of them are entire, but the lower ones are usually indented on both sides at the base. The fructifications are all over the back of the leaf, discharging a large quantity of yellow farina, with which the whole leaf will be often coloured.

Culture of the first two; The first two sorts grow naturally in the fissures and clefts of rocks in some parts of England, and they may be made to occupy similar places in gardens if the owner has an inclination for these kinds of plants. In the autumn, therefore, let the roots be carefully inserted in the crevices of moist rocks, old walls, ruins, &c. and they will sometimes grow, and not only increase the variety of plants, but prove ornamental to old ruins, or such rocky parts of the garden as are similar to those in which the plants are chiefly found growing in a state of nature. They will also grow in pots filled with a sandy, rubbishy earth.

of the third, The third sort is a native of England, growing naturally in moist, marshy places, and if the roots are taken up in the autumn, and planted in a moist, shady part of the garden, it will not only grow, but become of larger size than it is usually found in its natural place of growth.

and of the other sorts. The others being natives of distant parts, the roots must be set in tubs of native earth, in which they will grow and flourish, and in which they may be continued after their arrival, or turned out of the tubs, with the mould at the roots, into the places where they are designed to remain.

General direction. These are plants of singularity, and not destitute of beauty; but they are never sought after for gardens, except by those who are fond of all plants, and are for establishing a general collection. The East and West-India kinds also are not cultivated, but they may be preserved in a stove, and some species which are natives of Africa, will do very well in a green house, or under a hot-bed frame in winter; so that if a person is desirous of these plants, or a few of the more singular ones to add variety to his tender collection, he must procure them, planted in pots or tubs in their native country, and arrange them here as become plants from the hotter regions.

Titles. 1. Forked, or Horned Fern is titled, *Acrostichum frondibus nudis linearibus laciniatis*. Caspar Bauhine calls it, *Filicula saxatilis corniculata*; and John Bauhine, *Filix saxatilis*. It grows naturally in the fissures of rocks, on tops of mountains in Britain, and most of the northern parts of Europe.

2. Hairy Fern is, *Acrostichum frondibus sub-bipinnatis pinnis opposito-coadunatis obtusis subtus hirsutis basi superioribus*. In the *Flora Suecica* it is termed, *Polypodium fronde duplicato-pinnata pinnulis coadunatis obtusis subtus hispidis*; in the *Flora Lapponica*, *Polypodium duplicato pinnatum, pinnulis obtusis ... subtus villosum*. Plukenet calls it, *Polypodium ... Cambro-Britannicum*, and *Lonchitis aspera Ilvensis*; Morison, *Filicula Alpina ...*; and Ray, *Filix Alpina, pinnulis ... foliis subtus villosis*. It grows naturally on rocks in Wales, and most of the cold parts of Europe.

3. Marsh Fern is, *Acrostichum frondibus pinnatis pinnis pinnatifidis integerrimis*. John Bauhine calls it, *Filix mollis, sive glabra vulgari mas non ramosa accedens*; Ray, *Filix minor palustris repens*; Lobel, *Dryopteris*; and Parkinson, *Dryopteris, filix quernea repens*. It grows naturally in marshy places in England, and most of the northern parts of Europe.

4. Maryland Fern is, *Acrostichum frondibus pinnatis pinnis alternis linearibus apice serratis*. Petiver calls it, *Filix mariana, pinnulis ... angustissimis*. It grows naturally in Virginia and Maryland.

5. Virginian *Acrostichum* is, *Acrostichum frondibus pinnatis pinnis alternis ovatis crenatis sessilibus subtus argenteis*. Plukenet calls it, *Filix polypodium dicta minima Virginiana platyneuros*; Ray, *Asplenium Virginianum, polypodii facie*; and Morison, *Polypodium minus Virginianum, foliis brevibus subtus argenteis*. It grows naturally in Virginia.

6. Spanish *Acrostichum* is, *Acrostichum frondibus sub-bipinnatis pinnis opposito-coadunatis subtus hirsutissimis basi subdentatis*. Caspar Bauhine calls it, *Lonchitis folio ceterach*; Cammerarius, *Lonchitis aspera maranthæ*; and Plukenet, *Filicula aspera, lanugine hepatici coloris vestita*. It grows naturally in most of the southern countries of Europe.

Class and order in the Linnean system. *Acrostichum* is of the first order of the class *Cryptogamia*.

The fructifications are the only visible parts for observation, and they are so numerous, as to cover the whole disk of the leaves on the other side.

# CHAP. VI.

## *ACTÆA*, HERB CHRISTOPHER, or, BANE BERRIES.

WE are now entered upon another poisonous tribe, some of which are deemed as violent as the Aconite, whilst another species is held an antidote to the poison, and is said to be good against the deadly bite of the rattle-snake. This genus comprehends three distinct species, to which varieties belong, and they are called as follows:

Species. 1. The Common English Herb Christopher, or Bane Berries.

2. The

2 The Virginian Long-clustered *Actaea*
3 The Siberian *Actaea*

Varieties of the Common Herb Christopher

1 The Common Herb Christopher affords us three varieties, differing chiefly in the colour of their berries, viz the Black, the White, and the Red-berried

The Black-berried is most common with us being found plentifully growing in many parts of the north I have never yet heard of the White and Red growing with us in common, but in many parts of America they are found in plenty

Described

It hath a very thick root, furnished with many long fibres Its outward colour is black, but within it is of a yellow colour, and from this the leaves and flower-stalks arise The general leaf is large, being composed of several smaller standing by threes The division is so great, that no less than twenty-seven folioles constitute a full leaf, and these standing by threes on their own separate pedicle, are all supported by one common long slender foot-stalk The leaves are of a deep green, their edges are cut, and the whole makes a handsome appearance

This plant is seldom found to grow more than two feet high The flower stalk is garnished with leaves of the same composition as those that spring from the root, though smaller, and the flowers are produced at the top in small, branching spikes They are small, and of a fine white, are produced in May, and are succeeded by oblong, black shining berries, which will be ripe in September or October

The White and the Red-berried, with these, make a pretty variety, and their potency, as poisonous plants, is supposed not to be equal to the Black-berried sort

Description of the Long-clustered Virginian Actaea,

2 The Long-clustered Virginian *Actaea* is supposed to be the counter poison, and is said to be good against the bite of the rattle-snake This is a large growing plant, usually rising to upwards of four feet in height The leaves are large and fine, arising immediately from the root They are composed of several folioles, in the ternate way, and the whole form a grand leaf The flowers are produced in long spikes at the tops of the branches they are white, and the end of the spike naturally droops, or hangs downward It will be in blow in June, and will often continue to exhibit bloom until the end of July, but is seldom succeeded by seeds in England In America, this species goes by the name of Black Snake root, and is there in frequent use in the shops for many disorders

and of the Siberian Actaea

3 The Siberian *Actaea* is a lower growing plant, and has the beautiful appearance of our common Herb Christopher, but is of a very stinking nature The flowers are produced in a kind of panicles and are succeeded by a four capsuled fruit, containing the seeds This being a very foetid plant, is thought by many to be fit only for such places where general collections are making

Method of propagating them by seed,

All the sorts of *Actaea* are propagated by parting of their roots, and by sowing of the seeds

Beds for the seeds should be prepared of light earth, in a shady place, and they should be sowed soon after they are ripe The best way is to sow them in drills an inch deep, and having placed a peg at the end of each drill for a direction, the greater care may be taken the summer following in weeding them, for they will not always come up the first spring, and those seeds that are brought from abroad, are pretty sure of lying one year before they vegetate Until the plants come up, however, and afterwards, they must be kept clear of weeds and if the place is not naturally shady, the young plants must be covered with mats in hot weather, and watered now and then, according as the weather proves dry This is all the trouble they will cause the first summer after coming up In the autumn, or the spring following, the strongest plants may be set out for good, whilst the weaker may remain in the seed bed another year, to gain strength, by which time they will be good plants for transplanting

and by dividing of the roots

By dividing of the roots also, these plants are to be encreased The best time for this is the autumn, and, indeed, if a plant or two of each sort can be at first obtained, they will soon spread, and may be multiplied at pleasure

Proper situations

All these sorts are proper for wilderness quarters, for they all love shade, but it is the common Bane-berries that will flourish well under the drip of trees These, therefore may be planted any where with shrubs and trees, whilst the other species, which are more rare, may be made to occupy the open spaces in such works, or, may be planted in large borders amongst other perennial roots

Titles

1 The Common Herb Christopher is entitled, *Actaea racemo ovato, fructibusque baccatis* In the *Flora Lapponica* it is termed *Actaea caule inermi* Caspar Bauhine calls it, *Aconitum bacciferum*, Clusius, *Christophoriana*, Cornutus, *Aconitum baccis niveis*, and Morison, *Christophoriana Americana racemosa, baccis niveis & rubris*

The common Black-berried sort grows wild in England, and many parts of Europe, but the White and Red berried sorts are found growing only naturally in America

2 The Virginian Long-clustered This is, *Actaea racemis longissimis, fructibus unicapsularibus* Gronovius calls it, *Actaea racemis longissimis*, Plukenet, *Christophorianae facie herba spicata*, and Dillenius, *Christophoriana Americana procerior & longius spicata* It grows common in Virginia and Canada

3 Siberian This is, *Actaea racemis paniculatis fructibus quadricapsularibus* In the *Amoenitates Acad* it is termed, *Cimicifuga* Amman calls it, *Thalictroides foetidissimum, Christophorianae facie* It grows common in Siberia

Class and order in the Linnaean system

*Actaea* is of the class and order *Polyandria Monogynia*, and the characters are,

The characters

1 CALYX is a perianthium, composed of four roundish, obtuse, concave deciduous leaves

2 COROLLA consists of four deciduous petals that are longer than the calyx

3 STAMINA are about thirty slender filaments, which are broadest at the top, and have roundish, erect, didymous anthera

4 PISTILLUM consists of an oval germen, without any style, but a thickish, oblique, compressed stigma

5 PERICARPIUM is an oval, globular, smooth, unisulcated berry, containing one cell

6 SEMINA The seeds are semicircular, truncated in the inner side, and are arranged in a double series

# CHAP. VII

## *ADIANTUM*, MAIDEN-HAIR.

THE species of this genus which will bear our winters, are,

Species

1 True Maiden-hair
2 Shining Maiden-hair
3 Canada Maiden hair
4 Creeping American Maiden-hair

True Maiden hair,

1 True Maiden-hair The root is long, fibrous, black on the outside, and white within The leaves are decompound The stalks are slender black, glossy, naked for about three or four inches high, and from that to the top send forth the other parts which contribute to form the whole leaf These are pinnated, and arranged alternately, they are composed each of about four pair of folioles, which are terminated by an odd one These folioles are wedge-shaped, grow on short footstalks, are beautifully lobed or divided on the edges, are smooth on the upper surface, and soft to the touch The leaves carry their fructifications near the edges on the under side They are finely, though not strongly scented, and continue green all the year This plant affords the celebrated syrup called Capillaire, which is used in medicine It is a famous pectoral, is a great promoter of the discharge of tough phlegm, is good for the stone and gravel, removes obstructions of the viscera, and is also said to be good against the king's evil, and for wasting of hard old swellings

Shining Maiden hair,

2 Shining Maiden-hair The root is composed of numerous black fibres The leaves are supradecompound The stalks are hard, black, glossy, naked near the bottom, but branch about three or four inches from the ground into several divisions The folioles are almost of a black colour, smooth, shining, and grow alternately on black, smooth footstalks Their shape is a trapezium, and they are jointed, cut, and indented on their edges The whole leaf is large, shining, singular and beautiful, and receives no small additional beauty from its elegantly and finely polished black footstalk The fructifications are disposed under the incisures of the folioles on the under side

Canada Maiden hair

3 Canada Maiden hair The root is large, variously implicated, and of a fine shining black colour The general leaf is pedated The stalk is naked for five or six inches high, and then divides into two or three principal parts, which again, at intervals, divide into others, all of which are elegantly pinnated, but their directions are different, some grow erect, others horizontal, and the lower ones usually hang downward The folioles are trapeziform, obtuse, recurved, cut at the top, and arranged alternately along the midrib The fructifications are numerous on the back of the pinnæ, under the incisures at the top

and Creeping American Maiden hair

4 Creeping American Maiden-hair The root is thick, fibrated, and creeping The general leaf is compound The stalk is hard, tough, smooth, naked for about three or four inches high, and then adorned with the leaves, which are pinnated, and grow on smooth, polished footstalks The pinnæ are obtuse, and divided into three principal parts, which are again cut or jagged on their edges, and under these incisures are often found oval spots, which are the fructifications, and which occasion the edges to be curled inwards

Situations

The first sort grows naturally in Wales, and most of the southern countries of Europe Its natural situation is in the clefts of rocks, old walls, &c so that whoever is desirous of having it in his garden, should carefully dispose the roots in the crevices of rocks, old walls, ruins, and the like, where they will grow, and resist the cold of our severest winters They will also grow in pots filled with sandy, rubbishy earth, so that whoever is not provided with old walls, ruins, or rocks similar to the native places of this plant's growth, may easily preserve them that way

second,

The second sort grows chiefly naturally in Jamaica, but it is found growing in some parts of Scotland, and is hardy enough to resist the cold of our severest winters It may be planted in a light sandy ground, or in pots filled with light sandy earth, and either way it will flourish very well in gardens

third,

The third sort is extremely hardy It should have a light, loose, rich earth, and being thus planted, will grow to be near four feet high

and fourth sort

The root of the fourth sort creeps very much It is a native of some of the western parts of America, but will do very well here if planted in a dry light soil, in a warm well sheltered place

1 True Maiden-hair is entitled, *Adiantum frondibus decompositis foliolis alternis pinnis cuneiformibus lobatis pedicellatis* Sauvages calls it, *Adiantum ramis pinnatis, foliis circuli [illegible] crescentibus*, Caspar Bauhine, *Adiantum foliis coriandri*, Camerarius, *Adiantum*, Gerard, *Capillus Veneris verus*, and Parkinson, *Adiantum [illegible] Capillus Veneris verus* It is found in some parts of Wales, but grows plentifully in France, Spain, Portugal, and the southern countries of Europe, also in the East

2 Shining Maiden-hair is, *Adiantum frondibus supradecompositis foliolis alternis [illegible] incisis utrinque fructificationibus* In the *Hortus Cliffortianus* it is termed, *Adiantum fronde alternatim supradecomposita foliolis trapeziformibus [illegible] crenatis* Plumier calls it, *Adiantum ramosum [illegible] lucens & minus*, Sloane, *Adiantum nigrum ramosum [illegible], foliis magis trapezii in modum figuratis*, Plukenet, *Adiantum fruticosum coriandri folio, Jamaicense, [illegible] altum polytricho [illegible]* It grows naturally in Jamaica, and most of the West India Islands

3 Canada Maiden-hair is, *Adiantum [illegible] pedatis foliolis [illegible] pinnis [illegible] fructificantibus* Van Royen calls it, *[illegible] fronde bifida foliolis alternis pinnulis [illegible] recurvis superne incisis [illegible]* Gronovius, *Adiantum fronde supradecomposita [illegible] alternis alternis foliolis trapeziformibus*, [illegible] *Adiantum fruticosum Americanum [illegible] reflexis & in orbem expansis*, Caspar Bauhine [illegible]

*antum fruticosum Brasilienum*, and Cornutus, *Adiantum Americanum* It grows naturally in Canada and Virginia

4 Creeping American Maiden-hair is, *Adiantum frondibus compositis pinnis tripartitis obtusis incisis multiflora* Petiver calls it, *Adiantum triphyllum repens* It grows naturally in America

*Adiantum* is of the class and order *Cryptogamia Filices* and the fructifications are collected in oval spots, at the extremity of the leaves, on the under side, by which the joints, borders, or edges are reflexed or folded, and sometimes variously waved and curled — Class and order in the Linnæan system The characters

# CHAP. VIII

## *ADONIS*, BIRD's EYE

THE perennial species of this genus are usually called,

Species
1 The German *Adonis*
2 The Appennine *Adonis*

German Adonis described — 1 The German *Adonis* This species is now grown pretty common in our English gardens, and is chiefly valued on account of its early blowing, though the flower and the whole plant itself is elegant, and has properties enough to recommend it to a principal place in our choicest borders It is a low growing plant, seldom arising so high as two feet, and each stalk is terminated with a fine yellow flower, a little resembling some sorts of our single anemones The leaves of this species are elegant, long, narrow, of a pleasant green colour, and ornament the stalks in clusters, at proper distances If the root be strong, numbers of flower-stalks will arise from it, and as each will be crowned with a flower, they are delightful at so early a season, for they will be in blow in March, if the season is open, or early in April These flowers are succeeded by seeds which ripen well with us, and by which the plants are best propagated

Method of propagating this species — In August the seeds will be fit for gathering, and after having laid them in a dry airy place for a few days, sow them in a border facing the east, of good light earth, made fine Half an inch covering will be as much as they require, and in spring the plants will come up Weeding and watering must be afforded them all summer, at proper times, and in autumn, where they are too thick, they should be thinned by drawing out a proper share, which will do for other places But in order to have these flowers in perfection, it will be the best way never to remove the roots, for which reason I am for having the seeds sown in the places where they are designed to grow, and the removal to be made of such plants as come up too close, leaving a sufficient number only to stand

When this sort is to be propagated by the root, the best season for removing them is the autumn but plants of that kind never send out so many stalks, or produce their flowers so large and fine as those raised from seeds, which should also teach us not to give these plants the common removing of most perennial roots, but to let them remain for years undisturbed, loosening the ground near the root only annually, and keeping the beds in good order

The seeds of this plant may be sown in the spring, but then they seldom come up before the spring following, which is the reason of my directing their being sown as soon as they are ripe, for by such expeditious practice a year will be saved But before I quit this subject I must caution my reader, that if it should happen that the plants should not come up at the time expected, not to destroy the bed, but keep them in weeding all summer and if the seeds are good they will be pretty sure of coming up the spring after

This species grows common in many parts of Germany, and there the roots pass for the black hellebore of Hippocrates, and as such have been used in medicine, but by this time, I believe, most physicians are convinced this practice has been erroneous, the plant of that ancient writer being quite different from this

Appennine Adonis — 2 Appennine *Adonis* is with most persons in greater request than the other, for the flowers are larger, make a good show at a distance, and never fail to please on the closest examination The leaves are large and fair for these sorts, and of a fine deep green colour They are composed of several oblong pointed folioles, being divided in the pinnated way, and stand on purplish footstalks The flower-stalk is round and low, and tho' grown of a tolerable thickness, it is unable to support the flowers in an upright position The stalks are garnished with leaves, which are divided in an irregular manner They are besprinkled with little pellucid dots, and each of them is terminated by a large fair flower Its colour is yellow, and it will be as large as our single anemone The number of petals that belong to each flower is usually about fifteen, though sometimes they are found with not more than twelve These are broad, and expand themselves in a delightful manner They will be in blow in March, which makes them very valuable, and their propagation and management are exactly the same as the former — Culture

1 The German *Adonis*, and which is commonly called with us the Yellow Perennial Pheasant's Eye, is titled, *Adonis flore dodecapetalo, fructu ovato* Caspar Bauhine calls it, *Helleborus niger tenuifolius, buphthalmi flore*, and Clusius, *Buphthalmum Dodonæi, pseudo-helleborus niger* Dodonæus terms it simply, *Buphthalmum* It grows common in many of the mountainous parts of Germany, but is particularly found in great plenty in Prussia and Bohemia — Titles

2 Appennine *Adonis* is titled, *Adonis flore pentadecapetalo, fructu ovato* Morison calls it, *Helleborus niger fumariæ folio, flore magno* ... It grows common in Siberia, and on the Appennine Mountains

*Adonis* is of the class and order *Polyandria Polygynia*, and the characters are, — Class and order

1 CA-

The characters

1 CALYX is a perianthium composed of five obtuse, concave, coloured, deciduous leaves

2 COROLLA consists of five, eight, twelve, or more beautiful, oblong, obtuse, expanded petals

3 STAMINA are numerous, very short, subulated filaments, with oblong, inflexed antheræ

4 PISTILLUM consists of numerous germina, collected into a head, without any styles, but three very short pointed stigmas

5 PERICARPIUM There is none The receptacle is oblong, and holds the seeds in five series

6 SEMINA The seeds are numerous, angular, and irregular

# C H A P IX

## *ADOXA*, TUBEROUS MOSCHATEL, or HOLLOW-ROOT

In our tor[illegible] vations

ADOXA is a poor plant, but has something more than a merit after a general Collection to recommend itself to our care, for its leaves and flowers are finely scented, a little like those of musk It flourishes best in shade and under trees, and may therefore be made to cause a variety, in our wilderness works of any kind, and as it is a low plant, and requires little trouble, as well as being possessed of the above properties, it is really deserving of a place in any collection of perennial flower roots

Description of this plant

The root of this plant is of the tuberous kind It is white, toothed, and emits many small white fibres From this arise the leaves and the flower-stalks The leaves are composed of oblong segments, and much resemble those of the bulbous fumitory, their common footstalk is about three inches long The flower-stalk, which seldom rises above an inch higher, is also garnished with leaves, and is terminated by four or five flowers The stalk is slender, smooth, and of a pale green colour, and the leaves which ornament it are two in number They are placed opposite to each other, on short footstalks, at rather higher than half way, and they are of the same nature with those of the radical leaves, but smaller The flowers are small, and of a yellowish green colour They appear early in April, and are succeeded by small berries, which will be ripe in May

Method of propagating it

The propagation is by the berries and dividing the roots The berries should be sown, soon after they are ripe, in a place well prepared for them, in some part of the wilderness-quarters, or under some trees This plant requires no dung, the natural soil being the best, and the mould should only be made fine by digging, and all roots of trees and weeds should be picked out Then sow the seeds one inch deep, in patches, where they are to remain, for it will be the best way never to remove them At each patch place a stick for a direction, and keep some clear of weeds, whilst in others let the weeds grow, to see which will best succeed, for they will sometimes come up best if left wholly to Nature, which is not to be wondered at, as they grow naturally in many of our woods If the ground has been used to be kept clean by hoeing &c a mark must be always placed for the labourers, or they will be in danger of hoeing them up in the summer, for the leaves and flower stalks will be decayed by the beginning of June, and no more of the plant will be seen until it rises afresh for the next spring

This plant will also grow very well when transplanted, the best time for which is in May or June, on the decay of the leaves and stalks There are to have the like situation, and in such places they will grow and thrive without any further trouble

Titles

There being no other species of this genus, it stands with the name simply, *Adoxa* John Bauhine calls it, *Moschatellina foliis fumariæ bulbosæ*, Caspar Bauhine, *Ranunculus nemorum moschatellina dictus*, Tabernamontanus, *Fumaria bulbosa, sive tuberosa minima*, Gerard, *Radix cava minima viridi flore*, and Parkinson, *Ranunculus nemorosus moschatella dictus* It grows naturally in woods and shady places in most parts of Europe

Class and order in the Linnæan system The characters

*Adoxa* is of the class and order *Octandria Tetragynia*, and the characters are,

1 CALYX is a plane, permanent, bifid perianthium, placed below the germen

2 COROLLA consists of a single petal, cut into four oval, acute segments, that are longer than the calyx

3 STAMINA consist of eight subulated filaments, the length of the calyx, having roundish antheræ

4 PISTILLUM consists of a germen situated below the receptacle of the flower, having four simple, erect, permanent styles, with simple stigmas

5 PERICARPIUM is a globose umbilicated berry, containing four cells

6 SEMINA The seeds are single and compressed

## CHAP. X.

## *AGERATUM*, BASTARD HEMP AGRIMONY.

In rodu ry e . . . n

HOW wonderful is the variety of Nature in the vegetable kingdom! and how different from one another are those plants that must be collected to form one assortment or collection.

The present Division of this Work respects Perennial Flower-roots. *Achnia*, just before spoken of, is one, whose natural growth is no more than three or four inches in height, and which flowers early in the spring, and the leaves decay soon after. But this genus affords us one very tall growing species, that will rise with its flower-stalks to near six feet in height, and appears in full splendor at the end of autumn, thereby shewing how bountiful Nature is in her riches, by affording us plants of all sizes, different beauties, and times of flowering, that we may pick or choose, or rather make choice of such as will best answer our taste or purpose, in any part or whole of our intended decorations. The species under consideration is called, Perennial Bastard Hemp Agrimony, or, Tall *Ageratum*. The leaves are of an oval, heart-shaped figure, rough, and serrated on their edges. The stalk is smooth and erect, and, towards the top, puts out others by pairs. The flowers are produced in large tufts from the ends of the branches. They are of a snow-white colour, appear in October, but are seldom succeeded by ripe seeds in England. After the blow is over, the stalks should be cut up close to the roots, and cleared away, for, as they naturally die to the ground, without this, they will have a disagreeable look all winter. In the spring, the fresh ones rise for a succession.

This species de . . . ed

This species, as it is naturally a tall growing plant, should be stationed at the back of large borders, either amongst others of the same growth, or they may be planted in a row, at about a yard asunder, and the longer this is continued, the greater show will they make in October, when the general show of flowers is over, and we begin to set a greater value upon the flowery tribe, for these, being of a pure white, and produced in large tufts, not only look well of themselves, but they may be made to form an agreeable contrast of different colours that will be in blow at that time.

Proper situation

The propagation of this species is by seeds and parting of the roots.

Method of propagating this species.

By seeds the best plants are raised, but these must be procured from America, where they naturally grow, for I never yet knew them ripen in England. They should be sown in a bed of light earth, in a moist, shady place, and covered about half an inch deep, they will readily come up, and, in the autumn, may be planted out where they are designed to remain.

By seeds.

Parting of the roots may be done at any time, from the season of flowering, until the stalks get strong for the next blow, though the best season is in November, when the stalks decay. These seldom flower strong the succeeding autumn, but by the October following, they will be in their full glory. They will grow in almost any soil, but they chiefly delight in a good deep fat earth, that is moderately moist, and in such they will flower the strongest, and make surprising increase.

Parting of the root.

This species is entitled, *Ageratum foliis ovato cordatis rugosis, floralibus alternis, caule glabro*. In the *Hortus Cliffortianus* it is termed, *Eupatorium caule erecto, foliis cordatis serratis*, and in the *Hortus Upsaliensis*, *Eupatorium foliis ovatis serratis petiolatis, caule glabro*. Cornutus calls it, *Valeriana urticae folio, flore albo*, and Morison, *Eupatorium Canadense urticae foliis, flore albo*. It grows naturally in Canada and Virginia.

Titles.

*Ageratum* is of the class and order *Syngenesia Polygamia Aequalis*, and the characters are,

Class and order in the Linnaean System. The characters.

1. CALYX. The common calyx is oblong, and composed of many spear-shaped stalks, which are almost equal.

2. COROLLA. The general flower is uniform. The hermaphrodite florets are equal, numerous, tubulous, hardly longer than the calyx, and cut at their margin into five spread segments.

3. STAMINA are five very short capillary filaments, having a cylindrical, tubulous anthera.

4. PISTILLUM consists of an oblong germen, of a filiform style the length of the stamina, and two very slender, erect stigmas.

5. PERICARPIUM. There is none.

6. SEMINA. The seeds are single, oblong, angular, and each is crowned with its proper little cup, cut into five narrow pointed segments. The receptacle is naked, small, and convex.

## CHAP. XI.

## *ÆGOPODIUM*, HERB GERARD, GOUT-WORT, or WILD ANGELICA.

THERE is only one species of this genus, called by the various names of Herb Gerard, Gout-wort, Ash-weed, Wild Angelica, and Wild Master-wort. The root is tender, white, knotty, full of juice, and creeping. The stalk is round, striated, hollow, and branching in the manner of Master-wort, to which this plant bears much resemblance. The radical leaves are large, grow

D . . . ti . . . of the . . .

grow on long strong footstalks, and are composed of two or three pair of oblong, serrated, pointed foliols, which are terminated by an odd one. Those on the stalks consist of three foliols, which are serrated and pointed in the same manner, and they grow opposite by pairs at the joints. The flowers come out in convex umbels at the tops of the stalks and branches. They are of a white colour, appear in May and June, and the seeds ripen in August. This plant is said to be of singular service for the gout. It is used by stamping the roots, and applying them to the afflicted parts. It is also said to be good for hæmorrhages, swellings, and inflammations, but at present is little used.

which is said to be of service in the gout, &c.

Method of propagating it.

It is propagated by parting of the roots, which may be done any time in the autumn, winter, or early in the spring, before the leaves and stalks arise. It grows common in our ditches and hedges, which directs us to give it the worst and coldest part of the garden, when we are desirous of having a plant or two to be ready at hand for observation, or to cause variety among the other plants. When it is planted out it will require no trouble, except keeping it clean from weeds, cutting the old stalks away every autumn, and reducing the roots, as often as they are found to spread too far.

Titles.

This species is titled, *Ægopodium foliis caulinis summis ternatis*, and was the name formerly given to it, when other species were supposed to be of the genus, and made such a distinctive title necessary. Caspar Bauhine calls it, *Angelica sylvestris minor, seu erratica*, Dodonæus, *Herba Gerardi*, Rivinus, *Podagraria*, and Parkinson, *Podagraria vulgaris*. It grows common in hedges, ditches, gardens, and shady places in England, and most countries of Europe.

*Ægopodium* is of the class and order *Pentandria Digynia*, and the characters are,

Class and order in the Linnæan system. The characters.

1. CALYX. The general umbel is multiple and convex, the partial umbel is plane. There is neither general nor partial involucrum. The proper perianthium is very small.

2. COROLLA. The general flower is uniform. The florets consist each of five obovald, concave, equal petals, that are inflected at the tips.

3. STAMINA are five simple filaments, of double the length of the corolla, having roundish antheræ.

4. PISTILLUM consists of a germen situated below the flower, and two erect simple styles the length of the corollulæ, with capitated stigmas.

5. PERICARPIUM. There is none. The fruit is oblong, striated, and divided into two parts.

6. SEMINA. The seeds are two, oval, oblong, striated, convex on one side, and on the other plane.

# CHAP. XII.

## *AGRIMONIA*, AGRIMONY.

BESIDES the Agrimony of our pastures, that is so well known to every herb-woman, and whose virtues the afflicted in various diseases have so often experienced, there are,

Species.

1. Agrimony,
2. The Creeping Agrimony.
3. The Three-leaved Agrimony.

1. Agrimony. Of this there are three principal varieties.

Varieties of Agrimony.

Common Agrimony.
Small White Agrimony.
Sweet-scented Agrimony.

described.

Our Common Agrimony is known to be a fine, upright plant, rising with a stalk ornamented with many, large, pinnated leaves, and a beautiful spike of yellow flowers, to the height of two feet and a half.

The Small White differs from this in that the foliols are fewer and rounder, the flower-stalk seldom arrives to half the height of the other, and the flowers that compose the spike are of a white colour. This affords a variety, and, as such, is propagated by the general lovers of plants.

The Sweet-scented Agrimony, which is another celebrated variety of the Common Sort, is propagated, not only on account of its sweet odour, and fine flowers, but to be drank as a tea, for, being steeped and used as such, the drink is said to be very wholesome, and is by many thought to be agreeable. This sort will grow to be four feet high, or more, the leaves are pinnated, but large in proportion than the Common Agrimony, and the flower stalk branches into smaller, each of which supports a spike of yellow flowers. It must have a place in the perennial quarter, among the tall growers, and when propagated in quantities for use, the ground should be double-dug and made rich, and the plants should be set at two feet asunder. All these three sorts flower in June, and the seeds ripen in August and September.

Their culture.

The Common Sort is used in medicine. It is accounted aperient, detergent, and is employed in scorbutic disorders, debility and laxity of the intestines, &c. It also affords a diet drink, digested in whey, which is both palatable and wholesome to drink in the spring months.

Medicinal properties of the Common Sort.

2. Creeping Agrimony. This is a low growing plant, but has a very large thick creeping root. The leaves are pinnated, the foliols are long and narrow, and the whole has a graceful look. The flower stalk is also ornamented with pinnated leaves, and is very hairy. It is seldom seen higher than two feet, and the top is terminated by a short thick spike of flowers, all of which sit very close. The fruit that succeeds the flowers of all the preceding sorts, is very rough, but the fruit of this species is larger and rougher than the others, and will be ripe in autumn. To propagate this plant by the seeds, those should be sown immediately upon their being ripe, and they will come up in the spring, but this sort is readily to be had by the roots, that it is hardly worth while to wait the seeds, as they may soon be divided into any desired number.

Description of the Creeping.

3. The Three-leaved Agrimony differs much from any of the other species, not only as there are but three foliols on the footstalk, but because the seeds are not so thorn. And although the class to which this genus belongs, requires twelve stamina,

Of the Three-leaved Agrimony.

mina, the male organs of this species are only about seven in each flower, and the calyx also is fringed, and very singular The flowers of this species are succeeded by good seeds in our gardens, by which this and the former sorts may be all propagated, as well as by parting of the roots, the best season for both which is the autumn, though the roots will grow, if divided at any time of the year The seeds also may be sown at any time, though if they are kept out of the ground long, they will lie a whole year in the beds before they come up They require no nice part in the garden, for they are all very hardy, and will thrive in almost any soil or situation

Their culture

Titles

1 Agrimony is titled, *Agrimonia foliis caulinis pinnatis ... fructibus hispidis* This is the *Eupatorium* of the Greeks Caspar Bauhine calls it, *Eupatorium veterum, sive agrimonia* One or other of the varieties of this species are found by the sides of fields and roads, and in pasture-grounds or meadows in most parts of Europe

2 The Creeping Agrimony is titled, *Agrimonia foliis caulinis pinnatis impari petiolato, fructibus hispidis* Tournefort calls it, *Agrimonia orientalis ... repente, fructu ... spicam brevem & densè congestà* It is a native of the East

3 Three-leaved Agrimony is termed, *Agrimonia foliis caulinis ternatis, fructibus glabris* Caspar Bauhine calls it, *Agrimonia ...*, and others, *Agrimonoides* It grows naturally in woods and moist shady places in Italy

*Agrimonia* is of the class and order *Dodecandria Digynia*; and the characters are,

Class and order in the Linnæan system The characters

1 Calyx is a monophyllous perianthium, divided into five small, acute, permanent segments, placed on the germen, and is surrounded by another cup

2 Corolla consists of five plane, emarginated petals, with narrow ungues, which are inserted in the calyx

3 Stamina The filaments are of an uncertain number They are slender, shorter than the corolla, and are inserted in the calyx, and their antheræ are small, didymous, and compressed

4 Pistillum consists of a germen below the receptacle, having two simple styles the length of the stamina, with obtuse stigmas

5 Pericarpium There is none

6 Semina The seeds are roundish, and two in number

# CHAP XIII

## *AGROSTEMMA*, CAMPION, or WILD *LYCHNIS*

Species

We will here introduce,
1 Double Rose-Campion
2 Mountain Campion

Double Rose Campion described

1 Double Rose Campion The Gardener may perhaps wonder at finding the Rose-Campion ranked among the Perennials, as he has ever been used to treat it as a Biennial only, it arising from seeds in one summer viz the summer after flowering, producing seeds for its succession, and dying in the autumn This is the nature, indeed, of the Rose Campion in its Single state, and the Double is only a variety of this, differing in no other respect than in the fullness of the flowers A little art or care, however, in the management of this beautiful variety, will continue it for many years and as it never produces seeds, but was only at first accidentally obtained from the seeds of the Single, a more than ordinary eye must be had to it, or we shall soon be dispossessed of this flower, which is acknowledged by all to be very fine And as the Gardener will wonder to find this species ranked among the Perennials, so will the man of learning much regret to find the generical word altered to what it is now, *Agrostemma* The usual title for the Rose-Campion was, *Lychnis*, which was the name given it by the Greeks of old, and with good reason for the leaves of this plant afford a downy substance, that was often used by them for the wicks of lamps, and thus this plant originally obtained the name of *Lychnis*, from the Greek word λυχνος, which signifies *a lamp*, so properly was it first named, and so very improperly is that name made to comprehend a tribe of plants that are possessed of no such property

It appears that this plant, in its Single state, was known only to the Greeks of old, and that we owe the Double flower to later improvements in Gardening, and in this state we have it in two varieties

Varieties

The Double Red Rose-Campion
The Double Painted Lady

The leaves of all, whether in a Single or Double state, are of an oval lanceolate figure very downy, and soft to the touch The flower-stalks are weak, a ... to a foot or two in height, and are garnished by the same kind of downy leaves, standing by pairs at the joints The stalk naturally branches out into others, so that the main and all the side shoots are terminated by a flower Some value it in its Single state, but in its Double it demands respect, and challenges a place in our choicest gardens

described

Of raising these flowers

In order to continue this flower, let the root be taken up in the autumn, and slipt into as many parts as possible These being planted again will readily take root, will endure our severest winters, and will flower the summer following But as they are apt (though not so much as the Single seedlings) to run wholly into flower-stalks, which will put a period to their existence that autumn, some should be reserved in the nursery ground, that should not be permitted to flower, but as often as the flower-stalks arise, to nip them off This will occasion them to spread at the bottom, and form themselves into more heads, which may be made by dividing into as many good plants, and thus may these beautiful flowers be continued for years

The

The Single sort are three, the Deep red, the Pale-red, and the White-flowering Rose-Campion.

The seeds may be sown one year, they will readily come up, and will flower the next. After that they will scatter their seeds, and come up themselves, and these plants are generally better than those raised by art. Neither the Double nor the Single sorts are very nice in their soil, they will grow and thrive in any common garden mould, though the richer this is, the more luxuriant the plants will be.

Mountain Campion. 2. Mountain Campion is another species of this genus, but the least common of any. It was brought to us from Switzerland, where it grows common on those mountains, and is found to thrive best in the shade. The leaves are downy like the others, and the flower-stalks will rise only to about a foot in height. The flowers are of a fine red colour, and ornament the tops of the stalks in umbels. The time of flowering is June, and the seeds ripen in the autumn.

The seeds of this sort may be sown in the autumn soon after they are ripe, or the spring, in beds of fine earth, and when the plants are about two inches high, they may be removed to the places where they are designed to remain, and where they will call for no trouble except keeping them clean from weeds, and watering them in dry weather.

1. The Rose-Campion is titled, *Agrostemma tomentosa, foliis ovato lanceolatis, petalis integris coronatis*. In the *Hortus Cliffortianus* it is termed, *Coronaria*. Caspar Bauhine calls it, *Lychnis coronaria Dioscoridis sativa*, and Camerarius, *Lychnis*. It is a native of Italy.

2. Mountain Rose Campion is called, *Agrostemma tomentosa, petalis emarginatis*. Caspar Bauhine calls it, *Lychnis coronaria flore ...*, and Ray, *Lychnis umbellifera montana Helvetica*. It grows naturally on the Helvetian mountains.

*Agrostemma* is of the class and order *Decandria Pentagynia*, and the characters are, Class and order in the Linnæan system.

1. Calyx is a monophyllous, coriaceous, tubulous, permanent perianthium, divided at the edge into five narrow points.

2. Corolla consists of five petals, whose ungues are of the length of the tube of the calyx, and whose ... are ...

3. Stamina are ten awl-shaped subulated filaments, ... are fixed to the ... of the petals, and the others stand alternately between, having simple antheræ.

4. Pistillum consists of an oval germen, ... of five ... erect styles, the length of the stamina, with single stigmas.

5. Pericarpium is an oblong oval capsule, formed of five valves, and containing one cell.

6. Semina. The seeds are numerous, kidney-shaped, and dotted.

# CHAP. XIV.

## *AGROSTIS.*

THIS genus comprehends several of the grass tribe, many species of which ought by no means to be passed by, as it may give satisfaction to some persons (though they are not garden-plants) to know their titles and characters, especially such as are of English growth, and to be met with within the vortex of a morning's excursion. These are,

Species.
1. Fine Bent-Grass.
2. Brown Bent Grass.
3. Red Bent-Grass.
4. Creeping Bent-Grass.
5. Marsh Bent Grass.
6. Wood Bent Grass.
7. Small Bent Grass.
8. Reed *Agrostis*.
9. *Calamagrostis*.

Description of the Fine. 1. Fine Bent-Grass. This is an elegant grass of our meadows, rising with a slender stalk to about a yard high. The leaves are very narrow, and sheath the stalk near the bottom with their base, the upper part of the stalk to the flower is naked. The flowers are produced from the tops of the stalks, in large panicles. The branches, or rather foot-stalks, of the flower are extremely slender, and in a most elegant manner spread themselves in all directions, supporting the flowers at the end. The folicules are beardless, and their cups are awl-shaped, equal, coloured, and a little hispid to the touch. It will be in blow in July and August.

Brown. 2. Brown Bent Grass. This is another grass growing common in our meadows. The stalk is slender, weak, jointed, and (unless crowded with other plants) lies on the ground. The flowers are formed in panicles at the ends of the stalks. They are aristated, have brown-coloured cups, and are in perfection in July and August.

Red. 3. Red Bent-Grass. The flowers of this sort are disposed in loose pyramidical spikes. They are aristated, have long cups of a deep brown or red colour, and are in perfection in July.

Creeping. 4. Creeping Bent Grass. The radical leaves are numerous, a foot and a half long, and of a glossy green colour. The stalks are hollow, ... and not so tall as the radical leaves, and have leaves growing singly at the joint, surrounding it with their base, where they are ... inflated, forming, as it were, a swoln or bellied sheath to the stalks. The flowers come out from the tops of the stalks, in short spikes. They are of a greenish colour, soft to the touch, and are in perfection in August. There are several varieties of this species.

Marsh. 5. Marsh Bent Grass. The leaves are long, narrow, pointed, and of a light green colour. The stalks are jointed, hollow, lie on the ground, and strike root at the joints. The flowers come out in panicles from the ends of the branches. They are of a greenish colour, have no arista or awns, and the valves of the calyx are equal. It is in perfection in July.

Wood. 6. Wood Bent Grass. This is a very ... grass, growing naturally in some of our moist woods. The leaves are narrow, pointed, and ... the stalks with their base. The stalks are hollow,

low, jointed, and naked at the upper part. The flowers crown the stalks in panicles, having no arista. The calyces are oblong and equal. At first the corolla is shorter than the calyx, but it grows afterwards to be twice its length, which is a singularity not common to the other sorts. This species is in perfection in August.

and Small Bent Grass. 7. Small Bent Grass. This is a small elegant grass. The leaves are very narrow, the stalks slender, and the flowers crown the top in a slender branching panicle. They come out singly from the sides, and are arranged alternately. They appear in the summer with other grasses, and their composition agrees with the general characters of the genus.

of Rheed Agrostis. 8. Rheed Agrostis. The stalks are upright, smooth, hollow, and of different heights according to the different situations. The leaves are long, narrow, pointed, and of a pale green colour. The flowers come out in oblong panicles from the tops of the stalks, they are aristated, and the outer petal is hairy at the base. Their colour is a whitish brown, and they are in perfection in July and August.

and Calamagrostis. 9. *Calamagrostis*. The stalk of this species is smooth, hollow, and branching. The leaves are long, narrow, pointed, and their ends hang downwards. The flowers come out in close spikes from the ends of the branches, they are hairy, and each has a straight arista at the top, they are very glossy, of a silvery white, having frequently a mixture of green, and they are in perfection in July and August.

The first seven sorts are of English growth, the eighth and ninth are foreign plants, and are coveted by many who are fond of great variety of plants in their gardens. For they not only augment the Collection, but cause a pretty appearance by their fine glittering panicles of flowers, when in blow.

Method of propagating the sorts. They may be propagated by parting of the roots in the autumn when the stalks decay, or sowing the seeds in the spring. They should have a moist light earth, and be kept clean from weeds, and they will grow to a greater size, the panicles will be larger, glossy, and more beautiful.

The roots of the others may be taken up and planted, if a person is desirous of making a Collection of English grasses, or the seeds may be sown in the autumn or spring. The roots may be planted at any time of the year, though the best way will be to take them when they are in flower, that you may be sure of the sorts.

Titles. 1. Fine Bent Grass is titled, *Agrostis panicula capillari patente, calycibus subulatis æqualibus hispidiusculis coloratis, flosculis muticis*. In the *Flora Lapponica* it is termed, *Agrostis panicula tenuissima*. Caspar Bauhine calls it, *Gramen montanum, panicula spadicea delicatiore*, John Bauhine, *Gramen pratense vulgare, panicula fere arundinacea*, and Ray, *Gramen miliaceum locustis minimis, panicula fere arundinacea*. It grows every where in our meadows and pastures, and is found in plenty all over Europe.

2. Brown Bent-Grass is, *Agrostis calycibus coloratis, petalorum arista dorsali recurva, culmis prostratis subramosis*. Caspar Bauhine calls it, *Gramen supinum caninum paniculatum, folio varians*, and Scheuchzer, *Gramen paniculatum supinum ad infima culmorum genicula foliorum capillarium geniculis fasciculatis donatum*. It grows naturally in moist meadows and pastures in England and most parts of Europe.

3. Red Bent-Grass is, *Agrostis paniculæ parte florente patentissima, petalo exteriore glabro terminato arista tortili recurva*. Hudson calls it, *Agrostis panicula laxa colorata spiciformi, calyce flosculo triplo longiore, petalorum arista dorsali recurva*. In the *Flora Lapponica* it is termed, *Agrostis panicula inferiore verticillatim laxa, superiore coarctata*. Plukenet names it, *Gramen alopecuro accedens, ex culmi geniculis spicas cum petiolis longiusculis promens*, Tournefort, *Panicum serotinum arvense, spica pyramidata*, and Ray, *Gramen serotinum, sp. a la. a pyramidali*. It grows naturally in meadows and pastures in England, the Isle of Sheppey, and in Sweden.

4. Creeping Bent-Grass is, *Agrostis paniculæ ramulis divaricatis muticis, culmo ramoso repente, calycibus æqualibus*. Van Royen calls it, *Agrostis culmo repente, foliis radicalibus brevioribus, folii suprema vagina ventricosa, flosculis muticis*, also, *Agrostis culmo repente, vagina supremi folii ventricosa*. Vaillant terms it, *Gramen caninum supinum minus*, Scheuchzer, *Gramen radice repente, panicula densa spicata spadiceo viridi, locustis exiguis muticis*, and Ray, *Gramen montanum miliaceum minus, radice repente*. It grows naturally in moist meadows and pastures in England and most parts of Europe.

5. Marsh Bent-Grass is, *Agrostis panicula coarctata mutica, calycibus æqualibus hispiduscul s coloratis, culmo repente*. Petiver calls it, *Gramen miliaceum majus, panicula spadicea*, also, *Gramen miliaceum majus, panicula viridi*. It grows naturally in ditches, moist woods, and watery places in England and most parts of Europe.

6. Wood Bent-Grass is, *Agrostis panicula coarctata mutica, calycibus æqualibus. Virgines corolla brevioribus, fecundatis duplo longioribus*. Hudson calls it, *Agrostis panicula coarctata mutica, calycibus æqualibus, corolla ante florescentiam calyce breviore, postea duplo longiore*, and Ray, *Gramen miliaceum sylvestre, glumis oblongis*. It grows naturally in most woods in England.

7. Small Bent-Grass is, *Agrostis panicula mutica filiformi*. Guettard calls it, *Nardus panicula spicata, floribus solitariis alternis*, Dillenius, *Gramen spartium, capillaceo folio, minimum*, Caspar Bauhine, *Gramen minimum, paniculis elegantissimis*; John Bauhine, *Gramen minimum*, and Lobel, *Gramen minimum Anglo-Britannicum*. It grows naturally in Wales, France, and Germany.

8. Rheedy Grass is, *Agrostis panicula oblonga, petalo exteriore basi villoso, arista torta calyce longiore*. In the *Flora Lapponica* it is termed, *Agrostis culmo erecto, panicula contracta*. Petiver calls it, *Gramen miliaceum sylvestre, glumis oblongis*, Dillenius, *Gramen avenaceum, panicula acerosa, semine papposo*, and Scheuchzer, *Gramen avenaceum montanum, panicula angusta e dilutissimo fusco albicante & papposa*. It is not a native of England, but grows common in mountainous woodlands in most other countries of Europe.

9. Calamagrostis is, *Agrostis panicula incrassata, petalo exteriore toto lanato apice aristato, caule ramoso*. Scheuchzer calls it, *Gramen arundinaceum, panicula densa viridi argentea splendente aristata*. It grows naturally on the Alps of Helvetia and Verona.

Class and order in the Linnæan system. *Agrostis* is of the class and order *Triandria Digynia*, and the characters are,

The characters. 1. CALYX is a sharp pointed glume, composed of two valves, and containing one flower.

2. COROLLA is composed of two acuminated valves. They are hardly so long as the calyx, and one of them is larger than the other.

3. STAMINA are three capillary filaments, longer than the corolla, having furcated antheræ.

4. PISTILLUM consists of a roundish germen, and two reflexed hairy styles, with similar stigmas.

5. PERICARPIUM every where surrounds the seed.

6. SEMEN. The seed is single, roundish, and pointed at each end.

# CHAP. XV.

## *A I R A.*

ANOTHER sort of English grasses fall under the general term *Aira*, called,

Species 1 Crested Hair Grass
2 Purple Hair Grass
3 Water Hair Grass
4 Turfy Hair Grass
5 Grey Hair Grass
6 Mountain Hair Grass

Description of the Crested, 1 Crested Hair Grass. This is a small slender grass, that grows naturally in the mountainous parts of England. The flowers are produced in crested spikes that are a little hairy, they have seldom any arista, and the glumes are sharp-pointed, not of equal size, and frequently contain three flowers. They are of a silvery white, elegantly tinged with purple, soft to the touch, and will be in perfection in June, July, and August.

Purple, 2 Purple Hair Grass. This grows in moist turfy sterile places in many parts of England. The leaves are flat and sharp-pointed. The stalks are slender, and of a reddish brown, or purplish colour. The flowers are produced in long straitened panicles, they have no arista, and their other properties answer to the general characters. They are of a purplish colour, tho' they are sometimes bluish, and frequently have a mixture of those two colours blended together; their time of blow is from June to August.

Water, 3 Water Hair Grass. This is common by waters in many parts of England. The leaves are flat. The stalks are slender, hollow, prostrate, and strike root at the joints. The flowers are produced in spreading panicles, they have no arista, are smooth, and longer than the calyx, they are of a brownish colour, which will be deeper or lighter in different situations, and are in perfection in June, July, and August. This is often called Sweet Water Grass, because on being chewed, it is found to be possessed of a sweet-tasted juice.

Turfy, 4 Turfy Hair Grass. This is often called Corn Grass. The leaves are flat, thin, long, and slender, of ... The stalks are slender, hollow, jointed, ... and will grow to almost the same height. The flowers come out in roundish spreading panicles, the petals are hairy at their base, and have a short ... they are of the colour of the common Reed, and will be in perfection in June, July and August.

Grey, 5 Grey Hair Grass. This hath a kind of creeping root, sending forth several rushy, soft, ... leaves, among which arise the stalks, each supporting a panicle of bearded flowers at the top. These are of a grey colour, and are in perfection in June and July.

Mountain, 6 Mountain Hair Grass. The leaves are narrow, pointed, a little hairy, and about a foot long. The stalk is slender, weak, and about a foot and a half high. The panicle is situated at the top of the stalk in a loose, open manner, composed but of few flowers. These are of different colours in the different varieties, and are in perfection in June, July, and August. The principal varieties are, 1 The short leaved 2 The white cupped Varieties
3 The brown cupped 4 The purple.

These are all propagated in the manner of those Culture of the preceding genus.

1 Crested Hair Grass is titled, *Aira panicula spicata, calycibus subtriflosis pedunculo longioribus, petalis subaristatis inaequalibus*. Caspar Bauhine calls it, *Gramen, spica cristata subhirsuta*, and Ray, *Gramen parvum spica purpureo-argentea molli*. It grows naturally in England, Helvetia, and Gaul. Title

2 Purple Hair Grass is, *Aira foliis planis, panicula coarctata, floribus pedunculatis muticis convoluto subulatis*. In the *Flora Lapponica* it is termed, *Poa spiculis subulatis, panicula rara contracta*. Caspar Bauhine calls it, *Gramen arundinaceum enode ... sylvaticum*; Morison, *Gramen pratense serotinum, panicula rara purpurascente*, and Merret, *Gramen pratense, spica ... pendula*. It grows naturally in sterile, turfy, watery places and pastures in England, and most parts of Europe.

3 Water Hair Grass is, *Aira foliis planis, panicula patente, floribus muticis laevibus calyce longioribus*. Van Royen calls it, *Aira culmo inferiore repente flosculis muticis calyce longioribus alterno pedunculato*; Scheuchzer, *Gramen aquaticum ... laceum*; Caspar Bauhine, *Gramen caninum supinum paniculatum dulce*; Merret, *Gramen miliaceum fluitans suavis saporis*; and Parkinson, *Gramen exile tenuifolium canario simile, gramen dulce*. It grows naturally in overflowed pastures, by the sides of rivers, brooks, and ditches, in England, and most countries of Europe.

4 Turfy Hair Grass is, *Aira foliis planis, panicula patente, petalis basi villosis aristaque arista recta brevi*. In the *Flora Lapponica* it is termed, *Aira panicula longissima tenui*. Morison calls it, *Aira panicula patentissima, flosculis subaristatis ... basi villosis, foliis planis*; Caspar Bauhine, *Gramen segetum, panicula arundinacea*; Vaillant, *Gramen pratense paniculatum, locustis parvis splendentibus non aristatis*; Merret, *Gramen agrorum, latiore arundinaceo comosa panicula*; Gerard, *Gramen segetum*; and Parkinson, *Gramen segetum, panicula speciosa*. It grows naturally in woods, rich meadows and fruitful fields in England, and most countries of Europe.

5 Grey Hair Grass is, *Aira foliis setaceis summo spathaceo panicula ... obvolvente*. In the *Hortus Cliffortianus* it is termed, *Aira foliis setaceis, arista a basi glumarum calycem aequante*. Caspar Bauhine calls it, *Gramen foliis junceis, radice jubata*, and Ray, *Gramen ... ovinum ... molle*. It grows naturally in sandy places in England, and most of the southern parts of Europe.

6 Mountain Hair Grass is, *Aira foliis setaceis, culmis ... panicula divaricata, pedunculis flexuosis*. In the *Flora Lapponica* it is termed, *Aira panicula rara, calycibus albis*; also, *Aira panicula rara, calycibus fuscis*; in the *Flora Suecica*, *Aira foliis setaceis, panicula angustata, flosculis basi pilosis aristatis arista tortili longiore*. Ray calls it, *Gramen paniculatum locustis ... majus & perenne*; Scheuchzer, *Gramen ... panicula ...*

*num, foliis capillaceis brevibus, locustis purpureo-argenteis & aristatis*, also, *Gramen Alpinum nemorosum paniculatum, foliis angustissimis, locustis splendentibus aristatis* Caspar Bauhine stiles it, *Gramen nemorosum paniculis albis, capillaceo folio* It grows naturally in various places in England, and most of the other countries of Europe

Class and order in the Linnæan system The characters

*Aira* is of the class and order *Triandria Digynia*, and the characters are,

1 CALYX is a glume, composed of two oval, spear-shaped acute, equal valves, containing two flowers

2 COROLLA consists of two valves like those of the calyx

3 STAMINA are three capillary filaments, the length of the flower, having oblong antheræ, furcated at each end

4 PISTILLUM consists of an oval germen, and two setaceous, spreading styles, with hoary stigmas

5 PERICARPIUM There is none The seed is inclosed in the corolla

6 SEMEN The seed is nearly oval, and covered

# CHAP. XVI

## *AJUGA*, BUGLE.

Species

THE species of this genus are,

1 The Common Bugle

2 The Mountain Bugle, or Sickle-wort

3 The Red flowered Geneva Bugle

4 The Oriental Bugle

Description of the Common,

1 The Common Bugle grows very common in woods, meadows, and moist places It sends forth several side shoots from the root, which strike root, and by which it encreases very fast The leaves are of an oval figure, and brownish, their edges are indented, and they embrace the stalk with their base The stalk is single, and the flowers grow in whorls near the top, at certain distances from each other The common colour is blue, though there is a variety of it with white, and another with pale purple flowers These appear in April and May, and their seeds ripen in July

Mountain,

2 Mountain Bugle The leaves of this species are longer and narrower than those of the other, and their edges are angularly serrated The stalk is single, four-squared, hairy, and the flowers grow in whorls at certain distances from almost the bottom to the top Their colour is blue, though there is a variety of it with white, another with a pale red, and another with yellow flowers They appear in April and May, and bring their seeds to perfection about July

Red flowered Geneva,

3 Red flowered Geneva Bugle The leaves of this species are of an oblong figure, and very downy The flowers grow in whorls like the other, their colour is red, and their cups are very hairy There is a variety of this species with white flowers, which shew themselves about the time of the Common Bugle, and ripen their seeds accordingly

and Oriental Bugle

4 Oriental Bugle The leaves of this species are very hairy, oval, indented, and sit close to the stalks The stalks also are hairy, and the flowers are inverted Their colour is usually white, with a purple rim, though there is a sort of it with blue, and another with spotted flowers They blow in May, and ripen their seeds in July

Method of propagating these sorts

The first three sorts propagate very fast by the side shoots. These put out roots at the joints, which being taken off, and planted soon, become good plants

The fourth sort, called the Oriental Bugle, is rather tender, and encreases but slowly by off-sets, so that the best way is to sow the seeds in pots soon after they are ripe, and in the autumn place the pots under a hot-bed frame, to secure them from the severity of our winters When the plants are tolerably strong, a share of them may be set out in the places where they are to remain, which should be shady, naturally warm, and well sheltered, whilst another share should be set in separate pots, to be housed in winter, in case those abroad should be destroyed by the frost

The other sorts all like the shade and a moist soil, in which situation they will be in perfection, but are apt to encrease faster than one would desire, when so stationed

Medicinal properties

They are vulnerary herbs, especially the first, which is reckoned admirable in all cases of that nature

Titles

1 The Common Bugle is titled, *Ajuga stolonibus reptantibus* In the *Hortus Cliffort* it is termed, *Teucrium foliis obverse ovatis crenatis, caule simplicissimo, stolonibus reptatricibus* Caspar Bauhine calls it, *Consolida media pratensis cærulea*, Dodonæus, *Bugula* It grows naturally in England, and most of the southern part of Europe

2 Mountain Bugle This is titled, *Ajuga tetragono-pyramidalis* Caspar Bauhine calls it, *Consolida media cærulea Alpina*, John Bauhine, *Consolida media Genevensis*, Haller, *Bugula foliis angulose dentatis, caule simplici* It grows naturally in Wales, also in Germany, Sweden and Switzerland

3 Red-flowered Geneva Bugle This is titled, *Ajuga foliis tomentosis, calycibus hirsutis* Clusius calls it, *Bugula carneo flore* It grows naturally in the southern parts of Europe

4 Oriental Bugle This is, *Ajuga floribus resupinatis* Van Royen calls it, *Teucrium staminibus tubo corollæ brevioribus* Tournefort calls one sort of it, *Bugula orientalis villosa, flore inverso candido cum oris purpureis*, another, *Bugula orientalis villosa, flore inverso ceruleo albo macul is notato* It grows naturally in the East

Class and order in the Linnæan system The characters

*Ajuga* is of the class and order *Didynamia Gymnospermia*, and the characters are,

1 CALYX is a short, monophyllous, permanent perianthium, divided at the top into five parts

2 COROLLA is a ringent petal The tube is cylindrical and incurved, the upper lip is very small, erect, bifid and obtuse the lower lip is large, patent, trifid and obtuse, the middle segment is large and obcordated, the side ones small

3 STAMINA consist of four erect, awl shaped filaments,

filaments, two of which are longer than the others, with didymous antheræ

4 Pistillum consists of a germen, divided into four parts, a filiform style, the length and situation of the stamina; and two slender stigmas, of which the under one is the shortest

5 Pericarpium There is none The seeds are contained in the connivent calyx

6 Semina The seeds are four, and oblong

# CHAP XVII

## *ALBUCA*

THERE are only two species of this genus, called,

Species 1 The Greater *Albuca*

2 The Lesser *Albuca*

Greater 1 Greater *Albuca* The root is an oblong, roundish bulb, full of a viscous juice The leaves are spear-shaped, long, narrow, keeled, and flaccid The stalks are slender, and about twelve inches in height The flowers are six or seven, at the tops of the stalks They grow on long, slender footstalks, and hang drooping They are composed of six petals, of which the three interior are erect, the others spread open They are of a yellowish green colour, appear in July, but are not succeeded by seeds in England

and Lesser Albuca described 2 The Lesser *Albuca* The root is a small, roundish bulb. The leaves are awl-shaped, narrow, and spread in different directions The stalks are slender, and six or eight inches high The flowers come out from the tops of the stalks in close spikes They are of a green colour, having sometimes a small mixture of yellow They appear in July, but the seeds do not ripen in England

Method of propagating them Both these sorts are propagated by off-sets from the root, which should be taken off in August, when the stalks decay When they are planted out, they should be set in a light, dry, fresh earth, full upon the morning sun, and being thus stationed, they will bear the cold of our winters, and exhibit their bloom in the best manner

Titles 1 The Greater *Albuca* is titled, *Albuca foliis lanceolatis* In the former edition of the *Species Plantarum* it is termed, *Ornithogalum petalis alternis patentibus alternis erectis* Cornutus calls it, *Ornithogalum luteo virens Indicum.* It grows naturally at the Cape of Good-Hope

2 The Lesser *Albuca* is, *Albuca foliis subulatis* Herman calls it, *Ornithogalum Africanum, flore viridi altero alteri innato* It is a native of the Cape

Class and order in the Linnæan System *Albuca* is of the class and order *Hexandria Monogynia*, and the characters are,

The characters. 1 Calyx There is none

2 Corolla is six oval, oblong, permanent petals, the three outer are spreading, the interior are connivent

3 Stamina There are six triquetrous filaments the length of the corolla, of which three are fertile, narrow, though broad at the base, and higher-up folded on the sides These have versatile antheræ The other three, which are sterile, are the longest, are of a thicker substance than the fertile ones, and placed alternately with them, but have no antheræ There is a nectarium on each side the germen, lying under the lower parts of the filaments

4 Pistillum consists of an oblong, triquetrous, subpedicellated germen, a three-sided style, which is broad near the top, and a stigma composed of four parts, of which the middle one is three-sided and pyramidical, the other three are smaller, awl-shaped, and spreading

5 Pericarpium is an oblong, obtuse, triangular capsule, formed of three valves, and containing three cells

6 Semina The seeds are numerous, flat, broad, and lie over each other.

# CHAP XVIII

## *ALCEA*, The HOLLYHOCK.

Introduction to the Hollyhock THE Hollyhock, which was well known to the Ancients, and which, in its varieties, exhibits as gaudy a show as most of the flowering tribe, has of late years been propagated in great plenty by Gardeners, and lovers of gardening of almost all sorts, but commonness of any article, however valuable in itself, makes it for the most part disregarded, so the Hollyhock, shewing its profusion of flowers and varieties in almost every garden, begins now to be less esteemed, and whole delightful spikes are now to be seen only here and there in a garden, where the owner values a flower for its intrinsick properties, and is not actuated by the whim of custom, or the caprice of fashion, which will in time, perhaps, introduce the less deserving flowers in the greatest plenty, and will as immediately expel the most beautiful, and will hardly leave the traces of them behind.

This custom of alternately introducing and expelling of flowers, has this good effect at least, that we behold a banished sort in our gardens, after its long absence, with a redoubled pleasure, and our zeal in its culture is proportionably heightened; and this is what makes the custom or fashion of admitting or rejecting flowers so sedulously promoted by the Seedsmen, &c. Their seeds, by that means, alternately go off with the greater rapidity, and the spirit of trade is kept up chiefly by that means.

This fate has attended the Hollyhock perhaps more than any other plant in our gardens. Its extreme commonness, by its easy culture, has caused it to be rejected; but its admirable beauty would never suffer it to lie long disregarded; so that this plant, we may be pretty well assured, will (at least) by turns be always in esteem, and there are some situations and places in which it has a right to demand a residence from all lovers of gardening and taste.

This prerogative then is claimed by the Hollyhock in no gardens but what are large and extensive, and its residence should be in rows on the outside of large borders, under a strait hedge or pales, or near walls that are not too high. The chief care must be, to have the flowers as double as possible, and to cause them to blow in the strongest manner. The greatest variety also must be obtained in the different hues and colours of the flowers, which is easy enough done, by collecting the seeds from the different sorts; for they are of almost all colours, and the proper intermixture of them makes the show more perfect.

Method of raising the plants.

In order, therefore, to have a compleat blow of Hollyhocks, let the seeds be gathered from double flowers of the best colours. These should be carefully preserved in their capsules, in a dry place, until the beginning of April, when they should be taken out of their covers, and thinly sowed on a bed of good light mould, and a little earth sifted over them. They will soon come up, and in a few weeks after that, will be of a proper size for transplanting. The size of the young plants need not be so strictly attended to, as the weather; for a moist day, if possible, should be chosen for the purpose. They will immediately strike root, and soon appear vigorous and strong; but if a dry, parching summer should happen, they must, upon their being transplanted, be immediately well watered and shaded; and this watering and shade must be continued until they appear in a flourishing state. As this is to be the only time of their removal, so this must be from the seed-bed unto the place where they are designed to blow. It has been a custom to plant them out in the nursery way, a foot asunder, in order to stand to shew their flowers, and then to select the best of them for the pleasure garden. But this is a very bad custom; for plants removed after they have flowered, seldom rise in that graceful manner, or have half the majestic appearance of those that have been early, and but once transplanted from the seed-bed.

On a moist day then, having marked out a place for the purpose, and having the earth well prepared by digging, and clearing it from the roots of weeds, &c. let a line be drawn the whole length, and by this line, set your young plants from the seed bed at about a foot asunder. If the weather is moist, they will immediately take root, and if the weather should be otherwise, they may be planted in the evening, well watered, and afterwards shaded, and there will be little danger of their miscarrying. This being effected, the business is done for this season.

The spring following, these plants will arise for flowering, when a sufficient number of stakes should be provided to fasten them to, as they arise in height, and to secure them from being broken down by the winds. These stakes should be so artfully placed by the sides of the stalks, amongst the leaves, that they may be as hid as possible; for the natural beauty of the plant is greatly diminished by the stiff form of stakes appearing in view, drawn down or their support. In July they will shew their flowers, at the first appearance of which, all the single ones must be taken up and thrown away; and for this reason I have recommended the planting of them a foot asunder, that when the single and bad coloured ones are taken out, too great a gap may not appear in the rows. Otherwise, could we insure them all proving good, a foot and an half, or even two feet asunder, would not be too great a distance for these large leaved, tall growing plants. In double rows also they may be planted, if the seed bed will afford plants enough for the purpose. By this means the taking out of the single ones will not be so easily missed, and the show will be more striking and bold.

Propriety of situation.

Hitherto we have recommended these plants for the beauty of large borders, or to be planted near hedges, pales, or low walls; but they have an admirable effect in the middle of a large piece of ground that runs lengthways, upon each side of which is a walk. In this case, their propriety and beauty is still heightened, if the ground be rising in the middle, where they are planted, and a gentle descent is formed each way to the walks on either side. In such a situation, let three rows be planted the whole length of the bed, on the highest part of the ground, and as you walk on either side, you will be extremely delighted with these beautiful plants, thus situated, and appearing to such great advantage.

Time of blow.

These plants begin to blow early in July, and their flower stalks will arise to seven, eight or even nine feet in height, six or seven feet of which will be occupied by flowers, or flower-buds, and will continue to be produced for near three months. Each of the flowers considered singly, is as large as a rose. They closely garnish the stalk, form a beautiful spike, and afford variety enough by their own colours, which are of all sorts. The red and the white, the yellow and the purple, the black and the tawney, will interchangeably form the sweetest mixture; and the beauty of this mixture is still heightened by the different tints of the above colours in the different flowers. For there will be the deep crimson and the pale red, the straw colour and yellows of all degrees, some sorts approaching to black, and others lightly tinged with purple, some inclined to blue, and others finely variegated. These will appear (if the seed has been well chosen) in such a mixture, that Art would seem to have had an hand in their disposition; but Nature, which always baffles the works of Art, spontaneously gives us them in this pleasing view.

This will be the second year's blow of these flowers, and although they will continue for many years, you can hardly expect so fair a blow for the future, which has occasioned some to give this plant the appellation of a Biennial. Accordingly the curious will often raise a succession in another part of the garden, that every year they may have a blow of them in perfection, always eradicating the old roots, after they have blowed fair one year. But this is attended with great trouble and expence, and is to be practised by those only who have much garden-room. In order, therefore, to continue these roots for many years, let the stalks be cut down by the end of

Directions for continuing these roots many years.

September, the ground dug on each side the rows, and some rich earth added to mould up the plants, let such plants as have run wholly into stalks be pulled up, and the mould entirely taken away, and let some fresh rich soil be brought. Then supply these vacancies by plants from the seed-bed, for some few seeds (from the best sorts) should be sown every year, let a good ball of earth be taken with each out of the seed bed, and they will grow and flower with the others the succeeding summer, and thus may a show of these flowers be continued for many years.

The Hollyhock has been used to be joined to the Mallow tribe, but the characters of a distinct genus appearing in it, Linnæus has given it the name *Alcea*, which was the term formerly used for the Vervain Mallow.

Notwithstanding the variety of this genus is so great, it seems to admit but of two real species, which are distinguished among Gardeners by,

Species. 1. The Common Hollyhock.

2. The Fig-leaved Hollyhock.

Titles. 1. The Common Hollyhock is entitled, *Alcea foliis sinuato-angulosis*. Caspar Bauhine calls it, *Malva rosea, folio subrotundo*; Dodonæus, *Malva hortensis*. It is a native of the East.

2. The Fig leaved Hollyhock is called, *Alcea foliis palmatis*. This Caspar Bauhine terms, *Malva rosea folio ficus*. It grows also in the East, and can hardly be called a distinct species from the former, differing only in the shape of the leaves, which are so cut into deep segments, as to constitute what is called a pinnated leaf, but I am not certain whether this difference from seeds will always be invariably found.

Class and order in the Linnæan system. *Alcea* is of the class and order *Monadelphia Polyandria*, and the characters are,

The characters. 1. CALYX is a double perianthium, the outer cup is of one piece, and is divided at the top into six spreading, permanent segments, the inner is also monophyllous, larger than the other, and is cut into five permanent segments.

2. COROLLA consists of five large emarginated petals, which unite at their base, and are expanded at the top in a rose-like manner.

3. STAMINA are numerous filaments, which unite in their lower part, and compose a pentagonal column, higher they stand loose, and are crowned with kidney shaped antheræ.

4. PISTILLUM consists of a round germen, and of a short cylindrick style, that is terminated by about twenty setaceous stigmas.

5. PERICARPIUM is a round, depressed, articulated capsule, of many cells, which open on the inner part.

6. SEMEN. The seed is single, large, compressed, and kidney shaped.

# CHAP. XIX.

## *ALCHEMILLA*, LADIES MANTLE.

NO extraordinary beauty attends the flowers of the *Alchemilla*, but the leaves of all the sorts of this genus have charms to attract the attention, and demand respect. The species of this genus are,

Species. 1. Common Ladies Mantle.

2. Alpine Ladies Mantle.

3. The Smooth, Five leaved Ladies Mantle.

Common Ladies Mantle described. 1. The Common Ladies Mantle grows naturally in many of our moist pastures. It is used in medicine, the leaves being esteemed an admirable vulnerary and are very efficacious in stopping inward bleedings, &c. The root of this species is large and long, and furnished with many fibres of an astringent, bitter taste. The leaves rise immediately from the root, and are supported by long footstalks, they are roundish, of a pale, delicate green, and are about two inches in diameter. These roundish leaves are scalloped round the borders in a manner like the old fashioned mantles that had used to be worn by the ladies, which occasions this plant being called the Ladies Mantle. The flower stalks arise among the leaves to about the height of a foot, or more, they do not stand erect, they are round and thick, divide into many branches, and the leaves which garnish each joint are of the same nature with the radical ones, though smaller, and stand on short footstalks. The flowers have no petals, are of a greenish colour, and have, perhaps, the least beauty of any part of the plant. They will be in blow in June, and the seeds ripen in August.

Alpine Ladies Mantle. 2. Alpine Ladies Mantle. This admits of two notable varieties, called,

Its varieties. Cinque-foil Ladies Mantle.

Silvery-leaved Ladies Mantle.

described. Cinque-foil Ladies Mantle. This also is a small plant, but of a very elegant nature. The root has many fibres, and the leaves which rise immediately from thence, on pedicles about four inches long, are of a fine green on their upper surface, but of a silvery-white underneath. They are deeply cut into five parts, so as to form a digitated leaf, and each is serrated at the edges. The flower-stalks are about half a foot in length, are round, of a whitish colour, and procumbent. The leaves on these are like the radical ones, but smaller. The flowers are of a whitish-green colour, will be in blow in July, and the seeds ripen in the autumn.

Silvery leaved Ladies Mantle. This sort is of lower growth than the other, which has occasioned its being distinguished by some by the epithet *Minor*. The leaves are lobed, folded, acutely serrated, silky, and soft to the touch. The flowers are produced in small clusters, they are of the same kind of greenish colour, appear in July, and the seeds ripen in the autumn. The flowers are possessed of little beauty, but there is an elegance, on the whole, attending this plant that should induce any one to desire it, may occupy a place among his collection of perennials.

Smooth Five leaved described. 3. The Smooth, Five leaved Ladies Mantle grows naturally in Lapland, Sweden, and in several others of those cold parts. This is a very low plant. The leaves are quinate, smooth, and each of the lobes is cut into many segments. The flowers have as little beauty as any of the sorts and the desire of a general Collection is the chief cause of admitting them into a garden

Method of propagation, these sorts by dividing the roots

All these sorts are easily propagated by parting of the roots, which may be done at any time of the year, though autumn and the spring are the most eligible seasons for the purpose They grow admirably well when planted in the dead of winter, and if necessity should oblige them to be transplanted in the summer, their flower-stalks should be cut off, and they should be constantly supplied with shade and water in dry weather With this management they will grow and flourish very well

and by seeds

These plants are also easily raised by seeds the best time for sowing of which is the autumn, soon after they are ripe This work may also be done successfully in the spring, though it sometimes happens, when it is deferred till that time, that many of the seeds will remain until the spring after before they appear If therefore, a moderate crop should shew itself the summer after sowing, keep the beds clear of weeds all that season, and in the spring following an additional Collection of plants may be expected

When the plants are tolerably strong, remove them to the places where they are designed to remain A moist day should be chosen for the purpose, if possible, and if their destined situation be naturally moist and shady, it will be so much the better

Titles

1 Common Ladies Mantle is entitled, *Alchemilla foliis lobatis* In the *Hortus Cliffortianus* it is termed, *Alchemilla foliis palmatis*, and in the *Flora Lapponica*, *Alchemilla foliis simplicibus* Caspar Bauhine calls it, *Alchemilla vulgaris*, and Tournefort, *Alchemilla minor* It grows naturally in moist pastures in many parts of Europe

2 Alpine Ladies Mantle is called, *Alchemilla foliis digitatis serratis* Morison calls it, *Alchemilla perennis incana argentea, s sericea satinum provocans*, Ray, *Alchemilla Alpina pentaphyllos* Caspar Bauhine, *Tomentilla Alpina, foliis sericeis*, Parkinson, *Tomentilla argentea*, Gerard, *Pentaphyllum petrosum, heptaphyllum Clusii*; Tournefort, *Alchemilla Alpina pubescens minor*, and Hudson, *Alchemilla foliis lobatis, plicatis, acute serratis, sericeis* It grows common in the mountainous parts of Cumberland, Westmoreland, &c particularly near Penrith and Kendal, also on the Alps and other mountainous parts of Europe

3 Smooth Five-leaved Ladies Mantle is, *Alchemilla foliis quinatis multifidis glabris* Caspar Bauhine calls it, *Alchemilla Alpina quinquefolia*, and Boccone, *Alchemilla Alpina pentaphyllea minima, lobis fimbriatis* It grows naturally in the mountainous parts of Sweden, Lapland, &c

*Alchemilla* is of the class and order *Tetrandria Monogynia*, and the characters are, — Class and order in the Linnæan system

1 Calyx is a monophyllous, tubular, permanent perianthium, divided at the top into eight spreading parts, which are alternately smaller — The characters

Corolla There is none

3 Stamina are four small, erect, subulated filaments, placed on the brim of the calyx, having roundish antheræ

4 Pistillum consists of an oval germen, of a filiforme style which is the length of the cup, and inserted at the base of the germen, having a globose stigma

5 Pericarpium There is none The seed is contained within the neck of the calyx

6 Semen The seed is single, elliptical, and compressed

# CHAP. XX.

## *ALETRIS.*

The plant described

THERE is no English name for this genus, and the species here to be described is usually called the American *Aletris* The root is moderately large, and of a roundish figure The leaves spring from it in great plenty, they are spear shaped, sharp-pointed, nervose, and smooth Among these arises a single naked stalk, which is erect, taper, and striated near the top The flowers adorn the top of the stalk in a spike, they are thinly placed, grow alternately, have very short footstalks, and their colour is white, they come out in May, and if shaded will continue in beauty for some weeks

Of raising these flowers

This plant is easily propagated by dividing of the roots, the best time for which work is the beginning of autumn The strongest offsets may be set in the places where they are designed to remain, and many of them will flower the following year, but the smallest offsets should be planted in a bed in the nursery ground, at four inches distance from each other Many of the forwardest of these will be fit to plant out the autumn following, but the weakest of all should remain another year before they are set out for good

*Aletris* is titled, *Aletris acaulis, foliis lanceolatis membranaceis, floribus alternis* In the *Amæn Acad* it stands simply with the name, *Aletris* Gronovius calls it, *Hyacinthus caule nudo, foliis linguiformibus acuminatis dentatis*, and Plukenet, *Hyacinthus Floridanus spicatus* It grows naturally in North America — Titles

*Aletris* is of the class and order *Hexandria Monogynia*, and the characters are, — Class and order in the Linnæan system

1 Calyx There is none — The characters

2 Corolla is an oval, oblong, rough, sexangular petal, cut at the brim into six spear-shaped, pointed, patent, erect segments

3 Stamina are six awl-shaped filaments, the length of the corolla, having oblong, erect antheræ

4 Pistillum consists of an oval germen, a subulated style the length of the stamina, and a trifid stigma

5 Pericarpium is an oval, triquetrous, acuminated capsule of three cells

6 Semina The seeds are many.

# CHAP. XXI.

## *ALISMA*, WATER-PLANTAIN.

THERE are some species of this genus which grow naturally in standing water, and which, though never cultivated in gardens, may nevertheless be made to grow in such places where there is enough of them and a gentleman is desirous of having them stored with a large variety of other aquatic plants. These are called,

Species.
1. Great Water-Plantain.
2. Lesser Water-Plantain.
3. Creeping Water-Plantain.
4. Star-headed Water-Plantain.

Description of the Great.
1. Great Water-Plantain. The root is composed of numerous thread like fibres, collected together into a head. The leaves, which rise immediately from the root on footstalks, are large, oval, smooth, ribbed, pointed, and much resemble the Land-plantain. Among these the flower stalks rise, upright, firm, round, and grow to be three or four feet high. The flowers are produced from the top of the stalk, in a mazing plant. It then divides into numerous small branches, each of which divides into others for the support of the flowers. These are small, and of a white colour, appear in June and July, and are succeeded by three cornered capsules, containing ripe seeds, in September.

Lesser.
2. Lesser Water-Plantain. The root is composed of numerous fibres. The leaves rise immediately from the root on footstalks, they are long, narrow, spear shaped, and much resemble those of Narrow-leaved Plantain. Among these the flower stalks arise, they are slender, weak, and send forth several branches near the top for the support of the flowers, which are small, white, appear in June, July, and August, and are succeeded by round, rough, acuminated capsules, containing ripe seeds, in September.

Creeping.
3. Creeping Water-Plantain. This is a creeping plant, sending forth many slender fibres from the joints. From the same parts are also produced many oval obtuse leaves. The flowers grow on footstalks, which arise singly among the leaves. They are small, whitish, appear in July, and often continue in succession until the end of summer.

and Star-headed Water-Plantain.
4. Star-headed Water-Plantain. The root of this is composed of numerous thready fibres, collected into a head. The leaves are oblong, heart shaped, and grow on long slender footstalks. Among these the flower stalks arise to the height of about two feet. The flowers terminate the tops, and are produced from the sides in starry heads. They are small, of a white colour, appear in June and July, and are succeeded by six cornered capsules, containing seeds of a yellow colour when ripe, in the autumn.

Culture.
These plants are easily propagated by planting the roots in the mud of ditches, or standing water, in the autumn.

They may be also raised by sowing the seeds in such places, in the autumn, soon after they are ripe. A plant or two of a sort, for observation, will be sufficient; so that should they come up in great plenty, all but a few should be destroyed, leaving them for observation, and the adjacent parts of the pond for aquatics of the like nature.

Titles.
1. Greater Water-Plantain is titled, *Al[illegible] fo[illegible] [illegible] ovatis acutis, fructibus obtuse [illegible]gonis*. In the *Flora Lapponica* it is termed, *Al[illegible] [illegible]* [illegible]. Caspar Bauhine calls it, *Pl[illegible] [illegible] latifolia*, John Bauhine and Camerarius, *Plantago aq[illegible]*, and Gerard, *Plantago [illegible]tica major*. It grows naturally by river sides, lakes, and watery places in England and most parts of Europe.

2. Lesser Water-Plantain is [illegible] *lineari-lanceolatis*, [illegible]. In the *Hortus Cliffortianus* it is termed, [illegible] *globoso umbellato* [illegible]. Vaillant calls it, *Damasonium angustissimo plantaginis folio*, John Bauhine, *Plantago aquatica humilis angustifolia*, and Gerard, *Plantago aquatica [illegible]*. It grows naturally in watery places in England, and many parts of Germany and France.

3. Creeping Water-Plantain is, *Alisma foliis ovatis obtusis, pedunculis solitariis*. Vaillant calls it *Damasonium repens potamogetonis rotundifolii folio*, [illegible]lio, *Damasonium [illegible] cilis [illegible] ex geniculis*. Petiver terms it, *Ranunculus palustris, folio gramineo & [illegible]*. It grows naturally in ditches and lakes in England, Sweden, and Gaul.

4. Star-headed Water-Plantain is, [illegible] *cordato oblongis, floribus [illegible]* [illegible]. In the *Hortus Cliffortianus* it is termed, [illegible] *fructu [illegible]*. Caspar Bauhine calls it, *Plantago aquatica [illegible]*, Lobel, *Plantago aquatica minor [illegible]*, Dalechamp, *D[illegible]*, John Bauhine, *D[illegible]*, Gerard, *Plantago aqu[illegible]*, and Parkinson, *Plantago aqu[illegible]*. It grows naturally in ditches and standing pools in England and Gaul.

Class and order in the Linnaean system.
*Alisma* is of the class and order *Hexandria Polygynia*, and the characters are,

1. CALYX is a perianthium composed of three oval, concave, permanent leaves.
2. COROLLA is three large, roundish, plane, patent petals.
3. STAMINA are six awl shaped filaments shorter than the corolla, having [illegible] anthe[illegible].
4. PISTILLUM consists of [illegible] germina, having simple styles [illegible] stigmas.
5. PERICARPIUM consists of [illegible] compressed capsules, [illegible] together.
6. SEMEN. The seed is single and small.

CHAP.

# CHAP. XXII

## ALLIUM, GARLICK

WHOEVER considers the meaning of the word *Allium*, which is derived from the Greek verb αλεω, *to shun*, will perhaps wonder to find any species of a genus that requires such a term recommended as ornaments for the pleasure garden

Derivation of the name. The word *Allium* is properly constituted the term of this genus, because most people shun or avoid the smell of garlick, as a kind of nuisance Some species of it, however, bear very pretty flowers, and with these the eye must be entertained, whilst the nose must keep at its proper distance They are usually called,

Species.
1 The Broad-leaved Mountain Moly
2 Narrow leaved Moly, or Moly of Dioscorides
3 Broad-leaved White Moly of Theophrastus
4 The Lesser Moly with a Reddish Flower
5 Rush leaved Mountain Moly
6 Sweet Moly of Montpelier
7 Greater Mountain Garlick, with Leaves of the Narcissus
8 Lesser Mountain Garlick, with Narcissus Leaves
9 Small Triangular stalked Moly
10 Yellow Moly

To these may be added onions, leek, &c

Description of the Broad leaved Mountain, 1 The Broad-leaved Mountain Moly This is one of the best of the kind. The root is oblong and scaly, and sends forth many fibres, the leaves are broad, and the flower-stalks will rise to near a yard in height The flowers form a large roundish umbel, and they will be in blow in July

Dioscorides, 2 Dioscorides Moly The leaves of this sort are narrow, spear-shaped, and then under ones are hairy, but those on the stalks are smooth The flowers are very white, and produced in June in umbels

Theophrastus, 3 Theophrastus Moly The root is large and bulbous, like an onion, and the outer coat is black The leaves are broad and thick, and full of juice The stalk is round and upright, and bulbiferous, the flowers are of the lilly kind and produced in July This is supposed by many to be the sort mentioned by Homer, and is therefore called by some Homer's Moly

Lesser, 4 Lesser Moly with Reddish Flowers This is a low plant The leaves are of a thin contexture and are of the figure of a sword The stalk is naked, and produces an umbel of very fine flowers, of a reddish colour, which makes it a desirable variety by some

Rush leaved Mountain, 5 Rush leaved Mountain Moly The leaves of this sort are narrow, and of a rush-like appearance The stalk is round, and garnished with the like kind of small grassy leaves, and supports a round head of flowers, of a purplish colour The flowers however, which compose this head will be but few in number, and the appearance they make is very indifferent

Sweet, 6 Sweet Moly of Montpelier has narrow leaves, and the umbel of flowers forms nearly an even surface It has a smell somewhat like musk, which occasions its being called by some Musk Moly, by others the Sweet Moly of Montpelier, the place where it grows naturally

7 Greater Narcissus leaved Mountain Garlick



Greater, The upper part of the root of this species is a bulb of many scales, like an onion, but lower it runs into the ground, is oblong, and knotty like that of Solomon's seal The leaves are like those of the Narcissus, and the flowers are produced in July and August, they are of a purplish colour, and form a roundish head or umbel

and Smaller Narcissus leaved Mountain, 8 Smaller Narcissus leaved Mountain Moly The leaves of this sort are very narrow and channelled The stalk is naked, and the flowers stand erect, they are of a purplish colour, will be in blow in July or August, and form an umbel nearly with an even surface

Small Triangular stalked, 9 Small Triangular stalked Moly This is an humble plant the leaves and stalks are triangular, and the flowers, which are produced in small bunches, in June or July, are of little beauty

and Yellow Moly 10 Yellow Moly is the most cultivated in the flower garden of all the sorts It is a beautiful species, and very ornamental in any border of the pleasure-ground The root is a round white bulb, frequently single, but is often found double The leaves are usually two, and of a fine strong green colour, they surround one another at their bases, are near a foot in length, of a firm substance, and in figure nearly resemble those of the tulip Between these rises the stalk, of a foot or more in height It is round, smooth, and slender, but firm enough to support the umbel in an upright position Each floret is of a fine clear yellow colour, and its petals, which are six in number, are erect, though the three exteriors are more expanded than the others Numbers of these form the umbel, and each stands on its own separate footstalk in such a manner as to form nearly an even surface As these umbels are moderately large, and the flowers of so bright a yellow, the figure they make is pretty enough This sort flowers early in June

Methods of propagating these sorts The culture of the sorts of Moly is exceeding easy, for the offsets being taken off in the autumn, and planted where they are designed to remain, will soon become good plants, and will produce flowers for show, and fresh offsets (if necessary) for farther propagation The whole roots, every two or three years, should be taken up, and the strongest offsets planted afresh, otherwise they will every year flower weaker, and the little natural beauty many of them possess will be proportionably diminished

They may be also propagated by seeds, which should be sown in March They will easily come up, and in September they should be removed to the places designed for them, and by this method the best plants are often raised

Titles 1 Broad-leaved Mountain Moly is entitled, *Allium caule planifolio umbellifero, umbellâ rotundata, staminibus lanceolatis corolla longioribus, foliis ellipticis* Caspar Bauhine calls it, *Allium montanum latifolium maculatum* It grows naturally on the Helvetian and Italian Mountains

2 Narrow leaved Moly, or Dioscorides Moly, is titled, *Allium caule planifolio umbellifero, foliis inferioribus hirsutis staminibus subulatis* Caspar

 Bauhine

Bauhine calls it, *Moly angustifolium umbellatum*; and Clusius, *Moly Dioscoridis* It grows in Africa, Italy, and Spain

3 Theophrastus Moly is, *Allium caule plano folio umbellifero, ramulo bulbifero, staminibus simplicibus* Caspar Bauhine calls it, *Moly latifolium liliflorum* Linnæus supposes the *Caucason* of Lobel and old botanists to be a variety only of this species It grows naturally in Asia

4 The fourth sort is, *Allium caule plano folio umbellifero, umbellâ fastigiatâ, staminibus corollam æquantibus, foliis lævibus* Some have termed it, *Moly minus roseo amplo flore* It grows naturally near Montpelier

5 Rush leaved Mountain Moly is called, *Allium caule teretifolio umbellifero, foliis semiteretibus, staminibus tricuspidatis corolla longioribus* Clusius calls it, *Allium, sive Moly montanum purpureo flore* It grows naturally in Siberia and Italy

6 Musk Moly is titled, *Allium caule teretifolio umbellifero, umbellâ fastigiatâ subsexflorâ, petalis acutis, staminibus simplicibus, foliis setaceis* Many authors call it, *Moly moschatum, capillaceo folio* It grows naturally in several parts of France and Spain

7 The seventh species is, *Allium scapo nudo ancipiti, foliis linearibus subtus convexis lævibus, umbella subrotunda, staminibus subulatis* Caspar Bauhine calls it, *Allium montanum, foliis Narcissi, majus* It grows common in Sicily and Siberia

8 The eighth species is, *Allium scapo nudo ancipiti, foliis linearibus canaliculatis subtus subangulatis, umbellâ fastigiatâ* John Bauhine calls it, *Allium petræum umbelliferum*, and Caspar Bauhine, *Allium montanum, foliis Narcissi, minus* It grows naturally in moist places in several parts of Siberia

9 Small Triangular stalked Moly is entitled, *Allium scapo nudo triquetro* Tournefort calls it, *Allium caule triquetro*, Caspar Bauhine, *Moly parvum, caule triangulo* and Parkinson, *Moly caule & foliis triangularibus* It is a native of Spain

10 Yellow Moly is, *Allium scapo nudo subcylindrico, foliis lanceolatis sessilibus, umbellâ fastigiatâ* This species has gone among botanists by the various titles of, *Moly latifolium luteum, odore alii*, *Moly flavo flore*, *Moly montanum latifolium, flavo flore* &c It grows naturally upon Mount Baldus and the Pyrenees, also in Hungary, and some parts of France

*Allium* is of the class and order *Hexandria Monogynia*, and the characters are, Class and order in the Linnæan system

1 CALYX The flowers are included in one common, roundish, withering spatha The characters

2 COROLLA consists of six oblong petals

3 STAMINA are six subulated filaments, about the length of the corolla, with oblong, erect antheræ

4 PISTILLUM consists of a short three cornered germen, a simple style, and an acute stigma

5 PERICARPIUM is a very short, broad, trilobated capsule, of three valves and three cells

6 SEMINA The seeds are numerous, and of a roundish figure

# CHAP. XXIII

## *ALOE*

THERE is one species of this genus proper for this place, that has long gone among Gardeners by the name of *Iris Uvaria* It is a hardy plant, if not too tenderly raised and its culture and management is attended with very little trouble

This plant described

The leaves of this species are long, narrow, triangular, and spring directly from the root The stalks grow to about a yard high The flowers are produced in large imbricated spikes from the tops of the stalks, they are yellow, of a very disagreeable smell reflexed, and sit close to the stalk They appear in August and September, and sometimes are succeeded by good seeds, by which the propagation of this plant is best effected

Culture

The seeds should be sown soon after they are ripe, because if the business is deferred till spring, they sometimes do not come up before the spring following Sow them, therefore, in a warm border of sandy earth, in a well sheltered place, and in spring, when the plants come up, shelter them in bad weather, and keep them clean from weeds, water them frequently if the season should prove dry By August or September many of the plants will be of a proper size to set out, and that season is good for the purpose, nevertheless, lest an hard winter should happen, it will be advisable to let them remain in the seed-bed until spring, where they may be covered with mats, and protected from severe frosts Let this, then, be the management, and in the spring remove them to the places they are designed for, which should be naturally warm and well-sheltered, and if the soil happens to be of a dry sandy nature, they will be still less liable to be destroyed by the severity of bad winters

If the seeds cannot be sown before the spring, it would be advisable to do this on a moderate hotbed, for by the assistance of a little heat, they will soon come up They must be used to the full air as soon as possible, and in this bed they may stand all the next winter, to be covered with the glasses in bad weather, and in the spring may be set out for good as the others

Titles

This species is titled, *Aloe floribus sessilibus reflexis imbricatis prismaticis* In the *Hortus Cliffortianus* it is called, *Aloe foliis linearibus radicalibus membranaceis* Commelin and others term it, *Aloe Africana, folio triangulari longissimo & angustissimo, floribus luteis fœtidis* It is a native of the Cape of Good Hope

*Aloe* is of the class and order *Hexandria Monogynia*, and the characters are, Class and order in the Linnæan system

1 CALYX There is none The characters

2 COROLLA consists of an oblong single petal, divided at the top into six parts The tube is gibbous, and the limb is small, and spreads open

3 STAMINA are six subulated filaments, the

full length of the corolla, and inserted in the receptacle, having oblong incumbent antheræ.

4 PISTILLUM consists of an oval germen, a simple style the length of the stamina, and an obtuse trifid stigma

5 PERICARPIUM is an oblong three furrowed capsule, containing three cells, and opening in three parts

6 SEMINA The seeds are numerous and angular

## CHAP XXIV

### *ALOPECURUS*, FOX-TAIL GRASS

ANOTHER lot of grasses are comprehended in the term *Alopecurus* The perennials are,

Species

1 Meadow Fox-Tail Grass
2 Field Fox Tail Grass
3 Flote Fox Tail Grass
4 Bulbous Fox Tail Grass

Description of the Meadow,

1 Meadow Fox Tail Grass The root is composed of numerous white fibres, clustered together The radical leaves are long, narrow smooth, and pointed The stalks are upright, round, slender, smooth, of a purplish or pale green colour, about two feet high, and have three or four joints, at each of which is situated a leaf growing singly, and surrounding the stalk a great way up with its base The flowers come out from the ends of the stalks, in long spikes, almost in shape of a Fox Tail They are of a purplish colour, and their glumes are hairy, they appear in May, and the seeds ripen in June This is one of the common grasses of our meadows and pastures, and grows every where

Field,

2 Field Fox-Tail Grass The radical leaves are long, narrow, pointed, and of a pale green colour The stalks are upright, slender, round, smooth, two feet high, and have two or three joints, each having a single leaf, surrounding the stalk a great way up with its base The flowers come out from the tops of the stalks, in long, smooth, cylindrical spikes They appear in May and June, and the seeds ripen in June and July

Flote,

3 Flote Fox-Tail Grass This grows every where in waters and moist places The root consists of a multitude of white crooked fibres, clustered together The stalk is round, hollow, jointed, crooked, or bends in different directions at the joints, and strikes root at the joints The leaves are about half a foot long, grow singly at the joints, where they surround the stalk with their base, and are of a good green colour The flowers come out in long slender spikes, from the ends of the stalks, they are of a pale greyish green colour, and soft to the touch They appear in May and June, and continue to shew themselves until the end of autumn

and Bulbous Fox Tail Grass

4 Bulbous Fox-tail Grass The root of this is bulbous The stalk is upright, round, hollow, jointed, and two feet high The leaves are narrow, pointed, grow singly at the joints, and surround the stalk with their base The flowers are collected in cylindrical spikes at the tops of the stalks, they appear in May and June, and the seeds ripen soon after

Method of propagating them

The seeds of all these sorts should be carefully gathered when ripe, and kept in a dry place until the spring, when they may be sown, if a person chooses a general collection of grasses for his more immediate inspection and observation The roots also may be taken up and planted, the best time for which is when the plants are just out of flower, about such time as the seeds are ripe, because then you will be more certain that you have got the right sorts

1 Meadow Fox-Tail Grass is titled, *Alopecurus culmo spicato erecto, glumis villosis* Caspar Bauhine calls it, *Gramen Phalaroides majus, sive Italicum*, John Bauhine, *Gramen alopecuro simile glabrum cum pilis longis ex spicis in spica Onocordon*, Scheuchzer, *Gramen spicatum, spicâ cylindraceâ tenuissimâ longiore*, Van Royen, *Alopecurus culmo spicato erecto*, and Gerard, *Gramen Alopecuroides majus* It grows naturally in most meadows and pasture grounds in Europe Titles.

2 Field Fox-Tail Grass is *Alopecurus culmo spicato erecto, glumis nudis* Caspar Bauhine calls it, *Gramen typhoides, spicâ angustiore*, Barrelier, *Gramen typhinum, plantaginis spicâ, aristis geniculatis*, and Scheuchzer, *Gramen spicatum, spicâ cylindraceâ tenuissimâ longiore* It grows chiefly in the southern parts of Europe

3 Flote Fox-Tail Grass is *Alopecurus culmo spicato infracto* Van Royen calls it, *Alopecurus culmo infracto, aristis glumâ longioribus*, Caspar Bauhine, *Gramen aquaticum geniculatum spicatum*, Gerard, *Gramen fluviatile spicatum*, and Parkinson, *Gramen aquaticum spicatum* In the *Flora Lapponica* it is termed, *Alopecurus aristis gluma longioribus*, also, *Alopecurus aristis gluma æqualibus* It grows naturally in watery places in England, and most parts of Europe

4 Bulbous Fox Tail Grass is, *Alopecurus culmo erecto, spicâ cylindriceâ, radice bulbosâ* Ray calls it, *Gramen myosuroides nodosum*, and Barrelier, *Gramen typhinum phalaroides pilosâ spicâ, aquaticum bulbosum* It grows naturally in our meadows, and in most parts of France

*Alopecurus* is of the class and order *Triandria Digynia*, and the characters are, Class and order in the Linnæan system The characters

1 CALYX is a glume composed of two oval, spear shaped, concave, compressed, equal valves, containing one flower

2 COROLLA is one concave valve the length of the calyx, having a long arista inserted in its back near the base

3 STAMINA are three capillary filaments, having bifurcated antheræ

4 PISTILLUM consists of a roundish germen, and two cirrhose reflexed styles, longer than the calyx, with simple stigmas

5 PERICARPIUM The seed is surrounded by the corolla

6 SEMEN The seed is single, roundish, and covered

CHAP

# CHAP. XXV.

## *ALTHÆA*, MARSH-MALLOW

Species

THERE are three species of this genus
1 Marsh Mallow
2 Spanish Marsh-Mallow
3 Shrubby Marsh Mallow

Marsh Mallow. Varieties

1 Common Marsh-Mallow admits of three principal varieties
Common Marsh-Mallow of the Shops
Round-leaved Marsh-Mallow
Jagged-leaved Marsh-Mallow

described

Common Marsh-Mallow will grow to the height of about four or five feet The stalks are upright, round, robust, and downy. The leaves are large, downy, dentated on their edges, have the softness of velvet to the touch, and are placed alternately on strong footstalks The flowers are produced at the upper end of the stalks, from the wings of the leaves. They are a little like those of the Common Mallow though smaller and paler Their time of flowering is in July and August, and they are succeeded by good seeds in September or October, at which time the stalks decay, so that they must be entirely taken away, and the roots moulded up, to look handsome all winter, as well as to be in proper order to send out fresh shoots in the spring

The Round-leaved Marsh Mallow is a variety of this, and differs from it only in that the leaves are shorter and rounder, their position is the same, and their flowers and seeds are produced in the same manner

The leaves of the third sort are jagged, and as such the plant causes a variety, though the leaves are placed in the same manner as the other, and the flowers and seeds ripen alike The stalks lie down, and must be cleared off soon after the seeds are ripe

Uses of the roots

The roots of Marsh Mallow, outwardly applied are good for softening and maturing hard swellings, and a decoction of it is a fine diuretic and emollient, admirable for hoarsenesses, dysenteries, and nephritic complaints, &c

Spanish

2 The Spanish Marsh-Mallow is a very low trailing plant The stalks are ligneous, and very hairy The leaves also are hairy to a great degree, and grow on long footstalks, they are trifid, or deeply cut into three parts The flowers are small, and produced from the wings of the stalks, their appearance is a little like that of *Cistus*, but their lower part is possessed of a purplish colour They flower in July, and the seeds will be ripe in September This sort may not improperly be termed a biennial, as in common situations it seldom survives two years In order to have it last for a longer term, its situation must be naturally warm and dry, and the soil of a sandy nature, and for want of this, a mixture of lime rubbish and sand must be got, to be added to the common mould, where they are designed to continue

and Shrubby Marsh Mallow

3 The Shrubby Marsh Mallow is so distinguished from its woody stem, but strictly it is neither a shrub, a biennial, nor a perennial, and yet it is all of them This paradox in Nature, then would seem to puzzle any one to find its proper place and rank among plants upon our plan As a shrub it seems to demand a place in the shrubbery for its stem is woody, it will grow to the height of about five feet, and is very ornamental in those places, but it will seldom continue longer than two years and therefore is highly improper for a situation of that nature, as the death of any one of them will occasion a disagreeable vacancy or gap in a wilderness quarter It seems to stand now in the rank of a biennial, and indeed in some situations it is, but as in others it will continue for many years, some people will probably vote for its being termed a perennial I shall therefore treat of it here as a species of *Althæa*, under which article it comes of course, and I shall treat of others also of the like properties, leaving the judicious Gardener to dispose of them as he shall think proper

The species under consideration, then, has a large woody root, from which arises a stem to the height of six or eight feet, many side-branches issue from this stem, and these are garnished with leaves of different shapes The lower leaves are palmated, but those which occupy the upper part of the branches are digitated Some of them are deeply cut in a manner to resemble those of hemp, all of them are very hairy and rough, and they grow alternately on the branches The flowers are produced from the wings of the stalks, they are small and of a red colour and are succeeded by plenty of good seeds

Method of propagating these species

The sorts of the Common Marsh-Mallow may be propagated by parting of the roots but the best way of raising all the species is by sowing the seeds in the places where they are to remain, especially the two last sorts If these two are desired as biennials, sow the seeds in May, and not before, for if they are sown sooner, they will often flower the first year, which must of course be so late in the season as not to have time to bring the seeds to perfection but by sowing them in May, they will be good strong plants by the autumn, and will flower early the summer following, and thus the seeds will be perfected in great plenty for the purposes of a succession Where these plants are desired, they may continue for years, a quantity of lime-rubbish and sand must be mixed with the common mould, in a dry warm situation, and thus these plants may be made, with very little trouble, to continue and flower, and produce plenty of good seeds for many years

Titles

1 Marsh-Mallow of the Shops is titled, *Althea foliis simplicibus tomentosis* Caspar Bauhine calls it, *Althea Dioscoridis & Plinii*, also, *Althea folio rotundiore*, Ray, *Althea vulgaris similis folio et flore brevi*, Gerard, *Althea Ibiscus*, and Parkinson, *Althea vulgaris* It grows naturally in moist places in many parts of England, Holland, France, and Siberia

2 Spanish Marsh-Mallow is titled *Althea foliis trifidis palmatis hispidis stipulis glabris* Caspar Bauhine calls it, *Alcea hirsuta*, Barrelier, *Althea hirsuta minima, flore rubro, Hispanica* and Dalechamp *Alcea villosa* It grows common in Spain, Italy, France, and Austria

3 Shrubby Marsh Mallow is, *Althæa foliis inferioribus palmatis, superioribus digitatis* In the

Hortus

Ho ' s Cliffortianus it is termed, *Althæa foliis compositis palmis* Caspar Bauhine calls it, *Alcea cannabina*, and Clusius, *Alcea fruticosa cannabino folio* It grows common by the borders of woods in Hungary, Italy, and the south of France

Class and order in the Linnæan system. *Althæa* is of the class and order *Monadelphia Polyandria*, and the characters are,

1 CALYX is a double perianthium The exterior is formed of one leaf, and is unequally cut at the brim into nine small permanent segments, the interior is also of one leaf, which is divided into five, broad, acute, permanent segments

2 COROLLA consists of five heart-shaped plane petals, which coalesce at their base

3 STAMINA are numerous, which below coalesce, and form a cylinder, above they are loose, and are inserted into the column, on these are placed kidney-shaped antheræ

4 PISTILLUM consists of a round germen, a short cylindric style, with numerous setaceous stigmas, the length of the style

5 PERICARPIUM is an orbicular depressed capsule, of many cells

6 SEMINA The seeds are single, compressed, and kidney shaped

# CHAP. XXVI.

## *ALYSSUM*, MADWORT

AT first this seems to be a strange title for an ornamental plant in the pleasure garden, but the reader must be informed it was so termed on account of its virtues, being deemed a sovereign remedy for the bite of a mad dog, by being presented only to the diseased person, without any internal or external application

Derivation of the generic name. This genus was, therefore, styled *Alyssum*, of the Greek verb αλυσσω, *to be mad* a term than which nothing could be more proper, if it is possessed of the virtue it is said to have, namely, of curing madness by being barely looked upon This is asserted by Galen, but be that as it will, the species for our purpose are,

Species.
1 Rocky Madwort, or *Alysson* of Crete
2 Mountain Madwort
3 Narrow-leaved Madwort
4 Shrubby Hoary Madwort
5 Shrubby Prickly Madwort

Description of the Rocky, 1 Rocky Madwort is generally known among Gardeners by the name *Alysson* of Crete It is the most beautiful of all the sorts, and is richly deserving of a place in our choicest collections It is naturally a low spreading plant, and the leaves are spear-shaped, hoary, and their edges are waved, but free from serratures, they are long in proportion to their breadth, and they continue on the plant all winter But the flowers are the glory of this plant, these are of a bright-yellow colour, and are produced in panicles from the extremities of the branches They will be in blow in May, and as they cover the plant with their golden colour, the appearance is striking and delightful These flowers will be succeeded by seed, which ripen very well with us, and by which fresh plants may be raised

Mountain, 2 Mountain Madwort is a low plant, and the branches trail upon the ground The leaves are oblong, hoary, rough, and grow alternately on the branches The flowers are of a dark-yellow colour, and are produced at the ends of the branches, in small clusters They will be in blow in May or June, and sometimes (tho' not always) are succeeded by oblong seed vessels, full of good seeds

Narrow-leaved, 3 Narrow-leaved Madwort This is a small spreading plant The branches, which are slender, lie upon the ground and the leaves are very narrow and entire, they are rather of a lanceolate figure, are very hoary, and their edges are entire The flowers are white, and very beautiful, they are produced in small tufts, at the ends of the branches It will continue flowering the greatest part, nay sometimes all the summer, which, besides the beauty of its pretty white flowers, is an additional value to this plant

4 Shrubby Hoary Madwort This rises with a ligneous branching stalk to the height of about two feet The leaves are spear shaped, and very downy, their edges are entire, and they grow alternately on the branches The flowers are white, and are produced at the ends of the branches, in round bunches It will be in blow in June, and will continue flowering for four months The seeds will ripen, and will scatter themselves, and produce fresh plants without farther care Shrubby Hoary,

5 Shrubby Prickly Madwort arises with a ligneous stalk to the height of about two feet and the older branches are set with small prickles or spines The leaves of this sort are hoary, they are spear shaped, and are placed irregularly on the branches The flowers are white, and are produced in small clusters, at the ends of the branches, they will be in blow in May, will continue flowering some months, and will produce plenty of good seeds and Shrubby Prickly Madwort

All these sorts are easily propagated by slips or cuttings, the best time for which is the beginning of May They must be shaded and watered until they have taken root, and afterwards they will require no farther care than keeping them clear of weeds Method of propagating the for ... by cuttings,

These plants are all raised by seeds, which should be sown in March, and they will produce better plants than those raised from cuttings They will be fuller of branches, produce a greater bloom, and furnish more and better seeds for a succession and by seeds

The *Alysson* of Crete is very hardy, and will grow and flourish in almost any soil or situation, but it thrives best in a warm sandy place The others more peculiarly require such a situation, or they will be but short lived, they will grow naturally in rubbish, and on old walls, and if we have a rubbishy dry corner of the garden, and sow them there, they will continue to flower and produce good seeds for many years Proper soil and situations

Titles 1 The Alyssum of Crete is entitled, *Alyssum caulibus fruticosis paniculatis, foliis lanceolatis mollissimis tomentosis integris* Tournefort calls it, *Alyssum Creticum saxatile, foliis undulatis incanis*, and Boerhaave, *Alyssoides folio Leucoji incano, flore luteo* It grows naturally in Crete

2 Mountain Madwort is titled, *Alyssum ramulis suffruticosis diffusis, foliis punctato-echinatis* In the Hortus Cliffortianus it is termed, *Alyssum foliis lanceolatis obtusis incanis, caulibus procumbentibus, radice perenni* John Bauhine calls it, *Thlaspi montanum luteum* It grows common amongst rocks and ruins about Burgundy in France

3 Narrow leaved Madwort This is, *Alyssum foliis lanceolato-linearibus acutis integerrimis, caulibus procumbentibus perennantibus* Boccone calls it, *Thlaspi parvum, halimi angusto incano folio*, Herman, *Thlaspi, halimi folio, sempervirens* It grows naturally in dry, rocky places, in the southern parts of Europe

4 Shrubby Hoary Madwort This is, *Alyssum caule erecto, foliis lanceolatis incanis integerrimis, floribus corymbosis* Caspar Bauhine calls it, *Thlaspi fruticosum incanum*, Clusius, *Thlaspi incanum Machlinense* It grows naturally in dry, rocky places, in many parts of France, Italy and Spain

5 Shrubby Prickly Madwort This is titled, *Alyssum ramis floreis senilibus spinaeformibus nudis* Caspar Bauhine terms it *Thlaspi fruticosum spinosum* John Bauhine, *Leucojum f Thlaspi spinosum* It grows common in many parts of France, Italy, and Spain

*Alyssum* is of the class and order *Tetradynamia Siliculosa*, and the characters are, Class and order in the Linnæan system The characters

1 CALYX is a deciduous perianthium, composed of four oval, oblong, obtuse, connivent leaves

2 COROLLA consists of four petals, which are placed in the form of a cross, they are plane, and spread open above the calyx

3 STAMINA These are six filaments, of the length of the calyx though two of them are shorter than the others, and have a denticulation on their inner side The antheræ are erect

4 PISTILLUM consists of an oval germen, a simple style, the length of the stamina, and an obtuse stigma

5 PERICARPIUM is a globular, emarginated, compressed, bilocular pod

6 SEMINA The seeds are few, roundish and compressed

# CHAP XXVII

## *AMARYLLIS*, LILY-DAFFODIL

Introductory remarks AUTHORS have all along been dubious in the manner of ranging the species of this genus The flowers are of the Lily kind, hence some respectable Botanists have ranked them in the Lily train The roots, however, are like those of the Narcissus, and this has induced others to place them as species of that genus Tournefort, avoiding both these extremes, took a middle course, compounded the two words *Lilium* and *Narcissus*, and thereby constituted a fresh genus, and ranged the species of it under the term *Lilio Narcissus* Linnæus, the great reformer of the science, having established the distinctions of the genera, calls this *Amaryllis*, a sweet name, and which of old has been in use among Poets and Botanists of respect and renown The greatest part of the species of this genus, though they may keep alive in our warm borders, will not shew their flowers to perfection without artificial heat, so that these must come under the denomination of Stove plants Those that fall under this head are,

Species
1 The Guernsey Lily
2 Atamusco Lily
3 Autumnal Narcissus
4 Golden Vernal *Amaryllis*

Description of the Guernsey Lily, 1 Guernsey Lily We begin first with the Guernsey Lily, as being a flower exceeded by few in the vegetable world, and which, had not Nature denied it fragrance, would have been superior to most, if not any of the flowery tribe It is improperly called the Guernsey Lily, for the plant is a native of Japan, but some-how or other, the roots being (as is supposed) scattered by accident in that Island, grew, which so pleased the inhabitants by their flowers, that they propagate them all over the Island, where they make such amazing increase in their sandy soils, that they are the glory of their country, and we have large quantities of the bulbs sent over every year from thence for the enrichment of ours The flowers of the Guernsey Lily arise from the bulbs, before the leaves appear, they are supported on a naked, firm stalk, of about a foot in length At the top of this stalk is the spatha, or scabbard, and out of this proceed the flowers, of the most consummate beauty Each flower stands on its own proper footstalk, they are large, and the petals expand themselves to display all their charms Their colour is red of the greatest beauty and perfection, and they appear bespangled with gold The very organs of generation contribute to the beauty of these flowers, the filaments are of a pale and delicate red, with purple antheræ, and the style is gracefully terminated by a trifid purple stigma These flowers will be in their full glory in October, and after they are over, the leaves appear Those also are not without their beauties, they are of an oblong figure, moderately broad, of a beautiful green, are smooth, and seem peculiarly adapted to the nature and constitution of the species they are designed for

2 Atamusco Lily This also is a beautiful flower, but of a very inferior nature to the preceding Comparisons of this kind, however, with such plants as the Guernsey Lily, ought not to be admitted, but the Atamusco, standing alone, is a very desirable plant, and the more so, as its time of flowering varies from that of the former It will be in blow in May or June, and now and then in the autumn the bulbs will send forth their bloom The flowers are very large, but they arrive and Atamusco Lily

rise to no very great height, about half a foot being the usual length of the stalk, and one flower alone proceeds out of the spatha. Their colour at first is a delicate red, and then it is they are in their greatest beauty; but they die away to a pale, and almost a white colour; however being large, they have a fine appearance even in that state. And in Virginia and Carolina, where they grow plentifully in a state of nature, the richness of their appearance is said to be heightened by the different tints in the different stages of the flowers.

Of this there is a variety with purple flowers.

Varieties described. 3. Autumnal Narcissus. This admits of two principal varieties,

Yellow Autumnal Narcissus,

Double yellow Autumnal Narcissus.

Yellow Autumnal Narcissus. This is a very hardy species, and a very great ornament to gardens in the autumnal season. The Gardener has been long used to call it the Autumnal Narcissus, and by that name it still goes, which occasions my mentioning it under that title. But it has nothing to do with the Narcissus family; it may as well be called a *Pancratium*, *Colchicum*, or any other flower. The essential character in the Narcissus is the hollow nectarium, or the cup within the flower; this belongs to the whole tribe of those plants, but no such cup is to be found in this species; neither does it answer to the characters in the *Lilium*, the *Colchicum*, or the ..., as some would make it. This shews it to belong to another tribe, and therefore it is, according to the strictest laws of the science, ... under the present head *Amaryllis*. It flowers, as the title indicates, in the autumn; it will shew itself early in September, and will continue blowing until November or longer, if the weather should prove fine and mild. The flower-stalk is short, thick, smooth and green, and seldom grows to above three inches in height. A single flower bursts from the spatha, which soon after withers. The flower is large, and of a yellow colour. It is composed of six oblong broad, obtuse petals, and very much resembles that of the common yellow Crocus. With the flowers come up the leaves, which are of a pleasant green, and continue to grow and encrease all winter.

Double-yellow Autumnal Narcissus. This is a variety of the former sort, and by its multiplicity of petals, adds an additional splendor to our borders. Gardeners in general are fond of double flowers; a Botanist likes them in their single state. In these, the parts of generation are more perfect, and in those, they are often weakened, if not totally destroyed. In the plant under consideration, however, they are perfect and entire; the petals are of the same figure; they spread open in an agreeable manner like the other, and the plant retains the same form, and only glows in a higher degree, by the redundancy of its golden petals. What makes this flower still more valuable is, it continues in blow much longer than the single sort.

Golden Vernal Amaryllis described. 4. Golden Vernal *Amaryllis*. This, like the former, has usually been called the Yellow Narcissus, and has been distinguished from it only on account of its time of flowering, which will be in April and May; and though at that season plenty of flowers may be expected, yet it makes a very good variety among the low-flowering plants of our gardens. The flower-stalk is thick, short, and firm; and from a withering spatha comes a single flower, of a fine yellow colour. The petals are of equal size and shape, and the stamina are erect. The leaves are of a fine green, and they continue long before they die away from the bulb.

Culture. The culture of these species shall be considered next. And first of the Guernsey Lily. We receive the bulbs every year from Guernsey, and the time of their arrival is usually in July or August. Good and bad will be in them, notwithstanding the ... over; so that when a person has the convenience of a correspondent, it will be worth while to send directions of the best roots to be marked for his purpose. There will be always those that have not stood too long, or are grown into too large a clump since their removal; for the faces of these will be compressed by the great numbers growing in a body; but when they have not grown too long, the bulbs will be fewer, they will be more spherical, and more likely to flower strong. Let your orders run for them to be taken up as soon as the green leaves are decayed, and then let them be carefully picked up, and sent over.

Against the time of their arrival, the compost must be prepared. And for this, nothing more need be said than to desire the Reader to turn to the auricula compost. If he is a florist, he has plenty of it by him, and a better compost cannot be wished for, only with this difference, a third part more of drift-sand must be added. Guernsey is all, or is inclined to, a sandy soil. There they grow, and flourish in perfection. This, in some respect, has taught us their true culture, and experience demonstrates the practice to be right. A sufficient number of pots must be prepared, according to the number of the bulbs; fill them with this compost, and plant a single bulb in each pot. These pots are designed to form a bed, and having marked out a place, set them in rows. The breadth of this bed must be according to your own taste, or the conveniency of management, and the length of it must be according to the number of your pots. Let the pots be joined rim to rim, and fill the cavities between with any common garden mould; then hoop the beds, for the conveniency of covering them when too great a quantity of wet falls. By thus plunging the pots, the roots will be kept so cool and moist as to require little or no watering, which is very injurious to these plants; and by covering them, a redundancy of wet from the elements may be prevented, which otherwise might greatly injure, if not totally rot and destroy them.

In October, and sometimes earlier, the flower-buds will shew themselves, though but very sparingly, it is to be feared, all over the bed. If the greatest care has been taken in collecting the bulbs, not a quarter of them may be expected to blow; and if they are purchased of Seedsmen, who take them as they come, hardly three roots in twenty will shew their bloom. A few flowers here and there, however excellent in themselves, in that straggling manner, cannot be said to form a regular, grand appearance; and for this reason it is, I have directed them to be planted in pots, that the flowering sorts may be collected and placed together, to form a general blow. For this purpose, let a shed be provided; the auricula shed will be very proper. Let this be placed not too near walls, or large buildings, for thereby the flower-stalks would draw up too weak, and the flowers will be less beautiful. But they must have an open exposure, (such, nevertheless, as is guarded from strong winds) where they can have the benefit of the sun and air. Gentle waterings must now be frequently bestowed on them; the shed must be uncovered in fine weather, and constantly covered in rainy weather, which will greatly diminish the beauty of these flowers, and eclipse the dignity of their appearance. In hot weather also, they should be shaded from the heat

heat of the sun, for this will hasten their decay. With these precautions, these plants will glow in their utmost pride and lustre for near a month; they will strike every beholder with amazement, and will induce us to the most pleasing reflections on their nature, and that of their bountiful and all-wise Creator.

After the flowers are over, the pots should resume their former place, and here they may stand all the winter, with this management only, covering them in great rains and hard frosts. Here also they will have a beautiful appearance, by their fine green leaves which succeed the flowers, and will continue to grow all winter, and this management will be better than placing them in the green-house, or under hot bed frame, which always weakens the roots, and renders them less capable of flowering strong.

The operation must be repeated next year, and about the beginning of July, the top earth should be taken out of each pot, and fresh mould for the compost added. In October, more flowers, than in the preceding year, will probably shew themselves for the shed. And this work should be continued to be repeated for about four years, when the roots must be entirely taken up, and divided and planted again in fresh mould. The beginning of July is the time for this work, and a particular spot should be assigned for the off-sets, which need not be planted in pots, but in beds made of the like compost, at about four inches asunder. These off-sets may be expected to flower in about three years, and by this time, such plenty of flowering roots will be obtained, that a general blow of these delightful flowers may be every year exhibited.

All the other sorts are easy of culture, and a bulb or two of each being once obtained, they will propagate themselves fast enough. The Atamusco Lily indeed, must have a warm, dry, sandy soil, but the others will grow any where. They multiply very fast by off-sets, and these should be taken off, as soon as the green leaves are decayed, or, rather, let a plant stand four years, and then take up the whole root, which you will find to consist of many bulbs, some larger, some smaller. The larger may be planted out for immediate flowering, and the smaller off-sets in a place to succeed them. This work should be done as soon as the green leaves are decayed, for if it should be deferred, and much rain should fall, they will soon strike out fresh fibres, when it will be too late to recover them for that season, as the roots will be much weakened, which will cause them to flower very weakly, if at all, the ensuing season.

Method of raising these plants from seeds. Some people raise the plants from seeds, but this is hardly worth the while, as they encrease so fast by off-sets. When this is done, scatter the seeds thinly in any well cultivated warm border, and they will readily come up. Here they may stand two years, with only keeping them clear of weeds. After which, as soon as the green leaves are decayed, they may be taken up, and planted five inches asunder, when they may stand for flowering. If the soil be naturally sandy, it will be the better for them; if not, a few barrow-fulls may be added, and they will reward the trouble, by encreasing faster, and exhibiting fairer flowers. The Atamusco grows naturally in Virginia, and the others adorn the fields of Italy, Spain, and France. The soil of those countries is much inclined to sand, and this points out to us the culture of the native plants.

Titles. 1. Guernsey Lily is entitled, *Amaryllis spathâ multiflorâ, corollis revolutis, genitalibus erectis*. In the *Hortus Cliffortianus* it is, *Amaryllis spathâ multiflora, corollis æqualibus patentissimis revolutis, genitalibus longissimis*. Cornutus calls it, *Narcissus Japonicus, rutilo flore*, others, *Lilium Sarniense*. It grows naturally in Japan.

2. Atamusco Lily. This is titled, *Amaryllis spathâ uniflora, corollâ æquali, pistillo declinato*. Catesby calls it, *Lilio-Narcissus Virginiensis*; Lurrelier, *Lilio-Narcissus vernus angustifolius, flore purpurascente*; Plukenet, *Lilio-Narcissus uniflorus Carolinianus, flore albo singulari cum rubedine diluto*. It is a native of Virginia.

3. Autumnal Narcissus. This is, *Amaryllis spathâ uniflorâ, corollâ æquali, staminibus declinatis*. Clusius calls it, *Narcissus autumnalis major*, and Caspar Bauhine, *Colchicum luteum majus*. It grows in Thrace, Italy and Spain.

4. Golden Vernal Narcissus is called, *Amaryllis spathâ uniflora, corolla æquali, staminibus pistilloque rectis*. Tournefort calls it, *Lilio Narcissus luteus vernus*. It grows naturally in Spain and Portugal.

*Amaryllis* is of the class and order *Hexandria Monogynia*, and the characters are, (Class and order in the Linnæan system. The characters.)

1. Calyx is an oblong, obtuse, compressed, emarginated, withering spatha, that opens sideways.

2. Corolla consists of six spear-shaped petals. The nectarium consists of six very short squamulæ, situated on the outside of the base of the filaments.

3. Stamina are six subulated filaments, with oblong, incumbent, assurgent antheræ.

4. Pistillum is a roundish, furrowed germen, situated below the flower, a slender style, of about the length and breadth of the stamina, and a trifid slender stigma.

5. Pericarpium is an oval capsule, formed of three valves, and containing three cells.

6. Semina. The seeds are many and round. It is observable, that the inflexion of the petals, stamina, and pistil of the flowers of this genus, varies amazingly, in the different species.

CHAP.

## CHAP XXVIII

## AMMI, BISHOPS WEED

THERE is a perennial species of the Bishops Weed, of no extraordinary beauty, but which is, nevertheless, preserved in some gardens for the sake of variety The leaves are radical, large, and finely divided, and all the segments are shaped like a spear The stalk will grow to about a foot high, and it is garnished with the same kind of leaves as the radical ones, though smaller The flowers grow in umbels at the tops of the branches, they will be in blow in June, and their seeds ripen in August

*The plant described*

The culture of this plant is very easy Sow the seeds in the autumn, soon after they are ripe, in the places where they are designed to remain, and in the spring, where they come up too thick, thin them to about six or eight inches distance Almost any soil or situation will do for them, though they will continue longest in a dry, sandy, rocky, or rubbishy soil

*Culture*

This species is titled, *Ammi foliorum omnium laciniulis lanceolatis* John Bauhine calls it, *Daucus petraeus glaucifolius*, and Morison, *Ammi petraeum glaucifolium perenne* It grows naturally in Gallia

*Titles*

*Ammi* is of the class and order *Pentandria Digynia*, and the characters are,

*Class and order in the Linnaean system*

1 CALYX The universal umbel is composed of a great number of smaller The partial umbel is short, and thick set with flowers

*The characters*

The universal involucrum is composed of several narrow, pinnated, acute leaves, hardly the length of the umbel

The partial involucrum is composed of many narrow, acute, simple leaves, shorter than the umbelula

The proper perianthium to each flower is hardly discernible

2 COROLLA The universal corolla is uniform, the proper corolla is composed of five inflexed, cordated petals, of unequal size in the radius, but nearly equal in the disk

3 STAMINA are five capillary filaments, with roundish antheræ

4 PISTILLUM consists of a germen placed below the flower, and of two reflexed styles, with obtuse stigmas

5 PERICARPIUM There is none The fruit is round, small, striated, and is composed of two parts

6 SEMINA The seeds are two, they are striated, convex on one side, and on the other plane

## CHAP. XXIX.

## ANAGALLIS, PIMPERNEL

THE common Pimpernel is a well known weed in our gardens and fields It is of itself a beautiful little flower, and there are varieties of it that claim a place in our collection of annuals, but there is a species that will continue in a dry situation for several years, viz the upright lanceolate leaved Pimpernel

This is a very small growing plant The stalk is erect, hollow, will rise to about a foot high, and is of a pale green The leaves are spear-shaped, their edges are undivided, and they grow sometimes two, sometimes three at a joint The flowers are of a fine blue, and garnish the little stalks in plenty They grow from the wings of the leaves on long footstalks, will be in blow in May, and the seeds ripen a few weeks after the flowers are fallen

*Description of the plant*

The best culture of this sort is by the seeds, which, if sown soon after they are ripe, will readily come up, and if the winter should prove very wet and severe, it will be proper to cover them with mats in such sort of weather This precaution is only to be understood of very hard seasons, they bear our ordinary winters extremely well, especially if they have a dry soil, and a well-sheltered situation

*Culture*

This species is titled, *Anagallis foliis indivisis, caule erecto* In the *Hortus Cliffortianus* it is called, *Anagallis foliis lanceolatis* Caspar Bauhine calls it, *Anagallis caerulea, foliis binis ternisve ex adverso nascentibus*, and Clusius, *Anagallis tenuifolia monelli* It grows naturally at Verona

*Titles*

*Anagallis* is of the class and order *Pentandria Monogynia*, and the characters are,

*Class and order in the Linnaean system The characters*

1 CALYX is a permanent perianthium, divided into five acute, hollow segments

2 COROLLA is a rotated petal, divided into five oval, round, spreading parts

3 STAMINA are five erect filaments, shorter than the corolla, with simple antheræ

4 PISTILLUM consists of a globose germen, a filiforme, inclining style, and a capitated stigma

5 PERICARPIUM is a globular, circumcised capsule of one cell

6 SEMINA The seeds are numerous and angular



CHAP

# CHAP. XXX.

## *ANCHUSA*, BUGLOSS.

Introductory remarks. THE Common Buglofs is a well known plant, and our paths are garnifhed with it in plenty in many parts The flowers are exceeding beautiful, and their falutary ufes in medicine have been often experienced After this, the Reader will know to what family he is now got, it is the family of the Buglofs And the Common Buglofs fhould have been at the head of it, with all its varieties, in this place, were it not for the fhort duration of thofe plants in gardens, for however they may continue for feveral years by the hard, beaten, dry, fandy fides of highways, in gardens, where the foil is rich and fertile, they generally go off, after flowering ftrong, the fecond year from fowing, and as the varieties of this fpecies are fcarce, and exceeding beautiful, they fhall be referved for the Biennial tribe, where a more particular defcription of the Common Buglofs fhall be given

The fpecies more proper for this place are,

Species
1. The Italian Buglofs
2. The Oriental Buglofs
3. The Virginian Buglofs
4. The Downy *Fragaria*-fcented Buglofs
5. The Downy Montpelier Buglofs
6. The Broad-leaved Ever-green Buglofs

Defcription of the Italian. 1 The Italian Buglofs very much refembles our Common Buglofs It will rife with a rough, hairy branching ftalk to the height of about two feet The leaves are narrow, rough, hairy, and a little indented on their edges The flowers are produced in naked imbricated fpikes, two of them ufually grow together They are fmall, and of a red colour, will be in blow in June and July, and are fucceeded by good feeds a few weeks after This fort will not continue much longer than our Common Buglofs, unlefs the fituation be very dry and fandy

Oriental. 2 The Oriental Buglofs This hath weak, flender, trailing branches, which are garnifhed with hairy leaves of different figures and fizes, they are long and broad near the bottom of the plant, higher they are fmaller, and near the top they are fhort, and of a roundifh figure The flowers and the branches are produced alternately from the wings of the ftalks The flowers are of a yellow colour, will be in blow moft of the fummer months, and, if they are headed in July, will fhoot out afrefh, and continue flowering until the froft ftops them

Virginian. 3 Virginian Buglofs This ufually goes among the inhabitants of Virginia by the name of *Puccoon* It is a very pretty low growing early perennial, feldom growing higher than about nine inches, and, what is very different from the before-defcribed forts is, the ftalks are fmooth The flowers are produced from the fides of them without order, they are of a very fine bright yellow, and will be in blow early in the fpring

Downy Fragaria fcented. 4 Downy *Fragaria* fcented Buglofs. This will grow to about a foot high The ftalk is weak, flender, and downy The leaves alfo are very downy and hairy They are fpear fhaped, obtufe, grow alternately on the ftalks, and have the fmell of the *Fragaria* The flowers are produced from the upper parts of the branches in recurved fpikes They grow from the wings of the ftalks, and are very hairy their colour is a fine blue; and they have this fingularity, their ftamina are longer than the corolla

Downy Montpelier. 5 Downy Montpelier Buglofs This hath a red root, from which proceeds a fingle ftalk It will grow to be about a foot long, is weak, flender, downy, hairy, and often lies on the ground The leaves are hairy, downy, pear-fhaped, obtufe, and placed alternately on the ftalk. The flowers grow from the tops of the ftalks in fhort recurved fpikes Their colour is a bright purple; but the ftamina of this fpecies are not fo long as the corolla

and the Broad leaved Ever-green Buglofs. 6 Broad leaved Ever-green Buglofs This is a low, trailing plant The leaves are very broad, rough, hairy, and of a deep green The flowers are produced from the wings of the leaves in fmall fpikes, they are blue, and will be in flower for moft of the fummer months

Culture. The culture of thefe forts is very eafy, the chief thing is a proper fituation for them Moft of them grow in dry, uncultivated, fandy places, and fome of them, particularly the laft, will grow from the joints of old walls This teaches us to let them have as dry a part of the garden as poffible, and if it is not naturally fo, to raife the feeds at leaft a foot above the level of the garden, and add a good quantity of fea or drift fand If the fituation be naturally dry, warm, fandy, and rocky, it is the wifhed-for foil, and in fuch a place their roots will continue for many years If they are fown in good garden mould, they will grow very well, and flower ftronger, but their duration will be much fhorter Be the fituation, however, as it will, fow the feeds in the autumn, foon after they are ripe, for, if they are kept until the fpring, they will often lie until the fpring following, before they come up They fhould be fown in the places where they are to remain, and after they are come up, fhould be thinned to proper diftances They will then flower ftrong, and moft of them, after that, will fcatter their feeds, and come up without further trouble

Titles. 1 The Italian Buglofs is titled, *Anchufa racemis fubnudis conjugatis* Morifon calls it, *Buglossum anguftifolium minus*, Lobel, *Echii facie Buglossum minimum, flore rubente* It grows naturally in Italy and Germany

2 Oriental Buglofs This is titled, *Anchufa villofa-tomentofa, ramis floribufque alternis axillaribus, bracteis ovatis* Van Royen calls it, *Anchufa foliis avenuis, floribus folitariis ex alis ramorum, uti rami e caule*, Tournefort, and others, *Buglossum orientale, flore luteo* It is a native of the Laft

3 Virginian Buglofs This is titled, *Anchufa floribus fparfis, caule glabro* Gronovius calls it, *Anchufa lutea minor, quam alii Puccoon vocant*, Plukenet, *Anchufa minor lutea Virginiana, Puccoon indigenis dicta, qua fe pingunt Americani*, Morifon and Ray, *Lithofpermum Virginianum, flore luteo duplici amplior* It grows naturally in Virginia

4 Downy Fragaria-fcented Buglofs This is titled, *Anchufa tomentofa foliis lanceolatis, ftaminibus corolla longioribus* Barrelier calls it, *Pulmonaria mitis, Fragariae odore* It grows common at Algiers.

5 Downy

5 Downy Montpelier Bugloss This is titled, *Anchusa tomentosa, foliis lanceolatis obtusis, staminibus corolla brevioribus* In the former edition of the *Species Plantarum* it is called, *Lithospermum villosum, caulibus procumbentibus simplicibus* Caspar Bauhine terms it, *Anchusa pan ceis floribus*, and John Bauhine, *Anchusa Monspeliaca* It grows naturally at Montpelier, also, in some parts of the East

6 Broad-leaved Ever-green Bugloss This is titled, *Anchusa pedunculis diphyllis capitatis* Van Royen calls it, *Anchusa scapis diphyllis*, Caspar Bauhine and Morison, *Buglossum latifolium sempervirens*, and Gerard, *Borrago sempervirens* This is a native of ours, it grows naturally in Kent, and in several places near London, it grows also common in Spain

Class and order in the Linnæan system

*Anchusa* is of the class and order *Pentandria Monogynia*, and the characters are,

The characters

1 CALYX is an oblong, taper, permanent perianthium, divided into five acute parts

2 COROLLA is an infundibuliforme petal The tube is cylindrical, and the length of the calyx the limb is erect, patent, obtuse, and lightly cut into five segments The mouth is closed by five convex, prominent, oblong, connivent squamulæ

3 STAMINA are five very short filaments in the mouth of the corolla, with oblong, incumbent, covered antheræ

4 PISTILLUM consists of four germina, a filiforme style the length of the stamina, and an obtuse, emarginated stigma

5 PERICARPIUM There is none The calyx becomes larger, erect, and contains the seeds in its cavity

6 SEMINA are four in each cavity, they are oblong, obtuse, and gibbous

## CHAP XXXI

## *ANDROMEDA*

Species

THE perennials of this genus are,

1 Marsh Cistus, or, Wild Rosemary
2 Blue *Andromeda*
3 Clustered-leaved *Andromeda*
4 Imbricated-leaved *Andromeda*

Description of Wild Rosemary

1 Wild Rosemary The root is woody, fibrous, and creeping. The stalks are ligneous, tough, about a foot high, and divide into numerous slender branches The leaves are spear-shaped, their edges are reflexed, and they grow alternately on the branches The flowers come out in small clusters from the sides of the branches, they are small, oval, reddish, appear in June, and the seeds ripen in the autumn There is a variety of this with white flowers

Blue Andromeda

2 Blue *Andromeda* The root is tough, woody, perennial, and fibrous The stalks are rough, branching, brown, ligneous, and hardly a foot in length The leaves are narrow, plane, short, and obtuse, the flowers come out in small clusters from the sides of the branches They are oval, much resemble those of the *Arbutus*, appear in June and July, and the seeds ripen in the autumn

Varieties

The varieties of this species are,
The Deep Blue,
The Red,
The Purple,
The White *Andromeda*

3 Clustered leaved *Andromeda* The root is perennial, slender and fibrous The stalks are herbaceous, divide into a few branches, and grow to about a foot and half high The leaves are awl-shaped, and grow together in clusters at the sides of the stalks and branches The flowers come out from the ends of the branches on long single footstalks They are bell-shaped, appear in June and July, and the seeds ripen in September

4 Imbricated-leaved *Andromeda* The root of this is perennial, fibrous, and creeping The stalks are square, brownish, divide into a few branches, and grow to about a foot and half high. The leaves are short, obtuse, revolute, grow opposite, and hang *imbricatim* over one another in the range The flowers come out from the sides of the stalks on single slender footstalks, they are bell-shaped, appear about the time of the former, and the seeds usually ripen in the autumn

Culture

The first species grows naturally on boggy ground in the north of England, the others on the like places on the Alps of Lapland, so that the culture of these plants should not be attempted, unless where there is a similar situation, for, although the seeds will grow in a garden, yet, for want of a soil suitable to their nature, the plants will be but of short continuance

Whoever, therefore is possessed of a boggy, turfy spot, fronting the north especially, and in the shade, the ground may be prepared, and the plants cultivated both by the seeds and roots, in the manner that has been directed for raising the American species for the shrubbery, and to which, to avoid repetition, the Reader is referred

Titles

1 Marsh Cistus, or, Wild Rosemary, is titled, *Andromeda pedunculis aggregatis, corollis ovatis, foliis alternis lanceolatis revolutis* In the *Flora Lapponica* it is termed, *Andromeda foliis alternis lanceolatis margine reflexis* Buxbaum calls it, *Polifolia* Oeder, *Vitis idææ affinis polifolia montana*; Plukenet, *Erica humilis, rosmarini foliis, unedonis flore, capsulâ cistoide*, Ray, *Ledum palustre nostras, arbuti flore*; and Parkinson, *Rosmarinum sylvestre minus nostras* Its English situation is chiefly in Yorkshire, Lancashire, Westmoreland, and Cumberland, and it also grows naturally in most of the colder parts of Europe

2. Blue *Andromeda* is, *Andromeda pedunculis aggregatis, corollis ovatis, foliis sparsis linearibus obtusis planis* In the *Flora Lapponica* it is termed, *Andromeda foliis linearibus obtusis sparsis*; and in the *Amœnitates Academica*, *Andromeda varieg Norvegica* Buxbaum calls it, *Erica folio abietis, flore arbuti*. It inhabits the Alps of Lapland

3 Clustered leaved *Andromeda* is, *Andromeda pedunculis solitariis terminalibus, corollis campanulatis, foliis confertis subulatis*. In the *Flora Lapponica* it

is termed, *Andromeda foliis aciformibus confertis* It is a native of the Lapland Alps

4 Imbricated leaved Andromeda is, *Andromeda pedunculis solitariis ... foliis carinatis obtusis, et oppositis imbricatis ...* In the *Flora Suecica* it is termed, *Andromeda foliis quadrifariam imbricatis obtusis*, and in the *Flora Lapp Andromeda foliis quadrifariam imbricatis obtusis, ex alis floriferis* It grows naturally on the Alps of Lapland

# CHAP XXXII

## ANDROSACE

Remark — THIS genus stands without any English name, and the species under consideration have usually been called Sedums They grow naturally in the mountainous parts of the world, and are seldom propagated in any garden but where a general collection of plants is making For distinction sake I shall call them,

Species —
1 The Austrian *Androsace*
2 The Helvetian *Androsace*
3 The Pyrenean *Androsace*

Austrian Androsace, — 1 The Austrian *Androsace* is a very low growing plant The leaves are very narrow and smooth, and the flowers are produced in small umbels, these will be in blow in April, and the seeds ripen soon after the flowers are fallen

Helvetian Androsace, — 2 Helvetian *Androsace* This hath also very narrow and smooth leaves, but they are subulated or awl-shaped, whereas those of the former have more a grass-like appearance The stalk is low, seldom more than four inches high, and the flowers are many in the umbel They will be in blow in April, and their seeds ripen in May

There is another sort of this *Androsace* with ciliated leaves This Linnæus had arranged as a distinct species in his former work in his latter it stands as a variety only

Pyrenæan Androsace described — 3 Pyrenæan *Androsace* The leaves of this sort are very hairy, and the stalk hardly ever grows higher than three inches It is upright and hairy, and the flowers, which are produced in umbels, have hairy perianthiums They will be in blow in April, and their seeds ripen in May

Culture — The culture of these sorts is easy, they are only raised from seeds, and the sooner these are sown after they are ripe the better They will grow in almost any soil that is not too wet but if it is sandy, and the situation shady, it will be more agreeable to their nature In such places they will scatter their seeds, and the plants will come up in plenty without art or trouble

Titles — 1 The first species is titled, *Androsace foliis lanceolatis glabris, umbella involucris multoties longiore* Tournefort calls it, *Androsace Alpina perennis angustifolia glabra, flore singulari*, Caspar Bauhine and Ray, *Sedum Alpinum, gramineo folio, lacteo flore*, and Clusius, *Sedum minus XI* It grows naturally on the Alps of Austria

2 The second species is titled, *Androsace foliis subulatis glabris, umbella involucrum æquante* Tournefort calls it, *Androsace Alpina perennis angustifolia glabra & multiflora*; Caspar Bauhine, *Sedum Alpinum, angustissimo folio, flore carneo*, Plukenet, *Sanicula Alpina, angustissimo folio* The ciliated variety Haller calls, *Aretia foliis ciliatis linearibus, floribus umbellatis* It grows naturally on the Pyrenean and Helvetian mountains

3 The third species is titled, *Androsace foliis pilosis, perianthiis hirsutis* Haller calls it, *Aretia villosa, floribus umbellatis*, Caspar Bauhine, *Sedum Alpinum hirsutum, lacteo flore*, and Clusius, *Sedum minus X Alpinum II* It grows naturally on the Pyrennees

Class and order in the Linnæan system — *Androsace* is of the class and order *Pentandria Monogynia*, and the characters are

The characters — 1 CALYX The general involucrum is composed of many small leaves, and contains many flowers

The perianthium is a single, five cornered, erect, acute, permanent leaf, divided at the top into five segments

2 COROLLA is an hypocrateriform petal, the tube is oval, and is surrounded by the calyx, the limb is plane, and divided into five oval, oblong, obtuse, entire segments

3 STAMINA are five very short filaments, situated within the tube of the corolla, with oblong, erect, included antheræ

4 PISTILLUM consists of a globose germen, a very short filiforme style, and a globular stigma

5 PERICARPIUM is a globose capsule of one cell, opening five different ways at the top

6 SEMINA The seeds are numerous and roundish, on one side they are gibbous, on the other plane The receptacle is erect and free

CHAP.

# CHAP. XXXIII.

## *ANDRYALA*, DOWNY SOW-THISTLE.

*Species.*

THE perennial species of this genus are,

1. The Small Yellow Downy Sow-Thistle.
2. The Mountain Downy Sow-Thistle.

*Description of the Small Yellow Downy Sow Thistle,*

1. Small Yellow Downy Sow-Thistle. This will grow to about a foot high. The leaves are white and hairy, and of different figures; the lower leaves are large, and have indented edges; on the upper part of the stalk they are small, and their edges are entire. The stalk is upright and hairy, and is crowned by a small cluster of flowers. Their colour is a fine yellow; they will be in blow in July, but are not always succeeded by good seeds in these parts.

*and Mountain Downy Sow Thistle.*

2. Mountain Downy Sow-Thistle. This will grow to about twelve or fourteen inches high. The leaves are very silvery and woolly, of an oblong oval figure, and their edges are indented. The stalk is woolly, downy, branching, and ornamented with small, oval, downy leaves, which sit close. The flowers are produced singly from the ends of the branches; they are of a bright yellow colour, and very beautiful. They will be in blow in June, and sometimes continue flowering until the autumn, before which time the seeds from the first flowers will be ripe.

*Method of propagating these species.*

The propagation of these sorts is by the seeds. Sow them in the spring in a warm border of common garden-mould. When the plants come up frequently water them, keep them clean from weeds, and when they are too close, thin them. By June they will be of a proper size to transplant. Then having a bed prepared for the purpose, wait for a rainy day; and if no sign of this should happen, let the operation of removing them be performed in the evening. Set them at about five inches asunder, and give them a good watering; and if the weather proves hot, shade them with mats until they have taken root. In the autumn they should be transplanted to the flower-garden, and the summer following they will flower, and the latter sort never fail of producing good seeds. But as the first sort frequently miscarries, it is usually propagated by parting of the roots, as they naturally spread themselves under the surface of the ground, and these being taken off, immediately become good plants without further trouble.

These plants must have a dry light soil, especially the second sort. It is a mountainous plant, and will not live long in a moist rich situation.

*Titles.*

1. The Small Yellow Downy Sow-Thistle is titled, *Andryala foliis [illegible]*. In the *Hortus Cliffortianus* it is called, *Andryala foliis inferioribus dentatis summis integris*. Vaillant calls it, *[illegible] foliis inferioribus ad costam usque laciniatis*; and Caspar Bauhine, *Sonchus villosus luteus minor*. It grows naturally in Sicily and about Montpelier.

2. Mountain Downy Sow-Thistle. This is titled, *Andryala foliis oblongo-ovatis subdentatis lanatis, pedunculis ramosis*. Dalechampius calls it, *Hieracium montanum tomentosum*. It grows naturally in the southern parts of Europe.

*Andryala* is of the class and order *Syngenesia Polygamia Æqualis*; and the characters are,

1. CALYX is short, round, and hairy, and is composed of several equal subulated leaves.
2. COROLLA is uniform. The corollulæ are numerous and equal; each consists of a single, ligulated, linear leaf, indented in five parts; and these lie over each other in the imbricated way.
3. STAMINA are five very short capillary filaments, with cylindrical tubulous antheræ.
4. PISTILLUM consists of an oval germen, a filiforme style the length of the stamina, and two reflexed stigmas.
5. PERICARPIUM. There is none.
6. SEMINA. The seeds are oval and single. The pappus is hairy, and of the length of the calyx.

The receptacle is hairy and plane.

# CHAP. XXXIV.

## *ANEMONE*, The WIND-FLOWER.

*Introductory Remarks.*

THE real species of this genus are very numerous, and there is no end to the varieties principally belonging to those two sorts improperly called the Narrow-leaved and the Broad-leaved *Anemones*. From these two species, the prodigious variety that compose the Florist's collection are obtained. These in their original and natural state are Single flowers, growing wild by the sides of fields and woods in many parts of the East, from whence they were first introduced into our gardens, and from which flow, by happy culture, our amazing collection of Established flowers. These have been already treated of. But besides these, there are some species of the wild Wood *Anemones*, with varieties of double flowers, that adorn the Gardener's collection, are very beautiful, and excellently serve for the proper ornamenting of several places in the wilderness quarter, among shrubs and trees, making those places, as they are intended, to imitate a wild bespangled with its different produce, glowing in all natural luxuriancy and wildness. The principal of these come here of course for this purpose, and to join in the train, the *Hepatica* and *Pulsatilla* of old botanists are now added to this genus, each of which have many sorts. Perhaps it may surprise the Gardener when he is told, that these very different flowers are in reality no other than different species of the *Anemone*. I shall arrange the different sorts to be here treated of under such names as they have usually gone by, and by which they are still known among practical Gardeners; and they are,

Species.

1. The Narrow-leaved *Anemone* } Including all
2. The Broad-leaved *Anemone* } the varieties.
3. English Wood *Anemone*.
4. Blue or Mountain Wood *Anemone*, single and double.
5. The German Wood *Anemone*.
6. Virginian Wood *Anemone*.
7. Large-flowering *Pulsatilla*, or Pasque Flower.
8. Smaller Pasque Flower.
9. Siberian Pasque Flower.
10. Small-leaved Pasque Flower.
11. The *Hepatica*, including,
    The Single Red *Hepatica*.
    The Double Red *Hepatica*.
    The Single Blue *Hepatica*.
    The Double Blue *Hepatica*.
    The White *Hepatica*.
12. Yellow *Anemone*.
13. Alpine *Anemone*.
14. Canada *Anemone*.
15. Tyrolese *Anemone*.
16. Five-leaved *Anemone*.
17. Bastard *Ranunculus*.

Of all which in their order.

Narrow-leaved Anemone, 1. 2. The first species usually goes by the name of the Narrow-leaved *Anemone*, though it has a very large, fair, decompound leaf. It is distinguished by that name chiefly by the common Gardeners, each leaf being cut into a multitude of narrow segments, and also to distinguish it from the other species, whose segments are fewer and broader.

and Broad-leaved Anemone, described. The second species is with as great impropriety called the Broad-leaved *Anemone*, which name is used chiefly for distinction-sake, the segments being larger. The leaves of the first are very much divided, and those again are subdivided into others, the division always being in the ternate way, or by threes, more or less regularly. The second sort has digitated leaves, or of the finger-shape; and all of this sort, for distinction, though improperly, go by the name of Broad-leaved *Anemone*.

Remarks. It has been observed, that from these two species the multitude of varieties that compose our present valuable collection of *Anemones* are produced. They are the parents of all the rest, and their numerous offspring serve excellently for the ornamenting the different parts of the flower-garden, I mean to be planted in the usual way, without entering into the nice art and management of the florist, forming of their separate beds for show; for they are all very hardy, and common culture will do for them. And what can be more proper than all the single sorts, called the Poppy *Anemones*, to mix with the earliest spring flowers, to encrease the beauty of that collection? The double sorts also, if unremoved, will often flower at those early times; and as their colours are so perfect, their flowers so large, and their beauty so very great, we are as much indebted to the *Anemone* for the pleasure it affords, as to almost any other flower in nature.

The philosophical Gardener also must admire several of these plants for observation; the single sorts, which are established plants, and go by different names, shew their numerous stamens, thus proclaiming their class and order, whilst several of the double sorts shew Nature's beauty in the luxuriancy of culture. The proliferous *Anemone* is singular of the kind, the second flower being as large and fair as the first, and ought by all means to have a place amongst curious perennial flowers, whilst other curious sorts, such as the great Caledonian *Anemone*, &c. differing in form and appearance, equally beautiful and singular, should be here and there scattered, to shew the beauty of this genus in its wonderful species and sorts.

Wood Anemone, 3. The English Wood *Anemone*, which by old botanists was termed *Anemonoides*, has its various uses in gardening; and though not possessed of the splendor of the Oriental sorts, will look very beautiful in places adapted to its nature. It flourishes well among trees, and is very proper for wilderness quarters of all sorts.

The Common *Anemone* of our woods with a white flower, being to be met with in so many parts, is hardly worth propagating in any part of our works, particularly as there are varieties of it with double flowers, and those with different tinges which constitute another appearance, still retaining the general view of wildness they are designed to represent in those places.

In our woods there will be found some with reddish flowers, or those whose petals are stained on the outside with the delicate red of the peach bloom. These are to be removed into our wilderness quarters at the time of their being in blow, for it will be difficult to find their roots after their leaves and flower stalks are faded and gone. But above all, the variety with double flowers is most to be desired. It is really a full flower, fair and delicate, and often the red tinge is beautifully blended with the natural white of the petals. As this sort was accidentally obtained from seeds of the single sorts, and seldom produces seeds itself, it is encreased by the roots, which multiply very fast, and is now grown pretty common. The leaves of this species grow on long slender foot-stalks, and are of a pale green; they are divided by threes, and each of these parts again have their edges deeply cut. The flower-stalk rises single and undivided to the height of about half a foot, near the top of which stand three leaves placed nearly horizontally, being at right angles with the stalk, on longish foot-stalks, whose edges turn in so as nearly to form a tube. Above these is elevated the flower, on so slender a stalk that it appears drooping. The Double is of all the sorts the most valuable, and is really a fine flower; but whenever they are to be met with in tinges different from the very Common sort, they are to be selected, to encrease the variety where they are wanted, for they will grow and flower every where.

Blue Wood Anemone. 4. The Blue Wood *Anemone*, which is called by many the Mountain Wood *Anemone*, makes an excellent variety, whether in its single or double state.

The leaves, which grow on long slender foot-stalks, stand by threes, and are hairy, each of them has a shorter separate hairy foot-stalk. These lobules also are cut into three principal divisions, and those also deeply again on their edges. The flower-stalk rises single, and has terminated [illegible] leaves growing near the top, [illegible] curved foot-stalks, and in the bosom of these stands the flower, elevated upon a weak stalk, in a drooping posture. The [illegible] from the root

to

to the leaves is green, and moderately large, and for the immediate support of the flower, it is of a purplish colour, and much smaller.

The flowers in their single state are composed of about fourteen oblong petals, of a clear blue colour, in the middle of which are their numerous stamina.

This is a pretty flower in its single state, and if it is not wanted to ornament the ground in wilderness quarters, or the like, it ought to have a place in the borders with other perennial flowers, or it may be placed under an hedge, where it will grow and flourish exceeding well. Valuable, however, as this flower is, the double sort is much more so; for the petals being long in its double state, it forms a large flower, and makes a more than ordinary figure in places adapted to its nature, which, in short, are every where. But all these sorts ought chiefly to be appropriated to wilderness quarters, under hedges, and in places where few other things will thrive, that no part may be left unoccupied.

Germ. Wood Anemone.

5. The German Wood *Anemone* is so called, because it grows naturally in many parts of Germany, and is very ornamental to several of their woods. The leaves of this plant are divided in the ternate way, standing on long slender footstalks, and the flowers are large and white. The seeds are round and hairy, and will come up plentifully in any shady border, so that when a number of these is wanted to form a proper mixture in large quarters, this will be the most expeditious method to obtain them.

Virginian Wood Anemone.

6. Virginian Wood *Anemone* is so called, as being originally brought from Virginia. The leaves of this species are divided by threes. The main stalk branches out, and is ornamented with leaves as well as flowers. The stalks for the immediate support of the latter, are slender, naked, and long. The flowers are small, and of no figure. There are varieties of it, some with white, some with greenish petals, and which are succeeded by cylindrical spikes of hairy seeds.

Large-flowering Pasque Flower.

7. The Large-flowering Pasque Flower is a native of our own country, and flourishes in many of our heathy barren grounds, but it nevertheless vies in beauty with most plants we receive from abroad, and on which we bestow the nicest care and management.

The *Pulsatilla* has hitherto been deemed a distinct genus, but upon examination is found to be no other than a distinct species of the *Anemone*. The flowers cut a figure equal to most, and superior to many of the single Wind flowers, though so justly esteemed and sought after for the ornamenting borders, as well as for the sake of the seeds.

The root of this species is long and thick, and sends forth many pale and hoary leaves; these are hairy, and divided and subdivided into many small narrow segments in a most beautiful manner. The flower stalk is thick and hairy, and has a leafy involucrum, composed of many long narrow segments. These are of a light green, spread every way from the base, are hairy, or are possessed of a kind of down, which gives it a whitish colour. From this leafy involucrum rises the flower, terminating the stalk. This is truly of the *Anemone* kind, and has a variety of colours. It is very large and well shewing in the single state, but there is of it very full or double flowers. There are of this species, besides the double, varieties with white, yellow, and red flowers, but none equal its natural original colour, which is a fine bright purple; and with that it shines on Gogmagog Hills near Cambrige, Barnack-Heath, and Lowthorpe-Common near Stamford. With that colour also it glows in some dry pastures near Pontefract, in Yorkshire; and with such its original beauty also it decorates some of the Welsh mountains, and some other of our northern parts. In their single original state, the petals, which are large, are six in number; three of which being placed outward, and three within, form a flower nearly of a campanulate figure, and which hangs in a drooping manner. These petals are broad and thick; they are oblong, their ends are pointed, and the three innermost are of a deeper tinge than the others. In the middle of these stand their numerous stamina, forming a large tuft. These are succeeded by seeds, from which it may be raised in plenty, and varieties of sorts may be expected. It flowers in March and April, and is a fit companion with the Oriental *Anemone* in constituting some of the chief ornaments of the spring.

Smaller Pasque Flower.

8. Smaller Pasque Flower. The meadows, plains and dry sunny pastures in many parts of Germany are ornamented by this species, in the same manner as some of our heaths are by the former. There is a great resemblance between them, only this is of an humbler growth. The leaves are divided and subdivided the pinnated way into numerous narrow segments, though they are smaller than the other, and the flower-stalk shorter. It has near the top a kind of leafy involucrum, composed of very long narrow segments, and the flowers, which are naturally of a deep purple colour, droop in the same manner with our English sort. The brims of the petals are reflexed, forming a kind of bell-shaped figure, and their numerous stamina, forming a large tuft, fill the middle. These are succeeded by seeds, by which it is easily propagated, and by which variety of sorts may be obtained.

9. Siberian Pasque Flower is so distinguished, as being a native of that country. The leaves of this plant, which proceed from a thick fleshy root, attended with many fibres, are composed of several finger shaped lobes, which sit close, and are pointed, so that the whole makes a hand shaped appearance. The middle one of these is cut into three parts, but the side ones have seldom more than two. They are downy, which hoary look is an additional beauty to all leaves of such composition. The stalk which supports one flower will be about half a foot high, and the involucrum is placed at a greater distance from the flower than of the other sorts. This also is hairy, and very ornamental. The petals that compose the flower are large, white, and spread open, are hairy within-side, and their middle, in the usual way, is filled with their numerous stamina, forming a large tuft of a deep yellow colour. They will be in blow in March, or sooner, as the weather is, and the flowers will be succeeded by the usual sorts of seeds.

Smallage-leaved Pasque Flower described.

10. Smallage-leaved Pasque Flower flourishes fair in the barrenest woods and mountainous parts of other countries; and being of course very hardy, calls for no very nice part in the garden. This has a leaf a little resembling Smallage, which occasions its being so called among gardeners. They are pinnated in a plain simple way, and the stalk which supports the flower will arise to near a foot high. This also hath an hairy involucrum, very neat and upright, and the flower, differing from the drooping posture of the others, stands erect. It will be in blow in February or March, and its colour is a clear yellow. The middle has its large tuft of stamina, which are succeeded by seeds that will be ripe in June.

These are the cultivated sorts of the Pasque Flower, or *Pulsatilla* of old botanists; and before I proceed to the *Hepatica*, which was always held another

nother distinct genus, I shall give the method of their propagation

The first-mentioned species of this genus have been usually treated of among those flowers that are more peculiarly said to belong to the Florist's care There may be seen the method of raising them from seeds, or multiplying them by the root The Wood *Anemones* are to be raised the same way and their propagation is very easy The Pasque Flowers are for the most part possessed of long fleshy roots attended with many fibres, and require to be distinctly treated, with regard to their being multiplied that way, as also their propagation by seeds

Culture of the roots of Pasque Flowers

And first, the Pasque Flowers are to be propagated by the roots They are early-flowering plants, and like most others of that nature, their leaves and stalks decay early in the summer By the end of June these flowers will be seen to be in that state, and then, or in July, is the best time for transplanting them The utmost care must be used not to bruise or wound their roots in taking them up, and they are not to be divided into too small parts, which would cause them to flower weak, though if there be a tuft or head at the top of each root, it is a good plant, and though weak it will flower strong the second year This also will increase, and if left unremoved will produce numbers of flowers from each head, which may be parted the same way for multiplication at pleasure But notwithstanding, the end of June or July is the best time for parting those roots, it may be done at almost any time of the year, and this I mention, lest a person should not have an opportunity at that time September and October are good months for removing the plants, or indeed any time in the winter The worst season is just before, or when they are in flower, but even then they will grow so that a person is not to be discouraged, if he has his ground in readiness, for they ought, let them be removed when they will, to be planted again as soon as possible

by the roots,

All these sorts are natives of dry sandy pastures, barren woods, heaths, mountains, and the like; which teaches us that a sandy light soil is most agreeable to their nature so that if any particular spot is designed for these flowers, it will be a great addition, in preparing the bed, to mix with it a quantity of drift sand, and then the flowers will be larger, and the roots will multiply the faster

All these sorts are easily raised by seeds, which will be ripe the end of June, or in July, and the sooner they are sown after that the better A light compost should be procured for them at no very great trouble, for some common garden mould that is rich and good, having a little drift sand mixed with it, will answer very well though if some of the auricula compost be taken, some garden mould may be mixed with it to augment the quantity, and that will be much better for their reception A bed is to be made of this a foot deep, in any shady part of the garden, but not under the drip of trees, and the seeds should be sown in drills a quarter of an inch deep Pegs should be stuck at the end of each row, for a direction that more care in those lines may be used in weeding, for weeds must be immediately cleared off upon their first appearance If the season after sowing proves moist, the plants will come up in the autumn, but it will be best if they do not come up until the spring, for which reason no water should be given the beds after sowing until they appear When the plants come up, a little sprinkling of water should be given them every other evening, if the weather proves dry, and this will be all the trouble (except weeding) they will call for the first summer In July the leaves will decay but the small crown or bud at the top of each root will soon prepare to exhibit fresh leaves, and early in the spring they will be in their full strength When these leaves decay again which will be in June, or July, the roots should be taken up, for by that time they will be tolerably strong, when they should be planted in beds prepared at six inches asunder, and by the spring following many of them will flower, after which they may be removed into borders, or such parts of the pleasure garden they are designed to garnish

or by seeds

II The *Hepatica*, in all its varieties, is a well-known plant, and although there be the red, the white, the blue, the double red, the double blue, that have had titles by old botanists they are varieties only of the same species, and answer to the characters of the *Anemone* These join the numerous train of other *Anemones* in dressing out the spring, and though the flowers are small, they effectually do their part for they proceed early in pro[illegible] [illegible] [illegible] some standing [illegible] their low [illegible] [illegible] [illegible] for still heighten their excellence, and [illegible] the worth of these flowers [illegible] more proper, and indeed none is more common, than all the sorts to be planted in gu[illegible] fronting the sitting-room, to make a show, there with other early flowers They blow in February and March, and greatly contribute to the beauty of those months

The Hepatica described

The student, upon examining these plants, will find the root to be composed of numerous fibres, clotted together so as with difficulty to be separated The leaves are composed of three lobes, growing on long, slender, [illegible] footstalks Their edges are entire, [illegible] [illegible] and their under surface is of a whitish [illegible] The flowers often come out even before the leaves, [illegible] slender footstalks about four inches long Thirty, forty or even sixty of them will issue from one root, and will at once display their charms to every beholder, and as these decay, others will succeed them so that they will flower even until the beginning of April

In the general characters of the *Anemone* the botanist will find it thus expressed "There is no calyx" Upon examining these flowers he will find three leaves that he will take to be such He must be informed, however, that this is a leafy involucrum only, that is nearer the flower than in the *Pulsatilla* kinds Within this cup, or leafy involucrum, are placed the petals, that are of the above-mentioned colour in different sorts, and in their double state are arranged in a beautiful manner, so as to fill the flower The single sorts produce the seeds and by these they may be multiplied in plenty Indeed, this is by far the best way, for although they will sometimes grow by the roots, when taken up and divided, yet they often fail, and the expectation of many a true lover of them has been thus disappointed Nay, when this method is practised, if the roots are too much divided, it is great odds but the whole will be lost, and if they happen to live, or a share of them, the flowers are never so large and fine as those which the unremoved seedlings produce, so that the intelligent Gardener must be instructed to treat these plants as follows Let him chuse the seeds of the single blue, the peach-bloom colour, and the white, and let him preserve them in a dry place until the time of sowing This will be any time from the gathering the seeds until the March following, though it will be best to sow them about a week or ten days after, for then the plants will come up in the autumn, and will be by the autumn following nearly as strong

Remarks

Its culture

strong again as those that were sown in the spring, or even the August before. And although we dread a family of seedlings at the coming of winter, in many instances, on account of the havock the frost makes in throwing them out of the ground, &c. yet in these there is little to be feared on that head, for upon examining a plant after it has newly come up, it is found to have a root consisting of a long strong fibre struck down very deep, which will for the most part keep it in its position. And as even in their youngest state these plants are exceeding hardy, if they can be made to appear the autumn after the seeds are gathered and sown, almost a whole year will be saved. As these plants flower best if unremoved, let a proper place in the flower garden be pitched upon for them to grow in. If this place be in the shade, it will be the better, and if the soil be naturally strong and moist, the flowers will be always the larger, and the colours deeper. Ten days, therefore, after the seeds are gathered, and the soil is made light and fine by digging and well working, but not by sifting of it, for that will be improper, sow the seeds thinly about in different dots or spaces, according to the number of desired plants, sticking a peg down at each place for a direction, then sift over them a little of the auricula or the like compost, hardly a quarter of an inch thick. In the autumn many plants will come up, and in the spring more will appear. Keep them clean from weeds, and water them in dry weather all summer, and in the autumn mould them up with some of the rich compost. In the spring many of the strong plants will flower, so that the single ones, and those of bad colours, may be drawn out and thrown away, which will make room for the others, that they will not be too close. These also, as they arrive at maturity, will shew their flowers fair and strong, and when they are too close they may be taken up with a ball of earth, and planted immediately with the early sorts of the flowering tribe in any place. These will do very well, but those unremoved will always do best, and where perfection in flowers is desired, sowing of the seeds is the best method to obtain it.

Parting of the roots, and multiplying them this way, is to be done at any time, but is generally practised at their time of flowering. When this is to be done, do not divide them into more than two or three parts, and always observe never to remove any of these plants before they are got too large, which will hardly ever be, for it is naturally a small close-growing plant, and the larger it is, the greater burst of flowers will it show in its full glory and lustre.

Description of the Yellow, 12. Yellow *Anemone*. The root is tuberous and oblong, and of a dark brown colour on the outside, but whitish within. The radical leaves are large, roundish, lobed, indented on the edges, of a deep green on their upper side, but purplish underneath, and grow on long strong footstalks. The stalk is thick, about six inches high, and adorned with about three leaves, which are fairly cut and divided on their edges. The flowers come out singly from the tops of the stalks, and are large, single, and of a yellow colour; they appear in May, and the seeds ripen in August. The roots of this are to be parted, or the seeds sown like the common *Anemone*.

Wild Alpine, 13. Wild Alpine *Anemone*. The radical leaves are large, divided into many parts, and grow on long footstalks. The stalks are slender, about six inches high, and adorned with three supra-decompound leaves, which are elegantly cut into a multitude of narrow segments. The flowers come out singly from the tops of the stalks; they are of a white colour, appear in the spring, and are succeeded by hairy seeds, which ripen in the summer. It is propagated like the former.

Canada, 14. Canada *Anemone*. The root is creeping. The stalk is dichotomous, and about a foot high. The leaves consist of three principal parts, which are cut or jagged at the edges; they have no footstalks, grow opposite, and embrace the stalk with their base. The flowers come out singly from the divisions of the stalks on slender footstalks. They are of a white colour, and appear in May. This plant multiplies very freely by its creeping root.

Trifoliate, 15. Trifoliate *Anemone*. The stalk is single, and four or five inches high. The leaves are oval, undivided, serrated, and grow three together on the stalk. The flowers come out singly from the tops of the stalks; they are of a white colour, and appear about the same time with the former.

Five leaved Anemone, 16. Five-leaved *Anemone*. The leaves are quinate, oval, serrated, and very much resemble those of the common strawberry. The stalks are slender, and each supports a single flower at the top, which appears about the same time with the former.

and Bastard Ranunculus. 17. Bastard *Ranunculus*. The leaves are divided into many parts, which are beautifully cut at their edges. The stalks are slender, weak, and about five inches high. The flowers are one or two together at the tops of the stalks; they are of a yellow colour, appear in April and May, and the seeds ripen in July. The three last sorts are propagated by parting the roots, or sowing the seeds like the other kinds.

Titles. 1. The Narrow-leaved *Anemone* is entitled, *Anemone foliis radicalibus ternato decompositis, involucro folioso*. In the *Hortus Cliffortianus* it is called, *Pulsatilla foliis decompositis ternatis*. Cammeranus calls it simply, *Anemone*. It is a native of the East.

2. The Broad-leaved *Anemone* is, *Anemone foliis digitatis*. In the *Hortus Cliffortianus* it is called, *Pulsatilla foliis digitatis*. Dodonæus calls it simply, *Anemone*. It grows common in many parts of the East.

3. English Wood *Anemone* is, *Anemone seminibus acutis, foliolis incisis, caule unifloro*. Caspar Bauhine calls it, *Anemone nemorosa, flore majore*. Clusius, *Ranunculus sylvarum*, Gerard, *Anemone nemorum album*, and Parkinson, *Ranunculus nemorosus albus simplex*. It is common in most of our woods.

4. Blue Wood *Anemone* is entitled, *Anemone seminibus acutis, foliolis incisis, petalis lanceolatis numerosis*. This is the *Anemone, geranii Robertiani folio, cærulea*, of C. Bauhine. Parkinson calls it, *Ranunculus nemorosus, flore purpureo cæruleo*. It grows naturally in some of our woods, also on the Appennines and other mountainous parts of Europe.

5. German Wood *Anemone* is, *Anemone pedunculo nudo, seminibus subrotundis hirsutis*. In the *Hortus Cliffort.* it is, *Anemone seminibus setis plumosis terminatis*. This is the *Anemone sylvestris* of Clusius. It is a native of Germany.

6. Virginian Wood *Anemone* is, *Anemone pedunculis alternis longissimis, fructibus cylindricis seminibus hirsutis muticis*. Herman calls it, *Anemone Virginiana tertiæ similis, flore parvo*. Gronovius calls it, *Anemone caule ramoso, petalis lanceolatis*. It is a native of Virginia.

7. Large-flowering Pasque Flower is entitled, *Anemone pedunculo involucrato, petalis rectis, foliis bipinnatis*. In the *Hortus Cliffort.* and many botanic books of note, it stands with the title of, *Pulsatilla foliis decompositis pinnatis, flore nutante, limbo erecto*.

Caspar Bauhine calls it, *Pulsatilla folio crassiore & majore flore*. Cammerarius terms it simply, *Pulsatilla*. It grows common in many of the northern parts of Europe.

8. Small Pasque Flower is named, *Anemone pedunculo involucrato, petalis apice reflexis, foliis ... In the Hortus Cliffortianus it is termed, ... foliis ... Clusius calls it, ... flore*. It grows common in some parts of Germany, and is found on the plains of Sweden.

9. Siberian Pasque Flower is, *Anemone pedunculo involucrato, foliis ... Amman calls it, Pulsatilla, Anemone ... folio ... flore majore ...* It is a native of Siberia, the ... &c.

10. Smallage leaved Pasque Flower is, *Anemone pedunculo involucrato, foliis ... flore ...* Caspar Bauhine and others call it, *Pulsatilla, ... folio, ... flore majore*. It grows naturally on the Alps, and in the most barren woods and mountains of Switzerland.

11. *Hepatica* is now entitled, *Anemone foliis ... integerrimis*. In the *Hortus Cliffortianus*, and other of the early works of Linnæus, it has as a distinct genus, with the title simply, *Hepatica*; thus also it stands in the works of Gronovius and others. Caspar Bauhine calls it *Trifolium hepaticum flore simplici & pleno*. It grows naturally by the sides of woods, in forests, &c. in Germany and many parts of Europe.

12. Yellow Anemone is, *Anemone foliis ... lobatis ... involucro ... Hortus Cliffortianus* it is termed, *Pulsatilla ... petalatis*. Caspar Bauhine calls it, *Anemone ... folio, lutea, ... Clusius* names it, *Anemone ... latifolia I*. It grows naturally in Lusatia.

13. Alpine Anemone is, *Anemone foliis caulinis ... composita ... foliis, ... caulinis ... Haller calls it, ... caulibus ... foliis omnibus duplicato ... remotis*, Clusius, *Anemone ...* Caspar Bauhine, *Anemone Alpina alba major*, also, *Anemone Alpina alba minor*, also, *Pulsatilla flore albo*. It grows naturally on the Helvetian and Styrian Mountains.

14. Canada Anemone is, *Anemone caule ... foliis ... simplici ... foliis ...*. It grows naturally in Canada and Siberia.

15. Trifoliate Anemone is, *Anemone foliis ternatis ovatis ... caule unifloro*. John Bauhine calls it, *Anemone ... flore albo*, and Dodonæus, *Anemone trifolia*. It is a native of Gaul.

16. Five leaved Anemone is, *Anemone foliis quinis ... caule unifloro*. Plukenet calls it, *Ranunculus nemorosus, ... foliis ...*. It grows naturally in Virginia and Canada.

17. Bulbed *Ranunculus* is, *Anemone seminibus acutis, foliolis ... petalis ... caule ... flore*. Caspar Bauhine calls it, *Ranunculus nemorosus ...*, and John Bauhine *Ranunculus ... lutes ...*. It grows naturally in forests, pastures, and meadows in most of the northern countries of Europe.

*Anemone* is of the class and order *Polyandria Polygynia*, and the characters are, — Class and order in the Linnæan system. The characters

1. CALYX. There is none.

2. COROLLA consists of two or three orders of oblongish petals, there in each order, disposed in a series one over the other.

3. STAMINA are numerous capillary filaments, of about half the length of the corolla, having erect didymous antheræ.

4. PISTILLUM consists of numerous germina, collected into a head, having acuminated styles and obtuse stigmas.

5. PERICARPIUM. There is none. The receptacle is globose or oblong, and persistent.

6. SEMINA. The seeds are numerous, and acuminated, retaining the styles.

# CHAP. XXXV.

## *ANGELICA.*

Introductory observations. THE glory of this genus is the Common *Angelica* of our gardens, whose uses in the shops are well known, and whose admirable properties to form a sweetmeat are no less esteemed. This shall be reserved for the kitchen-garden, as it requires a particular treatment for those purposes. The species of inferior virtue, and of very little beauty, are,

Species.

1. Wild English *Angelica*.
2. Purple Canada *Angelica*.
3. Shining Canada *Angelica*.

Description of the Wild English. 1. Wild English *Angelica* grows common in our woods, watery grounds, and moist meadows. At a distance it has some resemblance to the Garden *Angelica*, but is not possessed of near so strong an odour. The leaves are large and pinnated, the folioles are of an oval lanceolated figure, and their edges are serrated, the stalk is strong and upright. From the wings of the leaves come out the general flower stalks; these are long and branching, and support the flower at the top, in a large compound umbel. The flowers are whitish, small, and numerous, each has its separate footstalk, they will be in blow in July, and produce good seeds in September.

Purple Canada. 2. Purple Canada *Angelica* will grow to about four feet high. The leaves are large, and of a blackish-green, they are pinnated, and the extreme pair of lobes are joined. The stalks are very robust, and many of them grow from a strong root. The ends are terminated by the flowers in umbels. Each individual flower is small, and of very little beauty; they will be in blow in June and July, and ripen their seeds in September.

and Shining Canada Angelica. 3. Shining Canada *Angelica* is also a large-growing plant. The leaves are finely pinnated, and of a polished green. The folioles are of an oval figure ... of an equal size,

size, and their edges are deeply serrated. A strong root will send forth many stalks, which will grow to upwards of a yard in height. They are robust and smooth, and produce their flowers in large compound umbels, in June and July, which will be succeeded by good seeds in September.

Method of propagating these sorts. To propagate these plants, watch for the first ripe seeds succeeding the first-blown flowers, and as soon as they are ripe, which will often be in August, lay them for a few days in an airy place to dry, then sow them in a border of any common garden mould. They will readily come up, and in the spring they must be transplanted to the places where they are designed to flower. This should always be the moistest part of the garden, where they will thrive amazingly. The English *Angelica* should be set at about two feet distance, whilst the Canada sorts should be allowed a yard. You must be careful to preserve seeds for a succession, for they are plants of no very long duration, three or four years being the usual period to their existence, if they are permitted to flower freely; but by cutting the stalks down as they shoot in May, fresh heads will be formed from the roots, and the plants continued in that manner for several years.

Titles. 1. The Wild English *Angelica* is titled, *Angelica foliis æqualibus ovato-lanceolatis serratis*. Caspar Bauhine calls it *Angelica sylvestris major*. Dodonæus and others, *Angelica sylvestris*. It grows naturally in woods and moist places in England, and several of the colder parts of Europe.

2. Purple Canada *Angelica* is titled, *Angelica extimo foliorum pari coadunato, foliolo terminali petiolato*. Cornutus calls it, *Angelica Canadensis atropurpurea*. It grows naturally in Canada.

3. Shining Canada *Angelica* is termed, *Angelica foliolis æqualibus ovatis inciso-serratis*. Cornutus calls it, *Angelica lucida Canadensis*. It grows naturally in Canada.

Class and order in the Linnæan system. *Angelica* is of the class and order *Pentandria Digynia*; and the characters are,

1. CALYX. The general umbel is roundish, and contains many small ones; the partial umbel, when in flower, is perfectly round.

The general involucrum is composed of three or five leaves; the partial is small, and consists of eight leaves.

The perianthium is very small, and indented in five parts.

2. COROLLA. The general corolla is uniform. The partial is composed of five spear-shaped, plane, incurved, caducous petals.

3. STAMINA consist of five simple filaments, longer than the corolla, with simple antheræ.

4. PISTILLUM consists of a germen placed below the flower, and two reflexed styles, with obtuse stigmas.

5. PERICARPIUM. There is none. The fruit is roundish, angular, solid, and divisible into two parts.

6. SEMINA. The seeds are two, oval, surrounded with a border, plane on one side, convex on the other, and have three lines running lengthways.

## CHAP. XXXVI.

## *ANTHEMIS*, CHAMOMILE.

Introductory remarks. WERE the eye to be continually feasted with the gaudy flowers in their superb dresses, their value would gradually diminish, and so dazzling a view would soon pall the imagination. Indulgent Nature has guarded against this evil, and with the most splendid has mixed those of humbler diet. (though of equally wonderful workmanship) to enhance the charms of one another, form a proper mixture, and raise our astonishment and gratitude. Of the humbler sort is the family of the Chamomile, a very numerous offspring, inferior in beauty of flowers, but of great singularity respecting their leaves, and admirable for the virtues and useful properties of some of them. They form a moderately-large list of annuals and perennials, and those for this place are,

Species. 

1. Common Chamomile.
2. Sea Chamomile.
3. Hoary Sea Chamomile.
4. Alpine Chamomile.
5. Italian Chamomile.
6. Portugal Chamomile.
7. Pellitory of Spain.
8. Siberian Chamomile.
9. German Ox-Eye.

These are all distinct perennial species of *Anthemis*, and include several varieties.

Common Chamomile. 1. Common Chamomile is known every where. The leaves are admirably compounded, and are composed in such a manner, and are of so fine a green colour, that in the spring of the year they have a refreshing look. It is chiefly cultivated for its medicinal properties; but there are two varieties of it worth propagating for the sake of their flowers alone. One is the Common Double Chamomile, which is of great beauty, and is the Chamomile flower in its full state. The other variety is the Large Double Chamomile, which is a perfectly full flower, is as large as a *Chrysanthemum*, and of a pure white.

Culture. This species is propagated by parting of the roots, or planting the slips in any of the summer months. These will readily grow, and the operation must be renewed every two years, otherwise the flowers will shew a tendency to degenerate, and will soon become single. A sufficient number of slips, therefore, should be planted for the purpose of the flowers, and the rest should be thrown away; for it is observable that these flowers are not so powerful in medicine as the Single ones, though so often used; so that for medicinal purposes the Single more especially should be planted.

Sea Chamomile. 2. Sea-Chamomile. This grows naturally on the sea coasts of Italy and France. The stalks are branching, and of a purplish colour. The leaves are pinnated, finely divided, dotted, and of a fleshy substance. The flowers are white, appear in July, and continue the succession all summer.

Hoary Sea, 3. Hoary Sea Chamomile. The stalk of this species is branching, and garnished with plane, obtuse, winged leaves, which are of a thickish consistence, and hoary, like wormwood. The flowers are white, grow on hairy footstalks, and continue to blow from Midsummer till October.

Alpine, 4. Alpine Chamomile. The leaves of this sort are pinnated and composed of several narrow entire segments. The stalk is hairy, and supports a single flower. The petals are of an oval figure, white, and expand themselves very agreeably. They will be in blow in July and August, and afford good seeds in the autumn.

Italian, 5. Italian Chamomile is a small bushy species. The leaves are plane, winged, and much divided. The segments are narrow, trifid, and acute, and the whole is very beautiful. The flowers are large, and of a white colour; each is supported by a very long footstalk. They will be in blow in July and August, and afford good seeds in the autumn.

and Portugal Chamomile, 6. Portugal Chamomile. The leaves of this species are single, and of an oval lanceolated figure, their edges are crenated, a little hairy, obtuse, and they are placed alternately on the branches. The stalk is erect, and is terminated by the flowers; these are yellow, will be in blow in July and August, and ripen their seeds in September.

Pellitory of Spain, 7. Pellitory of Spain. This species has a long tap root, like a carrot, and from this proceed several branches of about a foot in length. The leaves are beautifully divided into numerous small narrow parts, and they are placed irregularly on the branches. From the sides of the main stalk a few smaller are produced, and each of them is terminated by a single large, beautiful flower. The petals are large, oblong, within of a pure white, and purple on their outside. They will be in blow in June and July, but are seldom succeeded by good seeds, unless the season proves warm and dry; when this happens, they will be ripe in August.

Siberian Chamomile, 8. Siberian Chamomile. This arises with a branching stalk to the height of about two feet. The leaves are hoary, beautifully divided in the manner of milfoil, but larger. The flowers are produced singly on long footstalks; they are white, and much resemble those of the common Ox-Eye Daisy; will be in blow in June, and continue flowering all summer and autumn.

and German Ox Eye described. 9. German Ox Eye. This has bipinnated leaves, which are serrated and downy on their under side. The stalks will grow to be a yard or more in height, and divide into several branches, each of which is terminated by a corymbus of flowers. In general they are white, though there is a sort with yellow, and another with mixed coloured flowers; these will be in blow in June, and often continue flowering until the frosts stop them.

Method of propagating these sorts by cuttings, All these sorts are easily propagated by slips, which being planted in a shady border, in any of the summer months, will grow and become good plants by the autumn, when they may be removed to the places designed for them.

and by seeds. They are also easily raised by seeds. Sow these in the spring, and cover them with a quarter of an inch of fine mould; and when the plants are about three or four inches high, remove them, on a moist day, or for want of that in an evening, with a ball of earth to each root, to the places where they are designed to remain; though if the seeds are sown in the places where the plants are designed to flower, and, where they come up too close, thinned to proper distances, the plants, by being unremoved, will flower stronger.

1. The Common Chamomile is titled, *Anthemis foliis pinnato-compositis linearibus acutis subvillosis*. Van Royen calls it, *Anthemis foliis pinnato decompositis laciniis setaceis*; Caspar Bauhine, *Chamaemelum nobile, sive Leucanthemum odoratius*; Dodonaeus, *Chamaemelum odoratum*; Cammerarius, *Chamaemelum Romanum, flore multiplici*; and Tournefort, *Chamaemelum odoratum vernum, folio crassiore, flore magno*. It grows naturally in meadows and pasture grounds in most parts of Europe. Titles.

2. Sea Chamomile is titled, *Anthemis foliis pinnatis dentatis carnosis nudis punctatis, caule prostrato, calycibus subtomentosis*. Micheli calls it, *Anthemis maritima annua odorata praecox, flore albo, calyce purpurascente*; Caspar Bauhine, *Matricaria maritima*; and John Bauhine, *Chamaemelum maritimum*. It grows naturally at Montpelier and in Italy.

3. Hoary Sea-Chamomile is titled, *Anthemis foliis pinnatifidis obtusis planis, pedunculis hirsutis foliosis, calycibus tomentosis*. Vaillant calls it, *Chamaemelum, coronopi folio, tomentosum*; and Boerhaave, *Chamaemelum maritimum incanum, folio absinthii crasso*. It grows naturally on the sea-coasts of Greece.

4. Alpine Chamomile is titled, *Anthemis foliis dentato pinnatis linearibus integerrimis, caule villoso uniflore, petalis spathulatis*. Tilli calls it, *Chamaemelum Alpinum saxatile perenne, flore albo singulari, caule ligneo*. It grows naturally on Mount Baldus.

5. Italian Chamomile is, *Anthemis foliis pinnato multifidis planis, laciniis linearibus acutis trifidis, pedunculo longissimo*. John Bauhine calls it, *Absinthium montanum, chamaemeli flore magno*; Vaillant, *Chamaemelum Alpinum, abrotani folio*; Boccone, *Bellis montana, chrysanthemi Cretici folio*; and Ray, *Bellis pumila monanthos, foliis nasturtii pratensis*. It grows naturally in Italy and Switzerland.

6. Portugal Chamomile is titled, *Anthemis foliis simplicibus ovato-lanceolatis repando crenatis*. Tournefort calls it, *Chrysanthemum Lusitanicum, agerati folio*; and John Bauhine, *Chrysanthemum parvum, sive bellis lutea parva latifolia*. It grows naturally in Portugal and Spain.

7. Pellitory of Spain is, *Anthemis caulibus simplicibus unifloris decumbentibus, foliis pinnato-multifidis*. Shaw calls it, *Chamaemelum speciosum flore, radice longa fervida*; and Caspar Bauhine, *Pyrethrum flore bellidis*. It grows naturally in Arabia, Syria, Crete, Apulia, Thuringia, Bohemia, &c.

8. Siberian Chamomile is titled, *Anthemis foliis bipinnatis lacinulis linearibus integris, pedunculis nudis longissimis*. Miller calls it, *Achillea foliis pinnatis foliolis linearibus lanceolatis versus summitatem acutis*; Boerhaave, *Leucanthemum folio absinthii*; *Alpinum crassum*; and Gmelin, *Pyrethrum foliis duplicato-pinnatis pinnulis incisis, pedunculis unifloris, caule procumbente*. It grows naturally in Siberia.

9. German Ox Eye is, *Anthemis foliis bipinnatis serratis subtus tomentosis, caule corymboso*. Caspar Bauhine calls it *Buphthalmum tanaceti minoris foliis*; Lobelius, *Chrysanthemum foliis tanaceti*; and Plukenet, *Bellis Alpina, pumila, folio elatior*. It grows naturally in Germany and Sweden.

*Anthemis* is of the class and order *Syngenesia Polygamia Superflua*; and the characters are, Class and order in the Linnaean system. The characters.

1. CALYX is hemispherical, and composed of numerous narrow scales that are nearly equal.

2. Co-

2 COROLLA The compound flower is radiated. The hermaphrodite flowers are tubulous and numerous in the disk, the female flowers occupy the radius. The proper hermaphrodite flower is infundibuliforme, erect, and indented in five parts at the top. The female flowers are each spear-shaped, ligulated, and sometimes indented in three parts.

3 STAMINA of the hermaphrodite flowers are five very short capillary filaments, with a tubulous cylindric anthera.

4 PISTILLUM of the hermaphrodite flowers consists of an oblong germen, a filiforme style the length of the stamina, and two revolute stigmas.

5 PERICARPIUM. There is none.

6 SEMINA. The seeds of the hermaphrodite and female flowers are single and oblong.

The receptacle is paleaceous and conical.

## CHAP. XXXVII.

## *ANTHERICUM*, SPIDERWORT.

THE species of this genus proper for our borders are, *Species*

1 Bulbine *Anthericum*
2 Oriental *Anthericum*
3 Revolute-flowered *Anthericum*
4 Ramose stalked Plain flowered *Anthericum*
5 Single stalked Plain flowered *Anthericum*
6 *Liliastrum Anthericum*, or St Bruno's Lily
7 Scotch Asphodel
8 Marsh Alpine Asphodel

*Bulbine,* 1 Bulbine *Anthericum*. This species was formerly arranged under the article *Bulbocodium*, and under that head it stands in Hudson's *Flora Anglicana*, and is usually called Mountain Saffron, or Alpine *Bulbocodium*. This plant has very much the appearance of a Crocus. The root is a small round bulb, covered with a rough hairy bark, from this issues a flower like the Crocus, in an erect posture. It has a foot-stalk, however, about three inches long, and the leaves, which are short and narrow, are placed alternately on it. The flowers are white in the inside of the petals, but without they are of a very bad red colour; they will be in blow in March and April, and the seeds will be ripe about six weeks after.

*Oriental,* 2 Oriental *Anthericum*. The root of this species is a small bulb, from which issue a few narrow, smooth leaves, nearly the length of the stalk. This is single, and the top of it is ornamented with a corymbus of flowers, their number is about five. The intermediate footstalk supports a single flower, but the lateral footstalks have each two flowers, their colour is white. The stamina are shorter than the corolla, and the style than the stamina.

*Revolute flowered,* 3 Revolute-flowered *Anthericum*. This will grow to be about two feet high. The leaves are flat, rough, and compressed, and the stalk is very branching. The flowers are produced in loose spikes at the ends of the branches, they are white, and the petals are turned backward to the footstalk. They will be in blow in June and July, and their seeds ripen in September.

*Ramose,* 4 Ramose-stalked plain flowering *Anthericum*. The leaves of this species are plain. The stalk is branching, and will grow to be two feet high. The flowers are produced from the ends of the branches in loose spikes, they are white, and their petals do not turn backward as do those of the preceding sort. They will be in blow in July, and their seeds ripen in September.

*and Single stalked Plain flowering,* 5 Single-stalked plain flowering *Anthericum*. This species hath plain leaves, and an undivided stalk, which will grow to about a foot and a half high. The top of it supports a loose spike of white flowers, which are small, and the petals are not reflexed; they will be in blow in July, and their seeds ripen in September.

*and Liliastrum Anthericum* 6 *Liliastrum Anthericum*, or St Bruno's Lily. The leaves of this species are plain, upright, and firm. The stalk is single, and will grow to a foot or more in height; the top of it is ornamented with the flowers, hanging on one side of it. These are white, bell-shaped, and possessed of an agreeable odour. They will be in blow in June, at which time they should be shaded, or they will continue but about three or four days in beauty.

*Scotch* 7 Scotch Asphodel. This is also called the Lancashire Asphodel, because growing naturally in that county. Its situation is usually upon boggy ground, so that it is of very little use in gardening, unless such a place should happen in some part or other of our works. The leaves are narrow, and shaped like a sword. The stalk will grow to about six inches high, and is garnished with a few leaves. The flowers ornament the top of it in a loose spike; their colour is yellow, and their stamina are hairy.

*and Marsh Alpine Asphodel, described* 8 Marsh Alpine Asphodel. This is also a boggy plant. The leaves are ensiforme and narrow. The stalk rises about six inches high, and the top of it is garnished with the flowers. These are yellow, and have this singularity, the perianthium is trilobate, the filaments are smooth, and the pistil is trigynous.

*Methods of propagating the different sorts.* The two first sorts are propagated by parting of the roots. This should be done in the summer, soon after the leaves are decayed. The roots should remain unremoved for at least four years, or the off-sets will be very few; so that as they increase but slowly that way, the best method will be to sow the seeds.

This should be done in the autumn, on a border of fine light mould, in a shady well-sheltered place. They should be sown thinly on this bed, and about three quarters of an inch of fine fresh mould sifted over them. In the spring the plants will come up, and their growth must be forwarded by watering in dry weather, and weeding as there shall be occasion. When the leaves begin to decay, watering must be left off, and in the autumn the surface of the earth must be stirred, and about half an inch of fresh mould sifted over them. The spring after the plants will come up strong, and when their leaves are decayed, take them up, and plant them where they

they are intended to flower, which they will do in a spring or two after.

The third, fourth, and fifth sorts are also best propagated by sowing the seeds in the autumn. The situation should be warm, and the bed light and sandy. In the spring the plants will come up; and when the leaves decay, they must be taken up, and planted in a bed prepared for that purpose, consisting of light sandy mould, in a warm well-sheltered place. In this bed they may stand one year, and may then be removed to the places they are designed for, which ought to be naturally warm and well-sheltered, otherwise they are subject to be killed by severe frosts.

St Bruno's Lily is to be raised by seeds this way, but it may be encreased fast enough by parting of the roots. This work should be done in the autumn; and in order to have plenty of off-sets, let the plants remain undisturbed for three or four years. The smaller off-sets should be set in a bed in the nursery ground, for a year, to gain strength, whilst the stronger should be planted where they are designed to flower, which will be the summer following.

There are two varieties of this species, called the *Major* and the *Minor*, and by parting of the roots the difference may be kept up. They should have a sandy soil and an open exposure, and the flowers should be shaded when in blow to continue them longer in beauty.

The seventh and eighth sorts grow naturally upon bogs in many of the northern parts of the world, and are with difficulty preserved in gardens. If, therefore, a boggy or marshy piece of ground should happen in the circle of your works, early in the winter trench the ground, throw the turf in ridges, and let it be wholly exposed to frost and weather. In the spring turn it over, and continue this, now and then, all summer. In the autumn throw it into its natural level, and sow the seeds thinly over it, covering them down with about three quarters of an inch of the fine mould. They will pretty readily come up and flower, and will be useful in ornamenting such places as are hardly fit for any thing else.

Titles. 1. *Bulbocodium Anthericum*, or Mountain Saffron, is titled, *Anthericum foliis planiusculis, scapo unifloro*. In the former edition of the *Species Plantarum* it is titled, *Bulbocodium foliis subulato-linearibus*. Ray calls it, *Bulbocodium Alpinum juncifolium, flore unico intus albo extus squalide rubente*. C. Bauhine and others term it, *Pseudo-Narcissus gramineo folio*. It grows naturally upon Snowdon-Hill in Wales, and in several of the northern parts of Europe.

2. Oriental *Anthericum* is, *Anthericum foliis planis, scapo simplici, floribus corymbosis*. Tournefort calls it, *Bulbocodium Græcum, myosotidis flore*. It is a native of the East.

3. Revolute-flowered *Anthericum* is, *Anthericum foliis planis, scapo ramoso, corollis revolutis*. Tournefort names it, *Asphodelus foliis compressis asperis, caule patulo*. It is not certainly known where this plant grows in a state of Nature.

4. Ramose-stalked Plain-flowered *Anthericum* is, *Anthericum foliis planis, scapo ramoso, corollis planis, pistillo recto*. In the *Flora Suecica* it is termed, *Anthericum foliis planis, corollis planis deciduis*. Guettard calls it, *Anthericum caulibus ramosis, foliis planis*. Caspar Bauhine, *Phalangium, parvo flore, ramosum*; and Cammerarius, *Phalangium majus*. It grows common in most of the southern parts of Europe.

5. Plain flowered *Anthericum*, with a single or unbranching stalk, is named, *Anthericum foliis planis, scapo simplicissimo, corollis planis, pistillo declinato*. Guettard terms it, *Anthericum caulibus non ramosis, foliis planis*. Caspar Bauhine, *Phalangium, parvo flore, non ramosum*; and Lobel, *Phalangium non ramosum*. It grows naturally in Switzerland, France, and Germany.

6. St Bruno's Lily is, *Anthericum foliis planis, scapo simplicissimo, corollis campanulatis, staminibus declinatis*. In the former edition of the *Species Plantarum* it is termed, *Hemerocallis scapo simplici, corollis hexapetalis campanulatis*. Caspar Bauhine calls it, *Phalangium magno flore*; Clusius, *Phalangium Allobrogicum majus*; and Dalechamp simply, *Phalangium*. It grows common on the Savoy and Helvetian Mountains.

7. Scotch Asphodel is, *Anthericum foliis ensiformibus, filamentis lanatis*. In the *Flora Lapponica* it is termed, *Anthericum scapo folioso laxe spicato, filamentis villosis*. Caspar Bauhine calls it, *Pseudo-asphodelus palustris Anglicus*; and Dodonæus, *Asphodelus luteus palustris*. It grows naturally on boggy and marshy ground in Lancashire, Scotland, and most of the northern parts of Europe.

8. Marsh Alpine Asphodel is, *Anthericum foliis ensiformibus, perianthiis trilobis, filamentis glabris, pistillis trigynis*. In the *Hortus Cliffortianus* it is termed, *Anthericum filamentis lævibus, perianthio trifido*; and in the *Flora Lapponica*, *Anthericum scapo nudo capitato, filamentis glabris*. Caspar Bauhine calls it, *Pseudo asphodelus Alpinus*. It grows common on the mountains of Switzerland, Lapland, and Siberia.

*Anthericum* is of the class and order *Hexandria Monogynia*; and the characters are, Class and order in the Linnæan system.

1. CALYX. There is none. The character.
2. COROLLA consists of six oblong, obtuse, patent petals.
3. STAMINA are six erect subulated filaments, with small, incumbent, four-furrowed antheræ.
4. PISTILLUM consists of a blunt three-cornered germen, a simple style the length of the stamina, and an obtuse three-cornered stigma.
5. PERICARPIUM is an oval, smooth, trisulcated capsule of three cells.
6. SEMINA. The seeds are angular and numerous.

CHAP

# CHAP. XXXVIII.

## *ANTHOCEROS.*

FOR the satisfaction of the Botanist it may not be improper to mention the species of this genus, though they are of no use to the Gardener. Their number is three, and they are commonly named,

Species.
1. Spotted *Anthoceros*
2. Smooth *Anthoceros*
3. Multifid *Anthoceros*

Description of the Spotted,
1. Spotted *Anthoceros*. The leaves, each of which constitutes a distinct plant, are small, oblong, undivided, hollowed on the edges, thin, shining, and form a circular tuft about the same place. The fructifications arise from the surface of the leaves, surrounded by oblong, cylindrical, monophyllous sheaths. These are first slender and elegant, but thicken by degrees, and splitting longitudinally discover the antheræ loaden with yellow farina. The female parts appear in form of spots, or little warts, on the surface of the leaves of the same plant, or on distinct plants, which when mature open in six parts, discover their sex, and finally ripe seeds. This species flowers in April, and the seeds ripen in June.

Smooth,
2. Smooth *Anthoceros*. The leaves are small, oblong, thin, transparent, sinuated, of a bright green colour, and arise without order about the spot. The fructifications arise from several parts of the leaves, having slender monophyllous cups, which are a little waved on their edges. From these arise extremely long awl-shaped antheræ, which, when ripe, open with two valves, and discover a greenish farina. This flowers in May and June.

and Multifid Anthoceros.
3. Multifid *Anthoceros*. The leaves of this species are narrow, pinnatifid, glossy, of a thin consistence, and a deep-green colour. The fructifications arise from the surface of the leaves, in monophyllous cups. They have long antheræ, and the farina is of a yellowish colour. They shew themselves in April and May, and the seeds ripen in June and July.

Culture.
These are not cultivated plants, nevertheless, if a person is desirous of having them near at hand for observation, he should dig up a large quantity of mould containing the roots, and whatever grows with them. This he should preserve as whole and undivided as may be, and should lay it in a properly excavated place, in a most shady part of the garden, and being thus removed, the plants will grow, and present their fine, transparent, elegant, smooth leaves, attended by their fructifications, every spring. If they happen to like their situation, they will spread amazingly.

Titles.
1. The first species is titled, *Anthoceros frondibus indivisis sinuatis punctatis*. Dillenius calls it *Anthoceros foliis minoribus magis laciniatis*, Micheli, *Anthoceros minor foliis magis carinatis atque eleganter crenatis, subtus incurvatis*, and Ray, *Lichenastrum gramineo pediculo, & capitulo, oblongo, bifurco*. It grows common in moist shady places in England and Italy.

2. The second species is, *Anthoceros frondibus indivisis sinuatis lævibus*. In the *Hortus Cliffortianus* it is termed, *Anthoceros*. Dillenius calls it, *Anthoceros foliis majoribus minus laciniatis*, Micheli, *Anthoceros major*; and Buxbaum, *Lichen hepaticus, pediculis gramineis*. It grows naturally in England, and many parts of Europe and America.

3. The third species is, *Anthoceros frondibus bipinnatifidis linearibus*. Dillenius terms it, *Anthoceros folio tenuissimo multifido*. It is a native of Germany.

Class and order in the Linnæan system. The characters.
*Anthoceros* is of the class and order *Cryptogamia Algæ*, and the known characters are,

I. The Male Flower is sessile.

1. CALYX is monophyllous, subcylindrical, truncated, and entire.
2. COROLLA. There is none.
3. STAMINA. There is never a filament: but there is one very long awl-shaped anthera, composed of two valves. The farina is affixed to a free capillary receptacle.

II. The Female Flower is sessile in the same or separate plant.

1. CALYX is formed of one leaf, divided into six spreading parts.
2. SEMINA are usually three, naked, roundish, and lodged in the bottom of the calyx.

# CHAP. XXXIX.

## *ANTHOXANTHUM.*

This plant described.
OF this genus is that well known useful grass of our meadows and pastures, and too often in our gardens, called Vernal or Spring Grass. The root is composed of a number of white fibres. The leaves are about half a foot long, a quarter of an inch broad, and of a good green colour. The stalks are slender, smooth, jointed, and eight or ten inches high. The flowers come out from the tops of the stalks, in oval, oblong, loose spikes; they are usually of a yellowish green colour, and appear early in May.

The Gardener must be cautious to hoe up this grass as often as the plants appear, while they

they are young, for they will soon get large flowers, and shed their seeds, and if not early taken off, will so effectually stock the ground with good seeds as to be some years before it is perfectly cleared of them.

The husbandman, also, should be cautious in gathering the seeds of the true kind of this grass for his farm, for it is an admirable grass for cattle of all sorts, comes early in the spring, and is one of the most useful early grasses we have.

Of raising these plants. The seeds are usually sown in the spring, with barley or oats; but it is the best way to sow them alone, and if the ground is made fine by good ploughing, and the seeds be slightly harrowed in with a light harrow, having nothing to incommode their growth, they will readily come up, and soon cover the face of the earth. The seeds may be sown in the autumn, or any time in the summer, as soon as they can be procured, and the ground got in readiness to receive them.

Titles. This Grass is titled, *Anthoxanthum spica ovata oblonga, flosculis subpedunculatis arista longioribus*. In the *Hortus Cliffortianus* it is termed, *Anthoxanthum flosculis diandris*, and in the *Flora Suecia*, *Anthoxanthum*. Caspar Bauhine calls it, *Gramen pratense, spica flavescente*, John Bauhine, *Gramen anthoxanthon spicatum*, Morison, *Gramen alopecurum vernum pratense, spica flavescente*, and Ray, *Gramen vernum spica brevi laxa*. It grows naturally in all our meadows and pastures, and in the like situations all over Europe.

Class and order in the Linnæan system. *Anthoxanthum* is of the class and order *Diandria Digynia*, and the characters are,

The characters. 1. Calyx is a glume composed of two valves, containing one flower. The valves are oval, acuminated, concave, and the inner one is the largest.

2. Corolla is a glume of two valves of equal length with the larger calycinal valves, and each valve emits a small arista from the lower part of its back. There is a slender cylindrical nectarium, formed of two oval leaves, surrounding one another.

3. Stamina are two long capillary filaments, with long bifurcated antheræ.

4. Pistillum consists of an oblong germen and two filiforme styles, with simple stigmas.

5. Pericarpium. There is no other pericarpium than the glume of the corolla, which adheres to the seed.

6. Semen. The seed is single, taper, and pointed at each end.

# CHAP. XL.

## *ANTHYLLIS*, KIDNEY-VETCH, or LADIES FINGER.

THIS genus affords us two species for this place.

Species. 1. Mountain *Anthyllis*, or Purple Milk Vetch.
2. Northern *Anthyllis*, or Ladies Finger.

Mountain. 1. Purple Milk Vetch is a very pretty flower in our gardens. The branches are small, weak, and trailing, and they are garnished with pinnated leaves, which are composed of an equal number of lobes, are hairy, and of a whitish green colour. The flowers terminate the branches in globular heads; they are of a purple colour, very showy and beautiful, will be in blow the latter end of May and June, and afford plenty of seeds in the autumn.

and Northern Anthyllis described. 2. Northern *Anthyllis*, or Ladies Finger. Of this there are two remarkable varieties, called the Yellow and the Scarlet-flowering Woundwort. The stalks of these are small and slender. The leaves are pinnated, and composed of an unequal number of narrow spear-shaped lobes, growing by pairs, and terminated by an odd one, which is longer than the others. The flowers terminate the branches. In the scarlet variety they are generally collected into double heads, in the yellow sort they are for the most part single. They will be in blow in June and July, and produce plenty of good seeds in the autumn.

Method of propagating these sorts by seeds, The best way of propagating these sorts is by sowing the seeds in the autumn, soon after they are ripe. In the spring they will come up, when they must be kept clean from weeds, thinned where they come up too close, watered in dry weather; and in the autumn transplanted to the places where they are designed to flower, which they will do the summer following.

and by dividing the roots. They may also be propagated by parting of the roots, but these plants never look so well or flower so strong as those raised from seeds.

Titles. 1. Mountain *Anthyllis* is titled, *Anthyllis herbacea, foliis pinnatis æqualibus, capitulo terminali secundo, floribus obliquatis*. Haller names it, *Vulneraria foliis pinnatis æqualibus, sub umbellâ palmatis*. Barrelier, *Astragalus incanus tomentosus, pallido globoso flore, Italicus*. Caspar Bauhine, *Astragalus villosus, flore globoso*, and Dalechamp, *Astragalus purpureus*. It grows common on the mountains in the south of France, Italy, and Austria.

2. Northern *Anthyllis* is, *Anthyllis herbacea, foliis pinnatis inæqualibus, capitulo duplicato*. In the *Hortus Cliffortianus* it is termed, *Anthyllis foliis pinnatis, foliolis plurimis, terminali majore*. Caspar Bauhine calls it, *Loto affinis vulneraria pratensis*, Tabernæmontanus, *Lagopodium flore luteo*, and Dillenius, *Vulneraria rupina, flore coccineo*. It grows naturally in several of our dry pastures, and in such places in most of the northern parts of Europe.

Class and order in the Linnæan system. *Anthyllis* is of the class and order *Diadelphia Decandria*, and the characters are,

The characters. 1. Calyx is an oval, oblong, inflated, hairy, permanent monophyllous perianthium, divided at the top into five unequal parts.

2. Corolla is papilionaceous. The vexillum is long, and reflexed on both sides. The alæ are oblong, and shorter than the vexillum. The carina is like the alæ, is long, and compressed.

3. Stamina are ten filaments, which rise together, with simple antheræ.

4. Pistillum consists of an oblong germen, a simple style, and an obtuse stigma.

5. Pericarpium is a small roundish pod, of two valves, inclosed by the calyx.

6. Semina are one or two only.

CHAP.

# CHAP. XLI.

## *ANTIRRHINUM*, SNAP-DRAGON, or CALVES-SNOUT.

Introductory Remarks. BESIDES the usual plants arranged under this genus, there are now added to it the *Asarina*, or Bastard Asarum, the *Linaria*, or Toad-flax, the *Elatine*, or Fluellin, and some others. So that it is now very comprehensive, and contains a large number of species, many of which are very ornamental flowers for our gardens, and figure in our perennial and annual borders. The annuals bear the greatest proportion in the list, and the perennials are,

Species.
1 Snap-dragon.
2 Common Toad-flax.
3 Sweet-scented Toad-flax.
4 Toad-flax of Dalmatia.
5 Four-leaved Austrian Toad-flax.
6 Blue English Toad-flax.
7 Great Sweet-scented Purple Toad-flax.
8 Toad-flax of Gibraltar.
9 Ivy-leaved Toad-flax, or, *Cymbalaria*.

Snap-dragon described. 1. Snap-dragon is what we see growing on old walls in many parts of England; there it will last for years, but in our rich gardens it is seldom of long continuance. The leaves are spear-shaped, smooth, and grow on short footstalks. The flowers are large and spacious, and their varieties are very great, insomuch that of this species there are,

Varieties.
The Common Red Snap-dragon.
The White Snap-dragon.
The Yellow Snap-dragon.
The Broad-leaved Pale flowering Snap-dragon.
The White-mouthed Red Snap-dragon.
The [illegible] and Red Snap-dragon.
The White and Red Snap-dragon.
The Italian White flowering Snap-dragon.
The Purple Snap-dragon.
The Variegated Snap-dragon.

Method of propagating them. There are many more varieties of these sorts, which differ in the tints or colour of their flowers, or size of their leaves, and more still may be obtained by sowing of the seeds from the best sorts. In order for this, therefore, let seeds be sowed from those of the largest flowers, the longest spikes, and the finest mouthed. Sow them in April or May, in the poorest border of the nursery; the plants will readily come up, and in the autumn they should be set out where they are to flower, which will be the summer following. This thing, however, the Gardener must observe, if he chuses to continue the plants for several years: He must plant them in a dry, sandy, or rubbishy soil, and must frequently crop the flowers, to cause them to shoot out from the bottom. By this means they may be continued. But to have them in the greatest perfection, the best way is to consider them as biennials only, and plant them out in a very rich part of the garden; they will then flower amazingly strong the summer following; the figure they will make, especially at a distance, will be very grand, and as in such a soil most of the plants will die away after flowering, the best way will be to eradicate the whole, after having gathered seeds from the best sorts, and prepare the ground for the reception of other sorts for succession.

These sorts will continue the succession themselves, if you chuse it. They will scatter their seeds, which will come up all over the garden, and will rise from the crevices of old walls, buildings, &c. Any of the sorts with extraordinary good properties may be continued by planting of the slips or cuttings during any of the summer months: they will readily grow; and when planted out, they should be set in a dry, poor, rubbishy soil.

The Variegated Snap-dragon is esteemed by many on account of its beautiful striped leaves. It is to be continued in this variety, by planting of the cuttings in a shady border in the summer; and a few plants should be potted, to be housed in winter; this being rather of a tenderer nature than the other sorts, and is sometimes destroyed at that season.

Description of the Common. 2. Common Toad-flax has a slender, creeping root, which spreads itself under ground to a great distance, and sends up stalks from all parts. These will rise to about a foot and half high, are upright, branching, and garnished with many narrow, spear-shaped, grey-coloured leaves growing in clusters. The flowers terminate the branches in spikes, they sit close to the stalks, are yellow, and will often be in blow from June to the end of the summer.

This sort is much used in medicine; and an ointment being prepared by a mixture of it with hog's lard and the yolk of an egg, is said to be good against the piles.

Sweet-scented. 3. Sweet-scented Toad-flax. The stalks of this species are numerous, branching, and will grow to be two feet high. The leaves are very narrow, whitish, and garnish the stalks in clusters. The flowers grow in loose spikes from the ends of the branches. Their colour is a pale blue; they are sweetly scented, and will continue flowering from June to the end of the summer.

Dalmatian. 4. Dalmatian Toad-flax. This is a large growing plant. It will rise to up a yard or more high, and the stalk is strong and woody. The leaves are broad, spear-shaped, smooth, sessile, and placed alternately on the branches. The flowers are large, and terminate the branches in loose spikes; their colour is a deep yellow, and each flower has its separate short footstalk. They will be in blow in July, and rarely produce seeds with us. This is a very fine plant, and requires a different culture from the other sorts, which shall be explained.

Four-leaved Austrian. 5. Four-leaved Austrian Toad-flax. This plant hardly grows to a foot high. The stalks are many, and diffused. The leaves are short and narrow; their colour is greyish. At the bottom of the stalks they grow by fours, but higher, they are placed opposite. The flowers terminate the branches in short, loose spikes; they are of a pale yellow, but the chaps of the petal are of a bright gold colour. They will be in blow in June, but are not always succeeded by good seeds with us.

Blue English. 6. Blue English Toad-flax. This is a weed in many parts of England. It will grow to about two feet high. The stalks are many, erect, and branching. The leaves are narrow, and grow in whorls round the bottom of the stalks, but higher, they are placed by pairs, or singly. The flowers adorn the ends of the branches in long, loose spikes. They will be in blow from June to the end of the summer, and afford plenty of good seeds in the autumn. Of this species there are several varieties, particularly one with yellow flowers, is worthy of notice.

Great Sweet-scented Purple. 7. Great Sweet-scented Purple Toad-flax. This plant will grow to a yard high. The stalks are many, and some which proceed the flowers are erect, the others bend on every side. The leaves are spear-shaped, narrow, and long, they grow without order on the stalks, sometimes by fours, at others by pairs and singly, they are smooth, and their colour is greyish. The flowers terminate the branches in long, loose spikes, their colour is purple, they are finely scented, will be in blow from June to the end of the summer, and in the autumn will afford good seeds in plenty. Of this species there are two or three varieties, particularly one with a blue flower, is worthy of notice.

Gibraltar. 8. Gibraltar Toad-flax. The stalks of this plant are weak, slender, succulent, and seldom grow to be a foot long. The leaves also are succulent, spear-shaped, short, and narrow, their colour is greyish, and they are placed at the bottom of the stalks opposite, but higher irregularly. The flowers terminate the tops of the stalks in small tufts, they sit close, their colour is yellow, striped with purple, having also the chaps and spur of a dark purple. They will be in blow in June and July, and very seldom produce seeds in England.

Ivy-leaved Toad-flax. 9. Ivy-leaved Toad-flax, or *Cymbalaria*. This grows naturally in the crevices of old walls and buildings, as well as gardens, and will thrive in any place or situation. The stalks are round, weak, and put out roots from the joints, by which they fasten themselves to every thing they come near. The leaves are cordated, of a dark green colour, divided into five parts, and placed alternately on the branches. The flowers are small, and produced from the wings of the leaves on short footstalks. Their colour is purple, and they will continue to flower and produce seeds during the whole course of the summer months.

Culture. The fourth and the eighth sorts are best propagated from seeds, which should be procured from the places where they naturally grow. These should be sown in the spring, in a light, sandy, shady border. When they come up, they must be frequently refreshed with water, and thinned when they appear too close. In August, if a moist day should happen, carefully take them up, with a ball of earth to each root, and set them in the places where they are designed to remain. This must be well-sheltered, dry, sandy, and warm, or they will be pretty sure of being destroyed in the winter; so that, unless your situation is naturally such, it will be proper to pot a few of the plants, and preserve them under an hot-bed frame, or in the green-house, all winter, to secure the sorts, if the others should be destroyed. They may be encreased by parting of the roots, or planting cuttings in any of the summer months, though the plants raised from seeds are always the best.

The others are all exceeding hardy, and will grow in any soil or situation. They may be encreased by parting of the roots, or sowing of the seeds, and when, by either of these ways, you have once obtained a stock, they will sow themselves, and come up in plenty without further trouble.

Titles. 1. Snap-Dragon is titled, *Antirrhinum corollis ecaudatis, floribus spicatis, calycibus rotundatis*. In the *Hortus Cliffortianus* it is called, *Antirrhinum foliis lanceolatis petiolatis, calycibus brevissimis, racemo [illegible]*. Caspar Bauhine calls it, *Antirrhinum majus, rotundiore folio*, another sort of it he calls, *Antirrhinum luteo flore*, and a third, *Antirrhinum majus alterum, folio longiore*. Boccone calls it, *Antirrhinum latifolium pallido amplo flore*. Dodonæus, *Antirrhinum*. It grows naturally in several of the southern parts of Europe.

2. Common Toad-flax. This is titled, *Antirrhinum foliis lanceolato-linearibus confertis, caule erecto, spicis terminalibus sessilibus floribus imbricatis*. In the *Hortus Cliffortianus* it is called, *Antirrhinum foliis lanceolato-linearibus sparsis*. Guettard terms it, *Antirrhinum foliis lanceolato-linearibus sparsis, caulibus [illegible] brevioribus*. Caspar Bauhine calls it, *Linaria vulgaris lutea, flore majore*, and Fuchsius, *Osyris*. It grows naturally by the road-side in many parts of Europe.

3. Sweet-scented Toad-flax. This is titled, *Antirrhinum foliis linearibus confertis, caule nitido paniculato, pedunculis spicatis nudis*. Caspar Bauhine calls it, *Linaria capillaceo folio, odora*, and John Bauhine, *Linaria cærulea Monspessulana*. It is a native of France, and is found also growing in some parts of Kent.

4. Dalmatian Toad-flax. This is titled, *Antirrhinum foliis alternis cordatis amplexicaulibus*. Miller calls it, *Linaria foliis lanceolatis alternis, caule fruticoso*. Caspar Bauhine, *Linaria latifolia Dalmatica, magno flore*, and John Bauhine, *Linaria maxima, folio lauri*. It grows naturally in Crete and Armenia.

5. Four-leaved Austrian Toad-flax. This is titled, *Antirrhinum foliis quaternis lineari-lanceolatis, caule diffuso, floribus racemosis calcaratis*. Caspar Bauhine calls one sort of it, *Linaria quadrifolia supina*; another, *Linaria cærulea repens*, a third, *Linaria foliis carnosis cinereis*. It grows naturally in Austria, Helvetia, and Syria, also, upon Mount Baldus and the Pyrenees.

6. Blue English Toad-flax. This is titled, *Antirrhinum foliis sub-binatis linearibus inferioribus quaternis, calycibus pilosis viscidis, floribus spicatis, caule erecto*. Van Royen calls it, *Antirrhinum foliis linearibus alternis recurvis, ramis caule brevioribus*. Caspar Bauhine, *Linaria arvensis cærulea*, *Linaria pumila, foliolis carnosis, flosculis minimis flavis*, and, *Linaria quadrifolia lutea*, and Columna, *Linaria tetraphylla lutea*. It grows naturally in our fields and meadows, also, in Italy and France.

7. Great Sweet-scented Purple Toad-flax. This is titled, *Antirrhinum foliis quaternis linearibus, caule floribus erecto spicato*. In the *Hortus Cliffortianus* it is called, *Antirrhinum foliis linearibus sparsis, nectariis subulatis recurvis, floribus laxè spicatis*. John Bauhine calls it, *Linaria purpurea magna*, Caspar Bauhine, *Linaria purpurea major odorata*, and Dodonæus, *Linaria altera purpurea*. It grows naturally near Mount Vesuvius.

8. Gibraltar Toad-flax. This is titled, *Antirrhinum foliis lanceolatis sparsis inferioribus oppositis, nectariis subulatis, floribus [illegible]*. Dillenius calls it, *Linaria triphylla Hispanica*. It grows naturally on the rocks about Gibraltar.

9. Ivy-leaved Toad-flax. This is termed, *Antirrhinum foliis cordatis quinquelobis alternis, caulibus procumbentibus*. Caspar Bauhine and others call it, *Cymbalaria*. It grows naturally upon old walls about Paris, Basil, Harlem, &c.

Class and order in the Linnæan system. *Antirrhinum* is of the class and order *Didynamia Angiospermia*, and the characters are,

The characters. 1. CALYX is a monophyllous perianthium, deeply cut into five oblong, permanent segments.

2. COROLLA is a ringent petal. The tube is oblong and gibbous, the limb is bilabiated. The upper lip is bifid and reflexed on both sides, the lower lip is trifid and obtuse. At the base of the flower is situated the nectarium. It is prominent, subulated, and obtuse.

3. STAMINA. The filaments are four, and about

about the length of the corolla They are included in the upper lip two of them are shorter than the other, and their antheræ are connivent

4 PISTILLUM consists of a roundish germen, a simple style, the length and situation of the stamina, and an obtuse stigma

5 PERICARPIUM is a roundish, obtuse, bilocular capsule

6 SEMINA The seeds are numerous and angular.

## CHAP. XLII

## APHYLLANTHES

This species described

THERE is only one species of this genus, called *Aphyllanthes* The root is slender, tough, fibrous and creeping The leaves are numerous at the root, about two or three inches long, narrow, of a thin contexture, and soon decay The stalk is round, smooth firm, naked, and without a joint The flowers come out singly from the tops of the stalks, growing in imbricated cups They are of an elegant blue colour, appear in June and July, and the seeds ripen in September

Method of propagating it

This species is propagated by sowing the seeds in the spring in beds of light earth made fine When the plants come up they should be kept clean from weeds, and frequently watered in dry weather In July, or early in August, they should be removed to the place where they are designed to remain In doing of this, preserve a ball of earth to each root, and after they are set out, give them a good watering Repeat this at intervals, if dry weather makes it necessary, and keep them constantly shaded until they are established in their own situation They will then call for no trouble, except keeping clean from weeds, and the summer following they will flower, and perfect their seeds

This species may be also propagated by parting of the roots This is best done in the autumn, though it may be effected with success in the winter, or early in the spring Before the stalks shoot up for flowering they should always have a light, dry, sandy soil, and after they are set out, will require no trouble, except keeping them clean from weeds

Titles

There being no other species of this genus, it stands singly with the name *Aphyllanthes* Caspar Bauhine calls it, *Caryophyllus cæruleus Monspeliensium*, and John Bauhine, *Aphyllanthes Monspeliensium* It grows naturally in rocky, sterile, mountainous places in the south of France

Class and order in the Linnæan system The characters

*Aphyllanthes* is of the class and order *Hexandria Monogynia*, and the characters are,

1 CALYX is imbricated, and composed of several spear shaped glumes, which are formed each of a single valve

2 COROLLA consists of six oval petals, which spread open at top, but have narrow, erect ungues, that converge, and form a tube near the bottom

3 STAMINA are six setaceous filaments, shorter than the corolla, having oblong antheræ

4 PISTILLUM consists of a three-cornered turbinated germen, a filiforme style the length of the stamina, and three oblong stigmas

5 PERICARPIUM is a turbinated, triangular capsule, containing three cells

6 SEMINA The seeds are ovate

## CHAP XLIII.

## APOCYNUM, DOGS BANE.

Introductory Remarks

THE hardiest species of *Apocynum* are not of the lowest esteem in our gardens, the fineness of their leaves, their procerity of growth, the singular construction of their flowers, together with their ease of culture, cause them to be much admired and sought after They are indiscriminately called Canada Dogs Bane, a term proper enough for two of the species, as they grow naturally in that country, but very improperly applied to a third, which grows only in a state of nature in some of the Mediterranean islands

I will not, therefore, put the Gardener out of his old way, but use, as nearly as possible, his accustomed terms, and call them,

Species.

1 The Oval, or, Tutsan leaved Canada Dogs Bane

2 The Oblong leaved Canada Dogs Bane

3 The Venetian Willow leaved Dogs Bane

Description of the Tutsan-leaved Canada

1 Tutsan leaved Canada Dogs Bane This hath a thick, creeping root, from which arise several upright, thick, firm, smooth, brownish stalks, of about a yard, or four feet high The leaves are large, smooth, nearly oval, and of a firm consistence They are of a strong green, a little veined, and grow opposite by pairs at the joints The flowers terminate the stalks in large tufts or umbels each flower is of one leaf, divided into five parts at the brim, and the nectarium is singular

singular and conspicuous The real ground of the flower is white, but the nectarium is purple, reddish, of a chocolate colour, or some tints of the like nature Numbers of these will be collected together into a head, so that they form a moderately large umbel, of a proportionate bigness with the size of the plant They will be in blow in July, but I never knew them to be succeeded by good seeds

Oblong leaved Canada.

2 Oblong leaved Canada Dogs Bane This hath a thick, creeping root, from which arise several upright, firm, reddish stalks, to the height of two or three feet The leaves grow opposite by pairs at the joints They are smooth, oblong, and when broken, emit a kind of milky juice The flowers terminate the branches in panicles They are inferior to those of the former sort, and of a greenish-white colour, each individual flower is inconsiderable, and the panicles are small They will be in blow in July, and seldom produce good seeds with us

and Venetian Willow leaved Dogs Bane.

3 Venetian Willow leaved Dogs Bane This also hath a creeping root, which sends forth several herbaceous, upright stalks, about two feet high The leaves grow opposite by pairs they are smooth, and of an oval, lanceolate figure The flowers adorn the tops of the stalks in branches There are two varieties of them, one is purple, the other white flowers Each separate flower is larger than any of the other sorts, though they will not be so numerous in the bunches as the first sort, but their colours being more distinct and brighter, constitute a better flower They will be in blow in July and August, and never produce any seeds

Method of propagating these sorts.

These sorts are all propagated by the joints from their creeping roots, they may be taken off at any time in the autumn, winter, or spring Almost any soil or situation will do for them, and they require no more trouble, than the usual course of keeping the garden clean from weeds, and taking off the stalks in the autumn, when they decay, which would otherwise look unsightly, for they constantly die to the ground at the latter end of the year, and rise again in the spring

Titles.

1 Tutsan leaved Canada Dogs Bane is titled, *Apocynum caule rectiusculo herbaceo, foliis ovatis utrinque glabris, cymis terminalibus* In the *Hortus Cliffortianus* it is termed, *Apocynum foliis ovatis.* Van Royen calls it, *Apocynum caule erecto annuo, foliis ovatis*, Boccone, *Apocynum Canadense, foliis Androsæmi majoris* It grows naturally in Canada and Virginia

2 Oblong leaved Canada Dogs Bane This is titled, *Apocynum caule rectiusculo herbaceo, foliis oblongis, paniculis terminalibus* Gronovius calls it, *Apocynum foliis ovatis acutis subtus tomentosis*, Morison, *Apocynum Canadense ramosum, flore e viridi albicante, siliqua tenuissima*, and Plukenet, *Apocynum Canadense maximum, flore minimo herbaceo* It grows naturally in Canada and Virginia.

3 Willow-leaved Venetian Dogs Bane This is titled, *Apocynum caule rectiusculo herbaceo, foliis ovato-lanceolatis* In the *Hortus Cliffortianus* it is termed, *Apocynum foliis ovato-lanceolatis* Caspar Bauhine calls it, *Tithymalus maritimus, purpurascentibus floribus*, and Lobel, *Tithymalus maritimus Venetorum insulæ* It is a native of an island near Venice

Class and order in the Linnæan system.

*Apocynum* is of the class and order *Pentandria Digynia*, and the characters are,

The characters.

1 Calyx is a small, erect, monophyllous, permanent perianthium, divided at the top into five acute segments

2 Corolla is of one leaf, it is roundish, bell-shaped, and divided at the top into five parts, which turn backwards The nectarium consists of five oval corpuscules surrounding the germen

3 Stamina are five very short filaments, with five oblong, erect, acute, connivent, bifid antheræ

4 Pistillum consists of two oval germina, hardly any style, and a roundish stigma, that is larger than the germen

5 Pericarpium consists of two long, acuminated follicules, containing one cell

6 Semina The seeds are numerous, small, and crowned with long down The receptacle is very long, awl-shaped, rough and free

# CHAP XLIV

## *AQUILEGIA*, COLUMBINE

Species.

THIS genus consists of three species only

1 The Common Columbine of our gardens

2 The Mountain Columbine

3 The Dwarf Canada Columbine

Description of the Common,

1 The Common Columbine is a well-known plant, and the various forms it assumes from seeds are almost endless A description of the plant is this The root is large and fibrous The stalk is upright, slender, branching, hairy, and will grow to be two or three feet high The leaves are large, composed of many parts, and usually disposed by threes, without any order or regularity The flowers appear in May from the ends of the branches, they are numerous, and their varieties are amazing great, insomuch that from the same seed there will be some with blue flowers, some with red, others with white, purple or chesnut others will be sweetly variegated, some spotted, others again on the same plant will have the flower, or one part of it self-coloured, the other part will afford them tinged or spotted in the most elegant manner The form also of the flowers will be different, some will be single, others double, some will be short, round, and compact, others loose and long In some the nectarium, which is a conspicuous part of this flower, will be obliterated by the multiplicity of petals, in others, the nectaria are predominant Hence the names Horn Columbine, Rosy Columbine, &c have been variously given to express the different sorts Neither is their variety

all

Double Starry Columbine
Long Spiked Cytisus
Double White Crow foot.

all the excellence they consist of, but they are large flowers, and very showy. The plants are no ramblers, of a size proper for any garden, and easy of culture; and these with the other considerations conspire to encrease their value, and heighten them in our esteem.

Culture of this species

In order, therefore, to continue them in the greatest perfection, fresh plants must be raised every four or five years; for it is observable, that young plants always exhibit the finest flowers; and as the plants get old, they frequently run away from the colours, and from the pitch or elegance in variegation become plain. The seeds must always be gathered from flowers of the best properties, that is, the largest, the doublest, those of the best colours, and best mixed. On the same plant, flowers with these properties will often be found, and others of an indifferent nature. These must be constantly clipped as they appear, and the best only saved for seeds.

The seeds should be sown in the autumn or the spring, either of which is a very good season. Any border of common mould made fine, will do for the purpose, and the plants will require no trouble, except keeping them clean from weeds, until they are fit to remove. Against this time, let a bed be prepared for their reception in a conspicuous part of the garden, for they are deserving of such notice, and in a moist day, or some evening, remove the plants to this bed, planting them in rows at a foot asunder. The next summer the plants will flower, and the summer after that, will be in their utmost perfection. Those which shew bad colours or properties, should be eradicated at first, and the remaining sorts should be constantly kept clean of weeds, and have the ground dug between the rows every winter; and this is all the trouble these elegant plants will require. In two or three years after this, you will find them begin to degenerate; so that you must not neglect to gather seeds time enough, to keep up the succession in perfection and splendor.

Mountain,

2. Mountain Columbine grows wild in many of our woods and hilly grounds. The leaves are composed of many parts, that are also very much divided. The stalks are slender, branching, and terminated by the flowers, which are larger than those of the Garden Columbine, will be in blow in May and June, and ripen their seeds in September.

and Dwarf Canada Columbine described

3. Dwarf Canada Columbine is chiefly valuable on account of its early flowering, which will be in April. It is a pretty little plant, about a foot high. The stalk is slender and branching. A single flower, of a red colour, terminates each branch. The stamina are longer than the petals, and the nectaria are straight. This sort perfects its seeds in August. There is a variety of it, that will grow almost to the size of the Garden Columbine, and flowers in May.

Method of propagating these species

These sorts are propagated by sowing the seeds like the Garden Columbine, and in the autumn following removing them to the places where they are designed to flower, which they will do the spring after. All these plants have a very pretty effect, not only in flower-gardens, but in wilderness quarters, among shrubs, &c. so that the worst sorts may be appropriated to such places, in which they are sometimes thought to be more proper than better flowers; as they have an artless look, and appear in the ease and simplicity of Nature's own attire.

Titles

1. The Garden Columbine is titled, *Aquilegia nectariis incurvis*. In the *Hortus Cliffortianus* it is called simply, *Aquilegia*. The varieties of it have titles in Authors as distinct species. Caspar Bauhine calls one, *Aquilegia sylvestris*; another, *Aquilegia hortensis simplex*; a third, *Aquilegia hortensis multiplex, flore magno*; a fourth, *Aquilegia hortensis multiplex, flore inverso*; a fifth, *Aquilegia flore roseo multiplici*; and a sixth, *Aquilegia degener virescens*. It grows naturally in some of our woods, and is found in mountainous, woody and bushy grounds in several parts of Europe.

2. Mountain Columbine. This is titled, *Aquilegia nectariis rectis, petalo lanceolato brevioribus*. Caspar Bauhine calls it, *Aquilegia montana magno flore*. It grows naturally in Westmoreland.

3. Dwarf Canada Columbine. This is titled, *Aquilegia nectariis rectis, staminibus corolla longioribus*. Gronovius calls it, *Aquilegia corollâ simplici, nectariis fere rectis*; Cornutus, *Aquilegia pumila præcox Canadensis*; and Morison, *Aquilegia præcox Canadensis, flore externe rubicundo medio luteo*. It grows naturally in Canada and Virginia.

Class and order in the Linnæan system

*Aquilegia* is of the class and order *Polyandria Pentagynia*; and the characters are,

The characters,

1. CALYX. There is none.

2. COROLLA consists of five spear-shaped, oval, plain, patent, equal petals, besides which are the nectaria. These are five in number, equal, and grow alternately with the petals, each of them is horned, grows wider upwards, is rising on the outside, opens obliquely, and is annexed to the receptacle within; the lower part is lengthened into a long tube, that is incurved and obtuse at the end.

3. STAMINA are numerous, subulated filaments, having oblong, erect antheræ. The outer filaments are shorter than those within, and the antheræ are the length of the nectaria.

4. PISTILLUM consists of five oval, oblong germina, terminated by subulated styles, longer than the stamina, with erect, simple stigmas. There are ten short, rough kind of scales, that surround and separate the germina from each other.

5. PERICARPIUM consists of five cylindrical, parallel, upright, pointed capsules; each is of one valve, and opens at the top on the inside.

6. SEMINA. The seeds are numerous, shining, oval, carinated, and annexed to the suture where the vessel opens.

# CHAP. XLV.

## *ARABIS*, BASTARD TOWER MUSTARD.

Introductory remarks.

THE species of this genus have been understood variously by authors. Some of them have been taken for Gilliflowers, some for Mouse Ear, Rocket, Tower Mustard, and the like. The real English name of this genus is Bastard Tower Mustard; so that when we find the above names, we must understand them to mean no more than improperly to express one or other of the species of Bastard Tower Mustard. After this hint, they shall be arranged here by the names they have usually had, for by them the gardener will best know what plants we are treating of; and the titles that follow their culture will direct the more curious to their proper appellation in [illegible].

Under this genus, then, the Gardener will find,

Species.

1. The White Erect Spring Gilliflower.
2. The Trailing Spring Gilliflower.
3. The Codded Mouse-Ear.
4. The Smooth Lyrate-leaved Mouse-Ear.
5. Virginian Rocket.
6. Broad-leaved Tower Mustard.
7. Danes Violet-leaved Gilliflower.

Description of the White Erect Spring

1. The White Erect Spring Gilliflower. This has a creeping root, that spreads itself under the surface of the ground to a considerable distance. The radical leaves are oval, indented, and grow many together in a circular manner, forming themselves into a kind of head. From the center of this head of leaves the flower-stalks arise; these will be about a foot high, upright, and are garnished with broad leaves placed alternately, and which surround the stalk with their base. The flowers terminate the stalks in loose bunches; their colour is white; they will be in blow in March or April, and are succeeded by long flat pods full of [illegible] seeds.

and Trailing Spring Gilliflower.

2. Trailing Spring Gilliflower. This hath always been held as a distinct species, but Linnæus has made it a variety only of the former. It differs from it chiefly in this: The stalks are large, diffuse, and branching; they trail on the ground, and are adorned with large indented leaves that embrace the stalk with their base. The flowers are white, like the other, and are succeeded by long flat pods full of seeds.

Codded,

3. The Codded Mouse-Ear grows naturally in several parts of England. It is a very low plant. The leaves are spear-shaped, entire, and are placed on footstalks on the branches. These grow to about four or five inches high. The flowers are white, and grow alternately on the stalks. They flower early in the summer, and are succeeded by long slender pods full of small round seeds.

and Smooth Lyrate-leaved Codded Mouse-Ear.

4. Smooth Lyrate-leaved Codded Mouse-Ear. This also is a [illegible] inches high. The radical leaves are lyre-shaped and smooth; those on the stalks are spear-shaped, narrow, and smooth. The flowers grow nearly the most the length of the stalk; they are white, and larger than the other sort, and are succeeded by the same kind of seeds.

Virginian Rocket.

5. Virginian Rocket. The radical leaves are oblong and broad, and a little resemble those of the Daisy. The stalk is erect, will grow to upwards of a foot in height, and is garnished with spear-shaped, indented, smooth leaves. The flowers ornament the upper parts of the stalks in naked spikes; the largest spike always terminates the main branch, whilst two or three smaller from the upper wings adorn the sides a little lower. Their colour is white, and they are succeeded by compressed [illegible] pods full of seeds.

Broad-leaved Tower Mustard

6. Broad-leaved Tower Mustard. This will grow to about a foot high. The leaves are very broad, hairy, [illegible], and embrace the stalk with their base. The flowers are of a very bad white, formed in loose spikes, and grow alternately on the branches. It flowers in April or May, and the pods that succeed are long, narrow, and hang down [illegible]. These pods contain very good seeds.

and Danes Violet-leaved Gilliflower.

7. Danes Violet-leaved Gilliflower. The radical leaves of this species are broad, indented, and often [illegible] at their edges. The stalk will grow to upwards of a foot high, and is garnished with long spear-shaped hairy leaves, that closely embrace it with their base. The flowers are of a very pale white or yellow, and terminate the stalks in loose spikes. They will be in blow in May, and in July are succeeded by long, flat, narrow, declined pods, full of flat, brown, ripe seeds.

Method of propagating these sorts.

The best way of propagating all these sorts is by the seeds, which should be sown in the autumn soon after they are ripe; they will then readily come up, and become good plants soon, and most of them will flower the year following.

The first and second sorts encrease so fast by their creeping roots, that it will not be worth while to sow their seed, if a root or two of each can be obtained, for by them you will soon get stock enough. These plants are not only pretty in flower gardens, but also in shrubberies or wilderness quarters, where they grow very well, and have a delightful effect by their early flowers among the shrubs and trees.

Proper situation.

The others will often grow upon old ruins, rubbish, or buildings, which directs us to sow their seeds in a dry, sandy, or rubbishy spot; and indeed without such a situation, they are very short-lived in a garden; but for this they make amends themselves by sowing their seeds, and continuing the succession without further trouble.

Titles.

1, 2. The first and second sorts, though so widely different in appearance, are varieties only of the same species. Their common title is, *Arabis foliis amplexicaulibus dentatis*. The first sort is titled by Van Royen *Arabis foliis amplexicaulibus dentatis, caule erecto simplici*. In the Flora Lapponica it is termed, *Arabis caule simplici, foliis ovatis [illegible]*. Caspar Bauhine terms it, *Draba alba siliquosa repens*, and Clusius, *Draba alba siliquosa*. The second sort Van Royen titles, *Arabis foliis amplexicaulibus dentatis, caule diffuso ramoso*. Caspar Bauhine calls it, *Draba alba siliquosa*, and Clusius, *Draba 2*. They grow naturally on the Helvetian, Austrian, and Lapland mountains.

3. Codded Mouse-Ear. This is titled, *Arabis foliis petiolatis integerrimis*. In the Hortus Cliffortianus it is termed, *Turritis foliis lanceolatis integris petiolatis*.

tiolet s, a' √ort in ra aot in. foli arus Caspar Bauhine calls it, Bu fi poftions fimilis filiquosa major, and others, Pilosella filiquosa It grows on old walls, sandy, and gravelly soils in England, and most of the northern parts of Europe

4 Smooth-leaved Codded Mouse Ear This is titled, Arabis foliis glabris radicalibus lyratis caulinis linearibus Gronovius calls it, Chen anthus caule ... foliis ... lanceolatis, infimis ... It grows naturally in Canada

5 Virginian Rocket This is, Arabis foliis caulinis lanceolatis dentatis glabris Plukenet calls it, ... Gronovius, Turritis foliis lanceolatis ... radicalibus ... siliquis compressis ... It grows naturally in Virginia and Canada

6 Broad-leaved Tower Mustard This is titled, Arabis foliis amplexicaulibus, siliquis ... linearibus, calycibus ... Allamand calls it, Turritis ... hirsuta, siliquis ...

7 Dame's Violet-leaved Gilliflower This is titled, Arabis foliis amplexicaulibus, siliquis decumbentibus ... calycibus ... Sauvages calls it, Turritis caule simplici, foliis lanceolatis subdentatis glabris Guettard, Turritis perrato ... foliis lanceolatis obsolete dentatis, Tournefort, Leucojum ... folio, Boccone, Brassica ... floribus, albido flore, nutante siliqua, and Clusius Turrita major, Plateau It grows naturally in Switzerland, Hungary, Gaul, and Sicily

Arabis is of the class and order Tetradynamia Siliquosa, and the characters are, Class and order in the Linnæan system. The characters.

1 CALYX is a deciduous perianthium, composed of four parallel connivent leaves, the two opposite are large, oblong, acute, concave, and gibbous, the other two are narrow and erect

2 COROLLA consists of four oval patent petals placed in form of a cross, and of the length of the calyx

There are four nectariums each of them is a kind of reflexed scale affixed to the receptacle

3 STAMINA There are six erect subulated filaments, two of them are the length of the calyx, the other four are much longer, and the antheræ are heart shaped and erect

4 PISTILLUM consists of a taper germen the length of the stamina, without any style, but an entire obtuse stigma

5 PERICARPIUM is a long, narrow, compressed pod

6 SEMINA The seeds are many, roundish, and compressed

## CHAP. XLVI

## ARALIA, BERRY-BEARING ANGELICA.

BESIDES the Angelica tree already treated of, there are two hardy herbaceous species of this genus, whose stalks die to the ground every autumn, and fresh ones are produced from the roots every spring These are called,

Species 1 The Leafy-stalked, or Canada Berry-bearing Angelica

2 The Naked-stalked or Virginian Berry-bearing Angelica

The Leafy stalked Berry-bearing Angelica, 1 The Leafy-stalked Berry bearing Angelica rises with a round thick, jointed, smooth, branching stalk to the height of three or four feet The leaves grow alternately, are very large, and are composed of a great number of large, oval, pointed lobes that are serrated on their edges From the wings of the leaves the flowers are produced in roundish umbels placed on smooth footstalks, they are of a greenish colour at first, but become whiter afterwards They will be in blow in June, and are succeeded by round channeled berries, which will be first red, but when full ripe in the autumn of a black colour, and of a sweet taste

and Naked stalked Berry-bearing Angelica described 2 The Naked-stalked Berry bearing Angelica This rises with an upright branching stalk to a yard or better in height The leaves grow immediately from the root, are very large, branching, and have long footstalks, they usually consist of three divisions, each of which is composed of five serrated lobes From among these the stalks are produced in the spring, in June they are terminated in round umbels of whitish flowers, and these are succeeded by small black berries, which will be ripe in October

Culture These are both very hardy plants, and not only proper for large gardens, but wilderness-quarters, shrubberies, or to be stationed by the sides of woods which are much frequented, for they will grow very well among trees, and by their large compounded leaves have a majestic look, and in the autumn their berries in such places have a pleasing effect Proper situation.

They are propagated by dividing of the roots, or sowing the seeds The roots spread very much, so that they encrease fast enough that way Let these be divided in the autumn, and let the offsets be planted immediately in the places where they are designed to remain Culture.

By seeds also they readily rise These should be sown very thin in the autumn, and they will come up early in the spring All summer they will require no more trouble than keeping them clean from weeds, and thinning them where they are too close, and in the autumn they may be planted out, like the off-sets, in the places where they are designed to remain

1 The Leafy-stalked Berry-bearing Angelica is titled, Aralia caule folioso herbaceo lævi In the Hortus Cliffort it is termed, Aralia ex alis florifera Cornutus calls it, Panaces carpimon five racemosa Canadensis, and Morison, Christophoriana Canadensis racemosa et ramosa It grows naturally in Canada Title

2 The Naked-stalked Berry-bearing Angelica is titled, Aralia caule nudo, foliis binis ternatis Colden calls it, Aralia caule nudo, ... repente, and Plukenet, Christophoriana Virginiana, zarzæ radicibus surculosis & fungosis It grows naturally in Virginia

CHAP

# C H A P XLVII

## *ARBUTUS*, The STRAWBERRY-TREE

THERE are three low species of this genus, the culture of which is hardly ever attempted in gardens, but which are very stackish emule vines, and afford pretty for those whose thrift is for a general collection of plants, and who may happen to have a situation suitable to their nature. These are usually called,

Species 1. *Uva Ursi*, or Common Bearberry,

2. The Berry of Acadia,

3. *Vitis Idaea*, or Common Mountain Bilberry.

Description of the Common Bearberry, 1. *Uva Ursi*, or Common Bearberry. The stalks of this species are ligneous, divide into numerous branches, which are covered with a reddish bark, procumbent, and about a foot and a half or two feet in length. The leaves are oval, thick, smooth on the edges, of a strong green colour, and remain on the plant all winter. The flowers come out in clusters from the ends of the branches, they are of a greenish white colour, appear in May and June, and are succeeded by roundish black berries, which ripen in July. There is a variety with purple flowers, and another with red fruit.

Bilberry of Acadia, 2. The Bilberry of Acadia is a native of the country from which it is named. It grows naturally on boggy ground there, and that directs us to its situation when attempted to be propagated by us. Its branches are ligneous, trailing, and about two feet in length. The leaves are of an oval figure, and have their edges slightly serrated. They grow alternately on the branches, and in degree bear some resemblance to those of the *Alaternus*. The flowers are produced from the wings of the leaves, in small loose bunches; they appear in May and June frequently, and are succeeded by fruit in England. In the country where they grow naturally, they bear plenty of berries, which are eaten by the inhabitants.

and Common Mountain Bilberry. 3. *Vitis Idaea*, or Common Mountain Bilberry, as its title imports, grows naturally on the Alps, in Lapland, and in many other cold countries. This is also a low ligneous plant, with slender trailing branches. The leaves are of a whitish colour, and of an oblong figure, they are rough, and have their edges serrated. The flowers are produced from the wings of the leaves on slender footstalks, they appear in May and June, and are succeeded by black berries about the size of our common Bilberry, and in the places where they grow naturally are eaten as fruit, and much liked by the inhabitants.

Culture The best manner of raising these three sorts, if a person should happen to desire them, is, to obtain the berries from the places where they naturally grow, which are to be sent over well preserved in sand. These plants are found growing upon bogs on the sides of high mountains, which are for many months covered with snow; they are also seen growing in low, moist, swampy ground; but bogs and wet grounds are not so common to them in their native countries, for they are sometimes found growing upon sound ground, among moss, &c. in the barrenest sandy soils. These hints direct us to the place they should have with us, as well as their culture; for if there be a boggy place by the side of an hill or rising ground, it is a proper for the purpose. If it be on the north side, it will be the better, and without this it will not be worth while to attempt to raise them. The soil designed for the seeds should be turned over many months before, so that the sward, or whatever grows there, may be perfectly rotted. The soil being thus obtained, the mould, if boggy, should be fresh turned over, and be made as fine as it is capable of, and the seeds should be sown about half an inch deep. Leave the place then wholly to nature, nor should a weed be pulled up, nor the moss cleared off, and in the second spring you will find the young plants, if the seed was good, and the soil agrees with them, with whatever grows there. They may be thinned where they come up too thick, and this is the only way of raising these plants for them to continue with us. The plants coming up from seeds thus sown, have all demonstration that they like the soil, and they will afterwards grow and flourish in this place as well perhaps as in their native countries.

1. The *Uva Ursi*, or Common Bearberry, is entitled, *Arbutus caulibus procumbentibus, foliis integerrimis*. John Bauhine calls it, *Radix Idaea putata, & Uva Ursi*, and Clusius *Uva Ursi*. It grows in the northern parts of Europe, also in Canada, and many parts of America. Titles

2. The Bilberry of Acadia is, *Arbutus caulibus procumbentibus, foliis ovatis, ... foribus sparsis, baccis polyspermis*. This is the *Vitis Idaea Acadiensis* ... of Tournefort. It grows naturally in Acadia.

3. The *Vitis Idaea*, or Mountain Bilberry, is, *Arbutus ... procumbentibus, foliis rugosis serratis*. C. Bauhine calls it, *Vitis idaea foliis oblongis albicantibus*. Clusius and others, *Vitis Idaea*. It grows common on many mountainous parts of England, also on the Alps of Lapland, Switzerland, and Siberia.

C H A P

# CHAP. XLVIII

## *ARENARIA*

SEVERAL species of inconsiderable note are comprehended under the term *Arenaria*. The more lasting kinds are usually called,

1 Sea Chick-Weed, or Sea Pimpernel
Species 2 Tetraquetrous *Arenaria*
3 Many stalked *Arenaria*
4 Bavarian Saxifrage
5 Rock Chick-Weed
6 Mountain Chick Weed
7 Fine-leaved Chick Weed
8 Larch-leaved Chick-Weed
9 Striated Chick-Weed
10 Grand-flowered Chick-Weed

Description of the Sea Chick Weed, 1 Sea Chick-Weed The root is long, slender, jointed, and strikes deep into the ground The stalks are jointed, slender, about five or six inches long, divide into several branches, and spread themselves on the ground The leaves are oval, acute, fleshy, and of a pale or bluish green The flowers come out a few together from the tops of the stalks, having distinct footstalks; they are small, starry, and of a yellowish green colour; they appear in June and July, and the seed ripen in August and September

Tetraquetrous, 2 Tetraquetrous *Arenaria* The stalks of this species divide into several branches, which, unless supported, lie on the ground The leaves are oval, hollowed, recurved, and lie over each other four different ways The flowers come out singly on footstalks from the ends of the branches; they are small, starry, and of a greenish colour; they appear in June and July, and the seeds ripen in the autumn

and Many stalked Arenaria, 3 Many-stalked *Arenaria* The stalks of this plant are numerous from the root, slender, and trailing The leaves are oval, spear-shaped, nervose, sessile, and acute The flowers come out from the upper parts of the stalk, on short slender footstalks; their petals are undivided, and larger than the segments of the calyx They appear in June and July, and the seeds ripen in September

Bavarian Saxifrage 4 Bavarian Saxifrage The stalks are thick, succulent, branching, and five or six inches long The leaves are nearly cylindrical, taper, fleshy, and obtuse The flowers come out one or two together from the ends of the branches on footstalks; they are of a white colour, and the petals are spear-shaped They appear in June and July, and the seeds ripen in September

Rock, 5 Rock Chick-Weed The stalks are slender, divide into several branches, and lie on the ground The leaves are awl-shaped, smooth, slender, and of a bluish green The flowers come out in panicles from the tops of the stalks; they are of a white colour, appear in July, and the seeds ripen in September There is a variety with spotted flowers

Mountain, 6 Mountain Chick-Weed The stalks are very long and procumbent The leaves are spear-shaped, narrow, and rough The flowers are moderately large, and of a whitish green; they appear in July, and the seeds ripen in September

Fine leaved, 7 Fine-leaved Chick-Weed The stalks are slender, weak, and branching The leaves are awl-shaped, narrow, and very elegant The flowers come out in panicles from the ends of the stalks; they have simple footstalks, and their petals are shorter than the segments of the calyx They appear in June and July, and the seeds ripen in August and September

Larch leaved, 8 Larch leaved Chick-Weed The stalk is slender, tough, and almost naked on the upper parts The leaves are narrow, bristly, and come out in bunches in the manner of those of the Larch-tree The flowers are elegant, of a blue colour, grow on simple footstalks, and have hairy cups They shew themselves in August, and the seeds ripen in the autumn The other varieties of this species are, the White, the Yellow, and the Whitish Green flowered

Striated, 9 Striated Chick-Weed The stalks divide into a few branches, and grow to be five or six inches high The leaves are slender, narrow, and erect The flowers are very beautiful, resemble those of Mouse Ear, and have oblong striated cups They appear in August, and the seeds ripen in the autumn

and Grand-flowered Chick-Weed, 10 Grand-flowered Chick-Weed The radical leaves are narrow, pointed, and form a cluster at the crown of the root The stalk is slender, about four or five inches high, and closely garnished with narrow awl-shaped leaves The flowers come out singly from the tops of the stalks; they are very large for flowers of this sort, starry, and of a beautiful appearance Their time of blowing is mostly in July and August, and the seeds ripen in the autumn

Method of propagating the species. They are all propagated by sowing the seeds soon after they are ripe, in the places where they are to remain When they come up, they should be hoed to proper distances, and to a proper quantity, for three or four plants of each sort will be sufficient to be ready for observation, and this being done, they will require no trouble, except keeping them clean from weeds

Titles 1 Sea Chick-Weed, or Sea Pimpernel, is titled, *Arenaria foliis ovatis acutis carnosis* Caspar Bauhine calls it, *Alsine litoralis, foliis portulacæ*, Buxbaum, *Telephium maritimum, portulacæ folio* and Gerard, *Anthyllis lentifolia seu alsine cruciata marina* It grows naturally on the sea shores of England, and other countries in the north of Europe

2 Tetraquetrous *Arenaria* is, *Arenaria foliis ovatis carinatis recurvis quadrifariam imbricatis* It is a native of the Pyrenees

3 Many-stalked *Arenaria* is, *Arenaria foliis ovatis nervosis sessilibus acutis, corollis calyce majoribus* Haller calls it, *Alsine foliis lanceolatis, petalis integris calyce majoribus* It grows naturally on the Helvetian and Pyrenean mountains

4 Bavarian Saxifrage is, *Arenaria foliis semi-cylindricis carnosis obtusis, petalis lanceolatis, pedunculis terminalibus subbinatis* Seguier calls it, *Alsine Alpina, foliis teretibus obtusis, flore albo*, and Ray, *Saxifraga Bavarica* It grows naturally in Bavaria

5 Rock Chick Weed is, *Arenaria foliis subulatis, caulibus paniculatis, calycum foliolis ovatis* Guettard calls it, *Arenaria foliis subulatis, calycinis laciniis membrana auctis obtusis*, Sauvages, *Spergula foliis aciformibus densis, ramis reversis subnudis*, Herman, *Alsine glabra, tenuissimis foliis, floribus albis*,


5 C

*albis*, Tournefort, *Alsine saxatilis, laricis folio, minor & minori flore*, Plukenet, *Alsine caryophyllodes tenuifolia, flore albo punctato*, Ray, *Alsine pusilla pulchro flore, folio tenuissimo nostras & Saxifraga pusilla caryophylloides flore albo pulchello*, and Vaillant, *Alsine saxatilis & multiflora, capillaceo folio* It grows naturally in rocky mountainous places in England, Germany, Helvetia, France, and Spain

6 Mountain Chick Weed is, *Arenaria foliis lanceolato-linearibus foliis caulibus sterilibus longissimis procumbentibus* It grows naturally in the mountainous parts of the south of Gaul

7 Fine-leaved Chick-Weed is, *Arenaria foliis subulatis, caule paniculato, pedunculis simplicibus, capsulis erectis, petalis calyce brevioribus* Guettard calls it, *Arenaria foliis subulatis, calycis laciniis membranaceis ipsis angustiore acutissimus*, and Caspar Bauhine, &c *Alsine tenuifolia* It grows naturally in dry, sandy, and gravelly places in England, Italy, Gaul, and Switzerland

8 Larch-leaved Chick-Weed is, *Arenaria foliis setaceis, caule superne nudiusculo, calycibus subhirsutis* Haller calls it, *Alsine foliis fasciculatis, petalis simplicibus, calyce hirsuto* Caspar Bauhine, *Alsine Alpina, pinuo folio*, Vaillant, *Lychnoides, junipero folio, perennis*, and Ray, *Alsine caryophylloides tenuifolia montana, lato flore* It grows naturally in mountainous places in England, Switzerland, France, and Germany

9 Striated Chick Weed is, *Arenaria foliis linear bus erectis oppressis, calycibus oblongis striatis* Caspar Bauhine calls it, *Auricula muris, pulchro flore, folio tenuissimo* It grows naturally on the Alpine parts of Austria

10 Grand-flowered Chick-Weed is, *Arenaria foliis subulatis strictis radicalibus confertis, caulibus unifloris* Allioni calls it, *Alsine uniflora & grandiflora, foliis acuminatis, petalis integris* It grows naturally on the Alps, and other mountainous parts of Europe

*Arenaria* is of the class and order *Decandria Trigynia*, and the characters are,

1 CALYX is a perianthium composed of five oblong, acuminated, patent, permanent leaves

2 COROLLA is five oval petals

3 STAMINA are ten awl-shaped filaments alternately interior, having roundish antheræ

4 PISTILLUM consists of an oval germen, and three erect reflex styles, with thickish stigmas

5 PERICARPIUM is an oval covered capsule, containing one cell, and opening in five parts at the top

6 SEMINA The seeds are many, and kidney-shaped

# CHAP XLIX.

## ARETHUSA.

Species

OF this genus are,

1 Bulbose Arethusa

2 Ophioglossoide *Arethusa*, or Adder-tongue leaved Bastard Hellebore

3 Lily leaved Bastard Hellebore

Description of Bulbose Arethusa

1 Bulbose *Arethusa* The root consists of two roundish bulbs The stalk is tender, round, succulent, and about four or five inches high The leaves are smooth, of a thickish substance, and form a sheath to the stalk with their base The flowers come out singly from the tops of the stalks, arising from a two leaved spatha, they are long, purplish, and shew themselves in April and May

Adder-tongue leaved Bastard

2 Adder-tongue-leaved Bastard Hellebore This is often called Virginian Bastard Hellebore The root is fibrous The stalks are round, tender, upright, and adorned with two leaves only. One of the leaves belongs to the stalk, the other stands at the top of it, and serves for a spatha. The cauline leaf is oval and oblong, and the spathaceous leaf is flat, and spear-shaped At the top of this is situated the flower, which is of a reddish colour, and appears in May and June

and Lily leaved Bastard Hellebore

3 Lily-leaved Bastard Hellebore The root is palmated and fibrous The stalk is single, upright, tender, and five or six inches high The leaves are spear shaped, smooth, thick, and the lower one surrounds the stalk with its base At the top of the stalk is situated the spathaceous leaf This also is spear-shaped, and out of it arises one irregular lily-like flower, consisting of six petals Three of them petals are long, narrow, and of a dull purple; the other three are short, and of a reddish colour They appear in May and June, and the stalks decay soon after the leaves are past

These plants grow naturally in moist places in North America; so that whoever is desirous of having them, should procure the roots to be planted in tubs of earth when the stalks decay, which is in summer, after they have done flowering When they arrive in England, they should be turned out with the mould at the roots into some moist, sandy, shady place, but the first and the last sort should remain unmolested, suffering the natural herbage of the place to spring up with them, and they will then arise annually, and shew their flowers in the manner of our Orchis's or Satyrions The second sort is better adapted to garden culture, and may be encreased by parting the roots They are all very hardy, and will do extremely well provided the situation be moist enough, and the soil light and sandy, and not subject to bind and crack, as is the property of strong soils through dry weather in summer Culture

1 The first species is titled, *Arethusa radice bulbosa, scapo vaginato, spatha diphylla* In the *Acta Upsal* it is termed, *Serapias bulbis subrotundis, caule unifloro* Gronovius calls it, *Arethusa*, also, *Orchid affinis aquatica verna exigua*, and Plukenet names it, *Helleborine mariana monanthos, flore longo purpurascente liliaceo* It grows naturally in watery places in Virginia and Canada Titles

2 The second species is titled, *Arethusa radice fibrosa, scapo folio ovali, foliolo spathaceo lanceolato* In

In the *Hortus Cliffortianus* it is termed, *Cypripedium folio caulino ovato oblongo terminal. lanceolato plano* Plukenet calls it, *Helleborine Virginiana, ophioglossi folio*, and Morison, *Helleborine Virginiana diphylla* It grows in watery places in Virginia and Canada

3 The third species is, *Arethusa radice subpalmatâ, scapi folio, foliologue spathaceo, lanceolatis petalis, exterioribus adscendentibus* Gronovius calls it, *Serapias radicibus palmato-fibrosis, caule unifloro*, and Catesby, *Helleborine uni folio caulem ambiente, flore unico hexapetalo tribus petalis longis angustis obscurè purpureis, cæteris brevioribus roseis* It grows naturally in marshy places in most parts of North America

Class and order in the Linnean system. The characters. *Arethusa* is of the class and order *Gynandria Diandria*, and the characters are,

1 CALYX is a foliaceous spatha There is no perianthium

2 COROLLA is ringent, and composed of five oblong nearly equal petals; two of them are exterior, and all of them meet at top, and form the figure of an helmet There is a monophyllous nectarium, tubular at the base, and divided into two parts, the lower lip is reflexed, broad, rough, and propendent, the upper lip is narrow, tender, adheres to the style, and is hooked at the point

3 STAMINA are two very short filaments, sitting on the top of the pistil, having oval compressed antheræ

4 PISTILLUM consists of an oblong germen situated below the flower, an oblong incurved style surrounded by the interior lip of the nectarium, and an infundibuliforme stigma

5 PERICARPIUM is an oblong, oval, capsule formed of three valves, containing one cell, and opening in the angles

6 SEMINA The seeds are numerous and acerose

# CHAP L

## *ARETIA*

The plant described. THERE is only one species of this genus, called *Aretia* The root is thick, fibrous, and lasting The stalks arise immediately from the root, are about two or three inches high, and each is terminated by a flower The leaves are small, oblong, spear-shaped, and of a pale green The flowers come out singly from the tops of the stalk, they are salver-shaped, small, whitish, and there are some varieties which are brown, and others of a whitish green They appear in May, and the seeds ripen in June

Culture This species is propagated by sowing the seeds, as soon as they are ripe, in the places where they are to remain The land should be light, dry, and sand, , and when the plants come up, they will require no trouble, except keeping them clean from weeds By the end of April or May following the forwardest plants will flower If the seeds, when ripe, are permitted to scatter, they will frequently produce others, and this genus, though so small a plant, if it likes the soil and situation, will soon overspread a large spot in the garden, if not reduced and kept within bounds by good hoeing and management

Titles Though there be no other species of this genus, it stands by the distinctive name Haller gives it, that is, *Aretia villosa, scapis unifloris* In the *Amænitates Academicæ* it is termed, *Androsace caulescens, foliis alternis pedunculis unifloris* It is a native of Vallesia

Class and order in the Linnean system The characters *Aretia* is of the class and order *Pentandria Monogynia*, and the characters are,

1 CALYX is a monophyllous, bell shaped, permanent perianthium, cut into five obtuse segments

2 COROLLA is an hypocrateriform petal The tube is oval, and the length of the calyx The limb is divided into five obоval segments

3 STAMINA are five very short conical filaments in the middle of the tube, having erect acutish antheræ

4 PISTILLUM consists of a roundish germen, a filiforme style the length of the tube, and a capitated depressed stigma

5 PERICARPIUM is a capsule composed of five valves, and containing one cell

6. SEMINA The seeds are five

# CHAP. LI

## *ARISTOLOCHIA*, BIRTHWORT

Introductory Remarks.

MOST of the ſpecies of this genus were well known to the Ancients, and the accounts they give us of their great efficacy with child-bearing women, is altogether incredible. Their power is very great and uſeful in many diſorders, and that ſpecies of it called Snake Root, is a cure for the bite of the rattle ſnake, and other poiſonous ſerpents. Due reflection on the goodneſs of the All wiſe Creator ſhould not be paſſed by unnoticed, but his mercies magnified, in ordering theſe plants to abound in thoſe countries where ſuch noxious animals are to be dreaded. With us they are very uſeful in many caſes, they are imported from abroad, and are to be met with in the ſhops. I will, therefore, enumerate the ſorts, and put the Reader in a method how he may meet with them in his garden.

The hardy ſorts, (for there are ſeveral that are tender) are,

Species.

1. Round-rooted Birthwort.
2. Long-rooted Birthwort.
3. Hairy Birthwort.
4. Virginian Snake Root.
5. Upright Birthwort.

Deſcription of the Round rooted,

1. Round-rooted Birthwort. The ſhape of the roots is like thoſe of the common *Cyclamen*, but they will often grow to a larger ſize. From theſe ſpring a few weak, trailing ſtalks, about a foot and a half long. The leaves are heart-ſhaped, round, and obtuſe, they have no footſtalks, and are placed alternately on the branches. The flowers are produced ſingly from the wings of the leaves, they are long, narrow, of a faint yellow, with a dark purple end. They will be in blow in June and July, and ripen their ſeeds in the autumn.

Long-rooted,

2. Long-rooted Birthwort. The root of this plant is like that of a carrot, and from this iſſue a few weak, trailing branches, about a foot and a half long. The leaves are heart ſhaped, obtuſe, entire, and grow on ſhort footſtalks alternately on the branches. The flowers are produced ſingly from the wings of the leaves. Their colour is a dark purple. They will be in blow in June or July, and are ſucceeded by good ſeeds in the autumn.

and Hairy Birthwort.

3. Hairy Birthwort. This alſo hath a large, long tap root, like a carrot. The ſtalks are weak, hairy, and lie on the ground, without ſupport. The leaves are oblong, and very hairy. The flowers are very large, are produced from the wings of the leaves in June and July, and are ſucceeded by good ſeeds in the autumn.

Virginian Snake-Root,

4. Virginian Snake-Root. This hath ſeveral weak, round, flexible, procumbent ſtalks. The leaves are heart-ſhaped, oblong, plain, and are placed without order on the branches. The flowers grow ſingly from the wings of the leaves, they are long, crooked, and of a reddiſh colour. They will be in blow in June and July, and perfect their ſeeds in the autumn.

and Upright Birthwort.

5. Upright Birthwort. This hath a creeping root, which ſoon ſpreads itſelf to a great diſtance, and over-runs every thing that is near it. Theſe roots produce ſtalks, as they extend themſelves. They are ſingle, upright, firm, jointed, and will grow to about a foot and a half high. The leaves are heart-ſhaped, broad, and grow alternately at the joints on long footſtalks. The flowers are produced from the wings of the leaves in June and July, they are of a pale yellow colour, and are often ſucceeded in the autumn by ripe ſeeds.

The ſtalks of all theſe ſorts die to the ground in the winter, and new ones are produced in the ſpring. They are all of them uſed in medicine, and their virtues are very great. The firſt and the ſecond ſorts are of ſovereign uſe to women in labour, by promoting delivery. They are ſalutary againſt agues or poiſon, and very ſerviceable to thoſe who are troubled with ſhortneſs of breath, pains in the ſides, cramps, &c. They are remarkable for their drawing property, and the Gardener muſt remember, that thorns ſtruck into the fleſh, are extracted by a poultice of theſe roots. Medicinal properties of theſe ſpecies.

The Snake Root cures the bite of the rattle-ſnake, by chewing and ſwallowing ſome, and applying more to the wounded part. The roots are imported from Virginia and Carolina, and are ſold for various purpoſes in medicine with us.

The culture of the fifth ſort is not to be miſſed of. Take a piece of the root at any time of the year, but eſpecially in the autumn, winter, or ſpring, plant it in the worſt part of the garden, and it will grow, and ſoon extend itſelf to a conſiderable diſtance. There is little beauty in it, and it is chiefly propagated in phyſic-gardens for medicinal uſes. Culture

The other ſorts are propagated by ſeeds, which ſhould be ſown in the autumn in pots filled with light ſandy freſh earth. The pots ſhould be placed in a warm ſituation, and at the ſetting in of hard froſts, ſhould be removed into the green houſe, or under an hot bed frame, but when the weather becomes mild, ſhould reſume their former ſtation. About the middle or latter end of March, a moderate hot-bed ſhould be in readineſs, on this the pots ſhould be placed, filling up the vacancies with any common mould. This will ſoon bring up the plants, and as they appear, they muſt have frequent waterings, conſtant ſhade in the heat of the day, and as much free air as the weather will permit, to prevent their drawing weak. As the heat of the bed abates, they muſt be inured to the open air, and their ſituation need not be altered until the next ſpring, ſo here they may ſtand, ſhading them with mats in hot weather all ſummer, and covering them with the glaſſes in froſty weather all winter. About March, the plants ſhould be ſhaken out of the pots, and each ſhould be ſet in a ſmall pot filled with light, ſandy earth. This being done, their ſtation ſhould be under a frame, to be covered in bad weather. All ſummer the glaſſes ſhould be wholly taken off, but they muſt be ſhaded in the heat of the day with mats, and muſt have frequent waterings, however, this watering muſt be left off in the autumn, when the ſtalks decay. At the approach of bad weather, the glaſſes muſt be placed on the frames, and with that protection they muſt remain all winter. In the ſpring they muſt be planted out where they are to remain, which ſhould be in a bed of good, freſh, light earth, in a warm, well ſheltered place. If the ſummer ſhould prove dry, by ſeeds

they

they should be often watered, and kept constantly clean from weeds, and in the winter, if the weather is likely to be very severe, the beds should be hooped, to be covered with mats, to screen them from the frost, which is very apt to destroy them The summer following these plants will flower, and in the autumn afford good seeds, which should always be sown soon after they are ripe, because, if kept until spring, they frequently fail, or at least remain a whole year before they come up

Titles 1 Round rooted Birthwort is titled, *Aristolochia foliis cordatis subsessilibus obtusis, caule infirmo, floribus solitariis* In the *Hortus Cliffortianus* it is termed, *Aristolochia, caule infirmo ramoso, foliis cordatis integerrimis, floribus solitariis erectis* Caspar Bauhine calls it, *Aristolochia rotunda, flore ex purpura nigro* Another sort of it he terms, *Aristolochia rotunda, flore ex albo purpurascente* Clusius calls it *Aristolochia rotunda*, and Cammerarius simply, *Aristolochia* It grows naturally in Italy, Spain, and in some parts of France

2 Long rooted Birthwort This is titled, *Aristolochia foliis cordatis petiolatis integerrimis obtusiusculis, caule infirmo, floribus solitariis* Caspar Bauhine calls it, *Aristolochia longa vera* Another sort of it he terms, *Aristolochia longa Hispanica* Clusius calls it, *Aristolochia longa* It grows naturally in Italy, France, and Spain

3 Hairy Long-rooted Birthwort is titled, *Aristolochia foliis cordatis obtusiusculis hirtis, floribus solitariis pendulis recurvatis subtruncatis* Tournefort calls it, *Aristolochia longa subhirsuta, folio oblongo, flore maximo* It is a native of the Levant

4 Virginian Snake Root is titled, *Aristolochia foliis cordato-oblongis planis, caulibus infirmis super*è *flexuosis teretibus, floribus solitariis* In the *Materia Medica* it is titled, *Aristolochia caulibus infirmis angulosis flexuosis, foliis cordato-oblongis planis, floribus recurvis solitariis* Plukenet calls it, *Aristolochia pistolochia, sive serpentaria Virginiana, caule nodoso*, and Morison, *Aristolochia polyrhizos Virginiana, fructu parvo pentangulari* It grows naturally in Virginia, and other parts of America

5 Upright Birthwort This is titled, *Aristolochia foliis cordatis, caule erecto, floribus axillaribus confertis* In the *Hortus Cliffortianus* it is termed, *Aristolochia caule erecto simplicissimo foliis cordatis petiolatis, floribus lateralibus confertis* Caspar Bauhine calls it, *Aristolochia clematitis recta*, Clusius *Aristolochia clematitis vulgaris* It grows naturally in Austria, Gallia, and Tartary

Class and order in the Linnæan system The characters *Aristolochia* is of the class and order *Gynandria Hexandria*, and the characters are,

1 Calyx There is none

2 Corolla is a single, tubulous, irregular petal, the base is swelling and round, the tube is cylindrical and oblong, the limb is dilated, and the lower part of it hangs out like a tongue

3 Stamina There are no filaments, but six quadrilocular antheræ, which grow to the under part of the stigma

4 Pistillum consists of an oblong, angular germen, situated below the flower, of hardly any style, and a concave, roundish stigma, that is divided into six parts

5 Pericarpium is a large, sexangular capsule, of six cells

6 Semina The seeds are numerous, incumbent, and depressed

---

# CHAP. LII

# *ARNICA.*

Introductory Remarks THERE is no English name for *Arnica*, and the species of it have generally been supposed to belong to the Leopards Bane Some, indeed, have taken them for sorts of Dandelion, because there is some distant resemblance between the flowers of one and the other, and one species of it has been called by many an After The sorts, however, that are chiefly proper for this place, are known by the names of,

Species 1 Mountain Leopards Bane

2 Scorpion Leopards Bane

Description of the Mountain, 1 Mountain Leopards Bane Of this species there are two remarkable varieties One is called the Plantain-leaved Mountain Leopards Bane, the other, the Alpine Narrow-leaved Leopards Bane These are both very hardy perennials, and greatly esteemed in medicine The roots are large, thick, and succulent, and spread themselves all about From these grow the leaves, the figure of which is oval, their edges are free from serratures, and they a little resemble those of Plantain The leaves of the second variety are spear-shaped Between these arise the flower stalks They will be about a foot and a half high, and are garnished by a few pair of leaves that grow opposite to each other A single flower terminates each stalk The flowers are large, yellow, and not unlike those of the Dandelion They will be in blow in April and May, and are succeeded by oblong seeds, crowned with down, by which they are conveyed to a great distance

and Scorpion Leopards Bane 2 Scorpion Leopards Bane This hath a thick, jointed, fleshy, irregular root, having many offsets, contorted various ways, and this, together with the notion that such a root must necessarily cure the bite of a scorpion, has occasioned this species being distinguished by the above name From these roots rise several stalks garnished with leaves, growing alternately, having their edges finely serrated The flowers terminate the stalks, they are of the radical, composite kind, and are succeeded by oblong seeds, crowned with down, by which the wind conveys them to a great distance

Method of propagating them These plants are easily propagated by off sets from the roots or seeds They love a moist soil, and a shady situation, and the best time for dividing the roots, and sowing the seeds, is the autumn, though it may be done very well in the spring The roots and the seeds will readily grow, and after having once flowered, the wind will sow the seeds all over the garden, and plants will come up in improper places, which must either be transplanted to some other garden, or hoed down like weeds

Titles

1 The Mountain Leopards Bane is titled, *Arnica foliis ovatis integris caulinis geminis oppositis* In the *Flora Suecia* it is termed, *Doronicum foliis caulinis oppositis* in the *Flora Lapponica, Doronicum foliis oblongis ovalibus* Caspar Bauhine calls it, *Doronicum, plantaginis folio, alterum* The Alpine Narrow-leaved sort is termed in the *Flora Lapponica, Doronicum foliis lanceolatis* Tabernæmontanus calls it, *Caltha alpina.* They grow naturally on mountainous ground, also in meadows in Germany, and most of the colder parts of Europe

2 The Scorpion Leopards Bane is titled, *Arnica foliis alternis serratis* Caspar Bauhine calls it, *Doronicum radice scorpii brachiati*, Dalechamp, *Doronicum brachiatâ radice* It grows naturally in the moist upland grounds of Austria and Switzerland The *Doronicum radice dulci* of Caspar Bauhine is a variety of this species

Class and order in the Linnæan system

*Arnica* is of the class and order *Syngenesia Polygamia superflua*, and the characters are,

The characters.

1 CALYX The common calyx is shorter than the corolla, and is composed of several spear-shaped, erect scales, placed one over another

2 COROLLA is radiate and compound The hermaphrodite flowers are most numerous in the disk, and the female flowers in the radius are about twenty

Each hermaphrodite floret is tubulous, erect, and divided at the top into three or five parts

The female flowers are spear-shaped, long, patent, and are indented in three parts at the end

3 STAMINA The stamina of the hermaphrodite flowers are five very short filaments, with oblong antheræ, which join in a cylinder. These male flowers have five erect, awl-shaped filaments, but no antheræ

4 PISTILLUM in the hermaphrodite and female flowers is alike, and consists of an oblong germen, a single style the length of the stamina, and a bifid stigma

5 PERICARPIUM There is none

6 SEMINA The seeds of the hermaphrodite flowers are single, oblong, and crowned by long, hairy down

The seeds of the female flowers are like those of the hermaphrodite, but have no down

The receptacle is naked

# CHAP LIII

## *ARTEMISIA,* MUGWORT

Introductory remarks

AS the weakest, and seemingly meanest flower displays, upon close examination, the wonderful workmanship of the all-wise Creator, as well as the most splendid and gaudy, our gardens should not be wholly destitute of those plants which afford not the most tempting appearance Accordingly, the disposition of the ground ought to be such for the reception of the flower-roots, that the most showy, or those that are called good flowers ought to be stationed in the most conspicuous place of view, whilst the others should be placed at a distance, or in beds surrounding the choicest part of the flower garden, for the nicer observations of the Botanist, or such lovers of Nature, who are led to due contemplations, from the amazing contrivance and variety in all her works

The species of *Artemisia* are to be for this distant, or back part of the flower-garden, for the Reader must be acquainted, that under this genus are arranged the Mugworts, the Wormwood, the Southernwood, and all the vast variety that belongs to them, plants of no very great beauty as flowers, but nevertheless of some singularity, and many of them of admirable virtue and use

Of the species then for this place, there are,

Species.

1 The Common Mugwort
2 The Common Field Southernwood
3 The Wormwood
4 Tansey-leaved Mugwort
5 Siberian Narrow-leaved Mugwort
6 Helvetian Mugwort
7 Tartarian Southernwood
8 Roman Wormwood
9 Sea Wormwood
10 Lavender leaved Sea Wormwood
11 Alpine Wormwood
12 Male Southernwood

These are all of them distinct species, and comprehend many sorts, which differ in size, or some respect or other

1 The Common Mugwort is far from being a bad plant, but what are chiefly valued of it in gardens, are its two varieties, the Silver-striped, and the Gold-striped Mugwort The leaves are large, and finely divided The segments are acute; and the whole leaf is downy underneath The Silver-striped is pleasingly variegated with white, the Gold with yellow, and they are not apt to run away from their colour, which makes them more valuable The stalks among these leaves rises upright and firm, it is garnished with leaves, and the flowers are produced from the upper part These grow in single spikes, will be in blow in June, and the seeds ripen soon after As the variegated sorts are the kinds chiefly preserved in flower-gardens, they are continued and encreased only by parting of the roots, while the plain sort may be multiplied without end by the roots or seeds Common Mugwort,

2 Common Field Southernwood The Southernwood of our gardens is a kind of shrub, and permitted to join in our wilderness quarters This is a distinct species from that, of a disagreeable smell, and is found growing naturally in some parts of England The leaves are finely divided into a multitude of very narrow segments, not much unlike those of fennel Among these arise several small, tough branches, full of flowers They are adorned with smaller leaves at the joints, composed of many segments, and the flowers grow in spikes from almost every part Their colour is yellow, and they will be in blow in August Common Field Southernwood,

3 Wormwood The Wormwood grows chiefly about towns and villages, under walls, by the sides of ways, and on banks and dunghills in many parts of England, and is seldom cultivated in gardens The leaves are very much divided, and are beautiful, with an hoary look The flowers grow from the sides of the stalks They are Wormwood,

are nearly globular, hang down, and produce ſeeds enough to over-run a garden

Tanſey-leaved Mugwort. 4 Tanſey-leaved Mugwort The leaves of this plant are divided in the manner of Tanſey Their upper ſurface is bright and ſhining, but their under is downy, thoſe on the ſtalks are ſmall, pinnated, and have footſtalks The flowers grow in ſingle ſpikes, they are ſmall, and afford plenty of ſeeds ſoon after they are fallen

Siberian Narrow-leaved Mugwort, 5 Siberian Narrow-leaved Mugwort The leaves of this ſpecies are ſingle, ſpear-ſhaped, narrow, ſmooth on their upper ſurface, but downy underneath, they are of a ſtiffiſh ſubſtance, and their edges are acutely ſerrated The ſtalks grow to about two feet high, and are garniſhed with ſmall, ſpear ſhaped, ſerrated leaves The flowers grow from the wings of the leaves, near the top, they are produced ſingle, but lower, they are formed into ſmall ſpikes Their colour is yellow, and they are ſoon ſucceeded by plenty of ſeeds

Helvetian Mugwort, 6 Helvetian Mugwort This is a very low-growing plant The leaves are ſmall, palmated, and divided into ſeveral beautiful ſegments They are ſilky, of a ſilvery white, and are placed on footſtalks on the branches, they are ſingle, downy, and will grow to about eight or ten inches high The flowers terminate the ſtalks in kind of umbels, their colour is yellow, they have downy cups, and are placed on very ſhort footſtalks This is a pretty little perennial, and by its ſilvery leaves eſpecially, cauſes reſpect in any place

Tartarian Southernwood, 7 Tartarian Southernwood The leaves are ſingle, ſpear-ſhaped, ſmooth, and entire, they are finely ſcented, and in this the chief excellence of this plant conſiſts The flowers grow from the upper parts of the ſtalk They are compoſed of about half a dozen female florets, and twice that number of hermaphrodite, but are little regarded on their account

Roman Wormwood, 8 Roman Wormwood The leaves are compoſed of many narrow parts, that are downy on their under ſide The ſtalks grow to about a foot and a half long, and are plentifully garniſhed with leaves and flowers The flowers are produced from the wings of the leaves, their colour is yellow, they are ſmall, and hang downward, will be in blow in July or Auguſt, and ripen their ſeeds ſoon after

Sea Wormwood, 9 Sea Wormwood The leaves of this ſpecies are very downy, and divided into many parts The ſtalks are ſmall, and the flowers are produced from the ſides in ſmall ſpikes, growing alternately There are ſeveral ſorts of it, and ſome of them are finely ſcented They have variouſly gone by the names of Belgic Sea Wormwood, French Sea Wormwood, German Sea Wormwood, Sweet ſcented Sea Wormwood, Creeping Sea Wormwood, &c They grow upon many of the ſea-coaſts, but particularly France and Spain They flower in July and Auguſt, and produce plenty of ſeeds ſoon after

Lavender leaved Sea Wormwood, 10 Lavender-leaved Sea Wormwood Of this plant alſo, there are a great many ſorts growing naturally on moſt of the ſea ſhores of the ſouthern parts of Europe They are low-growing plants The leaves on the ſtalk are ſpear-ſhaped, hairy, and their edges are entire, but the radical leaves are very much divided Some of theſe ſorts have leaves that are moderately broad, others very narrow, and ſome much reſemble thoſe of Mugwort The flowers grow alternately from the ſides of the ſtalks, in a drooping manner They flower at the time with moſt of the other ſorts, and produce plenty of ſeeds for increaſe

Alpine Wormwood, 11 Alpine Wormwood There is great variety of this ſort, which vary alſo very much in different ſituations, and the natural appearance in their uſual places of growth alters very much by good culture in our gardens The leaves are pinnated, and very downy, ſome of them are of a ſilvery white, and ſilky, whilſt others are quite green The ſtalks of ſome are proſtrate, others riſing, and the flowers alſo differ in ſize They blow at the uſual time, and their ſeeds ripen in plenty This ſpecies comprehends the Dwarf Alpine, the Hoary Wormwood, the Creeping Roman Wormwood, the Silvery-leaved Oriental Wormwood, the Narrow Downy leaved Large-flowering Oriental Wormwood, the Scentleſs Oriental Wormwood, the Green Wormwood, &c all of which have been reckoned as diſtinct ſpecies by antiquated Botaniſts

and Common Southernwood deſcribed. 12 Common Southernwood This ſpecies, though a kind of ſhrub, is uſually planted by the outſide of flower gardens, for the improvement of noſegays, it being poſſeſſed of a ſtrong odour, which, to many, is very agreeable It is a well-known plant, and is eaſily propagated by cuttings The beſt time for planting them is Auguſt or September, though they will grow at any time of the year, and if the ſituation is ſhady, very few of them will fail growing, let the ſoil be what it will

Culture. The other ſorts alſo are eaſily propagated They come up plentifully from ſeeds, or may be ſpeedily encreaſed by cuttings or ſlips from the roots The roots may be divided at any time of the year, though the beſt ſeaſon is autumn and ſpring The cuttings ſhould be planted in April or in Auguſt, in a moiſt, ſhady border, and the beſt time for ſowing the ſeeds is the autumn, ſoon after they are ripe

As they are not much regarded, unleſs for medicinal purpoſes ſo they call for little trouble in their culture, for, beſides that they may be encreaſed with the utmoſt facility the above way, they come up readily themſelves from ſcattered ſeeds and there are very few of them, if they like the ſoil and have once flowered, that will not, for the future, afford you plants enough

Titles. 1 The Common Mugwort is titled, *Artemiſia foliis pinnatifidis planis inciſis ſubtus tomentoſis, racemis ſimplicibus, floribus ovatis radio quinquefloro* In the *Hortus Cliffortianus* it is termed, *Artemiſia foliis pinnatifidis planis laciniatis, floribus erectis* Caſpar Bauhine calls it, *Artemiſia vulgaris major*, John Bauhine, *Artemiſia vulgaris* It grows common in England, and moſt parts of Europe

2 Common Field Southernwood is titled, *Artemiſia foliis multifidis linearibus, caulibus procumbentibus virgatis* Caſpar Bauhine calls it, *Abrotanum campeſtre*, Cammerarius, *Ambroſia altera* It grows naturally in ſandy, gravelly ſoils in England, and moſt parts of Europe

3 Wormwood is titled, *Artemiſia foliis compoſitis multifidis, floribus ſubgloboſis pendulis receptaculo villoſo* Gmelin calls it, *Abſinthium incanum, foliis compoſitis latiuſcule multifidis, floribus ſubgloboſis pendulis* Caſpar Bauhine calls it, *Abſinthium Ponticum ſive Romanum, officinarum ſive Dioſcoridis* Cammerarius calls it ſimply *Abſinthium* It grows naturally by the ſides of paths, on banks, dunghills, &c in moſt parts of Europe

4 Tanſey leaved Mugwort is titled, *Artemiſia foliis bipinnatis ſubtus tomentoſis nitidis pinnis tranſverſis, racemis ſimplicibus* Gmelin calls it, *Artemiſia radice perenni, foliis pinnatis pinnatifidis inciſis ſerratis, calycibus ſubrotundis viribus nutantibus* It grows naturally in Siberia

5 Siberian Narrow-leaved Mugwort is titled, *Artemiſia foliis lanceolatis ſubtus tomentoſis integerrimis dentatiſque, florum radio ſub quinque floro* Gmelin calls it, *Artemiſia foliis planis lanceolato-linearibus*

*linearibus inferioribus ſæpe ex pinnato-dentatis* It grows naturally in Siberia

6 Helvetian Mugwort This is titled, *Artemiſia foliis palmatis multifidis ſericeis, caulibus adſcendentibus, floribus glomeratis ſubfaſtigiatis*. Haller calls it, *Artemiſia floribus umbellatis, foliis petiolatis palmatis ſericeis*, and Caſpar Bauhine, *Abſinthium Alpinum candidum humile* It grows naturally in Helvetia and Vallesia

7 Tartarian Southernwood This is titled, *Artemiſia foliis lanceolatis integerrimis* Tournefort calls it, *Abrotanum lini folio acriori & odorato*, Caſpar Bauhine, *Dracunculus hortenſis*, and Dodonæus, *Draco herba* It grows naturally in Tartary and Siberia

8 Roman Wormwood is titled, *Artemiſia foliis multipartitis ſubtus tomentoſis, floribus ſubrotundis nutantibus receptaculo nudo* Caſpar Bauhine calls it, *Abſinthium Ponticum tenuifolium incanum*, and Dodonæus, *Abſinthium tenuifolium* It grows naturally in Hungary, Myſia, and Thrace

9 Sea Wormwood is titled, *Artemiſia foliis multipartitis tomentoſis, racemis cernuis, floſculis femineis ternis* Van Royen calls it, *Artemiſia foliis compoſitis multifidis, racemis ſimplicibus alternis, floribus oblongis ſeſſilibus* Caſpar Bauhine calls it, *Abſinthium ſeriphium Belgicum*, alſo, *Abſinthium ſeriphium Germanicum* It grows on the ſea ſhores in many parts of Europe

10 Lavender-leaved Sea Wormwood This is titled, *Artemiſia foliis caulinis lanceolatis integris radicalibus multifidis, floſculis femineis ternis* Caſpar Bauhine calls it, *Abſinthium maritimum, lavendulæ folio*; Dodonæus, *Abſinthium anguſtifolium*, and Columna, *Abrotanum latifolium rarius, artemiſiæ folio* It grows on the ſea ſhores of the ſouthern parts of Europe

11 Alpine Wormwood This is titled, *Artemiſia foliis pinnatis, caulibus adſcendentibus hirſutis, floribus globoſis cernuis receptaculo papposo* Gmelin calls it, *Artemiſia foliis pinnatis piloſis, ramis adſcendentibus floribus oblongis ſubereƈtis* Another ſort of it he terms, *Abſinthium viride, foliis multifidis linearibus* Plukenet calls it, *Abſinthium Ponticum repens & ſupinum*, Boccone, *Abſinthium pumilum paneum minus, argenteo ſericeo folio*, Caſpar Bauhine, *Abſinthium Alpinum incanum*, and Tournefort, *Abſinthium orientale tenuifolium argenteum & ſericeum, flore magno* It grows naturally among rocks, &c in Siberia

12 Male, or Common Southernwood This is titled, *Artemiſia foliis ramoſiſſimis ſetaceis, caule ereƈto ſuffruticoſo* Caſpar Bauhine calls it, *Abrotanum mas anguſtifolium majus*, and Dodonæus, *Abrotanum mas* It grows naturally on the mountainous parts of Syria, Galatia, Cappadocia, Italy, and about Montpelier in France

# C H A P. LIV.

## *ARUM*, WAKE ROBIN, or, CUCKOW PINT.

Introductory Remarks THE great ſingularity of the ſpecies of this genus, renders them worthy of a place in any garden They are widely different from the reſt of the flowering tribe, and the diſpoſition of their flowers gives a freſh inſtance of the various ways with which Nature has bountifully adorned our gardens and fields The hardy ſpecies are,

Species 1 The Common *Arum*, Wake Robin, or, Cuckow Pint

2 Virginian *Arum*

3 Appennine *Arum*

4 Italian Narrow-leaved *Arum*

5 Italian Broad-leaved *Arum*, or *Ariſarum*

6 Dwarf American *Arum*

7 Trifoliate *Arum*

8 Dragons

Deſcription of the Common, 1 The Common *Arum* has a pretty effeƈt early in the ſpring, by its beautiful green leaves Theſe are ſmooth, haſtated, and their edges are entire They are of a ſhining green, though there are two or three varieties of it The leaves of one are ſpotted with dark ſpots, thoſe of another ſort are finely veined with white, and another ſort is ſpotted with white and black The white-veined kind grows much larger than the Common *Arum*, and is the ſort that is chiefly preſerved in gardens In the center riſes the ſtalk, ſupporting a large ſpatha, which opening, diſcovers the flowers, having a long red column placed above them They will be in blow in April, and after the ſpatha is withered, and the flowers are paſt, there ſucceeds them a multitude of red berries at the top of the ſtalk, which are the ſeeds, and which will be ripe in July

Virginian, 2 Virginian *Arum* The leaves of this ſpecies are haſtated and acute, though they are a little inclined to a cordated figure Between theſe riſe the flowers They have ſhort footſtalks, and will be in blow in May, though they rarely produce ſeeds in our gardens This is a ſmaller plant, of much inferior beauty to our Common *Arum*, and muſt have a warm ſituation, or it will be liable to be deſtroyed by the ſeverity of our winters

Appennine 3 Appennine *Arum* There are two or three ſorts of this ſpecies, all of which are very low plants The leaves in general are haſtated, and have ſhort footſtalks, though there are of it ſome with round leaves, and others that differ a little in their ſhape The flowers riſe immediately from the root, they are very inconſiderable, will be in blow in April, and when they ripen their ſeeds, which is not common with us, it will be about July

Italian Narrow leaved, 4 Italian Narrow-leaved *Arum* This alſo is a ſmall plant The leaves are ſpear-ſhaped and narrow The flowers grow immediately from the roots, are very inconſiderable, will be in blow in April, and ſeldom produce good ſeeds in theſe parts

Broad leaved Italian, 5 Broad-leaved Italian *Arum* This is nearly upon a ſtamp with the two foregoing ſorts The leaves are heart-ſhaped, oblong, and broad The ſpatha is oſhd, and the ſpadix is incurved It flowers in April, and the ſeeds rarely ripen here Theſe three ſorts have been uſually called *Ariſarum*, or Friers Hood, that being the generical word which

which, among old Botaniſts, was made to comprehend their ſpecies

Dwarf American

6 Dwarf American *Arum* This is a very low plant The leaves and flowers are ſeldom above eight or nine inches from the ground The leaves are pedated, they are compoſed of ſeveral ſpear-ſhaped lobes, having their edges entire The ſpadix rears its head above the ſpatha, and the flowers are very much like thoſe of our Common *Arum* It ſeldom is in blow before June, and very rarely produces ſeeds in these parts

and Three leaved Arum deſcribed

7 Three-leaved *Arum* This alſo is a ſmall plant The leaves are uſually two from each root from which they grow immediately on long footſtalks Each leaf is compoſed of three oblong, broad, pointed lobes, of a greyiſh green, having red veins Between theſe grows the flower, which is of various colours in the different varieties, though the moſt common is purple, and there is of it the green and the white The ſpatha is very beautiful, its inſide is uſually purple, ſweetly variegated with white They will be in perfection in June, but they ſeldom produce ſeeds with us

Deſcription of the Dragons

8 Dragons Theſe are large-growing plants, and there are ſeveral varieties of them, but the Silver and the Gold-ſtriped Dragons are the moſt eſteemed, and much ſought for in our gardens Their ſingularity, more than their beauty, cauſes them to be reſpected The roots are large and fleſhy, and the ſtalk will grow to a yard in height These are ſpotted in the manner of a ſnake's belly, which, to ſome, is an offenſive look, whilſt others again are much pleaſed with ſuch ſtrange ſingularity The leaves are pedated; they are large, ſmooth, and each is compoſed of ſeveral ſpear-ſhaped lobes, having their edges entire The ſpadix is very large, and ſhaped like a club It grows erect, and is for the moſt part of a fine purple The ſpatha alſo is purple, and large, ſo that when in full blow, theſe plants have an auguſt look They flower in June and July, and produce ripe, red ſeeds in September, about which time the ſtalks decay, and freſh ones will be put up late the following ſpring

Theſe plants have a ſtrong, diſagreeable ſcent, which occaſions their being baniſhed from gardens by many They are greatly eſteemed in medicine, being found ſerviceable in many caſes, on which account they are propagated by ſome in great plenty

It is ſaid, that no ſerpent will come near a perſon who has any part of theſe plants about him

Method of propagating theſe ſpecies by ſeeds

All theſe ſorts are to be raiſed by ſeeds, though the uſual way of propagating them is by parting of the roots The beſt time for this is the autumn, ſoon after the leaves decay The ſeeds ſhould be ſown in the autumn, ſoon after they are ripe, becauſe, if they are kept until ſpring, they uſually remain a year in the ground before they come up The ſeeds of the foreign ſorts muſt be procured from the places where they naturally grow Theſe ſhould be ſown as ſoon as they arrive, in pots filled with light earth After this, ſet them in the ſhade until the ſpring following, and in dry weather frequently water the pots In March, plunge the pots into a moderate hot-bed, this will ſoon bring up the ſeeds, uſe them to the air as much as poſſible, and draw out the weakeſt where they are too cloſe In the autumn, when the leaves decay, let each plant have a ſeparate pot, and in the winter ſet them in the green-houſe, or under a hot-bed frame In the ſummer following, plunge the pots up to the rim in a ſhady part of the garden, and about Auguſt or September turn the plants out of the pots into the places where they are deſigned to remain This ſhould be in a well-ſheltered place, for they are ſometimes deſtroyed by the ſeverity of our winters



1 Wake Robin is titled, *Arum acaule, foliis haſtatis integerrimis, ſpadice clavato* Caſpar Bauhine titles three ſorts of it, calling one, *Arum vulgare non maculatum*, another, *Arum venis albis*, and a third, *Arum maculatum, maculis candidis ſive nigris* Fuchſius calls it ſimply, *Arum* We have it common in our hedges and woods Titles.

2 Virginian *Arum* This is titled, *Arum acaule, foliis haſtato cordatis acutis, angulis obtuſis* It grows naturally in the moſt parts of Virginia

3 Appennine *Arum* This is titled, *Arum acaule, foliis haſtatis, ſpathâ declinata filiformi-ſubulata* Tournefort calls it, *Ariſarum flore in tenuem caudam abeunte*, Boccone, *Ariſarum minus proboſcideum* Barrelier, *Ariſarum latifolium minus repens ceſpitoſum* It grows naturally on the Appennine Mountains

4 Italian Narrow leaved *Arum* This is titled, *Arum acaule, foliis lanceolatis, ſpadice ſetaceo declinato* Caſpar Bauhine calls it, *Arum anguſtifolium* It grows naturally near Rome, alſo in Dalmatia, the Eaſt and in ſome parts of France

5 Broad leaved Italian *Arum* This is, *Arum acaule, foliis cordato oblongis, ſpathâ bifidâ, ſpadice incurvo* Caſpar Bauhine calls it, *Ariſarum latifolium majus*, alſo, *Ariſarum latifolium alterum*, and Cluſius, *Ariſarum latifolium* It grows naturally in Italy, Portugal, France and Spain

6 Dwarf American *Arum* This is titled, *Arum foliis pedatis foliolis lanceolatis integerrimis ſuperantibus ſpatham ſpadice breviorem* Herman calls it, *Arum polyphyllum minus & humilius*, Plukenet, *Arum, ſive ariſarum Virginianum, dracontii folio pene viridi longo acuminato* It grows naturally in America

7 Three leaved *Arum* This is titled, *Arum acaule, foliis ternatis, floribus monoicis* Caſpar Bauhine calls it, *Dracunculus, ſive ſerpentaria triphylla Braſiliana*, Moriſon, *Arum, ſive ariſarum triphyllum minus pene atro-rubente, Virginianum*, and Plukenet, *Arum, ſive ariſarum minus marianum, flore & pene ex pallido vireſcente* It grows naturally in Virginia

8 The Dragons is titled, *Arum foliis pedatis foliolis lanceolatis integerrimis æquantibus ſpatham ſpadice longiorem* In the *Hortus Cliffortianus* it is termed, *Arum foliis palmatis foliolis undecim lanceolatis integerrimis intermediis majoribus, ſpadice clavato* Caſpar Bauhine calls it, *Dracunculus polyphyllus*, Dodonæus, *Dracontium* It grows naturally in the ſouthern parts of Europe

*Arum* is of the claſs and order *Gynandria Polyandria*, and the characters are, Claſs and order in the Linnæan ſyſtem The characters

1 CALYX The ſpatha is of one leaf, large, and oblong It is convoluted at the baſe, connivent at the top, compreſſed in the middle, and coloured within

The ſpadix is ſimple, club ſhaped, and a little ſhorter than the ſpatha It is coloured, and ſupports the germina

2 COROLLA There is none

3 STAMINA There are no filaments, but there are two rows of nectaria, about the middle of the ſpadix, that are thick at their baſe, and terminate in ſlender cirrhi, and between them are the antheræ, which are numerous, four ſquared, and ſit cloſe to the body of the ſpadix

4 PISTILLUM conſiſts of numerous oval germina at the baſe of the ſpadix, having hairy ſtigmas, without any ſtyles

5 PERICARPIUM conſiſts of the like number of globoſe, unilocular berries

6 SEMINA The ſeeds are many, and roundiſh

# CHAP. LV.

## *ARUNDO*, The REED.

Species

OF this genus there are,
1. The Common Marsh Reed, or Reed Grass.
2. The Branched Reed Grass.
3. The Small Reed Grass.
4. The Sea Reed Grass.
5. The Indian Reed.

Remarks.

The first four sorts grow naturally in many parts of England, and are never propagated in gardens, unless for philosophical observation in some marshy out-part of the garden. The first species, however, the Gardener is much indebted to, for its great services in defending his tender plants in the winter, by the admirable hedges it forms. The fifth is the species for the Gardeners propagation, which has a singular and lofty look, when planted either among tall-growing perennials, or singly, in the moistest parts of the garden. There are two sorts of it,

Varieties.

The Common Indian Reed.
The Variegated Indian Reed.

Description of the Common,

Both belong to one species, though the Common Sort will grow to a much greater height than the other. It will arrive to twelve or fourteen feet high. The stalks are large, jointed, and round. The leaves are large and long, and the flowers are produced in diffused panicles; they flower in August, and in the autumn the stalks decay, and a fresh one succeeds them from the same root in the spring, which, by the autumn, will have made such amazing shoots as the former.

and Variegated Indian Reed.

The Variegated sort differs from the other only in that the leaves are variegated, and the whole plant of much smaller growth. The stalk seldom rises higher than six feet. The leaves also are narrow, but being variegated, are thought to have a pretty effect by those who are fond of such sort of plants.

Both these sorts are hardy enough to resist the cold of our severest winters, and the moistest parts of the garden must be allotted them.

Method of propagating these sorts.

They are propagated by dividing of the roots in February or March. They will readily grow, but will not arrive the first year to near the height they will the summer following. They encrease pretty fast; so that if they are left undisturbed for some years, and they like their situation, a large number of these strong reeds will arise from the same root, which in the autumn may be cut down near the bottom, and afterwards used as walking-sticks, fishing rods, &c.

1. The Common Marsh Reed is titled, *Arundo calycibus quinquefloris, paniculâ laxâ*. In the *Flora Suecia* it is termed, *Arundo paniculâ laxâ, flosculis quinis*. Sauvages calls it, *Arundo paniculâ laxâ, calycibus sebbifloris*; Caspar Bauhine, *Arundo vulgaris, sive phragmites Dioscoridis*. It grows naturally in rivers and lakes in most parts of Europe. Titles.

2. Branched Reed Grass is titled, *Arundo calycibus unifloris, culmo ramoso*. Caspar Bauhine calls it, *Gramen arundinaceum, paniculâ molli spadiceâ, majus*. It grows naturally in moist woods, hedges, and marshes, in most parts of Europe.

3. Small Reed Grass. This is titled, *Arundo calycibus unifloris, paniculâ erectâ, foliis subtus glabris*. Scheuchzer calls it, *Gramen arundinaceum paniculatum montanum, paniculâ spadiceo-viridi, semine papposo*. It grows naturally in most parts of Europe.

4. Sea Reed Grass. This is titled, *Arundo calycibus unifloris, foliis involutis mucronato pungentibus*. Caspar Bauhine calls it, *Gramen sparteum spicatum, foliis mucronatis longioribus*. It grows naturally near the sea-shores of Europe and America.

5. The Indian Reed is titled, *Arundo calycibus trifloris, paniculâ diffusâ*. In the *Hortus Cliffortianus* it is termed, *Arundo sativa*; and the spotted sort is called, *Arundo indica laconica versicolor*. Caspar Bauhine calls it, *Arundo sativa, quæ Donax Dioscordis*. It grows naturally in Spain and Portugal.

*Arundo* is of the class and order *Triandria Digynia*, and the characters are, Class and order in the Linnæan system.

1. CALYX is an erect glume, formed of two oblong, pointed valves, containing one or more flowers. The characters.

2. COROLLA is formed of two oblong, acuminated valves. These are of the length of the calyx, and have at their base a downy matter, which rises almost the length of the flower.

3. STAMINA consist of three capillary filaments, with bifurcated antheræ.

4. PISTILLUM consists of an oblong germen, and two capillary, reflexed, hairy styles, with simple stigmas.

5. PERICARPIUM. It has no other pericarpium than the corolla, which grows to the seed.

6. SEMEN. The seed is single, oblong, pointed, and has long down at the base.

# CHAP. LVI.

## *ASARUM*, ASARABACCA

Introduction to observations

THE different sorts of *Asarum* afford more pleasure from their singularity than their real beauty, and some of them, especially the English sorts, are more worthy of cultivation for the sake of their uses in medicine than any properties they are possessed of for ornamenting the Flower Collection They cause, however, variety, and as they are as useful for the philosopher's inspection as any of the most gaudy sorts, they claim a place here of course in the Collection of Perennials The distinct hardy species of *Asarum*, then, are,

Species

1 English Asarabacca
2 Canada Asarabacca
3 Virginian Asarabacca

English,

1 English Asarabacca is pretty well known, being common in many gardens, where it is chiefly cultivated for its uses in medicine It is an emetic, and a great sternutative It is recommended in the gout and dropsy, and several other chronic disorders, and is also a very powerful emmenagogue The roots of this species are oblong, thick, fleshy, and creeping, sending forth numerous fibres From these immediately arise the leaves, on short footstalks, they are kidney-shaped, auriculated, thick, smooth, and of a deep green colour The flowers also arise immediately from the roots, on still shorter footstalks, so that they are hid by the leaves, and must be sought for when desired They are of a purplish colour, will be in blow in May, and the seeds that succeed them will be ripe in July or August

Canada,

2 Canada Asarabacca sends forth its leaves and flowers from the root The leaves are moderately large, and stand on pretty long footstalks They are hairy, and their figure is reniforme; but instead of being bluntly rounded at the two extremities like the former, these are pointed The flowers grow in the same manner as the former, and their outside is of a greenish tinge, they will be in blow in May, and the seeds ripen in August

and Virginian Asarabacca, described

3 Virginian Asarabacca. The leaves of this species are of a cordated figure Their extremity is very much rounded, and their footstalks are very long They are smooth, and their upper surface is veined a little like those of the autumnal *Cyclamen* The flowers stand on long footstalks, and are of a deep purple colour, they will be in blow in May, and the seeds will be ripe in August

Method of raising these plants

All these sorts may be encreased at pleasure by dividing the roots, at almost any time of the year, though the autumn is rather the best season, and nothing more need be observed than to plant the English sort in a moist shady place The other sorts, also, love the shade, but they must have a place well protected, being more tender, otherwise they will be liable to be destroyed by the severity of our winters

Titles

1 English Asarabacca is termed, *Asarum foliis reniformibus obtusis binis* It is by numerous authors named, *Asarum foliis subcordatis petiolatis* Caspar and John Bauhine, Cammerarius, and Ray, call it simply, *Asarum* Parkinson terms it, *Asarum vulgare* It grows naturally in woody places, particularly in Lancashire

2 Canada Asarabacca is termed, *Asarum foliis reniformibus mucronatis* Gronovius calls it, *Asarum foliis subcordatis petiolatis*, Morison, *Asarum Canadense, mucronato folio*, and Cornutus, *Asarum Canadense* It is a native of Canada

3 Virginian Asarabacca is titled, *Asarum foliis cordatis obtusis glabris petiolatis* This is the *Asarum Virginianum, pistolochiæ foliis subrotundis, Cyclaminis more maculatis* It grows common in Virginia, Maryland, and Carolina

Class and order in the Linnæan system The characters

*Asarum* is of the class and order *Dodecandria Monogynia*, and the characters are,

1 CALYX is a thick, coloured, bell-shaped, permanent perianthium, formed of a single leaf, and lightly cut into three erect reflexed segments
2 COROLLA There is none
3 STAMINA are twelve subulated filaments, about half the length of the calyx, with oblong antheræ, fastened in the middle to the filaments
4 PISTILLUM consists of a germen at the bottom of the calyx, having a cylindric style the length of the stamina, and a stellated stigma cut into six reflexed segments
5 PERICARPIUM is a coriaceous capsule of about six cells
6 SEMINA The seeds are numerous and oval

CHAP.

# C H A P   LVII

## *ASCLEPIAS*, SWALLOW-WORT

Species

OF this genus there are,

1 Common White Swallow-Wort
2 Black Swallow-Wort
3 Syrian Dogsbane
4 Purple Upright Horned Dogsbane
5 Carolina Purple Dogsbane
6 Variegated flowered Dogsbane
7 Small Upright Canada Dogsbane
8 Hairy Virginian Dogsbane
9 Hairy New England Dogsbane
10 Siberian Mountain Swallow-Wort
11 Narrow leaved Maryland Swallow-Wort

Description of the Common White

1 Common White Swallow Wort hath a strong fibrous root, from which arise several slender upright, jointed, single stalks, to the height of about two feet The leaves are of an oval lanceolated figure, acute pointed, and grow opposite by pairs on short footstalks From the wings of the leaves the flowers are produced in small clusters, their colour is white, they will be in blow in June, and ripen their seeds in September The root of this sort is a common drug in the shops

and Black Swallow Wort;

2 Black Swallow Wort has several weak slender, twining stalks, which will grow to be about four feet long The leaves are oval, spear-shaped, smooth, and grow opposite by pairs The flowers rise from the wings of the leaves, in small clusters, their colour is black, they will be in blow in June, and ripen their seeds in the autumn

Syrian,

3 Syrian Dogsbane has a creeping root, from which arise several strong, upright, unbranching stalks, to the height of about four feet The leaves are large, oval, and oblong, they are of a thick consistence, of a dusky green colour on their upper surface, but downy underneath, and grow opposite by pairs on the stalks The flowers grow in small umbels, from the wings of the leaves, they are of a bad purple colour, and hang drooping, but are finely scented They will be in blow in July, and are succeeded by ripe seeds in the autumn

Purple Upright Horned

4 Purple Upright Horned Dogsbane The stalks of this sort are single or unbranching, and will grow to about two feet high The leaves are of an oval figure, hairy on their under side, and placed opposite by pairs The flowers are produced from the tops of the stalks, in upright umbels, they are of a fine purple colour, and have erect nectaria, called Horns, they will be in blow in July, but are seldom succeeded by seeds in our gardens

Carolina Purple,

5 Carolina Purple Dogsbane The stalks are single, and will grow to be about a yard high The leaves are oval, hairy on their under side, and grow opposite by pairs on the stalks The flowers grow in upright umbels, but the nectaria are declining, they are of a very bad purple colour, will be in blow in July, but are rarely succeeded by good seeds

Variegated flowered,

6 Variegated-flowered Dogsbane This species in America is called *Wisank*, which name has been adopted by some of our Gardeners, others have called it the Old American Dogsbane The stalks are upright, firm, unbranching, and will grow to about a yard high The leaves grow opposite by pairs, on short reddish footstalks, they are of an oval figure, rough, and their colour is a coarse green, with a reddish midrib The flowers grow from the tops of the stalks, in large umbels, supported by very short downy footstalks Each separate flower is rather small, but being finely variegated with red or crimson, having a whitish ground, and being produced in large tufts, they make a pretty appearance They often flower late in the autumn, and if the plants are set in pots, and removed into the greenhouse, they will frequently shew them selves in winter, when few other flowers appear on which account this is preserved by some as a greenhouse plant, though it will grow abroad in a warm soil and situation

Small Upright Canada

7 Small Upright Canada Dogsbane The stalks are erect, will grow to a foot and a half in height, and branch a little near the top The leaves are spear-shaped, smooth, and grow opposite by pairs on the lower part of the stalk, but where the division is made, usually three leaves are produced The flowers terminate the stalks in umbels, their colour is purple, they will be in blow in August, but are seldom succeeded by good seeds in these parts This, like the former, must have a warm situation, or it will be found too tender to live abroad through our hard winters, on which account it will be adviseable to keep a few plants of each sort in the greenhouse

Hairy Virginian

8 Hairy Virginian Dogsbane This sort has several weak, decumbent, hairy stalks, about a foot and a half long The leaves also are hairy, oval, and grow opposite, on very short footstalks The flowers terminate the branches in close umbels, they are of an orange colour, will be in blow in August, and sometimes bring their seeds to perfection A few plants of this sort also should be preserved in the greenhouse, as a very severe winter will often destroy all those that are planted abroad, let their situation be ever so well defended

and Hairy New England Dogsbane

9 Hairy New-England Dogsbane has a large tuberous root The stalks are upright, hairy, and grow to about two feet high The leaves are narrow, spear-shaped, hairy, and grow alternately on the branches The flowers are produced from the upper parts and ends of the stalks, in simple umbels, they are of an orange colour, will be in blow in August, and are sometimes succeeded by good seeds

of the Siberian Mountain

10 Siberian Mountain Swallow Wort has several weak decumbent stalks, about a foot and a half long The leaves are very narrow revolute, and spear-shaped The flowers grow in small tufts from the tops of the stalks, they blow in August, but do not always produce good seeds with us

and Narrow leaved Maryland Swallow Wort

11 Narrow-leaved Maryland Swallow-Wort The stalks of this sort are slender and upright The leaves are very narrow, and grow in whorls round the stalks The flowers grow in umbels, at the extremities of the stalks, their colour is white, they will be in blow in July, but are rarely

are

succeeded by good feeds in England This sort must have a warm situation, or it will be in danger of being destroyed by a hard winter

Method of propagating these sorts by dividing the roots,

All these sorts are easily propagated by dividing of their roots, the best season for which is the autumn, about such time as their stalks decay, though they will grow if removed any time in the winter or spring They all love a dry soil and a well-sheltered situation, which is especially necessary for the more tender sorts, to ensure their living abroad in our winters

and by seeds

They may be also raised from seeds These, except the common sorts, must be procured from the places where they naturally grow, but as they encrease very fast by their roots, it is hardly worth the while to be at this trouble This rule, however, will not hold good for them all for the eighth and ninth sorts should be always raised from seeds These should be sown in the spring in a hot-bed, and after the plants are come up, should have as much air as possible, to prevent their drawing weak, and must be sparingly watered They must be hardened to the full air when the weather will permit, and after that they should be planted in pots which ought to be plunged up to the rims in a shady part of the kitchen-garden, and in the autumn should be removed into the greenhouse, or placed under a hot-bed frame, to be all winter In the spring the plants may be turned out of the pots, with the mould, into the places where they are designed to flower, though it would be adviseable to shift a few of them into larger pots, to be kept as greenhouse plants, for the security of the sorts But as their roots are large and fleshy, they do not succeed so well in pots as in the open air, if the winters should happen not to prove too severe

This method of raising them from seeds will hold good with all the other foreign sorts, but the Common White and Black Swallow-Worts require no more trouble than sowing the seeds in a common bed, thinning them to proper distances, and keeping them clean from weeds

Titles.

1 The Common White Swallow-Wort is entitled, *Asclepias foliis ovatis basi barbatis, caule erecto, umbellis proliferis* In the *Flora Suecia* it is termed, *Asclepias caule erecto simplicissimo herbaceo, foliis cordato lanceolatis, racemis conglomeratis alternis*, and in the *Hortus Cliffortianus*, *Asclepias caule erecto annuo, foliis ovato-lanceolatis, floribus confertis* Caspar Bauhine calls it, *Asclepias albo flore*, and Dodonæus, *Vincetoxicum* It grows naturally in Germany, and some other parts of Europe

2 Black Swallow-Wort is, *Asclepias foliis ovatis basi barbatis, caule superne subvolubili* Van Royen calls it, *Asclepias caule subvolubili herbaceo, foliis ovato lanceolatis floribus confertis patentissimis*, Caspar Bauhine, *Asclepias nigro flore*, and Cammerarius, *Vincetoxicum flore nigro* It grows naturally on the hills near Montpelier

3 Syrian Dogsbane is, *Asclepias foliis ovalibus subtus tomentosis, caule simplicissimo, umbellis nutantibus* In the *Hortus Cliffortianus* it is termed, *Asclepias caule erecto simplici annuo, foliis ovato-oblongis subtus incanis, umbellâ nutante* Cornutus calls it, *Apocynum majus Syriacum rectum*, and Clusius, *Apocynum Syriacum* It grows naturally in Virginia

The *Asclepias foliis lanceolato ellipticis, caule simplici glabro, nectarii corniculis conniventibus* of the *Amænitates Academicæ* is a variety of this species

4 Purple Dogsbane with Upright Horns is, *Asclepias foliis ovatis subtus pilosiusculis, caule simplici, umbellis nectariisque erectis*. Dillenius calls it, *Apocynum floribus amæne purpureis, corniculis sursum erectis* It grows naturally in North America

5 Carolina Purple Dogsbane is named, *Asclepias foliis ovatis subtus villosis caule simplici, umbellis erectis, nectariis resupinatis* Dillenius calls it *Asclepias floribus obsolete purpureis, corniculis resupinatis*, and Herman, *Apocynum erectum Noveboracense, foliis minus incanis, flore ex obsoleto dilute purpurascente* It grows naturally in Carolina

6 Variegated flowered Dogsbane is entitled, *Asclepias foliis ovatis rugosis nudis, caule simplici, umbellis subsessilibus pedicellis tomentosis* Dillenius calls it *Apocynum erectum Americanum, Hispanicum*; Caspar Bauhine, *Asclepias Virginiana*, and Plukenet, *Apocynum Americanum erectum tuberosa radice non incanum, foliis rigidioribus latis subrotundis, floribus albis intus purpureis, summo caule corymbum magnum efformantibus* It is a native of North America

7 Small Upright Canada Dogsbane is, *Asclepias foliis lanceolatis caule superne diviso, umbellis erectis geminis* Van Royen calls it, *Asclepias caule erecto ramoso annuo foliis lanceolatis, umbellis terminalibus erectis pluribus*, and Cornutus, *Apocynum minus rectum Canadense* It grows common in Canada and Virginia

8 Hairy Virginian Dogsbane is, *Asclepias foliis villosis, caule decumbente* Gronovius terms it, *Asclepias caule decumbente hirsuto, foliis ovatis obtusis villosis subsessilibus* It grows naturally in Virginia

9 Hairy New England Dogsbane is, *Asclepias foliis alternis lanceolatis caule divaricato piloso* In the *Hortus Cliffortianus* it is termed, *Asclepias caule erecto divaricato villoso, foliis lanceolatis, umbellis simplicibus terminalibus* Herman names it, *Apocynum Novæ Angliæ hirsutum, tuberosa radice, floribus aurantiis* It grows common in North America

10 Siberian Mountain Swallow-Wort is *Asclepias foliis revolutis lineari-lanceolatis oppositis ternatisque, caule decumbente* Amman calls it, *Asclepias montana humilis, radice longius prosepente, lini foliis* It is a native of Siberia

11 Narrow leaved Maryland Swallow-Wort is, *Asclepias foliis revolutis linearibus verticillatis, caule erecto* Gronovius calls it, *Asclepias foliis verticillatis linearibus setaceis*, and Plukenet, *Apocynum Marianum erectum, lineariæ angustissimis foliis umbellatum* It grows common in Virginia

Class and order in the Linnæan system

*Asclepias* is of the class and order *Pentandria Digynia*, and the characters are,

The characters

1 Calyx is a small permanent perianthium, cut at the top into five acute segments

2 Corolla is a petal divided into five oval acuminated segments, which are somewhat reflexed There are five nectaria, which encompass the parts of fructification These are of an oval figure, and from the base arises a kind of horn, whose point turns towards the filaments The corpusculum, which surrounds the parts of fructification, is of a truncated form, and inclosed by five scales, opening by as many fissures at the sides

3 Stamina There are hardly any filaments, but five acute antheræ, that are inserted in the truncated corpusculum of the nectaria, within the scales

4 Pistillum The germina are two, oval, and acuminated The styles are hardly discernible, and the stigmas are simple

5 Pericarpium consists of two large, oblong, acuminated, swelling pods Each of them is formed of a single valve, and contains one cell

6 Semina The seeds are numerous, imbricated, and crowned with down

# CHAP. LVIII.

## *ASCYRUM*, St. PETER's WORT.

WE must not wholly pass by *Ascyrum*, for though the species of it are of no very great beauty, yet that the least variety, which possesses must planter or taste, would condemn an omission of that nature, is an unpardonable error. The species, then, are,

Species. 1. Oval-leaved *Ascyrum*, or St. Andrew's Cross.

2. Oblong-leaved *Ascyrum*, or Bastard St. John's Wort.

3. Hairy *Ascyrum*.

Oval. 1. Oval-leaved *Ascyrum*. The stalks of this sort are slender, round, about half a foot high, and divide into two smaller near the top. The leaves are small, oval, and grow opposite by pairs. The flowers are produced in loose spikes from the division of the branches; they are of a yellow colour, but small, and of little beauty.

and Oblong-leaved Ascyrum described. 2. Oblong-leaved *Ascyrum*, or Bastard St. John's Wort, will grow to about a foot and a half high. The stalks are flat and woody. The leaves are oblong, smooth, and narrow; they are glandulous at their base, and placed on the branches without any foot-stalks. The flowers are yellow, and four or five of them growing together, terminate the branches. Each of them is composed of four petals, which are hollow, and they seldom produce seeds in England.

Varieties. There are two or three varieties of this sort, but their differences are inconsiderable, except that of a dwarf sort, which grows to little more than half a foot high.

Hairy Ascyrum. 3. Hairy *Ascyrum*. The stalks of this species are woolly, upright, firm, and will grow to about a yard in height. The leaves are exceeding hairy, and their figure is oblong. The flowers terminate the branches. Each is composed of four leaves, and their colour is yellow; they are very much like those of the Common St. John's Wort, and are sometimes succeeded by good seeds.

Culture. All these sorts are easily encreased by planting of the cuttings in a shady border, or laying down the branches. Either way they will readily take root, and as many plants as you could wish for may be easily obtained.

Their station should be among such plants as are raised more for philosophical observation than beauty; or if there is a shrubbery, they would not be improperly fixed there, among the small-growing sorts, for they are of a kind of shrubby nature themselves, and the value of a Collection is always enhanced by variety, though the plants themselves seem to many inconsiderable and mean.

1. St. Andrew's Cross is titled, *Ascyrum foliis ovatis, caule tereti, paniculâ dichotomâ*. In the *Hortus Cliffortianus* it is termed, *Ascyrum foliis ovatis*. Plukenet calls it, *Hypericoides ex terrâ Mariana, floribus exiguis luteis*. It grows common in Virginia. Titles.

2. Bastard St. John's Wort is, *Ascyrum foliis oblongis, caule anceps, ...* Brown calls it, *Ascyrum fruticosum minus, floribus ...*, Plumier, *Hypericoides frutescens erecta, flore luteo*, and Plukenet, *Hypericum pumilum sempervirens, caule compresso ... ad bina latera acuto, flore luteo tetrapetalo*. It grows common in Virginia and Jamaica.

3. Hairy *Ascyrum* is termed, *Ascyrum foliis hirsutis, caule stricto*. Plukenet names it, *Hypericum Virginianum frutescens pubescens*. It is a native of Virginia.

*Ascyrum* is of the class and order *Polyadelphia Polyandria*, and the characters are, Class and order in the Linnæan system.

1. CALYX is an erect four-leaved perianthium. The two outer leaves are very small, narrow, and opposite; the two interior are large, plane, and cordated. The characters.

2. COROLLA consists of four oval petals. Of these the two outer are large and placed opposite, the two interior are smaller.

3. STAMINA consist of numerous setaceous filaments connected at their base into four parts, with roundish antheræ.

4. PISTILLUM consists of an oblong germen, a very small style, and a simple stigma.

5. PERICARPIUM is an oblong acuminated capsule, formed of two valves, and inclosed by the larger leaves of the calyx.

6. SEMINA. The seeds are numerous, small, and roundish.

# CHAP. LIX.

## *ASPERULA*, WOODROOF.

THE perennials of this genus are,

Species. 1. Common Woodroof.

2. Italian Woodroof.

3. Swedish Woodroof.

4. Squinancy Wort.

5. Rock Squinancy-Wort.

1. Common Woodroof. The root is slender, fibrous, and creeping. The stalks are weak, square, jointed, send out a few side-branches near the top, and grow to about a foot and a half long. The leaves are spear-shaped, oblong, narrow, pointed, of a dark green colour, and eight of Description of the Common.

of them grow at each joint, surrounding the stalks in a radiated manner. The flowers come out in clusters from the ends of the stalks and side branches, they are of a white colour, and very fragrant, they appear in May, and the seeds ripen in July.

This plant is said to be a good vulnerary, and is accounted salutary in palsies, epilepsies, obstructions of the liver, &c.

The leaves, as well as flowers, are of an agreeable odour, this they impart to liquors, and being steeped in wine, give it a fine flavour.

Italian, 2 Italian Woodroof. The stalks of this species are weak, jointed, square, send forth branches alternately, and are about a foot and a half high. The leaves are broad, oval, spear-shaped, smooth, and four grow together at a joint. The flowers come out in bunches from the end of the stalks and branches, they shew themselves in May and June, and the seeds ripen in July.

and Swedish Woodroof, 3 Swedish Woodroof. The stalk of this sort is weak, flaccid, square, jointed, branching, and, unless supported, lies on the ground. The leaves are narrow, and near the bottom of the plant grow six at a joint, higher up four only surround the stalk, in a radiated manner, at each joint. The flowers come out in bunches from the ends of the main stalk and branches, they are of a white colour, appear in May and June, and the seeds ripen in July.

and of the Squinancy, 4 Squinancy Wort. The root is long, hard, black, woody, and strikes deep into the ground. The stalks are slender, weak, square, jointed, six or eight inches long, for the most part procumbent, and strike root at the joints. The leaves are narrow, smooth, and grow four at a joint, except near the tops of the stalks, where there are two only, placed opposite. The flowers come out in umbels from the ends of the stalks, they are of a pale-red colour, appear in June, July, and August, and the seeds ripen in the autumn.

There is a variety of this, with white flowers.

This species is admirable for the cure of squinancies, either taken inwardly, or by external application.

and Rock Squinancy Wort. 5 Rock Squinancy-Wort. The stalks are upright, square, jointed, and eight or ten inches high. The leaves are spear-shaped, narrow, smooth, and quaternate. The flowers are tubular, mostly trifid, and of a red colour, they appear in June and July, and the seeds ripen in September.

Methods to propagate these species. These plants are all encreased by parting of the roots, which may be done any time of the year, though the best season is the autumn.

They may be also propagated by seeds, which may be sown in the autumn or spring. When the plants come up, they must be thinned where they are too close, and duly watered in dry weather, and when they are fit to remove, should be pricked out in beds at a small distance from each other, where they may stand until the autumn, and then be transplanted to the places in which they are designed to remain.

They are all extremely hardy, will grow in any soil or situation, and when they are once set out for good will call for no trouble, except keeping them clean from weeds.

1 Common Woodroof is called *Asperula foliis octonis lanceolatis, florum fasciculis pedunculatis*. In the *Hortus Cliffortianus* it is termed, *Asperula foliis octonis, floribus pedunculo caulinis*. Caspar Bauhine calls it, *Asperula seu Rubeola montana odorata*; Gerard, *Asperula*; and Parkinson, *Asperula odorata*. It grows common in woods and shady places in England, Germany, and Sweden. Title

2 Italian Woodroof is, *Asperula foliis quaternis ovato lanceolatis, floribus fasciculatis terminalibus*. Van Royen terms it, *Asperula foliis quaternis ovato-lanceolatis, ramis alternis*; and Caspar Bauhine, *Rubia quadrifolia & lato folio laevis*. It is a native of the Italian and Helvetian Mountains.

3 Swedish Woodroof is, *Asperula foliis linearibus, inferioribus senis, intermediis quaternis, caule flaccido, floribus trifidis*. In the *Flora Suecica* it is termed, *Asperula foliis quaternis linearibus, floribus trifidis*. Haller names it, *Rubeola quadrifolia, caule ramoso flaccido, floribus trifidis*; Morison, *Galium album tripetalum*; and Tabernæmontanus, *Gallium album*. It grows naturally on the dry rocky parts of Sweden, Thuringia, Gaul, and Siberia.

4 Squinancy-Wort is, *Asperula foliis quaternis linearibus superioribus oppositis stipulatis, caule erecto, floribus quadrifidis*. Van Royen terms it, *Asperula foliis linearibus quaternis, summis oppositis*; Haller, *Rubeola foliis quaternis, seminibus glabris, floribus umbellatis*; Caspar Bauhine, *Rubia cynanchica*; Columna, *Gallium montanum latifolium cruciatum*; Tabernæmontanus, *Gallium album minus*; Tournefort, *Rubeola vulgaris quadrifolia lævis, floribus purpurascentibus*; Gerard, *Cynanchica*; and Parkinson, *Asperula repens Gesneri, sive Saxifraga altera Cæsalpini*. It grows naturally in dry mountainous places, especially in chalky soils, in England, Germany, Helvetia, France, and Italy.

5 Rock Squinancy Wort is *Asperula foliis quaternis lanceolato-linearibus, caule erecto, floribus sæpius trifidis*. Caspar Bauhine calls it, *Rubia cynanchica saxatilis*. It grows naturally on the Pyrenees.

*Asperula* is of the class and order *Tetrandria Monogynia*, and the characters are, Class and order in the Linnæan system

1 CALYX is a small perianthium, placed on the germen, and indented in four parts.

2 COROLLA is a funnel-shaped petal. The tube is cylindrical and long, the limb is divided into four oblong, obtuse, reflexed segments. The characters

3 STAMINA are four filaments placed at the top of the tube, having simple antheræ.

4 PISTILLUM consists of a didymous roundish germen, situated below the flower, and a filiform style, divided at the top into two parts, each part being crowned by a capitated stigma.

5 PERICARPIUM consists of two juiceless, globular berries, growing together.

6 SEMINA. The seeds are single, large, and roundish.

CHAP

# CHAP. LX.

## *ASPHODELUS*, ASPHODEL, or KING's SPEAR.

THERE are no more than three diſtinct ſpecies of this genus at this time known, yet they admit of ſeveral varieties, all of which are pretty flowers; and their being eaſy of culture, makes them ſtill more valuable and deſirable in our gardens. Theſe ſpecies are called,

Species.

1. Yellow Aſphodel.
2. Fiſtular, or Hollow-leaved Aſphodel.
3. White Aſphodel.

Deſcription of the Yellow.

1. Yellow Aſphodel. The root of this ſpecies is compoſed of numerous, thick, fleſhy, yellow fibres, connected to one common head. From this head iſſue numerous, long, narrow, angular, hollowed, ſharp pointed, greyiſh leaves. The flower ſtalk will grow to be two feet and a half high; it is upright, round, firm, and garniſhed with numerous leaves like the radical one, but ſmaller. The flowers are numerous, and form a long ſpike from the middle of the ſtalk to the top; they are of a pure yellow, and expand themſelves in a ſtar like manner. Each flower is of ſhort continuance, but there will be a ſucceſſion of them on the ſame ſpike for a month or ſix weeks, inſomuch that the ſame ſtalk will at once ſhew you flower-buds opening, flowers full blown, flowers fading, and large ſeed-veſſels (like berries) with their ſeeds almoſt ripe. They will be in blow in June, and often from an off-ſet of the ſame plant freſh flowers will ariſe in September, which will continue to ſhew themſelves until the froſt ſtops them.

Fiſtular,

2. Hollow leaved Aſphodel. The root is compoſed of many thick fleſhy fibres. The leaves are numerous, and form a large tuft; they are narrow, ſubulated, ſtriated, hollowed, and ſharp-pointed. The ſtalk is ſmooth, and deſtitute of leaves; it is branching, and the top of it is adorned with the flowers. Theſe are white and ſtarry, with a few purple lines on the outſide; they will be in blow in July, and their ſeeds ripen in Auguſt or September.

and Great White Aſphodel.

3. Great White Aſphodel. The root of this ſpecies is compoſed of many thick fleſhy fibres, to which hang many tuberous, oblong parts. Theſe are collected into one common head, and from this iſſue a large number of ſword-ſhaped, hollowed, ſharp pointed leaves. The ſtalk is round, ſmooth, and naked; in ſome varieties it is ſingle, in others branching. The flowers adorn the top, in a long ſpike; each flower is large and ſpreading; it is of a pure white on the inſide, but without a line of purple runs down the middle of the ſegment. They will be in blow in June, and their ſeeds ripen in Auguſt.

Uſeful properties of this plant.

The roots of this ſpecies are of a very diſagreeable acrid taſte, though they ſeem to have been eſculent among the antient Greeks. Heſiod mentions this; and Theophraſtus acquaints us that their juices were corrected by roaſting, and were made ſtill more palatable by a proper mixture with figs. Some have contended for the Star of Bethlehem to be the Aſphodel of Heſiod, but it ſeems to be paſt a doubt, that this is the ſpecies. It grows common in Greece, Italy, Spain, &c. and anſwers to the character given of it by Theophraſtus.

Method of propagating theſe ſorts.

All theſe ſorts are eaſily propagated by parting of the roots; the beſt time for which is the autumn. The ſtrongeſt off-ſets will flower the ſummer following; ſo that they ſhould be immediately ſet out where they are deſigned to remain; whilſt the weaker off-ſets may be removed to the nurſery-ground for a year, and then planted out for good the autumn following.

Theſe plants ſhould remain unremoved at leaſt four years; for by that time they will have made great encreaſe, and will produce many ſtalks adorned with their fine ſpikes of flowers, and cauſe a more noble and ſplendid ſhow. The ſmaller off-ſets will alſo produce flowers to ſucceed thoſe of the ſtronger parts of the root; ſo that from the ſame plant there will often be a ſucceſſion of flowers from June to November.

Theſe plants are alſo raiſed from ſeeds. Sow them in the autumn, ſoon after they are ripe. In the ſpring they will appear; and when they come up too cloſe, draw out the weakeſt, and let the others remain in the bed for one year. Then plant them out in the nurſery ground, in beds at ſix inches aſunder from each plant. In theſe beds they may ſtand all ſummer, and in autumn the ſtrongeſt plants may be ſet out for good. Plants raiſed from ſeeds will be much ſtatelier, the flowers larger, and the purple rib on the outſide often of a deeper and finer colour.

Titles.

1. Yellow Aſphodel is titled, *Aſphodelus caule folioſo, foliis triquetris fiſtuloſis*. Caſpar Bauhine calls it, *Aſphodelus luteus flore & radice*; and Cammerarius, *Aſphodelus fœmina*. It is a native of Sicily.

2. Fiſtular leaved Aſphodel is, *Aſphodelus caule nudo, foliis ſtrictis ſubulatis ſtriatis ſubfiſtuloſis*. Van Royen calls it, *Aſphodelus caule nudo, foliis ſtrictis*; Caſpar Bauhine, *Aſphodelus foliis fiſtuloſis*; and Cluſius, *Aſphodelus minor*. It grows naturally in Crete, France, and Spain.

3. White Aſphodel is termed, *Aſphodelus caule nudo, foliis enſiformibus carinatis lævibus*. In the *Hortus Cliffortianus* it is named, *Aſphodelus caule nudo, foliis laxis*. Caſpar Bauhine calls one ſort of it, *Aſphodelus albus ramoſus mas*, and another, *Aſphodelus albus non ramoſus*. Cluſius terms it, *Aſphodelus*. It grows naturally in France, Italy, Spain, Portugal, Auſtria, &c.

Claſs and order in the Linnæan ſyſtem. The characters.

*Aſphodelus* is of the claſs and order *Hexandria Monogynia*; and the characters are,

1. CALYX. There is none.

2. COROLLA conſiſts of one leaf cut into ſix plane, ſpear ſhaped, patent ſegments. The nectarium is globular, ſituated at the baſe of the petal, and compoſed of ſix ſmall connivent valves.

3. STAMINA are ſix ſubulated arched filaments, inſerted in the valves of the nectarium. Theſe are alternately ſhorter, and have oblong, incumbent, aſſurgent antheræ.

4. PISTILLUM conſiſts of a roundiſh germen ſituated within the nectarium, a ſubulated ſtyle of the ſituation of the ſtamina, and a truncated ſtigma.

5. PERICARPIUM is a globular, fleſhy, trilobate capſule, of three cells.

6. SEMINA. The ſeeds are many, triangular, and gibbous on one ſide.

CHAP.

# CHAP. LXI.

## *ASPLENIUM*, SPLEENWORT, or MILT-WASTE.

THE species of this genus are such as grow for the most part in the fissures of rocks, on old walls, in old wells, damp places, &c. and are not garden plants. For the satisfaction of the Botanist, however, I shall enumerate the hardiest species under the names they are generally known by; and these are,

Species.
1. Spleenwort.
2. Hart's Tongue.
3. Italian Hart's Tongue.
4. Common Maidenhair.
5. Sea Maidenhair.
6. White Maidenhair, or Wall Rue.
7. Green Maidenhair.
8. Black Maidenhair.

All these, except the third species, are natives of England, and afford great pleasure to the curious student of Nature in his philosophical observations.

Description and Medicinal uses of the Spleenwort.
1. Spleenwort. The root is composed of a multitude of black slender fibres, much implicated or interwoven one with another. The leaves, which are all distinct plants, rise immediately from the root, are about four inches long, and three quarters of an inch broad; they are pinnatifid, the segments join in one body at the base, and they are arranged alternately along the mid-rib, which is naked at the bottom, and terminated by an odd lobe or segment. The leaves, or rather the plants, are of a thickish substance, of a pale-green colour on their upper side, and soft and downy underneath, where their fructifications are situated.

This plant is deemed pectoral and diuretic, and is employed in nephritic cases, and the cure of the jaundice; but is said to be of very little force in removing the spleen, though so celebrated for that purpose by Dioscorides and other antient writers.

Hart's Tongue.
2. Hart's Tongue. The root is composed of long, black, slender fibres, platted together. The leaves, or rather plants, rise many together, standing on black hairy footstalks; they are simple, undivided, heart-shaped at their base, pointed at the extremity, eight or ten inches long, an inch and a half broad, of a fine glossy green colour on their upper side, and streaked and rough on the back by the fructifications, where they are disposed in numerous short oblique lines.

This plant is recommended in the bloody-flux, and *pro fluvium ventris*, and is said to be a remedy for the bite of serpents. It was also formerly held in more request against the spleen than our modern practitioners now will allow it deserves.

Italian Hart's Tongue.
3. Italian Hart's Tongue. The root is like the former. The leaves are simple, heart-shaped, hastated, and composed of five undivided lobes, and grow on smooth footstalks. The fructifications are arranged in oblique lines on the back. Its medicinal qualities are nearly similar to the preceding.

Common.
4. Common Maidenhair. The root is a cluster of slender black fibres. The leaves, or rather plants, stand on round, slender, brittle, black, glossy stalks; they are pinnated, and about half a foot long. The pinnulæ are roundish, crenated, stand opposite, are smooth, of a bright glossy strong green colour, are terminated by an odd foliole, and carry their fructifications on their back.

This plant is a good pectoral, and is used in infusion or decoction, with an addition of liquorice, for the expectoration of tough phlegm, and disorders of the breast through too great acrimony of the juices. It is also substituted in room of the true Maidenhair in preparing the famous syrup called Capillaire, for which it does very well, so as hardly to be distinguished, especially if there be a small addition of orange-flower water.

Sea.
5. Sea Maidenhair. The fibres of the root are like hairs, black, extremely numerous, and amazingly implicated and entangled one with another. The leaves stand on glossy, slender, brown or blackish footstalks; they are pinnated, and the pinnæ are obovil, elegantly serrated or crenated obtuse, and wedge-shaped at their base; they are of a firm substance, terminated by an odd one, stand opposite (or nearly so) along the midrib, and the fructification on their back is of a rusty iron colour.

White.
6. White Maidenhair, or Wall Rue. The fibres of the root are as fine as hairs, numerous, and variously interwoven and clotted together. The leaves are small, elegant, decompound, and grow on dark brown or blackish footstalks. These footstalks rise naked to two or three inches high, and then send forth several branches, each of which is terminated by partial leaves, finely divided in the manner of the true maidenhair of the shops, or (as some fancy) the rue of our kitchen gardens. The folioles are of a thickish substance, rigid, wedge-shaped, of a pale-green colour on their upper side, and brownish underneath, where their fructifications are situated.

This species is a fine pectoral diuretic, is recommended in nephritic complaints, and is said to be good for the cure of ruptures in young children.

and Green Maidenhair.
7. Green Maidenhair. The fibres are as fine as any of the other sorts, and are clotted together in the same manner. The leaves are pinnated, and about four or five inches long. The pinnæ are roundish, truncated at their base, of a deep, strong, shining-green colour, and terminated by an odd one, and the lower ones are the smallest.

Varieties.
There are two or three varieties of this species, called, the Larger, the Small, and the Branching Green Maidenhair. They are all possessed of the same qualities, which are nearly similar to those of the Common Maidenhair.

Black Maidenhair described.
8. Black Maidenhair. The fibres of the root of this species are considerably thick, black, and interwoven one with another. The leaves are doubly, and frequently triply pinnated. The folioles are ranged alternately, and the pinnæ are spear-shaped, oval, cut, and serrated on their edges. The whole leaf is almost triangular; the upper side is of a dark green colour, and the under

under is dusted over with a fine yellow or saffron-coloured farina belonging to the fructification. The stalk is hard, rigid, black, glossy, and raised four, five, or six inches high, and then branches out for the support of the different parts which form the whole leaf.

There are several varieties of this species, all of which are used in medicine, their qualities being nearly similar to the Common Maidenhair.

Culture. This last sort will grow if planted in a shady place, and so will the second if the soil be stony or of a sandy nature. The others also will grow in rubbishy situations, or they may be preserved in pots filled with light, sandy, rubbishy earth, or they may be artfully inserted in the crevices of rocks, old walls, ruins, &c. where they will enrich the variety of the vegetable collection, and shew Nature by exhibiting her own favourite productions from such places.

Titles. 1. Spleenwort is titled, *Asplenium frondibus pinnatifidis lobis alternis confluentibus*. John Bauhine calls it, *Asplenium, s. Ceterach*, and Caspar Bauhine, *Ceterach officinarum*. It grows naturally from the fissures of moist rocks, old walls, &c. in England, Wales, France, Italy, and in the East.

2. Hart's Tongue is, *Asplenium frondibus simplicibus cordato-lingulatis integerrimis, stipitibus hirsutis*. Van Royen calls it, *Asplenium frondibus ensiformibus integris basi cordatis inflexis, petiolis hirsutis*, Caspar Bauhine, *Lingua cervina officinarum*, also, *Lingua cervina multifido folio*, John Bauhine, *Phyllitis crispa*, Plukenet, *Phyllitis, s. lingua cervina maxima, undulato folio auriculato per basin*, also, *Phyllitis, s. lingua cervina crispa, folio multifido, ramosa*, Morison, *Lingua cervina medio folio nervo in aculeum abeunte*, and Gerard, *Phyllitis*. It grows naturally in shady rocky situations in England and most parts of Europe.

3. Italian Hart's Tongue is, *Asplenium frondibus simplicibus cordato-hastatis quinquelobis integerrimis, stipitibus laevibus*. Caspar Bauhine calls it, *Hemionitis vulgaris*, and Clusius, *Hemionitis vera*. It grows naturally in Italy and Spain.

4. Common Maidenhair is, *Asplenium frondibus pinnatis pinnis subrotundis crenatis*. Caspar Bauhine calls it, *Trichomanes, s. Polytrichum officinarum*, also, *Trichomanes minus & tenerius*. Plukenet names it, *Adiantum maritimum segmentis subrotundis*, Tournefort, *Trichomanes foliis eleganter incisis*, Parkinson, *Trichomanes*, and Gerard, *Trichomanes mas*. It grows naturally in the crevices of rocks, old walls, and shady places in England and most parts of Europe, also in the East.

5. Sea Maidenhair is, *Asplenium frondibus pinnatis pinnis obovatis serratis superne gibbis obtusis basi cuneatis*. John Bauhine calls it, *Chamæ filix marina Anglica*, Caspar Bauhine, *Filicula maritima ex insulis Stachadis*, Parkinson, *Filix marina Anglica*, and Gerard, *Filicula petræa fœmina, sive Chamæ filix marina Anglica*. It grows common on the sea-rocks in England and America.

6. White Maidenhair, or Wall Rue, is, *Asplenium frondibus alternatim decompositis foliolis cuneiformibus crenulatis*. C. Bauhine calls it, *Ruta muraria*, John Bauhine, *Adiantum album tenuifolium, rutæ murariæ accedens*, Tabernæmontanus, *Adiantum album*, and Cammerarius, *Paronychia*. It grows naturally in the chinks of rocks, old walls, &c. in England, and most countries of Europe.

7. Green Maidenhair is, *Asplenium frondibus duplicato-pinnatis pinnis obovatis crenatis foliolis inferioribus minoribus*. Hudson terms it, *Asplenium fronde pinnatâ pinnis subrotundis basi truncatis*; Caspar Bauhine, *Trichomanes ramosum majus & minus*. John Bauhine, *Trichomanes ramosum*, and Gerard, *Trichomanes fœmina*. It grows naturally in rocky moist places in the north of England and Wales.

8. Black Maidenhair is, *Asplenium frondibus subtripinnatis foliolis alternis pinnis lanceolatis inciso-serratis*. Van Royen calls it, *Asplenium frondibus duplicato pinnatis, foliolis inferioribus majoribus foliolis ovatis superne crenatis*, Caspar Bauhine, *Adiantum foliis longioribus pulverulentis, pediculo nigro*, John Bauhine, *Adiantum pulcherrimum*, Dodonæus, *Dryopteris nigra*, Gerard, *Onopteris mas*, and Parkinson, *Adiantum nigrum vulgare*. It grows naturally in shady places, on old walls, &c. in England, France, and Italy.

*Asplenium* is of the Fern kind, and belongs to the Class *Cryptogamia*. (Class in the Linnæan system)

The fructifications are disposed in straight lines under the disk of the leaf.

# CHAP. LXII.

## *ASTER*, STARWORT.

Introductory remarks. THERE is hardly a genus that affords a greater number of beautiful hardy perennials than *Aster*. They are of different heights, and afford amazing variety by the difference of their leaves and manner of growth. The flowers are produced in plenty on all of them, their colours are mostly lively, and the generality of them coming late in the autumn, when the show of other flowers is chiefly past, makes their appearance more acceptable and welcome. The real hardy species are,

Species.
1. Italian Starwort, called *Amellus*.
2. Sea-Starwort, called *Tripolium*.
3. Alpine Starwort.
4. Siberian Starwort.
5. Broad-leaved American Starwort.
6. Bushy Daisy-Starwort.
7. Belvedere-leaved Starwort.
8. Linaria-leaved Starwort.
9. Flax-leaved Starwort.
10. Narbonne Starwort.
11. Virginian Single-stalked Starwort.
12. White Virginian Starwort.
13. Waved-leaved Starwort.
14. New-England Starwort.
15. Bushy Heath-like Starwort.
16. Broad leaved Autumnal Starwort.
17. Rough Lanceolate-leaved American Starwort.
18. Marsh Virginian Starwort.

19. Muta-

19 Mutable Starwort
20 Late White Carolina Starwort
21 New Holland Starwort
22 Catesby's Virginian Starwort
23 Oval flowered Starwort

Theſe are all diſtinct ſpecies, and comprehend above twice the number of varieties, all which are admirably found to enrich our gardens.

Deſcription of the Italian Aſter.

1 The Italian *Aſter* will grow to about two feet high. The ſtalks are numerous, upright, firm, and branching. The leaves are rough, ſpear-ſhaped, and obtuſe, they have three conſpicuous veins, and their edges are entire. The flowers adorn the ends of the ſtalks in the autumn. The florets in the center are of a golden yellow, but the rays of the flowers are of a fine blue, they make a lovely appearance when in full blow. But what makes the value of this plant ſtill greater, it will often afford you flowers in December, when few others are to be met with.

Virgil has pleaſingly deſcribed this plant in his fourth Georgick. It ſtands there with the name *Amellus*, which we are given to underſtand was a cant name only in uſe among the common people, and unknown to the botaniſts of thoſe times. In our gardens it has gone frequently by the title *Aſter Atticus*, and that this Attick *Aſter* is the *Amellus* of Virgil is plain, becauſe it anſwers exactly to the deſcription given of that plant by that poet, and grows common in the meadows of Italy, Sicily, Narbonne, and moſt of the ſouthern parts of Europe, where it is, as that author obſerves, eaſy to be met with.

Sea.

2 Sea Starwort grows naturally on the ſea ſhores in many parts of Europe. The leaves are ſpear ſhaped, fleſhy, ſmooth, and entire. The flowers terminate the ſtalks in a corymbus, their colour is blue, and they will be in blow in the autumn. This ſpecies by many botaniſts is called *Tripolium*.

Alpine.

3 Alpine Starwort. Of this plant there are many varieties, which differ ſo greatly in appearance, that they have been taken for diſtinct ſpecies, and have been titled by old botaniſts accordingly. The parent of them all is a low plant, ſeldom riſing to a foot in height. The radical leaves are moderately broad, ſpear ſhaped, and obtuſe. The ſtalk is unbranching, and garniſhed with leaves of the ſame form, but narrower, the top of it is crowned by a ſingle, large, blue flower, which will be in its full luſtre early in July.

Siberian.

4 Siberian Starwort. The ſtalks of this plant are ſtriated. The leaves are broad, ſpear-ſhaped, veiny, rough, and ſerrated at the upper parts. The flowers grow in umbels, the footſtalks are downy, and each ſupports a ſingle flower, which will be in blow in July or Auguſt.

Broad leaved.

5 Broad-leaved American Starwort. The ſtalks of this plant are very infirm and ſend forth many ſide-branches ſpreading one from another. The leaves are broad, oval, and their edges ſerrated. The flowers grow on footſtalks, each ſupporting one flower, their colour is white, and they appear the latter end of the ſummer.

Buſhy.

6 Buſhy Starwort. The ſtalks divide into a multitude of narrow branches, which divide into others, and form a very buſhy plant. The leaves are very narrow, and their edges are entire. The flowers grow in looſe panicles, the footſtalks are narrow, ſtriated, and each ſupports a flower, the rays are of a clear white, but the diſk is yellow, and they have ſome reſemblance of thoſe of the Common Daiſy, though ſmaller. This ſort flowers in October.

Belvedere leaved.

7 Belvedere-leaved Starwort. The ſtalks of this plant are ſlender, angular, and a little branching. The leaves are narrow, a little rough, and their edges are entire. The flowers ornament the ends of the branches in longiſh ſpikes, they are of a whitiſh blue colour, and will be in blow in the autumn.

Linaria leaved.

8 Linaria leaved Starwort. This ſpecies hath ſeveral tough ſtalks of a purple colour, the leaves are narrow, rough, carinated, acute, and of a fine green. A few flowers terminate the branches, they are of a deep violet colour, have leafy footſtalks, and will be in blow in October.

Flax leaved.

9 Flax-leaved Starwort. The ſtalks of this plant will grow to about four feet high, and ſend forth many branches from the ſides. The leaves are narrow, acute, and entire, they grow alternately, and embrace the ſtalk with their baſe. The flowers terminate the branches, their colour is blue, and they make their appearance in Auguſt and September.

Narbonne.

10 Narbonne Starwort. This plant is called by many the Blue Cluſter-flowering *Aſter*. The ſtalks are erect, branching, and will grow to near two feet high. The leaves are numerous, long, narrow, entire, and of a duſky green. The flowers terminate the branches in cluſters, their colour is blue, and they will be in blow in Auguſt.

Virginian Single ſtalked.

11 Virginian Single ſtalked Starwort. This will grow to about four feet high, and the ſtalk is ſingle, or unbranching. The leaves are of an oblong oval figure, entire, downy, and ſit cloſe to the ſtalk. The flowers are produced at the top of it in a kind of ſpike, their colour is blue, and they will be in blow in October.

White Virginian.

12 White Virginian Starwort. The ſtalks of this ſpecies will grow to near a yard high. The leaves are very narrow, and grow alternately. A ſingle flower terminates each ſtalk. There are two or three varieties of it, though the moſt common is white, which will be in blow in November.

Waved-leaved.

13 Waved leaved Starwort. The ſtalks of this plant are branching, and will grow to about a yard high. The leaves are heart-ſhaped, waved, downy underneath, and embrace the ſtalk with their baſe. The flowers grow in looſe ſpikes, they are of a whitiſh blue colour, and will be in blow in September.

New England.

14 New England Starwort. The ſtalks of this plant are hairy, and will grow to four or five feet high. The leaves are placed alternately, are ſpear ſhaped, entire, and half ſurround the ſtalk with their baſe. The flowers are produced at the tops of the ſtalks, are very large, of a violet purple colour, and will be in blow in September.

Buſhy Heath like.

15 Buſhy Heath-like Starwort. This plant will grow to about a yard high, and the branches divide in ſuch plenty as to form a very buſhy plant. The leaves are very narrow and entire. The flowers are ſmall, whitiſh, and very inconſiderable. They will be in blow in October.

Broad leaved autumnal.

16 Broad-leaved autumnal Starwort. This ſpecies hath ſeveral ſlender branching ſtalks, which will grow to about two feet high. The leaves are heart-ſhaped, pointed, and their edges are finely ſerrated. The flowers grow in panicles at the ends of the branches, their colour is white, and they will be in full blow in September.

Rough Lanceolate-leaved.

17 *Rough Lanceolate leaved American Starwort.* The ſtalks of this plant are upright, firm, of a purple colour, and will grow to about a yard high. The leaves are ſpear ſhaped, rough, and half ſurround the ſtalk with their baſe. The flowers terminate the ſtalk in a kind of corymbus. Their colour is a pale blue, and they will be in blow in October.

18. Marſh-

Marsh Virginian, 18 Marsh Virginian Starwort. This plant hath a very slender, erect, and almost naked stalk, that sends forth a few side-branches. The leaves are spear-shaped, obtuse, entire, and a little like those of the common Daisy. The flowers are whitish, and appear early in summer.

Mutable, 19 Mutable Starwort. This species grows to about a foot high. The leaves are broad, spear-shaped, and their edges are serrated. The flowers are produced in panicles, the rays of which are of a deep purple, but the flowers of the disk have this mutable property, that being yellow on their opening, they die away, or alter to a purple colour. This sort flowers in November.

Late White Carolina, 20 Late White Carolina Starwort. This is a tall growing plant. It will often arrive to the height of six feet, and send forth several branches from the sides. The leaves are narrow, spear-shaped, and a little serrated. The flowers grow in spikes from the ends of the branches, they are of a white colour, small, and will be in full blow in November.

New Holland, 21 New Holland Starwort. The stalks of this species are upright, firm, and will grow to about four feet high. The leaves are spear-shaped, a little serrated, and grow close to the stalk with their base. The flowers grow in kind of umbels, they are of a pale violet colour, and will be in full blow in September.

and Catesby's Virginian Star Wort. 22 Catesby's Virginian Starwort. The stalks of this plant usually grow to about a yard in height, and put forth many branches from the sides. The leaves are narrow, spear-shaped, rough, and reflexed. The side branches are each of them terminated by a large blue flower, which will be in full perfection in November.

Oval flowered Aster. 23 Oval-flowered *Aster*. The stalk of this plant will grow to five or six feet high. The leaves are small, those on the stalks are entire, but those on the branches are spear-shaped and entire. The flowers grow from the sides of the branches on short footstalks, they are of an oval figure, the disk being very convex. The rays are white, and very short, the florets in the disk are pale, and have yellow styles. This sort flowers in November, and if the weather proves open, will continue flowering until after Christmas.

The culture of all these sorts is exceeding easy.

Culture. It is done by dividing of the roots any time in the autumn, winter, or spring, though the autumn is the most eligible season.

The roots of many of them, particularly the common sorts, spread very much. Of all these spreading sorts, a small part of the root only should be planted, and it will grow up and flower the autumn following. The spring after it will shoot out a greater number of stalks, and the year following still more; which makes it necessary to reduce these plants every three years, or they will be too rambling and bushy. At the doing of this, the best way will be wholly to take up the roots, and after having planted a few off-sets of each for a succession, to throw the others away.

All the least spreading sorts may remain five or six years unremoved, during which time, if you want a few plants for other parts of the garden, you may easily take off some off-sets from any of them, which being planted will soon become good plants.

These sorts are easily encreased by the cuttings, which if planted in a moist shady border of loose earth will readily take root, but this method is hardly worth practising, as the very least spreading sorts will soon produce you off-sets enough.

The early flowering sorts produce seeds, so that if you chuse to raise them this way, they should be sown in the autumn as soon as they are ripe. But you need not be anxious about this, for they will scatter themselves, come up in amazing plenty, and afford still greater variety of colours at the time of flowering.

1 The Italian Starwort is titled, *Aster foliis lanceolatis obtusis scabris trinerviis integris, pedunculis nudiusculis corymbosis, squamis calycinis obtusis*. In the *Hortus Cliffort* it is termed, *Aster foliis lanceolatis scabris sem amplexicaulibus subserratis, calycibus laxis squamis lanceolatis*. Caspar Bauhine calls it, *Aster Atticus cæruleus vulgaris*; Dodonæus, *Aster Atticus*, and others, *Amellus Virgilii*. It grows plentifully in Italy, and most of the southern parts of Europe. Titles

2 Sea Starwort is, *Aster foliis lanceolatis integerrimis carnosis glabris, ramis inæqualibus, floribus corymbosis*. Ray calls it, *Aster maritimus Tripolium dictus*, Caspar Bauhine, *Tripolium majus cæruleum*, and Dodonæus, *Tripolium*. It grows naturally on the sea-shores and salt marshes in many parts of Europe.

3 Alpine Starwort is titled, *Aster foliis lanceolatis hirtis radicalibus obtusis, caule simplicissimo unifloro*. Caspar Bauhine calls it, *Aster montanus cæruleus, magno flore, foliis oblongis*, another sort of it he terms, *Aster Atticus Alpinus* [illegible], a third, *Aster Atticus cæruleus Alpinus*, and a fourth, *Aster hirsutus Austriacus cæruleus, magno flore, foliis subrotundis*. It grows naturally in Austria, Vallesia, Helvetia, and the Pyrenean mountains.

4 Siberian Starwort is, *Aster foliis lanceolatis venosis scabris extimo serratis, caulibus strictis, pedunculis tomentosis*. Gmelin calls it, *Aster foliis ovatis oblongis supra serratis, caulibus strictis, pedunculis unifloris umbellatis*. It grows naturally in Siberia.

5 Broad-leaved American Starwort is titled, *Aster ramis divaricatis, foliis ovatis serratis, floribus integerrimis obtusiusculis amplexicaulibus*. Gronovius calls it, *Aster caule infirmo, foliis ovatis acuminatis integerrimis, pedunculis unifloris nudis, calycibus simplicibus*, and Plukenet, *Aster americanus latifolius albus, caule ad summum bracteato*. It is a native of Virginia.

6 Bushy Daisy Starwort. This is, *Aster foliis linearibus integerrimis, caule paniculato, floribus terminalibus*. Herman calls it, *Aster Novæ Angliæ, linariæ foliis, chamæmeli floribus*, Plukenet, *Aster Americanus multiflorus, flore albo bellidis disco luteo*. It grows naturally in North America.

7 Belvedere-leaved Starwort. This is titled, *Aster foliis, sublinearibus integerrimis, pedunculis foliolosis*. Plukenet calls it, *Aster Americanus Belvedere foliis, floribus ex cæruleo albicantibus, spicis longis*. It grows naturally in North America.

8 Linaria-leaved Starwort. This is, *Aster foliis linearibus integerrimis mucronatis scabris carinatis, pedunculis foliolosis*. Plukenet calls it, *Aster Americanus frutescens saturejæ foliis scabris floribus amplis saturate violaceis*, Ray, *Aster Marilandicus, conyzæ ni folis angustioribus, in caule crebris mordicantis, floribus in summitate paucis*. It grows naturally in North America.

9 Flax-leaved Starwort is titled, *Aster foliis linearibus acutis integerrimis, caule corymboso ramosissimo*. Morison calls it, *Aster Tripolii flore, angustissimo & tenuissimo folio*. It is a native of North America.

10 Narbonne Starwort. This is titled, *Aster foliis lanceolato linearibus strictis integerrimis planis, floribus corymbosis fastigiatis, pedunculis foliolosis*. Sauvages calls it, *Aster caule erecto umbellifero, ramis simplicibus, foliis ligulatis*; Caspar Bauhine, *Aster tripolii flore*, Barrelier, *Aster angustifolius, tripolii flore*, and Lobel, *Aster minor Narbonensium, tripolii flore, linariæ foliis*. It grows naturally in Hungary, Spain, and France.

11 Virginian Single-stalked Starwort. This is, *Aster caule simplicissimo, foliis oblongo ovatis tomentosis*

*rentesis sessilibus integerrimis, racemo terminali* It grows naturally in Virginia

12 White Virginian Starwort is, *Aster floribus terminalibus solitariis, foliis linearibus alternis* It is a native of Virginia

13 Waved leaved Starwort This is titled, *Aster foliis cordatis amplexicaulibus undulatis subtus tomentosis floribus racemosis adscendentibus* Herman calls *Aster Novæ Angliæ purpureus, virgæ aureæ facie & foliis undulatis*, and Morison, *Aster Virginianus corosus, foliis latioribus & flosculis minimis cæruleis* It grows naturally in North America

14 New England Starwort This is, *Aster foliis lanceolatis alternis integerrimis semi-amplexicaulibus, floribus confertis terminalibus, caule hispido* Herman calls it, *Aster Novæ Angliæ altissimus hirsutus, floribus amplis purpuro-violaceis* It grows naturally in New England

15 Bushy Heath like Starwort This is titled, *Aster foliis linearibus integerrimis, caule paniculato, pedunculis racemosis, pedicellis foliosis* Dillenius calls it, *Aster ericoides dumosus* It is a native of North America

16 Broad leaved autumnal Starwort is titled, *Aster foliis cordatis serratis petiolatis caule paniculato* Morison calls it, *Aster latifolius glaber humilis ramosissimus, flore parvo cæruleo, foliis ad basin cordatis*, and Cornutus, *Aster latifolius autumnalis* It grows naturally in America and Asia

17 Rough Lanceolate leaved American Starwort This is titled, *Aster foliis semi-amplexicaulibus lanceolatis serratis scabris, pedunculis alternis subunifloris, calycibus arctum superantibus* Herman calls it, *Aster Americanus latifolius paniceis caulibus* It grows in North America

18 Marsh Virginian Starwort This is titled, *Aster caule subnudo filiformi subramoso, pedunculis nudis foliolis radicalibus lanceolatis integerrimis obtusis* It grows naturally in marshy places in Virginia

19 Mutable Starwort This is titled, *Aster foliis lanceolatis serratis calycibus squarrosis, panicula profastigiata* Herman calls it, *Aster Novi Belgii latifolius paniculatus, floribus saturate violaceis*, and Plukenet *Aster cæruleus Americanus non fruticosus procumbens angustifolius humilis, flore amplo floribundus* It grows naturally in North America

20 Late White Carolina Starwort is, *Aster foliis lanceolato-linearibus nudis serratis, pedunculis foliosis, caule racemoso, calycibus erectis* Morison calls it, *Aster Virginianus cauliculus frutescens parvis floribus albis tradescanti* It grows naturally in North America

21 New Holland Starwort is titled, *Aster foliis lanceolatis subserratis sessilibus, caule paniculato, ramulis unifloris solitariis, calycibus squarrosis* Herman calls it, *Aster Novæ Belgiæ latifolius umbellatus, floribus dilute violaceis* It grows naturally in Virginia and Carolina

22 Catesby's Virginian Starwort is titled, *Aster caule corymboso, foliis lingulatis reflexis, floribus solitariis, calycibus squarrosis* Gronovius calls it *Aster foliis lanceolatis, semi-amplexicaulibus crenatis scabris, ramis confertis foliosis*, Dillenius, *Aster grandiflorus asper squamis effusis*, and Martin, *Aster Virginianus pyramidatus, bugloss foliis asperis, calycis squamulis foliaceis* It grows common in North America Catesby first brought the seeds from Carolina, which occasions its being called by Gardeners after his name

23 Oval flowered Starwort This is titled, *Aster floribus ovatis disco recurvis longiore* Dillenius calls it, *Aster ericoides, in flore nigræ umbone* It grows common in North America

*Aster* is of the class and order *Syngenesia Polygamia Superflua*, and the characters are, 

1 CALYX The common calyx is imbricated, being composed of several scales lying over each other

2 COROLLA is compound and radiated The hermaphrodite flowers which compose the disk are numerous, funnel shaped and divided at the top into five spreading segments The female flowers in the radius are tongue-shaped, and are indented at the end in three parts

3 STAMINA The stamina of the hermaphrodite flowers are five very short capillary filaments, with a cylindric tubulous anthera

4 PISTILLUM of the hermaphrodite flowers consists of an oblong germen, a filiforme style the length of the stamina, and a patent bifid stigma In the female flowers the pistil is an oblong germen, a filiforme style, and two oblong revolute stigmas

5 PERICARPIUM There is none

6 SEMINA The seeds are single, oval, oblong, and crowned with down

Class and order in the Linnean System The characters

# CHAP. LXIII

## *ASTRAGALUS*, LIQUORICE-VETCH, or, MILK-VETCH

THE species of this genus are very numerous, and consist chiefly of hard annual and perennial flower-roots The perennials are,

Species

1 Yellow Oriental Milk-Vetch
2 Purple Oriental Milk-Vetch
3 Thuringian Milk-Vetch
4 Goat's Rue-leaved Milk-Vetch.
5 Carolina Milk-Vetch
6 Canada Milk-Vetch
7 Yellow Austrian Milk-Vetch
8 Dwarf Yellow Milk-Vetch
9 English Milk-Vetch, or Wild Liquorice
10 Syrian Milk Vetch
11 Small hoary Purple Milk-Vetch
12 Alpine Milk-Vetch
13 Mountain Milk Vetch
14 Round podded Siberian Milk Vetch
15 German Milk-Vetch
16 Hairy Yellow flowered Siberian Milk-Vetch
17 Helvetian Milk-Vetch

1 The Yellow Oriental Milk-Vetch rises with several upright stalks to about a yard in height The leaves are large and pinnated The pinnæ are numerous, though they are placed but thinly on the mid-rib, their figure is oval, and in each leaf they are terminated by an odd one The flowers are produced in clusters from the wings of the leaves almost the whole length of the stalks They are large, of a bright yellow colour, will

Description of the Yellow Oriental.

will be in blow in July, and sometimes, though not very commonly, will be succeeded by good seeds in the autumn.

Purple Oriental. 2. Purple Oriental Milk-Vetch. The stalks of this species are erect and hairy. The leaves are large, pinnated, and the pinnæ are pointed. The flowers grow in round heads from the wings of the leaves on very long footstalks; their colour is purple; they will be in blow in July, and now and then bring their seeds to perfection in our gardens in the autumn.

Hungarian. 3. Hungarian Milk-Vetch. This plant sends forth several erect hairy stalks, that will grow to about two feet high. The leaves are pinnated, and very woolly. The pinnæ are of an oval figure, consist of several pair in each leaf, which are always terminated by an odd one. The flowers are produced from the wings of the leaves in close spikes; their colour is yellow; they will be in blow in June, and are succeeded by oval-shaped hairy pods, which will have ripe seeds in September.

Goat's Rue leaved. 4. Goat's Rue leaved Milk-Vetch. This species hath several smooth erect stalks. The leaves are pinnated, and composed of near twenty pair of lobes; these are oval, and are terminated by an odd one. The flowers are produced from the wings of the leaves, in long spikes which hang downwards. They are of a whitish colour, having some tinge of yellow; will be in blow in June and July, and the seeds ripen in September. The pods are triangular, and sharp-pointed.

Carolina. 5. Carolina Milk-Vetch. This species hath several erect stalks, that will grow to about a yard in length. The leaves are large, being composed of near twenty pair of oval smooth lobes, besides the odd one that terminates the leaf. The flowers are produced from the wings of the leaves in spikes. Their colour is a yellowish green; they will be in blow in August, and very seldom bring their seeds to perfection in our gardens.

Canada. 6. Canada Milk-Vetch. The stalks of this plant are very irregular, and will grow to about two feet high. The leaves are large, the pinnæ are oval, and hairy on the under side. From the wings of the leaves the stalks are produced in spikes. Their colour is a yellowish green; they will be in blow in July, and are succeeded by cylindrical pointed pods, containing ripe seeds, in the autumn.

Yellow Austrian. 7. Yellow Austrian Milk-Vetch. The stalks of this plant are slender, will grow to about a yard long, and lie flat on the ground. The leaves are pinnated, and grow alternately. The pinnæ are small, of an oval figure, and consist of about ten pair, with an odd one. The flowers are produced from the wings of the leaves in small loose spikes. They are yellow, will be in blow in July, and are succeeded by roundish pointed pods, containing ripe seeds in the autumn.

Dwarf Yellow. 8. Dwarf Yellow Milk-Vetch. This hath a few erect stalks, that will hardly grow to a foot high. The leaves are large in proportion, and often composed of thirteen or fifteen pair of oval obtuse pinnæ. From the wings of the leaves the footstalks are produced that support the flowers. These are longer than the leaves, and the flowers grow in roundish heads at the top. Their colour is yellow; they will be in blow in July, and are succeeded by ripe seeds, contained in roundish pods, in the autumn.

English. 9. English Milk-Vetch, or Wild Liquorice. This is the common Wild Liquorice that is found growing in great plenty in lanes and woods in many parts of England, and is seldom admitted into gardens. The root is creeping, and the stalks are procumbent. The leaves are oval, and the flowers of a pale yellow. They appear in June and July, and their seeds, contained in three-cornered arched pods, ripen in the autumn.

Syrian. 10. Syrian Milk-Vetch. The stalks of this plant will grow to about two feet high, but they must be supported as they arise, or they will trail on the ground. The leaves are very narrow, spear-shaped, hairy, and a little downy. The flowers are large, and are produced in tufts at the end of long footstalks that rise from the wings of the leaves. They blow in July, and are succeeded by oblong, erect, hairy, downy pods, which will sometimes contain ripe seeds in the autumn.

Small hoary Purple. 11. Small Hoary Purple Milk-Vetch. This species hath several weak procumbent stalks, scarcely four inches in length. The leaves are pinnated, and the lobes are narrow, downy, and sit close to the mid-rib. The flowers are large for so small a plant, of a purple colour, and grow in loose spikes. Their time of flowering is June, and their seeds will be fit to gather in August.

Alpine. 12. Alpine Milk-Vetch. The stalks of this plant are seldom more than four or five inches long, and they lie on the ground. The leaves are pinnated, and a little resemble those of the Common Vetch. The flowers are produced from the wings of the leaves in loose pendulous spikes. They blow in July, and are succeeded by acute hairy pods, containing ripe seeds, in the autumn.

Mountain. 13. Mountain Milk-Vetch. The stalks of this plant are about two or three inches long. The leaves are pinnated; the pinnæ are narrow, sit close to the mid-rib, and are terminated by an odd one. The flowers are produced in loose erect spikes; their colour is purple; they will be in blow in June, and are succeeded by oblong crooked pods, containing ripe seeds, in August.

Round podded Siberian. 14. Round-podded Siberian Milk-Vetch. This plant hath no stalk at all. The root is creeping, and from that the leaves immediately arise, which are pinnated; the pinnæ are oval, arranged by pairs along the mid-rib, and are terminated by an odd one. Among these the flower-stalks arise; these will be about the length of the leaves, and the flowers grow at the top in cylindrical spikes. Their colour is yellow; they will be in blow in June, and they are succeeded by roundish inflated pods full of greenish seeds, which will be ripe in the autumn.

German. 15. German Milk-Vetch. This species hath no stalk, and the leaves spring immediately from the roots; they are pinnated, being composed of several pair of obtuse lobes, that are terminated by an odd one. Among the leaves the flower-stalk arises. It is erect, longer than the leaves, and crowned by a spike of blue flowers, which will be in perfection in June, and perfect their seeds in the autumn. The pods of this species are erect, inflated, awl-shaped, and hairy.

Yellow flowered Siberian. 16. Yellow-flowered Siberian Milk-Vetch. This plant hath no stalk. The leaves are hairy, and composed of several pair of oval obtuse lobes, that are terminated by an odd one. Among these arises a naked, hairy, upright stalk, supporting a close spike of large yellow flowers, which will be in blow in June, and ripen their seeds in the autumn.

Helvetian Milk-Vetch. 17. Helvetian Milk-Vetch. This species hath no stalk, and the leaves, which spring immediately from the root, are composed of several pair of hairy acute lobes. The flower-stalk seldom rises upright, and the top of it is garnished with the flowers. These are yellow, having a stain of purple near the base. They flower in July, and are succeeded by very hairy rough pods, containing ripe seeds.

Method of propagating them. The propagation of all these sorts is very easy. It is done by sowing the seeds in the spring in the places where they are to remain. They will readily come up, and require no farther trouble than keeping them clean from weeds, and thinning them where they appear too close. All of these, like the Milk-Vetch, though at the same time

they

they delight in an open exposure. This also should be naturally warm, and well defended from cutting winds, especially, for the Carolina and Canada species, which are rather tender while young. For these, indeed, it would not be amiss to sow the seeds in pots, and put them in a shelter for a winter or two, and afterwards turn them out in the spring, with the mould at the roots, into the places where they are designed to remain.

Titles. 1. The Yellow Oriental Milk-Vetch is titled *Astragalus caulescens* [illegible] *foliolis ex orbiculato* [illegible]. Tournefort calls it *Astragalus orientalis* [illegible] *flore luteo*; and Dillenius, *Astragalus Orientalis Cicer* [illegible]. It grows naturally in the East.

2. The Yellow Oriental Milk-Vetch is titled, *Astragalus caulescens* [illegible] *longissimis* [illegible]. Tournefort calls it, *Astragalus orientalis* [illegible] *flore purpureo*. It grows in the East.

3. Hungarian Milk-Vetch is titled, *Astragalus caulescens* [illegible] *leguminibus subulatis pilosis*. Amman calls it, *Astragalus* [illegible] *floribus* [illegible]; and Caspar Bauhine, *Cicer* [illegible]. It grows naturally in Hungary and Siberia.

4. Goat's-Rue-leaved Milk-Vetch. This is titled *Astragalus* [illegible] *leguminibus* [illegible]. Tournefort calls it, *Astragalus orientalis* [illegible] *flore* [illegible]; and Amman, *Astragalus* [illegible] *caule* [illegible]. It is a native of Siberia.

5. Carolina Milk-Vetch is titled, *Astragalus caulescens erectus* [illegible] *pedunculis* [illegible]. Van Royen calls it, *Astragalus floribus* [illegible]; and Dillenius, *Astragalus* [illegible] *flore* [illegible]. It is a native of Carolina.

6. Canada Milk-Vetch is *Astragalus caulescens* [illegible] *leguminibus* [illegible] *foliolis* [illegible]. Tournefort calls it, *Astragalus Canadensis, flore viridi flavescente*. It grows naturally in Canada and Virginia.

7. Yellow Austrian Milk-Vetch is *Astragalus caulescens* [illegible] *leguminibus subglobosis inflatis mucronatis pilosis*. Caspar Bauhine calls it, *Cicer sylvestre, foliis* [illegible] *majus*; and Camerarius, *Cicer sylvestre*. It grows naturally in Austria and Italy.

8. Dwarf Yellow Milk-Vetch. This is titled, *Astragalus* [illegible] *erecto-patulis foliolis* [illegible] *leguminibus subrotundis*. Caspar Bauhine calls it, *Cicer, foliis oblongis* [illegible]. It grows naturally in Siberia, Helvetia, and Thuringia.

9. English Milk-Vetch, or Wild Liquorice, is titled, *Astragalus caulescens prostratus, leguminibus* [illegible] *foliis ovalibus pedunculo longioribus*. In the *Hortus Cliffort.* it is termed, *Astragalus* [illegible] *caulibus procumbentibus*. Morison calls it, *Astragalus luteus* [illegible] *vulgaris*; and Caspar Bauhine, *Glycyrrhiza sylvestris, floribus luteo-pallescentibus*. It grows naturally in England, and most parts of Europe.

10. [illegible] Milk-Vetch. This is titled, *Astragalus caulescens procumbens* [illegible] *leguminibus* [illegible]. Caspar Bauhine calls it, *Astragalus* [illegible]; and Morison, *Astragalus* [illegible] *floribus* [illegible]. It grows naturally in Siberia.

11. Sea [illegible] Purple Milk-Vetch is, *Astragalus* [illegible] *procumbens, floribus* [illegible] *tomentosis*. Plukenet calls it, *Astragalus* [illegible], and Ray, *Cicer montanum* [illegible]. It is a native of England.

12. Alpine Milk-Vetch is titled, *Astragalus caulescens* [illegible] *pedunculis racemosis*, [illegible] *utrinque* [illegible]. In the *Hortus Cliffort.* it is termed, *Astragalus pedunculis* [illegible] *in Flora Lapp. Astragalus Alpinus* [illegible]. Scheuchzer calls it, *Astragalus Alpinus* [illegible]. It grows naturally on the Alps of Lapland and Switzerland.

13. Mountain Milk-Vetch. This is titled, *Astragalus acaulis, scapis folio longioribus, floribus* [illegible] *leguminibus ovatis, acuminato* [illegible]. John Bauhine calls it, *Astragalus quadam montanus* [illegible]; Caspar Bauhine, *Onobrychis* [illegible] *floribus* [illegible] *purpurascentibus* [illegible]; and Clusius, *Onobrychis*. It grows naturally in Helvetia and Valesia.

14. Round-podded Siberian Milk-vetch is titled, *Astragalus acaulos, scapis folia aequantibus, leguminibus* [illegible] *subglobosis* [illegible]. In the *Amoenitates Acad.* it is termed *Astragalus acaulos, leguminibus* [illegible] *globosis*. It is a native of Siberia.

15. German Milk-Vetch. This is titled, *Astragalus* [illegible], *scapo* [illegible] *foliis longiore, leguminibus* [illegible] *villosis erectis*. Amman calls it, *Astragalus non ramosus, villosus & incanus spicatus, floribus purpuro-violaceis*; Haller, *Astragalus totus* [illegible]; and Zinn, *Phaca pedunculis radicatis* [illegible], *foliolis ex ovato acutis* [illegible]. It grows in Siberia.

16. Hairy Yellow-flowered Siberian Milk-Vetch is, *Astragalus acaulis hirsutus, scapis erectis* [illegible] *foliolis ovatis obtusis villosis*. Amman calls it, *Astragalus, tragacanthae folio, non ramosus, floribus luteis*. It is a native of Siberia.

17. Helvetian Milk-Vetch is titled, *Astragalus acaulos, calycibus leguminibusque villosis, foliolis acutis*. Haller calls it, *Astragalus acaulos, foliis* [illegible], *calyce & fructu villoso*. It grows naturally in Helvetia, Oelandia, and Germany.

Class and order in the Linnæan system. *Astragalus* is of the class and order *Diadelphia Decandria*, and the characters are,

The characters. 1. CALYX is a tubular monophyllous perianthium, divided at the top into five acute segments.

2. COROLLA is papilionaceous. The vexillum, which is longer than the other parts, is upright, obtuse, emarginated, and reflexed on the sides. The alæ are oblong, and shorter than the vexillum. The carina is emarginated, and the length of the alæ.

3. STAMINA. The filaments are ten in number, nine of them join in a body, and one stands singly; their position is nearly upright, and the antheræ are roundish.

4. PISTILLUM consists of a taper germen, a subulated ascendant style, and an obtuse stigma.

5. PERICARPIUM is a pod of two cells.

6. SEMINA. The seeds are reniform.

CHAP.

# CHAP. LXIV.

## *ASTRANTIA*, BLACK MASTERWORT.

THERE are only two species of this genus:

Species.

1. The Great Black Masterwort.
2. The Small Black Masterwort.

The Great Black

1. The Great Black Masterwort. The roots of this species are large, spreading, black without, but white within. The radical leaves are large, and divided into five broad, oblong, pointed lobes, which are deeply serrated on their edges. Their colour is a dark green on their upper surface, but paler under, and they grow from the roots on long firm footstalks. From among the leaves the flower-stalks arise. These are round, striated, upright, firm, and will grow to about two feet high. At each joint stands a single leaf, composed of three sharp pointed sawed lobes, and the top of it is crowned by the flowers, the colour of which is a greenish white. They are produced in compound umbels at the end of every branch; the small umbels stand upon long footstalks; and the leaves that compose the involucrum are spear-shaped, sharp pointed, of a purplish colour, and extend beyond the rays of the flower; though this is not a permanent property; for sometimes they are short and narrow, of a whitish colour, or green, and now and then they appear variegated with both. It flowers in the summer, and produces plenty of seeds early in the autumn.

and Small Black Masterwort described.

2. The Small Black Masterwort has a large, spreading root, though the flower-stalk will not rise higher than about a foot. The leaves are what is called digitated, or shaped like the hand, each of them being composed of seven or eight deeply serrated lobes, which spread out like the fingers. The flowers are produced at the extremities of the branches in compound umbels. The leaves that compose the involucrum are very narrow, and often of a whitish colour. It flowers in the summer, and the seeds ripen soon in the autumn.

Method of propagating these species.

The propagation of these sorts is by dividing of the roots any time in the autumn, winter, or spring, though the former is the more eligible season. As they spread much by their large roots, they should be entirely taken up every three or four years, and the best off-sets planted afresh, throwing the remainder away. Thus they will always look neat and compact, which is a great article to be observed in all spreading flowers, as they would otherwise soon form a wild and slovenly look. They are very hardy plants, and as any soil and situation will do for them, and being flowers of no great beauty, the very worst part of the garden should be assigned them.

They may be also easily raised from seeds. The best time for sowing of these is in the autumn, soon after they are ripe. When the plants come up, they should be kept clean from weeds, and in the autumn may be transplanted to the places where they are designed to remain.

Titles.

1. The Great Black Masterwort is titled, *Astrantia foliis quinquelobis lobis trifidis*. In the *Hortus Cliffortianus* it is simply termed, *Astrantia*. Caspar Bauhine calls it, *Helleborus niger, saniculæ folio*; and Dodonæus, *Veratrum nigrum*. It grows naturally on the Alps; also in several parts of Switzerland, Bohemia, &c.

2. The Small Black Masterwort is titled, *Astrantia foliis digitatis serratis*. Haller calls it, *Astrantia foliis digitatis septenis integris dentatis*; Caspar Bauhine, *Helleborus, saniculæ folio, minor*; and Boccone, *Helleborus minimus Alpinus, Astrantiæ flore*. It grows naturally on the Helvetian, Hetrurian, and Pyrenean Mountains.

Class and order in the Linnæan system. The characters.

*Astrantia* is of the class and order *Pentandria Digynia*, and the characters are,

1. CALYX. The general umbel is composed of about three or four rays, the partial of many.

The general involucrum is formed of leaves duplicate to the rays; the partial of about twenty leaves, that are spear-shaped, patent, equal, coloured, and longer than the umbel.

The proper perianthium is acute, erect, permanent, and cut at the top into five segments.

2. COROLLA. The general flower is uniform. The proper corolla is composed of five bifid, erect petals, that are bent inwards.

3. STAMINA consist of five simple filaments, the length of the corollulæ, with simple antheræ.

4. PISTILLUM consists of an oblong germen, situated below the flower, and of two erect, slender styles, with simple patent stigmas.

5. PERICARPIUM is an oval, obtuse, striated fruit, divided into two parts.

6. SEMINA. The seeds are two, oval, oblong, and rough.

# CHAP. LXV.

## *ATHAMANTA*, SPIGNEL.

Introductory Remarks.

THE species of this genus being more remarkable for variety than beauty, are seldom admitted into gardens for the sake of their flowers. But the real son of Science may, perhaps, think it unpardonable to pass them by wholly unnoticed; for his sake chiefly, therefore, they are thus enumerated.

Species.

1. Common Spignel, Meu, Bald, or, Bawd-money.
2. Candy Carrot.
3. Sicilian Carrot.
4. Mountain Stone Parsley.
5. Broad-leaved Mountain Parsley.
6. Siberian Spignel.

These are the names they have usually gone by among old Botanists, Herbalists, &c. which I shall along chuse to retain as much as possible, because by them they are always most known. Their modern names follow for the satisfaction of those who more closely apply themselves to the science.

Common Spignel,

1. Common Spignel. This is the sort used in medicine. The stalks will grow to about a foot high. They are round, striated, and divide into smaller branches near the top. The radical leaves are large, and grow on long footstalks. Each is composed of a multitude of very narrow leaves, finer than those of fennel; they grow close together, are of a deep green, and look very beautiful. The leaves on the stalks are like the radical ones, but smaller. The flowers terminate the stalks in umbels. Their colour is white; they will be in blow in June, and are succeeded by oblong, smooth seeds, which will be ripe in August. The root of this species has been greatly esteemed as an alexipharmac, but is now less used than formerly.

Candy,

2. Candy Carrot. The stalks are branching, and will grow to upwards of two feet high. The radical leaves are large, and composed of a multitude of narrow, plain, hairy segments, not much unlike those of fennel. The flowers terminate the stalks in large, compound umbels. Their colour is white, they will be in blow in June, and are succeeded by oblong, hairy seeds, which will be ripe in September.

and Sicilian Carrot,

3. Sicilian Carrot. The stalks of this species are round, upright, firm, branching, and will grow to a yard high. The leaves are divided into a multitude of narrow segments, and the radical ones are bright and shining; those on the stalk are a little hairy, and their manner of growth is alternately. The flowers terminate the stalks in compound umbels; they are close and compact at their first appearance, but afterwards they spread open, and display their number of rays, standing on short, hairy footstalks. The flowers are white; they will be in blow in July, and are succeeded by hairy, ripe seeds in the autumn.

Mountain Stone,

4. Mountain Stone Parsley rises with several upright, round, striated, thickish stalks, to the height of about a yard. The leaves are bipinnated, and large, being composed of a multitude of broadish, serrated lobes. They are of a pale green on the upper surface, but whitish underneath; and the whole leaf is very beautiful. The flowers terminate the stalks in large hæmispherical umbels. Their colour is white; they will be in blow in July, and are succeeded by hairy seeds, which will be ripe in the autumn.

and Broad-leaved Mountain Parsley;

5. Broad-leaved Mountain Parsley will grow to a yard or better in height. The leaves are large, being composed of a multitude of oval, acute, serrated, or jagged lobes, that spread themselves various ways. The flowers terminate the stalks like the others; their colour is whitish; they will be in blow in July, and ripen their seeds in the autumn.

and Siberian Athamanta described.

6. Siberian *Athamanta* hath a slender, single, angular, furrowed stalk, about a foot high. The leaves are sub-bipinnated, glossy, and the pinnæ lie over each other in the imbricated way. The flowers are produced from the upper part of the stalk in exceeding close umbels; their colour is white; they will be in blow in June, and ripen their seeds in September.

Method of raising these plants.

These sorts are all easily propagated by sowing of the seeds; the best time for which is the autumn, soon after they are ripe. They are all very hardy, and will require no farther trouble, than keeping them clean from weeds, and if they are sown in the places where they are to remain, thinning them to proper distances. If they are raised in the seminary, a moist day should be made choice of, in the latter end of the summer, or the beginning of autumn, and they should be carefully taken up with a ball of earth to each root, and transplanted to the places where they are designed to remain. They will readily take root, and the summer following will flower, and ripen their seeds in the autumn.

Titles.

1. The Common Spignel is titled, *Athamanta foliolis capillaribus, seminibus glabris striatis*. Caspar Bauhine calls it, *Meum foliis anethi*; and Dodonæus simply, *Meum*. It grows naturally in England, Italy, Switzerland, and Spain.

2. Candy Carrot is titled, *Athamanta foliolis linearibus planis hirsutis, petalis bipartitis, seminibus oblongis hirsutis*. Haller calls it, *Libanotis foliis tenuissime pinnatis, laciniis petiolatis*; Caspar Bauhine, *Daucus Alpinus, multifido longoque folio*; John Bauhine, *Daucus Creticus, semine hirsuto*; and Cammerarius, *Daucus Creticus*. It grows naturally in Switzerland.

3. Sicilian Carrot. This is titled, *Athamanta foliis inferioribus nitidis, umbellis primordialibus subsessilibus, seminibus pilosis*. In the *Hortus Cliffortianus* it is termed, *Athamanta foliolis multifidis planis, seminibus villosis*; and Zanoni calls it, *Daucus secundus Siculus, sophiæ folio*. It is a native of Sicily.

4. Mountain Stone Parsley is titled, *Athamanta foliis bipinnatis planis, umbellis hæmisphæricis, seminibus hirsutis*. Haller calls it, *Libanotis pinnulis circa costam decussatis*; Caspar Bauhine, *Libanotis minor, apii folio*; and Plukenet, *Daucus montanus, pimpinellæ saxifragæ hircinæ folio*. It grows naturally in England and Germany.

5. Broad-leaved Mountain Parsley. This is, *Athamanta foliis divaricatis*. Haller calls it, *Selinum pinnis ad angulos obtusos pinnatis, pinnulis incisis non serratis*; Caspar Bauhine, *Apium montanum*,

*tanum, folio ampliore*, and Clusius, *Oreoselinum*. It is a native of Germany.

6. Siberian Spignel is titled *Athamanta foliis sub-bipinnatis foliolis dorsum imbricatis, umbellis lenticularibus*. It grows naturally in Siberia.

Class and order in the Linnæan system. *Athamanta* is of the class and order *Pentandria Digynia*, and the characters are,

The characters. 1. CALYX. The general umbel spreads open, and composed of many rays; the partial of fewer.

The general involucrum is composed of several narrow leaves, that are rather shorter than the rays.

The partial is linear, and about the same length with the rays.

2. COROLLA. The general flower is uniform; the proper corolla is composed of five inflexed, heart-shaped petals, that are nearly equal.

3. STAMINA are five capillary filaments, the length of the corolla, with roundish antheræ.

4. PISTILLUM consists of a germen situated below the receptacle, and of two distant styles, with obtuse stigmas.

5. PERICARPIUM. There is none. The fruit is oval, oblong, striated, and divided into two parts.

6. SEMINA. The seeds are two. Their figure is oval, striated, plain on one side, and convex on the other.

## C H A P. LXVI.

## *A T H A N A S I A.*

OF this genus is one perennial, commonly called,

Species described. Sea Cud-weed.

The stalks are upright, soft, woolly, and about eight or ten inches high. The leaves are spear-shaped, obtuse, short, white, downy, and soft to the touch. The flowers come out in roundish bunches from the tops of the stalks. They are of a yellow colour, appear in June and July, and the seeds ripen in the autumn.

Culture. This species is propagated by parting of the roots, or sowing of the seeds. The work for both may be performed in the autumn or spring. When they are set out, they should have a light, dry soil, an open situation, and they will afterwards require no trouble, except keeping them clean from weeds.

Titles. This species is titled, *Athanasia pedunculis unifloris subcorymbosis, foliis lanceolatis indivisis crenatis obtusis tomentosis*. In the former edition of the *Species Plantarum* it is termed, *Filago tomentosa, corymbo subramoso, foliis oblongis obtusis crenatis*; in the *Hortus Cliffortianus*, *Santolina corymbo terminali subdiviso, foliis oblongis integerrimis obtusis*. Caspar Bauhine calls it, *Gnaphalium maritimum*; and Morison, *Chrysanthemum perenne gnaphaloides maritimum*. It grows naturally on sea-shores in most of the southern parts of Europe.

Class and order in the Linnæan system. *Athanasia* is of the class and order *Syngenesia Polygamia Æqualis*, and the characters are,

The characters. 1. CALYX. The general calyx is oval, and imbricated with several spear-shaped, compact scales.

2. COROLLA. The general flower is uniform, and longer than the calyx. The hermaphrodite florets are numerous, equal, infundibuliforme, and cut at the top into five acute, erect segments.

3. STAMINA are five short, capillary filaments, having a cylindrical, tubular anthera.

4. PISTILLUM consists of an oblong germen, a filiforme style rather longer than the stamen, and a bifid, obtuse stigma.

5. PERICARPIUM. There is none.

6. SEMINA. The seeds are single, oblong, and furnished with a short, paleaceous down.

The receptacle is paleaceous. The paleæ are spear-shaped, and longer than the seeds.

## C H A P. LXVII.

## *ATRACTYLIS*, DISTAFF THISTLE.

THERE are only three species of this genus, one is an annual, another a biennial, and the third a perennial. The perennial species is usually called,

Species described. Prickly Gumbearing *Cnicus*, or, Carline Thistle.

This is a very low plant. The leaves rise immediately from the root; they are narrow, sinuated, prickly on their edges, and lie flat on the ground. Among these is placed the flower without any stalk. It is of the compound, radiated kind, and the flowers are numerous. The calyx that contains them is prickly; the rays are white, but the florets in the disk are of a yellowish colour. It will

will be in blow in July, but never perfects its ſeeds in our gardens

Method of propagating theſe ſpecies

The propagation of this ſpecies is by ſeeds Theſe may eaſily be procured from Italy, where the plants naturally grow, and having obtained them, nothing more is to be done, than to plant them in a light, warm, ſandy border, and a well-ſheltered place, for without ſuch a ſituation, if you raiſe ever ſo many plants, one of our hard, froſty winters will put an end to your whole ſtock

The beſt way will be to ſow them where they are to remain, though they will bear tranſplanting very well, if required Cover the ſeeds a quarter of an inch deep, and thin them when they come up too cloſe All the ſummer they will want nothing but weeding, and a little refreſhment with water now and then in dry weather, and in winter it will be neceſſary to prick ſome furze-buſhes round the beds, to break the edge of the black froſts, if they ſhould happen Thus, if your ſituation is naturally warm and well ſheltered, and they have alſo this additional protection, your plant may be continued for many years

Titles

This ſpecies is titled, *Atractylis flore aculi* Tournefort calls it, *Cnicus, carlinæ folio, acaulos gummifer aculeatus*, Caſpar Bauhine, *Carlina acaulos gummifera*; Alpinus, *Carduus pinea Theophraſti*, and Columna, *Chameleon albus Dioſcoridis* It grows naturally in Italy and Crete

Claſs and order in the Linnæan ſyſtem

*Atractylis* is of the claſs and order *Syngeneſia Polygamia Æqualis*, and the characters are,

The characters

1 CALYX The exterior is compoſed of ſeveral narrow, prickly leaves The common calyx is oval and imbricated, and compoſed of many oblong, ſpear-ſhaped, connivent ſcales, that have no ſpines

2 COROLLA is compound and radiated The hermaphrodite florets, which are numerous in the diſk, are tubular, funnel-ſhaped, and cut in the top into five ſegments The hermaphrodite florets in the radius are tongue-ſhaped, and indented at the ends in five parts

3 STAMINA of the florets, both in the diſk and radius, are five very ſhort capillary filaments, with a cylindrical, tubular anthera

4 PISTILLUM of the florets in the diſk conſiſts of a very ſhort germen, a filiforme ſtyle the length of the ſtamina, and a bifid ſtigma

5 PERICARPIUM There is none

6 SEMINA The ſeeds are turbinated, compreſſed, and crowned with a fine downy plume

The receptacle is plain and hairy

# CHAP LXVIII.

## *ATROPA*, DEADLY NIGHT-SHADE and MANDRAKE

Introductory Remarks

THE Deadly Night-ſhade and the Mandrake were never, until lately, conſidered as two ſpecies of one and the ſame genus The Mandrake has always ſtood alone, and Linnæus, in his former works, following the path of preceding Botaniſts, placed it as a diſtinct genus, calling it, as uſual, *Mandragora*, without any epithet or deſcriptive title But, upon cloſer examination of this plant, the characters are found exactly to anſwer to thoſe of *Atropa*, on which account, in the laſt edition of the *Species Plantarum*, it is placed there as the firſt ſpecies of that genus, the old generic name *Mandragora* being now cancelled, or made obſolete

The Mandrake, then, and the Deadly Night-ſhade are the two only hardy perennials that belong to this genus, and it is for the ſake of the former, that the word *Atropa* is introduced into this place

Deſcription of the Mandrake,

1 The Mandrake then has a very large tap root, which very often divides or becomes forked in a manner ſo as to occaſion its being fancied by ſome to repreſent the legs, thighs and other parts of the human body Hence ſo many ſtrange ſtories have been formed of this plant, and ſo many cheats and impoſitions been palmed on the public Heads have been carved to anſwer the purpoſe of making it a complete Mandrake, or a figure repreſenting the human body Nay, the roots of other plants, ſuch as briony, have been framed into human figures, with which to cheat the public, and ſerve the turn of impoſtures Theſe roots are long with numerous fibres, and will ſtrike a yard, or deeper, into the ground They are as large as a parſnip, and are ſometimes ſimple, like other tap-roots, and ſometimes forked, or divided into two or more branches Its colour is a pale brown on the outſide, but white within, and it is very durable, being ſuppoſed to remain ſound for half a century, or longer The top of it is crowned with the leaves Theſe are numerous, about a foot long, five inches broad in the middle, pointed, and of a dark green They have no footſtalks, are a little waved on their edges, and have a ſtrong diſagreeable ſcent The flowers riſe immediately from the roots among the leaves, on footſtalks about three inches long They are moderately large, and of a whitiſh green colour, will be in blow in March or April, and are ſucceeded by large, yellowiſh berries, containing ripe ſeeds, in July The berries are ſometimes round, and ſometimes ſhaped like a pear The name Male Mandrake has been uſed to expreſs the more common ſort with round berries, whilſt the pear ſhaped ſort has been uſually called the Female Mandrake

The Mandrake has been accounted poiſonous Theophraſtus affirms this, but it is nevertheleſs beyond all doubt that the plant is not only innocent, but wholeſome and ſerviceable in many caſes, if not taken in too great quantities Mandrakes are ſaid to have vaſt power in procuring fruitfulneſs to women, and certainly their nature was better known to the Iſraelitiſh women of old, who ſo earneſtly deſired them, than to many of our learned Explainers of the ſacred Text What laboured pages have been filled to prove, that by the Mandrake in Scripture is meant ſome other fruit, becauſe

cauſe they could not conceive how any perſon could be fond of this; ſerving only to prove theſe learned Commentators altogether ignorant of natural hiſtory, and of thoſe herbs which Nature has deſigned for the benefit of mankind. Now ſuch *learned* Divines muſt know, that the fruit of Mandrakes is not only innocent, but alſo very palatable, when boiled and mixed with ſpices. But be this as it may, the power of the Mandrake, as a uterine deobſtruent, is univerſally acknowledged, and was well known to the Ancients, and no doubt Rachel was well acquainted with its virtues as ſuch, which made her ſo earneſtly deſire it.

and Deadly Night-ſhade

2 Deadly Night-ſhade. This ought never to be admitted into gardens, where there are children, becauſe of the poiſonous quality of the berries, which are of a very beautiful black, and very tempting to ſuch little Innocents, whoſe reaſon is not yet ſtrong enough to direct their conduct. Where there are no children, a plant or two may be had for philoſophical obſervation, and to occaſion variety, as they look pretty in the autumn, by their gloſſy jet-black berries. The ſtalks are branching, of a purpliſh colour, and will grow to a yard or four feet high. The leaves are large, oval, entire, and grow alternately on the branches. The flowers are very numerous, they grow from the wings of the leaves ſingly on long footſtalks, they are large, and of a campanulated figure, their inſide is of a duſky purple colour, and their outſide is reddiſh. It flowers moſt part of the ſummer, and the leaves are of a jet or poliſhed black. They are about the ſize of a black cherry, pulpy, and of a diſagreeable ſweetiſh taſte. The Deadly Night-ſhade, properly prepared, is now found to be uſeful in many caſes, and its power in curing cancerous diſorders is amazingly great. If a perſon is deſirous of a plant or two of this ſort, he may take an off-ſet from ſome root in the autumn or ſpring, and it will readily grow, or he may ſow a few ſeeds in ſome place where they are deſigned to remain, and he will ſoon have plants enough.

Culture

With regard to the Mandrakes, their culture is effected by ſowing of the ſeeds. The beſt time for this is the autumn, ſoon after they are ripe. A light, ſandy, deep ſoil is moſt proper for their roots to ſtrike into. It ſhould be dug four feet deep, and the ſeeds ſhould be ſown, and covered over with about half an inch of fine mould. In the ſpring the plants will come up, and when they come up too cloſe, the weakeſt muſt be drawn out, leaving the ſtrongeſt at about a foot diſtance from each other. They will every year get ſtronger and ſtronger, and will bring their flowers and ſeeds to great perfection.

Titles.

1 The Mandrake is titled, *Atropa acaulis, ſcapis unifloris*. In the *Hortus Cliffortianus*, &c. it is called, *Mandragora*. Caſpar Bauhine calls it, *Mandragora fructu rotundo*, and Dodonæus, *Mandragoras*. It grows naturally in Italy, Crete, Portugal and Spain.

2 Deadly Night-ſhade. This is titled, *Atropa caule herbaceo, foliis ovatis integris*. In the *Hortus Cliffortianus* it is called, *Atropa*. Caſpar Bauhine terms it, *Solanum melanocerafus*, and Cluſius, *Solanum lethale*. It grows naturally in England, Italy, and Auſtria.

Claſs and order in the Linnæan ſyſtem

*Atropa* is of the claſs and order *Pentandria Monogynia*, and the characters are,

1 CALYX is a monophyllous, bulbous, permanent perianthium, divided at the top into five acute ſegments.

The characters

2 COROLLA is a ſingle bell-ſhaped petal. The tube is very ſhort. The limb is ventricoſe oval, longer than the calyx, and divided at the top into five equal, ſpreading ſegments.

3 STAMINA are five ſubulated filaments, ariſing from the baſe of the petal. They are of the length of the corolla, connivent at their baſe, but at the top ſpread from each other, and are crowned by thickiſh, aſſurgent antheræ.

4 PISTILLUM conſiſts of a ſemi-oval germen, a filiforme ſtyle the length of the ſtamina, and a capitated, aſſurgent, tranſverſe, oblong ſtigma.

5 PERICARPIUM is a globoſe, bilocular berry, placed on a large calyx.

The receptacle is carnoſe, convex, and reniforme.

6 SEMINA. The ſeeds are reniforme and numerous.

## C A P. LXIX.

## *A V E N A*, O A T S.

Of this genus there are ſome ſpecies whoſe roots do not periſh after they have ſeeded, but remain all winter, and ſhoot up freſh ſtalks in the ſpring. Theſe are uſually called,

Species

1 Tall Oat Graſs.
2 Meadow Oat Graſs.
3 Yellow Oat Graſs.

Tall,

1 Tall Oat Graſs. The root is a cluſter of ſmall tubes clotted together, and ſending forth long, ſlender fibres from their baſe. The leaves are long, moderately broad, pinnated, and of a deep green colour. The ſtalk is round, hollow, jointed in two or three places, at each of which is ſituated a ſingle leaf, ſheathing the ſtalk a great way up with its baſe. The flowers come out in long ſpikes from the top of the ſtalks. They are of a green colour, and being long and ſlender, naturally bend with their own weight. They appear chiefly in July and Auguſt.

Meadow,

2 Meadow Oat Graſs. The leaves are long, flat, and pointed. The ſtalk is jointed and hollow, two feet high, and a ſingle leaf ſurrounds it a good way up from every joint. The flowers are produced from the top in nodding, ſpiked panicles, and are moſt common in the month of July.

and Yellow Oat Graſs deſcribed

3 Yellow Oat Graſs. The leaves and ſtalks of this ſpecies anſwer to the characters of moſt other ſorts of graſſes. The one being long narrow, and pointed, the other round, jointed, and hollow, having one leaf growing ſingly at each joint, and ſurrounding it with their baſe. The flowers

are

are produced from the tops of the stalks in loose panicles. They are of a pale, yellow colour, and are most common in July.

None of these sorts are propagated plants, and I mention them only for the satisfaction of those, who might expect to see their titles in a work of this nature.

Titles

1. Tall Oat Grass, or Knotty Dogs Grass, is entitled, *Avena paniculata, calycibus bifloris, flosculo hermaphrodito mutico, masculo aristato*. Dalechamp calls it, *Gramen avenaceum, panicula ramosa, semine papposo*; Guettard, *Avena calycibus bifloris, panicula laxa spicata, petiolis prioribus fasciculatis*; Ray, *Gramen avenaceum elatius, juba longa splendente*; Caspar Bauhine, *Gramen nodosum avenacea, radice tuberibus praedita*; Gerard, *Gramen caninum nodosum*; and Van Royen, *Avena panicula patente, calycibus bifloris altero flosculo aristato*. It is common in our meadows and pastures, and grows naturally in most countries of Europe.

2. Meadow Oat Grass is titled, *Avena spica [illegible], calycibus quinquefloris*. In the *Flora Lapponica* it is termed, *Avena [illegible], calyce spiculis breviore*. Guettard calls it, *Avena panicula spicata, spiculis [illegible] culmo appressis*; Gmelin, *Avena calycibus [illegible] floris, panicula [illegible], foliis planis*; Ray, *Gramen avenaceum montanum, spica simplici, aristis recurvis*; also, *Gramen avenaceum glabrum, [illegible] purpureo-argentea splendente*; and Caspar Bauhine, *[illegible]*. It grows naturally in dry meadows and pasture grounds in England, and in all countries of Europe.

3. Yellow Oat Grass is titled, *Avena panicula laxa, calycibus trifloris brevibus, flosculis omnibus aristatis*. Ray calls it, *Gramen avenaceum pratense elatius, panicula flavescente, locustis parvis*; and Morison, *Gramen avenaceum, spica sparsa flavescente, locustis parvis*. It grows naturally in meadows and pastures every where in England, and in most parts of France and Germany.

*Avena* is of the class and order *Triandria Digynia*, and the characters are, Class and order in the Linnæan system. The character

1. CALYX is a glume, consisting of two large, loose, ventricose, spear-shaped, acute, beardless valves, and for the most part contains several flowers.

2. COROLLA is of two valves. The lower valve is the size of the calyx, but broader; it is rounded, ventricose, pointed at both ends, and emits from the back a single, twisted, reflexed, geniculated arista.

3. STAMINA are three capillary filaments, having oblong, bifurcated antheræ.

4. PISTILLUM consists of an obtuse germen, and two hairy, reflexed styles, with simple stigmas.

5. PERICARPIUM. The corolla closely surrounds the seed, opens in no part, and serves for the pericarpium.

6. SEMEN. The seed is single, slender, oblong, pointed at both ends, and marked with a longitudinal furrow.

## CHAP. LXX.

## *AZALEA*, AMERICAN HONEYSUCKLE.

THERE are two species of this genus, which, though seldom propagated in gardens, are natural plants, and worthy of good culture and management; called, Species

1. Lapland Honeysuckle.
2. Procumbent Alpine Honeysuckle.

Lapland, 1. Lapland Honeysuckle. This species hath a low woody stem, seldom growing to a foot high. The branches are numerous, compound, and nearly erect. The leaves are small, oval, spotted, hollowed, and terminate the branches in clusters, ten or a dozen of them usually growing together. Among the leaves come out long purple-coloured flowers, on short, reddish footstalks. They appear in June and July, and the seed ripens in the autumn.

and Procumbent Alpine Honeysuckle described. 2. Procumbent Alpine Honeysuckle. The stalks are ligneous, about a foot long, divide into a multitude of branches, and lie flat on the ground. The leaves grow by pairs, are small, and very much resemble those of the common thyme. The flowers are of a flesh-colour; they come out from the wings of the leaves in June or July, and are succeeded by ripe seeds in the autumn.

Method of propagating the sorts. These sorts are propagated by sowing of the seeds in the spring, in a shady, moist place. When the plants come up, they require no trouble, except keeping them clean from weeds, and watering them in dry weather. After they have grown one or two years, they may be removed to the places where they are to remain.

They are also propagated by layers. If the young branches are laid down in the spring, they will have struck root by the autumn following, and may then be removed to their destined habitation. The slips also will grow if planted in a moist, shady border in the spring; and by this means plenty of plants may be soon obtained. These plants require a moist, shady situation. They grow naturally in the cold, mountainous parts of the world, and a similar situation, if possible, should be allowed them among shrubs or trees in our plantations.

1. Lapland Honeysuckle is titled, *Azalea foliis adspersis punctis excavatis*. In the *Flora Suecica* it is termed, *Azalea ramis compositis suberectis*; and in the *Flora Lapponica*, *Azalea maculis ferrugineis subtus adspersa*. It grows naturally on the Alps of Lapland. Titles

2. Procumbent Alpine Honeysuckle is titled, *Azalea ramis diffuso procumbentibus*. Boccone calls it, *Chamærhododendros supina ferruginea, thymi folio, Alpina*; Caspar Bauhine, *Chamæcistus serpyllifolia, floribus carneis*; and Oeder, *Chamæcistus VII*. It grows naturally on the Alps of Europe.

# CHAP. LXXI.

## *BALLOTA*, BLACK HOREHOUND

Species. OF this genus are,

1 Stinking Black Horehound.

2 White Stinking Horehound

3 Woolly Stinking Horehound

Stinking Black, 1 Stinking Black Horehound The stalks are square, thick, hairy, and about a yard high The leaves are heart-shaped, serrated, of a dusky green, and grow opposite on short footstalks The flowers come out in clusters from the wings of the leaves at the upper parts of the stalks They are of a reddish purple colour, having acuminated cups They appear in July and August, and the seeds ripen in the autumn

White Stinking, 2 White Stinking Horehound The stalks are square, jointed, hairy, and two or three feet high The leaves are heart shaped undivided, serrated, and grow opposite to each other at the joints The flowers come out from the wings of the leaves for about half the length of the stalks They are of a white colour, having truncated cups They appear in July, and the seeds ripen in the autumn

and Woolly Stinking Horehound described 3 Woolly Stinking Horehound The stalks of this plant are square, jointed, and covered with a white woolly matter The leaves are composed of three or five obtuse lobes, are smooth on their upper side, hairy underneath, and grow opposite to each other at the joints The flowers are produced in whorls round the upper parts of the stalks They are large, and of a white colour, appear in July and August, and the seeds ripen in the autumn The two first sorts appear common in England, and are not cultivated plants, the other is preserved in some gardens

Culture These sorts are all raised by sowing the seeds in the spring, in beds of common mould made fine When the plants come up, they should be thinned where they grow too close, and be kept clean from weeds, which is all the trouble they will require

Titles 1 Stinking Black Horehound is entitled, *Ballota foliis cordatis indivisis serratis, calycibus acuminatis* In the *Hortus Cliffortianus* it is termed, *Ballota* Fuchsius calls it, *Ballote*, Caspar Bauhine, *Marrubium nigrum fœtidum*, Gerard, *Marrubium nigrum*, and Parkinson, *Marrubium nigrum fœtidum, Ballote Dioscoridis* It is common by waysides in England, and most countries of Europe

2 White Stinking Horehound is, *Ballota foliis cordatis ... serratis, calycibus subtruncatis* Cammerarius calls it, *Ballote*, and Tournefort, *Ballote flore albo* It grows naturally in England, and most countries of Europe

3 Woolly Stinking Horehound is titled, *Ballota foliis palmatis dentatis, caule lanato* Amman calls it, *Ballote foliis geranii laciniatis* ... It grows naturally in Siberia

*Ballota* is of the Class and Order *Didynamia Gymnospermia*, and the characters are, Class and order in the Linnæan System The characters

1 CALYX is a monophyllous, tubular, hypocrateriforme, five-cornered decemstriated, permanent perianthium, indented in five parts at the top There is an involucrum under the whorls, composed of several narrow leaves

2 COROLLA is one ringent petal The tube is cylindrical, and the length of the calyx The upper lip is erect, oval whole, crenated, and concave The lower lip is obtuse, and cut into three segments, of which the middle one is the largest, and indented at the end

3 STAMINA are four awl shaped filaments, of which two are shorter than the others, inclining towards the upper lip, and shorter than it having oblong, lateral antheræ

4 PISTILLUM consists of a quadrifid germen, a filiforme style, in situation and figure like the stamina, and a slender bifid stigma

5 PERICARPIUM There is none The seeds are lodged in the calyx

6 SEMINA The seeds are four, and of an oval figure

# CHAP. LXXII

## *BARTSIA*

Species OF this genus are two perennials, called,

1 Mountain Eye bright Cow-wheat

2 Virginian *Bartsia*

Mountain Eye bright Cow wheat, 1 Mountain Eye-bright Cow wheat The stalks are slender, square, hairy, and a foot and half high The leaves are heart-shaped, obtuse, serrated, hairy, sessile, and grow opposite to each other The flowers come out from the wings of the leaves almost the whole length of the stalks They are of a red colour, appear in June, and continue in succession until the end of August

and Virginian Bartsia described 2 Virginian *Bartsia* The stalks are slender, herbaceous, and a foot and half high The leaves are narrow, have two indentures on each side, and grow alternately The flowers come out in spikes from the tops of the stalks They are of a pale red colour, appear in July, and the seeds ripen in the autumn

The

Culture. The first sort grows common in England, and is rarely admitted into gardens; the other is propagated chiefly on account of its being of foreign extraction. They are both easily raised by sowing the seeds in the spring, in beds of common mould made fine. The plants will readily come up, and require no trouble, except thinning them where they are too close, and keeping them clean from weeds.

Titles. 1. The first species is titled, *Bartsia foliis oppositis cordatis obtuse serratis*. In the *Flora Lapponica* it is termed, *Euphrasia caule simplici, foliis cordatis obtuse serratis*. Ray calls it, *Euphrasia rubra Westmorlandica, foliis brevibus obtusis*; Oeder, *Pedicularis genus montanum*; Caspar Bauhine, *Clinopodium Alpinum hirsutum*, also, *Teucrium Alpinum, coma purpureo caerulea*; and Haller, *Staehelina*. It grows naturally in many parts of England; also on the Alps of Lapland, Helvetia, and other mountainous parts of Europe.

2. The second sort is titled, *Bartsia foliis alternis linearibus utrinque bidentatis*. In the *Hortus Cliffortianus* it is termed *Bartsia foliis alternis*. Plukenet calls it, *Pedicularis f. crista galli affinis Virginiana, ajugae multifido folio, apicibus coccineo, floribus pallidis, in spicam congestis*; and Morison, *Horminum, tenui coronopi folio, Virginianum*. It grows naturally in Virginia.

Class and order in the Linnean system. *Bartsia* is of the class and order *Didynamia Angiospermia*, and the characters are,

The characters. 1. CALYX is a monophyllous, tubular, permanent perianthium, cut at the top into two emarginated, coloured segments.

2. COROLLA is one ringent petal. The upper lip is slender, upright, long, and entire. The lower lip is small, reflexed, trifid, and obtuse.

3. STAMINA are four letaceous filaments the length of the upper lip, of which two are a little shorter than the other, having oblong approximate antheræ lying under the tip of the upper lip.

4. PISTILLUM consists of an oval germen, a filiform style longer than the stamina, and an obtuse, nutant stigma.

5. PERICARPIUM is an oval, compressed, acuminated capsule, formed of two valves, and containing two cells.

6. SEMINA. The seeds are numerous, angular, and small.

## CHAP. LXXIII.

## *BELLIS*, The DAISY.

Introductory remarks. THAT little flower which occupies our meadows in such amazing plenty, called the Daisy, is the only perennial of this genus. In its single state, it adorns our untouched pastures, and, together with the cowslip and the crow flowers, seems more than ordinarily to rejoice in the spring of the year. What sheets of these flowers are presented to our view the beginning of May! How enchanting the sight which Nature displays at that season! Amazing as it is, it is too often disregarded by the toiling Peasant; and the Admirer of Nature's works is principally exhilarated by such a scene. He at once sees in it the dignity of the appearance, and the greatness and goodness of the Author, in so pleasing as well as wonderful manner thus cloathing the fields; and is naturally led to thanksgiving and praise, as in the Hymn of Eve.

> How chearful along the gay mead,
> The Daisy and Cowslip appear,
> The flocks, as they carelessly feed,
> Rejoice in the spring of the year.
>
> The myrtles that shade the gay bowers,
> The herbage that springs from the sod,
> Trees, plants, cooling fruits and sweet flowers,
> All rise to the praise of my God.
>
> Shall man, the great master of all,
> The only insensible prove?
> Forbid it fair Gratitude's Call,
> Forbid it, Devotion and Love.
>
> The Lord, who such wonders can raise,
> And still can destroy with a nod,
> My lips shall incessantly praise,
> My soul shall be wrapt in my God.

Our meadows possess the Daisy in its single state, though there seems to be two varieties of it there; one with a white flower, and another whose rays are red, or more or less tinged with that colour. Our gardens enjoy it in its double state. Those flowers have been first of all accidentally obtained from the seeds of one or other of the single sorts, and which have been continued and improved by good culture ever since; so that we can now boast,

Species.
1. The Common Double Daisy.
2. The Double Red Daisy.
3. The Double White Daisy.
4. The Double Red and White Daisy.
5. The Double Variegated Daisy.
6. The Double-painted Lady Daisy.
7. The Double quilled Daisy.
8. The Double-pyed Quilled Daisy.
9. The Double Red Coxcomb Daisy.
10. The Double White Coxcomb Daisy.
11. The Double Speckled Coxcomb Daisy.
12. The Proliferous, or, Hen and Chickens Daisy.

There are still more varieties than these in colour, and the Doubleness of all is as great as possible. The Quilled and the Coxcomb sorts are less perfect flowers, but are admired on account of their being scarcer than the others, and causing some singularity in their appearance; whilst the Proliferous Daisy, commonly called by Gardeners the Hen and Chickens Daisy, is the most wonderful of all. From a large fair, and full double flower there issue several small ones, all standing on slender footstalks, attending and forming an agreeable ornament to their common parent. This Daisy is supposed to be originally obtained from the seeds of the large Red.

Culture. The culture of these sorts is by dividing of the roots root. It may be done at any time of the year, but the autumn is the best season for the purpose, and if performed then, they will flower strong the spring following. They are not nice in their apartment, for they will grow in almost any soil or situation; tho they thrive best in the shade, and a fresh earth. The most eligible way is to plant them in rows by the sides of walls, for in that manner their charms will be more conspicuous, as a few odd roots of these plants are too often disregarded. The roots should be transplanted every other autumn, which will keep them in their double and full beauty, whereas, if they are neglected for many years, they are too apt to become single, and run again into the common sorts.

Titles The D is titled, *Bellis hepo do*. In the *Hortus Cliffort* it is termed *Bellis hapo nude flo o*. Caspar Bauhine calls it, *Bellis sylvestris minor*; and Dodonæus, *Bellis sylvestris*. These titles belong to it in its single state. The Double or garden sorts are anciently called by old Botanists *Bellis hortensis flore pleno*, *Bellis hortensis*, *flore albo bull o*, *Bellis hortensis rubra*, *f... multiplex fil osa*, *Bellis hortensis prolifera*, and the like. This familiar species grows in pastures in most parts of Europe.

*Bellis* is of the class and order *Syngenesia Polygamia Superflua*, and the characters are, Class and order in the Linnæan system The characters

1. CALYX. The common calyx is simple, erect, and composed of a double series of small, equal, spear-shaped leaves.

2. COROLLA is radiated and discous. The hermaphrodite florets in the disk are numerous, funnel-shaped, and cut into five parts at the top.

The female flowers in the radius are tongue-shaped, and have three indentures at the end.

3. STAMINA, in the hermaphrodite flowers, are five very short capillary filaments, with a tubular cylindrical anthera.

4. PISTILLUM, in the hermaphrodite flowers, consists of an oval germen, a simple style, and an emarginated stigma.

In the female flowers it consists of an oval germen, a filiforme style, and two spreading stigmas.

5. PERICARPIUM. There is none.

6. SEMINA. The seeds both of the hermaphrodite and female florets are single, oval, and compressed.

The receptacle is conic and naked.

# CHAP. LXXIV.

## *BETONICA*, BETONY.

THERE are three species only of this genus, all of which are perennials, and plants of some singularity, tho' of very little beauty, and rarely introduced to any but botanic gardens. These are,

Species
1. Wood Betony.
2. Oriental Betony.
3. Mountain Betony.

Description of the Wood, 1. Wood Betony is a plant of admirable virtue, and much used in medicine. The leaves are large, bold, hairy, indented, of a dark green, and grow on long footstalks. The stalks are four square, sometimes rough, and will grow to about a foot or a foot and a half high; and the flowers terminate the stalks in spikes. The varieties of them are,

Varieties
The Purple-flowered Betony.
The Red Betony.
The White-flowered Betony.

They will be in blow in June and July, and ripen their seeds in August or September.

Oriental 2. Oriental Betony. The leaves of this plant are very long, narrow, hairy, of a pale green, indented, and grow on long footstalks. The stalk is thick, square, of a pale green, and will grow to about a foot and a half high. These stalks are ornamented with leaves growing opposite by pairs, and from the bosom of these leaves arise a few flowers; but the stalk is terminated by plenty of them growing in a large spike very close together. Their colour is a light purple; they will be in blow in June, and ripen their seeds in August.

and Mountain Betony 3. Mountain Betony. Of this species there are several varieties; some of very low growth, others with leaves nearly triangular, and shorter spikes of flowers. The colour of the flowers also is different. The most common is yellow, but there are of it the white and the red. They flower in June and July, and ripen their seeds in August.

Method of propagating these sorts These plants are all easily raised by sowing the seeds in the spring, or in a bed of common mould, in a shady place. When they come up too close, draw out the weakest, and keep them clean from weeds until the autumn, when they may be removed to the places where they are designed to remain.

By dividing of the roots also these plants are to be encreased. The best time for this is the autumn, though they will grow if removed any time in the winter or spring.

These plants all love the shade and a moist soil, so that if you can afford them such a situation, it will be more suitable to them than any, and they will flourish better.

Titles 1. The Wood Betony is titled, *Betonica spica interrupta*, *corollæ ... labii intermedia ...*. Dodonæus calls it simply, *Betonica*; C. Bauhine, *Betonica purpurea*. ... It grows naturally in most parts of Europe.

2. Oriental Betony. This is titled, *Betonica spica integra*, *corollarum lacinia labii intermedia integerrima*. Tournefort calls it, *Betonica orientalis*, *angustifolio ...*

*angustissimo & longissimo folio* It grows naturally in the East

3 Mountain Betony This is titled, *Betonica spica lasi foliosa, corollis galea bifidâ* Caspar Bauhine calls it, *Horminum minus album, Betonicæ facie*, also, *Betonicæ folio, capitulo alopecuri*, John Bauhine, *Betonicæ folio alopecuros quorundam*, Barrelier, *Betonica montana lutea*, and Ray, *Horminum Alpinum luteum, Betonicæ spicâ* It grows naturally on the mountainous parts of Italy, France, Austria, &c

Class and order in the Linnæan System The characters

*Betonica* is of the class and order *Didynamia Gymnospermia*, and the characters are,

1 CALYX is a tubular, cylindrical, aristated, monophyllous, permanent perianthium, divided into five parts at the top

2 COROLLA is a ringent petal, the tube is cylindrical and incurved; the upper lip is roundish, erect, plain, and entire, the lower lip is cut into three segments, of which the middle one is broad, roundish, and emarginated

3 STAMINA are four subulated filaments, two of which are shorter than the others, and incline towards the upper lip Their antheræ are roundish

4 PISTILLUM consists of a germen divided into four parts, a style of the figure and size of the stamina, and a bifid stigma

5 PERICARPIUM There is none The seeds are contained in the calyx

6 SEMINA. The seeds are oval, and four in number

# CHAP LXXV.

## *BORAGO*, BORAGE.

THERE is only one Perennial of this genus, called, Perennial Borage of Constantinople

Perennial Borage of Constantinople, described

This hath a thick spreading root, from which arise several large, heart shaped leaves on long hairy footstalks Among these proceed the flower-stalks, which will grow about two feet high, and divide near the top into branches or footstalks, supporting the flowers in kind of panicles They are of a pale blue colour, the petals turn backward, they will be in blow in April, and perfect their seeds in May or June

Method of propagating it

This plant is easily propagated either by the root or seeds Sow the seeds soon after they are ripe, and they will readily come up, or take a few pieces of the root any time in the autumn or spring, and they will readily grow and become good plants

These plants should have a dry rubbishy situation, which will cause them to flower with greater certainty early in the spring, and in such a soil they will not spread so fast by their roots, for in a rich soil they will soon over-run a pretty large spot

In order to keep these plants within bounds, they should be taken up every two or three years, when a sufficient quantity of off-sets should be planted again for a succession, and the rest should be thrown away The best time for this work is in the autumn

Titles.

The Perennial Borage of Constantinople is titled, *Borago calycibus tubo corollæ brevioribus, foliis cordatis* Tournefort calls it, *Borago Constantinopolitana, flore reflexo cæruleo, calyce vesicario* It grows naturally near Constantinople

Class and order in the Linnæan System The characters

*Borago* is of the class and order *Pentandria Monogynia*, and the characters are,

1 CALYX is a permanent perianthium, divided into five parts

2 COROLLA is a single rotated petal the length of the cup, the tube is shorter than the calyx, the limb is rotated, plain, and divided into five acute parts, the mouth is crowned by five obtuse indented prominences

3 STAMINA are five connivent awl-shaped filaments, with oblong connivent antheræ affixed to their inner-side in the middle

4 PISTILLUM consists of four germina, a filiforme style longer than the stamina, and a simple stigma

5 PERICARPIUM There is none The calyx is large and inflated

6 SEMINA The seeds are four, roundish, rough, and inserted longitudinally in the hollowed receptacle

# CHAP. LXXVI

## *B R I Z A*

Species.

THIS genus comprehends some well grown grasses, called,

1 Common Quaking-Grass
2 Small Quaking-Grass
3 Great Quaking-Grass
4 Love-Grass

Description of the Common.

1 Common Quaking-Grass This is frequently called Cow Quakes, and Ladies Hair. The root is composed of a multitude of short greyish fibres. The leaves form a cluster at the crown of the root, are grassy, and about four or five inches long. The stalk is slender, jointed, bent, garnished with one or two leaves which surround it with their base. The flowers are numerous at the tops of the stalks, and are collected in form of small oval spikes, each spike having a very slender footstalk. This occasions the whole to be set a-trembling by the least breath of wind. They are of a fine brown, or purple, and are to be found in our meadows in June.

Small,

2 Small Quaking-Grass. The leaves are small and grassy, and form a tuft at the crown of the root. The stalks are slender, jointed in two or three places, six or eight inches high, and have leaves growing singly at the joint, surrounding it with their base. The flowers are produced in panicles at the tops of the stalks, and are collected in small triangular spikes. Each of these spikes is supported by a very weak slender footstalk, which occasions the like tremulous motion with the former on the least gust of wind. It will be in flower in June.

and Great Quaking-Grass,

3 Great Quaking-Grass. The leaves are numerous at the root, and near a foot long. The stalks are slender, jointed, and about two feet long. The flowers are produced in panicles at the tops of the stalks; the little spikes of which the panicles are composed, are heart-shaped, and contain about seventeen floscules; they grow on slender weak footstalks, like the former, and being large, have a better effect by their tremulous property.

and Love-Grass.

4 Love-Grass. The leaves are of a whitish green colour, and five or six inches long. The stalk is jointed in two or three places, is furnished with leaves growing singly at the joints like the radical ones, but narrower, and grows to about a foot high. The flowers terminate the stalks in panicles; the spikes are spear-shaped, moderately long, of a bright white colour, and each contains about twenty florets; but being supported by strong footstalks, they are destitute of that tremulous property peculiar to the former species.

Culture.

The first two sorts are common in our meadows and pastures; the other two are natives of foreign countries. Whoever is inclined to propagate them may do it by sowing the seeds in the autumn, soon after they are ripe, or the spring following.

Titles.

1 Common Quaking-Grass is titled, *Briza spiculis ovatis, calyce flosculis* [illegible] Caspar Bauhine calls it, *Gramen tremulum majus*; John Bauhine, *Gramen tremulum*; Parkinson, *Gramen tremulum seu phalaris minor* [illegible] *purpurea et flavescens*; and Gerard, *Phalaris pratensis*. It grows common in England, and most parts of Europe.

2 Small Quaking-Grass is, *Briza spiculis triangulis, calyce flosculis* [illegible]. Caspar Bauhine calls it, *Gramen tremulum minus*, *panicula* [illegible] and Ray, *Gramen tremulum minus, panicula* [illegible] *locustis parvis triquetris*. It grows naturally in Jersey, Helvetia, and Italy.

3 Great Quaking-Grass is, *Briza spiculis cordatis, flosculis septendecim*. Caspar Bauhine calls it, *Gramen tremulum maximum*. It grows naturally in Italy and Portugal.

4 Love-Grass is, *Briza spiculis lanceolatis, flosculis viginti*. Gerard calls it, *Briza panicula* [illegible] *spicata, spiculis lanceolatis*; Gronovius, *Uniola* [illegible] *bus diphyllis, spiculis ovato-lanceolatis*; Caspar Bauhine, *Gramen paniculis elegantissimis*; and Tournefort, *Gramen eragrostis* [illegible]. It grows naturally in most of the southern countries of Europe.

Class and order in the Linnæan system.

*Briza* is of the class and order *Triandria Digynia*; and the characters are,

The characters.

1 CALYX is a glume composed of two heart-shaped, concave, equal, obtuse valves, containing many flowers, which are collected into a heart-shaped distichous spike.

2 COROLLA is two valves. The lower valve is of the size and shape of the calyx, and the upper one is small, plain, roundish, and closes the other.

3 STAMINA are three capillary filaments, having oblong antheræ.

4 PISTILLUM consists of a roundish germen, and two capillary recurved styles, with plumose stigmas.

5 PERICARPIUM. The corolla is all the pericarpium; it contains the seed, and opens for its dismission when ripe.

6 SEMEN. The seed is single, roundish, compressed, and small.

# CHAP. LXXVII

## *B R O M U S*

THIS genus comprehends another lot of grasses, called,

Species.
1. Tall Brome-Grass.
2. Spiked Brome-Grass.
3. Crested Brome-Grass.
4. Purging Brome-Grass.

Tall, 1. Tall Brome-Grass. The leaves are very long, near an inch broad, and end in a sharp point gradually to a point. The stalks are thick, smooth, hollow, jointed, and four or five inches high. The flowers come out in loose nodding panicles from the ends of the stalks; they appear chiefly in July and August.

Spiked, 2. Spiked Brome-Grass. The stalks are slender, and grow to about two feet high. The flowers are produced from the sides of the upper parts of the stalks in upper spikes, which are placed alternately on very short footstalks, and are mostly in June and July.

Crested, 3. Crested Brome-Grass. The stalks of this plant are seldom more than eight or ten inches high. The flowers are situated at the top in broad, oval, depressed, imbricated spikes. They appear in July, and the seeds ripen in August.

and Purging Brome Grass described. 4. Purging Brome-Grass. The stalks are upright, thick, firm, and six or eight feet high. The leaves are very long, near [illegible] broad, ending gradually to a point, and are of a good green. The flowers are collected in loose flexuose nodding spikes; they appear in July and August, and the seeds ripen in the autumn.

The first and second sorts grow common under hedges, in woods, &c. in England, and are not propagated; the third and fourth, being of foreign extraction, are sometimes cultivated, especially the fourth sort, which rises with large upright stalks, and broad leaves, in the manner of our reed, and makes a bold appearance in some places.

Method of propagating them. They are all easily propagated by sowing the seeds in the spring in moist rich earth; and when the plants come up they will require no trouble, except thinning them where they are too close, and keeping them clean from weeds.

Titles. Tall Brome Grass is entitled, *Bromus panicula nutante, spiculis quadrifloris aristis brevioribus.* Vaillant calls it, *Gramen sylvaticum glabrum, panicula recurva*; Van Royen, *[illegible]*; Caspar Bauhine, *Gramen [illegible]*. It grows naturally in woods and hedges in England, and most parts of Europe.

2. Spiked Brome-Grass is, *Bromus [illegible]*. In the *Flora Lapp.* it is termed, *[illegible] spicato, spicis [illegible]*. Caspar Bauhine calls it, *Gramen [illegible]*. It grows naturally in woods, meadows, and pastures in England, and most parts of Europe.

3. Crested Brome-Grass is, *Bromus spiculis [illegible] spicis [illegible] compressis*. Gmelin calls it, *[illegible]*, and Buxbaum, *[illegible]*. It grows naturally in Siberia and Tartary.

4. Purging Brome-Grass is, *Bromus panicula nutante [illegible], foliis [illegible] pilosis, glumis [illegible]*. It is called in *Gramen bromoides catharticum*. It grows naturally in Canada.

*Bromus* is of the class and order *Triandria Digynia*; and the characters are,

Class and order in the Linnæan System. The characters.

1. CALYX is a glume composed of two oval, oblong, acuminated, patent, beardless valves, of which the interior one is the smallest, containing many flowers collected in a spike.

2. COROLLA is of two valves, the lower valve is the largest, of the size and shape of the calyx, concave, obtuse, bifid, and below the tip emits a straight arista or awn. The upper valve is small, spear-shaped, and has no arista.

3. STAMINA are three capillary filaments shorter than the corolla, having oblong antheræ.

4. PISTILLUM consists of a turbinated germen, and two short, hairy, reflexed styles with simple stigmas.

5. PERICARPIUM. The corolla closely surrounds the seeds, and opens in no part.

6. SEMEN. The seed is single, oblong, convex on one side, and sulcated on the other.

CHAP.

## CHAP LXXVIII

## *BUBON*, MACEDONIAN PARSLEY.

Species

OF this genus there are,

1 The Common Macedonian Parsley

2 The Rigid Bubon

The Macedonian Parsley.

1 The Macedonian Parsley has hardly a right to this place, for it flowers but once, and then dies, neither ought it to be ranked among the annuals or biennials, because in our gardens it is often several years before it is brought to flower, during which time many leaves are formed from the root, growing on moderately long footstalks, which divide into smaller, and support the lobes These are of an oval-rhomb figure, of a bright green, and their edges are indented. The flower stalk proceeds from the middle of the leaves, is branching, and will grow to about a foot and a half high The flowers grow in umbels at the extremity of the branches, their colour is white, they will be in blow in July, and perfect their seeds in the autumn

The seeds of this sort are much used in medicine, they are esteemed an excellent carminative, and join in the composition of Venice treacle

and Rigid Bubon described

2 Rigid Bubon This is a regular perennial, the root continuing for many years The flower-stalk rises to about a foot high The leaves are narrow, rigid, and short The flowers terminate the stalks in umbels, they are of a white colour, small, appear in June, and ripen their seeds in September

Method of propagating these species

Both these plants are easily raised by sowing of the seeds in a warm border of light earth in the spring When the plants come up too close, they must be thinned, and afterwards nothing more need be done than keeping them clean from weeds The second sort will blow the second year, and continue to flower annually, but the first sort will be three, four, and sometimes more years before it shoots up to flower, after that it always dies away

These plants must have a well-sheltered situation, as well as a light, sandy, dry soil, or they will be liable to be destroyed by bad weather

1 The first sort is titled, *Bubon foliolis rhombeo ovatis crenatis, umbellis numerosissimis* Caspar Bauhine calls it, *Apium Macedonicum*, and Lobel, *Petroselinum Macedonicum* It grows naturally in Macedonia Titles

2 The second sort is titled, *Bubon foliolis linearibus* Boccone calls it, *Ferula durior sive rigidis & brevissimis foliis* It grows naturally in Sicily

*Bubon* is of the class and order *Pentandria Digynia*, and the characters are, Class and order in the Linnæan system The characters

1 CALYX The general umbel is composed of about ten smaller, of which the shortest are placed in the middle

The partial umbel is composed of about fifteen or twenty rays

The general involucrum is composed of five spear shaped, pointed, equal, spreading, permanent leaves

The proper perianthium is small, permanent, and indented in five parts

2 COROLLA The general corolla is uniform, and each floret consists of five spear-shaped inflexed petals

3 STAMINA are five simple filaments the length of the florets, with simple antheræ

4 PISTILLUM consists of an oval germen situated below the flower, and of two reflexed styles, with obtuse stigmas

5 PERICARPIUM There is none The fruit is oval, striated, and separable into two parts

6 SEMINA The seeds are two, oval, striated, hairy, convex on one side, and on the other plain

## CHAP LXXIX

## *BUFONIA*

Bastard Chick weed described

THERE is only one species of this genus, commonly called Bastard Chick weed

The root is slender, flexible, white, and fibrous The stalk is slender, round, upright, jointed, branching, and six or eight inches high The leaves are long, narrow, grassy, pointed, of a pale green, and grow by pairs at the joints The flowers come out from the wings of the leaves, almost the whole length of the branches, they are small, and of a whitish colour, appear in May and June, and are succeeded by small black seeds, which ripen in July and August

Whoever is inclined to propagate this species, may easily effect it by sowing the seeds soon after they are ripe, they will grow in almost any soil or situation, and after they come up will require no trouble, except thinning them to proper distances, and keeping them clean from weeds

As there is no other species of this genus, its name is simply *Bufonia* Ray calls it, *Alsinoides*, Magnol, Titles

Magnol, *Hermaria, angustissimo gramineo folio, erecta*, and Plukenet, *Alsine polygonoides tenui folia, flosculis ad longitudinem caulis ve ... spicam dispositis* It grows naturally in England, France, and Spain

Class and order in the Linnæan system. The characters

*Pistonia* is of the class and order *Tetrandria Digynia*, and the characters are,

1 CALYX is an erect permanent perianthium, composed of four awl shaped leaves, having carinated membranaceous edges

2 COROLLA is four oval, emarginated, erect, equal leaves, that are shorter than the calyx

3 STAMINA are four equal filaments the length of the germen, having didymous antheræ

4 PISTILLUM consists of an oval compressed germen, and two styles the length of the stamina, with simple stigmas

5 PERICARPIUM is an oval compressed capsule, formed of two valves, and containing one cell

6 SEMINA The seeds are two, oval, compressed, and convex on one side

# CHAP. XC

## *BULBOCODIUM*, MOUNTAIN SAFFRON

Spanish Meadow Saffron described

THERE is only one species of this genus called the Spanish Meadow Saffron The root is a small bulb covered with a brown skin The leaves are spear shaped and concave In the midst of these stands the flower, on a very short footstalk It has the appearance of a Crocus, and its colour is a purple It will be in blow in March or April, and the seeds will be ripe in a few weeks after

Culture

By these seeds plenty of plants may be easily raised, for they do not encrease very fast by offsets For this purpose, let a border be prepared in a well sheltered shady place If the ground is naturally moist, the bed must be raised at least a foot above the level, it should consist of fresh, light, undunged earth, the seeds should be scattered over it, and then some mould sifted over them three quarters of an inch deep The time for this work is the autumn In the spring the plants will come up, at which time they should be constantly cleared of weeds, and watered in dry weather When the leaves begin to decay, watering must be left off; and that is all the trouble they will require the first summer

In the autumn, let the surface of the earth be stirred, and some fresh mould sifted over them about half an inch deep When the plants appear in the spring, water them in dry weather, and when the leaves are decayed take them up, and set them where they are designed to flower Some of them will probably shew themselves the spring following, but the far greater part will not flower before the spring after that

They are also propagated by offsets In order to have plenty of these, the roots should not be disturbed till three or four years The time for taking them up is when the leaves are decayed, and they may be divided and planted again immediately, or kept in a dry airy place until October, when they should be set again in a well-sheltered shady place

Titles,

This species is titled, *Bulbocodium foliis lanceolatis* Clusius calls it, *Colchicum vernum*, and Caspar Bauhine, *Colchicum vernum Hispanicum* It grows naturally in Spain

Class and order in the Linnæan system The characters

*Bulbocodium* is of the class and order *Hexandria Monogynia*, and the characters are,

1 CALYX There is none

2 COROLLA is funnel shaped, and composed of six erect, lanceolate, concave petals, having very long narrow ungues

3 STAMINA are six subulated filaments inserted into the neck of the petals, with incumbent antheræ

4 PISTILLUM consists of an oval, obtuse, three cornered germen, a filiforme style longer than the stamina, with three oblong, erect, channelled stigmas

5 PERICARPIUM is a triangular acuminated capsule of three cells

6 SEMINA The seeds are numerous and angular

# C H A P. XCI.

## *B U N I A S.*

THERE is no Engliſh name for this genus, but the Perennial ſpecies that belongs to it is uſually called, the Oriental *Bunias*

*Deſcription of the Oriental Bunias*

The radical leaves are of an oblong figure, numerous, ſpreading, and their edges are deeply cut or indented, not much unlike thoſe of Dandelion The ſtalks ariſe from among them to the height of two feet, or more, they are very branching, and at the joints are garniſhed with oblong ſharp pointed leaves, that are eared at the baſe, and ſit cloſe, without any footſtalks The flowers are produced in looſe ſpikes from the ends of the branches, are yellow, and reſemble thoſe of the Common Cabbage, they will be in blow in June, and in September are ſucceeded by ripe ſeeds, contained ſingly in oval, gibbous, warted pods

*Culture*

This is a very hardy Perennial, and its propagation is very eaſy Sow the ſeeds in the ſpring where they are to remain, and when the plants come up too cloſe, thin them to proper diſtances, and keep them clear from weeds, the ſummer following they will flower, and in the autumn will perfect their ſeeds

This ſpecies is titled, *Bunias ſiliculis ovatis gibbis verrucoſis*. In the *Hortus Upſal* it is termed, *Bunias foliis retrorſum ſinuatis* Van Royen calls it, *Crambe foliis pinnato-haſtatis*, and Tournefort, *Crambe orientalis, dentis leonis folio, erucaginis facie* It grows naturally in the Eaſt, and in Ruſſia *Title*

*Bunias* is of the claſs and order *Tetradynamia Siliquoſa*, and the characters are, *Claſs and order in the Linnæan ſyſtem*

1 CALYX is a perianthium compoſed of four oval, oblong, patent, deciduous leaves

2 COROLLA conſiſts of four petals placed in form of a croſs, they are oval, double the length of the calyx, erect, and joined at their baſe *The characters*

3 STAMINA conſiſt of ſix filaments the length of the calyx, (of which the two oppoſite are rather ſhorter than the others) with erect antheræ that are bifid at their baſe

4 PISTILLUM conſiſts of an oblong germen, without any ſtyle but an obtuſe ſtigma

5 PERICARPIUM is an irregular, ſhort, oval, oblong pod, having four angles, one or other of which is pointed

6 SEMINA The ſeeds are one or two, and of a roundiſh figure

# C H A P XCII.

## *BUNIUM,* PIG-NUT, or, EARTH-NUT

THERE is only one ſpecies of this genus, called Pig-Nut, or Earth-Nut, Earth-Cheſnut, Kipper-Nut, or Hawk Nut, by all which names it reſpectively goes in different places

*Deſcription of the Pig Nut or Earth Nut*

The root is large, roundiſh, ſolid, eſculent, browniſh without, white within, and ſends forth fibres from the bottom and ſides The ſtalks are upright, green, channelled, compreſſed, branching near the top, and a foot and a half high The leaves are beautifully divided into a multitude of narrow ſegments, and the radical ones ſpread on the ground, thoſe on the ſtalks are ſmaller, and grow ſingly at the joints The flowers come out in umbels from the ends of the main ſtalk and ſide-branches, they are of a white colour, appear in May and June, and the ſeeds ripen in July

The root of this ſpecies is ſaid to afford great nouriſhment to the human body, eſpecially if boiled or roaſted If eaten raw, their taſte is not much unlike that of the Cheſnut, which has occaſioned its having, in ſome parts, the name of Earth Cheſnut In ſome places they are roaſted in a manner ſimilar to Cheſnuts, in others boiled and buttered, in either caſe they may be made into an agreeable diſh, and being in ſome degree pectoral, diuretic, and extremely wholeſome and nouriſhing, it is ſomewhat ſurprizing that they are not more ſought after and known than they ſeem to be

This ſpecies is eaſily propagated by planting the roots about the end of July, when the ſtalks decay, or the ſeeds may be ſown at that time They ſhould have a light dry, undunged earth, and if it has been newly broke up, the roots will be larger, and better taſted *Method of propagating*

There being no other ſpecies of this genus, it ſtands with the name ſimply *Bunium* Sauvages calls it, *Bunium bulbo globoſo*, Caſpar Bauhine, *Bulbocaſtanum majus, folio apii*, Lobel, *Nucula terreſtris*, Gerard *Bulbocaſtanum majus et minus*, and Parkinſon, *Nucula terreſtris major* It grows naturally in meadow and paſture grounds in England, France, and Germany

*Bunium* is of the claſs and order *Pentandria Digynia*, and the character are, *Claſs and order in the Linnæan ſyſtem*

1 CALYX The general umbel is multiple, and compoſed of near twenty rays The partial is ſhort and cloſe ſet *The characters*

The

The general involucrum is composed of several short narrow leaves The partial is setaceous, and the length of the umbellulæ. The proper perianthium is extremely small

2 COROLLA The general flower is uniform, the florets are all fertile, and each has five inflexed, heart-shaped, equal petals

3 STAMINA are five simple filaments shorter than the corolla, having simple antheræ

4 PISTILLUM consists of an oblong germen situated below the receptacle, and two reflexed styles with obtuse stigmas

5 PERICARPIUM There is none The fruit is oval, and divided into two parts

6 SEMINA The seeds are two, oval, convex on one side, and plane on the other.

## CHAP XCIII

## *BUPHTHALMUM*, OX-EYE.

FOUR principal species of *Buphthalmum* present themselves for this place They are,

Species

1 Maritime Ox-eye
2 Hairy Willow-leaved Ox-eye
3 Smooth Willow-leaved Ox eye
4 American Ox eye

Description of the Maritime,

1 The Maritime Ox eye is a plant about a foot high The stalk is very branching and woody The leaves are narrow, hairy, and wedge shaped The flowers are produced from the ends of the branches, they are radiated, and of a yellow colour, will be in blow early in summer, and continue flowering until the end of autumn, and sometimes the greatest part of the winter if the plants are housed but they are rarely succeeded by good seeds in our gardens

Hairy Willow leaved,

2 Hairy Willow leaved Ox eye The stalks are hairy, slender, branching, and will grow to about two feet high The leaves are spear shaped, hairy, and their edges are slightly serrated The flowers are produced from the ends of the branches, in June and July, they are of a bright yellow colour, radiated, and will be succeeded by ripe seeds in the autumn

Smooth Willow leaved

3 Smooth Willow-leaved Ox eye This hath several slender branching stalks, about two feet high The leaves are spear-shaped, narrow, smooth, and their edges slightly indented The flowers are radiated, and their colour is a bright yellow, they are produced from the ends of the branches in June and July, and are succeeded by ripe seeds in the autumn

and American Ox eye

4 American Ox eye The stalks of this plant will grow to a yard or more in height The leaves are placed opposite by pairs at the joints, are heart shaped, serrated, have three longitudinal veins, and one side of the base is shorter than the other The flowers are radiated, large, and of a bright yellow colour They appear at the extremities of the branches in July and August, and ripen their seeds in the autumn

Method of propagating them

The propagation of all these sorts is very easy, though the first sort requires tender management to continue it through our winters, it being pretty certain of being destroyed if bad weather happens, the plants, therefore, must be set abroad in a dry, warm, well sheltered place, and on the first approach of frost must be covered with hand glasses in nights while it lasts, and if the frost should be severe, straw or litter must be laid about the glasses, and also over them, to prevent the frost from penetrating the ground These glasses must be constantly taken off as the weather gets fine, and with this management the plants may be continued abroad for many years for they want only to be protected from hard frosts, and such plants will be healthier, and flower better than those that have been housed in the winter This sort is raised by planting of the cuttings, for it rarely produces good seeds in England The cuttings must be planted in pots in the summer, which must be immediately removed into the green-house, where, the windows being open, and being placed where no sun can come at them, they will readily strike root, and when you perceive this, they must be set abroad, or otherwise they will draw up weak and tender In the winter it would be advisable to place them near the green-house, or a hot bed frame, to be removed into them in bad weather, and when spring approaches, turn them out of the pots, with the mould at the roots, into the places where they are to remain and in the course of all subsequent winters manage them as above directed

The others are all exceeding hardy plants, and propagate themselves very fast by their roots so that with regard to them nothing more is to be done than to take off a few offsets, or divide the roots in the autumn or spring, and plant them where they are designed to remain About every third year the roots must be taken up and divided, to keep them within bounds at which time plant the best off-sets, and throw the others away

They are also very readily propagated by sowing of the seeds in the autumn, soon after they are ripe, or in the spring, but they multiply so fast by the roots, as to cause this method to be not worth putting into practice

Titles.

1 The Sea Ox eye is titled, *Buphthalmum calycibus obtuse foliosis pedunculatis, foliis alternis spatulatis, caule herbaceo* Boccone calls it, *Aster supinus lignosus siculus, conyzæ odore*, Barrelier, *Aster supinus luteus Massiliensis*, Clusius, *Aster 2, supinus*, Caspar Bauhine, *Aster luteus supinus*, and Tournefort, *Asteriscus maritimus perennis patulus* It grows naturally on the Mediterranean shores

2 Hairy Willow leaved Ox eye This is titled, *Buphthalmum foliis alternis lanceolatis subserratis villosis, calycibus nudis, caule herbaceo* Caspar Bauhine calls it, *Aster luteus major foliis succisæ*, Clusius, *Aster* [illegible], and Micheli, *Asteroides* [illegible] It grows naturally in the Alpine parts of Austria Helvetia &c

3 Smooth Willow leaved Ox eye This is titled, [illegible] *sub-* [illegible]

*dentatis glabris, calycibus nudis, caule herbaceo* Tournefort calls it, *Aster oides Alpina salicis folio*, Caspar Bauhin, *Aster luteus angustifolius*, and Morison, *Chrysanthemum perenne nudis, salicis glabro folio, ramosum* It grows naturally on the Alps of Italy and Austria

4 American Ox-eye is titled, *Buphthalmum calycibus foliosis, foliis oppositis ovatis serratis trinerviis, caule nervoso* Gronovius calls it *Helianthus foliis ... ferratis, pedunculis longissimis*, Martin, *Corona solis Caroliniana, parvis floribus, foliis trinerviis amplo aspero, pedunculo alto*, Plukenet, *Chrysanthemum, scrophulariæ folio, Americanum*, and Morison, *Chrysanthemum Virginianum, foliis globis scabris ... Virginianis*. It grows naturally in North America

Class and order in the Linnæan system. The characters

*Buphthalmum* is of the class and order *Syngenesia Polygamia Superflua*, and the characters are,

1 CALYX The general calyx is imbricated and various in the different species

2 COROLLA is radiated and compound The hermaphrodite florets which compose the disk are numerous, funnel-shaped, and cut at the top into five spreading segments

The female flowers in the radius are long, tongue-shaped, patent, and are indented at the top in three parts

3 STAMINA of the hermaphrodite florets are five very short capillary filaments, terminated by a tubulous cylindrical anthera

4 PISTILLUM, in the hermaphrodites, consists of an oval compressed germen, a filiforme style the length of the stamina, and a thick simple stigma

In the females it consists of a double-headed germen, a filiforme style, and two oblong stigmas

5 PERICARPIUM There is none

6 SEMINA The seeds of the hermaphrodite florets are single, oblong, and their border is cut into many parts

The seeds of the female flowers are single, compressed, and emarginated

The receptacle is paleaceous and convex

# CHAP XCIV

## *BUTOMUS*, The FLOWERING-RUSH, or, WATER GLADIOLE

OF this genus there is only one known species, and that affords us two varieties

The White flowering Rush

The Red-flowering Rush

Description of the White, and Red Flowering Rush

Both these are very beautiful flowers, and although they are found common, particularly the Red sort, growing in watery places in many parts, they are well worth cultivating in gardens, in such parts as are fitted to their nature, for they will not only help to occupy such places properly, and contribute greatly to the setting them off, but are proper flowers to be gathered to adorn rooms in flower-pots, &c

The root of this species is thick, oblong, and sends out many fibres, that are short in proportion to the strength of the leaves and flower-stalks it produces The leaves are long and flaggy, and the flower stalk will arrive to the height of four, five, or six feet This is strong, thick and smooth, and the flowers ornament the top they form an umbel, and will be in blow in June, July, and August They will be succeeded by good seeds

The White flowering sort is the least common, though the Red is most beautiful

Method of propagating these species

In order to propagate these sorts, procure some roots in August or September, after they have done flowering, from such watery places where they naturally grow, then in some boggy part of the garden, or at the edge of some pond, or by the side of a river, or the like, plant them carefully, observing not to set them too deep, next shade them, and if the autumn should prove dry, so as in a great measure to drain off the moisture, give them constant watering With this care they will take root, grow well, and flower, and afterwards will call for no farther trouble, for if the plants are neglected, they seem to flower fairest among the weeds which such places naturally produce

They may be also propagated by seeds, which should be sown in watery places in the autumn soon after they are ripe, and then left to nature These will often come up, but it is not a certain method, for unless the place be pretty well suited to the nature of the plant, your hopes this way will be disappointed

The best way therefore is to propagate them by the root, and then the different sorts of the Red and White may be preserved, for they will vary by seeds

The seeds ought nevertheless to be attempted, for if there is plenty of boggy ground, and they should happen to take, the seedling plants will be the best

Titles

This genus is entitled *Butomus*, and is so called, it is said, because the oxen are fond of this plant, notwithstanding they have their mouths wounded by the sharp edges of the leaves, it being formed of the two Greek words, βους, an Ox, and τεμνω, to cut C Bauhine calls it, *Juncus floridus major*, John Bauhine, *Juncus floridus*, Morison, *Sedo affinis, umbellata palustris*, and Dodonæus, *Gladiolus aquatilis* It grows common in the Langton brooks, and adorns the sides of the river Welland a great way It is also found in watery places in most parts of Europe

Class and order in the Linnæan system The characters

*Butomus* is of the class and order *Enneandria Hexagynia*, and the characters are,

1 CALYX The flowers grow in a single umbel, and have an involucrum composed of three leaves

2 COROLLA consists of six roundish concave petals

3 STAMINA

3 STAMINA are nine subulated filaments, with double lamellated antheræ

4 PISTILLUM consists of six oblong pointed germina, with single stigmata

5 PERICARPIUM consists of six oblong, erect, pointed capsules, formed each of a single valve, and opening inwards

6 SEMINA The seeds are numerous, oblong, cylindrical, and obtuse

# CHAP XCIV

## CACALIA, FOREIGN COLTSFOOT

Species

THIS genus affords us,

1 Alpine Coltsfoot

2 Virginian Coltsfoot

3 Canadian Sweet scented Coltsfoot

4 Perennial Groundsel

Description of the Alpine

1 Alpine Coltsfoot The varieties of this species are,

Varieties

The Hoary Alpine Coltsfoot

The Green leaved Alpine Coltsfoot

The Thick Hairy-leaved Alpine Coltsfoot

The Narrow-leaved Alpine Coltsfoot

All these varieties have thickish spreading roots, from which arise the leaves standing on single foot-stalks; they are generally reniform, or heart-shaped, and are of the different properties the varieties express Among them arise the stalks, which are about a foot and a half, or two feet high, according to the sorts The flowers are produced in small umbels They are of a purple colour in its different tints They come out the beginning of June, and are succeeded by oblong, downy seeds

Virginian

2 Virginian Coltsfoot This hath a thick, fleshy root, or many tubers, which spreads their under the ground all around The stalks are strong, and grow to be four or five feet high The leaves are roundish, heart shaped, smooth, sinuated, indented, and placed alternately on the stalks The flowers grow in umbels at the ends of the stalks They are of a greenish yellow colour, come out in July and August, and are succeeded by ripe seeds in October soon after which the stalks die to the ground, and fresh ones arise from the roots in the spring

Canadian Coltsfoot

3 Canadian Sweet scented Coltsfoot This hath a creeping root, which spreads all around The stalks rise in the spring, and will grow to be seven feet high The leaves are roundish, sagittate, and sharply sawed on their edges, their upper surface is a strong bright green, but they are paler underneath, and grow alternately on the stalks The flowers terminate the stalks in umbels, their colour is white, they come out in August, and are succeeded by oblong ripe, downy seeds in October, soon after which the stalks decay

Perennial Groundsel

4 Perennial Groundsel The root is creeping, and extends itself to a considerable distance The stalks are angular, herbaceous, and are to be six or seven feet high The leaves are spear-shaped, ... broad, serrated, and decurrent The flowers are of a whitish yellow, or sulphur colour, they come out in July and August, and the seeds ripen in October, soon after which the stalks decay, and new ones arise from the roots in the spring

Culture

There is no ... in the culture of all these sorts Divide the roots when you will, or how you will, and every bit of them will grow, though the best time for the work is the autumn

These plants will also propagate themselves by seeds ... ripen in the autumn, and, being crowned with down, are often wafted by the winds to a considerable distance, where they will come up, and soon become good plants, and may be either suffered to remain, or be removed in the autumn to such places where they are wanted to flower They grow in all soils and situations, though they delight most in shade, and in a moist, fat earth

Titles

1 Alpine Coltsfoot is titled, *Cacalia foliis reniformibus ... denticulatis ... calycibus ... floribus* Van Royen calls it, *Tussilago caule ramoso* Caspar Bauhine terms one sort of it, *Cacalia foliis crassis hirsutis*, another, *Cacalia foliis cutaneis acutioribus & glabris* In like manner Clusius names one sort, *Cacalia incano folio*, and another, *Cacalia glabro folio* Lobel calls it simply, *Cacalia* It grows naturally on the Helvetian and Austrian Mountains

2 Virginian Coltsfoot is titled, *Cacalia caule herbaceo, foliis subcordatis dentato-sinuatis, calycibus ...* Morison calls it, *Cacalia Virginiana glabra, foliis deltoidibus ... sinuatis ...*, Gronovius, *Porophyllum foliis ...*, and Plukenet, *Nardus Americana ...* It grows naturally in Virginia and Canada

3 Canadian Sweet-scented Coltsfoot This is titled, *Cacalia caule herbaceo, foliis hastato-sagittatis denticulatis ... petiolis superne dilatatis* It grows naturally in Virginia and Canada

4 Perennial Groundsel is titled, *Cacalia caule herbaceo, foliis lanceolatis serratis decurrentibus* Morison calls it, *Solidago foliis lanceolatis serratis decurrentibus, caule angulato*, Vaillant, *Senecio perennis ...*, Morison, *Virga aurea ...* radice repente ..., and John Bauhine, *Virga aurea ... latifolia* ... It grows naturally in the southern ...

Class and order in the Linnæan system

*Cacalia* is of the class and order *Syngenesia Polygamia Æqualis*, and the characters are,

The characters

1 CALYX The common calyx is simple, oblong, cylindrical

2 COROLLA is tubulous and compound ... florets are funnel shaped, and divided at the top into five erect segments

3 STAMINA consist of five very short capillary filaments, having a tubular, cylindrical antheræ

4 PISTILLUM consists of an oblong germen, a filiform style the length of the stamina, and two oblong, revolute stigmas

5 PERICARPIUM There is none

6 SEMINA The seeds are single, oblong, and crowned with long hairy down

... ... plant, and ...

CHAP

# CHAP. XCVI.

## CACHRYS

THERE is no English name for this genus, the species, which are two in number, are usually called,

Species

1 The French *Cachrys*

2 The Spanish *Cachrys*

French,

1 French *Cachrys* has a large, thick, fleshy root, which strikes deep into the ground The stalk is round, hollow, striated, jointed, and grows to about a yard high The leaves are bi pinnate, being beautifully composed of a multitude of narrow, acute segments The radical leaves are exceeding large, and make a fine show Those on the stalks are composed of the like parts, but are smaller The flowers terminate the stalks in very large umbels in June, their colour is yellow, and they are succeeded by small, smooth, furrowed seeds, which will be ripe in September

and Spanish Cachrys described

2 Spanish *Cachrys* The root is thick, strikes deep into the ground, and is possessed of a agreeable odour The leaves are bipinnate, and composed of many acute, narrow segments, arranged in a beautiful manner Among these arises the stalk to four or five feet high It is smooth, jointed, and the top of it is crowned by the flowers in large umbels Their colour is yellow, they come out in June, and are succeeded by oblong fungous, rough, channelled seeds, which will be ripe in September

Culture

These plants are easily propagated by sowing of the seeds, soon after they are ripe, in the places where they are to remain If you chuse to have them luxuriant and large, the earth should be rich, deep for the roots to strike into, and the situation should be shady, and in such a situation they should be thinned after they come up, to within a yard distance from each other every way, for you cannot expect to see these plants in their full beauty if they are close

If the seeds are sown in the autumn they will come up in the spring, and after that nothing more is to be done, than to thin them to their proper distances, keep the ground clean from weeds, and water them in dry weather for the first summer The plants being left in rows a yard asunder, the ground between the rows should be dug in the winter, and the summer following the plants will flower, and perfect their seeds The stalks always die down to the ground in the autumn, and fresh ones arise from the roots in the spring, and their after management is no more than to clear the stalks off when they begin to decay, dig the ground between the rows in the winter, and keep it constantly free from weeds in the summer

Titles

1 The French *Cachrys* is titled, *Cachrys foliis bipinnatis, foliolis acutis ... fiats, seminibus sulcatis laevibus* Morison calls it, *Cachrys semine fungoso sulcato ... minore, foliis peucedani angustis*, and John Bauhine, *Libanotis ferulae folio, semine angulosa* It grows naturally near Montpelier, and also in Sicily

2 Spanish *Cachrys* This is titled, *Cachrys foliis bipinnatis, foliolis linearibus acutis, seminibus sulcatis hispidis* Morison calls it, *Cachrys semine fungoso sulcato ... peucedani latifoliis* Caspar Bauhine, *Hippomarathrum Creticum*, and Boccone, *Hippomarathrum Siculum* It grows naturally in Spain and Sicily

Class and order in the Linnaean system

*Cachrys* is of the class and order *Pentandria Digynia*, and the characters are,

The characters

1 CALYX The general umbel is multiple, the partial is similar

The general involucrum is composed of many narrow, spear shaped leaves The partial consists of the like narrow segments

The proper perianthium is hardly discernible

2 COROLLA The general flower is uniform The florets consist each of five spear shaped, plain ish, equal petals, that are nearly erect

3 STAMINA consist of five simple filaments the length of the corolla, having simple antheræ

4 PISTILLUM consists of a turbinated germen situated below the flower, and of two simple styles, the length of the corolla, with capitated stigmas

5 PERICARPIUM is a roundish, oval angular, obtuse, large fruit, separable in to two parts

6 SEMINA The seeds are two, large, fungous, convex on one side, and plane on the other

# CHAP. XCVII

## *CALTHA*, DOUBLE MARSH MARYGOLD

Introductory Remarks

THE *Caltha*, which is so very ornamental to those parts of our meadows which lie near the sides of brooks and rivers, and is found generally to abound in such places almost without exception, affords us a double variety worthy of culture in our best gardens. In its single state it is a fine flower. The petals are large, the yellow is clear and good, and, were it not for its commonness, it would be much sought after. But in its double state the improvement is great, and the petals are so multiplied, as to form a large, fair, full flower, which will continue in blow for two months, or more. The first flower generally appears the beginning of May, and in cool seasons the whole month of June has been graced with its bloom. In its single state in our meadows, the flowers appear earlier, even in April, and they are what have been usually gathered for strewing before the doors on the eve of May-day, to usher in that welcome month. Amongst the common people, they usually go by the name of Marchblobs, and this double sort, by the less knowing ones, is distinguished by no other name than the Double Marchblob. The plant being now sufficiently pointed out, is known to all; a further description, therefore, is unnecessary, so that I shall proceed to its culture.

Culture

And for this, reason directs us to allow it as moist a place as possible in our gardens. This will be very proper, and if it be planted in the shade, it will be much better. But such a situation is not absolutely necessary, for I have known it flourish, and flower fair and well, in a dry, parching situation, near the top of a high hill, so that a person should not be discouraged from planting this beautiful perennial in any part where he has room for it, but ought nevertheless to remember, that it is a double variety only of that well-known lover of moist places, the Marsh Marygold, and should treat it accordingly.

Title.

As there is only one species of this genus, a descriptive title would be absurd. It is called, therefore, *Caltha*, and to this the flower, whether in its single or double state, belongs. John Bauhine calls it, *Caltha palustris*, Caspar Bauhine also terms it the same, and distinguishes the two sorts by adding, for the single one, *flore simplici*, and for the double, *flore pleno*. This genus is by some former Botanists termed *Populago*, who also reckon two sorts of it, a *Major* and a *Minor*. In Parkinson's Herbal it is called, *Caltha palustris vulgaris simplex*, and in Gerard's, *Caltha palustris major*. It grows naturally in moist, watery places, and by the sides of rivers almost every where.

Class and order in the Linnæan system

*Caltha* is of the class and order *Polyandria Polygynia*, and the characters are,

The characters

1. CALYX. There is none.
2. COROLLA consists of five large, oval, plain, patent, concave petals.
3. STAMINA are numerous filiforme filaments shorter than the corolla, with compressed, obtuse, erect antheræ.
4. PISTILLUM consists of several oblong, compressed, erect germina, having no styles, but simple stigmas.
5. PERICARPIUM consists of the like number of short acuminated, patent, bicarinated capsules, which open at the upper suture.
6. SEMINA. The seeds are numerous, of a roundish figure, and adhere to the upper suture.

# CHAP. XCVIII

## *CAMPANULA*, BELL FLOWER

THE *Campanula* is a very extensive genus, and affords us several hardy perennials, annuals, and some green-house plants, besides rampions for kitchen use, &c. Of the first sort there are,

Species

1. Pyramidical *Campanula*, or, Bell Flower
2. Lesser Round-leaved Bell Flower
3. Peach-leaved Bell Flower
4. Giant Throatwort
5. Great Throatwort, or, Canterbury Bells
6. Lesser Throatwort, or, Canterbury Bells
7. Hispid *Campanula*, or, Bell Flower.
8. Oriental Bell Flower.
9. Creeping Bell Flower
10. Dwarf Pyramidical Bell Flower
11. Small Alpine Bell Flower
12. Ivy-leaved Bell Flower

Description of the Pyramidical.

1. The Pyramidical *Campanula*, or, Bell Flower, is frequently called Steeple Bell Flower, and is by far the noblest plant of all the species before enumerated. It is cultivated not only for the ornament of gardens, but to adorn rooms, &c. and being placed in chimneys, and their stalks properly spread, they shew themselves to very great advantage, and have a fine effect. The roots of this sort are large, tuberous, and

and ma[illegible] The stalks are thick, firm, smooth, upright, and will grow to be four or five feet high The leaves are oval, smooth, a little serrated [illegible] the lower ones are much larger than those higher on the stalks The flowers are large [illegible] the stalks for above half their length Short branches also are frequently put forth from the sides of the stalks, full of flowers, so that they form on the whole, a kind of pyramid Each of them is large, and shaped like a bell, and on the whole, they cause a striking effect The most common colour is blue, though there is a variety of it with white flowers, both of which will be in blow a good part of the summer, and perfect their seeds in the autumn There is also a variety with double flowers, which at present is not very common

Round leaved 2 Round-leaved Bell Flower This hath a small, fibrous root, from which arise several roundish leaves, like those of the violet, which spread on the ground From the midst of these spring the stalks, they are slender, branching, and garnished with a few narrow leaves The flowers terminate the branches that are produced from the tops of the stalks, they are bell shaped, of a blue colour, though there is a variety with white flowers They will be in blow in June and July, and ripen their seeds in August

Peach-leaved Bell Flower, 3 Peach-leaved Bell Flower The stalk of this plant is angular, channelled, and will grow to about two feet high The leaves are long, narrow, a little indented, of a shining green, and not unlike those of the peach tree The flowers are produced from the upper parts of the stalks on short footstalks, the time of their blow is June and July Of this species the varieties are,

Varieties The Single Blue
The Single White
The Double Blue
The Double White

The double sorts have been accidentally obtained from seeds, and since they have been introduced into our gardens, the single kinds have been very little regarded

Giant Throatwort 4 Giant Throatwort This hath a thick, fleshy root, possessed of a milky juice, which sends forth several single, taper, strong, upright stalks, to the height of six or seven feet The leaves are broad, oval, spear shaped, serrated, and grow alternately The flowers are produced singly from the wings of the upper leaves on short footstalks They will be in blow in June and July, and ripen their seeds in September Of this sort there are,

Varieties The Blue
The Purple
The White
The Double Blue, or Purple
The Double White

Great Throatwort 5 Great Throatwort The stalks of this species are robust, upright, hairy, angular, and send out a few short side branches The leaves are oval, oblong, stiff, hairy, and indented The flowers grow on trifid footstalks from the wings of the leaves They will be in blow in June and July, and ripen their seeds in the autumn Of this species the varieties are,

Varieties The White
The Blue
The Purple
The Double White
The Double Blue and Purple
The Double Purple

Lesser Throatwort; 6 Lesser Throatwort The stalks are angular, hairy, and grow to about a foot, or a foot and a half high The leaves are oval, oblong, obtuse, and are placed alternately on the stalks without any footstalk The flowers are bell shaped, and terminate the stalks in round bunches They grow also by threes from the wings of the leaves Their colour is a bright purple, they will be in blow in July, and ripen their seeds in the autumn

Hispid, 7 Hispid Bell Flower The stalks of this plant are hispid, and unbranching The leaves are pear-shaped, and narrow The flowers terminate the stalks in oblong bunches, and appear about the same time with the former

Oriental, 8 Oriental Bell Flower The stalks are very diffuse The lower leaves are nearly oval, smooth, and entire The flowers are produced from the wings of the leaves and ends of the branches in July, but do not always perfect their seeds in England

Creeping, 9 Creeping Bell Flower The root of this plant creeps along the ground, and, if permitted, will soon spread itself to a considerable distance The stalks are but a few inches long, slender, and unbranching The leaves are oval, smooth, obtuse, [illegible] a little crenated on their edges Each stalk is terminated by one considerable large flower growing in a very rough cup

Dwarf Pyramidical 10 Dwarf Pyramidical Bell Flower This grows only to about a foot and a half high The leaves are [illegible] shaped, smooth, sharp pointed, and serrated The flowers grow in bunches from the upper parts of the stalks, they are drooping, the pistil of each is longer than the corolla, and the calyx has leaves that are [illegible], and very sharp pointed

Small Alpine 11 Small Alpine Bell Flower The stalks are single or unbranching, and seldom grow higher than a foot The leaves are narrow, oblong, obtuse, entire, hairy, and whitish on their upper side The flowers grow singly from the wings of the leaves on long footstalks, and the time of their appearance is about June or July

Ivy-leaved Bell Flower 12 Ivy-leaved Bell Flower The stalks of this species are loose and slender The leaves are heart shaped, smooth, five lobed, grow on footstalks, and most resemble those of ivy The flowers are small and of a blue colour They grow from the tops of the branches in June and July, and ripen their seeds in September

Culture The culture of all these sorts is exceeding easy It is to be effected by parting the roots in September, or sowing of the seeds in the spring The double sorts are to be encreased no other way than by parting of the roots, and the single sorts rise so freely from seeds, that many of them, particularly the Throatworts, will sow themselves after they have once flowered, and come up like weeds all over the adjacent parts The strongest offsets from all the double kinds, particularly the Double Peach leaved Bell Flowers, should be every other year taken off, and planted afresh, and if this work be done in September, they will immediately take root, and flower [illegible] the summer following [illegible], the old roots will [illegible] dwindle away, and flower weaker and weaker every year

The first sort, called the Pyramidical *Campanula* or Steeple Bell Flower [illegible] it is chiefly raised in pots to adorn halls and large rooms in the summer, will require close attendance to bring the plants to perfection for such uses, and, indeed, unless their culture is constantly attended to, you will soon be out of the sorts, for the roots are but of short duration So that whoever is desirous of having a never-failing supply of these plants in the summer must never fail to use the proper means for their multiplication and encrease, that fresh plants may always be at hand, with which to pleasure his friends, or or to succeed those that are in a state of decay, or whose chief beauty is past.

In order, therefore, to have these plants in perfection, they must be raised from seeds; for although they grow readily by dividing of the roots in the autumn, yet plants raised that way are vastly inferior in beauty, or majestic appearance, to those raised from seeds. So that if a person is desirous of excelling in the *Campanula*, he must submit to the more tedious method of raising them this way.

In order to obtain good seeds for the purpose, let a few plants be set out in the warmest border of the garden, and when they come into flower, cover them when heavy rains happen with handglasses. Take these constantly off on the return of fair weather; but all along let them have the kindly benefits of a few sprinkling showers as they shall happen. If this protection is carefully observed, your seeds will ripen freely in the autumn; but for want of it, the plants rarely produce seeds, there being nothing so destructive to the parts of generation in these flowers, as too much wet, which often happens when the plants are in full blow. The plants also that are set out for seed, should be seedling plants, or such as are raised from seedling plants; for by continually dividing of the roots from year to year, they will be every year less and less fertile, and will in time become entirely barren. So that when some seedling plants, or those that are nearly allied to such, cannot be obtained for you to raise your own seeds, the best way will be to procure the seeds from France or Italy, where they ripen them with greater certainty.

Having provided yourself with a sufficient quantity of seeds, let them be sown as soon as possible after you have them, whether it be in the autumn, winter, or spring. The autumn is the best time for the purpose, soon after the seeds are ripe; and if it is deferred until the spring, the plants often will not come up before the spring following. They should be sown in pots or boxes, or in a well prepared bed of light, fresh earth, in a well-sheltered place, and should be covered over with about half an inch of the finest, fresh, light mould. If the business is performed in the autumn, the beds must be hooped, to be covered with mats in frosty weather, and also in very heavy rains, which would work out the seeds; but this matting ought not to be put on, unless very hard frosts require it. Against small frosts, the beds may be guarded by pricking round them some furze-bushes; and when the weather sets in harder, then the mats must be applied; but all must be taken away on the return of mild weather. If the seeds are sown in pots or boxes, it may be sufficient to remove them into the green-house, or to place them under an hot bed frame, during the continuance of such inclemencies, remembering always to set them abroad again in a warm, well-sheltered part of the garden as soon as the weather will permit. In the spring the plants will come up, when nothing more is to be done than to keep them clean from weeds, and to water them now and then, if the weather should prove very dry; and as they daily get longer, they should be shaded from the violent heat of the sun in the middle of the day, permitting it only to shine on them until about ten o'clock in the morning. With this care, your plants will be grown to be tolerably strong by September, at which time their leaves will begin to decay.

This is the season for their removal into the nursery-bed, which should be in the warmest and best-defended part of the garden. The mould should be naturally dry and sandy, and for want of this, the beds must be raised five or six inches above the alleys. Drift sand should be added to the natural mould, to make it light. Having thus prepared your beds, the plants must be taken up with care, and in these they should be planted about four inches asunder, so deep that the crowns or tops of the plants may be about half an inch under the surface of the bed. This being done, the beds must be hooped, though they need not be covered with mats, unless very hard frosts set in; it will be sufficient to protect them from slight frosts by pricking round the beds some furze-bushes. In very hard frosts, however, they must always be covered with mats: they must also be screened in very rainy weather, for much wet is very liable to rot the roots.

With this care they must go through the winter, and in the spring they should have all the benefit of the sun, dew, and air. Weeding as often as is necessary must be observed; and watering, as the season calls for it, must be afforded them. When the sun gets powerful, they should be shaded about ten o'clock in the morning; and thus assisted in their vegetable progress, they will be very considerable by September. In October, when the leaves are decayed, the beds should be cleaned up, the surface should be stirred, and a fresh stratum of about half an inch of fine mould spread over the plants. During winter, and the summer following, they must be protected and encouraged as before; and in the autumn after that, they may be removed to the places where they are designed to remain.

These places should be in three different parts of the garden. A share of them should be set out among other tall-growing plants, to make a show in the flower-garden the succeeding summer; a share should be set out under a south wall, or hedge, in order to save seeds for a succession, for from such seedling plants there will be the greatest certainty of procuring good seeds; and another share must be planted in large pots, to adorn halls, &c. The strongest plants should be kept for the pots. They should be sheltered in the winter from hard frosts and heavy rains; and when their flower-stalks in the summer are advanced pretty nigh, they should be spread against a slight frame provided for the purpose, to which being fastened in a fan-like manner, the flowers will show to a greater advantage. If the rooms are very close, it will be of great advantage to these plants, and cause them to continue their beauty longer, if in evenings they are set abroad for the benefit of the air, under some shed or cover that can protect them only from the rains, and let them resume their stations in the rooms against the next morning.

In transplanting of these plants, the greatest care must be always taken to wound the roots as little as possible; for on being wounded, they emit a milky juice, which running freely, greatly weakens the plants. They love a light, sandy, good fresh earth, but dung is hurtful to them; which should caution all raisers of these flowers not to kill them with such kindness.

1. The Pyramidical Bell Flower is titled, *Campanula foliis ovatis glabris subserratis, caule erecto paniculato ramulis brevibus*. In the *Hortus Cliffortianus* it is termed, *Campanula foliis ovatis margine cartilagineo crenatis, caule ramosissimo angustato*. Tournefort calls it, *Campanula pyramidata altissima*; and Caspar Bauhine *Rapunculus hortensis, latiore folio, sive pyramidalis*. It is not certain in what part of the world it grows naturally. Titles.

2. Round leaved Bell Flower. This is titled, *Campanula foliis radicalibus reniformibus, caulinis linea*

*linearibus* Caspar Bauhine mentions three sorts of it One he terms, *Campanula minor rotundifolia vulgaris*, another, *Campanula minor rotundifolia Alpina*, and a third, *Campanula Alpina linifolia cærulea* It grows naturally on heathy, barren ground in England, and many parts of Europe

3 Peach leaved Bell Flower This is titled, *Campanula foliis radicalibus obovatis caulinis lanceolato-linearibus subserratis sessilibus remotis* Caspar Bauhine calls one sort of it, *Rapunculus persicifolius, magno flore*, another, *Rapunculus nemorosus angustifolius, magno flore, major*, and Clusius terms it, *Campanula persicæ folio* It grows naturally in many of the northern countries of Europe

4 Giant Throatwort is titled, *Campanula foliis ovato-lanceolatis, caule simplicissimo tereti, floribus solitariis pedunculatis, fructibus cernuis* Caspar Bauhine calls it, *Campanula maxima, foliis latissimis* It grows naturally in many of our hedges and forests

5 Great Throatwort, or, Canterbury Bells This is titled, *Campanula caule angulato, foliis petiolatis, calycibus ciliatis, pedunculis trifidis* In the *Hortus Cliffortianus* it is termed, *Campanula foliis radicalibus cordatis, calycibus ciliatis*, and Caspar Bauhine calls it, *Campanula vulgatior, foliis urticæ, vel major & asperior* It grows naturally in the hedges of England, and other parts of Europe

6 Lesser Throatwort, or Canterbury Bells This is titled, *Campanula caule angulato simplici, floribus sessilibus, capitulo terminali* In the *Hortus Cliffortianus* it is termed, *Campanula foliis lanceolato-ovatis crenatis, ramis capitulo florali terminatis* Caspar Bauhine calls it, *Campanula pratensis, flore conglomerato*, and Herman, *Trachelium Alpinum, floribus conglomeratis, foliis asarinæ rigidis & hirsutis* It grows naturally in our meadows, and many other parts of Europe

7 Hispid *Campanula*, or, Bell Flower, is titled, *Campanula hispida, racemo oblongo terminali, caule simplicissimo, foliis lanceolato-linearibus* Caspar Bauhine calls it, *Campanula foliis echii*, and John Bauhine, *Alopecurus Alpinus quibusdam, echium montanum Dalechampii* It grows naturally on the Alps of Hercynia

8 Oriental Bell Flower This is termed, *Campanula foliis subovatis glabris integerrimis, caulibus diffusis* Tournefort calls it, *Campanula saxatilis, foliis inferioribus bellidis, cæteris nummulariæ* It grows naturally in the East

9 Creeping Bell Flower This is titled, *Campanula caulibus unifloris, foliis obovatis glabris integerrimis subciliatis*, and Allionus calls it, *Campanula plerumque multicaulis uniflora, foliis ovatis sessilibus integerrimis* It grows naturally on the Alps

10 Dwarf Pyramidical Bell Flower This is titled, *Campanula foliis lanceolatis serratis lævibus, floribus racemosis secundis nutantibus, calycibus serratis*, and Alpinus calls it, *Campanula pyramidalis minor* It grows in the mountainous parts of Italy

11 Small Alpine Bell Flower This is titled, *Campanula caule simplici, pedunculis unifloris axillaribus diphyllis* Caspar Bauhine calls it, *Campanula Alpina pumila lanuginosa*, and Clusius, *Trachelium pumilum Alpinum* It grows naturally on the Alps of Schneeberg

12 Ivy-leaved Bell Flower This is titled, *Campanula foliis cordatis quinquelobis petiolatis glabris, caule laxo* Læfling calls it, *Campanula foliis subrotundis quinquangularibus basi emarginatis glabris, floribus solitariis*, and Caspar Bauhine, *Campanula cymbalariæ vel hederæ folio* It grows naturally in England, and some of the southern countries of Europe

*Campanula* is of the class and order *Pentandria Monogynia*, and the characters are, (Class and order in the Linnæan system The characters)

1 Calyx is a perianthium placed on the germen, divided into five acute, erect, patent parts

2 Corolla consists of a single bell-shaped petal, impervious at the base, and divided at the top into five broad, acute, spreading segments In the bottom of the flower is the nectarium, formed of five acute, connivent scales

3 Stamina consist of five very short capillary filaments, inserted in the top of the valves of the nectarium, with very long compressed antheræ

4 Pistillum consists of an angular germen placed below the receptacle, a filiforme style longer than the stamina, and an oblong, thick stigma, divided into three revolute segments

5 Pericarpium is a roundish, angular capsule, of three or five cells, each having a like number of holes for letting out the seeds when ripe

6 Semina The seeds are numerous, and small

## CHAP. XCIX.

## *CARDAMINE*, LADIES SMOCK.

THE perennials of this genus are pretty little plants, well deserving of a place in any collection of flowers, and some of them, in their double state, are highly ornamental, and admirably adapted to beautify the garden The species are, (Species)

1 The Common Ladies Smock, or, Cuckow Flower

2 The Daisy-leaved Ladies Smock

3 The Asarum-leaved Ladies Smock

4 The Rock Ladies Smock

5 The Reseda-leaved Ladies Smock

6 The Alpine Three-leaved Cress, or, Ladies Smock

7 Bitter Cresses, or, Ladies Smock

8 Virginian Ladies Smock

1 The Common Ladies Smock, or, Cuckow Flower, is what adorns our meadows in such great profusion in May In the state it is there found, we have no occasion to introduce it into our gardens, for we have enough of it every where, but the varieties of it are for our purpose, which are, (Description of the Common)

The

Varieties. The Large Round-leaved Ladies Smock.
The Single Purple Ladies Smock.
The Double White Ladies Smock.
The Large Double Purple Ladies Smock.

These sorts should be planted in the shade, and in a moist part of the garden, where the flowers will be larger and more beautiful than in any other situation.

Daisy-leaved. 2. Daisy-leaved Ladies Smock. This is a low plant, about six inches high. The leaves are simple, oval, entire, a little resembling those of the Common Daisy, and spread upon the ground. Among these the flower-stalk rises. It is weak, slender, and garnished with a few leaves, sitting close, without any footstalks. The flowers are produced on the upper parts of the stalks. They are small, white, come out in May, and are succeeded by very large, long pods, full of reddish seeds.

Asarum-leaved. 3. Asarum-leaved Ladies Smock. This hath a creeping root, which sends forth many roundish, heart-shaped leaves, that spread themselves on the ground. From among these the flower-stalk rises to about a foot in height. The flowers are produced at the top, come out in May, and are succeeded by long pods full of seeds.

Rock. 4. Rock Ladies Smock. The leaves are oblong, simple, and their edges are indented. The stalks are very slender, weak, and support a few flowers in May, which are succeeded by ripe seeds in about a month or six weeks after they are fallen.

Reseda-leaved. 5. Reseda-leaved Ladies Smock. The lower leaves of this species are oval and undivided; the upper leaves are composed of three lobes. The stalk rises but to about half a foot high, and supports a few small flowers, which are succeeded by pods like the former.

Alpine Three-leaved. 6. Alpine Three-leaved Ladies Smock. This spreads itself by its small, creeping stalks, which strike root into the ground as they extend in length. The leaves are trifoliate; the folioles are obtuse, and placed on longish footstalks in the manner of the common field-clover. Among these the flower-stalks arise. They are weak, almost naked, and grow but to little more than half a foot high. The flowers ornament the tops of the stalks in great plenty. They are white, come out in May, and are succeeded by long pods, containing the seeds.

Bitter, 7. Bitter Ladies Smock. The leaves of this species are pinnated, and the folioles are angular, and of a roundish figure. The flower-stalks support a few flowers at the top; they are moderately large, and are succeeded by long pods full of seeds. There is a variety of this with double flowers, which is much sought after.

and Virginian Ladies Smock. 8. Virginian Ladies Smock. The leaves of this species are pinnated, and lie flat on the ground; the folioles are numerous along the mid-rib, and have an indenture near the base. The stalks are almost bare of leaves, but the few with which they are sometimes garnished, are spear-shaped and entire. The flowers are white, and are succeeded by compressed pods.

Culture. The double sorts are all propagated by parting of the roots, and the others are propagated the same way, or by seeds. The seeds should be sown soon after they are ripe, in a shady border; and the best time for parting of the roots is in the autumn.

Either way they are to be multiplied exceedingly; for they are very hardy, and require no trouble, except keeping them clean from weeds. They will grow in almost any soil or situation, though a strong moist land suits them best.

Titles. 1. The Common Ladies Smock is titled, *Cardamine foliis pinnatis, foliolis radicalibus subrotundis, caulinis lanceolatis*. In the *Flora Suecica* it is termed, *Cardamine foliis pinnatis, foliolis subrotundis integris*; in the *Flora Lapponica*, *Cardamine foliis pinnatis, caule erecto*. Dodonæus calls it, *Flos cuculi*; Caspar Bauhine, *Nasturtium pratense, magno flore*; also, *Nasturtium pratense, flore rotundiore, flore majore*. It grows naturally in most pastures in most parts of Europe.

2. Daisy-leaved Ladies Smock. This is titled, *Cardamine foliis simplicibus ovatis integerrimis petiolis longis*. Caspar Bauhine calls it, *Nasturtium Alpinum, bellidis folio, minus*; and Clusius, *Plantula Cardamines æmula*. It grows naturally in England, also in Lapland and Switzerland.

3. Asarum-leaved Ladies Smock is titled, *Cardamine foliis simplicibus subcordatis*. Morison calls it, *Nasturtium Alpinum, palustre rotundifolium, radice repente*; and Caspar Bauhine, *Nasturtium Alpinum, bellidis folio, majus*. It grows naturally on the Alps of Italy.

4. Rock Ladies Smock is titled, *Cardamine foliis simplicibus oblongis dentatis*. Dillenius calls it, *Cardamine petræa Cambrica, nasturtii facie*; and Plukenet, *Nasturtium petræum*. It grows naturally on the sides of rocks in England, Wales, and Sweden.

5. Reseda-leaved Ladies Smock is titled, *Cardamine foliis inferioribus indivisis, superioribus trilobis*. Caspar Bauhine calls it, *Nasturtium Alpinum minus resedæ folio*. It grows naturally on the Helvetian and Pyrenean Mountains.

6. Alpine Three-leaved Ladies Smock is titled, *Cardamine foliis ternatis obtusis, caule subnudo*. Haller calls it, *Cardamine foliis ternatis*; Clusius, *Cardamine Alpina trifolia*; and Caspar Bauhine, *Nasturtium Alpinum trifolium*. In the *Flora Lapponica* it is termed, *Cardamine foliis ternatis crenatis, caule simplici*. It grows naturally in woods, by the sides of hills, and in shady places in Lapland and Switzerland.

7. Bitter Ladies Smock is titled, *Cardamine foliis pinnatis, axillis stoloniferis*. Haller calls it, *Cardamine foliis pinnatis foliolis subrotundis angulosis*; and Caspar Bauhine, *Nasturtium aquaticum majus & amarum*. It grows naturally in meadows and moist places in England, and most of the southern countries of Europe.

8. Virginian Ladies Smock is titled, *Cardamine foliis pinnatis foliolis lanceolatis basi unidentatis*. Gronovius calls it, *Alyssum foliis radicalibus pinnatis in orbem positis caulinis lanceolatis, siliculis compressis*; and Plukenet, *Nasturtium, bursæ pastoris folio Virginianum, flore albo, siliquâ compressâ*. It grows naturally in Virginia.

Class and order in the Linnæan System. *Cardamine* is of the class and order *Tetradynamia Siliquosa*, and the characters are,

The characters. 1. Calyx is a perianthium composed of four small, oval, oblong, obtuse, subpapulous, gibbous, deciduous leaves.

2. Corolla consists of four petals placed cross-wise. The petals are oblong, obovate, spread open, and have erect ungues twice the length of the calyx.

3. Stamina are six awl-shaped filaments, with small, oblong, heart-shaped, erect antheræ. The two opposite filaments are twice the length of the cup; the other four are rather longer.

4. Pistillum consists of a very slender, cylindrical germen, the length of the stamina, and an obtuse, capitated stigma, there being no style.

5. Pericarpium is a long, cylindrical, compressed, bilocular pod, opening spirally, and casting out the seeds, when ripe, with an elastic force.

6. Semina. The seeds are many, and roundish.

CHAP.

# CHAP. C.

## *CARDUUS*, THISTLE.

Introductory remarks.

THOUGH Thistles are generally looked upon as weeds, and very troublesome weeds in pastures, gardens, and fields, yet they are in reality very curious plants, and worthy of the strictest attention and observation. Many species are rare plants, and deserve admission into such gardens, where a collection of plants is making.

I shall, therefore, mention the Common Sorts, that the Gardener may know what it is that he hoes down with such industry and disdain, together with those of foreign growth, that he could wish to cultivate with satisfaction and pleasure. The annuals are reserved for another department. The perennials of this genus are,

Species.

1. The Marsh Thistle.
2. English Soft, or, Gentle Thistle.
3. Melancholy Thistle.
4. Dwarf Carline Thistle.
5. Italian Thistle.
6. Tartarian Thistle.
7. Narrow-leaved Austrian Thistle.
8. Carolina Thistle.
9. Tuberous Thistle.
10. Lapland Thistle.
11. Melancholy Thistle of Montpelier.
12. Siberian Thistle.

Description of the Marsh,

1. The Marsh Thistle grows naturally in moist meadows, woods, and pastures, in most parts of England, and is never cultivated in gardens. The leaves are narrow, decurrent, indented, and prickly on their edges. The flowers are reddish, erect, and grow in bunches on footstalks that have no prickles.

English Soft,

2. English Soft, or, Gentle Thistle, is another English Thistle, that grows naturally in moist places. The stalk is slender, stiff, downy, and grows to about a foot and a half high. The leaves are spear-shaped, indented, and unarmed with prickles. The flowers are collected into moderately large heads, and have prickly cups. There are three or four varieties of this species differing in one respect or other.

Melancholy,

3. Melancholy Thistle. This is another Thistle of English production. Its habitation is on mountainous and heathy ground, and it is very rarely admitted into gardens. The root is creeping, the stalk upright, unarmed with prickles, and branching a little near the top. The leaves are spear shaped, downy underneath, indented, and embrace the stalk with their base. The prickles are unequal and ciliated. The flowers terminate the plant in the usual way, and they are succeeded by large woolly, or downy heads, containing the seeds.

Dwarf Carline,

4. Dwarf Carline Thistle is an English Thistle, but nevertheless of great singularity and beauty. The root is large, often dividing into branches near the top, producing tufts of leaves from each head. The leaves are green, deeply cut, very prickly, and spread themselves on the ground. In the midst of these rises the flower without any stalk, or, at furthest, with an exceeding short one. Its colour is purple, growing in a large scaly cup. It comes out in July, August, and sometimes in September, and is succeeded by a large, downy head, containing the seeds. There is a variety of this with white flowers, and both ought to be admitted into every good collection of plants.

Italian,

5. Italian Thistle. This species grows to about a foot and a half high. The radical leaves are sinuated, those on the stalk are decurrent, pinnatifid, downy, and prickly. The flowers are of a purple colour, and grow on short, naked, downy footstalks, having oblong imbricated cups. They come out in July, and the seeds ripen in September. This plant being of foreign growth, is coveted by some, though it is of no superior beauty to many of our English sorts.

Tartarian,

6. Tartarian Thistle rises with an upright stalk to about two feet high. The leaves are decurrent, pinnatified, unarmed with prickles, are very downy on both sides, especially the under, where they are white. The flowers are moderately large, grow in scaly cups in July, and are succeeded by downy heads, containing the seeds. There are many varieties of this species, some having simple, undivided stalks, others which branch out very much. Some have small purple flowers, and others larger, and of a paler colour. They generally ripen in July and August, and perfect their seeds in September.

Narrow leaved,

7. Narrow leaved Austrian Thistle. The stalks of this species are branching, and grow to near a yard high. The leaves are decurrent, spear shaped, narrow, and possessed of soft spines. The flowers are produced on very long, woolly footstalks, each footstalk supports one flower, which is moderately large, having a long, narrow, imbricated cup.

Carolina,

8. Carolina Thistle. This rises with an upright, branching stalk, to a very great height. The leaves are pinnatifid, serrated, have no prickles, are downy underneath, and sit close without any footstalk. The flowers terminate the branches in July or August, and are succeeded by woolly heads, containing ripe seeds in September or October.

Tuberous,

9. Tuberous Thistle. The root of this species hath many fleshy knots, or tubers, like those of asphodel. The stalk is free from prickles. The leaves are moderately broad, finely divided, nearly decurrent, and prickly. The flowers are produced singly in cups that have no prickles, and the time of their appearance is July or August.

Lapland,

10. Lapland Thistle hath a creeping, knotty root, from which rises a stalk to the height of four or five feet. The leaves are spear-shaped, ciliated, jagged, and embrace the stalk with their base. The top of it is terminated by one or two flowers, which are succeeded by downy heads, full of smooth seeds.

Melancholy,

11. Melancholy Thistle of Montpelier rises with an upright stalk to the height of about two feet, or more. The leaves are green on both sides, of a firm substance, whole, ciliated, spear-shaped, and embrace the stalk with their base. The flowers grow singly on footstalks on the upper part of the plant, and are succeeded by downy heads, containing the seeds.

Siberian

12. Siberian Thistle. This grows to about the

the height of the former, and to which it seems nearly allied. The leaves are spear-shaped, downy underneath, broad, indented, prickly, and embrace the stalks with their base. The flowers grow singly on long foot-stalks; their colour is white, they have cylindrical caps, and are succeeded by a feathery down, among which are lodged the seeds.

These Thistles are all propagated by sowing of the seeds, either in the autumn, soon after they are ripe, or the spring. They should be sown in the places where they are to remain; and when they come up, nothing more is to be done, than thinning them to proper distances, and keeping them clean from weeds.

They may be also propagated by parting of the roots; the best time for which work is the autumn; but the plants raised this way will not be near so strong and beautiful, as those that are produced immediately from the seeds.

Titles. 1. Marsh Thistle is titled, *Carduus foliis decurrentibus dentatis margine spinosis floribus congestis erectis, pedunculis inermibus*. Van Royen calls it, *Carduus foliis lineari-lanceolatis ... spinosissimis, caule crispo spinoso, floribus erectis*; Caspar Bauhine, *Carduus palustris*; Morison, *Carduus spinosissimus ... angustifolius palustris*; and Dalechamp, *Carduus polyacanthos angustifolius*. It grows naturally in marshy and shady places in England, and most countries of Europe.

2. English Soft, or, Gentle Thistle. This is titled, *Carduus foliis decurrentibus lanceolatis, denticulatis ... calyce spinoso*. Lobel calls it, *Cirsium Anglicum*; and Caspar Bauhine, *Cirsium ... singulari capitulo magno, sive incanum varie dissectum*. It grows naturally in marshy places in some parts of England.

3. Melancholy Thistle. This is titled, *Carduus foliis amplexicaulibus lanceolatis denticulatis spinulis inaequalibus ciliatis, caule inermi*. Haller calls it, *Cirsium foliis ... lanceolatis serratis subtus tomentosis*; Caspar Bauhine, *Cirsium singulari capitulo squamato, vel incanum alterum*; also, *Carduus mollis, foliis ...*; and John Bauhine, *Cirsium Anglicum, radice ... fibrosa, folio longo*. It grows naturally in England and Siberia.

4. Dwarf Carline Thistle is titled, *Carduus acaulis, calyce glabro*. Caspar Bauhine calls it, *Carlina acaulis, minore purpureo flore*; and John Bauhine, *Chamaeleon exiguus*. It grows naturally in England, and many parts of Europe.

5. Italian Thistle is titled, *Carduus foliis decurrentibus pinnatifido-sinuatis ... spinosis, pedunculis ... tomentosis*. Barrelier calls it, *Carduus nemorosus ...*; and Triumphetti, *Carduus ...*. It grows naturally in the south of Europe.

6. Tartarian Thistle is titled, *Carduus foliis decurrentibus pinnatifidis linearibus integerrimis inermibus, pedunculis fultis tomentosis*. It grows naturally in Tartary.

7. Narrow-leaved Austrian Thistle is titled, *Carduus foliis decurrentibus lanceolatis serratis subspinosis ciliatis nudis, pedunculis longissimis lanuginosis uni-floris*. Haller calls it, *Carduus foliis rigidis ... spinosis, scapo longo unifloro*; Caspar Bauhine, *Cirsium ... angustifolius*; also, *Cirsium singularibus capitulis parvis*; and Clusius, *Cirsium ... montanum*. It grows naturally in Austria, Helvetia, and the south of France.

8. Carolina Thistle is titled, *Carduus foliis sessilibus ... serratis inermibus, caule ramosissimo, ... subserratis*. Dillenius calls it, *Cirsium altissimum, ... folio, ... tomentoso*. It is a native of Carolina.

9. Tuberous Thistle is titled, *Carduus foliis ... pinnatifidis ... spinosis, caule ... solitariis*. Sauvages calls it, *Carduus foliis ... spinis ...*; Lobel, *Carduus bulbosus Monspeliensium*; Caspar Bauhine, *Carduus pratensis, asphodeli radice, latifolius*; also, *Carduus pratensis, asphodeli radice, foliis ... incisis*; Tabernaemontanus titles it, *Jacea ... sive tuberosa*. It grows naturally in Bohemia, Austria, Helvetia, and in some parts of France.

10. Lapland Thistle. This is titled, *Carduus foliis amplexicaulibus lanceolatis ... integris ... caule subunifloro, calyce inermi*. In the *Flora Lapponica* it is termed, *Carduus calyce inermi, foliis lanceolatis margine ciliatis*. Caspar Bauhine calls it, *Cirsium ... asphodeli radice*. It grows naturally in Lapland and other cold parts of Europe.

11. Melancholy Thistle of Montpelier is titled, *Carduus foliis subamplexicaulibus lanceolatis integris serraturis spinoso-setaceis, pedunculis unifloris*. Gmelin calls it, *Carduus calycibus inermibus acutis, foliis utrinque viridibus firmis integerrimis ...*; Caspar Bauhine, *Cirsium angustifolium ... laciniatum*; and Clusius, *Cirsium Pannonicum ... pratense*. It grows naturally near Montpelier, also in Switzerland and Siberia.

12. Siberian Thistle is titled, *Carduus foliis amplexicaulibus lanceolatis serraturis spinoso-setaceis, floribus ...*. It grows naturally in Siberia.

*Carduus* is of the class and order *Syngenesia Polygamia Aequalis*; and the characters are, Class and order in the Linnaean System.

1. CALYX. The common calyx is ventricose and imbricated, being composed of numerous scales that are spear-shaped, sharp-pointed, and prickly. The characters.

2. COROLLA. The compound flower is tubulous and uniform. The florets are each infundibuliform, monopetal. The tube is slender, the limb erect, and divided at the top into five narrow, equal segments.

3. STAMINA are five very short capillary filaments, having a cylindrical, tubular anthera the length of the corolulae, and indented in five parts at the top.

4. PISTILLUM consists of an oval germen, a filiform style longer than the stamina, and a simple, awl-shaped, naked, emarginated stigma.

5. PERICARPIUM. There is none. The calyx becoming connivent, encloses the seeds.

6. SEMEN. The seed is solitary, oboval, four-cornered, and crowned with very long down. The receptacle is plain and hairy.

# CHAP. CI.

## *CAREX*, CYPEROIDE-GRASS

Introductory Remarks

THIS genus comprehends a multitude of uncultivated plants, the greatest part of which grow naturally in ditches, bogs, moist woods, by the sides of rivers, and watery places in different parts of the world I shall therefore only mention the names of the English species, in order to introduce the titles and generical characters, for the satisfaction of those who may expect to find them in this place The British species of this genus then are,

Species

1 Dioecious *Carex*, or Bastard Cypress-Grass
2 Small Capitated *Carex*, or Bastard Cypress-Grass
3 Flea *Carex*
4 Panicled *Carex*
5 Naked *Carex*
6 Sea *Carex*
7 Rough *Carex*
8 Great *Carex*
9 Prickly *Carex*
10 Grey *Carex*
11 Long leaved *Carex*
12 Yellow *Carex*, or Hedge-hog Grass
13 Round headed *Carex*
14 Vernal *Carex*.
15 Pink *Carex*
16 Turfy *Carex*
17 Pale *Carex*
18 Loose *Carex*
19 Bastard *Carex*
20 Brown *Carex*
21 Bladder *Carex*
22 Hairy *Carex*

They may be found in blow from May until the end of summer

Titles

1 The first species is entitled, *Carex spicâ simplici dioica* Micheli calls it, *Cyperoides parvum, culmibus et foliis tenuissimis triangularibus, spicâ longiore capsulis oblongis*, Morison, *Gramen cyperoides minimum, spicâ simplici cassa*, and Ray, *Gramen cyperoides minus, ranunculi capitulo longiore* It grows naturally on the tops of bogs and moist places in England, and most countries of Europe

2 The second species is, *Carex spicâ simplici androgynâ ovata superne mascula, capsulis imbricato patulis* Micheli calls it *Cyperoides parvum, culmibus et foliis tenuissimis triangularibus, spicâ subrotunda*, and Morison, *Gramen cyperoides minimum, ranunculi capitulo simplici asperiore rotundo* It grows naturally on turfy bogs, and moist places in England and Lapland

3 The third is, *Carex spicâ simplici androgynâ superne masculâ, capsulis divaricatis retroflexis* In the *Hortus Cliffortianus* it is termed, *Carex spicâ simplici androgynâ*, in the *Flora Lapp* *Carex spica unica* Ray calls it, *Gramen cyperoides minimum, seminibus deorsum reflexis pulicisformibus* It grows naturally in marshy places in England, and most parts of Europe

4 The fourth is, *Carex spiculis androgynis, racemo composito* Haller calls it, *Carex spicâ paniculata*, Caspar Bauhine, *Cyperus longus inodorus sylvaticus*, Scheuchzer, *Cyperus Alpinus longus nodorus, panicula ferruginea minus sparsa*, and Ray, *Gramen cyperoides palustre, spicâ longiore laxâ* It grows naturally in wet woods, rotten turfs, and uliginous Alpine places in England, and most of the southern countries of Europe

5 The fifth is *Carex spicâ compositâ, spiculis ovatis sessilibus approximatis alternis androgynis nudis*. In the *Flora Lapp* it is termed, *Carex spicis sessilibus confertis androgynis* Scheuchzer calls it, *Gramen cyperoides, spica e pluribus spicis* [illegible] Seguier, *Carex angustifolia, caule triquetro, spicis pluribus elegantibus* [illegible], and Caspar Bauhine, *Gramen cyperoides palustre majus, spica divisa* It grows naturally in wet places in England, and most countries of Europe

6 The sixth is, *Carex spicâ compositâ, spiculis androgynis* [illegible] Micheli calls it, *Carex* [illegible] *repente, caule triquetro, spica spadicea*, Plukenet, *Gramen cyperoides e* [illegible] *in arenosis nascens*, and Loetel, *Gramen cyperoides minus repens, spica divisa* It grows chiefly on the sea sands in most countries of Europe

7 The seventh is, *Carex spicâ compositâ distichâ nuda spiculis androgynis oblongis contiguis, culmo nudo* Haller calls it, *Carex spicis teretibus acutis alternis sessilibus contingentibus*, and Ray, *Gramen cyperoides elegans, spicâ compositâ asperiore* It grows naturally in uliginous places in most countries of Europe

8 The eighth is, *Carex spicâ supra decompositâ inferne laxiore spiculis androgynis ovatis sessilibus glomeratis superne masculis* Caspar Bauhine calls it *Gramen cyperoides palustre majus, spicâ compacta*, Gerard, *Gramen palustre cyperoides*, and Parkinson, *Gramen cyperoides palustre majus* It grows naturally by rivers and waters in most countries of Europe

9 The ninth is, *Carex spiculis subovatis, sessilibus remotis androgynis, capsulis acutis divergentibus spinosis* Guettard calls it, *Carex spicâ* [illegible] *compactis obscure alternis, culmo nudo compresso*, Micheli, *Carex nemorosa, spinosa radice, angustifolia minima, caule exquisite triangulari, spicâ brevi interrupta*, Ray, *Gramen cyperoides spicatum minimum, spicâ divulsa aculeata*, Caspar Bauhine, *Gramen nemorosum spicis parvis asperis*, and Parkinson, *Gramen cyperoides echinatum minimum* It grows naturally in marshes, moist woods and forests in England and most parts of Europe

10 The tenth is, *Carex spiculis subrotundis remotis sessilibus obtusis androgynis, capsulis ovatis obtusiusculis* In the *Flora Lapp* it is termed, *Carex spicis parvis, remotis sessilibus subovatis* [illegible] Loetel calls it, *Gramen cyperoides spicis curtis articulis* It grows naturally in moist woods, hedges, &c in England, and most of the northern countries of Europe

11 The eleventh is, *Carex spiculis ovatis sessilibus remotis androgynis, foliis caulinis culmum aequantibus* Guettard calls it, *Carex spicis foliosis in alis sessilibus*, and Ray, *Cyperoides angustifolium*,

*stifolium, spicis sessilibus in foliorum alis* It grows naturally by the sides of ditches, and moist shady places in most countries of Europe

12 The twelfth is, *Carex spicis confertis subsessilibus subrotundis mascula lineari, capsulis acutis recurvis* In the *Flora Lapp* it is termed, *Carex spicis ad apicem tribus sessilibus femineis subrotundis, capsulis acutis recurvis* Tournefort calls it, *Gramen cyperoides palustre aculeatum, capitulo breviore*, Caspar Bauhine, *Gramen cyperoides aculeatum Germanicum* minus and Gerard, *Gramen palustre echinatum* It grows naturally in bogs, marshy grounds, and moist places in most countries of Europe

13 The thirteenth is, *Carex spicis terminalibus confertis subrotundis, mascula oblonga* Plukenet calls it, *Gramen cyperoides tenuifolium, spicis ad summitatem caulis sessilibus globulorum æmulis*, and Ray, *Gramen cyperoides, spicis brevibus congestis folio molli* It grows naturally in meadows and moist places in most countries of Europe

14 The fourteenth is, *Carex spicis tribus ovatis sessilibus alternis, mascula oblonga* In the *Flora Lapp* it is termed, *Carex spicis tribus ad apicem sessilibus, femineis ovatis atris* Ray calls it, *Gramen cyperoides minimum*, Caspar Bauhine, *Gramen caryophylleum foliis, spica divulsa*, and Parkinson, *Gramen spicarum foliis caryophylleis* It is a native of most parts of Europe

15 The fifteenth is, *Carex spicis pedunculatis ... femineis ..., capsulis obtusiusculis ...* Ray calls it, *Gramen cyperoides foliis caryophylleis, spicis e ... oribus & tumidioribus ... compactis* It grows naturally in moist places in most parts of Europe

16 The sixteenth is, *Carex spicis erectis cylindricis ... sessilibus mascula terminali, culmo triquetro* Morison calls it, *Gramen cyperoides caryophyllatum, folio longiore & angustiore, spicis sessilibus compactis erectis* It rises out of the turf in bogs and marshy places in most parts of England

17 The seventeenth is, *Carex spicis pendulis mascula ..., femineis ... imbricatis, capsulis confertis obtusis* In the *Flora Lapp* it is termed, *Carex spicis tribus pedunculatis erectis remotis, mascula & femineis* Plukenet calls it, *Cyperoides polystachyon flavicans, spicis brevibus prope summitatem caulis* It inhabits moist places in most parts of Europe

18 The eighteenth is, *Carex spicis remotissimis subsessilibus, bractea vaginante, capsulis angulatis mucronatis* Ray calls it, *Gramen cyperoides spicis parvis longissime distantibus* It is a native of moist turfy places in most parts of Europe

19 The nineteenth is, *Carex spicis pendulis, pedunculis geminatis* Caspar Bauhine calls it, *Gramen cyperoides spica pendula breviore*, Parkinson, *Cyperus pseudo cyperus spica pendula breviore*, and Gerard, *Pseudo-cyperus* It grows by ditches in most parts of Europe

20 The twentieth is, *Carex spicis ... fasciculis pluribus femineis subsessilibus, capsulis obtusiusculis* Gerard calls it, *Gramen cyperoides* John Bauhine, *Gramen cyperoides cum paniculis nigris*, and Parkinson, *Gramen cyperoides majus latifolium & angustifolium* It is common by waters in most countries of Europe

21 The twenty-first is, *Carex spicis masculis pluribus, femineis pedunculatis, capsulis inflatis acuminatis* In the *Flora Lapp* it is termed, *Carex spicis plurimis florescentibus tenuibus, fructiferis crassis*, also, *Carex culmo longissimo, spicis tenuibus remotis* Ray calls it, *Gramen cyperoides sylvaticum tenuius spicatum* It grows naturally in wet woodlands and watery places in England, and most countries of Europe

22 The twenty second is, *Carex spicis remotis masculis pluribus femineis subpedunculatis erectis, capsulis hirtis* Morison calls it *Cyperoides polystachyon lanuginosum*, and Parkinson, *Gramen cyperoides Norvegicum parvum lanosum* It is common in moist meadows and pastures in England, and most countries of Europe

*Carex* is of the class and order *Monoecia Triandria*, and the characters are, Class and order in the Linnæan system The characters

I Male flowers are collected in a spike

1 CALYX is an oblong imbricated amentum, composed of several spear-shaped, acute, concave, permanent scales, each containing one flower

2 COROLLA There is none

3 STAMINA are three setaceous erect filaments longer than the calyx, having long, narrow, erect antheræ

II Female flowers

1 CALYX The amentum is as in the male

2 COROLLA There are no petals, but an oval, oblong, permanent, inflated perianthium, contracted upwards, and indented in two places at the top

3 PISTILLUM consists of a triquetrous germen within the nectarium, and a very short style, with two or three awl-shaped, incurved, long, pointed, downy stigmas

5 PERICARPIUM There is none The seed is lodged in the nectarium, which becomes large for the purpose

6 SEMEN The seed is single, triquetrous, oval, and acute.

CHAP

## CHAP CII

## *CARLINA,* CARLINE THISTLE

THERE are two Perennials of this genus called,

Species

1 The Stalkless Carline Thistle

2 The Corymbous-flowered Carline Thistle

Description of the Stalkless

1 The Stalkless Carline Thistle The root of this plant is large, thick, white, and of a sweet scent The leaves are finely jagged or divided, very prickly, about six inches long, and spread their leaves on the ground In the midst of these comes out the flower, without any stalk, or at most with a very short one Its colour is white, though there is a variety of it with red flowers Both sorts are very large, close in the evenings, and in rainy or misty weather, but expand in sunshine They make their appearance in July, and their seeds ripen in September

and Corymbous-flowered Carline Thistle

2 The Corymbous-flowered Carline Thistle The root of this species is thick, fleshy, and strikes deep in the ground The leaves are large, very prickly, and sit close, without any footstalk The stalk is upright, and divides near the top into a few branches The flowers are produced from the ends of the branches in a corymbus, they are of a golden yellow colour come out in July, and their seeds ripen in the autumn

There is a variety of this with small flowers, collected into little heads and another with a larger branching stalk, producing the flowers in a kind of umbel

Method of propagating these species

These plants are propagated by sowing the seeds in the spring in the places where they are to remain When the plants come up, nothing more need be done than to thin them to proper distances, and keep them clear from weeds, and if very dry weather should happen, refresh them with water now and then in the evenings By the autumn they will become strong good plants, and the summer following they will flower and perfect their seeds

Titles

1 The Stalkless Carline Thistle is titled, *Carlina caule unifloro, flore breviore* Caspar Bauhine calls it, *Carlina acaulos, magno flore albo*, and Clusius, *Chameleon albus* It grows naturally on the mountainous parts of Italy and Germany

2 The Corymbous Carline Thistle is titled, *Carlina caule multifloro subdiviso, floribus sessilibus, calycibus radio flavis* Caspar Bauhine calls it, *Acarna capitulis parvis luteis in umbella*, Columna, *Acarna capitulis umbellata*, Ray, *Carlina sylvestris multicaulis, flore flavo, radice perenni*, and Tournefort, *Carlina lutea, flore aureo, perennis* also, *Carlina parvis capitulis, e tactyl s folio & facie* It is a native of Italy

Class and order in the Linnæan system The characters

*Carlina* is of the class and order *Syngenesia Polygamia Æqualis*, and the characters are,

1 CALYX The common calyx is ventricose and imbricated The scales are numerous, loose, acute, long, patent, bright, coloured, and the inner ones shaped in a circular order, so as to resemble the radius of a compound flower

2 COROLLA The compound flower is uniform The florets are funnel-shaped, having a very slender tube and divided at the top into five parts

3 STAMINA are five very short capillary filaments, having a cylindrical tubulous anthera

4 PISTILLUM consists of a very short germen, a filiform style the length of the stamina, and an oblong bifid stigma

5 PERICARPIUM There is none

6 SEMEN The seed is single, taper, and crowned with a branching feathery down

## CHAP CIII

## *CARPESIUM.*

Italian Carpesium described

OF this genus there is a good Perennial for the flower garden, called Italian *Carpesium* The root is composed of many thick fibres The stalk is upright, firm, bending at the top, and two or three feet high The leaves are long, hairy, and serrated at their edges The flowers come out from the tops of the stalks, attended by a few leaves, which are smaller than the others, more acute and soft to the touch, they are moderately large, of a yellow colour, and hang drooping, they appear in July and August, and the seeds ripen in the autumn

Method of propagating it

This is easily propagated by parting of the roots any time in the autumn, winter, or spring, before the stalks rise They should have a fresh light soil, and shady situation and when they are set out, will require no trouble, except keeping them clean from weeds, and reducing the roots as often as they get too large

Title

This species is titled, *Carpesium floribus terminalibus* In the *Hortus Upsal* it is termed simply, *Carpesium* Vaillant calls it, *Bupthalmum ... folio, flore cernuo*, Caspar Bauhine, *Aster Atticus, foliis ... flore ... molliceus*, Columna, *Aster ...*, and

and Morison, *Chrysanthemum conyzoides cernuum, foliis circa florem crebrius* It grows naturally in Italy

Class and order in the Linnæan system The characters. *Carpesium* is of the class and order *Syngenesia Polygamia Superflua*, and the characters are,

1 CALYX The general calyx is imbricated The exterior leaves are the largest spreading, and reflexed The interior are short and equal

2 COROLLA The compound flower is equal The hermaphrodite florets in the disk consist each of one infundibuliform petal, cut at the top into five spreading segments

The female florets in the radius consist each of one tubular petal, cut at the top into five connivent segments

3 STAMINA of the hermaphrodites, are five very short filaments, having a cylindrical anthera

4 PISTILLUM of the hermaphrodites, consists of an oblong germen, a simple style, and a bifid stigma

The pistillum of the females is similar to that in the hermaphrodites

5 PERICARPIUM There is none

6 SEMINA of the hermaphrodites are obovall and naked The seeds of the females are similar to those of the hermaphrodites

The receptacle is naked

## CHAP. CIV.

## *CARTHAMUS*, BASTARD SAFFRON

Species THE Perennials of this genus are,

1 Bastard Saffron of Tangiers
2 Spanish Bastard Saffron
3 Smooth Bastard Saffron of Mount Lupus
4 Prickly Bastard Saffron of Mount Lupus
5 Corymbous-flowered Bastard Saffron

Description of the Bastard, 1 Bastard Saffron of Tangiers The stalk of this plant is upright, branches very little, and grows to about a foot and a half high The radical leaves are pinnated, but those on the stalk are pinnatifid, each segment ending in a prickle or sharp point One flower only terminates the stalks, the several florets of which it is composed are collected into a large scaly cup Their colour is blue, they appear in June and July, but are very rarely succeeded by good seeds in our gardens

Spanish Bastard, 2 Spanish Bastard Saffron The stalk is single, channelled, hairy, of a purplish colour, and grows to about two feet high The leaves are spear-shaped smooth on their upper surface, indented, prickly, and downy underneath One flower only terminates each stalk, having a large, leafy, prickly calyx, the colour of the florets is blue, and they have black antheræ They will be in full blow in June or July, and sometimes, though not very frequently, are succeeded by ripe seeds in our gardens

Smooth Bastard, 3 Smooth Bastard Saffron of Mount Lupus The stalk of this plant is upright, smooth, and grows only to about a foot high The leaves are unarmed with prickles The radical leaves are indented, and those on the stalks pinnated The flowers terminate the stalks, and are collected in large scaly cups Their colour is blue, and in favourable seasons the seeds ripen very well

Prickly Bastard, 4 Prickly Bastard Saffron of Mount Lupus The stalk of this plant is hairy, channelled, and grows to about six or eight inches high The leaves are narrow, as long as the plants, deeply cut or winged, and each segment ends in a sharp spine or prickle The flowers are collected into large scaly heads at the tops of the stalks, one flower only terminates one stalk, its colour is blue, it will be in blow in June, and is very rarely succeeded by good seeds with us

and Corymbous flowered Bastard Saffron. 5 Corymbous-flowered Bastard Saffron The stalks of this plant are upright, channelled, branching, and grow to about two feet high The leaves are large, prickly, hoary, and the whole plant has an appearance not much unlike the Globe-Thistle The flowers are numerous, and grow in roundish bunches, their colour is blue, they come out in June or July, and in favourable seasons are succeeded by good seeds in our gardens

Method of propagating it These sorts are all propagated by parting of the roots, the best time for which is the autumn, though it may be done with very good success early in the spring They should have a dry soil, and a warm situation, and in such places there will be a better chance of their perfecting their seeds, which, if they can be obtained, is the best way of raising these plants, especially for the fourth sort, which rarely puts out off-sets, and encreases very slowly that way

Having got good seeds, sow them about the end of March in a border of light, sandy, fresh earth, when the plants come up thin them where they appear too close, water them in dry weather, keep them clean from weeds all summer, and in the autumn, on a moist day, they may be removed, preserving a ball of earth to each root, into the places where they are designed to remain

Titles 1 Bastard Saffron of Tangiers is titled, *Carthamus foliis radicalibus pinnatis, caulinis pinnatifidis, caule unifloro* Morison calls it, *Carduus cæruleus erectus, cnici foliis dissectioribus* It grows naturally in the country of Algiers

2 Spanish Bastard Saffron is titled, *Carthamus foliis lanceolatis spinoso-dentatis, caule subunifloro* Caspar Bauhine calls it, *Cnicus cæruleus asperior*, and Clusius, *Cnicus alter cæruleo flore* It grows naturally in the corn-fields of Spain

3 Smooth Bastard Saffron of Mount Lupus is titled, *Carthamus foliis inermibus radicalibus dentatis, caulinis pinnatis* Vaillant calls it, *Carthamoides cærulea humilis & mitior*; and Morison, *Carduncellus montis Lupi minor spec.* It grows naturally in France

4 Prickly Bastard Saffron of Mount Lupus is titled, *Carthamus foliis caulinis linearibus pinnatis*

*natis longit ta ne plantæ* Sauv ig s calls it, *Carthamus fol s caule longioribus lig il tis pinnatifidis*, Van Royen, *Carthamus foli s red ce tus f iperne ferratis, inferne den atis ca h s dentato-pinnatis*, Herman, *Cr cus ceru eus hu t l s mo tis Lupi*, Lobel, *Carduncellus monti Lupi*, and Caspar Bauhine, *Eryngium montanum minimum, capitulo magno* It rows naturally in France, especially about Montpelier

5 Cory nbous flowered Bastard Saffron s t the, *Carthamus floribus cory nbosis numerosis* In the *Ho t is Cliffortia* us it is termed, *Echinops floribus fasciculatis, c l cibus multifloris* Dalechamp calls it *Chamæleon niger*, Caspar Bauhine, *Chamæleon niger umbellatus, flore cæruleo hyacinthino*, and Morison, *Carduus chamæleon di tus cap tulis plurimis n oribus cæruleis corymbosis ui a f fitis* It grows naturally in the pl ins of Apulia, Thrace, Lemnos, &c

*Carthamus* is of the class and order *Syngenesia Polygamia Æqualis*, and the characters are,

1 CALYX The common calyx is oval, and compofed of numerous leafy fcales, which are broad at their bafe, and fpread open

2 COROLLA The compound flower is uniform The florets are each a funnel-shaped petal, having the limb divided into five erect parts that are nearly equal

3 STAMINA are five very fhort capillary filaments, with a cylindrical tubular anthera

4 PISTILLUM confifts of a very fhort germen, a filiforme ftyle longer than the ftamina, and a fimple ftigma

5 PERICARPIUM There is none The calyx becomes connivent, and encloses the feeds

6 SEMEN The feed is fingle

The receptacle is plain and hairy

Class and order in the Linnæan System The characters

## CHAP CV

## *CASSIA*, WILD SENNA

Description of the Cassia, or Wild Senna

THERE is one fpecies of this genus that is a Perennial, and will live abroad in a warm fituation in our gardens, called Perennial Cassia, or Wild Senna of Maryland

The root is compofed of many black fibres The ftalks rife in the fpring, and die to the root in the autumn They are many, upright, and grow in the fummer to the height of about two feet The leaves are pinnated, the foliolés are oval, oblong, equal, fmooth, and each leaf confifts of eight or nine pair, beautifully arranged along the mid rib The flowers grow from the ends of the branches in loofe fpikes, are of a fine yellow colour, and make a beautiful appearance, they come out in July, but are very feldom, if ever, fucceeded by feeds in our gardens

Method of propagating it

This plant is propagated by fowing of the feeds, which are to be procured from America, and if they are fown in the fpring in a border of light earth, they will readily come up In the autumn a fhare of the plants may be drawn out, and planted in different parts of the garden, leaving the others in the feed-bed at about a foot and a half from each other Thofe in the feed bed will flower the ftrongeft the fummer following, for though thefe plants will grow on being removed, they feldom do fo well afterwards, which fhould caution thofe who have their ground in readinefs, to drop a few feeds in the places where the plants are defigned, gently covering them over with mould, and placing a ftick for a direction to prevent the young plants or feeds being deftroyed thro' inattention in clearing of the garden, in fhort, every expedient fhould be ufed to have this fpecies in perfection, for it is a very beautiful plant, and no garden that makes any pretenfions to a Collection fhould be without it

Titles.

The Perennial Cassia, or Wild Senna of Maryland, is titled, *Cassia foliis octojugis ovato-oblongis æqualibus, glandula bafeos petiolorum* Dillenius calls it, *Cassia mimofæ foliis, fi iqua hi fu a*, and Martin, *Cassia Marilandica, pinnis foliorum oblongis, calyce floris reflexo* It grows naturally in Virginia and Maryland

*Cassia* is of the class and order *Decandria Monogynia*, and the characters are,

Class and order in the Linnæan System The characters

1 CALYX is a perianthium compofed of five lax, concave, coloured deciduous leaves

2 COROLLA confifts of five roundifh concave petals, the lower ones being larger, patent, and more diftant than the others

3 STAMINA are ten declinated filaments, of which the three loweft are the longeft, and the three upper ones the fhorteft The three lower antheræ are large, arched, beaked, and open at the point, the four lateral antheræ open without any beaks, and the three upper ones are very fmall, and have hardly any pollen

4 PISTILLUM confifts of a long, pedunculated, taper germen, a very fhort ftyle, and an obtufe afurgent ftigma

5 PERICARPIUM is an oblong pod, having tranfverfe partitions

6 SEMINA The feeds are roundifh, and affixed to the upper future

## CHAP CVI

## *CATANANCHE*, PERENNIAL CANDY LION's FOOT, or BLUE GUM CICORY.

The plant described

THE Perennial Candy Lion's Foot hath a thick, tough, fibrous root The radical leaves are long, hairy, jagged on their edges, and lie flat on the ground Between these the flower-stalks arise to the height of about two feet, they divide into several branches, and are garnished with a few small hairy, jagged leaves The branches are all terminated by flowers, one head only belongs to a foot-stalk or small branch, they are of a fine blue colour, having purple bottoms, golden antheræ, and silvery cups, they continue in succession from the end of May until September, before which time ripe seeds from the first blown flowers may be gathered This is an elegant species, but there is a variety of it with double flowers, that is much sought after by the curious

Method of propagating the sorts

The single sort is to be propagated by the seeds, and both single and double are easily multiplied by parting of the roots

The seeds should be sown in March, in a bed of light sandy earth, and when the plants come up, the weakest should be drawn out, leaving the others at about three inches asunder When the plants are got tolerably strong they may be removed, with a ball of earth to each root to the places where they are designed to remain, which should be well sheltered, sandy, warm, and dry, otherwise they will be liable to be destroyed by severe weather, for which reason many plant them in pots, and keep them under shelter for a winter or two, before they set them out in the full ground

The roots may be slipt or divided any time in the autumn or spring, when the slips may be directly set in the places where they are to remain, or be planted in the nursery at six inches asunder, to remain there until the autumn following, by which time they will be good plants

When they are planted out for good, always observe that the soil be naturally dry, and the situation well defended, and when they are once set out, let them remain unremoved for five or six years, for this will cause their roots to be large, and send forth many stalks for flowering, making thereby a greater shew by the large quantity of bloom they will produce

Titles

The Perennial Candy Lion's Foot, or Blue Gum Cicory, is titled, *Catananche squamis calycinis inferioribus ovatis* Vaillant calls it, *Catananche cærulea, semiflosculorum ordine simplici*, Caspar Bauhine, *Chondrilla cærulea, cyani capitulo*, and Dodonæus, *Chondrillæ species tertia* It grows naturally in Candia, France, Italy, and Spain

Class and order in the Linnæan system

*Catananche* is of the class and order *Syngenesia Polygamia Æqualis*, and the characters are,

The characters

1 CALYX The common calyx is imbricated, turbinated, bright, and permanent

2 COROLLA The general flower is plain and uniform The florets are each one truncated tongue-shaped petal, that is deeply indented in five parts at the top

3 STAMINA are five very short capillary filaments, having a cylindric, pentagonal, tubular anthera

4 PISTILLUM consists of an oblong germen, a filiforme style the length of the stamina, and two revolute stigmas

5 PERICARPIUM There is none The calyx closes at the top, and holds the seeds

6 SEMINA The seeds are single, compressed, and crowned with a five-pointed pappus

The receptacle is paleaceous

## CHAP. CVII.

## *CENTAUREA*, CENTAURY.

THIS genus swallows up numerous genera of old botanists, so that the number of real species, exclusive of their varieties, must of course be very great The principal perennials belonging to it go by the various names of,

Species.

1 Greater Centaury
2 Yellow Alpine Centaury
3 *Eruca*-leaved Centaury
4 Creeping Blue-Bottle
5 Bitter Blue-Bottle
6 *Jacea*, Common Knapweed, or Matfellon
7 Great Knapweed, or Matfellon
8 Oriental Knapweed
9 Finland Knapweed
10 Mountain Blue-Bottle, or Blue Batchelor's Button
11 Knapweed of Ragusia
12 White Mountain Knapweed
13 Siberian Centaury
14 Evergreen Centaury
15 Hoary *Stoebe*
16 *Behen*
17 White Elecampane leaved Centaury
18 Woad-leaved Centaury

19 Cone-bearing Centaury
20 Cichory-leaved Knapweed
21 Sicilian Knapweed
22 Rock Knapweed
23 Yellow Prickly headed Knapweed
24 Italian *Stoeve*
25 Great Auſtrian Centaury
26 Naked-ſtalk Knapweed
27 Knapweed of Tangier
28 Winged ſtalk Thiſtle of Crete
29 Shrubby Centaury

Greater Centaury. 1 Greater Centaury The Greater Centaury is a very hardy, ſtrong plant The leaves are pinnated and large, the folioles are ſerrated, run along the mid-rib, and their colour is a bright-green The radical ones are long, and ſpread on the ground thoſe of the ſtalks are ſmaller, though of the ſame form, and grow ſingly from the joints of the plants The ſtalks are branching, pointed, upright, and grow to be ſix feet high The flowers are produced ſingly from the ends of the branches, they are of a kind of purple colour, and are longer than the calyx, they come out in July, and the ſeeds ripen in autumn

Yellow Alpine Centaury. 2 Yellow Alpine Centaury The leaves of this ſpecies are long, pinnated, ſmooth, entire, and of a glaucous colour The ſtalks are upright, branching, grow to be four or five feet high, and are garniſhed with ſmall leaves at the joints The flowers grow ſingly from the ends of the branches, their colour is yellow, they come out in July, and their ſeeds ripen in the autumn

Eruca leaved Centaury. 3 *Eruca* leaved Centaury This plant frequently goes by the name of Greater *Stoeve* The radical leaves ſpread themſelves around, are ſpear-ſhaped, indented, ſoft, and woolly The ſtalks riſe to about four feet high, are branching, and garniſhed with ſmall leaves at the joints The flowers are purpliſh, and grow in ſingle heads from the ends of the branches, they come out in July, and ſometimes the ſeeds ripen in the autumn

Creeping Blue Bottle. 4 Creeping Blue Bottle The root of this ſpecies is creeping, and ſpreads itſelf under the ſurface of the mould to a conſiderable diſtance The ſtalks are angular, ſmooth, and branching The leaves are ſpear-ſhaped, indented, and ſmooth on the ſurface, but have a rough border The flowers grow on long, naked, ſlender footſtalks, they are ſmall, have ſilvery cups, come out in June, and ſometimes are ſucceeded by ripe ſeeds

Bitter Blue Bottle. 5 Bitter Blue Bottle The root of this ſpecies is creeping, and the ſtalks (unleſs ſupported) will lie on the ground The leaves are broad, ſpear ſhaped, and entire The flowers grow ſingly on longiſh footſtalks, and are of a fine purple colour, they are moderately large, come out in July and in favourable ſeaſons are ſucceeded by ripe ſeeds in our gardens

Variety. There is a variety of this ſpecies, with long, narrow, hoary leaves, which at preſent is rather ſcarce in our gardens

Jacea. 6 *Jacea*, Common Knapweed, or Matfellon The radical leaves are long, ſpear ſhaped, ſinuated, indented, and of a blackiſh green colour The ſtalk riſes to about a yard high, is garniſhed with leaves, and divides near the top into a few angular branches Each of theſe is crowned by a ſingle head of flowers, of a purple colour, they come out in May and June, and the ſeeds ripen in the autumn

Great Knapweed. 7 Great Knapweed, or Matfellon The leaves are very long, pinnatifid, and the pinnæ are large, ſpear-ſhaped, indented, and of a dark-green colour The ſtalks are large, hairy, branching, and grow to be four or five feet high The flowers are very large, and of a beautiful purple colour, they come out in June and July, and the ſeeds ripen in the autumn

Oriental Knapweed. 8 Oriental Knapweed The radical leaves are very long, and each is compoſed of numerous, ſmooth, ſpear ſhaped pinnæ The ſtalks are branching, grow to be five feet high, and are garniſhed with leaves of the ſame form with the radical ones, but ſmaller The flowers are produced from the ends of the branches, in large ſcaly heads, they grow ſingly on their reſpective footſtalks, and the edges of the ſcales of the cups are ciliated, their colour is yellow, they come out in June, and ſometimes continue in ſucceſſion until the end of Auguſt, ſoon after which ripe ſeed, from the firſt-blown flowers, may be gathered

Finland Knapweed. 9 Finland Knapweed The radical leaves are long and undivided The ſtalks are branching, and garniſhed with a few ſmall narrow leaves The flowers are white, are produced in hairy heads in June and July, and the ſeeds ripen in the autumn

Mountain Blue-Bottle. 10 Mountain Blue-Bottle, or Blue Batchelor's Button This ſpecies hath a creeping root, from which ariſe many ſimple ſtalks to the height of about a foot and half, adorned with leaves The leaves are ſpear ſhaped hoary, and decurrent, and the flowers are produced in oblong heads on the tops of the ſtalks, their colour is blue, they come out in May and June, and their ſeeds ripen in Auguſt

Varieties. There is a dwarf variety of this ſort, and another with broad hoary leaves

Knapweed of Ragufia. 11 Knapweed of Raguſia This is often called the Silvery Knapweed, and in ſome places it goes by the name of the Snowy Mountain *Stoeve* The leaves are pinnatifid, and white with down The folioles are oval, obtuſe, entire, and the exterior ones are the largeſt The ſtalks are upright, ſtiff, branching, and perennial The flowers grow from the ſides of the branches on ſhort footſtalks, they are of a bright yellow colour, and have fine hairy cups; they come out in June and July, and are very ſeldom ſucceeded by good ſeeds in our gardens This ſpecies is rather tender, ſo muſt have a dry rubbiſhy ſoil, in a well ſheltered place

Culture. It may be propagated, like the other, by dividing the roots or ſowing the ſeeds, but it is uſually encreaſed by planting the ſlips or cuttings If theſe are ſet in pots, plunged up to the rims in a ſhady place, in any of the ſummer months, they will readily grow In the autumn they ſhould be ſet in a well-ſheltered place, to be ſcreened from ſevere weather, and in the ſpring ſhould be turned out, with the earth at the roots, into the places where they are to remain

White Mountain Knapweed. 12 White Mountain Knapweed This alſo is rather a tender plant, and ſhould have the ſame favourable treatment as the former The leaves are exceeding white, downy, and compoſed of numerous narrow ſegments The ſtalks are upright, branching near the top, and grow to about a yard high Each of the branches is terminated by a head of purple flowers, growing in hairy cups, they come out in June, and ſometimes the ſeeds ripen in the autumn

Proper ſituation. For want of a very dry rubbiſhy ſoil, in a warm well-ſheltered place, it would be adviſeable to have a few of theſe plants in pots, to be removed into the greenhouſe, or ſet under a hotbed-frame in ſevere weather, otherwiſe there will be great danger of loſing this ſort in the winter

Siberian Centaury. 13 Siberian Centaury The radical leaves are

are pinnatifid and downy. The lobes are spear-shaped, white, decurrent, and the outer one is the largest. The stalks are simple, downy, furrowed, declining, and garnished with a few downy undivided leaves. The flowers grow singly in large, swelling, hairy cups, from the tops of the stalks; their colour is purple, and their appearance is usually in June and July.

Evergreen Centaury.

14. Evergreen Centaury. The stalks of this species are upright and perennial. The leaves are spear-shaped, serrated, and continue all the winter. The flowers are produced in hairy cups, at the ends of the branches; they frequently come out in May, and sometimes this plant will exhibit its bloom in the autumn.

Soil and situation.

This species should have an exceedingly warm situation and a dry soil, or it will be liable to be destroyed by our winter's frosts; on which account a few plants should be set in pots, to be removed under cover in hard weather, like those of the tenth and eleventh sorts.

of Hoary Stoebe.

15. Hoary *Stoebe*. The leaves are pinnatifid, hoary, and the segments are narrow and entire. The stalks are upright, branching, about a yard high, and adorned with winged leaves, growing singly at the joints. The flowers grow singly from the ends of the branches, in oblong, scaly, hairy cups; their colour is purple; they make their appearance in June, and the seeds ripen in August.

Behen.

16. *Behen*. The radical leaves are lyre-shaped, and spread on the ground. Among these arise the stalks, adorned with a few leaves, which embrace it with their base. The flowers are produced from the ends of the branches, in rough scaly cups; their colour is yellow; they come out in July, and sometimes are succeeded by ripe seeds in autumn.

White Elecampane leaved Centaury.

17. White Elecampane-leaved Centaury. The leaves are oval, oblong, slightly indented on their edges, downy underneath, and grow nearly erect, in the manner of those of elecampane. The stalks grow to about a foot and a half high, and are crowned by the flowers, growing singly in large scaly heads; their colour is purple; they come out in July, and in favourable seasons are succeeded by ripe seeds in our gardens.

Woad leaved Centaury.

18. Woad-leaved Centaury. The leaves of this species are large, resembling those of woad. They grow erect, are long, undivided, and form themselves into great tufts. Among these the flower-stalks rise to the height of four or five feet; they are garnished with leaves growing singly at the joints, which are smaller than the radical ones, and are decurrent, having wings or borders running from one to the other. The stalks divide into a few branches near the top, and each of these is terminated by a single head of flowers; their colour is yellow, having scaly cups of a silvery whiteness; they come out in July, and are very rarely succeeded by good seeds in our gardens.

Cone bearing Centaury.

19. Cone-bearing Centaury. The leaves of this species are downy, and the radical ones are spear-shaped, but those on the stalk are pinnatifid. The stalk is unbranching, and grows to about a foot and a half high. The top of it is crowned by a single head of flowers; their colour is a bright-purple, and the cup in which they are contained is very large, scaly, broad at the base, and narrow at the top, where the flowers make their appearance, so as not to be much unlike the cone of the pine-tree. The flowers will be in full blow in June, and the seeds will be ripe in August or early in September.

Culture.

This species is to be propagated very slowly from the root; the seeds therefore should be sown, soon after they are ripe, in a border of common earth. They will readily come up, and require no trouble except thinning them where they are too close, and keeping them clean from weeds until the autumn following, when they may be transplanted to the places where they are designed to remain.

Cichory-leaved Knapweed.

20. Cichory-leaved Knapweed. The leaves of this species are undivided, decurrent, serrated, and prickly. The stalk is winged, having membranes running from the base of one leaf to the other. The top of it is crowned by a head of flowers; these are of a purple colour, and their appearance is in June or July.

Culture.

This species is best propagated from the seeds, and it should have a dry light soil and a well sheltered situation.

Sicilian Knapweed.

21. Sicilian Knapweed. The radical leaves of this species are lyre-shaped, hoary, indented, and rough; those on the stalk are spear-shaped. The flowers terminate the stalks in large, oval, scaly, prickly cups; their colour is yellow, and their appearance about the time of the former.

Rock Knapweed.

22. Rock Knapweed. The leaves of this species are bipinnated and composed of many narrow parts, which often divide or branch into others. The flower-stalk is a little angular, divides sometimes into a few branches near the top, and grows to about a foot and a half high. The flowers are of a yellow colour, present themselves at the top of their scaly cups in June, and are sometimes succeeded by ripe seeds in August.

Situation.

This must have a dry sandy soil and a warm situation.

Yellow Prickly-headed Knapweed.

23. Yellow Prickly-headed Knapweed. The leaves of this species are bipinnated. The stalks are angular, and divide into a few branches near the top, and each of these is crowned by a prickly head of yellow flowers.

Italian Stoebe.

24. Italian *Stoebe*. The leaves of this species are deeply sinuated on their edges, in the manner of the large saws, are moderately large, soft, and woolly. The stalks will grow to be four or five feet high, and are adorned with woolly leaves, like the radical one, but smaller. The flowers are of a pale yellow colour, and shew themselves in large heads at the ends of the branches in June, and sometimes continue in succession through July and August.

Great Austrian Centaury.

25. Great Austrian Centaury. The leaves of this species are spear-shaped, soft, hairy, cut into many segments, and spread flat on the ground. The stalks grow to near a yard high, and are adorned with leaves at the joints, which are spear-shaped and entire. The flowers grow singly in large heads from the ends of the branches; they are of a golden-yellow colour, and their cups are prickly; they come out in July and August, and are never succeeded by ripe seeds in our gardens. It may be propagated by parting of the roots, and should have a dry soil, otherwise the roots are apt to rot in the winter.

Naked-stalked Knapweed.

26. Naked-stalked Knapweed. The first leaves which come out are nearly oval and entire, but the others are spear-shaped, and indented at their base. The stalk is simple, and sometimes entirely naked; at others it is found with one or two narrow leaves, that are indented at their base. The top of the stalk is crowned by one prickly head of flowers; their colour is a reddish-purple, and their time of blow is June or July.

Knapweed of Tangiers.

27. Knapweed of Tangiers. The leaves of this species are spear-shaped, undivided, rigid, serrated, and prickly on their edges. Among these the flower-stalks rise, each supporting one flower,

flower, their colour is blue, and they grow in oblong prickly cups

Winged Stalk Thistle of Crete. 28. Winged Stalk Thistle of Crete. The leaves of this species are downy, sinuated, prickly, and decurrent. The stalks appear winged, from the membranes running from the base of one leaf to another. The flowers are small, and the heads or cups in which they are collected are bristly and prickly; they make their appearance in June and July, and the seeds ripen in the autumn.

Shrubby Centaury. 29. Shrubby Centaury. The root is creeping. The stalks are ligneous, and about two or three feet long. The leaves are spear shaped, smooth, obtuse, and grow on the stalks in great plenty. The flowers are a bright purple, and grow from the tops of the stalks, in large scaly heads; they come out in May, and sometimes continue in succession until the end of September.

Variety. There is a variety of this, with white flowers.

Culture. The culture which differs from the general management of these plants has been pointed out under such sorts as require it; the propagation of all the others is from seeds, or dividing the roots. In some kinds the seeds of several sorts will not ripen in England, and a few species never produce any ripe seeds at all. These are, then, to be procured from the places where they grow naturally; and in the spring all the sorts should be sown in beds of light earth, in a shady part of the seminary. When the plants come up, they must be thinned to proper distances, kept clean from weeds, watered in dry weather, and by the autumn they will be strong plants, and may then be removed to the places where they are designed to flower, which will for the most part be the summer following. But in order to ensure their flowering this summer the more effectually, the best way will be to get the seeds of such as ripen here in the ground in the autumn, and the plants will be forwarder by some weeks than those raised in the spring.

They are also propagated by parting of the roots. The best time for this work is the autumn, but it may successfully be done any time in the winter or spring, before they begin to shoot up for flowering.

Titles. 1. Greater Centaury is titled, *Centaurea calycibus inermibus squamis ovatis, foliis pinnatis foliolis decurrentibus serratis*. Caspar Bauhine calls it, *Centaurium majus, folio in lacinias plures diviso*; and Clusius, *Centaurium majus i vulgare*. It grows naturally in Tartary and on Mount Baldus.

2. Yellow Alpine Centaury is titled, *Centaurea calycibus inermibus squamis ovatis obtusis, foliis pinnatis glabris integerrimis impari serrato*. Caspar Bauhine calls it, *Centaurium Alpinum luteum*; and Cornutus, *Centaurium majus luteum*. It is a native of Baldus.

3. Eruca-leaved Centaury is, *Centaurea calycibus inermibus squamis lanceolatis foliis lanceolatis subdentatis lanuginosis*. Tournefort calls it, *Jacea foliis erucae lanuginosis*; Vaillant, *Amberboi, erucae folio, majus*; and Caspar Bauhine, *Stoebe major, foliis erucae mollibus lanuginosis*. The place of its native habitation is uncertain.

4. Creeping Blue Bottles, *Centaurea calycibus serratis, foliis lanceolatis subpetiolatis dentatis, pedunculis filiformibus aphyllis*. Tournefort calls it, *Jacea orientalis, cyani folio, flore parvo, calyce argenteo*. It is a native of the East.

5. Bitter Blue-Bottle is titled, *Centaurea calycibus serratis, caulibus decumbentibus, foliis lanceolatis integerrimis*. Caspar Bauhine calls it, *Cyanus repens latifolius*; Lobel, *Cyanus repens*; and Boccone, *Jacea saxatilis, longo incano angusto Lechrysi Cretici folio*. It grows naturally in Italy and the south of France.

6. *Jacea*, Common Knapweed, or Matfellon, is titled, *Centaurea scariosis lauris, foliis lanceolatis radicalibus sinuato-dentatis, ramis angulatis*. Caspar Bauhine calls it, *Jacea nigra pratensis latifolia*; Gerard, *Jacea nigra*; and Ray, *Jacea nigra mas, tomentosa, laciniata*. The *Jacea nigra angustifolia, lithospermi arvensis foliis, calice aspero & l..*, of Caspar Bauhine is a variety of this species. It grows naturally in meadows and pastures in England and several parts of Europe.

7. Great Knapweed, or Matfellon, is titled, *Centaurea calycibus ciliatis, foliis pinnatifidis pinnis lanceolatis*. Gerard calls it, *Jacea major*; Parkinson, *Jacea nigra vulgaris laciniata*; Dalechamp, *Scabiosa major*; and Caspar Bauhine, *Scabiosa major, squamatis capitulis*; also, *Scabiosa major altera, squamatis capitulis*. It grows naturally in meadows, fields, and pastures in England and most of the northern parts of Europe.

8. Oriental Knapweed. This is titled, *Centaurea calycibus squamis ciliatis, foliis pinnatifidis pinnis lanceolatis*. In the *Hortus Upsaliensis* it is termed, *Centaurea calycibus ciliatis, foliis pinnatis glabris foliolis lanceolatis integerrimis*. Haller calls it, *Cyanus foliis radicalibus partim integris, partim pinnatis, bracteis calycis ovalis, flore sulphureo*. It grows naturally in Siberia.

9. Finland Knapweed is titled, *Centaurea calycibus recurvato plumosis, foliis indivisis*. In the *Hortus Cliffortianus* it is termed, *Centaurea calycibus ciliatis ciliis setaceis recurvatis*. Clusius calls it, *Jacea 4 Austriaca, capite villoso*. Caspar Bauhine, *Jacea latifolia & angustifolia, capite hirsuto*; also, *Jacea alba, hirsuto capite*. It grows naturally in Finland, Austria, and Switzerland.

10. Mountain Blue Bottle, or Blue Batchelor's Button, is titled, *Centaurea calycibus serratis foliis lanceolatis, decurrentibus, caule simplicissimo*. Boccone calls it, *Cyanus montanus, caule folioso, capitulo oblongo*; Lobel, *Cyanus major*; Caspar Bauhine, *Cyanus montanus latifolius, sive verbasculum cyanoides*; also, *Jacea integrifolia humilis*. It grows naturally on the Austrian and Helvetian Mountains.

11. Knapweed of Ragusia. This is entitled, *Centaurea calycibus ciliatis, foliis tomentosis pinnatifidis, foliolis obtusis ovatis integerrimis exterioribus majoribus*. Morison calls it, *Jacea Cretica lutea, foliis cineris*; Zan, *Jacea arborea argentea Ragusina*; and Barrelier, *Stoebe montana nivea, capite cardui, subrotundis foliorum lobis*. It grows naturally in Crete, and many parts bordering on the Mediterranean.

12. White Mountain Knapweed is titled, *Centaurea calycibus ciliatis terminali sessilibus, foliis tomentosis bipinnatifidis lobis acutis*. Caspar Bauhine calls it, *Jacea montana candidissima, Stoebes foliis*; and Triumphetti, *Jacea cineraria laciniata, flore purpureo*. It is a native of Italy.

13. Siberian Centaury is titled, *Centaurea calycibus ciliatis, foliis tomentosis indivisis pinnatifidisque integerrimis, caule declinato*. Gmelin calls it, *Centaurea calycibus ciliatis subrotundis, foliis pinnatis & integris foliolis simplicissimis extremo maximo*. It is a native of Siberia.

14. Evergreen Centaury is named, *Centaurea calycibus ciliatis, foliis lanceolatis serratis inferioribus hastatis*. Morison terms it, *Jacea Lusitanica sempervirens*. It grows common in Lusitania.

15. Stoebe is titled, *Centaurea calycibus ciliatis oblongis, foliis pinnatifidis linearibus integerrimis*. Caspar Bauhine calls it, *Stoebe incana, cyano similis, tenuifolia*; and Clusius, *Stoebe Austriaca humilis*. It is a native of Austria.

16. Behen is titled, *Centaurea calycibus scariosis,*

*sis, foliis radicalibus lyratis lobis oppositis, caulinis amplexicaulibus*. Vaillant calls it, *Rhaponticoides lutea, foliis inferioribus dissectis, cæteris carthami*; Caspar Bauhine, *Serratulæ affinis, capitulo squamoso luteo ut & flore*, and John Bauhine, *Behen album*. It grows naturally in Asia.

17. White Elecampane-leaved Centaury is, *Centaurea calycibus scariosis, foliis ovato oblongis denticulatis integris petiolatis subtus tomentosis*. Dodonæus calls it, *Rha, sive Rhei ut existimatur*; and Caspar Bauhine, *Rhaponticum folio helenii incano*, also, *Rhaponticum angustifolium incanum*. It grows naturally on the Alps of Switzerland and Verona.

18. Woad leaved Centaury is titled, *Centaurea calycibus scariosis, foliis decurrentibus indivisis integerrimis*. Commeline calls it, *Centaurium majus orientale erectum, glasti folio, flore luteo*. It grows naturally in Siberia and several parts of the East.

19. Coniferous Centaury is titled, *Centaurea calycibus scariosis, foliis tomentosis radicalibus lanceolatis, caulinis pinnatifidis, caule simplici*. Caspar Bauhine calls it, *Jacea montana incana, capite pini*, and Lobel, *Chamæleon non aculeatus*. It grows naturally in the rocky and gravelly parts about Montpelier in France.

20. Cichory-leaved Knapweed is, *Centaurea calycibus setaceo-spinosis, foliis decurrentibus indivisis serrato-spinosis*. Ray calls it, *Jacea foliis cichoreis, caule alato, flore purpureo*. It grows naturally on Mount Argentarius.

21. Sicilian Knapweed is titled, *Centaurea calycibus ciliato spinosis, foliis decurrentibus lyratis inermibus incanis, capitulis terminalibus*. Mignol calls it, *Jacea Sicula, cichorei folio, flore luteo, capite spinoso*. It is a native of Sicily.

22. Rock Knapweed is titled, *Centaurea calycibus ciliatis spinosis, foliis bipinnatis linearibus*. Caspar Bauhine calls it, *Jacea laciniata lutea*, and Columna, *Jacea montana minima tenuifolia*. It is a native of Italy.

23. Yellow Prickly-headed Knapweed is, *Centaurea calycibus ciliatis inermi-spinosis, foliis bipinnatifidis, caule angulato*. Caspar Bauhine calls it, *Jacea lutea, capite spinoso*, and Clusius, *Jacea luteo flore*. It grows naturally in Spain, Italy, and the south of France.

24. Italian *Stoebe*. This is titled, *Centaurea calycibus setula reflexa spinosis glabris, foliis lyrato runcinatis, serratis*. Morison calls it, *Jacea major, foliis cichoraceis mollibus flore stramineo*, Caspar Bauhine, *Jacea major, foliis cichoraceis mollibus lanuginosis*, and Clusius, *Stoebe Salmantica* I. It grows naturally in the south of Europe.

25. Great Austrian Centaury is, *Centaurea calycibus setaceo-spinosis, foliis lanceolatis petiolatis inferne dentatis*. Boerhaave calls it, *Centaurium majus, folio molli acuto laciniato, flore aureo magno, calyce spinoso*. It grows naturally in many of the southern parts of Europe.

26. Naked-stalked Knapweed is, *Centaurea calycibus setaceo-spinosis, foliis runcinatis supra subdentatis, caule simplici nudiusculo unifloro*. Hermann calls it, *Jacea folio cerinthes, pannonica, flore, e rubro violaceo*; and Barrelier, *Jacea inbacea, capite rubro spinoso*. It grows naturally in Italy.

27. Knapweed of Tangiers is, *Centaurea calycibus margine spinosis, foliis lanceolatis radicalibus serrato-subspinosis, caulibus unifloris*. Haller calls it, *Cyanus foliis ellipticis dentatis rigidis, floribus cæruleis oblongis*, and Herman, *Cnicus perennis cæruleus Tingitanus*. It grows naturally about Tangier.

28. Winged-stalk Thistle of Crete is, *Centaurea calycibus setaceo-spinosis, foliis decurrentibus-sinuatis spinosis*. Caspar Bauhine calls it, *Carduus tomentosus, capitulo minore*; John Bauhine, *Carduus galactites*, and Tournefort, *Carduus Creticus non maculatus, caule alato*. It grows common in the south of Europe.

29. Shrubby Centaury is titled, *Centaurea calycibus inermibus oblongis, foliis lanceolatis obtusiusculis glabris, caule frutescente*. Caspar Bauhine calls it, *Cyanus repens angustifolius*, Tournefort, *Jacea frutescens, plantaginis folio, flore albo*, and Vaillant, *Rhaponticoides frutescens, oleæ folio*. It grows naturally in Crete, and in the East.

*Centaurea* is of the class and order *Syngenesia Polygamia Frustranea*, and the characters are, Class and order in the Linnæan system

1. CALYX. The common calyx is imbricated, roundish, and the scales are variously terminated.

2. COROLLA. The compound flower varies in appearance in the different species. The hermaphrodite florets are many in the disk, the female florets are fewer in the radius, but they are larger and more loosely disposed. The characters

The hermaphrodite florets are each of one petal. The tube is slender, the limb ventricose, oblong, erect, and terminated by five narrow erect segments.

The female florets are each of one petal. The tube is recurved, slender, and enlarges gradually, the limb is oblong, oblique, and unequally divided.

3. STAMINA are five very short capillary filaments, having a cylindrical tubular anthera, the length of the corollula.

4. PISTILLUM of the hermaphrodite florets consists of a small germen, a filiforme style the length of the stamina, and an obtuse stigma. The pistil of the female florets consists of a very small germen, without any stigma, and hardly any style.

5. PERICARPIUM. There is none. The connivent calyx encloses the seed.

6. SEMINA. The seeds of the hermaphrodite florets are single, the female florets are barren. The receptacle is setose.

CHAP

# CHAP. CVIII.

## *CERASTIUM*, MOUSE-EAR CHICKWEED.

Species. THE species of this genus are named,

1 Corn Mouse Ear Chickweed.
2 Mountain Mouse Ear Chickweed.
3 Creeping Mouse Ear Chickweed, or Sea-Pink.
4 Austrian Mouse-Ear Chickweed.
5 Marsh Mouse-Ear Chickweed.
6 Broad-leaved Mouse-Ear Chickweed.
7 Woolly Mouse-Ear Chickweed.
8 Shrubby Mouse Ear Chickweed.

Description of the Corn, 1 Corn Mouse-Ear Chickweed. This is by some called the Wild Pink, by others the Wild Sea-Pink. The root is fibrous and tough. The stalks are slender, short, weak, and lie on the ground. The leaves are narrow, spear-shaped, obtuse, smooth, and of a whitish-green colour. The flowers are produced from the ends of the stalks, in May and June; they are of a whitish colour, and are succeeded by ripe seeds in July or August.

Mountain, 2 Mountain Mouse-Ear Chickweed. This species has a creeping root, which sends forth several weak stalks, that divide into smaller branches. The flowers are large, and of a snowy whiteness; they come forth in June, and the seeds ripen in August.

Creeping, 3 Creeping Mouse-Ear Chickweed. The general name for this species used to be the Sea-Pink, and was formerly cultivated for edgings in gardens. It is a creeper, both with respect to the roots and branches, for the latter are weak, slender, lie on the ground and strike root from the joints. The leaves are hoary, spear shaped, and grow opposite to each other at the joints. The flowers are white, and produced from the ends and sides of the stalks on slender footstalks; they come out in May, and the seeds ripen in July.

Austrian, 4 Austrian Mouse-Ear Chickweed. The stalks of this species are weak, smooth, and procumbent. The leaves are narrow, smooth, and sharp pointed. The flowers grow one or two only on a footstalk; they are yellow, large, and very beautiful, come out in June, and are succeeded by round capsules containing the seeds.

Marsh, 5 Marsh Mouse-Ear Chickweed. This species grows common in our marshy grounds, by the sides of rivers and moist places, and is never brought into gardens unless to afford variety in some moist and watery parts. The root is creeping, full of fibres, and sends forth many round slender-jointed stalks. The leaves are heart-shaped, sessile, and grow opposite to each other at the joints. The flowers grow singly from the tops of the branches; they are small, whitish, come out in May and June, and are succeeded by long capsules containing the seeds.

Broad-leaved, 6 Broad-leaved Mouse-Ear Chickweed. The stalks of this species are slender, short, and a little branching. The leaves are oval, broad, downy, and garnish the plant in great plenty. The flowers grow singly from the tops of the branches; they are of a purplish colour, come out in June and July, and the seeds ripen in September.

Woolly, 7 Woolly Mouse-Ear Chickweed. The stalks of this species are slender, lie on the ground, and strike root at the joints. The leaves are oblong, spear-shaped, and downy. The flowers grow from the ends and sides of the branches, on branching footstalks; they come out in June, and are succeeded by globular capsules, containing ripe seeds, in August.

and Shrubby Mouse-Ear Chickweed. 8 Shrubby Mouse-Ear Chickweed. The stalks of this species are ligneous, perennial, and (unless supported) lie on the ground. The leaves are narrow, spear-shaped, rigid, and slightly covered with hair. The flowers are produced from the upper parts of the stalks in June and July, and the seeds ripen in August or September.

Proper situation. These sorts are all exceeding hardy, and will grow in any soil or situation. They are most of them natives of rocky mountains and sandy parts of the world, and therefore proper for such places which frequently happen in gardens in romantic situations of an extensive nature. They will grow exceeding well from the crevices of old walls, and are proper for grottos, in which places they will strike root, constantly flower, and have a very pretty effect.

They may be encreased by sowing of the seeds, or parting of the roots, and in doing of this you can hardly miss of the right way, especially if the seeds are sown in the spring, and the roots parted in the autumn.

Titles. 1 Corn Mouse-Ear Chickweed is titled, *Cerastium foliis lineari-lanceolatis obtusis glabris, corollis calyce majoribus*. In the *Hortus Cliffortianus* it is termed, *Cerastium foliis calycibusque hirsutis*. Vaillant calls it, *Myosotis arvensis hirsuta, flore majore*; and Caspar Bauhine, *Caryophyllus arvensis hirsutus, flore majore*. It is a native of England, and most of the southern countries of Europe.

2 Mountain Mouse-Ear Chickweed is, *Cerastium foliis ovato-lanceolatis, caule [illegible], capsulis oblongis*. In the *Flora Suecica* it is termed, *Cerastium foliis ovato-lanceolatis, corollis calyce majoribus*; and in the *Flora Lapponica*, *Cerastium corollis calyce majore*. Van Royen calls it, *Cerastium foliis lanceolato-[illegible], caule [illegible] flore*; and Ray, *Alsine myosotis [illegible] flore amplo niveo, repens*. It grows naturally in England, and in mountainous parts in most countries of Europe.

3 Creeping Mouse-Ear Chickweed, or Sea-Pink. This is titled, *Cerastium foliis [illegible], pedunculis ramosis, capsulis [illegible]*. In the *Hortus Cliffortianus* it is termed, *Cerastium [illegible] procumbens*. Van Royen calls it, *Cerastium [illegible] perenne procumbens, foliis lanceolatis tomentosis*; Vaillant, *Myosotis arvensis, polygoni folio*; Columna, *Ocymoides [illegible]*; and C. Bauhine, *Lychnis [illegible] repens*. It is a native of Gaul and Italy.

4 Austrian Mouse-Ear Chickweed is, *Cerastium foliis [illegible] bus connatis glabris, pedunculis [illegible], capsulis globosis*. Scheuchzer calls it, *Alsine [illegible] folio*; and Burser, *Caryophyllus holosteus alpinus, foliis [illegible] glabris [illegible], flore magno*. It grows naturally on the Austrian Mountains.

5 Marsh

5 Marsh Mouse-Ear Chickweed is titled, *Cerastium foliis* [illegible] *floribus solitariis, ramis pendulis* Caspar Bauhine calls it, *Alsine aquatica major*, and John Bauhine *Alsine major repens perennis* It grows naturally by brook sides and watery places in England, and most parts of Europe

6 Broad-leaved Mouse-Ear Chickweed is titled, *Cerastium foliis ovatis subtomentosis, ramis sub-unifloris, capsulis globosis* Caspar Bauhine calls it, *Caryophyllus holosteus Alpinus latifolius* It is a native of the Alps of Switzerland

7 Woolly Mouse-Ear Chickweed is titled, *Cerastium foliis oblongis tomentosis, pedunculis ramosis, capsulis globosis* Sauvages calls it, *Cerastium foliis lanceolato-lineatis subhirsutis, corolla calycem superante*, Caspar Bauhine, *Caryophyllus holosteus tomentosus latifolius*, also, *Caryophyllus holosteus tomentosus angustifolius* Ray terms it, *Alsine myosotis lanuginosa Alpina grandiflora, seu auricula muris villosa, flore amplo membranaceo* It is a native of Granada, and is also found in some parts of Wales

8 Shrubby Mouse-Ear Chickweed is titled *Cerastium caule perenni procumbente, foliis* [illegible] *subulatis* Tournefort calls it, [illegible] *tenuissimo folio* [illegible] It grows naturally in the south of Europe

*Cerastium* is of the class and order *Decandria Pentagynia*, and the characters are

1 CALYX is a permanent perianthium composed of five oval, spear-shaped, acute, patent leaves

2 COROLLA consists of five bifid, obtuse, erect, patent petals, about the same length with the cup

3 STAMINA These are ten slender filaments, shorter than the corolla They are alternately shorter, and have roundish antheræ

4 PISTILLUM consists of an oval germen, and five capillary, erect styles the length of the stamina, having obtuse stigmas

5 PERICARPIUM is an oval, cylindrical, or else a globular, obtuse capsule It consists of one cell, and opens at the top

6 SEMINA The seeds are many and roundish

Class and order in the Linnæan System. The characters

# CHAP CIX

## CERATOPHYLLUM

OF this genus are two common species, which grow naturally in ditches and ponds almost every where, called,

Species

1 Rough-horned Pond Weed
2 Smooth-horned Pond Weed

Rough-horned,

1 Rough-horned Pond Weed The root is fibrous, and strikes deep into the mud The stalks are about two feet long, creeping, and usually wholly immersed under the water The leaves are numerous, rough to the touch, of a dusky green colour, and divided into four segments, called Horns The flowers come out from the wings of the leaves They are small, greenish, and are to be found in the greatest plenty in July

and Smooth-horned Pond Weed described

2 Smooth-horned Pond Weed The stalks are like the preceding generally immersed, and strike root into the mud from the sides The leaves are smooth and branch out into six, eight, or more segments called Horns The flowers are produced from the wings of the leaves They are small, greenish, and appear about the same time with the former

Titles

1 The first species is entitled, *Ceratophyllum foliis dichotomo bigeminis, fructibus trispinosis* Vaillant calls it, *Hydroceratophyllum folio aspero quatuor cornibus armato*, and Loesel, *Equisetum sub aqua repens, foliis bifurcis* It grows naturally in ditches and ponds all over Europe

2 The second species is titled, *Ceratophyllum foliis dichotomo-trigeminis, fructibus muticis* Vaillant calls it, *Hydroceratophyllum folio lævi octo cornibus armato* It is common in waters in most parts of Europe

*Ceratophyllum* is of the class and order *Monoecia Polyandria*, and the characters are,

Class and order in the Linnæan System The character

1 Male Flowers

1 CALYX is a perianthium, divided into many equal, awl-shaped segments

2 COROLLA There is none

3 STAMINA are from sixteen to twenty scarcely conspicuous filaments, having oblong, erect antheræ, which are longer than the calyx

2 Female Flowers

1 CALYX is a perianthium, divided into many awl-shaped, equal segments

2 COROLLA There is none

3 PISTILLUM consists of an oval, compressed germen, without any style, but an obtuse, oblique stigma

4 PERICARPIUM There is none

5 SEMEN is an oval, unilocular, acuminated nut.

# CHAP. CX.

## *CERINTHE*, HONEYWORT

THERE are only two species of this genus, and that which belongs to this place is usually called,

Species described. *Cerinthe Minor*, or, Smaller Honeywort

The stalks are slender, and grow to about two feet high. The leaves are undivided, embrace the stalks with their base, and are of a bluish green colour. The flowers are of a yellow colour, come out in June and July, and the seeds ripen in September.

There is a notable variety of this species of larger growth, having leaves spotted and indented. It flowers and ripens the seeds at about the same time with the former.

Culture. The propagation of these sorts is by sowing the seeds in the autumn, soon after they are ripe, though it may be done with good success in the spring following. After the plants have flowers, they will shed their seeds and constantly afford a full stock without further trouble. These plants always shewed themselves but of short duration in my gardens, but I have been informed, that in some mountainous situations their roots will continue for many years.

Titles. *Cerinthe Minor*, or, Smaller Honeywort, is titled, *Cerinthe foliis amplexicaulibus integris, fructibus geminis, corollis acutis clausis*. Haller calls it, *Cerinthe foliis caulem amplexantibus, floribus profunde quinquefidis*, Caspar Bauhine, *Cerinthe Minor*, and Clusius, *Cerinthe Minor* ſ *quarta*. The variety with spotted, indented leaves in the former edition of the *Species Plantarum*, stood as a distinct species with the title of, *Cerinthe foliis amplexicaulibus emarginatis, corollis acutis clausis*. Caspar Bauhine names this, *Cerinthe* ſ *Cynoglossum montanum majus*. They are both found growing in Austria, and several of the southern countries of Europe.

Class and order in the Linnæan System. *Cerinthe* is of the class and order *Pentandria Monogynia*, and the characters are,

1 CALYX is a permanent perianthium, divided into five oblong, equal parts.

2 COROLLA is a bell-shaped petal. The tube is thick and short. The limb is tubular, ventricose, and rather thicker than the tube. It is cut at the brim into five segments, and the mouth is open and pervious.

3 STAMINA are five very short, awl-shaped filaments, with acute, erect antheræ.

4 PISTILLUM consists of a germen divided into four parts, a filiforme style the length of the stamina, and an obtuse stigma.

5 PERICARPIUM. There is none. The seeds are inclosed in the calyx.

6 SEMINA. The seeds are two, osseous, nearly oval, plain on one side, and convex on the other.

# CHAP. CXI.

## *CHÆROPHYLLUM*, WILD CHERVIL.

Introductory Remarks. THE Wild Cicely, or, Cow Weed, and Wild Chervil of our fields and pastures, belong to this genus, and also some other sorts that are extirpated as weeds from gardens. The following perennials, however, though of no extraordinary beauty, cause variety, and, as such, may claim a place in our collection of plants.

Species.
1 Golden-seeded Wild Chervil
2 Hairy White and Red-flowered Wild Chervil
3 Aromatick Wild Chervil

Description of the Golden-seeded. 1 The Golden seeded Wild Chervil sends forth several hairy leaves cut into many segments. From among these arise the stalks to about two feet high. The flowers adorn their crowns in spreading umbels. Their colour is white, and they are succeeded by yellow, striated seeds.

Hairy White and Red-flowered. 2 Hairy White and Red-flowered Wild Chervil. The stalks of this species are equal, channelled, and will grow to about a yard high. The leaves are exceeding hairy, and composed of numerous broad segments, so that they form a large, and finely-divided leaf. The flowers terminate the stalks in very large umbels. Some of them are of a red colour, others white, and often the same umbel will exhibit flowers of both these colours, on which account this sort is chiefly valued.

Aromatick Wild Chervil. 3 Aromatick Wild Chervil. The stalks of this species are equal, and of a strong scent. The leaves are large, and composed of many heart-shaped, oval, serrated, hairy segments, which emit a kind of aromatick odour. The flowers are formed into large, spreading umbels, at the tops of the stalks. They appear in June or July, and are succeeded by oblong, pointed fruit, containing the seeds.

Culture. A few plants of all these sorts will be sufficient for the largest garden, and in order to raise them, let some seeds be sown in any part of it, soon after they are ripe, they will readily come up, and soon after that, the weakest should be drawn out, leaving only a few of the strongest plants for observation and variety. These plants will often

often scatter their seeds, from which plenty of fresh plants will rise, and give you more stock than you desire

Titles

1 The Golden-seeded Wild Chervil is titled, *Chaerophyllum caule aequali foliolis incisis seminibus coloratis striatis* Morison calls it, *Myrrhis perennis alba minor, foliis hirsutis, semine aureo*, and Haller, *Myrrhis caule geniculato perenni, foliis subhirsutis, seminibus flavis obscure striatis* It grows naturally in Germany

2 Hairy White and Red-flowered Wild Chervil This is titled, *Chaerophyllum caule aequali, foliolis incisis acutis, seminibus fibrillatis* In the *Hortus Cliffortianus* it is termed, *Chaerophyllum foliolis dissectis, petiolis ramisque venosis utrinque membranaceis* Morison calls it, *Cerefolium latifolium hirsutum album & rubrum*, John Bauhine, *Cicutaria latifolia hirsuta*, and Haller, *Myrrhis seminibus strictis longissimis* It grows naturally in Switzerland

3 Aromatick Wild Chervil is titled, *Chaerophyllum caule aequali foliolis cordatis serratis integris* In the *Hortus Cliffortianus* it is titled, *Chaerophyllum foliolis lanceolato-ovatis serratis integris* Boccone calls it, *Cerefolium, rugoso angelicae folio, aromaticum*, and Rivinus, *Angelica podagrariae folio* It grows naturally in Istria

*Chaerophyllum* is of the class and order *Pentandria Digynia*, and the characters are,

Class and order in the Linnaean System The characters

1 CALYX The general umbel is patent The partial is composed of nearly the like number of rays

There is no general involucrum The partial involucrum is composed of about five spear-shaped, concave reflexed leaves, almost the length of the umbellulae The proper perianthium is obsolete

2 COROLLA The general corolla is nearly uniform The florets have each five inflexed, heart-shaped petals, of which the exterior ones are rather the largest

3 STAMINA consist of five simple filaments the length of the umbellulae, with roundish antherae

4 PISTILLUM consists of a germen situated below the flower, and two reflexed styles, with obtuse stigmas

5 PERICARPIUM There is none The fruit is oval, oblong, pointed, and divided into two parts

6 SEMINA The seeds are two, one being in each of the parts They are oblong, attenuated at the top, convex on one side, and plain on the other

# CHAP CXII

## *CHARA*

Introductory Remarks

Of this genus are four distinct species, all of which grow naturally in ditches, standing waters, and moist places in England, and are never cultivated plants I introduce them here for the sake of the curious Botanist, and not for the common Gardener's observation They are called,

Species

1 Common *Chara*, or, Stinking Water Horsetail

2 Brittle *Chara*, or, Coralline Horsetail

3 Prickly *Chara*

4 Smooth *Chara*

Common,

1 Common *Chara* The root is fibrous and creeping The stalks are round, slender, smooth, striated, jointed, branching, partly procumbent, and two or three feet long The leaves are small, oblong, and cut or jagged on their edges The seeds are small, oval, glossy, and the whole plant has a disagreeable smell

Brittle

2 Brittle *Chara* The stalks are numerous, round, jointed, striated, a foot and a half high, and armed with thick, strong spines at the joints The leaves are long, narrow, of a greyish colour, and come out all round the stalks at the joints The whole plant is extremely brittle, and of a coralline taste when chewed

Prickly,

3 Prickly *Chara* The stalks are numerous, slender, branching, round, procumbent, and beset with a great number of long, slender prickles The leaves are long, narrow, slender, and stand thick at the joints The whole plant is of a greyish green colour, and creeping under the water

and Smooth Chara described

4 Smooth *Chara* The stalks are slender, hollow, jointed, less brittle than any of the sorts, and have no spines at the joints The leaves are numerous, long and narrow, and usually of a brownish green colour

Titles

1 Common *Chara*, or, Stinking Water Horsetail, is titled, *Chara caulibus inermibus frondibus interne dentatis* In the *Flora Lapponica* it is termed, *Chara vulgaris* Van Royen calls it, *Chara caulibus laevibus*, Vaillant, *Chara vulgaris foetida* and Caspar Bauhine, *Equisetum foetidum sub aquâ repens* It grows naturally in ditches and standing waters in most parts of Europe

2 Brittle *Chara*, or, Coralline Horsetail, is titled *Chara aculeis caulinis ovatis* Morison calls it, *Equisetum fragile majus subcinereum aquis immersum*, Plukenet, *Equisetum sive Hippuris lacustris, foliis mansu arenosis*, and Gerard, *Equisetum sive hippuris coralloides* It grows naturally in ditches and standing water in most countries of Europe

3 Prickly *Chara* is titled, *Chara aculeis caulinis capillaribus confertis* In the *Hortus Cliffortianus* it is termed, *Chara caulibus aculeatis* Vaillant calls it, *Chara major, caulibus spinosis*, and Plukenet, *Equisetum sive hippuris muscosus sub aqua repens* It grows naturally in ditches, &c in most countries of Europe

4 Smooth *Chara* is titled, *Chara caulibus ... inermibus diaphanis superne latioribus* Ray calls it, *Chara transfluens minor flexilis* It grows naturally in ditches and ponds in England, and most countries of Europe

*Chara* is of the class and order *Cryptogamia Algae*, and all the known characters are,

Class and order in the Linnaean system The characters

1 CALYX is very small, and composed of two leaves

2 COROLLA There is none

3 STAMINA

3 STAMINA There are no filaments, but there is one globular anthera affixed to the receptacle

4 PISTILLUM consists of an oval germen, and three broadish stigmas without any style

5 PERICARPIUM There is none

6 SEMEN The seed is single, oval, and oblong

# CHAP CXIII

## *CHEIRANTHUS*, STOCK JULY FLOWER and WALL FLOWER.

Introductory remarks

THE two celebrated species of the *Cheiranthus* are what have been long known by the names of Stock July Flower and Wall Flower, names very vague and uncertain, and which convey no manner of idea of the plants they express To call a plant July Flower, can be no proper distinction, as thousands of plants will be in blow in that month, and to call a plant a Wall Flower is equally ridiculous, because many old walls in one part or other exhibit in bloom a no very inconsiderable share of the flowering tribe

They are known, however, by those names to the whole world They have been in use for ages to express them by The plants themselves are common, and the very mention of the names conveys a direct idea of the plants meant by them So that I shall not endeavour to put the Gardener out of his old road, but shall treat of these two noted species under the well known titles of,

Species

1 The July Flower, or, Stock Gilliflower
2 The Wall Flower

Stock July Flower described

At first the Stock July Flower ought in one sense to be ranked as a biennial, for this rises the first year, and in the second is in its full glory, and, like the hollylocks, frequently dies off in the autumn But as it will often continue for many years, we will grant it a place with its brethren, the Wall Flowers, with this precaution to the Gardener, not to depend upon it as such, but annually to raise his flowers for a succession, and consider them as biennials only

The root of the Stock July Flower is white, fibrous, and thick The plant in some of the varieties will grow to near a yard in height The stalk is woody and tough It is single, branching regularly near the top, and covered with a light down The leaves are spear shaped, their edges are entire, they are covered with a downy matter, and their colour is a kind of bluish green The branches are terminated by the flowers, which grow in loose spikes, and possess the utmost purity of fragrance, but that is often tainted by the scent arising from the stalks and leaves, for these, when heated, themselves emit a disagreeable odour, which too often overpowers the natural sweetness of the flower itself

This species varies without bounds in colouring, but the most remarkable varieties are,

Varieties

The Purple Red, or, Queen stock Gilliflower
The Deep Red, or, Brumpton Stock July Flower
The White Stock July Flower
The [illegible] Stock July Flower
The Cheiranthus Wall [illegible] *Cheiranthus*
[illegible], tendencies, and properties It is in their double state we chiefly admire them, and if care be taken in gathering of the seeds the chance for double flowers will be great enough From the full double flowers no seeds can be expected, the parts of generation being obliterated by the multiplicity of petals The seeds gathered from single flowers will for the most part produce single flowers again So that we must search for such flowers as are not either entirely single, or full double The natural number of the petals is four, so that whenever we find a flower with more than four petals, it has a tendency towards a double state Let such flowers, therefore, be marked for the seeds, observing always to preserve those flowers that have the most petals, for the greater the certainty will be of the seeds And I have known Semi-double produce such seeds, as to raise plants among which a single one was hardly to be found

Culture

Having, therefore, obtained good seeds from the proper sorts, sow them in May, and not earlier for if they are sown before, they will be grown too luxuriant before the winter comes on, and if it should happen to be a severe one, or very wet, the plants will be destroyed At the first appearance of the seedlings, they are subject to be destroyed by insects, if the weather happens dry, like turneps and radishes They must, therefore, be constantly watered in such weather, covered with mats in the heat of the day, always uncovered in the evenings, and in the night the dews and rain must be admitted, if it should happen Keep your beds clean from weeds, and when the seedlings are about an inch and a half high, transplant them to a dry, ungunged well-sheltered bed, set them at about a foot asunder, and the May following they will treat you with a profusion of their fragrant flowers, of different colours and odours, when the best flowers should be again marked for their seeds to keep up the succession, for the greatest share of these plants will die in the autumn

In order, therefore, to have them perennial, sow the seeds on a dry, rubbishy, or sandy spot of the garden, let them remain untransplanted, and the roots will strike deep into the ground, and being less liable to be destroyed by frost or wet, the stalks will become woody, and remain for years, constantly exhibiting their bloom in summer and autumn, and will continue to produce flowers if the earlier part of the winter should prove mild, until Christmas

These plants are also propagated by planting of the slips in a shady, moist place, in the summer months, and this is by many used for the finest and best double flowers but is a method not worth putting into practice, for plants thus raised

raised always look unthriving, hardly ever flower freely, and the name St ted July Flower seems with propriety to belong to the Whereas those from seeds appear healthy and strong, the flowers be large, and if the seed has been saved with tolerable care, there will be no fear of having D ers enough However, this w n y ven the to n, that one good double flower raised from seed is worth twenty, as they usually come, when propagated from slips or cuttings

The Queen Stock is one of the lowest-growing sorts It seldom rises to more than about a foot high, and will be covered with flowers of a pale but luscious red, w a grant The wh kinds grow rather t , and will be more subject to die in moist cold places, than any of the others

The Brompton Stock is one of the highest-growing kinds It will d to eight, long spike wh ed with large and grand flowers, of a deep red, which make a fine appearance

The Variegated sorts are ch fing These generally grow taller, are more woody and branching than the other sorts, and will remain for years in a dry situation Their stripes are of different colours, and they appear like flowering shrubs among the different parts of our gardens

The Clustered Wall-leaved *Cheiranthus* is a species of itself, but as it belongs to this it may The root is The stalk is thick, n ed, and erect The leaves terminate the top of it in large clusters The are sessile and recurved, are waved on their edges, and very downy They are spear shaped, but their points are obtuse The flowers are purple, and grow from the sides of the stalks in pale They resemble the other sorts of the Stock July Flower, to which this species is so nearly allied, that it can hardly be called more than a variety of them This must have a very dry, warm situation, or there will be great loss losing it the first winter, and it generally dies the autumn after it has flowered

Wall Flower described — Of Wall Flowers The variety of the Wall Flowers is not, the parent of them all is the Common Wall Flower, or Single Yellow July Flower, that grows naturally on the old walls at Leicester, and many other parts of England The root of this plant is long, ligneous, and tough The stalks also are tough and woody; their height will be different in different situations and soils, they are branches that are irregular, and are covered with a whitish bark The leaves are spear-shaped, smooth, and acute The flowers are produced in spikes from the ends of the branches They are yellow, very fragrant, and show themselves in full blow from old walls during most of the summer months This common and neglected plant is the parent of the following varieties

Varieties
The Winter Wall Flower
The Common Double Wall Flower
The Dwarf Double Wall Flower
The Large-growing Double Wall Flower
The Bloody Wall Flower
The Double Bloody Wall Flower
The Old Double Bloody Wall Flower
The White Wall Flower
The Cream-coloured Wall Flower
The Variegated Wall Flower

All these sorts are valuable in our gardens The first sort is a flower and will not only blow in spring, but fresh bloom in November, and if the season proves mild, will continue flowering the greatest part of winter

The other sorts are well known, but it is the Double Bloody Wall Flower that note esteem The White, the Cream-colour d, and the Variegated, are varieties, and by saving of the seeds, more varieties may be still obtained, with spikes of flowers larger, than from plants raised old way

Culture. In order, therefore, to raise these plants from seeds, let such be saved as have the best properties, that is, the largest, the most healthy and regular-growing plants, which have the deepest colour, and more than four petals in the flower Let all the single flowers be picked off, and leave only as to form combs, be preserved for seed

Sow the seeds in the spring, in any soil or situation, and they will readily come up Keep them clean from weeds, water them now and then, and when they are about two or three inches high, plant them out where they are designed to remain If the soil is naturally good, the plants will be very luxuriant, look healthy, and have a great height The flowers also will be larger and finer than if planted in a poor soil, but they will be more liable to be destroyed by wet and bad weather, so that if you desire they should continue, and are contented to see them in a less perfect state, the best way will be to sow the seeds in the most hungry, gravelly, rubbishy, dry part of the garden, and let them remain unremoved When this is done, thin them where they come up too thick, place the flowering plants at about a foot distance from each other and, as they show their flowers and spread, make still more room, by pulling up the worst, and throwing them away

By slips also these plants are easily propagated Plant them in May, in a shady border, and water them until they have taken root, keep them clean from weeds all summer, and in the autumn remove them to the places where they are designed to blow This management suits the nature of the Wall Flower better by far than the Stock Gilliflower, and, indeed, is the best method of multiplying the valuable kinds of these plants

Titles 1 The Stock July Flower is titled, *Cheiranthus foliis lanceolatis integerrimis obtusis incanis, siliquis apice truncatis compressis, caule suffruticoso* Caspar Bauhine calls it, *Leucojum, incano folio, hortense*, and Lobel, *Viola alba & purpurea* It grows naturally on the sea coasts of Spain

The Clustered Wall-leaved *Cheiranthus* is titled, *Cheiranthus caule indiviso, foliis confertocapitatis recurvis undulatis* It is not certain where this plant flourishes in a state of nature

2 The Wall Flower This is titled, *Cheiranthus foliis lanceolatis acutis glabris, ramis angulatis* Caspar Bauhine has given titles to several of the varieties as real species, and distinguished them by the terms, *Leucojum luteum vulgare*, *Magno flore*, *Grandiore flore*, *Pleno flore*, and the like Dodonaeus calls it, *Leucojum luteum* It grows naturally on old walls in England, Switzerland, France and Spain

Class and order in the Linnaean system. *Cheiranthus* is of the class and order *Tetradynamia Siliquosa*, and the characters are,

The characters. 1 CALYX is a compressed perianthium, composed of four spear-shaped, concave, erect, connivent, deciduous leaves, of which the two outer are swelling at their base

2 COROLLA consists of four roundish petals longer than the calyx, and placed opposite, in form of a cross

3 STAMINA consist of six subulated, parallel filaments the length of the calyx, two of which are between the globous leaves of the calyx, and are rather shorter Their antheræ are erect, bifid at the base, and acute and reflexed at the top

A nectariferous glandule surrounds the base of the shorter filaments

4 PISTILLUM consists of a four-cornered prismatick germen the length of the stamina, and marked on both sides with a kind of glandule, a very short, compressed style, and an oblong, thickish, divided, reflexed, permanent stigma

5 PERICARPIUM is a long, compressed pod

6 SEMINA The seeds are numerous, suboval, and compressed.

## CHAP. CXIV.

## *CHELIDONIUM*, CELANDINE.

THERE is only one Perennial species of this genus called Celandine It is a plant well known in medicine, and consists of two notable varieties, which usually go by the names of,

Varieties — The Common Greater Celandine

The Jagged leaved Celandine

Celandine described — Celandine hath a thick, knobby root, which, being broken, emits a yellow juice The stalks are round, hairy, branching, jointed, and grow to two feet, or a yard high The leaves are large, and composed of many folioles, which are indented or jagged on their edges The flowers are of a golden yellow colour, come out from the tops of the stalks in May and June, and the seeds ripen soon after the flowers are fallen

These sorts are admirable in medicine, on which account they are chiefly valued They grow common in lanes and road-sides in many parts of England, and ought not to be admitted into gardens, except where there are very extensive collections, and even then, unless there be no plants to be found near at hand for observation and use For they are by no means captivating, being possessed of a strong, disagreeable odour, which to most people is highly offensive The time of gathering these plants for medicinal uses is May, when they are in full flower

Culture — They are propagated by sowing of the seeds soon after they are ripe, and if it be in the spring, or any other time of the year, they will grow When the plants come up, the weakest should be drawn out, leaving any desired number for observation or use After they have once flowered, plants in plenty will arise from scattered seeds, if you chuse to let them remain unmolested until they are ripe

Titles — Celandine, or the Greater Celandine, or the Perennial Celandine, is titled, *Chelidonium pedunculis umbellatis* In the *Hortus Cliffortianus* it is termed, *Chelidonium pedunculis multifloris* Caspar Bauhine calls it, *Chelidonium majus vulgare*, and Fuchsius, *Chelidonium majus*

Caspar Bauhine terms the Jagged leaved kind, *Chelidonium majus, foliis quernis*, and Clusius calls it, *Chelidonium majus, folio laciniato*

Class and order in the Linnæan system — *Chelidonium* is of the class and order *Polyandria Monogynia*, and the characters are,

The characters — 1 CALYX is a roundish perianthium, composed of two oval, concave, obtuse, caducous leaves

2 COROLLA consists of four large, roundish, plane, patent petals, that are narrow at their base

3 STAMINA There are about thirty filaments, plane, broadest at the top, shorter than the corolla, and have oblong, compressed, obtuse, erect, didymous antheræ

4 PISTILLUM The germen is cylindrical, and the same length with the stamina. The style is wanting The stigma is capitated and bifid

5 PERICARPIUM is a cylindrical pod, formed of one or two valves

6 SEMINA The seeds are numerous, small, oval, and smooth

## CHAP CXV.

## *CHELONE.*

WE have here some fine autumnal flowering plants, which coming after the general blow of flowers is past, makes them desirable The species are,

Species — 1 The Virginian Smooth *Chelone.*

2 The Virginian Hairy *Chelone*

3 The Penstlemon *Chelone*

Virginian Smooth — 1 Virginian Smooth *Chelone* Of this species there are two remarkable varieties, one with a white, and another with a beautiful rose-coloured flower, which blow late in the autumn, and would make this species as valuable as most, were it not for its thick, creeping roots which spread themselves all around, and over-run small plants

plants that are near them From theſe roots, in every place where they run, riſe the ſtalks, which are about two feet high, and are ſmooth and channelled The leaves are ſpear-ſhaped, pointed, ſerrated, and grow oppoſite by pairs at the joints The flowers terminate the ſtalks in ſpikes The white flowering ſort is very pretty, but the other is a delightful plant, for in ſome they are of a deep red, in others paler, and in others a bright purple Each flower is compoſed of a ſingle petal, which is ringent They flower in Auguſt, September, and ſometimes in October and November, and though they ſhow themſelves ſo late in the ſeaſon, good ſeeds may be often gathered

Hairy Virginian,

2 Hairy Virginian *Chelone* The root of this ſpecies is ſpreading, and the ſtalks will grow to about the height of the former, they are very hairy, and garniſhed by hairy, ſpear-ſhaped leaves at the joints The flowers terminate the ſtalks in ſpikes They are of ſeveral varieties, ſuch as the White, the Red, the Pale Blue, and the Purple They flower in September, October, and November, and will often produce good ſeeds

and Penſtlemon Chelone deſcribed

3 Penſtlemon *Chelone* The roots of this ſpecies are not creeping like the others, and are of ſhort continuance, ſeldom laſting longer than two or three years The ſtalks are upright, branching, and will grow to about a foot and a half high The leaves are ſpear-ſhaped, oblong, and pointed, they grow oppoſite by pairs, and embrace the ſtalks with their baſe From the diviſions of the ſtalks the flowers are produced in ſhort, looſe ſpikes They are ſmall, of a purple colour, will be in blow in June and July, and their ſeeds ripen in the autumn

Culture

The culture of this laſt ſort is beſt performed by ſeeds Theſe ſhould be ſown in the autumn, ſoon after they are ripe for if they are kept until ſpring, they ſeldom grow that year In May or June the plants will be fit to remove This ſhould be done by preſerving a ball of earth to each root, and ſetting them in a dry, ſhady place, and the ſummer following they will flower

As theſe plants are often of ſhort continuance, you ſhould not neglect to ſow the ſeeds, or you will ſoon be out of the ſort, and indeed this ſpecies might not improperly be conſidered as a biennial, as it always flowers ſtrong the ſecond year, and though it ſometimes continues, it ſeldom ſhews itſelf in perfection after

The other ſorts are propagated faſt enough by parting of the roots in the autumn, neither is it worth while to ſow the ſeeds, though if this be done in the autumn, they will readily grow, and ſome varieties, reſpecting the colouring of the flowers, may be expected They will grow in any ſoil or ſituation

1 Virginian Smooth *Chelone* is titled, *Chelone foliis lanceolatis ſerratis ſummis oppoſitis* Tournefort calls it, *Chelone acadienſis, flore albo* Gronovius, *Chelone floribus ſpecioſis pulcherrimis, coloris roſæ damaſcenæ*, Ray, *Digitalis Mariana, perſicæ folio*, and Plukenet, *Digitalis Mariana ſpicatis denſis floribus rigidis & anguſtis foliis, ſummo ſtegmate triquetro* It grows naturally in Virginia and Canada [illegible]

2 Virginian Rough *Chelone* This is titled, *Chelone caule foliiſque hirſutis* Gronovius calls it *Anonymos flore pallide cæruleo digitalis inſtar in ſummis cauliculis diſpoſito, foliis alternis hirſutis*, Plukenet, *Digitalis Virginiana, parvo caule ſcabris foliis flore amplo palleſcente*, and Banister, *Digitalis flore pallido tranſparente, foliis & caule lanugine imbutis* It grows naturally in Virginia

3 Penſtlemon *Chelone* This is titled, *Chelone foliis amplexicaulibus panicula dichotoma* Miller calls it, *Aſarina caule erecto, foliis lanceolatis amplexicaulibus, panicula dichotoma*, Moriſon, *Dracocephalus latifolius glaber, lyſimachiæ lineæ foliis* and Micheli, *Penſtlemon* It is a native of Virginia

Claſs and order in the Linnæan ſyſtem

*Chelone* is of the claſs and order *Didynamia Angioſpermia*, and the characters are,

The characters

1 CALYX is a very ſhort permanent perianthium of one leaf, divided at the top into five oval ſegments, which are erect

2 COROLLA is a ringent petal The tube is cylindrical, and very ſhort The mouth is inflated, oblong convex above, and plane below The upper lip is obtuſe and emarginated The lower lip is lightly trifid

3 STAMINA are four filaments incloſed in the back of the corolla, of which the two ſide ones are a little longer than the others, with hairy bent antheræ There is the rudiment of a fifth filament between the upper ones

4 PISTILLUM conſiſts of an oval germen, a ſlender ſtyle the length and ſituation of the ſtamina, and an obtuſe ſtigma

5 PERICARPIUM is an oval capſule of two cells

6 SEMINA The ſeeds are numerous, roundiſh, and have a membranaceous border

# CHAP. CXVI.

## *CHENOPODIUM*, GOOSEFOOT.

Species

OF this genus are,

1 Common Engliſh Mercury, Good Henry, or, All Good

2 Penſylvania Gooſefoot

Common Engliſh Mercury,

1 Common Engliſh Mercury, or, All Good This ſpecies grows common among rubbiſh, by way-ſides, and in uncultivated places in many parts of England It is never propagated for its beauty, though a plant or two are ſometimes admitted into a garden, to be ready for obſervation, and ſometimes it is cultivated in moderate plenty for kitchen ſervice, being a fine eſculent, by ſome preferred to ſpinach, and is dreſſed for the ſame purpoſes at table The ſtalks are thick, ſtriated,

striated, and grow to about two feet high. The leaves are large, triangular, ... and grow on long footstalks. The flowers are produced from the tops of the stalks in close spikes; they are of a yellowish green colour; come out in June, July, and August, and ... the seeds ripen in the ... of ... or brown.

2. The ... Goosefoot is more to be ... of foreign extraction, than for any ... The stalks grow to about a foot ... high. The leaves are oval, oblong, and indented. The flowers grow in close clusters from the ... of the stalks; they are small, having no petals, of an herbaceous colour, come out in July, and ... the seeds ripen in September.

Culture. These ... are propagated by sowing of the seeds ... will do for the former; but the latter should have a dry, warm, well-sheltered situation. After the plants come up, nothing more need be done, than to draw out the weeds, leaving ... to stand to flower.

If the Common Mercury is to be raised for culinary purposes, the ground should be well dug, and the seeds sown in drills, two feet asunder, or else scattered all over the ground, and when the plants come up, those in the drills should be thinned to ... distance, and the other should be hoed leaving them a foot asunder every way. By this practice, your Mercury will come to perfection, and will present itself in great plenty to those who are disposed to prefer it before spinach and the like vegetable esculents.

1. Common English Mercury, or, All Good, is titled, *Chenopodium foliis triangulari-sagittatis integerrimis, spicis compositis aphyllis*. Caspar Bauhine calls it, *Lapathum unctuosum ... latifolium ...*; John Bauhine, *Bonus Henricus* ...; Tournefort, *Lapathum unctuosum*. It grows ... in England, and most countries of Europe.

2. Pensylvania Goosefoot is titled, *Chenopodium foliis ovato-oblongis ... racemis aphyllis*. Dillenius calls it, *Chenopodium ... scop. folio, ...*. It grows naturally in Pensylvania and Bonaria.

*Chenopodium* is of the class and order *Pentandria Digynia*; and the characters are, Class and order in the Linnæan System. The characters.

1. CALYX is a pentaphyllous perianthium, composed of five oval, concave leaves.

2. COROLLA. There is none.

3. STAMINA are five awl-shaped filaments, situated opposite to the leaves of the calyx, and about their length, having roundish didymous antheræ.

4. PISTILLUM consists of an orbiculated germen, a short style divided into two parts, and an obtuse stigma.

5. PERICARPIUM. There is none. The calyx closing, becomes pentagonal, and encloses the seed.

6. SEMEN. The seed is single, round, and depressed.

# CHAP. CXVII.

## *CHERLERIA.*

Species described. THERE is only one species of this genus, called *Cherleria*. The stalks are thick, tender, and six or eight inches high. The leaves are of a thickish consistence, of a greyish green colour, and grow alternately. The flowers are produced in clusters from the tops of the stalks; they are small, of a yellow colour, appear in July and August, and the seeds ripen in the autumn.

Culture. This species is propagated by parting of the roots, which may be done any time in the autumn, winter, or spring. It should have a light, dry soil, and a shady situation, and will then require no farther trouble, except keeping them clean from weeds.

Titles. This being the only species of this genus, it is named singly, *Cherleria*. Plukenet calls it, *Lychnis Alpina, muscosis foliis densius stipatis, floribus parvis, calyce aureo*; Morison, *Sedum montanum perpusillum luteum*; and Parkinson, *Sedum montanum perpusillum, luteolis floribus*. It grows naturally on the Helvetian and Vallesian mountains.

*Cherleria* is of the class and order *Decandria Trigynia*; and the characters are, Class and order in the Linnæan System. The characters.

1. CALYX is a perianthium, composed of five spear-shaped, concave, equal leaves.

2. COROLLA. There is none.

There are five small, emarginated nectariums, placed circularly.

3. STAMINA are ten awl-shaped filaments, the alternate ones being fastened to the back of the nectariums, having simple antheræ.

4. PISTILLUM consists of an oval germen, and three styles, which are bent backward, and have simple stigmas.

5. PERICARPIUM is an oval capsule, formed of three valves, and containing three cells.

6. SEMINA. The seeds are two or three, and kidney-shaped.

## CHAP. CXVIII.

## *CHONDRILLA*, GUM SUCCORY.

THERE is but one species of this genus, usually called,

Rushy Viscous Gum Succory.

Species described. The roots are large, thick, and full of viscous juice. They strike deep into the ground, and spread themselves under the surface to a considerable distance. From these arise many pinnatifid leaves, which are long, and finely divided. The stalks are slender, limber, and tough like rushes. They grow to about three feet high, and are garnished with leaves which are spear-shaped, narrow, and entire. The flowers are produced from the tops of the stalks and branches, are of a pale yellow colour, and much resemble those of lettuce. They come out in July, and are succeeded by ripe, downy seeds in September.

Culture. Take any part of the root, and plant it either in the autumn, winter, or spring, and it will readily grow, will soon spread itself, and strike so deep into the ground that you will find some difficulty to keep it from encreasing too fast upon your hands.

It may be also propagated by sowing of the seeds in the spring, but this method is not worth putting into practice, as it is to be multiplied so speedily, and so easily, by breaking the roots, and planting the divided parts.

Titles. There being no other species of this genus, it stands singly with the name *Chondrilla*. Whereas Van Royen calls it, *Chondrilla foliis radicalibus pinnatifidis, caulinis lanceolatis integris*; Tournefort, *Chondrilla juncea*, Caspar Bauhine, *Chondrilla juncea viscosa arvensis*, and John Bauhine, *Chondrilla viminea*. It grows naturally in Germany, Helvetia, and France.

Class and order in the Linnæan system. *Chondrilla* is of the class and order *Syngenesia Polygamia Æqualis*; and the characters are,

The characters. 1. CALYX. The common calyx is calyculated, and cylindrical. The scales are many, narrow, and equal, except a few at the base, which are very short.

2. COROLLA is imbricated and uniform. The florets are each one tongue-shaped, narrow, truncated petal, that is indented in four or five parts at the top.

3. STAMINA are five very short capillary filaments, having a cylindrical, tubular anthera.

4. PISTILLUM consists of an oval germen, a filiform style the length of the stamina, and two reflexed stigmas.

5. PERICARPIUM. There is none. The seeds are inclosed in the calyx.

6. SEMINA. The seeds are single, oval, compressed, rough, and crowned with simple stipitated down.

The receptacle is naked.

## CHAP. CXIX.

## *CHRYSANTHEMUM*, CORN MARYGOLD.

OF this genus are,

Species. 1. The Greater Daisy, or, Common Ox-eye.

2. Creeping Daisy.

3. Corymbiferous Daisy.

4. Lesser Mountain Ox-eye.

5. Grass-leaved Ox-eye.

6. Oriental Ox-eye.

7. Greater Mountain Daisy.

8. Alpine Ox-eye.

9. Serrated *Chrysanthemum*.

10. Bipinnated *Chrysanthemum*.

Description of the Greater. 1. The Greater Daisy, or, Common Ox-eye, is found growing naturally in our meadows and pastures almost every where. It is therefore never cultivated in gardens; but were it a scarce plant, it would be deemed an ornament to few in our collections. The radical leaves are broad, indented, and spread upon the ground; the upper ones are oblong, narrow, serrated, and embrace the stalks with their base. The stalks grow to be near two feet high, and each of them is crowned with a fair, large, white flower, of the elegant shape of the common daisy, but much larger. They come out in June, and are possessed of little or no smell or odour.

Creeping. 2. Creeping Daisy hath a creeping root, which soon spreads itself under the surface of the ground to a considerable distance. The lower leaves are broad, serrated, and lie on the ground; but those on the stalks are narrow, spear-shaped, serrated, and sharp pointed. The stalks grow to near a yard high, and divide into a few branches near the top. Each of these is terminated by a fine large, white flower, not unlike the former. There is a variety of this with jagged leaves, and another with a large double flower, both of which are greatly esteemed. They all flower in July and August.

3. Corymbiferous Daisy. The leaves of this species are pinnated, and the pinnæ are gashed and serrated. The stalks grow to about a yard and

and a half high, and the flowers are produced in kind of umbels at the top There is a variety of this plant with small, and another with large flowers, all of which come out in June and July

This species has little or no odour, and is frequently called the Scentless Tansey

Lesser Mountain, 4 Lesser Mountain Ox-eye The lower leaves of this species are rather broad, spear shaped, and serrated, but those on the stalks are narrow and entire The stalks are slender, grow to about a foot high, and in June each of them is terminated by one large white flower The seeds ripen in August, and by them this species is frequently raised

Grass leaved, 5 Grass leaved Ox-eye The root of this species sends forth many long grass like leaves, among which arise several small stalks, about a foot and a half high Each stalk is terminated by one large white flower in June, but the seeds seldom ripen in our gardens

and Oriental Ox eye 6 Oriental Ox eye The leaves of this species are oval, oblong, serrated and of a balsamic odour Among these the flower-stalks rise to about a foot and a half high, and in July or August each of them is crowned with a large, fine flower, of a strong odour

Greater Mountain Daisy 7 Greater Mountain Daisy The radical leaves of this species are large palmated, and the folioles are finely cut into many segments Among these the stalks arise to three or four feet high They are branched, and adorned with leaves that are beautifully divided The flowers are produced from the ends of the branches, standing on long, naked footstalks Their colour is white, and not unlike those of the Common Ox-eye They make their appearance in July, and others continue in succession until the autumn, by which time good seeds may be gathered from the first-blown flowers This sort is chiefly raised from the seeds, because such plants are finer, and flower stronger, than those from divided roots

Alpine Ox eye 8 Alpine Ox eye The leaves of this species are cuneiform, downy, and divided into several parallel, entire, acute, distant segments The stalks are stoloniferous, those which support the flowers are simple, about six inches long, and each of them is crowned by one flower, which comes out in June There is often a succession of these for three months

Patinated, 9 Patinated *Chrysanthemum* The stalks of this species are very short, thick, lie on the ground, and strike root at the joints The leaves are small, hoary, and divided into many narrow, acute, parallel, entire segments The flowers grow singly from the sides of the stalks on long footstalks, their colour is yellow, and there is often a succession until the end of September

and bipinnated Chrysanthemum described 10 Bipinnated *Chrysanthemum* The leaves of this species are divided into many spear shaped, serrated, hairy segments The stalks grow to about a foot and a half high, and are garnished with a few bipinnated leaves, like the radical ones, but smaller The flowers come out singly from the wings of the leaves on long, naked footstalks Their colour is yellow, and their appearance is about the same time with the former

Culture These sorts are all propagated by dividing of the roots This may be done successfully any time in the winter or spring, though the best season for it is September, that they may have time to take well to the ground, before the winter frosts come on The business should be done on a moist day, and for want of that, the ground should be well soaked with many tubs of water early in the morning In the evening it will be in good order to receive the plants These should be set together, if designed to make a show, at distances according to their size The largest should be set in the back line, and should be at least two feet asunder, the others a foot and half, and the smallest growers should not be from each other more than one foot Thus may these perennials be stationed to make a show of themselves, which will be both lively and beautiful, whilst a few remaining plants of every sort may be placed at random in the different parts of our works

There is hardly any of them which do not in general perfect their seeds well in our gardens, and from them the best plants are raised Let the seeds, therefore, be carefully gathered as soon as they are ripe, then spread them in an airy, dry room, for six days, and in that time they will be dry enough to put up Let each sort have its own separate bag, let them be all numbered, and hung up in a dry room until the spring In March, sow the seeds in beds of light, fine mould, covering them half a quarter of an inch deep, and in about a month or six weeks, your plants will appear, at which time, be sure to refresh them with water, if dry weather should happen Pick out the weeds as they arise, and when the plants come up too close, draw out the weakest All summer they will require no trouble, except keeping them clean from weeds, and watering them in dry weather In September they may be removed to the places where they are designed to remain, and if a ball of earth be preserved to each root, they will the sooner take to the ground, and flower strong the summer following

1 The Greater Daisy, or, Common Ox-eye, is titled, *Chrysanthemum foliis amplexicaulibus oblongis superne serratis, inferne dentatis* In the *Flora Lapponica* it is termed, *Chrysanthemum foliis oblongis serratis* Tournefort calls it, *Leucanthemum vulgare*, Caspar Bauhine, *Bellis sylvestris, caule folioso, major*, Gerard, *Bellis major*, and Parkinson, *Bellis major vulgaris, sylvestris* It grows naturally in meadow and pasture-grounds in most parts of Europe

2 Creeping Daisy is titled, *Chrysanthemum foliis lanceolatis superne serratis utrinque acuminatis* Plukenet calls it, *Bellis Americana procerior ramosa, flore amplissimo*, Morison, *Bellis major, ramosa repente, foliis laciniosis serratis* and Ray, *Aster foliis profunde dentatis & quasi laciniatis, ramosus*, also, *Bellis Americana frutescens ramosa* It grows naturally in North America

3 Corymbiferous Daisy is titled, *Chrysanthemum foliis pinnatis incisoserratis, caule multifloro* Tabernæmontanus calls it, *Tanacetum leucanthemum*, and Caspar Bauhine *Tanacetum montanum inodorum, minore flore*, also, *Tanacetum inodorum, flore majore* It grows naturally in the woody, mountainous, woodland parts of Hungaria, Bohemia, Helvetia and Siberia

4 Lesser Mountain Ox eye is titled, *Chrysanthemum foliis imis spathulato-lanceolatis serratis, summis linearibus* Tournefort calls it, *Leucanthemum montanum minus*, and John Bauhine, *Bellis montana minor* It grows naturally near Montpelier

5 Grass-leaved Ox-eye is titled, *Chrysanthemum foliis linearibus subintegerrimis, caule simplicissimo* Tournefort calls it, *Leucanthemum gramineo folio*, and Magnol, *Bellis montana, graminea folio* It grows naturally near Montpelier

6 Oriental Ox-eye is titled, *Chrysanthemum foliis ovatis oblongis serratis* Tournefort calls it, *Leucanthemum orientale, costi hortensis folio*, and Vaillant, *Bellioides balsamitæ majoris facie & odore* It grows naturally in the East

7 Greater Mountain Daisy is titled, *Chrysanthemum foliis imis palmatis foliolis linearibus pinnatifidis* Magnol calls it, *Bellis montana major*, fo-

*lus chrysanthemi Cretici angustioribus*, and Tournefort, *Leucanthemum montanum, foliis chrysanthemi* It grows naturally about Montpelier

8 Alpine Ox-eye is titled, *Chrysanthemum foliis cuneiformibus pinnatifidis laciniis integris caulibus unifloris* Caspar Bauhine calls it, *Chamæmelum Alpinum*, Haller, *Pyrethrum foliis omnibus longe petiolatis palmatis incanis*, and Clusius, *Leucanthemum Alpinum tenuifolium* It is a native of the Helvetian mountains

9 Pectinated *Chrysanthemum* is titled, *Chrysanthemum foliis pinnatis linearibus parallelis acutis integerrimis, pedunculis solitariis unifloris* Barrelier calls it, *Chamæmelum montanum incanum absinthoides Italicum* It is a native of Spain and Italy

10 Bipinnated *Chrysanthemum* is titled, *Chrysanthemum foliis bipinnatis serratis villosis* Gmelin calls it, *Pyrethrum foliis duplicato pinnatis pinnulis incisis, pedunculis unifloris* It is a native of Siberia

*Chrysanthemum* is of the class and order *Syngenesia Polygamia Superflua*, and the characters are, Class and order in the Linnæan system

1 Calyx is hemisphærical and imbricated The characters

2 Corolla is compound and radiated The hermaphrodite florets are numerous in the disk, and each consists of one funnel-shaped petal the same length with the calyx, and divided at the top into five spreading segments The females in the radius are ligulated, oblong, and indented at the top in three parts

3 Stamina are five very short capillary filaments, having a cylindrical, tubular anthera

4 Pistillum in the hermaphrodite florets consists of an oval germen, a filiform style that is longer than the stamina, and two revolute stigmas In the female florets it consists of an oval germen, a slender style, and two obtuse, revolute stigmas

5 Pericarpium There is none

6 Semina The seeds of the hermaphrodite florets are single, oblong, and have no down The seeds of the female florets are like those of the hermaphrodite

The receptacle is naked, punctated, and convex

# CHAP CXX

## *CHRYSOCOMA*, GOLDYLOCKS.

THE herbaceous species of this genus usually go by the appellations of, Species

1 German Goldylocks
2 Siberian Goldylocks
3 Canada Goldylocks
4 Tartarian Goldylocks

1 German Goldylocks The root of this species is very hardy, and sends forth several erect, round, stiff stalks, to about a foot or fifteen inches high The leaves are narrow, smooth, of a light green, and garnish the stalks in great plenty The stalks divide near the top into numerous, slender footstalks, each of which supports a head of flowers, so that there being many of them, every stalk is terminated by a large bunch of flowers, growing in a kind of umbel They are of a bright yellow colour, and make a fine appearance at a distance They come out in July, and the seeds ripen in September Description of the German,

2 Siberian Goldylocks The root of this species is creeping and spreads itself under the surface to a considerable distance The stalks are erect, stiff, and divide into a few branches near the top The leaves are stiff, spear shaped, rough, sharp pointed, and each has three veins running from the base to the extremity The flowers ornament the tops of the stalks, growing in loose panicles They are large, yellow, come out in June and July, and the seeds ripen in September There is a variety without rays Siberian,

3 Canada Goldylocks The stalks of this species are smooth, erect, and a little angular The leaves are spear-shaped, narrow, smooth, sharp-pointed, trinervous, and grow alternately The flowers terminate the stalks in a corymbus; each branch consists of many heads, which, being large, make a fine appearance They come out in July, and the seeds ripen in the autumn Canada,

4 Tartarian Goldylocks The stalks of this species are herbaceous, upright, and divide into several slender, upright branches, near the top The leaves are hoary, spear shaped, and hairy The flowers grow in umbels at the tops of the stalks Their colour is yellow, and they make their appearance about the same time with the former and Tartarian Goldylocks

These plants are propagated by dividing of the roots, the best time for which is the autumn, soon after the stalks decay, though it may be done successfully any time in the winter or spring They love best a light, dry soil, though they are very hardy, and will grow in almost any place, let the soil or situation be what it will Culture

They are also propagated by sowing the seeds in the spring on a bed of light, fresh earth The mould should be made exceeding fine, and drills should be made across the bed at about three inches asunder In these the seeds should be thinly scattered, and covered over with hardly a quarter of an inch depth of the finest mould In about six weeks the plants will appear, at which time you must afford them water, if the weather proves dry, to promote their coming up All summer they must be kept clean from weeds, and watered as often as there shall be occasion; and in the autumn they may be removed into the nursery, planting them in beds six inches distance from each other Here they may stand until the autumn following, when they may be removed to the places where they are designed to remain

Some

Some of them will flower the summer following, though the greatest part will not exhibit their bloom until the year after that, on which account they must stand in the nursery-beds two years, if necessary, before they are planted out for good.

Titles

1. Common Goldylocks is titled, *Chrysocoma herbacea, foliis linearibus glabris, calycibus laxis*. In the Hortus Cliffortianus it is termed, *Chrysocoma caule simplici*. Haller calls it, *Chrysocoma foliis ... pedunculo sub flore incrassato*, Columna, *Chrysocoma Dioscoridis & Plinii*, Lobel, *Linosyris nova*, Clusius, *Osyris austriaca*, and Caspar Bauhine, *Linaria, aureo capitulo luteo, major*. It grows naturally in Germany, France, and Italy.

2. Siberian Goldylocks is titled, *Chrysocoma ... foliis lanceolatis trinerviis punctatis ...*. Gmelin calls it, *... foliis ... lanceolatis integerrimis trinerviis ...*, and Amman, *Conyza ... foliis ... & nervosis, floribus luteis umbellatis*. It is a native of Siberia.

3. Canada Goldylocks is titled, *Chrysocoma herbacea, foliis ... lanceolatis glabris, floribus corymbosis*. It is a native of Canada.

4. Tartarian Goldylocks is titled, *Chrysocoma herbacea, foliis ... calycibus ...*. Gmelin calls it *Aster ... calyce ... foliis ... lanceolatis, flor... ...*, and Amman, *Conyza ... floribus luteis umbellatis, ... folio*. It grows naturally in Tartary and Siberia.

*Chrysocoma* is of the class and order *Syngenesia Polygamia Æqualis*; and the characters are, — Class and order in the Linnæan System. The characters

1. CALYX. The common calyx is imbricated, and composed of many narrow sharp-pointed scales, of which the outer ones are convex.

2. COROLLA. The compound flower is tubulous, and longer than the calyx. The florets are numerous, tubular, funnel-shaped, equal, and divided at the top into five revolute segments.

3. STAMINA are five very short filiform filaments, having a cylindrical tubular anthera.

4. PISTILLUM consists of an oblong, coronated germen, a short filiform style, and two oblong, depressed, involute stigmas.

5. PERICARPIUM. There is none.

6. SEMINA. The seeds are single, oval, oblong, compressed, and crowned with hairy down.

The receptacle is plane and naked.

# CHAP. CXXI.

## *CHRYSOSPLENIUM*, GOLDEN SAXIFRAGE.

THERE are only two species of this genus, both perennials, which are called,

Species

1. Common Golden Saxifrage.
2. Alternate-leaved Golden Saxifrage.

Common

1. Common Golden Saxifrage. The root is creeping, and puts forth numerous, slender fibres. The stalks are weak, tender, hairy, branching a little, and about six inches long. The leaves are roundish, crenated, hairy, and grow opposite to each other on short footstalks. The flowers are produced from the wings of the leaves on the upper parts of the branches. They grow on short footstalks, and are of a golden yellow colour, come out in March, April, and May, and the seeds ripen in June and July.

and Alternate-leaved Golden Saxifrage described.

2. Alternate-leaved Golden Saxifrage. The root is creeping, and full of slender fibres. The stalks are very tender, green, hairy, branching a little, and grow to about six or eight inches high. The leaves are oblong, roundish, crenated, hairy, ..., of a pale green, and grow alternately on long footstalks. The flowers are small, and of a bright yellow colour. They come out from the tops of the plants in April and May, and the seeds ripen soon after.

Culture

These two little elegant plants grow naturally in shady woods, bogs, and moist places in many parts of England, which teaches us to search out for them such a situation in our garden, if we would have them in perfection. If such a situation is wanted, the Gardener need not be discouraged, for they will grow very well in shady borders, or they may be planted in moist places in the wilderness among the trees, where they will flourish, and shew their flowers early in the spring, before the leaves of the trees are fully out.

The propagation is by parting of the roots, the best time for which is autumn. Previous to this work, the ground should be dug, made fine, and early in the morning should have a good soaking of water, if the place is not naturally wet and moist, and in the evening plant the roots. In doing of this, carefully spread the fibres, and let the tops of the roots be covered with about a quarter of an inch of the finest mould. If the place is not naturally shady, place some small boughs at a proper distance towards the south; then your plants will be protected from injuries which the sun may occasion, they will readily take to the ground, and early in the spring they will put up, exhibit their bloom, and make a pretty appearance. The wilderness among the trees, or in any place that is shady and moist enough for them to grow to perfection.

They may be also propagated by sowing of the seeds. This should be in the summer soon after they are ripe. The ground should be ..., and the seeds must be thinly sown and lightly raked in. The plants will soon come up, and if it be in the garden they must be kept clean from weeds, and duly watered; if on a boggy, moist part, that suits their nature, from the time of sowing the seeds, you need not be anxious about their safety, for there the ... will ... along with the native weeds, will seem to rejoice in such company, and in the spring will shew their bloom with that native ... and beauty Nature designed them.

Titles

1. Common Saxifrage, which is also often called Opposite-leaved Saxifrage, is titled, *Chrysosplenium foliis oppositis*. Tournefort calls it, *Chrysosplenium foliis ... rotundis auriculatis*. Tabernæmontanus, *Chrysosplenium ...*, *Saxifraga aurea*, Dodonæus, *Saxifraga aurea*, Caspar Bauhine,

Saxifraga

*Saxifraga rotundifolia aurea*, Dalechamp, *Saxifraga Romanorum*, and Moriſon, *Alchemilla rotundifolia aurea hirſuta*. It grows naturally in moiſt, ſhady places in England, Germany, and in Canada.

2. Alternate-leaved Golden Saxifrage. This is titled, *Chryſoſplenium foliis alternis*. In the *Hortus Cliffortianus* it is termed, *Chryſoſplenium*, and in the *Flora Lapponica*, *Chryſoſplenium foliis amplioribus auriculatis*. Tournefort calls it, *Chryſoſplenium foliis pediculis oblongis inſidentibus*, Ray, *Saxifraga aurea, foliis pediculis oblongis inſidentibus*, and Moriſon, *Sedum paluſtre luteum majus, foliis pediculis longis inſidentibus*. It grows naturally in moiſt ſhady places in England, Germany, and Sweden.

Claſs and order in the Linnæan ſyſtem. *Chryſoſplenium* is of the claſs and order *Decandria Digynia*, and the characters are,

The characters. 1. CALYX is a permanent perianthium, divided into four or five oval, coloured, patent ſegments.

2. COROLLA. There is none. The coloured calyx is all the flower.

3. STAMINA are eight or ten very ſhort, erect, awl-ſhaped filaments, placed in an angular receptacle, having ſimple antheræ.

4. PISTILLUM conſiſts of a germen ſituated below the flowers, and two awl-ſhaped ſtyles, the length of the ſtamina, with obtuſe ſtigmas.

5. PERICARPIUM is a two beaked bipartite capſule of one cell, formed of two valves, and ſurrounded by a green cup.

6. SEMINA. The ſeeds are numerous, angular, ſharp-pointed, and ſmall.

## CHAP. CXXII.

## *CICHORIUM*, SUCCORY, or ENDIVE.

THE Wild Succory of the ſhops, which grows ſo plentifully in lawns and borders of fields in many parts of England, ought not wholly to be paſſed by, as it is a beautiful flower, and in ſome countries, where it does not grow naturally, much reſpected.

This ſpecies deſcribed. The root is thick, and hung with many fibres. In ſome ſituations it will remain for many years, though in others its duration will not be longer than two or three years. The ſtalk is branching, and will be a yard or more in height. The leaves are deeply cut, and the ſegments ſharp pointed; they riſe directly from the roots, as well as the ſtalks, where they ſit cloſe, without any footſtalks. The flowers are of a fine blue colour, large, and are produced from the ſides of the ſtalks, without any pedicles. They will be in blow in June and July, and ripen their ſeeds in September.

Culture. It is propagated by ſowing the ſeeds in May. After the plants come up, thin them to two feet diſtance, keep them clean from weeds, and they will flower ſtrong the ſummer following.

Titles. Wild Succory is titled, *Cichorium floribus geminis ſeſſilibus, foliis runcinatis*. In the *Hortus Cliffortianus* it is termed, *Cichorium caule ſimplici*. Caſpar Bauhine calls it, *Cichorium ſylveſtre, ſive officinarum*, and Cammerarius, *Intybus ſylveſtris*. It grows naturally by road ſides in moſt parts of Europe.

Claſs and order in the Linnæan ſyſtem. *Cichorium* is of the claſs and order *Syngeneſia Polygamia Æqualis*, and the characters are,

The characters. 1. CALYX. The common calyx is calyculated and imbricated, the ſcales are narrow, ſpear-ſhaped, and equal.

2. COROLLA. The flower is plane and uniform. The florets are placed in a circle, and each conſiſts of a tongue ſhaped truncated petal, deeply indented in five parts.

3. STAMINA conſiſt of five very ſhort capillary filaments, with a cylindrical, five cornered, tubulous anthera.

4. PISTILLUM conſiſts of an oblong germen, a filiforme ſtyle the length of the ſtamina, and two revolute ſtigmas.

5. PERICARPIUM. There is none. The ſeeds are contained in the connivent calyx.

6. SEMEN. The ſeed is ſingle and compreſſed. The receptacle is paleaceous.

# CHAP. CXXIII

## *CICUTA*, WATER-HEMLOCK

THOSE who are fond of abundance of plants will of course admit the species of *Cicuta* into the watery and moist parts of their gardens. The species are three in number only, and are usually named,

Species

1. English Long-leaved Water-Hemlock.
2. Canada Water-Hemlock.
3. Virginian Water-Hemlock.

Description of the English Long-leaved Water Hemlock

1. English Long-leaved Water-Hemlock. This species always grows in water, and the culture of it should never be attempted in a garden, unless there is a pond, or some water for its reception; in such places it will have a very pretty effect among others of the watery breed.

The root sends forth numerous slender black fibres into the mud. The stalks will grow to be four feet high, and are large, hollow, and branching. The leaves are winged, composed of many long, narrow, serrated folioles, and grow on long sheathing footstalks. The flowers are produced in large umbels, from the ends of the branches, they are of a yellowish-green colour, come out in June and July, and are succeeded by small channelled seeds like parsley, which will be ripe in September. This plant is said to be a strong poison.

Method of propagating this sort

It is propagated by throwing the seeds into the water, soon after they are ripe, and if the place is suitable for them they will come up, and about the second summer after will shew their flowers.

The roots also may be planted in such places, but the plants seldom do so well as those raised from seeds. Where the water is not deep, it will have the best effect, as it will the better shew itself for observation. It grows naturally in a shallow pool on Hounslow-Heath, and whoever is possessed of such places in any part of his estate, he may beautify them with these wonderful products of Nature.

Description of the Canada

2. Canada Water-Hemlock. The stalks of this species are hollow, angular, and branching. The leaves are large, and beautifully divided into a multitude of minute, narrow, plane segments. The flowers grow in large umbels from the ends of the branches, and are succeeded by channelled seeds, which will be ripe in the autumn.

and the Virginian Water Hemlock

3. Virginian Water-Hemlock. This is often called Virginian Angelica. The stalks are large, hollow, and branching. The leaves also are large, and have membranaceous footstalks. The folioles are spear-shaped, acuminated, and sharply serrated. The flowers grow in large umbels from the ends of the branches, their colour is white, they come out in June and July, and are succeeded by small channelled seeds, which have the taste and smell of cinnamon, and will be ripe in the autumn.

Method of propagating these species

These two last plants are natives of watery places in their respective countries, but they will grow very well with us in a shady moist earth. In such a situation, therefore, let the ground be well dug and made fine, and then in the autumn thinly sow the seeds, soon after they are ripe, and slightly rake them in. In the spring the plants will come up, and then is the time to thin them where they appear too close. Weeding must always be attended to as often as you find it necessary, and watering in dry weather, for these plants especially must not be omitted, and this is all the trouble they will require.

About the second or third summer after sowing, the plants will shew their flowers, and in the autumn perfect their seeds.

Titles

1. English Long-leaved Water Hemlock is titled, *Cicuta umbellis oppositifoliis, petiolis marginatis obtusis*. In the *Hortus Cliffortianus* it is termed simply, *Cicuta*; and in the *Flora Lapponica*, *Cicuta aquatica*. Caspar Bauhine calls it, *Sium erucæ folio*; Gerard, *Sium alterum, olusatri facie*; and Parkinson, *Sium majus alterum angustifolium*. It grows naturally in pools and watery places in England and most parts of Europe.

2. Canada Water Hemlock. This is titled, *Cicuta ramis bulbiferis*. Gronovius calls it, *Ammi foliis in lacinulas capillaceas ..., caule angulato*; and Ray, *Umbellifera aquatica, foliis in minutissima & plane capillacea segmenta divisis*. It grows naturally in Canada and Virginia.

3. Virginian Water Hemlock is titled, *Cicuta foliorum serraturis mucronatis, petiolis membranaceis apice bilobis*. Gronovius calls it, *Ægopodium foliolis lanceolatis acuminatis serratis*; Plukenet, *Angelica Canadensium elatior, olusatri folio, flore albo, seminibus luteis striatis, cuminum odore & sapore*; and Morison, *Angelica Virginiana, foliis acutioribus, semine striato ..., cumini sapore & odore*. It is a native of Virginia.

Class and order in the Linnæan system. The characters

*Cicuta* is of the class and order *Pentandria Digynia*; and the characters are,

1. CALYX. The general umbel is roundish, and composed of numerous equal radii. The partial umbel also is roundish, and composed of many equal bristly rays.

   There is no general involucrum, but a partial one, composed of several short bristly folioles.

   The proper perianthium is hardly discernible.

2. COROLLA. The general flower is uniform. The florets consist each of five oval inflexed petals, which are nearly equal.
3. STAMINA are five capillary filaments, longer than the corolla, having simple antheræ.
4. PISTILLUM consists of a germen situated below the flower, and two filiforme persisting styles, longer than the corolla, with simple stigmas.
5. PERICARPIUM. There is none. The fruit is nearly oval, striated, furrowed, and divisible into two parts.
6. SEMINA. The seeds are two, oval, convex, striated on one side, and plane on the other.

## CHAP CXXIV.

## *CIRCÆA*, ENCHANTERS NIGHTSHADE

THERE are only two real species of this genus, called,

Species
1 Common Enchanters Nightshade
2 Alpine Enchanters Nightshade

Common Enchanters Night shade
1 Common Enchanters Nightshade The root is creeping, tough, and full of fibres The stalks are upright, round, and grow to about a foot and a half high The leaves are large, heart-shaped, pointed, slightly indented, of a dark-green colour on their upper surface, but paler under, and grow opposite to each other, on pretty long footstalks Each stalk is terminated by one long range of flowers, and smaller spikes also branch out from the sides, they are small, and of a white colour, come out in June and July, and the seeds ripen in August and September

Variety
There is a notable variety of this species, called the Canada Enchanters Nightshade The stalks are strong, erect, and advance to four or five feet high The leaves are very broad The flowers are white, and grow in very long loose spikes

Alpine Enchanters Night-shade
2 Alpine Enchanters Nightshade The root of this species is creeping, fibrous, and tough The stalks are weak, slender, and grow only to about six inches high The leaves are like those of the former, but smaller, and are indented on their edges The flowers come out from the tops of the stalks, in single loose spikes, they are very small, white, appear in June and July, and the seeds ripen in August

Culture
These sorts are easily propagated by dividing of the roots, the best time for which is the autumn, though it may be done successfully at any other season of the year They grow naturally in shady woods and moist places, which admonishes us, that they will relish best such a situation in our gardens, though we need not be anxious about success in propagating them, for though they like a moist shady situation the best, yet they will grow very well in any soil or situation, and no aspect comes amiss to them

Titles
1 Common Enchanters Nightshade is titled *Circæa caule erecto, racemis pluribus* In the *Hortus Cliffortianus* it is termed simply, *Circæa* Caspar Bauhine calls it, *Solani folia Circæa lutetiana major*, Lobel, *Circæa Lutetiana*, and Parkinson, *Circæa Lutetiana major* Tournefort names the Canada variety, *Circæa Canadensis latifolia, flore albo* It grows naturally in England, most parts of Europe, and North-America

2 Alpine Enchanters Nightshade is titled, *Circæa caule adscendente, racemo unico* In the *Flora Lapponica* it is termed, *Circæa calyce colorato* Caspar Bauhine calls it, *Solani folia Circæa Alpina* and Columna, *Circæa minima* It grows naturally on the sides of mountains in most of the cold parts of Europe

Class and order in the Linnæan system
*Circæa* is of the class and order *Diandria Monogynia*, and the characters are,

The characters
1 CALYX is a perianthium consisting of two oval, concave, deflexed, deciduous leaves

2 COROLLA consists of two obcordated, equal, patent petals, which are rather shorter than the leaves of the calyx

3 STAMINA are two erect capillary filaments the length of the calyx, having roundish antheræ

4 PISTILLUM consists of a turbinated germen situated below the flower, a filiform style the length of the stamina, and an obtuse emarginated stigma

5 PERICARPIUM is a turbinated, oval, rough, hispid, bilocular, bivalvate capsule, that opens from the base to the top

6 SEMINA The seeds are single, one being in each cell of the capsule, they are of an oblong figure, and narrowest at the base

## CHAP. CXXV.

## *CISTUS*, ROCK-ROSE.

OF this genus there are,

Species
1 Common Dwarf *Cistus*, or Little Sunflower
2 Prickly cupped Dwarf *Cistus*
3 Appennine Dwarf *Cistus*
4 Dwarf Mountain *Cistus*
5 Hairy Dwarf *Cistus*
6 Thyme leaved Dwarf *Cistus*
7 *Serpillum* leaved Dwarf *Cistus*
8 Moneywort Dwarf *Cistus*
9 Narrow-leaved Dwarf *Cistus*
10 Scaly-leaved Dwarf *Cistus*
11 Canada Dwarf *Cistus*
12 Plantain leaved Dwarf *Cistus*
13 Oeland Dwarf *Cistus*
14 *Marum* leaved Dwarf *Cistus*
15 White Spanish Dwarf *Cistus*
16 Italian Dwarf *Cistus*
17 Helvetian Dwarf *Cistus*
18 Heath-leaved Dwarf *Cistus*

19 Um

19 Umbellated Dwarf *Ciſtus*

Common Dwarf Ciſtus. 1 Common Dwarf *Ciſtus*, or Little Sunflower. This hath numerous ſlender, tough, trailing, ligneous ſtalks, covered with a brown bark. The leaves are oblong, green, a little hairy on their upper ſide, downy underneath, and grow oppoſite to each other on the branches. The flowers are produced thinly on the tops of the ſtalks, growing on moderately-long footſtalks; their colour is yellow; they come out in June and July, and the ſeeds ripen in Auguſt and September.

Varieties. There are two notable varieties of this ſpecies, called,

The Broad-leaved White-flowered Dwarf *Ciſtus*.
The Roſy Dwarf *Ciſtus*.

Prickly-cupped Dwarf Ciſtus. 2 Prickly-cupped Dwarf *Ciſtus*. The ſtalks of this ſpecies are ſhrubby, ſhort-jointed, upright, and ſend forth many branches from the ſides. The leaves are oblong and narrow, having reflexed borders; they are of a bright-green on the upper ſide, but downy underneath, and grow oppoſite to each other. The flowers are produced in ſmall cluſters from the ends of the branches; they are of a golden yellow colour, come out in July, and the ſeeds ripen in the autumn.

Variety. There is a variety of this, with white flowers.

Appennine Dwarf Ciſtus. 3 Appennine Dwarf *Ciſtus*. The ſtalks of this ſpecies are ligneous, tough, and ſpread themſelves every way. The leaves are ſpear-ſhaped, oblong, and downy. The flowers are large, and grow from the ends of the branches in June and July, and the ſeeds ripen in Auguſt and September.

Varieties. The varieties of this ſpecies uſually go by the names of,

White German Dwarf *Ciſtus*.
Yellow German Dwarf *Ciſtus*.
There is alſo another variety, called,
Stone Dwarf *Ciſtus*.

The ſtalks of this ſort are more erect than the others, and the flowers are whiter.

They uſually retain their difference from ſeeds, ſo that if you ſow the ſeeds of either of them, you may be pretty ſure of having the ſame ſorts again.

Mountain. 4 Dwarf Mountain *Ciſtus*. The ſtalks of this ſpecies are procumbent, tough, and ſhrubby. The leaves are oblong, oval, and of an hoary whiteneſs. The flowers are white, come out from the tops of the ſtalks in June and July, and the ſeeds ripen in Auguſt. This will ſometimes continue the ſucceſſion of blow until the end of ſummer.

Hairy. 5 Hairy Dwarf *Ciſtus*. The ſtalks of this ſpecies are ligneous, tough, and lie on the ground. The leaves are ſpear-ſhaped, oval, hairy, downy underneath, and grow oppoſite to each other. The flowers are collected into ſmalliſh heads, at the tops of the ſtalks; their colour is white, and they often continue to ſhew themſelves the greateſt part of the ſummer.

Thyme leaved. 6 Thyme-leaved Dwarf *Ciſtus*. The ſtalks of this ſpecies are ligneous, trailing, and about half a foot in length. The leaves are oval, narrow, hoary, and grow oppoſite to each other. The flowers are produced in ſmall cluſters from the ends of the ſtalks; their colour is white; they come out in June and July, and the ſeeds ripen ſoon after. This ſpecies muſt have a dry ſandy ſoil and a warm ſituation, otherwiſe its continuance will be but of ſhort duration.

Serpillum leaved. 7 *Serpillum*-leaved Dwarf *Ciſtus*. The ſtalks of this ſpecies are ſlender, ligneous, and lie on the ground. The leaves are oblong, hairy, and of a very dark-green colour. The flowers are of a golden yellow, and ſweetly ſcented; they come out in July, and the ſeeds ripen in September.

Moneywort. 8 Moneywort Dwarf *Ciſtus*. The ſtalks of this ſpecies are long, ſhrubby, divide into many branches, and trail on the ground. The lower leaves are round, and thoſe on the branches are of an oval figure; their upper ſurface is a light-green colour, but they are greyiſh underneath, and have ſeveral conſpicuous veins running from the baſe of each leaf. The flowers are large, and of a white colour; they come out in cluſters from the ends of the branches in July and Auguſt, and the ſeeds ripen in September.

Narrow leaved. 9 Narrow-leaved Dwarf *Ciſtus*. The ſtalks of this ſpecies are ſlender, trailing, ligneous, and tough. The leaves are oblong, oval, hairy, and grow oppoſite to each other. The flowers are ſmall, and of a yellow colour; they grow from the ends of the branches in ſmall looſe ſpikes; their appearance is in June and July, and the ſeeds ripen in Auguſt and September.

Scaly leaved. 10 Scaly leaved Dwarf *Ciſtus*. The ſtalks of this ſpecies are ligneous, four-cornered, and erect. The leaves are oval, ſpear-ſhaped, of a thickiſh ſubſtance, ſcaly on their ſurface, and grow on footſtalks. The flowers grow many together from the ends and ſides of the branches; their appearance is in July, and the ſeeds ripen in the autumn. This muſt have a dry, light ſoil, and a warm ſituation.

Canada. 11 Canada Dwarf *Ciſtus*. The ſtalks of this ſpecies are ſlender, herbaceous, and weak. The leaves are ſpear-ſhaped, and grow alternately on the ſtalks. The flowers grow in ſmall looſe ſpikes from the ends of the ſtalks; their colour is yellow, and they appear in July or Auguſt.

Plantain leaved. 12 Plantain-leaved Dwarf *Ciſtus*. The ſtalks of this ſpecies are thick, ſhort, and ſend forth ſeveral ſhort branches from the ſides. The radical leaves are oval, trinervous, and woolly; thoſe on the ſtalks are ſmooth, ſpear-ſhaped, and placed alternately. The flowers are pretty large; they come out from the ends of the branches in June and July, and the ſeeds ripen in Auguſt and September.

Oeland. 13 Oeland Dwarf *Ciſtus*. The ſtalks of this ſpecies are ſlender, ligneous, and procumbent. The leaves are oblong, ſmooth on both ſides, and grow oppoſite to each other. The flowers are moderately large, and their petals are indented; they come out about the ſame time with the former, and the ſeeds ripen accordingly.

Marum leaved. 14 *Marum*-leaved Dwarf *Ciſtus*. The ſtalks of this ſpecies are ſlender, ſhrubby, and branching. The leaves are oblong, oval, ſpear-ſhaped, hairy on their upper ſurface, and woolly underneath. The flowers come out from the ends and ſides of the branches in July and Auguſt, and the ſeeds ripen in the autumn.

White Spaniſh. 15 White Spaniſh Dwarf *Ciſtus*. The ſtalks of this ſpecies are ligneous and procumbent. The leaves are oval, hairy, very hoary, white on their under ſide, and grow to each other. The flowers are pale, and grow in kind of umbels; they come out in June and July, and the ſeeds ripen in September.

Italian. 16 Italian Dwarf *Ciſtus*. This is a ſlow erect, ſhrubby plant, ſending forth ſeveral ſpreading branches oppoſite to each other. The leaves alſo grow oppoſite, and are on both ſides armed with ſtrong prickly hairs or briſtles. The lower leaves are of an oval figure, and have ſo ſtalks, but thoſe on the upper parts of the plant are ſpear-ſhaped, and ſit cloſe without any footſtalks. The flowers grow in looſe ſpikes from the ends of the branches; they are of a pale-yellow colour, their petals are ſlightly indented, and their cups are hiſpid.

17 Hi-

Helvetian. 17. Helvetian Dwarf Cistus. The stalks are ligneous, trailing, and about a foot long. The leaves are narrow, hairy on their borders, and grow alternately. The flowers grow singly on footstalks, from the upper parts of the stalks; they are of a fine yellow colour, and sometimes continue to shew themselves from June to the end of summer.

Heath-leaved. 18. Heath-leaved Dwarf *Cistus*. The stalks of this species are erect, woody, and about a foot and a half high. The leaves are narrow, smooth, and grow in bunches alternately, from the sides of the stalks. The flowers grow in clusters on the tops of the plants; they are of a fine yellow colour, pretty large, and shew themselves in June, July, and August.

and Umbellated Dwarf Cistus described. 19. Umbellated Dwarf *Cistus*. The stalks are ligneous, short, and lie on the ground. The leaves are narrow, and placed opposite to each other. The flowers come out in umbels from the tops of the stalks, and their appearance is about the same time with the former.

Culture. These plants are propagated by seeds, or by cuttings or slips taken from the root. When the latter method is to be practised, the cuttings should be planted in pots, and the pots set in the greenhouse, in a shady place; and if they are duly watered, they will soon take root, and may any time afterwards be turned out with the mould into the places where they are to remain.

This method is to be understood of those species which are of a woody nature, with respect to those which are herbaceous, or have creeping roots, the roots may at any time be divided, either in the autumn, winter, or spring, and every bit will grow, and soon give increase enough.

But the first best method of propagating all the sorts is by sowing the seeds, which they ripen every year as regularly as hardy annuals.

The best way will be to sow the seeds, in the spring, in the places where they are to remain, and after the plants come up, to thin them to proper distances, for such plants will be longer than those that have been removed. But it may be done with greater expedition by sowing the seeds in a moderate hotbed, for this will bring them forward, and cause them to shoot strong from the first. About Midsummer, in the first moist weather that happens, they should be taken out of the beds, with a ball of earth to each root, and planted in the places where they are designed to remain, observing always to shade and water them at first as often as you find it necessary.

Most people keep a plant or two of each of the tenderest sorts in the greenhouse, to preserve the kinds; but for this there is no necessity; for they every year produce such large quantities of seed, that a few of each sort may be easily collected, to be sown in the spring, to raise a fresh supply, in case an unfavourable winter should put a period to the old plants. Neither is there an absolute necessity of gathering the seeds every autumn, though it would be a piece of prudence not to neglect it; for they will continue in the vessels until the spring of the year, the time for sowing them; insomuch that I have frequently collected good seeds in the spring from dead plants, that had been killed in the winter, and thus raised a fresh supply in abundance.

Proper soil and situations. They all like a sandy, chalky, light, dry soil, and a shady situation; and in such places they will last for many years. But as they are so easily raised from seeds, the best way will be to set them in any place as shall happen, and be careful to gather seeds for a succession, the same as you would biennials, and other short-lived plants.

These plants have a pretty effect in any place, and they should be stationed in plenty along the sides of the wilderness quarters where they will shew themselves to advantage, and be [illegible] ornamental, especially in mornings, when they will be covered with bloom, though in afternoons they assume rather a [illegible] aspect, [illegible] petals of some of the flowers will be [illegible] off, others quite gone, and, [illegible] of human life, and which [illegible] conduce to good reflections and observations.

1. Common Dwarf *Cistus*, or Little Sun Flower, is titled, *Cistus suffruticosus* [illegible], *stipulis lanceolatis, foliis oblongis* [illegible]. In the *Hortus Cliffortianus* it is termed, *Cistus stipulis* [illegible], [illegible] Caspar Bauhine calls it, *Chamaecistus vulgaris flore luteo*; John Bauhine, *Helianthemum* [illegible], [illegible]; Parkinson, *Helianthemum vulgare*; Gerard, *Helianthemum* [illegible] *flore luteo*; and Camerarius [illegible] *Panax* [illegible]. It grows naturally in dry pastures and mountainous places in England and most parts of Europe.

2. Prickly-cupped *Cistus* is, *Cistus suffruticosus* [illegible] *hispidis*. Gronovius calls it, *Cistus foliis* [illegible] *lanceolatis* [illegible]; Le Monnier, *Cistus foliis* [illegible]; Caspar Bauhine, *Cistus* [illegible]; [illegible] *Helianthemum* [illegible] *flore* [illegible]; and Clusius, [illegible]. It grows naturally in Spain and Narbonne.

3. Apennine *Cistus* is, *Cistus suffruticosus*, [illegible] *foliis lanceolatis* [illegible]. [illegible] calls it, *Helianthemum* [illegible]; and Dillenius, *Helianthemum* [illegible] *foliis* [illegible] *oblongis*, [illegible]. It grows naturally on the Appennine and Italian Mountains.

4. Dwarf Mountain *Cistus* is titled, *Cistus* [illegible] *stipulatus* [illegible], *foliis oblongo* [illegible]. Plukenet calls it *Cistus* [illegible]; Ray, *Cistus* [illegible]; and Dillenius, *Helianthemum* [illegible]. It grows naturally upon Prendown hills in Somersetshire.

5. Hairy Dwarf *Cistus*. This is, *Cistus suffruticosus* [illegible], *foliis lanceolatis* [illegible]. Clusius calls it, *Chamaecistus* [illegible]; Caspar Bauhine, *Chamaecistus foliis* [illegible]; John Bauhine, *Helianthemum flore* [illegible] *angusto* [illegible]; also, *Helianthemum* [illegible], [illegible]; and Sauvages, *Cistus stipulis* [illegible], *Cistus foliis villosis lanceolatis*, [illegible]. It grows naturally near Montpelier.

6. Thyme-leaved Dwarf *Cistus* is titled, *Cistus suffruticosus*, *stipulis* [illegible], *foliis* [illegible] *oppositis* [illegible]. Barrelier calls it, *Chamaecistus* [illegible] *folio*, [illegible]. It grows naturally in the south of France and Spain.

7. Serpyllum-leaved Dwarf *Cistus* is titled, *Cistus* [illegible], *stipulatus*, [illegible]. Caspar Bauhine calls it, [illegible]; [illegible] *serpilli folio* [illegible] *odorato*; [illegible]. It grows naturally on the Alps of [illegible] and Stiria.

8. [illegible]

*ovatis* Magnol calls it, *Cistus humilis, five Chamæcistus nummulariæ folio*, and John Bauhine, *Helianthemum nummulariam accedens* It grows naturally, near Montpelier

9 Narrow-leaved Dwarf Cistus is, *Cistus suffruticosus procumbens stipulatus, foliis ovato-oblongis subpilosis, petalis lanceolatis* Ray and Dillenius call it, *Helianthemum vulgare, petalis florum perangustis* It is a native of England, and grows naturally in the meadows near Croydon

10 Scaly leaved Dwarf Cistus is, *Cistus suffruticosus stipulatus, foliis oblongis squamis orbiculatis* Barrelier calls it, *Cistus humilis, floribus conspicuis, ... mineris foliis* It is a native of Spain

11 Canada Dwarf *Cistus* is, *Cistus herbaceus ..., foliis omnibus alternis lanceolatis, caule ...* It is a native of Canada

12 Plantain leaved Dwarf *Cistus* is, *Cistus ex... perennis, foliis radicalibus, ovatis trinerviis tomentosis, ... glabris lanceolatis summis alternis* Sauvages calls it, *Cistus perennis, foliis ... appressis villosis summis glabris*, Buxbaum, *Helianthemum, plantaginis folio, perenne*, Caspar Bauhine, *Cistus folio plantaginis*, and John Bauhine, *Tuberaria nostras*, also, *Tuberaria major* It grows naturally in Spain and Italy

13 Oeland Dwarf *Cistus* is, *Cistus suffruticosus procumbens exstipulatus, foliis oppositis oblongis utrinque ... petiolis ciliatis, petalis emarginatis* In the *Flora Suecica* it is termed, *Cistus caule procumbente, foliis oblongis utrinque, stipulis nullis* It grows naturally on the rocks of Oeland

14 Marum-leaved Dwarf *Cistus* is entitled, *Cistus suffruticosus exstipulatus, foliis oppositis ob... planis, subtus incanis* John Bauhine calls it, *Helianthemum Alpinum, foliis pilo... marum Tuchsii*, Haller, *Helianthemum foliis ad terram congestis superne pilosis, inferne tomentosis* and Barrelier, *Helianthemum luteum, thymi ... folio* It is a native of Switzerland and some parts of Italy

15 White Spanish Dwarf *Cistus* is titled, *Cistus suffruticosus exstipulatus procumbens, foliis oppositis oblongis villosis ... floribus subumbellatis* Sauvages calls it, *Cistus foliis ovatis subtus incanis, ... caule procumbente*, Caspar Bauhine, *Chamæcistus foliis ... incanis*, John Bauhine, *Chamæcistus foliis ... cinereis*, Clusius, *Chamæcistus* 3 Seguier, *Helianthemum Alpinum ... folio nigricante & hirsuto*, and Barrelier, *Helianthemum ... flore pallido* It grows naturally in France and Spain

16 Italian Dwarf *Cistus* is, *Cistus suffruticosus exstipulatus, foliis oppositis hispidis inferioribus ovatis, superioribus lanceolatis, ... petalis ...* Barrelier calls it, *Helianthemum serpylli folio ... flore pallido, Italicum* It is a native of Italy

17 Hungarian Dwarf *Cistus* is, *Cistus suffruticosus procumbens exstipulatus, foliis alternis ... petiolis ... scabris ...* In the *Flora Suecica* it is termed, *Cistus caule procumbente, foliis ...* Guettard calls it, *Helianthemum foliis ... alternis, ... hispidis, pedunculis ... caule ... folio* Sauvages, *Cistus fruticosus procumbens, foliis ... calycibus ...dis, floribus ...*, Caspar Bauhine, *Chamæcistus, ericæ folio, luteus humilior*, and John Bauhine, *Helianthemum tenuifolium glabrum, luteo flore, per humum sparsum* It grows naturally in Switzerland, Gothland, and France

18 Heath leaved Dwarf *Cistus* is, *Cistus suffruticosus adscendens exstipulatus, foliis alternis ... lineari... glabris, pedunculis ...* Caspar Bauhine calls it, *Chamæcistus ericæ folio, luteus elatior*, and John Bauhine, *Helianthemum tenuifolium glabrum erectum, luteo flore* It grows naturally near Montpelier

19 Umbellated Dwarf *Cistus* is, *Cistus suffruticosus procumbens exstipulatus, foliis oppositis linearibus, floribus umbellatis* Guettard calls it, *Cistus foliis linearibus non stipulatis, caule florali umbellato lignoso* Caspar Bauhine, *Cistus Ledo foliis thymi* and Clusius, *Ledon* X It grows naturally in France and Spain

# CHAP CXXVI

## CLAYTONIA

Species

THIS genus admits of two species only

1 Virginian *Claytonia*

2 Siberian *Claytonia*

Virginian

1 Virginian *Claytonia* The root is tuberous and small The stalks are slender, and grow but to about three inches high The leaves are narrow, succulent, about two inches long, and of a deep-green colour The flowers are produced from the ends of the stalks, in April, their colour is purple, and there is a variety with white flowers spotted with red The seeds ripen in June, soon after which the stalks die to the ground, and fresh ones arise from the roots early in the spring

and Siberian Claytonia described

2 Siberian *Claytonia* The root is fibrous The leaves are oval, smooth, nervous, broad at the top, and narrow at the base The stalk is round, about three inches high, and adorned with two oval leaves standing opposite to each other, without any footstalk The flowers are large, of a delicate red, and very beautiful in the spring, when they make their appearance

Culture

These plants are propagated by dividing the roots, the best time for which is in the latter part of the summer, when the stalks decay They love a light dry soil, and should be set in a well-sheltered situation, and when this is done, they will require no farther trouble except keeping them clean from weeds

They are also readily propagated by seeds These should be sown in the beginning of autumn, soon after they are ripe, in the places where they are designed to remain They will readily come up, and if the winter should happen to be severe, it would be proper to stick some furze-bushes round them for their defence

In

In the spring the plants must be thinned where they are too close and the weeds constantly plucked up as they arise, and this is all the trouble these plants will require

If they do not come up so close as to injure one another, the thinning may be deferred until the leaves decay, and then the drawn plants may be made to ornament other places for these plants bear removing at that season very well

Titles 1 Virginian *Claytonia* is titled, *Claytonia foliis* ... Plukenet names it, *Ornithogalo affinis* ... *flore purpureo pentapetalo de* ... and Gronovius simply, *Claytonia* It grows common in Virginia, from whence the seeds were sent by Mr Clayton, in honour of whom this genus is thus named

2 Siberian *Claytonia* is, *Claytonia foliis ovatis* In the Stockholm Acts it is termed, *Limnia* It grows common in Siberia

*Claytonia* is of the class and order *Pentandria Monogynia*, and the characters are, Class and order in the Linnæan system

1 CALYX is a two leaved oval perianthium, that is transverse at the base The characters

2 COROLLA consists of five oval, oblong, emarginated petals

3 STAMINA are five awl-shaped recurved filaments, a little shorter than the corolla, having oblong incumbent antheræ

4 PISTILLUM consists of a roundish germen, a simple style the length of the stamina, and a trifid stigma

5 PERICARPIUM is a roundish elastic capsule composed of three valves, and containing three cells

6 SEMINA The seeds are three, and are roundish

# CHAP. CXXVII

## *CLEMATIS*, VIRGIN's BOWER

THE greatest part of this genus are climbers, and fit to cover arbours, and diversify wilderness quarters, woods, hedges, &c but besides those already treated of, there are three beautiful species which grow erect, called,

Species 1 Upright White Climber

2 Upright Blue Climber

3 Maritime Climber

Upright White Climber 1 Upright White Climber The stalks of this species are upright, and grow to be about three feet high The leaves are pinnated, being composed of three or four pairs of oval, spear-shaped, entire folioles, besides the odd one which terminates them and they grow opposite to each other on the stalks The flowers are produced in umbels from the tops of the stalks, their colour is white, and each consists of four or five spreading petals, they make their appearance in June, and the seeds ripen in the autumn

Variety There is a variety of this species, of lower growth and with smaller leaves, but it hath, nevertheless, larger flowers, on which account it is much esteemed

Upright Blue 2 Upright Blue Climber The stalks of this species are erect, firm, slender, fluted, branching a little, and grow to be three or four feet high The leaves are large, oval spear shaped, smooth, entire, and grow opposite to each other at the joints without any footstalks The flowers come out from the upper parts of the plant, on long footstalks, they are large, of a fine violet colour, their petals are thick, and hang drooping they will be in full blow in June, and the seeds ripen in September

and Maritime Climber described 3 Maritime Climber This is a low creeping plant The stalks are unbranching and six cornered. The leaves are pinnated, being composed of about five pair of narrow, stiff smooth folioles, and they grow opposite to each other at the joints The flowers are produced from the tops of the stalks, on slender footstalks, they are moderately large, whitish, come out in June and July, and sometimes the succession continues to the end of summer

Culture These sorts are all propagated by dividing the roots, the best time for which is the autumn, though it may be done successfully in the winter or spring They multiply very fast, so that every other year the roots should be taken up, and reduced to a proper size, planting those again that have two or three good buds at the top of each

Soil and situation They are all very hardy, will grow in any soil or situation, and are highly proper to mix in the shrubbery, where they will shew their flowers in the vacancies among the lower trees to advantage, and in those places have a pretty effect

Titles 1 Upright White Climber is named, *Clematis foliis pinnatis foliolis ovato-lanceolatis integerrimis, caule erecto, floribus pentapetalis tetrapetalisque* Caspar Bauhine terms it, *Flammula recta* and Camerarius, *Flammula* It grows common on the hilly parts of Austria, Pannonia, Tartary, and the south of France

2 Upright Blue Climber is, *Clematis foliis simplicibus sessilibus ovato lanceolatis, floribus cernuis* Caspar Bauhine calls it, *Clematitis cærulea erecta* and Clusius, *Clematis cærulea Pannonica* It grows naturally in Hungary and Tartary

3 Maritime Climber is, *Clematis foliis pinnatis linearibus, caulibus simplicibus hexagonis* Caspar Bauhine calls it, *Clematis maritima repens* It grows naturally on the sea-shores of Italy and the south of France

# CHAP. CXXVIII.

## *CLINOPODIUM*, FIELD-BASIL.

THERE are only three species of this genus, called,

Species.

1. Common Field Basil.
2. Hoary Field-Basil.
3. Rough-leaved Field Basil.

Common Field Basil.

1. Common Field-Basil. The root is fibrous. The stalks are square, slender, hairy, branching a little near the top, and grow to about a foot and a half high. The leaves are oval, hairy, of a pale green colour, and grow opposite to each other at the joints. The flowers grow in whorls round the upper parts of the stalks, and each branch is terminated with a head of the flowers; they appear in June and July, and the seeds ripen in the autumn.

Varieties.

The varieties of this species are,

The Purple flowered.
The Red flowered.
The White flowered.
The Greater broad-leaved Field Basil.
The Rough-leaved Field Basil, having the whorls placed at a great distance from each other, commonly called the Ægyptian Field-Basil.

Hoary.

2. Hoary Field-Basil. The root is fibrous. The stalks are square, hoary, branching a little near the top, and grow to about two feet high. The leaves are oval, spear-shaped, serrated, hoary, strongly (and to some very agreeably) scented, and grow opposite by pairs at the joints [illegible] footstalks. The flowers terminate the stalks in flat tufts or heads, and others surround it at the joints a little lower; their colour is a pale-purple, and the lowest tufts are always the largest; they come out in July, and the seeds ripen in the autumn.

This plant is said to be an antidote against the bite of the rattle-snake; hence the name Snake-weed is given to it by the inhabitants of America, where it grows naturally.

Rough-leaved Field Basil described.

3. Rough-leaved Field-Basil. The stalks of this species are square, hairy, branching near the top, and grow to upwards of two feet high. The leaves are rough, hairy, serrated, and grow opposite by pairs at the joints. The flowers come out from the wings of the leaves, on each side of the stalk, on slender hairy footstalks; they are collected into small roundish heads; their colour is white, and they much resemble those of scabious; they make their appearance in September, and are rarely succeeded by seeds in our gardens.

Varieties.

There are three or four varieties of this species, some of which grow to upwards of three feet high, whilst others hardly ever arrive at the height of above a foot.

This sort must have a dry warm soil and a well-sheltered situation, otherwise it will not live through our winters; so that it would be advisable to set two or three plants in pots, to be housed in winter, to preserve the sorts, in case a severe winter should put a period to those [illegible] planted abroad.

Culture.

All these kinds are easily propagated by sowing of the seeds [illegible] of the roots. The best time for [illegible] the autumn; and [illegible] should be sown in the spring on a slight hotbed, to bring them forward. When they come up, they must be thinned where they appear too close, have plenty of air, and frequent waterings; they must afterwards be inured by degrees to the full air, when the glasses should be entirely taken off both night and day.

They need not be removed from the hotbed, but stand there until the autumn, by which time they will be strong plants, and may be then set out for good.

They all [illegible] dry soil and a warm situation; [illegible] on, but this must be more peculiarly granted to the third sort, as well as the throwing a few of the plants in pots, to ensure the continuance of the species.

1. Common Field Basil is titled, *Clinopodium capitulis subrotundis hispidis, bracteis setaceis*. In the *Hortus Cliffortianus* it is termed, *Clinopodium foliis ovatis, capitulis verticillatis*. Caspar Bauhine calls it, *Clinopodium origano simile*; and Camerarius, *Clinopodium*. The Ægyptian variety stands in Miller's Dictionary with the title, *Clinopodium foliis ovatis rugosis verticillis omnibus distantibus*. It grows common in England, and several parts of Europe, Canada and Egypt.

2. Hoary Field Basil is, *Clinopodium foliis subtus tomentosis, verticillis explanatis, bracteis lanceolatis*. Van Royen names it *Clinopodium foliis lanceolatis [illegible], verticillis [illegible]*; Dillenius, *Clinopodium [illegible] foliis [illegible] odoratum*; Morison, *Clinopodium [illegible] non [illegible], verticillis majoribus, floribus brevioribus [illegible]*; Plukenet, *Clinopodium [illegible] foliis capitulis [illegible]*; and Ray, *Origanum [illegible] ad summitatem caulium [illegible]*. It is a native of North America.

3. Rough-leaved Field-Basil. This is titled, *Clinopodium foliis rugosis, capitulis [illegible]*. Dillenius calls it, *Clinopodium rugosum, capitulis scabiosae*; Plukenet, *Scabiosae [illegible], chrysanthemi [illegible]*; Sloane, *[illegible]*; [illegible] *[illegible] floribus [illegible]*; Ray, *[illegible]*; and Plumier, *[illegible]*. It grows in Carolina and Jamaica.

Class and order in the Linnæan system.

*Clinopodium* is of the class and order *Didynamia Gymnospermia*; and the characters are,

1. CALYX. The involucrum is composed of a multitude of hairs, the length of the calyx, and is placed under the whorl or cluster of flowers.

The perianthium is monophyllous, cylindrical, slightly incurved, and divided into two lips. The upper lip is broad, reflexed, trifid, and acute; the under lip is cut into two narrow inflexed segments.

2. COROLLA is one ringent petal. The tube is short, and gradually widening to the mouth. The upper lip is erect, concave, obtuse, and indented; the lower lip is obtuse, and divided into three segments, of which the middle is the broadest and indented.

3 STAMINA are four filaments under the upper lip, of these two are shorter than the others, and all have roundish antheræ

4 PISTILLUM consists of a quadripartite germen, a filiforme style the length and situation of the stamina, and a simple, acute, compressed stigma

5 PERICARPIUM There is none The seeds are contained in the calyx

6 SEMINA The seeds are four, and oval

# CHAP CXXIX.

## *CLYPEOLA*, CLYPEATED MUSTARD

THERE are only two species of this genus, one of which is an annual, the other a perennial The perennial species is usually called Maritime Treacle Mustard, or *Alysson* The stalks of this species are numerous, tough, spreading, branching, and grow to about a foot and a half high The leaves are narrow, green on their upper side, but hoary underneath, and sit close to the branches without any footstalks The flowers terminate the branches in long spikes, having a roundish tuft at the end, they are small, white, come out in June, and the seeds ripen in September

This plant described

Culture

This sort is propagated by sowing of the seeds, in the spring, in the places where they are to remain When the plants come up, nothing more need be done than to thin them to proper distances, and keep them clean from weeds They will grow in any soil or situation, provided it be not too rich and moist, in such a station they are sometimes destroyed by hard weather in winters, but in poor, hungry, sandy, or gravelly soils, similar to that in which they naturally grow, they will be less luxuriant, will flower, perfect their seeds every year, and bid defiance to our keenest frosts

The seeds may be also sown on a bed of light sandy earth, and in the autumn the plants may be removed to the places where they are wanted, but removed plants seldom do so well as those that have never been disturbed

Titles

This species is titled, *Clypeola siliculis bilocularibus ovatis dispermis* Caspar Bauhine calls it, *Thlaspi alysson dictum mariti mum*, and Tabernæmontanus, *Thlaspi Narbonense, centunculi angusto folio* It grows naturally on the sea shores and sandy gravelly parts of Italy, France, and Spain

Class and order in the Linnæan System

*Clypeola* is of the class and order *Tetradynamia Siliculosa*, and the characters are,

The characters

1 CALYX is a permanent perianthium, composed of four oval oblong leaves

2 COROLLA is cruciforme, and consists of four oblong entire petals, which have ungues rather longer than the calyx

3 STAMINA There are six filaments shorter than the corolla, of which the two opposite ones are the shortest, the antheræ are simple

4 PISTILLUM consists of a roundish compressed germen, a simple style, and an obtuse stigma

5 PERICARPIUM is an orbicular, compressed, erect pod, composed of two valves

6 SEMINA The seeds are round and compressed

# CHAP CXXX.

## *CNICUS*, FOREIGN THISTLE

Species

THE species of this genus are,

1 Meadow *Cnicus*
2 Dwarf *Cnicus*
3 Prickly Alpine *Cnicus*
4 Jagged-leaved Meadow *Cnicus*
5 Pyrenean *Cnicus*
6 Nodding *Cnicus*
7 Fish *Cnicus*

Description of the Meadow,

1 Meadow *Cnicus* The stalks of this species are smooth, striated, branching near the top, and grow to be four feet high The radical leaves are pinnatifid, very large, long, and spread themselves on the ground all around, those on the stalks are heart shaped, entire, serrated, prickly, and embrace the stalk with their base The flowers terminate the stalks in clusters, their colour is a whitish yellow, they grow in moderately large heads, have scaly cups, come out in June, and their seeds ripen in September

Dwarf,

2 Dwarf *Cnicus* This is, as the name imports, a very low plant The leaves are oblong, narrow, sessile, and clustered together The stalk supports one flower only, sitting in a largish scaly cup, it comes forth in June or July, and the seeds ripen in the autumn

Prickly Alpine

3 Prickly Alpine *Cnicus* The stalk of this species is upright, single, and grows to about four feet high The leaves are so sinuated as to have

have the appearance of a pinnated leaf, they are very prickly, and embrace the stalk with their base. The flowers come out from the extremity of the stalk without any footstalk, and are surrounded by a cluster of broad, prickly, yellow-coloured leaves; they make their appearance in June, and the seeds ripen in September.

Jagged-leaved Meadow. 4 Jagged-leaved Meadow *Cnicus*. This species grows to be two or six feet high. The leaves are jagged, or deeply cut into a multitude of spear-shaped, prickly, ciliated segments, and embrace the stalk with their base. The flowers are purple, and hang drooping in glutinous or clammy cups; they come out about the same time with the former, and ripen their seeds accordingly.

Pyrenean. 5 Pyrenean *Cnicus*. This grows to about the height of the former. The leaves are pinnatifid, serrated, and have no prickles. The flowers are produced in June or July, from the ends of the branches, having cups composed of scales which are spear-shaped, membranaceous, and sharp-pointed.

Nodding. 6 Nodding *Cnicus*. The root of this species is composed of large fleshy fibres. The stalks are robust, striated, reddish, send out many short side branches, and grow to be six or eight feet high. The leaves are large, heart-shaped, serrated, of a deep green colour on their upper side, and white underneath. The lower ones have very short footstalks, and the upper ones embrace the stalk with their base. The flowers are produced singly from the ends of the branches; the florets are collected into globular heads, having cups composed of scales, which end in sharp spines; the flowers are of a yellowish colour; they come out in June, and the seeds ripen in September. The young stalks of this plant are by some people boiled, and preferred to many other vegetables. In Siberia, where the plant grows naturally, it is one of the common esculents of the country.

and Fish Cnicus. 7 Fish *Cnicus*. The stalk of this species is simple, but branches near the top, and grows to about three feet high. The leaves are spear-shaped, undivided, indented, and decurrent; they are of a hoary whiteness, and at every indenture are placed two long yellowish spines. The flowers are produced from the ends of the branches, in oval, woolly, prickly cups; their colour is yellow, but as they are nearly concealed by the calyx, they make but a small show; they will be in blow in July and August, and the seeds ripen in the autumn. The spines of this plant resemble the bones of some sort of fish, which occasioned this species being distinguished by the name of Fish *Cnicus*.

Culture. All these sorts are best propagated by sowing of the seeds, soon after they are ripe, in the autumn, though they will grow very well if they are kept until the spring. After the plants come up, nothing more is to be done except keeping them clean from weeds, and thinning them where they appear too close.

The largest plants ought not to be left more than four feet from each other, and the others at proportionably less distances, and if the ground be dug between them in the winter, they will arise to a greater height, and flower stronger for it the summer following.

They may be also propagated by parting the roots in the autumn or spring; but the plants will be for the most part weak, and of inferior beauty to those raised from seeds.

1 Meadow *Cnicus* is titled, *Cnicus foliis pinnatifidis carinatis nudis bracteis subcoloratis integris concavis*. Caspar Bauhine calls it, *Carduus pratensis latifolius*; also, *Cirsium latissimum*. Clusius terms it, *Carduus pratensis*. It grows common in meadows, hedges, and woods in many of the northern parts of Europe. Titles.

2 Dwarf *Cnicus* is termed, *Cnicus caule unifloro, foliis subulatis imbricatis sessilibus confertissimis, calyce inermi*. Caspar Bauhine names it, *Carduus mollis, folio oblongo, cirsii capitulo*; and Clusius, *Carduus mollior humilis longifolius* [illegible]. It is a native of Sneeberg.

3 Prickly Alpine *Cnicus* is, *Cnicus foliis* [illegible] *sinuato-pinnatis spinosis*, [illegible] *foliolis* [illegible]. Caspar Bauhine terms it, *Carlina polycephalos* [illegible], Haller, [illegible] *spinosissimum, floribus* [illegible], and Gmelin, [illegible]. It grows common on the Helvetian, Austrian, and Tartarian Mountains.

4 Jagged-leaved Meadow *Cnicus* is, *Cnicus foliis amplexicaulibus* [illegible] *nutantibus glutinosis*. Caspar Bauhine styles it, *Carduus pratensis*, [illegible] *laciniatis*; Plukenet, *Carduo-cirsium* [illegible] *foliorum* [illegible] *spinis* [illegible]; Tournefort, *Cirsium* [illegible], and Dalechamp, [illegible]. It grows common in the meadows and hilly parts of Austria and Gaul.

5 Pyrenean *Cnicus* is named, *Cnicus foliis* [illegible], *squamis calycinis* [illegible]. In the *Hortus Cliffortianus* it is termed, *Carduus* [illegible], *foliis pinnatifidis* [illegible], *squamis calycinis* [illegible]. Morison styles it, *Centaurium majus, foliis* [illegible]. It is a native of the Pyrenean Mountains.

6 Nodding *Cnicus* is, *Cnicus foliis cordatis, petiolis crispis spinosis amplexicaulibus, floribus cernuis*. Gmelin styles it, *Carduus foliis excordato lanceolatis margine serratis & spinosis, squamis calycinis membranaceis, laceris spinosis, capitulis nutantibus*. It is a native of Siberia.

7 Fish *Cnicus* is named, *Cnicus foliis decurrentibus lanceolatis indivisis, calycibus pinnato-spinosis*. In the former edition of the *Species Plantarum* it is termed, *Carduus foliis lanceolatis dentatis ciliatis decurrentibus spinis marginalibus duplicatis*. Van Royen styles it, *Carduus caule alato spinoso, foliis spinosis, spinis duplicibus*. Caspar Bauhine, *Acarna major, caule folioso*; also, *Acarna humilis, caule folioso*; Clusius, *Carduus* [illegible] *Salmanticensis*; and Dalechamp, *Picnomon Cretae salonensis*. It grows common in the fields of Spain.

*Cnicus* is of the class and order *Syngenesia Polygamia Aequalis*, and the characters are, Class and order in the Linnaean system.

1 CALYX. The general calyx is oval and imbricated, the scales being oval and sharp pointed. The characters.

2 COROLLA. The compound flower is tubulous and uniform. The florets are funnel-shaped, oblong, and divided at the top into five erect segments, that are nearly equal.

3 STAMINA are five very short capillary filaments, having a cylindrical tubular anthera.

4 PISTILLUM consists of a short germen, a filiform style the length of the stamina, and an oblong emarginated stigma.

5 PERICARPIUM. There is none. The calyx closing contains the seed.

6 SEMEN. The seed is single, and crowned with down.

The receptacle is plain and hairy.

## CHAP CXXXI

## *COCHLEARIA*, SCURVY-GRASS, or, SPOON-WORT

THERE are only two Perennials of this genus,

Species

1 Common Horse Radish

2 Low Hoary Dittander

Description of the Common Horse Radish

1 The Common Horse-Radish is a well-known plant, and allowed by most to exhibit more beauties at the table, with proper company, than it does when in full flower in the garden, which brings it of course into the articles belonging to the Kitchen Garden

and Low Hoary Dittander

2 Low Hoary Dittander This is the usual name of this species, it being formerly reckoned a *Lepidum* It is the *Lepidum Draba* of the former edition of the *Species Plantarum*, but closer examination than heretofore, places it under *Cochlearia*

The root is fleshy and creeping The stalks are weak and will grow to about a foot and a half high The leaves are spear shaped, indented, hoary, and embrace the stalks with their base The flowers grow at the ends of the branches in bunches, they are small, and of a white colour, they will be in blow in June, July, and August, and sometimes in September, and afford plenty of seeds in the autumn

There is a variety of this species of much lower growth, and with leaves that are less hoary

Culture

They are propagated by dividing of the roots any time in the autumn or winter, though the former is the more eligible season Any soil or situation will do for them, though they love the shade, and every two years the roots should be taken up and reduced or the plants will become too rambling and unsightly

Titles.

This species is titled, *Cochlearia foliis caulinis lanceolatis dentatis amplexicaulibus* In the *Hortus Cliffort.* it is termed, *Lepidum foliis lanceolatis amplexicaulibus dentatis* Caspar Bauhine calls it, *Draba umbellata, five major, capitulis donata*, and Clusius, *Draba vulgaris* It grows naturally in Austria Gaul, and Italy

Class and order in the Linnæan System

*Cochlearia* is of the class and order *Tetradynamia Siliculosa*, and the characters are,

The characters

1 CALYX is a perianthium composed of four oval, concave, deciduous leaves

2 COROLLA consists of four oval, patent petals, placed in form of a cross, they are doubly the size of the calyx, and have narrow ungues

3 STAMINA consist of six subulated filaments the length of the calyx, of which the two opposite are shortest, with obtuse, compressed antheræ

4 PISTILLUM consists of a cordated germen a very short, simple, permanent style, and an obtuse stigma

5 PERICARPIUM is a cordated, gibbous, compressed, scabrous, bilocular pod, fastened to the style

6 SEMINA The seeds are about four in each cell

## CHAP CXXXII

## *COLCHICUM*, MEADOW-SAFFRON.

Introductory Remarks

THE singular look of *Colchicum* is much admired by most people The flowers appear in the autumn without any leaves attending them, hence the appellation Naked Ladies has been applied to them They are of the Crocus kind, and though the number of species are but three in reality, yet they admit of many varieties of different kinds and doubles, and are very ornamental among the low-growing plants of the like nature in the autumnal season

The species of this genus are,

Species

1 The Common Meadow Saffron

2 The Mountain *Colchicum*

3 The Waved-leaved chequered *Colchicum*

Common Meadow Saffron,

1 The Common Meadow Saffron This may properly be called Common, for a term of distinction from the others, as we have it growing common in our meadows and gardens By the power of good culture, different colours and various kinds of doubles are produced The root is an oblong roundish bulb, frequently compressed, and covered with a dark-brown bark The leaves and flowers appear at different seasons, the leaves come out in March, and decay in June, they will grow to near half a foot in length, are in breadth about an inch, and their colour is a deep green, the leaves being gone, no appearance of a plant is to be found until the beginning of September, and then the flowers burst forth immediately from the root, entirely naked and defenceless The tube of the flower, like that of the Crocus, is long, and supplies the place of a footstalk, it grows erect, widens gradually, and near the top divides into six large segments Their colour is different in the different varieties, and the leaves differ in their breadth and size, insomuch that we have of this species,

Varieties

The Purple Meadow Saffron

The-

The White Meadow Saffron
The Pale Purple Meadow Saffron
The Variegated Meadow Saffron
The Many flowering Purple Meadow Saffron
The Many flowering White Meadow Saffron
The Double Purple Meadow Saffron
The Double Red Meadow Saffron
The Double White Meadow Saffron
The Broad leaved Meadow Saffron
The Striped-leaved Meadow Saffron

With this vast variety is our autumn adorned, and our borders enriched by their singular as well as beautiful appearance

Mountain

2 Mountain *Colchicum* Of this there are but few varieties, and the leaves succeed the flowers much sooner than those of the former sort The root is a small bulb, covered with a very dark brown bark From this spring the leaves, soon after the flowers are past, they are long, narrow, and spreading, and shew themselves of a fine green during the winter season In summer these die off and in September, and sometimes sooner, the naked flowers appear, they are of a reddish colour, the segments are long and narrow, and the stamina are yellow

and Chequered Colchicum described

3 Chequered *Colchicum* Of this there are the Waved leaved and the Plain leaved sorts, which have been ranked by old botanists as distinct species The root is an oblong flattish bulb The leaves are broad, and of a deep green colour, in some varieties they are undulated, in others plain, they come up in the spring, and go off in June The flowers appear the beginning of September, they arise naked like the others, are large, grow erect, and the segments are very long and beautiful They are chequered like the Fritillaries, and the chequer-work consists of different colours; the Pale Crimson, the Blood Red, and the White, often combine to form their flowers in such great beauty and perfection as is pretty well known

Method of propagating these species

The propagation of these plants is by dividing of the roots, and sowing the seeds The proper season for dividing the roots is the summer, after the leaves are decayed, if they have stood undisturbed for some years, they will have formed themselves into large bunches, and afford plenty of bulbs for use Beds may be formed for the different varieties, which will be very beautiful, but if they are planted singly about the garden, a small stick should be placed by each bulb, for a mark to prevent their being dug up or destroyed by labourers, or persons employed to work in the garden, which is too frequently the case They require as little trouble as almost any plants, and are so hardy that the roots will flower unplanted, lying only on the surface of the ground

By seeds fresh varieties may be obtained After the flowers are faded, the vessels that contain the seeds slowly raise themselves, they may be found among the green leaves in the spring, but will not arrive at maturity till about June In the autumn let the seeds be sown in boxes or pots, and then be placed under a warm hedge all winter, in the spring they will come up, at which time the morning sun only, until about ten o'clock, should be allowed them Watering in dry weather must be afforded them, and after the leaves are decayed a little fresh mould must be sifted over them, and they should be then placed in the shade all summer At the approach of winter let them resume their old situation under the warm hedge, and in the spring, as the days get long, let them have the morning sun until ten o clock After the leaves are decayed, plant them out where they are designed to flower The soil should be fresh and good, and if their situation is screened from the afternoon sun it will be the better Thus may these plants be raised by seeds, and by this method fresh varieties may be expected

Titles

1 The Common *Colchicum* is entitled, *Colchicum foliis planis lanceolatis erectis* Caspar Bauhine calls it, *Colchicum commune*, and Parkinson and Gerard, *Colchicum Anglicum purpureum et Anglicum album* It is found growing naturally in several of our rich meadows and pastures

2 Mountain *Colchicum*. This is titled, *Colchicum foliis linearibus patentissimis* Clusius calls it, *Colchicum montanum* It grows naturally in Spain and Portugal

3 Chequered *Colchicum* This is termed, *Colchicum foliis undulatis patentibus* Morison calls it, *Colchicum Chioense floribus fritillariæ instar tessulatis, foliis undulatis* It is a native of the Levant

Class and order in the Linnæan System The characters

*Colchicum* is of the class and order *Hexandria Trigynia*, and the characters are,

1 CALYX There is none

2 COROLLA is of one leaf The tube is angular, and rises directly from the root, and the limb is divided into six spear-shaped, oval, concave, erect segments

3 STAMINA are six subulated filaments shorter than the corolla with oblong incumbent antheræ, which are formed of four valves

4 PISTILLUM consists of a germen that is buried in the root, of three filiforme styles the length of the stamina, with their reflexed channelled stigmas

5 PERICARPIUM is a trilobate obtuse capsule of three cells, having a suture on the inside

6 SEMINA The seeds are many, roundish, and rough

CHAP

# CHAP. CXXXIII.

## *COLLINSONIA.*

THERE is but one ſpecies of this genus, called *Collinſonia*, in honour of my late worthy and ingenious friend Peter Collinſon, Eſq. F. R. S. who firſt introduced this plant into the Engliſh gardens.

Collinſonia deſcribed. The root is ſpreading, the ſtalk ſquare, upright, and grows to three or four feet in height. The leaves are heart-ſhaped, ſerrated, and grow oppoſite to each other. The flowers grow from the ends of the ſtalks, in looſe ſpikes; they are of a pale red colour, come out in July, and the ſeeds ripen in the autumn.

Culture. It is propagated by parting of the roots in the autumn, by which means it may be encreaſed very faſt. It loves a moiſt rich ſoil and a ſhady ſituation; and if thus ſtationed, it will grow to a greater height, and produce larger and proportionably longer ſpikes of flowers.

It may be alſo raiſed from the ſeeds, which ſhould be ſown in a bed of fine mould in the ſpring. When the plants come up too cloſe, they ſhould be thinned to three inches diſtance; all ſummer they ſhould be kept clean from weeds, watered in dry weather, and in the autumn they may be removed to the places where they are deſigned to remain.

Title. There being no other ſpecies belonging to it, it is named ſimply, *Collinſonia*. It grows naturally in the woods and moiſt parts of Virginia, Canada, Penſylvania, and Maryland.

*Collinſonia* is of the claſs and order *Diandria Monogynia*; and the characters are,

Claſs and order in the Linnæan ſyſtem. The characters. 1. CALYX is a monophyllous, tubular, permanent, bilabiated perianthium. The upper lip is broad, trifid, and reflexed; the lower lip is more erect, is awl-ſhaped, and divided into two parts.

2. COROLLA conſiſts of one unequal petal. The tube is funnel-ſhaped, and much longer than the calyx. The limb is divided into five parts; the upper ones are ſhort, obtuſe, and two of them are reflexed; the under lip is long, and cut into many capillary ſegments.

3. STAMINA are two ſetaceous, very long, erect filaments, with ſimple, incumbent, compreſſed, obtuſe antheræ.

4. PISTILLUM conſiſts of an obtuſe quadrifid germen, with a large gland, a briſtly ſtyle the length of the ſtamina, and inclining to one ſide, and an acute bifid ſtigma.

5. PERICARPIUM. There is none. The ſeed is contained in the bottom of the calyx.

6. SEMEN. The ſeed is ſingle and roundiſh.

# CHAP. CXXXIV.

## *COMARUM,* MARSH CINQUEFOIL.

THERE is but one ſpecies of this genus yet known, uſually called Red Marſh Cinquefoil.

Red Marſh Cinquefoil deſcribed. The root is thick, woody, and poſſeſſed of numerous black fibres. The ſtalks are round, reddiſh, two or three feet long, and often lie on the ground. The leaves are each compoſed of five lobes, though ſometimes there will be ſix or ſeven; these lobes are oblong, ſerrated, hoary underneath, and join at their baſe, ſtanding on pretty long footſtalks. The flowers are produced from the upper parts of the ſtalks, three or four growing together on ſhortiſh footſtalks; they are of a reddiſh-purple colour. Their botanical characters ſhew their ſtructure; they make their appearance in July, and the ſeeds ripen in the autumn.

Proper ſoil. This plant grows naturally in boggy and marſhy places, and its ſtation in a garden ſhould be in ground of a ſimilar nature, otherwiſe its culture will not be worth the attempting; though it will grow in a moiſt ſhady place, where the ſoil is deep and good.

Culture. It is propagated by parting of the roots, the beſt time for which buſineſs is the autumn. Previous to this operation, the ground of the bog ſhould be well dug, and cleared from the roots of all weeds; then having your ſetts in readineſs, plant as many of them as you would chuſe, at about a yard aſunder. It will be proper to ſhade them at firſt, if the work be done early in the autumn; but afterwards they will call for no trouble, not even weeding, for they will riſe with the natural herbage of the place, flower ſtrong, and perfect their ſeeds every year. There is a variety of it, with thick hairy leaves.

They are alſo propagated by ſeeds. The ground muſt be made as fine as the nature of the place will admit of, and the ſeeds ſown in the ſpring, covering them down with about half an inch of the boggy ſoil. At firſt the ground muſt be kept clear from weeds, until they get about four inches high, when the weeding may be diſcontinued, for they will be ſtrong enough to defend themſelves from injuries of that nature.

Titles. There being no other ſpecies of this genus, it

stands with the name simply, *Comarum*. Caspar Bauhine calls it, *Quinquefolium palustre rubrum*, Tournefort, *Pentaphylloides palustre rubrum*, Gerard, *Pentaphyllum rubrum palustre*, and Ray, *Pentaphylloides palustre rubrum crassis et villosis foliis, [illegible] et tuberosum* It grows naturally in many boggy ground, and standing waters in England, and most parts of Europe

Class and order in the Linnæan system: *Comarum* is of the class and order *Icosandria Polygynia*, and the characters are,

1 CALYX is a large, coloured, permanent, monophyllous perianthium, divided into three spreading segments, which are alternately smaller

2 COROLLA is five oblong acuminated petals, much smaller than the calyx, and inserted in it

3 STAMINA are twenty awl shaped persisting filaments inserted in the calyx, and of the length of the flower, having moon-shaped deciduous antheræ

4 PISTILLUM consists of numerous, small, roundish germina, collected into a head, having short simple styles arising from their sides, and simple stigmas

5 PERICARPIUM There is none The common receptacle of the seeds is a large, fleshy, permanent fruit of the figure of a [illegible]

6 SEMINA The seeds are numerous, sharp pointed, and adhere to the fruit

## CHAP CXXXV

## *CONVALLARIA*, LILY of the VALLEY, and SOLOMON's SEAL

THE Lily of the Vale, and Solomon's Seal, being now found to be of the same family, the species of this genus stand thus,

Species

1 Lily of the Valley
2 Solomon's Seal
3 Narrow-leaved Solomon's Seal
4 Many-flowered Solomon's Seal
5 Racemous Solomon's Seal
6 Stellated Solomon's Seal
7 Three-leaved *Convallaria*
8 Two leaved *Convallaria*, or Least Lily of the Valley

Description of the Lily of the Valley

1 Lily of the Valley is universally admired for the extreme fragrance of the flowers The root is oblong, white, fibrous, and creeps under the surface of the ground From this the leaves come out by pairs, one of which is for the most part taller than the other, they are narrow at the base, broadest in the middle, and diminish gradually to the end, they are from four to six inches long, have several longitudinal veins, and their real colour is a deep green, though in some situations they assume a paler aspect The foot-stalks of the flowers rise immediately from the roots by the sides of the leaves, they are naked, grow to about six inches high, and from the middle to the top the flowers are ranged in a single series, they have crooked footstalks, hang drooping, and the general characters indicate their structure They appear in May, and the seeds ripen in the autumn This is often called May Lily, from the time of its flowering

Virtues of this plant

The flowers are of excellent virtue, they afford a valuable exhilarating cordial, are admirable in conserves, and good for those who are struck with palsies, apoplexies, cramps, &c and are said often to afford great ease to those who are afflicted with the gout The varieties of this excellent species are,

Varieties

Common White Lily of the Valley
Red Lily of the Valley
Striped Lily of the Valley
Double White Lily of the Valley
Double Variegated Lily of the Valley

The flowers of the Red Lily of the Valley are the least of all the sorts, and less valuable, tho not very common, the Striped and the Double kinds are truly excellent, especially the [illegible] the flowers being delightfully striped with purple and white

Soil and situation

These sorts grow naturally in woods and shady places, so their situation in a garden should be as similar as possible, they love a light loose soil, and when that happens, they make amazing progress, and produce great plenty of flowers In a rich soil also they increase very fast The leaves will be very large, but the flowers for the most part but very few

Culture

The propagation is by parting of the roots, the best time for which is the autumn If the soil is loose and good, they should be set at a foot and a half asunder, and they will soon meet, if strong and in bad heart, nearer After they are planted they will require no trouble, except keeping them clean from weeds, until the roots are all matted one among another, when a fresh bed should be planted in a different spot of the garden, as before, and when that is in perfection the others may be destroyed, to make room for something else

This work must be repeated about every fourth or fifth year, otherwise the flowers will be very small, and of inferior beauty to those growing from single plants

Solomon's Seal

2 Solomon's Seal The root is thick, fleshy, white, creeping, jointed, knotty, and [illegible] The stalks are edged, [illegible], about [illegible] feet long, and [illegible] at the bottom, [illegible] adorned at the top, where they turn downwards, with oblong, [illegible] ribbed leaves, [illegible] one side of the stalks, while the other is [illegible] with the flowers, they grow singly, and [illegible] the stalks with their [illegible] The flowers come out from the wings of the leaves, but turn to the opposite side of the stalks, they have [illegible] crooked footstalks, and hang drooping, are white at the bottom, but green at the top, they appear

in May, and the seeds ripen in the autumn. The varieties of this species are,

Varieties

Common Solomon's Seal
Purple stalked Solomon's Seal
Sweet scented Solomon's Seal
Double flowered Solomon's Seal

Narrow leaved

3. Narrow-leaved Solomon's Seal. The root is oblong, white, jointed, and fibrated. The stalks are slender, angular, upright, and a foot and a half, or two feet high. The leaves are long, narrow, smooth, of a bluish green, and grow in whorls round the stalks at the joints. The flowers come out from the joints on short footstalks; they are small, and usually grow four or five together on a footstalk. The bottom of the flowers is white, but the brim is green; they appear in May and June, and the seeds ripen in the autumn.

and Many flower'd Solomon's Seal

4. Many flowered Solomon's Seal. The root is thick, white, jointed, creeping, and fibrated. The stalks are taper, firm, and grow upwards of two feet high. The leaves are smooth, broad, of a dark green colour, and embrace the stalks with their base. The flowers grow many together on footstalks, which come out from the wings of the leaves; they are of a greenish-white colour, come out in May and early in June, and the seeds ripen in September. The varieties of this species are,

Varieties

The Large Broad-leaved Many flowered Solomon's Seal
The Dwarf Multiflorous Solomon's Seal
The Sweet-scented Multiflorous Solomon's Seal
The Double Multiflorous Solomon's Seal

Racemous or Branching

5. Racemous or Branching spiked Solomon's Seal. The stalks of this plant are upright, firm, and grow to near a yard high. The leaves are oblong, pointed, ribbed, of a pale green colour, grow alternately, and sit close without any footstalk. The flowers are produced in branching spikes from the ends of the stalks; they are of a pale-yellow colour, come out in May and June, and are rarely succeeded by seeds in our gardens.

Stellated Solomon's Seal

6. Stellated Solomon's Seal. The stalks are firm, and two feet high. The leaves are oblong, numerous, of a pale-green colour, and embrace the stalks with their base. The flowers grow in single spikes from the extremities of the stalks; they are of a pale-yellow colour, come out early in June, and are succeeded by small red berries, which will be ripe in the autumn.

Three leaved

7. Three-leaved *Convallaria*. The stalk of this plant is slender, firm, and about a foot and a half high. The leaves are oval, oblong, ribbed, and embrace the stalks with their base. The flowers grow in single spikes from the ends of the stalks; they come out in May and June, and are very rarely succeeded by seeds in our gardens.

Two leaved Convallaria described

8. Two leaved *Convallaria*, or Least Lily of the Valley. The root is slender, white, fibrous, and creeping. The stalks are upright, slender, and grow to about half a foot high. The radical leaves are heart shaped, and arise from the roots on footstalks; those on the stalks are few in number, seldom being more than two, which are situated one above another. The flowers grow in loose spikes at the ends of the stalks; they are white, and finely scented; they come out in May, and are succeeded by small red berries, which will be ripe in the autumn.

Method of propagating them

All these sorts are propagated by parting of the roots the best time for which is the autumn, when the stalks decay; though they are very hardy, and will grow if removed at any time of the year. When they are planted they will call for no trouble, except keeping them clean from weeds, and reducing their roots every three or four years, for they multiply very fast, and unless kept within bounds will overspread all small plants that may grow near them.

Virtues of the root of the Common Solomon's Seal

The root of the Common Solomon's Seal is of great fame for closing of green wounds, knitting of bones, curing of bruises, and clearing away black or blue marks occasioned by falls or blows; in short it is one of the best vulneraries we have, and is applied in form of a poultice to the wounded parts.

Titles

1. Lily of the Valley is titled, *Convallaria scapo nudo*. Gerard calls it, *Lilium convallium*; Parkinson, *Lilium convallium flore albo*; Caspar Bauhine calls the sorts by the various names of *Lilium convallium album*, *Lilium convallium [illegible]*, *Lilium convallium latifolium*, and *Lilium convallium flore rubente*. It grows naturally in England, and most of the northern countries of Europe.

2. Solomon's Seal is titled, *Convallaria foliis alternis amplexicaulibus caule ancipiti, pedunculis axillaribus subunifloris*. In the *Flora Suecica* it is termed, *Convallaria foliis alternis, floribus axillaribus*. Sauvages calls it, *Convallaria foliis alternis, pedunculis pendulis unifloris*; Caspar Bauhine, *Polygonatum floribus ex singularibus pediculis*; also, *Polygonatum latifolium flore majore odoro*. It grows naturally in woods and hedges, by the sides of hills and shady places in England, and in most of the northern countries of Europe.

3. Narrow leaved Solomon's Seal is titled, *Convallaria foliis verticillatis*. Dodonæus calls it, *Polygonatum alterum*; Caspar Bauhine, *Polygonatum angustifolium non ramosum*; also, *Polygonatum angustifolium ramosum*. It grows naturally in forests, hills, precipices, and plains, in most of the northern parts of Europe.

4. Many-flowered Solomon's Seal is titled, *Convallaria foliis alternis amplexicaulibus, caule tereti, pedunculis axillaribus multifloris*. Sauvages calls it, *Convallaria foliis alternis, pedunculis pendulis multifloris*; Caspar Bauhine, *Polygonatum latifolium maximum*; and Clusius, *Polygonatum latifolium 1*. It inhabits the like places with the former, and is found in most of the northern parts of Europe.

5. Racemous Solomon's Seal is, *Convallaria foliis sessilibus, racemo terminali composito*. In the *Hortus Cliffortianus* it is termed, *Convallaria foliis alternis, racemo terminali*. Van Royen calls it, *Convallaria racemo composito*; Cornutus, *Polygonatum racemosum*; Morison, *Polygonatum ramosum & racemosum spicatum*; and Plukenet, *Polygonatum racemosum Americanum, [illegible] foliis amplissimis*. It grows naturally in Virginia and Canada.

6. Stellated Solomon's Seal is titled, *Convallaria foliis amplexicaulibus plurimis*. Morison calls it, *Polygonatum Virginianum erectum spicatum, flore stellato*; and Cornutus, *Polygonatum Canadense spicatum fertile*. It is a native of Canada.

7. Three leaved *Convallaria* is titled, *Convallaria foliis amplexicaulibus ternis, racemo terminali simplici*. Gmelin calls it, *Convallaria floribus racemosis, foliis ovatis oblongis caulinis*; and Amman, *Phalangium veratri foliis*. It inhabits the woods of Siberia.

8. Two leaved *Convallaria*, or Least Lily of the Valley. This is titled, *Convallaria foliis cordatis*. Caspar Bauhine calls it, *Lilium convallium minus*; and Cammerarius, *Gramen Parnassi*. It is a native of most of the northern parts of Europe.

Class and order in the Linnæan system

*Convallaria* is of the class and order *Hexandria Monogynia*, and the characters are,

The characters

1. CALYX. There is none.

2. COROLLA is one smooth bell-shaped petal, having the limb cut into six obtuse, patent, reflexed segments.

3. STAMINA are six awl-shaped filaments inserted in the petal, shorter than it, terminated by oblong erect antheræ.

4. Pis-

4 PISTILLUM consists of a globular germen, a filiforme style longer than the stamina, and an obtuse three-cornered stigma

5 PERICARPIUM is a round berry containing three cells, and spotted before it is ripe

6 SEMINA The seeds are single and roundish

# CHAP CXXXVI

## *CONVOLVULUS*, BINDWEED

THE sorts of *Convolvulus* which come of course in this place are,

[illegible] 1 Common Perennial Bindweed

2 Larger White Bindweed, or Bear bind

3 Syrian Bindweed, or Scammony

4 Tuberous Esculent rooted Bindweed, or Spanish Potatoes

5 *Linaria*-leaved Blue flowering Bindweed

6 *Linaria*-leaved Red flowering Bindweed

7 *Linaria*-leaved Clustered-flowering Bindweed

Des[illegible] of the Common [illegible] 1 Common Perennial Bindweed comes of course in this Collection, for it is a Perennial in the [illegible] sense, it is such a Perennial as you cannot easily get rid of, and of all the weeds infesting a garden, this is perhaps the most difficult to destroy The most service, therefore, that I can be of to the Gardener, is to tell how this is to be done, and for this there is only one good way that I know of, which is by pulling them up with the hand They will soon rise again, for the roots creep deep in the ground, even below the soil, and are by Gardeners in wrath called the Devil's Guts, but as they appear, let this work be repeated, and they will get weaker and weaker after every time of their pulling up, until they are finally destroyed, and this work will be more troublesome, and require longer perseverance, when they have taken possession of box edgings, shrubs, trees, or the like This plant, nevertheless, has its uses in gardening, for the flowers are delightful, they are of different colours, white, red, and many of them are sweetly variegated, and on a summer's day the plant glows with a profusion of these flowers I have let a tuft of them stand by the edge of a pond, or the corner of a slope, where the grass is constantly mowed and kept in order, and it has had a sweet effect The flowers have been taken for our most valuable Perennials, and would, if it was not for their commonness, during the time of snow, be inferior to few of them They should be admitted, however, on no terms, unless it be in this manner, in proper places in well shorn grass, and there, like a tuft of hair on the head of old Time, they will have a more singular effect, and by their glow of flowers a more beautiful look When the chief flower is over, the next time the walks are mowed let them partake of the fate of the other grass, and let not the remains of them appear, and in the next spring tufts of the like nature may be let at pleasure

[illegible] White, 2 Large White Bindweed, or Bear bind This is a very fine plant in wilderness quarters, where it should be stationed among the shrubs and trees as a climber, it will twine about, and show itself at the very top of those that are twelve or fourteen feet high The leaves are [illegible]-shaped, and the flowers grow singly from the sides of branches, and being large, fair, and of a pure white, they have a pretty effect in such places where climbers show to advantage They also may be made to shew themselves to advantage in gardens, by placing long sticks for them to twine about, but they will soon over-run the [illegible], and become a very troublesome weed to eradicate Some gardens are more infested with this species than the former, and when this happens, the best way of destroying them is by hand-weeding, as for that There will be the sooner destroyed, on account of the roots being thick, and full of a milky juice, which being broken, flows out and weakens the plant, and this being repeated, it soon becomes exhausted, and dies

3 Syrian Bindweed This is the [illegible] [illegible] of the shops The roots are large, thick, and full of a milky juice, upon wounding the root, the milk flows, and it is from this the scammony is collected These roots send forth many slender branches about four feet in length, they trail upon the ground, and are ornamented with narrow sagittated leaves The flowers are produced from the sides of the branches, they are of a pale-yellow colour and each footstalk supports two or three flowers They will be in blow in June and July, and the seeds ripen in the autumn

4 Tuberous Esculent rooted Bindweed This [illegible] is propagated in Spain and Portugal for the same purpose potatoes are by us, and we have them [illegible] imported from thence under the name of Spanish potatoes They will not do, however, with us to be cultivated for those purposes, all that we should desire of them is a few plants only, for variety and observation, and these may be obtained by planting the roots in the same manner we do potatoes They will send forth many trailing creeping stalks, about four feet long These will have heart-shaped angular leaves, and sometimes, if the situation is [illegible], warm, and the autumn proves favourable, they will produce flowers, but to obtain them more certainly, the best way will be to plant them in the spring on a hotbed, and protect them all [illegible], by glasses at the approach of cold weather

5 *Linaria*-leaved Bindweed The stalks of [illegible] the plant are erect, and will grow to about two or three feet in height The leaves are very narrow and pointed, they are [illegible] hoary, and [illegible] to the [illegible] The flowers are produced from the sides of the stalks in June and July, the footstalks are very short, and each usually supports two flowers which are of a pale blue colour, and seldom ripen their seeds with us

6 *Linaria*-leaved Red flowering Bindweed This [illegible]

[illegible]

roots of this plant send forth upright branching stalks to the height of about two feet The leaves are long narrow, and sit close to the stalks The flowers are produced from the sides of the stalks on long footstalks, four or five of them will grow on each peduncle, they are of a delicate red colour, and spread open They are produced in June and July, but rarely ripen their seeds here

Linear-leaved Clustered flowering Bindweed — 7 *Linear*-leaved Clustered flowering Bindweed This is a low growing plant, seldom rising higher than a foot The stalks are branching, and the leaves narrow and silky The flowers are produced from the ends and sides of the branches in small clusters, they are small, and of a red colour This plant rarely produces good seeds with us

Culture — Nothing more need be said of the culture of the two first sorts, and what has been said of the Spanish Potatoes may be sufficient The other sorts are all to be propagated by seeds The Syrian Bindweed ripens its seeds here, but those of the other sorts must be procured from the countries where they grow naturally All of them should be sown in a soil that is naturally dry and warm, and the situation well sheltered, here let them stand without removing, thin them to proper distances, keep them clear of weeds and here they will flower, soon after which the stalks decay, when they should be cleared off and the ground treated up In the spring you may expect fresh stalks to arise from the roots in due course and order

Titles — 1 Common Perennial Bindweed is entitled, *Convolvulus foliis sagittatis utrinque acutis, pedunculis unifloris* Caspar Bauhine calls it, *Convolvulus minor arvensis* It grows common in our fields, and too often in our gardens

2 Large White Bindweed, or Bear bind This is entitled, *Convolvulus foliis sagittatis postice truncatis, pedunculis tetragonis unifloris* Caspar Bauhine calls it, *Convolvulus major albus* It grows naturally in hedges in most parts of Europe

3 Syrian Bindweed, or Scammony This is, *Convolvulus foliis sagittatis postice truncatis pedunculis teretibus subtrifloris* Morison calls it, *Convolvulus Syriacus, sive Scammonia Syriaca* It grows common in Syria

4 Tuberous Esculent rooted Bindweed This is, *Convolvulus foliis cordatis hastatis quinquenerviis, caule repente hispido tuberifero* Ray calls it, *Convolvulus indicus vulgo Patates dictus*, and others, *Batatas* It grows naturally in both the Indies

5 *Linaria* leaved Bindweed is *Convolvulus foliis linearí lanceolatis acutis, caule ramoso erecto pedunculis multifloris* Tournefort calls it, *Convolvulus linariæ folio assurgens* It grows common in its varieties, in Italy, Sicily, and some parts of France

*Convolvulus* is of the class and order *Pentandria Monogynia* and the characters are, — Class and order in the Linnæan System. The characters

1 CALYX is a small, oval, connivent, obtuse, permanent perianthium, it is formed of one leaf, and divided into five segments at the top

2 COROLLA is of one leaf which is bell-shaped, it is large, plicated, spreading, and appears to be composed of five lobes

3 STAMINA The stamina are five subulated filaments about half the length of the corolla, with oval compressed antheræ

4 PISTILLUM is a roundish germen, and a filiforme style the length of the stamina, with two oblong broadish stigmas

5 PERICARPIUM is a roundish capsule, formed of one, two, or three valves

6 SEMINA The seeds are roundish, their outside is convex, and their inside angular

## CHAP CXXXVII.

# *CONYZA*, FLEA-BANE

Species — OF this genus there are,

1 Pyrenean Flea-Bane

2 White Cretan Flea Bane

3 Maryland Flea-Bane

4 Carolina Flea Bane

Description of the Pyrenean Flea Bane — 1 Pyrenean Flea-Bane The root is thick and fibrous The stalks are upright, firm, winged, and divide upwards into many slender branches The leaves are oval, oblong, rough, and embrace the stalks with their base The flowers come out from the ends of the branches in round bunches, their colour is yellow, they make their appearance in July, and the seeds ripen in the autumn, soon after which the stalks die down to the ground, and fresh ones arise in the spring

Culture of this species — This is easily propagated by parting of the roots, or sowing of the seeds The best time for parting of the roots is the autumn, about the time the stalks decay

The time for sowing the seeds is the spring A bed of light sandy earth should be prepared for their reception, and after they come up the weakest should be drawn out, leaving the others about three inches asunder All summer they will require no trouble, except keeping them clean from weeds, and watering them in dry weather, and in the autumn they may be transplanted to the places where they are designed to remain The greatest part of them will produce flowers the summer following

Soil — They will shew themselves the best in a rich soil, but in such a soil the roots are apt to rot in wet winters, so that, in order to continue the sort, the seeds should be constantly sowed for a succession, or the plants set in a dry, sandy, sunny soil, and being thus stationed, they will continue to flower and perfect their seeds for many years

White Cretan Flea Bane — 2 White Cretan Flea Bane The stalk of this plant is shrubby, branching, and grows to about six or eight inches high The leaves are soft, oval, downy, and of a silvery whiteness The flowers

flowers are produced, two or three together from the ends and ſides of the branches on long woolly footſtalks, which have ſmall oval, white leaves placed alternately They are of a dirty-yellow colour, come out in July, and are very rarely ſucceeded by ſeeds in our gardens

Culture of it. This ſort is propagated by planting the ſlips in June or July, in pots filled with light, ſandy, freſh earth The pots ſhould be immediately ſet in the green-houſe, in a ſhady part, the plants ſhould be well watered, which ſhould be conſtantly repeated every day until they have taken root, this will be in about a month, and when you find your plants in a growing ſtate, they ſhould be taken out of the green-houſe, and the pots plunged up to the rim in a ſhady part of the garden, but not under the drip of trees Here they may ſtand until the end of autumn, but for the firſt winter they ſhould have protection from the froſts It will be adviſeable, therefore, to ſet them under an hotbed-frame, in the green-houſe, or under ſome ſlight ſhelter, and in the ſpring they may be turned out, with the mould at the roots, into the places where they are deſigned to remain

Proper ſoil. The ſoil ſhould be naturally warm, ſandy, dry, and well defended, otherwiſe your plants will be liable to be killed by the winter froſts, on which account it would be adviſeable to have a few plants kept in the houſe every winter, to propagate from, in caſe thoſe abroad ſhould be deſtroyed, for this is a very beautiful ſpecies, and makes a ſingular and ſtriking appearance by its ſilvery white leaves

Mary-leaved, 3 Mary-leaved Flea Bane The root of this plant is ſpreading, fibrous, and ſends forth ſeveral herbaceous ſtalks to the height of about two feet The leaves are broad, ſpear-ſhaped, and ſlightly ſerrated on their edges The flowers are finely radiated, and produced in roundiſh bunches, their colour is white, they appear in July, and the ſeeds ripen in the autumn

and Carolina Flea-Bane deſcribed 4 Carolina Flea-Bane The ſtalk of this ſpecies is ſlender, ſtriated, winged, having membranes running from the baſe of one leaf to another The leaves are narrow, ſpear ſhaped, decurrent, downy underneath, and ſawed on their edges The flowers are produced in ſmall ſpikes from the different parts of the plant, their appearance is uſually in July, and ſometimes there is a ſucceſſion until the end of September

Culture These ſorts are propagated by parting of the roots, the beſt time for which is the autumn, when the ſtalks decay They ſhould be ſet in a light, dry, warm ſoil, in a well-ſheltered place, and in ſuch a ſituation they will flower in perfection, and with greater certainty perfect their ſeeds

They may be alſo encreaſed by ſeeds Theſe ſhould be ſown in the ſpring, in a bed of light fine mould When the plants come up they muſt be thinned to about three inches diſtance from each other All ſummer they muſt be conſtantly weeded and watered in dry weather By the autumn they will be grown to be ſtrong plants, and may be then ſet out for good, and the ſummer following the ſtrongeſt of them will flower

Variety There is a variety of the laſt ſort, with whiter leaves, which is rather tender, and ſhould be preſerved in the green-houſe during winter

Titles 1 Pyrenean Flea Bane is titled, *Conyza foliis ovato-oblongis amplexicaulibus* Plukenet calls it, *Eupatoria conyzoides maxima Canadenſis, foliis caulem amplexantibus* It grows naturally in Canada and on the Pyrenees

2 White Cretan Flea Bane is titled, *Conyza foliis ovatis tomentoſis, floribus conferτis, pedunculis lateralibus terminalibuſque* Tournefort calls it, *Conyza Cretica frutescens, folio molli candidiſſimo tomentoſo*, Bauhin, *Conyza tomentoſa, folio ſubrotundo*, Boccone, *Aſter tomentoſus luteus verbaſci folio*, and Barrelier, *Jacobæa Cretica incana, argenteo ſubrotundo folio* It inhabits Crete

3 Maryland Flea-Bane is titled, *Conyza foliis lanceolatis ſubſerratis, corollis radiatis* Plukenet calls it, *Aſter Marilandicus, ptarmicæ capitulis flore albo, baccharidis Monſpelienſium folio et effigie* It grows naturally in North America

4 Carolina Flea-Bane is titled, *Conyza foliis decurrentibus lanceolatis ſerrulatis, caule virgato, floribus ſpicatis ſparſis congeſtis* In the *Amænitates Academicæ* it is termed, *Gnaphalium virgatum* Plumier calls it, *Conyza altera, foliis bullatis anguſtis, alato caule*, Brown, *Conyza anguſtifolia ſubincana, caule alato, ſpicâ multiplici, floribus inferioribus ternatis ſuperioribus paucioribus*, and Sloane, *Helichryſum caule alato, floribus ſpicatis* It grows naturally in Carolina and Jamaica

Claſs and order in the Linnæan ſyſtem *Conyza* is of the claſs and order *Syngeneſia Polygamia Superflua*, and the characters are,

The characters 1 Calyx is oblong, ſquarroſe, imbricated, and compoſed of many acute ſcales, of which the outer ones ſpread open

2 Corolla is compound The hermaphrodite florets in the diſk are numerous, tubular, funnel-ſhaped, and cut at the brim into five ſpreading ſegments The female florets occupy the border, each of theſe is funnel-ſhaped, and divided at the top into three parts

3 Stamina of the hermaphrodite florets are five very ſhort capillary filaments, having a cylindrical tubular anthera

4 Pistillum of the hermaphrodite florets conſiſts of an oblong germen, a filiforme ſtyle the length of the ſtamina, and a bifid ſtigma

The piſtillum of the female florets conſiſts of an oblong germen, a more ſlender ſtyle than thoſe of the hermaphrodites, of about the ſame length, and two very ſlender ſtigmas

5 Pericarpium There is none The ſeeds are contained in the cloſed calyx

6 Semina The ſeeds of both the hermaphrodite and female florets are ſingle, oblong, and crowned with down

The receptacle is naked and plane

CHAP

# CHAP. CXXXVIII.

## *COREOPSIS*, TICKSEED.

Species.

THE Perennials of this genus are,

1. Alternate-leaved Virginian Corn Marigold.
2. Ternate-leaved *Coreopsis*, or Virginian *Chrysanthemum*.
3. White American *Coreopsis*.
4. Verticillate *Coreopsis*.

Description of the Alternate-leaved Virginian Corn Marigold.

1. Alternate-leaved Virginian Corn Marigold is a hardy ſtrong Perennial. The ſtalks will grow to be ten feet high, and proportionally robuſt. The leaves are ſpear-ſhaped, ſerrated, and grow alternately on ſhort footſtalks, having borders or wings running from the baſe of one to the other. The flowers come out from the ends of the branches, growing two or three together on a footſtalk; they are yellow, and much reſemble thoſe of the Sunflower, but ſmaller. They appear in Auguſt and September, but are not ſucceeded by ſeeds in our gardens.

Ternate-leaved,

2. Ternate-leaved *Coreopſis*, or Virginian *Chryſanthemum*. The ſtalks are round, ſmooth, firm, jointed, and grow to be ſix feet high. The leaves are for the moſt part trifoliate, ſmooth, and grow oppoſite to each other at the joints. The flowers terminate the ſtalks in bunches, having long footſtalks; the rays are of a pale yellow colour, but the middle is a dark-purple; they come out in July, and are ſeldom ſucceeded by good ſeeds in our gardens.

White American,

3. White American *Coreopſis*. The ſtalks of this plant are herbaceous, ſmooth, climbing, and divide into many ſlender branches. The leaves are for the moſt part trifoliate, ſmooth, and their edges ſerrated. The flowers come out from the ends and ſides of the branches on footſtalks; the rays are of a pure white, but the middle is purple; they appear in July and Auguſt, but are ſeldom ſucceeded by good ſeeds in our gardens.

and Verticillate Coreopſis.

4. Verticillate *Coreopſis*. The ſtalks of this plant are upright, firm, angular, grow to about a yard high, and ſend forth branches by pairs oppoſite to each other. The leaves are beautifully divided into a multitude of narrow parts, and adorn the ſtalks at the joints. The flowers are produced from the ſides of the branches, on long ſlender footſtalks oppoſite to each other; the rays are of a bright yellow colour, and the middle is a dark-purple. They come out in July, and ſometimes continue in ſucceſſion until the froſt ſtops them.

Culture.

All theſe ſorts are eaſily propagated by parting of the roots, the beſt time for which is the autumn, when the ſtalks decay. They ſhould be ſtationed according to their ſize; and after they are planted out, will require no trouble, except keeping them clean from weeds, and clearing away their dead ſtalks at the approach of winter; for the ſtalks die to the ground every year, and freſh ones ariſe in the ſpring. The firſt ſort is very hardy, and will grow in any ſoil and ſituation; but the others, eſpecially the third, ſhould have a dry ſoil, and a warmer expoſure. The flowers of all are very beautiful; and what ſtill enhances their value is, they will often continue in ſucceſſion until the froſt ſtops them in the winter, when the ſtalks decay.

Soil and Situation.

Titles.

1. Alternate-leaved Virginian Corn Marigold is titled, *Coreopſis foliis lanceolatis ſerratis alternis petiolatis decurrentibus*. Van Royen calls it, *Coreopſis foliis ſerratis*; Plukenet, *Chryſanthemum Virginianum, caule alato, ramoſius, flore minore*; and Moriſon, *Chryſanthemum Canadenſe bidens, alato caule*; alſo, *Chryſanthemum Virginianum, alato caule, bidens altiſſimum folio aſpero, flore minore ſerotino*. It grows naturally in Virginia and Canada.

2. Ternate-leaved *Coreopſis*, or Virginian *Chryſanthemum*, is titled, *Coreopſis foliis ſubternatis integerrimis*. Van Royen calls it, *Rudbeckia foliis compoſitis integris*; and Moriſon, *Chryſanthemum Virginianum, folio acutiore lævi trifoliato, ſ. anagyridis folio*. It grows naturally in the ſhady moiſt parts of Virginia.

3. White American *Coreopſis* is, *Coreopſis foliis ſubternatis cuneatis ſerratis*. Brown calls it, *Coreopſis ſcandens, foliis ſerratis ternato-pinnatis, receptaculo nudo*; and Herman, *Chryſanthemum Americanum, cicerris folio glabro, belidis majoris flore*. It grows naturally in America.

4. Verticillate *Coreopſis* is titled, *Coreopſis foliis compoſito-pinnatis linearibus*. Gronovius calls it, *Coreopſis foliis verticillatis linearibus multifidis*; Vaillant, *Ceratocephalus delphinii foliis*; and Plukenet, *Chryſanthemum Marianum, ſcabioſæ tenuiſſime diviſis foliis, ad intervalla conſertis*. It is a native of Virginia.

Claſs and order in the Linnæan ſyſtem.

*Coreopſis* is of the claſs and order *Syngeneſia Polygamia Fruſtranea*; and the characters are,

The characters.

1. CALYX. The common calyx is compoſed of a double ſeries of leaves; the outer ones, being about eight in number, are ſmalleſt, and placed circularly; the inner are large, membranaceous, and coloured.
2. COROLLA is radiated and compound. The hermaphrodite florets, which are ſituated in the diſk, are tubular, and indented at the top in five parts.

   The female florets, being about eight in number in the radius, are tongue-ſhaped, large, ſpreading, and indented in four parts.
3. STAMINA of the hermaphrodites are five very ſhort capillary filaments, having a cylindrical tubular anthera.
4. PISTILLUM of the hermaphrodites conſiſts of a compreſſed germen, a filiforme ſtyle the length of the ſtamina, and a ſlender, acute, bifid ſtigma.

   In the females the piſtil conſiſts of a germen ſimilar to that of the hermaphrodites, but no ſtyle nor ſtigma.
5. PERICARPIUM. There is none.
6. SEMINA of the hermaphrodite florets are ſingle, orbicular, convex on one ſide, and hollow on the other, having a membranaceous border, and two horns at the top.

The female florets are abortive.

The receptacle is paleaceous.

CHAP.

# C H A P. CXXXIX.

## C O R N U C O P I Æ.

THERE is only one species of this genus, an oriental grass, called *Cornucopiæ*.

Cornucopiæ described. The root is a cluster of tough, thick, spreading fibre. The leaves are about a foot long, narrow, pointed, stiff, and of a pale-green colour. The stalk is round, smooth, and about a foot and a half, or two feet high. The flowers come out from the tops of the stalks in clusters, and are very large for these kind of flowers; they appear in June and July, and the seeds ripen in August.

Culture. This species is propagated by sowing the seeds in the autumn, soon after they are ripe, or the spring following. The soil should be naturally moist, light and good; and after the plants come up they will require no trouble, except thinning them where they are too close, and keeping them clean from weeds.

Titles. This being the only species of the genus, it is termed, *Cornucopiæ*. Petiver calls it, *Juncus ... vaginatus polycephalus*; and Scheuchzer, *Gramen orientale ... viridis proveniens, capitulo inflexo*. It grows naturally about Smyrna.

Class and order in the Linnæan system. *Cornucopiæ* is of the class and order *Triandria Digynia*; and the characters are,

The characters. 1. CALYX. The common perianthium is a very large funnel-shaped leaf, crenated at the mouth, and containing many flowers.

The glume is composed of two oblong, obtusely acuminated, equal valves, and contains one flower.

2. COROLLA is one valve, which in shape, size, and situation is similar to the valves of the calyx.

3. STAMINA are three capillary filaments, with oblong antheræ.

4. PISTILLUM consists of a turbinated germen, and two capillary styles with curled stigmas.

5. PERICARPIUM. There is none. The corolla includes the seed.

6. SEMEN. The seed is single, turbinated, convex on one side, and plane on the other.

# C H A P. CXI.

## CORNUS, DOGWOOD.

THE herbaceous species of this genus are usually called,

Species. 1. Dwarf Honeysuckle.

2. Canada *Pyrola*.

Dwarf Honeysuckle. 1. Dwarf Honeysuckle. The root is slender, tough, and creeps much under the surface of the ground. The stalks are herbaceous, about a foot high, and send forth branches opposite to each other. The leaves are oval, spear-shaped, sharp pointed, ribbed, and grow opposite to each other on the stalks. The flowers come out from the ends and divisions of the branches; they are small, whitish, appear in May and June, and are succeeded by clusters of red berries, which will be ripe in the autumn.

and Canada Pyrola described. 2. Canada *Pyrola*. The root is slender, creeping, and fibrated. The stalk is herbaceous, tender, and divides into no branches. The leaves are oval, spear-shaped, and pointed. The flowers come out from the ends of the stalks in June and July, and are succeeded by roundish berries, which will be ripe in the autumn.

Culture. These plants propagate themselves very fast by their creeping roots, so that nothing more need be done than to get some of the roots in the autumn, and set them in the places where they are designed to remain. If the situation agrees with them, they will soon make good encrease; if not, though they should live at first, their continuance will be but for a short time.

They love a light, loose, moist earth, and a shady situation, and being thus stationed will make great encrease.

They may be also propagated by seeds. These should be sown in the autumn in the like situation, having dug the ground, and cleared it of all roots of trees, weeds, or the like, and made every thing fine, the seeds should be covered about half an inch deep, and pegs thrust down for a direction to prevent their being destroyed when the ground is hoed. The weeds should be carefully picked up with the hands whilst the plants are young; but when they are well established in their situation, you may let them all grow together; for the plants will grow, flower, and produce their seeds among the weeds, if the ground be light and mountainous, that being the situation in which they chiefly delight.

1. Dwarf Honeysuckle is titled, *Cornus herbacea, ramis binis*. Dillenius calls it, *Cornus pumila herbacea*,

*Lerbacea* [illegible] *renum* [illegible] Caspar B[illegible] hine, [illegible] and Pl[illegible]non, [illegible] It grows naturally in England, Sweden, Russ[illegible] and Norway

2 Canada *Pyrola* is titled, *Cornus herbacea* [illegible] *nullis* Caspar Bauhine calls it, *Pyrola alsin[illegible] flore, Brasiliana* It inhabits Canada

## CHAP CXLI

## *CORONILLA,* JOINTED-PODDED *COLUTEA*

Species [illegible]

T[illegible] are two herbaceous perennial species of this genus, called,

1 [illegible]

2 [illegible] *Coronilla*

Description of the Least Coronilla [illegible]

1 Least *Coronilla* [illegible] The stalks are slender [illegible] the ground The leaves are pinnated, and each of them is composed of about nine pair of [illegible] shaped folioles, ranged along the [illegible] The flowers are yellow, come out from the ends of the stalks in pairs, and are succeeded by angular [illegible] pods, containing ripe seeds, in August [illegible]

Its propagation

This species is [illegible] propagated by sowing of the seeds in the spring, in a bed of light fresh earth When the plants come up, they should be thinned to three inches asunder, and all summer they must be kept clean from weeds, and watered in dry weather Early in the autumn they should be taken up, with [illegible] of earth to each root, and set in a warm, dry, well sheltered place, [illegible] summer following [illegible] then seeds

[illegible]

2 Variable-flowered *Coronilla* The root is [illegible], and creeping The stalk is [illegible], slender, round, hardly able to support itself in an erect position, and three or four feet [illegible] leaves are smooth, of a pale-green colour [illegible] with eight or ten pair of obtuse oblong folioles, besides the odd one with which they are terminated, and grow alternately on the stalks The flowers grow in bunches from the [illegible] of the leaves and the ends of the stalks, [illegible] upon longish footstalks

Varieties

There are two or three varieties One is of a fine deep purple colour on its first appearance, and [illegible] light purple, and then to a white Another variety is strong crimson, and in another the standard is crimson, and wings white, both these vary to pale or white colours, and have sometimes a slight tinge or a few streaks of the original They all appear in June, July, and August, and are succeeded by numerous, long, erect, taper pods, containing ripe seeds, in the autumn

Culture

It is propagated by parting of the roots in the autumn, also by sowing of the seeds in the manner of the preceding species, but this is very hardy, no soil or situation comes amiss to it, especially if it be shady

Titles

1 The Least *Coronilla* is titled, *Coronilla procumbens, foliolis novenis lanceolatis, stipulis oppositi[illegible] emarginatis, leguminibus angulatis nodosis* Caspar Bauhine calls it, *Ferrum equinum, siliqua in summitate*, and Dalechamp, *Lotus* [illegible] It grows naturally in Italy, France and Spain

2 Variable-flowered *Coronilla* is titled, *Coronilla herbacea, leguminibus erectis teretibus torosis numerosis, foliolis plurimis glabris* Caspar Bauhine calls it, *Securidaca Dumetorum major, flore vario, siliquis articulatis*, Clusius, *Securidaca* 2 *altera species*, and Tournefort, *Coronilla herbacea flore vario* It grows naturally among bushes, in thickets, &c in France, Denmark, Lusatia and Bohemia

## CHAP CXLII

## *CORTUSA,* BEAR's EAR SANICLE

[illegible]

Of this genus there are only two species, called,

1 Bear's Ear Sanicle of Matthiolus

2 Bear's Ear Sanicle of Gmelin

[illegible]

1 [illegible] Sanicle of Matthiolus The root is composed of numerous fibres, collected into a head at the top, from this head issue many large, oblong, heart-shaped leaves, which are much indented and cut on the edge Among these arise the round naked flower-stalks, to the height of about six inches The flowers grow in [illegible] bels at the top, each floret having its own [illegible]

rate footstalk, they hang drooping, and then characters shew their structure They are of a fine red colour, having often in the middle a circle of white or yellow, they come out in April and May, but are very rarely succeeded by seeds in our gardens

and Bear's Ear Sanicle of Gmelin described

2 Bear's Ear Sanicle of Gmelin The leaves are heart shaped, oblong, cut or indented, and arise from the root in a large tuft The flower-stalk is naked, and grows to about four inches high The flowers are of a pale red colour, and [illegible] in an umbel at the top of the stalk, but they are small (their cups exceeding them in length), and altogether of inferior beauty to the former sort They appear in April and May, but very rarely produce seeds with us

These plants are natives of the rocky and mountainous parts of the world, so that in order to have them in the garden, the most hungry, lean, sandy, and shady spot should be assigned them The mould should be made fine, and having procured good seeds, they should be sown early in the spring, and slightly raked in When the plants come up they must be constantly kept clean from weeds, and when they are of sufficient strength they will, like the Common Bear's Ear, produce their flowers in the spring

They may be also propagated by parting of the roots, the best time for which is the autumn The roots should be set in a dry, sandy, shady spot, for they will not live long in the rich cultivated parts of the garden

Some persons plant them in pots filled with sandy undunged earth, and if these are set in the shade, and watered in the summer, they will live in that manner for many years

1 Matthiolus's Bear's Ear Sanicle is titled, *Cortusa calycibus corollis brevioribus* In the *Hortus Cliffortianus* it is termed, *Cortusa foliis cordatis, petiolatis* Clusius calls it, *Cortusa Matthioli*, and Caspar Bauhine, *Sanicula montana latifolia* [illegible] It grows naturally on the Alps of Austria and Siberia

2 Gmelin's Bear's Ear Sanicle is titled, *Cortusa calycibus corollam excedentibus* It inhabits Siberia

*Cortusa* is of the class and order *Pentandria Monogynia*, and the characters are,

1 CALYX is a small, patent, permanent perianthium, divided into five obtuse parts, which are reflexed at the top

2 COROLLA is one rotated petal The tube is very short, the limb is broad, plane, and divided into five roundish segments, at the base of which are situated five prominent tubercles

3 STAMINA are five obtuse [illegible], antherae bilamellated, obtuse, erect [illegible]

4 PISTILLUM consists of an oval germen, a filiforme style, and a simple stigma

5 PERICARPIUM is an oval, oblong, [illegible] nated, unilocular capsule, formed of two valves having their [illegible], and [illegible] longitudinally on each side

6 SEMINA The seeds are numerous, oblong, obtuse, and small

## CHAP CXLIII

## *COTYLEDON*, NAVEL-WORT, KIDNEY-WORT, or WALL PENNY-WORT

THERE is a hardy species of this genus which bids defiance to our cold, called,

Species

1 The Prickly Cotyledon
2 Common Wall Pennywort

Prickly Cotyledon

1 The Prickly *Cotyledon* It is not unlike the Houseleek of our walls The leaves are oblong, fleshy, pointed, and each of them is terminated by a spine Among these the flower-stalk rises to about four inches high, each of them supports four or five whitish flowers, which make their appearance in April and May, and sometimes are succeeded by good seeds in our gardens

Culture

It is propagated by parting of the roots any time in the autumn or winter It will grow in almost any soil, but must have a shady situation, and it resists the severest cold much better than it can the heat of our summer's sun

It is also propagated by sowing the seeds soon after they are ripe, in a shady place, they will readily come up, and after they have stood one year, they may be removed to the places where they are designed to remain

Common Wall Pennywort described

2 Common Wall Pennywort Of this species here are several varieties, both with respect to the roots and flowers, the roots of some being thick and in a manner bulbous, others [illegible], and others again very knotty, and full of large tubers The flowers of some are whitish, others reddish, some streaked, but the most beautiful, as well as most common of all the sorts, is the yellow-flowered, and which is distinguished by some with the name of Golden Cotyledon The leaves are round, fleshy, full of juice, indented, and grow on footstalks which are inserted in the middle Among these the flower stalks rise to different heights in different situations, in some places they not being more than four or five inches, in others near a yard long, the bottom of it is ornamented with a few small leaves growing alternately, the top is crowned with the flowers growing in a long spike, they come out in June, and at other times of the year They are succeeded by seeds, which scattering, will afford plants for a succession without further trouble

This species grows upon old walls, buildings &c in many parts of England, and the use of it in Gardening is to ornament the like places such as old ruins grottos, old walls, rocks, &c and an l f the feeds ar l t l n the crevices or m u'. or luch places th s ll grow, and the pla ts will ever af er ret in th t situation

1 Pr el Cot, de is titled, *Cotyledon fol o oblongis l ob-nuc o ul s, ca ie ft cato* It i hi- b s Seen

2 Common Wall Penny wort is titled, *Cotyledon f li cu llato f s , cre o dentatis alternis, r h ramojo, fu tens erectis* Van Royen calls it, *Coty-l lon fo us peltets*, Dodart, *Cotyleaon fore lut o radice repente* Morison, *Cotyledon revere tuber, lo g i repe te*, also, *Cot, don luteum u abi' catum spicatum radice repente, majus*, also, *Sedum luteum murale spicatum, folio umbil ato rotunda*, Cam me-rarius names it, *Umbili s i peus*, Clusius, *Coty'e on umbilicus v r s*, Caspa Bauhine, *Cotyledon m r* and John Bauhine, *Cotyledon vera, radic ubero'*. It grows n turally in England, Spain, Portugal, and J uca

*Cotyledon* is of the cl s and order *Decandria Pentagynia*, and the characters are,

1 CALYX is a small monophyllous perianthium, cut into five acute parts at the top

2 COROLLA is a bell-shaped petal div ded at the bottom into five segments The nectar m co n sists of a concave scale, and is situated at the base of all the germini

3 STAMINA are ten awl shaped fila ents he ne ate, having erect, four furrowed anthera.

4 PISTILLUM consists of five oblong tapering germen, terminating in an awl-shaped style long than the stamina, and having simple stigmas

5 PERICARPIUM consists of five oblong, ventricose, acuminated capsules, each of which is formed of one valve, and opens longitudinally on the inner side

6 SEMINA The seeds are many and small

Class and order in the Linnæan system The characters

# CHAP CXLIV

## *CRAMBE*, SEA COLEWORT

Species

OF this genus there are,

1 Common English Sea Colewort

2 Oriental Sea Colewort

Description of the Common English

1 Common English Sea Colewort The root is thick, white, and spreads itself under the su-face of the ground The radical leaves are broad, thick, smooth brittle, of a greyish or whitish green colour, divided at the edges into many obtuse parts, and they spread themselves on the ground The stalks are thick, smooth, branching, about a foot and a half or two feet high, and are adorned with small leaves growing singly at the joints The flowers are produced from the ends of the branches in kind or loose spikes, their colour is white, the general characters indicate their struc-ture, they appear in June, and the seeds ripen in the autumn There is a variet, of this species with jagged leaves and another with yellowish flowers

and Oriental Sea Colewort

2 Oriental Sea Colewort The leaves of this plant are cut alternately to the mid-rib, and each of the parts is again alternately cut into many segments, they are rough, of a greyish colour, and the radical ones spread themselves on the ground The stalks are upright smooth, branch ing, and grow to be two feet high The flowers are produced from the tops of the stalks in pa nicles, they are small, white, come out in June, and the seeds ripen in the autumn

Method of propagating these sorts

These plants are easily propagated by sowing of the seeds, which may be done in the autumn, soon after they are ripe, or in the spring When the plants come up, they should be thinned to about a foot and a half distance every way, and this, except keeping them clean from weeds, is all the trouble they will require

They will grow in any soil or situation, though they delight most in a light, sandy, or gravelly earth

Titles

1 English Sea Colewort is titled, *Crambe folus cauleque glabris*. In the *Hortus Cliffortianus* it is termed, *Crambe foli s cordat s et fpis carnosis* Cas-par Bauhine calls it, *Brassica m ritima monosp rmos*, Lobel, *Brassica marina sylvestris multiflora mono spermos*, Tournefort, *Crambe maritima brassicæ folio*, Parkinson, *Brassica marina monospermos*, and Gerard, *Brassica marina Anglica* It grows naturally on the sandy sea-shores in England, and most of the northern countries of Europe

2 Oriental Sea Colewort is, *Crambe foli s sca-bris, caule glabro* Van Royen calls it, *Crambe folus & scholis alternatim pinnatifidis*, and Tour-nefort, *Rapistrum orientale, acanthi folio* it is a native of the East

Class and order in the Linnæan system The characters

*Crambe* is of the class and order *Tetradynamia Siliquosa*, and the characters are,

1 CALYX is a perianthium composed of four oval, channelled, patent, deciduous leaves

2 COROLLA consists of four petals placed cru-ciformly, these are large, obtuse, broad, patent, and have ungues about the same length with the calyx

3 STAMINA The filaments are six, two of them are the length of the calyx, the other four are longer, and divided at the top into two parts The antheræ are simple, and placed on the exterior segment of the filaments

There is a melliferous glandule on each side, between the corolla and the longer stamina

4 PISTILLUM consists of an oblong germen and a thickish stigma, there being no style

5 PERICARPIUM is a roundish dry berry

6 SEMEN The seed is single and roundish

CHAP

## CHAP CXLV

## *CREPIS,* BASTARD HAWKWEED

Species.

OF this genus there are,
1 Sicilian Bastard Hawkweed
2 Siberian Bastard Hawkweed

1 Sicilian Bastard Hawkweed The leaves are ... indented, crenated, smooth, and of a pale-green colour The stalk is naked, and grows to about four or five inches high The flowers come out, two or three together, from the tops of the stalks, they are of a yellow colour, and the general characters ... the titles indicate their composition, they appear in June, and the seeds ripen in July and August

and Siberian ... wed ... ed

2 Siberian Bastard Hawkweed The stalks of this species are rough, branching, and about a foot and a half high The lower leaves are oblong, indented, and have winged indented footstalks, but the upper are spear-shaped indented, and embrace the stalks with their base The flowers come out from the ends and sides of the branches, on their own separate footstalks, they are of a yellow colour, appear in June and July, and frequently again in the autumn

Varieties

There are several varieties of this species differing chiefly with respect to the size of the plants and the indentures of the leaves, some being of taller growth, others lower, the leaves of some being deeply sinuated, others slightly indented, and some serrated They all blow about the same time, and the seed ripen soon after the flowers are fallen

Method of propagating these species

These sorts are easily raised by sowing the seeds soon after they are ripe, or in the spring When they come up they should be thinned where they appear too close All summer they should be kept clean from weeds, and in the autumn be removed to the places where they are to remain The summer following they will flower and perfect their seeds, which, if permitted, will be blown about by the winds to a considerable distance, and produce plants all over the garden

1 Sicilian Bastard Hawkweed is titled *Crepis ... foliis ... incisis ... polio ... flosculis ...* Boccone terms it, *Hieracium ... glabrum, ... ... folio*, and others, *Hieracium ... pumilum, ...* It is a native of Sicily

Siberian Bastard Hawkweed is, *Crepis foliis oblongis amplexicaulibus ... dentatis, ... ...* In the ... it is termed, *Crepis foliis ... dentatis, ... alatis ...* Gmelin ... it, *Hieracium ... ramoso, foliis ... petiolis, ... lanceolatis ... ... ...* It grows common on the ... of Siberia

*Crepis* is of the class and order *Syngenesia Polygamia Æqualis*, and the characters are,

1 C... is double The outer is very short, patulous, and deciduous, the inner ... is oval, sulcated, permanent, and has narrow ... narrow leaves

2 COROLLA is uniformly imbricated The floscules are numerous, and equal each consists of a single ligulated, linear, truncated petal, cut in five parts at the top

3 STAMINA are five very short capillary filaments, having a cylindrical tubular anthera

4 PISTILLUM consists of an oval germen, a filiforme style the length of the stamina, and two reflexed stigmas

5 PERICARPIUM There is none

6 SEMEN The seed is single, oblong, and crowned with a stipulated hairy down

The receptacle is naked

## CHAP CXLVI.

## *CRESSA*

Description of the plant

THERE is only one species of this genus, called *Cressa* The stalks are slender, weak, and trailing The leaves are small, oval, pointed, and hoary The flowers come out each in a kind of spike, from the tops of the stalks, they are of a reddish purple colour appear in June and July, and the seeds ripen in the autumn

Culture

This species is raised by sowing the seeds in the spring They must have a light sandy soil, and a well sheltered situation, and after the plants come up, must be thinned where they are too close, and kept clean from weeds all summer, and the summer following they will flower and perfect their seeds, which will ... and produce fresh plants without farther trouble

There being no other species of this genus, its name is simply, *Cressa* ... Tournefort, ... *palustris ... ... folio*, C Bauhin ... *... ... ... folio*, and ... ... It grows common in Italy and ...

C a s and order in the Linnæan system the characters

*Cressa* is of the class and order *Pentandria Digynia*, and the characters are,

1 CALYX is a permanent perianthium, composed of five oval, obtuse, incumbent leaves

2 COROLLA is one hypocrateriforme petal The tube is the length of the calyx, and swelling near the base, the limb is divided into five oval, acute, patent segments

3 STAMINA are five long capillary filaments, sitting in the tube of the corolla, having round antheræ

4 PISTILLUM consists of an oval germen, and two filiforme styles the length of the stamina, with simple stigmas

5 PERICARPIUM is an oval capsule, a little longer than the calyx, formed of two valves, and containing one cell

6 SEMEN The seed is single, oval, and oblong

## CHAP CXLVII.

## *CRITHMUM*, SAMPHIRE

THERE are only two species of this genus, one of which is a biennial, the other a perennial, called Samphire, or Smaller Sea Fennel

This plant described

The root is thick, knotty, strikes deep into the ground, is of a pleasant and delightful odour, and agreeable to the taste The stalks are round, thick, succulent, fleshy, branching, and grow to be two feet high The leaves are large, being compound of many thick, oblong, spear-shaped, fleshy segments, they are full of juice, spicy, saltish to the taste, and their succulent footstalks embrace the stalks with their base The flowers come out in round umbels, from the ends of the branches, they are of a yellow colour, appear in July, and the seeds ripen in the autumn

The leaves of this sort afford an excellent pickle, and are admirable in sallads

Culture

It grows naturally on our sea coasts, and delights in sandy, gravelly, and rocky situations, so that whoever is possessed of such places should make the ground fine by good digging, clearing off all weeds, &c and in the autumn should sow the seeds, soon after they are ripe, covering them only a quarter of an inch deep When the plants come up, they should be kept weeded at first, and be thinned where they are too close Afterwards they will require no farther care, their strong roots will strike deep into the ground or crevices of the rocks, if such a situation is allotted, and they will flower every year, produce seeds, and afford you plenty of leaves for use

Virtues of the leaves

The leaves, eaten in pickle or sallads, are exhilarating to the spirits, comfortable to the stomach, create an appetite, and are a fine diuretic

Titles

This species is titled, *Crithmum foliolis lanceolatis carnosis* Caspar Bauhine names it, *Crithmum, s. fœniculum maritimum minus* Lobel, *Feniculum marinum s empetrum, s calcifraga*, Gerard, *Crithmum marinum* and Parkinson, *Crithmum marinum vulgare* It grows common on the sea shores of England, and most countries of Europe

Class and order in the Linnæan System The characters

*Crithmum* is of the class and order *Pentandria Digynia*, and the characters are,

1 CALYX The general umbel is hemispherical, and the partial of the same figure

The general involucrum is composed of numerous spear-shaped, obtuse, reflexed leaves, the partial is narrow, spear-shaped, and the length of the umbellula

The proper perianthium is very small

2 COROLLA The general flower is uniform The florets are all fertile, and consist each of five oval, inflexed, and nearly-equal petals

3 STAMINA are five simple filaments longer than the corolla, having roundish antheræ

4 PISTILLUM consists of a germen situated below the flower, and two reflexed styles with obtuse stigmas

5 PERICARPIUM There is none The fruit is oval, compressed, and divided into two parts

6 SEMINA The seeds are two, elliptical, compressed, and striated on one side

# CHAP. CXLVIII

## *CROCUS*, SAFFRON.

*Introductory remarks*

THERE is but one real species of *Crocus*, though such numbers of varieties of it are found in our gardens. They are of that train of plants which usher in the spring, a few of the sorts only excepted, which are reserved to crown the autumn. They are most of them well-known plants, and the gaudy show they make when we view them from our windows, at a time the chilling cold forbids us to walk abroad, has often afforded us pleasure. The Autumnal Crocuses also are very beautiful; and all of them being low plants, and easy of culture, they are at once adapted for the smallest, as well as to figure in plenty in the largest gardens. The subject naturally divides itself into two heads:

*Divisions*

The Spring *Crocus*.
The Autumnal *Crocus*.

*Spring Crocus*

The Spring *Crocus*. The root is a small roundish bulb, white within, and covered with a brown bark. The leaves are many, long, and narrow; they are usually of a deep-green colour, with a whitish stripe along the middle. The flowers come out with or before the leaves; each has a very long tube, which serves the place of a stalk, and is surrounded with a thin ragged membrane. The flower is large, widens gradually, and divides into six large, oblong, oval, obtuse segments; these have the appearance of so many distinct petals; they open in the morning and middle of the day, but naturally close in evenings or in rainy weather; they will be in blow in February, and their seeds will be ripe in May.

This is the Spring *Crocus*, and of this there are the following varieties:

*Varieties*

The Early Wild *Crocus*.
The White *Crocus*.
The Purple striped White *Crocus*.
The Blue striped White *Crocus*.
Small Blue *Crocus*.
Blue *Crocus* with a Large Flower.
Blue Purple-striped *Crocus*.
Purple *Crocus*.
Yellow *Crocus*.
Yellow Black-striped *Crocus*.
Yellow *Crocus* striped with Purple.
Ash coloured *Crocus*.
Cream coloured *Crocus*.
The Little White Narrow-leaved *Crocus*.
White *Crocus* with a Purple Bottom.
Pale Blue *Crocus* with a Purple Bottom.
Great Violet *Crocus*.
Polyanthos *Crocus*.
Double Golden *Crocus*.
Double Blue *Crocus*.
Double striped *Crocus*.

These are the principal varieties of the *Crocus*, their differences are the effect of culture from seeds, for they are all but one species, and doubtless many more varieties may be easily obtained, if we would sow the seeds from the best flowers; but they all encrease so very fast by the roots, that it is a method hardly worth putting into practice.

*Culture*

The best way therefore, is, to get a few bulbs of the different varieties, and you will soon have plants enough. In planting of them, observe to set those together which flower at the same time, for there is a good deal of difference in the flowering; the early sorts will be in blow in February, and others again will not be in perfection before April. Mix the varieties, also, so as to cause the best effect, and let them be planted in beds marked out for the purpose; for when thus disposed they make a good show, and look much better than when set singly about the gardens. After the flowers are past, the leaves will grow to a great length, and it is too frequently the practice to cut them off; let this be never permitted, for the roots will be thereby greatly weakened, and the flowers the succeeding spring proportionably small. When the leaves are decayed, then is the best time for taking up the roots; at which time you should clean them, and lay them in an airy place for a few days; after that, put them into paper bags, to be ready for planting, which may be done at any time before spring you please, though the autumn is the more eligible season for the purpose.

They will grow and flourish well in any soil or situation; and if a large quantity of bulbs is wanted, the best way is to let them remain three or four years before they are removed, and by that time they will be formed into large bunches, and will afford prodigious encrease.

*Autumnal Crocus*

The Autumnal *Crocus*. The variety of the Autumnal Crocuses is not very great, neither do they encrease so fast by the bulb as the Spring kinds. They are all of them, however, very beautiful; and their having a spring-like appearance, puts you in mind of that reviving season, when Nature, in other respects, seems to be in a total decay. They appear when the summer flowers are over, and the fall of the leaf begins; then they rear their humble heads, and become more welcome by the singularity of their appearance. At this season we have,

*Varieties*

The Small Blue Autumnal *Crocus*.
White Autumnal *Crocus*.
Autumnal *Crocus* with a Whitish blue Flower.
Purple Autumnal *Crocus*.
Large Rush leaved Purple Autumnal *Crocus*.
Saffron.

The names, as they here stand, shew in what respect these sorts differ from each other; so that I shall single out the Saffron for a more circumstantial description, and which will, with very little variation, belong to them all.

*Saffron described*

The root of the Saffron differs little from those of the Spring Crocuses. It is a smallish bulb, white within, and covered with a brown dry bark; it is frequently double, and from the base run many fibres. The flowers come out before or with the leaves, and on their first appearance are wrapped in a thin flimsy membrane, which divides and lets them out. The leaves are long, narrow, and of a very deep green colour, with a membranaceous hollow line running lengthways. The flower rises immediately from the root standing upon its long tube; it widens gradually, and near the top is divided into six large, oval, obtuse segments. These have the appear-

appearance of petals, and their colour is a bluish-purple In the center of the flower is a slender style, placed on a roundish germen, this style has three stigmas, of a reddish-yellow colour, and these stigmata produce the Saffron of the shops

Culture The Autumnal Crocus's are all propagated by the roots, for they never produce any seeds here A part of the garden should be appropriated to these and the like kinds, such as *Colchicum*, Autumnal *Narcissus*, *Cyclamen*, &c They should not be disturbed oftener than every three or four years, if you want much encrease, and almost any soil or situation will do for them And thus, with so little trouble, may these plants be encreased, and made to adorn our gardens, and represent spring, at a time when the show of most flowers is past and gone But there is a particular method of propagating Saffron for use It is this

Method of propagating and preparing Saffron for use Make choice of a good, light, dry, rich ground, of an open exposure Let this be fallowed the year before; or if it has borne a crop of oats or barley it will do very well If it has been cropped, as soon as that is gathered let it be ploughed, and in the spring, about Lady-Day, the ploughing must be repeated, and let this ploughing be as deep as the soil will permit In May, let the ground be enriched with a large quantity of good rotten dung, spread it equally all over the place, and then plough it in About the end of June let the ploughing be repeated, and the ground will be in proper order for the reception of the plants

The best time for planting them is July, and the bulbs should be set in lines three inches asunder The ground should be squared out into beds, drills drawn for the purpose, and the roots covered over about two inches deep A large quantity of bulbs ought to be got in readiness, for in planting of them in that manner, it will take near sixteen bushels to an acre

Weeds of all sorts must be cleared off as they come up In September the Saffron flowers will appear, and this is the time for gathering them The morning is the time for the work, and a sufficient number of hands are to be employed to perform it Baskets are to be procured to receive them, and the business must be repeated every morning until the season is over, for there will be a succession of flowers constantly shewing themselves, which must as repeatedly be plucked off, and the ground cleared of them if possible before ten o'clock The remainder of the day is to be employed in picking out the stigmata, or what is usually called the Chives (for these are the Saffron), and the other parts of the flowers are to be thrown away as useless

This work being effected, the chives are then dried on a kiln This is done, first, by spreading an haircloth, and upon that some sheets of white paper, on the hearth, and then laying on the wet chives near three inches thick The chives are then covered with white paper and six or eight flannel cloths or doubled blankets The fire is then lighted, and a board with a large weight on it is laid over the whole, to press it down

At this time the greatest difficulty is, to preserve the chives from scorching they require a strong heat to make them sweat freely, and if this be too powerful they are in danger of being spoiled

They suffer this heat for about an hour, by which time the chives will be formed into a cake The covering is then to be taken off, and the contiguous Saffron, the edges of the cake are to be raised and the paper is to be laid on as before, a fresh board is fitted over this, and the whole is turned upside-down This side also will require the same heat for about an hour longer, and by that time the danger of scorching the cakes will be over

After that they are to have a very gentle heat, are to be pressed down with the usual weights, and to be turned every half-hour until dry, which will be in about twenty two hours longer

They frequently sprinkle the cakes with small beer to make them sweat, and sometimes two linen cloths are used next the cake, instead of paper The best fuel for the purpose is charcoal.

The quantity of Saffron produced on an acre will be very different The first year after ploughing it will often be very inconsiderable, sometimes there will not be more than a pound or two of dried Saffron, and if it should contain three or four pounds weight when ordered, it is thought a good crop The next crop will be better, and ten or a dozen pounds may be expected to be collected, and the third crop still more Twelve or fourteen, sometimes even sixteen pounds of good dried Saffron have been produced from an acre of the third crop

With regard to the drying in, it generally takes five pounds of wet Saffron to make one of dry, and at the latter end of the crop, six pounds of wet Saffron will produce one of dry only

This is the process of the three years crop; after that, the roots are to be taken up, divided, and planted afresh, the time for which is about the Midsummer following The method of doing this is various Sometimes it is done by digging, and picking up the roots, sometimes by a forked hoe the roots are drawn out, and frequently, in large quarters of them, the ground is ploughed, and then harrowed several times over, all which time a sufficient number of hands are employed to gather the roots as they are turned up

The roots are then to be cleaned, and the largest and best of them laid by themselves to be planted afresh, whilst the long-pointed, and all the carrot-rooted ones, should be thrown away

Saffron is cultivated in several places in England, but no where in such plenty as at Saffron-Walden in Cambridgeshire, and the adjacent parts

It has been observed, that there is but one real species of *Crocus*, its title is, *Crocus spathâ univalvi radicali, corollæ tubo longissimo* Most writers have made many species of it, and there are but few who have not considered the Spring and the Autumnal kinds as distinct species The Spring *Crocus* is usually named, *Crocus vernus latifolius*, and many have rested with that title to express all the varieties The Saffron is termed by Morison and others, *Crocus autumnalis sativus* They all are natives of the Helvetian and Pyrenean Mountains, also of the like kind of situations in Portugal, and some other places Titles.

*Crocus* is of the class and order *Triandria Monogynia*, and the characters are, Class and order in the Linnæan system The characters

1 Calyx is a monophyllous spatha

2 Corolla is of one leaf The tube is very long, and the limb is divided into six erect, equal, oval, oblong segments

3 Stamina are three subulated filaments, shorter than the corolla, with arrow-shaped stigmas

4 Pistillum consists of a roundish germen situated below the flower, a slender style the length of the stamina, and three twisted serrated stigmas

5 Pericarpium is a roundish trilobate capsule, of three cells

6 Semina The seeds are numerous and roundish

CHAP

# CHAP. CXLIX.

## *CROTALARIA*

Description of this plant.

THERE is one perennial only of this genus, called the White *Crotalaria* The stalk is herbaceous, smooth, and about two feet high The leaves are composed each of three spear-shaped oval folioles The flowers grow in a thyrse at the top of the stalks, they are of a white colour, come out in July, and are succeeded by short turgid pods containing the seeds

Culture

This species is propagated by sowing the seeds in a dry, warm, well-sheltered place, in the spring Where the plants come up too close the weakest must be drawn out, and all summer they must be kept clean from weeds, and frequently watered in dry weather By the autumn they will be grown to be good plants, and the strongest of them will flower the summer following.

Titles

This species is titled, *Crotalaria foliis ternatis lanceolato-ovatis, caule lævi, herbaceo, racemo terminali* Martin terms it, *Anonis Caroliniana perennis non spinosa, foliorum marginibus integris, floribus in thyrso candidis* It is a native of Carolina.

Class and order in the Linnæan system

*Crotalaria* is of the class and order *Diadelphia Decandria*, and the characters are,

The characters

1 CALYX is a large perianthium divided into three segments, of which the two upper are spear-shaped, and lean on the vexillum, the other is spear-shaped, concave, trifid, and supports the keel

2 COROLLA is papilionaceous

The vexillum is large, heart-shaped, and depressed on the sides

The alæ are oval, and much shorter than the vexillum

The carina is sharp-pointed, and the same length with the alæ

3 STAMINA are ten united filaments, having simple antheræ

4 PISTILLUM consists of an oblong, reflexed, hairy germen, a simple style, and an obtuse stigma

5 PERICARPIUM is a short, turgid, unilocular pod, formed of two valves

6 SEMINA The seeds are kidney shaped and roundish

# CHAP CL

## *CRUCIANELLA*, PETTY-MADDER.

Species

OF this genus there are,

1 The Maritime Petty-Madder,

2 Petty-Madder of Montpelier,

which will continue for years in some soils and warm situations

Description of the Maritime,

1 Maritime Petty Madder The stalks of this species are ligneous, perennial, square, hairy, about a yard long, and (unless supported) lie on the ground The leaves are spear-shaped, rigid, acute, and quaternate, being disposed by fours at the joints, in a radiated manner The flowers grow opposite to each other, and are of a dull-yellow colour, having black antheræ; they are closed in the day-time, but open in evenings, and are very fragrant

2. Montpelier Petty Madder

2 Petty Madder of Montpelier The stalks of this species are diffuse, moderately thick, procumbent, and possessed of branches which grow alternately from the sides The leaves are oval, rigid, acute, and on the lower parts of the stalks four grow together in a radiated manner, at the joints, but at the upper parts the joints are adorned with five or six, disposed round it in the same manner The flowers grow in spikes from the ends of the branches, having naked footstalks, they are of a whitish colour, come out in June and July, but being small make little show

Method of propagating these plants

These sorts are propagated by sowing the seeds in the spring, in the places where they are designed to remain The ground should be made fine, cleared of all roots, weeds, &c and the seeds covered about a quarter of an inch deep When the plants come up they must be thinned to proper distances, kept clean from weeds, and watered in dry weather As the stalks advance in height, they must be tied to sticks, otherwise they will lie on the ground, and the beauty of their appearance be greatly diminished

They may also be propagated by parting the roots, the best time for which is the autumn, though it may be done successfully in the winter or early in the spring When the roots are first set out, they should be watered and shaded, and afterwards, keeping clean from weeds, and repeating the watering occasionally, is all the trouble they will require

Soil and situation

They love a light dry, warm earth, and a well sheltered situation, and being thus stationed, their safety and beauty will be the better ensured

Titles

1 Maritime Petty-Madder is titled, *Crucianella procumbens suffruticosa foliis quaternis, floribus*

*oppositis quinquefiam* Sauvages calls it, *Crucianella erecta, foliis quaternis, corollâ ad solem conniventе*, and Caspar Bauhine, *Rubia maritima* It grows naturally in Crete, and the South of France

2 Petty Madder of Montpelier is, *Crucianella procumbens, foliis acutis caulinis quaternis ovatis, rameis subquinatis linearibus, floribus spicatis* Sauvages calls it, *Crucianella repens, foliis senis, spicis longis*, and Magnol, *Rubia spicata repens* It grows naturally near Montpelier and in Palestine

Class and order in the Linnæan system The characters

*Crucianella* is of the class and order *Tetrandria Monogynia*, and the characters are,

1 CALYX is a perianthium consisting of two spear-shaped, pointed, rigid, connivent, compressed leaves

2 COROLLA is one funnel-shaped petal The tube is cylindrical, slender, and longer than the calyx The limb is cut into four sharp pointed inflexed segments

3 STAMINA are four filaments placed at the mouth of the tube, having simple antheræ

4 PISTILLUM consists of a compressed germen situated between the calyx and the corolla, a bifid filiform style the length of the tube, and two obtuse oblong stigmas

5 PERICARPIUM consists of two capsules growing together

6 SEMEN The seed is single and oblong

# CHAP. CLI

## *CUCUBALUS*, BERRY-BEARING CHICKWEED.

THIS genus affords very few species that are cultivated for the sake of their flowers Some of them are great ramblers, whilst others again are termed weeds in the fields, but as those who first after a general collection of plants may complain on not finding such as are for their purpose under this head, I shall enumerate the sorts, and assign them their proper places in the different parts of the garden, &c

Species

1 Berry-bearing Chickweed
2 Bladder Campion, or, White Corn Campion, or, Spattling Poppy, or, White *Behen*
3 Dover Campion
4 Spanish Campion, or, Catch-Fly
5 Rocky, or, Pine-leaved Campion
6 Virginian Clove *Lychnis*
7 Tartarian *Lychnis*
8 Catholick *Lychnis*
9 Soft Maritime *Lychnis*
10 Reflexed-spiked *Lychnis*

Berry Bearing Chickweed described

1 Berry-bearing Chickweed ought to be stationed amongst trees in the wilderness quarters, for it is a climbing plant, and when trees are near to the support of its branches, will arise to the height of about six feet The branches are numerous, spreading, and, where no trees are near, trail on the ground The leaves of this plant grow opposite, they are of an oval figure and pointed and resemble those of Chickweed The stalks are round and jointed, and send out side-branches, two from every joint, standing opposite, so that the whole are numerous spreading, and diffused The flowers are small, white, and each is composed of five petals, which are placed at a distance from each other; the cup is of a bell-shaped figure, and very much inflated This plant will be in blow in June, and the flowers are succeeded by oval, black, juicy berries, which will be ripe in the autumn

Culture

It may be propagated by the roots, or sowing the berries and the very worst part of the garden or wilderness should be assigned it

Bladder Campion

2 Bladder Campion This is the *Behen album* of the shops, whose roots are esteemed cordial, cephalick, alexipharmick, &c It is a rambler, and no more than a plant or two should be admitted into the very worst part of the garden The stalks are round, smooth, jointed, and will grow to about two feet in length they are numerous, and often form themselves into large bunches The leaves are of an oval figure, and stand two at a joint, they are for the most part smooth, though they sometimes are found a little hairy, and their colour is a light-bluish-green The flowers are white, and their cups are nearly globular, they are smooth, reticulated, inflated, and venose, and the fruit that succeeds the flower is a capsule of three cells

Culture

This is to be propagated any way, but is with much difficulty to be eradicated, when once obtained

Miller has made several distinct species of this sort, which appear to be varieties only, and which differences are hardly worth keeping up or observing in a species so little qualified for ornamenting any part of the flower garden

Dover Campion

3 Dover Campion is so called from growing naturally on Dover Cliffs This is a low-growing plant, seldom rising to more than a foot in height The stalks are undivided, and ornamented with leaves placed opposite, these are long, narrow, and reflexed at their base The flowers are produced from the sides of the stalks on footstalks, they are of a pale-red colour, have long striped cups, and will be in blow in July The seeds ripen in September

Varieties

There are several varieties of this species, that are found growing chiefly on mountainous parts, and which are seldom or never cultivated but will nevertheless arise easily from seeds, which must be shaded from the time of being sowed, until they are grown to be strong plants

Spanish Campion

4 Spanish Campion is a dioecious species, having the male and female flowers on different plants They are pretty tall-growing plants, but the females seldom arise so high as the males The leaves are oblong, but narrow at their base, and broad at their extremity The male stalks will arise to a yard or more in height, but the female seldom above two feet The stalks are jointed, and from these exudes a glutinous matter, which will hold fast flies and small insects The leaves at the joints are long, narrow, and grow from every

every one of them opposite by pairs. The flowers are produced in small clusters, they are of a greenish colour, possess little beauty, blow in June, and the female flowers will be succeeded by seeds that ripen in the autumn, by which plenty of plants may be easily obtained.

Proper soil. It grows naturally on gravelly land in many parts, which shew that a dry soil should be given it in our gardens.

Description of the Rocky or Pine-leaved Campion. 5. Rocky, or, Pine-leaved Campion may be called annual, biennial, or perennial, according to its situation in the garden. Let it be sown in the [illegible] or rich earth, in a moist situation, and the leaves, [illegible], will be [illegible] with juices as to be pretty sure of drooping at the coming in of the winter frosts. Sow the seeds there in the spring, in a dry, warm place, and they will come up, stand the following winter well, flower the succeeding summer, and probably die the next winter; but sow them in a very dry, gravelly, rocky, or even in the little earth on the top of old decayed stone walls, and there they will grow, and last for many years, bidding defiance to almost any weather that shall happen. The leaves of this species are of a very thick consistence, succulent, and of an oval figure; their size is different, according to their different situations, and the height of the stalk will vary accordingly in a rich moist earth. The flowers are small, and of a greenish colour; they will shew themselves sooner or later, according to the strength of the plant, though the usual time of flowering is in June, and they will often be succeeded by ripe seeds.

Virginian Clove. 6. Virginian Clove Lychnis. The stalks of this plant are herbaceous, slender, and about a foot high. The leaves are smooth, of a deep-green colour, sharp pointed, and four of them stand round the stalks, growing together at each joint. The flowers are white, fringed, and grow opposite to each other from the joints of the upper part of the plant, on long footstalks. They appear in June, and in favourable seasons are succeeded by ripe seeds in our gardens.

Tartarian. 7. Tartarian Lychnis. The stalks are undivided, and grow to about a foot high. The leaves are oval, pointed, of a pleasant green colour, and much resemble those of hyssop. The flowers are produced in spikes at the tops of the stalks, their colour is white, they come out in July, and sometimes the seeds ripen in the autumn.

Catholic. 8. Catholick Lychnis. The stalks of this plant are round, thick, viscous, send out branches from the sides, and grow to about a yard high. The leaves are spear-shaped, oval, and pointed. The flowers are produced in panicles from the ends of the branches, hang drooping, and the petals are divided into two parts. Their colour is herbaceous, they come out in June and July, and the seeds ripen in the autumn.

Soft Maritime. 9. Soft Maritime Lychnis. From the root of this species issue several rigid, upright stalks, which are a little downy, soft to the touch, and about a foot high. The lower leaves are spathulate, but the upper ones are spear-shaped; they are of a fleshy substance, spread open, are [illegible] at the top, [illegible], and soft to the touch. The flowers come out in forked panicles, their colour is white, and their petals are cut nearly into two parts; they appear in June and July, and the seeds ripen in the autumn.

This species must have a dry, rubbishy, or sandy soil, it being apt to rot in moist seasons in a moist rich earth.

and Reflexed spiked Lychnis described. 10. Reflexed spiked Lychnis. The stalks of this species are round, jointed, and about a foot and a half high. The leaves are spear-shaped, narrow, and of a light green colour. The flowers are small, and of a [illegible] colour. They grow in reflexed spikes, having very short footstalks, appear in June and July, and the seeds ripen in the autumn.

Culture. All the species of this genus may be propagated by division of the roots in the autumn; but the best way is to have recourse to the seeds. These should be sown in the spring, in the places where they are to remain. After they come up, they should be thinned to proper distances, kept clean from weeds, and watered in very dry weather, which is all the trouble they will require.

Titles. 1. Berry bearing Chickweed is titled, Cucubalus calycibus campanulatis, petalis distantibus, pericarpiis coloratis, ramis divaricatis. In the Hortus Cliffortianus it is termed, Cucubalus caule ramosissimo, [illegible] globoso. Caspar Bauhine calls it, Alsine scandens baccifera; and Dodonaeus Alsine repens. It grows naturally in hedges, woods, forests, &c. in England, Tartary, Germany, France, and Italy.

2. Bladder Campion, or, White Corn Campion, &c. is titled, Cucubalus calycibus [illegible] glabris, [illegible] corollis [illegible]. In the Hortus Cliffortianus it is termed, Cucubalus floribus [illegible], caulibus [illegible] [illegible] [illegible]. [illegible] Behen [illegible] Camerarius, Parkinson, [illegible] Lobel, [illegible], Gerard [illegible] [illegible], and Parkinson, Papaver spumeum [illegible] Behen album vulgo. It grows common in fields, dry meadows, and pastures in England, and in most of the northern parts of Europe.

3. Dover Campion is titled, Cucubalus floribus [illegible] [illegible] [illegible] [illegible] [illegible]. Van Royen calls it, Cucubalus [illegible] [illegible] [illegible] [illegible] [illegible] [illegible]; [illegible] Tournefort, Lychnis orientalis [illegible] [illegible], and Ray Lychnis [illegible] flore [illegible]. It grows naturally on mountainous parts in England, Sweden, Italy, and also on [illegible] [illegible].

4. Spanish Campion, or, Catchfly, is titled, Cucubalus floribus dioicis, petalis linearibus integris. Caspar Bauhine calls it, Lychnis viscosa, flore [illegible] [illegible]; [illegible] and Gerard, [illegible] [illegible]; and Parkinson, [illegible] [illegible] [illegible]. It grows naturally in sandy gravelly soils in England, Austria, Valesia, Silesia, and Siberia.

5. Rocky, or, Pine-leaved Campion is titled, Cucubalus [illegible] [illegible] carnosis. Tournefort calls it, Lychnis maritima [illegible] [illegible] folio [illegible], [illegible] [illegible] [illegible], [illegible] Polemonium [illegible] [illegible]. It grows naturally [illegible].

6. Virginian Clove Lychnis is titled, Cucubalus foliis quaternis. Colden calls it, Lychnis foliis [illegible], Gronovius, Silene foliis [illegible], and Ray, Lychnis [illegible] Virginianus, [illegible] [illegible] quaternis ex singulis geniculis [illegible] ampliori [illegible] [illegible]. It grows naturally in Virginia and Canada.

7. Tartarian Lychnis is titled, Cucubalus petalis [illegible], [illegible] [illegible] [illegible] [illegible] [illegible], [illegible] [illegible]. [illegible] calls it, Lychnis [illegible] [illegible] [illegible]. It grows common in Tartary and Russia.

8. Catholick Lychnis is titled, Cucubalus petalis bifidis, [illegible] [illegible], floribus [illegible]. Van Royen calls it, Silene [illegible] [illegible], caule [illegible], [illegible] [illegible] [illegible]. It grows common in Italy and Sicily.

9. Soft Maritime Lychnis is titled, Cucubalus [illegible]

*petalis semibifidis, paniculâ bracteatâ dichotomâ, caule foliisque hoiosericeis ramealibus spatulatis* Tournefort calls it, *Lychnis maritima pulverulenta, folio carnoso* It grows naturally in the maritime parts of Italy

10 Reflexed-spiked *Lychnis* is titled, *Cucubalus floribus spicatis alternis secundis subsessilibus, corollis obsoletis nudis* Magnol calls it, *Lychnis sylvestris alba spicâ reflexâ* It grows naturally near Montpelier

Class and order in the Linnæan system. The characters.

*Cucubalus* is of the class and order *Decandria Trigynia*, and the characters are,

1 CALYX is a monophyllous, tubulous, permanent perianthium, indented in five parts at the top

2 COROLLA is composed of five petals The ungues are the length of the calyx, the limb is plane, and the laminæ in some species are bifid

3 STAMINA are ten awl-shaped filaments, alternately inserted in the ungues of the petals, being terminated by oblong antheræ

4 PISTILLUM consists of a longish germen, and three awl shaped styles longer than the stamina, with oblong downy stigmas, which turn contrary to the sun's motion

5 PERICARPIUM is a covered, acuminated, trilocular capsule, opening at the top in five parts

6 SEMINA The seeds are many, and roundish

## CHAP CLII

## CUNILA.

Species described

OF this genus is one perennial, usually called, Virginian Field Basil

The stalks are upright, brown, tough, and a foot and a half high The leaves are oval, pointed, serrated, smooth, and finely scented The flowers come out in roundish bunches from the tops of the stalks, they are small, whitish, and appear in July and August

Culture.

This plant is propagated by parting the roots, or planting the slips or cuttings in a moist shady place, in any of the summer months In dry weather they must be duly watered, especially at first, and they will soon strike root, and become good plants

Titles

This species is entitled, *Cunila foliis ovatis serratis, corymbis terminalibus dichotomis* In the former edition of the *Species Plantarum* it is termed, *Satureja foliis ovatis serratis, corymbis terminalibus dichotomis* Micheli calls it, *Hedyosmos*, Gronovius, *Thymus foliis ovatis acuminatis serratis, corymbis lateralibus terminalibus pedunculatis*, Plukenet, *Calamintha mariana, mucronatis rigidioribus & crenatis foliis, flosculorum calyculis villis argenteis summo margine fimbriatis*, and Morison, *Calamintha erecta Virginiana mucronato folio glabro* It grows naturally in Virginia

Class and order in the Linnæan system The characters

*Cunila* is of the class and order *Diandria Monogynia*, and the characters are,

1 CALYX is a monophyllous, cylindrical, decemstriated, permanent perianthium, indented in five parts at the top

2 COROLLA is one ringent petal The upper lip is erect, plane, and emarginated The lower lip is divided into three roundish segments

3 STAMINA There are two filiforme filaments, and two rudiments of filaments, having roundish, didymous antheræ

4 PISTILLUM consists of a germen divided into four parts, a filiforme style the length of the stamina, and a bifid acute stigma

5 PERICARPIUM There is none The seeds are lodged in the calyx

6 SEMINA The seeds are four, oval, and small

## CHAP CLIII.

## CYCLAMEN, SOW-BREAD

Introductory Remarks.

THE English name of this genus is almost unknown to our Gardeners, and the flowers which it comprehends universally go by the name of *Cyclamen*. They are all included in one species, and, like the *Primula*, the tulip, &c vary much by seeds, and beautiful sorts by that method may be annually obtained The principal kinds which we are ambitious of improving, are,

Varieties

The Winter-flowering *Cyclamen*

The Spring White flowered *Cyclamen*

The

The Spring Purple-flowered *Cyclamen*.
The Spring Red-flowered *Cyclamen*.
The Autumnal flowering *Cyclamen*.
The Common Persian *Cyclamen*.
The White Persian *Cyclamen*.
The Large-flowering Sweet-scented Persian *Cyclamen*.
The Small rooted, or, Chesnut-rooted *Cyclamen*.

Culture. These sorts are invariable, to be continued by dividing of the roots, though they are pretty permanent from seeds, and the varieties to be obtained that way chiefly respect the size or figure of the leaves, the largeness and colour of the flowers, and their different degrees of scent. The roots of all, except the last, are large, orbicular, fleshy, compressed lumps which send forth fibres from the sides, and the leaves of some are small, and grow on short footstalks from the root. Others are large and rounded, some heart-shaped, others angular in different degrees, which are usually called Ivy leaved *Cyclamen*, some are remarkably black in the middle, some lighter, and others green. The flowers of some are small, others large, some with purple tops and crimson bottoms, some with the purest white and purple bottoms, which is the common property of the Persian *Cyclamen*, some are nearly all red, others all white, others purple, some are remarkably finely scented, others dispossessed of any fragrance. In short, this species sports in varieties, and no less than thirty different sorts are found in some catalogues, which, nevertheless, are all included under the principal varieties of the species above-mentioned, and keep most true to their time of blowing, and the grand colour of their flowers.

These sorts are continued by dividing of the roots, the best time for which is the summer, soon after the leaves decay. I would by no means advise the cutting the roots into too many parts, for this occasions them to rot, but if that does not happen, and they grow, they will be weak for a long time, and be several years before they come to be good plants, so that the best way will be only to cut the root through the middle, making of each root two plants, and these will readily grow, be strong, and produce flowers in abundance. The Persian varieties are more tender than the others, and should have a dry, light, sandy soil, otherwise the wet will rot them, and the place should be well sheltered, otherwise they will suffer from the severity of our winters, on which account they are generally set in pots, to be placed under a frame or some cover in winter. But when the situation is favourable, this trouble will be found unnecessary, for if the soil is naturally dry, sandy, light, and the situation well defended and aslant, that the wet may easily drain off, they will live for years in such a situation, and nothing but uncommon unpropitious seasons can hurt them.

Notwithstanding these beautiful and elegant flowers are to be propagated by splitting of the roots down the middle, yet the encrease by that means goes on but slowly, and the most expeditious and the best method of raising *Cyclamens* is from the seeds, by which means only a multitude of fine plants may be had, and a variety of new and valuable kinds obtained.

In order therefore to obtain *Cyclamens* from the seeds, let them be gathered from those which have the best properties, that is, those of the most perfect colours, and most opposite to each other, the largest and the most fragrant, from which there will be a great chance of obtaining the most sweet scented sorts in return. The seeds ripen in the different sorts from July to the end of August, and having gathered them from these select sorts, lay them in an airy place for four or five days to dry, and then sow them in boxes filled with a rich, light, fresh earth, cover them only a quarter of an inch deep, and immediately set them in a shady place, but not under the drip of trees, all summer. As weeds appear, constantly pick them out, if dry weather happens, frequently sprinkle the mould in the boxes, and at the end of summer, as the days get short, and the rays of the sun less powerful, alter their situation, so that they may receive the morning sun to eleven of the clock. About the middle of October, remove them to a south aspect, and here let them stand until the middle or end of November, or till signs of bad weather approach, which sometimes does not happen until after Christmas. When you perceive cold or very wet weather to approach, remove them under an hot-bed frame, to be covered with the glasses in evenings, but always open the glasses in the day time in mild weather, and on all favourable occasions. Early in December you may expect the plants from the first sown seeds to appear, but the Persian kinds, which ripen their seeds later in the year, frequently lie until February and some times March, before they come up. When their green leaves appear, they must have plenty of air to prevent their drawing weak, and must be frequently watered. This watering must be observed till the leaves decay, which for the first come up sort is usually in May, and the Persian and late kinds about a month after, but as soon as ever you find their leaves decaying, watering must be totally discontinued. The protection of the hot-bed frame and glasses must be afforded the plants until all danger from bad weather is over, and then the boxes may be set out in the open air, in a place where they may receive the morning sun to ten of the clock only. In this situation they may remain all summer, with no other trouble than keeping them clean from weeds. In the autumn a quarter of an inch depth of rich light earth should be sifted over the plants, and the boxes removed into their south situation, where they may receive the benefit of the whole day's sun. Here they may stand till November, when they should be placed under the hot-bed-frame as before. In the autumn the green leaves will appear, and at that time watering must be re-assumed, if dry weather makes it necessary, and when the plants are set under the frames, they must be protected only from frosts and heavy rains, always opening the glasses in mild weather, and at all favourable opportunities. In the spring they may be set in a place where they may receive the morning's sun only until eleven o'clock. Here they must be frequently watered, kept clean from weeds and when their leaves decay, which will be in June, they will be of a proper age to set out for good. They should be planted in beds four feet wide, and in length proportionable to the number of the plants. The soil should be naturally dry, in good heart, but not dunged, and naturally sandy; and for want of this, four or five barrows full, or more if the bed be dry, must be brought in, and properly mixed with the mould of each bed. The plants should be then set a foot and a half distance from each other every way, covering the crowns with about an inch or two depth of mould. All summer they must be kept clean from weeds, and in the winter the beds must be hooped, to shield the plants from the violence of the hard frosts. As the hot weather in early summer advances, they will have frequent waterings, but when the leaves decay, watering must be discontinued. In the autumn, half an inch depth of fine sandy mould should be sifted over the beds, in the winter they must be hooped in very hard frosts, and by the autumn following the Autumnal

nal flowering kinds will begin to ſhew their bloom; the Winter-flowering ones will ſucceed them, and thoſe of the Spring will follow in due order But this will be but ſparingly this year, the year following they will exhibit more bloom, and you muſt not expect to have a general and real good ſhow of theſe flowers until the plants have been raiſed five years from the ſeeds, eſpecially the Perſian kinds, which are longer before they come to perfection than the others Hooping the ſecond winter after they have been planted out may be diſcontinued to the Common Spring and Autumnal-flowering kinds, for they will be then very hardy The Winter-flowering kinds alſo are hardy, but the beds ſhould be hooped, to be covered with mats when they are in bloom, otherwiſe, a ſudden ſnow falling will prevent the agreeable and ſingular appearance they would make in that dreary and dead ſeaſon of the year The Perſian kinds muſt always be hooped in winter, to be covered in unfavourable ſeaſons, or elſe there will be great danger of their being deſtroyed either by wet or hard froſt And, indeed, if a low frame be made, the length and depth of the bed, for the glaſſes to be drawn in mild weather, and ſhut in hard rain and froſts, it will be much better than by covering of mats When the ſoil is naturally moiſt, ſtrong, and damp, the planting of the Perſian *Cyclamen* abroad is impracticable, they muſt be then ſet in pots, and houſed every winter, as greenhouſe plants, but the flowers of theſe will be vaſtly inferior to thoſe which grow in the open ground, neither are they ſo prolific of ſeed So that when an unfavourable ſituation and ſoil oblige us to have recourſe to pots, to preſerve the plants through the winter, early in the ſpring they ſhould be placed under an hotbed-frame, the glaſſes muſt be conſtantly raiſed in mild weather, and by thus granting them all poſſible protection, and ſlightly ſprinkling them with water in dry weather, they will flower in the ſpring, and many will ripen their ſeeds in July or Auguſt

The waiting four, five, or even ſix years, before you can have a general ſhow of theſe flowers from ſeeds, perhaps, may be diſcouraging to ſome perſons, but they muſt be conſoled by the pleaſing hope and expectation, that ſome of the ſtrongeſt plants will ſhow their bloom earlier, and that when they are in full perfection, they will exhibit a ſhow which will make ample ſatisfaction for all preceding trouble and length of time, a ſhew beautiful and ſtriking to the greateſt degree, and which very few Gardeners were formerly acquainted with

*Cyclamen*, or Sow bread, is titled, *Cyclamen corollâ retroflexâ* In the *Hortus Cliffortianus* it is termed, *Cyclamen* The varieties of this genus among old Botaniſts go by the different names of, *Cyclamen hederæ folio*, *Cyclamen orbiculato folio inferne purpuraſcente*, *Cyclamen foliis cordatis ſerratis*, *Cyclamen radice caſtaneæ magnitudinis*, *Cyclamen hyeme & vere florens, folio angoloſo amplo, flore albo, baſi purpurea*, *Perſicum dictum*, &c &c &c It grows naturally in dry, warm, ſhady places in Auſtria, Tartary, and ſeveral of the ſouthern parts of Europe — Titles.

*Cyclamen* is of the claſs and order *Pentandria Monogynia*, and the characters are, — Claſs and order in the Linnæan ſyſtem

1 CALYX is a roundiſh permanent perianthium, cut into five oval ſegments — The characters

2 COROLLA is monopetalous The tube is nearly globular, is ſmall, nutant, and much larger than the calyx The limb is large, and divided into five ſpear-ſhaped ſegments, which are bent backward The neck is prominent

3 STAMINA are five very ſmall filaments inſerted in the tube of the corolla, having ſtraight acute antheræ, which are connivent in the neck of the corolla

4 PISTILLUM conſiſts of a roundiſh germen, a ſtraight filiforme ſtyle longer than the ſtamina, and an acute ſtigma

5 PERICARPIUM is a globular, unilocular, covered fruit, opening in five parts at the top

6 SEMINA The ſeeds are many, oval, and angular

The receptacle is oval and free

## CHAP. CLIV

## *CYNANCHUM.*

BESIDES the climber of this genus already treated of, there is a perennial of upright growth, uſually called the Erect *Cynanchum*, or Roundiſh-leaved Dogs Bane

This plant deſcribed — The ſtalks are upright, ſlender, branching, and grow to about a yard high The leaves are broad, heart ſhaped, pointed, ſmooth, and grow oppoſite to each other The flowers come out in ſmall branches from the wings of the leaves on branching footſtalks They are ſmall, of a white colour, appear in July and Auguſt, and are ſucceeded by oblong taper pods, but the ſeeds ſeldom ripen in our gardens

Culture. — It is propagated by parting of the roots, which may be done in the autumn, when the ſtalks decay, or early in the ſpring before they ſhoot up freſh from the roots

It is alſo propagated by ſowing of the ſeeds, when good ones can be obtained A bed of light ſandy earth muſt be made fine, and the ſeeds ſown in the ſpring, covering them a quarter of an inch deep with the fineſt mould When the plants appear, they muſt be frequently watered, and when the weather grows hot ſhould be ſhaded in the heat of the day The bed all ſummer muſt be kept clean from weeds, watering muſt be afforded the plants, as the ſeaſon makes it neceſſary; and in the autumn they may be removed to the places where they are deſigned to remain

This ſpecies is rather tender, ſo the ſoil muſt be — Proper ſoil and ſituation.

be naturally dry and warm, and the situation well defended, otherwise there will be a great hazard of losing your plants in hard weather, on which account it would be advisable to have a few set in pots, to be housed in the winter, to keep up the stock, in case those abroad should be destroyed

This species is titled, *Cynanchum caule erecto divaricato, foliis cordatis glabris* Caspar Bauhine calls it, *Apocynum folio subrotundo*, and Clusius, *Apocynum latifolium* It grows naturally in Syria

# CHAP CLV.

## *CYNARA*, ARTICHOKE

THE Artichoke and Cardoon of our kitchen-gardens are two notable species of this genus Besides these, there are two other Perennials which are cultivated in some curious gardens, called,

Species

1 Wild Artichoke of Spain

2 Stalkless *Cynara*

Description of the Wild Artichoke of Spain,

1 Wild Artichoke of Spain The stalks are upright, firm, and about a foot high The leaves are pinnatifid, prickly, downy underneath, and longer than the stalks The flowers are large, of a fine blue colour, and the cups are composed of oval shaped scales which spread open The whole has the appearance of an artichoke, but the scales of these plants have not that agreeable substance at their bottoms which those of the others possess This species will be in blow in July, and in warm dry seasons the seeds will be ripe in September

and Stalkless Cynara

2 Stalkless *Cynara* The leaves are large, pinnated, free from spines, and smooth on their upper side Among these the flowers rise immediately from the roots, without any foot-stalk, or, at most, with a very short one The flowers are large of a fine blue colour, and finely scented, they come out in July, and in favourable seasons the seeds ripen in the autumn

Method of propagating them

These plants are both raised by sowing the seeds in the spring, in a bed of light rich earth Where the plants come up too close, the weakest should be drawn out, leaving the others at four inches asunder They must be watered if dry weather happens, be regularly cleared from weeds, and in July should be taken up with balls of earth to their roots, and removed to the places where they are designed to remain, observing to water and shade them until they have taken root The Stalkless *Cynara* is tender, so that a few of the plants should be set in pots to be housed in winter, and turned out into the open ground in the spring Both kinds will flower the summer following, but if a wet season should happen, some hand-glasses must be elevated over those designed for seed, to guard them from the wet, otherwise they will not ripen in this country Both these species are perennial in their own countries, but with us they generally die soon after they have flowered, which makes the saving of the seeds the more necessary to be attended to

Titles

1 Wild Artichoke of Spain is titled, *Cynara foliis spinosis pinnatifidis subtus tomentosis, calycibus squamis ovatis* Clusius calls it, *Carduus sylvestris Baeticus*, Plukenet, *Carduus Tingitanus, flore magno caeruleo, foliis contractioribus, antea spinis caeruleo, spinis duriusculis*, and Morison, *Carduus humilis Tingitanus caeruleus, magno strobilo, tenuius laciniatus* It grows naturally in Spain and some parts of Africa

2 Stalkless *Cynara* is, *Cynara acaulos, foliis pinnatis inermibus supra glabris* Tilli calls it, *Cynara acaulos, Tunetana, Tingitana dicta, magno flore suaviter olente* It is a native of Barbary

Class and order in the Linnaean system

*Cynara* is of the class and order *Syngenesia Polygamia Aequalis*, and the characters are,

The characters

1 Calyx The general calyx is ventricose, and composed of numerous roundish, fleshy, canaliculated, pointed scales

2 Corolla The compound flower is tubulous and uniform The florets are nearly equal, and each consists of one funnel-shaped petal, having a slender tube, and an erect oval limb, divided at the top into five narrow segments

3 Stamina are five very short capillary filaments, having a cylindrical tubulous anthera indented in five parts

4 Pistillum consists of an oval germen, a filiforme style longer than the stamina, and a simple, oblong, emarginated stigma

5 Pericarpium There is none

6 Semen The seed is single, oblong, oval, four cornered, compressed, and crowned with long down

The receptacle is naked

CHAP

# CHAP. CLVI.

## CYNOGLOSSUM, HOUND's TONGUE.

THERE are two perennial species of this genus, viz.

Species.

1. The Common Hound's Tongue,
2. The Creeping Hound's Tongue, or Low Spring Navel-Wort,

which ought not to be passed over in this place.

Common Hound's Tongue described.

1. Common Hound's Tongue. The root is large, thick, black on the outside, white within, and of a sweetish nauseous taste. The radical leaves are large, broad, oval, spear-shaped, hoary, velvety to the touch, and of a very disagreeable smell. The stalks are round, hairy, firm, and grow to about two feet high. The leaves adorn them in plenty, and are long, narrow, pointed, hoary, and strongly scented. The flowers adorn the ends and sides of the branches for a good way down; they are small, of a dark-red or purple colour, appear in June and July, and the seeds ripen in the autumn.

Its uses in medicine.

The roots of this species are used in medicine, being esteemed [illegible] and narcotic; and they are said (when roasted and applied to the parts) to give ease to the piles.

Creeping Hound's Tongue described.

2. Creeping Hound's Tongue. This is a small creeping Perennial. The branches are slender, trailing, and put out roots from the joints. The leaves are heart-shaped, smooth, of a light green colour, and grow on long footstalks. The flowers come out in loose panicles from the divisions of the stalks; they are of a fine blue colour, come out in March, and often continue in succession until the end of May, but are seldom succeeded by good seeds in England.

Culture.

The first sort grows common by road sides in many parts of England, and is not often admitted into gardens. It is propagated by sowing the seeds in the autumn, soon after they are ripe, or in the spring. When the plants come up they must be thinned to proper distances; and this, except keeping them clean from weeds, is all the trouble they will require. The summer following they will flower and perfect their seeds, soon after which the roots generally die; nevertheless, I have ranked these plants among the perennials, because in some dry gravelly soils they will continue for many years.

When this plant is propagated for medicinal purposes, the ground should be double dug, that there may be room for the roots to strike deep, and grow large, they being the most valuable parts of these plants, though the leaves, in some cases, are said to have salutary effects.

The second sort propagates itself by trailing and rooting at the joints. Any or all of these taken off in the spring, winter, summer, or autumn, will grow and soon produce fresh plants in the like manner. They grow naturally in woods in foreign countries, and if we afford them a shady situation, they will continue to exhibit their flowers for a long time in the spring.

1. Common Hound's Tongue is titled, [illegible]. Titles.
Van Royen calls it, *Cynoglossum foliis [illegible] lanceolato-[illegible]*; Caspar Bauhine, [illegible]; also, *Cynoglossum [illegible]*; also, *Cynoglossum [illegible]*; and John Bauhine, *Cynoglossum folio [illegible]*. In the *Hortus Cliffortianus* it is termed, *Cynoglossum foliis [illegible]*. Its situation is chiefly by the sides of roads and beaten paths, and it is found in such places in most countries of Europe.

2. Creeping Hound's Tongue, or Low Spring Navel-Wort, is, *Cynoglossum repens, foliis radicalibus [illegible]*. Morison calls it, *Borrago minor [illegible], folio [illegible]*; Caspar Bauhine, *Symphytum [illegible]*; and Tournefort, *[illegible] pro [illegible] Symphyti folio*. It grows naturally in woods and at the roots of mountains in Portugal and Spain.

*Cynoglossum* is of the class and order *Pentandria Monogynia*; and the characters are, Class and Order in the Linnæan System.

1. CALYX is an oblong permanent perianthium, divided into five acute parts.
2. COROLLA is one funnel-shaped petal, the length of the calyx. The tube is cylindrical, and shorter than the limb. The limb is obtuse, and cut into five segments. The faux is closed by five convex, prominent, connivent squamulæ. The Character.
3. STAMINA are five very short filaments situated in the mouth of the corolla, having roundish naked antheræ.
4. PISTILLUM consists of four germina, a subulated persisting style the length of the stamina, and an emarginated stigma.
5. PERICARPIUM. There is none. The arilli are four, roundish, rough, and depressed.
6. SEMINA. The seeds are four, oval, gibbous, sharp-pointed, and smooth.

CHAP.

# CHAP. CLVII.

## *CYNOSURUS.*

THIS genus affords us two perennial graſſes, which are well known, called,

Species
1 Creſted Dog's Tail Graſs
2 Blue Dog's Tail Graſs

Creſted,
1 Creſted Dog's Tail Graſs The root is compoſed of a multitude of white fibres cluſtered together The leaves are ſhort, and not unlike the common meadow-graſs The ſtalks have two or three joints, grow about two feet high, and are garniſhed with leaves about four or five inches long, growing ſingly at the joints, and ſurrounding it a great way with their baſe The flowers come out in long bending ears or ſpikes, having pinnatifid bracteæ, they are of a pale-green colour, and flouriſh in June, July, and Auguſt

and Blue Dog's Tail Graſs deſcribed
2 Blue Dog's Tail Graſs The root is compoſed of many ſlender fibres The leaves are ſhort The ſtalks are round, jointed, and frequently of a brown or purpliſh colour The flowers come out from the tops of the ſtalks in ſhort, thick, compact ſpikes, attended by undivided bracteæ, they are of a purpliſh blue colour, and come to perfection in June and July

Culture
In order to obtain theſe two graſſes in their true kinds, the roots ſhould be taken up in the ſummer, while they are in flower, or before the ſtalks decay, or the ſeeds may be gathered when they are ripe, and either ſown immediately, or kept until the ſpring

Titles
The firſt ſpecies is titled, *Cynoſurus bracteis pinnatifidis* Caſpar Bauhine calls it, *Gramen pratenſe criſtatum, ſ ſpica criſtata lævi*, alſo, *Gramen criſtatum*, John Bauhine, *Gramen criſtatum*, Parkinſon, *Gramen criſtatum Anglicum*, and Ray, *Gramen criſtatum quadratum, ſ quatuor criſtatum glumarum verſibus* It grows common in all our meadows and paſtures, and is found in the like ſituations all over Europe

The ſecond ſpecies is, *Cynoſurus bracteis integris* Caſpar Bauhine calls it, *Gramen glumis variis*, and Ray, *Gramen parvum montanum ſpicâ craſſiore purpuro-cæruleâ brevi* It grows naturally in moiſt paſtures and meadows in England, and moſt countries of Europe

*Cynoſurus* is of the claſs and order *Triandria Digynia*, and the characters are, — Claſs and order in the Linnæan ſyſtem

1 CALYX The involucrum is partial, lateral, large, and uſually compoſed of three leaves — The characters.

The glume conſiſts of two narrow, ſharp-pointed, equal valves, and contains many flowers

2 COROLLA is compoſed of two valves The outer one is concave and longer than the other, the inner is plane and has no ariſta

3 STAMINA are three capillary filaments, with oblong antheræ

4 PISTILLUM conſiſts of a turbinated germen, and two hairy reflexed ſtyles with ſimple ſtigmas

5 PERICARPIUM There is none The ſeed is cloſely ſurrounded and covered by the corolla

6 SEMEN The ſeed is ſingle, oblong, and pointed at each end

# CHAP. CLVIII.

## *CYPERUS*

THERE are ſeveral ſpecies of this genus growing naturally in warmer parts of the world, and there are a few which are natives of Britain, or ſome of the neighbouring countries Theſe are called,

Species
1 Long Cyperus, or Engliſh Galangale
2 Yellow *Cyperus*
3 Brown *Cyperus*

Deſcription of the Long
1 Long *Cyperus*, or Engliſh Galangale The root is thick, knotty, implicated, long with tubers, of a blackiſh colour without, whitiſh within, of a warm taſte, and an agreeable odour The leaves are carinated, long, and narrow The ſtalks are three-ſquare, ſmooth ſtriated, full of pith, and two or three feet high The flowers come out from the tops of the ſtalks in large, leafy, ſupradecompound panicles, compoſed of numerous ſpikes growing alternately on naked footſtalks, they appear chiefly in July, though they are to be met with occaſionally all the remaining part of the ſummer

The root is carminative and ſtomachic, and frequently uſed in medicine

2 Yellow *Cyperus* The root is long, ſlender, and creeping The leaves are ſlender, carinated, and five or ſix inches long The ſtalks are three-ſquare upright, naked, and about ſix inches high The flowers come out from the tops of the ſtalks in large, ſupradecompound leafy panicles, compoſed of numerous, ſhort, compreſſed, ſpear-ſhaped ſpikes, they are of a yellow colour, and appear in July and Auguſt — Yellow,

3 Brown *Cyperus* The leaves are carinated, narrow, rough, and five or ſix inches long The ſtalks are naked, three-ſquare, upright, and ſix or eight inches high The flowers come out from the — and Brown Cyperus.

the tops of the stalks in leafy supradecompound panicles, composed of several very narrow compressed spikes, growing on simple unequal footstalks, they are of a dark-brown or black colour, and come to perfection in July

Culture None of these sorts are cultivated plants, if a person chooses it, however, he may easily effect it, by sowing the seeds in the spring, or parting of the roots, and must allot them some moist wet place for their residence

Titles 1 Long *Cyperus* is entitled, *Cyperus culmo triquetro folioso, umbellâ foliosâ supradecomposita, pedunculis nudis, spicis alternis* Caspar Bauhine calls it, *Cyperus odoratus radice longâ, five Cyperus officinarum* It grows naturally in marshy places in England, France, and Italy

2 Yellow *Cyperus* is, *Cyperus culmo triquetro nudo, umbellâ triphyllâ, pedunculis simplicibus inæqualibus, spicis confertis lanceolatis* Dalibard calls it, *Cyperus culmo triquetro nudo, paniculâ foliosâ supradecomposita, spicis confertis distiche compressis*, Tournefort, *Cyperus minimus, paniculâ sparsâ flavescente*, Morison, *Cyperus minor pulcher, paniculâ latâ compressâ sucoflavescente*, and Caspar Bauhine, *Gramen cyperoides minus, paniculâ sparsâ subflavescente* It grows naturally in the bogs of Ireland Helvetia, Italy, France, and Germany

3 Brown *Cyperus* is, *Cyperus culmo triquetro nudo, umbellâ trifidâ, pedunculis simplicibus inæqualibus, spicis confertis linearibus* Dalibard calls it, *Cyperus culmo triquetro nudo, paniculâ diphyllâ supradecomposita, spicis strigosioribus confertis distiche compressis*, Tournefort, *Cyperus minimus, paniculâ sparsâ nigricante*, Morison, *Cyperus minor pulcher, paniculâ compressâ nigricante*, and Caspar Bauhine, *Gramen cyperoides minus, paniculâ sparsâ nigricante* It grows naturally in most places in Helvetia, France, and Germany

Class and order in the Linnæan system The characters *Cyperus* is of the class and order *Triandria Monogynia*, and the characters are,

1 CALYX is a distichous imbricated spike, composed of many oval, carinated, plane, inflexed scales separating the flowers

2 COROLLA There is none

3 STAMINA are three very short filaments, with oblong sulcated antheræ

4 PISTILLUM consists of a very small germen, a very long filiforme style, and three capillary stigmas

5 PERICARPIUM There is none

6 SEMEN The seed is single, triquetrous acuminated, and has no hairs

# CHAP CLIX

## *CYPRIPEDIUM*, LADIES SLIPPER.

Species THERE are only two real species of this genus, called,

1 Fibrous-rooted Ladies Slipper

2 Bulbous Ladies Slipper

Description of the Fibrous rooted Ladies Slipper 1 Fibrous-rooted Ladies Slipper The root is thick, knotty, fibrated, and creeping The stalks are upright, firm, hairy, and about a foot high The leaves are large, oval, spear shaped, ribbed, and sit close, growing alternately, without any footstalks The stalk is terminated by one large flower, shaped like a slipper, from whence it took its name They are of different colours in the different varieties, and the general characters indicate their structure, they appear in June, and the seeds ripen in August, soon after which the stalks decay, and fresh ones arise in the spring The principal varieties are,

Varieties Deep Purple Ladies Slipper

Pale Purple Ladies Slipper

Golden Ladies Slipper

Larger Yellow flowered Ladies Slipper

Red Ladies Slipper

Various-flowered Ladies Slipper

All these sorts are more or less streaked or spotted in different parts with opposite colours, which causes their beauties to be more conspicuous the closer they are examined

Bulbous Ladies Slipper described 2 Bulbous Ladies Slipper The root is a roundish bulb The leaves are few, they rise directly from the root, and are of a roundish figure From the root also the flower-stalk comes forth, it grows to about three or four inches high, and the top of it is crowned by one flower, it appears in May or June, and the seeds ripen in August, soon after which the plants and leaves decay

Culture These sorts are said to be with difficulty preserved in gardens, but with very little reason The first sort creeps very much under the surface, and every joint of the root will grow, especially if taken off about the time the stalks decay

The bulbs of the other species also must be transplanted at the same time, and very early in the spring, and if the weather be open in the winter, they will shew good signs of growth They naturally love the shade, a cool situation, and an undunged soil, and being thus stationed they will continue for many years, and annually exhibit their elegant flowers

The seeds also may be sown in such places soon after they are ripe and covered over with about a quarter of an inch of the finest mould When the plants come up they must be kept clear from weeds, and be now and then watered for the first year during their time of growth, but when the leaves decay watering must be discontinued After the first season they will require no trouble; for if they are situated on the side of a hill, which they admirably like, as the common produce of such places is generally low, they will shew themselves among the weeds, and become delightful, as appearing to be sent there by the hand of Nature only

1 Fibrous-rooted Ladies Slipper is titled, *Cypripedium radicibus fibrosis, foliis ovato-lanceolatis caulinis* In the *Flora Lapp* it is termed, *Cypripedium foliis ovato lanceolatis* Dodonæus calls it, *Calceolus Marianus*, Caspar Bauhine, *Helleborine flore rotundo, sive Calceolus*, Gerard, *Calceolus Mariæ*, Parkinson, *Elleborine major, seu Calceolus Mariæ*, Plukenet *Helleborine calceolus dicta Mariana, caule ... flore luteo minore*, Ammann, *Calceolus minor, ... rio*, Cornutus, *Calceolus Marianus Canadensis*, Gmelin *Calceolus foliis ovato-lanceolatis*, also, *Calceolus foliis ovatis ... latis*, Morison, *Helleborine ... calceolus flore luteo majore*, also, *Helleborine flore majore purpureo* It grows naturally in woods, thickets, &c in England, and in most of the northern parts of Europe, Asia, and America

2 Bulbous Ladies Slipper is, *Cypripedium bulbo ... oso, folio subrotundo radicali* In the *Flora ...* it is titled, *Cypripedium folio subrotundo* ... calls it, *Serapias scapo unifloro*, Rudbeck, *Orchis Lapponensis monofolia* It grows naturally in Lapland, Russia, and Siberia

*Cypripedium* is of the class and order *Gynandria Diandria*, and the characters are, — Class and order in the Linnæan System

1 CALYX is a spatha — The characters

2 COROLLA is four or five long, spear-shaped, narrow, erect, patent petals The nectarium is situated between the petals, is very broad, shaped like a shoe or slipper, inflated, hollow, and obtuse, having the upper lip small, oval, plane, and inflexed

3 STAMINA are two very short filaments resting on the pistil, having erect antheræ, which are concealed under the upper lip of the nectarium

4 PISTILLUM consists of a long contorted germen situated below the flower, a very short style adhering to the upper lip of the nectarium, and an obsolete stigma

5 PERICARPIUM is an oval, obtuse, three-cornered, three-furrowed capsule, formed of three valves, and containing one cell

6 SEMINA The seeds are numerous and small

## CHAP CLX

## *CYTISUS*, BASE TREE-TREFOIL

THE species of this genus proper for the flower garden are, — Species

1 Low Downy *Cytisus*

2 Silvery *Cytisus*

3 *Linaria*-leaved *Cytisus*

1 Low Downy *Cytisus* This plant hath a tough strong root, which strikes deep into the ground The stalks are weak, slender, scarcely a foot long, and, unless supported, lie on the ground The leaves are oblong, smooth on their outside, downy underneath, and grow by threes upon longish footstalks The flowers are collected in small heads at the ends of the branches, they are of a deep yellow colour, and have a cluster of leaves under them, they appear in June, and are succeeded by flat downy pods, containing ripe seeds, in September — Low Downy ...

2 Silvery *Cytisus* The root is tough, and strikes into the ground like the former The stalks are weak, lie on the ground, and are very little more than six inches in length The leaves are small, spear-shaped, of a silvery whiteness, and grow by threes on the stalks The flowers come out two or three together from the ends of the branches, but from the wings of the leaves they grow singly, they are of a pale-yellow colour, have very short footstalks, appear in July, and in warm seasons the seeds ripen in the autumn — Silvery ...

3 *Linaria*-leaved *Cytisus* The root of this plant is tough, white, and strikes deep into the ground The stalks are ligneous, slender, angular, and put forth several weak four-cornered branches The leaves are simple, and spear-shaped The flowers are small, and of a yellow colour, they come out from the ends and sides of the branches in July, and sometimes the seeds ripen in the autumn — and Linaria-leaved Cytisus described

All these sorts are easily propagated by sowing of the seeds in the spring, in the places where they are designed to remain, for they do not bear transplanting well The soil should be naturally dry and warm, the aspect upon the south, and the situation well defended If they are thus stationed they will for the most part perfect their seeds, but if a very wet season should happen, which prevents the seeds from ripening, a few hand-glasses should be elevated over those designed for seed, to protect them from the wet, and then, unless the season is to the last degree cold and unpropitious, the seeds will ripen — Culture

After the plants come up, all the trouble they require is, drawing out the weakest where they are too close, keeping the ground clean from weeds, and watering in dry weather As the stalks shoot out for flowering, which will be the second summer after sowing, tie them to some short sticks, to prevent the flowers lying on the ground, which would not only have a slovenly look, but prevent the seeds from ripening

1 Low Downy *Cytisus* is titled, *Cytisus floribus umbellatis terminalibus, ramis decumbentibus, foliolis ovatis* Caspar Bauhine calls it, *Cytisus supinus, foliis infra & siliquis molli lanugine pubescentibus*, also, *Cytisus supinus, foliis incano lanugine infernis pubescentibus*, and Clusius, *Cytisus 7 species altera* It grows naturally in Siberia, Sicily, Spain, and Italy — Titles

2 Silvery *Cytisus* is, *Cytisus floribus subsessilibus, foliis tomentosis herbaceis, stipulis minutis* Sauvages calls it, *Cytisus acaulis, floribus ... foliolis ... lanceolatis*, Caspar Bauhine, *Lotus fruticosus incanus siliquosus*, Lobel *Lotus alpinus fruticosa Narbonensis incana*, and John Bauhine, *Trifolium argenteum, floribus luteis* It grows naturally in Italy, and the South of France

3 *Linaria*-leaved *Cytisus* is, *Cytisus foliis simplicibus lanceolato linearibus ramis angulatis* Tournefort calls it, *Barba jovis, linariæ folio, flore luteo parvo* It grows in most of the Mediterranean islands

CHAP

## CHAP CLXI

## *DACTYLIS*

THERE are only two species of this genus, called,

Species 1 Smooth Cock's Foot Grass

2 Rough Cock's Foot Grass

Smooth, 1 Smooth Cock's Foot Grass The stalk is round hollow, jointed, of a whitish colour, and two or three feet high The leaves are broad, very long, and smooth, except on their edges, which are a little rough The flowers come out in spikes from the tops of the stalks, they are rough, and ranged on one side, they appear in July, August, and September

and Rough Cock's Foot Grass described 2 Rough Cock's Foot Grass This is a common grass of our meadows and pastures The leaves are narrow, pointed and rough The stalks are slender jointed, round, hollow, and a foot and a half high The flowers come out in spikes from the tops of the stalks, are very closely set together, and arranged in one direction, they are of a reddish colour, and appear from June until the end of summer

Culture Whoever is inclined to propagate these grasses, may do it by sowing the seeds in the autumn as soon as they are ripe, or the spring following The first is rather a scarce grass, growing but sparingly in England, and other parts of the world, the second is to be found almost every where in most countries of Europe

Titles 1 The first species is titled, *Dactylis spicis sparsis secundis subulatis numerosis* Ray calls it, *Spartum Essexianum, spica gemina*, and Gronovius, *Gramen montanum, spica crassa dactyloide terminali, echinata, candido, also, Dactylis spicis alternis secundis subulatis erectis approximatis, calycibus subulatis* It grows in England, Portugal, Canada, and Virginia

2 The second species is, *Dactylis panicula secunda glomerata* In the *Flora Suecica* it is termed *Cynosurus panicula secunda glomerata* and in the *Hort Cliff Poa flosculis conferta* ... C Bauhine calls it, *Gramen spicatum, folio aspero*, Parkinson, *Gramen pratense spica latiore* ... and Morison, *Gramen paniculatum* ... *rum*. It is found in most parts of Europe

Class and order in the Linnæan system Dactylis is of the class and order *Triandria Digynia*, and the characters are,

1 CALYX is a compressed, carinated, acute glume, composed of two valves, one of which is longer than the flower the other shorter

the characters 2 COROLLA is an oblong, compressed, carinated, acute glume

3 STAMINA are three capillary filaments the length of the corolla, having bifurcated antheræ

4 PISTILLUM consists of a turbinated germen, and two capillary, patent, hairy styles, with simple stigmas

5 PERICARPIUM There is none The corolla includes the seed, and discharges it when arrived at maturity

6 SEMEN The seed is single, naked, depressed on one side, and convex on the other

## CHAP CLXII

## *DATISCA*, BASTARD HEMP

THERE are only two species of this genus, called,

Species 1 Smooth Bastard Hemp

2 Rough Bastard Hemp

Smooth, 1 Smooth Bastard Hemp This rises with strong, herbaceous, smooth, upright stalks, to the height of about four feet The leaves are pinnated, each being composed of three large, acute-pointed, serrated folioles, which are terminated by an odd one, their colour is a light-green, and they grow alternately on the stalks The flowers come out from the wings of the leaves on long loose spikes, they are males and females on different plants, and like most of these sorts make a little shew They make their appearance in June, and the females are succeeded by three-cornered capsules, containing ripe seeds in September

and Rough Bastard Hemp described 2 Rough Bastard Hemp The stalks of this plant are strong, upright, hairy, and grow to be five or six feet high The leaves are pinnated like the other, and grow alternately on the stalks The flowers are produced from the sides of the stalks like the former, and the females are succeeded by oblong triangular capsules, containing ripe seeds, in the autumn

Methods of propagating these sorts Both these sorts are easily propagated by sowing the seeds in the autumn, soon after they are ripe In the spring the plants must be thinned where they croud each other, drawing out the weakest All the summer they must be kept clean from weeds, and in the autumn may be removed to the places where they are designed to remain

Soil and situation They are hardy, and will grow in almost any soil or situation, but they do best in a moist rich earth that is much shaded

They are also propagated by parting the roots This should be done in the autumn, when the stalks decay, no art need be used in the performance, divide them any how, plant them out like the seedlings, and they will grow

Titles 1 Smooth Bastard Hemp is titled, *Datisca caule lævi* In the *Hortus Cliffor.* it is termed, *Cannabina foliis pinnatis* Caspar Bauhine calls it, *Luteola herbæ facie*, also, *Luteola herba foliis cannabinis*, and Alpinus, *Cannabis lutea sterilis*, also, *Cannabis lutea sterilis*, also, *Cannabis lutea Cretica* It grows naturally in Crete

2 Rough

2 Rough Bastard Hemp is, *Datisca caule hirsuto* It grows common in Pensylvania

Class and order in the Linnæan system *Datisca* is of the class and order *Dioecia Polyandria*, and the characters are,

The characters

I Male Flowers

1 CALYX is a perianthium composed of seven narrow, equal, acute leaves

2 COROLLA There is none

3 STAMINA The filaments are hardly discernable but the antheræ, which are about fifteen in number, are oblong, obtuse, and much longer than the calyx

II Female Flowers

1 CALYX is a small, erect, permanent perianthium, situated above the germen, and indented in two parts

2 COROLLA There is none

3 PISTILLUM consists of an oblong germen longer than the calyx, and of three short bipartite styles, with simple, oblong, hairy stigmas, the length of the germen

4 PERICARPIUM is an oblong, triangular, trivalvate, tricuspidated capsule of one cell

5 SEMINA The seeds are numerous, small, and adhere to the three sides of the capsule

## CHAP CLXIII

# *DELPHINIUM*, LARKSPUR

THERE are two perennial species of this genus,

Species 1 The Siberian Larkspur or Bee flower

2 The Silesian Larkspur or Bee fower

Siberian Larkspur 1 Siberian Larkspur The stalks are upright, firm, and two, three, or four feet high The leaves are smooth, hoary, consist of many narrow parts, and grow alternately on the stalks The flowers come out singly, or seldom more than two, on the upper parts of the plant, on long footstalks, they adorn the stalks a great way down, are of a blue colour, and have a bearded dark coloured nectarium in the center, forming the appearance of a bee in the flower, which has occasioned this species being termed the Bee Larkspur, they come out in June and July, and in favourable seasons the seeds ripen in autumn

Varieties There are several varieties of this species, which are very beautiful One seldom grows higher than about a foot, called the Dwarf Bee-Larkspur, another has beautiful purple stalks, and broader segments to the leaves, another has leaves like Aconite, being composed of about five lobes, divided at the edges into obtuse segments, and another has yellow flowers The names of these among Gardeners are,

The Dwarf Bee-Larkspur

Purple-stalked Bee-Larkspur

Aconite-leaved Portugal Bee Larkspur

Yellow Bee Larkspur

Culture They are continued in their varieties by dividing the roots, the best time for which is the autumn, when the stalks decay

Silesian Larkspur 2 Silesian Larkspur The stalks of this species are upright, hairy, hollow, purplish, and five or six feet high The leaves grow on long footstalks, and are divided into numerous segments, which spread open like the hand The segments are large, hairy, of a dusky green colour, and cut at the extremities into a few acute points The flowers come out from the tops of the stalks and branches in long spikes, they are of a purplish blue colour, having a two-leaved bearded nectarium, resembling a bee, like the former species, they appear in July and August, and the seeds ripen in the autumn

Its propagation This species is propagated by parting the roots, like the former sort; but the best way of raising all the kinds is from seeds, which will not only afford you the finest plants, but by that practice fresh varieties are often obtained

Sow the seeds, then, the first week in April, in beds of light rich earth, made fine, scatter them thinly, and slightly rake them in, then give them a good watering, if the weather is dry If no rain happens, water the bed twice a week, and in about five weeks your plants will come up At this time the weeds, which will intrude along with them, must be carefully picked out, and where the plants shew signs of crowding each other, they must be thinned, leaving them at three inches distance every way All summer watering must be afforded the plants, as often as dry weather makes it necessary, weeds must be pulled up as they arise, and in the autumn the plants may be removed to the places where they are designed to remain They are hardy, and will grow in almost any soil or situation, though they affect shade that is under the drip of trees, and a good, fresh, light earth

Titles 1 Siberian Larkspur is titled, *Delphinium nectariis diphyllis labellis integris, floribus subsolitariis, foliis compositis linearibus multipartitis* Amman terms it, *Delphinium elatius submanum perenne, floribus amplis azureis*, also, *Delphinium humilius angustifolium perenne, flore azureo*, and Tournefort, *Delphinium Lusitanicum glabrum, aconiti folio* It is a native of Siberia

2 Silesian Larkspur is, *Delphinium nectariis diphyllis labellis bifidis apice barbatis, foliis incisis, caule erecto* In the *Hortus Cliffortianus* it is termed, *Delphinium nectariis diphyllis, foliis peltatis multipartitis acutis* Amman calls it, *Delphinium perenne, aconiti folio ampliori, floribus cæruleis*, Caspar Bauhine, *Aconitum cæruleum hirsutum, flore consolidæ regalis*, and Clusius, *Aconitum lycoctonum, flore delphinii Silesiacum* It grows common in Siberia, Helvetia, and Silesia

*Delphinium* is of the class and order *Polyandria Trigynia*; and the characters are,

1 CALYX There is none

2 COROLLA consists of five unequal petals, disposed orbicularly The upper one is more obtuse on the back part than the others, and extends behind into one long, straight, obtuse, tubular tail, called the Spur the others are oval, spear-shaped, spreading, and nearly equal

The nectarium is situated in the center of the petals, towards the upper part It is bifid at the top, and has a tail or horn extended from the hinder part, which penetrates into the tube of the upper petal or spur, and which serves it as a scabbard or sheath

3 STAMINA The filaments are numerous, small, awl-shaped, broadest at the base, and inclining towards the upper petal The antheræ are small and erect

4 PISTILLUM The germina are oval, usually three in number, and support the styles, which are the length of the stamina, and have simple reflexed stigmas

5 PERICARPIUM consists of the like number of oval, awl-shaped capsules, which are composed of one valve, and open on the inner side

6 SEMINA The seeds are many and angular

# CHAP. CLXIV

## *DENTARIA*, TOOTHWORT, TOOTHED VIOLETS, or CORALWORT

ALL the species of this genus are hardy perennials, and called,

Species

1 Three-leaved Toothwort
2 Bulbiferous Toothwort, or Coralwort
3 Five-leaved Toothwort

Description of the Three leaved

1 Three-leaved Toothwort This species has a thick, fleshy, tuberous, knobbed root, from which arise the stalks, these are round, upright, firm and grow to about a foot high The radical leaves are composed of three large, broad, oval, serrated folioles, growing on long strong footstalks, those on the stalks are narrower, and three whole leaves usually come out from one point, making the number of folioles nine from the same quarter The flowers adorn the tops of the stalks, in loose spikes, they are small, of a palish-green colour, and their general characters indicate their structure, they make their appearance in May, sometimes earlier, and are succeeded by long slender pods, containing ripe seeds, in August

Bulbiferous,

2 Bulbiferous Toothwort, or Coralwort The root of this species is tuberous, toothed, craggy like coral, and full of a sharp disagreeable juice The stalks are slender, and grow only to about a foot high The radical leaves are pinnated, each being composed of three pairs of narrow, acute-pointed, jagged, hemp-like folioles, besides the odd one with which they are terminated The leaves on the lower part of the stalks are composed each of five of the like kind of folioles, and on the upper part, near the flowers, the leaves are simple The flowers are small, purplish, come out from the tops of the stalks, and among them small tubers or bulbs, which, falling to the ground, grow and commence good plants The flowers appear in May, and are succeeded by narrow taper pods, containing ripe seeds, in August

and Five-leaved Toothwort

3 Five-leaved Toothwort Of this species there are several varieties, some having rough leaves, others smooth, some white flowers, some blue, others purple, &c The roots of all are thick, full of tubers, fleshy, and full of juice The stalks in general grow to about a foot and a half high The leaves are digitated, and each is composed of five long acutely-serrated folioles, though in some varieties the lower leaves have seven, and they grow on long strong footstalks The flowers come out in kind of clusters, from the tops of the stalks, they are small, and of different colours in the different varieties, they appear in May, and are succeeded by long slender pods, full of round seeds, which ripen in August

These sorts all grow naturally in woody, mountainous, shady places, which teaches us that as similar a situation as may be should be afforded them in our gardens Let, therefore, a moist light soil be pitched on, in a shady place, let it be made fine, and let the seeds, soon after they are ripe, be sown on it, and slightly raked in The plants will then readily come up, whereas, if they are kept until the spring, they will sometimes lie until the second year before they appear When they come up they require no trouble, except thinning where they crowd each other, keeping clean from weeds, and watering in dry weather In the autumn they may be removed into the places where they are designed to remain, which ought to be a light soil, naturally moist, and in the shade Culture.

They are also propagated by parting the roots This should be done early in October, and a similar situation to that for the seedlings should be assigned

The Bulbiferous Toothwort is also propagated by planting the bulbs which are produced from the sides of the stalks As they fall off they should be carefully gathered, and planted in a light, moist, shady place, just covering them over with the finest mould, they will then readily grow, and soon commence good plants

1 Three leaved Toothwort is titled, *Dentaria foliis ternis ternatis* Van Royen calls it, *Dentaria foliis omnibus ternatis*, Caspar Bauhine, *Dentaria triphyllos*, Gesner, *Coralloides triphyllos*, and Columna, *Ceratia Plinii* It grows common in the sterile, shady, mountainous parts of Austria and Italy Titles

2 Bulbiferous Toothwort, or Coralwort, is,

*Dentaria foliis inferioribus pinnatis, summis simplicibus.* Caspar Bauhine terms it, *Dentaria heptaphyllos baccifera*, also, *Dentaria coccifera, foliis ptarmicae.* Clusius names it, *Dentaria IV bacci-fera*, and Gerard, *Dentaria bulbifera.* It grows common in the shady parts of parks, forests, &c in England, and most of the southern parts of Europe.

3 Five-leaved Toothwort is, *Dentaria foliis summis digitatis.* Haller terms it, *Dentaria foliis septenis, superioribus quinatis*, Gesner, *Dentaria foliis summis quinatis*, Tournefort, *Dentaria pentaphyllos, foliis asperis*, Caspar Bauhine, *Dentaria pentaphyllos*, also, *Dentaria heptaphyllos*, also, *Dentaria pentaphyllos foliis mollibus*, and Clusius, *Dentaria heptaphyllos*, also, *Dentaria 6 pentaphyllos.* It grows common on the Alps, and in mountainous shady places in several parts of Europe.

Class and order in the Linnæan system. *Dentaria* is of the class and order *Tetradynamia Siliquosa*, and the characters are,

The characters. 1 CALYX is a perianthium composed of four oval, oblong, parallel, connivent, obtuse, deciduous leaves.

2 COROLLA is cruciforme, and consists of four roundish obtuse petals, which are slightly indented, and have ungues the length of the calyx.

3 STAMINA consist of six awl-shaped filaments the length of the calyx, of these, two are shorter than the others, and the antheræ peculiar to them all are heart shaped, oblong, and erect.

4 PISTILLUM consists of an oblong germen the length of the stamina, a very short thick style, and an obtuse emarginated stigma.

5 PERICARPIUM is a long, taper, bivalvate, bilocular pod.

6 SEMINA. The seeds are many, and nearly oval.

# CHAP. CLXV.

## *DIANTHERA.*

THERE is one species of this genus which comes of course in this place, called, American *Dianthera*. The root is fibrous.

Description of this plant. The stalks are weak, simple, herbaceous, erect, and about four or five inches long. The leaves are roundish, hairy, of a dark green colour, and finely scented. The flowers are produced in single alternate, oval spikes, from the sides of the stalks. They are whitish, or of a reddish-purple colour, and their general characters indicate their structure, they appear in July, but are very rarely succeeded by seeds in England.

Culture. This species is propagated by parting of the roots the latter end of September. They must have a dry, light, sandy soil, and should be set on the side of some sloping ground, where the wet may freely pass off, otherwise there will be great danger of their rotting in winter. For want of such a situation, the ground should be elevated in some convenient place, in order to plant them, some forked sticks also should be stuck round the plants, and hand glasses set near, in order to cover them when very wet weather happens, and with this management they may be continued many years, for they are very hardy with respect to cold.

They may be also raised from seeds, which should be procured from America. These ought to be brought forward in the spring by a gentle hotbed, and when the plants are fit to remove, they should be set in a bed of light earth, about four inches distant from each other. This bed should be hooped, in order to protect the plants from violent rains, and in the autumn, or (if you choose it) the spring, or even autumn after that, they may be removed to the places where they are designed to remain, observing always, in taking them up, to preserve a ball of earth to each root, and breaking as few of the fibres as possible.

Titles. This species is titled, *Dianthera spicis solitariis alternis.* Gronovius terms it simply, *Dianthera*, and Plukenet, *Gratiolae affinis Floridana, foliis floribus & capsulis in spicâ dispositis, pedunculis e foliorum alis enatis.* It is a native of Virginia and Florida.

Class and order in the Linnæan system. The characters. *Dianthera* is of the class and order *Diandria Monogynia*, and the characters are,

1 CALYX is a monophyllous, tubular, permanent perianthium, divided into five spear shaped equal segments, which are of the length of the tube.

2 COROLLA is a ringent petal. The tube is short, the upper lip is plane, reflexed, bifid and obtuse, the lower lip is divided into three oblong, obtuse, distant segments, of which the middle one is the broadest.

3 STAMINA are two filiforme filaments, affixed to the back of the corolla, and of the length of the upper lip, having oblong, double antheræ, one of which is rather higher than the other.

4 PISTILLUM consists of an oblong germen, a filiforme style the length of the stamina, and an obtuse stigma.

5 PERICARPIUM is a bivalvate bilocular capsule, alternately compressed at the top and the bottom, and which opens elastically for the discharge of the seeds.

6 SEMINA. The seeds are flat, and single in each cell.

# CHAP CLXVI

## *DIANTHUS*, The CLOVE JULY FLOWER, or CARNATION

Introductory remarks

THE most considerable ornamental part of this genus is included in one species, which has been already amply treated of among the Prize-Flowers, as being the principal of those that fall more immediately under the Florist's care and protection But besides that species, what a world of varieties does this genus afford us, both for beauty and use! There is no end of the sorts of Carnations, or Cloves, neither is there any end of the variety of Pinks, and the sorts of Sweet-Williams are numberless in their varieties The other species, indeed, are more inconsiderable, but there is an elegance attending many of them I shall, therefore, arrange them in a regular manner, with one title only, and under that shall point out the different varieties, by double flowers, and the like, as I go along, and which are known by distinct names among Gardeners, for were they to be arranged as they are commonly called, the real species and the varieties would be blended together in so confused a manner, that the young student would hardly know how to distinguish them The principal of these I shall, therefore, first treat of, whilst the more inconsiderable species will follow of course, to be treated of in succession

The real species (attended by their varieties) of this genus, then, are,

Species

1 Clove July Flower
2 Pink
3 Sweet William
4 Deptford Pink
5 Mountain Pink
6 Wild Pink of the Forests
7 Stone-Pink
8 Alpine Pink
9 Maiden Pink
10 Montpelier Pink

Clove July Flower

1 The Clove July Flower, as has been more than once observed, is what has given rise to the profusion of Carnations which now adorn our gardens It is termed the July Flower because it chiefly flowers in the month of July, and the name Clove is added, because its fragrance a little resembles the spicy flavour of the clove Where no regular collection of stand and prize flowers is making, the gentleman is contented with a quantity of them for embellishing his flower garden, and indeed the number of these, which are what the florist calls indifferent flowers, is so great, that were he only to be possessed of two layers of a sort, they would be sufficient to stock a large spot Some, however, he must have, for beauty, nosegays, and observation, and these should be as different as possible Some Flakes and Bizarres should form a bed of themselves, which will make a noble show, some Picquettes and Painted Ladies should form another, whilst another bed or two should consist wholly of the true original kind of Cloves, in its Double state, which may be for use, for syrup, &c as well as afford pleasure from their fine flowers and spicy odours Some large clusters should be here and there placed to shew the variety they cause that way, and the owner may be brought into a more curious management of these, by first trying to blow them in the manner directed for the florist A board fixed at the top of the stick, for a few good flowers, will answer the end of a shed, to protect them from the inclemencies of the weather, and, better than boards, glasses (judiciously made) made be used, and by these may be given to the flowers sun or shade, in any part, as it is wanted, covering them with a cabbage leaf, or the like Almost every gardener knows how to make these glasses, they having been long used in different parts All these, with a few single flowers, the better to shew their stamina, will be sufficient of this species They may be multiplied, and placed here and there, according to the taste of the owner, and the manner of their propagation is either from layers or seeds

2 The Pink What a world of varieties belongs to this species, and what different colours do they exhibit! The whole of them afford a good collection of flowers, and from the earliest to the latest blowers, considerable part of the summer is occupied by them They are all well-known plants, and, besides their spicy fragrance, look well any how As an ornament to the edge of a large border, many of them are very proper, and what a glorious sight is it to behold a long row of these plants in full blow! This is the best manner, indeed, of shewing many of them to advantage, though they look well when four or five of them are planted near each other, to form little patches here and there about the garden They should be disposed according to the time of flowering, that as one sort goes off, another may appear in its full lustre and glory They are now grown so common, though nevertheless beautiful on that account, that every Gardener knows them, and they are chiefly distinguished among them by these strange names, which I shall enumerate, beginning with those that flower first, and mention them as they succeed in order

The Pink

The Little Milkmaid This is a small white single Pink, and is the earliest of all the sorts

Varieties

The Damask Pink This is a semi-double Pink, of a reddish-purple colour, remarkable for its fragrance

The White Shock Pink This is a very white Pink, and remarkable for having the edges of the petals more fringed than common

The Paper Pink This flowers so near to the time of the former that it can hardly be said to succeed it Its colour is a pure-white, it is of high fragrance, and the borders of the petals are much less jagged than those of the former

Browne's Pheasant-Eye seems rather to lead the van of that tribe, and the other sorts of Pheasant-Eyes, which consist of more than fourteen, flower about that time

The Monstrous Pheasant Eye rather succeeds This is a prodigious large broken flower The first that appears will always be the largest and

at

if this be planted in a light soil of rich fat earth, and only one or two permitted to blow, they will be as large as the Whole blowing Carnations

To the Monstrous Pheasant Eye succeeds the Cob-Pink This sort is of a fine red colour, of a fine fragrance, and the flower-stalks arise to above a foot high

Browname's Pink, and several others without any name, will be now in blow, and the show is continued by the Pinks called the Old Man's Head, the Painted Lady, &c until the Carnations are in splendor The last of these, indeed, are Carnations, but let them be ranked as they please, they are really fine flowers for borders, nosegays, &c and ought to be in plenty in every large garden These are the chief sorts known to Gardeners, but there are numerous others, which are yearly raised from seeds to encrease the variety These may be easily obtained, and the collection encreased at pleasure But before I proceed to the next article, I shall close this with giving the true method of propagating Pinks, and this is to be done,

1 By layers
2 By slips
3 By seeds

Method of propagating these pieces by layers, 1 By layers This is the most sure and certain method, and is a practice I would for the most part advise Numbers of layers in a little time may be made, and the sorts may be kept separate The method is, by making a slit at the joint, proceeding in the same manner as with the Carnation These, being weak, will have no need of pegs to keep them down, and being hilled up with a little mould will readily strike root, and these layers will be the very best plants, and will be proper for any place

slips, 2 By slips Many, nay, all of the sorts will grow this way, but success is not always to be depended upon, for if the weather comes dry and hot afterwards, all the watering in the world will not preserve great part of them from going off It is in some cases, however, the most expeditious way, and if the weather proves moist and cloudy, most of them may be reasonably expected to grow When this method is to be practised, then make choice of some moist weather July and August are proper months for the work, and as the weather clears up, shade them from the heat of the sun After they have taken root, which will be in a week or two if at all, they will require no trouble This method may be practised with your weakest trailing Pinks, with good success, but when there are only few plants to be encreased, the surest and best method is layering

and seed 3 By seeds This method is practised chiefly for the sake of raising fresh varieties, and also where they are used for edgings, for the seeds being sown to any stated distance will come up regularly, and flower and make a good show without ever removing The raising of the Single Pink is always practised this way, and, to make the show more valuable, gather your seeds from those which have the finest eyes, and these will again reward your attention with fairer flowers These seeds may be sown any time after they are ripe, though the usual way is to stay until spring Sow them in drills, covering them a quarter of an inch deep The other seeds, collected from the best flowers, and sown with a design to encrease the collection of sorts, may be sown in beds of any tolerable garden mould, and covered about a quarter of an inch deep, and they will soon come up in prodigious plenty In August they may be pricked out in beds at a few inches distance, and the summer following they will flower, when the best sorts may be preserved and encreased, and the worst thrown away

Sweet William 3 The next species of this genus to be considered are the Sweet Williams, and of these as great a variety may be obtained as of any of the sorts, but these are not so much tried for, the Sweet Williams being in general looked upon as common and indifferent flowers But this is a very great mistake, for altho' it be not very uncommon to find Sweet-Williams in gardens, yet it is rather unusual to see a proper show of them disposed to advantage, and to suppose it an indifferent flower is doing it injustice, for whoever examines the meanest of them with any attention will find it display numerous charms and beauties

Directions for ... vantage ... display of these flow... In order to make a proper show of these flowers, therefore, collect your seeds from some of the best flowers, the most beautifully bespangled, variegated, and those of the finest eyes Different shades of these sorts may be found without end, but those of the brightest colours only should be marked for the purpose Some of the deep scarlet and blood red should be chosen, for these have a delightful effect among the lighter coloured finely tufted flowers All indifferent flowers growing near these should be early plucked as they first shew themselves, to keep the seeds of the best sorts pure, which would be liable to be impregnated by the contiguous sorts These seeds will be ripe early in autumn, against which time prepare a long border of common garden mould made fine Then, near the edge of this border, mark out a place for the seeds, the whole length Let this be about a foot in breadth, let it be made fine ... with a little hand-rake, and draw ... each side for the direction of sowing the seeds This being done, sow the seeds very thin, the whole length, if it be an hundred yards it will be the better, then rake them in with the hand-rake as you do onions or leeks, and do but just cover them with the mould, and in two or three weeks the plants will come up By the end of October they will become good strong plants, when they may be thinned where they come up too thick and the drawn plants will serve for other places In the spring keep them clear of weeds, water them in dry weather, and in July they will flower, but the blow will not be in perfection until the July following Then will the sight be striking and enchanting, then you will behold a most glorious show of these flowers for a considerable length, in which, even upon nice examination, you will hardly find two exactly alike Here you will see the different shades, and their different colours, some bright, some deep, and some paler, all uniting to form, as it were, at a small distance, the appearance of one continued flower, glowing the whole length of the bed, for at the time of their blow they will be produced in such profusion as to cover the space they occupy, and hardly any thing but flowers dazzling the eyes will appear This is the perfection of these flowers, and this easy method is to be pursued to effect it Miller directs the sowing these seeds in the spring, it may be done, but then you lose a year by it, for they will not flower before the July twelvemonth after, and the Gardener's art is to bring things to forwardness as much as possible

This is the perfection of this flower in its Single state, and which will afford variety not only by the flowers but their leaves, some being very broad, some very narrow, which have been distinguished by different names by common Gardeners, and which it is thought proper to acquaint the more intelligent Gardener now, that

such

such differences are only seminal variations, and that the usual name Sweet-William is applicable to them both.

Varieties. There are three varieties of this species, with Double flowers, that are greatly esteemed; one of which is called the Mule, from the strange supposition that one or more of the Sweet-Williams, fecundating the seeds of a Carnation, from those seeds this impregnation came forth this flower. The leaves of this variety are narrow; the flowers are very double, of a bright red colour, and possessed of some fragrance. The second sort goes by the name of the Double-rose Sweet-William. These are complete full flowers, of a fine rose-colour, and possess a fragrance that makes them very desirable. The other Double Sweet-Williams have large double flowers, of a purplish colour; but as it bursts the pods, it is of all the sorts least admired.

Culture. All these Double sorts may be propagated by slips, planting them any time in moist weather in a shady place; but as they sometimes fail this way, the most certain method would be to layer them, and these will be sure to have good roots, and may be removed to any place.

Proceed we next to the other sorts of Pinks in their order, all which of themselves are distinct species.

Description of the Deptford, 4. The Deptford Pink. This is so called because it grows wild in a meadow near Deptford in Kent. It is of the Sweet-William kind, and produces its flowers in close bunches. The root is tough, and composed of many fibres. The stalks are slender, lie on the ground, and strike root at the joints. The flowers are red; they appear in July, and are soon succeeded by ripe seeds, by which this species may be propagated, sowing them in the manner of the Sweet-Williams, at any season from the time of their ripening until the spring.

Mountain, 5. Mountain Pink. This species, as the title imports, grows wild upon mountainous and rocky parts. It is a small elegant species. The leaves are very short and grassy, and of a light colour. The flowers are single, small, white, and have an elegant circle of purple surrounding the eye, which contributes chiefly to the beauty of this species, and makes it to be most admired.

Wild, 6. Wild Pink of the Forests. This is a very small Pink, which grows wild in dry stony places. The flowers come out singly, are of a pale-red colour, and the edges of the petals cut into many points. This species produces seeds in plenty, by which it may be propagated.

Stone, 7. The Stone Pink. This grows naturally in sandy, dry places, old walls, and the like, in many parts of England. The leaves are small and narrow. The flowers arise singly on the tops of the stalks; they are of a pale colour, and make little shew, though they are very sweet scented. Their cups have oval scales, and their petals are cut into many points. This species produces seeds in plenty.

Alpine, 8. Alpine Pink grows naturally upon the Alps and other parts. This is a dwarf Pink, with short blunt leaves, which are moderately broad. The stalk supports one single flower, with crenated petals. The flowers are of a pale-red colour, very small, and, like some of the preceding, desired only when a general collection of the different species of plants is making.

Maiden, 9. Maiden Pink. This is a very low plant, having numerous short subulated leaves. The flowers are small, and of a red colour, having their petals crenated, and the calyx hath very short scales. This is a native of ours, growing common on rocky dry ground in the north.

and Montpelier Pinks. 10. Montpelier Pink. The leaves are very narrow, and of a bluish-green colour; the stalks are slender, jointed, and about six inches high. The flowers come out singly on long footstalks; their exterior leaves are awl-shaped, and the petals are deeply cut into many narrow segments; they appear in July, and the seeds ripen in September.

Method of propagating them. The culture of all these last-mentioned species is very easy; for upon sowing the seeds they will come up almost any where, especially if the land be of a stony nature. The best way will be to sow the seeds where they are to remain, for the seedling plants, unremoved, produce their leaves and flowers rather stronger, though at best they are very low, dwarfs, and what in general they would term very insignificant plants. They bear removing very well, however, and may be encreased by parting of their roots. So this is all that is necessary to be said about them, the glory or our collection consisting chiefly in the varieties of the three first species, the Clove Pink being reckoned among the annuals. I shall, therefore, now proceed to give their botanic titles in the order they stand:

1. The Clove July Flower is titled, *Dianthus floribus solitariis, squamis calycinis subovatis brevissimis, corollis crenatis*. Caspar Bauhine names it, *Caryophyllus hortensis simplex flore majore*; also *Caryophyllus altilis major*; also, *Caryophyllus flore pleno*; also, *Caryophyllus maximus ruber*, &c. ... In the *Hortus Cliffortianus* it is termed, *Caryophyllus flore pleno ex squamis calycis ... longissimis ...*; also, *Caryophyllus spicam frumenti referens*. Haller calls it, *Tunica angustifolia ... petalis serratis*; and Seguier, *Caryophyllus ... flore rubro ... calyce ... brevibus ...*. It grows common in Italy and on the Alps of Switzerland. 1. Clove,

2. The Pink. This is, *Dianthus floribus solitariis, squamis calycinis ... binis, corollis crenatis*. Ray terms it, *Caryophyllus minor repens nostras*. Caspar Bauhine, *Caryophyllus simplex supinus latifolius*; and John Bauhine, *Betonica coronaria, &c. Caryophyllus minor, flore ... repens*. It is found growing in meadows, pastures, &c. in England and several other parts of Europe.

3. Sweet William. This is, *Dianthus floribus aggregatis fasciculatis, squamis ... lanceolatis ... foliis lanceolatis*. Caspar Bauhine distinguishes the Broad-leaved sort by the title, *Caryophyllus hortensis barbatus latifolius*; and the other he styles, *Angustifolius*. Dodonæus terms it, *Armeria ... altera*. This species is of uncertain origin.

4. Deptford Pink. This is, *Dianthus floribus aggregatis fasciculatis, squamis calycinis lanceolatis ... tubum æquantibus*. Caspar Bauhine names it, *Caryophyllus barbatus sylvestris*; and Lobel, *Armeria sylvestris altera*. It grows common in barren places in many parts of Germany, France, and Italy; also in England, particularly near Deptford in Kent, &c.

5. Mountain Pink. This is, *Dianthus floribus ... squamis calycinis lanceolatis ovatis ... corollis crenatis*. In the *Hortus Upsaliensis* it is termed, *Tunica ramosior, flore ... cum corolla purpurea*. It is a native of England, growing common on Cheddar Rocks in Somersetshire, and other rocky and mountainous parts.

6. Wild Pink of the Forests. This is *Dianthus ... squamis calycinis ... brevissimis corollis multifidis fauce pubescentibus*. In the Upsal Garden it is named, *Dianthus floribus solitariis, petalis multifidis, basi ...*; and in the Cliffort Garden *Dianthus petalis ...*. Caspar Bauhine terms it, *Caryophyllus sylvestris, floribus ...*; and Clusius, *Caryophyllus*

*ophyllus* [illegible] *species* [illegible] It grows common in forests, and the [illegible] ground, in many parts of Europe.

7 Stone-Pink is, *Dianthus* [illegible] *multifidis, foliis* [illegible] Ray terms it, [illegible] *flore* [illegible] *singulari*, Caspar Bauhine, [illegible] Clusius, *Caryophyllus* [illegible] and Dodonæus, [illegible] *flos tenuis*. It grows naturally in dry sandy places, and sometimes on old walls. It is found on Chedder Rocks, and in many parts of the North of England.

8 Alpine Pink This is, *Dianthus caule* [illegible] *floro, corollis* [illegible] *squamis calycinis* [illegible] Caspar Bauhine terms it, *Caryophyllus* [illegible] *latifolius*, and Clusius, *Caryophyllus* [illegible] It is a native of the Alps, and grows also in some parts of Austria, &c.

9 Mule Pink. This [illegible] *Dianthus caule* [illegible] *floro, corollis* [illegible] *squamis calycinis* [illegible] Caspar Bauhine terms it, *Caryophyllus* [illegible] *multiflorus*, and Dalechampius, [illegible] *flore* [illegible] It grows common about Montpelier in France.

10 Montpelier Pink is, *Dianthus floribus solitariis* [illegible] *calycinis subulatis tubum æquantibus, petalis multifidis*. It grows naturally near Montpelier and Verona.

*Dianthus* is of the class and order *Decandria Digynia*, and the characters are, Class and order in the Linnæan System. The characters.

1 CALYX is a long, cylindrical, striated, permanent perianthium, the mouth of which is erect and divided into five segments. The base is surrounded with four squamulæ, of which two are lower than the others.

2 COROLLA consists of five petals. The ungues are narrow, the length of the calyx, and inserted into the receptacle. The limb is plane, spreading, obtuse, and crenated.

3 STAMINA are ten subulated filaments the length of the calyx, having oval, oblong, compressed, incumbent antheræ.

4 PISTILLUM consists of an oval germen, and of two subulated styles longer than the stamina, with recurved acuminated stigmas.

5 PERICARPIUM consists of a cylindric covered capsule of one cell, opening four ways at the top.

6 SEMINA. The seeds are numerous, roundish, and compressed. The receptacle is free and four-cornered, and about half the length of the pericarpium.

# CHAP. CLXVII.

## DIAPENSIA.

THERE are only two species of this genus, both Perennials, called,

Species.

1 Lapland Diapensia.

2 Helvetian Diapensia.

Description of the Lapland

1 Lapland *Diapensia*. The root is fibrous and white. The leaves are narrow, obtuse, of a thin consistence, and a pale green colour. The stalks are but two or three inches long, jointed, usually procumbent, and adorned with tufts of small leaves at the joints. The flowers come out on slender pale green coloured footstalks from the joints. Each footstalk sustains one flower only, which is large, of a white colour, and appears in July, August, and often in the autumn.

and Helvetian Diapensia.

2 Helvetian *Diapensia*. The stalks are taper, and two or three inches long. The leaves are numerous, imbricated, and of a pale green colour. The flowers come out from the sides of the stalks, on very short footstalks, they are large, of a white colour, appear in July and August, and the seeds ripen in the autumn.

Method of propagating them

Both these sorts are propagated by parting of the roots in the autumn, or sowing of the seeds soon after they are ripe, or in the spring following. They are extremely hardy, will flourish in the most exposed places, on the north sides of hills, and after they are set out will require no trouble, except keeping them from being over-run with weeds.

Titles

1 The first species is titled, *Diapensia floribus pedunculatis*. In the *Flora Lapponica* it is termed simply, *Diapensia*. It grows common on the Alps of Lapland.

2 The second species is, *Diapensia floribus sub-sessilibus*. Haller terms it, *Aretia caulibus ceres-bis, foliis* [illegible] *floribus sessilibus*. It is a native of the Helvetian Mountains.

Class and order in the Linnæan System. The characters.

*Diapensia* is of the class and order *Pentandria Monogynia*, and the characters are,

1 CALYX is a perianthium composed of eight leaves, of which the five interior ones are placed circularly, the others imbricatim, and all of them are equal in size, oval, obtuse, erect, and permanent.

2 COROLLA is one hypocrateriform petal. The tube is cylindrical, open, and the length of the calyx, the limb is cut into five obtuse segments.

3 STAMINA are five compressed, narrow, short filaments, placed at the incisures of the segments, having simple antheræ.

4 PISTILLUM consists of a roundish germen, a cylindrical style the length of the stamina, and an obtuse stigma.

5 PERICARPIUM is a roundish capsule, formed of three valves, and containing three cells.

6 SEMINA. The seeds are many and roundish.

## CHAP. CLXVIII.

## *DICTAMNUS*, WHITE DITTANY, or *FRAXINELLA*.

This plant described. THERE is only one species of this genus, called White Dittany, or *Fraxinella*. The root is possessed of many long, strong white fibres, which strike deep into the ground. The stalks are round, clammy to the touch, and grow to be two or three feet high. The leaves are long, pointed, and grow alternately on the stalks. The foliols consist of about four or five pairs, besides the terminating odd one; they are oblong, smooth, pointed, have a longitudinal furrow on their upper side, and sit close to the midrib. The flowers are produced from the tops of the stalks, in a large pyramidical spike; they are of different colours in the different varieties, and the general characters in some of them still the same; they appear in May and June, and the seeds ripen in September.

The varieties of this species are,

Varieties. The Purple.

The White.

The Striped-flowered.

Described. These sorts are exceedingly ornamental, very hardy, and (considering their easy culture) may be justly ranked among the best perennials we have in the garden. The stalks and leaves are of different tinges in the different varieties. The stalks of the Purple are covered are of a purplish colour, and the leaves of a dark green. The stalks and leaves of the White-flowered are of a very light-green colour, and so are the rest. They are often clammy, especially the foot-stalks of the flowers, and are possessed of a strong odour, which is to many agreeable, to others loathsome. The root is the chief part used in medicine, and is much extolled as a cephalic.

Culture. It is propagated by parting of the roots, which may be done either in the autumn, winter, or early in the spring, before the flower-stalks rise.

But the best way of raising these plants is by sowing of the seeds. This should be done in the autumn, soon after they are ripe, in a bed of good garden mould made fine. In the spring the plants will come up. All summer they will require no trouble except thinning where they are too close, watering in dry weather, and keeping the ground free from weeds. Early in the autumn they should be removed into the nursery, planting them in beds six inches asunder. Here they may remain for one, or (if you choose it) two years, before they are planted out for good; for they will not flower before the third, and many of them the fourth year, after they have come up from seeds.

Soil and situation. They are all exceedingly hardy, and scarcely any soil or situation comes amiss to them.

Titles. There being no other species of this genus, it stands with the name simply, *Dictamnus*. Caspar Bauhine calls it *Dictamnus albus vulgo Fraxinella*, and others, *Fraxinella*. It is a native of Germany, France, and Italy.

Class and order in the Linnæan system. *Dictamnus* is of the class and order *Decandria Monogynia*; and the characters are,

The characters. 1. CALYX is a very small deciduous perianthium, composed of five oblong sharp-pointed leaves.

2. COROLLA consists of five oval, spear-shaped, pointed, unequal petals, of which two are turned upward, two are placed oblique to the sides, and one turns downwards.

3. STAMINA are ten awl-shaped, spotted, unequal filaments the length of the corolla, and placed between the two lateral petals, having assurgent four-cornered antheræ.

4. PISTILLUM consists of a five-cornered germen, a short simple recurved style, and an acute assurgent stigma.

5. PERICARPIUM consists of five compressed, bivalvate, acuminated capsules, which coalesce on their inner part, but spread open at the tops.

6. SEMINA. The seeds are oval, hard, smooth, and nearly round.

## CHAP. CLXIX.

## *D O D A R T I A*.

This plant described. THERE are but two species of this genus, one is an Indian plant, the other is called The Oriental *Dodartia*. The root is creeping, and spreads itself to a great distance. Several erect, compressed, branching stalks arise from it, about a foot and a half high. The leaves are long, narrow, fleshy, smooth, and entire; their colour is a deep-green, and they grow opposite to each other on the branches. The flowers are produced singly from the joints of the stalks, sit close, are long, and of the lip kind; they are of a deep-purple, will be in blow in July, and sometimes are succeeded by good seeds in the autumn.

Culture. This sort multiplies itself amazingly by its creeping roots. Any part of these being taken off, and planted either in the spring, autumn, or winter,

winter, they will readily grow, and soon over-spread a large pot, especially if the soil be light and dry. These plants should be transplanted every two or three years, or their roots reduced, and kept within distance.

*Titles.* This species is titled, *Dodartia foliis linearibus integerrimis glabris*. In the *Hortus Cliffortianus* it is called simply, *Dodartia*. Tournefort terms it, *Dodartia orientalis, flore purpurascente*. It grows common upon Mount Ararat in Armenia, and in Tartary.

*Class and order in the Linnæan system. The characters.* *Dodartia* is of the class and order *Didynamia Angiospermia*; and the characters are,

1. CALYX is a monophyllous, campanulated, permanent perianthium, divided at the top into five parts.

2. COROLLA is of one petal, and ringent. The tube is cylindrical, deflexed, and much longer than the calyx. The upper lip is small, emarginated, and rises. The lower lip is patent, broad, trifid, obtuse, and twice as long as the other. The middle segment is narrow.

3. STAMINA are four filaments, with small, roundish, didymous antheræ. They incline to the upper lip, and two of them are shorter than the others.

4. PISTILLUM consists of a roundish germen, a subulated style the length of the stamina, and an oblong, compressed, bifid, obtuse stigma.

5. PERICARPIUM is a globular capsule of two cells.

6. SEMINA. The seeds are numerous and small.

# CHAP. CLXX.

## *DODECATHEON, MEADIA.*

THERE is only one species of this genus, named *Meadia*, or Virginian Bear's Ear.

*This plant described.* The root is perennial, fibrous, and, if of long standing, sends forth a large tuft of leaves in the spring, which are smooth, almost half a foot long, and three inches broad; they grow erect on their first coming out, but afterwards, as the heat encreases, they become flaccid by the sun, and spread themselves on the ground. Among the leaves arise the flower-stalks, which are fewer or more in number in proportion to the age of the root; they are smooth, naked, and grow to be eight or nine inches high. The flowers come out in [illegible] from the ends of the stalks, having a [illegible] leaved involucrum; each has its own separate, long, slender, recurved footstalk, so that their position is drooping; they are of a purple colour, with a mixture of red, and the general characters shew their structure; they appear in May, and are succeeded by ripe seeds in July, soon after which the stalks and leaves decay, and [illegible] in the spring.

*Origin of the name.* The name *Meadia* was given to this plant by Catesby, in honour of Dr. Mead, but was altered to *Dodecatheon* by Linnæus, he being unwilling [illegible] should bear the name of a person so little skilled in botanic knowledge.

*Culture.* It is propagated by seeds and dividing the roots. The seeds should be sown in pots filled with light, loose, but fresh earth, in August, soon after they are ripe. The pots should be set in the shade, be watered if dry weather happens, and many of the plants will come up in the autumn. All winter they should be set in a warm well-sheltered place, and in the spring the remainder of the seeds will come up. They must be then set in the shade, be duly watered in dry weather, and about July the leaves will decay. The roots should be now taken up, and planted in beds of light loose earth, in a shady situation, at about six inches distance from each other, where they may stand and flower, or be transplanted (after they have stood one year) to other places where they are wanted.

By parting of the roots, also, they are propagated, the best time for which business is August, when the leaves are decayed. The plant is extremely hardy with respect to cold, and likes the shade, and a loose free earth that is rather moist. Here it will encrease very fast by offsets, the roots will soon become large, and six, eight, or nine stalks will frequently be produced from one root, bearing umbels of beautiful flowers at the top.

*Title.* There being no other species of this genus, it is termed simply, *Dodecatheon*, which is a name that was formerly given by Pliny to a yellow-rooted primrose. Catesby terms it, *Meadia*; and Plukenet, *Auricula ursi Virginiana floribus boraginis instar nostratis, cyclaminum more reflexis*. It is a native of Virginia.

*Class and order in the Linnæan System. The character.* *Dodecatheon* is of the class and order *Pentandria Monogynia*; and the characters are,

1. CALYX. The involucrum is composed of many small leaves, and contains [illegible] flowers. The perianthium is monophyllous, permanent, and cut at the top into five long reflexed segments.

2. COROLLA is monopetalous, and divided into five very long [illegible] reflexed segments. The tube is shorter than the calyx, and the limb reflexed backward.

3. STAMINA are five very short obtuse filaments, sitting in the tube, having arrow-shaped antheræ, connected into a beak.

4. PISTILLUM consists of a conical germen, a filiforme style longer than the stamina, and an obtuse stigma.

5. PERICARPIUM is an oval oblong capsule, containing one cell, and opening at the top.

6. SEMINA. The seeds are many and small. The receptacle is small and free.

CHAP.

# CHAP. CLXXI

## *DORONICUM*, LEOPARD's BANE

THERE are only three species of this genus: *Species*
1. Broad-leaved Leopard's Bane.
2. Plantain-leaved Leopard's Bane.
3. Wild Daisy-leaved Leopard's Bane.

*Broad-leaved Leopard's Bane described.* 1. Broad-leaved Leopard's Bane is often called the Scorpion Leopard's Bane. The root is thick, fleshy, knotty, creeping, white, and fibrated. The radical leaves are broad, heart-shaped, hairy, and grow on long footstalks. The flower-stalks are upright, channeled, hairy, put out some small erect stalks near the top, grow to near a yard in height, and are possessed of a few heart-shaped leaves, which closely embrace it with their base. The flowers grow singly at the tops of the stalks; they are large, yellow, and their general characters indicate their structure; they appear in May and June, and are succeeded by ripe downy seeds in July, which the wind will blow all about the garden where there are plenty of these plants.

*Variety.* There is a variety of this species, with a branching stalk; and another with a still more knotty toothed root, which probably gave occasion to this species being called the Scorpion Leopard's Bane, from the resemblance the root is supposed to have to a scorpion.

*Qualities of this species.* This sort is supposed to be a deadly poison to hounds, wolves, dogs, sheep, oxen, swine, &c. and all four-footed beasts of most sorts; but nevertheless is harmless to mankind, if taken inwardly, green or dried; it is used in medicine, and is a sovereign remedy against the bite of scorpions.

*Description of the Plantain-leaved.* 2. Plantain-leaved Leopard's Bane. The root of this species is thick, fleshy, and fibrated. The leaves are oval, acute, slightly indented, and the radical ones greatly resemble those of Plantain; those on the stalks are smaller, grow alternately, and embrace the stalk with their base. The stalks rise to about two feet high, and each of them is crowned by a large yellow flower; they will be in blow in May and June, and are succeeded by downy seeds, which will be ripe in July.

*and Wild Daisy-leaved Leopard's Bane.* 3. Wild Daisy-leaved Leopard's Bane. The leaves of this species are hairy, and shaped like those of the Lesser Daisy. The stalk is simple, naked, and about a foot high. One flower only crowns each stalk; the border is white, having a yellow disk; it will be in blow in June, and the seeds ripen in July.

*Variety.* There is a variety of this species, with large broad leaves, stalks near two feet high, and red and white flowers.

*Culture.* All these sorts are propagated by parting of the roots, which may be done with success in the autumn, winter, or spring, before the stalks shoot up for flower. They will grow in almost any soil or situation, though they will grow longer and flourish in a more lively and healthy look, if the situation be moist, light, and shady.

They are also propagated by sowing of the seeds; the best time for which is the summer, soon after they are ripe. If dry weather should happen, the beds must be frequently watered; and if they are shaded also, the plants will come up the sooner. After their appearance in the seed-bed, they will occasion no manner of trouble except drawing out the weakest where they are too close, and keeping them clean from weeds. Early in the spring the strongest plants may be taken up, with a ball of earth to each root, and set in the places where they are designed to remain, whilst the weakest may be left alone until the next autumn, to gain strength, before they are taken up and planted out for good.

All these sorts, after having once flowered in a garden, will scatter their seeds, which will come up, and often afford more plants than are desired. They may be easily hoed up, however, leaving an ordinary number remaining in proper places; and these unremoved plants will frequently be stronger, and produce finer flowers, than those which have been regularly raised, and transplanted from the seed-bed.

*Titles.* 1. Broad-leaved Leopard's Bane, or Scorpion-rooted Doronicum, is titled, *Doronicum foliis cordatis obtusis denticulatis, radicalibus petiolatis caulinis amplexicaulibus*. In the *Hortus Cliffortianus* it is termed, *Doronicum foliis cordatis denticulatis, caule ramoso*. Caspar Bauhine calls it, *Doronicum maximum, foliis caulem amplexantibus*; also, *Doronicum radice scorpii*. Clusius, *Doronicum VII. Styriacum*; also, *Doronicum latifolium*; and Dodonæus, *Aconitum Pardalianches*. It grows on the Helvetian, Pannonian, and Valesian Mountains.

2. Plantain-leaved Leopard's Bane is, *Doronicum foliis ovatis acutis subdentatis, ramis alternis*. Caspar Bauhine calls it, *Doronicum plantaginis folio*. Dalechamp, *Doronicum minus officinarum*; and Tournefort, *Doronicum plantaginis folio*. It grows naturally in Spain, Portugal, and France.

3. Wild Daisy-leaved Leopard's Bane is, *Doronicum scapo nudo simplicissimo unifloro*. Micheli calls it, *Bellidiastrum Alpinum, foliis brevioribus oblongis, caule palmari, flore albo*. Caspar Bauhine, *Bellis sylvestris media, caule carens*; Clusius, *Bellis media*; and Wentz, *Bellis caule pedali, sive bipedali, foliis magnis latis, floribus rubris & albis*. It grows naturally in shady places on the Alps and Pyrenean Mountains.

*Class and order in the Linnæan system.* *Doronicum* is of the class and order *Syngenesia Polygamia Superflua*; and the characters are,

*The characters.* 1. CALYX. The general calyx is composed of a double series of lanceolate, awl-shaped, erect, equal leaves, about the length of the rays of the flower.

2. COROLLA is compound and radiated. The hermaphrodite florets in the disk are numerous, funnel-shaped, and divided at the top into five spreading segments. The female florets in the radius are tongue-shaped, long, and indented at three parts at the top.

3. STAMINA of the hermaphrodites consist of five very short capillary filaments, having a cylindrical tubular anthera.

4. PISTILLUM of the hermaphrodites consists of an oblong germen, a filiform style the length of the stamina, and an elongated stigma.

That

That of the females consists of an oblong germen a filiforme style the length of the hermaphrodites, and two reflexed stigmas

5 PERICARPIUM There is none

6 SEMINA The seeds of the hermaphrodites are single, oval, compressed, sulcated, and crowned with hairy down

The seeds of the females are single, oval, sulcated, slightly compressed, and crowned with hairy down

The receptacle is naked and plane

# CHAP. CLXXII

## *D R A B A.*

THERE are only two species of this genus which may be properly called perennial

Species

1 Alpine *Alysson*

2 Pyrenean *Draba*

Description of the Alpine Alysson,

1 Alpine *Alysson* This is known in many parts by the name of Alpine Houseleek The leaves are spear-shaped, entire, short, narrow, very hairy, and collected in small heads in the manner of houseleek From each head comes out a naked flower-stalk, which hardly grows to be two inches high The flowers grow at the top in loose spikes, their colour is yellow, and the general characters indicate their structure, they appear so early as March or April, and are succeeded by broad compressed pods, containing ripe seeds, in June

and Pyrenean Draba

2 Pyrenean *Draba* The root of this species puts forth small ligneous stalks from the top, each of which is crowned by a tuft of leaves placed imbricatim The leaves are small, wedge or tongue shaped, trilobate, and some of them will be divided into five lobes The flowers grow on short naked footstalks, their colour is purple, they appear in March, and are succeeded by ripe seeds in June

Methods of propagating these sorts

These sorts are easily propagated by parting the heads, and planting them in a moist shady place The best time for this work is early in the autumn, that they may strike root before the frost comes on They will then flower the spring after, and produce seeds the summer following Both sorts are very hardy, and require no culture except keeping them clean from weeds

They are also raised by sowing the seeds, soon after they are ripe, in the summer The beds should be watered if dry weather happens, and also be hooped to be covered with mats in the heat of the day The plants will then readily come up, and some of the strongest may be set out in the autumn, either in beds, or the places where they are to remain This will make room for the smaller plants in the seed-bed, which, by the next autumn, will be of proper strength to be planted out for good

Titles

1 Alpine *Alysson*, or Alpine Houseleek, is termed, *Draba scapo nudo simplici, foliis lanceolatis integerrimis* Tournefort names it, *Alysson Alpinum hirsutum luteum*, Caspar Bauhine, *Sedum Alpinum hirsutum luteum*, Columna, *Leucoium luteum Aizoo des montanum*, Morison, *Bursa pastoris Alpina rosea lutea*, and Oeder, *Alysson Dalechampii* It grows common on the Alps, and other mountainous parts of Europe

2 Pyrenean *Alysson* is, *Draba scapo nudo, foliis cuneiformibus trilobis* Tournefort names it, *Alysson Pyrenaicum perenne minimum, foliis trifidis* It inhabits the Pyrenees

Class and order in the Linnæan system The characters

*Draba* is of the class and order *Tetradynamia Siliculosa*, and the characters are,

1 CALYX is a perianthium composed of four oval, concave, erect, spreading, deciduous leaves

2 COROLLA is tetrapetalous and cruciform, being composed of four oblong patent petals, placed cross-wise

3 STAMINA are six filaments, four of which are the length of the calyx, the other two are shorter, all having simple antheræ

4 PISTILLUM consists of an oval germen, a very short style, and a capitated plane stigma

5 PERICARPIUM is an elliptical, oblong, compressed pod, containing two cells

6 SEMINA The seeds are few, small, and roundish

CHAP.

# CHAP CLXXIII.

## *DRACOCEPHALUM*, DRAGON's HEAD

Species

THE Perennials of this genus proper for this place are,

1 American Dragon's Head,
2 German Dragon's Head
3 Austrian Dragon's Head
4 Swedish Dragon's Head, or *Ruyschiana*
5 Siberian Dragon's Head

American, 1 American Dragon's Head The stalk is upright, firm, striated, ridged, purplish near the top, and grows to about three feet high The leaves are spear-shaped, pointed, serrated, sessile, and usually grow opposite by pairs at the joints The flowers are produced in long spikes from the tops of the stalks, their colour is purple, and the general characters indicate their structure they appear in July, and often continue in succession until September, but are very rarely succeeded by good seeds in England

German 2 German Dragon's Head The stalk of this plant is striated, branching, and about three feet high The leaves on the lower part of the plant are oval, oblong, and slightly jagged on their edges, those on the upper part of the plant are spear-shaped, narrow, indented, prickly, and sharp pointed The flowers grow in kind of spikes from the ends of the branches, they appear in July, and often continue in succession until the end of summer

Austrian, 3 Austrian Dragon's Head This rises with an upright, hairy, branching stalk, to about two feet high The leaves are narrow, jagged, and prickly The flowers grow in spikes on the upper parts of the stalks, they are large, and of a blue colour, appear in July, and are sometimes succeeded by ripe seeds in the autumn

Swedish, 4 *Swedish* Dragon's Head The stalk is smooth, divides into a few branches, and is about two feet high The leaves are spear-shaped, narrow, of a fine green colour, and their edges are undivided The flowers grow in long spikes from the ends of the stalks, they are large, and of a bright blue colour, appear in July, and the seeds sometimes ripen in the autumn

and Siberian Dragon's Head described 5 Siberian Dragon's Head The stalks are upright, square, and about two feet high The leaves are heart-shaped, oblong, serrated, sharp-pointed, and grow opposite to each other at the joints The flowers are produced in whorls round the upper parts of the stalks they appear in July, and often continue in succession until the end of autumn

Culture The first is the most beautiful of all the sorts, and is deserving of a place in every good garden It is easily propagated by dividing of the roots, which ought to be in the autumn, that they may be well rooted before the winter comes on, in order to shoot up early for flowering in the spring In common it grows chiefly near rivers and moist places, and in the shade, which teaches, that if a like situation be afforded them, they will proportionably thrive better, the flowers will be larger, and the whole plant be more beautiful and healthy

The others also are propagated by parting of the roots, which ought also to be done in the autumn, though the work may successfully be performed in the winter, or before the stalks shoot up in the spring They are all very hardy, tho' they thrive best in the shade

They are all raised also by sowing of the seeds, but as the first sort rarely ripens in England, they should be procured from America, where the plants grow naturally The seeds of all the sorts, if they are good will come up in the open ground, nevertheless the best way will be to sow them on a slight hot-bed in the spring When the plants come up they must have much air, frequent waterings, and be hardened to the air by degrees When this is effected, the strongest plants may be removed to the places where they are designed to remain, but the others should be set in beds in the nursery ground, at about four inches distance from each other The beds must then be hooped, and shaded with mats until the plants have taken root, watering must be duly afforded them at first, and when once they are established in their new situation, they will require no trouble, except keeping them clean from weeds, and watering if the weather should prove long dry, until the autumn following, when they will be strong plants, of proper size to be removed to their final destination, and if this is done early in the autumn, and they are shaded and watered at first, they will strike root directly, and flower strong the summer following

Titles 1 American Dragon's Head is titled, *Dracocephalum floribus spicatis, foliis lanceolatis serratis* In the *Hortus Cliffort* it is termed, *Dracocephalum foliis simplicibus, floribus spicatis* Breynius calls it, *Dracocephalum*, Morison, *Dracocephalum angustifolium, folio glabro serrato*, Boccone, *Pseudo-digitalis persicæ foliis*, Dodart, *Digitalis Americana purpurea, foliis serratis*, and Barrelier, *Lysimachia galericulata spicata purpurea Canadensis* It grows naturally in North America

2 German Dragon's Head is *Dracocephalum floribus subspicatis, foliis caulinis ovato oblongis incisis, rameis lineari-lanceolatis denticulato spinosis* In the *Amœn Acad* it is, *Dracocephalum floribus oppositis, bracteis lanceolatis integerrimis foliis lanceolatis mucronatis dentatis*, in Act [illegible] *Dracocephalum foliis ex lanceolato-linearibus [illegible] dentatis* It grows naturally in Siberia

3 Austrian Dragon's Head is, *Dracocephalum floribus spicatis, foliis bracteisque [illegible] spinosis* In the *Hortus Cliffort* it is, *Hyssopus spicis interruptis* Hermann calls it, *Hyssopus austriacus, magno flore, folio chamæpityos*, Ammann, *Ruyschiana hirsuta, foliis laciniatis*, Caspar Bauhin, *Chamæpitys cærulea Austriaca*, and Clusius, *[illegible] Austriaca* It grows naturally in Austria

4 Swedish Dragon's Head, or *Ruyschiana*, is, *Dracocephalum floribus spicatis, foliis bracteisque lanceolatis indivisis [illegible]* In the *Hortus Upsal* it is termed, *Dracocephalum foliis [illegible] integerrimis, floribus spicatis* Ammann calls it, *Ruyschiana glabra, foliis integris*, Boerhaave, *Ruyschiana flore cæruleo magno*, Rivinus, *Pseudochamæpitys Austriaca*, and Morison, *[illegible] rida, amplo flore cæruleo* It grows naturally in Siberia and Sweden

5 Siberian Dragon's Head, *Dracocephalum floribus [illegible], foliis [illegible] oblongis [illegible]* In the [illegible]

*Hortus Upsal* it is termed, *Nepeta corymbis geminis pedunculatis axillaribus, foliis cordato-oblongis acuminatis serratis* Buxbaum calls it, *Cataria montana foliis veronicæ pratensis* It grows naturally in Siberia

Class and Order in the Linnæan System The Characters

*Dracocephalum* is of the class and order *Didynamia Gymnospermia*, and the characters are,

1 CALYX is a very short, monophyllous, tubular, permanent perianthium

2 COROLLA is one ringent petal The tube is the length of the calyx The mouth is large, oblong, inflated, gaping and a little compressed behind The upper lip is arched, complicated, and obtuse, the lower lip is divided into three segments, of which the two side ones are erect, and the middle ones turn downward, are small, roundish, prominent behind, and indented at the top

3 STAMINA are four awl-shaped filaments, two being rather shorter than the others, situated under the upper lip of the corolla, having heart-shaped antheræ

4 PISTILLUM consists of a four-parted germen, a filiforme style of the situation with the stamina, and a fine, acute, bifid, reflexed stigma

5 PERICARPIUM There is none The seeds are contained in the bottom of the calyx

6 SEMINA The seeds are four, triquetrous, oval, and oblong

# C H A P. CLXXIV

## *DRACONTIUM*, The DRAGON PLANT

THERE are two hardy species of this genus, called,

Species

1 Land Dragons

2 Water Dragons

Land Dragons described

1 Land Dragons The root is thick, white, fleshy, heavy, and fibrated The radical leaves are large, spear-shaped, and grow on long spotted footstalks The flower-stalks are upright, firm, thick, smooth, spotted with various coloured spots in the manner of a snake or adder, and grow to be two feet high On the top of the stalks is situated a long spatha, which is yellowish on the outside, but crimson within, and opening longitudinally discovers the spadix This is long, thick, and of a blackish colour The seeds are at first green, but when ripe of a bright scarlet This plant flowers in June and July, and the berries will be ripe in September

Varieties

There are two or three varieties of this species, differing chiefly in the size of the plants, but the largest and best spotted are always to be preferred

Water Dragons described

2 Water Dragons The root is thick, long-jointed and creeping The leaves are nearly heart-shaped, roundish, smooth, concave, and grow on long footstalks The stalks are round, upright, and about six inches high The spatha is small, and of a whitish colour The spadix is very short, greenish at first, and exhibits its cluster of berries of a bright scarlet, when ripe in the autumn

Culture

These sorts are propagated by parting of the roots in the autumn, when the stalks decay The Land Dragon is very hardy, and will grow in almost any soil or situation, but it chiefly likes the shade The Water Dragons grow naturally in watery places in America, which teaches us that the moistest part of the garden must be assigned it here

By seeds also the plants are raised These should be sown as soon as they are ripe in the autumn, and the plants, after they come up, may remain in the seed-beds two years before they are removed, then in the autumn they should be taken up and planted in beds nine inches distance from each other, here they may stand a year, and then be planted out for good Some of the strongest will flower the year following, though the generality of them will not come to such maturity under four years from the seed

Titles

1 The Land Dragon is titled, *Dracontium foliis lanceolatis* It grows naturally in Siberia

2 The Water Dragon is, *Dracontium foliis subrotundis concavis* Gronovius calls it, *Calla aquatilis, odore alii vehemente predita*, and Catesby, *Arum Americanum betæ folio* It grows naturally in standing waters and marshy places in Virginia and Carolina

Class and Order in the Linnæan System The Characters

*Dracontium* is of the class and order *Gynandria Polyandria*, and the characters are,

1 CALYX The spatha is boat-shaped, coriaceous, large, and consists only of one valve The spadix is simple, cylindrical, and covered on all sides with the parts of fructification There is no real calyx

2 COROLLA consists of five oval, concave, obtuse, equal, coloured petals

3 STAMINA in each floret are seven narrow, depressed, erect, equal, filaments longer than the corollula, having quadrangular, oblong, obtuse, erect, didymous antheræ

4 PISTILLUM consists of an oval germen, taper straight style the length of the stamina, and an obsolete three-cornered stigma

5 PERICARPIUM is a roundish berry

6 SEMINA The seeds are many

# CHAP CLXXV

## *DROSERA*, SUN-DEW, or *ROSA SOLIS*

THIS genus is very ornamental to the boggy or marshy part of our works. The species are,

Species

1. The Round-leaved Sun Dew, or *Rosa Solis*.
2. Long-leaved *Rosa Solis*, or Sun Dew.
3. Portugal Sun-Dew.
4. African *Rosa Solis*.
5. Cape *Rosa Solis*, or Sun Dew.

Round-leaved Sun Dew

1. Round-leaved Sun Dew is a small and elegant plant. The leaves are round, hollow, hairy, reddish, grow on slender footstalks, and on the surface, even in the hottest weather, are possessed of a real fluid liquor standing in drops, which occasions a most singular as well as beautiful look, especially when the sun shines full upon them, the drops being then most conspicuous and transparent. The flower-stalks are round, naked, and grow to about four inches high. The flowers come out in spikes from the tops of the stalks, each has its separate short footstalk, and the flowers for the most part turn one way. Their colour is white, and the general characters indicate their structure; they appear in May or June, and the seeds ripen in July or August.

Long-leaved Rosa Solis,

2. Long-leaved *Rosa Solis*. The leaves are oblong, hairy, reddish, and possessed of the like pellucid drops with the other. The stalks are round, upright, and grow to be five or six inches high. The flowers are moderately large, have footstalks, and adorn the tops of the stalks in a long series; their colour is white, and they appear, and the seeds ripen about the same time with the former.

Portugal Sun-Dew,

3. Portugal Sun-Dew. The leaves are awl-shaped, convex underneath, and much resemble those of the smaller *asphodel*. The stalks are slender, upright, and grow to about six inches high. The flowers are decandrous, and terminate the stalks in May, but are rarely succeeded by seeds in England.

African,

4. African *Rosa Solis*. The leaves are long, spear-shaped, pointed, very hairy, of a red colour, frequently tinged with crimson or purple, and possess on their surface large transparent drops, which are more conspicuous and glittering when the sun shines full upon them. The stalks are upright, naked, firm, purplish, though frequently brown, and grow to near a foot high. The flowers terminate the stalks in short spikes, are small, and of a snowy white colour; they appear in June, and are never succeeded by seeds in England.

and Cape Rosa Solis described.

5. Cape *Rosa Solis*. The leaves are spear-shaped, long-pointed, and their surface is spangled with dewy drops, which are very transparent in the sun's heat. The stalks are simple, upright, thin, and garnished with narrow leaves growing alternately. The flowers terminate the stalks in close spikes; they are moderately large, of a milky whiteness, appear in June, but are not succeeded by seeds in England.

Variety

There is a variety of this species with purple flowers.

Culture

The first two sorts are natives of England, and ripen their seeds with us; the seeds of the others must be procured from the places where they



grow naturally, if a person is desirous of cultivating these wonderful plants.

Soil and situation proper for them

The situation for them should be a bog, or some moist and watery place where the soil is light, sandy, and full upon the sun, which places are often found within the compass of gardens, when they are carried on to any tolerable extent.

Let the turf, moss, or whatever is the produce of the bog, or moist, sandy, watery place, be first pared off; then let the surface be stirred a few inches deep. If this work be done in autumn, let it be repeated three or four times in the winter, and in the spring let the seeds be sown, stirring the ground previous to the operation, as before. Scatter the seeds thinly about, and sift over them a small quantity of light sandy earth, but not more than will be sufficient to cover them half a quarter of an inch deep. From this time leave them to nature, pull up no weeds as they arise; the plants will come up with the natural herbage of the place, will seem to rejoice in such company, and are very conspicuous by their transparent glittering drops, which excite wonder and admiration in all beholders, especially in the hot sun, which refines their beauty on, and adds a glittering lustre to their charms.

The African sorts seldom survive the winter, and indeed very rarely flower here, but it is the leaves which constitute the great value of these plants, and on this account seeds should be annually procured from abroad, to enrich the collection, where there are proper situations to receive them.

Titles

1. Round-leaved Sun Dew is entitled, *Drosera scapis radicatis foliis orbiculatis*. Caspar Bauhine calls it, *Ros solis folio rotundo*; John Bauhine, *Ros solis*; and Ray, *Rorella rotundifolia perennis*. It grows naturally in marshy boggy grounds in England, and in many parts of Europe, Asia, and America.

2. Long-leaved *Rosa Solis* is, *Drosera scapis radicatis, foliis oblongis*. Caspar Bauhine calls it, *Ros solis folio oblongo*; Parkinson, *Ros solis sylvestris longifolius*; and Ray, *Rorella longifolia perennis*. It inhabits the like places with the former species, and is with good reason supposed by many to be only a variety of it.

3. Portugal Sun-Dew is, *Drosera [illegible] foliis subulatis [illegible] floribus decandris*. Morison calls it *Ros solis Lusitanicus, foliis asphodeli [illegible]*. It grows naturally in Lusitania.

4. African *Rosa Solis* is, *Drosera [illegible] foliis [illegible]*. Burman calls it *Drosera foliis [illegible] floribus [illegible]*, *Ros solis Africanus [illegible]*, and Hermann, *Ros solis Africanus [illegible] & longo*. It grows naturally in Africa.

5. Cape *Rosa Solis* is, *Drosera [illegible] foliis [illegible]*. Burman calls it *Drosera [illegible]*; Breynius, *Ros solis folio [illegible] flore [illegible]*; and Ray, *Ros solis [illegible]*. It grows naturally at the Cape of Good Hope.

 Drosera

Class and order in the Linnæan system. The characters.

*Drosera* is of the class and order *Pentandria Pentagynia*, and the characters are,

1. CALYX is a monophyllous permanent perianthium, cut at the brim into five erect acute segments

2. COROLLA is infundibuliforme, rather larger than the calyx, and consists of five oval obtuse petals

3. STAMINA are five awl-shaped filaments the length of the calyx, having small antheræ.

4. PISTILLUM consists of a roundish germen, and five simple styles the length of the stamina, with simple stigmas

5. PERICARPIUM is an oval capsule containing one cell, and opening with five valves at the top

6. SEMINA The seeds are many, small, and nearly oval

# CHAP. CLXXVI

## D R Y A S

Species

THERE are only two species of this genus, both natives of Britain, called,

1. Cinquefoil *Avens*
2. Mountain *Avens*

Cinquefoil.

1. Cinquefoil *Avens* The root is composed of [illegible] long, tough, [illegible] fibres The [illegible] leaves are compounded of five oblong [illegible]-shaped, pointed sharply-serrated lobes, which join at their base, and grow on long footstalks The stalks are slender, upright, herbaceous, garnished with leaves at the joints, and divide into a few branches near the top The flowers are produced from the ends of these branches, they are of a yellow colour, small, and each consists of five petals, they appear in May, June, and July, and afford plenty of seeds for succession

and Mountain Avens described

2. Mountain *Avens* The root is thick, woody, tough, creeping, and of a dark-brown or blackish colour The stalks are ligneous, tough, procumbent, of a reddish colour, and six or eight inches long The leaves are simple, oblong, serrated, rough, hoary underneath, and grow alternately on the stalks The flowers are produced singly on long hairy footstalks, they are very large and [illegible], each possesses eight petals, and they are of a snowy-white colour They make their appearance in May, and often continue in succession until August, before which time ripe seeds from the [illegible] flowers may be obtained

Culture

Both sorts are easily raised by parting of the roots in the autumn, winter, or spring, especially the first sort, which creeps under ground, and may be multiplied that way at a great rate

They are natives of the northern parts of the world, and grow on shady mountainous places, which teaches us, that as similar a situation as possible should be assigned them in our works

They are also raised by seeds These should be sown soon after they are ripe in a bed of light moist earth, in a shady place, they will come up in the autumn, stand the severity of the winter, and in the spring may be pricked out in small beds, in a shady place, four inches asunder Here they may stand all summer, with the usual care of weeding and watering in dry weather, in the autumn following they should be removed to the places where they are designed to remain, and the summer after they will flower and perfect their seeds

1. Cinquefoil *Avens* is titled *Dryas floribus pentapetalis, foliis pinnatis* John Bauhine calls it, *Caryophyllata pentaphyllea*, Caspar Bauhine, *Caryophyllata Alpina quinquefolia*, and Gerard, *Caryophyllata Alpina quinquefolia* It grows naturally in Scotland, and several of the northern parts of Europe Titles

2. Mountain *Avens* is, *Dryas octopetala, foliis simplicibus* Caspar Bauhine calls it, *Chamædrys Alpina, cisti flore*, John Bauhine, *Chamædrys Alpina, flore fragariæ albo*, Ray, *Caryophyllata Alpina chamædryos folio*, Clusius, *Chamædrys 3 [illegible] montana*, Oeder, *Leucas Chamædrys Alpina*, Parkinson, *Chamædrys spuria montana cisti flore*, and Gerard, *Teucrium Alpinum, cisti flore* It grows naturally in the mountainous parts of Ireland, Lapland, Switzerland, Austria, Siberia, &c

*Dryas* is of the class and order *Icosandria Monogynia*, and the characters are, Class and order in the Linnæan system The characters

1. CALYX is a monophyllous perianthium, divided either into eight or five narrow, oblong, equal, patent segments, which are a little shorter than the corolla

2. COROLLA consists of eight or five oblong, emarginated, patent petals, which are inserted in the calyx

3. STAMINA consist of numerous, very short, capillary filaments inserted in the calyx, [illegible] small antheræ

4. PISTILLUM consists of numerous small germens formed into a cluster, having [illegible] styles inserted into their sides, with simple stigmas

5. PERICARPIUM There is none

6. SEMINA The seeds are numerous, [illegible] compressed, and furnished with very long hairy styles

CHAP

# CHAP. CLXXVII.

## *ECHINOPHORA*, PRICKLY PARSNEP.

THERE are only two species of this genus yet known, called,

Species. 1. Prickly Sampire, or Sea Parsnep.
2. Carrot-leaved *Echinophora*.

Description of the Prickly Sampire. 1. Prickly Sampire, or Sea Parsnep. The root is creeping, long, thick, really is large as a carrot, and said to be very wholesome and good eating. The stalks are thick, fleshy, jointed, upright, and divide into a few branches near the top. The leaves are composed of numerous awl-shaped folioles, which are thick, entire, and terminate in spines. The flowers come out in umbels from the ends of the branches having prickly involucra, their colour is white, they appear in June, and the seed ripen in the autumn.

There is a variety of this species with reddish flowers.

The young leaves of these plants are said to afford a very wholesome and excellent pickle.

and Carrot-leaved Echinophora. 2. Carrot-leaved *Echinophora*. This hath a creeping root, that spreads itself under the surface to a considerable distance. The stalks are thick, ligneous, jointed, and send forth branches opposite to each other from the joints. The leaves have no prickles, are composed of a multitude of segments, and assume the appearance of the garden Carrot. The flowers come out from the ends of the branches in small umbels, their colour is white, they appear in July, but are rarely succeeded by ripe seed in England.

Culture. They are both propagated by parting of the roots, either in the autumn, winter, or early in the spring, before the stalks shoot up for flowering. They should have a dry, light, sandy earth, and the situation should be well defended, otherwise they will be liable to be destroyed by the winter frosts.

By seeds the first sort is best raised. These should be sown soon after they are ripe in the places where they are designed to remain; nevertheless, if the place is not naturally warm and well defended, the spring is the best time for sowing them, as a hard winter, in exposed places, frequently kills the young plants that come up in the autumn.

If the roots are designed to be eaten, the ground should be dug deep, that they may have room to strike in, be larger, and more fit for the table. After the plants come up, they should be thinned to proper distances. This, except keeping the ground clean from weeds, is all the trouble they will require.

1. Prickly Sampire or Sea Parsnep, is titled, *Echinophora foliolis subulatis spinosis integerrimis*. Wachendorf calls it, *Echinophora foliis decompositis*; Van Royen, *Caucalis caule lignoso foliis subulato-spinosis integerrimis*; Caspar Bauhine, *Crithmum maritimum spinosum*; Tournefort, *Echinophora maritima spinosa*; Parkinson, *Pastinaca marina*; and Gerard, *Crithmum spinosum*. It grows naturally on the sea shores in England, and in many other parts, particularly the borders of the Mediterranean. Titles.

2. Carrot-leaved *Echinophora* is, *Echinophora foliolis incisis inermibus*. Wachendorf calls it, *Echinophora foliis supradecompositis*; Van Royen, *Caucalis caule lignoso, foliis incisis*; Caspar Bauhine, *Pastinaca sylvestris angustifolia, flore albo*; and Columna, *Pastinaca Echinophora Apula*. It grows naturally in the maritime parts of Apulia.

*Echinophora* is of the class and order *Pentandria Digynia*, and the characters are, Class and order in the Linnaean system. The characters.

1. CALYX. The general umbel is composed of many smaller, of which the intermediate ones are the shortest.
   The general involucrum is composed of several leaves, which end in sharp spines.
   The partial is of a turbinated figure, composed of one leaf, and cut into six unequal acute parts. The proper perianthium is small, permanent, and indented in five parts.
2. COROLLA. The general umbel is difform. The floscules have each five unequal spreading petals.
3. STAMINA are five simple filaments with roundish antheræ.
4. PISTILLUM consists of an oblong germen situated below the flower, and two simple styles with simple stigmas.
5. PERICARPIUM. There is none.
6. SEMINA. The seeds are oblong, and about two in number.

CHAP.

# CHAP. CLXXVIII.

## *ECHINOPS*, GLOBE THISTLE.

Species.

THERE are two Perennials of this genus, usually known by the names of,

1. Greater Globe Thistle.
2. Smaller Globe Thistle.

Description of the Greater Globe Thistle.

1. Greater Globe Thistle. The stalks are upright, thick, firm, striated, branching, and grow to be three or four feet high. The leaves are large, rough, woolly, white underneath, sinuated, and a little prickly on their edges. The flowers come out from the ends of the main stalk and the branches, in large round heads; their colour is white; they appear in June and July, and the seeds ripen soon after the flowers are fallen.

Variety.

There is a variety with blue flower.

Smaller Globe Thistle described.

2. Smaller Globe Thistle. The stalks are upright, firm, white, downy, and grow to about a foot and a half high. The leaves are large, smooth on the upper side, downy underneath, and beautifully ... divided into a multitude of segments, each of which ends in a spine. The flowers terminate the stalks in globular heads; their colour is blue; they appear in June and July, and the seeds ripen soon after the flowers are fallen.

Variety.

There is a variety with white flowers.

The roots of both these species are large, fleshy, strike deep into the ground, and will continue for many years; nevertheless, it may not be improper to treat them as biennials, because they always flower the second summer from seeds, and will at that time be in their greatest beauty.

Culture.

In the spring, therefore, let the seeds be sown ... in the places where the plants are designed to remain; almost any soil or situation will do for them; and when the plants come up, they should be thinned to proper distances. All summer they should be kept clean from weeds, and by the autumn they will be grown to be strong plants, formed of large bunches of leaves proceeding immediately from the root. In the spring they will ... up for flowering, and after the flowers are ..., the seeds will soon ripen and fall off, and will come up in such plenty that ... culture ... need be attempted; for they will always maintain the succession, let the soil or situation be what it will, without any other trouble than thinning them where they are too close, and hoeing them down when they appear in improper places.

Titles.

1. The Greater Globe Thistle is titled, *Echinops capitulis globosis, foliis pubescentibus*. In the former edition of the Species ... it is termed, *Echinops ... foliis ...*; in the *Hortus Cliffort.* *Echinops ... capitulis, ... foliis ...*. John Bauhine calls it, *Echinops ...*; Caspar Bauhine, *Carduus sphærocephalus ...*; and Dalechamp, *Crocodilion*. It grows naturally in Italy and ... Asia.

2. Smaller Globe Thistle is, *Echinops capitulis globosis, foliis supra glabris*. In the *Hortus Upsal.* it is, *Echinops ... flore*. Caspar Bauhine calls it, *Carduus sphærocephalus ...*; Lobel, *... , Dalechamp, Crocodilion ...*; ... *foliis ... capitulis ...*; also, *Echinops ... ruthenus ...*. It grows naturally in dry places in Italy, France, and Siberia.

Class and order in the Linnæan system.

*Echinops* is of the class and order *Syngenesia Polygamia Segregata*, and the characters are,

The Characters.

1. CALYX. The general cup is composed of many awl-shaped reflected scales, and contains many flowers.

   The perianthium of each flower is oblong, imbricated, angular, and consists of many awl-shaped, erect, permanent leaves.

2. COROLLA consists of one petal infundibuliforme petal the length of the calyx, divided at the top into five reflexed patent segments.

3. STAMINA are five very short capillary filaments, having a cylindrical tubular antheræ, indented in five parts.

4. PISTILLUM consists of an oblong germen, a filiforme style the length of the corolla, and a double, oblong, deflexed, revolute stigma.

5. PERICARPIUM. There is none.

6. SEMEN. The seed is single, oval, oblong, narrow at the base, and obtuse and hairy at the top.

CHAP.

# CHAP. CLXXIX.

## *ECHIUM*, VIPER's BUGLOSS

**Species** THE hardy ſpecies of this genus are,

1 Common Viper's Bugloſs
2 Italian Viper's Bugloſs
3 Portugal Viper's Bugloſs

**Deſcription of the Common Viper's Bugloſs** 1 Common Viper's Bugloſs The ſtalks are erect, ſimple, rough, and covered with many tubercles The radical leaves are about a foot and a half high, moderately large, rough, and hairy, thoſe on the ſtalks are ſmaller, ſpear ſhaped, and very rough The flowers are produced in ſpikes from the ſides of the ſtalk, they are of a blue colour, appear in July, and the ſeeds ripen in September

**Varieties** There is a variety with purple, another with white, and a third with reddiſh flowers

**Italian** 2 Italian Viper's Bugloſs The ſtalks are erect, hairy, often finely ſpotted, and grow to near two feet high The leaves are ſpear-ſhaped, narrow, pointed, hairy, and uſually of a pale-green The flowers are produced in ſpikes from the ſides of the ſtalks, they are ſmall, and of a bluiſh-white colour, they appear in July, and the ſeeds ripen in September

The flowers of this ſpecies vary into white, blue, and purple, the leaves of ſome will be broader than others, and the ſpikes of flowers longer, neither will their ſtamina be always of equal length with the corolla

**and Portugal Viper's Bugloſs** 3 Portugal Viper's Bugloſs The ſtalks of this plant are undivided, upright, and grow to about two feet high The radical leaves are a foot long, about two inches broad, and covered with ſoft hairs, thoſe on the ſtalks are ſmaller, ſpear ſhaped, ſilky, and ſoft to the touch The flowers come out in ſhort ſpikes from the ſides of the ſtalks, they appear in July, and the ſeeds ripen in the autumn

The roots of theſe plants are of a tough hard nature, and in ſome ſituations will continue for many years, whilſt in others they die, eſpecially the firſt two ſorts, the ſecond year after ſowing, ſoon after the plants have flowered and perfected their ſeeds

**Culture** They are all raiſed by ſowing the ſeeds in the ſpring, in the places where they are to remain After they come up they will require no trouble, except thinning them where they appear too cloſe, and keeping them clean from weeds The ſummer following they will flower, and perfect their ſeeds, and though the roots ſhould die, yet freſh plants will ariſe from ſcattered ſeeds, which will maintain the ſucceſſion without further trouble They delight in gravelly ſandy ſoils, and will grow on the tops of old walls, &c and where a ſimilar ſituation is wanted, the plants ſhould be conſidered as biennials, and the ſeeds of the firſt two ſorts regularly ſowed in the places where you could wiſh to have the plants, every year, obſerving always, when they have done flowering, and the ſeeds are ripe, to dig up and plant the ground with ſomething of an oppoſite nature the ſpring following

**Titles** 1 Common Viper's Bugloſs is titled, *Echium caule tuberculato hiſpido, foliis caulinis lanceolatis hiſpidis, floribus ſpicatis lateralibus* Caſpar Bauhine calls it, *Echium vulgare* It grows naturally by way ſides, and in ſandy barren paſtures, arable land, &c in England, and moſt parts of Europe

2 Italian Viper's Bugloſs is, *Echium caule erecto piloſo, ſpicis hirſutis, corollis ſubæqualibus, ſtaminibus longiſſimis* In the former edition of the *Species Plantarum* it is termed *Echium corollis vix calycem excedentibus margine ciliosis* Camerarius calls it, *Echium flore albo*, and Caſpar Bauhine, *Echium majus & aſperius flore albo*, alſo *Lycopſis* It grows naturally in ſandy ſterile paſtures, by road-ſides, &c in England, Italy, and the South of France

3 Portugal Viper's Bugloſs is, *Echium corollis ſtamine longioribus* Van Royen calls it *Echium caule ſimplici, foliis caulinis lanceolatis ſericeis, floribus ſpicatis lateralibus*, and Tournefort, *Echium, ampliſſimo folio, Luſitanicum* It grows naturally in the South of Europe

**Claſs and order in the Linnæan Syſtem** *Echium* is of the claſs and order *Pentandria Monogynia*, and the characters are,

**The characters** 1 CALYX is an erect, permanent perianthium, divided into five awl-ſhaped ſegments

2 COROLLA is one bell ſhaped petal The tube is very ſhort The limb is erect, obtuſe, widens gradually, and is divided into five unequal ſegments, the two upper ones are longer than the reſt, the lower one is the ſmalleſt, acute, and reflexed

3 STAMINA are five awl-ſhaped, unequal, declinated filaments the length of the corolla, having oblong incumbent antheræ

4 PISTILLUM conſiſts of four germens, a filiform ſtyle the length of the ſtamina, and an obtuſe bifid ſtigma

5 PERICARPIUM There is none The ſeeds are contained in the calyx

6 SEMINA The ſeeds are four, roundiſh, and obliquely acuminated

# CHAP. CLXXX.

## *E L A T I N E.*

OF this genus there is one species, growing common in our bogs and ditches, called, Whorled-leaved *Elatine*, or Water-Wort.

*The plant described.* The root consists of many long white fibres, which strike deep into the ground. The stalks are numerous, round, smooth, branching, and spread themselves in various directions. The leaves are narrow, and grow in whorls round the stalks at the joints. The flowers come out from the ends and sides of the upper parts of the stalks, are small, and whitish; they appear in July and August, and the seeds ripen in the autumn.

This is not a cultivated plant, but grows in ditches, bogs, and watery places in England, France, &c.

*Titles.* This plant is titled *Elatine foliis verticulatis*. Sauvages calls it, *Elatine foliis emersis linearibus, immersis capillaceis*; Caspar Bauhine, *Equisetum palustre, linariæ scopariæ folio*; Vaillant, *Alsinastrum galli folio*; and Tournefort, *Alsinastrum gratiolæ folio*. It grows naturally in the above situation in England, France, and Germany.

*Class and order in the Linnæan system.* *Elatine* is of the class and order *Octandria Tetragynia*; and the characters are,

*The characters.* 1. CALYX is a perianthium cut larger than the corolla, consisting of four roundish, plane, permanent leaves.

2. COROLLA is four oval, obtuse, sessile, patent petals.

3. STAMINA consist of eight filaments the length of the corolla, having simple antheræ.

4. PISTILLUM consists of a large, round, depressed germen, and four erect, parallel styles the length of the stamina, having simple stigmas.

5. PERICARPIUM is a large, round, depressed capsule, composed of four valves, and containing four cells.

6. SEMINA. The seeds are many, lunulated, erect, and surround the receptacle rotatum.

# CHAP. CLXXXI.

## *ELEPHANTOPUS*, ELEPHANT's FOOT.

THERE are only two species of this genus, called,

*Species.* 1. Downy-leaved *Elephantopus*.
2. Rough-leaved *Elephantopus*.

*Downy,* 1. Downy-leaved *Elephantopus*. The stalks are upright, firm, very branching, and about a foot high. The radical leaves are large, oval, nervose, woolly, and lie on the ground; those on the stalks are smaller, narrower, and more acute pointed. The flowers come out by pairs from the ends of the branches, having a long, four-leaved involucrum; they are small, of little beauty, shew themselves in July, but are not succeeded by ripe seeds in England.

*and Rough-leaved Elephantopus described.* 2. Rough-leaved *Elephantopus*. The stalks are erect, branching, and about a foot and a half high. The leaves are oval, oblong, serrated, very rough, and the radical ones lie flat on the ground. The flowers come out in small heads from the ends of the branches; they are of a pale-purple colour, appear in July, and are sometimes succeeded by ripe seeds in England.

*Culture.* These plants are propagated by sowing the seeds in the spring, in pots filled with light fresh earth. The pot should be then plunged up to the rims in a hotbed, and after the plants are fit to be removed, each should be set in a separate pot; they should be next plunged up to the rims, as before, and watered and shaded until they have taken root. From this time they are to be hardened to the air by degrees; and when this is effected, they should be set abroad in a shady well-sheltered place. Here they may remain until the early frosts come on, when they should be removed under shelter for the first winter. In the spring a share may be planted in the open ground, in a warm well-sheltered place, whilst the others should still be continued in the pots, to be removed under shelter in frosty weather, which is liable to destroy the second sort. The first is more hardy; and though the root is naturally perennial, yet in England it is very subject to die after the plants have flowered strong in the manner of biennials.

*Titles.* 1. Downy-leaved *Elephantopus* is titled, *Elephantopus foliis ovatis tomentosis*. Brown calls it, *Elephantopus erectus hirsutus, foliis inferioribus ovatis utrinque productis floribus oblongis, capitulis alaribus*. It grows naturally in Virginia and Carolina.

2. Rough-leaved *Elephantopus* is, *Elephantopus foliis oblongis scabris*. Brown calls it, *Elephantopus erectus foliis oblongo-ovatis rugosis serratis floralibus cordatis amplexicaulibus terminalibus*; Dillenius, *Elephantopus conyzæ folio*; Breynius, *Bidens frutescens foliis oblongis utrinque acuminatis venosis & lanuginosis*; and Plukenet, *Baccharides Ind. or. affinis, semine & flor. bus in capitulis latis, ad caulium cymas*. It grows naturally in many parts of America.

*Elephan-*

Class and order in the Linnæan system The characters

*Elephantopus* is of the class and order *Polygamia Segregata*; and the characters are,

1 CALYX The involucrum is large, permanent, and contains many flowers

The perianthium is oblong, composed of many spear-shaped, subulated, erect, sharp-pointed scales, placed imbricatim, and each contains four flowers

2 COROLLA is tubulous and compound The florets are monopetalous, tongue shaped, narrow at the tip, and divided into five equal segments

3 STAMINA are five very short capillary filaments, having a cylindrical tubular anthera

4 PISTILLUM consists of an oval coronated germen, a filiforme style the length of the stamina, and two slender patent stigmas

5 PERICARPIUM There is none

6 SEMINA The seed is single, compressed, and crowned with bristly down

The receptacle is naked

## CHAP. CLXXXII

# E L Y M U S

Species

OF this genus are a few grasses, called,

1 Sea Lyme Grass
2 Pensylvanian *Elymus*
3 Siberian Wheat
4 Canada Secale Grass
5 Virginian Barley
6 Bearded Wheat Grass

Sea Lyme Grass.

1 Sea Lyme Grass The leaves are of a glutinous white colour, broad at the bottom and diminish gradually to a point, which is very sharp and pungent The stalks are round hollow, jointed, and sheath with the lower part of the leaves, which grow singly at the joints The flowers are produced from the tops of the stalks, in long, erect, downy spikes, and appear chiefly in May and June

Pensylvanian Elymus.

2 Pensylvanian *Elymus* The leaves are broadest at the bottom, pointed, striated, about foot long, and of a pale-green The stalks are round, hollow, jointed, and two or three feet high The flowers are produced from the tops of the stalks in spreading pendulent spikes, and appear chiefly in June and July

Siberian Wheat.

3 Siberian Wheat The leaves are as broad at the bottom as our English wheat, but their height is only about foot and a half The stalks are round, jointed hollow, and a yard high The flowers come out from the tops of the stalks in long, aristated, pendulent spikes, and appear in July and August

Canada Secale Grass

4 Canada Secale Grass The leaves are long, narrow, pointed, and of a pale green The stalks are upright, round, hollow, jointed, and three or four feet high The flowers are produced from the tops in nodding spikes, and appear in July and August

Virginian Barley,

5 Virginian Barley The leaves are narrow, pointed, and eight or ten inches long The stalk is round, hollow, jointed, of a pale green, and about a foot high The flowers are produced from the tops of the stalks in erect spikes, and appear about the same time with the former

Bearded Wheat-Grass

6 Bearded Wheat Grass The leaves are narrow, pointed, and of a greyish green The stalks are round, hollow, jointed, and two or three feet high The flowers turn in the stalks in nodding spikes, and appear in June and July

Culture

If a person is desirous of a plant or two of these sorts to be ready for observation, they may be easily raised by sowing the seeds soon after they are ripe, or parting the roots at any time of the year

Title

1 The first species is titled, *Elymus spicâ erectâ arctâ, calycibus tomentosis flosculo longioribus* In the *Flora Suecica* it is termed, *Secale junceis geminatis* Van Royen calls it, *Triticum floris acuminatis pungentibus*, Ray *Gramen caninum maritimum, spicâ triticeâ, nostras*, Caspar Bauhine, *Gramen caninum maritimum spicatum* and Parkinson, *Gramen caninum geniculatum maritimum spicatum* It grows naturally on the sea shores of England, and those belonging to most countries of Europe

2 The second species is, *Elymus spicâ pendulâ patulâ, spiculis persolutis, ... tenuis* It grows naturally in Pensylvania

3 The third species is, *Elymus, spicâ pendulâ arctâ, spiculis binatis calyce longioribus* Gmelin calls it, *Triticum radice perenni, spiculis binis longissime aristatis* It grows naturally in Siberia

4 The fourth species is, *Elymus spicâ nutante patulâ, spiculis inferioribus ternatis, superioribus binatis* Morison calls it, *Gramen secalinum majus altissimum Virginianum* It grows naturally in Canada

5 The fifth species is *Elymus spicâ erectâ, spiculis binatis involucro longioribus* Gronovius calls it, *Hordeum flosculis omnibus hermaphroditis, involucris flosculos crassitie et longitudine superantibus* It grows naturally in Virginia

6 The sixth species is, *Elymus spicâ aristatâ arctâ, spiculis ... involucro ... geminis* In the former edition of the *Species Plantarum* it is termed, *Triticum calycibus subulatis quadriflorus aristatis* Morison calls it, *Gramen caninum non repens elatius, spicâ aristatâ*, and Vaillant, *Gramen loliaceum, fibrosa radice, aristis donatum* It grows naturally in England, and most countries of Europe

Class and order in the Linnæan System The characters

*Elymus* is of the class and order *Triandria Digynia*, and the characters are,

1 CALYX The common receptacle is elongated in form of a spike

The glume is composed of four awl-shaped leaves arranged in a double series, two of them being situated under each spicula

2 COROLLA is composed of two valves, the exterior

exterior one is the largest, aristated, and sharp-pointed, the interior one is plane

3 STAMINA are three very short capillary filaments, having oblong antheræ, which are bifid at their base

4 PISTILLUM consists of a turbinated germen, and two divaricated, hairy, inflexed styles, with simple stigmas

5 PERICARPIUM The seed is wrapped up in the corolla

6 SEMEN The seed is single, narrow, and covered

## CHAP CLXXXIII

## *EMPETRUM*, BERRY-BEARING HEATH, CROW, or CRAKE BERRIES

THERE are two species of this genus, called,

Species

1 Procumbent Berry-bearing Heath

2 Upright Berry-bearing Heath

Description of the Procumbent,

1 Procumbent Berry bearing Heath This goes by the names of Black-berried Heath, Crow-berries, and Crake-berries The stalks are woody, slender, tough, of a reddish colour, and lie on the ground The leaves are numerous, narrow, [illegible], usually grow by threes or fours, and are of a dark green colour The flowers come out in plenty from the sides of the branches, they are small, of a greenish-white colour, appear in May, June, and July, and often continue in succession all summer, and are succeeded by black berries about the size of the Juniper, full of a purple juice Of these berries the heathcocks are remarkably fond, and these birds will for the most part be found in places where plenty of these plants naturally grow

and Upright Berry bearing Heath

2 Upright Berry-bearing Heath The stalks are upright, woody, brittle, branching, a foot and a half high, and covered with a dark coloured bark The leaves are numerous, short, narrow, grow usually by threes, and are of a dark-green colour The flowers are small, come out from the upper parts of the branches in June and July, and are succeeded by very white transparent berries, which ripen in the autumn

Method of propagating them

These sorts are propagated by layers or sowing the seeds The branches of the first sort frequently strike root from the sides, as they lie on the ground, and if the branches of the others are laid in the ground in the autumn, they will have taken good root by the autumn following, and may then be removed to the places where they are designed to remain They both require a moist soil, and [illegible] taking the layers be careful to preserve as much mould to the roots as possible, and let them be well watered and shaded until they have taken root, after that they will require no trouble, except pulling up the weeds which may annoy and obstruct them If they are planted upon bogs, in which situation they thrive admirably well, the turf, or whatever grows upon the place, should be first pared off, and the soil stirred or dug, and made as fine as it can be They will readily grow in such places, requiring no trouble not even weeding, and will appear very beautiful among the natural herbage of the place

They are also raised by seeds These should be sown in a moist shady place in the autumn, when they are full ripe, otherwise they will lie in the ground until the second spring after sowing before they make their appearance When the plants come up, keep them clean from weeds all summer, and frequently water them in dry weather. Repeat this the summer following, and when the plants are about two years old, they will be of proper size to be set out for good The seeds also may be sown in the places where they are to remain, and if it is a boggy ground, they will often come up among the herbage of the place, as if they spontaneously grew there, nevertheless if the place is apt to produce large weeds, or any strong growing plants, they should be all plucked up as they arise at first, otherwise they will choak the seedlings, and destroy your expectations This work should in some measure afterwards be repeated, which should admonish us to set these plants in such boggy ground only where the produce of the place is small and inconsiderable

If they are planted in the pleasure-garden for observation, they should have a shady situation, and be frequently watered in dry weather, and here they will grow very well, and annually produce plenty of flowers and fruit

1 Procumbent Berry-bearing Heath is titled, *Empetrum procumbens* In the *Flora Lapp* it is termed, *Empetrum* Caspar Bauhine calls it, *Empetrum vaccifera procumbens nigra*, Clusius, *Erica baccifera*, Tournefort, *Empetrum* [illegible] *fructu nigro*, Parkinson, *Erica baccifera nigra*, and Gerard, *Erica baccifera procumbens* It grows naturally in the moist mountainous parts of Derbyshire, Yorkshire, Lancashire, and in the like situation in Lapland, and most of the cold parts of Europe Titles

2 Upright Berry-bearing Heath is, *Empetrum erectum* Tournefort calls it, *Empetrum* [illegible] *fructu albo*, Caspar Bauhine, *Erica erecta*, [illegible] *candidis*, and Clusius, *Erica coris folio* X It grows naturally in Lusitania

*Empetrum* is of the class and order *Dioecia Triandria*, and the characters are, Class and order in the Linnæan system

I Male

1 CALYX is a perianthium divided into three oval permanent segments The characters

2 COROLLA consists of three oval, oblong, withering

withering petals, which are narrow at their base, and larger than the segments of the calyx

3 STAMINA are three very long capillary, hanging filaments, having short erect antheræ divided into two parts

II Females

1 CALYX is the same as in the males

2 COROLLA is the like kind of petals as the males

3 PISTILLUM consists of a depressed germen, a very short style, and nine reflexed patent stigmas

4 PERICARPIUM is a round, depressed, unilocular berry

5 SEMINA The seeds are nine in number, placed circularly, gibbous on one side, and angular on the other

## CHAP CLXXXIV

## *EPIGÆA*, TRAILING ARBUTUS

THERE is only one species of this genus, called *Epigæa*, or Trailing *Arbutus*

Description of the plant — The stalks are ligneous, lie on the ground, and strike root at the joints The leaves are oval, oblong, undivided, rough, waved on their edges, and grow on long slender footstalks The flowers come out from the ends of the branches in loose bunches, their colour is white, and the general characters indicate their structure, they appear in July, but are not succeeded by ripe seeds in England

Culture — This species propagates itself very fast by striking root from the joints of the stalks as they lie on the ground, and which, if left unmolested, would soon overspread a large spot of ground, but by being taken off in the autumn, will not only keep the other plants within due bounds, but also will become good plants, and fit for any place where they are wanted They chiefly love a moist soil, and a shady situation, which also should be well sheltered, to ensure their safety through our severe winters

Titles — There being no other species of this genus it is called simply, *Epigæa* Micheli calls it, *Memecylum*, Gronovius, *Arbutus foliis ovatis integris, petiolis laxis longitudine foliorum*, and Plukenet, *Pyrolæ affinis repens fruticosa, foliis rigidis scabritie exasperatis, flore pentapetaloide fistuloso* It grows naturally in Virginia and Canada

Class and order in the Linnæan system — *Epigæa* is of the class and order *Decandria Monogynia*, and the characters are,

The characters —

1 CALYX is a permanent double perianthium The exterior part is composed of three oval, spear-shaped, sharp pointed leaves, the interior is longer than the exterior, erect, and divided into five spear-shaped acuminated segments

2 COROLLA is one hypocrateriforme petal The tube is cylindrical, hairy within, and a little longer than the calyx The limb is patent, and divided into five oval oblong parts

3 STAMINA are ten filiforme filaments the length of the tube, and affixed to the base of the corolla, having oblong acute antheræ

4 PISTILLUM consists of a globular hairy germen, a filiforme style the length of the stamina, and an obtuse quinquifid stigma

5 PERICARPIUM is a subglobose, depressed, five-cornered capsule, containing five cells

6 SEMINA The seeds are many and roundish The receptacle is large, and divided into five parts

## CHAP. CLXXXV.

## *EPILOBIUM*, WILLOW HERB, or FRENCH WILLOW.

OF this genus there are,

Species —

1 Rose Bay Willow Herb, or French Willow

2 Broad leaved Willow Herb, or Siberian Willow

3 Hairy Willow Herb

4 Smooth-leaved Willow Herb

5 Narrow-leaved Willow Herb

6 Marsh Willow Herb

7 Mountain Willow Herb.

Rose Bay Willow Herb — 1 Rose Bay Willow Herb, or French Willow Of this species there are two principal varieties,

Varieties — The White, and

The Red French Willow

The roots are thick, white, and spread themselves in

in a little time to a great distance The stalks are thick, smooth, three or four feet high, and in the White variety are of a pale green, in the Red of a purplish colour, the difference of colour also in the leaves in the different varieties is preserved The leaves are long, narrow, terminate in a point, and much resemble those of the Willow tree The flowers are produced in long spikes from the ends of the main stalks and branches they are large, finely arranged on their separate pedicles, appear in June, and from fresh springing-up suckers often shew themselves in the autumn

These are the most beautiful of all the species of this genus, and are chiefly cultivated to adorn chimneys, flower pots, &c for which purposes they are admirably adapted, but they are altogether improper for small gardens, as they will, if permitted, soon overspread the whole spot, and destroy whatever grows near them In any cold abject part of the garden they will thrive exceedingly well, continue in such places longer in flower, and be ready to cut to adorn the rooms in the house, or to remain to ornament such places where few things will grow and thrive

Broad leaved

2 Broad-leaved Willow Herb, or Siberian Willow The root is thick, white, and creeping like the former The stalks are thick, upright, firm, and grow to be five or six feet high The leaves are spear shaped, oval, downy, soft to the touch, and grow alternately The flowers come out in long spikes from the ends of the stalks, they are very large, of a reddish-purple colour and shew themselves about the same time as the former

and Hairy Willow Herb

3 Hairy Willow Herb Of this species there are two principal varieties, called,

Small-flowered Hairy Willow Herb

Large-flowered Hairy Willow Herb, or Codlings and Cream

Varieties described

Small flowered Hairy Willow Herb The stalks are upright, hairy, very brittle, branching, and about four feet high The leaves are spear-shaped, hairy, decurrent, waved and serrated on their edges, and the lower ones grow opposite to each other The flowers are produced in bunches from the ends of the stalks, they appear in June, but are small, and inferior in beauty to those of

The Large-flowered Willow Herb, or Codlings and Cream This grows by the sides of brooks, rivers, ditches, &c and is well known all over England The stalks are upright, firm, branching, brittle, and about four feet high The leaves are spear shaped, serrated, decurrent, hoary, of a whitish green, soft to the touch, and remarkable for emitting a scent like coddled apples The flowers are produced from the ends of the stalks and branches in June, they are large, of a reddish-purple colour, and well known to every one

Smooth leaved,

4 Smooth-leaved Willow Herb The stalks are slender, smooth, brittle, branching, and about a foot and a half high The leaves are oval, spear-shaped indented, smooth, and grow opposite to each other on short footstalks The flowers are produced from the wings of the leaves near the ends of the branches on their own separate footstalks, they are small, of a purplish colour, shew themselves in June and July, and frequently in August and the autumn

This is rather a short lived species, for tho' the root will sometimes continue many years, yet they frequently die in the autumn, soon after the plants have flowered and perfected their seeds They will, however, sometimes sow themselves, come up, and maintain the succession, if the soil is moist and suitable

Narrow leaved,

5 Narrow-leaved Willow Herb The stalks are slender, square, upright, and put forth branches by pairs opposite to each other The leaves are narrow, spear-shaped, indented, and near the bottom of the plant grow opposite, but near the top frequently come out singly, and without order The flowers are produced in spikes from the upper parts of the main stalk and branches, they come out from the wings of the leaves, and ornament the stalks for a considerable length, they are rather small, of a beautiful red colour, appear in May, June, and July, and sometimes shew themselves in the autumn

6 Marsh Willow Herb The stalks are upright, square, and send forth branches by pairs opposite to each other The leaves are spear-shaped, entire, and grow opposite by pairs on the stalks The flowers are produced in spikes from the upper parts of the stalks and branches, are of a reddish colour, and their petals are indented, they appear about the same time with the former, on their native marshy wet grounds, and when in gardens will frequently shew themselves in the autumn

7 Mountain Willow Herb This hath a creeping stalk, which strikes root, and soon spreads itself to a considerable distance The leaves are oval, spear-shaped, smooth, entire, and grow opposite to each other The flowers are produced from the wings of the leaves, they are small, have bifid petals, appear in June, and, like most other creeping plants, will continue to shew themselves occasionally from fresh suckers the greatest part of the summer and autumn

and Mountain Willow Herb described

All these species, the second excepted, grow naturally in one part or other in England, and their situation is usually by the sides of rivers, moist hedges, ditches, and spungy marshy places on the sides of hills, so that whenever they are admitted into gardens, as similar a situation as possible should be assigned them, though they will do very well in dry ground, and flourish, yet not in such beautiful luxuriance, as in a gravelly and sandy soil, if the situation be shady They are all propagated by parting of the roots, which may be done at any time successfully in the autumn, winter, or early in the spring before the stalks rise

Soil and situation proper for them

Method of propagating these species

These plants are also raised by seeds, which should be sown in the summer or autumn, soon after they are ripe, the mould should be well pulverised, and the bed be in the shade When the plants come up they must be duly watered, if dry weather makes it necessary, and this work must be occasionally repeated during the succeeding summer, weeding must be all along observed, and in the autumn the plants will be of sufficient strength to be removed to the places where they are designed to remain, and will flower strong the summer following

After all, some of these sorts encrease so very fast by the roots, that it requires more trouble to keep them within bounds, than to propagate them, whilst the others will shed their seeds, and produce plants often in improper places, so that when once a garden is furnished with them, the trouble to keep them in due bounds, and in proper situations, will be greater than to multiply the roots by art

1 Rose Bay Willow Herb, or French Willow, is titled, *Epilobium foliis sparsis linearı lanceolatis, floribus inaequalibus* In the *Flora Suecica* it is termed, *Epilobium floribus difformibus, pistillo declinato*, in the *Flora Lapp* *Epilobium foliis lanceolatis integerrimis* Caspar Bauhine calls it, *Lysimachia Chamaenerion dicta angustifolia*, also, *Lysimachia Chamaenerion latifolia*, also, *Lysimachia Chamaenerion dicta Alpina* John Bauhine terms it, *Lysimachia*

Titles

*Speciosa*

*speciosa, quibusdam onagra dicta, siliquosa*, and Parkinson, *Chamænerion flore Delphinii* It grows naturally in England, and most of the northern parts of Europe

2 Broad-leaved Willow Herb, or Siberian Willow, is, *Epilobium foliis alaternis lanceolato-ovatis, floribus inæqualibus* It grows naturally in Siberia

3 Hairy Willow Herb is, *Epilobium foliis oppositis lanceolatis serratis decurrenti-amplexicaulibus* Caspar Bauhine calls it, *Lysimachia siliquosa hirsuta, flore parvo*, also, *Lysimachia siliquosa hirsuta, magno flore* Hudson distinguishes the Small-flowered variety by the name, *Epilobium foliis lanceolatis undulato-serratis decurrentibus inferioribus oppositis, caule subsimplici, racemo terminalibus*, and the variety called Codaled Apples by the name, *Lysimachia foliis lanceolatis serratis subdecurrentibus inferioribus oppositis, caule ramoso*, and Fuchsius, *Lysimachia purpurea* It grows naturally in moist places in England, and most countries of Europe

4 Smooth leaved Willow Herb is, *Epilobium foliis oppositis ovatis dentatis* Caspar Bauhine calls it, *Lysimachia siliquosa glabra major*, Dodonæus, *Pseudo-lysimachium purpureum primum*, Gerard, *Lysimachia campestris*, and Parkinson, *Lysimachia siliquosa major* It grows naturally in moist mountainous places in England, and most parts of Europe

5 Narrow-leaved Willow Herb is, *Epilobium foliis lanceolatis denticulatis imis oppositis, caule tetragono* Caspar Bauhine calls it, *Lysimachia siliquosa glabra minor*, and Tabernæmontanus, *Lysimachia minor* It grows naturally by the sides of ditches and rivulets in England, and most countries of Europe

6 Marsh Willow Herb is, *Epilobium foliis oppositis lanceolatis integerrimis, petalis emarginatis, caule erecto* In the *Flora Lapp* it is termed, *Epilobium foliis linearibus*, also, *Epilobium foliis lanceolatis ramosè florens* Caspar Bauhine calls it, *Lysimachia siliquosa glabra angustifolia* It grows naturally in moist marshy places in England, and most parts of Europe

7 Mountain Willow Herb is, *Epilobium foliis oppositis ovato lanceolatis integerrimis siliquis sessilibus, caule repente* In the *Flora Suecica* it is termed, *Epilobium foliis ovalibus superioribus attenuatis*, and in the *Flora Lapp* *Epilobium foliis ovato oblongis integerrimis* Haller calls it, *Epilobium, foliis ellipticis obtuse lanceolatis, totum leve*, Scheuchzer, *Chamænerion Alpinum, alsines foliis*, Boccone, *Lysimachia siliquosa nana, prunellæ foliis*, and Ray, *Lysimachia siliquosa glabra minor latifolia* It grows naturally by the sides of rivulets in England, also on the Alps of Lapland, and Switzerland

Class and order in the Linnæan system The characters

*Epilobium* is of the class and order *Octandria Monogynia*, and the characters are,

1 CALYX is a perianthium composed of four oblong, acuminated, deciduous, coloured leaves

2 COROLLA is four roundish, patent, emarginated petals

3 STAMINA are eight awl-shaped filaments, which are alternately shorter, and have oval, compressed, obtuse antheræ

4 PISTILLUM consists of a very long cylindrical germen placed below the receptacle, a filiforme style, and a thick, quadrifid, obtuse, revolute stigma

5 PERICARPIUM is a very long, cylindrical, striated capsule formed of four valves, and containing four cells

6 SEMINA The seeds are numerous, oblong, and crowned with down

The receptacle is very long, tetragonous, free, flexile, and coloured

# CHAP CLXXXVI.

## *EPIMEDIUM*, BARREN WORT.

THERE is only one species of this genus, called in English, Barren Wort

This plant described

The root is creeping, and soon spreads itself to a considerable distance The footstalks of the radical leaves are long, and divide into three branches near the top, each of which supports three heart-shaped folioles, that are rigid, sharp pointed, of a pale green colour on their upper-side, and hoary or whitish underneath The flower-stalks are round, woody, firm, often crooked, and grow to about a foot high The flowers are produced from the tops of the stalks on footstalks, each of which supports three flowers, except near the extremity, where there are sometimes two only, and one flower alone usually crowns the top They are small, but very elegant, and their structure is indicated in the general characters They are of a purple colour, having a mixture of yellow and a bright red, they appear in May and June, and sometimes the seeds ripen in August, soon after which the leaves and stalks decay, and fresh ones arise early in the spring

Culture

This sort is propagated by parting of the roots, the best time for which is early in the autumn, as soon as the stalks are decayed It is very hardy, and will grow in almost any soil or situation, but makes the greatest progress in a rich light earth

Title.

There being no other species of this genus, it is titled simply, *Epimedium* It grows naturally on the Alps, and other mountainous parts of the world

Class and order in the Linnæan system The characters

*Epimedium* is of the class and order *Tetrandria Monogynia*, and the characters are,

1 CALYX is a perianthium composed of four small, deciduous, oval, obtuse, concave, patent leaves, which are placed directly under the petals

2 COROLLA is four oval, obtuse, concave, patent

tent petals, and four cyathiforme nectariums, which are as large as the petals, and incumbent on them

3 **Stamina** are four awl-ſhaped filaments preſſing on the ſtyle, having oblong, erect, bilocular antheræ, opening longitudinally with two valves.

4 **Pistillum** conſiſts of an oblong germen, a ſhort ſtyle the length of the ſtamina, and a ſimple ſtigma

5 **Pericarpium** is an oblong, pointed, bivalvate pod, containing one cell.

6 **Semina** The ſeeds are many, and oblong

## CHAP CLXXXVII

## *EQUISETUM*, HORSE-TAIL

THE ſpecies of Horſe-Tail go by the reſpective names of,

Species 1 Wood Horſe-Tail
2 Corn Horſe-Tail
3 Marſh Horſe-Tail
4 River Horſe-Tail
5 Smooth Horſe-Tail
6 Rough Horſe-Tail, or Shave-Graſs

Wood 1 Wood Horſe-Tail, The root is ſingle, jointed, ſtrikes deep into the ground, and ſends forth fibres from the ſides The ſtalks are round, channelled, rough, about two feet high, and compoſed of many tubular joints inſerted into one another The leaves are long, ſlender, briſtly, and grow in bunches oppoſite to each other at the joints The fructifications are produced in ſpikes from the tops of the ſtalks, are in perfection in April and May, and frequently in June

Corn, 2 Corn Horſe-Tail The root is ſingle, jointed, and ſends forth fibres from the baſe The ſtalks are numerous, jointed, a foot and a half high, and of a deep green colour The leaves are long, thick, jointed, angular, very rough to the touch, and of a deep green colour The fructifications are found on naked ſtalks, and they appear ſo early as March and April

Marſh, 3 Marſh Horſe-Tail The root is creeping, jointed, ſpreads itſelf to a conſiderable diſtance, and ſends out fibres from the joints The ſtalks are ſimple, thick, ſtriated, angular, upright, jointed, and two feet high The leaves are narrow, briſtly, very rough, and grow in bunches from the joints The fructifications are found in form of ſpikes at the tops of the ſtalks, and are in moſt perfection in June

River, 4 River Horſe-Tail The root is thick, ſpreading, jointed, and ſends forth fibres from every joint The ſtalks are numerous, thick, ſtriated, hollow, jointed, and four or five feet high The leaves are long, briſtly, ſtriated, frequently eight or ten inches long, and grow twenty and thirty together in cloſe whorls round the ſtalk at every joint The fructifications are found at the tops of naked ſtalks in the form of oval ſpikes, and are to be met with chiefly in May and June This is the grandeſt and moſt ſtriking of all the ſpecies of Horſe-Tail

Smooth, 5 Smooth Horſe-Tail The root is ſlender, jointed, and creeping The ſtalks are ſimple ſmooth, and naked The fructifications are found in oblong ſpikes at the tops of the ſtalks, and they are to be met with in June

and Rough Horſe-Tail deſcribed 6 Rough Horſe-Tail, or Shave-Graſs The root is long, roundiſh, creeping, and of a duſky colour The ſtalks are round, tubular, jointed, ſtriated, rough, thickeſt at the baſe, obtuſely pointed, naked, two or three feet high, and uſually of a browniſh-purple near the bottom The fructifications are at the tops of the ſtalks, in large, oblong, oval ſpikes, they are of a brown colour, very broad, and are to be met with from June to the end of Auguſt

There are ſeveral varieties of this ſpecies, ſome being finely variegated, ſome branching near the baſe, and others with ſimple naked ſtalks They are all very rough, and uſed by artificers for poliſhing or ſmoothing their works on wood, horn, ivory, and ſometimes on braſs and copper, all theſe it poliſhes very well, and is ſaid to have the like effect in ſome degree on iron itſelf Hence the name Shave-Graſs has been long in uſe for this plant Varieties

All theſe are plants of great ſingularity, and would be deemed beautiful, were it not for their being common They are not cultivated, but the propagation may nevertheleſs be effected, if a perſon ſhould be deſirous of a few of each to be ready for obſervation, by planting the roots in the autumn in ſome moiſt ſhady place

1 Wood Horſe-Tail is titled, *Equiſetum caule ſpicato, frondibus compoſitis* Van Royen calls it, *Equiſetum ſetis ramoſis internodio multoties longioribus*, Caſpar Bauhine, *Equiſetum ſylvaticum tenuiſſimis ſetis*, alſo, *Equiſetum paluſtre tenuiſſimis & longiſſimis ſetis*, Ray, *Equiſetum ſylvaticum procumbens ſetis uno verſu diſpoſitis*, Gerard, *Equiſetum ſylvaticum*, and Parkinſon, *Equiſetum, omnium minus, tenuifolium* It grows naturally in woods and moiſt ſhady places in England, and moſt of the northern countries of Europe Title

2 Corn Horſe-Tail is, *Equiſetum ſcapo fructificante nudo, ſterili frondoſo* In the *Flora Suecica* it is termed, *Equiſetum ſcapo fructificante nudo, caule ſterili, ramis compoſitis*, in the *Flora Lapp Equiſetum arvenſe* Van Royen calls it, *Equiſetum ſetis ſimplicibus internodio multoties longioribus*, Guettard, *Equiſetum ſetis quadrangularibus internodio longioribus, caulibus reptantibus* Caſpar Bauhine, *Equiſetum arvenſe, longioribus ſetis*, Fuchſius, *Equiſetum minus*, and Gerard, *Equiſetum ſegetale* It grows naturally in moiſt fields and meadows in moſt parts of Europe, and the Eaſt

3 Marſh Horſe-Tail is, *Equiſetum caule angulato, frondibus ſimplicibus* Van Royen calls it, *Equiſetum ſetis ſimplicibus internodio vix ſuperantibus*, Lobel, *Equiſetum paluſtre*, and Caſpar Bauhine, *Equiſetum paluſtre brevioribus ſetis*, alſo, *Equiſetum paluſtre minus polyſtachyon* It grows naturally

naturally on bogs and moiſt places in moſt parts of Europe

4 River Horſe-Tail is, *Equiſetum caule ſtriato, frondibus ſubſimplicibus* In the *Flora Lapp* it is termed, *Equiſetum fluviatile* Haller calls it, *Equiſetum caule non ſulcato latiſſimo, verticillis denſiſſimis*, Caſpar Bauhine, *Equiſetum paluſtre, longioribus ſetis* Gerard *Equiſetum majus*; and Parkinſon, *Equiſetum majus paluſtre* It grows moſtly by the ſides of lakes, rivers, and in watery places in moſt countries of Europe

5 Smooth Horſe-Tail is, *Equiſetum caule ſubnudo lævi* Van Royen calls it, *Equiſetum ſcapo nudo ſimpliciſſimo*, and Ray, *Equiſetum nudum lævius noſtras* It grows naturally in rotten boggy grounds and moiſt places in moſt countries of Europe

6 Rough Horſe-Tail is, *Equiſetum caule nudo, ſcabro baſi ſubramoſo* In the *Flora Lapp* it is termed, *Equiſetum hyemale* Cammerarius calls it, *Equiſetum*, Caſpar Bauhine, *Equiſetum foliis nudum ramoſum*, alſo, *Equiſetum nudum minus variegatum Baſilienſe*; alſo, *Equiſetum foliis nudum non ramoſum ſ junceum* Gerard, *Equiſetum nudum* Parkinſon, *Equiſetum junceum ramoſum*, alſo, *Equiſetum junceum ſ nudum*, and Petiver, *Equiſetum lævi pæne nudum* It grows naturally in woods and moiſt places in moſt countries of Europe

*Equiſetum* is of the claſs and order *Cryptogamia Filices*, and all that can with certainty be known of its fructifications is, that they are arranged in an oval oblong ſpike, and that each is of a rounded figure, plane, peltated at the top, and opens in various angles from the baſe (Claſs and order in the Linnæan ſyſtem)

# CHAP. CLXXXVIII.

## *ERICA*, HEATH.

(Remarks) THE different ſpecies of this genus are very elegant plants, the Common Heath or Ling of our barren heaths not excepted, and would, were it not for their commonneſs, be in high eſteem, and thought richly deſerving of a place in any collection of plants I ſhall therefore enumerate the principal hardy ſpecies, that my readers may know what they are, and may, if they pleaſe, ſelect the moſt rare, or introduce a few plants of all the ſorts into their gardens

The ſpecies of this genus are, (Species)

1 Common Heath, or Ling
2 Portugal Heath
3 Herbaceous Heath
4 Small-leaved Heath
5 Spaniſh Heath
6 Greeniſh Purple flowered Heath
7 Croſs leaved Heath
8 Tree Heath
9 Pale Purple-flowered Heath
10 Rough-leaved Heath
11 Hungarian Heath
12 Fir-leaved Heath
13 Iriſh Heath, or Iriſh Whorts

(Deſcription of the Common Heath) 1 Common Heath, or Ling The ſtalk is woody, tough, ſlender, very ramoſe, and about two feet high The leaves are ſmall, oblong, triquetrous, erect, and grow oppoſite to each other The flowers come out from the ſides of the branches near the upper parts, they are ſmall, of a bright red colour often inclining to a purple, they appear early in the ſummer, and often continue in ſucceſſion until the end of autumn

(Variety) There is a variety of this ſpecies with white flowers

(Portugal,) 2 Portugal Heath The ſtalks are ligneous, tough, divide into numerous ſlender branches covered with a pale-brown bark, and grow to near two feet high The leaves are ſhort, ſmooth, grow by threes, and have a white longitudinal line on their under ſide The flowers are roundiſh and angular, and come out in naked umbels from the ends of the ſtalks, they are of a pale blue colour, and continue to ſhew themſelves great part of the ſummer

(Herbaceous,) 3 Herbaceous Heath The ſtalks are herbaceous, ſlender, and lie on the ground The leaves grow by threes, are ſmall, triquetrous, and ſpreading The flowers come out from the ſides of the branches, they are ſmall, bell-ſhaped, and ſhew themſelves moſt of the ſummer months

4 Small-leaved Heath The ſtalks are many, ſlender, ligneous, tough, hardly a foot high, and ſend forth branches, which are covered with a whitiſh bark The leaves are very ſmall, narrow, ſmooth, numerous, and adorn the ſtalks by threes nearly their whole length The flowers are produced in looſe ſpikes from the ends of the ſtalks, their figure is rather oblong, and their colour is purple, they appear in May, and will at times ſhew themſelves all ſummer

(Spaniſh,) 5 Spaniſh Heath The ſtalks are erect, woody, tough, and ſend forth many ſlender branches, which are of a white colour The leaves grow by threes, are ſmall, ſpreading, and uſually fall off early in the autumn The flowers grow in kind of whorls round the ſtalks, ſitting cloſe without any footſtalks, they are of an herbaceous colour, bell-ſhaped, and, like the preceding, come out great part of the ſummer

(Greeniſh Purple-flowered,) 6 Greeniſh Purple-flowered Heath This hath a ligneous, tough, branching ſtalk, which grows to about a foot high The leaves are ternate, ſpear-ſhaped, and lie over each other imbricatim The flowers are produced in kind of ſpikes from the ends of the branches, they are of an oval figure, and are all turned one way, their colour is a greeniſh-purple, and they continue in ſucceſſion a long time in the ſummer

(and Croſs-leaved Heath, deſcribed.) 7 Croſs leaved Heath The ſtem is woody, branching, and nearly procumbent The leaves are awl-ſhaped, of a dark-green, a little hairy, patent, and grow four round the ſtalks, two being placed oppoſite to two croſs-wiſe The flowers come

come out in clusters from the ends of the branches, they are nearly round, of a fine bright red colour, and usually appear in July and August.

Variety. There is a variety of this species with white flowers.

8. Tree Heath. The stem is erect, woody, branching, downy, and grows to upwards of a yard high. The leaves are quaternate, narrow, and spreading. The flowers come out in clusters from the ends of the branches, they are of an oval figure, white, and usually shew themselves in July and August. There is a variety with pale red flowers. They must have a light dry soil, and a well-sheltered situation, or they will be in danger of being destroyed by a severe winter. They are very beautiful plants, the largest of all the kinds of Heath, and are well adapted to figure in the shrubbery with other plants of the same growth.

Pale Purple flowered, 9. Pale Purple-flowered Heath. The stalks are woody, branching, and lie on the ground. The leaves grow five together round the branches at the joints. The flowers come out from the sides of the branches near the ends, they are of an oval figure, a pale purple colour, and shew themselves in May.

Rough leaved 10. Rough leaved Heath. The stem is woody, branching, two feet high, and covered with a blackish bark. The leaves are small, oblong, rough, ciliated, reflexed on the edges, spreading, and placed by threes on the branches. The flowers come out in whorled bunches from the ends of the branches, they are large, oval, of a bright-purple colour, and shew themselves in May, and frequently about the end of September.

Hungarian 11. Hungarian Heath. This is a small, procumbent, ligneous plant. The leaves are quaternate, triangular, small, smooth, and patent. The flowers come out from the sides of the branches near the top, they are oblong, of a pale red colour, and shew themselves early in the summer.

Fir-leaved, 12. Fir leaved Heath. The stalks are shrubby, slender, tough, divided into many branches, and grow to about a foot and a half or two feet high. The leaves grow five together at the joints round the stalks, they are moderately long, narrow, pointed, and much resemble those of the common Fir-tree. The flowers are produced in great plenty from the ends and sides of the branches, their figure is cylindrical, and they are of a faint-purple colour, they appear early in the summer, and will frequently, on different plants, shew themselves at the end of autumn.

and Irish Heath or Irish Whorts 13. Irish Heath, or Irish Whorts. The stalks are shrubby, branching, hairy, and covered with an iron-coloured bark. The leaves are oval, spear-shaped, entire, slightly hairy, of a pale green colour on their upper side, hoary underneath, and grow alternately on the branches. The flowers are produced in bunches from the ends of the branches, they are moderately large, and succeeded by roundish berries containing the seeds.

All these are hardy and distinct species of this genus, which admit of numerous varieties, differing in the size and narrowness of the leaves, and colour of the flowers, but upon examining all of them minutely, they will be found to agree to the titles belonging to one or other of the above kinds, except the African sort, of which there are no less than twenty-three distinct species, and which are too tender to live abroad in our climate in winter.

Method of propagating them They are all easily propagated by suckers, layers, or cuttings. Those sorts that throw out suckers should have them taken off and planted early in the autumn, that they may be established in their new situation before the frosts come on, which would otherwise probably throw them out of the ground. When they are to be encreased by layers, the young branches should be layered in the autumn, and by the autumn following they will have struck good root, and may be removed to the places where they are designed to remain. By cuttings or slips also they will grow. These should be taken off about the end of April, or in May, and planted in beds of light and finely pulverised earth. The beds should be then hooped and covered with mats, both night and day, for a week or more, as you see occasion, nevertheless opening an end of it occasionally, to admit a due proportion of air. The plants must be constantly and regularly watered until they have taken root, and after that they will require no trouble, except weeding and watering in dry weather. In the bed they should remain for two summers, by which time they will be grown to be good plants, and in the autumn may be removed (observing to continue a ball of earth to each root) to the places where they are designed to remain.

They are also propagated by seeds, which is the best, though the slowest way of raising these plants. Sow the seeds as soon as they are ripe, in beds of the finest mould, for if they are kept until the spring, they are usually a whole year before they come up. The day after sowing them give the bed a good watering, hoop it, and cover it with mats, continue the watering as you find occasion, and many of the plants will come up in the autumn, and the rest will make their appearance in the spring. All summer keep them clean from weeds, and water them in dry weather, and the spring following plant them out in beds six inches asunder. Here let them stand two years, and then remove them with care to the places where they are designed to remain.

Most of these plants thrive best in a light sandy earth, though some flourish most in a moist and spungy ground, as may be collected from their places of residence, which follow their titles, but notwithstanding that, they are not over-nice in their fare, for they will grow almost every where. Those from Portugal, and the southern parts of Europe, ought to have a dry and well-sheltered situation. Proper soil and situation

The African sorts differ little in appearance from those above-mentioned; and whoever is inclined to propagate them should procure the seeds from Africa, and sow them in pots filled with light sandy earth. The spring following they should be plunged into a hot-bed, to promote their sprouting. When the plants are fit to be removed, each should be set in a separate pot, and plunged up to the rim in a shady part of the garden, there to remain until October or November, if the weather is mild, and then be removed into the green-house. The spring following a share may be set abroad, and treated as green-house plants, and the rest turned out of the pots, with the mould at the roots, into a dry, warm, well sheltered place, and they will sometimes survive the cold of our temperate winters, be stronger plants, and produce larger and better flowers than those preserved in pots.

1. Common Heath or Ling, is titled, *Erica antheris bicornibus inclusis, corollis inæqualibus campanulatis mediocribus, foliis oppositis sagittatis*. In the *Hortus Cliffor.* it is termed, *Erica foliis quadrifariam imbricatis triquetris glabris erectis, corollis inæqualibus calyce brevioribus*. Caspar Bauhine calls it, *Erica vulgaris glabra*, also, *Erica myricæ folio hirsuto*, Ray, *Erica vulgaris hirsuta*; and Parkinson, *Erica vulgaris*. It grows naturally Titles

in

in a sandy, barren, uncultivated soil in England and most parts of Europe

2 Portugal Heath is, *Erica antheris bicornibus exsertis, corollis globosis umbellatis, foliis ternis cerosis glabris* Lœfling calls it, *Erica foliis acerosis glabris ternis, corollis ovatis, staminibus breviorbus terminalibus* It inhabits Lusitania

3 Herbaceous Heath is, *Erica antheris bicornibus inclusis, corollis campanulatis mediocribus secundis, foliis ternis, quetris patulis* Caspar Bauhine calls it, *Erica procumbens herbacea*, and Clusius, *Erica coris folio 8* It inhabits the southern parts of Europe

4 Small-leaved Heath is, *Erica antheris bicornibus inclusis, corollis ovatis racemosis foliis ternis glabris* Guettard calls it, *Erica foliis linearibus ternis, floribus globoso oblongis laxe spicatis*, Lœfling, *Erica foliis acerosis glabris ternis, corollis oblongo-ovatis staminibus longioribus verticillato-racemosis*, Caspar Bauhine, *Erica humilis, cortice cinereo, arbuti flore*, Clusius, *Erica coris folio 6* and Gerard, *Erica tenuifolia* It grows naturally in dry, woody, and heathy grounds in England and several other parts of Europe, and in the East

5 Spanish Heath is, *Erica antheris bicornibus inclusis, corollis campanulatis longioribus, foliis ternis patentibus, ramis albis* Sauvages calls it, *Erica erecta, foliis ternis floribus ad alas sessilibus verticillatis*, Caspar Bauhine, *Erica major scoparia, foliis deciduis*, and Lobel, *Erica scoparia, flosculis herbaceis* It grows naturally in Spain, and the South of France

6 Greenish Purple-flowered Heath is, *Erica antheris bicornibus inclusis, corollis ovatis longioribus, racemis corymbosis secundis foliis ternis* In the *Hortus Cliffort* it is termed, *Erica foliis lanceolatis oppositis imbricatis, floribus uno versu racemosis* Caspar Bauhine calls it, *Erica major, floribus ex herbaceo purpureis*, and Clusius, *Erica coris folio 3* It is a native of Portugal

7 Cross-leaved Heath is, *Erica antheris bicornibus inclusis, corollis subglobosis confertis folio longioribus, foliis quaternis ciliatis patentibus* In the *Hortus Cliffort* it is termed, *Erica foliis subulatis ciliatis quaternis, corollis globoso-ovatis terminalibus confertis* Caspar Bauhine calls it, *Erica ex rubro nigricans scoparia*, and John Bauhine, *Erica Brabantica folio coridis hirsuto quaterno* It grows naturally in moist heathy grounds in England, and most of the northern parts of Europe

8 Tree Heath is, *Erica antheris bicornibus inclusis, corollis campanulatis longioribus, foliis quaternis patentissimus, caule subarboreo tomentoso* Sauvages calls it, *Erica erecta, foliis quaternis floribus spicato-racemosis*, Van Royen, *Erica foliis acerosis linearibus patentissimis, corollis ovatis, staminibus brevibus*, and Caspar Bauhine, *Erica maxima alba* It grows naturally in the south of Europe

9 Pale Purple-flowered Heath is, *Erica foliis in summitate q...., caule procumbente* Caspar Bauhine calls it, *Erica procumbens dilute purpurea*, John Bauhine, *Erica foliis corios, flore purpureo di...o is coloris*, and Clusius, *Erica coris folio 7* It inhabits the south of Europe

10 Rough-leaved Heath is, *Erica antheris simplicibus inclusis corollis ovatis irregularibus, floribus terno racemosis, foliis ternis ciliatis* Lœfling calls it, *Erica foliis ovatis ciliatis ternis, corollis ovatis apice tubulosis irregularibus verticillato-racemosis*, Caspar Bauhine, *Erica hirsuta Anglica* Clusius, *Erica 12*, Gerard, *Erica vulgaris hirsuta*, and Parkinson, *Erica vulgaris hirsutior* It grows naturally on heathy grounds in England and Portugal

11 Hungarian Heath is, *Erica antheris simplicibus exsertis, corollis ovatis sublongioribus, foliis quaternis triangularibus patentibus glabris* Caspar Bauhine calls it, *Erica procumbens, ternis foliis, carnea*, and Clusius, *Erica coris folio 9* It grows naturally in the sandy parts of Hungary, Switzerland, and on Mount Baldus

12 Fir-leaved Heath is, *Erica antheris simplicibus bifidis exsertis, corollis cylindricis, foliis quinis patentibus* John Bauhine calls it, *Erica, foliis coris, multiflora*, Caspar Bauhine, *Erica maxima purpurascens, longioribus foliis*, and Lobel, *Erica juniperifolia dense fruticans Narbonensis* It grows naturally in uncultivated places in England, the south of France, and in the East

13 Irish Heath, or Irish Whorts, is, *Erica racemo terminali, foliis alternis subtus tomentosis* Tournefort calls it, *Erica Cantabrica, flore maximo, foliis myrti subtus incanis*, Ray, *Erica S. Dabeci Hybernis*, Petiver, *Erica Hybernica, foliis myrti pilosis subtus incanis*, and Hudson, *Vaccinium racemis nudis, foliis integerrimis revolutis lanceolato ovatis, subtus tomentosis* It grows naturally in the Hibernian mountains

*Erica* is of the class and order *Octandria Monogynia*, and the characters are, Class and order in the Linnæan system The characters

1 CALYX is a permanent perianthium, composed of four oval, coloured, erect leaves

2 COROLLA is a bell shaped swelling petal, divided into four parts at the brim

3 STAMINA are eight capillary filaments fixed to the receptacle, having bicornate antheræ

4 PISTILLUM consists of a roundish germen, a straight filiforme style longer than the stamina, and a coronulated, four-cornered, quadrifid stigma

5 PERICARPIUM is a roundish, covered capsule, smaller than the calyx, formed of four valves, and containing four cells

6 SEMINA The seeds are numerous and small

CHAP.

# CHAP. CLXXXIX

## *E R I G E R O N.*

Species

THE perennials of this genus are,

1 Viſcous *Erigeron*, or Great Sweet Flea-Bane
2 Philadelphian Flea-Bane
3 Blue-flowered Flea-Bane
4 Blue Alpine Flea-Bane
5 Lapland *Erigeron*
6 Graſs-leaved *Erigeron*
7 Tuberous-rooted Flea-Bane.

Deſcription of the Viſcous Erigeron,

1 Viſcous *Erigeron*, or Great Sweet Flea-Bane The ſtalk is thick, upright, branching, glutinous, and grows to about a yard high The leaves are oval, oblong, hairy, ſeſſile, grow alternately, and in warm weather exude a viſcous matter The flowers are produced ſingly from the ends and ſides of the branches in long footſtalks, they are yellow, finely ſcented, and the general characters indicate their ſtructure, they appear in July, and the ſeeds ripen in September

and Philadelphian Flea Bane

2 Philadelphian Flea-Bane The ſtalk is upright, a little branching, and grows to about a foot high The leaves are ſpear-ſhaped, rough, ſlightly ſerrated, and embrace the ſtalk with their baſe The flowers are produced in ſmall bunches from the tops of the ſtalks, their rays are of a white colour, and yellow in the center, they ſhew themſelves in July and Auguſt, and the ſeeds ripen in the autumn

Variety

There is a variety of this ſpecies with purple flowers

Blue flowered,

3 Blue-flowered Flea-Bane The root is yellow, hot and biting to the taſte The ſtalks are upright, uſually undivided, and grow to about a foot and a half high The leaves are ſpear-ſhaped, long, narrow, rough, of a bad green colour, and grow alternately The flowers come out alternately from the tops of the ſtalks, growing ſingly on their reſpective footſtalks, they are of a pale-blue colour, appear in Auguſt, and in September the ripe ſeeds will be wafted about with the wind

Blue Alpine Flea-Bane

4 Blue Alpine Flea Bane The ſtalks are upright, firm, and grow to be two feet high The leaves are long, ſpear-ſhaped, ſerrated, and grow alternately on the ſtalks Two or three flowers only are generally produced from the ends of the ſtalks, they are of a blue colour, appear in July or Auguſt, and are ſoon ſucceeded by ripe ſeeds, covered by a kind of browniſh iron-coloured down

and Lapland Erigeron deſcribed

5 Lapland *Erigeron* The ſtalk is ſlender, hairy, and about nine inches high The leaves are oblong ſpear-ſhaped, entire, whitiſh underneath, and grow alternately The flowers only crown the top of each ſtalk, they are moderately large, yellowiſh, and have hairy cups, they appear in July, and are ſoon ſucceeded by ripe ſeeds covered with down, and blowing about with the wind

Variety

There is a variety of this plant covered with purpliſh-coloured rays

Graſs-leaved Erigeron

6 Graſs-leaved *Erigeron* The ſtalks are ſlender, and grow only to three or four inches high The leaves are narrow, rough, ciliated, and placed alternately One flower only crowns the top of each ſtalk, their colour is white, they appear often in June, and the ſeeds ripen ſoon after the flowers are fallen

Variety

There is a variety of this ſpecies with hardly any ſtalk at all, the flower ariſing immediately from the root on a ſhort footſtalk

Tuberous rooted Flea Bane

7 Tuberous-rooted Flea-Bane The root is thick, fleſhy, and tuberous The ſtalks are ligneous, ſhort, tough, and ſend forth a few ſingle branches from the ſides The leaves are ſpear-ſhaped, entire, narrow, ſtiff, and grow on ſhort footſtalks The flowers come out ſingly from the ends of the branches, they are of a yellow colour, ſhew themſelves in Auguſt, and are ſucceeded by ripe downy ſeeds in the autumn

Methods of propagating theſe plants

All theſe ſorts are propagated either by parting of the roots, or ſowing the ſeeds They are very hardy, ſo that although the autumn is the beſt time for dividing the roots, it may ſucceſsfully be done any time in the winter or ſpring, before the ſtalks ſhoot up for flowering They will grow in almoſt any ſoil or ſituation, but they chiefly delight in a light freſh earth in a ſhady place

Great number of plants may be ſoon raiſed by ſeeds Theſe ſhould be ſown in the autumn, or end of ſummer, ſoon after they are ripe, in beds of light earth They ſhould be ſcattered with an even hand, and ſlightly raked in If dry weather happens the beds ſhould be watered, and before the end of autumn numbers of plants will be found to have made their appearance, and the reſt will come up in the ſpring, When they come up too cloſe, the weakeſt ſhould be drawn out to make room for the others, the weeds muſt be carefully cleared away as often as they appear Watering in dry weather muſt be afforded the plants, and by the autumn they will become ſtrong, and of proper ſize to remove to the places where they are deſigned to remain This removal ſhould be made early in the autumn, that they may be eſtabliſhed in their new ſituation before the froſts come on, and the ſummer following the ſtrongeſt plants will flower and perfect their ſeeds, whilſt the weakeſt frequently remain until the ſecond ſummer after removal before they ſhew their bloom

Plenty of plants will alſo riſe ſpontaneouſly from ſcattered ſeeds after they have once flowered in a garden, for theſe ripen freely, and being crowned with down are often wafted by the wind to a conſiderable diſtance, and generally come up where they happen to fall, ſo that having once obtained a few of theſe plants, they will afford you offſpring enough without any trouble, except keeping them clean from weeds, and hoeing them down where they come up in improper places

Titles

1 Viſcous *Erigeron*, or Great Sweet Flea-Bane, is titled, *Erigeron pedunculis unifloris lateralibus, foliis lanceolatis denticulatis calycibus ſquarroſis, corollis radiatis* In the *Hortus Cliffortianus* it is termed, *Aſter foliis ſerratis, pedunculis ſimplicibus*

*plicibus lateralibus unifloris longitudine folii foliosi*, Caspar Bauhine calls it, *Conyza mas Theophrasti, major Dioscoridis*, Dodonæus, *Conyza major* It grows naturally in Italy, France, and Spain

2 Philadelphian Flea-Bane is, *Erigeron caule multifloro, foliis lanceolatis subserratis, caulinis semiamplexicaulibus* It grows naturally in Canada

3 Blue-flowered Flea-Bane is, *Erigeron pedunculis alternis unifloris* In the *Flora Lapp* it is termed, *Erigeron vulgare* Caspar Bauhine calls it, *Conyza cærulea acris*, Columna, *Amellus montanus æquicolorum*, Parkinson, *Conyza odorata cærulea*, and Tournefort, *Aster arvensis cæruleus acris* It grows naturally in dry meadows and pasture grounds in England, and most parts of Europe

4 Blue Alpine Flea Bane is, *Erigeron caule sub bifloro, calyce subhirsuto* Caspar Bauhine calls it, *Conyza cærulea Alpina major*, John Bauhine, *Asteri montano purpureo similis globulariæ* It grows naturally in the Helvetian mountains

5 Lapland Erigeron is, *Erigeron caule unifloro, calyce piloso* In the *Flora Lapp* it is termed, *Aster caule unifloro, foliis integerrimis, calyci villoso subrotundo* Haller calls it, *Aster caule unifloro, calyce tomentoso* It grows naturally on the Alps of Lapland and Switzerland

6 Grass-leaved Erigeron is, *Erigeron caule unifloro, foliis linearibus ciliatis scabris* Gmelin calls it, *Aster caule unifloro longitudine foliorum lineatum*, and Amman, *Aster acaulos alpinus foliis gramineis* It grows naturally in Siberia

7 Tuberous-rooted Flea Bane is, *Erigeron foliis linearibus, ramis unifloris, caule suffruticoso* Caspar Bauhine calls it, *Chondrilla bulbosa Syriaca, foliis angustioribus*, also, *Chondrilla bulbosa Syriaca, foliis latioribus*, Sauvages, *Erigeron caule subunifloro foliis lanceolato-linearibus rigidis, radice tuberosa*; Clusius, *Chondrilla altera Dioscoridis putata*, Morison, *Conyza marina*, also, *Aster conyzoides Gesneri*, and Magnol, *Conyza tuberosa lutea, foliis angustis & rigidis* It grows naturally in Syria, France, &c

Erigeron is of the class and order *Syngenesia Polygamia Superflua*, and the characters are, — *Class and order in the Linnæan system* — *The characters*

1 CALYX The general calyx is imbricated, cylindrical, and oblong The scales are awl-shaped, erect, and nearly equal

2 COROLLA is a compound radiated flower The hermaphrodite florets are in the disk, each of them is funnel-shaped, and cut into five segments at the top The female half florets compose the rays, these are tongue shaped, narrow, erect, and for the most part entire

3 STAMINA, of the hermaphrodites, are five very short capillary filaments, having a tubular cylindrical anthera

4 PISTILLUM of the hermaphrodites, consists of a very small germen crowned with down, that is longer than the corollula, a filiforme style the length of the down, and two oblong revolute stigmas

The pistillum of the females, consists of a small downy germen, a capillary style the length of the down, and two very slender stigmas

5 PERICARPIUM There is none

6 SEMINA The seeds of the hermaphrodite florets are small, oblong, and crowned with long down

The seeds of the female florets are similar to those of the hermaphrodites

# CHAP CXC.

## *ERINUS*

THIS genus affords us one hardy species called, Alpine *Erinus*

*This plant described* The radical leaves are small, oblong, serrated, of a dark-green colour, grow in tufts, and lie on the ground The stalk is about two inches high, and the flowers come out from the top in loose erect bunches Their colour is purple, and the general characters indicate their structure, they appear in May, and the seeds ripen in July

*Variety* There is a variety of this species with white flowers

*Culture* These plants are propagated by parting of the roots, which may successfully be done in the autumn, winter, or early in the spring; though the early part of autumn, or the latter end of summer, is preferable They will grow in almost any soil or situation, but they chiefly like the shade, and a moist residence

They are also propagated by seeds, which should be sown in beds of fine light earth, soon after they are ripe; the beds must be hooped, to be covered with mats in the heat of the day, and watered as often as dry weather makes it necessary About the end of August your plants will come up, at which time watering must be duly afforded them, the beds must be constantly covered in the heat of the day, but the mats must be always taken off at night, and in all cloudy, misty, and rainy weather The weeds must be picked out as they arise About the middle or end of September the shading the plants with mats should be discontinued, for by that time the warmth of the sun will refresh them, and do them good On the approach of winter it would be advisable to stick some furze bushes round the bed, if the situation is not well defended, to break the keen edge of the sharp frosts, or the beds being already hooped, may be covered with mats in such weather, the more effectually to ensure their safety All the summer following watering must be afforded them, as often as there shall be occasion, the weeds must be regularly drawn out as they appear, shade should be granted them if it can conveniently be done, and by the autumn they will be of proper strength to be removed to the places where they are to remain

Titles

This species is titled, *Erinus floribus racemosis* Sauvages calls it, *Erinus* Caspar Bauhine, *Ageratum serratum Alpinum*, Dalechamp, *Ageratum purpureum*, and Barrelier, *Ageratum minus saxatile, flore albo* It grows naturally on the Helvetian and Pyrenean mountains, and in the south of France

Class and order in the Linnæan system The characters

*Erinus* is of the class and order *Didynamia Angiospermia*, and the characters are,

1 Calyx is a permanent perianthium, composed of five equal, erect, spear-shaped leaves

2 Corolla is one unequal petal The tube is oval, cylindrical, reflexed, and the length of the calyx The limb is plane, and divided into five nearly equal obcordated segments

3 Stamina are four very short filaments situated within the tube of the flower, of which the two opposite are a little longer than the others, and the antheræ peculiar to all of them, are small

4 Pistillum consists of an oval germen, a very short style, and a capitated stigma

5 Pericarpium is an oval bilocular capsule, covered by the calyx, and opening two ways

6 Semina The seeds are numerous and small

## CHAP CXCI

## *ERYNGIUM*, ERYNGO, or SEA-HOLLY.

Species

Of this genus there are,

1 Eryngo, or Sea-Holly
2 Common Eryngo
3 Amethystine Eryngo
4 Small Eryngo
5 Alpine Eryngo.
6 Broad leaved Plane Eryngo.
7 Virginian Eryngo.
8 Oriental Eryngo

Description of the Eryngo or Sea-Holly

1 Eryngo, or Sea-Holly The root is thick, fleshy, long, creeping, and strikes deep into the ground The radical leaves are large, roundish, sinuated, plicated, prickly, of a bluish white colour, and grow on long stiff footstalks, those on the stalks are smaller, but prickly, of the same shape, and embrace the stalk with their base The stalks are smooth, round, thick, tough, branching, of a bluish green colour, and grow to about a foot and a half high The flowers come out from the ends of the branches, in roundish prickly heads, being surrounded by narrow, stiff, prickly leaves, which are disposed radiatim, they are of a whitish blue colour, appear in July, and the seeds ripen in September, soon after which the stalks die to the ground, and fresh ones arise in the spring

Its use in Medicine

This is a plant of great virtue, especially the root, which is of great force in medicine, and said to be good for the cholic, stone and gravel, convulsions, epilepsies, &c also to be an antidote to the bite of serpents, and to give great ease to those who are much afflicted with cramps, &c

Common Eryngo

2 Common Eryngo The root is thick, fleshy, blackish on the outside, white within, and strikes deep into the ground The radical leaves are pinnated, divided into three principal parts, serrated, and prickly on their edges The stalks are round, striated, tough, branching, and about two feet high The flowers come out from the tops of the stalks, in roundish clusters, being surrounded with six small, rough, prickly leaves, they are of a blue colour, appear in July, and the seeds ripen in September

Variety

There is a variety with white, and another with yellowish flowers

Its use in medicine

The root of this also is candied, is a great pectoral, deobstruent, and much used in decoctions, &c

Amethystine Eryngo

3 Amethystine Eryngo. The radical leaves are digitated, and cut into numerous segments, all of which end in a small spine The stalks grow to about two feet high, and are adorned with leaves which are smaller and more beautifully divided than the radical ones, and the upper part is of the colour of an amethyst The flowers are also of that colour, but in a finer and more perfect degree, they appear in July, and the seeds ripen in September

Variety

There is a variety of this, with more rounded leaves, and larger heads of flowers, of a pale-blue colour

Small,

4 Small Eryngo The radical leaves are oblong, plane, and cut on their edges The stalk divides into branches by pairs, and grows to about nine inches high The flowers are produced in small heads from the divisions of the branches, sitting close, without any footstalks, they are of a white colour, appear in July, and the seeds ripen in September

Alpine,

5 Alpine Eryngo. The radical leaves are heart-shaped, oblong, and plane, but those on the stalks are cut into many winged and prickly points, almost to the mid-rib The stalks send forth branches from the sides, and grow to be two or three feet high The flowers terminate the stalks, in nearly cylindrical heads; they, together with the upper parts of the stalks, are of a bright-blue colour, they appear in July, and the seeds ripen in September

and Broad-leaved Plane Eryngo

6 Broad-leaved Plane Eryngo The radical leaves are broad, oval, plane, and indented on their edges, those on the stalks are cut into many segments, each of which terminates in a small spine The stalks grow to be two or three feet high, and divide into a few branches near the top The flowers are produced in oval heads from the ends of the stalks, they are of a purplish blue colour, have their separate footstalks, which (together with the upper parts of the stalks of the plant) are of the same fine purplish blue colour, appear in July, and the seeds ripen in September

Variety

There is a variety of this species, with white flowers,

flowers, which is of inferior beauty to the other, the upper parts of the ſtalks being white, and the leaves of a pale green colour.

Virginian Eryngo. 7. Virginian Eryngo. The radical leaves of this ſpecies are narrow, long, gladiated, ſerrated, prickly, and grow many together from the root, in the manner of ſome of the Aloes, or Adam's Needles; thoſe on the ſtalks are ſmall, and ſlightly indented. The ſtalks are ſtrong, ſimple, grow to about a foot high, and ſend forth many footſtalks near the top. The flowers are produced in ſmall heads from the ends of theſe footſtalks; they are of a bluiſh-white colour, appear in June and July, and the ſeeds ripen in September.

Its virtues. This plant is of great ſervice in curing the bite of the rattle ſnake. Hence the name Rattle ſnake-weed is generally applied to it in the countries where thoſe venomous reptiles abound.

8. Oriental Eryngo. The radical leaves are heart-ſhaped, oval, indented, and grow on ſtrong footſtalks; thoſe on the ſtalks are palmated, auriculated, and bend backward. The ſtalks divide into many branches, and grow to be two or three feet high. The flowers come out in ſmall conical heads from the ends or wings of the branches, on footſtalks; they are of a blue colour, appear in July, and the ſeeds ripen in September, ſoon after which the root very often decays.

Methods of propagating theſe ſorts. Theſe ſorts are all raiſed by parting the roots, or from ſeeds. The roots ſhould be planted when the ſtalks decay in the autumn, and they will readily take to the ground, and flower well the ſummer following; whereas, if the work is deferred until the ſpring, they will be very weak all the ſummer after. All of them, except the ſeventh ſort, love a dry, gravelly, or ſandy ſoil; and with reſpect to the firſt and ſecond ſorts, whoſe roots are candied, and uſed in medicine, a gravelly or ſandy ſoil is more eſſentially neceſſary for them, otherwiſe their roots will be of little value; and indeed, with all the art which can be uſed to promote their perfection in the gardens, the roots are vaſtly inferior to thoſe which are collected from the places where the plants grow naturally, which is near the ſea, in low, ſandy, gravelly places, which are frequently over-run with ſea-water.

They are alſo raiſed by ſeeds; but as they do not always ripen in wet ſeaſons, if ſuch weather ſhould happen, let a few glaſſes be fixed over the tops of the flowers when in blow; and let this method be continued as often as very wet weather makes it neceſſary, until the ſeeds are ripe, which will be (if theſe precautions are uſed) in September. Let the ſeeds be carefully gathered, and laid by in a dry airy room until the ſpring. Then let them be ſown in the places where the plants are deſigned to remain; for as moſt of the roots ſtrike deep into the ground, they will flower better if left undiſturbed than if they had been removed. When they come up they will require no trouble, except being kept clean from weeds; and the ſummer following they will flower, and (if the ſeaſon proves favourable) perfect their ſeeds.

Though all the ſorts may be raiſed this way, yet more caution ſhould be uſed for the ſeventh ſpecies, which is rather tender at firſt, and requires more water than all the other ſorts put together. Let, therefore, the ſeeds be ſown in pots, in the ſpring, filled with light ſandy earth, and let the pots be plunged into a hotbed, to facilitate their growth. When they come up give them plenty of air and frequent waterings; and when they are fit to remove, let each be ſet in a ſeparate pot, and let them be again plunged up to the rims in a hotbed. Let them be duly watered and ſhaded until they have taken root; then let them be hardened to the open air by degrees; and when this is effected, let the pots be plunged up to the rims in a ſhady part of the garden, to keep the mould cool. In winter they ought to be removed to a warm well ſheltered place; and if hard froſts ſeem to ſet in, ſhould be protected under a hotbed frame, or ſome other cover. In the ſpring they ſhould be taken out of the pots, with the mould at the roots, and ſet in the places where they are deſigned to remain, which ought to be a moiſt ſandy ſoil; and if the place be well ſheltered, they will often continue for many years, and annually produce flowers and ſeeds.

The eighth ſort often dies ſoon after it has flowered and perfected its ſeeds; ſo that altho' the roots will ſometimes continue for many years, yet if the ſoil or ſituation is not ſuitable, the ſeeds ſhould be regularly gathered, ſowed, and the plant conſidered as a biennial.

Titles. 1. Eryngo, or Sea-Holly, is titled, *Eryngium foliis radicalibus ſubrotundis plicatis ſpinoſis capitulis pedunculatis*. Caſpar Bauhine terms it, *Eryngium maritimum*; and Cluſius, *Eryngium marinum*. It grows common in the ſandy gravelly ſea-ſhores of England and other parts of Europe.

2. Common Eryngo is, *Eryngium foliis amplexicaulibus pinnato-laciniatis*. Caſpar and John Bauhine call it, *Eryngium vulgare*; Cluſius, *Eryngium campeſtre vulgare*; and Gerard, *Eryngium Mediterraneum*. It grows in uncultivated places, chiefly near the ſea, in England, Germany, France, Italy, and Spain.

3. Amethyſtine Eryngo is, *Eryngium foliis trifidis baſi ſubpinnatis*. Caſpar Bauhine terms it, *Eryngium montanum amethyſtinum*; Beſler, *Eryngium totum cæruleum*; and Barrelier, *Eryngium minus trifidum Hiſpanicum*. It is a native of the Lycian and Appennine Mountains.

4. Small Eryngo is, *Eryngium foliis radicalibus oblongis inciſis, caule dichotomo, capitulis ſeſſilibus*. Caſpar Bauhine terms it, *Eryngium planum minus*; and Cluſius, *Eryngium puſillum planum*. It grows common in Spain and in the Eaſt.

5. Alpine Eryngo is, *Eryngium foliis radicalibus cordatis oblongis, caulinis pinnatifidis, capitulis ſubcylindricis*. Caſpar Bauhine terms it, *Eryngium Alpinum cæruleum, capitulis Dipſaci*; and Lobel, *Eryngium cæruleum Geneven.* It is a native of the Helvetian and Italian Mountains.

6. Broad leaved Plane Eryngo is, *Eryngium foliis radicalibus ovalibus planis crenatis, capitulis pedunculatis*. Caſpar Bauhine terms it, *Eryngium latifolium planum*; and Cluſius, *Eryngium Pannonicum latifolium*. It is a native of Ruſſia, Poland, Auſtria, and Switzerland.

7. Virginian Eryngo is, *Eryngium foliis gladiatis ſerrato ſpinoſis, floralibus indiviſis, caule ſimplici*. In the *Hortus Cliffortianus* it is termed, *Eryngium foliis gladiatis utrinque laxe ſerratis, denticulis ſubulatis*. Gronovius names it, *Eryngium foliis gladiatis, utrinque laxe ſerratis ſummis tantum dentatis ſubulatis*; and Plukenet, *Eryngium Americanum, yuccæ folio, ſpinis ad oras molliuſculis*; alſo, *Eryngium lacuſtre Virginianum, floribus ex albido cæruleis, caule & foliis ranunculi flammei minoris*. It is a native of Virginia.

8. Oriental Eryngo is, *Eryngium foliis radicalibus cordatis, caulinis palmatis, auriculis retroflexis, paleis tricuſpidatis*. Gronovius terms it, *Eryngium foliis radicalibus ovatis crenatis petiolatis, capitulis pedunculatis*; Moriſon, *Eryngium Syriacum ramoſius, capitulis minoribus cæruleis*; and Boccone, *Eryngium capitulis pſyllii*. It grows common in the Eaſt, Sicily, and Spain.

*Eryngium*

Class and order in the Linnæan system. The characters.

*Eryngium* is of the class and order *Pentandria Digynia*, and the characters are,

1. CALYX. The florets are situated on one common conical receptacle, having a plane involucrum, composed of many leaves.

The proper perianthium is composed of five erect acute leaves, which are placed on the germen, and exceed the corolla in height.

2. COROLLA. The general flower is roundish and uniform. The florets are pentapetalous, each being composed of five oblong petals, whose extremities are turned towards the base.

3. STAMINA are five straight capillary filaments, longer than the florets, having oblong antheræ.

4. PISTILLUM consists of a hispid germen and two straight filiforme styles the length of the stamina, with simple stigmas.

5. PERICARPIUM is an oval fruit, divided into two parts.

6. SEMINA. The seeds are oblong and taper.

# CHAP. CXCII.

## ERIOPHORUM.

Species.

THE species of this genus are,

1. Common Cotton-Grass.
2. Hare's-Tail Rush.
3. Virginian Cotton-Grass.
4. Maryland Cotton-Grass.
5. Alpine Cotton-Grass.

Description of the Common Cotton Grass,

1. Common Cotton-Grass. The root is fibrous, and of a reddish-brown colour. The leaves are grassey, flat, pointed, and six or eight inches long. The stalks are round, smooth, rushy, and about a foot high. The flowers are produced from the tops of the stalks in spiked panicles, and when the seeds are ripe the heads are covered with a considerable quantity of soft, downy, cottony matter, of the purest white colour; they appear about the end of May, and continue in succession until July.

Hare's Tail-Rush,

2. Hare's-Tail-Rush. The root is composed of a multitude of brown fibres, which strike deep into the earth. The leaves are slender, rushy, sharp-pointed, and grow in clusters at the crown of the root. The stalks are round, taper, striated, tender, surrounded by many leaves at the bottom, and six or eight inches high. The flowers are collected in spikes at the tops of the stalks; they have no beauty, but when the seeds are ripe the heads are very hoary, soft to the touch, and very elegant, being covered with a soft, white, downy matter. They appear so early as February, and continue in succession until May.

Virginian,

3. Virginian Cotton-Grass. The leaves are grassy, flat and sharp pointed. The stalks are taper, compressed, and garnished with leaves about half their length. The flowers are collected in close compact panicles at the tops of the stalks; they are covered with a soft matter, which at first is of a gold or yellow colour, but afterwards becomes brown, and less beautiful. They appear in April, and continue in succession for a month or more.

and Maryland Cotton Grass

4. Maryland Cotton Grass. The leaves are narrow, grassey, and six or eight inches long. The stalks are taper, and adorned with leaves to the very top. The flowers come out in loose branching panicles from the tops of the stalks; they are very hairy, woolly, and of a reddish-yellow colour; they appear in April, and continue in succession until the end of May.

and Alpine Eriophorum

5. Alpine *Eriophorum*. The leaves are slender, triangular, and four or five inches long. The stalks are triangular, naked, soft, pithy, and five or six inches high. The flowers come out from the tops of the stalks in short erect spikes; they are furnished with a fine, soft, white, cottony matter, and are in perfection in April and May.

Culture.

These plants grow on bogs in different parts, and are not cultivated; they may be raised, however, by sowing the seeds soon after they are ripe, in the like situation. They are rendered singular, and very beautiful, by the long downy matter with which the seeds are furnished, and on which account the foreign sorts are raised in some extensive gardens.

Titles.

1. The first species is titled, *Eriophorum culmis teretibus, foliis planis, spicis pedunculatis*. In the *Flora Lapp.* it is termed, *Eriophorum spicis pendulis*. Caspar Bauhine calls it, *Gramen pratense tomentosum, paniculâ sparsa*; Gerard, *Gramen tomentarium*; Parkinson, *Gramen junceum lanatum, vel juncus bombycinus*; and Tabernæmontanus, *Linagrostis*. It grows naturally on turfy boggy places in England, and most countries in Europe.

2. The second species is titled, *Eriophorum culmis vaginatis teretibus, spica scariosa*. In the *Flora Lapp.* it is termed, *Eriophorum spicâ erectâ, caule tereti*. Caspar Bauhine calls it, *Gramen tomentosum Alpinum et minus*; also, *Juncus Alpinus capitulo lanuginoso, s. Schœnolagurus*; and Parkinson, *Gramen juncoides lanatum alterum Danicum*. It grows naturally on bogs in England, and most of the cold and sterile parts of Europe.

3. The third species is, *Eriophorum culmis foliosis teretibus, foliis planis, spicâ erecta*. Gronovius calls it, *Eriophorum spicâ compactâ erectâ foliaceâ, caule compresso*; Plukenet, *Gramen tomentosum Virginianum, paniculâ magis compactâ aureo colore perfusa*; and Morison, *Gramen tomentosum, capitulo ampliore fusco et foliaceo*. It grows naturally in Virginia.

4. The fourth species is, *Eriophorum culmis teretibus foliosis, paniculâ supradecompositâ proliferâ, spiculis subternis*. Gronovius calls it, *Scirpus paniculatus, foliis floralibus paniculam superantibus*; Plukenet, *Cyperus miliaceus ex provinciâ Mariland.*, *paniculâ villosa aureâ*; and Ray, *Cyperus miliaceus Marilandicus, spicis semiferis magis, confertis ru-*

*bentibus lanuginosis* It grows naturally in North America

5 The fifth is, *Eriophorum culmis nudis triquetris, spicâ pappo breviore* In the *Flora Lapp* it is termed, *Eriophorum spicâ erectâ, cauli triquetro*, Scheuchzer calls it, *Linagrostis juncea Alpina, capitulo parvo tomento rariore*, and Caspar Bauhine, *Juncus Alpinus bombycinus* It grows naturally on the Alps, and other mountainous parts of Europe

Class and order in the Linnæan system The characters

*Eriophorum* is of the class and order *Triandria Monogynia*, and the characters are,

1 CALYX The spike is imbricated on every side The scales are oval, oblong, plane, inflexed, membranaceous loose, acuminated, and separate the flowers from each other

2 COROLLA There is none

3 STAMINA are three capillary filaments, with oblong erect antheræ

4 PISTILLUM consists of a very small germen, a filiforme style the length of the scales of the calyx, and three reflexed stigmas which are longer than the style

5 PERICARPIUM There is none

6 SEMEN The seed is triquetrous, acuminated, and furnished with long hairs

# CHAP CXCIII

## *ERYSIMUM*, HEDGE-MUSTARD.

Species

OF this genus there are,

1 Jack by the Hedge, or Sauce Alone

2 Winter Cress, or Rocket

3 Hawkweed-leaved *Erysimum*

Jack by the Hedge,

1 Jack by the Hedge, or Sauce Alone The stalk of this plant is slender, herbaceous, and little more than a foot high The leaves are heart-shaped, broad, serrated, pointed, of a light-green colour, and taste and smell like garlick The flowers come out from the ends and sides of the stalks near the top, they are small, of a white colour, appear in June and July, and are succeeded by long narrow pods full of small seeds, which are of a black colour when ripe

This plant was formerly eaten as a sallad herb, which gained it the appellation of Sauce Alone, and is now much relished by some, who prefer it to many kinds of esculents It is in eating in March and April, and those who are fond of it, may find it by the sides of hedges, ditches, among bushes, and in many uncultivated places, without being at the trouble of cultivating it in the garden

Winter Cresses,

2 Winter Cress, or Rocket The stalks are round, herbaceous, branching, and grow to about a foot and a half high The leaves are lyre-shaped, broad, smooth, green, and the radical ones spread themselves on the ground The flowers are produced from the ends of the branches, they are small, of a yellow colour, appear in May, and are succeeded by narrow pods containing the seeds, which are of a reddish colour when ripe The leaves are green all winter, and much relished by many as a wholesome sallad herb

Varieties

There is a variety of this species with oblong undivided leaves, and others with roundish leaves of a thick consistence, which differences are pretty permanent from seeds

and Hawk weed leaved Erysimum described

3 Hawkweed leaved *Erysimum* The stalks are slender, herbaceous, and little more than a foot high The leaves are spear-shaped, serrated, and of a light-green colour The flowers are produced from the ends of the stalks, they are small, of a pale yellow colour, appear in June and July, and are succeeded by long narrow pods, containing ripe seeds, soon after

Culture.

All these sorts are propagated by sowing the seeds soon after they are ripe, they chiefly delight in the shade, and a moist soil, though they will grow any where; and if the seeds are permitted to scatter, will become a troublesome weed in the garden

Titles.

1 Jack by the Hedge, or Sauce Alone, is titled, *Erysimum foliis cordatis* Tournefort calls it, *Hesperis allium redolens*, Gerard, *Alaria* It grows naturally by the sides of hedges, ditches, shady places, &c in England, and most parts of Europe

2 Winter Cress, or Rocket, is, *Erysimum foliis lyratis extimo subrotundo* In the *Flora Lapp* it is termed, *Erysimum foliis basi pinnato-dentatis apice subrotundis* Caspar Bauhine calls it, *Eruca lutea latifolia sive barbarea*, John Bauhine, *Barbarea*, Ray, *Barbarea foliis minoribus & frequentius sinuatis*, Tournefort, *Sisymbrium, erucæ folio glabro, minus & procerius*, also *Sisymbrium orientale, barbareæ facie, folio subrotundo* It grows naturally in ditches, moist meadows, and watery places in England, and most parts of Europe

3 Hawkweed-leaved *Erysimum* is, *Erysimum foliis lanceolatis serratis* Caspar Bauhine calls it, *Leucojum luteum sylvestre hieracifolium*, and Ray, *Leucojum sylvestre inodorum, flore parvo pallidiore* It grows naturally in Gaul

Class and order in the Linnæan system The characters

*Erysimum* is of the class and order *Tetradynamia Siliquosa*, and the characters are,

1 CALYX is a perianthium composed of four oval, oblong, deciduous, coloured leaves

2 COROLLA is cruciforme The petals are four in number, oblong, plane, obtuse at the top, and have erect ungues the length of the calyx There is a double nectarium situated between the shorter filaments

3 STAMINA are six filaments the length of the calyx, of which the two opposite are the shortest, having simple antheræ

4 PISTILLUM consists of a narrow four cornered germen the length of the stamina, a very short style, and a small capitated permanent stigma

5 PERICARPIUM is a long, narrow, square, bivalvate pod, containing two cells

6 SEMINA The seeds are many, small, and roundish

## CHAP. CXCIV.

## *ERYTHRONICUM*, DOG's TOOTH VIOLET.

THERE is only one known species of this genus, though it affords many varieties, to adorn our borders early in the spring. They are all of them low, elegant, and beautiful, and are adapted to figure with Crocusses, and the like tribe in that early season.

Description of this plant. The root is fleshy, white, and fancied by some to be shaped like a tooth; hence the name Dog's Tooth hath been applied to this plant. By that name it has gone of old, and our gardeners have added the name Violet, calling it, Dog's-Tooth Violet, a term equally vague and inexpressive. From this tooth-shaped root arise two leaves; in some varieties they are oval, in others narrow and spear shaped; they enclose the flower, at first embrace each other, and afterwards fall opposite on the ground. These leaves are of a fleshy substance, and beautifully marbled, spotted, or variegated with brown, black, or purple, all over their surface. The flower-stalk rises with the leaves, or before them; it is naked, round, tender, and will grow to about four or five inches high. At the top of the stalk is placed the flower, in a drooping manner; it is very large for a small plant, exceeding elegant, and is composed of six spear-shaped petals, which turn backward. The stamina add great beauty to this plant, and are conspicuous enough; the filaments are white, and have their purple antheræ dusted with silver; the style also is white, large, and closely surrounded by the purple stamina. In short, the whole is very singular, elegant, and fine, and its coming up in so early a season enhances its value, and causes it to be sought after with great eagerness. It will be in blow early in April or March, at which time our borders glow with them in their full lustre and pride. For there are,

Varieties.
The Common Red Dog's Tooth Violet.
The Pale-Red Dog's Tooth Violet.
The Blood-Red Dog's Tooth Violet.
The White Dog's Tooth Violet.
The Yellow Dog's Tooth Violet.
The Crimson Dog's Tooth Violet.
The Purple Dog's Tooth Violet.
The Narrow-leaved White Dog's Tooth Violet.
The Narrow-leaved Red Dog's Tooth Violet.
The Narrow-leaved Purple Dog's Tooth Violet.
The Narrow-leaved Whitish-purple Dog's Tooth Violet.

These are the principal sorts of the Dog's Tooth Violet, and they are to be preserved in their varieties, and multiplied by parting of the roots. This work should be done in summer, after the leaves are decayed, though the plants will grow if removed at any time of the year. They do not send forth their off-sets very plentifully, so that their encrease this way is not very great.

Culture. These plants are propagated by seeds; by this means a large quantity of plants may be obtained, and fresh varieties expected. In order for this, let the seeds be gathered from plants of the red colour, such as Crimson, Deep Red, Purple, and Yellow; though the seeds of these will not always produce the same again, for there will be the White, Pale red, and others of a bad colour; however, there is always the best chance of having good flowers of seeds gathered from plants of the best properties.

The best time for sowing the seeds is in August or September. This must be done in a shady warm border, and the seeds must be covered over about half an inch deep. In the spring the plants will appear, when all weeds must be carefully plucked up as they arise, and the young plants must be frequently refreshed with water in dry weather. When the leaves are decayed, sift over them a little fine earth, and in the spring following, when the plants come up, water them often. As soon as you perceive the leaves to decay, leave off watering, keep the beds clean from weeds, and this is all the management they will require until they shew their flowers, which will be in about four years. When they flower, those with bad colours should be plucked up, and thrown away; those also with singular good properties should be marked for a place of distinction in the flower-garden; and all of them may be removed to the places of their destination any time between Midsummer and Michaelmas.

As there are no other species of this genus, it stands simply with the title *Erythronicum*. The varieties are found by different names among old botanists. Caspar Bauhine calls the Broad-leaved kind, *Dens canis latiore rotundioreque folio*; and the Narrow-leaved sort he terms, *Dens canis angustiore longioreque folio*; and the colour of the flower is also added, such as, *flore ex purpurâ rubente—flore ex albo purpurascente*; and the like. It grows naturally in Italy, Hungary, Virginia, &c.

*Erythronicum* is of the class and order *Hexandria Monogynia*; and the characters are, — Class and order in the Linnæan system. The characters.

1. Calyx. There is none.
2. Corolla consists of six oblong, spear-shaped, acuminated petals, which turn backward, and are alternately incumbent upon another at their base. The nectaria are two obtuse callous tubercles, adhering to the alternate interior petal near the base.
3. Stamina are six subulated filaments, with their oblong antheræ.
4. Pistillum consists of a turbinated germen, a simple style shorter than the corolla, and a triple, patent, obtuse stigma.
5. Pericarpium is a roundish capsule of three cells.
6. Semina. The seeds are many, oval, flat, and pointed.

# CHAP. CXCV.

## EUPATORIUM, HEMP AGRIMONY.

Species

OF this genus there are,

1 Common Hemp Agrimony, or Dutch Agrimony
2 Hyssop leaved Hemp Agrimony
3 Round leaved Hemp Agrimony
4 Sessile leaved Hemp Agrimony
5 Long leaved Hemp Agrimony
6 Trifoliate Hemp Agrimony
7 Purple Hemp Agrimony
8 Spotted Hemp Agrimony
9 Blue Hemp Agrimony
10 Perfoliate Hemp Agrimony
11 Aromatick Hemp Agrimony
12 Climbing Hemp Agrimony

Description of the Common.

1 Common Hemp Agrimony, or Dutch Agrimony The stalks are round, upright, of a reddish or purplish green colour, and grow to about three feet high The leaves are digitated and large The folioles are oblong, indented, and of a pale-green colour The flowers come out in large clusters from the tops of the stalks and branches, they are separate, small, and of a pale-red colour appear in July and August, and are soon succeeded by downy seeds, which will be wafted by the wind to a considerable distance It grows common by water, and in moist places in many parts of England, it is deemed an admirable vulnerary, is good for the jaundice, and being boiled in wine and water, is said to be of great virtue in removing tertian agues

Hyssop leaved,

2 Hyssop-leaved Hemp Agrimony The stalks are round, upright, send out branches by pairs opposite, and grow to about three feet high The leaves are spear-shaped, narrow, entire, trinervous, of a light-green colour, and grow opposite to each other on the stalks The flowers come out two or three together on long footstalks from the ends of the branches, they are moderately large, and of a white colour, they appear in October, and are not followed by ripe seeds in England

Round leaved,

3 Round-leaved Hemp Agrimony The stalks are upright, close jointed, and about a foot high The leaves are roundish, heart-shaped, serrated, of a light-green colour, and sit close, having no footstalks The flowers terminate the stalks in loose panicles, they are small, of a white colour, appear in June and July, and in favourable seasons the seeds ripen in the autumn

Sessile-leaved,

4 Sessile-leaved Hemp Agrimony The stalks are upright, jointed, send forth a few branches near the top, and grow to about two feet high The leaves are spear-shaped, slightly indented, of a whitish green colour, and embrace the stalks with their base The flowers come out from the tops of the stalks in kind of loose panicles, they are white, appear in July and August, and are sometimes followed by ripe seeds in the autumn

Long leaved,

5 Long-leaved Hemp Agrimony The stalks are upright, ligneous, firm, branching near the top, and grow to be four or five feet high The leaves are spear-shaped very long, narrow, slightly serrated, and of a whitish green colour The flowers adorn the tops of the stalks in plenty, they are moderately large, white, appear in July and August, and are sometimes succeeded by ripe seeds in the autumn

Trifoliate,

6 Trifoliate Hemp Agrimony The stalk is erect, firm, jointed, branching near the top, and three or four feet high The leaves are oval, spear-shaped, serrated, and grow three together at the joints The flowers are produced from the ends of the stalks in kind of loose panicles, they are of a bluish red colour, appear in July and August, and are sometimes followed by ripe seeds in the autumn

Purple,

7 Purple Hemp Agrimony The stalks are erect, taper, firm, purplish, and grow to be four or five feet high The leaves are spear-shaped, oval, unequally serrated, rough, oblique to the footstalks, of a dark green colour, and grow by fours in whorls round the stalks The flowers come out from the ends of the stalks in roundish bunches, their colour is purple, they appear in July and August, but are seldom succeeded by ripe seeds in England

Spotted

8 Spotted Hemp Agrimony The stalks are erect, firm, two feet and a half high, purplish, and marked with numerous, dark, purple-coloured spots. The leaves are spear-shaped, rough, a little downy, equally serrated, and usually placed by fives round the stalks The flowers terminate the stalks in roundish clusters, they are of a pale purple colour, appear in July and August, and in warm seasons are succeeded by ripe seeds in the autumn

Blue,

9 Blue Hemp Agrimony The root is more creeping than any of the other sorts, and sends forth numerous stalks to the height of about two feet The leaves are heart-shaped, oval, obtusely serrated, and grow on pretty strong footstalks The flowers terminate the stalks in corymbose bunches, they are of a fair purple colour, appear in July and August, and sometimes in September and October, but, like most other creeping plants, are seldom succeeded by seeds

Perfoliate

10 Perfoliate Hemp Agrimony The stalks are upright, hairy, and grow to about two feet and a half high The leaves are long, sharp-pointed, rough, hairy, downy underneath, grow opposite, and join at their base, so as to appear as one leaf, having the stalk thrust through it The flowers are produced in small clusters from the upper parts of the plant, each cluster having its separate footstalk, their colour is white, they appear in July, and are frequently succeeded by ripe seeds in our gardens

Aromatick

11 Aromatick Hemp Agrimony The stalks are erect, firm, send out upright branches from the joints, and grow about a yard high The leaves are oval, oblong, trinervous, rough, serrated, grow on short footstalks, and are possessed of an agreeable aromatick odour The flowers terminate the main-stalk and side-branches in clusters, their colour is white, they appear in August and September, but are rarely succeeded by seeds in England

and Climbing Hemp Agrimony,

12 Climbing Hemp Agrimony The stalks are slender, twining, and, if supported, will grow to be five feet high The leaves are heart shaped, indented, acute, and grow opposite to each other at the joints The flowers are produced in clusters, growing on long footstalks from the joints, two footstalks are usually produced from each

each joint, which adorn the plant in that manner nearly the whole length, their colour is white; they appear in September and October, but are never succeeded by seeds in England

Variety There is a variety of this species with purple flowers, both of which are very beautiful, and deserving of a place in every good collection of plants

Method of propagating them All these sorts are easily propagated by dividing of the roots, the best time for which is the autumn, though it may be done successfully in the winter, or early in the spring, before the stalks shoot up for flowering They are all very hardy, and love a moist soil and a shady situation, except the last, which should be planted in a warm dry place, and frequently watered in the summer, otherwise it will be so late in the season before it flowers, that the buds will be in danger of being destroyed by the early frosts before they open This sort should always have sticks thrust into the ground for it to twine about, and with respect to the others, they will require no trouble, except keeping them clean from weeds, digging the ground about them in winter, and reducing the roots every two or three years, as often as you find them spread too fast The stalks always die to the ground in the autumn, and fresh ones arise in the spring, on which account they should be always cleared off when they decay, to keep up the spirit of neatness, and make room for fresh ones to flourish the summer following

They are also raised by seeds, which should be sown about the middle of March, in beds of light earth made fine If very dry weather should happen, the beds must be watered twice a week, they should also be hooped, to be shaded with mats as the sun encreases in strength, and the growth of the seeds will be greatly promoted When the plants come up, they should be thinned where they are too close, kept clean from weeds all the summer, duly watered as often as dry weather makes it necessary, and by the autumn they will be fit to remove to the places where they are designed to remain

The seeds of the Common Hemp Agrimony, and those which ripen early in the autumn, may be sown as soon as they are ripe, and they will grow better, and the plants be forwarder, than if they were kept until the spring before they were committed to the ground, or if you choose to give yourself no trouble about raising them regularly, the early sorts will sow themselves, and produce perhaps more plants than you could wish to have raised

Titles 1 Common Hemp Agrimony, or Dutch Agrimony, is titled, *Eupatorium foliis digitatis* Caspar Bauhine calls it, *Eupatorium cannabinum*, Fuchsius, *Eupatorium adulterinum*, Ray, *Eupatorium cannabinum folio integro, seu non digitato*, and Gerard, *Eupatorium cannabinum mas* It grows naturally by waters in England, and most parts of Europe

2 Hyssop-leaved Hemp Agrimony is, *Eupatorium foliis lanceolato-linearibus trinerviis subintegerrimis* Dillenius calls it, *Eupatorium Virginianum, folio angusto, floribus albis*, Morison, *Eupatorium Virginianum, flore albo, hyssopi foliorum æmulum*, and Plukenet, *Eupatoria hirsuta, hyssopi foliorum æmula, Virginiana* It is a native of Virginia

3 Round-leaved Hemp Agrimony is, *Eupatorium foliis sessilibus distinctis subrotundo cordatis* Plukenet calls it, *Eupatoria valerianoides Virginiensis, trissaginis folio absque pediculis*, and Morison, *Cacalia foliis rotundioribus ad caulem sessilibus* It inhabits Virginia and Canada

4 Sessile-leaved Hemp Agrimony is, *Eupatorium foliis sessilibus amplexicaulibus distinctis lanceolatis* Morison calls it, *Eupatorium Virginianum, flore albo, foliis menthæ angustioribus sessilibus minutim dentatis* It is a native of Virginia

5 Long leaved Hemp Agrimony is, *Eupatorium foliis lanceolatis nervosis inferioribus extimo subserratis, caule suffruticoso* Morison calls it *Eupatorium Virginianum, longissimis & angustissimis foliis* It grows naturally in Pensylvania

6 Trifoliate Hemp Agrimony is, *Eupatorium foliis ternis* Gronovius calls it, *Eupatorium caule erecto, foliis ovato-lanceolatis serratis petiolatis ternatis*, and Ray, *Eupatorium cannabinum, foliis in caule ad genicula ternis Marilandicum* It grows naturally in Virginia

7 Purple Hemp Agrimony is, *Eupatorium foliis quaternis scabris lanceolato-ovatis, inæqualiter serratis rugosis petiolatis* Colden calls it, *Eupatorium foliis verticillatis*, Gronovius, *Eupatorium foliis ovato-lanceolatis obtuse serratis in petiolis desinentibus*, Cornutus, *Eupatorium enulæ folio*, and Morison, *Eupatorium Canadense elatius, longioribus foliis rugosis integris et caulibus ferrugineis* It grows naturally in many parts of North America

8 Spotted Hemp Agrimony is, *Eupatorium foliis quinis subtomentosis lanceolatis æqualiter serratis venosis petiolatis* In the *Hortus Cliffortianus* it is termed, *Eupatorium foliis lanceolato ovatis serratis petiolatis* Herman calls it, *Eupatorium Novæ Angliæ, urticæ foliis, floribus purpurascentibus, caule maculato* It is a native of North America

9 Blue Hemp Agrimony is, *Eupatorium foliis cordato-ovatis obtuse serratis petiolatis, calycibus multifloris* Gronovius calls it, *Eupatorium foliis cordatis serratis petiolatis*, Dillenius, *Eupatorium scorodoniæ folio, flore cæruleo*, and Plukenet, *Eupatorium Marianum, scrophulariæ foliis, capitulis globosis, colore cælestino* It grows naturally in Virginia and Carolina

10 Perfoliate Hemp Agrimony is, *Eupatorium foliis connato perfoliatis tomentosis* Plukenet calls it, *Eupatorium Virginianum, salviæ foliis longissimis acuminatis, perfoliatum*, and Morison, *Eupatorium Virginianum, mucronatis rugosis et longissimis foliis, perfoliatum* It grows naturally in standing waters and moist places in Virginia

11 Aromatick Hemp Agrimony is, *Eupatorium foliis ovatis obtuse serratis petiolatis trinerviis, calycibus simplicibus* Gronovius calls it, *Eupatorium caule erecto ramoso, foliis ovatis obtuse serratis petiolatis*, and Plukenet, *Eupatoria valerianoides, flore niveo, Teucrii foliis cum pediculis, Virginiana* It grows naturally in Virginia

12 Climbing Hemp Agrimony is, *Eupatorium caule volubili, foliis cordatis dentatis acutis* Plumier calls it, *Conyza scandens, solani folio anguloso*, and Plukenet, *Clematitis novum genus, cucumeris folio, Virginianum* It grows naturally in watery places in Virginia

*Eupatorium* is of the class and order *Syngenesia Polygamia Æqualis*; and the characters are, Class and order in the Linnæan system

1 CALYX The common calyx is oblong and imbricated The scales are narrow, spear-shaped, unequal, and erect The characters

2 COROLLA The compound flower is uniform The florets are funnel-shaped, and cut at the top into five spreading segments

3 STAMINA are five very short capillary filaments, having a tubular cylindrical anthera

4 PISTILLUM consists of a very small germen, and a long straight filiforme bifid style, with small stigmas

5 PERICARPIUM There is none

6 SEMINA The seeds are oblong, and crowned with long feathery down

The receptacle is naked

CHAP

# CHAP. CXCVI.

## *EUPHORBIA*, BURNING THORNY PLANT.

Species. OF this genus there are,
1 Aleppo Spurge
2 Sea Spurge
3 Portland Spurge
4 Belgic Spurge, or *Pithyusa*
5 Sweet Spurge
6 Italian Spurge
7 Apios Spurge
8 Portulacoide Spurge
9 Ipecacuanha Spurge
10. Rough-fruited Spurge
11 Hairy Spurge
12 Oriental Spurge
13 Coralloide Spurge
14 German Spurge
15 Calabrian Spurge
16 Marsh Spurge
17 Knotty-rooted Spurge, or Irish Spurge
18 Dendroide Spurge, or Tree Tithymel
19 Amygdaloide Spurge
20 Red Spurge
21 Wood Spurge

Aleppo. 1 Aleppo Spurge This hath a very creeping root, which sends forth several stalks that divide by pairs, and grow to about a foot and a half high The leaves are oval, spear shaped, pointed, and the lower ones are bristly, but those above are smooth, and resemble the Narrow-leaved Myrtle The flowers are produced from the divisions of the stalks, in large quinquifid umbels, their colour is yellow, and the general characters indicate their structure, they appear in June and July, and sometimes in September and October, but are very rarely succeeded by good seeds in England

Sea. 2 Sea Spurge The root is thick, woody, simple, and sends forth several upright stalks, which are of a reddish colour, and grow to about a foot and a half high The leaves are numerous, small, narrow, of a thickish substance, and closely garnish the stalks all round in an imbricated manner. The flowers are produced in large umbels from the tops of the stalks, they are yellowish, appear in June and July, and the seeds ripen in August and September

Portland. 3 Portland Spurge The root is thick, tough, strikes deep into the ground, and sends forth several thickish stalks to the height of about a foot The leaves are narrow, spear-shaped, and reflexed The flowers are produced in umbels from the ends of the stalks, and commonly consist of five divisions, they are of a yellowish colour, appear in June and July, and the seeds ripen in August and September

Though the root of this species will sometimes continue for three or four years, it frequently dies soon after the seeds are ripe, after this you need not be very anxious, for the seeds scattering will afford you plants enough for a succession without any trouble

Belgic. 4 Belgic Spurge, or *Pithyusa* The stalks are upright, a little branching, and about a foot high The leaves are spear shaped, short, sharp-pointed, shaped like those of Juniper, and lie over each other imbricatim The flowers are produced from the ends of the stalks in umbels, divided into five parts, each of which is again divided into two smaller; they are of a yellowish-green colour, appear in June and July, and the seeds ripen soon after

Sweet. 5 Sweet Spurge. The stalks are feeble, and grow but to about ten inches high The leaves are spear-shaped, entire, and obtuse The flowers are produced in quinquifid umbels from the ends and sides of the stalks, their colour is red, they appear in June and July, and sometimes in August, and the seeds ripen in September or earlier

Italian. 6 Italian Spurge This is a low plant, about eight or ten inches high The leaves are spear-shaped, obtuse, rough on their edges, and hairy underneath The flowers are produced in the like kind of umbels with the former from the ends and sides of the stalks, they are of a reddish colour, appear in June and July, and are succeeded by hispid capsules containing the seeds

Apios. 7 Apios Spurge The root is knobbed, thick, fleshy, and sends forth a few stalks, which grow to about a foot and a half high The leaves are oblong, hairy, and grow alternately all round the stalk The flowers come out in umbels like the former from the divisions of the stalks, and are small, and of a greenish-yellow colour, they appear in July, but are seldom succeeded by good seeds in England

Portulacoide. 8 Portulacoide Spurge The stalks are erect, divide by pairs, and grow to about two feet high The leaves are oval, undivided, retuse, and of a bluish-green colour The flowers come out singly on footstalks from the wings of the leaves, they are of a greenish colour, appear in July, but are seldom succeeded by good seeds in England

Ipecacuanha. 9 Ipecacuanha Spurge The stalks of this plant are upright, divided by pairs, and grow to about two feet high The leaves are spear-shaped, undivided, and of a bluish green colour The flowers come out singly from the wings of the stalks on footstalks, they are of a greenish colour tipped with yellow, and frequently shew themselves in April and May

Rough-pointed. 10 Rough-fruited Spurge. The stalks are upright, divided by pairs near the top, and full of a milky juice The leaves are spear shaped, slightly serrated, hairy, and downy underneath The flowers are produced from the tops of the plants in umbels, composed of five principal parts, each of which is again divided into two or three smaller, they are of a greenish-yellow colour, appear in July and August, and are succeeded by very rough, hairy, warted fruit, containing the seeds

In some moist rich soils this species should be treated as a biennial, the plant generally dying after it has flowered and perfected its seeds; you need not be very anxious, however, about a succession; for if the seeds are permitted to scatter, they will grow and produce plants enough.

Hairy. 11 Hairy Spurge. The stalks are ligneous, tough, milky, and about three feet high The leaves are spear-shaped, a little hairy on both sides, serrated near the extremities, and grow alternately on the stalks The flowers come out in umbels from the tops of the plant, they are of a yellow colour, appear in July, and are succeeded by rough hairy capsules containing the seeds.

Oriental. 12. Oriental Spurge. The stalks grow to be a yard high, are thick, succulent, smooth, covered with a purple bark, and divide by pairs near the top. The leaves are oblong, spear-shaped, smooth, and of a dark-green colour. The flowers are produced in quinquifid umbels from the divisions of the stalks; they are large, of a greenish-yellow colour, appear in June, and are succeeded by roundish capsules, containing ripe seeds, in August.

Coralloide. 13. Coralloide Spurge. The stalks are woody, smooth, dichotomous, grow to be six feet high, and are covered with a red bark. The leaves are spear-shaped, obtuse, smooth, and grow alternately. The flowers come out in quinquifid umbels from the divisions of the branches; their colour is yellow, they appear in July, and are succeeded by roundish rough capsules containing the seeds.

As the seeds of this plant, in all situations, do not ripen in England, it is generally propagated by planting the cuttings in a shady border. They will readily strike root, but as this species is rather of a tender nature, a share of them should be transplanted into pots filled with light earth in September, to be removed under shelter in winter, to keep up the stock in case those abroad should be destroyed by the frosts, which is pretty sure to be the case should the winter prove severe.

German. 14. German Spurge. The stalks are slender, smooth, milky when broken, and about a foot and a half high. The leaves are spear-shaped, narrow, smooth, thick, and of a bluish-green colour. The flowers come out in umbels, composed of many parts, from the ends and divisions of the stalks; they are of a yellow colour, appear in June and July, and sometimes later, and are succeeded by smooth capsules containing the seeds.

15. Calabrian Spurge. The stalks are thick, succulent, green, grow but to about a foot high, and are marked with scars or cicatrices when the leaves have fallen off. The leaves are spatula-shaped, fleshy, concave, rough on their borders, sharp-pointed, spreading, and of a glaucous green colour. The flowers terminate the stalks in large eight-parted umbels; they are of a yellow colour, appear in June and July, and are succeeded by smooth capsules containing the seeds.

This plant is rather tender, and may be raised from seeds or cuttings like the former, and a few plants should be always set in pots to be housed in winter, in case those abroad should be destroyed by hard weather.

Marsh. 16. Marsh Spurge. The stalk is thick, ligneous, smooth, and about three feet high. The leaves are spear-shaped, thick, and of a whitish green colour. The flowers are produced in multifid umbels from the upper parts of the plant; they are of a greenish yellow colour, appear in June, and the seeds ripen in August.

Knotty rooted. 17. Knotty-rooted Spurge. This species is frequently called Irish Spurge. The root is thick, knotty, and fibrated. The stalks are upright, unbranching, and about a foot high. The leaves are broad, oblong, entire, and grow alternately all round the stalks. The flowers come out in small umbels, which are divided into six parts, from the tops of the stalks; they are of a yellow colour, appear in June, and are succeeded by rough warted capsules, containing ripe seeds, in August.

Dendroide. 18. Dendroide Spurge, or Tree Tithymel. The stem is upright, woody, branching, and grows to be five or six feet high. The leaves are oblong, pointed, of a light-green colour, and grow alternately on the branches. The flowers are produced in umbels, divided into many parts, from the divisions of the branches; they are small, of a yellow colour, appear in July, but are not always succeeded by ripe seeds in England.

This species is rather tender, and should have the same culture and management as the thirteenth and fourteenth species.

Amygdaloide. 19. Amygdaloide Spurge. This rises with an upright shrubby stalk to about a yard in height. The leaves are of a thickish substance, obtuse, and continue all the year. The flowers are produced in close multifid umbels from the sides of the stalks. The perianthium is of a greenish-yellow colour, but the petals of the flowers are black; they will be in blow in May and June, and are succeeded by ripe seeds in July.

Red. 20. Red Spurge. The stalk is round, thick, smooth, perennial, three or four feet high, and covered with a reddish bark. The leaves are long, spear-shaped, entire, a little downy, and placed alternately on every side of the stalk. The flowers come out in multifid umbels from the ends and sides of the stalks; their colour is purple, they appear in June, and the seeds ripen in August.

There is a variety of this species with yellow flowers.

and Wood Spurge described. 21. Wood Spurge. The stalk is round, smooth, thick, woody, perennial, and about three or four feet high. The leaves are spear-shaped, long, entire, and much resemble those of the former species. The flowers are produced in five-pointed umbels, each part being composed of two smaller umbels, from the upper parts of the plant; they are of a purplish colour, appear in June and July, and the seeds ripen in September.

Method of raising them. These sorts are all propagated either by parting of the roots, planting the cuttings, or sowing the seeds. Some of the roots are creeping, and soon spread themselves to a considerable distance; such plants are generally least productive of seeds, and their usual culture is by parting of the roots in the autumn, by which means they may be encreased fast enough.

Some have thick, tough, and woody roots. These plants are generally short-lived, the whole plants often dying as soon as the seeds are perfected. They should have been ranked among the biennials, were it not that they frequently send forth young shoots near the ground, and the stalk becoming woody, will continue many years, and resist the cold of our severest winters. These are propagated by planting of the slips in any of the summer months, the spring, or the autumn; and such plants will be hardier than those raised from seeds.

by slips, By cuttings these, and indeed all the preceding sorts may be propagated. These should be planted in any of the summer months, be shaded and watered until they have taken root, and afterwards they will require no care except keeping them clean from weeds.

cuttings, They are also propagated by seeds, and by this way the best, most healthy, and beautiful plants are to be obtained. The seeds must be sown in the autumn, soon after they are ripe, otherwise they will frequently lie a whole year before they come up. They should be sown in the places where they are designed to remain, and after they make their appearance, will require no trouble but thinning them to proper distances, and keeping them clean from weeds, except the sorts mentioned that are rather of a tender nature, and must have some of the plants housed in winter,

and seeds.

winter, and the rest planted in warm well sheltered places to ensure their safety

Titles 1 Aleppo Spurge is titled, *Euphorbia umbellâ quinquefidâ dichotoma, involucellis ovato-lanceolatis mucronatis, foliis inferioribus setaceis* Morison calls it, *Tithymalus foliis inferioribus capillaceis superioribus myrto similibus*, and Alpinus, *Tithymalus Cyparissius* It grows naturally in Crete and Aleppo

2 Sea Spurge is, *Euphorbia umbellâ subquinquefidâ bifida, involucellis cordato-reniformibus, foliis sursum imbricatis* In the *Hortus Cliffortianus* it is termed, *Euphorbia inermis, foliis setaceo linearibus confertis, umbellâ universali multifidâ partialibus ramosis bifidis* Caspar Bauhine calls it, *Tithymalus maritimus*, Camerarius, *Tithymalus paralios*, Gerard, *Tithymalus paralios*, and Parkinson, *Tithymalus paralius seu maritimus* It grows naturally on the sandy sea-shores in England, and the like situations in most parts of Europe

3 Portland Spurge is, *Euphorbia umbellâ quinquefida dichotoma, involucellis subrotundatis concavis, foliis lineari-lanceolatis acutis glabris patentibus* Barrelier calls it, *Tithymalus montanus, esulæ fol...., minor, Italicus*, and Ray, *Tithymalus maritimus minor, Portlandicus* It grows naturally on sandy sea-shores, particularly on that part which joins Portland to Devonshire

4 Belgic Spurge, or *Pithyusa*, is, *Euphorbia umbellâ quinquefida bifida, involucellis ovatis mucronatis, foliis lanceolatis infimis involutis retrorsum imbricatis* Dalechamp calls it, *Pithyusa*, Caspar Bauhine, *Tithymalus foliis brevibus aculeatis*, and Boccone, *Tithymalus maritimus, juniperi folio* It grows naturally in sandy ground in Germany, France, Italy, and Spain

5 Sweet Spurge is, *Euphorbia umbellâ quinquefidâ bifida, involucellis subovatis, foliis lanceolatis obtusis integerrimis* Caspar Bauhine calls it, *Tithymalus montanus non acris*, and Lobel, *Pithyusa Esula minor altera, floribus rubris* It grows naturally in shady places in Italy, France, and Germany

6 ...n Spurge is, *Euphorbia umbellâ quinquefida ... , involucellis ovatis, foliis lanceolatis obtusis subtus villosis* Columna calls it, *Tithymalus epithymi fructu*, and Caspar Bauhine, *Peplos altera species* It grows naturally in Italy

7 Apios Spurge is, *Euphorbia umbellâ quinquefidâ bifida, involucellis obcordatis* Caspar Bauhine calls it, *Tithymalus tuberosa pyriformi radice*, and Clusius, *Tithymalus tuberosa radice* It inhabits Crete

8 Portulacoide Spurge is, *Euphorbia dichotoma, foliis integerrimis ovalibus retusis, pedunculis axillaribus unifloris folia æquantibus, caule erecto* Tewil calls it, *Tithymalus perennis, portulacæ folio* It is a native of Philadelphia

9 Ipecacuanha Spurge is, *Euphorbia dichotoma, foliis integerrimis lanceolatis, pedunculis axillaribus unifloris folia æquantibus, caule erecto* Gronovius calls it, *Tithymalus, flore exiguo viridi, apicibus flavis, antequam folia emittit florens* It is a native of Virginia, &c

10 Rough-fruited Spurge is, *Euphorbia umbellâ quinquefidâ subtrifida bifida, involucellis ovatis, foliis lanceolatis serrulatis villosis, capsulis verrucosis* Guettard calls it, *Euphorbia inermis, foliis linearibus, umbellâ universali trifidâ triphyllâ, partialibus trifidis, propriis dichotomis diphyllis, foliolis subrotundis* Caspar Bauhine calls it, *Tithymalus myrsinites, fructu verrucæ simili*, and, *Tithymalus foliis subhirsutis ad caulem ellipticis, subfloribus binis subrotundis* It grows naturally in Gaul, Switzerland, Italy, and the East

11 Hairy Spurge is, *Euphorbia umbellâ quinquefidâ trifida bifida, involucris ovatis, petalis integris, foliis lanceolatis subpilosis apice serrulatis* Gmelin calls it, *Euphorbia foliis alternis ex ovali-lanceolatis, umbellis diphyllis subtrifloris, capsulis ... caule simplici*, Barrelier, *Tithymalus palustris villosus mollior erectus*, Caspar Bauhine, *Tithymalus incanus hirsutus*, and Magnol, *Tithymalus Characias pratensis ...* It is a native of Siberia

12 Oriental Spurge is, *Euphorbia umbellâ quinquefidâ quadrifida dichotoma, involucellis ... acutis, foliis lanceolatis, involucro universali quinquefido lanceolato, partiali tetraphyllo subrotundo, propriis diphyllis*, and Tournefort, *Tithymalus orientalis, salicis folio, caule purpureo, flore magno* It is a native of the East

13 Coralloide Spurge is, *Euphorbia umbellâ quinquefidâ trifidâ dichotoma, involucellis ovatis, foliis lanceolatis, capsulis lanatis* In the *Hortus Upsal* it is termed, *Euphorbia inermis fruticosa, foliis lanceolatis, involucro universali quinquefido, partialibus triphyllis, reliquis bifidis* Boerhaave calls it, *Tithymalus arboreus, cum cortice ..., folio latiore, pericarpio barbato* It grows naturally in Sicily, Mauritania, and the East

14 German Spurge is, *Euphorbia umbellâ multifidâ bifida, involucellis subrotundatis, petalis subdentatis, ramis sterilibus, foliis uniformibus* In the *Hortus Upsal* it is termed, *Euphorbia inermis foliis lanceolato-linearibus involucri universalis foliis ovato acutis partialibus semi-orbiculatis* Sauvages calls it, *Euphorbia inermis, foliis lingulatis patulis ad umbellam, quinis ovato oblongis acutis, bracteis trigonis*, Magnol, *Tithymalus lithospermi majoris folio*, and Dalechamp, *Esula minor* It grows naturally in Germany and France

15 Calabrian Spurge is, *Euphorbia umbellâ subquinquefidâ bifida, involucellis subovatis, foliis spatulatis patentibus carnosis mucronatis margine scabris* In the *Hortus Cliffort* it is termed, *Euphorbia inermis, foliis superioribus reflexis latioribus lanceolatis, umbellâ universali trifidâ, partialibus bifidis* Sauvages calls it, *Euphorbia inermis, foliis ligulatis spinula terminatis ad umbellam duodenis, bracteis trigonis spinula terminatis*, Caspar Bauhine, *Tithymalus myrsinites latifolius*, and Clusius, *Tithymalus myrsinites legitimus* It grows naturally in Calabria, and the south of France

16 Marsh Spurge is, *Euphorbia umbellâ multifidâ subtrifida bifida, involucellis ovatis foliis lanceolatis, ramis sterilibus* In the *Hortus Cliffort* it is termed, *Euphorbia foliis lanceolatis, umbellâ universali multifidâ polyphyllâ partialibus trifidis triphyllis, propriis dichotomis* Caspar Bauhine calls it, *Tithymalus palustris fruticosus*, and Dalechamp, *Esula major* It grows naturally in Germany and Sweden

17 Knotty rooted Spurge, or Irish Spurge, is, *Euphorbia umbellâ sexfidâ dichotoma, involucellis ovalibus, foliis integerrimis, ramis nullis, capsulis verrucosis* Caspar Bauhine calls it, *Tithymalus latifolius Hispanicus*, Dillenius, *Tithymalus Hibernicus, vasculis muricatis erectis*, and Barrelier, *Tithymalus Hybernicus* It grows naturally in Hibernia, Siberia, Austria, and the Pyrenees

18 Dendroide Spurge, or Tree Tithymal, is, *Euphorbia umbellâ multifidâ dichotoma, involucellis subcordatis primoribus triphyllis, caule arboreo* Caspar Bauhine calls it, *Tithymalus myrtifolius arboreus*, and Cammerarius, *Tithymalus dendroides* It grows naturally in Italy, Crete, and several islands of the Archipelago

19 Amygdaloide Spurge is, *Euphorbia umbellâ multifidâ dichotoma, involucellis perfoliatis orbiculatis, foliis obtusis* Caspar Bauhine calls it, *Tithymalus Characias amygdaloides*, John Bauhine, *Tithymalus sylvaticus toto anno folia retinens*, and Parkinson, *Tithymalus Characias vulgaris* It grows naturally in woods and hedges in England, France, and Germany

20 Red Spurge is, *Euphorbia umbellâ multifidâ*

*fidâ bifida, involucellis perfoliatis emarginatis, foliis lanceolatis integerrimis, caule perenni* In the *Hortus Cliffort* it is termed, *Euphorbia inermis, foliis lanceolatis, umbellâ universali multifidâ, partialibus dichotomis, involucris semibifidis perfoliatis* Caspar Bauhine calls it, *Tithymalus Characias rubens peregrinus*, Clusius, *Tithymalus Characias* 1 and Gerard, *Tithymalus Characias Monspeliensium* It grows naturally in woods and hedges in England, France, Spain, Italy, and Germany

21 Wood Spurge is, *Euphorbia umbellâ quinquefidâ bifida, involucellis perfoliatis subcordatis retiusculis, foliis lanceolatis integerrimis* Columna calls it, *Tithymalus lunato flore*, and Caspar Bauhine, *Tithymalus sylvaticus lunato flore* It grows naturally in the southern parts of Europe

Class and order in the Linnæan System The characters

*Euphorbia* is of the class and order *Dodecandria Trigynia*, and the characters are,

1 CALYX is a monophyllous, ventricose, coloured, permanent perianthium, indented in four, and, in a few species, in five parts at the edge

2 COROLLA is four or five turbinated, thick, gibbous, truncated, permanent petals, unequally situated, alternate with the segments, and affixed by their ungues to the edge of the calyx.

3 STAMINA are twelve or more filiforme articulated filaments, inserted in the receptacle, and longer than the corolla, having didymous roundish antheræ

4 PISTILLUM consists of a roundish three-cornered germen, and three bifid styles with obtuse stigmas

5 PERICARPIUM is a roundish, trigonous, trilocular capsule, which opens with an elastic force for the discharge of the seeds

6 SEMINA The seeds are single and roundish

## CHAP. CXCVII

## *FERULA*, FENNEL-GIANT.

Species

THE species of this genus are,

1 Common Fennel-Giant
2 Glaucous Fennel-Giant
3 Fennel-Giant of Tangier
4 *Ferulago*, or Sicilian Fennel Giant
5 Oriental Fennel-Giant
6 Spignel leaved Fennel-Giant
7 Istrian Fennel-Giant
8 Canada Fennel-Giant
9 Asa Fœtida

Description of the Common Fennel Giant

1 Common Fennel Giant The root is very long, thick, and full of a milky juice The radical leaves are large, composed of a multitude of long, narrow, undivided segments, of a pale but bright-green colour, and spread on the ground. The stalk is very robust, round, hollow, jointed, grows to be ten or twelve feet high, and is adorned with leaves divided like the radical ones, but smaller The flowers come out from the ends and sides of the stalks in large roundish umbels, they are of a yellow colour, and the general characters shew their construction, they appear in June and July, and are succeeded by ripe seeds in September

The whole plant is of a strong smell, and acrid taste The gum called *Sagapenum*, or *Serapinum* of the shops is the concreted juice of this plant The stalks, when dry, are admirable for lighting of fires, and the pith is so very flammatory that it will burn like tinder, catching fire from the smallest sparks of the flint

Glaucous Fennel-Giant

2 Glaucous Fennel-Giant The root is long, thick, and juicy The radical leaves are large, glaucous, and divided into a multitude of narrow plane segments The stalks are upright, large, jointed, hollow, and grow to be seven or eight feet high The flowers are produced in umbels from the ends and sides of the branches, they are of a yellow colour, appear in June and July, and the seeds ripen in September

Fennel Giant of Tangier

3 Fennel Giant of Tangier The root is very large, thick, and juicy The leaves are composed of a multitude of jagged parts, each of which is divided into three unequal segments, the whole leaf is of a glossy-green colour, large, and the radical ones spread themselves on the ground The stalks are upright, strong, hollow, and grow to be eight or ten feet high The flowers come out in large umbels from the ends and sides of the stalks, they are of a yellow colour, appear in July, and the seeds ripen in September

4 Sicilian Fennel-Giant, or *Ferulago* The root is thick, long, and full of yellow juice. The leaves are pinnatifid, and the pinnæ are plane and trifid, they are of a dark green colour, and the radical ones spread themselves on every side The stalks are upright, round, hollow, and seven or eight feet high The flowers come out from the ends and sides of the stalks near the top, in roundish umbels, their colour is yellow, they appear in June and July, and the seeds ripen in September. Sicilian,

The *Galbanum* of the shops is the hardened juice of the root of this plant

5 Oriental Fennel-Giant The leaves are finely divided, and each of them possesses a multitude of beautiful segments, which are bristly, and of a pale-green colour The stalks are upright, firm, hollow, and grow to about three feet high The flowers come out in small umbels from the ends and sides of the stalks, they are of a yellow colour, appear in July, and the seeds ripen in September Oriental,

6 Spignel-leaved Fennel Giant The leaves are composed of a multitude of appendiculated and bristly foliole; the radical ones are large, spreading, and grow on angular channelled footstalks, those on the stalks are small, elegant, and surround them at the joints The stalks are upright, firm, jointed, send out side-branches by pairs from the joints, and grow to about a yard high Spignel leaved,

The

The flowers terminate the stalks in large umbels, they are of a yellow colour, come out in July, and the seeds ripen in September

Istrian 7 Istrian Fennel-Giant The leaves are composed of a multitude of folioles that are narrow, entire, and have appendages on both sides The stalks are upright, firm, full of pith, and about a yard high. The flowers are produced in small umbels at the joints, sit close, and have hardly any footstalk, they are yellowish, appear about the same time with the former, and the seeds ripen accordingly

and Canada Fennel Giant 8 Canada Fennel Giant The leaves are much divided, large, and of a most chearful bright or glossy-green. The stalks are upright, firm, pithy, and about a yard high The flowers come out from the ends and sides of the stalks in umbels; they are small, yellowish, appear in July, and the seeds ripen in September

Assa-Fœtida 9 Assa Fœtida The root is very thick, fleshy, full of juice, and strikes deep into the ground The leaves are composed of several folioles, which are sinuated, obtuse, and of a strong disagreeable odour The stalks are very thick, pithy, ten or twelve feet high, and divide into many branches for the support of the flowers These, as well as the main stalks, are terminated with the flowers growing in small umbels The flowers are of a greenish yellow colour, appear in July, and are succeeded by flat yellowish seeds, which ripen in September, and are then of an agreeable odour

The root of this plant being wounded, sends forth a strong gummy liquor or juice, which being dried is that stinking drug of the shops called *Assa Fœtida*

Method of propagating them All these sorts are possessed of thick, fleshy, juicy roots, which strike deep into the ground, so that, in order to have the plants in full perfection, a deep rich soil should be appropriated to them; in which they will grow to near double the height than in a soil of an opposite nature The Common Fennel-Giant, for instance, in some situations, will not grow higher than six feet, and in some rich deep earth will shew itself upwards of fourteen feet high But notwithstanding a good deep earth is better for the full growth of these plants, the roots, especially if it be of a moist nature, seldom continue so long as they do in a poorer soil, particularly the third sort, which in some situations generally dies soon after the seeds are perfected

The culture of all of them is extremely easy Sow the seeds in the autumn, soon after they are ripe, or in the spring, in the places where they are designed to remain When the plants come up they must be thinned to proper distances, leaving them three, four, or five feet asunder, according to their size Keeping them clean from weeds must be observed all summer, and digging the ground between the roots should be performed in the autumn or winter The summer following they will flower and perfect their seeds, soon after which the stalks die to the ground, and fresh ones arise in the spring The stalks should be regularly cleared off every autumn, and the ground between the plants should be then dug In doing of this, be careful not to dig too near the roots, lest they should be bruised, for if they are ever so little wounded the juice will flow, which will cause the root to become weak, and little qualified to push forth vigorous shoots for the summer following

Titles. 1 Common Fennel Giant is titled, *Ferula foliolis linearibus longissimis simplicibus* Caspar Bauhine calls it, *Ferula fœmina Plinii*, and Dodonæus, *Ferula* It grows naturally in most of the southern parts of Europe

2 Glaucous Fennel Giant is, *Ferula foliis supradecompositis foliolis lanceolatis inferne nervosis planis* John Bauhine calls it, *Ferula folio glauco, semine lato oblongo* It grows naturally in Italy and Sicily

3 Fennel Giant from Tangier is, *Ferula foliolis laciniatis lacinulis tridentatis inæqualibus nitidis* Herman calls it, *Ferula Tingitana, folio latissimo lucido* It grows naturally in Spain and Barbary

4 Sicilian Fennel Giant, or *Ferulago*, is, *Ferula foliis pinnatifidis pinnis linearibus planis trifidis* Caspar Bauhine calls it *Ferulago latiore folio*, and Morison, *Ferula latiore folio* It is a native of Sicily

5 Oriental Fennel Giant is, *Ferula foliorum pinnis basi nudis, foliolis setaceis* Tournefort calls it, *Ferula orientalis, folio et facie cachryos* It is a native of the East

6 Spignel leaved Fennel Giant is *Ferula foliorum pinnis utrinque appendiculatis foliolis setaceis* Tournefort calls it, *Laserpitium orientale, folio mei, flore luteo* It grows naturally in the East

7 Istrian Fennel Giant is, *Ferula foliis appendiculatis, umbellis subsessilibus* Van Royen calls it, *Ferula foliorum alis utrinque auctis foliolis linearibus integerrimis, umbellis terminatricibus subsessilibus*, Caspar Bauhine, *Libanotis ferulæ folio & semine*, and Lobel, *Panax asclepium, ferulæ facie* It grows naturally in Istria, Sicily, Portugal, and Spain

8 Canada Fennel Giant is, *Ferula lucida Canadensis* It grows naturally in Virginia and Canada

9 Assa Fœtida is, *Ferula foliis alternatim sinuatis obtusis* Kæmpfer calls it, *Assa Fœtida Disgunensis umbellifera ligustico affinis* It grows naturally in Persia

*Ferula* is of the class and order *Pentandria Digynia*, and the characters are, Class and order in the Linnæan system The characters

1 Calyx The general umbel is globular The partial is of the same figure The general involucrum is caducous The partial is small, and composed of several narrow leaves The proper perianthium is scarce distinguishable

2 Corolla The general corolla is uniform The florets have each five oblong erect petals, which are nearly equal

3 Stamina are five filaments the length of the corolla, with simple antheræ

4 Pistillum consists of a turbinated germen situated under the cup, and two reflexed styles with obtuse stigmas

5 Pericarpium is an elliptical, plane, compressed fruit, divided into two parts, and marked on each side with three prominent lines

6 Semina The seeds are two, large, elliptical, plane, and striated on each side The

# CHAP. CXCVIII

## *F E S T U C A.*

THIS genus comprehends many graſſes, ſuch as the,

Species.

1 Sheep's Feſcue Graſs
2 Hard Feſcue Graſs
3 Purple Feſcue Graſs
4 Amethyſtine Feſcue Graſs
5 Small Feſcue Graſs
6 Tall Feſcue Graſs
7 Flote Feſcue Graſs
8 Arabian Feſcue Graſs
9 Spaniſh Feſcue Graſs
10 Paleſtine Feſcue Graſs

Sheep's Feſcue,

1 Sheep's Feſcue Graſs The leaves are narrow, compreſſed, briſtly, and of a dark green The ſtalks are almoſt naked, ſquare, and ſix or eight inches high The flowers come out in panicles from the tops of the ſtalks They are ariſtated, arranged in one direction, and are to be met with at all times of the ſummer, but more eſpecially in June and July There are ſeveral varieties of this ſpecies, particularly the Proliferous Graſs, the ſpikes of which ſend forth young plants before the ſeeds are ripe

Hard Feſcue,

2 Hard Feſcue Graſs The leaves are ſlender, hard, and briſtly The ſtalks are weak, jointed, and about a foot high The flowers come out in panicles from the tops of the ſtalks, and the ſpikes of which the panicles are compoſed are arranged in one direction They appear chiefly in June, but are occaſionally to be met with all ſummer and the autumn

Purple Feſcue

3 Purple Feſcue Graſs The leaves are narrow, briſtly, and form a cluſter at the crown of the root The ſtalks are rounded on one ſide, but flat on the other, and grow to eight or ten inches high The flowers are produced in panicles from the tops of the ſtalks, they are ariſtated, rough, arranged in one direction, and are to be met with principally in June

Amethyſtine Feſcue,

4 Amethyſtine Feſcue Graſs The leaves are very narrow, briſtly, but moderately long The ſtalks are upright, ſlender, and a foot and a half high The flowers are produced from the tops of the ſtalks in panicles They are almoſt deſtitute of ariſtæ, look one way, and are principally to be met with in June and July

Small Feſcue,

5 Small Feſcue Graſs The leaves are ſlender, pointed, five or ſix inches long, and of a deep green The ſtalks are ſlender, weak, and trailing The flowers come out from the tops of the ſtalks in upright panicles, the ſpikes are nearly oval, and have no ariſtæ, and they are to be met with in Auguſt

Tall Feſcue

6 Tall Feſcue Graſs The leaves are broad at the bottom, diminiſh gradually to a point, and are two feet long The ſtalks are thick, round, jointed, and three or four feet high The flowers are produced from the tops of the ſtalks in upright panicles The ſpikes are almoſt deſtitute of ariſtæ, and all bend one way They are in the greateſt perfection in July, though they are frequently to be met with the end of ſummer, and in the autumn

Flote Feſcue

7 Flote Feſcue Graſs This hath a long, round, creeping root, which ſends forth fibres from the joints The ſtalks are long, crooked, and variouſly implicated with one another The leaves are broad and coarſe, but, nevertheleſs, much reliſhed by horſes, and grow alternately The flowers come out in ramoſe, erect panicles, from the tops of the ſtalks The ſpikes are taper, beardleſs, and placed on ſhort footſtalks They are of a whitiſh colour, and appear in June and July

8 Arabian Feſcue Graſs The root is long, thick, and creeping under the ſurface The ſtalks are upright, round, moderately ſtrong, and five or ſix feet high The leaves are long, ſharp-pointed, and grow alternately The flowers are collected in ſpikes, which adorn the tops of the ſtalks a great length, they grow alternately, have no ariſtæ, and each ſpike contains ſix flowers, which will be in perfection in July — Arabian Feſcue,

9 Spaniſh Feſcue Graſs The radical leaves are taper-edged, and about a foot long The ſtalks are ſlender, taper, have two or three tumid joints, grow to be four feet high, and have ſhort channelled leaves placed alternately The flowers are produced from the tops of the ſtalks in downy, ſpike like panicles, and appear in June and July — Spaniſh Feſcue,

10 Paleſtine Feſcue Graſs This riſes with an upright, branching ſtalk, to three or four feet high The leaves are long, awl ſhaped, grow ſingly at the joints, and form a ſheath for the ſtalk with their baſe a conſiderable way up The flowers are produced from the tops of the ſtalks in erect, branching panicles The ſpikes of which they are compoſed are long, carinated, beardleſs, and ſit cloſe to the ſtalks They will be in blow in July, and the ſeeds ripen ſoon after — and Paleſtine Feſcue Graſs deſcribed

The ſeven firſt ſorts are very common in our paſtures, meadows, and fields The three laſt are of foreign growth, and are raiſed for the ſake of obſervation, in ſome curious collections of plants — Culture

They are all propagated by ſowing the ſeeds ſoon after they are ripe, or the ſpring following, and after the plants come up, they will require no trouble, except reducing them to a proper number, and keeping them clean from weeds

1 Sheep's Feſcue Graſs is titled, *Feſtuca panicula ſecundâ coarctatâ ariſtatâ, culmo tetragono nudiuſculo, foliis ſetaceis* In the *Flora Lapponica* it is termed, *Poa ſpiculis ovato anguſtis ariſtato-acuminatis* Van Royen calls it, *Poa foliis ſetaceis, paniculâ ramoſâ, floribus petiolatis antrorſum ſpectantibus, glumis ſubulatis*, Caſpar Bauhine, *Gramen foliis junceis brevibus majus, radice nigrâ*, Loeſel, *Gramen criſtatum, paniculis nigricantibus*, Vaillant, *Gramen capillaceum, locuſtis pinnatis non ariſtatis* The Proliferous Oat Graſs is in the *Flora Suecica* termed, *Feſtuca ſpiculis viviparis* Scheuchzer calls it, *Gramen paniculatum ſparteum alpinum paniculâ anguſtâ ſpadiceo viridi, proliferum* The Common Sheep's Feſcue Graſs grows in dry, hot, ſandy places, all over Europe, but the ſort called Proliferous Oat Graſs is found chiefly on the Alps of Lapland, Helvetia, Scotland, and Wales — Titles

2 Hard Feſcue Graſs is titled, *Feſtuca panicula ſecundâ oblongâ, ſpiculis ſexfloris oblongis lævibus, foliis*

*foliis setaceis* Van Royen calls it, *Festuca paniculâ nutante inferne ramosa spicis adscendentibus bifidis, foliis setaceis*, Ray, *Gramen pratense, paniculâ duriore laxâ unam partem spectante*, and Caspar Bauhine, *Gramen tenue durius culmum & pene junceum* It grows naturally in dry meadows and pastures all over Europe

3 Purple Fescue Grass is, *Festuca paniculâ secundâ scavrâ, spiculis sexfloris aristatis, flosculo ultimo mutico, culmo semiterete* Scheuchzer calls it, *Gramen alpinum pratense, paniculâ duriore laxâ spadiceâ locustis majoribus* It grows naturally in dry sterile places all over Europe

4 Amethystine Fescue Grass is, *Festuca paniculâ flexuosâ, spiculis secundis inclinatis sulcatis, foliis setaceis* Scheuchzer calls it, *Gramen montanum, foliis capillaribus longioribus, paniculâ heteromalla spadiceâ et velut Amethystinâ* It grows naturally in England, Gaul, and Italy

5 Small Fescue Grass is, *Festuca paniculâ erectâ, spiculis subovatis muticis, calyce flosculis majore, culmo decumbente* Scheuchzer calls it, *Gramen montanum avenaceum, locustis muticis tumentibus, pilosum*, Morison, *Gramen triticeum palustre humilius, spicâ mutica breviore*, and Ray, *Gramen avenaceum parvum procumbens, paniculis non aristatis* It grows naturally in sterile places all over Europe

6 Tall Fescue Grass is, *Festuca paniculâ secundâ erectâ, spiculis subaristatis exterioribus teretibus* Van Royen calls it, *Festuca paniculâ spicatâ, spiculis uno versu inclinatis submuticis*, Morison, *Gramen loliaceum, spicâ divisa, pratense majus*, Barrelier, *Gramen spartum, spicâ brizæ paniculatâ & corniculatâ*, Vaillant, *Gramen paniculatum elatius, spicis longis muticis squamosis*, Caspar Bauhine, *Gramen arundinaceum, spicâ multiplici, calamagrostis*, Buxbaum, *Gramen pratense majus locustis tumidis*, and Ray, *Gramen arundinaceum aquaticum, paniculâ avenaceâ* It grows in the most fertile meadows and pastures in England, and most countries of Europe

7 Flote Fescue Grass is, *Festuca paniculâ ramosâ erectâ, spiculis subsessilibus teretibus muticis* In the *Hortus Cliffort* it is termed, *Poa spiculis oblongis erectis* Caspar Bauhine calls it, *Gramen aquaticum fluitans multiplici spicâ*, Morison, *Gramen loliaceum fluitans, spicâ longissimâ divisa*, and Gerard, *Gramen fluviatile* It grows naturally in ditches and watery places all over Europe

8 Arabian Fescue-Grass is, *Festuca paniculæ ramis simplicibus, spiculis subsessilibus* It grows naturally in Arabia and Palestine

9 Spanish Fescue-Grass is, *Festuca paniculâ spiciformi pubescente foliis filiformibus* It grows naturally in Spain

10 Palestine Fescue Grass is, *Festuca paniculâ erectâ ramosâ, spiculis sessilibus carinatis muticis* It grows naturally in Palestine

*Festuca* is of the class and order *Triandria Digynia*, and the characters are, Class and order in the Linnæan system The characters

1 Calyx is an erect glume composed of two valves, and containing many flowers, which are collected in form of a slender spike The valves are awl-shaped, acuminated, and the lower one is the smallest

2 Corolla consists of two valves, the lower valve is the largest, taper, sharp pointed, and shaped like the calyx, but exceeds it in size

3 Stamina are three capillary filaments shorter than the corolla, having oblong antheræ

4 Pistillum consists of a turbinated germen, and two short reflexed styles with simple stigmas

5 Pericarpium The corolla closes, and closely surrounds the seed in every part

6 Semen The seed is single, slender, oblong, pointed at both ends, and marked with a longitudinal furrow

# CHAP CXCIX

## *FRAGARIA*, The STRAWBERRY.

BESIDES the Strawberry so noted in our kitchen-gardens, there is a species which is a pretty little plant, and ought not to be excluded our collection, (especially in those parts where it does not grow naturally) called, the Barren Strawberry

Description of this plant This plant sends forth some weak decumbent shoots, which strike root, and produce fresh plants as they go along The leaves are like the Fruit-bearing Strawberry, but less, they are soft, hairy, slightly indented, and of a pale or whitish-green colour The flowers grow singly from the wings of the leaves, on long hairy footstalks; they resemble the Common Strawberry, though smaller, and are succeeded by a barren juiceless fruit of no value

Culture It is propagated by dividing of the roots, the best time for which is the autumn A plant or two only will be sufficient for observation, for it grows naturally in many of our woods, heaths, &c and indeed when it is found growing near at hand in a state of nature, the introducing it into the garden as a perennial may be omitted

This species is titled, *Fragaria caule decumbente repente* Caspar Bauhine calls it, *Fragaria sterilis*, Titles Morison, *Fragaria sterilis, sive minime vesca hirsuta, minime incana*, and Lobel, *Fragaria sylvestris minime vesca sive sterilis* It grows naturally in England and Switzerland

*Fragaria* is of the class and order *Icosandria Polygynia*, and the characters are, Class and order in the Linnæan system The characters.

1 Calyx is a plane monophyllous perianthium, divided at the top into ten segments

2 Corolla is five roundish patent petals inserted in the calyx

3 Stamina are twenty awl shaped filaments that are shorter than the corolla, inserted in the calyx, and have moon shaped antheræ

4 Pistillum

4 PISTILLUM consists of numerous small germina, collected into a head, and simple styles inserted in the sides of the germens, having simple stigmas.

5 PERICARPIUM There is none The common receptacle of the seeds is roundish, oval, pulpose, soft, large, coloured, truncated at the base, and deciduous

6 SEMINA The seeds are numerous, very small, sharp pointed, and scattered over the superficies of the receptacle

# CHAP. CC.

## *FRANKENIA*

Species OF this genus are,

1 Smooth Sea Heath

2 Hairy Sea Heath

Smooth, 1 Smooth Sea Heath The root is woody, of a blackish colour, and very bitter to the taste The stalks are ligneous, round, smooth, trailing, of a reddish colour, and ten or twelve inches long The leaves are slender, short, blunt, smooth, and grow in clusters at the joints The flowers come out singly from the ends of the branches, they are small, of a reddish-purple colour, appear in August and September, and the seeds ripen in October

and Hairy Sea Heath described 2 Hairy Sea Heath The root is woody, long, and of a white colour The stalks are hairy, six or eight inches long, and partly procumbent The leaves are spear-shaped, short, and grow six or eight together at a joint The flowers come out in clusters from the ends of the branches, they are of a white colour, appear in July and August, and the seeds ripen in the autumn

Culture. These sorts are raised by sowing the seeds in some dry, warm, sandy part of the garden, in the spring of the year, and after the plants come up they will require no trouble, except thinning them where they are too close, and keeping them clean from weeds

Titles 1 Smooth Sea Heath is titled, *Frankenia foliis linearibus basi ciliatis* Van Royen calls it, *Frankenia foliis confertis*, Sauvages, *Frankenia foliis aciformibus congestis* Guettard, *Franca floribus solitariis sessilibus, foliis prismaticis triangularibus*, Micheli, *Franca maritima supina saxatilis glauca ericoides sempervirens, flore purpureo*, Tilli, *Anthyllis repens Italica, thymi foliis, rubente flore, polygoni facie*, Barrelier, *Polygonum fruticosum supinum ericoides cinereum, thymi folio, Hispanicum*, Caspar Bauhine, *Polygonum maritimum, foliis serpylli*, John Bauhine, *Cal. s vermiculari marinæ non dissimilis planta*, and Ray, *Lychnis supina maritima ericæ facie* It grows naturally in maritime parts of England, and the southern countries of Europe

2 Hairy Sea Heath is, *Frankenia caulibus hirsutis, floribus fasciculatis terminalibus* Micheli calls it, *Franca maritima supina multiflora candida, caulibus hirsutis, foliis quasi vermiculatis*, Caspar Bauhine, *Polygonum Creticum thymi folio*, and Tournefort, *Alsine Cretica maritima supina, caule hirsuto, foliis quasi vermiculatis* It grows naturally in Crete and Apulia

*Frankenia* is of the class and order *Hexandria Monogynia*, and the characters are, Class and order in the Linnæan system The characters

1 CALYX is a monophyllous subcylindrical, decagonal, permanent perianthium, divided at the top into five acute spreading segments

2 COROLLA is five petals Their ungues are the length of the calyx The limb is plane, and the laminæ are roundish and patent. The nectarium is inserted in the respective ungues of the petals

3 STAMINA are six filaments the length of the calyx, having roundish didymous antheræ

4 PISTILLUM consists of an oblong germen, a simple style the length of the stamina, and three oblong, erect, obtuse stigmas

4 PERICARPIUM is one oval capsule, composed of three valves, and containing one cell

6 SEMINA. The seeds are many, oval, and small

CHAP

# CHAP. CCI.

## *FRITILLARIA*, FRITILLARY.

*FRITILLARIA* now ſwallows up many genera of authors It contains the Fritillary, *Petilium, Corona Imperialis*, and *Lilio Fritillaria* of Tournefort, Boerhaave, and others, ſo that the Gardener will find, under this head, a conſiderable ſhare of bulbous ſpring flowering plants, which he has been uſed to ſeek for under other titles The flowers that belong to this genus may be divided into three claſſes, viz

Species
1 Crown Imperials
2 Fritillaries
3 Perſian Lilies

### 1 Of Crown Imperials

Crown Imperials deſcribed — The Crown Imperials are well known plants, and originally took their name from the tuft or bunch of leaves above the flowers This tuft has very improperly been called a crown, though the flower itſelf has a majeſtick look, and if any thing, it ought to be called the King of the earlieſt bulbous-flowering tribe that adorn the ſpring, as it grows much taller than any other It is in every reſpect of a larger ſubſtance, ſtands among them with an air of majeſty, and ſeems to demand obedience and reſpect

The varieties with which it adorns the ſcene are numerous, and their number is ſtill annually encreaſed by good culture and management In its original ſtate it is of a duſky red colour This is the parent of them all It was brought into Europe from Conſtantinople about two hundred years ago, it ſoon became pretty common in our gardens, its grand appearance ſoon made it noticed, and its hardineſs and eaſe of culture ſoon rendered it common It encreaſes very faſt by the roots and ſeeds, and from hence new varieties have been formed, ſo that our gardens now have in tolerable plenty,

Varieties
The Old Crown Imperial
The Golden Crown Imperial
The Lemon-coloured Crown Imperial
The Gold-ſtriped Crown Imperial
The Bright-red Crown Imperial
The Late Red Crown Imperial
The Majeſtick Crown Imperial
The Double yellow Crown Imperial
The Double-red Crown Imperial
The Triple Crown Imperial
The Broad-leaved large-flowering Crown Imperial
The Gold Striped-leaved Crown Imperial
The Silver Striped-leaved Crown Imperial

All theſe varieties adorn our gardens in the ſpring, they uſher in the tall flowering tribe, and demand the attention of all

But let us ſee what a Crown Imperial is The root we find to be a large, thick, round bulb, compoſed of many juicy ſcales, it is of a yellow colour, here and there a little tinged with purple, and of a very diſagreeable ſtrong ſmell The ſtalk will grow to a yard or more in height; its colour is a light-green, and it is very thick, firm, and ſucculent The leaves are long and narrow, in proportion to ſuch a ſtalk; of a light green colour, ſmooth, and their edges are entire The flowers ſurround the ſtalks near the top on ſhort footſtalks; they are of a campanulated figure, large, and bend downwards, each of them is compoſed of ſix petals. At the baſe of each petal is the nectarium, which is a cavity filled with a honey-like juice, and the general characters of the flower indicate the ſtamina and other parts Above this noble general flower, compoſed of ſo many florets ſurrounding the tops of the ſtalks in this pleaſing pendulous manner, is a very large tuft of leaves, which are long, narrow, and pointed; and this is what is called the Crown, and gives an air of majeſty to the whole plant Such is the Crown Imperial, a plant which will be in blow the beginning of April, a time when no other of the tall growing flowers make their appearance The ſeeds will be ripe in July, and from theſe all the varieties have been obtained, and by theſe more may be eaſily added The method is tedious; ſix or ſeven years will elapſe before they are brought to flower in perfection, but if any one is poſſeſſed of this patience, and has leiſure for ſuch a performance, he may raiſe them in the following manner

Method of obtaining varieties — Let ſeeds be gathered from the largeſt and beſt plants, ſuch as are poſſeſſed of the moſt flowers, and the brighteſt colours, for I would have no ſeeds from your duſky reds, or bad yellows, which will probably produce others of the like diſagreeable tints Sow them in boxes in the autumn filled with rich light earth; ſet them in a well-ſheltered place, and in the ſpring they will come up Keep them clean from weeds, water them frequently, and as the days encreaſe in length ſet them entirely in the ſhade In theſe boxes let them remain all ſummer, and in October ſift over them a little freſh earth, let them have their former ſituation all winter, and in the ſpring, when the plants come up, give them now and then a little watering In July the leaves will decay, or ſooner Againſt that time let a bed be prepared of good light earth In this plant the largeſt bulbs a foot aſunder, and let them ſtand until they ſhew their flowers The ſmaller bulbs may be ſcattered on another bed together with the mould on which they grow, and ſome freſh earth ſifted over them an inch and a half thick The year following take up the bulbs in July, and plant them in beds a foot aſunder Here let them ſtand until they ſhew their flowers; when thoſe of the beſt properties ſhould be marked out for the flower-garden, and the worſt, after having flowered two or three ſeaſons, and ſhewed no ſigns of altering for the better, ſhould be thrown away

Manner of propagating theſe plants — The moſt general way to propagate theſe plants is by offsets, and by this way the varieties in their perfection may be continued The beſt time for this buſineſs is July, the ſtalks will then be in a ſtate of decay, and the bulbs ripe for removing When this is done, the ſmaller bulbs ſhould be planted by themſelves in the nurſery-ground, to gain ſtrength, and the ſtrongeſt planted in the borders, to keep up the ſucceſſion of flowering They ſhould not be removed oftener than every four or five years If you want great encreaſe, and the ground is not ready for their reception, they will keep good two or three months in a cool place,

place, or if laid in sand. Almost any soil will suit them, though they thrive best in a deep, fat, garden mould; there their stalks will rise to a greater height, and shew their flowers in greater majesty and perfection.

In a general shew of Crown Imperials as in tended, and many strong bulbs in their numerous varieties are provided for the purpose, they should be planted at near a yard distance from each other, especially if the soil is rich and good, for many of them will grow to be upwards of four feet high, and their majestic appearance will be diminished if they are crowded.

## 2. Of FRITILLARIES.

Fritillaries described. No one at first view can hardly be made to believe that the Fritillary, in species only of the same genus with the Crown Imperial: their appearance is vastly different, and their nature and composition seem to be of a different sort; but Science, in its improved state, has now taught us, that they are of the same fraternity, and that the generic distinctions are found to belong equally and alike to both these plants. The botanists seem to admit of but two real species, though so many imaginary ones have been formed and titled by botanists. These in a general sense may be called,

Varieties. The Alternate-leaved Fritillary.
The Opposite-leaved Fritillary.

The great variety which we see in our gardens belong to one or other of these species, and the many sorts which the Dutch catalogues contain, are all of them expressed by these two names, the Opposite and the Alternate-leaved Fritillary. They are all justly ranked among the best sorts of our early bulbous flowers, and are a great ornament to our borders in the spring; for there is a delicacy as well as great beauty attending them, and their inverted flowers, in such great variety, have a striking effect at so early a time of the year as the greatest part of them will be in blow. But let us examine the two species distinctly, and, 1.

described. The Alternate-leaved Fritillary. The root is a white, depressed, succulent bulb. The stalk will grow to about a foot in height: it is upright, slender, round, and of a brownish green colour, often tinged with purple. The leaves are but few, long, and narrow, and grow in the alternate way. At the top of the stalk hang one or more flowers, which are large, very beautiful, and of different colours, sizes, and properties, according to the varieties of this species.

2. The Opposite-leaved Fritillary. This hath a double, soft, fleshy, naked bulb. The stalk will be of different heights in the different varieties; the mean is about a foot; it is round, and erect, but slender. The leaves are long and narrow, though broader than the preceding sort, and their colour is a deep green; they grow by pairs on the lower part of the stalk, but higher, and stand alternately. This is the regular position of the leaves of all the varieties that belong to this species. At the top of the stalk hang the flowers, which are large, bell-shaped, and of different colours, sizes, and properties, according to the different varieties of this species.

These are the two species which comprehend the vast variety of our Fritillaries, and from hence arise the early Purple, the late Purple, the Red, Green, White, Black, Yellow, Double, Umbelliferous, and the different sorts of the chequered and spotted Fritillaries. Besides these, there are differences in their leaves, height of their stalks, and time of flowering. Some ornament our gardens in March, others again will shew themselves in blow even in June. Some have broad leaves, others narrower. The stalks are longer or shorter as it happens, and the different tinges of the different leaves and stalks still cause a greater variety of the flowers.

Numerous, however, as the varieties are, their number is still encreased by the industry of the Dutch, who spare no pains, as they want no patience, in raising these and most other bulbous plants from seeds. In order to obtain the same success with them in this laudable emulation let such plants be marked out for seeds as have the best properties; that is, such as have large flowers of good colour, and the stalks with the fewest leaves. In the beginning of August sow them in pots or boxes of rich garden mould, then place them in the shade, and all winter let them have a well-sheltered warm place. In the spring the plants will come up, at which time keep them clean from weeds, water them frequently, set them in the shade as the heat encreases, and here they may stand with this management all summer. In the autumn take up all the roots, and plant them at about four inches asunder, in a bed of light earth prepared in a well-sheltered place; at the same time do not throw the mould away in which they grew, but scatter it in another bed, and sift over it some fresh soil, about an inch and a half deep, and then the smallest bulbs will be saved. In these beds they may remain until they flower, which will be in about two or three years, and when they blow, mark those with the best properties to be taken up to be planted in the flower-garden. The time of flowering also should be marked, and they should be classed in different beds accordingly; for nothing is more ridiculous than to plant the early blowers with the late flowering kinds. When they are set out in these beds for good, they should be allowed the distance of about a foot, and they need not be removed oftener than every three or four years, by which time they will have made amazing increase, for they multiply very fast by offsets. The time for removing them is in the summer, when the stalks are decayed; against which time beds should be provided for their immediate reception, for they will not bear to be kept long out of the ground; and with this ease may these beautiful plants be encreased at pleasure. Culture.

## 3. Of PERSIAN LILIES.

Of these there are but few varieties, and their appearance is altogether very different from any of the beforementioned sorts. It is a distinct family in this tribe, and the number and disposition of the flowers make it both elegant and striking. The Dwarf and Common Persian Lily are the chief sorts that compose it, and little variation of their natural colour from seeds may be expected, so that it is not worth while to propagate them that way in hopes of variety. The best method is to obtain first of all a few plants, and after that they will multiply very fast by the roots. The root is a large, round, whitish bulb. The stalk is round, upright, firm, and will grow to about a yard in height. This is the size of the Common Persian Lily; the Dwarf variety will hardly grow to half that height. The leaves are long, narrow, pointed, obliquely waved, and grow on every side of the stalk. The flowers themselves terminate the stalk in a large pyramidical spike; they have footstalks, and are placed in a pendulous manner, like the other species of this genus. Each flower is but small in proportion to the others. They spread wide at the brims, and their colour is a deep purple; of this there are different tinges, the inside of all are paler than the outside, Persian Lilies described.

outside and a greenish cast is commonly found at the base of the petals These plants make a fine variety in our flower-gardens, and it is a species worthy of all care and management We received it from Susa almost two hundred years ago, and ever since it has been encreased and carefied in our gardens

Culture

It is to be propagated by seeds or by offsets, in the same manner as the Fritillaries, though the seeds should be procured from abroad, as they seldom produce them good with us

Titles

1 The Crown Imperial is titled, *Fritillaria racemo comoso inferne nudo, foliis integerrimis* In the *Hortus Cliffort* it is called, *Petilium foliis caulinis* Caspar Bauhine calls it, *Lilium, sive Corona Imperialis*, Clusius, *Lusai* It grows naturally in Persia

2 The Alternate Leaved Fritillary is, *Fritillaria caule subunifloro, foliis omnibus alternis* Caspar Bauhine calls it, *Fritillaria præcox purpurea variegata*, and Renealm, *Meleagris* It grows naturally in England, also in Italy, France, and Austria

3 Opposite-leaved Fritillary is termed, *Fritillaria caule multifloro, foliis infimis oppositis* Caspar Bauhine calls it, *Fritillaria flore minore*, Clusius, *Fritillaria Pyrenæa* It is a native of the Pyrenees

4 Persian Lily, *Fritillaria racemo nudiusculo, foliis obliquis* Dodonæus calls it, *Lilium Persicum*, and Clusius, *Lilium Susianum* The Dutch kind is expressed by *Fritillaria racemosa, seu Lilium Persicum minus* It grows naturally in Persia

Class and order in the Linnæan system

*Fritillaria* is of the class and order *Hexandria Monogynia*, and the characters are,

The characters

1 Calyx There is none

2 Corolla is of a campanulate figure, broad at the base, and composed of six oblong parallel petals at the base of each petal is a cavity, and that is the nectarium

3 Stamina are six subulated filaments presting upon the style, with oblong, erect, four-cornered antheræ

4 Pistillum consists of an oblong three-cornered, obtuse germen, a simple style longer than the stamina, and a triple, spreading, obtuse stigma

5 Pericarpium is an oblong, obtuse, trilobate capsule of three cells

6 Semina The seeds are numerous they are flat, semiorbiculated externally, and placed in a double order

# CHAP. CCII.

## FUMARIA, FUMATORY.

Species

THERE are of this genus,

1 Tuberous Fumatory
2 Bulbous Fumatory
3 Evergreen Perennial Fumatory
4 Nine-leaved Fumatory

Description of the Tuberous

1 Tuberous Fumatory The root is fleshy, about the size of a nutmeg, and full of insipid juice The leaves are composed of three principal parts, each of which is divided into smaller, having narrow folioles deeply cut into three segments, they rise immediately from the root, their number is usually about three or four only, and they grow on slender footstalks The flower-stalk is wholly destitute of leaves, and grows to about nine inches high The flowers are seldom more than five or six, and form a kind of loose spike at the top of the stalk, they are of a dull white colour, and the general characters shew their composition, they appear in May, but are very seldom succeeded by seeds in England

and Bulbous Fumatory

2 Bulbous Fumatory Of this plant there are three notable varieties, viz

Hollow Bulbous-rooted Fumatory
Greater Solid Bulbous-rooted Fumatory
Smaller Solid Bulbous-rooted Fumatory.

Varieties described

Hollow Bulbous-rooted Fumatory The root is large, fleshy, and hollow in the middle The leaves divide into many parts, and the folioles are short, obtuse, and of a light green colour The stalk is simple, grows to about six inches high, and is adorned with one or two leaves near the bottom The flowers are produced in spikes from the tops of the stalks they are of a reddish-purple colour, appear in May, and are very rarely succeeded by seeds in England

Greater Solid Bulbous rooted Fumatory The root of this plant is large, round, solid, and of a yellow colour The leaves are composed of many parts, like the former, and the radical ones grow on slender footstalks The stalks are undivided, usually naked, a little angular, and grow to about four or five inches high The flowers are produced in spikes at the tops of the stalks, they are of a purple colour, appear in April, and are seldom succeeded by seeds in England

There is a sort of this variety with greenish flowers

Smaller Solid Bulbous-rooted Fumatory The root is a small, round, simple, solid, fleshy bulb The leaves branch out into many divisions, and the folioles are small, and of a light-green colour The stalks are simple, angular, and grow but to about four inches high The flowers are produced in single spikes from the ends of the stalks, they are of a reddish-purple colour, appear early in April, but are rarely followed by good seeds in England

Evergreen Perennial Fumatory

3 Evergreen Perennial Fumatory The root is fibrous, and sends forth several angular stalks, which divide into numerous branches, and grow to about nine inches high The leaves are very much divided, and composed of numerous, small, obtuse folioles of a dark green colour The flowers come out in panicles from the ends of the branches, they are small, of a bright-yellow colour, appear early in the spring, and often continue in succession all summer

Varieties

There is a variety of this plant with whitish, and another with pale-yellow flowers, all of which continue green during the winter, and frequently

quently flower at that season, if the weather is mild and open

4 Nine leaved Fumatory The root is fibrous, but I am not certain whether it is a perennial, or if it decays soon after the seeds are perfected, certain it is, however, that when once a plant has flowered it will continue its succession by scattered seeds, and be every year found as a perennial in or about the same spot, though it be on the top of an old wall, where this plant will grow very well The stalks are slender, divide into numerous branches, and lie on the ground The leaves are triternate, each being composed of nine heart-shaped folioles, which are small, and of a light-green colour The flowers are produced in kind of panicles from the sides of the branches, they are small, of a greenish-white colour, appear early in summer, and often continue in succession to the end of autumn

*and Nine leaved Fumitory*

The first two species, including their varieties, are propagated by offsets from the roots These should be taken off in the summer, when the leaves decay, they should be planted in a light soil, have a shady situation, and they will resist the severest cold The leaves arise early in the autumn from their roots, continue green all winter, and early in the spring the flower-stalks come out, but the flowers very rarely produce good seeds, neither do they multiply very fast by offsets from the roots, so that wherever the seed can be procured it should be preserved with all diligence by those who are fond of these spring flowering plants As soon as the seeds are ripe they should be gathered, and spread on a sheet of white paper, to lie for a few days to dry, and then sown in pots or boxes filled with light sandy earth, the boxes should be set in the shade, and the mould watered as often as dry weather makes it necessary In about five or six weeks the seeds will come up, and if any weeds appear with them, they must be carefully drawn out, otherwise, when their roots get strong, they will draw up the young plants with them In the autumn the leaves of the plants will decay, the surface of the mould should be then stirred, and about half an inch depth of the finest mould sifted over the top This being done, they should be set in a well-sheltered place (but not under the drip of trees) for the winter In the spring they should be removed into the shade, watered as often as dry weather makes it necessary, and constantly weeded in summer, about the middle of which season the leaves will decay The bulbs should be now taken up and planted in beds four inches asunder, where they may stand one or two years, according to the strength of the plant, and then be set out in the places where they are designed to remain

*The method of propagating them*

The last two sorts are propagated by sowing the seeds soon after they are ripe They will readily come up in any soil or situation, flower the summer following, scatter their seeds, and soon produce you more plants than you could wish for They will grow upon old walls, ruins, buildings, &c and are a very proper ornament for such places where they are designedly introduced into a garden

1 Tuberous Fumatory is titled, *Fumaria scapo nudo* In the Memoirs of the Royal Academy at Paris it is termed, *B cucullata Canadensis, radice tuberosâ squamata* Cornutus calls it, *Fumaria tuberosa insipida*, Plukenet, *Fumaria siliquosa, radice grumosa, flore bicorporeo ad labia conjuncto, Virginiana*, and Boerhaave, *Capnorchis Americana* It grows naturally in Virginia and Canada *Titles*

2 Bulbous Fumatory is, *Fumaria caule simplici, bracteis longitudine florum* In the *Hortus Cliffort* it is termed, *Fumaria caule simplicissimo diphyllo floribus calyce destitutis* Fuchsius calls it, *Pistolochia*, Caspar Bauhine, *Fumaria bulbosa, radice cavâ, major*, also, *Fumaria bulbosa, radice non cavâ major*, also, *Fumaria bulbosa, radice non cavâ, minor* It grows naturally in forests and shady places in many parts of Europe

3 Evergreen Perennial Fumatory is, *Fumaria siliquis linearibus tetragonis, caulibus diffusis acutangulis* In the *Hortus Cliffort* it is termed, *Fumaria caule ramoso, siliquis oblongis, radice perenni* Caspar Bauhine calls it, *Fumaria lutea*, Dalechamp, *Fumaria lutea montana*; and Plukenet, *Fumaria Tingitana, radice fibrosâ, perenni, flore ex albo flavescente, siliquis curtis* It grows naturally in Mauritania, Italy, and France

4 Nine-leaved Fumitory is, *Fumaria foliis triternatis foliolis cordatis* Tournefort calls it, *Fumaria Hispanica saxatilis, foliis amplioribus cordiformibus, semine compresso*, Boccone, *Fumaria enneaphyllos Hispanica saxatilis*, and Plukenet, *Fumaria radice fibrosâ, foliis ad petiolum sinuatis crassioribus* It grows in the concavities of rocks, and stony barren places in Spain and Sicily

*Fumaria* is of the class and order *Diadelphia Hexandria*, and the characters are, *Class and order in the Linnaean system*

1 CALYX is a perianthium composed of two small, deciduous, equal, erect, acute leaves placed opposite *The characters*

2 COROLLA is oblong, tubular, and ringent The upper lip is plane, obtuse, emarginated, and reflexed The nectarium is situated at the base, it is prominent and obtuse The lower lip is in all respects like the upper, but keeled at the base The nectarium is carinated, and less prominent than that at the base of the upper-lip The faux is four-cornered, obtuse, and perpendicularly bifid

3 STAMINA are two equal, broad, acuminated filaments included in the two lips, each filament being terminated by three antheræ

4 PISTILLUM consists of an oblong, compressed, acuminated germen, a short style, and a round, erect, compressed stigma

5 PERICARPIUM is a short pod containing one cell

6 SEMINA The seeds are roundish

CHAP

# CHAP. CCIII.

## GALANTHUS, The SNOW-DROP

THE commonness of the Snow-Drop makes it little regarded by many, and its ease of culture too frequently neglected, but due reflection would teach them better, for whoever considers the Snow-Drop properly, must view it in a very desirable light It is small and elegant, and of as different a nature as possible to the rambling kind, it is compact, and full of flowers at the time of blow, which is a season when hardly any other flowers are to be met with, and to see how it rears its head among the snow, challenging to shew colours with it in the perfection of whiteness, is at once a very pleasing, bold, and daring look

This plant described

Of the Snow-Drop there is only one real species, but that is divided into three varieties

Varieties

The Single Snow-Drop
The Semi-double Snow-Drop
The Full-double Snow Drop

All these are beautiful, and each has its time of flowering The Single Snow-Drop leads the van, and will often shew itself in January, then follows the Semi-double, and after that the Double, which will not entirely have done flowering before March has entered on his blustering reign They all grow delightfully in uncultivated places, and here Nature intends them to appear in the greatest lustre Their beauty is much diminished by being planted singly in gardens, or for edgings, as is commonly practised, but to see them burst forth even through the turf in large bunches, there they shew themselves as Nature designed them By this is not meant that they should be excluded the garden No, they are to share in our borders, and at the same time are to adorn our wilderness quarters, borders of our woods, closes of resort, and uncultivated borders of all sorts The Single, though not so large a flower, is as valuable as the Double, on account of its early appearance, and they are all to be so stationed as to shew themselves in one or other of the varieties for as long a time as possible

But let us examine this plant more closely And here we find the root to be a small coated bulb, blackish without, white within, and very juicy The leaves are long, narrow, and of a bluish-green colour Among these rises the flower-stalk, which is naked, angular, of a pale-green colour, and will grow to about four or five inches in height At the top of the stalk is the spatha, from which issues a single flower, that hangs down It is composed of three hollowed petals, and the nectarium, which also consists of three parts The petals are of a pure white colour, but the nectarium near the bottom is tinged with green The nectarium constitutes a considerable share in this flower, it is of a firmer substance than the petals, and the three parts of which it is composed are placed alternately with the petals, and have a very good effect In short, the whole is a very delicate flower, and the effect is more wonderful by its bold and unshaken appearance at so rigorous a season

Single Snow-Drop described

The Snow-Drops are propagated by parting of the roots. They will grow at any time of the year, but the best season for it is in June, when the leaves are decayed The roots should not be divided oftener than every four or five years, that they may form themselves into large clumps, for then they appear in their best form They will keep out of the ground until autumn, if required, and when planted I would advise the placing at least half a dozen bulbs together, for by the modern method of planting them singly, they have for a year or two a very straggling insignificant look

Method of raising them

As this genus is divided into no species, the Snow-Drop stands simply with the title *Galanthus* Old writers have called it, *Leucojum bulbosum*, those of later date, *Narcisso-leucojum* Renealme terms it, *Erangelia*, and others have greatly erred in classing of this flower, the true *Leucojum* having six petals, and no nectarium, and is a very different plant from the Snow-Drop It is a native of the Alps, and frequently found at the bottoms of mountains in many parts of Italy, Austria &c

Titles

*Galanthus* is of the class and order *Hexandria Monogynia*, and the characters are,

Class and order in the Linnæan system

1 CALYX is an oblong, obtuse, compressed, withering spatha, that opens sideways

The characters.

2 COROLLA consists of three oblong, obtuse, concave, loose, spreading petals of equal size, and the nectarium, which is cylindrical, and composed of three parallel, obtuse, emarginated leaves about half the length of the petals

3 STAMINA are six very short capillary filaments, with oblong acuminated, connivent antheræ

4 PISTILLUM consists of an oval germen situated below the flower, a filiforme style longer than the stamina, and a simple stigma

5 PERICARPIUM is an oval, three-cornered, obtuse capsule of three cells

6 SEMINA The seeds are numerous, and of a roundish figure

## CHAP. CCIV.

## *GALEGA*, GOAT's RUE

THE species of this genus proper for this place is the common Goat's-Rue of the shops

The plant described. The root is thick, white, composed of many strong fibres, and sends forth several striated hollow stalks, which grow to the height of about a yard The leaves are pinnated, and each consists of six or seven pair of narrow, spear-shaped, entire, smooth folioles, terminated by an odd one The flowers come out from the wings of the leaves in spikes, their colour is a pale blue, and the general characters indicate their structure, they appear in June, and are succeeded by long taper pods, containing ripe seeds, in August

Varieties. There is a variety of this species with white, one with striped leaves, and another with larger leaves, larger and longer spikes of flowers, and thicker pods

Medicinal properties of this plant. The juice of Goat's Rue is good for killing the worms in children, expelling of poison, and is a great preservative against pestilential disorders, it is a fine sudorifick, an excellent pectoral, a powerful febrifuge, and useful in malignant diseases of most kinds

The young leaves were formerly eaten as sallad herbs with oil and vinegar, and also boiled as greens to be eat with meat; but now the many admirable esculents of the kitchen-garden have made them in a great measure disused for those purposes

Culture. They are raised by sowing the seeds any time in the autumn or spring When the plants come up they should be thinned to proper distances, and kept clean from weeds, and this is all the trouble they will require If the seeds are permitted to scatter, they will come up spontaneously, and afford you plenty of plants for any purpose Nevertheless, when large quantities of these plants are to be raised for medicinal purposes, the seeds should be sown in beds of fine mould, and when the plants are fit to remove, they should be set in rows in double dug ground, at about a foot and a half asunder The ground should be dug between the rows every winter, constantly kept clean from weeds in the summer, and this will cause them to shoot vigorously, and become of the best perfection for use

Titles. This species is titled, *Galega leguminibus strictis erectis, foliolis lanceolatis striatis nudis* In the *Hortus Cliffort* it is termed, *Galega* Caspar Bauhine calls it, *Galega vulgaris* It grows naturally in Spain, Italy, and Africa

Class and order in the Linnæan System. *Galega* is of the class and order *Diadelphia Decandria*, and the characters are,

The characters. 1 CALYX is a small, tubular, monophyllous perianthium, cut into five awl-shaped equal parts

2 COROLLA is papilionaceous The vexillum is large, oval, and reflexed The alæ are oblong, and almost as long as the vexillum The carina is oblong, compressed, gibbous, erect, and acute

3 STAMINA are diadelphous, nine filaments being joined in a body, the other standing singly, having oblong antheræ

4 PISTILLUM consists of a slender oblong germen, and a rising style shorter than the germen, with a small terminal punctum

5 PERICARPIUM is a long, compressed, striated, acuminated pod

6 SEMINA The seeds are many, oblong, and kidney-shaped

## CHAP CCV

## *GALEOPSIS*, HEDGE-NETTLE.

OF this genus there is only one species that is a perennial, which is usually called, Yellow Nettle Hemp

The plant described. The stalks are hollow, angular, and about a foot or more in length The leaves are oval, pointed, acutely serrated, and grow on footstalks by pairs on the branches The flowers are of a golden-yellow colour, they grow in whorls round the stalks among the leaves, each whorl consists of six flowers, which have a four leaved involucrum They will be in blow in May and June, and afford good seeds in July and August

Culture. The propagation of this plant is by its creeping root, a bit of which being taken off in the autumn, winter, or spring, will soon afford you as much of this sort as you can desire

It may easily be propagated by sowing the seeds, which should be in the worst part of the garden, soon after they are ripe After the plants come up you should destroy them all with the weeds, except three or four plants for observation or variety, for that will be a sufficient number to retain of this species

Titles. Yellow Nettle Hemp is titled, *Galeopsis verticillis sexfloris involucro tetraphyllo* In the *Hortus Cliffort* it is termed, *Leonurus foliis ovatis serratis acutis*

*acutis* Caspar Bauhine calls it, *Lamium folio oblongo luteum* and Dodonæus, *Urtica iners tertia, sive Lamium flore luteo* It grows naturally in woods and shady places in England, and most parts of Europe

Class and order in the Linnæan system The characters

*Galeopsis* is of the class and order *Didynamia Gymnospermia*, and the characters are,

1 CALYX is a monophyllous tubulous perianthium, divided into five parts, which end in long, sharp, bearded points

2 COROLLA is ringent The tube is short, and the limb open The faux is rather broader than the tube, and the length of the calyx, it is sharply indented above the base of the lower-lip, below it is concave The upper-lip is roundish, concave, and serrated at the top The lower lip is trifid, the two side segments are roundish, and the middle one, which is the largest, is crenated

3 STAMINA are four subulated filaments inclosed in the upper-lip, with roundish bifid antheræ

4 PISTILLUM consists of a quadrifid germen, a filiforme style the length and situation of the stamina, and a bifid acute stigma

5 PERICARPIUM There is none The seeds are contained in the bottom of the calyx

6 SEMINA The seeds are four

# CHAP. CCVI.

## *GALIUM*, LADIES BED STRAW, or CHEESE RENNET

THE perennials of this genus go by the respective names of,

Species

1 Common Yellow Ladies Bed-Straw, or Cheese-Rennet
2 Wild Madder, or Great-branching Madder
3 Mountain Ladies Bed Straw.
4 Glaucous Ladies Bed Straw
5 Purple Ladies Bed-Straw
6 Narrow leaved Red Ladies Bed Straw
7 Cross-Wort Meadow-Madder
8 Round leaved Madder
9 The Least Goose-Grass
10 Smooth Flax-leaved Madder
11 Bearded Madder
12 Broad-leaved Red Ladies Bed-Straw
13 White Marsh Ladies Bed-Straw
14 Marsh Goose-Grass
15 Rock Ladies Bed-Straw
16 Dwarf Ladies Bed Straw
17 Least Ladies Bed-Straw

Description of the Common Yellow Ladies Bed Straw,

1 Common Yellow Ladies Bed-Straw, or Cheese Rennet The root is creeping The stalk is round, weak two feet long, tender, and sends forth short floriferous branches by pairs from the joints The leaves are elegant, narrow, furrowed, and eight of them usually surround the stalk in a star-like manner at a joint The flowers come out in long clusters from the ends of the stalks and branches, they are of a beautiful yellow colour, make their appearance in May, June, and July, and frequently shew themselves afresh in the autumn

Wild or Great branching Madder

2 Wild, or Great branching Madder The root is creeping The stalks are long, slender, flaccid, and send forth several branches by pairs, which are spreading, and lie on the ground The leaves grow eight together from the sides of the stalks, they are oval, narrow, slightly serrated, smooth, shining, sharp-pointed, and spreading The flowers come out in clusters from the ends of the main-stalk and branches, they are of a white colour, appear in May and June, and often continue in succession the greatest part of the summer

Mountain

3 Mountain Ladies Bed Straw The stalks are small, weak, procumbent, rough, and send forth floriferous branches by pairs from the sides The leaves grow four or five together, are narrow, sharp pointed, and smooth The flowers are produced in clusters from the ends of the main stalk and branches, they are of a white colour, appear in May and June, and often again at different times of the summer

and Glaucous Ladies Bed-Straw

4 Glaucous Ladies Bed-Straw The stalks are weak, jointed, smooth, and a foot and a half long The leaves are narrow, of a grey colour, and surround the stalks in whorls at the joints The flowers are produced on forked footstalks from the ends and sides of the stalks, their colour is yellow, and they appear great part of the summer

Variety

There is a variety of this plant with white flowers

Purple

5 Purple Ladies Bed Straw The stalks are slender, partly procumbent, and about two feet long The leaves are narrow, bristly, and grow in whorls round the stalks The flowers are produced from the ends and sides of the stalks on long footstalks they are of a blackish purple colour, and shew themselves great part of the summer

and Narrow-leaved Ladies Bed-Straw

6 Narrow-leaved Red Ladies Bed-Straw The stalks are slender, about a foot long, nearly upright, and send forth branches by pairs from the joints The leaves are narrow, spreading, and grow in whorls round the stalks The flowers are produced in clusters from the ends and sides of the branches on short footstalks, they are of a dark red colour, and shew themselves at different times in the summer

and Cross wort Madder described

7 Cross-wort Madder The stalks are nearly erect, smooth, very little branching, and about two feet high The leaves are spear-shaped, acute, trinervous, smooth, and four of them surround the stalks at the joints The flowers come out in whorls round the stalks, and terminate the branches in small clusters, they are of a white colour, appear in June, July, and all summer,

ſummer, and are ſucceeded by rough ſeeds, which ripen in due order of ſucceſſion.

Round leaved Madder,

8. Round-leaved Madder. Of this ſpecies there are two varieties, one with a ſmooth, and another with a rough ſtalk. The leaves of both ſorts are oval, and ſurround the ſtalks by fours at the joints, but thoſe of the firſt variety are ſmooth and obtuſe, whereas the leaves of the latter are rough, hairy, ciliated, and prickly. The flowers come out in cluſters from the ends and ſides of the branches, they are ſmall, of a white colour, and appear moſt of the ſummer months.

Leaſt Gooſe Graſs,

9. The Leaſt Gooſe Graſs. This is a low plant, riſing with ſeveral ſmall, weak, ſquare, rough-jointed ſtalks, which grow to about a foot long. The leaves are ſpear-ſhaped, narrow, ſharp pointed, rough, and ſeven of them uſually ſurround the ſtalks in a ſtar-like manner at the joints. The flowers come out from the ends and ſides of the branches, growing two or three together on naked footſtalks, they are ſmall, and of a yellow colour, appear greateſt part of the ſummer, and are followed by rough ſeeds. There is a variety of this with dark-purple coloured flowers.

Smooth Flax leaved,

10. Smooth Flax-leaved Madder. The ſtalks of this ſpecies are ſmooth, ſlender, ſend forth branches by pairs, and grow to about a foot high. The leaves are ſpear-ſhaped, ſmooth, ſtiff, and eight or nine of them ſurround the ſtalks at the joints. The flowers are produced in panicles from the tops of the ſtalks, they are ſmall, and of a white colour, appear great part of the ſummer, and are followed by ſmooth, double berries, each containing two large ſeeds.

and Bearded Madder;

11. Bearded Madder. The ſtalks of this ſpecies divide into numerous branches, which are ſmooth, and entangle one among another. The leaves are ſpear-ſhaped, mucronated, ſmooth on both ſides, except on their edges which are rough, and four of them ſurround the ſtalks at the joints. The flowers grow in panicles from the tops of the branches, they are ſmall, and three uſually grow together on a footſtalk. Their colour is whitiſh, having yellow antheræ, and each of them is cut into four bearded, ſharp-pointed ſegments. They appear in May and June, and again in the autumn, and are ſucceeded by ſmooth, double berries, each containing two large, ſmooth, kidney-ſhaped ſeeds.

Broad leaved Red,

12. Broad-leaved Red Ladies Bed-ſtraw. The ſtalks of this ſpecies are upright, firm, and about two feet high. The leaves are ſpear-ſhaped, oval, broad, rough underneath, equal, and four of them ſurround the ſtalks at the joints. The flowers come out in ſhort panicles from the upper parts of the plant. They make their appearance in June, and other parts of the ſummer, and are ſucceeded by ſmooth ſeeds, which ripen in about a month after the flowers are fallen.

and White Marſh Ladies Bed ſtraw,

13. White Marſh Ladies Bed-ſtraw. The ſtalks of this ſpecies are ſlender, ſmooth, ſend our numerous branches by pairs oppoſite from the ſides, and, unleſs ſupported, lie on the ground. The leaves are oval, equal, ſmooth, and four ſurround the ſtalks at the joints. The flowers are produced in great plenty from the ends and ſides of the branches, they are ſmall, of a white colour, and ſhew themſelves moſt of the ſummer months.

Marſh Gooſe Graſs,

14. Marſh Gooſe Graſs. The ſtalks of this ſpecies are ſlender, herbaceous, and about a foot and a half high. The leaves are ſpear-ſhaped, ſharply ſerrated, ſtiff, mucronated, and ſix of them grow together round the ſtalks. The flowers are produced in great plenty from the upper parts of the plant, they are ſmall, of a white colour, and ſhew themſelves during moſt of the ſummer months.

Rock

15. Rock Ladies Bed-ſtraw. The ſtalks of this ſpecies are weak, very much branching, and lie on the ground. The leaves are oval, obtuſe, and ſix of them ſurround the ſtalks at the joints. The flowers are very ſmall, they come out from the ends and ſides of the branches in June, and continue to ſhew themſelves the greateſt part of the ſummer months.

Dwarf

16. Dwarf Ladies Bed-ſtraw. The ſtalks of this ſpecies are ſlender, weak, branching, five or ſix inches long, and lie on the ground. The leaves are ſpear-ſhaped, mucronated, ſmooth, and eight of them ſurround the ſtalks at the joints. The flowers come out in little cluſters from the ends and ſides of the branches, they are of a fine yellow colour, and ſhew themſelves great part of the ſummer months.

and Leaſt Ladies Bed-ſtraw deſcribed

17. Leaſt Ladies Bed-ſtraw. The ſtalks of this ſpecies are numerous, angular, hairy, ſend out a few branches alternately, and grow to about four or five inches long. The leaves are ſpear-ſhaped, narrow, acute, hairy, and ſix or eight of them grow in whorls round the ſtalks. The flowers have footſtalks, which divide by pairs, and they form themſelves into panicles at the ends of the ſtalks. They are moſtly of a yellow colour, appear at different times of the ſummer, though chiefly in June and July.

Proper ſituation

Many of theſe ſorts grow wild in many parts of England, and are hardly ever admitted into gardens. Some of them, however, are very beautiful plants, and, were it not for their commonneſs, would be in the higheſt eſteem; for what can be more beautiful than the Common Ladies Bed-ſtraw in its profuſion of flowers, glowing in their golden luſtre, when in full blow? Others again have their beauties, but it is not intended that the Engliſh ſorts ſhould be introduced into the garden as ornamental plants, we find them in our fields and hedges. They are mentioned here, that the Gardener and Botaniſt may know what they are, and may, if they pleaſe, appropriate the worſt part of the garden for a plant or two of each ſort, to be ready for obſervation, whilſt thoſe of foreign growth, though of no greater beauty, may have a better apartment, becauſe ſcarcer plants, and ſuch as will not occur for obſervation, unleſs they are afforded at leaſt the ſlight culture of hardy perennials.

Culture

All the ſorts have roots, which are more or leſs creeping, and by theſe they are ſpeedily propagated any time, either in the autumn, winter, or early in the ſpring. They chiefly delight in the ſhade and a good earth, there they will grow taller, and produce their flowers in greater abundance, but they will do very well any where, and no ſoil or ſituation comes amiſs to them.

The ſorts of Ladies Bed-ſtraw, particularly the Common Yellow Ladies Bed-ſtraw, being uſed as rennet, have the property of turning milk into cheeſe curd, and in many parts they are uſed for that purpoſe, and preferred before every thing elſe for producing the fineſt flavoured cheeſe. Hence the name Cheeſe-rennet is very ſignificantly applied to theſe plants.

Titles

1. The Common Yellow Ladies Bed-ſtraw, or, Cheeſe-rennet, is titled, *Galium foliis octonis linearibus ſulcatis, ramis floriferis brevibus*. In the *Flora Lappon.ca* it is termed, *Galium caule erecto, foliis plurimis verticillatis linearibus*. Caſpar Bauhine calls it, *Gallium luteum*, and Dodonæus, *Gallium*. It grows naturally by way-ſides, the borders of fields, and in dry places in England, and moſt countries of Europe.

2. Wild

2 Wild Madder, or, Great Branching Madder, is titled, *Galium foliis octonis ovato linearibus subserratis patentissimis mucronatis, caule flaccido, ramis patentibus* In the *Hortus Cliffortianus* it is termed, *Galium foliis pluribus acutis, caule flaccido, ramis patentissimis* Caspar Bauhine calls it, *Mollugo montana angustifolia ramosa, seu Gallium album latifolium*, also, *Rubia sylvestris lævis* Lobel names it, *Mollugo Belgarum*, and Gerard, *Rubia sylvestris* It grows naturally in hedges and leafy grounds in England, and many parts of Europe

3 Mountain Ladies Bed-straw is titled, *Galium foliis subquaternis linearibus lævibus, caule devili scabro, seminibus glabris* Haller calls it, *Galium caule recto, foliis senis infernè canaliculatis*, and Ray, *Mollugo montana minor gallio albo similis* It grows naturally in England and Germany

4 Glaucous Ladies Bed-straw is titled, *Galium foliis verticillatis linearibus, pedunculis dichotomis summo caule floriferis, caule lævi* Boccone calls it, *Gallium saxatile, glauco folio*, and Caspar Bauhine, *Rubia montana angustifolia* It grows naturally in Tartary, Switzerland, Austria, and the South of France

5 Purple Ladies Bed-straw is titled, *Galium foliis verticillatis linearibus setaceis, pedunculis capillaribus folio longioribus* Columna calls it, *Gallium nigro purpureum montanum tenuifolium* It grows naturally in Italy

6 Narrow-leaved Red Ladies Bed-straw is titled, *Galium foliis verticillatis linearibus patulis, pedunculis brevissimis* Caspar Bauhine calls it, *Galium rubrum*, and Clusius, *Galium rubro flore* It is a native of Italy

7 Cross wort Meadow Madder is titled, *Galium foliis quaternis lanceolatis trinerviis glabris, caule erecto, seminibus hispidis* Caspar Bauhine calls it, *Rubia pratensis lævis, acuto folio* John Bauhine, *Rubia erecta quadrifolia*, and Ray, *Mollugo montana erecta quadrifolia* It grows naturally in sterile places in England, and most of the northern parts of Europe

8 Round-leaved Madder is titled, *Galium foliis quaternis ovalis aculeato-ciliatis, seminibus hispidis* Morison calls it, *Rubia semine duplici hispido, latis & hirsutis foliis*. In the former edition of the *Species Plantarum* it is named, *Galium foliis quaternis ovatis lævibus obtusis, panicula dichotoma, seminibus hispidis* Caspar Bauhine stiles it, *Rubia quadrifolia s rotundifolia lævis*, John Bauhine, *Rubia quadrifolia, semine duplici hispido*, and Haller, *Aparine cruciata* It grows naturally in the Helvetian and Styrian Mountains

9 The Least Goose-Grass is, *Galium foliis verticillatis linearibus, pedunculis bifidis, fructibus hispidis* Van Royen calls it, *Aparine foliis lineari-lanceolatis acuminatis flaccidis, corollis fructu minoribus*, Tournefort, *Gallium pariense tenuifolium, flore atro purpureo*, and Ray, *Aparine minima* It grows naturally in sterile parts in England and France

10 Smooth Flax leaved Madder is, *Galium foliis octonis lanceolatis lævibus, panicula capillari* Morison calls it, *Mollugo pumila, alsines mollioris folio*, and Boccone, *Rubia lævis linifolia floribus albis montis virginis* It grows naturally in Italy

11. Bearded Madder is, *Galium foliis quaternis lanceolatis æqualibus margine scabris, caule ... petalis caudatis, seminibus glabris* It grows naturally in Germany, Italy, and some parts of France

12 Broad leaved Red Ladies Bed-Straw is, *Galium foliis quaternis lanceolato-ovatis æqualibus subtus scabris, caule erecto fructibus ...* It grows naturally in Italy, Portugal, and Spain

13 White Marsh Ladies Bed-Straw is, *Galium foliis quaternis obovatis inæqualibus, caulibus diffusis* In the *Flora Lapp* it is termed *Galium caulibus diffusis, foliis quaternis ...* Caspar Bauhine calls it, *Gallium palustre album*, Gerard, *Gallium album*, and Parkinson, *Mollugo ...* *... varietas minor* It grows naturally by brook-sides and moist places in England and most parts of Europe

14 Marsh Goose-Grass is, *Galium foliis ... lanceolatis retrorsum serratis ... mucronatis ..., corollis fructu majoribus* Van Royen calls it, *Aparine foliis lineari-lanceolatis ... corollis fructu majoribus*, Ray, *Mollugo montana minor gallio albo similis* Petiver, *Gallium album ...*, and John Bauhine, *Rubia ...* In the *Flora Lapp* it is termed, *Aparine ... palustris parisiensis, flore albo* It grows naturally in moist sterile places in England, and most countries of Europe

15 Rock Ladies Bed-Straw is, *Galium foliis senis obovatis obtusis, caule ramosissimo procumbente* In the *Hortus Cliffortianus* it is termed, *Galium caule ramosissimo, foliis quinis obversè ovatis*, and Jussieu, *Gallium saxatile supinum, molliore folio* It grows naturally on rocky stony grounds in some parts of Spain

16 Dwarf Ladies Bed-Straw is, *Galium foliis octonis lanceolatis mucronatis serrato aculeatis glabris ..., fructibus reflexis* In the *Hortus Upsal* it is named, *Galium foliis senis cuneiformi-lanceolatis mucronatis glabris* Tournefort calls it, *Gallium saxatile minimum supinum & pumilum, flore luteo* It grows naturally in Muscovy

17 Least Ladies Bed-Straw is, *Galium foliis octonis hispidis linearibus acuminatis subimbricatis, pedunculis dichotomis* Caspar Bauhine calls it, *Rubeola saxatilis* and Magnol, *Aparina minima s rubia saxatilis minima* It grows naturally in mountainous places in England, and many parts of Europe

*Galium* is of the class and order *Tetrandria Monogynia*, and the characters are, Class and order in the Linnæan system

1 CALYX is a very small perianthium, situated on the germen, and indented in four parts The characters

2 COROLLA is one rotated petal, having no tube, but divided almost to the bottom into four acute parts

3 STAMINA are four awl-shaped filaments shorter than the corolla, having simple antheræ

4 PISTILLUM consists of a didymous germen situated below the flower, and a filiform semi-bifid style the length of the stamina, with globular stigmas

5 PERICARPIUM consists of two juiceless, globular berries, which are joined together

6 SEMINA The seeds are single, large, and kidney-shaped

# C H A P. CCVII

## *GENISTA*, BROOM.

THE perennials of this genus are,
Species 1 Sagittated Broom
2 Leaſt Oriental Broom
3 Flax-leaved Dwarf Broom

Theſe are ſmall beautiful plants, and deſerve a place in any collection

Sagittated, 1 Sagittated Broom The ſtalks are herbaceous, perennial, green, lie on the ground, and divide into ſeveral flat jointed branches, whoſe ſides are edged like a ſword The leaves are oval, ſpear-ſhaped, ſmall, and grow ſingly at the joints without any footſtalks The flowers come out from the ends of the branches in cloſe ſpikes, their colour is yellow, they appear in June, and are ſucceeded by ſhort pods which ripen in September

Leaſt Oriental, 2 Leaſt Oriental Broom The ſtalks are very ſlender, branching, ſtriated, hairy, and ſpread themſelves every where on the ground The leaves are ciliated and ſpear-ſhaped The flowers come out in ſhort ſpikes from the ends of the branches, their colour is yellow, they appear in June, and are ſucceeded by ſhort pods, each containing ripe ſeeds, in the autumn

and Flax leaved Dwarf Broom, deſcribed 3 Flax-leaved Dwarf Broom The ſtalk is ligneous, and ſends forth ſeveral angular erect branches, which are covered with a ſoft white bark The leaves are narrow, ternate, ſeſſile, of a ſilvery white colour, and downy underneath The flowers come out in ſpikes from the ends of the branches, their colour is yellow, they appear in June, and are ſucceeded by ſhort hairy pods, which ripen their ſeeds in September

All theſe ſorts are propagated by ſowing the ſeeds in the ſpring, in the places where they are to remain When they come up they muſt be thinned where they appear too cloſe, conſtantly kept clean from weeds, watered in dry weather, and this is all the trouble they will require Its propagation

The firſt ſort will grow in any ſoil or ſituation, but the laſt two muſt be ſet in a dry, ſandy, warm, well-ſheltered place, or they will rarely perfect their ſeeds, and be in great danger of being killed in winter by hard weather Proper ſoil and ſituation

1 Sagittated Broom is titled, *Geniſta ramis ancipitibus articulatis, foliis ovato-lanceolatis* Caſpar Bauhine calls it, *Chamæ geniſta ſagittalis*, John Bauhine, *Geniſta herbacea ſ Chamæ ſpartium*, and Cammerarius, *Chamæ-geniſta ſagittalis Pannonica* It grows naturally in ſterile ſandy parts in Germany and Gaul Titles

2 Leaſt Oriental Broom is, *Geniſta foliis lanceolatis ciliatis, ramis proſtratis ſtriatis piloſis* Tournefort calls it, *Geniſta orientalis minima humifuſa foliis ſubrotundis ad oras piloſis* It grows naturally in the Eaſt

3 Flax-leaved Dwarf Broom is, *Geniſta foliis ternatis ſeſſilibus linearious ſubtus ſericeis* Tournefort calls it, *Cytiſus argenteus linifolius inſularum Stæchadum* It reſides in Spain and in the Eaſt

# C H A P CCVIII

## *GENTIANA*, GENTIAN, or, FELL-WORT.

THE perennials of this genus are uſually called,
Species 1 Bell-ſhaped *Gentianella*
2 Funnel-ſhaped *Gentianella*, or Vernal *Gentianella*
3 Ciliated *Gentianella*, or Autumnal *Gentianella*
4 Swallow-wort-leaved Gentian.
5 Calathian Violet
6 *Saponaria* leaved Gentian
7 Hairy Virginian Gentian.
8 Yellow Gentian
9 Purple Gentian
10 Spotted Gentian
11 Croſs-wort Gentian

Bell ſhaped, 1 Bell-ſhaped *Gentianella* The ſtalks of this ſpecies are ſlender, and ſeldom more than two or three inches long The leaves are oblong, ſpear-ſhaped, pointed, and grow oppoſite to each other, ſitting cloſe, without any footſtalks The flowers are remarkably large and beautiful, and grow erect on the tops of the ſtalks Their figure is that of a bell, but cut into five ſegments at the brim, and their colour is a deep azure blue They ſhew themſelves in May, and ſometimes again, if wet weather happens, in the autumn

2 Funnel ſhaped *Gentianella*, or Spring *Gentianella*. This is a very low plant, having hardly any ſtalk at all. The radical leaves are numerous, broad, and acute The flowers grow ſingly on the tops of their ſhort ſtalks, they are large, their poſition is uſually upright, their figure is infundibuliforme, and they are cut at the top into five ſegments Their colour is a deep elegant blue, they appear in the ſpring, and frequently again in the autumn and Funnel ſhaped Gentianella deſcribed

There

Variety. There is a variety of this species with smaller leaves and flowers, but usually taller stalks.

Ciliated, or Autumnal Gentianella described. 3. Ciliated, or Autumnal *Gentianella*. This also is a low perennial, the stalks being slender, and seldom more than three or four inches high. The leaves are small, narrow, pointed, and grow opposite to each other on the stalks. The flowers are very large, and of a deep and elegant blue colour; their figure is hypocrateriforme, and they are cut into four segments only at the brim, which are hairy on their inside. They sometimes shew themselves at different times of the year, but their regular time of blow is July and August.

Culture. These three sorts are usually propagated by dividing of the roots in the autumn, winter, or spring. By this method they may be encreased very fast; but the best way of rearing these plants is from the seeds. These should be sown in a border of fine rich mould, and only raked in; the best time for which is the latter end of summer, or soon after they are ripe. When they come up, they must be regularly kept clean from weeds, and watered as often as dry weather shall make it necessary. The following summer, and in the autumn, they should be set in beds at about three inches asunder. The autumn after that, each plant should be taken up, with a good ball of earth to the root; then set them in the places where they are designed to remain, and the summer following they will produce greater plenty, and more beautiful flowers, than such plants as have been raised from off-sets. These plants are often set in rows by way of edging for borders; here they have a very good effect; but the best way is to plant them in beds, each containing eight or ten rows, at four or five inches asunder; and being thus stationed, they will form a grand show when in blow, and be captivating to every beholder. They must have a rich, loamy earth; and the fresher the soil is, the more suitable it will be to their natures.

Swallow-wort-leaved Gentian described. 4. Swallow-wort-leaved Gentian. The stalks of this species are upright, and grow to about a foot high. The leaves are oval, spear-shaped, pointed, smooth, have five longitudinal veins, grow opposite to each other, and embrace the stalk with their base. The flowers come out from the wings of the leaves on each side of the stalk on short footstalks; they are moderately large, bell-shaped, and of an elegant blue colour. They make their appearance in June and July, and the seeds ripen in September.

Culture. This is propagated by parting of the roots, and sowing of the seeds, like the former; but it should have a moist, loamy earth, and be seldom removed, if you expect it to blow strong and fair.

Calathian Violet, 5. Calathian Violet. The stalks of this species are upright, and about a foot in height. The leaves are narrow, smooth, pointed, and grow opposite to each other without any footstalks. The flowers are produced on footstalks alternately from the upper parts of the plant; they are pretty large, bell-shaped, and of a deep blue colour. They make their appearance in some situations in August; in others, they do not shew themselves before September or October.

Saponaria-leaved, 6. *Saponaria*-leaved Gentian. The stalks of this species are upright, slender, and about a foot high. The leaves are oval, spear-shaped, trinervous, sessile, and grow opposite to each other on the stalks. The flowers are long, swelling, bell-shaped, divided at the brim into five segments, and stand erect. They are of an exquisite blue colour, and usually shew themselves in June and July.

Hairy Virginian, 7. Hairy Virginian Gentian. The stalks of this species are slender, upright, and about a foot high. The leaves are oblong, acuminated, hairy, and grow opposite to each other. The flowers are bell-shaped, ventricose, erect, cut at the brim into five parts, and usually shew themselves about the same time with the former.

and Yellow Gentian described. 8. Yellow Gentian. The root of this species is very thick, yellowish, and very bitter to the taste. The stalks are upright, firm, and grow to be three or four feet high. The radical leaves are moderately large, oval, oblong, pointed, stiff, have five longitudinal veins, and are of a yellowish-green colour. The leaves on the stalks are like the radical ones, but smaller, and they grow opposite by pairs at the joints, embracing the stalks with their base. The flowers are produced in whorls at the joints from the upper parts of the plant, standing on short footstalks; and each consists of one rotated petal, deeply divided into five parts. They are of a pale yellow colour, appear in July and August, at which time they are very beautiful, and greatly ornamental to the garden.

Medicinal Properties. It is the root of this species that is used in medicine, and which is deemed stomachic, restorative, sudorific, as well as good against poison and the plague; it is also used in intermitting fevers, and other disorders. It is an ingredient in treacle, one of the principal ingredients in bitters, and a good vulnerary when externally used for wounds. The word Gentian, or, as the generical word is, *Gentiana*, is formed from the Greek word γεντιανή, and is of long standing, being so named from one of the kings of Illyria, who is supposed to have first discovered the virtues of these plants.

Proper situation. As the root of this species is large, and strikes deep into the ground, the soil should be naturally deep, moist, and good.

Culture. It is propagated by sowing the seeds in the autumn, soon after they are ripe, on some rich, moist ground, double dug, and made fine. When the plants come up, which will be in the spring, they should be thinned to a foot asunder every way. All summer they should be kept clean from weeds, and duly watered in dry weather. In the autumn every other plant should be taken up, to form a fresh plantation, leaving the others to flower, without being removed. The plants should be taken up with care, and set in rows a foot and a half asunder. They will require no trouble, except keeping the ground clean from weeds, watering in dry weather, and digging between the rows in the winter. This will cause them to succeed very well; but they will not flower so strong as those plants that have not been removed; which teaches us, if there is conveniency for so doing, always to raise these plants where they are designed to remain. They seldom flower two years together, and sometimes not oftener than every third year; and they generally shew themselves the end of July or August. The seeds ripen in the autumn, soon after which the stalks decay.

Purple, 9. Purple Gentian. The root of this species is thick, fleshy, and bitter to the taste. The stalks are upright, firm, and three or four feet high. The lower leaves are oval, and grow on footstalks; but those on the upper parts of the plant are narrow, pointed, and sit close. The flowers grow in whorls round the upper parts of the stalks; they are bell-shaped, and cut into five segments at the brim; they are of a purple colour, appear in August, and the seeds ripen in October.

and Spotted Gentian described. 10. Spotted Gentian. The stalks of this species are upright, firm, jointed, and grow to about two or three feet high. The leaves are narrow, spear-shaped, and grow opposite by pairs at the joints. The flowers come out from the ends of the stalks by threes, each growing on its own

own separate footstalks, they are bell shaped, and cut at the brim into five parts like the former. Their ground colour is yellow, but they are beautifully spotted with purple spots, they appear about the end of July, or in August, and the seeds ripen in the autumn.

*Cross-wort Gentian described.* 11 Cross-wort Gentian. This is one of the lower kinds of Gentian, the stalks being weak, and seldom more than six inches long. The leaves are spear-shaped, smooth, sessile, of a dark green, grow opposite by pairs, and each pair crosses the other like the leaves of Cross-wort. The flowers are produced in clusters from the ends of the stalks, and in whorls lower down from the joints, they sit close, and their brims are cut into four segments only, they are of a high blue colour, appear in May, and frequently shew themselves afresh in the autumn.

*Culture.* This sort hath a creeping root, by which it multiplies very fast; the others also may be propagated by off-sets, which should be planted in the autumn when the stalks decay; but as all of them, for the most part, ripen their seeds pretty well, the best way will be to raise them from the seeds. These should be sown in the autumn, soon after they are ripe, and the sorts with large fleshy roots should be sown in the places where they are designed to remain, but the others may be raised in beds, and afterwards removed in the manner of the first three sorts. They all like the shade, fresh land, and a moist situation, and, being thus stationed, they will shew themselves to best advantage.

*Titles.* 1 Bell-shaped *Gentianella* is titled, *Gentiana corolla quinquefidâ campanulatâ, caulem excedente*. In the *Hortus Cliffortianus* it is termed, *Gentiana corollâ campanulatâ caulem longitudine excedente*. Caspar Bauhine calls it, *Gentiana Alpina latifolia, magno flore*, also, *Gentiana Alpina angustifolia, magno flore*. It grows naturally on the Helvetian, Austrian, and Pyrenean Mountains.

2 Funnel shaped *Gentianella*, or Spring *Gentianella*, is titled, *Gentiana corolla quinquefidâ infundibuliformi caulem excedente, foliis radicalibus confertis majoribus*. Haller calls it, *Gentiana flore verno tubuloso, foliis ad terram congestis acutis*, Caspar Bauhine, *Gentiana Alpina verna major*, and Clusius, *Gentianella verna minor*. It grows naturally on the Helvetian, Austrian, Rhetian, and Pyrenean Mountains.

3 Ciliated *Gentianella*, or Autumnal *Gentianella*, is titled, *Gentiana corollis quadrifidis margine ciliatis*. In the *Hortus Cliffortianus* it is termed, *Gentiana corollis hypocrateriformibus laciniis margine barbatis*. Columna calls it, *Gentianella cærulea fimbriata angustifolia autumnalis*, Caspar Bauhine, *Gentiana angustifolia autumnalis minor, floribus ad latera pilosis*, also, *Gentianella cærulea oris pilosis*. It grows naturally on the Mountains of Helvetia, Italy, and Canada.

4 Swallow-wort-leaved Gentian is titled, *Gentiana corollis quinquefidis campanulatis oppositis sessilibus, foliis amplexicaulibus*. In the *Hortus Cliffortianus* it is termed, *Gentiana floribus lateralibus solitariis sessilibus, corollis erectis*. Haller calls it, *Gentiana foliis ovato lanceolatis, floribus campanulatis in alis sessilibus*, and Caspar Bauhine, *Gentiana asclepiadis folio*. It grows naturally in the Helvetian, Pannonian, and Mauritanian Mountains.

5 Calathian Violet is titled, *Gentiana corollis quinquefidis campanulatis oppositis pedunculatis, foliis linearibus*. In the *Hortus Cliffortianus* it is termed, *Gentiana floribus terminalibus raris, corollis crenatis plicatis, foliis linearibus*. Caspar Bauhine calls it, *Gentiana angustifolia autumnalis major*, also, *Gentiana palustris angustifolia*, Parkinson, *Gentiana autumnalis Pneumonanthe dicta*, and Gerard, *Pneumonanthe*. It grows naturally in some of our meadows, also in moist pastures in most parts of Europe.

6 Saponaria-leaved Gentian is titled, *Gentiana corollis quinquefidis campanulatis ventricosis verticillatis, foliis trinerviis*. Gronovius calls it, *Gentiana floribus ventricosis campanulatis erectis quinquefidis, foliis ovato-lanceolatis*, Plukenet, *Gentiana major Virginiana, floribus amplis oblongis*, and Morison, *Gentiana Virginiana, saponariæ folio, flore cæruleo longiore*. It grows naturally in Virginia.

7 Hairy Virginian Gentian is titled, *Gentiana corollis quinquefidis campanulatis verticillatis, foliis trinervis*. Gronovius calls it, *Gentiana floribus ventricosis campanulatis erectis quinquefidis, foliis oblongis acuminatis lævibus villosis*. It grows naturally in Virginia.

8 Yellow Gentian is titled, *Gentiana corollis quinquefidis rotatis verticillatis, calycibus spathaceis*. In the *Hortus Cliffortianus* it is termed, *Gentiana floribus lateralibus confertis pedunculatis, corollis rotatis*. Caspar Bauhine calls it, *Gentiana major lutea*, and Cammerarius, *Gentiana*. It grows naturally on the Norwegian, Helvetian, Appennine, Austrian, and Pyrenean Mountains.

9 Purple Gentian is titled, *Gentiana corollis quinquefidis campanuliformibus verticillatis, calycibus truncatis*. Haller calls it, *Gentiana corollis campaniformibus verticillatis, foliis imis petiolatis ellipticis*, Caspar Bauhine, *Gentiana major purpurea*, Gesner, *Gentiana major, flore purpureo*, and Cammerarius, *Gentiana major alba*. It grows naturally on the Helvetian, Pyrenean, and Norwegian Mountains.

10 Spotted Gentian is titled, *Gentiana corollis quinquefidis campanulatis punctatis verticillatis, calycibus quinquedentatis*. Caspar Bauhine calls it, *Gentiana major, flore punctato*. It grows naturally on the Helvetian, Siberian, Austrian, Stirian, and Rhetian Mountains.

11 Cross-wort Gentian is titled, *Gentiana corollis quadrifidis imberbibus, floribus verticillatis sessilibus*. In the *Hortus Cliffortianus* it is termed, *Gentiana floribus confertis terminalibus, corollis quadrifidis imberbibus, interjecto denticulo*. Caspar Bauhine calls it, *Gentiana cruciata*, and Cammerarius, *Gentiana minor*. It grows naturally on the Pannonian, Helvetian, and Appennine Mountains.

*Class and order in the Linnæan system.* *Gentiana* is of the class and order *Pentandria Digynia*, and the characters are,

*The characters.* 1 CALYX is a perianthium, divided into five oblong, acute, permanent segments.

2 COROLLA is one petal, which varies in figure. It is, however, usually tubular at the base, and divided at the top into four or five segments.

3 STAMINA are five awl-shaped filaments, shorter than the corolla, having simple antheræ.

4 PISTILLUM consists of an oblong, cylindrical germen, and two oval stigmas, there being no style.

5 PERICARPIUM is an oblong, round, pointed, bivalvate capsule, containing one cell.

6 SEMINA. The seeds are numerous and small.

CHAP.

# CHAP. CCIX.

## GERANIUM, CRANE's BILL.

Species

THE hardy perennials of this genus are,
1. Tuberous Crane's Bill.
2. Long-rooted Sweet-smelling Crane's Bill.
3. English Spotted Crane's Bill.
4. Knotty Crane's Bill.
5. Striated Crane's Bill.
6. Mountain Crane's Bill.
7. Marsh Crane's Bill.
8. Crow-foot Crane's Bill.
9. Silvery Crane's Bill.
10. American Spotted Crane's Bill.
11. Siberian Crane's-Bill.
12. Bloody Crane's Bill.

Description of the [illegible]

1. Tuberous Crane's Bill. This plant hath a large fleshy root, from which arise several branching stalks to about a foot and a half high. The leaves are divided into many parts, the segments are narrow, subdivided, and obtuse. The flowers grow two together on a footstalk, their colour is purple; they come out in June, and ripen their seeds in July and August.

Long-rooted [illegible] smelling

2. Long-rooted Sweet-smelling Crane's Bill. This hath a long, thick, fleshy root, from which arise several branching stalks to the height of about a foot. The leaves are composed each of five lobes, which are divided into many short crenated segments; they are of a light-green colour, smooth, and garnish the stalk at the joints. The flowers grow from the ends of the branches in large inflated cups, on footstalks supporting only two flowers, but there being many together they form a considerable bunch. The petals are moderately large, and of a bright-purple colour; they are in their full beauty in May and June, and the seeds ripen in July and August. The whole of this plant is finely scented.

English Spotted,

3. English Spotted Crane's Bill. This rises with an upright stalk that is almost naked at the top to about a foot high. The leaves are large, and each is composed of about five serrated lobes; they grow from the bottom of the plant on long footstalks, but higher up the stalks they sit close. The flowers are produced from the ends of the branches, two only grow together on a footstalk; their colour is a dark-red or purple, being somewhat white or spotted in the middle; they come out in June, and the seeds ripen in August. This plant is strongly (and to some disagreeably) scented.

Knotty,

4. Knotty Crane's Bill. The stalks are of a purple colour, jointed, branching, and grow to about eight inches high. Each of the leaves is composed of about three serrated lobes; those on the lower part of the plant have footstalks, but higher up the stalks they sit close. The flowers grow two together on a footstalk from the ends of the branches; they are moderately large, of a pale purple colour, come out in June, and their seeds ripen in August.

Striated,

5. Striated Crane's Bill. The stalks are small and branching. The leaves are composed each of five lobes, have brownish or iron-coloured spots, and are hairy. Two flowers only grow together on a footstalk; their ground colour is white, but they are beautifully veined with a reddish purple; they come out about the same time as the former, and often continue their blow for a long time.

Mountain,

6. Mountain Crane's Bill. The stalks are upright, and grow to about nine inches high. Each of the leaves is composed of five serrated lobes; they have footstalks on the lower part of the plant, but those on the upper-parts of the stalks have none, and they grow opposite to each other from the joints. The flowers grow two together on a footstalk from the upper-parts of the plant; they are of a fine blue colour, come out in May and June.

Marsh,

7. Marsh Crane's Bill. The stalks are of a reddish colour, and grow to about a foot long. The leaves are composed of five lobes, which are cut at their edges. The flowers grow from the upper-parts of the plant on very long footstalks; they are of a blood red colour, appear in May and June, and the seeds ripen in July and August.

Crow-Foot Crane's Bill.

8. Crow-Foot Crane's Bill. This plant is very common in our meadows, and is one of the most beautiful sorts of Crane's Bill we have. The stalks grow to two or three feet high. The leaves are cut, or divided into many acute parts, like those of the field Crow Foot. The flowers are large, and of a delightful blue colour, two only grow together on one common footstalk. They come out from the upper parts of the plant in May and June, and the seeds ripen in July or August.

Varieties

There is a variety of this with white, and another with variegated flowers, both of which are inferior in beauty to the old original true blue.

Silvery Leaved,

9. Silvery Crane's Bill. The root of this species is very thick and long, the outside is very black, but it is of a fine white within; it divides into several parts near the top, from which the leaves and flower stalks proceed. The leaves are nearly target shaped, and consist of about seven trifid parts, are white, with a silvery down, and grow on long round footstalks. From among these the flower stalks arise. They are shorter than those of the leaves, and each of them supports two flowers, which are pretty large for so small a plant; their petals are indented, and their colour is pale-red, with some streaks of purple. They come out in June and July, and are succeeded by short beaks, but they very rarely produce ripe seeds in our gardens.

American Spotted,

10. American Spotted Crane's Bill. The stalks are erect, divide by pairs, and grow to be about a foot high. The leaves are divided into five parts, which are cut on their edges; they have longish footstalks at the bottom of the plant, but higher they sit close, and grow opposite to each other. The flowers are produced from the divisions or the branches on long naked footstalks, each supports two flowers, which are of a pale blue or purple colour; they come out in June, and sometimes are succeeded by ripe seeds in our gardens.

Siberian

11. Siberian Crane's Bill. This hath several spreading stalks, about a foot long. The leaves are divided into five acute, pinnated parts, grow opposite to each other, and have long slender footstalks. The flowers are produced from the wings of the [illegible] footstalks; each

each supports only one flower, which is of a whitish colour, having purple stripes, comes out in June, and the seeds ripen in July or August.

Bloody Crane's Bill. — Bloody Crane's Bill. The root is thick, fleshy, fibrous, and sends forth many weak slender stalks, which, unless supported, will lie on the ground. The leaves are round, and each of them is composed of five parts, which are trifid. The flowers are produced from the sides of the stalks on long hairy foot-stalks, each supports only one flower, which is large, of a deep red or purple colour; it comes out in June and July, and ripens its seeds in September.

Varieties. There is a variety of this plant with striped flowers, another with erect stalks, and a third with deeply jagged leaves.

These sorts are all extremely hardy, and their culture is very easy. The foreign sorts seem to give no way to our winter frosts, and there is hardly any situation or soil but they will thrive in; they delight in the shade, where they will exhibit their bloom most fair, and indeed the other sorts will have a more perfect look, if their situation be shielded in the middle of the day at least from the hot beams of the sun.

Method of propagating them. They are propagated by parting of the roots and sowing of the seeds. The best time for parting of the roots is in the autumn, tho' it may be done at any time with success in the winter or spring. With respect to the seeds, the plants will for the most part sow themselves, and raise plants in abundance, without any trouble or art, except thinning them where they are too thick, and keeping them clean from weeds.

When the plants are not allowed this freedom, the best way will be to sow the seeds, soon after they are ripe, in a shady border or light fresh earth; they will come up in the autumn, and the spring following may be pricked out in beds four inches distance from each other. Here they may stand with keeping clean from weeds, and watering in dry weather all summer, and in the autumn may be removed to the places where they are designed to remain.

Titles. 1. Tuberous Crane's Bill is titled, *Geranium pedunculis bifloris, foliis multipartitis laciniis linearibus subdivisis obtusis*. Caspar Bauhine calls it, *Geranium tuberosum majus*, and Lobel, *Geranium bulbosum*. It grows naturally in England and Italy.

2. Long-rooted Sweet-smelling Crane's Bill is, *Geranium pedunculis bifloris, calycibus inflatis, pistillo longissimo*. Caspar Bauhine calls it, *Geranium batrachioides odoratum*; and John Bauhine, *Geranium batrachioides longius radicatum odoratum*. It is a native of Italy.

3. Spotted English Crane's Bill is, *Geranium pedunculis bifloris foliis [illegible] [illegible] subangulatis, caule erecto, petalis undulatis*. In the *Hortus Cliffort*. it is termed, *Geranium pedunculis bifloris alternatim caule integro superne nudo ufcalo insidentibus*. Caspar Bauhine calls it, *Geranium montanum fuscum*; also, *Geranium batrachioides hirsutum, flore atro-rubente*; and Clusius, *Geranium 1 pullo flore*. It grows naturally in England, also on the Helvetian and Hungarian mountains.

4. Knotty Crane's Bill. This is, *Geranium pedunculis bifloris, foliis caulinis trilobis integris serratis summis subsessilibus*. Clusius calls it, *Geranium 5 nodosum Plateau*, Caspar Bauhine, *Geranium nodosum*, and John Bauhine, *Geranium magnum folio trifido*. It grows naturally in the mountains of Cumberland, and in some parts of France.

5. Striated Crane's Bill. This is, *Geranium pedunculis bifloris, [illegible] foliis quinquelobis lobis medio dilatatis, petalis [illegible] reticulatis*. Parkinson calls it, *Geranium Romanum versicolor striatum*. It is a native of Italy.

6. Mountain Crane's Bill. This is titled, *Geranium pedunculis bifloris, foliis subpeltatis quinquelobis [illegible], caule erecto, petalis emarginatis*. Caspar Bauhine calls it, *Geranium batrachioides, folio aconiti*, and Clusius, *Geranium 2 batrachioides minus*. It grows naturally in the woodland parts of England, and most of the northern countries of Europe.

7. Marsh Crane's Bill. This is, *Geranium pedunculis bifloris longissimis declinatis, foliis quinquelobis acutis, petalis integris*. Dillenius calls it, *Geranium batrachioides palustre, flore [illegible]*. It grows naturally in Russia and Germany.

8. Crow-Foot Crane's Bill is, *Geranium pedunculis bifloris, foliis subpeltatis multipartitis pinnatolaciniatis rugosis acutis, petalis integris*. Caspar Bauhine calls it, *Geranium batrachioides, Gratia Dei Germanorum*, Clusius, *Geranium 3 batrachioides majus*, and Parkinson, *Geranium batrachioides flore caeruleo*. It grows naturally in meadows in England, and most of the northern countries of Europe.

9. Silvery Crane's Bill. This is, *Geranium pedunculis bifloris, foliis subpeltatis septempartitis trifidis tomentoso sericeis, petalis emarginatis*. Caspar Bauhine calls it, *Geranium argenteum Alpinum*, and John Bauhine, *Geranium argenteum montis Baldi*. It grows naturally on the top of mount Baldus.

10. American Spotted Crane's Bill. This is titled, *Geranium pedunculis bifloris, caule dichotomo erecto, foliis quinquepartitis [illegible] fis summis sessilibus*. Dillenius calls it, *Geranium batrachioides Americanum maculatum, floribus obsolete caeruleis*. It grows naturally in Carolina, Virginia, and Siberia.

11. Siberian Crane's Bill. This is titled, *Geranium pedunculis subunifloris, foliis quinquepartitis [illegible] foliolis pinnatifidis*. It grows naturally in Siberia.

12. Bloody Crane's Bill. This is titled, *Geranium pedunculis unifloris, foliis quinquepartitis trifidis orbiculatis*. In the *Hortus Cliffort*. it is termed, *Geranium pedunculis simplicibus unifloris*. Caspar Bauhine calls it, *Geranium sanguineum, maximo flore*, Clusius, *Geranium 7 haematodes*, and Dillenius, *Geranium haematodes Lancastriense, flore eleganter striato*. It grows naturally in England and most parts of Europe.

Class and order in the Linnæan system. *Geranium* is of the class and order *Monadelphia Decandria*, and the characters are,

The characters. 1. CALYX is a perianthium composed of five oval, acute, concave, permanent leaves.

2. COROLLA is five large, obcordated, or else oval, patent petals.

3. STAMINA. The filaments are ten in number, awl-shaped, alternately longer, are shorter than the petals, and have oblong versatile antheræ.

4. PISTILLUM consists of a five-cornered rostrated germen, a subulated permanent style longer than the stamina, and five reflexed stigmas.

5. PERICARPIUM. There is none. The fruit is in form of a bird's beak, and contains five cells.

6. SEMINA. The seeds are single, and kidney-shaped.

CHAP.

# CHAP. CCX

## *GEUM*, AVENS, or HERB-BENNET

THERE are five species of this genus, called,

Species 1 Common Avens, or Herb Bennet
2 Water Avens
3 Mountain Avens
4 Virginian Avens
5 Creeping Avens

Description of the Common Avens 1 Common Avens, or Herb Bennet The root is thick, fibrated, reddish within, and of an aromatick odour The leaves are large, rough serrated, and of a dark green colour The stalks are round, upright, hairy, divide into a few branches near the top, and grow to about a foot high The flowers come out from the ends of the branches, standing erect, they are of a yellow colour, moderately large, and the general characters indicate their structure, they appear in May and June, and the seeds ripen in July and August

Its uses in medicine It is the root of this species which is used in medicine, being cephalic, alexipharmac, and good for colics, fluxes, &c The young leaves of this plant afford a wholesome pot-herb, and the roots being dried and laid among cloaths, preserve them from the moth, and afford them an agreeable odour

Water Avens 2 Water Avens The root is thick, fleshy, and hung with numerous fibres The radical leaves are large, lyrated, hairy, and grow on long footstalks The stalk grows to about a foot high, and is garnished with leaves singly at the joints, which are jagged, consist of about three lobes, and sit close, without any footstalks The flowers come out from the ends of the branches, hanging downwards, they are of a purple colour, appear in May and June, and the seeds ripen in July

Varieties There is a variety of this species with red, and another with large yellow flowers There are also several varieties, differing in respect to the size of the plant, largeness or roundness of the leaves, &c most of which have been titled as distinct species by old botanists

Mountain Avens 3 Mountain Avens The root is thick, fleshy, fibrated, and creeping The radical leaves are composed of several pair of pinnæ, terminated by an odd one, that is large and roundish, they are all rough, hairy, indented, and grow on strong footstalks The stalks are slender, about a foot high, and adorned with narrow, longish, sharp pointed leaves The flowers are produced singly from the ends of the stalks, growing erect, they are moderately large, of a golden-yellow colour, appear in June, and the seeds ripen in August

Varieties There are several varieties of this species, particularly one which seldom grows higher than four inches, called the Dwarf Alpine Avens

Virginian 4 Virginian Avens The stalks are upright, divide into a few footstalks near the top, and grow to near a foot and a half high The lower leaves are trifoliate, but those on the upper-parts of the stalks are simple The flowers come out singly on the small footstalks which are produced from the upper-parts of the plant, they are small, of a white colour, appear in June, and the seeds ripen in August

The root of this species is not possessed of that aromatick odour which most of the other kinds have

and Creeping Avens 5 Creeping Avens The stalks lie on the ground, and strike root at the joints The leaves are composed of several pair of folioles, which are uniform, jagged, and downy on their under-side The flowers come out on footstalks from the joints, opposite to the parts which have struck root into the ground, they are of a fine yellow colour, appear in June, and often continue in succession until the end of summer

Methods of propagating these sorts These sorts are all propagated by dividing of the roots, which may be done at almost any time of the year, but the best season for it is the autumn They will grow in any soil and situation, but chiefly delight in the shade and moist places

They are also propagated by seeds These should be sown in the autumn, soon after they are ripe, in beds of any common mould made fine When the plants come up they must be thinned where they appear too close, kept clean from weeds, and watered in dry weather all summer, and by the autumn they will be grown to be strong plants, they may be then taken up with a ball of earth to each root, and set in the places where they are designed to remain

Titles 1 Common Avens, or Herb-Bennet, is titled, *Geum floribus erectis, fructu globoso villoso aristis uncinatis nudis, foliis lyratis* Caspar Bauhine calls it, *Caryophyllata vulgaris*, and Dodonæus, *Caryophyllata* It grows naturally in woods, hedges, and shady places in England, and most parts of Europe

2 Water Avens is, *Geum floribus nutantibus, fructu oblongo aristis plumosis* In the *Flora Lapp* it is termed, *Geum rivale* Lobel calls it, *Caryophyllata septentrionalium*, Gerard, *Caryophyllata montana purpurea*, Parkinson, *Caryophyllata montana palustris purpurea*, and Caspar Bauhine, *Caryophyllata aquatica nutante flore*, also *Caryophyllata aquatica altera* It grows naturally in moist places in England, and most countries of Europe

3 Mountain Avens is, *Geum flore inclinato solitario, fructu oblongo aristis plumosis* [illegible] Haller calls it, *Caryophyllata pinnis consertis crenatis, extimis subrotundis, tubis rectis*, Camerarius, *Caryophyllata montana*, Caspar Bauhine, *Caryophyllata Alpina lutea*, also, *Caryophyllata Alpina minor*, and Barrelier, *Caryophyllata Alpina minima, flore aureo* It grows naturally on the Alps, and other mountainous parts of the world

4 Virginian Avens is, *Geum floribus erectis, fructu globoso aristis uncinatis nudis, foliis ternatis* Hermann calls it, *Caryophyllata Virginiana, albo flore minore, radice inodora* It grows naturally in Virginia and Siberia

5 Creeping Avens is, *Geum foliolis uniformibus incisis alternis minoribus, flagellis reptantibus* Haller calls it, *Caryophyllata flagellis foliosis*, Caspar Bauhine, *Caryophyllata Alpina, apii folio*, and Barrelier, *Caryophyllata Alpina tenuifolia, flore luteo longius radicata* It grows naturally in Switzerland

Geum

Class and order in the Linnæan system. *Geum* is of the class and order *Icosandria Polygynia*, and the characters are,

The characters. 1 CALYX is a monophyllous perianthium cut half way down into ten segments, which are nearly erect, and alternately small and acute

2 COROLLA consists of five roundish petals, having narrow ungues the length of the calyx, and inserted into it

3 STAMINA are numerous awl-shaped filaments the length of the calyx, into which they are inserted, having short, roundish, obtuse antheræ

4 PISTILLUM consists of numerous germens collected into a head, having long hairy styles inserted in their sides, and crowned by simple stigmas

5 PERICARPIUM There is none The common receptacle of the seeds is oblong, hairy, and placed on the cup, which is reflexed

6 SEMINA The seeds are numerous, compressed, hispid, and have the long geniculated styles adhering to them

# CHAP. CCXI

## *GLADIOLUS*, CORN-FLAG

Remarks. THE far greatest part of the species of the *Gladiolus* are natives of Africa, and too tender to live in these parts without protection in winter The Gardener has been used, however, to the Common Gladiole or Corn Flag in his borders, and been proud of shewing it in its greatest variety and perfection They are often distinguished by three classes, those with flowers hanging one way on the stalk, those with flowers in two series, and the larger broad-leaved tall-flowering sorts These by many have been supposed to be three distinct species, but they are varieties only of one, seeds saved from one plant will sometimes produce them all, and among them several other numbers of varieties will be found The real species for this place then are,

Species. 1 The Common Gladiole, or Corn Flag

2 The Russian Gladiole

Description of the Common Corn Flag. 1 The Common Corn-Flag The root is large, tuberous, of a yellowish colour, and covered with many brown skins The leaves are ensiform, or shaped like a sword they are of a fresh green colour, and embrace each other at their base Between these arises the flower-stalk, which is smooth, round, erect, and of different heights in the varieties, though its usual height is about two feet, the top of it is garnished with the flowers, and the varieties are,

Varieties. The Common Red Corn-flag, with flowers on one side the stalk

The Purple Corn-Flag, with flowers on one side the stalk

The White Corn Flag, with flowers on one side the stalk

The Deep Crimson Corn Flag, with flowers on one side the stalk

Red Corn-Flag, with flowers in a double series

White Corn-Flag, with flowers in a double series

Broad-leaved Purple Corn Flag

Broad-leaved Crimson Corn Flag

These are the chief varieties of the Common Corn Flag, they will be in blow in June, and their seeds ripen in August

Of the Russian Corn Flag. 2 Russian Corn Flag This has the same kind of leaves with the other sort The stalk rises in the same manner, but the disposition of the flowers is different, they are placed very close to each other, and imbricated, or placed over each other like scales The flowers are but small, and the figure they make is inferior to the best varieties of the Common Corn Flag

Culture. All these sorts are to be propagated by parting of the roots, the best time for which work is the summer, when the stalks decay If it be necessary, the roots will keep good for two months before they are planted, if laid in a dry room, and when you set them, little regard need be paid to the soil or situation, for they will grow and flourish almost any where

This is the common method of propagation, but the finest plants are always raised from seeds In order for this, let seeds be saved from those plants that have the firmest stalks, the most flowers, and the finest colours The larger tall-growing sorts are the best kinds of these species, let seeds be chiefly collected from these, but do not wholly exclude the others In the autumn sow them in a well-managed border of common mould, and sift over the seeds about half an inch of the same kind of earth In the spring the plants will come up, and in the summer, after the leaves are decayed, they should be taken up and planted at about five inches distance, in beds prepared for the purpose, and here they may stand until they flower, which will be in about two years more

Titles. 1 The Common Corn-Flag is titled, *Gladiolus foliis ensiformibus, floribus distantibus* Van Royen calls it, *Gladiolus caule simplicissimo, foliis ensiformibus*, Caspar Bauhine, *Gladiolus floribus uno versu dispositis*, and Rivinus simply, *Gladiolus* It grows common in most of the southern parts of Europe

2 The Russian Corn-Flag is titled, *Gladiolus foliis ensiformibus, floribus imbricatis* It grows naturally in Russia

Class and order in the Linnæan system. *Gladiolus* is of the class and order *Triandria Monogynia*, and the characters are,

The characters. 1 CALYX For the calyx there are a few vague spathæ, each of which is composed of two valves

2 COROLLA consists of six oblong obtuse petals, which unite at their base, and form there a short crooked tube, the three upper ones bend towards each other, but the three under spread open

3 STAMINA

3 STAMINA are three ſubulated filaments inſerted into every other petal, and covered by the connivent petals Their antheræ are oblong

4 PISTILLUM conſiſts of a germen ſituated below the flower, a ſingle ſtyle the length of the ſtamina, and of a trifid concave ſtigma.

5 PERICARPIUM is an oblong ventricoſe capſule, nearly trigonal, obtuſe, formed of three valves, and containing three cells.

6. SEMINA The ſeeds are many, roundiſh, and covered with a calyptra.

## CHAP. CCXII.

## *GLAUX*, SEA MILK-WORT, or BLACK SALT-WORT.

THERE is only one ſpecies of this genus, called, Sea Milk-Wort, or Black Salt-Wort, and by ſome Sea Chickweed

This plant deſcribed

The root is ſmall, full of fibres, and creeps under the ſurface of the ground The ſtalks are numerous, ſlender, five or ſix inches long, partly procumbent, and ſtrike root from the joints when they lie on the ground The leaves are ſmall, oval, oblong, of a thickiſh conſiſtence, a bluiſh-grey colour, and grow oppoſite to each other, ſitting cloſe, without any footſtalk The flowers come out from the wings of the leaves on both ſides the ſtalk almoſt its whole length, they are ſmall, of a purpliſh colour, appear in May, and continue in ſucceſſion for a long time, but the ſeeds which follow the firſt-blown flowers will be ripe in June

Varieties

There is a variety of this ſpecies with white flowers, another with flowers of a greeniſh-white, and a third with red and white ſtriped flowers

Its virtues.

This ſpecies is frequently uſed by ſuckling women, who covet it for the encreaſe of their milk, for which purpoſe theſe plants are ſaid to be very good, and to have gained the appellation of Milk-Wort, from the extraordinary quantity of milk they will afford to ſuch ſuckling-women as uſe them They may be uſed as a tea, or taken in broths, &c It grows common on our ſandy ſea ſhores, but thrives very well in gardens

Culture

It is eaſily propagated by parting of the roots, or taking up ſuch branches as have lain on the ground, or ſtruck root This work is beſt done in Auguſt or September, though it may be performed with ſucceſs at any time of the year It delights in a light ſandy ſoil, but will nevertheleſs grow in any ſoil or ſituation

This plant is eaſily raiſed by ſeeds, which ſhould be ſown ſoon after they are ripe in beds of light ſandy earth, and ſlightly raked in If dry weather ſhould happen, let the beds be watered, and in a little time your plants will come up All ſummer keep them clean from weeds, and the ſpring following let the ſtrongeſt be taken up and planted in beds a foot aſunder. By the autumn the remaining plants will be ſtrong enough to remove, and may be then ſet in the places where they are deſigned to remain

Title.

There being no other ſpecies of this genus, it ſtands with the name ſimply *Glaux* In the *Flora Lapp* it is termed, *Glaux foliis elliptico-oblongis* Caſpar Bauhine calls it, *Glaux maritima*, Loeſel, *Alſine bifolia, fructu coriandri, radice geniculatâ*, and Gerard, *Glaux exigua maritima* It grows naturally on the ſea-ſhores of England

Claſs and order in the Linnæan ſyſtem The characters

*Glaux* is of the claſs and order *Pentandria Monogynia*, and the characters are,

1 CALYX There is none

2 COROLLA is an erect, bell-ſhaped, permanent petal, divided into five obtuſe, revolute ſtigmas

3 STAMINA are five awl-ſhaped erect filaments the length of the corolla, having roundiſh antheræ

4 PISTILLUM conſiſts of an oval germen, a filiforme ſtyle the length of the ſtamina, and a capitated ſtigma.

5 PERICARPIUM is a roundiſh acuminated capſule, formed of five valves, and containing one cell

6 SEMINA The ſeeds are five, and roundiſh The receptacle is large, roundiſh, and hollowed by the ſeeds

## CHAP. CCXIII.

## *GLECOMA*, GROUND IVY, or GILL.

THERE is only one species of this genus, which is the Ground Ivy of our banks and hedges.

*This plant described.* The stalks are slender, square, procumbent, and strike root from the joints as they lie on the ground. The leaves are roundish, broad, kidney-shaped, hairy, crenated, and grow opposite by pairs at the joints. The flowers come out from the wings of the leaves on footstalks; they are of a blueish-purple colour, and the general characters indicate their structure; they appear early in April, and continue in succession until the end of summer.

*Varieties.* There is a variety of this plant with white, another with red, and a third with blue flowers, all of which are bitter to the taste, and possessed of the like kind of strong agreeable odour with the common sort.

*Culture.* Whoever is inclined to cultivate these kinds, may do it by parting the roots at any time of the year, but especially in the autumn, which is the best season. They spread about and encrease amazingly; and a plant or two only will be sufficient to be ready for observation, unless cultivated for medicinal purposes in such parts where they are not found growing naturally.

*Titles.* There being formerly supposed to be more species of this genus, Ground Ivy was distinguished by the name *Glecoma foliis reniformibus crenatis*, which is the title it now bears. Caspar Bauhine calls it, *Hedera terrestris vulgaris*, also *Hedera terrestris montana*; Gerard calls it, *Hedera terrestris*; Tournefort, *Calamintha humilior, folio rotundiore*; and Fuchsius, *Chamæcissus*. It grows naturally in woods, hedges, banks, &c. in England, and most of the northern parts of Europe.

*Class and order in the Linnæan system.* *Glecoma* is of the class and order *Didynamia Gymnospermia*; and the characters are,

*The character.* 1. CALYX is a monophyllous, tubular, cylindrical, striated, small, permanent perianthium, divided at the brim into five acute unequal segments.

2. COROLLA is one ringent petal. The tube is slender and compressed. The upper lip is erect, obtuse, and semi bifid. The lower lip is patent, large, obtuse, and divided into three segments, of which the middle one is largest and indented.

3. STAMINA. The filaments are four, under the upper lip, two of which are shorter than the other, and each pair of antheræ are connivent in form of a cross.

4. PISTILLUM consists of a quadrifid germen, a filiforme style under the upper lip, and a bifid acute stigma.

5. PERICARPIUM. There is none. The seeds are contained in the calyx.

6. SEMINA. The seeds are four, and oval.

## CHAP. CCXIV.

## *GLOBULARIA*, BLUE DAISY.

THE perennials of this genus are,

*Species.*
1. Common Blue Daisy.
2. Naked-stalked Blue Daisy.
3. Prickly Blue Daisy.
4. Heart-leaved Blue Daisy.
5. Oriental Blue Daisy.

*Description of the Common.* 1. Common Blue Daisy. The radical leaves are broad, nervous, smooth, of a thick consistence, and indented in three parts at their extremities. The stalks are round, striated, usually reddish, six, eight, or sometimes ten inches high, and adorned with narrow leaves, which are spear-shaped, smooth, and entire. The flowers are collected in round heads at the top of the stalk; they are of a beautiful blue colour, and the general characters indicate their structure. They appear in June, and are succeeded by seeds which ripen in autumn.

*Naked-stalked.* 2. Naked-stalked Blue Daisy. The leaves are oblong, spear-shaped, smooth, and of a dark-green colour. The stalk is single, round, slightly striated, naked, and grows to about eight or ten inches high. The flowers terminate the stalk, being collected there in round heads; they are of a pale, but elegant blue colour; they appear in June, and the seeds ripen in autumn.

*Prickly.* 3. Prickly Blue Daisy. The radical leaves are crenated, prickly, numerous, and of a deep green colour. The stalks grow to be six or eight inches high, and are adorned with leaves which are entire, and sharp or prickly-pointed. The flowers terminate the stalk in a globular form; they are of a blue colour, appear in June, and are succeeded by ripe seeds in autumn.

*Heart-leaved.* 4. Heart-leaved Blue Daisy. The leaves of this species are numerous, small, short, heart-shaped, and indented at the extremity. The flower stalks are slender, and grow to about four

four or five inches high, at the top of which stand the flowers in globular heads, they are of a blue colour, appear in June, and the seeds ripen in September

and Oriental Blue Daisy 5 Oriental Blue Daisy The stalk is herbaceous, single, almost destitute of leaves, and grows to be near a foot high The radical leaves are pretty broad, oval, spear-shaped, and entire, but the few leaves on the stalk are very small, spear-shaped, and placed alternately at a good distance from one another The heads of the flowers grow alternately from the upper parts of the stalk, and they sit close, having no footstalks, they appear in June and July, and in favourable seasons the seeds ripen in autumn

Manner of propagating these plants This last sort is rather tender, but the first four are all extremely hardy, and may be planted in the coldest situation They are all propagated by parting the roots early in autumn The first four should be set in moist, shady, and the most exposed places, but the situation of the last should be not only warm, dry, and well defended, but a few plants should be set in pots, to be preserved under a hot-bed frame or some shelter during the winter, to continue the sort, in case the plants abroad should be destroyed by the severity of the season

They are also propagated by sowing the seeds in the spring in beds of light earth made fine When they come up, the trouble they will call for is, to draw out the weakest where they crowd each other, to keep the ground clean from weeds, and afford them water in dry weather all the summer In the autumn they may be removed to the places where they are designed to remain, observing to plant the first four sorts in moist cool places, and one share of the plants of the fifth sort in the warmest situation, and another share in pots, to keep up the stock, in case those abroad should be destroyed by hard weather

Titles 1 Common Blue Daisy is titled, *Globularia caule herbaceo, foliis radicalibus tridentatis, caulinis lanceolatis* In the *Hortus Cliffort* it is termed, *Globularia caule folioso, foliis ovatis integerrimis* Cammerarius calls it, *Aphyllanthes anguillare*, Caspar Bauhine, *Bellis cærulea, caule folioso*, Tabernæmontanus, *Bellis cærulea Apula*, also *Bellis cærulea Monspeliaca* It grows naturally in Germany, Italy, France, and many other parts of Europe

2 Naked-stalked Blue Daisy is, *Globularia caule nudo, foliis integerrimis lanceolatis* Tournefort calls it, *Globularia Pyrenaica, folio oblongo, caule nudo*, Morison, *Scabiosa bellidis folio humilis, caule nudo, radice non repente*, and Caspar Bauhine, *Bellis cærulea, caule nudo* It grows naturally on the Alps and Pyrenees

3 Prickly Blue Daisy is, *Globularia foliis radicalibus crenato-aculeatis caulinis integerrimis mucronatis* Tournefort calls it, *Globularia spinosa*, and Caspar Bauhine, *Bellis cærulea spinosa*, also *Bellis spinosa, flore globoso* It grows naturally on the mountains of Granada

4 Heart-leaved Blue Daisy is, *Globularia caule subnudo, foliis cuneiformibus tricuspidatis, intermedio minimo* In the *Hortus Cliffort* it is termed, *Globularia foliis radicalibus cuneiformibus retusis dentatis, denticulo intermedio minimo* Caspar Bauhine calls it, *Bellis cærulea montana frutescens*, Tournefort, *Globularia Alpina minima, origani folio*, Morison, *Scabiosa bellidis folio humilis, caule nudo, radice repente, folio cordato*, also *Scabiosa, bellidis folio, Pyrenaica minima* It grows naturally in Pannonia, Austria, Helvetia, and the Pyrenees

5 Oriental Blue Daisy is, *Globularia caule subnudo, capitulis alternis sessilibus, foliis lanceolato-ovatis integris* Tournefort calls it, *Globularia Orientalis, floribus per caulem sparsis* It grows naturally in Natolia

Class and order in the Linnæan system *Globularia* is of the class and order *Tetrandria Monogynia*, and the characters are,

The characters 1 CALYX The common perianthium is of the length of the florets The proper perianthium is monophyllous, tubular and cut at the top into five acute permanent segments

2 COROLLA The general flower is nearly equal The florets consist each of one petal, which is tubular at the base, and divided at the top into five parts, which form a kind of upper and lower lip The upper lip is narrow, short, and divided into two segments, the lower lip is cut into three large equal segments

3 STAMINA are four simple filaments the length of the corollulæ, having an erect incumbent antheræ

4 PISTILLUM consists of an oval germen, a simple style the length of the stamina, and an obtuse stigma

5 PERICARPIUM There is none The proper calyx becomes connivent, and encloses the seeds

6 SEMINA The seeds are single and oval

# CHAP CCXV

## *GLYCYRRHIZA*, LIQUORICE.

THERE are only three species of this genus

Species 1 Smooth-podded *Glycyrrhiza*, or Common Liquorice

2 Hairy-podded Oriental Liquorice

3 Hedge-hog Liquorice

Smooth-podded Glycyrrhiza described 1 Smooth-podded *Glycyrrhiza*, or Common Liquorice The root is thick, long, creeping, strikes deep into the ground, is brownish without, yellowish within, and full of a pleasant sweet pectoral juice The stalks are round, firm, hairy, viscous, and grow to be four feet high The leaves are large and pinnated, each being composed of several pair of oval folioles, which are terminated by an odd one, they are a little clammy, and frequently of a dark-green colour The flowers are produced in erect spikes from the wings of the leaves, they are of a pale-blue colour,

colour, appear in July, and are ſucceeded by ſhort ſmooth pods containing the ſeeds.

Medicinal properties. The juice of liquorice is balſamic, detergent, and ſo fine a pectoral, that it bears a principal part in all compoſitions for coughs and diſorders of the ſtomach. Spaniſh juice is the inſpiſſated juice of liquorice.

Deſcription of the Hairy Oriental. 2. Hairy Oriental Liquorice. The root is thick, ſtrikes deep into the ground, and has a ſweetiſh taſte. The ſtalks are upright, firm, and a yard high. The leaves are pinnated, each being compoſed of five pair of folioles, which are terminated by an odd one. The flowers are produced from the wings of the leaves in July, and are ſucceeded by hairy pods, which are larger than thoſe of the former ſort, and contain ripe ſeeds in autumn.

and the Hedge-Hog Liquorice. 3. Hedge-Hog Liquorice. The root is thick, yellow within, and replete with a ſweet juice. The ſtalks are upright, firm, tough, glutinous, and grow to be four or five feet high. The leaves are pinnated, each being compoſed of about five pair of oval, oblong, clammy folioles, which are terminated by an odd one. The flowers come out from the wings of the leaves, in very ſhort cloſe ſpikes; they are ſmall, and of a blue colour, appear in July, and are ſucceeded by ſhort round prickly compact pods, containing ripe ſeeds, in autumn. This was the true *Glycyrrhiza*, or Liquorice, of the Greeks.

The laſt two ſorts are propagated in the ſame manner as the firſt, and as the firſt is raiſed in large quantities for medicinal purpoſes, I ſhall deſcribe the proceſs, and lay down proper rules to be obſerved in order to obtain a good plantation of liquorice.

Proceſs for forming a plantation of liquorice. The firſt thing principally to be regarded is the ſoil. This ſhould be naturally deep, looſe, light, dry, freſh, and rich, but not fattened with dung; for tho' liquorice will grow in rich dunged ſoils, it is generally black, frequently cankered, and of inferior value.

If the land is worn out with tillage, or the like, it muſt then be heartened with dung thoroughly rotten, mixed with lime, coal-aſhes, or ſoot. In rich ſandy ſoils liquorice will ſucceed; but in damp, wet, clayey ſituations the culture of liquorice ſhould never be attempted.

Having fixed upon a proper ſpot for the liquorice plantation, the firſt thing to be done is to prepare the ground properly; and that is by digging it as low as the ſoil will allow, which ought to be three ſpades deep at leaſt, if you expect to have the fineſt liquorice in return. September or October is the time for the work; and having well prepared the ground by ſuch double and triple digging, the next thing is to procure the ſets. Theſe ſhould be taken from the ſides of the old roots, be ſix or eight inches long, and ſhould have at leaſt one or two good eyes belonging to each. Having a ſufficient quantity of ſets in readineſs, and the ſurface of the mould levelled and made fine, the next proceſs is the planting. In order for this, let four rows be drawn a foot and a half from each other, and in theſe rows plant your ſets at a foot and a half diſtance from each other; an iron dibble is a proper inſtrument for the purpoſe; and they muſt be ſet ſo deep, that the eye or bud of each ſet ſhould be level with the ground. The four rows being thus planted, a bed is formed with ſets at a foot and a half diſtance from each other every way. An interval of two feet muſt be ſet off for an alley, and a ſecond bed muſt be planted with four rows in like manner; then a third, &c. until the whole is finiſhed. This being compleated, the alleys ſhould be dug up one ſpade's depth, to draw off the redundant moiſture, and the mould laid on the beds; and this will raiſe the ſoil about two inches above the eyes of the ſets. The ſurface muſt be next raked level and ſmooth, the alleys and beds muſt be neated up, and the buſineſs is done.

In winter, if hard froſts ſet in, cover the beds over with ſome looſe litter; but be careful to take it away early enough when the froſts are gone. In the ſpring hoe up the weeds as they appear; and let this work be repeated at proper intervals all ſummer; and the winter following, in very hard weather, let the beds be covered with looſe litter as before. In the ſpring, before the ſhoots ariſe, looſen the mould between the plants with a narrow ſpade, and dig up the mould in the alleys between the beds; and if ſoot or coal aſhes can be procured, ſprinkle it with the hand over the beds, and it will greatly invigorate and ſtrengthen the plants. During the ſummer, keep the ground clean from weeds; and let this be obſerved the ſummer after, and at the end of that, the plants being then three years old, the roots will be of proper age to be taken up for uſe. Every autumn the ſtalks ſhould be cut down to the ground, when they are in a decaying ſtate; and at that time, in the third autumn after planting, the roots ſhould be taken up. It ſometimes happens, in ſuitable land, that liquorice roots are taken up when two years old; but, notwithſtanding that, I am pretty certain the owner would be well paid for his waiting another year by the greater abundance the beds will yield. If the land ſhould not be very ſuitable to the plants, and at the end of three years you find the roots ſmall, and weak in proportion, they muſt nevertheleſs be then taken up; for after they have grown longer than three years, they become ſticky, often cankered, black-coated, and of little value.

Method of taking up the roots. The manner of taking the roots up is by opening a trench on the outſide of the plants the whole depth the roots ſtrike, and then trenching the whole ground in the like manner, having proper perſons in readineſs to take up the roots, as they are looſened by the ſpade.

Management of the land afterwards. The ſummer after the roots are taken up, the land ſhould lie fallow, be well manured with dung that is thoroughly rotten, and lime, and be three or four times well ploughed; and if the land has never borne any liquorice before, you may proceed to plant it afreſh in the autumn. After the ſecond crop is off, it ſhould not be planted again with liquorice, but the ſummer following it will bear an amazing crop of oats. The next ſummer it may be made to bear wheat; but the ſummer after that it ſhould lie fallow, and be well dunged. The fourth ſummer it may bear barley, the fifth wheat again; the ſixth it ſhould lie fallow, be well dunged with perfectly rotten dung mixed with lime, and then in the autumn be planted afreſh with liquorice ſets. A ſufficient number of ſpots muſt be aſſigned for the liquorice plantation, that they may ſucceed each other in order, and a regular ſale be made every year.

Encreaſe and profit. The encreaſe is amazing, and the profits very great, if the ſoil be ſuitable, no leſs than three thouſand pounds weight being known to grow on an acre, which has been ſold for upwards of ſixty pounds.

The moſt noted places for liquorice plantations in England, are Pontefract in Yorkſhire, and Godalmin in Surry.

It has been recommended by ſome to ſow onions, lettuces, or the like, when the liquorice plantation

plantation is first made. But this is very bad advice, for they will suck the heart of the land as bad as weeds, and by taking away that nourishment which ought to be communicated to the liquorice, cause it to become weaker, less juicy, and of inferior value. In order, therefore, to have your liquorice in perfection, suffer nothing to grow among it, keep it perfectly clean from weeds, and take up the roots as soon as the stalks are decayed, not earlier, or late in the spring, as is sometimes practised, for then they will shrivel, abate in weight, and be more liable to decay.

Titles

1. Common Liquorice is titled, *Glycyrrhiza leguminibus glabris, stipulis nullis*. Caspar Bauhine calls it, *Glycyrrhiza siliquosa & Germanica*, and Dodonaeus, *Glycyrrhiza vulgaris*. It grows naturally in Germany, Italy, France, and Spain.

2. Hairy-podded Liquorice is, *Glycyrrhiza leguminibus hirsutis, foliolo impari petiolato*. Tournefort calls it, *Glycyrrhiza Orientalis, siliquis hirsutissimis*. It is a native of the East.

3. Hedge-hog Liquorice is, *Glycyrrhiza leguminibus echinatis, foliis stipulatis*. Caspar Bauhine calls it, *Glycyrrhiza capite echinato*, Cammerarius, *Dulcis radix*. It is a native of Tartary.

Class and order in the Linnaean system

*Glycyrrhiza* is of the class and order *Diadelphia Decandria*, and the characters are,

The characters

1. CALYX is a monophyllous, tubular, permanent, bilabiated perianthium. The upper lip is divided into three narrow segments, the middle one of which is the broadest, and cut into two parts. The lower lip is narrow and undivided.

2. COROLLA is papilionaceous. The vexillum is oval, spear-shaped, upright, and long. The alae are oblong, and shaped like the carina, but are a little larger. The carina is dipetalous and acute.

3. STAMINA are diadelphous, nine filaments are joined in a body, the other stands single, and their antherae are roundish and simple.

4. PISTILLUM consists of a short germen, an awl-shaped style the length of the stamina, and a rising obtuse stigma.

5. PERICARPIUM is an oval, or else an oblong pod, which is compressed, acute, and contains one cell.

6. SEMINA. The seeds are kidney-shaped, and very few.

# CHAP. CCXVI.

## *GNAPHALIUM*, CUDWEED.

Species

THE species of this genus which may be cultivated abroad, are,

1. Mountain Cudweed, or Cats-foot.
2. Low Alpine Cudweed.
3. American Cudweed.
4. Plantain-leaved Cudweed.
5. Red-flowered Goldilocks.
6. Narrow-leaved *Stœchas*.
7. Oriental Goldilocks, or Eternal Flower.
8. Sweet-scented Eternal Flower.

Mountain Cudweed described

1. Mountain Cudweed, or Cats-foot. This is a low plant, sending forth shoots from the side, which strike root, and soon spread about to a considerable distance. The leaves are narrow at the base, rounded at the extremity, of a hoary white colour, and lie on the ground. The stalks for the support of the flowers are simple, hoary, and about four inches high. A single corymbus of flowers terminates each stalk; they appear in May and June, and frequently again in autumn.

Its varieties

The varieties of this species are,
The White-flowered Mountain Cudweed.
The Purple-flowered.
The Variegated.
The Long-leaved Mountain Cudweed.

It is the cups of all the species of *Gnaphalium* which constitute the greatest beauty of their flowers; these are permanent, glossy, and shining, and often look beautiful after the flowers have been gathered some years.

Description of the Low Alpine,

2. Low Alpine Cudweed. This is a low plant, sending forth short shoots from the sides, which strike root at the joints. The radical leaves are spear-shaped, smooth, and greenish on their upper side, but very white and downy underneath, and lie on the ground. The stalks are simple, downy, about three inches high, and adorned with about three or four narrow spear-shaped leaves. The flowers are collected into small naked heads at the tops of the stalks; they are of a dull red colour, appear in May and June, and often again in autumn.

American,

3. American Cudweed. This in many places is called Live-for-ever. The root is creeping, and soon spreads itself to a considerable distance. The radical leaves are moderately broad, oval, spear-shaped, pointed, and white, with a coarse down; but the leaves on the stalks are narrow, spear-shaped, acuminated, and grow alternately. The stalks are thick, soft, woolly, grow to about a foot and a half high, and divide into several branches near the top, for the support of the flowers. A corymbus of flowers terminates each of the branches, having moderately large permanent silvery calyces; they appear in June and July, at which time if they are gathered in a dry day, they will not fade for some years. Hence the names, Live-for-ever, Everlasting, Eternal, &c. have been used for this plant. They should be gathered when they first appear, otherwise they grow yellow in the middle, and lose their beauty.

Plantain-leaved,

4. Plantain-leaved Cudweed. This species sends runners from the side, which strike root, and make more encrease than could be wished. The radical leaves are oval, woolly, and large, but those on the stalk are narrow, and grow alternately. The stalks are simple, hoary, and about half a foot high. The flowers form a



 corymbus

corymbus on the top of the stalk, they are small, and of a white colour, appear in June and July, and frequently at the end of summer and in the autumn

5 Red-flowered Goldylocks The radical leaves are narrow, wooly, obtuse, entire, and spread on the ground The stalks are wooly, grow to about six inches high, and are adorned with leaves like the radical ones, but narrower and sharp-pointed The flowers are collected in corymbous bunches, which come out alternately from the upper part of the stalk, they are of a soft and delicate red colour, and display their beauties in the month of June

6 Narrow-leaved *Stoechas* The stalks of this plant are ligneous, grow to be two or three feet high and divide into many slender branches, which are covered with a white bark The leaves are narrow, green on their upper side, but hoary underneath, and are placed without order all over the plant The flowers form a compound corymbus at the ends of the branches, they are small and of a yellow colour, appear in May, and often continue in succession until the end of summer

7 Oriental Goldylocks, or Eternal Flower This species includes many varieties, the principal of which go by the names of,

Narrow-leaved Immortal Flower
Broad-leaved Immortal Flower
Dwarf Oriental Immortal Flower

Narrow-leaved Immortal Flower The stalks are ligneous, white, divide into a few irregular branches, and grow to about a yard high The leaves are long, narrow, spear-shaped, and downy on both sides The flowers terminate the branches in a compound corymbus, there are the Silvery White and the Golden-Yellow kinds, they appear in June, and often continue in succession all summer

Broad-leaved Immortal Flower The lower leaves are broad, spear-shaped, obtuse, grow many together, and are of a downy white on both sides The stalks grow to about a foot and a half high, send forth a few downy side-branches, and are adorned with leaves like the radical ones, but smaller The flowers grow in compound bunches at the ends of the stalks, they are of a golden yellow colour, appear in June, continue a long time in succession, and frequently alter to a reddish colour as they die away

Dwarf Oriental Immortal Flower The stalks are short ligneous, and put forth many heads, from which the flower-stalks proceed The leaves are wooly on both sides, narrow, and adorn the plant in great plenty The flower-stalks grow to be eight or ten inches long, and each of them is terminated by a compound corymbus of flowers, they are moderately large, of a bright yellow colour, appear in May, and often continue in succession until the end of summer

This is the most beautiful variety belonging to this species, and is one of the most common sorts in Portugal and Spain, where it is propagated to ornament their churches in winter, and from whence we frequently receive it in England to adorn our ladies, who purchase them for those purposes The flowers of all the sorts should be gathered before they are too ripe, a dry afternoon should be selected for the purpose, and they will then continue beautiful for many years

8 Sweet-scented Eternal Flower The stalks are woody, divide into several irregular branches, which are winged, and grow to about a yard high The leaves are oblong, obtuse, pointed, of a dark green colour on their upper side, but hoary underneath, and decurrent, having membranes running from the base of each leaf along the stalk The flowers come out from the ends of the branches in compound close corymbous bunches, they are small, and of a bright gold colour at first, but die to a dark, dull yellow, and lessen in beauty, they appear in May and June, and often continue in succession until the end of summer This sort frequently produces seeds in England

The first four sorts are extremely hardy, and will thrive in any soil or situation They increase amazingly by the roots and shoots, which strike root at the joints These may be taken from the old plants at any time of the year, more especially in the autumn, and set in the places where they are designed to remain, when the greatest trouble they will occasion will be to keep them within due bounds

The first sort is propagated by parting of the roots in the autumn, but it increases slowly, though it is an elegant plant, and deserving of a place in any collection of flowers It is tolerably hardy, but must have a dry light soil, a good exposure, and a well sheltered situation, to ensure its safety through our winters

The sixth sort is propagated by planting the slips where they are to remain in any of the summer months They must be well shaded and watered until they have taken root, and afterwards they will require no trouble, except keeping them clean from weeds, provided the situation be dry, warm, and well defended

The seventh and eighth species, including their varieties, are generally reckoned green-house plants, but the reason of their being introduced here, is on account of the extraordinary beauty they will assume when planted in the full ground, more than when confined in pots and housed, and that they will live through our moderate winters, provided the situation be warm and good Let, therefore, the warmest the lightest, and the dryest soil, in the best sheltered place, be appropriated to them, and their propagation is by planting of the slips in the manner of the former However, for safety sake, let a sufficient number of plants be removed into pots, to be housed in the winter, whereby the kinds may be increased, provided those abroad should be destroyed by hard weather

1 Mountain Cudweed, or Cat's Foot, is titled, *Gnaphalium sarmentis procumbentibus, caule simplicissimo, corymbo simplici terminali, floribus dioicis* In the *Flora Lapp* it is termed, *Gnaphalium caule simplicissimo, floribus coloratis terminato* Gerard calls it, *Gnaphalium montanum purpureum & album*, Parkinson, *Gnaphalium montanum flore pes cati*, Caspar Bauhine names it, *Gnaphalium montanum, flore rotundiore*, also, *Gnaphalium montanum, longiore flore & folio*, and Dodonæus, *Pilosella minor* It grows naturally in dry sterile places in England, and most countries of Europe

2 Low Alpine Cudweed is, *Gnaphalium sarmentis procumbentibus caule simplicissimo, capitulo terminali aphyllo, floribus oblongis* Haller calls it *Gnaphalium latiore folio, caule non ramoso, spica nuda fusca terminato*, Caspar Bauhine, *Gnaphalium Alpinum minus*, and Scheuchzer, *Filago Alpina minor erecta* It grows naturally on the Alps of Lapland and Switzerland

3 American Cudweed is, *Gnaphalium herbaceum, foliis linearis lanceolatis acuminatis alternis, caule superne ramoso, corymbis fastigiatis* Caspar Bauhine calls it, *Gnaphalium latifolium Americanum*, John Bauhine, *Gnaphalium Americanum*, and Parkinson, *Argyrocome sive Gnaphalium Americanum* It grows naturally in some of our meadows and pastures, as well as in most parts of North America

4 Hun-

4 Plantain-leaved Cudweed is, *Gnaphalium sarmentis procumbentibus, caule simplicissimo, foliis radicalibus ovatis mucronatis* Gronovius calls it, *Gnaphalium stoloniferum repens, caulibus longissimis, foliis ovatis ...*, and Plukenet, *Gnaphalium plantaginis folio, Virginianum* It grows naturally in Virginia

5 Red-flowered Goldylocks is, *Gnaphalium fruticosum, foliis sublanceolatis tomentosis sessilibus, corymbis alternis conglobatis, floribus globosis* Boerhaave calls it, *Elichrysum flore suaverubente* The place of its natural growth is not known

6 Narrow-leaved Stœchas is, *Gnaphalium fruticosum, foliis linearibus, ramis virgatis, corymbo composito* Caspar Bauhine calls it, *Elichrysum sive Stœchas citrina angustifolia*, Morison, *Helichrysum sive chrysocome angustifolia vulgaris*, Barrelier, *Chrysocome sive Stœchas citrina minor*; and Dodonæus, *Stœchas citrina* It grows naturally on dry barren hills in Germany, France, Spain, and the East

7 Oriental Goldylocks, or Eternal Flower, is, *Gnaphalium fruticosum, foliis lineari-lanceolatis sessilibus, corymbo composito, pedunculis elongatis* In the *Hortus Cliffortianus* it is termed, *Gnaphalium foliis confertis angusto lanceolatis, caule fruticoso, corymbo composito* Caspar Bauhine calls it, *Elichrysum orientale*, Commeline, *Elichrysum Africanum frutescens, angustis & longioribus foliis incanis*, and Morison, *Helichrysum frutescens latifolium, flore comubifero toto aureo* It grows naturally in Africa

8 Sweet-scented Eternal Flower is, *Gnaphalium herbaceum ... occurrentibus obtusis mucronatis ut inque tomentosis ...* Plukenet calls it, *Elichrysum latifolium ... caule, ...mum* It is not certain where this plant naturally grows

*Gnaphalium* is of the class and order *Syngenesia Polygamia Superflua*, and the characters are,

1 Calyx The general calyx is round, shining, imbricated The scales are oval, connivent, and loosely arranged

2 Corolla is composed of numerous hermaphrodite and female florets in the same calyx The hermaphrodite florets are tubular, funnel-shaped, and cut at the brim into five segments, which are reflexed The female florets have no corolla

3 Stamina, in the hermaphrodites, are five very short capillary filaments, having a tubular cylindrical anthera

4 Pistillum, in the hermaphrodites consists of an oval germen, a filiforme style the length of the stamina, and a bifid stigma

In the females it consists of an oval germen, a filiforme style the length of the hermaphrodites, and a bifid reflexed stigma

5 Pericarpium There is none The calyx is permanent and glossy

6 Semina, of the hermaphrodites, are single, oblong, small, and crowned with down

Those of the females are similar to those of the hermaphrodites

The receptacle is naked

Class and order in the Linnæan system The characters.

# CHAP CCXVII

## *GRATIOLA*, HEDGE HYSSOP

Species

THE many species of this genus are,

1 Common Hedge Hyssop

2 Virginian Hedge Hyssop

3 Peruvian Hedge Hyssop

Common Hedge Hyssop described

1 Common Hedge Hyssop This plant hath a thick, white, fleshy, jointed, fibrated root, which creeps under the ground, and soon spreads itself to a considerable distance The stalks are upright, square, often reddish near the ground, and grow to about a foot high The leaves are spear-shaped, narrow, serrated, and grow opposite to each other on the stalks The flowers come out on footstalks from the wings of the leaves at the joints, they are of a pale-yellowish colour, and the general characters indicate their composition They appear in June, and are sometimes succeeded by seeds, which ripen in September

Variety

There is a variety of this species with flowers of a pale-blue or white colour

The whole plant is intolerably bitter, is a violent cathartic and emetic, and used in infusions for dropsies, jaundices, &c

Virginian

2 Virginian Hyssop The stalks are upright, and grow to about a foot high The leaves are spear-shaped, obtuse, slightly indented on their edges, and grow opposite to each other on the stalks The flowers come out on footstalks from the wings of the leaves at the joints, their colour is white, they appear in July, but are rarely succeeded by seeds in England

and Peruvian Hedge Hyssop described

3 Peruvian Hedge Hyssop The stalk is slender, weak, jointed, and about eight or ten inches high The leaves are oval, oblong, serrated, and grow opposite to each other The flowers come out from the wings of the leaves on each side the stalks, on very short footstalks, they are small, of a white colour, appear in July, but are rarely succeeded by seeds in England

All these sorts grow in moist places, or such as have been overflowed with water, which teaches us to allow them a moist part of the garden, and, if possible, a shady situation

Culture.

They are propagated by parting of the roots, the best time for which is the autumn, when the stalks decay After they are set out they will require no trouble, except keeping them clean from weeds, and duly watering them in dry weather

Titles

1 Common Hedge Hyssop is titled, *Gratiola floribus pedunculatis, foliis lanceolatis serratis* Caspar Bauhine calls it, *Gratiola centauroides*, John Bauhine, *Gratiola*, and Morison, *Digitalis minima Gratiola dicta* It grows naturally in moist

moist meadows

mountainous places in Germany, France, and Italy

2 Virginian Hedge Hyssop is, *Gratiola foliis lanceolatis obsolete subdentatis* It grows naturally in Virginia

3 Peruvian Hedge Hyssop is, *Gratiola floribus subsessilibus* Feuill calls it, *Gratiola latiore folio, flore albo* It grows naturally in moist places in Peru

Class and order in the Linnæan System The characters

*Gratiola* is of the class and order *Diandria Monogynia*, and the characters are,

1 CALYX is an erect perianthium, divided into five awl-shaped permanent segments

2 COROLLA is one unequal petal The tube is angular, and longer than the calyx The limb is small, and divided into four parts, of which the upper one is the broadest, indented, and reflexed, the others are straight and equal

3 STAMINA There are four awl-shaped filaments shorter than the corolla, of which the two lower ones are short and steril, the other two, which are inserted in the tube of the petal, are lower, and have round sh antheræ

4 PISTILLUM consists of a conic germen, a straight awl-shaped style, and a stigma with two lips, which close after fecundation

5 PERICARPIUM is an oval, acuminated, bivalvate capsule, containing two cells

6 SEMINA The seeds are many, and small

# CHAP CCXVIII

## GUNDELIA

THERE is only one species of this genus, but it admits of two notable varieties, called,

1 Downy-headed *Gundelia*
2 Smooth-headed *Gundelia*

Downy

1 Downy-headed *Gundelia* The stalks are upright, branching near the top, and grow to be about a foot and a half high The leaves resemble those of the Prickly Bear's Breech, being large, nearly of the same form, and each indenture on their edges terminating in a spine, they are long near the bottom of the plant, smaller higher up, and some of them are cut almost to the mid rib The flowers come out from the ends of the branches in conical heads, having at their base a series of narrow prickly leaves placed circularly, they are of a purple colour, and the general characters indicate their structure, they appear in July, but are very seldom succeeded by ripe seeds in England

and Smooth leaved Gundelia described

2 Smooth headed *Gundelia* The stalks, leaves, and flowers are like the former, but the heads are destitute of that soft down or cottony matter which the others possess Both sorts arise indiscriminately from the same seeds, so that if you can procure good seeds from either kind, you will be pretty sure of having plenty of both in return

Method of raising them

They are propagated by sowing the seeds, which must be procured from the places where the plants naturally grow, for they rarely ripen well in England The seeds should be sown early in the spring in beds of light fresh earth The beds should be the places where the plants are designed to flower, for they do not bear removing well When they come up, they will require no trouble during the summer, except thinning them to proper distances, and keeping them clean from weeds At the approach of hard weather in winter let some gorse bushes be stuck round the beds, to break the edge of the black frosts, and with such slight protection they will live through our winters, provided the soil be naturally dry The summer following they will flower, at which time it may be proper to cover them with glasses, to prevent the wet from falling on them, which would otherwise rot the germen, and destroy the seeds If this precaution is used, the seeds will sometimes advance to maturity, to continue the kinds, if not, the seeds must be constantly procured from abroad Indeed the plants are richly deserving of that expence, being very beautiful, and ornamental at the time of flower, but though the root in some places will last for many years, it generally dies after the plant has flowered in our gardens

There being no other species of this genus, it stands with the name simply *Gundelia* Tournefort calls it, *Gundelia orientalis acanthi aculeati folio, capite glabro*, also, *Gundelia orientalis, acanthi aculeati folio, flosculis intensè purpureis, capite araneosa lanugine obsito* Morison names it, *Eryngium Syriacum foliis chon elloides longis et spinosis*, and Rauwolf, *Silybum Dioscoridis Hacub el carracg scrap ens* It grows naturally in Armenia, Syria, and Aleppo The

*Gundelia* is of the class and order *Syngenesia Polygamia Segregata*, and the characters are, Class and order in the Linnæan System The characters

1 CALYX The general calyx consists of the circle of long narrow leaves which surround the receptacle of the flower

2 COROLLA The general flower is uniform The hermaphrodite florets are equal, and five in each division Each floret is one clavated petal that is swelling at the top, and cut into five erect segments

3 STAMINA are five very short capillary filaments, having a long, cylindrical, tubular anthera

4 PISTILLUM consists of an oval germen immersed in the receptacle, crowned with small scales, a filiforme style longer than the corolla, and two revolute stigmas

5 PERICARPIUM There is none The seeds are contained in the receptacle

6 SEMINA The seeds are single, roundish, and sharp-pointed

CHAP

# CHAP. CCXIX.

## GYPSOPHILA.

THERE is no English name for this genus, and the species go by the respective titles of,

Species

1. Clustered-flowered *Gypsophila*.
2. Creeping *Gypsophila*.
3. Prostrate *Gypsophila*.
4. Fastigiate *Gypsophila*.
5. Tall *Gypsophila*.
6. Globular-flowered *Gypsophila*.
7. Downy *Gypsophila*.
8. Paniculated *Gypsophila*.
9. Perfoliate *Gypsophila*.
10. Rigid *Gypsophila*.
11. Saxifrage *Gypsophila*.

Clustered-flowered Gypsophila described.

1. Clustered-flowered *Gypsophila*. The leaves are numerous at the root, narrow, sharp-pointed, and recurved. The stalks grow a foot high, are jointed, branching near the upper part, garnished with leaves placed opposite, and frequently there are clusters of smaller attendant on them at the joints. The flowers come out from the ends of the branches in close bunches; they are small, and of a white colour, appear in July, and are succeeded by ripe seeds in September.

Creeping.

2. Creeping *Gypsophila*. The root is creeping, and sends forth numerous awl shaped, flat, grass-like leaves. The stalks are simple, about a foot high, and adorned with leaves placed opposite at the joints. The flowers are numerous at the ends of the stalks; they are small, and of a purplish colour, appear in July, and the seeds ripen in September.

Its varieties.

There is a variety of this species with white flowers, and another with flowers which are white on their inside and red without.

Prostrate Gypsophila.

3. Prostrate *Gypsophila*. The stalks are diffuse, smooth, taper, purplish at the joints, about a foot long, and lie on the ground. The leaves are spear-shaped, smooth, and rise in clusters from the roots. The flowers are produced in panicles; they are of a white colour, appear in June and July, and the seeds ripen in September.

Its variety.

There is a variety of this with purplish coloured flowers.

Fastigiate,

4. Fastigiate *Gypsophila*. The stalks are branching near the top, and grow to about a foot high. The leaves are narrow, spear shaped, and obsoletely three-cornered. The flowers come out from the ends of the branches in fastigiate bunches; they are of a white colour, appear in June and July, and are succeeded by ripe seeds in September.

Tall,

5. Tall *Gypsophila*. The stalks are thick, jointed, and three or four feet high. The leaves are spear-shaped, trinervous, and straight. The flowers terminate the stalks in roundish bunches; they are of a white colour, appear in July, and are succeeded by seeds which ripen in autumn.

Globular-flowered,

6. Globular-flowered *Gypsophila*. The stalks are simple, jointed, and about a foot and a half high. The leaves are narrow, taper, and grow in clusters from the root and sides of the stalks. The flowers are globose, and of a white colour; they appear in June and July, and are followed by ripe seeds in autumn.

Downy,

7. Downy *Gypsophila*. The stalk is round, downy, and about a foot high. The leaves are spear shaped, moderately broad, trinervous, and downy. The flowers are white, appear in July, and the seeds ripen in autumn.

Paniculated

8. Paniculated *Gypsophila*. The stalks are ligneous, tough, jointed, and about a foot and a half high. The leaves are spear shaped, acute, rough on their edges, and of a blueish-green colour. The flowers are produced in panicles from the tops of the plant; they are dioicous, small, and of a white colour; they appear in July, and are followed by ripe seeds in autumn.

Perfoliate

9. Perfoliate *Gypsophila*. The stalks are herbaceous, jointed, and about a foot and a half high. The leaves are oval, spear shaped, and embrace the stalk with their base. The flowers are produced from the ends of the stalks in kind of panicles; they are small, whitish, and have angular bell shaped cups; they appear in June and July, and are succeeded by ripe seeds in autumn.

Rigid,

10. Rigid *Gypsophila*. The stalk is dichotomous, and hardly a foot high. The leaves are narrow, spear-shaped, flat, and grow opposite to each other at the joints. The flowers grow two together on a footstalk; they are of a whitish colour, their edges are indented, and they have bell-shaped cups; they appear in June and July, and are succeeded by ripe seeds in September.

and Saxifrage Gypsophila described

11. Saxifrage *Gypsophila*. This species hath a creeping root, which sends forth several slender branches that lie on the ground. The leaves are narrow, awl shaped, and grow opposite to each other at the joints. The flowers are of a reddish colour, indented on their edges, and have angular cups; they appear in July, and are followed by seeds which ripen in the autumn.

Its variety

There is a variety of this species with white flowers.

These are all hardy plants, and annually produce flowers and plenty of seeds, by which they are best propagated.

Manner of propagating these plants

In the spring sow your seeds in a bed of common earth made fine. If dry weather happens after sowing, water the beds, and cover them with mats in the heat of the day, and in about six weeks your plants will come up. All summer they will require no trouble, except keeping them clean from weeds, and watering them in dry weather. In autumn the plants may be taken up, with a ball of earth to each root, and set in the places where they are designed to remain; and the summer following they will flower and produce ripe seeds.

Titles.

1. The first species is titled, *Gypsophila foliis mucronatis recurvatis, floribus aggregatis*. In the *Hortus Upsal.* it is termed, *Saponaria calycibus pentaphyllis, floribus aggregatis, foliis mucronatis canaliculatis recurvis*. Caspar Bauhine calls it, *Caryophyllus saxatilis, ericæ foliis, umbellatis corymbosis*. It grows naturally on the Alps, Pyrenees, and near Montpelier in France.

2. The second species is, *Gypsophila foliis lanceolatis, petiolis emarginatis, staminibus pistillo brevioribus*

... Hortus Cliffort. it is termed, ... , foliis ... planis, ex ... . ... calls it, Saponaria foliis ... ; ... , Buxbaum, ... folio, flore ... ; ... caryophylloides ... astragantis, and Caspar Bauhin, Caryophyllus saxatilis, foliis ... . It grows naturally in the mountainous parts of Siberia, Austria, Helvetia, and the Pyrenees.

3. The third species is, Gypsophila foliis lanceolatis ... , caulibus diffusis, petalis ... campanulatis oblongis ... . It is supposed to grow naturally on the Alps.

4. The fourth species is, Gypsophila foliis lanceolatis ... , ... obtusis ... . In the Flora Suecica it is termed, Saponaria ... , corymbus fastigiatis, foliis ... adnascente. Haller calls it, ... petalis ovatis, ... glaucis ... ; Caspar Bauhine, Caryophyllus saxatilis, ... corymbosis, and Mentzelius ... angustifolium ... . It grows naturally on the rocks of Gotland, Bornholm, and Helvetia.

5. The fifth species is, Gypsophila foliis lanceolatis ... . In the Hortus Upsal. it is termed, Saponaria calycibus ... , corymbis ... lanceolatis, caule adscendente. It grows naturally in Siberia.

6. The sixth species is, Gypsophila foliis linearibus, ... conferti s teretibus. In the Hortus Cliffort. it is termed, Saponaria caule simplici, foliis linearibus ... conjectis teretibus. Caspar Bauhine calls it, Saponariae lychnidis folio, flosculis ... , and Barrelier, ... glauco flore. It grows naturally in Spain.

7. The seventh species is, Gypsophila foliis lanceolatis subtus ... tomentosis, caule pubescente. Barrelier calls it, Linum sylvestre latifolium, flore albicante. It is a native of Spain.

8. The eighth species is, Gypsophila foliis ... scabris, floribus ... , corollis revolutis. It grows naturally in the deserts and stony parts of Tartary and Siberia.

9. The ninth species is, Gypsophila foliis ovato-lanceolatis semiamplexicaulibus. In the Hortus Cliffort. it is termed, Saponaria foliis lanceolatis, calycibus campanulatis angulatis. Dillenius calls it, Spergula ... , foliis inferioribus ... superioribus ... . It grows naturally in Spain and in the East.

10. The tenth species is, Gypsophila foliis ... lanceolatis planis, caule dichotomo, pedunculis ... floris, petalis emarginatis. In the Hortus Cliffort. it is termed, Saponaria caule dichotomo, foliis subulatis planis. Sauvages calls it, Saponaria caule brachiato, capillaceo folio, calyce campanulato, floribus sparsis, and Dalechamp, Tunica minima. It grows naturally near Montpelier.

11. The eleventh species is, Gypsophila ... , calycibus angulatis, squamis ... , corollis ... . In the former edition of the Species Plantarum it is termed, Dianthus calycibus ... , squamis calycinis lanceolatis ... , foliis subulatis. Van Royen calls it, Dianthus radice repente, ramis decumbentibus, foliis ... ; Haller, Dianthus calyce ... ; Caspar Bauhine, Caryophyllus saxifragus ... , Caryophyllus sylvestris, flore minimo, and Barrelier, Lychnis pumila caryophyllata, ... . It grows naturally in Austria, Helvetia, and Gallia.

Gypsophila is of the class and order Decandria Digynia, and the characters are, Class and order in the Linnæan system. The characters.

1. CALYX is a bell-shaped, angular perianthium, divided into five parts.

2. COROLLA is five oval, obtuse, patent, sub-sessile petals.

3. STAMINA are ten awl-shaped, patent filaments, with roundish antheræ.

4. PISTILLUM consists of a subglobose germen, and two filiform styles, with simple stigmas.

5. PERICARPIUM is a globular capsule, composed of five valves, and containing one cell.

6. SEMINA. The seeds are many and roundish.

# CHAP. CCXX

## HEDYSARUM, FRENCH HONEYSUCKLE.

THE perennials of this genus which will endure the open air, are, Species.

1. Canada French Honeysuckle.
2. Alpine French Honeysuckle.
3. Siberian Astragalus.
4. Low Spanish Hedysarum.
5. Rock St. Foin, or Cock's Head.
6. Common St. Foin, or Cock's Head.

1. Canada French Honeysuckle. The root is long, slender, and strikes deep into the ground. The stalks are herbaceous, weak, and about two feet high. The radical leaves are simple, but those on the stalk are trifoliate. The flowers come out in loose spikes from the ends and sides of the branches, they appear in July, and are succeeded by rough, jointed, triangular pods, containing ripe seeds in autumn. Description of the Canada French Honeysuckle.

The varieties of this species are, Its varieties.

The Red-flowered.
The White.
The Purple.

2. Alpine French Honeysuckle. The stalks are slender, nearly erect, and about a foot high. The leaves are pinnated, of a pale-green colour, and grow alternately at the joints. The flowers are produced from the upper parts of the plant in loose spikes, they are large, and of a fine purple colour, appear in July, and are succeeded by smooth, jointed, pendulent pods, containing ripe seeds in autumn. Alpine French Honeysuckle.

3. Siberian Astragalus. The stalks are herbaceous, branching, erect, flexuose, and grow to about two feet high. The leaves are pinnated, large, of a light green colour, and grow alternately at Siberian Astragalus.

at the joints The flowers come out from the ends and sides of the branches in pendulent bunches, they are of a bright purple colour, appear in July, and are succeeded by ripe seeds in autumn

*Its variety.* There is a variety of this species with white flowers.

*Low Spanish Hedysarum.* 4 Low Spanish *Hedysarum* The stalks are ligneous tough, and about eight or nine inches high The leaves are pinnated, large, and almost as long as the stalk The flowers are produced from the upper parts of the plant in smooth spikes, the vexillum of each flower is very short, and the carina is large, broad, and obtuse, they appear in July, and are succeeded by short pods, each containing one seed, which ripens in autumn

*Rock St Foin.* 5 Rock St Foin The leaves are pinnated, long, and much resemble those of the smaller vetches The stalks are very short, tough, and only about four or five inches high The flowers come out in loose spikes from the ends of the stalks, they are of a white colour, appear in July, and are succeeded by monospermous pods, which ripen their seeds in autumn

*Common St Foin.* 6 Common St Foin, or Cocks Head The roots are moderately thick, stringy, tough, and, if the soil will permit, will strike ten or twelve feet deep into the ground The stalks are weak, herbaceous, and usually two feet long, though sometimes in good soils they will grow to be four or five feet in length The leaves are pinnated and large, being composed of about eight or ten pair of folioles, which are terminated by an odd one The folioles are of an oval figure, and are arranged opposite to each other along the midrib The flowers come out from the sides of the stalks in spikes, growing on long naked footstalks, they are of an elegant red colour, appear in June, and are succeeded by roundish, compressed, prickly pods, each containing one seed, which ripens in September

*Its varieties.* The other varieties of this species are,

The White flowered.

The Purple

The Blue

The Striped-flowered St Foin

*Method of propagation.* All these sorts require a dry soil, otherwise their roots are apt to rot in the winter Their propagation is by sowing the seeds in the spring in the places where the plants are to remain When they come up, they will require no trouble, except thinning them to proper distances, and keeping them clean from weeds Many of them will flower the first summer, but the second year they will flower strong, and perfect their seeds

The first five sorts being of foreign growth, are coveted by those who are fond of a general collection of plants The fifth is an indigenous plant of Britain, the famous St Foin in Husbandry, and is propagated to great advantage in gravelly, poor, and chalky land, for the fodder of cattle, both when green or dried

*Laws for raising St Foin.* I shall therefore lay down the laws for raising St Foin, a plant by many thought to be superior to most herbs (Lucern not excepted) for cattle, and which may be cultivated to amazing advantage on some soils which will hardly bear any-thing else

*Proper soil.* Let the soil, therefore, for your St Foin be chalky, gravelly, poor, and dry, for in such soils it may be cultivated to most advantage It will succeed in all these soils, but it most delights in a ground that is rich, deep, and in good heart Nevertheless, do not attempt the cultivation of it in a fertile meadow, or a rich moist earth, for in such places the roots of St Foin will probably rot in a year or two, whereas in dry, chalky, gravelly, and beggarly lands, they will continue for upwards of twenty years, and be of great value in such places, which would otherwise produce little or nothing

Having pitched upon a spot for the purpose, let it be well ploughed, and harrowed several times over with a good harrow, to break all the clods, and pulverise the earth Then, in the beginning of March, proceed to sow your seeds, either *Two methods of sowing the seed.*

By Broad-cast, or

In Drill.

Broad cast is the method by which farmers have been used to sow their seeds of all sorts, and very few of them can hardly ever be made to pursue any other method, especially as it seems to belong to the practice of gardening rather than husbandry, which sowing seeds or setting plants in drills certainly does Broad cast in general is attended with the least trouble for all sorts of seeds, but then much seed may be ever saved by drill-sowing, which is an argument with some indigent farmers to practise that method with their horse peale and beans, when the seed is dear *Broad cast method considered.*

With regard to St Foin, it may be sowed with success both ways, if the soil is naturally light, if it is not, the drill-sowing ought to be practised, because there is a certain depth in which the seed of St Foin ought to be covered, to enable it to come up properly, and which can be more effectually observed in drills than when covered with the harrow

Half an inch is the most proper depth in which the seed should lie under ground If it is much deeper, in a strong soil, very little of it will grow, if it lies on the surface, it will strike root at first, but then it soon dries off, and comes to nothing

In light land the seeds will grow, if covered several inches deep, and in such soils the Broadcast may be used, but the sooner the business is dispatched, the greater quantity of seeds will be wasted

Two bushels of seed ought to be sown on an acre, for although a fourth part of that quantity would be sufficient, provided all were to grow and come up at proper distances, yet so many of the seeds will be buried, others lie on the surface, and so many of the plants probably be destroyed by the grub which frequently takes these plants when in the second leaf, that it will not be safe to sow fewer seeds than two bushels on each acre *Proper quantity to be sown.*

After the plants come up, they must be hoed, and thinned to proper distances, which ought to be twelve inches, or more, or nearer together, according to the soil Few farmers can be persuaded to agree to such thinning, as they think it is doing nothing but cutting up the crop, but they should be told, that without thinning, if the seeds were good and had succeeded, the plants would be so thick that one part would choak the other, and they should be reminded to consider, that a plant growing singly or alone, will assume an extraordinary luxuriance and beauty over others which are weak by their crowding, and much entangling with, one another Your St Foin, therefore, must be left at such a distance from one another, that the roots may have room to thicken and spread, as well as strike deep into the ground, and land occupied with plants thus judiciously disposed, will exert its vigour, and afford you encrease in the greatest abundance *Management after the plants are come up.*

When the plants are thinned with hoeing, dry weather should be made choice of for the purpose, and then all the weeds must be destroyed, and the repetition of hoeing down the weeds must be made as often as it is found necessary all

all summer, and even ever after; for if they are permitted to grow among the St. Foin as some slovenly farmers do, they will not only draw the nourishment which the roots of the St. Foin should have, but by choaking and crowding the plants whilst in their growing state, will otherwise prodigiously weaken and destroy it.

St. Foin is admirably raised by Drill sowing. The drills should be drawn a foot asunder from each other, and not deeper than an inch deep; the seeds should be then dropped into these rows, three or four inches distance from each other, and covered down about half an inch deep. If the seeds are good the plants will come up too close, so that there will be some to spare, in case the grub should attack them when in the second leaf. When all danger from the grub is past, the plants should be thinned in the rows to about the same distance with the former, and managed accordingly.

Directions for sowing the seeds.

Necessary cautions.

The first summer and winter it is thought dangerous to eat the Saint Foin on the ground by cattle, lest, by treading, their feet should harden the ground about them, hurt the crown of the roots, and injure the plants: let it therefore be mowed as it is wanted, and carried off the ground as soon as possible, that the roots may be at liberty to shoot up afresh. A small crop must be expected the first year; but if the plants are left singly at about the above distances, the encrease will be proportionably greater the second and succeeding years, and the roots will continue sound and good, and afford you St. Foin for upwards of thirty years, which otherwise would have rotted, and no traces of St. Foin would have been left in a third part of that time, provided the plants had never been thinned, but left crowding and choaking each other.

and general observations.

When St. Foin is designed for hay, it should be mowed early in June, before it comes into flower, for then the hay will be fine and good, tho' the quantity be less; whereas if the St. Foin is old before it is cut, the hay will be very coarse, and of little value for cattle of any sort.

Soon after the St. Foin is cut, it should be taken off the ground to be made, that the roots may shoot up afresh for a second crop; for two crops of St. Foin may be annually obtained even on poor land, though not in so great abundance as if the land had been rich and good.

It is observable, that St. Foin hay is always the best when there is the least rain, provided the weather be not very wet; cloudy weather and drying winds give the hay an agreeable sweetness, and a heightened flavour for cattle. Small rain hardly does it no harm, which is a property superior to what Lucern possesses. A small quantity of rain falling on Lucern turns it black, the leaves fall off, and the stalks become mouldy and good for little; but Saint Foin is never wholly spoiled by rain, until it can be said to be rotten on the ground.

After all, the greatest excellence in Saint Foin is when eaten green, it being then universally liked by all cattle. It affords abundance of milk to the cow; excellent butter is obtained in consequence of their feeding on it; and as it rises early in the spring, it becomes highly advantageous to such as deal in milch cows at that season. It purges cattle in the spring, cleanses their bodies, and frees them from disorders which they may have contracted through long confinement, cold weather, and dry food. Cows eating greedily of it are not so liable to be dew-blown as by the eating of clover; though they sometimes meet with a kind of surfeit, when first turned into a good pasture of Saint Foin in the spring. It is admirable for feeding black cattle in the autumn; sheep at that season will fatten in a very little time, but then care must be observed to take them off early enough, or they will eat the plants too low, weaken the roots, and greatly injure the succeeding crop; as well as by trampling and hardening the earth about the roots, retain the moisture, and cause them to rot.

By the end of October, or middle of November, the whole spot ought to be cleared of cattle; though if they are small cattle, such as sheep, and the season is dry, as it often happens at that time, and there be much St. Foin left, such small cattle may be continued until the middle or end of December, and they will, by manuring the ground, be of great service to the future St. Foin.

When St. Foin is designed for seed, it should be left untouched until the seeds which succeed the first blown flowers are ripe. This is the time to cut St. Foin for seed; for if it be left uncut until the seeds on the tops of the spikes are ripe, those that were first formed, and which are always the best, will have fallen and be lost; but by cutting it early, that is as soon as the seeds at the bottom of the spike are ripe, none of the seeds will be lost, for the others will ripen after being cut, and will in every respect become good seeds for use.

When the straw, seeds, and every part of your St. Foin is well dried, it should be mowed in the barn, or stacked in some convenient place until a little before the seed is wanted, and then the seed should be threshed out for use; for if it be done much earlier, it will heat, rot, and the greater part be good for nothing.

When necessity obliges it to be threshed in the field, or as soon as it is carried in the summer, the manner of preserving the seed until the spring is, by spreading a layer of straw in a convenient place, then laying on it a stratum of seeds, then another layer of straw, then seeds again, and so on alternately. This will keep them cool, their colour will be fine, and they will be as good in the spring as those that are just threshed out from the mow.

1. Canada French Honeysuckle is titled, *Hedysarum foliis simplicibus ternatisque, floribus racemosis*. Van Royen calls it, *Hedysarum foliis verticalibus simplicibus, caulinis ternatis, floribus laxe spicatis, leguminibus undulatis*. Cornutus, *Hedysarum triphyllum Canadense*; and Morison, *Onobrychis major perennis Canadensis triphylla, siliquis articulatis asperis triangularibus*. It grows naturally in Virginia and Canada. Titles.

2. Alpine French Honeysuckle is, *Hedysarum foliis pinnatis, leguminibus articulatis glabris pendulis caule erecto*. Amman calls it, *Hedysarum saxatile siliquâ levi floribus purpureis*; and Caspar Bauhine, *Onobrychis semine clypeato lævi*. It grows naturally in Siberia and Helvetia.

3. Siberian *Astragalus* is, *Hedysarum foliis pinnatis, stipulis vaginalibus, caule erecto flexuoso, floribus racemosis pendulis*. In the former edition of the *Species Plantarum* it is termed, *Astragalus canlescens erectus, stipulis vaginantibus*. Haller calls it, *Astragalus caule erecto ramoso, spicâ purpurea nutente terminato*. It grows naturally in Siberia and Helvetia.

4. Low Spanish *Hedysarum* is, *Hedysarum foliis pinnatis, caule suffruticoso corollarum vexillis carinâ, alisque vexillo brevioribus leguminibus monospermis*. It is a native of Spain.

5. Rock Saint Foin, or Cock's Head, is, *Hedysarum foliis pinnatis leguminibus monospermis corollarum alis brevissimis, scapis subradicalibus*. Tournefort calls it, *Onobrychis saxatilis, foliis viciæ angustioribus et longioribus aquis extensis*. It grows naturally on the Alps, and in several parts of Germany, Italy, and France.

6. Common

6. Common Saint Foin, or Cock's Head, is, *Hedysarum foliis pinnatis, leguminibus monospermis aculeatis corollarum alis calyce brevioribus, caule elongato* In the *Hortus Cliffort* it is termed, *Hedysarum foliis pinnatis, leguminibus subrotundis* Caspar Bauhine calls it, *Onobrychis, foliis viciæ, fructu echinato, major*; also, *Onobrychis incana, foliis longioribus* John Bauhine names it, *Polygalon Gesneri*; Lobel, *Caput gallinaceum Belgarum*; Gerard, *Onobrychis seu caput gallinaceum*, and Parkinson, *Onobrychis vulgaris* It is found growing on chalky, dry, warm land in England, France, Bohemia, and Siberia

Class and order in the Linnæan system The character is

*Hedysarum* is of the class and order *Diadelphia Decandria*, and the characters are,

1 CALYX is monophyllous perianthium, half cut into five awl-shaped, erect, permanent segments

2 COROLLA is papilionaceous and striated The vexillum is oval, oblong, reflexed, compressed, and indented at the top The alæ are oblong, narrow, and straight The carina is compressed, obtuse, and bifid at the base

3 STAMINA are ten inflexed filaments, nine of which are joined in a body, the other stands separate, having roundish compressed antheræ

4 PISTILLUM consists of a small, narrow, compressed germen, an awl-shaped inflexed style, and a simple stigma

5 PERICARPIUM is a jointed pod The articulations are roundish, compressed, and each contains one seed

6 SEMINA The seeds are reniforme and single

# CHAP. CCXXI

## *HELENIUM*, BASTARD SUN-FLOWER.

THERE is only one species of this genus, called, Bastard Sun-Flower

This plant described

The root is thick, large, spreading, and sends forth several robust, winged upright stalks, which divide near the top, and grow to about six feet high The leaves are narrow, spear-shaped, smooth, entire, and decurrent, the membranes running from the base of each, forming what used to be called the wings of the stalks The flowers come out singly from the divisions of the stalks, on naked footstalks, they are of a golden-yellow colour, like the Sun-Flower, but smaller, their rays are long, and their properties are shewn in the general characters, they appear in July, and continue in succession until the end of autumn

Varieties

There is a variety of this plant with hairy, and another with short serrated leaves

Culture

They are all propagated by parting of the roots, and by this method the differences with respect to the varieties are kept up The time for parting of the roots is any time in the autumn, winter, or early in the spring before the stalks shoot up for flowering They love a moist light earth, and a shady situation Being thus stationed, they will produce plenty of flowers every summer, and be extremely ornamental until the end of autumn

These plants are easily raised by seeds, but as they seldom ripen in England they must be procured from the countries where the plants naturally grow

The seeds should be sown early in the spring on a slight hotbed, to bring them up, otherwise they will often continue until the second year before they make their appearance As soon as they shew themselves, you must give them plenty of air, frequent waterings, and when you have got a sufficient crop above ground, harden them to bear the open air as soon as possible When this is effected, and the plants are fit to remove, let them be taken up on some moist day, and set in beds at about ten inches distance from each other, shade them at first, keep them clean from weeds, and water them as often as dry weather makes it necessary all summer, and by the autumn they will be grown to be strong plants, and may then be removed to the places where they are designed to remain The next summer they will flower, and sometimes, though not very often, perfect their seeds The roots need not be removed oftener than every third year, and if very dry weather should happen in any summer, even old plants, which have stood two or three years, should be watered, and it will cause them to produce a larger quantity of flowers in return

Titles

There being no other species of this genus, it stands with the name simply, *Helenium* In the *Hortus Cliffort* it is termed, *Helenium foliis decurrentibus* Morison calls it, *Chrysanthemum Americanum perenne, caule alato, folio angustato glabro*, Plukenet, *After floridanus aureus, caule alato*, and Cornutus, *After luteus alatus* It grows naturally in moist woods and shady cool places in most parts of North America

Class and order in the Linnæan system. The characters

*Helenium* is of the class and order *Syngenesia Polygamia Superflua*, and the characters are,

1 CALYX The general calyx is simple, monophyllous, patent, and divided into many parts

2 COROLLA is compound and radiated The hermaphrodite florets are numerous in the disk The female florets are in the radius, and of the same number with the segments of the calyx The hermaphrodite florets are tubular, shorter than the calyx, and indented in five parts at the top The female florets are tongue-shaped, longer than the calyx, and cut at the extremity into three segments

3 STAMINA, of the hermaphrodites, are five very short capillary filaments, having a cylindrical, tubular anthera

4 PISTILLUM, of the hermaphrodites, consists of an oblong germen, a filiforme style the length of the stamina, and a bifid stigma

The pistillum in the females consists of an oblong,

oblong germen, a very short style, and a bifid stigma

5 PERICARPIUM There is none

6 SEMINA The seeds of the hermaphrodites are single, angular, oboval, and crowned with small fine-pointed down

The seeds of the females are similar to those of the hermaphrodites

The receptacle is naked and convex.

## CHAP. CCXXII

## *HELIANTHUS*, SUN-FLOWER.

THE great annual Sun-Flower is a well known plant, and the glory of this genus, but besides that there are the following perennials

Species

1 The Many flowered Sun Flower
2 The Tuberous Sun Flower, or Jerusalem Artichoke
3 The Decapetalous Sun-Flower
4 The Strumous Sun Flower
5 The Tallest Sun Flower
6 The Giant Sun-Flower
7 The Smooth leaved Sun Flower
8 The Narrow leaved Sun-Flower
9 The Creeping American Sun-Flower
10 The Black Carolina Sun-flower

Description of the Common Perennial Sun Flower

1 The first sort is the Common Perennial Sun Flower, and is usually planted in wilderness-works, shrubberies, and in large borders of the pleasure-garden, it is not near so tall and large as the annual Sun Flower, yet is a fine plant The stalks are upright, green, hairy, and divide into a multitude of branches to support the flowers The leaves are large, the lower ones are heart-shaped, and the upper ones oval The flowers are numerous, and terminate the branches, they are large, of a bright-yellow colour, will flower in July and often continue in succession of bloom until the frost stops them Of this sort there are the Single and Double, both of which have their beauties though the Double is generally preferred

Jerusalem Artichoke

2 The second sort is the Jerusalem Artichoke, which, when it has once got possession of a garden, is not easily to be extirpated The stalks grow to eight or ten feet high The leaves are of an oval cordated figure, and the flowers grow from the extremities of the branches, they are small, and of a yellow colour, but are propagated more for the use of their roots than the figure they make in a garden

Decapetalous

3 The third sort grows to about four feet high The lower part of the stalk is smooth The leaves are spear shaped The flowers terminate the stalks in the manner of the Common Perennial flower, but the rays of each flower consist of ten petals only

Strumous

4 The fourth sort has a large, swelling spindle-shaped root, from which the stalks rise to eight or ten feet high The leaves are exceeding broad, and the flowers are produced late in the autumn

Latest Sun Flower

5 The fifth sort will grow to be ten feet high The stalks are smooth, purplish, and grow close together The leaves are spear shaped, broad, rough, nervous, and placed alternately on moderately long footstalks

Varieties

There are two or three varieties of this species respecting the rays of the flowers, but the difference is inconsiderable, and those of the brightest colours are always preferred

Giant

6 The sixth sort grows but to about the height of the former The stalks are green, are very rough The leaves are long, narrow, triple nerved, rough, serrated, close at their base, and grow alternately The flowers generally grow drooping The rays of each consist of about twenty petals, which are bifid at the top, and there will be a succession of them until the frost stops them

Smooth leaved,

7 The seventh sort has a smooth grey coloured stalk about four or five feet high The leaves are spear-shaped, smooth, serrated, trinervous, and grow opposite to each other on the stalks The flowers are produced on smooth footstalks in the autumn, and the number of rays are about thirteen

Narrow-leaved,

8 The eighth sort has very narrow rough leaves placed alternately The flowers are small, and produced late in the autumn, on long slender footstalks

Creeping American

9 The ninth sort has a creeping root, from which proceed several purplish stalks to the height of five or six feet The leaves are oval, oblong, trinervous, rough, and placed opposite without any footstalks The flowers are small, yellow, and formed into forked panicles, having rough footstalks.

and Black Carolina Sun Flower

10 The tenth sort has rough, oval, crenated leaves, with three nerves growing opposite to each other on winged footstalks The flowers are small, and the scales of the calyx erect, and about the length of the disk of the flower, which is almost of a black colour This sort flowers in September

All these sorts have a very pretty effect in large gardens, and from July to the end of autumn one or other of them will shew themselves in bloom, and though they have not the majestic look of the annual Sun flower, yet being scarcer and less robust, they form a more delicate appearance, and on that account are by many preferred

Method of propagating these sorts

They are easily propagated by dividing of the roots, which may be done any time in the winter or spring, but the best season is the autumn, when their blow is over, and the stalks decay They will then flower strong the summer following and after having stood two or three years, the roots of the most spreading sorts must be reduced by taking them entirely up, preparing the ground afresh, and planting the best offsets again for the succession

1 The

Titles

1 The Common Perennial Sun-Flower is titled, *Helianthus foliis inferioribus cordatis trinervatis superioribus ovatis* In the *Hortus Cliffort* it is termed, *Helianthus radice tereti inflexa perenni* Caspar Bauhine calls it, *He ium Indicum ramosum*, Tabernæmontanus *Corona solis minor femina*, Morison, *Chrysanthemum Americanum majus perenne, flor s folis fouis et floribus* It grows naturally in Virginia

2 The second sort is titled, *Helianthus foliis ovato-cordatis triplinerviis* In the *Hortus Cliffort* it is termed, *H nthus radice tuberosa* Caspar Bauhine calls it, *H e um Indicum tuberosum*, and Columna, *Flos solis Farnesianu* It grows naturally in Brasil

3 The third sort is titled, *Helianthus cau lem le i, foliis triplinerviis lanceolato cor s, radiis decapetalis, pedunculis sc bris* It grows naturally in Canada

4 The fourth sort is titled, *Helianthus radice fusiformi* Morison calls it, *Chrysanthemum Canadense fou m t ssimu a*, Boccone, *Chrysanthemum Canadense lat folium elatiu*, and Hermar, *Chrysanthemum Canadense st unojum ulgo* It is a native of Canada

5 The fifth sort is titled, *Helianthus foliis alternis ta rusc i lanceolatis scabris, pet s c lat s, caule stricto scabro* Morison calls it, *Chrysanthemum Virginianum altissimum, p nceis caulibus* It grows naturally in Pensylvania

6 The sixth sort is titled, *Helianthus foliis alternis lanceolatis scabris bas ciliatis, caule stricto scabro* Gronovius calls it, *Helianthus foliis lanceolatis sessilibus*, Morison, *Chrysanthemum Virginianum altissimum angustifolium, p nice s caulibus*, and Plukenet, *Chrysanthemum Virginianum, elatius angustifolium, caule lu suto viridi* It grows naturally in Virginia and Canada

7 The seventh sort is titled, *Helianthus foliis oppositis trinerviis lanceolatis serratis l evibus, caule pedunculisque glabris* It grows naturally in Virginia

8 The eighth sort is titled, *Helianthus foliis alternis linearibus* Petiver calls it, *Flos solis ma-iicus, foliis alternis angustissimis secoris* It grows naturally in Virginia

9 The ninth sort is titled, *Helianthus foliis oppositis sessilibus ovato oblongis ti nerviis panicul dicotoma* Morison calls it, *Chrysanthemum Virginianum repens, foliis asperis binat m sessilibus a u m nati.* It grows in many parts of North America

10 The tenth sort is titled, *Helianthus foliis oppositis spatulatis crenatis, tripa te s scabri, squam s c ly in s, c s lo itudin dis* Dillenius calls it, *Coro a s lis m nor, c fco a orul*, and Morison, *Coron sol s Carolin pr s flu , fo-lus trine c rpo p o h o lo* It grows naturally in Virginia and Carolina

*Helianthus* is of the class and order *Syngenesia Polygamia Frust* and the c r cters are,

1 CAL ... The general cal x is imbricated and expanded, and is composed of man, oblong pointed scales, that are broad at their base, and turned down

Class and order in the Linnæan System

The characters

2 COROLLA is radiated and compound The hermaphrodite florets in the disk are numerous, cylindrical, no longer than the general cup at the base th swelled, rounded, and depressed, and at the top are cut into five acute spreading parts

The female flowers in the radius are very long, tongue shaped, and entire

3 STAMINA In the hermaphrodite flowers the stamina consist of five cloathed filaments the length of the tube, with a cylindrical tubular anthera

4 PISTILLUM, in the hermaphrodite flowers, consists of an oblong germen, a filiforme style the length of the florets, and a bipartite reflexed stigma

5 PERICARPIUM There is none

6 SEMINA The seeds, which follow the hermaphrodite only (the females being imperfect, and consequently unfruitful), are oblong, four-cornered, and obtuse

The receptacle is paleaceous, large, and plane

# CHAP CCXXIII

## HELLEBORUS, BLACK HELLEBORE.

Species

THE species of this genus are,

1 Black Hellebore, or Christmas Rose

2 Winter Aconite

3 Wild Black Hellebore

4 Great Black Hellebore, Bear's Foot, or Setter Wort

5 Trifoliate Hellebore

Description of the Black Hellebore.

1 Black Hellebore, or Christmas Rose The root is thick, fleshy, and spreading The leaves are pedated, and rise immediately from the roots, on thick, strong, round, fleshy footstalks; each is composed of about seven or eight folioles, which are large, of a thickish substance, smooth, obtuse, and serrated The flowers come out immediately from the roots, singly, on thick fleshy footstalks, which are reddish near the base, and for the most part naked, though sometimes they are adorned with one small, oval, concave leaf or two near the top The flower is large and beautiful, its colour is white, and sometimes dies to a fine red or purple, it disdains our cold, and shews itself at Christmas, or soon after, and continues beautiful, in spite of all weather, through the month of January and part of February, regaling us at a time when few flowers, except such as are under shelter, are to be met with

The root is the true black Hellebore of the antients, it is deobstruent, and a violent purgative

Culture

It is propagated by parting of the roots, which may be done at any time of the year It is extremely

tremely hardy, and will grow in any soil or situation, though, in order to have it flower early, it should be planted in a light rich soil, full upon the sun, in a warm [illegible] sheltered place, otherwise the flowers will be few, and often not shew themselves before the middle of February.

Culture. It is also propagated by seeds, when they ripen, which is not very often in our gardens. When you perceive the seeds to fall by the flowers, let them be carefully gathered, and laid in a dry airy place for a few days to harden, then sow them in boxes filled with light earth, and place the boxes in the shade. If dry weather happens, frequently water them, and in a little time your seeds will come up. All summer keep them clean from weeds, and repeat the watering as often as dry weather makes it necessary. In the autumn set the boxes in a warm well-sheltered place, full upon the sun, and in March take up your plants, and set them in beds four inches distance from each other. Here they may stand all summer, with the usual care of weeding and watering, and in the autumn may be removed to the places where they are designed to remain, which ought to be near the parlour, and placed in view to regale the beholders with their pleasing flowers at so unexpected a season.

Winter Aconite. 2. Winter Aconite. The roots small, bulbous, and of a brown colour. The leaves rise on slender short footstalks; they are of a strong agreeable green colour, and divided into many parts. The flowers shew themselves above the leaves by the end of January, or early in February; they are of a golden yellow colour, and very ornamental at that early season.

Culture. This is propagated by parting of the roots, the best time for which is June, when the leaves decay. As the roots are small, not less than a dozen or fourteen should be set in the same place, otherwise the show will be inconsiderable. The flowers make an agreeable mixture with Snow Drops, and such others as can be collected to come in at that season, and their situation should be near windows or places of resort, that they may be easily seen.

Wild. 3. Wild Black Hellebore. The leaves are digitated, each being composed of about nine long, narrow, serrated lobes, which join at their base; the radical ones grow on long thick footstalks, and their colour is a dark green. The stalks grow to about a foot high, divide into a few branches near the top, and are adorned with a few small, narrow, serrated leaves, which sit close, without any footstalk. The flowers come out from the ends and divisions of the branches; they are of a greenish colour, appear in January and February, and are succeeded by plenty of good seeds, which ripen in May.

Great Black Hellebore. 4. Great Black Hellebore, Bears Foot, or Setter-Wort. By these names respectively, in different parts, this species is known, and in some places it goes by the name of Oxheel. The stalks are slender, narrowest near the ground, divide into several spreading branches, and grow to about two feet high. The leaves are pedated, large, and of a dark green colour, the folioles are long, narrow, smooth, serrated, and about nine in number to each leaf. The flowers are numerous at the ends of the branches; they are of a green colour, and often tipped with purple; they appear early in winter, and the seeds ripen in the spring.

Varieties. There is a variety of this species with longer leaves and stalks, which in some places is known by the name of Dalmatian Black Hell-bore, and another with trifoliate leaves, called the Three-leaved Bears Foot.

The roots are often given to kill worms in children, but the practice is dangerous, several children of late years having been poisoned by injudiciously taking inwardly the dried leaves of these plants. This should warn all people for the future from using this drug to kill the worms in children.

Trifoliate Black Hellebore. 5. Trifoliate Black Hellebore. The leaves are trifoliate, arise from the roots on strong footstalks, and are of a dark-green colour. Among these rise the flower stalks, each supports one flower, of a whitish or pale green colour, which appears in winter, but is not succeeded by seeds in such plenty as the two preceding sorts.

Culture. The third and fourth sorts are propagated by sowing the seeds as soon as they are ripe, in beds of common mould made fine. The plants will then readily come up, and require no trouble, except thinning them where they are too close, keeping them clean from weeds all summer, and by the autumn they will be grown strong enough to be removed to the places where they are designed to remain.

Some of these sorts should be planted among the shrubs in the wilderness-quarters, where they will have a pretty effect by their green flowers in the winter season. They are extremely hardy, and no soil or situation comes amiss to them; and after they have once flowered and perfected their seeds, if they are permitted to scatter, such swarms of plants will come up all around, as to cause as much trouble as weeds to reduce them to a proper number, and within bounds.

The fifth sort is propagated by parting of the roots, or sowing the seeds, in the manner of the first sort; but it requires a light dry soil, and a warm situation.

Titles. 1. Black Hellebore, or Christmas Rose, is titled, *Helleborus scapo subunifloro subnudo, foliis pedatis*. In the *Hortus Cliffortianus* it is termed, *Helleborus scapo flore sero subnudo, petiolo communi bipartito*. Caspar Bauhine calls it, *Helleborus niger flore roseo*, and Clusius, *Elleborus niger, legitimus*. It grows naturally in Austria, Hetruria, the Alps and Appennine mountains.

2. Winter Aconite is, *Helleborus flore folio insidente*. Morison calls it *Helleborus ranunculoides praecox tuberosus, flore luteo*, and Caspar Bauhine, *Aconitum unifolium bulbosum*. It grows naturally in Lombardy, Italy, and the Appennine mountains.

3. Wild Black Hellebore is, *Helleborus caule multifloro folioso, foliis digitatis*. In the *Hortus Cliffortianus* it is termed, *Helleborus caule aequali foliosa, foliis radicalibus caulem tamen superantibus*. Caspar Bauhine calls it, *Helleborus niger hortensis, flore viridi*, Cammerarius, *Elleborum nigrum alterum*, Parkinson, *Helleboraster minor, flore non-euante*, and Gerard, *Helleboraster minor*. It grows naturally in woods, meadows, and mountainous places in England, and several parts of Europe.

4. Great Black Hellebore, Bears Foot, or Setter-Wort, is, *Helleborus caule multifloro folioso, foliis pedatis*. In the *Hortus Cliffortianus* it is termed, *Helleborus caule inferne angusto multifolio multifloro, foliis caule brevioribus*. Caspar Bauhine calls it, *Helleborus niger foetidus*, Lobel, *Helleboraster maximus*, and Morison, *Helleborus niger trifoliatus*. It is found sometimes in meadows and pasture-grounds, but for the most part in hedges in England, Germany, Switzerland, and Gaul.

5. Trifoliate Hellebore is, *Helleborus scapo unifloro, foliis ternatis*. It grows naturally in the woods of Canada and Siberia.

Class and order in the Linnaean system. *Helleborus* is of the class and order *Polyandria Polygynia*, and the characters are,

1. CALYX. There is none.

2. COROLLA consists of five large, roundish, obtuse

obtuse petals. Their nectaria are many, very short, tubulated, and placed circularly; they are narrowest below, and divide at the top into two lips, which are erect, indented, and the interior one is the shortest.

3. STAMINA are numerous awl-shaped filaments, with compressed antheræ, which are narrowest below, and stand erect.

4. PISTILLUM consists of several compressed germens, having awl-shaped styles, with thickish stigmas.

5. PERICARPIUM consists of several compressed bicarinated capsules, of which the lower carina is the shortest, and the upper convex, and open for the discharge of the seeds.

6. SEMINA. The seeds are many, round, and affixed to the suture.

## CHAP. CCXXIV.

# HELONIAS.

THERE are only two species of this genus, called,

Species. 1. Bullated Helonias.
2. Asphodeloide Helonias.

Description of the Bullated, 1. Bullated *Helonias*. The stalks are upright, thick, firm, and two or three feet high. The radical leaves are spear-shaped, and moderately broad; but those on the stalk are narrow, and grow alternately. The flowers come out in spikes from the tops of the stalks; they are small, and bullated, appear in August, and the seeds sometimes ripen in the autumn.

and Asphodeloide Helonias. 2. Asphodeloide *Helonias*. The stalks are undivided, and grow to be two feet high. The leaves are narrow, smooth in the middle, but have a rough border, grow erect, and are placed alternately on the stalk. The flowers are produced from the tops of the stalks in long loose spikes; they are of a white colour, appear in July and August, and the seeds ripen in the autumn.

Culture. These species are propagated by parting of the roots, the best time for which is the autumn, that they may be established in their new situation before winter. They require a moist soil, especially the first sort, and both of them love the shade. After they are planted out they will require no trouble, except keeping them clean from weeds.

They may also be raised from seeds, which should be sown in the spring in beds of light earth made fine. When the plants come up, they must be thinned where they are too close, kept in good weeding, and duly watered in dry weather all summer; and in the autumn they may be taken up, with a ball of earth to each root, and set in the places where they are designed to remain.

1. The first species is named simply, *Helonias*. In the *Amænitates Acad.* it is termed, *Helonias foliis radicalibus lanceolatis*. Plukenet calls it, *Ephemerum phalangoides Virginianum flosculis arbuteis bullatis in spicam congestis*. It grows naturally in moist places in Virginia and Pensylvania. Titles.

2. The second species is, *Helonias foliis caulinis setaceis*. It grows naturally in Pensylvania.

*Helonias* is of the class and order *Hexandria Trigynia*; and the characters are, Class and order in the Linnæan system.

1. CALYX. There is none. The characters.

2. COROLLA is six oblong, equal, deciduous petals.

3. STAMINA are six awl-shaped filaments a little longer than the corolla, having incumbent antheræ.

4. PISTILLUM consists of a roundish three-cornered germen, and three short reflexed styles, with obtuse stigmas.

5. PERICARPIUM is a roundish trilocular capsule.

6. SEMINA. The seeds are roundish.

# CHAP. CCXXV.

## *HEMEROCALLIS*, DAY-LILY, or LILY-ASPHODEL

THIS genus consists of two well-known [illegible] called,

Sorts 1 The Yellow Day Lily
2 The Red Day Lily

Yellow Day Lily described 1 The Yellow Day-Lily has strong fibrous roots, to which hang several oblong tubers of a yellowish colour. The leaves are long, narrow, hollowed, and pointed. The stalk is slender, naked, upright, firm and grows to about two feet high; [illegible] the top it divides into a few [illegible] each of which supports a large flower of the Lily kind. They are of a bright yellow colour, and possessed of an agreeable odour; it will be in blow in June, and the seeds ripen in August.

Varieties There is a variety or two of this plant respecting the size or growth, but in every other respect they correspond.

Red Day-Lily described 2 Red Day-Lily. This is a large spreading plant. The fibres are strong and fleshy, and the tubers are large and oblong. From this rise many leaves near a yard in length, which are hollowed, pointed, and turn back near the top. The flower-stalk is naked, firm, thick, and will often grow to about a yard high. Near the top it divides into a few branches, which contain the flowers. These are of the Lily kind, and large. It is called the Red Lily, but this is very improper, for the colour is a composition of a red, brown, and copper colour. In short, in that respect it is not very desirable, for the colour is dull, and [illegible] mixture [illegible] those sorts. The stamina are large, and possessed of much copper-coloured farina, which is emitted from the antheræ in great plenty on being touched, and has often afforded much merriment to the Gardener, who causing the flowers to be smelt to by the unknowing ones, the farina has discharged itself in such plenty over their faces, as to stain them of a copper colour. It flowers in June, and the seeds ripen in August.

Method of propagating them These sorts are all propagated by parting of the roots, the best time for which is the autumn, though they will grow at any season of the year. If parted in the autumn, the largest offsets will flower the succeeding summer, and may be immediately planted where they are to remain; but the smaller should be set in the nursery-ground for a year, to gain strength, and then be planted out for good. These plants should be removed and reduced every three years, or they will get too large for small gardens, especially the second sort, which is a spreading, over-bearing plant.

They may be easily raised from seeds sown in the autumn, soon after they are ripe; for if they are kept until the spring they will often lie until the spring following before the plants appear. When the plants come up, keep them clean of weeds, frequently water them in dry weather, and in the autumn plant them in the nursery ground in beds at a foot asunder. In these beds they may remain one year, and be then planted out where they are designed to flower, which will be, in the strongest plants, the summer following.

1 Yellow Day Lily is titled, *Hemerocallis corollis flavis*. In the *Hortus Upsal.* it is called, *Hemerocallis scapo ramoso, corollis monopetalis*; in the *Hortus Cliffort. Hemerocallis radice tuberosa, corollis monopetalis*. Gmelin calls it, *Hemerocallis radice tuberosa, corollis monopetalis luteis*; Clusius, *Lilio-asphodelus luteo flore*; Caspar Bauhine, *Lilium luteum, asphodeli radice*. It grows naturally in most parts of Hungary and Siberia. Titles

2 The Red Day Lily is titled, *Hemerocallis corollis fulvis*. Clusius calls it, *Lilio-asphodelus puniceus*; and Caspar Bauhine, *Lilium rubrum, asphodeli radice*. It grows naturally in China.

*Hemerocallis* is of the class and order *Hexandria Monogynia*; and the characters are, Class and order in the Linnæan system.

1 CALYX. There is none.

2 COROLLA is an infundibuliforme campanulated petal, deeply cut into six parts. The tube is short, and the limb patent and reflexed. The character.

3 STAMINA are six subulated declinated filaments the length of the corolla, though the upper ones are somewhat shorter than the others, with oblong, incumbent, assurgent antheræ.

4 PISTILLUM consists of a roundish sulcated germen, a filiforme style the length and situation of the stamina, and an obtuse, three-cornered, assurgent stigma.

5 PERICARPIUM is an oval, trilobous, trigonal capsule of three cells.

6 SEMINA. The seeds are numerous and roundish.

CHAP

## CHAP. CCXXVI.

## *HERNIARIA*, RUPTURE-WORT.

OF this genus there are two abiding species, called

Species

1. Sea Rupture-wort
2. Shrubby Rupture-wort

Sea Rupture-wort

1. Sea Rupture-wort. The stalks are tough, slender, and lie on the ground. The leaves are oval, pointed, glossy, of a thickish substance, and a little resemble those of wild thyme. The flowers come out in clusters from the sides of the branches almost their whole length; they are small, and of a yellowish-green colour; they make their appearance in May and June, and frequently shew themselves at the end of summer and in autumn.

and Shrubby Rupture-wort described

2. Shrubby Rupture-wort. The stalks are ligneous, branching, and lie on the ground. The leaves are oval, pointed, hairy, and of a pale-green colour. The flowers come out in clusters from the sides of the stalks at the joints; they are small, yellowish, and shew themselves the greatest part of the summer.

Method of propagating them

Both these sorts are easily propagated by the slips or cuttings, or dividing the roots. They should be planted in the spring in a shady place, and they will readily grow. All summer they must be kept clean from weeds, be frequently watered in dry weather, and in the autumn may be removed to the places where they are designed to remain.

They are also propagated by seeds, which they produce in abundance. Sow these soon after they are ripe, in a bed of any common mould made fine, and they will readily come up. Here they may stand, with the usual care of weeding and watering in dry weather, until they are of proper strength to be removed to the places where they are designed to remain. They are plants of very little beauty, and chiefly covet..d by those who are fond of all sorts of plants.

Titles.

1. The first species is, *Herniaria lenticulata*. Caspar Bauhine calls it, *Polygonum minus lenticulatum*, also, *Polygonum minus lentifolium*. Plukenet terms it, *Polygonum maritimum longius radicatum nostras serpyllifolio crasso nitente*. Bauhin names it, *Campoonata frutescens, foliis latis & angustis*. Parkinson, *Polygonum minus Monspeliense*, and Petiver, *Polygonum foliis circinato*. It grows naturally on the sea shores in England, also near Montpelier in France, and the Escurial in Spain.

2. Shrubby Rupture-root is, *Herniaria caulibus fruticosis, floribus quadrifidis*. Caspar Bauhine calls it, *Herniaria fruticosa, viticulis lignosis*, and John Bauhine, *Polygonum hernia ie folio & facie, perennis radice*. It grows naturally in Spain.

Class and order in the Linnæan system. The characters.

*Herniaria* is of the class and order *Pentandria Digynia*, and the characters are,

1. CALYX is a monophyllous, permanent perianthium, coloured on the inside, and divided into five acute, spreading segments.
2. COROLLA. There is none.
3. STAMINA are five minute awl-shaped filaments, situated between the segments of the calyx, having simple antheræ. There are five other filaments, which are sterile, and placed alternately with them.
4. PISTILLUM consists of an oval germen, a very short style, and two acuminated stigmas the length of the style.
5. PERICARPIUM is a very small covered capsule, situated in the bottom of the calyx.
6. SEMINA. The seeds are single, oval, acuminated, and bright.

---

## CHAP. CCXXVII.

## *HESPERIS*, DAME's VIOLET, or ROCKET.

MOST of the species of *Hesperis* are remarkable for their fragrance, especially in evenings, when the circumambient air will be replete with their odours. Hence the word *Hesperis*, which signifies the Evening, was originally given to these plants. All of them are of short duration. The longest livers might not improperly be termed biennials; but as by some care and management they may be preserved for several years, I will introduce some of them into this place, and these shall be,

Species.

1. The Common Garden Rocket
2. The Unsavory Rocket
3. The Hungarian Mountain Rocket
4. The Siberian Rocket

The Common Garden Rocket described

1. The Common Garden Rocket will grow to about two feet high. The stalks are round, upright, firm, and hairy. The leaves are of an oval,

and lanceolate figure, they are rough, large, and pointed their edges are serrated, their colour is a fresh green, and they sit close to the stalks The flowers are produced in large spikes at the tops of the branches, and in smaller from the wings of the leaves, they will be in blow in June, and the single sorts will produce good seeds in September This is the Garden Rocket, and of this species are the following varieties

Varieties

The Single White Garden Rocket
The Single Crimson Garden Rocket
The Single Purple Garden Rocket
The Double White Garden Rocket
The Double Purple Garden Rocket
The Purple and White Garden Rocket

Of these the double sorts are the most beautiful, but the single kinds are possessed of the highest fragrance, on which account a larger share of them should be planted near rooms, or in pots, for the sake of their odours The ladies have always been remarkably fond of these plants, and have much distinguished them with a place in their bed-chambers, dressing-rooms, and apartments Hence the name Dame's Violet is supposed originally to be given to them

The Unsavory Rocket

2 The Unsavory Rocket This is a distinct species, but very much resembles the Sweet-scented Garden Rocket It will grow to about two feet high The stalk is round, upright, and firm The leaves are spear shaped, serrated, acute-pointed, and sit close to the branches The flowers terminate the branches in spikes, the calyces are uncoloured, and the petals of the flower are obtuse, without that pointed indenture which is peculiar to the petals of the other sort; the stamina, also, are shorter than the tube of the flower, and in these the specific differences chiefly consist Of this species there are the following varieties

Varieties

The Single White
The Single Purple
The Double White
The Double Purple

Mountain Rocket

3 Mountain Rocket This plant rises with upright hairy stalks to about two feet and a half high The leaves are spear-shaped, pointed, and much resemble those of the Common Garden Rocket, but are larger The flowers are produced in June, from the top of the stalk, in kind of loose panicles, they are small and of a pale colour, but are possessed of the highest degree of fragrance imaginable, on which account they are in the highest esteem in all parts, and much cultivated to exhilarate the different apartments of ladies, &c in most countries

and Siberian Rocket described

4 Siberian Rocket is a tall plant, it will grow to about four feet high The leaves are spear-shaped, long and narrow, and beautifully serrated The stalks are upright and firm, and the flowers ornament the tops They are of a purple colour, and each is composed of four obtuse entire petals This is a very fine species, and makes a good variety among other plants of the same growth

Culture of the single sorts

The Single sorts I would advise the Gardener to consider as biennials only, except the sorts with striped flowers, which must be treated as the Double kinds Let him, therefore, sow the seeds in April, in a border where he would chuse to have the plants flower, for they will do better by not being disturbed The soil should be fresh, and the seeds sown thinly over it, and then covered down with a quarter of an inch of fine-sifted mould Where the plants come up too thick, thin them, and the drawn plants may be made to ornament some other part of the garden Plants thus raised will flower strong in June, or the beginning of July, and will afford you plenty of seeds for a succession in September

The Mountain Rocket is more tender than the other sorts, and liable to be destroyed by the severity of our winters Let, therefore, a few seeds be sown in pots, that they may be set in the green-house during that season, and let the situation for the others be naturally dry and warm, so will they be less liable to be destroyed, and your expectations frustrated of a blow of these flowers, from which, more than their beauty, their excellence is derived

Manner of propagating the double sorts

Let us now take a view of the Double sorts And for this, in order to continue them for many years, the roots should be divided every autumn But to encrease them in plenty, let the following method be taken Plant a sufficient number of them in a shady part of the seminary, and when the flower-stalks are advanced to about half their growth, cut them off near the ground This will cause the roots to shoot out afresh, and by the sides of the stalks several heads for the continuance of the plant may be expected to grow These, therefore, should be divided in the autumn, and this is the best method of encreasing these plants

The cuttings also will grow, so that at the time you head the plants, let the bottom parts of the cuttings be set in a moist shady border Water them frequently in dry weather, and now and then stir the mould about them to admit the influences of the dew and rain Several of these will become good plants, though the generality of them will be weak and sickly, and a large share of them canker and rot And although this is a practice much recommended by Gardeners, I ever found, that the best plants were always to be obtained from dividing those roots which had been headed before

Titles

1 The Garden Rocket is titled, *Hesperis caule simplici erecto, foliis ovato-lanceolatis denticulatis, petalis mucrone emarginatis* Caspar Bauhine calls it, *Hesperis hortensis*, Dodonæus, *Viola matronalis* It grows naturally in Italy

2 Unsavory Rocket This is titled, *Hesperis caule simplici erecto, foliis sessilibus dentatis, petalis obtusis* Caspar Bauhine calls it, *Hesperis sylvestris inodora*, Clusius, simply, *Hesperis* It grows naturally in some parts of England, also, near Vienna and Montpelier

3 Mountain Rocket This species is termed, *Hesperis caule hispido ramoso patente* Caspar Bauhine calls it, *Hesperis montana pallida odoratissima*, Cammerarius, *Hesperis Pannonica* It grows naturally in Hungary and Austria

4 Siberian Rocket is titled, *Hesperis caule simplici, foliis lanceolatis dentato-serratis, petalis obtusissimis integris* It grows naturally in Siberia

Class and order in the Linnæan system

*Hesperis* is of the class and order *Tetradynamia Siliquosa*, and the characters are,

The characters

1 Calyx is a deciduous perianthium, composed of four narrow lanceolate leaves, which converge toward their tops, but open at the bottom, the two opposite ones are prominent near the base

2 Corolla is composed of four oblong petals in form of a cross These are bent obliquely, and have long narrow ungues about the length of the calyx

3 Stamina These are six subulated filaments about the length of the tube Two of these are much shorter than the other The antheræ are very narrow, erect, and reflexed at their points

4 PISTILLUM There is a prismatic, four-cornered germen, without any style, but an upright oblong stigma, split at the base, and connivent at the top

5 PERICARPIUM is a long, compressed, plane, striated, bilocular pod

6 SEMINA The seeds are numerous, oval, and compressed.

## CHAP CCXXVIII

## *HENCHERA*

THERE is only one species of this genus, commonly called American Sanicle

This plant described

The root is fibrous, strong, and sends forth numerous leaves, which form a large bunch on the crown The leaves are pretty large, almost round, indented, and grow on long slender foot stalks The flower stalks arise among the leaves from the root, are almost naked, and grow to about a foot and a half high The flowers come out in panicles from the tops of the stalks, they are of a dark purple colour, appear in May and June, and are sometimes succeeded by ripe seeds in August or September

Method of propagating it

It is chiefly propagated by parting the roots in autumn, but a greater number of plants may be sooner raised from seeds when they ripen well Sow the seeds therefore in March, in a bed of light earth in a shady place Water the beds frequently, and when the plants come up, thin them where they are too close Keep them clean from weeds, and water them, if the weather should prove dry, all summer, and in the autumn they may be removed to the places where they are designed to remain It loves a moist soil and a shady situation best, but it is extremely hardy, and will grow almost any where

Titles

There being no other species of this genus, it stands with the name simply *Henchera* Hermann calls it, *Cortusa Americana, flore squallide purpureo*, and Plukenet *Sanicula, s Cortusa Americana spicata, floribus squallide purpureis* It grows naturally in Virginia

Class and order in the Linnæan system The characters

*Henchera* is of the class and order *Pentandria Digynia*, and the characters are,

1 CALYX is a monophyllous, rounded perianthium, divided into five obtuse segments

2 COROLLA consists of five oval narrow petals the length of the calyx, and inserted in the edge of it

3 STAMINA are five awl shaped, erect filaments more than twice the calyx, with roundish antheræ

4 PISTILLUM consists of a roundish, semibifid germen, and two straight styles the length of the stamina, with obtuse stigmas

5 PERICARPIUM is an oval, acuminated, semibifid capsule, having two reflexed horns, and containing two cells

6 SEMINA The seeds are many and small

## CHAP CCXXIX

## *HIBISCUS*, SYRIAN MALLOW.

THE species of *Hibiscus* are, for the most part, tender annuals, or such whose lives are of a longer date, if preserved with the warmth and care of the stove Two species at least, however, we will venture to introduce in this place, their roots being perennial, tolerably hardy, and in warm seasons will exhibit their bloom fair and full and these are,

Species

1 The Oval Crenated-leaved *Hibiscus*

2 The Marsh Purple flowering *Hibiscus*

Description of the Oval Crenated-leaved,

1 The Oval Crenated-leaved *Hibiscus* The root of this plant sends forth single stalks to about two feet or a yard in height The leaves are of an oval figure, broad, and pointed, their edges are obtusely serrated, and they are downy underneath The flowers are produced from the sides of the branches on footstalks, they are large, and of a delightful purple colour, and when the season has been warm and suitable for them to blow fair, they have been of admirable beauty The stalks are annual, they perish at the approach of winter, and the roots send forth fresh ones the succeeding spring

and Marsh Hibiscus

2 Marsh *Hibiscus* This species also sends forth single herbaceous stalks from the root in the spring, to about the height of the former

The leaves are oval, subt lonate, and broad, their upper surface is of a fine green colour, but their under s downy The flowers are produced from the wings of the leaves they are large, of a bright-purple colour, and very beautiful The stalks, like those of the former species, die to the ground at the approach of winter, and fresh ones are produced in the spring They must therefore be cleared away from the roots as soon as they begin to decay, that the appearance of neatness and elegance may be kept up

Culture These plants are easily raised the greatest difficulty will be to make them blow fair Sow the seeds in the spring, on a moderate hot-bed, to facilitate their growth They will readily come up, and the usual care must attend them until they are of size to transplant A moist, or at least a cloudy day should be fixed upon for the purpose, and a naturally warm and well-sheltered place should be their station Water must be given them in dry weather, and shade from the great heat of the sun, until they have taken root, must not be neglected By the autumn they will be strong plants, and hardy enough to endure the cold of our winters, and by the autumn following, if the spring and summer have been mild and forward, they will shew their bloom

But as this depends upon a propitious season, in order to have a more certain blow of these flowers, let some of the roots, at the time of their removal from the seed-bed be set in pots, and let these be plunged up to the rims in a warm well sheltered place Clumps of annuals are recommended for most gardens, and some situations more peculiarly call for such an ornament Where this is most wanted, let a hot-bed be made, strong and good, and let the pots be placed on this hot-bed, then fill up the cavities, and even over the rims of the pots that they may not appear After this, bring a sufficient quantity of mould to form a slope from the top of the hot-bed to the walk Here, then, will be a tumulus of any size or shape you please, and all over it plant such annuals as flower late in the autumn, and are proper to join in the assortment with our Syrian Mallow, which will then appear to be of the same family Thus these plants may be brought forward by the hot-bed, and made to enrich a clump of that nature, which every true lover of taste and gardening never fails to admire

1 Oval Crenated-leaved *Hibiscus* This species is titled, *Hibiscus foliis ovatis acuminatis serratis, caule simplicissimo, petiolis floriferis* In the *Hortus Cliffort* it is called, *Hibiscus foliis ovatis crenatis* Tournefort calls it, *Ketmia Africana populi folio* It grows common in Canada and Virginia Titles.

2 Marsh *Hibiscus* This species is titled, *Hibiscus caule herbaceo simplicissimo, foliis ovatis subtrilobis subtus tomentosis, floribus axillaribus* Caspar Bauhine calls it, *Althæa palustris*, Dodonæus, *Althæa hortensis, sive peregrina* It grows naturally in Canada and Virginia.

## CHAP. CCXXX

## *HIERACIUM*, HAWKWEED,

THERE are very few species of *Hieracium* that are not very pretty plants, and there are very few but what are weeds and unnoticed in the places where they grow naturally Our own country is ornamented with no less than eight distinct species of this genus, which contain in themselves more than forty different sorts Our hills, our dales, our dry banks and our highways, are garnished with some or other of them, and they heighten the colouring of the flowery show The different parts of the world have still other species that grow spontaneously in the like plentiful manner The principal species are,

Species
1 Orange Hawkweed, or Grim the Collier
2 Wall Hawkweed, or French Lungwort
3 Broad-leaved Pyrenean Hawkweed
4 Heart leaved Pyrenean Hawkweed
5 Moth Mullein-leaved Pyrenean Hawkweed
6 Mountain Hawkweed
7 Mouse ear Hawkweed
8 Narrow leaved Hawkweed
9 Upright Hawkweed
10 Gronovius's Hawkweed
11 Gmelin's Hawkweed
12 Broad-leaved Bushy Hawkweed
13 Narrow-leaved Bushy Hawkweed
14 Bohemian Hawkweed.
15 Holy Hawkweed
16 Cymose Hawkweed
17 Common Creeping Mouse ear

1 Orange Hawkweed is a very pretty small plant, and has been long cultivated in gardens on account of the flowers Hence the name Garden Hawkweed has been applied to it But it is more generally known among the common-people by the name of Grim the Collier, a phrase which has been in use for many generations, and which was first given it probably on account of the dark coal-ash colour of the calyx, for the flower itself is of a bright orange colour The leaves of this species are oblong, oval, entire, of a blackish-green colour, and very hairy The flower stalk will grow to about a foot high, it is very hairy, round, single, upright, and naked, at least is garnished with no more than one small leaf near the top At the top of this stalk grow the flowers in a corymbus, one flower usually appears first, which is always the most perfect and beautiful The cup is composed of many narrow dirty-looking scales, which occasioned the above cant-word for the plant The flowers are of a reddish orange colour, they will be in blow early in June, and there will be a succession of them for three months or more, during which time good seed may

Description of Orange Hawkweed

may be obtained from the ſtalks of the firſt flowers.

Wall Hawkweed.

2. Wall Hawkweed grows common upon old walls in ſome parts of England, but is nevertheleſs a very pretty flower, and on this account is often admitted into gardens. It ſends out ſeveral leaves from the root, which are of an oval figure, very hairy, and have their edges indented. The flower-ſtalks will riſe to about a foot high, and divide into ſeveral branches. Each of the ſmaller branches are terminated by a flower; they are large, of a fine yellow colour, and have a ſhowy look; they will be in blow in June, and their ſeeds ripen in Auguſt.

Its varieties.

Of this ſpecies there are ſix or ſeven varieties, differing in ſize, ſhape of their leaves, or in ſome reſpect or other.

Broad-leaved Pyrenean,

3. Broad-leaved Pyrenean Hawkweed. This ſpecies ſends forth ſeveral leaves from the root, which are broad, of an oval figure, greyiſh colour, and have their edges indented. The ſtalk divides into ſeveral branches, and is garniſhed with ſmaller oblong leaves, which half embrace it with their baſe; its height is about a foot. The flowers are produced in bunches from the tops of the ſtalks; they are ſmall, of a pale yellow colour, and make their appearance about the ſame time with the former.

Heart-leaved Pyrenean,

4. Heart-leaved Pyrenean Hawkweed. The leaves are heart-ſhaped, and their edges are indented. The ſtalk, which will grow to better than a foot high, divides into ſeveral branches, and is garniſhed with ſmaller leaves, which ſurround it with their baſe. The ſmaller ſtalks are hairy, and each ſupport a ſingle flower; it is large, of a fine yellow colour, will be in blow in May, and afford good ſeeds in July. Of this ſpecies there are ſeveral varieties.

Moth Mullein-leaved Pyrenean,

5. Moth Mullein-leaved Pyrenean Hawkweed. This ſpecies riſes with ſeveral erect ſtalks to about the height of the former. The leaves are ſpear-ſhaped, hairy, indented on their edges, and embrace the ſtalk with their baſe. The flowers grow from the wings of the ſtalks on ſhort footſtalks; they are yellow, will be in blow in June, but are ſeldom ſucceeded by good ſeeds here.

Mountain,

6. Mountain Hawkweed. The leaves are oblong, entire, and woolly. The ſtalks are ſlender, ſix or eight inches high, and ſometimes adorned with one or two very ſmall narrow leaves. The flowers come out ſingly from the tops of the ſtalks; they are large, have hairy cups, appear in May, June, and July, and often again in autumn.

Mouſe ear,

7. Mouſe ear Hawkweed. The leaves are oval, oblong, undivided, hairy, and of a green colour. From the ſide of the root ſeveral ſhoots proceed, which lie on the ground and ſtrike root; but the flower-ſtalk is nearly upright, naked, and about a foot high. The flowers are numerous on the tops of the ſtalks; they are of a pale-yellow colour, and make their greateſt ſhow in May and June.

Narrow leaved,

8. Narrow leaved Hawkweed. This ſpecies ſends forth ſide-ſhoots, which creep along the ground, and ſtrike root like the former. The leaves are ſpear-ſhaped, acute, and entire. The flower-ſtalk is erect, naked, hairy, and about half a foot high. The flowers are produced in ſmall panicles from the tops of the ſtalks; they are of a yellow colour, and appear about the ſame time with the former.

and Upright Hawkweed deſcribed.

9. Upright Hawkweed. The leaves are oval, broad, downy, and indented on their edges. The ſtalk is naked, upright, branching, and about a foot high. The flowers come out in kind of ſpikes from the ends of the branches; they are of a pale yellow colour, and the upper flowers blow firſt, which are by far the faireſt; they ſhew themſelves the end of May and the beginning of June, and the ſeeds ripen in July.

Its variety.

There is a variety of this ſpecies with ſingle ſtalks.

Gronovius's,

10. Gronovius's Hawkweed. The radical leaves are oval, obtuſe, entire, and hairy. The ſtalk is ſlender, erect, about a foot high, and furniſhed with one or two ſpear-ſhaped leaves, which ſit cloſe, and embrace it with their baſe. The flowers come out in panicles from the tops of the ſtalks; they appear in June and July, and often again in autumn.

Gmelin's,

11. Gmelin's Hawkweed. The radical leaves are oval, ſerrated, and ſmooth. The ſtalks are naked, and divide into a few branches near the top. The flowers grow ſingly on hairy foot ſtalks, and then form a panicle on the tops of the ſtalks; they appear in June, and the ſeeds ripen in July or Auguſt.

Broad-leaved Buſhy Hawkweed.

12. Broad-leaved Buſhy Hawkweed. The ſtalks are upright, ligneous, and about two feet high. The leaves are oval, ſpear-ſhaped, indented, and half embrace the ſtalk with their baſe. The flowers come out in panicles from the tops of the plant; they are of a yellow colour, appear in June and July, and the ſeeds ripen in Auguſt.

Its varieties.

There is a variety of this ſpecies with hairy leaves; a ſecond with ſmooth leaves; and a third of very low growth.

Narrow-leaved Buſhy Hawkweed.

13. Narrow-leaved Buſhy Hawkweed. The ſtalks are upright, hairy, brittle, and about a foot and a half high. The leaves are long, narrow, and indented on their edges. The flowers come out in kind of panicles from the tops of the ſtalks; they are of a yellow colour, appear in May and June, and the ſeeds ripen in July.

Its varieties.

There are ſeveral varieties of this ſpecies reſpecting the properties of the leaves, ſtalks, and flowers.

Bohemian,

14. Bohemian Hawkweed. The ſtalks are hairy, ramoſe, and about a foot and a half high. The leaves are very rough and hairy; the radical ones are ſpear-ſhaped, oval, and indented; but the others are heart-ſhaped, and embrace the ſtalk with their baſe. The flowers grow ſingly on footſtalks from the ends and ſides of the branches; they are large, and of a yellow colour, appear in June and July, and the ſeeds ripen in Auguſt.

Holy,

15. Holy Hawkweed. The leaves are lyre-ſhaped, indented, and obtuſe. The ſtalks are naked, ſlender, and about ſix or eight inches high. Each of the branches is terminated by a yellow flower, which will be in blow in June, and afford good ſeeds in Auguſt.

Cymoſe,

16. Cymoſe Hawkweed. The leaves are ſpear-ſhaped, long, acute, entire, erect, and rough and hairy on both ſides. The ſtalk grows to about a foot high, is hairy, eſpecially near the bottom, and garniſhed with one ſmall leaf only. The flowers come out in cymoſe bunches from the ends of the ſtalks; they are of a yellow colour, appear in May and June, and continue in ſucceſſion the greateſt part of the ſummer.

and Common Creeping Mouſe ear deſcribed.

17. Common Creeping Mouſe ear grows almoſt every-where, and is unknown to few. The root ſends forth leaves and ſtalks, which creep and ſtrike freſh root into the ground. The leaves are oval, entire, and downy underneath. The flower-ſtalks are ſlender, hairy, and grow to about ſix or eight inches high. The flowers are produced ſingly from the tops of the ſtalks; they are of a pale-yellow colour, come out in May and June, and are ſucceeded by ripe ſeeds in July.

The

Method of propagation. The propagation of all these sorts is so easy, that [illegible] cannot miss [illegible] in the autumn, or in the spring, and every offset will speedily become a good plant.

These plants are also propagated by seeds. Sow them in the autumn or in the spring. They will soon come up, and may be afterwards either thinned to proper distances, or transplanted to different parts of the flower garden.

The roots creep pretty much under the surface of the ground, so that in a little time they will overspread a large space. It will be necessary, therefore, to take the roots up every two or three years, and plant afresh as many offsets as you chuse, and throw the others away. These will flower stronger, and be much handsomer, than broad over-run patches of these plants.

They will also propagate themselves, for if the seeds are permitted to scatter, they will freely come up, and produce very good plants for any purpose.

Titles. 1. Orange Hawkweed is titled, *Hieracium foliis integris, caule [illegible] pilo[illegible]* Caspar Bauhine calls it, *Hieracium [illegible] floribus atro-purpurascentibus*, also, *Hieracium Alpinum [illegible] flore fusco*, Columna *Hieracium Germanicum*, Morison, *Pilosella [illegible] major Syriaca, flore [illegible] aurantiaco*. It grows naturally in the woods of Syria, Helvetia, and Austria.

2. Wall Hawkweed. This species is titled, *Hieracium caule ramoso, foliis radicalibus ovatis dentatis, caulino minore*. In the *Flora Lapp.* it is termed, *Hieracium caule ramoso, foliis ovatis [illegible]* Caspar Bauhine calls it, *Hieracium [illegible] folio pilosissimo*, also, *Hieracium [illegible] minus pilosum*, Tabernaemontanus, *Pulmonaria Gallica femina*, Ray, *Hieracium [illegible] hirsutum, folio longiore*, also, *Hieracium [illegible] hirsutum, folio longiore*. Gerard, *Pulmonaria Gallica [illegible] latifolia*, also, *Pulmonaria Gallica, [illegible] angustifolia*, and Parkinson *Hieracium murorum [illegible], quod est pulmonaria Gallorum Lobelii*. It grows naturally in woods, and on dry banks and old walls in England and most parts of Europe.

3. Broad-leaved Pyrenean Hawkweed. This species is titled, *Hieracium foliis radicalibus [illegible] [illegible] caulinis oblongis [illegible] amplexicaulibus*. Tournefort calls it, *Hieracium Pyrenaicum, foliis [illegible], latifolium*. It grows naturally on the Pyrenean mountains.

4. Heart-leaved Pyrenean Hawkweed. This species is titled, *Hieracium foliis amplexicaulibus cordatis subdentatis, pedunculis unifloris hirsutis, caule ramoso*. Tournefort calls it, *Hieracium Pyrenaicum rotundifolium amplexicaule*, also *Hieracium Pyrenaicum longifolium amplexicaule*. It grows naturally on the Pyrenees.

5. Moth Mullein-leaved Hawkweed. This species is, *Hieracium foliis lanceolatis amplexicaulibus dentatis, floribus solitariis, calycibus laxis*. Tournefort calls it, *Hieracium Pyrenaicum, blattariae folio, minus hirsutum*. It is a native of the Pyrenees.

6. Mountain Hawkweed is, *Hieracium foliis oblongis integris dentatis, scapo subnudo unifloro, [illegible] piloso*. In the *Flora Lapponica* it is termed, *Hieracium caule unifloro, calyce villoso*. Caspar Bauhine calls it, *Hieracium Alpinum pumilum, folio lanuginoso*, Ray, *[illegible] villosum Alpinum, flore magno singulari*, and Morison, *Pilosella [illegible] non repens Alpina [illegible] lanuginosa, [illegible]*. It grows naturally on the Alpine parts of Lapland, Britain, and Austria.

7. Mouse-ear Hawkweed is, *Hieracium foliis integris ovato-oblongis, stolonibus repentibus, scapo nudo unifloro*. Haller calls it, *Hieracium [illegible] [illegible] ovato-lanceolatis, scapo [illegible] unifloro*, Vaillant, *Hieracium pilosellae [illegible]*, and Caspar Bauhine, *Pilosella major, [illegible]*. It grows naturally on hills and in dry places in England and Sweden.

8. Narrow-leaved Hawkweed is, *Hieracium foliis integerrimis lanceolatis, scapo nudo multifloro, stolonibus repentibus*. In the *Hortus Cliffort.* it is termed, *Hieracium majus foliis integerrimis, caule repente, scapo nudo [illegible]*. Caspar Bauhine calls it, *Pilosella major erecta altera*, and Ray, *Pilosella [illegible] [illegible] angustis [illegible]*. It grows naturally in dry meadows and pastures [illegible] in England and most parts of Europe.

9. Upright Hawkweed is, *Hieracium foliis [illegible], scapo nudo [illegible]*. Haller calls it, *[illegible] foliis [illegible] tomentosis, [illegible], floribus [illegible]*, Caspar Bauhine, *Hieracium [illegible]*, also, *Pilosella [illegible] erecta*. John Bauhine names it *[illegible]*. It grows naturally in Helvetia, Hercynia, and Upland.

10. Gronovius's Hawkweed is, *Hieracium caule paniculato subnudo, foliis [illegible] ovalibus [illegible] pilosis*. Gronovius calls it, *Hieracium foliis radicalibus obverse ovatis [illegible] [illegible] amplexicaulibus, floribus [illegible]*, and Plukenet, *Hieracium [illegible], pulmonariae gallicae [illegible] folio*. It grows naturally in Virginia and Pensylvania.

11. Gmelin's Hawkweed is, *Hieracium [illegible] nudo paniculato, foliis radicalibus [illegible] serratis [illegible]*. Gmelin calls it, *Hieracium [illegible] dentatis, caulibus [illegible] pubescentibus, [illegible] [illegible] floribus*. It is a native of Siberia.

12. Broad-leaved Bushy Hawkweed is, *Hieracium caule erecto multifloro, foliis ovato-lanceolatis dentatis semiamplexicaulibus*. Caspar Bauhine calls it, *Hieracium fruticosum latifolium hirsutum*, John Bauhine, *Hieracium sabaudum [illegible]*, Parkinson, *Hieracium fruticosum latifolium glabrum*, and Ray *Hieracium, [illegible] majoris species hirsutus, foliis [illegible] dentatis plurimis [illegible], [illegible] singularis, [illegible]*. It grows naturally in woods, hedges, and shady moist places in England and Germany.

13. Narrow-leaved Bushy Hawkweed is, *Hieracium foliis linearibus [illegible] sparsis, floribus subumbellatis*. Caspar Bauhine calls it, *Hieracium fruticosum angustifolium majus*, Dalechamp, *Hieracium sabaudum*, Gerard, *Hieracium [illegible]*, and Petiver, *Pulmonaria angustifolia glabra*, also, *Pulmonaria [illegible]*. It grows naturally in woods, hedges, and dry pastures in England, and most countries of Europe.

14. Bohemian Hawkweed is, *Hieracium caule ramoso [illegible], foliis [illegible] radicalibus lanceolato-ovatis dentatis, caulinis [illegible] cordatis*. Caspar Bauhine calls it, *Hieracium Alpinum latifolium [illegible] magno flore*, Plukenet, *Hieracium Alpinum, [illegible] folio, pilosum, flore majore*, and Clusius, *Hieracium [illegible]*. It grows naturally on the Alps, and in the like situation in Switzerland, Bohemia, and the south of France.

15. Holy Hawkweed is, *Hieracium scapo nudo multifloro, foliis [illegible] dentatis*. It grows naturally in Palestine.

16. Cymose Hawkweed is, *Hieracium foliis lanceolatis integris pilosis, scapo subnudo basi piloso, floribus subumbellatis*. Vaillant calls it, *Hieracium pilosellae [illegible] majus [illegible] foliis, [illegible] luteis fere umbellatis*; Caspar Bauhine, *Hieracium mu-*

*terum angustifolium non sinuatum*, also, *Pilosella montana, hispida, parvo flore*, and John Bauhine, *Pilosella minore flore, hirsut or & elatior, non repens* It grows naturally in Germany, Russia, Denmark, and Switzerland

17 Common Creeping Mouse-ear is, *Hieracium foliis integris ovatis, subtus tomentosis, caule repente, scapo unifloro* Caspar Bauhine calls it, *Pilosella major repens hirsuta*, Cammerarius, *Pilosella major*, Gerard, *Pilosella repens*, and Parkinson *Pilosella minor vulgaris repens* It grows naturally in dry pastures in England and most part of Europe

Class and order in the Linnæan System The characters

*Hieracium* is of the class and order *Syngenesia Polygamia Æqualis*, and the characters are,

1 Calyx is composed of many very narrow unequal leaves placed lengthways, and incumbent

2 Corolla The general flower is imbricated and uniform The flosculi are numerous and equal, each of them is composed of a single, ligulated, linear, truncated petal, indented in five parts at the end

3 Stamina are five very short capillary filaments, with cylindrical, tubulous antheræ

4 Pistillum consists of an oval germen, a filiforme style the length of the stamina, and two recurved stigmas

5 Pericarpium There is none

6 Semina are single, obtusely four-cornered, short, and crowned with hairy down The receptaculum is naked

## CHAP CCXXXI

## *HIPPOCREPIS*, HORSE-SHOE VETCH.

IN this place may be mentioned Liquorice Hatchet Vetch, or Tufted Horse-shoe Vetch

This plant described

The root is woody, tough, and in poor soils will continue for many years The stalks are round, tough, hardly a foot long, and lie on the ground The leaves are pinnated, each being composed of five or six pair of oval, narrow folioles, which are terminated by an odd one, and are sweetish to the taste The flowers come out in clusters from the wings of the leaves on long footstalks, they are of a pale yellow colour, appear in June, and are succeeded by short, crooked, jointed pods, containing ripe seeds, in August

Its variety

There is a variety with deep-yellow flowers

Method of propagating it

This plant is propagated by sowing the seeds, where they are to remain, in the autumn, soon after they are ripe, or in the spring When they come up, they must be thinned to proper distances, and kept clean from weeds, and this is all the trouble they will require

Proper soil

They should have a poor hungry dry soil, and the roots will continue for many years, but in a rich, fat, moist earth, the plants will be more luxuriant, and generally die soon after the seeds are ripe In such situations, therefore, this species should be considered an annual

Titles

This species is titled, *Hippocrepis leguminibus pedunculatis confertis, margine exteriori repandis* In the *Hortus Cliffort* it is termed, *Hippocrepis leguminibus pedunculatis confertis, margine exteriori lobatis* Caspar Bauhine calls it, *Ferrum equinum Germanicum, siliquis in summitate*, Columna, *Ferrum equinum comosum, s capitatum*, Parkinson, *Ferrum equinum comosum*, and Gerard, *Hedysarum glycyrrhizatum* It grows naturally on dry chalky ground in England, Germany, France, and Italy

Class and order in the Linnæan system The characters

*Hippocrepis* is of the class and order *Diadelphia Decandria*, and the characters are,

1 Calyx is a monophyllous, permanent perianthium, indented in five parts, at the top of which the two upper ones are joined

2 Corolla is papilionaceous The vexillum is heart shaped, and supported by a narrow unguis the length of the calyx The alæ are oval, oblong, and obtuse The carina is moon-shaped, and compressed

3 Stamina are diadelphous, and erect

4 Pistillum consists of a slender, oblong germen, an awl shaped style, and a simple stigma

5 Pericarpium is a compressed, membranaceous, long, incurved pod, cut or hollowed from the under suture to the upper into many roundish sinus's, connected by obtusely three-cornered joints, displaying the figure of an horse-shoe

6 Semina The seeds are single in each joint, oblong, and incurved

# C H A P. CCXXXII.

## *H I P P U R I S.*

THERE is only one species of this genus, called Mare's Tail.

**This plant described.** The root is thick, creeping, jointed, and sends forth long fibres into the mud. The stalks are upright, round, hollow, jointed, largest at their base, and diminish gradually to a point. The leaves are short, bristly, and surround the stalk in a radiated manner at every joint. The fructifications are produced from the wings of the leaves at the joint, and they are to be met with in May and June.

This species grows naturally in ditches, bogs, by the sides of brooks, springs, and watery places, and is never cultivated.

**Titles.** As it admits of no other species, its name is singly *Hippuris*. Caspar Bauhine calls it, *Equisetum palustre, brevioribus foliis polyspermum*, Cammerarius, *Polygonum fœmina*, Gerard, *Cauda equina fœmina*, and Parkinson, *Equisetum palustre alterum brevioribus setis*. It grows naturally in England and most countries of Europe.

**Class and order in the Linnæan system.** *Hippuris* is of the class and order *Monandria Monogynia*, and the characters are,

**The characters.**

1. CALYX. There is none.
2. COROLLA. There is none.
3. STAMINA consist of one filament sitting on the receptacle of the flower, having a semibifid anthera.
4. PISTILLUM consists of an oblong germen, one awl-shaped erect style longer than the stamen, and an acute stigma.
5. PERICARPIUM. There is none.
6. SEMEN. The seed is single, roundish, and naked.

# C H A P. CCXXXIII.

## *HOLCUS,* INDIAN MILLET.

OF this genus are two noted grasses of our meadows and pastures, called,

**Species.**

1. Meadow Soft Grass.
2. Creeping Soft Grass.

Tho' the name Meadow is in use whereby to express these grasses, yet they grow on all sorts of dry land, rich pastures, and sandy and gravelly soils. They are very early grasses, give a grateful odour to hay, and a fine flavour to such mutton as has been fed chiefly upon them. It is not designed that they should be introduced into the garden. I mention them here for the sake of giving the titles and characters to the Botanist, that he may know what they are, and how to distinguish them properly in his morning recreations.

**Titles.** 1. Meadow Soft Grass is titled, *Holcus glumis bifloris villosis, hermaphrodito mutico, masculo aristâ recurvatâ*. In the *Flora Suecia* it is termed, *Aira foliis pubescentibus, paniculâ contractâ, flosculo hermaphrodito mutico, masculo aristâ uncinatâ, calyce breviore*; in the *Hort. Cliffort.* *Aira flosculo masculo aristato, femineo mutico*. Caspar Bauhine calls it, *Gramen pratense paniculatum molle*, Dalechamp, *Gramen lanatum*, and Ray, *Gramen miliaceum paniculatum molle*. It grows naturally in England and almost all countries of Europe.

2. Creeping Soft Grass is, *Holcus glumis bifloris nudiusculis, flosculo hermaphrodito mutico, masculo aristâ geniculatâ*. Morison calls it, *Gramen paniculatum molle, radice graminis caninæ repente*, Ray, *Gramen miliaceum aristatum molle*, Caspar Bauhine, *Gramen caninum longius radicatum*.

It grows naturally all over Europe.

**Class and order in the Linnæan system.** *Holcus* is of the class and order *Polygamia Monoecia*, and the characters are,

**The characters.**

### 1. HERMAPHRODITE FLOWERS.

1. CALYX is a rigid, beardless, bivalvate glume, containing one or two flowers. The exterior valve is oval, concave, large, and embraces the inner, which is oblong, and rolled in at the sides.
2. COROLLA is a slender, bivalvate, hairy glume, smaller than the calyx. The outer valve is for the most part furnished with a stiff arista, or awn, which is longer than the calyx, but the interior valve is beardless, and very small.
3. STAMINA are three capillary filaments with oblong antheræ.
4. PISTILLUM consists of a turbinated germen, and two capillary styles, with penicilliforme stigmas.
5. PERICARPIUM. There is none. The seed is wrapped up in the corolla.
6. SEMEN. The seed is single, oval, and covered.

### 2. MALE FLOWERS.

1. CALYX is a glume composed of two oval, spear-shaped, concave, beardless, acute valves.
2. COROLLA. There is none.
3. STAMINA are three capillary filaments with oblong antheræ.

CHAP.

## CHAP. CCXXXIV.

## *HORMINUM*, PYRENEAN CLARY.

THERE are only two species of this genus, one of which is a perennial, the other a biennial. The perennial species is usually called, Pyrenean Baum, or Plantain-leaved Wild Clary.

*This plant described*

This is a low plant, growing only to about a foot high. The leaves are heart-shaped, oval, obtuse, crenated, and not unlike some of our sorts of plantain. The stalks have hardly any leaves, but the flowers surround them in whorls; they are of a violet colour, appear in June, and ripen their seeds in August.

*Method of propagation*

This species is easily propagated by parting the roots, the best time for which is autumn. It will grow in almost any soil or situation, but if its station be shady, it will be more adapted to its nature.

By seeds also this sort may be raised in plenty. Sow them in the autumn as soon as they are ripe. The plants will soon come up, and in the spring prick them out in the nursery-bed nine inches from each other. Water and shade them until they have taken root, keep them clean from weeds all summer, and in the autumn remove them to the places where they are to remain.

*Titles*

This species is titled, *Horminum foliis cordatis obtusis, caule nudo*. In the *Hortus Cliffort.* it is called, simply, *Horminum*. John Bauhine terms it, *Callitrichum folio rotundo, flore nigro violaceo*; Tournefort, *Horminum Pyrenaicum, caule brevi, plantaginis folio*. It grows naturally on mount Baldus and the Pyrenees.

*Class and order in the Linnæan system*

*Horminum* is of the class and order *Didynamia Gymnospermia*; and the characters are,

*The characters*

1. CALYX is a monophyllous, bell-shaped, unequal, channelled perianthium, having two lips; the upper of which is broad, oval, spreading, and ends in three acute points; the lower lip is spear-shaped, and ends in two acute points.
2. COROLLA is a ringent petal. The tube is the length of the calyx. The upper lip is erect, concave, and semibifid. The lower lip is trifid, the middle segment being large and indented.
3. STAMINA. There are four awl-shaped, rising, incurved filaments, that are not longer than the corolla. Of these the two opposite ones are the shortest, and all have simple antheræ.
4. PISTILLUM consists of a quadripartite germen, a filiforme style the length of the stamina, and an acute, bifid stigma.
5. PERICARPIUM. There is none. The seeds are lodged in the calyx.
6. SEMINA. The seeds are roundish, and four in number.

## CHAP. CCXXXV.

## *HOTTONIA*, WATER VIOLET.

OF this genus there is a beautiful aquatic, called the Water Violet.

*This plant described*

Its habitation is in ditches and stinking waters, where it garnishes such places by its beautiful leaves and flowers. The root consists of numerous slender fibres, which are very long and strike into the mud. The leaves are finely divided into a multitude of narrow parts. Hence the name Water Milfoil is frequently applied to this plant. They are large, and some of them will be immersed, while others will lie flat upon the water. The flower-stalk rises to six or eight inches high; it is round, naked near the bottom, upright, and supports the flowers in whorls near the top. The flowers terminate each stalk in a small cluster, as well as surround it lower in a radiated manner, or in whorls placed at certain distances from each other; they are of a beautiful purple colour, appear in June and July, and the seeds ripen in August.

*Its varieties*

There is a variety of this plant with white flowers, and another with white flowers having yellow centers.

*Method of propagation*

It is propagated by plucking up the roots from the places where they naturally grow, and throwing them by handfuls into the water. They will frequently float some weeks, and at length strike root in the mud, and shew both their leaves and flowers in the most pleasing form the summer following.

They are also propagated by seeds. These should be gathered as soon as they are ripe, and thrown into the water in such places where you would chuse to have the plants come up. Being thus submerged, they will vegetate, strike root into the mud, and by degrees reach their heads above the water, and display the beauties of their little flowers. They make an amazing encrease, and if they take to and like their situation, they will soon overspread that part of the lake.

*Titles*

This species is titled, *Hottonia pedunculis verticillato-multifloris*. Caspar Bauhine calls it, *Millefolium aquaticum, seu viola aquatica, caule nudo*; also, *Millefolium aquaticum equisetifolium, caule nudo*. Parkinson terms it, *Millefolium aquaticum floridum, seu viola aquatica*; Gerard, *Viola palustris*; and Boerhaave, *Hottonia*. It grows naturally in ditches and standing-waters in England and most of the northern countries of Europe.

*Class and order in the Linnæan system*

*Hottonia* is of the class and order *Pentandria Monogynia*; and the characters are,

*The characters*

1. CALYX is a monophyllous perianthium, divided into five narrow spreading segments.
2. COROLLA is one hypocrateriforme petal. The tube is the length of the calyx. The limb is plane, and cut into five oval oblong parts, which are indented at the extremity.
3. STAMINA are five short, erect, awl-shaped filaments, placed in the tube opposite to the segments of the corolla, having oblong antheræ.
4. PISTILLUM consists of a globose, acuminated germen, a short filiforme style, and a globose stigma.
5. PERICARPIUM is a globular, acuminated, unilocular capsule, placed on the calyx.
6. SEMINA. The seeds are many and round. The receptacle is large and round.

CHAP.

# CHAP. CCXXXVI.

## HYACINTHUS, The HYACINTH.

*Introduction of the genus.*

THE profusion of varieties that adorn this genus, which are arranged as belonging to one species of it only, and which are the pride of the Dutch and Flemish Florists, and now much cultivated and carried by our own, is amply treated of among those flowers that are more peculiarly set apart for the Florist's care, called Shed Flowers; so that the different species which remain for this place are those whose properties make them valuable to all, as being useful and ornamental in their stations; and though a rigid Florist may overlook some of them as beneath his notice, yet the Botanist will ever respect them with honour, and hunt after the species as eagerly as the other will after an Oriental Hyacinth of the first properties. There were originally no very great number of species belonging to this genus, but the *Muscari* of old botanists is now partly joined to it; so that at present they constitute the following number, whose usual names are,

*Species.*

1. The English Hyacinth, or Hare-Bell of our woods and hedges.
2. The Red Spanish Hyacinth.
3. The Common Spanish Hyacinth.
4. Amethystine Hyacinth.
5. Oriental Hyacinth.
6. Musk Hyacinth.
7. Feathered Hyacinth.
8. Fair haired Hyacinth.
9. Common Grape Hyacinth.
10. Racemose Grape Hyacinth.
11. Orchoide Hyacinth.
12. Branching stalked Hyacinth.

*Description of the English Hyacinth.*

1. The English Hyacinth is so common that it is universally known; our woods and hedges are almost every where full of it, so that I believe we have greater plenty of it than of the common Wild Primrose. A plant or two should be ever ready at hand for the philosopher's observation, and except those, no others need be admitted into any part of our works. When they are desired, they should be stationed with the common Primrose, in woods and wilds, without the appearance of the assistance of art, to shew themselves as perfect as if Nature alone had thrown them there.

*Variety.*

There is however a sort of this plant with white flowers, which is on that account a cultivated plant, and these would not only be proper to mix with the others, but claim a place in borders, and in the collection of Perennial flowers.

*Red Spanish.*

2. The Red Spanish Hyacinth. This is called so only for distinction, as it grows naturally in Spain. It flowers about the same time with our Common Hyacinth, and has been by some supposed to be only a variety of it; but we do not find it growing in any part of England, in its natural state of wildness, that I have ever yet heard of. The leaves are narrower than those of our Hyacinth, less spear-shaped, and more erect. The flowers are ranged on one side the stalk. The petals are of the usual campanulated figure, and naturally nodding or bowing towards the earth. These are differences from the former sort. But what constitutes its greatest beauty is the colour of its flowers, which are of a delicate pale red. Neither have I ever seen any of this species with blue flowers, or indeed of any other colour; on that account it chiefly claims a place in any collection, and deserves all due attention and care.

*Common Spanish.*

3. The Common Spanish Hyacinth is a name also used only for distinction; and the epithet Common is given it, perhaps, because the flowers are of a blue colour; for though it grows naturally in Spain, it is not more common there than the other sort. This is a distinct species, but of so little beauty, that a third only after a general collection can make it desirable. The flowers are small, and nearly campanulate, though they have a different appearance; for the segments are divided almost to the bottom, and the three exterior ones are at a distance from the three interior. It flowers later than our Common sort, and the colour is of a very bad worn-out blue; insomuch that some botanists have called it the Hyacinth with an obsolete flower, and others, the late Spanish Hyacinth with a flower of a worn out colour, &c.

*Amethystine Hyacinth.*

4. The Amethystine Hyacinth is so named on account of its colour, being naturally that of the finest amethyst. I say naturally, for that is the true native colour, and with due attention and culture will be preserved; but for want of this they so far run away from their colour, that they soon lose that fine tinge, and become of a very bad blue or dusky-grey colour; so that good management must be bestowed upon this plant to preserve its original perfection. This management will be only to plant it in a rich sandy soil, and to remove it every other year, take off the offsets, and the like. But it may be brought to greater perfection by seeds; for the colours of plants raised this way, after they have blown one year, and come to their full strength, will be clearer, and much exceed any that are produced from old roots or offsets. The seeds will come up in a common border of sandy earth, though they will be some years before they flower. This method was formerly in practice, but now seems entirely laid aside, the Eastern Hyacinths only being thought deserving of this tedious practice. A few plants therefore of this species will be sufficient to join in the collection, which may be procured by offsets, or old roots; and if these are set out in the flower garden, in such quarters as require removing every other year, their flowers will be tolerably good, though not perhaps of that fine tint or tinge of the amethyst.

This plant flowers early in the spring, being often in blow by the end of February. The flowers garnish the top of a strong upright stalk about a foot high; the footstalk of each is weak, so that they hang in a drooping manner. The bottom part of each flower is cylindrical, and their top is deeply cut into six segments, which naturally turn back.

This species, from its early blowing, should always be planted in such borders or beds as are under the command of the sitting room, with hepaticas, crocus's, &c. to be seen from thence when the weather will not permit the ladies to indulge in their usual walk.

5. The

Oriental. 5 The Oriental Hyacinth is the sort which gives birth to that profusion of delightful varieties that are the pride of the Dutch and Flemish florists. Their due management and care have already been treated of; all that is necessary to be remarked here is, that as we have given general directions for raising and encreasing these varieties from seeds, and as perhaps not one in a thousand will hardly be found worth admitting into the collection of Hyacinths as compleat flowers, such as are not possessed of those properties to deserve the florist's nice management, may, nevertheless be planted out in beds or borders, where they will flower and encrease abundantly, and though their flowers, perhaps, may not be so fair as they would with better management, yet they will be ornamental, and equal in beauty many of the border flowers. Besides, they will be useful to be gathered to set in rooms, in which they will plentifully infuse their delightful odour. Constant care must be taken to remove them as soon as they begin to wither and decay, for they are often possessed of the opposite qualities; so that to make a room delightful indeed, a fresh supply should be brought every morning.

Musk Hyacinth. 6 The Musk Hyacinth. The genus under which this and its different species are arranged by old botanists, is termed *Muscari*, but being examined by the stricter eye of Science, they are found to belong to the Hyacinth, being real and distinct species of that genus, differing only in the form of the corolla; the one being oblong and tubulous, the other inflated and round. This species, which commonly goes by the name of the Musk Hyacinth, has a large tunicated bulb, which sends forth leaves seven or eight inches long, these are narrow, of a fine green colour, a thick consistence, furrowed, and end in obtuse points. The stalk of the flowers, which is about half a foot high, rises in the middle of these, the topmost half of which supports the flowers. The flower-buds appear in March, but will not be in full blow before the end of April. These flowers are of a rounded figure, and have their edges so reflexed as to resemble the shape of a pitcher; they are of a very bad blue or purple colour, as if in a fading state, which has occasioned some former botanists to distinguish it with the title, *Muscari obsoletiore flore*, it having naturally so bad an appearance, unless improved by culture. Indeed, as well as most plants, this assumes a finer air in proportion to its good management. For if planted in a good border of sandy earth, and kept removing every other year, taking away the offsets, &c. it will be of a tolerable good blue colour. It will grow almost any where, without any art; and tho' the colours of this sort will not be so good, yet it in some degree makes amends by perfuming the air to a considerable distance by its musky odours.

Varieties. These are the properties of the Common Musk Hyacinth; but there are three or four varieties of it that are cultivated plants, and encreased by the offsets, the chief of which is the Large Yellow-flowering Musk Hyacinth. It resembles the other in every respect, of which it is a variety, only the bulbs, leaves, flower-stalks, and flowers, are much larger. The flowers are finely scented, and of a delightful yellow colour.

This variety was originally obtained by seeds in Holland, and sold by the Dutch florists for many years at a great price; and even now, though it is in several collections, it is far from being common.

Another variety of this plant has yellow flowers at the top of the spike, and purple flowers at the bottom. These are larger than the common sort, and being equally sweet scented, make it very valuable.

Feathered. 7 The Feathered Hyacinth is very much admired as a bulbous perennial flower root. The leaves, which are seven or eight in number, are of a fine green colour, narrow, plane, smooth, and end in obtuse points. From between these the flower-stalk arises, the flower-buds appear early in April, and will be in full blow in May. The flower-stalk has more than two parts out of three garnished with flowers, which are produced in a panicled manner. The flowers stand upon footstalks, which are large and longer at the bottom, and each contain several small flowers, with feathered-like petals. These flowers are of a blue colour, with a tinge of purple, but are never succeeded by any seeds, being destitute of both the male and female organs of generation, called the stamina and germen. This is a very ornamental plant amongst perennial flowers; it will grow in any soil or situation, and will require now and then only to be removed, and the offsets taken off to be multiplied that way.

Fair-haired. 8 The Fair-haired Hyacinth, or Broad-leaved Purple *Muscari*. This bulb produces seven or eight leaves, of a good green colour, a foot or more in length; they are near an inch broad at their base, and diminish gradually to a point. From these comes out the flower-stalk, which makes its appearance the beginning of March, but the flowers are rarely in full blow before the beginning of May. The stalk rises to about a foot in height, and the flowers, as is usual, garnish the upper part of it; one half, however, at least they occupy, and grow on long footstalks, which place them in a horizontal position. These flowers have angular cylindrical petals, but the top of the stalk is terminated by a tuft, whose petals are oval, and destitute of the female parts. The bottom-parts of the flowers, however, are not barren, but produce good seeds, from which plenty of plants may be raised. But as this is a tedious practice, they being usually three years before they flower, the common method of their encrease is by offsets, though seedlings, when they come to blow, will afford you varieties, some with white, some with blue, and others with purple flowers, which is the original colour of this species.

Grape. 9 The Grape Hyacinth is a plant pretty well known, being to be found in most old gardens, where the neglect of management will by no means impair or weaken it; for it will encrease itself, both by seeds and roots, in spite of all weeds, and I have seen it flower fair and strong in places where a spade had not entered for some years. The bulbs of this species are small in proportion to the other sorts, and the leaves are more numerous; they are about half a foot long, very narrow, and almost round, but have a channel or gutter running lengthways, and if the edges which form this gutter were a little more incurved, it would be quite cylindrical. The flower-buds of this species appear the beginning of March, and they will be in full blow by the middle of April. The bottom part of the stalk is naked, in the usual manner, but the flowers at the top of it form a close spike. These flowers are round and uniform, but their edges turn in so as to form it into the shape of a pitcher; they sit close to the stalk, and have a strong scent, which to most people is very disagreeable, whilst some few again fancy it to be very fine. Blue is the usual colour of this species, though there are varieties with white and ash-coloured flowers, which are more sought after, as being less common, and they have all, except in the colour of their flowers, exactly the same properties.

Racemose Grape. 10 The Racemose Grape Hyacinth is another

species that sends forth from the bulbs many sword-shaped leaves that are much like a sedge, which are of a greeable dark green colour, and about half an inch broad and eight inches long. From the middle of these, in March, appear the flower buds, which will be in blow in April, though they do not have ... stalk, but the ... of a ... stalk, each flower is of a ... nature, and their colour is a very fine blue, but they have rather a dingy appearance.

Orchid. 11. The Orchoide Hyacinth is so called from the resemblance it has to an Orchis. This species is very unlike all the other sorts of the Hyacinth, and though singular enough, yet it directly belongs to that family, and no other. The bulbs are small, white, and each produces seldom more than two leaves, which are ... six or eight inches long, and two inches broad. Their edges are quite smooth, and end in obtuse points; they are of a fine ... green colour, and their upper surface is spotted with many dark purple spots. From between the leaves the flower-stalk will be seen to appear the beginning of March, and they will be in full blow by the beginning of April. The flower-stalk will grow to about a foot high; it is round, smooth, and, like the leaves, spotted with brown or purple. The flowers, in the usual manner, ornament the top half, forming a spike, and ... for an Hyacinth very singular, each is composed of a single petal, ... is more than of the usual size, but the upper part is irregularly and deeply cut into six segments. These flowers are not placed close, but at a little distance from each other; they ... of a dusky yellow colour on the outside, but ... are more ... the Engot.

This plant grows naturally in the woods at the Cape of Good Hope, and requires with us to be protected from frosts in winter; so that the places where they are planted should be covered with tanner's bark, leaves, litter, or any thing that will prevent the frost from penetrating their fibres, and should be removed again as soon as the frost is over. In February the beds should be looped, and covered with mats in bad weather, for if the winter has been tolerably open, by the end of that month the flower-buds will appear. These must be guarded until they blow, and always have as much air as possible. This will be better than setting them in the green-house, or under a hotbed frame, as has been recommended, for there they would be drawn up weak, and will hardly have strength enough to cause them to flower well. ... are frequently brought from the Cape, so that if a person wants a few plants to furnish his collection, they may be easily obtained. If he covets a number of plants, which is seldom wanted but by those who raise them for sale, the seeds will furnish him the soonest with plenty, and if he pursues the method directed for raising the sorts of the Oriental Hyacinth, he will have plants enough, if his seeds are good; but of these he must be more careful to preserve them from frosts, which will probably destroy them.

Branching-stalked Hyacinth, or Peruvian. 12. The Branching-stalked Hyacinth. The bulb, which is large and round, sends out six or eight leaves of about a foot in length; they are of a fine green colour, narrow, and their edges are incurved. The flower-buds appear in March, tho' they will not be in blow before May. The stalk branches or divides itself into several smaller ... of flowers, so that a large panicle is formed. The flowers are of a kind of purple colour, and their petals are cut into very fine wool or hair-like filaments, that turn back. It is to be propagated by the bulbs, and if set in a light soil and shady situation, will multiply itself very fast.

Culture. This is the method of propagating all the sorts of Hyacinths, observing always, however, the precautions relating to the Orchoide species, which comes from a warmer country, and requires more care. With regard to the raising such of these species as produce good seeds by that means, the business will be effectually done, if the method directed for raising the Eastern Hyacinth be observed. However, so much care need not be bestowed upon any of the sorts, except the eleventh; for if they are sown in a shady border of light common garden mould, they will come up, and grow very well, and after the bulbs are two years old, so that they begin to be tolerably large, they may be set out where they are to remain for flowering. This method is seldom practised, a few plants of each sort, to furnish a collection, being generally all that are desired, the chief stress lying upon the noble species, with all its varieties, called the Oriental Hyacinth. The nurserymen, however, who has a demand for great numbers of flower-roots, may have recourse to seeds, to ... the greater number of his customers with bulbs, whilst he who only may choose the other method as the ... and ... way of gaining supply. I shall proceed now to give the botanic titles of the species above enumerated.

Titles. 1. The Common English Hyacinth is titled, *Hyacinthus corollis campanulatis sexpartitis apice revolutis*. This is the *Hyacinthus oblongo flore caeruleus major*, of Caspar Bauhine, the *Hyacinthus Anglicus*, of Gerard; and the *Hyacinthus Anglicus, Belgicus, Hispanicus*, of Parkinson. It grows common not only in England, but in France, Italy, and Spain.

2. The Red Spanish Hyacinth is, *Hyacinthus corollis campanulatis sexpartitis, ... ...* Clusius calls it, *Hyacinthus Hispanicus*; and Caspar Bauhine, *Hyacinthus oblongo flore ... rubente minor*. It is a native of Spain.

3. The Common Spanish Hyacinth is, *Hyacinthus corollis ... ... subdeflexis, ... coalitis*. Caspar Bauhine terms it, *Hyacinthus obsoleto flore*; and Clusius, *Hyacinthus obsoleti coloris, Hispanicus serotinus*. It grows common in Spain and Mauritania.

4. The Amethystine Hyacinth is, *Hyacinthus corollis campanulatis, semisexfidis basi cylindricis*. Caspar Bauhine calls it *Hyacinthus oblongo caeruleo flore minor*; and John Bauhine, *Hyacinthus minor Hispanicus angustifolius*. It is a native of Spain.

5. The Oriental Hyacinth is, *Hyacinthus corollis infundibuliformibus semisexfidis basi ventricosis*. Caspar Bauhine calls it, *Hyacinthus Orientalis ...*; and Dodonaeus, *Hyacinthus Orientalis major et minor*. Of this older botanists have made numerous species, to which they have given titles, and which are justly proved to be varieties only. It grows naturally in Asia and Africa.

6. Musk Hyacinth is, *Hyacinthus corollis ovatis omnibus aequalibus*. Caspar Bauhine calls it, *Hyacinthus racemosus moschatus*; and Clusius, *Muscari obsoletiore flore*. It is a native of Asia.

7. The Feathered Hyacinth is, *Hyacinthus corollis subovatis*. In the Hortus Cliffort. it is termed, *Hyacinthus floribus paniculatis monstrosis*. Caspar Bauhine calls it, *Hyacinthus paniculis caeruleis*; and Columna, *Hyacinthus Sannicsius, paniculis comosis*. It grows common in some parts of France.

8. Hair-haired Hyacinth is, *Hyacinthus corollis angulato-cylindricis summis sterilibus longius pedicellatis*. Caspar Bauhine calls it, *Hyacinthus comosus major purpureus*; Sauvages, *Hyacinthus corollis globosis, summis pedunculatis, foliis ensiformibus*; and Cammerarius simply, *Hyacinthus*. It grows common in the fields in France, and the northern parts of Europe.

9. The

9 The Common Grape Hyacinth is, *Hyacinthus corollis globosis uniformibus, foliis canaliculato-cylindricis strictis* In the *Hortus Cliffort* it is termed, *Hyacinthus corollis globosis* Tournefort calls it, *Hyacinthus botryoides vulgaris*, Tournefort, *Muscari arvense, junifolium cæruleum minus*, Sauvages, *Hyacinthus corollis globosis, foliis in cylindrum convolutis*, Caspar Bauhine, *Hyacinthus racemosus cæruleus major*, and Clusius, *Hyacinthus botryoides purpureus* It is a native of Italy

10 Racemose Grape Hyacinth is, *Hyacinthus corollis ovatis summis sessilibus, foliis laxis* Caspar Bauhine terms it, *Hyacinthus racemosus cæruleus minor junceifolius*, and Clusius, *Hyacinthus botryoides* It grows naturally in many of the northern parts of Europe

11 Orchoide Hyacinth is, *Hyacinthus corollis sexpartitis, petalis tribus exterioribus brevioribus* This by Breynius is termed, *Hyacinthus Orchioides Africanus, major, bifolius maculatus, flore sulphureo obsoleto majore*, Buxbaum, *Orchis angustifolia maculata*, also, *Orchis Hyacinthoides, foliis, caule, et floribus maculatis* It grows naturally in Ethiopia

12 Branching-stalked Hyacinth is, *Hyacinthus, corollis lanatis, caule ramoso* The native place of this species is uncertain

*Hyacinthus* is of the class and order *Hexandria Monogynia*, and the characters are,

Class and order in the Linnæan system The characters

1 CALYX There is none

2 COROLLA consists of one campanulated petal, cut at the limb into six reflexed segments The nectarium consists of three pores full of honey, situated on the point of the germen

3 STAMINA are six short subulated filaments, having connivent antheræ

4 PISTILLUM The germen is roundish, tho' three cornered, and marked with three furrows The style is single, shorter than the corolla, and the stigma is obtuse

5 PERICARPIUM is a roundish, three-cornered, three-sided, trivalvate capsule, containing three cells

6 SEMINA The seeds are roundish

Lest the unexperienced young gardener should expect to find the different sorts of Starry Hyacinths treated of under this head, it may not be improper to inform him they belong to another genus called *Scilla*, under which an account of them will be given

# CHAP. CCXXXVII.

## *HYDROCHARIS*, FROG's BIT.

THERE is only one species of this genus, called, Frog's Bit

This plant described

The root is possessed of several long fibres The leaves are roundish, juicy, thick, and of a brownish-green colour The stalks are upright, slender, and three or four inches high The flowers are produced from the top of the stalk, they are of a white colour, moderately large, and finely scented, they appear in June and July, and the seeds ripen in August

They grow naturally in ditches, brooks, and standing waters, and are not cultivated

Titles

There being no other species of this plant, it is termed simply, *Hydrocharis* Caspar Bauhine calls it, *Nymphæa alba minima*, also, *Nymphæa alba minor*, Dodonæus, *Ranæ morsus*, and Ray, *Morsus ranæ, flore pleno odoratissimo* It is a native of most parts of Europe

Class and order in the Linnæan system The characters

*Hydrocharis* is of the class and order *Dioecia Decandria*, and the characters are,

I Male Flowers

1 CALYX The spatha is composed of two oblong leaves, and contains three flowers The perianthium consists of three oval, oblong, concave leaves with membranaceous borders

2 COROLLA is three large, roundish, plane petals

3 STAMINA are nine awl-shaped upright filaments, disposed in three orders, having simple antheræ

4 PISTILLUM is the rudiment only of a germen in the middle of the filaments

II Females

1 CALYX There is no spatha, and the flowers grow singly The perianthium is the same as the males

2 COROLLA is the same as the males

3 PISTILLUM consists of a roundish germen, and six compressed styles the length of the calyx, having bifid acuminated stigmas

4 PERICARPIUM is a coriaceous roundish capsule, containing six cells

5 SEMINA The seeds are numerous, small, and roundish

## CHAP. CCXXXVIII.

## *HYDROCOTYLE*, WATER NAVEL-WORT.

OF this genus there are,

Species.

1. Marſh Pennywort, or White Rot.
2. American Water Navel-Wort.

Deſcription of the Marſh Pennywort or White Rot.

1. Marſh Pennywort, or White Rot. The root is ſlender and creeping. The leaves are peltated, roundiſh, emarginated, and of a pale-green colour. The ſtalks are ſlender, round, and four or five inches high. The flowers come out from the tops of the ſtalks in kind of umbels; they are of a reddiſh colour, or white ſpotted with red; appear in May and June, and the ſeeds ripen in July.

This ſpecies is ſaid to occaſion the rot in ſheep, if they eat thereof.

and American Water Navel-Wort.

2. American Water Navel-Wort. The ſtalk is round, uſually purpliſh, lies on the ground, and ſtrikes root at the joints. The leaves are kidney-ſhaped, neatly lobed, and indented on their edges; they are of a thickiſh ſubſtance, and a deep-green colour. The ſtalks ariſe from among the leaves, and grow to be four or five inches high. The flowers come out from the tops of the ſtalks in umbels; they are of a pale reddiſh colour, and appear about the time of the former.

Culture.

The firſt ſpecies grows naturally on boggy ground in England, and is not cultivated; the other, being a foreigner, may be encreaſed by parting of the roots, which may be done at any time of the year. It ſhould have a moiſt ſoil and a ſhady ſituation, and will afterwards require no trouble, except keeping it clean from weeds.

Titles.

1. The firſt ſpecies is titled, *Hydrocotyle foliis peltatis, umbellis quinquefloris*. In the *Hortus Cliffortianus* it is termed, *Hydrocotyle foliis peltatis orbiculatis undique emarginatis*. Caſpar Bauhine calls it, *Ranunculus aquaticus, cotyledonis folio*; Lobel, *Cotyledon aquatica*; and Tournefort, *Hydrocotyle vulgaris*. It grows naturally in watery places in moſt countries of Europe.

2. The ſecond ſpecies is, *Hydrocotyle foliis reniformibus ſublobatis crenatis*. It grows naturally in North America.

*Hydrocotyle* is of the claſs and order *Pentandria Digynia*; and the characters are,

1. CALYX. The umbel is ſimple. The involucrum is uſually compoſed of four ſmall leaves. The perianthium is very ſmall.

2. COROLLA. The general flower is uniform in figure, though not in ſituation. The florets have each five oval, acute, patent, undivided petals.

3. STAMINA are five awl-ſhaped filaments ſhorter than the corolla, having extremely ſmall antheræ.

4. PISTILLUM conſiſts of an erect, compreſſed, orbiculated germen, and two ſhort awl-ſhaped ſtyles, with ſimple ſtigmas.

5. PERICARPIUM. There is none. The fruit is round, compreſſed, and divided tranſverſely into two parts.

6. SEMINA. The ſeeds are two, ſemiorbicular and compreſſed.

## CHAP. CCXXXIX.

## *HYDROPHYLLUM*, WATER LEAF.

THERE are only two ſpecies of this genus, called,

Species.

1. Virginian Water Leaf.
2. Canada Water Leaf.

Virginian Water Leaf deſcribed.

1. Virginian Water Leaf. The root is thick, fleſhy, reddiſh without, and white and juicy within. The leaves are pinnatifid, ſmooth, and riſe from the root on long footſtalks of a bright-green colour. The flower-ſtalk is round, ſlender, five or ſix inches high, and of a pale-green colour. The flowers come out from the ends of the ſtalks in cluſters; they appear in June, and are ſometimes ſucceeded by ripe ſeeds in the autumn. The varieties are,

Its varieties.

The Deep blue.
The Pale blue.
The Red.
The White.

2. Canada Water Leaf. The root is thick, fleſhy, and ſtrong. The leaves are lobed, angular, indented, veined, ſmooth, and of a bright-green colour. The flower-ſtalks are round, ſlender, and five or ſix inches high. The flowers are produced in cluſters from the tops of the ſtalks; the moſt common colour is white, though there are the blue and red varieties; they appear in June, and ſometimes the ſeeds ripen in Auguſt.

Culture.

Theſe plants are propagated by ſowing the ſeeds in the ſpring, in a moiſt ſhady border. If dry weather happens after the ſeeds are ſown, the beds muſt be conſtantly watered, and after the plants come up, that buſineſs muſt be repeated all ſummer, for they love moiſture; and this, except thinning them to proper diſtances, and keeping them clean from weeds, is all the trouble they

they will remain until September, when they should be taken up on a moist day, and set in the places where they are designed to remain, which ought to be in a moist situation, and in the shade.

They are also encreased by parting of the roots, the best time for which is early in the autumn, that they may have time to take to the ground before the frosts come on. When they are set out for good, they will require no trouble except keeping them clean from weeds, and watering in dry weather, which must be afforded them after they are established in their new quarters, or the flowers will be small, few in number, and bad coloured.

1. The first species is titled, *Hydrophyllum foliis pinnatifidis*. In the *Hortus Cliffort.* it is termed simply, *Hydrophyllum*. Morison calls it, *Dentariæ facie planta monopetalos, fructu rotundo, monospermon*. It grows naturally in Virginia.

2. The second species is, *Hydrophyllum foliis palmato-angulatis*. It grows naturally in Canada.

*Hydrophyllum* is of the class and order *Pentandria Monogynia*; and the characters are, Class and order in the Linnæan system. The characters.

1. CALYX is a permanent perianthium nearly as long as the corolla, and divided into five awl-shaped spreading segments.

2. COROLLA is a semicampanulated petal, cut into five erect, obtuse, emarginated segments. The nectarium is a fissure situated about the middle of the petal under each of the segments, closed by two longitudinal connivent lamellæ.

3. STAMINA are five awl-shaped filaments longer than the corolla, having oblong incumbent antheræ.

4. PISTILLUM consists of an oval acuminated germen, an awl-shaped style the length of the stamina, and a bifid, acute, patent stigma.

5. PERICARPIUM is a globular capsule, formed of two valves, and containing one cell.

6. SEMEN. The seed is single, round, and large.

# CHAP. CCXL.

## *HYOSCYAMUS*, HENBANE.

IN this place may be stationed, Species.

1. The Cretan Golden Henbane.
2. Siberian Henbane.

1. Cretan Henbane. The root is thick, woody, and strikes deep into the ground. The leaves are roundish, indented, acute, and grow on longish footstalks. The stalks are round, slender, branching, and about two feet long. The flowers come out from the sides of the branches on footstalks; they are large, of a bright-yellow colour, with a dark-purple base, appear in June, and often continue in succession until the end of September, before which time, ripe seeds from the first-blown flowers may be gathered. Description of Cretan.

2. Siberian Henbane. The root is thick, woody, and strikes deep into the ground. The stalk is round, branching near the top, and about two feet high. The leaves are oval, smooth, entire, and grow on footstalks. The flowers are large, and very beautiful; they come out from the sides of the branches in June and July, and are followed by seeds, contained in large, roundish, inflated cups, like the Alkekengi, and which ripen in the autumn. and Siberian Henbane.

The first species is generally treated as a biennial; but if the situation is dry, warm, and well-defended, and the plants are set in pots to be protected from hard frosts in winter, it will continue for many years.

They are both propagated by sowing the seeds in the autumn, soon after they are ripe, in boxes filled with light fresh earth. They may be left under a warm wall during the winter, but at the approach of frosty weather should be sheltered by a hotbed-frame. In the spring the plants will come up. Where they are too close, they must be thinned, weeded, and constantly watered in dry weather. About the end of July the plants will be fit to remove. A share of the first sort should be set in pots, to be preserved under cover, in case those abroad should be killed by bad weather; the rest should be set in the full ground in warm well-sheltered places, watered and shaded until they have taken root, in very frosty weather should be hooped or covered with mats, and the summer following they will flower, and perfect their seeds. Culture.

The seeds also may be sown in open borders in the autumn; but as they come up early in the spring, they are frequently taken off at that time by the spring frosts; and if the seed is kept until the spring before it is sown, it often lies a year before it comes up.

However, if you have plenty of seeds, let a share be sown in boxes as before, and the rest sown in a warm well sheltered place, where they are to remain; for these plants, though they will bear removing, thrive best if they are undisturbed. Protect them, at their first coming up, from the spring frosts; and when all danger of that kind is over, draw out the weakest, leaving the others a foot asunder. Keep them clean from weeds all summer, and stir the mould between the plants in the autumn. If you do not choose to be at the trouble of matting them, stick a double row of furze at a small distance round the bed, to take off the edge of the cutting frosts; and if the winter is not very severe, they will survive it, and flower much stronger the summer following than those that have been removed. This respects the first species; the other is extremely hardy, and will grow almost any where.

By cuttings also these plants may be raised. These should be planted in any of the summer months, in good light mould, in a shady place; they must be duly watered as often as dry weather makes it necessary, and in a few weeks they will take root and become good plants. A share of the

the first sort may be set in pots, to have treatment similar to the seedlings, whilst the rest may take their chance in the open air. If they survive the winter, they will flower strong the summer following, but will not be so productive of seeds as seedling plants.

Titles

1 The Cretan Golden Henbane is titled, *Hyoscyamus foliis petiolatis eroso dentatis acutis, floribus pedunculatis, fructibus pendulis*. Caspar Bauhine calls it, *Hyoscyamus Creticus luteus major*; also, *Hyoscyamus Creticus luteus minor*. Clusius, *Hyoscyamus albus Creticus*; and Alpinus, *Hyoscyamus aureus*. It grows naturally in Crete and the East.

2 Siberian Henbane is, *Hyoscyamus foliis ovatis integerrimis, calycibus inflatis subglobosis*. It grows naturally in Siberia.

Class and order in the Linnæan system

*Hyoscyamus* is of the class and order *Pentandria Monogynia*, and the characters are,

The characters

1 CALYX is a monophyllous, tubulous, permanent perianthium, ventricose at the bottom, and cut at the top into five acute segments.

2 COROLLA is an infundibuliforme petal. The tube is cylindrical and short. The limb is erect, patent, and cut into five obtuse segments, of which one is broader than the others.

3 STAMINA are five awl-shaped inclined filaments, with roundish antheræ.

4 PISTILLUM consists of a roundish germen, a filiforme style the length of the stamina, and a capitated stigma.

5 PERICARPIUM is an oval, obtuse, bilocular capsule, marked on each side with a line, and opening with a lid at the top, which falls off horizontally for the discharge of the seeds.

6 SEMINA. The seeds are numerous, and unequal.

# CHAP. CCXLI.

## HYOSERIS.

OF this genus there are,

Species

1 Stinking *Hyoseris*.
2 Radiated *Hyoseris*.
3 Virginian *Hyoseris*.

Description of the Stinking

1 Stinking *Hyoseris*. The root of this plant is thick, fleshy, fibrated, and very strongly and disagreeably scented. The radical leaves are large, pinnatifid, smooth, and the outer ones lie on the ground. Among these the flower-stalks arise, upright, simple, naked, smooth, and about five or six inches high. The flowers grow singly on the tops of the stalks, and are of a pale-yellow colour; they appear in June and July, and are succeeded by ripe seeds in September. This is often called Stinking Hawkweed.

Radiated

2 Radiated *Hyoseris*. The leaves are radiated, smooth, and divided almost to the midrib. The stalk is single, naked, and about four or five inches high. One flower only crowns each stalk; its colour is yellow, and like a small Dandelion; it shews itself in June and July, and is succeeded by ripe seeds soon after. This frequently goes by the name of Small Dandelion.

and Virginian Hyoseris

3 Virginian *Hyoseris*. The radical leaves are oval, spear-shaped, lyrated, and acute. The stalks are naked, smooth, upright, and six or eight inches high. The flowers grow singly on the tops of the stalks; they are of a deep-yellow colour, appear in July and August, and the seeds ripen in the autumn.

Method of propagation

These plants are easily propagated by sowing the seeds soon after they are ripe, or in the spring; though if they are kept until that time, they often lie a year before they come up. After they come up, they must be thinned where they are too close, drawing out the weakest; all summer they must be kept clean from weeds, and in the autumn may be transplanted to the places where they are designed to remain. The summer following they will flower, and perfect their seeds.

Titles

1 The first species is, *Hyoseris scapis simplicissimis unifloris, foliis pinnatifidis, seminibus nudis*. Vaillant calls it, *Taraxaconastrum dentis leonis folio, radice fœtidâ*; Caspar Bauhine, *Dens leonis tenuissimo folio*; Micheli, *Leontodontoides Alpinus glaber, erysimi folio, radice crassâ fœtidâ*; and Columna, *Hieracium fœtidum*. It grows naturally on the Alps of Italy and Upper Austria.

2 The second species is, *Hyoseris scapis unifloris nudis, foliis glabris runcinatis angulis dentatis*. Van Royen calls it, *Hyoseris foliis glabris hastato-pinnatis*. Vaillant, *Taraxaconastrum dentis leonis folio ad summitatem radiato*; and Caspar Bauhine, *Dens leonis minor, foliis radiatis*. It grows naturally in Spain and Narbonne.

3 The third species is, *Hyoseris scapis unifloris, foliis lanceolatis lyratis glabris*. It is a native of Virginia.

Class and order in the Linnæan system

*Hyoseris* is of the class and order *Syngenesia Polygamia Æqualis*, and the characters are,

The characters

1 CALYX. The general calyx is decaphyllous and calyculated. The scales are spear-shaped and erect.

2 COROLLA. The general flower is subimbricated and uniform. The florets are placed circularly, and each consists of one tongue-shaped, narrow, truncated petal, indented in five parts at the top.

3 STAMINA are five very short capillary filaments, with a cylindrical tubular anthera.

4 PISTILLUM consists of an oblong germen, a filiforme style the length of the stamina, and two reflexed stigmas.

5 PERICARPIUM. There is none.

6 SEMEN. The seed is single, oblong, compressed, the length of the calyx, and crowned with down.

The receptacle is naked.

# CHAP. CCXLII.

## *HYPERICUM*, St. JOHN's WORT

Species.

THE perennial species of this genus are,

1 Spreading Tutsan
2 Virginian St John's Wort
3 Upright Tutsan, or Park Leaves
4 Olympick St John's Wort
5 Oriental St John's Wort
6 Creeping St John's Wort
7 Pensylvania St John's Wort
8 St Peter's Wort
9 Common St John's Wort
10 Trailing St John's Wort
11 Mountain or Imperforate St John's Wort
12 Tutsan, or Hairy St John's Wort
13 Marsh St Peter's Wort
14 Upright St John's Wort
15 Pyrenean St John's Wort
16 Canada St John's Wort

Description of the Spreading Tutsan. 1 Spreading Tutsan This hath a spreading root, which sends forth numerous, square, slender, simple, herbaceous stalks, which are about a foot in length The leaves are oval spear-shaped, smooth, undivided, grow opposite by pairs, and sit close, without any footstalks The flowers are large, of a bright-yellow colour, have numerous stamina, and each of them five styles, they come out from the ends of the branches in June and July, and are succeeded by pyramidal capsules, containing ripe seeds, in the autumn

Culture. This species is propagated by dividing of the root, every bit of which will grow, and if left undisturbed for a few years will overspread a large space It is generally planted in the shrubbery, as it flourishes very well under trees, it is also useful in islolated woods, as it will exhibit its flowers in full beauty in such places, and will grow without any other culture in any soil or situation

Virginian. 2 Virginian St John's Wort The stalks are upright, square, three feet high, and send forth several small branches, which come out by pairs opposite to each other The leaves are oblong, spear-shaped, smooth, grow opposite by pairs, and embrace the stalks with their base The flowers are produced singly from the ends of the stalks, they are large, yellow, have numerous stamina the length of the petals, and five styles, they come out in July and August, but are very rarely succeeded by ripe seeds in England It is propagated by parting of the roots in the autumn

Upright. 3 Upright Tutsan, or Park Leaves This plant rises with an upright ligneous stalk to the height of about two feet, sending forth slender branches from the sides by pairs opposite to each other The leaves are oval, heart shaped, pointed, of a pleasant green colour, and grow opposite by pairs at the joints, without any footstalks The flowers come out in clusters from the ends of the branches, they are of a bright-yellow colour, have numerous stamina though only three styles, appear in June and July, and are succeeded by roundish black capsules, each having three cells, according to the number of the styles These capsules being black and roundish, have very much the appearance of berries, and contain ripe seeds in the autumn

Olympick. 4 Olympick St John's Wort This plant hath a spreading root, which sends forth several ligneous upright stalks about a foot in height The leaves are spear-shaped, small, and grow opposite to each other without any footstalks The flowers come out in small bunches from the ends of the stalks, and their colour is a bright-yellow There are numerous stamina of unequal lengths, some being longer and others shorter than the petals, and only three styles They appear in July and August, and are succeeded by oval capsules, containing three cells, answering to the number of styles These cells are filled with seeds, which in a warm season will ripen with us in the autumn

Oriental. 5 Oriental St John's Wort This plant hath several slender tough stalks, which grow to about a foot and a half high The leaves are oblong, indented, have no footstalks, and a little resemble those of the Common Sneezewort The flowers sometimes come out singly, sometimes two or three together from the tops of the stalks, their colour is yellow, they appear in July and August, but are seldom succeeded by good seeds in England

Creeping. 6 Creeping St John's Wort The root spreads itself to a great distance, and sends forth numerous, round, taper, herbaceous stalks to about a foot high The leaves are spear shaped, narrow, and obtuse The flowers are yellow, have numerous stamina, and three styles only, they come out in July and August, but are not succeeded by seeds in England

and Pensylvania St John's Wort described. 7 Pensylvania St John's Wort The stalks are herbaceous, erect, taper, smooth, and of a reddish colour The leaves are oval, oblong, smooth, obtuse, and embrace the stalks with their base Two or three flowers only come out together from the tops of the stalks, their petals are yellow, they are acute, have numerous stamina which are hardly so long as the petals, and three styles, they appear in July and August, but are rarely succeeded by seeds in England

St Peter's Wort. 8 St Peter's Wort This hath a strong, tough, ligneous, fibrated root, which sends forth several upright, square, herbaceous stalks, to the height of about a foot and a half The leaves are roundish, oblong, grow opposite to each other on the stalks, sit close, and often there are several small leaves growing from the same point, which they seem to cherish in their bosoms The flowers come out from the tops of the stalks on short footstalks, their colour is yellow, they appear in June and July, and are succeeded by ripe seeds in the autumn, which, if permitted to scatter, will produce plants enough

Common. 9 Common St John's Wort The stalks are upright, edged, send forth branches opposite to each other, and grow to about a foot and a half high The leaves are roundish, obtuse, grow opposite by pairs without any footstalks, and are possessed of many pellucid spots, which appear more distinct if held up to the light The flowers are produced all over the tops of the plants on slender footstalks, they are of a fine yellow colour, and make a beautiful appearance, they

they have numerous ſtamina, which are not quite ſo long as the petals, and three ſtyles only, they appear in June and July, and are ſucceeded by ripe ſeeds in the autumn, which, if permitted to ſcatter, will ſoon produce plants enough

Medicinal properties of the laſt five ſorts

Theſe laſt two ſorts are admirable in medicine They afford a tea which is a fine diuretic, and good againſt the ſtone The leaves, flowers, and tender ſhoots, being bruiſed in a mortar, are an admirable vulnerary, being uſeful for green and old wounds, contuſions of all ſorts, and even burns and ſcalds They afford a red juice, which was formerly ſerviceable in dyeing, but is now chiefly diſuſed on account of its ſoon fading

Trailing St John's Wort,

10. Trailing St John's Wort is a very low plant The ſtalks are ſlender, weak, about five or ſix inches long, and for the moſt part lie on the ground The leaves are ſmall, oblong, ſmooth, and grow oppoſite to each other on the ſtalks The flowers come out from the ends and ſides of the branches on ſlender footſtalks They are in colour and ſhape like the Common St John's Wort, though ſmaller, they appear in July and Auguſt, and are ſucceeded by ripe ſeeds, which, if permitted to ſcatter, will come up all over the garden, if it be a light, gravelly, or ſandy ſoil, in which it moſt delights

The virtues of this root are ſaid to be not at all inferior to thoſe of the former

Mountain

11 Mountain or Unperforate St John's Wort The ſtalk is erect, ſmooth, taper, and undivided The leaves are broad, ſmooth, and nearly oval The flowers come out from the tops of the ſtalks, they are of a fine yellow colour, have numerous ſtamina and three ſtyles, appear in July and Auguſt, and are ſucceeded by ripe ſeeds in autumn

and Tutſan St John's Wort, deſcribed

12 Tutſan, or Hairy St John's Wort The ſtalks are herbaceous, erect, and taper The leaves are oval, ſpear-ſhaped, downy, and grow on very ſhort footſtalks The flowers are trigynous, they come out from the tops of the ſtalks in July and Auguſt, and the ſeeds ripen in autumn

Marſh St Peter's Wort, deſcribed

13 Marſh St Peter's Wort The ſtalks are round, hairy, creeping, and ſtrike root at the joints. The leaves are round, whitiſh, hairy, and grow by pairs at the joints The flowers are ſmall, and of a yellow colour, two or three only come out together from the ends of the ſtalks They appear in July and Auguſt, and the ſeeds ripen in the autumn

Upright,

14 Upright St John's Wort The ſtalks are upright, round, firm, reddiſh, branching near the top, and about a foot and a half high The leaves are heart-ſhaped, oval, obtuſe, ſmooth, grow two oppoſite to each other, and ſurround the ſtalk with their baſe The flowers are produced in plenty from the ends and upper parts of the branches, they are of a fine yellow colour, and make ſo good a ſhow, as to occaſion this ſpecies being diſtinguiſhed by the title or The Fair or Beautiful St John's Wort They are trigynous, come out in July and Auguſt, and the ſeeds ripen in autumn, which, if permitted to ſcatter, will afford plants enough.

Pyrenean,

15 Pyrenean St John's Wort The ſtalks are ſlender, and lie on the ground The leaves are heart-ſhaped, roundiſh, and ſmooth The flowers are large, of a pale yellow colour, trigynous, and have their petals indented; they come out in July, and the ſeeds ripen in autumn

and Canada St John's Wort, deſcribed

16 Canada St John's Wort The ſtalks are herbaceous, ſmooth, quadrangular, and branching. The leaves are narrow, ſpear-ſhaped, ſmooth, and undivided The flowers grow in panicles at the upper parts of the plants, they are very ſmall, and each has its ſeparate footſtalk, they are of a yellow colour, have numerous ſtamina, and three ſtyles, they appear in July, and are ſucceeded by long conical red capſules containing the ſeeds

Method of propagation

All theſe ſorts are eaſily propagated by parting the roots, the beſt time for which is the autumn; though it may be done ſucceſsfully either in the winter or ſpring before the ſtalks ſhoot up for flowering They may be alſo propagated by ſowing the ſeeds, but this is not worth putting in practice, as they may be multiplied ſo faſt the other way They will grow in almoſt any ſoil or ſituation, but they love ſhade and the north ſide of the hill They grow naturally for the moſt part among buſhes, in woods, hilly and mountainous parts, and therefore are very proper to cover the ground between the trees in wilderneſs quarters The Marſh St Peter's Wort grows naturally upon bogs, which ſhould remind the Gardener to aſſign it the moiſteſt part in the plantation, though it is a moderate plant, and ſeldom admitted into gardens, unleſs where a general collection of all ſorts of plants is deſired

Titles

1 Spreading Tutſan is titled, *Hypericum floribus pentagynis, caule tetragono herbaceo erecto ſimplici, foliis lævibus integerrimis* In the *Hortus Cliffort* it is termed, *Hypericum floribus pentagynis, foliis ovato oblongis glabris integerrimis* Moriſon calls it, *Androſæmum flore & thecâ quinquecapſulari omnium maximus*, and Caſpar Bauhine, *Aſcyrum magno flore* It grows naturally in Siberia, Canada, and the Pyrenees

2 Virginian St John's Wort is, *Hypericum floribus pentagynis, calycibus obtuſis, caule fruticoſo, foliis lineari lanceolatis* In Miller's Dictionary it is termed, *Hypericum floribus pentagynis, calycibus obtuſis, ſtaminibus corollam æquantibus, caule erecto herbaceo* It inhabits Virginia

3 Upright Tutſan, or Park-leaves, is, *Hypericum floribus trigynis, pericarpiis baccatis, caule fruticoſo ancipiti* In the *Hortus Cliffort* it is termed, *Hypericum floribus trigynis, fructu baccato, foliis ovatis pedunculo longioribus* Ray calls it, *Hypericum maximum androſæmum vulgare dictum*, Caſpar Bauhine, *Androſæmum maximum fruteſcens*, Dodonæus, *Androſæmum*, Parkinſon, *Androſæmum vulgare*, and Gerard, *Clymenum Italorum* It grows naturally in moiſt places, chiefly in woods and hedges, in England, Italy, and the South of France

4 Olympic St John's Wort is, *Hypericum floribus trigynis, calycibus acutis, ſtaminibus corollâ brevioribus, caule fruticoſo* Wheeler calls it, *Hypericum montis Olympi*, and Tournefort, *Hypericum Orientale, flore magno* It grows naturally on mount Olympus, alſo on the Pyrenees

5 Oriental St John's Wort is, *Hypericum floribus trigynis, ſtipulis reflexis, foliis oblongis denticulato-crenatis* Tournefort calls it, *Hypericum Orientale, ptarmicæ foliis* It grows naturally in the Eaſt

6 Creeping St. John's Wort is, *Hypericum floribus trigynis, caule tereti repente, foliis lanceolato-linearibus obtuſis* Tournefort calls it, *Hypericum Orientale, polygoni folio* It grows naturally in the Eaſt

7 Penſylvania St John's Wort is, *Hypericum floribus trigynis, petalis calyce ſublongioribus, foliis oblongis amplexicaulibus obtuſis, caule tereti* It grows naturally in Penſylvania

8 St Peter's Wort is, *Hypericum floribus trigynis, caule quadrato herbaceo* John Bauhine calls it, *Hypericum aſcyron dictum, caule quadrangulo*, Caſpar Bauhine, *Hypericum vulgare majus, caule quadrangulo, foliis non perforatis*; and Dodonæus, Gerard, &c *Aſcyron* It grows naturally in moiſt hedges, meadows, &c in England, and moſt countries of Europe

9 Common

9 Common St John's Wort is, *Hypericum floribus trigynis, caule ancipiti, foliis obtusis pellucido-punctatis* Caspar Bauhine calls it, *Hypericum vulgare*, and Dodonæus, Gerard, &c *Hypericum* It grows naturally by the sides of ditches, among bushes, hedges, &c in England, and most parts of Europe

10 Trailing St John's Wort is, *Hypericum floribus trigynis axillaribus solitariis, caulibus ancipitibus prostratis filiformibus, foliis glabris* Guettard calls it, *Hypericum foliis ovatis, caulibus supinis*, Haller, *Hypericum humifusum foliis perforatis punctis in margine nigris*, Caspar Bauhine, *Hypericum minus supinum*, *s supinum glabrum*, Clusius, *Hypericum supinum III minimum*, Parkinson, *Hypericum minus supinum*, and Gerard, *Hypericum supinum glabrum* It grows naturally in dry meadows and gravelly soils in England, and most of the southern parts of Europe

11 Imperforate St John's Wort is, *Hypericum floribus trigynis, calycibus serraturis glandulosis, caule tereti erecto glabro, foliis ovatis* John Bauhine calls it, *Hypericum elegantissimum non ramosum, folio lato*, Hill, *Hypericum caule simplici elegans latifolium*; Columna, *Androsæmum campoclarense*, Caspar Bauhine, *Ascyrum, s Hypericum bifolium glabrum non perforatum*, and Fuchsius, *Ascyrum* It grows naturally on mountainous woody parts in England and most countries of Europe

12 Hairy St John's Wort is, *Hypericum floribus trigynis, calycibus serrato-glandulosis, caule tereti erecto, foliis ovatis subpubescentibus* In the *Hortus Cliffort* it is termed, *Hypericum floribus trigynis, calycum serraturis capitatis, caule tereti* Guettard calls it, *Hypericum foliis lanceolatis, calycinis laciniis linearibus*, Ray, *Hypericum majus, s Androsæmum Matthioli*, Caspar Bauhine, *Androsæmum hirsutum*, and Morison, *Androsæmum ascyron dictum, caule rotundo hirsuto* It grows naturally in thickets, hedges, by the sides of hills, mountains, &c in England, and most parts of Europe

13 Marsh St Peter's Wort is, *Hypericum floribus trigynis, caule tereti repente, foliis villosis subrotundis* Caspar Bauhine calls it, *Ascyrum supinum villosum palustre*, Clusius, *Ascyrum supinum elodes*, and Gerard, *Ascyron supinum ελώδες Clusii* It grows naturally in marshy spongy grounds in England and Gaul

14 Upright St. John's Wort is, *Hypericum floribus trigynis, calycibus serrato glandulosis, caule tereti, foliis perfoliatis cordatis glabris* Guettard calls it, *Hypericum foliis cordatis connatis, laciniis calycinis ovatis obtusis*, Haller, *Hypericum calyce serrato, foliis connatis*, Caspar Bauhine, *Hypericum minus erectum*, John Bauhine, *Hypericum pulchrum Tragi*, Gerard, *Hypericum quintum, s pulchrum Tragi*; and Morison, *Hypericum minus glabrum erectum pulchrum* It grows naturally in woods, hedges, and heathy ground in England and most of the southern countries of Europe

15 Pyrenean St John's Wort is, *Hypericum floribus trigynis, calycibus serrato-glandulosis, foliis cordato-orbiculatis glabris* Caspar Bauhine calls it, *Hypericum nummulariæ folio*, Plukenet, *Hypericum fere orbiculato folio, floribus amplis pallidè luteis, petalis in ambitu crenatis*; and Boccone, *Androsæmum supinum saxatile, nummulariæ folio aversa parte rubente* It grows naturally in the Pyrenean mountains

16 Canada St John's Wort is, *Hypericum floribus trigynis, foliis lineari-lanceolatis, caule quadrangulo, pericarpiis coloratis* It grows common in Canada

# CHAP. CCXLIII.

## *HYPOCHÆRIS.*

THERE is no English name for this genus, but the perennial species have been long called,

Species 1 Long rooted Hawkweed.

2 Spotted Hawkweed

Description of Long-rooted, 1 Long-rooted Hawkweed The root is extremely long, thick, tough, and of a white colour The radical leaves are numerous, and form a large tuft on the crown of the root; they are broad, runcinated, obtuse, rough, and the outer ones lie flat on the ground. The stalks are smooth, naked, branching, tough, and about a foot and a half high The flowers come out singly from the ends of the branches, they are large, very double, and of a golden yellow colour, they appear in June and July, and are succeeded by ripe seeds in August and September.

and Spotted Hawkweed. 2 Spotted Hawkweed. The radical leaves are very large, oval, indented, hairy, of a pale-green above, and whitish underneath The stalks are garnished with one or two small leaves only, are slender, hairy, and about a foot and a half high The flowers come out from the tops of the stalks, they are of a yellow colour, appear in June and July, and often continue in succession until the end of summer, before which time ripe seeds from the first-blown flowers will be flying about with the winds

Propagation of the first sort Both these sorts are propagated by sowing the seeds, but those of the first sort should be in the places where the plants are designed to remain, for the roots are thick, strike deep into the ground, and ought not to be disturbed The ground should be double dug previous to their reception, and the soil should be light and dry, otherwise the roots are apt to rot in winter After the plants come up, they will require no trouble, except thinning them where they are too close, and keeping them clean from weeds; and after they have once flowered and ripened their seeds, fresh plants will come up all over the garden from seeds which have been blown to a distance by the wind.

Propagation of the last sort. The seeds of the second sort may be sown in beds pretty close together. When they come up, they should be thinned to about three inches distance, should be kept clean from weeds all summer, be frequently watered in dry weather, and in the autumn may be set in the place where they are designed to remain. The summer following they will flower, and the seeds scattering will produce young plants in abundance. The best time for sowing the seeds is the autumn, though the work may be deferred successfully to the spring.

The second sort is also propagated by parting the roots, which may be done any time in the autumn, winter or spring, before the stalks shoot up for flowering. It will grow in any soil or situation, but thrives best in a moist shady place.

Titles. 1. Long-rooted Hawkweed is titled, *Hypochaeris foliis runcinatis obtusis, scapo ramoso nudo, pedunculis squamosis.* Caspar Bauhine calls it, *Hieracium, dentis leonis folio obtuso, majus*, also, *Hieracium dentis leonis folio hirsuto*, also, *Hieracium, dentis leonis folio, bulboso.* Lobel terms it *Hieracium Longius radicatum*, Dodonaeus, *Hieracium tertium* and Tabernamontanus *Hieracium VII.* It grows naturally in pasture grounds in England and many parts of Europe.

2. Spotted Hawkweed is, *Hypochaeris caule subnudo, ramo solitario, foliis ovato-oblongis integris, dentatis.* Caspar Bauhine calls it, *Hieracium alpinum latifolium hirsutie incanum, flore magno*, also, *Hieracium Alpinum, foliis dentatis, flore magno.* Clusius terms it, *Hieracium latifolium I.* Vaillant, *Hypochaeris hirsuta, endiviae folio, magno flore*, and Ray, *Dens leonis foliis integris, caule raro, foliis rigido, non crenatis fere.* It grows naturally in rough pastures in England and most of the northern countries of Europe.

Class and order in the Linnaean System. *Hypochaeris* is of the class and order *Syngenesia Polygamia Æqualis*, and the characters are,

The characters. 1. CALYX. The general calyx is roundish, imbricated, and swelling at the base. The scales are spear-shaped and acute.

2. COROLLA. The general flower is imbricated and uniform. The florets are numerous, equal, and each consists of one narrow, tongue-shaped, truncated petal, indented in five parts at the top.

3. STAMINA are five very short capillary filaments, having a cylindrical tubular anthera.

4. PISTILLUM consists of an oval germen, a filiforme style the length of the stamina, and two reflexed stigmas.

5. PERICARPIUM. There is none. The calyx closes, becomes round, and ends in a point.

6. SEMINA. The seeds are single, oblong, and crowned with stipitated feathery down.

The receptacle is paleaceous. The paleae are spear-shaped, narrow, and the length of the seeds.

# CHAP. CCXLIV.

## *HYSSOPUS*, HYSSOP.

Species. THE real species of this genus are,

1. Common Hyssop.
2. China Hyssop.
3. Canada Hyssop.

Description of the Common Hyssop. 1. The Common Hyssop is a fine aromatic, and often raised in great plenty for medicinal uses, as well as to adorn the flower garden. The stalks are ligneous, square at first but round afterwards, and grow to about a foot and a half high. The leaves are small, spear-shaped, and grow opposite, without footstalks. The flowers are produced in whorls round the upper parts of the stalk for a great length; they appear in July and August, and are succeeded by ripe seeds in September.

Its varieties. The varieties of this species are,

The Common Blue-flowered Hyssop.
The White-flowered Hyssop.
The Red-flowered Hyssop.
The Long-spiked Hyssop with large deep-blue flowers.
Curled-leaved Hyssop.
Striped-leaved Hyssop.

China. 2. China Hyssop. The stalks are square and branching. The leaves are oblong, crenated, and grow opposite by pairs. The flowers are produced from the joints in small clusters; they are of a blue colour, make their appearance in June and July, and are succeeded by ripe seeds in September.

and Canada Hyssop, described. 3. Canada Hyssop. The stalks are square, smooth, and grow to near four feet high. The leaves are heart-shaped, sharp-pointed, serrated, and grow opposite by pairs on short footstalks. The flowers terminate the stalks in thick spikes; they appear in July, and the seeds ripen in September.

Its varieties. The varieties of this species are,

The Yellow-flowered Canada Hyssop.
The Red-flowered Canada Hyssop.
The Purple-flowered Canada Hyssop.

Propagation of the first sort. The propagation of all these sorts is very easy. For the first sort, plant the slips in the spring on a shady border. Water them at the time of planting, and repeat it every other evening, if dry weather should make it necessary. In a little time they will strike root, and in the autumn may be removed to the places where they are designed to remain.

The first sort is propagated by seeds also. These should be sown about the end of March, on a bed of light dry earth open only to the morning-sun. If dry weather should succeed the sowing, the bed should be watered every third evening to bring the plants up. They will then soon appear, and numbers of weeds will shew themselves along with them; these must be carefully pulled up, and where the plants come up too close they must be thinned. In the autumn the strongest plants may be taken up with a ball a ball of earth to each root, and planted in the places where they are designed to remain, while the weakest may remain in the seed bed another year to gain strength

Propagation of the last two sorts

The last two sorts are propagated by dividing the roots This may be done either in the autumn or spring, though the more eligible season is the autumn, as soon as their stalks decay

They are also readily increased by seeds These should be sown in the autumn as soon as they are ripe In the spring they will come up, when they will call for no trouble, except thinning them where they appear too close, watering them in dry weather, and keeping them clean from weeds With affording them this small management they will by the autumn become good plants, and may at that time be removed to the places where they are designed to remain

Titles

1 Common Hyssop is titled, *Hyssopus spicis secundis* Caspar Bauhine calls it, *Hyssopus officinarum cærulea, sive spicata*, also *Hyssopus rubro flore*, and Dodonæus, *Hyssopus vulgaris* The place of its habitation is uncertain

2 China Hyssop is titled, *Hyssopus corollis subresupinatis, staminibus inferioribus corolla brevioribus* Haller calls it, *Cataria floribus ...s* It grows naturally in China

3 Canada Hyssop is, *Hyssopus caule acuto quadrangulo* In the *Hortus Cliffort* it is termed, *Prunella bracteis lanceolatis* Plukenet calls it, *Betonica larga, ana el tior, foliis scrophulariæ glabris, flore ochroleuco*, and Tournefort, *Sideritis Canadensis altissima, scrophulariæ folio, flore flavescente* It grows naturally in Canada and Virginia

Class and order in the Linnæan system

*Hyssopus* is of the class and order *Didynamia Gymnospermia*, and the characters are,

The characters

1 CALYX is a cylindrical, oblong, striated, monophyllous, permanent perianthium, cut into five acute parts at the top

2 COROLLA is a ringent petal The tube is cylindrical, narrow, and the length of the calyx The mouth is inclining The upper lip is erect, plane short, roundish, and emarginated The lower lip is trifid, the middle segment being obcordated, crenated, and acute, and the two side segments short and obtuse

3 STAMINA are four erect, distant filaments longer than the petal, two of which being shorter than the others, have simple antheræ

4 PISTILLUM consists of a quadripartite germen, a filiform style situated under the upper lip, and a bifid stigma

5 PERICARPIUM There is none The seeds are lodged in the calyx

6 SEMINA The seeds are oval, and four in number

# CHAP CCXLV

## *JASIONE*, SHEEP's SCABIOUS

THERE is only one species of this genus, but it admits of two principal varieties, one of which is of such short duration, that it may not improperly be called a biennial, or even an annual The root of the other sort continues for several years, and this for distinction sake I call Perennial *Jasione*

This plant described

The root is thick, hard, black, woody, and very tough The leaves are spear-shaped, narrow, sawed on their edges, hairy, and of a worn-out green colour The stalks are slender, rough, and eight or ten inches high The flowers come out singly from the ends of the stalks and branches, they are moderately large, of a pale-blue colour, appear in May and June, and the seeds ripen in August

Variety

The other variety mentioned answers to the general characters, but the root is more slender, single, strikes deep into the ground, and generally dies as soon as the seeds are ripe

Method of propagation

These plants are propagated by sowing the seeds in the spring, in beds of light fresh earth, where they are to remain When they come up, they will require no trouble, except thinning them to proper distances, and keeping them clean from weeds, and the next summer they will flower, and perfect their seeds

Titles

There being no other species of this genus, it stands with the name simply, *Jasione* In the *Hortus Cliffort* it is termed, *Jasione foliis linearilanceolatis obsolete serratis* Caspar Bauhine calls it, *Rapunculus scabiosæ capitulo cæruleo*, Columna, *Rapuntium montanum capitatum leptophyllon*, Dalechamp, *Aphyllanthes*, and Gerard, *Scabiosa minima bifida* It grows naturally on heathy hilly grounds in England and most parts of Europe

Class and order in the Linnæan system

*Jasione* is of the class and order *Syngenesia Monogamia*, and the characters are,

The characters

1 CALYX The general perianthium is composed of many narrow permanent leaves, including several florets annexed to short footstalks The proper perianthium is permanent, situated above the germen, and divided into five parts

2 COROLLA The florets consist each of five spear-shaped, erect petals, which are connected at their base

3 STAMINA consist of five short awl-shaped filaments, having five oblong antheræ, which are connected at their base

4 PISTILLUM consists of a roundish germen situated below the flower, a filiform style the length of the corolla, and a bifid stigma

5 PERICARPIUM is a roundish, five-angular, bilocular capsule, with the permanent calyx at the top

6 SEMINA The seeds are many, and almost oval

# CHAP. CCXLVI

## *IBERIS*, CANDY TUFT, or SCIATICA CRESS

*Species.*

I SHALL only select for this place,
1 Round-leaved Candy Tuft
2 Flax-leaved Candy Tuft
3 Rock Candy Tuft

*Description of Round-leaved Candy Tuft.*

1 Round-leaved Candy Tuft The radical leaves are round, fleshy, smooth, and crenated, but the upper ones are oval, oblong, smooth, entire, and embrace the stalk with their base The stalks are herbaceous, upright, and about five or six inches high The flowers are formed into round close umbels on the tops of the stalks, they are of a purple colour, appear in June, but are very seldom succeeded by seeds in our gardens

*Method of propagating it.*

This is a hardy perennial, and propagated by dividing the roots in the autumn, or sowing the seeds soon after they are ripe When the plants come up by the latter practice, they must be thinned to proper distances, and when they are encreased by either method, they must be constantly kept clean from weeds, and this is all the culture they require They will grow in almost any soil or situation, though they chiefly delight in the shade in moist places

*Flax-leaved,*

2 Flax-leaved Candy Tuft This species used to be called Portugal Treacle Mustard, and by that name it is now known in many places The stalks are herbaceous, erect, perennial, and hardly a foot high The radical leaves are narrow, smooth, and a little indented, but those on the stalk are entire, thinly disposed, and sit close, without any footstalks The flowers come out from the tops of the stalks in round bunches, they are of a purple colour, appear in May and June, but are rarely succeeded by seeds in England

*and Rock Candy Tuft described.*

3 Rock Candy Tuft The stalks are erect, ligneous, perennial, and about a foot high The leaves are spear-shaped, narrow, fleshy, acute, ciliated, and entire The flowers come up in umbels from the tops of the stalks, they are of a purplish colour, come out in May and June, and often continue in succession for many months, but the seeds very rarely ripen in our gardens

*Propagation of these two sorts.*

These are tender species, and must therefore be committed to the full ground with caution They will grow by cuttings, but the best way of raising them is from the seeds, which must be procured from the places where the plants naturally grow, for they very rarely ripen in England

*Method of raising them by seeds.*

The seeds should be sown in the spring, in pots or boxes filled with light earth, they should be then set in the shade, and be frequently watered All summer the plants must be kept clean from weeds, and watering, as often as dry weather makes it necessary, must be observed In September the pots should be set in a place where the plants may have the morning sun until eleven o'clock, and in the beginning of October, they should be set under a warm south wall, where they may have the benefit of the sun the whole day Here they may remain until the frosts come on, when they should be sheltered under a hot bed frame or some cover, but should always be set abroad again on the return of fine weather In the spring they should be planted out A share should be set in beds, at about nine inches distance from each other, whilst the remaining plants should be set in pots, to be housed in winter, to continue the sorts, in case the severity of that season should destroy those that were planted abroad

The beds should be made in the dryest, the warmest, and the best-sheltered places, and they should be hooped, to be covered with mats, to be protected from the frosts in bad weather Many of them will flower the summer following; but the summer after the blow will be general, and the appearance very beautiful, which the second will form by their numerous corymbous bunches, and the third from their flatter umbels of purple flowers

Plants raised from seeds, and set in the open ground, will be finer than those raised any other way, they will have larger bunches of flowers, and from them there will be a far better chance of obtaining good seeds in England Nevertheless, they may be propagated,

2 By cuttings, and this method is to be practised to encrease the number of plants, when a few plants only, and no seeds can be procured The cuttings should be planted in a warm, dry, well-sheltered place, during any of the summer months They must be shaded with mats, and watered until they have taken root, and in the autumn a few plants must be set in pots, to be housed in the winter, while the remainder should have treatment similar to the seedlings *Method of propagating them by cuttings*

In the same manner may be treated the Candy Tuft Trees, but as I always found them the best and safest in the green-house, I shall reserve them for that place

1 Round-leaved Candy Tuft is titled, *Iberis herbacea, foliis ovatis, caulinis amplexicaulibus lævibus succosis* Barrelier calls it, *Thlaspi montanum, serrato cepreæ folio, flore purpurascente umbellato*; Tournefort, *Thlaspi Alpinum, folio rotundiore carnoso, flore purpurascente*, and Haller, *Lepidium caule repente, foliis ovatis amplexicaulibus* It grows naturally on the Alps and in several parts of Switzerland *Titles*

2 Flax-leaved Candy Tuft is, *Iberis herbacea, foliis linearibus integerrimis, caule herbaceo paniculato, corymbis hemisphæricis* Tournefort calls it, *Thlaspi Lusitanicum umbellatum, gramineo folio, flore purpurascente* It grows naturally in Spain and Portugal.

3 Rock Candy Tuft is, *Iberis suffruticosa, foliis lanceolatis linearibus carnosis acutis integerrimis ciliatis* Caspar Bauhine calls it, *Thlaspi saxatile, vermiculato folio*, and Columna, *Lithonthlaspi III fruticosus, vermiculato acuto folio* It grows in dry stony places in Italy and France

*Iberis* is of the class and order *Tetradynamia Siliculosa*; and the characters are, *Class and order in the Linnæan System*

1 CALYX is a perianthium composed of four small, oval, concave, patent, equal, deciduous leaves *The characters*

2 COROLLA is tetrapetalous, and unequal The petals are oval, obtuse, patent, and have long erect ungues The two outer ones are by far the largest, the two interior petals are small and reflexed

3 STAMINA are six awl shaped, erect filaments, of which the two side ones are shorter than the others, having roundish antheræ.

4 PISTILL...

4. PISTILLUM consists of a roundish compressed germen, a simple short style, and an obtuse stigma

5 PERICARPIUM is an erect, roundish, compressed, emarginated pod, surrounded by an acute border, and containing two cells

6 SEMINA The seeds are nearly oval, and about two in each pod

# CHAP. CCXLVII.

## ILLECEBRUM, MOUNTAIN KNOT-GRASS.

THERE are of this genus,

Species

1 Verticillate Knot-Grass

2 Small Spanish Mountain Knot-Grass

3. Upright Mountain Knot-Grass

Verticillate,

1 Verticillate Knot Grass The stalks are round, jointed, usually of a reddish colour, spreading, and lie on the ground The leaves are small, oval, pointed, and grow opposite by pairs at the joints The flowers come out at every joint in kind of verticillate clusters; they are very small, of a white colour, appear in May and June, and the greatest part of the summer, and the first-blown flowers are soon followed by ripe seeds

Small Spanish Mountain

2 Small Spanish Mountain Knot-Grass The stalks are slender, jointed, spreading every way, and lie on the ground The leaves are small, of a pale-green colour, and grow opposite by pairs at the joints The flowers come out from the sides of the stalks almost their whole length, they are very small, white, and glossy, appear in May and June, and are succeeded by ripe seeds in July and August

and Upright Mountain Knot-Grass described

3 Upright Mountain Knot-Grass The stalks are upright, ligneous, and grow to about two feet high. The leaves are oval, oblong, pointed, and much resemble those of myrtle The flowers come out singly from the sides of the stalks, they are small, glossy, appear in June and July, and the seeds ripen in September

Culture

These plants are easily propagated by sowing the seeds in the autumn, soon after they are ripe, or in the spring When they come up, they will require no trouble, except keeping them clean from weeds, and thinning them where they are too close The first sort thrives best in moist shady places, but the situation of the last should be warm and well-defended

The third sort is also propagated by planting the cuttings, which if set in a shady border in any of the summer months, and duly watered, will grow, and may from thence be removed to the places where they are designed to remain

Titles.

Verticillate Knot-Grass is titled, *Illecebrum floribus verticillatis nudis, caulibus procumbentibus.* Van Royen calls it, *Illecebrum caulibus procumbentibus*, Vaillant, *Paronychia serpyllifolia palustris*, Caspar Bauhine, *Polygola repens nivea*, John Bauhine, *Polygonum parvum flore albo verticillato*, and Ray, *Polygonum serpyllifolium verticillatum* It grows naturally in moist pastures in England, and most parts of Europe

2 Small Spanish Mountain Knot-Grass is, *Illecebrum floribus bracteis nitidis obvallatis, caulibus procumbentibus* In the *Hortus Cliffort.* it is termed, *Herniaria squamis nitidis flores superantibus* Caspar Bauhine calls it, *Polygonum minus candicans*, and Clusius, *Paronychia Hispanica* It grows naturally in France and Spain

3 Upright Mountain Knot-Grass is, *Illecebrum floribus lateralibus solitariis, caulibus suffruticosis* Van Royen calls it, *Illecebrum caule erecto*, Lobel, *Polygonum herniariæ foliis*, and Tournefort, *Paronychia Hispanica fruticosa, myrti folio* It grows naturally in Spain

Class and order in the Linnæan system The characters.

*Illecebrum* is of the class and order *Pentandria Monogynia*, and the characters are,

1 CALYX is a pentangular perianthium, composed of five coloured, acuminated, permanent leaves

2 COROLLA There is none

3 STAMINA are five capillary filaments situated within the calyx, having simple antheræ

4 PISTILLUM consists of an oval acute germen, a short bifid style, and a simple obtuse stigma

5 PERICARPIUM is a roundish pointed capsule covered by the calyx, composed of five valves, and containing one cell

6 SEMEN The seed is single, large, roundish, and pointed at each end.

## CHAP. CCXLVIII.

## *IMPERATORIA*, MASTER-WORT.

OF this genus there is only one species, yet known, called Masterwort.

*The plant described.* The root is thick, fleshy, oblique, brown, rough on the outside, and white within; aromatic, strong, and acrid to the taste. The leaves are large, consist of three principal parts, (which are again divided into three smaller,) are serrated, of a dark green colour, rankly scented, and grow on strong hollowed footstalks. The stalk is thick, round, jointed, divides into a few branches, and is two or three feet high. The flowers are produced in large umbels from the ends of the branches; their colour is white, they appear in June, and the seeds ripen in August.

This plant is very strongly, and to most people very disagreeably scented. It is admirable, however, against infected air, and pestilential disorders of all sorts. The root, which is chiefly used in medicine, is a cordial, sudorific, and alexipharmick; it is good against dropsies, asthmas, colics, cramps, often cures the ague, and is an ingredient in many compositions.

*Culture.* This plant is best raised from seeds, which should be sown in the seminary in a bed of fine mould, in the autumn, soon after they are ripe. They should be sowed very thinly, and covered with no more than a quarter of an inch of the finest mould. In the spring the plants will come up, at which time they should be kept clean from weeds, and constantly watered in dry weather. By the middle of May they will be of proper size to be pricked out in the nursery. For this purpose, let a bed, of a size sufficient for the quantity of plants, be well dug in a moist shady place, and in this set your plants in rows at six inches distance from each other. Give them a good watering, and continue it if dry weather makes it necessary, for these plants delight in moisture; all summer keep them clean from weeds, and in the autumn they should be set out for good.

The ground for their reception should be naturally moist, rich, and double dug, and the plants should be set at a good distance from each other every way. Their after-management is to hoe the ground to destroy the weeds in summer, and lightly to dig the soil between the plants, so as not to disturb the roots, in winter; and this is all the trouble they will require.

Masterwort is also propagated by parting of the roots, the best time for which is the autumn. This method may suffice when a few plants only are wanted for observation; but when large quantities are to be raised for medicinal purposes, the best way will be always to have recourse to seeds.

*Titles.* There being no other species of this genus, it stands with the name simply, *Imperatoria*, a name by which it was well known to botanists of old. Cammerarius calls it, *Magistrantia*. It grows naturally on the Alps, Austria, Helvetia, &c.

*Class and order in the Linnaean system.* *Imperatoria* is of the class and order *Pentandria Digynia*; and the characters are,

*The characters.* 1. CALYX. The general umbel is plane. The partial umbel is plane. The general umbel has no involucrum. The partial has an involucrum composed of a few slender leaves, which are nearly as long as the umbel. The proper perianthium is obsolete.

2. COROLLA. The general flower is uniform. The florets have each five almost equal petals, which are emarginated and inflexed.

3. STAMINA are five capillary filaments with roundish antheræ.

4. PISTILLUM consists of a germen situated below the flower, and two reflexed styles with obtuse stigmas.

5. PERICARPIUM. There is none. The fruit is roundish, compressed, bordered, and separable into two parts.

6. SEMINA. The seeds are two, oval, furrowed on one side, and are surrounded by a broad border.

## CHAP. CCXLIX.

## *INULA*, ELECAMPANE.

THE Perennials of this species go by the respective names of,

*Species.*

1. Elecampane.
2. Sweet-rooted Starwort.
3. Hungarian Flea Bane.
4. British Flea Bane.
5. Middle Flea-Bane.
6. Willow-leaved Mountain Starwort.
7. Prickly-leaved Starwort.
8. German Starwort.
9. Sword-leaved Aster.
10. Golden Sampire.
11. Round leaved *Jacobæa*.
12. Mountain Starwort.
13. Squarrose-cupped Starwort.
14. Maryland Aster.

1. Elecampane.

Elecampane. 1. Elecampane. The root is thick, spreading, brown on the outside, white within, of a strong aromatic odour, but bitterish to the taste. The radical leaves are more than a foot long, broad, very rough, crenated, and hoary underneath: the leaves on the stalks are smaller, rough, downy underneath, and embrace the stalk with their base. The stalks are upright, thick, firm, four or five feet high, and divide into a few branches near the top. The flowers come out many together from the tops of the main-stalks, but usually singly from the ends of the lower branches; they are large, of a deep-yellow colour, appear in June and July, and are succeeded by narrow, four cornered, downy seeds, which ripen in September.

Medicinal properties of this plant. The root is in great esteem in medicine. It is an excellent pectoral, carminative, stomachick, and good against poisons, putrid air, and pestilential disorders; but for the latter purposes is inferior to the root of Masterwort.

In order to raise this species for medicinal purposes, let the seeds be thinly sowed in a bed of light moist earth made fine, the best time for which is the autumn, soon after they are ripe; let them be lightly raked in, and many of them will come up before the end of autumn and the rest will [illegible] in the spring. In May the largest plants will be fit to remove; and the others may remain two or three weeks longer, to gain strength. Let a moist, shady, rich part of the garden be appropriated for their reception; let the ground be double dug, the surface levelled and made fine, and on this let the plants be set in rows at two feet distance from each other. A moist day should be made choice of for the purpose; for want of which watering should be immediately applied, to settle the mould to the roots. This should be repeated, if dry weather continues, until they are in a growing state; after that they will require no trouble, except keeping them clean from weeds. The summer following they will flower, and perfect their seeds, soon after which the stalks decay, and this is the time for gathering the roots for use.

Its propagation. This species is extremely hardy, and may be propagated very speedily by parting of the roots in the autumn, winter, or spring, which method may suffice when a few plants only are wanted for a collection. But I advise the former process from seeds only, when quantities are to be raised for medicinal purposes, as the roots by that method being raised and gathered when only two years old, will be more juicy, and of greater force for any purposes in medicine. The roots will continue for many years, if left undisturbed; and the plants will spread, send up numerous stalks, and choke every thing that is near them. If the seeds also are permitted to scatter, they will grow, and being dispersed by the winds, will produce plants enough all over the garden.

Sweet-rooted Starwort. 2. Sweet-rooted Starwort. The root is thick, spreading, and when broken emits an agreeable odour. The stalks are upright, firm, branching near the top, and grow to about three feet high. The leaves are indented, hairy, and the radical ones are of an oval figure; the upper ones are spear-shaped, and embrace the stalk with their base. The flowers are produced thinly from the upper parts of the plant; they are small, and of a yellow colour; they appear in July, but are very rarely succeeded by ripe seeds in our gardens.

Hungarian. 3. Hungarian Flea Bane. The stalks are upright, hairy, two feet high, and branching near the top. The leaves are oblong, spear-shaped, hairy, entire, and embrace the stalk with their base. The flowers come out in close clusters from the ends of the stalks; they are small, of a yellow colour, they appear in July, but are rarely followed by good seeds in England.

British. 4. British Flea-Bane. This hath long been called British Flea-bane, though I never could learn that it was an indigenous plant [illegible] of Britain. The root is creeping, and if undisturbed spreads to a considerable distance. The stalks are round, two feet high, and send forth a few erect branches near the top. The leaves are lanceolate, woolly, [illegible] and embrace the stalk with their base. The flowers come out singly from the ends of the branches; they are large, of a deep yellow colour, and very beautiful; they appear in July and August, and are rarely followed by ripe seeds in Britain.

and Middle Flea Bane. 5. Middle Flea Bane. The stalks are rough, hairy, paniculated, and about a foot and a half high. The leaves are heart-shaped, oblong, rough, of a greyish colour, and embrace the stalk with their base. The flowers are disposed in panicles on the tops of the plant; they are moderately large, and of a yellow colour; they appear in July and August, and are followed by downy seeds, which will be ripe in September.

Willow leaved Mountain 6. Willow leaved Mountain Starwort. The radical leaves are produced in bunches from the root, are spear-shaped, smooth, and recurved. The stalks are angular, striated, two feet high, and divide into several branches, or rather foot-stalks, near the top. The flowers come out singly from the ends of these footstalks. They are moderately large, and of a yellow colour; they appear in June, July, and August, and are soon followed by ripe downy seeds.

and Prickly Starwort, described. 7. Prickly Starwort. The stalks are hairy, rough, round, and about a foot high. The leaves are spear-shaped, obtuse, rough, prickly, and half embrace the stalk with their base. The flowers come out singly from the ends of the branches; they are of a yellow colour, appear in July and August, but are rarely followed by ripe seeds in England.

Varieties. There are several varieties of this species, differing in the degree of roughness of the leaves, height of the stalks, and size of the flowers.

German Starwort. 8. German Starwort. The stalks are upright, divide into several short branches near the top, and grow to near four feet high. The leaves are spear-shaped, indented, rough, recurved, and embrace the stalks with their base. The flowers come out in close bunches from the ends of the branches; they are small, of a yellow colour, appear in June and July, and the seeds ripen in September.

Sword leaved Aster. 9. Sword leaved Aster. The stalks are numerous, slender, and about a foot high. The leaves are long, narrow, sharp pointed, nervose, smooth, and sit close to the stalk. The flowers are one or two only at the tops of the stalks; they are of a yellow colour, appear in July and August, and are sometimes succeeded by ripe seeds in September.

Golden Samphire. 10. Golden Samphire. The stalks are upright, thick, and grow to about a foot and a half high. The leaves are long, narrow, fleshy, succulent, and three-pointed. The flowers come out for the most part singly from the tops of the stalks; they are large, of a yellow colour, appear in July and August, and the seeds ripen in September.

Round leaved Jacobæa described. 11. Round-leaved *Jacobæa*. The stalks are simple, erect, hairy, and grow to about a foot high. The radical leaves are oval, blunt, serrated, obtuse, downy underneath, and grow on

footstalks

footstalks, those on the stalks are spear-shaped, less serrated, and sit close. The flowers come out singly from the tops of the stalks; they are large, of a deep-yellow colour, appear in July and August, and the seeds ripen in September.

Mountain

12. Mountain Starwort. The stalks are upright, and a foot and a half high. The leaves are spear-shaped, entire, covered with soft hairs, and sit close to the stalks. The flowers come out singly from the tops of the stalks; they are large, of a yellow colour, appear in July, but are rarely succeeded by ripe seeds in England.

and Squarrose Cupped Starwort

13. Squarrose cupped Starwort. The stalks are upright, round, smooth, and about a foot high. The leaves are oval, smooth, finely veined in the manner of net work, and slightly indented on their edges. The flowers come out singly from the tops of the stalks, which being gathered, several smaller arise a little lower on their own separate footstalks; their colour is yellow; they are finely scented, and grow in squarrose cups; they appear in July and August, but are rarely succeeded by ripe seeds in England.

and Maryland Aster described

14. Maryland Aster. The radical leaves are numerous, hairy, an inch broad, and near half a foot long. The stalks are upright, hairy, send forth several side branches, and grow to about a yard high. The leaves on these are spear-shaped, sessile, hairy, slightly serrated, and placed alternately on the branches. The flowers come out from the tops of the stalks on slender footstalks, and are furnished with one or two small narrow leaves, which are large, of a yellow colour, appear in July and August, but are seldom succeeded by ripe seeds in England.

Variety

There is a variety of this plant of lower growth, which produces the flowers in kind of umbels.

Manner of propagating them

The culture of all these sorts is as easy as the Asters; there are few of them which do not encrease very fast by the roots, and these being taken up, parted, and planted again in the autumn, in almost any soil or situation, will grow and flower the summer following.

They are also easily encreased by seeds, and by this method fresh varieties may be obtained. Sow the seeds in the autumn, as soon as they are ripe, in beds of light mould made fine, and slightly rake them in; some of them will appear in the autumn, the rest will come up in the spring. Keep them clean from weeds, water them in dry weather, and in May prick them out in beds at about four inches distance from each other; here let them stand until the autumn, and then remove them to the places where they are designed to remain.

Most of them may also be encreased by cuttings. These should be planted close together before they come into flower, in a moist shady place; many of them will grow, and in the autumn may be removed to the places where they are designed to remain.

The sorts which ripen their seed propagate themselves very fast that way; for all of them, when ripe, are furnished with down, by which they are wafted all over the garden, and though they may come up in improper places, yet they may be removed in the autumn to the places where they are wanted.

The respective removals should be made early in the autumn, that they may strike root before the winter season, and the summer following they will shoot stronger, and produce larger and finer flowers. Every autumn, when they have done flowering, the stalks should be cut up to the ground; and if they are set in rows, the ground between the rows should be dug and laid level and smooth, to look well all winter. The sorts which creep the most should be taken up every other year, proper offsets be planted again for the succession, and the rest thrown away; but the sorts which have less tendency to creep, may stand three or four years before they are removed.

At every removal they should be watered at first, if dry weather should happen; be ever afterwards kept clean from weeds; and this is all the trouble they will require.

1. Elecampane is titled, *Inula foliis amplexicaulibus ovatis rugosis subtus tomentosis, calycum squamis ovatis*. In the *Hortus Cliffortianus* it is termed, *Aster foliis ovatis rugosis amplexicaulibus subtus tomentosis, calycum squamis ovatis patulis*. Caspar Bauhine calls it, *Helenium vulgare*; Camerarius, Ray, Gerard, &c. *Helenium*; and Parkinson, *Helenium sive Enula campana*. It grows naturally in moist meadows and pastures in Germany. Title

2. Sweet-rooted Starwort is, *Inula foliis amplexicaulibus dentatis hirsutissimis radicalibus ovatis, caulinis lanceolatis, caule paucifloro*. Caspar Bauhine calls it, *Aster luteus, radice odorâ*; Columna, *Aster atticus species Apula*; and Morison, *Conyza altera Apula*. It grows naturally in France, Italy, and Germany.

3. Hungarian Flea-Bane is, *Inula foliis amplexicaulibus oblongis integerrimis hirsutis, caule piloso corymboso*. In the *Hortus Cliffortianus* it is termed, *Aster caule superne ramoso amplo foliis lanceolatis amplexicaulibus integris, calycibus laxis tomentosis*. Caspar Bauhine calls it, *Conyza Pannonica lanuginosa*; and Clusius, *Conyza 3 Austriaca*. It grows naturally in Austria.

4. British Flea-Bane is, *Inula foliis amplexicaulibus lanceolatis distincte serratis subtus villosis, caule ramoso villoso erecto*. Caspar Bauhine calls it, *Conyza affinis*; also, *Conyza aquatica, asteris flore aureo*; and Morison, *Conyza palustris repens, Britannica dicta*. It grows naturally in most parts of Germany.

5. Middle Flea-Bane is, *Inula foliis amplexicaulibus cordato-oblongis subtomentosis, caule villoso paniculato, squamis calycinis setaceis*. In the *Flora Suecica* it is termed, *Aster foliis semiamplexicaulibus oblongis, caule paniculato hirsuto, floribus lateralibus, squamis calycinis setaceis*. Gerard calls it, *Conyza media*; Caspar Bauhine, *Conyza media, asteris flore luteo, vel tertia Dioscoridis*; Tabernæmontanus, *Conyza 1*; and Fuchsius, *Calaminthæ tertium genus*. It grows naturally in moist places, ditches, and the banks of rivers in England, and most parts of Europe.

6. Willow-leaved Mountain Starwort is, *Inula foliis sessilibus lanceolatis recurvis serrato-scabris, floribus inferioribus altioribus, ramis subangulatis glabris*. In the *Flora Suecica* it is termed, *Aster foliis lanceolatis amplexicaulibus serrato-ciliatis glabris acuminatis recurvis, floribus solitariis, caule striato*. Caspar Bauhine calls it, *Aster montanus luteus, salicis glabro folio*; and Tabernæmontanus, *Buphthalmum alterum 1*. It grows naturally in most rough places in most of the northern parts of Europe.

7. Prickly-leaved Starwort is, *Inula foliis sessilibus lanceolatis recurvatis subserrato-scabris, floribus inferioribus altioribus, caule teretiusculo superne*. Dalechamp calls it, *Aster foliis lanceolatis subintegerrimis, caulibus simplicibus unifloris, squamis calycinis subulatis*; Caspar Bauhine, *Aster luteus, hirsuto salicis folio*; and John Bauhine, *Aster tertius Pannonicus Clusii luteus, folio hirsuto salicis*. It grows naturally in most parts of Germany.

8. German Starwort is, *Inula foliis sessilibus lanceolatis recurvis scabris, floribus subfastigiatis* ...

Gmelin

Gmelin calls it, *Aster fol's ... amplexicaulibus oris reflexis, ramis multifloris, calycibus oblongis laxis*, Caspar Bauhine, *Conyza ... Germanica*, and Haller, *Aster Ilmeting acus ... latifolius montanus, flore luteo parvo*. It grows naturally in most parts of Germany.

9 Sword-leaved After is, *Inula foliis sessilibus lanceolatis ... nervosis glabris sparsis, caule subunifloro*. Boccone calls it, *Aster montanus saxatilis luteus, angusto nervoso acuto & molli plantaginis folio, multicaulis*, and Caspar Bauhine, *Aster luteus, linariae rigido glabro folio*. It grows naturally in the Lower Austria.

10 Golden Samphire is, *Inula foliis linearibus carnosis ... cuspidatis*. In the *Hortus Cliffort* it is termed, *Aster flore terminali, foliis linearibus tricuspidatis*. Caspar Bauhine calls it, *Crithmum maritimum, colore aster's Attici*, Dodonaeus, *Crithmum chrysanthemum* and Ray, *Aster maritimus flavus, crithmum chrysanthemum dictus*. It grows naturally in the maritime parts of England, France, Portugal, and Spain.

11 Round-leaved *Jacobaea* is, *Inula foliis subserratis, subtus tomentosis radicalibus petiolatis ovatis, caule erecto unifloro*. Caspar Bauhine calls it, *Jacobaea rotundifolia incana*. It grows naturally in many parts of Germany, Italy, and France.

12 Mountain Starwort is, *Inula foliis lanceolatis hirsutis integerrimis, caule ... flore, calyce brevi imbricato*. Caspar Bauhine calls it, *Aster Atticus luteus montanus villosus ... flore*, and John Bauhine, *Aster angustifolius luteus*. It grows naturally in France, Italy, and Spain.

13 Squarrose-cupped Starwort is, *Inula foliis ovalibus ... bus ... subcrenatis, calycibus squarrosis*. Tournefort calls it, *Aster conyzoides odoratus luteus*, and Plukenet, *Aster luteus latifolius ... foliis rigidis ... crenatis*. It grows naturally in France and Italy.

14 Maryland After is, *Inula foliis sessilibus lanceolatis subserratis pilosis, pedunculis subunifloris subfuscis, foliolis linearibus*. In Miller's Dictionary it is termed, *Aster Carolinianus pilosus conyzae caeruleae foliis, floribus ... quasi umbellatim dispositis*. Plukenet calls it, *Aster luteus Marianus, salignis brevioribus foliis hirsutie pubescentibus, summo caule ramosus*. It grows naturally in North America.

*Inula* is of the class and order *Syngenesia Polygamia Superflua*, and the characters are,

Class and order in the Linnaean system. The characters.

1 CALYX. The general calyx is imbricated. The folioles are loose, spreading, and the outer ones are the largest, and of equal length.

2 COROLLA. The compound flower is radiated. The hermaphrodite florets are numerous in the disk, equal, and each consists of one funnel-shaped petal cut at the top into five segments, which are nearly erect.

The female florets are numerous in the radius, and each of them is narrow, tongue-shaped, entire ...

3 STAMINA, of the hermaphrodite florets, consist of five very short filiform filaments, crowned by five, narrow, cylindrical antherae, which coalesce at the top, but each ends at the bottom in two straight bristles, which ... the length of the filaments.

4 PISTILLUM, of the hermaphrodite florets, consists of a long germen, a filiform style the length of the stamina, and a bifid erect stigma.

In the females, it consists of a long germen, and a filiform style half divided into two parts, each of which has an erect stigma.

5 PERICARPIUM. There is none.

6 SEMINA. The seeds of the hermaphrodites are single, narrow, quadrangular, and covered by a simple down the length of the seed.

The seeds of the females are similar to those of the hermaphrodites.

The receptacle is plane and naked.

## CHAP. CCL.

## *IRIS*, FLOWER-DE-LUCE.

Remarks.

THE family of the *Iris*, great as it was before, is now much enlarged by the admission of many distant cousins into a nearer relationship; for the *Sisyrinchium*, *Xiphium*, and *Hermodactylus*, which used to be reckoned among botanists as distinct genera, are now found to belong to this fraternity, and to be no more than species only of this genus. A venerable and respectable name, therefore, stands the *Iris*, and our gardens are so enriched with its numerous offspring, that it is difficult to know which to begin with first. The early dwarf kinds put in for this claim, while the larger-growing *Iris's* demand the preference. The common Flag-flower of our meadows tells you that he is an indigenous plant, and therefore his name ought of course to stand first in the list, while the more rare and delicate-coloured kinds lay claim to this prerogative. Without paying any attention to the propriety and weight of these demands, I shall divide them into two classes.

I. The *Iris* with Bearded Flowers.

II. The Unbearded Flowering *Iris*.

Under these two heads I shall consider the different species of this extensive genus, and point out the principal varieties as I go on.

I. The species of *Iris* with Bearded Flowers are,

Species.

1 The Chalcedonian *Iris*.
2 The German *Iris*.
3 The Florentine *Iris*.
4 Elder scented *Iris*.
5 Rough leaved *Iris*.
6 Broad-leaved *Iris* with a naked stalk.
7 Broad leaved Hungarian *Iris*.
8 Broad-leaved Portugal *Iris*.
9 Dwarf Austrian *Iris*.

Description of the Chalcedonian Iris.

1 The Chalcedonian *Iris* with great propriety stands

stands first in the list, it being a species (if I may be allowed the expression) both wonderful, awful, and daring The flowers are of so singular a construction, and odd a colour, that they have struck terror into the innocent peasants, who could not be persuaded to enter their fingers into their seemingly hissing mouths, which has often afforded much merriment to the Gardener and his friends The root is fleshy, thick, and juicy The leaves are long, firm, and of a greyish green colour, their ends and edges are sharp, and six or eight of them will be growing together, surrounding one another at their base The stalk is round, thick, jointed, firm, and will grow to about two feet in height, at the top of which stands this formidable flower This is the largest of all the Iris's The three bending petals are quite black, except among a few lines of violet or purple, that spread themselves without order about them, the middle is black, hairy, and in the center there is a conspicuous jetty spot The three upright petals are of a thin texture, very broad, waved, and of a kind of lead colour mixed or variegated with black, white, grey, and dusky spots or streaks The whole flower has the appearance of three distinct heads, hence the name Chalcedonius has been given to this plant The petals are so constructed as to represent a mouth, and the stamina the tongues, which seem open, and hissing at all who approach them This wonderful species was brought from Constantinople almost two hundred years ago, it has flowered well with us ever since, and will be in blow in June, but the flowers never produce good seeds in England

German, 2 German Iris This hath a thick, jointed, spreading, fleshy root The leaves are long and broad, their edges are sharp, and their ends sharp pointed, they rise in clusters from the root, at their base embrace each other, and spread themselves upwards in the form of fans Amidst these arises the flower-stalk, which will grow to about two feet in height It is jointed, and at each joint stands a sessile leaf ornamented with many flowers, which grow at distances one above another, and the lower ones have footstalks, and all at first have their separate spatha or covering The reflexed or under petals are of a violet colour, and have very long beards down the middle towards the base On these lie the stamina The three upright petals are very broad, grow erect, and do their part in forming a beautiful flower This species is very common, it will be in full blow the beginning of July, the germen swells after the flowers are decayed, and in a few weeks will produce plenty of good seeds

Florentine, 3 Florentine Iris This is called by many the White German Iris, and indeed differs very little from it, except in the colour of the flowers The leaves and stalks form the like kind of appearance, though there are seldom above two or three flowers on a stalk, and upon a close examination of them we find the upper petals grow more erect, the stigmas also are more erect, and slightly serrated

Elder scented, 4 Elder scented Iris This species has very much the smell of elder, which occasions its being so distinguished The leaves are very broad, their edges are sharp, and the ends pointed. Amidst these rises the flower-stalk to about two feet in height The flowers shew themselves at the top of this, above the leaves, several of them will grow from the stalk, and they make a fine shew Their under petals are plane, and of a deep violet colour, their erect petals are emarginated, and of a pale blue colour The time of blow is June or July, though I never observed any seeds to follow the flowers

5 Rough leaved Iris This hath very broad rough leaves, which will grow to about a foot and a half long, and their ends are pointed Among these arises the flower-stalk, which will grow to near two feet in height, and is furnished with several flowers, which are of very bad colours The reflexed petals are of a dirty purple colour, with a mixture of yellow and white, and the erect petals are of a very disagreeable faith, yellow This sort flowers in June and July Rough leaved.

6 Broad-leaved Iris with a naked stalk The leaves of this species, like many others, are very broad, but the singularity is, the stalk is entirely free from leaves, or naked and the leaves and stalks grow to an equal height The flowers are very beautiful, of a bright purple colour striped with white, and their beards rather are of a purplish cast They will be in full blow before the end of May, and then large triangular capsules will produce good seeds by the beginning of August Broad-leaved,

7 Broad leaved Hungarian Iris This has a large, thick, knotty root The leaves are very long and broad, their edges sharp, and the ends pointed, they are numerous, and their colour is a bluish green Among these rises the stalk, (whose height will be about the same with the leaves) rounded upright, and firm, its colour is a pale green upwards, but purplish near the ground, and towards the bottom at the joints a small single leaf is placed, with its base surrounding the stalk The stalk produces several flowers, and near the top, without any order, into a few side branches or footstalks, which support a few flowers, and a single flower always terminates the main-stalk The flowers are large and beautiful, the upright petals are of a fine yellow colour, the lower ones are white, and striped with purple or crimson The three heads of the style are variegated with yellow and white, the bearded part is whitish towards the top, and yellow near the base This is the natural colour of this beautiful species, but there are varieties of it Some have their lower petals altogether white, some flesh-coloured, and others again of a crimson, with a few streaks of a lighter colour Broad leaved Hungarian.

These are the effects of culture, and doubtless more varieties might be obtained from seeds, but it is not common that they produce them good with us This sort will be in blow in June

8 Broad leaved Portugal Iris This species hath a thick, fleshy, knobbed root The leaves are very broad and short they are of a firm substance and bluish-green colour The flower-stalk is still shorter than the leaves, and seldom grows higher than half a foot It produces a few flowers One always crowns the main stalk, and sometimes another or two will branch out from the side near the top, They are of a deep-purple colour, their upper petals are lighter, and sometimes the lower ones are a little striped with yellow or a pale blue It will be in flower in May, but seldom produces seeds with us Broad-leaved Portugal,

9 Dwarf Austrian Iris This is one of the lowest kinds of the Iris's, and contains the most varieties of any species of this genus In its natural or original state, we find the root to be large, fleshy, knotty, and irregular, and frequently the top of it will be above the surface of the earth The leaves are many, and of a pale-green colour, they are moderately broad and pointed, of a firm substance, and about three or four inches in length Among these arises the flower-stalk, which will not grow to the height of the leaves Its usual height is from two to three inches, and the top of it supports a single flower, which will be of different colours in the different varieties Difference also is and Dwarf Austrian Iris describ

is found in the leaves and properties of the flowers as well as in their colours, inſomuch that of this ſpecies there are,

Its varieties

The Common Broad-leaved Dwarf *Iris*
Dwarf *Iris* with a pale purple flower
Dwarf *Iris* with a deep-purple flower
Dwarf *Iris* with a bluiſh flower
Dwarf *Iris* with a red flower
Dwarf *Iris* with a peach bloom ſweet-ſcented flower
Dwarf *Iris* with a white flower
Dwarf *Iris* with a variegated flower

Theſe are the principal varieties of the Dwarf *Iris*, and all of them more or leſs, are ſtained or veined with different tints, and form a ſet of very beautiful flowers, and being naturally of low growth, they are adapted for the ſmalleſt gardens, as well as to figure in plenty in the largeſt borders

Thus much for the Bearded kinds of *Iris* Proceed we, ſecondly, to the Unbearded ſpecies of this genus A liſt of theſe are,

The Unbearded ſpecies of Iris

1 The Common Flag Flower, or Yellow Flower de Luce
2 The Roaſt-Beef Plant
3 Narrow-leaved Siberian *Iris*
4 Penſylvania *Iris*
5 Virginian *Iris*
6 Martinico *Iris*
7 Stinking Meadow *Iris*
8 Auſtrian Graſs-leaved *Iris*
9 Dwarf Spring Virginian *Iris*

SECT III

10 *Iris Hermodactylus*, or Snake's-Head *Iris*

IV

11 *Iris Xiphium*, or Bulbous *Iris*

V

12 *Iris Perſica*, or Perſian *Iris*

VI

13 *Iris Siſyrinchium*

Deſcription of the Flag Flower

1 The Flag Flower, or Yellow Flower de Luce This is the Common Yellow Flag Flower of our meadows and ditches, a plant well known to every one, and needing little deſcription Nevertheleſs, let us lead our ſtudent to a cloſer examination of this common plant And here we find the root thick and ſpreading, the leaves enſiforme or ſword ſhaped, and of a limberer ſubſtance and deeper-green colour than many of the before-deſcribed *Iris's* The ſtalk we find upright, firm, and about a yard in height A few flowers ornament the top of it one above another, which ſucceed each other in blow The under petals we find drooping, but the bearded nectarium is wanting A great difference is alſo obſervable in the other petals, for they are leſs than the ſtigmas, and conſequently want the graceful appearance which is peculiar to the upright petals in the before deſcribed ſorts We find it in blow almoſt all over England in marſhy places, in June, and the flowers are ſucceeded by large three-cornered capſules containing the ſeeds

The Roaſt Beef Plant deſcribed

2 The Roaſt-Beef Plant This ſpecies alſo grows naturally by the ſides of ditches and brooks in ſome parts of England It has a large root, but is more fibrous than the former The leaves are enſiforme, and of a deep green colour Among theſe riſes the flower-ſtalk, it will grow to about the ſame height with the leaves, is angular on one ſide, and ſupports about two flowers, which are of a purple colour, and one is a little variegated The outer petals are reflexed in the uſual way, and the inner petals are about the ſame length with the ſtigmas The flowers are inconſiderable, and the greateſt value of this ſpecies ariſes from the ſcent of the leaves, which is very much like that of roaſt beef Hence the Gardener takes pride in ſhewing it as ſuch, and the company wonder to find the ſmell of ſo excellent an article as a piece of roaſt beef ſo exactly ſimilar in a leaf of this plant

Its variety

This ſpecies has a variety with ſtriped leaves, which deſerves cultivation on their account, for they ornament the garden all winter by the fine and lively ſhow they make

Theſe plants flower in June, and the ſeeds will be ripe in September

Narrow-leaved, Siberian,

3 Narrow leaved Siberian *Iris* The leaves are numerous, narrow, of a deep green colour, and will grow to about a foot and a half high Amongſt theſe riſes the ſtalk, which is round, upright, firm, and bears its head above the leaves, the top of it is garniſhed with two or three flowers one above another The reflexed petals are blue, with a white ſtripe in the place of the beard, the interior petals are of a pale blue colour, and grow erect It flowers in July, and affords ripe ſeeds in autumn

and Penſylvania Iris deſcribed

4 Penſylvania *Iris* The leaves are many and narrow, of a enſiforme figure and a deep green colour The ſtalk is about the ſame height with the leaves, round, taper, bending, and having two or three flowers placed near the top The falling petals are of a deep purple colour, with a white ſtripe in the place of the beard, the upright petals are of a light blue colour, and about the length of the ſtamina It flowers in June, and when the ſeed-veſſels ſwell after the flowers, which is not very common, the ſeeds will be ripe in autumn

Its varieties

Of this ſpecies there are ſeveral varieties, viz The Broad-leaved Penſylvania *Iris*, the Narrow leaved, the Penſylvania *Iris* with a crenated ſtyle, and another with the ſtyle not crenated They all flower at the ſame time

Virginian,

5 Virginian *Iris* The leaves are many, and of a bluiſh-green colour The flower-ſtalk is upright, firm, and angular, it ſupports near the top two or three flowers, one above another The bending petals are purpliſh, and the upright petals of a lighter colour They will be in blow in July, but are not always ſucceeded by good ſeeds with us

Martinico,

6 Martinico *Iris* This has many long narrow leaves, and the ſtalk ſupports two or three flowers at the top, which have a three cornered germen like the preceding ſort, and their colour is a kind of blackiſh yellow The petals are glandulous near the baſe This ſpecies flowers about Midſummer but ſeldom produces good ſeeds here

and Stinking Meadow Iris deſcribed

7 Stinking Meadow *Iris* This ſpecies ſends forth many narrow leaves from the root, which emit, on being broken, a very diſagreeable ſcent The flower-ſtalk rears its head juſt above the leaves, and ſupports three or four flowers, which grow one above another The bending petals are purple, with a white line down the middle and the upright petals are of a pale-blue colour

Its variety,

There is a variety of this ſpecies with leaves which are not poſſeſſed of that diſagreeable ſmell, but the flowers are the ſame with the others

They will be in blow in July, and afford good ſeeds in the autumn

Deſcription of the Auſtrian,

8 Auſtrian Graſs leaved *Iris* This ſpecies hath long, narrow, graſſy leaves, which are of a light-green colour, and will grow to about a foot in height The beauty of this ſpecies is greatly diminiſhed by the ſhortneſs of the flower-ſtalk, for it will hardly arrive to above half the length of the leaves The flowers are very ſmall, and two or three, one above another, are

uſually

usually produced on a stalk. The flower itself is very elegant, the hanging petals are of a light purple colour, striped with blue, and in the place of the beard is a broad stripe of yellow intermixed with streaks of purple; the upright petals are of a reddish purple, delightfully variegated with a kind of violet colour. These flowers emit an odour like some sorts of fresh-gathered plums, which to many is agreeable; they will be in bloom in July, and their seed will be ripe in the autumn.

and Dwarf Spring Virginian Iris

9. Dwarf Spring Virginian *Iris*. This species hath a fibrous root, and from that issue several narrow grass-like leaves, about nine inches long. The flower-stalk arises among them, is shorter than the leaves, and supports one flower only. The hanging petals are purple, and the interior ones of a pale-blue colour. They constitute a beautiful flower, and have additional value from the agreeable odour which they constantly emit. It will be in flower in May, but rarely produces seeds with us.

CULTURE of these *Iris's*.

Culture of the foregoing Iris's

The culture of all the foregoing species of *Iris* is very easy. Their large spreading roots point out their method of propagation, and call upon the Gardener to divide and multiply them at pleasure. This work may be done at any time of the year, for they are all very hardy; but the best time is August or September, in a moist day; they will then strike root immediately, and flower strong the summer following.

This parting of the roots is the usual way of propagating these plants; but in order to obtain fresh varieties, the seeds should be sown. Let these be gathered from flowers which have the best properties, that is, such as are large, deep-coloured, and well variegated. While the seed is ripening, if the weather comes dry, frequently water the roots; and when they are ripe, carefully cut off the heads, and lay them on a dry shelf for a few days. After that take the seeds out of their vessels, and preserve them for sowing. The best time for this is the beginning of September. Any border of common mould is sufficient; and if it has the morning aspect only, it will be so much the better. Let the seeds be scattered very thinly over the bed, and sift over them about half an inch of fine mould. In the spring the plants will appear; pull up all weeds as they rise with the hand, and often give them water in dry weather. In August thin the beds where the plants come up too thick. A moist day should be chosen for that purpose, and the plants should be set in another bed at five inches asunder, leaving the seedlings in their own bed at about the same distance. The business is then done; nothing more will be required than keeping them clean from weeds, and the strongest of them will shew their flowers in about two years after. This method of raising plants from seeds is rather tedious; but there is great pleasure in the expectation, and endless varieties, as well as the best plants, are for the most part to be raised this way.

Proceed we now to the other species of the *Iris*, which have been held as distinct genera by old authors, and which is my third division of the species of the Flower de Luce. And for this in the next place presents itself,

III. *Iris Hermodactylus*.

Iris Hermodactylus described

This species is usually called the Snake's Head *Iris*. The root is very large and tuberous, from whence arise a few leaves, which are long, narrow, and four-cornered. Among these arises the flower-stalk; the top of it is garnished with one flower only, which is small, and of a dark-purple colour. It will be in blow in May, but is seldom succeeded by seeds in these parts.

CULTURE of this *Iris*.

Its culture

In order to have this plant in perfection, the nature of the soil and situation should be regarded. The situation should be where they may receive the morning sun only; and the soil should be rich and light, but not very deep, for the roots naturally strike deep into the ground, and where there is depth of soil for it, they will run so low as to lose themselves. They will first of all get so low as to flower weakly, then they will run lower, and not flower at all, and after that they will strike so low as never to come up again. To prevent this, many have laid a stratum of rubbish, and then covered it with a proper depth of earth, in which to plant these roots; and this is no very bad practice.

These things being premised, the manner of propagating them will be soon shewn. It is by taking off the tubers, and planting them in beds, with the above conditions, at about six inches asunder. They should be placed about three inches deep, and the ground should be always kept clean from weeds. The best time for this is on the decay of the leaves, and the roots ought to be annually transplanted. Nevertheless, if you want great increase of these plants, they should remain undisturbed for about three years.

IV. *Iris Xiphium*, or Bulbous *Iris*.

There is an elegance peculiar to all the sorts of the Bulbous *Iris*, and they claim a place in the choicest collections of plants. A description of it should vary in the different varieties; but in general, the root is a large, roundish, fleshy bulb. The leaves are channelled, sharp pointed, and embrace the flower-stalk at their base. These are of different heights and sizes in the different varieties, and the flower-stalks are of lower growth; sometimes they will not rise to half the length of the leaves. Each stalk supports one, two, or three flowers, which are of the same construction with the other sorts of *Iris*. Of this species there are the following varieties:

Iris Xiphium described

The Common Blue Bulbous *Iris*.
The Violet Bulbous *Iris*.
The Purple Bulbous *Iris*.
The White Bulbous *Iris*.
The Yellow Bulbous *Iris*.
The Bulbous *Iris* with white exterior petals, and blue upright petals.
The Bulbous *Iris* with yellow reflexed petals, and blue upright petals.
The Striped Bulbous *Iris*.
The Broad-leaved Blue Bulbous *Iris*.
The Broad-leaved Purple Bulbous *Iris*.
The Broad-leaved Variegated Bulbous *Iris*.
The Spanish Sweet-scented Blue Bulbous *Iris*.
The Spanish Sweet-scented Purple Bulbous *Iris*.
The Spanish Sweet-scented Variegated Bulbous *Iris*, &c. &c.

All these sorts are now pretty common in our gardens, and more varieties may be easily obtained from seeds. Therefore, the

CULTURE of the Bulbous *Iris*

Its culture and propagation by seeds

is first from seeds. These should be gathered from those flowers that are large, have the brightest colours, and are the best variegated; and the first week in September is the best time for sowing them. A bed of light, rich, sandy earth should be got ready in a warm, well-sheltered place, open only to the morning sun; or if your quantity of seeds be small, it will be the best way

way to sow them in pots or boxes, that they may be removed at pleasure. In either case scatter them very thinly, and sift about half an inch or the same kind of light rich mould over them. In the spring the plants will come up, at which time weeding and watering in dry weather must be observed; and as the heat increases, those sown in the pots should be placed entirely in the shade, or at least they should have no more than the morning sun until about ten o'clock. In July the leaves will begin to decay; watering then must be left off, and after they are withered the leaves must be cleared away, and about half an inch of fresh mould sifted over the young bulbs. In the spring manage them as before, and in summer, when the leaves decay, take up the largest bulbs, and plant them in a bed prepared for the purpose in the nursery ground. This bed should be made of the same kind of light, sandy rich earth, and the bulbs should be set at about three inches asunder, covering them over about two inches above the crown. The year following the plants out of the seed-bed must be transplanted, by which time the strongest in the former bed will shew their flowers. Let them all remain, however, good and bad, undisturbed for three years; for they will vary often from the first blow. The promising sorts have often the succeeding year proved bad, and those with seemingly bad properties have afterwards shewn a different nature. By the third season their colours and properties will for the most part be settled, and then is the time to mark the best, to be used for the best purposes, and the worst to be thrown away.

All the time from sowing the seeds to the flowering of the plants, if the winters should prove very severe, it would be proper to have the beds hooped and matted in such weather. But this is only with respect to very hard long frosts. In general they will want no defence, for they are tolerably hardy, as it is taken for granted the situation is well defended; and if some furze-bushes are pricked round the bed, it will be defence enough from a common frosty winter.

I by no means approve of sowing the seeds in shallow pans, &c. as is recommended by many; for the mould so soon dries, let your watering be ever so frequent, that the leaves will decay sooner by some weeks, than if the plants were in beds. By that means the bulbs will be proportionably smaller; and though they may be somewhat rounder, yet for want of bulk they will neither flower so soon, nor so strong, as those plants which have had all the advantages of a rich, cool, and moist bed, a bed adapted to their nature, and more similar to the places of their native growth.

This is the best way of obtaining plenty and great variety of these plants. But,

Method of propagation by offsets. Secondly, these plants are to be propagated by the offsets, and a tolerable quantity may be soon obtained that way. Let two or three plants, therefore, of the different varieties be procured, and plant them three inches deep, in a border open to the morning sun only, of the same kind of light, rich earth, that has been recommended for the seedlings. Let the bulbs remain three years undisturbed; by that time they will have made amazing increase, as well as annually have afforded you flowers for beauty. The time for removing them and parting the roots is in summer, on the decay of the leaves. At this time the strongest bulbs should be planted in a bed by themselves, to flower the ensuing season, and the weaker offsets also by themselves for a succession.



V. *Iris Persica.*

Description of the Iris Persica. This is a Bulbous *Iris*: but I chuse to mention it distinctly, because it has been looked upon by many of our Gardeners as a Spring *Iris*, independent on the rest. This is one of the sweetest ornaments of the early spring; for there is a delicacy, beauty, and elegance in this flower which is hardly equalled by any; and the time of flowering, and the fragrance it possesses, conspire to force it to our notice and enhance its value. The root of this delightful plant is a large, oval, oblong bulb, with a filmy covering. From this arise the leaves and the flower, tho' the latter will often be in blow before the former appear, and both at first are covered with several whitish membranes, which are the continuance of the outer coats of the bulb. The leaves themselves grow much taller than the flower-stalk; they are narrow, hollowed, and sharp pointed; they have a strong longitudinal rib, surround the stalk at the base, and are of a greyish-green colour. The stalk is white and short, seldom growing higher than about three inches; and at the top of it stands the flower. A more elegant one cannot be conceived. The ground of the outer petals is a pearly white, tinged a little with blue, and sometimes of a faint red colour; they have along their middle a broad yellow line, ornamented with spots of a lively brown, and numerous streaks of a fine violet; at the bottom is one large deep purple spot, velvety, and surrounded with white in the most delicate manner. The upright petals are white, spread open, and have their edges serrated; and these, as also the divisions of the stigmas, are often elegantly streaked. Add to this, that it is possessed of a very fragrant smell, which compleats the character of this flower.

This delightful plant will be in full blow in February, and is highly proper to form a show with some hepaticas and crocus's, snow-drops, narcissus's, and the like. Among these it stands a delightful variety, and is of by far superior beauty.

CULTURE of the Persian *Iris*.

Its cultivation. The cultivation of this species is exactly the same with that of the foregoing sorts of the Bulbous *Iris*. It is to be increased by seeds in the same manner, and multiplied also like those, by dividing the roots in the summer soon after the leaves are decayed.

VI. *Iris Sisyrinchium.*

Iris Sisyrinchium described. This is the last division of the species of the *Iris*. It is of the unbearded kind, and admits of several varieties, which are arranged under three heads, viz.

Its varieties. The *Sisyrinchium Majus*.
*Sisyrinchium Medium*.
*Sisyrinchium Minus*.

The root is a double bulb, one of which is placed over the other in the manner of the saffron roots. The leaves are long, narrow, sharp pointed, channelled or hollowed, and of a deep-green colour. The stalk is round and firm, and will grow to six inches high. The flowers are of a fine purple or blue colour, which is deeper or paler according to the varieties. The reflexed petals are spotted with yellow in the bearded place; and the whole is a very elegant and beautiful flower.

Propagation of them. They are propagated in the same manner as the Bulbous *Iris*.

We come now to the titles of the different species of this extensive genus; and,

I. The Bearded Species.

Titles of the Bearded species. 1. The Chalcedonian *Iris* is titled, *Iris corollâ barbatâ, caule foliis longiore unifloro*. It is the *Iris*

*Iris S.J , flore ... allo ... ce..*, of Caspar Bauhine, Morison, and many others. Clusius calls it, *Iris ... ..o.i* It is a native of the East.

2 German *Iris* This species is titled, *Iris corollis barbatis caule foliis longiore multifloro, floribus inferioribus pedunculatis* Caspar Bauhine calls it, *Iris vulgaris Germanica, sive sylvestris* It grows naturally in Germany.

3 Florentine *Iris* is, *Iris corollis barbatis, caule foliis altiore ... flor..* Caspar Bauhine calls it, *Iris alba Florentina* and Ray, *Iris flore albo* It grows naturally in many of the southern parts of Europe.

4 Elder-scented *Iris* is termed, *Iris corollis barbatis, caule foliis altiore multifloro, petalis deflexis ... emarginatis* This is the *Iris latifolia Germanica ... odore*, of Caspar Bauhine, and the *Iris major latifolia* of Clusius It grows naturally in several of the southern parts of Europe.

5 Rough-leaved *Iris* is, *Iris corollis barbatis, caule foliis altiore multifloro, petalis deflexis ... plicatis, erectis emarginatis* Boerhaave calls it, *Iris folio lato rugoso, petalis repandis ... purpureo ... dimo ... & luteo ... ereo ... lutescentibus* It grows naturally in many of the southern parts of Europe.

6 Broad-leaved *Iris* with a naked stalk is, *Iris corollis barbatis, scapo nudo longitudine foliorum multifloro* Caspar Bauhine calls it, *Iris latifolia, caule aphyllo* It is not certain in what part of the world this species grows in a state of nature.

7 Broad-leaved Hungarian *Iris* is titled, *Iris corollis barbatis, caule subfolioso longitudine foliorum multifloro.* Caspar Bauhine calls it, *Iris latifolia Pannonica, colore multiplici*, Lobel, *Iris lutea variegata* It grows naturally in Hungary.

8 Broad-leaved Portugal *Iris* is, *Iris corollis barbatis, caule foliis breviore uniflore* Besler calls it, *Iris latifolia major*, Caspar Bauhine, *Chamæiris major saturate purpurea ...* It grows common in Portugal.

9 Dwarf Austrian *Iris* is termed, *Iris corollis barbatis, caule foliis breviore uniflore* It is the *Chamæiris minor* of Caspar Bauhine, Clusius, &c. It grows naturally in Austria.

II TITLES of the Unbearded Species of *Iris*

1 The Common Flag Flower of our brooks is titled, *Iris corollis imberbibus, petalis interioribus stigmate minoribus, foliis ensiformibus* Caspar Bauhine calls it, *Acorus adulterinus*, and Camerarius, *Acorum falsum.* It grows in England and most parts of Europe.

2 The Roast-Beef Plant is, *Iris corollis imberbibus, petalis interioribus patentissimis, caule uniangulato, foliis ensiformibus* Caspar Bauhine calls it, *Gladiolus fœtidus*, and John Bauhine, *Spatula fœtida, ...* It is a native of England.

3 Narrow-leaved Siberian *Iris* is, *Iris corollis imberbibus, germinibus trigonis, caule teretiusculo, foliis linearibus* Caspar Bauhine calls it, *Iris pratensis angustifolia non fœtida altior*, Clusius, *Iris angustifolia* It grows in the meadows of Austria, Helvetia, and Siberia.

4 Pensilvania *Iris* is, *Iris corollis imberbibus, germinibus subtrigonis, caule tereti flexuoso, foliis ... ... .* This is the *Iris Americana ... ... flore ... ..so*, and the *Iris Americana ... ... flore ...*, of Dillenius It grows common in Pensilvania, Virginia, and Maryland.

5 Virginia *Iris* is titled, *Iris corollis imberbibus, germinibus ... , caule ...* It grows naturally in Virginia.

6 Martinico *Iris* is *Iris corollis imberbibus, germinibus ..., foliis ... ...* This is the *... flore ... ...* of Plumier. It grows naturally in Martinico.

7 Stinking Meadow *Iris* is, *Iris corollis imberbibus, germinibus hexagonis ..., caule tereti, foliis ... ...* Caspar Bauhine calls it *Iris pratensis angustifolia, ...*, and Clusius, *Iris ...* It is common in the meadows of Germany.

8 Austrian Grass-leaved *Iris* is, *Iris corollis imberbibus, germinibus ..., caule ancipiti, foliis ...* Caspar Bauhine calls it, *Iris ... ... ...* It grows naturally at the bottom and sides of mountains in Austria.

9 Dwarf Spring Virginian *Iris* is, *Iris corollis imberbibus ... ... foliis ..., ... fibrosa* Plukenet terms it, *Iris Virginiana ...*, *... angustifolia, flore purpureo ...* It grows naturally in Virginia.

10 *Iris* ... is titled *Iris corollis imberbibus, ... ...* Morison calls it, *Iris tuberosa folio angulato* It grows naturally in Arabia.

11 *Iris* ..., *Iris corollis imberbibus, ... ..., foliis subulatis canaliculatis ... ...* Van Royen calls it, *Iris caule ..., foliis margine ... ..., corollis imberbibus* It grows naturally in Spain.

12 Persian *Iris* is *Iris corollis ... petalis ... patentissimis ... foliis ... canaliculatis ... longioribus* Van Royen calls it, *Iris caulis, foliis ... ..., corollis imberbibus* and Tournefort, *Iris ... Persicum præcox, flore variegato* It grows naturally in Persia.

13 *Iris Sisyrinchium* is, *Iris corollis imberbibus, foliis canaliculatis, bulbis ... superimpositis* This comprehends the *Sisyrinchium ...*, the *Sisyrinchium ...*, and the *Sisyrinchium ...* of authors.

*Iris* is of the class and order *Triandria Monogynia*, and the characters are, Class and order in the Linnæan system.

1 CALYX For the calyx there are only a few permanent spathæ, which separate the flowers.

2 COROLLA is composed of six oblong petals, the outer are reflexed, the three interior are erect, and more acute, and all of them join at their base.

3 STAMINA are three subulated filaments lying on the outer petals, with oblong, flat, depressed antheræ.

4 PISTILLUM consists of an oblong germen placed below the flower, of a very short simple style, and of a very large stigma divided into three broad segments resembling petals.

5 PERICARPIUM is an oblong, angular capsule of three cells.

6 SEMINA The seeds are many and large.

CHAP.

## CHAP. CCLI.

## *ISOPYRUM.*

THERE are only three species of this genus. One is an annual, the others often continue three or four years, but seldom longer, and these are called

*Species*

1 Thalictroide *Isopyrum*, or Italian Meadow Rue.
2 Aquilegioide *Isopyrum*, or Mountain Columbine.

*Description of Thalictroide, and Aquilegioide Isopyrum*

1 Thalictroide *Isopyrum*, or Italian Meadow Rue. The leaves are composed of many small, smooth folioles, and much resemble those of *Thalictrum*, or Meadow Rue. The stalks are upright, smooth, and about four or five inches high. The flowers are produced from the tops of the stalks; their number is not great; they are of a white colour, have their petals obtuse, appear in March and April, and are succeeded by ripe seeds in May and June.

2 Aquilegioide *Isopyrum*, or Mountain Columbine. The leaves are nearly of the same composition with the flowers, but rather larger, and of a bright green colour. The stalks are upright, and about six inches high. Two or three flowers only come out from the tops of the stalks, which are small, and of a white colour; they appear in April, and the seeds ripen in June.

*Method of propagation*

These plants are propagated by sowing the seeds, soon after they are ripe, in a shady place. When they come up, they will require no trouble, except thinning them to proper distances, watering them in dry weather, and keeping them clean from weeds. The spring following [illegible] of them will flower, and the rest remain until the second spring before they exhibit their bloom. After they have flowered, the plants often die; but as they frequently continue three or four years, or longer, I thought proper to introduce them into this place, with this further consideration, that after they have once flowered and perfected their seeds fresh plants will spontaneously rise, so that though the old ones die, the succession will be kept up without any trouble, except the usual care of thinning them where they are too close, and keeping them clean from weeds. They will grow in any soil or situation, but delight most in the shade, and in moist places.

1 The first species is titled, *Isopyrum* [illegible] *ovatis, petalis obtusis*. Boccone calls it, [illegible]; Caspar Bauhine, *Ranunculus* [illegible]; and Clusius, *Ranunculus* [illegible]. It grows naturally on the mountainous parts of Italy and Germany.

2 The second species is, *Isopyrum* [illegible] *obsoletis*. Caspar Bauhine calls it, *Aquilegia montana*, [illegible]. It grows naturally on the Helvetian and Appennine mountains.

*Class and order in the Linnæan system*

*Isopyrum* is of the class and order *Polyandria Polygynia*, and the characters are,

1 CALYX. There is none.
2 COROLLA. There are five oval, equal, patent, deciduous petals, and five nectariums inserted in the receptacle, which are very short, equal, tubular, and divided at the top into three lobes, of which the outer one is the largest.
3 STAMINA are numerous capillary filaments, shorter than the corolla, having simple antheræ.
4 PISTILLUM. The germens are many and oval. The styles are simple and the length of the germens. The stigmas are obtuse, and of the same length as the stamina.
5 PERICARPIUM consists of many [illegible], recurved capsules, each containing one cell.
6 SEMINA. The seeds are many.

## CHAP. CCLII.

## *JUNCUS*, RUSH.

*Introduction*

THOUGH rushes cause no concern to many Gardeners, unless it be to destroy them, yet such Gardeners as have tasted the sweets of botanical knowledge, and made further advancements in the science, may be pleased to be acquainted with the different sorts of Rushes, even though their culture should never come into practice through the whole course of their works.

*Species*

The distinct species of this genus are,

1 Sea Hard Rush.
2 Round Headed Rush.
3 Common Soft Rush.
4 Hard Rush.
5 Least Soft Rush.
6 Trifid Rush.
7 Moss Rush, or Goose Corn.
8 Jointed Rush.

9 Nodose

9 Nodose Rush
10 Bulbose Rush
11 Toad Rush
12 Swedish Rush
13 Two-flowered Rush
14 Three-flowered Rush
15 Common Hairy Wood Rush or Grass.
16 Small Hairy Wood Rush
17 White Rush
18 Spiked Rush

Sea Hard Rush described. 1 Sea Hard Rush This species hath a thick, strong, clustered root, which strikes deep into the ground The stalk is naked, taper, sharp pointed, and three or four feet high The flowers come out in panicles from the tops of the stalks, having a prickly two-leaved involucrum, they appear in July, and are succeeded by oval, three-lobed, bright capsules, containing the seeds

Its uses This species is propagated in Holland, on the banks near the sea, to prevent the mould being washed away by the tide, which purpose it answers amazingly, the roots clotting together, sinking deep into the ground in those loose soils, and keeping them from being disturbed by the water These rushes, when full grown, are very hard, tough, and proper for ladies' work-baskets, for which use they are cut in Holland, dried, sold, and worked up

Description of Round headed, 2 Round headed Rush The root consists of numerous, long, thick brown fibres The stalks are round, slender, slightly striated, very pithy, and two or three feet high The flowers come out from the sides of the stalks in round, compact clusters or heads, they are numerous in the cluster, and of a pale brown colour when ripe

Common Soft, 3 Common Soft Rush The root is composed of numerous, thick, brown fibres The stalks are naked, smooth, shining, soft to the touch, full of pith, and about a yard high The flowers are produced from the sides of the stalks near the top, they are of a deep-brown colour, and shew themselves by the sides of waters almost every-where in the summer

and Hard Rush 4 Hard Rush The root is composed of many thick, brown, clotted fibres, which strike deep into the ground The stalks are naked, hard, rough, tough, two or three feet high, sharp-pointed membranaceous, and usually incurved at the top. The flowers come out in panicles from the sides of the stalks near the top, they are of a pale-brown colour, and appear great part of the summer

Its uses This rush being hard and tough, is proper for baskets, and the like purposes, and the roots matting and clotting together, are proper to secure banks from slight inundations, for which uses, I am informed, this species is often used like the first in Holland

Description of Least Soft, 5 Least Soft Rush The stalk is slender, soft, pithy, about a foot high, and usually drooping or bent at the top The flowers are produced in panicles from the sides of the stalk, nearer the bottom than the top, they are small, of a brown colour, appear in June and July and are succeeded by bright, three-sided capsules, containing plenty of ripe seeds, in August

Trifid, 6 Trifid Rush The stalk is slender, naked, pithy, about a foot high, sharp pointed, and reflexed On the top of the upright part of the stalk are situated three flowers, attended by three small, narrow leaves, they are of a pale-brown colour, appear in July, and the seeds ripen in August

Moss, 7 Moss Rush, or Goose Corn The fibres are long, slender, tough, and issue from a large thick head The leaves are numerous, hard, rough, and of a brown colour The flowers come out in small heads from the tops and sides of the stalks, they are brownish, glossy, appear in May and June, and the seeds ripen in July

8 Jointed Rush The root is composed of a multitude of long, slender, tough, spreading fibres The stalks are nodose, jointed, striated, compressed, and usually a foot and a half high The leaves are long, narrow, articulated, pointed, and grow singly at the joints The flowers come out in kind of umbels from the tops of the stalks, they are small, brownish, have their petals obtuse, appear in May and June, and are succeeded by long, awl-shaped, three-sided capsules, containing the seeds Jointed,

9 Nodose Rush The root is a cluster of long, slender, tough fibres The stalks are nodose, jointed, compressed, and about a foot and a half high The leaves are long, narrow, jointed, finely articulated, and grow singly at the joints The flowers are produced in roundish heads from the tops of the stalks, they are of a brownish colour, have sharp pointed petals, appear in June, and are succeeded by oval capsules containing the seeds Nodose,

10 Bulbose Rush The root is thick, dense, and creeping The stalks are slender, compressed, and about a foot and a half high The leaves are narrow, smooth, convex, furrowed on their under sides, and channelled on their upper The flowers are produced in roundish bunches from the ends of the stalks, they appear in May and June, and are succeeded by oval, obtuse, glossy, brown capsules containing the seeds Bulbose,

11 Toad Rush The root is composed of numerous narrow fibres, and generally dies as soon as the seeds are perfected The leaves are long, narrow, tough, and pliant The stalks are angular, forked, and grow only to about six or eight inches high The flowers come out singly from the sides of the branches, and sit close, having no footstalks, they are small and of a brown colour, appear in May and June, and are followed by ripe seeds in July and August and Toad Rush

Its varieties There is great variety of this species, differing in size, procerity, or one respect or other They are chiefly annual, or biennial, except one sort called the Creeping Toad Rush, which spreads itself about to a considerable distance

12 Swedish Rush This is a low elegant rush, growing in the marshy parts of Sweden The leaves are upright, narrow, awl-shaped, smooth, depressed, and six or eight inches long The stalks are round, simple, smooth, erect, and about the height of the leaves The flowers come out two or three together from the tops of the stalks The outer petals are narrow, acute, concave and purple on their outside, but the interior ones are of a pale brown colour The filaments are filiform, the antheræ yellow, the germen large, and the style white, and crowned by three reflexed stigmas They shew themselves the end of May and June, and are followed by oval, three-sided, bright, brown capsules, containing ripe seeds, in July and August Swedish,

13 Two-flowered Rush The leaves are awl-shaped, narrow, tough, and pliant The stalks are upright, smooth, and about a foot high At the top of each stalk is situated a glume containing two flowers, which shew themselves about the same time with the former Two flowered,

14 Three flowered Rush The leaves are flat narrow, and blunt pointed The stalks are upright, smooth, and six or eight inches high At the top of the stalk is situated a glume, containing three brown flowers Three flowered,

15 Common

Common Hairy Wood, 15 Common Hairy Wood Ruſh or Graſs The leaves are long, broad, flat, rough, and hairy The ſtalks are ſlender, rather taller than the leaves, and at the top divide into many branches, or rather footſtalks, for the ſupport of the flowers The flowers come out ſingly from the tops and alſo the ſides of theſe footſtalks, forming themſelves into roundiſh, thin, looſe bunches, they are of a reddiſh brown colour, and appear about the ſame time with the others

Small Hairy Wood, 16 Small Hairy Wood Ruſh The leaves are flat, pointed, rough, and hairy The ſtalks are ſlender, upright, and adorned about the middle with one ſmall, narrow, rough, hairy leaf The flowers come out in roundiſh heads from the tops and ſides of the ſtalks, they are of a browniſh colour, having yellow antheræ, and look very beautiful at the time of blow, which is in June

White, 17 White Ruſh The leaves are narrow, flat, and hairy The ſtalks are ſlender, round, and about a foot high The flowers come out in roundiſh bunches from the tops of the ſtalks, they are of a ſnowy-white colour, and very beautiful when in blow, which is in June

and Spiked Ruſh deſcribed 18 Spiked Ruſh The leaves are broad, flat, pointed, and riſe many together from the root The ſtalks are ſlender, about a foot and a half high, and divide at the top into ſeveral branches, each of which ſupports a ſpike of flowers Theſe are of a blackiſh brown colour, and appear about the ſame time with the former

Varieties Every one of theſe ſpecies admits of numerous varieties, moſt of which have been titled as diſtinct ſpecies by old botaniſts, as will be ſhewn with the titles

Propagation. If a perſon is deſirous of a plant or two of each ſort in his collection, to be at hand for obſervation, they may be propagated by parting the roots in the autumn, winter, or ſpring, or by ſowing the ſeeds ſoon after they are ripe But as Ruſhes in general are a nuiſance to the huſbandman, whoſe greateſt care is to deſtroy them, I propoſe mentioning the various ways of deſtroying them

Ruſhes are not always an indication of bad land I have known them in plenty in rich paſture grounds, growing chiefly in the furrows, and it is in ſuch lands as theſe that the huſbandman is ſo deſirous of deſtroying them, that the land may be better occupied with more uſeful herbage for his ſtock

Methods of deſtroying Ruſhes The firſt and moſt eaſy method of deſtroying Ruſhes is by conſtantly mowing them down as they ariſe In the whole vegetable world there are but few plants which may not be ſubdued by this inſult, they get weaker and weaker at every decapitation, till at length their roots being weary, and too weak to ſhoot out afreſh, they die, and the ground becomes cleared It is thus in a great meaſure with Ruſhes By mowing them down in the ſpring as they ariſe, and often repeating the mowing, they get weaker and weaker, though it is impoſſible wholly to deſtroy them this way in ſome ſoils where they naturally abound in great plenty

Another method of deſtroying Ruſhes is by ſowing pigeon-mulch moderately thick all over the place in the ſpring This will weaken them the firſt ſummer, but not kill them The repetition, therefore muſt be made the ſpring following, and the ſpring after that, and by conſtantly purſuing this method every year, in moſt ſoils, Ruſhes may be ſubdued, and the land improved

Lime ſown in this manner is ſtill of greater force to deſtroy Ruſhes Soot, alſo, and ſea coal aſhes have the ſame tendency, but in all of them the repetition muſt be annually made, and continued for many years before the ground can be cleared

Another method of deſtroying Ruſhes is by plucking them up by the roots Proper forks with ſharp tines ſet cloſe together, muſt be uſed for this purpoſe, and June and July are the beſt ſeaſon for the work The roots will then ſoon dry, and being laid in heaps and burnt, they become good manure to enrich thoſe places from whence they were taken Draw the roots up, however, as carefully as you can The ſpring following freſh plants will appear, ſo that this is a work which muſt be annually repeated for a long time before your ground can be wholly cleared from Ruſhes

In all theſe caſes the land muſt be drained, for this will give great aſſiſtance to any of the former practices The land alſo ſhould be duly and regularly rolled, and it will help to ſubdue them All theſe operations, jointly and ſeparately, muſt be more or leſs annually repeated ever after, for though the ground ſhould appear perfectly cleared of them, yet in a little time they will riſe afreſh, and no human induſtry can make the interval of their diſappearing permanent in ſuch places where nature deſigned them to grow

1 Sea Hard Ruſh is titled, *Juncus culmo ſubnudo tereti mucronato, panicula terminali, involucro diphyllo ſpinoſo* Sauvages calls it, *Juncus culmo pungente, paniculâ ex foliis ſolitarii axilla*, Guettard, *Juncus paniculâ univerſali culmo breviore infime coarcta, ſecundariis partialium laxis, capſulis triquetro-ſubovatis nitentibus*, alſo, *Juncus panicula univerſali culmo longiore, ſecundariis laxis longe pedunculatis, media precipua* Caſpar Bauhine names it, *Juncus acutus, capitulis ſorghi*, John Bauhine, *Juncus parvus cum pericarpiis rotundis*, and Ray, *Juncus acutus maritimus Anglicus* It grows naturally in wet marſhy places on the ſea ſhores in England, France, and Italy Titles.

2 Round headed Ruſh is, *Juncus culmo nudo ſtricto, capitulo laterali* Caſpar Bauhine calls it, *Juncus lævis, paniculâ non ſparſâ*, Scheuchzer, *Juncus lævis, paniculâ conglomeratâ*, Ray, *Juncus lævis vulgaris paniculâ compactiore*, Lobel, *Juncus lævis glomerato flore*, and Cammerarius, *Juncus* It grows naturally in moiſt meadows and paſtures in England and moſt of the northern countries of Europe

3 Common Soft Ruſh is, *Juncus culmo nudo ſtricto, panicula laterali* In the *Flora Lapponica* it is termed, *Juncus culmo nudo acuminato ad baſin ſquamato, floribus ſeſſilibus*, alſo, *Juncus culmo nudo acuminato ad baſin ſquamato, floribus pedunculatis* Scheuchzer names it, *Juncoides Alpinum, floſculis junci conglomeratis atro-fuſcis*, Caſpar Bauhine, *Juncus lævis, paniculâ ſparſa, major*, Ray, *Juncus lævis vulgaris paniculâ ſparſa noſtras*, Dodonæus, Gerard, &c *Juncus lævis* It grows naturally by the ſides of waters in England and moſt parts of Europe

4 Hard Ruſh is, *Juncus culmo nudo, apice membranaceo incurvato, paniculâ laterali* Sauvages calls it, *Juncus culmo nudo, paniculam arcuatim tegente*, Guettard, *Juncus paniculâ univerſali laterali culmo longiore, ſecundariis ſparſis*, and Caſpar Bauhine, *Juncus, acumine reflexo, major*, alſo, *Juncus, acumine reflexo, alter*, alſo, *Juncus acutus, paniculâ ſparſâ* It grows naturally in paſtures and by way ſides, &c in England and moſt parts of Europe

5 Leaſt Soft Ruſh is, *Juncus culmo nudo filiformi nutante, panicula laterali* Caſpar Bauhine calls it, *Juncus lævis, paniculâ ſparſâ, minor*, Ray, *Juncus parvus, calamo ſupra paniculam longius*

*gins prominulo.* It grows naturally in marshy, turfy, boggy places on the sides and tops of the mountains in England and most parts of Europe.

6. Trifid Rush is, *Juncus culmo trifido, foliis* [illegible] *tribus.* Caspar Bauhine calls it, *Juncus, acumine reflexo, minor & trifidus,* and Scheuchzer, *Juncus* [illegible] *trifidum.* It grows naturally on the alpine parts of Lapland, Helvetia, and the Pyrenees.

7. Moss Rush or Goose Corn, is, *Juncus culmo* [illegible]*, foliis setaceis, capitulis glomeratis aphyllis.* Van Royen calls it, *Juncus foliis setaceis, culmo nudo, capitulis glomeratis terminalibus.* Ray, *Juncus montanus palustris.* Caspar Bauhine, *Gramen junceum, foliis & spica junci,* and Lobel, *Gramen junceum, folio* [illegible]. It grows naturally in heathy, rushy places, in England, and most of the northern countries of Europe.

8. Jointed Rush is, *Juncus foliis nodoso-articulatis, petalis obtusis.* Van Royen calls it, *Juncus foliis articulosis, panicula inaequali, capitulis* [illegible]*, capsulis* [illegible]*.* [illegible] *foliis articulosis floribus umbellatis,* Caspar Bauhine, *Gramen junceum, folio articulato, aquaticum,* also, *Gramen junceum, folio articulato sylvaticum,* also, *Gramen junceum, folio articulato, cum* [illegible]*.* Scheuchzer names it, *Juncus Alpinus, folio articuloso,* and Micheli, *Juncus foliosus, foliis* [illegible] *nodosis.* It grows naturally in woods, moist pastures and meadows, in England, and most countries of Europe.

9. Nodose Rush is, *Juncus foliis nodoso articulatis, petalis mucronatis.* Gronovius calls it, *Juncus foliosus minor, pericarpiis ovatis, Americanus,* Plukenet, *Gramen junceum elatius, pericarpiis ovatis,* and Morison, *Gramen junceum Virginianum, calyculis paleaceis* [illegible]*.* It is a native of North-America.

10. Bulbose Rush is, *Juncus foliis* [illegible] *canaliculatis, capsulis obtusis.* Van Royen calls it, *Juncus foliis angulatis, culmo* [illegible]*, panicula terminali proliferа, capsulis ovatis,* Gronovius, *Juncus foliis linearibus canaliculato concavis, capsulis triangularibus,* Morison, *Gramen junceum junci* [illegible] *panicula,* Barrelier, *Juncus repens* [illegible] *minor,* Caspar Bauhine, *Gramen junceum, foliis & spica junci,* and John Bauhine, *Juncus parvus cum pericarpiis rotundis.* It grows naturally in heathy, moist, sterile pastures, and by way-sides in England, and most parts of Europe.

11. Hairy Rush is, *Juncus culmo dichotomo, foliis angulatis, floribus solitariis sessilibus.* In the *Flora Lapponica* it is termed, *Juncus palustris* [illegible]*, panicula laxissima.* Scheuchzer calls it, *Gramen nemorosum, calyculis paleaceis, repens,* also, *Gramen nemorosum, calyculis paleaceis,* [illegible]*,* also, *Gramen* [illegible]*, calyculis paleaceis, spicatum* [illegible]*.* Caspar Bauhine names it, *Gramen nemorosum, calyculis paleaceis,* also, *Gramen hirsutum* [illegible] *minimum.* Barrelier takes it, *Gramen* [illegible] *angustifolium majus,* Ray, *Gramen junceum* [illegible] *Anglo-Britannicum,* and Lobel, *Holosteum.* It grows naturally in meadows, pastures, and wet places in England, and most parts of Europe.

12. Swedish Rush is, *Juncus foliis setaceis depressis* [illegible]*, pedunculis geminis terminalibus,* [illegible] *solitariis subbifloris.* It grows naturally in woods and marshy places in Sweden.

13. Two flowered Rush is, *Juncus folio subulato, glumis bifloris terminalis.* It grows naturally on the Alps of Lapland.

14. Three-flowered Rush is, *Juncus foliis* [illegible]*, glumis trifloris terminalibus.* In the *Flora Lapponica* it is termed, *Juncus* [illegible] *terminante.* Caspar Bauhine calls it, [illegible]. It grows naturally on the Alps of Lapland.

15. Common Hairy Wood Rush or Grass is, *Juncus foliis planis pilosis, corymbo ramoso.* In the *Flora Lapponica* it is termed, *Juncus foliis planis, culmo paniculato, floribus sparsis.* Van Royen calls it, *Juncus foliis planis, pedunculis* [illegible]*.* Caspar Bauhine, *Gramen nemorosum hirsutum latifolium majus,* also, *Gramen hirsutum* [illegible] *majus.* Barrelier names it, *Gramen luzulae angustifolium* [illegible]*,* Scheuchzer, *Gramen hirsutum nemorosum angustifolium,* [illegible] also, *Gramen nemorosum hirsutum* [illegible]*,* Morison, *Gramen hirsutum* [illegible]*, vulgare.* It grows naturally in woods in England and most parts of Europe.

16. Small Hairy Wood Rush is, *Juncus foliis planis subpilosis, spicis* [illegible] *pedunculatis.* In the *Hortus Cliffortianus* it is termed, *Juncus foliis planis, panicula* [illegible]*,* in the *Flora Lapponica,* [illegible] *planis,* [illegible]*,* Caspar Bauhine calls it, *Gramen hirsutum,* [illegible] also, *Gramen hirsutum, capitulo* [illegible]*.* Scheuchzer names it, [illegible] also, *Junco ides* [illegible]*, capitulo glomerato,* also, *Junco ides latifolium* [illegible] *glabratum, panicula sub luteo splendente.* Tournefort calls it, *Juncus* [illegible]*, capitulis* [illegible]*,* Micheli, *Juncus* [illegible] *nemorosum villosum* [illegible]*, capitulis floribus candidis &* [illegible]*,* also *Junco ides Bohemicum, panicula* [illegible]*,* [illegible] *tendente* [illegible]*,* and Ray, *Gramen hirsutum* [illegible]*, panicula junceа compacta.* It grows naturally in meadows and pastures in England and most parts of Europe.

17. White Rush is, *Juncus foliis planis subpilosis, corymbis* [illegible]*, floribus fasciculatis.* Haller calls it, *Juncus foliis planis angustissimis, panicula* [illegible]*, floribus longioribus albis,* Scheuchzer, *Juncus montanum nemorosum, flore* [illegible]*,* and Caspar Bauhine, *Gramen hirsutum angustifolium* [illegible]*, panicula* [illegible]*.* It grows naturally on the Bohemian, Helvetian, and Rhetian mountains, also in the South of France.

18. Spiked Rush is, *Juncus foliis planis, spica racemosa nutante.* Haller calls it, *Juncus Alpinus latifolius, panicula racemosa nigricante pendula.* It grows naturally on the Lapland Alps.

*Juncus* is of the class and order *Hexandria Monogynia*, and the characters are, Class and order in the Linnaean system.

1. CALYX. The glume is composed of two valves. The perianthium consists of six oblong, acuminated, permanent leaves.

2. COROLLA. There is none. The coloured leaves of the calyx nearly resemble and are often taken for the corolla.

3. STAMINA are six very short capillary filaments, having oblong erect antherae the length of the perianthium.

4. PISTILLUM consists of a triquetrous, acuminated germen, a short filiform style, and three long, slender, hairy, reflexed stigmas.

5. PERICARPIUM is a covered, three-cornered, trivalvate capsule containing one cell.

6. SEMINA. The seeds are few, and roundish.

# CHAP. CCLIII.

## IXIA.

THE ſpecies of the *Ixia* are moſt of them tender plants, and there are only two that I know of which will do for the perennial flower garden. They are,

[Species.] 1. The Italian *Ixia*.

2. The Chineſe *Ixia*.

[Deſcription of the Italian Ixia.] 1. The Italian *Ixia* has all along, until of late, been taken for a crocus, and was ranked as a ſpecies only of that genus by Linnæus in his earlier works. The root is a ſmall browniſh bulb, and from this iſſue ſeveral narrow leaves. The flower-ſtalk is exceeding ſhort, and ſupports a ſingle flower; it is large, and very much like a crocus. There are varieties of it, viz. the pale blue with a white bottom, the variegated, and the white. [Its varieties.]

[The Chineſe deſcribed.] 2. The Chineſe *Ixia*. This is a tall growing plant, and will riſe to about two feet high. The root is tuberous, knotty, and ſends forth many fibres. The leaves are enſiform, and will be more than a foot long; they have ſeveral longitudinal ribs, and embrace the ſtalk with their baſe. The flower-ſtalk is ſmooth, firm, and jointed, and will grow to two feet high, or more. Near the top it divides into ſmaller branches, between which is placed a ſingle flower on a longiſh footſtalk. The branches alſo divide again in the like dichotomous manner, and each is crowned by a flower. Theſe flowers are large, each being compoſed of ſix equal petals; their ground colour is yellow, which is moſt elegantly ſpotted with orange colour. They will be in blow in July, and ſometimes bring their ſeeds to maturity in the autumn.

[Method of propagating them.] Both theſe ſorts are eaſily propagated by parting of the roots. The time for the firſt ſort is in ſummer on the decay of the leaves; and for the latter in the autumn, when the flower-ſtalks begin to die away. The firſt ſpecies is very hardy, and will grow in any ſoil or ſituation; but the other is rather tender, and muſt have a warm dry border in a well-ſheltered place, otherwiſe it will be deſtroyed by the ſeverity of our froſts in the winter.

[Method of raiſing them by ſeed.] By ſeeds alſo the Chineſe *Ixia* is ſometimes propagated. Theſe ſhould be ſown in the ſpring, on a good hot-bed. As they come up, they muſt have as much free air as poſſible, to prevent their drawing weak. All ſummer they muſt have frequent watering, and weeding muſt be conſtantly obſerved. In the autumn the plants ſhould be taken up, and ſet in pots filled with good, light, freſh mould. At the approach of bad weather, they ſhould be placed in the green-houſe, or under a hot-bed frame, but ſhould be conſtantly ſet abroad again as the weather gets mild. In the ſpring they ſhould be turned out of the pots, with the mould at the roots, into the like well-prepared warm border as was directed for the offſets.

[Titles.] 1. The Italian *Ixia* is titled, *Ixia ſcapo unifloro breviſſimo, foliis linearibus*. Tournefort calls it, *Bulbocodium crocifolium, flore magno allo fundo luteo*. It grows naturally on the Alps of Italy.

2. The Chineſe *Ixia*. This ſpecies is titled, *Ixia foliis enſiformibus, floribus remotis, panicula dichotoma, floribus pedunculatis*. Amman calls it, *Bermudiana radice carnoſa, floribus maculatis, ſeminibus piſiformibus obductis*. It grows naturally in India.

[Claſs and order in the Linnæan ſyſtem. The character.] *Ixia* is of the claſs and order *Triandria Monogynia*; and the characters are,

1. CALYX. For the calyx there are oblong, permanent ſpathæ, which encloſe the germen.

2. COROLLA conſiſts of ſix oblong, equal, ſpear-ſhaped petals.

3. STAMINA conſiſt of three ſubulated filaments ſhorter than the corolla, and ſituated at equal diſtances, with ſimple antheræ.

4. PISTILLUM conſiſts of an oval, three-cornered germen placed below the receptacle of the flower, a ſingle erect ſtyle the length of the ſtamina, and a thick trifid ſtigma.

5. PERICARPIUM is a roundiſh, three-cornered capſule of three cells.

6. SEMINA. The ſeeds are roundiſh.

# CHAP. CCLIV

## *LAMIUM*, DEAD-NETTLE, or ARCH-ANGEL

Species

THE perennials of this genus are,

1 White Dead-Nettle, or Arch-angel
2 Italian Dead-Nettle
3 Siberian Dead Nettle
4 Garganean Dead-Nettle
5 Hungarian Dead-Nettle

Description of the White Dead Nettle

1 White Dead Nettle, or Arch-angel The root is white and creeping The stalks are square, partly procumbent, and a foot and a half or two feet long The leaves are heart-shaped, oblong, pointed, rough, serrated, and grow opposite to each other on footstalks The flowers come out in whorls from the joints the whole length of the stalk, they are of a fine white colour, appear the greatest part of the summer, but in May they are in the best bloom

This is a well known and troublesome weed in gardens, and is mentioned here only to exercise the Botanist in his studies, and recommend a plant for his inspection, the due observation of which will greatly familiarize him to the nature of the characters of the class and order to which it belongs

Medicinal properties

This species is used in medicine, a conserve is made of the flowers, which also when distilled afford a liquor of a very wholesome and exhilarating nature

Italian,

2 Italian Dead-Nettle The stalks are square, jointed, partly procumbent, and about a foot and a half long The leaves are heart-shaped, pointed, grow opposite by pairs, and are of a light-green colour on the borders, but white in the middle The flowers grow in whorls, five on one side and five on the other, at the joints, almost the whole length of the stalks, they are of a purple colour, appear in May, often continue in succession the greatest part of the summer, and the seeds ripen in plenty

Siberian,

3 Siberian Dead-Nettle The stalks are smooth, square, of a purplish colour, and often two feet long The leaves are heart-shaped, rough, serrated, and grow opposite to each other at the joints The flowers grow in whorls, consisting of about four or five on each side, at the joints, the whole length of the stalk, they are of a red colour, and appear about the same time with the former

Garganean

4 Garganean Dead-Nettle The stalks are thick, square, and about a foot high The leaves are heart-shaped, hairy, obtuse, and grow opposite to each other on longish footstalks The flowers come out in whorls, many together, at a joint, almost the whole length of the stalks, they are of a pale-purple colour, appear in May, and continue in succession all summer Ripe seeds of this species may be gathered in July

and Hungarian Dead Nettle

5 Hungarian Dead Nettle The stalks are thick, square, jointed, and two feet high The leaves are heart-shaped, unequally serrated, and grow opposite by pairs at the joints The flowers surround the stalks at the joints, they are large, of a fine purple colour, appear in May and June, and, like the others, often continue to shew themselves throughout the whole summer The seeds of this species ripen in our gardens

Culture

These sorts are all propagated by parting of the roots, the best time for which is the autumn, that they may have time to take to the ground before the winter comes on, and be in condition for shooting up early the spring following They are hardy, and will grow in almost any soil or situation, but they delight most in the shade, and a rich, light, fresh earth

They are also propagated by seeds, which should be sown in a shady border If dry weather happens, the beds should be every third evening watered, and this will soon bring up the plants, at which time they should be thinned where they appear too close, and be cleared from weeds

During the remaining part of the summer, if dry weather happens, they should be watered every other evening, the weeds duly drawn out as they arise, and by the autumn some of the largest plants will be fit to remove, but the others should remain until the spring, let, therefore, some of the largest plants be drawn out, and removed to their proper places, and in the spring let the rest be transplanted to the respective situations designed for them Many will flower the autumn following and the weakest plants will exhibit their bloom in full perfection the May following

The Gardener need not be told, that this culture respects the last four sorts, nor be reminded with regard to the first, that when it has got possession of his garden, he should be careful to pick out the least parts of the root, when digging the ground, for every bit of it will grow, and what trouble does this plant, as well as Couch-Grass, afford, when it gets into the roots of other trees, and entangles itself with their fibres?

Titles

1 White Dead Nettle, or Arch-angel, is titled, *Lamium foliis cordatis acuminatis petiolatis, verticillis vigintifloris* Caspar Bauhine calls it, *Lamium album non fœtens, folio oblongo*, Gerard, *Lamium album*, Parkinson, *Lamium vulgare album, sive Archangelicum flore albo*, and Camerarius, *Galeopsis* It grows naturally under old walls, among rubbish, &c but its chief delight is in neglected gardens, and in such places it thrives amazingly, in England, and most countries of Europe

2 Italian Dead-Nettle is *Lamium foliis cordatis acuminatis, verticillis decemfloris* Caspar Bauhine calls it, *Lamium albâ lineâ notatum*, also, *Lamium maculatum*, and Columna, *Lamium Plinii* [illegible] It is a native of Italy

3 Siberian Dead Nettle is, *Lamium foliis cordatis rugosis, caule* [illegible]*, calycibus glabris longitudine corollæ* Plukenet calls it, *Lamium purpureum fœtidum, folio parvo acuminato, flore majore*, Boccone, *Lamium* [illegible] *rugoso folio, flore rubro*, Caspar Bauhine, *Lamium purpureum non fœtens, folio oblongo*, and John Bauhine, *Galeopsis flore purpurascente majore, folio non maculato* It grows naturally in Italy and Siberia

4 Garganean Dead Nettle is *Lamium foliis cordatis pubescentibus*, [illegible] In the Memoirs of the Royal Academy at Paris it is termed *Lamium* [illegible] It is called *Lamium* Garganicum

*Garganicum suoincanum, flore purpurascente labio superiore crenulato* It grows naturally on Mount Gargan in Italy

5 Hungarian Dead-Nettle is, *Lamium foliis cordatis inæqualiter argutè serratis, corollis fauce inflatâ, calyce colorata* Caspar Bauhine calls it, *Lamium maximum sylvaticum alterum*, Tilli, *Lamium montanum saxatile fermè glabrum, flore amplo purpureo labio inferiore crenulato*, and Clusius, *Galeopsis maxima Pannonica* It grows naturally in Pannonia and Italy

Class and order in the Linnæan system The characters

*Lamium* is of the class and order *Didynamia Gymnospermia*, and the characters are,

1 CALYX is a monophyllous, tubular, permanent perianthium, cut at the top into five segments, which are bearded, and nearly equal

2 COROLLA is one ringent petal The tube is cylindrical, and very short The limb is gaping The mouth is inflated, globous, and compressed, being dentated on each side The upper lip is arched, roundish, obtuse, and entire The lower lip is short, obcordated, indented, and reflexed

3 STAMINA are four awl-shaped filaments situated under the upper lip, of which two are longer than the others, having oblong hairy antheræ

4 PISTILLUM consists of a quadrifid germen, a filiforme style [illegible] and an acute bifid stigma

5 PERICARPIUM There is none The seeds are lodged in the calyx

6 SEMINA [illegible] are four, short, triquetrous, and convex on one side

# CHAP CCLV

## *LASERPITIUM*, LASER-WORT

ALL the species of this genus are hardy perennials, and go by the respective names of,

Species

1 Broad leaved Laser-Wort
2 Trilobate Laser-Wort
3 Great Laser-Wort
4 Narrow leaved Laser-Wort
5 Daucoide Laser-Wort
6 Mountain *Siler*
7 Peucedanoide Laser Wort
8 Oriental Laser-Wort
9 Montpelier Laser-Wort

Description of the Broad leaved,

1 Broad-leaved Laser Wort The root is thick, white, and strikes deep into the ground The radical leaves are large, and composed of numerous folioles, which are heart shaped, cut on their edges, of a light green colour on their upper side, and bluish underneath The stalk is round, striated, firm, branching, and adorned with leaves, which are placed alternately at the joints The flowers come out from the tops of the plant in very broad umbels, each separate flower is small, and of a white colour, they appear in June and July and are succeeded by beautiful membranaceous seeds, which will be ripe in September The whole plant is full of an acrid juice, which flowing, turns to a resinous substance

Trilobate,

2 Trilobate Laser-Wort This hath a thick root, which strikes deep into the ground The radical leaves are large, grow on long footstalks, and spread themselves on the ground The folioles of which they are composed are moderately broad, obtuse, and each is divided into three lobes, which are cut or jagged at the ends they are of a pale-green colour, and the whole leaf is acrid to the taste, and not unlike those of the Colombine, but larger The stalks are upright, firm, branching, and three or four feet high The flowers come out from the ends and sides of the branches in flat umbels, each separate flower is small, and of a whitish colour, they appear in June and July, and the seeds ripen in August and September

Great,

3 Great Laser-Wort The root is thick, fungous, greyish on the outside, white within, and when broken emits an agreeable odour The radical leaves are large and spreading, each is composed of numerous wedge-shaped folioles, which are of a light green colour, and divided into several parts at the top The stalks are round, firm, striated, grow to be six or eight feet high, and are garnished with a few leaves, which grow alternately at the joints The flowers come out from the ends and sides of the branches in large umbels, each flower is moderately large and of a white or yellow colour, they appear in July, and are succeeded by yellowish membranaceous seeds, which ripen in September The juice of this plant turns to a very acrimonious gummy substance

Narrow leaved,

4 Narrow-leaved Laser Wort The root is thick, fungous, white within and extends itself to a considerable distance The radical leaves grow on long footstalks, which being unable to support them in an upright position, the lower ones lie on the ground, the folioles are spear shaped, entire, and of a light green colour The stalks are round, striated, hollow, branching, and four or five feet high The flowers come out in umbels from the tops of the plant, they are moderately large, appear about the same time with the former, and the seeds ripen accordingly This species also is replete with acrimonious matter

and Daucoide Laser Wort

5 Daucoide Laser Wort The radical leaves are composed of numerous spear shaped, entire folioles, and much resemble those of Wild Carrot, they grow on long weak footstalks, and spread themselves to a considerable distance on the ground The stalks are striated, angular, branching, four or five feet high, and adorned with leaves, which grow alternately at the joints The flowers come out in umbels like the former, and are succeeded by villous, downy, membranaceous seeds, which ripen in September

Mountain Siler

6 Mountain *Siler* The radical leaves are large, spreading, and composed of numerous oval,

ov , ipen th , on stalks, which h ne entire, and grow to rot ttu s The h k e o m l itr d, i or ning thice or four feet high, and a rned w th a te v l es growing th t t is nice he i unca one cut in ller . The flowers come out in u t umbels f on he top of the plant, they appear about the same time with the others, and the seeds ripen accordingly.

Pe ce da no us, 7 Peucedanoide Laser-Wort. The radical leaves are com of the many narrow, spear-shaped, veined, and distinct foloboles, g e on long foot-stalks and the under ones lie on the g o t . The a re upright firm branching, and four or five feet high. The flowers come out in umbels, like the others, they appear about the same time, and the seeds ripen accordingly.

O ental 8 Oriental Laser-Wort. The leaves are compound in a very beautiful manner, the folioles narrow, ... but very elegant. The stalk is upright, firm ..., and five or six feet high. The flowers come out in large umbels from the top of the plant in July, and are succeeded by flat ... seeds, which ripen in the autumn.

... M ... described 9 Montpelier Laser-Wort. The leaves are heart-shaped, hairy, obtuse, ... over hairy foot-stalks, and constitute a ... not much unlike that of one sort of Parsnep. The stalks are upright round, jointed, and garnished with leaves at ... The flowers are produced in umbels about the same time with the other sorts, and the seeds ripen about six weeks after the flowers are fallen.

All these sorts were formerly used in medicine, but are now in a great measure out of request.

Culture There are numerous varieties of all these species, and even the same sort will vary by culture, and the soil which it is made to inhabit; some of them growing two or three feet taller in a rich suitable earth, than they will in a ... or in opposite nature. The roots of all these plants are large, and strike deep into the ground, which teaches us that the ground for their reception should be double dug. In the autumn therefore, when the seeds are ripe, let a piece of ground, in a rich light part of the garden, be prepared by double digging, the surface made smooth, and the whole trodden up, ... sow the seeds in patches at a yard distance from each other; place a stick at each patch for a direction, and leave them until the spring. In the spring the plants will come up, and with them plenty of weeds; these must be drawn out, and soon after all the plants, except one, being the strongest, by each stick; for if the ground is good, and double-dug in the manner it ought, the plants should not be nearer than one yard distance from each other. The crown plants may be removed to another situation, but if there is room for it at first, all the plants should be raised from seeds in the places where they are designed to remain; for the roots being large and long, are frequently broken or damaged by transplanting. Besides, should they suffer but little that way, yet it ... a check to the plants, and a removed plant hardly ever grows to the size, or is so luxuriant and beautiful as those which have never been removed. Indeed this is in great the case with most plants that have thick roots, which extend far and strike deep into the earth.

The weakest plants being taken away, and one the strongest, only left at each stick, our beds are furnished with unremoved plants growing at a yard distance from each other. All summer they must be kept clean from weeds, and in the autumn the ground between the rows must be dug. The summer following the plants will flower, and perfect their seeds, soon after which the stalks die down to the ground, and fresh ones arise again in the spring. In every autumn, therefore, let the stalks be cut up close to the roots, the ground between the rows be dug, and the beds ... up. In every summer let the weeds be ... up as they arise, and a repetition of these respective articles annually is the true culture of these plants, and all the trouble they will require.

Though a yard is ordered to be the distance of these plants, it must be understood as a medium only, the largest sorts should be four feet asunder, whilst two feet, or two feet and a half, will be a sufficient distance for the smaller ...

1 Broad-leaved Laser-Wort is titled, *Laserpitium foliis cordatis ... inciso-serratis*. Caspar Bauhine calls it, *Libanotis latifolia altera, ...*, ... *Laserpitium* ..., and Dodonaeus, ... It grows naturally in Germany, and many parts of Europe. Titles

2 Trilobate Laser-Wort is, *Laserpitium foliis ... trilobis ...* Van Royen calls it, *Angelica ... foliis superioribus ...*, and Caspar Bauhine, *Libanotis latifolia ...*, ... It grows naturally on Mount Gargan.

3 Great Laser-Wort is, *Laserpitium foliis ... integerrimis ...*. In the *Hortus Cliffort.* it is termed, *Laserpitium foliolis ... aequalibus*. Van Royen calls it, *Laserpitium foliolis ... sessilibus ...* Caspar Bauhine, *Laserpitium Gallicum*, John Bauhine *Laserpitium, ...*, and Ray, *Laserpitium ... angustifoliis ... latitudine ... dissectis*. It grows naturally in most of the southern parts of Europe.

4 Narrow-leaved Laser-Wort is, *Laserpitium foliolis lanceolatis integerrimis sessilibus*. Morison calls it, *Laserpitium ... angustifolium ...*, and Haller, *Laserpitium foliis ... petiolis oppositis*. It is a native of the southern parts of Europe.

5 Dauco Laser-Wort is *Laserpitium foliolis lanceolatis ...* Van Royen calls it, *Laserpitium foliis ... patentissimis*, Breynius, *Laserpitium ...*, and Rivinus, *Laserpitium ...* It grows naturally in several parts of Germany.

6 Mountain Siler is, *Laserpitium foliolis ovato-lanceolatis integerrimis petiolatis*. Caspar Bauhine calls it, *Ligusticum ... foliis ...*, and Matthiolus, *Siler montanum*. It grows naturally in France, Austria, and Helvetia.

7 Peucedanoide Laser-Wort is, *Laserpitium foliolis linearibus ...*. ... calls it, *Laserpitium ... segmentis ...*, and Plukenet, *Laserpitium ... integris*. It grows naturally in ... Mount Baldo.

8 Oriental Laser-Wort is, *Laserpitium ...*. Tournefort calls it, *Cachrys orientalis, ... foliis ... plano*. It grows naturally in the East.

9 Montpelier Laser-Wort is, *Laserpitium foliolis obliquis cordatis, ... hispidis*. Morison calls it, ..., Caspar Bauhine, *P... folio*, and Dodonaeus ... It grows naturally ...

*Laserpitium* is of the class and order *Pentandria Digynia*, and the characters are,

1 Calyx. The general umbel is ..., and the number of rays, of which it is composed, is from twenty to forty. The partial ... The general involucrum ... leaves. The proper perianthium is small, and indented in five parts. The character

2 COROLLA The general flower is uniform, and each floret has five inflexed, heart shaped, patent petals that are nearly equal

3 STAMINA are five setose filaments the length of the corolla, having simple antheræ

4 PISTILLUM consists of a roundish germen situated below the flowers, and two thick, acuminated, distant styles, with obtuse patent stigmas

5 PERICARPIUM There is none The fruit is oblong, separable into two parts, and angular, with eight longitudinal membranes

6 SEMINA The seeds are two, large, oblong, semicylindrical, plane on one side, and on the back and edges ornamented with four membranes

## CHAP CCLVI

## *LATHRÆA*

Species

THE species of this genus are,

1 *Squamaria*, or Great Tooth-Wort
2 *Anblatum*
3 *Phelypæa*
4 *Clandestina*

Squamaria described

1 *Squamaria*, or Great Tooth Wort The root is thick, spreading, and composed of a multitude of thick succulent scales which lie over each other The stalk is upright, simple thick, tender, succulent, brittle, surrounded by a thin skin, and four or five inches high The leaves are small, roundish, thick, and a few of them come out from the lower parts of the stalks The flowers ornament the tops of the stalks a great way down, all hanging one way, they are of a whitish purple colour, and appear in May and June

Variety

There is a variety of this species with reddish flowers

Anblatum,

2 *Anblatum* The root is composed of a multitude of thick fleshy fibres The stalk is upright thick, soft, four or five inches high, and covered with a thin brown skin The leaves are short, brown, fleshy, and four or five only are found on each stalk The flowers come out in spikes from the tops of the stalks, they are of a dusky-brown or purplish colour, appear in June, and often continue to shew themselves until the end of August

and Phelypæa described

3 *Phelypæa* The root is fleshy, white, and tender The stalks are simple, thick, brittle, and four or five inches high The leaves are small, and appear in membranes on the lower parts of the stalks The flowers adorn the top in kind of spikes, they are bell shaped, spreading, of a yellow colour, and appear in May and June

Variety

There is a variety of this species with scarlet flowers

Clandestina described

4 *Clandestina* The stalks are thick, and divide into a few branches even lower than the surface of the ground The flowers come out singly from the ends of the branches, growing erect just above the soil, they are moderately large, of a purple colour, and shew themselves in May and June

Varieties

There are several varieties of this species, the stalks of some growing higher out of the ground than others, some have no leaves, others a few leaves that are heart shaped, the flowers of some are blue, others purple, and some again have a mixture of purple and blue

Culture

I have not yet propagated any of the species of this genus, but I make no doubt that if the roots, with the contiguous mould, were taken up and planted in a light rich soil, in a shady place, they would grow, and shew their flowers the summer following nay it is, I think, past all probability, that even those species which are of foreign growth taken up in the same manner, and planted in pots, might be brought over to England, and then turned out of the pots with the mould at the roots into the places where they are designed to remain which should be in a light airy earth, shaded with trees of any sort

Titles

1 Squamaria or Great Tooth-wort, is titled, *Lathræa caule simplicissimo, corollis pendulis, labio inferiore trifido* Caspar Bauhine calls it, *Orobanche radice dentata major*, John Bauhine, *Anblatum cordi sive Aphyllon* and Mentzelius *Orobanche aphyllos radice squamosa, foliis et floribus clandestinis* It grows naturally in shady woods and lawns in England, and most of the colder parts of Europe

2 *Anblatum* is, *Lathræa caule simplicissimo* ... Tournefort calls it, *Anblatum* ... *flore purpureo* It grows naturally in the East

3 *Phelypæa* is, *Lathræa corollis* ... Morison calls it, *Orobanche* ... *Phelypæa Lusitanica* ... *flore coccineo* It grows naturally in the shady parts of Portugal

4 *Clandestina* is, *Lathræa caule ramoso subterraneo, floribus* ... Gerard calls it *Lathræa* ... Tournefort, *Clandestina flore subcæruleo*, Ray, *D*... *purpureo* ... *ramosa, flore purpureo* Caspar Bauhine, *Orobanche* ... Morison, *Orobanche* ... and Dalechamp, *Dentaria* ... It grows naturally in shady places in Italy, France, and the Pyrenean mountains

Class and order in the Linnæan system

*Lathræa* is of the class and order *Didynamia Angiospermia*, and the characters are,

The characters

1 CALYX is a monophyllous, bell shaped, strait, permanent, deeply cut at the brim into four parts

2 COROLLA is one ringent petal The tube is longer than the calyx The upper lip is concave, galeated, and broad but narrow and crooked at the point The lower lip is less, reflexed obtuse,

tube, and cut into three segments. The nectarium is a very short emarginated gland, depressed on both sides, and inserted in the receptacle.

3. STAMINA are four awl-shaped filaments the length of the corolla, having oblate, depressed, connivent antheræ.

4. PISTILLUM consists of a globose compressed germen, a filiforme style the length and situation of the stamina, and a truncated stigma.

5. PERICARPIUM is a roundish, elastick, obtuse but pointed capsule, formed of two valves, containing one cell, and covered with the large patent calyx.

6. SEMINA. The seeds are few, and roundish.

## CHAP. CCLVII.

## LATHYRUS, CHICKLING-VETCH.

THE most noted perennial species of this genus, and which best deserves propagating in a garden, is,

1. The Broad-leaved Everlasting Pea.

Broad-leaved Everlasting Pea described. This hath a thick membranaceous stalk, which will grow to be eight or ten feet long. The claspers are attended by two leaves, which are spear-shaped, and terminate the midrib. By the help of these claspers it climbs above bushes, and has a delightful effect in gardening, for the flowers are numerous, large, and of a red or purple colour; they grow many together on long foot-stalks, and show themselves at the tops of trees at a great distance. Neither does the worth of this plant wholly center in the fineness of the flowers; their long continuance in beauty also enhances its value; for it will begin flowering sometimes in June, and continue the succession of blow through July, August, September, October, and sometimes November; before which time good seeds from the first blown flowers may be gathered. The stalks decay on the first frost that comes, and in the spring fresh shoots from the root proceed to renew its splendor, and display its autumnal charms.

This is the principal perennial *Lathyrus* for our gardens; the other species of less note are,

Species.
2. Round-leaved Everlasting Pea.
3. Narbonne Chickling-Vetch.
4. Marsh Chickling-Vetch.
5. Siberian Chickling-Vetch.
6. Common Yellow Vetchling, or Everlasting Tare.
7. Tuberous-rooted Chickling-Vetch.
8. Hairy-podded Vetch.
9. Crimson Grass Vetch.

Narrow-leaved Everlasting Pea. 2. Narrow-leaved Everlasting Pea. This is a very fine showy plant, and would be highly esteemed were it not for the broad-leaved sort, which is much preferable to it. It grows common in woods and hedges in many parts of England; and whenever it is designed for a garden, its usual station is near some shrub or tree for it to climb upon. Over these, by the assistance of its claspers, it will rear its head, and exhibit a goodly shew of moderately large well-looking flowers. The stalk is not so thick as the Broad-leaved sort, but it has, like that, membraneous wings running from joint to joint. The leaves are composed of two narrow sword-shaped lobes, from the midrib of which come out the claspers. The flowers grow many together on long foot-stalks; they are of a reddish purple colour, having the wings and keel of a lighter colour, and in some varieties they are white. They will be in blow in July, August, and September, and afford good seeds in September and October.

Narbonne. 3. Narbonne Chickling-Vetch. The stalk will grow to be six feet long. The leaves are composed sometimes of two, and sometimes of four spear-shaped lobes, terminated by claspers. Each footstalk supports many flowers, which are small, of a bluish colour, will be in blow in June and July, and ripen their seeds in the autumn.

Marsh. 4. Marsh Chickling-Vetch. This grows naturally on boggy ground in Charley forest, near Leicester, and in several parts of England, but is rarely admitted into gardens. The leaves are composed of several narrow lobes, from which the claspers are produced. The flowers grow many on a footstalk; they are of a pale-purple or bluish colour, will be in blow in July, and ripen their seeds in the autumn.

and Siberian Chickling described. 5. Siberian Chickling-Vetch. This hath several angular stalks that are garnished with leaves, composed of five or eight pair of oval, oblong, acute lobes, having claspers. The flowers grow many together on long footstalks; they are of a violet colour, will be in blow in July, and ripen their seeds in the autumn. The pods that succeed these flowers are very much like those of the garden Pea.

Common Yellow Vetchling. 6. Common Yellow Vetchling, or Everlasting Tare. This plant hath several slender climbing stalks. The leaves are each composed of two spear-shaped lobes, having single claspers. The flowers grow many on each footstalk; they are of a bright yellow colour, and very beautiful; but are rarely admitted into gardens, not only as the plant itself is very common among our hedges and bushes, but because the roots spread themselves so fast, so deep into the ground, and at so great a distance, as to make it difficult to eradicate them when they have once taken possession.

and Tuberous described. 7. Tuberous-rooted Vetch. This hath a pretty large, brown, tuberous, creeping root, which is excellent, and is for this property esteemed in many parts, but particularly by the Dutch, who find great demand for them in large quantities to sell. From these roots rise many weak trailing branches, which have no membraneous wings from joint to joint like most of the other species of this genus. The leaves are composed of two oval lobes, which are terminated by claspers. The flowers grow on weak footstalks; they are of a deep red colour, and seldom bring their seeds to perfection; which, in which is not so necessary in this species, as it renders itself by its keeping it ots.

Hairy-podded.

8. Hairy podded Vetch. The stalks are few, and will grow to about two feet long. The leaves are composed of two narrow spear-shaped lobes, ending with clasps. The flowers grow two on a footstalk; they are of a purple colour, and succeeded by rough hairy pods containing the seeds.

and ... described.

9. Crimson Grass-Vetch is never propagated in gardens; it grows naturally among the grass in our meadows, and I mention it here for the pleasure of those whose taste directs their walks in the summer-season through the flowery meads, that when they meet with it they may know what it is. It will grow to about a foot and a half high, and has no clasps. The stalks are upright. The leaves are long, narrow, and grow singly at the joints. The flowers grow from the upper parts of the stalk on slender footstalks; they come out from the joints, and each stalk for the most part sustains a single flower only; their colour is a bright red, or crimson; they will be in blow in May or June, and the seeds ripen in July or August.

Manner of propagating them.

The best way of propagating all these sorts is by sowing the seeds, which may be done either in the autumn or spring. As the plants begin to make their shoots, proper sticks must be placed for their support. The Everlasting Peas may be sown near arbours, or trees of any sort to climb upon, and they will have a very good effect; the other sorts should be stuck with sticks, according to their height; but as they are chiefly introduced for variety, a few of each sort will be sufficient.

The Tuberous rooted sort multiplies amazingly by the roots; so that whoever is fond of them to eat, may soon be supplied in plenty that way, especially if the soil be fresh and light.

Titles.

1. Broad-leaved Everlasting Pea is titled, *Lathyrus pedunculis multifloris, cirrhis diphyllis, foliolis lanceolatis, internodiis membranaceis*. Caspar Bauhine calls it, *Lathyrus latifolius*; John Bauhine, *Lathyrus major latifolius, flore purpureo, speciosior*. It grows naturally in the woods near Cambridge, and in a few other parts of England. It grows also in such places, and among hedges, in many parts of Europe.

2. Narrow-leaved Everlasting Pea. This is titled, *Lathyrus pedunculis multifloris, cirrhis diphyllis, foliolis ensiformibus, internodiis membranaceis*. Caspar Bauhine calls it, *Lathyrus sylvestris major*; and Clusius, *Lathyrus sylvestris*. It is more common than the former sort in England, and most parts of Europe.

3. Narbonne Chickling-Vetch is, *Lathyrus pedunculis multifloris, cirrhis diphyllis tetraphyllisque, foliolis lanceolatis, internodiis membranaceis*. Sauvages calls it, *Lathyrus pedunculis multifloris, cirrhis diphyllis, foliolis gramineis trinerviis, internodiis membranaceis*; and John Bauhine, *Lathyrus major Narbonensis angustifolius*. It grows among woods, hedges, and by the sides and bottoms of mountains in most parts of Europe.

4. Marsh Chickling-Vetch is titled, *Lathyrus pedunculis multifloris, cirrhis polyphyllis, stipulis lanceolatis*. In the *Flora Lapp.* it is termed, *Lathyrus foliis pinnatis, pedunculis multifloris*. Caspar Bauhine calls it, *Lathyrus peregrinus, foliis viciæ, flore subcæruleo pallidè purpurascente fere*; and Plukenet, *Vicia Lathyroides, sive Lathyrus viciæformis*. It grows in moist woods and meadows in England, and several of the northern parts of Europe.

5. Siberian Chickling-Vetch is, *Lathyrus pedunculis multifloris, cirrhis polyphyllis, stipulis ovatis basi acutis*. Haller calls it, *Vicia pedunculis multifloris, foliis ovatis, stipulis maximis*. It grows naturally in Siberia.

6. Yellow Vetchling, or Everlasting Tare, is, *Lathyrus pedunculis multifloris, cirrhis diphyllis simplicissimis, foliolis lanceolatis*. Caspar Bauhine calls it, *Lathyrus sylvestris luteus, foliis viciæ*; John Bauhine, *Lathyrus luteus sylvestris Dumetorum*; and Haller, *Lathyrus foliis binis acutis, capreolo non ramoso*. It grows in the meadows in most parts of Europe.

7. Tuberous rooted Chickling-Vetch is, *Lathyrus pedunculis multifloris, cirrhis diphyllis, foliolis ovalibus, internodiis nudis*. Caspar Bauhine calls it, *Lathyrus arvensis repens tuberosus*; and Fuchsius, *Apios*. It grows naturally in the corn-fields of Tartary and Geneva.

8. Hairy podded Vetch is, *Lathyrus pedunculis bifloris, cirrhis diphyllis, leguminibus hirsutis, seminibus scabris*. Caspar Bauhine calls it, *Lathyrus angustifolius, siliqua hirsuta*; and John Bauhine, *Lathyrus siliquâ hirsuta*. It is a native of England, and most other countries of Europe.

9. Crimson Grass Vetch is, *Lathyrus pedunculis unifloris, foliis simplicibus, stipulis subulatis*. In the *Hortus Cliffort.* it is termed, *Lathyrus foliis solitariis lentiformibus*. Caspar Bauhine calls it, *Lathyrus sylvestris minor*; and Magnol, *Lathyrus angustifolius erectus, folio singulari, sine capreolis, Nissoli*. It is common in England and France.

Class and order in the Linnæan system.

*Lathyrus* is of the class and order *Diadelphia Decandria*; and the characters are,

The character.

1. CALYX is a monophyllous, bell-shaped perianthium, cut at the top into five spear-shaped acute segments, of which the two upper are the shortest.

2. COROLLA is papilionaceous. The vexillum is heart-shaped, large, and reflexed at the point and sides. The alæ are oblong lunulated, short, and obtuse. The carina is semiorbicular, and of the size of the wings.

3. STAMINA are ten filaments, nine of which are joined in a body, the other stands single, with roundish antheræ.

4. PISTILLUM. The germen is oblong, narrow, and compressed. The style is upright, plane, broad towards the upper part, and has an acute point. The stigma is hairy.

5. PERICARPIUM is a long, compressed, acuminated pod of two valves.

6. SEMINA. The seeds are roundish.

There is a great affinity between this genus and the garden Pease.

## CHAP. CCLVIII

## *LAVATERA*

The plant described. THERE are many species of the *Lavatera*, but that which is proper for our purpose in this place is called the Thuringian *Lavatera*, the name originally given it by Cammerarius, from the country where it naturally grows

The roots of this species are long, and furnished with many fibres From these, every spring, arise many stalks, which grow to about a yard in height and which constantly die away at the approach of winter The leaves are broad and angular, though rather roundish, or inclined to an heart-shaped figure at the lower part of the plant, but those that adorn the stalks are deeply and irregularly indented, they stand on long footstalks, and their colour is a pale green

The flowers are of the Marshmallow kind, and very large, they grow from the joints of the stalks, and are chiefly of crimson-purple colour, though they will be often of different tinges

Varieties. There are varieties of this species, some with pale-red, and others with white flowers The time of flowering is July and August, and they will be succeeded by plenty of good seeds in the autumn, soon after which the stalks decay

Culture. From these seeds the plants are best propagated, sow them, therefore, early in the spring, in a border of light fine earth, and sift over them a little mould a quarter of an inch thick They will readily come up, and require no other care than weeding and watering until the autumn, at which time plant them in the places where they are designed to remain Afterwards the ground about them must be dug every year, and the roots moulded up This must be done in the autumn, when the decayed stalks are taken away, and this is all the trouble they will require But it will be necessary, if a person is particularly fond of these plants, to raise fresh ones from seeds, as he sees occasion, and to extirpate the old roots, for the seedlings, at their first coming into blow, will always produce the fairest and largest flowers When the succession is continued this way, be sure let the blow be alternately in different parts of the garden

This species is entitled, *Lavatera caule herbaceo, fructibus denudatis, calycibus incisis* Cammerarius calls it, *Althea Thuringiaca*, Dillenius, *Althaea Thuringiaca grandiflora*, Van Royen, *Lavatera foliis inferioribus cordato-subrotundis, superioribus lobatis crenatis, calycibus utrinque incisis, caule herbaceo*, and Caspar Bauhine, *Althaea flore majore* It grows naturally by hedge-sides in Pannonia, Thuringia, Tartary, and Sweden Titles.

## CHAP. CCLIX.

## *LEDUM*, MARSH *CISTUS*.

THERE is only one species of this genus, called, Marsh *Cistus*, or Wild Rosemary

Description of the Marsh Cistus. The root is tough, creeping, and woody The stalks are ligneous, slender, branching, greyish, and grow to about two feet high The leaves are narrow, hairy underneath, of a brownish green or iron colour, and clammy to the touch The flowers come out in roundish bunches from the ends of the branches, they are of a reddish colour, and the general characters indicate their structure, they appear in May and June, and are followed by roundish capsules, containing ripe seeds, in August or September

Culture. The root of this plant being creeping, sends forth suckers in abundance, which may be taken up any time in the autumn, winter, or spring, and set in the nursery in rows at about fifteen inches asunder Here they may stand one year, by which time they will be proper plants to be set out for good Their situation ought to be in a marshy or boggy part of our works, for in such places they are found growing spontaneously in a state of nature; though they do extremely well in the garden, provided the places be moist, and in the shade

Titles. There being no other species of this genus, it stands with the name simply, *Ledum* In the *Flora Suecica* it is termed, *Ledum foliis linearibus subtus hirsutis, floribus corymbosis* Caspar Bauhine calls it, *Cistus ledon foliis rosmarini ferrugineis*, and Cammerarius, *Rosmarinum sylvestre* It grows naturally on bogs and marshy, wet places in England, and most of the northern parts of Europe

Class and order in the Linnaean system. *Ledum* is of the class and order *Decandria Monogynia*, and the characters are,

The characters. 1 CALYX is a very small monophyllous perianthium, indented in five parts at the top

2 COROLLA is five oval, concave, patent petals

3 STAMINA

3 STAMINA are ten filiform patent filaments the length of the corolla, having oblong antheræ

4 PISTILLUM consists of a roundish germen, a filiform style the length of the stamina, and an obtuse stigma

5 PERICARPIUM is a roundish capsule, containing five cells, and opening in five parts at the base

6 SEMINA The seeds are numerous, small, oblong, narrow, and pointed at each end

## CHAP CCLX

## *LEMNA*, DUCK MEAT

THERE are four distinct species of this genus, which are occasionally to be met with in our ponds, called,

Species

1 Common Duck Meat
2 Greater Duck Meat
3 Convex Duck Meat
4 Ivy-leaved Duck Meat

Description of the Common,

1 Common Duck Meat The root is a single fibre fastened to about the middle of the leaf The leaves are small, roundish, flat, and green on both sides The flowers are produced from the sides of the leaves, they are of a whitish-green colour, and are to be met with (though very rarely) in the month of June

Greater,

2 Greater Duck Meat The root consists of about ten or twelve slender fibres fastened to about the middle of the leaf The leaf is three times as large as the former sort, is almost oval, broader, and more rounded at one end than the other, of a thick consistence, a bright-green colour on the upper side, and a delicate purple underneath The flowers are to be met with in June and July

Convex,

3 Convex Duck Meat The root is a very long slender fibre fastened to about the middle of the leaf The leaf is large, rounded, and broader at one end than the other, of a thick fleshy substance, convex underneath, of a pale-green colour on the upper side, but still paler on the lower and convex part Its flowers are pretty frequent, and to be met with in June or July

and Ivy leaved Duck Meat

4 Ivy-leaved Duck Meat The root is a long, slender, white fibre The leaves are oblong, spear-shaped, trisulcated, and lobed in the manner of some Ivy, and grow on footstalks The flowers are to be met with in May and June

Titles.

1 Common Duck Meat is titled, *Lemna foliis sessilibus utrinque planiusculis, radicibus solitariis* Micheli calls it, *Lenticula minor monorhiza, foliis subrotundis utrinque viridibus*, Cammerarius, *Lens palustris* Caspar Bauhine, *Lens palustris, vulgaris*, and Parkinson, *Lens palustris, seu aquatica vulgaris* It grows in still waters in most countries of Europe

2 Greater Duck Meat is, *Lemna foliis sessilibus, radicibus confertis* Micheli calls it, *Lenticula major polyrhiza inferne atro-purpurea*, and Ray, *Lenticula palustris major* It grows naturally in ditches in England, and most countries of Europe

3 Convex Duck Meat is *Lemna foliis sessilibus subtus hemisphæricis, radicibus solitariis* Micheli calls it, *Lenticula palustris major, foliis ... convexa, fructu polyspermo* It grows naturally in ponds (though not very common in England) in most countries of Europe

4 Ivy leaved Duck Meat is *Lemna foliis petiolatis lanceolatis* Sauvages calls it, *Lemna foliis lanceolatis extremis decussatis*, Micheli, *Lenticula ... ramosa monorhiza, foliis oblongis pediculis longioribus donatis*, Caspar Bauhine, *Lenticula aquatica trisulca*, Gerard, *Hederula aquatica*, and Parkinson, *Ranunculus hederaceus aquaticus* It grows naturally in ditches and standing waters in England, and most countries of Europe

*Lemna* is of the class and order *Monoecia Diandria*, and the characters are, Class and order in the Linnæan system The characters

I Hermaphrodite Flowers

1 CALYX is a large, roundish, obtuse, depressed, entire, monophyllous, spreading perianthium, dilated obliquely outwardly, and opens sideways

2 COROLLA There is none

3 STAMINA are two awl-shaped incurved filaments the length of the calyx, having globular didymous antheræ

4 PISTILLUM consists of an oval germen, a short style, and an obsolete stigma

5 PERICARPIUM is abortive

II Female Flowers in the same plant with the male.

1 CALYX The same as the hermaphrodite

2 COROLLA There is none

3 PISTILLUM consists of a subovated germen, a short permanent style, and a simple stigma

4 PERICARPIUM is a globular but pointed capsule, containing one cell

5 SEMINA The seeds are few, oblong, almost as long as the capsule, pointed at each end, and situated on one side

# C H A P. CCLXI.

## *LEONTICE*, LION's LEAF.

Species. OF this genus there are,

1. Grecian Lion's Leaf.
2. Cretan Lion's Leaf.

Description of the Grecian, 1. Grecian Lion's Leaf. The root is thick, tuberous, as big as a small turnep, and covered with a dark-brown bark. The leaves are pinnated. The folioles are small on the midrib, and rise immediately from the roots on slender footstalks about six inches long. The stalks are tender, round, naked, upright, and six or eight inches high. The flowers come out from the upper parts of the stalks in kind of spikes; they are of a yellow colour, appear early in April, but are not succeeded by seeds in England.

and Cretan Lion's Leaf. 2. Cretan Lion's Leaf. The root is tuberous, large, greyish without, greenish within, and covered with many protuberances. The leaves are large, growing on foot-stalks which divide into three parts, forming in the whole a decompound leaf. The folioles are indented, ribbed, and of a bluish green colour. The stalks are round, slender, branching near the top, green, but often streaked with a purple colour, and adorned with leaves like the radical ones, but smaller, growing singly at the joints. The flowers come out in spikes from the ends of the branches; they are of a pale-yellow colour, appear in April, but are not succeeded by seeds in England.

Culture. These sorts are both propagated by seeds, which must be procured from the places where the plants naturally grow; and in order to continue them good, they should be kept in sand or dry mould until their arrival. As soon as possible afterwards, let them be thinly sown in beds of light, dry, fresh earth, in a warm well-sheltered place. Let the beds be hooped at the approach of winter, to be covered with mats in frosty weather; at the first sign of which, let two or three rows of gorse be stuck thick round the bed, to ensure its safety. In the spring the plants will come up, and where they are too close the weakest should be drawn out, otherwise they will cramp the roots of one another, and impede their growing in size. The weeds must be pulled up as they arise, and twice a week, if dry weather happens, the plants should have water. This work should be repeated until about midsummer, when their leaves decay, and then no watering should be allowed them until the autumn following. The beginning of October sift over the beds half an inch of the finest mould, and in November, or sooner, if you apprehend danger, let the gorse be stuck round the beds as before, and hoops be placed for the support of the mats, which must always be applied in frosty weather, but be constantly removed on the return of the mild season. In the spring, and until midsummer, weeding and watering must be observed as before, and in July, when the leaves are decayed, a share of the plants may be drawn out, and removed to other places, leaving the others at about a foot asunder in the beds.

The after-management of these plants is the same as the preceding. They must be protected from hard frost in winter, have a light, dry, fresh earth in the fall, in a warm well sheltered place, for they do very ill in pots; and being thus stationed their roots may be continued for many years, and will annually produce flowers, which are for the most part the finest from such plants as have never been removed.

1. Grecian Lion's Leaf is titled, *Leontice foliis pinnatis petiolo communi simplici*. Tournefort calls it, *Leontopetalum foliis costæ simplici innascentibus*; Caspar Bauhine, *Leontopetalum apii, folio quernis*; and Ray, *Cacalia genus Leontopetalon dictum*. It grows naturally in the corn fields of Greece, where it flowers about Christmas. Titles.

2. Cretan Lion's Leaf is, *Leontice foliis decompositis petiolo communi trifido*. Tournefort calls it, *Leontopetalon foliis costæ ramosæ innascentibus*; and Caspar Bauhine, *Leontopetalon*. It grows naturally in Apulia, Hetruria, and Crete.

*Leontice* is of the class and order *Hexandria Monogynia*, and the characters are, Class and order in the Linnæan system. The characters.

1. CALYX is a deciduous perianthium composed of six narrow patent leaves, which are alternately smaller.

2. COROLLA is six oval acute petals twice the length of the calyx. The nectarium is constituted of six oval, equal, patent leaves, fixed on short footstalks to the base of the petals.

3. STAMINA are six very short filiforme filaments, having erect, bilocular, bivalvate antheræ, which open at the base.

4. PISTILLUM consists of an oblong oval germen, a short taper style inserted obliquely to the germen, and a simple stigma.

5. PERICARPIUM is a globular, acuminated, hollow, inflated, succulent berry, containing one cell.

6. SEMINA. The seeds are few …

# CHAP CCLXII

## *LEONTODON*, DANDELION

THE species of this genus are,

Species

1 Common Dandelion
2 Golden Dandelion
3 Bulbose Dandelion
4 Autumnal Dandelion, or Yellow Devil's Bit
5 Tuberose Dandelion
6 Rough Dandelion
7 Hispid Dandelion

Description of the Common Dandelion

1 Common Dandelion The root is thick, strikes deep into the ground, and becomes very troublesome to the Gardener, especially when it has taken good possession of a gravel walk The leaves are runcinated, smooth, and when broken emit a milky juice The stalk is smooth, hollow, and eight or ten inches high, and replete with a milky juice The flowers grow singly on the tops of the stalks, they are large, of a golden-yellow colour, appear at all times of the summer, and soon after they are fallen are succeeded by very beautiful globular heads of seeds situated in the receptacle, crowned by stipitated feathered down, diverging from the center like rays from a luminous body, and which are soon displaced by the wind The varieties of this species are,

Varieties

Broad-leaved Dandelion
Long Narrow-leaved Dandelion
Round-leaved Dandelion
Jagged-leaved Dandelion

Golden,

2 Golden Dandelion The leaves are runcinated, smooth, and much resemble those of the Common Dandelion, but are smaller, and more obtuse The stalk is smooth, hollow, striated, and six or eight inches high The flowers grow singly on the tops of the stalks, they are of a bright copper colour in the front, but red underneath, and are situated in brownish dark-coloured cups, they appear in May and June, and are succeeded by ripe seeds, which will be blown off by the winds

Bulbose,

3 Bulbose Dandelion, or *Chondrilla* of the Greeks The root is thick, fleshy, of a yellowish brown colour on the outside, but white within The leaves are oblong oval, smooth, and slightly indented on their edges The stalk is round, hollow, six or eight inches high, and rough near the top, they grow singly on the tops of the stalks, are of a yellow colour, appear in May and June, and the seeds ripen in July

Autumnal

4 Autumnal Dandelion, or Yellow Devil's Bit The root is composed of numerous fibres, which issue from a small knob, or head, which usually appears as if broken or bitten off The leaves are long, narrow, spear-shaped, smooth, and indented on their edges The stalks are slender, branching, and eight or ten inches high The flowers come out from the ends of the branches, they are small, and of a yellow colour, their appearance is generally the latter end of the summer or autumn, they are nevertheless soon followed by ripe seeds, furnished with a stipitated feathery down

Tuberose,

5 Tuberose Dandelion The root is composed of numerous, small, fleshy tubers, like those of Asphodel The leaves are runcinated, rough, and hairy The flower-stalks come out from among the leaves, and rise to about five or six inches high The flowers grow singly at the ends of the stalks, they are of a yellow colour, having very rough hairy cups, they appear in May and June, and are succeeded by ripe seeds in July and August

Rough,

6 Rough Dandelion The root is thick, fleshy, and strikes deep into the ground The leaves are long, spear-shaped, sinuated, rough, and hairy The stalks are naked, hairy, and about six inches high The flowers grow singly at the tops of the stalks, having erect hairy cups, they are moderately large, of a fine yellow colour, and are double, they appear in July and August, before the end of which months ripe seeds from the first-blown flowers may be gathered

and Hispid Dandelion described

7 Hispid Dandelion The root is thick, white, fleshy, and strikes deep into the ground The leaves are long, narrow, hoary, sinuated, rough, and the hairs are furcated, whereas those of the preceding species are simple The stalks are naked, simple, and about six or eight inches high The flower grow singly on the tops, having erect hispid cups, they are of a yellow colour, appear about the same time with the former, and the seeds ripen accordingly

Method of propagation

These sorts are all best raised by sowing the seeds soon after they are ripe, in beds of any common mould made fine When they come up, they will require no trouble, except thinning them where they are too close, and keeping them clean from weeds, they bear transplanting extremely well, so may be removed to any place, though they thrive best if undisturbed The Common Dandelion is a very fine flower, and were it scarce, would be ranked among our most valuable plants The jagged-leaved sort is found in some collections merely on account of that variety, and all the sorts of it are wholesome eating, and afford an admirable sallet herb, if properly prepared by blanching in the spring, the method of performing which, comes of course among the articles of the Kitchen garden

Titles

1 Common Dandelion is titled, *Leontodon calyce inferne reflexo, foliis runcinatis denticulatis lævibus* Tournefort calls it, *Dens leonis latiore et rotundiore folio*, Caspar Bauhine *Dens leonis, latiore folio*, also, *Dens leonis angustiore folio*, Ray, *Dens leonis montanus angustifolius*, and Fuchsius, *Hedypnois* It grows naturally in meadows, pastures, and neglected gardens in England, and most countries of Europe

2 Golden Dandelion is, *Leontodon foliis runcinatis scapo subunifolio, calyce hispido* Haller calls it, *Taraxacum foliorum dentibus triangularibus, fine subrotundo*, Ray, *Dens leonis foliis extremo subrotundis, floribus aureis*, and Columna, *Hieracium alterum minus* 4 It grows naturally on Mount Baldus, and the Helvetian mountains

3 Bulbose Dandelion is, *Leontodon foliis oblongo-ovatis subdentatis glabris, calyce lævi, scapo sub[illegible] bato* Caspar Bauhine calls it, *Chondrilla bulbosa*, Sauvages, *Taraxacum calyce toto erecto subu[illegible]*

VOL I 53 7 Q [illegible]

radice bulbosâ Lobel, Chondrilla pusilla marina lutea bulbosa, and Columna, Chondrilla altera Dioscoridis It grows naturally in Italy and the south of France

4 Autumnal Dandelion, or Yellow Devil's Bit, is, Leontodon caule ramoso, pedunculis squamosis, foliis lanceolatis dentatis integerrimis glabris In the Hortus Cliffort it is termed, Crepis foliis longis dentatis linearibus caule decurvato nudo Caspar Bauhine calls it, Hieracium, chondrillæ folio glabro, radice succisa, majus et minus, Fuchsius, Hieracium minus, Petiver, Hieracium præmorsum lacmatum, Parkinson, Hieracium minus præmorsa radice; and Gerard, Hieracium minus sive leporinum It grows naturally in meadow and pasture grounds in England, and most countries of Europe

5 Tuberose Dandelion is, Leontodon foliis runcinatis scabris, calyce hirto Vaillant calls it, Taraxaconoides (bonbril e folio hirsuto, asphodeli radice, Caspar Bauhine, Dens leonis asphodeli bulbosi, and Lobel, Chondrilla altera Dioscoridis Monspeliensium It is a native of France, and other parts of Europe

6 Rough Dandelion is, Leontodon calyce toto erecto, foliis dentatis hirtis pilis simplicissimis In the former edition of the Species Plantarum it is termed, Crepis foliis lanceolatis, dentato sinuatis hispidis, setis subulatis, scapo unifloro Caspar Bauhine calls it, Hieracium, dentis leonis folio, hirsutie asperum magis laciniatum, also, Hieracium, dentis leonis folio, hirsutum asperum minus laciniatum, and John Bauhine, Hieracium parvum hirtum, caule aphyllo, crepum alii siciatum It grows naturally in Helvetia, France and Spain

7 Hispid Dandelion is, Leontodon calyce toto erecto, foliis dentatis integerrimis hispidis pilis furcatis In the former edition of the Species Plantarum it is termed, Hieracium foliis integris, subdenticulatis lanceolatis scabris, scapo unifloro Sauvages calls it, Picris caule erecto, foliis hispidis dentatis denticulis integerrimis, also, Hieracium foliis dentatis villosis hirsutis subasperis, scapo nudo unifloro, calyce hirto, Caspar Bauhine, Hieracium montanum angustifolium nonnihil incanum, also, Hieracium montanum, dentis leonis folio, laciniatum lentiginoso folio, and Clusius, Hieracium VI montanum, also, Hieracium folio Hedypnoidis It grows naturally in the meadows and pastures of most of the northern countries of Europe

Leontodon is of the class and order Syngenesia Polygamia Æqualis, and the characters are Class and order in the Linnæan system The characters

1 CALYX The general calyx is imbricated and oblong The interior scales are narrow, parallel, and equal The exterior are fewer in number, and often reflexed towards the base

2 COROLLA The compound flower is imbricated and uniform The florets are numerous, equal, and each consists of one tongue-shaped, narrow, truncated petal, indented in five parts at the top

3 STAMINA are five very short capillary filaments, with cylindrical tubular antheræ

4 PISTILLUM consists of a subovated germen, a filiforme style the length of the corolla, and two revolute stigmas

5 PERICARPIUM There is none The calyx is oblong and straight

6 SEMEN The seed is single, oblong, rough, and crowned by a stipitated feathery down

The receptacle is naked and punctated

# CHAP. CCLXIII.

## *LEONURUS*, LION's TAIL.

Species

OF this genus we have,

1 English Mother wort

2 African Lion's Tail

3 Bohemian Lion's Tail

English Mother wort described

1 English Mother-wort is a plant of greater use in medicine than beauty in the garden, but it is nevertheless cultivated for variety as well as use in general collections of plants The stalks are strong, square, and grow to be four or five feet high The leaves are large, divided into three lobes, and grow opposite to each other at the joints on long strong footstalks The flowers grow in whorls just above the leaves, surrounding the stalks at the joints, they are of a reddish or purplish colour, come out in June or July, and continue in succession until September

Varieties

There is a variety of this species with white flowers, and another with curled leaves, which by some are much esteemed The whole plant is very strongly scented, and the stalks die to the ground in the autumn, and fresh ones arise in the spring

African,

2 African Lion's Tail This hath a perennial root, which sends forth several square stalks to about a yard in height The leaves are spear-shaped, serrated, and grow opposite to each other at the joints The flowers are scarlet, they appear in June and July, and will sometimes continue in succession all summer

3 Bohemian Lion's Tail This is a plant of about the same height with the former The leaves are oval, spear-shaped, serrated, and cut or divided nearly like those of the Common Mother-wort The flowers are produced in June or July, and surround the stalks, sitting close, having prickly cups and Bohemian Lion's Tail described

These sorts are all propagated by dividing of the roots in the autumn, and also by sowing the seeds soon after they are ripe They love a moist soil, and a shady situation Indeed the first sort grows common by ditches in many parts of England, and when it is introduced into gardens, it will scatter its seeds, which will come up in such plenty as to cause as much trouble as weeds to keep them down Culture

1 English Mother-wort is titled, Leonurus foliis caulinis lanceolatis trilobis Caspar Bauhine calls it, Marrubium cardiaca dictum, Ray, Cardiaca crispa, and Fuchsius, Cardiaca It grows naturally in England, and most parts of Europe Titles

2 African

2 African Lion's Tail is, *Leonurus foliis lanceolatis subserratis, calycibus septem dentatis* It grows naturally in India

3 Bohemian Lion's Tail is, *Leonurus foliis ovatis lanceolatis serratis, calycibus sessilibus spinosis* In the *Hortus Cliffort* it is termed, *Sideritis foliis ovatis & lanceolatis inciso-serratis* Boccone calls it, *Marrubiastrum foliis cataria* It grows naturally in Bohemia

Class and order in the Linnæan system The characters

*Leonurus* is of the class and order *Didynamia Gymnospermia* and the characters are,

1 Calyx is a monophyllous, tubulous, pentagonous, persisting perianthium indented in five parts at the top

2 Corolla is a ringent petal The tube is narrow, the limb gaping, and the faux long The upper lip is semi-cylindrical, long, concave, gibbous, rounded at the top, hairy, and entire. The lower lip is reflexed, and divided into three spear-shaped segments, which are nearly equal

3 Stamina There are four filaments concealed under the upper lip, of which two are shorter than the others Their antheræ are oblong, compressed, bifid, and incumbent

4 Pistillum consists of four germens, a filiforme style the length and situation of the stamina, and a bifid acute stigma

5 Pericarpium There is none The seeds are lodged in the calyx

6 Semina The seeds are four, oblong, convex on one side, and angular on the other

## C H A P CCLXIV.

## *LEPIDIUM*, DITTANDER, or PEPPER-WORT

A FEW plants of the following perennials of this genus are admitted into our gardens

Species

1 Broad leaved Dittander
2 Grass-leaved Dittander
3 Spanish Dittander

Broad-leaved,

1 The Broad leaved Dittander has a white creeping root, by which it multiplies very fast, and in some places is looked upon as a common weed in the garden From these rise the stalks, which will grow to be two feet high The leaves are different in their different situations, the lower leaves are broad, but spear shaped, their edges serrated, and they stand on long footstalks, the leaves on the upper parts of the stalks are long, narrow, sharp-pointed, and entire The flowers are produced from the tops of the branches in bunches, they are small, of a white colour, will be in blow in June and July, and ripen their seeds in the autumn

Grass leaved,

2. Grass-leaved Dittander This hath smooth taper stalks, which will grow to about the height of our common garden cress The radical leaves are pinnated or lyre-shaped The lower leaves on the stalks are serrated, but the upper ones are narrow, and entire The flowers are small, white, and contained in purple cups

and Spanish Dittander described

3 Spanish Dittander The stalks are of a kind of woody nature, but very short, single, and a little downy The leaves are awl-shaped, narrow, undivided, and acute The flowers are produced from the wings of the upper leaves, and ends of the branches, in bunches, their colour is white, but they are small, and of little figure

Culture

These sorts are propagated by parting of the roots any time in the autumn, winter, or spring, though the former is the more eligible season After they are planted out they call for no trouble, except keeping them clean from weeds, and dividing the roots every two years, at the same time planting the best offsets, and throwing the others away by this means they will be kept within due bounds, and made to shew themselves as handsome plants

Titles,

1 Broad-leaved Dittander is titled, *Lepidium foliis ovato lanceolatis integris serratis* Caspar Bauhine calls it, *Lepidium latifolium*, Parkinson, *Piperitis, sive Lepidium vulgare*, and Gerard, *Raphanus sylvestris officinarum* It is a native of England, growing chiefly in moist and shady places

2 Grass leaved Dittander is, *Lepidium foliis linearibus superioribus integerrimis, caule paniculato virgato, floribus hexandris* Tournefort calls it, *Thlaspi Lusitanicum umbellatum, gramineo folio, flore albo* It grows naturally in most of the southern countries of Europe

3 Spanish Dittander is, *Lepidium foliis subulatis indivisis sparsis, caule suffruticoso* Tournefort calls it, *Lepidium, capillaceo folio, fruticosum Hispanicum* It grows naturally in Spain

Class and order in the Linnæan system. The characters,

*Lepidium* is of the class and order *Tetradynamia Siliculosa*, and the characters are,

1 Calyx is a perianthium composed of four oval, concave, deciduous leaves

2 Corolla consists of four petals placed in form of a cross, which are oval, have very narrow ungues, and are double the length of the calyx

3 Stamina consist of six subulated filaments the length of the calyx, with simple antheræ The two opposite filaments are shorter than the others

4 Pistillum consists of a cordated germen, a simple style the length of the stamina, and an obtuse stigma

5 Pericarpium is a subcordated, subemarginated, compressed pod of two cells

6 Semina The seeds are oval, pointed, and narrow at their base

CHAP.

## C H A P. CCLXV.

## *LEUCOJUM*, The GREAT SNOW-DROP

Prefatory Remarks

THIS is the old generical name of the Common Winter Snow-drop of our gardens, which used to be ranked as a ſpecies of the Great Snow-drop the plant under conſideration. But the improvements of the ſcience have now taught us, that they are of a different family, and no kin to each other, only the general appearance of the flowers being a little alike, has led former botaniſts into the error of claſſing them together. Linnæus, the great reformer of the ſcience, knowing this, and indeed it wanted no very minute obſervation to find it out, as upon the leaſt examination they are found almoſt as different as can be, (the flowers of the Great Snow-drop conſiſting of ſix petals, without any nectarium, whereas thoſe of our Common Snow-drop conſiſt of three petals only, and a very ſingular nectarium in the middle of the flower) Linnæus, I ſay, who could not but obſerve ſo manifeſt a difference, has with great propriety ſeparated them, and formed them into two diſtinct genera. Our Common Snow-drop he has termed *Galanthus*, and the older name *Leucojum* he has retained for the larger kinds with ſix petals and no nectarium, a very proper name for either of them, its meaning being to expreſs a white violet, it being derived of the Greek words λευκον, white, and ἴον, a violet; and where words are given to plants with ſome meaning, that is really very beautiful, it figures ſome idea of the plant, and quickens our reſearches into the offſpring of the different genera. Theſe laws were better obſerved formerly than at preſent, many of the genera being ſo named as to convey no idea of the nature of the flowers, and often ſo foreign to the purpoſe, as to cauſe it a needleſs trouble to de[illegible] its original.

The ſpecies of this genus are,

Species

1. The Vernal Great Snow-drop.
2. The Summer Great Snow-drop.
3. The Autumnal Great Snow-drop.

Deſcription of the Vernal,

1. Vernal Great Snow-drop. The root is a large, oblong bulb, covered with a brown coat or bark. The leaves are long, obtuſe at their ends, and of a very fine green colour; they are flat, and five or ſix of them will grow from a ſtrong bulb. In the midſt of theſe riſes the flower ſtalk, which is naked and hollow, a little edged or channelled, of a lighter green than the leaves, and will grow to be about a foot high. At the top is a whitiſh ſpatha, which opening ſideways, diſcloſes one or two flowers; they have very much the look of a ſnow-drop without cloſe examination, hanging downward in the ſame manner, and being of the ſame kind of ſnowy-white colour, only their edges are tipped with green. They will begin to blow in March, and emit an odour which by many is thought [illegible].

Summer

2. Summer Great Snow-drop. This ſpecies flowers later than the other, though hardly late enough to entitle it to the name of a ſummer-flowering plant. The root is a large, oblong bulb, and the leaves are long, flat, broad, and of a fine green colour. The ſtalk is thick, naked, and hollow. At the top of it is the ſpatha, and from this proceed many flowers, all of which have ſlender footſtalks, and hang drooping in a ſnow-drop manner. The time of this plant's flowering is in the beginning of May.

and Autumnal Great Snow-drop

3. Autumnal Great Snow-drop. This ſpecies hath a large, oblong, yellowiſh bulb, from which iſſue many narrow leaves of a fine green colour. The ſtalk is naked and hollow, and will grow to about a foot high. At the top of it is the ſpatha, and from this proceed many flowers, hanging drooping by their long weak footſtalks; they are all of a fine white colour, and the end of each petal is tipped with green. The ſtamina are the ſame as the others, but the ſtyle of this ſpecies is very ſlender, whereas that in each flower of the others is clavated. It flowers in autumn.

Method of propagating them

All theſe ſorts multiply very faſt by the roots, ſo that having obtained a few bulbs of each, the ſtock will ſoon become great. They grow naturally in meadow grounds in many parts, and this teaches us, that a moiſt, rich ſoil in our gardens is moſt ſuitable to them. The time for removing the roots is in the ſummer after the leaves are decayed, but in order to [illegible] of offſets, they ſhould not be diſturbed oftener than every three or four years. By that time many bulbs may be expected growing together in a bunch, which being taken up and divided, the ſtrongeſt ſhould be ſet for flowering, and the weaker bulbs by themſelves, to ſucceed them in blow, which will be about the year following.

Theſe plants are eaſily raiſed by ſeeds. And for this purpoſe, having ſaved ſome good ſeeds, let them be ſown, about the end of Auguſt, in a warm border of light earth. Scatter them very thinly, and cover them over with about half an inch of fine mould. In the ſpring they will come up, and all ſummer will require no other trouble than weeding and watering in dry weather, which latter muſt be left off as ſoon as the leaves begin to decay. They may ſtand here two years, and on the decay of the leaf be taken up, and planted four inches aſunder in beds, and here they may ſtand to flower, which will be in about four years from the ſpring after ſowing. This is a tedious method, and hardly worth practiſing, but by this means the beſt plants will be obtained, they will flower ſtronger, many of them will conſiſt of a greater number of petals, and ſome double flowers may be expected to appear.

Titles

1. The Vernal Great Snow-drop is titled, *Leucojum ſpathâ uniflora, ſtylo clavato*. Cluſius calls it, *Leucojum bulboſum*, others, *Leucojum bulboſum vulgare*. It grows naturally in meadow grounds in many parts of Italy and Germany.

2. The Summer Great Snow-drop is titled, *Leucojum ſpathâ multiflora, ſtylo clavato*. Cluſius calls it *Leucojum bulboſum* [illegible], Renealme, *Polyanthemum*. It grows naturally in Pannonia, Hetruria, and in ſome places near Montpelier.

3. Autumnal Great Snow-drop is, *Leucojum ſpathâ* [illegible], *ſtylo filiformi*. Cluſius names it, *Leucojum bulboſum* [illegible], Renealme, [illegible]. It grows naturally in Luſitania.

I[illegible]

Class and order in the Linnæan system The characters

*Leucojum* is of the class and order *Hexandria Monogynia*, and the characters are,

1 CALYX is an oblong, compressed, obtuse, withering spatha, which opens on the flat side, and withers

2 COROLLA is of a spreading campanulate figure, and composed of six oval, plane petals, which coalesce at their base, and are of a thicker substance at their ends than in any other part

3 STAMINA are six very short bristly filaments, with oblong, obtuse, erect, four cornered antheræ

4 PISTILLUM consists of a roundish germen placed below the flower, of an obtuse, clavated style, and a setaceous, erect, acute stigma, longer than the stamina

5 PERICARPIUM is a turbinated capsule formed of three valves, and containing three cells

6 SEMINA The seeds are numerous and roundish

# CHAP. CCLXVI.

## *LIGUSTICUM*, LOVAGE.

Species

Of this genus are,

1 Common Lovage
2 Scottish Sea Parsley
3 Cornwal Saxifrage
4 Austrian Lovage

Common Lovage described

1 Common Lovage The root is large, thick, fleshy, strikes deep into the ground, and is of a hot taste and strong odour The radical leaves are very large, being composed of a multitude of broad folioles, oval at the top, and of a dark-green colour The stalk is round, thick, channelled, branching, and six feet high The flowers are produced from the ends of the branches in large umbels, they are of a yellow colour, appear in June and July, and are succeeded by oblong, furrowed seeds, which ripen in the autumn

Medicinal properties

Every part of this plant is used in medicine, especially the seeds, which are an admirable carminative and fine aromatic

Common Sea Parsley

2 Scottish Sea Parsley The root is thick but much smaller than the former, and strikes deep into the ground The leaves are biternate, and the folioles are short, broad, and indented on their edges The stalks are round, upright, striated, and about a foot and a half high The flowers come out in umbels from the tops of the stalks, they are small and of a yellow colour, appear in June and July, and are succeeded by oblong, channelled seeds that ripen in the autumn, at which time the root frequently dies

Cornwal Saxifrage,

3 Cornwal Saxifrage The root is thick, and strikes deep into the ground The radical leaves are ternate, spear-shaped, and entire, but those on the stalk are composed of many small, slender folioles, which are cut on their edges The stalks are upright, branching, and a foot and a half high The flowers come out in umbels from the ends of the branches, they are small and of a yellow colour, appear in June and July, and are succeeded by oblong, channelled seeds, which ripen in autumn

and Austrian Lovage, described

4 Austrian Lovage The root is thick, white, and penetrates deep into the earth The stalks are thick, firm, jointed, bent in different directions alternately at the joints, and grow to about two feet high The leaves are bipinnated and the folioles run into each other, they are smooth of a chearful green colour, and grow singly at the joints The flowers come out in umbels from the tops of the main stalks, as well as side branches or footstalks, which arise from the wings of the leaves at the joints They are small and of a white colour, appear in June and July, and are succeeded by oblong, channelled seeds, which ripen in autumn

Method of propagation

All these species are best propagated by sowing the seeds in the autumn soon after they are ripe The ground should be double dug, and in the spring, when the plants come up, they must be thinned to proper distances, which should be according to their growth, leaving the roots of the first sort three feet distant from each other, and the rest proportionably nearer They will bear transplanting very well, so that the young plants may be made to occupy a fresh spot, if they are wanted From this time they will require no trouble, except keeping them clean from weeds in summer, and digging the ground between the rows in winter They will then flower strong, and fresh plants from scattered seeds will spontaneously arise, which may be taken up and removed to any place where they are wanted

Titles

1 Common Lovage is titled, *Ligusticum* [illegible] Caspar Bauhine calls it, *Ligusticum vulgare*, and Morison, *Levisticum vulgare* It grows naturally on the Appennine mountains, also in Italy and Germany

2 Scottish Sea Parsley is, *Ligusticum foliis biternatis* In the *Hortus Cliffort* it is, *Ligusticum foliis duplicato ternatis*, in the *Flora Lapponica*, [illegible] Plukenet calls it, *Ligusticum* [illegible] Herman, [illegible] Tournefort, *Ligusticum Scoticum apii folio*, and Ray, *Apium Scoticum* [illegible] It grows naturally on cliffs near the sea-shores in England, Sweden, and Canada

3 Cornwal Saxifrage is, *Ligusticum foliis decompositis* [illegible] Ray calls it, *Sisymbrium tenuifolium* [illegible] and Petiver, *Saxifraga cornubiensis* It is a native of Cornwal

4 Austrian Lovage is, *Ligusticum foliis bipinnatis, foliolis confluentibus incisis integerrimis* Caspar Bauhine calls it, *Seseli montanum, cicutæ folio, glabrum*, and Clusius, *Seseli I montanum Pannonicum* It grows naturally in the Alpine parts of Austria

Class and order in the Linnæan system. The characters.

*Ligusticum* is of the class and order *Pentandria Digynia*, and the characters are,

1 CALYX The general umbel is multiple, the partial also is multiple. The general involucrum is membranaceous, and composed of seven unequal leaves, the partial also is membranaceous, but has only three or four leaves. The perianthium is small, and indented in five parts.

2 COROLLA The general flower is uniform. The florets have each five equal, plane petals, which are bent at the points, and carinated inwards.

3 STAMINA are five capillary filaments shorter than the corolla, having simple antheræ.

4 PISTILLUM consists of a germen situated below the flower, and two approximated styles with simple stigmas.

5 PERICARPIUM There is none. The fruit is oblong, angular, five-furrowed, and divided into two parts.

6 SEMINA The seeds are two, oblong, smooth, channelled on one side, and plane on the other.

# CHAP CCLXVII

## *LILIUM*, LILY

Introductory observation.

WHEN we admire with wonder the unlimited bounty of Nature in the enrichment of our globe, we reflect with astonishment on the vegetable train, their distinct genera, species, and varieties sent us for that purpose, and we with gratitude behold the greatest variety belong to those genera which are possessed of the greatest beauty and value. The *primula*, the tulip, the hyacinth, the narcissus, the [illegible], are all instances of this assertion, our sheds and our borders glow with them, and they demand the attention of the most incurious, as well as that of the professed botanist and florist. *Lilium* seems to join in the train, and claim a place among such valuable flowers as are possessed of this prerogative. It is, in all its species, strictly noble, majestic and grand, and accordingly Nature has enlarged the family, and drest up the retinue in a vast variety of pleasing forms. The White Lilies, the Orange Lilies, and Martagons, are the chief species that belong to it. I shall treat of them distinctly, and point out the principal varieties as I go along.

Species.

### 1 Of White Lilies.

Of White Lilies.

These are well known plants, and their uses and virtues in medicine have often been experienced by the afflicted in various disorders. Of this species there are,

Varieties.

The Common White Lily,
The White Lily with variegated leaves.
The Double White Lily.
The Purple striped Lily.
The Crimson-striped Lily.
The White Lily of Constantinople.
The Large-stalked Lily of Constantinople.

These are the principal sorts of the White Lily, from which, as from a common parent, they all proceed, the difference is the effect of culture, and the sport of Nature in plants from seed. The White Lily, the parent of them all, is found in most of our gardens, and its commonness makes it rather disregarded. The root is a large, white, squammous bulb. The leaves are of an oblong figure, long and broad, smooth, and of a pale, or rather a reddish-green colour, the outer leaves lie prostrate on the ground, but those more in the center of the plant are more erect. They are in perfection all winter, at which time they are very ornamental to our gardens, when few greens appear in their lively colours. The flower-stalk is thick, firm, and will grow to more than a yard in height. The leaves on this are very irregularly placed, oblong, waved, and tinged with brown. From the stalk proceed the flowers singly on short footstalks, they are very large, of a pure white colour, smooth within, and very fragrant. They frequently grow in a very large cluster at the top of the stalk, at which time their appearance is majestic and noble. The leaves on the stalk frequently wither before the flowers are in perfection, which makes that appear naked, but perfection is not to be found in every thing. Amends is amply made in these plants other ways, and they have excellences enough to be prized. The decay of the leaves is followed by that of the flowers and the stalk, and this is the best time for their removal.

The others all belong to this species, and afford an agreeable variety in our gardens. The Striped-leaved kind is the White Lily, but the leaves are beautifully variegated, and its value is more apparent in the winter season. All that time we may behold this plant from our parlours in all the bloom and vigour of spring and summer. It will be large, delightfully variegated, and appear to be fresh stamped with the healthy juices of the vernant spring, which is enlivening to all beholders when Nature in other respects looks inactive, and the scene dreary and waste. The stalk arises the same, and the flowers are the same with those of the fore-mentioned sort, and it in no respect forms any variety, except in its variegated leaves, whose excellences chiefly appear in the winter season.

The striped leaved.

The Double kind is still the White Lily, but the flowers are double. In most instances of this kind, it is looked upon as a perfection with the Gardener, but here it is a defect. As [illegible] the flower seldom opens [illegible], and the doubleness seems to be owing more to vitiated juices than the effects of good culture. Though they have more petals, they have not the [illegible] and

and livelineſs of the Single, neither are they poſſeſſed of that agreeable odour, ſo that nothing but variety can induce the culture of this ſort

Purple ſtriped,

The Purple ſtriped Lily is a good variety, and appears in all the health and vigour of a perfect plant The petals of the flower are ſweetly ſtriped with purple, and this would conſtitute a moſt valuable flower, were it not that the ſtain often runs through the flower, mixes with its ſnowy whiteneſs and impairs, and often alters it to a dull, diſagreeable colour

Crimſon ſtriped,

Crimſon ſtriped Lily is a better variety ſtill The petals are delightfully ſtriped with crimſon, without the natural whiteneſs being ſo liable to be deſtroyed, and when the ſtain diffuſes itſelf, it forms a bluſh or mixture both deſirable and new

White Lily of Conſtantinople,

White Lily of Conſtantinople The flower of the other ſorts are produced erect, but theſe hang down The leaves are narrower, the ſtalk is ſlenderer, and the flowers are ſmaller, than the upright ſort, but their flowers being produced in a pendulous manner, makes this a variety highly deſirable

and Large ſtalked Pendulous White Lily, deſcribed

Large-ſtalked Pendulous White Lily This will riſe with a very large, broad, flat ſtalk, which will be terminated by a large bunch of white pendant flowers Often a hundred or them will grow together on the ſame ſtalk, and the appearance they will make when thus collected may be eaſily imagined

Method of propagating them

Theſe ſorts are chiefly deſigned for large gardens, though the Lily with variegated leaves is planted any where to look beautiful in the winter They are all propagated by parting of the roots, by which method they may be increaſed very faſt The time for this is in the ſummer after the leaves and ſtalks are decayed It ſhould not be attended long after this, for almoſt on the firſt ſhower that happens, they will put forth freſh leaves, after which it will not be ſo well to remove them They will grow in almoſt any ſoil or ſituation, are hardy enough to endure our ſevereſt froſts, and their culture is attended with no other trouble than removing them, and taking off the offsets every three or four years

## 2 Of Orange Lilies

Of Orange Lilies

Of theſe there are greater variety than of the former ſorts, and the number is much increaſed by the Bulbiferous kind being added Variety alſo is occaſioned by the time of flowering, which is different in the different ſorts, ſo that from their firſt appearance to the end of the blow of the Late Bulbiferous Lily, great part of the ſummer months will be taken up

Varieties

Of Orange Lilies there are,
The Common Orange Lily
The Striped Red Lily
The Double Red Lily
The Dwarf Orange Lily
The Bulbiferous or Fiery Lily
Many-flowering Fiery Lily
The Great Broad leaved Bulbiferous Lily
The Small Narrow-leaved Bulbiferous Lily
The Greater Bulbiferous Lily with yellowiſh flowers
The Smaller Bulbiferous Lily
The Hoary Bulbiferous Lily
The Phœnician Lily
The Large Purple and Gold Lily
The Small Purple and Gold Lily
The Late-flowering Bulbiferous Lily

Many of theſe have been looked upon by old authors as diſtinct ſpecies, but they are now arranged under the preſent ſyſtem under one common title

The Common Orange Lily deſcribed

The Common Orange Lily is a well known plant, there being few of our gardens in which it does not occupy a place The root is a ſquamoſe bulb The leaves are oblong, narrow, of a blackiſh green colour, ſigned, ſhining, and placed irregularly on the flower ſtalks, which is thick, round, upright, and firm, and the flowers ornament the top in great plenty Theſe are large and of an orange colour, though of different tinges, ſome are of a deep bloody red, others paler, but the generality of them are what is commonly known by the name of Orange Colour They are formed like the White Lily, only their inſide is rough, whereas that of the White Lily is perfectly ſmooth

This is the ſuppoſed parent of all the other ſorts, and their names indicate in what reſpect they differ from each other The time of flowering, however, will be different in the different ſorts and it may not be amiſs to acquaint the Gardener with this, that the Dwarf Lilies are the firſt which ſhew themſelves in perfection, being frequently in full blow in May The common ſorts of Orange and Red Lilies will ſucceed them, and their time of flowering is in June and July The Late Bulbiferous Lily, which is by far the moſt beautiful of any of them, brings up the rear, and will often ſhew itſelf in perfection in September

Method of propagation

All theſe plants increaſe very faſt by dividing the root, but the Bulbiferous kinds may be increaſed in amazing plenty by planting the bulbs which grow upon the ſtalk Theſe will be produced in plenty from the boſom of the leaves, and if they are taken off and planted in a common border, they will flower ſtrong the ſecond year Nay, they will often drop off when come to perfection, ſow themſelves, and grow and become freſh plants The proceſs of culture in the increaſe of theſe plants is wonderful, but there are frequent inſtances of the like kind They are all raiſed very ſlowly by ſeeds, but all-bounteous Nature has made amends for that by cauſing theſe bulbs, which are all embryo plants, to grow on the ſtalk from the boſom of the leaves, by which their greateſt increaſe may be ſoon effected As Nature does nothing in vain, ſome have been induced to think, that theſe plants never produce good ſeeds, and that ſhe has ordered the increaſe that way But this is a very great miſtake, for all theſe ſorts are ſeminal varieties, and the bulbs on the ſtalk ſeem to be ſent only to expedite their increaſe, and to raiſe our wonder and gratitude

Proper ſituation

All theſe plants are not only ornamental to large borders, where they will grow and flouriſh in the greateſt perfection, but they will do very well in uncultivated places, under the drip of trees, &c if at firſt properly planted there, and the ground be well dug and looſened for their reception This makes them highly proper for wilderneſs quarters and borders of woods, where very few flowers will ſhew themſelves in any tolerable beauty

## 3 Of Martagons

Of Martagons

There are ſeveral diſtinct ſpecies of Martagons, beſides the variety of which each conſiſts The moſt noted variety is that called the Pomponey Martagon Of this ſpecies there are,

Varieties

The Common Pomponey Martagon
The Early Red Martagon
The White Martagon
The Common Martagon with double flowers
The Double White Martagon
The Red ſpotted Martagon

The

The Yellow Pomponey Martagon
The Yellow spotted Martagon
The White spotted Martagon
The Imperial Martagon
The Major Pomponey Scarlet Martagon
The Early Scarlet Martagon
The Late Pomponey Martagon

Besides these there are numbers of varieties, with names in the Dutch catalogues, which have been obtained by seeds, and which are still industriously increased by them

*The Pomponey Martagon described.* The Pomponey Martagon, in its common and natural state, is a very fine plant. The root is a large scaly bulb. The leaves are narrow, and grow without any order or regularity. The stalk will rise to about three or four feet high, and the flowers garnish the top of it in a pleasing manner, they are placed at a distance from each other on footstalks. The flowers hang in a drooping manner, have their petals reflexed or turned backwards, are of a high-red colour, and will be in blow in June. This is the Pomponey Martagon, and from this the other varieties have been obtained by seeds, which may still be increased by those who have an inclination to raise them this way.

*Culture.* The usual method of propagating them, and of multiplying the varieties in their real colours and properties, is by parting of the roots. This should be done soon after the stalks are decayed, which will be usually in August. The earlier sorts will be fit for removing sooner, but the later kinds will not be out of flower, and the stalk decayed, before September or October.

*Scarlet Chalcedonian,* 4. Scarlet Chalcedonian Martagon. This is also frequently called the Martagon of Constantinople, and among many Gardeners it goes by the name of Scarlet Martagon. The root is bulbous, and the leaves are numerous, of a lanceolate figure, ribbed, and a little hairy near their edges. The stalk is round, thick, and firm, though hollow within side, of a pale-green colour, spotted on the lower part with red, and will grow to near a yard in height. On the stalk the leaves are numerous, and placed without any order or regularity. The flowers garnish the top of the stalk in July; they are usually six or eight in number, and of the Martagon kind, their position being drooping, and the petals of all turning backwards; they are large, and of a most rich scarlet colour. This species is justly ranked among the best sorts of Martagons. There are several varieties of it, some have very large bunches of deep scarlet flowers, and others again flowers of a purple colour, all which are of great beauty and value.

*Superb,* 5. Superb Martagon. This species often goes amongst Gardeners by the name of Yellow Martagon. It is a very strong plant, and the stalk will grow to be near five feet high. The leaves are spear-shaped, and grow without any order or regularity on the stalk. The upper part of the stalk produces the flowers, which will be in such plenty, that there will be sometimes fifty or more at the head of each. They grow in a pyramidical form, and their appearance is noble; but they are possessed of a very disagreeable scent, which makes them less valued. Each individual flower is large, they have reflexed petals, are of a yellow colour, and spotted with blackish spots. They will be in blow in June or July, but should not be placed near walks of resort on account of their fœtid quality. This closes the species with leaves growing singly on the stalks.

*and Old Martagon described.* 6. The Old Martagon, or Turk's Cap. This is a well known plant, and has been a long inhabitant of our gardens. The leaves are moderately broad, and grow round the stalk in circles. The stalk will rise to about three or four feet high, and the circles of leaves are placed at proper distances. At the top of the stalk grow the flowers in loose spikes; they are of a dull purplish colour, and spotted with black.

*Its varieties.* There is a variety of this species with double flowers, which at present is rather a scarce plant. They will be in flower in June but their odour is not the most agreeable. There is also another variety of it with red flowers, which is usually called the Red Martagon, and has been looked upon by many as a distinct species. The stalks are hairy, the leaves narrow, and the spots on the flowers very few. The flower buds also are covered with a kind of down. It flowers rather earlier than the other sort, and is generally estimated of higher value. The Imperial Martagon, with a divided stalk, is also of this species, and a variety in more esteem than any of them.

*Canada Martagon described.* 7. Canada Martagon. This species hath a large, oblong scaly root, and the stalks will grow to be four or five feet high. The leaves are narrow and pointed, and placed in circles at certain distances round the stalk. The flowers are produced in plenty at the top, and are very different from the other Martagons, for the petals do not turn backward. They are shaped pretty much like the Red Lily, are of a yellow colour, and spotted with black.

*Its varieties.* There are several varieties of this species differing in the size and colour of their flowers. They all blow pretty nearly at the same time, which is about the latter end of July, or the beginning of August, at which time they are very ornamental.

*Kamptschatka,* 8. Kamptschatka Martagon. This species hath an oblong, scaly root, and the leaves surround the stalk in the same manner as the others. The flowers are yellow, grow erect, are a little spotted, and their petals sit close to the footstalks, they will be in blow in July, soon after which the stalks decay.

*and Pensylvania Martagon described.* 9. Pensylvania Martagon. This species hath a small, oblong, scaly, white root, from which springs a stalk, that will rise to about eighteen inches in height. The leaves are short, broad, and surround the stalk in the same manner as the others. Two flowers are usually produced at the end of the stalk, standing upon short footstalks, they are bell-shaped, and grow erect, like the Bulbiferous Lily. The petals themselves are spear-shaped, and placed on the footstalk, with long narrow ungues. They are of a bright-purple colour, spotted at the bottom with several dark purple spots. They will be in blow in July, and their flowers will be succeeded by good seeds in the autumn, by which fresh plants may be raised.

*Propagation of all the foregoing sorts.* All the foregoing species, with their varieties, are easily propagated by parting of the roots, which should be done in the summer after the stalks are decayed. The roots, after they are taken up, if there is a necessity for it, may be kept in sand, or in a cool place, for some months, or if they are to be sent to a distance, the best way will be to wrap them in moss. But never let this be done, unless the ground is not in readiness for their reception, or the like, for though the utmost caution be taken, the scales will shrink, and the roots be proportionably weakened according to the time they are kept out of the ground. They all delight in a dry,

*Proper soil.* rich soil; and if the spot designed for them be naturally moist, the beds must be raised; for too much moisture will often rot the roots. With regard to the soil itself, you need not be over-

solicitous,

solicitous, for there are few soils in which they will not grow and flourish. Though if it be a stiff clay and binding, the usual precaution of mixing with it coal-ashes, coarse sand, and the like, will be better to be observed.

Proper situation

They are all of them proper for large gardens and borders where there is room enough; and many of them, particularly the Common Martagon, may be mixed with small shrubs in the wilderness quarters, where they will have a very fine effect, and add additional lustre to the shrubbery.

Method of raising them by seeds

They are also to be propagated by seeds, by which method fresh varieties may be expected. Sow the seeds in autumn, soon after they are ripe, in pots or boxes provided for the purpose. The soil with which to fill the boxes should be fresh, sandy, rich, and light; and the seeds should be covered about half an inch deep. This being done, remove the pots into a well-sheltered warm place, where they may stand all winter; and if it be so situated that they can have the sun as it may happen all that season, it will be so much the better. In the spring the plants will come up; and as the days get long, and the heat of the sun encreases, they must be removed into the shade, and the morning-sun only until about ten o'clock should be allowed to shine on them. Frequent and gentle waterings must be allowed them, and the weeds must be pulled up as they appear; which is all the trouble they will require until August. At that time the bulbs should be taken up, and planted in beds provided for the purpose; but lest the smaller bulbs should be lost, scatter the mould all over the beds, and cover all down with good light mould made fine, about an inch thick. The situation of this bed must be naturally warm and well sheltered by neighbouring trees or hedges, and they will require no trouble in the winter, for it is not in the power of moderate frosts to hurt them much. If the beds have not this defence, it will be proper to hoop them, in order to cover them with mats in very severe weather. Early in the spring it will be necessary to sift over them about a quarter of an inch of fine mould, for several of the bulbs will probably be thrown out of the ground; and if moss should have grown on the surface, the surface should be loosened before the mould is sifted on them, and this work should not be deferred later than February. After this they will only require weeding and watering during the summer. In the autumn they are to be planted out in fresh beds, where they are designed to shew their flowers. The beds should be well worked, and the soil should be light and good; and in these beds plant them about nine inches asunder. Here let them stand until they shew their flowers, which will be in two or three years afterwards. Those which discover at first great beauty should be marked, in order to be removed into the flower-garden on the decay of the stalks; and this will make room for the others to grow and flourish. Those which discover little beauty should not be at first rejected, but let them stand three or four years before you finally extirpate them; for they will often put on a better face the second year than the first, and a third year than the second. As their properties demonstrate them to be excellent, take them up to make way for the others; and after this sort of weeding has been repeated for about three or four years, the residue may be thrown away as useless, or may be planted in wilderness quarters to take their chance.

Titles.

1. The White Lily is entitled, *Lilium foliis sparsis, corollis campanulatis, intus glabris*. It is called, *Lilium album, flore erecto, vulgare*, and *Lilium candidum*, by old authors. The varieties have gone by titles, as if distinct species. Thus the Pendulous Flowering sort is termed by Caspar Bauhine, *Lilium album, floribus dependentibus, sive peregrinum*. Gronovius calls another, *Lilium caule plano compresso*; and after this manner are most of the others named. It grows naturally in Palestine and Syria.

2. The Orange Lily is entitled, *Lilium foliis sparsis, corollis campanulatis erectis*. The varieties are variously called, *Lilium purpureo-croceum majus*, *Lilium bulbiferum latifolium majus*, *Lilium bulbiferum minus*, and the like. It grows naturally in Italy, Austria, and Silesia.

3. Pomponian Martagon. This species is titled, *Lilium foliis sparsis subulatis, floribus reflexis, corollis revolutis*. Gmelin calls it, *Lilium radice tunicatâ, foliis sparsis, floribus reflexis, corollis revolutis*. Clusius, *Lilium rubrum praecox*. It is a native of the Pyrenees, and grows common also in Siberia.

4. Chalcedonian Martagon is, *Lilium foliis sparsis lanceolatis, floribus reflexis revolutis*. Clusius calls it, *Lilium rubrum, sive miniatum Byzantinum*. Caspar Bauhine makes several distinct species of this sort. Lobel stiles it, *Hemerocallis Chalcedonica*. It grows naturally in Persia.

5. Superb Martagon is, *Lilium foliis sparsis lanceolatis, floribus ramoso-pyramidatis reflexis, corollis revolutis*. Catesby calls it, *Lilium, sive martagon Canadense, flore luteo punctato*. It grows naturally in North-America.

6. The Old Martagon, or Turk's Cap, is titled, *Lilium foliis verticillatis, floribus reflexis, corollis revolutis*. Dodonaeus calls it, *Lilium sylvestre*. It grows naturally in Siberia, Hungary, &c.

7. Canada Martagon is, *Lilium foliis verticillatis, floribus reflexis, corollis campanulatis*. Catesby calls it, *Lilium, sive martagon Canadense, floribus magnis flavis non reflexis*. Morison, *Lilium martagon Canadense maculatum*. It is a native of Canada.

8. Kampschatska Martagon is, *Lilium foliis verticillatis, flore erecto, corollâ campanulatâ, petalis sessilibus*. It grows naturally in Canada and Kamptschatska.

9. Pensylvania Martagon is termed, *Lilium foliis verticillatis, floribus erectis, corollâ campanulatâ, petalis unguiculatis*. It grows naturally in Pensylvania and Canada.

Class and order in the Linnaean system.

*Lilium* is of the class and order *Hexandria Monogynia*; and the characters are,

The characters.

1. Calyx. There is none.

2. Corolla is of a campanulated figure, and composed of six petals, which are narrow at their base, but gradually widen and become broad; their ends are obtuse, and in many of the species turn quite backward. These petals are of a thick substance, and their backs are keel-shaped. Each has a longitudinal line near the base; and this is the nectarium, which in some of the species is barbated, in others plane.

3. Stamina are six erect, subulated filaments, shorter than the corolla, with oblong, incumbent antherae.

4. Pistillum. The pistil consists of an oblong, cylindrical germen marked with six furrows, of a cylindrical style the length of the corolla, and a thick triangular stigma.

5. Pericarpium is an oblong, six-furrowed capsule, having a hollow, trigonal, and obtuse top, composed of three valves and containing three cells.

6. Semina. The seeds are numerous, flat, externally semi-orbiculated, and lie over each other in double order.

## C H A P. CCLXVIII.

## *LIMOSELLA*, The LEAST WATER PLANTAIN

THERE is only one ſpecies of this genus, called the Leaſt Water Plantain

*This plant deſcribed.*

The root is ſmall, and creeping The leaves are numerous, ſpear-ſhaped, and pointed at the extremity The ſtalk is ſlender, undivided, and about an inch or two high The flowers come out from the tops of the ſtalks, they are ſmall, of a white colour, and are to be met with in July, Auguſt, and September

*Titles*

This plant grows common in muddy places, but is never cultivated Being the only ſpecies of this genus yet known, it is named ſimply, *Limoſella* Caſpar Bauhine calls it, *Plantaginella paluſtris*, and Plukenet, *Alſine paluſtris repens, foliis lanceolatis, floribus perexiguis* It grows naturally in England, and moſt of the northern countries of Europe

*Claſs and order in the Linnæan ſyſtem The characters*

*Limoſella* is of the claſs and order *Didynamia Angioſpermia*, and the characters are,

1 CALYX is a monophyllous, upright, permanent perianthium, cut at the edge into five acute ſegments

2 COROLLA is one bell-ſhaped, erect, ſmall petal, cut at the brim into five acute ſpreading ſegments

3 STAMINA are four erect filaments ſhorter than the corolla, having ſimple antheræ

4 PISTILLUM conſiſts of an oblong obtuſe germen, a ſimple declining ſtyle the length of the ſtamina, and a globular ſtigma

5 PERICARPIUM is an oval capſule formed of two valves, and containing one cell

6 SEMINA The ſeeds are many, and oval

## C H A P. CCLXIX.

## *L I N U M*, F L A X

THERE are of this genus,

*Species*

1 Perennial Blue Flax
2 Viſcous Red Flax
3 Broad-leaved Hairy Flax
4 Narbonne Flax
5 Narrow-leaved Wild Flax
6 Auſtrian Flax
7 Virginian Flax
8 Broad-leaved Yellow Flax
9 Shrubby Flax
10 Tree Flax
11 Campanulated Flax
12 Maritime Flax
13 French Flax
14 Italian Flax

*Deſcription of the Perennial Blue,*

1 Perennial Blue Flax The ſtalks are numerous from a ſtrong root, upright, firm, branching near the top, and grow to be about four or five feet high The leaves are narrow, ſpear-ſhaped, acute, of a deep-green colour, and grow alternately The flowers come out in umbels from the ends of the branches, they are large, of a fine blue colour, appear in June and July, and are ſucceeded by obtuſe capſules, containing ripe ſeeds, in September

*Viſcous Red,*

2 Viſcous Red Flax The ſtalks are upright, branching near the top, and poſſeſſed of a viſcous or clammy matter The leaves are broad, ſpear-ſhaped, hairy, and have five conſpicuous veins running from the baſe towards the point The flowers come out from the ends of the branches in ſmall bunches, they are of a red colour, and appear about the ſame time with the former

*Broad leaved Hairy*

3 Broad-leaved Hairy Flax The ſtalks are round, thick, firm, hairy, branching near the top, and two feet high The leaves are broad, hairy, and grow alternately on the ſtalks The flowers come out alternately from the ſides of the branches, ſitting cloſe, having no footſtalks, they are large, of a deep blue colour, appear in June and July, and are ſucceeded by ripe ſeeds in September

*Narbonne*

4. Narbonne Flax The ſtalk is round, divides into ſeveral ſlender branches near the baſe, and grows to about a foot and a half high The leaves are ſpear-ſhaped, acute, rough, and come out ſparingly and without order from the ſides of the plant. The flowers are produced in kind of umbels from the ends of the branches, they are rather ſmall, and of a pale-blue colour, they appear in June and July, and are ſucceeded by ſmall capſules, containing ripe ſeeds, in September

*and Narrow leaved Wild Flax*

5 Narrow leaved Wild Flax The ſtalks are ſlender, divide into a few branches or rather footſtalks near the top, and grow to about a foot and a half high The leaves are narrow, moſtly, rough on their outſide, and come out without order The flowers come out a few together from the ends of the branches or footſtalks, they are of various colours

colours in the different varieties, appear in June and July, and are ſucceeded by ripe ſeeds in the autumn.

Varieties. There are numerous varieties of this ſpecies, differing chiefly with reſpect to the colour and ſize of the flowers; ſuch as the Blue, the White, Aſh-coloured, Purple, Violet, Stripe, Large Deep-blue, Great Purple, &c.

Auſtrian. 6. Auſtrian Flax. The ſtalks are ſlender, round, ſtriated, divide into a few ſlender footſtalks near the top, and grow to about a foot and a half high. The leaves are narrow, acute, and very ſparingly beſtowed on the plants. The flowers come out two or three together from the ends of the branches; they are of a blue colour, having round obtuſe cups; they appear about the ſame time with the former, and the ſeeds ripen accordingly.

Virginian. 7. Virginian Flax. The ſtalks are very ſlender, paniculated, and about a foot high. The radical leaves are oval, ſmooth, entire; but thoſe on the ſtalks are narrow, ſpear-ſhaped, grow alternately, and ſit cloſe to the ſides of the ſtalks. The flowers come out alternately from the ſides of the branches, having acute cups, and very ſhort footſtalks; they are of a yellow colour, appear in June and July, and are ſucceeded by globular capſules, containing ripe ſeeds, in the autumn.

Broad-leaved Yellow, 8. Broad-leaved Yellow Flax. The ſtalks are upright, firm, and divide into branches at the top by pairs. The leaves are broad, oblong, pointed, and ſit cloſe to the ſtalks. The flowers are produced in panicles from the tops of the ſtalks; they are of a yellow colour, and appear about the ſame time with the others.

and Shrubby Flax deſcribed. 9. Shrubby Flax. The ſtalks are ligneous, upright, firm, branching into footſtalks near the top, and are a foot and a half high. The leaves are narrow, rough, and acute. The flowers come out from the tops of the branches on ſlender footſtalks; they are moderately large, of a white colour, appear in July, but are not always ſucceeded by ripe ſeeds in England.

Variety. There is a variety of this plant with yellow flowers.

Tree, 10. Tree Flax. This plant hath a perennial fibrous root, which ſends forth ſeveral upright ligneous ſtalks, which grow to about a yard high. The leaves are wedge-ſhaped, broad, and placed without order. The flowers come out from the ends of the branches, on ſlender footſtalks; they appear in July, but are ſeldom ſucceeded by ripe ſeeds in England.

This plant muſt have a well-ſheltered ſituation, and a few plants ſhould be ſet in pots to be houſed in winter, to keep up the ſorts, leſt thoſe abroad ſhould be deſtroyed.

Campanulated. 11. Campanulated Flax. The ſtalks are ſimple, angular, and about four or five inches high. The leaves are roundiſh, narrow, and the lower ones ſpatula-ſhaped, and have a glandulous punctum on each ſide the baſe. The flowers come out three or four together from the tops of the ſtalks, on ſlender footſtalks; they are large, and of a yellow colour, appear in July, and are ſometimes ſucceeded by ripe ſeeds in the autumn.

Maritime, 12. Maritime Flax. The ſtalks are upright, ſmooth, two feet high, and divide into ſeveral branches near the top. The leaves are ſpear-ſhaped, and the lower ones grow oppoſite to each other, but thoſe on the upper parts of the plant are placed alternately. The flowers come out in ſmall bunches from the tops of the branches; they are of a yellow colour, and hang downward; they appear in July, and are ſucceeded by ripe ſeeds in the autumn.

French, 13. French Flax. The ſtalks are ſlender, white, and hardly a foot high. The leaves are narrow, ſpear-ſhaped, and placed alternately. The flowers come out from the tops of the ſtalks in ſmall panicles; they are of a yellow colour, appear in June and July, and the ſeeds ripen in the autumn.

and Italian Flax deſcribed. 14. Italian Flax. The ſtalks are angular, ſlender, ſmooth, ſtiff, and divide at the top into two or three parts. The leaves are narrow, ſpear-ſhaped, ſmooth, and grow alternately. The flowers come out ſingly from the joints, ſitting cloſe, having no footſtalks; they are of a yellow colour, and almoſt hid by their long, leafy, narrow cups; they will be in blow in June and July, and are followed by ripe ſeeds in the autumn.

Method of propagation. All theſe ſorts are eaſily propagated by ſowing the ſeeds in the ſpring, in beds of light, freſh, good earth. When they come up, they muſt be kept clean from weeds; and where they are too cloſe, when they are fit to remove, a ſhare of the plants may be drawn out with a ball of mould to each root, and ſet in other places where they are wanted: they muſt be ſhaded and watered until they have taken root, and after that they will require no trouble except keeping them clean from weeds. They all vary in their height, according to the goodneſs or poverty of the ſoil in which they are planted; and a proportionable greater number of ſtalks will ariſe from the roots, in proportion to their ſtrength, and the greater number of years they have remained undiſturbed. Moſt of them afford flax, of which linen may be made, but of a very inferior nature to that well-known cultivated plant called Flax, which is an annual, and comes of courſe to be treated of among others of ſuch a ſhort-lived nature.

Titles. 1. Perennial Blue Flax is titled, *Linum calycibus capſuliſque obtuſiuſculis, foliis alternis lanceolatis integerrimis*. In the *Hortus Upſal.* it is termed, *Linum alternis lanceolatis integerrimis, calycibus apice obtuſis, capſulis muticis*; in the *Hortus Cliffort.* *Linum perenne, ramis foliiſque alternis lineari-lanceolatis*. Moriſon calls it, *Linum perenne majus cæruleum, capitulo majore*; and Ray, *Linum ſylveſtre cæruleum perenne erectius, flore et capitulo majore*; alſo, *Linum ſylveſtre cæruleum perenne procumbens, flore et capitulo minore*. It grows naturally on barren land in England and Siberia.

2. Viſcous Red Flax is, *Linum foliis lanceolatis piloſis, quinquenerviis*. Caſpar Bauhine calls it, *Linum ſylveſtre latifolium, caule viſcoſo, flore rubro*. It grows naturally in France and Germany.

3. Broad-leaved Hairy Flax is, *Linum calycibus hirſutis acuminatis, ſeſſilibus alternis, caule corymboſo*. Moriſon calls it, *Linum ſylveſtre latifolium hirſutum cæruleum*. It grows naturally in Tartary and Auſtria.

4. Narbonne Flax is, *Linum calycibus acuminatis, foliis lanceolatis ſparſis ſtrictis ſcabris acuminatis, caule tereti, baſi ramoſo*. Caſpar Bauhine calls it, *Linum ſylveſtre cæruleum, folio acuto*; and Magnol, *Linum ſylveſtre anguſtifolium, cæruleo amplo flore*. It grows naturally in France, Italy, Spain, and Germany.

5. Narrow-leaved Wild Flax is, *Linum calycibus acuminatis, foliis ſparſis linearibus retrorſum ſcabris*. Haller calls it, *Linum perenne, foliis anguſtioribus, calycibus ariſtatis*; Caſpar Bauhine, *Linum ſylveſtre anguſtifolium, flore magno*; alſo, *Linum ſylveſtre anguſtifolium, floribus dilutè purpuraſcentibus vel carneis*; alſo, *Linaria, capillaceo folio, altera*; alſo, *Linum ſylveſtre, anguſtis et denſioribus foliis, flore minore*; Cluſius, *Linum ſylveſtre V. anguſtifolium*; alſo, *Lini ſylveſtris V. anguſtifolii aliud genus*; alſo, *Linum ſylveſtre VI. anguſtifolium*; Tournefort, *Linum ſylveſtre anguſtifolium, flore magno*.

*magno intus cæruleo*, also, *Linum sylvestre angustifolium, flore magno violaceo*, also, *Linum sylvestre angustifolium, flore magno lineis purpureis distincto*, also, *Linum sylvestre angustifolium, flore magno cæruleo et velut cinereo* also, *Linum angustifolium album, ramusculis per terram sparsis*, and Boccone, *Linum oxyphyllum multicaule* It grows naturally in dry meadows and pastures in England, France, and Germany

6 Austrian Flax is, *Linum calycibus capitulatis obtusis, foliis linearibus acutis* Jacquin names it, *Linum sylvestre II* and Caspar Bauhine, *Linum sylvestre angustifolium, foliis raris* It is a native of Lower Austria

7 Virginian Flax is, *Linum calycibus acutis alternis, capsulis muticis, pedunculis filiformibus, foliis alternis lanceolatis, radicalibus ovatis* Gronovius calls it, *Linum ramis, foliisque alternis lanceolatis sessilibus nervo longitudinali instructis* It grows naturally in Virginia and Pensylvania

8 Broad-leaved Yellow Flax is, *Linum calycibus subserratis scabris lanceolatis subsessilibus, panicula ramis dichotomis* Caspar Bauhine calls it, *Linum latifolium sylvestre luteum*, John Bauhine, *Linum latifolium luteum*, and Clusius, *Linum sylvestre III latifolium* It is a native of Austria

9 Shrubby Flax is, *Linum foliis linearibus acutis scabris, caulibus suffruticosis* Tournefort calls it, *Linum angustifolium fruticosum Valentinum, foliis rigidis et aculeatis* It grows naturally in some parts of France and Germany

10 Tree Flax is, *Linum foliis cuneiformibus, caulibus arborescentibus* Alpinus calls it, *Linum arboreum* It is a native of Italy and Crete

11 Campanulated Flax is, *Linum foliorum basi utrinque puncto glanduloso* Sauvages calls it, *Linum foliis imis spathulatis, floribus luteis*, Caspar Bauhine, *Linum sylvestre luteum, foliis subrotundis*, also, *Rapunculus nemorosus angustifolius, parvo flore*, John Bauhine, *Campanula lutea lini folia*, and Lobel, *Campanula lutea linifolia montis Lupi, flore volubili* It grows naturally in France

12 Maritime Flax is, *Linum calycibus ovatis acutis muticis, foliis lanceolatis inferioribus oppositis* Van Royen calls it, *Linum caule simplici, ramis foliisque inferioribus oppositis linearilanceolatis*, Guettard, *Linum foliis acutis, floribus racemosis*, Dodonæus, *Linum sylvestre*, Caspar Bauhine, *Linum maritimum luteum*, and John Bauhine, *Linum luteum Narbonense* It grows naturally in France, Italy and the East

13 French Flax is, *Linum calycibus acutis, foliis lanceolato-linearibus alternis, panicula pedunculis brevibus* Sauvages calls it, *Linum foliis linearilanceolatis, pedunculis bifidis, floribus luteis*, and Caspar Bauhine, *Linum sylvestre minus, flore luteo* It grows naturally near Montpelier

14 Italian Flax is, *Linum foliis floriferis oppositis lanceolatis, floribus alternis sessilibus, calycibus longitudine foliorum* Morison calls it, *Linum luteum singulari specula floridum*; and Columna, *Linum luteum sylvestre latifolium*. It grows naturally in the strong marshy meadows of Italy

*Linum* is of the class and order *Pentandria Pentagynia*, and the characters are, (Class and order in the Linnæan system.)

1 CALYX is a permanent perianthium, composed of five small, spear-shaped, acute, erect leaves

2 COROLLA is infundibuliforme, and consists of five large oblong petals, which are narrow at their base, but widen gradually towards the top, where they are broad, obtuse and spreading

3 STAMINA are five awl-shaped erect filaments the length of the calyx, having simple sagittated antheræ

4 PISTILLUM consists of an oval germen, and five filiforme erect styles the length of the stamina, with simple reflexed stigmas

5 PERICARPIUM is a globular five-cornered capsule, formed of five valves, and containing ten cells

6 SEMINA The seeds are single in each cell, oval, plane, acuminated, and smooth

## CHAP CCLXX

## *LITHOSPERMUM*, GROMWELL.

THE perennial species of *Lithospermum* are,

1 The Great Upright Gromwell

Species 2 The Smaller Creeping Gromwell

3 The Virginian Gromwell

Description of the Great Upright, 1 Great Upright Gromwell This plant will grow to near a yard high The stalk is upright, branching, round, hard, and firm The leaves are spear-shaped, rough, hairy, of a dusky-green colour, and placed alternately without any footstalks on the branches The flowers are produced from the joints in May, they are small, white, and are succeeded by whitish glossy seeds in July or August

Smaller Creeping, 2 Smaller Creeping Gromwell The stalks are not more than a foot in length, and naturally trail on the ground The leaves are spear shaped, long, narrow, and placed alternately on the stalks The flowers are produced from the ends of the stalks early in June, they are of a white colour, and are succeeded by smooth glossy seeds, which will be ripe in August

3 Virginian Gromwell This will grow to about a foot and a half high The stalks are hairy, and many of them arise from the root The leaves are nearly of an oval figure, veined, rough, hairy, and placed alternately, without any footstalks, on the branches The flowers are produced from the ends of the stalks in short reflexed spikes, their colour is white, they will be in blow in June, and ripen their seeds in September (Virginian Gromwell.)

Nothing can be easier than the culture of these plants Sow the seeds any where, in any soil or situation, soon after they are ripe, or in the spring, (Culture)

spring, and they will readily come up, and require no other trouble than thinning them to proper distance where they come up too close.

Titles 1 The Great Upright or Common Gromwell is titled, *Lithospermum seminibus lævibus, corollis calycem superantibus, foliis lanceolatis*. Caspar Bauhine calls it, *Lithospermum majus erectum*, and John Bauhine, *Lithospermum, sive milium solis*. It grows naturally on dry banks, and gravelly sandy places in some parts of England, and in the like places in many other parts of Europe.

2 Smaller Creeping Gromwell is, *Lithospermum seminibus lævibus, corollis calycem multoties superantibus*. Caspar Bauhine calls it, *Lithospermum minus repens latifolium*, and Clusius, *Lithospermum repens majus*. It grows naturally in woods, and by the sides of paths in many parts of England, Italy, and France.

3 Virginian Gromwell is, *Lithospermum foliis subovalibus nervosis, corollis acuminatis*. Gronovius calls it, *Lithospermum corollarum laciniis acuminatis bifidis*, Morison and Ray, *Lithospermum latifolium Virginianum, flore albido longiore*. It grows naturally in Virginia.

*Lithospermum* is of the class and order *Pentandria Monogynia*; and the characters are, Class and order in the Linnæan system

1 CALYX is an oblong, acute, permanent perianthium, divided into five subulated hollow segments. The character

2 COROLLA is an infundibuliforme petal the length of the calyx. The tube is cylindrical, the limb is slightly divided into five obtuse erect segments, the mouth is open.

3 STAMINA are five very short filaments, with oblong antheræ inclosed in the mouth of the corolla.

4. PISTILLUM consists of four germina, a filiforme style the length of the tube of the corolla, and an obtuse bifid stigma.

5 PERICARPIUM There is none. The calyx becomes patulous, long, and contains the seeds in its cavity.

6 SEMINA The seeds are four in each cavity, they are oval, pointed, smooth, and hard.

# CHAP. CCLXXI.

## *LOBELIA*, CARDINAL FLOWER.

Species THE perennials of this genus are,

1 The Scarlet Cardinal Flower

2 Blue Cardinal Flower

3 Water Gladiole

Scarlet Cardinal Flower 1 Scarlet Cardinal Flower. The root is thick, white, fleshy, fibrated and full of a milky juice. The stalks are erect, firm, and grow to be two feet high. The radical leaves are oblong, serrated, and of a dusky-green or dark purple colour on the upper side. The leaves on the stalks are spear-shaped, serrated, and placed alternate on short rootstalks. The flowers come out from the tops of the stalks in long spikes, they are large, of a beautiful scarlet colour, and the general characters after the titles indicate their structure; they appear in July and August, and in favourable seasons are succeeded by ripe seeds in the autumn.

Varieties There are two or three varieties of this species, but their chief difference is in the size of the plants, which is inconsiderable, the flowers of all being of a most delightful scarlet colour, and grow in long spikes almost half the length of the stalks.

Blue Cardinal Flower 2 Blue Cardinal Flower. This plant hath a fibrous perennial root, but not so thick and milky as the former. The radical leaves are oval, spear-shaped, smooth, and a little indented on their edges. The stalks are upright, firm, a foot and a half high, and adorned with leaves like the radical ones, but smaller. The flowers come out from the wings of the leaves almost half down the stalks; they are of a pale blue colour, having large cups that have reflexed edges, they appear early in July, and the seeds ripen in the autumn.

Varieties There are two or three varieties of this species, one of which has a deeper blue flower, and another has a fine violet-coloured flower.

and Water Gladiole described 3 Water Gladiole. The root is composed of many long narrow fibres. The leaves are long, narrow, hollow, green, sweet to the taste, and each has a longitudinal partition, dividing it into two cells. The stalks are round, naked, and of different heights, according to the situation or depth of the water in which the plant grows, for it usually rises to exhibit the flowers above the surface of the water. The flowers come out from the tops of the stalks on footstalks, they are of a white colour, having a mixture of blue, they appear in July and August, and are succeeded by ripe seeds in the autumn.

This species is often found growing several yards under the water; and the leaves being tender, and sweet to the taste, become admirable food for wild-ducks, which are so very fond of them, that they will always repair to such places where they can meet with them, so that wherever there is plenty of these plants, there will be sure of being plenty of those fowls.

Method of propagating them The first two sorts are in great esteem for their flowers, and are cultivated in all gardens where any pretension to a collection of plants is made. They are raised by sowing the seeds in the autumn, as soon as they are ripe, in pots filled with rich garden-mould, and the plants will then come up in the spring, whereas if the seeds are kept until the spring before they are sowed, they rarely come up before the spring following. When the seeds are sown, the pots must be set under a warm wall, full upon the sun, and when heavy rains come on must be removed into shelter, also when the frosts advance, they should be set under a hotbed-frame, or the like, frost and over moisture b[illegible] g[illegible] pots to the[illegible] beds, e[illegible]n before they vegetate [illegible] the return of mild weather they [illegible] be exposed to the [illegible], it being highly necessary to [illegible] them to come up strong [illegible] good colour [illegible] the spring When you find the plants coming up, they [illegible] be set under the hot bed-frame, to be covered in bad weather, should it happen [illegible] very sharp frosts frequently happen late in the spring, which would probably destroy all your seedlings, were they to be exposed to such inclemencies in that early state

When all danger from bad weather is over, the pots must be set abroad in a place where the plants may have the morning sun only until eleven o'clock, they must be frequently watered in dry weather, and by the beginning of June some of them will be large enough to remove These should be taken up with care, and set in small pots filled with rich fat earth, then the plants must be directly watered, and the pots plunged up to the rims in the common mould in a shady part of the garden, but not under the drip of trees The other seedlings also must be transplanted when they are larger, and treated in a similar manner All summer they must be watered in dry weather, the weeds picked out as they rise, and by the end of July, or early in August, the strongest plants will require to be shifted into larger pots, which must be filled with the like kind of light rich earth, for it cannot be too fat and good for these plants In shifting them, care must be taken not to disturb the mould about the roots, or to break the fibres These roots must be turned out of the pots with the mould, and having others half filled should be set in them, filling up the vacant parts, and gently pressing the whole close with the hand They should now have a slight watering, be set in the shade until September, then be removed where they can have the morning sun, and in October should be set in a warm well-sheltered place, where they can have the whole day's sun At the approach of hard frosts they must be placed under shelter, but ought always to be set abroad again on the return of mild weather In the spring a share of them should be turned out into the full ground, the rest must be shifted into still larger pots, and plunged up to the rims in the common mould, in a place where they may have the morning sun until eleven o'clock, they should be duly watered in dry weather, and as the spring advances, you will find them shooting up strong for flowering They will exhibit their bloom in July, but in August they will be in their utmost glory The spike will be half the length of the stalk In order to continue them longer in beauty, they should have absolute shade the whole day, except a sufficient number designed for seeds These should have the morning sun at first, and afterwards the day's sun, and protection from heavy rains, the more effectually to procure good seeds for the encrease of this beautiful plant

Another, but inferior way of encreasing these plants is by parting of the roots, which should be done in the autumn The offsets should be set in pots, should have similar treatment to the seedling plants all winter, and in the spring should be set in the common ground for flowering

These plants are also encreased by cuttings The lower parts of the stalks afford the best cuttings They should be planted in beds of rich earth, and covered close down with glasses, to facilitate their taking root When they are in a growing state, the glasses should be removed, and their after-treatment should be similar to the seedlings

The last two methods of propagation are inferior to that of raising them from seeds, so that whoever is desirous of having their plants in perfection should regularly sow the seeds, to raise plants for a succession, especially for the first sort, which seldom if ever flowers so beautifully again as it does the first time from seeds The greatest share of plants also should be set in the open ground, for plants thus situated will be stronger, their spikes longer, and the flowers larger and fairer than such as are confined in pots

The third species grows naturally in waters I have never propagated it, but entertain no doubt that if the seeds are gathered in the autumn, when they are ripe, and thrown into waters that have sandy or gravelly bottoms, which they like better than mud, they will grow and become great allurements to wild ducks, teal, wigeons, and the like kind of fowls, which will resort to such places in plenty for the sake of the leaves, as well as give ample satisfaction to the Botanist who will eagerly repair thither also to make observations on the whole plant, but more especially the flowers

1 The Scarlet Cardinal Flower is titled, *Lobelia caule erecto, foliis lanceolatis serratis, spica terminali* Morison calls it, *Rapuntium galeatum Virginianum, coccineo flore majore* and others, *Rapuntium maximum, coccineo spicato flore* It grows naturally in Virginia Titles

2 Blue Cardinal Flower is, *Lobelia caule erecto, foliis ovato lanceolatis crenatis, calycum sinubus reflexis* Morison calls it, *Rapuntium galeatum Virginianum, flore violaceo majore*, Douart, *Rapunculus Americanus, flore dilute cæruleo*, and others, *Trachelium Americanum, flore cæruleo* It grows naturally in the woods of Virginia

3 Water Gladiole is, *Lobelia foliis linearibus bilocularibus integerrimis, caule subnudo* In the *Flora Lapp* it is termed, *Lobelia foliis bilocularibus subulatis* Clusius calls it, *Gladiolus lacustris Dortmanni*, Caspar Bauhine, *Leucojum palustre, flore subcæruleo*, Gerard, *Gladiolus lacustris*, and Parkinson *Gladiolus lacustris Clusii, f Leucojum palustre, flore subcæruleo* It grows plentifully in Wales and most of the colder parts of Europe

*Lobelia* is of the class and order *Syngenesia Monogamia*, and the characters are, Class and order in the Linnæan system

1 CALYX is a small, monophyllous, withering perianthium, growing round the germen, and indented in five parts The characters

2 COROLLA is monopetalous, and a little ringent The tube is cylindrical, longer than the calyx, and divided longitudinally at the top The limb is divided into five spear shaped segments, of which the two upper are smallest, more reflexed, deeper cut, and constitute the upper lip, the other three are spreading, and larger

3 STAMINA are five awl-shaped filaments the length of the tube, having antheræ which coalesce at the top, and form an oblong cylinder, but at the bottom are divided into five parts

4 PISTILLUM consists of an acuminated germen situated below the flower, a cylindrical style longer than the stamina, and an obtuse hispid stigma

5 PERICARPIUM is an oval bilocular capsule, surrounded by the calyx, and opening at the top

6 SEMINA The seeds are numerous and small

CHAP

# CHAP. CCLXXII.

## LOLIUM.

OF this genus is a well-known graſs of our fields, called Red Darnel.

*The plant deſcribed.* The root is perennial. The leaves are narrow, pointed, and of a dark-green colour. The ſtalks are round, jointed, hollow, uſually of a reddiſh colour, and two or three feet high. The flowers come out in beardleſs ſpikes from the tops of the ſtalks; they are of a reddiſh colour, appear chiefly in June and July, and the ſeeds ripen in Auguſt.

*Titles.* This plant grows almoſt every where by way-ſides, &c. Its title is, *Lolium ſpicâ muticâ ſpiculis compreſſis multifloris*. In the *Hortus Cliffort.* it is termed, *Lolium ſpicis muticis*; in the *Flora Lapp. Lolium ſpicis compreſſis, radice perenni*. Caſpar Bauhine calls it, *Gramen loliaceum, anguſtiore folio & ſpica*; and Gerard, *Lolium rubrum*. It grows naturally in England, and moſt countries of Europe.

*Claſs and order in the Linnæan ſyſtem.* *Lolium* is of the claſs and order *Triandria Digynia*; and the characters are,

*The characters.* 1. CALYX. The glumes are each one awl-ſhaped permanent valve, containing the flowers, which form a long oblichous ſpike, ſitting cloſe to the ſtalk.

2. COROLLA conſiſts of two valves. The lower valve is narrow, ſpear-ſhaped, convoluted, pointed, and the length of the calyx. The upper valve is ſhorter, linear, more obtuſe, and concave upwards.

3. STAMINA are three capillary filaments ſhorter than the corolla, having oblong antheræ.

4. PISTILLUM conſiſts of a turbinated germen, and two capillary reflected ſtyles, with plumoſe ſtigmas.

5. PERICARPIUM. There is none. The ſeed is cheriſhed in the corolla, which opens, and ſends it forth when ripe.

6. SEMEN. The ſeed is ſingle, oblong, convex on one ſide, ſulcated, and plane on the other.

# CHAP. CCLXXIII.

## LOTUS, BIRD's FOOT TREFOIL.

*Species.* THE perennials of this genus proper for this place, are,

1. Common Engliſh Bird's Foot Trefoil.
2. Procumbent Meadow Bird's Foot Trefoil.
3. Maritime Bird's Foot Trefoil.
4. Linear podded Bird's Foot Trefoil.
5. Straight-podded Bird's Foot Trefoil.
6. Cytiſoide Bird's Foot Trefoil.
7. White Auſtrian Bird's Foot Trefoil.
8. Hairy Italian Bird's Foot Trefoil.

*Common Engliſh Bird's Foot Trefoil deſcribed.* 1. Common Engliſh Bird's Foot Trefoil. The root is long, creeping, and of a reddiſh colour. The ſtalks are ſlender, branching, herbaceous, procumbent, a little downy, and a foot and a half long. The leaves are of a greyiſh green colour, and like Trefoil, but have appendages or rather ſmall leaves at the baſe on each ſide the footſtalk. The flowers come out from the ſides of the ſtalk, growing three or four together, on long footſtalks; they are of a fine yellow colour, appear in June, and are ſucceeded by narrow taper pods, containing ripe ſeeds, in September.

*Varieties.* There are ſeveral varieties of this ſpecies. Some have narrow leaves, and ſtalks a yard long; ſome are pentaphyllous, and of a ligneous nature; while others again hardly grow to a foot high. They all, very much according to the goodneſs or poorneſs of the ſoil, encreaſe very faſt by the roots or ſeeds; which ſcattering, will ſpontaneouſly grow, and cauſe no trouble to the Gardener, except extirpating the redundant quantity.

*Procumbent Meadow,* 2. Procumbent Meadow Bird's Foot Trefoil. The ſtalks are herbaceous, ſlender, diffuſe, and about a foot long. The leaves are trifoliate, have appendages at their baſe, and are downy underneath. The flowers come out ſingly from the ſides of the ſtalk on longiſh footſtalks; they are of a yellow colour, appear in June and July, and are ſucceeded by membranaceous quadrangular pods, containing ripe ſeeds, in the autumn.

*Maritime,* 3. Maritime Bird's Foot Trefoil. The ſtalks are ſlender, trailing, and a foot and a half long. The leaves are trifoliate, ſmooth, and have two appendages or ſmaller leaves at the baſe of each footſtalk. The flowers come out ſingly from the wings of the ſtalk on long ſlender footſtalks; they are of a yellow colour, appear in June and July, and are ſucceeded by long pods, having at each corner a leafy membrane running the whole length of the pod, containing ripe ſeeds, in September.

*and Narrow podded Bird's Foot Trefoil deſcribed.* 4. Narrow-podded Bird's Foot Trefoil. The ſtalks are ſlender, branching, nearly upright, and from a foot to two feet long, according to the ſoil.

foil in which the plants grow The leaves are pentaphyllous, or rather trifoliate, having two small leaves at the base of each footstalk The flowers come out two or three together on alternate footstalks, they are of a yellow colour, appear in June and July, and are succeeded by long, narrow, erect pods, containing ripe seeds, in September

Straight podded Bird's Foot Trefoil described 5 Straight podded Bird's Foot Trefoil The stalks are upright, strong, ligneous, tough, branching near the top, three or four feet high, and covered with a purplish bark The leaves are trifoliate, hairy at the base of each footstalk, having a heart-shaped appendage or foliole, the others are wedge-shaped The whole leaf is of a light-green colour, hairy underneath, and situated singly at each joint The flowers are produced from the ends of the branches in roundish heads, they are of a pale red or flesh colour, appear in June and July, and are succeeded by smooth, straight, brown-coloured pods, containing ripe seeds, in September

Variety There is a variety of this species with white flowers

Cytisoide, 6 Cytisoide Bird's Foot Trefoil The stalks are numerous, slender, diffuse, and a foot and a half or two feet long The leaves are trifoliate, roundish, hoary, and appendiculated at their base The flowers come out in divided heads, growing on short footstalks, they are of a yellow colour, appear in July, and are succeeded by taper pods, containing ripe seeds, in the autumn

White Austrian, 7 White Austrian Bird's Foot Trefoil The stalks are smooth, slender, ligneous, branching, and three or four feet high The leaves are composed of five folioles, which are disposed in form of a hand, they are small, hoary, sit close to the branches, and are but thinly bestowed on the plant The flowers come out from the ends of the branches in small heads, the respective flowers are very small, and of a white colour, they appear in June, and are succeeded by short pods, containing ripe seeds, in the autumn

This being rather a tender species, must have a light, dry soil, and a well sheltered situation

and Hairy Italian Bird's Foot Trefoil described 8 Hairy Italian Bird's Foot Trefoil The stalks are perennial, hairy, branching, and three feet high The leaves are trifoliate, hoary, and have appendages to the base of the footstalks The flowers are collected into heads, which come out from the sides of the stalk on longish footstalks they are of a bad white colour, with a mixture of red, and have hairy cups, they appear in June and July, and are succeeded by short, oval, chesnut-coloured pods, containing ripe seeds, in the autumn

This is a still more tender species than the preceding, but may nevertheless be ventured abroad in warm well sheltered places

The first six species are easily raised by sowing the seeds in the autumn, soon after they are ripe, or in the spring After they come up they will call for no trouble except thinning them where they are too close, and keeping them clean from weeds

The seventh and eighth sorts being rather tender plants, should be more nicely managed They are best raised by sowing the seeds on a very slight hot bed in the spring When the plants are about three or four inches high, each should be set in a separate small pot filled with light fresh earth, and the pots should then be plunged up to the rims in the common mould, in a shady part of the garden Here they may remain, with the usual care of weeding and watering, all summer, and at the approach of frosty weather should be removed under shelter In the spring the plants may be turned out of the pots, with the mould at the roots, into the places where they are designed to remain, and here, if they are naturally dry and well defended, they will live many years But as it sometimes happens that they are killed by hard frosts, it will be adviseable to retain a plant or two of each sort in the pots to be housed in winter, in order to perpetuate the succession, in case those abroad should be destroyed by hard weather

They are also propagated by cuttings These should be planted, during any of the summer months, in beds of light earth, and if they are shaded and duly watered, they will readily take root In the autumn a share of them should be set in pots, observing to preserve a ball of earth to each root on the removal, to be housed in winter, and managed as the seedlings, whilst the others should be left to take their chance with the weather, as it shall happen

1 English Bird's Foot Trefoil is entitled, *Lotus capitulis depressis, caulibus decumbentibus, leguminibus cylindricis patentibus* In the *Hortus Cliffort* it is termed, *Lotus caule herbaceo, florum capitulo depresso, leguminibus decumbentibus teretibus* Caspar Bauhine calls it, *Lotus s melilotus pentaphyllos minor glabra*, also, *Lotus pentaphyllos flore majore luteo splendente*, also, *Lotus pentaphyllos fruticosus, tenuissimis glabris foliis*, also, *Trifolium corniculatum frutescens, tenuissimis foliis*, Ray, *Lotus pentaphyllos minor angustioribus foliis, fruticosior*, also, *Lotus corniculata major, ? ius hi suta*, also, *Lotus corniculata minor, foliis subtus incanis*, John Bauhine, *Lotus corniculata glabra minor*, and Gerard, *Trifolium siliquosum minus* It grows naturally in meadows, pastures, hedges and woods in England, and most parts of Europe Titles

2 Procumbent Meadow Bird's Foot Trefoil is, *Lotus leguminibus solitariis membranaceo quadrangulis, caulibus procumbentibus, foliis subtus pubescentibus* Caspar Bauhine calls it, *Lotus pratensis siliquosus luteus*, and Rivinus, *Lotus tetragonolobus* It grows naturally in moist meadows in most of the southern parts of Europe

3 Maritime Bird's Foot Trefoil is, *Lotus leguminibus solitariis membranaceo-quadrangulatis, foliis glabris, bracteis lanceolatis* Ray calls it, *Lotus siliquosa lutea, siliquis pinnatis strictioribus & longioribus*, and others, *Lotus tetragonolobus maritimus, flore luteo* It is a native of the maritime parts of Europe

4 Narrow-podded Bird's Foot Trefoil is, *Lotus leguminibus subbinatis linearibus strictis erectis, caule erecto, pedunculis alternis* Van Royen calls it, *Lotus leguminibus sæpius ternatis linearibus strictis erectis*, Caspar Bauhine, *Lotus pentaphyllos minor hirsutus, siliqua angustissima*, and John Bauhine *Lotus corniculata, siliquis singularibus s binis, tenuis* It is a native of Narbonne

5 Straight podded Bird's Foot Trefoil is, *Lotus capitulis subglobosis, caule erecto, leguminibus rectis glabris* Van Royen calls it, *Lotus caule fruticoso, florum capitulis globosis*, Caspar Bauhine, *Lotus siliquosus glaber, flore rotundo*, and Morison, *Lotus polyceratos frutescens hirsuta alba major latifolia, siliquis tenuibus, curtis rectis* It grows naturally in Calabria, Sicily, and the South of France

6 Cytisoide Bird's Foot Trefoil is *Lotus capitulis dimidiatis, caule diffuso ramosissimo, foliis tomentosis* Barrelier calls it, *Lotus siliquosa maritima lutea, cytisi facie* It grows naturally near the sea in most of the southern parts of Europe

7 White Austrian Bird's Foot Trefoil is, *Lotus capitulis aphyllis, foliis sessilibus quinatis* In the *Hortus Cliffort* it is termed, *Dorycnium foliis digitatis sessilibus* Lobel calls it, *Dorycnium Monspeliensium*, and Caspar Bauhine, *Trifolium album angustifolium, floribus ? capitulum congestis*

It

It grows naturally in Spain, Austria, and the South of France

8 Hairy Italian Bird's Foot Trefoil is, *Lotus capitulis hirsutis caule erecto hirto, leguminibus ovatis* In the *Hortus Cliffort* it is termed, *Lotus caule fruticoso, florum capitulis depressis, calycibus lanigeris* Caspar Bauhine calls it, *Lotus pentaphyllos siliquosus villosus*, and Morison, *Lotus polyceratos frutescens incana alba, siliquis erectis crassioribus et brevioribus rectis* It grows naturally in France, Italy, and the East

Class and order in the Linnæan system The characters

*Lotus* is of the class and order *Diadelphia Decandria*, and the characters are,

1 CALYX is a permanent monophyllous perianthium, cut at the top into five erect, equal, acute parts

2 COROLLA is papilionaceous The vexillum is roundish, and bent backward The alæ are roundish, broad, shorter than the vexillum, and meet at the top The carina is short, rising a little, acuminated, gibbous on the lower part, and closed above

3 STAMINA are diadelphous, nine are joined in a body, and one stands separate, having small simple antheræ

4 PISTILLUM consists of an oblong taper germen, a simple rising style, and an inflexed stigma

5 PERICARPIUM is a close cylindrical pod shorter than the calyx, formed of two valves, and containing one cell, but crammed with numerous partitions to keep the seeds separate

6 SEMINA The seeds are several, and cylindrical

## CHAP CCLXXIV.

## LUNARIA, MOON-WORT.

THERE is one species of this genus which may not improperly be introduced here, called the Sweet-scented *Lunaria*, or Broad-leaved Violet

The plant described

The stalks are upright, whitish, tough, branching, and grow to near two feet high The leaves are oval, spear-shaped, pointed, rough, and grow alternately on the stalks The flowers come out in spikes from the ends of the stalks, and are of an agreeable odour, they are of different colours in the different varieties, some being of a reddish-purple, some white, and others yellow, they make their appearance in June, and are succeeded by oblong flat pods, containing ripe seeds, in the autumn

Culture

This sort is propagated by sowing the seeds, either in the autumn, soon after they are ripe, or in the spring, though the former is preferable As the roots are very tough, and strike deep into the ground, the best way will be to sow them in the places where they are to remain, and they will be proportionably stronger plants than if they had been removed When they come up, they will require no other trouble than thinning them where they are too close, and keeping them clean from weeds, and they will flower the second summer after sowing They should have a light, dry, sandy, or rubbishy soil, and being thus situated, the roots will continue for many years, but in a rich moist earth they are subject to rot, and to be killed by hard winters The stalks die to the ground in the autumn, and rise again from the roots in the spring, and they will flower, and ripen their seeds every year Any desired number of plants may be easily obtained

Titles

This species is titled, *Lunaria foliis alternis* In the *Hortus Cliffort* it is termed, *Lunaria foliis cordatis* Caspar Bauhine calls it, *Viola lunaria major, siliquâ oblongâ*, and Clusius, *Viola latifolia Lunaria odorata* It grows naturally in the northern parts of Europe

Class and order in the Linnæan system The characters

*Lunaria* is of the class and order *Tetradynamia Siliculosa*, and the characters are,

1 CALYX is an oblong perianthium, composed of four oval, oblong, obtuse, connivent, deciduous leaves

2 COROLLA The corolla consists of four large, obtuse, entire petals, placed cruciforme

3 STAMINA consist of six awl shaped filaments (of which four are the length of the calyx, the other two a little shorter), having erect patent antheræ

4 PISTILLUM consists of a pedicellated, oval, oblong germen, a very short style, and an entire, obtuse stigma

5 PERICARPIUM is a large, elliptical, plane, compressed pod, situated upon a small footstalk terminated by the style, composed of two valves, and containing two cells

6 SEMINA The seeds are few, kidney-shaped, compressed, possessed of a border, and situated in the middle of the pod

# CHAP. CCLXXV.

## *LUPINUS*, LUPINE.

THOUGH the Gardener can hardly form any other idea of a Lupine than that of an annual, we shall introduce him to one species of this genus which will last for years, viz the Virginian Lupine

The plant described. The root is long, and strikes deep into the ground The stalks are upright, channelled, branching, and will grow to near two feet high The leaves are digitated, and each is composed of about eight spear shaped, obtuse, smooth lobes, they are a little hairy at their edges, join at their base, and are placed on long footstalks on the branches The flowers adorn the ends of the stalks in long loose spikes, each individual flower having its own separate short footstalk; they are of a pale-blue colour, will be in blow in June, and produce good seeds in August

Method of propagating it. This species is propagated by sowing of the seeds in the spring where they are to remain, for they do not like transplanting, so that little more is to be done after that, than to thin them where they come up too close and let them stand to flower This is a very pretty perennial, and will be very ornamental in June and July It has also this other good property If after a dry summer a moist autumn should happen, fresh stalks at that season will rise from the roots, which will continue to flower until the frost stops them Plants of this tendency should ever be valued, because by such we are entertained at a season when few other flowers appear This species should have a dry, light, sandy soil

The Virginian Lupine is titled, *Lupinus calycibus alternis inappendiculatis, labio superiore emarginato, inferiore integro* Gronovius calls it, *Lupinus calycibus alternis*, [illegible], Van Royen, *Lupinus* [illegible], and Morison, *Lupinus* [illegible] *Virginianus repens* It grows naturally in Virginia

*Lupinus* is of the class and order *Diadelphia Decandria*, and the characters are,

1 CALYX is [illegible] bind, monophyllous perianthium

2 COROLLA is papilionaceous The vexillum is cordated, roundish, emarginated and [illegible] sides reflexed and compressed The [illegible] nearly oval and [illegible] the length of the vexillum, they are not fixed to the carina, but join at their base The carina is narrow, [illegible], acuminated, entire, and the length of the alæ

3 STAMINA are ten filaments joined at their base, but above are distinct, and have roundish, oblong antheræ

4 PISTILLUM consists of a subulated, compressed, hairy germen, a subulated, rising style, and an obtuse stigma

5 PERICARPIUM is a large, oblong, coriaceous, compressed, acuminated, unilocular pod

6 SEMINA. The seeds are many, roundish, and compressed

It must be observed, that the figure of the calyx varies in the different species

# CHAP CCLXXVI.

## *LYCHNIS*, CAMPION

THE *Lychnis* affords us several species of fine flowy plants, very different in appearance, all hardy and easy of culture, and as such beloved by those who wish to have little trouble Most of them are well-known plants, and their usual names are as follow

Species

1 Scarlet *Lychnis*
2 Ragged Robin, Meadow Pink, Wild William or Cuckow Flower
3 Batchelor's Button
4 German Catch-Fly
5 Alpine *Lychnis*
6 Siberian *Lychnis*
7 Lapland *Lychnis*

1 Scarlet *Lychnis* Of this species there are two notable varieties, viz

Single Scarlet *Lychnis*
Double Scarlet *Lychnis*

Single Scarlet *Lychnis* is a very beautiful flower in its single state It rises with an upright stalk, round and firm, to the height of [illegible] four feet The stalk is hairy, [illegible] leaves are placed opposite by pairs at the joints, [illegible] at some of the joints, from the bosom of the leaves, issue out other smaller [illegible], [illegible] with leaves, though [illegible] like manner The main [illegible] nated by a large bunch of flowers [illegible] the side shoots will have [illegible] These will be in blow in June and July, [illegible] in August, and their seeds will be ripe in the autumn The most common colour of this flower is a fine scarlet, which is the most beautiful of all though there are varieties of it with flowers of a pale-red colour, and [illegible] that produces white bloom

To

To continue these [illegible] on the best way is to sow the seeds early in the spring. They [illegible] come up, [illegible] the following [illegible] in June, July, or August, they should be [illegible] where they [illegible] remain. The [illegible] flowers, [illegible] flower, [illegible] and [illegible] flower-stalks and [illegible] of flowers, than these plants [illegible] of the roots by which method [illegible] they are to be encreased.

Double [illegible] is a very great improvement of the Single, beautiful as the latter [illegible], its charms are enhanced in the former more than ten fold. The flowers are formed in very large bunches, and [illegible] they do not come out quite so early as the Single sorts, they continue longer in blow. They are of a deep-scarlet colour, and [illegible] the look of a deep blaze. The [illegible] was formerly called *Lychnis*, because the downy substance of its leaves was often used for lamps, torches, &c. We regret its being [illegible] to *Agrostemma*, as well as the species under consideration being arranged under the word *Lychnis*, because none of them are possessed of that property. But if any-thing can justify this arrangement, it must be this Double variety, which may very properly be termed *Lychnis*, from the Greek word λυχνος, light, the flower having some appearance of a flame.

This beautiful variety, as is common with most other double flowers, never produces any seeds, but may be encreased by parting of the roots, and also by planting cuttings of the flower-stalks. If the stalks are vigorous and strong, three joints will be a proper cutting, two of which are to be planted in the ground. If the joints be close, as it often happens, then take five joints, planting three of them in the ground. This work must be performed before the flowers appear, or the stalks get too woody, and they will more readily take root. They should be well watered after planting, and shaded. If the soil be fresh and good, and they are finally planted out into such ground, they will succeed better than in very rich, dunged, old garden mould, for in [illegible] soil they often canker, and soon die away.

2. Ragged Robin. Of this species there are two principal sorts, viz.

Common Ragged Robin.
Double Ragged Robin.

Common Ragged Robin is found almost every where in our meadows and pastures, and is never in its single state planted in gardens.

Double Ragged Robin is the former species in its improved double state. It forms a large fair flower, and is much coveted by all lovers of flowers. The stalks are slender, channelled, and will rise to about two feet in height. They are jointed, and at the joints stand the leaves, opposite by pairs. In some they are long, narrow, and spear-shaped. The flowers ornament the tops of the stalks, standing on long footstalks. Each of the petals is deeply cut into four narrow parts, and has a torn ragged look, which occasions the flower to be called by the name of Ragged Robin, though its true name is Meadow Campion. It also goes by the name of Meadow Pinks, Wild Williams, and Cuckow Flower. It flowers in May, and the seeds of the Single sort ripen in June, by which plenty of plants may be raised. The Double sort never produces seeds, but may be encreased by parting of the roots, slips, [illegible].

3. Batchelor's Button. The principal varieties of this species are,

Common Red.
Double Red.
Double White.

Common Red Batchelor's Button grows common all over England. The [illegible] of almost every ditch will afford you for [illegible] of this sort; it is therefore never propagated in gardens.

There is a single variety of this sort, with white flowers, and [illegible] cups.

Double Red Batchelor's Button is the very sort which grows so common, [illegible] its full [illegible] and the multiplicity of petals are such in addition, as to make it really a desirable [illegible]. The stalks will rise to about a yard in height, and branch out in a very irregular manner. At every joint stand the leaves by pairs. These are of an oval figure, but end in acute points, are rough, very hairy, have their edges entire, and are rather of an unpleasant green colour. The flowers grow in clusters at the ends of the branches; they are of a red colour with a tinge of purple, and appear in April and May. The male and female flowers grow upon separate plants.

Double White Batchelor's Button blows in May. The flowers stand singly on [illegible] footstalks. This is less common than the Red sort, and much less beautiful. Both sorts are to be propagated by dividing the roots, or slips; the best time for which is August or September, when a moist day, if possible, should be made choice of for the work; if not, the earth should be well watered, and the plants shaded, and they will soon take root.

4. German Catch-Fly. The varieties of this species are,

Common Single Red German Catch-Fly.
Double Red German Catch-Fly.

Common Single Red German Catch-Fly grows wild in Wales and some parts of the North. It is now totally banished gardens to make room for the

Double Red German Catch Fly. This is of no very long standing in our English gardens; but the beauty of its flowers, and its easy propagation, have now made it as common a perennial as any we have. It is a variety of the Single sort, from which it was first raised from seeds. The leaves are long, narrow, and possessed of a downy matter near their base, where they are of a purplish colour. The flower-stalks are singly, will be from a foot and a half to two feet in height, and are smooth and jointed. The leaves stand at the joints opposite by pairs. Towards the top of the stalks, under each joint, exudes a kind of viscous matter of so clammy nature, as to entangle flies and other small insects. Hence the name of Catch-Fly was given to this species. The flowers terminate the stalks in small clusters, and for several joints downwards very small flower-stalks arise which are also terminated by flowers. These make a very good show, being of a fine red or purplish colour, large, very double, and form [illegible] a sort of spike of a considerable length. They will be in blow in May, and, if the weather is cool, continue a considerable time in beauty; but if very parching weather happens, as it often does at that early part of the summer, unless they are shaded, the flowers will be soon over.

The Single sort is raised in plenty by the seeds; but the Double is to be encreased only by parting the roots, the best time for which is August, when every slip will grow, and soon become a good plant. These should be well watered and shaded on their planting out.

Lychnis?
Cultivation.

Double Lychnis described.

Culture.

Common Ragged Robin.

and Double Ragged Robin described.

Propagation.

Double Red Batchelor's Button described.

Method of propagation.

Common Single and Double Red German Catch Fly described.

Method of propagating them.

Alpine

D fcrip tion of Al, ine Lycl nis

5 Alpine *Lychnis* is a low-growing plant, feldom rifing to more than eight inches in height The leaves are fpear fhaped, fmooth, and of a deep-green colour The ftalks are erect, and jointed, and the leaves which garnifh them are like the radical ones but fmaller, and ftand oppofite by pairs at the joints The flowers are produced from the tops of the ftalks in roundifh bunches, they are of a purplifh colour, and each of the petals is bifid, or cut in the middle, they will be in blow early in June, and are fucceeded by feeds, which will be ripe in Auguft

Method of propagation

By thefe feeds plenty of plants may be raifed They are alfo to be encreafed by parting of the roots, the beft time for which is Auguft This plant is a native of many mountainous parts, but in our gardens thrives beft in a moift, rich earth, and loves the fhade

Defcription of Siberian Lychnis

6 Siberian *Lychnis* The flower-ftalks are dichotomous, and about a foot high The leaves are narrow, hairy, and grow oppofite at the joints The flowers are produced from the divifions as well as the tops of the ftalks, they are white, have bifid petals, appear in June, and the feeds ripen in Auguft, by which plenty of plants may be foon raifed, as well as the ftock encreafed by parting of the roots in autumn

Propagation

Lapland Lychnis defcribed

7 Lapland *Lychnis* rifes with a fingle ftalk fupporting the flowers The fingularity of this fpecies is, that the petals are fhorter than the calyx. The calyx is inflated, and much larger than any of the other forts It is a plant of no great beauty, but makes a variety amongft others

Propagation

It is to be encreafed by parting of the roots, and by feeds

Titles

1 Scarlet *Lychnis* is entitled, *Lychnis floribus fafciculatis faftigiatis* Cafpar Bauhine calls it, *Lychnis hirfuta, flore coccineo, major*, and Dodonæus, *Flos Conftantinopolitanus* It is a native of Tartary

2 Ragged Robin is ftiled, *Lychnis petalis quadrifidis fructu fubrotundo* Cafpar Bauhine calls it, *Caryophyllus pratenfis, flore laciniato fimplici, f flos cuculi*, alfo, *Caryophyllus pratenfis, flore pleno* Clufius calls it, *Odontitis Plinii*, Gerard, *Armoraria pratenfis mas*, and Parkinfon, *Lychnis plumaria fylveftris fimplex* It grows common in moift meadows in Europe

3 Batchelor's Button is termed, *Lychnis floribus dioicis* In the *Flora Lapponica* it is ftiled, *Cucubalus caule compofito, calycibus oblongo-ovatis* Cafpar Bauhine calls it, *Lychnis fylveftris, five aquatica purpurea fimplex*, alfo, *Lychnis fylveftris alba fimplex*, alfo, *Lychnis alba multiplex*, Tilli, *Lychnis fylveftris noctiflora alba fimplex, calyce ampliffimo*, and Clufius, *Melandrium Plinii genuinum* It grows by the fides of ditches almoft everywhere

4 German Catch-Fly is, *Lychnis petalis integris* In the *Hortus Cliffort* it is termed, *Silene floribus pentagynis, capfulis quinquelocularibus* Cafpar Bauhine calls it, *Lychnis fylveftris vifcofa rubra anguftifolia*, Clufius, *Lychnis fylveftris*, and Gerard, *Mufcipula anguftifolia* It grows in dry paftures in many parts of the North of Europe

5 Alpine *Lychnis* is, *Lychnis petalis bifidis, floribus corymbofis* In the *Flora Lapponica* it is termed, *Silene Lapponica Alpina, facie vifcariæ* Van Royen calls it, *Silene floribus corymbofis, caule erecto, foliis lanceolato linearibus, capitulum*, and Haller, *Silene floribus in capitulum congeftis* It grows common in the mountainous parts of Lapland, Switzerland, Siberia, and the Pyrenees

6 Siberian *Lychnis* is, *Lychnis petalis bifidis, caule dichotomo, foliis fubhirtis* It is a native of Siberia

7 Lapland *Lychnis* is, *Lychnis calyce inflato, corollâ calyce breviore, caule fubunifloro, flore hermaphrodito* In the *Flora Suecica* it is termed, *Cucubalus caule fimpliciffimo unifloro, petalis calyce brevioribus*, and in the *Flora Lapponica*, *Cucubalus caule fimpliciffimo unifloro, corollâ inclufa* It grows common in Lapland, Siberia, &c

Clafs and order in the Linnæan fyftem

The characters

*Lychnis* is of the clafs and order *Decandria Pentagynia*, and the characters are,

1 Calyx is a monophyllous, tubulous, membranaceous, permanent perianthium, indented at the top in five parts

2 Corolla confifts of five petals, their ungues are of the length of the calyx, their upper part is plane and broad, and frequently cut into fegments

3 Stamina are ten filaments longer than the calyx, alternately difpofed, and faftened to the ungues of the petals, having incumbent antheræ

4 Pistillum confifts of an almoft oval germen, and of five fubulated ftyles longer than the ftamina, with reflexed downy ftigmas

5 Pericarpium is a covered capfule approaching to an oval figure, formed of five valves, and containing only one cell

6 Semina The feeds are numerous and roundifh

CHAP

## CHAP. CCLXXVII.

## *LYCOPSIS.*

Species

OF this genus are,

1. German Wild Bugloss.
2. Oriental Bastard Bugloss.
3. Virginian Wild Bugloss.

Description of German Wild,

1. German Wild Bugloss. The root is creeping. The stalk is upright, and three feet high. The leaves are broad at the base, pointed, entire, and possessed of a white downy matter. The flowers come out from the tops of the stalks in inflated pendulent cups, they are almost of a black colour, appear in July, and the seeds ripen in the autumn.

Oriental Bastard,

2. Oriental Bastard Bugloss. The stalks are upright, branching, and two feet high. The leaves are spear-shaped, very rough and hairy. The flowers come out from the ends of the branches, sitting close, and are arranged in one direction; they are of a yellow colour, beautifully marked with dark purple-coloured spots, appear in July and August, and the seeds ripen in the autumn.

and Virginian Wild Bugloss.

3. Virginian Wild Bugloss. The stalks are upright, and about a foot high. The leaves are narrow, spear-shaped, downy, soft to the touch, and grow in clusters from the sides of the stalks. The flowers are produced from the tops of the stalks on short slender footstalks, are of a blue colour, appear in July and August, and the seeds ripen in the autumn.

Method of raising them.

They are propagated by sowing the seeds in the autumn soon after they are ripe. When the plants come up, they must be thinned where they appear too close, and be duly kept clean from weeds, which is all the trouble they will require. They may be also propagated by parting of the roots, which is best done in the autumn, that they may be established in their new situation before the frosts come on. They will then flower strong the summer following, and perfect their seeds, which if permitted to scatter, will not fail to afford plenty of plants for encrease.

Titles.

1. The first species is titled, *Lycopsis foliis integerrimis, caule erecto, calycibus fructescentibus inflatis pendulis*. Clusius calls it, *Echium flore pullo*, and Caspar Bauhine, *Echium sylvestre lanuginosum*, also, *Buglossum sylvestre majus nigrum*. It grows naturally in Tartary and most parts of Germany.

2. The second species is, *Lycopsis foliis lanceolatis hirsutis, caule ramosissimo erecto, floribus secundis sessilibus*. Tournefort calls it, *Lithospermoides Orientale, buglossi folio, flore luteo maculis atro purpureis notato*. It grows naturally in America.

Class and order in the Linnæan system.

*Lycopsis* is of the class and order *Pentandria Monogynia*, and the characters are,

The characters.

1. CALYX is a perianthium divided into five oblong, acute, patulous, permanent segments.
2. COROLLA is an infundibuliform petal. The tube is cylindrical and crooked. The limb is divided into five obtuse segments. Five convex, prominent, connivent scales close the mouth of the flower.
3. STAMINA are five very small filaments situated at the flexure of the tube of the corolla, having small covered antheræ.
4. PISTILLUM consists of four germens, a filiforme style the length of the stamina, and a bifid, obtuse stigma.
5. PERICARPIUM. There is none. The calyx becomes large and inflated, and contains the seeds.
6. SEMINA. The seeds are four, and nearly oblong.

## CHAP. CCLXXVIII.

## *LYCOPUS*, WATER HOREHOUND.

Species.

THERE are only two species of this genus, viz.

1. European Water Horehound.
2. Virginian Water Horehound.

Description of European

1. European Water Horehound. The root is slender, creeping, and sends down numerous slender fibres, which are of a blackish colour. The stalks are numerous, square, hairy, hollow, and about a yard high. The leaves are oblong, pointed, rough, but not hairy, deeply serrated on the edges, and grow opposite by pairs on the stalks. The flowers come out in clusters round the stalks at the joints, almost their whole length; they are small and of a white colour, appear in June, July, and August, and their seeds ripen in September and October.

and Virginian Water Horehound.

2. Virginian Water Horehound. The root is slender, long, jointed, creeping, and fibrated. The stalks are square, hollow, hairy, and near two feet high. The leaves are spear-shaped, serrated, hairy, of a pale-green colour, and grow opposite by pairs at the joints. The flowers come out in clusters round the stalks almost their whole length at the joints; they are small and of

of a white colour, appear in July and Auguſt, but are rarely ſucceeded by ſeeds in England

Theſe ſpecies are propagated by parting of the roots, the beſt time for which is the autumn, when the ſtalks decay The firſt grows naturally by ditches and ſtanding waters in many parts of England, which teaches us not to be over nice in finding out a place wherein to ſtation it, but to aſſign it the coldeſt, the moiſteſt, and the moſt abject part of the garden, where a plant or two are deſired to be admitted for the ſake of obſervation The ſecond ſort, being a native of America, is chiefly coveted on that account, but it has very little right to precedence on account of its ſuperior beauty It is propagated by parting the roots in the autumn, and loves the ſhade, and a rich moiſt ſoil

1 European Water Horehound is entitled, *Lycopus foliis ſinuato-ſerratis* In the *Flora Suecica* it is termed, *Lycopus foliis indiviſis*, in the *Hortus Cliffortianus*, *Lycopus* Caſpar Bauhine calls it, *Marrubium paluſtre glabrum*, Dalechamp, *Stachys Matthioli*, Tournefort, *Lycopus paluſtris glaber*, alſo, *Marrubium aquaticum*, and Parkinſon, *Marrubium aquaticum vulgare* It grows naturally by the ſides of rivers, lakes, in ditches, &c in England and moſt countries of Europe

2 Virginian Water Horehound is, *Lycopus foliis inæqualiter ſerratis* Gronovius calls it, *Lycopus foliis lanceolatis tenuiſſime ſerratis* It grows naturally in Virginia

*Lycopus* is of the claſs and order *Diandria Monogynia*, and the characters are,

1 CALYX is a monophyllous, tubular, permanent perianthium, cut at the top into five narrow acute ſegments

2 COROLLA is one unequal petal The tube is cylindrical, and the length of the calyx The limb is cut into four obtuſe ſpreading ſegments, of which the upper one is emarginated and broadeſt, and the lower one ſmaller

3 STAMINA are two filaments, rather longer than the corolla, and inclined towards its upper ſegment, having ſmall antheræ

4 PISTILLUM conſiſts of a quadripartid germen, a ſtraight filiforme ſtyle the length of the ſtamina, and a bifid reflexed ſtigma

5 PERICARPIUM There is one The ſeeds are lodged in the calyx

6 SEMINA The ſeeds are four and obtuſe

# CHAP CCLXXIX

## *LYSIMACHIA*, LOOSE STRIFE.

THE perennials of this genus are uſually called,

1 Yellow Willow Herb or Looſe Strife
2 Tufted Looſe Strife
3 Quadrifoliate Looſe Strife
4 Spotted Looſe Strife
5 Jlap-leaved Looſe Strife
6 Yellow Pimpernel of the Woods
7 Yellow Money Wort or Herb Two-pence
8 Purple Money Wort

1 Yellow Willow Herb or Looſe Strife The root is creeping, thick, jointed, of a reddiſh colour, and ſoon ſpreads itſelf to a conſiderable diſtance The ſtalks are upright, firm, fluted, three or four feet high, and divide into branches, or rather footſtalks, near the top, for the ſupport of the flowers The leaves are ſpear-ſhaped, pointed, ſmooth, ſeſſile, and grow three or four together at a joint The flowers grow in ſpikes, and are formed into panicles on the tops of the ſtalks they are of a beautiful yellow colour, and the general character ſhews their compoſition, they appear in June and July, and the ſeeds ripen in the autumn

This plant grows naturally in ditches and moiſt places in many parts of England, but is nevertheleſs a fine ſhowy plant for the moſt abject parts of large gardens, where hardly any thing elſe will thrive, and is propagated with the utmoſt facility by parting of the roots almoſt at any time of the year, but more eſpecially in the autumn

2 Tufted Looſe Strife The root is thick, jointed, fibrated, and creeping The ſtalks are upright, jointed, firm, and about a foot and a half high The leaves are oblong, narrow, pointed, ſeſſile, and grow oppoſite to each other at the joints The flowers come out on footſtalks on each ſide of the ſtalks from the wings of the leaves, they are formed into globular heads or cluſters on the tops of the footſtalks, they are of a yellow colour, appear in June and July, but are very rarely ſucceeded by ſeeds in England or any other country

3 Quadrifoliate Looſe Strife The root is fibrated and ſpreading The ſtalks are upright, jointed, undivided, and two or three feet high The leaves are broad, oval, acute, and four of them grow at each joint, ſurrounding the ſtalk in a ring-like manner Four flowers alſo are produced from each joint, coming out ſingly on ſlender footſtalks, they are of a yellow colour, and appear in July, but are rarely ſucceeded by ſeeds in England

4 Spotted Looſe Strife The root is creeping The ſtalk is ſlender, and about a foot high The leaves are ſpear-ſhaped, often marked with black ſpots, and grow three and ſometimes four together, ſurrounding the ſtalks at the joints The flowers come out ſingly on ſlender footſtalks, four of them ſurrounding the ſtalk at each joint they are ſmall and of a yellow colour, appear in June and July, and the ſeeds ripen in the autumn

5 Jlap-leaved Looſe Strife The root is creeping, and ſoon ſpreads itſelf under the ſurface to a conſiderable diſtance The ſtalks are numerous from a root of long ſtanding, erect, and two feet high The leaves are oblong, oval, ſpear-ſhaped, acute, veined on the under ſide, ſmooth,

smooth, and grow opposite by pairs on short channelled footstalks The flowers come out singly from the upper joints on long, slender, naked footstalks, they are small, of a yellow colour, and appear in June and July, but are seldom succeeded by seeds in this country

*Yellow Pimpernel of the Woods*

6 Yellow Pimpernel of the Woods The stalks are numerous, weak, and lie on the ground The leaves are oval, pointed, and grow opposite by pairs at the joints The flowers come out singly on long slender footstalks from the wings of the leaves on each side of the stalk, they are small and of a yellow colour, appear in May, June, and July, and the seeds ripen in August and September This is a woodland plant, of little beauty, and is rarely ever cultivated in gardens

*Yellow Money Wort,*

7 Yellow Money Wort The root is tender, small, and spreading under the surface of the ground The stalks are numerous, weak, trailing, and strike root at the joints as they lie on the ground The leaves are small, smooth, green, heart-shaped, roundish, and grow opposite by pairs at the joints The flowers come out singly from the wings of the leaves on short slender footstalks, they are small and of a yellow colour, appear in June and July, and the seeds ripen in the autumn This species is seldom cultivated in gardens

*and Purple Money Wort described*

8 Purple Money Wort The stalks are very slender, hardly half a foot long, trailing, and strike root as they lie on the ground The leaves are small, oval, roundish, smooth, and grow opposite by pairs at the joints The flowers come out singly from the wings of the leaves on slender footstalks, they are small and of a purple colour, appear in May, June, and July and the seeds ripen in August and September The culture of this species also is rarely ever practised in gardens

*Method of propagation*

These are all propagated, like the first species, by parting the roots in the autumn, and like that, delight most in the shade and a moist situation They may be also raised from seeds, but as some of them hardly ever produce any, and all multiply very fast by the root, that practice is seldom attempted When the seeds are to be sown, however, let it be in the autumn, as soon as they are ripe, for if they are kept until the spring, they frequently lie until the spring after before they come up When the seeds are sown in the autumn, the plants will come up in the spring They must then be thinned where they are too close, be kept clean from weeds, and constantly watered all summer, and in the autumn may be removed to the places where they are designed to remain

1 Yellow Willow Herb or Loose Strife is entitled, *Lysimachia paniculata, racemis terminalibus* In the *Flora Lapponica* it is termed, *Lysimachia foliis lanceolatis, corymbo terminali* Van Royen calls it, *Lysimachia foliis lanceolatis, racemo composito terminali*, Caspar Bauhine, *Lysimachia lutea major*, John Bauhine, *Lysimachia lutea*, and Ray, *Lysimachia lutea foliis brevioribus & obtusis, floribus in summitate congestis* It grows naturally at the sides of waters in England and most parts of Europe

2 Tufted Loose Strife is, *Lysimachia racemis lateralibus pedunculatis* In the *Flora Lapponica* it is termed, *Lysimachia ex alis foliorum thyrsiflora* Van Royen calls it, *Lysimachia racemis simplicibus lateralibus* Caspar Bauhine, *Lysimachia bifolia, flore globoso luteo*, Clusius, *Lysimachia lutea*, and Gerard, *Lysimachia lutea flore globoso* It grows naturally in moist places in England and most parts of Europe

3 Quadrifoliate Loose Strife is, *Lysimachia foliis ..., pedunculis quaternis ...* Gronovius calls it, *Lysimachia ... quaternis ...*, ... *Anagallis lutea, foliis ... stellatis*, and Plukenet, *Anagallis lutea, foliis & floribus ex eodem exortu quaternis, ex eque... ibus ... intervallis ...* It grows naturally in Virginia

4 Spotted Loose Strife is, *Lysimachia foliis ..., pedunculis ...* In the *Hortus Cliffort* it is termed, *Lysimachia foliis lanceolatis floribus solitariis* Caspar Bauhine calls it, *Lysimachia lutea ..., foliis ...* Clusius, *Lysimachia ...*, and Morison, *Lysimachia ... flore luteo, ...* It grows naturally among the reeds in Holland

5 ...-leaved Loose Strife is, *Lysimachia ..., floribus cernuis* Wachendorf calls it *Lysimachia foliis ovato lanceolatis ...*, ... others, *Lysimachia Canadensis, jalappae foliis* It is a native of Virginia and Canada

6 Yellow Pimpernel of the Woods is, *Lysimachia foliis ovatis acutis, floribus solitariis, caule procumbente* Caspar Bauhine calls it, *Anagallis lutea nemorum*, Clusius, *Anagallis*, Gerard *Anagallis lutea*, and Parkinson, *Anagallis flore luteo* It grows naturally in woods and moist shady places in England, France, and Germany

7 Yellow Money Wort or Herb Two pence is, *Lysimachia foliis subcordatis, floribus solitariis, caule repente* Caspar Bauhine calls it, *Nummularia major lutea*, Camerarius, *Anagallis ...*, Gerard, *Nummularia*, and Parkinson, *Nummularia lutea* It grows naturally in most places in England and most countries of Europe

8 Purple Money Wort is, *Lysimachia foliis ovatis acutiusculis, pedunculis folio longioribus, caule repente* Guettard calls it, *Lysimachia foliis ..., floribus solitariis longe pedunculatis*, Sauvages, *Lysimachia foliis ... planis, floribus ... pedunculatis, caule repente*, others, *Nummularia minor, purpurascente flore* It grows naturally on bogs and moist heathy ground in England, France, and Italy

*Lysimachia* is of the class and order *Pentandria Monogynia*, and the characters are, *Class and order in the Linnæan system*

*The characters*

1 CALYX is an erect, permanent perianthium, divided into five acute parts

2 COROLLA is one rotated petal There is hardly any tube, the limb being cut almost to the bottom into five oval oblong segments, which are flat and spread open

3 STAMINA are five awl-shaped filaments with acuminated antheræ

4 PISTILLUM consists of a roundish germen, a filiforme style the length of the stamina, and an obtuse stigma

5 PERICARPIUM is a globular, decemvalvate capsule, containing one cell

6 SEMINA The seeds are many, and angular

The receptacle is globose, large, and punctated

CHAP

# CHAP. CCLXXX.

## *LYTHRUM*, WILLOW HERB, or PURPLE LOOSE STRIFE.

Species.

THE perennials of this genus are,

1. Purple-ſpiked Looſe Strife, or Willow Herb.
2. Verticillate Looſe Strife.
3. Petiolated Looſe Strife.
4. Linear-leaved Virginian Looſe Strife.
5. Hyſſop-leaved Looſe Strife.

Purple ſpiked Looſe ſtrife.

1. Purple-ſpiked Looſe Strife, or Willow Herb. The ſtalks are numerous, angular, upright, purple coloured, and grow to be four or five feet high. The leaves are nearly cordated, oblong, ſpear-ſhaped, and uſually grow oppoſite by pairs, though ſometimes there will be three growing together, ſurrounding the ſtalk at the joint. The flowers come out in long ſpikes at the tops of the ſtalks and branches; they are of a beautiful reddiſh purple colour, appear in July, and are ſucceeded by ripe ſeeds in the autumn.

Its varieties.

There are many varieties of this ſpecies. The leaves of ſome are almoſt round, others are long and acute. The ſtalks of ſome are hexangular, others are quadrangular, and of different heights. The flowers of ſome are of a ſtrong red colour, others are of a purple in its different tinges.

Verticillate.

2. Verticillate Looſe Strife. The ſtalks are upright, firm, branching, and about two feet high. The leaves are oblong, downy underneath, and grow oppoſite by pairs on very ſhort footſtalks. The flowers are produced in whorls round the upper parts of the ſtalks; they are of a pale purple colour, appear in July, and the ſeeds ripen in the autumn.

Petiolated.

3. Petiolated Looſe Strife. The ſtalks are woolly, upright, and about two feet high. The leaves are linear, and grow oppoſite by pairs on footſtalks. The flowers come out from the wings of the leaves on the upper parts of the ſtalks; they are ſmall and of a pale-purple colour, appear in July, and the ſeeds ſometimes ripen in the autumn.

Linear-leaved Virginian,

4. Linear-leaved Virginian Looſe Strife. The ſtalk is ſlender, angular, erect, and about a foot high. The leaves are linear, entire, and grow oppoſite to each other. The flowers come out ſingly from the wings of the leaves on each ſide the ſtalk; they are ſmall and of a white colour, appear in July, and the ſeeds ripen in the autumn.

and Hyſſop leaved Looſe ſtrife, deſcribed.

5. Hyſſop-leaved Looſe Strife. The ſtalks are upright, divide into a few branches, and grow to about a foot high. The leaves are oblong, narrow, very much like thoſe of the Common Hyſſop, and grow alternately. The flowers come out ſingly, or two together, from the wings of the leaves almoſt the whole length of the branches; they are uſually of a bluiſh-purple colour, appear in June, and the ſeeds ripen in the autumn.

Varieties.

The chief varieties of this ſpecies are,

The Broad Oppoſite-leaved.
The Narrow-leaved.
The Red-flowered.
The Blue.
The Purple.

Method of propagation.

All theſe ſorts are propagated by parting of the roots, the beſt time for which is the autumn. They all love a moiſt rich ſoil and the ſhade, and being thus ſtationed, their ſtalks will be taller, their ſpikes longer, and the flowers larger and more beautiful. When they are planted out, they will require no trouble, except keeping the ground clean from weeds. This makes them valuable (eſpecially the firſt ſort, tho' a native of England, and moſt common) for large gardens, where a ſhow of flowers is required, and little expence is to be afforded.

They are alſo raiſed by ſeeds, which ſhould be ſown in the autumn, in beds of light earth ſoon after they are ripe; for if they are kept until the ſpring, they frequently lie a whole year before they come up. When the plants make their appearance, they muſt be thinned where they come up too cloſe. Watering in dry weather, and conſtant weeding, muſt be afforded them all ſummer; and in the autumn they will be proper plants to ſet out for good.

1. Purple-ſpiked Looſe Strife, or Willow Herb, is titled, *Lythrum foliis oppoſitis cordato lanceolatis, floribus ſpicatis dodecandris*. In the *Hortus Cliffort.* it is termed, *Lythrum foliis oppoſitis*, in the *Flora Lapponica*, *Lythrum floribus verticillatis*. Caſpar Bauhine calls it, *Lyſimachia ſpicata purpurea*; Cluſius, *Lyſimachia purpurea commun. major*; Moriſon, *Blattaria rubra ſpicata major, folio ſubrotundo*; Boccone, *Lyſimachia trifolia ſpicata purpurea*; alſo, *Lyſimachia quadrifolia purpurea, mollior bus & longioribus foliis*; and Tournefort, *Salicaria vulgaris purpurea, foliis oblongis*. It grows naturally by brook-ſides and moiſt places in England and moſt parts of Europe. Titles.

2. Verticillate Looſe Strife is, *Lythrum foliis oppoſitis ſubtus tomentoſis ſubpetiolatis, floribus verticillatis lateralibus*. Gronovius calls it, *Lythrum foliis oppoſitis, floribus verticillatis*. It grows naturally in Virginia.

3. Petiolated Looſe Strife is, *Lythrum foliis oppoſitis linearibus petiolatis, floribus dodecandris*. Gronovius calls it, *Lythrum foliis petiolatis*. It is a native of Virginia.

4. Linear-leaved Virginian Looſe Strife is, *Lythrum foliis oppoſitis linearibus, floribus oppoſitis hexandris*. Gronovius calls it, *Lythrum foliis linearibus, floribus hexandris ſolitariis*. It grows naturally in Virginia.

5. Hyſſop-leaved Looſe Strife is, *Lythrum foliis alternis linearibus, floribus hexandris*. In the *Hortus Cliffort* it is termed, *Lythrum foliis alternis*. Tournefort calls it, *Salicaria hyſſopi folio latiore*; Caſpar Bauhine, *Hyſſopi. fol.*; alſo, *Lyſimachia rubra non ſiliquoſa*; alſo, *Lyſimachia hyſſopifolia purpureo cærulea*. It grows naturally about watery and moiſt places in England, Germany, and France.

*Lythrum* is of the claſs and order *Dodecandria Monogynia*; and the characters are, Claſs and order in the Linnæan ſyſtem.

1. CALYX is a monophyllous, cylindrical, ſtriated perianthium, having at the top twelve denticles, which are alternately ſmaller. The characters.

2. COROLLA is ſix oblong, obtuſe, patent petals, inſerted by their ungues into the indentures of the calyx.

3 STAMINA are twelve filiforme filaments the length of the calyx, (the upper ones being shorter than the lower) terminated by simple assurgent antheræ

4 PISTILLUM consists of an oblong germen, an awl-shaped declining style the length of the stamina, and a rising orbicular stigma

5 PERICARPIUM is an oblong, covered, sharp-pointed capsule, containing one cell

6 SEMINA The seeds are numerous and small.

# CHAP. CCLXXXI.

## *MALOPE*, BASTARD MALLOW.

THERE is only one species of this genus, often called Betony-leaved Mallow

This plant described — The root is composed of many thick white fibres The stalks are numerous, about a foot long, and lie on the ground The leaves are oval, smooth on their upper side, and indented on their edges The flowers come out singly from the wings of the leaves on long footstalks, they are of a reddish-purple colour, and look like the Common Mallow, they appear in June and July, and the seeds ripen in August

Culture — The root will sometimes last for many years, but usually dies as soon as the seeds are perfected, these should therefore be sown, soon after they are ripe, in beds of light earth, in warm well-sheltered places, and the plants will immediately come up and flower the summer following They may also be sown in the spring, and the plants will flower in the autumn, but be too late to perfect their seeds In either case, if you choose to have the roots continued, cut the stalks close to the ground, as soon as the flowers begin to decay, and this will cause them to form fresh heads at the bottom, which will flower early the summer following Nevertheless, to have these plants in perfection, the seeds should be sown regularly every year, and when the plants have flowered and perfected their seeds, the roots should be dug up, and thrown away, as they will, if they survive, exhibit a bloom of inferior beauty to those of young plants in the seed-beds These plants when young may be removed, but they do best when undisturbed, therefore let the seeds always be sown in the places where they are to remain

Titles — There being no other species of this genus, it is named simply *Malope* Morison calls it, *Malva betonicæ folio*, and Boerhaaver, *Alcea betonicæ folio, flore purpureo violaceo* It is a native of Hetruria and Mauritania

Class and order in the Linnæan system — *Malope* is of the class and order *Monadelphia Polyandria*, and the characters are,

The characters — 1 CALYX is a double perianthium The exterior one is composed of three broad, cordated, acute, permanent leaves The interior is monophyllous, permanent, erect, and cut into five segments

2 COROLLA consists of five obcordated patent petals, which coalesce at their base

3 STAMINA are numerous filaments, which join into a cylinder at bottom, but are loose above, having reniforme antheræ

4 PISTILLUM The germina are many, and roundish, the styles the length of the stamina; and the stigmas setaceous and simple

5 PERICARPIUM consists of numerous roundish arilli, collected into a head

6 SEMINA The seeds are single, and reniforme

# CHAP. CCLXXXII.

## *MALVA*, MALLOW.

A FEW species of this genus, though deemed biennials, ought nevertheless to come in here, viz

Species 1 Common Mallow
2 Vervain Mallow
3 Jagged-leaved Vervain Mallow

Description of the Common Mallow 1 Common Mallow is so well known as to need no description Its root is thick, very tough, strikes deep into the earth, and greatly impoverishes the ground, if permitted to grow, so that good husbandry directs all gardeners and farmers to draw them out when young, otherwise the trouble will be very great, and if they are neglected, so that they flower, and the seeds scatter, the labour of extirpating the breed will be more than doubled the succeeding summer

Varieties There is a variety of this species with jagged leaves, and another with white flowers, both which are sought after for some collections

Culture They are propagated by sowing the seeds soon after they are ripe, and when the plants come to flower, several of the Common Mallows will shew themselves with them These must be carefully pulled up as the flowers and leaves make their appearance, and then the seeds of both kinds will be more certain of producing the like sorts in return These Mallows flower the second summer from seeds, but the roots do not always die when the seeds are perfected, for the most part they become woody, thick, and strong, and last for many years

Medicinal properties The root, leaves, flowers, and seeds of this plant are used in medicine A conserve is prepared from the flowers The leaves are used in fomentations, cataplasms, and emollient glysters, they are the first of the four emollient herbs, and decoctions of them are employed in dysenteries, sharpness of urine, and obtunding acrimonious humours

Common Vervain Mallow 2 Common Vervain Mallow The stalks are upright, branching, and about two feet high The leaves are beautifully cut or divided into many parts The flowers are like those of the Common Mallow, but of a bright-red colour, they appear in June and July, and the seeds ripen in the autumn

Varieties The varieties of this species are distinguished among Gardeners by the names of,

Smaller Vervain Mallow
Larger Vervain Mallow
Downy-leaved Vervain Mallow
White-flowered Vervain Mallow

These names in common use shew in what respect the varieties differ from each other

Its virtues This plant is a fine emollient, and nearly of the same quality with the preceding, but is less mucilaginous

Jagged-leaved Vervain Mallow described 3 Jagged-leaved Vervain Mallow The stalks hardly rise to the height of the preceding species The radical leaves are kidney-shaped, and their edges jagged or deeply cut into many narrow segments; but those on the stalks are composed of five principal, which are winged, and finely divided The flowers are shaped like the former species, and are of different colours in the different varieties, they appear in June and July, and the seeds ripen in the autumn

Varieties Besides the varieties respecting the colour of the flowers, there are,

The Round-leaved
The Curled-leaved
The Taller, &c

Method of propagation The best way of raising these sorts is to sow the seeds in March or April in beds of common mould made fine The seeds will soon come up, and if they are in the places where they are designed to flower, they must be thinned to about a foot and a half distance from each other, if not, when they are about three inches high they should be planted in rows at about the above distance in the places where they are to remain The next summer they will flower, and perfect their seeds, by which fresh plants may be raised but if the stalks are cut down, as soon as the best show of blow is over, and before the seeds are ripe, they will shoot out afresh from the root, and flower very well the next year

Titles 1 Common Mallow is titled, *Malva caule erecto herbaceo, foliis septemlobatis acutis, pedunculis petiolisque pilosis* In the *Hortus Cliffortianus* it is termed, *Malva caule erecto, foliis multipartitis* Caspar Bauhine calls it, *Malva sylvestris, folio sinuato*, Gerard, *Malva sylvestris*, and Parkinson, *Malva vulgaris* It grows common in England, and most parts of Europe

2 Common Vervain Mallow is, *Malva caule erecto, foliis multipartitis scabriusculis* Caspar Bauhine calls it, *Alcea vulgaris major*, Clusius, *Alcea vulgaris*, Gerard, *Malva verbenacea* and Parkinson, *Malva vulgaris, s Malva verbenacea* It grows naturally in England, France, and Germany

3 Jagged leaved Vervain Mallow is, *Malva foliis radicalibus reniformibus incisis, caulinis quinquepartitis pinnato-multifidis* Columna calls it, *Malva montana, s Alcea rotundifolia laciniata*, Caspar Bauhine, *Alcea folio rotundo laciniato*, also, *Alcea vulgaris minor*, and John Bauhine, *Alcea tenuifolia crispa* It grows naturally in hedges and pastures in England and France, also in India

Class and order in the Linnæan system the high tables *Malva* is of the class and order *Monadelphia Polyandria*, and the characters are,

1 CALYX is a double perianthium The exterior is composed of three heart shaped, acute, permanent leaves The interior is monophyllous, large, permanent, and cut at the rim into five broad segments

2 COROLLA consists of five obcordated, præmorsed, plane petals, which coalesce at their base

3 STAMINA are numerous filaments inserted in the corolla, which join at their base and form a cylinder, but spread open above, having kidney-shaped antheræ

4 PISTILLUM consists of an orbicular germen, a short cylindrical style, and many setaceous stigmas as long as the style

5 PERICARPIUM is a round depressed head, composed of numerous arilli fastened to the columnar receptacle, and opening on their inside

6 SEMINA The seeds are single, and kidney-shaped.

CHAP

# CHAP. CCLXXXIII

## *MARRUBIUM*, HOREHOUND

Species

OF this genus are,
1 Common Horehound.
2 Foreign Horehound
3 French Horehound
4 Spanish Horehound
5 Cretan Horehound
6 *Alysson*, or Galen's Mad-wort
7 *Pseudo-Dictamnus*, or Common Bastard Dittany.
8 Acetabulous Bastard Dittany

Common Horehound described

1 Common Horehound The root is woody, tough and fibrous The stalks are square, hoary, and about a foot high The leaves are roundish, indented, hoary, grow opposite by pairs, and are of a strong, and to most an agreeable odour The flowers come out in whorls round the stalks at the joints, they are small, of a faint purple or white colour, and the general characters shew their composition, they appear in June and July, and the seeds ripen in the autumn

Medicinal properties of this plant

The leaves of this plant are aperient, deobstruent, promote the secretion of the fluids, and are of signal service in humoural asthmas, old coughs, jaundice, dropsy, green sickness, &c

Foreign,

2 Foreign Horehound Of this species there are two principal varieties, the Broad-leaved and Narrow leaved The stalks of the Broad-leaved are thick, square, hoary, and a yard high The leaves are large, round, and white The stalks of the Narrow leaved are slender, square, hoary, and near a yard high The leaves, as the distinctive name imports, are narrower than the other variety, they are also longer, but, like that, white and hoary, and of an agreeable odour The flowers of both grow in whorls round the stalks, having bristly cups, they appear in June and July, and the seeds ripen in the autumn

and French Horehound described

3 French Horehound The stalks are slender, weak, downy, and about eight inches high The leaves are small, roundish, silky, white, and indented on their edges The flowers come out in whorls round the stalks, they are moderately large, of a purple colour, appear in July, and the seeds ripen in the autumn

Variety

This species also hath a variety of larger growth, but in other respects is very little different

Spanish,

4 Spanish Horehound The stalks are upright, hoary, and near two feet high The leaves are roundish, white, grow opposite, and are serrated on their edges The flowers come out in thick whorls round the stalks at the joints, having spreading sharp-pointed cups, they are of a pale-purple or white colour appear in June and July, and the seeds ripen in the autumn

and Cretan Horehound,

5 Cretan Horehound The stalks are upright, hoary, and about a foot high The leaves are nearly oval, woolly, indented at the top, and grow opposite by pairs The flowers come out like the other sorts in whorls at the joints, and the calycinal segments are awl-shaped, they appear about the same time with the former, and in favourable seasons the seeds ripen accordingly

Alysson,

6 *Alysson*, or Galen's Mad wort The stalks are upright, hoary, divide into a few branches, and grow to about a foot high The leaves are wedge-shaped, curled, hoary, and indented The flowers grow in small loose whorls round the stalks, having no involucrum, but the segments of the perianthium are stiff, prickly, and spread open The flowers are of a bluish purple colour, appear in May and June, and the seeds ripen in August

Galen says, this plant is a sovereign remedy for the bite of a mad dog

Pseudo-Dictamnus

7 *Pseudo Dictamnus*, or Common Bastard Dittany The stalks are woody, divide into numerous woolly branches, and grow to about two feet high The leaves are heart-shaped, round, hoary, and grow opposite to each other The whorls are small, white or purple, and the flowers continue in succession the greatest part of the summer, but are rarely succeeded by seeds in England

and Acetabulous Bastard Dittany, described.

8 Acetabulous Bastard Dittany The stalks are thick, very hairy, and about two feet high The leaves are heart shaped, concave, rough, and hoary The flowers grow in whorls round the stalks, but are in a manner hid by the many segments of the calyx, which in this species are membranaceous, large, and angular, their colour is a pale-purple, and they continue in succession great part of the summer, but the seeds seldom ripen in England

Proper soil

All these sorts should be planted in a poor, hungry, dry soil, and their continuance will be lasting

Method of propagation

The first six sorts are raised by sowing the seeds in the spring, in beds of high dry earth When the plants come up, they require no trouble, except keeping them clean from weeds, and thinning them where they are too close The seventh and eighth sorts are always propagated by cuttings These being set in any of the summer months will grow, but their situation should be naturally dry, warm, and well defended, or they will be liable to be killed by the winter frosts, on which account, a few plants of each should be set in pots to be housed in winter, to keep up the stock, in case those abroad should be killed by the severity of the weather Indeed, when the whole garden consists of rich moist earth, and is but ill defended, it would be in vain to plant them abroad In all such situations the plants should be potted, and ranked with the hardiest green-house plants The other sorts also, like these, will grow by cuttings, and if the soil is not naturally poor, rubbishy and dry, a plant or two of all the sorts except the first should be potted and housed, for the same reasons and for the same purpose as the two last

Titles

1 Common Horehound is entitled *Marrubium dentibus calycinis setaceis uncinatis* Caspar Bauhine calls it, *Marrubium album vulgare*, also, *Marrubium album villosum*, Clusius, *Marrubium vulgare*, and others, *Marrubium album* It grows naturally about villages, heaths, pathways, &c in England, and most of the northern countries of Europe

2 Foreign Horehound is, *Marrubium foliis cuneato-lanceolatis serratis, calycum denticulis setaceis* Caspar Bauhine calls it, *Marrubium album latifolium peregrinum*, also, *Marrubium album angustifolium peregrinum*, Clusius, *Marrubium album Pannonicum*.

*cum*, and Dalechamp, *Marrubium Creticum* It grows naturally in dry sterile places in Crete, Sicily, and Austria

3 French Horehound is, *Marrubium denticus calycinis setaceis rectis villosis* Barrelier calls it, *Marrubium album serico parvo & rotundo folio*, also, *Marrubium album Hispanicum majus* It grows naturally in France and Spain

4 Spanish Horehound is, *Marrubium calycum limbis patentibus, denticulis acutis* Hermann calls it, *Marrubium album rotundifolium Hispanicum*, and Barrelier, *Marrubium subrotundo folio* It grows naturally in Spain

5 Cretan Horehound is, *Marrubium foliis subovatis lanatis superne emarginato-crenatis, denticulis calycinis subulatis* Tournefort calls it, *Marrubium album candidissimum et villosum* It is a native of Crete

6 *Alysson*, or Galen's Mad-wort is, *Marrubium foliis cuneiformibus quinquedentatis plicatis, verticillis involucro destitutis* Morison calls it, *Marrubium album, foliis profunde incisis, flore caeruleo*, Caspar Bauhine, *Alysson verticillatum foliis profunde incisis*, and Clusius, *Alysson Galeni* It grows naturally in Spain

7 *Pseudo-Dictamnus*, or Common Bastard Dittany, is, *Marrubium calycum limbis plantis villosis, foliis cordatis concavis, caule fruticoso* Caspar Bauhine calls it, *Pseudo-Dictamnus verticillatus inodorus*, and Dodonæus, *Pseudo-Dictamnus* It is a native of Crete

8 Acetabulous Bastard Dittany is, *Marrubium calycum limbis tubo longioribus membranaceis angulis majoribus rotundatis* Caspar Bauhine calls it, *Pseudo-Dictamnus acetabulis Moluccæ*; and Barrelier, *Dictamnus falsus verticillatus, pericarpio conoide, Beeticus* It is a native of Crete

*Marrubium* is of the class and order *Didynamia Gymnospermia*, and the characters are, Class and order in the Linnæan system The characters

1 CALYX is a monophyllous, tubular, funnel shaped, decemstriated perianthium, having an equal spreading brim, indented in ten parts

2 COROLLA is one ringent petal The tube is cylindrical, the limb gaping, with a long mouth The upper lip is erect, linear, semi bifid, and acute, the lower lip is broad, reflexed, and divided into three segments, the middle one being broad and emarginated, the lateral ones acute

3 STAMINA are four filaments under the upper lip, of which two are longer than the others, having simple antheræ

4 PISTILLUM consists of a quadrifid germen, a filiforme style the length and situation of the stamina, and a bifid stigma

5 PERICARPIUM There is none The seeds are lodged in the calyx

6 SEMINA The seeds are four, and oblong

## CHAP. CCLXXXIV.

## *MATRICARIA*, FEVERFEW.

THE species of the genus for this place are,

Species
1 Sea Feverfew
2 Oriental Feverfew
3 Common Feverfew

Sea, 1 Sea Feverfew The stalks grow to about a foot long, and divide into many branches, which spread near the ground The leaves are bipinnated, the pinnæ are of a thickish substance, short, convex on their upper side, concave underneath, and their colour is a dark-green The flowers are produced in kind of umbels from the ends and sides of the branches, they are moderately large, of a white colour, appear in July, and the seeds ripen in the autumn

Oriental, 2 Oriental Feverfew The stalks are upright, branching, hoary, and about a foot and a half high The leaves are composed of a multitude of narrow segments, in the manner of Milfoil, they are large, usually conjunct, and of a silvery white colour The flowers come out singly from the sides of the branches on hoary footstalks, they are large, white in the radius, but yellow in the disk, and look like the flowers of Chamomile, they appear in July, and the seeds ripen in the autumn

and Common Feverfew described 3 Common Feverfew The stalks are upright, round, striated, firm, branching, and two or three feet high The leaves are compound, and each consists of about seven oval folioles, which are cut into several obtuse segments, and are of a yellowish green colour The flowers come out in plenty from the ends and sides of the branches, the rays are white, but they are yellow in the middle, they appear in June, and the seeds ripen in September

Its uses in medicine This plant is a most powerful uterine, a decoction of it with chamomile flowers and mugwort gives instant relief to hysteric complaints It is efficacious in most disorders attending the female sex, an admirable carminative, a great expeller of flatulent disorders, affords a fine warm stimulating bitter, and possesses most of the qualities of chamomile flowers, though perhaps in a weaker degree Outwardly applied, it is good against the St Anthony's fire, hot swellings, and inflammations of all kinds

For the flower-garden it is also much respected in its numerous varieties By good culture the flower becomes double, fistulous, and presents itself in other pleasing forms, insomuch that we have of it,

Varieties
The Sulphur-flowered Feverfew
Small Fistulous Feverfew
Large Fistulous Feverfew
Semi-double Feverfew
Full Double Feverfew.
Short-rayed Feverfew
Rayless Feverfew
Curled-leaved Feverfew

Culture These sorts are pretty permanent from seeds, if the plants are not too near each other in the beds Let the seeds therefore be gathered from the best kinds of the different sorts, and sown in the

the spring in beds of any common mould made fine, and slightly raked in The plants will soon come up, and when they are about three inches high, they may be either set out for good, or in beds prepared for the purpose, planting them at about six inches distance from each other When they have stood in beds a few weeks, every other should be taken out, and planted in those places where they are designed to make a show, for they are very beautiful plants, and would be inferior to few of our larger flowering kinds, were it not for the strong disagreeable odour which they possess If you are desirous of preserving the roots, cut the stalks down when the best flow er blow is over, and before the seeds are ripe, and the summer following they will shoot out afresh, and produce plenty of flowers

They are all propagated also by planting of the cuttings in the spring, or any of the summer months By this method the full doubles are kept in their perfect state, and the Curled-leaves, or any beautiful singularity which shall present itself, may be continued

Whoever is fond of these plants should have recourse to both methods of propagation, for they are often short-lived, the plant shewing itself frequently a biennial, though in some soils the root often continues for many years Recourse should be had to seeds to propagate those sorts which ripen them freely, and cuttings should be employed to continue any singularity, or to multiply those plants which by their doubleness are incapable of affording good seeds

The two first species are also propagated in the same manner The first is allowed a place in general collections, and the Oriental sort is admired for its beautiful silvery leaves It must have a light dry soil, and a warm situation, and being rather tender, a few plants should be set in pots, to be housed in winter, in order to continue the sort in case those abroad should be killed by bad weather

Titles. 1 Sea Feverfew is titled, *Matricaria receptaculis hemisphaericis foliis bipinnatis subcarnosis, supra convexis, subtus carinatis* Ray calls it, *Chamaemelum maritimum perenne humilius, foliis brevioribus crassis obscure virentibus* It grows naturally on the sea-shores of England, and in other the northern countries of Europe

2 Oriental Feverfew is, *Matricaria foliis bipinnatis, pedunculis sol...* Vaillant calls it, *Matricaria monol... ...* *foliis a gen eis pleniumque conjugatis*, and Tournefort, *Chamaemelum orientale ... ... folio* It is a native of the East

3 Common Feverfew, *Matricaria foliis compositis planis foliolis ovatis incisis, pedunculis ramosis* Caspar Bauhine calls it, *Matricaria vulgaris, seu sativa*, and Dodonaeus *Matricaria* It grows naturally about villages, in cultivated fields, by way sides, hedges, &c in England, and most parts of Europe

Class and order in the Linnæan system *Matricaria* is of the class and order *Syngenesia Polygamia Superflua*, and the characters are,

The characters 1 CALYX The general calyx is hemisphærical, the scales are linear, imbricated, and nearly equal

2 COROLLA The compound flower is radiated The hermaphrodite florets in the hemisphærical disk are numerous, and each consists of one funnel shaped petal, cut at the brim into five spreading segments The females in the radius are oblong, and indented in three parts at the top

3 STAMINA of the hermaphrodites, are five very short capillary filaments, having a cylindrical tubular anthera

4 PISTILLUM of the hermaphrodites, consists of an oblong naked germen, a filiforme style the length of the stamina, and a bifid patent stigma

In the females it consists of a naked germen, a filiforme style the length of the hermaphrodites, and ten revolute stigmas

5 PERICARPIUM There is none

6 SEMINA The seeds of the hermaphrodites are single oblong, and have no down The seeds of the females are similar to those of the hermaphrodites

The receptacle is naked and convex

## CHAP. CCLXXXV

## *MEDEOLA*, CLIMBING AFRICAN ASPARAGUS

THERE are only two species of this genus, one of which is tender, the other called Virginian *Medeola*, Lily or Little Martagon

This plant described The root is scaly, small, and fibrated The stalks are ligneous, tough, unarmed with thorns, and about a foot high The leaves are spear-shaped, and grow in whorls round the stalks The flowers come out from the tops of the stalks on slender footstalks, they are of a pale herbaceous colour, hang drooping, and the general characters indicate their structure, they appear in June, but are not succeeded by ripe fruit in England

Method of propagation It is propagated by parting of the roots, the best time for which is the autumn It is tolerably hardy, but requires a light fresh soil that is not too moist Being thus situated, you will have a better chance of offsets for encrease, for unless the soil and situation perfectly agree with it, it is very slow in affording its offsets

Titles. This species is titled, *Medeola foliis verticillatis, ramis inermibus* Gronovius calls it, *Medeola foliis stellatis lanceolatis, fructu baccato*, and Plukenet, *Lilium s martagon pusillum, floribus minutissime herbaceis* It grows naturally in Virginia

Class and order in the Linnæan system *Medeola* is of the class and order *Hexandria Trigynia*, and the characters are,

The characters 1 CALYX There is none

2 COROLLA is ſix oval, oblong, equal, patent, revolute petals

3 STAMINA are ſix awl-ſhaped filaments the length of the corolla, having incumbent antheræ

4 PISTILLUM conſiſts of three cornicula ted germens, and the like number of ſtyles, with thick recurved ſtigmas

5 PERICARPIUM is a roundiſh, trifid, trilocular berry

6 SEMINA The ſeeds are ſingle, and heart-ſhaped

# CHAP CCLXXXVI

## *MEDICAGO*, MEDICK

THE Perennials of this genus are,

1 Sea Medick

2 Yellow Medick

Species 3 Lucern, or Medick Fodder

Deſcription of the Sea Medick 1 Sea Medick The ſtalks are herbaceous, woolly, branching, about a foot long, and lie on the ground The leaves are trifoliate, and grow at the joints on ſhort footſtalks, the folioles are ſmall, wedge ſhaped, and downy The flowers come out from the ends and ſides of the branches in ſmall cluſters, they are of a bright yellow colour, appear in June and July, and are ſucceeded by round, ſnail-ſhaped downy, prickly pods, containing ripe ſeeds, in September

Yellow Medick 2 Yellow Medick The ſtalks are numerous, round, flexible, branching, about a foot and a half long, and lie on the ground The leaves are trifoliate, and of a deep green colour, the folioles are ſpear ſhaped, obtuſe, and ſawed towards the top The flowers come out from the ends and ſides of the branches in cluſters, they are of a yellow colour, and without ſcent, appear in June and July, and are ſucceeded by narrow moon ſhaped pods, containing ripe ſeeds, in September

and Lucern 3 Lucern hath a very thick ſtrong root, which, if not obſtructed, will ſtrike ſeveral yards into the ground The ſtalks are annual, numerous, round, upright, and grow from two to three feet or more in height, according to the ſoil in which the plants are ſtationed The leaves are trifoliate, the folioles are ſpear ſhaped, ſerrated near the top, an inch and a half long, and half an inch broad they are of a dark green colour, and grow alternately The flowers are arranged in ſpikes, which come out from the wings of the ſtalks on naked footſtalks, they are of a fine purple colour, and the general characters indicate their ſtructure, they appear in June and July and are ſucceeded by contorted pods, containing ripe ſeeds in September

Varieties The varieties of this ſpecies are,

Saffron coloured Flowered Lucern

Yellow flowered Lucern

Violet-coloured Lucern

Violet and Yellow-flowered Lucern

Striped flowered Lucern

Theſe varieties are preſerved in gardens by thoſe who are fond of numerous ſorts of plants, but it is the Purple-coloured ſort that is the moſt common, the freeſt ſhooter, and moſt generally cultivated for fodder

Method of propagating them All the above ſpecies are eaſily propagated by ſowing the ſeeds in the ſpring Two or three plants of a ſort will be ſufficient for obſervation, ſo that when the ſeeds come up, the weakeſt plants ſhould be drawn out, leaving only a deſired number of each kind, in their reſpective places

The varieties of Lucern may be continued in their different colours by layers, for if the young ſhoots are laid in the ground as they ariſe in the ſpring, they will ſtrike root, become good plants, and may be afterwards removed to the places where they are deſigned to remain

The Purple flowered Lucern is now cultivated in great plenty in many parts of England for the ſake of the fodder It was known to the antients, and its praiſes, cultivation, and uſes, were extolled by the firſt writer on huſbandry Its old name, the name by which it is found in Virgil, Columella, Palladius, &c is *Medica*, and was given to this plant it is ſaid, becauſe it was firſt brought from Media But be this as it will, it certainly grows in a ſtate of nature in Italy, France, Spain, and ſeveral parts of Europe, and the ſeeds might be gathered in any of thoſe countries for uſe, had none ever been received from Media We have it growing naturally in our meadows and paſtures in many places, ſo that we can boaſt that this celebrated plant claims Britain, as well as other countries, for its native reſidence, and that it is as much an indigenous plant of Britain as of Media

Lucern is cultivated as an article of huſbandry three different ways, all of which have their advocates, by

Broad Caſt

Drill Sowing

By Plants or Sets from the Nurſery

### Broad Caſt

The land ſhould have borne a crop or two of barley, oats, beans, or the like, that no ſward or roots of any kind may be found among it If it has lain fallow and been tolled the preceding ſummer, it will be ſo much the better, and for want of this, it ſhould be well manured with the beſt and ſtrongeſt dung that can be procured For though Lucern will grow upon poor, ſandy, hungry ſoil, it likes a rich, deep, light ſoil to ſport in, and in ſuch a ſituation it will be more luxuriant, and afford the repetition of cutting the oftener proportionably to be made Method of cultivating Lucern by Broad Caſt

The land muſt be prepared for the reception of the ſeeds by ploughing, which muſt be as deep as the nature of the ſoil will bear it The repetition of the ploughing muſt alſo be in proportion to the ſtrength of the ſoil In ſtubborn lands it muſt be very often ploughed croſs-ways, and harrowed with heavy harrows, to ſeparate the parts,

parts, and break the clods, in lighter soils less ploughing will be sufficient. In short, it must be ploughed and harrowed until the mould is made fine, and then the usual preparations that are necessary previous to a crop of barley, will for the most part be sufficient to prepare the soil properly for the reception of the seeds of Lucern.

A settled dry weather should be the time for the Lucern to be sown, because if much rain happens soon after the seed is committed to the ground, it is apt to burst, and your hopes of a crop are destroyed, on which account do not sow it too soon in the spring, nor yet too late, because it is subject to be destroyed by the fly, if very dry weather should happen when the plants are young. The beginning of April is certainly the best time for the work, if the weather will permit, but if the land is warm and light, the middle of March is a good season, though I would by no means sow it the beginning of March, or earlier, as is by some recommended, because these plants, when young, are liable to be taken off by the frosts, and very sharp spring frosts sometimes happen after the plants will or could have come up from such early sowings.

The manner of this performance is what is usually practised for sowing of clover. It must be scattered with an even hand, and twelve pounds of seed will be sufficient for an acre. No barley or oats should be sown among it, as is practised in France and many parts, for that will proportionably weaken it or destroy the crop. The Lucern should possess the strength of the whole land, and if the above quantity be uniformly sown, it will for the most part produce plants enough almost at proper distances to occupy the whole spot without much thinning.

When the seed is sown, it should be well harrowed with a light harrow, and after the plants are come up, the ground should be hoed to destroy the weeds, at which time the weakest plants should be cut up, where they appear too close. This work should always be performed in dry weather, that the roots may be effectually killed, and prevented from striking afresh.

In June the Lucern may be mowed, and if the ground has been neglected to be hoed, the sooner it is done the better, that the annual weeds rising up with it may be extirpated before they have flowered, shed their seeds, and poisoned the ground. If the ground has been kept clean from weeds, the mowing should be deferred until July, when it will begin to flower, then is the time to cut it for hay, which, when done, should be immediately carried off the ground, to be made in convenient places. The ground should be next hoed, and a promising second crop will soon present itself. This may be cut in the autumn, for two cuttings only should be made the first year, or it may be eat up by sheep, turning them in when the Lucern is grown from the first cutting to be about half a foot high. Here they may regale themselves until the end of summer, fatten and much improve the land through the effects of their constant residence, to the greatly forwarding and loading the crop for the summer following. In November the sheep should be taken off the land; and in February the ground between the rows should be hoed, to kill the rising weeds, and air the surface of the earth, the better to admit the benign influence of the sun, showers, and air, to exhilarate the Lucern crop.

In large tracts of Lucern harrowing will be sufficient, which should be done by a good strong harrow, to kill the weeds, and keep the ground clean. This is certainly a very good way for large quarters, as it is found by experiment to do very little damage to the roots of the Lucern; but if the weeds, by that method, are far from being all destroyed, the hoeing, as at first, should be repeated in small tracts, where it can be done, and the successive crops will sufficiently pay for the extraordinary trouble of the performance.

Early in May the Lucern will be fit to cut, and it will afford four crops, at proper intervals, during the summer. Or if it is necessary, sheep may be turned upon it in March, which may be continued until nearly the middle of April, and if they are then taken off, the crop will be grown strong enough to cut in June. Another cutting may be made in July, or early in August, and after that it may be eat up, when it is grown about six inches high, if necessary, by sheep or larger cattle, as before.

As the stalks of Lucern are annual, they always die to the ground at the approach of winter, so that when they cease to grow, which will be in November, the cattle should be all taken off the spot, otherwise they will eat off the crown of the buds, and greatly injure the ensuing crop. The ground between the rows should be hoed in February, the weeds must be constantly destroyed the following and all succeeding summers; and the Lucern being now grown strong, may be eaten upon the spot by any sort of cattle, and will afford you, if mowed, five successive crops in a year.

This first is the most natural, easy, and least expensive way of raising Lucern. Proceed we now to the second, which is by some recommended, and by many practised, namely, raising Lucern by

## Drill Sowing.

The land should be well ploughed, as before, pulverised, and in every respect made fit for the reception of the seeds, which being done, drills should be drawn across it at a foot and a half or two feet (according to the richness of the soil) distance from each other. The drills should be hardly half an inch deep, and in them the seeds should be thinly scattered, slightly covering them over with the finest mould out of the drills. By this method, it is urged, much seed may be saved, six or seven pounds being sufficient to sow an acre. Spaces between the rows must be left to hoe the ground, keep it clean, and stir the surface, to the great forwarding of the plants. If this method is practised, the ground should be hoed early after the appearance of the Lucern plants, that the weeds may be more effectually killed before they have got too big to strike root again, at which hoeing also the Lucern plants in the rows should be thinned where they come up too close, to prevent their choaking and destroying one another, which is always the case if they are over-crowded. The hoeing must be repeated as often as the rising of the weeds makes it necessary, and by the end of July the flowers will appear, when it should be cut for hay, and the after-management be the same as before. Manner of propagating Lucern by Drill Sowing,

I come now to the third method of propagating Lucern, namely,

## By Plants or Sets from the Nursery.

A nursery for the raising of the plants must be set apart for the purpose, which must be well dug, cleared from all roots and weeds, clods must be broken, and the whole made as fine as possible; its extent should be in proportion to the quantity of sets to be raised. Some are at the trouble of laying it out in beds, in order to sow the and by Plants or Sets from the Nursery.

the [illegible], leaving all vs between them, but as all [illegible] which is not absolutely necessary should be avoided, his nicety need not too much [illegible] adhered to, and the seeds may be sown all over the ground evenly and with an even hand, in the same manner as most elements for the kitchen garden are sowed. The last week in March or the first in April, are the best times to the purpose, provided the weather be fine and dry, and when the seeds are sown, they should be raked in, in the same manner you would carrots, onions, or the like. When the plants come up, they must be thinned where they are too close, and be constantly kept free from weeds all summer, and by August they will be grown to be strong plants, and highly proper to form the Lucern plantation. If the ground has been in tillage, and is in good heart, it may bear a crop of oats or barley the summer before; if not, it will be advisable to let it lie fallow, giving it the usual tilths that are necessary for a crop of wheat. If it has borne oats or barley, it should be deeply and well ploughed as soon as they are taken off, and if it has a second ploughing before the roots are planted, it will be the better. The last week in August is the best time for the purpose, and having the ground in good order, a sufficient number of hands should be in readiness to carry on the business with dispatch. Some should be taking the plants with the greatest care out of the seminary, others should be engaged in shortening the tap-roots, (which should be six, seven, or eight inches in length, according to their strength) and in cutting off the tops two inches above the crown, throwing the roots as they prune them into a tub full of fresh water provided for the purpose, if the weather is dry; if it be moist or rainy, they are as well without it. A third set should be employed in making the lines for the rows, a fourth in setting the plants, and a fifth in neating up the whole.

The rows in common should be two feet asunder, in better land a yard, and in good suitable soils a yard and four inches. The distance of the plants also in the rows should vary, according to the goodness or poverty of the soil. A foot in some is a good distance, in others they should be set a foot and a half, two feet, or more, asunder. If they should be set too far asunder, ground will be lost; if too near, they will rob one another, especially if a wet season should happen. The nature of the soil must be a direction for every one as to the proper distance at which to plant the Lucern.

Method of planting the sets

The usual method of planting the sets is by making a hole with a dibble or setting-stick, in the manner practised for cabbage plants, but the far better way is by making a nick at right angles with the spade, and planting them in the manner I have directed to plant seedling elms, and other forest-trees, from the seminary to the nursery. They should be set in an upright position, the tops of the crowns should be just covered with the mould, the soil should be well closed to the sides of the roots, and after the surface of the ground is levelled and made fine, the business is done.

The summer following the crop must not be expected to be in perfection, but it will improve yearly, and when arrived to its full growth, which will be the third year from planting, will afford five or six cuttings every summer. Horse or hand hoeing between the rows must be regularly used every February, and the weeds should be constantly destroyed as they arise, for by thus keeping the ground in stirring, clean from weeds, and managing every thing properly, it will bring forth in greater abundance.

Lucern defigned to be eaten green

Lucern seems peculiarly designed to be eaten green, it being very ill adapted for hay, notwithstanding its excellencies in that way have been so lavishly extolled. I do not pretend to say, but that when it happens to be made good, its virtues are very great, and that it may be of so great an heart as at once to serve for fodder and corn. But this I must assert, it is very rarely that it can be got well. Writers on this subject say, that after it is mown, it must lie in the swath, and be frequently turned. The stalks of this plant are known to be very juicy, and before they can be so sufficiently haved this way as to be fit to carry, a fortnight at least must be expected to elapse, before which time they will be nearly buried in the fresh shoots of the aftermath, and will proportionably damage the crowns of the roots where they lie for so long a season. The young shoots also arising from the roots all about them, will in a manner shade them, and keep the ground so cool, that the time of their being finally hayed will be protracted, so that Lucern should be taken off the ground as soon as possible after it is cut, and hayed in a convenient place. Add to this, that there will be a double expence of carriage, which argues strongly against any plant's general utility, that ought to be shifted from place to place with horses and waggons before it is finally brought home for use.

During the time it is making, a particular gloomy dry weather is also necessary to its well-doing. If very hot weather happens, the leaves, which are the finest parts of the plant, drop off. If little rain falls, the whole turns black, and is good for nothing. So that Nature does not seem to intend this plant, in these parts, for general use for hay, but its chief uses are, to be cut and eat green, for which purpose there is no plant in nature that is equal to it, if the soil is suitable.

The chief uses of Lucern pointed out

In the first place, it presents itself very early in the spring before other green fodder can be had, and becomes highly serviceable to suckling ewes who fatten their lambs, and the new-milched cows who fill their udders. The abundance it yields also is prodigious. Its affording so many distinct cuttings during the summer is a strong argument for raising this plant, the goodness of its nature, and the heart it is known to possess is another, and finally, as it may be raised on stony, sandy, burnt-up land, where hardly any-thing else will grow, its propagation should be earnestly enforced, especially in populous countries where such land abounds, that a greater abundance may be afforded the inhabitants for the encrease of milk, butter, cheese, &c.

Where the land is not naturally dry, light, and warm, or if not sandy and gravelly, I must own I cannot encourage any-one to begin a plantation of Lucern of any tolerable extent, as its success will be very precarious. If it is wet and cold, a dwindling crop only must be expected, and your Lucern will go off in two or three years. In strong loams and clays it does very ill, and I am fully persuaded, we have hardly any part of Leicestershire where Lucern can be propagated to greater profit than the natural herbage of the place.

Proper soil

In dry, sandy, gravelly soils, therefore, Lucern may be propagated to amazing advantage. It grows admirably in light mould on the tops of rocks, stone quarries, &c. obtruding its roots within the crevices of such places, and sending them deep in gravel and sand.

The propagation of Lucern in Britain, therefore,

fore, should be considered as partial, and no doubt it was from the above reasons that it gained so little ground when first brought into England from France about the year 1650 It made a bustle, indeed, about that time, but soon became neglected and forgot Of late years it has been extolled for fodder beyond any of the products of Nature, and very probably it is so on hot, parched lands, where hardly any-thing else will grow, especially if a dry summer should happen, when herbage of all kinds is scarce in England, this plant seems to resist the drought, and flourishes in the hottest seasons regardless of rain or cooling showers In the Spanish West-Indies it is propagated to great advantage, and will there bear cutting every eight days At Lima it is regularly brought to the market for sale, and it is past a dispute, that every part of the warmer climates of America where fodder is wanting may be supplied by Lucern, which being cultivated will grow and flourish more than in these parts of Europe, to the great benefit of the cultivators, as well as (if become general) of national advantage to such places

The broad cast method of cultivating Lucern to be preferred

Of all the three methods laid down for cultivating this plant, I prefer the first, namely, the broad-cast, because attended with least expence, and because, from many experiments lately made, it is found productive of the greatest crops At the first hoeing, the plants may be left at regular distances every-way, be no ways crowded in any part, yet full, and may be so made to occupy the whole space, that the earth will be burthened, but not overloaded, by its vegetable off-spring, whereas when the plants are in rows, a great share of them must be crowded, because they will grow large by having such large distances as three feet four inches between the rows inactive By those interstices also being unoccupied, a proportionable less quantity of Lucern will be had than its increase in height by the large spaces and regular hoeings between the rows

Method of propagating it by sets the worst method

The worst of all the methods of propagating Lucern is by sets from the nursery, because the most expensive and most discouraging to put in practice I do not say but that admirable crops may be had this way, and that the ground may be burthened to a nicety, but with all the art that can be used, it can be made so little superior, if equal, to the broad-cast, and the expence of it is so much the more extraordinary, that it is a practice which ought to be exploded for raising plantations of Lucern of any tolerable extent Indeed, I wonder how any one should think to enforce the general culture of Lucern by drill-sowing and sets from the nursery With gentlemen, indeed, these methods may probably be the more taking, and the novelty will put them upon trying the experiment But how trifling will the quantity of Lucern be which gentlemen will propagate for experiment and amusement! If the culture of Lucern becomes general, it must be performed by farmers, who have no money for experiments, nor hardly any ideas for any-thing out of the common road, and who, if it was necessary, could never be prevailed upon to pursue any other way of raising it than by broad-cast, the method which they have been bred up to, and by the fruitful crops of which they have hitherto paid their rents and maintained their families Tell the farmer of the virtues of Lucern, its excellence for cattle of all kinds, and that it may be mowed four or five times a year, he will listen to you with great attention and resolve to appropriate the greatest part of his farm to so useful an herb But when he enquires after its culture, and you acquaint him that the seeds must be sown in drills, or that sets must be raised in the nursery, and then planted out in lines at certain distances, he will only laugh at you His wonder and indignation still encrease, when you inform him, that if the hay through showers should be turned black and spoiled (as a certain author does) it may be brought to its true smell and taste by laying of salt over each stratum in the mow He then concludes you mad indeed and with a sneering laugh tells you, that he never heard talk of salting any thing but his beef and bacon

If, therefore, the culture of Lucern becomes general in England, it must be by broad-cast, which is the best as well as the cheapest and easiest method, whilst the other arts may be practised by those who have leisure for experiment, and are fond of such amusements

Proper quantity of Lucern to be propagated, and directions for cutting it

The quantity of Lucern propagated should be according to the number of cattle which are to be maintained, and as it should always be cut and carried green off the ground the cuttings, like those of underwood, should be made at proper intervals, taking a piece only at a time, and in such a manner that when the last cutting of the piece is made, that which had been cut first will be in good growth for a second operation Fifteen inches, or a foot and a half, is a proper height to cut it to be given green though the first cutting should be made when it is lower, and the last taller, that a succession may be regularly kept up, otherwise, when the last cutting is made, the cattle must starve, or have other supplies, while this kind of grass grows again for their relief

How long a plantation of it will last,

If it should be asked, how long a plantation of Lucern will last, it may be answered, that this depends upon the nature of the soil and situation in which it is stationed In a cold, damp, starved place, though it may grow at first, it will go off in three or four years; especially if there be couch-grass to incommode it, which usually grows in such places, and which is a mortal enemy to Lucern In dry, suitable soils, it can hardly be said ever to decay In such places it is known to flourish for half a century, and probably may last half a century longer, indeed, there is no period to be assigned for the decay of Lucern in a suitable soil and fair treatment, nay, with the foulest play, in such a situation, you can hardly kill it A Gentleman assured me, that having a small plantation of Lucern, and being willing to convert it into a garden, the Lucern was pulled up, and the ground double dug Notwithstanding, it came up all over the spot, and though it was cleared off as often as it made its appearance, fresh shoots still presented themselves, plainly shewing that there is no getting rid of Lucern, after it has once taken possession of a place suitable to its nature, until the roots, by having the crowns taken off by constant hoeing, are rendered so weak, that their efforts for fresh shooting become ineffectual, and they die of course under the constant repetition of such severe discipline

Proper soil and situation

But though Lucern will live long, it will abate in vigour, unless manured like other herbage This business should be performed in November, or early in December, as soon as the last cutting is over The richest, the strongest, and the best rotten dung should be got for the purpose, nevertheless, if your Lucern plantation is on an unfavourable soil which is cold, clayey, moist, or the like, it will be better to assist it with such manure as soot, lime, malt-dust, ashes, &c

Proper time to raise the seeds

With regard to raising the seeds of Lucern, this should be from the second cutting; for the first

first will grow too rank for the purpose, and be seldom productive of much seed, nay, from the second or any cutting much seed is rarely produced, and in unfavourable seasons hardly any at all. It is to be purchased, however, of the seedsmen all over England, who import it from abroad, and as the rates are so very reasonable as at about 8d or 9d per pound, it may be purchased cheaper than what it can be raised for at home, and as the seed is much better, the sowing seed for use is not worth the attempt.

Titles. 1. Sea Medick is titled, *Medicago pedunculis racemosis, leguminibus cochleatis spinosis, caule procumbente tomentoso*. Caspar Bauhine calls it, *Trifolium cochleatum maritimum tomentosum*, Clusius, *Medica marina*. It grows naturally on the shores of the Mediterranean Sea.

2. Yellow Medick is, *Medicago pedunculis racemosis, leguminibus lunatis, caule prostrato*. Caspar Bauhine calls it, *Trifolium sylvestre luteum, siliquâ cornutâ*, John Bauhine, *Medica sylvestris*, Clusius, *Medica flavo flore*, Gerard, *Trifolium luteum siliqua cornutâ*, and Parkinson, *Medica frutescens flavo flore Clusii*. It grows naturally on the borders of fields, by way-sides, and dry places in England and most parts of Europe.

3. Lucern or Medick Fodder is titled, *Medicago pedunculis racemosis, leguminibus contortis, caule erecto glabro*. Clusius calls it, *Medica legitima*, Morison, *Medica sativa*, and Lobel, *Foenum Burgundicum*. It grows naturally in warm places in England, France, Spain, &c.

## CHAP. CCLXXXVII.

## *MELIANTHUS*, HONEY FLOWER.

THERE are only two species of this genus, called

Species. 1. The Greater Honey Flower.
2. The smaller Honey Flower.

Description of the Greater. 1. The Greater Honey Flower. The root is thick, woody, and spreading. The stalks are ligneous near the bottom, hollow, knotty, irregular, of a whitish colour, and grow to be six or eight feet high. The leaves are large, and to the last degree beautiful. Each consists of about four or five pair of sharply-serrated folioles terminated by an odd one, a leafy jagged border runs on each side the midrib connecting the folioles. They embrace the stalk with their base, have stipulæ growing singly to the bottom of each footstalk, and are of a whitish, cheerful and luscious green colour. The flowers are produced in long spikes from the tops of the stalks, they are of a brownish chocolate colour, having a monophyllous, compressed nectarium, full of a honey juice, appear in June, and sometimes, though very rarely, are succeeded by ripe seeds in the autumn.

and Smaller Honey Flower. 2. Smaller Honey Flower. The root is thick and woody, but not so spreading under ground as the former. The stalks are ligneous, round, soft to the touch, branching a little, and four or five feet high. The leaves are composed of four or five pair of folioles terminated by an odd one, but they are not near so large as the former, they have stipulæ on each side their base, are of a dark-green colour on their upper side, whitish underneath, and on the whole are very beautiful. The flowers come out from the ends and sides of the stalks in loose hanging bunches, they are small, but answer to the characters of the former, their colour is a composition of green, saffron, and pale-red, the petals near the base are green and tipped with saffron colour, and the smelling part is a pale red, they appear in June, but are very rarely succeeded by seeds in England.

These species, being both natives of Africa, were deemed green-house plants, and treated accordingly, but they are now found to be tolerably hardy, as they will bear our common winters in dry, well-sheltered places, and display their utmost beauty when growing in the full ground, when their roots are unconfined by pots, and their stems assume their natural growth, without being drawn weak and disfigured through the confinement of a green-house.

They are easily propagated by the suckers, and the first species sends these forth in great plenty. They will begin to arise in the spring, and there will be a succession of them all summer. They may be taken up any time, when they are of proper strength, and are possessed of a fibre or two, and they will then be good plants to set out for good. Method of propagating them.

The second species does not send out suckers so freely as the first, but then the slips will grow, and by this means plenty of plants may be soon obtained. The cuttings should be taken off in any of the summer months, and planted in pots filled with light earth. The pots should be then set in the green-house, in a shady part of it, and the plants should be regularly watered. When you find them in a growing state, they must be taken out of the green-house, otherwise they will soon look sickly, and draw weak, and the pots must be plunged up to the rims in the common mould, in a shady part of the garden. Here they may stand until November, when they should be set in the house for the first winter with the hardiest green-house plants, and in the spring may be turned out of the pots, with the mould at the roots, into the places where they are designed to remain.

The soil for both kinds should be light, dry, and rubbishy, and the place warm and well defended; and when such a situation is wanted, some plants of each kind must be regularly kept in the green-house in winter, whereby the sorts may be encreased, in case those abroad should be destroyed by bad weather. Proper soil and situation.

1. The

Titles 1 The first species is called, *Melianthus stipulis solitariis petiolo adnatis* Herman calls it, *Melianthus Africanus* It grows naturally in Æthiopia

2 The second species is, *Melianthus stipulis geminis distinctis* Commelin calls it, *Melianthus Africanus minor fœtidus*, and Ray, *Melianthus Africanus minor fœtidus* It grows naturally in Æthiopia

*Melianthus* is of the class and order *Didynamia Angiospermia*, and the characters are,

Class and order in the Linnæan system The characters 1 CALYX is a large, unequal, coloured perianthium, divided into five segments, of which the two upper are oblong and erect The lower one is very short, gibbous, and bag-shaped, and the two others are spear-shaped, erect, and placed opposite

2 COROLLA is four spear-shaped, narrow, patent petals, connected at their sides, and reflexed on their points

The nectarium is monophyllous, very short, compressed on the sides, cut in the margin, situated in the lower segment of the calyx, and with it fastened to the receptacle

3 STAMINA are four awl-shaped, erect filaments the length of the calyx, of which the two inferior are rather shorter than the others, having cordated, oblong, quadrilocular antheræ

4 PISTILLUM consists of a gibbous, four-cornered germen indented in four parts, an erect, awl-shaped style the length and situation of the stamina, and a quadrifid stigma

5 PERICARPIUM is a quadrangular, semi-quadrifid capsule, the angles being distinct and acute, divided into distended cells by partitions, and opening between the angles for the discharge of the seeds

6 SEMINA The seeds are four, roundish, and fastened to the center of the capsule

# CHAP CCLXXXVIII

# *MELICA*

THERE are three species of this genus, viz

Species 1 Common Melic Grass

2 Tall Siberian Melic Grass

3 Ciliated Melic Grass

Description of Common, 1 Common Melic Grass The root is long, slender, and creeping The stalks are slender, round, hollow, jointed, purplish near the top, and about a foot and a half high The leaves are narrow, pointed, grow singly at the joints, and sheath the stalk with their base The flowers are produced from the tops of the stalks in simple, drooping panicles, they are smooth, of a purplish colour, and usually hang all on one side on weak slender footstalks, they appear chiefly in June and July, though they are sometimes met with in the end of summer and in the autumn

Tall Siberian, 2 Tall Siberian Melic Grass The stalks are round, hollow, jointed, and three feet high The leaves are like those of oats, but smaller, grow singly at the joints, and surround the stalk with their base The flowers come out in branching panicles from the tops of the stalks, they are smooth, having no arista, and appear in June and July

and Ciliated Melic Grass 3 Ciliated Melic Grass The stalks are slender, round, jointed, and about two feet high The leaves are long, narrow, grow singly at the joints, and are possessed of woolly matter near the base, where they form a kind of sheath to the stalks The flowers come out from the tops of the stalks in simple, loose, spreading spikes, they are very white and hoary, and appear in July

Method of propagation Whoever is inclined to have a few of these grasses to be ready for observation, may easily effect it by sowing the seeds in the autumn soon after they are ripe, or the spring following They will grow in any soil or situation, and will require no trouble except keeping them clean from weeds

1 The first species is titled, *Melica petalis imberbibus, panicula nutante simplici* In the *Flora Lapponica* it is termed, *Melica floribus suo culmo pendulis* Caspar Bauhine calls it, *Gramen montanum avenaceum, locustis rubris*, also, *Gramen montanum avenaceum spicatum*, also, *Gramen avenaceum, locustis rarioribus*, John Bauhine, *Gramen locustis rubris*, and Morison, *Gramen avenaceum spicâ muticâ rariore glumâ* It grows naturally in moist woods in England and most of the cold countries of Europe Titles

2 The second species is, *Melica petalis imberbibus, paniculâ ramosissimâ* Gmelin calls it, *Melica flosculis glabris, summo urceolari*, and Morison, *Gramen avenaceum, locustis rarioribus muticis, Virginianum majus* It grows naturally in Siberia and Canada

3 The third species is, *Melica flosculi inferioris petalo exteriore ciliato* Van Royen calls it, *Melica floribus horizontaliter patentibus*, Caspar Bauhine, *Gramen avenaceum montanum lanuginosum*, and Scheuchzer, *Gramen avenaceum, spicâ simplici, locustis densissimis candicantibus & lanuginosis* It grows naturally in sterile rocky places in most countries of Europe

*Melica* is of the class and order *Triandria Digynia*, and the characters are, Class and order in the Linnæan system

1 CALYX is a glume composed of two oval, concave, nearly equal valves, containing two flowers The characters

2 COROLLA is two oval, beardless valves, one being concave, the other plane

3 STAMINA are three capillary filaments the length of the flower, having oblong antheræ bifurcated at each end

4 PISTILLUM consists of an oval turbinated germen, and two setaceous, patent styles, with oblong, hairy stigmas

5 PERICARPIUM There is none The corolla includes the seed, and discharges it when ripe

6 SEMEN The seed is single and oval

# CHAP CCLXXXIX

## *MELISSA*, BAUM

THE Baum and the Calamint of old authors are now joined as proper species of *Melissa*, so that the perennials of this genus stand in order thus

Species

1 Common Baum
2 Grand flowered Baum, or More Excellent Calamint
3 Common Calamint
4 Field Calamint
5 Cretic Baum, or Hoary Basil leaved Calamint

The virtues of the Common Baum

1 The virtues of the Common Baum, both for kitchen and medicinal uses, are universally known and admired So refreshing is the smell of this plant, so delicious is the appearance of its variegated sorts on their first coming out, and so salutary and cooling is the tea, that were it for no other purposes, this herb would have a first claim to a place in gardens, but it serves for numberless uses in medicine, as well as culinary purposes, which causes it to be still more respected, and brings it of course into the kitchen garden Therefore, all that I shall recommend of it in this place is, to have a plant or two of the best variegated kinds among the perennials destined for observation, and they will give great pleasure by their sweetly variegated leaves, as well as answer the other purposes of botanical inspection

Grand-flowered Baum described

2 Grand-flowered Baum, or More Excellent Calamint This is a finely scented plant The stalks are upright, and grow to about a foot high The leaves are oblong, oval, hairy, indented, and grow opposite to each other at the joints The flowers are produced from the wings of the stalks on forked footstalks, they are large and of a purple colour, appear in June, and ripen their seeds in August

Common Calamint described

3 Common Calamint This species rises with several upright, square, branching, hairy stalks, to the height of about a foot The leaves are strongly scented, roundish, indented, and grow opposite to each other at the joints The flowers are produced from the sides of the branches on forked footstalks, they are of a bluish or purple colour, appear in July, and ripen their seeds in the autumn

Its variety

There is a variety of this species with white flowers

Field Calamint,

4 Field Calamint The stalks are hard, square, hairy, branching, and fall on the ground The leaves are rough, indented, and smell like Penny Royal The flowers are produced in whorls round the stalks, and are of a purple colour, their footstalks are forked, and longer than the leaves, they appear in June to the end of summer, and ripen their seeds in the autumn

and Cretic Baum described

5 Cretic Baum, or Hoary Basil-leaved Calamint The stalks are hard, slender, and about a foot long The leaves grow opposite at the joints, they are hoary, roundish, and a little resemble those of Basil The flowers terminate the branches in loose spikes, and grow from the sides of the stalks on very short single footstalks, they are of a white colour, appear in June, and ripen their seeds in August

Culture

All these sorts are easily propagated by dividing of the roots The best season for this work is the autumn, though they will grow if planted at any time of the year The fifth species seldom lasts longer than three years, but Nature has sufficiently provided for its succession, for if the seeds are permitted to scatter, they will come up, and afford a never failing supply of these plants, which will call for no trouble, except keeping them clean from weeds, and thinning them where they appear too close

Titles

1 Common Baum is titled, *Melissa racemis axillaribus verticillatis, pedicellis simplicibus* In the *Hortus Cliffort* it is termed, *Melissa floribus ex alis inferioribus sessilibus* Caspar Bauhine calls it, *Melissa hortensis*, Lobel, *Apiastrum, sive Melissophyllum* It grows naturally in Italy, and on the mountains near Geneva

2 Grand-flowered Baum, or More Excellent Calamint, is titled, *Melissa pedunculis axillaribus dichotomis longitudine folii* Caspar Bauhine calls it, *Calamintha magno flore*, Besler, *Calamintha montana præstantior* It grows naturally on the mountains of Tuscany and Austria

3 Common Calamint is titled *Melissa pedunculis axillaribus dichotomis longitudine foliorum* In the *Hortus Cliffort* it is termed, *Melissa floribus ex alis superioribus, pedunculo communi confertis* Caspar Bauhine calls it, *Calamintha vulgaris & officinarum Germaniæ*, Dodonæus, *Calamintha montana* It grows naturally in England, Italy, France, and Spain

4 Field Calamint This species is titled, *Melissa pedunculis axillaribus dichotomis folio longioribus, caule decumbente* In the *Hortus Cliffort* it is termed, *Melissa floribus ex alis superioribus, pedunculo dichotomo, caule procumbente* Caspar Bauhine calls it, *Calamintha pulegii odore, sive nepeta*, Boccone, *Calamintha montana præalta, pulegii odore* It grows naturally in England, Italy, and Germany

5 Cretic Baum, or Hoary Basil-leaved Calamint, is titled, *Melissa racemis terminalibus, pedunculis solitariis brevissimis* Caspar Bauhine calls it, *Calamintha incana, ocymi foliis*, Barrelier, *Calamintha, pulegii odore, minor*, Plukenet, *Calamintha Clinopodii Austriaci foliis, odore pulegii* It grows naturally in France and Spain

Class and order in the Linnæan System

*Melissa* is of the class and order *Didynamia Gymnospermia*, and the characters are,

The characters

1 CALYX is a monophyllous, subcampanulated, angular, striated, permanent perianthium formed at the top into two lips, the upper of which is plane, and indented in three reflexed, patent parts, the lower one is short, acute, and indented in two parts

2 COROLLA is a ringent petal The tube is cylindrical, and the mouth is gaping The upper lip is short, erect, arched, roundish, and indented The lower lip is cut [illegible] into three segments, of which the [illegible] is the largest

3 STAMINA

3 STAMINA are four subulated filaments, (two of which are the length of the corolla, the other two are about half as long) with small antheræ, which join by pairs

4 PISTILLUM consists of a quadrifid germen, a filiforme style the length of the corolla, situated with the stamina under the upper lip, and of a slender, bifid, reflexed stigma

5 PERICARPIUM There is none The seeds are contained in the calyx

6 SEMINA The seeds are oval, and four in number

# CHAP CCXC.

## MELITTIS, BAUM-LEAVED ARCH-ANGEL, or BASTARD BAUM

THERE is only one species of this genus, usually called Bastard Baum

*This plant described*

The root is hard and woody The stalk is thick square, upright, and two or three feet high The leaves are like baum, but frequently larger, grow opposite on footstalks, are of a blackish green colour, and very strongly scented The flowers come out from the wings of the leaves almost the whole length of the stalks, are of a white colour, appear in June, and the seeds ripen in August

*Its Varieties*

The varieties of this species are,
Small-leaved Bastard Baum,
Jagged-leaved Bastard-Baum.
Large White-flowered,
Purple-flowered, and
Variegared Bastard Baum

*Method of propagation*

It is propagated by parting of the roots, which may be done at any time of the year, but more especially in the autumn when the stalks decay

Cuttings planted in a shady border, in any of the summer months, and duly watered at first, will grow, and soon commence good plants

There being no other species of this genus, it is termed, simply, *Melittis* Caspar Bauhine calls it, *Lamium montanum, melissæ folio*, Gerard, *Melissa Fuchsii*, and Parkinson, *Melissophyllon Fuchsii* It grows naturally in woods and hedges in England, Helvetia, Germany, and the South of France

*Class and order in the Linnæan system The characters*

*Melittis* is of the class and order *Didynamia Gymnospermia*, and the characters are,

1 CALYX is a monophyllous, bell-shaped, open, straight, bilabiated perianthium The upper lip is emarginated and acute, the lower lip is the shortest, and cut into two acute segments

2 COROLLA is one ringent petal The tube is much narrower than the calyx The mouth is somewhat thicker than the tube The upper lip is erect, roundish, and plane The lower lip is patent, obtuse, and divided into three segments, the middle one being the largest, and crenated at the top

3 STAMINA are four awl shaped filaments under the upper lip, having connivent, bifid, obtuse antheræ, placed by pairs cross wise

4 PISTILLUM consists of a quadrifid germen, a filiforme style the length of the corolla, and a slender, bifid, reflexed stigma

5 PERICARPIUM There is none The seeds are lodged in the calyx

6 SEMINA The seeds are four, and oval

# C H A P. CCXCI

## *MENTHA*, MINT

Remarks. THERE are only fourteen diſtinct ſpecies of this genus, and no leſs than eleven of them are natives of our own country. Our ditches, our ponds, and the banks of our rivers and brooks abound with ſome or other of the ſorts; nay our arable land and paſtures are not always deſtitute of ſome ſpecies proper to their natures; ſo that they are ſeldom propagated in gardens, unleſs for ſalutary purpoſes, and kitchen uſes. Nevertheleſs there are hardly any of the ſpecies which have not varieties of ſome ſingularity; and it is theſe varieties only that we cultivate among our curious plants. The leaves of ſome are finely ſpotted with ſilver, and variegated with the pureſt white; others again are ſtriped with gold, and glow in a collection of variegated plants. The downy hoarineſs of ſome recommends them to our notice, whilſt the Red, the Orange-coloured, and the different tinges of others, attract our obſervation, and induce us to perſevere in continuing and improving the ſorts by culture, though the mother ſpecies is found in our garden ditch. The ſpecies of which one or other of theſe varieties are to be found, are,

Species.
1. The Common White Mint
2. Spear Mint
3. Round-leaved Mint
4. Curled Mint
5. Water Mint
6. Pepper Mint
7. Sweet Mint
8. Red Mint
9. Corn Mint, or Calamint
10. Smooth Mint
11. Canada Mint
12. Narrow-leaved Penny-Royal
13. Common Penny-Royal

Common White. 1. The firſt ſort grows naturally in moiſt places, and often goes by the name of Long-leaved Horſe-Mint. The ſtalks are ſquare. The leaves are oblong, hoary, ſerrated, and ſit cloſe, without any footſtalks. The flowers grow at the tops of the ſtalks in long ſpikes; they are of a whitiſh-red colour, and their ſtamina are longer than the corolla.

Spear. 2. The ſecond ſort is the well-known Spear Mint of our Kitchen Gardens, and like moſt of the others ſhould not be mentioned in this place, were it not to introduce its agreeable varieties, of which there are the Curled leaved, and Variegated.

Round leaved. 3. The third ſort is frequently called Round-leaved Horſe-Mint, and alſo *Menthaſtrum*. The leaves are large, round, crenated, rough, and ſit cloſe, without footſtalks. The flowers grow in ſpikes at the ends of the branches, and the whole plant is more ſtrongly ſcented than moſt of the other ſorts.

Curled. 4. The fourth ſort has leaves that are waved or curled; theſe are heart-ſhaped, indented, and ſit cloſe, without any footſtalks. The flowers are produced in capitated ſpikes; they are reddiſh, and in one variety moderately large and fair.

Water. 5. The fifth ſort has angular red-coloured ſtalks. The leaves alſo are oved, oval, ſerrated, and grow on footſtalks. The flowers are collected into roundiſh heads; their colour is a kind of purple, and their ſtamina are longer than the corolla.

Pepper. 6. The ſixth ſort is the well known Pepper Mint, from which that fine cordial Pepper-Mint water is prepared. The ſtalks are purpliſh, and branching. The leaves are oval, oblong, of a dark colour, ſerrated on their edges, and grow on footſtalks. The flowers terminate the ſtalks in roundiſh heads; their colour is purple, and their ſtamina are ſhorter than the petals.

Sweet. 7. The ſeventh ſort hath ſmooth purple ſtalks. The leaves are oval, and acutely ſerrated. The flowers grow in whorls round the tops of the ſtalks, under each of which two ſmall leaves are placed; their colour is a bright-purple, and their ſtamina are longer than the corolla.

Red. 8. The eighth ſort has angular red ſtalks. The leaves are oval, acute, ſerrated, and finely ſcented. The flowers grow in whorls round the upper-parts of the ſtalks; they are of a pale-purple colour, and their ſtamina are ſhorter than the petals.

Corn. 9. The ninth ſort is called Calamint, and is a finely-ſcented plant. The ſtalks grow only to about a foot high, and are weak and hairy. The leaves are of an oval figure, acute, and ſerrated. The flowers grow in whorls round the ſtalks; they are of a pale purple colour, and their ſtamina and petals are equal.

Smooth, 10. The tenth ſort hath weak trailing ſtalks rather more than a foot long. The leaves are ſmooth, oval, ſpear-ſhaped, acute, and entire. The flowers grow in whorls round the ſtalks; their colour is purple, and their ſtamina are longer than the petals.

and Canada Mint deſcribed. 11. The eleventh ſort is a native of Canada, very hairy, and grows to about two feet high. The leaves are ſpear-ſhaped, hairy, deeply ſerrated, and have footſtalks. The flowers are produced in whorls, and their ſtamina and corolla are equal.

Narrow leaved. 12. The twelfth ſort grows naturally near Montpelier to about two feet high. The leaves are narrow, thickiſh, and finely ſcented. The flowers are produced in whorls round the upper parts of the ſtalks; their general colour is purple, though there is a variety with white flowers, and their ſtamina are longer than the corolla.

and Common Penny Royal deſcribed. 13. The thirteenth ſort is the Common Penny Royal, or Pudding Graſs. This grows naturally in wet places in many parts of England, and is chiefly cultivated in gardens for giving a right flavour to hogs puddings. The ſtalks are roundiſh, and bend to the ground. The leaves are oval, obtuſe, and indented. The flowers grow in whorls round the ſtalks, and their ſtamina are longer than the corolla.

Culture. Theſe ſorts will all readily take root from the cuttings, ſo that when a plant ſhews itſelf of extraordinary beauty, by the ſtripes, or colour of the leaves, &c. the cuttings may be taken off, and being planted in a moiſt ſhady border will grow, and continue the plant in its beauty.

But

But the best way of propagating these sorts in general is by dividing of the roots Take a bit or two of any of them, in the autumn, winter, or spring, and they will readily grow, and soon make great increase. When these plants are designed only for observation, two or three of a sort will be sufficient, these should be reduced every two years, or they will become too large and rambling, and the best season for this work is September

Titles 1 The Common, or Long-leaved Horse Mint is titled, *Mentha spicis oblongis, foliis oblongis tomentosis serratis sessilibus, staminibus corolla longioribus* Caspar Bauhine calls it, *Mentha sylvestris, folio longiore*, and John Bauhine, *Menthastrum spicatum, folio longiore candicante* It grows naturally in England, Germany, and other parts of Europe

2 Spear Mint is, *Mentha spicis oblongis, foliis lanceolatis nudis serratis sessilibus, staminibus corolla longioribus* In the *Hortus Cliffort* it is termed, *Mentha spicis solitariis interruptis, foliis lanceolatis serratis sessilibus* Caspar Bauhine calls it, *Mentha angustifolia spicata*, and Gronovius, *Mentha aquatica spicata, foliis oblongis utrinque serratis acuminatis* It grows naturally in England and Germany

3 Round leaved Horse-Mint is, *Mentha spicis oblongis, foliis subrotundis rugosis crenatis sessilibus* Caspar Bauhine calls it, *Mentha sylvestr., rotundiore folio*, and John Bauhine, *Menthastrum, folio rugoso rotundiore, spontaneum flore spicato odore gravi* It grows naturally in England

4 Curled Mint is titled, *Mentha spicis capitatis foliis cordatis dentatis undulatis sessilibus, staminibus corollam æquantibus* Morison calls it, *Mentha crispa Danica sive Germanica speciosa*, and Rivinus, *Mentha crispa* It grows naturally in Siberia

5 Water Mint is titled, *Mentha spicis capitatis, foliis ovatis serratis petiolatis, staminibus corolla longioribus* Caspar Bauhine calls it, *Mentha rotundifolia palustris sive aquatica major*, and Dalechamp, *Sisymbrium sylvestre* It grows naturally in most parts of Europe

6 Pepper Mint is, *Mentha spicis capitatis, foliis ovatis serratis petiolatis, staminibus corolla brevioribus* Ray calls it, *Mentha spicis brevioribus & habitioribus, foliis menthæ fuscæ, sapore fervido piperis* It is a native of England

7 Sweet Mint is, *Mentha floribus verticillatis, foliis ovatis acutiusculis serratis, staminibus corollâ longioribus* Caspar Bauhine calls it, *Mentha crispa verticillata* It grows naturally in the southern parts of Europe

8 Red Mint is, *Mentha floribus verticillatis, foliis ovatis acutis serratis, staminibus corollâ brevioribus* Caspar Bauhine calls it, *Mentha hortensis verticillata, ocymi odore*, and John Bauhine, *Mentha verticillata minor acuta non crispa, odore ocymi* It grows naturally in England, and most of the southern countries of Europe

9 Corn Mint is titled, *Mentha floribus verticillatis foliis ovatis acutis serratis, staminibus corollam æquantibus* Morison calls it, *Mentha arvensis verticillata procumbens*, John Bauhine, *Calamintha arvensis verticillata*, and Gerard, *Calamintha aquatica* It grows naturally in England, and many parts of Europe

10 Smooth Mint is, *Mentha floribus verticillatis, foliis lanceolato ovatis glabris acutis integerrimis* Ray calls it, *Mentha aquatica exigua*, Fuchsius, *Mentha rotundifolia*, and Lobel, *Calamintha aquatica Belgarum & Matthioli* It grows naturally in England

11 Canada Mint is, *Mentha floribus verticillatis, foliis lanceolatis serratis petiolatis pilosis, staminibus corollam æquantibus* It grows naturally in Canada

12 Narrow-leaved Penny Royal is, *Mentha floribus verticillatis, foliis linearibus, staminibus corollâ longioribus* Caspar Bauhine calls it, *Pulegium angustifolium* It grows naturally about Montpelier in France

13 Common Penny Royal is, *Mentha floribus verticillatis, foliis ovatis obtusis subcrenatis, caulibus subteretibus repentibus, staminibus corollâ longioribus* Caspar Bauhine calls it, *Pulegium latifolium*, Gerard, *Pulegium regium*, and Parkinson, *Pulegium vulgare* It grows naturally in England and Germany

*Mentha* is of the class and order *Didynamia Gymnospermia*, and the characters are,

1 Calyx is a monophyllous, tubulous, erect, permanent perianthium, indented in five equal parts — Class and order in the Linnæan system

2 Corolla is an erect tubulous petal a little longer than the calyx The limb is nearly equal, and divided into four segments, the upper of which is the largest, and emarginated — The character

3 Stamina consist of four subulated, erect, distant filaments, of which the two nearest are the longest, with roundish antheræ

4 Pistillum consists of a quadrifid germen, an erect filiforme style longer than the corolla, and a patent bifid stigma

5 Pericarpium There is none The seeds are lodged in the erect calyx

6 Semina The seeds are small, and four in number

# CHAP. CCXCII.

## *MENYANTHES*, BOG-BEAN, or MARSH TREFOIL.

THIS genus admits of two perennials, usually called,

Species.

1. Bog Bean, or Marsh Trefoil.
2. Fringed Water Lily.

Bog Bean.

1. Bog-Bean, or Marsh Trefoil. The root is thick, jointed, long, white, and in moist boggy places spreads very much every way under the surface of the ground. The stalks are smooth, weak, and upright, and about a foot high. The leaves are trifoliate, and the folioles are large, smooth, shining, of a deep green colour, and much resemble those of the common garden Bean. The flowers come out from the tops of the stalks in long loose spikes; they are of a white colour, having a slight mixture of carnation red; and the general characters shew their structure; they appear in June, July, and August, and the seeds ripen in the autumn.

This is a very beautiful plant, on the first appearance of the flowers, and worthy of a place in boggy ground, when such happens to fall within the compass of our works.

and Fringed Water Lily described.

2. Fringed Water Lily. This plant grows chiefly in large ditches, ponds, and often rivers. The root is thick, spongy, jointed, and spreading. The stalks are tender, pithy, and about a foot high. The leaves are heart-shaped, roundish, and entire. The flowers come out in small bunches from the ends of the stalks; they are of a white or yellow colour, being finely fringed on their edges, appear in June, July, and August, and the seeds ripen in the autumn.

Culture.

Both these sorts are easily propagated by parting of the roots. Those of the first sort should be planted in bogs and moist places early in the autumn, and those of the second should be pegged down to the mud, by the sides of ditches or waters where you would chuse to have them grow. The spring following they will shoot up, exhibit their flowers about June, and if they like their situation, will soon make increase enough.

They are also propagated by sowing the seeds soon after they are ripe. The boggy ground for the first species should be well dug, and made fine, and the seeds sown and just covered with the mould. From this time they must be left to Nature, not a weed should be pulled up, and you will find the plants rise in the spring with the common herbage of the place, and in such company they will display their native beauties much better than when incommoded by such care and culture as is usually and necessarily given to most kinds of plants.

The seeds of the second species should be sown by the sides of waters where you would chuse to have them grow, and in the spring following they will come up. But for both these species seeds will be an unnecessary practice, where a sufficient quantity of roots may be easily obtained, as they will be surer of growing, and come earlier the speedier.

Titles.

1. Bog Bean, or Marsh Trefoil, is titled, *Menyanthes foliis ternatis*. Caspar and John Bauhine call it, *Trifolium palustre*. Tournefort, *Menyanthe palustre latifolium & triphyllum* [illegible]; and Gerard, *Trifolium paludosum*. It grows naturally in marshy boggy places in England, and most countries of Europe.

2. Fringed Water Lily is, *Menyanthes foliis cordatis integerrimis corollis ciliatis*. In the *Hortus Cliffort.* it is termed, *Menyanthe foliis orbiculatis, corollis margine laceris*. Caspar and John Bauhine call it, *Nymphæa lutea minor, flore fimbriato*. It grows naturally in waters in England, and most parts of Germany.

Class and order in the Linnæan system.

*Menyanthes* is of the class and order *Pentandria Monogynia*; and the characters are,

The characters.

1. Calyx is a monophyllous, erect, permanent perianthium, divided into five parts.
2. Corolla is an infundibuliforme petal. The tube is short, cylindrical, and funnel-shaped. The limb is deeply cut into five reflexed segments, which are spreading, hairy, and obtuse.
3. Stamina are five short awl-shaped filaments, having erect acute antheræ, which are bifid at their base.
4. Pistillum consists of a conical germen, a cylindrical style about the length of the corolla, and a bifid compressed stigma.
5. Pericarpium is an oval unilocular capsule, surrounded by the calyx.
6. Semina. The seeds are many, oval, and small.

CHAP.

# CHAP. CCXCIII.

## *MERCURIALIS*, MERCURY.

Species

OF this genus are,

1. Dog's Mercury.
2. Spanish Mercury.

Description of Dog's Mercury

1. Dog's Mercury. The root is slender, white, and spreading. The stalks are simple, upright, jointed, and about a foot high. The leaves are oblong, spear-shaped, very rough, of a dark-green colour, indented on their edges, and grow opposite by pairs on the joints. The flowers come out in spikes from the ends of the stalks; they are small, and of a yellowish colour; males and females are found on different plants, and the general characters shew their composition; they appear the beginning of summer, and often continue in succession until the end of autumn, long before which time good seed from the first-blown female flowers may be gathered.

Its uses in medicine

This plant was formerly used in medicine, but is now known to be poisonous; however, an annual of this genus still retains its reputation as a fine emollient, laxative, &c. It grows wild in hedges and woods almost all over England, and a few plants only are now and then admitted into gardens to be ready for observation.

Its propagation

It is propagated by parting of the roots, which may be done at any time of the year, but the best season is the autumn.

Spanish Mercury described

2. Spanish Mercury. The stalks are woody, branching, and about a foot and a half high. The leaves are oval, downy on both sides, and grow opposite by pairs. The flowers come out in spikes from the ends and sides of the stalks, and males and females distinctly are found on different plants; they appear in July, and the females are succeeded by ripe seeds in the autumn.

Culture

This plant will live several years if the soil be dry, light, or rubbishy, and the situation well-defended. It is easily raised by sowing the seeds, which must be in the autumn, soon after they are ripe; because if they are kept until the spring they often remain until the spring following before they make their appearance. When they come up they will require no trouble, except thinning them where they are too close, and keeping them clear from weeds. After they have once flowered, and the seeds are scattered, plenty of plants will spontaneously arise, and continue the succession without trouble; so that although it may be necessary to station these plants in a very rubbishy soil, to continue the same plants for four or five years, yet sow them where you will, there will always, after they have once shed their seeds, be plenty of plants for a succession, even should the old ones die off every winter after they have flowered and shed their seeds.

1. Dog's Mercury is titled, *Mercurialis caule simplicissimo, [illegible]*. Caspar Bauhine calls it, *Mercurialis mon[illegible] testiculata*, also, *Mercurialis montana spicata*, [illegible], also, *Cynocrambe [illegible]*; Ray, *Mercurialis perennis repens cynocrambe dicta*; Gerard, *Cynocrambe mas et femina*; and Parkinson, *Mercurialis sylvestris cynocrambe dicta vulgaris, mas et femina*. It grows naturally in woods and hedges in England, and most parts of Europe. Title

2. Spanish Mercury is, *Mercurialis caule suffruticoso foliis tomentosis*. Caspar Bauhine calls it, *Phyllon testiculatum*, also, *Phyllon spicatum*; and Clusius, *Phyllum Mas ficus*, also, *Phyllum femi[illegible]*. It grows naturally in Spain, Italy, and the South of France.

*Mercurialis* is of the class and order *Dioecia Enneandria*; and the characters are, Class and order in the Linnean system. The characters

I. Male Flowers.

1. CALYX is a perianthium divided into three oval, spear-shaped, concave, spreading segments.
2. COROLLA. There is none.
3. STAMINA are nine or twelve straight capillary filaments the length of the calyx, having globular didymous antheræ.

II. Females.

1. CALYX is as in the males.
2. COROLLA. There is none. There is an awl-shaped sharp-pointed nectarium situated on each side of the germen.
3. PISTILLUM consists of a roundish, compressed, hispid germen, furrowed on each side, and of two reflexed hispid styles, with acute, reflexed stigmas.
4. PERICARPIUM is a roundish, scrotiform, didymous capsule, containing two cells.
5. SEMINA. The seeds are single, and roundish.

# CHAP. CCXCIV.

## *MIMULUS*

OF this genus there is one beautiful perennial species, called Canada Perfoliate Fox-Glove.

The plant described. The stalks are upright, square, jointed, and about two feet high. The leaves are oblong, smooth, pointed, grow opposite, and unite at their base, surrounding the stalks at the joints. The flowers come out singly on each side the stalk from the bosom of the leaves at the joints; they are large, of a beautiful blue colour, and the general characters shew their structure; they appear in July, and are succeeded by ripe seeds in the autumn.

Culture. This species is propagated by parting of the roots, the best time for which is the autumn. It is a hardy plant, and will grow almost in any soil or situation, though it delights most in a rich light earth, and the shade.

It is also raised from seeds. These should be sown in the autumn, as soon as they are ripe, in a bed of common garden mould made fine. In the spring the plants will come up, at which time weeds must be carefully drawn out as they arise; and if dry weather happens, the plants must be frequently refreshed by water. Shade also should be afforded them, for the hot sun is often prejudicial to them in their infant state. When the plants are fit to remove, the strongest should be drawn out, and planted in a bed at about six inches distance from each other; this will make room for the others, which will be daily getting stronger in the seminary in order for removal. In the autumn they will be fit to transplant, and may be then set out for good, either in beds, or disposed occasionally here and there about the different parts of the pleasure-garden. The plants in the beds may stand until the autumn following before they are removed, by which time they will become strong plants fit for any place; though it will be advisable only to take out every other plant, that there may be a bed for show entirely of these flowers; which will be the case when every other plant is taken away, the remainder being left at twelve inches distance from each other.

Titles. This species is entitled, *Mimulus erectus foliis oblongis linearibus sessilibus*. Plukenet calls it, *Euphrasia Floridana, lysimachiæ glabræ lusquosæ foliis, quadrato caule, ramosior*, Gronovius, *Lysimachia galericulata* [illegible] *gratiola elatior non ramosa*; Boerhaave, *Gratiola Canadensis latifolia, flore magno cæruleo*; and Morison, *Digitalis perfoliata glabra, flore violaceo minore*. It grows naturally in Virginia and Canada.

Class and order in the Linnæan system. *Mimulus* is of the class and order *Didynamia Angiospermia*; and the characters are,

The characters. 1. CALYX is an oblong, prismatick, five-cornered, equal, permanent perianthium, indented in five parts at the top.

2. COROLLA is one ringent petal. The tube is the length of the calyx, the limb is bilabiated; the upper lip is erect, bifid, rounded, and reflexed on the sides; the lower lip is broad, and cut into three roundish segments, the middle one being the smallest; the palate is convex and bifid.

3. STAMINA are four filiforme filaments, two being shorter than the others, having bifid kidney shaped antheræ.

4. PISTILLUM consists of a conical germen, a filiforme style the length of the stamina, and an oval, bifid, compressed stigma.

5. PERICARPIUM is an oval, covered capsule, containing two cells.

6. SEMINA. The seeds are many, and small.

# CHAP. CCXCV.

## *MITELLA*, BASTARD AMERICAN SANICLE.

THERE are only two species of this genus, both perennials, called,

Species. 1. American *Mitella*.

2. Asiatick *Mitella*.

Description of the American Mitella. 1. American *Mitella* sends forth from the root many large heart-shaped, angular, indented leaves, some of which are obtuse, others acute, of a dark-green colour, hairy on both sides, and grow on long footstalks. The stalks are slender, round, hairy, about a foot high, and nearly in the middle have two small, acute, angular leaves placed opposite to each other. The flowers are produced in loose spikes at the ends of the stalks; they are small, of a whitish colour, and their edges are nicely fringed; they appear early in June, and are succeeded by roundish capsules, containing the seeds, which do not always ripen in England.

Its varieties. This species varies very much in the colour of the flowers, there being the White, Pale Red, Deep Red, and Purple.

Asiatick Mitella described. 2. Asiatick *Mitella*. The leaves are smaller than the other, less angular, and grow on shorter footstalks. The stalks are slender, about six inches

inches high, and are always destitute of leaves. The flowers come out in short spikes from the ends of the stalks, and are whitish and red in different degrees; they appear in June, but are rarely succeeded by seeds in our gardens.

These sorts are propagated by parting of the roots, the best time for which is the autumn. They love a light rich soil, and a shady situation, and when they are planted out will require no trouble except keeping them clean from weeds. They are very hardy with respect to cold; and when the roots are divided, it should not be into two small parts, as they will then flower proportionably weaker for a long time after.

Titles. 1. American *Mitella* is titled, *Mitella scapo diphyllo*. Menzelius calls it, *Cortusa Americana altera floribus minutim fimbriatis*; Hermann, *Cortusa Americana, spicato flore, petalis fimbriatis*; and Dodart, *Sanicula seu cortusa Indica, flore spicato fimbriato*. It grows naturally in most parts of North America.

2. Asiatick *Mitella* is, *Mitella scapo nudo*. It is a native of the northern parts of Asia.

Class and order in the Linnæan system. The characters. *Mitella* is of the class and order *Decandria Digynia*; and the characters are,

1. Calyx is a monophyllous, bell-shaped, permanent perianthium, cut at the top into five segments.
2. Corolla is five petals divided into many slender parts, and inserted into the cup.
3. Stamina are ten awl-shaped filaments, shorter than the corolla, and inserted in the cup, having roundish antheræ.
4. Pistillum consists of a roundish bifid germen, with scarce any visible styles, but two obtuse stigmas.
5. Pericarpium is an oval bivalved capsule, containing one cell.
6. Semina. The seeds are many.

## CHAP. CCXCVI.

## *MOLUCCELLA*, MOLUCCA BALM.

IN this place may come a species of this genus, called Shrubby Italian Molucca.

This plant described. The stalks are square, ligneous, prickly, send out branches by pairs, and grow to about two feet and a half high. The leaves are oval, downy, serrated, have footstalks, and grow two or three together on each side the stalks. The flowers come out in whorls round the stalks at the joints, having small bell-shaped, prickly cups; they are moderately large, of a red colour, and their upper lip is more than commonly rough and woolly; they appear in July and August, and sometimes the seeds ripen in the autumn.

Propagation. This species is raised by cuttings, which, if planted in any of the summer months, shaded, and regularly watered, will grow.

They may also be raised by seeds, which should be sown in beds of light sandy earth in the spring, and when the plants are fit to remove, each should be set in a separate small pot, and then plunged up to the rim in a shady part of the garden. At the approach of frosty weather in winter they should be removed into the green-house, or set under shelter for their winter lodgings; and in the spring a share should be turned out, with the mould at the roots, into the places where they are designed to remain. When these plants are set abroad, a dry, warm, sandy, rocky, or rubbishy soil must be allotted them, in a warm well-sheltered place, and being thus stationed, the stalks will become more woody, hard, and be less liable to be destroyed by bad weather in winter.

Title. This species is titled, *Moluccella calycibus subcampanulatis quinquefidis, corollis calyce longioribus*. Ray calls it, *Scordium spinosum, floris* [illegible] *galea lanuginosa villosa*. It grows naturally in Italy.

Class and order in the Linnæan system. The characters. *Moluccella* is of the class and order *Didynamia Gymnospermia*; and the characters are,

1. Calyx is a large, monophyllous, permanent, incurved, turbinated bell-shaped perianthium, having a broad spreading limb, indented or cut into five, six, seven, or eight sharp-pointed segments.
2. Corolla is monopetalous, ringent, and smaller than the calyx. The tube and mouth are short; the upper lip is erect, concave, and entire; the under lip is cut into three segments, the middle ones of which are heart-shaped, emarginated, and longer than the others.
3. Stamina are four filaments situated under the upper lip, of which two are shorter than the others, having simple antheræ.
4. Pistillum consists of a four-parted germen, a style the size and situation of the stamina, and a bifid stigma.
5. Pericarpium. There is none. The seeds are lodged in the calyx.
6. Semina. The seeds are four, truncated, convex on one side, and angular on the other.

CHAP.

# CHAP. CCXCVII.

## *MOMORDICA*, MALE BALSAM APPLE.

THERE is one species of this genus, with an abiding root, called, the Wild or Spurting Cucumber.

The plant described.

The root is thick, white, fleshy, bitter, and of a nauseous disagreeable taste. The stalks are numerous, thick, rough, angular, full of juice, branching, and trail on the ground. The leaves are nearly heart-shaped, oblong, of a thick consistence, rough, of a greyish colour, and grow on long rough footstalks. The flowers come out from the wings of the leaves on tender rough footstalks; they are of a pale yellow colour, with greenish bottoms, and like the common cucumber, there are found male and female flowers on the same plant; they appear in succession great part of the summer, and the females are succeeded by large, oval, greyish, rough, prickly fruit, which when ripe, especially when touched discharge their seeds and juice with such amazing force as to cause consternation in the innocent fingerers, as well as much laughter to the by-standers, who laid the bait for their merriment. From the spirting property of this plant it frequently is called, *Noli me Tangere*, a name in use for other plants which are possessed of such properties, though in ever so small a degree. This species is also in some places called Ass's Cucumber.

Medicinal properties of this plant.

The juice of this fruit affords the Elaterium of the shops, is a violent purge, and given chiefly in dropsical cases. When the fruit is designed for these purposes, it should always be gathered before it is ripe; for then the juice will flow in greater plenty, and the Elaterium be finer, and of more lasting virtue than such as is collected from full ripe fruit.

Manner of propagating it.

These plants are easily raised by sowing the seeds, soon after they are ripe, in the autumn, or in the spring, in beds of light mould made fine. When the plants are fit to remove, they should be taken up, with a ball of earth to each root, and set in rows, four feet asunder, in a dry warm part of the garden. They must be shaded and watered at first, and afterwards will require no trouble, except keeping them clean from weeds. They will flower every year, and produce plenty of fruit, which spirting seeds to a considerable distance will grow, and come up in such plenty as to afford you more plants than you can tell what to do with, so that you need not be over-anxious about the old roots, should they be killed by the frost, which is often the case, because there will be plants enough to supply their places without any trouble. If you are desirous of preserving your old roots, you should see that they are first of all stationed in a dry, light, sandy, gravelly, or rubbishy soil; and in such a station you may reasonably expect them to continue for six or eight years. In rich, moist, fat earth they are generally killed by the first hard frost that happens.

Titles.

This species is titled, *Momordica pomis hispidis, cirrhis nullis*. In the *Hortus Upsal* it is termed, *Momordica absque cirrhis*; in the *Hortus Cliffort. Momordica pomis ovalibus hispidis, foliis cordatis integris plicato-dentatis*. Caspar Bauhine calls it, *Cucumis sylvestris asininus dictus*; and Cammerarius, *Cucumis sylvestris*. It grows naturally in most of the southern parts of Europe.

Class and order in the Linnæan system.

*Momordica* is of the class and order *Monoecia Syngenesia*; and the characters are,

The characters.

I. Male Flowers.

1. CALYX is a monophyllous concave perianthium, cut into five spear-shaped spreading segments.

2. COROLLA is large, rough, veined, spreading, and adheres to the calyx.

3. STAMINA. The filaments are three, awl-shaped, and short; the antheræ are seated on both sides; those belonging to two of the filaments are bifid, the other is simple; they are formed into a compressed border, and have a reflexed line, containing the farina.

II. Female Flowers on the same plant with the Males.

1. CALYX is the same kind of perianthium as the males, but sits on the germen, and is deciduous.

2. COROLLA is the same as the males.

3. STAMINA. None. There are three very short filaments, without any antheræ.

4. PISTILLUM consists of a large germen situated below the flowers, of a single, columnar, taper, trifid style, and of three oblong gibbous stigmas.

5. PERICARPIUM is a large, oblong oval apple, containing three cells, and bursting open with an elastic force.

6. SEMINA. The seeds are many, and compressed.

CHAP.

# CHAP. CCXCVIII.

## *MONARDA.*

THERE are three hardy perennials of this genus, diſtinguiſhed by the names of,

Species
1 Canada *Monarda*
2 Penſylvanian *Monarda*, or Oſwego Tea
3 Virginian *Monarda*

Deſcription of Canada, 1. Canada *Monarda* The root is compoſed of numerous fibres, which are thick, ſtrong, and ſpreading The ſtalks are upright, firm, hairy, obtuſely angular, branching a little near the top, and grow to about a yard high The leaves are oblong, broad at their baſe, pointed, hairy, indented, and placed oppoſite by pairs on ſhort hairy footſtalks The flowers come out from the ends of the ſtalks and branches in roundiſh heads, each head having a large five-leaved involucrum, they are of a purple colour and the general characters ſhew their ſtructure, they ſhew themſelves in July, and the ſeeds ripen in the autumn

This plant, on being bruiſed, emits an agreeable odour

Penſylvanian, 2 Penſylvanian *Monarda*, or Oſwego Tea The root is creeping The ſtalks are upright, ſmooth, have four acute angles, ſend forth a few branches near the top, and grow to about two feet high The leaves are oval, ſpear-ſhaped, ſmooth, indented, and grow oppoſite by pairs on very ſhort footſtalks The flowers come out in large heads from the ends of the ſtalks and branches From this head frequently riſes a ſmaller, ſtanding on a naked footſtalk, and there is alſo another head or whorl ſurrounding the ſtalk at the joint immediately underneath, they are of a bright red colour, appear in July, and continue in ſucceſſion frequently until the end of September, but the ſeeds very rarely ripen in England

This plant is remarkable for its fine odour on being bruiſed, eſpecially the leaves, which are poſſeſſed of an exhilarating ſweetneſs Theſe leaves in North America are uſed as tea, and much reliſhed by the inhabitants Hence the name Oſwego Tea has been uſed in thoſe parts for this plant

and Virginian Monarda 3 Virginian *Monarda* This hath a ſtrong creeping root, which ſoon ſpreads itſelf to a conſiderable diſtance The ſtalks are quadrangular, branching a little near the top, and grow to about two feet high The leaves are oval, oblong, ſpear-ſhaped, pointed, ſerrated, ſmooth on both ſides, and grow oppoſite to each other on ſhort footſtalks The flowers come out in roundiſh heads from the ends of the ſtalks, and a few in all whorls alſo are produced from the ſides, ſurrounding the ſtalks at the joints, they are of a fine purple colour, appear in July, and often continue in ſucceſſion until the froſt ſtops them, but they are rarely ſucceeded by ſeeds in England

Method of propagating them All theſe ſorts are propagated by parting of the roots, which may be done with ſucceſs almoſt any time of the year though the beſt ſeaſon is the autumn Every bit will grow, and after they are ſet out for good will require no trouble, except keeping them clean from weeds, though they ſhould have a moiſt ſoil, and a ſhady ſituation, in order to continue them the longer in blow

They may alſo be encreaſed by ſlips or cuttings, which ſhould be ſet in a ſhady border in May, and duly watered at firſt, and they will readily grow They are all extremely beautiful, as well as a fine aromatic The ſecond ſort ought to be propagated plentifully in the kitchen garden, for the ſake of the leaves to afford tea, which is highly agreeable, refreſhing, and ſaid to be very wholeſome

The firſt ſort encreaſes ſlowly by the roots, but then it every year produces plenty of good ſeeds, by which it may be encreaſed with more expedition and leſs trouble than any other way Whoever, therefore, is deſirous of a ſtock of this ſpecies, let him ſow the ſeeds on a bed of light earth in the autumn, ſoon after they are ripe, becauſe if they are kept until the ſpring, they often lie until the ſpring after before they come up If they are ſown in the autumn they will come up early in the ſpring, when they will want no trouble, except thinning them where they are too cloſe, watering them in dry weather, and keeping them clean from weeds About the middle or end of May they ſhould be pricked out in beds of light earth in a moiſt ſhady place, at about ſix inches diſtance from each other, here they muſt be duly watered, eſpecially at firſt, and if the uſual care of weeding is afforded them all ſummer, they will by the autumn be grown to be good plants and then be of proper ſize to be removed to the places where they are deſigned to remain The ſummer following they will flower, and perfect their ſeeds by which any required additional ſtock of plants may be raiſed at pleaſure

When ſeeds of the other two ſorts are obtained, the plants are to be raiſed this way, but as they encreaſe ſo wonderfully by the roots, and every ſlip or bit of them will grow if ſet in the ſummer, the proceſs of raiſing them from ſeeds is altogether uſeleſs, unleſs it be at firſt, before you are furniſhed with plants, and can by no other ways obtain them

1 The firſt ſpecies is titled, *Monarda capitulis terminalibus, caule obtuſangulo* In the *Hortus Cliffort* it is termed, *Monarda*, in the *Amœnitates Acad Monarda mollis* Van Royen calls it, *Monarda floribus capitatis, caule obliquo*, Cornutus, *Origanum fiſtuloſum Canadenſe* and Moriſon *Chenopodium majus Virginienſe, foliis minus hirtis acutioribus, floribus fiſtuloſis* It grows naturally in Canada Title

2 The ſecond ſpecies is, *Monarda floribus capitatis, ſubdidynamis, caule acutangulo* In the *Hortus Cliffort* it is termed, *Monarda caule acute angulato, capitulis terminalibus* Buttner calls it, *Monarda floribus capitatis verticillatiſque, caule acute angulato, foliis lanceolato ſerratis glabris* It is a native of Penſylvania, and many parts of North America

3 The third ſpecies is, *Monarda floribus capitatis, foliis leviſſimis ſerratis* Gronovius calls it, *Monarda foliis ovato lanceolatis, verticillis lateralibus dichotomis corymboſis, foliis inæqualiter ſerratis* It grows naturally in Virginia

Class and order in the Linnæan system The characters

*Monarda* is of the class and order *Diandria Monogynia*, and the characters are,

1 CALYX is a monophyllous, tubular, cylindrical, striated, permanent perianthium, indented in five equal parts at the brim

2 COROLLA is one petal The tube is cylindrical, and longer than the calyx, the limb is ringent, the upper lip is straight, narrow and entire, the lower lip is broad, reflexed, and cut into three segments, the middle segment being long, narrow, and emarginated, and the lateral ones shorter and obtuse

3 STAMINA are two setaceous filaments the length of the upper lip, and involved in it, having erect compressed antheræ, which are truncated at the top, and convex below

4 PISTILLUM consists of a quadrifid germen, a filiforme style involved in the upper lip with the stamina, and a bifid acute stigma

5 PERICARPIUM There is none The seeds are lodged in the bottom of the calyx

6 SEMINA The seeds are four, and roundish

# CHAP. CCXCIX

## *M O N O T R O P A*

Species

OF this genus are two species

1 European *Monotropa* or Bird's Nest smelling like Primrose roots

2 American *Monotropa*

European

1 European *Monotropa*, or Bird's Nest smelling like Primrose roots This plant grows common in some of our English woods, and resides chiefly at the roots of trees The root is thick, and very long The stalks are thick, yellow, contorted, possessed of a few squamose membranes instead of leaves, and grow to about eight or ten inches high The flowers come out many together from the tops and sides of the stalks, they are small, of a yellowish white colour, and usually shew themselves in July After the flowers are fallen the stalks become blackish, and at that time especially have the smell of Primrose roots

and American Monotropa described

2 American *Monotropa* The root is thick, and long The stalks are slender, succulent, brown, and about six inches high The flowers come out singly from the tops of the stalks, they are of a brownish-yellow colour, large, and hang drooping

Culture

I have never cultivated either of these sorts, but make no doubt that if the roots are taken up from the places where they naturally grow, about the latter end of summer, when the stalks become black, and are planted among trees, especially at the roots, in the wilderness, that they will grow, and produce stalks and flowers the summer following

Whoever is desirous of obtaining the American sort, must procure the roots to be planted in tubs filled with the natural earth of the country When they come into England, they must be turned out, observing to disturb the roots as little as possible, into warm, light, dry well sheltered parts of the wilderness, among the trees, where it is past a probability but they will grow, and the stalks every year shoot up for flowering

They may also be propagated by seeds, which should be sown as soon as they are ripe among trees, especially the Beech tree, of which the first sort seems peculiarly fond

Titles

1 The first species is titled, *Monotropa floribus lateralibus octandris, terminali decandro* Caspar Bauhine calls it, *Orobanche quæ hypopithys dici potest*, Mentzelius, *Orobanche hypopithys lutea*, Morison, *Orobanche flore breviore duplici, verbasculi odore*, and Plot, *Orobanche verbasculi odore* It grows naturally in woods in England, Sweden, Germany, and Canada

2 The second species is, *Monotropa caule unifloro decandro* Gronovius calls it, *Monotropa flore nutante*, Morison, *Orobanche monanthos Virginiana, flore majore pentapetalo*, and Plukenet, *Orobanche Virginiana, flore pentapetalo cernuo* It grows naturally in Maryland, Virginia, and Canada

Class and order in the Linnæan system The characters

*Monotropa* is of the class and order *Decandria Monogynia*, and the characters are,

1 CALYX There is none

2 COROLLA is ten deciduous, oblong, parallel, erect petals, furrowed at their top, of which the alternately exterior ones are gibbous at their base, concave inwardly, and full of a honey juice

3 STAMINA are ten simple, erect, awl-shaped filaments, having simple antheræ

4 PISTILLUM consists of a roundish acuminated germen, a cylindrical style the length of the stamina, and an obtuse capitated stigma

5 PERICARPIUM is an oval obtuse, five-cornered capsule, composed of five valves

6 SEMINA The seeds are numerous, and paleaceous

CHAP.

# CHAP. CCC.

## *MORINA.*

THERE is only one species of this genus, usually called, Oriental *Morina*.

*Description of the Oriental Morina.* The root is large, oblong, taper, possessed of many thick fleshy fibres, and strikes deep into the ground. The radical leaves are very large, oblong, of a bright green colour on their upper side, but paler underneath, a little hairy, and divided at their edges, where they are armed with spines. The stalks are robust, upright, smooth, often of a purplish colour near the bottom, green and hairy at the top, grow to three feet high, and are garnished with three or four leaves at each joint, like the radical ones, but smaller. The flowers come out from the tops and sides of the stalks in small heads; they are of different colours in the different varieties, and the general characters shew their composition; they appear in July, and in favourable seasons the seeds ripen in the autumn.

*Varieties.* The varieties of this species are,

The White.
The Pale Red.
The Deep Red.
The Purple.

*Method of propagation.* It is propagated by sowing the seeds in the autumn, as soon as they are ripe, in the places where they are to remain. Previous to the sowing, the ground should be double dug, and made fine, that their long tap roots may with more facility strike deep into the ground, and send forth proportionally stronger stalks for flowering. When they come up, they should be thinned to about a foot and a half distance from each other, and all summer must be kept clean from weeds. In the autumn the ground between the plants should be stirred, and a little fresh mould sifted over the crowns, and in the summer following some of the strongest plants will flower, though the bloom will not be general from seeds until about the third summer, after which they will continue to exhibit their bloom every year, and require no trouble, except keeping them clean from weeds, stirring the ground between the roots every winter, and afterwards sifting a little fresh mould over the crowns of the plants, to encourage their luxuriancy.

It often happens that the seeds of this plant do not come up until the second year, especially if the business should be deferred until the spring; which should caution all Gardeners to let their beds remain undisturbed, only keeping them clean from weeds, during the following summer, and they will be pretty sure of a crop of plants the spring after.

It is customary with some to sow the seeds in different parts of the garden. When this is to be done, the places designed for them should be dug deep, and at each place a stick should be thrust down for a direction, to prevent the seeds being dug up, which is often the case, especially if they should happen to lie one year before they make their appearance.

*Titles.* There being no other species of this genus, it stands with the name simply, *Morina*. Tournefort calls it, *Morina orientalis, carlinæ folio*. It grows naturally in Persia.

*Class and order in the Linnæan System.* *Morina* is of the class and order *Diandria Monogynia*; and the characters are,

*The character.* 1. CALYX is a double perianthium. That of the fruit is placed below the other, is monophyllous, permanent, cylindrical, tubular, and cut at the top into several awl-shaped acute segments, the two opposite ones being longer than the others. The perianthium of the flower is monophyllous, permanent, tubular, and cut at the top into two emarginated, obtuse, erect segments.

2. COROLLA is a bilabiated petal. The tube is very long, slender near the base, but wide and large at the top, and is a little incurved. The limb is plane and obtuse; the upper lip is small, and semibifid; the lower lip is cut into three obtuse uniform segments, the middle one being the longest.

3. STAMINA are two setaceous parallel filaments, pressing upon the style, and shorter than the limb, having erect, heart-shaped, distant antheræ.

4. PISTILLUM consists of a globose germen situated under the receptacle of the flower, a filiforme style longer than the stamina, and a capitated, peltated, inflexed stigma.

5. PERICARPIUM. There is none.

6. SEMEN. The seed is single, roundish, stands in its own permanent cup, and is crowned with the empalement of the flower.

CHAP.

## CHAP CCCI

## *MYAGRUM*, GOLD OF PLEASURE.

THERE are only two perennial species of this genus, called,

Species

1 German *Myagrum*, or Gold of Pleasure

2 Alpine Gold of Pleasure

German Myagrum described

1 German *Myagrum*, or Gold of Pleasure The stalks are upright, stiff, branching, and about two feet high The radical leaves are very hard, spear-shaped, hairy, sinuated, indented, and spread on the ground, but those on the stalks are narrow, sharp-pointed, indented, and hairy The flowers come out in long, loose spikes from the ends of the stalks, they are of a yellow colour, appear in June and July, and are succeeded by short pods having two joints, in each of which is contained a single seed, which ripens in September

Its Varieties

There is a variety of this species with white flowers, and another with jagged leaves

Alpine Gold of Pleasure described

2 Alpine Gold of Pleasure The stalks are upright, branching near the top, and a foot and a half high The radical leaves are large, oval, rough, serrated, and form a roundish tuft at the root, but those on the stalks are spear-shaped and narrow The flowers come out in roundish bunches from the tops of the stalks, they are small and of a pale yellow colour, appear in June and July, and are succeeded by small, oval, smooth pods, containing ripe seeds in the autumn

Varieties

The varieties of this plant are,
The Dwarf
The Taller Alpine Gold or Pleasure.
Smooth leaved
Single-stalked
Jagged-leaved
White-flowered
The Purple

Method of propagation

These sorts are all propagated by parting of the roots at almost all times of the year, though the best season is the autumn They are very hardy, and will grow in almost any soil or situation, though they delight most in a light, moist earth, in the shade

They are also raised by sowing of the seeds in the autumn, as soon as they are ripe When they come up, they will require no trouble, except keeping them clean from weeds, and when they are of a size to transplant they may be removed to the places where they are designed to remain

Titles

1 The first species is titled, *Myagrum siliculis biarticulatis dispermis, foliis extrorsum sinuatis denticulatis* In the *Hortus Cliffort* it is termed *Crambe foliis lanceolatis dentato-sinuatis* Caspar Bauhine calls it, *Rapistrum monospermum* It grows naturally in Germany

2 Alpine Gold of Pleasure is, *Myagrum siliculis lentiformi-obovatis glabris, foliis oblongis serratis scabris, caule paniculato* Sauvages calls it, *Cochlearia foliis radicalibus lanceolatis serratis, caulinis linearibus*, Magnol, *Cochlearia perennis saxatilis minima*, Seguier *Alyssum Alpinum, foliis circa radicem subovatis serratis in orbem circumactis*, and Caspar Bauhine, *Thlaspi saxatile rotundifolium*, also, *Thlasp. Alpinum minus, capitulo rotundo*, also, *Thlaspi Alpinum majus capitulis rotundis* It grows naturally on the Helvetian mountains, also on mount Baldus, and in the South of France

Class and order in the Linnæan system.

*Myagrum* is of the class and order *Tetradynamia Siliculosa*, and the characters are,

The characters

1 CALYX is a perianthium composed of four oval, oblong, deciduous, concave, coloured leaves

2 COROLLA consists of four plane, roundish, obtuse petals, placed cruciforme

3 STAMINA are six filaments the length of the calyx, of which four are rather longer than the others, having simple antheræ

4 PISTILLUM consists of an oval germen, a filiforme style the length of the calyx, and an obtuse stigma

5. PERICARPIUM is an obcordated, compressed, rigid, bivalvate pod terminated by the style.

6 SEMINA The seeds are roundish

## CHAP CCCII

## *MYOSOTIS*, MOUSE-EAR SCORPION GRASS.

OF this genus is that well-known plant called Common Mouse-Ear Scorpion Grass

This plant described

The root is slender, composed of numerous fibres, often in some varieties of short duration, in others frequently lasting several years The stalks are round, slender, branching, and about a foot and a half high The leaves are rough, hairy, spear shaped, obtuse, and callous at their tops The flowers grow in long curled spikes at the ends of the branches, and are usually ranged one way, they are chiefly blue in its different tints, though they are sometimes white, and

and often spotted with yellow; they appear in May, and often continue to shew themselves great part of the summer.

Varieties

There are many varieties of this species, some of which grow in dry meadows and pastures, and others in bogs and standing waters; and when any of the sorts are introduced into the garden, they vary very much in appearance.

Method of propagation

They are easily propagated by sowing the seeds, soon after they are ripe. Almost any soil or situation will do for them; and when they come up, they will require no trouble, except thinning them where they are too close, and keeping them clean from weeds. When they have once flowered and perfected their seed, there will soon be more plants than you could wish for. These plants grow common everywhere, notwithstanding which it is worth while to raise a few in the garden, to see the great improvement that will be made on them by culture; the stalks in gardens being often thick and firm, the leaves broad, the flowers large and of the most beautiful blue colour; whereas in the native places of growth, the stalks are weak and partly procumbent, the leaves narrow and of a worn out green, and the flowers small and frequently ill-coloured.

Titles

This species is titled, *Myosotis seminibus nudis, foliorum apicibus callosis*. In the *Hortus Cliffort.* it is termed, *Myosotis foliis hirsutis*; also, *Myosotis foliis glabris*. Dalechamp calls it, *Myosotis hirsuta arvensis major*; also, *Myosotis glabra pratensis*. Caspar Bauhine stiles it, *Echium scorpoides arvense*; also, *Echium scorpoides palustre*; also, *Echium scorpoides minus, flosculis luteis*. Gerard names it, *Myosotis scorpoides hirsuta*; also, *Myosotis scorpoides palustris*; and Ray, *Myosotis scorpoides latifolia hirsuta*; also, *Myosotis scorpoides hirta minor*. It grows naturally in England and most parts of Europe.

Class and order in the Linnæan system

*Myosotis* is of the class and order *Pentandria Monogynia*; and the characters are,

The characters

1. CALYX is an oblong, erect, permanent perianthium, cut at the top into five acute segments.

2. COROLLA is one hypocrateriforme petal. The tube is cylindrical and short. The limb is plane, and cut into five emarginated, obtuse segments. The mouth is closed by five convex, prominent scales, which bend toward each other.

3. STAMINA are five very short filaments, situated in the neck of the tube, having very small, covered antheræ.

4. PISTILLUM consists of four germens, a filiforme style the length of the tube of the corolla, and an obtuse stigma.

5. PERICARPIUM. There is none. The calyx becomes greater, is erect, and contains the seeds in its cavity.

6. SEMINA. The seeds are four, oval, acuminated, and smooth.

# CHAP. CCCIII.

## *MYRIOPHYLLUM*, WATER MILFOIL.

THERE are only two species of this genus, called,

Species

1. Verticillated Water Milfoil.
2. Spiked Water Milfoil.

Verticillated

1. Verticillated Water Milfoil. The root is composed of a multitude of fine hairy fibres, which strike into the mud. The stalks are slender, round, green, jointed, and often rear themselves six or eight inches above the water. The leaves are long and beautifully pinnated, but diminish in size as they grow nearer the tops of the stalks. The folioles are numerous, long, narrow, of a deep-green colour, and five leaves usually grow together at a joint. The flowers come out in whorls round that part of the stalk which is out of the water at the joints; they are small, whitish, and consist of males and females on the same plant; they appear in July, and the seeds ripen in the autumn.

and Spiked Water Milfoil described

2. Spiked Water Milfoil. The stalks are slender, round, green, jointed, and rise a little above the water. The leaves are composed of a multitude of narrow segments, are large, and of a deep-green colour. The flowers come out in spikes from the tops of the stalks, the females being situated under the males in the same spike; they appear in June and July, and the females are succeeded by ripe seeds in the autumn.

Propagation, and Propagation

These plants delight chiefly in standing waters, and in such places they are found in many parts of England. Those who are desirous of storing their ditches or ponds with them, may procure the roots about the end of summer from the places where they naturally grow, and peg them down to the mud. They will then readily strike into it, and the spring following the stalks will advance up for flowering.

They may be also propagated by sowing the seeds in the mud, in the autumn, soon after they are ripe. But this is not so sure a method as the former, because, unless the place suits them, they rarely grow; whereas from the roots they may be propagated in almost any place, provided it be moist and watery.

Titles

1. Verticillated Water Milfoil is titled, *Myriophyllum floribus omnibus verticillatis*. Clusius calls it, *Myriophyllum aquaticum minus*; Caspar Bauhine, *Millefolium aquaticum, flosculis ad foliorum nodos*; Ray, *Pentapterophyllon aquaticum flosculis ad foliorum nodos*; and Parkinson, *Millefolium aquaticum minus*. It grows naturally in ditches and standing-waters in England and most parts of Europe.

2. Spiked Water Milfoil is, *Myriophyllum floribus masculis interruptè spicatis*. In the *Flora Lapponica* it is termed, *Myriophyllum*. Vaillant calls it, *Myriophyllum vulgare majus*; Tournefort,

*Potamogeton foliis pinnatis*, Caſpar Bauhine, *Millefolium aquaticum pennatum ſpicatum*, and Morison, *Potamogeton aquaticum pennatum minus, foliis ſingularibus leticulis ſocculis ſubjectis* It grows naturally in ſtanding waters in England and moſt countries of Europe

Claſs and order in the Linnæan ſyſtem The characters

Myriophyllum is of the claſs and order *Monoecia Polyandria*, and the characters are,

I Male Flowers

1 Calyx is a perianthium compoſed of four oblong, erect leaves

2 Corolla There is none

3 Stamina are eight flaccid filaments, longer than the calyx, having oblong antheræ

II Female Flowers ſituated below the Males

1 Calyx is a perianthium, as in the Males

2 Corolla There is none

3 Pistillum conſiſts of four oblong germens, having downy ſtigmas, without any ſtyles

4 Pericarpium There is none

5 Semina The ſeeds are four, and oblong

# CHAP CCCIV

## *N A P Æ A*

THERE are only two ſpecies of this genus, viz

Species

1 Hermaphrodite *Napæa*

2 Dioceous *Napæa*

Hermaphrodite

1 Hermaphrodite *Napæa* The root is fibrous, and creeps under the ground The ſtalks are firm, upright, ſmooth, poſſeſſed of a ſtringy bark, and grow to four or five feet high The leaves are palmated, and chiefly conſiſt of five principal lobes, which are acute pointed, cut into many ſpear-ſhaped ſegments, of a bright-green colour, ſmooth, and grow alternately on longiſh footſtalks The flowers come out from the ſetting-on of the leaves, growing three or four together on a footſtalk, they are of a white colour, and for the moſt part hermaphrodites, they appear in July, but are very rarely ſucceeded by ſeeds in England

and Dioecous Napæa deſcribed

2 Dioecous *Napæa* The root is compoſed of many thick, fleſhy fibres, which are connected at the top The radical leaves are palmated, very large, rough, hairy, divided into about ſix or ſeven lobes, which are cut or indented on their edges, and they grow on very long, thick, ſpreading footſtalks The ſtalks are robuſt, rough, hairy, branching, ſix or eight feet high, and garniſhed with leaves like the radical ones, but ſmaller, growing ſingly at each joint The flowers come out from the joints on long branching footſtalks, each footſtalk ſuſtaining many flowers, they are dioiceous, and the petals are of a white colour, they appear in July, and the ſeeds ripen in the autumn This ſpecies hath a ſtringy bark like hemp, of which an uſeful cloth might be made

Propagation of the firſt ſpecies

The firſt ſpecies is propagated by parting of the roots, the beſt time for which is the autumn They ſhould be ſet in a rich, deep earth, and a ſhady ſituation, and after they are planted out, they will require no trouble, except keeping them clean from weeds, until the roots are reduced, which ought to be every ſecond year

Propagation of the ſecond ſpecies

The ſecond ſpecies is beſt propagated by the ſeeds, which ripen here very freely Theſe ſhould be ſown in the ſpring in a bed of good earth made fine After the plants come up, they muſt be thinned where they appear too cloſe, be kept conſtantly clean from weeds, and watered in dry weather all ſummer, and in the autumn they will be ſtrong plants, and proper for removing to the places where they are deſigned to remain This, like the former ſpecies, delights moſt in a rich, moiſt earth, and a ſhady ſituation, and being thus ſtationed, the whole plant will be ſtronger, larger, and more beautiful

Titles

1 The firſt ſpecies is titled, *Napæa pedunculis nudis lævibus foliis glabris, floribus hermaphroditis* In the *Hortus Cliffort* it is termed, *Sida foliis palmatis, laciniis lanceolato-attenuatis* Herman calls it, *Malva Virginiana, ricini folio* It grows naturally in Virginia

2 The ſecond ſpecies is, *Napæa pedunculis involucratis angulatis, foliis ſcabris, floribus dioicis* Baniſter calls it, *Althæa magna aceris folio, cortice cannabino, floribus parvis, ſemina rotatim in ſummitate caulium, ſingula ſingulis cuticulis roſtratis cooperta ferens* It grows naturally in Virginia.

*Napæa* is of the claſs and order *Monadelphia Polyandria*, and the characters are,

1 Calyx is a monophyllous, urceolated, permanent perianthium, cut at the top into five parts

2 Corolla is five oblong, concave, looſe, patulous petals, connected at their baſe

3 Stamina are many capillary filaments, longer than the calyx, joined near the baſe into a cylindrical column, having roundiſh, compreſſed antheræ

4 Pistillum conſiſts of a conical germen, and a cylindrical ſtyle divided at the top into ten parts, each being crowned by a ſimple ſtigma

5 Pericarpium is an oval fruit incloſed in the calyx

6 Semina The ſeeds are ſingle, and reniforme

# CHAP. CCCV.

## *NARCISSUS*, DAFFODIL.

Introductory observations.

IT will be not a little difficult to treat of the *Narcissus*, in such a manner, as at once to give satisfaction to the botanist and the florist. The real species of this genus are not very numerous, but the varieties are almost endless. Linnæus, in his earlier works, has enumerated six only; but in the last edition of his *Species Plantarum*, he has made them to consist of thirteen, all of which he has distinguished by proper titles. To give these titles alone would prove of little satisfaction to the florist, who would say they were insignificant; and the many names he has been used to, the number he finds in the Dutch catalogues, and the distinctions and differences he has been accustomed to observe, induce him to treat the science with contempt, and exclaim against it as extremely defective. On the contrary, the real botanist, who walks strictly by the laws of science, smiles at the florist's names and distinctions, and would not have them admitted into the rules of art.

In order, therefore, to please both as well as I can, I shall first give the real species, and point out their varieties; and then lay down rules for raising the best kinds of the *Narcissus* in all their varieties and colours. I shall arrange them under the following heads:

Species.

1. The Daffodils.
2. The Jonquils.
3. The Poetic Daffodil.
4. The Polyanthos *Narcissus*.
5. Small Autumnal *Narcissus*.
6. Hoop-petticoat *Narcissus*.
7. Winter Daffodil.
8. Incomparable Daffodil.
9. Musk Daffodil.
10. Trilobate *Narcissus*.
11. Triandrous *Narcissus*.
12. *Narcissus Calathinus*.
13. Sweet-scented *Narcissus*.

### 1. Of Daffodils.

Of Daffodils.

Daffodils grow wild in many parts of England. Woods, coppices, and hedges, are their principal habitation, and there they shew themselves in their native simplicity and beauty. It is in the Single state we chiefly find them, though there are sometimes the Double, and numbers of varieties, promiscuously glowing near the same spot. In the same places will be also found the Pale and the Deeper Yellow, the Short and the Long-tubed kinds, the Dwarf, the Semi-double, the Double, and the vast train of varieties of these sorts; all of which have been in more esteem than they are now, tho' for what reason I can give no account; for if beauty, nay majesty of look, hardiness, ease of culture, and duration, have recommendation to a flower, these seem to demand our respect. I have seen, in old gardens that have been run over with grass, the houses in ruins and uninhabited for many years, these flowers in as much pride and gaiety, as in the best cultivated places. Great has been the variety of the sorts, and there they have shone forth in their native simplicity and ease, regardless of the attacks of weeds, grass, or cattle. In this manner I am inclined to think they have been introduced into woods; for whenever I have seen them growing in any tolerable variety in plantations, it has been contiguous to some old hall-house that has for many years been uninhabited or in ruins; so that we must not too precipitately conclude, wherever we find them, that that is their native place of growth. If there are variety of Doubles and different tinges, it is a certain sign that they have originally been brought there; for the Single and the Dwarf kinds only are chiefly found growing in these kingdoms in a state of nature.

Description of a Daffodil.

I come now to the description of a Daffodil. We find the root to be a large tunicated bulb, from which rise the leaves and the flower-stalk. The leaves are about a foot long, and half an inch broad, of a whitish-green colour with a bluish cast, and a little hollowed in the middle. The flower-stalk will grow to about a foot or more in height; it is nearly of the same colour with the leaves, hollow, and has two angles opposite to each other running lengthways. At the top of the stalk is the spatha, from whence proceeds the flower. The spatha is of a filmy substance, withering, and continues in a worn out, tattered condition, after the flower is blown at the top of the stalk. One flower alone grows from this spatha; it is large, and composed of one petal, which is cut at the top into six segments that spread open, or rather into six petals affixed to the nectarium. In the middle of the flower stands the nectarium. This hitherto Gardeners have erroneously called the cup. It stands erect, is shaped like a bell, and is of an equal length with the petal. The petal is of a pale-yellow, but the nectarium is of a golden or deep-yellow colour. It will be in blow early in April, and the flower is succeeded by a roundish capsule containing the seeds.

This is the Daffodil in its Single and most perfect state, and it is from this that the numbers of varieties of this species have arisen.

Its propagation by the bulb and by offsets.

The culture of the Daffodil is so easy, that you can hardly err. They are to be propagated by the bulb, and they increase by offsets. Remove them at any time of the year, and they will grow, though the best season is in August, when the leaves are decayed. Every four years the roots should be entirely taken up, cleaned, and divided, and then planted afresh. Almost any soil or situation will do for the common sorts, though the best kinds deserve a good place in a well cultivated border or rich mould.

Proper soil and situation.

Here they will increase very fast, and here may their number be multiplied, whilst the other sorts may have their station near walks in wilderness quarters, woods, &c.

Method of propagating it by seeds.

By seeds also these plants are to be increased. But this is a method not worth putting into practice; for though they will readily come up and grow, they will be seven or eight years before they come to flower. Whoever has leisure and inclination for this work, may sow the seeds in pans or boxes soon after they are ripe, which will

will be in July or August. Hence let him keep them clean from weeds, and let them stand for two years, by which time the roots will be grown to be pretty large. Let him then plant them out, six inches asunder, in a border prepared for the purpose, where they may stand until they shew their flowers.

It is taken for granted, that the seeds have been collected from the best sorts, and if this has been strictly attended to, the greater may be your expectation of finding fresh varieties of value appear.

## 2. Of Jonquils.

*Of Jonquil.* The family of the Jonquils is not so numerous, neither are the flowers so showy, as those of the preceding sorts; but they make ample amends for this defect by the fragrance they possess, and the delicate appearance they make. They are ranked among the sweetest flowers of the spring, and their culture being very easy makes them highly valuable.

Their variety consists only of about six or seven sorts. These are,

*Varieties.*

The Dwarf Jonquil with single flowers.
The Jonquil Major with single flowers.
The Starry Jonquil.
The White Jonquil.
The Yellow and White Jonquil.
The Semi-double,
The Double with sweet-scented flowers,—and
The Large Double Jonquil without scent.

The Double is in most esteem, though the others are not without their beauties. All are of equal fragrance, except the Large Double without scent; and the Starry sorts look delightful. Several of the flowers will be produced on a stalk; they expand their petals in the manner of rays, and by their nodding position on the top of the stalk afford an agreeable and pleasing aspect.

*Description of the Jonquil.* The description of the Jonquil is this: The root is a tunicated bulb covered with a brown bark. The leaves have a rush-like appearance, are of a fine deep bright green colour, and look round; but upon closer examination we find them to be furrowed along the middle. The flower-stalk is green and upright, and will grow to about a foot in height. At the top of it is the spatha, from whence the flowers proceed. Their number is more or less according to their varieties. In the Double sorts there are seldom more than two from a spatha, and very often no more than one. In the Single sorts it is common to have four, six or eight will often be produced, which makes some amends for their Single state.

*Method of propagating it.* The Jonquils are propagated by the bulbs. They delight in a good rich border, and if the soil be fresh, it will agree with them so much the better. Plant them singly in these places at six inches distance, and let them stand unremoved three or four years. Miller directs them to be shifted every year; but this is a very wrong practice, for seldom more than two or three leaves proceed from a bud, and often never a flower. And though good bulbs may be supposed seldom to fail of flowering, yet a single flower-stalk with two or three leaves has but a mean look; and though there be many bulbs planted in this way at proper distances, the whole will have a straggling and paltry appearance; whereas, by letting them remain, they will flower stronger the second year, the roots will encrease, and they will send forth numbers of leaves and many stalks of flowers, which on the whole will form a grand look. However, let them not stand longer than three or four years, as the roots will grow oblong, many of them will strike deep into the ground, and their power for flowering be greatly diminished. The best time for removing these bulbs is in August or September, soon after the leaves are decayed.

## 3. Of the Poetic Daffodil.

*The Poetic Daffodil described.* The Poetic Daffodil admits of very few varieties; the Purple-cupped, the Yellow-cupped, the Semi-double, and the Double White *Narcissus* of our gardens, being all that I know. They are all very hardy, and their odour is agreeable; which qualities together with the simplicity and beauty of their flowers, have occasioned their being so much taken notice of, and their praises to be celebrated by philosophers and poets in all ages. The root is a roundish bulb covered with a brown bark. The leaves resemble those of the Daffodil, but are rather longer and narrower, and have the same kind of light-green colour. Among these arises the flower-stalk, which is of a whitish green colour, hollow, rather flat, and a little edged. The top of it produces the spatha, and out of that issues a single flower, which seems to droop a little, or rather is placed in a nodding manner; it is of a pure white colour, and the petals are rounded at their edges, and expand themselves very agreeably. In the center is the nectarium, which is very short, and its edge is fringed. Sometimes the border of it is of a bright-purple, and in others again it is of a deep-yellow colour. But it is the Purple cupped sort that seems to be the celebrated *Narcissus* of the Greek and Roman poets. Pliny, in his description of the true original *Narcissus*, tells us, that the flower is white, and the cup purple; and by this no doubt he means the πορφυρο-ανθος of Theocritus and Theophrastus. Ovid seems to contradict all this, when he says,

——— *Croceum pro corpore florem*
*Inveniunt foliis medium cingentibus albis.*

This has much puzzled the critics, who have made many vain attempts to reconcile them; and being unable to effect it, Ovid has been condemned for his want of skill in botany. I really believe him to be a better poet than a botanist, but that he had any want of skill in the latter cannot be inferred from the above verses. The late improvements in the science have unravelled the mystery, and acquit our poet of impropriety and inattention. The specific differences of plants are now pretty well ascertained, and we are taught, that though there is only one species of the true ancient *Narcissus*, yet it admits of two varieties, viz. the Purple-cupped and the Yellow-cupped; nay, that the Semi-double and the Double are still that flower. These are varieties only of the same plant, and Ovid perhaps pitched upon the Yellow-centered one, either because it was his greatest favourite, or because it was most suitable to his verse. In later ages, as well as formerly, the colour of the cups has been peculiarly attended to in the description of this flower. Thus Dodonæus calls it, *Narcissus medio purpureus*, and Caspar Bauhine, *Narcissus albus circulo purpureo*. Dioscorides, indeed, mentions a *Narcissus* with a yellow cup, and doubtless that is the *Narcissus* of Ovid, a variety of the species under consideration. Linnæus, regardless of the colouring, has with great propriety named it, *Narcissus nectario limbo rotato brevissimo*. This will be a standing title for this species, and to this the varieties all belong. Ask for the modern title of the *Narcissus* which he says has a yellow cup, and it is that. Ask for the modern title of the *Narcissus* with a purple

purple cup, described by Dodonæus, Bauhine, and others, and it is the same. This is the modern title of that early-known and much admired *Narcissus* of Theocritus, Theophrastus, Sophocles, Dioscorides, Pliny, &c &c

Culture. The culture of the Poetic Daffodil is very easy Plant the bulbs in the autumn, winter, or spring, and they will readily grow and flower Almost any soil or situation will do for them, though they thrive best in a rich strong soil Every four years take them up again, part the roots, and plant them afresh, and let this always be done after the leaves are decayed They increase very fast by offsets, and plenty of them may be soon obtained, though it is the Double flowering *Narcissus* only that is in much repute with most of the modern Gardeners among us

### Of the Polyanthos *Narcissus*

Of the Polyanthos Narcissus. The Polyanthos is the most valuable of all the species of the *Narcissus* It admits of a very numerous train of varieties, which are every year improved and augmented by the care of the Dutch florists, who excel the world in their assiduity and management of all bulbous roots They distinguish them by names and titles in the same manner they do the hyacinth, and their catalogues afford us thirty or forty varieties, most of which are superbly distinguished From them it is we buy these flowers annually, and tho' we pay for them, we are nevertheless greatly indebted to their industry Our gardens glow with them, and our rooms are filled with their agreeable odours, and before the dreary season of the winter is past, how are we regaled with them in sweet perfection, forming a proper mixture with others in glasses in our rooms! To describe this species would be endless, for the description ought to follow the sorts in all their varieties The times of flowering also are different, some being very early, while others again draw up the rear of their brotherhood in flower The general description, however, is this

General description of it. The root is a large, roundish, brownish bulb From this the leaves arise, they are long, flat, narrow, a little hollowed, of an agreeable green colour, and of a firm consistence The flower-stalk is round, naked, upright, firm, and of different heights in the different sorts From the stalk proceed many flowers of different tinges, colours, and properties, in the different varieties The petals and the nectariums are generally of different colours, and Nature usually gives orange or straw-coloured nectariums to attend on petals of a fine yellow colour Again, when the petals are white, the nectariums are for the most part yellow, and this yellow will be deeper or paler as the variety happens In some, indeed, the nectariums and the petals are all of one colour, but these are always held of inferior value, except the Small flowering White Perfumed kind Of these there are four or five sorts The flowers are of a snowy-white colour, and small, but they are produced in such large bunches, as to form an appearance inferior to few, and their perfection of fragrance demands respect The Double sorts also are in high esteem They are mostly of an agreeable odour, and all in general of this species are proper for the ornamenting

Proper situation. rooms by being blown in glasses, as well as decorating the flower-garden by being planted in well-cultivated beds

### CULTURE of the Polyanthos *Narcissus*

Culture. This is performed two ways, viz by multiplying the roots from offsets, and by sowing of the seeds

If a person is desirous of having a few of these flowers [illegible] at once he must procure a sufficient quantity of bulbs These [illegible] from [illegible] of our seeds-men, or he [illegible] readily have them from Holland, or [illegible] own Gardeners [illegible] are curious in their propagation and management Let him have the proper names of each, and at the time of planting get them be [illegible] [illegible] and book [illegible] Let the philosophical botanist smile at the names, [illegible] he pleases, yet they will be amusing, and [illegible] in the sorts be [illegible] Four bulbs of a sort will be a pretty good stock, and with the management I shall direct him to, they will soon be multiplied to a great collection

Proper situation. The situation must be warm, and [illegible] defended from the winds, and if it receives the morning-sun it will be the better In such a place set the bed [illegible] If the soil is naturally good, bring out of the [illegible] of mould from an old hyacinth bed and two or three barrow fulls of dust [illegible] Scatter these over the bed, dig them in, and incorporate them well with the natural soil Here plant your bulbs, and they will grow and flower very well

Method of ordering this plant in great perfection. But to have them in the greatest perfection, mark out a place for the bed, and dig out the soil to the depth of three feet Then bring some rotten cow dung, tanners bark, or the remains of an old hyacinth bed and spread this over the bottom of the bed, that it may be after it is settled fourteen inches deep After this, bring the [illegible] compost, for that is very proper for these plants Spread this on the other stratum a foot and a half thick, and you will be got within four inches of the level of the soil of the garden Then smooth the surface, and mark the lines, and plant the bulbs eight inches asunder Set them in an upright position, and cover the crown over four inches deep, which will form a stratum of about six or seven inches above the other mould After that neat up your beds, and clean your alleys, and the business is done

I would not advise the planting of these bulbs before the latter end of September, or the beginning of October, because, if they are set earlier, they will spring too early in the spring, sometimes in January, and severe frosts happening afterwards, are often injurious, if not destructive to them

They will exhibit their blow in the spring and give an additional splendour to the garden by their variety and form The eye will behold them with delight, while the sense of smelling will be no less regaled by their agreeable and inoffensive odours, and the judgment confirmed which directs a man to improvements of this nature, and points out the path to these agreeable, innocent, and pleasing pursuits

After the flowers are fallen, and the leaves are entirely decayed, take them away, and neat up your beds Keep them constantly clean from weeds, and about once a month stir the surface of the bed with a trowel, the better to receive the kindly influences of the sun and air at the approach of winter Prick round the bed pretty close some furze bushes, which will be all the protection they will require against the frost In the spring they will exhibit their bloom afresh, which will be stronger than that of the preceding year, and these flowers in one or other of the sorts will appear for a month or more in full beauty When the leaves are decayed, and you are neating up your beds, you may take off some of the offsets without disturbing the old-

old roots, and plant them in a bed prepared for the purpose. This is a method practised by some, and which I by no means disapprove of, though I must own I rather chuse to let them all remain undisturbed for three years, then, after the total decay of the leaves, take them all up, and divide them. Preserve the flowering bulbs to be planted in a fresh for a succeeding blow, and the offsets according to their sizes in nursery-beds to gain strength.

This is the proper management of these flowers. By letting them stand three years, they will flower strong, and many stalks will be produced in a bunch; by letting them remain longer unremoved, they will be divided so much into offsets, that the very largest bulbs will be much compressed, and their force for flowering greatly abated.

We have supposed the beds to be only about three inches above the level of the garden. But the ingenious Gardener is not to understand this too literally. It is in dry soils and situations only that the beds are to be so little raised. In most wet places, in clays, or the like, the beds should be raised a foot, or a foot and half above the surface, and some made to keep up the mould; and the height of the bed should always be in proportion to the dampness of the place, in which the Gardener's judgment must always direct him.

By seeds also the Polyanthos *Narcissus* is to be propagated, and fresh varieties of it obtained. But before I enter upon this head, I must, in justice to the honest laborious Gardener, acquaint him, that it is not worth his while to put this method in practice. Six or seven years will elapse before the plants can be brought to shew their flowers in perfection. All the while, at intervals, much trouble and attention must be given; and when the bloom is exhibited, many bad flowers will appear among them, so that we have little to encourage us in these pursuits, but the pleasure from the expectation of fresh faces of value to add to our collection. Variety is a very agreeable object, and when that is of intrinsic worth and real goodness, the pursuit of it is truly commendable and praiseworthy. But the variety which the most sanguine expectations can be replete with from these productions, is but trifling in comparison to some other flowers. The tulip itself, I affirm, is not worth the raising from seeds, considering the low price which the best Dutch breeders may be purchased at, and yet the variety among them is a hundred fold more than what can be expected from any of the *Narcissus* kind. Purchase, therefore, a few bulbs of each kind, and manage them in the manner directed; and such as have leisure, inclination, and patience, to wait for their flowering from seeds, I advise to raise them in the following manner.

First, let them procure good seeds, all saved from the best kinds, with the best properties, and their hopes of success in obtaining valuable flowers will be the better grounded.

Let the seeds be sown early in July, in pots or boxes, and not in shallow pans, filled with good, light, rich earth, covering them down three quarters of an inch deep. Then set them in the shade in a well sheltered place, but not too near old walls, houses, buildings, or the like. In October place them where they can have the full sun, and at the approach of frosts set them in a warm, well sheltered place. If the frost should be severe, still defend them by pricking round them some furze-bushes, and if all this is not sufficient to keep out the frost, remove the pots into the green-house for that time, and as soon as it is over, set them abroad again. As the warm days in the spring advance, place them where they can have the morning-sun only until eleven o'clock, and by the beginning of April the plants will appear. Then plunge them up to the rims in the natural mould in the same situation, to keep them moist. Keep them clean from weeds, water them in dry weather, and, as the days get long, and the heat powerful, set them entirely in the shade. In June the leaves of the young seedlings will decay. At this time frequently stir the surface of the earth, to prevent the moss growing, and in the beginning of July, having cleared the surface from the old leaves, &c. sift over it some light fresh earth to about half an inch deep. Let them remain in the shade all the summer, but never water them after their leaves are decayed, and in the autumn place them where they can have the morning sun. In the winter let their situation be warm and sheltered from frosts, if possible; if not, prick plenty of furze-bushes round them to defend them. In summer let them have the management as before, and let this be repeated until the third year from sowing, by which time the bulbs will be grown to be moderately large, and it is not worth the while to remove them sooner.

When the green leaves are upon the decay, which will be in June, take up the plants, and plant the largest in beds prepared as before in lines five inches asunder. Scatter the smaller together with the mould promiscuously on another bed, sifting over them two or three inches deep of fresh mould. By this means none of the small bulbs will be lost. They will soon get strength, and as they encrease in size take them up on the decay of the leaf, and plant them in lines in beds prepared as before. In these beds let them all stand until they shew their flowers. After they have flowered two or three years, (for you must not be too precipitate in condemning them) the worst sorts should be taken up and thrown away, and those that are beautiful, and have really good properties, should be named, and their names or titles entered in a book, and properly numbered. The roots also should have a number-stick placed by them to direct to the plant, and afterwards should be treated as before directed for old roots.

Of the other species of the *Narcissus*.

5. The Small Autumnal *Narcissus*. This is a very beautiful small plant, and its flowering at different times from the others makes it esteemed, and much coveted to mix with others of the like nature which flower in the autumnal season. The bulb is very small, and the leaves are few and narrow. The stalk itself will not grow to above eight or nine inches high; it is jointed, and from the spatha proceeds a single flower only. The petals are of a snow-white colour, but the nectarium is yellow, very short, and singularly cut into six segments. This species must have a warm situation and a sandy, light soil, otherwise it will be liable to be destroyed in the winter by bad weather.

6. Hoop petticoat *Narcissus*. This name has been long in use among Gardeners for this species which it originally obtained from the form of the flowers, which are said to resemble that of the old fashioned hoop petticoats. This species hath a very small bulb, and the leaves are short and narrow, have a rush-like appearance, and are a little furrowed on one side. The flower stalk is slender and short, seldom

growing

growing higher than six inches, the top of it produces the spatha, and out of that issues one flower It is of a singular construction, for the petal is very short, hardly half an inch long, and the nectarium is more than two inches in length, it widens regularly from the base, and at the bottom is very broad, this occasions its being called the Hoop-petticoat *Narcissus* It flowers in April, but seldom produces seeds with us

Winter, 7 Winter Daffodil This species is mostly valued on account of its time of flowering, it being frequently in winter, when few flowers shew themselves abroad The bulb is rather small, and the leaves are much broader than what might be expected Among these grow the stalks to a foot in height, they are firm, and of a pale green colour A single flower issues from the spatha, and grows in a drooping manner, it is large, and of a fine yellow colour The petals are spear-shaped, and the border of the nectarium is cut into several segments, six is the usual number, but they will often be divided into twelve or more, and their edges appear fringed and curled, and look very beautiful

and Incomparable Daffodil described 8 Incomparable Daffodil This plant is a very near relation to the Common Daffodil, but the leaves are longer, and of a darker green colour The flowers are of two colours, the petals are white, and the nectarium of a deep-yellow colour

Varieties Of this species there are many varieties, and different degrees of doubleness are found among them The petals are not always white, in some varieties they are of a sulphur colour Their figure also is various Sometimes they are long and narrow, in others they are found shorter and rounder, and more disposed to grow in a globular form The nectarium is usually of a deep yellow colour, a campanulate figure, broad at the brim, and spreading, it is sometimes waved, and this, together with the petals of different colours, form a very good flower These flowers will be in blow in April, but the Double sorts only are in much esteem with our modern gardeners

Musk, 9 Musk *Narcissus* This plant is chiefly admired for its musky odour It consists of a single flower growing from the spatha in a drooping or nodding posture The petals are white, and the nectarium is yellow In the latter is the greatest singularity; it is of a cylindrical figure, and the brim turns backward, without being either waved, curled or indented

Trilobate, 10 Trilobate *Narcissus* This is a very near relation to the Jonquils, the leaves are narrow, of a rush-like appearance, and the stalk produces a few yellow flowers The singularity in this species is, the nectarium, which is bell-shaped, or rather of a cylindrical figure, is not waved or curled, but obtusely cut into three lobes This is a distinction differing from all the others, and sufficiently indicates a distinct species

and Triandrous Narcissus, 11 Triandrous *Narcissus* The leaves of this species are very narrow, channelled, and of a pale-green colour The flower-stalk also is very pale, and from the spatha proceeds seldom more than one flower, which is of a snowy-white colour The petals are of an oblong oval figure, and the nectarium is bell shaped The chief singularity in this species respects the stamina, which are for the most part only three in number Sometimes indeed a flower of this species is found possessed of six; but this is very rarely the case, the usual number being three only, they have yellow antheræ, and are shorter than the nectarium

Narcissus Calathinus, 12 *Narcissus Calathinus* This is a very fine species of the *Narcissus*, and very near a-kin to the *Polyanthos* kind before described The leaves are long, narrow, flat, and of a fine green colour The stalk is very robust, and the spatha contains many flowers These are large, and form a noble appearance, their colour is yellow, and their construction is much the same as the *Polyanthos Tazettæ*, but their petals are somewhat broader, and the ends more acute The nectarium is of a campanulate figure, the edge a little crenated, and about the length of the petals This is a very fine species, it is a *Polyanthos-Narcissus*, according to the meaning of that word, and has until lately been looked upon as a variety of it

13 Sweet-scented *Narcissus* The stalk of this species sometimes bears many flowers, at other times two or three flowers only will be produced from the spatha, and very frequently a single one only The flowers are exceedingly large and beautiful, they are altogether yellow, and the petals expand themselves in a ray-like manner The nectarium is bell-shaped, and the edge of it neither waved nor curled, but obtusely cut into six lobes The largeness of these flowers, their bright yellow colour, and the fragrance they possess, make it inferior to few, if any, of the beforementioned sorts and Sweet scented Narcissus described

All these species are propagated like the other sorts They will grow and flower exceeding well in a border of good light earth, and every three or four years they should be removed, their offsets taken off, and planted by themselves to gain strength The largest bulbs should be set in those places where they are designed to shew their flowers The best time for this is when the leaves are decayed The bulbs may be planted again immediately, or preserved in a dry room until September, October, or longer, by which means the time of flowering may be varied Method of propagation

The last two species are very valuable sorts, and though they will grow and flower very well in a common border, yet they are worthy of the nicest culture and management of the best *Polyanthos* kinds

We come now to the titles, and,

1 The Daffodil is named, *Narcissus spathâ uniflorâ, nectario campanulato erecto crispo æquante petala ovatâ* Dodonæus calls it, *Narcissus luteus sylvestris* The Double sort is called *Narcissus sylvestris multiplex*, and authors accordingly have pointed out the other varieties by titles suitable to them It grows naturally in woods and groves in England, France, Italy, and Spain Titles

2 The Jonquil This is entitled, *Narcissus spathâ multiflorâ, nectario hemisphærico crenato breviore petalis, foliis semiteretibus* Caspar Bauhine expresses one sort by the title, *Narcissus juncifolius, oblongo calyce, luteus major*, another he calls, *Luteus minor* Clusius and others name it in the like manner It grows chiefly in moist boggy lands in the East

3 Poetic Daffodil This is entitled, *Narcissus spathâ uniflora, nectario rotato brevissimo scarioso crenulato* It has been variously named by different authors, as has been before observed Caspar Bauhine calls the Double kind, *Narcissus medio purpureus multiplex* It grows naturally in England, and some parts of France

4 *Polyanthos Narcissus* This is entitled, *Narcissus spathâ multiflorâ, nectario campanulato truncato breviore petalis, foliis planis* Caspar Bauhine calls it, *Narcissus luteus polyanthos Lusitanicus*, and Clusius, *Narcissus latifolius flore prorsus albo* It grows naturally in Spain, Portugal, and some parts of France Its habitation is chiefly in moist places, and near the sea-coast

5 Small Autumnal *Narcissus* This is titled, *Narcissus spathâ uniflorâ, nectario brevissimo sexpartito* Caspar Bauhine calls it, *Narcissus albus autumnalis*

*autumnalis minimus*, and Clusius, *Narcissus serotinus* It grows naturally in Italy, Spain, and Barbary

6 Hoop-petticoat *Narcissus* This is titled, *Narcissus spatha uniflora, nectario turbinato petalis majore geniculatis aequantes* Clusius calls it, *Pseudo-Narcissus juncifolius 2, flavo flore* It grows naturally in Portugal

7 Winter Daffodil This is termed, *Narcissus spatha uniflora, nectario obconico erecto crispo fissido aequante petala lanceolata* John Bauhine calls it, *Bulbocodium minus*, and Barrelier, *Narcissus sylvestris pallidus minimus* It grows naturally in Spain

8 Incomparable Daffodil This is, *Narcissus spatha uniflora, nectario campanulato margine patulo crispo aequante petala* Caspar Bauhine calls it, *Narcissus albus, calyce flavo, alter* It grows naturally in many of the southern parts of Europe

9 Musk Daffodil This is called, *Narcissus spatha uniflora, nectario cylindrico truncato subrepando aequante petala oblonga* Caspar Bauhine calls it, *Narcissus albus, calyce flavo, moschati odore* It grows naturally in Spain

10 Trilobous Daffodil This is, *Narcissus spatha submultiflora nectario campanulato subtrifido integerrimo, dimidio breviore petalis* This is the *Narcissus angustifolius pallidus, calyce flavo*, of Caspar Bauhine and others It grows naturally in the southern parts of Europe

11 Triandrous Daffodil This is, *Narcissus spatha submultiflorâ, nectario campanulato crenulato, dimidio breviore petalis, staminibus ternis* Clusius calls it, *Narcissus juncifolius, albo flore reflexo* It grows naturally in the Pyrenees

12 *Narcissus Calathinus* This is, *Narcissus, spatha multiflorâ, nectario campanulato subcrenato aequante petala, foliis planis* It is the *Narcissus 9 angustifolius* of Clusius It grows naturally in the south of Europe, also in some parts of the East

13 Sweet-scented *Narcissus* This is, *Narcissus spathâ submultiflorâ, nectario campanulato sexfido levi dimidio breviore petalis* It grows naturally in many of the southern parts of Europe

*Narcissus* is of the class and order *Hexandria Monogynia*, and the characters are,

Class and order in the Linnæan system The characters

1 CALYX is an oblong, obtuse, compressed, withering spatha, that opens on one side

2 COROLLA consists of six oval, pointed, plane petals, which are inserted into the outside of the nectarium, a little above the base The nectarium is of one leaf, and of a cylindrical, funnel, or campanulate figure, which spreads open at the brim, and resembles a cup, the name by which it has been usually called

3 STAMINA are six subulated filaments affixed to the tube of the nectarium, they are shorter than the nectarium, and have oblong antheræ

4 PISTILLUM consists of a three-cornered, roundish, obtuse germen, situated below the flower, a filiforme style longer than the stamina, and a trifid concave, obtuse stigma

5 PERICARPIUM is a roundish, obtuse, three-cornered capsule, composed of three valves, and containing three cells

6 SEMINA The seeds are numerous, and of a roundish figure

## CHAP CCCVI.

# NARDUS

THIS genus affords a grass of English growth, not destitute of beauty, but of little use to the farmer, called Mat Grass

This plant described

The root is composed of a multitude of brownish fibres, and creeps under the ground The leaves form a pretty large cluster at the crown of the roots, they are small, narrow, and hardly six inches long The stalks are numerous, naked at the top, but surrounded at the base with the leaves, and grow to be six or eight inches high The flowers come out in long, narrow, upright, bearded spikes from the tops of the stalks, the valves are spear-shaped, rigid, and of a brownish colour; they appear in June and July, and the seeds ripen in September

Propagation

Whoever is desirous of a plant or two of this species, to be ready for observation, may easily obtain them by sowing the seeds as soon as they are ripe, or planting the roots in the autumn It grows common among bushes, on heathy ground, bogs, dry hills, and sterile places in England, so that no soil or situation can be too bad for it

Titles

This species is titled, *Nardus spicâ setaceâ rectâ* In the *Flora Lapp* it is termed, *Nardus spicâ lineari* Caspar Bauhine calls it, *Gramen sparteum juncifolium*, also, *Gramen sparteum Hollandicum, capillaceo folio, et minus*, and Parkinson, *Sparteum parvum Batavicum & Anglicum* It is a native of England, and most parts of Europe

Class and order in the Linnæan system The characters

*Nardus* is of the class and order *Triandria Digynia*, and the characters are,

1 CALYX There is none

2 COROLLA is formed of two valves The exterior is spear shaped, narrow, long, sharp pointed, and surrounds the other, which is very narrow, sharp pointed, and proportionally shorter

3 STAMINA are three capillary filaments shorter than the corolla, having oblong antheræ

4 PISTILLUM consists of an oblong germen, a single, long, filiforme downy style, and a simple stigma.

5 PERI

5 PERICARPIUM The corolla grows to the feed, and furrounds it, and ferves for a pericarpium

6 SEMEN The feed is fingle, narrow, efpecially near the top, long, covered, and pointed at each end

## CHAP. CCCVII.

## *NEPETA*, CAT-MINT, or NEP.

THE hardy perennials of this genus are, Species

1 Common Cat Mint, or Nep
2 Hungarian Cat Mint
3 Blue Cat-Mint
4 Little Red Cat Mint
5 Tall White *Sideritis*
6 Spiked Clary
7 Italian Cat-Mint
8 Cretan Cat-Mint
9 Tuberous Cat-Mint
10 Virginian Cat-Mint

Defcription of Common Cat Mint

1 Common Cat-Mint, or Nep The root is hardy and creeping The ftalks are upright, fquare, branching, and about two feet high The leaves are heart fhaped, indented, ferrated, hoary on their underfide, and grow oppofite by pairs on longifh footftalks The flowers are produced in fpikes from the tops of the ftalks, and under the fpikes are two or three whorls at certain diftances, growing on fhort footftalks, they are of a white colour, appear in July, and the feeds ripen in the autumn

Varieties

There are feveral varieties of this fpecies, called,

The Greater Cat Mint
The Smaller
The Narrow leaved
The Blue Flowered
The Purple, &c

They are all very fragrant, having a ftrong fmell between Mint and Penny-Royal Cats are very fond of this plant, and they will bite and roll themfelves on it as they will on *Marum* Hence the name Cat-Mint has been long in ufe whereby to exprefs it It is ufed in medicine, and its virtues are nearly fimilar to thofe of Mint and Penny Royal

Hungarian,

2 Hungarian Cat-Mint The root is creeping The ftalks are upright, fquare, branching near the top, and often a yard high The leaves are heart fhaped, indented, hoary, ftrongly fcented, and grow oppofite on footftalks at the joints The flowers come out in panicles from the tops of the plants, they are of a whitifh colour with a flight mixture of blue, appear in July, and the feeds ripen in the autumn

and Blue Cat Mint defcribed

3 Blue Cat-Mint The ftalks are upright, fquare, fend out a few flender branches from the fides, and grow to about two feet high The leaves are heart-fhaped, oblong, fmooth, indented, and grow oppofite on footftalks at the joints The flowers are produced in roundifh whorls, ftanding on footftalks at the joints, they are of a blue colour, appear in June and July, and the feeds ripen in the autumn

Varieties

There is a variety of this fpecies with white, and another with purple flowers



Little Red Cat Mint,

4 Little Red Cat-Mint The ftalks are flender, fquare, branching a little, and about eight or ten inches high The leaves are cordated, fpear-fhaped, narrow, indented, downy, and grow oppofite to each other at the joints The flowers come out in fmall bunches from the ends of the branches, they are of a delicate red colour on their firft appearance, but foon alter to a dirty white, they appear in June and July, and the feeds ripen in the autumn

and Tall White Sideritis defcribed.

5 Tall White *Sideritis* The ftalks are robuft, fquare, hairy, branching, and four or five feet high The leaves are heart fhaped, oblong, ferrated, and grow oppofite on very fhort footftalks The flowers come out in naked whorled fpikes from the ends of the branches, they are large, and of a white colour, they appear in July, and the feeds ripen in the autumn

Its variety

There is a variety of this fpecies with pale-red flowers

Spiked Clary defcribed,

6 Spiked Clary The ftalks rife to about two feet high The leaves are heart-fhaped, obtufe, flightly indented on their edges, and grow on longifh footftalks The flowers are formed into fpikes, growing in whorls round the tops of the ftalks, they fit clofe at the joints, and are almoft covered with a hoary down, they are of a pale-blue colour, appear in July, and the feeds ripen in the autumn

Variety

There is a variety of this fpecies with white flowers The whole plant fmells very much like Lavender

Italian,

7 Italian Cat-Mint The ftalks are erect, and about a foot high The leaves are heart-fhaped, obtufe, crenated on their edges, hoary, ftrongly fcented, and grow oppofite on footftalks The flowers come out in whorled fpikes from the tops of the ftalks, they fit clofe, without any footftalks, and the whorls are at a confiderable diftance from each other, they are of a white colour, but are almoft concealed by the numerous fpear-fhaped bracteæ which attend them, though the time of blow is nearly the fame with the former forts

Cretan,

8 Cretan Cat-Mint The ftalks are fquare, woolly, branching a little, and a foot and a half high The leaves are heart fhaped, obtufe, woolly, and grow oppofite at the joints The flowers come out in fpikes from the ends of the ftalks, attended by hairy heart-fhaped bracteæ, they fit clofe, are fmall, and appear about the fame time with the others

and Tuberous Cat-Mint defcribed

9 Tuberous Cat-Mint The root is thick, knobbed, and fends out long fibres from the fides The ftalks are flender, partly procumbent, about two feet and a half long, and fend out a few branches by pairs from the fides oppofite The

leaves are oblong, crenated, of a deep-green colour, sessile near the top of the plant, and grow opposite by pairs at the joints. The flowers come out in long whorled spikes from the ends of the stalks, attended by small, oval, coloured bracteæ; they sit close, are of a blue colour, and appear about July with the other sorts.

Varieties. There is a variety of an upright growth, and another with whitish flowers.

Virginian Cat-Mint described. 10. Virginian Cat-Mint. The stalks are upright, square, and two feet high. The leaves are spear-shaped, broad, hairy, and grow opposite by pairs. The flowers come out in large roundish heads from the tops of the stalks, and also in whorls lower down at the joints; they are of a white colour, and appear in July.

Variety. There is a variety of this species with pale-red flowers.

Method of propagating them. All these sorts are propagated by parting of the roots, which may be done at any time of the year, though the best season is the autumn, for they will then take to the ground before winter, and shoot up strong for flowering the summer following.

They may also be encreased by slips or cuttings. These should be planted in May, or early in June; and if they are shaded and watered at first, they will grow, and soon become good plants.

They may also be encreased by seeds. These should be sown as soon as they are ripe, and when they are fit to be transplanted, should be removed to the places where they are designed to remain. Seedling plants are always fruitful in good seeds from their first flowering, which scattering, will grow, and produce you more plants perhaps than you would wish for in the various kinds. This is not always the case of old roots which have been first raised from slips or offsets. They will grow in any soil or situation, though if it be rather dry and hungry, the plants will be less luxuriant, and more finely scented.

Titles. 1. Common Cat-Mint, or Nep, is titled, *Nepeta floribus spicatis, verticillis subpedicellatis, foliis petiolatis cordatis dentato-serratis*. In the *Hortus Cliffortianus* it is termed, *Nepeta floribus interrupte spicatis pedunculatis*. Caspar Bauhine calls it, *Mentha cataria vulgaris & major*; also, *Mentha cataria minor*; Dodonæus, *Cataria herba*; Gerard, *Mentha felina seu cataria*; and Parkinson, *Nepeta major vulgaris*. It grows naturally in England, and most parts of Europe.

2. Hungarian Cat-Mint is, *Nepeta floribus paniculatis, foliis cordatis petiolatis obsolete crenatis*. Van Royen calls it, *Nepeta caule paniculato, pedunculis partialibus ramosis multifloris*; Morison, *Nepeta Pannonica major et elatior*; and Caspar Bauhine, *Mentha montana verticillata*. It grows naturally in Pannonia.

3. Blue Cat-Mint is, *Nepeta verticillis pedunculatis corymbosis, foliis petiolatis cordato-oblongis dentatis*. Sauvages calls it, *Nepeta foliis ovatis petiolatis, floribus verticillis distincte spicatis glabris*; Barrelier, *Nepeta minor altera purpurea major, sparsa spicâ*; and Tournefort, *Cataria Hispanica, betonicæ folio angustiore, flore cæruleo*. It is a native of Spain.

4. Little Red Cat-Mint is, *Nepeta foliis cordato-lanceolatis dentatis tomentosis, floribus racemosis recurvis quinquefariis*. It is a native of the South of Europe.

5. Tall White Sideritis is, *Nepeta foliis cordato-oblongis sessilibus, floribus racemosis verticillatis nudis*. In the *Hortus Upsal* it is termed, *Nepeta foliis sessilibus nudis, calycibus fructûs ovatis æqualibus*. John Bauhine calls it, *Mentha cataria Hispanica, olim sideritis altissima, flore albo*. It grows naturally in Spain.

6. Spiked Clary is, *Nepeta foliis sessilibus verticillato-spicatis, verticillis tomentoso-involutis*. Boccone calls it, *Horminum spicatum lavendulæ flore et odore*. It grows naturally in Sicily.

7. Italian Cat-Mint is, *Nepeta foliis sessilibus verticillato-spicatis, bracteis lanceolatis longitudine calycis, foliis petiolatis*. Caspar Bauhine calls it, *Mentha cataria minor Alpina*. It grows naturally in Italy.

8. Cretan Cat-Mint is, *Nepeta spicis sessilibus terminalibus, bracteis subovatis aristatis, foliis cordatis obtusis*. Caspar Bauhine calls it, *Scordium alterum lanuginosius verticillatum*; and Alpinus, *Scordotis*. It is a native of Crete.

9. Tuberous Cat-Mint is, *Nepeta spicis terminalibus sessilibus, bracteis ovatis coloratis, foliis summis sessilibus*. Caspar Bauhine calls it, *Mentha tuberosa radice*; and Boccone, *Nepeta tuberosa spicata Hispanica*. It grows naturally in Spain and Portugal.

10. Virginian Cat-Mint is, *Nepeta foliis lanceolatis, capitulis terminalibus, staminibus flore longioribus*. In the *Hortus Cliffortianus* it is termed, *Clinopodium foliis lanceolatis, capitulis terminalibus*. Plukenet calls it, *Clinopodium, candicanti folio, floribus albis*; and Morison, *Clinopodium, flore albo, rariflorius, angustioribus foliis glabris, Virginianum*. It grows naturally in Virginia.

Class and order in the Linnæan system. The characters. *Nepeta* is of the class and order *Didynamia Gymnospermia*; and the characters are,

1. CALYX is a monophyllous, tubular, cylindrical perianthium, indented at the top in five acute parts.

2. COROLLA is one ringent petal. The tube is cylindrical and incurved, the limb gaping; the upper lip is erect, roundish, and emarginated; the lower lip is roundish, concave, large, entire, and a little indented at the edge.

3. STAMINA are four awl-shaped filaments, placed close together under the upper lip, two being shorter than the others, having incumbent antheræ.

4. PISTILLUM consists of a quadrifid germen, a filiforme style the length of the stamina, and a bifid acute stigma.

5. PERICARPIUM. There is none. The seeds are lodged in the cup.

6. SEMINA. They are four, and nearly oval.

CHAP.

# CHAP. CCCVIII.

## *NYMPHÆA*, WATER LILY.

Species — OUR rivers and brooks abound with two species of this genus, called,

1. Yellow Water Lily.
2. White Water Lily.

Yellow — 1. Yellow Water Lily. The root is large, of a spongy substance, knotty, long, thick, and often troublesome to the fishermen. The leaves rise immediately from the roots on long footstalks, and swim upon the surface of the water; they are very large, heart-shaped, smooth, and of a deep-green colour. The flowers come out singly on long footstalks; they are large, of a beautiful yellow colour, and just shew themselves above the surface of the water; they appear in July, and are succeeded by ripe seeds about the end of August, or early in September.

and White Water Lily described — 2. White Water Lily. The root is thick, knotty, of a spongy substance, usually black on the outside, white within, and sends forth numerous strong fibres, which strike deep into the gravel, sand, or mud. The leaves are heart-shaped, almost round, entire, of a thickish substance, juicy, lie floating on the top of the water, and are connected with the roots by long, round, smooth, spongy footstalks. The flowers come out singly on long, round, spongy footstalks; they are large, of a white colour, very fragrant, and beautifully shew themselves just above the surface of the water; they appear in June and July, and are succeeded by ripe seeds the end of August, or early in September.

Its virtues — The root of this species is narcotic; the flowers are recommended in alvine fluxes; and the seeds, used in decoctions or broths, promote chastity.

Culture — The last sort is not so common as the first, and when it occurs is one of the greatest ornaments that can happen to a river. The seeds are of a shining black colour, and when full ripe, sink to the bottom of the water; so that whoever is desirous of propagating this plant, should carefully watch the time of the seeds becoming ripe, which may be known by the opening of the large oval berries in which they are contained; and when he has got a sufficient quantity should throw them into his river, ponds, canals, lakes, ditches, or wherever he would chuse to have them grow; and if they like their situation they will come up the following spring, though it is generally two or three years before the plants begin to flower.

Titles — 1. Yellow Water Lily is titled, *Nymphæa foliis cordatis integerrimis, calyce pentaphyllo petalis majore pentaphyllo*. Caspar Bauhine calls it, *Nymphæa lutea major*; and Gerard, *Nymphæa lutea*. It grows naturally in rivers, brooks, and ditches in England, and most parts of Europe.

2. White Water Lily is, *Nymphæa foliis cordatis integerrimis calyce quadrifido*. In the *Flora Lapp.* it is termed, *Nymphæa calyce tetraphyllo, corolla multiplici*. Caspar Bauhine calls it, *Nymphæa alba major*; Gerard, *Nymphæa alba*; and Parkinson, *Nymphæa alba major vulgaris*. It grows naturally in rivers and sweet waters in England, and most parts of Europe and America.

Class and order in the Linnean system — *Nymphæa* is of the class and order *Polyandria Monogynia*; and the characters are,

The character — 1. CALYX is a perianthium composed of four large coloured, permanent leaves.

2. COROLLA consists of numerous petals (usually about fifteen) sitting on the side of the germen in more than a single series.

3. STAMINA are a very great number of short, plane, obtuse, crooked filaments, having oblong antheræ growing to their sides.

4. PISTILLUM. The germen is large and oval; there is no style; the stigma is orbicular, plane, peltated, sessile, permanent, marked with rays, and crenated on the border.

5. PERICARPIUM is a hard, oval, fleshy, rude, pulpy berry, narrowed or drawn together at the neck, crowned at the top, and containing many cells.

6. SEMINA. The seeds are many, and roundish.

CHAP.

# CHAP. CCCIX

## *OENANTHE*, WATER DROPWORT

Species. THE ſpecies of this genus are,

1 Common Water Dropwort.
2 Hemlock Water Dropwort
3 Proliferous Water Dropwort
4 Round-fruited Water Dropwort.
5 Pimpernel Water Dropwort

Common, 1 Common Water Dropwort The root is fibrous, and poſſeſſed of many oval fleſhy tubers hanging to their ends The ſtalk is round, ſtriated, hollow, branching, and about two feet high The radical leaves are large, and compoſed of a multitude of fine ſegments, thoſe on the ſtalks are cylindrical, hollow, and pinnated at the top The flowers come out from the tops of the ſtalks and branches in umbels, they are moderately large, cloſely ſet together, and of a white colour, they appear in July, and the ſeeds ripen in the autumn

This plant is of a poiſonous nature, but not ſo deadly as,

Hemlock, 2 Hemlock Water Dropwort The root is compoſed of many oblong, tuberous, taper, fleſhy parts, which reſemble parſneps, and are full of a yellowiſh acrid juice The ſtalks are robuſt, thick, ſtriated, hollow, jointed, branching, and grow to be four or five feet high The leaves are large, being compoſed of a multitude of obtuſe folioles in the manner of Hemlock, but their colour is a paler green The flowers come out in umbels from the tops of the ſtalks, they are of a white colour, appear in June and July, and the ſeeds ripen in September

The whole plant is full of a yellowiſh fœtid juice, of intolerable acrimony, and a deadly poiſon

This is one of the moſt poiſonous plants we have in nature The roots have been ignorantly gathered and eaten for Parſnep, and death has ſpeedily enſued And what wonder! for the juice in the ſmalleſt quantity taken inwardly, immediately brings on the moſt direful inflammatory ſymptoms of the moſt corroſive poiſon, a gangrene immediately enſues to the parts, and ſoon after death

No antidote againſt the poiſonous quality of this plant is yet known, which ſhould be a great caution to every one (eſpecially the poor, who are apt to eat any thing in time of ſcarcity) how they uſe plants which they are unacquainted with

Proliferous, 3 Proliferous Water Dropwort The ſtalks are round, ſtriated, jointed, hollow, and two or three feet high The leaves are compoſed of many folioles, of a light green colour The flowers are produced from the ends of the ſtalks in proliferous umbels, they are of a whitiſh colour, appear in June and July, and the ſeeds ripen in the autumn

Round fruited, 4 Round-fruited Water Dropwort The ſtalks are round, ſtriated, thick, jointed, hollow, and about a yard high The leaves are compoſed of many parts, the radical ones are large, and grow on ſtrong hollow footſtalks, but thoſe on the ſtalks are ſmaller, and diminiſh gradually as they approach the top of the plant The flowers come out from the tops of the ſtalks in umbels, they are white, appear in July, and are ſucceeded by a globular fruit, containing ripe ſeeds, in the autumn

and Pimpernel Water Dropwort deſcribed 5 Pimpernel Water Dropwort The ſtalks are angular jointed, and eight or ten inches high The radical leaves are bipinnated, and the folioles are oval, wedge-ſhaped, and cut on their edges, thoſe on the ſtalks are long, narrow, channelled, and undivided The flowers come out in unequal umbels from the tops of the ſtalks, they are of a white colour, appear in June and July, and the ſeeds ripen in the autumn

Culture Whoever is inclined to propagate theſe plants may eaſily do it by ſowing the ſeeds in the autumn in the places where they are to remain The ſoil cannot be too moiſt for their reception, and as the roots ſtrike deep into the earth, the ground ſhould be double dug When the plants come up, they will require no trouble, except thinning them to proper diſtances, and keeping them clean from weeds, but if the ground between the plants be dug in winter, it will cauſe the ſtalks to be more robuſt, taller, and the leaves and umbels of the flowers larger

Titles 1 Common Water Dropwort is titled, *Oenanthe ſtolonifera, foliis caulinis pinnatis filiformibus fiſtuloſis* In the *Hortus Cliffort* it is termed, *Oenanthe foliis caulinis fiſtuloſis teretibus* Caſpar Bauhine calls it, *Oenanthe aquatica*, Rivinus, *Oenanthe*, Gerard, *Filipendula aquatica*, Parkinſon, *Oenanthe paluſtris ſ. aquatica*, and Moriſon, *Oenanthe aquatica triflora, caulibus fiſtuloſis* It grows naturally by the ſides of ditches, brooks, rivers, and moiſt places in England, and moſt parts of Europe

2 Hemlock Water Dropwort is, *Oenanthe foliis omnibus multifidis obtuſis ſubæqualibus* Caſpar Bauhine calls it, *Oenanthe chærophylli foliis*, Lobel, *Oenanthe cicutæ facie, ſucco viroſo crocante*, John Bauhine, *Oenanthe ſucco viroſo, cicutæ facie*, *Lobelii*, Gerard, *Filipendula cicutæ facie*, and Parkinſon, *Oenanthe cicutæ facie Lobelii* It grows naturally by the ſides of rivers, brooks, ditches, and moiſt places in England, and moſt parts of Europe

3 Proliferous Water Dropwort is, *Oenanthe umbellularum pedunculis marginalibus longioribus ramoſis maſculis* In the *Hortus Cliffort* it is termed, *Oenanthe floſculis radiantibus ... prolifera* Van Royen calls it, *Oenanthe floſculis diſci ſeſſilibus radii pedunculo ramoſo elevatis*, and Caſpar Bauhine, *Oenanthe prolifera Apulia* It grows naturally in Sicily and Apulia

4 Round fruited Water Dropwort is, *Oenanthe fructibus globoſis* Tournefort calls it, *Oenanthe Luſitanica, ſemine craſſiore globoſo* It grows naturally in Portugal

5 Pimpernel Water Dropwort is, *Oenanthe foliolis radicalibus cuneatis fiſſis, caulinis integris linearibus longiſſimis canaliculatis* Caſpar Bauhine calls it, *Oenanthe Apii folio*, alſo, *Oenanthe pimpinellæ ſylveſtris folio, ſemine atriplicis*, John Bauhine, *Oenanthe ſtaphylini folio aliquatenus accedens*,

and

and Plukenet, *O... aquatic... pimpinellæ saxifragæ...* It grows naturally in ditches and about waters in England and most of the southern parts of Europe.

Claſs and order in the Linnæan Syſtem. The characters.

*Oenanthe* is of the claſs and order *Pentandria Digynia*; and the characters are,

1. CALYX. The general umbel has but few rays, the partial is compoſed of many ſhort ones. The general involucrum is ſimple, and compoſed of many leaves, which are ſhorter than the umbel; the partial alſo conſiſts of many ſmall leaves. The perianthium is permanent, and indented in five parts at the top.

2. COROLLA. The general flower is difform, and radiated. The flowers of the diſk are hermaphrodites, and ... ſhaped petals, ... of the ... unequal, ...

3. STAMINA are five ſingle filaments, with roundiſh antheræ.

4. PISTILLUM conſiſts of a ... germen ... below the flower, and two awl-ſhaped, permanent ſtyles, with obtuſe ſtigmas.

5. PERICARPIUM. There is none; the fruit is oval, crowned by the ... which ... into two parts.

6. SEMINA. The ſeeds are two, oval, convex, ſtriated on one ſide, plane on the other, and indented at the top.

# CHAP. CCCX

## *OENOTHERA*, TREE PRIMROSE

THERE are two perennials of this genus, called,

Species.

1. Low American Tree Primroſe.
2. Virginian Tree Primroſe.

Deſcription of Low American.

1. Low American Tree Primroſe. This ſpecies hath a perennial fibrous root, which ſends forth many oval ſpear-ſhaped, entire leaves, that are ſmall, and ſit cloſe to the crown of the root, having no footſtalks. The ſtalk is weak, ſlender, herbaceous, taper, about ſix or eight inches long, lying on the ground unleſs ſupported, and ornamented with a few ſpear-ſhaped, ſmooth, obtuſe leaves, which are of a light-green colour, and ſit cloſe to the ſtalks. The flowers come out ſingly from the wings of the leaves on very ſhort footſtalks; they are of a bright-yellow colour, appear in June and July, and are often continued in ſucceſſion through Auguſt and September. The capſules are ſmall, oval, obtuſe, and angular, and thoſe which ſucceed the firſt-blown flowers will be full of ripe ſeeds in the autumn.

and Virginian Tree Primroſe.

2. Virginian Tree Primroſe. The ſtalks are upright, ligneous, two or three feet high, and covered with a reddiſh purple coloured bark. The leaves are narrow, ſpear-ſhaped, and ſlightly indented on their edges. The flowers come out from the wings of the leaves, growing four or five together on a footſtalk; they are of a yellow colour, are remarkable for their very ſlender, narrow tubes, appear in July, often continue in ſucceſſion for two or three months, and are ſucceeded by capſules, having four acute angles, containing ripe ſeeds, in the autumn.

Method of propagation.

Both theſe ſpecies are propagated by ſowing the ſeeds, which ſhould be done in the autumn as ſoon as they are ripe, becauſe if they are kept until the ſpring, they often remain a full year before they come up. The ſoil ſhould be light, freſh, and dry, and the ſituation ſhould be warm and well defended. In the ſpring the plants will come up, when they ſhould be thinned where they are too cloſe, be regularly weeded, and conſtantly watered in dry weather all ſummer; and in the autumn they may be removed to the places where they are deſigned to remain. The ſummer following they will flower, and perfect their ſeeds, which, if permitted to



ſcatter, will produce freſh plants for a ſucceſſion without further trouble.

They are alſo encreaſed by parting of the roots, which may be done ſucceſsfully either in the autumn, winter, or ſpring. But as great plenty of plants may be eaſily obtained from ſeed, and as ſeedling plants are always the beſt, the latter method is hardly worth putting into practice, when there is an opportunity of encreaſing the plants the other way.

Titles.

1. Low American Tree Primroſe is titled, *Oenothera foliis lanceolatis obtuſis glabris ... floribus ..., capſulis acutis ...* In Miller's Dictionary it is termed, *Oenothera ... ... lanceolatis ... capſulis ...* Plukenet calls it, *...* Morison, *...*, and Ray, *Lyſimachia ...* It grows naturally in most parts of North America.

2. Virginian Tree Primroſe is, *Oenothera ... lanceolatis ſubdentatis, capſulis pedicellatis ... angulis racemo ...* Gronovius calls it, *Oenothera ... floribus ...*, and Tournefort, *Onagra anguſtifolia ... flore minore*. It grows naturally in Virginia.

Claſs and order in the Linnæan Syſtem. The characters.

*Oenothera* is of the claſs and order *Octandria Monogynia*; and the characters are,

1. CALYX is a monophyllous, deciduous perianthium, placed above the germen. The tube is cylindrical, ... and erect. The limb is cut into four oblong, ... deflexed ſegments.

2. COROLLA is four plane, obcordated petals, inſerted in the diviſions of the calyx, and about the ſame length with the ſegments.

3. STAMINA are eight crooked, awl-ſhaped filaments, ſhorter than the corolla, and inſerted in the tube of the calyx, having oblong, incumbent antheræ.

4. PISTILLUM conſiſts of a cylindrical germen ſituated below the calyx, a filiform ſtyle the length of the ſtamina, and a thick quadrifid, obtuſe, reflexed ſtigma.

5. PERICARPIUM is a cylindrical, four-cornered capſule, formed of four valves, and containing four cells.

6. SEMINA. The ſeeds are many, angular, ... The receptacle ... four ...

# C H A P. CCCXI.

## *ONONIS*, REST HARROW, or CHAMMOCK.

Species

OF this genus there are,

1 Common Rest Harrow, or Chammock
2 True Rest Harrow of the Antients
3 Creeping Rest Harrow
4 Spanish Purple Rest Harrow
5 Variegated Rest Harrow
6 Yellow Rest Harrow, called *Natrix*
7 Yellow Striped Rest Harrow, called *Natrix Pinguis*
8 Curled leaved Rest Harrow
9 Round leaved Rest Harrow

Description of Common Rest Harrow

1 Common Rest Harrow, or Chammock. This hath a strong tough root, which strikes deep into the ground, spreads itself all about, and is so strong as frequently to stop the husbandman's harrow, which occasioned the English appellation of Rest Harrow to be given to this plant. The stalks are ligneous, tough, round, hairy, clammy, about a foot and a half high, and send forth several branches from the sides, which are armed with sharp spines. The leaves on the lower part grow by threes among the flowers, singly; they are small, oblong, indented, and of a good green colour. The flowers come out from the sides of the branches the whole length; they appear early in summer, and often continue in succession until the end of autumn.

Varieties

The varieties of this species are,

The Pale-Red
The Purple
The White
The Thornless, with broad leaves, upright stalks, and red flowers
The Thornless with purple flowers
The Thornless with white flowers

These varieties in some gardens are admitted; but the Common sort, though very beautiful in itself, is denied admission into the pleasure-ground.

Medicinal properties of the root

The root of the Common sort is used in medicine. Being boiled in vinegar and water, it is good for the tooth-ach; the cortical part provokes urine, and is good for the stone; and the young shoots, taken early in the spring, afford a pleasant pickle.

True,

2 True Rest Harrow. The stalks are upright, ligneous, firm, about a foot high, and send forth several hooked branches, which are armed with long strong spines. The lower leaves grow by threes; higher they come out singly. The flowers come out singly from the sides of the branches on footstalks; they are large, of a reddish purple colour, appear in June, July, and August, and the seeds ripen in the autumn.

Creeping,

3 Creeping Rest Harrow. The root is creeping, tough, and spreads itself to a considerable distance. The stalks are tough, hairy, diffuse, about two feet long, and lie on the ground. The leaves are hairy and oval; the lower ones grow by threes, and the upper ones singly. The flowers come out singly from the wings of the leaves; they are of a purple colour, appear in July, and the seeds ripen in September.

Spanish Purple,

4 Spanish Purple Rest Harrow. The stalks are hardly a foot high, possessed of a viscous matter, and divide into a few branches near the ground. All the leaves are trifoliate, hairy, clammy, and grow on viscous hairy footstalks. The flowers come out from the sides of the branches almost the whole length; they are of a palish purple colour, and sit close, having no footstalks; they appear in July, and are succeeded by ripe seeds in the autumn.

5 Variegated Rest Harrow. The stalks are branching, diffuse, clammy, and about nine inches high. The leaves are simple, narrow, wedge-shaped, serrated, and grow on short footstalks. The flowers come out singly from the wing of the leaves, on short footstalks; they are moderately large, and beautifully striped with yellow; they appear in July and August, and the seeds ripen in the autumn. — The Variegated Rest Harrow described

There is a variety of this plant with yellow flowers. — Variety

6 *Natrix*, or Yellow Rest Harrow. The stalks are ligneous, tough, unarmed with spines, branching near the bottom, and about two feet high. The leaves are trifoliate, oval, hairy, and clammy to the touch. The flowers come out from the sides of the stalks almost their whole length; they are moderately large, of a bright-yellow colour, having some brown streaks, and grow singly on long footstalks; they appear in June and July, and are succeeded by ripe seeds in September. — Natrix,

7 *Natrix Pinguis*, or Yellow striped Rest Harrow. The stalks of this species are angular, branching, unarmed with spines, and grow to about two feet high. The leaves are trifoliate, broad, spear shaped, and oblong. The flowers are pretty large, and come out down the greatest part of the branches; their colour is a purple ground finely striped with yellow; they appear in June, July, and August, and the seeds ripen in the autumn. — Natrix Pinguis,

8 Curled leaved Rest Harrow. The stalks of this plant are ligneous, erect, a little downy, and clammy to the touch. The leaves are trifoliate, roundish, waved or curled, and their edges are indented. The flowers are large, yellow, and their outside is streaked with red; they come out in June and July, and the seeds ripen in the autumn. — Curled leaved,

9 Broad-leaved Rest Harrow. The stalks are shrubby, upright, jointed, and about a foot and a half high. The leaves are roundish, small, smooth, and trifoliate. The flowers come out from the wings of the leaves, three growing together on long slender footstalks; they are of a pale yellow colour, appear in June, and the seeds ripen in September. — and Broad leaved Rest Harrow described

Culture

All these sorts may be propagated by slips, or parting of the roots, in the autumn; but the best way of raising them is by sowing of the seeds, which ripen very well in England.

The seeds may be sown in the seminary, and the plants in the autumn following removed to the

the places where they are designed to remain; but the best way will be to sow the seeds at once in the places where they are to remain. The ground therefore should be [illegible] out, then well dug, and [illegible] rows, with a few seeds of each sort put into the ground, covering them over with about half an inch depth of mould, and afterwards thinning [illegible] into the ground, then [illegible] the seeds are sown in the middle or end of March, the plants will come up in May, when they will need no trouble, except keeping them clean from weeds, drawing out the weakest where they appear too close, and watering them in dry weather during the summer. By the autumn they will become strong plants; and if the situation is not well sheltered, and the soil naturally warm and dry, it will be proper to stick some furze bushes round those sorts which come from Spain and the Southern parts of Europe, to break the keen edge of our black frosts, should they happen. Here they may be protected even in a bleak situation, provided the soil is naturally dry and sandy, for the plants are tolerably hardy; and if they survive the winter, they will flower, and produce seeds the summer following. With regard to the English kinds, the most exposed, open, and worst soils should be allotted them, for they will grow every where, and barricade the place with their tough spreading roots in such a manner, as even to threaten to foil the labours of the ploughman, should he with his plough and horses attempt to molest them.

Titles. 1. Common Rest Harrow, or Cammock, is titled, *Ononis floribus racemosis geminis, foliis ternatis superioribus solitariis, ramis inermibus subvillosis*. The Prickly sort in the *Hortus Cliffort.* is termed, *Ononis floribus subsessilibus lateralibus caule spinoso*; and the Smooth sort *Ononis floribus subsessilibus solitariis lateralibus, ramis inermibus*. Caspar Bauhine calls the Common sort, *Ononis spinosa flore purpureo*; Gerard, *Ononis*, *J rvestr boris*; Fuchsius, *Ononis*. The Smooth sort Caspar Bauhine terms, *Ononis spinis carens purpurea*; Gerard, *Ononis non spinosa purpurea*; and Clusius, *Ononis mitior I*. This species in its varieties grows naturally in sterile pastures in England, and most parts of Europe. The Smooth sort is usually called in England Common Rest Harrow.

2. True Rest Harrow is, *Ononis floribus solitariis foliolo majoribus, foliis inferioribus ternatis, ramis laeviusculis spinosis*. Tournefort calls it, *Ononis legitima antiquorum*. It grows naturally in Italy, Portugal, and Spain.

3. C[illegible] Rest Harrow is, *On[illegible] diffusis, [illegible]* [illegible] *[illegible]* Tournefort calls it, *[illegible] procumbens, [illegible]*. It grows naturally on [illegible] in the Isle of Thanet [illegible] part of England, [illegible]

4. Spanish P[illegible] Rest Harrow is, *Ononis [illegible] floribus [illegible] petiolatis [illegible]* [illegible] it, *Ononis [illegible]* Tournefort, *Ononis [illegible]*; and John Bauhine, *[illegible]*. It grows naturally in Italy, Spain, and the South of France.

5. Variegated Rest Harrow is, *Ononis [illegible] foliis [illegible] floribus [illegible]*. Butcher calls it, *Ononis lutea, [illegible] gmus folio, minima*; and Tournefort, *Ononis non spinosa, flore luteo variegato, angustifolia [illegible]*. It grows naturally in the maritime parts of the South of Europe.

6. Natrix Rest Harrow is, *Ononis pedunculis [illegible] floris aristatis, foliis ternatis ovatis [illegible] integerrimis*. Caspar Bauhine calls it, *Ononis [illegible] spinis carens lutea [illegible]*; Camerarius, *Ononis lutea*; and Rivinus, *Natrix*. It grows naturally in Italy, Spain, and the South of France.

7. Narrow-leaved Natrix is, *Ononis pedunculis [illegible] floris aristatis, foliis ternatis lanceolatis, stipulis [illegible] integerrimis*. Caspar Bauhine calls it, *Ononis non spinosa, flore luteo variegato*; Dalechamp, *Ononis lutea non spinosa*, *Natrix [illegible]*; and Plukenet, *Ononis lutea [illegible], oxytriphylla ad foliorum petiolas cepreolata*. It grows common in most of the southern counties of Europe.

8. Curled-leaved Rest Harrow is, *Ononis fruticosa, foliis ternatis subrotundis [illegible]*; Magnol calls it, *Ononis Hispanica frutescens, folio rotundiore*; and Tournefort, *Ononis Hispanica frutescens, folio rosa [illegible]*. It is a native of Italy and Spain.

9. Round-leaved Rest Harrow is, *Ononis fruticosa, pedunculis triflores, calycibus triphyllo bracteatis, foliis ternatis [illegible]*. Caspar Bauhine calls it, *Cicer sylvestre latifolium triphyllum*; Dodonaeus, *Cicer sylvestre [illegible]*; and Lobel, *Cicer sylvestre [illegible]*. It grows naturally on the Helvetian mountains.

CHAP

# C H A P. CCCXII.

## *OPHIOGLOSSUM*, ADDER's TONGUE.

THERE is one English species of this genus of great use as well as singularity, called Adders Tongue.

This plant described.

The root is composed of many long fibres, which strike deep into the ground. From the top rises a single leaf, which is oval, thick, flat, of a beautiful green colour, and having a thick, green, succulent base or footstalk near three inches long. The stalk arises from the bottom of the leaf, supporting the fructification: it is small, tender, three or four inches high, and at the top is situated a long pointed capsule, called the adder's tongue, from the resemblance it is supposed to have to the tongue of that reptile. It appears in April and May, soon after which the leaves and stalks decay, and nothing more to be found until the spring following.

Medicinal properties of it.

This plant is one of the best vulneraries we have, and is well known to the country-people, who by its means effect great cures, though it is much neglected in the shops. An ointment made of it, with a mixture of butter and lard, is also given inwardly.

It grows naturally in moist meadows, heaths, and pastures, in many parts of England. Whoever is desirous of having it in his garden should dig up some large turfs very deep, containing the roots, about the end of May, or early in June, when the stalks decay, and place them in a moist part of his garden, and the spring following the plants will appear.

Method of propagating it.

This species is titled *Ophioglossum fronde ovato*. In the *Hortus Cliffort.* it is termed, *Ophioglossum folio ovato, spica disticha*. Caspar Bauhine calls it, *Ophioglossum*; also, *Ophioglossum vulgatum*; also, *Ophioglossum minus, subrotundo folio*; and Parkinson, *Ophioglossum*, *sive Lingua serpentina*. It grows naturally in England and most parts of Europe.

Titles.

*Ophioglossum* is of the natural class *Cryptogamia*, Order the 1st.

Class and order in the Linnæan system.

We know nothing of the flower and its different parts, but the fruit consists of a distichous capsule, divided into cells by numerous transverse articulations, each of which, when come to maturity, opens transversely for the discharge of the seeds.

The characters.

The seeds are numerous, very small, and nearly oval.

# C H A P. CCCXIII.

## *OPHRYS*, TWYBLADE, or TWAYBLADE.

OF this genus are,

Species.

1. Common Twyblade.
2. Least Twyblade.
3. Birds nest.
4. Coral *Ophrys*.
5. Spiral *Orchis*, or Triple Ladies Traces.
6. Crain *Ophrys*.
7. Dwarf *Orchis*.
8. Prussian *Orchis*.
9. Hooded *Orchis*.
10. Monophyllous *Ophrys*.
11. Yellow or Musk *Orchis*.
12. Alpine *Orchis*.
13. Green Man *Orchis*.
14. Insect *Orchis*.

Common,

1. Common Twyblade. The root consists of many thick, strong fibres. The leaves are two only, oval, broad, obtuse, veined, and grow opposite near the bottom of the stalk. The stalk is six or eight inches high, round, succulent, tender, green, and above the two leaves which are situated near the base quite naked. The flowers terminate the stalks in spikes, they are of a greenish colour, and their composition is such, that they form the appearance of gnats sitting on the stalks; they appear in May and June, the stalks decay in July and August, and fresh ones arise in the spring.

and Least Twayblade described.

2. Least Tway-blade. The root is a small bulb, sending forth many strong fibres. The stalk is round, slender, about four inches high, and garnished near the bottom with two small heart-shaped notched leaves placed opposite. The flowers terminate the stalks in spikes, they are small, herbaceous, and have a gnat-like appearance; they come out in June and July, and the stalks decay soon after.

Its variety.

There is a variety of this species with purplish saffron-coloured flowers.

Bird nest.

3. Birds nest. The root is composed of many long, slender, bulbous parts, clustered together. The stalks are thick, round, succulent, about a foot high, and surrounded and sheathed by the leaves almost the whole length. The flowers terminate the stalks in loose spikes, they are of a pale-brown colour, will be in blow in May and June, and the stalks decay about the end of August.

and Coral Ophrys.

4. Coral *Ophrys*. The root consists of many oblong, branching, bulbous parts, often of a very deep red colour. The stalk is upright, round, succulent, sheathed by being surrounded

by

by the leaves almost to the top, and grow to six or eight inches high The flowers come out in spikes from the tops of the stalks, they are of a white colour, and appear in May and June

Spiral Orchis

5 Spiral *Orchis*, or Triple Ladies Traces The root consists of many oblong bulbs clustered together The radical leaves are oval, pointed, ribbed, and form a cluster at the crown of the root The stalks are simple, tender, and about six inches high The flowers are produced in long spiral spikes from the tops of the stalks, they are small, of a white colour and an agreeable odour, and their appearance is generally in August

and Canada Ophrys described

6 Canada *Ophrys* The root is composed of a multitude of thick, fleshy fibres clustered together The radical leaves are long, narrow spreading, and form a large tuft at the crown of the root The stalk is thick, round, succulent, and adorned with a few short leaves, which surround it with their base almost to the top The flowers are produced in close spikes from the tops of the stalks, they are small in a drooping position, and usually shew themselves in July

Description of Dwarf,

7 Dwarf *Orchis* The root is a roundish bulb The leaves are spear-shaped, narrow, and two usually arise from the root Out of the middle of these proceed the stalk, which is naked, round, tender, and about five or six inches high The flowers come out in spikes from the tops of the stalks, they are small The lip of the nectarium is undivided, and the two outer petals are very narrow Their time of blowing is in July

Prussian,

8 Prussian *Orchis* The root is a round bulb The leaves are two, spear-shaped, and almost as long as the stalk The stalk is upright, naked, almost round at the bottom, but three-cornered near the top The flowers are five, six, seven, or eight at the top of the stalks The lip of the nectarium is very large, and of an oval figure, but the petals are narrow and reflexed They are of a yellowish-green colour, and appear about the same time with the former

and the Least Orchis

9 The Least *Orchis* The root is a small, oval bulb The leaves are spathulated, very rough on their borders, and three or four usually rise from the root, the outer ones being the shortest The stalks are almost naked, five-cornered, and three or four inches high The flowers are many, and form a loose spike at the top of the stalk, they are of a greenish-yellow colour, and appear in June and July

Monophyllous Ophrys described

10 Monophyllous *Ophrys* The root is a small, roundish bulb, sending forth a single leaf of an oval figure By the side of the leaf rises a tender, naked, succulent stalk to five or six inches high At the top of this stand a few flowers in form of a spike, they are of a greenish colour, and appear about the same time with the others

Yellow Orchis described

11 Yellow or Musk *Orchis* The root is a roundish bulb, and sometimes several of them will be clustered together The leaves are oblong, and usually about three or four at the crown of each root The stalk is slender, naked, and about six inches high The flowers are produced in spikes from the tops of the stalks, they are possessed of an agreeable musky odour, and usually appear in August

There are several varieties of this species, such as,

Varieties

The White-flowered,
The Yellow,
The Pale-green,
The Yellowish-green,
The Smooth-leaved —and
The Hairy leaved,

all which have a musky odour, and are very fragrant

Alpine

12 Alpine *Orchis* The root consists of two oval bulbs joined together at the top The leaves are long, slender, awl-shaped, and for the most part four at the crown of each root The stalk is slender, surrounded by the leaves at the bottom, but naked upwards, and grows to about four inches high The flowers are four or five only, growing alternately at the top of the stalk, they are of a pale green colour, and usually appear about the same time with the former

and Green Man Orchis described,

13 Green man *Orchis* The root is composed of several roundish bulbs The radical leaves are oblong, and usually three or four at the crown of each root The stalks are thick, upright, adorned with a few narrow leaves, and grow to a foot and a half high The flowers come out in loose spikes from the tops of the stalks, they are of a greenish colour, and their composition is such as to represent the figure of a naked man This singular species blows in June

Its variety

There is a variety of it with brownish flowers, which is also usually tinged with green

Insect Orchis, with its Varieties described

14 Insect *Orchis* This species comprehends numerous varieties, known by the respective names of,

The Fly *Orchis*
The Bee *Orchis*
The Beetle *Orchis*
Spider *Orchis*
The Larger Fly *Orchis*
The Larger Bee *Orchis*
The Smaller Yellow Fly *Orchis*
The Large Blue Fly *Orchis*
Large Green Fly *Orchis*
The Black Bee *Orchis*
Green winged Bee *Orchis*, &c

The roots of all are two roundish bulbs, with some fibres The leaves are oblong, usually pointed, though various in the different sorts The stalks are garnished with leaves, and are of different heights in the different varieties The flowers come out in spikes from the tops of the stalks, and their composition is such as to represent the various figures of flies, bees, &c. of different colours These wonderful plants will be in full blow in June

Method of propagation

Nature seems never to have designed these plants for the garden, as their greatest beauty is displayed in their natural places of growth, whether it be in woods, bogs, moist or dry land They may, however, be introduced into the cultivated garden, by taking up the roots about such time as the stalks decay, and planting them immediately in soil as nearly similar as possible to that they were brought from They will flower the summer following, but then they often look shabby, their spikes are for the most part imperfect, and their colour is frequently bad Where large tracts of gardening, however, are carried on, suitable situations in one part or other may be found for the respective sorts Let the plants, therefore, be marked, when in full blow, by placing a stick for a direction to the roots As soon as the stalks and leaves are decayed, which will be before the end of summer in most of the sorts, let a very large and deep turf be dug up, including the root and its whole contents, and let some little of a sufficient size be in readiness for the reception of the mould, to prevent its being broken or divided Then having brought them to the places where you would chuse to have them planted, let them be set in places similar to those from whence they were taken Let those which occupied bogs, have bogs, or at least a moist situation, those which were taken out of woods should be stationed in the wildernesses among trees, and those which occupied sandy or chalky hills or plains, ought to be planted among the grass in some dry open exposure In planting, let a hole of sufficient size be dug up, and carefully let in the turf in which the root is contained Let the surfaces of both be equal, close the parts carefully by filling the interstices with mould, and gently pressing the whole down with the foot, and then leave them to Nature

Early the summer following you will perceive them advance for flowering amidst the natural herbage of the place, and being surrounded by their own soil, they will be naturalized to it, and will exhibit their bloom for the most part in as great perfection as if they had never been disturbed Thus may these singular plants be made to grow, and ornament one part or other of large and extensive designs, which will not fail to give satisfaction and pleasure to the beholders But to introduce them into gardens as cultivated flowers, I think, had better never be attempted, because, though they do grow by observing the proper time of removing the roots, yet I always found them to be weak sickly, bad-coloured, and disqualified to afford that satisfaction to beholders which they expected, and which they would not fail to grant when growing wild in rutty neglected places, though they were at first brought there by the care and industry of the owners

Titles 1 Common Twayblade is titled, *Ophrys bulbo fibroso, caule bifolio, foliis ovatis, nectarii labio bifido* In the *Hortus Cliffort* it is termed, *Ophrys foliis ovatis*, Fuchsius calls it, *Ophrys*, Gerard, *Ophrys bifolia*, and Parkinson, *Bifolium sylvestre vulgare* It grows naturally in moist meadows, woods, and thickets, in England, and most parts of Europe

2 Least Twayblade is, *Ophrys bulbo fibroso, caule bifolio, foliis cordatis* In the *Flora Lapponica* it is termed, *Ophrys foliis cordatis* Caspar Bauhine calls it, *Ophrys minima*; John Bauhine, *Bifolium minimum*, and Mentzelius, *Ophrys minima, floribus purpureo croceis* It grows naturally in moist woods, turfy and heathy ground, in England, and most of the colder parts of Europe

3 Bird's Nest is, *Ophrys bulbis fibroso-fasciculatis, caule vaginato, nectarii labio bifido* In the *Flora Suecica* it is termed, *Neottia bulbis fasciculatis, nectarii labio bifido* Caspar Bauhine calls it, *Orchis abortiva fusca*, and Lobel, *Nidus avis* It grows naturally in woods and shady places in England, Sweden, France, and Germany

4 Coral Ophrys is, *Ophrys bulbis ramosis flexuosis, caule vaginato, nectarii labio trifido* In the *Flora Suecica* it is termed, *Neottia bulbis reticulatis, nectarii labio trifido*, in the *Flora Lapponica, Neottia radice reticulatâ* Caspar Bauhine calls it, *Orobanche radice coralloide*, Rudbeck, *Orobanche sueonum radice coralloide, flore albo*, Ruppier, *Orobanche spuria, s corallorhiza*, and Mentzelius, *Orobanche radice coralloide ruberrimâ* It grows naturally in the deserts of most of the northern countries of Europe

5 Spiral Orchis, or Triple Ladies Traces, is, *Ophrys bulbis aggregatis oblongis, caule subfolioso, floribus secundis, nectarii labio indiviso crenato* Caspar Bauhine calls it, *Triorchis alba odorata minor*, also, *Triorchis, s Tetrorchis alba odorata major*, John Bauhine, *Orchis spiralis alba odorata*, Lobel, *Testiculus odoratus*, and Micheli, *Orchiastrum æstivum palustre album odoratum* It grows naturally in dry pastures in England, France, and Italy

6 Canada Ophrys is, *Ophrys bulbis fasciculatis, caule folioso, floribus cernuis, nectarii labio oblongo integro acuto* It grows naturally in Virginia and Canada

7 Dwarf Orchis is, *Ophrys bulbo subrotundo, scapo nudo, foliis lanceolatis, nectarii labio integro, petalis dorsalibus linearibus* Gronovius calls it, *Ophrys scapo nudo, foliis radicalibus ovato-oblongis dimidii scapi longitudine*, Ray, *Pseudo orchis bifolia palustris*, Caspar Bauhine, *Chamæorchis latifolia*; and Parkinson, *Chamæorchis latifolia Zelandica* It grows naturally in marshy places in England, Sweden, Canada, and Virginia

8 Prussian Orchis is, *Ophrys bulbo subrotundo, scapo nudo trigono, nectarii labello ovato* Loeselius calls it, *Ophrys diphyllos bulbosa.* It grows common in the marshy parts of Prussia and Sweden

9 The Least Orchis is, *Ophrys bulbo subrotundo, scapo subnudo pentagono, foliorum apicibus scabris, nectarii labio integro* Ray calls it, *Orchis minima bulbosa*, and Plukenet, *Orchis bifolia minor palustris* It grows naturally in marshy places in England and Sweden

10 Monophyllous Ophrys is, *Ophrys bulbo subrotundo, scapo nudo, folio ovato, nectarii labio integro* Loeselius calls it, *Ophrys monophyllos bulbosa*, Mentzelius, *Monorchis ophioglossoides*, and Clusius, *Pseudo-orchis monophyllos* It grows naturally in moist woods and marshy grounds in Germany

11 Yellow or Musk Orchis is, *Ophrys bulbo globoso, scapo nudo, nectarii labio trifido cruciato* In the *Flora Suecica* it is termed, *Herminium bulbo supra radiato, nectarii labio trifido*, in the *Flora Lapponica, Herminium radice globosâ* Gmelin calls it, *Orchis radice subrotundâ, labello hastato*, Seguier, *Orchis trifolia, floribus spicatis herbaceis*, Loeſel, *Orchis coleo unico, s Monorchis flosculis pallide virentibus*, Micheli, *Monorchis*, Mentzelius, *Monorchis bifolia, flore pallide virente, Prussica* Caspar Bauhine, *Orchis odorata moschata, s Monorchis*, also, *Orchis lutea, hirsuto folio* also, *Triorchis lutea, folio glabro*, also, *Triorchis lutea altera* It grows naturally in sterile pastures and meadows in England and most countries of Europe

12 Alpine Orchis is, *Ophrys bulbis ovatis, scapo nudo, foliis subulatis, nectarii labio indiviso obtuso, utrinque unidentato* Caspar Bauhine calls it, *Chamæorchis Alpina, folio gramineo*, and Haller, *Orchis radicibus subrotundis, calcare nullo, foliis longis & perangustis* It grows naturally on the Alps of Lapland and Helvetia

13 Green Man Orchis is, *Ophrys bulbis subrotundis, scapo folioso, nectarii labio lineari tripartito, medio elongato bifido* In the *Acta R S Ups* it is termed, *Neottia bulbis subrotundis, nectarii labio quadrifido* Caspar Bauhine calls it, *Orchis, flore nudi hominis effigiem representans, femina*, and Columna, *Orchis antropophora oreades* Its residence is chiefly in chalky soils, growing naturally in such places in England, Italy, France, and Portugal

14 Insect Orchis is, *Ophrys bulbis subrotundis, scapo folioso, nectarii labio subquinquelobo* In the *Flora Suecica, &c* it is termed, *Cypripedium bulbis subrotundis, foliis oblongis caulinis* The varieties of this species stand with titles in the works of old botanists Thus, I *Myodes* Lobel calls, *Orchis myodes prima, floribus muscam exprimens*, and Caspar Bauhine, *Orchis muscæ corpus referens minor, galeâ & alis herbidis*, also, *Orchis muscam referens major*, also, *Orchis muscam referens lutea* Breynius stiles it, *Orchis muscam cæruleam majorem*

*jorem repreſentans*, alſo, *Orchis myodes lutea Luſitanica*, alſo, *Orchis myodes fuſca Luſitanica* II *Adrachnites* Lobel calls, *Orchis adrachnit s*, and Caſpar Bauhine, *Orchis araneum referens*, alſo, *Orcnis fucum referens, colore rubiginoſo*, alſo, *Orchis fucum referens major, foliolis ſuperioribus candidis & purpuraſcentibus*, alſo, *Orchis fucum referens, flore ſubvirente* Breynius ſtiles it, *Orchis ſcarabæum referens*, alſo, *Orchis cercopithecum exprimens Luſitanica* They grow naturally in meadows and paſtures in England and the ſouthern parts of Europe

Claſs and order in the Linnæan ſyſtem *Ophrys* is of the claſs and order *Gynandria Diandria*, and the characters are,

The characters 1 CALYX The ſpathæ are vague The ſpadix is ſimple There is no perianthium

2 COROLLA is five oblong, equal petals, which aſcend, join at the top, and form the appearance of a helmet.

The nectarium is dependent, longer than the petals, and keel ſhaped behind

3 STAMINA are two very ſhort filaments ſitting on the piſtil, having erect antheræ, covered by the interior border of the nectarium

4 PISTILLUM conſiſts of an oblong, contorted germen ſituated below the flower, a ſtyle growing to the inner border of the nectarium, and an obſolete ſtigma

5 PERICARPIUM is an oval, three-cornered, obtuſe, ſtriated capſule, formed of three valves, and containing one cell

6 SEMINA The ſeeds are numerous, and like duſt

## CHAP. CCCXIV.

## *ORCHIS.*

Species OF this genus are,

1 Common Butterfly *Orchis*
2 Spaniſh Butterfly *Orchis*
3 Hooded *Orchis*
4 Ciliated *Orchis*
5 Purple Late-flowering *Orchis*.
6 Globoſe *Orchis*
7 The Leſſer Lizard Flower
8 Female Foolſtones
9 Male Foolſtones
10 Little Purple-flowered *Orchis*.
11 The Man *Orchis*
12 Male Handed *Orchis*
13 Female Handed *Orchis*
14 Red Handed *Orchis*
15 Auſtrian Handed *Orchis*, or Elder *Orchis*
16 Sweet ſcented *Orchis*
17 Yellow Virginian *Orchis*
18 Roſe *Orchis*
19 Purple Bird's Neſt
20 American White-heeled *Orchis*

Deſcription of Common 1 Common Butterfly *Orchis* is of many ſorts The root conſiſts of two oblong, pear ſhaped bulbs The leaves, which riſe immediately from the root, are uſually two, though in ſome varieties they are three or four, they are ſhaped like thoſe of the Lily, often ſpotted, and of a pale-green colour The ſtalks are ſlender, furrowed, eight or ten inches high, and garniſhed with a few ſmall leaves, which embrace it with their baſe The flowers come out in looſe ſpikes from the tops of the ſtalks, they are of a white colour, very fragrant, and exhibit the appearance of an expanded butterfly This ſpecies blows in May and June

and Spaniſh Butterfly Orchis 2 Spaniſh Butterfly *Orchis* The root is compoſed of two roundiſh bulbs The leaves are oblong, and often four or five proceed from the root The ſtalk is upright, tender, and about nine inches high The flowers come out in looſe ſpikes from the tops of the ſtalks, are very large, and repreſent a butterfly with the wings expanded Their chief blow is in June

3 Hooded *Orchis* The root is compoſed of two round bulbs, which join together The radical leaves are two, and of an oval figure The ſtalk is upright, naked, and about eight or ten inches high The flowers come out in ſpikes from the tops of the ſtalks, having confluent petals forming the appearance of a hood, indented in three parts Deſcription of Hooded,

4 Ciliated *Orchis* The root conſiſts of two or three oblong bulbs, which are joined together at top The leaves are oblong, ſmooth, and of a pale-green colour The ſtalk is upright, moderately thick, yet tender, and a foot and a half high The flowers form a looſe ſpike at the top of the ſtalk, they are of a yellow colour, have the lip of the nectarium ſpear-ſhaped and ciliated, and are further remarkable for a very long yellow ſpur or heel The whole ſpike is large, and very elegant Ciliated,

5 Purple Late-flowering *Orchis* The root is compoſed of two oblong bulbs The radical leaves are oblong, narrow, and three or four are produced at the crown of the root The ſtalks are a foot high, and garniſhed with three or four narrow, erect leaves, which embrace it with their baſe The flowers come out in thick roundiſh ſpikes from the tops of the ſtalks, they are of a reddiſh-purple colour, having ſharp-pointed wings and long ſpurs, and appear in June and July Purple Late flowering,

6. Globoſe *Orchis* The root is compoſed of two conical bulbs joined together The leaves are oblong, ſmooth, and of a light green colour The ſtalks are upright, tender, and ſix or eight inches high The flowers are produced in ſhort cloſe ſpikes from the tops of the ſtalks, and appear about the ſame time with the former and Globoſe Orchis

7 The Leſſer Lizard Flower The root is two roundiſh bulbs joined together The leaves are narrow, three or four in number, and embrace the ſtalk with their baſe The ſtalk riſes to about ſix or eight inches high, and ſupports The Leſſer Lizard Flower deſcribed

at

at the top a short spike of dark-coloured or blackish flowers, which appear in June

There is a variety with white, and another with brownish grey-coloured flowers

This plant is possessed of a very disagreeable smell, not much unlike that of confined goats

8 Female Foolstones The root is two round bulbs joined together The leaves are oblong, smooth, nobbed, grow four or more at the root, and spread on the ground The stalk is eight or ten inches high, having a few narrow leaves, which embrace it with their base The flowers come out in spikes from the tops of the stalks in May and June, and are of different kinds, such as, the Purple, the Pale-red, the White, the Violet, the Flesh coloured, &c They are sometimes pretty large, and beautifully tinged with deeper spots in the various colours

9 Male Foolstones The root is two roundish bulbs joined together The leaves are oblong, smooth, spotted, and not much unlike those of the Lily The stalk is upright, thick, round, a foot high, and adorned with two or three narrow leaves, which embrace it with their base The flowers come out in long loose spikes from the tops of the stalks, they are usually of a reddish-purple colour, having deeper purple spots, and appear in May These flowers vary in their colour like the former, though not so common, are moderately large, have a fine appearance, and are very agreeably scented

10 Little Purple flowered Orchis The root is two small, oblong bulbs joined together The leaves are oblong, narrow, and surround the stalk, forming a kind of sheath, with their base The stalks are upright, slender, and six or eight inches high The flowers come out in spikes at the top, are usually of a purple colour, and finely spotted, they vary in their tinges, and one with a white nectarium is much admired This species flowers in May and June

11 The Man Orchis The root is a double bulb The leaves are smooth, oblong, five or six in number, and form a sheath to the stalk with their base The stalk is eight or ten inches high, and supports the flowers These flowers are formed into loose spikes having longish footstalks, and are very fragrant, they are of different varieties, and their composition is such as to exhibit the appearance of a naked man; their colours are different in the same flowers, viz ash coloured, red, brown, and sometimes an almost black has a principal share, and all are beautifully spotted or striped with still deeper marks in the various colours Their time of blow is June

12 Male Handed Orchis The root of this species is palmated, the bulbs being divided into four or five fingers, which spread open like the hand The stalks are thick, upright, succulent, and often a foot in height The leaves are large, broad, acute, smooth, free from spots, and embrace the stalk with their base The flowers come out in short close spikes from the tops of the stalks, they are large, of a red colour spotted with purple, and appear in May and June The colour of the flowers varies in the different sorts, and there is a kind with very slender stalks and narrow leaves

13 Female Handed *Orchis* The root is a double fleshy bulb, dividing into about four parts, which spread out like the fingers of the hand The stalk is upright, fleshy, spotted, and about a foot high The leaves are shaped like the former, but smaller and narrower, and further vary in being spotted all over with dark coloured spots The flowers come out in close spikes from the tops of the stalks, they appear in June, and the principal varieties are,

The Pale-purple
The Deep purple
The Rose-coloured
The White

14 Red Handed *Orchis* The bulbs are palmated like the former The stalks are succulent, tender, surrounded by the base of the leaves, and about a foot high The leaves are long, narrow, free from spots, and of a pale-green colour The flowers are formed into long beautiful spikes at the tops of the stalks, they are of several varieties, but the most beautiful is that of a bright glossy red colour without spots This species flowers in June

15 Austrian Handed *Orchis*, or Elder *Orchis* The root is a double bulb divided into seven straight fleshy parts The stalk is round, thick, tender, and about six inches high The leaves are oblong, smooth, pointed, free from spots, and embrace the stalk with their base The flowers come out in loose spikes from the tops of the stalks; their varieties are,

The White
The Red
The Red and White
The Purple

They appear in June, and smell like the flowers of Elder

16 Sweet-scented *Orchis* The bulbs are divided into five or six spreading parts The leaves are narrow, acute, short, and sit close to the stalk The stalks are succulent, tender, and about six inches high The flowers are formed into spikes at the tops of the stalks, are remarkable for their extraordinary fragrance, and appear in June

17 Yellow Virginian *Orchis* The bulbs are palmated The radical leaves are spear-shaped, broad, and eight or nine inches long The stalks are upright, tender, and ten or twelve inches high The flowers grow in narrow spikes at the tops of the stalks, are of a yellow colour, and appear about the same time with the former

18 Rose *Orchis* The bulbs are palmated The leaves are oblong, narrow, pointed, and smooth The stalks grow to about six or eight inches high The flowers are of an elegant rose colour, often marked with deeper-coloured spots

There is a variety with yellow spotted flowers

19 Purple Bird's Nest The root is composed of many thick, fleshy fibres, or long narrow bulbs bunched together The stalks are thick, purple-coloured, about a foot and a half high, and sheathed by the base of the leaves, which are also of a purple colour, narrow, and pointed The flowers form a thyrse at the tops of the stalks, are of a deep purple colour, and appear in June

20 American White heeled *Orchis* The root is composed of several oblong, fleshy parts The radical leaves are two, broad, of an oval figure, and a dark green colour The stalk is naked, and six or eight inches high The flowers are five or six only in the spike, but they are large and very elegant, the exterior petals being green, the middle of the flower blue, and the spur white

All these species are propagated by removing the roots when the stalks decay Nature seems not to have designed any of them for garden flowers, but they may be made to flourish extremely well in one part or other of large walks, with the natural herbage of the place, where the various kinds of dry grass ground, woods, wilderness, moist meadows, chalky and other soils, are

are to be found When therefore they are in full blow, let a stick be thrust down by each plant you would chuse to have removed for a direction, and in summer, when the stalks are decayed, let each plant be taken up with as much mould as possible, placed in a tub or basket and planted in a situation as nearly as possible similar to that it before grew in, that is, such as grow naturally on dry chalky land, let them be set on the side of some dry hill of a like nature, such as have been taken from the woods, let them be planted in the wilderness, or such as were removed from moist places, in the coolest part of our works After they are planted leave them to Nature, and they will grow and flourish extremely well with the natural herbage of the respective places They will also grow in cultivated gardens, if removed with the above care, but there they generally dwindle, look sickly, and in a little time die away

This method of propagation respects such of the species as are natives of our own country With respect to the foreign sorts, whoever is desirous of obtaining them, should procure them to be planted when the stalks decay in tubs or boxes, being careful to preserve the earth at the roots on the removal When they arrive, they may be turned out of the tubs, with the mould unbroken, into suitable places, in order to take their chance for growing with the other kinds

Ti l s. 1 Common Butterfly Orchis is titled, *Orchis bulbis indivisis, nectarii labio lanceolato integerrimo cornu longissimo, petalis patentibus* C... calls it, *Testiculi species*, Haller, *Orchis ... bus connatis, labello lingulato simplicissimo*, Gerard, *Orchis psycodes*, Parkinson, *Orchis sphegodes s testiculus vulpinus primus*, John Bauhine, *Orchis hermaphroditica bifolia*, and Caspar Bauhine, *Orchis alba bifolia minor, calcari oblongo*, also, *Orchis trifolia minor*, also, *Orchis bifolia altera*, also, *Orchis bifolia latissima* It grows naturally under bushes, and in rough pastures in England and most countries of Europe

2 Spanish Butterfly Orchis is, *Orchis bulbis indivisis, nectarii labio indiviso ante dilatato emarginato crenato cornu subulato, petalis conniventibus* Caspar Bauhine calls it, *Orchis papilionem expansum referens* It grows naturally in Spain

3 Hooded Orchis is, *Orchis bulbis indivisis, nectarii labio trifido, petalis confluentibus, cauli nudo* Gmelin calls it, *Orchis radice rotunda, cucullo tricentato* It grows naturally in Siberia

4 Ciliated Orchis is, *Orchis bulbis indivisis, nectarii labio lanceolato ciliato, cornu longissimo* Van Royen calls it, *Orchis nectarii labio lanceolato ciliato seta germine multo longiore*, Morison, *Orchis palmata elegans lutea Americana, cum longis calcaribus luteis*, and Ray, *Orchis Marylandica grandis et procera, floribus luteis, calcari longissimo lobulo fimbriato* It grows common in Virginia and Canada

5 Purple Late-flowering Orchis is *Orchis bulbis indivisis, nectarii labio trifido aequali integerrimo cornu longo, petalis sublanceolatis*, In the *Acta Upsal* it is termed, *Orchis bulbis indivisis, nectarii labio trifido antice bidentato cornu longo, petalis acuminatis*, in the *Hortus Cliffort Orchis radicibus subrotundis, bracteis flore brevioribus, nectarii labio trifido, seta longissima* Ray calls it, *Orchis purpurea, spicâ congestâ pyramidali*, and Caspar Bauhine, *Cynosorchis militaris montana, spica rubente conglomerata*, also, *Cynosorchis latifolia, hiante cucullo, altera*, also, *Cynosorchis latifolia spicâ compactâ* It grows naturally in chalky and sandy dry pastures in England, France, and Germany

6 Globose Orchis, *Orchis bulbis indivisis, nectarii labio trifido medio trilobo cornu brevi, petalis apice subulatis* Haller calls it, *Orchis radicibus conn s, spica brevi densa petalis caudatis*, and Caspar Bauhine, *Orchis flore globoso* It grows common in Helvetia

7 The Lesser Lizard Flower is, *Orchis bulbis indivisis nectarii labio ... fido reflexo crenato cornu brevi, petalis conniventibus* Sauvages calls it, *Orchis bulbis indivisis, labello trifido ... lacinula media longiore ... tis brevior*, Caspar Bauhine, *Orchis odorata ... minor*, also, *Orchis odore hirci minor, spica purpurascente*, Ray, *Tragorchis minor, flore fulginoso*, also, *Orchis barbata foetida minor, flo... albo*, and Lobel, *Tragorchis minor et verior germanica* It grows naturally in pasture grounds in England, and most of the southern countries of Europe, also in the East

8 Female Foolstones is, *Orchis bulbis indivisis, nectarii labio quadrifido crenulato cornu obtuso, petalis omnibus conniventibus* Van Royen calls it, *Orchis ... labello ... crenulato cornu obtuso*, Caspar Bauhine, *Orchis morio foemina*, Fuchsius, *Tragorchis ... minus*, Haller, *Orchis ... cucullo clauso ... crenulato*, and Gerard, *Cynosorchis morio foemina* It grows naturally in meadows, moist pasture, under bushes, in woods, &c in England, and most parts of Europe

9 Male Foolstones is, *Orchis bulbis indivisis nectarii labio quadrilobo crenulato cornu obtuso, petalis dorsalibus reflexis* Caspar Bauhine calls it, *Orchis morio mas, foliis maculatis* also *Orchis foliis sessilibus maculatis*, Cammerarius, *Testiculus 4* and Gerard, *Cynosorchis morio mas* It grows common in meadows and pastures in England, and most parts of Europe

10 Little Purple-flowered Orchis is, *Orchis bulbis indivisis, nectarii labio quadrifido punctis scabro cornu obtuso, petalis distinctis* Tournefort calls it, *Orchis militaris pratensis humilior*, Caspar Bauhine, *Cynosorchis militaris pratensis humilior*, Clusius, *Orchis Pannonica*, Gerard, *Cynosorchis minor Pannonica*, and Parkinson, *Cynosorchis militaris Pannonica* It grows naturally in dry pastures, and sterile and chalky soils in England, and most of the southern parts of Europe

11 The Man Orchis is, *Orchis bulbis indivisis, nectarii labio quinquefido ... scabro cornu obtuso, petalis confluentibus* Caspar Bauhine calls it, *Cynosorchis latifolia, hiante cucullo, major*, also, *Cynosorchis latifolia, hiante cucullo, minor*, also, *Orchis ... referens*, John Bauhine, *Orchis galea et alis cinerea*, also, *Orchis magna, foliis latis galea fusca vel nigricante*, Fuchsius, *Orchis mas latifolia*, Tournefort, *Orchis militaris major*, Columna, *Orchis zoophora cercopithecum exprimens* Parkinson, *Cynosorchis latifolia minor*, and Gerard, *Cynosorchis major altera* It delights in chalky soils, and grows common in meadows and pasture-grounds in England, and most of the temperate parts of Europe

12 Male Handed Orchis is, *Orchis bulbis subpalmatis rectis, nectarii cornu conico labio trilobo lateribus reflexo, bracteis flore longioribus* In the *Hortus Cliffort* it is termed, *Orchis radicibus palmatis, bracteis flore longioribus nectarii labio trifido, cornu germinibus breviore* Caspar Bauhine calls it, *Orchis palmata pratensis latifolia, longis calcaribus*, also, *Orchis palmata palustris latifolia*, also, *Orchis palmata montana altera*, also *Orchis palmata palustris maculata*, Gerard, *Palma Christi mas* and Parkinson, *Orchis palmata mas, sive palma Christi mas* It grows naturally in meadows and pastures in England, and most parts of Europe

13 Female Handed Orchis is, *Orchis bulbis palmatis ... nectarii cornu germinibus breviore*

*vicre l..o plano, pet..'s do. ia.ibu. datuis* Caspar Bauhine calls it, *O chis palmata pt a.e.sis ma culata*, also, *Orchis palmata montana n acu'ata*, Dodonæus, *Satyr um basilicum femina*, Gerard, *Palma Christi femina* and Parkinson, *Orchis palmata fœmina, f p.n. a Crrist fæmina, foliis maculatis* It grows com non in moist pastures and meadows in England, and most countries of Europe

14 Red Handed *Orchis* is, *Orchis bulbis pal matis, nectarii cornu setaceo ge min bus longiore labio trifido petalis duobus patentissimis* In the *Hortus Cliffort* it is termed, *Orchis radicibus palmatis, bracteis longitudine floris, nectarii labio trifido, seta germ nibus longiore* Caspar Bauhine calls it, *Orchis palmata minor, calcaribus oblongis*, also, *Orchis palmata angustifolia n inor*, also, *Orchis palmata pratensis max ma*, Fuchsius, *Satyrium basilicum mas*, Gerard, *Se.apias n.inor n entc fore*, and Parkinson, *Orchis palmata minor, fore rubro* It grows n turally in meadows and upland pastures in England, and most parts of Europe

15 Austrian Handed *Orchis* is, *Orchis bulbis subpalmatis rectis, nectarii cornu conico, labio ovato subtrilobo, bracteis longitudine floris* Caspar Bauhine calls it, *Orchis palmata, sambuci odore*, and Clusius, *Orcais Pannonica* 8 It grows naturally in Austria, and many parts of Europe

16 Sweet-scented *Orchis* is, *Orchis bulbis palmatis, nectarii cornu recurvo, labio ovato acuto, foliis linear bus* Caspar Bauhine calls it, *Orchis palmata angustifolia minor odoratissima* It grows naturally in Germany, France, and Italy

17 Yellow Virginian *Orchis* is, *Orcnis bulbis palmatis, nectarii cornu fusiform longitudine germinis, labio trifido integerrimo* Morison calls it, *Orchis palmata elegans lutea Virginiana, cum lo gis calcaribus lute s* It is a native of Virginia

18 Rose coloured *Orchis* is, *Orchis b lb s palmat s, nectarii cornu conico labio obsolete tı lobo serrato, petalis dorsalibus reflexis* Seguier calls it, *Orchis palmata lutea, floris labio maculato* It grows common in most parts of Europe

19 Purple Bird's Nest is, *Orcnis bulbis fasciculatis filiformibus, nectarii l b o ov. o i .egerrimo* Sauvages calls it, *Orchis radic bus ... tets flo e brev oribus, labello trifido oblongo, ... permınibus ... ore*, Caspar Bauhine, *O. ... a violacea*, Haller, *Limodorum*, Clusius, *Limo... Austriacum*, Gerard, *Nidus avis flore & caule purpureo violaceo*, and Parkinson, *Nidus avis purpureus* It grows naturally in dry meadows and shady places in England, Germany, France, and Italy

20 White-heeled American *Orchis* is, *Orchis nectarii cornu longitudine germinis labio ovali emarginato, caule aphyllo, fol.s ovalibus* Gronovius calls it, *Orch s foliis radicalibus bin. ovalibus, galea ... nectarii labio ovato integerrimo*, also, *Orchis foliis inferioribus ovat s superioribus ovato-oblongis, floribus ex al s super or bus*, and Clayton, *Orchis flore pulcherrimo magno speciso, nectarii galea saturati cæruleâ, calcari luteo, fol s amp s oblongo-ovatis saturate viridibus* It grows naturally in Virginia

*Orchis* is of the class and order *Gynandria Diandria*, and the characters are, C... and Order in the Linnæan System.

1 Calyx The spathæ are vague, the spadix is simple, there is no perianthium

2 Corolla is five petals, three of which are exterior, and two inner, they rise upwards, meet at top, and form a helmet

The nectarium is of one leaf, fixed to the lower side of the receptacle, between the division of the petals The upper lip is short and erect, the under lip is large, broad, and spreading, the tube is nutant, and shaped like a horn

3 Stamina are two very short slender filaments sitting on the pistil, having erect oval antheræ, situated under the upper lip of the nectarium

4 Pistillum consists of an oblong contorted germen situated below the flower, and a very short style fastened to the upper lip of the nectarium, with a compressed obtuse stigma

5 Pericarpium is an oblong, tricarinated, trivalvate capsule, containing one cell, and opening on the three sides, but joined at the top and bottom

6 Semina The seeds are numerous, small, and scrobiforme.

## CHAP. CCCXV.

## *ORIGANUM*, MARJORAM

THE hardy sorts of Marjoram are generally cultivated in kitchen gardens for broths and soups, and more frequently raised in plenty to give a fragrance to ointments, and for medicinal purposes But as in these species there are some singularities which the curious catch at, it might be thought improper were they to be omitted in this place

The hardy perennial sorts of Marjoram are,

Species
1 Common Wild Marjoram
2 Pot Marjoram
3 Winter Sweet Marjoram

Description of the Common Wild Marjoram

1 Common Wild Marjoram This rises with several square, hairy, ligneous stalks to the height of about a foot and a half The principal leaves are oval, and grow opposite on short footstalks, having several smaller attending them at the joints The flowers are produced from the ends and sides of the stalks, they grow in roundish spikes, and many of these will be clustered together so as to form a large panicle, their colour is a pale red, they come out in June and July, and ripen their seeds in the autumn

There is a variety of this species with beautifully-variegated leaves, one with white and another with purple flowers, and these sorts are chiefly coveted for the pleasure garden Var...

2 Pot Marjoram This hath several slender, ... ligneous stalks about two feet long The ... leaves are heart-shaped, oval, and grow on short

footstalks

root talks The flowers are produced in oblong spikes from the ends of the branches; many of these spikes are collected together so as to form a largish tuft; their colour is white, having a tint of purple; they appear in June and July, and ripen their seeds in the autumn

Its variety. Of this species there is a variegated variety that is much esteemed

Winter Sweet Marjoram described. 3 Winter Sweet Marjoram This hath many four-cornered, branching, hairy, purplish stalks about a foot and a half long The leaves are oval, obtuse, hairy, and grow opposite on short footstalks The flowers are produced in long clustered spikes; they are small, of a white colour, come out in July, and ripen their seeds in the autumn

Variety. This plant is often called Pot Marjoram, and there is a variety of it with variegated leaves, which is coveted for the pleasure garden

All these species are finely scented, and many prefer them for nosegays, especially the last, before any other aromatic whatever

Method of raising them. They are all easily propagated by dividing of the roots in the autumn, and will grow in any soil or situation, though they seem to like a dry soil best

They are also easily encreased by sowing the seeds, but this method is seldom practised, unless large quantities are wanted for kitchen and medicinal purposes

There is an oil prepared from these herbs that is admirable against the cramp

Titles. 1 Common or Wild Marjoram is titled, *Origanum spicis subrotundis paniculatis conglomeratis, bracteis calyce longioribus ovatis* In the *Hortus Cliffort* it is termed, *Origanum foliis ovatis, spicis laxis erectis confertis paniculatis* Caspar Bauhine calls it, *Origanum sylvestre*, John Bauhine, *Origanum vulgare spontaneum*, Gerard, *Origanum Anglicum*, and Parkinson, *Marjorana sylvestris* It grows naturally in England, and many parts of Europe and also in Canada

2 Pot Marjoram is, *Origanum spicis oblongis aggregatis hirsutis, foliis cordatis tomentosis* Caspar Bauhine calls it, *Origanum onites*, Gerard, *Marjorana major Anglica*, and Parkinson, *Marjorana lat folia, sive major Anglica* It grows naturally in many parts of England

3 Winter Sweet Marjoram is, *Origanum spicis longis pedunculatis aggregatis, bracteis longitudine calycum* Caspar Bauhine calls it, *Origanum Heracleoticum, cunila gallinacea Plinii*, and Lobel, *Orega, origanum Heracleoticum, cunila* It grows naturally in Greece, Italy, Portugal, and Spain

Class and order in the Linnæan system. *Origanum* is of the class and order *Didynamia Gymnospermia*, and the characters are,

The characters. 1 CALYX The involucrum is composed of several oval coloured leaves lying over each other The perianthium is various and unequal

2 COROLLA is a ringent petal The tube is cylindrical and compressed, the upper lip is erect, plane, obtuse, and emarginated, the lower lip is trifid, being cut into three nearly equal segments

3 STAMINA consist of four filiforme filaments the length of the corolla, of which two are longer than the others, having simple antheræ

4 PISTILLUM consists of a quadrifid germen, a filiforme style inclining to the upper lip of the corolla, and a bifid stigma

5 PERICARPIUM There is none The seeds are contained in the bosom of the calyx

6 SEMINA The seeds are oval, and four in number

# CHAP. CCCXVI.

## *ORNITHOGALUM*, STAR of BETHLEHEM.

Species. OF this genus are,

1 Common Star of Bethlehem
2 Broad-leaved Star of Bethlehem
3 Spiked Star of Bethlehem with a greenish flower
4 Spiked Star of Bethlehem with a white flower
5 Pyramidical or Largest-spiked Flower of Bethlehem
6 Yellow Star of Bethlehem
7 The Least Yellow Star of Bethlehem
8 Neapolitan *Ornithogalum*
9 Arabian *Ornithogalum*

Common. 1 Common Star of Bethlehem The root is a large, roundish, white bulb. The leaves are long, narrow, keel shaped, spreading, and marked with white streaks down the middle the whole length The stalks are about five inches high The flowers come out in umbels from the tops of the stalks, having long slender footstalks; the petals are of a milky-white colour within, but on the outside are marked with broad stripes of green; they appear in April and May, and are succeeded by roundish three-cornered capsules, containing ripe seeds, in July

Broad-leaved. 2 Broad-leaved Star of Bethlehem This is often called Alexandrian Lily The root is a very large roundish bulb The leaves are very broad, long, sword-shaped, and spread on the ground The stalk is upright, thick, firm, and sometimes near a yard high The flowers come out in long loose spikes from the tops of the stalks; they are large, extremely numerous in the spike, and of a fine white colour; they appear in June, but are not succeeded by ripe seeds in England

Spiked. 3 Spiked Star of Bethlehem with a greenish flower This is often called Onion Asphodel The root is a largish onion-like bulb The leaves are carinated, long, narrow, and spread on the ground The stalk is upright, naked, simple, smooth, and a foot and a half high The flowers come out in long loose spikes from the tops of the stalks, growing on long, slender, spreading footstalks,

footstalks, they are of a yellowish-green colour, and finely scented, they appear in May, and after the flowers are fallen, the footstalks by degrees become erect, to support the capsules, which contain ripe seeds in August

This plant is said to be of singular service against the yellow jaundice

Spiked, 4 Spiked Star of Bethlehem with a white flower The root is a moderate-sized, roundish bulb The leaves are narrow, and spreading The flowers are collected into oblong spikes at the tops of the stalks, they are of a white colour, and grow on footstalks, which spread out from the main stem, they appear in May and June, and are sometimes succeeded by ripe seeds in August

Pyramidical, 5 Pyramidical or Largest-spiked Star of Bethlehem The root is a very large oval bulb The leaves are long, keeled, and of a dark green colour The stalk is upright, firm, naked, and often a yard high The flowers grow on longish footstalks, and are collected into large pyramidical spikes at the tops of the stalks, they are of a white colour, appear in June, and are succeeded by roundish capsules, containing ripe seeds, in August

Yellow, 6 Yellow Star of Bethlehem The root is a small, viscous, roundish bulb The radical leaves are usually but two or three, they are keeled, half a foot long, and of a dark green colour The stalk is angular, naked, and about six inches high The flowers come out in umbels from the tops of the stalks, attended by two leaves like the radical ones, but smaller The flowers in the umbel are six or eight only, which grow on long slender footstalks, they are yellow, or of a bright-saffron colour on their inside, but on the outside usually striped with green, they appear so early as April, and are succeeded by small triangular capsules, containing ripe seeds, in July

Least Yellow Star of Bethlehem 7 The Least Yellow Star of Bethlehem The bulbs of this plant are small, not larger than pease The radical leaves are generally one or two only, narrow, keeled, greyish-coloured, and about four inches long The stalks are slender, angular, and three inches high The flowers come out in umbels from the tops of the stalks, attended by two narrow, keeled, greyish leaves, they are small, and grow on longish footstalks, are of a yellow colour within, but on the outside of a purplish green, they appear in May, and are succeeded by small triangular capsules, containing ripe seeds, in July or August

Neapolitan, 8 Neapolitan *Ornithogalum*, or Star Flower of Naples The root is a large, oblong compressed bulb The leaves are long, narrow, keeled, three or four in number, and of a dark green colour The stalks are upright, thick, succulent, and a foot and a half high The flowers come out in loose spikes from the tops of the stalks, they are white within, of an ash-coloured green on the outside, and tipped with white, they appear in April and May, and are succeeded by very large, roundish, triangular capsules, which will be so heavy before the seeds are ripe as to weigh down the stalk The seeds ripen in August

and Arabian Ornithogalum described. 9 Arabian *Ornithogalum* This is often called the Star-flower of Constantinople, also, Lily of Alexandria The root is a very large, roundish, flat-bottomed bulb The leaves are long, broad, keeled, of a deep-green colour, and embrace each other with their base The stalk is upright, firm, and a foot and a half high The flowers are produced in kind of umbels from the tops of the stalks, they are large, and of a white colour This species does not flower often in our climate, when it does, its bloom is usually in May

All these sorts are propagated by offsets from the roots, most of which will throw out abundance, if they are permitted to stand The best time for removing them, and taking off the offsets, is the end of July, or August, soon after the seeds are ripe, and the stalks and leaves are decayed They love a light fresh soil, but the most tender of them will grow in almost any soil or situation, provided it be not too wet They should all be transplanted every other year, and the roots cleared of all offsets, if you would chuse to have them blow large and fair, nevertheless, if encrease be your aim, you may let them stand three or four years, and the multiplication of the bulbs will be amazing, especially of the common sorts They are all in esteem on account of their being hardy, and, from the starlike appearance of the flowers, have a pretty effect with others about the same size Method of propagating them.

They are also propagated by sowing the seeds, but as they encrease fast by offsets, and the seedling plants are hardly to be brought to blow in less time than four years, the latter method is not worth putting into practice

1 Common Star of Bethlehem is titled *Ornithogalum floribus corymbosis, pedunculis scapo altioribus, filamentis emarginatis* Caspar Bauhine calls it, *Ornithogalum umbellatum medium angustifolium*; John Bauhine, *Ornithogalum vulgare et verius, major & minus*, and Gerard, *Ornithogalum vulgare* It grows common in meadows, pastures, and woods in England, Germany, France, and the East Titles.

2 Broad-leaved Star of Bethlehem is, *Ornithogalum racemo longissimo, foliis lanceolato ensiformibus* Caspar Bauhine calls it, *Ornithogalum latifolium & maximum* It grows naturally in Arabia and Egypt

3 Spiked Star of Bethlehem with a greenish flower is, *Ornithogalum racemo longissimo, filamentis lanceolatis, pedunculis floriferis patentibus æqualibus fructiferis scapo approximato* In the *Iter Scanicum* it is termed, *Ornithogalum racemo longissimo, filamentis dilatato-linearibus, capsulis erectis* Caspar Bauhine calls it, *Ornithogalum angustifolium majus, floribus ex albo virescentibus*, Haller, *Ornithogalum spica longissima, filamentis triangularibus*; Clusius, *Ornithogalum majus*, also, *Ornithogalum Pyrenaicum*, Gerard, *Asphodelus bulbosus*, and Parkinson, *Asphodelus bulbosus Galeni*, sive *Ornithogalum majus flore subvirente* It is a native of England, growing with us by way sides, meadows, and pastures, it also grows naturally on the Alps of Helvetia, Geneva, and the Pyrenees

4 Spiked Star of Bethlehem with a white flower is, *Ornithogalum racemo oblongo filamentis lanceolatis membranaceis, pedunculis floribusque patentibus* Caspar Bauhine calls it, *Ornithogalum majus spicatum, flore albo*, and Dodonæus, *Ornithogalum Narbonense* It grows naturally in the cultivated fields of France and Italy

5 Pyramidical or Largest spiked Flower of Bethlehem is, *Ornithogalum racemo conico, floribus numerosis adscendentibus* Caspar Bauhine calls it, *Ornithogalum angustifolium spicatum maximum* It grows naturally on the hills of Portugal

6 Yellow Star of Bethlehem is, *Ornithogalum scapo anguloso diphyllo, pedunculis umbellatis simplicibus* In the *Hortus Cliffort* it is termed, *Ornithogalum scapo diphyllo, pedunculis simplicibus terminalibus, filamentis omnibus subulatis* Caspar Bauhine calls it, *Ornithogalum luteum*, and Gerard, *Ornithogalum luteum seu cepe agraria* It grows naturally on the borders of cultivated fields, meadows, and pastures in England, and most countries of Europe

7 The Least Yellow Star of Bethlehem is, *Ornithogalum scapo angustoso diphyllo, pedunculis umbellatis*

*umbellatis ramosis* Caspar Bauhine calls it, *Ornithogalum luteum minus* It grows common on the borders of cultivated fields in most parts of Europe

8 Neapolitan *Ornithogalum*, or Star-flower of Naples, is, *Ornithogalum floribus secundis pendulis, nectario stramineo campaniformi* In the *Hortus Cliffort* it is termed, *Ornithogalum floribus secundis pendulis, filamentis latis emarginatis* Caspar Bauhine calls it, *Ornithogalum exoticum, magno flore minori innato*, and Clusius, *Ornithogalum Neapolitanum* It grows naturally about Naples

9 Arabian *Ornithogalum* is, *Ornithogalum floribus corymbosis, pedunculis scapo humilioribus, filamentis emarginatis* Caspar Bauhine calls it, *Ornithogalum umbellatum maximum*, and Clusius, *Ornithogalum Arabicum* It grows naturally in Arabia.

*Ornithogalum* is of the class and order *Hexandria Monogynia*, and the characters are, Class and order in the Linnæan system

1 CALYX. There is none

2 COROLLA is six spear-shaped petals, which are erect from the base to the middle, but above the middle plane and spreading, they are permanent, but lose their colour The characters

3 STAMINA are six erect filaments, dilated at their base, and shorter than the corolla, having simple antheræ

4 PISTILLUM consists of an angular germen, an awl-shaped permanent style, and an obtuse stigma

5 PERICARPIUM is a roundish, angular, trivalvate capsule, containing three cells

6 SEMINA The seeds are many, and roundish.

## CHAP. CCCXVII

## *OROBUS*, BITTER VETCH.

THE species of *Orobus* are all perennials, growing wild in woods and commons in different parts of the world. They are most of them very pretty flowers, and highly proper to join in our collection of perennials, and contribute much to the enrichment of the show in flower gardens of any sort I shall therefore arrange them thus.

Species.

1 The Vernal *Orobus*, or Bitter Vetch.
2 Tuberous-rooted Bitter Vetch
3 Narrow-leaved Bitter Vetch
4 Vetch-leaved Bitter Vetch
5 Pyrenean Bitter Vetch.
6 English Bitter Vetch
7 Bitter Vetch, called Bastard *Lathyrus*.
8 Bitter Vetch of Thrace
9 Siberian Bitter Vetch

These are all the species of this genus yet known, and which contain several varieties

Description of the Vernal Bitter Vetch

1 Vernal Bitter Vetch This is a low-growing plant The stalks are unbranching, and will grow to about a foot high The leaves are not large, though of the pinnated kind, the lobes are oval, and acutely pointed, at the bottom of the footstalk is situated a small leaf, which is by botanists called a *stipula*, and in this species is pointed a little like an arrow The flowers grow from the wings of the leaves on footstalks, they are of the butterfly kind, and disposed in short spikes; they flower in March, and sometimes in February, and are usually succeeded by good seeds in May or June.

Its varieties

*This species includes the following varieties:*

The Purple
The Deep-Blue
The Pale-Blue Bitter Vetch

It is observable, that the Deep-Blue sort is of a fine purple colour at its first appearance, and alters to a blue when in full blow

Tuberous Bitter Vetch described

2 Tuberous Bitter Vetch This grows naturally in many parts of England, and is called Wood Pease, and Heath Pease It has a thick knotty root, which in some varieties is very tuberous and fleshy From these roots rise the stalks, which are unbranching, angular, and about a foot long The leaves are pinnated, each being composed of about four pair of spear-shaped smooth lobes, at the base of each leaf is situated a semi-sagittated *stipula*, as in the former species The flowers grow from the upper parts of the stalks on long footstalks, their colour is red, but they die often to a purple, they will be in blow in April or May, and produce good seeds about June

Of this species there is a variety with variegated flowers, which grow in a moderately large spike Variety

3 Narrow-leaved Bitter Vetch This plant hath a single stalk, which is garnished with leaves composed of two or three pair of very narrow spear-shaped lobes, the stipulæ are awl-shaped The flowers grow in small spikes, their colour is yellow, and there is a variety of it with purplish flowers Narrow-leaved,

4 Vetch-leaved Bitter Vetch This hath several branching stalks that will grow to be two feet long The leaves stand singly at the joints, they are pinnated, and each is composed of about six pair of oblong oval lobes The flowers grow from the wings of the stalks on long footstalks, each of which usually supports five or six flowers, their colour is purple; they will be in blow in May, and ripen their seeds in July Vetch-leaved,

5 Pyrenean Bitter Vetch The stalks of this plant are smooth and branching, and will grow to about a foot and a half long The leaves are composed of two or three pair of spear-shaped lobes, which have strong veins running from the base to the point The flowers rise from the wings of the leaves on long footstalks, and are formed into a kind of loose spike, they are of a purple colour, will be in blow in May, and ripen their seeds in July Pyrenean,

6 English Bitter Vetch This hath several branching, English,

branching, hairy stalks about a foot and a half long, and trail on the ground The leaves grow singly at the joints, they are finely pinnated, each being composed of seven or eight pair of narrow lobes ranged close together along the midrib The flowers grow from the wings of the leaves in close spikes, their colour is purple, they will be in blow in June, and ripen their seeds in July or August

Bastard Bitter Vetch, 7 Bastard Bitter Vetch This plant hath a few erect branching stalks about a foot high The leaves grow opposite by pairs, and sit close to the stalks, they are oval, pointed, smooth, and of a shining green colour The flowers grow from the wings of the leaves on short footstalks, they are formed into spikes, and often several of them rise from the same place, their colour is a clear blue they will be in blow in June, and ripen their seeds in August

Bitter Vetch of Thrace, 8 Bitter Vetch of Thrace This plant hath an unbranching, hairy, trailing stalk The leaves grow by pairs, have footstalks, are of an oval figure, and very hairy The flowers adorn the tops of the stalks in small spikes, they are of a fine blue colour, and are succeeded by hairy pods, containing the seeds

and Siberian Bitter Vetch describ d 9 Siberian Bitter Vetch The stalks are unbranching, and grow to about a foot and a half long The leaves are composed of about four or five pair of oval oblong lobes, at the base of which is the stipula embracing the stalk The flowers grow from the wings of the leaves on short footstalks, their colour is purple, and being large they make a fine show, they will be in blow in April, and are succeeded by long inflated pods, which will have ripe seeds in June

Culture All these sorts are easily propagated by seeds, or by parting of the roots The seeds should be sown in the autumn, and they will readily come up the ensuing spring, whereas, if they are kept until the spring, they often lie in the ground until the spring after When the plants come up, keep them clean from weeds, water them in dry weather, and in July or August, if a moist day happens, plant them out in beds at about half a foot asunder The summer following keep them clean from weeds, and early in the autumn, on a moist day, remove them to the places where they are designed to flower, which will be the spring following

These plants are also encreased by parting of the roots, the best time for which is early in the autumn, when the stalks begin to decay The weakest offsets should be planted out in the nursery-ground, like the seedlings, to gain strength, for a year, whilst the strongest may be set out where they are designed to flower, which will be the spring following.

All these plants like a loose rich soil, and a shady situation, tho' they will grow and flourish almost any where, and their being so easy of culture, and pretty plants, makes them very valuable

Titles 1 The Vernal Bitter Vetch is titled, *Orobus foliis pinnatis ovatis, stipulis semisagittatis integerrimis, caule simplici* In the *Hortus Cliffort* it is termed, *Orobus caule simplicissimo, foliolis pluribus ovatis acutis* Caspar Bauhine calls it, *Orobus sylvaticus purpureus vernus* It grows naturally in woodlands in the northern parts of Europe

2 Tuberous-rooted Bitter Vetch is, *Orobus foliis pinnatis lanceolatis, stipulis semisagittatis integerrimis, caule simplici* In the *Hortus Cliffort* it is termed, *Orobus caule simplicissimo, foliolis pluribus lanceolatis integris* Caspar Bauhine calls it, *Astragalus sylvaticus, foliis oblongis glabris*, and Lobelius, *Lathyrus angustifolius, radice tuberosa* It grows naturally in meadows, pastures, woods, and hedges in England, and several of the northern parts of Europe

3 Narrow-leaved Bitter Vetch is, *Orobus foliis bijugis ensiformibus, stipulis subulatis, caule simplici* It grows naturally in Siberia

4 Vetch leaved Bitter Vetch is, *Orobus caule ramoso, foliis sejugis ovato oblongis* Caspar Bauhine calls it, *Orobus sylvaticus, viciæ foliis*, and Clusius, *Orobus Pannonicus* It grows in most of the northern parts of Europe

5 Pyrenean Bitter Vetch is, *Orobus caule ramoso, foliis bijugis lanceolatis nervosis, stipulis subspinosis* Tournefort calls it, *Orobus Pyrenaicus, foliis nervosis*, and Plukenet, *Orobus Pyrenaicus latifolius nervosus* It grows naturally on the Pyrenean mountains

6 English Bitter Vetch is, *Orobus caule ramoso hirsuto decumbente, foliis subseptemjugis* Ray calls it, *Orobus sylvaticus nostras* It grows naturally in the north part of England, and in Wales

7 Bastard Bitter Vetch is, *Orobus foliis conjugatis subsessilibus, stipulis dentatis* Amman calls it, *Lathyroides erecta, folio ovato acuminato, caeruleis viciæ floribus et siliquis, Sibirica* It is a native of Siberia

8 Bitter Vetch of Thrace is, *Orobus foliis conjugatis petiolatis, stipulis integris* In the *Hortus Cliffort* it is termed, *Orobus caule simplicissimo, foliolis binis ovatis* Boerhaave calls it, *Orobus latifolius repens, flore cæruleo, foliis et siliquis hirsutis*, and Buxbaum, *Orobus sylvaticus, foliis circa caulem auriculatis* It is a native of Thrace

9 Siberian Bitter Vetch is, *Orobus foliis pinnatis ovato oblongis, stipulis rotundato-lunatis dentatis, caule simplici* Caspar Bauhine calls it, *Orobus Alpinus latifolius* It grows in the mountainous parts of Siberia, also on the Pyrenean mountains

*Orobus* is of the class and order *Diadelphia Decandria*, and the characters are,

1 CALYX is a monophyllous, tubulous, withering perianthium, it is obtuse at the base, and divided at the top into five parts, the three lower segments being acute, and the two upper shorter and obtuse Class and order in the Linnæan system. The characters

2 COROLLA is papilionaceous. The vexillum is heart-shaped, and reflexed both at the point and sides, the alæ are connivent, assurgent, oblong, and almost as long as the vexillum, the carina is bifid, acuminated, and assurgent; the borders are connivent, parallel, and compressed, and the bottom is swollen.

3 STAMINA are diadelphous and rising Nine filaments join in a body, the other stands separate, their antheræ are oblong

4 PISTILLUM The germen is cylindric and compressed, the style is filiforme, bent, and rising, the stigma is narrow, downy, and fastened in the middle by the inner edge to the top of the style

5 PERICARPIUM is a long, taper, pointed pod of one cell

6 SEMINA The seeds are many, and round sh

CHAP.

# CHAP. CCCXVIII.

## *OROBANCHE*, BROOM RAPE.

Species.

OF this genus are,

1 Common Broom Rape
2 Branched Broom Rape
3 Smooth Broom Rape
4 Virginian Broom Rape
5 One-flowered Broom Rape

Deſcription of Common

1 Common Broom Rape The root is thick, ſcaly, fleſhy, fibrated, blackiſh without, and of a yellowiſh-purple colour within From this thick bulbous part ariſes an upright, thick, ſimple, brown-coloured, fleſhy ſtalk, to the height of about a foot The leaves are ſmall, pointed, of a brown colour, and ſit cloſe to the ſides of the ſtalks The flowers are produced from the tops of the ſtalks in ſpikes, they are of a yellowiſh-brown colour, and ſhew themſelves in the month of June

and Branched Broom Rape

2 Branched Broom Rape The ſtalk is thick, upright, branching near the top, and a foot high The leaves are ſmall, narrow, pointed, and ſit cloſe to the ſtalk. The flowers come out in ſpikes from the ends of the branches they are of a bluiſh colour, and uſually appear in June

Its varieties.

There is a variety of this ſpecies with white, and another with purpliſh flowers There is a difference alſo in the ſize of the flowers and plant, the flowers of ſome being nearly as long again as others The title, however, points out the ſtanding properties of this ſpecies, the chief of which are, that the ſtalks are branching, and the flowers are cut at the brim into five ſegments

Smooth,

3 Smooth Broom Rape The ſtalk is thick, ſimple, ſmooth, and of a bluiſh colour There are a few ſhort membranes by way of leaves, and ſome of the ſtalks have none at all The flowers are large, grow in ſpikes at the tops of the ſtalks, are of a purple colour, and appear about the ſame time with the former

Virginian

4 Virginian Broom Rape The ſtalk is thick, more ligneous than the other kinds, and divides into a few branches near the top The flowers are ſmall, indented in four parts at the top, and thinly arranged along the ſides of the branches

and One-flowered Broom Rape deſcribed

5 One-flowered Broom Rape The ſtalk is ſimple, five or ſix inches high, and wholly bare of leaves The flowers come out ſingly from the tops of the ſtalks, are large, deflexed, and of a pale-yellow colour

Its variety

There is a variety of this ſpecies with bluiſh flowers

Method of propagation

The firſt two ſpecies are natives of England, and have been reported to grow no-where but among Broom, and even at the very roots of that ſhrub But this is a miſtake for they have been found growing in dry meadows and paſtures where no Broom was to be ſeen I have never cultivated any of them, but I make no doubt, that if they are ſought for where they naturally grow, and the roots are taken up after they have flowered, with the mould at them, and ſet in dry light earth, they will take to ſuch ſoil, and ſhew their flowers the ſummer following

The laſt three ſpecies are of foreign growth, Whoever, therefore, is deſirous of theſe, muſt procure ſome to be planted in pots in their native countries, with the mould at their roots, and after their arrival, he may turn them out, together with the mould, in light, dry, well-ſheltered places, to take their chance for growing

How far theſe ſpecies are to be encreaſed by ſeeds, I am not certain, having never made experiments that way, whereſore I ſhall ſay no more of their culture than conjecturing, that, if good ſeeds are procured of all the ſorts, they may be made to grow and produce good plants, by ſowing them in light, dry, ſandy earth, in warm, well-ſheltered places

1 Common Broom Rape is titled, *Orobanche caule ſimpliciſſimo, pubeſcente, ſtaminibus ſubexſertis* In the *Hortus Cliffort* it is termed, *Orobanche caule ſimpliciſſimo* Sauvages calls it, *Orobanche caule ſimplici, bracteis longioribus*, Caſpar Bauhine, *Orobanche major caryophyllum olens*, Cluſius, *Orobanche I* and Lobel, *Rapum geniſtæ* It grows naturally in dry meadows and paſtures, but chiefly among Broom, in England and many countries of Europe Titles.

2 Branched Broom Rape is, *Orobanche caule ramoſo, corollis quinquefidis* In the *Hortus Cliffort* it is termed, *Orobanche caule ramoſo* Caſpar Bauhine calls it, *Orobanche ramoſa*, Cammerarius, *Orobanche* It grows naturally in tillage fields and dry ſoils in England and moſt parts of Europe

3 Smooth Broom Rape is, *Orobanche caule ſimpliciſſimo lævi, ſtaminibus exſertis* Sauvages calls it, *Orobanche caule ſimplici cæruleo, bracteis brevibus*, Caſpar Bauhine, *Orobanche majore flore*; and John Bauhine, *Orobanche magna purpurea Monſpeſſulana* It grows naturally near Montpelier

4 Virginian Broom Rape is, *Orobanche caule ramoſo, corollis quadridentatis* Gronovius calls it *Orobanche caule ramoſo, floribus alternantibus*, and Moriſon, *Orobanche minor Virginiana lignoſior, per totum caulem floribus minoribus onuſta* It grows naturally in Virginia

5 One-flowered Broom Rape is, *Orobanche caule unifloro, calyce nudo* Gronovius calls it, *Dentariæ, ſ anblato cordi aſſinis, flore pallide cæruleo*, Plukenet, *Gentiana minor aquatica, flore ſimplici amplo deflexo pallide flaveſcente*, Ray, *Orobanche aut helleborine aſſinis Marilandica, caule nudo, unico in ſummitate flore*, and Micheli, *Aphyllon* It is a native of Virginia

*Orobanche* is of the claſs and order *Didynamia Angioſpermia*, and the characters are, Claſs and order in the Linnæan ſyſtem

1 CALYX is a monophyllous, erect, coloured, permanent perianthium, cut at the top into five ſegments The characters

2 COROLLA is a ringent petal The tube is inclinated, large, and ventricoſe The limb is patent The upper lip is concave, wide, open, and

and emarginated, the lower lip is reflexed, and cut into three ſegments, which are nearly equal

3 STAMINA are four awl ſhaped filaments under the upper lip, two of which are longer than the others, having erect, connivent antheræ, which are ſhorter than the limb

The nectarium is a gland ſituated at the baſe of the germen

4 PISTILLUM conſiſts of an oblong germen, a ſimple ſtyle the length and ſituation of the ſtamina, and a ſemibifid, thick, obtuſe, nutant ſtigma

5 PERICARPIUM is an oval, oblong, acuminated, bivalvate capſule, containing one cell

6 SEMINA. The ſeeds are numerous, and ſmall

## CHAP. CCCXIX.

## ORVALA.

THERE is no Engliſh name for this genus, and only one ſpecies of it, expreſſed in the generical term *Orvala*

This plant deſcribed

The root is fibrous The ſtalks are thick, ſquare, hollow, jointed, and grow to about a yard high The leaves are heart ſhaped, roundiſh, rough, pointed, laciniated on their edges, and the lower ones grow on long footſtalks, but the upper ones ſit cloſer to the ſtalks The flowers come out in whorled cluſters from the joints of the upper parts of the ſtalk, they are large, of a fine purple colour, appear in May and June, and the ſeeds ripen in July and Auguſt

Method of propagation

This ſpecies is eaſily propagated by ſowing the ſeeds, ſoon after they are ripe, in beds of light, moiſt, rich earth, in a ſhady place They will come up in the autumn, and ſtand the winter very well In the ſpring a ſhare of them ſhould be tranſplanted to the places where they are deſigned to remain, leaving the ſtrongeſt plants in the bed at about two feet diſtance from each other These will flower in the autumn, but probably too late for the ſeeds to ripen; the others will flower the early part of the ſummer following, and will be ſucceeded by ripe ſeeds in about ſix weeks after the flowers are fallen

Titles

There being no other ſpecies of this genus it ſtands with the name ſimply *Orvala* Micheli calls it, *Papa Garganica, foliis urticæ oblongis & eleganter inciſis, flore purpureo* It is a native of Italy

Claſs and order in the Linnæan Syſtem

*Orvala* is of the claſs and order *Didynamia Gymnoſpermia*, and the characters are,

The characters

1 CALYX is a monophyllous, tubular, crooked perianthium, indented in five parts at the top, of which the lower denticles are the ſhorteſt

2 COROLLA is one ringent petal The tube is the length of the calyx The upper lip is oblong, arched and indented at the top The lower lip is divided into three ſegments, of which the lateral ones are indented in three parts at the top, the middle ſegment is reniforme, denticulated, and mucronated

3 STAMINA are four awl-ſhaped filaments the length of the corolla, ſecreted by the upper lip, two of which are longer than the others, having didymous antheræ.

4 PISTILLUM conſiſts of a germen divided into four parts, a ſimple ſtyle the length and ſituation of the ſtamina, and a bifid acute ſtigma

5 PERICARPIUM There is none The ſeeds are lodged in the bottom of the calyx

6 SEMINA The ſeeds are four, oval, and reniforme

CHAP

# CHAP CCCXX

## *OSMUNDA*, OSMUND ROYAL, or FLOWERING FERN

THE hardy species of this genus are,

Species
1 Moon-wort
2 Flowering Fern, or Osmund Royal
3 Rough Spleen-wort
4 Stone Fern
5 Northern Fern
6 Virginian Fern

Moon-wort described. 1 Moon-wort The root is composed of several slender, thready fibres, which are black on the outside, but yellow within, and strike deep into the ground From this rises a simple, round, thick, naked stalk, to the height of about six or eight inches About three or four inches from the base is situated one pinnated leaf, composed of about five or six pair of thick, succulent, moon-shaped folioles terminated by an odd one The stalk is slender above the leaf, and supports numerous seed-vessels, which are very elegant, and have a beautiful appearance They shew themselves in May and the early part of June

Flowering Fern described. 2 Flowering Fern, or Osmund Royal The root is composed of numerous fibres of a black colour, which are so implicated or interwoven one with another, as to form the appearance of a solid body in the shape of a heart The leaves are bipinnated, large, smooth, and of a pale-green colour The stalks grow to about a yard high, and divide at the top into many branches for the support of the flowers The seed vessels are numerous, and grow in clusters or spikes the whole length of the branches at the extremity of the leaves, differing in this respect from most others of the Fern kind, which carry their fructifications on the back This species flourishes in July and August

Rough Spleen wort describ d. 3 Rough Spleen-wort The root is large, thick, black, and has numerous fibres, which are implicated, or interwoven one among another The leaves are spear shaped, pinnatifid, and about a foot long The segments are long, narrow, run parallel to each other, are smooth on the upper side, and rough underneath These leaves are all the shew the plant affords It flourishes in July

Description of Stone. 4 Stone Fern The fibres are numerous, tough, and implicated The leaves are supra-decompound, and very large, the pinnæ are roundish, jagged and curled on their edges, and arranged alternately along the mid-rib This is an elegant Fern, and in its greatest beauty in July and August

Northern. 5 Northern or Norway Fern The fibres are thick, black, and very intricately interwoven and mixed with each other The leaves are pinnated, large, and grow on firm footstalks, which are naked for five or six inches from the ground The pinnæ are oblong, narrow, pinnatifid, often of a brown colour, and the whole leaf rises to be near two feet high The stalk is furrowed near the top, and there the fructifications are arranged in a double series, as well as on the back of the folioles, they are extremely numerous, and the whole plant is in perfection in July and August

And Virginian Fern. 6 Virginian Fern The root is fibrous, and possessed of many fleshy tubers, like those of Asphodel The stalk is simple, firm, striated, and about a foot high About five or six inches from the bottom is situated a leaf composed of numerous narrow parts, which are of a brownish-grey colour From the setting-on of this leaf the stalk is more slender, and divides at the top into several branches, each of which supports the seed vessels collected in close spikes

Method of propagating them. The first four species are natives of England, the last grows naturally in Russia, Norway, Sweden, and other northern parts of Europe, but is an elegant plant, and flourishes very well in our gardens. They are all propagated by parting of the roots, the best time for which is the early part of the autumn

The fourth sort grows naturally in the crevices of rocks, stone walls, &c and its culture in gardens is rarely attempted The others thrive extremely well, but delight most in the shade and a moist situation

Titles. 1 Moon wort is titled, *Osmunda scapo caulino solitario, fronde pinnata solitariâ* In the *Hortus Cliffort* it is termed, *Osmunda fronde pinnatâ caulinâ, pinnis lunulatis*, in the *Flora Lapponica*, *Osmunda folio pinnatifido, pinnis lunulatis* Caspar Bauhine calls it, *Lunaria racemosa minor & vulgaris*, also, *Lunaria racemosa major*, also, *Lunaria minor, rutaceo folio* Breynius names it, *Lunaria racemosa minor, adianti folio*, Cammerarius, *Lunaria minor*, and, *Lunaria tertior species* Ray stiles it, *Lunaria minor foliis dissectis*, and Gerard, *Lunaria minor* It grows naturally in some meadows, but delights chiefly in mountainous places, in England and most countries of Europe

2 Flowering Fern, or Osmund Royal is, *Osmunda frondibus bipinnatis apice racemiferis* In the *Flora Suecia* it is termed, *Osmunda scapo paniculato polyphyllo* in the *Hortus Cliffort Osmunda frondibus caulinis simpliciter pinnatis, pinnis lanceolatis* Plumier calls it, *Osmunda regalis*, *Filix florida*, Caspar Bauhine, *Filix ramosa non dentata florida*, Dodonæus, *Filix palustris*, Gronovius, *Filix florida*, *Osmunda regalis, foliis alternis, surculis semiauriferis*, Pluknet, *Filix non dentata florida, foliis claviformis & in summo caule seminibus occultis*, and Morison, *Filix botryitis, Filix florida major Virginiana, pinnulis non dentatis alternatim positis* It inhabits chiefly the sides of rivers and moist places, and in such is found growing in England, most countries of Europe, and in Virginia

3 Rough Spleen-wort is, *Osmunda frondibus lanceolatis pinnatifidis, laciniis confluentibus integerrimis parallelis* In the *Flora Suecia* it is termed, *Pteris frondae pinnatâ lanceolata, laciniis parallelis integerrimis* Van Royen calls it, *Pteris fronde pinnata, foliis linearibus parallelis*, Micheli, *Polypodioides vulgaris foliis angustis*, Caspar Bauhine, *Lonchitis minor*, Cammerarius, *Lonchitis aspera minor*, and Gerard, *Lonchitis aspera* It grows naturally in moist forests and heathy ground in England, Sweden, Germany, and the Pyrenees

4 Stone Fern is, *Osmunda frondibus supradecompositis, pinnis alternis subrotundis incisis* Caspar Bauhine calls it, *Adiantum foliis minutim in oblongum scissis, pediculo viridi* John Bauhine, *Adiantum album tenuifolium, rutæ murariæ accedens*, Ray, *Adiantum album Alpinum crispum*, Plukenet, *Adiantum album floridum, s. Filicula florida Anglica, foliis pluries fertatis acutis* It grows naturally out of rocks, old ruins, and in stoney places, in England, Helvetia, the South of France, and the Pyrenean mountains

5 Northern or Norway Fern is, *Osmunda frondibus pinnatis, pinnis pinnatifidis, scapo fructificante distincto* Caspar Bauhine calls it, *Filix palustris altera, fusco pulvere, hirsuta*, and Amman, *Filicastrum Septentrionale & palustre* It grows naturally in Norway, Russia, Helvetia, and Sweden

6 Virginian Fern is, *Osmunda scapo caulino solitario, fronde supra decompositâ* Gronovius calls it, *Osmunda fronde pinnatâ caulinâ, fructificationibus spicatis*; and Plumier, *Osmunda asphodeli radice* It grows common in Virginia and most parts of North-America

*Class and order in the Linnæan system.* *Osmunda* is of the class *Cryptogamia*, and belongs to Order the First, *Filices*

*The characters* The fruit is the only distinctly visible part of the fructifications, and consists of numerous globose, distinct capsules, arranged in spikes or clusters, which, when come to maturity, open horizontally for the discharge of the seeds

The seeds are numerous, very small, and of an oval figure

## C H A P CCCXXI

## *OSYRIS*, POET's CASSIA.

THERE is only one species of this genus, called Poet's *Cassia*

*This plant described* This species rises with a shrubby, branching stalk, to the height of about two feet The leaves are long, narrow, and sharp-pointed The flowers are small, of a greenish-yellow colour, appear in June, and are succeeded by middle-sized, roundish berries, which are of a bright-red colour when ripe

*Method of propagation* This shrubby plant grows naturally out of rocks, and in sandy, stoney places, in the different parts of the world, and ill relishes the culture of the garden It may be propagated, however, by sowing of the berries, which should be done in the autumn, as soon as they are ripe, in the places where they are designed to remain *Proper situation and soil* The situation should be on the side of some hill, where the soil is rocky, sandy, or gravelly They will be often two or three years before they come up, therefore, a stick should be placed at the time of sowing for a direction, and care should be taken not to disturb the place during that time When the plants make their appearance, they must at first be kept clean from weeds, but should afterwards be permitted to grow wild with the natural produce of the place Being thus situated, they will flower, and be delightful in the autumn by their beautiful red berries, but in gardens, though the shrub may be made to grow and flower, yet the berries, if ever there be any, always drop off while they are green, and before they come to maturity

*Titles* There being no other species of this genus, it stands with the simple name, *Osyris* Loefling calls it, *Osyris foliis linearibus acutis*, Caspar Bauhine, *Osyris frutescens baccifera*, Cammerarius, *Cassia poetica Monspeliensium*, Alpinus, *Cassia Latinorum*, and Gesner, *Cassia Monspelii dicta* It grows naturally in the South of France, Italy, Spain, and on Mount Libanus

*Class and order in the Linnæan system* *Osyris* is of the class and order *Dioecia Triandria*, and the characters are,

*The characters.*

I Male Flowers

1 Calyx is a monophyllous, turbinated perianthium, cut into three equal, oval, acute segments

2 Corolla There is none

3 Stamina are three very short filaments, having small roundish antheræ

II Female Flowers

1 Calyx is a small perianthium, as in the male, placed above the germen

2 Corolla There is none

3 Pistillum consists of a turbinated germen situated below the calyx, a style the length of the stamina, and a stigma divided into three spreading parts

4 Pericarpium is a globular, umbilicated berry, containing one cell

5 Semen The seed is a globular *ossiculum* filling the pericarpium

C H A P

# CHAP. CCCXXII

## *OXALIS*, WOOD SORREL

Species

THE hardy species of this genus are,
1 Common Wood Sorrel
2 Long-flowered Wood Sorrel
3 Violet Wood Sorrel

Common Wood Sorrel described

1. Common Wood Sorrel The root is thick, jointed, scaly, and spreading The leaves are trifoliate, heart-shaped, and grow on long, slender, reddish footstalks The flowers grow singly on slender, naked, reddish footstalks, and are usually of a white colour, with a tinge of pale-red, blue, or purple, they appear in April and May, and are succeeded by five-cornered capsules, which discharge the seeds with an elastic force when ripe

Medicinal properties of its leaves

The leaves of this species are a fine acid, superior to Sorrel, and therefore coveted by those who are fond of such herbs in their sallads They are not only wholesome, but a great strengthener of the stomach, and procure an appetite If beaten with sugar, they afford a conserve which allays thirst, and is a most useful refrigerant in fevers, and hot pestilential disorders, and if boiled with milk, they make an agreeable whey

The varieties of this species are,
The Large White
The Red
The Blue
The Purple
The Striped

Description of Long flowered

2 Long flowered Wood Sorrel The root is thick, scaly, and full of juice The leaves are trifoliate, each being composed of three bifid folioles, which join at their base, and sit close on slender footstalks The stalks are naked, single, and four or five inches high The flowers come out singly from the tops of the stalks, are remarkably long, appear in May, and are succeeded by five-cornered capsules, which discharge the seeds, on the least touch, with great violence

and Violet Wood Sorrel

3 Violet Wood Sorrel The root is large, fleshy, and scaly The leaves are trifoliate, each being composed of three obcordated folioles, which join at their base, and grow on slender footstalks. The stalks are naked, and support the flowers in kind of umbels at the top These flowers are of a dark-purple or violet colour, appear in May, and are succeeded by five-cornered capsules possessed of the elastic property of the former sorts

Method of propagation

These species are propagated by parting of the roots, which may be performed in the summer, after they have done flowering, or in the autumn

Proper situation

They love a moist, cool, shady situation; and being thus stationed, they will make amazing encrease, especially the first species, which will soon spread itself every-where, and become as a troublesome weed in the garden

Titles

1 Common Wood Sorrel is titled, *Oxalis scapo unifloro, foliis ternatis, radice squamoso articulatâ* In the *Flora Lapponica* it is termed, *Oxalis foliis ternatis, scapo unifloro* Caspar Baumine calls it, *Trifolium acetosum vulgare*, Dodonæus, *Trifolium acetosum*, Merret, *Trifolium acetosum vulgare, flore purpureo*, Gerard, *Oxys alba*, and Tournefort, *Oxys flore subcæruleo*, also, *Oxys flore purpurascente* It grows naturally in woods, and by the sides of hedges, in England and most of the northern parts of Europe

2 Long-flowered Wood Sorrel is, *Oxalis scapo unifloro, foliis ternatis semibifidis, lobis lanceolatis.* It grows naturally in Virginia

3. Violet Wood Sorrel is, *Oxalis scapo umbellifero, foliis ternatis obcordatis, calycibus apice callosis* Gronovius calls it, *Oxalis caule aphyllo, flore purpureo, radice tuberosâ rotunda*, and Plukenet, *Oxys purpurea Virginiana, radice lilii more nucleatâ* It grows common in Virginia and Canada

Class and order in the Linnæan system

*Oxalis* is of the class and order *Decandria Pentagynia*, and the characters are,

The characters

1 CALYX is a very short, permanent perianthium, divided into five acute parts

2 COROLLA is composed of five erect, obtuse, emarginated parts or petals, which join at their base

3 STAMINA are ten erect, capillary filaments, of which the outer ones are shorter than the others, having roundish sulcated antheræ

4 PISTILLUM consists of a pentangular germen, and five filiforme styles the length of the stamina, with obtuse stigmas

5 PERICARPIUM is a five-cornered capsule, containing five cells, and opening longitudinally at the angles

6. SEMINA The seeds are roundish

## CHAP. CCCXXIII.

## *PÆDEROTA.*

THIS genus comprehends a perennial species which was formerly supposed to be a Speedwell, called, *Bonarota*

This plant described — The root is fibrous and white The stalks are slender, weak, and a foot and a half high The leaves are oblong, deeply serrated, of a dusky-green colour, and grow opposite by pairs on the stalks The flowers come out in roundish bunches from the tops of the stalks, they are of a blue colour, appear in July and August, and the seeds ripen in the autumn

Culture — This is propagated by sowing the seeds in the autumn, soon after they are ripe, or the spring following, and when the plants are fit to remove, they may be stationed in the places where they are designed to remain

It is also encreased by parting of the roots, or planting of the cuttings in any of the summer months, which, if shaded and duly watered, will grow, and soon commence good plants

Titles — This species is titled, *Pæderota foliis serratis* In the former edition of the *Species Plantarum* it is termed, *Veronica corymbo terminali, foliis oppositis serrato-dentatis, calycibus linearibus* Caspar Bauhine calls it, *Chamædrys Alpina saxatilis*, and Micheli, *Bonarota* It grows naturally in the Austrian and Italian mountains

Class and order in the Linnæan system — *Pæderota* is of the class and order *Diandria Monogynia*, and the characters are,

The characters —
1 CALYX is a perianthium divided into five narrow, equal, patent, permanent segments

2 COROLLA is a subrotated, obtuse, quadrifid petal The upper lip is the broadest, and usually emarginated

3 STAMINA are two filiform rising filaments shorter than the corolla, having connivent, oval, acute, bivalved antheræ

4 PISTILLUM consists of an oval germen, and an awl-shaped, deflexed, permanent style the length of the stamina

5 PERICARPIUM is an oval capsule longer than the calyx, containing two cells, and opening at the top

6 SEMINA The seeds are many, and roundish.

## CHAP. CCCXXIV.

## *PÆONIA,* PEONY.

THERE are only two species of this genus, called,

Species —
1 Common Peony
2 Narrow leaved Peony

Description of Common Peony — 1 Common Peony The varieties of this species are so numerous, that upwards of twenty different sorts are enumerated by some authors This plant, in its natural state, has a root composed of several thick fleshy tubers, full of a clammy juice, which hang by strings to the main head The stalks are round, smooth, branching, and in rich soils a yard high The leaves are large, grow on long footstalks, and spread themselves every way, they are composed of several folioles, which are of an oblong figure, often cut into two or three segments, which are smooth, of a bluish-green colour on their upper side, and hoary underneath The flowers come out singly from the ends and sides of the branches, they are of a deep-red colour, and have numerous filaments in the middle, with yellow antheræ Between these are situated an uncertain number of large germina, covered with a whitish hairy down, these by degrees turn backward, and, when the seed is ripe, open lengthways, and in some sorts exhibit it in a most pleasing form

Medicinal properties of it — The roots, flowers, and seeds, are used in medicine, but more especially the roots, they are emollient, corroborant, serviceable in the yellow jaundice, obstructions in the viscera, pains in the kidneys, heat of urine, &c but above all, are more particularly used as an antiepileptic, and a curer of spasmodic complaints

Its varieties — The principal varieties are called,

Male Peony
Female Single Peony
Double Purple Peony
Double Red Peony
Double Black Peony
Double White Peony
Single Pale coloured Peony
Portugal Peony
Maidens Peony
Peony of Constantinople
Dwarf Peony

Male Peony described — Male Peony The folioles are large, nearly oval, with a gash or two on the side, of a dark strong green colour, but hoary underneath The flowers are single, and of little esteem, but the plant

plant is of high eſtimation from its manner of exhibiting the ſeeds. The capſules turn backward, open longitudinally, and diſplay their inſide of a bright-red colour, with the numerous round, and ſhining black ſeeds ſticking to the ſuture the whole length, and on the whole have a very ſingular, beautiful, and ſtriking appearance.

Female, Female Peony. This is of a paler-green colour than the former ſort, the folioles are narrower, and more cut on their edges. The flowers come out from the ends and ſides of the branches, but are ſmaller, of a deeper purple colour, and appear in May.

Double Purple, Double Purple Peony is one of the largeſt and moſt ſhining flowers we have in the garden; it is known every where, and much regretted on account of its falling petals, which begin to fall off, and give the flower a ſhattered appearance, almoſt as ſoon as it has attained to its beauty.

Double Red, Double Red Peony is hardly ſo large a flower as the former, but is much more valuable; for the petals do not drop off, but remain until the winter, before which they alter to a pale-red.

Double Black, Double Black Peony. This plant is like the former, but ſmaller; it is a very double flower, and retains its petals, which are of an elegant black colour at firſt, but become white before they wither and die away.

Double White, Double White Peony. The flowers of this plant are like the former, but ſmaller; the petals at firſt are of a faint black colour, but ſoon alter to a white, which they retain until the laſt.

The three laſt ſorts come into blow the end of May, or the beginning of June, and continue in beauty for ſix weeks, or longer.

Single Pale-coloured, Single Pale-coloured Peony. The leaves are of a whitiſh-green colour, the folioles pretty much divided, and a little hairy. The flowers are ſingle, of a bluſh-red colour, and come into blow the end of April or beginning of May.

Portugal, Portugal Peony. The ſtalk grows to about a foot high; the folioles are oval, of a pale-green colour on their upper ſide, and whitiſh underneath. The flower is ſingle and ſmall, of a bright-red colour, and finely ſcented.

and Maiden's Peony, Maiden's Peony. The ſtalks are lower than the former, and more branching; the folioles are oblong, often jagged on their ſides, ſmooth, of a ſtrong green colour on their upper ſide, and a little hairy underneath. The flowers are ſingle, of a pale red colour, and appear early in May.

Peony of Conſtantinople, Peony of Conſtantinople. The ſtalks are robuſt, often reddiſh, divide into a few branches, and are about a yard high. The leaves are compoſed of the like kind of folioles with the Common Peony, but larger, and cut on their edges. The flowers are ſingle at the ends of the main-ſtalks and branches; they are very large, of a blood-red or purple colour, and appear in May.

and Dwarf Peony deſcribed. Dwarf Peony. The ſtalks are ſlender, upright, ſingle for the moſt part, and eight or ten inches high. The folioles are narrow, of a pale-green colour, and grow on ſlender footſtalks. The flowers come out from the tops of the ſtalks; they are ſingle, of a white colour, having at firſt a tinge of red, and appear early in May.

There are ſeveral other varieties of this ſpecies, but their difference is ſo trifling as not to deſerve mentioning.

Narrow-leaved Peony deſcribed. 2. Narrow-leaved Peony. The root is thick, fleſhy, creeping, and full of a viſcous juice. The ſtalks are ſlender, upright, undivided, and about a foot high. The leaves are divided into a multitude of narrow ſmooth ſegments, have longiſh footſtalks, and are placed alternately. The flowers come out ſingly from the tops of the ſtalks; they are of a red colour, and appear in May and June.

Culture. All the Double kinds are propagated by parting of the roots, and the Single ſorts are alſo propagated by parting of the roots, and ſowing the ſeeds.

The beſt time for parting of the roots is Auguſt, in doing of which they ſhould not be divided into too ſmall parts; at leaſt there ought to be one good bud or eye to crown each offſet. The ground for their reception ſhould be double dug, and holes of ſufficient depth ſhould be made at two feet diſtance from each other; the roots ſhould be then put in, and the mould cloſed to the ſides, leaving the bud or crown equal with the ſurface of the earth. If the offſets are not too weak, the plants will flower the year following; the ſecond year they will flower ſtronger, and continue to exhibit more bloom every year, until they get too cloſe, and require to be removed, which need not be oftener than once in ſeven years. Though I have ordered them to be planted in beds at two feet diſtance from each other, this is recommended only in order to obtain a general ſhow of theſe flowers; they may be planted any where, for they are extremely hardy, flouriſh well in the ſhade, and are ornamental in wilderneſs-quarters, and under the drip of trees, where few other things will flouriſh.

All the Single kinds are encreaſed by ſeeds, and by this method new Doubles and freſh varieties are often obtained. The ſeeds ſhould be thinly ſown in Auguſt, ſoon after they are ripe, in beds of light rich earth, and covered down not quite half an inch deep. In the ſpring they will come up, and require no trouble, except keeping them clear from weeds, watering them in dry weather, and ſifting a little freſh mould over their tops in the autumn, for two years, for they will be too ſmall to remove before that time. Having ſtood two ſummers in the ſeed bed, in September let them be planted in the nurſery, previous to which let the ground be double-dug, made fine, and the roots removed with all care, being heedful not to break off their fibres, which by this time will be ſwelled, and tolerably large. They ſhould be planted about a foot aſunder, where they may remain until they flower, at which time, if any particular beautiful variety ſhews itſelf, it may be marked, and tranſplanted at the proper ſeaſon into the flower garden, whilſt the others may be uſed for medicinal purpoſes.

Its uſes in medicine. The roots of all the ſorts are promiſcuouſly uſed in medicine, being ſuppoſed to poſſeſs the ſame, or nearly the like kind of virtue; but the Male Peony is moſtly propagated for thoſe purpoſes. And ſo great was the opinion the Antients had of the virtue of this root, againſt epileptic complaints, that they believed the wearing it about the neck was a ſure preſervative againſt them. Galen aſſerts this, and ſays it is effectual for children, but orders it to be taken inwardly by grown perſons, for the cure or prevention of thoſe dreadful maladies.

Titles. 1. The firſt ſpecies is titled, *Pæonia foliolis oblongis*. Lobel calls it, *Pæonia mas*; alſo, *Pæonia femina*. Haller, *Pæonia foliis difformiter lobatis*; alſo *Pæonia foliis lobatis ex ovato lanceolatis*; and Caſpar Bauhine, *Pæonia communis, ſ. femina*; alſo, *Pæonia folio nigricante ſplendido, quæ mas*. It grows naturally in the foreſts and mountainous parts of Switzerland.

2. The ſecond ſpecies is, *Pæonia foliolis linearibus multipartitis*. Zinn calls it, *Pæonia laciniis foliorum linearibus*. It is a native of Ukrania.

Claſs and order in the Linnæan ſyſtem. *Pæonia* is of the claſs and order *Polyandria Digynia*; and the characters are,

The characters

1 Calyx is a small permanent perianthium, composed of five roundish concave, reflexed leaves, which are of an unequal size and situation

2 Corolla is five large, roundish, concave, spreading petals, which are narrow at their base

3 Stamina are numerous short, capillary filaments, with large, oblong, upright, quadrangular antheræ, containing four cells

4 Pistillum consists of two or three oval, erect, tomentose germina, having no styles, but oblong, compressed, coloured, obtuse stigma

5 Pericarpium consists of the like number of oval, oblong, reflexed, patent, tomentose capsules, composed of one valve, containing one cell, and opening longitudinally on the inner side

6 Semina The seeds are many, oval, glossy, and very beautiful

# CHAP CCCXXV

## *PANAX*, GINSENG

Species

Of this genus are two noted species, called,

1 Five-leaved *Panax*, or Ginseng

2 Three-leaved *Panax*

Five-leaved Panax described.

1 Five-leaved *Panax*, or Ginseng This celebrated plant has a fleshy taper root, about the size of a radish, tho shorter, and which usually divides into two parts near the bottom, it is brownish and roughish on the outside, yellowish within, of an aromatic agreeable odour, its taste rather acrid and bitter, but nevertheless of a grateful and acceptable flavour The stalk is single, smooth, usually of a reddish colour, a foot in height, and at the top divides into three or four footstalks for the support of the leaves The leaves are quinate, the folioles are spear-shaped, serrated, a little hairy, and of a pale-green colour The flowers come out in small umbels, growing on slender footstalks, which arise from the divisions of the stalks, they are of a greenish-yellow colour, and the general characters shew their structure, they appear in June, and are succeeded by compressed, heart-shaped, red berries, containing ripe seeds, in August

Its virtues

The root of this plant is said to be a remedy for all disorders, though its excellency consists chiefly in being an admirable restorative in decays from age, intemperance, and fatigues, it is a great strengthener of the stomach, creates an appetite, is good in consumptions, pleurisies, &c and is said to be a powerful provocative to venery

The Chinese and Tartars gather the roots with great caution, and dry them for sale, which they hold up at a great price The plant is now found growing naturally in North America, and may be procured in plenty if it is found deserving of it, and is proved to be possessed of those eminent virtues which the Chinese and Tartars affirm belong to it, but as they believe it to be a most powerful provocative to venery, it is to be feared they extol its sanative qualities too greatly, and, under a pretence of contributing to health and long life, many of them, it is to be feared, use it for bad purposes

Three-leaved Panax described

2 Three-leaved *Panax* This hath a small, taper, fleshy root, of an aromatic odour, and an agreeable sweetish taste The stalk is single, about six inches high, and divides at the top into three footstalks for the support of the leaves The leaves are trifoliate, the folioles are spear-shaped, long, narrow, deeply cut on their edges, and of a pale-green colour The flowers come out in small bunches on footstalks, which arise from the divisions of the stalks, they are very small, greenish, and appear about the same time with the former

Method of propagating them

These plants are propagated by sowing the seeds in the autumn, as soon as they are ripe, in beds of light fresh earth, covering them down with about half an inch of the finest mould The beds must be hooped, to be covered with mats in frosty weather in the winter, and in the spring (if the seeds are good) a share of the plants will come up, but the greatest part will probably not appear before the spring following And as it often happens that none of the plants come up the first spring, the beds must be all along kept clear from weeds, and if shaded in the heat of the day, and frequently watered in dry weather, it will be the better After the plants have made their appearance, they will require no trouble except thinning them where they are too close, and the usual care of weeding and watering, the summer after they will flower, and perfect their seeds, soon after which the stalks decay, and fresh ones arise in the spring

As these plants are dioecious, and the seeds are rarely found to be good, it seems necessary to have a sufficient quantity both of hermaphrodite and male flowers growing near each other, for the proper fœcundating the seed of the hermaphrodite flowers, and it is probable that for want of this so many seeds have miscarried, and the attempts of raising these plants proved fruitless, though the seeds, to all appearance, were perfectly fine, and well ripened

1 Five-leaved *Panax*, or Ginseng, is titled, *Panax foliis ternis quinatis* Catesby calls it, *Aureliana Canadensis*, Vaillant, *Araliastrum, quinquefolii folio, majus Ninsin vocatum*, and Trew, *Araliastrum foliis ternis quinquepartitis Ginseng, seu Ninsi officinarum* It grows naturally in Canada, Virginia, and Pensylvania Titles

2 Three-leaved *Panax* is, *Panax foliis ternis ternatis* Vaillant calls it, *Araliastrum, fragariæ folio, minus*, Trew, *Araliastrum foliis ternis tripartitis & quadripartitis*, and Plukenet, *Nastur-*

*tium Marianum, anemonæ sylvaticæ foliis, enneaphyllon, floribus exiguis* It is a native of Virginia

Class and order in the Linnæan System. *Panax* is of the class and order *Polygamia Diœcia*, and the characters are,

The characters. I Hermaphrodite Flowers on distinct plants

1 CALYX The umbel is simple, equal, and close, the involucrum is composed of several awl-shaped, small, permanent leaves, the proper perianthium is small and permanent

2 COROLLA The general flower is uniform the florets have each five oblong, equal, recurved petals

3 STAMINA are five very short caducous filaments, with simple antheræ

4 PISTILLUM consists of a roundish germen situated below the flower, and two small upright styles, with simple stigmas

5 PERICARPIUM is a heart shaped, umbilicated berry, containing two cells

6 SEMINA The seeds are single, heart shaped, acute, convex, and plane

II Male Flowers on different plants

1 CALYX The umbel is simple, round, and composed of many equal coloured rays, the involucrum is composed of several short-shaped, awl-shaped, equal in the number of outside rays, the perianthium is turbinated, whole, and coloured

2 COROLLA consists of five oblong, obtuse, narrow, reflexed petals, sitting on the perianthium

3 STAMINA consist of five filiforme filaments inserted in the perianthium, having simple antheræ

# CHAP CCCXXVI

## *PANCRATIUM*, SEA DAFFODIL.

THERE are several species of the *Pancratium* which are too tender to shew themselves to perfection in these parts without the benefit of the stove The hardy sorts are,

Species

1 The Common Sea *Pancratium*

2 The Illyrian *Pancratium*

Description of the Sea, 1 The Sea *Pancratium* The root is a very large oblong bulb, full of a thick juice, and covered with a blackish tough coat or skin The leaves are of an oblong figure, flat, and shaped like the tongue, they are surrounded at the bottom by a kind of sheath, and will grow to about a foot in length, six or eight of them arise from the bulb, and their colour is a bluish-green The flower-stalk is round, thick, and naked, will rise to a foot and half in height, and at the top has an oblong spatha or sheath, which opening sideways discloses the flowers, whose colour is white Six or eight of them ornament the top of the stalk, and each is supported by its own proper footstalk They are of the Daffodil kind, have a spreading nectarium, and six expanded petals, which, though their general colour is white, are often tinged or variegated with a fine green, the filaments also are white, but their antheræ are yellow, which still heightens their variety Their fragrance is delightful, and they will be in blow in September, but are never succeeded by seeds in these parts

and Illyrian Pancratium. 2 The Illyrian *Pancratium* The root is a very large oval bulb, covered with a dark tough coat or skin The leaves are ensiforme or shaped like a sword, will grow to about a foot and a half in length, and are about two inches broad, they are of a firm substance, and their colour is a greyish green The stalk is round, thick, naked, of a whitish colour, especially near the ground, very juicy or succulent, and will grow to about two feet in height At the top of this is the spatha, which opening discloses the flowers These will be six, eight, ten, and sometimes more in number, each has its separate footstalk, and they are moderately large Their colour is white, they are possessed of an agreeable fragrance, are shaped like the former sort, though the stamina are much longer than the nectarium, will be in blow in June or July, and are often succeeded by good seeds in the autumn

These sorts are best propagated by offsets, which the bulbs will send forth in tolerable plenty, if they remain undisturbed for three or four years, they thrive best in a light, rich, sandy soil, must have a warm situation, and be well sheltered, to defend them from the severe frosts, which otherwise would sometimes destroy them The leaves of the first sort decay in May or June, and that is the time for removing the bulbs, and dividing the offsets The best time to remove the other species is in September or October, when the seeds will be ripe, and the leaves and stalks decayed Plant the smaller offsets in beds by themselves, in the nursery, to gain strength, before they are brought into the pleasure ground, but the larger offsets may be planted where they are designed to flower, which may be expected the second season after removing Method of propagation

These plants may also be propagated by seeds, but this method is so tedious as not to be worth putting into practice for they can hardly be brought to flower under six or seven years from the time of sowing When this is to be done, however, let some good seeds be procured from the places where they naturally grow, though the latter sort frequently produces good seeds here, then sow them in pots or boxes, and manage them as has been directed for the *Polyanthos Narcissus*, which is the true method also to be pursued in the raising of these plants, and to which

which the reader, to avoid repetition, is referred.

*Titles.*

1. Sea Pancratium is entitled, *Pancratium spathâ multiflorâ, petalis planis, foliis lingulatis*. Caspar Bauhine calls it, *Narcissus maritimus*, and Morison, *Lilio-Narcissus albus maritimus minor*. It grows naturally on the sea coast of Spain, and in the South of France.

2. Illyrian Pancratium is, *Pancratium spathâ multiflorâ, foliis ensiformibus, staminibus corollâ longioribus*. Caspar Bauhine calls it, *Narcissus Illyricus liliaceus*. It grows naturally in Sclavonia, also in some parts of Sicily.

*Class and order in the Linnæan system.*

Pancratium is of the class and order *Hexandria Monogynia*, and the characters are,

*The characters.*

1. Calyx is an oblong, obtuse, compressed, withering spatha, that opens on one side.

2. Corolla is six spear-shaped petals, which are inserted into the outside of the tube of the nectarium above the base. The nectarium is a cylindrical funnel-shaped petal, the mouth of which is coloured, spreads open, and is cut into about a dozen segments.

3. Stamina are six subulated filaments inserted in the brim of the nectarium, with oblong incumbent antheræ.

4. Pistillum consists of an obtuse three-cornered germen situated below the flower, a filiforme style longer than the stamina, and an obtuse stigma.

5. Pericarpium is a roundish, three-cornered capsule of three cells.

6. Semina. The seeds are many, and of a globular figure.

## CHAP. CCCXXVII.

## *PANICUM*, PANIC-GRASS.

THERE are many species of this genus which are annuals, or such as grow naturally in warm countries, and will not thrive in England in the open air. There is one species, however, which is a perennial, a native of this country, and ought not wholly to be passed by unnoticed, called Creeping Panic Grass.

*Description of Creeping Panic Grass.*

The root is jointed, thick, and creeping. The stalks are round, slender, usually of a purplish colour, and about two feet high. The leaves are long, narrow, sharp-pointed, and embrace the stalk with their base. The flowers come out in spikes from the tops of the stalks, are four or five in number, and spread far asunder; they are of a purplish colour, appear in July, and the seeds ripen in August.

*Method of raising it.*

Whoever is inclined to have a plant or two of this grass, to be ready for observation, may plant the roots at any time of the year, but more especially in the autumn or spring, or he may sow the seeds as soon as they are ripe, or keep them until the spring, and they will grow, afterwards they will require no trouble, except reducing them to a proper quantity, and keeping them clean from weeds.

*Titles.*

This species is titled, *Panicum spicis digitatis patentibus basi interiore villosis, floribus solitariis, sarmentis repentibus*. Caspar Bauhine calls it, *Panicum dactylon, folio arundinaceo, majus aculeatum*; John Bauhine, *Gramen repens cum paniculâ graminis manæ*; Scheuchzer, *Panicum dactylon radice repente, officinarum*; Gerard, *Gramen dactyloides radice repente*; and Parkinson, *Gramen canarium ischæmi paniculis*. It grows naturally in England, and most of the southern parts of Europe, also in the East.

*Class and order in the Linnæan system. The characters.*

Panicum is of the class and order *Triandria Digynia*, and the characters are,

1. Calyx is a glume formed of three oval valves, of which one is smaller, and placed behind the others; and each glume contains one flower.

2. Corolla consists of two oval valves, one being smaller and flatter than the other.

3. Stamina are three very short capillary filaments with oblong antheræ.

4. Pistillum consists of a roundish germen, and two capillary styles with plumose stigmas.

5. Pericarpium. The corolla adheres to the seed, and serves for a pericarpium.

6. Semen. The seed is single, covered, roundish, and flattish on one side.

CHAP.

# CHAP CCCXXVIII

## *PAPAVER*, POPPY

BESIDES thoſe well known gaudy annuals called Poppies, there are of this genus ſome ſpecies whoſe roots will laſt for years in our gardens, and theſe are,

Species
1 The Alpine Poppy
2 The Welch Poppy
3 The Oriental Poppy

Alpine,
1 The Alpine Poppy is a ſmall plant of the mountains The leaves are doubly pinnated The ſtalk is ſlender, naked, rough, hairy, and ſupports a ſingle flower, which is ſmall, yellow, will ſhew itſelf in May, and be ſucceeded by very rough, prickly, roundiſh heads, containing the ſeeds

Welch,
2 The Welch Poppy The leaves are pinnated, and the lobes cut on their edges The ſtalks are ſmooth, ſlender, garniſhed with a few ſmall leaves on the lower part, and grow to about a foot high Each of them is terminated by a large yellow flower, which will be in blow in June, and is ſucceeded by an oblong ſmooth capſule containing the ſeeds, which are ſmall, and of a purpliſh colour

and Oriental Poppy deſcribed
3 The Oriental Poppy This plant hath a large thick root, which ſends forth ſtalks to the height of two or more feet The leaves are winged, very long, and the lobes ſerrated The ſtalks are very rough, hairy, and garniſhed on the lower part with a few leaves A ſingle flower is produced at the top of each ſtalk, its colour is a deep-red, it will be in blow in May, and be ſucceeded by a round ſmooth capſule full of purple ſeeds

Varieties
There is a double variety of this ſpecies, the colour of the flowers alſo will vary from ſeeds, and there is a ſort of it whoſe ſtalk and root uſually die after the ſeed is perfected

Culture
The culture of theſe ſorts is by ſowing the ſeeds, and parting of the roots, the beſt ſeaſon for doing both is the autumn Where the ſeedlings come up too cloſe they muſt be thinned to proper diſtances, and there they may ſtand without removing until they ſhew their flowers, during which time they will call for no other management than keeping them clean from weeds

The roots ſhould be parted early in the autumn, that they may take well to the ground before the winter comes on, they ſhould be planted immediately in the places where they are wanted, and the ſummer following they will exhibit their blow

Titles
1 The Alpine Poppy is titled *Papaver capſulis hiſpidis, ſcapo unifloro nudo hiſpido, foliis bipinnatis* Haller calls it, *Papaver perenne, foliis rigidiſſimis, ſpinosis, ... ſulco* Seguier, *Papaver Alpinum ſaxatile, ... foſo* Caſpar Bauhine, *Argemone ... foliis ... ea*, and Dalechamp, *Argemone minor ...* It grows naturally on the Pyrenean mountains, alſo in Switzerland and Auſtria

2 Welch Poppy is, *Papaver capſulis glabris oblongis, caule multifloro laevi, foliis ... incisis* Dillenius calls it, *Papaver Cambricum perenne, flore ſulphureo* Morison, *Argemone Cambro Britannica lutea, capite longiore glabro*, and Caſpar Bauhine, *Papaver erraticum Pyrenaicum, flore flavo* It grows naturally in Wales, alſo in ſome parts of England, and the Pyrenees

3 Oriental Poppy is, *Papaver capſulis glabris, caulibus unifloris ſcabris ſoliolis, foliis pinnatis ſerratis* Van Royen calls it, *Papaver foliis pinnatis, fructu globoſo*, and Tournefort, *Papaver orientale hirſutiſſimum, flore magno* It grows naturally in the Eaſt

Claſs and order in the Linnæan Syſtem
*Papaver* is of the claſs and order *Polyandria Monogynia*, and the characters are,

The characters
1 CALYX is an oval indented perianthium, compoſed of two oval, concave, obtuſe, caducous leaves

2 COROLLA conſiſts of four large, roundiſh, plane, ſpreading petals, which are narroweſt at the baſe, and the interior ſmall

3 STAMINA conſiſt of numerous ſhortiſh, capillary filaments, with oblong, compreſſed, erect, obtuſe antheræ

4 PISTILLUM The germen is large and roundiſh, there is no ſtyle, the ſtigma is target-ſhaped, radiated, and plane

5 PERICARPIUM is a large capſule of one cell, crowned by a large plane ſtigma, and opens under it at the top in ſeveral places

6 SEMINA The ſeeds are numerous, and ſmall

# C H A P. CCCXXIX

## *PARIETARIA,* PELLITORY.

THE perennials of this genus are usually called,

Species

1 Pellitory of the Wall
2 Small Oval-leaved Pellitory

Pellitory of the Wall described

1 Pellitory of the Wall The root consists of many thick, fleshy, reddish fibres, which strike into old walls or buildings, as well as hard, rocky, and stoney grounds, by the way sides The stalks are numerous, round, hairy, send forth a few branches from the sides, and grow to about a foot and a half or two feet long The leaves are spear shaped, oval, hairy, veined, of a dusky-green colour, and placed alternately The flowers come out in small clusters from the wings of the leaves, almost the whole length of the stalk, they are small, and of a greenish colour, they appear in May, continue in succession until the end of summer, and afford plenty of seeds for increase

Medicinal properties of this plant

This is one of the five emollient herbs The juice is a fine diuretic, and being tempered with white lead, affords an ointment that is admirable against St Anthony's fire and shingles, a decoction of it is good for nephritic complaints, and fomentations of it are used by the good women of the country, who hold this plant in high esteem, and by means of it are of service to the afflicted in various cases

Small oval leaved Pellitory described

2 Small Oval-leaved Pellitory This plant has numerous slender hairy stalks, about a foot long, and nearly erect The leaves are small, oval, hairy, and grow alternate The flowers are produced in small clusters all down the stalk, they are of a greenish colour, and appear great part of the summer

Titles

1 Pellitory of the Wall is titled, *Parietaria foliis lanceolato-ovatis alternis* Caspar Bauhine calls it, *Parietaria officinarum & Dioscoridis*, Camerarius *Helxine*, Gerard, *Parietaria*, and Parkinson *Parietaria vulgaris* It grows naturally out of walls, particularly old churches and ruinous buildings, also by way sides, among rubbish, &c in England, and most of the more temperate parts of Europe

2 Small oval-leaved Pellitory is, *Parietaria foliis ovatis, caulibus erectiusculis, calycibus trifloris, corollis hermaphroditis defloratis elongato-cylindricis* Caspar Bauhine calls it, *Parietaria minor, ocymi folio* It grows naturally in Palestine

Class and order in the Linnæan system

*Parietaria* is of the class and order *Polygamia Monoecia*, and the characters are,

The characters

I Hermaphrodites

1 CALYX The involucrum, containing two hermaphrodite flowers is plane, and composed of six folioles, of which the two opposite and exterior ones are the largest The perianthium is monophyllous, plane, quadrifid, obtuse, and about half the size of the involucrum

2 COROLLA There is none

3 STAMINA are four awl shaped filaments longer than the perianthium, having didymous antheræ

4 PISTILLUM consists of an oval germen, a filiforme coloured style, and a penicilliforme capitated stigma

5 PERICARPIUM There is none The seed is surrounded by the perianthium

6 SEMEN The seed is single, and oval

II Females

One female flower is situated between the two hermaphrodites within the involucrum

1 CALYX is the same as in the hermaphrodites

2 COROLLA There is none

3 PISTILLUM is the same as in the hermaphrodites

4 PERICARPIUM There is none The seed is wrapped up in the perianthium

5 SEMEN The seed is single and oval, like those of the hermaphrodites

CHAP

## CAAP CCCXXX

## *PARIS*, TRUE-LOVE, or ONE BERRY.

OF this genus there is only one species, called, Herb *Paris*, True-love, or One Berry

This plant described. The root is slender, jointed, and creeping The stalks are round, firm, and six or eight inches high The leaves are four in number, and grow near the top of the stalk, their figure is oval, spear-shaped, entire, and placed in form of a cross, or true-love-knot, which occasioned the plant being antiently called Herb True-love From the center of these four leaves arise the flowers, which are of a white or whitish-green colour, appear in May and June, and each of them is succeeded by one roundish-cornered black berry, which ripens in June or July

Medicinal properties of it. This plant is held narcotic and alexipharmac, the greatest force is in the root and fruit, though the leaves are in some degree possessed of these qualities

Culture. It is propagated by sowing the berries, soon after they are ripe, in a moist shady part of the wilderness-quarters, for they do ill in cultivated gardens After the seeds are sown, they should be left to Nature, and if the place agrees with them, they will grow and exhibit their flowers and fruit, and by their creeping roots soon spread themselves to a considerable distance

They may be also propagated by parting of the roots, soon after the seeds are ripe, they should not be parted into too small pieces, and if it is not at too great a distance it should be done with the spade, digging up as much mould as can be made to hang together The roots, with the mould disturbed as little as may be about them, should be then carefully set in such part of the wilderness-quarters, or in the woods, where you would chuse to have them grow

Titles. There being no other species of this genus, it stands with the single name *Paris* In the *Flora Lapp* it is termed, *Paris foliis quaternis* Caspar Bauhine calls it, *Solanum quadrifolium bacciferum*, Tabernæmontanus, *Aconitum salutiferum*, and Gerard, *Herba Paris* It grows naturally in woods, forests, and shady places in England, and most countries of Europe

Class and order in the Linnæan system. *Paris* is of the class and order *Octandria Tetragynia*, and the characters are,

The characters. 1 CALYX is a permanent perianthium, composed of four spear-shaped, acute, patent folioles, of the bigness of the flower

2 COROLLA consists of four awl-shaped, patent, permanent petals similar to the calyx

3 STAMINA are eight awl-shaped filaments, having long antheræ fastened to the middle on each side

4 PISTILLUM consists of a roundish four-cornered germen, and four patent styles with simple stigmas

5 PERICARPIUM is a roundish tetragonal berry, containing four cells

6 SEMINA The seeds are many, and lie over each other in a double series

## CHAP. CCCXXXI

## *PARNASSIA*, GRASS of PARNASSUS

OF this genus there is only one species, called, Grass of Parnassus

The plant described. The root is of a reddish-white colour, and hung with numerous slender fibres The radical leaves are oblong, heart-shaped at the base, pointed, smooth, of a pale green colour, and grow on long footstalks The stalks are numerous, slender, angular, eight or ten inches high, and adorned with one leaf only The leaf is shaped like the radical ones, but smaller, and surrounds the stalk with its base The flowers come out singly from the tops of the stalks, they are large, of a white colour, and very beautiful, they appear in July and August, and the seeds ripen in September

Medicinal properties. This plant is diuretic, and good for the stone and gravel

There is a variety of this species which is in high esteem with the curious

They are propagated by parting of the roots, which may be done any time in the autumn, winter, or early in the spring, before the leaves arise They must have a moist shady place, and will grow, flourish, and flower every year, but in dry hot soils they will do very ill unless shaded, and water be regularly afforded every evening in dry weather

Method of propagation. The Single sort is propagated by sowing the seeds This should be done in the autumn, soon after they are ripe, in beds of light rich earth

Some

Some of the plants will come up in the autumn, and the rest will remain until the spring. After their appearance, they should be thinned where they crowd each other, and if the place is not in the shade, the plants should be protected from the heat of the sun as it gets powerful in the spring, and this protection should be afforded them all summer; they must also be kept clean from weeds, and duly watered in dry weather. When the leaves decay, they may be taken up with a ball of earth to each root, and set in some moist shady part of the garden for their continuance.

Titles. There being no other species of this genus, it stands with the single name *Parnassia*. Caspar Bauhine calls it, *Gramen Parnassi albo simplici flore*; Cordus, *Hepatica alba*; Morison, *Pyrola roundifolia palustris, flore unico amplore*; Tournefort, *Parnassia vulgaris & palustris*; Gerard, *Gramen Parnassi*; and Parkinson, *Gramen Parnassi vulgare*. It grows naturally in moist meadows, watery and boggy places in England, and most countries of Europe.

Class and order in the Linnæan system. *Parnassia* is of the class and order *Pentandria Tetragynia*; and the characters are,

The characters.
1. Calyx is a perianthium divided into five oblong, acute, patent, permanent segments.

2. Corolla. The petals are five, roundish, emarginated, striated, concave, and spreading. The nectarii are five in number, each consists of a heart shaped, concave squamula, having at the edge thirteen styles, which are gradually taller, and respectively terminated with a globular bud.

3. Stamina are five awl shaped filaments the length of the corolla, having depressed incumbent antheræ.

4. Pistillum consists of a large oval germen, and four obtuse permanent stigmas, without any styles.

5. Pericarpium is a tetragonous oval capsule, formed of four valves, and containing one cell. The receptacle is quadrupled, and adheres to the valves.

6. Semina. The seeds are many, and oblong.

## CHAP. CCCXXXII.

## *PARTHENIUM*, BASTARD FEVERFEW.

THERE are only two species of this genus, one of which is an annual, the other a perennial, called, Virginian Bastard Feverfew.

The plant described. The stalk is upright, herbaceous, firm, but dies to the ground every autumn, and fresh ones arise in the spring. The leaves are large, oval, indented, rough to the touch, and whitish underneath. The flowers come out from the tops of the plant on foot stalks; they are of a white colour, but small, and of little beauty; they appear in July, but are rarely succeeded by ripe seeds in our gardens.

Culture. It is propagated by parting of the roots, which may be done successfully in the autumn, winter, or early in the spring, before the shoots arise. It is a hardy plant, and after it is set out will call for no trouble, except weeding, and clearing the decayed stalks from the roots every autumn.

Titles. This species is titled, *Parthenium foliis ovatis crenatis*. Dillenius calls it, *Partheniastrum helenii folio*; Plukenet, *Ptarmica Virginiana, scabiosæ Austriacæ foliis dissectis*; and Morison, *Ptarmica Virginiana, folio helenii*. It grows naturally in Virginia.

Class and order in the Linnæan system. *Parthenium* is of the class and order *Monoecia Pentandria*; and the characters are,

The characters.
1. Calyx. The general perianthium is simple, and composed of five roundish, plane, equal, patent folioles.

2. Corolla. The general flower is convex. The hermaphrodite florets in the disk consist each of one tubular erect petal, cut at the brim into five segments.

The females in the radius consist each of one tongue-shaped, oblique, obtuse, roundish floret, the length of that of the hermaphrodites.

3. Stamina of the hermaphrodites are five capillary filaments the length of the florets, having the like number of thickish antheræ, which can hardly be said to cohere with each other.

4. Pistillum of the hermaphrodites consists of a very small germen situated below the receptacle, and a capillary style without any stigma.

The females consist of a large turbinated cordated, compressed germen, situated below the flower, a filiform style the length of the corolla, and two filiform patent stigmas the length of the styles.

5. Pericarpium. There is none.

6. Semina of the hermaphrodites are barren; of the females are single, naked, heart shaped, and compressed.

## CHAP. CCCXXXIII.

## *PASSIFLORA*, PASSION FLOWER.

THE following species of this genus are perennials, and will live abroad in warm, well-sheltered places, through our moderate winters

Species
1 The Three-leaved Italian Passion-flower
2 The Yellow Virginian Passion-flower

Description of the Three leaved Italian

1 The Three-leaved Italian Passion-flower This species hath several slender, climbing stalks, which, by the assistance of the claspers that grow from the joints, will arise to about four feet high The leaves in general are composed of three thin, light-coloured lobes, they are of an oblong figure, serrated, join at their base, and grow singly from the joints, on short footstalks At the joints also the flowers are produced They come in early in the summer, and as the stalks advance in height fresh flowers as well as leaves are formed for the succession, so that there will be a continuance of them until the stalks decay, which will be at the end of autumn They grow on long footstalks, and their appearance is singular and elegant The five segments which compose the calyx are oblong, and of a pale-green colour, the five petals of the flower are white, and round the style is a double circle of rays, of a fine purple colour, the columna rises in the middle, supporting the female parts, and the male organs spread about with great singularity and beauty They are finely scented, but the continuance of each individual flower is very short It comes out in the morning, and the evening puts a period to its existence But Nature makes amends for this by granting a fresh supply the next day, which will continue to be made until the frost stops them The fruit rarely ripens, unless the plants are set in the stove, and then it appears to the last degree beautiful It is of the size of a moderate orange, and almost of the same colour, though paler At first it is green, till it assumes the orange colour when ripe, so that the same stalks will shew large pale orange coloured fruit from the first-blown flowers at its bottom, other fruit green and ripening higher upwards and flowers in their full perfection at its top Thus nobly adorned will this plant be when it succeeds properly, on which account it has a right to challenge our best culture and management

and The Yellow Virginian Passion Flower

2 The Yellow Virginian Passion-flower This is a more feeble plant than the other The stalks are very weak, slender, and put out claspers from the joints, by which they will rise to about a yard high The leaves are trilobate, each being composed of three smooth entire lobes, they are of a pale-green colour, thin, and about the size and shape of those of our common Ivy tree The flowers come out from the joints on shortish footstalks, are small, and of a bad yellow colour, so that though the scarcity of this plant may recommend it to our notice, it is vastly inferior in beauty to the former sort

Its propagation

The propagation of it however, is much easier, for it has a creeping root, by which it may be multiplied exceedingly at pleasure The best time for dividing the roots is the beginning of April They should be immediately planted in a dry, warm, sandy place, that is every where defended from the cutting winds of our winters, which, if not more severe than common, they will in such a situation be able to endure

Propagation of the first species

The first species is easily propagated by layers In performing this, nothing more need be observed than drawing down the young shoots as they are produced in the summer, and they will strike root, and soon become good plants In the autumn they should be taken off, and a share of them planted in the warmest and best-sheltered part of the garden, while the remainder should be set in pots, to be preserved under the hot-bed frame, to continue the sort, in case a very severe winter should happen

Propagation of them by seeds

By seeds also they are easily propagated These should be procured from America, for they rarely ripen here, unless the plants are set in the stove They should be sown in the spring on a moderate hot-bed From this they are to be removed into small pots, preserving a ball of earth to each root These pots should be set in a second hot-bed, and covered three inches deep with mould, to prevent the roots from scorching The interstices should be then filled up with common mould, and the plants should be watered, and kept shaded from the sun until they have taken root Water must be given them as often as there shall be occasion, and they must be hardened by degrees to the open air In June the pots should be taken from the hot-bed, and plunged up to the rims in a shady part of the garden Here they should stand until the end of autumn, when they should be removed under the hot-bed frame, to be preserved for the first winter In the spring they should be turned out of the pots, with the mould at the roots, into the places where they are to remain

As this plant is so delightful when garnished with flowers and ripe fruit, it is worth while to place a few of them in the stove; for the fruit very rarely sets, and much less arrives at perfection, without the assistance of artificial heat

The stalks of both these species die to the ground every autumn, and fresh ones are produced again in the spring

Titles.

1 The Three-leaved Italian Passion-flower is titled, *Passiflora foliis trilobis serratis* In the *Hortus Cliffort* it is termed, *Passiflora foliis semitrifidis serratis, basi duabus glandulis convexis, lobis ovatis* Herman calls it, *Granadilla Hispanis, flos passionis Italis*, Caspar Bauhine, *Clematis trifolia, flore roseo clavato*, and Morison, *Clematis trifolia, sive flos passionalis, flore viridi* It grows naturally in Virginia, the Brasils, and Peru

2 The Yellow Virginian Passion-flower is titled, *Passiflora foliis trilobis cordatis æqualibus obtusis glabris integerrimis*. In the *Hortus Cliffort.* it is termed, *Passiflora foliis cordatis trilobis integerrimis glabris, lateralibus angulatis* Gronovius calls it, *Passiflora foliis trilobis integerrimis, laciniis semiovatis acutis integerrimis glabris*, Morison, *Clematis passionalis triphyllos, flore luteo*, and Sloane, *Flos passionis minor, folio in tres lacinias non serratas minus profundas diviso* It grows naturally in Virginia and Jamaica.

## CHAP. CCCXXXIV.

## *PASTINACA*, PARSNEP.

THERE are only two species of this genus, one of which is the Parsnep of our kitchen gardens, and the other is called Illyrian *Costus*

Illyrian Costus described. The Illyrian *Costus* has a large, long, thick root, that sends forth a large, thick, hairy, round, rough, striated, branching stalk, to the height of about six feet The leaves will be sometimes near two feet long, and are composed of a multitude of large, broad, rough, hairy, serrated lobes, which being wounded emit a yellow juice The flowers are yellow, and terminate the branches in very large umbels, they will be in full blow in July, and ripen their large flat seeds in the autumn

Method of propagating it. This species is raised by sowing of the seeds in March, in the places where they are to remain When they come up, the plants should be thinned to a yard distance from each other; and this, except keeping them clean from weeds, will be all the trouble they will require

Titles. This species is titled, *Pastinaca foliis decompositis pinnatis* Caspar Bauhine calls it, *Panax Costinum*, Morison, *Panax Heracleum*, Tabernæmontanus, *Costum Illyricum* It grows naturally in Italy and Sicily

Class and order in the Linnæan system. *Pastinaca* is of the class and order *Pentandria Digynia*, and the characters are,

The characters. 1 CALYX The general umbel is multiple and plane, the partial also is multiple Neither of them have any involucrum, and the perianthium is scarce discernible

2 COROLLA The general corolla is uniform, and each flower consists of five spear-shaped, involute, entire petals

3 STAMINA consist of five capillary filaments, with roundish antheræ

4 PISTILLUM consists of a germen placed below the flower, and of two reflexed styles with obtuse stigmas

5 PERICARPIUM There is none The fruit is plane, compressed, elliptic, and divisible into two parts

6 SEMINA The seeds are two, elliptic, surrounded with a border, and nearly plane on both sides

## CHAP. CCCXXXV.

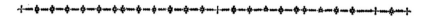

## *PEDICULARIS*, RATTLE, COXCOMB, or LOUSE-WORT.

OF this genus are,

Species

1 Red Rattle or Louse-wort
2 Rostrated Rattle
3 Swedish Rattle
4 Verticillate Rattle or Louse-wort
5 Siberian Purple Rattle or Louse-wort
6 Siberian Yellow Rattle
7 Helvetian Rattle
8 Imbricated Rattle
9 Hairy Rattle
10 Flesh-coloured Rattle
11 Lapland Rattle or Louse-wort
12 Leafy-spiked Rattle
13 Tuberous Rattle or Louse-wort

Red Rattle described. 1. Red Rattle or Louse-wort The stalks are tender, branching, partly procumbent, and eight or ten inches long The leaves are composed of many parts, which are finely divided or cut on their edges, and they are placed alternately on the branches The flowers come out singly from the sides of the stalks near the upper part, they are of a red colour, appear in May and June, and the seeds ripen soon after

Its properties. It is said that this plant causes sheep or whatever cattle feed thereon to become lousy Hence the name Louse-wort has been long in use to distinguish it It is held to be of great service for the cure of fistulas, hollow ulcers, and the bloody flux

Description of Rostrated. 2 Rostrated Rattle The stalk of this species divides into two or three branches, and grows to about a foot high The leaves are composed of numerous folioles, which are cut on their edges, and they are placed alternately The flowers come out thinly from the sides of the stalks, are of a purple colour, and have a long, pointed beak, they appear in May and June, and the seeds ripen in July

3 Swedish

Swediſh, 3 Swediſh Rattle. The radical leaves are cut almoſt to the mid-rib, and indented on their edges. The ſtalk is ſimple, naked, and ſix or eight inches high. The flowers come out by threes, ſurrounding the ſtalk at the upper part; they are ſmall, unpoſſeſſed of the gaping property of the other flowers of this genus, ſituated in indented cups, appear in May and June, and the ſeeds ripen in July.

Verticillated, 4 Verticillated Rattle. The ſtalk is undivided, tender, and ſix or eight inches high. The leaves are pinnated, and grow by fours, ſurrounding the ſtalk in the whorled manner. The flowers come out in ſpikes from the tops of the ſtalk; they appear in May and June, and frequently again in the autumn, and the ſeeds ripen very well in our gardens.

Siberian Purple, 5 Siberian Purple Rattle. The ſtalk is ſmooth, ſimple, and about a foot high. The leaves are ſpear-ſhaped, deeply ſerrated, and grow alternately. The flowers come out ſingly from the wings of the leaves at the upper parts of the ſtalks, having no footſtalks, and appearing as if thrown backwards; they are of a deep-purple colour, have the vexillum large and full, appear in June, and the ſeeds ripen in July.

Siberian Yellow, 6 Siberian Yellow Rattle. The ſtalk is ſimple, and ſix or eight inches high. The leaves are pinnatifid, ſerrated, and placed alternately. The flowers come out from the tops of the ſtalks in a roundiſh ſpike or head, are of a yellow colour, obtuſe, and the helmet is a little incurved and hairy on the border; they appear about the ſame time as the former, and the ſeeds ripen accordingly.

Helvetian, 7 Helvetian Rattle. The ſtalk is ſimple, and eight or ten inches high. The leaves are pinnated, and grow alternately. The flowers are formed into a thick cloſe ſpike at the top of the ſtalk, are of a dark red colour, have long ſtamina, and appear about the ſame time with the former.

Imbricated, 8 Imbricated Rattle. The ſtalk is ſimple, erect, and about a foot high. The leaves are almoſt divided to the mid-rib, and the ſegments are obtuſe, hang backward, and lie over each other *imbricatim*. The flowers come out from the tops of the ſtalks in kind of ſpikes; they are of a yellowiſh-red colour, appear in June and July, and frequently again in the autumn.

Hairy, 9 Hairy Rattle. The ſtalk is upright and undivided. The leaves are narrow, and indented ſo near the mid-rib as to appear pinnated. The flowers come out from the upper parts of the ſtalk, having hairy cups; they appear in July, and ſometimes in the end of ſummer.

Fleſh coloured, 10 Fleſh coloured Rattle. The radical leaves are large, pinnated, and the pinnæ are pinnatifid and ſerrated; thoſe on the ſtalks are only pinnatifid, and ſerrated on their edges, and are placed alternately. The ſtalks are ſimple, ſmooth, and a foot and a half high. The flowers come out from the tops of the ſtalks a great way down the ſides; they are of a fleſh colour, appear in June and July, and the ſeeds ripen in Auguſt.

Lapland, 11 Lapland Rattle. This ſpecies hath a ſimple ſtalk like the former, but of lower growth. The leaves are pinnatifid, and ſerrated on their edges. The flowers come out down the ſides of the upper parts of the ſtalks, are of a browniſh-red colour, and have bifid, obtuſe cups; they appear in June and July, and the ſeeds ripen in Auguſt.

Leafy ſpiked, 12. Leafy-ſpiked Rattle. The ſtalk is upright, firm, ſimple, and about a foot high. The leaves are ſemi-pinnated, and grow alternately. The flowers come out in cloſe, leafy ſpikes from the tops of the ſtalks; they are of a yellowiſh or ochre colour, appear in June or July, and frequently again, if much wet happens, in the end of ſummer or autumn.

and Tuberous Rattle 13 Tuberous Rattle. The root is hung with ſeveral fleſhy tubers in the manner of Drop-wort. The ſtalks are ſimple, and about ſix or eight inches high. The leaves are pinnated, and ſeldom more than two on a ſtalk, ſtanding ſingly, at certain diſtances from each other. The flowers are produced in ſpikes from the tops of the ſtalks, are of a yellow colour, appear in June and July, and the ſeeds ripen in Auguſt.

Method of propagating them These ſpecies are all propagated by the ſeeds, which ſhould be ſown in the autumn ſoon after they are ripe, or in the ſpring; and after they come up, they will require no trouble, except thinning them where they are too cloſe, and keeping them clean from weeds. The roots of ſeveral of them are frequently of no long continuance; but the ſucceſſion will be ſpontaneouſly kept up from ſcattered ſeeds, which will ariſe in great plenty after they have once ripened in a garden; ſo that you need not be over-anxious about their ſafety. They are ſeldom coveted for the flower-garden, and are found only in ſuch places where a general collection of plants is preſerved.

Titles, 1 Red Rattle or Louſe-wort is titled, *Pedicularis caule ramoſo, calycibus oblongis angulatis lævibus, corollis labio cordato*. In the *Flora Suecia* it is termed, *Pedicularis caule ramoſo, floribus ſolitariis calycibus quinquefidis*; in the *Flora Lapponica*, *Pedicularis caule ramoſo, floribus ſolitariis remotis*. Caſpar Bauhine calls it, *Pedicularis pratenſis purpurea*; Dodonæus, *Fiſtularia*; Gerard, *Pedicularis*; and Parkinſon, *Pedicularis pratenſis rubra vulgaris*. It grows naturally in moiſt woods, ſwampy heaths, and meadows, in England and moſt parts of Europe.

2 Roſtrated Rattle is, *Pedicularis caule ſubramoſo, corollis galeâ roſtrato-acuminatis, calycibus ſubhirſutis*. Haller calls it, *Pedicularis Alpina, foliis alternis, pinnulis inciſis, floribus ſparſis roſtratis purpureis*; Caſpar Bauhine, *Pedicularis Alpina, filicis folio, minor*; and Cluſius, *Alectorolophus Alpina III minor*. It grows naturally on the Alps of Auſtria and Helvetia.

3 Swediſh Rattle is, *Pedicularis caule ſimplici, floribus ternato-verticillatis, corollis clauſis, calycibus crenatis, capſulis regularibus*. In the *Flora Lapponica* it is termed, *Sceptrum Carolinum*. Van Royen calls it, *Pedicularis capſulis ſubrotundis regularibus*. It grows naturally in moiſt places in Sweden, Lapland, and Germany.

4 Verticillated Rattle is, *Pedicularis caule ſimplici, foliis quaternis*. Haller calls it, *Pedicularis Alpina, floribus purpureis ſpicatis, foliis pinnatis verticillatis*; Cluſius, *Alectorolophus Alpina II floribus purpureis*; and Caſpar Bauhine, *Filipendula montana altera*. It grows naturally in Siberia, Auſtria, and Helvetia.

5 Siberian Purple Rattle is, *Pedicularis caule ſimplici, foliis lanceolatis ſerratis crenulatis, floribus reſupinatis*. It grows naturally in Siberia.

6 Yellow Siberian Rattle is, *Pedicularis caule ſimplici, corollarum galeis margine villoſis*. Gmelin calls it, *Pedicularis caule ſimplici, foliis ſemipinnatis, pinnulis obtuſis acute ſerratis*. It grows naturally in Siberia.

7 Helvetian Rattle is, *Pedicularis caule ſimplici, ſtaminibus floris galeâ longioribus*. Haller calls it, *Pedicularis Alpina, foliis alternis pinnatis, floribus ex atro-rubentibus in ſpicam denſam congeſtis*. It grows naturally on the tops of the Helvetian mountains.

8 Imbricated

8 Imbricated Rattle is, *Pedicularis caule simplici, foliis pinnatis retro-imbricatis* In the *Flora Lapponica* it is termed, *Pedicularis caule simplici, foliis semipinnatis obtusis, laciniis imbricatis crenatis* Haller calls it, *Pedicularis caule erecto non ramoso, pinnis foliorum retroversis imbricatis*, and Caspar Bauhine, *Pedicularis Alpina, folio ceterach* It grows common on the Alps of Lapland and Helvetia

9 Hairy Rattle is, *Pedicularis caule simplici, foliis dentato-pinnatis linearibus, calycibus vestitis* In the *Flora Lapponica* it is termed, *Pedicularis caule simplici, calycibus villosis, foliis linearibus dentatis crenatis* It is a native of the Alps of Lapland

10 Flesh-coloured Rattle is, *Pedicularis caule simplici, foliis pinnatis serratis, calycibus rotundatis glabris, corollis galeâ incinatis acutis* It grows naturally in Siberia

11 Lapland Rattle is, *Pedicularis caule simplici, foliis pinnatifidis serratis, calycibus bifidis obtusis* In the *Flora Lapponica* it is termed, *Pedicularis caule simplici, foliis lanceolatis semipinnatis serratis acutis* It is common on the Alps of Lapland

12 Leafy-spiked Rattle is, *Pedicularis caule simplici, spicâ foliosa, corollis galeâ acutis emarginatis, calycibus quinquedentatis* It grows common on the Italian mountains

13 Tuberous Rattle or Louse-wort is, *Pedicularis caule simplici, calycibus crenatis, corollis galeâ rostrato-aduncis* Haller calls it, *Pedicularis Alpina, foliis alternis pinnatis, pinnulis pinnatis, floribus ochroleucis rostratis in spicam congestis*, Caspar Bauhine, *Filipendula montana, flore pediculariæ*; and Barrelier, *Alectorolophus montanus, flore luteo* It grows naturally on the Helvetian and Italian mountains

*Pedicularis* is of the class and order *Didynamia Angiospermia*, and the characters are, Class and order in the Linnæan system The characters

1 CALYX is a monophyllous, roundish, ventricose, permanent perianthium, cut at the brim into five equal segments

2 COROLLA is one ringent petal The tube is oblong, and gibbous The upper lip is galeated, erect, compressed, and indented, the lower lip is plane, patent, obtuse, and cut into three segments

3 STAMINA are four filaments the length of the upper lip, two of which are shorter than the others, having incumbent, roundish, compressed antheræ

4 PISTILLUM consists of a roundish germen, a filiforme style longer than the stamina, and an obtuse inflexed stigma

6 PERICARPIUM is a roundish acuminated, oblique capsule, containing two cells, and opening at the top

6 SEMINA The seeds are many, roundish, tunicated, and compressed

## C H A P. CCCXXXVI.

## *PEGANUM*, WILD SYRIAN RUE

THERE are only two species of this genus, called,

Species 1 *Harmala*, or Wild Syrian Rue.

2 Mountain Harmel

Description of Harmala 1 *Harmala*, or Wild Syrian Rue The root is thick, tough, and ligneous The stalks are upright, firm, branching, and grow to about a foot high The leaves are divided into a multitude of long, narrow segments, which are of a thick consistence, a dark-green colour, and have a disagreeable taste The flowers come out from the wings of the leaves near the tops of the branches, are large, and of a white colour, having yellow antheræ, they appear in July, and are succeeded by roundish, three cornered capsules, containing (in favourable seasons) ripe seeds in the autumn

and Mountain Harmel 2 Mountain Harmel The root is fibrous and spreading The stalks are numerous, upright, firm, and a foot and a half high The leaves are narrow, spear-shaped, pointed, and of a light green colour The flowers come out from the wings of the leaves near the upper parts of the stalk; they are of a white colour, appear in July, and are sometimes succeeded by ripe seeds in the autumn

There is a variety of this species with a yellow flowers Its variety

The first species grows naturally in loose, sandy places in the East, and should have here as similar a situation as possible It is propagated by sowing the seeds in the spring When the plants come up, they must be kept clean from weeds, and be frequently watered all summer In the autumn a share of them may be drawn out, and set in warm, well-sheltered, sandy places. The rest may be left in the seed bed, and provided this be naturally dry, warm and well defended, they will survive the cold of our winter, flower the summer following, and, if much wet does not happen, will perfect their seeds Proper situation and Propagation of the first species

The second species may be raised in the above manner, but it is usually propagated by parting of the roots, which may be done any time in the autumn, winter, or early in the spring It is extremely hardy, and after it is set out, will call for no trouble, except keeping it clean from weeds Propagation of the second species

1 *Harmala*,

Titles

1 *Harmala*, or Wild Syrian Rue, is titled, *Peganum foliis multifidis* In the *Hortus Cliffort* it is termed, simply, *Peganum* Caspar Bauhine calls it, *Ruta sylvestris, flore magno albo*, and Dodonæus, *Harmala* It grows naturally in the sandy parts of Syria

2 Mountain Harmel is, *Peganum foliis indivisis*. Amman calls it, *Harmala montana Daurica perennis multicaulis, polygalæ folio, flore albo*, also, *Harmala montana, polygalæ foliis, floribus luteis* It grows naturally in Siberia

Class and order in the Linnæan system The characters

*Peganum* is of the class and order *Dodecandria Monogynia*, and the characters are,

1 CALYX is a perianthium composed of five narrow, erect, acute, permanent leaves, of the same length with the corolla

2 COROLLA is five oblong, oval, erect, patent petals

3 STAMINA are fifteen awl shaped filaments, about half the length of the corolla, and dilated at the base in to a nectarium under the germen, having oblong, erect antheræ

4. PISTILLUM consists of a three cornered roundish germen, elevated on the receptacle from the base of the flowers, a filiforme taper style the length of the antheræ, and an oblong, triquetrous stigma

5 PERICARPIUM is a three-cornered, roundish capsule, composed of three valves, and containing three cells

6 SEMINA The seeds are many, oval, and pointed

## CHAP CCCXXXVII.

## *PEPLIS*, WATER PURSLANE.

OF this genus is a small plant, an inhabitant of moist and overflowed places, called Water Purslane

This plant described

The stalks are slender, square, jointed, usually of a reddish colour, partly procumbent, and strike root at the joints The leaves are roundish, obtuse, smooth, undivided on their edges, of a yellowish-green colour, and grow opposite to each other at the joints The flowers come out singly from the wings of the leaves at the joints, they are small, of a purple colour, and to be met with in August and September

Its cultivation

This species is an inhabitant of watery places, and is not cultivated Nevertheless, if a person is inclined to have a few plants to be ready for observation, he may take up the roots or cuttings and plant them in the mud, and they will readily grow

Titles

This species is titled, *Peplis floribus apetalis* Micheli calls it, *Glaucoides palustre, portulacæ folio, flore pupureo*, Caspar Bauhine, *Alsine palustris minor, serpyllifolia*, Gerard, *Alsine rotundifolia, s portulaca aquatica*, and Parkinson, *Alsine aquatica minor folio oblongo, s portulaca aquatica* It grows naturally in places which have been overflowed in winters in England and most countries of Europe

Class and order in the Linnæan system The characters

*Peplis* is of the class and order *Hexandria Monogynia*, and the characters are,

1 CALYX is a large, monophyllous, bell-shaped, permanent perianthium, cut into twelve segments at the top, which are alternately reflexed

2 COROLLA is six very small oval petals inserted in the mouth of the calyx

3 STAMINA are six short, awl-shaped filaments, with roundish antheræ

4 PISTILLUM consists of an oval germen, a very short style, and an orbicular stigma

5 PERICARPIUM is a cordated capsule containing two cells

6 SEMINA The seeds are many, three-sided, and small.

# C H A P. CCCXXXVIII.

## *PEUCEDANUM*, HOG's FENNEL, or SULPHUR-WORT.

Species

OF this genus are,

1 Common Hog's Fennel, or Sulphur-wort

2 Meadow *Sesel*

3 Alsace Carrot

Common Hog's Fennel described

1 Common Hog's Fennel, or Sulphur wort The root is composed of many thick, fleshy fibres, is blackish without, greenish within, of a strong disagreeable odour, and has usually at the top a tuft of hairy matter, formed of the fibres of decayed leaves These fibres are all full of a yellowish juice, which flowing is soon concreted, and has then the smell of sulphur or brimstone, which occasions this plant to be frequently called Sulphur wort The stalks are upright, firm, round, striated, jointed, and three or four feet high The leaves are composed of a multitude of long, narrow segments, nearly in the manner of fennel, but larger, they are smooth, of a deep green colour, and form a large and beautiful leaf The radical ones grow on strong channelled footstalks, and when bruised smell like brimstone The flowers come out in umbels from the ends of the branches, are small, of a yellow colour, appear in June, and are succeeded by flat, compressed, furrowed seeds, which ripen in the autumn

Medicinal properties of its root

The root is held to be stimulating and attenuating, diuretic, and a good promoter of expectoration

Varieties

The varieties of this species go by the names of German Hog's Fennel, Italian Hog's Fennel, French Hog's Fennel, &c which being of considerable difference, have been titled as distinct species by old botanists

Meadow Seseli described

2 Meadow *Seseli* The root is thick, blackish without, whitish within, full of juice, and divides into many parts The stalks are upright, round, firm, channelled, jointed, and two or three feet high The leaves are composed of many folioles, which are moderately broad, spear-shaped, pinnatifid, and of a blackish-green colour The flowers come out in umbels from the tops of the stalks, they are small, of a yellowish colour in front, but whitish on the outside, appear in June, and the seeds ripen in the autumn

Alsace Carrot described

3 Alsace Carrot The root is thick, fleshy, usually divides into two or three parts, and strikes deep into the ground The stalks are upright, firm, striated, jointed, and four feet high The leaves are large, and composed of many folioles, which are winged almost to the mid-rib, and the segments are again cut or divided into three obtuse parts The flowers come out in umbels from the tops of the stalks, are of a yellowish colour, appear in June, and the seeds ripen in the autumn

Method of propagation

They are all propagated by sowing the seeds, which may be done in the autumn or spring, though the autumn is the best season, because the seeds will be surer of growing The soil for their reception should be rich, and inclined to moisture, and the ground should be double dug for the roots to strike freely Being thus situated, the plants will grow to a larger size than if otherwise stationed

After they come up, they must be thinned to proper distances, which ought to be a foot and half asunder All summer they must be kept clean from weeds, and in the autumn, or early in the winter, the ground between the plants should be stirred by a slight digging This will greatly invigorate the plants for the summer after, when they will flower, and perfect their seeds

Title

1 Hog's Fennel or Sulphur-wort is entitled, *Peucedanum foliis quinquies tripartitis filiformibus linearibus* In the *Hortus Cliffort* it is termed, *Peucedanum foliis quinquies tripartitis, segmentis [illegible] integerrimis* John Bauhine calls it, *Peucedanum*, Caspar Bauhine, *Peucedanum Germanicum*, also, *Peucedanum Italicum*, and Parkinson, *Peucedanum vulgare* It grows naturally in marshy places in England, Germany, and the southern parts of Europe

2 Meadow *Seseli* is, *Peucedanum foliolis pinnatifidis, laciniis oppositis, involucro universali diphyllo* Caspar Bauhine calls it, *Seseli pratense*, and Dodonæus, *Siler [illegible] pratense* It grows naturally in meadows and moist places in England, Helvetia, France, and Germany

3 Alsace Carrot is, *Peucedanum foliolis pinnatifidis, laciniis trifidis obtusis [illegible]* In the *Hortus Cliffort* it is termed, *Selinum foliolis pinnatim laciniatis, laciniis trifidis obtusis* Caspar Bauhine calls it, *Daucus Alsaticus*, and John Bauhine, *Umbellifera [illegible] tica magna, umbella parte sublutea* It grows naturally in Germany

Class and order in the Linnæan system

*Peucedanum* is of the class and order *Pentandria Digynia*, and the characters are,

The characters

1 CALYX The general umbel is multiple, long, and slender, the partial is spreading

The general involucrum is small, and composed of several narrow, reflexed leaves, the partial is smaller

The proper perianthium is very minute, and indented in five parts

2 COROLLA The general flower is uniform The florets have each five oblong, entire, equal, incurved petals

3 STAMINA are five capillary filaments with simple antheræ

4 PISTILLUM consists of an oblong germen situated below the receptacle, and two small styles with obtuse stigmas

5 PERICARPIUM There is none The fruit is oval, surrounded with a border, striated on both sides, and divided into two parts

6 SEMINA The seeds are two, oval, oblong, compressed, convex on one side, marked with three ridges, and surrounded with a broad membranaceous border that is indented at the top

CHAP

## CHAP CCCXXXIX

## *PHACA*, BASTARD MILK-VETCH

THERE are only thr… species of this genus, viz

Species.

1 Portugal Bastard Milk-vetch
2 Alpine Bastard Milk-vetch
3 Siberian Bastard Milk-vetch

Description of Portugal Bastard,

1 Portugal Bastard Milk-vetch The root is thick, broad, black on the outside, horned, and strikes deep into the ground The stalks are numerous, ligneous, erect, hairy, and two or three feet high The leaves are pinnated, and the folioles are short and hoary The flowers come out in short spikes from the wings of the leaves, they are moderately large, of a white colour, appear in September and October, but are not succeeded by ripe seeds in England

Alpine Bastard,

2 Alpine Bastard Milk vetch The stalks of this species are numerous, smooth, erect, and three or four feet high The leaves are pinnated, of a bluish or whitish green colour on their upper side, and hoary underneath The flowers are produced in spikes from the wings of the leaves, are small, and of a yellow colour, they appear in August, September, and October, and are succeeded by oval, pendulent pods, in which through favourable seasons the seeds ripen in the autumn

and Siberian Bastard Milk vetch

3 Siberian Bastard Milk-vetch The leaves are pinnated, the pinnæ are digitated, hairy, and almost white on their under side They form a large tuft about the root Among these the stalks arise a few inches high, they are hairy, undivided, and support the flowers at the top The flowers are of a reddish purple colour, appear in July and August, and the seeds ripen in the autumn

Method of propagating them

These species are all best propagated from the seeds, but as those of the first species seldom ripen in England, they must be procured from abroad

The ground should be double dug, and made fine, and the seeds of the first two sorts should be sown five or six together in patches four or five feet asunder If all the seeds grow, the weakest plants should be drawn out, leaving only two or three in each patch Every autumn the stalks die to the ground, and fresh ones arise in the spring When they are decayed, they must be cut off close to the roots, the ground between the rows dug, and a little fresh mould laid over the tops of the roots, which will enable them to shoot more vigorously the summer following, and this is all the trouble they will require

The seeds of the third species may be sown in any open border of the flower-garden, and being a small plant, of great beauty and easy culture, it is deserving of a place in every collection

Titles

1 Portugal Bastard Milk-vetch is titled, *Phaca ca… …scens erecta pilosa, leguminibus te… cymbiformibus* Van Royen calls it, *Phaca leguminibus …* Caspar Bauhine, *Astragalus Boeticus lanuginosus, radice crassissimâ*, and Clusius, *Astragalus Baeticus* It grows naturally in Spain and Portugal

2 Alpine Bastard Milk-vetch is, *Phaca c… …lescens erecta glabra, leguminibus oblongis inflatis stipitatis* In the *Flora Suecica* it is termed, *Phaca frigida* Tilli calls it, *Astragaloides Alpina supina glabra, foliis acutioribus*, and Amman, *Astragaloides elatior erecta, vicia foliis, floribus luteis, siliquis pendulis* It grows naturally on the mountainous shady pa…s of Lapland, Siberia, and Italy

3 Siberian Bastard Milk-vetch is, *Phaca acaulis fol… …, pinnis digitatis* Amman calls it, *Astragaloides nana, non ramosa, floribus ca… … …* also, *Astragaloides hirsuta minor, non ramosa, floribus purpurascentibus* It grows naturally on the Alpine parts of Siberia

Class and order in the Linnæan System

*Phaca* is of the class and order *Diadelphia Decandria*, and the characters are,

The characters

1 CALYX is a monophyllous, tubular perianthium, indented in five parts at the brim
2 COROLLA is papilionaceous
The vexillum is obloval, large, and upright
The alæ are oblong, obtuse, and shorter than the vexillum
The carina is short, compressed, and obtuse
3 STAMINA are diadelphous filaments, crowned by roundish, rising antheræ
4 PISTILLUM consists of an oblong germen, an awl shaped, rising style, and a simple stigma
5 PERICARPIUM is an oblong, inflated pod, having the upper suture depressed towards the under
6 SEMINA The seeds are many, and kidney-shaped

CHAP.

## C H A P. CCCXL

## *PHALARIS,* CANARY GRASS.

Species.

THE folllowing graſſes are arranged under the generical term *Phalaris*, viz

1 Reed Canary Graſs
2 Bulboſe Canary Graſs
3 Aquatick Canary Graſs
4 Utriculated Canary Graſs
5 Cylindrical Spiked Canary Graſs

Deſcription of Reed Canary Graſs.

1 Reed Canary Graſs The root is jointed, fibrated, and creeping The ſtalks are round, jointed, ſmooth, four or five feet high, and like thoſe of reed The leaves are long, narrow, graſſy, of a deep-green colour, grow ſingly at the joints, and ſurround the ſtalk with their baſe The flowers come out from the tops of the ſtalks in oblong ſwelling panicles, often half a foot in length, they are of a purpliſh colour, or whitiſh, for there are both kinds, they are in full blow in July, and the ſeeds ripen in Auguſt

Variety.

Though this ſpecies is mentioned chiefly for the ſatisfaction of the botanical ſtudent, who might expect it in this place, yet there is a variety of it with beautifully-variegated leaves, worthy of the gardener's notice, and deſerving of a place in every good collection of plants

Bulboſe.

2 Bulboſe Canary Graſs The root is thick, knobbed, and fibrated The ſtalks are jointed in three or four places, and grow to about two feet high The leaves are narrow, pointed, and, as is uſual to graſſes, grow ſingly at the joints, ſurrounding the ſtalks with their baſe The flowers terminate the ſtalks in cylindrical panicles, they are of a pale green colour, having a mixture of white, and will be in perfection in July and Auguſt

Aquatick.

3 Aquatick Canary Graſs This hath a large, thick, bulbous root, ſending forth ſeveral long fibres, which ſtrike deep into the mud The ſtalks are round, jointed, hollow, and four or five feet high The leaves are hairy, proportionably larger than thoſe of the other ſort, grow ſingly at the joints, and ſurround the ſtalk in the uſual way. The flowers come out from the tops of the ſtalks in oval, oblong, ſpiciforme panicles, their glumes are large, carinated, and of a pale-green colour, and they are in perfection in July and Auguſt

Utriculated,

4 Utriculated Canary Graſs The ſtalks are ſlender, ſmooth, reddiſh at the joints, and two feet high The leaves are narrow, pointed, embrace the ſtalk with their baſe, and the upper leaf ſurrounds the ſpike of flowers in the manner of a ſpatha The flowers come out from this vagina formed by the leaf in ſpiked panicles, they are of a purple colour, and in perfection in June and July

and Cylindrical ſpiked Canary Graſs deſcribed.

5 Cylindrical-ſpiked Canary Graſs The ſtalk is round, ſlender, a foot and a half high, and jointed all the way up The radical leaves are eight or ten inches long, and a third of an inch broad; they are firm, rough to the touch, and of a pale greyiſh-green colour, thoſe on the ſtalks are ſimilar to the radical ones, but ſmaller, and embrace the ſtalk a great way up with their baſe The flowers come out from the tops of the ſtalks in a long, taper, cylindrical ſpike, ſhaped like a rat's tail, on a ſtrong plant, they are near four inches long, almoſt as thick as a man's little finger, of a greyiſh or light-brown colour, and are in perfection in June, July, and Auguſt

Culture.

None of theſe ſorts are propagated in gardens, except the Striped kind, for its beautifully-variegated leaves If a perſon is deſirous, however, to have a few plants at hand for obſervation, he may ſow the ſeeds ſoon after they are ripe, or in the ſpring, or the roots may be tranſplanted at any time of the year, when he can be ſure of the right ſorts, and by either method he will ſoon get plants enough

Titles.

1 Reed Canary Graſs is titled, *Phalaris paniculâ oblongâ ventricoſâ* In the *Flora Suecia* it is termed, *Phalaris paniculâ oblongâ*, in the *Hortus Cliffort Arundo foliis planis, paniculâ ſpicatâ, phalaridis ſemine* Ray calls it, *Gramen arundinaceum, aceroſa glumâ, Jerſejanum*, Caſpar Bauhine, *Gramen arundinaceum ſpicatum*, alſo, *Gramen aquaticum paniculatum latifolium*, alſo, *Gramen paniculatum, folio variegato*, and Parkinſon, *Gramen arundinaceum, aceroſâ glumâ, noſtras* It grows naturally on the banks of rivers, lakes, and moiſt places in England, and moſt parts of Europe.

2 Bulboſe Canary Graſs is, *Phalaris paniculâ cylindricâ glumis carinatis* Van Royen calls it, *Phalaris radice perenni*, and Ray, *Phalaris bulboſa, ſemine albo* It is a native of the Eaſt

3 Aquatic Canary Graſs is, *Phalaris paniculâ ovato-oblongâ ſpiciformi glumis carinatis lanceolatis* Barrelier calls it, *Gramen typhinum phalaroides majus bulboſum aquaticum*; and Buxbaum, *Gramen phalaroides hirſutum, ſpicâ longiſſimâ* It grows naturally in Italy and Egypt

4 Utriculated Canary Graſs is, *Phalaris paniculâ ſpicatâ, petalis ariſtâ articulatâ, vaginâ ſupremi folii ſpathiformi* Caſpar Bauhine calls it, *Gramen pratenſe, ſpicâ purpureâ ex utriculo prodeunte, ſ gramen folio ſpicam amplexante* It grows naturally in Italy

5 Cylindrical-ſpiked Canary Graſs is, *Phalaris paniculâ cylindricâ ſpiciformi* In the *Flora Suecia* it is termed, *Phalaris ſpicâ cylindricâ* Caſpar Bauhine calls it, *Gramen typhoides aſperum primum* It grows naturally in moſt countries of Europe

Claſs and order in the Linnæan ſyſtem. The characters.

*Phalaris* is of the claſs and order *Triandria Digynia*, and the characters are,

1 Calyx is a compreſſed obtuſe glume, compoſed of two valves, and containing one flower The valves are navicular, compreſſed, obtuſe towards the top, and have ſtraight edges, which are nearly parallel and connivent

2 Corolla is leſs than the calyx, and compoſed of two valves, the outer valve being oblong, convoluted, ſharp-pointed, and the interior one the ſmaller

3 Stamina are three capillary filaments ſhorter than the calyx, having oblong antheræ

4 Pistillum conſiſts of a roundiſh germen, and two capillary ſtyles with hairy ſtigmas

5 Pericarpium The corolla forms a kind of cruſt round the ſeeds, opens in no part, and is the pericarpium

6 Semen The ſeed is ſingle, covered, ſmooth, roundiſh, and pointed at each end

C H A P.

# CHAP. CCCXLI

## PHELLANDRIUM

THERE are only two species of this genus, usually called,

Species

1 *Mutellina*, or Alpine Spignel

2 Water *Phellandrium*.

Mutellina

1 *Mutellina*, or Alpine Spignel The stalk is thick, hollow, smooth, jointed, branching very little, and about two feet high The leaves are composed of a multitude of narrow acute segments, in the manner of Wild Chervil, the radical ones are large, and grow on long footstalks, but those on the stalks, which are seldom more than two or three, are smaller, and sit almost close The flowers come out in umbels from the tops of the stalks, they are of a purple colour, appear in July and August, and the seeds ripen in the autumn

and Water Phellandrium described

2 Water *Phellandrium* admits of two principal varieties, called,

Water Yarrow

Water Hemlock

Water Yarrow,

Water Yarrow has a tough slender root, which sends forth numerous fibres from the sides The stalks are round, striated, branching, and two or three feet high The leaves are large, branching, and composed of a multitude of narrow green parts, nearly in the manner of Milfoil The flowers come out in umbels from the tops of the stalks, they are of a white colour, appear in July and August, and the seeds ripen in the autumn

and Water Hemlock described

Water Hemlock This has a thick, jointed, tender root, sending forth numerous fibres from the joints, which are of a white colour, long, and strike deep into the mud The stalks are thick, upright, stiff, branching, hollow, striated, and four or five feet high The leaves are large, branching, and beautifully composed of narrow segments in the manner of Hemlock, they consist of many divisions, are near a foot long, almost as broad, and grow on strong channelled footstalks, those on the upper parts of the plant are smaller, and have shorter footstalks The flowers come out in small umbels from the ends and sides of the branches, they are of a white colour, appear in July and August, and the seeds ripen in the autumn, soon after which the whole plant generally dies

Culture

The first sort is found in curious collections of plants, the second sort, with both varieties, grows naturally in lakes and standing waters in most parts of England The first sort is propagated by sowing the seeds in the spring The ground should be rich, moist, and double-dug, and when the plants come up, they should be thinned to two feet distance from each other. All summer they should be kept clean from weeds, and in the autumn, or early part of the winter, the ground between the plants should be slightly dug, the plants then will rise strong and vigorous the summer following for flowering, and perfect their seeds in the autumn

If any one should be desirous of a few plants of the second species, he may gather the seeds in the end of summer, when they are ripe, and drop them in ditches and standing waters, and they will readily grow and flower the second year from the seed They will also grow in a moist part of the garden, if a person has room enough for all sorts of plants, and is desirous of a general collection

1 *Mutellina*, or Alpine Spignel, is titled, *Phellandrium caule subnudo, foliis bipinnatis* Haller calls it, *Seseli caule vix ramoso, umbella purpurea, pinnulis acute multifidis*, Caspar Bauhine, *Meum Alpinum, umbella purpurascente*, and John Bauhine, *Mutellina* It grows naturally in Helvetia and Carniola Titles.

2 Water *Phellandrium* is, *Phellandrium foliorum ramificationibus divaricatis* In the *Hortus Cliffort* it is termed simply, *Phellandrium* Matthiolus calls it, *Millefolium aquaticum*, Caspar Bauhine, *Millefolium aquaticum umbellatum, coriandri folio*, also, *Cicutaria palustris tenuifolia*, John Bauhine, *Phellandrium, vel cicutaria aquatica quorundam*, and Lobel, *Cicutaria palustris* It grows naturally in ditches, rivers, lakes, &c in England, and most parts of Europe

*Phellandrium* is of the class and order *Pentandria Digynia*, and the characters are, Class and order in the Linnæan System The characters

1 CALYX The general umbel is multiple, the partial is similar The general involucrum is wanting, the partial is composed of seven acute leaves the length of the umbellulæ The perianthium is small, permanent, and indented in five parts

2 COROLLA The general flower is nearly uniform, the distinct flowers are unequal, and each has five acuminated, heart-shaped, inflexed petals

3 STAMINA are five capillary filaments longer than the corolla, having roundish antheræ

4 PISTILLUM consists of a germen situated below the perianthium, and two awl-shaped, erect, permanent styles, with obtuse stigmas

5 PERICARPIUM There is none The fruit is oval, smooth, crowned with the perianthium and styles, and divided into two parts

6 SEMINA The seeds are two oval, and smooth

# CHAP. CCCXLII.

## *PHLEUM.*

THREE perennial grasses are comprehended in the word *Phleum*, called,

Species

1 Meadow Cat's Tail Grass.
2 Bulbous Cat's Tail Grass.
3 Alpine Cat's Tail Grass.

Description of the Meadow Cat's Tail Grass.

1 Meadow Cat's Tail Grass. The root is a multitude of very narrow, slender, white fibres, issuing from the base of the stalk. The stalk is slender, round, kneed or jointed, and about a foot and a half high. The leaves are, like most grasses, long, narrow, green, and pointed, the radical ones are near a foot long, the cauline ones are shorter, grow singly at the joints, and surround the stalk a great way up with their base. The flowers come out from the tops of the stalks in long cylindrical spikes, from a large healthy plant they will be five inches long, tolerably thick, and resemble, as some fancy, the tail of a cat. Their colour is at first green, but they alter to a kind of white, and are in perfection, with the other grasses in our meadows, chiefly in June and July.

Its variety.

There is a variety of this species of smaller growth, called the Smaller Cat's Tail Grass.

Bulbous

2 Bulbous Cat's Tail Grass. The root is bulbous, and hung with many slender fibres. The stalks are hollow, kneed or jointed and surrounded with vaginæ of the leaves, often lie on the ground, and strike root at the joints. The leaves are rough on their edges, but smooth on the other parts, and they sheath almost the whole stalk with their base. The flowers come out from the tops of the stalks in cylindrical spikes, and are to be found every where in our meadows and pastures during the season of hay-making.

and Alpine Cat's Tail Grass described.

3 Alpine Cat's Tail Grass. The fibres of the root are whitish, spreading, and not numerous. The stalks are slender, round, jointed, and about a foot high. The leaves are narrow, sharp-pointed, of a greenish green colour, and the cauline ones grow singly at the joints, surrounding the stalk with their base. The flowers come out from the tops of the stalks in short, thick, oval spikes; they are at first green, but almost black when full ripe.

Method of propagation

These sorts are best propagated by sowing the seeds, soon after they are ripe, or the spring. The third species is a native of the Alps, but the first two species grow common in our meadows and pastures, and are to be found almost every where.

Titles.

1 Meadow Cat's Tail Grass is titled, *Phleum spicâ cylindricâ longissimâ, culmo recto*. Caspar Bauhine calls it, *Gramen typhoides asperum primum*, also, *Gramen typhoides maximum, spicâ longissimâ*. Gerard, *Gramen typhinum majus, seu primum*; also, *Gramen typhinum minus*, and Parkinson, *Gramen typhinum medium, s. vulgatissimum*. It grows naturally in most parts of Europe.

2 Bulbose Cat's Tail Grass is, *Phleum spicâ cylindricâ basi sterili, culmo adscendente, radice bulbiferâ*. Barrelier calls it, *Gramen typhinum supinum tuberosum, spica asperâ*, Caspar Bauhine, *Gramen nodosum, spicâ parvâ*, also, *Gramen typhoides asperum alterum*. It grows naturally in most parts of Europe.

3 Alpine Cat's Tail Grass is, *Phleum spicâ ovato cylindrica*. Scheuchzer calls it, *Gramen typhoides Alpinum, spicâ brevi densâ et velut villosâ*. It grows naturally chiefly on mountainous places in most parts of Europe.

Class and order in the Linnæan system.

*Phleum* is of the class and order *Triandria Digynia*, and the characters are,

The characters.

1 CALYX is a bivalvate, oblong, narrow, compressed glume, opening with two points at the top, and containing one flower. The valves are straight, concave, compressed, truncated, equal, mucronated, and fold one over the other.

2 COROLLA is composed of two valves, and is shorter than the calyx, the outer valve is the largest, and surrounds the interior.

3 STAMINA are three capillary filaments longer than the calyx, having oblong bifurcated antheræ.

4 PISTILLUM consists of a roundish germen, and two capillary reflexed styles with plumose stigmas.

5 PERICARPIUM. There is none. The calyx and corolla include the seed.

6 SEMEN. The seed is single, and roundish.

CHAP.

# CHAP. CCCXLIII.

## *PHLOMIS,* JERUSALEM SAGE.

OF this genus we have the following perennials

Species

1 Oriental *Phlomis*
2 Sage-leaved *Phlomis*
3 Jagged-leaved *Phlomis*
4 Samian *Phlomis*
5 Narbonne *Phlomis*
6 Nettle-leaved *Phlomis*

Oriental,

1 Oriental *Phlomis* The radical leaves of this species are heart-shaped, downy on both sides, and grow in clusters on long downy footstalks, they can hardly be said to rise immediately from the root, for this puts forth some short, trailing, woolly branches, on which the clusters of leaves are situated without order Among these the flower-stalks arise, they are slender, about a foot high, and usually send out two side-branches opposite near the bottom The leaves on the stalks are oval, spear-shaped, downy, and those on the top are proportionably smaller than the lower ones The flowers are produced in whorls almost the whole length of the branches, they grow thinly in the whorls, and each flower stands separate, their colour is yellow, they appear in June and July, but are very rarely succeeded by seeds in England

Sage leaved,

2 Sage-leaved *Phlomis* The radical leaves are spear-shaped, long, woolly, soft, come out in tufts or bunches, and lie on the ground The stalks are slender, two feet high, and garnished with oval woolly leaves, growing opposite at the joints, and embracing the stalks with their base The flowers come out in whorls in the bosom of the leaves, they are yellow, and have a bristly radiated involucrum, they appear in July, and are rarely succeeded by seeds in England

Jagged leaved,

3 Jagged-leaved *Phlomis* The leaves are alternately pinnated, the lobes are small, jagged or cut on their edges, and the radical leaves continue all winter The stalks grow to a foot and a half high, and are ornamented with leaves like the radical ones, but smaller The flowers grow in whorls round the stalks, and have woolly cups, they are of a very dull-purple colour, appear in June, and are very seldom succeeded by seeds in England

Samian,

4 Samian *Phlomis* The leaves are heart-shaped, oval, pointed, downy, and have strong veins on their under side The stalks grow to about a foot and a half high, and have leaves like the radical ones, but smaller, growing opposite by pairs at the joints The flowers are produced in whorls round the stalks, having bristly involucrums, they are of a worn-out purple colour, appear in June and July, but are not succeeded by seeds in England

Narbonne,

5 Narbonne *Phlomis* The leaves are large, oval, oblong, and rough The stalks are square and downy The leaves grow opposite at the joints, without any footstalks The flowers are produced in whorls round the stalks, having hispid bristly involucrums, they are of a bright-purple colour, appear in June and July, and are rarely succeeded by seeds in England

and Nettle-leaved Phlomis described.

6 Nettle-leaved *Phlomis* rises with upright, herbaceous, four-cornered, purple-coloured stalks to the height of five feet or more The leaves are large, heart-shaped, pointed, rough, crenated, and grow opposite at the joints The flowers grow in whorls round the stalks, having awl shaped hispid involucrums, they are of a pale purple colour, appear in June and July, and are succeeded by ripe seeds in September

Culture.

All these sorts are easily propagated by slips from the heads, or dividing of the roots The best time for this performance is the beginning of September, for then they will immediately strike root, be well established before the frost comes on, and the strongest plants will flower the summer following The first four sorts should have a dry warm soil, and a well sheltered situation, especially the third and fourth, which are liable to be killed by very severe weather, on which account it would be adviseable to keep a plant or two of each sort in pots, to be housed in case such weather should happen, in order to gain fresh increase should those abroad be destroyed The fifth and sixth sorts are extremely hardy, and scarce any soil or situation comes amiss to them

The sixth sort is also propagated by the seeds, which ripen very well with us These should be sown in the spring in a bed of any common mould made fine, and slightly raked in When the plants come up, the weakest should be drawn out where they are too close, and the weeds, which will probably appear in plenty with the young plants, must be picked out, and if the weather is dry, the plants should be watered The repetition of weeding and watering all summer, as the growth of weeds and dry weather make it necessary, must be observed, and in the autumn the plants will be grown strong, when they should be taken up with care, and set in the places where they are designed to remain

This work should be done early in the autumn, that the plants may have time to be well established before the frosts come on, and the next summer they will flower and ripen their seeds

Titles.

1 Oriental *Phlomis* is titled, *Phlomis foliis radicalibus cordato sagittatis utrinque tomentosis villosis* Nissol calls it, *Phlomis orientalis foliis auriculatis incanis, flore luteo* It grows naturally in the East

2 Sage leaved *Phlomis* is, *Phlomis foliis lanceolatis tomentosis, floralibus ovatis, involucris setaceis lanatis* Sauvages calls it, *Phlomis foliis lingulatis utrinque tomentosis radiis involucri setaceis villosis*, Caspar Bauhine, *Verbascum angustis salviae foliis*, and Lobel, *Verbascum sylvestre foliis salviae tenuifolie* It grows naturally in the southern parts of Europe

3 Jagged leaved *Phlomis* is, *Phlomis foliis alternatim pinnatis foliolis laciniatis, calycibus tomentosis* Tournefort calls it, *Phlomis orientalis, foliis laciniatis* It is a native of the East

4 Samian *Phlomis* is, *Phlomis foliis cordatis subtus tomentosis, involucris subulatis strictis hispidis* In the *Hortus Cliffortianus* it is termed, *Phlomis involucr* [illegible]

*involucri radiis subulatis strictis* Sauvages calls it, *Phlomis radiis involucri setaceis trifidis, foliis cordatis* and Tournefort, *Phlomis Samia herbacea, folio lunariæ* It is a native of Samos

5 Narbonne *Phlomis* is, *Phlomis involucris setaceis hispidis, foliis ovato oblongis scabris, caule herbaceo* In the *Hortus Cliffort* it is termed, *Phlomis involucri radiis setaceis hispidis* Caspar Bauhine calls it, *Marrubium nigrum longifolium* It grows naturally in Persia, Tartary, and Narbonne

6 Nettle-leaved *Phlomis* is, *Phlomis involucris hispidis subulatis, foliis cordatis scabris, caule herbaceo* In the *Act Gatt* it is, *Phlomis foliis cordiformibus, galeâ lacerâ.* Amman calls it, *Phlomis urticæ foliis, glabra*; Buxbaum, *Galeopsis maxima, foliis hormini* It is a native of the plains of Siberia

## C H A P. CCCXLIV.

## *PHLOX, LYCHNIDEA,* or BASTARD *LYCHNIS.*

THIS genus comprehends many beautiful perennials, called,

Species

1 Paniculated *Lychnidea*, or Bastard *Lychnis*
2 Spotted *Lychnidea*, or Bastard *Lychnis*
3 Hairy *Lychnidea*
4 Carolina *Lychnidea*
5 Smooth Virginian *Lychnidea*
6 Divaricated *Lychnidea*
7 Oval-leaved *Lychnidea*
8 Subulated *Lychnidea*
9 Siberian *Lychnidea*

Paniculated 

1 Paniculated *Lychnidea* The stalk is herbaceous, smooth, of a light-green colour, sends forth a few branches from the sides, and grows to be two or three feet high The leaves are spear-shaped, broad, sessile, of a dark green colour, rough on their edges, and grow opposite by pairs on the branches The flowers grow in panicles at the tops of the stalks, and each part of it consists of a small roundish bunch of flowers, growing separate on distinct footstalks, they are of a pale-purple colour, and have long tubes, they appear in July and August, and the seeds frequently ripen in the autumn

and Spotted Lychnidea described

2 Spotted *Lychnidea* The stalks are upright, taper, rough, often purplish, and spotted with white, red, or black spots, send forth branches by pairs opposite near the top, and grow to be three feet high The leaves are spear-shaped, though cordated at the base, pointed at the extremity, smooth; grow opposite by pairs, and embrace the stalk with their base The flowers come out from the ends of the stalks and side-branches in tufts or bunches, that which crowns the main-stalk is large and elegant, the others are smaller, they are of a bright-purple colour, appear in July and August, but are rarely succeeded by seeds in England

Varieties

There is a variety of this species with pale-red, and another with white flowers

Hairy,

3 Hairy *Lychnidea* The stalks are single, slender, upright, and about a foot high The leaves are spear-shaped, narrow, acute, hairy, and sit close to the stalk The flowers come out in a loose corymbus from the tops of the stalks, they are of a reddish-purple colour, appear in June and July, but are very seldom succeeded by seeds in our gardens

4 Carolina *Lychnidea* The stalks are numerous from a strong root, and about two feet high Carolina, The leaves are spear-shaped, acute, smooth, shining, of a thickish substance, reflexed on their edges, sit close, and grow opposite by pairs on the stalks The flowers come out from the tops of the stalks in large roundish bunches, one of which always terminates the stalk, another grows lower, surrounding it in the verticillate way, and still smaller bunches terminate two slender side-branches, which are generally produced opposite to each other from the upper part of the stalk, they are of a purple colour, appear in July, and are rarely succeeded by ripe seeds in England

5 Smooth Virginian *Lychnidea* The stalks are upright, round, smooth, firm, two feet high, and send forth a few branches near the top The leaves are narrow, spear-shaped, pointed, perfectly smooth, of a pale green colour, and grow opposite to each other at the joints The flowers come out from the tops of the stalks in a corymbus, they are large, and of a reddish colour, appear in July, and are seldom succeeded by seeds in England

and Smooth Virginian Lychnidea described.

There is a variety of this species with large white flowers Variety

6 Divaricated *Lychnidea* The stalks are slender, weak, and divide into several branches, which spread in different directions The leaves are broad, spear shaped, smooth, soft to the touch, sessile, and on the main-stalk grow alternately on the branches opposite to each other The flowers come out from the ends of the branches in small loose bunches, they are of a pale blue colour, appear in May, but the seeds seldom ripen in England Divaricated,

7 Oval leaved *Lychnidea* The stalks are slender, two or three from the root, and about nine inches high The leaves are oval, rough, hairy, and grow opposite to each other on very short footstalks The flowers come out singly from the tops of the stalks, they are large, of a light-purple colour, appear in July, but are not succeeded by seeds in England Oval-leaved,

8 Subulated *Lychnidea* The stalks are slender, numerous from a strong root, and about a foot high The leaves are awl-shaped, hairy, and grow opposite to each other. The flowers come Subulated,

out

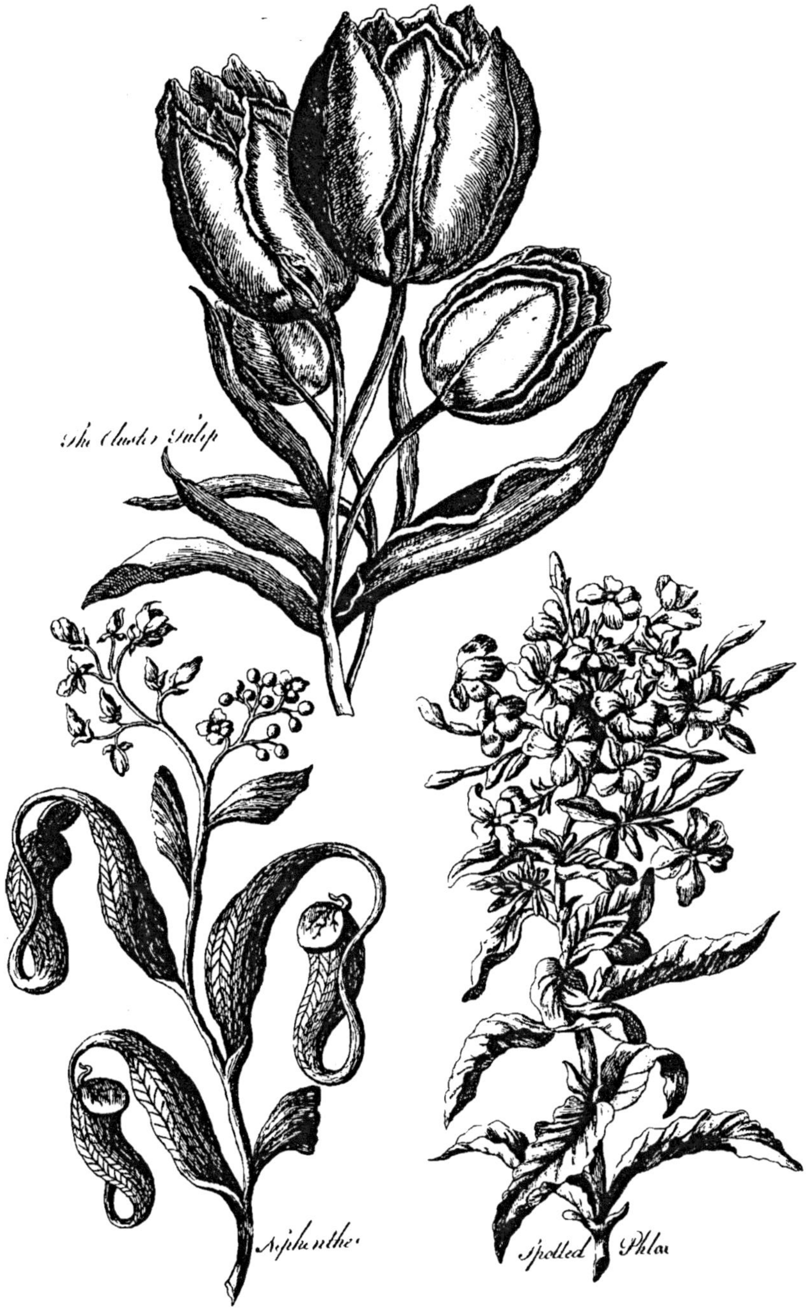
The Cluster Tulip
Nepenthe
Spotted Phlox

out from the wings of the leaves on the upper parts of the ſtalks, they are of a reddiſh or light-purple colour, appear in June and July, but are not ſucceeded by ſeeds in England

Siberian Lychnidea deſcribed

9 Siberian *Lychnidea* The ſtalks are weak, ſlender, and about a foot long The leaves are narrow, hairy, and of a light green colour The flowers come out by threes growing on footſtalks from the tops of the ſtalks, they are of a reddiſh purple colour, appear in June and July, and are not ſucceeded by ſeeds in England

Theſe ſorts are all beautiful perennials, and deſerving of a place in every good flower garden, where a quantity is not deſired, but only a ſelect number of the beſt and moſt beautiful plants for ſhew

Culture

They are all propagated by parting of the roots, many of which creep and encreaſe very faſt, and thoſe which are leaſt inclined to ſpread generally afford offsets enough for multiplication The beſt time for parting of the roots is when the ſtalks decay in the end of ſummer, and they will be the ſooner eſtabliſhed and leſs liable to be injured by froſts the ſucceeding winter When they are planted out, they will require no trouble except keeping them clean from weeds, and reducing the roots as often as they ſpread too far, they are very hardy, and will grow in any ſoil or ſituation, but are much more beautiful in freſh loamy earth in open places

They may alſo be multiplied by cuttings, and this method is moſtly practiſed on thoſe ſorts that have leaſt tendency to throw out offsets from the roots

By this method they may be more ſpeedily propagated if a large quantity is wanted The time for planting them is in May, as the ſtalks ſhoot up for flowering The ſtalks ſhould be cut as near the ground as may be, and having taken off the tops, leaving them about four or five inches long, let them be ſet in pots, many together, filled with good, freſh, loamy earth Let the pots be immediately ſet in the ground, the windows being open, and the cuttings well watered, their ſituation muſt be in ſome ſhady part of the houſe, and water muſt every other day be regularly afforded the cuttings This will cauſe them ſoon to ſtrike root, and when you perceive them to be in a good growing ſtate, they muſt be removed out of the houſe, (or they will ſoon be drawn too weak) and placed in a ſhady part of the garden At the approach of winter they ſhould be ſet under ſome warm hedge, in a well-ſheltered place, for their winter ſituation, or if the froſt ſhould ſet in very ſevere, they may be removed under ſhelter until it is over In the ſpring they may be planted out in different places allotted for them, ſome of them will flower in the ſummer, tho' perhaps but weakly, but the ſummer after that they will be ſtrong, and exhibit their bloom in perfection

Titles

1 Paniculated *Lychnidea* is titled, *Phlox foliis lanceolatis margine ſcabris, corymbis paniculatis* Dillenius calls it, *Lychnidea folio ſalicino*, and Plukenet, *Lyſimachia Virginiana umbellata maxima, lyſimachiæ luteæ floribus amplioribus* It grows naturally in North America

2 Spotted *Lychnidea* is, *Phlox foliis lanceolatis lævibus, racemo oppoſite corymboſo* Ray calls it, *Lychnoides Marilandica, foliis binis oppoſitis baſi & caulis coulem utrinque amplexantibus* It grows naturally in Virginia

3 Hairy *Lychnidea* is, *Phlox foliis lanceolatis villoſis, caule erecto, corymbo terminali* Ray calls it, *Lychnoides Marilandica, calycibus lanuginoſis, foliis anguſtis acutis*, and Plukenet, *Lychnidea umbellifera, blattariæ accedens Virginiana major repens, pſeudomelampyri foliis piloſis, flore pentapetaloide fiſtuloſo* It grows naturally in Virginia

4 Carolina *Lychnidea* is, *Phlox foliis lanceolatis lævibus, caule ſcabro, corymbis ſubfaſtigiatis* In Miller's Dictionary it is termed, *Lychnidea foliis lanceolatis ſeſſilibus glabris craſſis, caule erecto, floribus verticillatis terminalibus* Martyn calls it, *Lychnidea Caroliniana floribus quaſi umbellatim diſpoſitis, foliis lucidis craſſis acutis* It grows common in Carolina

5 Smooth Virginian *Lychnidea* is, *Phlox foliis linear lanceolatis glabris, caule erecto, corymbo terminali* Dillenius calls it, *Lychnidea folio melampyri* It is a native of Virginia

6 Divaricated *Lychnidea* is, *Phlox foliis lato-lanceolatis ſuperioribus alternis caule bifido, pedunculis geminis* Plukenet calls it *Lychnidea Virginiana, alſines aquaticæ foliis, floribus in ramulis divaricatis* It grows naturally in Virginia

7 Oval-leaved *Lychnidea* is, *Phlox foliis ovatis, floribus ſolitariis* Plukenet calls it, *Lychnidea fiſtuloſa Marilandica, clinopodii vulgaris folio, flore amplo ſingulari* It grows naturally in Virginia.

8 Subulated *Lychnidea* is, *Phlox foliis ſubulatis hirſutis, floribus oppoſitis* Plukenet calls it, *Lychnidea, blattariæ accedens Virginiana, minor repens, hirſutis camphoratæ foliis* It is a native of Virginia

9 Siberian *Lychnidea* is, *Phlox foliis linearibus villoſis, pedunculis ternis* It grows in the northern parts of Aſia

Claſs and order in the Linnæan ſyſtem

*Phlox* is of the claſs and order *Pentandria Monogynia*, and the characters are,

The characters

1 Calyx is a monophyllous, cylindrical, decangular, permanent perianthium, indented in five parts at the top

2 Corolla is one hypocrateriform petal The tube is cylindrical, crooked, longer than the calyx, and narroweſt near the baſe The limb is plane, and divided into five obtuſe equal ſegments, which are ſhorter than the tube

3 Stamina are five filaments ſituated within the tube, having antheræ placed in the mouth of the flower

4 Pistillum conſiſts of a conical germen, a filiform ſtyle the length of the ſtamina, and a trifid acute ſtigma.

5 Pericarpium is an oval trigonal capſule, formed of three valves, and containing two cells

6 Semina The ſeeds are ſingle, and oval.

## C H A P. CCCXLV

## *P H R Y M A.*

THERE is only one ſpecies of this genus, called, *Phryma* or *Leptoſtachia*

*The plant deſcribed*

The root is fibrated and perennial The ſtalks are ſquare ſmooth, branching, and nearly a foot and a half high The leaves are oval, acute, a little rough on the ſurface, ſerrated, and grow oppoſite to each other on ſhort footſtalks The flowers come out in ſpikes from the tops of the ſtalks, they are ſmall, and of a white colour, having a mixture of purple on the outſide, they appear in July and Auguſt, but are ſeldom ſucceeded by ſeeds in England

*Method of raiſing it*

It is propagated by parting of the roots in the autumn It loves a freſh light ſoil, and the ſhade, if the place is open, and after it is ſet out will require no trouble, except keeping clean from weeds, until the roots get too large, and muſt by tranſplanting be reduced to a proper ſize

It is alſo propagated by ſowing the ſeeds in the ſpring, in beds of light freſh earth made fine When the plants come up they ſhould be thinned where they are too cloſe, kept clean from weeds, watered in dry weather all ſummer, and in the autumn may be removed to the places where they are deſigned to remain

*Titles*

This being the only ſpecies of the genus, it is called ſimply, *Phryma* Micheli calls it, *Leptoſtachia*, Plukenet, *Amaranthi Siculi Bocconis ſpica, floribus parvis purpureis propendentibus, herbâ Floridanâ*, Petiver, *Verbena Mariana, roſæ Chinenſis folio, ſeminibus deorſum tendentibus*, and Gronovius, *Verbena racemoſa, pl ... ſimo, floribus ſeſſilibus, calycibus fructûs reflexis racemoque appreſſis* It grows naturally in North America

*Claſs and order in the Linnæan ſyſtem* *The characters*

*Phryma* is of the claſs and order *Didynamia Gymnoſpermia*, and the characters are,

1 CALYX is a monophyllous, cylindrical, bilabiated, ſtriated perianthium The upper lip is long, narrow, and trifid, the lower one is obtuſe and bifid

2 COROLLA is one ringent petal The tube is the length of the calyx, the upper lip is ſhort, ſtraight, emarginated, and nearly oval, the lower lip is large, more ſpreading, and divided into three ſegments, the middle one being the longeſt

3 STAMINA are four filaments, two on each ſide, having roundiſh connivent antheræ in the mouth of the corolla

4 PISTILLUM conſiſts of an oblong germen, a filiform ſtyle the length of the ſtamina, and an obtuſe ſtigma

5 PERICARPIUM There is none

6 SEMEN The ſeed is ſingle, oblong, a little taper, and furrowed on one ſide

## C H A P. CCCXLVI

## *P H Y S A L I S, A L K E K E N G I,* or W I N T E R C H E R R Y

*Species*

OF this genus there are,

1 Common *Alkekengi*, or Winter Cherry

2 Penſylvanian Winter Cherry

3 Virginian Winter Cherry

*Deſcription of the Common Alkekengi*

1 Common *Alkekengi*, or Winter Cherry The root is yellowiſh, long, and creeping The ſtalks are numerous, upright, jointed, and a foot and a half high The leaves are large, oblong, pointed, entire, have long ſh footſtalks, and are generally two together from the ſame point The flowers come out from the ſides of the ſtalks on ſlender footſtalks, they are of a white colour, appear in July, and are ſucceeded by round pulpy berries, incloſed in large inflated bladders, they are round, as large as ſome ſorts of cherries, and are of a beautiful red colour when ripe, which will be in the autumn

*Medicinal properties of this plant*

Theſe cherries are in high eſteem as detergent, aperient, diuretick, and highly recommended for heat of urine, voiding of bloody water, ulcers in the kidneys and bladder, and more eſpecially for expelling gravel They are alſo ſaid to be of ſingular ſervice againſt the gout, both in effecting a cure and preventing its return They may be alſo boiled in milk, and ſweetened with ſugar, or eaten raw

*Penſylvanian Winter Cherry deſcrib'd*

2 Penſylvanian Winter Cherry The root is perennial and ſpreading, though in a much leſs degree than the former ſort The ſtalks are numerous, a foot and a half long, herbaceous, a little angular, weak, and unleſs ſupported will lie on the ground The leaves are oval, obtuſe, acutely indented, of a pale-green colour and grow alternately on longiſh footſtalks The flowers come out from the wings of the ſtalks on

on slender footstalks; they are moderately large, of a pale yellow colour, having a dark-coloured bottom, appear in July and August, and are succeeded by round berries about the size of pease, which are of a red colour when ripe.

Variety. There is a variety of this species with oval yellow berries.

Virginian Winter Cherry described. 3. Virginian Winter Cherry. The root is creeping like the first sort. The stalks are numerous, herbaceous, smooth, divide into several slender branches near the top, and grow to about a foot high. The leaves are heart-shaped, oval, obtuse, entire, rough, a little downy, and have longish footstalks. The flowers come out from the wings of the stalks on slender footstalks; they are of a pale yellow colour, having purple bottoms, appear in June and July, and are succeeded by large, round, viscous berries, which are of a greenish yellow colour when ripe.

Propagation. The first sort is extremely hardy, will grow in any soil or situation, and spreads amazingly by the root, insomuch that in a small space of time, a single root, especially if the land be rich and light, will occupy several yards square. The propagation, therefore, is by parting of the roots, which may be done at any time of the year; and by this method thousands of plants may be soon raised.

They are also propagated by seeds, but as the former method is so expeditious, that of seeds is not worth putting into practice, unless when a person happens to have a few of the berries, and no opportunity of obtaining the roots. In this case let them be sown, as soon as possible, in a light dry place, and covered down with about half an inch depth of the finest mould. If the plants do not come up in the spring, for they will often lie a whole year before they make their appearance, let the ground remain undisturbed, and kept in clean weeding all summer, and in the autumn sift a little fine mould over the bed. When the plants are about three inches high, they may be set in the places where they are designed to remain, or stand in the seed-bed until the autumn, before they are set out for good.

The second and third sort are also propagated by parting the roots, or sowing the seeds in the spring. In either case, where the plants are set out, the soil should be naturally dry, light, and warm, and the situation well defended, or the plants will be liable to be killed by our frosty winters, especially the third species, which is the most tender of the two. It would be adviseable therefore to set a few plants of each sort in pots, to be housed with the hardiest green-house plants in the winter; thus the kinds may be preserved, in case the plants abroad should be destroyed by bad weather.

1. *Alkekengi*, or Common Winter Cherry, is titled, *Physalis foliis geminis integris acutis, caule herbaceo inferne subramoso*. In the *Hortus Cliffort.* it is termed, *Physalis caule simplici annuo, foliis integris geminatis, floribus solitariis*. Van Royen calls it, *Physalis radice perenni, foliis lanceolato-cordatis*; Caspar Bauhine, *Solanum vesicarium*; Tournefort, *Alkekengi officinarum*; and others simply, *Alkekengi*. It grows naturally in low moist places in Germany, Italy, and Japan. Titles.

2. Pensylvanian Winter Cherry is, *Physalis foliis ovatis subrepandis obtusis glabriusculis, floribus geminis, caule herbaceo*. In Miller's Dictionary it is termed, *Physalis radice perenni, caule procumbente, foliis ovatis acute dentatis, petiolis longissimis*. Rand calls it, *Alkekengi Virginianum perenne majus, flore luteo amplo, fructu minimo*. It grows naturally in Pensylvania and Virginia.

3. Virginian Winter Cherry is, *Physalis foliis geminis repandis obtusis subtomentosis, caule herbaceo superne paniculato*. In the former edition of the *Species Plantarum* it is termed, *Physalis foliis cordatis integerrimis obtusis scabris, corollis glabris*. Van Royen calls it, *Physalis radice perenni, foliis cordatis obtusis*; and Dillenius, *Alkekengi Bonariense repens, flore luteo magno fructu*. It is a native of Virginia and Buenos Ayres.

Class and order in the Linnæan system. *Physalis* is of the class and order *Pentandria Monogynia*; and the characters are,

The characters. 1. Calyx is a small, monophyllous, swelling, five-cornered perianthium, cut at the top into five acute permanent segments.

2. Corolla is one rotated petal. The tube is very short; the limb is large, plicated, and slightly divided into five short, broad, acute segments.

3. Stamina are five very small, awl-shaped, connivent filaments, having erect connivent antheræ.

4. Pistillum consists of a roundish germen, a filiform style rather longer than the stamina, and an obtuse stigma.

5. Pericarpium is a roundish bilocular berry, situated in a large, inflated, closed, five-cornered, coloured calyx. The receptacle is reniform and duplicated.

6. Semina. The seeds are many, reniform and compressed.

CHAP.

# C H A P CCCXLVII.

## *PHYTEUMA*, RAMPIONS.

Species

THE species of this genus are,

1 Round-headed Horned Rampion
2 Grass leaved Rampion
3 Spiked Rampion
4 Small Alpine Rampion
5 Comose Rampion
6 Pyramidical Rampion

Description of the Round headed Horned,

1 Round headed Horned Rampion The root is thick, fibrated, and perennial The radical leaves are heart-shaped, smooth and beautifully serrated; those on the stalks are long, narrow, serrated, and sharp pointed The stalks are upright, single, and two or three feet high The flowers come out from the tops of the stalks in roundish heads, they are of a purple colour, appear in June, and are succeeded by small roundish capsules, containing ripe seeds, in August or September

Grass-leaved,

2 Grass-leaved Rampion The root is perennial, thick, and fibrated The leaves are narrow, and undivided on their edges The stalks are upright, firm, and two or three feet high The flowers come out from the tops of the stalks in roundish heads or umbels, they appear in June and July, and the seeds ripen in August and September

and Spiked Rampion

3 Spiked Rampion The root is thick, white, and strikes deep into the ground The radical leaves are cordated, but those on the stalks are spear shaped, and serrated on their edges The stalks are thick, upright, and a yard high The flowers come out from the tops of the stalks in oblong spikes, they are of a blue colour, appear in June and July, and the seeds ripen in September

Varieties

There is a variety of this species with white, and another with purplish flowers

Small Alpine,

4 Small Alpine Rampion This plant hath a thick fleshy root, of a sweet taste The leaves are all spear-shaped, obtuse, and serrated on their edges The stalks are slender, upright, and about a foot high The flowers are but few on the tops of the stalks, and disposed in the manner of a spike, they are of a bluish-purple colour, appear in May and June, and are succeeded by ripe seeds in August or September

Comose,

5 Comose Rampion The root is thick, sweet, and esculent The radical leaves are heart-shaped, indented, and of a deep green colour, but those on the stalks are oblong, narrow, indented, and grow on long footstalks The stalk is slender, striated, and about a foot high The flowers terminate the stalks in close bunches, immediately under which is situated a cluster of long narrow leaves The flowers are of a bluish purple colour, appear in June, and the seeds ripen in September

and Pyramidical Rampion described

6 Pyramidical Rampion The root is thick, oblong, white, and esculent The radical leaves are large, and cut or sinuated almost to the midrib The stalk is thick, round, striated, three or four feet high, and adorned with leaves like the radical ones, but smaller The flowers come out from the tops of the stalks in pyramidical spikes, they are moderately large, and of a fine purple colour, appear in June and July, and the seeds ripen in the autumn

Propagation.

These plants are all propagated by sowing the seeds in the autumn, soon after they are ripe, in the places where they are designed to remain The mould should be fresh, dry, light, and double-dug, for the roots to strike deep, and cause the stalks and flowers to be stronger and larger They should be sown in drills made for the largest sorts two feet asunder, for the smallest a foot and a half, and the seeds covered with no more than a quarter of an inch depth of mould In the spring the plants will come up, when they must be thinned in the rows, leaving them half a foot asunder, or more, according to the sorts All summer they must be kept clean from weeds, and in October the ground between the roots should be dug, and the summer following they will flower strong, and perfect their seeds

The first two sorts are perennials, and so are the others in some light dry soils, but in rich, dunged, moist gardens, they seldom last longer than three years, especially the fifth sort, which is generally reckoned biennial, the plants for the most part dying soon after the seeds are ripe, so that whoever is desirous of having these plants in perfection, should be careful to sow the seeds at due intervals, the more effectually to maintain the succession properly

Titles.

1 Round headed Horned Rampion is titled, *Phyteuma capitulo subrotundo, foliis serratis radicalibus cordatis* Guettard calls it, *Phyteuma foliis oblongis, spicâ orbiculari*, Columna, *Rapuntium montanum rarius corniculatum*, Caspar Bauhine, *Rapunculus folio oblongo, spicâ orbiculari*, also, *Rapunculus umbellatus latifolius*, also *Rapunculus umbellatus angustifolius*, Gerard, *Rapunculus corniculatus montanus*, and Parkinson, *Rapunculus alopecuroides orbiculatus* It grows naturally in dry pastures in England, Italy, and Helvetia

2 Grass-leaved Rampion is, *Phyteuma capitulo subrotundo, foliis linearibus integerrimis* Van Royen calls it *Phyteuma foliis linearibus, floribus capitatis*, Caspar Bauhine, *Rapunculus umbellatus flore gramineo*, and Columna, *Rapuntium alterum angustifolium Alpinum* It grows naturally on the Helvetian, Italian, and Pyrenean mountains

3 Spiked Rampion is, *Phyteuma spicâ oblongâ, capsulis bilocularibus, foliis radicalibus cordatis* In the *Amœnitates Acad* it is termed, *Phyteuma spicâ oblongâ nudâ, foliis caulinis lanceolatis serratis* Guettard calls it, *Phyteuma foliis cordato-lanceolatis, spicâ oblongâ*, Caspar Bauhine, *Rapunculus spicatus* [illegible], Morison, *Rapunculus foliis cordatis, spicâ florum oblongâ*, and Morison *Rapunculus corniculatus spicatus, alopecuroides flore albo & cæruleo* It grows naturally on the Alpine parts of Helvetia, Austria, France and Italy

4 Small Alpine Rampion is, *Phyteuma capitulo subfolioso, foliis omnibus lanceolatis* John Bauhine calls it, *Rapunculus Alpinus parvus comosus*, and Haller, *Rapunculus foliis obtusis, spicâ paucifl...*

*pauciflorâ* It grows naturally on the Helvetian and Styrian mountains

5 Comose Rampion is, *Phyteuma fasciculo terminali-sessili, foliis dentatis radicalibus cordatis* Caspar Bauhine calls it, *Rapunculus Alpinus corniculatus*; and Plukenet, *Campanula sphærocephalus pervenusta, foliorum ad oras insignites dent culata* It grows naturally on Mount Baldus, the Alps, and Austrian mountains

6 Pyramidical Rampion is, *Phyteuma floribus sparsis, foliis pinnatis* Caspar Bauhine calls it, *Rapunculus Creticus, s pyramidalis altera* and John Bauhine, *Rapunculus Creticus, petrœus vel* It grows naturally in Crete

Class and order in the Linnæan system

*Phyteuma* is of the class and order *Pentandria Monogynia*, and the characters are,

1 CALYX is a monophyllous perianthium situated on the germen, and divided into five acute parts

The characters

2 COROLLA is monopetalous, starry, spreading, and divided into five narrow acute segments, which are recurved

3 STAMINA are five filaments shorter than the corolla, having oblong antheræ

4 PISTILLUM consists of a germen situated below the flower, a filiforme recurved style the length of the corolla and an oblong, three pointed, revolute stigma

5 PERICARPIUM is a roundish capsule containing three cells

6 SEMINA The seeds are many, roundish, and small

# CHAP. CCCXLVIII

## *PHYTOLACCA*, AMERICAN NIGHTSHADE.

THERE are two perennials of this genus, called,

Species

1 Virginian *Phytolacca*

2 Mexican *Phytolacca*

Virginian Phytolacca described

1 Virginian *Phytolacca*. The root is remarkably thick, fleshy, and divides into several thick fleshy fibres, which strike deep into the ground The stalks are thick, herbaceous, six or eight feet high, divide into many branches near the top, and are covered with a purplish bark The leaves are oblong, pointed, entire, of a deep-green colour in the summer, but alter to a purple in the autumn, and grow irregularly on short footstalks The flowers come out in bunches on long footstalks, which arise from the divisions of the stalks, they are small, and each flower has its separate pedicle, about half an inch in length, they are decandrous, of a purplish colour, appear in July and August, and are succeeded by round, depressed, furrowed, umbilicated berries, containing the seeds, which frequently ripen in the autumn

Uses

In America the young shoots are boiled and eaten as Spinach, and two spoonfulls of the juice is said to be an useful purge to the inhabitants there The juice, especially of the berries, affords a purple dye to linen or paper but some ingredients seem wanting to make it lasting

Mexican Phytolacca described

2 Mexican *Phytolacca* The stalks are thick, upright, herbaceous two or three feet high, and divide into a few short branches near the top The leaves are oval, spear-shaped, much veined, of a deep-green colour, and come out without order on strong footstalks The flowers are collected in spikes, sitting close at the top of footstalks, which arise from the sides of the branches opposite to the leaves, they are octandrous, of a white colour, appear in July and August, and are succeeded by flat, umbilicated, furrowed berries, containing ripe seeds, in the autumn

Culture

These plants are raised by sowing the seeds in the spring in beds of light rich mould, in warm well-sheltered places The roots of the first sort being very large, the ground more especially for that should be double-dug, to make way for them to strike in, and the stalks will be proportionably stronger and finer The plants of the first sort ought to be four or five feet distant from each other, but the others need not be left more than two feet asunder. They will flower the second year, and sometimes the first, from the seeds, and every autumn the stalks should be cut down to the crowns of the roots, the surface of the mould stirred, the beds neated up, a little fresh mould added, and the shoots will be more vigorous the summer following The roots of the second sort frequently die after the flowers are fallen, and the seeds ripened, so that whoever is desirous of continuing this sort, should be careful to sow the seeds at proper intervals

Titles

1 The first species is titled, *Phytolacca floribus decandris decagynis* Dillenius calls it, *Phytolacca vulgaris*, and Plukenet, *Solanum racemosum Americanum* It grows naturally in Virginia

2 The second species is, *Phytolacca floribus octandris octogynis* Dillenius calls it, *Phytolacca Mexicana, baccis sessilibus* It grows naturally in Mexico

Class and order in the Linnæan system

*Phytolacca* is of the class and order *Decandria Decagynia*, and the characters are,

The characters

1 CALYX There is none

2 COROLLA is five roundish, concave, patent petals, which are coloured, permanent, and inflexed at their extremities

3 STAMINA are ten, eight, or else twenty awl-shaped filaments the length of the corolla, having round sh lateral antheræ.

4 PISTILLUM consists of an orbicular depressed germen, divided on the outside, terminated by eight or ten very short, patent, reflexed styles, having simple permanent stigmas.

5 PERICARPIUM is an orbicular, depressed, umbilicated berry, having ten longitudinal furrows, and containing ten cells.

6 SEMINA. The seeds are single, reniform, and smooth.

# CHAP. CCCXLIX.

## *PICRIS.*

THERE is one species of this genus for this place, called Pyrenean *Picris*.

This plant described. The root is tough, yellowish, and fibrous. The stalks are upright, rough, hairy, and about a foot high. The leaves are oblong, pointed, hairy, sinuated, and indented on the edges. The flowers come out from the upper parts of the stalks on hairy footstalks, they are large, of a yellow colour, appear in June, July, and August, and the seeds ripen soon after the flowers are fallen.

Its propagation. It is propagated by sowing the seeds as soon as they are ripe, or the spring after, in any soil or situation, and they will readily grow. When they are fit to remove they may be transplanted to any place wanted, or they may remain in the beds, thinning them to proper distances, and keeping them clean from weeds. The summer following they will flower, and perfect their seeds, which being furnished with down will be dispersed by the winds, and plants will come up all over the garden by the casual falling of such scattered seeds.

Titles. This species is titled, *Picris perianthiis laxis, caule piloso, foliis dentato-sinuatis*. Herman calls it, *Hieracium Pyrenaicum, blattariæ folio, minus pilosum*. It grows naturally on the Pyrenees.

Class and order in the Linnæan system. *Picris* is of the class and order *Syngenesia Polygamia Æqualis*, and the characters are,

The characters.

1 CALYX is double. The exterior is large, and composed of five heart-shaped, plane, loose, connivent leaves. The interior is imbricated and oval.

2 COROLLA. The general flower is imbricated and uniform. The florets are all hermaphrodites, and each consists of one tongue-shaped, narrow, truncated petal, indented in five parts at the top.

3 STAMINA are five very short capillary filaments, having a cylindrical tubular anthera.

4 PISTILLUM consists of an oval germen, a style the length of the stamina, and two reflexed stigmas.

5 PERICARPIUM. There is none.

6 SEMINA. The seeds are single, ventricose, obtuse, and crowned with a feathery down.

The receptacle is naked.

# CHAP. CCCL.

## *PIMPINELLA*, BURNET SAXIFRAGE.

OF this genus are two perennial species, called,

Species.

1 English Burnet Saxifrage.
2 Foreign Burnet Saxifrage.

English Burnet Saxifrage described. 1 English Burnet Saxifrage admits of many varieties, but two more especially, called,

Varieties.

Great Burnet Saxifrage.
Small Burnet Saxifrage.

Great Burnet Saxifrage. Great Burnet Saxifrage. The root is thick, taper, strikes straight into the ground like a parsnep, and is not biting to the taste. The leaves are pointed, pinnated, and the radical ones

ones have three or four pair of oblong serrated folioles, terminated by an odd one They are of a dark-green colour, and grow on long footstalks, the cauline leaves are like the radical ones, but smaller, and those on the branches are still less, consisting only of two or three parts, which sit almost close The stalks are upright, hollow, jointed, firm, branching, and two feet high The flowers come out from the ends of the branches in small umbels, they are of a white, though sometimes of a red colour, appear in July, and the seeds ripen in the autumn

Small Burnet Saxifrage described

Small Burnet Saxifrage The root is slender, acrid, and strikes straight into the ground The leaves are pinnated, the radical ones are composed of three or four pair of deeply-cut folioles, terminated by an odd one, but those on the stalks are linear, some consisting of three, and others of five narrow parts The stalks are slender, hollow jointed, branching, and a foot and a half high The flowers come out in small umbels from the ends of the branches, they are of a white colour, appear in July, and are succeeded by warm acrid seeds, which ripen in the autumn

Medicinal properties of it

The root of this species (including both varieties) is in much esteem as a stomachic, resolvent, detergent, diuretic, diaphoretic, and alexipharmac It is used in cutaneous and scorbutic disorders, foulness of the blood, swelling of the glands, &c and is an ingredient in the *pulvis ari compositus* The virtues of this root are most perfect when extracted by distillation

Foreign Burnet Saxifrage described

2 Foreign Burnet Saxifrage The radical leaves are pinnated, and indented on their edges, those on the stalks are wedge shaped, and deeply cut into several segments The stalks are round, striated, hollow, jointed, and about a foot and a half high The flowers come out in umbels from the tops of the branches, they are of a white colour, appear in July and August and are succeeded by striated, warm, aromatick seeds, which ripen in the autumn

Method of propagation

These sorts are raised by sowing the seeds in the autumn, as soon as they are ripe, or in the spring The ground should be light, dry, and double dug, for the roots more freely to strike deep and the stalks will be proportionably larger and finer the following year When they come up they must be thinned to proper distances, and constantly kept clean from weeds, which is all the trouble they will require The second year, however, they will flower, and perfect their seeds

Titles.

1 English Burnet Saxifrage is, *Pimpinella foliis pinnatis; foliolis radicalibus subrotundis, summis linearibus* In the *Flora Suecica* it is termed, *Pimpinella foliolis subrotundis*, in the *Hortus Cliffortianus*, *Pimpinella* Caspar Bauhine calls it, *Pimpinella saxifraga major*, also, *Pimpinella saxifraga minor altera*, also, *Pimpinella saxifraga major, umbellâ candidâ*, also, *Pimpinella saxifraga major, umbellâ rubente*, also, *Pimpinella saxifraga tenuifolia*, Gerard, *Pimpinella saxifraga*, also, *Pimpinella seu saxifraga minor*, Parkinson, *Pimpinella saxifraga hircina major*, also, *Pimpinella saxifraga hircina minor*, Ray, *Pimpinella saxifraga minor, foliis sanguisorbæ*, and Hudson, *Pimpinella foliis pinnatis foliolis cordatis, impari trilobo* It grows naturally in woods, hedges, dry meadows, and pastures in England, Switzerland, France, and Italy

2 Foreign Burnet Saxifrage is, *Pimpinella foliis radicalibus pinnatis crenatis, summis cuneiformibus incisis* In the *Hortus Cliffortianus* it is termed, *Anisum foliis radicalibus pinnatis* Caspar Bauhine calls it, *Apium peregrinum, foliis subrotundis*, and Columna, *Daucus tertius Dioscoridis* It grows naturally in the sterile pastures of Italy

Class and order in the Linnæan System

*Pimpinella* is of the class and order *Pentandria Digynia*, and the characters are,

The characters

1 Calyx The general umbel is composed of many rays, the partial of yet more numerous, the involucrum is found to neither of them, the perianthium is very small

2 Corolla The general flower is nearly uniform, and each floret has five inflexed heart-shaped petals that are nearly equal

3 Stamina are five simple filaments longer than the corollula, having roundish antheræ

4 Pistillum consists of a germen below the flower, and two very short styles with roundish stigmas

5 Pericarpium There is none The fruit is oval, oblong, and divided into two parts

6 Semina The seeds are two, oblong, narrowest towards the point, convex, striated on one side, and on the other plane

CHAP

# C H A P. CCCLI.

## *PINGUICULA*, BUTTER-WORT.

THERE are four species of this genus, all perennials, called,

Species
1 Common Butter-wort, or Yorkshire Sanicle
2 Cornwall Butter-wort
3 Alpine Butter-wort
4 Hairy Butter-wort

Description of Common,

1 Common Butter-wort, or Yorkshire Sanicle The root is moderately thick, short, and fibrous The leaves are four or five at each root, of a thickish substance, soft, unctuous, full of juice, of a yellowish green colour, and the outer ones spread on the ground The flower-stalks are simple, naked, grow three or four from each root, and about five or six inches high The flowers come out singly from the tops of the stalks, they are of different varieties, such as the White, the Purple, the Blush, the Blue, and most frequently a mixture of these colours in the same flower, they appear in May and June, and the seeds ripen in July

Cornwall,

2 Cornwall Butter-wort The leaves are small, soft, grow four or five from the root, and the exterior ones lie on the ground The stalks are upright, slender, and three or four inches high The flowers come out singly from the tops of the stalks, are small, and generally of a pale flesh colour, they appear in May and June, and the seeds ripen in July and August

Alpine,

3 Alpine Butter-wort The leaves of this species are nearly tongue shaped, obtuse, fat and unctuous on the surface, of a pale green colour, and usually four or five grow from the root The stalks are simple, slender, grow two or three from the root, and four or five inches high The flowers come out singly from the tops of the stalks, and are generally of a white colour, having an elegant yellow spot in the middle, they appear in May and June, and the seeds ripen in July

and Hairy Butter wort

4 Hairy Butter-wort This is the smallest of all the species The root consists only of about four or five branching fibres The leaves are not an inch long, grow three or four from the root, are thickish, of an oily surface, and a pale green colour The stalks are single, two or three inches high, and covered with numerous fine soft hairs The flowers come out singly from the tops of the stalks, are small, and of a pale blue, red, or purple colour, they appear about the same time with the other species, and the seeds ripen accordingly

Method of propagating them

If any one chuses these little elegant violet-looking flowers within the vortex of his morning perambulation, he should mark out some moist or boggy parts where he would have them grow, and let the ground be well dug, and if this be repeated until the whole be made fine, and the turf rotted, it will be so much the better Then having procured some seeds of the different kinds, let them be sown as soon as possible in those places, covering them over with not half a quarter of an inch depth of mould Leave them then to Nature, the plants will come up with the herbage, and annually exhibit their flowers and unctuous leaves amongst the natural produce of the place

The roots may also be taken up when they have done flowering, with a spade-full of mould to each, and if planted with care in some moist, boggy parts of the garden, they will grow, and exhibit their bloom the May following

Titles.

1 Common Butter-wort, or Yorkshire Sanicle, is entitled, *Pinguicula nectario cylindraceo longitudine petali* Caspar Bauhine calls it, *Sanicula montana flore calcari donato*, John Bauhine, *Pinguicula Gesneri*; Gerard and Parkinson, *Pinguicula sive Sanicula Eboracensis* It grows naturally in moist, boggy places in many parts of the North of England, and in most other countries of Europe

2 Cornwall Butter-wort is, *Pinguicula nectario apice incrassato* Ray calls it, *Pinguicula flore minore carneo*; others, *Viola palustris pinguicula dicta* It grows naturally in Cornwall, also in Lusitania

3 Alpine Butter-wort is, *Pinguicula nectario conico petalo breviore* Ray calls it, *Pinguicula flore albo minore, calcari brevissimo* It grows naturally in great plenty on the Alps of Lapland, and is found, though more sparingly, in most of the northern parts of Europe

4 Hairy Butterwort is, *Pinguicula scapo villoso* Ray calls it, *Pinguicula Cornubiensis, flore minore carneo* It grows naturally in Cornwall, in many parts of Germany, Lapland, and most of the cold countries of Europe

Class and order in the Linnæan system

*Pinguicula* is of the class and order *Diandria Monogynia*, and the characters are,

The characters

1 CALYX is a small, acute, ringent, permanent perianthium The upper lip is erect and trifid, the lower lip is reflexed, and cut into two segments

2 COROLLA is one ringent petal The longer lip is straight, obtuse, supine, and cut into three segments, the shorter lip is more obtuse, more spreading, and cut into two segments There is a corniculated nectarium produced from the base of the petal

3 STAMINA are two cylindrical, crooked, rising filaments, shorter than the calyx, having roundish antheræ

4 PISTILLUM consists of a globose germen, a very short style, and a bilabiated stigma The upper lip is the largest, plane, reflexed, and covers the antheræ, the lower lip is shorter, very narrow, erect, and bifid

5 PERICARPIUM is an oval, unilocular capsule, compressed at the top, where it opens for the discharge of the seeds

6 SEMINA The seeds are many, and cylindrical

# CHAP CCCLII

## PISUM, The PEA.

The plant described

THERE is a perennial species of the Pea, which grows naturally in England, Canada, and some other parts of the world. It admits of two or three varieties, and the Canada sort is much larger than that which grows in England. The roots run far into the ground, the stalks are angular, the leaves are a little downy, and the flowers are produced many together on footstalks, and succeeded by a tolerable eatable pea.

Various conjectures upon the first discovery of it in England

This species, though it grows naturally in many parts of England, was taken little notice of before the year 1555, at which time there being nearly a famine, the poor, pinched with hunger, found these peas growing in amazing quantities by the sea-side, between Orford and Aldborough, in Suffolk, on a rocky, barren place, where nothing else could grow. They were supposed to be miraculously sent thither to preserve life, and the Bishop of Norwich, and many of the Nobility, as well as others, resorted to see them, who must be amazed to find them growing in such quantities in such places, where neither grass nor any other produce was ever seen. Some thought they were pease cast on shore by shipwreck, and others, no doubt, had their various conjectures. But all this was for want of knowing the nature of the plant. The root is perennial, strikes deep, and grows naturally among rocks and such places, and, without doubt, these pease were growing in the above-mentioned place ages before, though unnoticed until that time.

But be this as it will, History informs us, that in that year of scarcity there was a most amazing, if not a miraculous, crop of pease at this place, and that in the month of August, and afterwards, the poor resorted from all quarters, and gathered them in such plenty, as to lower the price of provisions.

Method of propagating it

This species is hardly ever propagated in gardens. But if a person has a dry, rocky, sandy part, he may for variety's sake sow a few of these pease therein, and they will strike the roots deep, and annually produce their flowers and fruit, though, for eating, this is reckoned one of the worst sort of pease yet known.

Titles

The title of this species is, *Pisum petiolis supra planiusculis caule angulato, stipulis sagittatis, pedunculis multifloris*. In the *Hortus Cliffort.* it is termed, *Pisum stipulis integerrimis*. Ray calls it, *Pisum marinum*, Morison, *Pisum spontaneum perenne repens humile*. It grows naturally on sandy places near the sea in many parts of Europe.

Class and order in the Linnæan system

*Pisum* is of the class and order *Diadelphia Decandria*, and the characters are,

The characters

1. CALYX is a monophyllous perianthium, cut into five acute, permanent segments, of which the two uppermost are the broadest.

2. COROLLA is papilionaceous. The vexillum is very broad, obcordated, reflexed, and indented, with a point.

The alæ, or wings, are roundish, connivent, and shorter than the vexillum. The carina, or keel, is compressed, semilunulated, and shorter than the wings.

3. STAMINA are diadelphous. The upper filament stands singly, is plane, and awl-shaped, the other nine, which are joined together, are cylindrical below the middle, and awl-shaped above. The antheræ of all are roundish.

4. PISTILLUM consists of an oblong, compressed germen, a triangular, rising, membranaceous style carinated in its upper part, and an oblong, hairy stigma.

5. PERICARPIUM is a large, long, taper pod, formed of two valves, and terminated by a rising point.

6. SEMINA. The seeds are many, and roundish.

# C H A P. CCCLIII.

## *P L A N T A G O.* P L A N T A I N.

Species. THE diſtinct ſpecies of this genus are,

1 Broad leaved Plantain
2 Aſiatic Plantain
3 Hoary Plantain
4 Talleſt Plantain
5 Rib-wort, or Rib wort Plantain
6 *Catanance* Plantain
7 White Spaniſh Plantain
8 Alpine Plantain
9 Narrow-leaved Plantain
10 Subulated Plantain
11 Jagged leaved Plantain.
12 Buck's-horn Plantain
13 Sea Plantain
14 Graſs-leaved Plantain
15 Shrubby Italian Plantain, or *Cynops*
16 African Plantain, or Jagged leaved Flea-wort

Broad leaved Plantain deſcribed. 1 Broad-leaved Plantain The root is thick, ſhort, and frequently ends abruptly, where it is hung with many long whitiſh fibres The leaves are oval, broad, obtuſe, ſmooth, and marked with three ſtrong longitudinal nerves on each ſide of the mid-rib The ſtalks are naked, upright, thick, round, a little hairy, and near a foot high. The flowers are arranged along the tops of the ſtalks in long, ſlender, cylindrical, imbricated ſpikes, they appear all ſummer, and are to be found every-where, eſpecially by way-ſides

Its uſes in medicine. The leaves and ſeeds are aſtringent, and recommended in hæmorrhages The leaves bruiſed, and applied to green wounds, effect a ſpeedy cure

Varieties. There are numerous varieties of this ſpecies, ſuch as,

The Small Broad-leaved,
The Long Green ſpiked,
The Purple,
The Short Oval-ſpiked,
The Roſe Plantain, &c

Deſcription of Aſiatic, 2 Aſiatic Plantain The leaves are oval, ſmooth, ribbed, and often indented near the baſe The ſtalks are angular and eight or ten inches high The flowers come out from the tops of the ſtalks in very long, ſlender, but not imbricated ſpikes, being placed at a ſmall diſtance from each other, they appear in June and July, and the ſeeds ripen in Auguſt

Hoary, 3 Hoary Plantain The leaves are oval broad, have ſeven ſtrong, longitudinal ribs, and are of a hoary-whitiſh green colour The ſtalks are round, naked, hoary, and eight or ten inches high The flowers come out from the tops of the ſtalks in ſhort, thick, oblong ſpikes, they appear in June, July, and Auguſt, and the ſeeds ripen in September

Talleſt, 4 Talleſt Plantain The radical leaves are four or five feet high, thick, ſtrong ſmooth, have five ſtrong ribs, and are a little indented on their edges The ſtalks are thick, hairy, angular, and a yard or more in height The flowers come out from the tops of the ſtalks in oblong, cylindrical ſpikes, they appear in July and Auguſt, and the ſeeds ripen in the autumn

Rib wort, 5 Rib wort, or Rib wort Plantain The leaves are ſpear ſhaped, and ribbed with five ſtrong longitudinal nerves The ſtalks are ſlender, angular, and ſix or eight inches high The flowers come out from the tops of the ſtalks in longiſh, naked ſpikes, and are to be ſeen every-where from June to the end of ſummer

Catanance, 6 *Catanance* Plantain The leaves are ſpear-ſhaped, ſlightly indented, downy underneath, and not ribbed like the former ſorts The ſtalks are round, taper, upright, and ſix or eight inches high The flowers come out from the tops in roundiſh, looſe, hairy ſpikes, they appear in July and Auguſt and the ſeeds ripen in September

White Spaniſh 7 White Spaniſh Plantain The leaves are ſpear ſhaped, narrow, oblique, hairy, and of a hoary whiteneſs The ſtalks are taper, hoary, and much taller than the leaves The flowers come out from the tops in oblong ſpikes, appear in July and Auguſt, and are ſoon ſucceeded by ripe ſeeds

Alpine 8 Alpine Plantain The leaves are narrow, flat or convex underneath, hairy, and of a blackiſh green colour The ſtalks are ſlender, round, and hairy The flowers come out from the tops in oblong ſpikes, hang drooping at firſt, but ſoon recover themſelves, and grow erect, they appear chiefly in July and Auguſt, and are ſoon followed by ripe ſeeds in plenty

Narrow leaved 9 Narrow-leaved Plantain The leaves are very numerous, narrow, flat on one ſide, convex on the other, and poſſeſſed of a downy or woolly matter near the baſe The ſtalks are taper, and ſix or eight inches high The flowers are produced in oblong ſpikes from the tops of the ſtalks, and appear chiefly in June and July, though they are ſometimes found in the autumn

Subulated 10 Subulated Plantain The leaves are numerous at the crown of the root, awl-ſhaped, ſlender, angular, acute, woolly near the baſe, and a little rough on the edges The ſtalks are taper, ſlender, and three or four inches high The flowers come out from the tops of the ſtalks in oval, oblong, ſmooth ſpikes, and appear in June and July

Jagged leaves 11 Jagged-leaved Plantain The leaves are ſpear-ſhaped, ſtriated, have five ſtrong longitudinal nerves, are downy underneath, and deeply cut or indented on the edges. The ſtalk is round, ſlender, and covered with a ſoft down The flowers come out from the tops of the ſtalks in ſmall ſpikes, and appear about the ſame time with the former

Buck's horn, 12 Buck's-horn Plantain The root is thick, long, white, and ſweet to the taſte The leaves are numerous at the crown of the root, and ſpread themſelves in all directions; they are narrow, and divided at the edges into ſeveral diſtant ſegments, ſo as to occaſion their being thought by ſome to bear the reſemblance of a ſtag's horn The ſtalks are ſlender, round, hairy, and four or five inches high The flowers are produced in long, ſlender ſpikes, appear in June, and continue in ſucceſſion frequently throughout the ſummer

Sea, 13 Sea Plantain The leaves are narrow, and have a few inciſures or gaſhes chiefly on one

ſide

side. The stalk is slender, upright, hairy, and five or six inches high. The flowers come out from the tops of the stalks in oval spikes, are of a brownish colour, and appear chiefly in July.

Grass-leaved, 14. Grass leaved Plantain. The root is composed of several long and thickish fibres. The leaves are numerous, awl-shaped, succulent, and two or three inches long. The stalks are only an inch or two in height. The flowers come out singly from the tops of the stalks, and are to be found chiefly in July.

Shrubby Italian, 15. Shrubby Italian Plantain, or Cynops. The stalks are ligneous, tough, hard, branching, eight or ten inches high, and covered with a purplish bark. The leaves are slender, awl shaped, entire, and a little hairy near the base. The flowers come out from the wings of the leaves on long footstalks, they are collected in small heads, attended by oval concave bracteæ, and appear chiefly in July and August.

and African Plantain 16. African Plantain, or Jagged-leaved Fleawort. The stalk is shrubby, erect, downy, branching, and about a foot high. The leaves are spear-shaped, striated, hairy, and deeply cut or indented on their edges. The flowers come out in spikes from the ends of the branches, are of a whitish colour, and have no bractea.

Method of propagation. The English species are never cultivated, but the foreign sorts, particularly the fourth, sixth, seventh, fifteenth, and sixteenth, are found in some curious gardens. They are propagated by sowing the seeds, in the spring, in beds of dry, light earth, in well-sheltered situations, and they will bear our winters very well. The second summer they will flower, and, if the season proves favourable, will perfect their seeds.

The 14th and 15th species may be also propagated by cuttings or slips, planted in any of the summer months. But though they are tolerably hardy in dry, warm, well-sheltered places, it will be adviseable to have a few of each species set in pots filled with light, sandy, fresh earth, to be housed in winters, in order to continue the sort in case those abroad should be destroyed by bad weather.

Titles. 1. Broad leaved Plantain is entitled, *Plantago foliis ovatis glabris, scapo tereti, spicâ flosculis imbricatis*. In the *Hortus Cliffort.* it is termed, *Plantago foliis ovatis glabris*, in the *Flora Lapponica, Plantago scapo spicato, foliis ovatis*. Camerarius calls it, *Plantago major*, Parkinson, *Plantago latifolia vulgaris*, and Caspar Bauhine, *Plantago latifolia sinuata*, also, *Plantago latifolia glabra minor*, also, *Plantago latifolia rosea, floribus quasi in spicâ dispositis*, also, *Plantago latifolia, spica multiplici sparsa*; also, *Plantago latifolia rosea, flore expanso*. It grows naturally by way-sides in England, most parts of Europe, and Japan.

2. Asiatic Plantain is, *Plantago foliis ovatis glabris, scapo angulato, spica flosculis distinctis*. It is a native of China and Siberia.

3. Hoary Plantain is, *Plantago foliis ovato-lanceolatis pubescentibus, spicâ cylindricâ, scapo tereti*. Clusius calls it, *Plantago major incana*, Gerard, *Plantago incana*, and Caspar Bauhine, *Plantago latifolia incana*, also, *Plantago latifolia hirsuta minor*, also, *Plantago latifolia incana, spicis variis*. It grows naturally by way-sides, and in sterile pastures in England and most countries of Europe.

4. Tallest Plantain is, *Plantago foliis lanceolatis quinquenerviis dentatis glabris, scapo subangulato, spicâ oblongo-cylindricâ*. Tilli calls it, *Plantago montana, crasso glabro canaliculato tenuioreque folio, profundissime radicata*. It is a native of Italy.

5. Ribwort, or Rib-wort Plantain, is, *Plantago foliis lanceolatis, spicâ subovatâ nudâ, scapo angulato*. Dodonæus calls it, *Plantago minor*; Gerard, *Plantago quinquenervia*, John Bauhine, *Plantago lanceolata*, and Caspar Bauhine, *Plantago angustifolia major*, also, *Plantago trinervia, folio angustissimo*; also, *Plantago angustifolia major, caulium summitate foliosâ*. Another variety of it is termed by Tournefort, *Plantago argentea angustifolia e rupe victoriæ*. It grows naturally every where in England and most parts of Europe.

6. Catanance Plantain is, *Plantago foliis lanceolatis obsolete denticulatis, spica subrotundâ hirsuta, scapo tereti*. Morison calls it, *Plantago angustifolia, paniculis lagopi*, and Rauwolf, *Plantago Catanance*. It grows naturally in France, Portugal, and Spain.

7. White Spanish Plantain is, *Plantago foliis lanceolatis obliquis villosis, spicâ cylindrica erectâ, scapo tereti foliis longiori*. Van Royen calls it, *Plantago foliis lanceolato-linearibus, scapo longitudine foliorum, spica oblonga*, Sauvages, *Plantago foliis lanceolato-linearibus, scapo foliis duplo longiore, spicâ oblongâ*, Clusius, *Holosteum Salmanticense majus*, Caspar Bauhine, *Holosteum hirsutum albicans majus*, and John Bauhine, *Holosteum hirsutum albicans minus*. It grows naturally in dry places in France and Spain.

8. Alpine Plantain is, *Plantago foliis linearibus, planis hirsutis, spicâ oblongâ erectâ*. Haller calls it, *Plantago foliis linearibus, spicâ oblonga*, and Caspar Bauhine, *Holosteum hirsutum nigricans*. It grows naturally on the Helvetian and Austrian mountains.

9. Narrow-leaved Plantain is, *Plantago foliis semicylindraceis integerrimis, basi lanatis, scapo tereti*. In the *Flora Lapponica* it is termed, *Plantago scapo spicato, foliis linearibus subtus convexis*. Caspar Bauhine calls it, *Coronopus maritimus major*, and Tournefort, *Plantago maritima major tenuifolia*. It grows naturally on some of our sea-shores, and is found also in the like situations in several other parts of Europe, also in North-America.

10. Subulated Plantain is, *Plantago foliis subulatis triquetris striatis scabris, scapo tereti*. Guettard calls it, *Plantago foliis triangulari-prismaticis*, Lobel, *Serpentina omnium minima*, and Caspar Bauhine, *Holosteum, strictissimo folio, minus*, also, *Holosteum Massiliense*. It grows naturally on the Mediterranean shores.

11. Jagged-leaved Plantain is, *Plantago foliis lanceolatis quinquenerviis dentato-serratis, scapo tereti*. Columna calls it, *Plantago Apula laciniata bulbosa*. It grows naturally in Apulia and Mauritania.

12. Buck's-horn Plantain is, *Plantago foliis linearibus dentatis, scapo tereti*. In the *Hortus Cliffort.* it is termed, *Plantago foliis linearibus pinnato-dentatis*. Dodonæus calls it, *Herba stella, seu cornu cervinum*, Caspar Bauhine, *Coronopus sylvestris hirsutior*, also, *Coronopus hortensis*. It grows naturally in gravelly, sandy places in England and most countries of Europe.

13. Sea Plantain is, *Plantago foliis linearibus subdentatis, scapo tereti, spicâ ovatâ, bracteis carinatis membranaceis*. Gerard calls it, *Plantago marina*, and Parkinson, *Plantago marina vulgaris*. Hudson stiles it, *Plantago foliis linearibus subdentatis, scapo tereti, spicâ cylindricâ, bracteis carinatis membranaceis*. It grows naturally on the sea marshes in England.

14. Grass-leaved Plantain is, *Plantago scapo unifloro*. Guettard calls it, *Plantago floribus femineis sessilibus ad exortum scapi unifloris maris*; Morison, *Gramen junceum, capitulis quatuor longissimis filamentis donatis*, and Tournefort, *Plantago palustris*

*palustris gramineo folio, monanthos Parisiensis* It grows naturally in moist, sandy places in England and most countries of Europe

15 Shrubby Italian Plantain, or Cynops, is, *Plantago caule ramoso fruticoso, foliis filiformibus integerrimis strictis, capitulis subfoliatis* In the *Hortus Cliffort* it is termed, *Plantago perennis, foliis integerrimis, caule ramoso diffuso* Morison calls it, *Psyllium sempervirens*, and Caspar Bauhine, *Psyllium majus supinum* It grows naturally in many parts of France and Italy

16 African Plantain, or Jagged-leaved Fleawort, is, *Plantago caule ramoso fruticoso, foliis lanceolatis dentatis, capitulis aphyllis* Caspar Bauhine calls it, *Psyllium, foliis crenatis, Indicum*, and Boccone, *Psyllium foliis laciniatis* It grows naturally in Sicily and Barbary

*Plantago* is of the class and order *Tetrandria Monogynia*, and the characters are, Class and order in the Linnæan system

1. Calyx is a very short, permanent, upright perianthium, divided into four parts

2 Corolla consists of one petal The tube is cylindrical, and globose The limb is depressed, and divided into four oval, acute segments The characters

3 Stamina are four very long, erect, capillary filaments, having oblongish, compressed, incumbent antheræ

4 Pistillum consists of an oval germen, a filiforme style hardly half the length of the stamina, and a simple stigma

5 Pericarpium is an oval capsule of two cells

6 Semina The seeds are many, and oblong

# C H A P CCCLIV.

## *PLUMBAGO,* LEAD-WORT.

THERE is only one hardy species of this genus, called European Lead-wort

This plant described — The stalks are slender, weak, channelled, branching, and about a yard high The leaves are spear shaped, rough, entire, and embrace the stalks with their base The flowers come out from the ends of the stalks and branches in small tufts or bunches, they are of a blue colour, appear in October, but are not succeeded by seeds in England

Varieties — There is a variety of it with white flowers, another with purple, and a third with smooth leaves

Medicinal properties of it — This species is very caustic, and often called Tooth-wort, from the extraordinary quality it is said to possess of curing the tooth ach

Its cultivation — It is propagated by parting of the roots, the best time for which is the end of autumn, when the stalks decay They should have a light, dry soil, and a warm situation, otherwise they will not flower When they are set out, they will require no trouble, except clearing the stalks off every autumn, digging the ground between the roots in winter, and keeping it clean from weeds in summer

Proper soil and situation

Titles — This species is titled, *Plumbago foliis amplexicaulibus lanceolatis scabris* Caspar Bauhine calls it, *Lepidium dentiliaria dictum*, and Columna, *Tripolium Dioscoridis* It is a native of most of the southern parts of Europe

*Plumbago* is of the class and order *Pentandria Monogynia*, and the characters are, Class and order in the Linnæan system

1 Calyx is a monophyllous, oval, oblong, tubular, pentagonal, rough, permanent perianthium, indented in five parts at the brim The characters

2 Corolla is one funnel shaped petal The tube is cylindrical, narrowest near the top, and longer than the calyx The limb is divided into five oval, erect, spreading segments

The nectarium consists of five very small, acuminated valves, in the bottom of the corolla, including the germen

3 Stamina are five awl shaped filaments sitting on the valves of the nectarium within the tube of the flower, having small, oblong, versatile antheræ

4 Pistillum consists of a very small, oval germen, a simple style the length of the tube, and a slender, five-pointed stigma

5 Pericarpium There is none

6 Semen The seed is single, oval, and included in the calyx

CHAP

# CHAP. CCCLV

## *POA.*

THIS genus comprehends numerous species of our meadow grasses, called,

Species
1 Common Meadow Grass
2 Great Meadow Grass
3 Narrow-leaved Meadow Grass,
4 Creeping Meadow Grass
5 Wood Meadow Grass
6 Reed Meadow Grass
7 Marsh Meadow Grass
8 Bulbose Meadow Grass

Description of Common, 1 Common Meadow Grass The fibres of the root are numerous, slender, whitish, and variously implicated The leaves are narrow, sharp pointed, and of a dark green colour The stalks are upright, slender, light, round, jointed in two or three places, and about a foot high The flowers come out from the tops of the stalks in panicles, each spike is composed of three flowers, which are downy at their base They come first into blow the end of May or early in June, and are to be found every where in our meadows and pastures until the end of summer

Great, 2 Great Meadow Grass The root is a tuft of numerous fibres variously interwoven or implicated one with another The leaves are moderately broad pointed, and of a strong-green colour The stalks are upright, round, jointed, and two feet and a half or three feet high The flowers come out in diffused panicles from the tops of the stalks, the spikes are oval, smooth, and each is composed of five flowers They are in blow chiefly in June

Narrow-leaved, 3 Narrow-leaved Meadow Grass The leaves are very narrow, and nearly awl-shaped The stalks are erect, taper, jointed, and two feet high The flowers crown the tops of the stalks in diffused panicles the spikes are downy, and each is composed of four flowers Their chief blow is in June and July

Creeping, 4 Creeping Meadow Grass The root is white, creeping, and hung with numerous, slender fibres The stalks are compressed obliquely The flowers come out from the tops in panicles, the spikes which compose the panicles are oval, smooth, and compressed, and each consists of three, or else six flowers They appear in June, and new stalks arising from the creeping roots will frequently shew fresh flowers in the autumn

Wood, 5 Wood Meadow Grass The root is creeping The stalks are slender, and incurved The flowers are produced in loose panicles from the tops, the spiculæ, or little spikes, are mucronated, rough, and carry only about two or three flowers They appear chiefly in June, but are to be found in woods and shady places all summer

Reed, 6 Reed Meadow Grass This is a very large grass The leaves are larger than those of wheat, and the stalks are upright, round, firm, jointed, and as thick as a reed The flowers come out from the tops of the stalks in diffused panicles, the various spikes are whitish, narrow, and each contains six flowers They appear chiefly in July and August The stalks strike fresh roots from the lower joints, and the leaves are often beautifully variegated with white and green

Marsh, 7 Marsh Meadow Grass This is a less grass than the former The leaves are narrow, of a whitish green colour, and rough on the under side The flowers come out from the tops in elegant diffused panicles, the spikes consist each of three or four flowers, and they are found chiefly in July and August

and Bulbose Meadow Grass 8 Bulbose Meadow Grass The bottom of the stalk is thick, knotted, or tuberous The stalks are slender, and incline to the ground The flowers are produced from the tops in spreading panicles, and each of the little spikes consists of four flowers They appear chiefly in June, but are to be found occasionally all summer

Varieties, There are numerous varieties of all these species, differing in some respect or other Upon nice examination, however, the difference in fact is inconsiderable, and chiefly founded on the different situations or soils in which they grow The titles specify the real distinct species, and, upon examining the different grasses, it may be easily seen to which of the titles they respectively belong

Propagation They are all raised by sowing the seeds, as soon as they are ripe in the summer, or spring following, or the roots may be transplanted, which you are sure of getting the right sorts

Titles 1 Common Meadow Grass is entitled, *Poa panicula subdiffusa, spiculis trifloris basi pubescentibus, culmo erecto tereti* Caspar Bauhine calls it, *Gramen pratense paniculatum medium*, and John Bauhine, *Gramen pratense minus* It grows naturally every where in our meadows and pastures, and in most other pastures of Europe

2 Great Meadow Grass is, *Poa panicula diffusa, spiculis quinquefloris glabris, culmo erecto tereti* In the *Flora Lapponica* it is termed, *Poa spiculis ovatis compressis muticis* Scheuchzer calls it, *Gramen pratense paniculatum majus*, Caspar Bauhine, *Gramen pratense paniculatum majus latiore folio*, and Gerard, *Gramen pratense* It grows naturally in the richest pastures in England and most other countries of Europe

3 Narrow-leaved Meadow Grass is, *Poa panicula diffusa, spiculis quadrifloris pubescentibus, culmo erecto tereti* In the *Flora Lapponica* it is termed, *Poa spiculis ovato oblongis, foliis subulatis* Caspar Bauhine calls it, *Gramen pratense paniculatum angustifolio* It grows naturally chiefly on the borders of fields, woods, and hedges, in England and most countries of Europe

4 Creeping Meadow Grass is, *Poa [illegible] secunda [illegible], culmo obliquo compresso* Caspar Bauhine calls it, *Gramen [illegible]*, Vaillant, *Gramen [illegible]*, and Scheuchzer, *Gramen [illegible] compresso [illegible]* It grows naturally in dry places in England, most parts of Europe, and in North America

5 Wood Meadow Grass is, *Poa [illegible] culmo incurvo* Dillenius calls it, *Gramen [illegible] paniculatum [illegible]*, Scheuchzer, *Gramen [illegible] Alpinum, [illegible]*

*ra totibus & angustioribus non aristatis*, Vaillant, *Gramen nemorosum, paniculis laxa, radice repente*, and Morison, *Gramen loliaceum Alpinum, paniculis exiguis & exiguis locustis compositum*. It grows naturally in woods, forests, and shady places, in England and most countries of Europe.

6. Reed Grass is, *Poa panicula diffusa, spiculis sessilibus muticis* in the *Act. Stockh.* it is termed, *Poa panicula diffusa, spiculis sexfloris linearibus muticis compressis*, in the *Hortus Cliffort.* *Poa paniculis contractis, spicis ovatis teretiusculis*. Caspar Bauhine calls it, *Gramen palustre paniculatum altissimum*, also, *Gramen aquaticum paniculatum latifolium*, and Gerard, *Gramen aquaticum majus*. It is common by waters in England and most parts of Europe.

7. Marsh Meadow Grass is, *Poa panicula diffusa, spiculis sexfloris, foliis subtus scabris*. Scheuchzer calls it, *Gramen paniculatum aquaticum angustifolium, panicula speciosa*, and Caspar Bauhine *Gramen palustre, panicula speciosa*. It is a native of the Helvetian and Italian marshes.

8. Bulbose Meadow Grass is, *Poa panicula secunda, patentiuscula, spiculis quadrifloris*. Guettard calls it, *Poa culmorum basi tuberosa*, Caspar Bauhine, *Gramen arvense, panicula crispa*, Plukenet, *Gramen arvense, panicula crispa longiore, rostratas*, Vaillant, *Gramen vernum, radice Ascalonica*, and Scheuchzer, *Gramen arvense angustifolium, panicula densa subrotunda, spiculis in panicula angustissimis*. It grows naturally in England, France, Spain, and in the East.

*Poa* is of the class and order *Triandria Digynia*; and the characters are, — Class and order in the Linnæan system. The characters.

1. CALYX is a beardless glume, composed of two oval acuminated valves, containing many flowers arranged in a double series, or disticheus, oval, oblong spike.

2. COROLLA is composed of two oval, acuminated, concave, compressed valves, roughish on their edges and rather longer than the calyx.

3. STAMINA are three capillary filaments with bifurcated antheræ.

4. PISTILLUM consists of a roundish germen, and two hairy reflexed styles with simple stigmas.

5. PERICARPIUM. The corolla surrounds the seeds and leaves for a pericarpium.

6. SEMEN. The seed is single, oblong, compressed, covered, and pointed at each end.

# CHAP. CCCLVI

## *PODOPHYLLUM*, DUCK's FOOT, or MAY APPLE.

THERE are two species of this genus, viz. — Species.

1. Common Duck's Foot, or May Apple.
2. Two leaved May Apple.

1. Common Duck's Foot, or May Apple. The root is thick, fleshy, succulent, spreading, and hung with many fibres. The stalks are single, grow to about five or six inches high, and then divide into two parts. The leaves are one to each part, roundish, peltated, smooth, of a light-green colour, composed of six or seven lobes, the upper ones being indented at the top, and join together at their base. The flowers come out singly from the divisions of the stalks on short footstalks. Even before they open they may be said to be very beautiful, being then guarded by a very large, upright, red coloured perianthium, but this falling discovers the flower, of a white colour, and composed of nine roundish concave petals with folded borders. They appear in May, and are succeeded by large, oval berries, which are of a reddish or yellow colour, and the size of the common hip of our hedges when ripe. — Common Duck's Foot described.

2. Two leaved May Apple. The leaves are two, nearly heart shaped, smooth, entire, and grow on footstalks. The stalk rises immediately from the root, and is five or six inches high. The flowers come out singly from the tops of the stalks, appear early in the summer, and are succeeded by the like kind of fruit with the former. — Two leaved May Apple described.

These species are propagated by dividing the roots, for which work the autumn is the best time. They will grow in almost any soil or situation, though they delight most in the shade and a good light earth. When they are planted out, they will require no trouble except keeping them clean from weeds, and reducing the roots to a proper size as often as they get too large. — Propagation. Proper situation and soil.

They may also be raised by seeds. These should be sown, soon after they are ripe, in beds of light, loamy earth made fine. When the plants come up, they must be thinned where they are too close, and kept clean from weeds, and when they are fit to remove, they may be set out in such places where they are wanted.

1. The first species is entitled, *Podophyllum foliis peltatis palmatis*. In the *Hortus Cliffort.* it is named, simply, *Podophyllum*. Catesby calls it, *Anapodophyllum Canadense*, Tournefort, *Anapodophyllum Canadense Morini*, and Mentzelius, *Aconitifolia humilis, flore albo unico campanulato, fructu cynosbati*. It grows in most parts of North-America. — Titles.

2. The second species is, *Podophyllum foliis binatis semicordatis*. It grows naturally in Virginia.

*Podophyllum* is of the class and order *Polyandria Monogynia*, and the characters are, — Class and order in the Linnæan system. The characters.

1. CALYX is a large, coloured, concave, upright perianthium, composed of three oval, concave, deciduous leaves.

2. COROLLA consists of nine rounded petals, having plaited or folded borders.

3. STAMINA are numerous, short filaments, with large, oblong, erect antheræ.

4. PISTILLUM consists of a roundish germen, without any style, but an obtuse, plaited stigma.

5. PERICARPIUM is an oval, unilocular berry, crowned by the stigma.

6. SEMINA. The seeds are many, and roundish. The receptacle is free.

CHAP.

# CHAP. CCCLVII.

## *POLEMONIUM*, GREEK VALERIAN, or JACOB's LADDER.

Of this genus there are two well-known species, called,

Species. 1. Greek Valerian, or Jacob's Ladder.

2. Creeping Greek Valerian.

Description of Greek Valerian. 1. Greek Valerian, or Jacob's Ladder. The stalks are upright, hollow, channelled, and about a foot and a half high. The leaves are pinnated, and consist of several pair of folioles ranged alternately along the mid-rib, and terminated by an odd one. The folioles sit close, are broadest at their base, and pointed. The lower leaves are very large, consisting of ten or twelve pair, besides the odd one, and they diminish gradually in size as they are stationed higher up the stalk. The flowers come out from the tops of the stalks in erect bunches, are chiefly blue, but of different colours in the different varieties; they appear in May and June, and are succeeded by oval, acute-pointed capsules containing ripe seeds in August.

Its varieties. The principal varieties of this species are,

The Common Blue,

The White,

The Variegated,

The Woolly-cupped;

all of which will occasionally rise from the same sort of seed.

Creeping Greek Valerian described. 2. Creeping Greek Valerian. This species hath a creeping root, which soon spreads itself to a considerable distance. The stalks are upright, branching, and about a foot high. The leaves are pinnated, and consist of several pair of folioles, which are narrow, placed alternately, and are of a deep green colour. The flowers are produced in bunches from the tops of the plants, growing on longish footstalks; they are small, of a light-blue colour, hang drooping, appear in May and June, and the seeds ripen in August. This species frequently exhibits flowers in the autumn.

Method of propagating them. Both these species may be propagated by parting of the roots, the best time for which is the autumn. This is the only way of continuing the variegated kinds, or any beautiful singularity which may shew itself by seeds; but, notwithstanding they may be encreased by parting of the roots, the best and most beautiful plants are always obtained from seeds.

In the spring, therefore, let a sufficient quantity of good seeds be sown on a bed of light earth made fine. They will soon come up; and when they are two or three inches high, it is customary to prick them out in beds at a small distance from each other, to grow there until Michaelmas. If they are too close in the beds, the strongest may be drawn out, and transplanted in the same manner; otherwise the trouble may be saved, for they will grow very well if they are not removed before Michaelmas. Such as have been pricked out must be duly watered until they have taken fresh root, and those in the beds also should have the same assistance in dry weather. Weeding must be observed all summer, and in the autumn the plants should be removed unto the places where they are designed to remain. The summer following the plants will flower, and perfect their seeds.

1. The first species is entitled, *Polemonium foliis pinnatis, floribus erectis, calycibus corollæ tubo longioribus*. In the *Flora Lapponica* it is termed, *Polemonium*. Caspar Bauhine calls it, *Valeriana cærulea*; Gerard, *Valeriana Græca*; Tournefort, *Polemonium vulgare cæruleum*. In the *Hortus Upsaliensis* a variety of it is named, *Polemonium calycibus lanatis*. It grows naturally in thickets in England and most parts of Europe, also in Asia. Titles.

2. The second species is, *Polemonium foliis pinnatis septenis, floribus nutantibus*. Gronovius calls it, *Polemonium foliis pinnatis, radicibus reptatricibus*. It grows naturally in Virginia.

*Polemonium* is of the class and order *Pentandria Monogynia*; and the characters are, Class and order in the Linnæan system. The characters.

1. Calyx is a monophyllous, cyathiform, permanent perianthium, cut at the brim into five acute segments.

2. Corolla is one rotated petal. The tube is shorter than the calyx, and closed by five valves, which are placed at the top. The limb is broad, plane, and divided into five obtuse, roundish segments.

3. Stamina are five filiforme, inclined filaments, shorter than the corolla, and inserted in the valves of the tube, having roundish, incumbent antheræ.

4. Pistillum consists of an oval, acute germen, a filiforme style the length of the corolla, and a trifid, revolute stigma.

5. Pericarpium is a three-cornered, oval, covered capsule, formed of three valves, and containing three cells.

6. Semina. The seeds are many, irregular, and acute.

# CHAP. CCCLVIII

## *POLYANTHES*, The TUBEROSE.

THE Tuberose belongs to that set of flowers which are in general esteem. Their tall growing stems beautifully set with flowers, sometimes to the number of twenty, or more placed in a natural agreeable manner, attract the attention of the beholders, and the extreme fragrance that is continually emitted from them treats you with further delight, and enhances their value. The roots are annually imported from Genoa, from whence also they are sent into Holland, and several parts of Germany. They flourish exceeding well in Italy, Sicily, Portugal and Spain; but with us the first frost that comes upon them puts a period to their existence. The varieties of it (or rather of the species) are,

The Common Tuberose,
The Dwarf Tuberose,
The Double-flowering Tuberose,
The Variegated-leaved Tuberose,

all of which are now grown pretty common, though it is the first-mentioned sort that we have imported in such plenty.

In treating, therefore, of the culture of these plants, I shall first consider the management of the roots we receive from abroad; and, secondly, shall direct the method of preserving them, and causing them to blow at home.

In regard to those roots that we import, the largest and firmest are to be preferred. They must be perfectly sound, and the fewer offsets they have the better. They usually arrive in February or March, and in order to have a succession of them, they must be planted at different times. For the first blow, let the roots be planted immediately on their arrival. For this purpose let a hotbed be prepared, with a good frame, a yard or more in the back, and of a proportional height in the front, and covered with a good rich light earth. That recommended for the Hyacinth is as good a compost as can be desired. The bed must be covered about eight inches deep, and when it is in a proper temper, cross lines must be drawn eight inches asunder both ways, and where they cross each other let two roots be planted very near together. Before this is done, the roots should be cleared of all the old skins, withered fibres, offsets, &c. and the tops of the roots should be just covered with the earth. At this time be cautious of watering, as it is not necessary to hasten the growth; and too much will rot them. The flower stems will soon shew themselves above ground, and at that time water is requisite to be given to cause them to grow firm and strong. Too much forcing will draw them weak, and the flowers will be few and insignificant, too little will have the same effect, and too little water will bring them into a weak and crumbling state. The heat of the bed, therefore, must be preserved and uniform; plenty of water must be given them as they require it, and the glasses must be raised, and as much air given them as possible, in all tolerable weather. When the stems are about a foot and a half high, let a stick be placed by each for its support from winds and accidents. In all mild weather take the glasses entirely off in the day-time, and at the approach of evening draw them on again. The beginning of May the frames may be entirely taken away, and the bed hooped, to be covered with mats only in the night. Watering them must not be neglected; and when the bells of the flowers begin to shew themselves, the plants should be carefully taken up, two of them together, with balls of earth to the roots, and planted in pots. The earth should be well settled to them, and after that they may be set in different places to flower, some in the green-house, hall, bed chamber, and places of resort, whereby you will be always regaled by their agreeable inoffensive sweets, that are continually emitted from their fragrant flowers. Roots thus managed will be in blow by the end of June.

For the second blow of these flowers, plant the roots the first week in April. The management of these will be attended with considerably less trouble than the former. They must have a hotbed frame and all, and the management must be the same as the others, only such nice attendance will be of shorter duration, as the days grow fine, and the danger from frosts will be soon over.

For the third blow, the roots should be planted the first week in May. They should have a moderate hotbed, and afterwards will require little protection, except hooping and covering them with mats at night during the first three weeks or month.

It is by planting the roots at these different seasons a show of the flowers may be continued from the end of June to the end of October.

This being the proper management of the roots we receive from abroad, let us consider, secondly, the manner of treating them at home, which is by offsets, the only method, indeed, of encreasing the Double-flowering and Striped-leaved Tuberoses. In this management the greatest care must be taken to keep the roots from the frost, and they will do exceeding well. Keep them carefully in dry sand all winter, and in the beginning of March plant them in a hotbed about three or four inches under the surface, protect them from frost and bad weather, by having the beds hooped, and well covered down with mats, when the weather is bad. Let them be wholly exposed when the heat is gradually increasing, weather permitting. This is the attendance they will require during the summer. In October or November the roots should be taken up, before which time, if you perceive the frosty air, cover them well down with mats in the evening. When you take up the roots, clean them, put them in dry sand, preserve them in a dry place until March, and then plant them as before. Some amongst of these will flower the following year, and most of the others the year after.

The

The Striped leaved sort is only preserved for variety, and the Double-flowering sort, though it makes a fine show with its double flowers, is not possessed of that heightened fragrance which is peculiar to the Single kind It is also attended with greater trouble in blowing, for as the flowers begin to open, they should be placed under a glass case, and preserved from rain, dews, &c which will diminish their beauty, if not wholly destroy them, on this account the Single sort is by many preferred

The Dwarf sort is so called for distinction, because it is of smaller growth, but it is of inferior value to the others, for that consists chiefly in the height of the spikes, and number of the flowers The Common Tuberose will grow to a yard or four feet high, and what can be conceived finer than a stalk garnished at the top by such a number of beautiful bell shaped flowers, placed alternately to the very top, the bottom flowers first opening, and others higher preparing to succeed them in their order In short, the Tuberose, as a flower for the entertainment of both senses, is of the first class, and universally admired

Titles As the Tuberose is the only species of this genus, it stands simply with the name *Polyanthes* Linnæus, in his former works, termed it, *Polyanthes floribus alternis*, Caspar Bauhine, *Hyacinthus Indicus tuberosus, flore narcissi*, and Clusius, *Hyacinthus Indicus, tuberosâ radice* It grows naturally in India, and from thence it was first sent into the several parts of Europe

Class and order in the Linnæan system *Polyanthes* is of the class and order *Hexandria Monogynia*, and the characters are,

The characters 1 CALYX There is none

2 COROLLA is an infundibuliforme petal, the tube is oblong, and incurved, and the limb is divided into six oval spreading segments

3 STAMINA are six thick obtuse filaments, terminated by linear antheræ that are longer than the filaments

4 PISTILLUM consists of a roundish germen situated in the bottom of the corolla, a filiform style, and a thick, trifid, melliferous stigma

5 PERICARPIUM is a roundish, obtusely three-cornered capsule, wrapped up in the base of the corolla, it is formed of three valves, and contains three cells

6 SEMINA The seeds are numerous, flat, semiorbicular, and disposed in a double series

## CHAP CCCLIX.

## *POLYGALA*, MILK-WORT.

Of this genus the following perennials present themselves for this place, called,

Species. 1 Common Milk-wort
2 Bitter Milk-wort
3 Shrubby Portugal Milk-wort
4 Dwarf Box Milk-wort
5 Senega Milk-wort, or Senega Rattle Snake-wort

Common Milk wort described 1 Common Milk-wort The root is long, white, and slender The stalks are simple, slender, herbaceous, six or eight inches long, and lie on the ground The leaves are narrow, spear-shaped, pointed at both ends, smooth, and of a bright-green colour The flowers come out from the ends of the stalks in crested spikes, they appear in June, and are succeeded by ripe seeds in August or September

There are numerous varieties of this species, the principal ones are,

Its varieties The Blue,
The Red,
The White,
The Violet-coloured,
The Striped

Bitter, 2 Bitter Milk wort The radical leaves are large, and almost of an oval figure The stalks are herbaceous, nearly erect, and six or eight inches high The flowers come out in crested spikes from the tops of the stalks, they are principally blue, though there are other varieties respecting their colour, they appear in June, and the seeds ripen in August or September

This plant is intolerably bitter to the taste

Shrubby Portugal, 3 Shrubby Portugal Milk-wort The stalks are slender, ligneous, about a foot high, green, and have the scars or marks of fallen leaves left on the bark The leaves are nearly oval, awl-shaped, small, narrow, sessile, placed alternately at a distance from each other, and soon fall off, leaving the mark of the base on the bark The flowers come out from the tops of the stalks in short spikes, they are large, and often of two or three colours, they appear in May and June, and the seeds ripen in August

Dwarf Box, 4 Dwarf Box Milk-wort The stalks are slender, ligneous, branching, and about a foot high The leaves are numerous, spear-shaped, smooth, of a firm substance, and a bright-green colour The flowers come out from the sides of the stalks near the upper part on short footstalks they are mostly white on the outside, but within are a mixture of purple and yellow, and very finely scented, they appear in May, and are sometimes succeeded by ripe seeds in England

and Senega Milk wort described 5 Senega Milk-wort, or Senega Rattle Snake-wort The root is thick, fleshy, and strikes deep into the ground The stalks are simple, slender, herbaceous, upright, and about a foot and a half high The leaves are spear-shaped, broad, and grow alternately The flowers are produced in spikes from the ends of the stalks, they are small, of a white colour, appear in July, but are seldom succeeded by seeds in England

Medicinal properties of it The root of this plant is an infallible cure for the bite of the rattle-snake, if used in time It is reduced

reduced to powder, about thirty grains taken inwardly, and a share applied to the wounded part. It is so certain a remedy, that the inhabitants, where those venomous creatures abound, carry it continually with them when they walk in the woods, with very little concern about being bitten. Its virtues in other respects are very great, tho' their known uses in medicine are not of very long standing with us. It is allowed to be a great purifier of the blood, a fine diuretic, diaphoretic, cathartic, frequently emetic, and used in hydropic cases, pleurisies, peripneumonies, and the like.

Culture. The first two sorts are easily propagated. Their seeds should be sown, soon after they are ripe, in any bed of common mould made fine, and when the plants come up, they will require no trouble except thinning them where they are too close, and keeping them clean from weeds.

The seeds of the third and fourth sort should be sown, as soon as they are ripe, in beds of light, unmerged, sandy earth, in shady well-sheltered places; because if they are kept until the spring, they rarely come up before the spring after. When they come up they must be kept clean from weeds, frequently watered in dry weather in summer, and in winter should be guarded against its over-severity by a double row of furze bushes stuck round the bed at about a yard distance.

When the seeds do not ripen in England, they must be procured from abroad, and then the best way will be to get them sown, as soon as they are ripe, in boxes filled with their native earth. When you receive the boxes, set them in a shady but warm place, and after the plants come up frequently refresh them with water. When they are about three or four inches high, they may be set in pots filled with light sandy earth, which should be then plunged up to the rims in some shady part of the garden. Here they may remain until the end of November, when they should be planted under a hotbed-frame, or some shelter, for their winter lodgings, observing always to give them full air, or set them abroad in mild weather, and in the spring they may be turned out of the pots, with the mould at the roots, into the places where they are designed to remain.

The fifth sort is propagated by sowing the seeds, which must be procured from America, as they very seldom, if ever, ripen here. The ground must be naturally warm, dry, light, sandy, and the place well defended; it must be double dug, and made as fine as possible, for the roots to strike more freely, and encrease in thickness. In winter, if the weather should be likely to prove severe, a double row of furze bushes should be stuck round, or some light litter laid on it, which should always be taken away on the return of fine weather, and this (except keeping them clean from weeds in summer) is all the trouble they will require.

Titles. 1 Common Milk-wort is titled, *Polygala floribus cristatis racemosis, caulibus herbaceis simplicibus procumbentibus, foliis lineari lanceolatis.* Van Royen calls it, *Polygala foliis lineari-lanceolatis, caulibus diffusis herbaceis*; Clusius, *Polygala vulgaris major*; Caspar Bauhine, *Polygala vulgaris*, also, *Polygala major*; Tournefort, *Polygala alba*; Ray, *Polygala myrtifolia palustris humilis et ramosior*; Boerhaave, *Polygala carnea*, also, *Polygala violacea*; and Gerard, *Polygala*. It grows naturally in dry, heathy, barren places in England, and most parts of Europe.

2 Bitter Milk wort is, *Polygala floribus cristatis racemosis, caulibus erectis simplicibus, foliis radicalibus obovatis majoribus.* Caspar Bauhine calls it, *Polygala vulgaris, foliis circa radicem rotundioribus, flore caeruleo, sapore admodum amaro*; and Vaillant, *Polygala buxi minoris folio.* It grows naturally on the mountainous parts of Gaul and Austria.

3 Shrubby Portugal Milk wort is, *Polygala floribus imberbibus racemosis, caulibus fruticosis, foliis minutissimis ellipticis.* Tournefort calls it, *Polygala Lusitanica frutescens, magno flore, foliis minimis.* It grows naturally in Spain and Portugal.

4 Dwarf Box Milk-wort is, *Polygala floribus imberbibus sparsis carina apice subrotundo, caule fruticoso, foliis lanceolatis.* Caspar Bauhine calls it, *Chamaebuxus flore Coluteae*; and Clusius, *Anonymos flore Coluteae.* It grows naturally on the mountainous parts of Austria, Helvetia, and Alsace.

5 Senega Milk-wort, or Rattle Snake-wort, is, *Polygala floribus imberbibus spicatis, caule erecto herbaceo simplicissimo, foliis lato-lanceolatis.* Gronovius calls it, *Polygala caule simplici erecto, foliis ovato lanceolatis alternis integerrimis, racemo terminali erecto*; and Ray, *Plantula Marilandica, caule non ramoso, spica in fastigio singulari e flosculis albis composita.* It grows naturally in Virginia, Pensylvania, and Maryland.

*Polygala* is of the class and order *Diadelphia Octandria*; and the characters are, Class and order in the Linnean system. The characters.

1 CALYX is a small perianthium composed of three oval, acute, permanent leaves; two of which are below the corolla, the other is above it.

2 COROLLA is papilionaceous as to the figure, but the number of petals are indeterminate.

The alae are large, oval, plane, and placed beyond the other parts of the corolla.

The vexillum is short, tubular, nearly cylindrical, and a little reflexed and bifid at the top.

The carina is concave, compressed, and ventricose towards the apex.

3 STAMINA are diadelphous filaments included in the carina, having eight simple antherae.

4 PISTILLUM consists of an oblong germen, a simple erect style, and a thickish bifid stigma.

5 PERICARPIUM is a turbinated, heart shaped, compressed capsule composed of two valves, and containing two cells.

6 SEMINA. The seeds are single, and oval.

CHAP

# CHAP. CCCLX.

## *POLYGONUM*, KNOT-GRASS.

*Species.*

Of this genus there are,

1. Greater Bistort, or Snake-weed.
2. Small Bistort, or Snake-weed.
3. Perennial Arsmart.
4. Virginian Arsmart.
5. Sea Knot-grass.
6. Oriental Buck-wheat.

*Description of the Greater Bistort.* 1. Greater Bistort, or Snake-weed. This hath a thick, oblique, contorted root, blackish on the outside, and reddish within. The stalk is round, simple, slender, jointed, and about two feet high. The leaves are oval, oblong, acuminated, and grow alternately on the stalks. The flowers come out from the tops of the stalks in short thick spikes; they are small, but of a whitish-red colour, appear in May and June, and the seeds ripen in July and August.

*Medicinal properties.* The root of this plant is a most powerful astringent, and is used both internally and externally for immoderate hemorrhages and other fluxes. It is also said to be good for healing sore mouths and fastening of loose teeth, by holding it in the mouth at repeated intervals for some time.

*Small Bistort.* 2. Small Bistort, or Snake-weed. The root is like the former, but smaller, and less vermicularly bent. The stalk is round, slender, jointed, and six inches high. The leaves are spear-shaped, and long for so small a plant; they are of a good green colour on their upper-side, tho' paler underneath, and those on the stalks grow alternately. The flowers come out in long spikes from the tops of the stalks; they are of a whitish-red colour, appear in June, and are succeeded by large reddish-coloured seeds, which ripen in August.

The root of this plant is possessed of the qualities of the former.

*Perennial Arsmart.* 3. Perennial Arsmart. The root is long, jointed, and fibrous. The stalks are weak, tender, and float in the water, or lie on the ground. The leaves are spear-shaped, long, narrow, pointed, and grow alternately. The flowers come out in spikes from the tops of the stalks; they are of a pale-red or purple colour, appear in June and July, and are succeeded by hard three-sided seeds, which ripen in September.

This plant grows in ditches and standing waters, but will nevertheless thrive very well by land, if planted in a moist soil, and a shady situation.

*Virginian Arsmart.* 4. Virginian Arsmart. The root is fibrous and spreading. The stalks are round, tough, and branching near the bottom. The leaves are of an oval figure, usually spotted, and grow alternately. The flowers come out in spikes from the ends of the branches; they are of a white colour, having frequently a light tinge of red or purple; they appear in July, and the seeds sometimes ripen in the autumn.

*Sea Knot-Grass.* 5. Sea Knot Grass. The root is long, slender, tough, and full of fibres. The stalks are ligneous, tough, white, jointed, perennial, and divide into numerous slender branches, which are also knotty, or full of joints. The leaves are oval, oblong, of a bluish-white colour, and saltish to the taste. The flowers come out from the wings of the leaves almost the whole length of the branches; they are small, of a whitish green colour, appear in July, and the seeds ripen in the autumn.

*and Oriental Buck-wheat described.* 6. Oriental Buck-wheat. This hath a woody, tough, fibrated, creeping root. The stalks are jointed, grow to about a yard high, and divide into numerous jointed branches, which spread themselves every way. The leaves are spear-shaped, narrow, pointed, smooth, and of a pale-green colour. The flowers are produced in loose spikes from the ends of the branches; they are of a white colour, appear in June, and the seeds ripen in September.

*Culture.* The first two sorts are propagated by parting of the roots in the autumn, and planting them in moist places. The third sort may be set by the sides of ditches, and the stalks will float in the water, and strike root at the joints, always making great encrease. It may be set in some moist shady part of the garden, where it will grow and flourish exceedingly well. The fourth, fifth, and sixth sorts will grow any where, though they like the shade and moisture; and their encrease is by parting of the roots in the autumn, winter, or early in the spring.

They are also propagated by sowing of the seeds, the best time for which is the autumn, soon after they are ripe. In the spring the plants must be thinned to proper distances; all summer they must be kept clean from weeds, and watered in dry weather; and in the autumn may be removed to the places where they are designed to remain.

*Titles.* 1. Greater Bistort, or Snake-weed, is titled, *Polygonum caule simplicissimo, monostachyo, foliis ovatis in petiolum decurrentibus*. In the *Hortus Cliffort.* it is termed, *Bistorta foliis ovato oblongis acuminatis*. Camerarius calls it, *Bistorta*; Caspar Bauhine, *Bistorta major, radice magis intortâ*; Gerard, *Bistorta major*; and Parkinson, *Bistorta vulgaris*. It grows naturally in moist places and meadows in England, and is common in the Helvetian and Austrian mountains.

2. Small Bistort, or Snake-weed, is titled, *Polygonum caule simplicissimo, monostachyo, foliis lanceolatis*. In the *Flora Lapp.* it is termed, *Bistorta foliis lanceolatis*. Amman calls it, *Bistorta montana minor, radice contortâ modicâ, flosculis in spicæ cacumine albis sterilibus, infernâ spicæ parte tuberculis proliferis turbinatis puniceis fecundâ*; Caspar Bauhine, *Bistorta Alpina minor*; also, *Bistorta media*; Haller, *Bistorta Alpina minima*; Gerard, *Bistorta minor*; Parkinson, *Bistorta minor nostras*; and Ray, *Bistorta minima Alpina, foliis imis subrotundis & minutissimè serratis*. It grows common in mountainous places in England, and most parts of Europe.

3. Perennial Arsmart is, *Polygonum floribus pentandris semidigynis, staminibus corollâ longioribus*. In the *Hortus Cliffort.* it is termed, *Persicaria florum*

*florum staminibus quinis corollam superantibus, stylo bifido*, in the *Flora Suecia*, *Persicaria floribus pentandris digynis, corollâ staminibus breviore*. Caspar Bauhine calls it, *Potamogeton salicis folio*, Ray, *Persicaria salicis folio perennis, potamogeton angustifolium dicta*; Gerard, *Potamogeton angustifolium*, and Parkinson, *Fontalis major longifolia*. It grows naturally in ditches and moist places in England, and most countries of Europe.

5. Virginian Arsmart is, *Polygonum floribus pentandris semidigynis, corollis quadrifidis inequalibus, foliis ovatis*. In the *Hortus Cliffort* it is termed, *Persicaria florum staminibus quinis, stylo duplici, corollâ quadrifida inæquali*. Wachendorf calls it, *Persicaria floribus pentandris digynis, corolla quadrifida inæquali*, and Morison, *Persicaria frutescens maculosa Virginiana, flore albo*. It grows naturally in Virginia.

Sea Knot-Grass is, *Polygonum floribus octandris trigynis axillaribus foliis ovali-lanceolatis sempervirentibus, caule suffrutescente*. Caspar Bauhine calls it, *Polygonum maritimum latifolium*, John Bauhine, *Polygonum marinum*, Cammerarius, *Polygonum maritimum*. Gerard, *Polygonum marinum maximum*, and Parkinson, *Polygonum marinum majus*. It grows naturally on the sea shores in England, also on the Mediterranean, Eastern, and Virginian shores.

6. Oriental Buck wheat is, *Polygonum floribus octandris trigynis racemosis, foliis lanceolatis, caule divaricato patulo*. In the *Hortus Upsal* it is termed, *Helxine foliis lanceolatis, caule diffuso*. Tournefort calls it, *Fagopyrum orientale ramosum & multiflorum, Persicariæ folio*, and Boccone, *Persicaria Alpina altera saxatilis, foliis durioribus acutis*. It is a native of Siberia and Corsica.

*Polygonum* is of the class and order *Octandria Trigynia*, and the characters are, Class and order in the Linnæan System. The characters.

1. CALYX is a turbinated perianthium, coloured on the inner side, and divided into five oval, obtuse, permanent segments.

2. COROLLA. There is none.

3. STAMINA are for the most part eight very short awl-shaped filaments, with roundish [illegible] bent anthers.

4. PISTILLUM consists of a triquetrous germen, and for the most part of three very short filiform styles with simple stigmas.

5. PERICARPIUM. There is none. The seed is wrapped in the calyx.

6. SEMEN. The seed is single, triquetrous, and acute.

# CHAP. CCCLXI.

# *POLYMNIA.*

THERE are only two species of this genus, called, Species.

1. Virginian *Polymnia*.
2. Canada *Polymnia*.

1. Virginian *Polymnia*. This plant rises with several robust stalks to the height of about five feet. The leaves are large, angular, sinuated, divided on the edges in the manner of those of the Oriental Plane tree, and grow opposite by pairs. The flowers adorn the upper parts of the plant in moderate plenty; they are of a yellow colour, appear in July, August, and September, but are not succeeded by seeds in England. Virginian and Canada Polymnia described.

2. Canada *Polymnia*. The stalks are upright, firm, and three or four feet high. The leaves are large, angular, hollowed on the edges, and grow alternately. The flowers come out from the tops of the plant on slender footstalks; they are of a yellow colour, appear in August and September, but are very rarely succeeded by seeds in England.

The stalks of both these species die to the ground every autumn, and fresh ones arise in the spring. They are propagated by parting of the roots, which should be done in the autumn, when the stalks decay; they love a light, fresh, moist soil, and an open situation, and being thus stationed the stalks will be stronger, and the flowers larger and fairer, than such as are produced in dry sandy soils in confined places. Its propagation.

1. The first species is titled, *Polymnia foliis oppositis hastato sinuatis*. In the *Hortus Cliffort* it is termed, *Osteospermum foliis oppositis palmatis*. Morison calls it, *Chrysanthemum perenne Virginianum majus, platani orientalis folio*, and Plukenet, *Chrysanthemum, angulosis platani foliis, Virginianum*. It grows naturally in Virginia. Titles.

2. The second species is, *Polymnia foliis alternis hastato-sinuatis*. In the *Amænitates Acad.* it is termed simply, *Polymnia*. It grows naturally in Canada.

*Polymnia* is of the class and order *Syngenesia Polygamia Necessaria*, and the characters are, Class and order in the Linnæan System. The characters.

1. CALYX consists of two parts. The general or outer calyx consists of five large, oval, spreading leaves; the superior is composed of ten cymbiform foliols, which stand erect.

2. COROLLA. The compound flower is radiated. The hermaphrodite flowers are many in the disk, and the females are five or ten in the radius.

Each hermaphrodite floret consists of one funnel-shaped petal, cut at the brim into five parts.

The females are each one tongue shaped petal, having three indentures at the top.

3. STAMINA of the hermaphrodites are five filaments, with a cylindrical tubular anthera that is a little longer than the corolla.

4. PISTILLUM of the hermaphrodites consists of a very small germen, a filiform style the length of the stamina, and an obtuse stigma.

In the females, it consists of a large oval germen, a filia filiforme ſtyle the length of the tube, and two acute ſtigmas

5 Pericarpium There is none

6 Semina of the hermaphrodite florets are none

Of the females they are ſingle, oboval, gibbous, naked, and ſlightly angular underneath The receptacle is paleaceous, convex, and imbricated The paleæ are oval, concave, obtuſe, and the length of the florets

## CHAP CCCLXII

## *POLYPODIUM*, POLYPODY.

THERE are numerous ſpecies of this genus, moſt of which are natives of the Indies, and not propagated in gardens The more hardy ſpecies, which are natives of Britain, or ſuch as are found in ſome collections, are uſually called,

Species
1 Common Polypody, or Wall Fern
2 Virginian Polypody
3 Great Polypody, or Spleenwort
4 Welch Polypody.
5 Wood Polypody
6 Sweet Polypody
7 Rock Polypody
8 Creſted Polypody
9 Male Polypody, or Fern
10 Female Polypody
11 Prickly Polypody
12 Stony Polypody
13 New York Polypody
14 Marginal-fruited Polypody
15 Bulbiferous Polypody
16 Brittle Polypody
17 Royal Polypody
18 Branched Polypody
19 Portugal Polypody
20 Golden Polypody

Deſcription of Common

1 Common Polypody, or Wall Fern The root is thick, long ſpreading, of a duſky-brown colour, full of tubercles, and hung with numerous ſlender fibres The leaves are all diſtinct plants, they are pinnatifid, and grow on naked footſtalks The ſtalks are naked for about five or ſix inches high, the pinnæ are broadeſt near the bottom, and diminiſh gradually to a point at the top, they are of an oblong figure, obtuſe, ſlightly ſerrated on their edges, of a dark-green colour on their upper-ſide, and beautifully ſpotted underneath with yellow dots, which are the fructifications of the plants

Virginian

2 Virginian Polypody The root is ſlender, ſmooth, creeping, and hung with numerous ſlender fibres The leaves or rather plants are numerous, five or ſix inches high, pinnatifid, and ſupported by ſtalks, which are naked about two inches from the ground The pinnæ are longeſt near the baſe, and diminiſh to a point like the preceding, they are of an oblong figure, obtuſe, ſlightly ſerrated, and ſmooth on both ſides

3 Great Polypody, or Spleen-wort The root is fibrous and ſtringy The leaves are pinnated, and about a foot high The pinnæ are lunulated, hairy, ſerrated on their edges, ſharp pointed, and grow on ſlender narrow footſtalks, which are naked for about two or three inches from the ground Great

4 Welch Polypody This plant is often called Jagged Polypody The ſtalks are naked for about two inches, and are adorned with the pinnæ on each ſide for about ſix inches in length, theſe are ſpear ſhaped, and their edges cut or jagged almoſt to the mid rib, they are of a browniſh green colour on their upper-ſide, but yellowiſh underneath by the farina of the fructifications Welch

5 Wood Polypody The leaves or rather plants are nearly bipinnated, the pinnæ are of different figures, but for the moſt part ſpear-ſhaped, pinnatifid, and hairy, the lower ones are reflexed, hang drooping, and are ſtationed on firm pale-coloured footſtalks The fructifications are numerous, ſpotted on the backs, and their colour is a yellowiſh brown Wood,

6 Sweet Polypody The leaves are nearly bipinnated, ſpear-ſhaped, and grow on paleaceous rigid footſtalks The folioles are cloſely ſet together, the lateral lobes are obtuſe, deeply ſerrated on their edges, and the whole plant, eſpecially the root, is of a ſtrong, and to many a very agreeable odour Sweet,

7 Rock Polypody This is a ſmall elegant Fern about three or four inches high, nearly bipinnated, and ſpear-ſhaped The folioles are ſhort, roundiſh, have two or three indentures on the edges, and are ſtationed on ſmooth, gloſſy, ſhort, ſlender footſtalks Rock,

8 Creſted Polypody The root is compoſed of a multitude of ſmall black fibres The leaves are nearly bipinnated, large, and in good ground three or four feet high The folioles are of an oval oblong figure, and the pinnæ are obtuſe, and acutely ſerrated at the top, they are ſupported by long ſtrong footſtalks, which are flat on one ſide, round on the other, and naked a foot and a half before the ſetting-on of the branches, the whole leaf is of a ſtrong green colour on the outſide, but paler and reddiſh underneath, through the effect of the fructifications Creſted,

9 Male Polypody, or Fern, is well known and Male Polypody

The leaves are bipinnated, large, and grow on paleaceous footstalks. The pinnulæ are obtuse, crenated on their edges, and of a yellowish-green colour.

Medicinal properties of this plant. The root of this Fern is used in medicine. It is aperient, and said to be good for destroying worms in the human body.

Female. 10 Female Polypody. The root is long, black, and creeping. The leaves are bipinnated, large, and grow on strong, upright, naked footstalks. The pinnulæ are spear-shaped and acute, but variously indented, some being cut almost to the mid rib, others possessed of slighter indentures, whilst others again are nearly entire.

The root is possessed of the same qualities with the former.

Prickly. 11 Prickly Polypody. The root is creeping. The leaves are bipinnated, large, and supported by strigose footstalks. The pinnulæ are lunulated, broad, ciliated, indented, and prickly; they have prickly appendages at the base, and the whole leaf is of a dark-green colour on the ourside, but dusty underneath, through the effect of the fructifications.

Stone. 12 Stone Polypody is a loose bipinnated Fern. The folioles are spear-shaped, and at a considerable distance from each other. The pinnæ also are remote, spear-shaped, and acutely sawed on their edges.

New York. 13 New York Polypody. This is a large bipinnated fern, elevated on a smooth strong footstalk, and grows about a yard high. The pinnæ are oblong, entire, close arranged, run almost parallel to each other, and the fructifications are numerous, in the form of little spots on the under-side.

Marginal. 14 Marginal Polypody. This is a bipinnated Fern about the size of the former. The pinnæ are oblong, sinuated, obtusely serrated towards the base, and are made remarkable by carrying their most conspicuous fructifications on the margin, or close to the edges on the under-side.

Bulbiferous. 15 Bulbiferous Polypody. The leaves are bipinnated and the folioles are arranged at a considerable distance from each other. The pinnæ are oblong, obtuse, serrated, and remarkable for carrying globules or little bulbs like berries on their under-side.

Brittle. 16 Brittle Polypody. This also is a bipinnated Fern. The folioles are remote, the pinnæ are roundish, cut or jagged on their edges, and the fructifications are in form of black spots underneath. The footstalk is slender, and of a very brittle nature.

Royal. 17 Royal Polypody. This is a very beautiful bipinnated Fern. The folioles are placed nearly opposite to each other, and the pinnæ are elegantly cut or jagged on their edges. It is of a light-green colour on the upper side, but yellowish underneath, by the abundance of the farina which will be dusted all over the bottom.

Branched. 18 Branched Polypody. The root is creeping, black, hairy, and very astringent. The stalks are upright, slender, naked for about a foot high, and then branch out into many divisions; these are pinnated, and the pinnæ are finely cut or divided almost to the midrib. The plant differs in height according to its different situation. In some places it is two feet and a half high, in others not a foot. The fructifications are in form of blackish spots on the under-side.

Portugal. 19 Portugal Polypody. The root is creeping, and hung with many fibres. The leaves are large, supradecompound, and supported by firm striated footstalks; the folioles are ranged alternately, and the pinnæ are oblong, and longitudinally pinnatifid.

and Golden Polypody described. 20 Golden Polypody. The root is very thick, fleshy, and creeps under the surface. The leaves are pinnated, and grow to a yard or more in height. The pinnæ are spear-shaped, entire, smooth, very long, of a bluish green colour on the upper side, and dotted with large golden spots, which are the fructifications, on the under-side.

This is the most admired of all the Polypodies, and much coveted for the gardens of the curious.

Method of propagating. All the preceding species are easily propagated by parting of the roots, which may be done successfully any time in the autumn, winter, or early in the spring. They should be stationed in places as similar as possible to their natural place of growth, which may be seen after their titles, and are all very hardy, except the last species, which should be planted in pots to be housed in bad weather in winter.

Titles. 1 Common Polypody, or Wall Fern, is entitled, *Polypodium frondibus pinnatifidis pinnis oblongis subserratis obtusis, radice squamata*. In the *Hortus Cliffort.* it is termed, *Polypodium fronde pinnatâ pinnis lanceolatis indivisis serrulatis alternis connato-sessilibus*; in the *Flora Lapp. Polypodium pinnatum, pinnis lanceolatis integris*. Dodonæus calls it, *Polypodium majus*; Caspar Bauhine, *Polypodium vulgare*, also, *Polypodium minus*; Gerard, *Polypodium*; and Ray, *Polypodium murale pinnulis serratis*. It grows naturally on old walls, in chinks of rocks, dry banks, and shady places in England, and most countries of Europe.

2 Virginian Polypody is, *Polypodium frondibus pinnatifidis pinnis oblongis subserratis obtusis, radice lævi*. Petiver calls it, *Polypodium minus vulgaris facie*; Plumier, *Polypodium radice tenui et repente*; and Morison, *Polypodium Virginianum minus, foliis obtusioribus*. It grows naturally in dry shady places in Virginia.

3 Great Polypody, or Spleen-wort, is, *Polypodium frondibus pinnatis pinnis lunulatis ciliato-serratis declinatis, stipitibus strigosis*. Caspar Bauhine calls it, *Lonchitis aspera*; Gerard, *Lonchitis aspera major*; and Parkinson, *Lonchitis aspera major Matthioli*. It grows naturally in fissures of rocks in Wales, and the North of England, also in Alpine situations in most countries of Europe.

4 Welch Polypody is, *Polypodium frondibus pinnatifidis pinnis lanceolatis lacero-pinnatifidis serratis*. Van Royen calls it, *Polypodium fronde pinnatifidâ foliolis lanceolatis sinuato pinnatifidis*; Morison, *Polypodium Cambro-Britannicum, foliis profundè dentatis*; Ray, *Polypodium Cambro-Britannicum, pinnulis ad margines laciniatis*; and Plukenet, *Filix amplissima, lobis foliorum incimatis, Cambrica*. It grows naturally out of Welch rocks, and in some parts of France.

5 Wood Polypody is, *Polypodium frondibus sub-bipinnatis foliolis infimis reflexis partialis pinnatâ quadrangulari coadunatis*. In the *Flora Lapp.* it is termed, *Polypodium pinnatum pinnis lanceolatis pinnatifidis integris inferioribus nutantibus*. Morison calls it, *Filix minor Britannica, pediculo pallidiore, alis inferioribus deorsum spectantibus*, and Petiver, *Filix non ramosa minor & sylvestris*. It grows naturally in the chinks of rocks, and moist, shady, woodland places in England, and most countries of Europe, also in Virginia.

6 Sweet Polypody is, *Polypodium frondibus sub bipinnatis lanceolatis foliolis confertis lobis obtusis serratis, stipite paleaceo*. Amman calls it, *Dryopteris rubrum Idæum spirans*. It grows naturally

rally in the chinks of rocks, and moist places in England and Siberia

7 Rock Polypody is, *Polypodium frondibus subbipinnatis lanceolatis foliolis subrotundis argute incisis, stipite laevi* Caspar Bauhine calls it, *Filicula fontana minor*, and Barrelier, *Adiantum fumarium durius crispum* [illegible] It grows naturally out of the clifts of rocks, old walls, &c in England and Siberia

8 Crested Polypody is, *Polypodium frondibus subbipinnatis foliolis ovato oblongis pinnis obtusiusculis apice acute serratis* In the *Flora Suecica* it is termed, *Polypodium fronde duplicato-pinnatâ pinnulis obtusis coadunatis crenatis.* Morison calls it, *Filix non ramosa major pinnulis latis densis lengiorul is in profundos a [illegible] arctis*, Plukenet, *Filix mas ramosa, pinnulis dentatis*, and Ray, *Filix montana ramosa minor argute denticulata* It grows naturally in woods and moist shady places in England, and most of the northern countries of Europe

9 Male Polypody, or Fern, is, *Polypodium frondibus bipinnatis pinnis obtusis crenulatis, stipite paleaceo* Caspar Bauhine calls it, *Filix mas non ramosa dentata*, Fuchsius, *Filix mas*, Gerard, *Filix mas non ramosa, pinnulis angustis rarisque profunde dentatis*, and Parkinson, *Filix mas vulgaris* It grows naturally on heaths, in woods, and stony grounds in England, and most parts of Europe

10 Female Polypody is, *Polypodium frondibus bipinnatis pinnulis lanceolatis pinnatifidis acutis* Morison calls it, *Filix mas non ramosa, pinnulis angustis raris ar [illegible], profunde dentatis* It grows naturally in moist places in England, and most of the colder parts of Europe

11 Prickly Polypody is, *Polypodium frondibus bipinnatis pinnis lunulatis ciliato-dentatis, stipite strigoso* Caspar Bauhine calls it, *Filix mas aculeata major*, Plukenet, *Filix mas non ramosa, pinnulis latis auriculatis spinosis*, and Ray, *Filix aculeata major, pinnulis auriculatis crebrioribus, foliis integris angustioribus* It grows naturally in shady places in England, and most countries of Europe

12 Stone Polypody is, *Polypodium frondibus bipinnatis foliolis pinnatifique remotis lanceolatis serie minis acuminatis* Caspar Bauhine calls it, *Filix montana major, s adiantum album, filicis folio* John Bauhine, *Filix rhaetica tenuissime denticulata*, and Clusius, *Filix pumila saxatilis altera* It grows naturally in mountainous stony places in England, France, and Germany

13 New York Polypody is, *Polypodium frondibus bipinnatis pinnis oblongis integerrimis parallelis, stipite laevi* It grows naturally in Canada

14 Marginal Polypody is, *Polypodium frondibus bipinnatis pinnis basi sinuato repandis fructificationibus marginalibus* It grows naturally in Canada

15 Bulbiferous Polypody is *Polypodium frondibus bipinnatis foliolis remotis pinnis oblongis obtusis serratis subtus bulbiferis* Van Royen calls it, *Polypodium fronde duplicato-pinnatâ, foliolis oblongis obtusis incisis dorso bulbiferis*, Plukenet, *Filix saxatilis Canadensium globulifera*, and Cornutus, *Filix baccifera* It grows naturally in Canada

16 Brittle Polypody is, *Polypodium frondibus bipinnatis foliolis remotis pinnis subrotundis incisis* Plukenet calls it, *Filix saxatilis caule tenui fragili*, Clusius *Filix pumila saxatilis 2*, and Caspar Bauhine, *Filix saxatilis non ramosa nigris maculis punctata* It grows naturally in dry stony places in England, and the colder parts of Europe

17 Royal Polypody is, *Polypodium frondibus bipinnatis foliolis suboppositis pinnis laciniatis* Vaillant calls it, *Filix regia, fun [illegible] pinnulis* It grows naturally in Gaul

18 Branched Polypody is, *Polypodium frondibus supradecompositis foliolis ternis bipinnatis* In the *Flora Lapp* it is termed, *Polypodium trifidum ramis pinnatis pinnis pinnatifidis* Caspar Bauhine calls it *Filix [illegible], pinnulis dentatis*, Clusius, *Filix pumila saxatilis*, and Gerard, *Dryopteris Tragi* It grows naturally in dry, rocky, woodland places in England, and most parts of Europe

19 Portugal Polypody is, *Polypodium frondibus supradecompositis foliolis alternis pinnis oblongis longitudinaliter pinnatifidis* Magnol calls it, *Filix Lusitanica polypodii radice* It grows naturally in Portugal

20 Golden Polypody is, *Polypodium frondibus pinnatifidis laciniis pinnis oblongis distantibus infimis patulis, terminali maxime, fructificationibus serialibus* In the *Hortus Cliffortianus* it is termed, *Polypodium fronde pinnatâ pinnis lanceolatis integerrimis basi connatis patulis terminali maximâ* Plumier calls it, *Polypodium majus aureum*, Petiver, *Polypodium maximum*, Sloane, *Polypodium altissimum*, and Morison, *Polypodium Jamaicense majus et elatius, alis longioribus punctis aureis aversâ parte notatis* It grows naturally in America

Class and order in the Linnaean system

*Polypodium* is of the class and order *Cryptogamia Filices*, and of this genus the fructifications appear in form of roundish spots on the under side of the leaf

# CHAP. CCCLXIII.

## PONTEDERIA.

OF this genus there is one species, which may be made to grow in the moist parts of our gardens, called, Virginian *Pontederia*.

This plant described. The stalks are thick, herbaceous, and about a foot high. The leaves are heart shaped, pointed, large, of a thick consistence, and grow on footstalks which embrace the stalk with their base. The flowers are produced in short close spikes from the tops of the stalks, bursting from a spatha which opens longitudinally; they are of a blue colour, appear in June, but are not succeeded by seeds in our gardens.

Method of propagating it. It is propagated by seeds, which must be procured from America. These should be sown in some moist boggy part of the garden made fine; and if the soil is not naturally light and sandy, some drift sand must be added. When the plants come up, the culture they require will be to thin them where they are too close, keep them clean from weeds, and to afford them abundance of water in dry weather, for the plant is naturally an aquatick, and in Virginia grows in places that are almost always overflowed with that element.

The roots also may be sent over planted in boxes or pots, and when they arrive here may be turned out, with the mould at the roots, into some light, boggy, moist, well sheltered place, where they will grow and annually produce flowers, though the seeds seldom ripen here.

Titles. This species is titled, *Pontederia foliis cordatis, floribus spicatis*. In the *Hortus Cliffort.* it is termed, *Ponteder a floribus spicatis*. Petiver calls it, *Gladiolus lacustris Virginianus cæruleus, sagittæ folio*. Morison, *Sagittæ similis planta palustris Virginiana, spicâ florum cæruleâ*; and Plumier, *Plantagini aquaticæ quodammodo accedens, floribus cæruleis hyacinthi spicatis*. It grows naturally in watery places in Virginia.

Class and order in the Linnæan system. *Pontederia* is of the class and order *Hexandria Monogynia*; and the characters are,

The characters. 1. CALYX is an oblong spatha opening sideways.

2. COROLLA is a tubular petal divided into two parts. The upper lip is straight, equal, and divided into three segments; the lower lip is reflexed, and divided into three equal segments.

3. STAMINA. There are six filaments, the three longest of which are inserted in the mouth of the corolla, the other three in the base; and their antheræ are oblong and erect.

4. PISTILLUM consists of an oblong germen situated below the corolla, a simple declining style, and a thickish stigma.

5. PERICARPIUM is a fleshy, conical, triangular, trisulcated, capsule, containing three cells.

6. SEMINA. The seeds are many, and roundish.

# CHAP. CCCLXIV.

## POTAMOGETON, POND-WEED.

FOR the sake of those who may be desirous of having the different sorts of Pond weed, and not to recommend them as cultivated plants, this genus is introduced in this place. The respective species are usually called by the several names of,

Species.
1. Broad-leaved Pond-weed.
2. Perfoliated Pond-weed.
3. Long-leaved Pond-weed.
4. The Greater Water *Caltrops*.
5. The Lesser Water *Caltrops*, or Frog's Lettuce.
6. Compressed Pond-weed.
7. Fennel leaved Pond-weed.
8. Grass-leaved Pond-weed.
9. Small Grass-leaved Pond weed.
10. Sea Pond-weed.

Broad-leaved Pond-weed described. 1. Broad-leaved Pond weed. The root is long, jointed, white, and fibrous. The stalks are very long, round, jointed, branching, and arise to the top of the water. The leaves are broad, oblong, oval, and grow singly at the joints on long footstalks; they are generally of a brownish-green colour, and part of them will be immersed in the water, and others lie floating on the surface. The flowers come out in spikes from the tops of the stalks; they are small, and of a light red, purple, [illegible] yellowish center, so [illegible] these waters, they appear chiefly in August, and the seeds ripen in the autumn.

[illegible] 2. Perfoliated Pond-weed. The root is creeping, long, and white. The stalks are slender, round, jointed, branching, and when near their heads three or four feet above the water. The leaves are heart-shaped, pointed, of a thin substance, ribbed, shining, and surround the stalk with their base. The flowers come out in spikes from the divisions of the stalks; they are small, of a whitish or yellowish colour, appear in June and July, and the seeds ripen in September.

[illegible] 3. Long-leaved Pond-weed. The root is thick, round, creeping, jointed, and sends forth fibres from the joints, which strike deep into the mud. The stalks are moderately thick, round, jointed, and shew their tops above the surface of the water. The leaves are spear-shaped, long, narrow, sharp-pointed, and shining. The flowers come out from the tops of the stalks in close spikes; they are small, of a reddish colour, appear chiefly in June, but frequently shew themselves in subsequent months, and in the autumn.

The Greater 4. The Greater Water Caltrops. The stalks are thin, flat, reddish, bending various ways, and strike root from the lower joints. The leaves are spear-shaped, curled, waved, serrated on their edges, of a reddish green colour, and grow alternately on the stalks, though opposite, by pairs, near the ends of the branches. The flowers come out a few together, forming a spike, from the wings of the leaves near the top of the plant, on short thickish footstalks; they are of a reddish colour, and appear chiefly in June and July.

and the Lesser Water Caltrops described 5. The Lesser Water Caltrops, or Frog's Lettuce. The stalks are slender, round, kneed or jointed, bending various ways, and branching near the top. The leaves are spear-shaped, pointed, serrated, slightly waved, and grow opposite to each other at the joints. The flowers come out by pairs on slender footstalks, are of a whitish-green colour, and appear chiefly in July.

Description of Compressed 6. Compressed Pond-weed. The stalk is compressed, almost flat, branching, jointed, and immersed in the water. The leaves are narrow, obtuse, a little waved, long, thin, longitudinally ribbed, and grow alternately on the stalks, but opposite near the tops of the branches, where the flowers are produced. The flowers come out in short spikes from the wings of the leaves, are small and greenish, having a little red in the middle, and appear chiefly in June and July.

Fennel-leaved 7. Fennel-leaved Pond-weed. The root is long, slender, fibrous, and strikes deep into the mud. The stalks are weak, bending various ways, several feet long, according to the depth of the water, and divide into many branches, especially near the top. The leaves are composed of many long, narrow, acute segments, which run nearly parallel to each other, join at their base, and grow alternately on weak, slender footstalks. The flowers come out in slender spikes from the upper parts of the plant; they are small and white, having a little yellow in the center, and flourish chiefly in June and July.

Grass-leaved, 8. Grass-leaved Pondweed. The stalks are weak, branching, and immersed in the water. The leaves are narrow, spear-shaped, sessile, and grow alternately. The flowers come out in small spikes from the upper parts of the plants, and appear chiefly in June and July.

Small Grass-leaved, 9. Small Grass-leaved Pond-weed. The stalk is taper, slender, weak, and branching. The leaves are narrow, grassy, and grow sometimes opposite to each other, and sometimes alternately at a considerable distance. The flowers are produced from the wings of the leaves on the upper parts of the plant, appear in June, and continue in succession until the end of summer.

10. Sea Pond-weed. The stalks divide into very numerous branches, floating in the water. The leaves are narrow, grassy, grow alternately, and surround the stalk with their base. The flowers come out in small bunches from the upper parts of the plant, are moderately large, and appear chiefly in August. and Sea Pond-weed

All these species grow naturally in ditches, standing waters, ponds, &c. and are not cultivated plants. Nevertheless, if any person is desirous of furnishing his ditches or distant waters with these plants for his observation, it may be easily effected by inserting the roots in the mud at any time of the year; or, if the seeds of the respective sorts be gathered when they are ripe, and thrown into the water, they will grow, especially if the bottom be full of mud. Method of propagation

1. Broad-leaved Pond-weed is entitled, *Potamogeton foliis oblongo ovatis petiolatis natantibus*. In the *Flora Lapponica* it is termed, *Potamogeton foliis ovato oblongis natantibus*. Caspar Bauhine calls it, *Potamogeton rotundifolium*; Gerard, *Potamogeton latifolium*; and Parkinson, *Potamogeton major latifolia vulgaris*. It grows naturally in lakes and rivers in England and most parts of Europe. Titles

2. Perfoliated Pond-weed is, *Potamogeton foliis cordatis amplexicaulibus*. Ray calls it, *Potamogeton perfoliatum*; Caspar Bauhine, *Potamogeton foliis latis splendentibus*; Gerard, *Potamogeton III Dodonaei*; and Loekl [illegible] *majus alterum*. It grows naturally in lakes and rivers in England and most countries of Europe.

3. Long-leaved Pond-weed is, *Potamogeton foliis lanceolatis planis in petiolos desinentibus*. Caspar Bauhine calls it, *Potamogeton foliis angustis splendentibus*; John Bauhine, *Fontalis lucens major*; Ray, *Potamogeton aquis immersum, folio pellucido, lato oblongo, acuto*; and Gerard, *Potamogeton longis acutis foliis*. It grows naturally in rivers, lakes, and ditches, in England and most parts of Europe.

4. Greater Water Caltrops is, *Potamogeton foliis lanceolatis, alternis undulatis serratis*. Caspar Bauhine calls it, *Potamogeton foliis crispis, seu Lactuca ranarum fasciis plantis*; John Bauhine, *Potamogeton, seu Fontinalis crispa*; Gerard, *Tribulus aquaticus minor quercus floribus*; and Parkinson, *Tribulus aquaticus minor [illegible]*. It grows naturally in waters almost every-where.

5. Lesser Water Caltrops, or Frog's Lettuce, is, *Potamogeton foliis lanceolatis oppositis sub undulatis*. Gerard calls it, *Potamogeton foliis lanceolatis confertis undulatis, caulibus longe ramosis*; Caspar Bauhine, *Potamogeton longo serrato folio*; John Bauhine, *Potamogeton, seu fontalis media lucens*; Gerard, *Tribulus aquaticus minor, moscatellae floribus*; and Parkinson, *Tribulus aquaticus minor alter*. It inhabits chiefly slow rivulets in England and most countries of Europe.

6. Compressed Pond-weed is, *Potamogeton foliis linearibus obtusis, caule compresso*. Haller calls it, *Potamogeton caule plano, foliis gramineis undulatis, spica exigua*; Ray, *Potamogeton caule compresso, foliis gramineis caninis*. It grows naturally in ditches and rivers in England and most parts of Europe.

7. Fennel-leaved Pond-weed is, *Potamogeton foliis setaceis parallelis approximatis distichis*. Van Royen calls it, *Potamogeton foliis linearibus acutis longissimis alternis confertis*; Caspar Bauhine, *Potamogeton gramineum ramosum*; Ray, *Potamogeton millefolium, seu foliis gramineis ramosum*; and Gerard,



9 A

rard, *Millefolium aquaticum*. It grows naturally in ditches, lakes, and rivers, in England and most countries of Europe.

8 Grass-leaved Pond-weed is, *Potamogeton foliis lineari-lanceolatis alternis, stipulis ... latiori... us*. Ray calls it, *Potamogeton gramineum latifolium, foliis ... dentatis stipatis*, and Petiver, *Potamogeton gramineum latum*. It grows naturally in ditches and standing-waters in England and most parts of Europe.

9 Small Grass-leaved Pond-weed is, *Potamogeton foliis ... oppositis alternisque distinctis, basi ... bus*. Van Royen calls it, *Potamogeton foliis linearibus alternis ...*, Caspar Bauhine, *Potamogeton minimum, capillaceo folio*, ... *Potamogeton gramineum tenuifolium*, and Vaillant *Potamogeton pusillum, gramineo folio ...*. It grows in ditches and standing-waters in England and most parts of Europe.

10 Sea Pond-weed is, *Potamogeton foliis linearibus alternis distinctis internodiis vaginantibus*. Boccone calls it, *Potamogeton pusillum ...*, Plukenet, *Potamogeton ma... ramosissimum, grandiusculis capitulis, capillaceo folio*, and Petiver, *Potamogeton fæniculaceum*. It grows naturally in sea ditches in England and other parts of Europe.

*Potamogeton* is of the class and order *Tetrandria Tetragynia*, and the characters are, Class and order in the Linnæan system. The characters.

1 CALYX. There is none.

2 COROLLA consists of four roundish, obtuse, concave, erect unguiculated petals.

3 STAMINA are four very short, plain, obtuse filaments with short didymous antheræ.

4 PISTILLUM consists of four oval, acuminated germens, with obtuse stigmas, there being no styles.

5 PERICARPIUM. There is none.

6 SEMINA. The seeds are four, roundish, acuminated, gibbous on one side, and compressed and angulated on the other.

# CHAP. CCCLXV.

## *POTENTILLA*, CINQUEFOIL.

THE perennials of this genus are, Species.

1 Common Cinquefoil, or Five-leaved Grass.
2 Silvery Cinquefoil.
3 Rough Cinquefoil.
4 Stipulated Cinquefoil.
5 Golden Cinquefoil.
6 Canada Cinquefoil.
7 White Cinquefoil.
8 Spring Cinquefoil.
9 Small Rough Cinquefoil.
10 Small White Cinquefoil.
11 Seven-leaved White *Potentilla*.
12 Red Cinquefoil.
13 Yellow Upright Cinquefoil.
14 Silver-weed, or Wild Tansy.
15 Siberian Silver-weed.
16 Multifid *Potentilla*.
17 Strawberry *Potentilla*.
18 Upright Bastard Cinquefoil.
19 Snowy *Potentilla*.
20 Short-stalked *Potentilla*.
21 Shrub Cinquefoil.

1 Common Cinquefoil, or Five-leaved Grass. Common Cinquefoil described. The root is thick, woody, and hung with strong fibres. The stalks are round, slender, lie on the ground, and strike root at the joints. The leaves are digitated, and composed of about five oblong, serrated folioles, which join at their base, and grow alternately on long footstalks. The flowers are produced singly on long, slender footstalks, are moderately large, of a fine yellow colour, appear in June, and frequently continue in succession until the end of summer.

The root is chiefly used in medicine, being astringent, and serviceable in diarrhœas and other fluxes. Its use in medicine.

2 Silvery Cinquefoil. Description of Silvery. The stalks are upright, branching, and about a foot high. The leaves are composed of five wedge-shaped folioles, which are cut on their edges, and downy or hoary underneath. The flowers come out from the tops of the stalks on slender footstalks; they are of a yellow colour, appear in June and July, and the seeds ripen in August and September.

3 Rough Cinquefoil. Rough. The stalks are slender, rising, and about a foot long. The radical leaves are composed of seven folioles, those on the stalk of five. They are wedge-shaped, furrowed at the top, and hairy on their under side. The flowers come out singly on long slender footstalks, are of a yellow colour, and appear chiefly in June and July.

4 Stipulated Cinquefoil. Stipulated. The stalks are slender, smooth, divided into a few branches near the top, and have broad, emarginated stipulæ, growing singly, and surrounding it with their base. To these are joined the leaves, which are of the digitated form, and consist each of eight or nine narrow, spear-shaped folioles, which are smooth, and slightly serrated on the edges. The flowers come out singly on longish footstalks, are of a yellow colour, and appear about the same time with the former.

5 Golden Cinquefoil. Golden. The stalks are slender, jointed, partly procumbent, and about eight or ten inches long. The radical leaves are composed of five folioles, those on the stalks of three, and all of them are acutely serrated, sharp pointed, and very soft and silky to the touch. The flowers come out singly on long slender footstalks, are large, of a golden-yellow colour, appear in June and July, and frequently again in the end of summer and in the autumn.

There is a variety of this species with beautifully-spotted flowers. Its variety.

6 Canada Cinquefoil. Description of Canada. The stalks are round, slender, jointed, hairy, and six or eight inches long. The radical leaves are quinate, the folioles are nearly oval, sharply serrated, downy on the

the upper ſide, ſoft and hairy underneath, and grow on white hairy footſtalks. The flowers are yellow, and appear in July.

*White*

7. White Cinquefoil. The ſtalks are round, ſlender, jointed, hairy, lie on the ground, and ſtrike root at the joints. The leaves are digitated, and conſiſt of five oblong ſerrated lobes, which are greeniſh on their upper ſide, but very hoary and ſilky underneath, and grow on long, hairy footſtalks. The flowers come out immediately from the root on long, ſlender footſtalks; they are of a white colour, appear in June, and continue in ſucceſſion, from freſh plants occaſioned by the runners, until the end of ſummer.

*Spring,*

8. Spring Cinquefoil. The ſtalk is ſlender, lies on the ground, and ſtrikes root at the joints. The radical leaves are quinate, acutely ſerrated, and retuſed; thoſe on the ſtalks are ternate. The flowers are of a yellow colour, grow on long, ſlender footſtalks, and appear chiefly in May and June.

*Small Rough,*

9. Small Rough Cinquefoil. The ſtalks are very ſlender, lie on the ground, and are covered with a ſoft, downy matter. The leaves are quinate, wedge-ſhaped, ſerrated, hoary, and ſoft and ſilky to the touch. The flowers are yellow, and ſhew themſelves chiefly in July.

10. Small White Cinquefoil. The ſtalks are upright, and four or five inches high. The leaves are quinate, ſerrated, greeniſh on their upper ſide, and ſoft and downy underneath. The flowers come out many together [illegible] of the ſtalks, are of a white colour, [illegible] in June and July.

11. Seven-le[illegible] [illegible] are erect, eight or ten inches high, [illegible] with few ternate leaves, [illegible] and downy. The flowers come [illegible] branches from the tops of the ſtalks, are very ſmall, of a white colour, and appear in June and July.

*Red,*

12. Red Cinquefoil. The leaves are quinate, of a ſilvery whiteneſs, a ſilky ſoftneſs, and have three indentures at the top. The ſtalks are ſoft, downy, and four or five inches high. The flowers come out ſingly from the tops of the ſtalks, are large, of a fine red colour, and appear in June and July.

*and Yellow Upright Cinquefoil deſcribed.*

13. Yellow Upright Cinquefoil. The ſtalks are upright, branching near the top, and about a foot high. The leaves are compoſed of ſeven ſpear-ſhaped, ſerrated folioles, which are green, and a little hairy on both ſides. The flowers terminate the ſtalks in corymboſe bunches; they are pretty large, of a yellow colour, and appear in July.

*Its variety.*

There is a variety of this ſpecies with white flowers.

*Silver-weed deſcribed.*

14. Silver-weed, or Wild Tanſey. The ſtalks lie on the ground, and ſtrike root at the joints. The leaves are long, and pinnated; they conſiſt of eight or nine pair of oblong, narrow, ſerrated folioles terminated by an odd one, and are of a ſilvery whiteneſs, eſpecially underneath. The flowers come out ſingly on longiſh footſtalks, are large, and of a beautiful yellow colour; they appear chiefly in June and July, but often ſhew themſelves in the end of ſummer and the autumn.

*Medicinal properties of it.*

This plant was formerly held aſtringent and vulnerary, but is very ſeldom uſed at preſent.

*Siberian Silver-weed deſcribed.*

15. Siberian Silver-weed. The ſtalks are ſix or eight inches long, and lie on the ground, but have little tendency to creep or ſtrike root as they lie. The leaves are bipinnated; the pinnulæ are narrow, ſhort, entire, white and ſilky on both ſides. The flowers have hairy footſtalks, grow alternately, are of a yellow colour, and appear in June and July.

*Multifid,*

16. Multifid *Potentilla*. The ſtalks are ſlender, and lie on the ground. The leaves are cut into many narrow ſegments, which are ſmooth, and downy underneath. The flowers come out ſingly on ſhort footſtalks, are of a yellow colour, and appear in June and July.

*and Strawberry Potentilla deſcribed.*

17. Strawberry *Potentilla*. This ſpecies hath a thick, ſleſhy, covered root, hung with long ſilk brown fibres. The ſhoots lie on the ground, and ſtrike root at the joints in the manner of the Barren Strawberry. The leaves are ſometimes ternate, and ſome are compoſed of two or three folioles, which are terminated by an odd one; the folioles are oval, ſerrated, hairy, grow oppoſite on the mid-rib, and the terminal one is the largeſt. The flowers grow on ſlender, hairy footſtalks, are of a white colour, and like the Small Strawberry; they appear in May and June.

*Upright Baſtard Cinquefoil deſcribed.*

18. Upright Baſtard Cinquefoil. The leaves are collected into diſtinct heads at the tops of the roots; they are pinnated, being compoſed of three pair of roundiſh folioles terminated by an odd one, are crenated on their edges, and ſupported by long footſtalks. From each head riſe one or two upright ſtalks to about nine inches high, which are adorned with a few trifoliate leaves placed alternately. The flowers come out two or three together on footſtalks from the tops of the ſtalks; they are of a white colour, reſemble [illegible] the Strawberry, and appear in June.

[illegible] ſlender [illegible] at the joints, [illegible] ſerrated [illegible] their edges, hairy, and white, with [illegible] on their under ſide. The flowers [illegible] on ſlender footſtalks, are moderately large, of a white colour, and appear in June.

*Its Variety.*

There is a variety of this ſpecies with beautiful yellow flowers.

*Short-ſtalked Potentilla*

20. Short-ſtalked *Potentilla*. The ſtalk is very ſhort, and decumbent. The leaves are trifoliate, rough, hairy, wedge-ſhaped, obtuſe, indented on their edges, and very downy on both ſides. The flowers are very large, of a yellow colour, and appear in June.

*and Shrub Cinquefoil deſcribed.*

21. Shrub Cinquefoil. This is a beautiful flowering ſhrub, and ſhould have been arranged in that department, but was omitted by miſtake. The ſtalks are woody, divide into numerous ſpreading branches, and grow to about three or four feet high. The leaves are compoſed of five oblong, narrow, entire, acute-pointed folioles, which are of a pale green colour on their upper ſide, whitiſh underneath, and grow alternately on whitiſh, hairy, channelled footſtalks. The flowers come out from the ends and ſides of the branches on ſlender, round, downy footſtalks; they are large, of a yellow colour, appear in June and July, but, though natives of England, are very rarely ſucceeded by ſeeds in gardens.

*Propagation of this laſt ſpecies.*

This ſhrubby ſpecies is propagated by laying down the branches, or planting the ſlips or cuttings, in the autumn or ſpring. If the propagation is by cuttings, the ground ſhould be in the ſhade, naturally moiſt, and well dug; and if they are planted any time in the autumn, winter, or early in the ſpring, they will readily grow. In the autumn or winter following the ſtrongeſt plants may be removed to the places where they are deſigned to remain, whilſt the weakeſt may be ſet in the nurſery ground at a ſmall diſtance from each other, and by the autumn following they will be good plants, fit for removal.

If the operation is performed by layers, the trouble then is only pegging down the young branches,

branches, and covering a little mould over them. They will then readily strike root, and in the autumn or winter following they must be taken up, trimmed and planted in the nursery way, to remain there for a year, before they are removed to the places of their final destination.

Method of propagating the species. All the other species of Cinquefoil are propagated by parting of the roots, which may be done in the autumn. They may be also propagated by seeds, which should be sown as soon as they are ripe. Many of them propagate themselves very fast by their runners, which strike root at the joints, and cause fresh plants; and those which have this tendency in a less degree, generally produce the best seeds, and may soon be plentifully raised that way. The species of English growth are generally looked upon as weeds, where-ever they are met with, though they are not without their beauties, were they less common. The other species, which are natives of distant countries, are more prized, and are sought after to enlarge the collections of the Curious.

Titles. 1 Common Cinquefoil, or Five leaved Grass, is entitled, *Potentilla foliis digitatis, caule repente, pedunculis unifloris*. In the *Hortus Cliffort.* it is termed *Potentilla foliis digitatis ..., pinnulis serratis, caule repente*. Caspar Bauhine calls it, *Quinquefolium majus repens*, Fuchsius, *Quinquefolium majus luteum*, Gerard, *Quinquefolium majus*, and Parkinson, *Pentaphyllum vulgatissimum*. It is found almost every-where in England and most countries of Europe.

2 Silvery Cinquefoil is, *Potentilla foliis quinatis cuneiformibus incisis subtus tomentosis, caule erecto*. In the *Flora Suecica* it is termed, *Potentilla foliis digitatis, caule erecto corymboso*, in the *Hortus Cliffort. Potentilla foliis digitatis inciso serratis, caule erecto*. Caspar Bauhine calls it, *Quinquefolium folio argenteo*, and Cammerarius, *Pentaphyllum minus*. It grows naturally in dry, gravelly pastures and meadows, by way sides, &c. in England, and most countries of Europe.

3 Rough Cinquefoil is, *Potentilla foliis septenatis quinatisque cuneiformibus incisis pilosis, caule adscendente*. Caspar Bauhine calls it, *Quinquefolium montanum erectum hirsutum*. It grows naturally on the Pyrenees, and in the South of France.

4 Stipulated Cinquefoil is, *Potentilla foliis septenatis ... stipulis dilatatis ... stipulis in ...*. Gmelin calls it, *Potentilla foliis novenis stipulis in ...*. It grows naturally in Siberia.

5 Golden Cinquefoil is, *Potentilla foliis radicalibus quinatis serratis acuminatis, caule ..., caule declinato*. Haller calls it, *Potentilla foliis quinatis acute serratis, ... petiolis ...*, and Caspar Bauhine, *Quinquefolium minus repens alpinum aureum*. It grows naturally on the Helvetian mountains.

6 Canada Cinquefoil is, *Potentilla foliis quinatis villosis, caule adscendente hirsuto*. Morison calls it, *Quinquefolium Canadense minimus*. It grows naturally in Canada.

7 White Cinquefoil is, *Potentilla foliis quinatis apice conniventi-serratis, caulibus filiformibus procumbentibus, receptaculis hirsutis*. Haller calls it, *Quinquefolium album*, Caspar Bauhine, *Quinquefolium album majus alterum*, Clusius, *Pentaphyllum majus, flore albo*, and Gerard, *Quinquefolium sylvaticum majus, flore albo*. It grows naturally in Wales, also on the Stirian, Austrian, and Pannonian mountains.

8 Spring Cinquefoil is, *Potentilla foliis radicalibus quinatis acute serratis retusis, caulinis ternatis, caule decumbente*. In the *Flora Lapponica* it is termed, *Potentilla foliis quinatis incisis, caule assurgente*. Caspar Bauhine calls it, *Quinquefolium minus repens luteum*, and John Bauhine, *Montanus, Pentaphyllum, seu quinquefolium minus*. It grows naturally in dry, cold, sterile pastures in England and most parts of Europe.

9 Small Rough Cinquefoil is, *Potentilla foliis radicalibus quinatis cuneiformibus serratis, caulinis suboppositis, ramis filiformibus decumbentibus*. Clusius calls it, *Quinquefolium IV flavo flore, 2 species*, Caspar Bauhine, *Quinquefolium minus repens lanuginosum luteum*, also, *Quinquefolium ... hirsuta*. John Bauhine names it, *Pentaphyllum parvum hirsutum*, and Gerard, *Pentaphyllum incanum minus repens*. It grows naturally in England, Austria, Helvetia, and on mount Baldus.

10 Small White Cinquefoil is, *Potentilla foliis quinatis apice conniventi-serratis, caulibus multifloris erectis, receptaculis hirsutis*. Caspar Bauhine calls it, *Quinquefolium album caulescens*, also, *Quinquefolium album minus alterum*, and Clusius, *Quinquefolium II minus, albo flore*. It grows naturally on the Helvetian, Austrian, and Stirian mountains.

11 Seven leaved White Potentilla is, *Potentilla foliis septenis obovatis serratis tomentosis, caule erecto, petalis calyce brevioribus, receptaculis ...*. It grows common on the Alps, Pyrenees, and other mountainous parts of Europe.

12 Red Cinquefoil is, *Potentilla foliis quinatis tomentosis conniventi-tridentatis, caulibus unifloris, receptaculis lanatis*. Boccone calls it, *Heptaphyllum argenteum Alpinum trifoliatum fol. ...*, Caspar Bauhine, *Trifolium Alpinum argenteum, persici folio*, and Seguier, *Chamaedryes Alpina argentea sericea, persici flore*. It grows naturally on mount Baldus.

13 Yellow Upright Cinquefoil is, *Potentilla foliis septenatis lanceolatis serratis utrinque subpilosis, caule erecto*. In the *Hortus Upsal.* it is termed, *Potentilla foliis digitatis, caule erecto corymboso*. Caspar Bauhine calls it, *Quinquefolium rectum luteum*, and Dodonaeus, *Quinquefolium alterum vulgare*. It grows naturally on the borders of fields in France and Italy.

14 Silver-weed, or Wild Tansey, is, *Potentilla foliis pinnatis serratis, caule repente*. Caspar Bauhine calls it, *Potentilla*, Dodonaeus and Gerard, *Argentina*, and Ray, *Pentaphylloides argentina dicta*. It grows naturally in poor, starved pastures in England and most countries of Europe.

15 Siberian Silver-weed is, *Potentilla foliis bipinnatis utrinque tomentosis, segmentis parallelis approximatis, caulibus decumbentibus*. Haller calls it, *Potentilla foliis pinnatis hirsutis, pinnis tredecim ovatis crenatis decurrentibus*, and Gmelin, *Potentilla foliis duplicato pinnatis, pinnulis linearibus integerrimis brevibus*. It grows naturally in Siberia.

16 Multifid Potentilla is, *Potentilla foliis bipinnatis, segmentis integerrimis distantibus subtus tomentosis, caule decumbente*. Buxbaum calls it, *Pentaphylloides repens, foliis pinnatis*, and Amman, *Pentaphylloides supinum minus, folio glabro non serrato*, also, *Pentaphylloides supina minor, foliis alatis hirsutis varie dissectis*. It grows naturally in Siberia, Tartary, and Cappadocia.

17 Strawberry Potentilla is, *Potentilla foliis pinnatis ternatisque, extimis majoribus, flagellis reptantibus*. Gmelin calls it, *Potentilla foliis ternatis hirsutis utrinque virentibus, lobulis accessoriis*, and Haller, *Potentilla foliis novenis palmatis apice serratis*. It is a native of Siberia.

18 Upright Bastard Cinquefoil is, *Potentilla foliis pinnatis alternis, foliolis ovatis ovatis crenatis, caule erecto*. Caspar Bauhine calls it, *Quinquefolium fragiferum*, and John Bauhine, *Pentaphylloides erectum*. It grows naturally in the mountainous parts of Germany.

19 Snowy

19. Snowy *Potentilla* is, *Potentilla foliis ternatis inciſis ſubtus tomentoſis, caule adſcendente* Haller calls it, *Potentilla foliis ampliter crenatis ſubtus tomentoſis*, and Amman, *Fragaria ſterilis procumbens, foliis betonicæ inſtar ſerratis* It grows naturally on the Alps of Lapland and Siberia

20 Short-ſtalked *Potentilla* is, *Potentilla foliis ternatis dentatis utrinque tomentoſis, ſcapo decumbente* Moriſon calls it, *Fragaria ſterilis ſylveſtris ſericea ſ incana*, and Caſpar Bauhine, *Fragariæ affinis ſericea incana* It grows naturally in France and Siberia

21 Shrub Cinquefoil is, *Potentilla foliis pinnatis, caule fruticoſo* Moriſon calls it, *Pentaphylloides rectum fruticoſum Eboracenſe*; Amman, *Pentaphylloides fruticoſa elatior*, and Ray, *Pentaphylloides fruticoſa* It grows naturally in Yorkſhire and ſeveral parts of the North, alſo, in Oelandia and Siberia

*Claſs and order in the Linnæan ſyſtem*

*Potentilla* is of the claſs and order *Icoſandria Polygynia* and the characters are,

*The characters*

1 Calyx is a monophyllous, planiſh perianthium, divided into five ſegments, which are alternately ſmaller, and reflexed

2 Corolla is five roundiſh, patent petals, inſerted by their ungues into the calyx

3 Stamina are twenty awl-ſhaped filaments, inſerted in the calyx, and ſhorter than the corolla, having elongated, lunulated antheræ

4 Pistillum conſiſts of numerous ſmall germens collected into a head, and numerous ſtyles the length of the ſtamina, and inſerted into the ſides of the germens, having obtuſe ſtigmas

5 Pericarpium There is none The common receptacle is roundiſh, ſmall, permanent, covered with ſeeds, and included in the calyx

6 Semina The ſeeds are numerous, and acuminated

## CHAP. CCCLXVI

## *POTERIUM*, GARDEN BURNET

*Species.*

HERE we find,

1 The Common Burnet of our Kitchen Gardens

2 The Sweet-ſcented Burnet

*Uſes of the Common Burnet*

1 The uſes of the Common Burnet for ſallads, cool tankards, or in medicine, are well known, and occaſion this plant in ſome parts to be propagated in great plenty It is, however, very beautiful, and on this account, even where plants are raiſed with no other view than for obſervation, a few of Burnet ought to join in the collection

*Deſcription of it*

The root is perennial, and ſends forth many fine, pinnated leaves These are of a lively-green colour, have long footſtalks, the pinnæ ſerrated on their edges, and are in number about ſix or ſeven pair, beſides the odd one that terminates them The ſtalks are many, upright, branching, angular, and grow to about a foot and a half high The flowers terminate the branches in oblong ſpikes, growing on long, ſlender footſtalks There will be found males and females in the ſame ſpike They are of a purpliſh-red colour, have long filaments, and yellow antheræ They come out in June, and the females are ſucceeded by ripe ſeeds in the autumn

*Sweet-ſcented Burnet deſcribed*

2 Sweet-ſcented Burnet. The ſtalks are taper, upright, and grow to about two feet high The leaves are like agrimony, finely ſcented, and each is compoſed of about three or four pair of oblong lobes terminated by an odd one, they have their edges ſerrated, and are for the moſt part placed alternately along the mid-rib The flowers are produced from the upper parts of the ſtalks on long footſtalks, which divide into ſmaller ones, each ſupporting a ſmall head or ſpike, they will be in blow in July, and have ripe ſeeds in the autumn

*Method of propagating them*

Theſe ſpecies are eaſily raiſed by parting of the roots in the autumn But the beſt way is by ſeeds, which may be ſown either in the autumn or ſpring, and after the plants come up, nothing need be done, except thinning them where they appear too cloſe, and keeping them clean from weeds They bear tranſplanting very well; ſo that the plants which are drawn to make room for the others, may be uſed to form a bed in another part The ſecond ſpecies frequently dies after it has perfected its ſeeds, ſo that, unleſs you intend regularly to ſow the ſeeds to continue the ſucceſſion, you ſhould nip off ſome of the ſtalks before they come to flower. This will cauſe them to ſhoot out afreſh from the roots, and preſerve them for a blow the next ſeaſon.

*Titles.*

1 Common Burnet is titled, *Poterium inerme, caulibus ſubanguloſis* There are ſeveral varieties of it, one of which Caſpar Bauhine terms, *Pimpinella ſanguiſorba minor hirſuta*, another, *Pimpinella ſanguiſorba minor lævis*; and another, *Pimpinella ſanguiſorba inodora* Van Royen calls it, *Poterium inerme, filamentis longiſſimis*, and Camerarius, *Pimpinella ſanguiſorba* It grows naturally in England and moſt parts of Europe

2 Sweet ſcented Burnet is titled, *Poterium inerme, caulibus teretibus ſtrictis* In the *Hortus Upſal* it is termed *Poterium agrimonoides* Van Royen calls it, *Poterium inerme filamentis flore vix ſuperantibus*, Moriſon, *Pimpinella agrimonoides*, and Barrelier, *Pimpinella agrimonoides odorata* It grows naturally near Montpelier in France

*Claſs and order in the Linnæan ſyſtem*

*Poterium* is of the claſs and order *Monoecia Polyandria*, and the characters are,

*The characters*

I Male Flowers forming a ſpike

1 Calyx is a perianthium, compoſed of three oval, coloured, caducous leaves

2 Corolla is compoſed of four oval, concave, patent, permanent petals, which coaleſce at their baſe

3 Stamina are numerous long, capillary, flaccid filaments, with roundiſh, didymous antheræ

II Female Flowers in the ſame ſpike

1 Calyx is the like perianthium with that of the male

2 Corolla is a wheel-ſhaped petal The tube is ſhort, and roundiſh The limb is divided into four oval, plane, reflexed, permanent ſegments

3 Pistillum conſiſts of two oval, oblong germina, and two capillary, coloured, flaccid ſtyles the length of the corolla, with pencil-ſhaped, coloured ſtigmas

4 Pericarpium is a berry contained in the indurated tube of the corolla

5 Semina The ſeeds are two

## C H A P CCCLXVII

## *PRENANTHES.* WILD LETTUCE.

Species

OF this genus are,
1 Ivy-leaved Wild Lettuce
2 Narrow-leaved Wild Lettuce
3 Purple Wild Lettuce
4 Canada Wild Lettuce
5 White Wall Lettuce
6 Creeping Wall Lettuce

Deſcription of Ivy leaved,

1 Ivy-leaved Wild Lettuce The ſtalk is upright, firm, round, branching near the top, and a foot and a half high The leaves are ſerrated, and ſawed like the Sow-Thiſtle, but the extremity is compoſed of three broad flat lobes, like ſome leaves of Ivy; they are ſoft and tender, of a pale green colour on their upper-ſide, whitiſh underneath, grow alternately, and embrace the ſtalk with their baſe The flowers come out in panicles from the tops of the ſtalks, they are very ſmall, of a yellow colour, appear in July, and are followed by downy ſeeds, which ripen ſoon after

Narrow leaved

2 Narrow-leaved Wild Lettuce The leaves are long, narrow, tender, and undivided on their edges The ſtalks are upright, branching, and about a foot high The flowers come out in the manner of the former ſort from the tops of the plant, they are ſmall, and of a purple colour, appear in July, and the ſeeds ripen in Auguſt

Purple,

3 Purple Wild Lettuce The ſtalks are upright, round, firm, and three or four feet high The leaves are ſpear ſhaped, and a little indented towards the ends The flowers are produced in panicles from the tops of the ſtalks, they are of a bluiſh-purple colour, appear in July and Auguſt, and the ſeeds ripen in September

and Canada, Wild Lettuce

4 Canada Wild Lettuce The ſtalks are upright, firm, and riſe to four feet or more in height The lower leaves are large, long, divided chiefly into three lobes, though ſome of them are five-lobed, and a little indented on their edges The flowers come out from the ends and ſides of the ſtalks in ſmall bunches, they are of a pale-yellow colour, appear in July, and are ſucceeded by downy ſeeds, which ripen in September

Variety

There is a variety of this ſpecies with pale-purple flowers

Its virtues

The root of this plant is alexipharmac, and particularly ſerviceable in expelling the venom of the rattle ſnake

5 White Wall Lettuce The root is thick and fleſhy The ſtalk is ſingle, covered with a reddiſh bark, and grows to be two or three feet high The leaves are haſtated, angular, rough, and cut on their edges The flowers come out in ſmall bunches from the upper parts of the ſtalks, they are of a ſnowy-white colour, and hang drooping, they appear in Auguſt and September, and in favourable ſeaſons the ſeeds ripen in the autumn White Wall Lettuce deſcribed

There is a variety of this ſpecies with pale-purple flowers, which will be in blow in October Variety

6 Creeping Wall Lettuce The root is creeping, and ſoon ſpreads itſelf to a conſiderable diſtance The ſtalks are upright, branching a little near the top, and about a foot and a half high The leaves are trilobate, and grow alternately on the ſtalks The flowers come out in kind of panicles from the tops of the ſtalks; they are ſmall, of a yellow colour, appear in June and July, and frequently again in the autumn Creeping Wall Lettuce deſcribed

Theſe plants are, with the utmoſt facility, propagated by ſowing the ſeeds, ſoon after they are ripe, in beds of common mould made fine In the ſpring, after they come up, they muſt be thinned where they are too cloſe, and kept clean from weeds and having once flowered and ripened their ſeeds, plants will come up all over the garden from ſcattered ſeeds, which will be waſted to a conſiderable diſtance by the wind Its culture

1 Ivy-leaved Wall Lettuce is entitled, *Prenanthes floſculis quinis, foliis runcinatis* Caſpar Bauhine calls it, *Sonchus lævis laciniatus muralis, parvis floribus*, John Bauhine, *Lactuca ſylveſtris murorum flore luteo*, Cluſius, *Sonchus lævis vulgatior 2*, Gerard, *Sonchus lævis muralis*, and Parkinſon, *Sonchus lævis alter parvis floribus.* It grows naturally on old walls, and in ſhady woods and foreſts in England, and moſt countries of Europe Titles

2 Narrow leaved Wild Lettuce is, *Prenanthes foliis linearibus integerrimis* Vaillant calls it, *Prenanthes anguſtifolius, flore purpureo*, and Juſſieu, *Chondrilla anguſtiſſimo longiſſimo integroque folio* It grows naturally on the Alps, and other mountainous parts of Europe

3 Purple Wild Lettuce is, *Prenanthes floſculis quinis, foliis lanceolatis denticulatis* Cluſius calls it, *Sonchus lævior Pannonicus 4 purpureo flore*, Caſpar Bauhine, *Lactuca montana, purpureo-cæruleo,*

*cæruleo, major*, and Columna, *Sonchus montanus purpureus tetrapetalos* It grows naturally on the mountainous forests of Germany, Helvetia, and Italy

4. Canada Wild Lettuce is, *Prenanthes flosculis quinis, foliis trilobis, caule erecto* Vaillant calls it, *Prenanthes Canadensis altissima, foliis variis, flore luteo*, and Plukenet, *Sonchus elatius, f dendroides Virginianus, ad in modum articulatis foliis, ramosissimus, floribus luteis pentapetalis* It grows common in Canada and Virginia

5 White Wild Lettuce is, *Prenanthes flosculis plurimis, floribus nutantibus subumbellatis, foliis hastato angulatis* Plukenet calls it, *Prenanthes Nov Anglicanus, chenopodii foliis, radice bulbosa, sanguineo caule, floribus racemosis candidissimis*, and Gronovius, *Prenanthes ... flore albo purpureo deorsum ... spicatim ad caulem dispositio, foliis ...*, *caule singulari* It grows naturally in Carolina Virginia, and Pensylvania

6 Creeping Wild Lettuce is, *Prenanthes repens, foliis trilobis* It is a native of Siberia

*Prenanthes* is of the class and order *Syngenesia Polygamia Æqualis*, and the characters are, — Class and order in the Linnæan system The characters

1 Calyx is smooth, and made nearly cylindrical by equal scales, which have at their base a few short ones that are unequal

2 Corolla. The general flower consists of from five to eight equal florets, placed circularly, and each floret consists of one tongue-shaped truncated petal, indented in four parts at the end

3 Stamina are five very short capillary filaments, having cylindrical tubular antheræ

4 Pistillum consists of an oval germen, a filiforme style longer than the stamina, and a bifid reflexed stigma

5 Pericarpium There is none The cylindrical calyx becomes slightly connivent at the top, and contains the seeds

6 Semen The seed is single, heart-shaped, and crowned with a hairy down

The receptacle is naked

## CHAP CCCLXVIII

## *PRIMULA*, The PRIMROSE

Introductory observations

NUMBERS of genera govern more real species, but none have so many varieties as the *Primula* The *Auricula Ursi* or old botanists is now found justly to belong to the Primrose; and accuracy, as well as the laws of the science, obliges us to rank it with that under one common title of *Primula*, insomuch that by the joining of these families, which before were supposed to be distinct, the largest train of attendants of course mix in the common herd What numbers of the *Polyanthos* kind! what numbers of the *Auricula*! and these are still to be multiplied by seeds, for in these articles especially there are no limits to culture

More than a thousand varieties of the *Polyanthos* Primrose have I had at once in blow in a single bed, and nearly that number of *Auriculas* and doubtless other florists can boast, besides the sorts that are established plants, and named, many others to be added to the number So that without doubt from those two distinct species of the *Primula* grow many thousands of varieties, indeed they may be encreased without end The care of these, in their improved state, is the province of the florist, for which we have given him the best directions What remain to be treated of under this article, are such plants as are either to adorn a flower-border, mix in our wilderness walks, or be planted near at hand for observation, nosegays, and the like The distinct species are,

Species

1 The Primrose
2 The *Auricula Ursi*, or Bear's Ear
3 Bird's Eye
4 The Least *Primula*
5 Narrow-leaved *Primula*
6 Oblong-leaved *Primula*
7 Cordated *Primula*

1 The Primrose Of this species are the following varieties — The Primrose Varieties

The Common Primrose of our hedges and woods,
The Paper White Primrose,
The Cowslip,
The Oxslip,
The Double Yellow Primrose,
The Double White Primrose,
The Double Crimson Primrose,
The Double Cowslip,
The Proliferous Oxslip

Though some of these sorts are not very common, yet they are so easily known, being a multiplication of the petals only of the sorts that are most known and common, that their description is needless

Description of the Common

The Common Primrose of our woods is seen almost every where in the spring, so that we have no occasion for it in any collection, unless in such parts of our wilderness works where Nature, in her wildest state, is to be represented, and the beauty of the woodland introduced It would not be doing her proper honour not to mention this flower, for she is the parent of all our innumerable varieties, and all our beautiful Primroses and *Polyanthus*'s are supposed originally to spring from her This plant, however, has its beauties and excellent properties, and were it not so common, would be highly regarded

and Paper White Primrose

The Paper White Primrose is sometimes found in our woods growing naturally with the others of of which it is a seminal variety, but as it is not common, it is a cultivated plant, and much more so than the sorts of Red Primroses, and the like, which have the general appellation of wild plants All these sorts then flourish in woods, and under hedges and trees, and our wilderness-quarters should have plenty of the White and Red sorts, with a few of the Yellow But let the Red sorts be well selected, before they are planted Let their colour be bright and lively, for they are often painted of such faint, disagreeable, pale reds, that they look rather unwholesome than ornamental, so that if those of a good red cannot be procured, the places are better without the others

The Cowslip. The Cowslip of our pastures is well known Its uses in medicine, and its cordial wine, the invalid has often experienced Nature designed these flowers for an open exposure, and therefore teaches us that they are not, like the Primrose, to grow in our wilderness-works; however, a tuft or two round the edges removes the appearance of art at a greater distance, and tho' they are such common plants, in that manner they will look very well There are, however, varieties of this sort besides the Double that are cultivated, and would do well to mix in that manner by the edges of our plantations, particularly the Scarlet sort, which should be made to grow in a state of wildness in such open places, and amongst such other plants as are designed to make such a representation

Oxslip. The Oxslip of our pastures is also well known, and is to be found growing in common with the Cowslip, though here and there only, for Nature has given us so few plants of it, that it may be said to be rather rare

It was probably this plant that induced Linnæus to class the Primrose, Cowslip, and Oxslip as one species only, making them varieties only of one another For in this plant we see the flower of the Primrose growing upon the stalk of the Cowslip, which stalk naturally grows stronger and larger in proportion, as it were properly to sustain its larger flowers, and this has occasioned former botanists to distinguish it by the epithet *Elatior*

This plant seems to be a mongrel breed between the Primrose and Cowslip, but it is more beautiful, and by far a better looking flower than either, tho' Nature has denied it that agreeable odour which both the former are possessed of This plant may be made to mix with Cowslips in any of our works, or be made to grow in wilds, besides which it claims a place in our best borders of perennial flowers, where it will be larger, and shew to great advantage

Double Yellow, and Double White Primrose described. The Double Yellow and Double White Primrose are delightful plants They are as double and large as a Cinnamon Rose, and in the time of flowering rise up from every part of the root in such plenty as almost to cover the leaves

Their Culture. These plants are propagated by parting of the roots; and when a stock is once obtained, great care must be taken to preserve them, or all of them will soon be lost They should be planted in a shady border made rich with neat's dung mixed with drift-sand, or in the compost directed for the *Polyanthos* Primroses; and even in this they will not live long, if neglected They are naturally weak plants, in proportion to the other Primroses Their leaves are small, the fibres of the roots are slender, and fewer in number; the footstalks of the flowers are weak, and the flowers themselves very large and full, which, perhaps, may contribute considerably to weaken the other parts, so that after they have done flowering, they generally appear in a declining if not a dying state The root will have multiplied itself into several heads, all of which will be weak and languid, especially if they have stood unremoved more than a year In order, therefore, to keep up a stock of these beautiful flowers, let the shady border be made as rich as possible, and there let the offsets be planted Every year, soon after they have done blowing, take up the roots, and, having parted them, plant them again in a like kind of rich border This will cause their weak and almost fibreless heads to encrease the few remaining fibres, and strike out fresh ones from the sides in this fresh, loose, rich mould, and they will accordingly shoot out leaves, and soon resume the appearance of healthy plants These will blow well the spring following, after which the work must be repeated They will stand, indeed, two years unremoved, but this will be attended with great hazard and loss, and I must inform the reader, that I planted a bed of them to see the event They got weaker by degrees, and at the end of three years not a single plant was to be found living; the leaves above, and the fibres below the scaly part always decaying for want of removal Hence, then, let the intelligent Gardener disregard Mr Miller's advice, to plant them in wilderness works for show, as if they were as hardy and durable as the other Primroses, as it will soon prove the loss of his whole stock thus planted, and convince him that Mr Miller is very ignorant of their true nature and culture

Double Crimson Primrose described. The Double Crimson Primrose is the glory still of this tribe It is every whit as large and double as the others, and of a most delicate, true, and perfect crimson

Culture. This plant requires the same management as the others, though it is of a more tender nature, for in severe winters it will be taken off by bad weather; so that a few of them ought always to be potted, to be set in the green house, or under a hotbed-frame, in the severity of winter and then, though all the rest should die, the breed will be preserved, and may soon be encreased, by parting of the roots, to a great quantity If they are potted at the usual time the others are planted out, the pots should be set up to the brims in natural mould, in a shady place, until the bad weather comes on, when they should be removed as above

A sufficient number of roots of these three sorts, to form a large bed, all planted together, will have a most enchanting look, and tho' here are no great variety of colours, yet they will on the whole equal any bed of the *Polyanthus* of the like size But if this should not be allowed, we may say surely, it will make a delightful contrast with those beautifully variegated kinds

Double Cowslip. The Double Cowslip is more hardy in its double state than any of the Primroses, tho' it is inferior in doubleness to none of them Reason must dictate to us that the flowers are not so large, but this is in some measure counterbalanced by so many of them standing on their separate footstalks on one common stem Culture will make these larger; and if they have a rich, shady, moist border, they will be more fair in proportion Dividing of the roots is their propagation, and no good border should be without a few They blow later than the Double Primroses, and are therefore not proper to form a bed with them, but should bear a part with the Common Oxslip, and also with the

Proliferous Oxslip. Proliferous Oxslip This plant is not double, like the others, but one flower rises out of the bosom of the other, as the Common sort from its calyx, so that it is composed of two petals

petals of equal size and form, one above another. The flower is destitute of a calyx, and the under flower supplies its place. It is an agreeable variety, and grows larger by culture. Its station should be with the other sorts in borders for show or observation; and it will be really pleasing to see how the sport of Nature will abound with singularities of such pleasing forms.

Auricula Ursi Varieties. 2. *Auricula Ursi*, or Bear's Ear. Of this species are,

Common Bear's Ear
Double Yellow Bear's Ear
Double Buff-coloured Bear's Ear
Double Purple Bear's Ear

Common Bear's Ear. The Common Bear's Ear. This plant is of various colours, and in its natural state of wildness is very beautiful, and finely scented. But such a profusion of varieties are now obtained by seeds, that, when arranged in a collection under proper management, they form a show surpassing any thing the flowery tribe can produce. The ordering of these is chiefly the business of the florist; and the botanist, when engaged in this work, loses that superior title, and, with respect to these, is mentioned as a florist. All these beautiful (and almost infinite in number) varieties are supposed to come originally from one common Yellow *Auricula*, though Caspar Bauhine, and some other botanists, will have the Purple to have a share; nay, he mentions a Round-leaved and a Narrow-leaved sort, and another with a variegated flower, as being distinct species. But, doubtless, these are only varieties of one another; neither is it very important whether our grand stock proceeds originally from the Yellow or Purple, as from neither of them now, nor indeed from any self-coloured flower, we collect seeds to encrease our number, but from those of the best properties in their improved state in our hands. The Common *Auricula* then, is mentioned here with respect, and, were not the sorts so much improved, would be highly esteemed; for it is a luscious flower, and inferior to none in agreeable odour. They are of various colours, and should have their station in borders or open beds; but not under the drip of trees, which will soon weaken, if not destroy them. A couple of plants of the different Self-coloured ones should be obtained, when a person has no inclination to commence florist; and indeed when he has, as the finest cultivated sorts are either by nature or nursing tender, and are to grow in pots, with a design to make a show in a shed, a few of the Common sorts should ornament his borders in the open ground. When once, therefore, a person is engaged in raising these flowers from seeds, he will have such a number of Self-coloured ones, and such as will not be esteemed good enough to be admitted in a collection, as will furnish his most extensive borders, &c. These will be always useful for nosegays, the plants will be hardier, and they will require no other culture than common border flowers.

and the Double Bear's Ear described. The second, third, and fourth varieties are the Common *Auriculæ* in their Double state. The best sorts of these are as double as the Primrose, tho' each flower is hardly half so large. It is contrary to the laws of some florists to admit these double flowers into their collection, to be shewn on the bed with those of the best properties. But if these laws were to be less rigorously regarded, it would be so much the better; for they are deserving of it, and their multiplicity of petals gives them so different a look from all the others, that they at once set themselves off, and the others, however fine, they are joined with. For when they are thus mixed, the eye is relieved, after beholding a flower of the first properties, by seeing another as opposite as possible, and equally wonderful in its way. Perhaps by this I may incur the censure of some florists. I don't mind that; I love to have them mixed together, and the effect never can be bad. However, every person, without exception, will be glad of them for borders in the flower garden. Here they will grow, having a tolerable good soil, with no more than common culture; though if the border be shady (but not by the hanging-over of trees) and has a free air, they will thrive and flower the better.

Thus have we given our intelligent pupil a full account of this great genus the *Primula*, including the *Auricula* of old authors, which of right belongs to its family, and laid before him their whole nature, with the management of their different offspring, whether they are endowed with such properties as may entitle them to the highest places of honour, or should remain in lower stations, to be serviceable that way. Proceed we now to the other species.

3. Bird's Eye. This plant grows common in the North of England. It has a scaly head, (like the Common Primrose, though smaller) which shoots out into a number of long fibres. The leaves are smooth, indented on their edges, and of a pale-green colour. The flowers are produced in the spring, growing many upon one common stalk, each having its separate pedicle; their colour is naturally red, though there are found varieties with white flowers. The roots being parted, and set in an open shady border, will thrive and multiply very fast. Bird's Eye.

4. The Least *Primula*. This plant grows naturally on the Alps, and other mountainous parts of Europe. The leaves are very small, wedge-shaped, of a thick consistence, indented on their edges, and of a pale green colour. The flowers are produced in the spring, standing many together, and are much larger than the leaves from which they grow. Least.

5. The Narrow-leaved *Primula*. The leaves are narrow, entire, of a thick consistence, and of a pale-green colour. The flowers are produced in the spring, sitting close, in tolerable plenty; they are sessile, and their cups are about as long as the tube of the corolla, whose limb is divided into five oval oblong segments. Narrow-leaved,

This plant also grows naturally on the Alps, and other mountainous parts.

6. Oblong Entire-leaved *Primula* has fleshy smooth leaves, with edges entire. The flowers are produced in the spring, and are usually of a pale-red colour, though it has different varieties, which may be encreased by seeds. Oblong Entire-leaved,

7. Cordated *Primula*. The leaves are lobated, crenated, nearly heart-shaped, and grow on short strong footstalks; they are unlike any of the sorts of the *Primula*, though they perfectly agree in their flowers. and Cordated Primula described.

All these sorts love a rich sandy soil, in a shady border, where there is a free air. Here they will grow, thrive, and flower strong, and may be multiplied by parting of the roots at pleasure. Culture.

1. The Primrose is titled, *Primula foliis dentatis rugosis*. John Bauhine calls it, *Primula veris odorata, flore luteo simplici*; Caspar Bauhine, *Verbasculum pratense odoratum*; also *Verbasculum pratense vel sylvaticum inodorum*; also, *Verbasculum sylvestre majus, singulari flore*; Clusius, *Primula veris, pallido flore, humilis*; also, *Primula veris, pallido flore, elatior*. It grows in the woods, meadows, and pastures of Europe. Titles.

2. *Auricula Ursi*, or Bear's Ear, is titled, *Primula foliis serratis glabris*. In the *Hortus Cliffortianus* it

it is termed, *Primula foliis serratis carnosis glabris*. Caspar Bauhine calls it, *Sanicula Alpina lutea*, also, *Sanicula Alpina purpurea*, also *Sanicula Alpina, foliis rotundis*, also, *Sanicula Alpina, flore variegato*, also, *Sanicula Alpina angustifolia*, also, *Sanicula Alpina, foliis quasi ferina adspersis*. It grows naturally in the Helvetian and Styrian mountains.

3. Bird's Eye is titled, *Primula foliis crenatis glabris, floribus limbo plano*. Clusius calls it, *Primula veris rubro flore*, and Caspar Bauhine, *Verbascum umbellatum Alpinum minus*. It is found in plenty growing naturally in many parts of the North of England, and most of the colder countries of Europe.

4. The Least Primula is, *Primula foliis cuneiformibus dentatis minimis corollis longe minoribus*. Caspar Bauhine calls it, *Sanicula Alpina minima carnea*, Clusius, *Auricula Ursi 8 minima*. It is a native of the Alps, and other mountainous parts of Europe.

5. The Narrow leaved Primula is, *Primula foliis linearibus integerrimis, floribus sessilibus*. In the Aman. Acad. it is termed, *Primula flore subsessili foliis linearibus*. Caspar Bauhine calls it, *Sedum Alpinum exiguis foliis*, Tournefort, *Auricula Ursi Alpina gramineo folio, jasmini lutei flore*. It grows naturally on the Pyrenean and Italian mountains.

6. Oblong Entire leaved Primula is, *Primula foliis integerrimis glabris oblongis, calycibus tubulosis obtusis*. Haller calls it, *Primula foliis glabris carnosis integerrimis*, Caspar Bauhine, *Sanicula Alpina rubescens, folio non serrato*, and Clusius, *Auricula Ursi 4*. It grows naturally on the Helvetian, Styrian and Pyrenean mountains.

7. Cordated Primula is, *Primula foliis petiolatis cordatis sublobatis crenatis*. It is a native of Siberia.

Class and order in the Linnean system. *Primula* is of the class and order *Pentandria Monogynia*, and the characters are,

1. Calyx. The involucrum is composed of many small leaves, and contains many flowers.

The characters. The perianthium is of one leaf, tubulous, five-cornered, permanent, and divided into five acute erect segments.

2. Corolla consists of a single petal. The tube is cylindrical, and the length of the calyx; the limb is patent, and divided into five obcordated obtuse segments.

3. Stamina are five very short filaments, placed within the neck of the corolla, having acute, erect, connivent antheræ.

4. Pistillum consists of a round germen, a slender style the length of the calyx, and a globular stigma.

5. Pericarpium is an oblong capsule almost the length of the perianthium, containing one cell, and opening in ten places at the top.

6. Semina. The seeds are small, and numerous.

# CHAP. CCCLXIX.

## *PROSERPINACA.*

There is only one species of this genus, called, *Proserpinaca*.

The plant described. The root is thick, creeping, and fibrous. The stalks are slender, round, taper, and about a foot and a half high. The leaves are spear-shaped, serrated, and grow alternately. The flowers come out singly from the wings of the leaves; they are small, and have no petals; they appear in July and August, but are rarely succeeded by seeds in England.

Culture. This is propagated by parting of the roots in the autumn, and flourishes best on bogs or marshy grounds. For want of these, it must have the moistest part of the garden, and be constantly supplied with water in dry weather.

Titles. There being no other species of this genus, it is named simply, *Proserpinaca*. Micheli calls it, *Trixis*. It grows naturally in the marshy parts of Virginia.

Class and order in the Linnean System. *Proserpinaca* is of the class and order *Triandria Trigynia*, and the characters are,

The character. 1. Calyx is a perianthium situated above the germen, and consists of three erect, acuminated, permanent leaves.

2. Corolla. There is none.

3. Stamina are three awl shaped patent filaments the length of the calyx, having didymous, oblong, acute antheræ.

4. Pistillum consists of a large triquetrous germen situated below the cup, having no style, but three thick downy stigmas the length of the stamina.

5. Pericarpium. There is none.

6. Semen. The seed is single, oval, triquetrous, trilocular, and terminated by the closed calyx.

CHAP.

# CHAP. CCCLXX.

## PRUNELLA, SELF-HEAL.

*Species.*

THERE are three species of this genus, all perennials, called,

1. Common Self-heal.
2. Jagged-leaved Self-heal.
3. Hyssop-leaved Self-heal.

*Common Self-heal described.*

1. Common Self-heal. The stalks are upright, thick, square, hollow, and eight or ten inches high. The leaves are oval, oblong, of a blackish-green colour, and grow opposite to each other on footstalks. The flowers come out in spikes from the tops of the stalks; they are of a blue colour, appear in May, and continue to shew themselves from different plants in different situations until the end of summer.

*Varieties.*

There is a variety of this species with white, and another with very large blue flowers.

*Its virtues.*

This species is held as a most admirable vulnerary, and was originally called Self-heal, from its great power of healing. It is very good for sore mouths, and is much employed in hæmorrhages, alvine fluxes, &c.

*Jagged-leaved Self-heal described.*

2. Jagged-leaved Self-heal. The stalks are upright, square, branching, and about a foot high. The leaves are oval, oblong, the lower ones jagged on the edges, and grow on longish footstalks; those on the upper part are spear-shaped, indented only on their edges, and have short footstalks. The flowers come out in spikes from the tops of the stalks; they are of a blue colour, and appear great part of the summer.

*Variety.*

There is a variety of this species with white flowers.

*Hyssop-leaved Self-heal described.*

3. Hyssop-leaved Self-heal. The stalks are hairy, and eight or ten inches high. The leaves are spear-shaped, narrow, hairy, and grow opposite on very short footstalks. The flowers come out in spikes from the tops of the stalks; they are of a white or blue colour, appear in June, and the greatest part of the summer.

*Method of propagating them.*

These sorts are all propagated by seeds, which ripen well here, and may be sown in the autumn, as soon as they are ripe, or the spring following. The first grows every where in our meadows and pastures, and is not cultivated; the others are very hardy, and will grow in almost any soil or situation, though they delight most in moist places, and the shade.

*Titles.*

1. Common Self-heal is titled, *Prunella foliis omnibus ovato-oblongis petiolatis*. In the *Hortus Cliffort.* it is termed, *Prunella bracteis cordatis*. Dodonæus calls it, *Brunella*; Caspar Bauhine, *Brunella major, folio non dissecto*; also, *Brunella cærulea, magno flore*; and Clusius, *Brunella i. non vulgaris*. It grows naturally in most pastures of Europe.

2. Jagged-leaved Self-heal is, *Prunella foliis ovato-oblongis petiolatis, summis quatuor lanceolatis dentatis*. Clusius calls it, *Brunella ii. non vulgaris*; Caspar Bauhine, *Brunella folio laciniato*; also, *Brunella major, folio laciniato*; and Vaillant, *Brunella [illegible] folio, flore cæruleo*. It grows rather sparingly in the pastures of Europe.

3. Hyssop-leaved Self-heal is, *Prunella foliis lanceolato-linearibus ciliatis subsessilibus*. Caspar Bauhine calls it, *Brunella hyssopifolia*; and Morison, *Brunella angustifolia [illegible] hirsutior*. It grows naturally in the south of France.

*Class and order in the Linnæan system.*

*Prunella* is of the class and order *Didynamia Gymnospermia*; and the characters are,

*The characters.*

1. CALYX is a monophyllous, permanent, bilabiated perianthium. The upper lip is plane, broad, truncated, and slightly indented in three parts; the lower lip is the narrowest, erect, acute, and semibifid.

2. COROLLA is one ringent petal. The tube is short and cylindrical, the mouth oblong; the upper lip is concave, whole, and narrow; the lower lip is reflexed, and divided into three obtuse segments.

3. STAMINA are four awl-shaped bifurcated filaments, of which two are rather longer than the others, having simple antheræ inserted in one side only, below the point.

4. PISTILLUM consists of a germen divided into four parts, a filiforme style inclining with the stamina towards the upper lip, and an emarginated stigma.

5. PERICARPIUM. There is none. The seeds are lodged in the calyx.

6. SEMINA. The seeds are four, and nearly oval.

# CHAP. CCCLXXI.

## *PTERIS*, BRAKES, or FEMALE FERN.

Species

OF this genus are,

1 Female Fern, or Brakes.

2 Dark-purple *Pteris*

3 Siberian *Pteris*

Female Fern,

1 Female Fern, or Brakes, is known every where The root is creeping, and spreads itself all around The stalks are upright, firm, naked for two feet high, and then divide into branches, each forming in the whole a supradecompounded leaf, frequently four feet high The folioles are pinnated The pinnæ are spear-shaped, smooth, of a light-green colour on the upper side, but whitish, and frequently a little downy underneath The stalks rise from the ground in May, and the whole plant is in perfection in August

Dark-Purple,

2 Dark-Purple *Pteris* The stalk is of a blackish purple colour, glossy, finely polished, naked for six or eight inches high, and then divides into branches, forming in the whole a decompounded leaf The pinnæ are spear-shaped, and the terminal one is very long, they are often rolled in on their edges, smooth, and of a dark shining green colour on their upper side, and brownish underneath.

and Siberian Pteris described

3 Siberian *Pteris* The stalks are upright, smooth, naked, six or eight inches high before the setting-on of the branches Each leaf, or rather plant, consists of three principal parts, of different colours in the different varieties The pinnæ are cut or jagged almost to the midrib, and the principal varieties are the Dark-green, the Ferrugineous, and one of a brownish green on the upperside, and a silvery white underneath They are all finely dusted underneath, and are plants of singularity and beauty

Its varieties

The first sort seems to be too common in England, over running large tracts of heathy ground, and rendering it of little value It is generally known by the common people by the name of Brakes, and they are cut down in the autumn to burn for the sake of the ashes, which are made into balls, and sold to afford a ley for washing of cloaths

The other two are rare plants, and found in some curious gardens They are propagated by parting of the roots in September or October, and must have a light moist soil, and a shady well-sheltered situation Culture

1 Female Fern, or Brakes, is entitled, *Pteris frondibus supradecompositis foliolis pinnatis pinnis lanceolatis infimis pinnatifidis superioribus minoribus* Caspar Bauhine calls it, *Filix ramosa major, pinnulis obtusis, non dentata*, and Fuchsius, *Filix femina* It grows naturally in woods and heaths in most countries of Europe Titles

2 Dark Purple *Pteris* is, *Pteris frondibus decompositis pinnatis, pinnis lanceolatis terminalibus longioribus* Gronovius calls it, *Pteris adianti facie, caule ramulisque pediculis politiore nitore nigricantibus* It grows naturally in Virginia

3 Siberian *Pteris* is, *Pteris frondibus quinquangularis trifoliatis pinnis pinnatifidis lateralibus bipartitis* In the *Hortus Cliffort* it is termed, *Pteris fronde simplici quinquangulari producta tripartita intermedia trifida lateralibus bipartitis* Plumier calls it, *Hemionitis profunde laciniata ad oras pulverulenta*, Sloane, *Hemionitis foliis atro-virentibus maxime dissectis, s Filix geranii Robertiani folio*, Plukenet, *Filix hemionitis Americana, petiolis et foliis profunde laciniatis*, and Morison, *Adiantum monophyllum Americanum, foliis profunde laciniatis ad oras pulverulentum*, also, *Adiantum monophyllum Antegoanum, ad oras pulverulentum planum in modum divisum lacinia media longius producta* It grows naturally in Siberia and Jamaica

*Pteris* is of the class and order *Cryptogamia Filices* and of this genus the fructifications are collected in a line, surrounding the border of the leaf on the under side Class and order in the Linnæan system

CHAP

# CHAP. CCCLXXII.

## *PULMONARIA*, LUNG-WORT.

OF this genus are six distinct species of perennials, called,

Species. 1. Common Spotted Lung-wort, or Bugloss Cowslips.
2. Narrow-leaved Lung-wort.
3. Virginian Lung-wort.
4. Siberian Lung-wort.
5. Sea Bugloss.
6. Rough Lung-wort.

Description of Common Spotted Lung-wort. 1. Common Spotted Lung-wort, or Bugloss Cowslips. The stalk is hairy, angular, frequently of a purplish colour, and eight or ten inches high. The radical leaves are broad, oval, rough, hairy, and spotted with broadish whitish spots on the upper side, and grow on long, strong, rough footstalks. The leaves on the stalks are smaller, and grow alternately. The flowers come out in small bunches from the tops of the stalks; some of them are of a red colour, some purple, and others blue in the same bunch; they appear in April and May, and the seeds ripen in June and July.

Its variety. There is a variety of this species with white flowers.

Its uses in medicine. The root and leaves of this plant are pectoral, and particularly serviceable in coughs, consumptions, and disorders of the lungs. Hence the name Lung-wort was originally given to this plant. The leaves are an admirable pot-herb in the spring.

Narrow leaved, 2. Narrow-leaved Lung-wort. The radical leaves are spear-shaped, long, narrow, and hairy. The stalks rise to about a foot high, and are adorned with still narrower leaves, which embrace it with their base. The flowers are produced in bunches from the tops of the stalks; they are at first opening of a red colour, but soon alter to a lively blue; they appear in April and May, and the seeds ripen in June and July.

Virginian, 3. Virginian Lung-wort. The root is thick, fleshy, and fibrated. The stalks grow to about a foot and a half high, and divide into several short branches near the top. The lower leaves are long, spear-shaped, obtuse, smooth, of a light-green colour, and grow on short footstalks; the upper leaves are smaller, and sit close to the stalks. The flowers come out in clusters from the tops of the stalks. The varieties are the Blue, Red, Purple, and White; they appear in April and May, and the seeds ripen in June and July.

and Siberian Lung-wort, 4. Siberian Lung-wort. The radical leaves are heart-shaped, smooth, and of a glaucous colour; those on the stalks are oval. The stalk grows to about a foot high, and divides into a few branches near the top. The flowers come out in roundish bunches from the tops of the stalks; they are blue, red, and purple, and usually hang downward; they appear in the spring, like the former, and the seeds ripen accordingly.

Sea Bugloss, 5. Sea Bugloss. The stalks are more branching than any of the former sorts, and lie on the ground. The leaves are oval, glaucous, and grow on strong footstalks. The flowers are of a blue or purple, or a mixture of both colours in the same flower; they appear in July, and are succeeded by smooth seeds, which ripen in the autumn.

and Rough Lung-wort described. 6. Rough Lung-wort. The stalks are simple, upright, taper, very rough, and about a foot high. The leaves are heart-shaped, entire, smooth on the upper side, but very rough underneath, and grow alternately on footstalks. The flowers come out in bunches from the tops of the stalks, having rough cups; they are of a purplish colour, and grow erect; they appear in April and May, and the seeds ripen accordingly.

Culture. These sorts are all easily propagated by parting of the roots; the best time for which is the latter end of the summer, or early in the autumn, that they may take to the ground before winter comes on, in order to be strong and early the spring following. They are extremely hardy, and will grow in almost any soil or situation; but all of them delight most in a fresh loamy earth, and the shade.

They may also be propagated by seeds, which may be sown in the autumn or spring, after they are ripe, in beds of common mould, in the open quarter of the seminary. After they come up the usual care of thinning where they are too close, keeping clean from weeds, and watering in dry weather, is all the culture they will call for until the end of summer or autumn, when they must be set out for good.

Titles. 1. Common Spotted Lung-wort, or Bugloss Cowslips, is titled, *Pulmonaria foliis radicalibus ovato-cordatis scabris*. Caspar Bauhine calls it, *Symphytum maculosum, seu Pulmonaria latifolia*; Tournefort, *Pulmonaria vulgaris latifolia, flore albo*; and Clusius, *Pulmonaria I. non maculoso folio*. It grows naturally in forests, and such situations, in England and most parts of Europe.

2. Narrow-leaved Lung-wort is, *Pulmonaria foliis radicalibus lanceolatis*. Clusius calls it, *Pulmonaria 5. Pannonica*. It grows naturally in Pannonia, Helvetia, and Sweden.

3. Virginian Lung-wort is, *Pulmonaria calycibus abbreviatis, foliis lanceolatis obtusiusculis*. Gronovius calls it, *Pulmonaria calyce brevi, corolla tubo longiore, pedunculis quinquefloris*; Trew, *Pulmonaria foliis ovatis glabris, scapo flexo*; and Plukenet, *Symphytum, seu Pulmonaria non maculata, foliis glabris acuminatis, flore pallide caeruleo*. It grows naturally in Virginia.

4. Siberian Lung-wort is, *Pulmonaria calycibus abbreviatis, foliis radicalibus cordatis*. It grows naturally in Siberia.

5. Sea Bugloss is, *Pulmonaria calycibus abbreviatis, foliis ovatis, caule ramoso procumbente*. In the *Hortus Cliffort.* it is termed, *Cerinthe foliis ovatis petiolatis*. Dillenius calls it, *Cerinthe maritima procumbens*; Plukenet, *Cynoglossum procumbens glaucophyllum maritimum*; Morison, *Cynoglossum perenne maritimum procumbens*; and Ray, *Echium marinum*. It grows naturally on the sea shores of England, and the northern countries of Europe.

6. Rough Lung-wort is, *Pulmonaria foliis cor-*

*datis, caulinis p l sis supra lenibus* It grows naturally on the mountains of Istria.

Class and order in the Linnæan system. The characters.

*Pulmonaria* is of the class and order *Pentandria Monogynia*, and the characters are,

1 CALYX is a monophyllous, five-cornered, permanent perianthium, indented in five parts at the top

2 COROLLA is one infundibuliforme petal The tube is cylindrical, and the length of the calyx the limb is cut into five obtuse, erect, patent segments

3 STAMINA are five very short filaments in the mouth of the corolla, having erect connivent antheræ

4. PISTILLUM consists of four germens, a filiforme style shorter than the calyx, and an obtuse emarginated stigma

5 PERICARPIUM There is none The seeds are lodged in the bottom of the calyx.

6 SEMINA The seeds are four, roundish, and obtuse.

## C H A P CCCLXXIII.

## *PYROLA*, WINTER-GREEN

Species

THE species of this genus are,

1 Common Winter-green
2 Lesser Winter-green
3 Tenderer Winter green
4 Umbellated Winter green
5 Spotted Winter-green
6 One flowered Winter-green

Description of Common Winter green

1 Common Winter-green The root is fibrous and white The leaves are five or six from the root, almost round, of a thick consistence, entire, of a deep-green colour, smooth, glossy, and grow on long footstalks The stalk is simple, slender, upright, eight or ten inches high, and adorned with a few acute leaves near the top The flowers are produced from the tops of the stalks in loose spikes, they are large, white, spreading, and very beautiful, they appear in June and July, and the seeds ripen in September

Medicinal properties

This species is an admirable vulnerary, whether applied outwardly by way of cataplasm or poultice, or taken inwardly in decoctions for wounds and bruises in the inward parts

Lesser,

2 Lesser Winter-green The root is small and creeping The leaves are roundish, serrated, and grow on shortish footstalks The stalks are upright, slender, and four or five inches high The flowers come out from the tops of the stalks in loose spikes, they are of a white colour, appear in July and August, and the seeds ripen in the autumn

Tenderer,

3 Tenderer Winter-green The root is small, and creeping under the surface The leaves are oval, acute-pointed, serrated, of a thin consistence, soft to the touch, a dark but shining green colour, and grow on short footstalks The stalk is slender, frequently bending near the top, and five or six inches high The flowers are arranged along one side of the stalk only at the top, they are of a pure white colour, appear in June and July, and the seeds ripen in September

Umbellated,

4 Umbellated Winter green The root is woody, and creeping The leaves are oblong, serrated, of a thick consistence, and a bright shining green colour The stalks are upright, ligneous, and eight or ten inches high The flowers grow four or five together at the tops of the stalks on their own separate peduncles, forming kind of small umbels, they are of a whitish-purple colour, appear in July, and the seeds ripen in the autumn

5 Spotted Winter green The root is woody, and creeping The stalks are ligneous, and about a foot and a half high The leaves are oblong, sharply serrated, acute pointed, stiff, have a broad white midrib, white veins underneath, and are sometimes irregularly spotted with dark-coloured dots, in the manner of the leaves of *Arbutus* The flowers come out two or three together on peduncles, which arise from the extremity of the stalks, they are pale-coloured, and small, appear in June and July, and the seeds ripen in the autumn Spotted,

6 One-flowered Winter-green The root is slender, perennial, and creeping The radical leaves are small, roundish, of a thickish substance, and grow on short footstalks The stalk is simple, upright, and three or four inches high The flowers come out singly from the tops of the stalks, they are large, of a fine white colour, and very beautiful, they appear in June and July, and the seeds ripen in September and One flowered Winter green described

These sorts are propagated by parting of the roots in September or October Their station should be in the most exposed places, and the earth should be fresh and undunged When they are set out, they should remain unmolested from the gardener's care, but the natural herbage, moss, &c of the place should be suffered to grow with them Being thus preserved they will live for many years, but do very ill with rich mould and garden culture, for which they seem not by Nature to be designed Propagation

1 Common Winter green is entitled, *Pyrola staminibus adscendentibus, pistillo declinato* In the *Flora Lapponica* it is termed, *Pyrola staminibus & pistillis declinatis*, in the *Hortus Cliffort Pyrola foliis subrotundis, scapo racemoso* Van Royen calls it, *Pyrola foliis integerrimis*, Caspar Bauhine *Pyrola rotundifolia major*, Colden, *Pyrola Noveboracensis*, Gerard, *Pyrola* and Parkinson, *Pyrola nostras vulgaris* It grows naturally in woods, heaths, and forests in the North of England, and most of the northern countries of Europe Titles

2 Lesser Winter-green is, *Pyrola floribus racemosis dispersis, staminibus pistillisque rectis* Haller calls it, *Pyrola tuberis recta minor, folio frequentius serrato*,

*ferrato, ſpicâ breviore & denſiore*, Caſpar Bauhine, *Pyrola folio minore et duriore*, and Rivinus, *Pyrola minor* It grows naturally in woods, &c. in the North of England, and moſt of the cold parts of Europe

3 Tenderer Winter-green is, *Pyrola racemo unilaterali* In the *Flora Lapp* it is termed, *Pyrola floribus uno verſu ſparſis* Caſpar Bauhine calls it, *Pyrola folio mucronato ferrato*; Cluſius, *Pyrola ſecunda tenerior*, and Parkinſon, *Pyrola tenerior* It grows naturally in woods, heaths, and foreſts in England, and moſt of the northern parts of Europe

4 Umbellated Winter-green is, *Pyrola pedunculis ſubumbellatis* Caſpar Bauhine calls it, *Pyrola fruteſcens arbuti folio*, and Cluſius, *Pyrola 3 fruticans* It grows naturally in woods in Europe, Aſia, and North America

5 Spotted Winter-green is, *Pyrola pedunculis bifloris* Gronovius calls it, *Pyrola petiolis apice biflis ... floris*, Petiver, *Pyrola Marilandica minor, folio mucronato arbuti*, and Plukenet, *Pyrola Mariana arbuti foliis anguſtioribus, trifoliatâ ad meatum ſervum ... albâ ... que per longitudinem decurrent* It grows naturally in the woods of North America

6 One flowered Winter-green is, *Pyrola ſcapo unifloro* Caſpar Bauhine calls it, *Pyrola rotundifolia minor*, Moriſon, *Pyrola ſingulari flore amplio*, and Oeder, *Pyrola 4* It grows naturally in woods in moſt of the northern countries of Europe

Claſs and order in the Linnæan ſyſtem

*Pyrola* is of the claſs and order *Decandria Monogynia*, and the characters are,

The characters

1 CALYX is a ſmall permanent perianthium, divided into five parts

2 COROLLA is five roundiſh, concave, patent petals

3 STAMINA are ten awl-ſhaped filaments ſhorter than the corolla, having large, nutant, two-horned antheræ

4 PISTILLUM conſiſts of a roundiſh angular germen, a permanent filiforme ſtyle longer than the ſtamina, and a thickiſh ſtigma

5 PERICARPIUM is a roundiſh, depreſſed, pentagonal capſule, containing five cells, and opening in the angles

6 SEMINA The ſeeds are numerous, and paleaceous

# CHAP. CCCLXXIV.

## QUERIA

THERE are two ſpecies of this genus, one of which is a perennial, called, Canada Queria

This plant deſcribed

The root is fibrous The ſtalk is dichotomous, upright, ſlender, taper, and eight or ten inches high The leaves are ſpear-ſhaped, oval, entire, frequently ſpotted with brown ſpots, and grow oppoſite to each other The flowers come out ſingly from the diviſions of the ſtalks on very ſhort footſtalks, they are ſmall, of a greeniſh colour, appear in July and Auguſt, but are ſeldom ſucceeded by ripe ſeeds in England

Propagation of it

This plant is beſt propagated by ſowing the ſeeds on a ſlight hotbed in the ſpring When the plants come up they muſt have plenty of air, and be frequently watered, and when they are fit to remove, muſt be taken up with a ball of earth to each root, and ſet in beds eight or ten inches diſtant from each other Here they muſt be ſhaded until they have taken root, be duly watered in dry weather, kept clean from weeds all ſummer, and in the autumn may be removed to the places where they are deſigned to remain

Titles

This ſpecies is titled, *Queria floribus ſolitariis, caule dichotomo* Gronovius calls it, *Mollugo foliis oppoſitis, ſtipulis quaternis, caule dichotomo* It grows naturally in Canada and Virginia

Claſs and order in the Linnæan ſyſtem

*Queria* is of the claſs and order *Triandria Trigynia*, and the characters are,

The characters

1 CALYX is an upright permanent perianthium, compoſed of five oblong, acute, pointed leaves, of which the outer one is recurved

2 COROLLA There is none

3 STAMINA are three ſhort capillary filaments with roundiſh antheræ

4 PISTILLUM conſiſts of an oval germen, and three ſtyles the length of the ſtamina, with ſimple ſtigmas

5 PERICARPIUM is a roundiſh capſule compoſed of three valves, and containing one cell

6 SEMEN The ſeed is ſingle

# CHAP. CCCLXXV

## *RANUNCULUS*, The CROW-FLOWER, or BUTTER CUPS.

*Introductory observations.* THE *Ranunculus* hath a prodigious number of species, a large share of which grow wild in fields, waters, and pasture grounds in England, whilst another part occupy the like places in foreign countries. The number of varieties produced from the Persian species afford the greatest pleasure, as being by far the most beautiful. These have been already treated of; but there are many sorts belonging to the other species of this genus, that are both beautiful, and worthy of culture and regard; and these are chiefly such as have distinguished themselves by the multiplicity of their petals, and are what we call Double Flowers; for the commonest weed in its double state is a pleasing singularity, and immediately upon becoming such demands culture. So that out of this number of species I shall select those which are worthy of being preserved, either on account of their double flowers, or as being natives of distant countries, and are for that reason alone propagated in the English gardens. The species, then, as they are commonly called, are,

*Species.*

1. Grass-leaved Crowfoot.
2. The Plantain-leaved Crowfoot.
3. Portugal Crowfoot.
4. Cretan Crowfoot.
5. Sweet Wood Crowfoot, or Goldilocks.
6. Mountain Crowfoot.
7. Illyrian Crowfoot.
8. Rue-leaved Crowfoot.
9. Round-rooted Crowfoot.
10. Creeping Crowfoot, or Butter-cups.
11. Upright Crowfoot.
12. Oriental Crowfoot.
13. Oriental Aconite-leaved *Ranunculus*.
14. Pile-wort.
15. Great Spear-wort.
16. Lesser Spear-wort.
17. Lapland Crowfoot.
18. Montpelier Crowfoot.
19. Helvetian Crowfoot.
20. Water Crowfoot.
21. Ivy-leaved Water Crowfoot.
22. Asiatic Crowfoot.

*Grass-leaved Crowfoot Varieties.* 1. Grass-leaved Crowfoot. There are two principal varieties of this species, viz.

The Single Grass-leaved Crowfoot.
The Double Grass-leaved Crowfoot.

*Description of it.* There is an elegance attending this species even in its single state, but it is the double sort which is the delight of the Gardener. The root is bulbous. The leaves are long and narrow, grassy, of a dark-green colour, and sit close to the stalks. The stalk is upright, slender, and divides near the top into a few branches, each of which is crowned with a small yellow flower. It will be in blow about the time our common Crow-flowers first paint the pastures and meadows with their yellow hue. The flowers of the Grass-leaved sort are a little like those, though smaller, and rather of a paler yellow colour. The Double sort is very full, and justly reckoned a good flower; and its being at present not very common, still enhances its value.

*Plantain-leaved Crowfoot described.* Plantain-leaved Crowfoot, which is naturally a mountainous plant, will shew itself to a much greater advantage by the common culture of the garden; and although even there it will seldom be found so high as two feet, in its natural place of growth it hardly ever aspires to the height of one. The leaves are narrow and small, of an oval figure, have their ends pointed, are smooth, of a light colour, and embrace the stalk at their base. The stalk rises from eight inches to near two feet high, according as it likes the soil and culture, and the top divides into two or three slender branches, each supporting a single flower. The flowers are white, and will appear in April. *Proper situation.* If it be planted in a rich, shady border, there it will shew itself in the greatest perfection, as a plant worthy of such care.

*Portugal Crowfoot described.* 3. Portugal Crowfoot is a very low flower, though it springs from a very large fleshy root, like that of the Yellow Asphodel. The leaves are few, broad, and of a thickish consistence; and, what is not very common, they are in many places inflated, or rise into small tubercles. They are of a pale-green colour, an oval figure, and their edges are serrated. The stalks rise from the middle of these leaves; they are small, naked, very tender, and of a very light-green colour, but often with a tinge of red near the bottom. Each of these stalks supports a single flower, which is large, of a golden-yellow colour, and, desireable as it may be in its Single state, is still more so in its Double; for there are both varieties. The single naked stalk which supports each flower seldom arises to half a foot high; so that this is one of the lower species of the Crowfoot. But the flower is large and fair in proportion, and what makes it still more valuable is its time of flowering; for if the winter be mild and open, it will shew itself some time or other in that dreary season.

*Proliferation.* This species requires a warm, rich border, and in the Double sort, in its luxuriancy, the stalk will be continued from the center of one flower, and support another smaller, of the like form and beauty. In this state it claims the name (with propriety) of the Proliferous *Ranunculus*; but as other species of the *Ranunculi* are endowed with this property, the distinction will not be sufficient, unless the word Portugal be added. That being the name the Common Single sort has usually gone by since the time of Dodonaeus, is still used by our Gardeners at this day.

*Cretan Crowfoot described.* 4. Cretan Crowfoot has a root like the Asphodel. From this rise several broad, large leaves, which are kidney shaped, crenated, almost divided into five lobes, hairy, and have long, hairy footstalks. This is the nature of the radical leaves, or those arising immediately from the root. Those leaves that grow on the flower-stalk are each of them divided into three lobes, which

which are of a spear-shaped figure, and have their edges free from serratures. Two or three of these leaves will be upon each stalk, to which they sit close. The stalk rises to near a foot in height, and the top naturally branches out into footstalks, each of which supports one flower only. The flowers are of a pale-yellow colour, large, and fair, though I have never yet met with a double one of this species. If planted in a rich, warm border, it will be in blow by the end of May or beginning of June. The roots are rather tender, so that, if the frost sets in very severely in winter, it will be proper, to ensure their safety, to spread over them some loose litter, leaves of trees, tanners bark, or the like.

Proper situation.

5. Sweet scented Wood Crowfoot. This species is commonly known by the name of Golden-haired Crowfoot, and is often called Goldilocks. The radical leaves are broad, roundish, kidney-shaped, and have their edges crenated and often jagged, some indeed so deeply as nearly to be divided into lobes. The leaves growing on the flower stalk are very small, narrow, and shaped like the hand. The stalk rises to about a foot in height, and divides as it grows into smaller stalks, each of which support a yellow flower. This will be in blow in April, and the single sort is by many as much admired as the double, for the middle is filled up by a large tuft of filaments which strike the attention, and it is from these filaments this species acquires the name of Golden-haired Crowfoot, or Goldilocks. But besides the charms afforded by their beauty whether in a double or single state, these flowers are possessed of an agreeable fragrance, on all which accounts this plant is worthy of culture. If it is planted in a shady place, in almost any soil, it will grow and flourish exceedingly, for it is a native of our country, and is frequently seen under hedges and in woods.

Description of Sweet scented Wood Crowfoot.

Proper situation.

6. The Mountain Crowfoot claims the first praise of all the species belonging to this genus, for there is an elegance and a delicacy peculiar to the leaves, stalks, and flowers, that justly entitles it to the rank, or appellation, of being called one of the prettiest of the perennial flowering tribe. The leaves are of a pale green colour, soft, and smooth, their upper surface is of a bluish cast, whilst their under is tinged with purple. They are large, and each is composed of five spear-shaped lobes, which are deeply cut and notched. The middlemost of these lobes is largest, and stands distinct on a footstalk, and a short footstalk also on each side supports the other four lobes. The leaves have all a strong mid rib, and large veins. In the spring, whilst they are young, a finer leaf can hardly be conceived, for the purple and bluish tinge gives it a peculiar delicacy, and this is sometimes stronger on the main footstalk, which is long, proportionably large, and smooth. The flower-stalk will arise to about two feet high, and sometimes higher, if the soil be rich and light. It is smooth and elegant, and claims praise from its easily dividing or branching out into others for the support of the flowers. These divisions are few, but sufficient to afford flowers enough to prevent the imputation of a deficiency of them, nor yet so many, as to raise a just complaint, as in some others, of too great a redundancy. To add to their perfection, these stalks are garnished, at each division, with a single leaf like those from the root, though smaller. The flowers are of a pure-white colour, and very double, the petals are regularly disposed, and though they form no very large, yet they constitute a regular, complete, and very desireable flower. It will be in full blow the beginning of June.

Description of the Mountain

7. The Illyrian Crowfoot is so called, because it is supposed to have been first brought from that into this country. This species hath whitish and downy leaves, each of which is composed of three narrow, spear-shaped lobes, whose edges are entire, they rise from a tuberose root. The stalks are slender, round, and rise to about a foot or a foot and a half in height. This divides near the top into other smaller ones for the support of the flowers. On these stalks a few small leaves are irregularly placed. The flowers are of a pale yellow colour, and being not very common, make a pretty variety amongst other perennial flower-roots in a cool, shady garden.

and Illyrian Crowfoot.

8. Rue leaved Crowfoot. This species hath a tuberose root, from whence arise a few large, decompound leaves, being cut or divided into many parts, like those of Rue. These leaves are very delicate, soft, smooth, and justly admired. The flower stalk rises to about a foot in height, is ornamented with a single leaf of the same nature with the others, but smaller, and the end of it is crowned by one flower. This in its best state is very double, large, of a bright yellow colour, and will be in blow by the beginning of June. Even in its single state this is a very desirable plant, for, besides its beautiful leaves, which are inimitable, it will produce a large, fair flower, composed of twelve or more petals. There is also another agreeable variety, the outside of the petals of whose flowers is of a bluish or red colour, and their inside white.

Rue leaved Crowfoot described.

This species is rather tender, and requires a warm, well-sheltered place, or it will be liable to be destroyed by hard frosts, though it is not a little that will hurt it, but to ensure its safety, if the frosts should set in very severe, it will be proper to spread over it a little loose litter, or the like.

Proper situation.

9. Round-rooted Crowfoot. The root of this species consists of a roundish bulb. It is also called the Onion and the Turnep-rooted Crowfoot, by which names it is known and distinguished by different Gardeners. From this root arise several compound leaves, like those of the Common Crowfoot, though smaller, and of a dusky, worn out green colour. Among these grow several slender, erect stalks, to about a foot high, which elevate the flowers. Those are chiefly of a pale yellow colour, very double, and will be in blow the beginning of May. The single sort is found common in our meadows and pasture grounds. This directs us to bestow no extraordinary culture on it, for it will do very well in any part of the garden, though, if the situation be shady, the beauty of its fine double flowers will be longer continued.

Round-rooted Crowfoot described.

Proper situation.

10. Creeping Crowfoot. This is the common Creeping Crowfoot of our fields and pastures, and it is in its double state that our Gardeners covet it. In this state it is a very full flower, and, being of so bright a yellow, very beautiful. But every one cannot but know how pleasing a fine double Crowfoot must be, even in its single state, were it not for its commonness, it would be much esteemed. Having got a plant or two of the double sort, then, the chief business will be to keep them within bounds, for being exactly the Common Crowfoot, though with a double flower, their trailing shoots, striking root at every joint, will soon overspread every thing near it. These shoots, therefore, must be nipped off as they grow, and the whole plant kept within bounds.

Creeping Crowfoot described.



11. Upright

Upright Crowfoot deſcribed. 11 Upright Crowfoot demands garden culture on account of its double flowers, though it is no other than the common Upright Crowfoot of our fields or meadows in that improved ſtate. The leaves are much divided, and of a darker green colour than the Creeping ſpecies, and the ſtalk, growing more erect, ſhews the flower to greater advantage. At the bottom the leaves have long footſtalks, many points, and are divided by threes; thoſe which grow on the top of the flower ſtalk are cut, to the very bottom, into linear or narrow ſegments. The ſtalk, which is taper and round, branches near the top into ſmaller ones, each of which is adorned by a fine double flower. It will be in blow in May, and continue a month or ſix weeks to exhibit its flowers in ſucceſſion. If it be planted in a thick, ſhady border, it will ſhew itſelf in its proliferous ſtate, viz. from the middle of the flowers, others growing equally as double, though ſmaller.

Proper ſituation.

Deſcription of Oriental. 12 Oriental Crowfoot has not been long introduced into our gardens; nay, it is a plant that ſeems to be altogether unknown to Botaniſts not very remote from the preſent times. It is beautiful, and eaſy of culture, and its being rather new renders it more worthy of notice. The root is fibrous. The leaves are large, growing upon long footſtalks, and their colour is a whitiſh-green. The footſtalks of the leaves are hollowed, and each of the leaves is divided into many long, narrow ſegments, on which ſome looſe cottony matter is found. The ſtalks riſe to a foot or more in height, divide near the top into footſtalks for the ſupport of the flowers, and are ornamented with leaves growing alternately, of the ſame nature with thoſe growing from the root, but ſmaller. The flowers are of a pale-yellow colour, and moderately large; but I have not yet ſeen any double variety of this ſpecies. Each flower is compoſed of five oval, ſpreading petals in the Crow-flower way, which have their middles filled up by their numerous ſtamina. It will be in blow by the end of May, and as the ſeeds ripen freely, it would be worth while to ſow them annually, to try for the double ſort, which when once obtained would be a ſufficient reward for much induſtry and pains. In ſuch an attempt we have very little doubt of ſucceſs, as there is no genus whoſe ſpecies ſo naturally ſport in this kind of luxuriancy as that of the *Ranunculus*.

and Oriental Aconite leaved Crowfoot. 13 Oriental Aconite leaved Crowfoot is ſo called chiefly to diſtinguiſh it from the former ſpecies, for the leaves of both are multifid, or cut into many points. This ſpecies alſo has not been long diſcovered. Tournefort firſt found it growing in the Levant, and has deſcribed and entitled it, Oriental *Ranunculus*, with an Aconite leaf, and a very large flower. The ſtalk riſes to a foot or more in height, and, beſides the flower, it is garniſhed with two leaves placed alternately, and ſitting cloſe. It will be in blow in May. The flower is large, being compoſed of five ſpreading, oval, yellow petals. In its ſingle ſtate it is very beautiful, and as in this it is large and fair, if it could be obtained in its luxuriant doubleneſs, few plants would be more eſteemed; therefore, as it ripens its ſeeds well with us, it would not be unworthy a Gardener's care to attempt it.

Pile wort deſcribed. 14 Pile wort. The root is ſtringy, and hung with many tubers. The leaves are heart-ſhaped, angular, ſmooth, of a bright deep-green colour, and grow on ſtrong footſtalks. The ſtalks are ſimple, naked, and four or five inches high. The flowers come out ſingly from the tops of the ſtalks, are large, of a bright-yellow colour, appear in February, March, and April, and the ſeeds ripen in May.

It varies. There is a variety of this ſpecies with double flowers.

Medicinal property of its root. The root is ſaid to be a ſovereign remedy for the piles.

Deſcription of Great 15 Great Spear-wort. The ſtalk is upright, thick, jointed, hollow, two or three feet high, and divides into a few branches near the top. The leaves are ſpear-ſhaped, long, of a ſhining green colour, and ſit cloſe to the ſtalks. The flowers come out from the ends and ſides of the branches on ſlender footſtalks; they are large, of a beautiful yellow colour, appear in May and June, and the ſeeds ripen in July.

and Leſſer Spear-wort. 16 Leſſer Spear-wort. The ſtalk is round, jointed, hollow, branching, and about a foot and a half high. The leaves are oval, ſpear-ſhaped, of a lucid green colour, and grow on footſtalks at the joints. The flowers come out from the ends and ſides of the branches on ſlender footſtalks; they are ſmall, of a yellow colour, appear in May and June, and continue in ſucceſſion until the end of ſummer.

Deſcription of Lapland, 17 Lapland Crowfoot. The ſtalk is ſlender, ſimple, and four or five inches high. The radical leaves are palmated, but thoſe on the ſtalks ſit cloſe, and are divided into many ſegments. The flowers come out ſingly from the tops of the ſtalks, are of a yellow colour, and appear in May and June.

Montpelier, 18 Montpelier Crowfoot. The ſtalk is ſimple, hairy, almoſt naked, and eight or ten inches high. The leaves are divided into three parts, and crenated on the edges. The flowers come out ſingly from the tops of the ſtalks, are very large, and appear about the ſame time with the former.

and Helvetian Crowfoot. 19 Helvetian Crowfoot. The ſtalks are ſlender, round, and about ten inches high. The leaves are beautifully divided into many ſegments, in the manner of thoſe of Coriander. The flowers are uſually two at the tops of the ſtalks, of a whitiſh-purple colour, and appear in May and June.

Water 20 Water Crowfoot. The ſtalks are ſlender, divide into numerous branches, and ſwim in the water. The leaves which are immerſed are finely cut into a multitude of narrow ſegments, nearly in the manner of Cammomile. Thoſe which are above the water are generally roundiſh, and indented on their edges. The flowers come out from the ſides of the branches, rearing up their heads above the water on diſtinct footſtalks; they are of a white colour, finely ſcented, and in full blow in May, June, and July.

and Ivy leaved Water Crowfoot deſcribed. 21 Ivy-leaved Water Crowfoot. The ſtalks are creeping, and ſtrike root at the joints. The leaves are roundiſh, and compoſed of three entire lobes, in the manner of thoſe of Ivy. The flowers are of a white or yellow colour, and appear in May and June.

Their Varieties. There are ſeveral varieties of theſe laſt two ſpecies, none of which are cultivated, as they grow naturally in ponds, ditches, ſlow rivulets, and ſtanding-waters, almoſt every-where; and which I mention here for the ſatisfaction of thoſe who may be deſirous of knowing their names.

Aſiatic Crowfoot deſcribed. 22 Aſiatic Crowfoot is the ſpecies already treated of among the Selected Flowers, and it includes the numerous varieties which fall more immediately to the Floriſt's care. A few of each ſort, however, the Gardener muſt have in his borders or beds of perennials, to compleat his collection. No particular compoſt will be neceſſary for them; they will grow, flouriſh, and flower very well in almoſt any common garden mould. The beſt way, however, is to plant them with

Its propagation.

with annuals, as their roots ought yearly to be taken up and set again; but if they are planted amongst the perennials that are to be removed every other year, they will often flower twice very well without removing.

*Propagation of all the other species.*

The propagation of all the other species is very easy. They multiply exceedingly by the roots, so that these being parted any time in the autumn or spring, plenty of new plants may be obtained, which will be ready for a division of the like nature after standing two years more. Any common garden mould will do for all of them, and any situation, except for the few species before particularized, which are rather tender; though, if they could have shade, that great preserver of flowers, their blow will continue longer in beauty.

The titles of the real species are as follow:

*Titles.*

1. The Grass-leaved *Ranunculus*, or Crowfoot, is titled, *Ranunculus foliis lanceolato-linearibus sessilibus, caule erecto, radice bulbosâ*. Caspar Bauhine terms it, *Ranunculus, gramineo folio, bulbosus*; also, *Ranunculus montanus, folio gramineo, multiplex*; John Bauhine, *Ranunculus pumilus, gramineis foliis*. It grows naturally on the Pyrenees, and in France.

2. Plantain-leaved Mountain *Ranunculus* is, *Ranunculus foliis ovatis acuminatis amplexicaulibus, caule multifloro, radice fasciculata*. Caspar Bauhine calls it, *Ranunculus montanus folio plantaginis*; and Mentzelius, *Ranunculus dulcis, foliis latis rapistri perfoliatis, floribus albis*. It grows wild on the Alps and Appennine mountains.

3. Portugal *Ranunculus* is, *Ranunculus foliis ovatis serratis, scapo nudo unifloro*. This is the *Ranunculus Lusitanicus* of Dodonæus, and the *Ranunculus grumosâ radice* of Clusius. Caspar Bauhine calls it, *Ranunculus latifolius bullatus, asphodeli radice*. It grows common in Portugal and Crete.

4. Cretan *Ranunculus* is, *Ranunculus foliis radicalibus reniformibus crenatis sublobatis, caulinis tripartitis lanceolatis integerrimis, caule multifloro*. Caspar Bauhine terms it, *Ranunculus, asphodeli radice, Creticus*; Clusius, *Ranunculus Creticus latifolius*; Van Royen, *Ranunculus foliis radicalibus cordato-subrotundis, caulinis tripartitis, sessilibus lanceolatis integerrimis*. It is a native of Crete.

5. Sweet-scented Wood *Ranunculus* is, *Ranunculus foliis radicalibus reniformibus crenatis incisis, caulinis digitatis linearibus, caule multifloro*. Caspar Bauhine calls it, *Ranunculus nemorosus, sive sylvaticus, folio subrotundo*; and Dalechamp, *Ranunculus I sylvestris*. It grows naturally in moist pasture grounds in most parts of Europe.

6. Mountain *Ranunculus* is, *Ranunculus foliis omnibus quinatis lanceolatis inciso-serratis*. Clusius calls it, *Ranunculus montanus IV*. and Caspar Bauhine makes three distinct species of it, calling one, *Ranunculus montanus, aconiti folio, albus, flore majore*; another, *flore minore*; and this double sort, *flore albo multiplici*; and which Clusius distinguishes also by a separate title, calling it, *Ranunculus pleno flore albo*. It grows naturally on the Alps, and in several mountainous parts of Switzerland and Austria.

7. Illyrian Crowfoot is, *Ranunculus foliis ternatis integerrimis lanceolatis*. Caspar Bauhine terms it, *Ranunculus lanuginosus angustifolius, grumosâ radice, major & minor*; Clusius, *Ranunculus grumosâ radice IV*. It grows naturally in Illyria, Italy, France, and Hungary.

8. Rue-leaved Crowfoot is, *Ranunculus foliis supradecompositis, caule simplicissimo unifolio unifloro, radice tuberosâ*. This is the *Ranunculus rutaceo folio, flore suave rubente*, of Caspar Bauhine and Morison; and the *Ranunculus præcox I. rutæ folio*, of Clusius. It is found growing wild in the mountainous parts of Austria, and also in the Levant.

9. Bulbous-rooted Crowfoot is, *Ranunculus calycibus retroflexis, pedunculis sulcatis, caule erecto, foliis compositis*. In the *Hortus Cliffort.* it is termed, *Ranunculus radice simplici globosâ*. Lobel calls it, *Ranunculus bulbosus*. It grows common in meadows and pasture-grounds in England and most countries of Europe.

10. Creeping Crowfoot is, *Ranunculus calycibus patulis, pedunculis sulcatis, sarmentis repentibus, foliis compositis*. In the *Hortus Cliffort.* it stands with the title, *Ranunculus foliis ternatis, foliolis petiolatis trifidis, medio productiore, caule multifloro*. Caspar Bauhine terms it, *Ranunculus pratensis repens hirsutus*; others, *Ranunculus pratensis*. It grows almost every-where in Europe.

11. Upright Crowfoot is, *Ranunculus calycibus patulis, pedunculis teretibus, foliis tripartito multifidis summis linearibus*. In the *Hortus Cliffort.* &c. it stands with the title, *Ranunculus foliis peltatis quinquangularibus multipartitis, laciniis linearibus, caule multifloro*. This is the *Ranunculus pratensis erectus acris* of Caspar Bauhine and others. It grows almost every-where in our meadows and pastures, and in most pastures of Europe.

12. Oriental Crowfoot is entitled, *Ranunculus seminibus spinoso-subulatis recurvis, calycibus reflexis foliis multifidis*. It is a native of the East.

13. Oriental Aconite-leaved Crowfoot is, *Ranunculus caule erecto bifolio, foliis multifidis, caulinis alternis sessilibus*. Tournefort entitles it, *Ranunculus Orientalis aconiti folio, flore maximo*. It is a native of the East.

14. Pile-wort is titled, *Ranunculus foliis cordatis angulatis petiolatis*. Caspar Bauhine calls it, *Chelidonia rotundifolia minor*; also, *Chelidonia rotundifolia major*; and Fuchsius, *Chelidonium minus*. It grows naturally in meadows and cold spongy pasture-grounds almost every-where.

15. Great Spear-wort is, *Ranunculus foliis lanceolatis, caule erecto*. Caspar Bauhine calls it, *Ranunculus latifolius palustris major*; Tabernæmontanus, *Ranunculus lanceolatus major*; Plukenet, *Ranunculus flammeus, latiori plantaginis folio, marginibus pilosis*; Gerard, *Ranunculus flammeus major*; and Parkinson, *Ranunculus palustris flammeus major*. It grows naturally in moist places in England and most of the northern parts of Europe.

16. Lesser Spear-wort is, *Ranunculus foliis ovato-lanceolatis petiolatis, caule declinato*. In the *Flora Lapponica* it is termed, *Ranunculus foliis ovato-oblongis integerrimis, caule procumbente*. Caspar Bauhine calls it, *Ranunculus longifolius palustris minor*; also, *Ranunculus palustris, foliis serratis*. Dodonæus names it, *Flammula Ranunculus*; Gerard, *Ranunculus flammeus minor*; and Parkinson, *Ranunculus palustris flammeus minor, sive angustifolius*. It grows naturally in moist places in England and most parts of Europe.

17. Lapland Crowfoot is, *Ranunculus calyce hirsuto, caule unifloro, foliis radicalibus palmatis, caulinis multipartitis sessilibus*. John Bauhine calls it, *Ranunculus minimus Alpinus luteus*. It grows naturally on the Alps of Lapland and Helvetia.

18. Montpelier Crowfoot is, *Ranunculus foliis tripartitis crenatis, caule simplici villoso subnudo unifloro*. Caspar Bauhine calls it, *Ranunculus saxatilis, magno flore*. It grows naturally about Montpelier.

19. Helvetian Crow-foot is, *Ranunculus calycibus hirsutis, caule bifloro, foliis multifidis*. In the

the *Flora Lapponica* it is termed, *Ranunculus caule unifloro, calyce hirsuto* John Bauhine calls it, *Ranunculus montanus purpureus, calyce villoso*, and Barrelier, *Ranunculus Alpinus, coriandri folio, flore albo-purpurascente* It grows naturally on the Alps of Lapland and Helvetia

20. Water Crowfoot is, *Ranunculus foliis submersis capillaceis, emersis subpeltatis* In the *Flora Lapponica* it is termed, *Ranunculus foliis inferioribus capillaceis, superioribus peltatis*, in the *Flora Suecica*, *Ranunculus foliis submersis capillaceis*, and in the *Hortus Cliffort Ranunculus foliis omnibus capillaceis circumscriptione rotundis* Dodonæus calls it, *Ranunculus aquatilis*, Caspar Bauhine, *Ranunculus aquaticus, folio rotundo & capillaceo*, also, *Ranunculus aquaticus capillaceus*, also, *Millefolium aquaticum cornutum majus*, also, *Millefolium aquaticum, foliis abrotani, ranunculi flore & capitulo*, also, *Millefolium aquaticum, foliis fœniculi, ranunculi flore & capitulo* Van Royen stiles it, *Ranunculus foliis omnibus capillaceis circumscriptione orbiculatis*, Plukenet, *Ranunculus aquaticus albus, circinatis tenuissime divisis foliis*, Haller, *Ranunculus foliis capillaceis circumscriptione vagis inferioribus*, and Columna, *Ranunculus trichophyllos aquaticus medio luteus* It grows naturally in ditches, standing-waters, and rivulets, in England, and most parts of Europe

21 Ivy-leaved Water Crowfoot is, *Ranunculus foliis subrotundis trilobis integerrimis, caule repente* Caspar Bauhine calls it, *Ranunculus aquaticus hederaceus luteus*, John Bauhine, *Ranunculus hederaceus rivulorum se extendens, atra macula notatus*, and Ray, *Ranunculus aquatilis hederaceus albus* It grows naturally in waters in England, France, and Germany

22 Asiatic Crowfoot is, *Ranunculus foliis ternatis biternatisque, foliolis trifidis incisis, caule inferne ramoso* In the *Hortus Cliffort* it is termed, *Ranunculus foliis tripartitis laciniatis, caule inferne ramoso, radice tuberosa* Caspar Bauhine calls it, *Ranunculus, grumosa radice, ramosus*, also, *Ranunculus grumosa radice, flore flavo vario*, also, *Ranunculus grumosa radice, flore albo*, also, *Ranunculus grumosa radice, flore albo leniter rubente*, also, *Ranunculus grumosa radice, flore niveo*, also, *Ranunculus grumosa radice, flore Phœniceo minimo simplici*, also, *Ranunculus asphodeli radice, flore sanguineo*, also, *Ranunculus, asphodeli radice, flore subphœniceo rubente*, also, *Ranunculus, asphodeli radice, prolifer miniatus* It grows naturally in Asia and Mauritania

*Ranunculus* is of the class and order *Polyandria Polygynia*, and the characters are, Class and order in the Linnæan system. The characters

1 CALYX is a perianthium, composed of five oval, concave, coloured leaves

2 COROLLA consists of five bright, obtuse petals, having very small ungues The nectarium is a small cavity in each petal above the ungues

3 STAMINA The stamina are numerous filaments, about half the length of the petals, having erect, oblong, obtuse, didymous antheræ

4 PISTILLUM consists of numerous germina collected into a head, without any styles, but very small, reflexed stigmas

5 PERICARPIUM There is none The seeds are fastened to the receptacle by very short pedicles

6 SEMINA The seeds are numerous and irregular, of an uncertain figure, and have their points reflexed

✠✠✠✠✠✠✠✠✠✠✠✠✠✠✠✠✠✠✠✠✠✠✠✠✠

## C H A P. CCCLXXVI.

## *RESEDA*, BASTARD ROCKET.

THERE are a few perennials of this genus that should be stationed with others of the like kind in our gardens, and they are,

Species.
1 The Spanish Narrow-leaved Bastard Rocket
2 The Spanish Waved leaved Bastard Rocket
3 The Spanish Pinnated-leaved Shrubby Bastard Rocket

Description of Spanish Narrow leaved,
1 The Spanish Narrow-leaved Bastard Rocket This species grows naturally on the Spanish mountains, and is there accounted a low growing plant In our gardens, the stalks, which are slender and few, will grow to a foot and a half in length The leaves are very narrow, awl-shaped, obtuse, entire, hoary, and placed very thinly on the plant The flowers are produced from the tops of the stalks in spikes, they are of a whitish colour with a tinge of purple, have no footstalks, will be in blow in May or June, and ripen their seeds in August

Spanish Waved leaved,
2 Spanish Waved-leaved Bastard Rocket The stalks will grow to about a foot high, are upright, angular, striated, and grow close together The radical leaves, as well as those which ornament the stalks, are pinnated, the pinnæ are spear-shaped, decurrent, acute, and waved The flowers terminate the stalks in long spikes, and are of a white colour, having yellow antheræ, they flower in May or June, and ripen their seeds in August or September

and Spanish Pinnated leaved Shrubby Bastard Rocket
3 Spanish Pinnated leaved Shrubby Bastard Rocket The root is large, woody, and sends forth a few smooth, ligneous, striated stalks The leaves are pinnated, and each is composed of about five or seven lobes, which are spear-shaped, decurrent, smooth, and recurved at the points The flowers are produced in spikes from the upper ends of the stalks, they are of a white colour, and each of them has five or six trifid petals, and about eleven stamina

Method of propagating them
The culture of these species is very easy Sow the seeds in the autumn soon after they are ripe, and they will more readily come up than if kept until

until the ſpring Where you find they come up too cloſe, pull out the weakeſt, and let the others remain for flowering, which will be the ſecond ſummer from the time of ſowing

Titles 1 The Spaniſh Narrow leaved Baſtard Rocket is titled, *Reſeda foliis ſubulatis ſparſis* Caſpar Bauhine calls it, *Reſeda alba minor*, Cluſius, *Seſamoides Salmanticum parvum*, Tournefort, *Seſamoides flore albo, foliis caneſcentibus* It grows naturally in Spain

2 Spaniſh Waved-leaved Baſtard Rocket is titled, *Reſeda floribus trigynis tetragyniſque, calycibus quinquepartitis, foliis pinnatis undulatis* Barrelier calls it, *Reſeda minor, foliis inciſis* It grows naturally in Spain

3 Spaniſh Pinnated-leaved Shrubby Baſtard Rocket is, *Reſeda foliis pinnatis apice recurvis, floribus tetragynis, calycibus quinquepartitis patentibus, caule baſi ſuffruticoſo* It grows naturally in Spain

Claſs and order in the Linnæan ſyſtem *Reſeda* is of the claſs and order *Dodecandria Trigynia*, and the characters are,

The characters 1 CALYX is a monophyllous perianthium, divided into ſeveral acute, erect, permanent ſegments

2 COROLLA conſiſts of ſome unequal, and for the moſt part trifid petals the upper of which is gibbous at the baſe, of the ſame length with the calyx, and contains an honey juice

The nectarium is a plane erect gland, placed on the upper ſide of the receptacle, between the ſtamina and the upper petal, connivent with the baſe of the petals, and dilating from the ſides

3 STAMINA are about fifteen ſhort filaments, with erect obtuſe antheræ the length of the corolla

4 PISTILLUM conſiſts of a gibbous germen, and ſome very ſhort ſtyles with ſimple ſtigmas

5 PERICARPIUM is a gibbous angular capſule, that is open between the ſtyles, and contains one cell

6 SEMINA The ſeeds are numerous, reniforme, and faſtened to the angles of the capſule.

# CHAP CCCLXXVII.

## *RHEUM*, RHUBARB.

OF this genus are four hardy ſpecies, called,

Species
1. Common Rhubarb
2. Chineſe Rhubarb
3. Tartarian Rhubarb
4. Currant Rhubarb

Common Rhubarb deſcribed 1 Common Rhubarb The root is very large, thick, brachiated, of a reddiſh-brown colour on the outſide, and yellow within The leaves are very large, heart-ſhaped, ſmooth, and grow on thick, ſtrong, reddiſh footſtalks, which are ſlightly channelled on the under ſide The ſtalk is upright, thick, hollow, ſtriated, jointed, often of a purple colour, two or three feet high, and adorned with leaves growing ſingly, without any footſtalks at the joints The flowers are produced from the tops of the ſtalks in thick cloſe ſpikes, they are of a white colour, appear early in June, and are ſucceeded by large, brown, triangular ſeeds, which ripen in Auguſt

Its virtues The root of this ſpecies is aſtringent, and affords a gentle purge, and the young ſtalks cut in the ſpring are made into agreeable tarts

Chineſe, 2 Chineſe Rhubarb The root is very thick, brachiated, ſtrikes deep into the ground, of a duſky colour on the outſide, and yellow within The leaves are very large, oblong, pointed, curled on the edges, a little hairy on their upper ſide, have ſtrong veins on the under, and grow on plane equal footſtalks The ſtalk is thick, firm, ſtriated, jointed, hollow, four feet high, and adorned with leaves growing ſingle, and ſitting cloſe at the joints The flowers come out in long and numerous ſpikes or bunches from the tops of the ſtalks, they are of a white or greeniſh-yellow colour, appear in May or early in June, and the ſeeds ripen in Auguſt

This Rhubarb is imported from China and might be raiſed to national advantage in this kingdom, though the grain and colour of our growth is not ſo fine as thoſe we receive from abroad

3 Tartarian Rhubarb The root is thick, large, and very yellow within The leaves are very large, heart-ſhaped, ſublobed, obtuſe, ſmooth, ribbed on the under ſide, indented on their edges, and grow on long footſtalks, which are of a pale-green colour, and flat on one ſide The ſtalk is large, thick, jointed, four or five feet high, of a pale green colour, and at each joint garniſhed with one leaf, ſitting cloſe, without any footſtalk The flowers come out in panicles from the tops of the ſtalks, hanging downward, they are of a white colour, appear in May, or early in June, and the ſeeds ripen in Auguſt Tartarian

The root of this plant is the fineſt, yelloweſt, and moſt compact of all the ſorts of Rhubarb, and beſt deſerves propagation for medicinal purpoſes It is extremely hardy, and flouriſhes well in our gardens, but I never yet found the root of ſo fine a grain, or ſo well coloured, as that imported from abroad

4 Currant Rhubarb The root is thick, fleſhy, and ſtrikes deep into the ground The leaves are very broad, warted on the ſurface, have numerous protuberances, are curled on their edges, of a purpliſh-green colour, grow on ſhort footſtalks, and ſpread themſelves near the ground. The ſtalks riſe to three or four feet high, ſupporting the and Currant Rhubarb deſcribed.

the flowers at the top, they appear in June, and are ſucceeded by triangular ſeeds, ſurrounded by a deep red or purple-coloured pulp, aſſuming the appearance of berries, which ripen in the autumn

Culture

In order to raiſe theſe plants to perfection, ſome good land ſhould be pitched upon for the purpoſe, it ſhould be light, but yet loamy, freſh, and not too moiſt The ſeeds muſt be ſown in the autumn, as ſoon as they are ripe, in the places where they are deſigned to remain, and, previous to their being committed to the ground, it ſhould be double dug, in order for the root to ſtrike more freely downward, and the whole made as fine as poſſible Having prepared the land the ſeeds ſhould be ſcattered thinly all over it, and raked in with a good iron rake In the ſpring the plants will come up, and when they are about two inches high, they muſt be thinned to proper diſtances, which ſhould be about a foot from each other At this time all weeds muſt be kept down, and that theſe may be more effectually deſtroyed, the work ſhould always be performed in dry weather In about a month or ſix weeks time the ground will probably call for a ſecond hoeing, to deſtroy the weeds, and at this time every other plant muſt be taken away, or rather the ſmalleſt, leaving the plants two feet or two feet and a half diſtant from each other every way Thoſe plants that are taken up may be planted again, if they are wanted, for they grow very well on removal, though the roots will not grow ſo large as thoſe that have never been diſturbed After the ſecond hoeing the weeds muſt be cut up as often as they ariſe, when the leaves do not defend themſelves, and in the autumn the ground ſhould be ſlightly dug between the plants, but not ſo near them as to diſturb the roots

A repetition of hoeing down the weeds muſt be obſerved every ſummer, and every winter the ground ſhould be made clean, and the ſurface ſtirred between the plants The third ſummer they will flower, and perfect their ſeeds for further encreaſe, if neceſſary, but the roots ſhould remain ſeven or eight years, if you would chuſe to have them large and good

The ſtalks of the firſt ſort only are peeled in the ſpring, and made into tarts, for which purpoſe alone this ſpecies is deſerving of culture

Title

1 Common Rhubarb is entitled *Rheum foliis glabris, petiolis ſubſulcatis* In the *Hortus Cliffort* it is termed, *Rheum*, in the *Hortus Upſal Rheum foliis glabris* Alpinus calls it, *Raponticum*, and Caſpar Bauhine, *Raponticum folio lapathi majoris glabro* It grows naturally in Scythia and Thrace

2 Chineſe Rhubarb is, *Rheum foliis ſubvilloſis undulatis petiolis æqualibus* In the *Hortus Upſal* it is termed, *Rheum foliis ſubvilloſis* Amman calls it, *Rhabarbarum folio longiori hirſuto criſpo, florum thyrſo longiori et tenuiori* It grows naturally in China and Siberia

3 Tartarian Rhubarb is, *Rheum foliis ſublobatis obtuſiſſimis glaberrimis argute denticulatis glabris* In Miller's Dictionary it is termed, *Rheum foliis cordatis glabris marginibus ſinuatis ſpicis arcuatis nutantibus* It grows naturally in China and Tartary

4 Currant Rhubarb is, *Rheum foliis granulatis, petiolis æqualibus* Dillenius calls it, *Lapathum orientale, aſpero et verrucoſo folio, Ribes Arabibus dictum*, Breynius, *Lapathum orientale tomentoſum rotundifolium, Ribes Arabum dictum*, Pocock *Lapathum orientale aſperum, folio ſubrotundo, fructu magno purpureo*, Rauwolf, *Ribes Arabum*, and Caſpar Bauhine, *Ribes Arabum, foliis petaſitidis* It grows naturally on Mount Libanus, and other mountainous parts of the Eaſt

Claſs and order in the Linnæan ſyſtem

*Rheum* is of the claſs and order *Enneandria Hexagynia*, and the characters are,

The characters

1 Calyx There is none

2 Corolla is one impervious petal narrowed at the baſe, and cut at the top into ſix obtuſe ſegments, which are alternately ſmaller

3 Stamina are nine capillary filaments inſerted in the corolla, and of the ſame length with it, having oblong, obtuſe, didymous antheræ

4 Pistillum conſiſts of a very ſhort three ſided germen, ſcarce any viſible ſtyles, and three reflexed plumoſe ſtigmas.

5 Pericarpium There is none

6 Semen The ſeed is ſingle, large, trique trous, bordered, and acute.

CHAP

## CHAP. CCCLXXVIII.

## *RHEXIA.*

OF this genus there are two perennials, called,

Species

1. Virginian *Rhexia*
2. Maryland *Rhexia*

Virginian

1 Virginian *Rhexia*. The ſtalk is upright, four-cornered, hairy, and about a foot high. The leaves are ſpear-ſhaped, hairy, and grow oppoſite to each other. The flowers come out two or three together on footſtalks from the ends and ſides of the ſtalks near the top; they are of a red colour, appear in June, but are rarely ſucceeded by ſeeds in England.

and Maryland Rhexia deſcribed

2 Maryland *Rhexia*. The ſtalk is upright, near a foot high, and cloſely ſet with iron-coloured ſtinging hairs. The leaves are ſpear-ſhaped, grow oppoſite, and are poſſeſſed of the like kind of iron-coloured ſtinging hairs with thoſe of the ſtalk, but finer. The flowers come out one or two together on footſtalks from the tops of the plant; they are of a red colour, appear in June, but are rarely ſucceeded by ſeeds in England.

Culture

Theſe plants are raiſed from ſeeds procured from abroad; they ſhould be ſown as ſoon as poſſible in pots filled with freſh, light, ſandy earth. In the ſpring the pots ſhould be plunged into a hotbed, which will effectually bring up the ſeeds; after which they muſt have air, frequent waterings, and be hardened as ſoon as poſſible to be ſet abroad. When this is effected, and the plants fit to remove, they ſhould be taken up with a ball of earth to each root, and ſet in a warm, dry, light, well-ſheltered place, reſerving a few for pots, to be houſed in winter, in caſe bad weather ſhould threaten the deſtruction of thoſe that are ſet abroad. The ſummer following they will flower; but as they are frequently of ſhort duration, ſeldom living longer than three or four years with us, proviſion, at proper intervals, of ſeeds for a ſucceſſion ſhould be regularly made from abroad.

Titles.

1 The firſt ſpecies is entitled, *Rhexia foliis ſeſſilibus ſerratis calycibus glabris*. Plukenet calls it, *Aliſanus vegetabilis Caroliniānus*; alſo, *Lyſimachia non papposa Virginiana, tuberariæ foliis hirſutis flore tetrapetalo rubello*. It grows naturally in Virginia.

2 The ſecond ſpecies is, *Rhexia foliis ciliatis*. Plukenet calls it, *Lyſimachia non papposa, terræ Marianæ, leptonuros, flore tetrapetalo rubello, folio et caule hirſutie ferruginea hiſpidis*. It grows common in Maryland, and the Braſil Iſlands.

Claſs and order in the Linnæan ſyſtem. The characters

*Rhexia* is of the claſs and order *Octandria Monogynia*; and the characters are,

1. CALYX is a monophyllous, tubular, oblong, permanent perianthium, ſwelling below, and divided at the top into four ſegments.
2. COROLLA is four roundiſh patent petals inſerted in the calyx.
3. STAMINA are eight filiforme filaments, having declining, ſulcated, linear, obtuſe, verſatile antheræ.
4. PISTILLUM conſiſts of a roundiſh germen, a ſimple declining ſtyle the length of the ſtamina, and a thick oblong ſtigma.
5. PERICARPIUM is a roundiſh capſule in the belly of the calyx, formed of four valves, and containing four cells.
6. SEMINA. The ſeeds are numerous, and roundiſh.

## CHAP. CCCLXXIX.

## *RHODIOLA*, ROSE-ROOT.

OF this genus there is only one ſpecies, called Roſe-root.

Deſcription of it

The root is thick, knotted, fleſhy, and when bruiſed emits the agreeable odour of the Damaſk Roſe. The ſtalks are upright, thick, ſucculent, and eight or ten inches high. The leaves are numerous, oblong, ſerrated, thick, ſucculent, of a grey colour, and come out alternately from every ſide of the ſtalk. The flowers come out in cluſters from the tops of the ſtalks; they are of a yellowiſh-green colour, and finely ſcented; they appear in June, July, and frequently in Auguſt, and the ſeeds ripen in the autumn.

Method of propagating it.

It is eaſily propagated by parting of the roots, which may be done in the early part of autumn, or the ſpring, or any time of the ſummer.

It is alſo multiplied by cuttings. Theſe ſhould be taken off in one of the early ſummer months, and, being ſucculent, ſhould be laid a few days in an airy place for the wounded parts to heal over, otherwiſe there will be great danger of their rotting. The cuttings ſhould be then planted in pots of light freſh earth, and ſet in a ſhady part of the green-houſe; a little water ſhould be afforded them to ſettle the mould, which muſt be occaſionally repeated, though but ſparingly, until

until they are in a growing state When they are arrived at this, they must be taken out of the green-house, and set in any convenient part of the garden, and in the autumn may be turned out of the pots, with the mould at the roots, into the places where they are designed to remain, which may be in any exposed situation, provided the ground be dry, and not too rich

If the cuttings are planted in the open ground, they will grow, especially if they are shaded, and covered with hand-glasses, so that when the convenience of a green-house is wanting, this method may be practised with probable hopes of success

Titles

There being no other species of this genus, it stands with the single name *Rhodiola* Caspar Bauhine calls it, *Rhodia radix*; Morison, *Telephium luteum minus, radice rosam redolente*, Tournefort, *Anacampseros, radice rosam spirante, major*, also, *Anacampseros, radice rosam spirante, minor* It grows naturally on the mountainous parts of Britain, Austria, Helvetia, and Lapland

Class and order in the Linnæan system

*Rhodiola* is of the class and order *Dioecia Octandria*, and the characters are,

I Male Flowers

The characters

1 Calyx is an erect, concave, obtuse, permanent perianthium, divided into four parts

2 Corolla is four oblong, obtuse, erect, patent, deciduous petals, which are much longer than the calyx, and four erect emarginated nectariums, which are shorter than the calyx

3 Stamina are eight awl-shaped filaments longer than the corolla, having simple antheræ,

4 Pistillum consists of four oblong, acuminated germens, with obsolete styles and stigmas

II Females

1 Calyx is a perianthium as in the males

2 Corolla is four rude, erect, obtuse, permanent petals equal with the calyx, and three or four nectariums like those of the males

3 Pistillum consists of four oblong acuminated germens, having straight simple styles, with obtuse stigmas

4 Pericarpium consists of four corniculated capsules, which open in the inner side

5 Semina The seeds are many, and roundish

## CHAP CCCLXXX

## *RUBIA*, MADDER

THERE are only two species of this genus, called,

Species

1 Cultivated Madder
2 Wild Madder

Description of Cultivated

1 Cultivated Madder The root is long, thick, jointed, spreading, succulent, tender on the outer part, tough within, of a reddish colour, and an acute, sweetish, bitterish taste The stalks are thick, square, jointed, rough, being covered with hooked spines, weak, procumbent, send out branches by pairs from the joints, which again branch into others in the like manner, and are four, five, six, or even eight feet long, according to the goodness of the soil in which they grow The leaves are oblong, spear-shaped, pointed, smooth on the upper side, but rough on the midrib underneath, and grow usually six at each joint, sitting close, and surrounding the stalk in a radiated manner The flowers come out in bunches from the sides of the branches at the joints; they are of a yellow colour, appear in June, but are rarely followed by ripe seeds in England

and Wild Madder

2 Wild Madder The root is long, slender, spreading under the surface, of a brownish colour, and of an austere taste The stalks are weak, jointed, procumbent, and about two feet long The leaves are four at each joint, short, pointed at the ends, smooth on the outside, and rough underneath The flowers come out in clusters from the ends and sides of the branches, they are small, of a yellow colour, appear in July and August, and the seeds ripen in the autumn

Its variety

There is a variety of this species with white flowers

Medicinal properties of it

The roots of both these sorts are used in medicine, being detergent and aperient, they are also used in dying, but it is the first species which is cultivated in such amazing plenty in some parts for the dyer's purposes

In order to obtain a crop of Madder, the first thing to be considered is a soil and situation proper for the purpose, for although Madder will grow in almost any soil or situation, it must not be expected to be cultivated for profit in this kingdom, unless the soil be in every respect suitable to its nature

Proper soil and situation

The soil should be a rich deep mould, inclining to sand, but not over light; rather moist, fresh, and the situation low and open On such a spot, all probable hopes of the highest success may reasonably be expected to attend your plantation of Madder

Propagation of it

If the quantity of Madder to be planted is but small, the ground should be double dug, working the turf to the bottom, in the manner that has been directed for preparing the nursery-ground for planting If very large plantations of Madder are to be made, ploughing may serve, though the Madder will never thrive so well on ploughed, as it will on double-dug ground

If the ground be double dug, it must be immediately before the planting of the Madder, if it is prepared by ploughing, it should be done

the

the autumn before, ploughing it as deep as may be with a very strong plough, then ploughing it again cross-wise, to break the clods, and separate the parts All winter it may lie in this manner, to be pulverised with the frost, snow, rain, sun, and air, and in the spring, just before the plantation is made, which may be in April and May, it should be ploughed afresh, and then well harrowed, to make the surface as smooth and even as possible, after which the business of planting may be proceeded on

For this purpose lines should be drawn the whole length of the ground at an interval of two feet, and the plants set with an iron dibble at a foot and a half distance from each other The sets, which are suckers from the old plants, may be taken off soon after they appear above ground and as much root as may be should be preserved to each set, which will cause them more readily to take to the ground, and shoot with greater vigour All summer they must be kept clean from weeds, and in the autumn the stalks will die These are seldom taken off the ground In small plantations, which are laid out in beds, they are covered with mould from the alleys In larger plantations they are suffered to rot upon the ground, in order to protect the plants from the injuries of bad weather, restore to the earth the nourishment they had before deprived her of, and grant the plants fresh supplies for vigorous acting If the stalks are cut off, the ground between the rows should be slightly dug, and two inches of fresh mould laid over the tops of the roots In the spring the shoots will rise up afresh, and the summer after require very little weeding except at first, as the stalks will then smother all weeds that may grow among them The third summer still less trouble will be required, and the October following the roots will be fit to take up for use But though I mention three summers for the growth of Madder, it must not be understood that Madder will not be fit to take up earlier, for it is sometimes taken up the second, and even first year after planting, in general the crop ought to stand three years undisturbed, as the yielding will then be proportionally in greater abundance

Method of raising Madder by seeds

Madder plantations are also made by seeds, which is a method preferred by most on the Continent, where the seeds ripen well, but with us this is rarely attempted, because the seeds seldom ripen in England Nevertheless, although the plants multiply so fast by suckers, it will be worth while to procure the seeds from abroad, because the best plants are raised by them, and if they are never removed, the best Madder will in consequence ensue

If the plantations are not to be over-large, the best way will be to prepare the land, and sow the seeds with no intention to remove the plants If the plantations are to be very extensive, the most eligible way will be to raise a sufficient quantity of plants in seed beds, in order to furnish them, that the expence of keeping so large a tract of ground free from weeds, and affording the plants suitable culture for a year or two longer than what will be necessary for plantations which are formed at first from the sets, may be saved The autumn, soon after the seeds are ripe, if their situation is warm and well defended, or the spring following, are both good seasons for sowing the seeds, and if they are sown in beds, nothing more need be done after the plants come up, than to thin them where they are too close, and keep them clear from weeds all summer, and in the autumn they will be proper plants to be set out for good, which may be done in the manner directed for the suckers

As the best Madder is generally obtained from unremoved plants, the roots by being undisturbed growing large, and striking deep into the earth, that method is now practised by those who value themselves on exhibiting the best Madder

The ground for the reception of the seeds should be double dug, but not below the natural depth of the mould, and if ploughing is to be the preparation, it must be ploughed as deep as may be, two or three times in different directions, that the parts may be more separated Well harrow it with a heavy harrow, that the clods may be broken, and then again with light harrows, the better to pulverise the surface, finally, it should be raked over with good iron rakes, to make the surface smooth, level, and even, for the reception of the seeds

The seeds may be sown by broad cast, but if there be a scarcity of seed, it may be made to hold out by sowing it in drills two feet asunder This practice will save much seed, but the trouble and expence of drawing the lines, making the drills, and sowing the seeds, will be the greater

If the seeds are sown by broad cast, they should be scattered thinly with an even hand, and harrowed in with light harrows When the plants come up they must be hoed in the manner of turneps, leaving them at about a foot and a half distance from each other every way At this hoeing the weeds must be carefully destroyed, and the more effectually to accomplish this business, it should be performed in dry weather In about a month or six weeks the business of hoeing down the weeds must be repeated, for no weeds must be suffered to grow among the Madder, and a third or fourth hoeing also must be made, as there shall be occasion

The distribution of the stalks is various by different people some chusing to let them lie and rot on the ground, in order to restore to the earth in the winter that virtue the plants had extracted from it in the summer others, to cut the stalks off green the latter end of summer, to become fodder for cattle This latter practice weakens the roots, but by this means a useful crop of fodder is saved, for Madder is very nourishing to most cattle, and is what they are extremely fond of, especially cows, who eat it greedily, and to whom it affords much milk, which will be of a reddish cast

If regard only is had to the Madder roots, I think the best way will be to cut off the stalks at the end of October, when they decay, and then to stir the whole surface of the ground with the hoe, drawing a little fresh mould over the crown of each root Thus the roots will be refreshed with all necessary supplies, and they will shoot forth strong the succeeding spring, unmolested by straw lying slovenly to rot on the ground, under pretence of restoring it to its first heart Hoeing every year in the summer, and the like practices in winter, must be annually repeated, and the third or fourth year, from seeds, the roots of the Madder will be of proper size to be taken up

Method of taking up Madder roots

The method of taking up the roots is by opening a trench on the outside two feet broad, and as deep as the Madder roots have struck into the ground, two feet more must be set off for the next trench, and the mould of the second must be thrown into the first trench, as is practised in the manner of trenching or double-digging of land for the first planting, all the while having

having a sufficient number of hands in readiness to pick up every bit of the roots, that no part may be lost.

After the roots are taken up, they will be immediately fit for use, without the trouble of drying and pulverising them, as is usually practised.

Manner in which the roots are used in dyeing

The manner of using them fresh is by first washing them, then cutting them in small pieces, pounding them in a wooden or stone mortar, and throwing them into a copper with the water luke-warm. When the water is near scalding hot, the cotton should be put into the copper, and worked about for three quarters of an hour, the liquor all that time being kept from boiling, yet never less hot to a degree of scalding; afterwards the liquor is made to boil well for three quarters of an hour more, and the dyeing is then finished. This liquor is said to be much finer than that which is made from the best Dutch ground Madder; so that every dyer ought to have a Madder plantation of his own ready at hand, in order to use the roots fresh, the design of drying and reducing them to powder being chiefly for sending them to distant parts for the purpose of dyeing, where the culture of Madder is not practised.

Four pounds of fresh Madder must be allowed after this rate to one pound of dry Madder, and this is the proportion to be observed in procuring an equal dye.

When the Madder is not intended to be used fresh, the roots should be carried as soon as possible, and placed under a shed to dry, the shed should be open at the sides, to admit a free current of air, and only covered to protect them from the wet. When the mould at the roots is well dried, which will be in a few days, it should be carefully rubbed off, and when the roots are first sufficiently dried by this gentle method, they are next to be carried to the kiln, where they must be further dried, and reduced to powder. They are then threshed, and the parts of different degrees of goodness separated, and carried to a mill or pounding-house; and when this is effected, it is put up in casks to be sent to the different parts of the world to be ready for use.

Cautions

The mills, &c. are various in different parts, and every planter pleads for his own being the best, because he is most used to it. These mills are very expensive to erect, which should caution every one from building his mill or pounding-house before he is certain his land is so far suitable to the growth of Madder, that a sufficient quantity may be raised to keep it in good motion, in proportion to the expence. And for this there is but little encouragement from the repeated experiments which have been made on the cultivation of Madder in this kingdom, few of them yet having ever answered according to expectation, though tried with all the various ways of practice used in Zealand, and other parts of the world where Madder is cultivated to such great advantage. I mention this as a caution for persons not over-precipitately to enter deeply into the practice, before they are certain every thing is suitable for the purpose, which may be known by raising a little in small quantities, in different parts, for experiment only. I could mention a very curious man, zealous for the promotion of public utility, and who had acquired a considerable fortune in the Woad-way, that was almost reduced to necessity thro' his over zeal for Madder-planting, though carried on with all the care and caution of foreign practice.

Land that is suitable to Madder may be made to bear two crops of it successively, after that it will produce amazing crops of oats or barley, and may be kept in tillage with good management, dunging and lying fallow at proper intervals, for nine years, and will then be again in good condition for a fresh crop of Madder.

Madder seems to be possessed of ... subtility of parts. If taken inwardly, it tinges the urine of a deep red colour; and in one experiment it is found to have had the like effect on the bones of animals that had eaten it, all of them were changed to a deep red, though the flesh and other parts remained unaltered; and though the bones were first macerated many weeks in water, and afterwards steeped and boiled in spirit of wine, yet they lost none of their colour, nor communicated the least tinge to the liquor. This should induce one to think that Madder is deserving of the nicest enquiry and experiment, with respect to its medicinal virtues, as well as dyeing qualities. | ... ex ... Ma...

1 Cultivated Madder is entitled, *Rubia fol... subsenis*. Sauvages calls it, *Rubia perennis, foliis sæpius quinis*; Caspar Bauhine, *Rubia sylvestris aspera*; also, *Rubia tinctorum sativa*; Gerard, *Rubea tinctorum*, and others, *Rubia hortensis*. It grows naturally in Italy, and the South of France. | Titles

2 Wild Madder is, *Rubia foliis quaternis*. Hermann calls it, *Rubia quadrifolia asperrima lucida peregrina*; and Parkinson, *Rubia sylvestris*. It is a native of England, but is not known to grow naturally in any other part of the world.

*Rubia* is of the class and order *Tetrandria Monogynia*, and the characters are, | Class and order in the Linnæan system

1 CALYX is a very small perianthium situated above the germen, and indented in four parts. | The characters

2 COROLLA is one bell-shaped petal without a tube, divided into four parts.

3 STAMINA are four awl-shaped filaments shorter than the corolla, having simple antheræ.

4 PISTILLUM consists of a didymous germen situated below the calyx, and a filiform style bifid at the top, with capitated stigmas.

5 PERICARPIUM consists of two smooth berries joined together.

6 SEMEN. The seed is single, roundish, and umbilicated.

CHAP

# CHAP. CCCLXXXI

## *RUBUS*, The BRAMBLE.

THERE are a few herbaceous perennials of this genus, which may have a place in some out corners of our gardens or wilderness-works, to be at hand for observation, where they are wanted, but they have not beauty enough to gain admission among the flowering tribe in the best parts of the pleasure garden, neither would such a situation be suitable to their natures. They are called,

Species

1. Stone Bramble.
2. Dwarf Bramble.
3. Cloud Berry.
4. *Dalibarda*.

Stone

1. Stone Bramble. This plant hath a small, reddish, herbaceous stalk, which trails upon the ground, and puts out roots from the joints. The leaves are trifoliate, and of a fine green colour, the lobes are large, serrated, and grow on long slender footstalks. The flowers are produced from the ends of the branches in May or June; they are of a white colour, and are succeeded by a small reddish fruit, which will be ripe in August, and is of a very agreeable flavour.

and Dwarf Bramble,

2. Dwarf Bramble. The stalks are upright, smooth, and grow to about three or four inches high. The leaves are trifoliate and small. The flowers grow singly from the tops of the stalks; they are of a purple colour, and are succeeded by small, red, fragrant fruit, which has the taste and smell of a common Strawberry.

Cloud Berry,

3. Cloud Berry. The stalks grow to about eight inches high. The leaves are simple, lobed, and being only two to garnish the stalks, they are placed at a distance from each other, are moderately large, tough, serrated, and grow from the joints on long footstalks. The stalk is crowned by one flower, which is of a purple colour, and is succeeded by black fruit not unlike the mulberry, on which account the name Dwarf Mulberry has been usually applied to this plant.

and Dalibarda described.

4. *Dalibarda*. This hath a creeping root, which sends forth several herbaceous trailing stalks, that strike fresh root as they lie on the ground. The leaves are simple, a little hairy, heart-shaped, obtuse, crenated, and grow on long footstalks. From among the leaves rises a naked stalk supporting one flower, which is of a white colour, and resembles those of the common Blackberry.

Culture

The first and fourth sorts are propagated by parting of the roots, and grow tolerably well in gardens, but the other two are with difficulty made to grow in any place where they do not spontaneously arise. They grow naturally upon bogs and the like sort of ground, and may be successfully introduced into such places, whenever they happen within the limits of our works. If a bog, therefore, should be found any where within the bounds of the garden, early in the spring throw up the middle of it in ridges, covering the turf, or burying it that it may rot. As the weeds begin to shoot out afresh, turn the ridges at random, keeping the turf, or whatever grows on it, underneath to rot. Let this be repeated once or twice more in the summer, as you find it necessary, and by the time the fruit is ripe let it be dug, and the surface laid smooth and level; then having procured some good ripe fruit, sow them in patches, six or eight in a patch, and cover them with about an inch depth of the same mould, for other mould must by no means be added to the natural soil of the bog.

The spring following some of the plants will come up, but the greatest part generally lie a whole summer before they appear. In either case, as they come up, and indeed from the time of their being sowed, let no weeds be disturbed, they thrive best when growing with the common produce of the spot, and in conjunction with such company they more pleasingly indicate that case of growth which they assume when found in a state of nature.

1. The Stone Bramble is titled, *Rubus foliis ternatis, flagellis nudis reptantibus herbaceis*. This is *Rubus caule repente annuo, foliis ternatis*, *Flora Lapp.* n. 200. It grows naturally on stony mountainous grounds in England, and most countries of Europe. Titles.

2. Dwarf Bramble is, *Rubus foliis ternatis, caule inermi unifloro*. In the *Flora Lapp.* it is termed, *Rubus caule unifloro, foliis ternatis*. Buxbaum calls it, *Rubus humilis flore purpureo*, and Amman, *Rubus trifolius humilis non spinosus, sapore et odore fragariæ, fructu rubro polycocco*. It grows naturally in Bothnia, Siberia, and Canada.

3. Cloud Berry is, *Rubus foliis simplicibus lobatis, caule inermi unifloro*. In the *Flora Lapp.* it is termed, *Rubus caule trifolio unifloro, foliis simplicibus*. Caspar Bauhine calls it, *Chamærubus foliis ribes*, and Clusius, *Chamæmorus*. It is a native of England, and other parts of Europe.

4. *Dalibarda* is, *Rubus foliis simplicibus cordatis indivisis crenatis, scapo aphyllo unifloro*. In the former edition of the *Species Plantarum* it is called simply, *Dalibarda*. It grows naturally in Canada.

## CHAP CCCLXXXII

## *RUDBECKIA*, DWARF SUN-FLOWER.

Species

OF this genus are,
1 Jagged-leaved Dwarf Sun flower
2 Rough Dwarf Sun-flower
3 Purple Dwarf Sun-flower
4 Narrow-leaved Dwarf Sun flower
5 Opposite-leaved Dwarf Sun-flower

Jagged leaved Dwarf Sun flower described

1 Jagged-leaved Dwarf Sun-flower The stalks are upright, firm, and grow to six, seven, eight, or nine feet high The lower leaves are usually compoled of five principal parts, and all of them are deeply cut into acute parts, or jagged, sometimes to the mid-rib The leaves on the stalk are smaller, and some of them are undivided The flowers come out from the tops of the plants on long, naked footstalks, they are of a yellow colour, and much resemble a Single Sun-flower, but are smaller, they appear in July, August, and sometimes in September, soon after which the stalks die to the ground, and fresh ones arise in the spring

Of this species there are several varieties, called,

Varieties

The Broad Jagged-leaved Sun-flower
The Narrow Jagged-leaved Sun flower
The Purple-stalked Jagged leaved Sun-flower
The Small-flowered Jagged leaved Sun-flower, &c &c

Propagation of them

They hardly ever produce seeds in England, but are easily propagated by parting of the roots, the best time for which is the autumn, when the stalks decay They are all very hardy, and proper furniture for shrubberies, and they may be set in the borders of woods to which walks lead, as they delight in the shade, and will be very ornamental to such places, though seen at a distance

Rough Dwarf Sun flower described

2 Rough Dwarf Sun-flower The stalks rise to about a foot and a half high The leaves are undivided, oblong, oval, rough, and hairy The flowers come out singly on long, naked foot-stalks, are of a yellow colour, and moderately large, they much resemble a Sun flower, the rays being broad, indented, and of a fine yellow colour, having a purple prominent center or middle They come out in July, and continue to shew themselves sometimes to the end of autumn, and sometimes they produce good seeds in our gardens

Propagation of it

This species is propagated by dividing the heads, the best time for which is the autumn, when the stalks decay This work must be sedulously attended to every two or three years, or you will lose the species, for without due culture, it will go off in about four or five years It must also have a dry soil, and a warm situation, otherwise it will be liable to be killed the first winter after planting This species, in many parts of England, is known by no other name than the Dwarf Sun-flower, by which title it usually goes

Purple Dwarf Sun flower described

3 Purple Dwarf Sun-flower The stalks will grow to about two feet, or more, in height The leaves are undivided, spear-shaped, oval, smooth, veined, and grow alternately on the stalks The flowers come out singly, in July and August, on long, slender footstalks They are of two or three varieties, the rays of one are long, reflexed, and of a fine peach colour, having a dark, purple coloured middle, which gradually rises in a pyramidical manner, and is at the top of a flaming-yellow colour, the rays of another are purple-coloured, and very long, and a third variety has broader leaves than either They are all very valuable, and usually go by the name of Dwarf Carolina Sun-flower

Culture

It is more difficult to propagate this species than the former, because the roots do not send out heads in the same manner, so that it can be encreased but slowly The culture of it, however, is by dividing the roots, the best time for which is the autumn Indeed, the plants sometimes produce good seeds; and when this happens, a good stock may be soon raised by sowing them in a border of light earth in the spring, and in the autumn removing the plants to the places where they are designed to remain

Description of Narrow leaved Dwarf

4 Narrow-leaved Dwarf Sun-flower The stalks are upright, firm, and about two feet high The leaves are long, narrow, rough, entire, and grow opposite to each other The flowers are of a fine yellow colour, having a dark-red or purple middle, they appear about the middle of July, and continue in succession until November, but the seeds do not ripen in our gardens

and Opposite leaved Sun flower

5 Opposite-leaved Sun flower The stalks are upright, and about the height of the former species The leaves are spear-shaped, oval, serrated, and grow opposite to each other The whole flower is yellow, the rays and disk also being of that colour The plant will be in blow in July and August, and sometimes continue to shew its bloom through September and October

Method of propagating them

Both these last species are of short duration, frequently dying soon after they have flowered, therefore, to continue them, the stalks should be cut down in May as they shoot up, in order to cause them to encrease in the root When this proves successful, they may be parted in the autumn, and must have a light, dry soil, and a warm situation

They are also propagated by seeds These should be procured from the countries where the plants naturally grow In the spring they should be sown on a slight hot-bed to bring them forward, and, when they are of a size to transplant, may be removed, with a ball of earth to each root, to the places where they are designed to remain, and the summer following they will flower

Titles.

1 Jagged-leaf Dwarf Sun-flower is titled, *Rudbeckia foliis compositis laciniatis* Morison calls it, *Chrysanthemum Americanum perenne, foliis di-visis dilutius virentibus, majus*, Caspar Bauhine, *Doronicum Americanum, laciniato folio*, and Cornutus, *Aconitum helianthemum Canadense* It grows naturally in Virginia and Canada

2 Rough Dwarf Sun flower is, *Rudbeckia foliis indivisis spatulato-ovatis triplinerviis, radii petalis emarginatis* Buttner calls it, *Rudbeckia, ramis indivisis unifloris, foliis ovato-lanceolatis, hirtis*, Gronovius, *Rudbeckia foliis lanceolato ovatis alternis indivisis, petalis radii integris*, Dillenius,

*Oli-*

*Obeliſcotheca integrifolia radio aureo, umbone atro-rubente*, and Plukenet, *Chryſanthemum helenii folio, umbone floris grandiuſculo prominente*. It grows naturally in Virginia and Canada.

3. Purple Dwarf Sun-flower is, *Rudbeckia foliis lanceolato-ovatis alternis indiviſis, petalis radii bifidis*. Plukenet calls it, *Chryſanthemum Americanum, doronici folio, flore Perſici coloris, umbone magno prominente ex atro-purpureo viridi & aureo fulgente*; Morison, *Dracunculus Virginianus latifolius, petalis florum longiſſimis purpuraſcentibus*, and Petiver, *Polarium*. It is a native of Virginia and Carolina.

4. Narrow-leaved Dwarf Sun-flower is, *Rudbeckia foliis oppoſitis linearibus integerrimis*. In the former edition of the *Species Plantarum* it is called, *Coreopſis foliis linearibus integerrimis*. It is a native of Virginia.

5. Oppoſite-leaved Dwarf Sun-flower is, *Rudbeckia foliis oppoſitis, lanceolato-ovatis ſerratis, petalis radii bifidis*. It grows naturally in Virginia.

Claſs and order in the Linnean ſyſtem. *Rudbeckia* is of the claſs and order *Syngeneſia Polygamia Fruſtranea*, and the characters are,

The characters. 1. CALYX. The common calyx is compoſed of two orders of plain, broad, and ſhort ſcales.

2. COROLLA is compound and radiated. The hermaphrodite florets in the diſk are tubulous, funnel-ſhaped, and indented in five parts at the brim. The female florets in the radius are very long, ſpear-ſhaped, plane, and have two or three indentures at the top.

3. STAMINA, in the hermaphrodite florets, are five very ſhort capillary filaments, having a cylindrical tubular anthera.

4. PISTILLUM, in the hermaphrodite florets, conſiſts of a four-cornered germen, a filiforme ſtyle the length of the corollulæ, and a revolute ſtigma divided into two parts.

The piſtil for the female florets is a very ſmall germen, without either ſtyle or ſtigma.

5. PERICARPIUM. There is none.

6. SEMINA. The ſeeds of the hermaphrodites are ſingle, oblong, and crowned with down which has four indentures.

The female florets produce no ſeeds.

The receptacle is paleaceous, conic, and longer than the common calyx. The paleæ are of the length of the ſeeds, erect, channelled, concave, and deciduous.

# CHAP. CCCLXXXIII.

## RUELLIA.

OF this genus there is one ſpecies that may be ſtationed among the perennials in a warm corner of the garden, called Virginian Ruellia.

The plant deſcribed. The root is fibrous and perennial. The ſtalks are four-cornered, jointed, and about a foot high. The leaves are oval, and grow oppoſite at the joints on ſhort footſtalks. The flowers come out from the wings of the leaves on very ſhort footſtalks, ſurrounding the ſtalk at the joints; they are of a pale-purple colour, appear in July, and the ſeeds ripen in the autumn.

Culture. It is raiſed by ſowing the ſeeds on a hot-bed in the ſpring, and when the plants are fit to remove, they ſhould be tranſplanted to ſome warm, dry part of the garden, where, if they are watered and ſhaded at firſt, they will grow, ſtand the cold of our moderate winters, and flower and perfect their ſeeds the ſummer following. Nevertheleſs, as they are ſometimes deſtroyed by very ſevere weather, a few plants ſhould be ſet in pots, to be houſed, if ſuch weather ſhould threaten deſtruction to thoſe which are abroad.

Titles. This ſpecies is entitled, *Ruellia foliis petiolatis, floribus verticillatis ſubpetiolatis*. In the *Hortus Cliffort* it is termed, *Ruellia foliis petiolatis, fructu ſeſſili conferto*. Dillenius calls it, *Ruellia ſtrepens, capitulis comoſis*. It grows naturally in Virginia and Carolina.

Claſs and order in the Linnæan Syſtem. *Ruellia* is of the claſs and order *Didynamia Angioſpermia*, and the characters are,

The characters. 1. CALYX is a monophyllous, permanent perianthium, divided into five linear, acute, ſtraight ſegments.

2. COROLLA is one irregular petal, the neck of the tube being patulous and inclining, and the limb divided into five obtuſe, ſpreading ſegments, the two upper ones of which are more reflexed than the others.

3. STAMINA are four filaments placed in the wide part of the tube, connected by pairs, and having ſhort antheræ.

4. PISTILLUM conſiſts of a roundiſh germen, a filiforme ſtyle the length of the ſtamina, and a bifid, acute ſtigma.

5. PERICARPIUM is a taper, bilocular, bivalved capſule, pointed at both ends, and burſting with an elaſtic force for the diſcharge of the ſeeds when ripe.

6. SEMINA. The ſeeds are few, roundiſh, and compreſſed.

# CHAP CCCLXXXIV

## RUMEX, DOCK.

Introduction

THERE are no leſs than twenty-ſeven different ſpecies of Dock, ten of which grow naturally in our own country, but none of them merit introduction into the garden, except the Patience Dock, the Sorrel-tree, and Sorrel The Sorrel belongs to the kitchen garden, the Sorrel-tree to the green-houſe, and Patience Dock claims a right to be ſtationed here

Patience Dock and its varieties deſcribed

The Patience Dock is alſo called Patience Rhubarb, and Monk's Rhubarb There are two varieties of this ſpecies, one with oblong, heart-ſhaped leaves; the other with rounder and ſhorter leaves, and it is to this latter ſort that the appellation of Monk's Rhubarb is generally applied The roots are very large, thick, and ſtrike deep into the ground; they are yellow within, but their outſide is of a dark-brown colour The leaves are a foot long, broad, and have long, ſtrong, thick, reddiſh footſtalks The ſtalks are ſtriated, upright, firm, and will grow to about a yard high, they are garniſhed at each joint with a leaf like the radical one, though ſmaller, and more acutely pointed Their upper parts are adorned with the flowers Theſe are produced in cloſe, upright ſpikes, are of a white colour, appear in May or June, and ripen their ſeeds in the autumn

Propagation of them

Theſe ſorts are beſt raiſed by ſowing of the ſeeds, the ſeaſon for which ſhould be the autumn, ſoon after they are ripe They ſhould have a rich, looſe, deep ſoil, and, to cauſe the plants to be very large, ſhould be ſown in the places where they are to remain When they come up, nothing more is to be done than to keep them clean from weeds, and thin them to a good diſtance from each other Such plants will flower ſtronger, and produce larger leaves or ſtalks than thoſe that have been removed

They are alſo propagated by dividing of the roots The beſt time for this work is the autumn They will readily grow, and ſoon become good plants, though they will, for the moſt part, be greatly inferior to thoſe that are raiſed from ſeeds

This ſpecies is titled, *Rumex floribus hermaphroditis, valvulis integerrimis unica granifera, foliis cordatis* Caſpar Bauhine calls it, *Lapathum hortenſe, folio oblongo*, Dodonæus, *Lapathum ſativum* It grows naturally in Italy — Title

*Rumex* is of the claſs and order *Hexandria Trigynia*, and the characters are, — Claſs and order in the Linnæan ſyſtem

The characters

1 CALYX is a perianthium compoſed of three obtuſe, reflexed, permanent leaves

2 COROLLA conſiſts of three oval, connivent, permanent petals, which are larger than thoſe of the cups, but very much like them

3 STAMINA conſiſt of ſix very ſhort, capillary filaments, with erect, didymous antheræ

4 PISTILLUM conſiſts of a turbinated, three-cornered germen, three capillary, reflexed ſtyles from the chinks of the connivent petals, and large, laciniated ſtigmas

5. PERICARPIUM There is none The connivent, three-cornered corolla contains the ſeed

6 SEMEN The ſeed is ſingle, and three-cornered

# CHAP CCCLXXXV

## RUPPIA

THERE is only one ſpecies of this genus, commonly called Sea Graſs

This plant deſcribed

The root is long, thickiſh, jointed, and creeping The ſtalk is ſingle, round, ſlender, and five or ſix inches high The leaves are narrow, graſſy, acute-pointed, grow alternately, and ſurround the ſtalk with their baſe The flowers come out from the ſides of the ſtalks on leafy footſtalks, and are to be met with in July, Auguſt, and September

This is not a cultivated plant, being found chiefly in ditches near the ſea, and other moiſt places which are frequently covered over with ſea-water

There being no other ſpecies of this genus yet known, it ſtands with the ſingle name *Ruppia* Micheli calls it, *Bucciferа maritima, foliis acutiſſimis*, Ray, *Potamogeton maritimum, granis ſ longior bus foliis, fructu fere umbellato*, alſo, *Potamogeton m i t'm n pyſillum alterum*, Plukenet *Potamogeton maritimum puſillum alterum, ſeminibus ſingulis longis pediculis inſidentibus*, Caſpar Bauhine, *Gramen maritimum fluitans cornutum* It grows naturally in England and moſt countries of Europe — T i.

*Ruppia* is of the claſs and order *Tetrandria Tetragynia*, and the characters are, — Claſs and order in the Linnæan ſyſtem

1 CALYX

The characters.

1 CALYX is a very ſmall ſpatha, ſcarcely diſtinguiſhable from the vagina of the leaves

The ſpadix is awl-ſhaped, ſimple, ſtraight at firſt, but crooked when the fruit is ripe with which it is loaded, arranged in a double ſeries

2 COROLLA There is none

3 STAMINA There are no filaments, but nevertheleſs there are four, ſeſſile, equal, roundiſh, ſubdidymous antheræ

4 PISTILLUM conſiſts of four or five oval, connivent germens, without any ſtyles, but with obtuſe ſtigmas

5 PERICARPIUM There is none The ſeeds ſit on their own proper, ſlender footſtalks, which are as long as the fruit

6 SEMINA The ſeeds are four or five in number, oval, oblique, and crowned by two plane, rounded ſtigmas

# CHAP. CCCLXXXVI.

## *RUTA*, RUE.

Flax leaved Rue

THE Flax leaved Rue is the ſpecies intended for this place. There are three principal varieties of it, viz

Its varieties.

The Spaniſh Flax-leaved Rue

The Mountain Round leaved Rue

The Oriental Small flowered Rue

Deſcription of it

The Rue of our kitchen gardens has very large decompound leaves, but thoſe of this ſpecies are whole The leaves of the firſt ſort are long, narrow, entire, and grow ſingly on the ſtalks, thoſe of the ſecond ſort are roundiſh and undivided, and thoſe of the third ſort are narrow, and a little like thoſe of Toad Flax The flowers grow from the tops of the ſtalks in kind of panicles, appear in July and Auguſt, and ſometimes (though not always) ripen their ſeeds in the autumn

Culture

Theſe ſorts are raiſed by ſowing of the ſeeds in March on a bed of light, ſandy earth, ſifting over them about a quarter of an inch of the like fine mould Where the plants come up too cloſe, draw out the weakeſt Water the bed if dry weather happens, and keep it clean from weeds, and in a moiſt day after the plants are of proper ſize to remove, plant them out in beds in the nurſery ground at ſix inches aſunder Water them until they have taken root, and in the autumn they may be removed into the places where they are deſigned to remain Their ſituation ſhould be naturally dry, ſandy, and well-ſheltered, otherwiſe they are very liable to be deſtroyed by our cold winters On this account ſome plants ſhould be ſet in pots, to be placed in the green-houſe in winter, to preſerve the ſort Care alſo ſhould be taken to obtain good ſeeds for a ſucceſſion, namely, by covering the plants when in flower, and afterwards with glaſſes, if very wet weather ſhould happen, and by giving them all poſſible aſſiſtance of this kind, for without ſuch treatment, if a wet, cold autumn ſhould happen, they rarely perfect their ſeeds

Titles

This ſpecies is titled, *Ruta foliis ſimplicibus indiviſis* In the *Hortus Cliffor* it is termed, *Ruta foliis ſimplicibus ſolitariis* Boccone calls it, *Ruta ſylveſtris linifolia Hiſpanica*, Buxbaum, *Ruta montana, foliis integris ſubrotundis*, Tournefort, *Ruta Orientalis, Linariæ folio, flore parvo* It grows naturally in Spain

*Ruta* is of the claſs and order *Decandria Monogynia*, and the characters are,

1 CALYX is a ſhort, permanent perianthium, divided into five parts

2 COROLLA conſiſts of four oval, patent petals, having narrow ungues

3 STAMINA are ten patent, awl-ſhaped filaments the length of the corolla, with very ſhort, erect antheræ

4 PISTILLUM conſiſts of a gibbous, cruciform, furrowed germen, having ten points at the baſe, an erect, ſubulated ſtyle, and a ſimple ſtigma

5 PERICARPIUM is a gibbous five lobed capſule, containing five cells, and opening at the top in five parts

6 SEMINA The ſeeds are numerous, reniform, angular and rough

CHAP

# CHAP CCCLXXXVII.

## *SAGITTARIA*, ARROW-HEAD.

OF this genus there is a well-known species of our brooks and ditches, called Arrow-head

This plant described. The root is thick, fungous, white, fibrous, and strikes deep into the mud The leaves are shaped like an arrow, acute, and rise on very long, round, thick, fungous footstalks The stalks are thick, roundish, striated, fungous, and rise above the leaves The flowers come out in whorls from the tops of the stalks, and are of a beautiful white colour, having purple antheræ; they appear in July, and the seeds ripen in September

There are many varieties of this species, called,

Varieties. The Greater Water Arrow-head
The Lesser
The Small Broad-leaved
The Small Narrow-leaved
The Various-leaved, &c

Method of propagation. If any one is inclined to have this species in his ponds, ditches, or standing-waters, he may effect it by scattering some seeds into the water, or planting the roots in the mud

Titles. This species is entitled, *Sagittaria foliis sagittatis acutis* Dodonæus calls it, *Sagitta minor*, Caspar Bauhine, *Sagitta aquatica minor latifolia*, also, *Sagitta aquatica minor angustifolia*, also, *Sagitta aquatica major* Loesel names it, *Sagitta aquatica foliis variis* It grows naturally in ditches, rivers, lakes, &c in England and most parts of Europe

Class and Order in the Linnæan System. *Sagittaria* is of the class and order *Monoecia Polyandria*, and the characters are,

The characters.

I Male Flowers

1 CALYX is a permanent perianthium composed of three oval, concave leaves

2 COROLLA is three roundish, obtuse, plane, patent petals, which are much larger than the calyx

3 STAMINA are about twenty-four awl-shaped filaments collected into a head, having erect antheræ the length of the calyx

II Female Flowers situated below the Males

1 CALYX is a perianthium like that of the males

2 COROLLA The same as the males

3 PISTILLUM consists of numerous compressed germens collected into a head, having very short styles, with acute, permanent stigmas

4 PERICARPIUM There is none The seeds are collected in a roundish head

5 SEMINA The seeds are numerous, oblong, compressed, and surrounded lengthways with a broad membranaceous border.

# CHAP. CCCLXXXVIII.

## *SALICORNIA*, JOINTED GLASS-WORT, or SALT-WORT.

OF this genus there are three perennial species, called,

Species.
1 Greater Jointed Glass wort
2 Lesser Jointed Glass-wort
3 Tamarisk Jointed Glass-wort

Description of Greater, 1 Greater Jointed Glass wort The stalks are shrubby, upright, jointed, with acute articulations branching from the bottom, and eight or ten inches long The leaves are short, succulent, and of a purplish-green colour The flowers come out from the joints near the upper parts of the branches, but they are extremely small, appear in July and August, and the seeds ripen in the autumn

Lesser, 2 Lesser Jointed Glass-wort. The stalks are thick, succulent, jointed, having obtuse articulations, branching, and five or six inches long The leaves are small, and succulent The flowers come out in oval spikes from the upper parts of the branches, are extremely small, of a yellowish-green colour, appear in July and August, and the seeds ripen in the autumn

and Tamarisk Jointed Glass wort. 3 Tamarisk Jointed Glass-wort The stalks are shrubby, branching, and the articulations are cylindrical The leaves are narrow, round, and succulent The flowers are produced in very slender spikes like the former species, appear about the same time, and the seeds ripen accordingly.

Propagation. These plants are seldom propagated, but grow wild on the sea-shores, where they are gathered, dried, and burnt for the ashes, which, with the Common Glass wort, are used for making of glass Nevertheless, if the seeds are sown in a light, sandy place, in the spring, they will grow, or the cuttings may be planted in the shade in any of the summer months, and the stock will be soon encreased

1 The

Titles

1 The first species is entitled, *Salicornia caule erecto fruticoso* Caspar Bauhine calls it, *Kali geniculatum majus* Sauvages, *Salicornia sempervirens*, Ray, *Salicornia ramosior procumbens, foliis brevibus purpurascentibus* It grows naturally on the sea-shores of England and most others of Europe

2 The second species is, *Salicornia articulis obtusis basi incrassatis, spicis ovatis* Caspar Bauhine calls it, *Kali geniculatum minus* It is a native of Arabia

3 The third species is, *Salicornia articulis cylindricis, spicis filiformibus* Buxbaum calls it, *Kali arborescens, tamarisci facie* It grows on the Caspian and Median shores

Class and order in the Linnæan system the characters

*Salicornia* is of the class and order *Monandria Monogynia*, and the characters are,

1 CALYX is four cornered, truncated, swelling, and permanent

2 COROLLA There is none

3 STAMEN is one simple filament, longer than the calyx, having two oblong, didymous, erect antheræ

4 PISTILLUM consists of an oval, oblong germen, a simple style placed under the stamen, and a bifid stigma.

5 PERICARPIUM There is none The calyx becomes more inflated, and contains the seed

6 SEMEN The seed is single

# CHAP CCCLXXXIX

## *SALIX*, WILLOW.

Introductory observations

THERE are some species of this genus that are either herbaceous, or such low, ligneous plants as are not fit to be ranked among the shrubs These plants, however, ought not wholly to be passed by unnoticed, not only in order to give every one an account of the most inconsiderable species of this genus, but also because the philosopher, and the gentleman of an unlimited thirst after the works of Nature, may probably be tempted to admit a few of each sort to such suitable parts of their plantations in which they could wish to find them stationed These species, then, are,

Species

1 Herbaceous Willow
2 Myrsinite Willow
3 Lapland Willow
4 Round-leaved Dwarf Willow
5 Round-leaved Eared Willow
6 Sand Willow
7 Creeping Willow
8 Brown Willow
9 Rosemary-leaved Willow
10 Woolly leaved Dwarf Willow
11 Incubaceous Willow
12 Thyme-leaved Willow

Description of Herbaceous,

1 Herbaceous Willow This species hath a creeping, fibrated root, which sends forth several slender, weak, herbaceous branches, that spread themselves on the ground The leaves are round, smooth, and have their edges serrated The flowers come out in the spring, they are only small katkins, and the females are succeeded by downy seeds, which will be ripe in the summer

Myrsinite

2 Myrsinite Willow The root is creeping, woody, and fibrated The stalks are ligneous, slender, and covered with a brownish bark The leaves are small, oval, venose, glossy on the upper side, greyish underneath, and serrated on their edges The flowers grow in thick spikes, and turn to a light down, which is wafted about every-where by the wind

Lapland,

3 Lapland Willow The stalks are ligneous, very tough, and about two feet high The leaves are nearly oval, smooth on their upper side, glaucous underneath, and slightly serrated at their edges The flowers come out among the leaves in the spring, and the females are succeeded by downy seeds, which ripen well in England

Round leaved Dwarf,

4 Round-leaved Dwarf Willow The stalks are slender, ligneous, tough, round, and of a brown colour The leaves are oval, obtuse, undivided at their edges, smooth on their upper side, and curiously wrought or marked like fine net-work underneath The katkins come out in the spring, and the seeds ripen in August

Round-leaved Eared,

5 Round leaved Eared Willow The stalks are slender, ligneous, round, tough, and about a foot and a half long The leaves are oboval, hairy on both sides, entire, downy underneath, and have ears or appendices at their base The katkins are small, come out in the spring, and the seeds ripen about the time of the former

and Sand Willow.

6 Sand Willow This is a low willow growing in marshy places as well as sandy ground The leaves are hoary, acute, entire, slightly hairy on their upper side, and downy underneath The katkins are small, and appear and ripen their seeds nearly with the former

Creeping Willow described

7 Creeping Willow This species hath a small, creeping root, which spreads itself under the surface of the earth to a considerable distance The stalks are slender, hardly a foot and a half long, trail on the ground, and strike root from the sides The leaves are narrow, spear-shaped, and hairy on both sides This species seldom produces flowers, but when they do appear, it is early in the spring, and they soon alter to light down, like the other species.

Variety.

There is a variety of this species with roundish leaves, which are soft and woolly on their under sides

Description of Brown Willow

8 Brown Willow The root is woody, fibrated, and of a black colour The stalks are slender, hardly a foot and a half long, and covered with a brown bark The leaves are small, narrow, spear-shaped, entire, smooth, of a bright-green colour on their upper side, and downy underneath Among these come out the flowers, they are small, appear early in the spring, and soon afford plenty of down wafted about by the wind

*Roſe-mary-leaved,* 9 Roſemary-leaved Willow The root is creeping The ſtalks are ſlender, about a foot and a half long, and, if permitted to lie on the ground, ſtrike root at the ſides The leaves are numerous, narrow, ſpear ſhaped, undivided, have no footſtalks, are of a ſilvery whiteneſs, and ſoft to the touch Among theſe come out the flowers in the ſpring, and they are ſucceeded by downy ſeeds

*Wooly leaved Dwarf* 10 Woolly-leaved Dwarf Willow The ſtalks are upright, woody, and grow to about two feet high The leaves are oval, broad, acute, entire, woolly on both ſides, and grow on very ſhort footſtalks The flowers come out from the ſides of the branches early in the ſpring, and the females are ſucceeded by downy ſeeds like the others

*Incubaceous,* 11 Incubaceous Willow The root is creeping The ſtalks are ſlender, ligneous, about two feet long, covered with a brown bark, and not ſo weak as to lie on the ground, nor yet ſtrong enough to ſupport themſelves in an upright poſition The leaves are ſpear-ſhaped, undivided, bright, and downy underneath The flowers come out in roundiſh ſpikes early in the ſpring, and are followed by downy ſeeds like the other ſorts

*and Thyme leaved Willow deſcribed* 12 Thyme-leaved Willow The ſtalks are herbaceous, weak, and about ſix inches in length The leaves are ſmall, oval, obtuſe, ſmooth, ſlightly ſerrated, and of a lucid green colour Among theſe, ſmall whitiſh flowers come out in the ſpring, which are ſucceeded by downy like the others

*Conſervations* It ought not to be underſtood, that the above-mentioned ſpecies are deſigned to mix in the flower-garden, or to join in any ornamental collection They are only enumerated to make it known that there are ſuch plants, and what they are, in order that any perſon may, if he pleaſes, propagate them in an appropriated ſpot for his obſervation and philoſophical inſpection And, indeed, where there is extent of room, a proper and remote place ſhould be aſſigned theſe and other ligneous uncultivated plants which will occur in the courſe of his work By this means a very large extent of the vegetable kingdom will be at hand, the wonders of the Almighty in a greater meaſure diſplayed, and the ſoul elevated to higher degrees of praiſe and thankſgiving

*Proper ſoil* A moiſt ſoil ſuits the moſt general part of them, particularly thoſe that grow in the northern parts of Europe And as it is not abſolutely neceſſary that this place ſhould be near to an habitation, there are few gentlemen who may not have it in their power to appropriate a proper ſpot for the culture and management of theſe hitherto uncultivated plants

Some, which will occur in the courſe of this work, require a ſandy ſituation, perhaps on the top of an high hill, or the declivity of a rock Such places ſhould be deſtined for thoſe plants that will flouriſh no-where elſe, whilſt a large ſhare, which will thrive only on bogs and low marſhy ground, ſhould have every part thereof ſacredly kept ſeparate, diveſted of all common trees and ſhrubs, and appropriated ſolely to the culture and management of ſuch boggy plants as grow naturally only in diſtant parts of England or foreign countries

Then, in the compaſs of a morning's walk in a gentleman's environs, the wild produce of the Alps of Lapland, and other northern parts, may be found to grow and abound, while the more enchanting flowering tribe are ſeen to glow in a well cultivated ſpot called the Pleaſure-garden, deſigned for conſtant obſervation and uſe

*Culture* The culture of the above-mentioned Willows is very eaſy Every ſlip or cutting will grow, if planted in the ſpring The roots alſo, if cut into pieces, and planted juſt beneath the ſurface of the earth, will ſhoot up, and ſoon become good plants But ſuch minute practices will be for the moſt part unneceſſary to be followed; for wherever they grow naturally, good plants may be taken up with roots at them, and theſe being ſet in a ſoil as ſimilar as poſſible to that they were taken from, commence ſpeedily the moſt perfect plants

The creeping ſpecies muſt have their roots reduced, and kept within bounds The trailers alſo muſt be ſupported, or their branches, lying on the ground, will ſtrike root, and ſoon ſpread too far They ſhould be conſtantly kept clean from weeds, that the plants may the better ſhew what they are Thus, with ſuch eaſy culture, may a ſight of theſe wild plants be had at any time for obſervation

1 Herbaceous Willow is titled, *Salix foliis ſerratis glabris orbiculatis* Caſpar Bauhine calls it, *Salix ſaxatilis minima*, Boccone, *Salix Alpina lucida repens, alni rotunda folio* It grows naturally on Snowdon Hill and in Weſtmoreland, alſo on the Alps of Lapland and Switzerland *Titles*

2 Myrſinite Willow is, *Salix foliis ſtrictis glabris ovatis venoſis* Haller calls it, *Salix myrtilli folio, ſpicâ craſſiſſimâ*, Scheuchzer, *Salix Alpina, foliis anguſtioribus ſplendentibus ſerratis*, and Tilli, *Salix Alpina pumila repens, foliis oblongis exiguis ſuperne ſplendentibus, inferne virentibus creberrimis & tenuiſſimis crenis* It grows naturally on the Alps of Lapland, Switzerland, and Italy

3 Lapland Willow is, *Salix foliis ſubſerratis glabris ſubdiaphanis ſubtus glaucis, caule ſuffruticoſo* In the *Flora Lapponica* it is termed, *Salix foliis ſerratis glabris obovatis*, alſo, *Salix foliis integris glabris ovatis confertis pellucidis*, alſo, *Salix foliis ſerratis glabris lanceolatis utrinque acutis* It grows naturally on the ſandy plains of Lapland

4 Round-leaved Dwarf Willow is, *Salix foliis integerrimis glabris ovatis obtuſis* In the *Flora Lapponica* it is termed, *Salix foliis integris glabris ovatis ſubtùs reticulatis.* John Bauhine calls it, *Salix pumila, folio rotundo*, and Haller, *Salix pumila, folio rotundo integerrimo, julo gracili* It grows naturally on the Alps of Lapland and Switzerland

5 Round-leaved Eared Willow is, *Salix foliis integerrimis utrinque villoſis obovatis appendiculatis* Dillenius calls it, *Salix folio rotundo* [illegible], and Ray, *Salix caprea pumila folio ſubrotundo, ſubtùs incano* The reſidence is chiefly in woods and hedges in England and moſt of the northern parts of Europe

6 Sand Willow is, *Salix foliis integris ovatis acutis, ſupra ſubvilloſis, ſubtùs tomentoſis* In the *Flora Lapponica* it is termed, *Salix foliis integris ſubtus villoſis ovatis acutis* Haller calls it, *Salix foliis integris utrinque hirſutis lanceolatis*, Caſpar Bauhine and Ray, *Salix pumila, foliis utrinquè candicantibus & lanuginoſis* It grows naturally in ſandy paſtures in England and moſt parts of Europe

7 Creeping Willow is, *Salix foliis integerrimis lanceolatis utrinquè ſubpiloſis, caule repente* Caſpar Bauhine calls it, *Salix pumila brevi anguſtoque folio incano*, alſo, *Salix Alpina pumila rotundifolia repens, inferne ſubcinerea*, John Bauhine, *Salix pumila anguſtifolia infernè lanuginoſa*; Cluſius, *Salix pumila latifolia I* and Parkinſon, *Salix humilis anguſtifolia repens* It grows naturally in moiſt places in England and Sweden

8 Brown Willow is, *Salix foliis integerrimis ovatis, ſubtus villoſis nitidis* John Bauhine calls it, *Salix pumila folio utrinque glabro*; Caſpar Bauhine, *Salix pumila linifolia incana*, Parkinſon, *Salix pumila anguſtifolia recta*, and Gerard, *Chamæ tea*,

*mæ .ea, five faux pum'a* It grows naturally in moift, heathy places in England and moft countries of Europe

9 Rofemary leaved Willow is, *Salix folus integerrimis lanceolato-linearibus fr ctis feffil. is fubtus tomentofis* Cafpar Bauhine calls it, *Salix humilis angustifolia*, Lobel, *Saux humi is repens angustifolia*, and Ray, *Salix pumila rhamni fecunda Clufii folio* It grows naturally in moift, mountainous parts in England and moft parts of Europe

10 Woolly-leaved Dwarf Willow is, *Sal x folus u'rinque lanatis fubrotundis acutis* Cafpar Bauhine calls it, *Salix humus latifolia erecta* In the *Flora Lappon ca* it is termed, *Salix folus n tegris fubtus villofis lanceolato-ovatis utr nque acutis* It grows naturally on the Alps of Lapland

11 Incubaceous Willow is *Sal x folus integerrimis lanceolatis, fubt is villofis nitidis, ftipulis ovatis acutis* Van Royen calls it, *Sal x fol is ovato-lanceolatis integerrimis, ramis decumben ib us, radice reptatrice*, Guettard, *Salix folus integris ovatis aliquot linearum longis, caulibus vix affurgentibus*, and Haller, *Salix pumila, folus ellipticis integerrim.s, fubtus glaucis, fpicâ rotundiore* It grows naturally in watery places in moft parts of Europe

# CHAP. CCCXC.

## *SALSOLA*, GLASS-WORT.

THERE are two perennials of this genus, called,

Species 1 Spanifh Glafs wort

2 Proftrate Afiatic Glafs wort

Defcription of Spanifh 1 Spanifh Glafs-wort The ftalks are ligneous, jointed, perennial, branching, and grow to about a yard high The leaves are oval, flefhed, acute-pointed, hoary, and grow in clufters from the fides of the branches The flowers grow from the upper parts of the branches between the leaves, they are very fmall, having no petals, but the feeds which fucceed them are large, fpiral, and covered by the leaves of the calyx

and Proftrate Afiatic Glafs wort 2 Proftrate Afiatic Glafs-wort The ftalks are ligneous, branching, and, unlefs fupported, lie on the ground The leaves are narrow, hairy, and have no prickles The flowers grow in roundifh clufters from the fides of the branches, but they are fmall, and of no figure

Method of propagating them Both fpecies are propagated by the flips or cuttings in the fpring Thefe fhould be fet in pots filled with light, fandy earth, and the pots muft be immediately plunged up to the rims in a fhady part of the garden In the autumn they fhould be removed into fhelter for their winter lodging, and in the fpring turned out of the pots, with the mould at the roots, into the places where they are defigned to remain

The foil fhould be naturally dry, light, and fandy, and the fituation well defended, otherwife they will be liable to be deftroyed by our frofts On this account it would be advifeable to keep a plant or two of each fpecies in the pots, to be preferved in the green-houfe through the winter, to be ready to afford a frefh ftock, fhould the others be killed by the frofts Proper foil and fituation

1 Spanifh Glafs-wort is titled, *Salfola fru tefcens, folus ovatis acutis carnofis* Lœfling calls it, *Salfola fruticofa, floribus fpicatis alternis folitarus*, Buxbaum, *Kali fruticofum, ericæ folio*, and Barrelier, *Kali geniculatum aphyllanthes, galvis paleacei s flofculis, Hifpanicum* It is a native of Spain Titles

2 Proftrate Afiatic Glafs-wort is, *Salfola frutefcens proftrata, folus linearibus pilofis inermibus* Lœfling calls it, *Salfola lignofa, ramis filiformibus adfcendentibus, floribus conglomerato-fpicatis* It grows naturally in Afia and Spain

L

CHAP.

# CHAP CCCXCI.

## *SALVIA*, SAGE

Introduction

THE Common Sage of our kitchen-gardens is univerſally known, and its virtues are ſo great as to cauſe the culture of it to become general, there being very few gardens where Sage is not to be found

The other ſpecies of this genus are commonly found in gardens deſigned for a general collection of plants, and in theſe the following perennials may be expected viz

Species

1 Common Engliſh Wild Clary, or *Oculus Chriſti*
2 Meadow Clary
3 Tuberous-rooted Clary
4 Auſtrian Wild Clary
5 Syrian Wild Clary
6 Glutinous Clary
7 Indian Sage

Deſcription of the Common Engliſh Wild Clary

1 The Common Engliſh Wild Clary, or *Oculus Chriſti*, hath ſeveral ſlender, ſquare, hairy ſtalks, about a foot long The leaves are rough, ſinuated, and of a dark green colour, the lower ones have moderately long footſtalks, while thoſe that garniſh the upper parts of the plant join the ſtalks with their baſe The flowers are produced from the tops of the branches in whorled ſpikes, a principal ſpike terminates each ſtalk, whilſt two or three ſide ſpikes are produced from the wings of the leaves a little lower They are ſmall, of a blue colour, appear in June and July, and are ſucceeded by ripe ſeeds in Auguſt and September The ſeeds of each flower are four in number, ſitting in the calyx; they are round, of a blackiſh colour, and are very powerful in clearing of the eye, when injured by any-thing falling into it

Method of uſing the ſeeds to clear the eye

The uſual method of relief is, by putting of the ſeed into one corner of the eye, keeping the eye lid cloſe down, and gently moving the ſeed to the moth or duſt that may have happened there, and the ſeed being poſſeſſed of a glutinous quality, whatever is in the eye will ſtick to it, and the cauſe of the diſagreeable ſenſation will be removed without the leaſt injury to that tender part

Meadow Clary deſcribed

2 Meadow Clary The ſtalks are ſquare, hairy, and about a foot high The leaves are heart-ſhaped, oblong, and deeply indented, thoſe on the lower part of the plant have moderately long, hairy footſtalks, but thoſe on the upper part embrace the ſtalk with their baſe The flowers terminate the branches in ſpikes, are of a blue colour, very ſweet, appear in June and July, and ripen their ſeeds in September

Its variety

There is a variety of this ſpecies with broad, obtuſe, hoary leaves, and large white flowers

Deſcription of Tuberous rooted,

3 Tuberous-rooted Clary The root is hung with tubers in the manner of Aſphodel The ſtalks are red, and grow to about two feet high The leaves are heart-ſhaped, oval, rough, and downy The flowers are blue, and contained in prickly cups

Auſtrian Wild,

4 Auſtrian Wild Clary This ſpecies grows to about a foot and a half high The leaves are ſpear-ſhaped in an heart-like manner, biſerrated, waved, and ſpotted The flowers are ſmall, appear in June or July, and ripen their ſeeds in the autumn

Syrian Wild

5 Syrian Wild Clary The ſtalks are hairy, and about a foot long The leaves are heart ſhaped, oblong, downy, rough, ſtrongly-ſcented, and appear as if eaten on the edges The flowers are white, have bilabiated cups, and ſtamina about the length of themſelves

and Glutinous Clary

6 Glutinous Clary The ſtalks are poſſeſſed of a glutinous matter that ſticks to the finger The leaves are glutinous, heart ſhaped, ſagittated, ſerrated, acute, of a yellowiſh green colour, and grow on footſtalks about four inches long The flowers are yellow, appear in July and ripen their ſeeds in Auguſt The whole plant is clammy, and very ſtrongly ſcented

Indian Clary deſcribed.

7 Indian Sage The ſtalk is four cornered, and riſes to four feet high The lower leaves are heart-ſhaped, long, and acutely crenated Thoſe on the upper parts of the ſtalks are ſmaller, and grow oppoſite by pairs at the joints, without any footſtalks Half the length of the ſtalk is adorned by the flowers, they grow in whorls at a conſiderable diſtance from each other, have no leaves under them, are of a blue colour, appear in May, and ripen their ſeeds in July

Method of propagation

All theſe ſpecies are eaſily propagated by parting of the roots, or ſowing of the ſeeds, the beſt time for both which works is the autumn, though the ſeeds will grow very well if kept until the ſpring They require no other culture than keeping them clean from weeds, and, when raiſed from ſeeds, thinning them where they come up too cloſe Moſt of the ſpecies, after they have once flowered, will ſhed their ſeeds, if you neglect cutting down the ſtalks before they are ripe, which will grow, and produce, perhaps, more plants than you would deſire The Indian ſpecies ſhould have a dry ſoil, and it will live through our winters, let the expoſure be what it will

Titles

1 Common Engliſh Clary is titled, *Salvia foliis ſerratis ſinuatis læviuſculis, corollis calyce anguſtioribus* In the *Hortus Cliffort* it is termed, *Salvia foliis pinnatim inciſis ſcabris* Caſpar Bauhine calls it, *Horminum ſylveſtre, lavendulæ flore*, Barrelier, *Horminum ſylveſtre minus, inciſo folio, flore azureo*, and Triumfetti, *Horminum, verbenacæ laciniis, anguſtifolium*, It grows naturally in England and many parts of Europe, alſo in the Eaſt.

2 Meadow Clary is, *Salvia foliis cordato oblongis, ſummis amplexicaulibus, verticillis ſubnudis, corollis galea glutinoſis* In the *Hortus Cliffort* it is termed, *Salvia foliis ovatis inciſo crenatis, verticillis ſubnudis* Caſpar Bauhine calls it, *Horminum pratenſe, foliis ſerratis* In the *Amœnitates Academicæ* a variety of this ſpecies ſtands with the title of, *Salvia agreſtis foliis cordatis, ſummis amplexicaulibus, corollarum galeâ labium æquante* Caſpar Bauhine calls this, *Horminum pratenſe niveum, foliis incanis*, It grows naturally in England and moſt countries of Europe

3 Tuberous rooted Clary is, *Salvia foliis cordato ovatis rugoſis tomentoſis, calycibus hiſpidis, radice tuberoſâ* Triumfetti calls it, *Horminum ſanguineum, aſphodeli radice*, Barrelier, *Horminum ſylveſtre*

*sylvestre majus haemotodis glabrum, flore caeruleo, Italicum* It is a native of Italy

4 Austrian Wild Clary is, *Salvia fol. s cordato lanceolatis undatis biserratis maculatis acutis, bracteis coloratis flore brevioribus* Caspar Bauhine calls it, *Horminum sylvestre salvifolium majus maculatum*, Clusius, *Horminum sylvestre V altera species* It grows naturally in Lower Austria and Bohemia

5 Syrian Wild Clary is, *Salviae foliis cordato-oblongis, erosis staminibus corollam aequantibus* Barrelier calls it, *Horminum sylvestre majus, flore albo, integris foliis* It grows naturally in Syria

6 Glutinous Clary is, *Salvia foliis cordato-sagittatis serratis acutis* Caspar Bauhine calls it, *Horminum luteum glutinosum*, and Clusius, *Horminum sylvestre secundum* It grows naturally in most parts of Europe

7 Indian Sage is *Salvia foliis cordatis acute crenatis, summis sessilibus verticillis subnudis, remotissimis* Tournefort calls it, *Sclarea Indica, floribus variegatis* It is a native of India

*Salvia* is of the class and order *Diandria Monogynia*, and the characters are,

Class and order in the Linnæan system. The characters

1 Calyx is a tubulous, striated, monophyllous perianthium, wide at the mouth, bilabiated, and erect

2 Corolla is a single petal The tube towards the upper part is large and compressed The limb is ringent The upper lip is concave, compressed, incurved, and indented The lower lip is broad and trifid, the middle segment being large, roundish, and indented

3 Stamina are two very short filaments split into two parts, one of which is longer than the other, lies under the upper lip of the flower, and supports the anthera, the other is shorter, and has an obtuse head

4 Pistillum consists of a quadrifid germen, a filiforme long style of the situation of the stamina, and a bifid stigma

5 Pericarpium There is none The seeds are contained in the calyx

6 Semina The seeds are roundish, and four in number

# CHAP. CCCXCII.

## *SAMBUCUS*, ELDER.

THERE is one herbaceous species of this genus, called *Ebulus*, Dwarf Elder, Wallwort, or Dove-wort, and it admits of two principal varieties, viz

Common Dwarf Elder

Jagged leaved Dwarf Elder

Common Common Dwarf Elder The root is strong, thick, tough, creeping, and soon spreads itself to a considerable distance The stalks are thick, a little woody, green, striated, full of pith, and grow to be three or four feet high The leaves are large, pinnated, and much resemble those of the Common Elder-tree The folioles are very long, indented, sharp-pointed, and of a deep-green colour, their number is about six or seven pair, which are placed opposite along the midrib, besides the odd one with which they are terminated, and they are very strongly and disagreeably scented The flowers come out in umbels from the ends of the stalks, they are large, spreading, of a fine white colour, though often tipped or spotted with red, appear in July, and are succeeded by black berries which will be ripe in the autumn

and Jagged leaved Dwarf Elder described

Jagged leaved Dwarf Elder This is not so strong a plant as the former The root is smaller, and less creeping, the stalks are more slender, and of lower growth, the leaves are not so large, and their edges are beautifully cut, jagged, or divided into narrow segments The flowers are white, terminate the stalks in large spreading umbels in July, and are succeeded by black berries, which will be ripe in the autumn.

Medicinal properties of it

This plant is admirable in dropsies, and frequently gives ease in the gout It is a fine diuretic, aperient, and of great efficacy in freeing the body from all watery, as well as ill and unwholesome humours The roots and berries are chiefly used and taken inwardly for these purposes, whilst the leaves, used as a cataplasm, are good for taking down hard swellings, &c and are admirable in fomentations for swellings and hurts of all kinds

Method of propagation

Both sorts are easily propagated by parting of the roots, the best time for which is the autumn Every oit will grow, and no soil or situation comes amiss to them The greatest difficulty will be to keep them within bounds, especially the first sort For this purpose, the offsets should be regularly dug up as they arise, and once every two years or every third year at farthest, the whole should be dug up, and any desired number of plants set at a yard distance from each other, if required for use, otherwise two plants of either sort will be sufficient for variety and observation

Titles

*Ebulus*, or the Dwarf Elder, is titled, *Sambucus cymis trifidis, stipulis foliaceis, caule herbaceo* In the *Flora Suecia* it is termed, *Sambucus caule herbaceo simplici* Caspar Bauhine calls it, *Sambucus humilis, s Ebulus*, also, *Sambucus humilis, s Ebulus folio laciniato* Gerard and Parkinson call it, *Ebulus sive sambucus humilis*, and Fuchsius, *Ebulus* It grows naturally in hedges and by way-sides in England and most parts of Europe

## C H A P. CCCXCIII

## *SAMOLUS*, ROUND-LEAVED WATER PIMPERNEL.

OF this genus there is only one species, called, Round-leaved Water Pimpernel

This plant described — The root consists of a number of thick, white fibres The stalk is round, smooth, upright, and about a foot high The radical leaves are shaped like those of the common Daisy, but those on the stalks are shorter, rounder, and grow alternately, they are of a thickish substance, smooth, entire, and of a pale-green colour The flowers come out in kind of loose spikes from the tops of the stalks, they are of a white colour, appear in June and July, and the seeds ripen in August

Culture — Whoever is inclined to propagate this plant, may easily effect it by sowing the seeds, soon after they are ripe, or the spring following, in some moist part of the garden After the plants come up, they will require no trouble, except thinning them where they are too close, watering in dry weather, and keeping them clean from weeds The second summer they will flower, and perfect their seeds, soon after which the plants generally die; but if the seeds are permitted to scatter, fresh ones for a succession will arise without further trouble

Titles. — There being no other species of this genus, it is named simply, *Samolus* Caspar Bauhine calls it, *Anagallis aquatica, rotundo folio non crenato*, Morison, *Alsine aquatica, foliis rotundis beccabungæ*, John Bauhine, *Samolus Valerandi*, Gerard, *Anagallis aquatica rotundifolia*, and Parkinson, *Anagallis aquatica 3 Lob fol o subrotundo non crenato* It grows naturally in watery places in England, and most parts of Europe, Asia, and America

Class and order in the Linnæan system. Linnæan characters — *Samolus* is of the class and order *Pentandria Monogynia*, and the characters are,

1 CALYX is a perianthium situated above the germen, obtuse at the base, and divided into five upright permanent segments

2 COROLLA is one hypocrateriform petal, the tube is short, patulous, and the length of the calyx, the limb is plane, and divided into five obtuse parts, having at the base of the sinus five very short connivent squammulæ

3 STAMINA are five very short filaments, one being placed between each segment of the petal, with connivent covered antheræ

4 PISTILLUM consists of a germen situated below the receptacle, a filiforme style the length of the stamina, and a capitated stigma

5 PERICARPIUM is an oval unilocular capsule surrounded by the calyx

6 SEMINA The seeds are many, oval, and small

The receptacle is round and large

## C H A P. CCCXCIV

## *SANGUINARIA*, PUCCOON.

THERE is only one species of this genus, usually called Puccoon

This plant described — The root is tuberous, hung with many fibres, of a dirty-brown colour on the outside, and yellowish within The leaves are large, roundish, cut or indented on their edges, of a greyish-green colour, and grow on moderately long footstalks The stalk is slender, low, naked, and usually reddish near the ground The flowers come out singly from the tops of the stalks, they are large, of a pure white colour, appear in April and May, and the seeds ripen in July

Varieties — There is a variety of this species with semi-double, and another with full double flowers, in high esteem with the curious

Its propagation — This plant is propagated by parting of the roots, the best time for which is July, when the leaves and stalks decay They will grow in any soil, but should have a shady situation, in order to continue the flowers the longer in blow, and after they are set out, they will require no trouble, except keeping them clean from weeds

They may also be raised by seeds, but this is a tedious method, as they will be four or five years before they come into blow this way, nevertheless, by experiments of this nature fresh varieties are often obtained, which will recompense the patient horticultor for the exercise of that virtue

The root, leaves, and stalk, are full of a yellowish

lowish juice, of a strong disagreeable smell, with which the Indians paint themselves

Titles. There being no other species of this genus, it is named simply, *Sanguinaria*. Cornutus calls it, *Chelidonium majus Canadense acaulon*, Parkinson, *Ranunculus Virginiensis albus*, Dillenius, *Sanguinaria minor, flore simplici*, also, *Sanguinaria major, flore simplici*, also, *Sanguinaria major, flore pleno*. It grows naturally in North America.

Class and order in the Linnæan System. *Sanguinaria* is of the class and order *Polyandria Monogynia*, and the characters are,

The characters. 1 CALYX is a two-leaved, oval, concave, caducous perianthium, shorter than the corolla

2 COROLLA is eight oblong, obtuse, spreading petals

3 STAMINA are many simple filaments shorter than the corolla, having simple antheræ

4 PISTILLUM consists of an oblong compressed germen, without any style, but a thick, bisulcated, permanent stigma

5 PERICARPIUM is an oblong ventricose capsule, formed of two valves, and pointed at each end

6 SEMINA. The seeds are many, roundish, and acuminated.

## CHAP. CCCXCV.

# *SANGUISORBA*, GREATER WILD BURNET.

THERE are only three species of this genus, called,

Species.
1 Common English Wild Burnet
2 Greater American Wild Burnet
3 Lesser American Wild Burnet

English Wild Burnet described. 1 English Wild Burnet. The root is composed of many long thick fibres, of an acrid bitter in taste. The leaves are pinnated, each being composed of five or six pair of oblong, pointed, serrated, smooth, glossy folioles, arranged by pairs along the midrib, and terminated by an odd one. The stalks are upright, round, striated, branching, three feet high, and adorned with leaves like the radical ones, but smaller, growing alternately at a considerable distance from each other. The flowers come out from the ends of the branches in thick, close, oval spikes; they are of a brown colour, appear in June and July, and the seeds ripen in August.

Its variety. There is a variety of this plant of larger growth, and ... ... leaves.

Greater American Wild Burnet described. 2 Greater American Wild Burnet. The root is thick, long and of a whitish colour. The leaves are pinnated, and the radical ones more than a foot long; each consists of eight or ten pair of heart-shaped, oblong, serrated folioles terminated by an odd one. The stalk is upright, firm, branching, four feet high, and adorned with a few small leaves placed alternately. The flowers come out from the ends of the branches in long spikes; they are of a greenish white colour, appear in July, and the seeds ripen in September.

Variety. There is a variety of this species with red flowers.

Lesser American Wild Burnet described. 3 Lesser American Wild Burnet. The leaves are composed of five or six pair of smooth folioles terminated by an odd one. The stalks are upright, smooth, branching, and about two feet high. The flowers come out from the ends of the branches in short cylindrical spikes; they are of a red colour, appear in July, and the seeds ripen in August and September.

Method of propagation. These sorts are easily raised by sowing the seeds in the autumn, soon after they are ripe. Many of the plants will come up before winter, the others in the spring, soon after which they must be thinned where they come up too close. All summer they must be kept clean from weeds, watered in dry weather, in the autumn they may be removed to the places where they are designed to remain; and the next summer they will flower and perfect their seeds.

They are also easily propagated by parting of the roots, which is best effected in the autumn, though it may be done successfully in the winter, or early in the spring, before the stalks arise. They are extremely hardy, and thrive best in a cold moist soil, and a shady situation.

Titles. 1 The first species is entitled, *Sanguisorba spicis ovatis*. Caspar Bauhine calls it, *Pimpinella sanguisorba major*; John Bauhine, *Sanguisorba major flore spadiceo*, also *Sanguisorba minor*. Dodonæus, *Pimpinella sylvestris, sive Sanguisorba major*; Gerard, *Pimpinella sylvestris*; Parkinson, *Pimpinella major vulgaris*; and Boccone, *Pimpinella major rigida parvâ et triculata subnuda*. It grows naturally in meadows and some moist pastures in England, and most parts of Europe.

2 The second species is, *Sanguisorba spicis longissimis*. Morison calls it, *Pimpinella sanguisorba Canadensis major, spicâ longiore albâ*; and Cornutus, *Pimpinella maxima Canadensis longius spicata*. It grows naturally in Canada.

3 The third species is, *Sanguisorba spicis cylindricis*. Zinn calls it, *Sanguisorba tetrastemon, staminibus tubo longioribus, spicis cylindricis*; Zanoni, *Pimpinella minor de Canadà*; and Morison, *Pimpinella Canadensis major, spicâ breviore rubrâ, foliis lævibus*. It grows naturally in Canada.

Class and order in the Linnæan system. *Sanguisorba* is of the class and order *Tetrandria Monogynia*, and the characters are,

The characters. 1 CALYX is a perianthium composed of two very short caducous leaves placed opposite to each other

2 COROLLA

2 Corolla is one rotated petal divided into four oval obtuse segments, which cohere at their base

3 Stamina are four filaments the length of the corolla, broadest near the top having small roundish antheræ

4 Pistillum consists of a four-cornered germen placed between the calyx and the corolla, a very short filiforme style, and an obtuse stigma

5 Pericarpium is a small capsule containing two cells

6 Semina The seeds are small

# CHAP. CCCXCVI.

## *SANICULA*, SANICLE.

THERE are three species of this genus, called,

Species

1 Common Sanicle
2 Maryland Sanicle
3 Canada Sanicle

Description of Common Sanicle

1 Common Sanicle The root is composed of many fibres, of a black colour on the outside, and white within The radical leaves are simple, roundish, divided into five principal parts, of a dark-green colour, and grow on long footstalks The stalks are round, smooth, of a brownish colour, divide into a few branches near the top, and are about a foot high The flowers come out in small tufts or umbels from the ends of the branches, they are of a white colour, appear in May and June, and the seeds ripen in August

Variety

There is a variety of this species with pale flesh-coloured flowers

Its virtues

This species is held as a good vulnerary, and much recommended for diet drinks, decoctions, and vulnerary potions for the cure of wounds or inward hurts of most sorts

Maryland

2 Maryland Sanicle The root of this species also is black, and hung with many fibres The radical leaves are large, roundish, divided into seven unequal lobes, serrated on their edges, and grow on long slender footstalks The stalks are round, upright, of a purplish-brown colour, glossy, and divide into branches by pairs near the top The flowers come out in small umbels from the ends and divisions of the branches, they are small, and consist of male flowers and hermaphrodites, the male flowers having footstalks, but the hermaphrodites none, they appear in June and July, and the seeds ripen in the autumn

and Canada Sanicle described

3 Canada Sanicle The leaves are large, and divided into many parts, the radical ones grow on long footstalks The stalks are round, upright, brownish, divide into a few branches near the top, and are two or three feet high The flowers come out in small tufts or bunches from the ends of the branches, they are of a white colour, appear in June and July, and the seeds ripen in the autumn

Culture

These plants are all propagated by parting the roots or sowing the seeds The roots may be parted any time in the autumn, winter, or early in the spring before the stalks arise, and the seeds may be sown as soon as they are ripe, or the spring following After they come up, they must be thinned where they are too close, duly watered in dry weather, and kept clean from weeds In the autumn they may be removed to the places where they are designed to remain, and the summer following they will flower, and perfect their seeds They will grow in almost any soil or situation, but delight chiefly in moisture and the shade

Titles.

1 Common Sanicle is titled, *Sanicula foliis radicalibus simplicibus, flosculis omnibus sessilibus* In the *Hortus Cliffort* it is termed simply, *Sanicula* Gronovius calls it, *Sanicula flosculis omnibus sessilibus*, Caspar Bauhine, *Sanicula officinarum*, Camerarius, *Diapensia*, Gerard, *Sanicula, sive diapensia*, and Parkinson, *Sanicula vulgaris, sive diapensia* It grows naturally in woods and under hedges in England, and most countries of Europe

2 Maryland Sanicle is, *Sanicula flosculis masculis pedunculatis, hermaphroditis sessilibus* In the *Hortus Upsal* it is named, *Sanicula foliis septilobatis inæqualibus, flosculis masculis pedunculatis* Ray calls it, *Sanicula Marilandica, caule et ramulis dichotomis, echinis minimis in eodem communi pediculo ternis* It grows naturally in Maryland and Virginia

3 Canada Sanicle is, *Sanicula foliis radicalibus compositis, foliolis ovatis* Tournefort calls it, *Sanicula Canadensis, amplissimo laciniato folio* It grows naturally in Virginia and Canada.

Class and order in the Linnæan system

*Sanicula* is of the class and order *Pentandria Digynia*, and the characters are,

The characters

1 Calyx The general umbel is composed of about four rays only, the partial of numerous ones, clustered together, and collected into a roundish head

The general involucrum surrounds only the outside, the partial surrounds the whole, and is shorter than the florets The perianthium is very small

2 Corolla The general flower is uniform, and each floret has five compressed inflexed petals

3 Stamina are five simple erect filaments twice the length of the florets, having roundish antheræ

4 Pistillum

4 PISTILLUM consists of a hilod germen situated b lo th receptacl , d two awl shaped reflexed styles with acute stigmas

5 PERICARPIUM There is non The fl is oval, acute, rough, and divided into two parts

6 SEMINA The seeds are two, convex and situated on one side, and plane on the other

# CHAP CCCXCVII

## SANTOLINA, LAVENDER-COTTON

THERE are of this genus called,

Species 1 Common Lavender Cotton

2 Rosemary leaved Lavender-Cotton

3 Chamomile leaved Lavender-Cotton

4 Alpine Lavender Cotton

Common Lavender Cotton described 1 Common Lavender Cotton The stalk is woody, two feet high, and divides into several ligneous tough, slender, whitish branches The leaves are long, slender, whitish, strongly scented, and quadrifariously indented The flowers come out singly from the tops of the branches on long naked footstalks; they are of a yellow colour, appear in June and July, and the seeds ripen in September

Its virtues The seeds, leaves, and flowers of this plant kill worms in children, and are useful against poisonous serpents and venomous beasts.

Rosemary leaved Lavender-Cotton described 2 Rosemary leaved Lavender-Cotton There are several varieties of this species, differing in the height, colour of the leaves, or in some other respect or other The stalks are woolly, branching, and in some varieties not more than a foot, in others upwards of a yard in height The leaves are hoary, narrow, in some sorts long, and in others short, some are hoary to a degree of whiteness, others are green, and closely arranged, and others are more loosely disposed on the branches The flowers come out singly on footstalks from the upper parts of the plant, they are yellow in its different stages, some being of a very pale yellow, straw or sulphur colour, and others of a deep bright yellow, they appear in July and August, and the seeds ripen in the autumn

Culture These two sorts are easily propagated by planting of the slips in any of the summer months, they should be duly watered and shaded at first, and in the spring following removed to the places where they are designed to remain They are often introduced into the evergreen wilderness-quarters, amongst the lowest shrubs, where, by their hoary leaves, and other singularities, they have a pretty effect, if they are judiciously arranged, and properly kept trimmed, in order to shew them to advantage

They may also be propagated by sowing the seeds, in the spring, in any border of common mould made fine After they come up, they should be constantly kept clean from weeds, and watered in dry weather, and in July or August, according as they are in forwardness, should be pricked out in the nursery at a few inches asunder, and in spring following the strongest plants may be removed to the places where they are to remain, whilst the weakest may stand longer, to grow to a proper size, before they are planted out for good

Chamomile leaved, 3 Chamomile-leaved Lavender Cotton The stalk is herbaceous, hairy, divides into numerous branches, and is eight or ten inches high The leaves are downy, and composed of many narrow segments in the manner of those of Chamomile The flowers come out singly from the ends of the branches on long footstalks, they are of a yellow colour, appear in July and August, and the seeds ripen in the autumn

and Alpine Lavender Cotton described. 4 Alpine Lavender Cotton The stalks are unbranching, herbaceous, and eight or ten inches high The leaves are bipinnated, of a glaucous colour and in some sorts very white and hoary The flowers come out singly from the tops of the stalks, they are of a yellow colour, appear in July, and the seeds ripen in the autumn

Culture These two sorts are propagated by parting of the roots, the best time for which is the early part of the autumn that they may be established before the frost comes on

They may be also propagated by sowing the seed in the spring When the plants come up, they should be thinned where they are too close, kept clean from weeds all summer, frequently watered in dry weather, and on the first autumnal rain should be removed to their final destination, observing to preserve a ball of earth to each root, and to be assiduous in other necessary precautions which are peculiar to careful gardeners

Titles 1 Common Lavender-Cotton is titled, *Santolina pedunculis unifloris, foliis quadrifariam dentatis*. Caspar Bauhine calls it *Abrotanum fœmina, foliis teretibus*, Camerarius, *Abrotanum fœmina vulgare*, and others, *Chamæcyparissus* It grows naturally in most of the southern countries of Europe

2 Rosemary leaved Lavender Cotton is *Santolina pedunculis unifloris, foliis linearibus integris tuberculatis* Clusius calls it *Abrotanum fœmina 4*; and Caspar Bauhine, *Abrotanum fœmina, foliis rosmarini, majus*, also, *Abrotanum fœmina, foliis rosmarini, minus*, also, *Abrotanum fœmina viride*, also, *Abrotanum fœmina, flore majore, foliis villosis et incanis* It grows naturally in Spain

3 Chamomile leaved Lavender-Cotton is, *Santolina pedunculis unifloris, foliis bipinnatis, caule ramosissimo villoso*. Vaillant calls it, *Santolina perennis, chamæmeli folio, caule ramoso* It grows naturally in Italy and Spain

4 Alpine Lavender-Cotton is, *Santolina pedunculis unifloris, foliis bipinnatis, caulibus simplicibus*



Micheli

Micheli calls it, *Santolinoides Alpina saxatilis, foliis glaucis et veluti argenteis, floribus luteis*, and Barrelier, *Pyrethrum alterum minus, cespitosâ radice, anthemidis flore, Italicum* It grows naturally on the mountainous parts of Italy

Class and order in the Linnæan system The characters

*Santolina* is of the class and order *Syngenesia Polygamia Æqualis*, and the characters are,

1 CALYX The general calyx is hemispherical and imbricated, the scales are oval, oblong, acute, and appressed

2 COROLLA The compound flower is uniform, and longer than the calyx The hermaphrodite florets are numerous, equal, funnel-shaped, and cut at the top into five revolute segments

3 STAMINA are five very short capillary filaments, having a cylindrical tubular anthera

4 PISTILLUM consists of a tetragonous oblong germen, a filiforme style the length of the stamina, and two oblong, depressed, truncated stigmas

5 PERICARPIUM There is none

6 SEMINA The seeds are single, oblong, four cornered, and have no down

The receptacle is paleaceous, and almost plane. The paleæ are concave

# CHAP CCCXCVIII

## SAPONARIA, SOPE-WORT.

Species

THE perennials of this genus are,

1 Common Sope wort
2 Ocymoide Sope wort
3 Yellow Sope-wort

Common Sope wort described

1 Common Sope-wort The root is creeping, jointed, reddish on the outside, and soon spreads itself to a considerable distance The stalks are round, smooth, jointed, thick, and two or three feet high The leaves are oval, spear-shaped, pointed, smooth, have three longitudinal ribs on the under-side, and grow opposite to each other at the joints The flowers come out from the tops of the stalks in kind of umbels, they are of a whitish-red or purplish colour, appear in July, and often continue in succession until the end of summer

Its varieties

There is a variety of this species with double flowers, another with concave leaves, short, thick, swelling joints, and purple flowers

Medicinal properties of this plant

The root and leaves of this species are used in medicine The root is held aperient, corroborant, and sudorific The leaves also have their sanative qualities, and being boiled in water afford a sope like froth, nearly of equal goodness with the solution of real sope for washing or cleansing of cloaths

Ocymoide

2 Ocymoide Sope-wort The root is thick, whitish, and creeping The stalks are jointed, divide by pairs, and unless supported lie on the ground The leaves are narrow, pointed, of a pale-green colour, and grow opposite to each other at the joints The flowers come out in kind of umbels from the tops of the stalks, they are of a whitish-red or purplish colour, and grow in hairy cylindrical cups, they appear in July, and frequently continue in succession until the end of summer

and Yellow Sope-wort described

3 Yellow Sope wort The stalks are jointed, partly procumbent, and eight or ten inches long The leaves are narrow, channelled, and grow opposite to each other at the joints The flowers come out in umbels from the tops of the stalks, they are of a yellow colour, having black filaments, appear in July and August, and frequently in September and October

Method

All these sorts are propagated by parting of the roots, the best time for which is the autumn, though it may be done successfully at any season of the year, they are extremely hardy but thrive best in cold, moist, shady places and, after they are set out require no trouble, except keeping them clean from weeds, and reducing the roots as often as they spread too far

Titles

1 Common Sope-wort is entitled, *Saponaria calycibus cylindricis, foliis ovato lanceolatis*. Camerarius calls it, *Saponaria vulgaris*, Caspar Bauhine, *Saponaria major lævis*, also, *Saponaria concava Anglica*, John Bauhine, *Gentiana folio convoluto*, Ray, *Lychnis saponaria dicta*, also, *Lychnis saponaria dicta, folio convoluto*, Gerard, simply, *Saponaria*, and Parkinson, *Saponaria vulgaris* It grows naturally in England and some middle countries of Europe

2 The second species is, *Saponaria calycibus cylindricis villosis, caulibus dichotomis procumbentibus* Caspar Bauhine calls it, *Lychnis vel Ocymoides repens montanum* and John Bauhine, *Saponaria minor quibusdam* It grows naturally in Helvetia, Italy, and the south of France

3 The third species is, *Saponaria calycibus teretibus, corollis coronatis, floribus subumbellatis, foliis sublinearibus canaliculatis* Allion calls it, *Lychnis floribus umbellatis ochroleucis, petalis ovatis, filamentis nigris*, Columna, *Globularia lutea montana*, Caspar Bauhine, *Bellis montana globoso luteo flore*, Barrelier, *Lychnis lutea montana, globulariæ capite & facie*, and Boccone, *Lychnis rubra, globulariæ capitulo* It grows naturally on the Alps

Class and order in the Linnæan system The characters

*Saponaria* is of the class and order *Decandria Digynia*, and the characters are,

1 CALYX is a monophyllous tubular, permanent perianthium, indented in five parts at the top

2 COROLLA is five petals The ungues are narrow, angular, and the length of the calyx, the limb is plane, broad, and obtuse

3 STAMINA are ten awl-shaped filaments the length

length of the tube of the corolla, and inserted alternately into the ungues of the petals, having oblong, obtuse, incumbent antheræ

4. PISTILLUM consists of a taper germen, and two straight parallel styles the length of the stamina, with acute stigmas

5 PERICARPIUM is a cylindrical covered capsule the length of the calyx, containing one cell

6 SEMINA The seeds are many, and small. The receptacle is free.

## CHAP. CCCXCIX.

## *SARRACENIA*, SIDE-SADDLE FLOWER

THERE are only two species of this genus, called,

Species 1 Purple *Sarracenia*

2 Yellow *Sarracenia*

Purple, 1 Purple *Sarracenia* The root is fibrous, and strikes deep into the ground The leaves are large, hollowed like pitchers, irregularly swelling or bunched behind, of a firm substance, beginning from a small base, and widening by degrees to the neck in an upright position, and are capable of holding a considerable quantity of water Among the leaves rise the flower-stalks, which are round, naked, upright, and a foot and a half or two feet high The flowers grow singly on the tops of the stalks, they are large, of a fine purple colour, and hang drooping, they appear in June, and the seeds ripen in the autumn

and Yellow Sarracenia described 2 Yellow *Sarracenia* The leaves are numerous from a strong root, hollow, stand on a slender base, widen gradually to the top, and grow to be three feet high The stalks are naked, and two or three feet high The flowers grow singly on the tops of the stalks, they are of a yellow colour, appear in June and July, and the seeds sometimes ripen in the autumn

Variety There is a variety of this species with green flowers

These plants are much admired for the great singularity of their leaves and flowers, but as they are natives of moist, rotten, boggy places in America, they are with some difficulty preserved in our gardens The most speedy way of procuring them is from America, where tubs should be ready to be filled with the contiguous mould of the plants, and the plants then taken up with as much mould as possible to the roots, when they will grow, and suffer little from the removal From this time they must be constantly watered, and when the plants arrive in England, they may be turned out of the tubs, with the mould at the roots, into the places where they are designed to remain

Proper soil and situation Their situation in England should be in a soft, black, rotten, spongy earth, in a low vale well sheltered with hedges and trees It is observable, that in such places very hard frosts have little effect on them These are the places for our *Sarracenia*, but as frost is a fatal enemy to them, when such weather threatens they should have an additional guard of furze bushes, or some covering, to keep it out; and with that protection they will live and flower many years

For want of such a situation the plants may be continued in the tubs, or whatever they are planted in, set in the shade, constantly watered in summer, and in winter protected from frost by a hotbed frame, or some cover, and in this manner they may be preserved many years

1 The first species is titled, *Sarracenia foliis gibbis* Catesby calls it, *Sarracena foliis brevioribus latioribus*, Morison, *Coilophyllum Virginianum, breviore folio, flore purpurascente*, Plukenet, *Bucanephyllum Americanum limonio congener dictum*, and Caspar Bauhine, *Limonium peregrinum, foliis forma floris aristolochiæ* It grows in most parts of North America Titles

2 The second species is, *Sarracenia foliis strictis* In the *Hortus Cliffort* it is termed, *Sarracena foliis rectis* Catesby calls it, *Sarracena foliis longioribus & angustioribus*, Morison, *Coilophyllum Virginianum, longiore folio erecto, flore luteo*, Plukenet, *Bucanephyllum elatius Virginianum, Limonio congeneris altera species elatior, foliis triplo longioribus*, and John Bauhine, *Thuris limpidi folium* It is found in most parts of North America

*Sarracenia* is of the class and order *Polyandria Monogynia*, and the characters are, Class and order in the Linnæan system

1 CALYX is a double perianthium The lower one is composed of three very small, oval, deciduous leaves, the upper one is composed of five large, suboval, coloured, deciduous leaves The characters

2 COROLLA is five oval inflexed petals covering the stamina, having oval, oblong, straight ungues

3 STAMINA are numerous small filaments, with simple antheræ

4 PISTILLUM consists of a roundish germen, a very short cylindrical style, and a clypeated, peltated, quinquangular, permanent stigma covering the stamina

5 PERICARPIUM is a roundish capsule, containing five cells

6 SEMINA The seeds are many, roundish, acuminated, and small

CHAP.

# CHAP. CCCC.

## *SATUREJA*, SAVORY.

Species

HERE comes of course,
1. Winter Savory.
2. Virginian Savory.

Winter,

1. Winter Savory. This plant rises with shrubby branching stalks to the height of about a foot. The leaves are narrow, and grow many together at the joints. The flowers are produced from the wings of the leaves on short footstalks; their colour is white, with a reddish tint; they appear in June, and ripen their seeds in the autumn.

and Virginian Savory described.

2. Virginian Savory. This plant rises with a stiff, erect, angular, branching stalk, to the height of about a foot and a half. The leaves are spear-shaped, stiff, pointed, and smell like Pennyroyal. The flowers terminate the stalks in roundish heads; their colour is white; they appear in July; and sometimes (though not very common) ripen their seed in the autumn.

Culture.

These sorts are easily propagated by planting the slips in any of the summer months; they should be shaded and watered until they have taken root, and afterwards they will require no further trouble except keeping them clean from weeds. They require a dry soil, to resist our severest winters, and thus stationed, they are liable to be hurt by no weather.

Title.

1. Winter Savory is titled, *Satureja pedunculis dichotomis lateralibus solitariis, foliis lineari-lanceolatis mucronatis*. In the *Hortus Cliffortianus* it is termed, *Melissa foliis linearibus integerrimis*. Caspar Bauhine calls it, *Satureja montana*; and Rivinus, *Satureja perennis*. It grows naturally in Italy, and the South of France.

2. Virginian Savory is, *Satureja capitulis terminalibus, foliis lanceolatis*. In the *Hortus Cliffortianus* it is termed, *Clinopodium foliis lanceolatis acuminatis, capitulis terminalibus*. Hermann calls it, *Satureja Virginiana*. Morison, *Pulegium erectum Virginianum angustifolium, floribus in cymis dispositis*; Plukenet, *Clinopodium, pulegii angustifolio rigidiore folio, Virginianum flosculis in cymis dispositis*; and Boccone, *Origanum Virginiana*. It grows naturally in Virginia.

Class and order in the Linnæan system.

*Satureja* is of the class and order *Didynamia Gymnospermia*; and the characters are,

1. CALYX is a monophyllous, tubulous, striated, erect, permanent perianthium, indented at the top into five unequal erect segments.

2. COROLLA is a ringent petal. The tube is cylindrical, and shorter than the calyx; the faux is simple; the upper lip is erect, obtuse, acutely indented, and of the same length as the lower lip; the lower lip is patent, and divided into three obtuse segments, of which the middle one is rather the largest.

3. STAMINA are four setaceous distant filaments the length of the upper lip, of which the two lower ones are rather the shortest, with connivent antheræ.

4. PISTILLUM consists of a quadrifid germen, a bristly style the length of the corolla, and two bristly stigmas.

5. PERICARPIUM. There is none. The seeds are contained in the bosom of the calyx.

6. SEMINA. The seeds are roundish, and four in number.

CHAP.

# CHAP. CCCCI.

## *SATYRIUM.*

Species OF this genus are,
1 The Lizzard-flower, or Goat-stones
2 Frog Satyrion, or *Orchis*
3 Black Satyrion
4 White Satyrion
5 Creeping Satyrion, or Bastard *Orchis*

Lizzard flower, 1 The Lizzard-flower, or Goat-stones The root consists of two large bulbs joined together The leaves are large, broad, oblong, obtusely pointed, ribbed, and surround the stalk with their base The stalk is upright, thick, tender, and often two feet high The flowers are formed into large loose spikes on the tops of the stalks, the parts are curiously divided, and at the bottom of each is a long beard hanging down, their predominant colour is a reddish purple, but there are other varieties which are curiously spotted or variegated with white, and often green The time of their appearance is June and July The whole plant has a strong smell of goats

Frog 2 Frog Satyrion, or *Orchis* The root consists of two small bulbs, which divide into fingers that spread out like those of the hand The leaves are small oblong, obtuse, and surround the stalk with their base The stalk is slender, weak, and eight or ten inches high The flowers grow in long spikes at the top, they are small, and greenish, with a mixture of white and purple, though they are of various colours in the different varieties, and some of them are so divided as to exhibit the appearance of little frogs, which occasioned its being called Frog Satyrion It blows in May, and continues to exhibit its bloom through the month of June

Black, 3 Black Satyrion The bulbs are palmated The leaves are narrow, and embrace the stalk with their base The stalks are about nine inches high The flowers are formed into thick short spikes at the tops of the stalks, they are of a very dark or blackish-purple colour, and come into blow the beginning of June

White, 4 White Satyrion The root is composed of many small bulbs joined together The leaves are spear-shaped, and embrace the stalks with their base The stalks arise to about eight inches high The flowers are collected in a short thick spike at the top of the stalk, they are of a whitish green colour, and appear in June

and Creeping Satyrion describ d 5 Creeping Satyrion The root is composed of many thick, fleshy, jointed fibres, which creep and spread themselves under the surface The radical leaves are broad, oval, smooth, and ribbed The stalk is slender, six or eight inches high, and garnished with a few narrow leaves, which embrace it with their base The flowers form a narrow spike at the tops of the stalks, they are of a whitish colour, prettily spotted with deep-red and dark-coloured spots, and appear in May and June

Variety There is a variety of this species, with the leaves beautifully spotted with black and white spots

Culture The first four species are propagated in the manner of the *Orchis*, and delight most in uncultivated places, they therefore should be stationed, like the different species of the *Orchis*, in such various parts of the Gardener's province as tally best with their native places of growth In such places they will exhibit their bloom fair, and encircle the family of the *Orchis* and *Ophrys*, to which they will (without a close observation) appear to belong

The fifth sort propagates itself fast enough by its creeping roots If the parts are divided any time about the end of summer, or early in the autumn, they will readily grow, they may be planted in any part of the flower-garden, though they delight most to be stationed among trees in cool shady places

Titles 1 The Lizard flower or Goat-stones, is titled, *Satyrium bulbis indivisis, foliis lanceolatis, nectarii labio trifido, intermedia lacinia elongata oblique præmorsa* Caspar Bauhine calls it, *Orchis barbata, odore hirci, breviore latioreque folio*, John Bauhine, *Orchis barbata foetida*, Gerard, *Tragorchis maximus* & *Tragorchis mas*, and Parkinson, *Tragorchis maximus et Tragorchis mas* It delights most in chalky soils, and grows naturally in Kent and several parts of France

2 Frog Satyrion, or *Orchis*, is, *Satyrium bulbis palmatis, foliis oblongis obtusis, nectarii labio lineari trifido intermedio obsoleto* In the *Flora Lapp* it is termed, *Satyrium foliis oblongis caulinis* Caspar Bauhine calls it, *Orchis palmata, flore viridi*, also, *Orchis palmata batrachites*, Lobelius, *Orchis palmata, flore galeato rubente ad virorem*; Gerard, *Satyrium batrachites alterum*, and Ray, *Orchis palmata minor, flore luteo viridi* It grows naturally in dry pastures, and under bushes in England, and most of the colder parts of Europe

3 Black Satyrion is, *Satyrium bulbis palmatis, foliis linearibus, floribus resupinatis, nectarii labio indiviso ovato* Van Royen calls it, *Satyrium foliis linearibus*, Caspar Bauhine, *Orchis palmata angustifolia Alpina, nigro flore*, Cammerarius, *Palma Christi minor*, and Haller, *Palmata angustifolia, flore supinato, calcare brevissimo* It grows common on the Alps of Lapland and Switzerland

4 White Satyrion is, *Satyrium bulbis fasciculatis, foliis lanceolatis, nectarii labio trifido acuto, lacinia intermedia obtusa* Haller calls it, *Orchis palmata Alpina, spica densa albicante* Michelius, *Pseudo-orchis Alpina, flore herbaceo*, and Ray, *Orchis palmata thyrso specioso longo, dense stipato ex albicante* It grows naturally in meadows and moist places in England, and most parts of Germany

5 Creeping Satyrion, or Bastard *Orchis*, is, *Satyrium bulbis fibrosis, foliis ovatis radicalibus, floribus secundis* In the *Flora Lapp* it is termed, *Satyrium foliis ovatis radicalibus* Caspar Bauhine calls it, *Pseudo orchis*, Cammerarius, *Orchis minor, flosculis albis, radice repente*, Loeselius, *Pyrola angustifolia polyanthos, radice geniculata*, Gmelin, *Epipactis foliis ovatis radicalibus*, and Mentzelius, *Orchis radice repente, foliis maculis*



nigris

*..gi s et albis adspersis* It grows naturally in woods in Sweden, England, Siberia, and Helvetia

Class and order in the Linnæan system The characters

*Satyrium* is of the class and order *Gynandria Diandria*, and the characters are,

1 CALYX The spathæ are vague, the spadix is simple, there is no perianthium

2 COROLLA is five petals, three of which are outer, the other two inner, they rise upwards, meet at top, and form a helmet, the nectarium is of one leaf annexed to the lower side of the receptacle between the division of the petals, the upper lip is short and erect, the lower lip is plane, hangs down, is prominent behind, and at the base shaped like the scrotum

3 STAMINA are two very short slender filaments sitting on the pistil, having oval antheræ covered by the upper lip of the nectarium

4 PISTILLUM consists of an oblong contorted germen situated below the flower, a very short style fastened to the upper lip of the nectarium, and a compressed obtuse stigma

5 PERICARPIUM is an oblong, unilocular, tricarinated, trivalvate capsule, opening under the keels three different ways, but fastened at the top and bottom

6 SEMINA The seeds are numerous, small, and scobiform

# CHAP CCCCII

## SAURURUS, LIZARD's TAIL.

THERE is only one species of this genus, called, Lizard's Tail

The plant described

The root is fibrous, whitish, and creeping under the surface of the ground The stalks are moderately thick, furrowed, and a foot and a half or two feet high The leaves are heart-shaped, smooth, obtuse-pointed, veined underneath, and grow alternately on footstalks The flowers come out from the wings of the leaves at the upper parts of the stalks in taper recurved katkins, the katkins are about two inches long, and of a yellowish colour, they appear in July, but the seeds rarely ripen in England

Method of propagation

This species is easily propagated by parting of the roots, which may be done at any time of the year, but more especially in the autumn, winter, or early in the spring, before the stalks arise It is very hardy, and will multiply exceedingly, especially if it has a moist rich soil, and a shady situation

Titles

There being no other species supposed formerly to belong to this genus, it stands with the distinctive name, *Saururus foliis cordatis petiolatis, amentis solitariis recurvis* Van Royen calls it, *Saururus foliis profunde cordatis ovato-lanceolatis, spicis solitariis*, and Plukenet, *Serpentaria repens, floribus stramineis spicatis, bryoniæ nigræ folio amphiore pingui, Virginiensis* It grows naturally in Virginia

Class and order in the Linnæan system The characters

*Saururus* is of the class and order *Heptandria Trigynia*, and the characters are,

1 CALYX The amentum is oblong, and covers the flowers The proper perianthium is of one leaf, oblong, lateral, coloured, and permanent

2 COROLLA There is none

3 STAMINA are seven long capillary filaments, with oblong, erect antheræ

4 PISTILLUM consists of four oval, acuminated germens, having no styles, but stigmas which are fastened to the interior lip of each germen

5 PERICARPIUM consists of four oval berries, each containing one cell

6 SEMEN The seed is single, and oval

CHAP.

# CHAP CCCCIII

## *SAXIFRAGA*, SAXIFRAGE

THIS genus comprehends many perennials, such as,

Species
1 *Cotyledon* Saxifrage
2 Yellow Saxifrage
3 Pensylvanian Saxifrage
4 Narrow-leaved Saxifrage.
5 Sedoide Saxifrage
6 Hairy Kidney-wort
7 Thick-leaved Saxifrage
8 Mountain Sengreen
9 Spotted Saxifrage
10 Wedge-leaved Saxifrage
11 Hairy Saxifrage
12 Opposite leaved Saxifrage
13 Autumnal Saxifrage
14 Yellow Mountain Sengreen
15 Round leaved Mountain Sanicle
16 White Saxifrage, or Sengreen
17 Small Mountain Sengreen
18 Trifid Sengreen
19 London Pride, or None-so-pretty

Description of Cotyledon Saxifrage. 1 *Cotyledon* Saxifrage The leaves are tongue-shaped, serrated, of a whitish green colour, spreading, and placed circularly on the crown of the root The stalk is upright, slender, branching, and eight or ten inches high The flowers are produced in panicles from the tops of the stalks, they are of a white colour, and though small yet very beautiful, and shew themselves chiefly in June

Varieties. There are a great many varieties of this species, differing in the leaves, flower stalks, or in some respect or other

Yellow, 2 Yellow Saxifrage The leaves are tongue-shaped, cartilaginous, serrated, and grow in clusters at the top of the root The stalks are upright, branching, and about a foot high The flowers come out in long spikes from the ends of the branches, they are large, of an elegant saffron colour with a mixture of purple, and appear about the same time with the former

Pensylvanian, 3 Pensylvanian Saxifrage The leaves are spear-shaped, long, have small denticles on their edges, are thickish, of a deep-green colour, and spread near the ground The stalks are naked, paniculated, and a foot and a half high The flowers come out in small heads from the ends and sides of the branches, they are small, of a whitish green colour, and appear in June

Narrow leaved, 4 Narrow leaved Saxifrage The leaves are numerous, smooth, awl-shaped, pointed, and lie over each other imbricatim The stalks are about four or five inches high, clammy to the touch, and adorned with three or four very small narrow leaves placed alternately The flowers come out singly from the tops of the stalks, they are moderately large, of a white colour veined with red, and appear in June

and Sedoid Saxifrage, 5 Sedoide Saxifrage The radical leaves are tongue shaped, and disposed in a circular direction on the crown of the roots The leaves on the stalk are spear-shaped, some of them are placed opposite to each other, and others grow alternately The stalks are slender, clammy, and five or six inches high The flowers come out from the tops of the stalks on slender footstalks, they are of a kind of buff or yellow colour, and appear in May and June

Hairy Kidney wort, 6 Hairy Kidney-wort The leaves are spear-shaped, pointed, hairy, and serrated on their edges The stalks are naked, divided into a few branches, and grow to about six or eight inches high The flowers come out from the tops of the stalks in small bunches, they are of a white colour, with a mixture of red or purple spots, and appear in June and July

Thick-leaved Saxifrage, 7 Thick-leaved Saxifrage The leaves are oval, retuded, smooth, obsoletely serrated, fleshy, almost half an inch in thickness, and grow on thick fleshy footstalks The stalk is wholly naked, and about a foot high The flowers come out in roundish panicles from the tops of the stalks, they are moderately large, of a purplish colour, and appear in June and July

Mountain Sengreen, 8 Mountain Sengreen The leaves are nearly oval, indented on the edges, and lie close to the root The stalk is simple, naked, and about five or six inches high The flowers come out from the tops of the stalks in roundish compact clusters, they are of a white colour, and appear in July and August

Spotted, 9 Spotted Saxifrage The leaves are roundish, white, indented on their edges, and placed circularly round the top of the root on long smooth footstalks The stalk is slender, naked, branching near the top, and about a foot high The flowers are produced in panicles from the tops of the stalks, they are of a white colour spotted with red or purple spots, and appear in June, July, and August

Wedge-leaved, 10 Wedge-leaved Saxifrage The leaves are wedge-shaped, obtuse, bend backward, and have indentures on their edges The stalk is naked, branching, and about a foot high The flowers come out in panicles, they are white, with a mixture of red, and appear in July

Hairy, 11 Hairy Saxifrage The leaves are heart-shaped, oval, retused, cartilagineous, and acutely crenated on their edges The stalks are naked, hairy, branching, and eight or ten inches high The flowers come out in panicles from the tops of the stalks, the petals are white, but the pistil of the flowers is red, their blow is in June and July

Opposite leaved, 12 Opposite leaved Saxifrage The leaves on the stalks are small, oval, opposite, of a brown in green colour, and lie over each other imbricatim in the range The stalks are slender, procumbent, and often strike root at the joints as they lie on the ground The flowers come out singly from the ends of the branches they are large of a deep blue or purple colour, and appear in March and April

and Autumnal Saxifrage described 13 Autumnal Saxifrage The radical leaves are spear-shaped, and grow in clusters at the crown of the roots The stalks are about six or [illegible] inches long, and adorned with narrow, ciliated leaves, [illegible] close, [illegible] ranged alternately from the top to the bottom. The flowers come out in clusters from the tops of the stalks; they are of a yellow colour spotted with red on the inside, and appear the latter end of summer, or the early part of autumn.

Yellow Mountain Sengreen.

14. Yellow Mountain Sengreen. The stalks [illegible], trailing, and four or five inches long. The leaves are narrow, awl-shaped, smooth, [illegible], and sparingly bestowed on the stalks. The flowers come out in small clusters from the ends of the stalks; they are of a yellow colour, and appear in July and August.

Round-leaved Mountain Sanicle.

15. Round-leaved Mountain Sanicle. The stalks are upright, channelled, branching, hairy, and a foot high. The leaves are kidney-shaped, roundish, sharply indented on their edges, and grow on footstalks. The flowers come out in panicles from the tops of the stalks; they are small, of a reddish colour, or spotted with red, and appear in May and June.

and White Saxifrage described.

16. White Saxifrage. The roots are like grains of [illegible], and of a reddish colour. The leaves are kidney-shaped, hairy, indented, and grow alternately on long footstalks. The stalks are upright, thick, channelled, branching, hairy, and about a foot high. The flowers come out from the ends of the branches in small clusters; they are of a white colour, and appear in April, May, and June.

Medicinal property of this.

The root of this plant is diuretic, and, being boiled in wine and drank, is good against the stone, gravel, and strangury, cleanses the kidneys, and helps most complaints in those parts.

Small Mountain Sengreen,

17. Small Mountain Sengreen. The radical leaves are narrow, some of them simple, others trifid, and grow in clusters at the crown of the roots. The stalk is upright, almost naked, and three or four inches high. The flowers come out two or three from the tops of the stalks; they are small, and shew themselves chiefly in August.

Trifid Sengreen,

18. Trifid Sengreen. The radical leaves are narrow, trifid, and grow on footstalks at the crown of the roots. From the sides of these come out [illegible] shoots, which lie on the ground, and strike root, and from the middle of the lower arise the flower-stalks, which are upright, branching, adorned with a few leaves only, and possessed of a viscous clammy matter. The flowers are produced from the tops of the stalks in May and June, and frequently again the latter end of summer, and the autumn.

and London Pride described.

19. London Pride, or None-so-pretty. The leaves are numerous, obovate, some of them are nearly retused, others not, crenated on their edges, and grow on broad, flat, furrowed footstalks, which are ciliated with a kind of hairy down. The stalks are naked, slender, stiff, brittle, hairy, of a reddish purple colour, and grow to about twelve or fifteen inches high. The flowers come out in panicles from the upper parts of the stalks; they are of a white colour spotted with red, and have red pistils; they are in blow chiefly in June and July.

Method of propagating them.

These sorts are all propagated by parting of the roots, which may be done at any time of the year, but is best effected soon after they have done flowering in the summer or autumn, when the [illegible] decay; they will then soon take to the ground, and form good heads for flowering the summer following. They are all extremely hardy, and will grow in almost any soil or situation, tho' they delight most in the shade, and moist places, where their leaves will be of a better colour, they will be larger, the stalks fuller of flowers, and continue longer in blow.

1. Cotyledon Saxifrage is titled, *Saxifraga foliis [illegible] radicalibus aggregatis [illegible] angulatis [illegible]*. In the *Flora Suecica* it is termed, *Saxifraga [illegible] crenatis, [illegible]*. [illegible] *Saxifraga foliis [illegible]*; in the *Flora Lapponica*, *Saxifraga [illegible] marginatis [illegible]*. Ilekere calls it, *Sedum [illegible] montanum [illegible], flore [illegible]*; Morison, *[illegible]*; Caspar Bauhine, *Cotyledon [illegible], foliis oblongis serratis*; [illegible], *Cotyledon [illegible]*; Tournefort, *Sedum [illegible] folio, flore albo, [illegible]*; [illegible], *Saxifraga, [illegible] Pyrenaica*; Dodonæus, *[illegible]*; Gerard, *[illegible] Pyramidale, [illegible]*; and Seguier, *[illegible], sed [illegible]*. It grows naturally on the Alps, and other mountainous parts of Europe.

2. Yellow Saxifrage is, *Saxifraga foliis [illegible] caulibus [illegible]*. Haller calls it, *Saxifraga [illegible] limbo [illegible], floribus [illegible]*. It grows naturally on the Helvetian and Italian mountains.

3. Pensylvanian Saxifrage is, *Saxifraga foliis [illegible], floribus [illegible]*. Gronovius calls it, *Saxifraga foliis [illegible] dentatis, [illegible] racemoso floribus confertis capitatis*; Colden, *Saxifraga Noveboracensis*; Dillenius, *Saxifraga Pensylvanica, floribus [illegible]*; and Plukenet, *Sanicula Virginiana alba, folio oblongo mucronato*. It grows naturally in Virginia, Pensylvania, and Canada.

4. Narrow-leaved Saxifrage is, *Saxifraga foliis aggregatis [illegible] subulatis [illegible], caule subnudo unifloro*. Seguier calls it, *Saxifraga Alpina foliis glaucis acutis, monanthos caule foliofo*; and Caspar Bauhine, *Sedum Alpinum, [illegible] flore*. It grows naturally on the Alps, and other mountainous parts of Europe.

5. Sedoide Saxifrage is, *Saxifraga foliis caulinis aggregatis alternis oppositisque [illegible] lanceolatis, flore pedunculato*. Seguier calls it, *Saxifraga Alpina [illegible], foliis linguiformis [illegible], flore ochroleuco*. It is a native of the Alps and other mountainous parts of Europe.

6. Hairy Kidney-wort is, *Saxifraga foliis serratis, caule nudo ramoso, petalis acuminatis*. In the *Flora Suecica* it is termed, *Saxifraga foliis lanceolatis [illegible], caule nudo simplici*; in the *Flora Lapponica*, *[illegible] myosotis, [illegible] fere [illegible]*. Morison calls it, *Sedum montanum [illegible] dentato folio, flore albo [illegible]*; Tournefort, *Geum palustre minus, foliis oblongis [illegible]*; Ray, *Cotyledon aquatica hirsuta*; and Oeder, *Sedum Alpinum IV*. It grows naturally in the mountainous parts of the North of England, Wales, Helvetia, and Lapland.

7. Thick-leaved Saxifrage is, *Saxifraga foliis [illegible] retusis obsolete serratis petiolatis, caule nudo, panicula conglomerata*. Gmelin calls it, *Saxifraga foliis ovatis [illegible] crenulatis, caulibus nudis*. It is a native of the Siberian mountains.

8. Mountain Sengreen is, *Saxifraga foliis obovatis crenatis [illegible], caule nudo, floribus congestis*. In the *Flora Suecica* it is termed, *Saxifraga foliis subovatis crenatis, caule nudo, floribus capitatis*; in the *Flora Lapponica*, *Saxifraga caule nudo simplici, foliis elliptico-subrotundis crenatis, floribus capitatis*. Gronovius calls it, *Saxifraga foliis cordato-ovalibus crenatis, corollâ albâ, caule hirsuto aphyllo*; Ray, *Saxifraga foliis oblongo-rotundis dentatis, floribus compactis*; Plukenet, *Sempervivum minus dentatum*; and Oeder, *Sedum III*.

It

It grows naturally on the Welch and Lapland mountains, also in Virginia and Canada.

9. Spotted Saxifrage is, *Saxifraga foliis subrotundis dentatis longius petiolatis, caule nudo.* Morison calls it *Sedum bicorne serratum, pulmonare folio rotundiore, floribus punctatis.* It grows naturally in Siberia.

10. Wedge-leaved Saxifrage is, *Saxifraga foliis cuneiformibus obtusis apice denticulatis, caule nudo paniculato.* John Bauhine calls it, *Cotyledon altera olim Mattbioli*; and Gesner, *Cotyledonis tertia species quædam.* It grows naturally on the Styrian mountains.

11. Hairy Saxifrage is, *Saxifraga foliis cordato-ovalibus retusis cartilagineo crenatis, caule nudo paniculato.* Magnol calls it, *Geum folio circinato acute crenato, pistillo floris rubro.* It is a native of the Pyrenees.

12. Opposite-leaved Saxifrage is, *Saxifraga foliis caulinis ovatis oppositis imbricatis, summis ciliatis.* In the *Flora Lapponica* it is termed, *Saxifraga foliis ovatis quadrangulo imbricatis, ramis procumbentibus.* Caspar Bauhine calls it, *Sedum alpinum, ericoides purpurascens*; Tournefort, *Saxifraga alpina ericoides, flore cæruleo.* It grows naturally out of the rocks on the mountainous parts of Wales, the Pyrenees, Lapland, and Switzerland.

13. Autumnal Saxifrage is, *Saxifraga foliis caulinis linearibus ciliatis, radicalibus aggregatis.* Haller calls it *Saxifraga foliorum marginibus ciliatis, floribus luteis maculosis*; Breynius, *Saxifraga angustifolia autumnalis, flore luteo guttato, foliis in margine crenatis*; Caspar Bauhine, *Sedum Alpinum floribus luteis maculosis*; and Morison, *Sedum angustifolium autumnale, flore luteo guttato.* It grows naturally in moist places in England, Prussia, and Switzerland.

14. Yellow Mountain Sengreen is, *Saxifraga foliis caulinis linearibus subulatis sparsis nudis inermibus, caulibus decumbentibus.* In the *Flora Suecica* it is termed, *Saxifraga foliis linearibus sparsis glabris*; in the *Flora Lapponica*, *Saxifraga foliis subulatis sparsis.* Caspar Bauhine calls it, *Sedum Alpinum, flore pallido*; Clusius, *Sedum minus VI.* Ray, *Sedum montanum Alpinum luteum nostras.* It grows naturally in Westmoreland and on mount Baldus, and on the Alps of Lapland and Styria.

15. Round-leaved Mountain Sanicle is, *Saxifraga foliis caulinis reniformibus dentatis petiolatis, caule paniculato.* Van Royen calls it, *Saxifraga foliis reniformibus acute crenatis, caule ramoso foliosa*; Caspar Bauhine, *Sanicula montana rotundifolia major*; and Camerarius, *Sanicula Alpina.* It grows naturally on the Helvetian and Austrian mountains.

16. White Saxifrage or Sengreen is, *Saxifraga foliis cuneiformibus tridentatis, caule ramoso erecto.* Caspar Bauhine calls it, *Sedum tridactylites, alba*; John Bauhine, *Saxifraga alba, annua, foliosa*; Camerarius, *Saxifraga tridactylites*; and Parkinson, *Saxifraga Ruta muraria.* It grows naturally in meadows and pastures in England and most countries of Europe.

17. Small Mountain Sengreen is, *Saxifraga foliis radicalibus aggregatis, caule nudo; foliis integris, tridentatis, caule ramoso, rudo, floribus.* Haller calls it, *Saxifraga foliis simplicibus & trifidis, caule pene aphyllo pauciflora*; Segnier, *Saxifraga foliis partim integris partim trifidis*; Caspar Bauhine, *Sedum tridactylites Alpinum minus*; and Gesner, *Sedum montanum Alpina lutea.* It grows naturally in the mountainous parts of Westmoreland, Lapland, Helvetia, and the South of France.

18. Trifid Sengreen is, *Saxifraga foliis caulinis linearibus integris trifidisve stolonibus procumbentibus, caule erecto nudiusculo.* In the *Hortus Cliffort* it is termed, *Saxifraga procumbens, foliis linearibus integris trifidisque.* Haller calls it, *Saxifraga foliis omnibus angustis petiolatis apice tridentatis, caule scaposo ramoso trifido*; Caspar Bauhine, *Sedum Alpinum, trifido folio*; Van Royen, *Saxifraga procumbens, foliis linearibus integris trifidis & quinquefidis*; Tournefort, *Saxifraga muscosa trifido folio*; and Plukenet, *Sedum Alpinum laciniatis ajugæ foliis.* It grows naturally in mountainous parts of the North of England, and on the Helvetian, Austrian, and Pyrenean mountains.

19. London Pride, or None-so-Pretty, is, *Saxifraga foliis ovatis subretusis cartilagineo crenatis, caule nudo paniculato.* In the *Hortus Upsal* it is termed, *Saxifraga foliis cuneiformibus retusis cartilagineo sinuato serratis margine acutis, caule paniculato.* Tournefort calls it, *Geum folio subrotundo minori, pistillo floris rubro.* It grows naturally on some of the Welch mountains, and in Ireland.

*Saxifraga* is of the class and order *Decandria Digynia*, and the characters are, Class and order in the Linnæan system.

1. CALYX is a short, monophyllous, permanent perianthium, divided into five acute parts. The characters.

2. COROLLA is five patent petals, which are narrow at their base.

3. STAMINA are ten awl-shaped filaments with roundish anthera.

4. PISTILLUM consists of a roundish, acuminated germen, and two short styles with obtuse stigmas.

5. PERICARPIUM is an oval, birostrated capsule, containing one cell, and opening between the points.

6. SEMINA. The seeds are numerous, and small.

# C H A P. CCCCIV

## *SCABIOSA*, SCABIOUS

*Species*

THE perennial species of Scabious are,
1 Common Field Scabious
2 Alpine Scabious
3 Narrow-leaved Shrubby Scabious
4 Devil's Bit
5 Lesser Field Scabious
6 Silvery Scabious
7 Grass-leaved Scabious
8 Shrubby Cretan Scabious
9 Yellow German Scabious

*Common Field Scabious described*

1 Common Field Scabious The root is thick, white, fibrous, and long The stalks are round, rough, hairy, branching, and two or three feet high The leaves are oblong, hairy, variously jagged at their edges, of a brownish green colour, and grow opposite to each other at the joints The flowers come out from the ends and sides of the branches on naked footstalks, they are of a beautiful blue colour, appear in July and August, and the seeds ripen in September

*Variety*

There is a variety of this species with reddish, and another with purple flowers

*Its uses in medicine*

This species is used in medicine as an aperient, sudorific, and expectorant

*Alpine*

2 Alpine Scabious The root is strong, fibrous, and strikes deep into the ground The stalks are large, firm, channelled, branching, and four or five feet high The leaves are pinnated, and composed of about four or five pairs of spear shaped, serrated, acute pointed lobules, terminated by an odd one The flowers come out on naked footstalks from the ends and sides of the branches, are of a whitish yellow colour, appear in June and July, and the seeds ripen in the autumn

*and Narrow leaved Shrubby Scabious described*

3 Narrow-leaved Shrubby Scabious The stalks are upright, firm, divide into a few branches, and grow to about two feet high The leaves are pinnatifid, narrow, and of a pale-green colour The flowers come out singly from the ends and sides of the branches on naked footstalks, are of a snowy white colour, and appear in July, but are seldom succeeded by ripe seeds in England

*Devil's Bit described*

4 Devil's Bit The root is thick, short, blackish, and ends abruptly as if it had been bit off, which has occasioned the name Devil's Bit to have been long in use for this plant The stalks are single, upright, jointed, and two feet high The leaves are oval, spear shaped, smooth, and grow opposite to each other at the joints The flowers come out from the tops and sides of the upper parts of the stalks on short footstalks, they are of a blue colour, appear in June, July and August, and the seeds ripen soon after the flowers are fallen

*Its variety*

There is a variety of this species with hairy leaves and purple flowers

*Medicinal properties of it*

A decoction of this species, used as a gargarism, is admirable for the cure of sore throats It is good against poisons, and is said to be noways inferior to the Common Field Scabious in sanative qualities

*Lesser Field,*

5 Lesser Field Scabious The root is thick, white, and long The radical leaves are nearly oval, and crenated on their edges, those on the stalks are pinnated, and grow opposite to each other The stalks are round, rough, branching, hairy, and about a foot high The flowers come out from the ends and sides of the branches on naked footstalks, are of a blue or purple colour, appear in June and July, and the seeds ripen in August and September

*Silvery,*

6 Silvery Scabious The stalk is slender, and divides into a few weak branches which spread on every side The leaves are of a silvery-white colour, and the lower ones are divided into many spear-shaped parts, but the upper ones are small, and undivided The flowers come out from the ends and sides of the branches on long, smooth, naked footstalks, they are very small and pale, appear in July and August, and the seeds ripen in the autumn

*Grass leaved,*

7 Grass-leaved Scabious The stalks are herbaceous, tender, and a foot and a half high The leaves are narrow, spear shaped, entire, and of a silvery-white colour underneath The flowers come out from the wings of the leaves on slender footstalks, are of a blue colour, appear in July and August, and the seeds ripen in the autumn

*and Shrubby Cretan Scabious described*

8 Shrubby Cretan Scabious The stalk is ligneous, branching, knotty, and two or three feet high The leaves are numerous, spear-shaped, entire, smooth, and of a whitish green colour The flowers come out from the ends and sides of the branches on naked footstalks, are of a blue colour, appear in July and August, but are seldom succeeded by seeds in England

*Variety of it*

There is a variety of this species with pale-purple flowers

*Description of Yellow German Scabious*

9 Yellow German Scabious The radical leaves are pinnatifid, large, and spread on the ground, those on the stalk are pinnated, narrow, and cut on their edges The stalk is upright, firm, and about two feet high The flowers come out from the upper parts of the stalks on long footstalks, are of a yellow colour, appear in July, and the seeds ripen in the autumn

*Method of propagating the eighth species*

The eighth is the most tender of all these species, and is propagated by planting the slips or cuttings in any of the summer months They must be shaded and duly watered until they have taken root, and in the autumn they may be removed, observing to preserve a ball of earth to each root, into the places where they are designed to remain The soil should be naturally light, dry, warm, and the place well defended, otherwise they will be liable to be destroyed by our winters For this reason, at the time of the removal a few plants should be set in pots, to be housed in bad weather, in order to preserve the sorts in case those abroad should be destroyed

*Propagation of the other species*

The other species are all propagated by parting of the roots or sowing of the seeds The roots are best parted in the autumn or latter end of summer, when the stalks decay, and they will then soon take to the ground, and shoot forth strong for flowering the summer following

But the way to obtain the best plants is by seeds

seeds. Let them, therefore, be sown in the spring, in beds of light earth made fine. Sift over them a little fine mould; and, if dry weather should follow the performance, give them in evenings a slight watering. This will keep the ground cool and moist, and speedily bring up the seeds. Soon after their appearance they must be thinned where they are too close, must be duly watered in dry weather all summer, and kept clean from weeds; and in the autumn they may be removed to the places where they are designed to remain. The summer following they will flower, and perfect their seeds. The ninth species frequently dies soon after it has flowered; so that its seeds should be regularly gathered at proper intervals to be sown, to continue the sort in perfection and plenty. They all love a moist, loamy soil and the shade best; though they will grow in almost any soil or situation. The first, fourth, and fifth species grow common in our poor meadows and pastures, and are seldom cultivated. They are, nevertheless, beautiful flowers, and, were it not for their commonness, as deserving of culture as many other perennials of our gardens.

Titles. 1. Common Field Scabious is entitled, *Scabiosa corollulis quinquefidis radiantibus, caule hispido, foliis pinnatifidis, incisis, apicibus...*. Tabernamontanus calls it, *Scabiosa ... ensis*; Caspar Bauhine, *Scabiosa pratensis hirsuta*; John Bauhine, *Scabiosa major communior hirsuta, folio laciniato*; Haller, *Scabiosa caule & foliis hirsutis, ... superioribus ... pinnatis*; Gerard, *Scabiosa major vulgaris*; and Parkinson, *Scabiosa vulgaris pratensis*. It grows naturally in meadows and the borders of fields in England and most countries of Europe.

2. Alpine Scabious is, *Scabiosa corollulis quadrifidis æqualibus ... superioribus cernuis, foliis pinnatis, foliolis ... serratis*. Caspar Bauhine calls it, *Scabiosa Alpina, foliis centaureæ majoris*. It grows naturally on the Helvetian and Italian mountains.

3. Narrow-leaved Shrubby Scabious is, *Scabiosa corollulis quinquefidis æqualibus, squamis calycinis ... foliis pinnatifidis*. Clusius ... calls it, *Scabiosa frutescens ... folia elata*, also, *... folio ...*. It is a native of Narbonne.

4. Devil's bit is, *Scabiosa corollulis quadrifidis æqualibus, ... approximatis, foliis lanceolato-ovatis integerrimis*. Caspar Bauhine calls it, *Succisa glabra*; also, *Succisa hirsuta*; Cammerarius, *Succisa*; ... Ray, *Scabiosa radice succisa, flore globoso*; Gerard, *Morsus diaboli*; and Parkinson, *Morsus diaboli vulgaris, flore purpureo*. It grows naturally in meadows and pasture-grounds in England and most countries of Europe.

5. Lesser Field Scabious is, *Scabiosa corollulis quinquefidis radiantibus, foliis radicalibus ovatis crenatis, caulinis pinnatis ...*. Caspar Bauhine calls it, *Scabiosa, capitulo globoso, major*; also, *Scabiosa capitulo globoso, minor*; Cammerarius, *Scabiosa minor*; Gerard, *Scabiosa minor, sive Columnaris*; and Parkinson, *Scabiosa minor campestris*. It grows naturally on dry mountainous pastures in England and most parts of Europe.

6. Silvery Scabious is, *Scabiosa corollulis quinquefidis, foliis pinnatis, laciniis lanceolatis, pedunculis ... longissimis*. Tournefort calls it, *Scabiosa Orientalis argentea, foliis ... oribus ...*; and Vaillant, *Asterocephalus perennis argenteus ... cæruleo*. It grows naturally in the East.

7. Grass-leaved Scabious is, *Scabiosa corollulis quinquefidis, foliis linearibus lanceolatis integerrimis, caule herbaceo*. Caspar Bauhine calls it, *Scabiosa argentea angustifolia*; John Bauhine, *Scabiosa graminea argentea*; and Vaillant, *Asterocephalus argenteus graminifolius, flore cæruleo*. It grows naturally on the mountainous parts of Helvetia, and on mount Baldus.

8. Shrubby Cretan Scabious is, *Scabiosa corollulis quinquefidis, foliis lanceolatis confertissimis ... integerrimis, caule fruticoso*. Caspar Bauhine calls it, *Scabiosa stellata, folio non dissecto*; Tournefort, *Scabiosa Cretica frutescens auriculæ ursi folio*; and Vaillant, *Asterocephalus frutescens leucoj folio longiore angusto*. It grows naturally in Crete.

9. Yellow German Scabious is, *Scabiosa corollulis quinquefidis radiantibus, foliis ... bus pinnatis, radicalibus bipinnatis, petiolis perfoliatis*. Sauvages calls it, *Scabiosa corollulis quinquefidis, foliis pinnatis, foliolis lanceolatis sup... incisis*; Caspar Bauhine, *Scabiosa multifido folio, flore flavescente*; and Clusius, *Scabiosa VII*. It grows naturally in dry meadows and pastures in Germany.

Class and order in the Linnæan System. *Scabiosa* is of the class and order *Tetrandria Monogynia*; and the characters are,

The characters. 1. CALYX. The common perianthium is patent, composed of many leaves, and contains many flowers. The folioles are placed on the receptacle, and surround it in various series, the inner ones being gradually the smaller.

The perianthium is double, and both are fixed on the germen. The outer perianthium is short, membranaceous, plicated, and permanent; the inner is divided into five awl-shaped, capillary segments.

2. COROLLA. The florets have each one tubular petal, cut at the brim into four or five segments.

3. STAMINA are four weak, awl-shaped, capillary filaments, with oblong, incumbent antheræ.

4. PISTILLUM consists of a germen situated below the receptacle, and surrounded by a vagina in the manner of a calyx, a filiforme style the length of the corolla, and an obtuse, obliquely emarginated stigma.

5. PERICARPIUM. There is none.

6. SEMEN. The seed is single, oval, oblong, and crowned by the calyx.

## C H A P CCCCV

## *SCANDIX*, SHEPHERD's NEEDLE, or VENUS COMB

THERE is one perennial of this genus, which usually goes by the name of Sweet Cicely, or Sweet Fern

*This plant described*

The root is large, thick, and has the taſte of Aniſeed The ſtalks are hairy, fiſtular, and will grow to be four or five feet high The leaves are large, and very much reſemble thoſe of Fern, on which account ſome have given this plant the appellation of Sweet Fern The flowers terminate the ſtalk in umbels, are of a white colour, and very fragrant, they will be in blow in May or June, and ripen their ſeeds in July These are long, angular, furrowed, and, like the root, have the flavour of Aniſeed

*Propagation of it*

This ſpecies is of exceeding eaſy culture Sow the ſeeds in any ſoil or ſituation, and they will readily come up, after which nothing more is to be done, than to thin the plants to proper diſtances, and keep them clean from weeds When they have once flowered, they will afford you a conſtant ſupply from ſcattered ſeeds, which will come up without any trouble

*Titles*

This ſpecies is titled, *Scandix ſeminibus ſulcatis angulatis* Caſpar Bauhine calls it, *Myrrhis major, Cicutaria odorata*, and Dodonæus, *Myrrhis* It grows naturally in Germany and Italy

*Claſs and order in the Linnæan ſyſtem*

*Scandix* is of the claſs and order *Pentandria Digynia*, and the characters are,

*The characters*

1 CALYX The general umbel is long, and compoſed of few rays, but the partial conſiſts of many

There is no general involucrum, but the umbellulæ have a partial one, compoſed of five leaves about the ſame length with themſelves

The proper perianthium is hardly diſcernible

2 COROLLA The general corolla is deformed, and radiated There are both hermaphrodite and female flowers Thoſe in the diſk are each of them compoſed of five inflexed, heart-ſhaped, equal petals, thoſe in the radius have five inflexed, heart-ſhaped, unequal petals

3 STAMINA conſiſt of five capillary filaments with roundiſh antheræ

4 PISTILLUM conſiſts of an oblong germen ſituated below the flower, and of two permanent, ſubulated ſtyles the length of the ſmalleſt petal, with obtuſe ſtigmas

5 PERICARPIUM There is none The fruit is very long, awl-ſhaped, and conſiſts of two parts

6 SEMINA The ſeeds are two, one being lodged in each of the parts They are awl ſhaped, ſulcated, convex on one ſide, and plane on the other

## C H A P. CCCCVI.

## *SCHEUCHZERIA*, LESSER FLOWERING RUSH

THERE is only one ſpecies of this genus, called the Leſſer Flowering Ruſh

*This plant deſcribed*

The root is ſlender, jointed, and creeping under the ſurface of the ground The radical leaves are narrow, pointed, three or four inches long, and of a pale-green colour The ſtalk is round, ſingle, jointed, five or ſix inches high, and adorned with leaves growing ſingly at the joints, and ſurrounding it with their baſe The flowers come out ſingly from the upper parts of the ſtalks on ſlender footſtalks, they are of a greeniſh-yellow colour, moderately large, appear in July and Auguſt, and the ſeeds ripen in the autumn

*Propagation of it*

This ſpecies is propagated by parting of the roots at any time of the year, but more eſpecially in the autumn, when the flowers are paſt, they will then ſoon take to the ground, and ſhoot forth ſtrong for flowering the ſummer following

It is alſo propagated by ſowing the ſeeds in the ſpring, in beds of light, moiſt earth After the plants come up, they muſt be kept clean from weeds all ſummer, and duly watered in dry weather, and in the autumn they may be removed to the places where they are deſigned to remain

*Proper ſituation*

This ſpecies grows naturally on bogs and in watery places in the northern parts of Europe This directs us to aſſign it ſome damp, cold, and moiſt

moist part of the garden, which will suit its nature better than a warmer place

Titles

There being no other species of this genus yet known, it stands with the name, simply, *Scheuchzeria*. Caspar Bauhine calls it, *Juncus floridus minor*; Scheuchzer, *Junco affinis palustris*; and Lobel, *Gramen junceum aquaticum, semine racemoso*. It grows naturally in moist places in Lapland, Helvetia, Sweden, and Prussia

Class and order in the Linnæan system The characters

*Scheuchzeria* is of the class and order *Hexandria Trigynia*, and the characters are,

1 CALYX is a perianthium composed of six oblong, acute, reflexed, patent, permanent leaves

2 COROLLA There is none

3 STAMINA are six very short, flaccid, capillary filaments, with long, upright, compressed, obtuse antheræ

4 PISTILLUM consists of three oval, compressed germens the length of the calyx, no styles, but oblong stigmas, which are obtuse at the top, and adhere to the germen on the outside

5 PERICARPIUM consists of three roundish, compressed, inflated, reflexed, distinct, bivalved capsules

6 SEMINA The seeds are single, and oblong

# CHAP. CCCCVII

## SCHOENUS

Species

THE English species of this genus are,

1 Long rooted Bastard *Cyperus*
2 Black-headed Bog-rush
3 Brown Bastard *Cyperus*
4 Compressed Bastard *Cyperus*
5 White-flowered Rush-grass

Description of Long rooted Bastard Cyperus

1 Long rooted Bastard *Cyperus*. The root is thick, long, creeping, and of a blackish colour on the outside. The leaves are numerous at the crown of the root, long, carinated, prickly on the back and edges, broad at the bottom, and diminish gradually to a point. The stalks are upright, taper, jointed, and four or five feet high. The flowers come out in panicles from the tops of the stalks, are in perfection in July and August, and are succeeded by small, black, glossy seeds, which ripen in September

Black headed Bog-rush described

2 Black-headed Bog-rush. The root is fibrous, and of a black colour. The leaves are smooth, triangular, and six or eight inches long. The stalk is round, naked, smooth, purplish near the base, and a foot and a half high. The flowers are produced from the tops of the stalks in oval heads, are of a blackish-brown colour, appear in June, and are succeeded by whitish, glossy seeds, which ripen in August

Description of Brown

3 Brown Bastard *Cyperus*. The leaves are grassy, narrow, pointed, and four or five inches high. The stalks are slender, taper, naked, and eight or ten inches high. The flowers are collected at the tops of the stalks in the form of double spikes; they are small, of a brownish colour, appear in July, and the seeds ripen in August

and Compressed Bastard Cyperus

4 Compressed Bastard *Cyperus*. The root is creeping, slender, and fibrated. The leaves are grassy, narrow, pointed, and eight or ten inches high. The stalks are roundish, three cornered, naked, and twelve or fifteen inches high. The flowers come out from the tops of the stalks in distichous, compressed spikes; they are of a brown colour, appear in July, and are succeeded by small, greyish, glossy seeds, which ripen in August

White flowering Rush grass described

5 White-flowering Rush-grass. The root consists of a few blackish fibres collected into a head. The leaves are numerous, setaceous, and eight or ten inches long. The stalks are rigid, firm, almost three-square, leafy, and about a foot high. The flowers come out in bunches from the upper part of the stalk; they are of a fine bright white colour, appear in July, and the seeds ripen in August

Method of propagation

These grasses grow naturally by waters, and in boggy, marshy places in many parts of England, and are not cultivated. Nevertheless, if any one is desirous of having a few plants to be ready for observation, it may be easily effected by parting of the roots at any time of the year, or sowing the seeds, as soon as they are ripe, in the autumn or spring following, observing to allow them some moist, damp part of the garden for their residence

Titles

1 Long rooted Bastard *Cyperus* is entitled, *Schoenus culmo tereti, foliis margine dorsoque aculeatis*. Scheuchzer calls it, *Pseudo-cyperus palustris, foliis & carina serratis*; Caspar Bauhine, *Cyperus longus inodorus Germanicus*; and Morison, *Cyperus longus inodorus major, foliis & carina serratis*. It grows naturally in marshy places in most countries of Europe

2 Black-headed Bog-rush is, *Schoenus culmo tereti nudo, capitulo ovato, involucri diphylli valvulâ alterâ subulatâ longâ*. Morison calls it *Juncus lævis minor, panicula glomerata nigricante*; Magnol, *Juncus lithospermus semine*; Scheuchzer, *Junco affinis capitulo glomerato nigricante*; and Merret, *Gramen sparteum nigro capitulo*. It grows naturally in bogs, and moist, turfy places in most parts of Europe

3 Brown Bastard *Cyperus* is, *Schoenus culmo tereti nudo, spicâ duplici, involucri valvula majore spicam æquante*. Morison calls it, *Gramen cyperoides minimum, ex sophylis proliferi capitulo simplici squamato*; Ray, *Junceolo accedens gramen folia plantula, capitulis armeriæ proferens*. It grows naturally in marshy places in England and Gothland

4 Compressed Bastard *Cyperus* is, *Schoenus culmo subtriquetro nudo, spicâ disticha, involucro monophyllo*. Micheli calls it, *Cyperoides non una spicata, radice repente, caule rotundo ... spica* ...

*[illegible] disticha, [illegible] e neo*, Plukenet, *Gramen cyperoides spica simplici compressa distichâ* It grows naturally in England, Helvetia, and Italy

5 White-flowered Rush-grass is, *Schoenus culmo subtriquetro folioso, floribus fasciculatis, foliis setaceis* In the *Hortus Cliffort* it is termed, *Schoenus flosculis fasciculatis* Morison calls it, *Cyperus palustris hirsutus minor, paniculis albis*, Micheli, *Cyperella palustris, capitulis umbellatis primum albis, deinde fulvis*; Plukenet, *Gramen Junceæ accedens glabrum, in palustribus proveniens, paniculatum*, Scheuchzer, *Gramen cyperoides palustre leucantremum*, and Merret, *Gramen cyperoides, albis glumis* It grows naturally in marshy, boggy places in England and most of the northern countries of Europe

Class and order in the Linnæan system

*Schoenus* is of the class and order *Triandria Monogynia*, and the characters are,

The characters

1 CALYX is a glume composed of two large, erect, attenuated, permanent valves, and contains many flowers

2 COROLLA is six, spear-shaped, acute, connivent, permanent petals, which are unequal in situation, nearly imbricated in their disposition, and the outer ones are the shortest

3 STAMINA are three capillary filaments, with oblong, erect antheræ

4 PISTILLUM consists of an oval, triquetrous, obtuse germen, a setaceous style the length of the stamina, and a slender, trifid stigma

5 PERICARPIUM There is none The seed is contained in the corolla, which becomes loose, and discharges it, when ripe

6 SEMEN The seed is single, suboval, glossy, obscurely three-cornered, and thickest in the upper part

# C H A P. CCCCVIII.

## *S C I L L A*, S Q U I L L.

Introductory to its cultivation

THE several species of this genus, with their varieties, are pretty ornaments in the flower-garden They have a genteel appearance when in blow, without the rambling look of many of the sorts of perennial flowers, and as their culture is easy, and they will grow in almost any soil or situation, they are much coveted by all, and greatly preferred by those who have not room for a general collection, because many of them together will require to occupy but a small space Of this nature, a number of species, with their varieties, may be selected, in the course of this work, to afford a field of entertainment to the curious lover of flowers, in the compass of a few borders, properly disposed, in a small space of garden for them

The different species of the *Scilla*, then, are usually called,

Species

1 The Common Squill, or Sea Onion
2 The Lily Hyacinth
3 The Italian Star Hyacinth
4 The Peruvian Hyacinth
5 The Byzantine, or Borage-flowered Star Hyacinth
6 The Vernal Star Hyacinth
7 The Autumnal Star Hyacinth
8 The Single-leaved Star Hyacinth

Common Squill described

1 Common Squill, or Sea Onion The root of this species is a large tunicated bulb, from the bottom of which issue many long fibres The coats of this bulb lie over each other like those of our Garden Onion, they are thick, and full of a slimy, acrid juice The leaves are about a foot and a half long, and three inches broad at the bottom, from which they gradually diminish to a point, they are of a thick consistence, juicy, and of a delightful bright-green colour Thus they continue all winter, but die in the spring when the flower stalk arises This flower-stalk, which is green, succulent, and round, will arise from two feet to a yard in length The flowers ornament the top to near half way down, the bottom being naked, they compose a thyrse of a pyramidical form, are white, and each individual floret has a star like appearance, being composed of six petals with acute points that spread open

Varieties

There are two sorts of this species, one with a red, and another with a white root, which have induced some persons to believe they are distinct species, but we have reason to suppose they are accidental varieties only, though most virtue is attributed to the White-rooted sort

Medicinal properties and propagation of it

The use of these bulbs as an emetic and detergent is well known They may be made to flower in gardens, though not continued there long, by planting them in grit or sea sand at the time of their leaves decaying, throwing over them now and then salted water, and with this management they may be kept for a few years, if they are protected from frost in the winter But this is hardly worth while If a person has got the bulbs, they may be easily made to flower once in that manner, which may be sufficient to satisfy the curiosity

The Lily Hyacinth described

2 The Lily Hyacinth is so called from the resemblance it has in its root and leaves to the Common Lily It hath the same kind of squamous bulb, from the bottom of which issue several long fibres, it is yellow, and the scales are thick, and full of juice The leaves much resemble those of the Lily in figure, though they are much smaller The flower-stalk will arise to about a foot in height, it is round, succulent, green, and has its top ornamented with flowers of a starry figure. These are usually of a beautiful blue colour, and their time of blowing is June

Varieties

There are the White and the Red flowering Lily Hyacinth, which have been classed by some as distinct species, but they are varieties only Nevertheless, they are equally valuable to the Gardener, as they encrease the number of his sorts,

ſorts, and as the White and Red Flowering ſorts are not ſo frequent, a great reſpect is ſhewn them on that account, though the colours are not near ſo good of the ſort.

*The Italian Star Hyacinth deſcribed*

3. The name of Italian is uſed for the third ſpecies only by way of diſtinction, for it is not altogether certain, that it flouriſhes in its wild ſtate in any part of that country. Beſler calls it, *Hyacinthus ſtellaris Italicus*, but it does not appear that he met with it otherwiſe than in gardens, ſo that it might be as well titled the Engliſh, as it has for many years been an old inhabitant of our gardens. The root of this ſpecies, differing from the others, is a ſolid bulb, white, roundiſh, and ſends out many fibres from the baſe. The leaves are obtuſe, pointed, tolerably broad, ſtriated, and of a pale-green colour. The ſtalk is round, thick, and of a pale-green colour, it will be near a foot in length, and the top is ornamented with a large, broad, conical tuft of flowers. Theſe will be in blow the beginning of May, and each floret is compoſed of ſix oval petals, which by expanding themſelves have the appearance of rays of a ſtar which they form.

*Varieties*

Of this ſpecies there are two varieties, viz. the Blue and the Grey, both equally valuable, as being equally common, and of equal culture.

*Deſcription of the Peruvian*

4. Peruvian Hyacinth. Of this ſpecies there are two principal varieties, viz. the blue and the White. The root is a ſolid bulb, large, ſound, compact, and covered with a brown coat, its ſhape is inclined to an oblong, and its baſe is prominent, ſending from thence many long, thick fibres. The leaves are few, ſeldom exceeding five in number, but they are very beautiful, being of a fine ſhining green colour. They are about half a foot or more in length, hollowed, and conſiderably broad at their baſe, tho narrower upwards. Theſe leaves ſpring from the bulbs in the autumn, and would be more delightful in the winter, were it not for their natural ſpreading property over the ground, for thus they are ſubject to have their fine ſhining-green colour concealed by the beſpattered dirt occaſioned by the heavy rains, which is too often their fate, and to which they would not be ſo liable, were their poſition more erect. The flower-ſtalks are about as high as the leaves are long, they are thick, ſucculent, of a pale-green colour, and ornamented at top with a large cluſter of flowers forming the figure of a cone, their footſtalks being larger downwards, and diminiſhing gradually to the top. Each of theſe flowers is compoſed of ſix petals, which ſpread open in a ſtar like manner. Both the Blue and the White ſorts flower at the ſame time and have exactly the ſame properties. Their time of blow is in May, and their ſeeds will ripen in July or Auguſt, ſoon after which the green leaves will ſhoot out afreſh from the bulbs.

*Byzantine*

6. The Byzantine, or Borage-flowered Star Hyacinth. This ſpecies goes by different names amongſt Gardeners, ſome calling it the Early Star Hyacinth, and others the Vernal, which is a meaning of the ſame import, but either of theſe is very proper for any of the ſorts of this tribe, as they are moſt of them vernal, or early flowering plants. Others again, who are better acquainted with the original, call it the Byzantine Hyacinth, Byzantium being the place of its native growth, from whence it was introduced into our gardens above 170 years ago. I have met with ſome Gardeners who have never heard of any of theſe names, and yet are well acquainted with the plant, and with them, and not improperly as a diſtinction, it goes by the name of the Borage-flowered Hyacinth, from the reſemblance the flower hath to thoſe of the Common Borage, and it has been diſtinguiſhed by a title of the ſame meaning by ſome former botaniſts of note. The root is a large, ſolid, fleſhy bulb, which is nearly round, and of a purpliſh colour. The leaves are few, being ſeldom more than four or five, they are about a foot in length, hardly an inch broad, hollowed, channelled, of a delightful ſhining green colour, which is often ſullied by the daſhing of the mould in heavy rains, and for the moſt part lie upon the ground. The ſtalks, which will be two or three according to the ſtrength of the root, will be of different heights, the ſtrongeſt ariſing to near a foot, the others proportionably ſhorter; they are hardly round, being a little ridged, and are of a purpliſh colour, tender, full of juice, and have their top terminated by a ſpike of flowers, each of which reſembles that of our Common Borage. Theſe flowers ſtand ſingly on ſlender foot-ſtalks, on which account they are a little drooping. Each is compoſed of ſix petals, that ſpread open with great uniformity and beauty. They are oblong, end in acute points, and are of a clear ſky-blue colour. This ſpecies flowers in March, and the ſeeds will be ripe by the end of May.

*Vernal Star*

6. Vernal Star Hyacinth. Of this ſpecies there are two principal varieties, viz. the Blue and the White. The root is roundiſh and ſolid, but rather a ſmall bulb, which ſends forth two leaves only beſides the flower-ſtalk. Theſe leaves are of a delightful ſhining-green colour, channelled, hardly an inch broad, and about half a foot in length. Between theſe the flower-ſtalk ariſes, which is alſo channelled, ſlender, tender, and full of juice. The top is ornamented by a tuft of flowers on longiſh footſtalks, which are ſlender, but of ſufficient ſtrength to ſupport the flowers in an erect poſition. The flowers are but thinly placed on the ſtalk, and though thoſe neareſt the baſe are on moderately long footſtalks, they gradually diminiſh in length to the top. Each is compoſed of ſix petals, and they ſpread open in the uſual beautiful ſtar-like manner. The flowers appear early in March, and are blue or white according to their nature in the variety, their ſtamina are either blue or white according to the colour of the petals they belong to, and their ſeeds will be ripe by the end of May or beginning of June.

*Autumnal Star*

7. The Autumnal Star Hyacinth. The root conſiſts of a ſmall, round, white, ſolid bulb. From this proceed a few ſmall, ſlender, linear leaves, about half a foot in length, which come out in September, and remain green all winter, but die away in the ſpring. In the center of theſe leaves ariſes the flower-ſtalk, the ſtrongeſt of which will be about the length of the leaves, and when there is more than one, it is proportionably ſhorter and has fewer flowers. The flowers that ornament the top of the ſtalk grow in a ſmall corymbus, and have naked footſtalks, which ariſe one over the other the length of the flower. Each floret is ſmall, and of a pale-blue colour, and the petals are expanded in the uſual ſtar like manner. It will be in blow the beginning of September. This ſpecies is chiefly valued on account of the flowers coming out at this unuſual ſeaſon, alſo, on account of the leaves, which will be green and in a growing ſtate during the whole courſe of the winter months.

*and Single-leaved Star Hyacinth*

8. Single-leaved Star Hyacinth. This ſpecies hath a ſmall, roundiſh, ſolid bulb, from whence grows a ſingle, roundiſh leaf. The ſtalk is tender, roundiſh, and riſes to about the height of ſix or ſeven inches. The top is ornamented with white ſtarry flowers, they are ſmall, and appear early in the ſpring, but ſeldom continue in blow longer

longer than in forming it, and the seeds are ripe in a few weeks after.

Culture. The culture of these sorts is very easy, and they will multiply themselves very fast by their offsets. A common border of garden mould will do for them all. To have them in perfection, they should be removed every two or three years, and their offsets cleared off and planted out. They also will flower and become good plants the second year after.

Any of them are easily raised from seeds, but this is hardly worth while, for they will be four or five years after they come up, before they flower. If any person chuses to practise this method, it may be done by sowing them an inch deep, in October, in common fine garden mould. In the spring they will come up, and require no other trouble during two years than keeping them clean from weeds, at which time they should be taken up and planted in beds at six inches asunder, where they may remain until they flower, which will be in two or three years after.

Dr. Hill says, the way to have the colours of these plants in perfection is, to raise them from seeds; for which purpose he orders a strange compost made of toad's dung, &c. But what he advances is as absurd as the compost he recommends; for seedlings of the *Scilla*, as well as the *Hyacinthus*, will not have one in twenty when they come to flower that will have their colours perfect, or, as he terms it, of a *celestial blue*; and when the sorts are good they are best preserved, and with much more expedition multiplied, by offsets.

Title. 1. The Common Squill, or Sea Onion, is entitled, *Scilla nudiflora, bracteis refractis*. Caspar Bauhine calls it, *Scilla vulgaris, radice rubrâ*; also, *Scilla radice albâ*; and Clusius, *Scilla Hispanica*. It grows common on the sandy sea shores in Spain, Sicily, and most of the warm parts of Europe.

2. The Lily Hyacinth is, *Scilla radice squamatâ*. Caspar Bauhine calls it, *Hyacinthus stellaris, folio & radice lilii*; and Tournefort, *Lilio-hyacinthus vulgaris, flore cæruleo*. It grows common in Spain, Portugal, the Pyrenees, &c.

3. Italian Hyacinth is, *Scilla radice solidâ, corymbo conferto hemisphærico*. Caspar Bauhine calls it, *Hyacinthus stellatus spicatus cinereus*; Besler, *Hyacinthus stellaris Italicus*; and Clusius, *Hyacinthus stellatus cinerei coloris*. It is of uncertain original.

4. Peruvian Hyacinth is, *Scilla radice solidâ, corymbo conferto conico*. C. Bauhine calls it, *Hyacinthus Indicus bulbosus stellatus*; and Clusius, *Hyacinthus bulbosus Peruanus*. It grows common in Lusitania.

5. The Byzantine, or Borage-flowered Star Hyacinth is, *Scilla floribus lateralibus alternis subnutantibus*. C. Bauhine calls it, *Hyacinthus stellaris cæruleus amœnus*; and Besler, *Hyacinthus stellaris Byzantinus*. It grows naturally in Byzantium.

6. Vernal Star Hyacinth is, *Scilla radice solidâ, floribus erectiusculis paucioribus*. C. Bauhine calls it, *Hyacinthus stellaris bifolius Germanicus*; Fuchsius, *Hyacinthus cæruleus minor*; and Clusius, *Hyacinthus stellaris, albo flore*. It grows naturally in France and Germany.

7. The Autumnal Star Hyacinth is, *Scilla radice solidâ, foliis filiformibus linearibus, floribus corymbosis, pedunculis nudis adscendentibus longitudine floris*. Sauvages calls it, *Scilla radice solidâ, [illegible] multifloro, floribus capitatis*; and Clusius, *Hyacinthus autumnalis minor*. It grows common in France, Spain, and Germany, also in many parts of England.

8. The Single-leaved Star Hyacinth is, *Scilla folio teretiusculo, latere [illegible]spicato*. John Bauhine calls it, *Bulbus monophyllus, flore albo*. It grows naturally in Lusitania.

Class and order in the Linnæan System. *Scilla* is of the class and order *Hexandria Monogynia*, and the characters are,

The characters. 1. CALYX. There is none.

2. COROLLA consists of six oval and very patent petals.

3. STAMINA are six subulated filaments about half the length of the corolla, with oblong incumbent antheræ.

4. PISTILLUM consists of a roundish germen, a single style the length of the stamina, and a simple stigma.

5. PERICARPIUM is a nearly oval, smooth, three-furrowed capsule, formed of three valves, and containing three cells.

6. SEMINA. The seeds are many, and roundish.

# CHAP. CCCCIX.

## *SCIRPUS*, RUSH GRASS.

THE English species of this genus are usually called,

Species.
1. Club Rush.
2. Dwarf Club Rush.
3. Least Upright Club Rush.
4. Floating Club Rush.
5. Bull Rush.
6. Round headed Bull Rush.
7. Pointed Bull Rush.
8. Round-rooted Bastard *Cyperus*.
9. Millet *Cyperus*-Grass.

Description of the Club 1. Club Rush. The root is slender, fibrous, and creeping. The stalks are round, smooth, full of a spungy pith, usually reddish at the bottom, and about a foot or a foot and a half high. The flowers terminate the stalks in oval spikes; they are of a brown colour, and appear in July.

and Dwarf Club Rush. 2. Dwarf Club Rush. The root is creeping, and scaly. The stalks are naked, striated, reddish near the bottom, and five or six inches high. The flowers come out from the tops of the stalks in small

small short heads, and are in greatest plenty in July

Least Upright. 3 Least Upright Club Rush The stalk is slender, naked, taper, setiforme, and four or five inches high The flowers terminate the stalk in small oval spikes, and are in greatest plenty in August

and Floating Club Rush 4 Floating Club Rush The stalks are leafy, flaccid, taper, and six or eight inches long The flowers terminate the stalks in small imbricated spikes, and are most common in July and August

Bull Rush, 5 Bull Rush The root is thick, creeping, of a blackish-red colour on the outside, and white within The stalks are numerous, thick, round, taper, smooth, without knots, full of a white spongy pith, of a strong green colour on the outside, and five or six feet high The flowers are collected in oval imbricated spikes growing on naked footstalks, they are harsh to the touch, of a dark-brown colour, and are in full blow in July and August

Round headed, 6 Round-headed Bull Rush The stalk is round, taper, naked, green, full of pith, and of different heights in different situations The flowers are collected in roundish imbricated spikes, at the base of which are situated two unequal, sharp-pointed leaves, and their time of blow is July

and Pointed Bull Rush, 7 Pointed Bull Rush The stalk is triangular, rigid, but yet soft to the touch, naked, and terminates in a very sharp point The flowers come out in roundish naked spikes from the sides of the stalks near the top, and appear in July and August

Round rooted Bastard Cyperus, 8 Round rooted Bastard Cyperus The root is round, knotty, hard, fibrated, and creeping The stalks are triangular, and two or three feet high The flowers are produced in panicles at the tops of the stalks, and appear chiefly in August

and Millet Cyperus-Grass described 9 Millet Cyperus Grass The stalks are triangular, a foot and a half or two feet high, and adorned with sharp-pointed leaves, which grow singly at the joints, and surround it with their base The flowers are collected in leafy umbels composed of many small imbricated spikes at the tops of the stalks, and appear in July

Method of propagating them None of these species are cultivated plants, but may nevertheless be easily effected, if a person is desirous of having a few of them, in some boggy or moist parts of his ground by planting the roots at any time of the year, but more especially in the autumn, soon after they have done flowering

Titles. 1 Club Rush is entitled, *Scirpus culmo tereti nudo, spicâ subovatâ terminali* Van Royen calls it, *Scirpus culmo nudo, spicâ terminali subovata*, Tournefort, *Scirpus equiseti capitulo majore*, Caspar Bauhine, *Juncus palustris, capitulo equiseti, major*, and Loesel, *Juncellus cyperoides capitulo simplici* It grows naturally in ditches, rivers, bogs, and moist places in England, and most countries of Europe

2 Dwarf Club Rush is, *Scirpus culmo striato nudo, spicâ bivalvi terminali longitudine calycis, radicibus squamulâ interstinctis* In the *Flora Lapp* it is termed, *Scirpus folio culmi unico* Tournefort calls it, *Scirpus montanus capitulo breviore*, Ray, *Juncus parvus palustris, cum parvis capitulis equiseti*, and Caspar Bauhine, *Gramen junceum, foliis et spicâ junci, minus* It grows naturally in moist places in most countries of Europe

3 Least Upright Club Rush is, *Scirpus culmo tereti nudo setiformi, spicâ ovatâ terminali bivalvi seminibus nudis* Van Royen calls it, *Scirpus magnitudine aciculæ*, Scheuchzer, *Juncus minimus, spicâ breviore squamosa spadiceâ*, Plukenet, *Juncellus minimus, capitulis equiseti*, and Morison, *Juncellus omnium minimus, capitulis equiseti* It grows naturally in waters and moist places in most countries of Europe

4 Floating Club Rush is, *Scirpus culmis teretibus nudis alternis, caule folioso flaccido* Guettard calls it, *Scirpus foliis linearibus planis, alternatim fasciculatis spicâ terminali*, Van Royen, *Scirpus caule folioso flaccido, scapis alternis capitatis* Tournefort, *Scirpus equiseti capitulo minori*, Caspar Bauhine, *Juncellus, capitulis equiseti, minor fluitans*, and Ray, *Gramen junceum clavatum minimum* It grows naturally in ditches, ponds, and moist places in England, France, and Germany

5 Bull Rush is, *Scirpus culmo tereti nudo, spicis ovatis pluribus pedunculatis terminalibus* Van Royen calls it, *Scirpus spicis copiosis*, Caspar Bauhine *Juncus maximus, seu scirpus major*, Tournefort, *Scirpus palustris altissimus*, Parkinson, *Juncus lævis maximus*, and Gerard, *Juncus aquaticus maximus* It grows naturally in rivers, brooks, and standing waters in most countries of Europe

6 Round headed Bull Rush is, *Scirpus culmo tereti nudo, spicis subglobosis glomeratis pedunculatis, involucro diphyllo inæquali mucronato* Sauvages calls it, *Scirpus panicula folio foliosa, spicis globosis pedunculatis lateralibus*, Caspar Bauhine, *Juncus acutus maritimus, capitulis rotundis*, Scheuchzer, *Scirpoides maritimum capitulis sparsis glomeratis*, Tournefort, *Scirpus maritimus, capitulis rotundis glomeratis*, Parkinson, *Juncus acutus maritimus alter*, and Dalechamp *Holoschænus* It grows naturally on the sea shores of England, and most of the southern countries of Europe

7 Pointed Bull Rush is, *Scirpus culmo triquetro nudo acuminato laterali, spicis conglomeratis* Micheli calls it, *Scirpo cyperus maritimus* Caspar Bauhine, *Juncus acutus maritimus, caule triquetro rigido et molli* and Plukenet, *Juncus acutus maritimus, caule triquetro rigido, mucrone pungente* It grows naturally on the sea-shores and by the sides of waters in England, Italy, Helvetia, and Virginia

8 Round rooted Bastard Cyperus is, *Scirpus culmo triquetro, panicula conglobatâ foliaceâ, spiculorum squamis trifidis intermediâ subulatâ* Van Royen calls it, *Cyperus culmo triquetro, panicula foliaceâ, pedunculis simplicissimis, spicis confertis*, Guettard, *Cyperus panicula subsessili, capitulis subovatis*, Caspar Bauhine, *Cyperus rotundus inodorus Germanicus*; also, *Cyperus rotundus inodorus Anglicus*, also, *Gramen cyperoides, paniculâ sparsâ, majus*, Scheuchzer, *Cyperus paniculâ compactâ, e spicis teretibus cassoribus compositâ*, and Micheli, *Scirpo-cyperus paluster, radice repente nodosa inodorâ, panicula sparsâ, capitulis majoribus* It grows naturally on the sea shores, and by the sides of rivers in most countries of Europe

9 Millet Cyperus-Grass is, *Scirpus culmo triquetro foliosa, umbellâ foliaceâ, pedunculis nudis supradecompositis, spicis confertis* Van Royen calls it, *Cyperus culmo triquetro, panicula foliosâ, pedunculis nudis supradecompositis, spicis confertis*, Caspar Bauhine, *Gramen cyperoides miliaceum*, Loesel, *Gramen arundinaceum, foliis acutissimis, paniculâ multiplici, aperta face*, and Parkinson, *Pseudocyperus miliaceus* It grows naturally in moist woods and watery places in most countries of Europe

Class and order in the Linnæan system *Scirpus* is of the class and order *Triandria Monogynia*, and the characters are,

The characters 1 Calyx The spike is every way imbricated The scales are oval, plane, and infexed, separating the flowers

2 COROLLA There is none

3 STAMINA are three longish filaments with oblong antheræ

4 PISTILLUM consists of a very small germen, and a long slender style, with three capillary stigmas

5 PERICARPIUM There is none

6 SEMEN The seed is single, three-sided, acuminated, and hairy

## CHAP. CCCCX.

## *SCLERANTHUS,* GERMAN KNOT-GRASS, or *KNAWEL.*

THERE is only one perennial of this genus, called, Perennial *Knawel*

The root is long, tough, and whitish The stalks are numerous, round, slender, jointed, hoary, branching, and lie on the ground The leaves are oblong, narrow, pointed, hoary, grow opposite by pairs, and embrace the stalk with their base The flowers come out in clusters from the ends and divisions of the branches, they are of a white colour, appear in July and August, and the seeds ripen in the autumn

The plant described

This plant is propagated by sowing the seeds in some dry sandy parts of the garden where they are to remain, and after the plants come up they will require no trouble, except thinning them where they are too close, and keeping them clean from weeds

Method of propagation

This species is titled, *Scleranthus calycibus fructus clausis* Ray calls it, *Knawel incanum, flore majore, perenne*, Tabernæmontanus, *Polygonum minus polycarpon*, and Tournefort, *Alchimilla gramineo folio, majori flore* It grows naturally in sandy gravelly places, dry banks, &c. in England, and most countries of Europe

Titles

*Scleranthus* is of the class and order *Decandria Digynia*, and the characters are,

Class and order in the Linnæan system The characters

1 CALYX is a monophyllous, tubular, permanent perianthium, divided into five acute segments

2 COROLLA There is none

3 STAMINA are ten very small, awl-shaped, erect filaments sitting in the calyx, with roundish antheræ

4 PISTILLUM consists of a roundish germen, and two erect capillary styles the length of the stamina, with simple stigmas

5 PERICARPIUM is a slender oval capsule situated in the bottom of the cup

6 SEMINA The seeds are two, convex on one side, and plane on the other

## CHAP CCCCXI.

## *SCOLYMUS,* GOLDEN THISTLE.

THIS genus consists of two species, one of which is an annual, the other a perennial, called the Golden Thistle

The root is thick, fleshy, and strikes deep into the ground The stalks are thick, send out many branches from the sides, grow to about a yard high, and have leafy borders running from joint to joint, which are indented, and armed with spines The leaves are stiff, jagged, thick on their borders, and possessed of spines The flowers are produced from the ends of the branches, they are of a golden-yellow colour, appear in July, and the seeds ripen in the autumn

This plant described

This plant is propagated by sowing the seeds, early in the spring, in the places where they are to remain When they come up, they will require no trouble, except thinning them where they are too close, and keeping them clean from weeds The ground should be fresh, undunged, naturally light and dry, and the place open and full

Method of propagating it

full upon the sun, and being thus stationed, there will be a greater probability of the seeds ripening in the autumn

Titles. This species is titled, *Scolymus foliis margine incrassatis* Sauvages calls it, *Scolymus vivax* Caspar Bauhine calls it, *Scolymus chrysanthemos*, Clusius, *Scolymus Theophrasti Hispanicus*, and Dodonæus, *Carduus chrysanthemos* It grows naturally in France, Italy, and Sicily

Class and order in the Linnæan system. The characters. *Scolymus* is of the class and order *Syngenesia Polygamia Æqualis*, and the characters are,

1 Calyx The general calyx is imbricated and oval The valves are numerous, spear-shaped, loose, and acute

2 Corolla The compound flower is imbricated and uniform The hermaphrodite florets are numerous, equal, and each has one tongue-shaped, narrow, truncated petal, lightly indented in five parts at the top

3 Stamina are five very short capillary filaments, having a cylindrical tubular anthera

4 Pistillum consists of an oblong germen, a filiform style longer than the stamina, and two reflexed stigmas

5 Pericarpium There is none

6 Semina The seeds are single, rather oblong, triangular, pointed at the base, and have no down

The receptacle is paleaceous and convex The paleæ are roundish, plane, indented in three parts at the top, and are longer than the seeds, which they separate from each other

# CHAP. CCCCXII.

## *SCORZONERA*, VIPER's GRASS

THE species of this genus are chiefly cultivated for physical uses, or for culinary purposes, in our kitchen gardens On these accounts they are excellent, and those and other good properties attend their flowers The most durable sorts shall have a place here, which are,

Species.
1 Broad Sinuated-leaved Viper's Grass
2 Dwarf Broad-leaved Viper's Grass
3 Grass leaved Viper's Grass
4 Downy Oval leaved Viper's Grass
5 Purple Viper's Grass
6 Narrow-leaved Viper's Grass
7 Oriental Viper's Grass

Description of the Broad Sinuated-leaved. 1 The Broad Sinuated leaved Viper's Grass This has a large tap root as big as a small carrot, covered with a dark brown coat, white within, brittle, and possessed of a milky juice The stalk is robust, round, smooth, branching, and grows to about a yard high The leaves are long, sharp pointed, sinuated, and embrace the stalks with their base The flowers grow from the ends of the branches, they are large, of a bright-yellow colour, will be in blow in June and July, and ripen their seeds in August or September

Dwarf Broad leaved. 2 Dwarf Broad-leaved Viper's Grass This hath a tap-root like the former, though smaller The stalk grows only to about a foot and a half high, and is almost naked The leaves are large, plane, and very much veined One large yellow flower terminates each of the branches, it appears in June and July, and ripens its seed about a month after

Grass-leaved, 3 Grass-leaved Viper's Grass The root of this plant is large and thick The stalks are branching, and will grow to about two feet high The flowers are of a pale-yellow colour, and one is situated at the top of each of the branches; they flower in June or July, and ripen their seeds about a month after

4 Downy Oval leaved Viper's Grass The stalk is upright, single, and very downy The leaves are of an oval figure, white, downy, full of veins, and sharp-pointed; they grow alternately, and embrace the stalk with their base The flowers come out singly, for the most part, from the wings of the leaves near the tops of the stalks, they appear about the usual time, and ripen their seeds soon after Downy Oval leaved,

5 Purple Viper's Grass The stalks are taper and branching The leaves are narrow, awl-shaped, plane, entire, and placed alternately on the branches The flowers grow on slender footstalks, they are of a pale purple colour, and appear about the same time with the former Purple,

6 Narrow-leaved Hungarian Viper's Grass The stalks are simple, hairy, and grow to about a foot high The leaves grow close together, they are narrow, awl shaped, and almost as long as the stalks The flower is large, its colour is yellow, having a tinge of purple on the under-side, and flowers about the same time as the former Narrow-leaved,

7 Oriental Viper's Grass The stalks are very short The leaves are smooth, and deeply indented The flowers are yellow, and appear about the time of the former and Oriental Viper's Grass

All these plants are raised by sowing of the seeds in the spring, in beds of light dry earth double dug, they should be sown thinly, and covered over with about half an inch of fine mould When the plants come up too close, they should be thinned to proper distances, which ought to be always according to the size of the plants, and afterwards they will require no trouble, except keeping them clean from weeds By the autumn the roots will be grown very large, Culture

and

and the summer following they will flower strong, and perfect their seeds soon after

Title

1 The Broad Sinuated leaved Viper's Grass is titled, *Scorzonera caule ramoso, foliis amplexicaulibus integris serrulatis* Caspar Bauhine calls it, *Scorzonera latifolia sinuata*, and Clusius, *Scorzonera major Hispanica* 1 It grows naturally in Spain and Siberia

2 Dwarf Broad-leaved Viper's Grass is, *Scorzonera caule subnudo unifloro, foliis lato lanceolatis nervosis planis* Caspar Bauhine calls it, *Scorzonera humilis latifolia nervosa*, and Clusius, *Scorzonera humilis lat fol a Pannonica* It grows naturally in Hungary, and several of the northern countries of Europe

3 Grass leaved Viper's Grass is, *Scorzonera foliis lineari ensiformibus integris carinatis* Buxbaum calls it, *Scorzonera Lusitanica, gramineo folio, flore pallide luteo*, and Gmelin, *Scorzonera caule ramoso, foliis linearibus acuminatis carinatis, calycibus acutis* It grows naturally in Siberia and Portugal

4 Downy Oval-leaved Viper's Grass is, *Scorzonera foliis ovatis nervosis tomentosis integerrimis sessilibus* Tournefort calls it, *Scorzonera orientalis latifolia nervosa candidissima & tomentosa* It grows naturally in the East

5 Purple Viper's Grass is *Scorzonera foliis linear-subulatis integris planis, pedunculis cylindricis* Gmelin calls it, *Scorzonera caule ramoso tereti, foliis linearibus acuminatis, calycibus obtusiusculis*, and Caspar Bauhine, *Scorzonera angustifolia subcærulea* It grows naturally in Siberia, Austria, and several parts of Germany

6 Narrow leaved Viper's Grass is, *Scorzonera foliis subulatis integris, pedunculo incrassato, caule simplicissimo, basi villoso*. Caspar Bauhine calls it, *Scorzonera angustifolia prima*, Clusius, *Scorzonera humilis angustifolia Pannonica* 3 and Barrelier, *Tragopogon pin fol um Hispanicum* It grows naturally on the hilly parts of Spain, Austria, and some parts of France

7 Oriental Viper's Grass is, *Scorzonera foliis sinuatis denticulatis acutis, caulibus subunifloris* It grows naturally in the East

Class and order in the Linnæan system

*Scorzonera* is of the class and order *Syngenesia Polygamia Æqualis*, and the characters are,

The characters

1 CALYX The general calyx is imbricated, long, and nearly cylindrical

1 COROLLA The general flower is imbricated and uniform The florets are many, and the outer ones are longest, each of them consists of one tongue-shaped, narrow, truncated petal, indented at the top in five parts

3 STAMINA consist of five very short capillary filaments, with a cylindrical tubular anthera

4 PISTILLUM consists of an oblong germen, a filiforme style the length of the stamina, and two reflexed stigmas

5 PERICARPIUM There is none The calyx becomes oval and connivent

6 SEMINA The seeds are single, oblong, striated, and crowned with a feathery down

The receptacle is naked

# C H A P. CCCCXIII.

## *SCROPHULARIA*, FIG-WORT.

Species

THE perennial species of this genus are,

1 Maryland Fig wort
2 Knobby-rooted Fig wort
3 Water Fig-wort, or Betony
4 Auriculated Fig wort
5 Balm-leaved Fig wort
6 Oriental Fig-wort
7 Elder-leaved Fig wort
8 Lucid Fig wort
9 Nettle leaved Fig wort

Description of Maryland

1 Maryland Figwort The root is thick, knobbed, and spreading under the surface The stalks are quadrangular, upright, and two or three feet high The leaves are heart-shaped, rounded at the base, sharply serrated on their edges, and grow opposite to each other The flowers come out in long loose spikes from the tops of the stalks, they are of a greenish colour, appear in July, and the seeds ripen in the autumn

and Knobby-rooted Fig-wort

2 Knobby rooted Fig-wort The root is full of knobs, whitish, and spreading under the surface of the ground The stalks are four-cornered, upright, hollow, purplish, and a yard high The leaves are heart shaped, serrated, of a brownish-green colour on the upper side, but pale underneath, have a strong disagreeable odour, and grow opposite by pairs on the stalks The flowers are collected in long loose spikes at the tops of the stalks, they are of a purple colour, appear in June and July, and the seeds ripen in August

Its use in medicine

The leaves and root of this species are used in medicine, and said to be excellent against scrophulous disorders, and for the cure of the piles

Variety

There is a variety of this species with striped leaves

Water Fig-wort described

3 Water Fig-wort, or Betony The stalks are thick, firm, square, hollow, of a brown colour, have a thin acute membrane running from joint to joint, and are three or four feet high The leaves are heart-shaped, obtuse, crenated on their edges, and grow opposite to each other on short footstalks The flowers come out in loose spikes from the tops of the stalks, they are of a reddish-purple colour, appear in June and July, and the seeds ripen in August

There

Variety. There is a variety of this species with variegated leaves.

Auriculated. 4. Auriculated Fig-wort. The stalks are strong, upright, smooth, cornered, and three or four feet high. The leaves are heart-shaped, oblong, appendiculated at the base, serrated on the edges, green on the upper side, whitish underneath, and grow opposite to each other on the stalks. The flowers come out in loose spikes from the tops of the stalks; they are of a green-purple colour, appear in June and July, and the seeds ripen in September.

Baum-leaved. 5. Baum-leaved Fig-wort. The stalks are upright, firm, hollow, and four feet high. The leaves are heart-shaped, doubly serrated on their edges, and grow opposite to each other on short footstalks. The flowers come out from the tops of the stalks in loose compound spikes; they are of a reddish green colour, appear in July and August, and the seeds ripen in the autumn.

Oriental. 6. Oriental Fig-wort. This creeps much by the root. The stalks are upright, hollow, and two or three feet high. The leaves are spear-shaped, narrow, acutely serrated, and grow on short footstalks. The flowers come out from the tops of the stalks in compound loose spikes or bunches; they are of a brown colour, appear in May and June, and the seeds ripen in the autumn.

Elder-leaved. 7. Elder-leaved Fig-wort. The stalks are square, firm, hollow, four-cornered, smooth, and three or four feet high. The leaves are large, of different shapes, jagged, and irregularly cut on the edges. The flowers come out from the wings of the leaves at the upper parts of the stalks on forked footstalks; they are large, and of a purple colour, having a mixture of green; they appear in June and July, and the seeds ripen in the autumn.

Lucid. 8. Lucid Fig-wort, or Broad-leaved Dog's Rue. The root has many fleshy fibres. The stalks are upright, smooth, green, cornered, and about three feet high. The lower leaves are large, bipinnated, smooth, and of a lucid green colour; the upper leaves are narrow, jagged, or variously cut on the edges, and grow on long footstalks. The flowers come out in loose slender spikes from the tops of the stalks; they are of a purplish colour, with a mixture of white and some green; they appear in June and July, and the seeds ripen in September.

and Nettle-leaved Fig-wort described. 9. Nettle-leaved Fig-wort. The stalks are upright, slender, hollow, and about two feet high. The leaves are heart-shaped, pointed, and acutely serrated; the lower ones grow opposite to each other, and the upper ones are placed alternately. The flowers come out two together on footstalks from the wings of the leaves; they are of a dull red or purple colour, appear in June or July, and the seeds ripen in August.

All these sorts are extremely hardy, and will grow in almost any soil or situation, but they delight most in moist places, and the shade.

Culture. They are propagated by parting of the roots, which may be done in the autumn, soon after they have done flowering, or early in the spring, before the stalks arise; and after they are set out, will require no trouble, except keeping them clean from weeds.

There are varieties of most of them with variegated leaves; and in order to continue them in perfection, they must have a dry, light, and barren soil; and being thus stationed, the stripes will be large, and the colours strong and beautiful.

They are also raised by seeds, and by this method the best plants are generally obtained. The seeds should be sown in the autumn, soon after they are ripe; and if the land be moist and good, the stalks will be stronger and taller by some feet, the spikes longer, and the flowers larger and fairer. After they come up they will require no trouble, except thinning them where they are too close, keeping them clean from weeds, and reducing the roots, as often as they become too spreading, and without bounds.

1. Maryland Fig-wort is titled, *Scrophularia foliis cordatis serratis acutis basi rotundatis, caule obtusangulo*. Gronovius calls it, *Scrophularia foliis cordatis oppositis, racemo terminali*; and Ray, *Scrophularia Marilandica, longo profundius serrato urticæ folio*. It is a native of Virginia. Titles.

2. Knobby-rooted Fig-wort is, *Scrophularia foliis cordatis trinerviatis, caule acutangulo*. In the Hortus Cliffort it is termed, *Scrophularia foliis cordatis, racemo terminali*. Caspar Bauhine calls it, *Scrophularia nodosa fœtida*; Cammerarius, *Scrophularia*; Gerard, *Scrophularia major*; and Parkinson, *Scrophularia vulgaris*. It grows naturally in moist woods and hedges in England, and most countries of Europe.

3. Water Fig-wort, or Betony, is, *Scrophularia foliis cordatis petiolatis decurrentibus obtusis, caule membranis angulato, racemis terminalibus*. Guettard calls it, *Scrophularia foliis cordatis petiolorum alis decurrentibus*; Caspar Bauhine, *Scrophularia aquatica major*; Cammerarius, *Scrophularia fœmina*; Gerard, *Betonica aquatica*; and Parkinson, *Betonica major*. It grows naturally in moist places in England, Helvetia, and Gaul.

4. Auriculated Fig-wort is, *Scrophularia foliis cordato-oblongis basi appendiculatis subtus tomentosis, racemis terminalibus*. Tournefort calls it, *Scrophularia betonicæ folio*; Barrelier, *Scrophularia aquatica montana mollior*; and Lobel, *Betonica aquatica septentrionalium*. It grows naturally in Spain.

5. Baum-leaved Fig-wort is, *Scrophularia foliis cordatis duplicato-serratis, racemo composito*. Tournefort calls it, *Scrophularia melissæ folio*; and Plukenet, *Scrophularia scorodoniæ folio*. It grows naturally in England and Lusitania.

6. Oriental Fig-wort is, *Scrophularia foliis lanceolatis serratis petiolatis caulinis ternis, racemis oppositis*. Van Royen calls it, *Scrophularia foliis lanceolato linearibus acute serratis inferne incisis, racemo composito*; and Tournefort, *Scrophularia orientalis, foliis cannabinis*. It grows naturally in the East.

7. Elder-leaved Fig-wort is, *Scrophularia foliis interrupte pinnatis cordatis inæqualibus, racemo terminali pedunculis axillaribus geminis dichotomis*. Van Royen calls it, *Scrophularia foliis difformibus, pedunculis axillaribus aggregatis*; Alpinus, *Scrophularia sambucifolia*; Caspar Bauhine, *Scrophularia foliis laciniatis*; Morison, *Scrophularia sambuci foliis, capsulis maximis*; and Ray, *Scrophularia Lusitanica, maximo flore, foliis dissectis*. It grows naturally in Spain, Portugal, and the East.

8. Lucid Fig-wort is, *Scrophularia foliis inferioribus bipinnatis glaberrimis, racemis bipartitis*. Caspar Bauhine calls it, *Scrophularia foliis filicis modo laciniatis, sive ruta canina latifolia*; Boccone, *Scrophularia saxatilis lucida, laserpitii Massiliensis folio*; and Tournefort, *Scrophularia glauco folio in amplas lacinias diviso*. It grows naturally in Crete, and the East.

9. Nettle-leaved Fig-wort is, *Scrophularia foliis cordatis superioribus alternis, pedunculis axillaribus bifloris*. Caspar Bauhine calls it, *Scrophularia urticæ folio*; and Cammerarius, *Scrophularia peregrina*. It grows naturally in Italy.

Class and order in the Linnæan system. *Scrophularia* is of the class and order *Didynamia Angiospermia*; and the characters are,

1. CALYX.

The characters

1 CALYX is a monophyllous permanent perianthium, divided into five short rounded segments

2 COROLLA is one unequal petal The tube is globular, large, and inflated, the limb is small, and divided into five parts The two upper segments are the largest, and stand erect, the two lateral ones are spreading, and the lower one is reflexed

3 STAMINA are four linear declining filaments, of which two are longer than the others, having didymous antheræ

4 PISTILLUM consists of an oval germen, a simple style the length of the stamina, and a simple stigma

5 PERICARPIUM is a roundish, acuminated, bilocular capsule, formed of two valves, and opening at the top

6 SEMINA The seeds are many, and small

# C H A P. CCCCXIV.

## *SCUTELLARIA,* SKULL-CAP.

Species

THE species of this genus are,

1 Oriental Skull-cap
2 Alpine Skull-cap
3 Siberian Skull-cap
4 Canada Skull cap
5 English Skull cap, or Hooded Willow-herb
6 Lesser English Skull-cap, or Hooded Willow-herb
7 Swedish Skull-cap
8 Germander-leaved Skull-cap
9 Hyssop leaved Skull-cap
10 Italian Skull cap
11 Tallest Skull cap
12 Cretan Skull cap

Oriental,

1 Oriental Skull cap The stalks are weak, ligneous, divide into many branches, and, unless supported, lie on the ground The leaves are nearly triangular, jagged almost to the midrib, of a light-green colour on the upper side, downy underneath, and grow opposite to each other on slender footstalks The flowers come out in short spikes from the ends of the branches, they are of a bright yellow colour, appear in June and July, and the seeds ripen in August and September

Alpine,

2 Alpine Skull cap The stalks are shrubby and trailing The leaves are heart shaped, oval, and deeply cut and crenated on the edges The flowers come out from the tops of the stalks in roundish, four-cornered, imbricated spikes, they are of a fine violet colour, and have a white lip, they appear in June, July, and August, and the seeds ripen in the autumn

Siberian

3 Siberian Skull-cap The stalks are shrubby, and trailing The leaves are heart shaped, acute-pointed, smooth on both sides, and deeply cut or serrated on their edges The flowers come out from the ends of the stalks in rounded, four-cornered, imbricated spikes, they are large, of a white colour, appear in June, July, and August, and the seeds ripen in the autumn

Canada,

4 Canada Skull cap The stalks are weak, slender, lie on the ground, and strike root at the joints The leaves are oval, spear-shaped, serrated, smooth, and grow on short footstalks The flowers come out in loose leafy spikes or bunches from the sides of the stalks, they are small, appear in June, and often continue in succession until the end of summer

English,

5 English Skull-cap, or Hooded Willow-herb The stalks are tender, weak, and trailing The leaves are cordated, spear-shaped, crenated on the edges, of a dark-green colour, and grow opposite to each other on very short footstalks The flowers come out from the wings of the leaves, they are small, of a blue colour, appear in July and August, and the seeds ripen in the autumn

Lesser,

6 Lesser English Skull-cap, or Hooded Willow-herb The stalks are small, tender, square, and send forth a few branches by pairs from the sides The leaves are heart-shaped, oval, almost entire, and grow opposite to each other on very short footstalks The flowers come out from the wings of the leaves, almost the whole length of the stalks and branches, they are small, and of a purple colour spotted on the inside with white, they appear in July and August, and the seeds ripen in the autumn

Swedish,

7 Swedish Skull-cap The stalks are tender, and trailing The lower leaves are hastated, the upper ones sagittated, their edges are undivided, and they grow opposite to each other on the stalks The flowers come out two or three together from the wings of the leaves, they are of a blue colour, appear in July and August, and the seeds ripen in the autumn

Germander leaved

8 Germander-leaved Skull-cap The stalks are upright, four-cornered, branching and about two feet high The leaves are oval, and the lower ones obsoletely serrated on the edges, but the upper ones are entire, and sit close, having no footstalk The flowers come out from the wings of the leaves a great way down the upper parts of the branches, they are of a fine blue colour, spotted on the inner side, appear in June and July, and the seeds ripen in the autumn

and Hyssop leaved Skull cap described

9 Hyssop-leaved Skull-cap The stalks are slender, square, branching a little, and about a foot and a half high The leaves are spear-shaped, narrow, hairy, and grow opposite on very short footstalks The flowers come out from the wings of the leaves at the upper part of

of the stalks, they are small, of a blue or purplish colour, appear in July and August, and the seeds ripen in the autumn

10 Italian Skull-cap The stalks are four cornered, hairy, firm and about a foot and a half or two feet high The leaves are nearly heart shaped serrated, hairy, and grow opposite to each other The flowers come out from the tops of the stalks in long spikes, they are moderately large, of a purple colour, appear in June and July, and the seeds ripen in August — Italian Skull-cap described

There is a variety of this species with white flowers — Variety

11 Tallest Skull-cap The stalks are strong, send out a few slender branches from the sides, and grow to be four feet high The leaves are heart-shaped, oblong, acuminated, serrated, and of a dark green colour The flowers are produced from the tops of the stalks and branches in naked spikes they are of a purple colour, appear in June and July, and the seeds ripen in the autumn — Tallest,

12 Cretan Skull-cap The stalks are woody, send forth a few slender branches from the sides, and grow to be two feet high The leaves are heart-shaped, obtuse, bluntly serrated, of a light-green colour on the upper side, and hoary underneath The flowers are produced from the tops of the stalks in long thick spikes, they are of a white colour, appear in July, and the seeds ripen in the autumn — and Cretan Skull-cap described

These sorts are all best raised from seeds, which should be sown in the autumn, soon after they are ripe In the spring, when the plants are all up, they should be thinned where they are too close, and kept clean from weeds, which is all the culture they will require The cuttings also will grow, if planted before they come into flower, about the beginning of June, in a shady place, and duly watered By this means the plants may be multiplied, but they will be always of inferior beauty to such as have been raised from seeds — Propagation

1 Oriental Skull-cap is titled, *Scutellaria foliis incisis subtus tomentosis, spicis rotundato tetragonis* Van Royen calls it, *Scutellaria foliis pinnatifidis*, Tournefort, *Cassida orientalis, folio chamædryos, flore luteo*, also, *Scutellaria orientalis incana, foliis laciniatis, flore luteo* It grows naturally in the East, and in America — Titles

2 Alpine Skull cap is, *Scutellaria foliis cordatis inciso-serratis crenatis, spicis imbricatis rotundato-tetragonis* In the *Hortus Cliffort* it is termed, *Scutellaria foliis ovatis, spicis imbricatis* Caspar Bauhine calls it, *Teucrium Alpinum inodorum, magno flore* It grows naturally on the Helvetian mountains

3 Siberian Skull-cap is, *Scutellaria foliis cordatis inciso serratis acutis glabris, spicis imbricatis rotundato-tetragonis* Tournefort calls it, *Cassida Alpina supina, magno flore albido* It grows naturally in Siberia and Tartary

4 Canada Skull-cap is, *Scutellaria foliis lævibus carina scabris, racemis lateralibus foliosis* Van Royen calls it, *Scutellaria foliis cordato-lanceolatis serratis, pedunculis multifloris*, Gronovius, *Scutellaria foliis ovato lanceolatis petiolatis, racemis foliosis*, and Morison, *Scutellaria palustris repens Virginiana major, flore minore* It grows naturally in Canada and Virginia

5 English Skull cap, or Hooded Willow-herb, is, *Scutellaria foliis cordato lanceolatis crenatis, floribus axillaribus* Caspar Bauhine calls it, *Lysimachia cærulea galericulata, sive gratiola cærulea*, Dalechamp, *Lysimachia galericulata*, Tournefort, *Cassida palustris vulgatior flore cæruleo*, and Parkinson *Lysimachia cærulea, sive latifolia major* It grows naturally by watery places in England, and most countries of Europe

6 Lesser English Skull cap, or Hooded Willow herb, is, *Scutellaria foliis cordato ovatis subintegerrimis, floralibus oblongis* Tournefort calls it, *Cassida palustris minima, flore purpurascente*, Ray, *Lysimachia galericulata minor*, and Gerard, *Gratiola latifolia* It grows naturally in marshy places in England

7 Swedish Skull-cap is, *Scutellaria foliis integerrimis inferioribus hastatis, superioribus sagittatis* Rivinus calls it, *Scutellaria folio non serrato* It grows naturally in Sweden

8 Germander-leaved Skull cap is, *Scutellaria foliis sessilibus ovatis inferioribus obsolete serratis superioribus integerrimis* Gronovius calls it, *Scutellaria foliis integerrimis*, Plukenet, *Scutellaria cærulea Virginiana, lamium aut potius Teucrii folio minore*, and Ray, *Scutellaria Teucrii folio, Marilandica* It grows naturally in Virginia and Canada

9 Hyssop-leaved Skull cap is, *Scutellaria foliis lanceolatis* Petiver calls it, *Cassida Mariana hyssopifolia* It grows naturally in Virginia

10 Italian Skull-cap is, *Scutellaria foliis subcordatis serratis, spicis elongatis secundis* Columna calls it, *Cassida*, Caspar Bauhine, *Lamium peregrinum, sive scutellaria* It grows naturally about Florence and Leghorn

11 Tallest Skull cap is, *Scutellaria foliis cordato-oblongis acuminatis serratis, spicis secundis* Tournefort calls it, *Scutellaria orientalis altissima, urticæ folio* It grows naturally in the East

12 Cretan Skull cap is, *Scutellaria villosa, foliis cordatis obtusis obtusiusque serratis, spicis imbricatis bracteis setaceis* Tournefort calls it, *Cassida Cretica fruticosa, folio catariæ, flore albo* It grows naturally in Crete

*Scutellaria* is of the class and order *Didynamia Gymnospermia*, and the characters are, — Class and order in the Linnæan system

1 Calyx is a very short, monophyllous, tubular perianthium, having an entire brim, and an incumbent squammula, which covers the mouth after the flower is fallen — The characters.

2 Corolla is one ringent petal The tube is very short, and bent backward, the mouth is long, and compressed, the upper lip is concave, and divided into three segments, the middle segment being concave and emarginated, the two side ones plane and acute, the lower lip is broad, and emarginated

3 Stamina are four filaments secreted under the upper lip, of which two are longer than the others, having small antheræ

4 Pistillum consists of a germen divided into four parts, a filiforme style the situation and length of the stamina, and a simple, recurved, acuminated stigma

5 Pericarpium There is none The calyx being closed by the incumbent squammula, becomes helmet-shaped, triquetrous, contains the seeds, and opens in the lower edge for their discharge, when ripe

6 Semina The seeds are four, and roundish

# CHAP. CCCCXV.

## *SEDUM*, LESSER HOUSE-LEEK

THE perennial species of this genus are,

Species

1 Orpine, or Live-long
2 *Anacampseros*, or Smaller Round leaved Orpine
3 *Aizoon*, or Yellow Siberian Orpine
4 Small Creeping Orpine
5 Palestine *Sedum*
6 Reflexed *Sedum*, Yellow Stone-crop, or Prick madam
7 Rock Stone-crop
8 Spanish *Sedum*
9 White Stone-crop
10 Common Wall Stone-crop, or Wall-Pepper
11 Insipid Stone crop

Orpine described

1 Orpine, or Live long The root consists of many fleshy tubers, among which are numerous long fibres The stalks are upright, round, smooth, succulent, and a foot and a half to two feet high The leaves are oval, oblong, of a thickish substance, succulent, serrated, of a greyish or bluish green colour, and come out closely, but without order, all round the stalks The flowers come out in corymbous bunches from the tops of the stalks, they appear in July, and the seeds ripen in the autumn

Varieties

The principal varieties of this species are,
The White Flowered,
The Small Purple,
The Great Purple,
The Broad leaved,
The Great Spanish, &c

The roots of all these are composed of the like kind of fleshy tubercles The stalks and leaves are more or less tinged with green, red, or purple, according to the varieties, and they are of different heights, and the flowers of different colours, as their names distinguish, which are the chief differences in which these varieties consist

Medicinal properties of it

This species is held vulnerary, astringent, and good for old sores, ulcers, and mitigating of pains, by bruising the leaves or roots, and applying them to the afflicted parts They are also said to take away corns, if applied to them in this manner But notwithstanding the great things said of this plant, it is seldom used in medicine, and very little regard is paid to it in the present practice

Culture

This plant is propagated by planting the cuttings in any of the summer-months

Anacampseros described

2 *Anacampseros*, or Smaller Round leaved Orpine The root is fibrous, and the stalks trail on the ground The leaves are roundish, wedge-shaped, and grow alternately on the stalks The flowers terminate the stalks in a corymbus, they are of a purple colour, appear in July, and sometimes the seeds ripen in the autumn

Culture

This is a very beautiful plant, and continues green all the year It is propagated by parting of the roots, or planting the slips or cuttings in a moist place

Aizoon described

3 *Aizoon*, or Yellow Siberian Orpine The root is composed of many tubercles and fleshy fibres The stalks are numerous, round, succulent, upright, and about a foot high The leaves are spear-shaped, plane, of a thick substance, partly serrated on the edges, and grow alternately on every side the stalk The flowers are produced from the tops of the stalks in flat bunches, they are large, of a bright yellow colour, appear in June and July, and the seeds ripen in August

Culture

This plant is propagated like the former

Small Creeping Orpine described

4 Small Creeping Orpine The stalks are procumbent, and strike root from the sides into the ground The leaves are wedge-shaped, concave, and slightly indented on their edges The flowers terminate the stalks in flat bunches, they are of a purple colour, appear in July, and often continue in succession through August and September

Culture

This plant is propagated by parting of the roots at any time of the year

Palestine Sedum described

5 Palestine *Sedum* The root consists of many thick fleshy fibres The radical leaves are spathulated, spear-shaped, acute, smooth, entire, and form a large bunch at the crown of the root The stalk is simple, adorned with a few narrow, acute-pointed leaves near the bottom, and grows to about six or eight inches high The flowers come out in long loose spikes from the tops of the stalks, each footstalk generally carrying two flowers, they shew themselves in June and July, and sometimes the seeds ripen in the autumn

Culture

It is propagated by parting of the roots like the other sorts

Reflexed Sedum described

6 Reflexed *Sedum*, Yellow Stone-crop, or Prick-madam The root is small, and tender The stalks are slender, succulent, and trailing The leaves are awl shaped, succulent, acute-pointed, and of a whitish-green or greyish colour The flowers come out from the tops of the stalks in reflexed spikes or bunches, they are of a bright yellow colour, appear in July and August, and the seeds ripen in September

Culture

This plant is propagated like the former kinds

Rock Stone crop

7 Rock Stone crop The stalks are slender, purple, and trailing The leaves are awl-shaped, short, of a glaucous colour, quincuncarially imbricated, and the lower ones fall off on being touched The flowers come out from the tops of the stalks in roundish bunches they are of a bright-yellow colour, appear in July and August, and the seeds ripen in the autumn

and Spanish Sedum described

8 Spanish *Sedum* The leaves are taper, succulent, acute, of a glaucous colour, and the radical ones grow in clusters at the crown of the root The stalks are slender, round succulent, and four or five inches high The flowers come out in bunches from the tops of the stalks, they are downy, and of a white colour, they appear in June, July, and August, by which time the seeds,

seeds, which succeed the first flowers, will be ripe

White. 9 White Stone-crop. The stalks are slender, trailing, and eight or ten inches long. The leaves are oblong, obtuse, taper, sessile, spreading nearly horizontally, and grow alternately on the stalks. The flowers come out from the tops or the stalks in branching tufts or bunches; they are of a white colour, appear in June, July, and August, and the seeds ripen in September.

Common Wall, 10 Common Wall Stone-crop, or Wall Pepper. The stalks are slender, round, succulent, and five or six inches high. The leaves are short, pointed, thick, and succulent. The flowers come out from the tops of the stalks in bunches; they are of a yellow colour, appear in June, July, and August, and the seeds ripen in the autumn.

and Insipid Stone crop described. 11 Insipid Stone-crop. The stalks are thick, succulent, and short. The leaves are nearly oval, succulent, and imbricated in six rows or directions. The flowers come out from the upper parts of the stalks in tufts or bunches; they are moderately large, and of a yellow colour; they appear in July and August, and the seeds ripen in the autumn.

Propagation. The first, second, third, fourth, fifth, sixth, and eighth sorts are preserved in some curious gardens; but the others are seldom admitted, as they grow naturally on the tops of walls, rocks, old ruins, and the like. They may be easily propagated by parting of the roots, or planting the cuttings; and they may be made to occupy the tops of any walls, provided there be the least mould for the roots to strike into. They are admirably adapted for preserving the coping of mud-walls; and for this purpose the roots should be ranged along the tops in three rows, when the mortar for the preservation of the coping is first laid on.

The seeds also may be sown on the copings of such walls when they are first made, where they will grow, and become greatly preservative to such kind of fences.

Titles. 1 Orpine, or Live-long, is titled, *Sedum foliis planiusculis serratis, corymbo folioso, caule erecto*. In the *Hortus Cliffort.* it is termed, *Sedum foliis planiusculis patentibus serratis, corymbo terminali*. Caspar Bauhine calls it, *Telephium vulgare*; also, *Telephium purpureum majus*; also, *Telephium purpureum minus*; also, *Telephium latifolium peregrinum*. John Bauhine, *Anacampseros maxima*; Fuchsius, *Telephium album*; Haller, *Sedum foliis ovalibus serratis, umbellis in alis foliorum*; Clusius, *Telephium Hispanicum*; Gerard, *Crassula, s. faba inversa*; and Parkinson, *Telephium, s. crassula major vulgaris*. It grows naturally in dry places in England, and most countries of Europe.

2 *Anacampseros*, or Smaller Round-leaved Orpine, is, *Sedum foliis cuneiformibus integerrimis, caulibus decumbentibus, floribus corymbosis*. Sauvages calls it, *Sedum foliis spatulatis integris, umbella terminali*; Caspar Bauhine, *Telephium repens folio deciduo*; John Bauhine, *Anacampseros minor, rotundiore folio, sempervirens*; and Clusius, *Telephium 6 Cepæa Plantii*. Its native place is not certain.

3 *Aizoon*, or Yellow Siberian Orpine is, *Sedum foliis lanceolatis serratis planis, caule erecto, cymâ sessili terminali*. In the *Hortus Upsal.* it is termed, *Sedum foliis planis serratis, corymbo folioso*. Amman calls it, *Anacampseros flore flavo*. It grows naturally in Siberia.

4 Small Creeping Orpine is, *Sedum foliis cuneiformibus concavis subdentatis aggregatis, ramis repentibus, cymâ terminali*. Buxbaum calls it, *Anacampseros minor repens, flore purpureo*; and Amman, *Sedum minus repens, chamædryos foliis, e singulis foliorum alis radices gerens*. It grows naturally in Tartary.

5 Palestine *Sedum* is, *Sedum foliis radicalibus fasciculatis spatulato lanceolatis, caule subnudo simplicissimo*. It grows naturally in Palestine.

6 Reflexed *Sedum*, Yellow Stone-crop, or Prick-madam, is, *Sedum foliis subulatis sparsis basi solutis, inferioribus recurvatis*. Caspar Bauhine calls it, *Sedum minus luteum, folio acuto*; also, *Sedum minus luteum ramulis reflexis*. Gerard, *Aizoon scorpioides*; also, *Sedum minus hæmatoides*; and Parkinson, *Vermicularis scorpioides*. It grows naturally on walls and old buildings in England, and most countries of Europe.

7 Rock Stone-crop is, *Sedum foliis subulatis quinquefariam confertis basi solutis, floribus cymosis*. Dillenius calls it, *Sedum rupestre repens foliis compressis*; Ray, *Sedum minus e rupe S. Vincentii*; and Petiver, *Sedum minus Vincentii*. It grows naturally on St. Vincent's rock near Bristol, and on rocky stony places in most countries of Europe.

8 Spanish *Sedum* is, *Sedum foliis teretibus acutis radicalibus fasciculatis, cymâ pubescente*. Dillenius calls it, *Sedum Hispanicum, folio glauco acuto, flore albido*. It grows naturally in Spain.

9 White Stone-crop is, *Sedum foliis oblongis obtusis teretiusculis sessilibus patentibus, cymâ ramosâ*. Caspar Bauhine calls it, *Sedum minus teretifolium album*; Lobel, *Vermicularis, s. illecebra major*; Gerard, *Sedum minus officinarum*; and Parkinson, *Vermicularis flore albo*; also, *Vermicularis, s. crassula minor vulgaris*. It grows naturally on old walls, buildings, rocks, &c. in England, and most countries of Europe.

10 Common Wall Stone-crop, or Wall Pepper, is, *Sedum foliis subovatis adnato-sessilibus gibbis erectiusculis alternis, cymâ trifidâ*. Caspar Bauhine calls it, *Sempervivum minus vermiculatum acre*; Dodonæus, *Illecebra, s. sempervivum tertium*; John Bauhine, *Sedum parvum acre, flore luteo*; Gerard, *Vermicularis, seu illecebra minor acris*; and Parkinson, *Illecebra minor, s. Sedum tertium Dioscoridis*. It grows naturally on walls, old buildings, rocks, and sterile places in England, and most countries of Europe.

11 Insipid Stone-crop is, *Sedum foliis subovatis adnato-sessilibus gibbis erectiusculis sexfariam imbricatis*. Caspar Bauhine calls it, *Sempervivum minus vermiculatum insipidum*; and Camerarius, *Sempervivum minimum*. It grows naturally in dry places in England, and most countries of Europe.

*Sedum* is of the class and order *Decandria Pentagynia*; and the characters are, Class and order in the Linnæan System.

1 Calyx is an erect, acute, permanent perianthium, divided into five parts. The characters.

2 Corolla is five spear-shaped, pointed, plane, patent petals. There are five nectariums, each being a very small emarginated scale, inserted to the outward part of each germen near the base.

3 Stamina are ten awl-shaped filaments the length of the corolla, having roundish antheræ.

4 Pistillum consists of five oblong germens, terminating in slender styles, with obtuse stigmas.

5 Pericarpium consists of five patent, acuminated, compressed capsules, which are emarginated towards the base, and open longitudinally on the inner side.

6 Semina. The seeds are many, and small.

# C H A P. CCCCXVI.

## *SELINUM,* MILKY PARSLEY.

OF this genus there are,

Species.

1 Wild Milky Parſley of Pliny

2 Marſh Milky Parſley,

3. Caraway-leaved Milky Parſley

Deſcription of Wild,

1 Wild Milky Parſley of Pliny The root conſiſts of numerous fuſiforme parts, which multiply and ſpread in the ground The ſtalks are thick, ſtriated, of a purpliſh colour near the bottom, branching near the top, and grow to be five or ſix feet high The leaves are compoſed of numerous parts nearly in the manner of carrot, and when broken emit a milky juice The flowers come out in umbels from the tops of the ſtalks, they are of a whitiſh colour, having red on the outſide, appear in June and July, and the ſeeds ripen in Auguſt

Marſh,

2 Marſh Milky Parſley The root is ſingle, large, of a brown colour on the outſide, and full of an acrid, cauſtic, milky juice The radical leaves are large, being compoſed of a multitude of oblong narrow parts, they are of a dark-green colour, full of a milky juice, and ſupported by long footſtalks The flower ſtalk is round, jointed, branching near the top, five or ſix feet high, and adorned with leaves like the radical ones, but ſmall, and growing ſingly at the joints The flowers come out from the ends of the branches in large ſpreading umbels; they are of a white colour, having a tinge of red on the outſide of the petals, they appear in June and July, and the ſeeds ripen in Auguſt or September

and Caraway leaved Milky Parſley

3 Caraway-leaved Milky Parſley The leaves are compoſed of numerous folioles, which are ſharp pointed, and elegantly divided almoſt to the midrib The ſtalks are numerous, upright, furrowed, angular, and two or three feet high The flowers come out from the tops of the ſtalks in umbels, they are of a white colour all over, appear about the ſame time with the former, and the ſeeds ripen accordingly

Its variety

There is a variety of this plant with yellow flowers

Culture

Theſe ſorts are propagated by ſowing the ſeeds in the autumn, ſoon after they are ripe, or the ſpring following The ground ſhould be double-dug for their reception, if it be moiſt, freſh, and in good order, ſo much the better When the plants come up, they muſt be thinned to a foot or fifteen inches diſtance from each other, and when they are grown ſtronger, ſo that you may know which will be good plants, they ſhould have a ſecond thinning, leaving the ſtrongeſt plants at a yard diſtance from each other From this time, all the trouble they will require, will be to keep the ground clean from weeds in ſummer, and in order to cauſe them to ſhoot ſtrong, every winter to dig the ground between the plants, and lay a little mould over the crown of the roots The ſecond ſummer they will flower, and perfect their ſeeds, in order for further increaſe, if neceſſary

1 The firſt ſpecies is titled, *Selinum radice fuſiformi multiplici* Caſpar Bauhine calls it, *Apium ſylveſtre, latteo ſucco, turgens*, and Lobel, *Thyſſelium Plinii* It grows naturally in Germany Titles

2 The ſecond ſpecies is, *Selinum ſublacteſcens, radice unicâ* In the *Flora Lapp* it is termed, *Selinum paluſtre lacteſcens* Guettard calls it, *Selinum foliolis & laciniulis oblongo-linearibus*, and Caſpar Bauhine, *Seſeli paluſtre lacteſcens* It grows naturally in marſhy places in moſt of the northern countries of Europe

3 The third ſpecies is, *Selinum caule ſulcato acutangulo, involucro univerſali caduo, piſtillis fructûs reflexis* Gmelin calls it, *Selinum foliolis pinnatim laciniatis*, Rivinus, *Angelica tenuifolia*, and Caſpar Bauhine, *Carvifolia* It grows naturally in Siberia and Germany

*Selinum* is of the claſs and order *Pentandria Digynia*, and the characters are, Claſs and order in the Linnæan ſyſtem

1 CALYX The general umbel is multiple, plane, and ſpreading, the partial is the ſame The general involucrum is compoſed of many ſpear-ſhaped, narrow, reflexed leaves, the partial is ſimilar, patent, and the length of the florets, the proper perianthium is very ſmall The characters

2 COROLLA The general flower is uniform, and each floret has five inflexed, heart-ſhaped, unequal petals

3 STAMINA are five capillary filaments, with roundiſh antheræ

4 PISTILLUM conſiſts of a germen below the receptacle, and two reflexed ſtyles, with ſimple ſtigmas

5 PERICARPIUM There is none The fruit is compreſſed, plane, elliptical, oblong, ſtriated on both ſides, and divided into two parts

6 SEMINA The ſeeds are two, oblong, elliptical, plane on both ſides, ſtriated in the middle, and have membranaceous borders affixed to their ſides

# CHAP. CCCCXVII.

## *SEMPERVIVUM*, HOUSE-LEEK.

Species.

THE hardy species of this genus are,

1. Common Great House-leek.
2. Globular House-leek.
3. Rough House-leek.
4. Mountain House-leek.
5. Cobweb House-leek, or Cobweb *Sedum*.

Description of Common Great House-leek.

1. Common Great House-leek. The radical leaves are roundish, thick, succulent, pointed, convex on the outside, plane within, ciliated on the edges, spread themselves in a circular manner, and lie flat on the ground. The stalk is upright, thick, round, succulent, of a reddish colour, adorned with narrow, pointed, succulent leaves, and grows to about a foot high. The flowers come out from the tops of the stalks in reflexed bunches; they are of a reddish colour, appear in July and August, and the seeds ripen in the autumn.

Its virtues.

This species is a great cooler, and is good against the St. Anthony's fire, shingles, burns, scalds, inflammations, &c.

Culture.

This plant is propagated by the offsets, which it puts out in plenty from every side. If these are taken off at any time of the year, and planted on the tops of walls, thatched houses, or any mud copings of buildings, they will grow and thrive amazingly.

Globular House-leek described.

2. Globular House-leek. The leaves are numerous, narrow, ciliated, turn inward at the points, and form a compact globular body. The stalks are round, succulent, slender, and six or eight inches high. The flowers come out in bunches from the tops of the stalks; they are of a yellow colour, appear in July and August, and the seeds ripen in the autumn.

Variety of it.

There is a variety of this species with reddish flowers.

Culture.

This plant is propagated by the offsets, which are of a globular form, and being thrust out, or falling from the large heads, grow of themselves, and soon become good plants.

Rough House-leek described.

3. Rough House-leek. The leaves are thick, succulent, indented on the edges, and very rough and prickly at the tips. The stalks are upright, round, succulent, and eight or ten inches high. The flowers come out from the tops of the stalks in reflexed loose spikes or bunches; they are of a white colour, appear in July and August, and the seeds ripen in the autumn.

Culture.

This plant thrusts forth offsets from the sides, by which it is easily propagated, like the other sorts.

Mountain House-leek described.

4. Mountain House-leek. The leaves are oblong, pointed, thick, smooth, succulent, spreading, ciliated, but are not indented on the edges. The stalk is upright, round, succulent, branching near the top, adorned with narrow leaves, and eight or ten inches high. The flowers come out in spikes from the ends of the branches; they are of a deep red colour, having purple antheræ; they appear in July and August, and the seeds ripen in the autumn.

Culture.

This plant puts out offsets like the former sorts, the leaves of which are open and expanded, and by which it is easily propagated.

Cobweb House-leek described.

5. Cobweb House-leek. This species is commonly called Cobweb *Sedum*. The leaves are short, narrow, pointed, of a greyish colour, and have white fibres variously intersecting each other, in the manner of a spider's web, which gained it the appellation of Cobweb *Sedum*. The stalk is round, succulent, branching near the top, about six inches high, and garnished with narrow, awl-shaped, succulent leaves growing alternately. The flowers are ranged in rows along the sides of the branches; they are of a bright-red colour, having a deeper coloured longitudinal line down each petal, and yellow antheræ; they appear in June, July, and August.

The offsets of this plant are small, round, and compact, by which it is propagated like the former sorts. Culture.

All these kinds, like the first sort, will grow on the tops of houses, walls, &c. so that they may be made not only to occupy such places, but are highly proper for rock work, and become ornamental to such places as hardly any thing else will thrive in. For want of such places, they must be planted in a dry, sandy, rubbishy soil, or in pots filled with rubbishy earth, which is better adapted to their nature than the rich quarters in the open part of the garden.

1. Common Great House-leek is titled, *Sempervivum foliis ciliatis, propaginibus patentibus*. In the *Hortus Cliffort.* it is termed, *Sempervivum foliis radicalibus carnosis ciliatis, caulinis imbricatis membranaceis, corymbo racemoso reflexo*. Dodonæus calls it, *Sempervivum majus alterum, s. barba Jovis*; Caspar Bauhine, *Sedum majus vulgare*; and Gerard, *Sempervivum majus*. It grows naturally on buildings and barren hills in England, and most countries of Europe. Titles.

2. Globular House-leek is, *Sempervivum foliis ciliatis, propaginibus globosis*. In the *Hortus Cliffort.* it is termed, *Sempervivum foliis radicalibus in globum congestis ciliatis, propaginibus globosis*. Morison calls it, *Sedum majus vulgari simile, globulis decidentibus*; and John Bauhine, *Sedum vulgari magno simile*. It grows naturally in Siberia.

3. Rough House-leek is, *Sempervivum foliis caule petalisque apicibus hirtis*. Caspar Bauhine calls it, *Sedum majus montanum, foliis dentatis*; and Clusius, *Cotyledon altera montana*. It grows naturally on the Alps, and other mountainous parts of Europe.

4. Mountain House-leek is, *Sempervivum foliis ciliatis, propaginibus patulis*. Haller calls it, *Sedum rosulis liberis foliis lævibus*; Besler, *Sedum minus, flore rubente*; and Caspar Bauhine, *Sedum Alpinum, rubro magno flore*; also, *Sedum majus montanum, foliis non dentatis, floribus rubentibus*. This grows naturally on the Alps, Pyrenees, and Helvetian mountains.

5. Cobweb *Sedum* is, *Sempervivum foliis pilis intertextis, propaginibus globosis*. In the *Hortus Cliffort.* it is termed, *Sempervivum foliis radicalibus in globum congestis villis reticulatim connexis*. Columna calls it, *Sempervivum rubrum montanum gnaphalodes*; and Caspar Bauhine, *Sedum montanum tomentosum*. It grows naturally on the Alps of Italy, Pyrenees, and Helvetian mountains.

*Sempervivum* is of the class and order *Dodecandria Dodecagynia*; and the characters are, Class and order in the Linnæan system.

CALYX

The characters

1 CALYX is a concave permanent perianthium, divided into about twelve acute parts

2 COROLLA conſiſts of about twelve oblong, ſpear ſhaped, acute, concave petals a little larger than the calyx

3 STAMINA are about twelve awl-ſhaped ſlender filaments, with roundiſh antheræ

4 PISTILLUM conſiſts of about twelve erect germens placed circularly, terminating in the like number of patent ſtyles, with acute ſtigmas

5 PERICARPIUM conſiſts of about twelve oblong, ſhort, compreſſed capſules, ſituated in a circular direction, acuminated outwardly, and opening on the inner ſide

6 SEMINA The ſeeds are many, ſmall, and roundiſh

# C H A P. CCCCXVIII

## *SENECIO*, GROUNDSEL

THERE are ſome pretty annuals of this genus, and ſome very fine tender plants for our green houſe and ſtove The hardy perennials are few, and rather inconſiderable, and many of them grow unnoticed in our fields and meadows

Species.

The ſpecies proper for this place are,

1 Flax leaved Groundſel
2 Southern wood leaved Groundſel.
3 Canada Golden Rag wort
4 Broad-leaved Engliſh Rag-wort,
5 Marſh Rag wort
6 Hoary Alpine Rag-wort
7 German Ragwort

Flax leaved Groundſel deſcribed

1 The Flax leaved Groundſel has, until of late, been taken for a Golden rod, and ranked accordingly It riſes with an herbaceous, branching ſtalk to about a foot and a half in height The leaves are narrow, oblong, and entire The flowers terminate the branches in a corymbus, their colour is yellow, and their time of appearance the end of October or November, when moſt other flowers are paſt

Propagation

It is propagated by parting of the roots any time in the autumn, winter, or ſpring

Southern wood leaved Groundſel deſcribed

2 Southern wood-leaved Groundſel The ſtalks of this ſpecies will riſe to about two feet high The leaves are finely divided, and compoſed of a multitude of narrow ſegments The flowers terminate the branches in bunches, are of a yellow colour, will be in blow in July, and ripen their ſeeds in the autumn

Its propagation

This ſpecies is beſt raiſed from ſeeds, which ſhould be ſown in April on a bed of light, ſandy earth When the plants come up, they muſt be thinned, if too cloſe, and frequently watered, and in the autumn following they may be removed to the places where they are deſigned to flower, which will be the ſummer after

Deſcription of Canada Golden,

3 Canada Golden Ragwort The ſtalks will grow to about two feet high The radical leaves are heart ſhaped, crenated on their edges, of a purpliſh colour on their under ſide, and grow on long, ſlender, hairy footſtalks The leaves on the ſtalks are lyre ſhaped The flowers grow from the upper part of the ſtalks ſingly on long, ſlender footſtalks, they are of a yellow colour, will be in blow in June and July, and ripen their ſeeds in September.

Broad leaved Engliſh,

4 Broad-leaved Engliſh Rag wort This ſpecies hath a creeping root, from which ariſe ſeveral ſtalks that will grow to be four feet long The leaves are narrow ſpear-ſhaped, ſmooth, ſerrated on their edges, and grow alternately The flowers terminate the ſtalks in a corymbus, are of a yellow colour, will be in blow in July, and ripen their ſeeds in September

and Marſh Rag-wort deſcribed

5 Marſh Rag-wort This ſpecies grows in marſhy places, and on the ſea-ſhores, in England and many parts of Europe The ſtalks are channelled, grow cloſe together, and will riſe to about a yard in height The leaves are ſword ſhaped, hairy on their under ſide, and ſharply ſerrated on their edges The flowers grow from the upper part of the ſtalks on long, ſlender footſtalks, they are of a yellow colour, will be in blow in June and July, and ripen their ſeeds in September

Its variety

There is a variety of this ſpecies with very long, downy, ſerrated leaves, which by their hoary appearance have a very pretty effect among other plants of different tints

Hoary Alpine Rag wort deſcribed

6 Hoary Alpine Rag-wort This is a low plant, about a foot high The leaves are winged, notched, and covered on both ſides with a fine white, hoary down The flowers terminate the ſtalks in a corymbus, are of a yellow colour, and will be in blow in June, but are not always ſucceeded by good ſeeds in our gardens

Propagation of it

This is one of the prettieſt of all the ſpecies, on account of its low growth and downy white appearance, and may be eaſily propagated by ſlips any time in the autumn or ſpring

German Rag wort deſcribed

7 German Rag-wort riſes with ſeveral branching ſtalks to a yard or more in height The leaves are oval, ſpear-ſhaped, hairy underneath, and a little ſerrated on their edges The flowers terminate the ſtalks in a kind of umbels, are of a yellow colour, will be in blow in July, and ripen their ſeeds in the autumn

Method of propagation

All theſe ſpecies are eaſily encreaſed by parting of the roots any time in the autumn, winter, or ſpring, or they may be raiſed by ſeeds in the manner directed for the ſecond ſpecies

Titles

1 The Flax leaved Groundſel is titled, *Senecio corollis radiantibus, foliis linearibus integerrimis, corymbo ſubſquamato, caule herbaceo* In the *Hortus*

*tus Cliffort* it is termed, *Solidago foliis linearibus integerrimis, corymbo simplici* Caspar Bauhine calls it, *Linariæ aureæ affinis*, and Boccone, *Jacobæa linifolia Hispanica & Italica* It grows naturally in Spain and Italy

2 Southern-wood-leaved Groundsel is, *Senecio corollis radiantibus, foliis pinnato-multifidis linearibus nudis acutis, floribus corymbosis* Caspar Bauhine calls it *Chrysanthemum Alpinum, foliis abrotani multifidis*, and Clusius, *Chrysanthemum Alpinum II* It grows naturally on the Alps and Pyrenees

3 Canada Golden Rag-wort is, *Senecio corollis radiantibus, foliis crenatis, infimis cordatis petiolatis, superioribus pinnatifidis lyratis* Morison calls it, *Jacobæa Virginiana, foliis imis alliariæ glabris cærulescentibus valvareæ* It grows naturally in Virginia and Canada

4 Broad-leaved English Rag-wort is, *Senecio corollis radiantibus, floribus corymbosis, foliis lanceolatis serratis glabriusculis* In the *Hortus Cliffort* it is termed, *Solidago caule simplici, corymbo terminali, pedunculis partialibus alternis nudis longitudine folii* Fuchsius calls it, *Solidago Saracenica*, and Caspar Bauhine, *Jacobæa, subrotundo, minus, latinato folio* It grows naturally in England, Switzerland, and France

5 Marsh Rag wort is, *Senecio corollis radiantibus, foliis ensiformibus acute serratis subtus subvillosis, caule stricto* Guettard calls it, *Senecio foliis integris serratis*, Morison, *Jacobæa foliis longis integris & mucronatis*, and Caspar Bauhine, *Conyza palustris serratifolia* It grows naturally in marshy places in England and most parts of Europe

6 Hoary Alpine Ragwort is, *Senecio corollis radiantibus, foliis utrinque tomentosis subpinnatis obtusis, corymbo subrotundo* Caspar Bauhine calls it, *Chrysanthemum Alpinum incanum foliis laciniatis*, Clusius, *Chrysanthemum Alpinum I* and Barrelier, *Jacobæa alpina incana minor* It grows naturally on the Alps and Pyrenees

7 German Rag wort is, *Senecio corollis radiantibus octonis, foliis lanceolatis biserratis subtus villosis, caule ramoso* Haller calls it, *Senecio foliis ovato-lanceolatis subtus hirsutis, floribus umbellatis*, and Gmelin, *Solidago foliis lanceolatis serratis, floribus ad pedunculum summis* It flourishes in forests of Germany and Siberia

*Senecio* is of the class and order *Syngenesia Polygamia Superflua*, and the characters are,

Class and order in the Linnæan system The characters

1 Calyx is of a conic figure, truncated, and composed of a multitude of subulated scales, that are contracted above, and surrounded at the bottom with others that are broad and shorter

2 Corolla The compound flower rises higher than the calyx The hermaphrodite florets are numerous in the disk, are funnel-shaped, and each of them is cut at the top into five reflexed segments

The female flowers in the radius are tongue-shaped, oblong, and slightly indented at the top in three parts

3 Stamina of the hermaphrodite flowers are five very small, capillary filaments, having a tubular, cylindrical anthera

4 Pistillum, in both sorts, consists of an oval germen, a filiforme style the length of the stamina, and two oblong, revolute stigmas

5 Pericarpium There is none

6 Semina The seeds are single, oval, and winged with down The receptacle is plane and naked

## CHAP. CCCCXIX

## *SERAPIAS*, HELLEBORINE, or BASTARD HELLEBORE.

THERE are four distinct species of this genus, viz

Species

1 Helleborine, or Broad leaved Bastard Hellebore

2 Long-leaved Bastard Hellebore

3 Italian Bastard Hellebore

4 Spanish Bastard Hellebore

Description of Helleborine

1 Helleborine, or Broad-leaved Bastard Hellebore The root is composed of many thick, fleshy, juicy fibres The stalk is single, jointed, and about a foot high The lower leaves are oval, but the upper ones are spear-shaped and pointed, they are nervous, grow singly at the joints, and embrace the stalk with their base The flowers come out in kind of loose spikes from the tops of the stalks They are of the Orchis kind, and of different colours. The expanded wings are whitish, the nectarium in the middle is of a purplish colour, and the whole flowers in different parts are more or less tinged with green They will be in blow in June, July, and August, and the seeds ripen in the autumn

Long leaved Bastard Hellebore described.

2 Long-leaved Bastard Hellebore The root consists of several thick, fleshy fibres, full of juice The stalk is upright, round, tender, jointed, and about a foot high The leaves are spear-shaped, long, sharp-pointed, veined, of a bright-green colour, and grow singly at the joints, sitting close The flowers come out in loose spikes, growing alternately along the upper parts of the stalks, they are of a white colour, appear in June and July, and the seeds ripen in the autumn

Varieties

There are several varieties of this species, one in

in particular with purplish flowers, and another called the Marsh Bastard Hellebore, the flowers of which are a composition of purple, white, and yellow, the spreading parts being purplish, the nectarium in the middle called the fly, having a yellowish head striped with purple and a white body, and the pendulent lip fringed and of a white colour. They all flower nearly at the same time.

Italian

3. Italian Bastard Hellebore. The root of this species consists of two roundish, juicy bulbs joined together. The stalk is upright, round, succulent, and eight or ten inches high. The radical leaves are roundish, but those on the stalk are narrow, smooth, and grow alternately, embracing it with their base. The flowers come out from the tops of the stalks in small loose spikes, are of an iron colour, and the lip of the nectarium is remarkably long, smooth, and trifid; they appear in July and August, but it is uncertain whether the seeds ripen in England.

and Spanish Bastard Hellebore described

4. Spanish Bastard Hellebore. The root is a pair of roundish bulbs hung with many slender, whitish fibres. The stalk is upright, thick, firm, and a foot and a half high. The radical leaves are large and roundish, but those on the stalk are narrow, smooth, grow alternately, and embrace the stalk with their base. The flowers come out from the tops of the stalks in spikes, have slender footstalks, hang downwards, and the lip of the nectarium is remarkably large, trifid, and nearly heart-shaped; they will be in blow in July and August, but the seeds do not ripen in England.

Propagation of the first two species

All these species are nearly allied to the *Orchis*, and, like that, are with difficulty preserved in gardens. The first two species grow naturally in woods, hedges, and moist places in England, and may be taken up, when they have done flowering and the stalks decay, with a good quantity of mould to each root, and planted in similar situations, about the shrubbery, wilderness, or other out-works, and they will grow and flourish very well.

Propagation of the last two species

The last two species, being foreigners, must be first set with the mould at the roots in pots or tubs, and when they arrive in England, they must be turned out with the mould, disturbing the roots as little as possible, into the places where they are designed to remain, which ought naturally to be light, sandy, rather moist than dry, warm, and well sheltered.

Titles

1. The first species is titled, *Serapias bulbis fibrosis, floribus erectis bracteâ brevioribus*. In the *Flora Suecica* it is termed, *Serapias bulbis fibrosis, nectarii labio obtuso crenato petalis breviore*. In the *Hortus Cliffort.* *Serapias caule multifolio multifloro*. Cammerarius calls it, *Epipactis, seu helleborine*, and Caspar Bauhine, *Helleborine latifolia montana*, also, *Helleborine flore carneo*. It grows naturally in woods and rough places in most countries of Europe.

2. The second species is, *Serapias bulbis fibrosis, floribus erectis bracteâ longioribus*. Ray calls it, *Helleborine palustris, seu pratensis nostras*. Caspar Bauhine, *Helleborine angustifolia palustris, seu pratensis*, also, *Helleborine flore albo, seu damasonium montanum latifolium*, also, *Helleborine montana angustifolia purpurascens*. It grows naturally in most countries of Europe.

3. The third species is, *Serapias bulbis subrotundis, nectarii labio trifido acuminato petalis longiore glabro*. Sauvages calls it, *Satyrium radicibus subrotundis, cucullo clauso monopetalo, labello ovato-lanceolato*. Columna, *Orchis macrophylla*, and Caspar Bauhine, *Orchis montana Italica, flore ferrugineo, linguâ oblongâ*, also, *Orchis montana Italica, linguâ oblongâ alterâ*. It grows naturally in Italy, France, and Portugal.

4. The fourth species is, *Serapias bulbis subrotundis, nectarii labio trifido acuminato maximo basi barbato*. Rudbeck calls it, *Orchis montana Italica, linguâ trifidâ*. It grows naturally in Spain, Italy, and in the East.

*Serapias* is of the class and order *Gynandria Diandria*, and the characters are, Class and order in the Linnæan system. The characters

1. CALYX. The spathæ are vague. The spadix is simple. There is no perianthium.

2. COROLLA. The petals are five, oval, oblong, erect, spreading, but close at the top.

The nectarium is the length of the petals, hollowed at the base, melliferous, oval, gibbous below, but cut at the top into three segments, the middle one being heart-shaped and obtuse, the others acute.

3. STAMINA are two very short filaments sitting on the pistil, having erect antheræ placed under the upper lip of the nectarium.

4. PISTILLUM consists of an oblong, contorted germen situated below the flower, a style growing to the upper lip of the nectarium, and an obsolete stigma.

5. PERICARPIUM is an oval, obtusely three-cornered, tricarinated capsule, composed of three valves, containing one cell, and opening under the keels.

6. SEMINA. The seeds are numerous, and scrobiforme.

CHAP

# CHAP. CCCCXX.

## *SERRATULA*, SAW-WORT

THIS genus comprehends many hardy perennials, such as,

Species
1 Common Saw-wort
2 Italian Saw-wort
3 Mountain Saw wort, or Low Mountain Melancholy Thistle
4 Field Saw-wort, or Way Thistle
5 Willow-leaved Saw-wort
6 Many-flowered Saw-wort
7 New-York Saw-wort
8 Pensylvanian Saw-wort
9 Maryland Saw-wort
10 Squarrose Saw-wort or Tuberous Melancholy Thistle
11 Virginian Saw-wort, or Tuberous Knapweed
12 Spiked Saw-wort.
13 Siberian Saw-wort

Description of Common, 1 Common Saw-wort The stalk is upright, striated, branching near the top, and about two feet high The leaves are cut almost to the mid-rib, and each terminates in one broad lobe, they are smooth, elegantly serrated on their edges, and of a dark-green colour The flowers come out from the tops of the stalks in scaly heads There are the White and Purple-coloured varieties They appear in July and August, and the seeds ripen in the autumn

Italian, 2 Italian Saw-wort The stalk is upright, sulcated, firm, and four or five feet high The leaves are large, smooth, of a deep-green colour, cut almost to the mid-rib, and the terminal lobes are by far the largest The flowers come out from the tops of the stalks in scaly heads, are of a purple colour, appear in July, and the seeds ripen in the autumn

Mountain 3 Mountain Saw-wort Of this species there are many varieties differing in their height of growth, the properties of their leaves, colour of their flowers, &c The sort called Low Mountain Melancholy Thistle has two or three slender, channelled stalks, about a foot and a half high The lower leaves are oval, oblong, and indented, but the upper ones are narrow and entire The flowers come out from the ends of the branches in small bunches, they are of a purple colour, appear in June and July, and the seeds ripen in August

Field, 4 Field Saw-wort, or Way Thistle The root is black and creeping The stalk is upright, round, branching a little near the top, and two or three feet high The leaves are long, spear-shaped, narrow, indented, very prickly on their edges, and grow alternately on the stalks The flowers come out from the ends and sides of the branches in oblong, scaly heads, they are of a white colour, appear in July and August, and the seeds ripen in September

Willow leaved 5 Willow-leaved Saw-wort The stalk is upright, angular, branching near the top, and about a foot and a half high The leaves are narrow, spear-shaped, sessile, entire, downy underneath, and grow alternately The flowers come out in bunches from the ends of the branches, are of a red colour, appear in July and August, and the seeds ripen in the autumn

Many-flowered 6 Many flowered Saw wort The stalk is upright, angular, divides into numerous branches at the top, and grows to be three or four feet high The leaves are spear-shaped, long, entire, nearly decurrent, of a bluish-green colour on their upper side, and white and hairy underneath The flowers come out in roundish bunches from the ends and sides of the branches, are of a red or purple colour, appear in July and August, and the seeds ripen in the autumn

and New York Saw wort, 7 New-York Saw-wort The stalks are channelled, and seven or eight feet high The leaves are spear-shaped, oblong, serrated, soft and downy underneath, and sit close to the stalks The flowers come out from the ends and sides of the branches at the tops of the stalks, they are of a purple colour, appear in July and August, but the seeds seldom ripen in England

Variety There is a variety of this species with yellow flowers, of lower growth

Description of Pensylvanian, 8 Pensylvanian Saw-wort The stalk is branching, and four or five feet high The leaves are spear shaped, oblong, pointed, spreading, hairy on their under-side, and sit close to the stalks The flowers are produced in loose bunches from the ends of the branches, are of a pale-purple colour, appear in August and September, but are not succeeded by ripe seeds in England

Maryland 9 Maryland Saw-wort. The stalks are of a purple colour, channelled, and six or seven feet high The leaves are oval, oblong, pointed, serrated on their edges, and of a light-green colour The flowers come out in loose, roundish bunches from the tops of the stalks, are of a purple colour, appear in August, but are seldom succeeded by good seeds in England

Squarrose 10 Squarrose Saw wort This species is frequently called Tuberous Melancholy Thistle. The root is tuberous. The stalk is single, and about three feet high The leaves are narrow, stiff, entire, rough, and of a pale green colour on both sides The flowers come out alternately from the sides of the stalk near the top, and one larger head than the rest crowns the stalk, sitting close; they appear in August, but the seeds seldom ripen in England

Virginian 11 Virginian Saw wort, or Tuberous Knapweed The root is large and tuberous The stalk is upright, strong, channelled, and three or four feet high The leaves are narrow, spear-shaped, entire, and adorn the stalk in great plenty The flowers come out from the tops of the stalks in long, loose spikes, they are of a purple colour, appear in August, but are rarely succeeded by ripe seeds in England

Spiked, 12 Spiked Saw-wort The root is tuberous The stalk is single, and two or three feet high The leaves are narrow, smooth, ciliated at their base, sit close, and come out without order all round the stalk The flowers come out in long spikes from the tops of the stalks, are small, of a purple colour, appear in August, but are not succeeded by seeds in England

and Siberian Saw wort 13 Siberian Saw-wort The stalk is upright, sends forth a few branches alternately from the sides, and grows to about a foot and a half high The leaves are pinnatifid, spear shaped, acute, veined, and smooth on both sides The

flowers

flowers come out singly from the ends of the branches, are of a purple colour, appear in July and August, and the seeds ripen in the autumn

Method of propagation. All these species are easily propagated by parting of the roots, the best time for which is the early part of the autumn, that they may be established in their new situation before winter, and they will then rise early in the spring, and flower strong the summer following

They may be raised by seeds also, which is the best way of raising the tuberous rooted species The seeds should be sown in the autumn, as soon as they are ripe, or the spring following When they come up, they should be thinned where they are too close, kept clean from weeds, and watered in dry weather In the autumn the tuberous species should be set in beds at six inches asunder, to remain there for a year longer, but all the others may, the first autumn after they come up from seeds, be removed to the places where they are designed to remain

Proper situation. They are all extremely hardy, and proper ornaments for large flower-gardens, and well adapted to mix with flowering-shrubs in wilderness quarters, &c They may also be set in woods thro' which walks of pleasure are drawn, where they will be extremely ornamental, and require no trouble, except digging the ground about the roots in winter, to kill the contiguous weeds and invigorate the plants, and reducing the roots as often as they become too spreading, which need not be oftener than once in four or five years

Titles. 1 Common Saw wort is titled, *Serratula foliis lyrato-pinnatifidis, pinna terminali maxima, flosculis conformibus* Caspar Bauhine calls it, simply, *Serratula*, Gerard, *Serratula purpurea*, Parkinson, *Serratula vulgaris, flore purpureo*, and Boerhaave, *Serratula flore candido* It grows naturally in meadows and moist woods in England, and most of the northern countries of Europe

2 Italian Saw-wort is, *Serratula foliis lyrato-pinnatifidis, pinnâ terminali maximâ, flosculis radii femineis longioribus* Boccone calls it, *Serratula præalta centauroides montana*, and Gmelin, *Carduus inermis, foliis glabris pinnatis laciniâ extimâ maxima, capitulis squalidis* It grows naturally in Italy and Siberia

3 Mountain Saw-wort is, *Serratula calycibus subhirsutis ovatis, foliis indivisis* In the *Flora Suecia* it is termed, *Serratula foliis petiolatis, radicalibus ovato oblongis dentatis, caulinis integerrimis*; in the *Flora Lapp* *Serratula foliis ovato lanceolatis, radicalibus serratis, caule thyrsifloro* Gmelin calls it, *Cirsium inerme, foliis ex ovato-lanceolatis denticulatis infra lanugine candidis*, also, *Cirsium inerme, foliis linearibus utrinque viridibus, calycibus hirsutis* Plukenet names it, *Cardro-cirsium minus Britannicum, floribus congestis*, Morison, *Cirsium humile montanum, cynoglossi folio, polyanthemum*, also, *Cirsium polyanthemum, molli hastato folio* Haller stiles it, *Cirsium foliis triangularibus lunate dentatis*, Clusius *Carduus mollior II* and Caspar Bauhine, *Carduus mollis, lapathi foliis* It grows naturally in the mountainous parts of Wales, and the North of England, also, on the Alps of Lapland, Austria, Helvetia, and Siberia

4. Field Saw-wort, or Way Thistle, is, *Serratula foliis dentatis spinosis* In the *Flora Lapp* it is termed, *Carduus radice repente, foliis lanceolatis dentatis margine aculeatis* Columna calls it, *Ceanothus Theophrasti*; and Caspar Bauhine, *Carduus vinearum repens, sonchi folio*, also, *Carduus in avenâ proveniens* It grows naturally in fields and by way-sides in England and most countries of Europe

5 Willow leaved Saw-wort is *Serratula foliis lineari-lanceolatis alternis subtus niveis sessilibus integerrimis* Gmelin calls it, *Cirsium inerme erectum, foliis ex lineari-lanceolatis, infra candidis* It grows naturally in Siberia

6 Many-flowered Saw wort is, *Serratula foliis lanceolatis subtus villosis subdecurrentibus integerrimis, caule corymboso, calycibus cylindricis* Gmelin calls it, *Cirsium inerme, caulibus adscendentibus, foliis linearibus infra cinereis* It grows naturally in Siberia

7 New-York Saw-wort is, *Serratula foliis lanceolato-oblongis serratis penaulis* Dillenius calls it, *Serratula Noveboracensis maxima, foliis longis serratis*, Morison, *Serratula Noveboracensis altissima, foliis doriæ mollibus subincanis*, and Plukenet, *Centaurium medium Noveboracense luteum, solidaginis folio integro tenuiter crenato* It grows naturally in most parts of North America

8 Virginian Saw wort is, *Serratula foliis lanceolato-oblongis serratis patentibus subtus hirsutis* Dillenius calls it, *Serratula Virginiana, persicæ folio subtus incano*, Boccone, *Serratula præalta angusta, plantaginis aut persicæ folio*, and Plukenet, *Eupatoria Virginiana, serratulæ Noveboracensis latioribus foliis* It grows naturally in Virginia, Pensylvania, and Carolina

9 Maryland Saw wort is, *Serratula foliis ovato-oblongis acuminatis serratis, floribus corymbosis, calycibus subrotundis* Dillenius calls it, *Serratula Marilandica, foliis glaucis cirsii instar denticulatis*, and Plukenet, *Centaurium medium Marianum, folio integro cirsii nostratis more spinulis fimbriato* It grows naturally in Maryland, Virginia, and Carolina

10 Squarrose Saw-wort is, *Serratula foliis linearibus, calycibus squarrosis subsessilibus lateralibus acuminatis* Dillenius calls it, *Cirsium tuberosum, capitulis squarrosis*, and Morison, *Stoebe Virginiana tuberosa lat folia, capitulis sessilibus, squamis foliaceis acutis donatis* It grows naturally in Virginia

11 Virginian Saw wort, or Tuberous Knapweed, is, *Serratula foliis lanceolatis integerrimis, calycibus squarrosis pedunculatis obtusis lateralibus* Gronovius calls it, *Cirsium non ramosum, foliis lateralibus, flores ferens pauciores majores*, Plukenet, *Jacea altera non ramosa, tuberosa radice, foliis latioribus, flores ferens pauciores majores*, also, *Eupatorio affinis Americana bulbosa, floribus scariosis, capitulis contextis* It grows naturally in Virginia

12 Spiked Saw-wort is, *Serratula foliis linearibus basi ciliatis, floribus spicatis sessilibus lateralibus, caule simplici* Dillenius calls it, *Cirsium tuberosum, lactucæ capitulis spicatis*, Banister, *Jacea non ramosa, tuberosâ radice, floribus plurimum rigidis perangustis*, Plukenet, *Jacea angustifolia, tuberosâ radice, Virginiana*, and Morison, *Stoebe Virginiana tuberosa angustifolia, capitulis sessilibus* It grows naturally in North-America

13 Siberian Saw-wort is, *Serratula foliis pinnatifidis acutis glabris inermibus, squamis calycinis mucronatis, interioribus membranaceis* Gmelin calls it, *Carduus caule ramoso, foliis pinnatifidis, foliolis dentatis, squamis ex lanceolato spinosis* It grows naturally in Siberia

*Serratula* is of the class and order *Syngenesia Polygamia Æqualis*, and the characters are, Class and order in the Linnæan system.

1 CALYX The general calyx is oblong, nearly cylindrical, and imbricated The scales are smooth, spear shaped, and acute The characters.

2 COROLLA The general flower is tubular, and uniform The florets have each one funnel-shaped petal, the tube of which is inflexed, and the limb ventricose, and divided into five parts

3 STAMINA are five very short capillary filaments, having a cylindrical, tubular anthera

4 PISTILLUM consists of an oval germen, a filiforme stile the length of the stamina, and two oblong, reflexed stigmas

5 PERICARPIUM There is none

6 SEMEN The seed is single, and oval The down is sessile

CHAP

# CHAP CCCCXXI.

## SESELI.

Species. OF this genus are,

1 Mountain *Seſeli*, commonly called Mountain Saxifrage

2 Glaucous *Seſeli*, or Grey-leaved Fennel

3 Pimpinelloide *Seſeli*

4 *Seſeli* of Marſeilles, or Crooked Fennel

Mountain. 1 Mountain *Seſeli*, or Mountain Saxifrage The radical leaves are large, compoſed of many oblong ſolioles, and of a greyiſh colour The ſtalks are upright, round, ſmooth, about a foot and a half high, and garniſhed with very narrow leaves, having a long entire membrane embracing the baſe of each The flowers come out in umbels from the tops of the ſtalks, they are of a white colour, appear in July, and the ſeeds ripen in the autumn

Glaucous. 2 Glaucous *Seſeli*, or Grey-leaved Fennel The ſtalks are upright, ſlender, ſmooth and about two feet high The leaves are compoſed of many narrow ſegments, which are for the moſt part divided into two parts, they are of a glaucous colour, and a membrane embraces the baſe of each footſtalk The flowers come out in umbels from the tops of the ſtalks, their colour within is white, but on the outſide purpliſh, they appear in July and Auguſt, and the ſeeds ripen in the autumn

Pimpinelloide Seſeli. 3 Pimpinelloide *Seſeli* The leaves are pinnated, and the pinnæ are cut into many narrow plane ſegments, which are placed alternately The ſtalk is ſlender, weak, partly procumbent, and about a foot high The flowers come out in umbels from the tops of the ſtalks, they are of a white colour, appear in July and Auguſt, and the ſeeds ripen in the autumn

and Seſeli of Marſeilles deſcribed. 4 *Seſeli* of Marſeilles, or Crooked Fennel The ſtalks are thick, rigid, ſtriated, crooked at the joints, branching near the top and three or four feet high The ſolioles are narrow, and grow in bunches from the ſides of the ſtalks The flowers come out from the ends and ſides of the branches in ſmall umbels, they are of a yellow colour, appear in July and Auguſt, and the ſeeds ripen in the autumn

Method of propagation. Theſe ſorts are all propagated by ſowing the ſeeds in the autumn, ſoon after they are ripe, or the ſpring following, in the places where they are deſigned to remain The ſoil ſhould be neither over moiſt nor dry, and the ſituation open After the plants come up they muſt be thinned to proper diſtances, and conſtantly kept clean from weeds, which is all the trouble they will require The ſecond ſummer they will flower and perfect their ſeeds, which, if permitted to ſcatter, will frequently grow, and afford you more young plants than you would wiſh for

Titles. 1 The firſt ſpecies is entitled, *Seſeli petiolis rameferis membranaceis oblongis integris, foliis caulinis anguſtiſſimis* Caſpar Bauhine calls it, *Meum latifolium adulterinum*, and Moriſon, *Saxifraga montana minor Italica, foliis in breviores partes diviſis* It grows naturally in France and Italy

2 The ſecond ſpecies is, *Seſeli petiolis rameferis membranaceis oblongis integris foliolis ſingularibus binatiſque canaliculatis lævibus petiolo longioribus.* Tournefort calls it, *Fœniculum ſylveſtre, glauco folio*, Caſpar Bauhine, *Daucus, glauco folio, ſimilis fœniculo tortuoſo*, and Moriſon, *Saxifraga montana minor glauca et rigidior* It grows naturally in France and Italy

3 The third ſpecies is, *Seſeli caule declinato, umbellis nubilibus nutantibus* It grows naturally in moſt of the ſouthern countries of Europe

4 The fourth ſpecies is, *Seſeli caule alto rigido, foliolis linearibus faſciculatis* In the *Hortus Cliff.* it is termed *Oenanthe ſtriata rigida* Caſpar Bauhine calls it, *Seſeli Maſſilienſe, fœniculi folio*; and John Bauhine, *Fœniculum tortuoſum* It grows naturally in moſt of the ſouthern countries of Europe

Claſs and order in the Linnæan ſyſtem. *Seſeli* is of the claſs and order *Pentandria Digynia*, and the characters are,

The characters. 1 Calyx The general umbel is rigid, the partial is very ſhort, multiplex, and almoſt round There is no general involucrum, the partial conſiſts of one or two narrow acuminated ſolioles the length of the umbellulæ, the perianthium is very ſmall

2 Corolla The general flower is uniform, the florets have each five inflexed, heart-ſhaped, planiſh petals

3 Stamina are five awl-ſhaped filaments, with ſimple antheræ

4 Pericarpium There is none The fruit is oval, ſmall, ſtriated, and divided into two parts

5 Semina The ſeeds are two, convex and ſtriated on one ſide, and plane on the other

## CHAP CCCCXXII

## *SIBBALDIA.*

Species

THERE are two species of this genus, called,
1 Procumbent Bastard Cinquefoil
2 Upright Bastard Cinquefoil

Procumbent

1 Procumbent Bastard Cinquefoil The stalks are round, procumbent, and strike root as they lie on the ground The leaves grow by threes on the stalks, they are of a whitish green colour, soft or hairy on both sides, and indented in three parts at the extremities The flowers come out four or five together on footstalks, which arise from the joints, they are of a yellow colour, appear in July and August, and the seeds ripen in the autumn

and Upright Bastard Cinquefoil described

2 Upright Bastard Cinquefoil The stalk is erect, round, hairy, and eight or ten inches high The leaves are composed of five narrow folioles, which are of a light-green colour, and finely jagged or cut into many segments The flowers are produced in small clusters from the sides of the stalks, they are of a reddish colour, appear in July and August, and the seeds ripen in the autumn

Method of propagation

The first species is propagated by parting of the roots, and both of them by sowing the seeds in the autumn, soon after they are ripe, or the spring following After the plants come up they will require no trouble, except thinning them where they are too close, and keeping them clean from weeds

Titles

1 The first species is titled, *Sibbaldia procumbens, foliolis tridentatis* Sibbald calls it, *Fragrariæ sylvestris affinis planta, flore luteo*, and Plukenet, *Pentaphylloides fruticosum minimum procumbens, flore luteo* It grows naturally on the Alps of Lapland, Helvetia, and Scotland

2 The second species is called, *Sibbaldia erecta, foliolis linearibus multifidis* Amman calls it, *Pentaphylloides foliis tenuissime laciniatis, flosculis carneis* It grows naturally in Siberia

Class and order in the Linnæan system The characters

*Sibbaldia* is of the class and order *Pentandria Polygynia*, and the characters are,

1 CALYX is a monophyllous perianthium, divided into ten nearly spear-shaped, patent, permanent segments

2 COROLLA is five oval petals inserted in the calyx.

3 STAMINA are five capillary filaments shorter than the corolla, and inserted in the calyx, having small obtuse antheræ

4 PISTILLUM consists of five very short oval germens, with styles the length of the stamina arising from the sides, and crowned by capitated stigmas

5 PERICARPIUM There is none The calyx closes, and holds the seeds

6 SEMINA The seeds are a little oblong, and five in number

## CHAP. CCCCXXIII.

## *SIBTHORPIA*

OF this genus there is one Perennial, usually called Bastard Money-wort

This plant described

The root is creeping, and hung with many slender fibres The stalk is round, slender, branching, and lies on the ground The leaves are kidney shaped, nearly peltated, and crenated on the edges The flowers are produced from the sides of the stalks on slender footstalks, they are of a greenish-yellow colour, appear in July and August, and the seeds ripen in the autumn

Propagation of it

This is not a cultivated plant, it grows wild by the sides of ditches, rivers, brooks, and standing waters, in many parts of England Whoever is desirous of it, however, may part the roots at any time of the year, and on planting them in some moist ground, they will grow, and call for no trouble, except keeping them from being over run with tall weeds

Titles

This species is titled, *Sibthorpia foliis reniformibus subpeltatis crenatis* Petiver calls it, *Chrysosplenium Cornubiense*, and Ray, *Alsine spuria pusilla repens foliis saxifragæ aureæ* It grows naturally in moist places in Westmoreland, Devonshire, Cornwall, &c in England, and in the like situations in Portugal

Class and order in the Linnæan system The characters

*Sibthorpia* is of the class and order *Didynamia Angiospermia*, and the characters are,

1. CALYX is a monophyllous turbinated perianthium,

rianthium, divided into five oval, patent, permanent segments

2 COROLLA is one petal the length of the calyx, divided into five equal, patent, rounded segments

3 STAMINA are four capillary filaments, with heart-shaped, oblong antheræ

4 PISTILLUM consists of a roundish compressed germen, a thick cylindrical style the length of the flower, and a simple, capitated, depressed stigma

5 PERICARPIUM is a compressed, orbicular, biventricose capsule, formed of two valves, and containing two cells

6 SEMINA. The seeds are few, roundish, oblong, convex on one side, and plane on the other

## CHAP. CCCCXXIV

## *SIDERITIS*, IRON-WORT.

THE species of this genus proper for this place are,

Species
1 Perfoliate Iron-wort
2 Hyssop-leaved Iron-wort,
3 Montpelier Iron-wort
4 Hairy Iron wort
5 Hoary Spanish Iron-wort

Description of Perfoliate,

1. Perfoliate Iron-wort The stalk is herbaceous, upright, covered with prickly hairs, branching near the top, and about a yard high The leaves are oblong, heart-shaped, obtuse, strongly scented, and surround the stalk with their base The flowers come out in whorls round the upper parts of the stalks, having two heart-shaped pointed leaves under each whorl, they are large, of a whitish-yellow colour, appear in July and August, and the seeds ripen in the autumn

Hyssop-leaved,

2 Hyssop-leaved Iron wort The stalks are upright, branching, and a foot and a half high The leaves are spear shaped, smooth, entire, sit close to the stalks, and emit a strong odour when bruised The flowers come out in whorled spikes from the ends of the branches, they are of a yellow colour, appear in June and July, and the seeds ripen in the autumn

Montpelier,

3 Montpelier Iron-wort The stalks are ligneous, upright, simple, and about a foot and a half high The leaves are spear-shaped, acute, indented, and hairy underneath The flowers come out from the tops of the stalks in oval spikes, attended by oval, indented, prickly leaves, they are of a yellow colour, appear in July and August, and the seeds ripen in the autumn

Hairy,

4 Hairy Iron-wort The stalk is rough, hairy, and a foot and a half high The leaves are spear-shaped, obtuse, deeply indented, rough, and hairy The flowers come out in whorled spikes from the tops of the stalks, attended by heart shaped prickly bractea, they are of a yellow colour, appear in July and August, and the seeds ripen in the autumn

and Hoary Spanish Iron wort

5 Hoary Spanish Iron-wort The stalks are upright, square, woody, downy, and about a foot and a half high The leaves are spear-shaped, narrow, entire, white, and downy The flowers come out in whorled spikes from the tops of the stalks, attended by heart-shaped, hoary, indented, prickly, bracteæ, they are of a yellow colour, appear in June and July, and the seeds sometimes ripen in the autumn

Method of propagating them

The sorts are raised by sowing the seeds in beds of light earth in the spring, and when they come up, they must be thinned where they crowd each other, kept clean from weeds, watered in dry weather all summer, and in the autumn may be removed to the places where they are designed to remain They will all flower the summer following, and perfect their seeds The first sort frequently dies after the seeds are ripe, so that, to continue it in a regular succession, care must be taken to sow the seeds at proper intervals

The last sort must have a dry, sandy, or rubbishy situation, in a well-sheltered place, otherwise it will be liable to be destroyed by the severity of our winters

Titles

1 Perfoliate Iron-wort is titled, *Sideritis herbacea hispido-pilosa, foliis superioribus amplexicaulibus* Van Royen calls it, *Stachys foliis oblongis acutis amplexicaulibus serratis floralibus cordatis acutis integerrimis*, and Tournefort, *Sideritis orientalis, phlomidis folio* It grows naturally in the East

2 Hyssop leaved Iron wort is, *Sideritis foliis lanceolatis glabris integerrimis, bracteis cordatis dentato-spinosis, calycibus æqualibus* In the *Hortus Cliffort* it is termed, *Sideritis foliis lanceolato-linearibus sessilibus glabris* C Bauhine calls it, *Sideritis Alpina hyssopifolia*, and Clusius, *Sideritis VII* It grows naturally on the Alps and Pyrenean mountains

3 Montpelier Iron-wort is, *Sideritis foliis lanceolatis acutis dentatis, bracteis ovatis dentato-spinosis, calycibus æqualibus, spicis ovatis* C Bauhine calls it, *Sideritis foliis hirsutis profunde crenatis*, and Lobel, *Sideritis, s ferruminatrix Heraclea* It grows naturally about Montpelier

4 Hairy Iron-wort is, *Sideritis foliis lanceolatis obtusis dentatis pilosis, bracteis dentato spinosis, caule hirto, spicis interruptis elongatis* C Bauhine calls it, *Sideritis hirsuta procumbens*, and Clusius, *Sideritis III* It grows naturally in France, Italy, and Spain

5 Hoary Spanish Iron-wort is, *Sideritis suffruticosa tomentosa, foliis lanceolato linearibus integerrimis, floribus bracteisque dentatis* Tournefort calls it, *Sideritis Hispanica erecta, folio angustiore*; and

and Barrelier, *Hyssopus montana verticillata major* It grows naturally in Spain

Clafs and order in the Linnæan fyftem The characters

*Sideritis* is of the clafs and order *Didynamia Gymnofpermia*, and the characters are,

1 Calyx is a monophyllous, tubular, oblong perianthium, cut at the brim into five nearly equal acute fegments

2 Corolla is one almoft equal petal The tube is cylindrical and oblong, the mouth oblong and roundifh The upper lip is erect, narrow, and bifid, the lower lip is cut into three fegments, the middle one being round and crenated, the two fide ones fmaller than the upper lip, and more acute

3. Stamina are four filaments within the tube, (two being fhorter than the other), having roundifh two twin antheræ

4 Pistillum confifts of a quadrifid germen, and a filiforme ftyle a little longer than the ftamina, with two ftigmas; of which the upper one is cylindrical, concave, and truncated, and the lower one fhort and membranaceous

5 Pericarpium There is none The feeds are lodged in the calyx

6 Semina The feeds are four

## CHAP CCCCXXV.

## SIGESBECKIA

THERE are two fpecies of this genus, called,

Species

1 Oriental *Sigesbeckia*

2 Occidental *Sigesbeckia*

Oriental

1 Oriental *Sigesbeckia* The ftalks are upright, thick, branching, and two or three feet high The leaves are broad, ferrated on the edges, and grow on fhort footftalks The flowers come out from the ends of the branches, having hifpid fpreading cups, they are fmall, of a yellow colour, appear in July and Auguft, and the feeds ripen in the autumn

and Occidental Sigefbeckia defcribed

2 Occidental *Sigesbeckia* The ftalks are upright, thick, firm, winged, or made fquare with the decurrent footftalks of the leaves The leaves are fpear fhaped, oval, trinervous, ferrated, downy underneath, and grow oppofite to each other on footftalks, having membranes from one to the other The flowers come out in bunches from the tops of the ftalks, they are fmall, of a pale-yellow colour, appear in July and Auguft, and the feeds ripen in the autumn

Method of propagation

Thefe two forts are raifed by fowing the feeds in a hotbed in the fpring, and, when the plants are fit to remove, fhould be fet out on a moift day in fome warm, dry, well fheltered place Some of the forwardeft plants will flower the firft fummer, the weakeft not before the fummer following If the winter fhould prove fevere, they fhould be protected with mats, or fome covering, efpecially the firft fort, otherwife they will be liable to be deftroyed by our frofts

Titles

1 The firft fpecies is titled, *Sigesbeckia petiolis feffilibus, calycibus exterioribus linearibus majoribus patentibus* In the *Hortus Cliffort* it is termed fimply *Sigesbeckia* Buxbaum calls it, *Bidenti fimilis foliis latiffimis ferratis*, and Plukenet, *Cichorio affinis lapfana finica, menthraftri foliis, calyce fimbriato hifpido* It grows naturally in China and Media

2 The fecond fpecies is, *Sigesbeckia petiolis decurrentibus, calycibus nudis* Gronovius calls it, *Verbefina foliis ovatis petiolatis decurrentibus oppofitis, flofculis radiorum folitariis*; Ray, *Chryfanthemum Americanum, caule alato, foliis amplioribus binatis, floribus pallidè lutefcentibus parvis*, and Vaillant, *Eupatorio phalacron folio trinervi fcrophulariæ, caule alato* It grows naturally in Virginia.

Clafs and order in the Linnæan Syftem The characters

*Sigesbeckia* is of the clafs and order *Syngenefia Polygamia Superflua*, and the characters are,

1 Calyx The outer calyx confifts of five narrow, taper, patent, permanent leaves, which are longer than the flower The interior is nearly quinquangular, and compofed of feveral oval, concave, obtufe, equal leaves

2 Corolla The compound flower is femiradiated The hermaphrodite florets are many in the difk, the females are but few in the radius The hermaphrodite florets have each a funnel-fhaped petal indented in five parts at the top, the females are tongue-fhaped, broad, fhort, and indented in three parts at the extremity

3 Stamina, of the hermaphrodites, are five very fhort filaments, having a cylindrical tubular anthera

4 Pistillum, of the hermaphrodites, confifts of an oblong incurved germen the fize of the calyx, a filiforme ftyle the length of the ftamina, and a bifid ftigma

In the females, it confifts of an oblong incurved germen the fize of the calyx, a filiforme ftyle the length of the hermaphrodites, and a bifid ftigma

5 Pericarpium There is none

6 Semina of the hermaphrodites, are fingle, oblong, obtufely four-cornered, blunt, naked, and have no down

The feeds of the females are fimilar to thofe of the hermaphrodites

CHAP

# CHAP. CCCCXXVI.

## SILENE, CATCH-FLY, or VISCOUS CAMPION.

Species.

THE Perennials of this genus are,

1. Broad leaved Mountain Viscous Campion, or Nottingham Catch-fly.
2. Sea Campion.
3. Shrubby Campion.
4. Giant Campion.
5. Oriental Campion.
6. Virginian Campion.
7. Many-leaved Campion.
8. Saxifrage Campion.
9. Moss Campion.

Description of Broad leaved Mountain

1. Broad leaved Viscous Mountain Campion, or Nottingham Catch-fly. The stalks grow to about two feet high, and are viscous or clammy below the joints. The leaves are long, spear-shaped, and grow opposite to each other at the joints. The flowers come out from the wings of the leaves on pretty long footstalks, which support four or five flowers, and form a kind of panicle on the upper parts of the stalks; they hang drooping, and each has its own separate short footstalk; they are of a white colour, and their petals are cut into two parts; they appear in May, and the seeds ripen in August.

Sea,

2. Sea Campion. The stalks are slender, numerous, crooked, smooth, spread upon the ground, and are about a foot in length. The leaves are small, narrow, green, of a thickish substance, and grow opposite to each other. The flowers come out, two or three together, from the upper parts of the branches, on footstalks placed opposite to each other; their colour is white, having bifid petals; they make their appearance in May and June, and often continue to shew themselves until the end of autumn. The seeds of the first-blown flowers will be ripe in August.

Shrubby,

3. Shrubby Campion. The stalks are ligneous, divide into a few branches, and grow to about a foot high. The leaves are spear-shaped, smooth, and end in acute points. The flowers grow in small spreading panicles from the upper parts of the branches; they are of a greenish white colour, and their petals are bifid; they come out in June and July, and the seeds ripen in the autumn.

Giant, described,

4. Giant Campion. The stalks are smooth, round, and grow to about a yard high. The radical leaves are fleshy, roundish, downy, and hollowed like a spoon; those on the stalks are oval, narrow, downy, and grow by pairs, or else three or four together, round the stalk. The flowers grow in loose spikes from the tops of the stalks; they are of a whitish-green colour, and open only at night; the season of their appearance is June, and the seeds ripen in August.

Proper situation and soil.

This plant must have a dry, light, sandy soil, and a well-sheltered situation, in order to continue it for many years.

Oriental

5. Oriental Campion. The stalk is erect, herbaceous, channelled, and grows to about a foot and a half high. The leaves are narrow, spear-shaped, acute-pointed, smooth, and in the spring, before the stalks arise, form a large clustered head from the root. The flowers are produced from the wings of the leaves, two or three growing together on short footstalks; their colour is white; they expand only at night, grow erect, and the season of their appearance is July; but it is not often that they are succeeded by good seeds in our gardens.

Virginian

6. Virginian Campion. The stalks are viscous, upright, and about eight or nine inches long. The leaves are oblong, broad, spear-shaped, and blunt pointed. The flowers come out from the upper parts of the stalks in spreading panicles; they are of a fine red or crimson colour, appear in July, and often continue in succession until the end of August.

Many-leaved,

7. Many-leaved Campion. The stalks are round, jointed, branching, and about a foot and a half high. The leaves are narrow, small, downy, and grow many together in bunches. The flowers come out from the upper parts of the branches on short footstalks; they make their appearance in July, and the seeds ripen in the autumn.

Saxifrage

8. Saxifrage Campion. This plant hath a tough ligneous root, from which issue several smooth stalks to the height of about four or five inches. The leaves are narrow, smooth, acute, and grow opposite to each other. The flowers come out singly from the ends of the stalks on long slender footstalks; their petals are bifid, red underneath, and white above; they make their appearance in July, and the seeds ripen in the autumn.

and Moss Campion described.

9. Moss Campion. This is so called from the resemblance the plant has to moss. The leaves are small, and spread upon the ground in a moss-like manner. The flowers are small, and rise hardly to half an inch in height, so that this is a low perennial indeed. The flowers are of a dirty-white colour, will be in blow in May and June, and are succeeded by good seeds in July or August.

This being an exceeding low plant, the strictest care must be used in pulling up the weeds which grow, on their first appearance, otherwise they will soon overspread it, and endanger its being choaked up with them.

Culture

The third sort is propagated by planting the slips in the spring, which if watered and shaded at first will readily grow, and soon become good plants.

All the others are encreased by slipping the heads, or dividing of the roots, the best time for which is July and August, though it may be done successfully in the autumn, winter, or early in the spring, before the stalks shoot up for flowering.

They are also raised by sowing of the seeds, the best time for which is the autumn, soon after they

they are ripe, though if the work be deferred until the spring, the seeds will readily grow After the plants come up, they will require no trouble all summer, except thinning them where they are too close, keeping them clean from weeds, and watering them in dry weather If these precautions are taken, they will by the autumn be grown to be good plants, and may be then set out for good

Titles

1 Broad leaved Mountain Viscous Campion, or Nottingham Catch-fly, is titled, *Silene petalis bifidis, floribus lateralibus secundis cernuis, panicula nutante* In the *Hortus Cliffort* it is termed, *Silene foliis lanceolatis, caule paniculato, floribus nutantibus, calyce striato, corollis monogynia* Caspar Bauhine calls it, *Lychnis montana viscosa alba latifolia*, John Bauhine, *Polemonium petraeum Gesneri*, Gerard *Lychnis sylvestris alba IX Clusii*, and Parkinson, *Lychnis sylvestris alba, sive ocymoides minus album* It grows on the walls of Nottingham castle, and in stony mountainous parts and dry meadows in England, and most of the northern countries of Europe

2 Sea Campion is, *Silene petalis bifidis corollis subcoadunatis, floribus secundis, pedunculis oppositis trifloris, ramis alaternis* In the *Hortus Upsal* it is termed, *Silene petalis bifidis coronatis corolla coadunata, calycibus erectis raris pilosis* Caspar Bauhine calls it, *Lychnis maritima repens*, John Bauhine, *Lychnis marina Anglicana*, Morison, *Lychnis perennis angusti folia maritima Anglica procumbens*, Gerard, *Lychnis marina Anglica*, and Parkinson, *Lychnis marina repens alba* It grows naturally on the sea-shores of England, also in Tartary

3 Shrubby Campion is, *Silene petalis bifidis, caule fruticoso, foliis lato-lanceolatis, panicula trichotoma* In the *Hortus Cliffort* it is termed, *Silene caule folioso fruticoso foliis linearis lanceolatis acutis glabris, capsulis ovatis* Caspar Bauhine calls it, *Lychnis myrtifolia behen albo similis*, Commeline, *Ocymoides fruticosum*, and Boccon, *Saponaria frutescens cereus foliis, ex Sicilia* It grows naturally in Sicily and Germany

4 Giant Campion is, *Silene foliis radicalibus cochleariformibus confertissimis, caule subaphyllo* Wachendorf calls it, *Silene foliis obovatis crassis, limbis corollae bifidis a sole revolutis*, and Walther, *Lychnis Graeca, flore [illegible] foliis & facie flore albo* It grows naturally in Africa

5 Oriental Campion is, *Silene petalis bifidis, floribus pedunculatis, oppositis bracteis erectioribus, foliis lanceolatis caule glaucis* In the *Hortus Cliffort* it is termed, *Silene caule folioso bi[illegible]*, *foliis lanceolatis acutis glabris, calycibus erectis* Tournefort calls it, *Lychnis orientalis, buplevri folio* It inhabits Persia

6 Virginian Campion is, *Silene calycibus floris cylindricis villosis, panicula dichotoma* Gronovius calls it, *Lychnis flore simplici speciosa coccineo, foliis oblongis acuminatis adversis, caule viscoso* It is a native of Virginia

7 Many-leaved Campion is, *Silene foliis fasciculatis setaceis ramorum florentium oppositis* Caspar Bauhine calls it, *Lychnis sylvestris, plurimis foliis [illegible]*, and Clusius, *Lychnis sylvestris VIII* It grows naturally in Pannonia, Austria, and Bohemia

8 Saxifrage Campion is, *Silene caulibus unifloris, pedunculis longissimis caule, foliis glabris, floribus hermaphroditis feminesque* Caspar Bauhine calls it, *Caryophyllus saxifragus*, John Bauhine, *Saxifraga antiquorum quibusdam*, and Seguier, *Lychnis minima saxifraga* It grows naturally on the mountainous parts of Gaul and Italy

9 Moss Campion is, *Silene acaulis* In the former edition of the *Species Plantarum* it is termed, *Cucubalus acaulis* Caspar Bauhine calls it, *Lychnis Alpina pumila, folio gramineo*, John Bauhine, *Muscus Alpinus, lychnidis flore*, Ray, *Lychnis Alpina minima*, and Gerard, *Caryophyllus pumilus Alpinus* It grows naturally on the mountainous parts of England, Lapland, Austria, Helvetia, and the Pyrenees

*Silene* is of the class and order *Decandria Trigynia*, and the characters are, Class and Order in the Linnaean System

1 CALYX is a monophyllous, tubulous, permanent perianthium, indented in five parts at the top The Characters

2 COROLLA consists of five petals Their ungues are narrow, and the length of the cup, the limb is plane, obtuse and often bifid The nectarium is composed of two denticles, situated in the neck of each petal, constituting a crown to the faux

3 STAMINA are ten awl-shaped filaments, alternately inserted in the ungues of the petals, having oblong antheræ

4 PISTILLUM consists of a cylindrical germen and three simple styles longer than the stamina, with stigmas which are inflexed contrary to the sun's motion

5 PERICARPIUM is a cylindrical, close, trilocular capsule, opening five ways at the top

6 SEMINA The seeds are many and reniforme

CHAP

# CHAP. CCCCXXVII.

## SILPHIUM, BASTARD CHRYSANTHEMUM.

THE hardy species of this genus are usually called,

Species.
1. Sun-flower-leaved *Astericus*.
2. Maryland *Chrysanthemum*.
3. Trifoliate *Chrysanthemum*.
4. Jagged-leaved American *Bidens*.

Sun flower leaved Astericus. 1. Sun flower-leaved *Astericus*. The stalk is upright, thick, firm, hispid, frequently spotted with purple, and grows to be three or four feet high. The leaves are undivided, rough, serrated on the edges, and the lower ones grow alternately; but the upper ones are placed opposite, and sit close to the stalk. The flowers come out from the tops of the stalks on long slender foot stalks; they are of a yellow colour, and, though smaller, not much unlike the Common Perennial Sun-flower; they appear in August, but are rarely succeeded by seeds in England.

Maryland, 2. Maryland *Chrysanthemum*. The stalks of this species are upright, firm, and grow to about a yard high. The leaves are oblong, serrated, and grow opposite by pairs on very short foot-stalks. The flowers come out from the tops of the stalks on slender foot-stalks; they are of a yellow colour, appear in August, but the seeds rarely ripen in England.

and Trifoliate Chrysanthemum, 3. Trifoliate *Chrysanthemum*. The stalks are thick, hard, firm, of a purplish colour, divide into several branches near the top, and grow to be five or six feet high. The leaves are oblong, rough, sharply serrated, and about the middle of the stalk grow by threes at a joint, though lower they are generally placed by fours, and at the top by pairs, sitting close to the stalks. The flowers come out singly on long footstalks from the ends and sides of the branches; they are of a yellow colour, appear in July and August, and sometimes the seeds ripen in the autumn.

and Jagged leaved American Biden described. 4. Jagged-leaved American *Bidens*. The stalks are very thick, simple, taper, smooth near the bottom, but rough and hairy near the top, and grow to be eight or ten feet high. The leaves are very large, pinnatifid, jagged, rough, grow alternately, and embrace the stalk with their base. The flowers come out from the tops of the stalks on their own separate footstalks; they are of a yellow colour, appear in August, but the seeds rarely ripen in England.

Culture. All these sorts are propagated by parting of the roots in the autumn, when their stalks decay. They are extremely hardy, and proper ornaments for large gardens, wilderness-quarters, frequented woods, &c. When mixed with Sun-flowers, Asters, and other tall-growing perennials, they have a very good effect.

Titles. 1. The first species is titled, *Silphium foliis indivisis sessilibus oppositis inferioribus alternis*. In the *Hortus Cliffort.* it is termed simply, *Silphium*. Van Royen calls it, *Silphium foliis oppositis*; and Dillenius, *Astericus corona: foliis forma et facie*. It grows naturally in Virginia and Carolina.

2. The second species is, *Silphium foliis oppositis lanceolatis acute serratis*. Gronovius calls it, *Silphium foliis oppositis petiolatis serratis*; and Plukenet, *Chrysanthemum Marianum, virga aurea Americanae foliis, florum petalis oriaentalis*. It grows naturally in Virginia.

3. The third species is, *Silphium foliis ternis*. Morison calls it, *Chrysanthemum Virginianum, foliis asperis trilobis, quaternis ad genicula sitis*. It grows naturally in Virginia.

4. The fourth species is, *Silphium foliis alternis pinnatifidis sinuatis*. It grows naturally in many parts of North America.

Class and order in the Linnæan system. *Silphium* is of the class and order *Syngenesia Polygamia Necessaria*; and the characters are,

The characters. 1. CALYX is oval, imbricated, and squarrose. The scales are oval, oblong, permanent, prominent, and reflexed in the middle.

2. COROLLA. The compound flower is radiated. The hermaphrodite florets in the disk have each one funnel shaped petal, indented in five parts at the top.

The females in the radius are spear-shaped, very long, and usually indented in the parts at the extremity.

3. STAMINA of the hermaphrodites are five very short capillary filaments, having a cylindrical tubular anthera.

4. PISTILLUM of the hermaphrodites consists of a very slender taper germen, a long, filiforme, hairy style, and a simple stigma.

The females consist of an obcordated germen, a short simple style, and two setaceous stigmas as long as the style.

5. PERICARPIUM. There is none.

6. SEMINA of the hermaphrodites are none. The females are single, obcordated, and have a membranaceous, two horned, indented border.

The receptacle is paleaceous, and the paleæ are linear.

CHAP.

# CHAP CCCCXXVIII.

## *SINAPIS*, MUSTARD.

THERE is one species of this genus which is a Perennial, called, the Pyrenean Mustard

This plant described. The stalks are smooth, and slender The radical leaves are large, deeply runcinated, smooth, of a light-green colour, with a whitish midrib, and on the whole very much resemble those of Dandelion The leaves on the stalks are smooth, and spear-shaped The flowers are produced in bunches from the ends of the branches, they are small, yellow, and succeeded by straight, rough, striated, hairy pods, containing the seeds

Culture. This species is easily propagated by dividing of the roots in the autumn or spring, and it loves a light soil, and a shady situation

These plants may also be raised in plenty by seeds, which should be sown in March in a border of light earth, and when they come up too close, draw out the weakest After that keep them clean from weeds, and water them now and then in very dry weather, and this is all the trouble they will require until the autumn, when they may be removed to the places where they are designed to remain

Titles. This species is titled, *Sinapis siliquis striatis scabris, foliis runcinatis lævibus* Tournefort calls it, *Erysimum, dentis leonis folio, perenne Pyrenaicum* It grows naturally on the Pyrenean mountains

Class and order in the Linnæan system. *Sinapis* is of the class and order *Tetradynamia Siliquosa*, and the characters are,

The characters.

1 CALYX is a perianthium composed of four cruciform, patent, narrow, concave, channelled, deciduous leaves

2 COROLLA consists of four roundish, plane, patent, entire petals, placed in form of a cross The nectaria are four, and of an oval figure; one is situated on each side between the short stamen and the pistil, and one between the long stamina and the calyx

3 STAMINA are six erect awl shaped filaments, of which the two opposite are the length of the calyx, the other four are rather longer, with erect, patent, pointed antheræ

4 PISTILLUM consists of a taper germen, and a style the length of the germen and altitude of the stamina, with a capitated entire stigma

5 PERICARPIUM is an oblong, torulose, rough, bilocular pod, opening with two valves

6 SEMINA The seeds are many, and globose

# CHAP. CCCCXXIX.

## *SISON*, BASTARD STONE PARSLEY

THE more lasting species of this genus are,

Species

1 Common Bastard Stone Parsley
2 Canada Myrrh
3 Verticillated *Sison*

Common Bastard Stone Parsley described. 1 Common Bastard Stone Parsley The root is taper, hung with many fibres, and strikes deep into the ground The stalks are slender, upright, branching, and two or three feet high The leaves are pinnated, indented, serrated of a bright green colour, and a strong agreeable odour The flowers come out from the ends of the branches in small erect umbels, they are of a white colour, appear in June and July, and the seeds ripen in the autumn

Its Medicinal properties. The seeds of this species are of a hot agreeable aromatick smell and taste, a composition in the Venice treacle, and used in medicine as a carminative and a diuretic, and emmenagogue

Canada Myrrh. 2 Canada Myrrh The stalk is upright, branching a little, and about a foot and a half high The leaves are trilobate, each being composed of three oval, pear shaped, and serrated folioles, they are of a lucid green colour, grow on hairy footstalks, and have a membranaceous cover hair surrounding the stalk at their base The flowers come out in umbels from the ends and sides of the stalks, they are of a white colour, appear in June and July, and the seeds ripen in August

and Verticillated Sison described. 3 Verticillated *Sison* The stalk is thick, swelling, jointed, branching near the top, and about two feet high The leaves are elegantly divided into a multitude of narrow segments, which grow in whorls round the stalks at the joints The flowers are produced in umbels from the ends of the branches, they are moderately large, and of a purplish colour on the outside, but white within; they appear in May and June, and the seeds ripen early in August

Culture. These sorts are all raised by sowing of the seeds, the best time for which is the autumn, soon after they are ripe The ground should be double-dug, and the situation moist and shady In the spring they must be thinned where they are too close, and constantly kept clean from weeds, which is all the trouble they will require

The roots of the first sort are frequently of no very

very long continuance, but if the seeds are permitted to scatter, there will be plants enough for a succession. The other sorts also will shed their seeds, by which means plants, more than may be wished for, will frequently arise.

Titles. 1. The first species is entitled, *Sison foliis pinnatis, umbellis erectis*. In the *Hortus Cliffort.* it is termed, *Sison foliis pinnatis*. Caspar Bauhine calls it, *Sison quod amomum officinis nostris*; Dodonæus, *Petroselinum Macedonicum Fuchsii*; Tournefort, *Sium aromaticum sison off.* and Parkinson, *Sison vulgare, vel amomum Germanicum*. It grows naturally in woods, hedges, and moist places in England.

2. The second species is, *Sison foliis ternatis*. Morison calls it, *Myrrhis Canadensis trilobata*; and Rivinus, *Myrrhis Canadensis*. It grows naturally in North America.

3. The third species is, *Sison foliolis verticillatis capillaceis*. Sauvages calls it, *Carum foliolis setaceis verticillatis, radice napiformi*; also, *Bunium bulbis oblongis*; Dalechamp, *Oenanthe foliis pinnatis foliolis linearibus laciniatis*; Caspar Bauhine, *Daucus pratensis millefolii palustris folio*; Dalechamp, *Daucus pratensis*; and Tournefort, *Carvi foliis tenuissimis, asphodeli radice*. It grows naturally on the Alps and Pyrenees.

Class and order in the Linnæan system. *Sison* is of the class and order *Pentandria Digynia*; and the characters are,

The characters. 1. Calyx. The general umbel is composed of about six rays, and the partial of about ten, all of which are unequal. The general involucrum consists of four unequal leaves; the partial is similar; the perianthium is scarce discernible.

2. Corolla. The general flower is uniform, and each floret has five spear-shaped, planish, inflexed petals.

3. Stamina are five capillary filaments the length of the corolla, having simple antheræ.

4. Pistillum consists of an oval germen situated under the flower, and two reflexed styles, with obtuse stigmas.

5. Pericarpium. There is none. The fruit is oval, striated, and divided into two parts.

6. Semina. The seeds are two, oval, convex and striated on one side, and plane on the other.

## CHAP. CCCCXXX.

## *SISYMBRIUM*, WATER-CRESS.

Species. THE Perennials of this genus are,
1. Common Water-Cress.
2. Pyrenean Radish.
3. Water Rocket.
4. Water Radish.
5. Fine-leaved Rocket.
6. Wall Rocket.
7. Yellow Rocket.
8. Yellow *Draba*.

Common Water Cress described. 1. Common Water-Cress. The stalks are round, hollow, branching, and a foot and a half high. The leaves are pinnated, being composed of about four or five pair of folioles, which are terminated by an odd one; they are smooth, of a thickish substance, nearly heart-shaped, and of a warm, agreeable, bitter taste. The flowers come out in loose spikes from the ends of the branches; they are small, of a white colour, appear in June, and the seeds ripen in July.

Medicinal properties of it. This species is admirable against the scurvy, a fine diuretic, and a purifier of the blood; on which accounts it is eaten by many as a sallad-herb in the spring. It grows naturally by springs, rivulets, ditches, and in watery and moist meadows in most parts of England; from which places it is generally gathered for use.

Culture. Its culture, however, is worth effecting in the gardens, in such places where it does not happen to grow naturally. It is easily propagated by sowing the seeds, soon after they are ripe, in some moist part of the garden, and after they come up will require no trouble, except keeping them clean from weeds. The roots also may be planted in some moist part of the garden, and they will grow and flourish the spring following, and afford good crops for the table. The seeds also may be sown by ditches, brooks, rills, ponds, &c. and they will grow, and soon supply the table with this kind of wholesome agreeable sallad.

Pyrenean Radish, 2. Pyrenean Radish. The stalks are hollow, branching near the top, and a foot and a half high. The lower leaves are lyre-shaped, but the upper ones are bipinnated, and embrace the stalk with their base. The flowers come out from the tops of the stalks in loose spikes; they are of a yellow colour, appear in June and July, and the seeds ripen in August.

Water Rocket, 3. Water Rocket. The stalk is erected, branching, partly procumbent, and a foot and a half or two feet long. The leaves are pinnated, long, and the folioles are spear-shaped, and serrated on the edges. The flowers are produced in loose spikes from the ends of the branches; they are of a yellow colour, appear in June and July, and the seeds ripen in August.

Water Radish, 4. Water Radish. The stalk is weak, procumbent, and strikes root into the mud. The leaves are long, moderately broad, and cut almost to the midrib. The flowers come out from the tops of the stalks on longish footstalks; they are of a yellow colour, appear in June and July, and the seeds ripen in August.

This plant grows naturally in waters, but is not cultivated.

and Fine leaved Rocket described. 5. Fine-leaved Rocket. The stalks are branching, and about a foot and a half high. The lower leaves are elegantly divided into a multitude of tender segments, but the upper ones are entire.

The flowers are produced in loose spikes from the tops of the stalks, they are of a white colour, appear in July and August, and the seeds ripen in September

Wall Rocket described

6 Wall Rocket The stalk is nearly upright, rough, juicy, hairy, naked, and about eight or ten inches high The leaves are spear-shaped, smooth, and deeply indented or serrated on the edges The flowers come out in loose spikes from the tops of the stalks, they are large, of a yellow colour, appear in June, and the seeds ripen in August

Its variety

There is a variety of this species with beautifully jagged leaves

Yellow Rocket,

7 Yellow Rocket The stalks are smooth, simple, naked, and six or eight inches high The leaves are cut almost to the midrib, long, narrow, and a little hairy The flowers come out from the tops of the stalks in loose spikes, they are of a yellow colour, appear in June and July, and the seeds ripen in August

and Yellow Draba described

8 Yellow *Draba* The stalks are many from a strong root, branching, and about three feet high The leaves are spear-shaped long, broad, serrated, of a deep-green colour, and grow alternately The flowers are produced in loose spikes from the tops of the stalks, they are small, of a yellow colour, appear in June and July, and the seeds ripen in August

Culture

These sorts are propagated by sowing the seeds soon after they are ripe, or the spring following They will grow in any soil or situation, though the inhabitants of moist places should have similar allotments, in order to cause them to flourish properly They will all sow themselves after the seeds have once ripened, and produce more plants than could be wished for

They may be also propagated by parting of the roots, which may be done at any time of the year, but more especially the latter end of summer, when the stalks decay

Titles

1 Common Water Cress is titled, *Sisymbrium siliquis declinatis, foliis pinnatis foliolis subcordatis* Fuchsius calls it, *Sisymbrium cardamine*, Caspar Bauhine, *Nasturtium aquaticum supinum*, John Bauhine, *Sisymbrium cardamine, seu nasturtium aquaticum*, Gerard, *Nasturtium aquaticum, sive crateve Sium*, and Parkinson, *Nasturtium aquaticum vulgare* It grows naturally in England, and most countries of Europe, also in America, and the East

2 Pyrenean Radish is, *Sisymbrium siliquis subovatis, foliis inferioribus lyratis, superioribus bipinnatifidis amplexicaulibus, stylis filiformibus* Morison calls it, *Raphanus minimus repens luteus foliis tenuiter divisis*, and Allion, *Alyssum foliis pinnatis multiformibus, floribus racemosis luteis* It grows naturally on the Helvetian and Pyrenean mountains

3 Water Rocket is, *Sisymbrium siliquis declinatis, foliis pinnatis foliolis lanceolatis serratis* Caspar Bauhine calls it, *Eruca palustris nasturtii folio, siliquâ oblongâ*, also, *Eruca quibusdam sylvestris repens, flosculo luteo*, also, *Eruca sylvestris minor, luteo parvoque folio*, Fuchsius, *Eruca sylvestris*, and Gerard, *Eruca aquatica* It grows naturally in England, France, and Germany

4 Water Rocket is *Sisymbrium siliquis declinatis oblongo-ovatis, foliis pinnatifidis serratis* In the *Flora Suecica* it is termed, *Sisymbrium foliis pinnatifidis serratis*, in the *Hortus Cliffort Sisymbrium foliis infimis capillaceis, summis pinnatifidis*, also, *Sisymbrium foliis simplicibus dentatis serratis* Caspar Bauhine calls it, *Raphanus aquaticus, foliis in profundas lacinias divisis*, also, *Raphanus aquaticus, rapistri folio*, also, *Raphanus aquaticus alter*, Vaillant, *Sisymbrium aquaticum foliis variis*, Haller, *Sisymbrium foliis imis integris ovatis serratis, superioribus pinnatis*, and Gerard, *Rapistrum aquaticum* It grows naturally in waters in England, and most of the northern countries of Europe

5 Fine leaved Rocket is, *Sisymbrium foliis integerrimis infimis tripinnatifidis, superioribus integerrimis* Caspar Bauhine calls it, *Sinapi tenuifolio*, and John Bauhine, *Eruca tenuifolia perennis* It grows naturally in Italy, Gaul, and Helvetia

6 Wall Rocket is, *Sisymbrium subacaule, foliis lanceolatis sinuato serratis levigatis, scapis subscabris adscendentibus* Ray calls it *Eruca Monensis laciniata lutea*; and Caspar Bauhine, *Eruca sylvestris minor lutea, bursæ pastoris folio* It grows naturally in sandy places in England, Italy, and Gaul

7 Yellow Rocket is, *Sisymbrium acaule, foliis pinnato-dentatis subpilosis* Dillenius calls it, *Eruca Monensis laciniata, flore luteo majore*, and Tournefort, *Eruca perennis et saxatilis, radice crassâ e rupe Victoriæ* It grows naturally in sandy places in the Isle of Anglesey

8 Yellow *Draba* is, *Sisymbrium foliis lanceolatis dentato serratis caulinis* Caspar Bauhine calls it, *Draba lutea siliquis strictissimis*, and Cammerarius, *Arabis quibusdam dicta planta* It grows naturally on the mountainous parts of Helvetia and Italy

*Sisymbrium* is of the class and order *Tetradynamia Siliquosa*, and the characters are, Class and order in the Linnæan system

1 CALYX is a perianthium composed of four spear shaped, narrow, patent, coloured, deciduous leaves The characters.

2 COROLLA is tetrapetalous and cruciform, the petals are oblong, patent often smaller than the calyx, and have very small ungues

3 STAMINA are six filaments longer than the calyx, of which the two opposite ones are rather the shortest, having simple antheræ

4 PISTILLUM consists of an oblong filiform germen, a very short style, and an obtuse stigma

5 PERICARPIUM is a long, incurved, gibbous taper pod, composed of two valves, and containing two cells

6 SEMINA The seeds are many, and small

CHAP

# CHAP. CCCCXXXI.

## SISYRINCHIUM

THERE is only one real species of the *Sisyrinchium*, but there are two or three varieties which differ very greatly. Those proper for this place are known among Gardeners by the names of,

Species
1. The Bermuda *Sisyrinchium*.
2. The Virginian *Sisyrinchium*.

Bermuda,
1. The Bermuda *Sisyrinchium*. The root is fibrous. The leaves are sword-shaped, and embrace the stalk at the bottom; they are of a firm substance, will grow to about half a foot in length, and their colour is a deep green. The flower-stalk will rise rather higher than the leaves; it is sword-shaped, being possessed of two longitudinal borders, and the top of it is ornamented by the flowers. These will be about half a dozen in number; their colour is a deep blue, with yellow bottoms; they are placed upon short footstalks; each is composed of six oval, pointed, spreading petals; they will be in blow in June; and each is succeeded by an oval obtuse capsule, containing the seeds.

and Virginian Sisyrinchium described
2. Virginian *Sisyrinchium*. The root is fibrous. The leaves are sword-shaped, but shorter and narrower than the former species; their edges are entire, and their colour is a light-green. The flower-stalk will grow to about the height of the leaves; they have two longitudinal borders or edges, and the top is ornamented with the flowers. The number of these is seldom more than two; they are of a blue colour, and grow on short footstalks; they will be in blow in June, and the flowers are succeeded by oval capsules, containing the seeds, which will be ripe about September.

Method of propagating them
The culture of these sorts is very easy. The first method is by parting of the roots; the best time for which work is September. A moist day, if possible, should be made choice of; and if the situation designed for them is shady, and the soil fresh and light, it will be more agreeable to their nature, and they will shew themselves to greater perfection.

These plants are also propagated by seeds. Sow them in the same kind of shady borders in September, and sift over them some fine light mould about half an inch deep. In the spring the plants will come up, and have the appearance of grass; so that in weeding them care must be taken to avoid mistakes. Thin them where they come up too close, and now and then give them a little water. By the autumn they will be grown to be strong plants, and may be transplanted to the places they are designed for; and the generality of them may be expected to flower the summer following.

Titles.
1. The first species is titled, *Sisyrinchium caule foliisque ancipitibus*. Plukenet calls it, *Sisyrinchium Bermudiense, floribus parvis ex cæruleo et aureo mixtis*; and Dillenius, *Bermudiana iridis folio, radice fibrosâ*. It grows naturally in Bermuda.

2. The second sort, which is common in Virginia, is termed by Plukenet, *Sisyrinchium cæruleum parvum, gladiato caule, Virginianum*; and Dillenius, *Bermudiana graminea, flore minore cæruleo*.

Class and order in the Linnæan system
*Sisyrinchium* is of the class and order *Gynandria Triandria*; and the characters are,

The characters
1. CALYX is a spatha composed of two compressed, keel-shaped, pointed leaves.
2. COROLLA consists of six oblong, oval, erect, pointed, spreading petals.
3. STAMINA are three very short filaments, with bifid antheræ affixed to the style.
4. PISTILLUM consists of an oval germen situated below the flower, a subulated style shorter than the corolla, and a trifid reflexed stigma.
5. PERICARPIUM is an oval three-cornered capsule, formed of three valves, and containing three cells.
6. SEMINA. The seeds are roundish, and numerous.

# CHAP. CCCCXXXII.

## *SIUM*, WATER PARSNEP.

Species

THE ſpecies of this genus are,
1 Common Water Parſnep
2 Creeping Water Parſnep
3 Ninzin
4 Rigid *Sium*
5 Perennial Biſhop's Weed
6 Trifoliate Water Parſnep

Common

1 Common Water Parſnep The ſtalk is upright, thick, firm, branching, and five or ſix feet high The leaves are large and pinnated, being compoſed of oblong, broad, ſerrated fo lioles, terminated by an odd one The flowers come out in large umbels from the ends of the branches, they are of a pale-yellow colour, appear in June and July, and the ſeeds ripen in Auguſt

and Creeping Water Parſnep,

2 Creeping Water Parſnep The ſtalks lie on the ground, and ſtrike root at the joints The leaves are pinnated, and the folioles are oblong, pointed, ſerrated, and of a light-green colour The flowers are produced in umbels from the joints, they are of a white colour appear in June, July, and Auguſt, and the ſeeds ripen in September

Ninzin.

3 Ninzin The root often divides in the manner of mandrakes, ſo that the upper-part becomes like the body, and the two branches reſemble the legs of a man Hence the name Ninzin has been uſed for this plant in China, where it naturally grows, that word ſignifying in the Chineſe language (as it is ſaid), *reſemblance of man* The ſtalks are thick, round, ſtriated, jointed, branching, and will grow to about two feet high The leaves are of different figures, ſome being entire, others pinnated, and thoſe on the top of the ſtalks trilobate, they are ſmooth, of a bright-green colour, and grow alternately at the joints The flowers are produced in umbels from the tops of the branches, they are ſmall, of a white colour, and are ſucceeded by reddiſh bifid ſeeds, a little like thoſe of Aniſe A kind of tubercle alſo is produced from the upper-parts of the plant, about the ſize of peaſe, which being planted, when arrived to their full maturity, will grow, and become freſh plants

Rigid Sium,

4 Rigid *Sium* The ſtalk is rigid, upright, and branching The leaves are pinnated, each conſiſts of about five or ſix pair of ſpear ſhaped lobes terminated by an odd one, they are for the moſt part entire, though ſome of them will be a little ſerrated, they are ſtiff, ſmooth, and their footſtalks channelled The flowers are produced in umbels at the ends of the branches, but are ſmall, and of little figure

Perennial Biſhop's Weed,

5 Perennial Biſhop's Weed This hath a creeping, thick, fleſhy root, of the taſte of *Eryngo* The ſtalks are upright, branching, and grow to about two feet high The leaves are ſmall, narrow, decurrent, join together, and embrace the ſtalk with their baſe The flowers are produced in large flat umbels, their colour is white; they appear in July, but are not often ſucceeded by good ſeeds in our gardens

and Trifoliate Water Parſnep deſcribed

6 Trifoliate Water Parſnep. The ſtalks will riſe to about two feet high The radical leaves are trifoliate, large, and of a ſhining-green colour, but thoſe on the ſtalks are bipinnated The flowers are produced in umbels in July, their colour is yellow, and they are for the moſt part ſucceeded by good ſeeds in the autumn

Method of propagation

All theſe ſorts are propagated by the ſeeds, which ſhould be ſown in the autumn, or the ſpring, in the places where they are to remain After they come up they will call for no culture, except keeping them clean from weeds, and thinning them to about a foot and a half diſtance from each other

They are alſo propagated by offsets from the roots in the autumn, and indeed the fifth ſort encreaſes by this method ſo faſt, that it would be needleſs to attempt its propagation any other way They are plants of very little beauty, ſo that not more than two or three of a ſort ought to find a place in our largeſt gardens, unleſs cultivated for medicinal uſes, the firſt ſort being ſaid to be a very fine cordial, and uſeful in many diſeaſes

Titles

1 Common Water Parſnep is titled, *Sium foliis pinnatis, umbelus terminalibus* Caſpar Bauhine calls it, *Sium latifolium*, alſo, *Sium, ſ apium paluſtre, foliis oblongis* It grows naturally on the banks of rivers, ſides of meadows, and moiſt places in England, and moſt countries of Europe

2 Creeping Water Parſnep is, *Sium foliis pinnatis, umbellis axillaribus ſeſſilibus* Moriſon calls it, *Sium aquaticum procumbens, ad alas floridum* It grows naturally in rivers, brooks, and ditches almoſt every-where in England, and moſt countries of Europe

3 Ninzin is titled, *Sium foliis ſerratis pinnatis rameis ternatis* Kæmpfer calls it, *Siſarum montanum, Coraenſe, radice non tuberoſâ* It grows naturally in China

4 Rigid *Sium* is, *Sium foliis pinnatis foliolis lanceolatis ſubintegerrimis* Gronovius calls it, *Pimpinella foliolis lanceolatis glabris acuminatis ſæpius integerrimis, rarius ſerratura notatis*, and Moriſon *Oenanthe maxima Virginiana, pæoniæ feminæ foliis* It grows naturally in Virginia

5 Perennial Biſhop's Weed is titled, *Sium foliolis linearibus decurrentibus connatis* Caſpar Bauhine calls it, *Eryngium arvenſe, foliis ſerratis*, and Moriſon, *Ammi perenne repens* It grows naturally in moſt parts of Germany, and in the Eaſt

6 Trifoliate Water Parſnep is, *Sium foliis radicalibus ternatis, caulinis bipinnatis* [illegible] calls it, *Myrrhis foliis paſtinacæ lætè [illegible]*, and Zan, *Daucus, paſtinacæ folio, [illegible]* It grows naturally in Sicily

Claſs and order in the Linnean Syſtem

*Sium* is of the claſs and order *Pentandria Digynia*; and the characters are,

The characters

1 CALYX The general umbel is different in the different ſpecies, the partial is plane and patent, the general involucrum is compoſed of many ſpear ſhaped, reflexed leaves, which are ſhorter

shorter than the umbel, the partial is composed of many small narrow leaves, the proper perianthium is very small

2 COROLLA The general corolla is uniform, and each of the flowers consists of five inflexed, heart-shaped, equal petals

3 STAMINA consist of five simple filaments, with simple antheræ

4 PISTILLUM consists of a very small germen situated below the flower, and two reflexed styles, with obtuse stigmas.

5 PERICARPIUM There is none The fruit is small, oval, roundish, striated, and separable into two parts

6 SEMINA The seeds are two, streaked, oval, plane on one side, and convex on the other

# CHAP. CCCCXXXIII.

## *SMYRNIUM*, ALEXANDERS.

OF this genus there is one Perennial, called, Virginian *Smyrnium*

The plant described. The stalk is round, smooth, firm, branching a little, and five or six feet high The radical leaves are triternate, oblong, oval, smooth, entire, and of a glaucous green colour, those on the stalks are for the most part trifoliate, and they grow on footstalks at the joints The flowers are produced in umbels from the tops of the stalks, they are of a white or yellowish colour, appear in June and July, and the seeds ripen in August.

Method of propagation This plant is propagated by sowing the seeds, soon after they are ripe, in the places where they are to remain When the plants come up, they must be thinned to proper distances, and afterwards kept clean from weeds, which is all the trouble they will require

Titles This species is titled, *Smyrnium foliis caulinis duplicato ternatis integerrimis* Gronovius calls it, *Smyrnium foliis caulinis ternatis petiolatis foliolis oblongo ovatis integerrimis* It is a native of Virginia

Class and order in the Linnæan system *Smyrnium* is of the class and order *Pentandria Digynia*, and the characters are,

The characters 1 CALYX The general umbel is unequal, and the partial is erect There is no involucrum The perianthium is so small as to be scarce discernible

2 COROLLA The general flower is uniform The florets have each five spear-shaped, slightly inflexed, carinated petals

3 STAMINA are five simple filaments the length of the corolla, having simple antheræ.

4 PISTILLUM consists of a germen situated below the calyx, and two simple styles, with simple stigmas

5 PERICARPIUM There is none The fruit is nearly globular, striated, and divided into two parts

6 SEMINA The seeds are two, lunulated, marked with three streaks, convex on one side, and plane on the other

# CHAP CCCCXXXIV

## *SOLDANELLA*, SOLDANEL.

OF this genus there is only one species yet known, called Soldanel

The plant described. The root is fibrous and spreading The leaves are roundish, nearly kidney-shaped, of a dark-green colour, and grow on long footstalks The stalk is naked, and about four or five inches high The flowers come out, two or three together, from the tops of the stalks, they are of a blue colour, appear in April and May, and the seeds ripen in July

Its variety. There is a beautiful variety of this species with white flowers

Culture. This species is propagated by parting of the roots, the best time for which is August, or early in September, that they may be established in their new situations before the winter frost comes on If the weather should prove hot, they must be shaded and duly watered until they have taken root, and afterwards they will require no trouble, except keeping them clean from weeds The soil should be in good heart, loamy, naturally moist, and in the shade, otherwise this species thrives very ill in this country

They may also be raised by seeds These should be gathered as soon as they are ripe, and laid in an airy place for a few days to dry, then sow them in pots or boxes filled with a light good earth, a little mould should be sifted over them, and they should be set in places wholly in the shade, but not under the drip of trees The next day, if no rain happens, they should be watered, and if the weather continues to prove dry, watering in small quantities should be repeated three times a week This will effectually bring up the seeds, so that before the end of autumn, the greatest share of plants will be above ground Weeds must be duly picked out, as they arise and when the frosts begin to threaten, the pots should be placed under a hotbed-frame, or some shelter, but always be set abroad again in mild open weather In the spring the remaining part of the seeds will come up Watering must be afforded the plants as often as dry weather makes it necessary, and when all danger of frost is over, the pots should be plunged up to the rims in some shady place Here the plants may remain, with the usual care of weeding and watering, until August, or the beginning of September, when they may be set out in the places where they are to remain

Titles. There being no other species of this genus, it is named simply, *Soldanella* Caspar Bauhine calls it, *Soldanella Alpina rotundifolia*, and Camerarius, *Soldanella Alpina* It grows naturally on the Pyrenean, Austrian, and Helvetian mountains

Class and order in the Linnæan system. *Soldanella* is of the class and order *Pentandria Monogynia*, and the characters are,

The characters.

1 CALYX is an upright permanent perianthium, divided into five spear-shaped segments

2 COROLLA is one bell-shaped petal, widening gradually, and jagged at the brim

3 STAMINA are five awl-shaped filaments, having simple antheræ

4 PISTILLUM consists of a roundish germen, a filiform permanent style the length of the corolla, and a simple stigma

5 PERICARPIUM is an oblong, taper unilocular capsule, obliquely striated, and opening in ten denticles at the top

6 SEMINA The seeds are numerous, acuminated, and small

The receptacle is columnar, and free

# CHAP. CCCCXXXV.

## *SOLIDAGO*, GOLDEN-ROD

THE variety of Golden rods is very great More than fixty forts may be found with titles in different authors, which are reduced by Linnæus to twelve fpecies only, and thofe are,

Species

1 The Common Englifh Golden rod
2 Flefhy Smooth-leaved New-York Golden-rod
3 Narrow-leaved Canada Golden-rod
4 Talleft Late American Golden-rod
5 Lateral-flowered Golden-rod
6 Smooth Maryland Golden-rod
7 Mexican Golden rod
8 Canada Golden rod with a Fig wort Leaf
9 Broad leaved Canada Golden-rod
10 Pyrenean Golden-rod
11 Penfylvanian Golden-rod
12 New-York Golden rod

Thefe are the real and diftinct fpecies of this genus, and to one or other of them the amazing variety of Golden rods that is found in our gardens belongs

Common Englifh Golden-rod defcribed

1 The Common Englifh Golden-rod has feveral angular, flender ftalks, a foot and a half or two feet in length The lower leaves are oval, fpear-fhaped, and their edges are ferrated, thofe on the ftalks are narrow, entire, and grow clofe, without any footftalks The ftalks divide near the top into fmaller branches, all of which are terminated by erect clufters or fpikes of flowers, which are of a golden-yellow colour, and look very beautiful in Auguft and September, when they are in their greateft perfection

Varieties

There are three or four varieties of this fpecies, one of which has purple ftalks, and is of taller growth, another has very broad, ferrated leaves, a third has exceeding narrow leaves, with hardly any ferratures, and a fourth is of low growth, feldom rifing higher than a foot All thefe have titles, as if diftinct fpecies, in old authors

Defcription of Smooth Flefhy leaved New-York,

2 Smooth Flefhy-leaved New York Golden-rod This fpecies hath feveral red ftalks, which will grow to be fix feet high The lower leaves are thick, of a flefhy fubftance, fpear-fhaped, fmooth in the middle, but have a rough border, with three confpicuous veins running length-ways, and are of a deep-green colour The upper leaves are narrower, quite fmooth, flefhy, have entire edges, and diminifh in fize as they are placed higher on the ftalks The flowers form a large panicle at the tops of the ftalks The fpikes are erect, and the flowers are clofely fet, numerous, and of a bright-yellow colour; fo that at the time of flowering they make a very fine fhow They blow late in the autumn, and continue flowering great part of the winter, if very hard frofts do not fet in

Narrow leaved Canada,

3 Narrow leaved Canada Golden-rod This fpecies hath feveral fmooth, round ftalks, that will grow to about two feet high The leaves are narrow, rough, fharp pointed, fit clofe to the ftalks, are a little ferrated, and have three longitudinal veins The tops of the ftalks are adorned with a fpecious, roundifh panicle of flowers; the upper fpikes are erect, but the lower ones are reflexed, their colour is yellow, and they flower in July and Auguft

Talleft Late American,

4 Talleft Late American Golden rod There are fo many varieties of this fpecies which differ fo much among themfelves, that a defcription of one can hardly convey a fufficient idea of the others They go, among Gardeners, by the names of New-England Golden-rod, Large Hairy Golden-rod, Rough Maryland Golden rod, &c The ftalks are numerous, round, fmooth, and grow in general to about four or five feet high The leaves are fpear-fhaped, rough, have hardly any ferratures on their edges, and no longitudinal veins, like many of the other forts The panicles are very large and round The fpikes are very clofely fet with flowers, and in fome varieties they fpread very much, and are reflexed, in others they grow more compact They are of a yellow colour, and blow in September and October

Lateral-flowered,

5 Lateral-flowered Golden-rod This fpecies grows only to about a foot and a half high The leaves are narrow, foft to the touch, pointed, and have not their edges ferrated The fpikes of flowers are produced from almoft the bottom of the ftalk on long, fingle branches, and continue to be produced from the fide to the top, the branches diminifhing in length in proportion as they get nearer the top, fo that the whole forms a very large roundifh panicle of flowers Thefe are of a yellow colour, and will be in blow in September

Smooth Maryland

6 Smooth Maryland Golden rod The ftalks are fmooth, flender, and will grow to about a foot and a half high The leaves are fpear-fhaped, narrow, pointed, fmooth, and indented The flowers form a corymbous panicle at the top of the ftalk, are of a yellow colour, and will be in blow in September

Mexican,

7 Mexican Golden-rod This fpecies hath feveral oblique, fmooth, brown ftalks, that will grow to about a foot and a half in length The leaves are fpear-fhaped, fmooth, and entire The flowers are produced from one fide of the ftalk in fpikes, having leafy footftalks, their colour is yellow, and they fhew themfelves in Auguft and September

and Canada Golden-rod

8 Canada Golden-rod with a Fig-wort Leaf This fpecies hath a flender, fmooth, flexuofe ftalk, about two feet long The leaves are oval, fharp-pointed, and their edges are ferrated The flowers are produced from the fides of the branches in bunches; they are of a pale-yellow or brimftone colour, and are in their greateft perfection in September

Varieties,

There are three or four varieties of this fpecies, differing in the fize of their leaves, colour of their flowers, times of flowering, or the like, but they are eafily feen to be of the fame kind, for the difference in the leaves is very inconfiderable, and the colour of the flowers hardly to be regarded, the one being more of a yellow than the other, and fhewing itfelf a little earlier in the feafon

Broad leaved Canada Golden-rod defcribed

9 Broad-leaved Canada Golden-rod The ftalks are upright, angular, and will grow to about two feet long The leaves are broad, of an oval figure, fharp-pointed, and their edges

are

are ſerrated. The flowers are produced in ſhort, ſingle ſpikes from the wings of the leaves; their colour is yellow, and they flower in September.

*Pyrenean Golden rod deſcribed.*

10. Pyrenean Golden-rod. This is a very low plant, riſing with a few ſingle ſtalks to the height of about a foot. The leaves are ſpear ſhaped, narrow, and their edges are entire. The flowers are produced from the wings of the leaves, each footſtalk ſupporting one flower, which will be in blow in Auguſt.

*Varieties.*

There are two or three varieties of this ſpecies, one has very large flowers, and another is of a deeper-yellow colour, and appears later.

*Deſcription of Penſylvanian*

11. Penſylvanian Golden rod. This ſpecies hath ſeveral upright, firm ſtalks, that ſend forth branches alternately from the ſides. The leaves are oval, exceeding rough, and rigid. The flowers form a corymbus at the ends of the branches, are of a yellow colour, and will be in blow in September.

*and New-York Golden rod.*

12. New-York Golden-rod. This ſpecies hath a few naked, branching ſtalks, that will grow to near a foot and a half high. The radical leaves (for the ſtalks are naked) are oval, oblong, rough, and grow on moderately ſtrong footſtalks. A few flowers terminate the branches, they are large, yellow, and blow in September.

*Method of propagation.*

All theſe ſpecies are very hardy, and you cannot err in their culture. Divide the roots any time in the autumn, winter, or ſpring, and they will readily grow, though the autumn is the more eligible ſeaſon, as the plants removed then will flower ſtronger than thoſe removed in the ſpring, if the ſummer ſhould prove dry. The largeſt growing ſorts are very ornamental to the edges of wilderneſs quarters, woods, &c. near walks of reſort. When they are deſigned for ſuch places, dig the ground well for about a yard ſquare, and then ſet in a good ſtrong plant. Keep it in weeding for the firſt two months in the ſpring, and afterwards leave it to chance and Nature. It will conſtantly ſhew its flowers in the autumn, though the place be uncultivated, and appear as if Nature originally deſigned it for that ſpot, though not ſo luxuriantly as in a well cultivated garden.

The lower ſorts are by no means proper for theſe places. A few plants of each ſhould be ſtationed in the flower-garden, and all of them ſhould be kept within bounds by reducing the roots of thoſe that are apt to ſpread faſt, every two or three years, for the beauty of theſe plants is to have a few ſtems only, as they will always ſhew their flowers larger and in greater perfection than when they are crowded.

The ſeeds of the earlier-flowering ſpecies will often ripen, by which plants may be eaſily raiſed that way. Sow them in the autumn as ſoon as they are ripe, and the ſpring and ſummer following, when the plants come up, keep them clean from weeds, water them now-and-then in dry weather, and thin them where they come up too cloſe. In September plant them in the nurſery ground at about half a foot diſtance from each other, and the September after that remove them to the places where they are deſigned to remain.

This method is hardly worth putting into practice, as theſe plants may be encreaſed ſo readily and ſpeedily by dividing of the roots, and alſo as little variety may be expected in the colouring of the flowers.

*Titles.*

1. The Common Engliſh Golden-rod is titled, *Solidago caule ſubflexuoſo, racemis paniculatis erectis confertis*. In the *Hortus Cliffort.* it is termed, *Solidago caule erecto, racemis alternis erectis*, in the *Flora Lapponica*, *Solidago floribus per caulem ſimplicem undiquè ſparſis*. Caſpar Bauhine calls it, *Virga aurea latifolia ſerrata*, John Bauhine, *Virga aurea vulgaris latifolia*. It grows naturally in England and moſt parts of Europe.

2. Smooth Fleſhy-leaved New-York Golden rod is titled, *Solidago foliis lanceolatis ſubcarnoſis glaberrimis margine ſcabriuſculis, paniculâ corymboſâ*. Herman calls it, *Virga aurea Noveboracenſis glabra, caulibus rubentibus, foliis anguſtis glabris*, Moriſon, *Virga aurea Canadenſis, foliis carnoſis non ſerratis, latioribus & anguſtioribus*, and Plukenet, *Virga aurea, ſive ſolidago procerior Americana, caule multiplici*. It is common in ſeveral parts of North-America.

3. Narrow-leaved Canada Golden-rod is titled, *Solidago paniculato-corymboſa, racemis recurvatis, floribus adſcendentibus, foliis trinerviis ſubſerratis ſcabris*. Plukenet calls it, *Virga aurea anguſtifolia, paniculâ ſpecioſâ, Canadenſis*, Moriſon, *Virga aurea Americana, foliis ſerratis anguſtis ſubtus nervoſis*. It grows naturally in Canada and Virginia.

4. Talleſt Late American Golden-rod is, *Solidago paniculâ corymboſâ, racemis recurvis, floribus adſcendentibus, foliis enerviis ſerratis*. Martin calls it, *Virga aurea altiſſima ſerotina, paniculâ ſpecioſâ patulâ*, another ſort of it he terms, *Virga aurea Marilandica, ſpicis florum racemoſis, foliis integris ſcabris*. Boerhaave calls it, *Virga aurea Novæ Angliæ altiſſima, paniculis nonnullùm reflexis*, Dillenius, *Virga aurea Americana hirſuta, radice odoratâ, &c*. It grows naturally in North-America.

5. Lateral-flowered Golden-rod is, *Solidago paniculâ corymboſâ, racemis recurvis adſcendentibus, caule infernè ramoſo floriferoque*. It is a native of North-America.

6. Smooth Maryland Golden-rod is, *Solidago paniculâ corymboſâ, racemis ſuprà denſioribus, caule glabro lævi*. Dillenius calls it, *Virga aurea Marilandica, cæſiâ glabrâ*, and Ray, *Virga aurea Marilandica, foliis longis anguſtis acutis, ramis ſive virgulis floriferis è foliorum alis exeuntibus longa ſerie*. It grows in North-America.

7. Mexican Golden-rod is, *Solidago caule obliquo, pedunculis erectis foliolatis ramoſis, foliis lanceolatis integerrimis*. Caſpar Bauhine calls it, *Virga aurea Mexicana*, Tournefort, *Virga aurea, limonii folio, paniculâ uno verſu diſpoſitâ*. It is a native of Mexico.

8. Canada Golden-rod with a Fig-wort Leaf is titled, *Solidago caule flexuoſo, foliis ovatis acuminatis ſerratis, racemis lateralibus ſimplicibus*. Herman calls it, *Virga aurea Canadenſis, aſteriſci folio*, and Plukenet, *Virga aurea montana, ſcrophulariæ folio*. It grows in Canada.

9. Broad-leaved Canada Golden-rod is titled, *Solidago caule erecto, foliis ovatis acuminatis ſerratis, racemis lateralibus ſimplicibus*. Plukenet calls it, *Virga aurea, latiſſimo folio, Canadenſis glabra*. It grows naturally in Canada.

10. Pyrenean Golden-rod is, *Solidago caule ſimpliciſſimo, foliis caulinis integerrimis, pedunculis axillaribus unifloris*. Moriſon calls it, *Virga aurea humilis Alpina*, Herman, *Virga aurea omnium minima, floribus maximis*, and Plukenet, *Virga aurea montana, bunchalis pumila*.

11. Penſylvanian Golden-rod is termed, *Solidago foliis caulinis ovatis ſcabris, ramis alternis faſtigiatis, corymbis terminalibus*. Herman calls it, *Virga aurea Novæ Angliæ, lato rigidoque folio*. It grows naturally in Penſylvania.

12. New-York Golden-rod is, *Solidago foliis radicalibus ovato-oblongis petiolatis, caule nudiuſculo ramoſo faſtigiato*. It grows naturally in North-America.

*Claſs and order in the Linnæan ſyſtem.*

*Solidago* is of the claſs and order *Syngeneſia Polygamia Superflua*, and the characters are,

*The characters.*

1. CALYX. The common calyx is oblong and imbricated,

imbricated, being composed of several oblong, narrow, connivent, sharp pointed scales

2 COROLLA is radiated The hermaphrodite florets are numerous in the disk, funnel shaped, and cut at the top into five spreading segments

The female florets in the radius are tongue-shaped, and indented in three parts

3 STAMINA, in the hermaphrodite flowers, are five very short capillary filaments, with cylindrical, tubular antheræ

4 PISTILLUM, in the hermaphrodite flowers, consists of an oblong germen, a filiforme style the length of the stamina, and a bifid, patent stigma

The pistil in the female flowers is an oblong germen a filiforme style, and two revolute stigmas

5 PERICARPIUM There is none

6 SEMINA The seeds are single, oblong, and crowned with hairy down

The receptacle is plain, and naked

## CHAP CCCCXXXVI

## SONCHUS, SOW-THISTLE.

Species

OF this genus are,

1 Tree Sow thistle
2 Marsh Sow-thistle
3 Maritime Sow-thistle
4 Pyrenean Sow-thistle
5 Siberian Sow-thistle
6 Canada Sow thistle

Description of Tree,

1 Tree Sow thistle The root is very thick, hard, and hung with a few fibres The stalk is thick, woody, very robust, and eight or ten feet high The leaves are long runcinated, and a little heart shaped at their base The flowers come out from the tops of the stalks on very rough, hispid footstalks, they are large, of a beautiful yellow colour, appear in July and August, and are soon succeeded by ripe downy seeds, which the wind will be blowing about to a considerable distance The whole plant is possessed of a milky juice

Marsh,

2 Marsh Sow thistle The root is white, thick, and spreading The stalks are upright, smooth, crested, and five or six feet high The leaves are long, runcinated, and embrace the stalks with their base The flowers come out from the tops of the stalks in kind of umbels, have very rough footstalks, are of a yellow colour, and about the size of the Common Sow-thistle, they appear in August, and are soon succeeded by downy seeds like the former

Maritime

3 Maritime Sow-thistle The root is white, thick, and creeping The stalks are thick, upright, crested, and five or six feet high The leaves are long, spear-shaped, sharply indented, and embrace the stalks with their base The flowers are produced from the tops of the stalks on naked footstalks, are of a yellow colour, appear in July and August, and are soon followed by ripe downy seeds like the former

Pyrenean,

4 Pyrenean Sow-thistle The stalks of this species are thick, upright, firm, and six feet high The radical leaves are two feet long, runcinated, smooth on their upper side, veined, and rough underneath, but those on the stalks are shorter, narrower, and more acute The flowers come out in panicles from the tops of the stalks, are large, have naked footstalks, and are of a blue colour, they appear in July and August, and the seeds ripen in September

Siberian,

5 Siberian Sow thistle The stalks are upright, smooth, and two or three feet high The leaves are spear shaped, undivided, glaucous underneath, and sit close to the stalks The flowers are produced from the tops of the stalks in roundish bunches, are of a blue colour, appear in August, and the seeds ripen in September

and Canada Sow thistle

6 Canada Sow-thistle The stalks are very robust, upright, and eight or ten feet high The leaves are runcinated, large, of a pale-green colour on their upper side, and glaucous underneath The flowers are produced in bunches from the tops of the stalks, growing on long, hairy, clammy footstalks, they are of a blue colour, appear in August, and the seeds ripen in September

Method of propagation

These species are all propagated by sowing the seed, soon after they are ripe, or the spring following When the plants come up, they must be thinned to proper distances, and this, except keeping them clean from weeds, is all the trouble they will require When the seeds have ripened, they will be conveyed by the winds to a considerable distance, by means of which plants in all parts of the garden will frequently arise If you would chuse to have them in perfection, they should have a rich, moist earth, for by being thus stationed, they will be almost as large again as when situated in a soil of an opposite nature

Proper soil

Titles

1 Tree Sow-thistle is titled, *Sonchus pedunculis calycibusque hispidis subumbellatis, foliis runcinatis basi cordatis* In the *Flora Suecica* it is termed, *Sonchus pedunculis calycibusque hispidis, floribus congestis*, in the *Hortus Cliffort Sonchus foliis lanceolato-oblongis dentatis, floribus congestis hispidis* Caspar Bauhine calls it, *Hieracium majus, folio sonchi*, *Hieracium sonchites*, John Bauhine, *Sonchus repens, multis hieracium majus*; Fuchsius, *Hieracium majus*, and Gerard, *Sonchus arborescens* It grows naturally in fields and hedges in England, and most countries of Europe

2 Marsh Sow thistle is, *Sonchus, pedunculis calycibusque hispidis subumbellatis, foliis runcinatis basi sagittatis* In the *Hortus Upsal* it is termed, *Sonchus pedunculis calycibusque hispidis, floribus distanti-corymbosis*, in the *Hortus Cliffort Sonchus caule erecto, foliis pinnato hastatis apiceque hastatis, floribus*

*ribus congestis villosis* Clusius calls it, *Sonchus lævior Austriacus V altissimus*, Ray, *Sonchus in-cubitalis, folio cuspidato*, Caspar Bauhine *Sonchus asper arborescens*, and Gerard, *Sonchus arborescens alter* It grows naturally in meadows and moist places in England, France, Italy, and Germany

3 Maritime Sow-thistle is, *Sonchus pedunculo nudo, foliis lanceolatis amplexicaulibus indivisis re-trorsum argute dentatis* Caspar Bauhine calls it, *Sonchus angustifolius maritimus*, and Ray, *Chondrilla paniculata longifolia sinuata leniter spinosa* It grows naturally in the south of Europe

4 Pyrenean Sow thistle is, *Sonchus pedunculis squamatis, floribus paniculatis, foliis runcinatis* Vaillant calls it, *Lactuca Alpina glabra acanthi folio, flore magno cæruleo* It grows naturally on the Pyrenees

5 Siberian Sow-thistle is, *Sonchus pedunculis squamatis, foliis lanceolatis indivisis sessilibus* Gmelin calls it, *Sonchus foliis lanceolatis sessilibus [illegible] dentatis, floribus corymbosis, caulibus glabris*, and Amman, *Lactuca salicis folio, flore cæruleo* It grows naturally in Siberia, Finland, and Sweden

6 Canada Sow thistle is, *Sonchus pedunculis hispidis, floribus racemosis, foliis runcinatis* Gronovius calls it, *Chondrilla foliis pinnato-hastatis denticulatis* It grows naturally in Canada

*Sonchus* is of the class and order *Syngenesia Polygamia Æqualis*, and the characters are, Class and order in the Linnæan system The characters

1 CALYX The common calyx is ventricose, globous, and composed of many narrow unequal scales

2 COROLLA The general flower is imbricated and uniform The hermaphrodite florets are numerous, equal, and each consists of one tongue shaped, narrow, truncated petal, indented in five parts at the top

3 STAMINA are five very short capillary filaments, having a cylindrical tubular anthera

4 PISTILLUM consists of a suboval germen, a filiforme style the length of the stamina, and two reflexed stigmas

5 PERICARPIUM There is none The calyx closes at top, forms the figure of a depressed, acuminated globe, and contains the seeds

6 SEMINA The seeds are single, oblong, and furnished with hairy down

The receptacle is naked

# C H A P CCCCXXXVII

## S O P H O R A.

THERE are two Perennials of this genus, called,

Species

1 Oriental *Sophora*
2 Virginian *Sophora*

Oriental

1 Oriental *Sophora* The root is creeping The stalks are numerous from an old root, upright, and three or four feet high The leaves are pinnated, being composed of numerous, oblong, hairy folioles, arranged along the midrib, and terminated by an odd one The flowers come out from the ends and sides of the stalks in close erect spikes, they are small, of a pale-blue colour, appear in July, and the seeds sometimes ripen in the autumn

and Virginian Sophora described

2 Virginian *Sophora* The stalks are many from a strong root, branching from the bottom, weak, and procumbent The leaves are composed of three roundish smooth folioles, which join at the base, and grow on very short foot stalks The flowers are produced from the ends and sides of the branches in short spikes, they are of a yellow colour, appear in July, and the seeds frequently ripen in the autumn

Culture

These plants are propagated by parting of the roots, which may be done in the autumn, winter, or early part of the spring The first sort is extremely hardy, but the second should have a dry light soil, and a warm situation After they are planted out they will require no trouble, except keeping them clean from weeds, and reducing the roots as often as they become too spreading

They are also raised by seeds, which should be sown in the spring in beds of common mould made fine, and covered about half a quarter of an inch deep If dry weather should happen after sowing, it would be adviseable to water the beds three times a week, the more effectually to bring up the seeds When they appear, the plants must be thinned where they are too close, kept in weeding and watering all summer, and in the autumn may be removed to the places where they are designed to remain

1 The first species is titled, *Sophora foliis pinnatis foliolis numerosis oblongis villosis, caule herbaceo* In the *Hortus Cliffort* it is termed simply, *Sophora* Tournefort calls it, *Ervum orientale alopecuroides perenne, fructu longissimo*; and Buxbaum, *Glycyrrhiza siliquis nodosis quasi articulatis* It is a native of the East Titles

2 The second species is, *Sophora foliis ternatis subsessilibus foliolis obovatis glabris* Gronovius calls it, *Cytisus foliis fere sessilibus, calycibus bractea triplici auctis*, and Plukenet, *Cytisus procumbens Americanus, flore luteo, ramosissimus, qui anil suppeditat* It grows naturally in Virginia

*Sophora* is of the class and order *Decandria Monogynia*, and the characters are, Class and order in the Linnæan system The characters

1 CALYX is a short, monophyllous, bell shaped perianthium, divided at the top into five oblique obtuse segments

2 COROLLA is papilionaceous, and consists of five petals The vexillum is oblong, gradually broader, straight, and reflexed on the sides The alæ are two, oblong, and appendiculated at their base

baſe The carina is navicular, and compoſed of two petals like thoſe of the alæ, having the lower edges joined together

3 STAMINA are ten diſtinct parallel, awl-ſhaped filaments the length of the corolla, and hid in the carina, having very ſmall aſſurgent antheræ.

4 PISTILLUM conſiſts of an oblong taper germen, a ſtyle the ſize and ſituation of the ſtamina, and an obtuſe ſtigma

5 PERICARPIUM is a long, ſlender, nodoſe, unilocular pod

6 SEMINA The ſeeds are many, and roundiſh

## CHAP. CCCCXXXVIII

## *SPARGANIUM*, BUR-REED.

Species

THERE are only two ſpecies of this genus yet known, called,

1 Great Bur-reed
2 Little Bur-reed

Great

1 Great Bur-reed The root is compoſed of a multitude of long thick fibres The radical leaves are numerous, upright, triangular, two or three feet long, and of a bright green colour The ſtalk is round, thick, tender, ſometimes branching, ſometimes ſimple, and about the height of the leaves The flowers come out in round bur-like cluſters from the ends and ſides of the ſtalks and branches, they appear in July, and the ſeeds ripen in Auguſt

and Little bur-reed deſcribed

2 Little Bur-reed The leaves are plane, and float on the water or lie on the mud The ſtalks are unbranching, round, and four or five inches high The flowers are collected in few roundiſh ſpikes at the top of the ſtalk, they are to be met with chiefly in July, and the ſeeds ripen in September

Theſe are not cultivated plants, growing naturally in waters and moiſt places in moſt parts of England, and even in the coldeſt parts of the whole earth

Titles

1 The title of the firſt ſpecies is, *Sparganium foliis erectis triquetris* Dodonæus calls it, *Platanaria, ſ. Butomon*, Caſpar Bauhine, *Sparganium ramoſum*, alſo, *Sparganium non ramoſum* It inhabits chiefly the coldeſt parts of Europe

2 The ſecond ſpecies is titled *Sparganium foliis decumbentibus planis* In the *Flora Lapp* it is termed, *Sparganium foliis natantibus plano-convexis* Dillenius calls it, *Sparganium non ramoſum minus*, Haller, *Sparganium foliis complanatis natantibus ſpicis, pauciſſimis*, and Ray, *Sparganium minimum* It grows naturally in ditches, ſtanding waters, lakes, and ſlow flowing brooks and rivers in moſt of the northern countries of Europe

Claſs and order in the Linnæan ſyſtem

*Sparganium* is of the claſs and order *Monoecia Triandria*, and the characters are,

The characters

I Male Flowers, which are numerous, and collected into a roundiſh head

1 CALYX The common amentum is roundiſh, conſtant, and cloſely imbricated on every ſide The perianthium conſiſts of three narrow deciduous leaves

2 COROLLA There is none

3 STAMINA are three capillary filaments the length of the corolla, having oblong antheræ

II Female Flowers

1 CALYX The ſame as the Males The general receptacle is roundiſh

2 COROLLA There is none

3 PISTILLUM conſiſts of an oval germen, terminating in a ſhort awl-ſhaped ſtyle, crowned by two acute permanent ſtigmas

5 PERICARPIUM is a juiceleſs drupe, angular below, and pointed at the top

6 SEMINA The ſeeds are two oſſeous, oblong, oval, angular nuts

CHAP

## CHAP. CCCCXXXIX.

## *SPERGULA*, SPURREY.

OF this genus there is one Perennial called, Knotted Spurrey, or English Marsh Saxifrage.

This plant described. The root is composed of a multitude of very fine fibres. The stalks are slender, upright, jointed, mostly undivided, and four or five inches high. The leaves are very narrow, awl-shaped, smooth, and a large tuft of them is formed at the crown of the root, but they grow opposite on the stalks at the joints. The flowers come out from the tops of the stalks on simple footstalks; they are of a white colour, and moderately large and beautiful; they appear in July and August, and the seeds ripen in the autumn.

Culture. This species is propagated by parting of the roots in the autumn, or sowing of the seeds, which may be done in the autumn, soon after they are ripe, or the spring following. In either case, all the trouble they require will be only watering them in dry weather, and keeping them clean from weeds until the autumn following, when they should be removed to the places where they are designed to remain. As this plant grows naturally in marshy situations, it directs us to assign it the moistest shady part of the garden.

Titles. This species is titled, *Spergula foliis oppositis subulatis, laevibus, caulibus simplicibus*. In the *Hortus Cliffort.* it is termed, *Spergula foliis oppositis pedunculis simplicibus*. Caspar Bauhine calls it, *Alsine nodosa Germanica*; John Bauhine, *Arenaria*; Plukenet, *Alsine palustris, ericae folio, polygonoides, articulis crebrioribus, flore albo pulchello*; Loesel, *Polygonum, foliis gramineis, alterum*; Gerard, *Alsine palustris, foliis tenuissimis, seu saxifraga palustris Anglica*; and Parkinson, *Saxifraga palustris Anglica*. It grows naturally in moist places in England, and most of the colder countries of Europe.

*Spergula* is of the class and order *Decandria Pentagynia*; and the characters are, Class and order in the Linnæan system. The characters.

1. CALYX is a perianthium composed of five oval, obtuse, concave, patent, permanent leaves.
2. COROLLA is five oval, concave, patent, undivided leaves, larger than those of the calyx.
3. STAMINA are ten awl-shaped filaments, shorter than the corolla, having roundish antheræ.
4. PISTILLUM consists of an oval germen, and five erect, reflexed, filiforme styles, with thickish stigmas.
5. PERICARPIUM is an oval covered capsule, formed of five valves, and containing one cell.
6. SEMINA. The seeds are many, globular, depressed, and surrounded with an indented rim.

## CHAP. CCCCXL.

## *SPIRÆA*.

THE herbaceous species of this genus are,

Species.
1. The Queen of the Meadows, or Meadow Sweet.
2. Virginian Meadow-Sweet.
3. Drop-wort.
4. Goat's Beard.

Queen of the Meadows described. 1. Queen of the Meadows, or Meadow Sweet, is found in most meadows in England. The root is thick, of a blackish or dark-red colour, sweet-scented, and spreading. The stalk is upright, firm, brittle, of a reddish purple colour, and three or four feet high. The leaves are very large and pinnated; the folioles are rough, indented, of a dark-green colour on their upper-side, white underneath, and consist of about two or three pair, besides the odd one with which they are terminated, which is the largest, and usually divided into three lobes. The flowers terminate the stalks in large cymose bunches; they are of a white colour, and agreeably scented; they appear in July, and the seeds ripen in the autumn.

Varieties. Were it not for the commonness of this plant, it would be deemed one of the best flowers we have; but there are varieties of it which are not very common, and which no good collection of flowers ought to be without, namely, the Double Meadow-Sweet, and the Striped-leaved Meadow-Sweet; the flowers of the first sort being double, the bunches large, and of a good white colour colou They make a noble show, and are very grateful to the smell, many preferring this kind of sweet before most others The striped sort is of lower growth, and the bunches of flowers smaller but the leaves are longer, and finely striped with bright-yellow colour, and afford great beauty to those who are fond of variegated plants

Virginian Meadow Sweet. 2 Virginian Meadow Sweet The stalks are upright, branching, and little better than a foot high The leaves are t ... though near the top they are sometimes single, and in pairs, they are sharply ... acute-pointed, and their upper surface is of a bright-green colour ... they are paler underneath The flowers terminate the stalks in loose ... formed of numerous, long, slender spikes, they have slender foot-stalks, and each of them is possessed of five spear-shaped petals, they are of a ... white colour, appear in July, and the seeds ripen in September

and Drop-wort described. 3 Drop-wort The root is composed of numerous ... having many large oval tubers ... to them The leaves are pinnated, each being composed of several serrated lobes, which are placed alternately along the midrib, they are large, of a dark-green colour and spread themselves on the ground Among these arises the flower stalk to the height of about a foot, it is slender, striated, hollow, erect, and ornamented with only one or two small leaves The flowers crown the top in cymose bunches, they are large, of a good white colour, and each has its separate footstalk, they appear in July, and the seeds ripen in the autumn

This plant in its single state is very ornamental, but there is a variety of it with double flowers which no good collection ought to be without

Varieties. There is also another sort with longer narrower leaves, taller stalks, and often larger bunches of flowers

Goat's Beard described. 4 Goat's Beard The leaves are supradecompounded, being composed of several doubly-winged leaves, each having three or four oblong serrated folioles, which are terminated with an odd one The stalks are upright, firm, and about a yard high The flowers terminate the stalks in loose panicles, their colour is white, they appear in July, and the seeds sometimes (though not often) ripen in the autumn

Culture. These species are all propagated by parting of the roots, and indeed this is the only way of multiplying them in the Variegated and Double kinds The best time for this work is the autumn though it may be done successfully in the winter, or early in the spring, before the flower-stalks arise They will grow in any soil or situation, though they chiefly delight in the shade, and moist places The Variegated Meadow-Sweet should have a hungry gravelly soil, to ... ... ... ... often watered if dry weather should happen, or they will die ...

They are also propagated by seeds which should be sown ... soon after they are ripe In the spring the plants will come up, when they should be thinned where they appear too close, kept clean from weeds all summer, frequently watered if dry weather make it necessary, and in the autumn they may be removed to the places where they are designed to remain

Titles. 1 The Queen of the Meadows, or Meadow-Sweet, is titled, *Spiraea foliis pinnatis impari majore lobato, floribus cymosis* Caspar Bauhine calls it, *Barba capri floribus compactis*, Clusius, *Ulmaria*, Parkinson, *Ulmaria vulgaris*, Dodonaeus and Gerard, *Regina prati* It grows naturally in meadows and moist shady places in England, and most parts of Europe

2 Virginian Meadow Sweet is, *Spiraea foliis ternatis serratis, floribus ... maculatis* In the *Hortus Cliffort* it is termed, *Filipendula foliis ternatis* Plukenet calls it, *Ulmaria major trifolia, flore ... Virginiana*, and Morison, *Ulmaria Virginiana trifolia, floribus ... longis & acutis* It grows naturally in Virginia and Canada

3 Drop-wort is, *Spiraea foliis pinnatis foliolis ... serratis, caule herbaceo, floribus cymosis* In the *Hortus Cliffort* it is termed, *Filipendula foliis pinnatis foliolis uniformibus* Caspar Bauhine calls it, *Filipendula vulgaris*, Cammerarius John Bauhine, Gerard, Parkinson, &c *Filipendula* It grows naturally in meadows and pasture-grounds in England, and most countries of Europe

4 Goat's Beard is *Spiraea foliis supradecompositis, spicis paniculatis, floribus dioicis* Van Royen calls it, *Aruncus*, Caspar Bauhine, *Barba caprae floribus oblongis*, and Cammerarius, *Barba caprae* It grows naturally on the mountainous parts of Austria and Alvernia

# CHAP. CCCCXLI

## *STACHYS*, BASE HOREHOUND

Species

OF this genus there are,

1 Marsh *Stachys*, or Clown All-heal
2 Alpine *Stachys*, or Mountain Hedge-nettle
3 German Base Horehound
4 Base Horehound of Candia
5 Viscous Base Horehound of Crete
6 Prickly Base Horehound of Crete
7 Oriental Base Horehound

Description of Marsh Stachys

1 Marsh *Stachys*, or Clown All-heal This is a most admirable vulnerary, and ought to be in every garden on account of its great power in curing green wounds Gerard gives us some extraordinary cases, and the reason for his naming it Clown All-heal The root is possessed of many tubers The stalks are channelled, hairy, and grow to about two feet high The leaves are rough, spear shaped, narrow, indented, and grow opposite by pairs without any footstalks The flowers grow in clusters round the tops of the stalks their colour is purple, with a few spots of white, they will be in blow in August, and perfect their seeds in the autumn

Its virtues

If any one belonging to the garden should accidentally cut themselves, let them immediately bruise this herb into a poultice, mix with it a little hog's grease, apply it to the wounded part, and he will find that a cure will soon be effected This plant may be found in marshy watery places, and by the sides of rivulets, in many parts of England

Alpine Stachys,

2 Alpine *Stachys* The stalks are downy, and very hairy The leaves are of an oval spear shaped figure, indented at their base, and of a yellowish green colour The whorls consist of many flowers, they are of a kind of iron colour, will be in blow in August, and the seeds ripen in the autumn

German Base Horehound

3 German Base Horehound This is a dispensatory plant, of great efficacy in curing green wounds The root is full of tubers The leaves are crenated, oblong, and hoary The stalks are square, hoary, firm, and will grow to be two feet high The flowers surround the upper-part of the stalk in clusters, their colour is red, they will be in blow in July, and ripen their seeds in August or September

Base Horehound,

4 Base Horehound of Candia The leaves are oblong, rough, and of a pale-green colour The stalks grow to about two feet high, and are very rough, but not so woolly as the former The flowers grow in whorled clusters at the tops of the stalks, their colour is purple, and they will be in blow in July and August

Viscous Base Horehound of Crete,

5 Viscous Base Horehound of Crete This is a very branching plant, and hardly a foot high The stalks are four-cornered, slender, and smooth The leaves are spear shaped, smooth, and but thinly placed on the plant The stalks and leaves are possessed of a sticky or clammy matter, and have very much the smell of *Bitumen* The flowers grow in whorls round the stalks, their colour is a bad white they will be in blow in July, and ripen their seeds in September

6 Prickly Base Horehound of Crete This is a branching plant, about a foot and a half high The leaves are spear-shaped, oblong, white, and hairy The stalks are square, and every branch is terminated by a sharp spine The flowers grow from the tops of the branches, they are of a palish-blue colour, will be in blow in July and August, and ripen their seeds in the autumn

Prickly Base Horehound of Crete

7 Oriental Base Horehound This plant will grow to a yard or better in height The leaves are oval, spear-shaped, downy, and have a very foetid smell The flowers are produced in whorls round the tops of the stalks they will be in blow in July or August, and ripen their seeds in the autumn

and Oriental Base Horehound described

Culture

These sorts are all propagated by seeds, which should be sown in March in some well-prepared bed in the seminary Any common garden mould will do for them, but if it be fresh, light, and sandy, it will be better As the plants come up, they must be constantly kept clean from weeds, and as the dry weather comes on, if they are now and then refreshed with water, it will greatly forward their growth When they are of proper size to remove, another bed should be prepared of light earth, and if it be in a shady situation, it will be so much the better Into this bed your plants must be removed, placing them at about four or five inches from each other. They will readily take root, but until that is done, it will be necessary to shade them, and constantly supply them with water, and after that they will require no more trouble until the autumn, at which time the plants should be taken up, with a ball of earth to each root, and set in the places where they are designed to remain They will then flower strong the summer following, and produce plenty of seeds in the autumn

The fourth, fifth, sixth, and seventh sorts require a dry, warm, light soil, in a well sheltered place, or they are liable to be destroyed by our winters, so that it will be necessary to have a plant or two of each sort set in pots, to be removed into the green-house, or set under a frame, during the winter, to preserve the sorts, if hard weather should happen And this precaution is more necessary to the fifth sort, which is naturally so tender as hardly to bear our ordinary winters abroad, let its situation be what it will

Titles

1 Marsh *Stachys* is titled, *Stachys verticillis sexfloris, foliis linearі lanceolatis semi amplexicaulibus* In the *Hortus Cliffort* it is termed, *Stachys foliis linear i-lanceolatis sessilibus basi emarginatis* Caspar Bauhine calls it, *Stachys palustris foetida*, and Tabernaemontanus, *Stachys aquatica* It grows in moist places in England, and most parts of Europe

2 Alpine *Stachys*, or Mountain Hedge Nettle, is, *Stachys verticillis multifloris, foliorum serraturis apice cartilagineis, corollis labio plano* In the *Hortus Upsal* it is termed, *Stachys verticillis a o- ... multifloris*,

*decem-floris, caule villoso*, in the *Hortus Cliffort* *Stachys foliis lanceolato ovatis basi emarginatis, verticillis tomentosis* Plukenet calls it, *Stachys latifolia major, foliis obscure virentibus, flore galeato ferrugineo*; and Caspar Bauhine, *Pseudo-stachys Alpina* It grows naturally in Germany and Switzerland

3 German Base Horehound is, *Stachys verticillis multifloris, foliorum serraturis imbricatis, caule lanato* In the *Hortus Upsal* it is termed, *Stachys verticillis quadragin a-floris, caule lanato*; in the *Hortus Cliffort* *Stachys foliis oblongo cordatis, floribus verticillatis* Caspar Bauhine calls it, *Stachys major Germanica*, and Fuchsius, *Stachys* It grows naturally in England, and most parts of Germany

4 Base Horehound of Candia is, *Stachys verticillis multifloris, calycibus pungentibus, caule hirto* This is, *Stachys folio obscure virente, flore purpurascente, Walth Hort* 108 t 19 Caspar Bauhine calls it, *Stachys Cretica* It grows naturally in Crete

5 Viscous Base Horehound of Crete is, *Stachys ramis ramosissimis, foliis lanceolatis glabris* Morison calls it, *Sideritis glutinosa bitumen redolens*, and Zan, *Sideritis viscosa Cretica bitumen redolens* It is a native of Crete

6 Prickly Base Horehound of Crete is, *Stachys ramulis spinâ terminatis.* Caspar Bauhine calls it, *Stachys spinosa Cretica*, and Clusius, *Gaidarothymo* It grows naturally in Crete

7 Oriental Base Horehound is, *Stachys foliis tomentosis ovato-lanceolatis floribus verticillo brevioribus* Tournefort calls it, *Stachys orientalis altissima fœtidissima* It grows naturally in the East

*Stachys* is of the class and order *Didynamia Gymnospermia*, and the characters are, Class and order in the Linnæan system The characters

1 CALYX is a monophyllous, tubulous, angular, permanent perianthium, divided into five sharp-pointed segments

2 COROLLA is a ringent petal The tube is very short, and the mouth oblong; the upper-lip is erect, nearly oval, hooked, and sometimes indented, the lower lip is large, reflexed at the sides, and trifid, the middle segment is large, and indented

3 STAMINA The filaments are awl-shaped, and four in number, two of them are shorter than the others, and their antheræ are simple

4 PISTILLUM consists of a four-pointed germen, a filiforme style the length of the stamina, and a bifid acute stigma

5 PERICARPIUM There is none

6 SEMINA The seeds are four, angular, and oval

# CHAP. CCCCXLII.

## STÆHELINA.

THERE are only two species of this genus One comes out of Ethiopia, and is tender, the other grows naturally in the South of France, and will bear our winters, if properly situated, this is called, Purple *Stæhelina*

The plant described The stalk is upright, woody, slender, and about a foot and a half high The leaves are narrow, slightly indented, and when bruised, emit an agreeable odour The flowers are collected in oblong heads at the ends of the stalks, they are of a purple colour, and finely scented, they appear in July and August, and the seeds ripen in the autumn

Culture This plant is best raised from the seeds, which should be sown in the spring, in the places where the plants are to remain When they are about two inches high, the strongest should be drawn out, and set in such places where they are wanted, leaving the others at proper distances in the seed-bed The soil in which the seeds are sown, and to which the others are removed, ought to be naturally dry, light, and sandy, and the situation well sheltered, otherwise they will be destroyed by our frosts in winter, so that when such a situation is not to be had, a share of the plants should be set in pots, to be housed in bad weather, to continue the sort in case those abroad should be destroyed

The second summer they will flower, and perfect their seeds; soon after which, if the soil in which they grow is rich and good the greatest share of the plants generally die, if the situation is sandy, dry, and hungry, the plants will be less luxuriant, and frequently continue many years.

Titles This species is titled, *Stæhelina foliis linearibus denticulatis, squamis calycinis lanceolatis, pappo calycibus duplo longiore* Van Royen calls it, *Gnaphalium caule fruticoso, foliis linearibus denticulatis, capitulis oblongis*, Magnol, *Stœchas odorata purpurea*, John Bauhine, *Stœchadi citrinæ affinis, capitulis oblongis*, Caspar Bauhine, *Elichrysum sylvestre, flore oblongo*, Barrelier, *Chamæ-chrysocome prælongis purpureisque jaceæ capitulis*, and Tournefort, *Jacea capitata, rosmarini folio* It grows naturally in France and Spain

*Stæhelina* is of the class and order *Syngenesia Polygamia Æqualis*, and the characters are, Class and order in the Linnæan system The characters

1 CALYX is oblong, cylindrical, and imbricated The scales are spear-shaped, coloured, and erect

2 COROLLA The composite flower is tubulous The hermaphrodite florets are equal, monopetalous, and infundibuliform, having a bell-shaped brim, divided into five equal acute segments

3 STAMINA in each are five capillary filaments, having a cylindrical tubular anthera

4 PISTILLUM consists of a very short ger-

men,

men, a filiforme style, and a double, oblong, obtuse, erect stigma

5 Pericarpium There is none

6 Semen The seed is single, three cornered, short, and crowned by a long branching down

The receptacle is paleaceous and plane The paleæ are very short and permanent

## CHAP CCCCXLIII

## *STATICE*, THRIFT, or SEA PINK.

Species OF this genus are,

1 Thrift, or Sea Gillyflower
2 Sea Lavender
3 Heart-leaved Sea Lavender
4 Matted Sea Lavender
5 Tartarian Sea Lavender
6 Siberian Sea Lavender
7 Golden Sea Lavender
8 Flexuose Sea Lavender
9 Grecian Sea Lavender

Description of Thrift or Sea Pink 1 Thrift, or Sea Pink, or Sea Gillyflower The root is thick, oblong, fibrated, and spreading The leaves are collected in heads or tufts, which branch out from the root, they are numerous long, narrow, pointed, grassy, and of a dark green colour The stalks are numerous, slender, naked, and grow to be six inches high The flowers come out in globular heads from the tops of the stalks, their original colour is a pale-red, though there are now great varieties of it, they appear in May, and continue in succession the greatest part of the summer, but their greatest beauty will be in the beginning of June

Varieties The varieties of this species are,

Pale-red Thrift,
Scarlet Thrift,
White Thrift,
Large Red flowered Mountain Thrift,
Large White Mountain Thrift,
Least Sea Thrift, or Sea Pink

Culture These sorts are propagated by the roots at any time of the year, but the best season is the autumn, when they have done flowering They are extremely hardy, will grow in any soil or situation, and require no trouble, except keeping them clean from weeds, and reducing the roots every two or three years

The Common Thrift with Red flowers, called Scarlet Thrift, is the most beautiful of all the sorts, and was formerly planted for edgings to large borders, to which nothing is more proper where Box is not used Indeed where no edging is wanted, a good show of these flowers has a fine appearance, and is to be obtained only by setting the plants in a long row, for being low plants, if they are set singly, or a few together, as it were in patches, about the garden, the appearance is so paltry, that they will be pretty sure of being disregarded But by arranging them in a long line by the sides of the walk, their appearance will be striking, and their beauties being continued to a long extent, will have a fine effect To make this as perfect as possible, the rows should be planted at six inches distance from each other, and a set of plants should be in readiness in the nursery, to make good such as may have failed in the rows The sort should be the Bright-red, or Scarlet, but a few of the White, for variety, may be admitted They should not be removed oftener than every three years, for the show of flowers will be greater when the rows become broad, and nearly approach each other and when they are in blow, as the first flowers decay, their stalks should be constantly cut up to the bottom with scissars, or the like, otherwise their withered dead heads and stalks will much injure the beauty of those in bloom, and have a very dull, indolent, and disagreeable look

Sea Lavender described 2 Sea Lavender The root is oblong, thick, reddish and fibrated The radical leaves are oval, spear-shaped, of a thickish substance, smooth, of a dark-green colour, and grow on thick footstalks The stalk is round, firm, branching, and a foot or more in height The flowers come out in spikes from the ends of the branches, they are of a pale-blue colour, and all ranged one way; they appear in July, and are succeeded by oblong seeds, which ripen in the autumn

There is great variety of this species, such as,

Varieties The Great Sea Lavender,
The Olive-leaved Sea Lavender,
The Least Sea Lavender,
Deep blue Sea Lavender,
White-flowered Sea Lavender,
Late flowered Sea Lavender

Heart leaved, 3 Heart-leaved Sea Lavender The leaves are small, heart-shaped, smooth, thick, of a greyish colour, and spread themselves on the ground The stalks are naked, slender, branching and five or six inches high The flowers come out in crooked panicles on the tops of the stalks, they are small, of a pale red colour, appear in August, but are not succeeded by seeds in our gardens

Matted, 4 Matted Sea Lavender The leaves are wedge-shaped The stalks are slender, branching, matted together, and lie on the ground The flowers come out in panicles from the ends of the branches, they are of a pale-blue colour, appear in July and August, and are succeeded by ripe seeds in the autumn

and Tartarian Sea Lavender described 5 Tartarian Sea Lavender The leaves are long, broad, spear-shaped, ribbed, and sharp-pointed The stalks divide into a few branches, and grow to about eight or ten inches high The flowers

flowers are produced in short spikes from the ends of the branches, they are of a white colour, appear in August and September, but are not succeeded by seeds in England

Variety of it. There is a variety of this species with pale blue flowers

Siberian, 6 Siberian Sea Lavender The leaves are vaginant, narrow, and spear shaped The stalks are woody, naked, branching near the top, and grow to be two feet high The flowers are collected in small heads at the sides of the branches, they grow alternately and sit close, having no footstalks, they are of a pale-blue or white colour, appear in August and September, but are rarely succeeded by ripe seeds in England

Golden, 7 Golden Sea Lavender The stalks are ligneous, round, leafy, strong, branching, and eight or ten inches high The leaves are long narrow, and awl shaped The flowers come out in roundish bunches from the ends of the branches, having cups of a golden yellow colour, they appear in August, but are rarely succeeded by seeds in England

Flexuose, 8 Flexuose Sea Lavender The stalks are weak, flexuose, branching, naked, and eight or ten inches long The leaves are oval, pointed, nervose, and rise from the root on short strong footstalks The flowers come out in corymbous bunches from the ends of the branches, they appear in August and September, but the seeds rarely ripen here

and Grecian Sea Lavender described. 9 Grecian Sea Lavender The root is thick, woody, long, and tough The stalks are naked, ligneous, and divide into several slender branches near the top The leaves are awl shaped, rough on their edges, and each terminates in a rigid thorn, or prickly point, and they are placed mori-c tin The flowers are produced in panicles from the tops of the stalks, they are of a whitish colour, often having a mixture of blue, and they appear about the same time with the former

Method of propagating them. These sorts are all propagated by sowing the seeds, which must be procured from the places where they ripen, for hardly half of them ripen their seeds well in England As soon as possible after they are ripe, on their arrival, let them be sown in beds which have the benefit of the sun only in the morning-part If the seeds are sown soon after they are ripe, most of the plants will come up in the spring, if the business is deferred until the spring, the seeds frequently lie until the spring following before they make their appearance When they come up, they must be frequently watered, and kept clean from weeds all summer, and in the autumn may be removed to the places where they are designed to remain, which ought to be in a light dry earth, warmly situated, for there they will have a better chance of ripening their seeds for further propagation

They are also easily encreased by slips or cuttings These should be planted in a moist light earth, in the spring, or any of the summer months, and watered and constantly shaded until they have taken root When they are in a good growing state, the shade may be removed, and the plants exposed to the full sun Watering, except on very long dry intervals, may be omitted, for they will do with very little water after they have taken well to the ground Weeding must be afforded them all summer, and in the autumn they may be removed, being careful to preserve a ball of earth to each root, and set in the places where they are designed to remain

Titles. 1 Thrift, or Sea Gillyflower, is titled, *Statice scapo simplici capitato, foliis linearibus* Morison calls it, *Limonium aphyllocaulon gramineum globosum*, Caspar Bauhine, *Caryophyllus montanus major, flore globoso*, also, *Caryophyllus montanus minor*, Tournefort, *Statice montana minor*, Gerard, *Caryophyllus marinus minimus Lobelii*, and Parkinson, *Gramen marinum minus* It grows naturally in meadows and plains, chiefly near the sea, in England, and most countries of Europe, also in North America

2 Sea Lavender is, *Statice scapo paniculato tereti, foliis lævibus* In the *Hortus Cliffort* it is termed, *Statice caule nudo ramoso* Caspar Bauhine calls it, *L. [illegible]*, also, *L[illegible] rus, [illegible] folio*, also, *L[illegible]*, Ray *Limonium [illegible]*, also, *Limonium [illegible] [illegible] floribus in spicas [illegible]*, Gerard terms it simply, *Limonium*, and Parkinson, *Limonium majus vulgatius* It grows naturally on the sea-shores of England, and most parts of Europe, also in Virginia

3 Heart-leaved Sea Lavender is, *Statice scapo paniculato, foliis spathulatis retusis* Caspar Bauhine calls it, *Limonium maritimum minus, foliis cordatis*, and Barrelier, *Limonium maritimum cordatum, folio retuso* It grows naturally on the shores of the Mediterranean sea

4 Matted Sea Lavender is, *Statice scapo paniculato prostrato, ramis sterilibus retroflexis nudis, foliis cuneiformibus* Sauvages calls it *Statice foliis obverse-ovatis, ramis nudis bifurcatis, intricatis*, Plukenet, *Limonium minus, virgulis reticulatis se invicem implicantibus*, and Ray, *Limonium reticulatum* It grows naturally on the sea shores of England, and other parts of Europe

5 Tartarian Sea Lavender is, *Statice scapo dichotomo, foliis lanceolatis mucronatis, floribus alternis distantibus* Tournefort calls it, *Limonium orientale, plantaginis folio, floribus umbellatis*, and Amman, *Limonium elatius, plantaginis foliis procumbentibus in aculeum terminatis, floribus albis spicatis* It grows naturally in Tartary

6 Siberian Sea Lavender is, *Statice caule fruticoso, superne nudo ramoso, capitulis sessilibus, foliis lanceolatis vaginantibus* Gmelin calls it, *Statice foliis e lanceolato linearibus, caulinis basi vaginantibus, capitulis alternis sessilibus* It grows naturally in Siberia.

7 Golden Sea Lavender is, *Statice caule fruticoso foliosa ramoso, foliis subulatis* Gmelin calls it, *Statice caulibus fruticosis teretiusculis, foliis subulatis caulinis, floribus ex corymboso-fasciculatis*, and Amman, *Limonium [illegible] ephedræ facie, calycibus florum aureis* It grows naturally on the mountainous parts of Dauria.

8 Flexuose Sea Lavender is, *Statice scapo ramoso flexuoso, corymbis terminalibus, foliis nervosis* Gmelin calls it, *Statice foliis ovalibus muticis nervosis, caule nudo alternatim ramoso flexuoso, corymbis terminalibus* It grows naturally in Siberia

9 Grecian Sea Lavender is, *Statice scapo paniculato, foliis subulatis mucronatis* Van Royen calls it, *Limonium foliis caulinis subulatis pungentibus*, Tournefort, *Limonium orientale frutescens, caryophylli folio in aculeum rigidissimum abeunte*, also, *Limonium Græcum junperi folio*, Buxbaum, *Limonium cæspitosum, foliis aculeatis*, and Alpinus, *Echinus, sive tragacantha altera* It grows wild in the deserts of Greece and Media

Class and order in the Linnæan system. *Statice* is of the class and order *Pentandria Pentagynia*, and the characters are,

The characters. 1 CALYX The common perianthium is of different structure in the different species The proper perianthium is monophyllous and funnel shaped, the tube is straitened, the limb is plicated and entire

2 COROLLA is infundibuliform, and consists of five petals, which are narrowed below, but above are broad, obtuse, and spreading

3 STAMINA are five awl-shaped filaments shorter than the corolla, and adnate to the ungues

ungues of the petals, having incumbent antheræ

4 Pistillum consists of a very small germen, and five filiforme distant styles, with acute stigmas

5 Pericarpium There is none The seed is contained in the calyx

6 Semen The seed is single, small, roundish, and coronated with its proper calyx

# CHAP. CCCCXLIV

## *STELLARIA*, GREAT CHICKWEED.

THE Perennials of this genus are usually called,

Species 1 Greater Stick-wort
2 Lesser Stick-wort
3 Broad-leaved Stick-wort
4 Two-flowered Stick-wort

Greater, 1 Greater Stick-wort The root is small, jointed, creeping, and hung with many fibres The stalks are tender, round, full of joints, and lean towards the ground The leaves are narrow, spear shaped, slightly serrated, and grow opposite to each other at the joints The flowers come out in plenty from the tops of the stalks on slender footstalks, they are of a white colour, their petals are bifid, and they are disposed in a radiated manner, they appear in April, May, and June, and the seeds ripen in July

Lesser, 2 Lesser Stick-wort The root is small, fibrated, and creeping The stalks are slender, knotty, weak, and partly procumbent The leaves are narrow smooth, entire, and grow opposite to each other at the joints The flowers come out in panicles from the tops of the stalks, they appear in June, July, frequently at the end of summer, and in the autumn

Broad leaved, 3 Broad-leaved Stick-wort The stalks are thick, jointed, and two feet high The leaves are broad heart-shaped, and grow opposite on footstalks at the joints The flowers are jagged, and come out from the tops of the stalks on branching footstalks, they appear chiefly in July and August, and are occasionally to be met with in September and the autumn

and Two flowered Stick wort described 4 Two flowered Stick-wort The root is slender, and fibrous The leaves are small, awl-shaped, and form a tuft at the crown of the root The stalks are slender, partly naked, and four or five inches high The flowers come out, two together, on footstalks, from the tops of the stalks, they appear in June, July, and August, and frequently again in the autumn

Method of propagation The first three sorts are natives of England, and are not cultivated, though the other, being a foreigner is admitted into some collections They are to be propagated by parting of the roots in the autumn, and should have some moist shady part of the garden for their situation

They may be also raised by seeds, which should be sown soon after they are ripe, and when the plants are fit to remove, they should be transplanted to the places where they are designed to remain

The 1 Greater Stick-wort is titled, *Stellaria foliis lanceolatis serrulatis, petalis bifidis* In the *Hortus Cliffort* it is termed, *Alsine foliis lanceolatis* Caspar Bauhine calls it, *Caryophyllus holosteus arvensis, flore majore*, and Gerard, *Gramen leucanthemum* It grows naturally in woods and hedges in England, and most countries of Europe

2 Lesser Stick wort is, *Stellaria foliis linearibus integerrimis, floribus paniculatis* In the *Flora Lapp* it is termed, *Alsine foliis linearibus* Caspar Bauhine calls it, *Caryophyllus arvensis glaber, flore minore*, also, *Caryophyllus holosteus Alpinus angustifolius*, also, *Alsine aquatica Media*, John Bauhine, *Alsine longifolia uliginosis proveniens locis*, Tabernæmontanus, *Gramen floridum minus*, Dillenius, *Alsine, folio gramineo angustiore, palustris*, Ray, *Caryophyllus holosteus arvensis medius*, Gerard, *Gramen Leucanthemum alterum*, and Parkinson, *Gramen leucanthemum minus* It grows naturally in meadows, pastures, woods, and hedges in England, and most parts of Europe

3 Broad-leaved Stick-wort is, *Stellaria foliis cordatis petiolatis, paniculâ pedunculis ramosis* Morison calls it, *Alsine montana folio smilacis instar, flore laciniato*, Caspar Bauhine, *Alsine montana latifolia, flore laciniato*, also, *Alsine altissima nemorum*, and Columna, *Alsine montana hederacea maxima* It grows naturally in woods and hedges in England, and most countries of Europe

4 Two flowered Stick-wort is, *Stellaria foliis subulatis scapis sub-bifloris, petalis emarginatis, germinibus oblongis, calycibus striatis* In the *Flora Lapp* it is termed, *Sagina ramis erectis bifloris*, in the *Flora Suecica*, *Moehringia scapis bifloris*, in the *Amæn Acad* *Stellaria foliis subulatis, calycibus striatis, germinibus oblongis, floribus corymbosis* Seguier calls it, *Alsine polygonoides, foliis brevibus, flore albo* It grows naturally on the Alps of Lapland

Class and order in the Linnæan system The characters *Stellaria* is of the class and order *Decandria Trigynia*, and the characters are,

1 Calyx There is none

2 Corolla is one infundibuliforme permanent petal The tube is long and slender the limb is divided into four or five oval lobes

3 Stamina are eight or ten very short filaments, with oblong antheræ

4 Pistillum consists of an oval germen, a very short permanent style, and a capitated stigma

5 Pericarpium There is none

6 Semen The seed is single, rostrated, and glossy

CHAP

## CHAP. CCCCXIV.

## *STIPA*, WINGED SPIKE GRASS.

Species. OF this genus there are,
1. Feather Grass.
2. German *Stipa*.
3. Spanish *Stipa*.
4. Virginian *Stipa*.

Description of Feather Grass. 1. Feather Grass. The root is a multitude of slender fibres clotted together. The leaves are very narrow, upright, a foot and a half long, of a dusky green colour, and form a large tuft at the crown of the root. The stalks are slender, and elevate the flowers above the leaves, and when the seeds are ripe are of exquisite beauty; their aristæ are hairy, with a feathery downy matter, which will be bending in different directions, and afford a singular appearance to all beholders. I do not recollect any one plant in the garden that has been more admired than this Grass.

German, 2. German *Stipa*. The leaves are numerous, rushy, stiff, and marked with a longitudinal furrow. The stalks are round, slender, jointed, and a foot and a half high. The flowers come out from the tops of the stalks in simple spikes; they have long, naked, crooked aristæ; they appear in July and August, and the seeds ripen soon after.

Spanish, 3. Spanish *Stipa*. The leaves are like thread, and five or six inches long. The stalks are small, round, weak, and six or eight inches long. The flowers come out in leafy panicles from the tops of the stalks; their aristæ are hairy near the bottom, and they are in most perfection in June and July.

and Virginian Stipa described. 4. Virginian *Stipa*. The leaves are broad at the bottom, diminish gradually to a point, and are eight or ten inches long. The stalks are slender, round, smooth, hollow, jointed, and a foot high. The flowers come out in panicles from the tops of the stalks; their aristæ are naked, contorted, and jointed near the base, and are in perfection in July and August.

Culture. These sorts are raised by sowing the seeds soon after they are ripe, or the spring following. The first sort is admired by many on account of its great singularity and beauty. It may be encreased by parting of the roots, but the best plants are always raised from seeds. These should be sown in some moist part of the garden; and when the plants come up, they must be thinned where they are too close, watered in dry weather, kept clean from weeds the summer following, and in the autumn may be removed to the places where they are designed to remain. Their situation should be in the shade, and the soil rich and moist; and being thus stationed, they will be better, larger, and more strong than if otherwise assigned.

Titles. 1. Feather Grass is titled, *Stipa aristis lanatis*. Van Royen calls it, *Festuca aristis paniculæ circiter longitudine plumosis*; Tournefort, *Gramen spicatum, aristis pennatis*; Caspar Bauhine, *Gramen sparteum pennatum*; and Clusius, *Spartum Austriacum pennatum*. It grows naturally in Westmoreland in England, Austria, Gaul, and Sweden.

2. German *Stipa* is, *Stipa aristis nudis incurvatis, calycibus semine longioribus*. Caspar Bauhine calls it, *Festuca longissimis aristis*; and Ray, *Gramen avenaceum montanum, spicâ simplici, aristis recurvis*. It grows naturally in Germany and Gaul.

3. Spanish *Stipa* is, *Stipa aristis basi pilosis, panicula spicatâ, foliis filiformibus*. Caspar Bauhine calls it, *Gramen sparteum paniculâ comosa*; and Clusius, *Spartum herba Plinii*. It grows naturally in sandy places in Spain.

4. Virginian *Stipa* is, *Stipa aristis nudis, calycibus semen æquantibus*. Gronovius calls it, *Andropogon folio superiore spathaceo, pedunculis lateralibus oppositis unifloris, aristis flexuosis*. It grows naturally in Virginia.

Class and order in the Linnæan system. *Stipa* is of the class and order *Triandria Digynia*; and the characters are,

The characters. 1. CALYX is a loose acuminated glume, composed of two valves, and containing one flower.

2. COROLLA consists of two valves. The exterior is terminated by a very long, wreathed, straight arista, articulated at the base; the interior valve is the length of the exterior, linear, and has no arista.

3. STAMINA are three capillary filaments, with linear antheræ.

4. PISTILLUM consists of an oblong germen, and two hairy styles united at the base, with downy stigmas.

5. PERICARPIUM. The glume grows to the seed.

6. SEMEN. The seed is single, oblong, and covered.

CHAP.

# CHAP CCCCXLVI

## *STRATIOTES*, WATER SOLDIER.

THERE is only one species of this genus, called Water Soldier, also Water Aloe, Water Housleek, and Fresh-water Soldier

This plant described

The root consists of several long thick fibres, each having a tuft of smaller fibres at the ends The leaves are numerous, ensiforme, truncated, pointed, sharply serrated or prickly on the edges, of a greyish colour, and eight or ten inches long The stalks come out from among the leaves, and are seldom more than five or six inches long The flowers are produced singly from the tops of the stalks, they are of a white colour, appear in June and July, and the seeds ripen in September

Method of propagation

They may be encreased by throwing the plants in the spring into ponds or standing waters of any sort, they will float about for some time, and afterwards strike root in the mud In the autumn they disappear, but rise again the spring following

They may be also propagated by seeds, which should be thrown into the water in different places, in the autumn, soon after they are ripe, and they will grow and furnish the ponds with a sufficient stock of these curious plants

Titles

This species is titled, *Stratiotes foliis ensiformi-triangulis ciliato-aculeatis* In the *Flora Lapp* it is termed simply, *Stratiotes*, Lobel calls it, *Stratiotes militaris aizoides*, Caspar Bauhine, *Aloe palustris*, Ray, *Stratiotes foliis aloes, semine longo*; Gerard, *Militaris aizoides*, and Parkinson, *Stratiotes, sive militaris aizoides* It grows naturally in waters in England, and most of the northern countries of Europe

Class and order in the Linnean system The characters

*Stratiotes* is of the class and order *Polyandria Hexagynia*, and the characters are,

1 CALYX The spatha is composed of two compressed, obtuse, connivent, permanent leaves, carinated on each side, and containing one flower The perianthium consists of an erect deciduous leaf, divided into three parts

2 COROLLA is three obcordated, erect, patent petals, twice the size of the calyx

3 STAMINA are twenty filaments the length of the perianthium, and inserted into the receptacle, having simple antheræ

4 PISTILLUM consists of a germen situated below the receptacle, and six bipartite styles the length of the stamina, with simple stigmas

5 PERICARPIUM is an oval covered capsule, attenuated at each end, a little hexangular, and containing six cells

6 SEMINA The seeds are many, oblong, and crooked

# CHAP. CCCCXLVII

## *SUBULARIA*, AWL-WORT.

THERE is only one species of this genus, called Awl-wort

The plant described

The root is fibrous and white The leaves are rushy, round, pointed, soft to the touch, and five or six inches long The stalks are upright, thick, soft, and tender The flowers are collected in roundish heads, they are small, of a white colour, and are soon followed by oval pods, containing a few small yellowish seeds

This plant grows naturally in waters, and is never cultivated

Titles

There being no other species of this genus, it stands with the name, simply, *Subularia* Buxbaum calls it, *Alyssum palustre, foliis junci*, Plukenet, *Graminifolia aquatica, thlaspeos capitulis rotundis septmento siliculam dirimente*, Morison, *Gramen junceum hybernum, thlaspeos capitulis*, and Ray, *Subularia erecta juncifoliis acutis mollibus*, also, *Juncifolia sub aquis nascens, cochlear æ capsulis* It grows naturally in lakes, rivers, and overflowed places in England, and most of the northern countries of Europe

Class and order in the Linnean system The character.

*Subularia* is of the class and order *Tetradynamia Siliculosa*, and the characters are,

1 CALYX is a perianthium composed of four oval, concave, patent, deciduous leaves

2 COROLLA is cruciforme, and consists of four oboval entire petals, which are a little larger than the leaves of the calyx

3 STAMINA

3 STAMINA are six filaments shorter than the corolla, of which the two opposite are shortest, having simple antheræ

4 PISTILLUM consists of an oval germen, a very short style, and an obtuse stigma

5 PERICARPIUM is an obovał, compressed, undivided pod, containing two cells

## CHAP. CCCCXLVIII.

## *SWERTIA.*

THERE is one Perennial of this genus, called Marsh Gentian

The root is fibrous, and of a yellowish colour The stalk is upright, round, firm, jointed, usually reddish near the base, and a foot and a half high. The leaves are ribbed, the lower ones are broad, oval, and have footstalks, but the upper ones are narrower, sessile, and grow opposite to each other on the stalks The flowers are produced in plenty from the tops of the stalks, growing on slender footstalks, they are of a blue colour, elegantly spotted or streaked with black, appear in July and August, and the seeds ripen in the autumn

This plant described

This species is propagated by sowing the seeds in April, in some moist part of the garden When the plants come up, they must be thinned where they crowd each other, all summer they must be kept clean from weeds, duly watered in dry weather, and in the autumn may be removed to the places where they are designed to remain, which should be moist and shady

Culture

This species is titled, *Swertia corollis quinquefidis, foliis radicalibus ovalibus* In the *Hortus Cliffort* it is termed simply, *Swertia* Caspar Bauhine calls it, *Gentiana palustris latifolia*, Monnier, *Gentiana corollarum laciniis nectario gemino notatis*, Clusius, *Gentiana XII punctato flore*; and Gerard, *Gentiana Penne minor*. It grows naturally in Wales, Helvetia, Bavaria, and Gaul

Titles

*Swertia* is of the class and order *Pentandria Digynia*, and the characters are,

Class and order in the *Linnæan* system

1 CALYX is a plane permanent perianthium, divided into five spear shaped segments

The character.

2 COROLLA is one petal There is no tube, the limb is plane, and divided into spear-shaped segments, which are larger than the calyx, and connected by their ungues

The nectariums are ten, two being in form of hollowed points, surrounded with fine erect hairs at the bottom of every segment of the corolla.

3 STAMINA are five awl shaped, erect, patent filaments shorter than the corolla, having incumbent antheræ

4 PISTILLUM consists of an oval oblong germen, no style, but two simple stigmas

5 PERICARPIUM is a taper capsule pointed at each end, formed of two valves, and containing one cell

6 SEMINA The seeds are numerous, and small.

## CHAP. CCCCXLIX.

## *SYMPHYTUM*, COMFREY.

OF this genus there are three species, called,

Species

1 Common Comfrey

2 Tuberose Comfrey

3 Oriental Comfrey

1 Common Comfrey The root is thick, black on the outside, white within, full of a viscous juice, and strikes deep into the ground The stalk is upright, thick, hairy, very rough, branching near the top, and about three feet high The leaves are very large, oval, spear-shaped, pointed, decurrent, rough to the touch, and of a pale-green colour The flowers come out in bunches from the tops of the stalks, they hang downward, and are of different colours in the different varieties, they appear in June and July, and the seeds ripen in August

Common Comfrey described

The varieties of this species are,

Varieties
The Purple,
The Blue,
The White,
The Yellow,
The Red

Medicinal properties
The root of this species is used in medicine, and greatly answers in quality to those of Marshmallows, but the mucilage is said to be stronger

Tuberous,
2 Tuberose Comfrey The root is composed of many thick fleshy tubers, joined together by fleshy fibres, and full of a slimy juice The stalks are rough, hairy, a foot and a half long, and usually incline towards the ground The leaves are long, narrow, pointed, rough, hairy, [illegible], the lower ones grow alternately, but those under the flowers are placed opposite The flowers come out in bunches from the tops of the stalks, they are of a pale-yellow colour, appear in June and July, and the seeds ripen in August

and Oriental Comfrey described
3 Oriental Comfrey The root is thick, juicy, black on the outside, and white within The stalks are thick, rough, branching near the top, and a foot and a half or two feet high The leaves are oval, very rough, hairy, and grow on short, rough, hairy footstalks The flowers come out in pendulent bunches from the tops of the stalks; they are of a blue colour, appear in March and April, but are seldom succeeded by seeds in England

[illegible]
There is a variety of this species with white flowers

Propagation
These sorts are all very hardy, and are propagated by parting of the roots which is best done in the autumn They will grow any where, though they love a moist, rich, deep soil best

The first sort is sometimes raised in plenty for medicinal purposes The ground should be then double-dug, and the plants set two feet asunder every way During the summer they must be kept clean from weeds, and in the winter the ground between the plants should have a slight digging, and this will cause them to become larger, and better for use

These plants are with difficulty extirpated in places where the ground is to be converted to other purposes, for the roots being brittle break into numerous pieces, and being of a dark colour [illegible] round, and every bit of them [illegible] so deep into the ground [illegible] below the common [illegible] into the clay, [illegible] when the common mould is cleared of every bit of the root, yet the smallest part lodged in the clay below will rise through a stratum of mould upwards of a yard deep, and if neglected will soon again overspread the whole spot A constant repetition of hoeing them down will at first weaken them, and at length destroy them

These plants are also raised by seeds, which should be sown in the spring in beds of common mould made fine When the plants come up, they must be thinned where they are too close, kept clean from weeds all summer, watered in dry weather, and in the autumn may be removed to the places where they are designed to remain

Titles
1 Common Comfrey is titled, *Symphytum foliis ovato-lanceolatis decurrentibus* Caspar Bauhine calls it, *Symphytum consolida major*, Gerard, *Consolida major, flore purpureo*, Parkinson, *Symphytum majus vulgare*, and Merret, *Symphytum flore purpureo* It grows naturally in moist shady places in England, and most countries of Europe

2 Tuberose Comfrey is, *Symphytum foliis summis oppositis* Caspar Bauhine calls it, *Symphytum majus, tuberosa radice*, and Cammerarius, *Symphytum radice tuberosa* It grows naturally in Germany, France, and Spain

3 Oriental Comfrey is, *Symphytum foliis ovatis subpetiolatis* Tournefort calls it, *Symphytum orientale, folio subrotundo aspero, flore cæruleo*, also, *Symphytum Constantinopolitanum, boraginis folio & facie, flore albo* It grows naturally on the sides of rivers near Constantinople

*Symphytum* is of the class and order *Pentandria Monogynia*, and the characters are,
Class and order in the Linnæan system The characters

1 CALYX is an upright, pentagonal, permanent perianthium, divided at the brim into five acute segments

2 COROLLA is one bell-shaped petal The tube is very short, the limb is tubular, ventricose, a little thicker than the tube, and divided at the brim into five obtuse reflexed segments, the opening is guarded by five awl shaped rays, which are shorter than the limb, and connive into the form of a cone

3 STAMINA are five awl shaped filaments, placed alternately with the rays of the aperture, having erect, acute, covered antheræ

4 PISTILLUM consists of four germens, a filiform style the length of the corolla, and a simple stigma

5 PERICARPIUM There is none The calyx becomes larger, and contains the seeds

6 SEMINA The seeds are four, gibbous, sharp pointed, and have their apices connivent

CHAP

# CHAP. CCCCL.

## *TANACETUM*, TANSEY.

THE perennials for the open borders of this genus are,

*Species*

1 Common Tanſey
2 Coſtmary, or Alecoaſt
3 Siberian Tanſey
4 Oriental Tanſey

*Deſcription of Common Tanſey*

1 Common Tanſey The root is tough, creeping and fibrous The ſtalks are upright, thick, channelled, divide into a few erect branches near the top, and grow to about a yard high The leaves are large, bipinnated, ſerrated, of a deep-green colour, and ſtrongly, and to moſt people very agreeably, ſcented The flowers come out from the ends of the branches in umbels, they are of a deep-yellow colour, appear in July and Auguſt, and the ſeeds ripen in the autumn

*Varieties*

The principal varieties of this ſpecies are,
The Curled-leaved,
The Scentleſs,
The Variegated

The Variegated kind is deſerving of a place in any collection as an ornamental plant, on account of its beautiful variegated leaves, and the Curled-leaved alſo merits the ſame reſpect, on account of its large, double or curled leaves, and its heightened fragrance

*Medicinal properties*

Tanſey is in great eſteem both for culinary and medicinal purpoſes For the firſt, it is uſed by ſome as a ſallad-herb in the ſpring, to mix with eggs, and to give a flavour to cakes, puddings, &c For the latter, being a warm wholſome bitter, it is deemed a good pectoral, uſeful in hyſterics, and for ſuppreſſion of urine The root, prepared with honey and ſugar, and taken faſting for a certain time, is ſaid to be very good againſt the gout The ſeeds, leaves, and flowers are held anthelmintic, being a certain remedy to deſtroy worms of all ſorts that are incident to the human body

*Coſtmary deſcribed*

2 Coſtmary, or Alecoaſt The root is thick, hard, fleſhy, and creeping The ſtalks are round, ſtriated, branching, of a whitiſh green colour, and grow to about a yard in height The leaves on the ſtalks are oval, ſerrated, and of a greyiſh green colour, but the radical ones are entire The flowers come out in kind of umbels from the ends of the branches, they are ſmall, and of a yellow colour, appear in Auguſt, but are rarely ſucceeded by ripe ſeeds in England

*Its uſes in medicine*

The whole plant is of an agreeable odour, and was formerly in great eſteem for ſteeping in ale, which was drank by girls for the green-ſickneſs, and by many for the worms, gripes, bloody-flux, dropſy, &c

*Siberian*

3 Siberian Tanſey The root is thick, creeping, and fibrous The ſtalks are upright, herbaceous, and two feet high The leaves are pinnated, the pinnæ are narrow, tender, ſome are entire, and others cut at the ends into two or three points The flowers come out in umbels from the ends and ſides of the ſtalks in a corymbus, they are ſmall, of a yellow colour, appear in June and July, and the ſeeds ripen in the autumn

*and Oriental Tanſey deſcribed*

4 Oriental Tanſey The ſtalks are upright, ſimple, herbaceous, downy, and a foot and a half or two feet high The leaves are bipinnated, elegant, white, and hoary The flowers come out from the tops of the ſtalks in oval bunches, they are of a yellow colour, appear in July and Auguſt, but are rarely ſucceeded by good ſeeds in our gardens

*Culture*

Theſe ſorts are all propagated by parting of the roots, which may be done at any time of the year, but more eſpecially in the autumn, winter, or early in the ſpring, before the ſtalks ariſe They will grow in almoſt any ſoil or ſituation, and after they are ſet out will call for no trouble, except keeping them clean from weeds, and clearing off the old ſtalks as they decay in the autumn

They are alſo raiſed by ſeeds, which ſhould be ſown in the ſpring, in beds of light freſh earth When the plants come up, they ſhould be thinned where they appear too cloſe, frequently watered if dry weather makes it neceſſary, and conſtantly kept clean from weeds. In July or Auguſt they may be tranſplanted to the places where they are deſigned to remain, or pricked out in beds at a foot diſtance from each other, to remain there for another ſeaſon, that the roots may get ſtrong before they are removed to the places of their final deſtination

*Titles*

1 Common Tanſey is titled, *Tanacetum foliis bipinnatis inciſis ſerratis* In the *Flora Lapp* it is termed, *Tanacetum foliis pinnatis planis pinnis ſerratis* Caſpar Bauhine calls it, *Tanacetum vulgare luteum*, alſo, *Tanacetum foliis criſpis*, Dalechamp, *Athanaſia, ſ Tanacetum*, and Dodonæus, *Tanacetum criſpum* It grows naturally in the borders of fields, road ſides, &c in England, and moſt countries of Europe

2 Coſtmary, or Alecoaſt, is, *Tanacetum foliis ovatis integris ſerratis* Caſpar Bauhine calls it, *Mentha hortenſis corymbifera*, Dalechamp, *Coſtus hortenſis*, and others, *Balſamita* It grows naturally in Italy, and the ſouth of France

3 Siberian Tanſey is, *Tanacetum foliis* [illegible] *laciniis linearibus filiformibus, corymbis* [illegible], *caule herbaceo* Gmelin calls it, *Tanacetum foliis pinnatis multifidis laciniis linearibus* [illegible] It grows naturally in Siberia

4 Oriental Tanſey is, *Tanacetum foliis bipinnatis tomentoſis, corymbo ovato compoſito* In the *Hortus Cliffort* it is termed, [illegible] *ſimplici, corymbo compoſito ovato terminali* Tournefort calls it, *Abſinthium orientale incanum tenuifolium, floribus lateis in capitulum congeſtis & ſurſum ſpectantibus* It is a native of the Eaſt

*Claſs and order in the Linnæan ſyſtem*

*Tanacetum* is of the claſs and order *Syngeneſia Polygamia Æqualis*, and the characters are,

1 CALYX

The characters

1 CALYX is hemispherical and imbricated The scales are acute and compact

2 COROLLA The hermaphrodite florets are numerous, and tubular in the disk The females are a few in the radius Each hermaphrodite flower has one funnel-shaped petal, cut at the top into five reflexed segments The female florets are trifid

3 STAMINA, of the hermaphrodites, are five very short capillary filaments, crowned by a cylindrical tubular anthera.

4. PISTILLUM, of the hermaphrodites, consists of a small oblong germen, a filiforme style the length of the stamina, and a bifid revoluted stigma.

In the females, it consists of an oblong germen, a simple style, and two reflexed stigmas

5 PERICARPIUM There is none

6. SEMINA The seeds are single, oblong, and naked.

The receptacle is convex, and naked.

# CHAP. CCCCLI

## TELEPHIUM.

OF this genus there is one species, called, True Orpine of Imperatus

The plant described. The root is thick, hard, of a yellowish colour on the outside, white within, and furnished with a few thick spreading fibres The stalks are numerous, round, slender, green, eight or ten inches long, and lie on the ground The leaves are small, oval, smooth, stiff, of a greyish colour, and grow alternately The flowers come out from the ends of the branches in short, thick, reflexed spikes, they are of a white colour, appear in June and July, and the seeds ripen in the autumn

Culture. This species is propagated by sowing the seeds in the autumn, soon after they are ripe, in the places where they are designed to remain The soil should be light and dry, and the situation open Many of the plants will come up before winter, the rest in the spring, when they should be thinned where they are too close, leaving them about eight inches asunder every way All summer they must be kept clean from weeds, and many of the plants will flower in the autumn The summer following the blow will be general, and the seeds will ripen, which, if permitted to scatter, will soon over stock the ground with these plants

Title. This species is titled, *Telephium foliis alternis* Van Royen calls it, *Telephium foliis oblongo-ovatis, racemis secundis terminalibus*, Caspar Bauhine, *Telephium repens, folio non deciduo*; also, *Cistus folio marjoranæ*, and Clusius, *Telephium legitimum Imperati*

Class and order in the Linnæan system. *Telephium* is of the class and order *Pentandria Trigynia*; and the characters are,

The characters. 1 CALYX is a perianthium the length of the corolla, composed of five oblong, obtuse, concave, carinated, permanent leaves

2 COROLLA is five oblong, obtuse, erect petals, which are narrowest at the base

3 STAMINA are five awl-shaped filaments shorter than the corolla, having incumbent antheræ

3 PISTILLUM consists of a three-sided acute germen, without any style, but three acute patent stigmas

5 PERICARPIUM is a short three-sided capsule, formed of three valves, and containing one cell.

6 SEMINA The seeds are many, and roundish

The receptacle is free, and half the length of the capsule

CHAP.

# CHAP CCCCLII

## TETRAGONOTHECA

THERE is only one species of this genus, called, which tolerates *Tetragonotheca*

The plant described. The stalks are upright, thick, branching near the top, and about two feet high. The leaves are large, oblong, hairy, rough, slightly serrated, grow opposite by pairs, and embrace the stalk with their base. The flowers come out singly from the ends of the branches; they are large, of a yellow colour, appear in August, and in favourable seasons the seeds ripen in the autumn.

Culture. This species is propagated by sowing the seeds in some open bed of good, light, fine earth. When the plants come up, they must be thinned where they are too close, kept clean from weeds all summer, and in the autumn may be removed to the places where they are designed to remain. They must have a very light, dry, warm soil, and a well sheltered situation, otherwise they are liable to be destroyed by the severity of our winters. The second summer they will flower, and sometimes the seeds ripen in the autumn, but this seldom happens, unless the soil and season be very favourable, and as the plant in England seldom lives longer than three or four years, care should be taken at proper intervals to procure the seeds from abroad.

Titles. This being the only species of this genus, it is named, *Tetragonotheca*. Dillenius calls it, *Tetragonotheca Helianthi facie maxima folio*. It grows naturally in Virginia.

Class and order in the Linnæan System. *Tetragonotheca* is of the class and order *Syngenesia Polygamia Superflua*, and the characters are,

The characters.
1 CALYX. The general calyx is large, and divided into four triangular, heart-shaped, plane, spreading segments.

2 COROLLA. The flower is radiated. The hermaphrodite florets are numerous in the disk. The females are twelve in the radius. The hermaphrodite florets are funnel-shaped, and cut at the brim into five reflexed segments.

The females are tongue-shaped, equal, trifid, and acute.

3 STAMINA, of the hermaphrodites, are five very short capillary filaments, having a cylindrical tubulous antheræ.

4 PISTILLUM of the hermaphrodites consists of a roundish germen, a filiform style the length of the stamina, and a reflexed stigma.

In the females, it consists of a roundish germen, a filiform style the length of the hermaphrodites, and two revoluted stigmas.

5 PERICARPIUM. There is none.

6 SEMEN of the hermaphrodites is single, roundish, and has no down.

Of the females, it is single, nearly oval, and has no down.

The receptacle is paleaceous.

# CHAP CCCCLIII.

## TEUCRIUM, GERMANDER

THIS is a very extensive genus, comprehending many genera of old Botanists. The most hardy species are,

Species.
1 Common Germander
2 Shining Germander
3 Water Germander
4 Yellow Germander, or Tree Germander
5 Cretan Germander
6 Spanish Germander
7 Siberian Germander
8 Canada Germander
9 Hircanian Germander
10 Wood Sage
11 Campanulated Germander
12 Bastard Ground Pine
13 Mountain Poly
14 Lavender-leaved Mountain Poly
15 Pyrenean Mountain Poly
16 Dwarf Mountain Poly
17 Capitated Mountain Poly
18 Common *Marum*, or Syrian Mastick

Common Germander described. 1 Common Germander. The root is slender, fibrous, and creeping. The stalks are four-cornered, tough, hairy, branching, and spread on the ground. The leaves are oval, crenated on the edges, and grow opposite on short footstalks. The flowers come out from the sides of the branches near the top; they are of a reddish colour,

colour, though there are varieties with white, and also with purplish flowers; they appear in June and July, and the seeds ripen in the autumn.

[illegible] This plant is held [illegible], diuretic, [illegible] good [illegible] employed in [illegible], and has been found serviceable in the gout, hydropical and various sorts of chronical disorders.

[illegible] 2. Shining Germander. The root is creeping, and sends forth several upright smooth stalks, which are of a [illegible] green colour. The leaves are oblong, [illegible], nervose, smooth, of a shining green colour, and grow on footstalks. The flowers come out, two together, from the wings of the leaves, on each side the stalks, almost their whole length; they are of a purple colour, appear in June and July, and the seeds ripen in September.

and Water Germander described. 3. Water Germander, or Scordium. The root is creeping. The stalks are square, branching, hairy, and [illegible]. The leaves are oblong, indented, hairy, of a pale-green colour, and grow opposite by pairs. The flowers come out, [illegible] two together, from the wings of the leaves at the joints; they are small, and of a red or purple colour; they appear in July and August, and the seeds ripen in the autumn.

Medicinal properties. This plant has much the taste of garlick, and is held [illegible], diuretic, and [illegible]. It is said to be good against poisons, and [illegible] by way of cataplasm, gives ease to the gout, cures ulcers, and is serviceable in [illegible] and many other chronical disorders.

Culture. These three sorts are propagated by parting of the roots, which may be done at any time of the year, but more especially in autumn, winter, or spring. Slips also planted in the spring will grow as readily as Sage. The seeds also may be sown, and thereby plenty of plants will be obtained. They all love a rich moist soil, and [illegible] the third species, which [illegible] should [illegible] be thus stationed.

[illegible] 4. Yellow [illegible] Germander. The stalks [illegible] branching, and a foot and a half [illegible]. The leaves are heart-shaped, a little waved, [illegible] of a deep-green colour, and [illegible] footstalks. The flowers come out from [illegible] the leaves almost the whole length of the branches; they are small, appear [illegible] and the seeds ripen in the autumn.

[illegible] of this species are,

The White-flowered,

The Yellow,

The Purple-flowered.

[illegible] 5. Shrubby Cretan Germander. The stalks are [illegible], upright, hoary, and about a foot high. The leaves are small, oval, heart-shaped, rough, unequally serrated, hoary, and grow on short footstalks. The flowers come out in upright [illegible] from the tops of the stalks; they are of a [illegible] purple colour, appear in July, and the [illegible] in the autumn.

[illegible] These two sorts are propagated by cuttings, which may be planted in any of the summer months, and if they are shaded and duly watered will readily grow. They must have a light dry soil, and a well sheltered situation, otherwise they will be liable to be destroyed by our winters, for which reason a few plants should be set in pots, to be occasionally housed, to continue the sorts, in case those abroad should be destroyed through the severity of the weather.

Spanish Germander described. 6. Spanish Germander. The stalks are herbaceous, square, tolerably erect, and about two feet high. The leaves are narrow, pointed at both ends, and [illegible] pointed.

The flowers come out in bunches from the sides of the stalks, almost their whole length; they are of a red colour, appear in June and July, and the seeds ripen in the autumn.

Culture. It may be propagated by parting of the roots, setting the slips, or sowing the seeds, like the first three sorts, and will grow in almost any soil or situation.

Siberian, 7. Siberian Germander. The stalks are slender, square, herbaceous, and a foot and a half high. The leaves are oval, serrated, of a strong green colour on their upper-side, a little hoary underneath, and grow on short footstalks. The flowers grow by threes on footstalks, which come out singly from the wings of the leaves; they are small, of a purple colour, appear in June and July, and the seeds ripen in the autumn.

Canada, 8. Canada Germander. The stalks are upright, and a foot and a half high. The leaves are oval, spear-shaped, equally serrated, plane, and downy underneath. The flowers come out in [illegible] from the tops of the stalks; they are small, and of a whitish or reddish colour; they appear in July, and the seeds ripen in the autumn.

and Hircanian Germander described. 9. Hircanian Germander. The stalks are thick, square, dichotomous, and three feet high. The leaves are heart-shaped, oblong, obtuse, indented on their edges, and grow on short footstalks. The flowers come out from the tops of the plant in long spiral, thick spikes; they are small, of a reddish colour, appear in July and August, and the seeds ripen in the autumn.

Wood Sage, 10. Wood Sage. The root is creeping. The stalks are woody, four-cornered, firm, jointed, and grow to about a foot and a half high. The leaves are heart-shaped, slightly serrated on their edges, and grow opposite on short footstalks. The flowers come out in long spikes from the tops of the stalks; they are of a greenish white colour, having purple antheræ; they appear in July, and the seeds ripen in the autumn.

Campanulated Germander, 11. Campanulated Germander. The stalks are herbaceous, about a foot long, and trail on the ground. The leaves are smooth, of a deep green colour, grow opposite to each other, and are cut almost to the midrib into many segments. The flowers come out singly from each side the stalk; they are of a white colour, appear in June and July, and the seeds ripen in September.

and Bastard Ground Pine described. 12. Bastard Ground Pine. The root is thick, and of a whitish colour. The stalk is herbaceous, tender, and divides from the root into many slender, spreading branches. The leaves are hairy, and composed of three principal parts, each of which is cut into three or more narrow entire segments. The flowers come out singly on footstalks opposite to each other from the sides of the stalks; they are of a white colour, appear in June and July, and the seeds ripen in September.

Culture. These three sorts are propagated by planting the slips, sowing the seeds, or parting the roots, like the first sorts.

Mountain Poly described. 13. Mountain Poly. The stalks are herbaceous, a little woolly, branching, and trail on the ground. The leaves are oblong, obtuse, downy, indented on their edges, and sit close, having no footstalk. The flowers come out in spikes from the ends of the branches; they are of a yellow colour, but in some varieties white; they appear in June and July, but are seldom succeeded by ripe seeds in England.

Varieties. There are many varieties of this species, but the flowers of most of them are either white or yellow.

Lavender leaved 14. Lavender leaved Mountain Poly. The [illegible] is ligneous, tough, and hung with many spreading

spreading fibres The stalks are ligneous, weak and partly procumbent The leaves are spear-shaped, entire, of a deep green colour on the upper side, but whitish underneath, and grow opposite to each other by pairs The flowers come out from the ends of the branches in a corymbus, they are small, of a white colour, appear in June and July, and are very seldom succeeded by seeds in England

Pyrenean

15 Pyrenean Mountain Poly. The stalks are ligneous, slender, trailing, hairy, and covered with a purplish bark The leaves are wedge-shaped, but rounded at the extremity, are of a thick consistence, hairy, and crenated on the edges The flowers terminate the stalks in a corymbus. There are the Purple, the White, and the Purple and White sorts They appear early in summer, and continue in succession until the autumn, but the seeds seldom ripen in our gardens

Dwarf

16 Dwarf Mountain Poly The stalks are slender, very downy, and lie on the ground The leaves are narrow, plane, and come out together in small spreading clusters The flowers are collected in small heads at the extremity of the stalks, they appear in June, July, and August, but are rarely succeeded by ripe seeds here

Capitated

17 Capitated Mountain Poly The stalks are upright, ligneous near the bottom, branching, and about a foot high The leaves are spear-shaped, narrow, downy, indented on the edges, and of a thickish consistence The flowers are collected in roundish heads or bunches, which come out from the ends of the branches on footstalks they are of a white colour, appear chiefly in June and July, and the seeds seldom ripen here

Method of raising varieties

There are many varieties of all these sorts, or species of Mountain Poly, and their number may be encreased by sowing the seeds, which is the best way of raising these plants, but as these rarely ripen in England, they must be procured from the places where the plants naturally grow Having therefore procured a quantity of good seeds of the respective sorts, let them be sown in the spring, in beds of light fresh earth, made fine, and a little of the finest mould sifted over them Give the beds a slight watering twice a week, if the weather should prove dry and the seeds in about a month or five weeks will make their appearance When they come up, the weeds must be carefully drawn out as they arise, the plants frequently refreshed with water, and when they crowd each other let them be thinned In July, or early in August the plants will be fit to remove, then, on a moist day, let each be taken up, with a ball of earth to the root, and planted in the places where they are designed to remain The soil should be naturally dry, light, undunged and here they will live for many years Nevertheless if there be plants enough, a share of them may be planted in the richest parts of the garden, and they will be more luxuriant, and flower proportionably stronger, but every part of these plants being replete with juice, and becoming more herbaceous and tender, thro' their free manner of growing, great part of them may be expected to be destroyed, should the winter prove very severe

Common ... coloured

18 Common Marum, or Syrian Mastick The stalk is wooly, upright, firm, divides into numerous slender, ligneous, hoary branches, and grows to a foot and a half or two feet high The leaves are small, oval, entire, pointed at both ends very hoary underneath, and grow opposite to each other at the joints The flowers come out in spikes at the ends of the branches, they are of a bright red colour, appear in July, but are seldom succeeded by seeds in England

This plant is very strong, and to most people very agreeable, scented It is generally treated as a green-house plant, but will do very well abroad, if planted in a dry warm soil, in a well-sheltered place It is a fine aromatic, and affords an essential oil, very penetrating and acrimonious

Culture

Its propagation is extremely easy The slips or cuttings being planted in any of the summer months, shaded at first, and duly watered, will readily grow These cuttings may be set close together, and if the weather should prove hot, cover them with mats at first When they are in a good growing state, the mats may be omitted by degrees, and in the autumn or spring following the plants may be taken up, with a ball of earth to each root, and set in the places where they are to remain The situation may be among the lowest trees in the Evergreen shrubbery, or many of them may be made to form a bed in a warm well-sheltered place, planting them at about six or eight inches distance one from another, ... Thus they will make a very elegant figure when in blow, but will be liable to be destroyed by cats, who are fond of the plants, and will seldom let them pass unmolested when there are numbers of plants growing together

Notwithstanding this plant is recommended to the open air in warm well sheltered places, a sufficient quantity should be set in pots, to be treated as hardy green-house plants, where they will not only look very beautiful, but will be ready to afford encrease, in case a more than ordinary severe winter should destroy those that are planted abroad

Titles

1 Common Germander is entitled, *Teucrium foliis cuneiformi ovatis incisis crenatis caulibus ... floribus ... petiolatis* Rivinus calls it, *Chamaedrys*, Caspar Bauhine, *Chamaedrys major repens*, also, *Chamaedrys minor repens*, and Gerard, *Chamaedrys major latifolia* It grows naturally in England, Helvetia, France, and Germany

2 Shining Germander is, *Teucrium foliis ovatis acute incisis ... floribus axillaribus geminis, caule ...* Magnol calls it *Chamaedrys Alpina frutescens, folio splendente* It is common in France and Germany

3 Water Germander, or *Scordium*, is *Teucrium foliis oblongis sessilibus dentato-serratis, floribus geminis axillaribus pedunculatis, caule diffuso* In the *Hortus Cliffort* it is termed, *Teucrium foliis ovato lanceolatis serrulatis sessilibus, floribus ... * Caspar Bauhine calls it, *Scordium*, Gerard, *Scordium ...*, and Parkinson, *Scordium legitimum* It grows naturally in moist marshy places in the Isle of Ely, and most parts of Europe

4 Yellow, or Tree Germander is *Teucrium foliis cordatis obtuse serratis, floralibus integerrimis concavis, caule fruticoso, floribus ternis* In the *Hortus Cliffort* it is termed, *Teucrium foliis subovatis crenatis, floribus laxe spicatis pedunculatis, caule fruticoso* Caspar Bauhine calls it, *Teucrium*, Morison, *Chamaedrys fruticosior, flore ochroleuco*, Clusius, *Teucrium vulgare fruticans ...*, and Plukenet, *Teucrium lucidum, parvo folio flore ... purpureo* It grows naturally in Italy, Sicily, Malta, France and Spain

5 Cretan Germander is, *Teucrium foliis ovatis ... caulibus ... ramentis reflexis* Clusius calls it, *Teucrium Creticum*, Barrelier, *Teucrium fruticosum incanum Creticum, flore purpureo*, and Tournefort, *Chamaedrys fruticosa Cretica, flore purpureo* It grows naturally in Crete

6 Spanish

6 Spanish Germander is, *Teucrium foliis ovatis utrinque acutis superne serrato dentatis, floribus racemosis* In the *Hortus Cliffort* it is termed, *Teucrium foliis ovatis utrinque, acutis utrinque bidentatis, verticillis laxis* Tournefort calls it, *Chamædrys multiflora tenuifolia Hispanica* It grows naturally in Spain

7 Siberian Germander is, *Teucrium foliis ovatis ... petiolis foliaribus trifloris, bracteis linearilanceolatis* Gmelin calls it, *Teucrium chamædryos folio, flore parvo purpureo* It grows naturally in Siberia

8 Canada Germander is, *Teucrium foliis ovato-lanceolatis serratis, caule erecto, racemo terminali, verticillis hexaphyllis* Gronovius calls it, *Teucrium foliis lanceolatis serratis petiolatis, floribus solitariis*, and Tournefort, *Chamædrys Canadensis, urticæ folio subtus incano* It grows naturally in Canada

9 Hircanian Germander is, *Teucrium foliis cordato-oblongis obtusis, caule brachiato dichotomo, spicis longissimis terminalibus sessilibus spiralibus* Haller calls it, *Teucrium foliis cordatis crenatis petiolatis, spicis oblongis densissimis* It is common in Hircania

10 Wood Sage is, *Teucrium foliis cordatis serratis petiolatis, racemis lateralibus secundis, caule erecto* Van Royen calls it, *Teucrium foliis cordatis crenatis petiolatis, spicis laxis secundis*, Rivinus, *Scordonia*; Caspar Bauhine, *Scordium alterum, sive salvia sylvestris*, Gerard, *Scorodonia, sive salvia agrestis*, and Parkinson, *Scorodonia, sive scordium alterum quibusdam, et salvia agrestis* It grows naturally in woods and thickets in England, Helvetia, France, and Germany

11 Campanulated Germander is, *Teucrium foliis multifidis, floribus oppositis* Van Royen calls it, *Teucrium foliis cuneiformibus trifidis laciniis divisis, floribus solitariis*, Boerhaave, *Teucrium, calyce campanulato, laciniatum, flore parvo subcæruleo*, and Tilli, *Teucrium supinum perenne palustre Apulum glabrum, foliis laciniatis, flore albo* It is common in the East, and in Apulia

12 Bastard Ground Pine is, *Teucrium foliis ... partitis trifidis linearibus integerrimis, floribus pedunculatis solitariis oppositis, caule patulo* Caspar Bauhine calls it, *Chamæpitys spuria, multifido folio, lamii flore*; Clusius, *Pseudo-chamæpitys*, and Cammerarius, *Chamæpitys alia* It grows naturally in Spain

13 Mountain Poly is, *Teucrium capitulis subrotundis, foliis oblongis obtusis crenatis tomentosis sessilibus, caule prostrato* Clusius calls it, *Polium montanum* 5 Columna, *Hyssopum Dioscoridis*, and Caspar Bauhine, *Polium montanum luteum*, also, *Polium montanum album*, also, *Polium montanum supinum alterum*, also, *Polium montanum supinum Venetum* It grows naturally in Italy, Portugal, France, and Spain

14 Lavender-leaved Mountain Poly is, *Teucrium corymbo terminali, foliis lanceolatis integerrimis subtus tomentosis* In the *Hortus Cliffortianus* it is termed, *Teucrium foliis lanceolatis integerrimis petiolatis, spicis laxe subrotundis* Caspar Bauhine calls it, *Polium, lavendulæ folio*, and Rivinus, *Ajuga folio integro* It grows naturally in dry sandy places in most parts of France and Germany

15 Pyrenean Mountain Poly is, *Teucrium corymbo terminali, foliis cuneiformi-rotundatis crenatis* In the *Hortus Cliffort* it is termed, *Teucrium foliis suborbiculatis crenatis, spicâ laxâ orbiculatâ depressâ* Van Royen calls it, *Teucrium foliis cuneiformibus crenatis, corymbo terminali, foliolis floralibus linearibus*, Tournefort, *Polium Pyrenaicum supinum, hederæ terrestris folio*, and Boccone, *Polium saxatile purpureum chamædryoides, amplâ comâ* It grows naturally on the Pyrenees

16 Dwarf Mountain Poly is, *Polium capitulis sessilibus terminalibus, foliis linearibus planis quadrifariis consertis, caule procumbente tomentoso* Tournefort calls it, *Polium Hispanicum montanum pumilum, rosmarini folio, flore rubro*, and Barrelier, *Polium montanum pumilum rubrum, viridi stæchadis folio* It grows naturally in Spain

17 Capitated Mountain Poly is, *Teucrium capitulis pedunculatis, foliis lanceolatis crenatis tomentosis, caule erecto* Barrelier calls it, *Polium montanum album serratum latifolium*, Caspar Bauhine, *Polium maritimum erectum Monspeliacum*, and John Bauhine, *Polium Monspeliacum* It grows naturally in Spain

18 Common Marum, or Syrian Mastick, is, *Teucrium foliis integerrimis ovatis subtus tomentosis utrinque acutis racemis secundis, calycibus villosis* In the *Hortus Cliffort* it is termed, *Teucrium foliis ovatis utrinque acutis integerrimis, floribus solitariis utrinque digestis* John Bauhine calls it, *Marum cortusi* It grows naturally in the kingdom of Valencia

*Teucrium* is of the class and order *Didynamia Gymnospermia*, and the characters are, Class and order in the Linnæan system The characters

1 Calyx is a monophyllous permanent perianthium, gibbous at the base, and cut at the brim into five nearly equal acute segments

2 Corolla is one ringent petal The tube is cylindrical, short, and incurved at the top The upper lip is erect, and deeply divided into two acute segments, the lower lip is divided into three segments, the lateral ones being the figure of the upper lip, and nearly erect, the middle one is large and roundish

3 Stamina are four awl-shaped filaments longer than the upper-lip of the corolla, and prominent between the segments, having small antheræ

4 Pistillum consists of a germen divided into four parts, a filiforme style the size and situation of the stamina, and two slender stigmas

5 Pericarpium There is none The seeds are lodged in the calyx

6 Semina The seeds are four, and roundish

CHAP.

# CHAP. CCCCLIV.

## THALICTRUM, MEADOW RUE.

THE species of this genus are all perennials, and go by the respective names of;

Species.

1 Great Meadow Rue.
2 Lesser Meadow Rue.
3 Mountain Meadow Rue.
4. Stinking Meadow Rue.
5 Tuberous Meadow Rue.
6 Canada Meadow Rue.
7 Dioecious Meadow Rue.
8 Purple Meadow Rue.
9 Siberian Meadow Rue.
10 Narrow-leaved Meadow Rue.
11 Shining Meadow Rue.
12 Contorted Meadow Rue.
13 Columbine-leaved Meadow Rue, or Feathered Columbine.

Great Meadow Rue described.

1. Great Meadow Rue. The root is thick, yellow, and creeping. The stalks are upright, firm, hollow, round, furrowed, smooth, and five or six feet high. The leaves are composed of many folioles, most of which are cut into three segments; they are of a deep-green colour, smooth, and grow alternately at the joints. The flowers come out in erect panicles from the tops of the stalks, are of a greenish-white colour, appear in June and July, and the seeds ripen in August.

Variety.

There is a variety of this species with yellow flowers.

Description of Lesser,

2. Lesser Meadow Rue. The root is small and creeping. The stalks are weak, branching, and about a foot high. The leaves are usually divided into six parts, are thin, tender, acute, and grow alternately on the stalks. The flowers come out from the tops of the stalks in loose, nodding panicles; they are small, of a yellowish colour, appear in July and August, and the seeds ripen in September.

Mountain,

3. Mountain Meadow Rue. The root is fibrous and creeping. The stalks are simple, almost naked, and about six or eight inches high. The leaves are small, obtuse, smooth, and glossy. The flowers are produced from the tops of the stalks in loose, single spikes; they are small, whitish, and appear in May.

Stinking,

4. Stinking Meadow Rue. This is a low plant, rising with a slender, branching stalk to the height of about six inches. The leaves are composed of a multitude of small folioles, which are indented, downy underneath, and of a strong, disagreeable odour. The flowers are produced from the tops of the stalks in loose panicles, are small, of a whitish-green colour, and appear in June.

Tuberous,

5. Tuberous Meadow Rue. The root is hung with many knobs or tubers, in the manner of Asphodel. The stalk is upright, almost naked, branching a little near the top, and a foot and a half high. The leaves are small, indented in three parts at their top, smooth, of a greyish colour, and grow singly under the division of the stalk at the top. The flowers come out in bunches from the ends of the branches, are of a white colour, moderately large, appear in June and July, and the seeds ripen in August.

6. Canada Meadow Rue. The root is thick, fibrous, and of a dark-brown colour. The stalks are upright, firm, smooth, purplish near the bottom, branching toward the top, and three or four feet high. The leaves are smooth, of a greyish colour, and much resemble those of the Common Columbine. The flowers come out in large panicles from the tops of the stalks, are of a white colour, appear in June and July, and the seeds ripen in August. Canada,

7. Dioecious Meadow Rue. The root is fibrous and spreading. The stalks are upright, naked almost to the top, and about a foot high. The leaves are composed of many small, indented folioles, are of a greyish colour, and grow singly under the flowers. The flowers are produced in bunches from the tops of the stalks; they are dioecious, being males and females on different plants, and appear in June and July. Dioecious,

8. Purple Meadow Rue. The stalks of this species are upright, purplish coloured, and about a foot and a half high. The leaves are divided into three principal parts, are of a glaucous colour, and grow alternately on the stalks. The flowers come out from the tops of the stalks in loose panicles; they hang drooping, are of a purplish colour, have yellow stamina, and appear in June. Purple,

9. Siberian Meadow Rue. The stalks are slender, jointed, branching a little near the top, and about a foot high. The leaves are divided at the base into three principal parts; they grow alternately at the joints, and the folioles of which they are composed are very small, of a glaucous colour, and tender. The flowers come out from the tops of the stalks in loose, nodding panicles; they are small, of a yellow colour, appear in June and July, and the seeds ripen in August. Siberian,

10. Narrow-leaved Meadow Rue. The stalks rise to two or three feet high. The general leaf is moderately large, and the folioles of which it is composed are very narrow, spear-shaped, entire, and elegant. The flowers come out in panicles from the tops of the stalks, are small, of a greenish-white colour, and appear in June and July. Narrow leaved,

11. Shining Meadow Rue. The stalks are upright, channelled, and three feet high. The leaves are narrow, of a fleshy substance, and a lucid-green colour. The flowers are collected in panicles at the tops of the stalks, are of a yellowish-white colour, appear in July, and the seeds ripen in August. Shining,

12. Contorted Meadow Rue. The stalk is upright, edged, and a foot and a half high. The leaves are composed of many narrow segments, and grow alternately at the joints. The flowers are numerous at the tops of the stalks, of a white colour, appear in July, and are succeeded by triangular, contorted seeds, which will be ripe in August. and Contorted Meadow Rue.

Columbine leaved Meadow Rue described

13 Columbine leaved Meadow Rue This species hath long gone among Gardeners by the name of Feathered Columbine The stalks are upright, thick, firm, taper, and three or four feet high The leaves are large, and much like those of the Columbine The flowers come out in large panicles from the tops of the stalks, are of a white colour, appear in July, and are succeeded by straight, triangular, pendulent seeds, which will be ripe in August

Variety

There is a variety of this species with purple stalks and flowers

Method of propagation

These are all extremely hardy plants, and the roots of many of them creep very much under the surface, so that their propagation is easy The roots may be parted at any time of the year, but the best season is the autumn, when the stalks decay The roots will then soon get established in their new possessions, and shoot forth strong for flower the spring following

They may also be raised by seeds These may be sown in the autumn, soon after they are ripe, or the spring following, and when the plants are fit to remove, they may be set in the places where they are designed to remain But as they are so easily encreased by parting of the roots, that method of propagating them is most generally followed

Proper soil and situation

They love moist soils and the shade, and being thus situated, they will grow larger than if stationed in a soil of an opposite nature

Titles

1 Great Meadow Rue is titled, *Thalictrum caule folioso sulcato, panicula multiplici crecta* In the *Flora Lapp* it is termed, *Thalictrum pratense* Dodonæus calls it, *Thalictrum magnum*, Caspar Bauhine, *Thalictrum majus, siliqua angulosa striata*, also, *Thalictrum majus flavum, floribus luteis, s glauco folio*, Gerard, *Thalictrum, seu thalictrum majus*, and Parkinson, *Thalictrum vulgare* It grows naturally in meadows, by the sides of rivers, and in moist places, in England and most of the northern parts of Europe

2 The Lesser Meadow Rue is, *Thalictrum foliis sexpartitis, floribus cernuis* In the *Flora Suecia* it is termed, *Thalictrum caule folioso, foliolis caulinis acutis, panicula divaricatâ, floribus nutantibus* Caspar Bauhine calls it, *Thalictrum minus*, Tabernæmontanus, *Ruta pratensis minor*, and Ray, *Thalictrum montanum minus, foliis latioribus* It grows naturally in moist meadows and pastures in England and most countries of Europe

3 Mountain Meadow Rue is, *Thalictrum caule simplicissimo subnudo, racemo simplici terminali* In the *Flora Lapp* it is termed, *Thalictrum caule subnudo simplici, foliolis obtusis* Morison calls it, *Thalictrum montanum minimum præcox, foliis splendentibus*, and Ray, *Thalictrum minimum montanum atro-rubens foliis splendentibus* It grows naturally on the Alps of Lapland and Arvonia

4 Stinking Meadow Rue is, *Thalictrum caule paniculato filiformi ramoso folioso* In the *Hortus Cliffort* it is termed, *Thalictrum caule filiformi ramosissimo, in paniculam dispersa, subjectis foliolis* Caspar Bauhine calls it, *Thalictrum minimum fœtidissimum* It grows naturally in Helvetia, Valesia, and the South of France

5 Tuberous Meadow Rue is, *Thalictrum floribus pentapetalis, radice tuberosâ* Tournefort calls it, *Thalictrum minus, asphodeli radice, magno flore*; Herman, *Thalictrum minus, grumosâ radice, floribus majoribus*, Morison, *Ranunculus thalictri folio, asphodeli radice*, and Caspar Bauhine, *Oenanthe hederæ foliis* It grows naturally in Spain and on the Pyrenees

6 Canada Meadow Rue is, *Thalictrum floribus pentapetalis, radice fibrosâ* Cornutus calls it, *Thalictrum Canadense*, Morison, *Thalictrum majus, foliis aquilegiæ, flore albo*, and Parkinson, *Thalictrum Americanum* It grows naturally in Canada

7 Dioecious Meadow Rue is, *Thalictrum floribus dioicis* It grows naturally in Canada

8 Purple Meadow Rue is, *Thalictrum foliis tripartitis, caule foliis duplo altiore, floribus cernuis* Morison calls it, *Thalictrum Virginianum elatius glaucum, staminibus purpurascentibus* It grows naturally in Virginia and Canada

9 Siberian Meadow Rue is, *Thalictrum foliis tripartitis, foliolis subreflexis argute incisis, floribus cernuis* Seguier calls it, *Thalictrum Alpinum minus saxatile, rutæ folio, staminibus luteis* It grows naturally in Siberia

10 Narrow leaved Meadow Rue is, *Thalictrum foliolis lanceolato linearibus integerrimis* Caspar Bauhine calls it, *Thalictrum pratense, angustissimo folio* It grows naturally in Germany

11 Shining Meadow Rue is, *Thalictrum caule folioso sulcato, foliis linearibus carnosis* Pluknet calls it, *Thalictrum minus lucidum libanotidis coronariæ folio*, Tournefort, *Thalictrum minus alterum Parisiensium, foliis crassioribus & lucidis*, and Clusius, *Thalictrum I vel pratense* It grows naturally in France and Spain

12 Contorted Meadow Rue is, *Thalictrum fructibus pendulis triangularibus contortis, caule subaneipiti* In the *Amænitates Academicæ* it is termed, *Thalictrum hybridum seminibus contortis* It grows naturally in Siberia

13 Columbine-leaved Meadow Rue, or Feathered Columbine, is, *Thalictrum fructibus pendulis triangularibus rectis, caule tereti* In the *Hortus Cliffort* it is termed, *Thalictrum seminibus triangularibus pendulis, stipulis caulinis* Caspar Bauhine calls it, *Thalictrum majus, florum staminibus purpurascentibus*, and John Bauhine, *Thalictrum majus, folliculis angulosis, caule lævi* It inhabits Scania and Helvetia

Class and order in the Linnæan system The characters

*Thalictrum* is of the class and order *Polyandria Polygynia*, and the characters are,

1 Calyx There is none

2 Corolla is four roundish, obtuse, concave, caducous petals

3 Stamina are numerous compressed filaments, which are broadest in the upper parts, longer than the corolla, and have long, erect antheræ

4 Pistillum consists of numerous roundish, pedicellated germens, with thickish stigmas

5 Pericarpium There is none

6 Semina The seeds are many, sulcated, and oval

CHAP

## CHAP. CCCCLV.

## *THAPSIA*, DEADLY CARROT, or SCORCHING FENNEL

Species

OF this genus there are four species, called,
1 Hairy Deadly Carrot, or Scorching Fennel
2 Carrot-leaved Scorching Fennel
3 Digitated Scorching Fennel
4 Trifoliate Scorching Fennel

Hairy Deadly Carrot described

1 Hairy Deadly Carrot, or Scorching Fennel This species hath a thick, fleshy tap-root, like a carrot, it is black without, white within, and full of a bitterish, acrid, milky juice The stalk is round, striated, spongy, jointed, divides into a few branches near the top, and grows to about three feet high The leaves are large, and composed of many long, thick, broad, pointed, hairy, indented segments; they are of a light-green colour, a little downy, and the radical ones spread on the ground The flowers are produced from the ends of the branches in large umbels, are of a yellow colour, appear in June, and the seeds ripen in August

Description of Carrot-leaved,

2 Carrot-leaved Scorching Fennel This species hath a thick, taper root, blackish without, white within, full of an acrid juice, and grows to about two feet high The leaves are composed of many folioles, which are cut into numerous segments, that are narrowest at their base, and stand opposite to each other, they are rough, hairy, and possessed of a glutinous, clammy matter The flowers come out from the tops of the stalks in umbels, are of a yellow colour, appear in July, and the seeds ripen in September The whole plant has a strong, disagreeable odour

Digitated,

3 Digitated Scorching Fennel The root is as thick as a large raddish, yellowish on the outside, white within, and full of an acrid, milky juice The stalk is upright, naked, branching a little near the top, and two or three feet high The leaves are digitated, hairy, and the folioles are cut into a multitude of very narrow segments The flowers are produced in small umbels from the ends of the branches, are large, of a yellow colour, appear in July, and the seeds ripen in September

and Trifoliate Scorching Fennel

4 Trifoliate Scorching Fennel The root is about the thickness of middle-sized raddish, juicy, and strikes deep into the ground The stalk is upright, slender, unbranching, jointed, of a purplish colour, and about two feet high The radical leaves are heart-shaped, but those on the stalk are trifoliate, the folioles are oval and indented, and one leaf only is situated at each joint The flowers are produced from the tops of the stalks in umbels, are of a purple colour, appear in July, and the seeds ripen in September

Varieties

There are several varieties of these species, some being of taller growth than others, a second sort being more hairy, a third having larger leaves, the segments broader and more spreading, and a fourth, larger and finer umbels of flowers

Culture

They are all propagated by sowing the seeds, which is best done in the autumn, soon after they are ripe. They should have a light, fresh earth, and the ground should be double dug for their reception, that the roots may strike deep with more facility They are best sown in drills, two feet asunder for the lowest growers, but three feet for the largest, and they should be lightly covered with the finest mould In the spring, when the plants are all up, they should be thinned to four or five inches distance Here they may stand, with the usual care of weeding and watering in dry weather, all summer, and in the autumn they must be thinned to their proper distances, which should be a foot and a half, or two feet, from each other, in the lines, according to their sizes The drawn-out plants may be made to occupy any other spot where they are wanted, for they bear transplanting well In the spring, the ground between the rows should be dug, and in doing of this let great caution be observed not to injure the roots, and they will then shoot up strong for flowering the summer following In the autumn, when the stalks are decayed, they should be covered up to the crown of the roots, the ground should be dug between the rows, and a little fine mould laid over the tops of the roots This is to be their constant management in winters, and weeding will be the only trouble they will call for in summer, and with such treatment they will every year flower strong, and perfect their seeds

1 Hairy Deadly Carrot, or Scorching Fennel, is titled, *Thapsia foliolis dentatis villosis basi coadunatis* Caspar Bauhine calls it, *Thapsia latifolia villosa*, and Clusius, *Thapsia I* It grows naturally in France, Italy, Spain, and Portugal Titles

2 Carrot-leaved Scorching Fennel is, *Thapsia foliolis multifidis basia ngustatis* Caspar Bauhine calls it, *Thapsia carotæ folio*, and John Bauhine, *Thapsia carotæ effigie* It grows naturally in Spain

3 Digitated Scorching Fennel is, *Thapsia foliis digitatis, foliolis bipinnatis setaceo-multifidis.* Van Royen calls it, *Thapsia foliis pinnatifidis linearibus ad pedunculum communem radiatis*, Morison, *Thapsia tenuifolia, petiolis radiatis*; John Bauhine, *Thapsia Turbit Garganicum, semine latissimo*, Caspar Bauhine, *Panax Asclepium, semine folioso*, and Columna, *Panax Asclepium Apulum* It grows naturally in Apulia

4 Trifoliate Scorching Fennel is, *Thapsia foliis ternatis ovatis* Gronovius calls it, *Sium folio infimo cordato, caulinis ternatis, omnibus crenatis.* It grows naturally in Virginia

*Thapsia* is of the class and order *Pentandria Digynia*, and the characters are, Class and order in the Linnæan system The characters

1 CALYX The general umbel is large, and consists of about twenty rays, which are nearly of equal length The partial consists of the like number of rays, which are nearly equal

There is no involucrum

The perianthium is scarce discernible

2 COROLLA The general flower is uniform, and each floret has five spear shaped, incurved petals

3 STAMINA

3 STAMINA are five capillary filaments the length of the corolla, having simple antheræ

4 PISTILLUM consists of an oblong germen situated below the calyx, and two short styles, with obtuse stigmas

5 PERICARPIUM There is none The fruit is oblong, surrounded longitudinally with a membrane, and divided into two parts

6 SEMINA The seeds are two, large, oblong, convex, pointed at both ends, and have on each side a large, flat, undivided border

# CHAP. CCCCLVI.

## THESIUM.

Species

OF this genus are two perennials, called,

1 Flax-leaved *Thesium*, or Bastard Toad Flax

2 Umbellated *Thesium*

Flax leaved Thesium described

1 Flax leaved *Thesium*, or Bastard Toad Flax The root is hard, fibrous, white, and spreading The stalks are slender, woody near the bottom, of a pale-green colour, and a foot and a half or two feet high The leaves are narrow, spear-shaped, long, and resemble those of Flax The flowers are produced in panicles at the tops of the stalks, are small, of a white colour, appear in June and July, and the seeds ripen in August

Variety

There is a variety of this species with yellow flowers

Umbellated Thesium described

2 Umbellated *Thesium*. The stalks are upright, send forth branches alternately near the top, and grow to be two or three feet high The leaves are oval, spear-shaped, undivided, and grow alternately The flowers are produced in umbels from the tops of the stalks, are of a yellow colour, appear in July and August, and the seeds ripen in the autumn

Method of propagating them

These species are propagated by sowing of the seeds, which should be done in the spring, in beds of light earth made fine They should be covered hardly an eighth part of an inch deep, and if the weather should prove dry afterwards, the beds should be watered in evenings After the plants come up, they will require no trouble, except keeping them clean from weeds all summer and in the autumn they may be removed to the places where they are designed to remain The summer following they will flower, and perfect their seeds

They may also be encreased by parting of the roots, the best time for which is the autumn, though it may be done successfully in the winter, or early in the spring

Both species are extremely hardy, will grow in any soil or situation, but thrive best in light, sandy places

Titles

1 The first species is titled, *Thesium paniculâ foliatâ, foliis lineari-lanceolatis* In the *Hortus Cliffort* it is termed, simply, *Thesium* Sauvages calls it, *Thesium floribus sparsis*, Caspar Bauhine, *Linaria montana, flosculis albicantibus*, also, *Onobrychis IV lutea* Morison names it, *Sesamoides procumbens montanum, linariæ folio, floribus albicantibus*, Clusius, *Anonymos lini folio*, Gerard, *Linaria adulterina*, and Parkinson, *Pseudo linaria montana alba* It grows naturally in dry mountainous pastures in England and most countries of Europe, also in the East

2 The second species is, *Thesium floribus umbellatis, foliis oblongis* Plukenet calls it, *Centaurium luteum alcyro des Virginianum* It grows naturally in the dry pastures of Virginia and Pensylvania

Class and order in the Linnæan system

*Thesium* is of the class and order *Pentandria Monogynia*, and the characters are,

The characters

1 CALYX is a monophyllous, turbinated, permanent perianthium, divided into five nearly spear-shaped, erect, obtuse segments

2 COROLLA There is none The calyx is coloured on the inner side, and by some taken for a corolla

3 STAMINA are five awl-shaped filaments, shorter than the calyx, and inserted in the bottom of the segments, having roundish antheræ

4 PISTILLUM consists of a germen situated below the cup, a filiforme style the length of the stamina, and a thickish, obtuse stigma

5 PERICARPIUM There is none The seed is lodged in the calyx

6 SEMEN The seed is single, roundish, and covered

CHAP

## CHAP. CCCCLVII.

## *THLASPI*, MITHRIDATE MUSTARD, or TREACLE MUSTARD.

OF this genus there are two perennials, called,

Species.
1. Perennial Mithridate Mustard.
2. Mountain Mithridate Mustard.

Description of Perennial: 1. Perennial Mithridate Mustard. The root is slender, fibrous, and creeping. The stalks are slender, six or eight inches long, and incline to the ground. The leaves are oblong, sagittated, and hoary. The flowers are produced in spikes from the tops of the stalks, are small, and of a white or yellow colour; they appear in June or July, and the seeds ripen in August.

and Mountain Mithridate Mustard: 2. Mountain Mithridate Mustard. The root is creeping. The stalks are slender, branching a little, and five or six inches long. The radical leaves are wedge-shaped, smooth, and entire; the upper ones are sagittated, and embrace the stalk with their base. The flowers are produced from the ends of the branches in loose spikes; they are small and of a white colour, appear in June and July, and the seeds ripen in August.

Method of propagation: Whoever is inclined to propagate these plants may easily effect it by sowing the seeds, soon after they are ripe, in any soil or situation; and after the plants come up, they will require no trouble, except keeping them clean from weeds.

Titles: 1. The first species is titled, *Thlaspi siliculis subrotundis pilosis, foliis caulinis sagittatis villosis*. Caspar Bauhine calls it, *Thlaspi villosum, capsulis hirsutis*; John Bauhine, *Thlaspi capsulis hirsutis*; and Ray, *Thlaspi vaccariæ incano folio perenne*. It grows naturally in mountainous places in Wales, France, and Italy.

2. The second species is, *Thlaspi siliculis obcordatis, foliis glabris, radicalibus carnosis obovatis integerrimis, caulinis amplexicaulibus, corollis calyce majoribus*. Sauvages calls it *Thlaspi siliculis obverse cordatis, foliis imis spathulatis, summis amplexicaulibus sagittatis*; Caspar Bauhine, *Thlaspi Alpinum, bellidis cæruleæ folio*; also *Thlaspi montanum, glasti folio, minus*; John Bauhine, *Thlaspi foliis globulariæ*; Column, *Thlaspi montanum, bursæ pastoris fructu*; and Gerard, *Thlaspi incanus alter supini varietas*. It grows naturally on rocky, mountainous places in England, Helvetia, Austria, France, and Italy.

Class and order in the Linnæan system: *Thlaspi* is of the class and order *Tetradynamia Siliculosa*; and the characters are,

The characters:
1. CALYX is a perianthium composed of four oval, concave, erect, spreading, deciduous leaves.
2. COROLLA is cruciforme, and composed of four obovil petals, which have narrow ungues, and are twice the length of the calyx.
3. STAMINA are six filaments about half as long as the corolla, (the two opposite being a little shorter than the others,) having acuminated antheræ.
4. PISTILLUM consists of a roundish, compressed, emarginated germen, a simple style the length of the stamina, and an obtuse stigma.
5. PERICARPIUM is a compressed, obcordated, emarginated pod, having a style the length of the indenture, and containing two cells.
6. SEMINA. The seeds are many, nutant, and affixed to the sutures.

## CHAP. CCCCLVIII.

## *THYMBRA*, MOUNTAIN HYSSOP.

OF this genus there are only two species, called,

Species.
1. Spiked Macedonian Mountain Hyssop.
2. Verticillated Mountain Hyssop.

Spiked Macedonian: 1. Spiked Macedonian Mountain Hyssop. The stalk is woody, divides into several ligneous branches, and grows to about a foot high. The leaves are long, narrow, acute, grow opposite by pairs, and are possessed of a fine and agreeable odour. The flowers are produced from the ends of the branches in thick, close spikes; they are of a purple colour, appear in June and July, and the seeds ripen in the autumn.

and Verticillated Mountain Hyssop described: 2. Verticillated Mountain Hyssop. The stalk is woody, sends forth several slender, ligneous branches, and grows to about a foot high. The leaves are narrow, spear-shaped, entire, spotted, and finely scented. The flowers are produced in whorled ſpikes from the ends of the branches; they are of a purple colour, and ſit cloſe to the ſtalks; they appear in June and July, and the ſeeds ripen in the autumn.

Propagation. They are propagated by ſowing the ſeeds on a ſlight hotbed in the ſpring. When the plants are fit to remove, each ſhould be ſet in a ſeparate pot filled with light earth; the pots ſhould be then ſet in the ſhade, and the following winter the plants muſt be protected from froſts under ſome cover. The ſpring after they may be removed to the places where they are deſigned to remain, reſerving nevertheleſs a few in the pots, to be houſed in winter, in order to continue the ſorts in caſe thoſe abroad ſhould be deſtroyed by bad weather. Their ſituation abroad ſhould be well ſheltered, and the ſoil naturally warm; and if it is of a ſandy gravelly nature, it will be the better.

Titles. The firſt ſpecies is titled, *Thymbra floribus ſpicatis*. Barrelier calls it, *Thymbra ſpicata verior Hiſpanica*; Plukenet, *Thymum majus longifolium, ſtœchadis foliaceo capite purpuraſcente, piloſum*; Moriſon, *Hyſſopus capitata Africana, ſatureja rigido hirſuto folio*; and Dodart, *Satureja hirſuta purpurea olibani*. It grows naturally in Spain, Macedonia, and Mount Libanus.

2. The ſecond ſpecies is, *Thymbra floribus verticillatis*. Caſpar Bauhine calls it, *Hyſſopus anguſtifolia montana aſpera*; and Dalechamp, *Hyſſopus montana*. It grows naturally in many of the ſouthern countries of Europe.

Claſs and order in the Linnæan ſyſtem. *Thymbra* is of the claſs and order *Didynamia Gymnoſpermia*; and the characters are,

The characters. 1. Calyx is a monophyllous bilabiated perianthium. The upper-lip is the broadeſt, and cut into three equal ſegments; the lower lip is narrower, and divided into two parts.

2. Corolla is ringent. The tube is nearly cylindrical; the upper-lip is plane, ſtraight, ſemibifid, and obtuſe; the lower lip is plane, and cut into three nearly equal ſegments.

3. Stamina are four filiforme filaments placed by pairs; the lower pair being a little the ſhorteſt, having two-lobed antheræ under the upper-lip.

4. Pistillum conſiſts of a quadrifid germen, a ſlender ſemibifid ſtyle, and two acute ſtigmas.

5. Pericarpium. There is none.

6. Semina. The ſeeds are four.

## CHAP. CCCCLIX.

## *THYMUS*, THYME.

THE ſpecies of Thyme are uſeful both in the kitchen, phyſic, and flower garden; and therefore I ſhall begin with them here, as they are very uſeful for edgings, or, if planted ſingly among other plants of the like nature, for obſervation. And beſides this, ſome of them have a further claim to this place, as they are preferred by many to join in noſegays, before any other herb in uſe for thoſe purpoſes. The real ſpecies of Thyme therefore are,

Species.
1. *Serpyllum*, or Wild Thyme.
2. Common Garden Thyme.
3. Spaniſh Thyme.
4. Portugal Spear leaved Thyme.
5. Portugal Hairy-leaved Thyme.
6. Maſtich Thyme, or *Marum*.

Of moſt of theſe ſorts there are great varieties; and,

Serpyllum deſcribed. 1. *Serpyllum*, or Wild Thyme. This is the Wild Thyme of our paſtures and heaths, and is the parent of the following ſorts:

Varieties.
Broad leaved Mother of Thyme,
Narrow-leaved Mother of Thyme,
Broad leaved Hairy Mother of Thyme,
Great Purple Wild Thyme,
Rock Thyme,
Scentleſs Wild Thyme,
Lemon Thyme,
Walnut-tree-leaved Scented Thyme,
Shrubby Wild Thyme,
Hoary Thyme,
Variegated Wild Thyme.

Theſe are all accidental varieties; and there will be no certainty, by ſowing the ſeeds of any of the ſorts, of obtaining the like again. Some plants may be expected, but the generality of them will be the Common Wild Thyme, and other or freſh varieties of that ſpecies; ſo that to continue the ſorts perfect, recourſe muſt be had to planting of ſlips from the roots, which may be done with great ſucceſs at any time of the year, but eſpecially in the autumn or ſpring.

Common Thyme deſcribed. 2. Common Thyme. This is the Common Thyme of our kitchen-gardens, and is often raiſed in great plenty for medicinal uſes. There are ſeveral varieties of it, which are divided into two claſſes, called, the Broad-leaved and Narrow-leaved ſorts.

Culture. They are all eaſily raiſed by planting the ſlips in the ſpring, in beds at about ſix or eight inches diſtance from each other, or by ſowing the ſeeds; the latter of which methods is preferable where large quantities are raiſed for kitchen or medicinal purpoſes, as fine young ſeedling plants are of greater force than thoſe raiſed from ſlips taken from old roots.

Spaniſh Thyme. 3. Spaniſh Thyme. There are ſeveral varieties of this ſpecies, but the moſt common has a ſhrubby erect ſtalk, adorned with long narrow leaves, which are ciliated at the baſe. The flowers terminate the branches in ſpikes; they come out in the ſummer, but are not always ſucceeded by good ſeeds in our gardens.

4. Portugal

Portugal Spear leaved,

4 Portugal Spear-leaved Thyme. This hath a low woody stalk, sending forth many stiff hoary branches, about half a foot long. The leaves are small, spear-shaped, narrow, hoary, and grow opposite to each other. The flowers are produced from the ends of the branches in large imbricated heads, though there is a variety of it with heads of flowers very small; their colour is white, they appear in July, and in favourable seasons are succeeded by good seeds in the autumn.

Portugal Hairy leaved,

5 Portugal Hairy-leaved Thyme. The stalks are erect, woody, hairy, and about half a foot long. The leaves are narrow, bristly, hairy, and grow in clusters at the lower-part of the stalks, but higher come out by pairs. The flowers terminate the branches in large scaly heads, the bractea, or leafy scales, are acutely indented, and the flowers are of a purple colour; they appear in July, but it is very rare that they are succeeded by seeds in England.

and Mastick Thyme described

6 Mastick Thyme, or *Marum*. The stalks are shrubby, branching, and grow to about a foot and a half high. The leaves are oval, obtuse, hoary and finely scented. The flowers are produced from the tops of the branches in roundish downy whorls, and there are two varieties of them, the White and Red; they come out in June, but are never succeeded by seeds in England.

Culture

The last four sorts are easily propagated by planting the slips or cuttings in any of the summer months; they should be set at four inches distance from each other, in a shady place, and duly watered until they have taken root. In the autumn remove them to the places where they are to remain, observing always to let them have a dry light soil, and a well sheltered situation, otherwise they will be liable to be destroyed by our hard frosts. For want of such a situation, it would be advisable to plant a few of each sort in pots, to be housed in winter, that in case bad weather should destroy those abroad, these may afford fresh cuttings to continue the succession.

Titles

1 *Serpyllum*, or Wild Thyme, is titled, *Thymus floribus capitatis, caulibus decumbentibus, foliis planis obtusis basi ciliatis*. In the *Hortus Cliffort.* it is termed, *Thymus repens, foliis planis, floribus verticillato spicatis*. Caspar Bauhine calls it, *Serpyllum vulgare minus*; and Dodonæus, *Serpyllum vulgare*. The varieties of it have titles in old authors expressive of their properties, such as, *Serpyllum vulgare majus*, *Serpyllum vulgare, flore albo*, *Serpyllum vulgare, flore amplo*, *Serpyllum angustifolium glabrum*, *Serpyllum vulgare hirsutum*, *Serpyllum foliis citri odore*, and the like. It grows naturally all over England, and most parts of Europe.

2 Common Garden Thyme is, *Thymus erectus, foliis revolutis ovatis, floribus verticillato spicatis*. Caspar Bauhine calls one sort of it, *Thymus vulgaris, folio tenuiore*; another, *Thymus vulgaris, folio latiore*. Dodonæus calls it, *Thymum durius*. It grows naturally in Spain, Italy, and the South of France.

3 Spanish Thyme is, *Thymus floribus verticillato-spicatis, caule suffruticoso erecto, foliis linearibus basi ciliatis*. Caspar Bauhine calls it, *Serpyllum folio thymi*; John Bauhine, *Thymo vulgatiori rigidiori simile*; Barrelier, *Thymum angusto longioreque folio*; and Clusius, *Serpyllum sylvestre Zygis Dioscoridis*. It grows naturally in Spain.

4 Portugal Spear-leaved Thyme is, *Thymus capitulis imbricatis magnis, bracteis ovatis, foliis lanceolatis*. Tournefort calls it, *Thymus Lusitanicus cephalotos, squamis capitulorum amplioribus*; Barrelier, *Tragoriganum, dictamni capite, Hispanicum*. It grows naturally in Portugal and Spain.

5 Portugal Hairy-leaved Thyme is, *Thymus capitulis imbricatis magnis, bracteis dentatis, foliis setaceis pilosis*. Tournefort calls it, *Thymus Lusitanicus, folio capillaceo villoso, capite magno purpurascente oblongo*; also, *Thymus Lusitanicus, folio capillaceo villoso, capite magno purpurascente rotundo*. It grows naturally in Portugal.

6 Mastick Thyme, or *Marum*, is, *Thymus verticillis lanuginosis, dentibus calycinis setaceis pilosis*. Caspar Bauhine calls it, *Sampsucus, sive Marum Masticen redolens*; and Dodonæus, *Marum vulgare, sive clinopodium*. It grows naturally in Spain.

Class and order in the Linnæan system

*Thymus* is of the class and order *Didynamia Gymnospermia*, and the characters are,

The characters

1 CALYX is a monophyllous, tubular, permanent perianthium, divided into two lips, having the mouth hairy and closed. The upper-lip is broad, plane, erect, and indented in three parts; the lower-lip ends in two bristles of equal lengths.

2 COROLLA is a ringent petal. The tube is the length of the calyx, the mouth small, the upper-lip is short, plane, erect, emarginated, and obtuse; the lower lip is longer, broader, patent, obtuse, and cut into three segments, of which the middle one is broadest.

3 STAMINA are four incurved filaments, of which two are longer than the others, having small antheræ.

4 PISTILLUM consists of a quadripartite germen, a filiform style, and a bifid acute stigma.

5 PERICARPIUM. There is none. The seeds are lodged in the calyx.

6 SEMINA. The seeds are small, roundish, and four in number.

CHAP.

# CHAP. CCCCLX.

## *TIARELLA.*

THERE are only two species of this genus, called,

Species 1 Heart-leaved *Tiarella*

2 Trifoliate *Tiarella*

Description of Heart leaved 1 Heart-leaved *Tiarella* The root is fibrous, and creeping The radical leaves are numerous, heart-shaped, and grow on slender footstalks The stalks are naked, slender, and about four or five inches high The flowers come out from the tops of the stalks in loose spikes, they are small, of a greenish-white colour, appear in May and June, and frequently ripen in the autumn

and Trifoliate Tiarella 2 Trifoliate *Tiarella* The root is fibrous, and creeping The radical leaves are trifoliate, and grow on footstalks near the crown of the root The stalks are slender, rough, hairy, five or six inches high, and garnished with two or three small leaves at certain distances from each other The flowers are produced from the tops of the stalks in loose spikes, they appear in May, but are seldom succeeded by ripe seeds in England

Culture These sorts are propagated by parting of the roots, the best time for which is the autumn, though it may be done with success at any time of the year They are extremely hardy, and will grow any where, but delight most in moisture and the shade, and when they are set out will require no trouble, except keeping them clean from weeds, and reducing the roots as often as they become too spreading

1 The first species is titled, *Tiarella foliis cordatis* In the *Hortus Cliffort* it is termed, *Mitella scapo nudo* Herman calls it, *Cortusa Americana, flore spicato, petalis integris* It grows naturally in Asia and America. Titles

2 The second species is, *Tiarella foliis ternatis* In the *Amæn Acad* it is termed, *Mitella foliis ternatis* It grows naturally in Asia

*Tiarella* is of the class and order *Decandria Digynia*, and the characters are, Class and order in the Linnæan system

1 CALYX is a perianthium divided into five oval, acute, permanent parts The characters

2 COROLLA is five oblong petals inserted in the calyx

3 STAMINA are ten filiforme filaments longer than the corolla, and inserted in the calyx, having roundish antheræ

4 PISTILLUM consists of a bifid germen, ending in two short styles, tipped with simple stigmas

5 PERICARPIUM is an oblong capsule, composed of two valves, and containing one cell

6 SEMINA. The seeds are many, oval, and glossy

# CHAP. CCCCLXI.

## *TORMENTILLA*, TORMENTIL.

OF this genus there are only two species, called,

Species 1 Upright Tormentil, or Septfoil

2 Creeping Tormentil

Description of Upright Tormentil 1 Upright Tormentil, or Septfoil The root is very thick, tuberous, knobbed, black without, white within, and hung with numerous slender fibres The stalks are slender, weak, hairy, usually reddish, and about a foot long The leaves are oblong, narrow, serrated, and grow seven together at the joints The flowers come out from the ends and sides of the branches on long slender footstalks, they are of a yellow colour, appear in June and July, and the seeds ripen in August

Medicinal properties The root is one of the most agreeable, as well as best astringents the vegetable world affords

Creeping Tormentil described 2 Creeping Tormentil The stalks are jointed, slender, trail on the ground, and strike root at the joints The leaves are deeply cut at the edges, of a good green colour, and grow on footstalks at the joints The flowers come out from the wings of the leaves at the joints, they are of a yellow colour, appear in July, and the seeds ripen in September

Propagation These sorts are propagated by parting of the roots, which may be done at any time of the year, but more especially in the autumn They will grow in any soil or situation, and when they are set out will require no trouble, except keeping them clean from weeds, and reducing the roots as often as they become too spreading

1 Upright Tormentil, or Septfoil, is titled, *Tormentilla caule erectiusculo, foliis sessilibus* Cammerarius calls it simply, *Tormentilla*, and Caspar Titles

Bauhine,

Bauhine, *Tormentilla sylvestris* It grows naturally on commons and dry pastures in England, and most countries of Europe

2 Creeping Tormentil is, *Tormentilla caule repente, foliis petiolatis* In the former edition of the *Species Plantarum* it is termed, *Tormentilla caule repente* Morison calls it, *Pentaphyllum minus viride, flore aureo tetrapetalo, radiculas in terram e geniculis dimittens*, Plot, *Pentaphyllum reptans alatum, foliis profundius serratis*, and Plukenet, *Pentaphyllum aureum minus, sylvaticum, nostras, foliis tripartito-divisis ex cauliculorum geniculis radicescens* It grows naturally in woods and commons in England

Class and order in the Linnæan system

*Tormentilla* is of the class and order *Icosandria Polygynia*, and the characters are,

The characters

1 CALYX is a monophyllous plane perianthium, divided into eight segments, which are alternately smaller, and more acute

2 COROLLA is four plane obcordated petals, inserted by their ungues into the calyx

3 STAMINA are sixteen awl-shaped filaments half the length of the corolla, and inserted in the calyx, having simple antheræ

4 PISTILLUM consists of eight small germens collected into a head, with filiforme styles the length of the stamina, and inserted into the sides of the germens, crowned by obtuse stigmas

5 PERICARPIUM There is none The receptacle of the seeds is small, and surrounded by the calyx

6 SEMINA The seeds are eight, oblong, and blunt pointed

# CHAP CCCCLXII

## *TOZZIA*

OF this genus there is only one species, called, *Tozzia*

The plant described

The root is thick, squammous, almost round, and hung with many long fibres at the base The stalks are square, and about a foot high The leaves are oval, pointed, slightly indented, have no footstalks, and grow opposite by pairs at the joints The flowers come out singly from the wings of the leaves on short footstalks, they are small, of a yellow colour, appear in June and July, and the seeds ripen in August or September

Its propagation

This species is propagated by offsets from the root, which should be taken off when the stalks decay, and set in the nursery-ground four inches from each other Here they may stand for one or two years, and may then be removed to the places where they are designed to remain They are extremely hardy, and will grow in almost any soil or situation, but delight most in moisture and the shade

This species may be also raised by seeds, which should be sown in pots or boxes, soon after they are ripe, and set in a warm well-sheltered place for the winter In the spring they must have the morning-sun only till ten o'clock, and after the plants come up must be frequently refreshed with water As the days advance in length, they must be removed totally into the shade, kept clean from weeds, watered as often as dry weather shall make it necessary, and in the autumn should be set in beds in the nursery like the offsets, and managed accordingly

Titles

There being no other species of this genus, it stands with the name simply, *Tozzia* Micheli calls it, *Tozzia Alpina lutea, alsines folio, radice squamatâ*; Caspar Bauhine, *Euphrasia lutea alsinefolia, radice squamatâ*, Mentzelius, *Dentaria buguloides, radice globosâ, squamulis myontoideis, Alpina*, Morison, *Orobanche buglossoides, radice rotundâ, squamulis myontoideis, Alpina*, and Columna, *Anonyma, f Gregorii, radice dentariæ* It grows naturally in most rough places on the Pyrenean, Austrian, Helvetian, and Italian mountains

Class and order in the Linnæan system

*Tozzia* is of the class and order *Didynamia Angiospermia*; and the characters are,

The characters

1 CALYX is a very short, monophyllous, tubular, permanent perianthium, indented in five parts at the top

2 COROLLA is one ringent petal The tube is cylindrical, and longer than the calyx, the limb is patent, the upper-lip is bifid, the lower-lip trifid, all the segments being rounded, and nearly equal

3 STAMINA are four filaments hid under the upper-lip, having roundish antheræ

4 PISTILLUM consists of an oval germen, a filiforme style the length and situation of the stamina, and a capitated stigma.

5 PERICARPIUM is a globular capsule, composed of one valve, and containing one cell

6 SEMEN The seed is single, and oval.

## C H A P CCCCLXIII

## *TRACHELIUM*, BLUE UMBELLIFEROUS THROAT-WORT

THERE is only one ſpecies of this genus, uſually called, Blue Umbelliferous Throat-wort.

The plant deſcribed. The root is thick, fleſhy, perennial, and furniſhed with many ſpreading fibres The ſtalks riſe to a foot and a half high The leaves are oval, ſpear ſhaped, ſerrated, and pointed The flowers are produced in umbels from the tops of the ſtalks, they are of a fine blue colour, appear in June and July, and the ſeeds ripen in September

Culture. This is propagated by ſowing the ſeeds in the autumn, ſoon after they are ripe, in beds of light undunged earth Many of the plants will come up before winter, the reſt in the ſpring, and where they appear too cloſe, let them be thinned to proper diſtances All ſummer they muſt be kept clear from weeds, but they will do without watering even in very dry weather, and in the autumn they may be removed to the places where they are deſigned to remain

Proper ſituation. Their ſituation ſhould be in a dry ſandy place, where they will continue for many years, but in rich moiſt ſoils they will periſh ſoon after they have perfected their ſeeds They flouriſh very well on the tops of walls, old buildings, ruins, and the like, and when they are deſigned to occupy ſuch places, the ſeeds ſhould be lodged between the chinks or crevices of the buildings, and they will grow, and the plants live longer in ſuch places than in any ſoil whatſoever in the full ground

Titles. There being no other ſpecies of this genus, it is named ſimply, *Trachelium* In the *Hortus Cliffort* it is termed, *Trachelium foliis ovatis ſerratis, caule umbellâ terminato* Van Royen calls it, *Trachelium foliis ovatis ſerratis, corymbis compoſitis*, and Caſpar Bauhine, *Cervaria valeriano-des cærulea* It grows naturally in ſhady places in Italy and the Eaſt

Claſs and order in the Linnæan ſyſtem. *Trachelium* is of the claſs and order *Pentandria Monogynia*, and the characters are,

The characters.

1 CALYX is a very ſmall perianthium, ſituated above the germen, and divided into five parts

2 COROLLA is one infundibul forme petal The tube is cylindrical, very long, and ſlender, the limb is ſmall, and divided into five oval, concave, ſpreading ſegments

3 STAMINA are five capillary filaments the length of the corolla, having ſimple antheræ

4 PISTILLUM conſiſts of a three-ſided roundiſh germen ſituated below the cup, a filiforme ſtyle double the length of the corolla, and a globular ſtigma

5 PERICARPIUM is a roundiſh, obtuſe, trilobed capſule, formed of three valves, and containing one cell

6 SEMINA The ſeeds are numerous, and very ſmall

## C H A P. CCCCLXIV.

## *TRADESCANTIA*, VIRGINIAN SPIDER-WORT

OF this genus there is one hardy ſpecies, called, Virginian Spider-wort

The plant deſcribed. The root is thick, and furniſhed with many ſpreading fibres The radical leaves are numerous, two feet long, about half an inch broad, pointed, and ſurround one another at the baſe The ſtalk is upright, round, thick, ſmooth, green, jointed, two or three feet high, and adorned with narrow graſs-like leaves, growing ſingly at the joints The flowers come out in cluſters from the tops of the ſtalks, they are large and beautiful, but very fugacious, appearing early in the morning, but fading in the full ſun frequently before noon, however, the ſucceſſion is renewed every morning, ſo that their beauties continue to be exhibited for a month or more They chiefly blow in June, and are ſucceeded by ſeeds, which ripen in the autumn

The

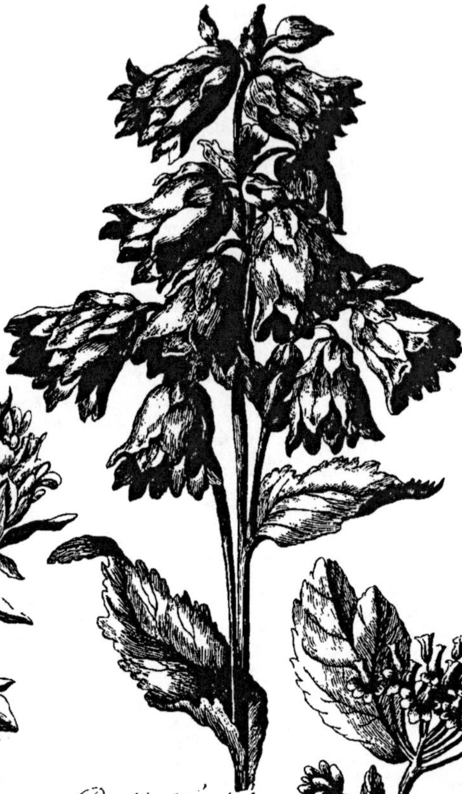

Double Tracheleum.

Purple Shrub Trefoil

Corymbous lobated Spiræa

Varieties The varieties of this species are,
The Pale-blue,
The Deep blue,
The Purple,
The Red,
The White

Culture They are propagated by parting the roots in the autumn, or by sowing the seeds in the spring, in a bed of common mould made fine. When the plants come up, they must be thinned where they are too close, kept clean from weeds all summer, and in the autumn may be removed to the places where they are designed to remain.

Titles This species is titled, *Tradescantia erecta lævis, floribus congestis*. In the *Hortus Cliffort* it is termed simply, *Tradescantia*. Caspar Bauhine calls it, *Allium, seu moly Virginianum*; and Morison, *Ephemerum phalangoides non repens Virginianum gramineum*. It grows naturally in Virginia.

Class and order in the Linnæan System. *Tradescantia* is of the class and order *Hexandria Monogynia*; and the characters are,

The characters. 1. CALYX is a perianthium composed of three oval, concave, patent, permanent leaves.

2. COROLLA is three large, plane, orbicular, equal, patent petals.

3. STAMINA are six filiforme, upright, hairy filaments, the length of the calyx, having reniforme antheræ.

4. PISTILLUM consists of an oval, obtusely three-cornered germen, a filiforme style the length of the stamina, and a three-cornered obtuse stigma.

5. PERICARPIUM is an oval, trivalved, trilocular capsule, covered by the calyx.

6. SEMINA. The seeds are few, and angular.

# CHAP. CCCCLXV.

## *TRAGOPOGON*, GOAT's BEARD.

Of this genus there is one lasting species, called, the French Goat's Beard.

This plant described. This is a low perennial, the stalk rising only to four or five inches high. The leaves are deeply indented, in the manner of those of Dandelion, but they are very rough and downy. The flowers are large, purple underneath, and their upper-parts are of a pale-yellow colour; they will be in blow in June or July, and their seeds ripen in the autumn.

Varieties. There are two or three varieties of this species; one has a sulphur-coloured flower, and another has leaves that are more deeply jagged on the edges.

Method of propagation. They are propagated by parting of the roots in the autumn or spring; they love a light soil, and a shady situation, and being thus stationed, they will call for no trouble, except keeping them clean from weeds.

Title. This species is titled, *Tragopogon calycibus monophyllis corollâ brevioribus inermibus, foliis runcinatis*. Caspar Bauhine calls it, *Hieracium asperum, flore magno dentis leonis*; John Bauhine, *Hedypnois Monspessulana*; Barrelier, *Hieracium sulphureum, incisis foliis, montanum*; and Dalechamp, *Hieracium magnum*. It grows naturally in Spain and Narbonne.

Class and order in the Linnæan system. *Tragopogon* is of the class and order *Syngenesia Polygamia Æqualis*; and the characters are,

The characters. 1. CALYX. The general calyx is simple, and composed of eight spear-shaped equal leaves, which are alternately larger, and join at the base.

2. COROLLA. The general flower is imbricated and uniform. The florets are many, and each consists of a tongue shaped truncated petal, indented at the top in five parts.

3. STAMINA consist of five very short filaments, with a cylindrical tubular anthera.

4. PISTILLUM consists of an oblong germen, a filiforme style the length of the stamina, and two revolute stigmas.

5. PERICARPIUM. There is none. The seeds are contained in the swoln connivent calyx.

6. SEMINA. The seeds are single, oblong, slender at both ends, angular, rough, and crowned by a feathery down.

The receptacle is naked, plane, and rough.

## C H A P CCCCLXVI.

## *TRIENTALIS*, CHICKWEED-FLOWERED WINTER-GREEN.

THERE is only one species of this genus, called, Chickweed-flowered Winter-green

The plant described — The root is composed of numerous long, white fibres The radical leaves are spear-shaped, pointed, entire, and about an inch and a half long The stalk is round, smooth, slender, about four or five inches high, and garnished at the top with six or seven small leaves, growing circularly on short footstalks The flowers come out from the tops of the stalks on long slender footstalks, they are of a white colour, appear in May and June, and the seeds ripen in July

Method of propagation — This plant grows naturally in woods, commons, &c and is not propagated Its culture, however, may be easily effected by sowing the seeds, soon after they are ripe, in some moist shady place, and after the plants come up, they will require no trouble except keeping them clean from weeds

Titles — This species is titled, *Trientalis foliis lanceolatis integerrimis* In the *Hortus Cliffort* it is termed simply, *Trientalis* Caspar Bauhine calls it, *Pyrola, alsines flore, Europaea*, also, *Pyrola, alsines flore, minor Brasiliana*; John Bauhine, *Herba Trientalis*, and Ray, *Alsinanthemos* It is a native of England, and most of the northern countries of Europe

Class and order in the Linnean system — *Trientalis* is of the class and order *Heptandria Monogynia*, and the characters are,

The characters —
1 Calyx is a perianthium composed of seven spear shaped, pointed, patent, permanent leaves
2 Corolla is stellated, plane, and consists of one petal, divided to the very base into seven oval spear-shaped parts
3 Stamina are seven capillary filaments the length of the calyx, and inserted into the corolla, having simple antheræ
4 Pistillum consists of a globular germen, a filiforme style the length of the stamina, and a capitated stigma
5 Pericarpium is a capsular, juiceless, globular berry, containing one cell
6 Semina The seeds are few, and angular The receptacle is large, and excavated for the reception of the seeds

## C H A P. CCCCLXVII

## *TRIFOLIUM*, TREFOIL.

Species — OF this genus are,
1 Honeysuckle Trefoil, or Clover
2 White Trefoil, or Dutch Clover
3 Tall Oriental Trefoil
4 Mountain Trefoil
5 Swedish Trefoil
6 White Meadow Trefoil
7 Downy Trefoil
8 Strawberry Trefoil

Honeysuckle Trefoil described — 1 Honeysuckle Trefoil, or Clover The stalks are slender, branching, hairy, and about two feet high Each of the leaves consists of three large folioles, which join together at the base, and grow upon long slender footstalks The flowers come out in tufts, shoots, or spikes, from the ends of the branches, they are monopetalous, of a reddish-purple colour, and frequently replete with a honey juice, they appear in May, are in full blow in June, and are to be met with occasionally in our meadows and pastures until the end of summer

Varieties — There are many varieties of this species, but that with purple leaves, and the White flowered Clover, are the only sorts that are introduced into gardens

White Trefoil — 2 White Trefoil, or Dutch Clover. This plant is of lower growth than the former, but exceeds it in value for laying-down of ploughed land, it grows closer, the roots spread themselves, strike root at the joints, and soon overspread the whole spot, though the seeds be sown thinly at first, and as it is deemed the most excellent food for cattle, fattens them the soonest, and causes them to give the greatest quantity of milk, it is now used more than any of the sorts, for the laying-down the ploughed lands upon the enclosure of common fields

Tall Oriental Clover — 3 Tall Oriental Clover The stalks are upright, hollow, and two or three feet high The foliolets are obversely oval, and serrated on the edges The flowers come out in roundish heads supported by long footstalks, they are of a white colour, appear in May, and continue in succession until September

Thus

This is by many supposed to be a variety only of the former species

Mountain. 4 Mountain Trefoil The root is thick, and sweet to the taste The leaves are composed of three narrow spear shaped folioles, and form a large tuft at the crown of the roots The stalks are simple, undivided, and five or six inches high The flowers come out in roundish heads from the tops of the stalks, they are large, appear early in summer, and frequently shew themselves in September and the autumn

Swedish, 5 Swedish Trefoil The stalk is upright, branching, and two feet high The leaves are oval, oblong, spear shaped, and slightly serrated on the edges The flowers come out from the ends of the branches in roundish hairy spikes, they are of a red colour, appear in June and the seeds ripen in August

White, 6 White Meadow Trefoil The stalks are upright, branching, and about two feet high The leaves are spear-shaped, and serrated on the edges The flowers are produced from the ends of the branches in short roundish spikes, they are of a white colour, appear in June and July, and the seeds ripen in August

Downy, 7 Downy Trefoil The stalks are slender, branching, and recumbent The leaves are oval, obtuse, smooth, and indented The flowers are produced in small heads from the wings of the leaves on very short footstalks; their cups are very downy inflated, and obtuse, they appear in June, and the seeds ripen in August

and Strawberry Trefoil described 8 Strawberry Trefoil The stalks lie on the ground, and strike root at the joints The leaves are roundish, and a little serrated on the edges The flowers are collected into roundish heads, standing on long slender footstalks, they are of a whitish-blush colour, and appear chiefly in July and August

The heads of this species bear some resemblance to Strawberries, hence the name Strawberry Trefoil has been applied to the plant

Culture These sorts are all raised by sowing the seeds in the spring If the seeds are good they will quickly come up, and after that they will require no trouble, except thinning them when they are too close, and keeping them clean from weeds

Titles 1 Honeysuckle Trefoil, or Clover is titled, *Trifolium spicis subvillosis, cinctis stipulis oppositis membranaceis, corollis monopetalis* In the *Hortus Cliffort* it is termed, *Trifolium spicis villosis, caule diffuso, foliolis integerrimis*, in the *Flora Lapp Trifolium pratense, flore monopetalo* Caspar Bauhine calls it, *Trifolium pratense purpureum*, Ray, *Trifolium pratense purpureum minus foliis cordatis*, also, *Trifolium purpureum majus sativum, pratense simile*, Gerard, *Trifolium pratense*, and Parkinson, *Trifolium pratense vulgare* It grows naturally in meadows and pastures in England, and most countries of Europe

2 White Trefoil, or Dutch Clover, is, *Trifolium capitulis umbellatibus, leguminibus tetraspermis, caule repente* In the *Hortus Cliffort* it is termed, *Trifolium capitulis subrotundis, flosculis pedunculatis, leguminibus tetraspermis, caule procumbente* Caspar Bauhine calls it, *Trifolium pratense album* and Rivinus, *Trifolium repens* It grows naturally in meadows and pastures all over Europe

3 Tall Oriental Trefoil is, *Trifolium capitulis umbellatibus, leguminibus tetraspermis, caule adscendente* Vaillant calls it, *Trifolium orientale altissimum, caule fistuloso, flore albo* It grows naturally in the East

4 Mountain Trefoil is, *Trifolium scapo nudo, leguminibus dispermis pendulis, foliis linearibus-lanceolatis* In the *Hortus Cliffort* it is termed, *Trifolium scapo nudo simplicissimo foliis linearibus lanceolatis* Caspar Bauhine calls it, *Trifolium Alpinum, flore magno, radice dulci*, and Haller, *Anonis* [illegible] *floribus longissimis, foliis non serratis* It grows naturally on the Helvetian and Italian mountains

5 Swedish Trefoil is, *Trifolium spicis subglobosis villosis terminalibus* [illegible], *caule erecto, foliis lanceolatis serrulatis* Van Royen calls it, *Trifolium spicis villosis subovatis, caule erecto, foliis ovato-oblongis integerrimis*, Caspar Bauhine, *Trifolium montanum purpureum majus*, Clusius, *Trifolium majus*, and John Bauhine *Trifolium majus non album sed rubrum* It grows naturally in most countries of Europe

6 White Meadow Trefoil is, *Trifolium spicis subimbricatis* [illegible], *vexillis subulatis emarcescentibus, calycibus* [illegible], *caule erecto* In the *Flora Suecica* is termed, *Trifolium capitulis terminalibus, corollarum vexillis subulatis, caule erecto, foliis lanceolatis serrulatis* Caspar Bauhine calls it, *Trifolium montanum album*, and Fuchsius, *Trifolium pratense album* It grows naturally in dry meadows and pastures in most countries of Europe

7 Downy Trefoil is, *Trifolium capitulis sessilibus globosis tomentosis, calycibus inflatis obtusis* Magnol calls it, *Trifolium fragiferum tomentosum*, and John Bauhine, *Trifolium glomerulis tomentosis per caulium longitudinem* It grows naturally in France, Italy, Portugal, and Spain

8 Strawberry Trefoil is, *Trifolium capitulis subrotundis, calycibus inflatis bidentatis reflexis, caulibus repentibus* Caspar Bauhine calls it, *Trifolium capitulo spumoso aspero minus*, also, *Trifolium fragiferum Frisicum*, John Bauhine, *Trifolium caule nudo, glomerulis glabris*, Gerard, *Trifolium fragiferum*, and Morison, *Trifolium fragiferum purpureum folio oblongo* It grows naturally in moist meadows and pastures in England, Sweden, and Gaul

*Trifolium* is of the class and order *Diadelphia Decandria*, and the characters are, Class and order in the Linnæan system The character.

1 CALYX is a monophyllous, tubular, permanent perianthium, indented in five parts at the top

2 COROLLA is papilionaceous The vexillum is reflexed, the alæ are shorter than the vexillum, the carina is shorter than the alæ

3 STAMINA are diadelphous filaments, three being joined in a body, the other single, having simple antheræ

4 PISTILLUM consists of a nearly oval germen, an awl shaped rising style, and a simple stigma

5 PERICARPIUM is a short pod formed of one valve

6 SEMINA The seeds are very few and roundish

## CHAP. CCCCLXVIII

## *TRIGLOCHIN*, ARROW-HEADED GRASS.

OF this genus there are only two species, called,

Species
1 Arrow headed Grass
2 Sea Spiked Grass

Description of Arrow-headed, 1 Arrow-headed Grass The leaves are numerous at the crown of the root, round, hollow, erect, and about six inches long The stalks are round, unbranching, upright, and about a foot high The flowers are produced in loose spikes from the sides of the stalks almost half their length, they are of a greenish colour, and appear chiefly in July and August

and Sea Spiked Grass 2 Sea Spiked Grass The leaves are numerous, narrow, flat on the upper side, rounded underneath, of a dusky-green colour, and about six inches long The stalks are round, rushy, green, and eight or ten inches high The flowers are produced in spikes from the tops of the stalks, they are of a greenish colour, and appear in May and June

These grasses grow naturally in some meadows and pastures, and are never cultivated

Titles 1 The first species is titled, *Triglochin capsulis trilocularibus sublinearibus* In the *Flora Lapp* it is termed, *Triglochin fructu tenui* Caspar Bauhine calls it, *Gramen junceum spicatum, s Triglochin*, John Bauhine, *Gramen Triglochin*, Dalechamp, *Calamagrostis IV*, Tournefort, *Juncago palustris & vulgaris*, Micheli, *Juncago maritima perennis, bulbosa radice*, Barrelier, *Juncago maritima*, and Gerard, *Gramen marinum spicatum* It grows naturally in moist meadows and pastures in England, and most countries of Europe

2 The second species is, *Triglochin capsulis sexlocularibus ovatis* In the *Flora Lapp* it is termed, *Triglochin fructu subrotundo* Micheli calls it, *Juncago palustris et maritima perennis, fructu breviore quinque capsulari*, Caspar Bauhine, *Gramen junceum & spicatum alterum*, and Lobel, *Gramen marinum spicatum* It grows naturally in the salt marshes in England, and the like situations in most countries of Europe

*Triglochin* is of the class and order *Hexandria Trigynia*, and the characters are, Class and order in the Linnæan system

1 CALYX is a perianthium composed of three roundish, obtuse, concave, deciduous leaves The characters

2. COROLLA is three oval, concave, obtuse leaves, similar to those of the calyx

3 STAMINA are six very short filaments, having the like number of antheræ, which are shorter than the corolla

4 PISTILLUM consists of a large germen without any style, but three or more reflexed plumose stigmas

5 PERICARPIUM is an oval, oblong, obtuse capsule, containing the like number of cells as there are stigmas

6 SEMINA The seeds are single, and oblong

## CHAP. CCCCLXIX

## *TRILLIUM*, THREE-LEAVED NIGHTSHADE, or HERB TRUE-LOVE of CANADA

THERE are three species of this genus, called,

Species
1 Nodding flowered Carolina *Trillium*
2 Canada *Trillium*
3 Virginian *Trillium*

Nodding-flowered Carolina Trillium, 1 Nodding-flowered Carolina *Trillium* The root is thick, tuberous, and possessed of many fibres The stalk is simple, naked, and about six inches high The leaves are three, at the top of the stalk, they are oval, smooth, of a deep-green colour, and grow spreading from each other, in the form of a triangle, on short footstalks The flowers come out singly on short nodding footstalks, arising from the center of the three leaves, they are of a whitish-green colour on the outside, and a kind of flesh colour within, they appear in April, and the seeds ripen in July

2 Canada

Canada

2 Canada *Trillium* The stalk is upright, and about a foot high The leaves are three in number, at the top of the stalk, they are of a deep-green colour, and disposed in the manner of the former The flowers come out singly on erect footstalks, which arise from the center of the leaves, they are greenish on the outside, and purplish within, they appear in April or May, and are succeeded by roundish succulent berries, which ripen in July or August

and Virginian Trillium described

3 Virginian *Trillium* The stalk is smooth, usually of a purplish colour, and eight or ten inches high. The leaves are long, sharp-pointed, and three of them are situated at the top of the stalk, in the manner of the former The flowers are situated singly in the bosom of the leaves, having no footstalk, their petals are long, narrow, and their position upright, the outer ones, which are the leaves only of the calyx, are green, the other of a dark purple, they appear about the same time with the former, and the seeds ripen accordingly.

Culture

These are best propagated by sowing the seeds, soon after they are ripe They often remain two years before they come up, during which time the ground must be kept clean from weeds When the plants come up, the usual care of watering them in dry weather, and keeping them clean from weeds, must attend them, and in the autumn they may be transplanted to the places where they are designed to remain

Their situation should be moist and shady

Titles

1 The first species is titled, *Trillium flore pedunculato cernuo* Catesby calls it, *Solanum triphyllum, flore hexapetalo carneo*, and Colden, *Paris foliis ternis, flore pedunculato nutante* It grows naturally in Carolina

2 The second species is, *Trillium flore pedunculato erecto* In the *Amæn Acad* it is termed, *Paris foliis ternis, flore pedunculato erecto* Caspar Bauhine calls it, *Solanum triphylium Brasilianum*, Cornutus, *Solanum triphyllum Canadense*, and Morison, *Solano congener triphyllum Canadense* It grows naturally in Virginia

3 The third species is, *Trillium flore sessili erecto* Gronovius calls it, *Paris foliis ternatis, flore sessili erecto*, Plukenet, *Solanum Virginianum triphyllum, flore tripetalo atro purpureo in foliorum sinu, absque pediculo, sessili*, and Catesby, *Solanum triphyllum, flore hexapetalo tribus petalis purpureis, cæteris viridibus reflexis* It grows naturally in Virginia and Carolina

Class and order in the Linnæan system

*Trillium* is of the class and order *Hexandria Trigynia*, and the characters are,

The characters

1 CALYX is a perianthium composed of three oval, patent, permanent leaves

2 COROLLA is three suboval petals, somewhat larger than the calyx

3 STAMINA are six awl shaped upright filaments shorter than the calyx, having oblong antheræ of the same length

4 PISTILLUM consists of a roundish germen, and three filiforme recurved styles, with simple stigmas

5 PERICARPIUM is a roundish berry, containing three cells

6 SEMINA The seeds are many, and roundish.

## CHAP. CCCCLXX.

## *TRYOSTEUM*, FEVER ROOT, Dr TINKER's WEED, or FALSE IPECACUANHA.

OF this genus there are only two known species, called,

Species.

1 Perfoliate *Triosteum*

2 Narrow-leaved *Triosteum*

Perfoliate

1 Perfoliate *Triosteum* The root consists of numerous, thick, fleshy, rough, contorted fibres The stalks are woody, firm, jointed, and about two feet high The leaves are oblong, broad, grow opposite by pairs at the joints, and embrace the stalk with their base The flowers are produced in whorls, sitting close in the bosom of the leaves, having no footstalks, they are small, and of a dark-red or purplish colour, they appear early in June, and are succeeded by round yellow berries, which ripen in the autumn

and Narrow-leaved Triosteum described

2. Narrow-leaved *Triosteum* The stalks are herbaceous, jointed, and about a foot and a half high The leaves are spear shaped, long, narrow, and grow opposite at the joints The flowers come out singly from the wings of the leaves on short footstalks, they are of a yellow colour, appear in June, and the seeds ripen in the autumn

Medicinal properties

The roots of both these species are emetic, and frequently substituted in the room of the true *Ipecacuanha*, they pass in America by the name of Dr Tinker's Weed, who first discovered their use and virtue

Culture

They are propagated by sowing the seeds in the autumn, soon after they are ripe, in beds of light earth The seeds sometimes remain in the ground until the second spring after sowing before they make their appearance, which directs us to let the ground remain unmolested, only kept clean from weeds When the plants come up they must be shaded, kept clean from weeds, duly watered all summer, and in the autumn may be removed to the places where they are designed to remain

They are also propagated by parting of the roots, which may be done in the autumn, or early in the spring, before the stalks arise Their situation

situation should be moist, and in the shade, otherwise they will make very little progress

Titles

1 The first species is titled, *Triosteum floribus verticillatis sessilibus* Dillenius calls it, *Triosteospermum, latiore folio, flore rutilo* It grows naturally in the woods of North America

2 The second species is, *Triosteum floribus oppositis pedunculatis* Gronovius calls it, *Lonicera humilis hirsuta, caule obsolete rubente quadrato, foliis lanceolatis adversis, flore luteo ad alas unico* and Plukenet, *Periclymenum herbaceum rectum Virginianum* It grows naturally in Virginia

Class and order in the Linnæan System The characters

*Triosteum* is of the class and order *Pentandria Monogynia*, and the characters are,

1 Calyx is a permanent perianthium situated above the germen, and divided into five spear-shaped parts, which are as long as the corolla

2 Corolla is one tubular petal The limb is shorter than the tube, it is erect, and divided into five roundish lobes, the lower ones being the smallest

3 Stamina are five filiforme filaments the length of the corolla, having oblong antheræ

4 Pistillum consists of a roundish germen situated below the calyx, a cylindrical style the length of the stamina, and a thickish stigma

5 Pericarpium is an oval, nearly three-cornered, trilocular berry

6 Semen The seed is single, osseous, obtusely three-cornered, sulcated, and obtuse

## CHAP CCCCLXXI

## *TRITICUM*, WHEAT

OF this genus there are three perennials, called,

Species

1 Couch Grass, Quick Grass, Dog's Grass, or Wheat Grass

2 Rush Wheat Grass

3 Sea Wheat Grass

Common Couch Grass described

1 The first is the Common Couch Grass, Quick Grass, Dog's Grass, or Wheat Grass This is that well known troublesome grass which overspreads all neglected gardens, fields, &c and affords so much toil to the gardener and husbandman to eradicate it out of his possessions It is too well known to need any description, but the root, troublesome as it is to the gardener, is of excellent virtue, being a fine diuretic and attenuant, and is frequently used in medicine, but principally in aperient spring-drinks for sweetening of the blood

Medicinal properties

The other two species are insignificant grasses, which are never cultivated, so that I shall pass them over with barely giving their titles, for the satisfaction of those who may expect to find them in this place

Titles

1 The first sort is titled, *Triticum calycibus subulatis quadrifloris acuminatis* In the *Flora Lapp* it is termed, *Triticum radice repente, foliis viridibus* Caspar Bauhine calls it, *Gramen caninum arvense, s Gramen Dioscoridis*, Ray, *Gramen spica triticea repens vulgare, caninum dictum*, Gerard, *Gramen caninum*; and Parkinson, *Gramen caninum vulgatius* It grows every-where in tillage-fields in England, and all other countries of Europe

2 The second is titled, *Triticum calycibus truncatis quinquefloris, foliis involutis* Caspar Bauhine calls it, *Gramen tritic. spicâ mutic similis* It grows naturally in most of the southern countries of Europe, and in the East

3 The third is titled, *Triticum calycibus multifloris, flosculis mucronatis, spicâ ramosâ* Van Royen calls it, *Poa paniculâ ramosa, floribus alternis sessilibus*, Caspar Bauhine, *Gramen maritimum paniculâ loliaceâ*, and Scheuchzer, *Gramen loliaceum, paniculâ ramosâ, maritimum* It grows naturally in the maritime parts of France and Gaul

*Triticum* is of the class and order *Triandria Digynia*, and the characters are,

Class and order in the Linnæan System The characters

1 Calyx is a glume composed of two oval obtuse, concave valves, and containing about three flowers

2 Corolla is two nearly equal valves, as large as the calyx The exterior valve is ventricose and pointed, and the interior one is plane

3 Stamina are three capillary filaments, having oblong bifurcated antheræ

4 Pistillum consists of a turbinated germen, and two capillary reflexed styles, with plumose stigmas

5 Pericarpium There is none The corolla cherishes the seed, opens, and sends it forth when ripe

6 Semen The seed is single, oval, oblong, obtuse at both ends, convex on one side, and furrowed on the other

CHAP

# CHAP. CCCCLXXII

## *TROLLIUS*, GLOBE *RANUNCULUS*.

THERE are only two species of this genus, distinguished by the names of,

Species

1 The European Globe Flower

2 The Asiatic Globe Flower

European

1 The European Globe Flower This species goes under different names in different places In some parts it is called the Globe *Ranunculus*; in others, the Double Crow-flower, and the Globose Crow-foot Others, again, know it by no other name than *Locker Gowlans*, and many call it the Troll flower, *Trollius* The Gardener now will be certain what this species is which is under consideration, and he may be instructed that the most natural English name for this plant is the Globe Flower, is referring to no other genus, and to distinguish it from the other, the word European should be added, which makes it a compleat title The European Globe Flower hath a small root, composed of several black fibres, from which spring several leaves, with long footstalks, of a fine deep-green colour, these in their general figure are nearly round, but they are cut almost to the bottom into five principal parts, which are also divided, and deeply notched at the edges The flower-stalk rises to about two feet in height, it is usually of a pale-green colour, smooth, round, hollow, and is divided into branches near the top, for the support of the different flowers, besides which it is ornamented with leaves, that sit close, having no footstalks The stalks divide into a few other branches only, that are smaller near the top, and each is crowned by a large, yellow, globular flower, standing naked, with great singularity and beauty, on its own separate footstalk Each flower is composed of several large concave petals, which so turn inwards, that they appear folded or rolled up together; and thus they constitute at first a perfect sphere or globe, being entirely closed at the top, and which afterwards expands, and opening, discloses the stamina, but still retaining its round shape, though not in so perfect a degree The petals that compose each flower are generally ten or twelve, they are of a golden yellow colour The plant will be in blow by the beginning of June, and the seeds ripen in August

and Asiatic Globe Flower described

2 The Asiatic Globe Flower This plant hath not such a just right to that appellation as the first species, for the petals spread open, in the essential characters, however it differs in no respect from that, proving itself thereby to be of the same family, and for distinction is called the Asiatic *Trollius*, or Globe Flower The leaves are large, growing upon long footstalks, and their colour is a pale but fine green, they resemble those of the Aconite, and are divided like them, being cut into larger and not so many parts as the former sort As the petals do not converge like the other, the stamina have a very pretty effect in this flower, and the nectaria are very singular These flowers are of an elegant saffron colour, and will be in blow in May, tho' they will not always produce seeds

This species naturally loves moisture, so that it should be planted in a cool shady border, where it will be more vigorous, flower stronger, and be most likely to produce seeds, which, in such a situation, it sometimes does to perfection — Proper situation and soil

Both these species are easily propagated by parting of the roots, or sowing the seeds September is the best season for the former, though it may be done any time in the winter or spring, and they will grow very well, and as a couple of plants of each sort will be sufficient to join in the collection, if the offsets can be obtained, this will be the easiest and best way When more plants are wanted, or they are raised for sale, the most expeditious way of having plenty is to sow the seeds A rich border of common garden mould made fine, in a cool part of the garden, is proper for them, and if they are covered hardly half an inch deep, they will come up, and grow exceedingly well They may be sown soon after they are ripe, or kept until the end of February, the latter of which I rather prefer, because if they are sown early in August they often come up that autumn, and are liable, without the care of covering in winter is bestowed on them, to be thrown out of the ground by the frosts When they are planted out finally, the worst and coldest part of the garden should be allotted them Our Globe Flower grows common by the sides of ditches in Wales, and many parts of the North, which directs us to its culture and situation in gardens, and the Asiatic sort is no less fond (if the term may be allowed) of such low life, but which nevertheless ought to enhance its esteem with the Gardener, for growing and flourishing where most other plants will not, they thereby keep the meanest part not unoccupied, or destitute of ornament and splendor — Method of propagating them

Titles.

1 The European Globe Flower is titled, *Trollius corollis conniventibus nectariis longitudine staminum* In the *Flora Suecia* it is termed, *Helleborus flore clauso erecto petalato, caule simplicissimo*, in the *Hortus Cliffort* *Helleborus foliis angulatis multifidis, flore globoso* Gerard calls it, *Ranunculus globosus*, Dodonæus, *Ranunculus flore globoso*, and Caspar Bauhine, *Ranunculus montanus aconiti-folio, flore globoso* It grows common in many parts of the North of England, and Wales, by the sides of mountains, ditches, and woods, and in such places it is also found in Sweden, and in many parts of Germany

2 The Asiatic Globe Flower is titled, *Trollius corollis patentibus, nectariis longitudine petalorum* Buxbaum calls it, *Trollius humilis, flore patulo*; Tournefort, *Helleborus niger orientalis, ranunculi folio, flore nequaquam globoso*, and Amman *Helleborus aconiti folio, flore globoso croceo* It grows naturally in Siberia and Cappadocia

*Trollius* is of the class and order *Polyandria Polygynia*, and the characters are, — Class and order in the Linnæan system

1 CALYX There is none

The characters



10 I 2 COROLLA

2 Corolla conſiſts of about fourteen nearly oval connivent petals, and nine narrow, plane, incurved, umbilicated nectaria, that are perforated near the baſe on the inſide

3 Stamina are numerous briſtly filaments ſhorter than the corolla, having erect antheræ

4 Pistillum conſiſts of numerous germina, ſitting cloſe in a columnar form, having no ſtyle, but are terminated by pointed ſtigmas

5 Pericarpium conſiſts of numerous oval capſules, collected into a head

6 Semina The ſeeds are ſingle

## CHAP CCCCLXXIII.

## *TULIPA*, The TULIP

THIS delightful genus, which affords ſuch endleſs variety for the Floriſt, is poſſeſſed of about one or two more real ſpecies than that to which that prodigious variety belongs, and which would be looked upon as excellent flowers, were they not ſo much out ſtripped in beauty by theſe uncommonly elegant and well-known flowers

The Tulip, with its few real ſpecies, but almoſt infinite varieties, that ſo much engage the attention of the curious, is of Turkiſh extraction, and has been known in Europe a little more than two hundred years Geſner mentions a Tulip that he ſaw in blow at Augſburg in the year 1559, which was raiſed from ſeeds brought from Conſtantinople Indeed it is no wonder that ſo fine a flower ſhould employ the ſkill of the beſt gardeners in its increaſe, for not very long after, we find many ſorts of the Tulip mentioned by botanic writers, all which appear to be but poor flowers in compariſon of our preſent ſorts And though I mention theſe as poor flowers, it muſt be comparatively only; for the very worſt ſort, were they not outſtripped by ſuch a profuſion, has charms enough to recommend it So large a flower elevated upon a firm and elegant ſtalk, compoſed of ſuch large broad petals, let their figure or colour be what it will, would be very engaging, whilſt backed with novelty Whether diligence was afterwards uſed in procuring bulbs from their native places of growth, and whether the few plants then in Europe were multiplied by ſeeds, is not certain It was not long, however, before they became pretty well known to authors, and the ſorts became ſo different, that I make no doubt, beſides the varieties of our own raiſing, ſeveral ſorts were ſent us from abroad For Cluſius, about twenty years after, mentions a Double Tulip, which probably had been ſent into Europe by the bulb This was but a poor Tulip, as Tulips go now, being compoſed of a double ſeries of petals, and its colour was a bad green Beſler, who wrote after this, mentions two more Double Tulips, one with a red, and another with a yellow flower, whence it appears, that the Double Tulips are nearly of as long ſtanding as any in the European gardens

*Whence and when Tulips were firſt introduced into and cultivated in Europe*

From the extraordinary beauty of this flower, it has led many to fancy it to be the Lily of the Field mentioned by our Saviour, where he ſays, that "Solomon, in all his glory, was not arrayed like one of them" But theſe perſons ſhould conſider that the very meaneſt flower, which the Almighty has cloathed in his wiſdom, exceeds any thing that Art can reach in human contrivance It does not appear, however, that the Tulip ever grew naturally in Judea, nor, tho' it is a plant of ſuch ſingular beauty that it was ever known to the antients at all The Greeks make no mention of it, neither is there any word in all that language by which we can ſuppoſe they mean to expreſs it, though it was a native of their own country, and in many parts abounded in its native luxuriancy and wildneſs What makes this more extraordinary is, that the Greeks were remarkable for their botanic ſkill in the former ages (if the term for ſo early an age may be allowed), were great admirers of plants, and very ſtudious of their virtues and uſes This has induced ſome to believe, that the plant which Theophraſtus has praiſed ſo much (though without any real deſcription) for its invigorating qualities, muſt be the Tulip But this is a wild conjecture, for it does not appear that any part of the Tulip, either bulb, ſtalk, leaves, or flower, is or ever was poſſeſſed of ſuch qualities Neither is there any plant deſcribed by him, that can in any reſpect be made to belong to the Tulip, nor does it appear that that great botaniſt, his cotemporaries, predeceſſors, or ſucceſſors, knew any thing of this plant Thoſe perſons judge more reaſonably, who think the plant thus celebrated is the *Ginſeng* of our times, the virtues of which, Theophraſtus ſays, an Indian taught him

*Enquiry whether this plant was known to the antients*

As this plant was ſo little known to the antients, it is no wonder we find it undeſcribed It is uncertain how long the word Tulip has been uſed for this flower It ſeems to be formed of the Turkiſh word *Tulpent*, which, it is ſaid, ſignifies a turban But why it ſhould be called the Tulip, or Turban-flower, is not eaſy to gueſs, as its figure is very unlike the covering uſed by the Turks called the Turban Beſides, the title of Turban flower is given to another plant How long this genus hath been named Tulip, and with what propriety it is ſo named, is hardly worth while to examine further Certain it is, it has been ſtiled ſo with us, as long as we have known the flower, and it is diſtinguiſhed in the works of the moſt able Botaniſts under the words *Tulipa*, and *Tulipa Turcarum*, names expreſſive

*Obſervations upon the origin of the name*

pressive of the country, but which convey no *real idea of the flower.*

This rare and choice plant, which is now grown so common, and in such perfection in the different varieties established by culture, began, soon after it was known, to be much desired, and no doubt a seed or an offset was hardly lost, without its encrease being forwarded with all care. But by no people was it propagated with greater zeal than the Dutch. The varieties became soon so numerous and different in themselves, that they appeared as distinct species, and were arranged with different classes or assortments according to their time of flower, &c. These were distinguished by the Early Blowers, and the Late Blowers. The zeal of the people for this flower rose at length to such a height that no price for one of them was too great, and hence, was thought too extravagant. This phrenzy raged till the year 1637 when it began to abate, by the timely interposition of the States of Holland and West Friezeland, who limited the price of these flowers, in their best state, as has been before observed.

**Extravagance of the Dutch in cultivating this flower.**

The Early species were the sort of Tulips that was so much coveted in the above-mentioned period, and for the bulbs of which formerly such extravagant prices were given. All the Early sorts fall very short in number and beauty of those called Late Blowers, which are now with good reason become the most cultivated, and which are propagated by the Dutch, English, and other florists, with much industry and art. They bestow great pains in breaking them from the breeders, and bringing the colours of this most delightful flower to perfection, the method of which I have already given. The Florist, the Botanist, and Gardener, now must see what remains, including the commonest of these sorts, for his observation in the flower garden, and they are,

**Observation on the Early and Late Blower.**

**Species.**

1. The Early Sweet-scented European Tulip.
2. The Turkish Tulip, including all the sorts.

1. The Early Sweet-scented European Tulip.

**1. Early Sweet-scented European Tulip described.**

*This plant, though of our own growth, seems* to have been long overlooked. When once it came to be taken notice of, it was coveted by all lovers of flowers; but it propagated itself so very fast by the roots, that it soon grew common, and the Turkish Tulip becoming easy to be purchased, and outstripping it so much in beauty, the former was neglected by most, as of small value. It may be seen, however, in almost every place where it has been planted, for there is no killing it. A garden that has for many years been over-run with weeds and neglected will still show this flower in perfection. It will multiply itself by the roots, in all deserted uncultivated places; and it will arise with its leaves and flowers among the thickest rubbish and weeds, bidding defiance to all obstructions, and seeming to outvie them in low life.

The leaves of this sort are long and narrow, spear-shaped, of a pale-green colour, and end in acute points. The flowers will be ripe early in April; they stand upon a weak slender stalk in a drooping manner, are small in respect to a Tulip, and have a property which belongs to few of that tribe, viz. being *possessed of an agreeable odour.* Their petals end in acute points, and meet at the ends, which occasions its going by the cant name of Snake's-head, it being in shape a little like the head of that reptile.

This is a species that no good collection of flowers should be without; and though it has not the splendor of the Turkish Tulip, yet it is rather an elegant plant, and its coming so early, and being possessed of fragrance, are properties that ought to be taken into consideration in the estimate of its value.

2. The Turkish Tulip, in its numberless varieties, affords pleasure to all, whether Botanist, Gardener, or Florist. What has been said of them, perhaps, might serve for all; neither is there any thing material to be added here, for a person's own judgment will direct him how to dispose a few of them to advantage in the pleasure-ground, where no general collection of flowers is aimed at.

**Turkish Tulip described.**

The Early sorts, as has been observed, naturally demand a place in well sheltered beds that are in view of the sitting room, telling the beholders, that they are the van-guard only of a large troop which is to follow in order.

**Proper situation.**

The Double Tulips, and the Broken flowers, are fit for any place, tho' they do best in an open exposure, and not under the drip of trees. These should be planted in borders of the flower garden; and to encrease the variety, a few of that well-known Tulip called the Parrot, should be mixed with them. In wilderness-quarters and wilds the meanest Tulips should be set, and left for years in an uncultivated state. Broken flowers with the properties of Tulips, would be out of character for such places, were they to succeed in them. The Common Red, and the Common Yellow, with their acute pointed petals, shew real Nature here. If these are carelessly set amongst trees, in the middle of the quarter, they will, when unremoved for years, easily produce their flowers, and add an air of gaiety and beauty to such places, yet still retain their native simplicity.

It is not uncommon, in a collection of breeding Tulips, to find a few with stalks in a strange luxuriance, dividing it to several branches, thereby forming a large cluster of these fine flowers. I have had seven fine flowers growing upon one stalk in this manner, and which have broken into fine stripes. They are chiefly the Baquettes that are most liable to this sport of Nature, which, when it happens, forms a most singular and wonderful, as well as beautiful and majestic plant. These are to be marked, and placed separately in the flower-border, in the richest soil, and they will form a large bough, which will excite admiration.

**Remarkable properties of some sorts.**

*As this is accidental and a variety only, they* are liable to lose that branching property, and the year following to appear regular, with their single flower and stalk. But though they are liable, they are not very subject to return in that manner, for I have had them flower for many years together in large clusters, and many of their offsets, when they came to blow, have appeared in the same clustered manner, tho' I ever observed, that the most branching Tulip, if left in the ground all summer, always produced its flowers the succeeding spring on a single upright stem, in the usual way; so that when this singularity appears, they must be regularly taken up, as soon as the leaves are decayed, and when planted again must always be set in the richest soils, which will more probably continue them in that uncommon state. These particularly must be early supported as they advance in height, or they will be pretty sure of being broken off by the winds before they come to perfection.

The Florist has had enough of the culture of all the sorts of the Tulip, and the Gardener will find they will multiply themselves fast enough by the bulb. As we suppose what we have treated of to be only border flowers, they may share in the same kind of culture, and will do

**Culture.**

very

very well to be removed every other year, except the Cluster-Tulips above-mentioned. At the time of removal their offsets should be taken off, and they may be set immediately again with other flower-roots. Such red and common Tulips as are planted among trees in wilderness-works, may be left purely to Nature; they will flower every year, their bunches grow larger, and will be very ornamental without trouble.

[Titles] 1. The Early Sweet-scented European Tulip is titled, *Tulipa flore subnutante, foliis lanceolatis*. Caspar Bauhine calls it, *Tulipa minor lutea Italica*, also, *Tulipa minor lutea Gallica*. It grows naturally in Italy, and the South of France.

2. The Turkish Tulip is, *Tulipa flore erecto, foliis ovato-lanceolatis*. In the *Hortus Cliffort* it is termed simply, *Tulipa*. Caspar Bauhine calls it, *Tulipa genus fere totum*, and others, *Tulipa Turcarum*. It grows naturally in Cappadocia.

[Class and order in the Linnæan system. The characters] *Tulipa* is of the class and order *Hexandria Monogynia*, and the characters are,

1. CALYX. There is none.
2. COROLLA. The corolla is bell-shaped, and composed of six oblong, oval, erect, concave petals.
3. STAMINA are six very short awl-shaped filaments, with quadrangular, oblong, erect, distant antheræ.
4. PISTILLUM is a large, oblong, roundish, three-cornered germen, without any style, but a triangular, three-lobed, permanent stigma.
5. PERICARPIUM is a three-cornered capsule, composed of three valves, and containing three cells.
6. SEMINA. The seeds are many, plane, semicircular, and lie over each other in a double series.

## C H A P. CCCCLXXIV

## *TUSSILAGO*, COLT's FOOT.

[Species] THE perennials for this place are,

1. Common Colt's Foot.
2. Alpine Colt's Foot.
3. *Anandria*, or Siberian Colt's Foot.
4. Lapland Colt's Foot.
5. Common Butter-Bur.
6. Small-white Butter Bur.
7. Long-stalked Butter-Bur.

[Common Colt's Foot described] 1. Common Colt's Foot. The root is long, white, and creeping under the surface. The stalks are simple, thick, tender, hollow, imbricated, and five or six inches high. The flowers come out singly from the tops of the stalks; they are large, of a pale-yellow colour, and very beautiful; they appear in March and April, and are succeeded by downy seeds, which ripen soon after. The leaves arise after the flowers are past; they are very large, nearly heart-shaped, angulated, indented, hoary, and grow on strong footstalks; they continue until the autumn, when they die to the roots, and fresh ones arise in the spring.

[Medicinal properties] This species is held pectoral, is frequently used in decoctions, and the dried leaves are a principal ingredient in the British Herb Tobacco.

The flowers have sufficient beauty to entitle this plant to a place in any garden; but it grows wild every where, and when once it has taken possession of a garden, creeps so fast by the roots, as soon to overspread every thing that is near it.

[Alpine,] 2. Alpine Colt's Foot. The root is small, and creeping. The stalk is almost naked, upright, hollow, and three or four inches high. The flowers come out singly from the tops of the stalks; they are of a purple colour, appear in March and April, and are followed by downy seeds, which ripen soon after. The leaves are almost round, crenated, smooth, of a dark bright-green colour on their upper-side, downy underneath, have footstalks about three inches long, and continue until the end of autumn, when they die, and fresh ones arise in the spring.

[Siberian,] 3. *Anandria*, or Siberian Colt's Foot. The stalk is about three or four inches high, and supports one flower at the top. The leaves are lyrated, oval, and grow close to the ground. The flowers appear early in the spring, and are soon changed into down; but the leaves continue all summer.

[and Lapland Colt's Foot] 4. Lapland Colt's Foot. The stalk is upright, imbricated, downy, and supports a few flowers at the top, growing in a kind of thyrse. The leaves are oval, acute, white, and downy underneath. The flowers come out in March or April, and soon fade; but the leaves continue all summer.

[Common Butter-bur described] 5. Common Butter-Bur. The root is thick, fleshy, and creeping just below the surface of the earth, blackish without, white within, strongly scented, hot, and bitterish to the taste. The stalks are hollow, thick, about six inches high, arise early in the spring, and support the flowers, growing on oval spikes at the top. The flowers are of a purplish colour, appear in March, and are soon over. When the flowers are past, the leaves come up; they are large, about two feet broad, roundish, heart-shaped at the base, cut into angles on their edges, downy on the underside, and grow on thick strong footstalks; they continue all summer, in the autumn decay, and every spring fresh ones arise after the flowers are past.

[Its use] The roots are aperient, deobstruent, and good against fevers and pestilential disorders.

6. Small

*Small White,*

6 Small White Butter-Bur The stalks are almost naked, about three inches high, and sustain a small bunch of white flowers at the top, they appear early in the spring, and after they are past the leaves arise, and continue all summer, at the end of which they decay, and fresh ones arise the spring after

*and Long stalked Butter-Bur described*

7 Long stalked Butter-Bur The stalks are thick, hollow, tender, six or eight inches high, and support the flowers in an oblong thyrse at the top; they appear in March, and after they are past, the leaves arise, as of the other sorts

*Culture*

There is no missing of the culture of any of these sorts Plant the roots at any time of the year, but especially in the autumn and every bit of them will grow They chiefly like moisture and good ground, and being thus situated they will encreafe perhaps faster than you would desire

*Titles*

1 Common Colt's Foot is titled, *Tussilago scapo imbricato unifloro, foliis subcordatis angulatis denticulatis* Caspar Bauhine calls it, *Tussilago vulgaris*, Clusius, &c *Tussilago* It grows naturally in most places in England, and most countries of Europe

2 Alpine Colts Foot is, *Tussilago scapo subnudo unifloro, foliis cordato-orbiculatis crenatis* Caspar Bauhine calls it, *Tussilago Alpina rotundifolia glabra*, also, *Tussilago Alpina rotundifolia canescens*, and Clusius, *Tussilago Alpina 1 flore purpureo*, also, *Tussilago Alpina 2* It grows naturally on the Helvetian, Austrian, Bohemian, and Siberian mountains

3 *Anandria*, or Siberian Colt's Foot is, *Tussilago scapo unifloro subsquamoso erecto, foliis lyrato-ovatis* In the *Amœn. Acad* it is termed simply, *Anandria*, in the *Hortus Upsal Tussilago scapo unifloro, calyce clauso* Gmelin calls it, *Tussilago scapo unifloro, calyce subaperto* It is a native of Siberia

4 Laponian Colt's Foot is, *Tussilago thyrso fastigiato, flosculis radiatis* Gmelin calls it, *Tussilago scapo nudo tecto floribus spicatis radiatis, foliis infra nervis acutis* Haller, *Petasites scapo paucifloro, foliis subtus tomentosis albissimis*, and Caspar Bauhine, *Cacalia tomentosa* It grows naturally in the hollows and valleys belonging to the Alps of Lapland, Helvetia, and Siberia

5 Common Butter-Bur is, *Tussilago thyrso ovato, flosculis omnibus hermaphroditis* Cammerarius calls it, *Tussilago major*, Caspar Bauhine, *Petasites major et vulgaris*, Gerard, *Petasites*, and Parkinson, *Petasites vulgaris* It grows common in moist meadows and pastures in England, and several parts of Europe

6 Small White Butter-Bur is, *Tussilago thyrso fastigiato, flosculis femineis nudis paucis* Caspar Bauhine calls it, *Petasites minor*; and Cammerarius, *Petasites flore albo* It grows naturally on the Alps, and other mountainous parts of Europe

7 Long stalked Butter Bur is, *Tussilago thyrso oblongo, flosculis femineis nudis plurimis* Dillenius calls it, *Petasites major, floribus pedunculis longis insidentibus*, and Buxbaum, *Petasites in medio majoribus flosculis, reliquis minoribus* It grows naturally in some meadows near Loughborough, and is common in Holland, and many parts of Germany

*Class and order in the Linnæan system. The characters*

*Tussilago* is of the class and order *Syngenesia Polygamia Superflua*, and the characters are,

1 CALYX The general calyx is cylindrical, and composed of fifteen or twenty narrow, spear-shaped, equal scales

2 COROLLA The compound flower is various The florets are either all hermaphrodites, or else hermaphrodites only in the disk An hermaphrodite floret is one funnel shaped petal, cut at the brim into four or else five acute reflexed segments, which are longer than the calyx

The female florets, where there are any, are tongue shaped, narrow, whole, and longer than the calyx

3 STAMINA of the hermaphrodites are five very short capillary filaments, having a cylindrical tubular anthera

4 PISTILLUM of the hermaphrodites, consists of a short germen, a filiform style longer than the stamina, and a thickish stigma.

Of the females, it consists of a short germen, a filiforme style the length of the hermaphrodites, and a thickish bifid stigma

5 PERICARPIUM There is none

6 SEMEN of the hermaphrodites is single, oblong compressed, and crowned with hairy stipitated down

The seeds of the females, if there are any, are similar to those of the hermaphrodites

The receptacle is naked

## CHAP. CCCCLXXV.

## *TYPHA*, CAT's TAIL, or REED-MACE.

THERE are only two species of this genus yet known, called,

Species
1 Great Cat's Tail, or Reed-Mace
2 Narrow-leaved Cat's Tail

Great
1 Great Cat's Tail, or Reed-Mace The root is hard, thick, creeping, of a white colour, and possessed of numerous fibres The leaves are flaggy, nearly sword-shaped, sharp on the edges, and three or four feet long The stalks are round, smooth, glossy, firm, naked, and five or six feet high The flowers terminate the tops of the stalk in a most dense spike, they appear in July, and the seeds ripen in September

and Narrow leaved Cat's Tail described
2 Narrow-leaved Cat's Tail The root is white, creeping, and hung with many fibres The leaves are semi-cylindrical, smooth, and of a dark-green colour The stalk is round, upright, firm, and naked The flowers are produced in spikes from the tops of the stalks, they appear about the same time with the former, and the seeds ripen accordingly

Culture
These plants grow common in our ditches, brooks, and standing waters, but are never cultivated Nevertheless, if a person is desirous of having a few of them to be ready for observation, it may be easily effected by planting the roots in the autumn, in some ditch or moist place, or by sowing the seeds soon after they are ripe.

Titles
1 The first species is titled, *Typha foliis subensiformibus, spicâ masculâ femineâque approximatis* Caspar Bauhine calls it, *Typha palustris major*, Gerard simply, *Typha*, and Parkinson, *Typha palustris maxima* It grows naturally in England, and most countries of Europe

2 The second species is, *Typha foliis semicylindricis, spicâ masculâ femineâque remotis* In the *Hortus Cliffortianus* it is termed simply, *Typha* Caspar Bauhine calls it, *Typha palustris, clavâ gracili*, also, *Typha palustris minor*, John Bauhine, *Typha palustris media*, and Parkinson, *Typha minor*. It grows naturally in England, and most countries of Europe

*Typha* is of the class and order *Monoecia Triandria*, and the characters are, Class and order in the Linnaean system

I Males terminating the stalk The characters

1 Calyx The common amentum is cylindrical, dense, and constant. The perianthium consists of three bristly leaves

2 Corolla There is none

3 Stamina are three capillary filaments the length of the calyx, having oblong pendulent antheræ

II Females closely surrounding the Stalk, and situated below the Males

1 Calyx consists of soft downy hairs

2 Corolla There is none

3 Pistillum consists of an oval germen, an awl-shaped style, and a capillary permanent stigma

4 Pericarpium There is none The fruit are numerous, and constitute a cylinder

5 Semen The seed is single, oval, retains the style, and sits on the capillary down

## CHAP CCCCLXXVI

## *VACCINIUM*, WHORTLE-BERRY

OF this genus are,

Species
1 The Common Bilberry, or Whortle-Berry
2 Great Bilberry-Bush
3 White Bilberry
4 Red Whorts, or Whortle-Berries
5 Cranberry
6 Marsh Virginian Whortle-Berry

Common Bilberry
1 The Common Bilberry, Black Wort, or Whortle-Berry The stalk is shrubby, angular, branching, and about two feet high The leaves are oval, oblong, slightly serrated, smooth, and of a dark green colour The flowers come out singly on footstalks from the ends and sides of the branches; they are of a greenish-white colour, appear in April and May, and are succeeded by those large and well-known eatable berries, called Bilberries, Black-Whorts, or Whortle-Berries

2 Great Bilberry Bush The stalk is woody, branching, and three feet high The leaves are oval, entire, veined, of a thin contexture, and whitish underneath The flowers grow singly on their own separate and distinct footstalks, they are of a whitish-purple colour, appear in April and May, and are succeeded by large berries, which ripen in July Great Bilberry-Bush

3 White Bilberry The stalks are woody, branching, White Bilberry

branching, and a foot and a half or two feet high The leaves are oval, entire, and downy underneath The flowers come out in small clusters from the ends and sides of the branches, they are of a greenish white colour, appear in May and are succeeded by berries which are at first green, and afterwards of a white colour when ripe

Red Whorts, 4 Red Whorts, or Whortle-Berries The stalks are very slender, branching, and seldom more than six inches high The leaves are oval, smooth, of thick consistence, spotted underneath, and continue green all the year The flowers are produced in clusters from the ends of the branches, they are of a reddish colour, appear in April and May; and are succeeded by juicy berries, which are of an elegant red colour when ripe

The berries of this species are highly esteemed for tarts

Cranberries, 5 Cranberries The stalks are slender, long, and lie almost flat on the ground, and strike root as they lie The leaves are small, oval, entire, and their edges turn backward The flowers are produced from the upper parts of the branches on long slender footstalks, they are of a red colour, appear in May and June, and are succeeded by those celebrated berries for tarts, called Cranberries, which ripen in the end of July and August

and Marsh Virginian Whortle Berry described 6 *Marsh Virginian Whortle-Berry* The stalks are slender, rough, imbricated, trailing, and strike root as they lie on the ground The leaves are oval, entire, and their edges turn backward The flowers are produced from the upper parts of the branches on slender footstalks, they are of a greenish-white colour, appear in May, and are succeeded by very large red berries, which seldom ripen in England

None of these are what are properly called cultivated plants, but may be made to grow in suitable soils and situations The first four sorts grow naturally in cold, but light sandy woods, heaths, &c the last two on bogs, and marshy and sturbed soils, which have very little produce except them and moss

Culture In order to cultivate the last two, let the bogs be well dug, and kept clean from weeds the first part of the summer, and when the berries are well ripened, sow them in patches, covering them over with a quarter of an inch depth of earth only From this time let the place remain undisturbed, pull up no weeds, and in the spring, or the spring following, for they sometimes lie two years, the Cranberry plants will arise, and by the creeping branches will propagate themselves fast enough The sixth sort, being a native of Virginia, the seeds must be procured from thence, kept in sand, and sown as soon as possible after their arrival The first four sorts may be raised in the same manner, if the soil be suitable, otherwise, though the plants come up, they will make very little progress, and by degrees will decay, and come to nothing

All these sorts may be propagated by taking up the roots from the places where they naturally grow, with a large quantity of mould to them, and planting them in a similar situation, they will frequently grow in such places, and soon make great encrease but for gardens their culture is not worth the attempt

Titles 1. The Bilberry Shrub is titled, *Vaccinium pedunculis unifloris, foliis serratis ovatis deciduis, caule angulato* Caspar Bauhine calls it, *Vitis idæa foliis oblongis crenatis fructu nigricante*, John Bauhine, *Vitis idæa angulosa*, Dalechamp, *Myrtillus Germanica & vitis idæa*, and Gerard, *Vaccinia nigra* It grows naturally in woods in most of the northern countries of Europe

2 The Great Bilberry-Bush is, *Vaccinium pedunculis unifloris, foliis integerrimis ovalibus obtusis* In the *Flora Suecia* it is termed, *Vaccinium foliis ovalibus integerrimis deciduis*, in the *Flora Lapp Vaccinium foliis annuis integerrimis* Caspar Bauhine calls it, *Vitis idæa foliis subrotundis exalbidis*; John Bauhine, *Vitis idæa magna quibusdam, s myrtillus grandis*, Clusius, *Vitis idæa II*; Gerard, *Vitis idæa foliis subrotundis major*, and Parkinson, *Vaccinia nigra fructu majore* It grows naturally in mountainous places in England, and some other of the northern countries of Europe

3 White Bilberry is, *Vaccinium pedunculis simplicibus, foliis integerrimis ovatis subtus tomentosis.* It grows naturally in Pensylvania

4 Red Whortle-Berry is, *Vaccinium racemis terminalibus nutantibus, foliis obovatis revolutis integerrimis subtus punctatis* In the *Flora Lapp* it is termed, *Vaccinium foliis obverse ovatis perennantibus* Caspar Bauhine calls it, *Vitis idæa foliis subrotundis non crenatis, baccis rubris*, John Bauhine, *Vitis idæa sempervirens fructu rubro*, Gerard, *Vaccinia rubra*, and Parkinson, *Vaccinia rubra buxeis foliis* It grows naturally in mountainous places in the North of England, and most of the cold countries of Europe

5 Cranberry is, *Vaccinium foliis integerrimis revolutis ovatis, caulibus repentibus filiformibus nudis* In the *Flora Suecia* it is termed, *Vaccinium ramis filiformibus, foliis ovatis perennantibus, pedunculis simplicibus, stipulâ duplici*, in the *Flora Lapp Vaccinium ramis filiformibus repentibus, foliis ovatis perennantibus* Caspar Bauhine calls it, *Vitis idæa palustris*, John Bauhine, *Oxycoccus, seu vaccinia palustria*; Gerard, *Vaccinia palustria*, and Parkinson, *Vaccinium palustre* It grows naturally on bogs, and cold, moist, turfy places in the North of England, and most of the colder countries of Europe

6 Marsh Virginian Whortle-Berry is, *Vaccinium foliis integerrimis revolutis ovatis, caulibus repentibus filiformibus hispidis* Plukenet calls it, *Vitis idæa palustris Americana, oblongis splendentibus foliis, fructu grandiore rubro plurimis intus acinis referto*, and Ray, *Vitis idæa palustris Virginiana, fructu majore* It grows naturally on bogs and moist places in most countries of North America

*Vaccinium* is of the class and order *Octandria Monogynia*, and the characters are, Class and order in the Linnæan system

1 Calyx is a very small perianthium situated above the germen The characters

2 Corolla is one bell-shaped petal, divided at the brim into four revoluted segments

3 Stamina are eight simple filaments, having two horned antheræ, opening at the point, and furnished with two spreading aristæ on the outside

4 Pistillum consists of a germen situated below the calyx, a simple style longer than the stamina, and an obtuse stigma

5 Pericarpium is a globular umbilicated berry, containing four cells

6 Semina The seeds are few, and small

CHAP

# C H A P. CCCCLXXVII.

## *VALANTIA*, CROSS-WORT.

Species

OF this genus are two perennials, called,
1 Common Croſs-wort, or Mug-weed
2 Smooth Italian Croſs-wort

Common Croſs-wort deſcribed

1 Common Croſs-wort, or Mug weed. The root conſiſts of ſeveral ſmall, ſlender, yellowiſh fibres. The ſtalks are numerous, ſquare, weak, hairy, jointed, partly procumbent, and about a foot long. The leaves are broad, ſhort, obtuſe, hairy, and four ſurround the ſtalk in a radiated manner at every joint. The flowers come out in ſmall cluſters from the wings of the leaves, they are of a yellow colour, appear in May and June, and the ſeeds ripen in July and Auguſt.

Its uſes in medicine

This ſpecies is held a good vulnerary, whether applied outwardly by way of poultice, or uſed by decoction for inward bruiſes.

Smooth Italian Croſs-wort deſcribed

2 Smooth Italian Croſs-wort. The ſtalks are ſquare, ſmooth, partly procumbent, and bout a foot long. The leaves are oval, ſpear-ſhaped, ciliated, ſmooth, and four of them are diſpoſed in a radiated manner at every joint. The flowers come out in ſmall cluſters from the ſides of the ſtalks, they are of a yellow colour, appear in June and July, and the ſeeds ripen in Auguſt.

Proper ſituation

Theſe ſpecies are propagated by ſowing the ſeeds ſoon after they are ripe. When they come up they will require no trouble, except keeping them clean from weeds, and after they have flowered, and the ſeeds are ſcattered, a ſucceſſion of plants, more than could be wiſhed for, will ſpontaneouſly ariſe.

Titles

1 The firſt ſpecies is titled, *Valantia floribus maſculis quadrifidis, pedunculis diphyllis*. In the *Hortus Cliffortianus* it is termed, *Galium foliis quaternis, floſculis in alis confertis*. Caſpar Bauhine calls it, *Cruciata hirſuta*, Gerard, *Cruciata*, and Parkinſon, *Cruciata vulgaris*. It is common by hedges and buſhes in England, Germany, Helvetia, and Gaul.

2 The ſecond ſpecies is, *Valantia floribus maſculis quadrifidis, pedunculis dichotomis aphyllis, foliis ovalibus ciliatis*. Caſpar Bauhine calls it, *Gallium latifolium glabrum*, alſo, *Cruciata glabra*. It grows naturally in Auſtria and Italy.

Claſs and order in the Linnæan ſyſtem. The characters,

*Valantia* is of the claſs and order *Polygamia Monoecia*, and the characters are,

I Hermaphrodite Flower

1 CALYX is very ſmall.
2 COROLLA is one plane petal, divided into four oval acute ſegments.
3 STAMINA are four filaments the length of the corolla, having ſmall antheræ.
4 PISTILLUM conſiſts of a large germen ſituated below the flower, and a ſemibifid ſtyle the length of the ſtamina, with capitated ſtigmas.
5 PERICARPIUM is coriaceous, compreſſed, and reflexed.
6 SEMEN. The ſeed is ſingle, and globular.

II Male Flower

1 CALYX. There is ſcarcely any.
2 COROLLA is one plane petal, divided into three or four oval acute ſegments.
3 STAMINA are the like number of filaments the length of the corolla, having ſmall antheræ.
4 PISTILLUM conſiſts of a ſmall germen ſituated below the flower, having a very ſmall obſolete ſtyle and ſtigma.
5 PERICARPIUM is abortive.
6 SEMEN. There is none.

## CHAP. CCCCLXXVIII.

## *VALERIANA*, VALERIAN

Species

OF this genus there are,
1 Garden Valerian
2 Great Wild Valerian
3 Red Valerian
4 Marsh Valerian
5 Mountain Valerian
6 Celtick Valerian, or Celtick Nard
7 Tuberous Valerian
8 Stone Valerian
9 Pyrenean Valerian

Garden,

1 Garden Valerian hath many thick, jointed, fleshy, strong scented, creeping roots, which send forth several round, smooth, hollow, branching stalks, to the height of about a yard The radical leaves are oblong, and undivided, those on the bottom of the stalks are jagged, those higher up on the stalks are pinnated, they are smooth, of a pale green colour, and grow opposite by pairs at the joints The flowers grow in umbels, and are of a white colour; they crown the stalks and smaller branches in May and June, and are succeeded by oblong downy seeds soon after

This species is highly valued in medicine, and goes by the name of *Phu* in the shops

Great Wild,

2 Great Wild Valerian The roots are long, fleshy, and collected into heads, from whence the stalks proceed, they are channelled, hollow, hairy, and grow to about two feet high The radical leaves, as well as those of the stalks, are pinnated, and each is composed of about six or seven pair of lobes, besides the odd one which terminates them, they are sharp-pointed, hairy, and grow opposite by pairs at the joints The flowers are produced in kind of umbels from the tops of the stalks and small side branches, which come out opposite to each other, they are tinged with purple on the outside, will be in blow in May and June, and ripen their seeds soon after

This species also is valuable in medicine, and it is observable, that the roots have greater force, when collected from the places where they naturally grow, than when propagated and brought to a larger size in the garden, which should admonish us, if they are to be raised in plenty for medicinal purposes to grant them a hungry or undunged part of the garden

Red

3 Red Valerian This hath a thick, woody, spreading root, which sends forth smooth, round, hollow, branching stalks, to the height of two or three feet The leaves are smooth, spear-shaped, pointed, and grow for the most part by pairs at the joints, though sometimes there will be three or four from the same joint The branches are produced by pairs, and these, together with the main stalk, are all terminated by the flowers, they grow in moderately large clusters, and tho' their usual colour is red, yet there are of it the White and Pale Flesh-coloured varieties They flower most part of the summer, and the seeds being scattered by the winds, will produce plenty of plants all over the garden, nay, they will come up in the crevices of old walls and buildings, so that they are often industriously put between the stones of ruins, grottos, &c which growing, flower strong, and have a good effect most part of the summer

Marsh,

4 Marsh Valerian This pretty little plant adorns our bogs and moist grounds, and is seldom cultivated in gardens, it ought, however, to find admittance among other perennials, especially in those places where it does not grow naturally The roots are slender, and creeping The stalks are upright, and will grow to about a foot or a foot and a half high The radical leaves are undivided, but those on the stalks are pinnated, being composed of six or seven pair of lobes, terminated by an odd one, which grow opposite at the joints A few side branches are produced near the top of the stalks by pairs, and these, together with the main-stalks, are terminated by the flowers, they grow in clusters, and their colour is a kind of whitish red or purple, they flower in May and June, and ripen their seeds soon after

and Mountain Valerian,

5 Mountain Valerian The stalks are single, and grow to about half a foot long The leaves are oval, oblong pointed, and slightly indented at the edges The flowers are produced from the tops of the stalks in May and June, and ripen their seeds soon after

Celtick Nard,

6 Celtick Nard The stalks grow to about half a foot long, lie on the ground, and put out fresh roots from the joints, which become large, rough, and scaly The leaves are oblong, oval, obtuse, and entire The flowers are produced from the ends of the stalks in kind of loose spikes, they are of a whitish, yellowish, or pale-red colour, they will be in blow in May and June, though they very seldom bring their seeds to perfection in our gardens

Tuberous

7 Tuberous Valerian This hath a large, oblong, fleshy root, from which arise several spear-shaped entire leaves From among these spring the flower stalks, garnished with a few pinnated leaves, the tops of which are adorned with flowers in June, and they ripen their seeds in July or August

Stone Valerian

8 Stone Valerian The stalks will grow to about half a foot high The radical leaves are of an oval figure, and entire, but those on the stalks are spear-shaped, narrow, and indented The flowers terminate the branches in small tufts, they are of a kind of whitish red or purple colour, will be in blow in June, and ripen their seeds in August

and Pyrenean Valerian described

9 Pyrenean Valerian The root is fibrous The stalks are hollow, channelled, and will grow to about a yard high The radical leaves are heart-shaped, serrated, of a bright green colour, and smooth on the upper-side, but pale and hairy underneath, and have very long footstalks The leaves on the stalks are smaller, pointed, and often grow by threes near the top, on short footstalks The flowers terminate the main stalk and branches in kind of umbels, they are of a pale-red or flesh colour, will be in blow in June, and ripen their seeds in August

Culture. The first three sorts are propagated by parting of the roots, or sowing the seeds. The best time for parting of the roots is the autumn, though they will grow any time in the winter or spring. They ought to have a dry undunged soil, if the roots are raised for medicinal uses, but they will flourish in almost any soil or situation.

They are also propagated by sowing the seeds, soon after they are ripe; they will readily come up, and in the spring should be set out in a nursery-bed, at about nine inches from each other, and in the autumn may be removed to the places where they are designed to remain.

The fourth sort is propagated by the roots, which may be taken from our meadows or bogs soon after the flowers are past in the summer. They must have a very moist part of the garden, be well watered and shaded until they have taken root, and afterwards they will require no further trouble.

The fifth, sixth, seventh, and eighth sorts grow naturally on the rocky and mountainous parts of the world, so that to preserve them in our gardens, we must allot them a dry, light, sandy soil. In such a situation set the roots, or sow the seeds, and there will be a greater certainty of continuing these sorts in your garden.

The ninth sort, though a mountainous plant, grows well in vales and moist places. Their downy seeds are wafted to a considerable distance by the winds, which will come up without any art, after you are once furnished with a plant of this kind, though if you chuse a regular crop of it the seeds should be sown in the autumn, soon after they are ripe, and covered with about a quarter of an inch of the finest mould. In the spring the plants should be pricked out in the nursery-bed at about nine inches from each other, and in the autumn may be removed to the places where they are to remain.

It is also propagated by dividing of the roots, which may be done at almost any time of the year, but the best season is the autumn.

Titles. 1. Garden Valerian is titled, *Valeriana floribus triandris, foliis caulinis pinnatis, radicalibus indivisis*. In the *Hortus Cliffort.* it is termed, *Valeriana foliis infimis integris, proximis laciniatis; caulinis pinnatis*. Caspar Bauhine calls it, *Valeriana hortensis*. It grows naturally in Alsatia.

2. Great Wild Valerian is titled, *Valeriana floribus triandris, foliis omnibus pinnatis*. Caspar Bauhine calls it, *Valeriana sylvestris major*; and Dodonæus, *Valeriana sylvestris*. It grows naturally in England, and most countries of Europe.

3. Red Valerian is, *Valeriana floribus monandris caudatis, foliis lanceolatis integerrimis*. Caspar Bauhine calls it, *Valeriana rubra*, also, *Valeriana rubra angustifolia*, and Morison, *Valeriana marina latifolia major rubra*. It grows naturally in Switzerland, Italy, and the East.

4. Marsh Valerian is, *Valeriana floribus triandris dioicis, foliis pinnatis integerrimis*. In the *Hortus Cliffort.* it is termed, *Valeriana, foliis caulinis pinnatis, seu distincta*. Caspar Bauhine calls it, *Valeriana palustris minor*, also, *Valeriana Alpina minor*, and Morison, *Valeriana pratensis minor*. It grows naturally in England, and the East.

5. Mountain Valerian is, *Valeriana floribus triandris, foliis ovato oblongis subdentatis, caule simplici*. Haller calls it, *Valeriana foliis omnibus integris ex ovato-acuminatis leviter dentatis*, and Caspar Bauhine, *Valeriana montana, subrotundo folio*. It grows naturally on the Helvetian and Pyrenean mountains.

6. Celtick Valerian, or Celtick Nard, is, *Valeriana floribus triandris, foliis ovato-oblongis obtusis integerrimis*. Haller calls it, *Valeriana foliis ovatis obtusis minime dentatis*, Caspar Bauhine, *Nardus Celtica Dioscoridis*, John Bauhine, *Nardus Celtica*, and Cammerarius, *Spica Celtica fastigio floculorum ordine differens*. It grows naturally on the Helvetian and Vallesian mountains.

7. Tuberous Valerian is, *Valeriana floribus triandris, foliis lanceolatis integerrimis, caulinis basi pinnatis*. Caspar Bauhine calls it, *Nardus montana, radice olivari*, and Cammerarius, *Nardus montana, longius radicata*. It grows naturally in Dalmatia and Sicily.

8. Stone Valerian is, *Valeriana floribus triandris, foliis subdentatis, radicalibus ovatis, caulinis linearilanceolatis*. Caspar Bauhine calls it, *Valeriana Alpina nardo Celticæ similis*, Clusius, *Valeriana sylvestris Alpina 2 saxatilis*, and Plukenet, *Valeriana Alpina nardo Celticæ similis inodora*. It grows naturally on the Syrian, Austrian, and Italian mountains.

9. Pyrenean Valerian is, *Valeriana floribus triandris, foliis caulinis cordatis serratis petiolatis, summis ternatis*. Tournefort calls it, *Valeriana maxima Pyrenaica, cacaliæ folio*, Rivinus, *Valeriana Canadensis*, and Buxbaum, *Valeriana orientalis, aliariæ folio, flore albo*. It grows naturally on the Pyrenees.

Class and order in the Linnæan system. *Valeriana* is of the class and order *Triandria Monogynia*, and the characters are,

The characters. 1. CALYX is a kind of margin, or small border, placed upon the germen.

2. COROLLA is one petal. The tube is gibbous, and contains a honey juice. The limb is divided into five obtuse segments.

3. STAMINA consist usually of three, sometimes not so many, awl-shaped erect filaments the length of the corolla, with roundish antheræ.

4. PISTILLUM consists of a germen placed below the flower, a filiforme style the length of the stamina, and a thickish stigma.

5. PERICARPIUM is a coronated deciduous capsule, that does not open while on the plant.

6. SEMEN. The seed is single, and oblong.

CHAP.

## CHAP. CCCCLXXIX.

## *VALLISNERIA.*

THERE is only one species of this genus, called, *Valisneria*

The plant described. The root is thick, white, fibrated, and creeping The leaves are long, narrow, serrated at the top, and rise in clusters, in the manner of flags, from the crown of the roots The stalk is naked, slender, and spirally twisted in the manner of a cork-screw The flowers come out from the tops of the stalks, they are of a beautiful purple colour, appear in July and August, and the females are succeeded by long cylindrical capsules, containing the seeds

There is a variety of this species with small white flowers

This species grows naturally in ditches and standing waters in Italy, and is not deemed a cultivated plant But as the root is strong and

Its propagation. creeping, I make no doubt but if the heads were planted in the like situation in England, they will grow, and render beautiful small lakes or ditches that are situated in low vales, and kept warm through the defence of large hills and woods

Titles. There being no other species of it, it is termed simply, *Vallisneria* Micheli calls it, *Vallisneria palustris, algæ folio, Italica, foliis in summitate denticulatis, flore purpurascente*, also, *Vallisnerioides palustre, algæ folio, Italicum, foliis in summitate tenuissime denticulatis, floribus albis vix conspicuis*, and Boccone, *Potamogeton, algæ folio, Pisanum.* It is common in most parts of Italy

Class and order in the Linnæan system. *Vallisneria* is of the class and order *Dioecia Diandria*, and the characters are,

The character. I. Males

1 CALYX The common spatha is divided into two oblong, bifid, reflexed segments The spadix is compressed, and covered with flowers

2. COROLLA is one petal, having no tube, but divided into three oval and most spreading or reflexed segments

3 STAMINA are two erect filaments the length of the corolla, having simple antheræ

II Female.

1 CALYX. The spatha is long, cylindrical, erect, bifid at the top, and contains one flower The perianthium is placed above the germen, and divided into three oval segments

2 COROLLA is three linear, very narrow, truncated petals, a little shorter than the calyx The nectarium is a patent cuspis in each of the petals

3 PISTILLUM consists of a long cylindrical germen situated below the calyx, a very short style, and a stigma divided into three oval, semibifid, convex segments, which are longer than the calyx

4 PERICARPIUM is a long cylindrical capsule, containing one cell

5 SEMINA The seeds are numerous, oval, and affixed to the side of the capsule

## CHAP. CCCCLXXX.

## *VELLA,* SPANISH CRESS

THERE are only two species of this genus, one of which is an annual, the other is usually called Spanish Cress

This plant described. The stalks are upright, woody, and two feet high The leaves are oval, white, very rough, hairy, sit close to the stalks, and are of a greyish colour The flowers come out in bunches from the tops of the stalks, they are of a yellow colour, appear in July and August, and the seeds ripen in the autumn

Propagation. This species is propagated by sowing the seeds in the spring, in a light sandy place When the plants come up, they must be thinned to proper distances, kept clean from weeds, and the summer following they will flower, and perfect their seeds, which, if permitted to scatter, will afford plants for a succession, without further trouble

This species is rather of short duration, seldom lasting longer than about three years, but as plants will arise spontaneously from scattered seeds, much anxiety need not be had about its continuance

Titles. This species is titled, *Vella foliis integris obovatis ciliatis, siliculis erectis* Caspar Bauhine calls it, *Pseudo-cytisus flore leucoji luteo*, and Lobel, *Cytisi facie alysson fruticans quorundam* It grows naturally in Spain

Class and order in the Linnæan system. *Vella* is of the class and order *Tetradynamia Siliculosa*, and the characters are,

1 CALYX

The characters

1 CALYX is an upright cylindrical perianthium, composed of four linear obtuse, deciduous leaves

2 COROLLA is cruciform, and consists of four oval patent petals, having ungues the length of the calyx

3 STAMINA are six filaments the length of the calyx, (of which the two opposite ones are somewhat the shortest) having simple antheræ

4 PISTILLUM consists of an oval germen, a conical style, and a simple stigma

5 PERICARPIUM is a globular, entire, bilocular pod

6. SEMINA The seeds are few, and roundish

## CHAP. CCCCLXXXI.

## *VERATRUM*, WHITE HELLEBORE.

Species

THERE are three species of this genus, called,

1 Green-flowered White Hellebore

2 Dark red flowered White Hellebore

3 Yellow flowered White Hellebore

Description of Green flowered White Hellebore.

1 Green flowered White Hellebore The stalks are thick, round, branching from the very bottom, and three or four feet high The leaves are oblong, oval, nervous, and the lower ones are very large, but they become narrow, and diminish gradually in size as they are stationed towards the top of the plant The flowers come out from the ends of the branches in spikes, they are of a greenish white colour, appear in June and July, and the seeds ripen in September

Medicinal properties

The root of this species is used in medicine, and is the powerful sternutatory of the shops

Dark red,

2 Dark-red-flowered White Hellebore The stalks are thick, branching, and four or five feet high The leaves are very long, nervous, and of a yellowish-green colour The flowers come out in spikes from the ends of the branches, they are of a dark-red colour, appear in May and June, and the seeds ripen in August

and Yellow flowered White Hellebore described

3 Yellow-flowered White Hellebore The root is thick, and fleshy The radical leaves are oblong, spear-shaped, nervous, firm, smooth, and spread themselves on the ground The stalk is simple, ten or twelve inches high, and furnished with a few small sessile leaves, placed without order The flowers terminate the stalk in a close thick spike, they are small, of a yellow colour, appear in June and July, but are seldom succeeded by seeds in England

Culture

These sorts are all propagated by parting of the roots, the best time for which is the autumn They love a good rich earth, and a shady situation, and after they are finally set out, will require no trouble, except keeping them clean from weeds

They may be also encreased by seeds, which should be sown in beds of light earth, soon after they are ripe When the plants come up, they must be thinned where they are too close, watered in dry weather all summer, and in the autumn should be set in the nursery, in beds at about eight inches asunder Here they may stand for one or two years, before they are finally set out

Titles

1 Green flowered White Hellebore is titled, *Veratrum racemo supradecomposito, corollis erectis* Gmelin calls it, *Veratrum pedunculis corollâ erectâ patente brevioribus*, Caspar Bauhine, *Helleborus albus, flore subviridi*, and Clusius, *Helleborus albus, exalbido flore* It grows naturally on the mountainous parts of Russia, Siberia, Austria, Helvetia, Italy, and Greece

2 Dark-red-flowered White Hellebore is, *Veratrum racemo composito, corollis patentibus* Gmelin calls it, *Veratrum pedunculis corollâ patentissimâ longioribus*, and Caspar Bauhine, *Helleborus albus, flore atro-rubente* It grows naturally in warm dry places in Hungary and Siberia.

3 Yellow-flowered White Hellebore is, *Veratrum racemo simplicissimo, foliis sessilibus* Gronovius calls it, *Veratrum caule simplicissimo*, also, *Reseda foliis lanceolatis, caule simplicissimo* It grows naturally in Virginia and Canada

Class and order in the Linnæan system

*Veratrum* is of the class and order *Polygamia Monœcia*, and the characters are,

The characters

I Hermaphrodites

1 CALYX There is none

2 COROLLA is six oblong, spear shaped, serrated, permanent petals

3 STAMINA are six awl-shaped filaments half the length of the corolla, having quadrangular antheræ

4 PISTILLUM consists of three erect oblong germens, ending in a very short style, with simple stigmas.

5 PERICARPIUM consists of three oblong, erect, compressed capsules, each of which is formed of a single valve, contains one cell, and opens on the inside

6 SEMINA The seeds are many, oblong, membranaceous, and compressed

II Male Flowers.

1 CALYX is the same as in the males

2 COROLLA as in the males

3 STAMINA as in the males

4. PISTILLUM There appears a barren rudiment of a pistil

CHAP

# CHAP. CCCCLXXXII

## *VERBASCUM*, MULLEIN

Species

THE more durable ſpecies of this genus are,
1 Sage-leaved Black Mullein
2 Borage leaved Mullein
3 Phœnician Mullein
4 Prickly Mullein

Sage-leaved Black,

1 Sage-leaved Black Mullein The radical leaves are oblong, heart-ſhaped, crenated, downy underneath, and eight or ten inches long The ſtalk is angular, four or five feet high, and garniſhed with a few narrow, pointed, ſerrated leaves, growing irregularly on it The flowers come out in long ſpikes from the tops of the ſtalks, they are of a beautiful yellow colour, having purple antheræ, and are poſſeſſed of an agreeable odour, they appear in July, and the ſeeds ripen in the autumn

Borage leaved,

2 Borage leaved Mullein The leaves are oval, thick, hairy, crenated on the edges, and ſpread flat on the ground The ſtalks are ſlender, naked, four or five inches high, and divide into a few branches near the top The flowers come out ſingly from the ends of the branches they are large, of a blue colour, appear in May and June, and the ſeeds ripen in Auguſt

Phœnician,

3 Phœnician Mullein The radical leaves are oval, crenated, rough, and ſpreading The ſtalk is branching, almoſt naked, and about three feet high The flowers are produced from the ſides of the branches on ſhort footſtalks, they are of a bluiſh-purple colour, appear in June and July, and ſometimes the ſeeds ripen in the autumn

and Prickly Mullein deſcribed

4 Prickly Mullein The ſtalk is woody, hoary, five or ſix feet high, and crowned with ſpines The leaves are long, thick, ſpongy, of a whitiſh colour, and come out without order at a ſmall diſtance from each other on the ſtalks The flowers are produced in long ſpikes from the tops of the ſtalks, they are of a yellow colour, appear in June and July, and in favourable ſeaſons the ſeeds ripen in the autumn

Method of propagation

Theſe plants are beſt raiſed from ſeeds, which ſhould be ſown in the ſpring in beds of light earth made fine When the plants come up, let them be thinned where they are too cloſe, kept clean from weeds, and duly watered in dry weather all ſummer, and in the autumn they may be removed to the places where they are deſigned to remain

The firſt two ſorts are very hardy, and will grow in any ſoil or ſituation, but the other two muſt have a dry, light, ſandy earth, and a well-ſheltered place, otherwiſe they frequently die, eſpecially the third ſort, after they have flowered

They are alſo propagated by offſets, which ſhould be ſet early in the autumn, that they may have time to obtain good root before the froſts come on The plants will flower the ſummer following, but they are ſeldom ſo ſtrong or beautiful as the ſeedlings

Titles

1 Sage-leaved Black Mullein is titled, *Verbaſcum foliis oblongo cordatis petiolatis* In the *Hortus Cliffort* it is termed, *Verbaſcum foliis ovatis ſubtus incanis crenatis, ſpicâ laxâ rarius ramoſâ* Van Royen calls it, *Verbaſcum foliis ovatis crenatis ſubtus tomentoſis, caule angulato*, Caſpar Bauhine, *Verbaſcum nigrum, flore ex luteo purpuraſcente*, John Bauhine, *Verbaſcum nigrum, flore parvo, apicibus purpureis*, Lobel, *Verbaſcum nigrum ſalvifolium, luteo flore*, Gerard, *Verbaſcum nigrum*, and Parkinſon, *Verbaſcum nigrum vulgare* It grows naturally by way-ſides, &c in England, and moſt countries of Europe

2 Borage-leaved Mullein is, *Verbaſcum foliis lanatis radicalibus, ſcapo nudo* Van Royen calls it, *Cortuſa foliis ovatis ſeſſilibus*, Caſpar Bauhine, *Sanicula Alpina, foliis boraginis, villoſa*; and Dalechamp, *Auricula urſi myconi* It grows naturally on the Pyrenees

3 Phœnician Mullein is, *Verbaſcum foliis ovatis crenatis radicalibus, caule ſubnudo racemoſo* In the *Hortus Cliffort* it is termed, *Verbaſcum foliis ovatis crenatis nudis ſcabris, caule ramoſo* Moriſon calls it, *Blattaria perennis, flore violaceo*, and Caſpar Bauhine, *Blattaria purpurea* It grows naturally in Portugal and Spain

4 Prickly Mullein is, *Verbaſcum caule folioſo ſpinoſo, fruteſcente* Tournefort calls it, *Verbaſcum Creticum ſpinoſum fruteſcens*, Lobel, *Verbaſcum ſpinoſum Creticum*; Caſpar Bauhine, *Verbaſcum Creticum ſpinoſum incanum luteum*, and Alpinus, *Leucojum ſpinoſum* It grows naturally in Crete

Claſs and order in the Linnæan ſyſtem

*Verbaſcum* is of the claſs and order *Pentandria Monogynia*, and the characters are,

The characters

1 CALYX is a ſmall, monophyllous, permanent perianthium, divided into five erect acute parts

2 COROLLA is one wheel-ſhaped petal The tube is cylindrical, and very ſhort The limb is patent, and divided into five oval obtuſe ſegments

3 STAMINA are five awl ſhaped declining filaments ſhorter than the corolla, having roundiſh, erect, compreſſed antheræ

4 PISTILLUM conſiſts of a roundiſh germen, a filiforme inclining ſtyle the length of the ſtamina, and a thickiſh obtuſe ſtigma

5 PERICARPIUM is a roundiſh bilocular capſule, opening at the top

6 SEMINA The ſeeds are numerous, and angular.

# CHAP. CCCCLXXXIII.

## *VERBENA*, VERVAIN.

Species.

OF this genus there are,
1. Tall American Vervain.
2. Canada Nettle-leaved Vervain.
3. Low Virginian Vervain.
4. Carolina Vervain.
5. Creeping Vervain.

Tall American. 1. Tall American Vervain. The stalks are many, from a strong root, four-cornered, upright, and send forth short branches from the sides, and grow to five or eight feet high. The leaves are spear-shaped, deeply serrated, acute-pointed, and placed by pairs on slender footstalks. The flowers are produced in long, slender, sharp-pointed spikes, from the tops of the stalks; they are of a blue colour, appear in August, and the seeds frequently ripen in the autumn.

Canada Nettle-leaved. 2. Canada Nettle-leaved Vervain. The stalks are four cornered, upright, and about a yard high. The leaves are oblong, acute-pointed, serrated, and grow opposite by pairs on slender footstalks. The flowers are collected into slender paniculated spikes at the tops of the stalks; they are small, and of a white colour; they appear in July, and the seeds ripen in the autumn.

Virginian. 3. Virginian Vervain. The stalks are numerous, square, rigid, a little hairy, branching, and two or three feet high. The leaves are oblong, pointed, deeply jagged on the edges, and grow opposite to each other on long slender footstalks. The flowers are produced from the tops of the stalks in slender spikes; they are larger than the former sort, and of a pale blue colour; they appear in July and August, and the seeds ripen in the autumn.

Carolina. 4. Carolina Vervain. The stalks are upright, square, firm, and four or five feet high. The leaves are spear-shaped, obtuse-pointed, serrated on the edges, rough to the touch, and grow opposite to each other on very short footstalks. The flowers are collected in slender spikes at the tops of the stalks; they shew themselves in July and August, and in favourable seasons the seeds ripen in the autumn.

and Creeping Vervain described. 5. Creeping Vervain. The stalks trail on the ground, strike root at the joints, and soon spread themselves to a considerable distance. The leaves are oval, spear-shaped, serrated, and sit close to the stalks. The flowers come out in conical spikes, arising from the wings of the branches on long naked footstalks; they are of a yellowish-white colour, appear in August and September, and continue in succession until the frost stops them.

Method of propagating them. These plants are best raised by sowing the seeds, which may be done in the autumn, as soon as they are ripe, or the spring following. When the plants come up, they must be thinned where they appear too close, kept clean from weeds, duly watered all summer, and in the autumn may be removed to the places where they are designed to remain. The summer following they will flower, and perfect their seeds.

They are also propagated by parting of the roots, which is best done in the autumn, though it may, with success, be effected in the winter, or the early part of the spring. They love an open exposure, and the first sort delights in moisture. The soil for the second should be warm and dry; the two last should have a light soil, not over-moist, but will do very well in a dry soil, provided they be daily watered in dry weather.

1. The first species is titled, *Verbena tetrandra, spicis longis acuminatis, foliis lanceolatis.* Van Royen calls it, *Verbena foliis lanceolatis serratis, spicis filiformibus paniculatis*; and Hermann, *Verbena mas, recta altissima spica multiplici, urticæ foliis angustis, floribus cæruleis.* It grows naturally in most places in Canada. Titles.

2. The second species is, *Verbena tetrandra, spicis filiformibus paniculatis, foliis indivisis ovatis serratis acutis petiolatis.* Van Royen calls it, *Verbena foliis ovatis, caule erecto, spicis filiformibus paniculatis*; and Morison, *Verbena recta Canadensis, urticæ foliis.* It grows naturally in Virginia and Canada.

3. The third is, *Verbena tetrandra, spicis filiformibus, foliis multifido-laciniatis, caulibus numerosis.* It grows naturally in Virginia and Canada.

4. The fourth species is, *Verbena tetrandra, spicis filiformibus, foliis indivisis lanceolatis serratis, calycibus subsessilibus.* Dillenius calls it, *Verbena Caroliniensis, melissæ folio aspero*; and Ray, *Verbena Caroliniana, folio integro serrato scabro.* It grows naturally in North America.

5. The fifth species is, *Verbena tetrandra, spicis capitato-conicis, foliis serratis, caule repente.* Gronovius calls it, *Verbena caule repente, foliis oblongis superne crenatis, pedunculis solitariis capitatis.* It grows naturally in Virginia.

*Verbena* is of the class and order *Diandria Monogynia*; and the characters are, Class and order in the Linnæan system.

1. CALYX is a monophyllous angular tubular, linear, permanent perianthium, indented in five parts at the top.

2. COROLLA is one unequal petal. The tube is cylindrical, and the length of the calyx; the limb is patent, and cut into five round and nearly equal segments.

3. STAMINA are four very short setaceous filaments within the tube of the flower, two of which are longer than the other, having crooked, incurved antheræ.

4. PISTILLUM consists of a four-cornered germen, a simple filiform style the length of the tube, and an obtuse stigma.

5. PERICARPIUM. The seeds are contained in the calyx.

6. SEMINA. The seeds are either two or four, and of an oblong figure.

CHAP.

# CHAP. CCCCLXXXIV.

## *VERONICA*, SPEEDWELL.

OF this genus are the following perennials, viz.

Species.
1 Siberian Speedwell
2 Virginian Speedwell
3 Narrow-leaved Spiked Speedwell
4 Maritime Speedwell
5 Long-leaved Speedwell
6 Hoary Speedwell
7 Upright Spiked Male Speedwell, or Fluellin
8. Welch Speedwell
9 Male Speedwell of the Shops
10 Naked-stalked Speedwell
11 Daisy-leaved Speedwell
12 Shrubby Speedwell
13 Alpine Speedwell
14 Paul's Betony, Little or Smooth Speedwell
15 Common Brook Lime
16 Long-leaved Water Speedwell
17 Narrow-leaved Water Speedwell
18 Austrian Speedwell
19 Mountain Speedwell
20 Prostrate Speedwell
21 Wild Germander
22 Broad-leaved Wild Germander
23 Narrow-leaved Wild Germander
24 Denticulated Speedwell

Description of Siberian. 1 Siberian Speedwell. The stalks are upright, rough, hairy, and four or five feet high. The leaves are broad, oval, spear-shaped, and seven of them surround the stalk in a radiated manner at the joints. The flowers come out from the tops of the stalks in long spikes; they are of a blue colour, appear in July and August, and the seeds ripen in the autumn.

Virginian. 2 Virginian Speedwell. The stalks are upright, and four feet high. The leaves are spear-shaped, serrated, acute-pointed, and four or five surround the stalk in a radiated manner at each joint. The flowers are produced from the tops of the stalks in long, slender spikes, are of a white colour, appear in July and August, and the seeds ripen in the autumn.

Narrow-leaved Spiked. 3 Narrow-leaved Spiked Speedwell. The stalks are about three feet high. The leaves are long, narrow, serrated, acute, of a bright-green colour, and three of them usually surround the stalk at each joint. The flowers terminate the stalks in spikes, are of a blue colour, appear in June and July, and the seeds ripen in the autumn.

Maritime. 4 Maritime Speedwell. The stalk is erect, and about two feet high. The leaves are spear-shaped, unequally serrated, of a light green colour, and, for the most part, three of them surround the stalk at each joint. The flowers terminate the stalks in spikes, are of a bright colour, appear in July, and the seeds ripen in the autumn.

Long-leaved. 5 Long-leaved Speedwell. The stalks grow to a foot and a half or two feet high. The leaves are spear-shaped, serrated, pointed, of a lucid-green colour, and grow opposite to each other at the joints. The flowers terminate the stalks in long spikes, are of a blue colour, appear in June, and the seeds ripen in the autumn.

Hoary. 6 Hoary Speedwell. The stalks are erect, white, woolly, and about a foot high. The leaves are oblong, crenated, hoary, and grow opposite to each other at the joints. The flowers terminate the stalks in many slender, erect spikes, they are of a deep blue colour, and appear in June and July.

Upright Spiked Male. 7 Upright Spiked Male Speedwell, or Fluellin. The stalk is unbranching, and about a foot high. The leaves are oval, oblong, crenated, of a pale green colour, and grow opposite to each other. The flowers come out from the tops of the stalks in short spikes; they are of a blue colour, appear in June and July, and the seeds ripen in the autumn.

and Welch Speedwell. 8 Welch Speedwell. The stalk is erect, sends out a few branches from the sides, and grows to be ten or twelve inches high. The leaves are oblong, obtuse, serrated, rough, hairy, and grow opposite to each other. The flowers terminate the stalk and side-branches in long spikes, are of a pale blue colour, appear in June and July, and the seeds ripen in the autumn.

Male Speedwell of the Shops described. 9 Male Speedwell of the Shops. The stalks are weak, hairy, branching, partly procumbent, and strike out at the joints. The leaves are oval, serrated, and grow opposite to each other. The flowers are produced in spikes from the ends and sides of the branches; they are small, of a pale blue colour, often having a tinge of purple, appear in June, and the seeds ripen in August.

Medicinal properties of it. This species is a fine pectoral, an excellent vulnerary, and affords a tea that is good against the gout, rheumatism, scurvy, measles, and small-pox.

Description of Naked-stalked. 10 Naked-stalked Speedwell. The radical leaves are small, oval, hairy, and form a cluster at the crown of the root. The stalk is single, naked, and four or five inches high. The flowers terminate the stalk in a corymbus, are of a blue colour, and appear in June.

Daisy leaved. 11 Daisy-leaved Speedwell. The stalk is undivided, adorned with two leaves only, and eight or ten inches high. The leaves are oval, rounded at the extremity, narrower near the base, and much resemble those of the Daisy. The flowers terminate the stalk in a corymbus, are small, of a blue colour, and appear in June and July.

Shrubby. 12 Shrubby Speedwell. The stalks are ligneous, upright, branching, and eight or ten inches high. The leaves are spear-shaped, obtuse, smooth, and crenated on their edges. The flowers come out in a corymbus at the tops of the stalks, are of a purplish colour, and appear about the same time with the former.

and Alpine Speedwell. 13 Alpine Speedwell. The stalks are ligneous, partly procumbent, and about a foot and a half long. The leaves are oval, crenated on their edges, and grow opposite to each other on the stalks. The flowers come out in a corymbus from

from the extremity of the ſtalks, they are ſmall, have very rough, hiſpid cups, appear in June and July, and the ſeeds ripen in the autumn

*Paul's Betony deſcribed.* 14 Paul's Betony, Little or Smooth Speedwell The ſtalks are ſlender, trailing, branching, and ſtrike root at the joints The leaves are oval, ſmooth, crenated, and grow oppoſite to each other at the joints The flowers come out from the ends of the branches in kind of ſpikes, they are of a whitiſh colour, having a tinge of blue, appear in May and June, and the ſeeds ripen in Auguſt

*Common Brook Lime deſcribed.* 15 Common Brook Lime The ſtalks are round, thick, ſucculent, ſmooth, procumbent near the baſe, where it ſtrikes root from the joints into the mud, but riſes afterwards nearly in an upright direction, and grows to a foot or more in height The leaves are oval, plane, ſucculent, ſmooth, crenated, of a deep-green colour, and grow oppoſite by pairs at the joints The flowers come out in ſpikes from the wings of the leaves, are of a beautiful blue colour, appear in June and July, and the ſeeds ripen in Auguſt

*Medicinal properties of it.* This ſpecies is an excellent antiſcorbutic, and recommended to be eaten as a ſallad-herb in the ſpring

*Deſcription of Long leaved Water,* 16 Long-leaved Water Speedwell The ſtalk is thick, jointed, upright, branching, and two feet high The leaves are ſpear-ſhaped, ſerrated, and grow oppoſite to each other at the joints The flowers come out in looſe ſpikes from the wings of the leaves, are of a whitiſh blue colour, appear in July, and the ſeeds ripen in the autumn

*Narrow leaved Water,* 17 Narrow-leaved Water Speedwell The ſtalks are ſlender, and about a foot high The leaves are very narrow, ſpear ſhaped, entire, and grow oppoſite to each other The flowers come out from the wings of the leaves in looſe ſpikes, are of a blue colour, appear in June, and the ſeeds ripen in Auguſt

*Auſtrian,* 18 Auſtrian Speedwell The ſtalks are upright, thick, tough, ſend forth branches by pairs from the ſides, and grow to be three feet high The leaves are ſpear-ſhaped ſmooth, and elegantly jagged, or cut, almoſt to the mid-rib, into many ſlender ſegments The flowers come out in looſe ſpikes from the wings of the leaves, are of a blue colour, and appear in July and Auguſt

*Mountain* 19 Mountain Speedwell The ſtalk is ſlender, weak, and unable to ſupport itſelf erect The leaves are oval, rough, crenated on their edges, and grow oppoſite on footſtalks The flowers come out from the wings of the leaves in kind of looſe ſpikes, are ſmall, but few in the ſpike, and their cups are hairy, they appear in May and June, and the ſeeds ripen in Auguſt.

*and Proſtrate Speed-Well* 20. Proſtrate Speedwell The ſtalks are of a hardiſh ſubſtance, downy, and lie flat on the ground The leaves are oval, oblong, ſerrated, downy, and the lower ones have ſhort footſtalks, but the upper ones ſit cloſe The flowers come out from the wings of the leaves in long, looſe ſpikes, they are of a fine violet colour, appear in July, and the ſeeds ripen in September

*Wild,* 21 Wild Germander The ſtalks are weak, ſlender, cornered, jointed, and hairy The leaves are oval, rough, indented, grow oppoſite to each other, and ſit cloſe, having no footſtalks The flowers come out from the wings of the leaves in looſe ſpikes elevated on long footſtalks, they are of an elegant blue colour, appear in May, June, and July, and the ſeeds ripen in Auguſt and September

*Broad leaved Wild,* 22 Broad-leaved Wild Germander The ſtalks are ſlender, but firm and upright The leaves are heart-ſhaped, rough, indented, and grow oppoſite The flowers come out in long, looſe ſpikes or branches from the wings of the leaves, near the upper parts of the plant, they are of a bright-blue colour, and appear in May, June, and July

*and Narrow leaved Wild Germander deſcribed* 23 Narrow leaved Wild Germander The ſtalks are ſtiff, upright, and three or four feet high The lower leaves are oval rough, indented and obtuſe, but the upper ones are narrow and acute The flowers come out in long, cloſe ſpikes or bunches from the ſides of the ſtalks, are of a blue colour, and appear in June, July, and Auguſt

*Paniculated Speedwell deſcribed* 24 Paniculated Speedwell The ſtalk is ſlender, jointed, and uſually leans on one ſide The leaves are ſpear-ſhaped, ſerrated, and for the moſt part grow by threes at a joint The flowers come out in ſpiked panicles from the tops of the ſtalks, are of a deep blue colour, appear in July, and the ſeeds ripen in the autumn

*Method of propagation.* Theſe plants are all extremely hardy, and en creaſed with the utmoſt facility by parting of the roots, which may be effected at any time of the year, but is beſt done in the autumn The Brook Lime and Wild Germander are not cultivated but the others are deſerving a place in every good collection of flowers, where, by their long ſpikes and good colour, they will afford a beautiful variety The talleſt ſorts may be planted by the borders of the wilderneſs quarters, nay, even in woods, &c whilſt the lower kinds may be made to occupy open beds in the flower-garden *Proper ſituation* All of them like the ſhade and moiſture, and being thus ſtationed, their ſpikes will be larger, their colours more beautiful and they will continue much longer in blow, than if ſituated in places of an oppoſite nature

They may be alſo propagated by ſeeds Theſe ſhould be ſown in the autumn ſoon after they are ripe, or the ſpring following When the plants come up, they muſt be thinned where they appear too cloſe, be conſtantly kept clean from weeds, and, when they are fit to remove, may be tranſplanted to the places where they are deſigned to remain

*Titles* 1 Siberian Speedwell is titled *Veronica ſpicis terminalibus, foliis ſeptenis verticillatis, caule ſub hirſuto* Amman calls it, *Veronica ſpicata, foliis verticulatis diſpoſitis* It grows naturally in Dauria

2 Virginian Speedwell is, *Veronica ſpicis terminalibus, foliis quaternis quinisve* In the *Hortus Cliffort* it is termed, *Veronica foliis quaternis quinisve* Plukenet calls it, *Veronica Virginiana procerior, foliis ternis, quaternis, & etiam quinis caulem amplexantibus, ſpicis florum candidiſſimis* It grows naturally in Virginia

3 Narrow leaved Spiked Speedwell is, *Veronica ſpicis terminalibus, foliis ternis æqualiter ſerratis* Caſpar Bauhine calls it, *Veronica ſpicata anguſtifolia*, and Barrelier, *Veronica mas ſurrecta elatior* It grows naturally in Siberia, Thuringia, France, and Italy

4 Maritime Speedwell is, *Veronica ſpicis terminalibus, foliis ternis inæqualiter ſerratis* In the *Flora Suecica* it is termed, *Veronica floribus ſpicatis, foliis ternis*, in the *Hortus Cliffort Veronica foliis ſæpius ternis*; in the *Flora Lapp Veronica caule erecto, ſpicis pluribus, foliis lanceolatis ſerratis* Caſpar Bauhine calls it, *Lyſimachia ſpicata cærulea*, and Dodonæus, *Pſeudo-lyſimachium cæruleum* It grows naturally in the maritime parts of Europe

5 Long leaved Speedwell is, *Veronica ſpicis terminalibus, foliis oppoſitis lanceolatis ſerratis* Caſpar Bauhine calls it, *Veronica ſpicata latifolia*, Cluſius, *Veronica I elatior latifolia*, and Amman, *Veronica ſpicata longifolia altera*, alſo, *Veronica ſpicata,*

*spicata, urticæ folio* It grows naturally in Sweden, Austria, and Tartary

6 Hoary Speedwell is, *Veronica spicis terminalibus, foliis oppositis crenatis obtusis, caule erecto tomentoso* Van Royen calls it, *Veronica caule fruticoso, foliis oblongis, inferioribus crenatis petiolatis, superioribus sessilibus integerrimis*, and Amman, *Veronica spicata lanuginosa & incana, floribus cæruleis* It grows naturally in Ucrania and Samara

7 Upright Spiked Male Speedwell, or Fluellin, is, *Veronica spicâ terminali, foliis oppositis crenatis obtusis, caule adscendente simplicissimo* In the *Flora Suecia* it is termed, *Veronica floribus spicatis, foliis oppositis, caule erecto*, in the *Hortus Cliffort Veronica foliis oppositis, caule spicâ terminato* Caspar Bauhine calls it, *Veronica spicata minor*, Gerard, *Veronica recta minima*, and Parkinson, *Veronica erecta angustifolia* It grows naturally in meadows and pastures in England and most of the northern countries of Europe

8 Welsh Speedwell is, *Veronica spicis terminalibus, foliis oppositis obtuse serratis scabris, caule erecto* Ray calls it, *Veronica spicata Cambro-Britannica, bugulæ subhirsuto folio* It grows naturally in Wales, and but sparingly in other parts of Europe

9 Male Speedwell of the Shops is, *Veronica spicis terminalibus pedunculatis, foliis oppositis, caule procumbente* In the *Flora Suecia* it is termed, *Veronica floribus spicatis, foliis oppositis, caule procumbente*, in the *Flora Lapp Veronica caule repente, scapis spicatis, foliis oppositis ovatis strigosis* Caspar Bauhine calls it, *Veronica mas supina & vulgatissima*, Gerard, *Veronica vera & major*, and Parkinson, *Veronica mas vulgaris & supina* It grows naturally in common, woods, and sterile pasture grounds, in England and most countries of Europe

10 Naked stalked Speedwell is, *Veronica corymbo terminali, scapo nudo* Van Royen calls it, *Veronica foliis ovatis radicalibus, caule nudo*, Boccone, *Veronica Alpina pumila, caule aphyllo*, Plukenet, *Veronica ... saxatilis, cauliculis nudis*, and Caspar Bauhine, *Chamædrys Alpina minima ... sa* It grows naturally on the Alps and other mountainous parts of Europe

11 Dairy leaved Speedwell is, *Veronica corymbo terminali, caule adscendente diphyllo* Haller calls it, *Veronica caule non ramoso, floribus congestis terminato, foliis ... subasperis*, and Caspar Bauhine, *Veronica Alpina, bellidis folio* It grows naturally in Helvetia and on the Pyrenees

12 Shrubby Speedwell is, *Veronica corymbo terminali, foliis lanceolatis obtusiusculis, caulibus fruticulosis* Haller calls it, *Veronica foliis ovatis crenatis, fructu ovali floribus in summo caule purpurascentibus*, and Caspar Bauhine, *Veronica Alpina frutescens* It grows naturally on the Austrian, Helvetian, and Pyrenean mountains

13 Alpine Speedwell is, *Veronica corymbo terminali, foliis oppositis, calycibus hispidis* In the *Flora Suecia* it is termed, *Veronica floribus corymbosis terminalibus, calycibus hispidis*, in the *Flora Lapp Veronica caule floribus terminato, foliis ovatis crenatis* Van Royen calls it, *Veronica caule inferne procumbente fruticoso, foliis ovatis oppositis, racemo terminali*, and John Bauhine, *Veronica saxatilis* It grows naturally on the Alps and other mountainous parts of Europe

14 Paul's Betony, or Little or Smooth Speedwell is, *Veronica racemo terminali subspicato, foliis ovatis glabris crenatis* In the *Flora Suecia* it is termed, *Veronica floribus solitariis subcorymbosis, foliis ovatis glabris crenatis*, in the *Hortus Cliffort Veronica foliis inferioribus oppositis ovatis, superioribus alternis lanceolatis, floribus solitariis*, in the *Flora Lapp Veronica floribus sparsis, foliis ovatis crenatis glabris* Caspar Bauhine calls it, *Veronica pratensis serpyllifolia*, John Bauhine, *Veronica fœmina quorundam, aliis betonica Pauli serpyllifolia*, Gerard, *Veronica minor*, and Parkinson, *Veronica pratensis minor*. It grows naturally in meadows and pastures in England and in most countries of Europe, also in North America

15 Common Brook Lime is, *Veronica racemis lateralibus, foliis ovatis planis, caule repente* Van Royen calls it, *Veronica foliis oppositis lævibus crenatis, floribus racemosis lateralibus*, Gronovius, *Veronica foliis oppositis lævibus crenatis, floribus laxè spicatis ex alis*, Caspar Bauhine, *Anagallis aquatica major (in norque) folio subrotundo*, Dodonæus, *Anagallis aquatica*, Gerard, *Anagallis, sive Becabunga*, and Parkinson, *Anagallis aquatica vulgaris, sive Becabunga* It grows naturally in ditches and rivulets in England and most countries of Europe

16 Long leaved Water Speedwell is, *Veronica racemis lateralibus, foliis lanceolatis serratis, caule erecto* Caspar Bauhine calls it, *Anagallis aquatica major, folio oblongo*, Tabernæmontanus, *Berula major*, Ray, *Veronica aquatica longifolia media*, Gerard, *Anagallis aquatica minor*, and Parkinson, *Anagallis aquatica folio oblongo crenato*. It grows naturally in ditches and moist places in England and most parts of Europe, also in the East

17 Narrow leaved Speedwell is, *Veronica racemis lateralibus pedicellis pendulis, foliis linearibus integerrimis* Van Royen calls it, *Veronica foliis lineari-lanceolatis integris, racemis laxe floriferis*, Caspar Bauhine, *Anagallis aquatica angustifolia scutellata*, John Bauhine, *Anagallis aquatica angustifolia*, and Ray, *Veronica aquatica angustifolia minor* It grows naturally in watery places in England and most countries of Europe

18 Austrian Speedwell is, *Veronica racemis lateralibus, foliis lineari-lanceolatis pinnato-dentatis* Caspar Bauhine calls it, *Chamædrys Austriaca, foliis tenuissime laciniatis*, John Bauhine, *Chamædrys spuria tenuissime laciniata*, and Tournefort, *Veronica Cappadocica, foliis laciniatis* It grows naturally in Austria

19 Mountain Speedwell is, *Veronica racemis lateralibus paucifloris, calycibus hirsutis, foliis ovatis rugosis crenatis petiolatis, caule debili* Caspar Bauhine calls it, *Chamædrys spuria affinis rotundifolia scutellata*, Columna, *Alysson Dioscoridis montanum*, and Ray, *Veronica chamædryoides foliis pediculis oblongis insidentibus* It grows naturally in shady places in England, Italy and Germany

20 Prostrate Speedwell is, *Veronica racemis lateralibus, foliis ovato-oblongis serratis, caulibus prostratis* Caspar and John Bauhine call it, *Chamædrys incana spuria minor angustifolia* It grows naturally on the hills of Italy and Germany

21 Wild Germander is, *Veronica racemis lateralibus, foliis ovatis sessilibus rugosis dentatis, caule debili* In the *Hortus Cliffort* it is termed, *Veronica foliis oppositis plicatis dentatis, scapis ex alis inferioribus*, in the *Flora Lapp Veronica foliis cordatis sessilibus oppositis, racemis laxe floriferis*. Caspar Bauhine calls it, *Chamædrys spuria minor rotundifolia*, Dalechamp, *Hierobotane mas*, Gerard, *Chamædrys sylvestris*; and Parkinson, *Chamædrys spuria sylvestris* It grows naturally in meadows and pastures in England and most countries of Europe

22 Broad-leaved Wild Germander is, *Veronica racemis lateralibus, foliis cordatis rugosis dentatis, caule stricto* Van Royen calls it, *Veronica foliis oppositis plicatis dentatis, scapis ex alis superioribus laxe spicatis*, Buxbaum, *Veronica pratensis omnium maxima*, and Caspar Bauhine, *Chamædrys spuria major latifolia* It grows naturally in Helvetia, Bythinia, and Austria

23 Narrow-leaved Wild Germander is, *Veronica racemis lateralibus longissimis, foliis ovatis rugosis dentatis obtusiusculis, caule erecto* Haller calls it, *Veronica foliis imis cordatis superioribus angustioribus*; Caspar Bauhine, *Chamædrys spuria major angustifolia*; and Clusius, *Teucrii IV tertia species* It grows naturally in Germany

24 Paniculated Speedwell is, *Veronica racemis lateralibus longissimis, foliis lanceolatis ternis serratis, caule adscendente* Amman calls it, *Veronica angustifolia, floribus paniculatis* It grows naturally in Tartary

Class and order in the Linnæan System The characters

*Veronica* is of the class and order *Diandria Monogynia*, and the characters are,

1 CALYX is a permanent perianthium divided into four spear-shaped, acute segments

2 COROLLA is one wheel-shaped petal The tube is nearly as long as the calyx. The limb is plane, and divided into four oval segments, the lower segment being the narrowest, and the opposite one to that the broadest of any of them

3 STAMINA are two rising filaments, with oblong antheræ

4 PISTILLUM consists of a compressed germen, a filiforme declining style the length of the stamina, and a simple stigma.

5 PERICARPIUM is an obcordated capsule, compressed at the top, formed of four valves, and containing two cells

6 SEMINA The seeds are many, and roundish

# CHAP CCCCLXXXV

## *VICIA,* VETCH.

Introduction

THE Common Vetches, or Tares, are in themselves very pretty plants, and would be much valued in gardens, on account of their excellent uses, were it not for their commonness in the fields Our woods and our bushes afford some other species, that rear their heads among the branches, and garnish the shrubs in a pleasing taste In places where these species do not grow common, a few of them may be admitted into the garden, together with some others of foreign growth, that ought not to be omitted in our collection In the worst compartment of the garden, therefore, let there be planted,

Species

1 The Common Tufted Vetch
2 The Tufted Wood Vetch
3 The Hungarian Wood Vetch
4 The Thuringian Vetch
5 The German Shrubby Vetch
6 The English Hedge Vetch

Common Tufted

1 The Common Tufted Vetch has a weak, climbing stalk, five or six feet long The leaves are very pretty, being composed of about ten pair of spear-shaped lobes, which are of a whitish-green colour, and hairy, and the tendril terminates the mid rib The flowers are formed in long, imbricated spikes, grow on long footstalks, are of a clear-blue colour, will be in blow in July, and ripen their seeds in September

This species has a pretty effect where it grows naturally, and, were it not for its commonness, would be highly esteemed in gardens

and Tufted Wood Vetch described

2 Tufted Wood Vetch This species will grow, by the assistance of bushes, to be eight or nine feet high The foliage is very fine Each leaf is composed of about seven or eight pair of smooth, oval lobes, terminated by the tendril The flowers are many, large, and formed in long spikes; they grow from the wings of the stalks, blow in July, and ripen their seeds in September

Varieties

There are two varieties of these plants, one has a pale-blue flower, the other is white, having a few blue stripes They are both very pretty plants, and would be highly esteemed, were they difficult to come at

3 The Hungarian Wood Vetch This species climbs upon trees and bushes to a considerable height The stalks are angulated, striated, and tough The leaves are sessile, and composed of several pair of oval lobes, the lower ones joining the stalk The flowers grow on long pedicles from the joints of the stalks, are of a yellow colour, will be in blow in July, and ripen their seeds in the autumn Hungarian Wood Vetch described

There is a variety of this species with white flowers Variety

4 Thuringian Vetch This species will climb to six or eight feet high The leaves are composed of several pair of lobes, which are long, oval, pointed, and reflexed, and the lower ones grow distinct from the stalks The flowers grow from the wings of the leaves on footstalks, are of a purplish or blue colour, will be in blow in July, and ripen their seeds in the autumn Description of Thuringian,

5 German Shrubby Vetch This species hath kind of ligneous stalks, but they die in the autumn like the other sorts, and fresh ones arise from the root in the spring The root also is woody and creeping, and its stalks, which will not become woody before the end of the summer, will be about a yard long The leaves are composed of about eight or ten pair of lobes, they are oval, and their ends are acutely pointed The flowers are produced from the wings of the stalks in short spikes, they are of a pale-blue colour, will be in blow in July, and ripen their seeds in September German Shrubby,

6 English Hedge or Bush Vetch. This species will climb to the height of four or five feet The leaves are composed of about six pair of entire, oval, acute lobes The flowers are produced from the wings of the leaves on short footstalks, they are of a kind of bluish purple colour, will be and English Hedge or Bush Vetch

be in blow in July, and ripen their seeds in the autumn.

Propagation. These species are easily propagated by sowing the seeds. This may be done in the spring, but the autumn is the best season, soon after they are ripe, for then they will be surer of growing. As the plants advance in height, they must be supported with sticks, or their stalks will trail on the ground, look unsightly, produce few or no flowers, and in wet seasons rot. A few plants of a sort will be sufficient, and they ought never to be admitted into any but large gardens.

Proper situation. These plants are by Nature designed as ornaments to shrubberies or wilderness quarters, which places should never be without them, for there they will grow with all their native luxuriance and ease, climb upon the shrubs or bushes, and shew their flowers from their tops or sides in the most perfect and pleasing manner. They will add a gaiety and unartful beauty to the whole, and amply reward the little trouble they cause in first being introduced to their stations.

Culture. In all shrubberies, wilderness quarters, and borders of woods, through which are walks for recreation, let a few seeds of all these species be sown. Let the ground be well loosened and dug under the bushes you intend shall be for their support, and in the autumn, soon after the seeds are ripe, sow a few seeds in these little prepared spots under the bushes, leaving a stick for a direction or mark where they have been sown. In the spring they will come up, at which time they should be carefully kept clear of weeds, and, if the weather should prove very dry, now and then watered. After they are grown strong, and begin to climb, they will require no farther trouble, it will be out of the power of weeds to hurt them, and the bushes will afford them sufficient shade from the raging heat of the sun, and at the same time yield them that assistance for climbing they naturally stand in need of, and introduce them to that perfection they are by Nature designed to attain.

Titles. 1. Tufted Vetch is titled, *Vicia pedunculis multifloris, floribus imbricatis foliolis lanceolatis pubescentibus, stipulis integris*. In the *Hortus Cliffort.* it is titled, *Vicia pedunculis multifloris, stipulis utrinque acutis integris*. Caspar Bauhine calls one sort of it, *Vicia sylvestris spicata*, another, *Vicia multiflora*. Rivinus calls it, *Cracca*. It grows naturally in England and most parts of Europe.

2. Tufted Wood Vetch is titled, *Vicia pedunculis multifloris, foliolis ovalibus, stipulis denticulatis*. In the *Flora Lapponica* it is termed, *Vicia pedunculis multifloris, stipulis crenatis*. Plukenet calls it, *Vicia multiflora maxima perennis, tetro odore, floribus albentibus, lineis cæruleis notatis*. It grows naturally in woods, hedges, and bushes, in many parts of England, Germany, and Sweden.

3. Hungarian Wood Vetch is titled, *Vicia pedunculis multifloris, petiolis polyphyllis, foliolis ovatis, infimis sessilibus*. Caspar Bauhine calls it, *Pisum sylvestre perenne*, Clusius, *Pisum sylvestre*, and Rivinus, *Cracca flore ochroleuco*. It grows naturally in the woods of Hungary.

4. Thuringian Vetch is titled, *Vicia pedunculis multifloris, foliolis reflexis ovatis mucronatis, stipulis subdentatis*. In the *Flora Suecica* it is termed, *Vicia pedunculis multifloris, petiolis polyphyllis cirrhosis, foliolis alternis ovatis, stipulis dentatis*. Caspar Bauhine calls it, *Vicia maxima Dumetorum*, John Bauhine, *Vicia sylvatica maxima piso similis*; and Rivinus, *Cracca sylvatica*. It grows naturally in Thuringia.

5. German Shrubby Vetch is titled, *Vicia pedunculis subsexfloris, foliolis denis ovatis acutis, stipulis integris*. In the *Hortus Cliffort.* it is termed, *Vicia pedunculis multifloris, caule fruticoso*. Plukenet calls it, *Vicia multiflora cassubica frutescens, siliqua lata*. It grows naturally in Germany.

6. English Hedge Vetch is titled, *Vicia leguminibus pedicellatis subquaternis erectis, foliolis ovatis integerrimis, exterioribus decrescentibus*. In the *Hortus Cliffort. &c.* it is termed, *Vicia leguminibus adscendentibus, petiolis polyphyllis, foliolis ovatis acutis integerrimis*. Caspar Bauhine calls it, *Vicia sepium, folio rotundiore acuto*, and Rivinus, *Vicia sepium*. It grows naturally in the hedges of Europe.

Class and order in the Linnæan system. *Vicia* is of the class and order *Diadelphia Decandria*, and the characters are,

The characters. 1. CALYX is a tubulous, erect, acute, monophyllous perianthium, divided at the top into five parts.

2. COROLLA is papilionaceous. The vexillum is oval, indented, has a sharp point at the top, is reflexed on the sides, and has a compressed ridge down the middle. The two wings are oblong, erect, semicordated, and shorter than the vexillum. The carina is shorter than the wings, is compressed, and has an oblong claw divided into two parts.

3. STAMINA. The filaments are diadelphous, nine of them are joined in a body, the other stands alone. The antheræ are erect, roundish, and four-furrowed.

4. PISTILLUM consists of a long, narrow, compressed germen, a filiform rising style, and an obtuse stigma, bearded under the top.

5. PERICARPIUM is a long coriaceous, pointed pod, of one cell, that opens with two valves.

6. SEMINA. The seeds are many, and roundish.

CHAP.

# CHAP. CCCCLXXXVI.

## *VIOLA*, VIOLET.

THE Marſh Violet of our hedges, in its varieties, is the chief ſpecies for our gardens, on account of its well known agreeable odour; though there are others like them that are pretty little plants, which take up ſmall room in a garden, and afford variety of theſe low kinds. So that at the head of this tribe ſhall ſtand,

Species

1 Common Sweet-ſcented Spring Violet, or Marſh Violet.
2 Hairy Scentleſs Marſh Violet.
3 Marſh Violet.
4 Palmated-leaved Violet.
5 Pedated leaved Violet.
6 Pinnated leaved Violet.
7 Lanceolated-leaved Violet.
8 *Primula*-leaved Violet.
9 Dog's Violet.
10 Ceniſian Violet.
11 Mountain Violet.
12 Yellow Alpine Violet.

Common Marſh or Spring Violet deſcribed

1 Common Marſh or Spring Violet has a thick, fibrous, brown root from which riſe leaves, flowers, and creeping ſtalks. Theſe ſtalks trail upon the ground, ſtrike root at the joints, and by cutting the ſhoot become diſtinct plants. The leaves come out in cluſters; they are heart ſhaped, a little hairy, and have a moderately-long green footſtalk. Among the leaves come out the flowers; they grow on ſlender footſtalks ſhorter than thoſe of the leaves, are of a pale green colour, and often near the baſe are tinged with purple; they appear in March, and ſometimes earlier; and of them there are the following varieties.

Varieties

The Common Blue Violet,
The Pale-purple Violet,
The White Violet,
The Double Blue Violet,
The Double White Violet.

The Double ſorts are moſt valued, on account of the flowers, which are very large and double, and not ſo common as the other ſorts. They are very ſweet, but have not the heightened fragrance of the Single ſorts.

Culture

Violets are propagated by parting of the roots, or taking off the new plants formed by the trailing ſhoots. This may be done at any time of the year, but the beſt ſeaſon is the ſummer, if moiſt weather happens, after they have done flowering. They will ſoon become ſtrong plants, and produce a greater quantity of flowers the ſpring following than if the buſineſs was deferred longer.

They are alſo eaſily propagated by the ſeeds, which ripen in July or Auguſt, and ſhould be ſown ſoon after in a ſhady border of light earth. In the ſpring the plants will come up, and in about a month after may be tranſplanted to the places where they are deſigned to remain. Theſe always make the prettieſt plants, are the fulleſt of flowers, are not ſo inclined for the firſt ſeaſon to throw out their trailing ſhoots, and are in every reſpect the moſt elegant.

Its uſes in medicine

The medicinal uſes of the Violet are well-known. The ſyrup is a great cooler, laxative, and ſerviceable to children in many caſes.

Thus much for the Common Violet. Thoſe of inferior value are,

Hairy Scentleſs Marſh.

2 Hairy Scentleſs Marſh Violet. This grows common in ſome of our woods. The leaves are large, heart-ſhaped, and very hairy. The flowers are large, but without ſcent. In other reſpects it differs little from the Common Violet.

Marſh.

3 Marſh Violet. This grows naturally upon bogs, meadows, and marſhy grounds in many parts of England. The leaves are ſmall, ſmooth, and ſhaped like the kidney. The flowers are ſmall, of a pale blue colour, and uſually in full blow in June.

Palmated-leaved

4 Palmated-leaved Violet. The leaves are compoſed of five lobes, in ſuch a manner as to repreſent the hand and fingers; they are ſmall, a little downy, and thoſe on the lower-parts are ſometimes entire. The flowers are white; they appear in June, are ſmall, and have no ſcent.

Pedated-leaved

5 Pedated-leaved Violet. The leaves are ſhaped like the foot, and each is compoſed of ſeven lobes, which join at the baſe. The ſtalks are naked. The flowers are of three colours like thoſe of Heart's Eaſe, and have no ſcent; they appear in June, and never produce ſeeds with us.

Pinnated leaved,

6 Pinnated-leaved Violet. The leaves are very ſmall, and cut into many parts in ſuch a manner as to form a kind of winged leaf. The flowers ſtand on ſhort footſtalks; they are of a pale blue colour, and appear in June.

Lanceolated leaved,

7 Lanceolated leaved Violet. The leaves are ſpear-ſhaped, oval, deeply ſinuated, and grow on ſhort footſtalks. The flowers are large, of a bluiſh-purple colour, and without ſcent.

Primula-leaved,

8 *Primula*-leaved Violet. This hath cordated, oblong, obtuſe, crenated leaves, that have membranaceous footſtalks; by theſe they cauſe a variety with the other ſorts, but the flowers are trifling.

and Dog's Violet deſcribed

9 Dog's Violet. The leaves are of an oblong, cordated figure. The flowers grow on ſtalks about four or five inches long; they are of a pale-blue colour, have no ſcent, and will be in blow in April.

Its variety

There is a variety of this ſpecies with white flowers.

Ceniſian

10 Ceniſian Violet. This hath ſeveral ſlender creeping ſtalks. The leaves are ſmall, oval, ſmooth, entire, and placed on moderately long footſtalks. The flower is large, of a blue colour, and is produced ſingly on a long peduncle.

and Mountain Violet deſcribed

11 Mountain Violet. The ſtalks are erect, and grow to be upwards of a foot high. The leaves are heart ſhaped, and oblong. The flowers grow from the wings of the branches on long footſtalks; they are of a purple colour, and will be in blow in April or May.

Varieties

There is a variety of this ſpecies with pale blue flowers, and another with blue and white.

12 Yellow Violet. The leaves are of an oblong, oval figure, and their edges are indented. Among theſe ariſe the ſtalks to about four inches high; they are garniſhed with ſmall leaves, and the flowers are placed on them on long naked footſtalks; they are of the Heart's Eaſe kind, being yellow

yellow striped with purple, but there is a variety of it with purple flowers, and another with a bright yellow flower; they have no scent, and will flower most part of the summer.

Culture. These sorts are all propagated by dividing of the roots in the autumn A moist day should be pitched upon for the purpose, and they will readily grow and flower strong the spring or summer following

They are also propagated by seeds, which should be sown in the autumn, and they will come up early in the spring By Midsummer they will be good plants, and any time between then and Michaelmas may be set out for good

Titles. 1 Common Spring Violet is titled, *Viola acaulis, foliis cordatis, stolonibus reptantibus* In the *Hortus Cliffort* it is termed, *Viola acaulis, stolonibus teretibus reptantibus, pedunculis radicalibus* Caspar Bauhine calls it, *Viola martia purpurea, flore simplici odoro*, Renealme, *Viola odorata*, and Dodonæus, *Viola nigra, sive purpurea* It grows naturally in most parts of Europe

2 Hairy Scentless Violet is, *Viola acaulis, foliis cordatis piloso-hispidis* Morison calls it, *Viola martia hirsuta inodora*, and Ray, *Viola trachelii folio* It is found in some of our woods and hedges, and grows in such places in several of the colder parts of Europe

3 Marsh Violet is, *Viola acaulis, foliis reniformibus* In the *Flora Lapp* it is termed, *Viola foliis subrotundo cordatis, pedunculis radicatis* Morison calls it, *Viola palustris rotundifolia glabra* It grows naturally upon boggy and marshy grounds in England, and most of the northern parts of Europe

4 Palmated-leaved Violet is, *Viola acaulis, foliis palmatis quinquelobis dentatis indivisisque* Gronovius calls it, *Viola foliis palmatis sinuatis, stolonum reniformibus*, and Plukenet, *Viola Virginiana, platani fere foliis parvis & incanis* It grows naturally in Virginia

5 Pedated-leaved Violet is, *Viola acaulis foliis pedatis septempartitis* Gronovius calls it, *Viola foliis palmatis*, and Plukenet, *Viola Virginiana tricolor, foliis multifidis, cauliculo aphyllo* It is a native of Virginia

6 Pinnated leaved Violet is, *Viola acaulis, foliis pinnatifidis* Caspar Bauhine calls it, *Viola Alpina, folio in plures partes dissecto*, and John Bauhine, *Viola montana, folio multifido.* It is a native of Siberia

7 Lanceolate-leaved Violet is, *Viola acaulis, foliis lanceolatis crenatis* It grows naturally in Canada and Siberia

8 *Primula*-leaved Violet is, *Viola acaulis, foliis oblongis subcordatis, petiolis membranaceis* It grows naturally in Siberia and Virginia

9 Dog's Violet is, *Viola caule adultiore adscendente, foliis oblongo-cordatis* In the *Hortus Cliffort* it is called, *Viola caulibus adscendentibus fl · forte, foliis cordatis*; in the *Flora Lapp* *Viola foliis cordatis oblongis, pedunculis subradicatis* Caspar Bauhine calls it, *Viola martia inodora sylvestris*, and John Bauhine, *Viola cærulea maritima inodora sylvatica in acumine semen ferens* It grows naturally in England, and most parts of Europe

10 Cenisian Violet is, *Viola caulibus filiformibus indivisis prorepentibus, foliis ovatis petiolatis integerrimis glabris, stipulis indivisis, pedunculo solitario* Allionius calls it, *Viola foliis ovalibus integerrimis uniformibus, pedunculis caulinis* It grows naturally on the Cenisian mountains

11 Mountain Violet is, *Viola caulibus erectis, foliis cordatis oblongis* Van Royen calls it, *Viola foliis ovato-lanceolatis, caule erecto, stipulis dentatis*, Caspar Bauhine, *Viola martia arborescens purpurea*, Morison, *Viola erecta, flore cæruleo et albo*, and Cammerarius, *Viola arborescens* It grows naturally on the mountains of Lapland, Austria, and upon Mount Baldus.

12 Yellow Alpine Violet is, *Viola caule abbreviato, floris nectario subulato petalis longiore, foliis subovatis, stipulis dentatis* Caspar Bauhine calls it, *Viola montana lutea grandiflora*, Tournefort, *Viola montana cærulea grandiflora*, and Dalechamp, *Melanium montanum* It grows naturally on the Pyrenean and Helvetian mountains

Class and order in the Linnæan System. *Viola* is of the class and order *Syngenesia Monogynia*; and the characters are,

The characters. 1 Calyx is a very short, five-leaved, permanent perianthium The folioles are oval, oblong, erect, sharp at the top, obtuse at the base, equal in size, and differently disposed in different species.

2 Corolla is irregular, and formed of five unequal leaves The upper petal is broader than the others, obtuse, indented at the end, and has at the base a corniculated obtuse nectarium, which makes its way through the leaves of the cup, the two side petals are equal, opposite, straight, and obtuse, the lower pair are larger, and turned upwards

3 Stamina There are five very small filaments, two of which are placed at the upper petal, and penetrate the nectarium by their annexed appendages The antheræ are obtuse, they usually coalesce, and are edged with membranes

4 Pistillum consists of a roundish germen, a filiforme style beyond the antheræ, and an oblique stigma

5 Pericarpium is an oval, three-cornered, obtuse, unilocular capsule, formed of three valves

6 Semina The seeds are numerous, and oval

# CHAP. CCCCLXXXVII.

## *URTICA*, NETTLE.

Species

OF this genus are,

1 Common Stinging Nettle.
2 Hemp Nettle
3 Cylindrical Flowered Nettle.
4 Divaricated Nettle
5 Canada Nettle
6 Silvery Nettle

Common Stinging Nettle described

1 Common Stinging Nettle is too well known to need description It grows among old rubbish under walls, intrudes into neglected gardens, and is found almost every where about towns and villages Its great virtues, however, are equal to the commonness of the plant, and Nature seems to design this useful herb to be most general, by causing it to grow almost every where, that it may with convenience be found out, and gathered for use It is a fine diuretic, admirable for the cain-cough in children, good against inflammations of the lungs, pleurisies, stone, gravel, and brings speedy relief to those who have eaten and are affected by the poisonous qualities or mistaken Mushrooms or Hemlock It is an excellent pot-herb in the spring, and is in general used for that purpose among poor people, who (without doubt) receive great benefit from its sanative and cleansing property, as well as its serving as an excellent substitute for other expensive vegetable food

Medicinal properties

Hemp,

2 Hemp Nettle The stalks are upright, square, armed with stinging hairs, and five or six feet high The leaves are oblong, divided into three principal parts, which are deeply cut on the edges, stinging, and grow opposite to each other on long footstalks The flowers come out from the wings of the leaves in long katkins, they appear in July, and the seeds ripen in the autumn

Cylindrical Flowered,

3 Cylindrical Flowered Nettle The stalks are square, branching, and three or four feet high The leaves are oblong, nervose, serrated, and grow opposite on footstalks The flowers come out from the wings of the leaves in cylindrical, simple, undivided katkins, they appear in July, and the seeds ripen in the autumn

Divaricated,

4 Divaricated Nettle The stalks are upright, branching, and two or three feet high The leaves are oval, stinging, but in a less degree than the Common sort, and grow alternately on the stalks The flowers come out in compound, loose, divaricated bunches, they are of a greenish colour, and appear in July and August, but the seeds rarely ripen in England

Canada,

5 Canada Nettle The stalks grow to be two feet high The leaves are heart-shaped, oval, and grow alternately The flowers are produced in branching, distichous, upright katkins, from the tops of the stalks, they appear in August, and are seldom succeeded by ripe seeds in England

and Silvery Nettle described

6 Silvery Nettle The stalks grow numerous from a strong root, and grow to be three or four feet high The leaves are oval, but pointed at each end, serrated on the edges, of a deep green colour on the upper-side, but venose, and of a silvery-white underneath, and grow alternately on long slender footstalks The flowers come out from the tops of the stalks in loose spreading bunches, they appear in winter, but are not succeeded by seeds in England

Method of propagation

All these sorts may be propagated by parting of the roots, which may be done at any time of the year, but more especially in the autumn, winter, or early in the spring, before the stalks arise for flowering

They may be also propagated by sowing of the seeds, when good ones are to be procured, they should be sown in beds of light earth in the spring, and when they are fit to remove, may be transplanted to the places of their final destination The last sort is esteemed for the singular appearance it causes from its downy silvery leaves. The four preceding sorts are cultivated where a general curious collection of plants is attempted; but the first sort grows every where, and is always extirpated from gardens, and places of resort

Titles.

1 The Common Stinging Nettle is titled, *Urtica foliis oppositis cordatis, racemis geminis* In the *Flora Lapp* it is termed, *Urtica foliis cordatis, amentis cylindricis, sexu distincto*. Caspar Bauhine calls it, *Urtica urens maxima*; Dodonæus, *Urtica urens altera*, Gerard, *Urtica urens*, and Ray, *Urtica racemifera major perennis* It grows naturally in most countries of Europe

2 Hemp Nettle is, *Urtica foliis oppositis tripartitis incisis* Amman calls it, *Urtica foliis profunde laciniatis, semine lini* It grows naturally in Siberia

3 Cylindrical Flowered Nettle is, *Urtica foliis oppositis oblongis, amentis cylindricis solitariis indivisis sessilibus* Gronovius calls it, *Urtica foliis oblongis serratis, nervosis petiolatis*, and Sloane, *Urtica racemosa humilior iners* It grows naturally in most places in Canada, Virginia, and Jamaica

4 Divaricated Nettle is, *Urtica foliis alternis ovatis, racemis compositis divaricatis* Plukenet calls it, *Urtica racemosa major, Virginiana mitior, s minus urens* It grows naturally in Virginia and Canada

5 Canada Nettle is, *Urtica foliis alternis cordato ovatis, amentis ramosis distichis erectis* Morison calls it, *Urtica Canadensis racemosa mitior, s minus urens* It grows naturally in Canada and Siberia

6 Silvery Nettle is, *Urtica foliis alternis suborbiculatis utrinque acutis subtus tomentosis* Plukenet calls it, *Urtica racemifera maxima sinarum, foliis subtus argenteâ lanugine villosis* It grows naturally in China

Class and order in the Linnæan system

*Urtica* is of the class and order *Monoecia Tetrandria*, and the characters are,

The characters

### I Male Flowers

1 CALYX is a perianthium composed of four roundish, concave, obtuse leaves

2 COROLLA There are no petals, but in the center

center of the flower is situated a small, pitcher-shaped, undivided nectarium, that is permanent near the base

3 STAMINA are four awl-shaped patent filaments the length of the calyx, having bilocular antheræ.

II Female Flowers on the same or separate plants

1 CALYX is an oval, concave, erect, permanent perianthium, composed of two valves.

2 COROLLA. There is none

3 PISTILLUM consists of an oval germen, without any style, but a hairy stigma

4 PERICARPIUM There is none The calyx closes, and contains the seed

5 SEMEN The seed is single, oval, obtuse, compressed, and glossy.

## CHAP. CCCCLXXXVIII

## *UTRICULARIA*, WATER MILFOIL.

IN many of our standing waters, ditches, and ponds, are found,

Species. 1 Common Hooded Milfoil

2 Lesser Hooded Milfoil

Common, 1 Common Hooded Milfoil The root is thin, white, creeping, and possessed of small hollow knobs or tubers The stalks are slender, divide into numerous branches, lie flat in the mud, and strike root as they lie The leaves are finely divided into many spreading segments, and when the branches strike root are attended with round pellucid vesicles, or *utriculi* The flowers are elevated on long, simple upright footstalks, which arise from the sides of the branches, as they lie in the mud, they are six or eight in number, shaped like a hood, moderately large, of a beautiful yellow colour, and are generally to be met with in June and July

and Lesser Hooded Milfoil described. 2 Lesser Hooded Milfoil The root and stalks are slender and creeping The leaves consist of many narrow parts The flowers are small have a carinated nectarium, and are to be met with in June and July

These sorts grow common in ditches and standing waters, and are never cultivated

Titles 1 The first species is titled, *Utricularia nectario conico, scapo paucifloro* Rivinus calls it, *Lenticularia* Caspar Bauhine, *Millefolium aquaticum lenticulatum*; John Bauhine, *Millefolium aquaticum flore luteo galericulato*, and Gerard, *Millefolium palustre galericulatum*. It is common in most countries of Europe

2 The second species is, *Utricularia nectario carinato* Plukenet calls it, *Millefolium palustre galericulatum minus, flore minore*, and Ray, *Lentibularia minor* It grows naturally in most countries of Europe

*Utricularia* is of the class and order *Diandria Monogynia*, and the characters are, Class and order in the Linnæan system The characters.

1 CALYX is a perianthium composed of two very small, oval, concave, deciduous leaves

2 COROLLA is one ringent petal The upper-lip is plane, obtuse, and erect, the lower-lip is the largest, plane, and undivided The palate of the flower is heart-shaped, and a little prominent between the lips The nectarium is corniculated, and arises from the base of the petal

3 STAMINA are two very short crooked filaments, with small coherent antheræ

4 PISTILLUM consists of a globular germen, a filiforme style the length of the calyx, and a conic stigma

5 PERICARPIUM is a large globular capsule, containing one cell.

6 SEMINA The seeds are many

# CHAP. CCCCLXXXIX.

## *UVULARIA*

THERE are three species of this genus, called,

Species
1 Broad-leaved *Uvularia*
2 Perfoliate *Uvularia*
3 Sessile-leaved *Uvularia*

Description of Broad-leaved Uvularia.
1 Broad-leaved *Uvularia* The stalk is branching a little near the bottom, and grows to about two feet high The leaves are heart-shaped, oblong, smooth, acute-pointed, and embrace the stalk with their base The flowers come out singly from the wings of the leaves on long slender footstalks, they are of a yellow colour, and hang downward, they appear in April and May, but are seldom succeeded by seeds in England

Variety
There is a variety of this species with a white flower

Perfoliate
2 Perfoliate *Uvularia* The stalks are numerous from a strong root, slender, branching a little near the ground, and two or three feet high The leaves are oblong, pointed, smooth, grow opposite, and surround the stalk with their base. The flowers come out from the bosoms of the leaves on long slender footstalks, they are of a yellow colour, and hang drooping; they appear in April and May, but are rarely succeeded by seeds in England

and Sessile leaved Uvularia described.
3 Sessile-leaved *Uvularia* The stalks usually divide into two branches, which spread asunder The leaves are oval, spear-shaped, sessile, and grow alternately The flowers are elevated singly on long naked footstalks, they are of a yellow colour, and appear about the same time with the former

Culture
These plants are propagated by parting of the roots, which is best done in the autumn. They are very hardy, and will grow in almost any soil or situation

1 The first species is titled, *Uvularia foliis amplexicaulibus* Van Royen calls it, *Uvularia foliis cordato-oblongis*, Barrelier, *Smilax perfoliata ramosa, flore albo*, Caspar Bauhine, *Polygonatum latifolium ramosum*, and Clusius, *Polygonatum latifolium 4 ramosum* It grows naturally on the mountains of Silesia, Saxony, and Bohemia Titles

2 The second species is, *Uvularia foliis perfoliatis* In the *Hortus Cliffort* it is named simply, *Uvularia* Van Royen calls it, *Uvularia folio integerrimo*, Gronovius, *Uvularia caule perfoliato*, Morison, *Polygonum ramosum, flore luteo, majus*, and Caspar Bauhine, *Polygonatum latifolium perfoliatum Brasilianum* It grows naturally in Virginia and Canada.

3 The third species is, *Uvularia foliis sessilibus* Colden calls it, *Uvularia foliis sessilibus, flore unico* It grows naturally in Canada.

*Uvularia* is of the class and order *Hexandria Monogynia*, and the characters are, Class and order in the Linnæan system

1 CALYX There is none
2 COROLLA is six very long, oblong, spear-shaped, acute, erect petals The nectarium is a cavity in the base of each petal The characters.
3 STAMINA are six very short but broadish filaments, having long erect antheræ, about half the length of the corolla.
4 PISTILLUM consists of a roundish germen, and one semitrifid filiforme style longer than the stamina, crowned by simple reflexed stigmas
5 PERICARPIUM is an oval, triangular, acute capsule, containing three cells
6 SEMINA The seeds are many, roundish, and compressed

# CHAP CCCCXC.

## *YUCCA*, ADAM's NEEDLE

THERE are two species of this genus, which will live abroad in tolerably warm situations, called,

Species
1 Adam's Needle
2 Thready-leaved *Yucca*

Description of Adam's Needle,
1 Adam's Needle The stalk is thick, woody, branching, and two or three feet high The leaves are very long, narrow, stiff, of a dark or bluish-green colour, terminate in a long, strong, sharp, black spine, and are produced in great plenty The flowers come out in spikes from among the leaves; they are bell-shaped, and hang drooping, the colour on the inside is a clear white, but without the petals have purple stripes, they appear in August and September, but are not succeeded by seeds in our gardens

2 Thready-leaved *Yucca* The stalks are thick, woody, and about two feet high The leaves are and Thready leaved Yucca

are long, spear-shaped, of a dark green colour, blunt-pointed, and have many threads coming out from the sides, which hang downwards The flowers come out in spikes from among the leaves, they are shaped like those of the former, and hang downwards, they appear in August and September, and are not succeeded by seeds in England

Culture

These sorts are easily propagated by the offsets, or suckers, which they generally put out in great plenty After they are taken off, they should be laid by in a dry airy place for about four or five days, that the wounded parts may skin over, otherwise they will be liable to rot When the parts are skinned over, they should be set in pots filled with light sandy earth, and if they have the benefit of a slight hotbed, to facilitate their taking root, it will be the better They will grow, however, very well without this, and if it is afforded them, they must be soon hardened to the open air, and set abroad up to the rims in any part of the garden As the hard weather comes on in the winter, it will be proper to set the plants under a hotbed frame, or remove them into the green-house for the first winter, and in the spring they may be planted in the full ground, in the places where they are to remain The soil should be naturally dry and warm, and if the place is tolerably well defended, they will live through our winters, and soon become amazingly strong and firm plants

Proper situation

Both these sorts have a singular effect in the wilderness-quarters among other trees, and as in such places the trees generally keep one another warm, a few of them may be introduced here to add to the variety, if the soil is light and dry, but they will not live long in a stiff, moist, strong soil

These plants are also raised by seeds These should be procured from the places where they naturally grow, and sown in pots filled with light earth, and then plunged up to the rims in a moderate hotbed As the mould dries in the pots, they must be watered, giving it a very small quantity at a time, and in about six weeks the plants will come up They must then have plenty of air, and water sparingly, for too much water, in that early state, would rot them When the plants are fit to remove, which will be in about three weeks from their coming up, each should be set in its own separate small pot, filled with light sandy earth, they must be then plunged up to the rims in the hotbed, and the plants must be shaded and watered until they have taken root, after this they must be hardened by degrees to the open air, and then set abroad in a well sheltered place Here they may remain until November, and be then taken into shelter, or set in the green-house with the hardiest aloes and managed like them The similar management of hardy green house plants must attend them for about three years, by which time they will be grown to be strong plants, and may be set out in the open ground like the former

Titles

1 Adam's Needle is titled, *Yucca foliis integerrimis* In the *Hortus Cliffort* it is termed, *Yucca foliis margine integerrimis* Van Royen calls it, *Cordyline foliis pungentibus integerrimis*, Caspar Bauhine, *Yucca foliis aloes*, and Barrelier, *Yucca Indica foliis aloes* It grows naturally in Canada and Peru

2 Thready leaved *Yucca* is, *Yucca foliis serrato filamentosis* Gronovius calls it, *Yucca foliis lanceolatis acuminatis integerrimis margine filamentosis* Morison, *Yucca foliis filamentosis*, and Plukenet, *Yucca Virginiana, foliis per marginem ap prime filatis* It grows naturally in Virginia

Class and order in the Linnæan system

*Yucca* is of the class and order *Hexandria Monogynia*, and the characters are,

The characters

1 CALYX There is none

2 COROLLA is one bell-shaped petal, divided almost to the base into six large oval segments

3 STAMINA are six very short reflexed filaments, having very small antheræ

4 PISTILLUM consists of an oblong three-cornered germen, longer than the stamina, having no style, but an obtuse, pervious, three-furrowed stigma

5 PERICARPIUM is an oblong, triangular, trifid capsule, formed of three valves, and containing three cells

6 SEMINA The seeds are many, and lie over each other in a double order

## CHAP. CCCCXCI.

## *ZYGOPHYLLUM*, BEAN CAPER.

THE Common Bean Caper will flourish for many years in some dry situations

The plant described. The root is very thick, fleshy, white, and strikes deep into the ground The stalks are herbaceous, round, jointed, smooth, send forth a few green jointed branches from the sides, and grow to be four feet high The leaves are nearly oval, smooth, fleshy, of a bluish-green colour, and two or three of them grow together on one footstalk The flowers come out two or three together from the wings of the joints, on short footstalks, they are of a reddish colour on the outside, white within, appear in June and July, and are succeeded by oblong prismatical capsules, containing ripe seeds in the autumn

Its propagation. This plant is raised by sowing the seeds in a slight hotbed in the spring When the plants are fit to remove, each should be set in a separate pot, where they must be shaded and watered until they have taken root, and after that hardened by degrees to the open air When this is effected, let them be set abroad in some warm well sheltered place, where they may remain until the end of autumn At the approach of frost they should be set in the green house, or under a hotbed frame, or some cover, for the first winter, but should be always placed abroad again on the approach of mild weather In the spring they may be turned out of the pots into the places where they are designed to remain; in which, if the place be naturally dry, sandy, and full of a rubbishy earth, they will live for many years, and annually produce flowers and seeds

Titles. This species is titled, *Zygophyllum foliis petiolatis, foliolis obovatis, caule herbaceo* In the former edition of the *Species Plantarum* it is termed, *Zygophyllum capsulis prismatico-pentaedris*, in the *Hortus Cliffort Zygophyllum foliis petiolatis* Caspar Bauhine calls it, *Capparis portulacæ folio*, and Dodonæus, *Capparis Fabago* It grows naturally in Syria and Mauritania

Class and order in the Linnæan system. *Zygophyllum* is of the class and order *Decandria Monogynia*, and the characters are,

The characters.

1 CALYX is a perianthium composed of five oval, obtuse, concave, erect leaves

2 COROLLA is five obtuse emarginated petals, which widen gradually, and are somewhat longer than the calyx The nectarium is composed of ten connivent leaves, and includes the germen

3 STAMINA are ten awl shaped filaments shorter than the corolla, having oblong incumbent antheræ

4 PISTILLUM consists of an oblong germen, an awl-shaped style the length of the stamina, and a simple stigma

5 PERICARPIUM is an oval, five-cornered capsule, composed of five valves, and containing five cells

6 SEMINA The seeds are many, roundish, and compressed

# ADDENDA.

## CHAP CCCCXCII.

## *CINERARIA*

Species. OF this genus are,

1 Marsh Flea-bane
2 Mountain Ragwort
3 Siberian *Cineraria*
4. Glaucous *Cineraria*
5 Golden *Cineraria*
6 Sea Ragwort
7 Canada Sea Ragwort

Description of Marsh Flea bane. 1 Marsh Flea-bane The stalks are thick, crested, hairy, hollow, and four or five feet high The leaves are broad, spear-shaped, and the upper ones embrace the stalk with their base, the edges of the lower ones are sinuated and serrated, but in some varieties they are more jagged, or cut into many segments, and the upper leaves of all the sorts are entire, or nearly so, and sit more close to the stalks The flowers are numerous at the tops of the plant, growing on slender footstalks, they are of a yellow colour, appear in August, and are followed by narrow, four-cornered,

nered, downy ſeeds, which will be ripe, and will blow about with the winds in September and October

Mountain Ragwort deſcribed

2 Mountain Ragwort The ſtalks are thick, ſimple, creſted, hollow, and three or four feet high The leaves are oblong, ſpear-ſhaped, entire, hairy, ſeſſile, and of a hoary whiteneſs The flowers come out in ſmall umbels from the tops of the ſtalks, before they open they are of a dark red colour, but when in full blow of a bright yellow, they appear in June and July, and are ſucceeded by ripe downy ſeeds in Auguſt.

Varieties

There are ſeveral varieties of this ſpecies, the leaves of ſome being almoſt round, others heart-ſhaped, and others long and narrow, they differ alſo in the degrees of whiteneſs, and the indentures on the edges The height of the plant alſo varies, and particularly that variety called the Small Alpine Ragwort, growing to little better than a foot, whilſt others riſe with robuſt ſtalks to the height of five or ſix feet They all flower nearly at the ſame time, and the ſeeds ripen accordingly

Siberian,

3 Siberian *Cineraria* This hath a large, tuberous, yellowiſh root, from which riſe numerous, heart ſhaped, obtuſe, ſmooth, and indented leaves, growing on long footſtalks The ſtalk is adorned with one or two leaves only, it is round, thick, hoary, upright, unbranching, and two or three feet high The flowers come out in looſe ſpikes from the tops of the ſtalks, they are large, and of a yellow colour, appear in July and Auguſt, and are ſucceeded by narrow, quadrangular downy ſeeds, which ripen ſoon after the flowers are fallen

Glaucous,

4 Glaucous *Cineraria* The ſtalk is thick, undivided, upright, and a yard or more in height The leaves are heart-ſhaped, oblong, ſmooth, entire, of a glaucous colour, and embrace the ſtalk with their baſe The flowers are produced in ſpikes at the tops of the ſtalks, they are large, of a yellow colour, and appear about the ſame time with the former

and Golden Cineraria,

5 Golden *Cineraria* This riſes with ſeveral upright hairy ſtalks to the height of about two feet The leaves are ſpear ſhaped, ſerrated, hairy on the upper-ſide, and downy underneath The flowers come out in roundiſh bunches from the tops of the ſtalks, they are large, of a golden-yellow colour, appear in July and Auguſt, and the ſeeds ripen in the autumn

and Sea Ragwort deſcribed

6 Sea Ragwort The ſtalks are woody, branching, partly procumbent, about a yard long, and the young ſhoots are made delicate by a ſoft, hoary, ſilvery down The leaves are large and pinnatifid, and the ſegments are irregularly ſinuated or divided into other parts, they are of a thickiſh conſiſtence, ſmooth, ſoft, and of a bluiſh-green colour, duſted all over and made white with a moſt delicate ſilvery down The flowers come out in roundiſh bunches from the ends and ſides of the branches, they are of a yellow colour, and the rays turn backward, they appear in June, continue in ſucceſſion through the whole ſummer, and afford ripe ſeeds in the autumn

Its variety

There is a variety of this ſpecies with narrow leaves, finely divided, called the Narrow-leaved Sea Ragwort

Canada Sea Ragwort deſcribed

7 Canada Sea Ragwort The ſtalks are herbaceous, divide into ſeveral branches, are two or three feet long, die to the ground every autumn, and freſh ones ariſe in the ſpring The leaves are large, pinnatifid, and the ſegments ſinuated and a little hairy underneath, but they are not white and downy like the former ſort The flowers are produced in panicles from the tops of the plant, they are of a yellow colour, and the rays are ſpreading, but do not turn backward like thoſe of the former ſpecies, they appear in July, Auguſt, and September, and the ſeeds ripen in the autumn, ſoon after which the ſtalks decay

Method of propagating them

All theſe ſorts are to be raiſed by ſeeds, which ſhould be ſown in the autumn, as ſoon as they are ripe A part of the plants will come up in the autumn, the others will appear in the ſpring When they are all up, they ſhould be thinned where they are too cloſe, duly weeded and watered all ſummer, and in the autumn ſhould be removed to the places where they are deſigned to remain, and the ſummer following they will flower, and perfect their ſeeds

The firſt five ſorts, and the ſeventh are propagated by parting of the roots, the beſt time for which is the autumn When they are ſet out, they will require no trouble, except keeping them clean from weeds

The ſixth ſort is propagated by ſlips, which may be ſet in any of the ſummer months in a moiſt ſhady place, for want of that they ſhould be ſhaded and duly watered at firſt, and afterwards they will require no trouble, except keeping them clean from weeds, and in the autumn they may be taken up with a ball of earth to each root, and ſet in the places where they are deſigned to remain

A few plants of this ſpecies ſhould be ſet in the different quarters of the Evergreen wilderneſs, where they will have a pretty effect, by their ſilvery, hoary, large, and beautiful leaves, among the different tinges of green in that place, eſpecially in winter, when they diſplay a more than ordinary beauty by their leaves and young ſhoots, much more than what they afford by their flowers in ſummer, theſe being of little beauty, and the leaves at that ſeaſon appearing coarſer, or at leaſt being in a great meaſure diveſted of ſome of their delicacy and luſcious beauty

Titles

1 Marſh Flea-bane is titled, *Cineraria floribus corymboſis, foliis lato-lanceolatis dentato ſinuatis, caule villoſo* In the *Iter Scanicum* it is termed, *Othonna paluſtris*, in the *Hortus Cliffort Solidago foliis inferioribus lanceolatis ſerrato ſinuatis ſuperioribus integris amplexicaulibus* Moriſon calls it, *Jacobæa aquatica elatior, foliis magis diſſectis*, Caſpar Bauhine, *Conyza aquatica laciniata*, Gerard, *Conyza foliis laciniatis*, and Parkinſon, *Conyza helenitis foliis laciniatis* It grows naturally in ditches, marſhy and watery places in England, and moſt parts of Europe

2 Mountain Ragwort is, *Cineraria umbella involucrata, pedunculo communi nudiuſculo, foliis oblongis villoſis* Van Royen calls it, *Solidago foliis cordatis petiolatis dentatis*, Boccone, *Jacobæa montana, integro rotundo folio*, Haller, *Senecio foliis petiolatis cordatis ſerratis ſubtus incanis, floribus luteis e ſummo caule racemoſis*, alſo, *Senecio foliis lingulatis tomentoſis ſimpliciſſimis*; Caſpar Bauhine, *Jacobæa Alpina, foliis ſubrotundis ſerratis*, alſo, *Jacobæa Alpina laciniata, flore buphthalmi*, alſo, *Conyza incana*, alſo, *Jacobæa montana lanuginoſa anguſtifolia non laciniata*, Ray, *Jacobæa montana non laciniata noſtras*, Barrelier, *Jacobæa montana polyanthos, flore aureo, foliis longis et integris*, Gmelin, *Solidago foliis lanceolatis ſeſſilibus integris denticulatis, floribus umbellatis, involucro ſetaceo*, and Lobel, *Conyza helenitis mollis incana* In the former edition of the *Species Plantarum*, *Othonna integrifolia*, entitled, *Othonna foliis lanceolatis ſubdenticulatis villoſis, floribus umbellatis*, and, *Othonna helenitis*, entitled, *Othonna foliis lanceolatis integris ſubdentatis villoſis, floribus umbellatis*, are now found to be varieties only of this ſpecies

It

It grows naturally on the Pyrenean, Helvetian, Austrian, and Siberian mountains, also on the mountainous parts of England, and the South of France

3 Siberian *Cineraria* is, *Cineraria racemo simplici, foliis cordatis obtusis denticulatis lævibus, caule simplicissimo monophyllo* In the *Hortus Upsal* it is termed, *Othonna foliis cordatis, caule subnudo simplicissimo* Amman calls it, *Jacobææastrum cacaliæ folio*, Tournefort, *Jacobæa orientalis, cacaliæ folio*, Vaillant, *Jacobæoides ari crenato folio*, and Gmelin, *Solidago foliis cordatis sub rotundis dentatis petiolatis* It grows naturally in Siberia and the East

4 Glaucous *Cineraria* is, *Cineraria racemo simplici foliis cordatis integerrimis lævibus, caule simplicissimo* Gmelin calls it, *Solidago floribus spicatis, foliis subcordatis glaberrimis glaucis oblongo ellipticis amplexicaulibus* It is a native of Siberia

5 Golden *Cineraria* is, *Cineraria floribus corymbosis, foliis lanceolatis serratis subtus tomentosis* It grows naturally in Siberia

6 Sea Ragwort is, *Cineraria floribus paniculatis, foliis pinnatifidis tomentosis laciniis sinuatis, caule fruticescente* In the *Hortus Upsal* it is termed, *Othonna* 2, in the *Hortus Cliffort* *Solidago foliis pinnatifidis laciniis sinuatis, corymbis racemosis* Caspar Bauhine calls it, *Jacobæa maritima*, and Dodonæus, *Cineraria* It grows naturally on the Mediterranean sea-shores

7 Canada Sea Ragwort is, *Cineraria floribus paniculatis, foliis pinnatifidis subvillosis laciniis sinuatis, caule herbaceo* It grows naturally in Canada

*Cineraria* is of the class and order *Syngenesia Polygamia Superflua*, and the characters are, Class and order in the Linnæan system The characters

1 CALYX The general calyx is simple, and composed of many equal folioles

2 COROLLA The general flower is radiated The hermaphrodite florets are equal and numerous in the disk The female florets in the disk are stretched out like the tongue, and answer to the number of the leaves of the calyx Each hermaphrodite floret is funnel-shaped, and cut at the brim into five erect segments

The females are tongue shaped, and indented at the top

3 STAMINA of the hermaphrodites consists of five short slender filaments, having a cylindrical tubular anthera, divided at the top into five parts

4 PISTILLUM of the hermaphrodites consists of an oblong germen, a filiforme style the length of the stamina, and two erect stigmas

In the females, it consists of an oblong germen, a short filiforme style, and two oblong, obtuse, revolute stigmas

5 PERICARPIUM There is none

6 SEMINA of the hermaphrodites are single, narrow, quadrangular, and crowned with down.

The seeds of the females are like those of the hermaphrodite

The receptacle is naked, and almost plane

# C H A P. CCCCXCIII

## *H Y P O X I S.*

OF this genus is one hardy species, called, Hairy Star of Bethlehem

The plant described The root is a small roundish bulb, full of a viscous juice The radical leaves are narrow, grassy, hairy, and five or six inches long The stalks are slender, upright, angular, and about six inches high The flowers come out in small umbels from the tops of the stalks, growing on hairy footstalks, they are of a yellow colour on the inside, but striped with green on the out, they appear in May, and are succeeded by oval capsules, containing ripe seeds, in August

Culture This plant is propagated by offsets from the roots, and the best time for parting them is August, when the stalks and leaves decay They love a light fresh earth, but will grow in almost any soil or situation, provided it be not too wet

Titles This species is titled, *Hypoxis pilosa, capsulis ovatis* In the former edition of the *Species Plantarum* it is termed, *Ornithogalum scapo angulato, pedunculis umbellatis villosis* Van Royen calls it, *Ornithogalum scapo bifloro*, Gronovius, *Ornithogalum vernum luteum, foliis angustis hirsutis*, Petiver, *Ornithogalum Virginianum luteum*, and Plukenet, *Ornithogalum herbaceum luteum parvum Virginianum, foliis gramineis hirsutis* It grows naturally in Virginia and Canada

*Hypoxis* is of the class and order *Hexandria Monogynia*, and the characters are, Class and order in the Linnæan system The characters

1 CALYX There is none

2 COROLLA is one petal placed above the germen, and divided at the top into six oval, oblong, patent, permanent segments

3 STAMINA are six very short capillary filaments, having oblong antheræ

4 PISTILLUM consists of a turbinated germen situated below the flower, a filiforme style the length of the stamina, and an obtuse stigma

5 PERICARPIUM is an oblongish, trivalvate, trilocular capsule, crowned by the permanent corolla

6 SEMINA The seeds are many, and roundish

CHAP

## CHAP. CCCCXCIV.

## *MILIUM*, MILLET GRASS.

Species. OF this genus are,
1 Scattered-flowered Millet Grass
2 Clustered-flowered Millet Grass
3 French Millet Grass

Scattered-flowered, 1 Scattered-flowered Millet Grass This hath a jointed reddish root, which sends forth many slender fibres The stalks are slender, round, smooth, jointed, and about three feet high The leaves are long, narrow, bend backward, grow singly at the joints, and sheath the stalks a good way up with their base The flowers are produced in fine spreading panicles from the tops of the stalks, they are of a brownish colour, appear in July and August, and are succeeded by ripe seeds soon after

Clustered-flowered, 2 Clustered-flowered Millet Grass The stalks are round, jointed, hollow, and about a yard high The leaves are broad, long, bend backward at the tops, and embrace the stalks with their base The flowers come out in clusters from the tops of the stalks, they appear about the same time with the former, and the seeds ripen accordingly

and French Millet Grass described 3 French Millet Grass This is a very noble grass, rising with an upright firm stalk to the height of six feet. The leaves are large, and like those of oats or barley The flowers come out in bearded panicles from the tops of the stalks, they are of a white colour, and are succeeded by black, oval, glossy seeds, which ripen in the autumn

Culture The first two sorts grow naturally in woods, and are not cultivated in gardens, the last is deserving of a place, for it makes a fine variety with the grass kinds, being a tall, beautiful well-looking plant They are all propagated by sowing the seeds in the spring, but whether their roots are so durable as to entitle them to a place here, I am not certain, having no memorandum of their continuance

1 Scattered-flowered Millet Grass is titled, *Milium floribus paniculatis dispersis muticis* In the *Hortus Cliffort* it is termed, *Milium glumis diphyllis* Caspar Bauhine calls it, *Gramen sylvaticum, paniculâ miliaceâ sparsâ*, Gerard, *Gramen miliaceum*, and Parkinson, *Gramen miliaceum vulgare* It grows naturally in woods, forests, and shady places in England, and most parts of Europe Titles.

2 Clustered-flowered Millet Grass is, *Milium floribus paniculatis confertis* Scheuchzer calls it, *Gramen paniculatum Alpinum latifolium, paniculâ miliaceâ sparsa* It grows naturally in the woods of Helvetia

3 French Millet Grass is, *Milium floribus paniculatis aristatis* In the former edition of the *Species Plantarum* it is, *Agrostis paradoxa* Morison calls it, *Gramen avenaceum paniculatum Gallo provinciale, aquilegiæ semine* It is a native of Gaul

*Milium* is of the class and order *Triandria Digynia*, and the characters are, Class and order in the Linnæan system The characters

1 CALYX is a glume composed of two oval acuminated valves, containing one flower

2 COROLLA is two oval valves smaller than the calyx, and one is larger than the other

3 STAMINA are three very short capillary filaments, with oblong antheræ

4. PISTILLUM consists of a roundish germen, and two capillary styles with penicilliforme stigmas

5 PERICARPIUM The seed is covered by the petals of the flower, which serve for a pericarpium.

6 SEMEN The seed is single, and roundish



END OF THE FIRST VOLUME.

CPSIA information can be obtained at www.ICGtesting.com
Printed in the USA
BVOW01s1403051213

338281BV00007B/188/P

9 781170 971697